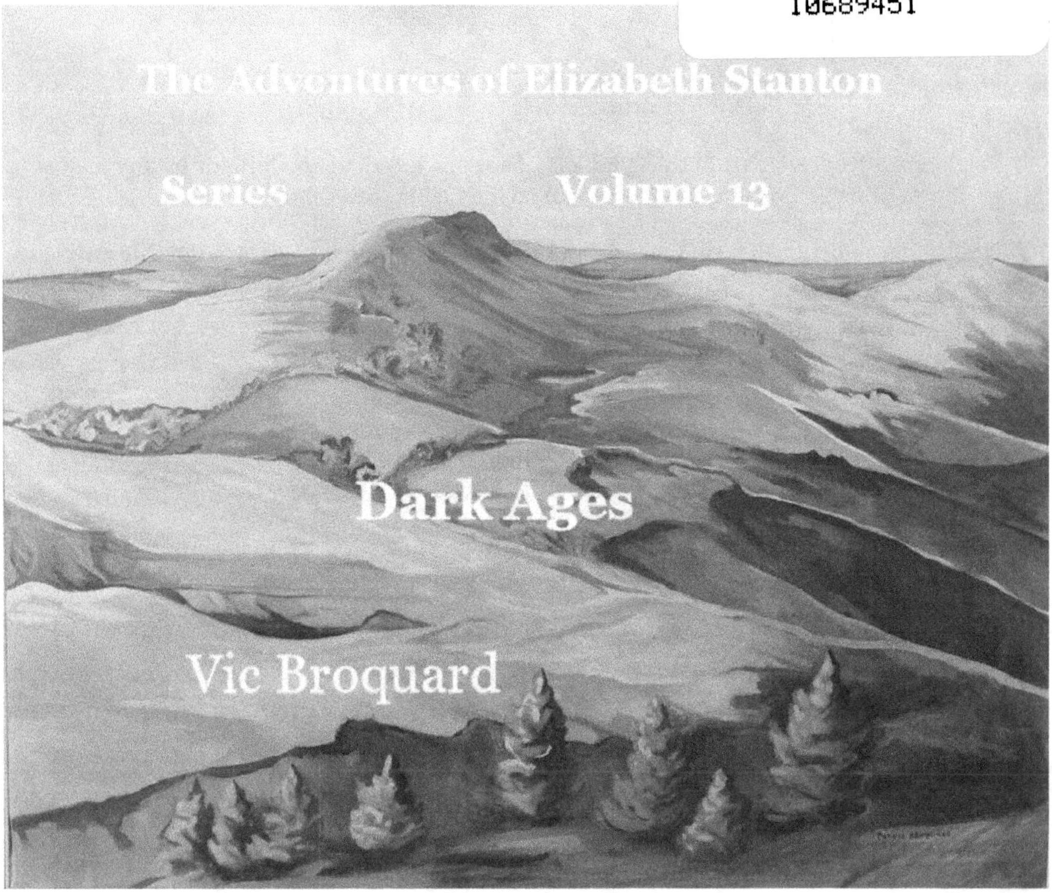

The Adventures of Elizabeth Stanton Series

Volume 13 Dark Ages

Vic Broquard

Published by:
Broquard eBooks
http://Broquard-eBooks.com
author@Broquard-eBooks.com
103 Timberlane
East Peoria, IL 61611

Artwork by Crooked Willow Studios

For Morgan and L. Ron Hubbard

Table of Contents

Chapter 1 The Die Is Cast
Chapter 2 Discovery and Counteractions
Chapter 3 The Genetic Modifications
Chapter 4 It begins on Megalos
Chapter 5 Megalos and Nobles
Chapter 6 The Fall of Demokritos
Chapter 7 The Greenway and Sea Prince Reactions
Chapter 8 What Once Was Juda Arad
Chapter 9 For Some, It Was Not Death
Chapter 10 Madness in Tashien
Chapter 11 Burning in Hell
Chapter 12 Long Range Plans Begin
Chapter 13 Battle for Sanity
Chapter 14 The Fall of Naxos, Arolas
Chapter 15 Escape
Chapter 16 The Walking Dead
Chapter 17 Exodus
Chapter 18 A Toehold in Tashien
Chapter 19 Skulls, Vengeance, and Pirates
Chapter 20 Joining Forces
Chapter 21 Ancient History
Chapter 22 Old Ways Die Hard
Chapter 23 Dreams
Chapter 24 An Idea Can Be Powerful
Chapter 25 The Groundwork Is Lain
Chapter 26 The Idea Grows
Chapter 27 And Grows
Chapter 28 And Arrives
Chapter 29 The Path Out of Darkness Begins
Chapter 30 A Naval Affair
Chapter 31 The Centurions
Chapter 32 The Rescue
Chapter 33 Raffaella and Eve Take Action
Chapter 34 Evolution of Women's Apparel
Chapter 35 Heavy Darkness Descends on Phindos
Chapter 36 In Phindos, For Some, the Darkness Grows
Chapter 37 The Path Out of Darkness Appears
Chapter 38 The Coming of Darkness Over Alia
Chapter 39 Help for Katerine and Annelise
Chapter 40 The Strange Case of Alexina Phanes
Chapter 41 Zeederlund, the Land That Time Forgot
Chapter 42 Culture Clash
Chapter 43 Heavy Darkness Over Alia

Chapter 44 Darkness Over Theos
Chapter 45 A Light in Trikala, Theos
Chapter 46 Baby Boom and Therapies
Chapter 47 The Saving of Phindos
Chapter 48 The Civil War of Theos
Chapter 49 Thrace Recovery
Chapter 50 Alia Has to Be Salvaged
Chapter 51 Salvaging Alia
Chapter 52 Alia Begins to Recover
Chapter 53 Alia Becomes a Done Checkmark
Chapter 54 Partholan Intervenes
Chapter 55 Just as Likely as Berwyn's Girls
Chapter 56 Brina Cerdwin of Bregia, Layamon
Chapter 57 Partholan's Request
Chapter 58 Be Careful What You Import
Chapter 59 Be Careful Whom You Meet
Chapter 60 Shipwrecked
Chapter 61 Nan Yan and We Take Responsibility
Chapter 62 The Rise of Philosophies
Chapter 63 Aberration Unhandled, Returns
Chapter 64 Flight to Safety
Chapter 65 From the Ashes
Chapter 66 Flight
Chapter 67 High Country Drug Overlords
Chapter 68 The Drug Lords' Plans
Chapter 69 Countermeasures
Chapter 70 Rescue
Chapter 71 Economic Collapse and the Desert Dwellers
Chapter 72 Blinded and the Search
Chapter 73 Traditions and Truth
Chapter 74 Criminals

Chapter 1 The Die Is Cast

Hammertharmalosis walked back to his office, his head slumped lower than normal, showing his age more so now than ever before. The orders of the Supreme Master still burned in his auditory senses, "You are hereby *ordered* to lead our last shipment to Planet X! And yes, you *must* assist the Greys and the plasticine with their last shipments! Yes, yes, do find out what happened to your colleague, but make *sure* the penal colony is secure! You are *not* to return here until you have made it secure. Do I make myself clear, geneticist?"

Yes, he'd been perfectly clear. Hammertharmalosis knew that he had no choice but to venture into space, leaving the home world behind. He also knew that he hated space travel, long months of sheer boredom. Worse, he would have to play host to their enemies! The very ones that they had fought for three and a half centuries now — fought to a stalemate, if underground rumors were to be trusted. Hammertharmalosis knew better than to trust them, however. He was a geneticist, a scientist. Actually, with the departure of Thranikansisnestoris, he was actually the last of the geneticists.

Didn't the Supreme Master realize that? If anything happened to him, this entire field of science would vanish from their civilization! "Your only purpose is to build effective, long lasting prison cells, nothing more!" The words of the Supreme Master still burned in his mind. A fighter, the Supreme Master was anything but a scientist. Did he know that if anything happened to Hammertharmalosis, then over a thousand years of careful genetic research and development would be utterly lost forever? Probably not, he cursed, but only the foul smelling air heard it. Years of bombardment had taken its toll on the landscape of his home world.

Why had not Thranikansisnestoris reported? He'd been gone nearly a year and a half now, more than enough time to get to Planet X, make the genetic modifications that the two had been devising for more than a score of years, and return safely. Though he was too afraid to admit it even to himself, something must have gone very wrong on their penal colony for his colleague to not have returned — nay, not even a subspace communication had been received. This he knew very well, having bribed a friend in the Interstellar Communications Office. No, if any message of any kind had come through, he would have heard about it, even if it was military oriented and not meant for his ears. He could not flush from his mind the nagging fear that something awful had happened to his colleague and he was being sent straight into the fire.

At least he had managed to get a squadron of two fighter captains to accompany him. He would have some protection, though he suspected that they were along only because he was chaperoning a pair of ships belonging to their archenemies. Still, something else bothered him, something the Supreme Master had said, and yet not said. This was to be the *last* shipment to the penal colony. Even their enemies were making their last runs as well. Why? "Have we really rid our society of all the undesirables?" he mused.

As he passed the rubble, which had once been their University, bombed by some Grey's attack a century ago, he spied several small mantis children scampering over the now grass-covered stones in search of food. Well, food was becoming a serious problem for non-combatants. Three plus centuries of continuous warfare had left their planet in shambles; little food was being cultivated any longer. What little was grown was being shipped off to their valiant soldiers who still fought for the homeland. Seeing the small hatchlings searching for scraps to eat, he answered his own question. Indeed, all the undesirables have been captured, shipped off to the penal colony on Planet X. His would be the last load, only fourteen thousand one hundred six, many of whom had been held in stasis cells for over a score of years now. Yes, the undesirables were now a thing of the past.

Ancestral memories came into his mind, those of the first years of the war. Images of thousands upon thousands of beings rounded up each week flowed through his mind. Avant garde thinkers, rebellious beings, even criminals were rounded up, implanted, and sent to Planet X, interred there forever in the genetically engineered mammalian prison cells created by the geneticists, refined for over a millennia by his ancestors and the other geneticists. A smile appeared; he was proud of his achievements and those of his ancestors. No one saw his smile, however. There were far too few of the mantises left these days.

He ducked down the crumbling stone stairway that led to his underground research laboratory. One day. One day was all he had to prepare for this momentous journey. Hardly enough time, he thought. Yet, he was a scientist. He forced his mind to concentrate upon the task at hand. Punching in his access code, he downloaded all of his research notes covering the many proposed modifications to their mammalian prison cells. For a moment, he wondered what old Thranikansisnestoris may have already implemented. Before he'd left, they had agreed upon which ones he would use. Still, without having heard back from Thranikansisnestoris, he had no idea which had been implemented, if any. Hence, he took all of his voluminous research notes, leaving nothing to chance. After all, Planet X was at the far edge of the galaxy. One could not just hop back here to pick up a forgotten note, not at these distances.

Next, he dialed into his computer the genetic materials that he would need. Operating under the assumption that his fellow geneticist had failed to make any of the needed alterations to the mammalian prison cells, he opted to play it safe. He ordered a complete stockpile of amino acids, powdered compounds, and a host of complex chemicals — a sufficient amount to rework all the mammalian cells on Planet X at least twice over. Not that he intended to fail and have to redo everything, rather, his computer simulations indicated that the current population growth of these lower life forms had greatly increased. While simulations were most worthy, he lacked real-time data for well over a century. He estimated that at most the error factor was two. That is, the mammalian cell population had more than doubled from his computer simulation.

He finished and pressed the Execute button. Somewhere near the mighty spaceport, he envisioned the great cranes now beginning their automatic loading programs, all computer controlled. When he arrived there in the morning, all of his supplies would have been already loaded into his ship. No mantis had to intervene, a marvel of their engineering skills. Now to pack his few personal effects.

Knock. Knock. A loud banging on his door brought him out of his reverie. "Enter," he called out, straightening himself up. He'd slept in his office during the night, something he was wont to do — far more these days. It was too disheartening to walk home past all the war-ravaged rubble of buildings and parks he'd known as a child or that his ancestors had known. After all, he did have all of his ancestor's memories as well as his own.

A lean, fit mantis entered. "Ah, there you are, Hammertharmalosis. I am Captain Restorislomas. Captain Jemalensis is already at the spaceport. I am to escort you there now. Let's get this pathetic mission over as soon as possible," he growled. It was plainly obvious to Hammertharmalosis that the fighters greatly disliked having to accompany him to their penal colony. There was no battle glory in that, not unless somehow they could goad the Grey and plasticine into attacking them on this trip.

An hour later, he climbed into his large space ship, a giant cigar shaped affair. His was a merchant ship. That his ship was an antiquated relic, rusted and barely flight-worthy bothered him not, only that his vitally needed supplies were all present. In addition, a second ancient merchant ship was there, loaded with the remainder of his supplies. This ship was being flown by remote control from his ship's computer and would tag along behind his. Nearby, his two fighter captains boarded their sleek, shiny one-mantis crafts, each loaded with firepower, though such was unlikely to be needed on this trip, which annoyed them both no end. "Yes, all here," he muttered to himself, "now for the pre-launch protocols." He set to work going mechanically down the list.

That theirs were the very last crafts to get the go ahead to take flight was lost upon him. Such was not the case with the two captains, who growled and cursed to each other over their fighter comm-link. Worse still, they would have to follow this pathetic geneticist's lead! Only Hammertharmalosis knew their precise destination. Planet X was not on any navigational charts, for good reasons too. He checked the thousands of stasis cells; all held their captured spiritual beings tightly. At last, he was given take off clearance, and he relayed it to his two guards.

Shortly, the voice of Captain Jemalensis came across the comm-link. "Okay, here are the rendezvous coordinates, Hammertharmalosis. Punch them in and fire on my mark." A few minutes later, the three craft accelerated to top speed for the aging, rusted, merchant ship. This also annoyed the two fighters, whose sleek ships could go at least twice as fast, perhaps more. When Hammertharmalosis clicked off his link, Jemalensis chatted to his partner. "Restorislomas, take heart. This mission should only be a month long. Just as soon as we get clearance to leave this Planet X, we'll use our max-drive. Damn, this is pathetically slow!" Both growled their agreement with the slow plodding of their ships.

The massive grey cargo ship of the Grey's was waiting for them as they arrived. Translation units in the four ships energized and the mechanical translation voice spoke, "Greetings. I am Captain N'Gar Kar of Arcturus. How soon do we get under way? How far is this Planet X anyway? I cannot get a fix on our signal beacon there."

After introducing himself, Hammertharmalosis replied that he too could not get a beacon fix. He found that troubling and dug out his navigational charts. "We must wait on the plasticine ship," he replied and set to work plotting a course by hand. He finished the work by the next day, grateful for the delay caused by the doll creatures.

Beep. Beep. The enemy-warning system activated, as the saucer shaped plasticine ship sailed up to the four ships. The translation unit barked mechanically, "Captain Dross here. We are ready to take our prisoners to the penal colony now, but I am having trouble getting a fix on our signal beacon there."

The two mantis captains and the Grey admitted that they were having similar problems.

"Follow me," Hammertharmalosis interrupted. He relayed the proper coordinates and the five ships headed off into the blackness and cold void of outer space.

It took Hammertharmalosis a full month of searching to find the proper star and then the blue-green penal planet. The others had become extremely annoyed and outright angry over the interminable delay in reaching their destination. Yet, he only grinned to himself. His ancestral memories were guiding him to the proper sun and planet, something that neither the Greys nor plasticine could ever do, for neither had the immense benefit of ancestral memories to guide them. This was a uniquely mantis trait, one which made them the superior beings, he thought.

As the five ships passed the scattered debris of the three signal beacons far above the planet, everyone became alarmed and switched to defensive protocols. Gun ports opened and implant beams were readied. No attack came, however.

Both Captains N'Gar Kar and Dross announced that they would dump their cargo of "frozen" spiritual beings into the ocean and then go check on their prison wardens. They were under orders to return home with all them, leaving no Grey or plasticine wardens on Planet X any longer. Both races were quite satisfied that this prison complex was fulfilling its mission perfectly. Not one of their exiled beings had yet to return to their home worlds, a fact that caused Hammertharmalosis to smile smugly once more. Of course, his mammalian prison cells were the perfect solution to unwanted spiritual beings.

The two mantis captains gave the all clear signal. Captain Jemalensis barked, "No signs of any space craft anywhere around Planet X. It is safe to deposit your cargos. However, something destroyed the signal beacons. Hence, follow hostile enemy protocols." All five ships concurred and began executing their own missions. Hovering high over the Med Sea, Hammertharmalosis released the Freezer Cage locks and watched the last of their unwanted spiritual beings descending towards the ocean far below his position.

After failing to make any contact with Thranikansisnestoris, Hammertharmalosis headed to their main base at Chichulain, where his fellow geneticist ought to be. The three ships landed before the complex hanger doors on a plain high atop the rugged mountains. Still, they saw no signs of life, though the large circle of stone heads surrounding the open, recessed, display arena unnerved the two fighter captains slightly. The three left their ships and walked up to the entrance. While he entered the override access code, the two captains drew their hand pistols, ready for trouble. As the gaping door opened, they insisted on entering first to make sure that the complex was safe for the scientist.

A few minutes later, both returned, their pistols holstered. "It's completely empty. Some small scout ships are inside, perhaps those belong to the missing geneticist," Captain Jemalensis suggested.

Hammertharmalosis asked the two to begin unloading his cargo while he went inside to try to figure out what had gone wrong for his fellow scientist. Nothing inside seemed damaged and it took him only minutes to get all the machinery back online once more. Next, he called up the various video logs and began to watch them. His fellow scientist had followed all the protocols and was leaving an accurate record for him, Hammertharmalosis thought.

When Thranikansisnestoris had arrived, he discovered a massive prison escape on Dorota, thousands of them. Per protocols, he had to eliminate the mammalian cells there and re-entrap the prisoners. "So far so good," Hammertharmalosis muttered to himself. Slowly the story unfolded. When the two captains finally joined him, grumbling about not signing on to be his workers, Hammertharmalosis explained the situation that his predecessor had encountered. "Massive prison escape," he began.

When he finished explaining what had happened to Dorota, the two captains looked very worried. "It isn't safe here. We need to go to Stage IV Alert. We'll deal with the physical security of this facility and check on the status of our 'guests.' You figure out what happened here after that. They probably killed your scientist friend," Captain Jemalensis both ordered and suggested. The mantis soldiers were more than a little concerned. They were on the ground inside a secure prison filled with millions of undesirables and criminals, while they were only two.

Hammertharmalosis nodded and returned to the video records. He heard the sounds of the four ships being brought inside the complex and the doors closing. He felt safe enough for the moment, plus the images of the captured mammalian cells were on the screen now. Intense pride filled him, for here were his and his ancestor's creations come to life!

Soon, he watched the video results of Version One. "Damn Thranikansisnestoris! He went ahead with the beaks after all! I told him that would not be a good modification. Ah, the female of the species does look good, except for the beak. Yes, I can see feeding and drinking is a monumental problem with those beaks. Yet, from the neck on down, their form does look good. The mammary glands definitely set them apart. See, I told you so, Thranikansisnestoris! Hobble the men and you slow their whole lives down. Perfect."

Later, he listened to the metallic voices from the language translator as the four attempted to explain the problems facing themselves in their new mammalian forms. Now he began to realize that Thranikansisnestoris realized that he had made a terrible mistake with the beaks and he smiled smugly to himself. "Thranikansisnestoris never did wholly listen to me." After listening to all their suggestions, the video then showed him "undoing" the changes. A bit later, he watched the Version Two modifications appear on the four mammalian cells.

Thranikansisnestoris' justifications played. "Ah yes, I see my error with the beaks. Now having had to follow the protocol and nuke Dorota, I must quickly create millions of new mammalian cells. It is fortunate that these four specimens have asked for enhanced sexual stimuli. That I must do anyway to ensure a million new mammalian cells in short order for those from Dorota."

Hammertharmalosis agreed, "Yes, my friend, you had no choice but to do what's needed to generate a million new mammalian cells. No fault there."

The video record continued to play. "Of course, I will not tell them that those changes, the enhanced sexual drives, will only last for a year or so. Cannot have millions more cells without prisoners for them, now can I?" He carefully evaluated their arguments, as did Hammertharmalosis, who came to the same conclusion.

"Yes, the female mammalian is correct. Sudden removal of arms from adult cells will cause irreparable mental harm, likely leading to suicide. We cannot have the females in short supply. That will totally damage and threaten the entire prison," Hammertharmalosis muttered to himself, agreeing with his fellow geneticist's conclusions, though he wondered what the solution could possibly be.

"Brilliant!" he commented as he heard the proposed solution. He watched in fascination as his fellow scientist extracted the images from the female mammalian cell and later returned with prototypes of the various devices. He watched with a smug satisfaction as the two female mammalian cells readily adapted to these devices.

As he looked over Version Two results, he worried about the lack of alterations on the male mammalian cells. "He should not have allowed the males to have virtually no alterations. Oh my no! That is not good. Still, I can see no other action that was done wrong. I wonder what happened to him." He paused to get something to eat and then resumed the video review. Apparently, all was going very well indeed. He saw the four mammalian cells being loading onto the ship and returned to their homes on this run. After that, the screen went dark; this was the last entry in the video log!

"Damn, something must have gone wrong on that last run," he mused, fretting that he still did not know the complete story. Just as he was about to turn the machine off, new images appeared. "What's this? Those are the same mammalian cells, but who are those two?" As he watched, he saw buttons being pressed as if by magic! Words were being spoken, but without the language translator, they were incomprehensible to him. Now he stared at the screen. Slowly, he realized that these mammalian cells were working on an "Undo" process!

Before long, his suspicions were confirmed! Somehow, these mammalian cells had been able to kill his fellow geneticist and had the intelligence to use his machine to fabricate new bacteria, which if used, would undo most of the genetic modifications that Thranikansisnestoris had introduced! Incredible and scary at the same time, if some of these prisoners had this kind of abilities, skills, and knowledge, then a massive prison outbreak could occur at any point it time. Reluctantly, yet fearful for his own safety, he reported these startling findings to his two captains, who were very much concerned, if not outright afraid as well. From this point on, they remained locked securely inside the cavernous fortress high atop the mountain.

Even more startling, the other two alien captains reported to Hammertharmalosis that their installations were either destroyed or uninhabited. The Grey's main outpost in the Appian Way was gone. However, their research facilities at the North Pole and the mantis facility in the middle of the Desert of Desolation were still fully operational, though they had been vacant for a very long period of time. However, they did report that they had fully restocked both with full supplies, just in case they ever needed to return here at some point in the distant future. The doll captain reported similar findings. Both aliens also took their leave of the three mantises, heading back to their home worlds, their mission of dumping off the last of their prisoners finished. They left the prison and its situation to the mantis creatures, wiping their hands of the whole mess.

When Hammertharmalosis finally finished reviewing all the video, the two captains insisted on knowing what he intended to do about the situation. "Oh my. Oh my, this is serious. We knew that modifications needed to be done, just not how serious the situation was here. Now we do. Gentlemen, I will put things to right in short order. We will avoid all the mistakes that Thranikansisnestoris made."

"Yes, but how long will it take?" Captain Jemalensis demanded to know immediately. He was getting more and more nervous about this whole assignment. Still, he was under orders to assist this geneticist. They'd face a court martial if they up and left him now.

"Not long. Oh my. Let's see. First, I must review the modifications and decide upon the ones to make. We must ensure that the mammalian cells do not kill themselves because of the modifications. That alone would guarantee a massive prison break. Oh yes it would. Give me a day to work this out. I believe that I will need your assistance in the implementation, unless you wish to wait here several months while I hatch a bunch of eggs to help me out."

"Yes, yes of course. We will help. Please, let's get this done and head home as soon as possible!" Captain Jemalensis replied. He did not intend to wait six months for eggs to hatch and the hatchlings to grow sufficiently to help with the situation. With escaped prisoners on the loose, both captains were rightly worried. Somehow, these prisoners had killed the other geneticist, perhaps even the other alien wardens!

Hammertharmalosis began his work of designing the new modifications. He felt a bit of freedom, he had no one to countermand his ideas about what modifications to make. Still, he could not help recalling that the mammalian cells would likely commit suicide if the modifications were intolerable. Ideally, all their previous ten centuries of modifications had been done on the unborn — that removed all chances for such traumatic actions. He realized that the female mammalian cell in the video was wise and quite right. If a cell suddenly woke up without their arm appendages upon which they had depended their whole lives, the mental trauma would be quite severe indeed, perhaps even an unrecoverable one. He knew then that the modifications that he was about to make would have to be palpable, at least somewhat.

Not even in question was the starting point, the old Dorota society. Female mammalian cells did not have arm appendages, which forced the male cells to care for them in ways not seen before. That had to be the starting point. Yet, the males also had to undergo a major modification. That had to be the error committed by his predecessor. What else could have caused such a catastrophe? For a time, the "what" remained elusive. He reviewed the hours of video once more. Then, he struck upon it. "Oh my, it was right here before my eyes all the time. Absolutely perfect. That will slow them all down, yet not keep them from making a living. Yes, indeed, perfect. Now what minor touches can I make? What would I like to see in these mammalian cells?" he mused, greatly relieved to have solved the worst of his problems.

Inadvertently, he allowed his own tastes in body forms to enter his grand plan. The mantis did not have separate sexes; each one was capable of generating fertilized eggs at any time they desired. Yet, these mammalian cells had been carefully designed to require a pair to procreate the species, further limiting their survival. That design criteria had been built-in ten centuries ago. He could not help but desire the female form to look quite different from the male of the species. His modifications would enhance just that. He grinned with satisfaction. Now he began to program in the computer his new designs.

This was tedious, delicate work, one that would not permit even the slightest mistake on his part. Indeed, this was the most critical aspect of genetic engineering, as he well knew. Fortunately, the computer and machine were programmed with this in mind. After entering his design criteria, the results were displayed on his video monitor in a rotatable, 3-D format. He reviewed the results carefully. Satisfied, he then began to input the minute details that were needed to modify genetically these mammalian cells. That work took him three tedious days to perform.

Meantime, he sent the two captains out on a counting-survey reconnoitering mission. He needed to know the precise number of mammalian cells and their distribution across Planet X. However, the protocols required that this survey be done from extreme altitude to avoid alerting the prisoners below. He knew that this was the very error that his predecessor had made, flying low and eventually having been detected by the prisoners, who then somehow responded to the perceived threat. That had to be avoided this time. Stealth was mandatory. The two captains were very glad to remain at the most extreme altitude that their instruments would tolerate.

They returned three days later with their computers filled with the raw data counts. "Oh good, good. You have done well," he complimented the two captains. He was in a good mood, having finished the modifications work. The machine was now manufacturing the needed quantities of the aerial born bacteria. "Gentlemen, the bacteria are being prepared. I will tabulate your data and have the computer work out the distribution mechanics. However, we must provide each home with the necessary items for the mammalian cells to survive. I have programmed the manufacturing machine to begin their construction. I need you boys to begin loading the two merchant ships."

"Well, that is good news. How long will it take us to finish this project and head for home?" asked Captain Jemalensis. This was the only question in both captain's minds. They wanted off this prison colony as soon as possible.

"When we begin the release of the bacteria, it will take it three days to work its effects upon the cells. By the time that it is finished, we must also have deposited a set of survival objects for each of them. Don't worry, that's what we have a computer for — to work out the optimum delivery methods."

He saw that this was not sufficient and added, "A week at most and you'll be on your way home. I may decide to stay around a while to make sure that all goes well and to document the results and their effectiveness. We do not want to have to make a return trip here, now do we?" He added that last to get them to agree with him, which they certainly did. He'd long ago learned that to enlist cooperation, one only had to get someone to agree with him a little.

Eagerly, the two headed off to begin loading the two ships. He smiled at how easily he had manipulated the two warriors. "They are not scientists — so easily manipulated," he mused and then set to work correlating the survey tabulations, entering them into the computer before him.

Now that the computer had actual data about the population and its distribution, he could begin the actual calculations. To avoid the low elevation distribution, which he concluded had caused his predecessor's downfall, he programmed a high altitude deployment. Of course, this would require a larger volume of the bacteria, and he allowed an extra day of shelf life to compensate for the greater length of time that it would take to reach the surface of the planet. The computer program then began its work, calculating the needed path of dispersal, the rate of flow, and ultimately the quantity of bacteria that must be made.

That required well over an hour's time to work out and would use all the supplies that he had brought along. He smiled as he realized that he had been right in making the estimates doubled in size. Now the computer had to work out the more difficult chore of object manufacturing and the delivery means. The computer suggested that using both merchant ships, only one full day would be required to encircle the planet with the bacteria. That was reassuring. However, the deployment of the survival items was going to be far more problematical he assumed, and he was right.

Over dinner, he shared the initial projections with his two warriors, hoping for some fresh ideas. "Using both ships, it will take us one day to dispense the bacteria planet-wide. However, assuming that we start out with both ships filled with the items, the computer suggests that it is going to take us almost three weeks to deliver the goods to every location, assuming that one of us stays behind to run the manufacturing machine while the others are making the delivery runs. Even so, half of that time will be wait time, waiting for the fabrication machine to make enough for the next run and then for us to reload the ships. I am open to any suggestions to speed this up."

The handling of cargo runs was not something in which Hammertharmalosis had any education at all. He was, after all, a highly skilled geneticist, not a common laborer. They discussed this unexpected setback for some time. Clearly, the two captains did not want to spend nearly another month here on this back hole, penal colony. Captain Jemalensis suggested, "Say, you are approaching this backwards. What we need to do is execute a standard in-flight reloading."

"Huh?" the confused geneticist muttered.

"We make all the needed items. We take a shipload into geosynchronous orbit and deposit the load there. We station them at key locations. Then, when all the items have been made, we execute the drops. When a ship uses up its supply, it merely tractors in the next load from orbit and continues on its way. We can program the whole operation into the ship's guidance center. In fact, we do not even need to be onboard the ships. It can all be done automatically, just like our army is re-supplied."

"Brilliant, oh my yes! Brilliant. Captain Jemalensis, can I turn this aspect of the mission over to you to program?" Hammertharmalosis could not believe his luck.

Knowing that this would cut weeks off their stay, both captains eagerly volunteered to handle the entire distribution of required items. Already they had both merchant ships fully loaded, and an hour later, they departed with the ships. Once in a stable geosynchronous orbit and at the precise locations dictated by their supply delivery program, the two captains pressed the eject button. Two enormous piles of tightly compacted items floated motionless in space, high above the blue-green world far below them, some twenty-two thousand two hundred twenty-five miles above the sea. Both onboard computers logged the location of the supply depot and activated a locator beacon, just in case.

Five days later, ten resupply depots were in orbit, ready for nearly instantaneous pickup. While Hammertharmalosis loaded his precious bacteria canisters into both ships, his captains finished loading the two ships with the last of the required items. Then, the geneticist transferred the bacteria delivery program to the ships' computers, and finally the captains activated the delivery program into the two computers as well.

"Gentlemen, in the morning, we begin and should be done in five days' time. You can head for home after that and report a job well done!" Hammertharmalosis exclaimed enthusiastically. "I will stay around a while longer, observe the results, and repair the signal beacon, just in case the Supreme Master wishes a return to Planet X."

"None too soon for us," Captain Jemalensis commented. "However, as a matter of security, in case something does go wrong, we cannot afford to have these mammalian cells returning here to this base and using your machine to undo your work."

"Very true. Very true. What are you suggesting?" he asked, fully aware that his predecessor had made this very mistake.

"We will set explosive devices here in the complex. One of us will have to return here in say five days to deactivate them. If we do not return, they detonate, blowing the whole complex to bits. The prisoners must not be allowed any means of escape."

"I like that. Please see to it, but you will have to show me how to deactivate it."

"Of course."

On October 21, 823, the two merchant ships left the complex at Chichulain, rising rapidly to a high altitude. One headed to the southern polar area, while the other headed to the northern polar zone. Once in position, the gas valves opened and the two ships began spiraling orbits around Tarra; the area covered by each spiral overlapped the previous one slightly, ensuring a uniform coverage of the surface far below. Because many sailing ships were at sea, even the oceans had to be covered. It was simpler just to lay down a uniform covering over the planet's surface than to attempt to hit only the locations in which the mammalian cells lived or were currently located, as with the ships at sea.

On October 22, the three mantises sat in the comfort of the cavern complex, monitoring the two merchant ships that had now begun the execution of the required-items delivery program. All on automatic, the three had little to do but to ensure the program worked as anticipated. All three relaxed. The prison outbreak was about to be totally contained, nothing could go wrong this time, nothing at all. Nothing had been left to chance this time. He'd avoided all the problems his predecessor had faced.

Chapter 2 Discovery and Counteractions

The evening of October 22, 823 began with all round celebrations for four young couples. "Yes, it's official. I'm pregnant," I announced to everyone as our large group gathered around the table for supper. Marco, my husband, leaned over me and kissed my head, a proud father to be. Squeals of joy erupted around me.

I guess I should explain a little. My name is Bethany Elizabet Bartiana Angela, and I'm now sixteen. I love long hair and mine now reaches the small of my back, jet-black, straight, and thick. My brown eyes have begun to lighten a little. I'm still growing and am now five-eleven, almost as tall as my husband is — Marco Angela, who is also sixteen and who is six-one now, a handsome man — well, I think so anyway. He has shoulder length brown hair that is starting to have a natural wave in it, and his eyes match his hair. Marco is a Protector and has been taking good care of me. I've come to depend heavily upon him during the last two years.

We live here in our large mansion or estate with our parents and siblings. My folks are Tito and Sofia Bartiana. Dad's thirty-three and mom's a year younger. I get my hair from dad, whose is as black as mine is, plus his eyes match his hair, and he's also quite tall as well. Dad is a foreman at Velona Steel, a company that makes steel in vast quantities. Sofia has wavy, shoulder length black hair and dark brown eyes. I get my eyes from her, she claims. She, too, is quite tall and is a musician, playing the violin in the All Velona Orchestra. She also sings, adding her alto voice to the Sunday church choir. We all attend the Church of the Three Holy Roses.

My oldest brother is Sergio, who is tall and fit at eighteen. He's been made Chief Detective Inspector for Velona. He has wavy black hair and is growing a moustache, though we tease him about it.

My youngest brother, Giovanni is also tall and seventeen now. He has let his black hair grow longer than Sergio's and it touches his shoulders, barely. Giovanni is not growing a moustache. Yes, Giovanni is still one of our two resident engineers, having been partially responsible for the incredible explosion of inventions during the last forty years, including his last life as Enyo, the inventor. He has finally made the commitment to carry on his work with the company he co-founded, the DAE Enterprises, which is responsible for innumerable incredible inventions.

I come next, at sixteen. My younger sister, Lucianna, is fifteen, and has shoulder length, wavy black hair. In her last lifetime, she was Arsenio, the inventor who helped Enyo or Giovanni, found the DEA Enterprises. Both Giovanni and Lucianna often tease each other about having somehow gotten each other's bodies this time around. Like Giovanni, Lucianna has resumed her position at DAE Enterprises, continuing her inventor career.

Marco's parents are Sandro and Marta Angela. Sandro is thirty-two and very blonde! His hair is nearly yellow and falls to his shoulders. His eyes are a rich blue and he is an electrician by trade. His wife Marta is a year younger and has lovely light brown hair and matching eyes. I think that she is even prettier than my mom, Sofia. Marta is the Head Librarian at the Laird Library of Velona having taken over the position from her mother, Natalie, who retired several years ago.

Their oldest is Lisa, who is now eighteen and has married my brother, Sergio. Last lifetime, these two were inseparable and are continuing their close relationship this life as well. Lisa is blonde like her dad and has her mother's eyes, light brown. She keeps her hair only shoulder length so that it does not interfere with her fighting skills. Yes, she is still the Protector of Sergio, as strange as this seems.

Marco comes next and then come their twins, Evelina and Valerio at sixteen. Evelina (who used to be my Renzo in previous lifetimes) is only five-eight, with lovely, straight blonde hair, as long as mine is actually. She has light blue eyes and keeps telling us that this lifetime, she is supposed to get it right, meaning learning how to be a woman properly, since last life, when she, as Dita, and I were married, we didn't have it right. Eve has married my brother Giovanni.

Her twin brother Valerio has short blonde hair and light blue eyes too, just like her. He used to be Len or Ilenakova, and is still a Protector as well. Both he and Renzo each took one of the two baby bodies when they were born. We are all very thankful that they did not fight each other for the male baby. Evelina accepted the fact that she would have to be a she this lifetime. Valerio married my young sister Lucianna.

All four of we young women are now pregnant and are expecting sometime during next June. I'm guessing that I'll be the last one to deliver a new bundle of joy in June. "See, I told you to keep at it," my sister Lucianna teased me. She'd been the first to discover that she was pregnant, announcing it about two weeks ago.

"I'm just glad that we've all got our arms back," I replied.

"No kidding!" exclaimed Eve. "Taking care of a baby is damnably hard without them."

"I just cannot imagine raising a family when you don't have arms," mom added. "Honestly, you four have been a handful!"

Marta chuckled and added, "You can say that again!" We kids all laughed.

We'd just returned recently from our trip to Chichulain, where we managed to fabricate a genetic cure to the "plague" which the mantis creature Nestor had dumped on our country, Velona, along with nineteen other nearby countries. He'd captured us and experimented on the four of us, that is, Marco, Eve, Giovanni, and myself. Fortunately, we'd been able to convince the mantis Nestor to alter his genetic modifications on all humans.

His Version One had been intolerable. We convinced him of that. Later, when he'd unleashed his revised genetic mutation bacteria upon us, we women all lost our arms, had our waists shrunk to around eighteen inches, had permanent makeup, and hypersensitive, long dangling ear lobes. The fellows only had comparable ear lobes. Yet we all had our body's sexual stimulus greatly enhanced so that there would be millions of new baby bodies created this year for the millions of spiritual beings whose bodies were vaporized when Nestor annihilated the island nation of Dorota.

We had managed to stop Nestor from spreading his bacteria across all of Tarra, containing it to the nineteen countries plus part of the huge country of Tashien. Later, we discovered Nestor had taken a female body in Tashien. With her help, we managed to operate the complex mantis machinery at their installation at Chichulain. She created a new bacteria mutation, which caused women's bodies to regrow their arms. As of today, we believe that nearly all women in the infected lands have had the cure. If not, the cure was on its way to them.

Life had finally returned to normal, though hardly anyone has yet redone their kitchens or doors. By that I mean when we lost our arms, Nestor provided replacement kitchens, which were low to the ground so that we women could cook using our feet. I think that nearly every woman was still a bit edgy about having the low kitchens removed, just in case our new-grown arms somehow failed. We'd all undergone a traumatic situation over a year ago, waking up one morning to find our bodies armless.

Yet, adaption had been the name of the game. I aided nearly all the women who were affected by publishing a book of tips on how to accomplish the things of life that we used to be able to do. Even today, I was still receiving piles of thank you letters in the daily post. During the past two weeks, I got the many articles compiled into a four hundred page book format. Even though the crisis was over now, I still intended to have it published. Further, I was working on a translation into the Demokritos language, for there were many unfortunate women in that far southern country who had lost their arms for various other reasons. I felt that it would give them some hope, if they wanted to change their life style from that of a Holy Woman of the Eighth Degree.

Lisa asked, "Bethany, have you and Marco picked out names yet? Sergio and I are going to call ours either Alessa Marta or Bartolo Sandro." Her parents smiled, delighted that their first grandson or daughter would share their names.

I giggled and replied, "Er, no, not yet. Maybe Bianca Sofia or Mario Tito?" Marco chuckled.

"But won't you get confused, Marco, if Bethany calls out Bianca?" asked Lucianna. "I mean that was your name last life, Bianca. I think that'd be confusing, I mean, if I called my son Arsenio. I wouldn't know if Valerio was calling me or him." She was so serious that we all laughed heartily; her face flushed. Me, I was very content with just living life now; all the horrors and mountainous stress of the last eighteen months was gone. If all of us women losing our arms was not bad enough, we had to endure it all while nearly starving to death. The dust cloud from the destruction of Dorota had obscured the sun, wiping out all crops for a half year. Only a desperate struggle to obtain food supplies from other unaffected countries had managed to keep us all alive. Now the current fall harvest had been the greatest in the history of the eight Sea Princes as well as the ten kingdoms of the Greenway. We had food supplies filling every available storage space.

In fact, Stefano West Po, our monarch, had to convert a dozen warehouses to the storing of our excess produce. Lucianna explained that the miraculous super-growth of all plants was caused by all the falling dust from Dorota. She called it a super plant growth supplement and not to expect such enormous yields in future years.

"I'm ready for desert, chocolate pie!" Eve declared, having eaten her meal rapidly just to get to the pie. Like me, she was a "chocaholic." None of the rest of us was even close to being ready for desert. "Hey, I'm a pregnant woman. I get to eat what I want now, since I am eating for two."

"Bet you don't share it with your baby," Lucianna teased her and we all laughed again. Eve looked miffed at first, but then realized the truth of her jest.

"Well, that's true. Maybe he or she won't like chocolate. Do you suppose?" Eve teased her back, adding to our supper's mirth. Oh, just to enjoy such simple banter felt good to me. I was only now realizing just how much stress I had been under these past eighteen months more or less. So were the others for that matter. Life's simple pleasures seemed huge to us all now.

Eve, in an attempt to hurry us all along towards desert, began to carry the dirty dishes back into the kitchen. She walked past the large, stacked pile of the dozens of yokes that we women had had to use just to be able to carry anything when only weeks ago we had no arms. She eyed them and felt intensely relieved that she did not have to use them any longer. I spied her glancing at them and I knew what she was thinking as well. I felt the same way.

Just to tease Eve all the more, Giovanni purposely ate slower than normal, attempting to drag it out as long as possible. Finally, her hands on her hips, Eve declared, "Giovanni! If you don't speed up right now, you get to sleep on the floor!" We all roared with laughter, all the more so when he made super-exaggerated eating motions as if hurrying up and yet going no faster than before.

Finally, Eve brought in the two chocolate pies that she had baked this afternoon, one in each hand. She sat one in front of mom and the other before herself. Carefully, she quartered the pie and then quartered it a second time, before scooping out two pieces for herself. Once more we chuckled and she stuck out her tongue at us, before diving into the rich brown desert, topped with whipped cream. "Heavenly," she mumbled with a very full mouth, causing us all to chuckle again.

Just then and without warning, three images appeared just to the right of our large dining room table. The Guardian, Linda, and Chaucer began to materialize their forms before us. Okay, I forgot, now they were calling themselves Macario, Raffaella, and Lucio Ines, leaders of their newly formed Church of God. Quickly, they made their bodies quite solid, knowing that we all related to real flesh and bone bodies and not to ghostly images. Yes, these three were quite powerful spiritual beings now.

"Excuse us, Bethany, everyone. Sorry about not giving you advanced warning. This is an emergency situation," Macario or the Guardian said quite seriously. Suddenly, I felt sick at my stomach, and it wasn't morning sickness or from having eaten too much chocolate pie! In all these centuries that I'd known him, he'd never made an appearance quite like this before.

I'm afraid that I replied rather foolishly, "Want some chocolate pie?" As the words came out, I immediately wished that I'd not said anything.

Marco came to my rescue, adding swiftly, "Drag up a chair and tell us the bad news, Macario. We can take it; we're all sitting down." His slight jest broke the ice. Macario actually grinned.

To our amazement, three chairs appeared before us and the three sat down in unison. Raffaella actually broke into a small chuckle. Then, the grin vanished from Macario's face, almost as suddenly as it had come.

"I'm afraid that I've terrible news, perhaps the worst news that I have ever been called upon to deliver in my whole existence," Macario began. I realized that he was trying to soften the blow that was about to come. My mind raced with possibilities, but Eve beat me to it.

"It's the mantis, isn't it?" Eve blurted out, sending a small dab of her chocolate pie flying onto her plate by accident. She shouldn't talk with her mouth so full, but no one was complaining.

"Yes, Eve, you are dead on. The mantises are back. Only this time, they are being cagier than before, far more careful. Let me explain more fully," Macario said softly. "We've been working on therapy sessions with some new members of our Church of God. We each had our patient moved out of their bodies, and we were drilling them on moving from place to place here on Tarra."

"And working on their perceptions," Raffaella added. She obviously thought that this was a significant detail that we needed to know.

He continued, "Actually, our patients were the first to point out the bacteria slowly descending upon all of Tarra. 'What is all this confetti falling around us?' my person asked me. That's when we all began to see the millions of tiny bacteria falling like an invisible rain down upon the entire planet. Here, I will Mind Link you all to me and show you what we saw earlier today." I felt the gentle touch as his mind overlaid mine, and I could not help but remember the loving times we'd shared centuries ago when we first met. He was then Jes Amir, the Great Messiah, and I, his wife.

We all saw our world from a vantage point miles above the surface. All around us, tiny glowing particles were raining down from some location far higher in the sky. At first, I thought it looked more like some cloud of golden glitter, but realized that was the sunlight reflecting off the tiny bacteria.

He continued, "Obviously, this time, the mantis released the bacteria from a very high altitude, avoiding detection from all of us here on the surface. At once, we three and several others went in search of the cigar shaped mantis spacecraft, but found none. Raffaella took a different approach. She worked out the path that was used to make the bacteria delivery, based upon the falling bacteria and such. She determined that two ships had been used and that they had woven a spiral path, beginning at both polar areas of Tarra, ending near the equator."

Raffaella continued, "Yes, my guess is that they began at the poles at least thirty-six hours ago and met at the equatorial zone some twelve hours ago — their payload delivered to all of Tarra." I felt a little sicker as I heard her conclusion, because it meant they had gotten to the whole planet this time.

Macario continued, "We continued our search today and we finally located the two ships, Bethany. They are probably identical to the one that Nestor used. At this time, they are some ten thousand miles above the surface, moving in slow, spiral orbits down from either polar area, as if retracing their previous routes. We observed them for quite some time, before we took additional actions."

Raffaella added, "I was the first to spot what the ships were doing. They are in the process of delivering another set of items, just as Nestor did before. The ships are depositing much the same things as before, kitchen items, yokes, and even strange looking shoes this time. As far as I can tell, every home is getting some of these items." We all knew just what this implied!

"After her discovery," Macario continued, "I decided to slip into one of the ships and confront the mantis. To my amazement, Bethany, the ship was entirely devoid of anyone! No mantis, no person, no being. I believe that the ships are somehow being controlled automatically."

She went on, "Our only conclusion is that the two ships are being somehow remotely controlled by the mantis and are making the necessary deliveries of the supplies, which will allow all people to potentially survive the coming genetic mutations. Hence, we've decided not to interfere just yet. If another mutation is coming, at least the mantises are somehow following the example that you helped Nestor set: provide items necessary for survival. Just how did these new mantises know that you and your friends worked this out with Nestor? Somehow, they must have discovered what you folks and Nestor had done, though I don't have any idea how they could have learned that."

"It bothered me so much that I went over to Tashien and checked up on Lin Zu. She's perfectly happily married and enjoying her life. I could detect no signs that the mantis had somehow found her and interrogated her about what she had done as Nestor."

For the first time, Lucio, that is Chaucer, spoke up. "While she was off doing that, I continued to monitor the two ships — well, one of them that is. I made an interesting discovery. After the ship had apparently unloaded all its cargo of household items, it made for a higher elevation location, not too far from where it had dropped off its last set of items. To my amazement, there floating in space was a huge cargo load of these items, all densely packed together. As I watched, the ship tractor-beamed the load into its hold and then dove back down to continue its methodical transport of sets of items to locations far below on Tarra. What an incredible feat of logistical supply, just incredible, all on automatic. Incredible. Anyway, I began to scout around and I discovered several more of these orbiting supply depots located further south of the one that the ship had just picked up. The only conclusion reachable is that the ships are programmed to deposit the items to everyone on Tarra in a timely, uniform manner."

Macario picked up the tale from here, "Based on all this, we've decided that the best course is to allow the ships to complete their task. If the mantis is planning some hideous genetic modifications on us all once more, we believe it best to allow them to deliver what they believe to be survival goods to all the humans on Tarra, before we take decisive action."

I finally spoke up, though I had to clear my throat first. "I agree. If the bacteria are now upon us all, then we'd best make sure that we get whatever things the mantis believe that we need to survive this. But where are the mantises now? How many of them are there?"

"We believe the most likely place would be Chichulain, although we don't know its location precisely. That's your ball game, so to speak," he replied. "We decided that we best not confront them until this delivery process is finished. If we attack them, we might somehow upset the delivery of the critical items, which might lead to the deaths of millions of people who will need them to be able to survive," Macario added his cautionary note.

"Yet, we have not been idle. We know that Tarra is a dumping ground for unwanted spiritual beings from three alien civilizations. Hence, the three of us also went looking for the possibility of 'new arrivals.' Good thing that we did. Bethany, at least another hundred thousand spiritual beings have been dumped onto Tarra! My worst fears have come true. All three alien races are back again!"

My mouth opened wide, but I couldn't think of any appropriate words to say. Eve did, "Damn them to hell!" she exclaimed. "Let me at them! I'll wring their necks!"

Macario smiled and continued, "I found that the doll creatures had dumped a load of 'frozen' beings into the waters east of Tashien. I believe that they use saucer shaped spacecraft and have visited their caves where the electronic devices were housed. However, as far as I can tell, none of the suppressive electronic devices have been repaired or activated. Perhaps they just visited there to see the current situation. I can find no trace of them now."

"I spotted a dump of 'frozen' beings in the eastern Med Sea," Raffaella added. "I checked around and discovered a couple of shepherds in the Langdoc region who were talking about having seen a strange flying ship over the Appian Way, visiting perhaps their old base there, which was destroyed centuries ago. Knowing that they also had bases in the Desert of Desolation and at the North Pole, I checked on those as well. Melted snow up north tells me that one of the Grey Creature's ships has definitely landed there within the past week or so. However, no one is at either location, they remain deserted."

"I spotted another batch of 'frozen' spiritual beings in the western Med Sea just off Velona," Lucio added. "It seems that all three alien races have just deposited more of their undesirables onto Tarra."

Lucianna spoke up, "Boy, I hope that they sent along some more engineers. We could use more fresh ideas. You know that I am about to make some machines that can fly, don't you?" Only Lucianna could find something positive in this incredible disaster befalling us."

"Well, maybe they left us some more artisans," mom added, taking a hint from her youngest daughter. "Lord knows that we could use more musicians, painters, and writers."

Macario grinned again. "Yes, we may well have some benefits from this, Sofia. We may well."

"So when do we obliterate them?" Eve broke in, ready to go into action immediately. She was quite annoyed that the mantises were back once more, though she was not actually angry. I'll give her that. Eve was one who never backed down from a fight, not ever, if she could help it.

"Patience, Eve. You will get your chance soon," he replied. "As we speak, I am organizing an attack force. In our group, we have sixteen very able spiritual beings. I came here tonight to also ask several of you to join us when we go after them."

"Absolutely! Just say when, and I am ready!" Eve replied.

"Eve, I would not think of going off to battle without you." She beamed and I had to smile at her enthusiasm. "Bethany, we'd like you to come as well. The rest of you are going to be most desperately needed here in Velona. I believe that eighteen of us ought to be able to wipe out these aliens. However, I would like to try to find out as much information about their current and future plans as possible, before we annihilate them, Eve."

"Okay, so when do we leave?" she asked eagerly, forgetting all about the remnants of the pie sitting before her plate.

"We're going to go there soon and spy on them," he replied.

"Hold on a second," Giovanni spoke up for the first time. "One thing that I have learned about the mantis is that they rely heavily upon electronics. We've seen that they have some kind of electronic sensors, which can detect spiritual beings when we touch their machines. Remember Eve, Bethany? When you touched Nestor's ship, he was alerted to your presence and blasted you both with some white energy beams, knocking you both unconscious."

"Wise point, Giovanni. I believe that I can slip into their cavern complex without activating their sensors. I will take that risk upon myself. If I fail and get blasted again, then Raffaella can take over the mission for me."

"But Eve and I know the inside layout, Macario. You don't," I protested slightly.

"I thought about that Bethany. I will be Mind Linked with you when I make the attempt. Only you must promise me that if we get detected, you will break the link before you get zapped as well." I swore that I would, though I wondered if I could react quickly enough to avoid getting myself in trouble again.

"So when do we go?" Eve asked eager to get into action once more.

He smiled, "Patience, Eve. Will an hour be sufficient for you?" She flashed him a grin.

"While we are gone, I would like the rest of you to alert all the other countries about the impending doom. Prepare them as much as possible for what's coming. As we find out more about what the mantises have in store for us, we will relay it to you here."

"But do we know what the mutations will be like this time?" asked Marco. Indeed, that was the key thought that most all of us were thinking. God, I hoped it would not be Nestor's original Version One formula. Life would be nearly unlivable if we were all spouting those enormous rounded beaks nearly a foot in diameter.

"We can make an educated guess, based upon the items being deposited in people's homes up north," Raffaella suggested. "Some of us could go there and take a peek before we head off to Chichulain. Eve, Bethany, care to join me? You know better than we what the items might suggest in the way of genetic body modifications."

Lucianna piped up, "Hey, it's a good thing that I've gotten my LD radio systems operational. Macario, do you realize that I can now talk directly with the ten kings of Greenway, the other monarch of the Sea Princes, Pian in Shansee, and even the Emperor down in Demokritos? We can let them all know about this attack in no time at all! Now if only I had my flying machines operational," she sighed, fretting that she'd been too idle this past year! Inventors! Honestly.

"Well done, Lucianna. Yes, the survival of the world may well hinge on how fast communications can be relayed to other countries," Macario complimented her. "While Raffaella, Eve, and Bethany are off examining the items, let's work out how we may best communicate this horrible news to the other world leaders."

Eve and I headed to the living room, plopping our bodies onto one of the sofas, where they would be safe while we headed off with Raffaella. Marco came to sit with us, watching over our bodies while we were away from them. Shortly, she and I moved out of our bodies, joining Raffaella, who allowed her mocked up body form to dissolve. We three headed off up north.

Meanwhile around the table, Giovanni suggested, "Well, we still have probably enough of our curing bacteria left to re-grow all the women's arms in the Greenway, the Sea Princes, and southern Tashien — that is, if this mutation causes them to wither away again. We made plenty of extra bacteria, just in case."

"That was wise of you. Yet this time it is planet-wide. Could you possibly make more of the bacteria?" Macario asked.

"Well, we still have Lin Zu around. I'm sure that we could ask her to help again. Eve is a master at punching in those weird buttons on the mantis machinery in Chichulain," he declared hopefully.

"Ah, excellent. Maybe we can somehow divert the brunt of this attack upon us all," he replied.

Mom spoke up, "You know, in the meantime, if this mutation causes we women to lose our arms again, we ought to get Bethany's little book of hints broadly published and into the hands of every woman on Tarra."

"Mom, they won't have hands," Lucianna pointed out.

"Dear, you know what I mean," Sofia scolded her daughter. "We found her suggestions absolutely lifesaving." They chatted about this for a while and Macario decided that if the bacteria were going to cause women to lose their arms again, he'd see that this was somehow done.

Although it was nighttime, Eve and I could tell that we were flying over the Greenway. Forests dotted the rolling farm fields as we headed northward. After a while, I spotted a dark mass ahead of us — the mountains — and realized that we must be in the very northern portion of the Greenway, perhaps the Karka Kingdom. At last, Raffaella took us down towards an isolated farmstead. We could see a dim light coming from some windows.

Following her lead, we moved right on through the walls and into the rural home. I know that I felt like a spy, intruding into some family's private life. I sincerely hoped that we would not be detected or that we would not intrude upon some very private moments of this family. Fortunately, we didn't.

A middle aged farmer and his wife were examining in detail the pile of objects, which had suddenly materialized in their front room earlier this day. Their older children were there as well. I guessed that four extended families lived here. I spotted five youngsters as well as the adults. My heart sank as I saw them examining the pile of things.

"Why are we getting another kitchen, mom?" one younger woman asked. "We already have one, yokes too. Aren't we all cured of the plague now? All of our arms are back, just like they said they would be."

"Rachel, I don't understand this either. Your father certainly made us far better yokes than these, though. I wonder where all this stuff came from?"

Her husband asked, "Didn't you see it all coming? I was out in the fields, but I didn't see any space ships flying overhead, like the last time. I didn't hear a thing either."

"No, John, I heard nothing either. I just walked in here and there it all was. Do you suppose that we are being attacked again?" her face showed heavy lines of fear.

"Betsy, I just don't know what to make of it, but I will keep our long guns loaded, just in case these aliens show up again. We can always make use of the new kitchen pots and pans, though I am not sure what we can do with all the kitchen sinks and shelves. I suppose I can find some use for them."

"Papa, you can use them in the house that you are building for Pete and me," Rachel spoke up. He grinned.

"Dear, these shoes. At least I think that these are shoes. I've never seen anything like them. Who could possibly wear such things?" his wife asked.

We'd seen enough and Raffaella motioned for us to leave. *Seen enough?* she asked, mentally. We had. We decided that we were now back home with our bodies and so we were. Amazing what skills and abilities a spiritual being actually has.

"Ah, back so soon?" Marco said as Eve's and my body reacted as we latched onto our heads once more.

My body instantly reflected my paled mood. He knew what I was going to say before I said it, as Raffaella manufactured a physical body near us. "Yes, they are getting kitchens made for armless women once more. Just like before, yokes and all that," I replied.

"What do you make of the shoes?" asked Eve. None of us had an answer for that, which didn't concern us anywhere near as much as the fact that this planet-wide mutation was going to be far worse than before. I expected that all women on Tarra would be affected this time, and there was nothing I could do to prevent it this time. It was already beginning, though the severity would likely hit them in the morning.

"We have to make more counter-bacteria," I replied, not answering her question. "Come on; let's go tell the others the dismal news."

I don't think that any of them were particularly surprised with our news, not given the fact that these were mantises. Their track record on Tarra was obvious to all of us in the room. Interestingly enough, I found that they had already contacted Stefano West Po, our monarch and close friend. He'd dashed over to our place at 42 Hampton Way. As we returned with our observations, Giovanni had finished briefing him on the situation. I could tell that he was very much impressed with Lucio and Macario.

"Damn, not again," Stefano cursed. "Any chance we can make more of your special anti-bacteria this time?" he asked looking at Eve and me.

I shrugged. "We can get Lin Zu to help us. Still, it will take us time, assuming the mantis leave enough of the stuff from which to make more bacteria. It took us nearly a year to get there, make it, and get back last time. Somehow, all the women of Tarra are going to have to make do until we do." Stefano looked incredibly glum.

"Damn, damn, damn," his anger burst out. "We can't get a single real break from these damnable aliens, can we? I guess that I'd better put out another countrywide alert again." We nodded. "Do I dare suggest that it might only be temporary this time? I mean if you women lose your arms again, the plan is to make new bacteria to counter it?" His eyes pleaded with us and me in particular.

"You know that we'll do all that we can to undo this coming mess, Stefano, but," my voice trailed off. I didn't want to say that we might not be able to counter it this time. My eyes caught my mother's. How could she live if she once again couldn't play her violin?

To my surprise, Macario answered him. "Stefano, that would be prudent. We do not as yet know the extent of their plans or whether we can counter the damage. It would not do to get everyone's hopes up only to dash them. Emotions will be raw as it is. However, Stefano, this time, you have the Church of God and us behind all of you. We will come through this bout of adversity. I give you my word on that." Coming from the Guardian, Stefano felt encouraged, and a little hope returned to him.

He then said, "Eve, Bethany, the others are ready. Shall we go check out Chichulain now?"

Since we had no idea how long we would be away from our bodies, Eve and I headed to our bedrooms. Eve suggested, "I think we ought to get into simple nightgowns. That will make it easier for Marco and Giovanni to look after our bodies while we're gone." I agreed with her. If we were only gone a few hours, that was one thing. If we were gone for days, Marco would have his hands full with taking care of my resting body. A few minutes later, she and I sailed out of our bodies and joined Macario, Raffaella, and Lucio. Shortly we five sailed up and out of our mansion, rising above our beloved Velona.

There I spotted another fifteen spiritual beings, some of whom I recognized, hovering awaiting us. We didn't actually communicate, but headed off towards Chichulain en mass, with Eve and me leading the way. We floated out over the huge ocean heading due southwest of Velona. I was in a hurry and set a very rapid pace. Before too long, we spotted the distant coastline of the western continent, which spanned both hemispheres of Tarra. The jungles of Wanakan lay north of us, as we headed across the vast unexplored interior of that continent. Far down at the southern tip was the country of the amazon women, Konstantin, where the women routinely amputated their men's arms, treating them as cattle, in a sort of perverse switch of the mantis experiments. I wondered how their society would fare if the women there lost their arms this time. I made a note to check on that aspect later on.

Around one in the morning, Eve and I spotted the cavern complex high atop the rugged mountains that lined the western edge of the central portion of the continent. There below us was the recessed arena with the stone heads of the previous generations of our human bodies, a shrine to the glories of the mantis genetic experiments.

Caution. We do not want to activate any of their warning devices, Macario sent to us all. *I have had some prior experiences with such. They activate when they sense the energy flows that we put out. If by accident we do trigger one or more of their alert devices, I want everyone to scatter to the four winds as fast as possible. We'll regroup later. Under no circumstances are any of you to stick around. I don't want to have to fish you out of the ocean as a frozen cube.*

I for one didn't relish being blasted unconscious again and readily agreed. He continued, *Right now, their two cargo ships are in the preprogrammed process of delivering the needed items to all homes on Tarra. We don't want to interrupt that. Rather, we need information. What are their ultimate plans for us — that sort of data are key? We must know before we act. I will be going inside by myself, but I have changed my mind and have decided that I will take Bethany with me. I will Mind Link with her so that she can show me the way and relay what I learn back to the rest of you. Eve, you link to her and then to the others here.*

One slight problem, Macario. We don't speak their language. Before, Nester always had some kind of translation devices on our heads so that we could communicate, I explained, worried that I had not thought of this before now. How could he possibly understand anything that the mantis might say — anything that he might overhear?

Leave that to me. I have my ways. I felt the Guardian's touch, as if he were giving me one of those smiling teases. *Show me the layout just inside those doors, please.* I did as he asked.

One moment, Macario was floating beside me and the next instant he had positioned both of us immediately inside the massive doors, through which their space ships had entered. We saw two smaller ships, silvery and sleek, bristling with what could only be gun turrets — fighter craft of some sort. A dim light illuminated the vast space. To his far right was the fabrication machine, which had made all the items that Nestor had given to us, such as the kitchens and yokes. The cavernous room seemed completely deserted.

Slowly, we made our way towards the heart of the complex, following my guidance. Before long, he spotted two mantises sleeping in one room. Then, near a view screen sat a third. He was monitoring the two cargo ships' progress, represented by two small blips on his 3-D screen, which showed Tarra as a blue-green globe.

We then continued moving around the complex. Intuitively, I knew that he wanted to know first how many mantises we were up against. He took his time and was very cautious, yet no further of these fifty-foot long mantis creatures appeared. We were facing three this time, not just one, but the three were adults. Nester had hatched a batch of offspring, but those children were very easy to exterminate. Strange choice of words, but at the time, that's how I felt — bugs to be exterminated.

Satisfied that there were only three of them, we moved back to the one staring at the monitor. I sensed Macario gently touching the mind of the mantis. However, the information he was able to see, that is the mental images of the creature, yielded nothing useful. Now we waited.

Suddenly, I had an idea. Those four metal headbands, which handled the interspecies communications when we were held prisoners here, were still lying on a workbench or perhaps those were some additional ones. I had him move back to that area, near the prison cell rooms in which we had been locked up. There were four of the devices. I noticed now that one had a tiny green light emitting spot on it, while the others had a tiny red light emitting spot. Guessing that green suggested the device had somehow been left turned on, I sent to him, *Bring the one with the green light into the room where the mantis is watching the screen. Hide it in some out of the way spot. I think that it is on and will be translating their language when they speak.*

Brilliant! He followed my suggestion. Soon, he positioned the device beneath some rubbish in one corner of the large room. We both extended a faint communication line to the headband. Now we had to wait until the others rose and conversations ensued.

Great idea! Eve sent to me. However, in doing so, she put a little too much energy into her communication line with me. Suddenly, an alarm triggered on the master console. However, luck was on our side! While the mantis reacted fearfully, jumping up and staring at the alarm, it suddenly ceased making its loud noise. Eve had instantly dropped her communication line with me. That was a narrow escape. A bit later, she quietly sneaked her communication line back to me once more, though she didn't dare send me an "I'm sorry."

Hours passed. At dawn, the other two rose and joined the one at the console. Now I could see that these two must be fighter types. Both were well armed with gun-like things strapped to their sides. That meant the one at the console must be the geneticist. We waited and began to listen in on their conversation. The translation unit was working perfectly.

"Twenty percent done. All is going perfectly, Captain Jemalensis. Tremendous idea of yours. Brilliant."

One of the fighters replied, "Of course Hammertharmalosis. Now does this mean that we can leave for home in four more days?"

"Oh yes, yes. Yes, you may. Since all is going so well, I don't see why you both cannot leave now. I can take it from here. Today, the entire population of mammalian prison cells will have been infected with my mutation bacteria and be displaying the beginning results. Unfortunately, those living near the equator will have undergone the complete mutation process before the ships deposit their necessary survival items. But that can't be helped. They won't die in one day's time."

Both fighters looked pleased, but Jemalensis spoke up, "As much as we'd like nothing better to do than go home, we are under orders to stay here until the mutation cycle is completed. Then, we can leave. Will you be coming back with us then?"

"I ought to stick around a little longer and verify all is going according to plan. After all, it is possible that I have made an error and will need to correct it," the one called Hammertharmalosis replied. "After all, I am the very last of the geneticists of our world. If I am gone, then there is no one else who knows anything about any of these creations. I must stay and fully document it — science and all that."

"Why? You know the Supreme Master has said that this would be the last trip here. We've sent the last of our undesirables. No more will be coming here. Even the Greys and the plasticines have made this their last trip here to the penal colony. We are all done and out of here. Why are you bothering with it?" asked Captain Jemalensis. "What's the point? The prisoners are in their cells, and with your modifications, they will stay that way. So why bother? Why waste your time? The project here on Planet X is finished, done, complete."

"Oh my. Dear fellow, science. Science. I am the last of our geneticists. We have learned much during the last millennia. Who knows, perhaps a century from now the Supreme Master will have need for our services again. I must make sure that all the data are properly catalogued so that we do not repeat the mistakes of the past. After all, look what it cost poor Thranikansisnestoris. No, we must have all the data from all our experiments properly logged for future research. We certainly do not want to have to start over again, now do we?"

With a resigned sigh, Captain Jemalensis said, "So be it. Have it your way. Still, we have to wait until the ships finish their runs. Four days it is. God, I can't wait until this menial task is done!"

"Well, take over for me. I am falling asleep on my perch. Say, you might check out that proximity alarm. It went off briefly during the night. Only beeped for about a second is all. Something may be wrong with it," the geneticist said. He walked away, heading into the same room in which the other two had been sleeping.

"Damn fool of a scientist! Those proximity alarms *only* go off if there is a free spiritual being around! I don't care if it was even for a second. Restorislomas, we must have some company nearby. Take the pulse gun and the hand-held alarm and search the cavern complex."

The other mantis radiated fear, no doubt of that! "Why don't you do it?"

"I'm monitoring the ships. Don't tell me you are afraid of some stupid prisoners, Restorislomas," he invalidated his fellow fighter. Yet, I could sense that he too was fearful.

"But they don't have bodies," he protested.

"Of course not. That's why we have the pulse guns. One zap and they are out like a light."

"Well, maybe we should just give a pulse cavern-wide first? Then, any of the prisoners who might be inside will be zapped. Perhaps I should do it outside too, just in case."

"Scared of your own shadow, eh? Well, go ahead. You don't need my permission to do it. Besides, you never can tell with these prisoners. After all, we're here because they are escaping their cells," Captain Jemalensis suggested.

Obviously, both mantises were afraid of us, which I found rather shocking. However, Macario instantly took us outside the cavern, and had all his group appear down at the seacoast. *Sorry about sounding the alarm,* Eve sent as our large group arrived on the sandy beach far below the mountain top.

No problem. We've learned that these two mantis fighters are terrified of us, Macario relayed. He also went over again what we had heard thus far, which we all found most interesting indeed. Perhaps once these mantises were eliminated, there would be no further threats to our world and us humans. I found that encouraging, if only we could find a way out of the mess that the mantis geneticist was making for us now.

A blinding flash of whitish light came from the mountaintop, not visible to human eyes, but highly visible to us. Had we been up there, I know that I would have been knocked unconscious once again. I began to wonder what kind of energy these creatures were using that made me so susceptible to being knocked out. Strange. Macario sent to me, *The energy is a very high frequency pulse in the aesthetics band.* This gave me something to ponder. We waited a while longer before resuming our stations. Very carefully, Macario took us back inside to our former position.

"Guess it was nothing after all. Honestly, Jemalensis, I am getting really spooked by this place. We are right smack in the middle of a penal colony full of some of the nastiest of beings. Gives me the willies down in my belly."

"Know what you mean. I'm antsy too. It is just two of us against millions of them. As long as we keep alert, we should be okay. Just a few more days of this and we're out of here. I'm not staying a moment longer than our orders dictated. If the silly geneticist wants to stick around here, why, it's his neck, not ours. Here, take over the monitor while I get something to eat."

Hours passed, but we learned very little more. Later, the geneticist rose and took over the monitoring process, while the two fighters headed for bed again. Fortunately for us, the geneticist liked to talk to himself, and we began to learn more details.

"Well, this time, good old Hammertharmalosis has done it properly. Thranikansisnestoris just had to deviate from our initial plans. I've taken care of that possibility. Oh my, imagine allowing these prisoners access to our machines here. Yet, I do wonder just how they managed to figure out how to operate this, our greatest invention ever. Well, we know some of the prisoners were geniuses who didn't know their places in society, always causing trouble. Probably those six were some of them. Well, I sure that I have fixed them good this time. Oh yes I did. After all, if I were them, I would have made extra bacteria just in case." He made a noise that seemed to translate as a chuckle, though we could not be sure.

"Well, I've taken care of that. Just let them try to use more of the bacteria they created to undo what Thranikansisnestoris did. Ha. I've engineered these bacteria not to accept that one. They can breathe in a whole canister of it, if they still have it around, and it'll do them no good at all. The prisoners are going to have to stay in their mammalian cells this time. No escaping on my watch. No sir. Not with Hammertharmalosis on the job. I wonder if I have considered every possibility, though?" I thought that I detected a bit of doubt in his mind. I wish that I dared tweak his mind a little, re-enforcing his doubts. Yet, I dare not do so.

On the other hand, I was crestfallen when I heard that our undo bacteria that we still had in sufficient quantity for our nineteen countries was going to be useless against his new one. We were simply stuck with whatever genetic modifications he was making — stuck with it until I could get Lin Zu back up here and perhaps fabricate other antidote bacteria. To say that I was afraid would not be accurate. Concerned and worried, yes. Fear played no role with me. Yet, I knew very well how terrified other women would soon become. Again, I felt helpless to change the course of these hideous events. If only we could have somehow blown up this entire cavern complex when we left it some months ago. . . Of course, I had no idea how we could possibly have blown it up. We'd have to have an enormous pile of our gunpowder, probably all that had ever been manufactured in the world to date.

Still, had we been able to somehow destroy this place or perhaps damage these machines, this mantis geneticist would not have been able to work his dirty work on us. Recrimination. Yes, that's precisely what I felt as the day dragged on interminably. Although we continued to monitor them, we learned little else of significance to our plight. We did hear about their continued warfare with the Grey and plasticine civilizations, a war that was well into its fourth century!

During the third night, Macario called a break from the monitoring. Again, to avoid detection, we all moved down the mountain to the sandy beach. *I've decided that we will take them out the moment that their cargo ships have finished depositing the needed items. Until the last folks get the things that they are going to need to survive, I simply cannot risk taking them out. If something should go wrong, some of our people will be in the most dire straits. It's just too risky to attack them before that point. I don't think that we'll learn much more useful information, but we'll keep on monitoring them.*

When the attack time comes, I will let you know. Just materialize inside and have at the three mantises. Let's make it quick and take no chances on the mantises activating their flash weapons. Remember, these creatures are fifty feet long and very strong for their size. Work together, divide up into three teams, and make your attack plans. When we strike, we must be swift. If we give them time to react, they will hit their flash weapons, stunning us all in an instant. I don't want to have to pluck you out of the ocean in a frozen cube. We all went through that on Dorota; once was bad enough for me. I sensed that these others knew precisely what he meant and wondered if being frozen into a cube was much different from the period of unconsciousness that Eve, Marco, Giovanni, and I had endured with Nestor. However, I didn't ask.

During the next days, we got additional confirmation from the mantises that indeed the Grey creatures and the plasticine dolls had abandoned this planet for good. However, we learned that they had re-supplied their bases of operation in the unlikely event that they did have to return. None of us knew precisely what that meant, but guessed they left food supplies and such.

Finally the last day came. We watched the monitor along with all three mantis creatures. The paths of the two blips representing the cargo ships drew closer and closer until they appeared to collide on the 3-D monitor. The agreed upon signal would be when the mantises stated that the supply process was completed. Obviously, the two fighter captains intended to make a hasty exit shortly after that. We waited patiently, though I wonder how Eve managed to have such patience, waiting all this time outside the cavern. I guess she was satisfied by being the relay point from me.

At last, Hammertharmalosis drew back from the monitor. "Ta da! Finished. Completed. Gentlemen, I am forever in your debt. Your supply operation worked incredibly efficiently. My compliments."

"Good. Then our job here is officially over. All has gone according to your plan, right geneticist?" Captain Jemalensis asked for verification and confirmation.

Macario took this as the opportunity to strike. He sent a single thought to the others waiting outside. *Attack.* Instantly, the others appeared in the room, setting off the warning alarms, indicating the invasion of spiritual beings that were using energy in some way. Before Macario or I could attack them ourselves, the others struck.

They struck with a brutality that I'd seldom seen! Eighteen powerful spiritual beings, including Eve, worked together, six on each mantis. Because of Eve's Mind Link to me, they all knew the precise location of each mantis and had worked out their attack strategy. I could tell Eve's attack. Hers was unique. Hammertharmalosis' head began spinning around and around in a circle. Of course, his neck snapped on the first revolution, but she continued it until his ugly looking head with the bulbous eyes and huge mandibles fell off onto the floor. Others ripped out the many appendages, keeping him from being able to react and press his pulse gun, which would have ended it for us right there.

One second after they appeared, gore and ooze from their dead bodies filled the room, body parts lay strewn about the room. *Well that's that!* Eve sent us all. *Guess we will have a mess to clean up when we bring our bodies here to manufacture the antidote.* That was an understatement!

Just then, we spotted the stunned fighters drifting up through the ceiling and out over Tarra. Macario sent several after them to watch what those spiritual beings did next. As we all suspected, the only thing that the two stunned, disoriented beings could do was to head off in search of baby bodies. They were about to suffer life now as humans, having to endure whatever the bacteria would be doing to us all.

However, we soon spotted Hammertharmalosis as he drifted upwards. Only he was not stunned. Rather, he was laughing hideously. Okay without a body, we picked up an energy flow from him that indicated he was hysterical. We felt a huge flow of the total irresponsible glee that accompanies complete insanity. I found it rather sickening to behold. We all moved out of the cavern to follow him and to make sure he caused no further trouble. From our experiences with Nestor, I knew that without a physical body, these mantis creatures were completely helpless, unable to do anything except to somehow search for a pregnant woman. They had a total compulsion to grab a new body, a monomania, and their sole urge at this point. Nothing else was in their minds, but we all made sure of that, though.

I guess in hindsight, all twenty of us following them was a very good thing. By the time that they reached the lower elevations, some explosive charges that we had not known were there suddenly detonated. We all heard a massive explosion behind us. Looking back, the entire top of the mountain rose into the air, turned into dust, then slowly drifted outwards like some giant balloon. All twenty of us froze to the spot, staring at this totally unexpected event.

At last, Eve sent, *Shit! Now we are **really** screwed!* Her exclamation woke us all up. At the moment, I didn't have a stomach, but I felt terribly sick at my stomach anyway, as I realized that now we had absolutely no way to create undo bacteria! Whatever genetic modifications this Hammertharmalosis had made to our bodies, we were stuck with it forever and planet-wide to boot!

During all these centuries that I had known Jes, the Guardian, Macario, I had never heard him curse or swear. Macario sent loudly, *Double shit! Damn him to hell!* Then he added less emotionally, *Yes Eve, we are really, really **screwed** this time. Let's head home and see how badly we are screwed.*

Chapter 3 The Genetic Modifications

We arrived home in the early morning of October 26, 823. I slipped silently into my body and began to see and sense what had become of it, fearing the very worst. Well, no arms. Somehow that didn't surprise me at all, that was a given, but what else had happened to our bodies? I sat up. I was still in my nightgown. Marco, who way laying at my side, roused. "Ah welcome home, my love." He sat up, wiping his sleepy eyes and then gave me a loving hug.

"What's the damage?" I whispered. "Say, your dangling ear lobes — they're gone!"

"Yes, so are yours. Damage? Oh, our feet mostly. You women are faring far better in that department than we men. Let me show you what's happened to your feet." He pulled back the covers, and I got a good look at my feet.

My arches were highly U-shaped, so much so that my heels were almost completely above the back ends of my toes, making the small feet of Tashien look positively large! Only my toes would touch the floor when I stood on them, the heels of my feet were a good six inches above the floor. I flexed my ankles. To my surprise, the toes went way back far beyond what ordinarily would have been a ballet dancer's en pointe.

"Lucianna claims that it is easier to get a fork up to your mouth this way. She also says that they are very springy, but that you almost have to wear these new special shoes if you are to do any walking." He held up my new shoes. Essentially, they looked like an enormous cork wedge with the tiny heel, perhaps a quarter inch around being within a half inch of the back of the toes, giving the overall appearance of incredibly tiny feet.

"Unreal," I managed to mutter, mostly shocked by what I was seeing. "What about you? How can yours be any worse?" I finally recovered and remembered what he'd suggested a moment ago.

"Look, ours are totally altered, for the worst, mind you." He showed me his feet or rather what was left of them. His foot was pointed straight downward; all of his toes now had the same length as his big toe and were fused together. The tips of his toes had a thick growth of padding flesh, and I saw at once that he would have to be walking on the tips of his toes like a ballet dancer and similar to what Nestor had devised in that awful Version One modification.

He added, "Can't bend my ankles much at all; we're forced to walk on our toes. It's impossible without these special wedge boots." He raised his pair up so I could see them up close. They looked more like ankle boots that laced up tightly over his feet and part way up his shins. Indeed, the tips of his toes were the only thing touching the ground! Yet the wedge of the boots had a bit of a heel behind the toes, again only about a half inch around and about an inch behind the toes.

"How can you fellows walk in them?" I asked, my heart going out to him as I recalled how he and Giovanni had struggled to walk in somewhat similar footwear during our brief period as Version One modifications.

"Almost impossible. We've been holding on to you women for balance and support for the last couple of days. You women can manage to get around easily, but we are in for a nasty time of it. The only positive thing is that the boots are steel re-enforced so we can't twist our ankles, and there is no pain. Valerio thinks that's partly due to the extra cushioning at the tips of our toes. Sergio believes that in time, we will get the hang of it, but we sure do move slowly. All this is certainly going to alter our entire lives and civilizations that's for darn sure."

"Damn," I replied, fighting hard to keep from crying. What else could I say? I felt horrible. Marco pulled me onto his shoulders, and I buried my head into his chest and cried a while. Finally, I pulled myself together and pulled back from him.

Sniffing, I asked, "So what else is now wrong with our bodies?"

"Well, all that gory makeup is gone; your eyes and lips are normal, that is, they are like they used to be before Nestor. As far as I can tell, this is all that the mantis altered in us males."

"Well, that's plenty bad for you fellows as it is." I thought that he was not telling me quite everything, perhaps breaking the news to me gently. Then, I noticed that my breasts seemed larger.

Marco noticed me noticing and added, "Well, there's going to be more of you to love. You're right; they are big, but not grotesque as in Version One. We think that since you are still growing, yours will get somewhat larger yet. Sofia's and Marta's are quite large; melons, they're calling them. Dresses are going to have to be altered, that's for sure. Plus your waist is probably even smaller than before. Lisa claims hers is now only twelve inches around."

"Pull up my nightgown, let me see, please." Marco pulled it off and tussled my hair for me. Yes, my breasts were three times as large as I recalled, but not unacceptable yet. I wondered how much larger they would become. My lower abdomen seemed to be slightly larger, but my waist muscles seemed even stronger, and I was definitely more flexible. I would have to wait and see about having lost inches around my waist, though. It was hard to tell, what with the larger bust and hips.

"Giovanni has speculated that the mantis has enlarged your lower body, moving some of your organs down, rather than just compacting everything like the tight lacing corsets women used to wear. He figures this will be far healthier for you. He's asked the Foundation to look into this when they get the chance," Marco added.

"Well, that is good. I once died in childbirth because I wore a tight corset since I was five years old. It really messed up my organs. I hope the mantis got it right or we women are all going to die in childbirth." Being pregnant had brought these ancient memories back to me now.

"One more thing, love," Marco added with a wry smile, "and this one you are going to actually like."

I gave him a queer look. So far, I had not liked any of this. "Well?"

"You hair has grown some, actually quite a lot. It's down to your ankles now. So has all the other women's hair — grown about two feet. Lucianna has had Valerio cut hers back to the way it was. So have the others, except Giovanni and I — we haven't cut yours or Eve's yet. We figured we'd wait and see if you like it this long first."

I could not help but smile. Okay, I am vain about my hair, all right? I love it long. Still, lacking arms made dealing with it a time consuming action. "Thanks, you're right in not cutting it. I guess we'll see how it goes. I hope you don't mind helping me with it."

Marco leaned over and gave me a passionate kiss. He whispered, "I don't mind helping you with anything. I just hope that you don't mind helping me as well. For a while, I need you to support me as I walk. Otherwise, it is incredibly difficult to manage on my own. Lucianna suggested that we try using crutches, but in the long run, we've got to learn to manage ourselves."

"You can count on me, Marco." I could not help but remember Eve's pronouncement, "We are really screwed." It seemed an understatement now. "Come on, get me sort of dressed and help me with the toilet. I'm really starving. Have you been feeding our bodies these past few days?" He grinned and began explaining how he and Giovanni had been looking after Eve and me like mother hens.

After donning the shoes, I rose and got my balance. So utterly weird, far worse than the tiny feet I'd had in Tashien. Marco, I quickly saw, had an even far harder time of it. Yet, I noticed that his legs and knees in particular seemed far more muscular than before, probably to support the extra stress being placed on his knees and legs. As I stood, my thick, black hair slipped down over me, nearly touching the floor. That I liked. He slipped his arm around me for support and together we began extremely slowly making our way out of our bedroom towards the kitchen and food.

I noticed that trying to walk without my shoes was awkward and a bit painful. The highly recurved middle arch of my foot was now perpendicular to the ground, bearing the weight of my body on that U-shaped arch. Yes, springy was one way to describe it, but painful too. With the strange shoes, which provided solid support beneath the heel and part of the arch, I felt no pain and could walk. Yet I could not walk normally. As I suspected, I was doing an exaggerated shuffle, really, taking no more than a three inch step at a time, which made even the shortest distances seem to take forever to cross. Our speed of travel was even slower than the fashionable women of Tashien who had intentionally broken their arches to get "small feet." Try it sometime. Try walking a distance and restricting yourself to only three inches forward with one step and you'll see what I mean.

Still, I was able to maintain balance, which is a whole lot more than I can say about poor Marco and the other fellows. He was extremely dependent upon me to keep his own balance, and even then, his free arm continually flailed about wildly. He did appreciate the fact that we were taking very small steps. However, I soon pointed out that once he got the hang of it, he would be able more likely to manage a foot at a time, perhaps.

As usual, our parents were already up and working together to make breakfast for us all. I realized suddenly that here we were, all grown up and married even, and yet our folks were still fixing us breakfasts, as if we were still youngsters! Mom saw me coming in and flashed me a brave smile, but tears swelled in spite of her attempts to put up a stalwart front. She wanted to give me a big hug, but dad was clinging to her for support, just as Marco was depending upon me. It was almost humorous watching mom with dad in tow moving at a snail's pace to come over to me to give me a welcoming home hug. Okay, I broke down and cried too, as we met and I threw my head onto mom's shoulders and dad's free arm slipped around my back.

While we were hugging, Giovanni and Eve entered, he hanging onto her for dear life. Her folks stopped their breakfast chores and moved to hug her as well. "We are really screwed this time, aren't we?" Eve finally said, while Giovanni wiped the tears from her cheeks as the four separated.

"That's an understatement, if I ever heard one," Valerio called out. He had just entered the kitchen, holding onto Lucianna for support. "How the hell are we to survive this mess?"

"Dear, watch your language," Marta scolded him. "We may be down, but we are not out yet."

"Hi Eve, Bethany," Sergio called out. He and Lisa were right behind Valerio and Lucianna. "Well, there is one good thing about all this. Crime ought to be nearly non-existent. I might be out of a job." Good old Sergio, always trying to find a bright spot in the midst of calamity.

"He's right," Lisa added, carefully watching both her steps and his. "Like this, a criminal cannot escape. Gosh, the fellows can barely walk. Don't worry, love, I've got you." He flashed her a loving glance and smile.

Marco and I finally got to the table. Although he still held on to me for support, he adjusted my chair for me and we sat down together. Unused to having my hair two feet longer than before, I had him drape it down on either side of my front. He and Giovanni watched each other, taking hints from each other, as he adjusted Eve's long golden locks. "Wow, Eve, love your hair," I could not help but comment. She beamed with satisfaction. Amazing how small things take on unusual proportions in crises.

Eve and I had been gone now for about five days, during which everyone else had been enduring these modifications, finding ways to adapt to them somewhat. I began to notice the little things. Now our fathers were constantly holding onto our mothers everywhere they went. As a result, they would use their hands so that our moms didn't have to try to use their feet as they had used to do. It was almost as if the two were now joined at the hips, so to speak, working together on almost everything, an inseparable pair.

When our folks finally came to the table with the pancakes, bacon, and eggs, ready to serve up a hearty breakfast, mom explained, "Bethany, Eve, as you can tell, things are very different this time around. Our men are unable to walk much on their own, and we are almost as bad with our feet. We've decided that the best way to get by for now is always to work together. Marta and I provide support so they can move around, and they use their arms and hands for what we need done. We work as a team now."

"Sofia's right, dear," dad backed her up, "we have to work together to get something done. I'm her arms and she's my support."

Sandro added, "Don't worry too much, Eve. We ended up crawling around on our hands and knees the first couple of days. But the last three days now, we've been walking, and if I do say so myself, we fellows are starting to get the hang of it. Honestly, dear, I do think that given time and your mother's patience, I will be able to manage on my own again, albeit at a snail's pace."

"Of course, the whole city is at a complete standstill," Sergio took up the briefing. He'd just decided that it was briefing time, though he paused to grab another bite. "None of us have any idea how anything is going to get done now. We are all just trying to cope and stay alive now."

I took a deep breath and then began to relay all that had happened and what we'd learned. To say that they were crushed by the news that the mantis had blown up the entire installation at Chichulain would be an understatement of some magnitude. I know that everyone was hoping and praying that we could again somehow find a cure for all this. Mom, for example, had made the best of it last time, knowing that Eve and I were off working on a cure. One by one, the harsh fact that this time there would be no cure sunk home. I could tell it in all their faces. You could hear a pin drop when I finished.

"We are so screwed!" Eve added once I'd finished.

Her mother, Marta, whispered, "Are we — are we looking at the end of the world then?"

I had to answer her, as I suddenly realized that this idea would be the most likely idea worldwide. "Marta, it is not the end of the world. I give you my solemn promise never to rest until I can find a way out of this mess. We are all still alive and very much healthy. We have our minds intact." I suddenly noticed that everyone had stopped eating and were staring at me, intent on my every word! What I said now would have a far-reaching impact upon all of my family and dear friends.

"Look, the mantis counted upon us humans being reactive. That is, we have the ability to react to drastic changes in our environment. Of course, we once again must do just that, find ways and means to adapt to our misfortunes. That is understandably the first action that we must all take, find alternate ways to accomplish what we must do to continue to live as an extended family and as a country and as a worldwide species. I freely admit that we are all in a very, very dangerous situation. The first action must be to forget about our normal habits and routines and all get in there and work together to handle the dangerous situation that we are facing, just like you are already doing."

"As we go along in this, we must all strive to keep our own personal ethics in solidly. For example, Eve, if our long hair begins to interfere with what we must do to help everyone, then we'll just have to cut it shorter. We can always let it grow out later. No sloughing off. As we go along handling the situation that we are facing, we must all reorganize our lives so that we don't keep on finding ourselves in a complete dangerous mess, day after day. This may mean maintaining a stockpile of groceries at all times. I don't know yet what all this may entail, I haven't yet seen all the danger that we are facing. If we all work together, I know that we can make it."

"Look, the people on Dorota managed to do very well for themselves. Yes, I know that their society had its faults, particularly in the arts, but they did survive and prosper. We can too, if we take the proper steps and actions, together as a group."

"Yet, this is most definitely not enough, just being reactive. Man is a sentient being, not some reactive dog that changes his life as his environment dictates. We are not puppets of the universe. I refuse to be a puppet slave. No, once we have the dangerous mess somewhat under control, we need to use our minds as part of the reorganization phase. We need to invent new things to aid us in our survival. Look, if women on Tarra are never going to have arms again, then we need new devices to help us survive better, like the yokes, for example. Perhaps something better than yokes can be invented." I rather ran down at this point, but my father broke the silence first. Tito began clapping, and at once all the fellows joined in while the gals stomped their feet.

"Well said, daughter, well said!" my father called out.

As the noise died down, Lucianna spoke up, "Hey, count me in on the new inventions angle! If I am never going to get my arms back, then I am certainly going to invent a whole lot of useful devices. Speaking of which, I've already had a brilliant idea, sis. I hate doing the laundry even when I had arms!" Mom chuckled. She was well aware of Lucianna's constant wiggling out of her turn doing the massive laundry each week when it was her turn. "So I've spent the last couple days dreaming up a solution. I believe that I can create a washing machine to do the washing for us without our having to do anything more than put the dirty things in it and then take them out. I promise to get right on it today even," she exclaimed.

Then, she added, "Okay, I will wait a while on my flying machines." I gave her a big smile of thanks. She had picked up on my meaning about getting one's own ethics in solidly and not doing other things that were not critical to our present situation.

Valerio spoke up, "You know, Bethany, you are inspirational! You are right on the money! If we and everyone else do just what you are suggesting, we can get out of this mess somehow! Say, you ought to go to Stefano with your ideas this morning. He is totally lost now. He's so overwhelmed by all this that he's not even made one speech to us all or even put out any word beyond his initial warning that the aliens were attacking us again. You are going to have to get Stefano propped up immediately or we are all doomed no matter what this extended family does."

"He hasn't?" I muttered. In a flash I realized how he must have been feeling about now, just like Marta, perhaps this was the beginning of the end of the world.

Sergio backed him up. "Look, during the last year, because of the situation then, many of those who did not own a radio have purchased one. So much valuable and timely information was first announced on radio that people have begun to depend upon them. Yet, this time, the radio has gone silent. All broadcasting stopped two days ago, probably because no one can get to the studio to operate the playback equipment. There haven't been any papers in the last four days either, probably the same reason. You have to get to Stefano immediately and work with him to get information out very soon. People are likely panicking, though I admit, none of us had ventured outside the mansion since this happened. We can't walk that far on our own yet."

"Okay, Marco and I will go to Stefano's as soon as we finish breakfast. Say Eve, why don't you and Giovanni go check up on our friends Tatiana and Wanda. It's only three blocks, and they might need some arms about now. Remember how we found them last time?"

"You got it," Eve replied. "After that, I'm taking Giovanni to his office at the DAE and help him get going on inventions."

"Don't worry, Bethany," Lucianna added, "Valerio and I will head there as soon as we finish breakfast. I want to get this washing machine idea going as soon as possible. If it works, we must make some for every household in Velona. That ought to spark some life into our women. At least it will do so for me. Then, mom can stop hounding me to do the laundry." Sofia chuckled, while most of us grinned.

A while later, I had Marco help me into one of Tatianna's designer dresses, which used to fit me perfectly. Now I faced two new problems, one of which I ignored. My waist was definitely smaller, and the hooks were very loose around my waist. However, my breasts were so much larger that he couldn't get the top on right. At last, he succeeded, but I looked like I was about to explode out of the top of my dress at any moment. He chuckled and teased me, "Ah, so much more of you to love now, my dearest." I gave him a playful hip-butt bump. I had him then tie a ribbon around the back of my hair so my long hair would stay put across my back, and we headed out.

At first, I could not believe how slow going it was — minutes just to reach the front door and an eternity to reach our garage. We decided to take our putt-putts. I could still operate my modified T-putt-putt, but Marco had a devil of a time operating the controls with his now tiny, pointed feet. Still, we managed to get them started and headed noisily out of our front gates.

As we drove along the streets to Stefano's estate, I was shocked utterly. Velona is home to well over a million inhabitants. At this time of day, mid-morning, the streets ought to have been packed with men, women, and children. Street-side shops ought to have been everywhere, swarming with business. Throngs ought to have been in the streets, to say nothing of motor vehicles, putt-putts, horse carriages, and wagons. We saw absolutely no one, not a single person was on the streets! I felt as if I had arrived in a lifeless world! I was shocked beyond words.

Stefano's gate was closed, but not locked. "Hey, I'll get the gate, Marco." I knew that he would have an awful time trying to open the gates, so I volunteered. Using my foot, I undid the latch, pushed the gates open, and climbed back on my three-wheeler, glad once more for Lucianna's modifications to our putt-putts. Marco shot me a thankful look and I gave him a grin. We had to work together now to survive, that was abundantly clear to me as we drove on up to his columned front entrance.

Two tall granite spires supported a fancy gable over his front doors, which were made from black teakwood. A pair of interlocking dolphins was carved ornately in each door. After parking our putt-putts, Marco again put his arm over my shoulders and we slowly moved up to the door. Marco knocked for us. Shortly, I heard a faint, "Come on in." It sounded like Caresa's voice, his wife. Marco opened the door and together we made our way slowly inside.

Just inside the entryway, we could see into their spacious front room. At the far end, Caresa and their daughter Andrea, now seven, were slowly making their way towards us. However, Stefano was on his hands and knees, trying to come to the door like a dog! I was shocked once more. Tears streamed down his face; he was humiliated beyond words. I understood though.

"Oh Bethany, Marco! So good of you to come by. It is the end of everything, isn't it? The whole world is dying, right?" Caresa burst out the only thought that was on her mind, probably for days now, I guessed.

"Oh don't be silly, Caresa. Of course, it's not the end of the world. A minor setback," I attempted to cast our calamity in less horrid terms. "You are looking well. My, how Andrea is growing up."

Andrea said, "Hi Bethany. Wow, your hair is even longer than mine is now. Did you know that my hair has grown a whole two feet in the last few days? I wonder if it will continue to grow like this. I hope it gets as long as yours is. I've lost my arms again; guess you have too. So has mommy. Will we get them back next year like before? Our feet are all messed up this time. Will they get fixed up too? I hope so, cause daddy can't even walk anymore," Andrea gaily chatted, eager for some company other than her parents, who looked more like ghosts of their former selves.

We had finally reached their couches, but before I sat down, I put my foot around Andrea, giving her a little hug. Marco did give her a proper hug for us both. Stefano finally managed to reach the couch and got himself onto it, barely able to face us.

"Well, I've come to report the bad news to you, Stefano, as well as enlist your aid," I began. "Andrea, this time, I am afraid that we will very likely not be getting our arms back anytime soon, if ever. Plus, for the time being, we will have to live with our feet the way that they are now. I hope our hair stops growing soon or mine will reach the floor. If it does, I may have to use my hair as a floor mop." Andrea giggled at my little jest, livening up the atmosphere of doom and gloom that permeated the room from the two adults.

I outlined what had happened with the mantis in full detail. When I finished, Stefano sighed, succumbing to his fate, "Then, that's it. There is no hope that our women will ever be able to get their arms back this time and our feet will always be like this. We are indeed doomed; it is the end of everything, just as I thought before."

I had to get him out of his wallowing self-pity or indeed all would be lost. "Stefano! Don't be silly! The world is not going to end. We all have our health, our bodies are fit, our minds are intact, and more importantly, the aliens have left Tarra for good. The mantis installation where they created the nasty bacteria is destroyed. The last living mantis geneticist is dead; they no longer have the knowledge or capability of mutating our human bodies ever again. There is a bright future for us, if we all apply the right condition, take the right actions, take them immediately and without fail!"

"Really? Bethany, I can't even walk anymore. No man can."

"Hey, I just got here," Marco retorted. "Obviously, I had to do some walking. Don't be silly. It is horribly awkward and quite a challenge, but if I can sort of do it with Bethany's help, so can you, man."

I decided now was the time to punch in what had to be done, repeating the gist of the speech I gave my family. "Look, the mantis counted upon we humans being reactive creatures. That is, we have the ability to react to drastic changes in our environment. Once again, we must do just that, find alternate ways and means to adapt to our misfortunes. That is understandably the first action that we must all take, to find alternate ways to accomplish what we must do to continue to live as ourselves, as our families, as a country, and as a worldwide species. I freely admit that we are all in a very, very dangerous situation. Of that, there can be no doubt in anyone's mind."

"Hence, the first action that we must all do is to forget about our normal habits and routines and all get in there and work together to handle this dangerous situation that we are all facing. That is the single most critical action we must do immediately. Now, as we go along in this, we must all strive to keep in our own personal ethics. For example, if my long hair begins to interfere with what I must do to help everyone, then I'll just have to cut it shorter. I can always let it grow out later. No sloughing off. As we go along handling the situation that we are facing, we must all reorganize our lives so that we don't keep on finding ourselves in a complete dangerous mess, day after day. This may mean maintaining a stockpile of groceries at all times. I don't know yet what all this may entail. I haven't yet seen all the danger that we are facing. If we all work together, I know that we can make it."

"The people on Dorota managed to do very well for themselves. I know that their society had its faults, particularly in their entire lack of the arts, but they did survive and prosper. We can too, if we take the proper steps and actions, together as a group."

"Yet, this is most definitely not enough, just our being reactive. We are sentient beings, not some reactionary dog that changes his life as his environment dictates. We are not some puppets of the universe. I refuse to be a puppet slave. No, once we have this dangerous mess somewhat under control, we need to use our minds as part of the reorganization phase. We need to invent new things to aid us in our survival. If women on Tarra are never going to have arms again, then we need new devices to help us survive better. Right at this moment, Lucianna is off at DAE inventing what she calls a washing machine, which will do the laundry washing for us. As she says, we just put the dirty clothes in and it washes them all for us. We need that and many more helpful inventions."

"Now as far as walking is concerned, my folks and family have already worked this out. We women can walk by ourselves fairly well, if slowly. So we have to help our fellows with walking. Marco puts his arm around me and I act as his support. It does work. Right now, at our place, wherever a fellow needs to go, his wife goes with him, supporting him. In fact, that's how they made breakfast for us today. Mom has become dad's support and goes everywhere with him and he uses his arms to help her cook and such. Teamwork, Stefano, that's what all men must have at this moment — someone to lean on to help support them while they walk."

Marco added his opinion to the mix, "She's right. We've been doing this for the last few days now. Everywhere I go, a woman is with me so I can use her for balance. It does work; that's how I got here today, leaning on Bethany. However, we have also noticed that as the days go by and we continue to practice walking, we are getting better and better at it. I do feel that soon I'll be able to manage to walk on my own without being utterly dependent upon Bethany here to keep my balance. I think that we will have to learn how to walk all over again. At least it rather seems that way to me. Have you tried walking while holding onto Caresa or Andrea?"

"Well, no," Stefano replied, his pride was wounded. "I mean, she's in such worse shape than I am, Andrea too. How can I ask to lean on them when they don't even have their arms to help them keep their balance?"

"We've got more toe support, silly," I answered that one. "Have you looked at their shoes? We have all our toes on the ground, while you're standing on the tips of your toes. We can keep our balance better. Come on, stand up, and try it. Caresa, let's show Stefano a thing or two." She grinned, eager to do anything to get her husband out of the horrific slump that he had been in for days now.

With effort and wobbling like mad, he rose. Caresa moved beside him and he quickly put his arm around her. Not to be left out, Andrea got up and came to his other side. Balancing on the two, Stefano began to take hesitant steps. Marco and I rose and joined them, giving them a model to follow or duplicate. "Yes, I know pathetically tiny steps. Takes forever to even get to the door, let alone any real distance, but see, you are doing it. Teamwork is required until you fellows can learn to walk on your own. I am hopeful that Marco is right, that with enough practice, you fellows can manage without us. Until then, we go everywhere you fellows need to go; only you need to lend us your hands as well."

We went around the living room a couple times. Andrea gaily exclaimed, "See, daddy, you can walk now. We just have to help you with it." Stefano slowly regained his self-worth, his self-respect. When we were finally back at the couches, he hugged his wife and daughter, whispering to them how much he loved them both. We allowed them this private moment and said nothing.

At last, Stefano said what I had been waiting to hear, "Okay, Bethany. You are an angel once more. Thank you. So what should I do first? So many things need immediate attention. What should be the first steps?"

I grinned; now he was back to battery, and I felt a bit of hope returning. "First, via the radio, we have to make a public address of the situation and what everyone must do. Second, we have to get whatever we say over the radio printed up in the paper and make sure that every household in the city gets a copy, as well as all the other towns and villages. That's enough for us to do in one day, considering the five times as slow rule, which now also applies to you fellows, not just to we women," I teased him. He knew what I meant. When we were struck with the plague over a year ago and we women lost our arms then, the mantra that everyone echoed was my advice that it took us five times as long to accomplish an action now as it did when we had arms.

"I don't think anyone is at the station now," he stated. "We'll need one of the fellows who knows how to operate the radio transmitter equipment. I'll call and find someone."

"When you do, tell him — no order him to bring his wife or girlfriend along with him to help him with the walking," I advised. Stefano grinned.

Sometime later, we were ready to head out to the studio. "We'll take my motor-car," Stefano offered.

"Okay, lean on me," Caresa said moving to his side. He looked quizzically at her, so she added, "Where you go, so go I."

"Me too," Andrea added, eager to help as well. With his arms around both, Stefano began to make his way to his front door. Marco and I followed behind them. I couldn't believe that we took nearly twenty minutes to finally get to their motor-car and going. Such a short distance too.

Now Stefano faced a new problem, the three floor pedals. Ordinarily, he used his feet, bending them at his ankles to operate them. Now his ankles didn't bend much at all and his feet were pointed. He had to make exaggerated body motions, extending and retracting his legs to operate the controls. I made a mental note to relay this to Giovanni and Lucianna. Perhaps they could devise some alternate type of controls. It would be nice if we women could drive the vehicles too.

"My god, there is no one on the streets!" Stefano exclaimed as we drove along. I knew that he now felt the same sense of urgency as we did. When we arrived, we found the station manager and his wife were already there. As expected, he depended utterly upon her to keep his balance as he moved around the equipment, getting the station ready to broadcast once more.

"Hey, Stefano! Say, it is possible to walk with Alesa's help. Good idea. I need another couple of minutes and then you are on the air. She's going to transcribe what you say, and then she and I will take turns repeating your words until suppertime. Okay?"

It was. I noticed that she had one of the low desks still in the main broadcasting room. Evidently, she had done the transcribing before. She saw me noticing it and whispered, "Don't worry. I can keep up, though I have to rewrite it more legibly once you are done." I gave her a knowing wink, and she flashed me a smile.

"Hello citizens of Velona, ladies, gentlemen, and children. This is Stefano West Po. I am sorry that I haven't been able to address you sooner. My only excuse is that I was as devastated by this plague as you are. But I am back to battery now. This address will be repeated throughout the day, and we'll try to get it also reproduced in the paper, delivered to every home in Velona as soon as possible. First, let me apprise every one of the situation. Yes, Tarra was once again attacked by the same aliens who attacked us not so long ago. Once again, they unleashed a powerful plague upon us all. By now, you are acutely aware of the plague's aftereffects. Our women are without arms. Men and women's feet are wildly altered for the worst."

"Unlike the last attack, we did not have any advanced warning of its coming. This time, the plague has affected every human being on the entire planet! Take heart, every woman in the world is in the same position as us, and likewise, every man is as well. At least we are not in imminent danger of starvation this time."

"What of the aliens? At this time, I am able to report our forces have annihilated all the aliens. Yes, those who unleashed this monstrous plague upon mankind are very dead. Further, their facility, which manufactured these plagues here on Tarra, has been completely destroyed, much as they did to Dorota. They will never again be able to unleash such terrible plagues upon any of us. There is some comfort in that at least. Further, we have learned that these aliens will not be returning to Tarra in the future. This plague was their last action against us. Again, I take some comfort in knowing that these monsters will never be coming back to Tarra."

"The bad news is indeed bad, however. Unlike last time, when our able citizens were able to manufacture an anti-dote to the plague's effects, at least for the women, this time, due to the nature of this plague, they tell me that it is highly unlikely that a full cure will be found, at least not in the near future, perhaps not even in my lifetime. I have our scientists' pledge that they will continue to work on a cure, but they are not hopeful at all at this time. Perhaps when we learn more, a way will become known, but that is merely my hopeful speculation. In short, our bodies are going to be as they are now. That is, all women of Tarra will be without their arms. Everyone's feet will be as they are now." He paused for dramatic effect and to let that sink into the audience's mind.

"Citizens, take heart. The world is *not* ending. As a very wise woman recently told me, look, the world is *not* going to end. We all have our health. Our bodies are fit; our minds are intact. More importantly, the aliens have left Tarra for good. There is a bright future for us, if we all work together, pull together, apply the right conditions, take the right actions, take them immediately and without fail!"

"She wisely pointed out to me, look, the mantis counted upon we humans being reactive creatures. That is, we have the ability to react to drastic changes in our environment. Once again, we must do just that, finding alternate ways and means to adapt to our misfortunes. That is understandably the first action that we must all take, to find alternate ways to accomplish what we must do to continue to live as ourselves, as our families, as a country, and as a worldwide species. I freely admit that we are all in a very, very *dangerous* situation. Of that, there can be no doubt in anyone's mind, certainly not in my mind."

"Hence, the first action that we must all do is to forget about our normal habits and routines. All of us must get in there and work together to handle this dangerous situation that we are all facing. That is the single most critical action we must do *immediately*. Now, as we go along in this, we must all strive to keep in our own personal ethics. No sloughing off. No excessive drinking binges. Don't put things off when you have time to do them now. As we go along handling the situation that we are facing, we must all *reorganize* our lives so that we don't keep on finding ourselves in a complete dangerous mess, day after day. This may mean maintaining a stockpile of groceries and petrol for our vehicles. I don't know yet what all this may entail, because I haven't yet seen all the dangers that we are facing. If we all work together, I know that we can make it."

"History has shown us that the people on Dorota managed to do very well for themselves. We know that their society had its faults, particularly in their entire lack of the arts for which Velona now leads the way, but they did *survive* and *prosper*. We can too, if we take the proper steps and actions, together as a group."

"Fellow citizens, it is not enough for us to be merely reactive to the changes in our bodies. Men and women are sentient beings, not some reactionary dogs that change their lives around as the environment dictates. We are not puppets at the strings and whims of the universe. I refuse to be a puppet slave. No, once we have this dangerous mess somewhat under control, we need to use our minds as part of the *reorganization* phase. We need to invent new things to aid us in our survival. If women on Tarra are never going to have arms again, then we need new devices to help them and us survive better. Right at this moment I am told, Lucianna Angela is off at DAE labs inventing what she calls a washing machine, which will do the laundry washing for us. As she says, we just put the dirty clothes in, and it washes them all for us. We need that and many more helpful inventions."

"Consider this a formal call for new ideas. The DAE alone do not have a monopoly on bright ideas for new inventions that will help our men and women. If you have an idea that you believe will aid us, I ask you to call either the DAE or my offices and tell us. I assure you that I or they will talk with you about your ideas."

"Now as far as walking is concerned, I freely admit that I have only been crawling around on my hands and knees since the plague struck us. Only this morning did a bright young woman and her husband show me the folly of my ways. Men, here is the secret to walking. Women can walk by themselves fairly well, if slowly. So women of Velona, it is your duty to help our fellows with walking. Have your man put his arm around you, and you act as his support. It does work beautifully. For the immediate future, wherever your husband, boyfriend, or fellow needs to go, you go with him, supporting him as he walks. It is a simple matter of teamwork between men and women. I do believe that she is right, that we men are facing having to learn how to walk all over again. I'm told that with practice, we will soon be able to get around on our own. However, until your man can do so on his own, I urge you women to go with him and support him. Fellows, this also means that you need to be her arms when she needs them as well. Teamwork goes both ways."

"As in our earlier crisis, you may expect to hear from me personally and quite frequently. I will see that the information also appears in our papers. Further, you may expect Mrs. Bethany Bartiana Angela to be sending out more of her incredibly helpful tips. In fact, the tip that I just gave you fellows came from her. I'll repeat it. fellows, we have to learn how to walk again. So fellows get your wives, mothers, girlfriends, or anyone of the fairer sex to help you learn by going along with you giving you her physical support and you help her with your hands."

"Finally, since not everyone has a radio or has it turned on just now, my message will be repeated over and over this afternoon. Please alert your friends and neighbors. It's time that we *take back* our lives. Thank you."

He nodded and the manager ended the broadcast. "Well, Bethany, Marco, Caresa, did I leave anything out?" he asked.

"Nope, good start. Now we had best get this published and help get your staff back on the job somehow," I replied, trying to anticipate what had to be done next.

We spent most of the rest of the day visiting the homes of his extended families, many of whom held key government positions, along with the newspaper publishers and the book publishers. With a little coaxing, we got the key men to begin getting their areas going once more, insisting that all had to have their wives tagging along with them just so that they could walk.

By the time that Marco and I finally returned home, my feet were slightly sore, but Marco's positively ached! Together, we stumbled along into the dining room, where he finally sat down. While we chatted with everyone else about our day's events, I had Marco remove his shoes, and I did my very best to massage his aching feet. Damn, if I only had hands, this would have worked wonders for him. Thankfully, Valerio saw what I was trying to do and he lent his hands. The relief on Marco's face was more than enough thanks for him.

As we dined, Marco fed me. "Hey, you helped me a whole lot today, so this is the very least I can do in return, dear." I grinned and accepted his assistance, though I knew in the future that I would be feeding myself using my feet and toes as before. Still, it was a nice gesture.

Eve reported that Tatiana and Wanda most definitely needed a bit of help. It seems that after their arms regrew, they had placed most of their cooking gear and supplies back on the higher shelves. Now they were unable to get to them. Giovanni, with Eve balancing him, got all their things brought down to lower, reachable locations. "She gave him a big kiss. Boy, did he blush," she added. He flushed again, as all eyes looked over at him.

He cleared his throat, "Well, you would too if a gorgeous blonde gave you a loving kiss. I can't get over how good she looks. Her hair is much longer as well, and she looks really good with it this long."

"As good as me?" Eve teased him.

He flushed again. "No, of course not. There is only one Eve, dearest." He gave her a kiss to shut her up. "Now then, Lucianna and I were the only ones at DAE today, excepting Eve and Valerio, of course. We did get a lot of work done on the washing machine design. It is a very doable project. I think that we will be able to get a company to begin manufacturing them within a month's time. Gang, let's start brain storming ideas that we can use to make life easier for our women folk."

"Hey, tomorrow," Sergio spoke up, "Lisa and I will begin manning the help phone lines once more. Any ideas that come in to us, we will relay to you."

"We should have one person in charge of collecting all the ideas and jotting them down," Lucianna suggested.

"I'll volunteer to do that," Lisa said, "after all I'll be one of the contact persons anyway. I'll get them together and to you two each night. Will that work out?" That was fine with the two inventors.

"Say, we already have a suggestion," Marco spoke up. "Today, Stefano drove us around to the various places we needed to go. He had a devil of a time using the three foot pedals. Can you re-engineer the foot controls somehow? Also, can you fix it up so that our women can drive the motor vehicles? If so, they could get around lots better." Lisa dashed off to get some paper and a pencil to jot down the first of the ideas. I say dashed, but that is figurative. At three inches a footstep, it was anything but a dash.

Again, our parents did the evening dishes, with our mothers supporting our fathers who actually did the work. They were definitely setting us an example of teamwork. Marco and I plopped down on a front room sofa. With my hair so long now, even though it was in a ponytail, I really had to swing my head around to get it to my front side before I sat down. Earlier today, I had forgotten to do it and had sat down on my hair. Ouch. I rather wished that it had taken its time growing this extra two feet, giving me time to get used to its new length.

While we were relaxing, Macario and Raffaella appeared again. First, he telepathically asked if they could meet with us and then both began materializing before us. Again, I was glad that they went all the way and appeared to have real fleshly bodies. I still had a hard time dealing with ghostly images. "Hi, we've got Stefano back to battery," I announced as they finished creating bodies and sat them down across the room from us in another sofa.

"Excellent, Bethany," Macario replied. "We've been busy too. If you will deliver your book of helpful hints to the publisher tomorrow, we will see that it is widely distributed across Tarra. Raffaella will see that it is translated into as many languages as needed."

"Hey, terrific. I know that those women who lucked out last time are definitely going to need the hints this time. I wonder. Did the mantis implant my memories on how to use some of the things, like the yokes?" I asked.

She shrugged her shoulders, and I noticed that she had not created arms on her body this time. However, both of their feet were normal, not misshapen as ours now were. "You probably are wondering why we've come again so soon," she asked. We nodded. I figured that it must not be super critical this time, since neither seemed worried or concerned.

"We've been examining many feet today, and we want your permission to examine yours, too, if you don't mind," she answered.

What a weird request, I thought. Well, maybe they needed to see close up what had happened to our feet. "Sure go ahead," I replied, curiously.

While she took off my shoes and began feeling mine, Macario did the same with Marco. "Valerio gave me a good massage. Honestly, Macario, my feet were aching fiercely when I got back today. Apparently, we cannot walk on our toes for too long a time. Bummer."

He nodded, but seemed preoccupied. After a few minutes, they traded places. "Hey, that tickles," I giggled as his hands moved along my steeply curved arches. He smiled but continued his observations.

Then, they put our shoes back on us and took their seats across from us once more. "So, what was that all about?" I asked, unable to contain my curiosity any longer.

"Well today, Raffaella and I have looked over at least a hundred sets of feet, male and female. So far, each observation has yielded the same result. Most curious. I only wish I knew if this effect will hold true for everyone on Tarra," he began.

"Okay, what effect?" I replied rather tartly. I wish that he'd just come out and say it. Our feet are doomed or whatever.

"I don't want to raise false hopes," he answered.

"Out with it, Macario. We can take it," I endeavored to get him to continue.

"Okay, Bethany. Please keep this to yourselves for now." After Marco and I promised, he said, "We both believe that the mantis geneticist has made an error in his mutations. Either that, or he has made a terrible miscalculation about our species, I mean your bodies."

"What do you mean?" Marco asked, becoming curious himself.

"Allow me to explain this fully, Marco. We humans are actually a composite of four parts. First, there is you, the immortal spiritual being, the personality, the individual himself. You are really all that is vital and important here. The other three parts are far less important. The second part is your mind."

"Sure that's obvious," he interrupted.

"Third, there is your actual flesh and blood body, which is really more of an engine that uses food as its fuel instead of petrol as do your motor-cars and putt-putts."

"Sure, and it is our bodies that are in real trouble now," Marco interrupted again.

"Very much so, Marco. Yet, there is a fourth component, the low-grade entity, the life force, which actually owns and runs your body, its engineer, so to speak. He keeps your body breathing, handles the digestion of food, and keeps your blood flowing."

"Oh yeh? Where is he? This engineer fellow? I only sense myself here," he replied.

"He resides in your stomach area. It is he, the engineer, who is carrying along the genetic blueprint of our bodies. It is he upon whom the mantis has been experimenting and working their modifications. It is he, the engineer, who has been called upon by their bacteria to alter the form and shape of the body, which he builds and runs."

"That's certainly interesting. I don't think that we've really been much aware of him, the engineer," Marco replied.

Macario smiled, "No indeed, mankind has not. In fact, I doubt very much that the mantis geneticists were all that aware of him either. And that is perhaps where the mantis made his mistake."

"What mistake?" I asked. This was fascinating information. I'd never considered this line of inquiry before. Surely, something had to be running our bodies, keeping them breathing and all that.

"Let me finish first," Macario gently admonished me for being hasty. "I am going to call him the engineer for want of any other term. Now the engineer's job is to equip the body for optimum survival, as he sees it. He's a rugged fellow, not easily harmed or deflected from his seemingly monomaniac drive to keep the body going properly. Over lifetimes, the engineer takes what is thrown at him that potentially can harm his creation, the body, and adapts the next generation of bodies that he builds to deal with that. For example, the Axemen live in the subpolar regions, where winters are long and harsh, fiercely cold, bitterly cold. To counter this, the engineers running those bodies up there have adapted their bodies to better deal with the climate. Their bodies are usually large and carry extra body fat to help insulate them from the cold. Have you ever seen a skinny Axeman? Nope. Further, most all had very thick hair, again to help them with the bitterly cold environment."

"Makes sense. But what has this to do with us?" I asked, following his argument but not seeing it leading anywhere.

"I'm getting to it, dear Bethany. The mantis has foisted off onto the engineers two modifications, which in fact are highly counter to the optimum survival of the engineer's body."

"Ah, our feet," I exclaimed.

He grinned, "Yes, our feet and also your thin waists. He makes his residence down there where it is now only twelve inches around. He feels horribly cramped. He was able more or less to adapt to being confined to a fourteen-inch waist, but that additional two-inch reduction has him fighting mad. In everyone we've examined today, their engineers are also very angry with the current state of your feet. The enforced modifications done without his consent has greatly angered the engineers of those hundreds of people. It is Raffaella's and my opinion that soon the engineers are going to rebel and reform their bodies differently all on their own."

"Wait. Are you saying that our body's engineers are going to undo the mess that our feet are in?" I asked in disbelief.

"Yes, Bethany, we both believe that is very likely going to occur, that and a resizing of your waistlines. Whether the engineers grow your waists back to fourteen inches or even larger, we can't guess yet, but I would not go having a bunch of new dresses made just yet. Hold off on it a little longer. What we don't know is how soon the engineers will rebel and start their reformation work. It could be days, weeks, or months. In any case, we both feel that the state that your feet are in right now will only be a temporary thing."

"Wow! That is the best news I've heard in days!" Marco exclaimed, greatly relieved, especially after today's workout.

"But what about our arms?" I asked what concerned me the most, obviously.

"I am afraid that the engineers have uniformly not considered the lack of arms critical to the survival of their bodies. I doubt very much that they will do anything about them. We can look to Dorota for a model, however. There, the doktors amputated the arms when the babies were born, and the engineers did nothing about their loss."

"Well, I guess that we can accept being armless, if we have our feet back to battery," I sighed. "After all, if we cannot even get around, life is going to be perfectly miserable."

"True. Raffaella and I have discussed this at length today. Our opinion is that if we give a few key engineers in any given country a nudge to get going on this undoing business, then as other engineers see this happening, they too will get going on their own undo operation. We feel that it is kind of like a herd of cattle. Where the leader goes, so goes the rest of the herd. Follow the leader style."

"Hey, that sounds plausible to me," I replied.

He grinned, "I thought that it would. With your permission, Raffaella and I would like to give you and your extended family here a gentle nudge in that direction. If it works, we will do so to many of the key leaders and personnel in all the countries, in hopes that we can start an avalanche of engineers working on undoing these genetic modifications of the mantis."

"You don't have to ask twice!" Marco replied eager to get it started, anything to get his feet back to normal. I could not help wishing our arms could be handled as well, though. Macario smiled and he and Raffaella set to work. I felt a gentle touch on my feet and a sharp electrical jolt in my stomach area.

"There, we're done. However, we have no idea how long it will take or how much discomfort you will experience or how you can manage during the transition period. Please keep us posted. I think it best to wait and see how this works out here in Velona and Barcella before we cover all of Tarra," Macario added. We both thanked them profusely and then called out for everyone else to join us.

We listened as Macario explained all this once more to everyone else. An hour later, after everyone had experienced their gentle nudges, the two left. Naturally, we all chatted about this unexpected news, going to bed far more hopeful than we had been since this whole thing started.

Chapter 4 It Begins on Megalos

Pope Pius I sat on his throne, his head cupped in his hands. Late night mass had ended, he'd barely been able to stand during his most holy ceremony. His feet ached, but he'd managed not to show fleshly weakness before the large assemblage of fellow priests, guards of his holy city, the Mano del Dio, and the holy nuns. He'd said late night mass every night since he'd become their pope so many years ago. Yet, never had his feet hurt so badly.

Were the rumors true? Had the northern plague finally reached this far south, to the island of Megalos? He doubted that very much, since by all reports those affected by the plague in the northern realms had recovered. Some said divine intervention was involved. After all, women did not lose their arms mysteriously, and they certainly did not have them somehow regrown, as if they had never lost them.

By now, it was a well-documented fact that over a year ago, some kind of plague had struck twenty northern countries, leaving them mutants. Women lost their arms, had their waists shrunk, and had some permanent makeup worn only by the painted whores of back alleys. Even the men had grown strange ear lobes, like the women, lobes that touched their shoulders. That was how any mutant could easily be recognized. Everyone now knew that. In spite of his papal orders, hardly anyone had any contact with the northern mutants any longer. Fear of contagion exceeded all other emotions. Rightly so, plague was a nasty affair, incurable, or so his physicians told him. Yet, now these very same whores had mysteriously regrown their arms. How was any of this possible? It had somehow to be Lord Jehosa's work, what else could explain it? Surely not these wild tales of aliens and flying ships in the sky.

Yes, many such reports had come to Megalos, but he gave them no credence. There were no such things as flying ships. Delusion. Man was easily deluded, seeing things that were not real, that were not there. Perhaps they had all smoked opium or perhaps the drug had been introduced into their food supply. That was far more likely in his mind than an admission of non-existent flying machines.

What troubled him the most was that now the plague was apparently beginning to affect Megalos. During the day, he'd been called to the nunnery right here in his own Holy City, Constanza City. Nun after nun had shown him her arms, arms that looked shriveled and shrunken. Panic-stricken women, these nuns were slowly becoming unable to care for their own basic needs, let alone the needs of the Holy Father, his priests, the Mano del Dio, and the city guards. Indeed, his manservant had to prepare his evening meal this evening.

Still, he took heart in the fact that the nun's ears appeared perfectly normal and no garish makeup had appeared upon their lips and eyes. Surely this was not the plague, which had struck those northern countries. The symptoms were not the same, he reasoned. Yet, tonight, tonight during the mass he was certain that something unspoken was occurring among his holy worshipers. The men walked in hesitant steps, as if their very own feet were aching somehow. The poor nuns cried throughout the entire mass, praying almost constantly, begging for absolution for their sins. Sins. Oh, the confessions that he and his fellow priests had taken from them afterwards. "Forgive me father, for I have sinned. I have forgotten to say my prayers when I rose this morning." Drivel. Not a single true sin had they heard this evening.

Still, something was going on, he was convinced of it. But what? In the north, the only plague effects upon their men had been that their ear lobes had lengthened and they had a heightened sexual drive. He felt his ears, normal as always. He felt no sexual urges at all, but he had never felt such towards the nuns in the first place. Young boys, well that was another matter — between himself and Lord Jehosa — a matter with which he fought every day of his adult life, unwilling to give in to those urges. Even now, the drive was no more than it had always been. Surely, the plague could not be affecting him or his men. Yet, something was, but what? He held his head and sighed, admitting that he had no idea. Instead, he began to pray to Lord Jehosa for guidance, guidance he would surely need on the morrow.

Dawn's first light rays shown through the stained glass window of the Holy Bedroom. Dust motes sparkled. The late fall day had come to sunny Megalos, bringing welcome relief from the slow cooking heat of the summer months. Indeed, in this land of broiling summers, these balmy fall days were welcomed by all. The welcoming sun found not the appreciating audience that it had for several weeks now.

Pope Pius I roused at first light, as he had every day of his life. He rose and stood to change from his plush, royal purple nightgown into his morning bathrobes, unaware of the change in his feet. No longer did his ankles bend; rather they were locked in a pointed down position, his toes pointing to the floor. As he stood, his whole body weight balanced on the tips of his toes like a ballet dancer en pointe.

Taken by complete surprise, he fell over, smashing his head against his oak table, jamming his outstretched right arm as it crunched into the floor.

Red ooze trickled down his forehead; pain throbbed in his elbow and shoulder. Pope Pius I cried out in pain, and then struggled to a sitting position, made all the more difficult by the weight of his rotund frame. His vice: he ate too much. His left hand sought the bump on his head. Feeling the wetness, he pulled his hand before his eyes. Red. I'm bleeding, he thought. He looked around for something on which to wipe his bloody hand. Finding nothing within reach, he used his nightgown and then felt his right arm. From the pain in his shoulder, he guessed that he may have broken something and at last called out loudly for help, trusting his manservant would enter shortly. He slept nearby and always rose with the dawn to assist His Holiness in dressing.

Aias had not entered yet. Strange, Aias had never been late a morning in his life. "Aias! Please, I need help." He called out, but stopped once more to wipe the tickling on his face, which only spread the gushing blood over his face. Now he purposely used a bottom corner of his gown to wipe his whole face, alarmed at the amount of red, which appeared on it as he pulled it away from his head. "Aias! Help!"

Relief! He heard the doorknob turning. Ah, Aias at last. "Aias, I've fallen. Help," he called out, certain that his manservant would appear in an instant. As the door opened, his eyes expected to see his faithful Aias, a tall, thin bronzed skinned man. He saw only open space beyond the door! Noise. He heard noise on the floor at the door, and at last, his eyes lowered to the floor at the doorway. Shock filled his mind.

Aias was entering, but was crawling on his hands and knees, like some cur of a dog in a back alleyway! His eyes were bloodshot; a clear wetness covered his face. "Aias! What's wrong?" Pope Pius I called out, forgetting his own plight, an innocent spill from his bed, and a careless one at that.

Aias moved dog style towards him, "I, I can't walk anymore!" He forgot to address His Holiness in the proper manner, so great was his despair. Pope Pius I ignored that and beckoned the man to come to him. "You're hurt! Let me get some water and bandages!" The pope felt his stomach going queasy on him as he watch the pitiful man crawling to his night stand to fetch the water pitcher and wash rags. Pushing and sliding them before him, Aias finally reached the pope. Quickly, he washed the blood off his face, but asked him to hold another rag to his head.

"My arm, I think it's broken," the faint voice of the pope whispered to Aias, who began examining the man's arm and shoulder.

"I think that it may just be dislocated. I have to get the doctors. Can you get back into your bed?" he asked. With an effort, the pope made the attempt, but again, his feet failed to work, and he slumped back onto the floor, like an overweight sack of potatoes. Aias, whose feet were likewise mutated, simply could not lift the man while he himself was confined to the floor on his hands and knees as well.

However, in their struggles to get him up onto the bed, Pope Pius I finally got his feet into a position where he could see them. His face told all to Aias, who in a flash realized that his pope had yet to see his own grossly mutilated feet. "Dear god! What has happened to my feet?" the pope wailed. "I can't bend them!"

"Like mine, Your Holiness. See?" Aias slid his feet around so that the pope could see that his were the same way. "I can only crawl now, but I will go get us some help. You sit here and hold that rag to your head." With that, Aias began his slow crawl towards the door and out, leaving the door wide open.

Pope Pius I stared long at his feet, even feeling them with his good left hand. Panic began to eat at his stomach, and he felt sick, but unable to reach the chamber pot. He heard the sliding of Aias now moving some distance away and more doors opening. Instead of bringing relief, the opened doors brought even more distress to His Holiness. Voices, terrified voices, screaming voices, sheer terror — all these and more echoed faintly into his bedroom and into his ears. Women, the nuns, were shrieking, wailing, crying out in terror and panic from their dorm rooms. Men's voices, thousands of them, crying out in horror floated into his room and ears, like some symphony from Lucifer's Realm! What was happening? Had the world gone insane? Had the Day of Judgment come? Slowly the notion that the Holy End of All Days had arrived crept into the back of his mind. He began reciting a litany of Holy Prayers.

How long he sat there, he had no idea. At last, several panic-stricken men came crawling into his room, Aias leading the way. The disabled men struggled mightily to get him up onto his bed. Then, the doctors began treating his head wound and discussing among themselves what must be wrong with his right arm. A searing blast of pain accompanied the repair of his dislocated shoulder, which brought immense relief at once. Finally, Pope Pius I felt able to speak.

"What is happening out there? The wailing, the screaming? Are we under attack?" he asked.

"Your Holiness, some are saying the Day of Judgment is upon us," one of his priests who had come with the doctors answered him, unsure of exactly how to answer His Holiness. Indeed, he had come seeking Holy Answers from his pope. "Our men, all of our men cannot walk any longer. Our feet —

they no longer bend; we cannot touch the floor. Our feet only point straight down; we cannot walk on the tips of our toes, though I tried, Your Holiness. We are forced to crawl now."

The pope felt another wave of nausea coming, but fought hard to suppress it. He had to set an example for the others. He was the Holy Father. His priest continued, "We entered the Holy Nunnery in answer to their screams." Quickly, the priest made the sign of the cross across his chest. "It is terrible. They, they, they are all afflicted horribly. All the Holy Sisters have lost their arms, and their feet are far more grotesquely distorted than ours are. Theirs are bent in some crazy U-shape. Only their toes touch the ground. Their heels lie six inches above the floor. They too cannot walk, and without arms, they cannot crawl. They lie wretchedly in their beds, resting in their own bodily fluids, unable to rise and use their chamber pots. Holy Father, has the Day of Holy Judgment indeed come unto us at last? Is this not the Final Days as spoken of in the Holy Gospels? What are we to do?"

"I, I must attend to our needs. Holy Mass, yes, we must gather in our most Holy Chapel and pray with all our hearts in these our final hours. Yes, gather everyone and I will come unto them," he replied, more mechanically than rationally.

"But you cannot crawl, not with your shoulder," a doctor protested. "Bring the chair with wheels for His Holiness!" Quickly, someone began crawling away to find it, and the pope cringed as he saw how the man had to move like some unwanted dog. Meanwhile, the others attempted to get him dressed in his grandiose attire that he always wore on the most important, the most holiest of times. Crawling made this difficult, especially when neither the pope nor those assisting him could stand. It was a mighty struggle to get him attired. By then, the man returned pushing the chair on wheels before him as he crawled into the pope's Holy Bedroom. Only with great effort were they able to get him up and into the chair, he wobbled something awful as they held him sort of on his feet, slipping the chair under him. The horridness of this simple action was not lost on the pope, who became even more convinced that the Holy Day of Judgment had indeed come.

Incongruous. Yes, that was how the pope finally saw them as the men began pushing him along in his chair, while they crawled along on the floor, pushing him ahead of themselves. The wails and cries of stark, unabated terror grew louder as they passed by the ornate pillars holding the vaulted ceiling of the passageway, which led to the Holy Nunnery here in the huge Constanza City complex. Their despair sent chills down his spine. He nearly panicked himself and was thankful that the others were pushing him along, away from that terror filled cacophony. He knew that he could not face them. He was not that strong of a man.

As they turned and headed down another long ornate hallway with great tapestries and magnificent paintings done by the finest artists of Megalos, his Supreme Prelate of the Mano del Dio came crawling up to him, as if some pitiful dog seeking a bone from his master. The pope noticed that the man's hands were bloodied as well as his knees. He'd been crawling far too much; a trail of blood marked his path up to the pope.

"Your Holiness, I bring terrible words. I sent out men to check on the nearby port city. All there are similarly affected. Women have no arms; men's feet are as ours, pointed like some overgrown fly. Women's feet are so curled that they cannot walk or stand. One of our Mano in Galantas has arrived; thank the Lord for horses! His feet too are gone, and he reports that it is the same in Galantas. Women's arms are gone; men's feet are frozen like inflexible sticks. Everywhere it is the same. Should I send out riders to the other cities on Megalos? Please, Your Holiness, I, your humble Supreme Prelate, beg for your Divine Wisdom. How can I protect you any longer when I too cannot walk but am forced to move as a dog?" He hung his head downward as a mastiff who knows that he has disobeyed his master and seeks forgiveness.

"You have done well, my son. Rise up, look not down, for the Day of Holy Judgment has come. Now the Faithful may rejoice, Lord Jehosa has come unto us at last, to take us, his Holy Faithful unto his bosom, unto his Holy Realm. Come. Rise. Gather all our faithful unto me. Together, we will sing praises unto Lord Jehosa until he comes at last to raise us up unto Heaven above." Pope Pius I felt an immense relief. There, he had said the words, and at last, he felt that he was doing the right action, the right thing. Confidence renewed, he bade the crawling faithful to carry out his request.

An hour later, the Inner Private Chapel was filled beyond capacity. Every man who was inside Constanza City had crawled into the chapel. The lucky ones had been able to find a seat on the hard pews and sat bravely facing their Holy Pope, who looked resplendent in his gold-lined purple robes, sitting before the Holy Altar, surrounded by Holy Images of the Great Messiah hanging from the Holy Cross, the Virgin Mother holding the product of the Immaculate Conception in her arms, and above both of these magnificent paintings and above the Holy Pope Pius I, hung from the vaulted and frescoed ceiling some hundred feet above their heads, the huge golden cross representing Lord Jehosa himself. No idol did these men ever attempt to use to display their God on high. Only the magnificent cross, signifying the load that man must bear if his precious soul were to gain entry unto Heaven above.

The whispered voices of the thousands of men echoed in the huge vaulted chamber, but were nearly drowned out by the distant wailing, screaming, and terror filled cries of some five hundred nuns, none of which had been brought to this final mass. At last, Pope Pius I rang his Holy Bell, which announced the commencement of High Mass as it always had. It brought comfort and resolve to the pope.

"All praise to Lord Jehosa as we, his most faithful followers gather here in his Most Holiest of Chapels on Tarra to celebrate the coming of the Day of Holy Judgment as foretold centuries ago in our Holy Gospels. Across our world, it has come at last. Our fleshly bodies are struck down, even as we slept. Judgment Day is at hand. Let us begin by unleashing our Holy Voices unto Lord Jehosa, let us welcome him into this Most Holy House of Prayer. Join me in singing Psalm 29." He began the chant and thousands of voices joined his; the sounds sent tingles of energy throughout his entire body, a feeling that he'd never felt before. He knew that Lord Jehosa had just touched him. Lord Jehosa was here, here in this very temple unto God!

Psalm after psalm the men sung, between which Pope Pius I said the Last Holy Mass and revealed that the Divine Light of Lord Jehosa was here in this Holy Chamber with them, beckoning them to come unto him. So powerful was his conviction, so desperate their situation that the Mano del Dio began to assist these, the Most Holy of Men to arise unto their Holy Salvation. Crawling on their blood soaked knees, oblivious to their own fleshly body's pain, they did their Holiest of Deeds. A simple knife slice across a throat whose bare neck was uplifted towards Heaven and Lord Jehosa helped these Most Worthy to ascend, this the Day of Holy Judgment.

An hour later, Pope Pius I finally heard only his own voice singing loudly the Last Psalm. A very bloody Supreme Prelate crawled up to him and whispered, "It is done. All the Faithful have Arisen unto Heaven. We are the last. Come, let us join Lord Jehosa at last, Your Holiness. Our long and arduous work is finally complete. Let us bask in the radiance of our Lord."

"Bless you my son, bless you, for you have done the Holy Work of Lord Jehosa." He made the sign of the cross over his prelate, cupped his hands in holy prayer, felt cold steel upon his throat, felt a warm wetness flowing down his chest and robes. Darkness came; he slipped out of his body, which now joined thousands of others here in the Holy Chapel. He waited patiently for the touch of Lord Jehosa, for the Hand of God to lift him up unto Heaven. Nothing. He waited patiently. Still nothing. He began to rise above the chapel and then found himself outside his church complex. All was bright and sunny. All was quiet. *I am here, your Most Holy Servant*, he called out, though without a voice. Nothing. Nothing at all, save several sea birds gliding in the sky, oblivious to the trials and tribulations of man. He waited. Day grew into night and still nothing. Had Lord Jehosa forsaken him? Had he been left behind, forgotten? Panic struck him.

Light. He saw the light. Something reacted within him. He was compelled to follow that light! Perhaps Lord Jehosa had finally come for him. There had been so many others to lift unto heaven. It had taken time, yes, that had to be it. He arrived at the light. Suddenly, he seemed to have all of his memories flying by in some mad jumble of disorder, yet nothing was here. Nothing was causing this. Still his memories — wait! Were these even his memories? A woman giving birth? He'd not been married. He grew more and more confused, until at last, he forgot who he was. Now only a single impulse flowed through his entire beingness. Find a new baby body. A command, a command that he could not disobey! He had to follow it. Find a new baby body. He shot off like a rocket to Megalos with that single thought in mind. He had no other thoughts, no other ideas. He could not resist that heavy command delivered by some monstrous head, which looked like a mantis, a giant one at that. He did not realize that the command had come from his past, some five centuries ago, a command buried deep within his own unconscious mind. Time had become a confused jumble for him. He had to find a new baby body. Nothing else mattered. Nothing.

Senator Aminta Akantha headed through the crowded streets of Galantas, the capital of Megalos, disgusted as usual. As one of only five female senators, her opinions were seldom counted, her ideas never accepted by the male dominated Senate. Indeed, she often felt as if she were just another object, brought into the Senate for looks. Men, she thought harshly to herself as she trudged along the streets, heading towards her home away from home. Elected as the Senator for West Edge, the small mountainous sector of the island close to the large continent of the Southlands, she had done her best these past four years to represent her constituents. All to little avail, she mused. Not one of her ideas had been accepted. The best that she had done was to cast useless vetoes on measures contrary to what she believed her constituents back home desired.

"Well, the Senate never does actually accomplish anything," she said to herself in disgust. She knew, as did everyone, that the true power, the true leadership of Megalos now resided in the pope of the Church of Jehosanity, whose headquarters was within his own private world of Constanza City down by the northern ocean port. It wasn't always this way; she remembered her history lessons. Once the Senate ruled, making the laws of the land, while the Emperor carried them out. Yet, that form of government had long ago disintegrated when the Emperors began to usurp the power of the Senate. Serves them right, she thought, because after that, the Pope usurped the reins of power from the Emperor. Touché, she thought.

What's the point of sticking around here any longer, she wondered as she passed a water boy calling out his wares. The day was warm and she ignored him, continuing her fast pace. The President today had rejected another of her proposed bills. That made fifty-two that he'd summarily dismissed out of hand. Had he even read her proposal? She doubted it very much. Give up? No way! Aminta was a fighter — she always had been, all of her twenty-four years.

She was still young, but not particularly attractive or so she always considered. Overly tall, she claimed, reaching all of six-two in her flat sandals. Aminta wore her wavy brown hair short enough that it didn't touch her shoulders, a necessity she thought during the heat of Megalos summers. Some claimed that she had a scathing tongue, but they deserved all her ire, she thought. Childless and widowed that was her cross to bear.

She'd lost her first one to a miscarriage and the second had died at birth. Four years ago, her Centurion husband had gone and gotten himself killed in a skirmish over in the Southlands. With little chance at finding a husband at her age and having lost both children, she solemnly and silently bore her cross. Still, she had been elected four years ago to represent the West Edge and had accepted the role cast for herself, believing then that she could perhaps make a difference in the Senate. Today, she accepted that as total naiveté. How could she have been so unobservant? Ah well, in two more years, she could quietly return to her inherited family country home. Of course, she had no idea what she would do once she had returned home.

At last, she reached the gated entrance to her small home here in Galantas. Senator security was important and she dug out her key to unlock the gates, but not before glancing over her shoulder to make sure no one was nearby. As soon as she had entered, she re-locked the gates and headed up the date tree-lined steps that led to her white marble temporary home away from home. The front portion had white marble sides with a red tiled roof; this section was the only secure portion, housing her bedroom and a combined small kitchen and dining room. The rear door opened onto the usual open aired buildings so common on Megalos. Marble columns held up an ornate domed ceiling, again covered with the familiar red tiles. Three sides were open to the air, but thin veils of curtains could be lowered. It was in these open areas where most residents of Megalos dwelled, obtaining some slight relief from the broiling summer sun and picking up the occasional sea breezes which reached this far inland, some fifty miles.

Her single servant woman called out from the open-air quarters, a mulato named Ari Nuo who was also twenty-four, "Dinner is in ten minutes, Miss Aminta." Ari traced her heritage to a black skinned slave woman named Nuo, who had born a daughter of one of the Senators. Her mother had now passed away and Ari was fending for herself. Of course, there were virtually no opportunities for employment for a mulato anywhere on Megalos, except as domestic servants. Ari, who dreaded becoming a play toy of some self-important man, had jumped at the chance to provide domestic service for Aminta when she had appeared in Galantas. The two had been together now for four years. Ari respected Aminta highly because she treated her like any other woman, ignoring her mulato heritage. Here inside their small home, she felt whole, like a real person. Once she stepped beyond those gates, her heritage always became enforced upon her again. Still, she bore it; going to the market was one of her domestic duties.

Although it was late October, the weather was still quite warm, some eighty degrees. A hint of the distant sea, which Ari had never seen, drifted through the open aired rooms where she finished preparing their evening meal. Ari wore the thinnest of togas, which allowed her dark brown form to be readily visible, but it was cool. Shortly, Aminta joined her, having changed from her grey toga indicative of a Senator into a similar gauze of a toga, which readily revealed her bronzed skin. Aminta smiled at Ari and proceeded to light the two candles on the perfectly laid out table. The two were wont to dine in style.

As they sat down to eat, Ari asked, "Miss Aminta, did they accept your proposal today?"

She sighed, "No, but then when has a man ever accepted anything that we women do?" Her words sounded harsh, but she meant every word. Ari grinned and nodded her complete acceptance of Aminta's declaration. Men were the root of all evil in the world, at least according to Ari.

Ari teased, "Well, I bet they would accept your proposal, if you proposed that the male Senators received a ten thousand gold piece raise, while the women Senators got only a hundred." Both women chuckled. A bit later, both women were full and sat back sipping their red wine.

"You know, I have been feeling so tired all day long, Miss Aminta. My arms feel like they weigh a ton. I must apologize for not getting all the dusting done today. I am just out of sorts today. Tomorrow I will be better."

"That's fine Ari. No problem, the dust can wait. There is always more dust. Say, come to think of it, my arms have been acting strangely all day today too. Somehow, they seem weak to me. Must be the weather. Fall's here now. Come on, I'll lend you a hand with the dishes and we can turn in early. I bet a good night's sleep will benefit us both greatly. Besides, tomorrow is Saturday; we've nothing to do but relax until Monday." Ari grinned and agreed.

Late the next morning, Aminta was aroused by a shriek coming from Ari's bed, one gauze curtain from hers here in the back open area. She struggled to sit up, but her arms didn't seem to be working right. Then she saw her arms and screamed as well. They seemed to be about half as long from shoulder to finger tips, as they had been when she went to bed last night. Worse, her upper arm muscles were almost gone, leaving little but skin on bone. She could barely move them. She struggled to her feet and nearly fell over. Glancing at her feet, she let out another sharp cry. Her feet were grossly malformed; the beginnings of some enormous U-shaped arch had formed. Hesitantly, she tried to stand on them and found that she could as long as she stood only on her toes. Her heel could no longer touch the ground. She tiptoed across the small bedroom, pushing aside the gauze veil that separated her bed from Ari's.

Ari was sitting up staring at her arms, which looked much like Aminta's. Her feet also looked malformed. The two women sat on Ari's bed and held onto each other crying for quite some time. "What is happening to us?" Ari finally managed to say.

"I don't know. I just don't know, but I do know that I am famished. Come on, let's help each other into the kitchen and see if we can make something to eat, Ari." Putting their withered arms over each other's shoulders, the two took small, hesitant steps toward the kitchen. They paused at the door, which was shut. It was not locked, but the doorknob became a barrier. They both attempted to turn it with their feeble arms, but neither had the strength to rotate it enough. For a minute, the two women panicked and began crying.

Finally, the fighter in her kicked in, and Aminta glared at the doorknob. She carefully sat down and began fiddling with it using her toes. Click. Finally, the knob rotated enough to open. Ari held it open. "Well, I don't want to have to do that again. Come on, let's find something that we can use to prop it open!" Together, they moved a small statue of some forgotten goddess into position, holding the door open. Slowly they made their way into the kitchen.

Sometime later, they managed to carry their breakfast out to the open aired table and ate, but only with extreme difficulty. Their arms barely were able to lift the fork and spoon up to their mouths. While they were eating, the ever-present street noises began to filter into their space. Only now, both women detected fear and panic among the voices. They picked up snatches of conversations.

"It's the plague!" "We've all gotten that northern plague!" "There is no cure." Repeatedly and in many different ways, they overheard similar conversations all morning long. Both women were terrified, but tried to maintain a brave face. They had no thoughts of leaving the home in search of a doctor. Everyone knew that there was no cure for a plague. One either succumbed or one survived. That was the way of plague.

"We'd better get lots of bed rest," Aminta suggested, trying to remember anything useful that she'd ever heard about illnesses. Sleep was often prescribed, hence her only positive suggestion. The two headed back to bed. For a time, Aminta could not sleep. She kept looking at her arms to make sure that they were still there. The street noise, which was normally loud of a Saturday, continued to filter into her ears, bringing with it all manner of wild speculations. None of which gave her any comfort. Now voices were saying that this was the Day of Holy Judgment come at last, whatever that meant. She was not a religious person. By late afternoon, the street noise died down, and she fell into a deep sleep finally.

Sunlight roused her. Aminta awoke from a strange, evil dream, a dream in which her arms had withered and her feet had become grossly malformed. She tried to sit up and found that her arms were not working. Eyes wide open, she looked for her arms and shrieked wildly. Her arms were now completely gone! Vanished! No trace remained that she had ever had arms attached to her bronze shoulders. Panic flooded over her entire body and she screamed.

Another scream brought her out of her panic — a nearby scream of terror. Ari! "Ari! Ari!" she called out. Yes, it was a terrified Ari screaming wildly from no more than ten feet from her bed. Aminta sat up. She still had her feet, only now they were even more twisted. "I'm coming, Ari!" she yelled and attempted to get to her feet.

Standing only on her toes, for no other part of her foot would touch the ground, she felt a great "springyness" in her feet. Very, very slowly and equally carefully, Aminta moved across the small bedroom and through the veil, which separated their two bedrooms. Ari was sitting up on her bed, just as armless as she was. The poor mulato was screaming wildly, shaking her head no-no-no. Aminta moved to her side and sat down beside her. Only then did Ari realize she was there and ceased her wild screaming. The two women laid their heads on each other's shoulders and cried together for quite some time.

Later, Aminta suggested, "Maybe if we eat enough, our arms will grow back, Ari. Didn't those women in the northern lands have their arms come back in time? I think that's what everyone was saying. If we go slowly, we can rather walk."

Without arms, they found making anything to eat impossible. However, they managed to get the block of cheese out and began gobbling it with their mouths — like a pair of mice, Aminta thought. Finally stuffed with cheese, they sat back looking at each other. Now they began to hear other women and even men screaming in terror. Based on the volume of the sounds, they could not tell if it was near neighbors or more distant ones. Aminta judged it was both. She strained her ears for any news, but concluded this plague had spread all over the city of Galantas, near and far from her small home. As soon as she realized this, she had a very sick feeling in her stomach. All Galantas was affected.

Ari whispered, "It's coming to an end, isn't it? Life, I mean. We are all dying, right?"

"I — I don't know, Ari. I don't know. We have only lost part of our bodies so far. Most of us is still here. Let's lie down. Perhaps sometime soon the doctors will come by with some medicine for us all. Surely, this plague is widespread, and they surely know so many of us have it. I'm sure eventually someone will come by to help us. You don't believe that Jehosanity crap about the End of Days do you?"

"No I don't. They won't even let me in their churches. It's not my religion. You think someone will come? Will they even help me? I mean give me medicines?" She didn't add that she had no religion.

Aminta caught the subtle clue from Ari. "If the doctors come with medicine, I will insist and demand they give some to you as well, if they do not. Trust me, Ari. I won't let you down. I think we're in this together, you and me." Ari smiled, greatly relieved to hear the encouraging words. She had picked the right person to work for this time.

Monday came and still no one had come by to check on them. Aminta didn't really expect that anyone would, however, especially when the entire world had been eerily silent since Sunday. Around three in the afternoon, both women were starving. They had managed to devour all the food that was in reach, low to the ground so to speak. They stood balanced precariously on their toes looking longingly at all the food on the higher shelves, away from the mice, which were a constant problem everywhere on Megalos. Open houses invited these guests. Aminta never did bother to get a cat.

Suddenly, a large pile of objects appeared in her front room. Poof. Right out of nowhere, the two women claimed. Ever so slowly because of their super arches, the two moved into the room to see what had just materialized. "Look, shoes," Aminta exclaimed. "What weirdly shaped shoes. You know, they might just fit our feet as they are now. I heard that up north during the plague things like this suddenly appeared. Come on; let's see if they fit us. Anything is better that the way we are now. My feet ache from this little bit of walking, like they are about to break in half."

With some effort, both women managed to slip their feet into the strange shaped shoes. When they stood up, the relief both felt shown on their faces. Ari exclaimed, "Ah, they fit and my feet finally don't hurt when I stand. I wonder if we can walk in them any better?"

The two walked around the room a bit testing them out, before Aminta commented, "We are going as slow as a snail! I can't take any step larger than maybe three inches! It will take forever to walk to the Senate from here."

Ari grinned, "Assuming there is still even a Senate." Both women chuckled, but Aminta began to wonder if Ari just might be right. They moved back to examine the large pile of things. Aminta sat down on the chair, which had a sloped writing surface about six inches from the floor; her feet moved over the flat surface. Suddenly, she had a vision of someone sitting here writing. Ari also saw a similar image in her mind.

"Say, Aminta, you could probably write your proposals using that desk. Oh! You have to write with your feet now. I have these strange visions."

"Me too, I saw myself, no — someone else I think, sitting here writing a page." Slowly, the two women began having other images float into their consciousness. Item by item, they began to see how it might be used by a woman with no arms. Aminta finally said, "Ari, it is a whole kitchen here that we might somehow be able to use. Only problem is, who can we get to install it?"

"More to the point, how can we get to all our food on those higher shelves, Aminta? We've got to figure that one out soon. I am getting terribly hungry again," Ari replied.

By suppertime, the two inventive women had arranged a series of boxes and chairs before the pantry walls and the kitchen stove and sink. Working together, they had retrieved most all their food supplies, piling them on to the counter top. Now the two began to stand on the boxes and chairs balancing each other with their bodies, while Ari attempted to use one foot to cook some supper. Well after nightfall, they finally finished their supper and headed to bed, exhausted from their day's efforts.

Tuesday came and they continued to aid each other, managing to cook two meals that day. Both women continued to hope that someone would come to assist them. Maybe they could beg and plead with them to install this strange kitchen somehow, which someone had given to them. No one came. Further, the eerie silence continued. No street sounds came into their ears, none at all.

Wednesday arrived and still no one came; no sounds echoed from the street. Normally, Mondays were Ari's market days. That is, she would visit the farmer's markets and the various shops, gathering up the week's supply of groceries. By Wednesday, they were beginning to run low of things to cook, especially perishables. Aminta realized that they were going to have to do something themselves, but what? Already the two had worked out how to use the awkward yokes to carry things. "Perhaps, Ari, we should try to go shopping together. We do need many things or we are going to be in major trouble. We're about out of food."

"Will it be safe for us? How can we possibly manage, Aminta? The men at the markets will need money, and we have no hands to give them the coins. Besides we have no hands to pick out what we need."

"We must use our feet, Ari. What other choice do we have? We haven't died yet; we've not lost any more parts of our bodies. I am way past needing a haircut, Ari. I've never allowed my hair to be this long! Good thing it is not summer or I would be sweating to death from such long hair." It reached down to the middle of her back. Ari's hair now reached the small of her back, since she usually allowed hers to fall over her shoulders. Neither could decide if they had lost anything more around their waists. Both had been concerned about finding themselves with such tiny waists, but so far, they could not tell that they'd actually lost some organs. They breathed, their blood flowed, and their digestive systems worked as always.

By now, they both had realized that working together they were able to accomplish what one could not do alone. They had bonded as never before. "Okay, I guess that we do not have any other choice, Aminta. But we will have to wear a toga; we can't go out in public as we are." Both women were completely naked and had been since waking up without their arms. This way, they could easily and readily use the chamber pots. Besides, they had no idea how to dress themselves. Now they had to tackle this detail.

Fortunately, togas were easy to slip into, especially when each woman helped the other. Aminta wore her official Senator toga. Instantly recognized by all, she calculated that no one would dare accost her or Ari while they were out. Such was a high crime in Galantas. Fixing breakfast and dressing to go shopping consumed the morning. Not until noon did the two finally step under their yokes and begin taking their tiny shuffling steps towards the front door.

After a few perplexing minutes working hard to get the doorknob to work, Ari slid part of a chair into the entrance way to keep the door from fully closing. A few more minutes and the shuffling women faced their next obstacle, the locked gates, designed to provide them some protection, but now it was a distinct barrier. Aminta had her keys in her money pouch, which she had draped over her neck. Actually, Ari had helped her get her head through the leather loop.

Both women sat down and Ari fished out the keys with her toes. Aminta spent a very frustrating half hour working with her feet to get the key into the lock and the lock undone. Both women let out a small cheer when the lock finally came loose. A bit later, bearing the yokes over their shoulders, the two finally set out down their street heading for the nearest open air market. After a bit, Ari complained, "At this speed, we are going to take all day getting there." Indeed the two could only take three-inch steps — anymore and they would lose their balance and take a tumble onto the hard stone pavement.

Aminta looked up, startled to hear Ari's voice. "Wait a second, Ari. Do you hear that?"

"What? I don't hear anything at all," she replied growing worried.

"Nothing. Silence. It is midday Wednesday and nothing. The street is completely empty. It's quiet everywhere! Is everyone else dead of the plague? Are we the only ones alive now?" Panic flooded through Aminta as she spoke what she felt. No sense in hiding or pretending now, not as they were. Ari took a deep inhale of breath, trying to calm her nerves.

The two walked on and at last reached the open market some five blocks from their home. The huge square was completely empty. No open shops. No farmers. Nothing. "What will we do now?" Ari asked becoming quite unnerved. So had Aminta. Never had the markets been completely deserted, not even on a holiday. Someone was always there, well except late at night that is.

"Hey, I have an idea. We are close to the President's house. Let's go to the President of the Senate. Surely, he'll have some ideas and can help us out. After all, I still am a fellow ruler, a colleague. This way," Aminta suggested and headed off to their left. After six thousand more tiny steps, they covered the five blocks to where President Demeter's estate lay. A high marble wall surrounded the complex. The two sat their yokes down at his front gates and peered inside. The huge house looked empty of life, but the gate was unlocked, which rather surprised Aminta. Well, he was the President, who would dare harm him or his family, she thought. She sat down and raised the latch to open the gate. As she got to her feet, a pack of large dogs came rushing across the grassy lawn. Growling and fighting viciously with each other, one grabbed whatever they had been fighting over and made a dash across the lawn before the two women. Three others dashed after him.

Aminta gasped and gagged; the dog was carrying a human arm! "Oh my god!" Ari exclaimed, just as shocked as her employer.

As the growling pack disappeared off to their left, probably ducking around the house, a child's voice came from the ajar front door. "Help me! It's safe now, but hurry." The two stared up at the front door and saw an eight year old girl, wearing no clothing but shoes similar to the ones the two women were wearing. She too had no arms, but was trying to wave to them with her head.

"Come on. We have to see what is wrong here," Aminta exclaimed and began moving as fast as she could up the path to the house. Ari was right behind her, but both women kept glancing to the right and left, fearful that the viscous dogs would return at any moment. Four hundred more hasty steps and the two finally reached the relative safety of the porch and the small girl, who was elated to see them.

"Come inside, the dogs won't bother us if we are inside, I expect," she said. "They are hungry too. We haven't eaten for days. Please help me."

"I'm Senator Aminta Akantha and this is my housekeeper Ari Nuo."

"Pleased to meet you," she replied using her best manners. "I am Desma Demeter. You've lost your arms too. I can't walk without wearing these shoes. Can you?"

"No, we can't either. Say, where is your father, President Demeter?" Aminta asked.

"He isn't moving any more, nor is mom. I can't wake either of them up. Please help me."

"Of course we will, Desma. Come on. Show me where they are. Perhaps Ari and I can wake them. We need our President now more than ever." Desma led them into a large study, but even before the entered the room, Aminta knew that smell, that awful smell of rotting, decomposing bodies. Ari gagged and didn't enter the room, but Aminta held her breath and followed Desma to the bodies.

"Papa said the world was ending and he stuck a knife in mom, but she kicked him and he fell over and the knife stuck in him too. I couldn't get it out of him. I tried but I don't have any arms anymore. We've got the plague, haven't we?" Desma put up a brave front, fighting back her grief. She had spent days and hours crying over her parents and now had come to accept the fact that they were not waking up. Aminta saw where the dogs had been at work. The arm was the President's right arm, ripped from his corpse by the starving pack of dogs. Eventually, the pack would return. She knew that they had to get Desma out of this house quickly.

"Where is your toga, Desma? We have to go now before the dogs come back." A scary half hour passed before they had her dressed and ready to go. Aminta did have the common sense to have Desma bring along her yoke however. Just as the three made it to the front door, three dogs came growling and snarling in from the open back portion of the home, making straight for the two corpses. Aminta took that as the sign to get out to the street, and the three took a hasty four hundred more tiny steps, before reaching the safety of the gates. As Aminta began to close them, one mastiff came dashing out of the front door after them, barking and snarling. She managed to slam the gate shut with her body, just in time. The dog jumped up and barked hideously at the three. Ari shrieked involuntarily. Quickly, the three headed on down the street, praying that the pack of dogs would remain inside.

A block later, they halted, staring at a terrible sight ahead of them. A dozen dead bodies, men and women, lay in a random pattern in the street. Carrion birds flapped over the bodies, pecking away, daring the three to approach their find. "What happened here?" Ari asked, trying to hold back from vomiting.

"I don't know, but let's go back the way that we came. Let's try down that way. Surely, we can find a grocery store somewhere."

Ari took a deep breath. "I always go to Bion's."

"Okay, lead the way, Ari." They ducked down another side street. Unfortunately before long, the street began a descent. After all, Galantas was sitting on the top of a mountain. Many streets were anything but level, especially in this wealthier section to the north. The heart of the city was mostly flat. The three found going downhill was exceedingly challenging. By the time that it leveled off, their knees were aching. "We've got to rest a spell, Ari. I can't go on any more." The three sat down on the curb, which smelled of urine. Folks dumped their chamber pots in the gullies at the side of the streets. Rain washed it into the sewers below the city, at least that's what Aminta was led to believe.

An hour later, they neared the butcher's shop. "What's that smell?" Ari asked.

"Smoke. It's smoke! Come on," Aminta urged. Soon the three reached the Bion's Butcher Shop, where Ari bought their fresh meat once a week. Flames were shooting out of the shop's roof. A man was laying part way out of the front door, half in, half out.

"That's Mr. Bion!" Ari cried. The three sat their yokes down and shuffled to him as fast as they dared, nearly losing their balance several times. It seemed to Aminta an eternity passed before they reached the fallen man. Blood seeped out from beneath him and he moaned a little. He was wearing some strange boots, which forced his feet into a ballerina's form, Aminta noticed.

"We've got to get him out of the fire," Aminta yelled.

"How? We don't have any arms to pull him," Ari wailed.

"Use your teeth, Ari. Bite down on his shirt. I'll bite down on his belt. Maybe we can pull him enough." Both women sat down and leaned over. They grabbed a hold of him and used their knees to pull him. Slowly, he slipped on out of the doorway. None too soon, though. As his feet cleared the doorway, part of the roof collapsed and would have crushed his legs had they not taken such hasty action. Now free of the burning building, they rolled him over to examine his wound. Someone had stabbed him in his guts. That much was plain. Working together and with Desma's helpful feet, they got his shirt off him and managed to tie it around the wound, slowing the bleeding for now. He finally came to.

"Help me," he said weakly.

"We are. You've been stabbed. Can you move? Someone has set your store ablaze," Aminta stated the obvious. He struggled and sat up, holding his wound with both hands.

"My shop! Why did they have to burn my shop?" He began to explain. A number of thieves came crawling into his shop demanding meat. He had only a small amount left; the delivery wagon had not come this week. Apparently, that was not enough, and one lad had stabbed him. Another dumped lantern oil over his empty counters and set it ablaze. He remembered trying to crawl out but had passed out.

"You have saved me? You must have," he finished up. "I recognize you. You come each week. Loin roast, right?" he recognized Ari.

She smiled. He remembered her. Few men ever remembered her, for she was an unmentionable, a mulato. "Yes, we came looking for food and found you half out of the door and your store burning. We got you out just in time. Your roof has collapsed."

He looked at her and a smile appeared, "But how? You have no arms any more. How could you do this?"

She grinned, "Aminta's idea. We gripped you with our teeth and used our legs to pull and slide you out. Say, why are you wearing such weird shoes? Has the plague struck you too?" she asked.

"It's my feet. Something is wrong with them. They are somehow fused into this position. Until somehow magically these boots appeared, I could not walk or stand on my feet. Now I can just barely stand, but not really walk. My wife is inside."

Suddenly, Aminta felt sick once more. Had they failed to rescue her as well? He saw her shocked face and added quickly, "No, she has passed away two days ago. She too lost her arms and she took a very bad fall. I crawled to her, but she'd hit her head on the stone basin. There was nothing I could do for her. Now at least she has had a proper burial. Her ashes will merge with Nature, as was her desire. She loved to grow plants, you see."

He looked back at the flames and sighed, "I suppose that you should have left me there. Now I have nothing left. No home, no tools, no wife, no clothes, nothing at all." His voice sank low.

"Oh don't be silly, Bion! You have your life and that is most precious. Come on. You can stay with us. We could use your arms around the place. Can you crawl?" Aminta asked.

"Maybe. Thank you, Senator. I will do all that you ask of me. I will try."

"Good, that's a better attitude. We need all the arms we have left around here. We do have one problem. We are out of groceries, mostly. That's why we are out and about, looking for supplies."

"Why don't we try Loukas? It's only two blocks from here, that way," he pointed.

"Right! Why didn't I think of that?" Ari chided herself for having forgotten that store. She'd often shopped there as well. Maybe it was all the confusion of the day that caused her lapse of memory.

Slowly the four headed on down the deserted street. Bion dragged himself along the ground, but was able to move far faster than the women were. This allowed him not to have to exert himself in his wounded state. As they approached Loukas, they noticed several more fires in the distance, not a good sign. As they headed up the short, paved path to the shop's door, Aminta heard the sound that she dreaded. A low growl stopped them all in their tracks. From the side of the building a large brown mongrel slunk forward, growling in defiance. His large canines dripped saliva onto the brown cobblestones. He hunkered down as if ready to spring at them any moment. Aminta had a vision of the dog ripping what was left of her body to shreds.

She had no weapons, nor could she have used them if she had. Bion sat up ready to protect them with his fists, and the three women moved behind him, frightened to death. Slowly, like a lion on the prowl, the dog crept forward, smelling the fresh blood from Bion's abdomen. He growled again and then it happened, just as Aminta had envisioned. The large dog charged forward towards them, Bion in particular, ready to rip into fresh meat. The dog looked half starved, she noted.

Bang! The loud sound of a long gun startled all four. Right before their eyes, the dog lurched to its right and fell lifelessly to the ground. A curl of smoke drifted across their vision, coming from their right. As the four turned to see who had fired this most welcome and timely shot, they spotted a young man on his knees shuffling his way towards them, a long gun in his hands, a grin on his face.

"Damn dogs anyway!" he called out. "Running in packs they are now. Are you folks all right? It's not safe to be on the streets without some protection. Tenth dog I've killed today. Name's Pavlos. You can thank me now," he said rather boisterously.

"Senator Aminta Akantha, my housekeeper, Ari, the late President's daughter, Desma, and our neighborhood butcher, Mr. Bion," Aminta replied formally. This fellow was a tad arrogant, she thought, but timely.

"I know Bakchos here. Figured you were one of those useless senators. Your toga. Ah well, so I rescued a worthless politician. However, we can't afford to lose our neighborhood butcher now can we, Bion Bakchos?" he replied.

Obviously, this man has some beef with senators, Aminta thought. Such arrogance. Still he had saved them and he didn't have to have done that. No one would have been the wiser. "Sorry about the worthless senators. I have fought them tooth and nail for years, but it doesn't really matter as the stupid Church of Jehosanity actually runs our country now. Why are you on your knees? So you shoot better that way? Sorry, I don't know the first thing about guns, though my late husband was a Centurion. Killed over in the Southlands by a spear, I was told. Still, we are grateful for your timely intervention. Is this grocery store open? We are most desperate to get some supplies." She didn't know why she felt compelled to tell this strange, arrogant man about her late husband. It just came out. Maybe it was the sight of the long gun in his hands, which he was now carefully reloading.

"Got the plague. Haven't you heard, senator? We all got the plaguep; though the damnable Jehosanity crowd thinks it's the end of all days or some such drivel. Yes, I got the plague too," he added, seeing her perplexed look. He slid his legs around, revealing his feet. He too wore the same strange boots that forced his feet to those of a ballerina. He was not pleased to have to reveal it to her. She sensed that he was embarrassed to have to show her his malformed feet. "All the men are like this. We can't walk anymore, if you haven't noticed," he added a bit harshly, defending himself and his humiliation at having become a cripple, crawling about like the dog he'd just shot.

"I'm sorry, Pavlos. Our feet are bad too and worse, we don't have our arms anymore. We are so helpless now. Please, could you possibly lend us a hand? We desperately need groceries and medical attention for Mr. Bion. Thieves broke into his store, robbed him, set his store ablaze, and stabbed him. We were just barely able to rescue him, pulling him out of the inferno. I'm afraid that's the best we can do to bandage him. No arms or hands. Please, can you help us a little," she begged.

"Of course, senator. Don't fret so. Those of us who are left have to help. How bad is it, Bakchos?" He crawled over to the butcher and began examining the wound. "Okay, into the store. You folks pick up what you need, and I'll see what I can find to fix up Bakchos here." She thanked him and they headed up to the door. Although it was locked, Pavlos forced the door open. "We can leave payment for what we take," he added, not wanting the senator to believe that he was a thief. "Never stole a thing in my life. I'm a falconer," he added just so there could be no mistake.

Inside, the three women set about trying to fill their yokes with supplies, while Pavlos crawled down the aisles looking for anything that might be useful in treating the butcher. "How are we supposed to pick up anything and put it into our baskets?" Ari asked, fighting against crying. Her handicap had once more reared its ugly head. Surrounded by all the food in the world, she could not pick up any of it."

"Use our feet as best we can, that's all we can do," Aminta answered her. Pavlos overhead her and slid along the floor to a vantage point from which he could observe their struggles. He was fascinated, curious, and mortified at the same time. Never would he wish such a calamity on anyone, let alone a woman. Yet, this was life now. The plague had come. He had to deal with it. He watched them for a minute. His fascination gave way to one of admiration. The useless senator was leading the way for the others, trying to make the best of their handicap, which he realized was so far beyond his own that he was embarrassed with his earlier harsh words towards her.

Then she spotted him watching her as she tried to get a five pound sack of flour down from the shelf with her foot. She failed. Her face flushed, but Aminta refused to give this arrogant man the satisfaction of seeing her fail. She sat down, slipped off her other shoe, and used both feet to move the sack into her basket. There, she thought to herself, I showed him! She wondered why she had to show him anything, but shook it off as Ari asked if they needed more sugar. When she had a chance to glance his way again, Pavlos had moved on off in search of medical supplies once more.

A half hour later, all three had their yoke baskets as full as they dared. Now came the moment of truth: could they possibly lift them and carry them home? As Aminta tried to lift hers with her shoulders, one basket was heavier than the other was, and she nearly spilled the lot. Pavlos saw it and spoke up, "Let me lend you a hand, senator. I think that the loads have to be balanced." Aminta was grateful for his assistance, watching closely as he adjusted her load several times before it hung properly across her shoulders. Then, he did the same for Ari and for little Desma, whose baskets were much smaller. Still the ten year old was determined to bring home food; she was weak with hunger.

Pavlos also saw this and tore open a sugar snack treat. "Here, Desma, you are going to need some energy to carry that heavy load home." Aminta watched as he held the treat for her as she eagerly gobbled it up and then a second one too. Aminta flashed Pavlos a grateful smile, which he returned.

"Okay, I got the supplies. We ought to leave some funds behind," he said.

"Take a couple of gold from my pouch please. That ought to cover it," Aminta asked. "It will take us another hour to for us to get the coins out." She exaggerated, but he understood.

"Lead the way ladies. I'm going to make sure that you all get safely home," he stated. "Besides, once there, I can treat Bakchos here."

It took them over an hour to get back to Aminta's small home. By now, all three women's feet were aching, unused to such work in their new U-shaped forms. Once inside, Aminta asked Pavlos to shut and lock the gate. "I'll feel safer with the gate locked. I know that it took us almost an hour to get it opened this morning, but with what we've seen today, it ought to be locked I think." He agreed and the five entered the house, struggling to get their heavily laden yokes through the comparatively narrow doorway. Pavlos grimaced as he watched and waited patiently for them to enter so that he and Bakchos could crawl on inside as well. His admiration for these brave women continued to grow on him.

Once inside, Pavlos asked them to boil some water. "First action is get Bakchos patched up. Then, let's see what we can do for some supper, okay?" he took charge. Aminta would have rather given the orders; it was her house, after all. Still, he had the priorities right. Bion had to be tended to first. Their stomachs could wait a while.

"We can get it boiling, but we need the stove lit first, and then you'll have to carry the pot; we can't manage that yet. Perhaps we will be able to do it after we find someone who can install all that kitchen stuff there. It just appeared, but we think we know how to use some of those things," Aminta explained.

An hour later, Bakchos sported a nicely bandaged lower chest, and the five sat crowded around Aminta's table, which was designed for two. The three women were very pleased when the men offered to feed them. Already Pavlos had done most of the work and cooking, greatly speeding everything along. Good thing too, since it was already dark outside. After they finished eating, she put Bakchos to bed in her inside bedroom and he rapidly fell asleep. She put Desma to bed on her own outdoor bed, promising her that she would soon join her.

The sleepy Desma asked, "Are you going to be my mother now?"

"Sure Desma, I would be honored to be your mother as long as you want me to." She gave her a loving kiss on her forehead, before joining Ari and Pavlos in the kitchen. Those two had finished the mountain of dirty dishes that the two women had been setting aside, unable to work out ways and means to wash them by themselves. Ari mostly pointed out what went where in the kitchen.

"I'm turning in, Aminta. Pavlos can have my inside bed close to Mr. Bion in case he needs something during the night," Ari said sleepily.

Her departure left Aminta alone with Pavlos for the first time since they met. In the kitchen, two oil lamps cast a warm glow on the two. She noticed his knees and hands for the first time. Until now, she had not realized the toll all that crawling at her expense had taken on him. "Here, let me tend to your knees and hands, Pavlos. Men were not made to crawl on stone. I'm sorry that you got so banged up on our account."

Using the last of the warm water, she used her feet to wipe off his bloody knees. He then put some salve on them, left over from treating Bion. He also smeared it over his hands as well. All the dishwashing had removed the blood and grim, but his palms were rather raw now.

"Thanks, Pavlos, for helping us today. I don't know what we would have done without your aid. You are welcome to stay the night or longer," she added and wondered why she added that last.

"You are most welcome, senator," he replied. "I'll stay the night. It's not safe to be out at night just now."

"Aminta, please, not senator. I too am disgusted with the usual senators. Please, just Aminta."

He smiled, "Okay, Aminta it is then."

"So, Pavlos, what do you do? I mean before this plague struck us all?" she wanted to know more about this young man. He was tall and slender with kindly blue eyes.

"Falconer. I raise falcons. I like nothing better than to be out in the open countryside and watch my birds fly and soar. There is no greater pleasure in the open freedom of the sky. Perhaps one day, man will be able to fly as well. I hope to be such a man." He was a romantic too, she thought to herself. The two chatted for quite some time before both began yawning and called it a night.

Aminta crawled into bed beside Desma, being as careful as possible not to wake her. That was made all the more difficult because of her lack of arms. She snuggled up to the young girl and gave her another kiss. For the first time in a long time, Aminta felt somehow whole and complete. Perhaps it was having Desma beside her.

At dawn, both Aminta and Ari rose as usual. The others were still sleeping so the two decided to fix breakfast for them. Once more, they had to slide the boxes and chairs back into position so that they could somehow get at the counter, stove, and shelves. Both women didn't notice that Pavlos and Bakchos had awakened and were watching them from their indoors bedrooms.

It took them well over an hour and a half to prepare bacon and griddle cakes, five times longer than Ari would have taken before the plague. Still, between them, they had done it and felt a sense of pride, when they at last called out, "Wake up, sleepyheads. Breakfast is served." The two men took this clue to pretend to wake up and join them.

Over breakfast, Pavlos commented, "Amazing what you can do in your kitchen. I would have figured that you would be completely helpless, you know."

"We very nearly are, Pavlos, but I'll be damned if I am going to just give up and die! We haven't lost everything to this damnable plague. If it is trying to kill me, I won't go down without a fight," Aminta replied.

"Ditto," Ari added. "Life has always been hard for the likes of me — you know mulato and all that."

"Hey, Ari, don't put yourself down like that!" Bakchos protested. "You cannot help what happened to your mother and father. You cannot change your body. I don't care if you are purple skinned. You are you, and folks ought to accept a person for who they really are."

Ari giggled, "Purple?" Bakchos grinned.

"Well, I can see that we need to get your kitchen installed right away," Pavlos changed the topic. "Bakchos, you any good with plumbing or is it only butchering that you are good at?" he teased.

"Ah, anyone can put these things in, Pavlos, though I suppose that we could emulate our illustrious senate and form up some committees to debate just how to do it. Perhaps in a year or two, we might be able to reach some consensus about how to proceed and then take another couple years to do it." Both men roared with the jest, Aminta did too, freeing Ari to join in. She had not been sure if Aminta took this as an insult. After all, she was a senator.

"Point taken, Senator Pavlos," Aminta stated formally. "Honestly, centuries ago, the dam up in the mountains failed. It used to bring fresh water down to Galantas, or so I am told. How many centuries now has the Senate been working on figuring out how to repair that dam? Still we must get our fresh water from the water wagons lumbering up from the coastal areas."

"Point taken, Senator Aminta," Pavlos echoed her and they all roared. Yes, the dam that my Lightning Circle had destroyed to make our escape from Megalos had still not been repaired.

"Speaking of water, if this plague has struck everywhere, we might not be getting any more water shipments. What the devil will we do then?" Aminta asked, suddenly realizing a very serious threat to their survival!

"Damn, Aminta, you are right! We may well run out of fresh drinking water! Hell, this is rapidly becoming a nightmare without end!" Pavlos replied.

After breakfast, the two men began work on installing the kitchen, removing the old counter, sink, and stove first. Two women helped as best they could. Desma wandered about the home examining her new surroundings.

By late afternoon, they finished the job. Now both women could easily reach everything while sitting in the chairs on rollers. "Okay, we'll see if we can fix supper now," Aminta suggested. While it still took them five times as long to do it, do it they did. With pride, they served up the hot meal, though the men did the carrying of the dishes to the small table.

Once dinner was done, Aminta asked, "Pavlos, have you tried to walk in your boots?"

"Yes, but I can't do it. It is just easier to crawl. I can't keep my balance."

"I think you should try again, Pavlos. Honestly, ballet dancers do it. I've seen them. Come on, you can lean on me. Even with my crippled up feet, I can sort of walk, if I take tiny steps. I think that you were meant to walk. Otherwise, why give you those weird boots?"

"But I can't do it," he protested.

"Maybe not alone, but now you have me. Come on, Ari, you work with Bakchos too. I am certain that they are not supposed to spend the rest of their lives crawling around. Already they've ruined their pants and knees. There's not a chance that we women can mend them. Come on, Pavlos. Lean on me. Give it a try."

"I can't Aminta. It's too embarrassing," he whispered, hoping the she'd get the message and shut up about it.

"Embarrassing? Embarrassing? Pavlos Rikles let me tell you about embarrassing! We can hardly do a damn thing for ourselves anymore. I can't brush my hair even, let alone get dressed without help. Ari and I have to have help with every damn thing in life now. Embarrassing — hell, we can't even feed ourselves. You don't know what embarrassing is until you try being in our shoes, Mr. Rikles. Now stand up and put your arm over my shoulders this very minute."

His face turned beet red. She'd struck him hard and he knew it. He struggled to his feet and his arm frantically latched onto her shoulders. She wobbled under the pressure but held him up. "So far so good. Now let's walk. Please, I can only take tiny steps, Pavlos." Quickly he found that her tiny steps were perfect for him. His were pitifully small as well. Around and around the small, enclosed portion of her home they went. Ari and Bakchos were right behind them, while Desma watched and encouraged them on.

"Ari, now I get it," Aminta suddenly realized, "it's like they have to learn how to walk all over again. Like a child learning to take their first steps. That's what's going on here."

"Hey, you might have something there, Aminta," Pavlos replied. It made sense now. This did feet as if he was learning all over how to walk.

"Don't your toes ache?" asked Ari, after they had walked around the room a couple times.

"Strange as this seems," Bakchos answered, "no. I think it is all that fleshy stuff that has grown onto the ends of our toes. Maybe it's meant to be a cushion or something."

"I think a few days of this and you fellows will be walking fine on your own," Aminta declared when they finished.

"Thanks, Aminta. I hope and pray that you are right. Crawling is grim," Pavlos replied.

The small group spent the next two days helping the men learn to walk. Finally, on the third day, they were once again in trouble. "Oh no, we are out of fresh water," Ari announced at breakfast.

"Well, the water wagon has not made its weekly trip to fill our cistern," Aminta concluded. "What are we going to do? We have to have drinking water. I don't know a darn thing about water supplies."

"I do," Ari broke in, "there ought to be large public cisterns in each major market square. If those are empty, then there is the main storage cistern on the southern edge of the city. If that is empty, then there is no water at all."

"Okay, assuming there is water in the nearest cistern, how are we going to transport it here?" Aminta asked. "We can't carry much in our yokes."

"We'll figure something out, Aminta. We'll just have to be resourceful," Pavlos offered a hopeful note. "Come on; we had best get going. We need to know if we are totally out of water as soon as possible. If so, we are going to have to leave the city or perish. This is serious, gang." Aminta didn't like the sound of his voice. She grew worried again, realized that she had ceased being worried these past couple of days, and wondered why. Nothing had changed, for she was just as helpless as that first day.

A few minutes later, the five set out on a search for drinking water. Aminta was very thankful to have Pavlos along as he easily opened the locked gate, saving her at least a half hour struggle. The five made quite a sight as they headed down the street. They walked five abreast, with Aminta on the far right, Pavlos with an arm over her shoulder and the other arm over Ari's shoulder. Bakchos had his arm over Ari and also over Desma on the far left. However, there was no one on the street to witness the sight.

As expected, their progress was pitifully slow, no more than their usual three inches a step. What mattered to the five was that they were walking, that they were doing it. Later reflection upon it all, Aminta would suggest that these five had a high survival desire. The universe would not do them in so easily.

"What is that awful stench?" asked Ari.

"Rotting corpses," Pavlos answered. As they turned a corner, ahead of them the street was filled with dead. Some showed signs of a conflict, a street battle perhaps? They could not tell. Pavlos had his long gun over his shoulder and felt confident that they would not be bothered.

"This is really spooky! Where is everyone?" Ari asked in a whisper.

"Probably staying indoors where it is safe," Bakchos suggested.

Two hours later having covered what ought to have been walked in some twenty minutes, they reached a major cistern, located in the center of a large deserted market square. However, it was not deserted. Ahead, they saw another man and woman, each holding on to each other, much like the five, struggling to carry a pair of buckets full of water.

The couple smiled as the five approached. "You need water too. There's still plenty. Any news?" the man asked.

"No news. Lots of dead though," Pavlos answered.

"Yes, some of the Church of Jehosanity men came around early on trying to kill us, saying the Day of Judgment had come. We kicked them out, but I know that they did kill our neighbors. Is anyone in charge anymore? Are we on our own? Is the plague everywhere? We thought about walking over to the Senate, but it's too far for us to manage just yet."

"Glad you kicked them out," Aminta answered. "I don't know who is in charge anymore. I am a senator but I've had absolutely no word either. I think we can safely assume that the plague has also stricken the coastal cities or else the water wagons would have already come. They are way late in deliveries."

"What are we to do?" asked the young woman. "If we run out of food and water, where are we to go and how?"

"I don't know. I truly don't know, but I aim to find out, once we get some water. We're totally out. Stay indoors as much as possible. There are wild dogs running around and perhaps packs of thieves too," she suggested. The woman flashed a grateful smile and the two continued their arduous trip home with their two precious buckets of water.

"We should have brought some buckets," Ari commented sadly, as they approached the cistern.

"We make do, Ari," Pavlos replied, looking around the large square. "Bingo! There is our answer," he pointed out a fire wagon across the way from the well. It was a pushcart affair used to ferry water to fires. He and Aminta made their way over to it. It was empty as expected. While he pulled, she pushed and soon had the small wagon beside the well. Now the real work began, and unfortunately, the women could find no way to help the men. The buckets had to be lowered and the crank turned countless times to raise the full bucket. Repeatedly, the men cranked up buckets full of water, dumping them into the waiting wagon. At last, the wagon was full.

"If only we had a horse," Pavlos teased, dreading what would come next. Standing on the tips of his toes, he knew that he could hardly pull anything.

"Well, we can't pull, Pavlos, but we can put our backs to it and push," Aminta suggested. With both men pulling and the three women pushing, the heavily laden wagon began moving. They stopped to rest five times before arriving back at Aminta's home. Emptying the wagon into the household cistern was the easiest task all day.

The next day, Aminta held a formal council. "Okay gang. Someone has to be in charge of Galantas and get things going again. We have to go find out who that is and get some action over here in our part of the city. We've got to get the dead somehow buried before we all get sick."

"Yes, that is quite reasonable, Senator," Pavlos reverted to his cynical views once more. "Under these circumstances, where do you propose that we go to find out who is in charge? Tell me that one, if you can."

"The mayor's house or office — that's the place to start. Come on, it's a bit of a walk, unfortunately, almost to the Senate building, I'm afraid. Bring your long gun, please."

"Wouldn't think of leaving the house without it, Senator," he teased her.

Normally, it was a brisk forty-five minute walk from her house to the Senate, perhaps only thirty-five to the mayor's home and a minute more to his main office building where the city was governed. They started out at nine that morning and finally arrived at the mayor's home around noon. Along the way, they saw hundreds of dead in the streets, on the curbs, and in yards and lots. The stench was becoming awful. Yet, they also saw a number of others active as well, most in search of either food or water. Twice, though, Pavlos had to shoot a wild dog that threatened them or others. Everywhere they went, those who were out, begged them for news and begged them for guidance. Where were their rulers? Sadly, Aminta had no answers, but continued to promise them that she would find out.

At the mayor's fancy estate, they were shocked to find his entire family had died. From the grizzly scene, Pavlos concluded that some madness had overwhelmed them. Most likely, the mayor himself had killed his wife, two daughters, and son, before slitting his own throat — so much for the mayor. A grim faced five headed on to the city offices.

Here they found the building was completely deserted. All signs pointed to the simple fact that no one had been here since the start of the plague, well over a week ago, but closer to two now. "Now what?" Pavlos asked, worried that they had made the long walk for nothing.

"We rest. I need to think," Aminta said, biting her lip. She sat down on the steps and began to work this out. "No one is running the city anymore. Mayor's dead. Offices have been closed since the beginning. Makes sense from all that we've seen, but it must be worse than that. Look, Galantas is the capital of Megalos. From here, the country is run, except for the control exerted upon us by the Church of Jehosanity from on down the coast. One would reason that since nothing has been done in nearly two weeks, our country is as of now leaderless."

"Why do you conclude that?" Pavlos asked.

"We are in an obvious crisis situation. The first principle that all leaders know is that in a crisis, they must communicate with the people in some manner. If they do not, the country goes out of their control. In spite of titles, they are no longer the leaders. Often, that communication comes by way of force, if men are in charge. You know, soldiers and guns and all that."

"So you don't think men make good leaders?" Pavlos snickered.

"Absolutely not! Look where male leadership has gotten our country? According to our history books, we used to be a glorious civilization, the rose of the world. Now look at us. We still haven't repaired the dam which used to provide us with endless water from the aqueducts that the original founders built."

"Point taken," he had to admit. "So now what?"

"Hell, we cannot even abandon ship!" Aminta suddenly realized. "If the whole world has gotten the plague, it is like this everywhere we could go!"

The five sat in stunned silence for some time. At last, Aminta remembered something. "There is one thing that we might try. I don't know if it will amount to anything, but we ought to try." All four looked at her, a slight hope in their eyes.

"Not so long ago, the Senate acquired one of the latest inventions of Velona. It is called LD radio. Apparently, this device allows one to talk to others over long distances. I was told that with it, we could talk to the leaders in Velona and many others in the northern countries. I think that we ought to try it and ask them for help. It can't hurt any. We're doomed anyway that we go now. We have no leaders. Unless we do something, thieves will eventually control everything."

Thirty minutes later, the five made their way into an office in the deserted Senate building. Already dust had accumulated on the marble seats on which she had sat weekdays for four years. "Yes, here it is. I wonder how it works?" The five looked around and found an instruction manual written in their own language. Aminta was worried that it had been written in the Velona dialect, which would have been the last straw, as none of them spoke that language.

With the men turning the crank, which generated electricity, Aminta sat down and used her foot to press the Talk button. "This is Megalos calling anyone. Please help. Anyone. Megalos calling anyone who can hear me. This is Megalos calling anyone. Is anyone out there? Can anyone hear me?" She talked in a similar vein for several minutes.

Suddenly a loud voice answered. Unfortunately, none could understand the voice; it spoke in the Velona dialect. Just as their hearts sank, the person spoke in a terrible version their language. "Velona here. Hang on a few minutes while I get someone who can speak Megalos." He repeated it several times and Aminta replied, "Thank you. We will be here."

Anxious minutes passed, while Aminta wondered what she should say. Velona was so far away and their need here too great. "Hello Megalos. Are you there?" The speaker bellowed loudly in their own tongue, although the woman did have a noticeable accent.

"Yes, we are here. Thank god we got through!"

"Hello, I am Bethany Bartiana Angela of Velona. Monarch Stefano West Po is also on the line, but he speaks poor Megalos dialect. I am translating for him. The plague has struck worldwide. How are you fairing down there? How can we help?" she asked, saying the word that Aminta desperately wanted to hear. Help.

She quickly outlined what little she knew: the state of women and men, the dead bodies, the lack of water, and mostly the fact that the country was likely leaderless at this time.

I began a lengthy reply. "First, Senator Aminta, you are not alone. The entire world has gotten the plague. I hate to tell you this, but every woman on Tarra has lost her arms and is just like yourself. Every man has to walk on their toes like a ballerina." I took my time and fully explained all that had happened including the fact that the perpetrators of the plague had been slain.

I outlined the steps that we had taken in Velona and explained about my book, which gave women thousands of helpful hints on how to carry on routine actions of life using alternate methods. "Don't ask me how, but in three days, you will receive a large supply of the books, translated into your language. I will see that they are also dropped off at your other major cities. Their distribution I have to leave up to you."

"You are not leaderless any longer. Stefano West Po hereby appoints you, Senator Aminta as the sole ruler of Megalos, until your people decide to elect other leaders. Now then, Monarch Aminta here is what you must do first."

"Have someone write down all that I've said that has happened to our world. Make enough copies of it and send out men on horseback to visit all the cities and then smaller towns. Make them your official news carriers. Part of the message to be delivered is that you are now the monarch and are in control. It is vital that the average person knows that someone is in control, even if that control is tenuous at best."

"Part of this is to explain to everyone that until your men learn to walk on their own, their women companions must accompany them, providing support while they walk. It takes time for them to relearn how to walk on their toes. Also, men have to now become the hands for the women, until you get my book and learn alternate ways. Yes, it is hard, but it can and has been done up here in the north."

"Your second action is to organize men to deal with the removal of all the dead. Perhaps a mass grave is in order or a mass cremation. If you do not do this soon, you will be facing massive outbreaks of disease and far more will die as a result. Thirdly, have the news carriers ask that all men and women attempt to resume their normal jobs as best they can. Forth, setup a hotline where people can go to request aid and assistance. Many women can be used to staff this hotline. Make use of your horses, since none of us can walk much at all. Finally, I want you to stay in daily touch with me and us in Velona. We will guide you at every step along the way. Stefano will be sending a caravel with some men and women who can help you later on, but it will take them a month to reach you. Until then, talk to us daily, say around noon. Oh yes, the inventor of this LD radio says that you ought to be able to transport it on a pushcart to your home, as where it is now is probably a good distance from your house."

I went over this several times to make sure Aminta had it straight. Yes, she thanked me profusely and promised to do what she could.

"Damn, Aminta, that was brilliant! Somehow, that woman up in Velona knows precisely what must be done! Every one of her points is so perfectly clear, so logical. Why didn't we think of those things? They are as plain as the nose on my face." Pavlos exclaimed.

"Hey, I found a pushcart. Let's get this life saver home!" Bakchos declared, enthused for the first time since the plague struck.

The next day, Pavlos and Bakchos found a pair of horses in a nearby stable. They mounted up and began going up and down the streets of Galantas, reading aloud this first official proclamation, outlining what had happened to the world and what was needed here in Galantas. Before noon, they had a dozen more men eager to lend a hand, so welcome was the news that someone was in charge and that there was the potential for survival. By the next day, Aminta was able to send off a dozen more riders to other cities, the first of which was the city, which supplied Galantas with its water supply.

The second day, more and more bodies began to be dumped out onto lawns, sidewalks, and the streets. Slowly at first and with women providing support, men began using wagons to load up the dead and to move them out of the city. Because of the sheer number of dead, Aminta opted for mass cremations. She knew that she had to dispose of the rotting bodies or face massive outbreaks of disease.

As the dead began to be hauled away, life crept back into the city. More and more men and women volunteered to help with the removal of the dead. Finally, she was able to organize patrols of men and women who went house to house. So many dead were still inside their homes.

On the fourth day, huge piles of the promised books appeared magically on her front porch. Once she announced that the books had arrived, for a week, men and women dropped by to obtain their copy. Aminta and Ari quickly devoured the book, eager to learn all that they could. Then both Pavlos and Bakshos read one and then read it aloud to Desma, who had only begun to read.

By the end of the fourth week after the plague did its dirty work, the five stood just outside the gate, watching people moving down the street. Shops had reopened. A few merchants resumed selling in the markets. Food had become available once more. More importantly, that very day, the local water wagon pulled up and refilled Aminta's cistern.

She was so elated, so happy to see the water wagon's return that Aminta leaned over and gave Pavlos a loving, passionate kiss. His arms encircled her and pulled her tightly to his body, returning her kiss in kind. When they pulled away, he asked her to marry him.

"I thought that you disliked Senators," she teased him.

"Well, you are not a Senator anymore. You are our Monarch. There's a difference," he teased back.

"Yes, I will, I thought that you would never ask, let alone kiss me," she replied.

"You are the one in control, remember that? Women ought to be our leaders this time."

"Thanks, that means a lot to me, Pavlos." She kissed him again.

Nearby, Bakchos was embracing Ari. Already he had asked her to marry him. She had protested, saying that she was a mulato, but he again denounced that idea. You are a fine woman. I am marrying a fine woman, that is all that I see —unless you are going to turn into a purple woman, because I am not sure that I would like that." Both chuckled and then embraced again.

Desma smiled, she knew now that she would have two parents again.

Chapter 5 Megalos and Nobles

Late October, Dimitris Macedon buttoned the last of the many fastenings on his elegant tuxedo. Made from the finest silk imported from Tashien, the suit had cost him a thousand gold. Yet for Dimitris, this was a mere pittance, a copper at best. Dimitris was perhaps the wealthiest nobleman on Megalos, measuring his fortune in the hundreds of millions. Passed down from generation to generation, Macedon Enterprises manufactured nearly all the army's weapons. With his parent's deaths two years ago, he'd inherited the entire fortune. His younger brother had died in an unfortunate plant explosion some ten years ago now and his sister had died during childbirth. Dimitris was thirty-five. He looked at his image in the full-length mirror. His lightly oiled black hair looked immaculate, as did his moustache, his pride and joy. Satisfied that he looked the part, he was ready to head off to the Grand Art Opening and then the Fall Dance.

He walked down the hallway to his wife's dressing room. "Dear are you ready yet?" he called out to her.

"Not quite, almost. Please go check on the children. Make sure that they are getting ready for bed, Dimi," Danae called out from her dressing room. He smiled. The children. They had a fine young boy and a gorgeous daughter, now nine and eight respectively. He headed on down the hallway to check on the kids.

As expected, their nanny was reading them their bedtime stories. As he entered, she stopped, knowing the two would race to their father. They did so, predictable children, she thought. After giving each a hearty hug and kiss, he told them, "Now you all obey Nanny Alesa and go to bed when she says. Mom and I are off to the Art Opening. In a few more years, you will both get to come with us. Now won't that be something." They cheered and agreed.

He left thinking such delightful children, so well behaved. Yes, he doted on his two children, but not as much as he doted on his gorgeous wife, Danae. How fortunate he had been to discover her, a gem among gems. She was thirty-four with silky, long black hair, a bronze complexion that was an artist's dream to paint. Already, six portraits of her hung around the mansion. Her sharp eyes never missed a thing and her mind, well let's just say that she was far smarter than he. Indeed, she was more than perfect in all ways. Married now fifteen years, he was still madly in love with her, and she with him.

If she had any fault at all, which he would never admit that she had, it was that she was an ardent worshiper of the Church of Jehosanity and had insisted and demanded upon becoming a Holy Woman of the Eighth Degree, which had been her only stipulation when he had proposed to her sixteen years ago. Unlike her devotion to the Church, he had no taste for organized religion of any type. Men fought, he supplied the weapons they needed. If there was a God, wars would have been outlawed — that was the argument that he always used.

As a Holy Woman, her upkeep was costly, which is why only those women who were married to wealthier men could become such a highly respected Holy Woman of the Church. Without arms, Danae was very dependent upon servants for all her needs, though when with Dimitris, he assisted her with all her needs. He loved to feed her breakfast in bed, though such nearly always resulted in far more happening afterwards. He smiled recalling their romp in bed after he'd brought her breakfast this morning.

He kept six women servants here at the mansion to wait on her needs at all times when he was not available. Yet only one would actually spend the night here, just in case she should need some assistance. Each of the six took turns spending the night. Only on Sunday nights was no one here. Dimitris never failed to be here those nights, business or no business. Yes, it cost three thousand gold for their salaries each month, but he didn't mind at all, as long as Danae received only the very best of care. Nothing was too fine for her.

As he approached her dressing room, the door opened, and she stepped out. "Perfect timing as always. How do I look, dear?" she asked demurely. She had bangs that fell close to her eyes, while her luxurious, silky, black hair fell to her waist. Tonight, she wore a jade green satin gown, strapless as always. She insisted on displaying her empty shoulders, for she was proud to be a Holy Woman. Her corset held her waist tucked in to about eighteen inches and the dress flared out some six feet around her, many petticoats holding it in a perfect style. She wore matching tall heels and the expensive, black silk hose imported from Tashien, each pair costing nearly fifty gold. She looked radiant and breathtaking.

"Absolutely perfect, as always, my dearest!" He leaned over and kissed her gently, being careful not to mess up her makeup. She wore matching jade earrings and a jade necklace adorned her neck, falling down to her well-defined cleavage. Danae smiled and Dimitris slid his arm around her waist, escorting the love of his life off to the Art Opening.

The opening was displaying a dozen paintings by the famous Demokritos artist Charon. If you had to ask how much each of these still life paintings cost, you could not afford one. All were so realistic that one felt that one could reach out and touch the flowers, trees, and water. "Oh Danae! You look simply marvelous tonight. New dress?" the wife of the gallery owner effused as Dimitris escorted Danae inside the packed gallery, filled with the wealthy of Galantas, although some had traveled here from distant cities just for this opening.

"So glad that you noticed. Why yes it is. I had it made especially for this opening. Jade is the official color of the Emperor and Empress of Demokritos," Danae replied, confident that her choice had been utterly perfect, quite unlike the garish red satin of her host. Dimitris gave a polite hug to the woman and quickly escorted Danae off to begin circulating around the room and viewing the paintings. He wondered if she would take a fancy to one of these.

One by one, Danae and Dimitris met and greeted other wealthy noblemen and women. Indeed, Danae was not the lone Holy Woman at the Art Opening. Twenty-four others were here as well. Only the wealthy could afford the servants needed to attend to the needs of a Holy Woman. The Church of Jehosanity had raised such women to a very high status in society. Merely to be seen with a Holy Woman meant the man was wealthy. While Danae would not admit it, women like herself were often seen as objects, status symbols of the wealthy.

Every Sunday at Mass, these Holy Women were given seats in the very front rows, the center of attention of all those within the Church. Their husbands had to sit behind them in the second row of pews. It was natural for these women to band together, visiting each other's homes as frequently as they could manage. Seldom did they interact with other women.

As a young girl attending services with her parents, she had seen the high honor bestowed upon such women and they elevated the status of their husbands. She swore that whenever she married that she would become a Holy Woman to help elevate her husband into the ranks of the finest of Galantas society. It was the very least that she could do to ensure that both of their social standings were nothing but the very best, the very highest.

Now fifteen years after she had made that supreme sacrifice when she got married, she had no misgivings about it, no second thoughts. Her marriage and the social status of her family were simply tops. Her husband was still madly in love with her, and she, he. Both doted over their two darling children. Life was perfect for the couple. Her six servants handled all of her many needs, including housekeeping and the family cooking.

Well, perhaps if boxed into a corner, Danae did have a gnawing thought about being a Holy Woman, one that was always in the back of her mind. Only in her most private of moments did she look at it, and then only fleetingly, refusing to allow the idea to flourish and ruin everything. Danae was too smart, too intelligent. Perhaps that was why she dared not allow this single dark thought from surfacing.

Dimitris quickly saw just how brilliant his charming, beautiful young wife actually was. She was a whiz with numbers and had an innate knack at knowing just the right action that needed to be taken in any given situation, social or business. Already he had made good use of her skills in his business, calling upon her services when a particular critical decision had to be made. Further, she had a skill that had become indispensable both in his personal life and in business. Danae could tell in an instant whether a person was telling the truth or was lying or attempting to withhold key facts. Some might call her a soothsayer, but neither of the two did. Danae simply could read the minute facial and physical manifestations that appeared when someone was not telling the truth or the whole of it.

Dimitris never withheld anything from her, nor did he ever do anything that he might not have wanted her to know. Right or wrong, the two shared everything with each other, the good and the bad, their successes and their failings. Perhaps that accounted for their loving marriage. Perhaps that also was why Danae kept her one dark doubt deeply buried. Besides, even if there was some truth in that dark thought, she could now do nothing about it. Yet that one dark thought was soon to sweep into prominence in their lives, rather like a freight train coming swiftly and certainly down the tracks.

An hour later and finished viewing the art, the two entered the Royal Festival Hall for the annual fall dance. Over a thousand crowded into the enormous ballroom, decked out in the oranges, browns, and greys of fall. The Women's Decorating League had spent days preparing the "atmosphere" of the hall. Anyone who was anybody attended the ball as well as many others who could afford the ten gold per couple entrance fee. Years ago, the Ball Committee had to institute this cover charge to keep riffraff from attending. In such a large crowd, the two dozen Holy Women stood out, primarily because all them usually chose to wear strapless gowns, proudly displaying their armless shoulders to the world.

When the assembled musicians finally began to play the first slow dance tune of the ball, Dimitris put his arms around Danae's waist, being careful as always to make sure they were beneath her luxurious long hair. His hands encircled her tiny waistline and their bodies touched, she resting her head on his shoulder as always. She whispered, "Remember, I wore my lower five inch heels tonight so I can take larger steps." Danae always reminded him of which heels she was wearing. Such was an important detail, if they were to be seen as a seamless pair. When she wore her Annelise heels with their towering seven-inch heels, she could only take the tiniest of steps. However, tonight she wanted to dance and chose to wear her lower five-inch heels. He smiled and nudged her body into motion, relishing the feel of her closeness to himself.

The two took frequent breaks this evening, by mutual consent. "Dear, I just don't know why my energy level seems so low tonight. My feet seem to be aching a bit," he whispered. She volunteered that hers were too, for no apparent reason, she thought. Still, they enjoyed their night out, and he deftly fed her some appetizers and shared a glass of wine with her. She marveled at just how well he knew what she needed when she needed it. Fifteen years of marriage will do that, she thought — that, and perhaps always being open and up front about what she needed and when she needed it. From her frequent chats with her other Holy Women friends, she knew that many of them did not share such a close relationship with their husbands. Indeed, some were down right awkward with their assistance to their wife's needs, claiming that's why they hired servants.

Partway through the evening, Danae whispered, "Dear, we are not the only ones who seem to be tiring early. I do believe nearly everyone is having troubles. I wonder what is going on?"

"Probably the weather. What else could it be?" he asked, baffled by the sudden notion that everyone else here might be having sore feet and ankles.

"Well, some older folks seem to be affected by weather. Perhaps you are right," Danae admitted.

Interestingly enough, by mutual consent, the dance ended an hour earlier than ever before. No one protested the early stopping time. By the time that Dimitris escorted Danae into their mansion estate near midnight, both were complaining of sore feet. While he went into his dressing room to change, Danae went into hers, where her night servant quickly undressed her.

"You are back so soon, madam," she said, loosening Danae's tight corset.

"Well yes, for some strange reason, our feet seem sore. Actually, everyone at the dance seemed affected too. Probably the weather, Dimi says."

"Me too. I almost fell asleep waiting for you to return. Here, sit down and I will massage your feet." For a few minutes, Danae was in heaven. "Forgive me, madam, but my arms are just so tired tonight. Will that be enough?" It was and she dismissed her for the night. Dressed in a thin silk gauze of a nightgown, Danae headed into their bedroom, where Dimitris was already waiting for her.

"How's your feet, dear?" she asked.

"Not so good." The dark cloud that was cradled in the deepest recesses of her mind nudged closer to the surface. Oh, how she desperately wanted to massage his feet, to return the ecstasy her maid had just given her. But how could she?

"Let me try with my feet, dear," she suggested hoping that somehow her feet might be able to give him some relief. She tried her best, but was unable to do a whole lot for him. Finally, she had to give up, turning instead to their usual bedtime games. She raked her long hair over his face and chest. Before long, their passions took over.

The next morning disaster began to strike. First, Dimitris fell out of bed, landing hard on the floor. His feet had given out completely and unexpectedly. His ankles refused to bend much at all, and his toes and feet were pointed downward. Their servant woman shrieked, and when Danae came into her room, she too cried out. Her arms were only half their usual size, nearly skin and bones. Danae insisted that she go immediately to the doctor's office. She led the servant to their carriage driver, who also was having major problems with his feet. Danae was shocked to see him crawling to the carriage, but he did fulfill his duty and took the servant off to find the doctor.

She went to check on their children, who ought to be out of bed by now. Again, she was shocked to find her son also unable to walk. He, however, ignored it and was playing with his toy soldiers on the floor. He had them lined up and was in the middle of a big battle, ignoring his mother completely. Her daughter sat on her bed, proudly staring at her shriveled arms. "Mom. Look, my arms are going away. I am going to be just like you! Isn't that just great!" She was not the least bit disturbed yet, anyway. Her daughter had always wanted to be just like her gorgeous mother. "Nanna can feed me today, just like you."

"Nanna has gone to the doctors. I think that dad will have to fix our breakfast and feed us both today," she replied. Her daughter grinned, liking that idea even better. Danae headed back to check on Dimitris, beginning to get very worried. Still, soon the other five servant women should be arriving, and surely, all would be set to rights then.

The servants didn't arrive and the two had a most difficult day. Poor Dimitris was forced to crawl about his mansion, tending the needs of both his wife and now his daughter as well. He had to prepare their breakfast himself as well as the remaining meals, a task for which he was ill suited to doing, having never really fixed a meal in his life. Danae, though she had not done so since she was nineteen, hovered over him, giving directions as best she could.

Oh, how she actually wanted to help them! The dark thought began to surface now. She was sick and tired of having others always helping her while she could not return the flow, the favor. She just could not help in return! By nightfall, she was dark with frustration, but Dimitris didn't notice it. He was too preoccupied with his own problems with his feet and now sore hands and knees.

The next day was even worse for everyone except her daughter, who proudly announced, "Mom, look! Now I am exactly like you! Isn't this just great?" Had their six servants been here, perhaps it would have been so. Under the circumstances, Danae felt a little sick. Her whole family desperately needed her help now, from dressing to fixing meals. She could do no more than stand around and make suggestions!

Since Dimitris could no longer get around easily, Danae darted around the house, trying to deal with the calamity. Still, she was now forced to walk on her toes. Her own feet were becoming very distorted; a strange U-shaped arch appeared and her heels no longer could touch the floor, making keeping her balance difficult. However, she found a temporary solution by wearing her highest Annelise heels. While they no longer fit her strange arch, at least they provided some support and she could walk about the house fairly well, though her stride was but a few inches.

Panic slowly grew. The five security guards who always patrolled the perimeter of the estate no longer came to work. Their carriage driver had brought the carriage back the other day, but had gone home to nurse his own problem feet and had not returned. None of the six servants had shown up at all, though a message had come from one yesterday, saying that her arms were giving her trouble. Danae's bronze face was nearly ashen when she finally returned to Dimitris, who was sitting sour-faced on the love seat.

"Well?" he asked hopefully.

"Gone. Dimi, we are alone! Only the four of us are here. They are all gone. What is going on? What is happening to us?" Danae asked, trying to restrain her growing fears and panic.

He was crushed! Deserted by all his servants in his hour of most desperate need, his face sank into his hands and he said nothing at all.

Danae needed him now more than ever, but what could she do to help him? "I know. I am going to walk down to the gate and call out to someone on the street and ask them to go for help. I'll be right back." Well, she lied. In these extreme Annelise heels, her speed of travel was akin to a snail. A half hour or more would be more like "be right back." She headed off to call for help.

Sometime later, her feet aching from the now ill-fitting shoes, she arrived at their gates. They were unlocked, a point that she failed to recognize until it was too late. The streets were utterly and completely empty. Although she could not open the gates and go out into the street for a better look, she stood there for several minutes. Not a person was outside. Further, she began to hear the distance cries of shock and terror coming from nearby homes and mansions. Here on the south side of the city, the estates were generally large. Still, she heard women screaming in terror and men's voices crying out in shock and fear. What was going on? Panic seeped into her stomach and she nearly fainted. Only with sheer will power did she manage to get her feet going again, doing a slow shuffling glide back into their mansion.

As she entered, she realized the incredible wisdom that Dimitris had shown the very day that they were married and she was brought here to the estate. Since she had become a Holy Woman, he had changed all the doorknobs to the newer bar style. "This way, you can open any door in the mansion," he had proudly explained. Indeed, as she pushed down on the latch and the mechanism released, she could use her toe to pull the door open. Only now did she realize how critical his action fifteen years ago had been.

After she explained what she had not seen and what she'd heard, Dimitris shrank deeper into his shell. Danae, who needed him, now more than ever before, slumped down beside him. Her dark thought now swamped her. How could she have been so foolish to have her arms removed? Her family needed her and she was completely helpless to assist them in any way! She always wanted to help others, not just be helped. Yet for fifteen years, she had been utterly swamped with others helping her and with no way at all of returning that help unto others. She broke down and began sobbing to herself. Beside her, he cried as well. Their world was ending.

How long they sat there neither knew. Their two children finally came into the room. They were very hungry. "Mom, when are we going to eat?" their son asked, having crawled into the room pretending that he was a scout soldier sneaking up on the enemy units. His sister, hobbling along on her toes, was an enemy unit. So far, he hadn't minded that his feet no longer worked. He could now play on the floors with impunity!

Tears in her eyes, she looked up. Somehow, a meal had to be prepared. "The children, Dimi. The children need us now." He looked up and tried to put on a brave face, failing utterly.

Just then, a man came crawling into their house. Danae recognized him at once from his ripped and torn robes. He was Mano del Dio, one of the protectors of the Holy Fathers. "Please, you must help us," she pleaded.

"What's going on?" Dimitris asked the man, who probably had the answers he desperately needed.

"Our Cardinal has sent me. The Holy Day of Judgment has come at last to Tarra! As foretold in our Holy Gospels, the day of our Judgment has finally come. The world is ending and Lord Jehosa is beckoning all the faithful souls unto Heaven," he replied.

"What's going on, man? Why is no one on the streets? Where is everyone?" Dimitris demanded to know. He hated the stupid Church of Jehosanity. While he had no choice but to accompany his wife every Sunday, he normally slept through the proceedings.

"Lord Jehosa is preparing your way unto Heaven as we speak. All women of Galantas have lost their arms, becoming Holy Women unto the Lord. All men have been struck down as even I, one of the faithful, have been reduced to crawling as a dog. The Day of Judgment is at hand. Prepare your souls to be lifted up into Lord Jehosa's Holy Realm. The Cardinal has sent me out among the Most Faithful to assist their souls in attaining Heaven above," the Mano del Dio replied. "All praise to Lord Jehosa. May he find your souls most worth of gaining entrance into his Holy Realm." With that, the short sword that he had been secretly withdrawing came out before him. In one swift motion, he severed the boy's throat. He crawled a few more inches and swung again, nearly slicing their daughter's head off. Danae shrieked!

Dimitris screamed, "You filthy assassin! You bastard!" He dove off the couch towards the man who was moving into position to strike Danae next. The two tumbled into a heap between the blood-covered bodies of the two children. Danae just screamed and screamed, as the horror of these few seconds hit home.

He was not a fighter, nor had he any defensive training, while the Mano del Dio was a highly trained assassin. Dimitris had no real chance and soon the assassin got the better of him. Just as he was about to deliver a killing strike to the prone Dimitris, Danae rose and swung her foot into the assassin's head. Afterwards, Dimitris claimed that it had been a miracle happening before his eyes.

Danae had been wearing her seven-inch Annelise heels so that she could just barely manage to walk. Her kick to the assassin's head was such that the tip of the spike entered his left ear. The force of the blow drove the spike almost completely into the man's head. Her subsequent fall to the floor broke the heel off her shoe, and she hit the blood-covered floor between the fallen bodies of her children quite hard, temporarily dazing her. The assassin slumped as dead weight on top of Dimitris.

Summoning his strength, he rolled the dead man off him and moved to his wife's side, lifting her up, holding her head against his chest. He cried uncontrollably. Both their adoring children were dead, drained of their life's blood, which formed an enormous pool around the two parents. Danae came to and saw that he was still alive, saw their two children and wailed uncontrollably. The two grieving parents sat there swamped in grief, unable to do anything but sob.

It was getting dark when the two finally pulled out of their intense shock and grief. The blood had become quite sticky now. "What has the Cardinal done?" she whispered. "He has betrayed us all. Dimi, I have been the biggest fool in the world to ever have believed in that wicked, evil Church! Please, please, I can't live with this. Take his sword and let me join our children."

His arms were still around her and he pulled her tightly into him. "Sh. Sh. The world has been betrayed by that Church, dear. Everyone has. You saved my life and yours too, Danae. That is a Holy Miracle. God will grant us more children in time. You will see. We are still young yet. God has shown his mercy on you and I. Sh. Sh. I love you still." She sobbed again, desperately needing to feel him clinging tightly to her body, though she wanted to cling to his as well, but was unable to do so.

Sometime later, she whispered, "We have to bury them properly, Dimi."

"I know, I know. I would like to bury them in our backyard, where they used to love to run and play." He broke down and began crying as memories came into his mind. Danae, likewise.

"It's my fault, Dimi. I saw that the gate was unlocked! I let the assassin in!" Danae suddenly realized her error.

"No, Mano del Dio is not stopped by a simple locked gate. It would have only slowed him down a minute maybe. Dear, you are blameless. Come, you go find some fitting clothes in which to bury our beloved children, while I drag this filth of the earth out into the street where the rats can feast upon his foul flesh." Grief had changed to anger. "When this is over, I promise you that the Cardinal and this foul Church will pay dearly for what they have done here today!"

Never has she seen him this angry, yet anger rose in her as well. "I want the Cardinal to suffer. Rip his arms off and blind him and cut out his foul tongue so that no one else can be affected by his foul, wicked, evil lies!"

"Right dear, we will destroy this evil, wicked church, you and I. Let's do it!" Both finally rose from the bloody mess on the floor. Limping, she headed off to find proper burial clothes, while be began slowly dragging the dead assassin out of their home. A half hour later, the corpse was deposited in the street. After spitting on it, he locked his gate and made his way back inside.

They chose a spot in their backyard where the children used to play. With three lanterns providing the illumination, the two set to work. Danae insisted on trying to help dig the grave. Eventually, she did, using her feet to push the dirt into a bucket, which he then lifted up and out of the hole. Around midnight, the two finally patted the top of the grave. "Rest now, dear children. We give you our word that your untimely deaths will not go un-avenged," he said his last words.

"You both were the very best children in the world. Now you can play soldier all you want. Dear, you look just like mommy. I am so proud of you both. Mommy will never, ever forget either of you. Rest in peace," Danae whispered her final farewell. A bit later, they collapsed on the sofa, utterly exhausted, physically and emotionally. They spent the entire next day cleaning up the mess in their front room. Blood seemed to be everywhere.

During their cleanup operation, a pile of objects suddenly materialized nearby. They ignored them until they finally finished their work. Although they had not realized it yet, they had been working together as a team all day, each doing what they could, though saying very little to each other. Their intense grief was still too raw.

Finally bathed and in clean garments, the two headed off to inspect the strange collection of objects. She wore the thinnest of gauze throw-over dresses, making it easy for them both to handle her needs. He wore only shorts, but had wrapped heavy wrappings around his knees, which were now bloodied and sore. Danae was drawn to the shoes first, because walking on her toes was most difficult. After slipping them on, she announced, "Wow. Perfect. Dimi, I can finally walk again without pain. Try yours on; maybe they will let you walk some."

"On my toes? Like a ballet dancer? I hardly think so, but I'll give it a try." He did and wobbled wildly about. Danae at once moved to his side and had him put his arm around her. Soon, both discovered that together, he could walk, albeit slowly and only with great care. He jested, "I feel like I have to learn to walk all over again." She grinned.

"What a weird writing desk," he commented.

"Oh, I just had a thought, dear. Perhaps that is for me. I keep seeing images in my mind of someone sitting there writing with their feet," Danae replied. Slowly, the two began to see uses for each of the items. He was the first to suggest that by using the yoke, she could carry things. Her dark thoughts of being unable to help anyone began to subside as she began to think that perhaps she was not entirely as helpless as she had been led to believe for the last fifteen years.

They spent the next day redoing their kitchen and for the first time in fifteen years, Danae prepared a meal. Her self-pride slowly returned, while his for her only grew rapidly.

In early November, they heard a crier out in the street reading some kind of proclamation or news. Supporting each other as they now did all the time, the two moved slowly out to their gate to listen to the man. They heard Monarch Aminta's recap of the news and what was needed to be done swiftly. Later, they hitched up their carriage and acquired one of the Bethany Books, as they quickly became known. Both read it cover to cover.

Finally, both decided that this new Monarch Aminta Akantha deserved their support and aid. He drove them in their carriage to meet with this woman and volunteer their services, such as they could. They found her in a small home, surrounded by some men and women from Velona.

"We're looking for Monarch Aminta Akantha. Dimitris and Danae Macedon here," he announced themselves.

"Wow. The Dimitris Macedon?" Aminta said, startled to hear that name.

"Yes, we've come to volunteer our help. We need to destroy the Church of Jehosanity. They murdered our two children," he said, fighting back welling tears; she too.

"Well, I am she. And you need not worry about that Church. They killed themselves too. There is not a priest of the Church in Galantas, and from what I have heard, the pope and all his men are dead as well. I think you need not worry about that any longer. They got what they deserved. Now then, I am so glad that you've come forward. We need all the help we can get right now." Turning to those from Velona she added, "They are the richest people in Galantas." He smiled, of course, he was, but he would give his fortune away to have his children back.

"Good riddance." Both seemed greatly relieved. "Monarch Aminta, there is one thing that I must say up front. Macedon Enterprises has always been heavily in the armament industry, making all manner of weapons for our armies and security forces. However, a sword that my companies made was used to slaughter our defenseless children. From now on, my companies will not manufacture another weapon of war. You have my sworn word on that. Other than that, Danae and I are volunteering to help in any way that we can."

Aminta grinned. "Right now, I know of no one who can eat or drink a sword. I like your decision, Dimitris. We are still trying to get things organized here." One of the Velona women whispered something to her. She smiled, "This is Gustavo and Tina West Po, cousins to the monarch of Velona and close friends of Bethany Bartiana Angela, who has saved our proverbial butts here on Megalos. They wish to offer some suggestions."

"Hi, Gustavo here. Sorry if my Megalos is a bit off. As you may know, Velona has come up with some marvelous inventions. With all our women now armless, we are doing everything possible to help them be able to do what's needed to live properly. For example, we've just invented a washing machine."

Tina took over, "It's so incredible, Danae. It sits low to the ground. We put the dirty clothes in it, using our feet of course. Put in some soap, push a button and presto, a half hour later all the clothes are clean. We only have to hang them out on clotheslines that we can reach." Danae smiled, thinking that would be a marvelous invention.

Gustavo continued, "For some time now, we have things called radios, which play music and over which Stefano, our monarch, can relay important news. You see, when this plague struck us, nearly everyone in our country knew about it and were told what to do and so on. Marvelous way to let all your people know what is going on within minutes of it happening."

"Then, there are the motor-cars and motor-wagons. They use an oil compound called petrol to run. They have replaced horse-drawn wagons in Velona. Even now, they are being adapted so that even a woman can be able to drive herself anywhere she wants to go, bring home a load of groceries, for example. Marvelous. Then for just scooting rapidly around the city, we have the putt-putts and the T-putt-putts especially for women. You should see Bethany as she drives madly around the city running her many errands. Any woman can drive a T-putt-putt."

"You bet," Tina added. "They are great for getting around. They even have baskets so we can carry things too. I'd be lost without mine, especially with our feet so distorted that we can barely walk."

"Plus," Gustavo continued, "we have the LD radios." At this point, Aminta gave a demonstration, allowing Dimitris and Danae to chat briefly with me up in Velona. They were impressed. He continued, "I've been telling Aminta here that you need at least one of these in every major city so that things of importance can be replayed rapidly."

"Whoa! Gustavo! I am sold! How do I bring these marvelous things to Megalos? I have money. I have factories. Name your price!" Aminta smiled, things were working out far better than she ever imagined possible. With Macedon on her side bringing all these incredible and valuable things to Megalos, everyone would win.

The two headed home late that night. He'd signed a contract to be allowed to manufacture all these inventions here in his own company plants. Instead of money, the contract called for small tithe payments on each item produced, due in iron ore, copper, coal, and other raw materials, which Velona desperately needed to vamp up its production. The only stipulation that Velona made was that the cost of the items had to be low enough so the average person could afford them.

What had surprised Dimitris the most was that these Velona folks had come prepared. A working model of each device was on board their caravel along with the detailed engineering plans required for their manufacture! His companies' jobs would be that of mere retooling so that production could begin swiftly. Now he realized that was the whole point. People were desperate. Products to make life livable had to be produced rapidly.

Danae expressed it well on their way home. "If we don't quickly get the things that we women in particular need in order to survive, all hell will erupt. Then it truly will be the end of everything." He leaned over and kissed her.

During the next week, he began to get his companies, which were sprawled over the island nation, back to battery. With men barely able to walk and some still needing the support of their wives or girlfriends, he had his work cut out for himself. However, first, he visited their carriage driver and his family, convincing him to return to his job at double his old pay. For a while, his wife had to come with him to help him walk. He then hired a second carriage driver for himself, since Danae now needed their old one.

She visited each of her former servant women to see how they were holding up. Two homes were deserted, evidently, they had not survived. Disheartened, she reread the Bethany Book and then had her driver take her to visit Aminta again.

"Aminta, thanks for seeing me. I know that you are terribly busy, but I've been going over Bethany's Book again. She does say that it is best if four of we women are in the same household. That way, we can help each other far better than going it alone."

"Yes, Ari and I have found that to be very true."

"Well, we could not help noticing that your house here is a bit small for all the government things you are trying to run from here. Dimi and I would like to make our mansion estate available for you. Come and move in with us and use our huge space to help run our city and country, at least until things get more organized. I am good with organizational things."

Aminta grinned, "Yes, I made a few inquiries about you, Danae. Is it true what I've heard that you can tell when someone is lying or not revealing the whole truth of a matter?"

"Sure, it's easy. Dimi uses my skill often in his business dealings. Why? Can you use it too? If so, I am very willing to help."

By late November, Aminta, Ari, Desma, Pavlos, and Bakchos moved into the Macedon estate, where fifty rooms were available. Now with space available, more work could be done, more help hired. The women were far better able to handle life together.

By December 1, the official death toll had finally been estimated. So many had died and no records kept, that it was just the best guess. Roughly, half of the people living on Megalos had perished during the plague. The Church of Jehosanity on Megalos no longer existed. Stefano and I held out some hope that the island nation would be able to pull out of the disaster, now that Aminta had taken charge and Macedon Enterprises were manufacturing critically needed products.

Mobility and communications were the key factors behind Stefano's and my thinking. We reasoned thus: hobbled as we all are, both men and women, walking to where we needed to go was out. Everyone needed some means of swifter mechanical transportation. Further, direct communication from their leaders was paramount to keep the average citizen well informed. Without rapid, meaningful, and timely communication from leaders, chaos would erupt and the country would fold up into lawless sections, where might made right. A Dark Age would befall those people. This, we had to avoid. Further, without being able to move around at least as swiftly as they did before the plague, people would give up. Goods would not be transported, and people would slowly starve in the towns and cities. The country would revert to a rural farmstead land, where the only way to survive was to grow and make your own food and goods. Again, a Dark Age would fall. Millions of lives would be lost.

Only this miracle had saved Megalos. Time would tell if we had acted swiftly enough to prevent its total collapse.

Chapter 6 The Fall of Demokritos

Late October, the plague had struck Demokritos hard. While Stefano and I had relayed the news to Emperor Karpos Omela, we had not heard anything from him in days. One of his daughters, Alexa, had married Flavio West Po and was living not too far from our estate in Velona. Both were twenty-four now and had a little girl, Roxane, who was one year old last month. I knew that Alexa would be terribly worried about her parents and siblings, so I had the two of them also monitoring the LD radio. So far, all further attempts to make contact with them in Kefall, the capital of Demokritos, had failed.

Working out plans to send aid to the Greenway kingdoms the morning of the 31st, I was surprised to feel the mental contact of two old, dear friends, Kallisto and Ania. I had not heard from them since they took off for Demokritos and new baby bodies some eighteen years ago.

Bethany? That you? Ania and Kallisto here.

Hi, it's about time that you checked in with me! How are you two? We're knee deep in trouble up north here.

Same here. Plague?

Yes, all women had lost their arms up here again. I proceeded to relay them all the news of the recent events.

We are a bit desperate ourselves. We hooked up with the king and queen of Arolas, here in Naxos. I'm called Anathia Tropos, Ana for short. I'm eighteen now. My sister is Kallisto, now called Callisto; she's seventeen. All hell has broken out down here. Sure looks like she and I are too late to salvage the country.

I asked, *What happened? We relayed the initial news to Emperor Karpos, but now we have not been able to establish contact with him for a week.*

The government has broken down. Here in Naxos, our dad didn't listen to us. Rioting has broken out. People are being killed right and left, some by their own hands, claiming Dooms Day has come. Right now, the palace here is being stormed. Dad's been killed; mom couldn't take it and jumped off a parapet. The guards are holding their own for a little while, but I'm sure the rebels will be taking this place very soon. We need some help. She and I are about to make our escape using the secret tunnels. We're going to try to make it to the coast and the big port of Andros. Can you find out if there is any caravel close enough to pick us up? Callisto thinks that we ought to stick it out somewhere. If we decide to do that, can you send a caravel here with some help?

I replied, *You got it. I'll let you know about nearby ships. Give me a few days to try to put something together to send down there, but it's going to take three months to get to you two. Can you hold out somewhere that long?*

We don't have much choice. From what little we've heard, the whole country is disintegrating. It's becoming as bad as Tashien was with all its overlords. Thanks, we gotta run; the palace gates just broke! More later. She broke the connection. I cursed. Well, now I had a better idea of what was happening down there and possibly, why we'd not heard back from the Emperor.

I dropped everything and headed off on my T-putt-putt to Stefano's LD radio installation, where Flavio and Alexa were monitoring it. I also wanted to consult Vitorre's large map of where all our ships were currently located, in case one was close to Andros. A quick glance at his wall-size map told all. What with the discrimination our ships were facing, that is, the attitude of 'we don't serve mutants,' it was difficult to supply our caravels for such a long voyage to the far southern continent. Not one was plying those southern seas, so much for immediate help. I headed on down the hall to the LD radio room.

Flavio looked up; he was holding their year old Roxana, putting her back to sleep. Alexa had finished nursing her; she looked up anxiously. She knew that I must know something; otherwise, I would have just telephoned. She looked more gorgeous by the year, I thought. Her straight, thick, blonde hair now flowed down to her ankles; her pale blue eyes, enchanting.

"Hi, I have some news, not good I am afraid. I have two old friends down in Demokritos. You may have heard us referring to them from time to time. Ania and Kallisto. They just contacted me from Naxos."

"Yes, I remember them," Flavio said. "How are they doing?"

"Not good. It seems that they are now the daughters of the king and queen of Arolas. Apparently, all hell has broken out in that kingdom. The king has been killed; the queen has also died. The rebels are storming the palace and have just broken the main gates. Those two are now fleeing by a secret tunnel. They have heard some scanty news that it is riots everywhere. It doesn't sound too good for your folks and family, Alexa. I wanted to give you the bad news personally."

She fought hard to hold back welling tears. Flavio put a free arm on her shoulders, a gesture of his support and commitment to her. He said, "Any chance we can catch a caravel for Demokritos?"

"Hang in there a while longer, Flavio. When we hear something more concrete, we'll see what we can do to get you down there. I know that you both want to help." He nodded, but said nothing.

Just then, the LD radio crackled. Alexa jumped! She recognized the voice of her younger brother, Alexio. "Demokritos calling Velona, Stefano? Anyone? Is anyone there? Calling Velona. Anyone in Velona. Please."

"Yes, it is us, Flavio and Alexa," he hit the transmit button rapidly.

Alexa leaned over and added, "It's me, little brother. What's happening? We are worried sick up here!"

"Can't talk long now. Palace is being stormed. Dad had a heart attack the day of the news. Mom fell off a wall. Akios tried to assume the throne and led an armed force out to try to put down the rioting. He's dead too. Long gun. Diona couldn't take it. No servants, no help, and with Akios gone, she went mad and killed her three kids and then herself. Pushed them off the very same parapet that mom used. Last I heard, Airla is safe with her husband, and I think that they may have gone into hiding. It's almost impossible to get anyone to take a message. No one can walk much. I can a little if I lean on Io. She and I are going to try to make a getaway. That's why I am calling."

I broke in, "Tell him to take the LD radio with him. Use it to keep in touch with us." Flavio relayed my message.

"Any ideas where we should try to go? I think the world has gone mad down here," he asked.

"Tell him to make for Andros, Arolas. Tell him that we will have him meet up with two of our people there. Stay off the main roads as much as possible. Take food and water with him if he can," I said as I thought fast.

After Flavio relayed it, Alexio replied, "Great! We have to go now. Very little time. We move so damnably slow now. We'll call when it's safe for us to do so. Love you, Alexa." The LD radio went silent. Alexa began crying and buried her head in his shoulders, while his arm encircled her.

"Stay by the radio. I'll see that food is sent to you both. I'm off to arrange a caravel for you two." He nodded and kissed his wife's head.

Down in Demokritos, it was late spring, equivalent to our May up here. Ana and Callisto had long known about the secret tunnel. Their father had told them about it and had shown them how to work the levers. When they were ten, he actually took them down the tunnel and the girls thought this was great fun. Now it would save their lives. Ana and Callisto had prepared for this flight several days ago. Both were Judgers and knew very well the path that the kingdom and country was following. The overall emotional tone level of Demokritos had been steadily dropping over the last couple of centuries. More recently, it had fallen so low that fascism had taken a foothold. Along with it came heavy propitiation, as the Emperor merely gave the populace what it desired. He had more than enough funds to dole out whatever pleased the people, and they in turn kept him on his throne.

Now given this plague, the overall emotions dropped further down. My mere guess was that of grief or perhaps even lower to that of a victim. The country was ripe for anarchy and chaos.

The two began making their plans the day that their dad refused to follow their advice. Armless once more, both knew that riding a horse would be far too difficult. Besides, they would need to take supplies along with them. If conditions were as bad as they suspected, there would be no inns in operation along the way. They opted for a plain carriage. The secret tunnel exited in an old royal warehouse, where repairs were made to palace carriages and wagons. Since the plague had pretty well immobilized everyone, they had been able to leave the two horses and carriage in the warehouse unattended. They had begged a friend to help them get the horses and wagon. Both felt sorry for him, as he had to crawl everywhere to help them get it all ready to go. He even helped them stock pile food, water, and blankets as well, but then, the young lad had managed to get himself shot during one of the many street fights between aspiring generals and would be overlords.

Already, the two had used their new yokes to gather up as many gold coins and gems that lay around the palace. Clothes were another matter. Both decided to forgo all dresses; they would be too hard to manage. Instead, they packed several changes of men's shirts and pants. In order to get their pants on, each had to help the other. Neither could do it alone. Before they contacted me, the two had positioned their yokes inside the tunnel. As the palace gates broke, the two slipped into the throne room. Ana used her foot to activate the lever, while Callisto kept watch. No one was around. Hardly any man could walk these days. While women could if they wore these new, strange shoes, most stayed in their rooms, fearing the worst. After all, they all felt utterly helpless since the plague struck.

The two young women ducked into the tunnel, and Callisto used her foot to activate the lever. The stone slid back into position leaving them in utter darkness. "Blue light!" Ana called out, followed by

Callisto. Two faint blue lights appeared, and the two sisters smiled at each other before stepping under their yokes. Now the long journey beneath the city began. An hour later, they stepped out into the warehouse. What should have been maybe a ten minute walk had taken far longer. Neither could manage more than a three-inch step at a time.

Their horses and carriage were just as they had left them. Now they carried their yokes to the carriage and struggled to get the door open and the yokes with their baskets inside. "Damn, this is difficult!" Callisto muttered. Working together, an hour later the two had their yokes and baskets inside. Callisto climbed up onto the driver's seat. To make sure that they could not lose the reins, they had had their helper securely tie them around a metal crossbeam. From here, they could gather up the reins and hopefully drive the horses. Even if the reins slipped from their feet, they would not go anywhere, and they'd just have to gather them up again. Neither had yet worked out just how they were going to manage controlling the horses with the reins, however. Ana used her foot to open the door and then put her body into pushing it wide enough for the carriage to pass.

She moved as quickly as she could to the carriage; it seemed terribly slow to her. At any moment, they expected to see someone coming looking for them. Climbing up the steps to the driver's seat without the use of your arms is indeed challenging. Ana took her time and at last made it. Now the two began to intertwine a set of reins around one leg. Each would control one pair. When they wanted to turn to the right, Ana would pull on hers. When going left, Callisto would pull hers. At least that was their plan. A bit of coaxing and the horses headed out the door, glad to be free of just standing around inside a warehouse for a couple of days.

"Right! No left! Damn, this is more difficult than it looks!" Callisto exclaimed, as the two veered from one side of the street to the other. Fortunately, almost no one was on the streets, no one except the rioters who all rode horses. Foot travel was almost impossible for everyone.

They had gone only a few blocks in safety when two riders with long guns came out of a side street and halted in front of them. "Jest where do yea think you ladies are going? You will make a fine pair of play dolls for us. That's all you women are good for now, isn't it? You can't do a damn thing for yourselves anymore. If you are nice to us, we will feed you some grub, that's after you show us a good time."

"Obviously we can do quite a lot for ourselves. Please get out of our way," Ana replied politely, but she and Callisto were readying their old Druwid spells. Both men began to maneuver their guns toward the two women. Zap! A pair of lightning bolts arced from the sky, striking both men, who went flying from their saddles. Boom! The echoing thunder startled the horses further. Their two mounts galloped off in two directions. Unfortunately, so did theirs.

Their carriage flew down the street, mostly out of control, while the two women fought hard to rein them in. At last, they gave that up and tried not to run into anything and head them down the streets that they desired. They had a bit of luck and didn't meet any other riders, and soon they left the last houses of Naxos behind them. By now, the horses had calmed down, and the two finally got them onto the main paved road that led to Arolas' largest port, Andros, almost due north of Naxos. The road paralleled the Pinos River all the way to the coast, some three hundred miles to the north.

The day was sunny and mild, a perfect spring day. Around them, the countryside was blossoming. Many farmers already had their crops sewn, a very promising action, since the plague had struck. At least there would be some crops maturing later in the year. In ordinary times, this would have been a very picturesque trip. Now, it was fraught with perils. "It's the towns along the way that are going to be our biggest problem," Ana broke the silence of their ride.

"True, gangs will be trying to control the cities by force. We should steer clear of all, including even the smaller villages, unless we want to kill again," Callisto added. "Trouble is, sis, this main road has tons of towns and villages between here and the port. I think that we are going to have to get off it pretty soon."

"If only we had a detailed map of the country around here," Ana complained. "Keep your eyes open for a side road to our right. I'm sure that there won't be another road this close to the river. We can go east until we get to another north road, follow the back roads all the way."

"That is if the back roads go all the way and we don't hit an obstacle like a small river without a bridge. Say, what are we going to feed the horses?" Callisto asked. Ana glared at her, they had forgotten that detail in their haste to get away.

An hour later, they found a side road eastward that looked promising and took it. Another hour later, they were heading north once more over a rural gravel road, much rougher traveling, but far safer they thought. Now there was only the occasional farmstead, usually adjoining the road. Their carriage looked terribly conspicuous out here, but they felt safer anyway. Probably no one was following them, there was no reason to — they had no intention of making a play for the throne of Arolas. They only wanted out to a place of safety, period.

As the sun began to set, they spotted a small patch of trees ahead and decided to spend the night here. With care, they managed to pull the carriage off the road and parked it between the trees, careful to have a straight shot back out. Also, there was quite a bit of fresh grass here as well, perfect for the horses. Now to dismount. Both looked at the ground and where they were at. In unison, they exclaimed, "Damn!" Then they broke into a laugh. How were they going to dismount? Climbing up had been treacherous, but going down would be even worse.

While they were discussing the best way to do it without falling and hurting themselves, they heard two riders coming down the road that they had just used. "Double damn! Company. Just what we don't need. Okay, ready spells," Callisto whispered.

"Maybe they won't see us. It is getting dark," Ana whispered back. They listened intently. The steady clop, clop began to slow down. Both held their breaths, silently urging the riders on their way. That didn't happen, instead the riders halted. They heard whispers and then a voice said, "That way." Damn, thought Ana, they are coming our way into these trees!

A minute later, the two riders reined in just in front of the two. Both women were relieved. They knew the two lads from their dad's court. They were the twins, Seth and Spyro Ridon, both spindly eighteen year olds. "Well, bet you thought that you could get away from us," Seth said with a sly grin on his face. Both had bowl-cut brown hair, making it nearly impossible to tell them apart.

Spyro added, "Not much chance of that, My Ladies," he did a fake courtly bow from his saddle, comical under other circumstances. The two were always clowning around, playing tricks on everyone that they could. Once they even managed to sneak sugar into their father's saltshaker, though they never saw the result of their mischief.

"Your loyal followers and admirers have come to your rescue," Seth continued.

"So what's the plan?" Spyro added, mischief in his voice.

"We are escaping the palace, silly. What do you think that we are doing? Mom and dad are both dead and the gates fell. We got out with our lives," Ana answered them.

"So what are you fellows doing way out here? Won't your folks be wondering where you are at?" Callisto added.

"Nah, we told them we were off seeing the world. Honestly, they were glad to see us go. I think that they have had enough of our jokes, really. No, we came after you to protect you both. Really," Spyro explained.

"You bet. We suspected that you two would never be taken alive in the palace. So we made our plans. We've been spying on you for days. We knew about the hidden carriage. We just didn't know when you would escape or how. How did you get out of there anyway? Never mind, probably a state secret. We heard the thunder but didn't see any storms or clouds for that matter and decided to check up. Your carriage was gone so we headed out in search of you two. Honestly, Ana, you have been very easy to follow, once we figured out which direction you were headed. So here we are, your royal rescuers are at hand," Seth said boldly with a bit of annoying ego in his voice.

"So what's the plan? Where are we headed? Are we stopping here for the night?" Spyro asked.

Ana tried to reason with them, "Listen fellows, this is very dangerous. Our lives are in danger. Mobs and brigands have seized control of most everything. If you get caught with us, you are likely to be killed. You should head back home right now."

"She's got spunk, didn't I tell you so?" Spyro commented.

"Yeh, I know. Look, you both are armless since the plague came. You need us now. We promise to behave, if that's what you are worried about. Don't get us wrong, Ana, we don't think that you are helpless like our mother and sister are. Obviously, you are not or you wouldn't have gotten this far on your own. Actually, Ana, we are both very impressed with you both, really we are. Besides, we like you two. You are not like the other court girls; you have spunk. We really do want to help you both with whatever it is that you are doing. Please, let us help you," Seth begged finally. Ana and Callisto, both excellent judges of human nature, knew that they were being both truthful and honest about their intentions.

"Okay, don't say that we didn't warn you. In truth, Seth, we could use a hand. It seems we overlooked one critical detail," Ana agreed.

The twins smiled. "What's that?" asked Seth.

"We can't figure out how to get ourselves down from here," she replied. The boys grinned.

The boys slid very slowly and carefully off their horses. Seth explained, "We have to be very careful. We have to walk on our toes and thus have to just touch the ground gently, but we have been practicing walking, though, figuring that we might have to do some to keep up with you. Hold on a minute while we tie up our horses."

"Okay, just sort of fall off into my arms and I will catch you, Callisto," Spyro said, holding his arms out, while Seth put his arms around him to support his brother. Callisto did as asked. She fell off the wagon and into his arms. All three nearly fell to the ground, before Seth managed to keep them all balanced. Then Ana came down.

"Thanks fellows," Ana said. "Well, we ought to make camp. We're starving. Did you fellow think to bring along any food?"

"Some dried stuff. Dare we risk a fire?" Seth asked.

They all thought better of it; they were still too close to Naxos. Walking on the soft, uneven ground was difficult for them all and quickly they paired up, Spyro holding onto Callisto and Seth, Ana. Together, they aided each other. Once they had a blanket spread out and had sat down, Ana told them what to fetch from the carriage. As dusk came, the fellows had the meager dinner spread out before the four.

"Er, do you want us to feed you?" asked Seth, slightly embarrassed for the first time in his life. Spyro kept his mouth shut, avoiding showing his.

"Only if you really want to, we are perfectly capable of feeding ourselves," Callisto demonstrated using her feet. Thus a tacit agreement was reached. The women would ask if they needed assistance.

A bit later, Seth asked, "Where are you planning to sleep? I mean it still gets chilly at night. We brought blankets. Want to all cuddle up to stay warmer?"

"Sure, it is tough for us to get our blankets out and arranged properly. It is wise for us all to snuggle up. We can't afford to get a chill," Ana replied. Soon, all four were rolled up in a tight bundle, destined to stay warm.

The stars were bright overhead. Seth asked again, "So what's the plan? Where are we heading?"

"To Andros for now. We may be able to catch a caravel to safety there. Perhaps not, but that is our first destination," she replied. That met with the boys' approval.

Next morning, with the helping hands of the boys, things went very smoothly. Seth and Spyro decided that they would take turns driving the carriage. Neither was sure why both women insisted on riding in the driver's seat with them, however. In time, they would learn why.

As they rode along Seth said, "Going to take us about two weeks to get there. We haven't got enough food to last that long."

"Neither do we. We'll cross that bridge when we come to it," Ana replied. "So tell me, Seth, why were you two keeping an eye out for us?"

Seth grinned, "We like you two. Honestly. And not because you both have really big knockers now. Have you seen the young ladies who surrounded your father's court in Naxos? Flakes, all them. Knock, knock." He teased childishly.

From his saddle beside them, Spyro answered. "No body."

"No body who?" Seth continued the jest.

"No body home," Spyro finished and the twins chuckled.

"Shallow, no thoughts, but how pretty they look," Seth added. "We, however, have always had our eyes on the two of you."

"Ever since we were about twelve," Spyro continued his brother's thought. "Now those two have a head on their shoulders."

"Smart, wise, sharp," Seth added.

"Never miss a darn thing. They see right through all the plays and positioning going on in King Tropos' court," Spyro continued.

"But most of all, you two have spunk which none of the other young ladies have. So when the plague first struck, we decided that we're going to be your Official Protectors. Then, things went weird, what with all the rioting and the killing of your dad. Hey, we are sorry about your folks. Really, we are. I mean he might not have been the best King of Arolas," Seth explained.

Spyro added, "No, the best ruler that we ever had was old Queen Alekto Pegasos some fifty years ago now. We studied her. She was a Holy Woman too, but she had class and a whole lot of spunk! History books tell how she got us back on the right path, though it obviously didn't last once she moved away."

"Right. Now, along come you two spunky gals and the plague. So we says, didn't we, Spyro, we says, 'Preserve that spunk!' Didn't we?" Seth asked. His brother nodded affirmative. Callisto didn't know whether to believe all this, but memories of those past times returned to her and Ana. Both had been there helping me out.

Ana melted a little, "Well, boys, it is terribly difficult for us now, and we certainly do appreciate your coming along to help. If you think it is all fun and games living without our arms, think again. It's torture, but by god, we're not going to give up and succumb. I do have to warn you both, right up front here. This is going to be dangerous. Our country and kingdom is collapsing in on itself. Probably nowhere is life now going to be fun and safe. Danger seems to follow us."

"Of course, it is dangerous, Anathia! That's why we came along, to be your Protectors," Seth declared. Ana and Callisto chuckled. "What's so funny about that? We have long guns and we know how to use them. We're not court dandies," Seth protested. He was going to say that they were real men, but decided that would be pushing it.

Callisto felt a tad ashamed of embarrassing the lads, "We were not laughing at you two. Sorry. It's just that while you think that you know us, trust me, you don't know the half of it. Sis and I were chuckling because it may well be the other way around, us protecting you."

"Ah, come on now," Seth said, not quite sure whether she was pulling his leg or that she was serious about it.

"Let's leave it at this, fellows. If later on you find being around us too dangerous, you have our permission to leave us for safety. Agreed?" Ana asked. Both boys nodded.

Four days passed uneventfully. Budding spring lay all around them. Shoots of the new crops appeared in some of the fields. Smoke curled from many of the farmsteads. Farm animals were plentiful, but few people were visible outside. A few farmers were attempting to do their chores, hobbling along their toes like some strange out of control ballet. They only saw two women outside the whole time. Any other spring, they knew that they should have seen hundreds outside doing chores, working the fields, or even children playing. The world had been turned upside down by this plague of the alien mantises.

"Come on, Anatoli. Help me carry this LD radio set. If we lose it, we are sunk, son. Io, you bring Leda. To the carriage quickly," Alexio ordered. He had taken charge of his family. Something in him had changed and Io liked the change in her husband. Until this plague and its horrors, Alexio had treated her as a perfect Holy Woman of the Eighth Degree, but little more. Now, he was really treating her as his wife and an integral part of his life. True, with the loss of all her servants, he had no choice but to feed her and look after her many needs, but he never had done so before. Now he looked upon her with a kindness that she'd never before seen in his eyes. Perhaps, she thought that it had something to do with her own efforts to do unheard of things for herself, like brushing her hair and Leda's, even attempting to help fix their meals. Still, the appearance of the strange things and the even stranger memories of how to use them had somehow changed her too. Maybe this was just the way it was with life, she mused, shuffling along with Leda beside her after the two struggling men.

Struggling they were, now so crippled up, forced to wear these strange boots, their feet unable to bend, forced to walk as ballerinas on their tiptoes. What had happened to her secure world? Had Lord Jehosa called for the End of All Days as some of dad's courtiers had proclaimed? No, they were still alive. It was just the madness of men that caused all this rioting.

In the Emperor's palace courtyard, the men put the radio set inside the large carriage and then helped Io and Leda climb inside. "Be careful, Anatoli," Leda whispered. "I'm like mom and can't help you very much." She was fourteen now, with her mother's long blonde hair. Hers, like her mother's, had grown some two feet in the last week. Hers was now down to the small of her back, which she relished, along with the sudden increase of her bust size. She felt that she was maturing rapidly, which she had been wishing for long and hard for two years now. Leda wanted to be grown up, like her mother. Io was thirty-two and her blonde hair had grown so long now that it had almost reached her ankles. What alarmed her most was not that her waist shrank so, but that her bosom had more than tripled in size. Still, Alexio seemed to enjoy the more of her, and she had stopped fretting about her "melons" as he'd called them.

"Don't worry, Leda," Anatoli called out to his sister. "I've got my long gun with me. I'll protect you and mom." He was fifteen now, but still thin and lean, still growing, as his father often told him. Time enough for the ladies later on. Well, that was fine with him, because he didn't like any of the young ladies who frequented his grandfather's court. They seemed to know only how to giggle and then at nothing. Air heads, he called them to Leda, who always laughed at his jest. Now he felt big and important. The world was coming to an abrupt end, or so many of the advisors had been saying. Well, something was happening; his feet were gone, replaced by vertical sticks, he called them. Worse, had all women everywhere lost their arms, becoming Holy Women of the Church? It seemed so; even Leda said so, but then, Leda had been just like their mom, though he could not see why anyone would want to become armless. Women — he knew that he just did not understand them at all. Now these riots — these he could understand. Men wanted more and more given to them. He'd seen that every day of his life in his grandfather's court. The more the old man gave his people, the more that they wanted from him, and no one actually seemed to *do* anything to earn it. Well, he had to admit that he had not done anything either, though he knew that his dad had been covertly doing all manner of things in secret from his grandfather, the Emperor. Yet, obviously, it had not been enough. Their world was crumbling around them.

Alexio and Anatoli carefully climbed into the driver's box. They checked their stash of long guns. Reassured that all ten were ready, barrels poking up like a stash of umbrellas, Alexio took the reins and slapped them across the backs of the two horses. They slowly rode across the courtyard and out of the wide-open palace gates. Once clear of them, he urged the horses into a gallop. He had no intention of being stopped by the mobs of rioters who wandered the streets of Kefall.

Three streets down and two over, they met their first challenge, a dozen men were sitting alongside the street, drinking from a stolen keg of ale. The charging carriage headed towards them. Some reacted by reaching for their guns, but thought better of impeding a dashing carriage, especially since one of them was holding a long gun. "That was close," Alexio called out to his son, who nodded.

They charged onwards, fleeing for their lives, though Alexio had not explicitly told his family this detail. They were scared enough as it was. He knew better. This was their dash for life. The rioters would soon take the Emperor's Palace, killing any of the royal families who were still there. God knows what they will do after that, he thought. The world may well be ending, but now his only thoughts and desires were somehow to get his incredibly brave, loving wife and dear children to safety, wherever that may be. He envied Alexa who had the good sense to get out of Demokritos a couple years ago, while the getting was good. A smile creased his lips as he thought of her, so good to hear her voice again even if so brief. She sounded well. This Velona must be a good place after all.

Street corner by street corner, the carriage raced down Athena Way, until at last, he neared Central Park, the designated rendezvous point. He held his breath as he approached. Wagons! Relief. Others were joining him! He pulled in the galloping horses and slowed the lathered beasts to a walk, pulling up alongside the other five wagons and a carriage.

"Hail Adonis! Well met. Everyone here?" Alexio called out. His close friend, thirty-seven year old Adonis Chylos waved from his wagon. His wife, Xanthe and their three of age children were sitting in the back of the stuffed wagon, a number of long guns ready for the man and his two boys.

"All set," he answered. Alexio waved to another of his friends, Aison Sopos and his wife Melina, who sat in the back of another wagon along with their two teenaged daughters. All three looked pale with fear and worry. Dio and Minta Mitrios were there as well, longtime friends of Io. She and their two teenaged daughters peered out of a carriage, while their son sat proudly beside their father on the high driver's seat. Damon Aerios and his wife Airla sat on another wagon, while their teenagers, a boy and girl, sat in the rear along with piles of supplies.

Two other young teens drove another pair of heavily laden wagons, while four more teens rode horses. Something close to fifty long guns was part of this whole collection. Alexio at last felt better about this daring escape. They would not be alone. Indeed, he'd talked with these, his closest friends, for several days. All had agreed with him, now was the time to escape the crumbling Kefall before it was too late and the mobs took control of everything. They had packed what they could take, necessities only, and were prepared to follow Alexio unquestioningly. The extra six teens, he learned that evening, were the betrothed or boyfriends of the six teenaged daughters, who refused to be left behind with the departure of their girlfriends. Young love, Alexio thought, brooks no barriers.

"Okay, let's get out of the city. We're heading towards Naxos and Andros. There we may expect some help. Let's roll," Alexio called out. The small group cheered and the wagons began falling in behind Alexio's. Once they were all in line, Alexio again urged the horses into a gallop. Anatoli picked up a long gun and held it at the ready. Soon, they made the turn onto the main paved northeast road that led finally to Naxos, Arolas. First, they had to get out of Kefall, Thrace. Then some two hundred miles across the countryside of Thrace would come the spectacular Lonki Basin walls and a steep climb up, out of the kingdom of Thrace, and into the kingdom of Arolas. It was a thousand miles to Naxos, a very long distance in normal times. He blocked that out of his mind, focusing on just getting everyone safely out of Kefall.

"Damn!" he swore without thinking. Ahead, rioters had attempted to block the main road by placing two empty wagons on either side. Well, there was a little room to get though down the center of the road. He spotted six men with long guns manning the barricade! "Damn! Start firing son," he yelled, grabbing one of the guns to his left.

The six thugs, startled by the sudden appearance of what seemed to be a whole convoy of wagons with men pointing and shooting guns at them, cowered behind the wagons for cover. Bang! Anatoli fired, dropping one. Alexio fired and missed. He couldn't aim and shoot while driving the horses. Still, he grabbed the next gun and fired in the direction of the thugs. Anatoli fired again and put a hole through another's hat, barely missing. Now the five remaining thugs dropped to the ground, unwilling to risk their necks any further. There were just too many coming through, that would be how they answered their boss. Bang! Behind him, he heard the others firing as well. Now past the barriers, he urged the team to their maximum speed, they had to get past these men!

A half hour later, open springtime countryside appeared finally. Alexio slowed the lathered horses down to a walk. Handing the reins to his son, he stood and looked behind their carriage. "Everyone's behind us," he called out. He yelled to Adonis who relayed the question on down. Soon, one of the teens on horseback came galloping up.

"Sir, no one is hurt. We got by them."

"Thanks, that is the best news today. As you drop back, tell the others well done! We now have a fighting chance!" Alexio called out, greatly relieved. So far, so good. He began reloading the six fired guns, before taking the reins once more.

An hour later, he spotted a town ahead and halted their little caravan. Carefully, he dismounted, cursing again his crippled feet. They did not bend or flex; thus, extreme care had to be exercised when getting down to the ground. Awkwardly, he stepped back to the others, who had now pulled up close and two abreast. They'd met no other travelers, unheard of in normal times.

"Town ahead. I'm worried about another road blockade," Alexio relayed his growing fear.

"I agree, Alexio. Too dangerous, what with the women and girls with us in the open wagons," Dio called out.

"Sir, how about some of us riding ahead and checking it out?" one of the teens whom Alexio didn't know asked. While he'd rather not risk their lives, the boy had a good idea. He gave the lad the go-ahead. While they rested the horses, two teens galloped on ahead to the town of some ten thousand.

Meanwhile, Alexio faced a new difficulty. Io and Leda needed to relieve themselves. So did many of the other women. All had to be helped down by their men or boyfriends; besides leg stretching was in order as well. In addition, the men and boys needed the assistance of the ladies to walk without wobbling and flailing like match-stick men.

Io spoke up, "Look, everyone, we have to go to the bathroom and this is no time for modesty. We can't do it ourselves and there is no privacy around. Alexio, lend me a hand please." While the men were embarrassed, they had no real choice but to openly deal with their wives and girlfriend's necessities of life. Io noticed that the men kept their eyes from roaming, a good sign she thought. What else could they do? Modesty had to take a back seat. Such were the times at hand.

When they all had finished, the two lads came galloping back. Alexio had been wise, the main road through the town as totally barricaded and guarded. "Okay, we have to get off this main road. It's side roads for us now."

"Hey, I know this area well, Alexio. What say I lead for a while?" Dio volunteered. Alexio was relieved and pulled his carriage in behind Dio's carriage. They backtracked a ways before taking a north road.

As the day waned, Io began to worry again. Actually, this was the very same worry that she had had ever since she and Alexio began planning their daring escape from Kefall. The normal long journey to Naxos meant more than a month sitting in a carriage and countless stops at inns along the way. This trip, there would be no inns. While the inns did most likely still exist, no one was now able to run them. Everyone was so crippled up. The maids and cooks could no longer do their work. Everything had come to a complete standstill, as if the world had come to its end. No, there would be no comfortable, warm inns for them, no hot, warm meals.

Her great fear was how would they manage? Sleeping in the carriage was Alexio's only plan. Food? Lots of dried beef, fish, and lamb, he'd suggested. Had he forgotten how chilly these late spring nights could be? And out in the open with no heat? As the sun lowered in the west, she began to worry again. She felt so helpless just now. No servants had shocked her to the very core of her beingness as a Holy Woman of the Eighth Degree. How was she to survive? She recalled how she had bawled like a silly baby in Alexio's arms. His words came back to her, he'd whispered, "I'm your arms and hands now, my dearest." Such comfort. Yet, he could not even stand on his own when he said that to her.

Now she had these memories of how she might be able to do some things, but they all revolved around those magically appearing things, around a low to the ground kitchen, none of which they had now. They were essentially camping out, something that she had never done in her life. Neither had Alexio. How would they manage?

The men decided to make camp by a small stream where the spring grasses had begun to grow. About a mile further on down the road was a small farmstead with a number of buildings. It seemed safe enough here, miles from the nearest town. The small group set about making camp for the night.

They had not gotten much done at all when a middle aged man came riding up on a donkey. "Hello. Name's Dorieus. My farm."

"Hello, I am Alexio, my wife, Io, our kids, my friends. Do you mind if we camp here? We are on our way to Naxos. Trying times. Had to leave Kefall."

He smiled, "Figures. Them city folks are nuts. Houses stacked upon houses. No space. Well, wife and I saw you coming down the road. Don't get many visitors down these roads here, only our neighbors and not many of them these days, plague and all. Any news about the plague?"

Alexio shared what he had heard from Flavio and Alexa. "Damn, the whole world? Say, is anything else going to happen to us? I mean are we going to lose more parts of our bodies? Is this the end of the world coming?" he asked.

"Hardly. I think we've lost all that we are going to lose. Now we just have to get used to how we are," Io bravely relied.

"Aye, that'll be hard enough. It can be done, you know. Getting by as we are. Got that kitchen fixed up for the misses. She's somewhat able to do some cooking now. Reckon in time, we'll find ways. Never thought that I'd be riding old Jack here, but I can't get around now without him. Say, why don't you put up in our barn for the night? Got plenty of hay left over from last year in there, and it's just going to waste. In ordinary times, the misses and I would ask you in for a hot meal and chat, but. . ."

"I know, we can't do much anymore," Io finished his thought for him. She'd not done any cooking for fifteen years or so; she'd not done anything but look pretty for Alexio. Inwardly, she cursed herself for having been such an utter fool! She'd been nothing but a pretty wallflower, and yet he had stuck by her all these years and now was risking everything to get her and the kids to safety.

"Yes, but, I didn't want to open heartbreaks," Dorieus said softly. "Still, maybe some of you fellows can manage to heat up something for your misses. We'd love to chat with ya. Don't get many travelers out here."

An hour later, their horses grazing in his barn, the whole group filled their host's front room and dining room. Several men, holding on to their wives and trying to follow their directions, were attempting to fix a hot dinner for everyone. Later, after a lot of news sharing, they threw their blankets on the floors of several rooms and slept in peace and quiet. Alexio noticed that the six young teens were looking after their fiancés or girlfriends. He felt pleased, so far so good.

Over breakfast the next day, Alexio and his friends held a council. It was some three hundred miles to the Lonki Basin walls. The only way for the wagons and carriage to climb the steep walls was on the main paved road. They decided to continue the back roads until they would be forced to get onto the main road. After talking with Dorieus, they decided to rely upon other friendly farmers each evening. "We ought to attempt to make thirty miles each day," Adonis stated. "Ten days and we'll be out of Thrace. Maybe things will be better in Arolas."

Melina pointed out, "Guys, we have enough food between us to last ten days. After that, somehow we are going to have to get more. I've no idea how. Probably no stores and markets are open now."

While they hitched up the horses, Alexio had Anatoli pedal the generator of the LD radio. Everyone gathered around curious. "Okay, when the needle gets to this point, it's ready to go. Yes, that's the right speed son; keep her steady. Alexio calling Velona. Demokritos calling Velona. Are you there? Anyone there? Alexio calling."

"Hey, hi, Flavio here. Alexa, it's him. Hi."

"Alexio! Are you okay? Io, the kids?" the worried voice of his sister came through loud and clear, though a little scratchy.

"Yes, we are fine. We've escaped Kefall. Bit harrowing, but we made it. I have four of my friends and their families with me and six of their daughter's boyfriends too. A small caravan. We are one day out of Kefall now, heading towards Naxos," Alexio told her.

"I am so relieved! Flavio and I will be coming down there in a caravel soon. We'll have one of these radios with us so we can keep in touch. Alexio, it will take us three months to get to you!"

"I know sis. We'll make it somehow. Going to take us a month at least to get to Naxos and then a couple more weeks to get to Andros."

"Hey, I am supposed to tell you, somehow you are to meet up with the two daughters of the late king of Arolas, Anathia and Callisto Tropos. They are now on their way to Andros as well. Bethany says that they can look after you until we get there," Flavio relayed my message.

Alexio misunderstood. "You mean there are some women who still have their arms?"

"Oh, no. They lost theirs too, but they are very able young women. Bethany says that you should trust them with your life."

"Okay. We had best get going. I'll try to make contact with you each morning about this time."

"We'll be here. I love you, little brother," Alexa added, before they signed off. She was greatly relieved to hear that they were somehow all right. She'd barely slept all night.

Ana, Callisto? Bethany here. Slight change in plans. Alexio Omela and his family along with four other families have managed to escape from Kefall. He's Alexa's brother. They are also heading to Andros. Keep an eye out for them and give them all the aid that you can. I'm going to send Flavio and Alexa down there shortly, but it's going to take three months to get to you.

Okay. Will do. We've picked up a couple of boys who are insisting on being our protectors. We can use their help. Hope we don't get them killed. Catch ya, Callisto replied.

"What was that?" asked Spyro, who was sitting beside the two women, driving the carriage.

He'd noticed that both of them had suddenly become "not quite there."

Callisto answered him truthfully, "Oh, we were chatting with our friend Bethany up in Velona. She told us to be on the lookout for some more folks who are fleeing from Kefall. She's sending a caravel for us, but it's going to take three months to get here."

"Come on, you just made all that up? Right?" he teased.

"No, we have the ability to telepathically talk to others," Callisto insisted.

"Naw, you can't. No one can do that, can they?" Spyro protested.

Yes I can! Silly boy. The words appeared in his mind. Spyro nearly dropped the reins, though because of the way that they were tied, it would not have mattered.

"My god! You can! Seth, she can," he said wide-eyed.

"I know, I just heard her too! Incredible. I told you these two had spunk!" Seth exclaimed from his saddle, riding alongside them.

An hour later, they approached a small village. While they thought about detouring around the village, Callisto said, "Why don't I just go over to the village and check it out first. If I don't see anything, we can just go right on through."

"Good idea. Say, there is far too much smoke coming from the village. I think something is wrong there," Ana said, suddenly becoming concerned.

"You want to borrow my horse?" asked Spyro, not fully grasping what she was planning.

"No silly. Bethany is the one who can ride horses. I mean that she rides them without her arms. No, I will leave my body here and move on ahead and check it out."

"You leave your body? What are you talking about?"

"Ana, you explain it. I'm off. I don't like the looks of that either. Way too much smoke for a few chimneys."

Ana grimaced, just like Callisto to take off leaving her to have to try to explain about spiritual beings and bodies and moving out of them. As expected, when she finished, Seth made his usual comment, "See, I told you they had spunk." She smiled; they had only one word for the unusual, spunk. Ah well.

Shortly, Callisto's body reactivated. "Damn! Damn! Double damn!" she swore loudly, startling both boys.

Ana, used to Callisto's sometimes harsh reactions, knew something awful was happening. "Brigands or whatever ahead. They are burning down the village. I saw dozens of dead men and boys littering the streets. Worse, they have dozens of women all tied together behind some wagons. Ana, we have to rescue them. I won't stand for such brutality!"

"Me either. Spyro, get these horses into a gallop. We have to set things right. Seth, ready your long gun, you are going to need it!" Ana called out. "Ready spells."

Callisto replied, "Right. No mercy to these dogs! Kill every last one of them!" Both Seth and Spyro were quite shocked at such a reaction from their "spunky" girls. They obeyed and the horses broke into a gallop, closing the distance to the rural village rapidly.

As they entered the village, Ana guessed that at one time the village was home to perhaps five hundred. Now half of the buildings were in flames, as they came charging down the main street into the village. Their half of the village was yet untouched by flames. Six wagons were parked in the middle of the street ahead of them. Women and girls were roped together in lines behind each wagon. Most of the wagons were loaded with stolen goods from the homes. Dead bodies of men, boys, and babies lay strewn about the street, lawns, and doorways.

Men were rummaging through the homes, confiscating what they desired, carrying the goods out to the wagons. Spyro pulled in the horses just behind the rear wagon with a half dozen women tied in a line behind it. Several men were walking to the wagons, their arms piled with stolen loot. I say walking, but wobbling on tiny steps would be more accurate.

Two lightning bolts arced into a pair of men, sending them flying, goods falling in a heap near where they had been standing. Boom! Boom! Thunder came. Bang. Bang. The twins took out two more. Each grabbed a second long gun and wildly looked around for more of the bandits.

Ana and Callisto each looked to one side, as if they were back to back. Soon, a half dozen more men came stumbling out of the houses, trying to walk and to raise their long guns. Something had gone terribly wrong for them. They had made sure that all resistance was eliminated before they had dismounted. On horseback, they could move at will as always. Yet, on foot, they could only just barely walk. Bang. Bang. Two more dropped. Two more lightning bolts arced. Boom! Boom! Peals of thunder shook the village.

Four remaining men attempted to run to their horses. Well, that would have been their intended action. Not anymore. Barely able to walk, they stumbled wildly, two fell onto the ground and began rapidly crawling towards their horses. The other two wildly flailed their arms, somehow managing to remain on their toes. Bang. Bang. They dropped. Two more lightning bolts arced followed by great peals of thunder. Both boys looked up at the sky, but saw only one billowing white cloud. Where was this fortuitous thunderstorm?

"Any more of them?" Ana called out to the shocked, numb women. "Any more of them?" she repeated herself. Finally, one woman shook her head no. "Seth, help me down, please." He complied, just barely able to catch her as she mostly fell off the carriage. Then, he helped Callisto down.

"We got to reload our guns, just in case," Spyro said, rapidly reloading his two long guns. Seth now did the same, while Ana and Callisto slowly made their way to the traumatized women. At least they could walk, if only three inches a step.

"Damn them anyway," Callisto said as she drew close to this back line of women. All were young. All were traumatized, shaking wildly, barely able to stand. A rope was tied around their waists leading to the one in front and in back of them and eventually to the rear of the wagon. "You are safe now. Sit down if you want to. We'll get you untied as soon as we can. Spyro, hurry up. We need you fellows to untie them," she called out.

Soon, the twins, an arm over each other for support, came slowly up to her, a long gun in their other arm. "We'll cover you fellows. Untie all them, please," Callisto ordered.

"But you can't hold my long gun," Spyro protested.

"Who do you think cast those lightning bolts? Us, silly, now untie them. We could, but it will take us forever to do it with our feet, please," she asked. Quickly, the twins began doing as she asked.

A while later, Callisto counted thirty-six women, the oldest was barely twenty-four, the youngest was fourteen. Flames roared from the burning homes. Ana had the women now sitting on the ground beside one of the wagons in a small group. "Is this all that are alive?" she asked incredulously.

An older woman named Kassi spoke up amid her crying, "Yes, they killed the rest of us, my babies, my parents." She broke down.

"Are there more of them? Are more bad men coming?" Callisto needed to know. Several shook their heads no.

One twenty-four year old woman with long brown hair got up and headed for one of the closest dead men. She began kicking him with her foot. "Bastard! Bastard! Foul bastard!" She shrieked in anger.

Ana grinned; she had an idea. "Okay, come on, all of you. Up on your feet. See her, go join her, kick those filthy bastards who did this to you. Come on, everyone, up and at it. You've got to go kick those bastards to death!" Slowly, as if rising from some deep trance, the women struggled to their feet and shuffled slowly over to four of the closest dead men. Their first kicks were mostly a gentle tap, as if they expected the men to jump up and attack them again. Since the bodies remained motionless, they began kicking harder and then harder still. Suddenly, they cursed and swore, their anger venting like smoke in a stiff breeze. Soon, their anger spent, they returned to the two women who had come to their rescue. Their grief was still raw, but they had done something to fight back, which made a huge difference to their mental well-being.

Callisto asked, "What happened here? What did they want? Where did they come from?"

One of the older women answered for them. "I'm Kassi. They came from Naxos. They rode into our village and killed all our men first. Our husbands tried to protect us, but they couldn't; they can barely walk. They said that we are now worthless and are to become their play toys. If we give them pleasure, they will feed us and give us a warm place to stay. We are useless for anything else but to give them pleasure. They are right; we are now so useless. We can't do anything anymore since the plague struck. We can only be men's playthings now. What else can we do? My husband has been feeding me and cooking our meals, even feeding my baby. I can't do anything, not even use the chamber pot by myself. Those men are right. We can only be their pleasure toys now and hope that they will feed us and keep us warm. What else is there for us now? We are lost."

"Didn't I say that this was what was going to happen down here?" Callisto growled to Ana. "Damn, damn, damn."

"Didn't you have some images in your minds about how to carry things with those yokes? How to write using the low desks? How to cook using those new kitchen things? Didn't you all get those things magically appearing in your houses?" Ana asked.

"I did." One woman answered. Another added, "Me too." Soon nearly all admitted that they had.

"Look, do you really want to spend your whole life being nothing but a play toy, a doll for some man to get his jollies off on you?" Callisto demanded of them.

"No, but what else is there now?" Kassi asked.

"We find alternate ways to do what we must do, just like those images in your minds," Callisto replied in a kinder, gentler voice. "It's hard, it takes us much longer to do anything, but by god, I will never be a play toy for some man. I'll kill him first!"

"But how will we survive now? We can't stay here. They will be back when these fail to return to

Naxos," Kassi asked.

"Pack up. You are coming with us. We are heading to some safe place," Callisto answered her, making up her mind that no way was she going to abandon these women.

Just then, they heard horses galloping towards them. "Shit! Already?" Callisto swore, she was exceedingly angry just now. She and Ana took a position ready to face the riders. The twins got down on their knees and steadied their long guns, cursing because they had only brought one long gun with them; their others were on the carriage and horses.

Six riders came galloping into town from the direction that the four had entered. "Wait! Don't shoot! That's my husband, Cleo," Kassi called out. Callisto breathed a sigh of relief, but the twins only lowered their guns, not ready to trust Kassi.

The shocked riders pulled up. Ordinarily, Callisto would have expected these husbands to rapidly dismount and rush to their wives. Such was not possible anymore. They rode as close as they dared, ignoring Ana, Callisto, and the twins. Cleo slowly dismounted but moved too quickly, falling to his knees, his feet unable to support him. He crawled as fast as he could towards her, and she took her tiny steps towards him as fast as she could. He threw his arms around her. Likewise, the other five young men found their wives among these remaining women and hugged them for dear life.

Finally, Cleo said, "My god! What happened, Kassi? We were trying our best to work the fields, saw the smoke, and came as fast as we could." Bawling nonstop, Kassi described what had happened, how the men came and shot all the villagers except the younger women, how they were told that their only purpose in life was to be pleasure toys for men. Finally, she described their incredible rescue by the four.

"Look, Cleo, it's not safe to remain here much longer. Kassi said that they would likely send out more men to find out why these have not returned. I want you to come with us to a place of safety. I have some friends who will be rescuing us, but we have to get going soon. We can't take on an army of these men," Ana explained as gently as she could. "We don't have time to bury the dead either."

"Let's get organized," Callisto added. "Are there any more wagons around here? If so, get all the horses and wagons you can find together. Ladies, let's go see if we can find some yokes in the houses which are not burning. Then, let's go through the houses and collect anything that we might find useful. fellows, find all the long guns, powder, and lead you can find. We have to protect these women. We are going to need cooking utensils to fix meals and eat with, so grab those too. Load up the wagons; time is precious."

"But we can't just leave them, we have to bury them," Kassi protested.

"Okay, we can't bury them because we can't dig enough graves. So let's give them our best send off and allow them to burn instead. Their ashes can nourish the very earth itself, helping to bring forth new life," Ana suggested, wisely.

With Callisto and Ana leading the way, the three dozen women began to catch on quickly, especially after finding a number of yokes in the undamaged homes. Mimicking the foot actions of the two, the women did their best, gathering up blankets, food, even pots, pans, plates, and silverware. All this took far longer than either wanted, but they soon saw that it could not be speeded up. Taking this many women with them meant that they had to have supplies, ways to prepare meals, clothing, and blankets for the cold nights.

The men found another six wagons and two dozen horses and got them into the lineup on the main street. By the time they were ready to leave, they had fifty long guns between the men, more than six a piece. It took vastly longer for the men to get the many fallen into one house. Late in the afternoon, they all gathered outside that house and held a funeral service. Then, the six villagers tossed torches into the home, setting it ablaze. Lamp oil ensured the fire would consume the bodies.

As they prepared to leave, Ana and Callisto faced a new problem. They had a dozen wagons plus their carriage and only eight men to drive them. "Now what do we do?" asked Callisto, as they stood surveying the problem. "One of us can drive our carriage, but that leaves three wagons."

"Wait a minute," Cleo spoke up. "What do you mean? You can drive your carriage? How? You have no arms."

"Feet, we still have feet," Callisto answered him. "Come; see how we have it fixed up. Maybe we can do something like this and some older women can manage to drive wagons too."

Cleo saw how the two managed the reins and the six set to work making similar changes to three of the wagons. Six of the older women volunteered and they watched carefully, as Ana and Callisto demonstrated how they had done it. To be on the safe side, the fellows also tied sturdy ropes from wagons driven by them to the wagons driven by their wives. That way, things could not get too far wrong. At last, they set out. Another pile of horses were tied in a long string behind the last wagon. Callisto and Ana took point, with Seth and Spyro driving two wagons loaded with supplies and women right behind them.

As they rode along, Ana made contact with me once again. *Bethany. Ana here. New development. It's as we feared. The country has fallen into anarchy. Roving bands of men are now raiding villages, capturing young women to become their sexual slaves. We've just rescued three dozen women, but six still have their husbands with them. I fear that we are going to be accumulating a whole lot more before your help gets here.*

Damn, you were right, Ana. You and Callisto are dead on the money. Well, I'll give you all the support I can muster. Will you be able to make it to the port? Will it be too dangerous to go there?

Don't know. We'll let you know. We have to deal with this bunch right now. More later.

An hour later, Kassi yelled from far behind us. "Hey, I have an uncle who has a farm where we could spend the night." Ana liked that idea and stopped the convoy to make some adjustments in their order, bringing Kassi up behind them so that she could lead the way. The sun was just setting as they pulled into the farmyard.

However, the farmhouse was completely empty, which unnerved Kassi. "Perhaps, they have gone to help some neighbors," Callisto suggested. "Come on; we have to find a way to fix supper for us all." Their first night was quite an experience for all. The women had no choice but to pitch in and figure out ways to help deal with fixing the meal. There were just not enough hands to go around, literally.

As the group finally sat down to eat and with most all the women struggling to feed themselves, a small sense of self-pride returned to them. They had done more in the past half day than they had ever imagined possible since the plague hit. While they were eating, Callisto said, "Ana, you know that we are going to have to give them therapy sessions, the sooner the better."

"I know, I've been thinking about that as we rode along today. Let's take Kassi and Cestis; they are the oldest. We'll do them right after supper," she suggested.

Later, as they sat around the remnant of the fire, wrapped in blankets by the men, everyone listened in as Callisto and Ana began the first of the therapy sessions. After explaining what they wanted the women to do, they asked them to return to the first moment today when they sensed something was wrong.

A couple of hours later, both women had taken the horrible loss of the day off and were now, as both Ana and Callisto expected, running out the plague, having lost their arms to it. The recent loss was hanging solidly onto the earlier loss. A while later, Kassi suddenly started laughing. "I was sitting there shocked, terrified, more afraid and scared than I have ever been in my life. My dad says, 'She's completely useless now. She can't do anything at all.' The hell I can! I felt like I was useless after that. Why, just look at what we all have done today! I am not useless, Cleo, I am not useless. I just need time to figure things out!"

Before long, the other woman was laughing as well, she had nearly the same experience. Callisto and Ana surmised that all the women would have something similar at the bottom of it all, unless they had to go further into their past, perhaps having once been a Holy Woman of the Eighth Degree. There was always that possibility.

After seeing the miracle results, everyone wanted therapy as well. As Callisto and Ana anticipated, the men and the two women wanted to help as well. The next night, they instructed the ten on how to do it and turned them loose on ten more women. They watched over the ten sessions, helping when someone got into trouble. The next night, these ten also wanted to help and that third night, all the remaining women received their therapy as well.

The fourth night, to the surprise of the men, Ana and Callisto had ten women give the men therapy sessions as well. After all, they too suffered loss from the plague.

The fifth day, they were again running low on supplies, but they had put another hundred twenty-five miles between them and the raided village. Until now, they had carefully bypassed other villages. In fact, they were halfway to Andros now. Cleo suggested that they might be able to resupply in the small town of Antos. He had once stopped there when his father had taken him on a trip to Andros.

They approached the town late that afternoon. Ana called a halt about two miles away. She and Callisto then left their bodies under the watchful eyes of Spyro and Seth, heading into Antos to see what lay ahead. They were gone for quite some time, causing the twins to begin to worry that something was wrong.

At last, they returned to their bodies, much to the relief of the twins. Callisto merely said, "Damn!" They guessed this meant trouble.

Ana guessed that originally Antos was home to five thousand. That is, there were approximately a thousand homes in the town, not counting businesses. Half of the homes were deserted; many had been ransacked. Close to fifty men, none older than fifty, were holded up in a bunch of houses at the southern edge of town. Not a woman was with them, according to Callisto. There was a graveyard just beyond the eastern edge of town, piled high with unburied corpses, young and old alike, men and women, according to Ana, who had checked it out.

"In the center of town are three large inns," Callisto began explaining, having sat down and sketching the layout with her heel in the dirt. "Inside, well, you won't believe it until you see it."

"No, please, we have to know," Seth begged. She gave him an annoyed glance.

"Okay, inside the many guest rooms they have women tied spread eagle on beds, gagged, and naked. Do I need be more graphic?" she asked. From the flushed looks on many of the men's faces, she had her answer. "Now then, it seems that this is all the mayor's doing. He's the sole person in charge. All the surrounding homes in a four-block radius are filled with his henchmen, hundreds of them. They have a lot of guns with them and there are dozens patrolling the streets, well not actually patrolling, more like sitting there watching it," Callisto corrected herself, desiring above all to be accurate. They'd probably all be killed rescuing these women, but she sure was going to try.

"We're ten, how can we possibly take on hundreds or more?" asked Cleo.

"We can't, unless you men wish to commit suicide," she replied. Cleo looked relieved, but Seth wasn't.

"Hey, we just cannot leave those poor women like that. We have to do something," Seth protested. Several others agreed with him.

"Count us in too," Kassi added. "I don't know what we can possibly do, but whatever it is, we'll try. Beasts!"

"Beast is an accurate description," Callisto grinned. "Lower than animals. No, I am not about to just leave. I have an idea. Ana and I found it curious that those men on the edge of town are so far from the others. I have a notion that perhaps they are against the mayor and his crowd, but have had their weapons taken away and banished to the far edge of town. Tonight, I want to make contact with them and see if this is the case. If so, let's get them involved. After all, I bet anything many of their wives and children are being held captive by the mayor and his band of vile beasts."

"Kill every last one of the beasts!" one woman called out. Others seconded her wish. Callisto smiled, right attitude, she thought.

"Okay, here's what we are going to do just as soon as it gets dark," Callisto began her explanation.

When evening came around six, the ten men, two of whom led Callisto and Ana on two horses, rode quietly up to the edge of town, where they dismounted. Behind them, several women followed bringing the rest of the women in a pair of now empty wagons. Ana and Seth headed to the first house, while Callisto and Spyro headed to the next one. The other men took up covering fire positions, in case anything went wrong. Ana nodded and Seth knocked on the door. Spyro followed suit.

Some fifteen minutes later, both couples came back outside and signaled the others. Soon, a number of men who were holed up in the two houses came out and made their way painstakingly slowly to nearby houses. About thirty minutes later, the women were in position with the wagons, loaded with all the remaining guns. Fifty-one young men now sat on the lawn there at the edge of Antos, waiting for instructions.

Just to make sure that everyone understood, Ana explained once more. "Okay, Callisto and I will head down the street and put to sleep everyman who is outside. Then, you are to gather up all the oil you can find and pour it over the doors of the houses and all around the sides. Remember, we don't torch them until everyone is in position. We only have fifty long guns and the enemy has many times that. We cannot allow them to come out shooting. Ladies, you know what to do once the bonfire starts?"

Kassi replied, "Right, we watch for any man who somehow gets out of the burning building and we kick them, stomp on them, smash their balls, anything. Count on us, we'll do it!" Ana had no doubt that they would, she grinned.

"Okay, let's get this rescue mission going." She and Callisto headed down the center of the street, although they moved very slowly. Well, so did everyone else, they realized. As long as the men were on foot, the ledger was balanced. Only if they were mounted were they in trouble. As they finally neared men sitting, while standing watch, they began casting their spells, causing the men to fall into a deep sleep. They would be dealt with shortly. Finally, they reached the far side of the inhabited zone and twenty men lay sleeping at their posts. The two backtracked and took up watch right in the middle of the zone, ready for any who might come outside to relieve those on guard duty.

After an hour, which seemed like an eternity, they began to see activity among the young men of the village. Oil was now being spread at the strategic locations. Twenty homes had to be covered in oil, and then action would follow. Hopefully, not too many would die rescuing these women, Ana hoped.

At eight, she received the signal that all was ready. Men with long guns were in position, the women ready. Callisto nodded her head in an exaggerated motion, giving the signal. Dozens of torches sprang to life. Moments later, the fronts of twenty buildings burst into flames, rapidly spreading to the surrounding sides, a wall of flames shooting up the sides. Callisto smiled, so far so good. How many men were inside the three inns remained unknown. Hence, they had fifteen long guns aimed at the three main entrances. All remaining guns were on the twenty houses, now fiery infernos.

As expected, some of the men inside detected the fires and tried to escape the flames. Those who came out in flames were left to burn. The few who manage to make a jump for it were either shot or were swarmed by the women, who kicked them mercilessly, until one of the men could get to them and finish him off. The sounds of the fire, screams, and gunfire brought men dashing out of the inn. Dashing is an exaggeration, hobbling out, using long guns as canes would be a better description. Bang. Our long guns fired, taking them out almost as fast as they appeared. After fifteen men fell, the main doors were closed, lights doused, and faces appeared at the windows, peering out.

Per Callisto's orders, her men were lying prone in the street, giving those inside a most difficult target to hit, especially in the moonless night. They tended to fire wildly at mere shadows. However, that was all that Callisto and Ana needed. Lightning bolts arced into the windows, sending them flying backwards, and most never to rise again. Soon an eerie silence fell. No more shots came from inside the three inns; no more men came dashing out of the infernos. Callisto allowed another ten minutes to pass, while she and Ana moved out of their bodies and into the inns.

They both knew that this action on their part had to be thorough and precise. Their untrained forces simply could not barge into an inn after those who remained inside. There would be too many dead as a result. Instead, the duo cast their sleep spells on the few men that they found still inside. A half hour later, they rejoined their bodies.

"Okay, Seth, we've done our job. This inn here has five more men inside, sleeping soundly. In you go, but be careful. It is possible to wake them up. That inn there has six men. That one there has seven, and the mayor is hiding on the top floor in a closet at the end of the hall. Have at it, boys," Callisto ordered.

"Spunky, really spunky," Spyro whispered to her as he began crawling to one of the inns.

Seth was right behind him and added, "Really very spunky!" Both Ana and Callisto grinned at the twins, though they could not see their smiles.

Callisto gave another huge head nod. Slowly all the other men and women began making their way to the three inns. By the time that the large group assembled before the inns, the fifteen men came back out, waving the all clear sign. Now everyone divided into teams and headed into the inns to rescue the women held captive. She went into the first of the rooms along with Spyro and several other men. "Damn!" she cursed. "Okay, get them untied and help them down into the large public bath. Once you fellows get them all down, fan out and see if you can find any towels, clothes, and their shoes anywhere. Be careful, their feet can't take much walking without their shoes." She turned and began heading out to her group of some sixteen women.

"Okay, the bath is this way. We have to get these poor women bathed. You know what I mean, get the filth washed off them, out of their hair, the works. The fellows will see about finding towels and clothes later on," she ordered.

By the time that the first of the terrified, traumatized women were led into the large public bath, Callisto and the sixteen other women had gotten themselves undressed and into the warm waters, ready to bathe the victims. Slowly, each woman was helped into the waters, and the women set to work, doing their best to wash them using their feet. Every now and then, one of them would have a bright idea about how to do it better and shared it with the others. By the end of this process, the original women had become quite good at giving another a bath. Their self-respect continued to grow.

An hour later on, it grew even more. The men had found not only dresses, shoes, and towels, but also hairbrushes, the new style ones that had been part of the magical appearing items. The women set to work on drying off the victims and brushing out their hair. Meantime, Seth and Spyro organized a food brigade among some of the men. When the women were finally presentable, Seth announced, "Dinner will be served in the dining room whenever you fair ladies are ready to dine." His teasing manner did bring a slight smile to a few of the victim's faces, though Callisto knew well that only therapy sessions would stand any chance of rehabilitating these women. There were so many of them.

Once everyone packed into the dining room, the local men began going from inn to inn in search of their wives, daughters, and relatives. Many tearful reunions highlighted the late evening meal. Callisto's next decision was where to have everyone sleep this night. No chance of going back into the inn's bedrooms. Their trauma was too raw for that. Instead, the locals brought in all manner of blankets. Everyone slept on the floors of the dining room that night.

The next morning, besieged with questions, Ana had everyone gather outside in the main street where she and Callisto could address everyone at the same time. She had done a quick head count. They had rescued close to four hundred women between thirteen and forty. Additionally, fifty-one husbands or boyfriends had helped them. Callisto sighed. Out of a town of about five thousand people, only a tenth survived! This was far worse than either she or Ana had anticipated!

"May I have everyone's attention," Ana spoke, Callisto stood beside her. "My name is Anathia

Tropos. My sister, Callisto Tropos. We organized this rescue attempt." Many in the crowd gasped, while others cheered.

Someone yelled out, "You're the king's daughters?"

Callisto whispered, "Shit!"

Ana answered, "Yes, the king and queen are dead, killed."

"So you are now our Queens?" someone else called out questioningly.

Neither Ana nor Callisto desired to become the queen of Arolas or to be the leaders. They had only wanted to get to a place of safety. Yet, there comes a time when personal desires have to be set aside for the greater good. Even though neither felt a strong attachment to Demokritos, they did feel such towards its people.

"There is no one around now who can appoint us your Queens. Anarchy rules," Callisto tried one last attempt to wiggle out of it.

"We'll appoint you," someone called out. Rapidly, the throng agreed.

Smiling, the two replied, "We accept. Arolas now has two queens. That being settled, here is what we intend to do. Our first action is to get us all to a place of relative safety. We have friends in Velona who will be coming to our aid. Callisto and I beg all of you to come join with us. We will see that every one of you gets our therapy sessions. Ask our fellow women and men about it when you get the chance. We do the therapy sessions each evening after we dine."

"Now I have learned that perhaps five hundred of your fellow townsfolk managed to flee to relatives in the country. Some of you may wish to do so now. That is fine too. However, I'd like to have some idea how many of you wish to continue with our group. We need to make preparations."

Ten men and women wanted to join their relatives in the surrounding countryside. That left exactly three hundred eighty-one women and forty-one more men who wished to join up. "Oh boy!" declared Callisto. "We're going to need a whole lot more wagons!"

Ana sent the fellows out searching for as many wagons as they could find, while she had the thirty-six women show the hundreds how to use the yokes. Then, they all fanned out. Objective: find all the yokes, shoes, hairbrushes, and other useful things the women would need. Ana began to realize that they were going to have to become relatively independent of the men. Women now outnumbered them nearly nine to one. No way could the men be responsible for four or five women at the same time. They were simply going to have to learn how to do some things for themselves, if they had not yet figured it out.

By noon, the women had caught on to the yokes and had made a large pile of needed items for their personal needs. Now they were busy raiding cupboards for food supplies. The men had rounded up wagons, they now had fifty wagons available along with an extra supply of some forty-six horses, which they saddled up and tied into long strings behind some of the wagons. Ana next had the men deal with reaching down things that the women thought necessary to bring along which were out of their reach.

By the time that they had gathered everything, it was really too late in the day to get started. Hence, another night was spent on the floors of the three inns. Yes, dinner and arranging bedding was once more organized chaos, but everyone did their best to help as they could. After the meal was finished, Ana organized the first of the therapy sessions, utilizing all the original thirty-six women. She decided that it might be best if the men dealt with the men and not the women who had been severely brutalized by men. Hence, only eight sessions were conducted that night for the men. She guessed it might take them two weeks to erase the hideous traumas of these women.

Bethany, Ana here. Er, it's worse than before. She outlined what had happened, and that she and Callisto had no choice but to don the mantle of leaders of Arolas, at least for now. *We need a safe, defensible place to hold up. See what you can figure out.* I promised to do what I could, glad that I was holding off sending Flavio and Alexa immediately to Andros. If they were going to try to re-establish law and order, they would need additional support instead of a mere rescue mission.

I checked around some, but found no one who knew much about Arolas. Annoyed with our lack of data, Marco and I decided to go have a firsthand look. That is, the next morning, we left our bodies sitting comfortably on the sofa and headed to Andros, Arolas. From a bird's eye view, the city looked quaint, like any Demokritos port city, minus people out and about. We spotted only a few. He and I decided to glide along the coastline both east and west of the port. Our caravels would need a place to put in and Ana and Callisto would need a defensible location. Nasty combination. It had to be along the coastline or nearly so. We had both just about given up when I spotted something.

Some twenty miles west of Andros along the coast lay the ruins of some fortification. The stonework seemed solid enough although it had been abandoned centuries ago. The small bay could hold two caravels at anchor at one time. Within a half mile on down the coast, clusters of very small fishing villages dotted the coastline. We zoomed up a bit and took in the overall landscape. Small farms lay in a random pattern across the semi-hilly landscape. We could see no large towns, certainly no large cities, though patches of forest cropped up here and there. The area was definitely rural in nature. My conclusion was that here they could stay in relative safety and with the potential for a local food supply.

I made contact with Ana and Callisto and via a Mind Link gave them a tour. *Hey, it looks perfect. We'll make for there,* Ana said, thanking me profusely. I had taken a big burden off her shoulders. Now she had a concrete destination. That evening, Ana made contact with me once more. She'd found out from one of the men that the place was the old ruins of Aran. Apparently, it was one of the first establishments in the country when the first settlers came to Arolas.

Now I had to relay this to Alexio, hoping that he would be able to find the place. They were just riding up the steep road the led over the edge of the Lonki Basin, the boundary between Thrace and Arolas. He had no idea of this place, but I told him when he got to the Pinos River, don't cross. Instead, head northward. Above all, I urged him to bypass all villages and certainly all towns or cities. "Hey, the farmers so far have been very kind and obliging," he said over the LD radio. Now it was time for us to work out just what to send them and to get Flavio and Alexa on their way.

Chapter 7 The Greenway and Sea Prince Reactions

Late October, at the Whitefield-Johns-Weston farmstead, located in an isolated valley far from Uru, Kingdom of Karka, the reaction was indicative of all the rural areas of the great breadbasket of the ten kingdoms of the Greenway. All had been through the first plague. These hardy pioneer men, women, and children had managed to learn alternative ways of getting what had to be done accomplished. Yes, a few like Tom and Elaine Whitefield had perished, but most had taken the calamity in stride, finding ways and means of carrying on with their lives.

For a year and a half, these extended families worked together to handle their growing farm. Of course, they had to make allowances, particularly in terms of the time that it took to accomplish tasks. Allie and Jean, the two older wives, led the way for their younger daughters, by insisting that they take notes on how long it now took to handle the canning of the garden produce, how long berry picking now took, the length of time that the women needed to put up the berry preserves, for example. Armed with this key data, this fall they would be better able to allot the necessary time to get the many fall chores done.

The men likewise made allowances. First, they always allowed their wives and children to see if there was some means by which they could carry out some action. Fetching the water from the well to water the garden, for example, had always been done by the mothers and daughters, while the men and boys worked the fields. The women put their heads together and with a little experimentation devised a plan. Using their yokes and balanced buckets, they got the water to the garden plots, all three of them. Each family had their own plot. Sitting on their butts and using their feet to manipulate copper cups whose handles hand been rotated ninety degrees, they were able to get the water to the crops which needed it.

While they had recently built a small water tower, which delivered fresh water under a little pressure to faucets in each home, the tower had to be refilled each month. Further, in case of emergencies, the wells all had hand cranks. Try as they might, the women had no way to effectively raise a heavy bucket of water. With pioneers, this was unacceptable. In an emergency, even the young girls might be called upon to fetch a bucket from the well. The men then put their heads together to devise an alternate method of drawing water buckets from the well. From the bucket at the bottom of the well, they rerouted the rope through a pulley at the top of the well house, and then ran it down to another pulley at the side of the well. Here it was attached to a waist high frame and tied off to a log. No possible way could the rope be lost by accidentally falling into the well, it was stopped at this frame and lower pulley. Attached to this were a large loop and a second log.

The women would simply walk up and straddle the rope with the log across their upper legs. They would walk some twenty-five feet out, pulling the water bucket up. At this other end was a large stump around which they could easily slip the loop in the rope, which then held the bucket. Then returning to the well, they used their foot to push the bucket over to the top surface of the stonework. After unhooking the rope from the handle, they could finally deal with the water using their yokes. Two buckets were always kept here, because loads always had to be balanced for the women. Keep it balanced was now a mantra for all, including the men and the boys.

Already, the extended families had gotten most of their fall harvesting done before the cure for that first plague was delivered to them. Yes, all eighteen living here were elated to see their arms returning the second week of October. Yes, it came as a shock to see them disappear once more by the middle of the fourth week.

"Well, that was short lived," Betsy declared flatly to Fran, who was a year older.

Fran giggled, "I guess those aliens never give up. Able, we will just have to show them that we don't give up either!"

Her husband agreed, "You bet dear. We never give up, right mom?" He looked up at his thirty-one year old mother, who grinned and nodded.

"Yes, thanks to our men-folk, we never quit. I admit when it first happened I was scared that we could not possibly make it," Jean responded.

"Admit it mom, you were scared," Able challenged her.

"Son, I have never been more scared in my whole life as I was those first few days. I hope you children learned a valuable lesson from that. When tragedies strike, fear is your enemy. Out here, there is no one to help you. Our nearest neighbors are seven miles away."

"We know mom, we were just as scared, too," Mary spoke up, she was her eldest daughter, Fran was now her daughter-in-law.

"Yes, dear, every one of you handled yourselves admirably well. We are all so very proud of the way you dealt with it," Jean praised them.

"Don't worry mom," Lilly added. She was the youngest girl here, now eleven. It was her parents who died. She still had the scars where her father had attempted to kill her when he went insane. Jean had taken her under her wing and Lilly now called her mom. "I am totally used to not having arms now. I really didn't know quite what to do with them when we got them back last week. It really is fine that we don't have them. Hank likes me anyway." Hank, Jean's youngest boy also eleven, hid his face, thinking "girls!"

"Right. We carry on with our lives as usual," Bill stated. The whole group was holding a family conference, now that the second plague had struck them so soon after finally regaining their arms.

"Only this time, it seems we women are going to have to help our man-folk a lot," Allie Weston finally nudged the talk down the path that the two sets of older parents had intended with this meeting.

"We know, mom," Fran said flatly, as if this were nothing at all. "They have to walk on their toes and while we can walk just fine, only very slowly. I've already promised Able that he can lean on me when he needs to walk somewhere. What I don't understand is if we are always going to have to walk with them while they do their chores, how will our chores get done?"

Allie smiled, "Good question. Henry?" She turned it over to her husband.

All eyes turned to him. Indeed, the young teens were very interested to hear the answer. Unable to walk, they had tried crawling, but that would never allow them to carry out the chores that needed to be done. "Kids, I think that it is this way. We fellows are going to have to learn to walk all over again. That's what it seems to me. I figure that in a couple weeks with we leaning on all of you women for support and balance, why we ought to have it worked out and can then go it alone. Meantime, when we finish our chores, we will be lending you a hand with yours. Where we go, you go. Where you go, we go. We are going to be a team of two. Now for the next week, we need to prioritize all the chores that we all do. Obviously, there will not be enough hours in a day to get them all done, so some will have to be put off until later. The cows have to be milked every day, but Mark, your room doesn't have to be cleaned each week."

"Yes! I'm for that!" his youngest son exclaimed; he hated cleaning his room.

"Now boys, we must take a tip from our women folk. From now on, we time how long it takes to do each chore around here. That way, we can plan ahead for next time," Henry issued his main order. "Yes, each of us will have to keep track of the time. No sloughing it off on the ladies. We keep our own records, fellows."

"Say dad, remember what the news said — that Stefano West Po and *the* Bethany said that we are all to do?" Fran changed the topic again. "Remember: 'reorganize our lives so that we don't keep on finding ourselves in a complete dangerous mess. New things must be invented to help.' Well, I am going to write her a letter and tell her what we need around here to help us all out."

Henry smiled, "Sounds like a good thing to do, Fran. What do we need invented around here?"

"Well, dad, wouldn't it be great if there was some kind of really big wagon with one of those motor engine things on it — like that fancy motor-truck that we saw two weeks ago in Uru, only lots bigger so you fellows can haul a whole lot more grain to Uru in one trip."

"Well, yes honey, but those things don't exist," he protested.

"Of course not dad, she's asking for ideas for new things that would help. Now wouldn't that help?" she countered.

"Say, while you are writing her," Betsy broke in, "how about a machine that does the sewing for us. It is hard to sew without hands. That's been the hardest thing I have to do — to try to make a new dress."

"Cool! I'll write that down too. Keep the ideas coming. I'll write her a long letter."

On October 31, I received a letter from Fran Weston-Johns from rural Uru. I could not help but smile as I read her lengthy letter. Besides telling me how they all were managing, which alone was uplifting, she had so many great ideas that I passed her letter on to Giovanni and Lucianna, who were elated at the great ideas. Both promised to get the DAE onto them as soon as possible.

Lucianna added, "Bethany, we are going to have to start advertising for more workers at the DAE. I'm looking at hiring at least a hundred more women and teaching them how to do drafting. With all these ideas and so many plans to draw up, Giovanni and I can't possibly keep up." Indeed, she did just that, added one hundred more women to their company. Many more would follow.

"Of course, there is one major fly in the butter," Giovanni pointed out.

"What?" Lucianna asked, wondering what she had missed. The ideas were great.

"Petrol. All these motorized vehicles need petrol. Right now, most comes from Fortress d'Grange and their petrol wells and refineries. If we make thousands more of these, then where's all the petrol to fuel them going to come from?"

"Okay, I can take a hint," I replied. "Tomorrow I will talk to Stefano and see about ways and means of getting more petrol. You get the things designed and built, I'll see about getting the fuel that will be needed. Fair trade?" They agreed.

The reaction of these three extended farming families was typical of that in the Greenway. However, in the larger cities not all was so pleasant. Here they suffered their greatest loss of life from the plague. Estimates put the death toll to the plague and its aftereffects there to over ten thousand men and women, nearly all were city folks.

The Sea Princes faired equally well, primarily because we had already survived and adapted to the first plague of Nestor. While most of us had our arms back for a little longer than those in the isolated sections of the Greenway, still dealing with the situation for over a year, women of the Sea Princes had made their adaptions to life, one way or another. In Velona, only a hundred perished because of the plague. An equal number died in Barcella, our close ally and neighbor.

Monarch Barbe Barcella's reaction was simply, "Crap! Not again. Aw well, we will continue to manage. What's the plan, Stefano?" As before, she slavishly followed our advice in all these matters. All that she asked was for us to manufacture more T-putt-putts and motor vehicles. "We'll need more mobility now. What can we do to help?"

True, commerce and life did shut down for a few days when the plague struck. However, slowly it all began returning. Within a month, all shops were open, goods flowing, markets bustling, albeit everything and everyone was now moving excruciatingly slowly. In those early days, I relayed Barbe's question to Giovanni and Lucianna, wondering if they had any ideas as well.

"We need more plants making the electricity generators — you know the stationary steam engines. The key to helping is providing electricity to homes and then to provide mass mobility to everyone, especially for women," Giovanni began his often spoken speech. "We need more plants making all manner of motorized vehicles, but we are holding back on that because there is only so much petrol that Fortress d'Grange can make. To be useful, city folks should have a refueling station within easy reach. Velona is almost there. The metal pipeline between d'Grange and Velona is almost done. When it opens, our petrol will become far more widely available and cheaper too. Bethany, get more petrol sources found. Only then will the making of bigger vehicles and more of all them become practical."

Like a wound up doll, he rattled on, "It takes money to start up a new manufacturing plant, whose goal is the production of large quantities at low consumer costs. What good is a T-putt-putt if they are too expensive for the average woman to purchase? What good would it do to design and build a motor-grain truck, if the cost of one was so great that the average farmer could not afford to buy one? You need to talk to those who have sufficient quantities of funds to invest in the new plants."

"Then, there is the infrastructure aspect. Let's take our new clothes washing machine, which is going to become widely available in December I think. While a new plant has to be designed to make them and employees hired and trained to build them, just having a machine sitting in your house is not enough. Having one implies that you have certain other things. In this case, it implies that you have electricity at your house, which implies that your house has been wired to an electrical generating plant somewhere, providing you the needed current. It also implies that you are hooked up to the pressurized running water system. Further, the dirty water has to go somewhere. That implies that your home has a connection to the city sewer lines, which assumes there is a sewer line. You see, Bethany, we are building upon what is already present."

"Giovanni, this all seems so interrelated and complicated, that I don't know where to begin," I replied, growing a bit frustrated. Life was not simple as it was two centuries ago.

"The place to start is to get Barbe and some of her more wealthy men and women to come to Velona on the train for a conference. I can arrange for the right Velona men and women to meet with them. I am sure that they can work out the details," Giovanni offered.

The second week of November, the meeting was held here in Velona. When Barbe returned home, she, her staff, and those financiers had a grand plan. Barcella would be constructing the world's first industrial park! Built from scratch, this ten square mile plot would boast all necessary infrastructure to support large scale manufacturing plants. A year from now, their plants began turning our large volumes of the various models of putt-putts, the new monster sized motor-grain trucks, and a new invention called the stream tractor, which would begin to modernize the farming industry in the Greenway.

Meanwhile, I needed to solve the petrol problem. At first, I cursed myself for not having followed and been deeply involved in all the developments of industry on Tarra. I was completely ignorant of this whole petrol thing, save I knew my T-putt-putt needed refueling periodically. The fellows always handled that aspect for me. Duh. Now I had to know all about this petrol stuff. Thank goodness for the telefono. I began to make calls and finally got in touch with Monarch Leroy d'Grange. He put me in touch with his staff. Eventually, I was given the name of the rock man, Dario Metrio, the one who had discovered all their sources of petrol. Unfortunately, he was a bit of a recluse and rather hard to locate.

After a few more telefono calls, I finally learned where he lived. Actually, he was in our sector, Velona. He had a place in the wild lands just south of Alta, our northernmost town. Louis d'Grange had a small horse ranch just north of Alta. Hence, I was familiar with the general area. I knew that south of there our land was full of steep, rocky gullies — a strange place for a permanent residence. Ah, well, I could see that I had to make a day trip if I was going to make any progress, well maybe a couple of days anyway.

Marco and I took our putt-putts to the train station. While I shuffled up to deal with purchasing our tickets — good practice using my feet to dig out the coins from my waist pouch, he worked on getting our machines onboard the flat car. We'd brought along lunch and had a picnic as we watched the countryside go by us on our way to Alta. Okay, we also took time out to snuggle and kiss, private time for ourselves.

I wasn't much use in helping him unload our vehicles, not unless I spooked the few workers around the station by "magically" lifting them off the flat car. Perhaps one day, we beings could be free to just use our native skills and not have to make our bodies do the things. At least a few people were out and about in Alta, a small town of five thousand at most. We smiled as we spotted quite a few women were helping men with their walking. Buggies were in widespread demand for even the shortest travel about town. Made sense, our walking speed was now nearly non-existent. Marco, his arm on me for support, headed us off to the main general store to ask for directions.

Marco remembered the storekeeper. Last lifetime as Bianca, she knew well the young man's father. Still, he knew better than to make such a comment. The owner answered Marco, "Ah, you can't miss him. He comes in once a month for supplies. Take the east track out of town. Keep going until there's no more road. There you'll find him. Rock Man, we call him around here. Collects rocks and knows all about them, though I can't see much use in that. Rocks is rocks." Marco added some snacks to our backpack and then we headed out to our putt-putts.

Our noisy vehicles caught everyone's attention, though, as well as startling several horses. Later, I learned that there was only one T-putt-putt in town. The blacksmith bought one for his wife to get around better last year. Well, I hoped that soon way more of them would be around for we women's use. Marco and I turned up a small dust cloud as we headed out of town on the dirt trail.

I could see at once that a motor-vehicle had traveled this track. The tire prints were unmistakable. We began to wonder if we should have spent the night in Alta before heading out to find the Rock Man. It was getting dark and still the dirt road ambled southeastward, though it was getting more and more winding and twisting, meandering its way in and around the many rocky gullies that dominated our most northern lands. Finally, we spotted a small wood frame house and a motor-truck parked outside. The track was barely visible here and obviously ended here. We'd made it.

The noise of our arrival brought the man out to see what was making the racket. He was a young man, perhaps twenty-two, which surprised me a little. I'd expected a middle-aged man for some reason. He must have worked on the petrol situation when he was a teen, I surmised. He was tall and spindly, even more so with the boots that he and Marco were forced to wear these days. He had bushy brown hair, rather unkempt and maybe a week's growth of beard. He was slipping up his suspenders as he stepped out of the door, looking quizzically at us.

We pulled up close to his porch so that we didn't have to walk as much. Funny how we now all unconsciously did just that — get our vehicles or horses as close to our destination as possible before stopping or dismounting. "Hello, Dario Metrio, the Rock Man?" I called out.

"Yep, that'd be me. Come to look for rocks? Kind of late in the day for that," he replied. He was not particularly handsome. His nose was slightly askew. Something about his eyes caught my attention: one was slightly higher than the other was.

"I am Bethany Bartiana Angela, my husband Marco Angela. We've come on behalf of Monarch Stefano. We are in dire need of your services it seems. Can we discuss it?"

"Sure come on in." We all had an awkward moment as Marco and I moved at our snail's pace to get up to his porch, up the step, and across the six feet to his door, where he was waiting to shake Marco's hand. Stump, stump, stump, went poor Marco's feet as he wobbled his way to Dario, holding securely onto me. That's twenty-four steps we had to take just to cross that short distance. Makes for pregnant, social pauses; damn the mantises anyway.

At last, he was able to shake Marco's hand, while holding on to the doorframe himself. I sensed that he had not been around women much, because he didn't quite know how to greet me. I just leaned a little into him and he got the idea of a brief hug. "Hope you don't mind the mess. Only gotten worse since the plague. I don't get around easily any more. Of course, I really didn't clean up much before, for that matter. Come on in. Had supper yet? I was just about to serve up mine. You can join me. I've got plenty fixed. I don't like to cook much, so I just made a big batch and eat it for a couple days."

His small home was filled with rocks! Where most people put books and knickknacks on their shelves, he put rocks. When those were full, they went onto the tables and chairs, the larger ones rested on the floor. He stumped his way into the kitchen and we followed. The men's feet made a hollow sound on his floor with each of their steps. I realized that his floor was merely raised a little off the ground. There was no basement to it.

Rocks also littered the kitchen. The two had to move a bunch out of the way so that Marco and I had a place to sit down. "Sorry about not having a low table. That's what you women need, right? I hope you can still somehow manage," Dario said, rather embarrassed about it. "I have never had a woman visiting me before. Sorry. You are the one who wrote that hint book, right?" he asked, stumping his way over to the table carrying a blackened stew pot.

"Yes, that's me."

"Wish you had hints for us fellows in getting around on our toes, but I reckon that is nothing to what our women are facing again."

"Sorry, the only clue I have is to have men lean on women for support and balance until you learn how to walk again. Sorry not much help on this one."

Marco realized that it would be very tough for me to get my feet up to the table and he began being my arms, that is, feeding me, allowing me to get to our business. "Dario, this time, we have no cure for the plague. I'm afraid all the women on Tarra are going to be like this from now on."

"Damn aliens anyway! Hope they rot in Hell," he swore.

"Anyway, women are going to need better ways to get around and to have machines to assist them with daily chores. Stefano and many other leaders along with the DAE are working on making T-putt-putts, for example, by the thousands. One day we hope that every woman will have one to help her get around more easily. The DAE is working on making a motorized washing machine to help women do the laundry. They have many ideas in the works, and Barbe Barcella is creating the very first industrial park, devoted to the manufacturing of more motorized vehicles to help us all out. All this mechanization depends upon one very key ingredient."

He chuckled, "No kidding. Petrol. You need more petrol and coal, right? I told d'Grange that he was eventually going to need to find more petrol fields, more petrol deposits. Did he listen to me? Nah, he was content with what he had."

"You are right. We need much more coal and particularly petrol. While there might be petrol in the Southlands or Demokritos, it is far too difficult to transport it up here to d'Grange. Stefano has given me the authority to ask you if you will immediately search the Sea Princes — that's all the sectors — to find more petrol deposits. You may write your own paycheck on this, carte blanche. This is utterly critical to all women of Tarra. We have to have mobility and things to help us survive better. Please, can you help?"

"All the sectors? Wow! That's a Rock Man's dream come true! You bet I will. I don't care much for the money. Got all I can use now. I'll need official papers from each sector giving me the authority to nose around. Need test drilling permits too, in case I find some likely spots. Now is a good time to start in, the leaves are gone. It's lots easier to see the rocks and land formations when the leaves are not obscuring things."

"I was hoping that you would. I took the liberty of getting the prospecting documents from all the sectors. They are in my pouch." Marco discretely retrieved them so that I didn't have to make an awkward bunch of motions to get them out. "When you are ready to go, Stefano wants you to take one of the new LD radio sets along with you. When you need more permits, like the test drilling one, call him up, and he'll see that they are issued. Honestly, all the rulers are behind this project. We are all facing the worst crisis ever. If we don't do everything we possibly can to help our women survive better, our whole civilization is doomed."

"Well, I think that we may already be doomed. Men can barely walk hardly anymore. Prospecting will be tough for me now, but I'll do my part. More coal means more electricity generators. I sure could use a small one out here. My biggest problem will be getting enough petrol for my motor-truck out front there. I'll have to have barrels delivered to key northern towns, where I can stop by and pick them up."

"No problem. Use the LD radio and Stefano will arrange a train to deliver the barrels to the needed sector and hauled by wagon to wherever you need them," I suggested.

"Perfect. I'll start in Barcella. I've already thoroughly covered all of Velona. Stefano has my field report. Not so good for us. Could be petrol here, like d'Grange, but it will take some very costly drilling to find it. We're sitting on an intrusion cap. Now I hope that in Barcella or Vito that intrusion will have lessened, making the petrol closer to the surface. I've already surveyed about half of Barcella too. I still have the extreme eastern quarter to go. That's where I'll start. Can you arrange for my truck to be transported to Barcella on the train? If so, I can get started tomorrow."

I thought this perfect and he set out to pack yet this evening. "You all can look at my fabulous rock collection while I'm stumping around packing." We did. Rocks were everywhere. He did show me his pride and joy. An amber crystal had an ancient fly creature perfectly preserved in its center. Now that I thought impressive.

The next day, Marco and Dario loaded our putt-putts onto the back of his motor-wagon and we drove into Alta. After an hour's wait, it and we boarded the southbound train for Velona. The following day, Dario was off to Barcella along with a dozen large barrels of petrol, enough to last him quite a while.

After helping the yard workers get his motor-wagon onto the flatcar, he climbed on too, sitting in his cab. This was a freight run, no place for passengers. Well, he was mostly freight, he thought. Slowly the train pulled out of the bustling Velona yards, moving from siding to siding until at last it pulled out onto the main line, heading eastward along the coastline of the Med Sea. Sitting in his motor-wagon's cab, he had a terrific view of the scenery. However, at the first stop, a woman wearing an engineer's uniform came slowly back to his flat car.

"Hi there. Luca said that we had a passenger riding in a motor-wagon. I'm Marcella, one of your engineers. Care to come ride a ways with us up in the engine?"

"Sure, I've always wanted to see how these great machines work. Coming, well slowly coming, that is, these darn feet."

"Yes, I know, Luca has the same problem. Our feet have made this a terribly difficult job. Lean on me, Luca does. Says it helps."

"Thanks, Dario Metrio. I am amazed. You can run the train?" he asked as he stumped along very carefully on the rocky railroad bed beside the tracks and train cars.

She chuckled. "Everyone thinks that a woman can't run the trains. Well, I'm proof that we can. Oh, I think you meant because of having no arms."

"I'm sorry. I don't mean to offend you, young woman. I've not been around women much, certainly not since the plague. I sometimes put my foot in my mouth, unintentionally."

"No problem, Dario. First, they used not to let women become engineers. I'm the best engineer on the line, so they had to change their rules. After the plague came, I can still do my job, though I admit that a few things Luca has to do for me, like shovel the coal into the firebox and deal with the heavy wrenches. Here we go. Watch your step; it's pretty steep."

"Hi, Luca Rinella," her husband shook Dario's hand and made sure that he made it up, before showing him around. "After this plague wiped out our feet, they put up this extra railing so we can catch ourselves if we start to fall, so it's pretty safe now. Marcella's going to get us going and then she'll let you drive a spell if you want. It's my turn to snooze a little."

Several hours later as they pulled into Barcella, Dario was back sitting in his cab. It wouldn't do to have the yardman see visitors up in the engine cab or so Marcella explained. She'd kindly loaned him her shoulders as he had walked back to the flat car. "Amazing what our women can do," he talked to his cab. He often talked to his cab and even the rocks around him. Who else did he have to talk to? He'd lived alone most of his adult life, primarily because most of time he'd been out collecting rocks or surveying them.

The yard workers unloaded his vehicle and he made sure that the precious barrels of petrol were loaded onto wagons destined for the northeastern towns and villages. Finally, satisfied, he revved up his motor and headed off up the northern spoke road. At the first junction, he took a right and followed the rim road to the next junction, where he turned left and headed north once more. Twice more he made his jog, until he came to the last town where his rock survey had ended sometime last December. Here in Bondeno, a dozen of his petrol barrels would be delivered.

He stopped at the delivery store and made arrangements for two barrels to be shipped further north to the last town called Lodi, population barely five thousand. From there he would be launching his detailed search, covering the remaining lands of Barcella over to its border with Vito. He was excited, for he was heading into new, unexplored areas, whose rocks he'd never seen. Of course, he knew that no other person shared his unabated enthusiasm for rocks. For him, rocks told interesting stories, though he wondered if some were actually true.

Dario's biggest problem when rock hunting and surveying was maps. While he had the best maps of Barcella and Vito with him, they only showed the areas up to the last towns of the sector. Beyond that, the map was blank. The rock structure was already well known in the settled lands. His job was to find new locations, which would likely yield more coal deposits and petrol supplies. Thus, he had to begin searching in these blank areas of the maps.

Ordinarily, he would drive his motor-wagon, laden with his supplies, as far as the tracks would permit. From there, he would hike on foot or for longer periods; he'd rent a packhorse and lead it, carrying his camping supplies. Now, all that had changed for the worst. He'd not said anything to that young woman who'd come to engage his services, but he could barely walk on flat ground. How could he possibly walk out in the rough countryside where he needed to be looking? "I'll take it slow and easy," he had decided when he had accepted her proposal.

Now as the track narrowed, he wondered if it would even be possible. He drove onward, but slowly, as the vehicle lurched to the left and right over a path never made for a motor-wagon. His plan now was to get as close as he could to minimize walking. He consulted his own maps. "Perfect, cab. We are almost to where we need to be. Last year, I left off my search about five miles west of here at the edge of the gorge. Just a little further cab and we'll make our camp." The motor groaned and struggled, pulling the vehicle up the sharply rising valley. Naked trees dotted the hills far off to the west — the very hill on which he had stood last December. He'd been there illegally, though. No one had given him permission to wander about the backcountry of Barcella. He'd just done it on his own. Now he had all the proper papers. Just a little ways more, he thought.

Bump! Suddenly, the vehicle stopped abruptly, knocking him into the steering wheel. The left rear wheel had fallen into a deep rut and stuck there. "Oh cab, what have we done now?" he said. "Oh dear." Turning off the motor, he carefully eased himself out of the cab and onto the rough, rocky ground. Holding on to the sides of the vehicle, he made his way to the rear to survey the problem. The wheel was in a deep rut, nearly up to its axle. Dario knew that he was in trouble now.

It was growing dark and getting chilly. He'd been stuck before and always found a way out. "Well, cab, looks like this is as far as we go tonight, but it's a strange place to make camp though. I should have stopped sooner, cab. Then, you know how excited I am to be out in the field again. I bet, cab, we are going to find some incredible rocks this trip. Want to bet me? No? Well that's okay, but I'm certain that it's a sure thing that we will come back loaded with rocks. Kind of wish that you were not stuck though."

An alto voice from behind him said, "Mister, who are you talking to? Are you stuck? Do you need some help?"

"Huh?" Dario turned around. A woman sat on a low, sturdy horse, perhaps fifty feet from him. She held the reins between her teeth. She repeated her three questions, talking through her teeth.

"Oh, forgive me. I was talking to my motor-wagon's cab. I always talk to my cab and rocks and things. Don't often have any people to talk to, you see. Yes, in my excitement to get this new adventure off, I wasn't watching what I was doing. My feet, you see. I can barely walk and so I was going to try to get my vehicle as far up this valley as possible, before I head off on foot. Rock hunting, rock surveying. Official business of Barcella, this time. I suppose that I could use some help. Where did you come from? Perhaps your husband could lend me a hand with this?"

"Back yonder, I've a small ranch there. Sorry, my dad died last spring. Nearest neighbors are seven miles back the way you came and over to the east a bit. I can ride over there and fetch them in the morning if you need them."

"I'm sorry about your father. You live alone out here? No, I've been stuck before. I'll manage in the morning, when I can see again. I will just have to make camp here."

"Yes. Lia, Lia Dovica. You can stay at my ranch tonight. If you don't mind lending me a hand with a few things, I'll fix you a square meal too." She had been considering this from the moment that she saw him. As independent as she was, there were still a few things that she just could not figure out ways to do them. Fortune had just dropped a man with hands in her lap. A few minutes and these annoying chores would be handled for her.

"Thank you very much. I'd like a warm place to sleep. Certainly, Lia, I'll be glad to help you. I know it must be so difficult for women these days. Mind you, I'm told that I don't relate to women very well. I don't mean to offend you, just keep in mind that I'm almost never around women very much. Heck, not even men, for that matter. Back home, the locals call me the Rock Man. I study rocks, you see. I collect them, survey rock formations, and talk to them."

She looked surprised, "Do they talk back to you?"

"Oh sure! Sometimes rocks have a marvelous story to tell, if one only listens to them. Ah then, most people never listen to a rock, much less talk to them. Why the stories some can tell." He was about to go on, when he realized it was getting quite dark.

"We'd better go," Lia interrupted him. "It's about a half mile on up the valley. Can you walk it?" Dario gave it his best try, but his arms went flailing wildly and his feet tried to negotiate the rocky surface. He couldn't see where he was even stepping.

"You're going to fall and break something, Dario. Here. Hold still." She nudged her horse up to him. "Climb up behind me. Peg can carry us both." She felt his hands feeling for the saddle. "Sorry, no saddle. I can't tighten cinches any longer. I have no choice but to ride bareback now. Here, I'm holding on tight. Grab hold of me and pull yourself up."

"Are you sure? I don't want to pull you off your horse."

"Not a chance. Grab my shoulders, yes. Now up you come." He tried hard not to pull on her, but simply had to do so. Once he finally was up, he wondered how he had avoided pulling her off the horse. It seemed incredulous that he hadn't.

"Thanks, Lia. I am in your debt. My adventure is off to a rocky start," he jested. She smiled, though he couldn't see it. As they headed up the valley, he began to slide off and quickly put his arms around her waist.

"Don't ride much do you?" she said between her teeth as she nudged Peg onwards.

"Well no. I often rent one to carry my things while I am out surveying, but I never ride. I am always on foot so I can be close to the rocks," he tried to explain, and gave up, concentrating on not falling off the horse.

Shortly a dim lantern appeared. He saw it illuminating faintly the front porch of her ranch home. She rode up to the porch. "Slide off here, but gently or you will damage your feet," she ordered. He did so, but still landed hard, falling on down to the ground, landing on his butt. She grinned, nudged Peg into her corral, and carefully slid off herself. He saw her foot swing up high around the horse's head and a bit later, the hackamore came off. "Thanks Peg. See you in the morning," she called out. Her mellow alto voice sounded almost musical, he thought. She slung the hackamore over her shoulder and slowly moved towards him.

"Here, lean on me and let's go inside. Supper is still on the stove," she said. He put his arm over her shoulders. Quickly, he discovered that walking was far easier like this. He opened her door, but saw that she could have done it herself. A sliding slat was the operating mechanism, one she could reach easily with her foot.

Inside, a number of lanterns illuminated the ranch house. She hung the hackamore on a peg just beside the door, where a half dozen more hung. "This way," she led him into the kitchen. The table was divided into halves. One half was barely six inches off the ground, while the other was a table's usual height. The whole counter-sink combination was low to the ground. She had a chair on wheels, which she sat down on and began sliding from pot to pot on her stove, stirring the stew a bit. Steam rose.

"Want me to carry the pots to the table?" he asked. He felt very ill at ease. He had never been around women very much at all and certainly not since they got the plague.

"Well, if you insist. I'll set another place while you carry them over," she replied, giving her chair a strong push, rolling halfway across the kitchen to where plates were neatly stacked. While he carefully lifted the two pots and slowly stumped his way awkwardly over to the table, she set a plate on the taller half of the table, then a fork, spoon, and finally a cup. She then slid herself over to her side of the table.

"Er, do you want me to dish out some stew onto your plate?" he asked, somewhat embarrassed.

She grinned, "Guests are supposed to be served first. Help yourself. Okay, you can fill up my plate for me, if you like. Obviously, I can do it myself or I'd have starved to death last year," she replied.

His face grew redder. "Sorry, I said I don't mean to offend. I've just never been around — well you know what I mean."

"Don't you have women in your country?" she asked confused.

"Oh sure. Millions of them. Well, I mean I live alone, far from the nearest town, that's Alta in the north of Velona. No women around me, you see." There, he'd finally made it make sense, he thought.

She seemed to accept his explanation and began to eat. He saw that she was about his own age, perhaps twenty-two. Her face was a bit weathered looking; her brown hair fell below her shoulders. Her eyes were a pale blue. She was wearing what had probably once been a heavy men's cotton shirt, whose sleeves had been removed and the openings sewn shut. Her pants were held up by two suspender-like affairs and looked to be originally men's pants. Instead of the usual fastenings, a large loop had been sewn onto the waistband, which looped around a button. Obviously, he thought, this made it easy for her to put on her own pants. She worn the same unusual shoes that every woman had been given rather mysteriously when the plague had come.

After they finished eating and were sipping their strong, black tea, she asked, "So Dario, what is it that you do with the rocks? Why do you survey them? It sounds rather silly. Rocks are everywhere."

"There are all kinds of rocks. Now my job this time is no secret. Monarchs Stefano West Po and Barbe Barcella have asked me to see if I can find more deposits of coal and petrol. You see, they want to create many more motorized vehicles to help women get around better, men too. They want to bring electricity to many more homes to help women. They are inventing a whole lot more machines to help. They told me about a thing that washes your clothes for you. Even a man would like that machine, but it needs electricity to work. To get electricity, they need more coal to burn in the steam engines that make it."

He continued, for he loved to talk about his work, his rocks. Lia seemed to be interested, he thought. "So they came to me, the Rock Man. I was the one who has found all the petrol deposits that Fortress d'Grange is pumping now. I once helped Vito find a new coal deposit that was easy to mine. You see, rocks tell me a story. Right here underneath your home lays a thick vein of coal. The problem is that the vein is far too far under the ground to make mining it practical. It is up to me to tell them where the coal lies close to the surface. I find things for them, you see."

"Can you find where other things like these come from?" she asked, fumbling with a pouch on a ledge behind her. Quickly, she gave up trying to open it and using her foot, tossed it across the table to Dario. "Open it up, I'm too slow. Good catch." She grinned; he caught it nicely.

"Impressive toss," he complimented her and opened the pouch. Inside were about a dozen raw gold nuggets. He smiled, "Gold. It's always gold or perhaps silver. Yes, I find those too, but those don't interest me much. I'm not into making lots of money. I mean if I don't make another gold coin as long as I live, then I still have more money now than I can ever spend. I use it to finance my travels, you see."

"I keep finding them in the shallow creek out back. It might be nice to know where they are coming from; might help me pay for my supplies," Lia explained.

"Sure, I'll have a go at it. I've got to survey all around here anyway. Might as well keep my eyes open for the source of these nuggets. Say, how do you survive out here? Farming?"

Lia laughed, "Do I look like a farmer?"

"Well, no, you look like, well I don't know exactly," he fumbled. He was going to say that she looked like a well bosomed young woman, but thought better of it. After all, he'd heard that all women were now well busted, since the plague.

"I raise horses. Dad and I used to do it, but now it's just me. I take a couple down to Lodi each fall, sell them, and use the funds to lay in what I need for the year. Actually, he puts it down as a big credit. I go to town about every four months, but only when I have to go. I don't like towns. I can't imagine why anyone would want to live all enclosed up like that. I need wide open spaces."

He grinned, "Me too. I need the wide open spaces because there is where the rocks are, not in some town."

She smiled back. Interesting man. "I used to train and break horses too, but since the plague last year, I can't really put a saddle on them. So I raise them and break them partway. I ride bareback and get them used to doing that before I sell them."

"I bet you love to ride then," he suggested.

A broad grin enveloped her face. "You bet I do. Why, I've ridden all this backcountry of Barcella and even into Vito quite a ways. I know every inch of the land up here! I never get lost. I am sometimes gone for weeks at a time. It used to drive my dad nuts with worry, but now that I am on my own, I take off whenever I feel like it. It's a shame that you don't ride."

"Oh, it's not that I don't like to ride, but I've rarely been on a horse. Usually, I am leading a horse, who is carrying my things. You see, I like to walk along and view the rocks and their formations close up. I carry my trusty pick and take samples every so often just to verify the stories the rocks might be telling me. I've been over every inch of the backcountry of Velona, all over d'Grange, and even Barcella here, up to that ridge line about five miles west of here. When I take off on one of my trips, I am sometimes gone for months at a time. Now this trip is extra special for me. I am charged with surveying all the Sea Princes from here, where I left off last December, clear down to Zargarb! Oh, the rocks that I shall be seeing! Gives me the shivers just imagining what I will find out there." Suddenly, he registered what she had just said, that she knew every inch of this area of Barcella and even that of Vito!

"Wait a second," he exclaimed, surprising her by his abrupt change. "You know all the lands around here on into Vito and beyond really well?"

"Yes, that's what I said. I often ride there. I know them like the back of my hand. Did you really mean to say that you are going to be going over all the back lands from here to Zargarb? All of it?" she asked, her mind traversing the possibilities.

"Why yes. That is my current mission, to survey every inch of the back lands down to Zargarb. The monarchs want to open up vastly more petrol fields and more coal mines to support their ever-growing industry. Yes, I have to map it all out. So you know all the lands around here. Fascinating." An idea formed in his head.

At the very same instant, both said, "Would you. . ." Both stopped. Then, they both said again, "Would you. . ." Again, they stopped and chuckled.

He minded his manners, suppressing his enthusiasm a moment, "Please, I'm interrupting you. Ladies first."

"No, you are the guest in my house. I should not be interrupting you. Please," she insisted.

"Okay, would you consider tagging along with me on this expedition of mine, being my guide for a while, at least until you need to return, or we go as far away as you care to go? Your assistance and guidance would be invaluable in my work." There, he'd said it. He'd never asked anything like this before and wasn't sure that he was right and proper in doing so. Still the lure of having a local guide who knew the total lay of the land would drastically speed up this first portion of his survey.

She laughed. "That is just what I was going to ask you — if you wouldn't mind my tagging along. I'd love to see the rest of the backcountry down to Zargarb. I'd give *anything* to do that! Anything. If you'll take me with you, I'll wash your clothes, cook your meals — anything to earn my keep." Then, she realized that she might be giving him the wrong idea and added, "Well, not anything. I mean I won't sleep in your bed, if you follow me."

He flushed. "Oh dear. No, I wouldn't think of ever asking anyone to do that! Oh no. Please, I am looking for a guide. You would be perfect. Your guidance will save me weeks here in Barcella and Vito. Once we get beyond where you've been, you can come back if you want, but if you want to keep on traveling with me, that is fine as well. I'd love to have some company, but then, you might not like me so much by then. Would you consider being my guide? I will of course recompense you appropriately for your services."

She laughed, "You want to pay me to do what I would give anything just to do? You have yourself a deal! When do we leave?"

"Well, I need to get my motor-wagon unstuck. I usually go off into the backcountry leading a packhorse. So I suppose we ought to get that ready and then head out. This is fantastic. You will be helping me so much, wow. This is great. But tomorrow, I still need to take care of those things for which you wanted my hands. Then, I can go get my truck unstuck."

"Well, I have all the horses you need here. Probably all the things you need to bring along too. How long will we be out at one time before returning to resupply?" Lia asked.

"Do you think that we can cover all the rest of the Barcella Sector in say two weeks? If so, let's begin with that. After that, I'll move my motor-wagon over into Vito and we can resume there. Oh this is going to be great."

Then he realized that he would be going out into the rough with an armless woman and he became flustered again. "Er, remember, I haven't been around women much, particularly since the plague came. I don't know what help you will need or when. Please don't think less of me because I miss doing something that I ought to be doing to help you, Lia."

"You've said that several times now, Dario. Look, dad taught me to be independent. He always said, "In the final analysis, Lia, the only person that you can count on is you. When the plague stuck me so hard, he pushed me even harder. Look, supposing you were me. What would you do when you needed some help?"

"Why I'd ask you. Is that what you mean?"

"Precisely. Dario, when I need some help, I will ask for it. Otherwise, assume that I do not need help. Yes, I am pitifully slow at nearly everything, but I do get it done. Just be considerate enough to allow me the time to do it. If you can do that, we'll get along just fine," Lia spelled it out for him.

"Deal."

By then, both were getting tired. She had him sleep in her father's bedroom that night. Next morning, while she fixed breakfast for them, she began to give him some projects to do for her, projects, which had been put off until now, when hands were available. Her old saddles were still plopped in the middle of her living room, where her father had last left them. They were too heavy for her to move them. Dario carried them and put them into a back room on the special saddle holders for her.

Most of the rest of the chores that she really needed help with involved mending. A loop needed to be reattached to a pair of pants. A rip in the knees of another needed a patch. While not skilled with a needle, he soon saw that skill was not needed. All of her clothing had belonged to her father and he had made all these adjustments just for her. He finished the last of her chores by the time she had finished their breakfast dishes.

"Thanks for mending all those things for me. Come on. I'll give you a ride down to your motor-wagon. It is too far to walk on your toes." They went outside. He marveled at her skill with her horses. She whistled and called out, "Peg. Here girl." The sturdy trail horse came trotting up to her. Soon she had the hackamore on and secured. He was amazed at how skillful this woman was with just her feet. She hopped up, wiggled her legs around, and soon sat up. After securing the reins in her teeth, she had him climb up.

A short ride later, he was back at his trusty vehicle. She dismounted and sat down to watch. She had no idea how he could possibly get the motor-wagon out of the deep rut that it was in. This, she told herself, she had to see. He got out his jack and cranked up the left rear axle, high enough so that the wheel was at ground level, if there had not been a hole there. Next, he began shoveling ground, filling in the hole. Once the hole was filled, he lowered the jack.

"Clever, Dario, clever. I would have never thought of that," Lia praised him.

"I'm independent too, Lia. I know precisely what you mean by it. Out here," he waved his arms around the area, "there is only me. I have to be able to deal with whatever comes up." She grinned, thinking that he did indeed know what it really meant to be independent. Lia liked this Rock Man. She'd never met anyone like him before, excepting perhaps her independent father.

As the two stood by Peg getting ready to return to the ranch, both began having stabbing pains in their feet. "What's happening?" Dario exclaimed, and then slumped to the ground, rubbing his aching feet. Lia also sat down rather hard, trying to get off her feet as well.

"My feet are aching. I can hardly stand, Dario. I think that we had better get ourselves back to the ranch quickly," Lia said. She was becoming a little alarmed. Were the alien bacteria causing more changes in her body? She could ill afford to lose any more parts!

He held on to her while she mounted. Fighting the pain, he finally rose and struggled to climb up behind her. Relief. Both felt fine riding back to the ranch home. Only when they dismounted did the intense pain return. Dario gave up and just crawled into the house. Lia couldn't crawl and managed to fight back tears of pain as she hobbled into her house. She made for the first thing she could find to sit on, the couch. He crawled up to her.

"What a pathetic pair we make," Dario took a stab at making light of their sudden plight. "Can I take a look at your feet? See what's happening to them? Gosh, I hope they don't turn into my kind of feet. I can barely get around."

"Please, if you would maybe massage them a little," Lia asked, fear starting to seep into her mind again. He took off her shoes and began massaging them. Her arches were gigantic, he noticed, like springs. As he rubbed them, they began to change, to reform, causing her even more pain. Then he just had to stop because his own feet were throbbing! He had to get his boots off fast. In doing so, he noticed that his ankles had a little more mobility than before.

Finally, he crawled up beside her. The two just sat on her couch. "Well, isn't this a fine pickle. Here I have found the ideal guide and am ready to head off on my glorious voyage of exploration, and we both end up hobbled up!" Dario complained. She managed a grin.

"As long as we are sitting here, are there any more projects that I could do for you? Did we get them all done?" he asked.

"Well, there is one other thing you might do," she replied hesitantly. "My hair. Dad used to cut it very short for me. Since this new plague struck, look how long it has grown! It's down to below my shoulders now and gets in the way. I can't use a scissors any more. I've tried, but no luck with them. Could you cut it short? I don't care what it looks like."

"Are you sure Lia? I mean, it looks really, really good on you. I can cut it if you like, but I think you look really good with your hair as long as it is."

Lia had never before had a man express a liking for how she looked. "You think it does look good on me? Really?"

"Yes, it kind of makes a balanced look about you." He wished he were more of an artist so that he could express himself better. Surely, there was a better way to describe her look.

"Well, okay. Let's leave it for now then," she replied. She felt an unusual emotion that she'd not felt before. She wasn't sure what it was exactly, only that it was nice.

The two sat on the couch chatting the rest of the morning, both a little too scared to look at their feet. A little after noon, both were getting hungry and both needed to use the chamber pots. They finally looked at their feet closely. Her steep arches were descending, and his ankles were bending significantly now, his arch starting to reform.

"Could our feet be returning to normal?" Dario asked incredulously.

"God, that would be heaven-sent!" Lia exclaimed. "Damn, I can't put any weight on my feet!" He couldn't either.

He got down on his knees and helped her to her knees. "We walk on our knees to the chamber pots and then the kitchen," he suggested. He'd just finished using it, when she called to him from her room.

"This is so utterly embarrassing, Dario. I need help. My feet hurt so badly that I can't even get my pants down." He crawled to her and was as discrete and gentle as he could be. He could scarcely believe just how awful she must be feeling about now.

"Come on, to the kitchen, my turn to rustle up something," he quickly changed the topic.

By dinnertime, their feet were one halfway back to normal! Over supper, Lia asked, "Do you suppose that my arms will come back too?"

"We could take a look, but the way your shirt goes on, you know, pull over, I'd have to pull it off, and, well, you know," his voice trailed off as his face flushed. Hers flushed too.

"How about feeling around my shoulders and see if you can feel anything growing out there? That's how they came back in October," Lia suggested. He did so, but both were disappointed. Her shoulders still had no traces of arms.

The next morning, their feet were back to normal feet, but still too sore to bear their weight. By the following morning, both could stand on their feet and both yelled and cheered for several minutes. "Glory ha le lu ya!" Dario exclaimed.

Now they had a new problem, shoes. She rummaged around and found her old flats, more like moccasins. "Boy you don't know what you have until you lose them," she declared triumphantly.

"What am I going to do? I have an old pair in my wagon. Guess I can crawl down there and fetch them."

"Hey, try on some of dad's old shoes. I haven't had the heart to toss them," Lia suggested. They fit quite well and he put on some of his old socks as well. "Great, take all his socks and shoes, please. I have no use for them anymore. Let's start packing! I'm ready to get riding."

Lia claimed that he now looked like some prospector. Various picks and small shovels hung from his waist. He led a packhorse of hers loaded with their camping equipment and food supply and a bit of grain for the horses too. As usual, he preferred to walk, while she rode on Peg. He marveled at how she too managed to pack along supplies. She had rigged a backpack, stuffed full of things. She explained that last year she experimented with it, determining just how heavy a load she could carry, still mount, and dismount safely.

"First, show me where you found your nuggets," he asked, and the two set off on his voyage of exploration. For a time, they wandered up the little creek behind her ranch. About a mile upstream, he halted. "Hop down and see the story that the rocks are telling us, Lia." She did, coming to his side. He pointed out the story. Here was a small, exposed vein of gold. Each year as erosion came, a bit more of the top soil and rock was removed, bringing with it bits of gold. "You have your own gold mine right here, if you want to dig a bit. The vein undoubtedly stretches back that way towards the Appian Way, probably for miles." He described more about the rocks and the vein. Then, they continued on their journey.

During the day, she watched him scampering over rock out-crops, picking away here and there, as excited as a little boy as he found some new rocks. Evenings, she cooked their main meal, after he set the fire up for her, and then did the dishes, while he made copious notes on his map of Barcella. Because it began to get quite chilly at night, the two bundled up together for warmth.

By the start of the last week of November, they had finished the Barcella portion of the survey. At last, he used his LD radio to relay what he'd found. One section of Barcella looked highly promising for an extensive coal mine. No petrol, however. Barbe was delighted and promised to send out a team to explore further the area he designated.

After re-supplying, refueling, moving the motor-wagon, and the horses, the two set out again, picking up where they had left off at the border. By now, Lia had a better idea of what he was looking for and she led him straight to pay dirt. "Eureka! This is it! Lia, I could kiss you. This is an easy to get to access point for petrol! Yahoo." She looked very pleased indeed.

"I always thought that this was just a messy place to avoid, black, icky oily stuff everywhere. So they make petrol from it? Who could have known that?" she exclaimed.

Dario used the LD radio to inform the monarch of Vito right away, as well as Stefano. For a century, Vito and Bonilla had been the slums of the Sea Princes. They'd seen the tremendous rise of wealth of Velona and neighboring Barcella. Even the other Sea Prince sectors had thrived, while they stagnated, overrun with roving bands of bandits. Why? For over a century now, the Church of Jehosanity had been running these countries. After they lost the Second Crusade, Barcella and Pieta had forced a change in rulers of these two countries. Slowly both countries were pulling out of their dark times. With the discovery of petrol in Vito complementing its huge coal reserves, Vito was finally going to prosper beyond its wildest imaginations.

After relaying the news, the two headed back from the motor-wagon to resume their survey from where they had left off at the petrol location. They had not gone many miles further, when a December snowstorm forced them to hunker down for a day. True, the snow would melt quickly, as it always did this far south, but for a whole day, travel was too treacherous. The two huddled together inside the small tent, wrapped in blankets trying to stay warm.

Lia looked at Dario, leaned over, and gave him a passionate kiss. "But, but, I thought. . ." he reacted very much surprised.

"Sh. I have fallen for you, Dario."

"Oh. Well, in that case, I can tell you what I have wanted to tell you for days, I've fallen for you! Where have you been all my life?" He returned her passionate embrace. On January 1, when they had to move the motor-wagon again, they made a short stop at the nearest church to get married. Then, it was back out into the back country once more.

By the time that they had surveyed the whole of the Sea Princes, he had found additional petrol locations. Vito boasted three sites, Bonilla, two, and Pieta, one. Pieta and Solamina had two additional coal mining locations. Zargarb, on the other hand, had three potential petrol sites, most rather close to the Arad. Now, Dario wondered about traveling across that desert land in search of more. However, the climate was tough, and he had not gotten permission and thought better of that idea.

After returning home, he and Lia split their days between his place in Velona and hers in Barcella. However, she did make him clean up his rock collections, and she helped him organize them too.

At least by January 824, Stefano, Barbe, and I felt more comfortable about our plans for the future. With enough supplies in the making, we may well be able to manufacture the products necessary to make lives easier to survive, especially for women. All was not doom and gloom around the world. Hope still survived in the north.

Chapter 8 What Once Was Juda Arad

Late October 823, about a year and a half since it last met, the Qaam Oikoumen met in Jerilum, Juda Arad. Qaam is the only sect of the ancient Jehosa religious order that survives today in the Arad. As always, they are staunch believers in the old ways, though there are no new ways any longer, not for centuries. Oikoumen is an ancient word that means the entire inhabited world. The Qaam Oikoumen is the highest religious authority of these people.

As it was last year, Jerilum was chosen as their place of meeting, not because it was a larger city in the Arad, nor because of its ancient traditions, nor because of its strategic position on the old north-south Centurion paved roadway. This time it was chosen because it was here centuries ago that those fleeing the Great Battle sought sanctuary and a new life.

Juda Arad and Velona have been staunch allies ever since the First Crusade for Religious Freedom centuries ago. With the startling discoveries of Messiah Bani el Marina and his wife Tamina some forty years ago, these alliance ties are even stronger. Indeed, within Velona and the Greenway lived the direct descendants of their Great Messiah Jes Amir himself. Of course, the wicked, evil Church of Jehosanity denied that Jes was a man, claiming instead that he was immaculately conceived as the Holy Son of God, come to redeem all mankind. One day, these ardent followers of the true Jehosa religion would rise up and reveal the utter lies of the evil Church destroying it forever. However, as was said back then, as now, "Now is not the time." These days, many questioned if ever there would be time!

Once more, this supreme council was called upon to meet the latest, most startling and shocking event. A plague had struck, sickening all these faithful followers of the ancient ways. This time, all their women folk had been struck, losing their arms and having their feet horrible malformed. Even worse, many claimed, though the claimants were male, that the men's feet were even more malformed, forcing men to walk on their toes, so difficult to do in the desert sands.

The many prophets and messiahs of the Arad called for this special session of the Qaam Oikoumen to rule on the meaning of this horrific plague and to give them the guidance, which they now desperately needed. Three old, wise men made up this group. Badar Tunis, sixty-one, was the eldest. His long bushy hair and enormous beard was nearly grey now. (No males of the Qaam sect ever removed their facial hair.) Hamir el Wad was the youngest member at fifty-six. Yaz Madi was sixty, with a hint of grey in his brown hair.

As before, for three days, they had listened to the arguments presented by dozens of messiahs and prophets and even concerned followers. Now here in Jerilum, with the stark reality of their own feet and inability to walk upright as men, the three met in private to reach their important decision, which would dictate how the entire Arad reacted to this catastrophe of unparalleled proportions.

As the eldest, Badar took charge. "First, let us review nothing but the absolute, provable facts — those which are directly observable by our people. Correct me if I misspeak or have an omission. Our women have lost all traces of their arms. Their waists are as tiny as the date tree. Their feet so malformed that they can only walk with the special shoes. Our men's feet are even more malformed, ankles unable to bend. We walk, if at all, on the tips of our toes. Other leaders of the world report the same has happened there. I can recite the litany of countries, which report this has happened to them, but I shall not, and instead merely stipulate that it appears worldwide. These things are clearly visible." The others agreed.

Badar pointed out, "I find it interesting that this time no one is claiming to have seen these supposed alien flying machines. We cannot assign all this to the unknown, the unseen, enemy that we know not of." Again, the others agreed.

"This then brings us to the assertion that all this was somehow the result of a second great plague. This time, Velona is not asserting that they have seen or killed some bacteria, while claiming that it is the cause. Yet, our messiah and prophet in Velona have sent us word that the Medical Research Foundation there in Velona has once more claimed to have found tiny bacteria which has caused this plague. Nothing seems to have come from this claim, however. No cure, for example. As before, I say the bacteria cannot be seen by our eyes. Our people cannot see for themselves these tiny things. Further, we again only have their word that it was these tiny things which caused the plague. Additions?"

Yaz added, "Fact, our women are wailing, wanting to know what they have done to deserve this torture. Likewise, men are seeking to know what it is that they are being punished for having done. Indeed, all of our people now firmly believe that they are being punished, but claim they know not why. All are asking why are we being punished? What have we done to deserve this? How are we to survive? This, too, is observable."

"Accepted. Are there any other directly observable facts that I have overlooked?" Badar asked.

Hamir spoke up, "Yes, we have all seen these strange, alien objects appearing in our homes. Our women cannot walk without wearing the shoes. Our men cannot walk without wearing the boots. Our messiah in Velona reports that these objects are similar, if not identical, to those that appeared during the first plague last year. These should be in the observable fact category." This was accepted by the other two.

Yaz added, "Some women have given birth since the infection struck. Their babies are similarly affected; baby girls have no arms. This is observable." This too they accepted.

"I know this is relatively minor, but the wives of the messiahs here in the Arad report that they can no longer fulfill their wifely duties to protect their messiah's back, to fight with him in his battles, to prepare his meals, or to sever him or his guests, as dictated by our Holy Scriptures," Yaz explained. This was accepted.

"Okay, let us move on into the realm of direct conclusion and speculation supported by the facts," Badar continued. "We can accept as speculation that some plague has caused this catastrophe to our bodies. We can conclude that we are all now mutations of the human race, since our offspring carry on our deformities."

"May I add another speculation?" Yaz asked. Badar nodded, "It is reported that our women somehow have strange notions of how these alien objects ought and should be used to help them recover life actions. Why should they have such thoughts? Would any of us have such thoughts if we suddenly found a pile of alien objects before us? I truthfully have had none." That was added to the supporting ideas.

Badar solemnly said, "Now we must determine what this all means and what we are to do about it. We have all studied our scriptures. We have listened to our venerable prophets. Yet, nowhere can I find any direct reference to our current tortures. Have any of you found something I may have missed?" They shook their heads, no.

He continued, "Some claim that this is the work of the devil, casting out the Unholy from our human race. This I discard, for it is the human race that is being discarded, including us, the Most Holy. We have heard the notion put forth that Lord Jehosa is now punishing the Unholy for their earthly sins and that Lord Jehosa has cast them out. Again, I say unto you, we cannot all be the Unholy. Some have suggested that Lord Jehosa has called forth the Days of Judgment and that we should pray and be prepared for his Holy Judgment upon us, which could happen at any time now. This may have some truth in it." The other two nodded that it did.

Yaz commented, "It is hard for many to accept that Lord Jehosa would not have intervened with his children, if this was an alien attack upon his children, especially we, his Most Holy Followers."

Hamir added solemnly, "So we are left with the idea that the Days of Judgment have arrived. It could be said that women are now being punished for their Original Sin. This they could accept. Yet, what of we men? Are we also being punished for our complicity in the Original Sin? If so, does this not mean the Days of Judgment are at hand?"

Badar answered, "Millennia ago, it is written after the Great War destroyed our lands, homes, and people, the survivors were led out of the Burning Desert unto the Arad, there to rebuild and avow their Faith in our Lord Jehosa, who thus spared their lives. Could it be that once again, we are facing another Great War and are being called upon to exodus unto a new land, there to reaffirm our undying faith in our Lord Jehosa?"

Yas asked, "It seems that we have two different possibilities from which to decide. Is this the opinion I am to draw? Could I propose yet a third?" They nodded and he explained, "Perhaps at this time, Lord Jehosa is in some way testing our strength of character and our faith. If so, is it not our duty as the Holy Leaders of Lord Jehosa to do all that we can to support our people, to help them find ways to regain their strength and prosperity, and to strengthen their faith in Lord Jehosa?"

Bandar then asked, "Three choices. How is it that we are to decide among these? Do we claim Original Sin and prepare ourselves for the Days of Judgment? If we do not and that day does come, will we not find ourselves wholly unprepared and thus be denied entrance into the Holy Realm? Or could it be another Great War in which Lord Jehosa is again asking us to exodus once more to a new land and begin anew? If we stay and do not go and if this is what our Lord is asking, are we not then failing to follow the Lord's Commandments? Or is this merely a test of our true faith in Lord Jehosa that we are to find ways to thrive and prosper in the face of the adversity of his test? If so and do not do this, are we then failing to obey our Lord God?"

The three men were silent. All three choices were equally possible. "Let us meditate upon this and pray for divine guidance," Bandar suggested. The next day, they still could not choose between the three equally plausible choices.

Yaz then made a suggestion. "Since even we, the Qaam Oikoumen, cannot decide which is our Lord's commandment, what if we take these three choices unto our people? Let us do all three. One of us will lead our followers on a Holy Exodus to a new land. One of us will prepare our believers for the Days of Judgment. One of us will remain and do what can be done so that our people who so believe may thrive and prosper. Three of us, three choices. Allow our people to meditate and search their own souls, make their own decision and join one of us three. Then, whichever one of the three is Lord Jehosa's Commandment, some of us will have obeyed it and our lives will not have been in vain."

Pragmatism won. That was then the final decision of the Qaam Oikoumen. The three proposed meanings of the events were carefully explained to all of those in the Arad. They were then given three days of meditation, after which they were asked to make their decision.

Hamir el Wad, being the youngest volunteered to lead the exodus unto a new land. Badar Tunis, being the eldest, volunteered to lead those who anticipated the Days of Judgment. Yaz Madi was left with attempting to find ways and means for those who stayed to flourish and prosper in spite of the calamity.

On November 5, 823, Hamir el Wad, began walking, leading a band of some forty thousand faithful followers out of Juda Arad, heading past New Bark and out into the Red Desert. They dropped out of all our knowledge after that. Badar collected another forty thousand faithful believers unto him in Jerilum. There, amid continuous Holy Prayers, they fasted until the Days of Judgment came unto them. By December, dust began covering their remains.

Yaz Madi collected to him all the worldly possessions that could be found. He listened to the women and his men attempted to follow their notions of low to the ground kitchens. Many women now had the luxury of several yokes, those preparing for the Days of Judgment gave up their yokes and shoes and possessions unto these who would remain behind. Thus, he shortly thereafter received forty thousand copies of Bethany's Hints translated into the Arad dialect.

In early December, when their feet returned to normal, they believed that Lord Jehosa had given them his answer, that their choice had been the right one. Men's lives returned to normal, but their women still suffered. So grateful for this Holy Miracle, the remaining Arad men began to adapt new attitudes towards their women, beneficial, positive ones.

Thus, Juda Arad lost two thirds of its meager population to the plague of 823.

Chapter 9 For Some, It Was Not Death

Some countries were not as utterly devastated as others were. True, the effects of the plague were horrible beyond words for everyone; still, some countries fared better than others did, some attributing it to their customs.

In the Northern Steppes, the land of the nomadic horsemen, only some of whom had recently begun settling in towns, the effects were moderated by their culture and lifestyle. Primarily hunters and gatherers by nature, even though their men were unable to walk, they could still ride and thus continue to hunt. Their women, traditionally the gatherers, found that they could still gather, using their yokes. They cooked over campfires and lived in domed hide huts. All this was manageable and untold thousands of the replacement kitchens went unused. Eventually, Stefano made a deal with the Czar and purchased all the unused kitchen appliances in return for mechanized vehicles, power generating engines for the cities, and basic food supplies for those in the cities.

Culturally, the biggest hurdle was faced by a few women of the Steppes, the bredas. These were highly respected women, the ones who actually bred the horses upon which their whole culture was based. The Czarina herself was a breda and the loss of their arms was all the more crushing to these breda women. Overnight, they saw their status as the highest respected women of their country drop to that of an ordinary woman. Thus, the Czar had no choice but to issue a tradition-bending new law. The breda could now have men of their choosing assist them in the ritual breeding of horses. Time will tell whether these women will retain the high respect that they deserve or whether the men they chose will eventually usurp their power.

There were a few casualties of the plague in the steppes, but they numbered less than two hundred, remarkable, considering the horribleness of the plague and its effects.

In the far north, Volksholm, home of the burly Axemen, the long, harsh winter had already come when the plague struck them. Unable to stand or move on the snow and ice while walking on their toes, men slipped and fell attempting to deal with life needs, such as bringing in more firewood. Likewise, the women's shoes held only slightly better footing in the snow and ice. Unlike the men, they had no way to keep their balance and simply could not go outside of their long houses. By the time that their feet returned to normal, one-half their population starved or froze to death, some slipping into the frigid waters of the fiords. Once able to walk again, the men quickly re-established control and began finding new ways to survive the disaster. Little else is currently known about their plight at this time, though more would become known later on.

Very different reactions came from Annelise on the opposite end of the far southern continent. Stefano notified King Hans about the plague when he notified all the other rulers, again via LD radio. A week later, he received word from King Hans; some of us thought it was comical, under the circumstances.

"Greetings Stefano. Yes, the plague has struck us as well. Our men are mortified, such hideously made shoes that they now have to wear. I am instructed by our Shoe Maker's Guild that they will soon commence construction of highly polished, shiny black boots for men, of the highest quality, naturally. Yes, the women's shoes are also being hastily reworked! Such ghastly designed shoes, our women are embarrassed to wear them. Again, expect that within a month, high quality women's shoes will once again become available. We will ship a load off to Velona as soon as possible. Please tell your fashionable women that ideal, high quality shoes are coming."

"As far as our women are concerned, yes, they were both shocked and overjoyed with these effects. Their loss of arms is most unfortunate, and we are anxiously awaiting Bethany's Hints so that our seamstresses can follow her advice and get back to work. Our women are enamored with their new tiny waistlines! Long has a fourteen inch seemed the ideal in beauty and form for which all women strove but so few made. Now they all have twelve-inch waists. Unfortunately, our tailors are now madly overworked, stepping in for all the seamstresses, in performing dress alterations. We still don't quite know what to make of the gargantuan breast sizes. Do not expect any shipments of new fine quality suits for quite some time. Our women must come first; I do hope you understand. Once all their dresses are properly refitted, then the tailors can resume fulfilling your orders."

Stefano replied, "Well that's good to hear, Hans, that your women love their new figures. Has anyone died as a result of the plague?"

"Oh my no, Stefano. On the contrary, while my wife is a bit put out by her sudden lack of arms, she is in love with her new waist size and is anxiously awaiting the proper alterations to show off her fine figure. Me, I am in love with her new bust size." In the background, we heard is wife chiding him royally on that point.

He continued, "Yes we will adapt down here, have no fear of that. However, Bethany's Hints will be most welcomed here, I assure you. We are installing the kitchens now and we men are doing our part until our women have a chance to read this fine book and learn their Alternate Ways of doing things. Patience, I keep telling everyone patience. Things have really slowed down here for men. We walk now as slowly as our fashionable women used to glide in their fine heels. Please let us know when we can expect Bethany's Hints. Give her Annelise's highest regards, our highest praise for a job well done. In time, we will be sending her a fine thank you present for her incredibly fine work."

Stefano promised to let him know when the books were ready, even though he had no idea about the books. The Guardian or Macario was handling that aspect. A week later millions of copies of my book arrived at King Hans' palace, all nicely translated into their dialect, compliments of Macario. One day, I must remember to ask him how all these books are being translated, published, and distributed in such short order and in such volume. I keep forgetting to ask.

On the other side of the world, in the equatorial jungles, the city-state of Wanakan simply vanished. We knew that they hunted for their food and grew some crops, but were heavy into gathering the bounty of the jungle. When one of our caravels arrived there in December, the entire city was deserted. Wanakan was a ghost town. Although they went into the city and looked around, they found a new mass grave, but little else. Tens of thousands of natives simply vanished without a trace. Not even their beloved pacas were found. I was now glad that we had imported pacas long ago; their wool was the finest in the entire world. Zargarb now produced the world's supply of paca wool. I have a strong suspicion that these people were forced to break up into smaller hunter-gatherer groups fleeing inland in search of sufficient food.

No one has much contact with the wild horsemen of Vladimir, cradled between two impassible mountain ranges, which protect Annelise to the east and Demokritos to the west. They are too warlike for our tastes and Velona only rarely trades with them. Hence, we don't know what happened in their land. I theorized that since their culture centered on horses, they somehow managed to survive the plague.

One of the first actions I took when we learned of the coming plague was to check with Vittore West Po. I needed to see if we had any ships anywhere near Konstantin, on the southern tip of the western continent, the land of the amazon women. Here, their culture was a mirror image of that being created by the mantis. These women outright amputated the arms of their male babies upon birth. Men in their society were mere objects, many working as human oxen, and the lucky few as the play toys for the women. As far as I knew, marriages as we knew them did not exist in that country.

As soon as I learned the plague would strike worldwide, I knew that Konstantin and their major port city of Kostya would be in the direst of straights. No one there would have any arms at all. Hence, I wanted somehow to get a ship to them, hoping that the crew, as few as they were, could somehow help prevent the total loss of their society. Besides, Kostya was the only major port on the western continent south of Wanakan where our ships could stop for provisions.

From Lucianna, I also knew that Stefano had installed LD radio on all of Velona's caravels. Thus, if one was close enough, we could direct them there and stay in communication with them upon their arrival, offering suggestions. The nearest caravel according to the giant map in Vittore's office was nearly a month away.

I grimaced. At least it was springtime down there. It could be worse and be the dead of winter. What if the bacteria re-grew their men's arms? After centuries of slavery and brutality, would these men reverse the roles and brutalize the women? I had all manner of wild notions floating through my head. Yes, their whole society was based upon aberration, derived originally centuries ago by women fleeing the mantis experimentations. I'd always hoped that in time, these men and women could get the therapy they needed to alter their society more towards an optimum one. Then, I am always trying to be optimistic.

On the morning of October 23, two twenty-year old roommates prepared themselves for today's assignment. Jelena brushed out her luxurious, waist length black hair, rose, and checked her appearance in her mirror. Her white paca dress was heavily embroidered with multi-colored flowers and leaves, her favorite. Her eyes were enchantingly green and observant. She glanced at her roommate and lover, Nika. She too had finished brushing out her waist length blonde hair. Her white paca dress had embroidered pacas randomly placed as though they were out in one of their pastures. Nika flashed Jelena a smile.

"Ready?" she asked. Jelena nodded.

Today, these two women of the First Leader Collective had the assignment of teaching the ten year old girls of Konstantin their political lessons. The two slipped into their sandal flats and headed out of the First Leader Domicile and into the streets of Kostya, Konstantin. The day was ordinary, as were most days. Some five thousand lived here in the city in Collective Domicile homes. They stepped out of the way of a small carriage pulled by two strong armless men clad only in loincloths about their waists. Armless men were the beasts of burden here in Konstantin. Horses, oxen, such beasts were unknown here at the extreme southern tip of the great western continent. This was an amazon society, had been for centuries.

The two entered the Education Hall and found the room where twenty-four ten year old girls were anxiously waiting for their teachers. They had been told that today, two women from the First Leader Collective would be addressing them. Everyone knew that the women of the First Leader Collective were the most important, powerful women in the country, hence, the young girls' excitement. Jelena and Nika entered looking their best and took their familiar bar stool style seats at the front of the room. Both loved this aspect of their duties.

Jelena spoke first. "Hello. I am Jelena and this is my mate, Nika. We are from the First Leader Collective." She allowed the girls to whisper their "ah's" but knew that the girls already knew this. "Today, we will begin by reviewing how our country is organized. The basic unit that all we women operate under is called a Collective, that is, always a group of twenty-four, like-minded, like-skilled women. Each Collective has a home called a Domicile, with twelve bedrooms, two women per room, a kitchen, dining room, living room, and of course a large bath." The girls giggled at the mention the bath; this they loved, as did most women. Bathing time was a fun, private time, carefree and theirs alone.

"How many of you know how many different Collectives there are?" Jelena asked. Several called out answers. "Right, we have nineteen different types of Collectives. Our Fighter Collective provides our defense against wild animals and even sometimes bad foreign men. Our Fisher Collective catches and processes fish from the wide ocean. The Boat Builder Collective builds our new boats. The House Builder Collective has very hard workers; they build all our Domiciles and other buildings. The Lumber Collective fells the trees and makes the wood, which others use for many purposes besides making more buildings. The Farmer Collective is very important, because they grow our many crops. Without them, we would all starve to death. Our Cloth Maker Collective turns paca wool into cloth and then cloth into these luxuriously soft dresses." Again, the girls giggled. Indeed, who didn't get sensual pleasure from just running their fingers over their dresses?

"Our Husbandry Collective raises our many domesticated animals, the paca, the sheep, the goats, the chickens, the rabbits. The Butcher Collective turns some of these into our meat which we love to eat. The Jewelers Collective makes our fine earrings, bracelets, and necklaces. Our Metal Worker Collective turns rocks and minerals into metals, and I'm sure that I do not know how that is done. Our Tool Maker Collective then takes the metals and makes useful products from them, from the weapons that our fighters use, to the tools that our Domicile builders use, to the silverware that we all use at meal times. Our Rope Makers Collective weaves the ropes that we use for so many things, such as drawing water from our wells. The Wagon Maker Collective builds the carriages and wagons, which are used to haul so many of the heavy loads. The Teamster Collective does all the heavy transportation work, moving loads of lumber from the north down to Kostya. They haul loads of grain from the many farms into town. Then, the Barrel Maker Collective builds our many water barrels and our many buckets, such as our scrub buckets." Again, the girls whispered, "eue." None liked the chore of scrubbing the floors.

"One of the more interesting ones is the Gatherer Collective, who wanders the great wide world north of us, gathering berries, nuts, and yes, even the wild flowers. Then, there are the Healers Collectives. Let us hope that we don't need their skills very often." The girls smiled. No one wanted to be hurt or sick. "Finally, there is the Leaders Collective. It is our job to write down our history, to educate all new girls in the customs of our country, and to provide the organization and leadership for all the other Collectives and our country."

Now Kika took over. "Today, there are one thousand eight hundred full and complete Collectives. With twenty-four women in each one, that means that there are forty-three thousand two hundred of us. Well, those do not yet count you young girls. Once you are fully educated and reach your twelfth birthday, you will be assigned to a Collective that suits you best, either replacing an ancient woman or in a brand new Collective. Yes, we are still growing larger each year."

"As a matter of record, each Collective also has six beasts of burden, armless strong men who are used to pull our plows in the fields or to pull our heavy wagons or to pull our carriages. Yes, that means that we keep ten thousand eight hundred of these nearly worthless, strong legged men, unless some of you want to spend your life pulling wagons and plows." A litany of "no's" echoed from the giggling girls.

"Ah but each Collective also keeps two of the finest, best looking, virile armless men as our breeders. Yes, it is most unfortunate for us that we women must have a seed from these men creatures in order for us to create new life within us. Sometimes, Nature can be perverse. Hence, each Collective keeps two around for this purpose. One day, you will be given opportunities to bear children of your own."

Nika continued. "There are many sets of each of these nineteen Collectives. Who can tell me which one has the most Collectives?"

"Right. The Farmer Collective has the most; five hundred complete Collectives. We need a lot of food." Everyone giggled. "The Barrel Makers and the Gatherers now have two hundred sets and the Husbandry Collective now numbers one hundred eighty sets. The Fighters, Fisher, and the Cloth Makers each have a hundred sets. Who has the fewest?" No one had that answer.

Nika smiled, "The Jewelers and the Leaders. We don't need that many earrings now do we? Likewise, we don't need tons of leaders either. Now then, within a Collective, who is the top authority?"

One girl called out, "The Matron."

"Right, the Matron is in charge of her Collective. Often she is either the eldest or the most skilled woman in that Collective. Now because there are so many sets of any given Collective, to be able to identify each one, we prefix a number. For example, Jelena and I are in the First Leader Collective. With a few exceptions, girls, just because your Collective has a high number, does not mean that others with lower numbers are more important or that your set is any less valuable. Usually it is just a number so everyone can know who is who, like our names."

"The only two exceptions are the Leader and Healer Collectives. Within the Healer Collective, the lowest number sets are our most skilled doctors. Within the Leader Collective, the set number indicates the organizational level over which that set leads. The First Leader Collective runs our whole country; we make the big decisions that have to be made. Ours is a huge responsibility. If we make an error, tens of thousands of you all suffer because of it."

Jelena and Nika continued their talk until noon, at which point the girls all dashed out of the room, heading off for lunch. As the two reached the street, Nika slid her arm around Jelena's waist, allowing Jelena's thick black hair to touch the back of her hand. Jelena smiled and slid hers around Nika's waist, careful to go beneath her long blonde hair as well. The sun beaming down upon their faces as they headed south to their Domicile. For them, the world was at peace and perfect in all ways. All was about to change however.

Jelena commented, "Well, at least they didn't ask leading questions about the men."

Nika chuckled, "Yes, we lucked out today. Say, Kiska and Lara are due pretty soon now. We ought to drop by their Domiciles and see how they are doing later today."

"Yes, we should. It is tough carrying a baby for nine months. Even tougher when it turns out to be a worthless boy and is killed. Yet, half of our children are these useless male babies. Two thirds of them have to be killed right after they are born. We only need a few strong beasts of burden and even fewer breeders, though I sometimes think we could have a whole lot more fun if we kept more breeders in each Domicile," Jelena teased.

Nika squeezed her backside. "I'm not good enough for you?" she teased. "No, seriously, I know what you mean. Worse luck, it is our turn to make the decisions for Niska and Lara. If they have boy children, we have to make the decision to keep them as beasts of burden or as breeders or dispose of them. Honestly, how can we look at a baby and tell if it will grow up with strong legs to pull wagons or if it will grow up to be handsome and virile?"

Jelena replied, "I don't know. I guess that is why we are getting this training ourselves. Ah, lunch is served." They entered the Queen's Palace, otherwise known as the First Leader Domicile.

As they joined the other two dozen women at the long table, their Matron, Queen Anastasia Toya called out to them in her distinctive alto voice, "How did it go with the girls today?"

"Fine, we did well," Nika replied. She liked the forty-one year old woman's long brown hair, though she preferred her own and Jelena's length, at least a foot longer than the Queen's. Still, both Nika and Jelena respected the immensely important decisions that always seemed to face Queen Anastasia.

That evening, Jelena and Nika entered their private bedroom and changed into their thin paca nightgowns. Each brushed out the other's long hair and then passionately embraced each other. Soon, they found themselves in their bed, intertwining their bodies and their hair, pleasuring each other most passionately. The next morning both women awoke and discovered that their arms were incredibly weak, very thin, their muscle tone gone. Even the length of their arms had seemed to shrink somehow! Still, they were able to use them.

When they joined the others for breakfast, which was late because the woman whose turn it was to cook also had the same problems with her arms, they found this the sole topic of fearful conversations. Before long, reports began arriving from all the Collectives. By noon, these top leaders knew that whatever was going on was affecting every woman in Konstantin! Queen Anastasia summoned all the First Healers to her meeting room, demanding to know what was going on and to find a cure immediately.

"Nika! No more talk of these plague rumors!" Queen Anastasia barked out, chiding her. Many had heard the rumors spread by the very few caravels that chose to dock at their port for water and food resupply. Last year some horrible plague had struck some far distant northern continent. At least that was the rumor going around, spread by the First Fighter Collective who had met with the crews, forcing their men to stay aboard their vessels, only allowing women, if any were onboard, ashore. Now, women were becoming scared and were reminded of this year-old rumor. Could it be happening here? Had these visitors brought the plague here?

Dr. Kisa calmed the Queen's fears. "Look, it has been three months since the last foreign ocean ship docked at Kostya. This cannot be the result of that encounter. We know that if someone who is ill contacts another person, the other may get ill with the disease within a week or two at the most, but never three months later. You are blameless in this matter, Queen Anastasia. Whatever this may be, it is not coming from those few outsiders who dock here for water."

"Well okay, but what is this? We need a cure fast. We can only just barely use our arms. Our strength is almost gone in them," she insisted.

Dr. Kisa sighed, "I don't know. We will continue to monitor it and try various cures." She departed to issue orders to her fellow doctors, though she held little hope. She had never seen anything like this, not ever.

All work was canceled this day, which only increase the women's fears and worries. Nika and Jelena spent most of the day in their bedroom, doing their best to pleasure each other, valiantly trying to relieve the ever-growing fears that they had. Like many others, they fell asleep and missed the evening meal entirely.

They awoke to screams of terror and wild screeching. Sitting up, they added their voices to those of the other twenty-two women in nearby bedrooms. All twelve rooms were off the one long hallway. The two women sat up side by side in their bed, armless, screaming in terror.

How long they screamed they could not tell. Finally, the shock began to lessen and Nika rose to use the chamber pot. Her feet were now deformed and she lost her balance from the unexpectedness of her feet on the floor and fell. Jelena saw her fall and struggled to get out of bed to help her. That's when she noticed the other changes in their bodies. Only her toes now touched the floor, her heels would never bend that far down. Her waist seemed to have disappeared utterly and her breasts were almost the size of her head. Peering down at Nika, she thought her lover's hair seemed longer. "Are you okay, Nika?" she fought hard to speak without panic in her voice.

Nika moaned and began to try to figure out how to get up. She sat up and looked up at Jelena, noticing the other changes in their bodies now. "What — what has happened to us?" Nika attempted to form a coherent question.

Jelena said the only concept that made the slightest sense, "Plague?"

Two things saved the day for the women in Konstantin this day. First, they only wore panties during their time of the month. All other times, at night they wore the loose fitting, easy slip on, paca gowns, while their day dresses were also easy slip on styles. Thus, Nika and Jelena were able to deal with the chamber pot, as did most other women that morning. Second, these women had not invented doorknobs. Instead, all doors were held shut by sliding latches, which were reachable by raising their feet a ways to operate them.

A while later, standing precariously only on their toes, their hair now reaching their ankles, the two managed to slide the latch and open their bedroom door. Taking but the tiniest of steps and trying wildly to keep their balance, the two headed into the large living room, as other pairs did the same. Their faces were uniformly ghostly white, while fear and terror knotted these women's stomachs.

Ordinarily, at the first scream, the entire First Fighter Collective would have come charging into the living room, weapons at hand, ready for combat. Jelena noticed that not one of their fighters had yet arrived. Her fears only grew as she began to realize that all women were being affected by this plague.

Everyone looked to Queen Anastasia for guidance or for anything at all. She in turn stared at the huge pile of strange things that filled the center of the room. Now Jelena and Nika saw them too. How had they not seen them when they entered? Both women were so confused, so frightened.

"Are, are we dying?" asked Ivanna. Jelena thought suddenly that must be what was happening. They were all dying a very slow death.

Queen Anastasia, fighting her own growing terror, knew only one thing. She was the Matron of this First Leader Collective and these women controlled all other Leader Collectives, who controlled the other eighteen hundred Collectives and thus the entire forty thousand-some women. If she allowed her panic to rule, her country was doomed. That and that alone, kept her focused for the time being.

"Ladies, don't be silly! We are not dying yet. What do you make of this pile of stuff? Did anyone hear anyone coming in during the night and depositing it? Did some caravel dock while we were sleeping and dump all this here? Where are our guards anyway? Ivanna, go find our guards. Have them see if a caravel is docked in our port. Come, ladies, let's see what all this mess actually is."

"These look like some kind of shoes," Anastasia decided. After some tries, she found a pair the fit her feet. "Well, now that is a whole lot better! Ladies, find some of these shoes that fit. My feet feel a thousand times better in them. At least they don't hurt anymore."

While the other women began following her lead, Nika whispered to Jelena, "How can she be so calm? I'm scared out of my wits!"

"We're goners if she doesn't lead us. Look, her face is as white as our sheets! She's just as terrified as we are. Come on, Nika, we have to be brave for all the others!" Finding a pair of shoes that fit and donning them made a difference. Now they discovered that they could stand without their feet arches hurting and they retained their balance slightly better.

Soon, they began to chat about what was here, recognizing some items quickly. Then, strange images began appearing to some and ideas began to flow freely. Desks for writing, cups that could be held by a foot, cooking utensils suited for use with a foot were pointed out and recognized. Julya was the first to realize how the yokes could be used, which brought a good deal of relief to Queen Anastasia, who finally saw how she and others could somehow carry things. That had been one of her prime concerns, how could they carry anything at all now. So much of life depended upon the simple action of carrying an object from here to there, she realized. At last, Natalya vocalized what many were realizing. "Hey, this all looks like a kitchen, but only one that is low to the ground. Maybe we are to cook with our feet now."

Jelena saw the truth of this, as the images swirled in her mind. "But how do we get it installed?" she asked without thinking.

"We will worry about that later, Jelena," Anastasia declared. Right now, she had no idea about how that could be done. "Okay, ladies. Here's what must be done immediately." She instructed each one of them to go to their subordinate Collectives and issue some orders. Everyone was first to find a pair of shoes that fit and find a yoke suited to their height. Second, any woman who still had her arms was to report to the Queen immediately. Third, using the yokes, everyone was to assist in moving the kitchen items that could be moved on into the kitchen. Fourth, using whatever means possible, the Collective as a group was to fix themselves something to eat.

Nika and Jelena headed out the front door along with the others, off to issue their first orders. It felt good to have a positive action to take, both thought. No one but themselves was outside. "Such tiny steps! Nika, it will take forever to walk anywhere. I have to be so darn careful."

"I know. I have a bump on my forehead from this morning," Nika replied, as the two made tiny shuffling steps towards the Domicile which they needed to visit.

Having issued their orders, the two headed back home. "Golly, our hair is so long! Look, it is down to the tops of our ankles. I hope that we don't trip over it," Nika said rather worriedly. She realized that no one would be able to cut it for her now.

A while later, they made it into the kitchen. Jelena bit into an apple and carried it over to the table. She sat down and tried her best to eat it, using only her mouth. She felt horribly embarrassed to be eating as the beasts of burden did, slopping up food with their mouths, like the animals that they were. Now she too was an animal and it scared her.

Anastasia kept hoping that one or more women who still had their arms would come racing into the room to save them all. None did. The breakfast had been a fiasco, but still they had eaten something. It was a start. For a while now, she would have time to think. Soon, though the many reports would start coming in to her. When any kind of major problem, calamity, natural disaster, or anything unusual occurred, the Collective Matrons would send full details up to their Leaders, who would in turn relay it on up the line. Eventually, the message would get to one of the women here in the First Leader Collective and thus to her. She estimated that by evening, she would have heard from all eighteen hundred Matrons and thus have a complete picture of this disaster. Until then, she had time to think.

Soon word did begin to trickle up to these twenty-four women. Jelena and Nika were kept almost constantly busy receiving messages during the day. At last, they began to sit at the low desks and struggled to jot down some key facts before they got lost in the nearly continuous stream of information coming up the lines from the various Matrons. "Well, I can sort of write," Nika whispered to Jelena.

"Damned hard and crude, but I think I can read what I've gotten down here. So many things are being reported!" Jelena replied. "It's more horrible than we ever imagined. Do you think that Sasha and Sonya will be able to cook us something? I can't imagine how?" Anastasia ordered Nika and Jelena to take over the reporting duties of those two women and sent them off to the kitchen with orders to somehow fix everyone supper. The two were the best cooks of the Domicile, Jelena knew. She loved their meals and hated her own. She was just not cut out to be a cook. Nika had no chance to answer, as another woman shuffled slowly up to her to report in.

That evening, the twenty-four women sat around the dining room table, working out how to eat the hot stew the two women had managed to fix. Sonya and Sasha had spent nearly six hours figuring out how to make it and then getting it done. The kitchen looked more like some chaotic warehouse now, with boxes places at seeming random locations. However, they were strategically located by the two women so that they could stand on them and get their feet over the pots and such. The potatoes still had their skins on them, because they had been unable to peel them. Still, their Collective heaped praises upon them for the hot meal.

Later, Queen Anastasia gathered everyone into the living room for a complete series of reports. Most carried their scribbled writings into the room by holding them in their mouths. One by one, each relayed the most important details that had been reported to them. The picture that emerged was almost beyond their comprehension.

Every woman, whether a few days old or sixty now had no arms. Their waists seemed to be no more than a foot around, causing much griping from those portly women who loved their "big woman" appearance. By all reports, their hair had grown two feet, but had now ceased its wild growth spurt. Breasts had become melons — that being the most frequently used term to describe them. Even the young girls had drastically larger breasts as well. Finally, their feet were all uniformly malformed in nearly identical ways. They walked on their toes with the strange shoes adding a little extra support by way of a heel placed almost at the back of their toes, just enough support so that they could more readily keep their balance while walking. No one reported being able to take more than a three-inch step at one time. Mobility had been reduced to nearly nothing.

Reports also included modifications to their beasts of burden and their breeders. It seems that their feet had undergone a different malformation. Their ankles would no longer bend and their feet were now pointed downwards. None could stand or walk, because that meant that they would be standing on the tips of their toes. Their beasts of burden could now barely move along on their knees only, making them useless as beasts of burden. However, there appeared to be special boots that would fit their strange malformed feet. Unfortunately, these had laced strings and thus required hands to put them on and lace them up securely. Thus far, no one had tried to do this for their animals.

Anastasia listened to these formal reports, although she had already heard most of them when they were being first reported to her comrades. When they finished, she knew that she had to give them guidance, but what? "We need more data. However, we must all take a lesson from Sonya and Sasha. Alone, we are helpless. As pairs, we may be able to care for our needs. Tonight, as you retire with your partner, work together as a team. See if together you can deal with our nightly actions. I believe that this will soon become our guiding principle: work in teams to accomplish what one used to do alone. Think on this. We will meet in the morning and discuss it further."

Nika and Jelena slowly shuffled into their bedroom, still wearing their nightgowns. "Well, our hair must be brushed," Jelena observed.

Nika chuckled slyly, "Hey, that's not all. She said we are to do our routine, nightly actions." She grinned mischievously. "I do love your hair and your breasts look incredibly inviting, my love."

Jelena returned her grin, "If I still had my hands, I would have found it impossible to keep mine off yours too! All day, I wanted to bed you, Nika. Come on, let's see if I can figure out how to use this new brush on your hair."

The next morning, the two worked together and managed to get out of their nightgowns and into their usual paca dresses, before heading out to join the others. Several others had also managed to change into presentable dresses. Everyone had gone around yesterday in their nightgowns. Somehow, Jelena felt more comfortable today, dressed as she had for so many years. Perhaps it was just being civilized.

"Well done for those of you who are dressed appropriately. Those in your nightgowns, go see if you can get changed. Work together. See, it can be done. Oh, Jelena, Nika, you are off to the maternity room. The shock has sent Lara and Kiska into labor. You will be needed there," Anastasia ordered.

Dutifully, the two headed off to perform their duties to the two young mothers. They had to cover five blocks this morning and both complained about their incredibly slow pace. "How many steps do we have to take anyway?" Nika complained. "This is taking forever. I do hope that we are not late, this being our first time and all."

"I know but I am going as fast as I dare. Oops, maybe a bit too fast," Jelena replied, frantically wiggling her body to keep from falling. "That's the weirdest sensation! Nika, my arms were flailing around like mad there and nothing was happening. They aren't there, but it felt like they were. God, I hate this."

"Oh! Think of the doctors! How can they deliver the babies now? What if one is a boy and we say keep it? How will they perform their surgery?" Nika began to realize plights far beyond their own.

When they arrived, Lara already had hers, a little girl. They found mother and daughter resting comfortably. Ten doctors were working together for these first two deliveries. Kiska was on the floor instead of the table. Now the two saw why. On the floor, the ten doctors were using their feet to help her deliver the baby. All ten were covered in blood, having a most trying time of it all.

The two chatted with Lara until they heard the cries of the newborn coming from the next room. One doctor motioned to them to come on in, moving her head in an exaggerated motion. The two entered. "Okay, leaders. A boy. What do we do with it?" Kiska was crying, grieved that hers had been carried for nothing, it being a useless boy baby. The two felt a bit sick but went close to have a look at the baby boy. The doctors tried to hold him up, but couldn't and just laid him down on the floor.

"How are we to tell?" whispered Nika.

"He looks so cute," Jelena whispered back. Here was new life wiggling about. Somehow, that he was a boy didn't seem to matter as much as the fact that it was life, new life. The hardened viewpoint of adult women also didn't seem to matter to her.

"Breeder," Jelena blurted out. No way did she want to see this tiny spark of life be extinguished. Kiska sighed and began crying; it had not all been for nothing after all. She would nurse a future breeder.

Doctor Kisa groaned. "Naturally, our first has to be a breeder. How are we to operate, Jelena? It was all that we could do as a team to deliver the babies. Now we have to perform surgery with our feet no less. We can't hold a knife. We can't stitch up the wounds. We can't wrap the bandages. How the blazes are we to do this?"

Another doctor said soothingly, "Well, it must be done. Let's see what is possible, shall we? After all, it is only a boy animal, not one of we valuable women." They tried to carry the baby to the operating table and gave that up. They fumbled around but couldn't figure out how to pick him up and carry him. Another pointed out that their feet couldn't reach the table anyway. Deciding to do the surgery on the floor, they began discussing how. Ordinarily, they would simply make a clean cut around the upper arm so that there was some fleshy skin to use to close the hole left after they got the arms out of their sockets. All felt that they could do none of this.

Finally, Doctor Kisa had an idea. "Look, the only possible way that we can do this now is to use field emergency methods. We can tie a tourniquet around the upper arm, say about here, if four of us work on pulling it tight to stop the blood flow. Somehow, we have to then slice off the arm just below the wrapping and then use hot metal to cauterize the wound. Just how we can cut the bone, I don't know. Our breeder here will become the first of a new breed of animal, one with little short arms, perhaps a few inches long. I can think of no other alternative, unless you all can. It's too risky to cauterize the shoulder if we simply remove the arm from its socket. He'll bleed to death before we can staunch it." The other doctors agreed.

"Jelena, you and Nika will have to relay all this to Anastasia. Tell her that we have no other option available to us now," Doctor Kisa ordered.

Jelena and Nika agreed and stepped out to be with Lara once more, awaiting the results. Suddenly, they heard the baby's terrified screams of intense pain. Jelena felt sick at her stomach. This sounded so much like pure torture to her. At last, the baby went unconscious, fortunately for her and Nika, who were unused to being around surgical doctors performing their work. Lara simply said, "Don't worry, it's only a boy animal, not one of us."

Jelena felt the urge to punch Lara in the mouth! It was a living person who was being brutalized in there, but she was brought sharply to the present as she realized that she had no arms with which to slap the young mother.

An hour later, Doctor Kisa reported that it had been successful. Konstantin now had another breeder who would have two-inch arms. The two headed back to their Domicile to report on the affair.

"Dear god! Our baby girls too? Damn!" Queen Anastasia exclaimed, hearing the two's report. "No matter about the animal breeder. Two-inch arms will be of no consequence. Come on, we must hold major discussions now."

The twenty-four women gathered in the living room. Anastasia began the meeting. "Whatever are we going to do now? From now on, all we women are going to be armless, just like our lowly animals that we have always kept! Yet the male babies are still coming with their arms, while our new baby girls have none! Ideas anyone?"

"Maybe we women are being punished for having so long been cutting off the arms of our males," suggested Ivanna. Suddenly, Jelena realized that there might well be truth in her suggestion! How many centuries now had they routinely removed baby boy's arms, while outright killing the other two-thirds that were born? Had the gods finally had enough and now afflicted them as they had afflicted their men? Suddenly, in her mind and many other women, this seemed so. Many others nodded their heads in agreement with this notion.

"So we are to assume that the gods are angry with us for treating the male animals as the true animals that they are? That we are now to suffer as we have made our animals suffer?" Anastasia called out feistily.

"Yes," Ivanna said meekly.

"Lamb dung! Ivanna, have you ever in your life seen a god hovering around here?"

Well, no one had seen a god or anything like that. Anastasia continued, "Don't be silly, Ivanna. There are no gods doling out their wishes on humans. We all know from our most ancient records that men, when they had arms, treated us like objects, sexual toys, meant only to give them pleasure. Do you really want to be relegated to being some man's toy, to answer to his every whim? To give up your own life and goals? I certainly think not!"

"Our records show that men, when they have arms, are always fighting, causing wars that devastate, killing innocent women and our children, raping us, pillaging, carting off women into bondage and slavery. Who brought us the killing long gun? Men from the other lands, men with arms. Have we not heard tales of their many brutal and savage wars? Their recent Second Crusade, a butchery of men, women, and children. No, give a man arms and you get fighting, wars, brutality beyond comprehension, slavery, rape, corruption — the list is endless! Yet, remove his arms, put we women in charge and do we get any of that wickedness? Never has there been a war in Konstantin. Whenever has a woman been raped, her virginity stolen along with her self-respect? Never." Anastasia wound down.

"But how are we to survive?" asked Natasha.

"Ah, now you are focusing on what is critical, Natasha," Anastasia complimented her. "How are we to survive? No longer can we do so many things. Our fighters are unable to use any of their many weapons, and they cannot perform their defensive duties. Our fishers may be able to find ways to maneuver their boats and perhaps bring in some fish — they hold out some hope for that. Our boat builders claim that there will likely be no more boats built. Our house builders, likewise, claim that they will be unable to build more homes and be unable to make most repairs that may be needed on our existing homes. Our lumber women claim that they will be unable to fell trees, let alone mill them into proper forms."

"Our farmers say that they may be able to somehow grow crops, though they will no longer have the use of their animals to pull their plows, since the beasts can no longer stand or walk. They suggest that we put them out of their misery with mercy killings, only our fighters are unable to do that at this time. Our cloth makers believe that in time they will be able to make more cloth, but are doubtful that they will be able to make new dresses. Ladies, preserve what you have."

"Our husbandry women suggest that they will be able to somehow keep our many domesticated animals alive and well and breeding, though it will be hard. Our butchers believe that they will be unable to do their job at all, since they cannot handle their knives any longer. No more fresh meat. Our metalworkers state that they cannot do their work, as have our tool makers. Our rope makers hold out some faint hope that they will be able to make more rope, given enough time. Our wagon makers and barrel makers have all but given up. Our teamsters no longer have their beasts to pull their wagons and are unable to load or unload them anyway. Our gatherers believe that once they become proficient with these yokes that they may be able to resume their usual work. We may have strawberries soon ladies, that's something positive at least. And we have heard today that our healers may yet be able to perform some of their activities."

"So this is where we stand. Unless we figure out something, no new houses, tools, barrels, lumber, fresh meat, for example. We have kitchens which some believe would allow us full use of our kitchens again, but alas, there is no way to get them installed. Worse, we have no defensive protection," Anastasia stated, heading to her key point, the one that she feared the most.

She lowered her voice for emphasis, all listened intently, "One man with arms can arrive at our port and take over our whole country! One man with arms can destroy our whole country, make us all his slaves, rape anyone of us any time he chooses, make us do whatever may take his fancy. One man with arms, just one."

The reality of her words sunk home to these leaders. All saw just how completely helpless their beast of burden were, to say nothing of their breeders, with whom many had spent some nights. Helpless they were, the women had total control of them. Now, one single man could take over their whole world and there was nothing that they could do about it!

"We cannot even run away! Three inch steps, ha," she further added to drive home her point. "A man with arms comes, and we cannot flee, we cannot fight, we can only do his bidding. We are doomed."

"Couldn't we just burn down the docks?" asked Tanya.

"Boats can anchor far off and the men can bring in their little boats anywhere along our sea shores, Tanya. I thought about that idea already."

"What about abandoning Kostya? Moving further away from the coast?" asked Natalya.

"We cannot build new buildings. Where would we live? We cannot carry much of anything. How would we move all of our possessions, our supplies, our tools, even though we are now unable to use them? How far can we get as slow as we must now go? Walking on the open, rough countryside may well be far too much for us to endure. Yes, we could try to abandon our big city here, but then where would we go? I am afraid that we are stuck here."

"We cannot pretend that this invasion problem doesn't exist, our fighters have already brought it up. We cannot ignore it. That is complete foolishness. We can all just give up and resign ourselves to becoming slaves to the first man with arms who desires to take control of us. We cannot flee, unless by fleeing you mean taking three-inch steps to a man's three-foot step. We no longer have the means to fight. I admit that I am at a total loss of what to do," Anastasia finally admitted to her subordinates. She sighed.

Silence was stunning. At last, Natalya suggested, "Maybe we could start letting our boy babies keep their arms. As they grow up, maybe we could teach them to be kind and compassionate to us women, to teach them to respect and honor us, to help us, and to be kind to us." She sounded so hopeful, Jelena thought. Could it be done? No more brutality against the baby boys?

"Nice idea, Natalya, but think it through. What happens to the boy when he grows up and learns the truth of what our perfect society has been doing to men for centuries? Will he not harbor animosity towards us for what we have done?" Anastasia countered. What seemed such a perfect solution suddenly went down in flames in the minds of these women leaders. In a way, they all shared and felt some guilt for their treatment of their men, two-thirds of which were outright murdered at birth.

Silence fell. After sometime passed, Anastasia spoke again. "I have been able to think of only one possibility, a very long shot, and we may not have enough time left for us to make it work." Everyone looked up out of their gloom. "Natalya may have given us a possible way out of this mess. She is right, if we concentrated our efforts on the new male babies as they grew up, trying to teach them to be good men and to treat us properly as we deserve, that might work. However, as soon as these boys reach the breeding age and see all their fellow men who are now our beasts of burden, they will rightly change their attitudes towards us."

"As of now, our ten thousand beasts are completely useless, consuming our precious food, which we may desperately need for ourselves later on. Suppose that tomorrow we got rid of all these useless men, remove them from Konstantin, leaving only the breeders left. Then, as the young men come of age, they will not witness firsthand what has been done to their kind in our past. Perhaps, they will remain kind and descent to us women. I don't know if they would allow us women to continue to rule, however. I suspect not, since they will have the arms and hands, and thus the upper hand in all this. This might be a way out for us, but it will take at least a score of years before that can happen, assuming many of us get pregnant soon."

Sasha spoke up, "But surely a man with arms will come to Kostya long before twenty years has past. The big ships come every few months, even though we do all that we can to discourage them from stopping here."

Sonya added, "She's got a point. I've seen how these outsiders react when they see our beasts of burden. They are repulsed. Surely, one of them will decide to take over our country long before twenty years. I think that we should go ahead and eliminate the useless beasts right now. That serves two purposes. One, it gets rid of useless mouths to feed, considering how hard it will be for us to make more food. Two, should outsiders come, they may not be so repulsed any longer. They seldom have seen our breeder men."

"If we do this, how will we cart their bodies away? Where will we put them? We cannot dig any graves anymore?" asked Tanya.

Jelena was thinking along a different line. "Here's another idea. This outer land of Velona. Those people have always treated us with respect. Why don't we ask them for help? Perhaps they will come and give us aid and not try to subjugate us."

"How do we contact them?" asked Anastasia, shooting down that idea. She did like Jelena's idea though. There was just no way to do it.

After more discussion, they agreed on one point: the useless beasts had to go. In the morning, the doctors handed out vials of poison. The cooks prepared a last meal for the now starving men and with great effort managed to get it to them. By the afternoon, Konstantin began trying to deal with ten thousand eight hundred dead men. It took them a week to roll the bodies to designated locations. They sat on their butts and used their legs to roll the dead along. Once there, great bonfires were lit and slowly the bodies were cremated. For a week, the stench around the country was nauseating, but all knew that this had to be done. They had to "wipe" their slate clean. Perhaps arriving men with arms would now no longer be so repulsed with them. Additionally, Anastasia quintupled the number of women allowed to breed during any one month.

The first week in November, within each Collective, the women set to work diligently trying all manner of ways to get their usual jobs and chores accomplished. As the days dragged on, ways were found to handle the little domestic duties, dressing, brushing hair, changing their bedding, even cooking and eating, what little there was left to cook. Meat had disappeared from their diet and their dried fish stocks were running low.

Ordinarily, when a Domicile ran low, one of their members would stop by a warehouse in Kostya and pick up more. Now however, the remaining stock in the warehouses was simply out of reach. Women looked longingly at the sacks of grain, flour, and the barrels of dried fish stacked neatly six or more feet above them on the massive rows of shelves and cried, unable to reach them now.

By mid-November, the situation grew more and more serious for the women. Many of those in the Gatherers Collectives were laid up having sprained their ankles and feet trying their best to search out fresh berries, fruits, nuts, anything the land might hold for them. The rough terrain had taken its toll on them.

Anastasia stood looking at the high shelves lined with lifesaving food supplies, just out of their reach. She had to do something. At last, she struck upon an idea and spent an hour moving the ladder by a row of flour sacks. "We can't climb it, please," Tanya begged her; she had accompanied Anastasia to this warehouse. Indeed, at first, she thought Tanya might be right. The bottom of her foot was only a few inches now, the length of her toes. The shoe's heel was almost touching the backs of her toes, where the arch began its monstrous recurve. Still, she tried. Carefully placing one foot on the round rung of the ladder, she leaned into it and stepped up. Slowly, ever so slowly, she began to climb up the ladder. It was precarious, with all her weight on the mere inches of her toes, and her feet ached from the attempt.

As she again put her weight on the next rung, her toes slipped. She flailed her arms wildly, trying frantically to hold on to the ladder, but her arms were not there. She fell. Tanya watched in horror as Anastasia fell to the floor, her head cracking on the stone floor making an ugly sound. Tanya screamed and screamed. Others came and eventually, several doctors came slowly shuffling into the warehouse.

Several hours passed, along with a great effort and some brilliant ideas by Jelena before they had Anastasia back in her Domicile and in her bed. Jelena's breakthrough had been to push her unconscious body onto a blanket and then, using their teeth to hold onto the blanket, slowly pull her body along. It had been quite an effort among some forty women to get their queen home. Now she was in the hands of the doctors.

Two days later, she regained consciousness and whispered to the doctor watching over her, "Summon my group to me." One by one the twenty-three other members of the First Leader Collective shuffled into the room. Anastasia managed a flickering smile as she saw her women gathering around her.

"I am not going to make it. As my last official order, I elect Jelena to be your next Matron. Jelena, do what you can to get help for our people. Do not let our women perish."

Crying bitter tears, Jelena said, "I promise, but you have to get better, Anastasia. You just have to." Anastasia didn't respond and lapsed into a coma. She passed away a day later. Her last act had been to pass on her torch of responsibility.

Jelena sat in her bedroom that night, allowing Nika to struggle with her long hair, knowing that in a while she would be doing the same for Nika. Life was so damnably hard now. "Why me, Nika? Why did she choose me? Tanya and others are older and wiser. Why me?"

Nika thought before answering. Perhaps it is better not to answer such a question unless you have an honest answer, she thought before one came to her, "When we were all meeting trying to decide what to do, perhaps she found your idea the best of all of ours. Contact Velona and beg for their help. I think she saw in you a chance for our new baby boys and for all of us. She probably heard how you were repulsed by our ancient practices of harming our baby boys that day with Kiska's boy. I think that she too saw this as wicked of us or perhaps a thing that should best be left in our past. We younger women want to give men a chance to do right by us. The older ones are not so inclined; at least that's what I think. There, your hair is as gorgeous as I can make it. My turn."

Each day, things grew only worse for the women. Each day, Jelena prayed that a ship from Velona would magically appear in their harbor. Each day, she silently cried as Nika brushed out her hair. The miracle of their feet returning to normal did not have the impact that Nika thought it would have had on her lover.

On December 1, Captain Armand Clement of the Smiling Prince spotted the harbor of Kostya. He had picked up a load of cereal grains in Annelise and was preparing to set sail towards Tashien when he got my call to divert to Kostya. A week out from there, he and his men's feet began aching so badly that he had no choice but to heave to and wait it out. After three days, miraculously their feet had returned to normal! After relaying this incredible news to us, he resumed his journey to Kostya.

"Captain, we are really supposed to help these amazons? They kill most of their boy children and maim the rest," a crew member protested.

"Aye, those rumors are true boys, but that is now in the past. They are human too and are probably in danger by now. I bet they will welcome you with open arms," the captain replied.

"Cap, they don't likely have arms no more," another crewman replied. All roared with laughter. Captain Armand was a well-educated man and had taken to the sea in hopes of making a quick fortune so that he could then settle down. He was now twenty-four and already had amassed nearly all that he had set out to acquire. A couple more voyages and he would retire from the sea and do what he wanted to do, build a home of his own design. Ever since he was a kid, he'd made drawing after drawing of his ideal house, changing his mind every so often as he spotted some architectural feature around Velona that caught his fancy.

He knew one thing that his crew was not considering. Make that two things. One, people can change, sometimes for the better, sometimes for the worse, but they can change. Two, anyone who lost their arms would be in great need, great enough to do almost anything to get the help that they needed.

Slowly the Smiling Prince tacked into the small harbor. He had heard stories spoken around the sea faring pubs about how amazon women in fighter garb would dash out to meet incoming ships. He half expected to see such fighters.

"Jelena! Jelena! A ship is coming! Jelena!" a guard came running into their living room.

Jelena smiled. It was so good to see her women folk able to walk and run normally again! She fought down her nervousness and followed her guard. This could be the beginning of the end of Konstantin and the beginning of her slavery or dare she hope otherwise? As she raced to the docks, she remembered and thought, "Dignified, be dignified. I am representing all our people now." She slowed down and began to walk down the wooden planks watching the caravel using only its tiny sail making a zig-zag path towards her. She saw tiny men on its deck, men with arms. She waited, holding her breath as it neared. At last, she saw the figurehead and the writing "Smiling Prince," but knew not the language.

"Wow! Look at that beauty," his bosun exclaimed, as they got their first glimpse at the woman standing on the docks waiting for them. She wore a white paca dress, heavily embroidered, well busted, as were all women they'd seen since the plague struck while they were heading to Annelise. Her rich black hair hung draped over her shoulders in front of her falling to her ankles, almost touching the ground. Captain Armand smiled, the woman had a big smile on her face, a very good sign he thought.

He ordered a crew member to fire up the LD radio and contact Bethany. He knew language would be somewhat of a barrier. At last, his crew hopped off, affixing the mooring lines and hauling out the gangplank. Captain Armand then stepped off the ship onto the docks. Another woman with blonde hair stood just behind this lovely woman, a protective stance he thought to himself.

"Hello. I am Captain Armand Clement. Do you speak my language?" She continued smiling but obviously didn't understand a word. "Velona?" he tried. That brought a reaction.

Jelena heard the man speak, but just could not understand a word. Her heart sank; how could they communicate their desperate needs? Then she heard the magic word that she did understand. Velona. She reacted. She grinned and repeated it several times. "I am our leader, Jelena. I am so glad that you have come."

Now it was Captain Armand's turn to be flustered. The words sounded vaguely familiar, but not quite. Then, he realized it must be a derivative of Demokritos. He replied in that tongue, "Captain Armand Clement of Velona. Can you understand me? Can you say again what you just said? I didn't quite get it."

"What a strange accent you have. Yes, I am our leader, Jelena. I am so glad that you have come from Velona. We need your help badly."

"Whoa. Slower please, ma'am. Will you come with me? I have Bethany on the radio. She speaks your language well. Please, this way." He repeated it several times before she understood.

"If I don't come back, Nika is to be the new leader of First Leader Collective," she whispered to her guard. Then, she hesitatingly followed this tall, thin man wearing the strange blue uniform. She hoped that he was not leading her into a trap, to catch her like a fly, rape her, and make her his slave. She tried to banish those thoughts as she stepped onto the ship, feeling its slow rocking motion.

He led her into the poop deck cabin where she heard a woman's voice and felt a tad more confident. "Here is our radio device. It lets us talk to Bethany who is back in Velona," he explained. A crewman continued peddling, generating the electricity the LD radio needed to operate.

"Bethany, Captain Armand here. I have the leader of Konstantin here with me. Jelena is her name. Please, go ahead. I am having a hard time understanding her."

"Hi Jelena. Am I speaking your language well enough for you to understand me? I am Bethany Bartiana Angela of Velona."

"Hi, I am Jelena, Bethany. You speak so much better than the man here does. I am so glad you have come. We are desperate for help. My people are dying of hunger because we cannot get to our food supplies stored on the higher shelves. We need help badly."

"I understand. I lost my arms too. All women on our world have lost their arms now. Have your feet returned to normal?"

"Yes, that is a miracle. Will our arms come back too?"

"No, I am afraid that we women are doomed to never have arms again. When I learned of this plague, I sent Captain Armand to you. He has a load of cereal grains to help feed your people. We in Velona want to help you and your people overcome this disaster. Each day, come aboard his ship and talk with me, okay? First, tell me what things your women need done right away. I will make sure that Captain Armand understands. He and his six men will help you with them. Alright?"

"Yes, you are saving us from dying. Our whole country thanks you. We have food supplies in our warehouses but they are out of our reach now. Can they fix up our kitchens? We think that we can use these mysterious kitchens to cook better. We have so many other needs, but these two are the most critical. Can they do these things for us?"

"Captain, did you follow all that?" He had gotten most of it and I filled in the missing bits. "Okay, Jelena, the captain and his men will start in on these things right now. Remember to come to this radio and talk to me tomorrow morning, okay?"

"Oh yes. Thank you, thank you for saving us." Jelena followed him out of the radio room and back onto the docks. She then led him to the first warehouse, while hundreds of other women now timidly began appearing, watching what was happening.

"Wow, I see your problem, Jelena. Okay, boys, bring everything down low. That'll keep you boys busy for a while. Their language is something like Demokritos, fellows."

"Aye, aye, captain," his boson saluted and began issuing orders to the other five men. Quickly, boxes, sacks, and barrels were lifted down and repositioned on the ground. As soon as they had repositioned everything in this warehouse, Jelena pointed out the other ten warehouses. At the same time, crews from the many Domiciles began pushing up carts, eagerly attempting to load some supplies onto their carts, and then push them back to their homes. All chatted excitedly and kept on thanking the crew members over and over. They began to enjoy all this freely given attention.

Jelena led Armand into her Domicile to show him the kitchen, which needed to be installed. "This is my bed mate, Nika." Once more, he was taken aback by how beautiful Nika was, her blonde hair also reaching her ankles. "Come, I'll show you our kitchen and what magical things came."

Later that day, Armand finally had their kitchen fixed up properly. His men had the food supplies all within reach of the women and a steady stream of women with pushcarts had gone in and out of the warehouses. Now he assembled his men in the fixed up kitchen and explained what they would be doing tomorrow. "If I understand this right, we have something like eighteen hundred kitchens to install, men." They groaned and he added, "You will find them most appreciative of your help." Their attitude changed, breaking into smiles. "Mind you sailors, keep your hands to yourselves." They laughed some more. Actually, having hundreds of women fussing over them fed their egos sufficiently. Each soon began to feel immense pride in being able to help these women.

For the next few days, I chatted every morning with Jelena. She readily told me their story, promising me that they no longer would harm their baby boys. "I believe that it is wrong to harm others, especially the babies. I hope that they don't grow up and harm us though. We do not trust men." I told her that I fully understood.

"Look, Jelena, you are right to worry about men. Some men would treat you just as you fear. Yet, there are also good men who will treat you right. Right now, my biggest fear for you is that, before you have enough good men to help and protect you, bad men will come and enslave you and your people."

"Yes, that is what so many have said. Just one bad man with arms can take over our whole country and enslave us all. That is what so many of us fear the most," Jelena replied.

"We think alike, Jelena. I am organizing a group of good men and sending them down to your country. They will help you and protect you until you no longer need them. It will take several months for them to get to you. Until they arrive, Captain Armand and his crew will stay with you and do all that they can to help you. Together, we will get through this horrible mess that we are all in now."

"How can we possibly thank you for all this?" Jelena asked.

"Jelena, you already have done the one single thing that I most desired."

"What could that be?" she asked confused. She'd done nothing yet.

"You and your people have stopped harming your boy babies. That is a monumental step forward in the right direction. Men and women have to learn to respect each other and to live with each other, help each other and not harm each other, especially now that all we women have lost our arms. Men must help we women keep our self-respect. If not, we and all mankind are doomed for extinction."

"Yes, I think I understand. I felt bad when the doctors harmed the first baby boy that I tried to save. We will do all that we can to help."

"I know that you will and we will do all that we can. I am sending along some of my helpful hints for you and your women. You may find some of the hints useful, suggesting alternate ways to do things that must be done."

Indeed, the next day, forty-three thousand two hundred copies of my book translated into their language appeared just outside her Domicile. While it took them time to get them all distributed, they read them and began ardently following the hints.

While the captain was forced to stay there for three more months, he and his crew didn't mind. I gave him enough extra pay that he could retire when he returned. His crew was elated at the generous compensation that they were going to receive. Before they returned home, they were going to earn it. There was so much in Konstantin that had to be done and only seven of them who could do it.

I know, compared to the tens of millions of people whom we could not help on Demokritos, forty thousand pales. Still, I thought this a small victory. Tashien was going to be another matter entirely.

Chapter 10 Madness in Tashien

Hindsight sometimes is one hundred percent. Looking back on it, I ought to have predicted these effects of the plague. Certainly, my old Judger friends had, Anathia and Callisto down in Demokritos. Hindsight also tells me that one able spiritual being thrown into a lion's pit become the lion's meal. Hindsight does not tell me why the two most densely populated areas of Tarra are also the lowest in overall emotional tones. Demokritos has an estimated population of seventy million or so. Originally, a country of seven kingdoms allied together; today it has become too huge for one centralized government. Their tone has slipped down to that of grief since the plague struck. Whether it bounces back up a little higher, time will tell, but I doubt that it will return to its pre-plague high of propitiation. As of December 823, the whole country had reverted to anarchy and chaos, no government at all.

The most populous country is Tashien with well over a hundred twenty million inhabitants. This was the country that used to be controlled by the doll creatures, otherwise called the plasticine by the mantis. Their continuous electronic bombardment had kept the spiritual being pinned at the depths of the human emotions, grief and below. When the continuous suppression was lifted a number of years ago, some rose up to anger, but most only climbed a little higher. Chaos reigned as dozens of overlords fought each other for control of land, farms, and cities. We intervened and attempted to establish a new way for the people of Tashien to rule themselves, a two parliamentary system, one local, one national. Several of my friends stayed there to see the change through.

Honestly, the incredible, cold-hearted cruelty and human degradation that we experienced there was shocking. I'd never been around such people before. I call them people, but they had to be from some other race; they'd lost their self-respect, their humanity, and had begun to enjoy sadism. Women were mere objects to these people. Dita (Eve now) and I had our feet wiped out, our arms amputated below our elbows, our legs cut off at the knees, addicted to opium, and finally left to freeze in the back of a wagon. When you lose your humanity, others pay an awful price.

Tashien is divided into four provinces. Tan Loc Province with Shansee its largest city is the southern one. Rice is one of their main agricultural exports. Our steam train line goes all the way from Velona to Shansee. North of Shansee is Wontun Province and the Imperial City of Zau, where the palace of the Emperor and Empress lies. North of there is Linyi Province. In the far north is Dong Province, largely uninhabited now, since the mass exodus almost a century ago. It is an ice province in which life is extremely harsh. Tan Loc Province has an estimated forty million inhabitants, having lost a great many in the first plague. Wontun Province now has about sixty-five million residents, while Linyi has the rest, some fifteen million.

In Zau, the High Parliament makes the laws of the country, while the Emperor and Empress enforce them. Each member is elected to six-year terms and can be re-elected. To guarantee continuity, the Emperor and Empress are also elected and serve a single ten-year term and cannot hold it a second time. Each province has a Low Parliament, which makes their local laws, which their elected Princess enforces. The Emperor and Empress control the Imperial Army, but each province has their own local militia as well as many local overlords, vying for power. That was the new government system that we helped establish. Until now, it has brought law and order out of the chaos of those times.

Down in Shansee, Princess Pian Ling Wu, whom I knew as Jemma, a Judger, was now thirty-one, her daughter, Misha, eleven. She carried out the law in the province. When the plague struck, she kept me informed nearly every day for a time. I had not been following nor had kept informed on the recovery that I had helped put in place in Tashien over sixty years ago. Now I realized that this had been a mistake on my part and spent hours on the LD radio catching up on over a half century of developments. Pian was most helpful and spent hours chatting with me. I should break this down into before plague and after plague situations.

Before the first plague struck, the new ruling system had worked out well. The elected Low and High Parliament members designed reasonable laws for the most part. The Emperor, Empress, and three local Princesses had seen to their implementation, backed by the newly formed Imperial Army and Local Militias of the Princesses. The utter chaos of a half century ago appeared gone, but was in fact merely swept under the rug, so to speak. Degradation of the magnitude found in Tashien cannot be solved, removed, or erased from men and women by mere passage and enforcement of laws or even moral codes for that matter. The root cause of the near total loss of self-respect in each person had to be handled, one person at a time.

To that end, De An had set up his Church of God, where therapy sessions were given. Through these sessions, individual spiritual beings had the opportunity to face their own personal trauma and decisions, which had put them into such a degraded situation. One on one, the Counselors, as the deliverers of the therapy sessions became known there, began to undo centuries of horrors. As I learned from Pian, De An had been very wise. He had cleverly arranged for the best possible protection of the Church of God and its vital Counselors by having members of the most powerful martial arts school in all Tashien as its guardians, the Olin Masters.

He had setup four initial Churches of God. Two were in Tan Loc Province. Master Liang Dhow and his wife Counselor Dia Son began the Church in Shansee, while Master Jian and his wife Counselor Mei Bi Li began the Nan Yan Church of God. Up in the Imperial City of Zau, Wontun Province, Master Ning Chou and his wife Counselor Chan Bao established their church. Further north in Linyi Province, Master Peng Dong and his wife Counselor Feng started the Lou Yang Church of God.

Of course, all these men and women I had known personally and counted as my friends, but age had claimed them all. Yet their work had flourished and prospered. Each Church of God, Pian explained, now boasted over a thousand members. Every day, dozens of therapy sessions were being delivered. However, I must point out that in Tan Loc Province, two thousand rescued spiritual beings out of forty million are but a drop in an ocean. That was the problem. Had the plague not come, perhaps a vastly different story could be told of Tashien.

From Pian, I learned that most of the members of the Church of God in Shansee were the wealthier members of their city. I began to see why, as these men and women tended to be slightly higher in emotional tone, having done something to amass their fortunes. Those who most needed the therapy were so degraded that they didn't recognize the vital nature that the therapy and the Church had to offer. When you are stuck in utter hopelessness, it is very difficult to recognize something which offers salvation. That was perhaps the underlying reason for what happened now, over a half century later when the plagues struck.

Don Ho was the youngest son of Overlord Ho, a ruthless, power hungry man. Wealthy, yes, but he always wanted more. He'd witness the coming to power of the Low Parliament and the reinstatement of their Princess and the rebuilding of her army. He'd witnessed the complete destruction of the overlord up in the city of Nan Yan. For years, Don was lectured by his father on how the rich and wealthy were taking control of their city, forcing their will and laws upon everyone, including the Ho's. "How dare these men whose only claim to power is their immense wealth, which allows them to buy all things and dictate to us!" his father drilled into the young, impressionable Don. "You must be strong and smart to take on the wealthy with their vast money, my son." That was his pronouncement the day he sent Don off to Lian's School of Martial Arts in Shansee.

Maybe his father had purposely sent him away to save his life. In later years, he occasionally thought so. Either that or he was preparing his son to obtain the revenge that he would never be able to achieve. Don preferred the latter idea, as it backed his own goals. He well remembered that day, October 29, 815 — the day the wealthy nobles-backed militia of the Princess stormed his father's stronghold in west Tan Loc Province, butchering his father, mother, sister, and two older brothers, destroying the last overlord who dared stand against their "new order." They had fought a valiant, but futile battle, according to all accounts.

Now penniless, but skilled in martial arts, Don Ho began his long road to revenge. He began naturally in the poor slums of Shansee, where his skill kept him alive and allowed him to dominate other young men. He began by establishing an extortion protection racket, demanding safe money from the pitifully poor merchants who attempted to eke out barest survival. Soon, he saw this as only aiding the wealthy, who ignored such petty things as long as such did not impact themselves. He changed his tactics, moving his racket into the middle zone, just above the slums. Quickly, the protection racket became quite profitable and his organization began attracting others who saw this as their chance to gain wealth and respect.

Don Ho realized almost at once that he and his ever-growing gang needed undying support of large numbers of people to act as an invisible buffer zone, protecting them. He well remembered that first announcement to his fifty gang members. "Starting today, one tenth of all that we take in shall be doled out to those in the slums." Oh, how his gang had protested that call. Yet, he had been right. Give the poor a constant handout and they will back you implicitly. By 823, any member of his extensive organization only had to appear anywhere in the slums of Shansee and they would be guarded, fed, and protected by several million people! In the slums, they were untouchable! Down there he now had ten safe houses where anyone could hang out in utter safety, should the army of the wealthy become too threatening.

Don Ho soon began to expand his activities from simple extortion. Such would never yield him his desired revenge. He added thieves to his payroll, sending them into the wealthier neighborhoods. Once strong enough, he quietly took over the opium trade in Shansee, where again his martial arts training served him well, as he personally eliminated the current drug lord. Once more, he enforced the strict rule that ten percent of their profits were doled out to those in the slums, who now began to see great benefits in supporting the illusive Don Ho.

I say illusive, because it was at this time that Don Ho changed his appearance. Why? He now set his sights closer to the target: the wealthy. Opium had given him just the entrance point he needed. Many wealthy liked to indulge in a high, now and then. They also, he discovered, loved to gamble and to enjoy the many pleasures of the houses of pleasure, of which the Purple Palace was the finest in Shansee. Now his target became two-fold. Bit by bit, his group began to infiltrate and take over the many gambling houses in Shansee, from cards to dice to cock fighting. By 820, he controlled them all, but focused his main thrust on the exclusive gambling houses. There, he had to dress the part and was never seen dressed in less than the finest suits that money could buy in Shansee.

Late 820 was a pivotal point for Don Ho. Three men controlled all the major houses of pleasure in Shansee. He planned carefully; his men had scouted the three men for months. At last, Don gave the order and joined one group to see to his plan's execution. Rapidly and under cover of a rainy night, he and his men slipped into the heavily guarded Purple Palace, eliminating the guards, who were taken by complete surprise. They had somehow gotten keys to the front doors. Actually, a purse of gold coins had gotten them the keys, simple.

He barged into the bedroom of Dian and told the startled man, "Sign here and you live, choose now." He held the pen towards Dian's hand. The paper was an official deed, signing over ownership of the Purple Palace and two others that Dian owned to him. The man refused and Don drove the pen into the man's eye, killing him instantly. Withdrawing the pen, he forged the man's signature, as his other men were currently doing with the two other major players. In one evening, Don Ho took over all the pleasure houses of Shansee.

His first action was to establish a free house of pleasure in the middle of the slums. If you walked into the Free Palace wearing a suit, you had to pay. If you walked in wearing peasant's clothing, everything in the house was free. The impact that this had on those in the slums was what you might well expect, greatly endearing Don Ho and his organization to those who lived there.

Until now, his revenge had been hit or miss, penny ante at best. Now, well now he was ready to begin for real! He needed three things to happen. One, he needed to get the wealthy noblemen and women hooked on gambling. Two, he needed them hooked on drugs. Three, he needed them hooked on constantly attending his many houses of pleasure. Once a wealthy man or woman was hooked on all three, he had their souls in his hands. Oh, what he would do to them then! He savored the coming delicious moments!

He began enticing them to the gambling houses by offering all manner of free amenities, such as gorgeous women to cling to them, free drinks for the entire night, free food but only the finest Shansee had to offer — all designed to lure them into his establishments, where slowly but surely he began to take away their money.

Both there and at the houses of pleasure, he had standing orders for those serving drinks to lace them lightly with opium when the customer was one of the wealthier men or women. He opened up high class opium dens as well. Just before the first plague of Nestor's struck Shansee, money was rolling in faster than his accountants could count it!

Now the houses of pleasure traditionally used special women to provide sensual pleasures, kami they were called. It was an honorable profession, not the lowly prostitutes of the streets, filthy and disease-ridden. No, these women had their arms bound behind them, the symbol universally recognized as an honored pleasure giver, clean and healthy. And these women were highly trained to deliver such pleasures. Sadistic tendencies ran deep in these people of Tashien, caused by centuries of the doll creatures' electronic suppression of emotional tones. Men and women craved sensations in this land, Don Ho made sure that they got it in volume. He did regret that the ancient art of the zen-kami had been outlawed for some sixty years now. That was the practice of removing a kami's arms at their elbows, then charging enormous fees for her most unusual services. Don Ho considered reviving them, but as yet had not found the means. To implement that, he would need the services of doctors and assistants. He'd only begun exploring that avenue when the first plague struck. When all the women of Shansee suddenly lost their arms, Don Ho believed that the gods had answered his prayers!

Additionally, Don Ho studied his opponents well. He knew that the wealthier women insisted on having the centuries old habit of having small feet. In ancient days, the women bound their feet when they were but children — a painful habit that had been outlawed long ago. Now, under the careful watch of a doctor, metal casings were fitted to a woman's feet and tightened, fracturing her arches, reforming and reshaping them. Only when her bones had healed were the casings removed, revealing feet in which only the toes could touch the ground. Her heels were highly elevated, and she needed to wear special shoes, ones whose heels almost touched the backs of her toes, giving the illusion of very tiny feet. Of course, the woman could only now take the tiniest of steps, in a shuffling sort of gait. However, tiny feet were the norm among all the Great Ladies of Tashien.

He made it a practice to hire only women with small feet and insisted all of his kami obtain such as well. They were very eager to have it done because it would elevate them to the status of a Great Lady. That he also paid for the operation and gave them a five hundred gold coin bonus certainly helped convince them to do it soon. His many kami looked so enticing now, that he personally bought them all the extremely expensive black silk hose and highly polished high-heeled shoes that they needed to wear. Wealthy men and women now saw the kami pleasure givers as being of their high status in society, Great Ladies. Business boomed.

When the first plague struck and all of his kami now really had no arms, he was elated! However, the women were not! Terrified and afraid, they continued to scream and cry that first day. He had to take action. While it was one thing for them to have their arms bound for several days, they had other unbound kami women caring for their needs. Every five days, they would be unbound and allowed to stretch cramped muscles and care for the needs of their other kami. Now, they had no arms at all and they were frightened to death. He had to take action.

He went from house to house, gathering all his kami together. "Yes, this is a calamity facing all women of Shansee. Together, my dear, lovely kami, we can get through this. First, your pay will quadruple to one hundred gold each night. Second, I will provide men, kind men, to look after your needs, to feed you, to bathe you, to dress you, to brush out your lovely long hair. Tell me your needs and I will see that they will be met." This went a very long way to calming his kami. He left standing orders that any man assigned to assisting the kami who molested, bothered, or harmed a kami would be summarily executed. Only one man had to be killed to set an example. Soon the kami were extremely happy women, with money, respect, and manservants. Of course, few of these women ever saw the "promised" gold.

He expected his pleasure house business to boom. It didn't. With every woman now armless, the exotic intrigue of his kami just wasn't there. Yes, business continued as normal with only a slight increase, but it didn't explode as he desired. He needed something different. Then, word came in October that a cure had been found. Women were ordered to certain locations to be given the cure that would regrow their arms. He again met with all his kami, offering them each a thousand gold bonus if they chose not to get their arms regrown, stating that they could always have it done later. This was a lie; of course, he had no idea if that was even possible. None had their arms regrown, for they loved their incredible good fortunes.

For a month after that, his business steadily grew. Then the second plague came and with it came word that there would be no cure this time. From now on, all women worldwide would be armless. Once more just as he was about to achieve his ultimate victory over the wealthy of Shansee, fate had slipped him another cruel curve! He had to have something even more exotic, more enticing, something that would really draw in the men and women into his pleasure houses.

This is not to say that as of October 823, Don Ho had not had successes in his revenge upon all the wealthy of Shansee. By no means not!

Just before the first plague came in June the previous year, Lin Li Sun had just finished her next painting. She sat back and admired her product. Two swans floated across a crystal clear lake lined with well-shaped evergreens. Perfect she thought. Lin Li was then eighteen years old, the daughter of a wealthy merchant. Her mother, always perfect and elegant, was her role model in many ways.

Lin Li had already undergone the procedure to have small feet like her mother. That was five years behind her now. Already, she had heaped the benefits from it. Whenever she went out in public, all eyes turned to her; she was a Great Lady. Like her mother, she dressed the part, even while painting. After all, who can say what Most Honorable Person might drop by their richly done home while she was painting? It would be a social affront of magnitude to appear dressed in some peasant rags covered with paint. She wore an elegant, silk, pencil style dress, which accentuated her youthful figure. Just enough of her expensive, fine, black silk hose was exposed by the small walking slit. Her highly polished, shiny black heels were instantly visible and admired everywhere she went. That she now had to exercise the greatest care in walking to keep her graceful balance was a small price to pay. Her steps were more of a shuffle, no more than a few inches a step. Her form-fitting, long pencil dress kept her from overstepping and taking a tumble. Indeed, so tight were these dresses, she could only put one foot twelve inches in front of the other while sitting down, with just barely enough ease to allow her to cross her legs at her knees. She had no chance of taking too big of a step and taking an inelegant tumble.

Lin Li was a gifted person, with an eidetic mind, able to recall the tiniest of details. Yet, she did not know what she wanted to do with her life. Getting married at fourteen did not interest her. She couldn't see herself as being a mother at fifteen and had rejected all of her Most Honorable Father's suggestions for marriage proposals. She could paint well, but she thought her works lacked fire and emotion though they looked mechanically sound. She had learned to play a flute, but she had already given that up as well. Her calligraphy was technically correct, yet lacked inspiration or so her master had told her before she gave that up as well. Now, she was into painting, enjoying technical mastery, but again lacking that spark of life that would truly make a painting. She sighed and rose, her heels announcing her slow, but steady progress from her studio room.

Already, her two older brothers had been killed. They had gaily joined the army, seeking fame and glory. Both had found a bullet instead. Now Lin Li was the last of her siblings. Upon their deaths, her Most Honorable Father had changed. His eyes were sunken as if all hope had left him. He took to going out at night, to where, her Most Honorable Mother would not say, though her eyes betrayed her. Lin Li guessed that he spent time at one of the houses of pleasure and perhaps a house of gambling. She'd once seen a chip from one of those places in his suit pocket, while she had been pressing it for him.

In early June, her Most Honorable Mother grew more and more morose with each passing day until finally she did not rise one morning. Lin Li shuttered as she remembered knocking and entering her room only to find her lifeless, cold body lying in the bed. Oh how she had promised her Most Honorable Father that she would look after him, cook his meals, and press his suits. His sorrowful eyes had pierced her soul. For an instant that June, she entertained thoughts of moving out onto her own, perhaps opening up an art studio of her own. They had money, lots of it; she could buy a small shop and sell her paintings. Yet, she had squelched that idea in favor of doing her right and proper duties for her father. That, as it turned out, had been a terrible mistake.

The day before the first plague struck, they had just finished dining on the supper that she had prepared for them, when someone knocked on their door. Her father sat unmoving in his chair, his eyes were dull, as if he were somewhere else. "I'll answer the door, Most Honorable Father," Lin Li said quickly, rose, and began her slow shuffle to the door, her heels click clicking on the polished hardwood floor. "Coming," she called out, knowing that it would take her minutes to go from their dining room all the way to the front door. As a little girl, she could have bounded there in seconds, but now as a Great Lady, she was forced to move mere inches with each step, careful inches or she could lose her balance and be forced to flail her arms about in a most inelegant manner. She'd done that many times while she had learned to walk again, after the procedure years ago.

She opened the door and saw a very elegantly dressed man, perhaps in his late thirties. His blue suit was extremely expensive, she noted. He was immaculately well groomed, not a black hair was out of place. His perfectly trimmed moustache transformed his face into male perfection, she thought, perhaps he might consent to sitting for a portrait one day. "Good evening, Most Honorable Great Lady Miss Lin Li Sun, I presume? I am Most Honorable Don Ho here to conduct some business with the Most Honorable Sun."

He saw an exquisitely dressed young woman of eighteen. He noticed her small feet, her luxurious, long, shiny black hair that reached to the small of her back, her perfectly manicured two-inch long, cherry red, painted nails, her unblemished complexion, and her angelic face. Lin Li, he thought, was a perfect specimen in all ways.

She bowed low to the man. "Please, come in Most Honorable Ho. Most Honorable Father is in our dining room. Allow me to take you to him," she extended her arm, as was the custom when greeting guests. He slipped his arm around hers. Lin Li noticed that he seemed comfortable walking at her side, which meant that he was used to escorting Great Ladies himself. Obviously he must be, since he was so handsome, so refined in his motions. For a moment, she wondered if her father was once more attempting to suggest her hand in marriage. She dismissed that notion, for he'd said nothing about that topic for over a year now.

The two did not speak as Lin Li slowly led Don Ho to their dining room. "Most Honorable Father, Most Honorable Don Ho has come to see you." She bowed low to her father and turned to leave the two men alone.

"Most Honorable Daughter, please stay," the icy cold voice of her father landed upon her back. So cold, she thought. Why? He had never had her remain in the presence of his meetings. She turned and faced the two men.

"Most Honorable Daughter, Most Honorable Don Ho has come to collect my debt to him."

"What are you talking about?" Lin Li asked. She had no idea what he was saying. What debt? Her father appeared not to want to say anything further. She looked from face to face, seeking an answer.

"Are you going to tell her or shall I?" Don Ho said softly and politely, with just a hint of covert hostility in his voice. He stood once again on the edge of yet another revenge victory, a sweet one at that! Her father muttered something incomprehensible, so Don spoke for him.

"It seems that the Most Honorable Sun has a serious gambling problem. Indeed, he has gambled away all of his extensive fortune. A wise man would have stopped when that happened. Alas, Most Honorable Great Lady Lin Li, he did not. He borrowed on his business to the point where he could no longer meet the moneychanger's monthly payment. Still, he could not control his urges. He has gambled away his magnificent home here, borrowing its full value from the moneychangers once again. Still he would not cease his gambling vice. Being the Most Honorable Man that I am, I took pity on the Most Honorable Sun and purchased up his moneychanger loans. Still that was not enough. I am afraid that he has made a fool out of me. I lent him a sizeable amount of funds, hoping that he would invest them in his business. Unfortunately, he again gambled even that away and once again cannot meet his obligations. Yet, he is a Most Honorable Man and has struck a bargain with Most Honorable Self. I am most saddened to be the one to tell you this, Most Honorable Great Lady Lin Li, but your father has sold you to me to cover his gambling debts. If you agree to come with me now, all of your Most Honorable Father's gambling debts will be forgiven once again. He can start out tomorrow fresh once more. If you do not agree, I will not force you to come with me. However, the moneychangers will come tomorrow and confiscate this home and its possessions, and you will both most unfortunately be thrown out into the street with only the clothes on your backs. All else, your Most Honorable Father has sold to the moneychangers."

Waves of shock and repulsion flooded her body and mind. She fought hard to keep her dinner down. "Father! Is this true? How could you?" she screamed, forgetting all manner of social refinements and protocols.

He did not answer her, staring unmoving at the empty plate before him, below apathy, below useless, a total and complete failure. That Don Ho spoke the truth slammed into her hard, like running into a stone wall. She grasped the table for support as her knees began to give out. Lin Li slumped into her chair.

Don Ho reveled in his complete and total victory over this ex-wealthy nobleman! Yet, he was extremely careful not to show any signs of it. He gracefully allowed her a moment to come to grips with this most shocking news. He was certain that she had known nothing of this at all. All the better for me, he thought.

At last, he decided that she was ready to hear more. "Most Honorable Great Lady Lin Li, I am a Most Honorable Business Man. I will treat you with the kindness and respect that you deserve. I will see that you continue to receive only the best, as fitting and proper for the Great Lady that you are. I have many fine establishments in which you may find a most profitable employment. It would grieve me most horribly to see a Most Honorable Great Lady such as yourself thrown out into the street like some petty slum rat. Please, you must allow me to come to your rescue. I give you my solemn word that you will be treated with honor and respect until you can get yourself established. Please, think of your Most Honorable Father and give him another chance. Do not forsake him. Be the Most Honorable Daughter that you are."

His words sounded like honey to Lin Li, whose mind was in turmoil. How could her father have betrayed her so? Betting her off as if she was a mere chip in some card game! Ho's offer seemed to provide the only way out.

Lin Li spoke, not for her father, but for her own sake. "Most Honorable Don Ho, I will accept your most gracious offer. I do not wish to remain in this house a moment longer. I have been betrayed by my own father!" Her words carried an acid sting, which Don savored, like a superb seasoning on a perfectly done steak. Her father still moved not a muscle.

Don came to her side, helped her up, and quietly escorted her out of the only home that she had known. He felt her body trembling and inwardly smiled. He carefully led her to his waiting carriage. She noticed that it too was one of the most expensive, regal carriages that she had ever seen, complete with gold-plated light fixtures, which glimmered in the early evening light from their enclosed, burning wicks. His strong hands lifted her up and into the carriage.

Once inside, the carriage began moving through the streets. Lin Li didn't even ask where she was being taken. He spoke, "Once we arrive, I will take you to an elegant bedroom, provide you with a little after-dinner wine, and allow you time to adjust to this great tragedy. In the morning over breakfast, we can talk about your future path. I understand that you are something of a painter." He attempted to console her for a short while.

"You are so kind. Yes, not a very good one, though," she struggled to say. He graciously allowed her to continue in silence. At the back entrance to the Purple Palace, he lifted her down from the carriage. Her pencil dress would not allow her to take such large steps nor could she easily keep her balance while doing so, unless he helped her. He led her inside. The back alleyway changed into an elegant hallway, golden light fixtures lined the walls. Plush purple carpet covered the floors. The walls were painted in a complimentary shade of purple as well. Holding her arm, he led her up the stairs to the third floor.

She saw another long, very elegantly done hallway with many side rooms. Into the first one, he led her. Well, at least she would be living in true luxury, she noted. Everything about the room spoke of lavish expense. Whoever Don Ho was, he certainly must have vast amounts of money and she began to relax. He left her a moment and returned with a golden tray, a bottle of very expensive wine, and a golden goblet. "Here, some of my finest wine. Sip please, this is not a guzzling type of wine," he grinned. She realized this was a touch of humor and managed a slight smile. "Sip, relax, sleep. We can talk more in the morning. Thank you for honoring me in my humble attempts to keep your Most Honorable Father and yourself from utter ruin." He bowed and left. The closing of the door seemed to her to be a closing of all her past eighteen years. In a way, it was.

She poured some wine, sipping it as she examined the confines of her room. One thing was certain: everything in here was far finer than anything she had ever seen before. From the slippery red satin sheets to the plush purple carpet, which held not the slightest trace of dirt or dust, everything was of the highest quality. All the fixtures in the room appeared to be made of gold! She sipped more and began to relax. Lin Li laid down on the soft bed.

Now the stark reality of what had happened, every nuance recorded forever in her mind, replayed itself. She cried and then felt very drowsy and drifted into sleep. She didn't hear the muffled voices as two men entered her room around midnight.

"Okay, she is out, doctor. Now do your handiwork. It should be a simple matter," Don Ho commented snidely. If this works out, this will be superb in all ways, he thought. I will have a product that no one else does and I will be able to parade my victories before the entire world, most importantly before all the other wealthy ones. He laughed, though the doctor didn't know why.

Yes, it was a simple matter, a simple, almost trivial operation, one for which he was being highly over paid. That aspect he liked. Perhaps Don Ho had a good idea here. This was such a gorgeous young woman. He set to work. Five minutes later, he finished. "Here, observe how they look for yourself. If they are not the proper shades, we can always try others, many others."

While the doctor held Lin Li's eyelids open, Don Ho looked down upon her lovely face and her new yellow-brown glass eyes. Perfect, he thought. It matches her skin tones brilliantly. "Well done, doctor. No one has such women in their pleasure houses. She will be most unique indeed." He saw vast sums of money now rolling in. Of course, the next day the plague struck, changing his plans once more.

Lin Li awoke and opened her eyes. It had to be morning, yet it was pitch black. Had someone turned off the lights while she slept? She struggled to get up. She felt her body and realized that she had slept in the dress and shoes that she had been wearing last night. Was it in the middle of the night? She was hungry and wide awake. "Hello. Is anyone there? Could someone please turn my night lights on?"

Presently, someone entered the room, though no light came. "Hello, I am Qian Mei. I am to help you with things now. It is morning time. The day is bright. Come, let us get you some breakfast." The woman had a kindly voice.

"But I can't see anything. Please, turn on the lights," Lin Li asked politely. "I was supposed to meet with the Most Honorable Don Ho this morning."

"It is very bright in here now, Lin Li. I am sure Don will visit you later this morning. Come, I will lead you. You have such pretty yellow-brown eyes now."

Panic struck her; her hands felt her eyes. They were cold, like glass. "What has happened to me?" she wailed.

"I am told that they removed your eyes and replaced them with these most beautiful new glass eyes. They do look so very good on you, Lin Li. Here take my arm. Let us get some breakfast. You will feel better now." Lin Li felt the warm, soft touch of the woman's hand on her arms and rose. Soon, she discovered that walking was now very treacherous; she was blind!

Lin Li never felt so utterly helpless in all her life. Dutifully, she allowed this young woman to feed her, brush her hair, and assist her with the chamber pot. However, soon her own arms began to tire. Even Qian Mei began complaining about her arms. Both decided to lie down for a while. While Lin Li cried herself to sleep, she did sleep for quite some time.

When she awoke, the complete darkness was still all that she could see. She moved her arms to her face, but could not feel them. She suddenly realized something was terribly wrong. After more frantic motions, she sensed that somehow her arms were completely gone! She shrieked and cried out terrified.

The door opened and a sober faced Don Ho entered. "I am so terribly sorry, Lin Li. There has been some kind of alien plague that has struck all of Shansee and many other countries, I am told. All of our women have lost their arms completely. Vanished, as if you never had any! We are all quite shocked. Please rest now. I must see what can be done about this plague. It has affected every one of my female employees. This is a complete disaster. However, rest assured that I will find a way to keep my word to all of you women in my employ. Please give me time to see what can be done. Rest now, Lin Li, please." She heard the door close and she began crying once more.

After a time, she began listening. At least that had not been taken away from her yet. She heard the muffled crying coming from many other rooms. Now she began to believe him. Were all women now armless and completely helpless? She cried once more.

He kept his word. Later in the day, a man entered and began caring for her needs. He led her down the hall to a room where she heard other women present: some sobbing, some whispering. She also heard sounds of eating and smelled hot food. Suddenly, she felt ravenous. The kind voiced man began feeding her, but it was so awkward. She could not see when he was bringing up another bite of food for her and had to listen to his clues. Around her, she heard the other women being fed. Now she felt that it must be true, they had lost their arms to the plague.

Once fed, the women began chatting and Lin Li learned they were armless along with other smaller modifications. She could not see her own small waist nor feel it, taking the word of these kindly women who told her how she looked. They took instant pity on her; for blind, she was in far worse shape than they were. As kami, they were used to not having the use of their arms for several days. Once Ho had made them their comforting offer, their fears and terrors abated. Yet for them, this new arrival could not even see and that endeared her to them. Many voices promised to help look after her, though they knew not how they could now lacking arms themselves.

In time, Lin Li was escorted into some room filled with many people. She often heard whispered comments about her exquisite beauty, though she had no idea what they meant or who these men and women might be. She was only told that no one would ever violate her virginity. The penalty for that was instant death. She took comfort then that no one was going to rape her, though she often was pleasured, though nearly always by these fellow women. Time passed by, she knew not how long. Lin Li had no way to keep track of it now. She was helpless and merely allowed others to move her body as they desired, depending wholly upon unseen men to handle her needs, which was always done with kind and gentle hands.

She knew from the feeling from the rest of her body that she was still wearing the fine silk hose, which she dearly loved. Her heels felt like the same ones that she had always worn. She could feel the fine silk of her pencil dress on her body and knew it was a pencil dress, her legs motion was severely limited by the tightness of the dress. Well, she needed that to help her avoid taking too large a step, now more than ever before, because she could not see what she was doing. She knew that her hair was being properly cared for, since she could still toss it about with her head. Now she loved to do just that, for it created a light sense of touch wherever her tresses landed, replacing sensory input from her absent arms and eyes.

Next, they had asked her to do something by herself! She was to walk around the room, smiling at these unseen people! "The floor is flat," a voice said. "Go very slowly and feel the objects so that you don't bump hard into things. Glide gracefully and smile." That first walk was terrifying. No one was holding on to her. She had no hands to feel her way. She took minuscule steps at first, perhaps an inch at a time. The voice encouraged her, "Yes, that is the way. Small steps. Remember to smile. You are very beautiful." Thus, Lin Li made her debut on the main floor of the Purple Palace.

After some time, she was led away. "Did you see their reactions, boss? You have struck gold with her! The lecherous dogs will pay anything for a repeat performance." Don Ho smiled, perfect in all ways. Yes, he now had new attractions that would draw huge paying crowds. He would be parading his victory prizes before the wealthy, who didn't even realize what Lin Li represented! He reveled in his revenge, eager to expand outward.

Then, the second plague struck, this time crippling up men as well. The first day, chaos ruled Don Ho's many establishments. None of his many women received their usual assistance as they rose for the day. Their calls and pleadings fell on minds too engrossed in their own problems to deal with theirs.

Poor Lin Li called and called for help. At last, one of the kami managed to get her door open. "Lin Li, it's me, Qian Mei. Something awful has happened again, Lin Li. We are not sure what just yet. None of our helper men is answering our calls. Maybe there is a way I can help you." The two struggled with the chamber pot. Mostly succeeding with that, Qian asked, "Would you feel better if you were sitting with the rest of us?"

"Oh please. Yes. It is so horrible just sitting here in the dark not knowing what is happening. Are you all right?"

"Yes, we kami are fine. Our shoes are a little loose, but that seems to be about all. Come on, follow me." She rose and took a couple of her tiny shuffling steps.

Lin Li got to her feet and froze. "Qian, Qian, I can't see you. Which way? The man always leads me."

"Sorry, Lin Li, I forgot. I don't have any hands. Maybe you can stay close to me and hear me as we go." Qian had no idea how she could do this otherwise; she too felt helpless to lead the blind woman along. Lin Li took little steps until she felt the back of Qian. Then the two did their slow shuffling walk. Qian kept encouraging her and telling her about the coming turns. At last, they entered a big commons area where a number of couches were filled with the many other kami who worked here at the Purple

Palace.

Qian now had another problem. While she could see where to sit down, Lin Li could not. She carefully directed her friend until finally Lin Li managed to sit down, rather awkwardly however. Now she listened in on the women's conversations and felt more relaxed than she ever had.

Around noon, two of their helpers came crawling in on their hands and knees. Qian began describing the awful way that their feet looked and that the men could no longer stand. They had brought the women some lunch, crudely made this time.

Later that night, three of their helper men returned stumping along wearing the mantis-created boots. Again, Qian described for Lin Li what she saw, before she was interrupted by the men offering her a bite. Once fed, one of these men insisted on getting Lin Li back into her bedroom for the night. She felt his reassuring arm around her waist, but soon felt the wild wiggling he did just to keep his balance while taking the small steps. The last thing she heard that night was the stumping sounds of his boots as he slowly made his way out of her room.

This was the start of many changes. Soon, Lin Li was told that because of the plague, she was going to be moved into a room with several other women who were like herself. That way, they all could be better cared for, at least that's what they were told. Meals now came only twice a day after that. Initially, Lin Li had no idea that she was now being housed in a dorm style room, complete with six beds in a row, thought more were added later on. A man led her into her new room, got her to her bed and helped her sit down.

She then heard other women being brought in as well, counting five more to herself. After hearing the door shut and no more action, Lin Li called out, "Who is there? I am Lin Li, can you see me?" A number of women's voices answered her, no.

"I am Mei Qing. I can't see. They tell me that I have yellow-brown glass eyes now. I don't have any arms either. I am totally helpless, Lin Li. How about you?" A chorus of me too's came from all sides of Lin Li.

One by one, the women introduced themselves to each other. They included Mei Qing, Ting Zhe, Ni Ton, Wen Lon Ton, and Xian Wong. Some of the last names sounded familiar to Lin Li. The Honorable Wongs had lived down the street from her and before she had her feet done, she used to play with their daughter. Could this be the same woman, she wondered.

Lin Li called out, "I knew a Xian Wong; we played together until I had my feet done."

Lin Li, is that really you? I wondered. We used to play with my rag doll."

"Yes, and I accidentally cracked its ceramic head. I'm sorry that I broke your doll." Now both women knew that here was their childhood friend. Lin Li now began telling her and the others all about what had happened to her.

What started out as a simple explanation took on a darker side for these women. One by one, the others related their stories. All were following the same pattern. Somehow, their fathers had gotten addicted to gambling and had lost everything to Don Ho. In order to save their fathers from debtor's prison, they had agreed to go away with Don Ho, who promised to treat them well and with respect and honor. Like Lin Li, they were given wine and fell asleep, only to wake up blind and in terror.

Lin Li had her eyes opened by these conversations, figuratively that is. She knew that she had not been violated, that is, raped. She asked the others if they had. None had; all claimed to have been treated well, wanting nothing, except of course that which could not be given back to them: eyes and arms. Still, this sounded like some kind of diabolical plot of Don Ho.

Some days later, Lin Li had no idea how many, the male voice explained. "The whole city has completely shut down. No man can walk much. No shops are open, no markets, and no stores. It is spooky. I stepped outside onto the Princess Path. Not a single person was on the street! No one!" Lin Li recalled times she had seen this main east-west street. Always, it had been packed with people and riks. Deserted? She felt afraid once more.

"I'm sorry, but Don Ho is now rationing our remaining food. We are all down to one meal a day. There is just no place to buy or steal any food. He's heard from Princess Pian that soon food supplies will be available, but when is anyone's guess. If no man can walk, how can anyone get any delivered? I surely don't know. I will do my best to bring you all that I can. I truly am sorry, but at least you six are eating something. We've heard that down in the slums, people are starving to death. This plague is becoming very dangerous indeed."

"Please," Lin Li begged. She couldn't see if he was waiting for her to speak or not and so continued, "Please find out all that you can about this plague and its effects. We really do want to know, but we can't see anything for ourselves. Please, sir." He promised and left them.

In her palace, further east on down the Princess Path, Princess Pian was trying to figure out how to deal with this new plague and its crippling effects. By the second week, she had to do something.

Dead bodies were starting to pile up in the streets down in the slums, she was told.

"Look, if you ride a horse, you can get around," she reasoned. After all, that's how she was getting her information now, from her guards who rode. "No shops or markets where people can get food are open. By now, everyone must be running out of food. If we do nothing, millions may starve to death. If we don't get the dead handled, we will be facing mass disease and illness among those who are still alive. We have to do something."

"Okay, let's have men take wagons and go around picking up the dead. Haul them off," she suggested. Someone countered that the men would be unable to dig enough graves to bury them, not with the way that their feet now were. That's when she got the idea of mass cremation. She ordered the dead to be taken a mile north of town and there to be burned.

Next, she ordered all of her militiamen who had horses or could get one to begin taking wagons to the known locations, which may yet have food supplies stored. Whatever they could find would be confiscated and loaded onto the wagons. They would leave a receipt for what was taken. Later on, the Princess could settle up the accounts. Then, the men were ordered to go up and down each street calling out to see if anyone needs food. Those that did were to be given some from the wagon.

By the end of the second week, she had a better idea of the food situation. Fortunately, it was fall harvest time throughout Tan Loc Province, early November. However, only about half of this year's crops had yet been brought in to markets. The farmers were just as laid up as the men in the city were. Still, her estimates suggested that they could get by without any new influx of food for another month, maybe two or three.

Nevertheless, men, women, and children continued to die all throughout Shansee. Her militia just could not reach enough of the millions of inhabitants frequently enough. Compounding the problem, some of her army men began to fall ill from handling of so many dead, decomposing bodies. Others out right deserted, heading off to try to help their own families who were now in dire need as well. Her work force continued to dwindle each week, only compounding the problems.

What started out as her humanitarian efforts to get food to her starving subjects turned violently ugly towards the end of November. With less than half of her men still working long hours in spite of their aching feet, more and more people had become desperate for something to eat, to feed their families. Now the wagons started being attacked and her soldiers killed, as angry mobs stumped or crawled up to them as they entered a block. The mobs grabbed everything edible, leaving the wagon and dead soldiers behind. Some even took the horses, hoping to butcher them for fresh meat!

During the last week of November, Pian was forced to hold up in her palace, while incredibly slow moving mobs of starving, angry citizens roamed the streets, looting any shop that held any remote possibility of housing food. Now army-less, Pian became rightly worried. Daily, she relayed what little more she had learned, now very little, only what her husband could see with his spy glass atop one of the palace buildings. To say that Princess Pian was under stress would be understating it!

When too much bad happens too quickly, one can become temporarily overwhelmed by it and make bad decisions, even if you are ordinarily quite able. On November 30, that happened to Pian. In the middle of the afternoon, she heard gunfire. She headed out of her palace throne room to see if anyone knew what that was all about. She shuffled slowly across the courtyard when one of her remaining aides came stumping along on his toes towards her. His face was ghastly white.

"He's dead! They shot your husband, Princess!" Pian gasped. Slowly, she headed to her aide, who then just as slowly led him to his body where he'd fallen from the roof. A bullet hole was visible in his chest; a blood pool lay around his mangled body. Pian vomited. The aide carefully helped walk her back into the throne room, where Misha, who now had turned twelve looked pale and scared. She'd heard the aide talking and had come here as fast as she could. Seeing her mother sobbing, she feared the worst. "He's dead. Your father's dead," Pian managed to sob to her daughter, who now began to cry as well. The poor aide could only offer them slight comfort.

After some time, Pian ordered someone to lay him in state and to see if there wasn't some wagon still around with which to carry him to the cemetery. She had no idea how anyone could bury him, though. She and Misha leaned their bodies into each other, resting their sobbing heads on each other's shoulders, letting their grief flow.

Near sunset, the aide returned just as Pian heard more gunshots nearby. "Princess, the mob is storming the palace walls! What shall we do? They think that we have a mountain of food inside here, yet we do not."

Pian felt completely overwhelmed now. Only a handful of guards remained and a few aides. She had long ago sent the service women home to their own families. "As long as the gates hold, we should be safe. The men probably cannot climb the walls with their crippled feet," she suggested, hoping that was so. Otherwise — well, that thought was too horrible to think.

A bit later, she heard the sounds of heavy banging on their front gates. She didn't need a guard to tell her what that meant. Eventually, the sturdy gates would succumb, and the mob would overrun her remaining guards. She and Misha would be at their mercy. Misha! She couldn't let anything happen to her daughter!

Just then, a guard came stumbling up to her. "Princess. A wealthy nobleman is at our rear gate in a carriage asking to enter. I have taken the liberty of allowing him inside. The mob is nowhere around that rear gate yet. He is on his way to see you now." She thanked him and wondered why a nobleman would so want to see her now, just as everything was about to crumble down around her.

Don Ho, wearing his finest suit, walked slowly into her throne room. He had spent days perfecting his walk. After all, dancers in the ballets often walked on their toes, why not he? Besides, he had to be the role model for all of his men. If he could walk well, then there was no reason his men also could not. Yes, he moved slowly, but gracefully, as if he'd always walked on his toes.

"Dear Princess Pian! I just heard that your husband has been shot and killed. The mob is about to break down your palace gates even as we speak. I have come to rescue you and your charming young daughter. I can take you to a place of relative safety until this mob action runs its course and it is safe for you to resume your duties. Will you accept my assistance, my Princess? We must act quickly; think of your daughter's safety."

Pian was grieving, overwhelmed, and confused. Yet, she knew that she had to get herself and most of all Misha out of immediate harm's way. "Thank you for your kind offer. Come on Misha, we have to make our escape now." Don Ho put a comforting arm around each still grieving woman. Together, he walked them to his coach and lifted each into the luxurious coach, before climbing in himself.

The ride to the back entrance of the Purple Palace was very short, barely a mile. "I have a room awaiting the both of you. I will hide you away until it is safe. I give you my word that I will look after both you and your daughter's needs, even though food is a little hard to come by now. We all have to tighten our bellies now." He chatted comforting words for the short ride to the rear door of the Purple Palace.

He helped them down, as they were forced to fall out of the carriage into his open arms, catching them under their massive breasts. Then, he took them inside into the lavish bedroom in which Lin Li had stayed her first night here. "Here, you will both be quite safe. I will guard you both with my life. I have left a little fine wine here for you both. Perhaps it will help settle your nerves and bring a restful sleep this night. Tomorrow we shall discuss what we must do next, my Princess."

Pian thanked him and he bowed and left the two alone. He had already poured two small golden cups with wine, the style of cups that he knew his women somehow managed to be able to use. "Mom, can I?" Misha asked. The two drank the wine and pulled back the bedding. While Pian missed her husband's hands, as he always helped her change, as well as Misha, tonight, she decided that they ought to sleep with their clothes on, just in case more bad trouble came and they had to evacuate this establishment.

Pian woke, but it was still completely dark. She didn't remember turning out the lights. Someone must have come in while they were sleeping. Misha. Was she okay? She rolled a little and felt her daughter at her side, and she also woke up. "Mom. It's totally dark in here."

"Someone, someone please, we need our lights relighted, please," Pian called out. She heard the door open and someone enter, a man, most likely from the stumping noise of his boots on the plush purple carpeting.

"Princess Pian, the lights are still on brightly. Welcome to a new, bright day. Both you and your daughter are now my guests. I have taken the liberty of replacing your eyes with new ones, which are far prettier than your old ones. Your new glass eyes are an exquisite yellow-brown, which matches your complexions most perfectly. Indeed, you both look extremely pretty now. If you will rise, I will lead you to the others like yourself. I believe that they are about to be fed their breakfast."

"What? What have you done to us?" Pian screamed. "I am your Princess."

"Mom! Are we blinded?" Misha called out, extreme fear radiated from her young voice.

"Well, that is one way of looking at it, Misha, though I am afraid that you both will be doing no more looking," he snickered as he savored yet another victory. She felt his hands getting her up and then Misha too. He gently ushered the two terrified women out of the room. Ahead, Pian heard voices and smelled hot food. Her stomach growled, although it was tied in a panic knot.

"Ladies, here come the latest additions to your group of most beautiful women with the magnificent yellow-brown eyes. Since none of you can actually see your new companions, allow me to introduce you to Princess Pian Ling Wu and her charming daughter Misha Wu. Dear Misha has just turned twelve. You might wish to wish her a most happy birthday, Most Honorable Ladies." Someone helped Pian sit down, and she heard her terrified daughter being sat down beside her. Someone touched her lips with some fish and rice. Mechanically, she ate.

Later, after the unseen someone had left, Lin Li called out, "Are you really our Princess Pian?" When she said that she was, the other women groaned. Their world was rapidly crumbling now.

"Now that went incredibly smoothly," Don Ho said to his second in command here at the Purple Palace. "I merely spread the rumor to those in the slums that the Princess was hoarding vast amounts of food in her palace, and they did the rest. Of course, suggesting that someone shoot her husband was mere icing on the cake." Both men chuckled. Indeed, for weeks now, Don Ho had been calling in favors from the grateful in the slums. All these years of doling out funds to those needy folks had paid off handsomely. They had gotten rid of the militia for him and now even made it possible to add the Princess herself to his growing collection. Now it was time to add many more women to his collection. Of course, all retained their virginity. Indeed so. One day down the road when he'd finished with his revenge, he planned to hold an auction, selling these magnificent yellow-brown eyed women to the highest bidders. Perhaps, though, he might keep one for himself. But until the auction, their virginity was paramount, for they'd fetch a far, far higher price that way.

"Mommy! I can't see. I'm scared. Please make him give me back my eyes. I can't live like this," Misha frantically cried out. Pian could only sob. She couldn't even see where her daughter was, let alone have her lean on her shoulders. She was too terrified to try to get up and walk; she couldn't see either.

Meanwhile, Lin Li, sensing their terror, which had to be similar to what she had felt, began to chat, telling them her story. When she finished, the other six talked as well. Somehow, the two found a little comfort in this. Although she didn't say anything, Pian was very much relieved to hear that in all the time that these blind women had been here, not one had been raped or molested in any way. In fact, they were fed and their needs attended too, they only had to call out and one of the men would come to assist them.

Not long after that, the men's feet returned to normal. Just days after that, farmers began returning to the city markets, bringing mountains of produce to sell or trade. Wagons of fall harvests began coming into the city. Yet now the city was without its rulers and anarchy reigned. He who was strongest controlled his section of the city.

During the next few days, although none of them could tell the days any longer, three more women joined them, all sharing the terror and fright that each had had. Pian recognized their names! Yan Ti, Hui Don, and Hong Zhau. All three were, if she remembered correctly, somewhere in their late teens or early twenties. More importantly, all were daughters of Low Parliament members!

I had not heard from Pian for days now. Worse, I could not reach her on the LD radio and began to grow worried. Her last reports were dismal to say the least. I sat down and decided to contact her by telepathy. I reached out and zoomed in on her unique wavelength. *Pian. It's Bethany here.* I was not prepared for the rush of terror, anger, and wild emotions that came back on the return of that communication line! Good thing I was sitting down.

Misha and I've been kidnaped by a man called Don Ho. He has blinded us. I think he drugged us and tore out our eyes and put in glass eyes. We are utterly and completely helpless, scared out of our wits. There are others here like us too. Bethany, please, please help me. Help us, I beg you.

That emotional charge nearly caused me to lose the connection! I focused my attention again. No wonder she had not been able to use her telepathy to contact me. You have to be able to focus your attention. I had her tell me all she knew, which she readily did. I pointed out that as long as she was being well treated and not molested, she should relax and learn all that she could about where she was being kept. She had no idea where she and Misha were now. She did calm down considerably, knowing that I knew of her plight. She was not alone any longer. I promised to check in with her every day, and she promised to get her emotional state under control.

I can still cast my ball of fire, but I dare not. I can't see where to put it and risk burning innocents or setting the whole place on fire. I can't use lightning bolts because I know we're indoors somewhere. Well, I can use my Judger spells. Okay, if they try anything nasty on us, I'll go ahead and modify their minds. Until then, perhaps it is best for them not to know that I can do these things.

I agree, Pian. That is wise for now. We'll work something out. From all indications, Shansee has returned to complete anarchy. It might take a small army to punch our way to you. We'll work on it.

Our only contact with Shansee now was via the trains, which still ran between Velona and Shansee. By the end of the year, we learned that an estimated two million people starved to death before the farmers were able to get their fall harvests delivered. Nearly all had lived in the larger cities. At this point, the food issue had stabilized. Men were out fishing once more; farmers markets were populated. Still, the city was in political chaos.

Via other means, word finally came to us about the situation in Wontun Province and Linyi Province. They were even harder hit, because their women had not suffered from the initial plague and had not already survived a year without their arms. Couple that shock with the food crisis and crippled men and you have a recipe for disaster.

Uncounted were the bodies, though rough estimates suggested many millions perished before

December when men's feet returned to normal. In Linyi Province, local government completely broke down. There the four elemental martial arts groups took control of the province. As yet, we do not know if this is good or bad. In Wontun Province, the Emperor and Empress survived, but now only have less than half of their Imperial Army intact. Various overlords have again risen to local power, primarily by doing what was necessary to provide food for the starving, endearing them to the population. Politically, a standoff arose between the High Parliament, Low Parliament of Wontun Province, the Emperor and Empress, and the two dozen provincial overlords. Stalemate. Neither side could effectively rule, and again chaos was the product.

On January 1, 824, I received another surprise telepathic message. We had been trying to figure out what to do about Pian, when it came.

Bethany? This is Fina. Remember me, the Protector of Jemma. Have I got the right Bethany?

Fina! Wow, yes, hello! Great to hear from you. How are you doing?

Not so good. Has the plague struck you? Here, we women have all lost our arms. For a while, men's feet were wiped out, but somehow they've recovered. I took a breath and filled her in completely on all that I knew up to this point, worldwide. For this key information, she was very grateful. News had only been trickling in, very patchy at best.

Well, I am an Olin Master now as well as a Counselor in De An's Church of God. I'm called Shu Wen Chou. My husband, Feng, runs the Olin Masters here in Zau. He's twenty-two and my body is twenty-one now. One of the smartest things that the Olin Masters did was to construct a walled fortress around our main complex. As a result, when all this chaos struck, all of us have been pretty well protected and insulated from the street fighting. Same should be true at the other three main Churches of God, you know in Nan Yan, Shansee, and Lou Yang.

She filled me in on more of the details of what had and was happening there in the Imperial City. None of it was good, however. She had contacted me to ask for some assistance and as usual, I promised her that I would do what I could.

We are an island of calm amid a turbulent sea. Perhaps this can be used, she suggested. She didn't have to tell me, though, that she felt guilty about leaving Jemma on her own this lifetime. Last lifetime, she pledged herself to protecting Jemma, who continued to help bring law and order to Zau. When their bodies grew old and passed on, her love of fighting and now the martial arts had taken over. She allowed Jemma to go her own way, while she pursued her own interests and was now an Olin Master herself. She volunteered her help in rescuing Pian.

Such was the state in Tashien as the new year began, far worse than I had ever imagined. Ania and Kali had been right. The lower toned societies had fallen into Dark Ages, unable to cope effectively with the results of the plague.

Chapter 11 Burning in Hell

In early October, life in Nuadilan, Cyrmy, also known as West Reach, was rich and bountiful. Harvest had begun, bringing long days of work for all. This day, two nineteen year old women were carrying a deer they had just shot deep in the northern woods back to Nuadilan. Friends since early childhood, Brina Gamce and Kaie Treva, long bows across their backs along with their quivers, carried the carcass between them. Both had well-muscled legs and powerful arms, developed from their many years with the long bows. They fancied themselves as *true* hunters, unlike the long gun shooters of today's world. Both women kept their hair cut as short as they dared, often teased as being too boyish. Brina's was jet black, while Kaie's was quite blonde, but both had blue eyes, though Brina's was darker. Both were tall, perhaps too tall, other women of Nuadilan sometimes suggested, when they were hinting that it was high time the two settled down and found a man.

"Aye, once again we proved the bow is mightier than the long guns," Brina commented as the two tromped through the trees, staggering now and then from the weight of their catch.

"Aye, one gunshot and the whole forest flees, where we are totally silent, as it should be. Who wants to eat meat fouled by the deer's fear from the loud shots? Ours is a silent, clean kill, tasty meat," Kaie replied.

"True indeed. Are we going thirds on this?" Brina asked, already knowing the answer. It was two years now since Kaie's older sister had lost her young husband in a hunting accident. Keelin had only been married four years when she was widowed and left to raise their daughter, young Shela, now five years old. Keelin Morgandy was twenty-one. Both she and her daughter had blonde hair as well. Unlike her younger sister, Keelin allowed hers to grow as long as it desired, now falling to the middle of her back. She'd never cut it and often teased her sister, who kept hers so darn short that she almost looked like a man. Since the devastating death of her husband, Keelin, had tried to provide for her daughter and herself by taking in laundry. Ends never met and for two years now, Kaie and Brina had been lending Keelin their support, often in terms of fresh meat, which was too expensive for Keelin's meager budget.

The Treva's lived next door to the Gamce's, while Keelin's home was a block away. Thus, the women remained close physically as well. Indeed, Brina and Kaie were never seen apart, except at bedtimes. Some men thought this was not right and took any opportunity to tease and intimidate the two young women. Few actually dared do it to their faces, though. The last lad who tried received a busted nose in return. Folks did respect the power and strength of these two women.

"Aye, we should. Keelin is having an awful time. Lord knows, I'd never take in men's filthy wash! Ewe! Think of what must be on their sheets and underpants!" Kaie teased. Both grinned, even though they were struggling under the heavy weight of the deer.

Later, the two women carried their deer through the streets of Nuadilan to their house. Many gave them nods of acknowledgment for their kill, especially other women. As usual, they headed on into the small back yard behind Keelin's small frame house. Here, they had the space to do the butchering, plus they already had their block and tackle tied to the lone oak tree, which shaded the yard. Keelin came out, wiping her redden hands on her apron. The long hours in hot soapy waters were slowly taking their toll on her hands. "You got one!" she exclaimed a bit surprised, though she shouldn't be, she thought. When had these two not returned with a kill?

"Aye, sis. Big one this time. Plenty of buttons and picks from this one's antlers and bones. Hope you are ready to dry a third of its meat, sis," Kaie grinned.

"You shouldn't have," Keelin protested as usual. Brina grinned too and that was the end of that. All three knew just how badly Keelin needed the meat. Winter was soon coming.

"Mommy, can I watch," little Shela asked.

"Yes, but stay out of their way. Those knives are sharp and don't get any blood on your dress, I have enough laundry to do," Keelin insisted.

The streets of Nuadilan were dark when the two hunters finally walked up to their front doors. After bowing to each other, a ritual that they had always done since they were five when entering at last their own homes and having to go their separate ways, they simultaneously entered their folk's homes. Their parents were now in their late forties and had given up chiding them for staying out so late. Their older brothers were long married and out on their own. Both women hung up their collection bags, quivers, and bow on the pegs beside the front door and headed into the living rooms where their parents were wont to sit of an evening, prepared to endure another round of why don't you this and that. Often this and that was find a man and settle down.

Their well-ordered world came to an end on October 23, just as it did for everyone else in the world. The first day when their arms had begun to wither and were weak, they speculated that perhaps the plague, which had struck the mainland last year had come to Cymry now. Both sets of parents chided them saying this was pure nonsense. Both had gone to check on Keelin and Shela that day, finding them in just as bad a shape. They even took pity on Keelin, whose arms were so weak that she would be unable to finish the laundry she had taken in. Both pitched in to help her get it done. On their way home, the two hunters made some plans.

"Look, if we do lose our arms like the women on the mainland, we ought to be prepared somehow. We should make sure that everything we need is in our hunting bags. We can sling them over our heads and shoulders and carry our things that way," Brina suggested. That night, they did just that, packing and re-packing what they thought was valuable in their leather bags, which had long loops. Ordinarily, they always slipped them over their shoulders before slipping on their quivers. Both women reasoned that these packs could carry what they needed should this really be the plague. Neither woman, however, had any real sense of what it would be like not to have their arms.

The next day, their universe and everyone else's changed. Shrieks and cries woke both; their mothers had already awakened to find their arms missing. The voices of their fathers added to their sudden fright. As they sat up and discovered their own helplessness, they too reacted with screams. Even their feet were mutilated, they thought at first, as they tried to stand and found that only their toes went flat on the floor.

They found their parents in complete shock and frightened out of their minds, which rather forced them to take charge. Even though their fathers were forced to crawl around on their hands and knees, they insisted that they get them out of their cotton nightgowns and dressed. Wisely, both women insisted on no panties and had their dads put their Sunday dresses on them. Why? Both intuitively realized that if they wore their usual leather pants, they could not possibly go to the bathroom by themselves. At least in a dress, they could manage this necessity.

While their fathers finally crawled off to try to silence the continuous screaming of their mothers, the two headed to their living rooms, discovering the pile of alien objects there. Both immediately went for the shoes. Ah, now they could walk, well sort of. Both fell a couple times, taking their normal strides. Undaunted, with effort they struggled back up and experimented some more. Suddenly, Brina thought of Kaie and begged her father to open their door for her. He was too busy and refused, so she sat down on her butt and spent ten minutes working the latch. When she finally went outside, she made sure that the door stayed wide open so she could get back inside later.

As Brina looked around, she saw no one outside! That had never happened before. She moved slowly over to Kaie's house and stood before the door, wondering how she could get inside. She was about to knock, when the door finally opened, revealing Kaie sitting on her butt, just as she had done to get her own door open. Kaie flashed a grin.

"Wise women think alike," Kaie said to her best friend, nodding her head to Brina's dress. She too had forced her father to put her Sunday dress on her.

"We gotta pee," Brina teased. Kaie smiled.

"Come on. We gotta go check on Keelin and Shela. I bet they are in a whole lot of trouble. They don't have any man in their house. Is your dad all crippled up too?" she asked.

Brina replied that he was. As the two began their slow, careful walk of the block to Keelin's home, they chatted about what had happened to everyone, speculating about what was going on, concluding that it had to be the plague. Brina pointed out that it must be a different plague, because the mainland plague had not harmed men.

"Damn, we can barely walk like this, Brina!"

"At least we can. Dad has to crawl. He can't even stand. Say, what happened to your hair? It is so long now and your boobs. Wow! Some knockers, Kaie," Brina exclaimed, finally noticing the other changes to her friend's body.

"Hey, yours too, look at the size of them. We both need haircuts!" Kaie added. "Damn! How are we going to get in? I hear them crying. Sis! We're coming!" she yelled as loudly as she could.

After a bit of a struggle and by working together, the two managed to get the door opened and awkwardly struggled to their feet once more, teetering on their toes to regain their balance. Inside, they found Keelin and Shela bawling like mad. Somehow, Keelin had gotten into Shela's bedroom and was lying beside her daughter. Their faces were wet, eyes bloodshot. Terror exuded from each.

"It's okay, sis. We're here. Calm down, please," Kaie ordered her older sister.

"We're completely helpless! Our lives are over! I wish we could just die. I can't live like this. Poor Shela, look at her! How can she live like this? Why didn't we just die? Why are we being tortured like this?" Keelin wailed away. If Kaie had had her hands, she would have slapped her sister to bring her out of it. Still, she echoed the same dark thoughts that she and Brina both were having. Why? How could they live like this?

At last, shoving such counter-productive thoughts out of her head, ever-practical Kaie ordered, "Sis, snap out of it. We have to get you changed and Shela too. Come on, we need you to help. We lost ours too. Now come on."

In many ways, the rest of this morning was vitally important for all four of them. Necessity had forced these four to begin to work together to get the two changed and dressed, to begin to do very necessary actions of life. After getting the two into Sunday dresses and into the new strange shoes, the four looked at what else was in the pile of things. Finding the hairbrushes, Brina and Kaie worked on Keelin's now long hair, then Shela's whose hair now fell to her knees.

Keelin then pointed out, "Okay, sis. I guess it's my turn to figure it out. Let me do your hair and Brina's. I do like it longer like this. It is far more attractive, sis." Kaie frowned. Her hair was now below her shoulders, longer than she had ever worn it, Brina's was too.

Shela then complained that she was starving. The three women sighed, realizing that somehow they had to fix something to eat. Again, the three worked together, throwing out various ideas and guesses and an hour later had something hot prepared. All four then sat down and stared at the plates sitting before them. "Do I eat like a doggie?" Shela asked.

Keelin began crying again, feeling that they were reduced to being nothing but dogs now. "Oh knock it off, sis. We still have our feet. How do you suppose all the women on the mainland manage to eat now? Come on; let's see if we can figure it out somehow. Maybe we are supposed to feed each other, I don't know," Kaie spoke up.

At last, they were full and Keelin suggested, "Kaie, do you suppose that mom and dad will let Shela and me come live with you and them again? Dad can then help us."

"Your old room is full of junk now, but I'm sure they would be glad to have you back, at least until this mess gets fixed," Kaie replied.

"You think we'll get our arms back?" Shela asked, hoping so.

Kaie didn't answer that, "Come on; let's go check on mom and dad." The four headed out into the street, but only after making sure that Keelin's door was propped open. They found their parents sitting on the floor, his arms around her. Both were dazed, their eyes red, hopelessness emanated from their faces. Already, they had given up and were waiting for the end to come.

While the sisters tried to get their parents up and active, they soon saw the futility of it. Both were resolved to wait for the end to strike them down. Both were convinced that they would soon be dead. "What's the matter with grandma and grandpa?" Shela asked, wondering why they just sat there on the floor and didn't get up.

"Maybe this isn't such a good idea, Kaie," Keelin whispered. The three women agreed and Keelin and her daughter headed back home, while Brina and Kaie headed over to check on Brina's folks, before heading back to Keelin's.

They found her parents faring little better. Her father was half-crazy ranting about, "Prepare yourselves. Partholan is coming to fetch us to the Underworld. He's coming any minute now. Partholan is nigh upon us now! Prepare yea, prepare yea. Death's scythe is falling upon us all. Cymry will be wiped clean of all of us very soon now."

"Oh good god!" Brina exclaimed. Quietly the two stepped outside. "Wait, let me get my things." She went back inside and using her teeth, she added a few more things to her hunting bag, and then slid it over her shoulder. Kaie took the hint and headed back into her house, likewise adding a few more things to hers, such as a hairbrush, drinking cup, and such. A bit of careful wiggling, her hunting bag slipped off the peg and over her head. Smiling with triumph, she joined her best friend. Together, they slowly walked the block to Keelin's place.

"Who's this Partholan he keeps ranting about?" Kaie asked.

"He's supposed to be the God of the Underworld or something. Mythological of course. Doesn't exist, but some say that he founded Cymry or some such nonsense. Honestly, I think my dad's cracked up."

"Hi again, sis. We're here to stay," Kaie said, much to the relief of Keelin, who now saw that the only help she would have for the immediate future was her sister and Brina.

Several days passed by. With each day, the four gained more confidence and worked out how to do more and more things. One could say that they had no choice but to try to figure out ways of doing the things that were needed to stay alive. That would be correct, for in their case, they had no one else to assist them. These four were fighters, tenaciously holding onto life.

On November 1, their world finally came to an end. It was midnight. Brina and Kaie were sleeping together in the Shela's bedroom, while Shela was sleeping with her mother. All four were sleeping naked, covers piled over themselves. It was just too much trouble to get into their nightgowns. Because Shela's bed was so narrow, Brina and Kaie were lying tightly together, chest to chest. Both young women were rather pleased with the touch, feel, and smell of each other's bodies. Something woke Brina from her dreams of Partholan, a nightmare sight of some giant of a man walking towards her from a cloud of thick smoke, beyond which her eyes could not penetrate. Smoke. She coughed and roused. Smoke. Smoke. She smelled real smoke.

Now, she heard distant screaming voices and became fully conscious. Had Partholan actually come? A thin gauze of smoke filled the room and she coughed again. Fire! Brina screamed loudly, "Fire! Wake up! Fire!" She got up and slipped on her shoes. Kaie woke, coughed, and recognized smoke too.

They had left a lantern going in the living room, serving as their nightlight. Had it caught the house on fire? The two shuffled to there, cursing their impossibly slow speed. No, the lantern still burned low, the lamp-blackened globe cast a dim light in the room. As always, they had left the front door open, and tonight that act probably saved their lives. Smoke was coming into the house from outside. Keelin and Shela slowly came into the room, fear on both their faces. "Oh thank god! I thought our lantern had caught the house on fire," Keelin said very much relieved.

However, they all now saw flickering yellow hues coming in from the front door and moved instinctively there to look outside. Nothing could have prepared them for the ghastly sight that met their eyes. Nuadilan was on fire! All around them, homes were burning. Here and there, they saw men crawling on their knees, escaping the flames. Several women stumbled onto the street, their hair and nightgowns flaming, their shrieks chilled the four to their bones, as they stood petrified. Voices screamed, "Partholan has come! Partholan has come!"

The worst fear of a town had come true, fire. With wooden buildings built so closely together, fire was the one thing that everyone feared. Normally, the men would band together, rush the water wagons to the blazes, and try to contain the flames. Now, the men could do nothing but crawl like pathetic mongrel dogs. Flames leapt from house to house right before their eyes. The four stared in complete disbelief until hot embers landed on the thatched room of Keelin's home.

"Oh my god! It's on your roof! Keelin, we have got to get out of here," Brina yelled.

"Gather up what we absolutely can't live without!" Kaie yelled. The four headed inside and sat down, hastily helping each other put on their now dirty Sunday dresses. Then, they went from room to room, picking a thing here and there, carrying them between their teeth back to their packs by the front door. About twenty minutes later, the blazing roof gave way, dropping a mass of flamed into the upper level of the home, their storage area. Part of it came on down, smashing to the floor close to where Keelin and Shela were trying to bring two water bags with them. Shela fell to the ground, the flames nearly touching her legs. The terrified girl could not get back onto her feet, continually trying to use the arms that she no longer had. Keelin just screamed and screamed for Shela to get up.

Brina was closest to the pair and moved as quickly as she could to help them. "Get up and get out of here, Keelin. I'll bring Shela," she yelled her orders. Sliding on her butt using her feet, Keelin's body obeyed, though her mind refused to work. Brina bit down on Shela's dress and began pushing off with her powerful legs. Slowly she dragged the terrified five year old out of the flames, just as more of the floor above them collapsed, crashing to the floor where the girl had lain moments before. Heat seared at Brina's face, but she continued pushing the two out of the room. At last, a safe distance away, she helped the girl to her feet and then struggled to get herself up as well. Both headed to the living room and the escape that beckoned to them from the opened front door.

As they got to the door, all three women wiggled and twisted with the leather hunting packs still hanging on the pegs. One by one, the straps slipped off and over the heads of the three women. Boom! Half of the ceiling thundered down, burying the two bedrooms in an explosion of fiery flames. The four headed out of the front door just as the remainder of the upper ceiling fell to the floor where they had just been standing. Hot, burning heat flew out at them, pushing their long hair out towards the street.

Moving as fast as their three-inch footsteps would allow, while wigging to maintain their balance as they tried to move too quickly, they got into the middle of the street and stopped horrified by the sights around them. In all directions, brilliant flames crackled and thrust their hungry tentacles upwards towards the sky above. To their right, part of a home collapsed, falling out into the street, jarring them into action once more. "We have to get out of the city!" Brina screamed. "This way." The four began their slow shuffle down the street, moving this way and that around the burning remains of other houses, parts of which had fallen onto the streets.

"Lead on, Brina. I'll keep an eye on the houses we pass. It's an inferno!" Kaie yelled. Keelin looked after Shela, urging her daughter to try her best to keep up with them. No doubt about it, Shela's short legs were slowing them all down, Keelin also knew that her daughter was only five and would tire soon. Would they all just leave her here to burn in this inferno from Hell?

For the four, their nightmare only grew worse, for Nuadilan had been built to withstand an assault. Wooden pilings forming a stockade encircled the city. Worse, there were now ten of these concentric stockade rings. Each ring had only four entrances and from ring to ring, the entrances were staggered so that an invading army, having just broken down one gate could not ride straight up to the next one. Instead, they would have to travel around an eighth of the distance to the next gate, attacked all the way from the inner ring. For the four and the others who were trying to flee the inferno, this protection threatened to keep them inside the burning city, roasting them alive like pigs on a hearth.

Twice, Brina found their way blocked by flames and fallen debris, forcing them to retreat and try for another gate. On the positive side, many men had crawled to the gates ahead of them and had opened them, trying to crawl their way to safety. Had the four arrived at a closed gate, they may have well been consumed by the heartless, relentless flames that were rapidly consuming the entire city of some forty thousand.

Worse, the four could only move excruciatingly slowly. Acrid smoke often blocked their vision, seared their eyes, which watered continuously now. "North Gate!" Brina screamed, trying to be heard above the blazing inferno around them. After an eternity in Hell, Brina finally stepped through the North Gate, setting foot just outside the outermost stockade, free from the all-consuming fires at last. Coughing and hacking, the other three stepped out beside her. It had taken them an hour to escape the city walls. "Come on, we're not safe yet," she ordered.

Now Brina and Kaie were on very familiar ground. Ever since they were ten, they had been out roaming the surrounding countryside. They knew every nook and cranny so to speak of the nearby forest. "Hey, we can camp at Shady Glen," Kaie called out. This was their name for a particularly secluded, picturesque spot, although at this time of year, many trees had already dropped their leaves. Most oaks still retained their browned leaves, however. The location was about three miles into the forest just north of Nuadilan.

Brina led them on unerringly. She or Kaie could find this spot in their sleep; it was their favorite spot to sit and daydream. While they didn't realize it yet, in their strange new heels, walking on the uneven, rough terrain would be exceedingly difficult, forcing them to move vastly slower. Nighttime only made matters worse, as they prepared to take some sixty thousand tiny steps.

They had not gone far before Shela fell, too exhausted to rise or continue. All along, Keelin feared this would happen. Now she was ready to just give up herself and sit with Shela until the end came at last. Perhaps this Partholan was real and would soon come to claim herself and her daughter.

"Okay, we're going to have to carry her," Kaie declared. "I'll go first. You two, see if you can get her up. I'll lean way over and try to carry her on my back." Ten frantic minutes later, Shela was now sitting on her aunt's back, her legs wrapped tightly around Kaie's chest just above her large breasts, which now had a real purpose, helping support the little girl. Kaie had to remain rather bent over, because Shela had no way to hang on.

"Damn, this is making walking almost impossible," Kaie whispered to Brina.

"Take it slow, one step at a time. When you get too tired, I'll take over," her dear friend suggested. Onward continued the women's nightmare, seemingly endlessly.

Dawn's first rays came just as they finally entered the sheltered glen. All three had taken turns carrying the child, exhausted beyond measure. Their feet ached and they simply collapsed upon the bed of soft leaves and fell into a deep sleep. They were at least still alive.

"Mommy, over here?" Shela roused the three women. It was now late afternoon. Shela had awakened to find herself in a small, secluded glen and had gone exploring. She found the small spring, which came bubbling nearby the glen and had been drinking the cool, clear water. Of course, she had knelt down and drank much as a dog might. Her hair had fallen in and was sopping wet.

The three rose and looked at each other. Their faces were covered with blackish smears. Soot covered their dresses, and their hair was a mess of tangles and soot. They laughed at their filthy appearance. Never had they ever been so dirty.

The three joined Shela but soon had to spit out black soot from their mouths. Soon they were also inhaling water in their noses and blowing out soot as well. For days afterwards, they still coughed up smoke residue. At least all four managed to get their faces cleaned off and their parched thirst quenched. Now they were hungry.

"Let's see what all we managed to bring with us," Brina suggested hopefully. Between the three of them, they estimated that they had perhaps three days of dried fish, carrots, and apples. Well, it was a start.

"So now what do we do?" Brina asked, while they were chewing on the fish. "We can't go back to Nuadilan. There's nothing left but ashes."

"Well," Keelin volunteered, "we could always go to our cousin's place up in the Highlands. I'm sure that Fergus d'Aine would take us in and help us out. Otherwise, I haven't got any ideas at all."

"That's a good twenty-five miles away and across the Daneas River," Kaie complained. "How far can we go on foot? The way our feet are now, it's almost impossible to walk at all. I can't carry Shela much more. My feet are still aching from last night. We can't make it on just two day's food."

"Across country, we have maybe only twenty-one more miles to go. If we can manage to walk three miles each day, we are looking at seven days with only food for two," Brina pointed out. "Surely, we can't starve to death in five days." She sounded a hopeful note.

"Well, if we just had our long bows," Kaie began to say, thinking of doing a little hunting to get some rabbits for meals. She realized that even if she had her bow, it would be useless to her now. That sharp realization brought tears to her eyes again. She'd never be able to shoot her bow again, nor even hunt.

Brina added, "How would we even butcher anything that we caught? I can't hold my knives any more. We have to think outside of our normal ways, that's all."

"Berries!" Keelin exclaimed. "We can perhaps find berries that are still around. Maybe we can find some wild roots too. Br. I am getting cold. We should have brought a blanket along."

"Damn, we are likely to freeze. It is now early November after all," Kaie added to their misery, knowing that snow was more than likely any day now, though it ought to have snowed already.

"We can use leaves as our blankets," Brina said suddenly inspired. "We travel by day and look for a place to spend the night where there are a lot of leaves, like right here. Come on, before it gets too dark." As night fell on Layamon, the four were snuggled close together and had used their feet to cover themselves with many of the leaves in the glen. Although still chilled, they didn't freeze. At dawn and after another long drink from the creek, they set out on their hike to the Highlands of Ruadan.

Late the sixth day, they finally encountered the gravel road that led on up into the Highlands. Ahead they saw the stone bridge over the wide Danaes River, which separated Layamon from the Highland of Ruadan. Another day ahead of them was the small town of Denholm, where their cousin lived. Years ago, the successive Kings d'Aine had lived there in a fortified castle. Now the castle was crumbling and the first heir to the throne, Fergus d'Aine and his wife Rona lived there.

On November 8, the four women staggered up to the gates of the old castle, hoping and praying that their cousin would save them. Half starved, completely filthy, the four looked as miserable as they felt. A gate man crawling about on his knees let them in and crawled off to inform Fergus. An anxious ten minutes passed, as the four waited until they saw their cousin, reduced to crawling himself, coming their way.

"Fergus! It's us, Keelin and Kaie. Please, we need your help! Nuadilan has burned to the ground!"

"Keelin? Kaie? Lassies, is that really you? Oh my god! Come on in, come, dear lassies. How did you get here? Burned? God, this is worse than I expected. Come, come lassies. Sorry, I canna walk anymore," the twenty-five year old highlander exclaimed.

His twenty-three year old wife, Rona, wearing the traditional Highlander plaid dress, came walking slowly up behind Fergus. Her five year old daughter, Tam, walked at her side. Behind her, another cousin, Zena, followed. She was twenty-four. All four had fiery red hair, a gift from their ancestor, Fionna of Cuch Glen, Ket Bethany's sister. Like Keelin, Zena was widowed, having lost her husband some years back. Fergus had kindly taken her in under his wing. Now he prepared to do the same with his cousins and their young friend.

"My god! What happened to you?" Rona exclaimed as she saw the four filthy women. While they were led inside the great hall, Kaie explained what had happened and how they got here. All the d'Aine's were very much impressed that they had somehow managed to walk all that distance and with no food or blankets.

Several hours later, after a long hot bath, dressed in simple plaid dresses, the four joined Fergus at his Great Table for a hot meal, which he had prepared. Most all of his staff had been sent to their own homes, attempting to deal with their own families. Only the old gate man remained. Fergus had been doing his best to tend to the needs of his wife, daughter, and sister, but it had been trying for him and for them as well.

Fergus had taken on the assignment from his father to rebuild the old ancestral castle here at Denholm. They'd been at the project for three years now. "Lassies, you are so lucky that we're here," he kept saying, thanking the stars that he had been here to rescue his cousins.

"Mommy, they have such red hair!" Shela whispered a bit too loud.

"Aye, little lassie, that we do indeed, and proud of it," Rona replied. Her flaming hair now fell to just below her knees, as did Zena's. Tam's was below her shoulders.

"Cousin, are we going to be safe here?" Keelin asked what most concerned her now.

Fergus sighed. "Lassie, nothing in this world of ours is certain, not anymore. After what yea have all been through, I'd like nothing more than to say you will be safe here for evermore, but lassie, but I just don't know anymore. Our food supply is about gone, though I suppose I can crawl into town and see about getting more, but no shops are open. Streets are deserted — been so since the plague struck. I know some have died. There are ghastly bodies in the streets. I sent off a dispatch rider to the king, my dad, some fifteen days ago, but haven't heard back. Should have heard something eight days ago. Must be terrible everywhere. We have some food reserves, but they are stored up high. I'm going ta need a ladder to get to 'em. Have ta see about that soon."

He went on, "People are a'doing crazy things now. Some claim that Partholan has come. Others of that damnable Church of Jehosanity are saying that the Days of Judgment have come, which I take it means pretty much the same thing — that the end of the world has come."

"Now enough of this gloomy talk, lassies. Rona, you take them up to the guest rooms and see that they get all settled in. I expect these lassies are tireder than tireder." Keelin smiled, now full for the first time in weeks, she was terribly sleepy. A while later, she fell sound asleep amid the soft comfort of a warm bed, secure finally.

In the next room, Kaie and Brina lay beneath the warm covers, their melon sized breasts touching each other. Brina whispered, "Kaie, I want you to know that I love you as the sister that I never had. I will always look after you. You can count on me, depend on me."

"I know, Brina, I love you too," she hesitated a moment and decided to risk all. "More than just a sister." She gave Brina a passionate kiss. "I've wanted to do that for years," she admitted, thankful that Brina could not see her blushing face in the near dark of the bedroom.

"Me too," Brina whispered back, suddenly elated and electrified. She returned Kaie's passionate kiss. "I love you too. Looks like you and I will never get a chance at a man now. What man in his right mind would want us like this? We're almost helpless. It's just you and me, Kaie. I will always be here for you."

"Me too, Brina. I'm here for you, just as if we were married. Honestly, no man is going to want us now. So it's got to be just you and me, together from now on." The two continued to let their long withheld passions flow.

Bang! Bang! Gunshots roused both women. They sat up and listened for more, their tranquility shattered in an instant. Screams. "That sounds like Rona! Come on!" Brina exclaimed, getting out of bed. The two were naked and paused for a moment, wondering if they ought to take time to get their new dresses on somehow. Rona screamed for help so they just slipped on their shoes and headed out of the room, hoping to follow the screams in this unfamiliar castle.

Keelin stepped out of her room, naked as well, little Shela right behind her, their faces twisted in fright once again. "We'll go see. You get dressed if you can," Kaie called out to her sister. Rona yelled again and the two took their bearings and headed towards the voice. Moving as quickly as they dared, the two took a couple of wrong turns before they ran into Zena, who had just gotten up as well. Like them, she had been unable to dress and was trying to walk as fast as she could, her flaming locks acting as a dress.

"This way," she called out, the two followed her, thankful for a guide at least. Minutes later, they walked out onto the cobblestoned commons. Ahead covered by her thick, curly red hair, Rona squatted. Nearby the broken parts of a long gun lay on the stones. As they drew closer, they saw that she was beside Fergus, who lay sprawled on the stones.

"He's been shot and he fell from up there," Rona wailed, as the three women arrived at her side. Fergus had a bleeding hole in his chest. He looked terrible, Brina thought. The three women squatted down beside the two.

"We're completely pathetic!" Brina whispered what she felt. Oh, how she longed to reach out with her hands to help Fergus in his time of need, to stop the bleeding, to carry him inside, to help him somehow. All she could do was squat down over him, watching the life flow from his body.

"I feel so helpless," Kaie whispered back. "What can we do?"

Just then, Fergus regained consciousness, "Rona! Rona, you must take our find to Bethany on the mainland. Promise me, Rona. You will take them all and our find to Bethany. Nothing is more important than that. Rona, promise me."

"I promise Fergus. I promise, but we have to help you somehow," Rona said as her crying continued unabated.

Perhaps he had not heard her, he whispered, "Promise me, Rona. Get our find to Bethany." He seemed to pass out or pass away; none could be sure; they had no hands to feel for a pulse.

If that wasn't enough, something came flying high over the walls, catching their attention. Then, another. Flaming torches! In horror, Rona saw them land on the newly thatched roof of the Great Hall. Brina and Kaie panicked again. They were being burned out of this home as well.

Outside, some man was yelling. "The Day of Judgment is at hand. Prepare to meet Lord Jehosa's Holy Wrath!" If this wasn't enough, the gates burst open and a rider wearing the blue tunic with white cross came charging in, burning torch in his hand, lobbing it onto the roof as well.

As he rode up towards the women, Brina's anger peaked. She jumped up right in front of his horse. The effect was just as she predicted. The spooked horse reared up high, the rider, unprepared, fell off the back, landing hard on the cobblestones. Brina and Kaie rushed towards him — rushed as fast as their tiny steps would allow. Brina kicked him as hard as she could in his crotch. Kaie stomped hard down on his exposed neck. Brina continued to kick and Kaie continued to stomp, as if venting their anger at the entire world!

"Stop, Brina. Stop. He's dead," Zena called out, moving to push her body into theirs to get them to cease.

"Bastard," Brina spat on him.

"Come on, we have to get dressed and get our things and get out of here before the place burns down," Zena ordered. "We have some time; we're on the first floor, and the fire is way up there on the fifth. Come on before it's too late. Already Rona was at the door heading inside; the three followed her. Already there were commotions out in the streets, and people were screaming Fire! Fire!

It took the women a while to get their new plaid dresses on and their few things packed. Brina then led Kaie, Keelin, and Shela back out into the courtyard, where they were surprised to find the old gate man had a wagon hitched for them. "I've loaded it with blankets, food, and water, lassies," he explained. "I'll drive yea out of here as soon as the Lady is ready."

With a good deal of wobbling and obvious pain in his toes, the old man helped the four into the back of the wagon. Not long after that, Rona, Tam, and Zena came out of the door, two large sacks draped across their shoulders. Brina smiled; they had taken her advice and stowed things in hunting bags, about the only way that they could now carry anything. "Quickly, quickly," the old man motioned to the three. It seemed like they were not moving; yet their strange shuffling motions indicated that they must be in action, so slow were their steps, Brina thought.

"We are utterly pathetic now, useless beyond useless. Why are we even bothering?" she thought to herself. After what seemed an eternity amid the growing flames behind them as the Great Hall was now totally in flames and wild cries of voices throughout the town behind them, the three got to the wagon. The old man again ignored the crippling pain in his feet, as he lifted each into the bed of the wagon. Now he hobbled his way back to the front ready to climb aboard and get these women to safety.

He didn't make it. Horse hooves upon the stone echoed loudly. Brina and Kaie, who were sitting with their backs to the driver's seat rose and turned to see yet another of these wicked Church of Jehosanity riders. In horror, they watch him aim it at the old man, "The Day of Holy Judgment is upon us all!" Bang! A puff of black-grey smoke appeared around the barrel. From the corner of her eye, Brina saw the old man fall to the ground.

At that instant the two horses bolted, pulling the wagon ahead into the rider. Frantically with one hand, he tried to pivot his horse around. Halfway turned, their horses and wagon banged into the butt of the horse, which reared suddenly to get out of the way. As if in slow motion, Brina saw the blue tunic sail through the air. An awful sounding crunch followed, ending that man's life, as the wagon pitched out into the street, wildly out of control.

All around them, buildings were in flames. People were fleeing their homes, men crawling upon the ground. Chaos was everywhere, which only spooked the horses all the more. On their own, they headed first down one street and then another, finally settling on the road that led south out of the city, the very road that the four had walked to get here yesterday.

"Come on, we have to stop them," Brina called out to Kaie. The two women climbed over the low railing and got onto the driver's bench. The reins were still there, tied to two posts. Now what?

"Try to wrap them around your leg and pull back," Brina suggested. With effort and a lot of wiggling, the two got their legs around the reins and pulled back feebly, all the while calling out, "Whoa, whoa, whoa." At last, the horses calmed down and began simply to walk along at a very slow pace. Brina and Kaie breathed a sigh of relief.

"Now what do we do?" Kaie called out. "What did Fergus want us to do? Where are we supposed to go now? No sense heading south, Nuadilan is gone."

Zena answered, "Fergus wanted us to go to the mainland. Velona, I think. Without old Argus, how are we to do that?"

"We make for the coast. No sense heading south. Let's try for Banna on the coast. Take the first left," Rona finally spoke up, coming out of her shock at last. "We make for the coast and hop a ferry to the mainland. It's three days to the coast along the Arranagh Creek. Have we got any money to buy passage?"

Money? Brina grinned. What good was money now? No store was open. The world was burning down. More importantly, you could not eat it. Thinking of food, she was suddenly hungry. A bit later, the two halted the horses and climbed into the bed, where the others had rummaged through what old Argus had packed for them. Brina and Kaie stared at the inviting apples.

Kaie had an idea. "Here, I'll hold it for you." Kicking off her shoes, using her feet, she got an apple up and held it for Brina to eat. Yes, she looked a bit silly, lying on her back, her feet up in the air supporting the apple, but Brina could now eat it easily. Grinning, the other women duplicated her.

"Lots easier eating it this way," Brina commented. For a while, they took turns feeding each other. Then, the two climbed over the back of the seat, wrapped their legs around the reins, and got the horses moving again.

An hour later, they came upon a small Layamon village. Smoldering ashes with curls of grey smoke drifted upwards. Only the clop-clop of their horses' hooves broke the eerie stillness surrounding this place. No one said a word, but Brina and Kaie had their legs full, attempting to steer the horses and wagon around the dead bodies lying here and there in the street. Everyone was glad when they left the other end of the village. Rona whispered, "I knew a dozen who lived there."

Later that afternoon, the two wisely detoured around the next town. When dusk began to fall, they halted and discussed what to do now. They could not unhitch the horses nor could they tie them up. Everyone feared losing them in the night if they climbed down and camped nearby. In the end, they decided not to part with their wagon, but sleep in it as they could. Brina and Kaie drove the horses off the road to where there was a good stand of grass and stopped, hoping the horses would be content to graze and not head off on their own while they slept.

After again helping each other to a meager supper, they managed to drag some blankets out and over themselves, all huddled up against each other for added warmth against the cold November night. So it went for two more days and nights, until they reached the small port of Banna. As they crested the last ridge and spotted the village against the sea, they breathed a sigh of relief. The village had not burned, not yet anyway.

Later they rode down the hill into Banna, but not a person was on the streets. Lights shone from windows, smoke drifted upwards from many chimneys, people still lived, but nothing was opened. Of course, they all knew why. They drove down to the small docks, where they spotted dozens of small fishing vessels, none of which could take them across to the mainland.

All but one, that is. The Kilberry read the name on the side of a single-masted sailing craft, a thirty-footer. It looked like it might do and they pulled the wagon up to it and stopped. "Now what?" asked Brina, who had never seen a boat before.

Rona declared, "Well, I should go make some inquiries. See if I can find the owner and book us passage."

"But we don't have a coin among us," Zena protested.

"We've a perfectly good wagon and horses. Trade, I hope." Rona carefully scooted down off the wagon, with the others watching how she did it. They watched as Rona moved slowly to the front door of a building, knocked on it with her foot and waited patiently. They were too far away to hear what was said, but since she moved on down the docks, they guessed whoever answered didn't own the boat.

A bit later, they spotted Rona returning. Behind her, a huge man followed them, his arm resting on the shoulders of another woman who was helping him keep his balance while walking on his toes. When she was close enough, she called out encouragingly, "This is Axel and his wife Sabrina. Axel will take us over to d'Grange in the morning, I hope." Brina and Kaie saw at once that he was one of the Axemen who had settled here on Cymry. He was huge, as far as they were concerned.

"Aye, fine wagon, good pair of horses. More than enough for me to risk it," Axel declared after looking over the horses and wagon.

Sabrina added, "You can stay in our guest room tonight. I am afraid it will be overly crowded, but I am so helpless now. If it weren't for my Axel here, I'd of died already. Have you any news to share?"

Axel helped them get their things unloaded and Rona let them have the remainder of their supplies in exchange for the hot meal the Axel fixed for them. They spent an hour relating all the dismal news, which shocked the two considerably. Before they left in the morning, Axel made sure that he had ample food prepared for Sabrina and that she could somehow manage for the two days that he'd be gone. She assured him that she would be all right.

"Oh my god!" Brina exclaimed as the bobbing vessel got underway. Without arms to hold onto anything at all, she was more than a little spooked. So were the others, for that matter. Axel told them to just lie down and perhaps sleep a little. He grinned at the landlubbers on their first voyage. He did cover them with a number of blankets. It was quite cold out here on the sea. Already ice had begun to build up around the edges of the docks. Another couple of weeks and he would not have been able to make this run. As it was, he was gaining a valuable wagon and horses, something that he had a suspicion he may well need, if things got any worse. At least he could flee inland with Sabrina now, though he would hate to leave his boat behind. Well, he could always build another boat, but he could not replace Sabrina, which is why he took this gamble of a late crossing to the mainland.

Late that day, he sailed into Fortress d'Grange, depositing them safely on the docks there. It was November 13. "What do we do now? Walk to Velona, wherever that is?" asked Brina, now totally lost and in a strange world full of towering stone fortress walls, mighty spires of stone, all facing the ocean. At least there were a few men and women about, the men leaning on the women for support.

Rona took charge. "Come on. It's time I used my heritage card. We must seek an audience with their monarch. If I recall Fergus right, it is Leroy d'Grange. Come on. Let's start asking people we see."

Sometime later, the small group was led into a lavish Great Hall. Trumpeters sounded and a man spoke loudly, "Rona d'Aine, First in Line to the Throne." She'd played the last card that she had. A middle-aged couple was dining, and the man rose awkwardly.

"Hail and well met, Rona d'Aine. Please, come join my wife and I. We were just having supper. Will you need some hands to help you eat?" he asked politely.

Rona smiled, her stomach desired food. "Thank you, sir. Yes, we are starving. We come seeking aid and bearing ill news, I am afraid. And yes, I surely don't know how we can possibly manage on our own."

Before long, several men, young and old, came slowly into the room, hanging on to wives or girlfriends for support. While they dined, Rona told him all that had happened and what the dying orders of her husband had been. Of course, he asked many probing questions and was aghast at the severity of the destruction occurring on Cymry.

"Of course, I need to report all this to Bethany and Stefano in Velona. If you will follow me, you can talk to her yourself," he said as they all finished. None of them had the slightest idea what he meant, but fell in behind him as he leaned on his wife and began heading to an adjoining room.

"Here is our LD radio system. It allows us to talk to anyone who has one of these, anywhere on Tarra."

"What are these strange torches? They burn but I see no flames?" asked Brina, baffled by the electric lights.

"Marvelous invention of the DAE down in Velona. Electric lights, they are called. d'Grange calling Velona. d'Grange calling Velona, come in please," he spoke into the device.

To say that the women were shocked when they heard my voice coming through the speaker would be an understatement. Brina let out a squeal of surprise. I said, "Hi Leroy, Bethany here, filling in for Stefano tonight. What's up?"

"I've got Rona d'Aine here from the Highlands of Ruadan. Lots of news from West Reach, all dismal, I'm afraid. Her husband, Fergus, was murdered a couple days ago and his dying words were orders to bring something to you. Shall I put her on?"

"Damn, murdered by whom?" I asked.

Leroy whispered, "Just talk normally, Rona."

She began hesitatingly, "Some Church of Jehosanity men shot him as they rode through our town torching our homes." Slowly, Rona related what had happened and that Fergus had ordered her to bring me something that they had found.

I replied, "Leroy, put them on the next train to Velona. I'll meet them at the station."

The next morning, the women stared at the huge steam engine and cars. Great clouds of steam and smoke rose into the clear blue sky. What wonder was this? The ten-hour trip was most memorable for all them. They had never seen anything like this before. When the train began its approach into Velona, the city, they were in even greater awe. The sheer size of our city dwarfed anything on Cymry. As they moved slowly through the city, they saw motor-wagons, motor-cars, noisy putt-putts and T-putt-putts driven by women such as them, armless, driving these three-wheeled vehicles about at a good clip using only their feet. Yes, there were also the usual horse drawn carriages and wagons too.

I met them at the station, with Marco at my side, his arm over my shoulders, beneath my very long hair. "Wow! Look at the flaming hair!" he whispered as they carefully climbed down from their car.

I yelled "Over here." Images of my sister Fianna when I was Ket Bethany came back into my mind. For a moment, I wondered what ever happened to her.

Rona d'Aine took charge, stepping a little before the others. "Hello. I'm Rona d'Aine."

"Hi, Bethany Bartiana Angela. My husband, Marco. I hope you enjoyed your first train ride. Come on, you are going to be staying at my mansion for a while. Such flaming red hair!"

She and Zena smiled. Theirs was nearly as long as my raven locks. I knew that we shared a love of long hair. "What is this thing that moves without horses?" she asked what they all wanted to know. I had Marco explain about the motor-car that he was helping us all into now. Engines and motors were not my specialty. As long as my T-putt-putt started, that's all I cared to know about them now.

While Marco drove us home, I pointed out the sights and explained about all the marvelous things that we had been taking for granted. "Oh, you all will just have to try out my T-putt-putt," I insisted. A while later, Marco helped us out and I moved close to him, so he could slide his arm over my shoulders. "Only way our fellows can walk is if we provide the balance support that they need. I figure in time, they will learn how to walk again, just as we have to learn new ways to do just about everything. Come on, I'll introduce you to the whole gang and then we can have some tea and see what Fergus so wanted me to see."

An hour later, with mom heading off with the two little girls to find things for them to play with, Rona, her companions, and I sat down for tea at our low tables. I showed them how to manage and they grinned and began to try it themselves. Rona then related her story more fully.

"Fergus and I took on the challenge of restoring the ancestral castle, which has been in decay for at least a century. What a project that has been, but now it's burned down." Tears of grief came and I allowed her time to regain her composure. "While we were doing the renovations, we chanced to uncover a secret chamber, where records were stored and came upon this scroll. We read it and decided that it must be very important. Fergus and I planned to bring it to you come spring. It is so hard to get a ship out of Cymry in the winter; everything is iced over. Then, he got killed. . ." She began to cry once more and I knew that soon I would have to run a therapy session for her and probably these others too.

"Look at the signatures first, then read it," she said softly.

I did so. It was signed, Lia Ines Amir and Fianna d'Aine! Boy did I ever have flashbacks! My delightful sister, Fianna! She'd married my friend Fergus and become Queen Fianna. Lia Ines, she was the incredible armless woman whom my son, Taliesin Amir, the famous bard and musician, had married something like two centuries ago. Voices from two hundred years in the past were now speaking to me in the present. My eyes watered, and I explained to Marco and the others the significance of the two names. Then, I read aloud the letter.

Dearest Bethany,

Lia Ines and I are on a spring vacation. It's May of 660 now. I am writing this because Lia has a hard time writing much, obviously. Anyway, Taliesin and Fergus have brought us to the Standing Stones near the city of Brea, where King Lachlan Laird used to rule and now her niece Cerys Laird is in charge. It's the same Standing Stones where that ancient Sacred Talisman of Lachlan appeared, the one that Fergus rescued and that you eventually handed down to Cerys.

Anyway, Lia Ines and I went off exploring these immense and mysterious stones, while the fellows went on into Brea on some business of their own. Mostly all this is Lia Ines' doing.

While we were wandering among the stones, she found one stone that seemed to draw her to it. There appeared to be a sort of human form molded into it, her kind of from, like that of an armless woman. She rather walked into the hollow spot, seeing if her body matched the shape. I was standing there beside her, thank god.

Anyway, the strangest thing happened to her and me. It seemed that the ground opened up and we fell far into the ground, though we landed as if we had not even taken a step. Lia Ines says that we were in an underground chamber, but I am not so sure. It was huge anyway. Then the strangest thing happened. It was as if some voice spoke to us, though we saw no one around us at all, yet the chamber was illuminated by means neither she nor I can explain.

Dalny? My long lost Dalny? Have you returned to me, my love? That's what it said to Lia Ines or rather what she says appeared in her mind. Lia Ines says this Dalny must be a woman, but she can't say why she thinks that.

Then Lia Ines says that she felt a mind or something touching hers. She felt intense sorrow and the idea: No, you are not my Dalny. Yet you so resemble her. Go now and I will look after you, you who are the image my long lost Dalny. After that, we appeared on the surface, not far from that same Standing Stone. She swears that there is some living being there that we encountered and a very, very old one at that.

We know that the Standing Stones are all on points of power, Fergus told us that, but you would know about that better than we do, brother. Lia Ines thinks that we have stumbled upon something that might be really, really important. Can there be beings around who do not have bodies? Lia Ines thinks that we ran into one. So I am writing all this down for you. I am not sure when I can get this letter to you, but we'll see that it does somehow get to you.

Your loving sister, Fianna d'Aine and your sister-in-law, Lia Ines Amir

Incredible. I had tears of joy and remembrance streaming down my cheeks, which Marco kindly dabbed with his handkerchief. I had to do a lot of explaining, not only for Marco's sake but also for the women who had endured such hardships to get this to me. I also realized that the dying Fergus also saw this as a way for his wife and child to survive this current calamity. Smart fellow.

Now on top of everything else that I was dealing with worldwide, this intriguing letter beckoned me to Cymry. I knew that I had to go. Why? The form! Lia Ines was as armless as we were. Why had her letter only now come to me, nearly two hundred years late? Was there yet a fourth alien race working behind the scenes? My curiosity was pricked rather badly.

However, I had to handle our new guests. Brina, Kaie, Keelin, and Shela had lost everything they owned. Penniless and with nowhere to live and no one to help them with their needs, I just had to step in. Perhaps in time, Fergus' brother, the King d'Aine, could help his widow, niece, and sister, Zena. Until then, they too needed my assistance in order to survive.

I then told them, "Okay, I cannot express my thanks enough for receiving this letter. It may well be vitally important to us all. In the meantime, all of you are my guests here in Velona. You may stay here with us as long as you desire. We will all help you in any way that we can. The starting point is to have each of you read my helpful hints book." Interestingly enough, when I went to get them some copies, bringing them back into the room using my small willow yoke, I found that somehow they had been translated into their own languages. The Guardian was certainly being most helpful!

We made up the guest bedroom and Giovanni and Eve moved in with Marco and me, giving their room to Brina, Kaie, Keelin, and Shela. We were a little crowded for the moment. After all the hustle and bustle of getting these guests settled in, Marco and I discussed the significance of the letter. He was as intrigued about it as I was. Yet, how could we get away and check it out right now? The world was crumbling and it was certainly anything but safe to journey across to West Reach now. How many things could I handle at one time, I wondered?

Chapter 12 Long Range Plans Begin

Most of November I spent coping with all the situations that continued to appear, while working closely with Stefano. He and I saw a bright future ahead, if only we took the right advance planning actions now. Modernization, Mobilization, Communication, and Electrification (or MMCE or "mc" as we pronounced it) became our guiding principle behind the countless decisions that we had to make. Across Tarra, only the Sea Princes had significant modern equipment and inventions. We had steam and petrol powered vehicles that allowed for faster, cheaper transportation of goods. We had radios, telefonos, and LD radios, whose tremendous benefits were only now being discovered in many other countries. Electricity promised us all a bright future, with homes having cheap electricity for lights and soon washing machines. Many more electrical devices were in the planning stage. Devices to help women were given top priority.

Our task was somehow to spread our technologies to the rest of Tarra, in hopes that MMCE would either help prevent a country from falling into Dark Ages or help them pull out of one. As we discovered that the two most populous countries were descending into the horrors of a Dark Age, that is Demokritos and Tashien, we began to see the impact this would have on the remaining countries. Demokritos had more caravels than all the other countries combined, the loss of that amount of shipping capacity would cripple the rest of the world.

As soon as the Rock Man's reports began arriving announcing the discovery of more coal and petrol sites, he and I reached a decision. "Look, we need more steam powered, steel ocean-going ships to replace the aging caravel fleets. Vito and Bonillo now have new coalfields to go along with their iron production. What if we set them up to become the manufacturers of new steam ships?" he suggested. "Besides giving their people immediate new jobs, in the long run, they can reap significant benefits." I agreed and Stefano began working with the two monarchs who jumped at the opportunity. While these ships often took five years to build, their lifetimes would be quadruple that of our smaller caravels. Stefano's plans called for the launching of thirty new ships during the next ten years, each one able to carry ten times the cargo of one of our caravels. With luck, this would help offset the anticipated loss of much of the Demokritos shipping.

Pieta with its copper mines was given contracts to begin production of the wire needed in the construction of electrical devices along with contracts to build thirty more giant electricity generating plants during the same ten year period. The objective was to have every town and city in the Sea Princes and the Greenway with a population of five thousand or more electrified within ten years. Solamina received contracts to build large quantities of the LD radio sets, the commercial radios, and the power transmitting stations. Here, the ten-year plan called for every household in the Sea Princes where electricity was available to have a radio. Every large town was to have their own LD radio so that the leaders of each country could be kept fully informed at all times. Finally, Zargarb was given contracts for the construction of steam-powered looms. Their goal was to mass produce cotton, wool, and paca cloth bolts, becoming the world's supplier of inexpensive cloth from which clothing could be made.

Barcella soon began manufacturing all manner of helpful household devices, beginning with the first production models of the clothes washing machines, followed in December with Lucianna's next bright idea, an electric vacuum machine designed for women to be able to easily clean their homes. I can count on my fingers how many times Lucianna sat down on her butt and used her feet to sweep at our house, though it was supposed to be one duty that we all took turns doing. Yes, I have no arms now. That gal was amazing; she always found a way out of that chore too!

One of the first foreign country situations I dealt with was that of Megalos, which had been our enemy for centuries, as far back as I could remember. With the total collapse of their government and the self-destruction of the Church of Jehosanity, when we received Senator Aminta's plea for help, Stefano and I saw an incredible opportunity to change our relationship with that large island nation. Immediately, he dispatched a caravel carrying the engineering plans and production models of many of our devices, knowing that their companies would love to be allowed to start producing these many items. When their wealthiest capitalist jumped at the opportunity, we then began our next move. There was always a month's delay, the sailing time between Velona and Megalos.

We both knew that Monarch Aminta's hold on the country was tenuous at very best. Once the men could walk again, some might attempt to regain control of the country. "Should we send her an army?" Stefano asked. "They could help enforce her rule. We don't want to lose her."

"Stefano, the Dark Ages will not be won by force of arms. She has lost the battle if we have to send our armed forces to help her. No, this war will be won by MMCE. If she cannot rapidly bring such positive changes to her nation, her own people will toss her out, one way or another. No, what we must do is to use everything in our power to help her achieve a speedy MMCE, so much so, that the ordinary person reaps the benefits that she is bringing. If so, her people will back her all the way. One thing that we can do immediately is get their dam rebuilt so that Galantas has its water supply back. That alone will make a tremendous impact on the people in their capital city. Lord knows, their Senate has spent centuries trying to rebuild it with no results. We need to send down a team of our engineers who can get their dam and aqueduct system repaired in short order. Ideas?"

He grinned. "Plus one to Bethany," he jested. "Are you sure that you don't want to be Monarch of Velona? You are more than qualified."

I laughed, "Oh no way! Look at all those people with whom you have to deal. No thanks. I'm happy to sit back and advise now and then." He chuckled.

A few days later, another caravel sailed to Megalos, carrying two engineers and a dozen stonemasons. He and I then talked to Monarch Aminta and told her that our engineers were on their way to repair their broken dam and aqueduct system. He suggested, "Monarch Aminta, you might begin to suggest to your citizens in Galantas that their old water system would be back working again by the first of the new year. That should give them something to look forward to and something more by which to measure your deeds and effectiveness as their new ruler, firming up your grassroots support." She thanked him at least a dozen times. Indeed, in late December when water flowed down the aqueduct system into Galantas for the first time in two centuries plus, the entire city turned out to cheer!

I also spent time at the Velona Banca del Dio, researching the accounts of the government of Megalos and that of the Church of Jehosanity there on Megalos. Armed with the facts, I again talked to her over the LD radio. "First, Monarch Aminta, since you are now the head of the government of Megalos, I have worked with the Banca del Dio here and they are prepared to transfer all the country's funds into a new account, which only you and those you choose have access to, is that acceptable?" She agreed and asked how much was there. "Thirty-five million in gold, more or less." She shrieked, shocked beyond belief. The Senate had always been shooting down her proposals to help the common people with projects that would benefit them, such as road improvement, stating lack of funds. She began to see the depth of the lies fomented upon her people.

"Now there is another matter. As you have explained to me, the pope and Church of Jehosanity have murdered countless of your people. At this time, they have all died. However, they have sizeable funds on deposit. The Banca del Dio is prepared to also transfer those funds over to you as reparations for their crimes against your people. I am afraid that other countries will also be submitting similar claims. The Banca will be using the funds in the Church's accounts in those countries to pay similar reparations there. Are you willing to accept these reparations from the Church as full and complete atonement for their many atrocities there on Megalos? If so, I will see that those funds are also transferred to your account."

"Yes, I will accept that. They've paid with their lives, but perhaps I can use such meager funds to assist those who have been directly harmed," she replied.

"Okay, in that case, I will see that another twenty-two million gold is transferred to your country's account."

"What? Twenty-two million?" I heard Pavlos quickly grabbing on to the shocked woman.

He said, "Forgive her, she is dumbfounded. What we can do for our people with such a fortune is staggering. On behalf of our Monarch, thank you, Bethany. Thank you!" I did hear her squeak a thank you in the background.

Later in the week, I heard back from the advisors that we had sent down there to help her. They reported that Monarch Aminta made a countrywide announcement that starting January 1, a massive road reconstruction project would commence, with a re-paving of all roads in need of repairs, long wanted but never constructed new roads would be built, construction for new public schools for every city and town with a population of five thousand or more would be begun in February, and that the government would be providing free education for all children through the age of fourteen. Further, construction would begin in March on government-sponsored hospitals to care for the sick and injured, again in every large town. Further, she announced that there would be no yearly taxes collected from any citizen during the coming year of 824 and if possible, none in 825.

When Stefano and I heard that news, he and I looked at each other. He said, "Well, if her people don't fully back her now, then nothing will!" He and I put a checkmark in the done column, a column labeled "Saved."

The second week of December, our feet were back to normal. We heard from Captain Armand Clement of the Smiling Prince, when he docked in Kostya, Konstantin. For several days, I talked with him and their new Queen Jelena, helping with the language barrier and getting a feel for what help we could provide. Jelena's fears were well-founded. One man could indeed take over their whole country now. We all held lengthy discussions about just what we could do to help them.

It was touchy. Their culture was vastly different from ours or any other country's for that matter. I argued that we did not have the right to enforce our morals and culture onto these women. We certainly could do so; there was nothing the women could really do about it if we did. "Look, no argument, we have to send men with enough guns to fight off any one making an attempt to conquer them. The men most likely will have their hands full of mundane things, felling trees, making logs, building homes, making tools, and so on. Yet, we can do more. We can lead by example. We can show them that men should accept half of the responsibility for raising their offspring. We can show them the benefits of a monogamous marriage, which may have to be altered slightly because undoubtedly they have lesbian relationships as an inherent cultural fact of life."

Stefano grinned, "What? You mean that we can't send lecherous men down there?" We chuckled. "Honestly, the temptation is going to be huge. I mean if we can send fifty men who might like to resettle there for many years, then that would mean a ratio of eight hundred sixty-four women to one man!"

"Yes, maybe we can find a hundred men who might be up for such a challenge. Now we're down to four hundred to one," I teased. "I think that a hundred men would be ample to defend the port and to deal with the heavier labor that the women used to do." He agreed.

It took us a month to find eighty men who were willing to tackle this interesting challenge. Half were skilled tradesmen who already had families. All signed a contract agreeing to work there for a period of five years for a stipend of three thousand gold per year, payable upon demand, though most likely when they returned. We sent along three LD radios, two hundred long guns, five of the fancy rapid-fire machine style guns, three cannonae, and plenty of ammunition. We also sent along a small steam engine electrical generator in hopes that a coal supply could be found there. A motor-wagon, a motor-car, and ten putt-putts of each type accompanied them, along with a generous supply of petrol. At least the women could see these inventions and the potential they offered.

Once I had the ball rolling, I realized that someone who was educated needed to oversee these various tradesmen. I chatted privately with Captain Armand. After telling him how it was going, that I expected to be sending a sizeable force, which would arrive there around March 1, 824, I explained, "Captain, I'd like to make you another deal. We need an educated, honorable man to oversee these men who will be coming to stay and help the women for a period of five years. I've checked your bank account. What would you say if I asked you to assume that role, say for five years? If so, I would triple your account balance immediately. If you find that it doesn't work out, you still keep these funds. Perhaps, you could spend part of these years building the house that you've dreamed about, you know, work out the bugs in it. When you return, you'll know precisely what to do."

"Triple? I can retire and never work again on that! Okay, I'll do it. Gladly, actually. These women are really quite kind, very bright, industrious, and have quite a civilization going here. Bit goofy in some ways though, but Jelena claims that they have changed their ways towards their baby boys. She has asked me for help in making sure the new boys that are born are raised properly. I'd rather like to help them with that. They are extremely fragile at this point, so horribly vulnerable. If we treat them right, show them that all men are not pigs, we may win the war." I agreed and relaxed, knowing that he had the right attitude for the job.

What to do about the Demokritos situation occupied far more of my attention during the early part of November, as the reports continued to arrive outlining the ever changing situation that Ana and Callisto and Alexio's groups were facing. It had gone from an initial caravel sent to pick up my two friends to more of a support role, as the two had rescued a large number of women and were planning to don the leadership role of their kingdom.

Stefano wanted to send a general and five thousand troops to help them. I vetoed that, at least for now, "Look, if we land that many troops on their soil, the people can easily twist that into an invasion from Velona attempting to conquer their kingdom. No, we wait on that until Ana and Callisto specifically ask for an army. Meantime, I will put a freeze on their Emperor's bank accounts and all the other kingdom's accounts. Make their new leaders go through the proper channels of verification to regain access to their funds. Keep thinking of ideas, MMCE shines the way, Stefano."

Later I relayed to Ana and Callisto that I had the Arolas accounts transferred to their names and that they had around twenty-five million in kingdom funds. Also, the Emperor's accounts held another thirty-five million, which I split into eighths, giving one portion to Alexio's group, since he represented what was left of the Imperial Court. The other portions I earmarked to give back to the seven kingdoms, adding another four million to Ann and Callisto's account. At least there were funds to continue their kingdom's operations. Yet, what to do for real help eluded me. Worse was the three-month voyage that it took to get there from Velona. What I decided to send now would not arrive there until the middle of

February, if I sent it immediately.

At last, Stefano made the decision for me. He duplicated our planned shipment of aid to Megalos, sending along engineers, plans, and working models of our key MMCE items, along with several more LD radios. He added some fifty soldiers to help protect the shipment and a generous supply of long guns and ammunition, just in case. Instead of the two planned caravels, he had to use three in order to be able to carry along enough food and fresh water for the three-month voyage. He continued to bypass all of our usual way ports in the Southlands. Thanks to their total embargo on re-supplying our ships because we were mutants, none of our caravels ever stopped in their ports, not for the last eight months.

I hoped this load would suffice. If they got there and needed to handle an evacuation instead, they could, because by then the space required by all the perishable supplies would be available. They could make a quick run over to Annelise and resupply there, as well as re-plan.

While I really wanted to take a quick trip over to the Highlands to check out this mystery at the Standing Stones, as December came, I knew that I'd have to put it off until spring. The ports on West Reach were now frozen over, except that of Bregia in the far south. However, that city had been torched and was out of commission for the time being. We'd received little other word from the large island just off our coast. Honestly, with Bregia out, there was little that we could do until the ice broke in the spring. By then, I'd be likely too far into my pregnancy to go, darn. I promised myself that we'd go in the summer, baby and all.

As the days went by in December, the situation in Shansee worsened. When I finally heard from Pian, my heart nearly burst for her. Eve and I knew well the sadism that ran deep and rampant in that country. Once again, it hit home to us and at the same Purple Palace to boot. That was the very place where she and I had first been mutilated when we were there trying to help them deal with the chaos some sixty plus years ago. Naturally, Eve wanted her and me to hop the next train to Shansee and raid the Purple Palace! I thought better of that, not just yet. We'd need an army if the reports of the anarchy there were true. Still, I had to help her and the four Church of God groups. The how eluded me just now.

Chapter 13 Battle for Sanity

Alexio struggled to walk the three hundred yards to the grain crib near the barns. He was fuming, fighting angry, and not because his arms were flying in all directions as he strove to keep his balance. Rather the scene that he'd just encountered in the farmhouse. He had followed the advice of Bethany and had carefully avoided all the villages and towns, traveling the back roads instead. While it had been slower and full of detours, thus far, it had been safe for his small group.

Each evening, they had relied upon the generosity and kindness of the local Arolas farmers. Often now, they had been able to lend a hand to these extended families, helping them deal with heavier work with which their wives had used to assist them. A meal and a night's shelter in a barn had readily been offered, not once, but every single night so far, much to the amazement of Alexio and his friends. Indeed, Alexio already had gained a deep insight to the rural people of his country, a viewpoint entirely lacking from all his years at the Emperor's Palace in Kefall.

He'd now seen a whole spectrum of human reactions to the plague. The worst, he knew he'd never be able to get out of his mind. One such scene would haunt him until his death. One evening they'd pulled into a farmstead that seemed deserted. Livestock had not been tended for weeks. Upon entering the farmhouse, the stench of decaying bodies was overwhelming, but the scene inside made the smell seem like perfume. A detective was not needed to ascertain what had happened. The elder farmer had taken a corn knife to the throats of his wife and children, all six of them. One was only a baby! Then, he'd propped his long gun between his legs and blown half of his head off. Sickening.

This evening, they'd witness a nasty scene while sharing dinner with a fine extended farming family. His eldest daughter, Zoe, had recently gotten married to Aesop, a neighboring farm lad. At the dinner table, he continued refusing to help her with anything, not even pulling out her chair so she could join the large gathering. Her embarrassed father had hastily gotten up and fumbled his way over to help her, glaring at his new son-in-law.

"What?" Aesop bickered. "Why bother? She's a useless, pathetic bitch now. I wish I'd never married her! Now I have an albatross around my neck. Damn her anyway. She has to fend for herself. All you damnable women have to fend for yourselves. You pathetic women! You are just using this as an excuse not to do a damn thing around the farm anymore. Well, I ain't falling for it. You can all go to hell. That's probably where you all belong anyway now. If you can't pull your own load around here, I sure as hell ain't going to pull it for you. You men — you are pathetic too, cow towing to their pathetic whimpering all the time. You make me sick. Feed your own damn self, Zoe!" He rose, knocking his chair over on its back, slapped her in the face, and stomped out of the dining room and out the front door, leaving an awkward, upsetting, embarrassing silence in his wake.

Zoe broke into tears, burying her head on the table. Her mother rose and moved to her side, leaning her body into her daughters, unable to put comforting arms around her. Her father shook his head sadly, uncertain what to do. "I'm sorry. You must forgive Aesop. He's young. All this has upset him." He tried to make less of the highly disturbing scene just played out before us all. Alexio fumed. Nothing could excuse such conduct!

"Excuse me, I'll be right back, Io," he whispered and kissed her on her forehead. Wobbling more than normal because Io wasn't at his side, he headed after the lad, determined to have a word with him. He spotted him heading into the grain crib and slowly followed him.

"There you are, Aesop. What the hell do you think you are doing, son?" he yelled, viciously.

"Putting those pathetic women in their places, damn them anyway," he replied caustically and defiantly.

"Do you have any idea who I am, son?" Alexio finally regained his composure. Anger ill-suited him, as he stood there looking at the lad who couldn't be but nineteen at the most. His anger left him.

"Some down on their luck travelers I suppose," he said accusingly.

"See this ring? I'm the Emperor's son, traveling on Imperial Business here in Arolas. I'm the most important man in the whole country, save only for Emperor Omela." He didn't mention that the Emperor was dead. As expected, this got the lad's complete attention!

"Look son, all of us are upset and angry over what has happened to all of our wives, women, and girls. Let me tell you something. I'm in communication with most all the countries on Tarra. This plague had affected every single last woman and girl in the entire world! Every one of them, everywhere, every country. It isn't going to go away. Their arms are not going mysteriously to grow back. Worse, baby girls have already been born and they too are just like their mothers. From now on, women on Tarra are going to have no arms and there is not a damn thing that you or I or anyone else can do about it, period! I know, Zoe is not what you bargained for in a wife. Son, what you wanted in a wife, none of we men can ever have again, not ever. So here, take my pistol. Go ahead, point it at your head, and pull the trigger. Put yourself out of your misery right now. Here, take it. Go ahead. Do it. None of us will ever be able to have a wife with arms, so go on; do it. End your life right now. Come on, blow your brains out." He kept pushing the pistol towards him. He didn't bother to tell the lad that it was not loaded. He seldom kept it loaded. The long guns were so much better than these pistols, why bother with them? He had it more for show.

"I, I don't want to shoot myself," Aesop muttered, refusing the gun. "I don't want to die. I wanted a real wife, that's all. You really the Emperor's son? From Kefall?"

"Of course I am. On my way to visit my sister coming down for a visit from Velona. So you want to live. I figured that you did. A real wife, eh? Well, someone who loves you, who will always be there for you, who will bear your children, who will do her part — is that it?"

"We were planning to start our own farm, raise a family. Now she can't even do a blessed thing for herself. I can't do it all by myself. She swore that she was going to do her half," Aesop answered. "We had all these great plans and ideas."

"Oh, I see. So you don't think of Zoe as just another possession, another thing to have, like another horse or sheep or chicken?" Alexio probed. "A thing to have around to mend your shirts, cook your meals, keep your house so you don't have to?"

"Well, that's women's work anyway, but she and I, we had all these plans. We were going to get our own parcel of land from my dad this summer. Zoe and I were going to build us our own house and grow pumpkins together."

"Oh, I see what you mean now. Yes, you two had admirable plans and goals worked out. I agree, those will make for an excellent future. Only now, she's lost all those goals and plans because they were in her arms, and those are now gone, leaving nothing but an empty shell walking around. I see, people carry their plans and goals in their arms, is that it?"

"Huh? Don't be stupid! Those things are in our minds. Only now she can't do a damnable thing anymore, and I'll have to do the work of both of us, and I can't do it. I can barely walk now."

"Excuse me. Yes, I see now. She still shares those same plans of getting the land, building a fine home, and growing vast fields of pumpkins."

"Sure, but now she can't do any of it. She is as helpless as her little baby sister who is one year old."

"Look, Aesop, she and all them have just suffered the most traumatic loss of their arms. She is in shock and is terrified. She needs you now more than ever. Real men do not desert their wives when their wives need them. That's part of what being a man means. Likewise, one day you may really need her help too. What's missing here is that none of this whole extended family has been giving their women time and help in learning new alternative ways of doing things, from getting dressed, to eating, to cooking, and most importantly helping around the farm to make it thrive. Come with me, son. I want to have you meet someone."

The two stumped over to the barn where their wagons were parked for the night. He had the lad peddle the generator while he began setting the controls. "Alexio calling Velona. Alexio calling Velona." A bit later, he said, "I need to talk with Bethany. No, it's not an emergency. Okay. We'll hang on."

Alexio began explaining the LD radio to the wide-eyed Aesop. The night operator rang me up on the telefono and I powered up the LD radio in our mansion. "Bethany here. Calling Alexio. Come in Alexio. Bethany here," I spoke rather sleepily into the large mouthpiece.

"Hi, sorry to bother you at night, but I need some help." He outlined the situation and introduced me to Aesop. I spent around a half hour telling him about how up north we women, in time, found alternate ways to do most everything. Based on what Alexio told me, these people had not even installed their replacement kitchen nor helped their women learn to use the yokes. Hence, I went into detail what needed to be done and what he could expect the women there to soon be able to do on their own.

An hour later, Alexio and Aesop reentered the farmhouse. The others were already finished eating and the menfolk were dealing with clearing the table. Aesop's face was bright, though he felt ashamed. "Zoe, I am truly sorry. I've been a complete jerk. We all have. All these things that appeared here, duh, we are supposed to install them for Zoe and the rest of you. You won't believe what I've been doing!" He excitedly began explaining about the LD radio and talking to some woman in Velona about everything.

Alexio and his group stuck around the next day, lending them a hand with all the work. Further, they lugged the LD radio inside and I spent another hour talking with all the women, covering with them as many of my hints as I could, especially those I had picked up from the rural farmers of the Greenway. Io and the others in Alexio's party also greatly benefitted from this as well. Once more, I knew the absolute necessity of somehow getting my hints books to these people. The how remained elusive.

By the time that Alexio and his group finally met up with Ana and Callisto's huge group, he had seen just about all possible reactions that men and women had had to the devastating, crippling effects of the plague. Alexio was a far wiser man when he met up with those two than he had been before he left.

Ana and Callisto continued their push towards the coast, using the back roads as much as possible. Several of their newly rescued people were familiar with the area and for several more days, they had little trouble making progress and avoiding towns and villages. Now some three days from the huge port city of Andros, they had no choice but to head back to the main road. Why? They had to find a bridge over the Pinos River if they were ever to get to the ruins at Aran.

"Damn, another town," Ana called out over her shoulder to Callisto, who was driving the wagon behind hers. Callisto pulled her wagon up beside Ana's to survey the sight with her sister. Worse, they heard gunfire in the distance. "Well, that can't be a good sign."

"Come on, we'd best see about getting these women out of here. Perhaps there is a side road up ahead," Callisto suggested. "We're totally out in the open with fields all around us. Not defensible," she pointed out. They alerted the men and few women who were driving the wagons behind them and then began moving forward once again.

They had gone barely a mile when they saw a group of riders galloping towards them coming from the town. "Hey, those look like our soldiers," Ana called out. The Arolas army wore bright red uniforms trimmed with green bars and blue slashes, making them look very visible and eye-catching which some said added to their authority. "Don't fire, they are our military men." They continued moving towards the oncoming group.

Before long, Ana and Callisto were able to grasp the situation coming their way. A group of ten soldiers was fleeing from a band of thirty mob members. They were obviously being chased out of the town and galloping for their lives. As the soldiers approached the long line of wagons loaded with mostly women, their captain yelled to them, "Flee! Flee! Flee for your lives!"

"The hell I am fleeing," Callisto replied. "Spells." She didn't bother to look at Ana, but focused on the approaching band of men, galloping all out towards them. Many carried long guns, but most held a sword in one hand. She surmised that they had already fired their guns and could not possibly have reloaded them while galloping after the soldiers. "Now!"

Two great balls of fire appeared in the midst of the charging mob, expanding outward encompassing the entire band. Shrieks and screams rose above the many hoof clops upon the gravel road. The ten soldiers reined in and turned around only to see this giant ball of flames totally obscuring the mob, which had been chasing them. Now a flaming, riderless horse appeared coming out of the inferno, then another and another at seemingly random locations.

"What the. . ." the captain attempted to say, unable to find words for what his eyes were seeing. More riderless horses galloped out and the flames subsided and then were gone, as if they had not been there at all. Smoldering bodies lay in a random pattern on the blackened gravel, most were men, but several were horses.

"Sorry about the horses, couldn't be helped," Callisto spoke at last. "Damned idiots anyway."

"What happened?" the captain finally was able to asked, wiping his hands over his eyes, staring in disbelief.

"Sorry about the horses," Callisto repeated. "Had to stop the mob before they could harm us. I take it that they were after you, captain?"

"Yes, that was incredible! Did you do that? Are you magicians or witches or what? Captain Jude Ioannis of the Arolas First Army. Who are you? Who are all these people?"

"Queen Callisto and Queen Anathia Tropos, your monarchs now, since our parents are dead," Callisto replied, not waiting for Ana to answer. "We've been rescuing brutalized women along the way. Heading for Andros."

"King Tropos is dead? Good god! No wonder we haven't had any word from Naxos! That explains a lot. But how did you do that?"

"Ana and I have our ways, Captain Jude. She and I are not to be messed with, if you take my meaning."

Ana probed for more key information, "Where are you stationed, captain? Were you attacked in yonder town?"

"Yes, Your Majesties. We're from the First Army Barracks not far from here. We've not had any resupply for weeks and food is running low. General Gyros send us into town to see what was causing the delay, figuring it was the plague. It struck us as well. None of we soldiers can walk. Our camp wives and women have been — well you know what I mean." He seemed embarrassed to come right out and say it: armless and probably helpless as well.

"We ran into a mob that controls the town — ambushed us, killed half my men. The general will take swift action; I'm sure, just as soon as we report in. You cannot continue toward Andros, Your Majesties. Please, come with us back to the barracks. I am sure that the general will want to speak with you immediately."

Ana realized that this was more like an order than a request. Yet, she began to see some benefits, perhaps these women could stay on the barracks for a time in relative safety. "Of course, captain, lead the way," she replied, nodding to Callisto.

Is this a safe move? Callisto sent her.

We should take the gamble. Think of the women who are with us. Maybe we will be able to use these soldiers to help us, Ana sent back.

The wagons backtracked a mile and took a west road and soon crossed over a stone bridge, one of the few crossings of the wide Pinos River along this stretch of the country. At last, they spied the huge First Army Barracks, a sprawling complex of crude stone buildings and many barns. As they approached the gates, they spied a number of sentries sitting on the ground. As the captain approached, they hastily got to their knees. None tried to stand.

"Take them to the northwest section, they can stay in the empty barracks there," Captain Jude explained. "Here, you two, take over the reins from these two women. Your Majesties, if you will step down and come with me please?" he ordered. "Oh, do you need a hand down?" he suddenly realized that they might not be able to climb down on their own.

They accepted his helping hands. Once down, they suggested he put his arms over their shoulders for support. He was a bit sheepish about it at first, but soon discovered that he could walk much better this way. They walked up to this first, large stone building, where another kneeling sentry opened the door for the two.

General Gyros sat at his big desk, a rather portly man. His red uniform looked freshly pressed. His black hair was nicely combed and his black eyes missed nothing. "Ah Captain Jude, you've returned at last. Looks like you have brought back more than just our needed supplies," he added, spying the two teenagers.

Snapping to attention, Captain Jude barked, "General Gyros, sir. I present Queens Anathia and Callisto Tropos, sir. Our king and queen are dead sir. They told me so sir."

"At ease, captain. What's this? King Tropos is dead? Who are you two teens anyway?" General Gyros demanded to know. He didn't believe a word of the captain.

"I'm Anathia Tropos and she's my sister, Callisto Tropos. Mom and dad are dead. Rioters killed them and stormed the palace a few days back. We've managed to escape the carnage in Naxos and were heading to Andros, when we stumbled upon your captain here and had to come to his rescue. We have been appointed the monarchs of Arolas and are working on ways to put down all this anarchy in the streets." *Get ready to tweak his mind if he doesn't believe us,* she sent to Callisto.

General Gyros studied the two women for a moment. "I reckon you who you say you are. You look different from when I last saw you at the formal parade last summer. You were on the stands with your folks."

Ana realized where she had seen him before. It was at the parade all right, but not in the reviewing stands. She and Callisto were wearing their red satin dresses, but were seated in a row below their parents. She pointed this out to the General, who grinned. "Aye, just a little test. You both look so different now, but then all our women do. I am so sorry about the loss of your parents. King Tropos was a fine leader. So now the government is in your hands?" he asked but then his face grew red; they had no hands. "Surely you wish to pass off the leadership to worthy men as soon as possible?" he asked.

"Thanks. No, we are officially now the reigning monarch of Arolas. What with all the vast mistreatment of our women, we feel it is our obligation to set things right." Ana described some of the horrors that they had encountered thus far.

"That is outrageous! We must put an end to such atrocities. Say, what did you mean by coming to the rescue of Captain Jude?" he remembered what Ana had said a bit ago. She realized that he was methodically dealing with the issues before him in a priority manner. Ana turned to Captain Jude and nodded for him to explain.

"Dear god! What the devil is happening to Arolas? What the devil? Balls of fire? That's not possible, captain!"

"I'm sorry, General. I did not want to destroy the horses, just the mob men," Callisto added innocently. "Ana and I are quite powerful. If you want a demonstration, we can oblige. We'll have to step outside, though, and find a place where no one will get hurt by it. No one ever messes with us, sir!"

Poor General Gyros. He greatly wanted to see such a demonstration, but his own embarrassment at having to get down on his hands and knees to crawl to the door prevented him. "Well, perhaps later on. Right now, we are dangerously low on supplies. Skala is two weeks late on their deliveries. I sent Captain Jude and twenty men into Skala to see why the delay. Now we know. I'll send in the whole damn army now!" He realized that it was too late in the day to mount an offensive.

"Captain Jude, send for all the captains. We'll plan our assault for the morning."

"General, we want to be part of the planning and its execution," Ana interrupted. "We anticipate that there will be a large number of women being mistreated in the town, if it's like the other towns we've passed through. Besides, Callisto and I can help reduce the number of your men who get hurt. If you don't believe us, talk to those that we brought with us. They can tell you in detail what we can do. We may not have arms, but we are more lethal than mere long guns. Go ask them."

Callisto was a bit baffled by what Ana was saying. Then, she worked it out. Ana needed to get these soldiers firmly behind us and use them to help them to retake control of Arolas, city by city. She smiled, liking the plan.

"Captain, please escort our Majesties to the guest quarters." To the two, he added, "I'm sorry. There is no courtly finery around here; this is an army barracks. You'll have to stay in plain housing."

"That will be fine with us general. We are not remotely interested in such matters. There are far more critical things that must be done," Ana answered. Again, she offered her shoulders to the captain as the three left. As they walked along, the two could not help notice how empty the complex seemed to be and commented upon it to Captain Jude.

"Aye, we've lost about half of our men. General Gyros has allowed many to have official Leaves of Absence to attend to their family's needs. The plague, you know. We have about ten thousand men here normally, but we are down to barely five thousand now," he explained.

"Just make sure that the general does speak to those that we've rescued, please, it's important," Ana begged him.

As they got to the guest barracks, Spyro and Seth were sitting on the doorstep waiting for them. The captain nodded to them, turned, and left. "Well, now what's the plan?" Seth asked, adding, "The food's atrocious." They helped the two women inside and a lengthy chat began.

The room was Spartan, but livable. At least they would be sleeping in a real bed tonight. After dark, Captain Jude knocked and asked them to come to the planning meeting. Seth and Spyro insisted on coming along. "Hey, we are their top advisors," Seth pointed out and Ana went along with his suggestion.

The general sat at his big desk, but now the room was filled with some fifty captains and majors. A table had been placed centrally and held a diagram of the town of Skala. Around the town, toy soldiers had been placed, probably marking the positions of his various units. After a brief explanation of the proposed military assault on the town, Ana and Callisto tried to alter it.

"Look," Ana explained, "if you go charging in there, many men are going to get killed. They have the advantage of cover from inside the buildings. Your men will be at a severe disadvantage. Unacceptable losses from your Monarchs' point of view. We need all of you alive. Here's a better idea."

General Gyros was not used to having his plans altered, especially by women and especially not now, when all the women were so helpless. Callisto wondered if he would be reasonable or pigheaded. So many of the soldiers were just that, egocentric oriented, especially those in command.

After Ana made her suggestions, Callisto spoke up. "General Gyros, captains. I want to say something too. You see, this plague has brought our country to an enormous cliff. Anarchy and chaos are breaking out everywhere in Demokritos. We are sliding down into an abyss from which we can never return. Hell is awaiting us all if we do not act swiftly to arrest this slide. The only thing that stands between utter Dark Ages here in Arolas and recovery are you men and us, Ana and me. Whole villages have already been wiped out in the madness that has come upon our people. The atrocities being committed daily in Arolas are almost beyond the imagination of us good people. If we do not act swiftly and precisely, Dark Ages will descend upon us. At this moment in time, barely five thousand of us stand between the coming Dark Ages and the light of survival. We cannot afford to lose many of you in this one small town. Please, allow us to do our job. We will not let you down. We are depending upon you and your men to save Arolas from destruction. Please."

General Gyros cleared his throat. "Well, it certainly cannot hurt any to give our Monarchs a chance. If they fail, we resort to the original plan. Now go inform your men. We ride at nine in the morning."

"Thank you, General Gyros," Ana said sincerely.

The next morning, Captain Jude brought up a wagon for the two women. "What's that for?" asked Callisto.

"For you, Your Majesties," he replied. "Surely you cannot ride a horse."

"Oh don't be silly. We are not that helpless. Bring us a pair of mounts and tie the reins together," she ordered. He obeyed, but in disbelief.

Holding the reins, he watched as Callisto put her chin on the saddle and stepped awkwardly up, wiggling into position, then bit down hard on the reins. "I'm all set." Ana followed suit, much to his amazement and shortly thereafter the general's. *If Bethany can do it, we can do it,* Callisto sent to Ana.

Beside them, Seth whispered to Spyro, "Spunky!" Both boys grinned.

Later, the boys helped the two dismount near the edge of the tree-lined town of Skala. The bright red uniforms flooded around the town, surrounding it. However, they stayed beyond long gun range for the moment, allowing the women time to do what they had suggested.

"Okay, fellows, watch over our bodies. Time for some action," Ana ordered. She and Callisto moved out of their bodies and moved into the town.

Just as we thought. They have guards posted. Let's take them out first, Ana sent. For several minutes, the two moved from area to area, putting the men on guard duty to sleep. Then, they headed into the heart of the city, surveying the actual situation, leaving behind some fifty sleeping men. As they expected, the thugs had taken over the heart of the town, the city hall building and the nearby inns, confiscating the best in the town for themselves. Greed was highly predictable. Satisfied that they had pretty well located the bulk of those in charge, they sent a telepathic message to the general. Presently, they spotted the mounted red uniforms moving into town. Some stopped to deal with the men who were mysteriously "sleeping" on guard duty.

The two kept watch, but as expected, the others in the town rapidly became aware of the many soldiers moving into positions around city hall and some five inns all within five blocks of each other. *Can we really do this?* Callisto asked.

Got any better ideas? Ana replied. She sent word to the general that they would deal with the closest inn first, farthest from the stone city hall building. The two went inside and began casting their illusions. Those inside believed that the building had somehow caught fire and that they were inside a raging inferno. The two were using the images they had of the previous fires they had used when freeing the women. As anticipated, terrified men began crawling like ants from a hole in the ground, crawling out into the awaiting guns of the soldiers.

Two men inside the inn seemed unaffected by their illusions and knocked windowpanes out with their long guns, preparing to fire upon the soldiers. Two lightning bolts arced from the sky, sending both men flying. General Gyros looked up at the simple white clouds in the sky and stared in disbelief, wiping his eyes.

Now gunfire began erupting from the nearby inns and the two moved over to the next inn. Once more they repeated their illusions with similar results, though they had to also fire off several more bolts. An hour later, only those hold up in the stone building remained un-captured. *Fire won't be believable here,* Callisto sent.

Let's see if we can sleep those near the doors and then while soldiers enter, keep on sleeping those closest to them. Ana sent and the two began implementing their plan. While not all men fell victim to their positive suggestion spell, enough did that the swarming soldiers quickly overpowered the few who attempted to hold the doors. Some shots were fired, but so many soldiers invaded the building at one time, the remainder threw down their guns and surrendered.

The two returned to their bodies and smiled. "Thanks fellows. Help us mount. Let's go see the results, shall we?" Ana asked Seth. A bit later, the four rode into the town, watching the many red uniforms going about their duties, mostly on their knees, however. By the time that they got to the inns, several were talking to their captains. A number of young women were found inside, being held prisoners. They had been raped repeatedly. General Gyros himself awkwardly walked inside, while Ana and Callisto were helped to dismount. Providing their shoulders to the boys, all four headed in after the general.

"Is it as bad as before?" Seth whispered to Ana.

"Not quite, but nearly so."

The general met them at the door. His bronze face was nearly ashen, very shaken by what he'd seen. "You were right. Can I leave them to you?" he asked. The two nodded and continued inside.

The general's justice was swift and effective. Long guns sounded for quite some time, while the four began assisting the traumatized women. Before long, husbands and boyfriends began arriving looking for their loved ones. Willingly they lent a hand with the task, many sending for other older women who had not been taken prisoner by the mobs to come and help as well. It was late afternoon before all the traumatized women had been bathed, clothed, and fed. Many were then taken home by their families, while older women volunteered to take the remaining ones into their care.

When the four finally emerged from the inn, Ana noticed that all the captured men were now gone. A large cremation fire now blazed just outside the town. Soldiers were loading their long overdue supplies onto wagons, overseen by a smiling General Gyros, sitting proudly on his horse. Spotting them, he called out, "Well done, Your Majesties, well done indeed. Lost only one man, incredible!" Ana and Callisto nodded and smiled. Both knew that now they had his complete support and that of his five thousand men. It was a start at least.

As they joined the general and his staff that evening for supper, Seth asked, "So what's the plan?"

"Yes, I must say that you two were brilliant, positively brilliant today. I simply do not know how you two managed all that. Yet, I saw the results with my own eyes," General Gyros added. "So what is next, Your Majesties?"

"We must take back control of Andros first. It is our only safe supply line to the outside world. We are going to need supplies," Ana replied, phrasing it in terms to which a general could easily relate. Lines of supply were crucial in any military operation.

"Excellent. Excellent. We can move out tomorrow," he suggested.

November 21, five thousand soldiers plus the four paused on the high ridge line looking down on the large port city of Andros, home to nearly two hundred fifty thousand people — that is, before the plague. Several caravels lay quietly moored to the docks. Hardly anyone was about. From this distance, perhaps a few were moving down at the docks. The general sent out a dozen riders, entering the city from several locations. Quickly, many returned.

"My god! Dead bodies are everywhere, sir! The stench is overwhelming," one soldier reported to his captain who rode near the general and the four.

"Damn, they didn't even have the common sense to dispose of the dead! General, we are likely going to find plenty of very ill people on our hands," Ana advised. "Tell your men to boil all their drinking water. Under no circumstance are they to drink water from the city or to eat anything that has not been thoroughly cooked, unless they want to get ill too."

"That bad? You can tell all this from here?" he asked. "So be it. You have not been wrong yet, Your Majesties." He quickly issued the orders and began sending hundreds of soldiers on down into the city, while the rest rode closer to the outer edges of the sprawling city. Now they too smelled the nauseating stench of the decaying corpses.

They waited about a quarter mile from the southern edge of the city, as slowly the scouts began making their reports. The general was unwilling to allow the four into the city or himself for that matter until they verified that there would be no armed resistance. Around two that afternoon, word came that the advanced scouts had made it all the way to the ocean. No one offered any resistance at all. Rather, they were being bombarded with pleas for help. Many were sick, they reported.

"My god. My god. What do we do now?" General Gyros asked rhetorically.

"Well, the first thing is to start disposing of the rotting corpses," Ana advised.

"Right. We can set up a place outside the city and begin cremation. We should go door to door. How many more bodies may still be inside? Probably many," he answered his own question.

"Good. As they go door to door, as they find the ill, we need them brought to a makeshift hospital. Callisto and I, with the help of our aides, can set about attempting to cure them."

"What? Are you telling me that you two are doctors too?" he asked amazed.

"No, but we know a good deal about healing," Callisto answered. "I think that we're going to need a lot of room for the sick and help with them as well. Perhaps, we can enlist some of the healthy city folk to lend a hand. Probably, your men will find many starving people as well. Have them locate the warehouses, which have food supplies. We'll need to get them distributed rapidly, I think."

"Good ideas. We'll find an empty warehouse and set it up as a temporary field hospital. I will make my division doctors at your disposal. Bet you didn't think that we had them," he teased Callisto.

"You got me on that one. Yes, all the doctors and nursing staff will be most definitely needed. I think that we have one enormous mess on our hands, well your hands, I seem to have misplaced mine now," she jested. The general stared at her a moment and then roared with laughter.

"I like you, Your Majesty. Well said. Let's get on it. Seth, take them to the field doctors and then lead them down towards the docks. We'll find you a warehouse as fast as possible," he ordered.

The four accompanied the five doctors and ten nurses, all men, as they slowly drove their wagons loaded with medical supplies through the streets. Often, they had no choice but to drive over the dead who were blocking the streets. As they approached the large docks, one soldier waved to them, he'd found them a reasonably empty warehouse. As the two women stood by watching the men unload the wagons, Ana suggested, "I suspect that we will be seeing mostly cholera and dysentery cases."

A doctor replied, "Astute observation. We will need much fluids. That means we are going to have to be boiling a whole lot of water. Nurses, as soon as we've finished unloading, fire up the portable stoves and get all the water boiling that you can. Find barrels in which we can put it to let the sterile water cool down. We are going to need vast amounts of safe drinking water. Wish we had vast amounts of chicken soup too."

They had no more than gotten all setup when the first cases began to arrive. Some were carried here on horseback by the soldiers; some were carried by their husbands. Later, wagons began bringing whole families. "What do we do?" asked Seth as the ill flooded into the warehouse.

"Watch what the doctors are doing. We will be sorting them out: cholera or dysentery. I hate to do this to you fellows, but we'll let you work on washing off the dysentery cases. Believe me, it has to be done and you will be helping save many lives," Ana replied.

A bit later, Seth cried out, "My god, she's covered in it!"

Ana grinned, "Yes, so do a good job, get her cleaned up."

It was well past midnight when one of the doctors came to relieve Ana and Callisto. Both were on their butts, using their feet to bathe the faces of the last two cholera victims. "Here, let me sterilize your feet and then you are ordered to go get some food and sleep." Sore and exhausted, the two allowed him to clean themselves up. They had worked nonstop along with all the others for close to nine hours now. The entire warehouse, as huge as it was, held sick men, women, and children, thousands of them.

Seth and Spyro joined them at the doors. "Food's this way," Seth said, exhausted himself. He'd lost count of the number of men and women he'd washed.

General Gyros spotted them coming out. He'd kept an eye on them though and knew they had all worked industriously along with his field doctors. He was more than impressed with his new monarchs. He still rode his horse, however. "Got a food station over here, Your Majesties. Got temporary beds set up for you as well. I'll give you a report while you eat." Ana flashed him a smile, too tired to say much at all.

They sat down, and at once, the boys began stuffing the hot meat into Ana and Callisto's mouths. No way were they going to make them use their feet, not after all that they had seen the two do for the last nine hours. Both Ana and Callisto smiled and thanked the two. The General slowly dismounted and got to a makeshift bench inches from where his foot hit the ground, trying hard not to look completely foolish. He still felt embarrassed by his feet.

"We have got all the dead hauled out of the city, we think. We'll be burning for days, I expect."

"How many?" Callisto asked, talking with her mouthful.

He sighed, "I think a third of the city. There were too many to count, far worse than any battlefield that I have ever seen or read about in our books. So many of them, children even. So many. Is our world ending? So many of the survivors now believe that is what's happening. After what I've seen here today, maybe it is."

"It would be if we had not come here," Ana pointed out. "I told you that we are perilously close to slipping into the Dark Ages. Here in Andros, we have arrested that slide. We'll know in a few days if we have been successful or not."

"Well, I think a quarter of the living is ill with something. Tomorrow, I'll start getting the others to work on useful projects. We found plenty of food in locked warehouses. Tomorrow, my men will start going house to house distributing it. What are we going to do when we find houses with no men now alive there?"

Ana sighed, "How about leaving one of your men with them? Keep a record of how many homes are manless. I think this will be critical. We women have to have at least one man in the household for now. Maybe later on, they can get by with a man only occasionally looking in on them, but not right away. Please, keep me posted on this detail."

"Okay, Your Majesty," he replied.

"Say, could you please just call me Ana? We really are not interested in all that useless court formality. Not now, not under these conditions."

"Aye, aye, Yo. . . Ana," he caught himself. She smiled and he grinned.

"Thanks, right now, we are just one of you. We have to survive and help others make it. Courtly manners are irrelevant. It's people that matter. Thanks for all you and your men have done here today. You are saving a whole city. Please relay that to your men. They are saving a whole city."

Again, he smiled, "You sure know how to make a soldier feel his actions are needed. I will do so, Yo. . . Ana," he again fought hard to break his formal habits.

The next day, everyone began complaining about their feet hurting, which slowed everything down even further. However, by the following day, men and women began rejoicing. A miracle was occurring: feet were returning to normal. By the third day, General Gyros walked proudly up to the four who were still attending to the many thousands who were ill.

"Ana, Callisto. Reporting in. All the dead have been disposed. I have now found a local man for each of the four hundred sixty-nine homes which lack a man in them. Most are relatives of one of the women who live there. Tomorrow, the markets and shops will open up for the first time since the plague struck."

"Excellent general."

"Just one tiny problem, Ana. My men are asking about their monthly pay. What should I tell them?"

"As soon as the Banca del Dio opens, we'll withdraw their pay. Send your paymaster to me when the Banca is ready for business. We have plenty of gold; no need to worry about pay," Ana answered him. From the look on his face, she knew that this had been a very great concern of his. She contacted me in Velona to assist with the communication to the Banca del Dio there in Andros. Ana knew that it would be three months at least until the paperwork from the main Banca del Dio in Velona got the documents to the Banca here.

In fact, this ultimately led to an overhaul in the entire Banca del Dio network. As rapidly as possible, each Banca branch was sent their own LD radio so that they could rapidly verify accounts and transactions worldwide.

The next day, Alexio and his group pulled into Andros and at last met up with Ana and Callisto. After many introductions, we held a long talk via the LD radio. I convinced Alexio, who wanted very much to help in any way that he could, to assume the mantle of Emperor for the time being. We all realized that Demokritos was just too big to be run by one man. Instead, we all decided that each kingdom ought to run its own affairs. The era of the Emperor was over. However, until law and order was restored, I convinced him to wear the Emperor's hat. Such would still convey additional authority that the common man would recognize and perhaps respect. He agreed to do it. General Gyros was extremely pleased to discover that he now had the Emperor of Demokritos with him as well. Io decided that an Empress was not really needed, but she would pretend so, if needed. She had much to deal with herself, especially later that day.

Again, Macario came though. A huge mound of Bethany's Hints suddenly appeared in the middle of the docks, nicely translated into their language. Ana had the soldiers begin delivering one to every woman in the city.

With so many deceased, including nobles and the mayor, Ana and Callisto appointed one of the local men who had spent long hours helping them with the many sick as the new temporary mayor. They instructed him to choose his own people to form up a staff to get the city going once more. In this arena, Ana and Callisto shone, for this was their specialty, being Judgers.

With so many empty homes, she and Alexio took over one abandoned estate, sufficiently large to house them all. This became their "palace," but really, it was their base of operations, as they put in more organization daily. By December 15, Ana, Callisto, and Alexio spent the day standing on a raised platform addressing crowds of city folk, explaining what had happened, who they were, and promising a bright future. Groups of ten thousand were assembled every hour throughout the day, until at last everyone in the city saw and heard these speeches. Communication was the key, Ana kept telling everyone.

Then, the three held a lengthy meeting with the wealthier men and women who had survived. They explained that mid-February a caravel from Velona would arrive bringing them the latest inventions along with detailed plans for their construction and an offer to allow them to begin manufacturing these items here in Andros. These men began to see that perhaps immense profits were to be had and hope rekindled in them as well, though most reserved judgment until they saw these inventions with their own eyes.

Next, Ana, Callisto, and Alexio met with General Gyros to plan their next move. He began sending out squads of twenty-four men, armed with stacks of Bethany's Books. Their task was to visit every farmstead within a hundred mile radius of Andros. He sent four squads similarly armed off to visit each village and town within that same radius. Their job was to deliver aid, news, and assistance, but also to be alert for mob-controlled towns. The instant they came across such, a courier was to report to the General, and we would then deal with it personally. Ana and Callisto insisted on being part of each retaking of a mob-controlled town, and the general was very willing to have their help. Thus far, he had only lost one man, utterly remarkable indeed.

He also sent off dispatches to two other very distant army barracks. The Second Army Barracks was close to the border with Thrace, some seven hundred miles as the crow flies from Andros, over a thousand by the main roads. The Third Army Barracks was nearly as far away to the east, patrolling the Katos Mountains, beyond which the wild horsemen of Vladimir ruled and occasionally raided coastal villages of Arolas. He knew well that come winter, they would likely be zeroing in on Naxos, what used to be their capital city and home to millions. Five thousand men could hardly deal with several million. He needed help, especially since the Fourth Army Barracks was located within Naxos, protecting the king's palace among other things. Obviously, they had failed to do that, and he had some suspicions that the general there might have seized control of the city for himself.

The many rescued women were given new homes in Andros and local men volunteered to look after them as needed. Each home had the new kitchen installed and the many doors adjusted so that women could use them. All were delighted to be given a free new home.

Ana and Callisto also issued some new laws, which the soldiers also disseminated as they traversed the country and towns. Besides announcing the new rulers, one proclamation stated that taxes were hereby rescinded until further notice. Another stated clearly that anyone who molested, raped, or harmed any woman would be summarily executed, unless they could prove extenuating circumstances but only in the case of harming her. Rape and molestation were outlawed under any circumstances. Further, Callisto added one of her own. Any man found guilty of kidnaping and binding a woman, such as they had seen being done in the villages on their way here would have his own arms removed as well as castrated. "Give them a taste of their own medicine," she declared. Ana grinned, knowing Callisto always did have a passion for the dramatic.

Thus, as the new year came, a tiny section of Arolas was finally back to a semblance of sanity. Order had been brought into the chaos in this small section of Arolas. Land mass wise, it was a twentieth of the country and hardly a scratch on all of what had been Demokritos. Still, Ana and Callisto were pleased that they had accomplished even this much. When they had left Naxos, they did not think that this much was actually possible.

As January rolled around, summer had now arrived. Along with it, feet were back to normal. "Expect more trouble now that men can walk again," Ana said to Callisto as the two women struggled to brush out each other's hair as they had done since they were little girls. Now of course, they were reduced to using their feet, but they had had plenty of experience with this in previous lifetimes.

"Agreed. The mobs who have taken over towns are now freed from their physical restrictions and that makes them all the more dangerous. Besides, by now they may have worn out their play things and will be trying to boldly replace them with new ones," Callisto replied harshly and crudely.

"We've got to put an end to it, sis, we just have to."

"You know, we ought to put those three hundred women who did that dab of therapy to work on the women of Andros. It would give them a really worthwhile project," Callisto mused.

"But we can't be looking over their shoulders if they run into trouble. We have to be ready to head off to help take the next town when the soldiers come back with word," Ana pointed out. "Still, I see your point. Why not? If someone hits a snag, we can always sort it out when we return. Let's do it."

It certainly didn't take much coaxing to get those women to do it. All were more than willing to do what they could with their limited knowledge of our therapy methods. In groups of ten, the two monarchs went over the key therapy details and let them begin. A citywide announcement proclaimed that trauma handling was available. One woman was put in charge of making the appointments and arrangements. By the end of the week, the three hundred plus women were each delivering at least one therapy session each day. Soon word spread of the miraculous results that they were achieving and an advanced sign up list began.

When I heard about what the two were doing, I relayed it to Raffaella. "You know, you ought to take advantage of this. If you had one of your knowledgeable Counselors down there, it might be a way to expand your Church of God," I suggested.

"I do believe that you are right. I'll see to it."

What I found interesting was that later Flavio and Alexa reported that, when they stopped at an uninhabited island to take on fresh water, a young woman named Zosime appeared there and asked for passage to Andros with them. She, they discovered, was a member of the Church of God, on her way to help with the needed therapy sessions. Thus, she arrived in mid-February along with the three caravels, providing her a reasonable and acceptable method of appearing in Andros. I detected the impressive hands of Macario at work.

After introducing herself to Ana and Callisto, they had a long talk. The next day, she was given an empty house and was introduced to the many women who were giving therapy sessions. Zosime then took over complete responsibility for these sessions. Further, she also gave Ana and Callisto a battery of sessions as well.

After the battery was finished, the three sat around having tea. Ana and Callisto saw that Zosime was an extremely able spiritual being. The teapot appeared to levitate and move itself from the kitchen into the living room. It poured their cups and even lifted itself up to Zosime's lips. The twenty year old smiled, "Just letting you know that you can count on me."

Ana and Callisto grinned, "You have us beat. Bethany and Eve can do that trick. We never quite got the hang of that, but we do many other things. Our feet can kill a man," Ana teased.

"That I know. Bethany told me about the training you had last lifetime. I just wanted you to know that I will be here to back you up," Zosime explained. Both Ana and Callisto felt somewhat more secure facing the future now. "When you get the country stabilized, I will work Macario's Advanced Therapy on you both. Perhaps you will regain far more that the mere lifting of a teacup." Her eyes twinkled; both looked forward to those future sessions. Zosime had given them something to look forward to in their own future.

Chapter 14 The Fall of Naxos, Arolas

Early May 824 as the fall colors once again turned the world into a mixture that few artists could ever hope to capture, Monarchs Anathia and Callisto Tropos neared Naxos, Arolas. Ana was driving the first of the new motor-wagons produced by the startup company Andros Vehicles. All the controls were within reach of her feet; gone were the foot pedals of the original models build in Velona years ago. All new models had to be able to be driven by women as well as men. Her boyfriend Seth Ridon sat beside her; he'd pulled navigation duty. Riding in the wagon bed Callisto and her boyfriend Spyro sat with their backs to the cab watching the multicolored leaves go by.

Their supplies filled the wagon bed. They had planned for a lengthy stay. During the past months, per the monarchs' orders, General Gyros and his First Army had slowly been expanding their perimeter of control. Originally an arc of about a hundred miles centered on their main port of Andros, now they had swept throughout all of Arolas and had encircled the huge capital city of Naxos. He had recalled the five thousand soldiers for whom he'd granted leaves when the plague struck and already three thousand had rejoined him. Actually, as they swept through more towns and villages freeing them from local gangs or merely helping the town get going once more, he found many of his soldiers there, helping their families. Two thousand of them, however, failed to report back and were counted as lost or missing.

Further, the other two generals who commanded the Second Army and the Third Army had received his dispatches. They were, naturally, very cautious, but agreed to meet with him and their new monarchs. Ana was prepared to alter their minds if need be, but once they were fully briefed, they swore allegiance to their new monarchs. Between the three army groups, they had finished off going from town to town, farmstead to farmstead. Dozens of gang or mob controlled towns and villages were freed, the guilty were merely executed on the spot. All women were then given their copy of Bethany's Hints. Somehow, more of the books kept appearing just when they were needed.

Ana and Callisto continued personally to assist the retaking of towns, which were under mob or gang control. Neither wished to lose more troops than necessary. Both feared the bloodbath that would arise when they finally got to Naxos, the largest city in the country. During these past three months, General Karpos and General Krates had personally witnessed the "miracles" created by their two young monarchs. If they had not been convinced before, they certainly were now. Flaming balls of fire, bolts of lightning, to say nothing of men mysteriously falling asleep accompanied the two teens.

All told, they now commanded twenty-four thousand soldiers. Yet there was one major caveat: border patrol. Arolas had one of the largest borders of any of the seven kingdoms of Demokritos. Their border with the neighboring Kingdom of Penelopus stretched for nearly twelve hundred miles. At least half of that had a natural barrier, the Pinos River. However, the remaining half was the shared Dark Forest. Here many bands of thieves made their homes. From these dense woods, they could strike and then retreat into woods so thick that they could not easily be found. At least the eight hundred mile border with Thrace had the natural barrier wall the Lonki Basin, which was passable only in a few key places, except on foot or possibly on horseback.

The problem with chaos is that it is unpredictable by nature, and it spreads like some nasty bacteria. The border communities and farms were constantly being raided by brigands from neighboring Thrace and to a lesser extent from Penelopus. Once the army had restored law and order, the two monarchs were forced to keep a strong force here to keep out the chaos spilling into Arolas from their neighbors. Fifteen hundred men now patrolled the huge border zone. The monarch posted many signs periodically along the border. They read: Anyone raiding Arolas from across our border will be hunted down and exterminated. The soldiers who were given the assignment of protecting the borders greatly appreciated this threat. They had carte blanche to take whatever actions they deemed necessary to track down the raiders.

The fall harvest was well underway as the motor-wagon roared up the road to Naxos and the waiting three generals. "Spunky driver," Seth teased Ana, who was driving perhaps a bit too fast.

"Hey, you navigate. I drive. God, what an invention!" Ana exclaimed, loving every minute behind the wheel. Actually, the four had been taking turns being the driver, with each getting a fifty-mile stretch. Naxos was only a couple hundred miles south of Andros, where they had begun their journey around ten this morning. Callisto had driven first, then Spyro. After they stopped for lunch, Seth took his turn, leaving Ana to be the one to drive the motor-wagon into the main army camp, where they were sure to draw a crowd of onlookers.

Shifting gears gave the women the most trouble, since it took both feet to operate the controls, one for the clutch and one for the gear shift lever and gas pedal. During the shifting periods, they had to hold the steering wheel steady with their heads and chins. Bit awkward, but quite manageable, once you had a bit of practice. "I'll never ride a horse again," Ana declared.

Seth commented dryly, "Until you run out of the petrol stuff, then you will be begging me for a horse, spunky." Both laughed. Around dusk, they pulled into the large, temporary army headquarters about three miles north of Naxos. Already the twenty thousand soldiers had moved into surrounding positions, totally encircling the whole city. As expected, the noisy motor-wagon drew a huge crowd as Ana pulled it up before the huge tents readily identifiable as belonging to the three generals. Even more were impressed when they saw that Ana was the one driving this strange beast.

Of course, Ana and Callisto had to take the three generals for a test drive and then allowed each to drive the vehicle around a bit. "Each of these can carry at least a ton of cargo and travels at a breathtaking speed of thirty miles an hour," Ana explained. "It took us only seven hours to get here from Andros." The generals were most impressed; they had taken seven days by horseback.

"How soon can your army expect delivery of many of these motor-wagons?" asked an enthused General Gyros.

"Andros Vehicles is making them at about two or three a week now," Callisto recited the latest figures that she'd heard. "When more raw materials become available, they hope to be able to make more each week. They are just getting started."

"Right," Ana took over. "At first, every other vehicle is being sent off to one of our towns and villages. Our goal is to have one of these in every town and village in Arolas as the town's vehicle for use by the folks. Callisto and I are paying for them out of our own pockets, but right now, only every other one that is made is being sent to the towns. The other ones are going to be given to you generals and your valiant army men. Later this week, they will be driven up here from Andros. I think the first shipment will amount to ten motor-vehicles. Getting enough petrol is our current biggest problem with them. I have assurances that in time, petrol will be in greater abundance."

"Well, thank you monarchs! I look forward to having them," General Gyros replied. Already the three men began seeing vast new uses for them. They could move their troops from point A to point B in one-tenth the time that they could by horse, to say nothing of fast resupply lines.

Once inside General Gyros' field command tent, Ana asked, "Okay, so what's the situation in Naxos?"

General Methodios paced his office at Fourth Army Headquarters in the heart of Naxos, Arolas. Paced was not a good word, the overweight man was on his knees. The plague had finally come to Demokritos. It was October 25, 823. During a crisis, the forty-one year old general always paced. He was determined to move about his office in spite of the dastardly plague turning his feet into matchsticks. Earlier that morning, he'd been awakened by the terrified shrieks of his wife. Bitch can't handle a damn thing, he thought as he recalled waking up beside her. Poor beast had no arms at all today, none, gone, nada. He himself had fallen flat on his face when he tried to rise and help her calm down. His feet refused to work. Well, that is not entirely true, he mused. They are match sticks now, yes, that's what he'd called them, after letting loose his own tirade of curses.

"You've got problems, lady? What about me? I can't even stand up. At least you can do that, woman, now let me be. I have a country to run. Arolas is a bit more important than you," he'd said angrily to her. Perhaps that was not the best thing to say to the woman, he now thought. She'd only wailed louder than before. So much so, that he'd just gotten dressed and headed to his office. The ignominy of it all, having to crawl to his office! Still, every other man he'd seen was also crawling. General Methodios took some comfort in that now, some ten hours later.

Slowly the reports had been coming into his office all day long now. His entire garrison of some ten thousand soldiers were lamed up just as he. Worse, all their wives, daughters, and servant staff were armless now. Actually, he was not terribly surprised with that; only yesterday, the women's arms looked like withered appendages of the dead. No, he'd really not been very surprised to see Clea armless this morning. Not that it really mattered, for she was just a wife and a pathetic one at that. She'd given him two daughters, which he had to scramble to get married off. No sons, not a blessed one, no one to carry on the tradition of the Methodios heritage of serving in the Arolas army, as his father and grandfather had done before him. Now that line would end with him.

Later in the day, word began arriving from around Naxos itself. Apparently, this plague was now citywide. The King had not responded to his requests for orders — not that he had truly expected such from old Tropos. He didn't care for the man personally, no gumption, a mere follower, a dandy on the throne. "Never had an original idea of his own," he grumbled to his walls. Citywide, yes, citywide. The right side of his mouth curled up as he realized the extent of the plague and its likely reaction. Total shutdown, that is what he had predicted to his aides when they came crawling in with the news from the city proper.

Maintain order. That's the first idea that entered his head. Around noon, he began issuing orders to the soldiers under his command. But then, he realized that if everything shut down, there would not be any need of that. Rather, he decided that he needed information. What was happening out there in the huge, sprawling city of several million people, covering twenty square miles or more? His orders were simple: "Fan out and cover the city and observe what is going on and report that back to me periodically."

Now word began coming back up the command lines to him. Of course, no one below him dared actually do anything about what they were witnessing. No orders. If he had taught his men one thing, it was only and always follow orders, his orders. His second orders were to find men who could cook and get the chow lines going before everyone mutinied. Besides, he was more than hungry now, ignoring the fact that he really ought to lose some fifty pounds, maybe more.

Around six that night, an aide brought him the first food he'd had all day, sliding a plate along before him as the man crawled into his office. Around nine, all reports continued to reflect a dead Naxos. That is, no shops had opened all day. No one but his soldiers was in the streets and they all rode horses to get about. However, wailing, screaming, and crying sounds came from all the residential areas, rather sickening many had reported. Satisfied all was as well as could be expected and leaving orders for breakfast to be served at eight the next morning, General Methodios crawled back to his home residence a block away.

He was not pleased with what he found. His wife was still sobbing. Bitch! Had she done nothing but sit in bed and cry all the damn day? Shit, she'd soiled his sheets! The stench was nauseating. "Couldn't you at least have got up and used the chamber pot?"

"I can't get my nightgown off or my panties down," she sobbed. "Please help me. Please. I can't do anything like this."

"Hell, I've been crawling around all day long. My hands and knees are raw. Oh the hell with it, woman!" He turned around and crawled back out of his residence and back to his office, where he summoned an aide to fetch him some blankets. He'd sleep in his office from now on — at least it didn't stink to high heaven. Besides, some important news might be arriving at any minute, he justified.

The next morning after breakfast, he began receiving some rather disturbing news. Apparently, some of the Church of Jehosanity men were going around notifying everyone that the Holy End of Days had come, that the Holy Day of Judgment was upon everyone. Subsequent reports added that apparently these men were helping some along, slicing their throats. What were their orders now?

General Methodios was not a religious man. The plague was proof enough that there was no such thing as a god. What kind of a god would allow this to happen to his people, his faithful? Certainly no god that Methodios wanted anything to do with, that's for sure. "Hell, let them kill them all," had been his orders. No sense risking his soldiers' lives on these ignorant churchmen.

Later that day, reports came to him concerning the old King. Apparently, the old fool had tried to ride out of his palace and talk sense to these religious fanatics and had gotten himself killed! Mobs of men were now taking to the streets. Slowly a smile began to spread over his face, a coy, smile that ended in a sneer. The king was dead. He had no sons, except the one known bastard son, whom was in exile for fear of his life. Naxos and all Arolas were now leaderless! That's what caused him to smile. Naxos, the heart of Arolas, was leaderless. From all reports, it was simply chaos in the streets. Who better to take the reins of the country than he?

True, there were three other generals, but their forces were hundreds of miles away. Given the situation, they were highly unlikely to come to Naxos. Who better than he, General Methodios, to become the next ruler? After all, had not the Emperors done something similar? Assuming control during a chaotic situation? Perfect. His orders, "Observe and report. Take no action."

"The essence of a successful coup is timing," he explained to his aides. "We wait, let the mobs and the church prepare the way for us. When the time is right, we step in and take over the city and the country. I shall be the next King of Arolas and the people will completely back us up." His aides smiled, knowing that if he became the ruler, their pockets would be well filled.

As the ensuing days passed by, General Methodios never left his office. Instead, he began pinning little flags onto his large map of Naxos. One flag read, October 26, mob smashed the palace gates. Another read, inspection of Church of Jehosanity on 9th Street found nothing but dead bodies, throats slashed. Dozens of flags indicated the conditions in various parts of the city. He was not even fazed when an aide reported that his wife had been discovered dead in her bed. He'd only grunted and told them to bury her somewhere and fumigate the house.

Two weeks after the onset of the plague, General Methodios finally decided to take action. Why? His men reported that the stench of the rotting corpses in the streets, yards, and homes was getting so bad that his soldiers were balking at going into certain sections of the city on their patrols. Secondly, their food supplies needed replenishing. His control of the army went only as far as he could both feed them and pay them. Lose both and he lost his soldiers — any general knew that.

Food? Well, that posed no real problem. Send their supply wagons and raid the storage warehouses. Pay? Problem. Cash on hand: enough for one more month. He issued orders to begin raiding the warehouses and for the paymaster to dole out his soldier's last two week's pay. Where to get more funds? That occupied his thoughts for several days. He could bash in the doors of the Banca del Dio, but it was general knowledge that the banks did not keep sizeable funds in their vaults. Rather, funds were transferred in timely fashion to his paymaster from the king's accounts, but the king was dead — shot in the streets by the mobs.

The answer was plain and simple. His forces would have to take over total control of Naxos and confiscate what they needed. Get the wealthy to "donate" to the pay of the soldiers who would be protecting them. "Makes sense, since we will be the only effective protection this city will now have," he told his aides, who agreed.

However, he also was forced to do something about the rotting corpses. The city was now so "ripe" that he smelled it even here in his office! Once the wagons finished bringing in the current round of food supplies, he ordered all his soldiers to use them to pick up the dead. "Go door to door and remove any dead. Tell the living that General Methodios is now in control of Naxos and to remain calm." As his aides left to issue the orders to the many majors and captains, he mused, "This coup is even easier than I ever imagined."

Now he began to sort through the enormous pile of dispatches that he'd been putting off for days. He picked up the first one. "Perfect format, yes, private initials, his sergeant's signature, his captain's signature and dispatch number and dispatch content category, perfect." He mused a moment on how wonderfully successful he had been getting his many subordinate officers to follow the precise military protocols on all dispatches. Indeed, they were now perfect. He finally read the message about some house having no men there and the five women were quite desperate for some aid. What should he do about it?

"Hell if I know! Aren't we all in trouble?" he cursed and tossed that one into another pile and grabbed the next one. A private asked, "On Marble Lane, a family was starving, totally out of food. What should be done?" He growled and tossed that one aside as well. What should be done? Lord knows, go out, and get some food from the markets and stores. The man's an idiot, he thought. The next dispatch asked him what to do about a family of eight who were all quite sick. Should the soldier send a doctor to them?

"Hell, that is just what you get when you have a government like our Emperor who does nothing but give handouts to everyone. Now the stupid peasants can't even take themselves to the doctor when they're sick. Idiots! The world has become populated with idiots, thanks to the Emperor's giveaways. Well, that's going to change right now!" General Methodios pounded the table. The piles of dispatches bounced in the air and settled back down, awaiting his hands.

By evening, his head was swimming with all the reported problems and requests for his guidance on what or how to deal with them. Hours ago, he grew tired of even calling out "idiots." At last, he just dumped the whole lot into the wastebasket. "Either they will solve their own petty problems or not. If they don't, we'll just haul them to the graveyard and good riddance to them. Ah well, where's my supper? Aide?" he yelled.

The next morning, the general was very ill, too weak even to send for an aide. Fortunately, one came crawling in with the morning dispatches and found him. A while later, a doctor came, though he too was sick. "Cholera," he pronounced. "General, drink lots of water. Half our men are down with it. I think that it came from carrying our food back in the wagons contaminated with all the rotting corpses." General Methodios groaned in agony, but didn't mention that those were his orders. Hell, he wasn't a doctor. If that was a problem, why didn't one of his doctors tell him? He was too weak now to say anything, but filed it away for later.

Two days before the plague struck, Mathias Nasses quietly entered his mansion, purposely quiet, hoping to miss the argument going on in their spacious living room. He'd heard them arguing as he entered and tried to tiptoe inside. Mathias was thirty-nine, immaculately oiled black hair, perfectly dressed at all times. He was reputedly the wealthiest man in Naxos, perhaps in all of Arolas many thought. He had inherited his fortune from his father whom he'd just buried some six months ago. Mathias owned the Nasses Clothier, a river-water powered factory that produced seventy-five percent of all cloth bolts in Arolas, both cotton, linen, and wool. The factories, one for each of the main products, lay just at the north end of his estate, a square nearly three miles on a side. The Pinos River marked the eastern border; the western edge was Nasses Avenue, running north-south at the very western edge of Naxos. He owned the Nasses Mills, a complex once again powered by the river at the southern edge of his estate. The mills ground all the various grains for Naxos. Nearby were the Nasses Grain Silos, where a large percentage of the grains were stored, once purchased from the outlying farmers and brought here usually during the fall harvest. Inside the city, he owned the Nesses Brass Foundry, which produced numerous brass household items. He also owned Nesses Imports, a company that imported fine clothing and other expensive items from all over the world. Yes, he was rich.

Yet, he was not rich in sons. His beautiful wife Sophia, a Holy Woman of the Eighth Degree, had given him three daughters before she finally had a son. She was a year younger, with long blonde hair and charming blue eyes. She was also the prima dona soprano in Arolas. Through her numerous connections, Mathias had become a well-known supporter of the Fine Arts of Naxos. Some said that Sophia had the voice of an angel, but Mathias thought that if there were such things as angels, Sophia looked like one. In his eyes, she was a spectacularly beautiful woman and he doted on her. If only she had borne more sons. His many businesses were taking up more and more hours of each day.

Sophia was wearing her restrictive Annelise corset and billowing hoop skirt. She always looked most presentable during the day. "Who knows when someone important might call? I must look my best for you, Mathias," she'd told him a hundred times, if not once. That she could barely walk in those Annelise heels bothered her not. As the prima dona, she prided herself on the example that she set for all the other vocalists and many artists of Naxos. Returning home, as he tried to sneak inside, he overheard Sophia lecturing their eldest daughter, Persephone, who was eighteen, engaged, and had her mother's angelic good looks. Her hair came from her father, jet black, luxurious and long. Sophia's was very blonde and long as well. Persephone, though a gorgeous young woman, was far more interested in raising and training horses, an activity in which she excelled. Already, they had something like fifty horses in various pastures on the expansive estate.

"Now Perse, you know that you absolutely must become a Holy Woman of the Eighth Degree when you marry Eros. Just look at all the tremendously beneficial things I have brought your father because of my high status. You owe your own high status in part to me as well. It is your duty and obligation as a Nasses to elevate your Eros as high as possible in our society. Besides, becoming a Holy Woman binds husband and wife for life. You must stop being so stubborn and self-centered. When you marry Eros, you must be ready to assist him in all ways. You owe it to Eros to be the very best that you can be, dear Perse, and there is no finer gift that you can give him than becoming a Holy Woman yourself! No more of this silly horse riding at all hours of the day. You must dress in your finest gowns during the day, just as I do each and every day."

"But mom! I can't even walk in those heels nor even breathe! I feel like I'm fainting all the time! I don't know how you can stand to wear them. Besides, I don't want to be a helpless wallflower like you are. You can't do anything for yourself; servants do everything for you. I don't want any part of being a Holy Woman. I've told you that a hundred times," she blasted her mother.

Sophia's eyes watered. True, she was so dependent on others for everything. Her daughter's words stung her. Still, she refused to give up, "You know very well that I am the prima dona vocalist in all Naxos! I've told you a thousand times that you have to wear the corset all the time along with the hoops and heels, if you are *ever* going to get used to them. That's all it takes — wear them all the time, and you'll get quite used to them. But no! I can only get you into them when you are going to a ball! No wonder you feel faint all the time. Honestly, I ought to have Mathias insist that you start wearing them all the time now. You are eighteen years old, not ten! Your twin sisters have been wearing them for years now, every day. You don't hear them complaining bitterly do you?"

Persephone knew that she could not win that point. Her two sisters were always going about the house wearing tight corsets, enormous ball gowns that flared out some twelve feet across, and wore those impossibly high Annelise heels. In fact, both had been very eager finally to be allowed to wear them when they turned fourteen. They had been wearing their outfits daily now for three years, constantly teasing her about being a tomboy. Hence, she countered, "You are only a Holy Woman because grandfather insisted you become one or he wouldn't let dad marry you! What kind of a choice is that? To be helpless all of your life?"

Fighting back tears, Sophia heard the door and called out, "Mathias? Mathias, please come here a minute. We have a problem with our eldest daughter." She carefully leaned her armless body forward as much as possible and rose to her feet, her long blonde hair slipping from around her back to her bosom. "Mathias?"

"Yes, dearest, just coming home," he called out and reluctantly turned right, walking into a hornet's nest, he thought. Sophia took a couple of her graceful, but tiny steps towards him so that her billowing dress would fall into its proper shape and look perfect for his eyes. She tossed her head first to one side and then the other, trying to get her long blonde hair to fall properly across her back. Perse rose reluctantly as well. He put his arms around Sophia and gave her a loving hug and kiss. Then, he moved over to Perse, gave her a hug, and kissed her forehead. She smelled of horses, but when hadn't she, he thought.

"Mathias, I have just been telling Perse that she is soon going to marry Eros. She simply must start dressing properly and elegantly and she must begin making preparations for becoming a Holy Woman of the Eighth Degree. Honestly, she simply must, Mathias. Just look at all the many benefits that she will be giving to Eros. Why, he will instantly be elevated into the very best of circles here in Naxos. How can Perse be so selfish not to do all that she can to help her new husband? Please, talk some sense in to your daughter, Mathias." She looked sternly at him.

He knew whenever she became *his* daughter, that Sophia was definitely angry and putting him in the hot seat. He sighed, hating to interfere in women's affairs, but in this household, he was surrounded with women's affairs nearly every day. If only they had had more sons. Sons could be reasonable, he thought. If he sided with Perse, there would be hell to pay with Sophia tonight. If he sided with Sophia, Perse would stomp off to her room and sulk all night, missing supper most likely. You can't win when you deal with women's affairs, that was his motto and guiding light. How to get out of this one?

"Perse, becoming a Holy Woman is a very important thing, and it is to be entered only with the full consent and wishes of both the husband and wife. Haven't I got that right, Sophia?" She nodded; she could not disagree with that key principle, as much as she would have liked to now. "So let's let that decision lie with Perse and Eros. Yet, Perse, you should try to look your very best more often now; after all, you are eighteen and about to be married. Surely, those outfits of yours take some getting used to, I'm told. Perhaps we can compromise on this, shall we, daughter? After all, Perse, you are as beautiful as your mother."

Perse realized that she had just gotten a major concession and decided not to risk her luck any further. "Okay dad. I'll change for supper." He looked at her sternly and she added further, "And I'll wear the darn gowns every day except when I need to work with the horses." He smiled and she knew that she had said enough to defuse the situation. He gave her a hug and whispered in her ear, "Thank you, gorgeous." She smiled; she loved it when he called her that. Of course, he'd been calling her that as long as she could remember, and more importantly, he didn't call Nikoleta or Dora that. This was a special word just for her, gorgeous. Well, she was far prettier than her sisters were — anyone could see that. She headed off to clean up and get into the awful outfit.

Mathias turned to his wife and again hugged her and gave her a passionate kiss, hoping she would forget about all this. She did; she always melted in his arms. "I love you, Mathias," she whispered.

"Love you too, my pretty angel," he replied, and relaxed, the first time since entering the door. Just then, they heard the telltale clicking of high heels on the polished marble floor. They turned to see the twins slowly gliding into the room, their arms around their boyfriends, who had come for dinner with them as usual. Sophia insisted that their children always bring their boyfriends or girlfriend, as in the case of their son Aristeides, to dinner each night. That way, all could become better acquainted with them.

Compared to Perse, the twins, Nikoleta and Dora, were quite plain. Perse had her mother's great beauty and facial structure. The twins were down right plain and looked a lot like their father. Early on, their seventeen year old identical twins wanted others to be able to tell them apart so that they could be themselves. Nikoleta allowed her light brown hair to grow long and wavy, falling below her shoulders, while Dora kept hers short, barely touching her shoulders. Both were wearing different colored satin hoop dresses, flaring out the required twelve feet. Their small, tightly corseted waists made their appearance even more striking. From their slow forward speed, he knew that the twins were wearing their Annelise heels as their mother always insisted.

He eyed them both as they slowly made their way into the room and over to their parents. Nikoleta was his chemistry whiz. She excelled in this arena. "Dad, I've just invented a new way to make a good quality Prussian Blue for the painters," she announced proudly. Her fingers with their long red nails also told him that she had been at her chemistry. Spots of deep blue remained on her hands, although she had washed them. Well, that was better than some of the side effects that her continual experimentation had caused. Once she'd blown up her small laboratory and nearly caught her own dress on fire. Another time, acid had totally ruined a dress, burning holes all over its front.

"Well done, my chem whiz," he replied, giving her a hug as she finally drew close.

"Evening sir," her boyfriend Doros Ranor said, shaking his hand. Doros was eighteen with black hair, which always looked as if it was in need of a cutting. He was a budding engineer and seemed a good match for his daughter. That Nikoleta was happy with Doros was enough for him to consent to their marriage. Besides, if Doros did become good at inventing, he could profit by it. "We are going to try to market her new mixture tomorrow. I believe that the painters will approve of her new mixture." He nodded and moved to greet Dora, who was behind the two, while Nikoleta and Doros gave a welcoming hug to Sophia.

"Hi dad," Dora said, giving him a hug. She was his little math whiz. She could add columns of numbers in her head! She had dutifully impressed her with her math skills when she was ten, finding a thousand gold error in one of his accounting reports. He investigated and discovered one of his employees had been skimming profits. He was fired. Ever since then, Dora examined his accounting records once a month.

"Evening sir," her boyfriend Euclid Kleides said formally shaking his hand. He was eighteen and had gotten a job teaching school. Again, he approved of the two; they also seemed a good match. True, he was the son of a miller, yet Dora was happy with him, and she would elevate him in social standing. Likewise with Doros, whose father was also an engineer not a nobleman. Like father, like son; still a marriage to Nikoleta would also raise the boy's position in Naxos' society.

While the small group began chatting with Sophia, their son Aristeides entered, escorting his girlfriend, Natasa Kissa. He was sixteen and being trained up to assist in the management of the many companies in the Nasses empire. He had short blonde hair, after his mother, and looked a bit effeminate, or so Mathias thought, but since he was his only son, he accepted the lad's looks. Still, he dressed immaculately, taking after his father. Natasa and Aristeides had been friends since they were children. Her home was at the south end of their estate, just across Miller Avenue, and at the corner of Nasses Avenue. She was the daughter of a marble contractor, yet love knows no social barriers. She was pretty with long brown hair. Natasa wore a brown satin ball gown; Aristeides had bought her several outfits on the quiet. Her parents could not afford such dresses and imported heels.

"Hi dad. All's well at the mills today. Say, dad, Natasa and I had a great idea. How about us holding a spring ball in our huge ballroom? We can hire the Alkyone Players; they are about the best dance music makers around. What do you think? I'm sure mom will go for it."

"Sure, ask her, son. If she agrees, then it is fine with me," he replied.

A bit later, Persephone came slowly into the room, her heels clicking on the marble floor. She looked radiant in her bright yellow ball gown, though she seemed to be having trouble both breathing and walking. He now saw what Sophia meant; Perse had better start wearing these outfits soon. "Is this better, dad?" she asked a bit huffily. Several servants had really hustled to get her into the outfit in such short a time. Worse, they had tightened the corset far too quickly, which only added to her discomfort.

He smiled and nodded to her. She turned to see what his nod meant and broke into a big smile. Eros Rikos had just entered. "Hi Eros!" she exclaimed and nearly stumbled as she tried to hurry over to him too quickly.

"Hey, easy does it in that dress, dear. You look really good, Perse," Eros replied, hanging his light coat on the coat pegs near the entrance of the living room. He wore an acceptable suit, but it was not an expensive one. Eros was a budding inventor of useful items or so he claimed. His father was a doctor. The lad was eighteen and quite handsome. Mathias saw what Perse saw in him, a kind, loving personality and who was also good looking. He'd long ago agreed to their marriage. Besides, it could not hurt to have a doctor as a relation. Eros slid his arm around Perse and escorted her towards the spacious dining room where everyone was gathering for supper.

Although they had been dining here for many weeks now, Eros, Doros, Euclid, and Natasa still felt a bit uneasy eating around Sophia. Yet, Mathias didn't seem to mind feeding his wife, holding her cup or glass up for her to sip. Rather, it seemed second nature to him. Still, the four young folks often stole quick glances their way. Worse, they had never dined where the table setting included two forks and two spoons, but their fiancés took that in stride, educating them on proper etiquette. Still, even after so many meals, they were still a bit nervous about it.

When the plague struck them all, chaos struck hard. Awakened by screams from Persephone's bedroom, followed by shrieks from Nikoleta's and Dora's, Mathias jumped out of bed, but fell flat on his face when his feet failed to work. It had been a hellish morning for him. He'd fought down his panic and talked calmly to his three daughters. Sophia, likewise shocked, though pleased at first, also helped calm the three down. He quickly handled their morning needs, got them dressed, and to the dinner table.

Only then did he discover that their servants had also been infected as well. "Don't panic, everyone, dad is just going to have to cook your breakfast." That turned sobbing faces into a slight smile, since they all knew that he couldn't cook.

Soon, he piled the eggs, rolls, tea, and pancakes onto the table. "No sense minding our manners this morning. Son, you have to assist. I'll feed your mom and Perse. You feed the twins. Relax daughters. I'll send for the doctor as soon as I can."

After they ate, the three teens felt a bit better, though they were still horrified. Sophia kept talking to them gently, telling them about all the wonderful things that had happened in her life because of having become a Holy Woman. It was her attempt at least to get her daughters to relax a bit. Meanwhile, Aristeides crawled off to check on Natasa, while Mathias visited with their many servants.

After only a brief discussion, he sent them all to their homes, via a pair of his many carriages. "Look, don't worry about us. Right now, you need to take care of your own families. Only come back when you are all well," he tried to sound hopeful. How they could possibly ever be well again when their arms had completely vanished was beyond him. What else could he say?

As he watched the last carriage heading out of their paved courtyard onto to Main Street, Eros, Doros, and Euclid came riding up. Their feet looked just like his and they wore no shoes. All had a most difficult time dismounting, but Eros had brought along the crutches he'd used when he had broken his leg two years back. While the others crawled inside, Eros was mostly able to walk, and Mathias asked, "Son, I think we need several more sets of crutches now."

"I'll get some for all of you, but first I have to check on my Persephone!"

By the time that he got inside, he heard her sobbing, "Eros! I've lost my arms! I am helpless as a baby now. Your feet? You can't walk either? What is happening to us all? I'm terrified."

"I won't leave you, Perse. I love you. I will be here for you, just as your dad is always there for your mom. Dad says it is an epidemic — the plague he thinks. Everyone's gotten it at the same time." She flashed him a brief smile and her tears began to dwindle. Mathias heard Euclid and Doros promising nearly the same thing to their fiancés too. He smiled, these boys were becoming real men, and he definitely approved of them now.

Aristeides came crawling in with Natasa walking slowly beside him. Her eyes were red and swollen, though she had stopped bawling when Aristeides came to her home. She was very pleased that he still wanted to marry her and was extremely glad that he offered to bring her here to stay with him. "Dad, mom, I've promised that Natasa can stay here with us, with me. Her dad has all he can do to take care of her mother."

Sophia replied, "I think that is a very good idea son. Boys, I do hope that your parents will allow you to also stay here with us so that you can help your fiancés with their needs now."

Mathias changed the topic, "Eros, come with me; take me to see your father. How many crutches can you get? Enough for all of us here?" He nodded, kissed Perse, and promised to return as soon as possible.

Later, while Eros began loading crutches into the carriage, Mathias spoke to the highly distraught Doctor Rikos. "Bloody epidemic! There is nothing that I can do for you, Mathias. Nothing. I've never seen anything like this before. There was some talk of a plague like this that struck up in the far northern continent. Maybe it has spread here as well. Is it okay with you if my son stays at your place? He wants to care for Persephone."

Mathias alleviated the doctor's worries on that issue and left. As he and Eros rode through the streets, they came across some of the blue robed Church of Jehosanity men riding by them. Their tunics were covered in blood, and they kept calling out, "Prepare yea. The Holy Day of Judgment has come unto us all. Prepare yea."

"What do they mean by that?" Eros asked. Mathias shook his head. He had no idea, but he didn't like the sounds of it. Once home again and able to get around on the crutches, which beat crawling on the floor, he loaded his long gun, just in case. The other boys had already headed home to fetch their things, and as soon as Mathias returned, Aristeides took the carriage from them and headed over to Natasa's home to fetch her things.

While Sophia and the girls were discussing what rooms the boys should use, a Mano del Dio man came crawling into the room. "Prepare yea. The Holy Day of Judgment is upon us all. He had drawn his very bloody sword and came crawling over towards Sophia. The man seemed crazed and she backed up slowly.

"Stop right there!" Mathias called out, grabbing his long gun.

The man turned and tried to crawl up to him, swinging his blade menacingly. "I'm following the Cardinal's orders. I am here to help you get to Lord Jehosa's Holy Realm quickly."

"Get out of here now!" Mathias yelled at him, though he tried to control his rising fears. The man again attempted to cut him with the sword and in backing up, he lost his balance and fell to the floor. The long gun went off and drilled a hole through the man's chest. A queer look appeared on the man's face; his sword dropped to the floor, and he slumped face down. A pool of red began seeping out onto the white marble floor from beneath him.

A shocked silence followed. "He — he — he was going to kill us! Mathias, he was going to murder us all!" Sophia exclaimed, breaking the silence.

"Daddy, what is going on?" Persephone cried out, becoming terrified once more.

Right then, Mathias realized the magnitude of what was and would be happening. It came to him in a sudden flash of insight — utter and complete chaos was going to engulf the whole city!

Thankfully, the other boys returned and were shocked to find a dead Mano del Dio man lying on the living room floor. After an explanation, Mathias had the four boys help him get the body out of the house, depositing it at the side of Nasses Avenue. Then, he locked the main gates. An hour later, they had the mess cleaned up.

He then cooked some late lunch for everyone, and the boys got their first experience dealing with their girlfriend's needs. Having seen Mathias feeding Sophia so many evenings, the boys quickly got the hang of it and were not too embarrassed by the whole thing. Over tea, Mathias finally spoke what was eating at his mind all this time.

"Everyone, may I have your attention. We're entering a crisis. With all men hobbled up, unable to walk, with all our women folk armless, assuming that this plague is citywide, we are in for major problems. We can expect that all stores, shops, businesses, and markets will be abandoned. No one will be reporting to work. If it also impacts the farmers around here, so none of the farmer's markets will be open either."

"Hey, where will we get food then?" asked Euclid, grasping the bigger picture before the others had.

"Precisely the problem," Mathias explained. "Expect rioting in the streets, mob actions, looting, the works. The real question will be what will our king do about it all? If he can somehow maintain order and somehow get the ample food reserves doled out, we should be okay."

They discussed the ramifications for a while and then they all headed off to get the newcomers settled. Mathias and Sophia decided that the boys should sleep in the girl's rooms. She knew very well how much she depended upon Mathias each evening, as well as when rising in the morning. Their daughters loved the idea, as did a very frightened Natasa. The parents kissed their daughters good night and gave a hug to Natasa. Mathias whispered in her ear, "You are taking this very bravely. I am proud of you, Natasa." She managed a faint smile.

The next day, Mathias took the boys out in the carriage to see what was happening. Were any shops open? How bad was this going to get? They returned very somber faced. "What's wrong, Mathias? How bad is it?" Sophia asked; she knew that look on her husband's face.

"King's been killed. A mob is storming the palace now. I've locked the gate; we should be safe enough. However, I'm going to get all our long guns out and at the ready. I believe that it is going to get really bad, dear, really bad."

Later that day, he took the boys and a wagon down to the river and followed it to the southern edge of his property where the huge mills were located. Ordinarily, this time of day, the mills would be in operation with many wagons coming and going. Not a soul was around — the mill buildings were deserted. Crutching their way inside, Mathias pointed out a dozen sacks of milled flour, which they loaded onto the wagon. With two hundred pounds of cornmeal and wheat flour, they could make plenty of bread. His idea was to find ways to hold out the coming storm.

When they returned, Sophia pointed out the huge pile of items that had mysteriously appeared in their living room. Already, the five women had discovered the strange shoes were easy for them to put on by themselves and most importantly, they could walk in them without all the pain that they had been having. The men balked at the strange boots that were apparently for them, since they'd be standing on their toes in them. "Hey, we are already trying to stand on our toes, maybe these will help somehow," the inventor Eros declared.

With everyone focusing their attention on this huge pile of strange things, the five women began having equally strange visions in their minds. At last, they opened up to the images that gave them clues. Even Sophia began to think about life differently. All her servants upon whom she had depended since she got married over nineteen years ago were no longer around. She just had to start doing some things to help. She cheered up the teens at her own expense, "Well, I've lived like this, armless, for more years than I had arms, yet I never did learn to do much for myself. Don't you think that it is high time that I learn to do some things for myself?"

Even Persephone giggled, which brought a smile to Sophia. She was making an impression on these teens, a good one. "Look, if I can live for nineteen years like this, you all are not going to perish any sooner. I think we just have to all work together somehow," Sophia added.

"Sir, do you have any fishing poles?" asked Eros. "We've got the river down there a few miles. We could go fishing every day and add to our food that way." Ideas for survival began flowing.

The second full week after the plague came, the streets became deadly quiet. Periodically, Mathias and one of the boys ventured a peek outside the estate. The sight was grim, dead lay randomly on the streets and lawns. No one was burying them. By the third week, they no longer ventured out; the stench was too strong. A soldier came by and asked questions dand Mathias asked him a dozen questions. All that he learned was that the plague was everywhere and that the king was dead. General Methodios had declared martial law and was in charge. The soldier insisted that they had nothing to worry about. Mathias didn't believe a word of that, because he knew the general, a power hungry, fat buffoon. Still as long as they could remain safe in his mansion, they could survive this. Their food stocks were holding out, what with the boys fishing every day.

The fourth week, they finally spotted soldiers with their wagons going around systematically picking up the rotting dead bodies. One asked if there were any dead here in his estate. Fortunately, there wasn't.

A couple of days later, Doctor Rikos came by for a visit. "Are any of you ill? You doing okay, son?" he asked of Eros. He explained that an epidemic of cholera and dysentery had broken out among the soldiers along with many who lived in the town. He urged them to boil their drinking water.

He also brought them news, none of it good. "Ma'am, your Church of Jehosanity is a thing of the past. All their nuns were found in their rooms, throats slit like pigs. All the priests and guards are dead too. Mobs have been looting all the stores, which used to sell food supplies of any kind. They come in after the soldiers finish looting them first. The soldiers are breaking into the places, loading up their wagons, and carting stuff off, probably to feed themselves. Once they're gone, men come crawling like ants, swarming over the remainder, carting off what's left. I think may be the end of the world has come. Worse, I just heard from a soldier that the Emperor was killed too. The plague has struck all of Demokritos, though I only know for sure that it has struck Thrace and Penelopus. Not been enough time to hear from the more distant kingdoms yet, but I sure don't know why they would have been spared." Mathias sent him home with a twenty-pound sack of flour and some fish, since the man had already nearly run out of anything at all to eat.

Early December, the entire family got a shock. As they were dining, Mathias heard a funny noise. "That is strange, come on boys, grab your guns, and let's check it out. Hobbling on their crutches and carrying their long guns, they headed to the front doors. "Damn!" Mathias cursed under his breath. Four thugs were attempting to break into his estate by forcing the lock on his gate.

"What do we do? We have to protect Perse," Eros whispered.

"Come on; let's scare them off. If they don't, then shoot to kill; we only got one shot at them," Mathias whispered back, regretting that they'd left their shooting bags with powder and shot back in the living room. They opened the doors and yelled at the thugs. Seeing five long guns pointed at them, the group dropped down on their hands and knees and crawled away as rapidly as they could go. "Dogs!" Mathias yelled at them.

After that fright, Mathias decided to post all-night guards. The five of them decided to share two-hour shifts throughout the nights. The girls chose to stay up with their boyfriends, promising that they would come wake everyone else if they trouble came. This proved a wise more, five more times during December, they had to scare off would be thieves attempting to break in to the estate.

Doctor Rikos came by at least once a week to visit his son and make sure that he was doing all right. General Methodios was now making use of his services as a local doctor. Thus, he became a fountain of current news. "Yes, Mathias, it is just as you suspected. More are dying every day. Hardly any business or shop has not been robbed. The soldiers bust in first, taking what they want. Once they leave the desperate follow in their wake. Dozens are dying every day. They've set up an emergency hospital in the king's old palace. I have to spend about four hours there a day. Not much I can do for them, I'm afraid, not unless the general doles out a whole lot more food. Honestly, Mathias, starvation is an awful way to go."

"What do the soldiers want besides food?" he asked.

"Coins, I think. Soldiers have to be paid somehow. I think that now there is very little difference between the mobs and the soldiers who are supposed to be protecting us," Doctor Rikos pointed out.

"Doctor, that is not a good sign. Soldiers have guns to back them up. If they become lawless, we are all doomed."

"Aye, I don't disagree with you there, Mathais. I once did a stint in the army myself, back in my youth. It's almost as if the soldiers here are treating Naxos as if it was a conquered city. You know, taking what they want, stealing food and valuables, though I reckon they won't be much interested in your valuables."

"No, what's a soldier going to do with paintings and sculptures? They can't sell them easily."

"True and you don't keep much gold around you place do you? They'll for sure come after that."

"Nope, just the wife's jewelry and my daughters'. We keep nearly everything in the Banca. Far safer."

"Yes, so many of us do. I think that's what is frustrating the general. He can't find enough to pay his men and that's one thing that I wanted to talk to you about, say in private or maybe with the boys here," the doctor said worriedly and softly. Mathias and the boys walked him outside, out of hearing range from the five women.

"Heard that now the soldiers are taking younger women off to their barracks. You know, raping them, making them into sex slaves or worse. Soldiers are prone to do that, you know," he whispered. His voice belied a deep resentment and fear of what the near future held.

"What? How dare they?" Mathias exclaimed growing more worried and angry at the same time, two conflicting emotions fought for dominance.

"Yes, I heard that they are going house to house stealing away the younger women. Heard that they took ten yesterday. Screaming and kicking, they didn't go easily, some have told me, though I expect many went willingly in hopes of getting food."

"Dad! That's immoral! I'll protect Perse with my life. No damnable soldier is going to take her away!" Eros declared, growing very angry now, which worried his father, of course.

"Son, you best be careful. Don't go messing with the soldiers; there are too many of them. I don't want to lose you, Eros, nor any of yours, Mathias," the doctor added, hoping Mathias would not take his remark the wrong way. It's just that Eros was his only son.

"I'll take good care of him. He's going to be my son-in-law, doctor," Mathias grinned, knowing how the man felt. He was worried about Aristeides as well. "We've got three square miles here in which we can hide out if the soldiers come. I'll keep him safe." The doctor shook his hand and then left.

"Sir, what are we going to do if the soldiers come? I'll kill them before I let them get their hands on Perse," Eros said spitting on the ground.

"I know, son, I know. I need to think. Come on. Let's let the women know about this. We can't keep it from them. They have to know the danger that we are all in now," Mathias explained.

The women's reactions were predictable, he thought, more fear and terror. He looked at Sophia and his daughters, so vulnerable, so helpless now. He had to protect them somehow. While the boys talked of opening fire on soldiers as they came up the driveway, he wracked his brain for alternatives, for a gunfight would be deadly for all them.

"Dad, we could use our riverboat and pack up everything and sail down river to safety," Aristeides suggested. Mathias did have a nice riverboat and had often taken the kids for boat rides on summer weekends.

"But where would we go? If it's like this everywhere else, what's the point?" asked Dora.

"Well, it the soldiers do come and we put up a fight, we are all going to be dead, sis!' Aristeides retorted. "That's the point."

"Dad, what about using my horse shelter down in the woods by your cloth factories? It is two miles from here across the pastures and hills. They'd never think of looking for us down there," Persephone ventured an idea.

Mathias hugged his eldest, "Brilliant, Perse. Brilliant. Yes, if the soldiers come, you fellows escort our women out the back and down to the patch of forest. Once you get over that first rise, you ought to be safe from all prying eyes. We need to post guards now day and night. You women must be prepared to head out of the house on a moment's notice, and quietly too. Come on fellows, we need to make some preparations down there. It'll be our secret retreat!" They spent the rest of the day hauling some blankets and supplies down to the old shelter. It wasn't much, but they could hide out there. Besides, it was summer now and the nights were warm.

December 15, 823 became known as Black Thursday, although the full details were days in reaching the group. Around noon, Eros, who was on guard duty, sent Perse to fetch everyone to the front porch. Gunfire had erupted, lots of it!

"What is going on, Mathias?" Sophia whispered frantic with worry. Was the end now drawing close? "Promise me that you will shoot me and our daughters if the soldiers break through and are after us. I can't bear that nor can I live with knowing our daughters will be so harmed. Please, promise me."

"I don't think it will come to that, Sophia," Mathias answered. He had no idea what was going on, and he couldn't possibly shoot his wife or their children. Dear god, has it come down to this? Parents forced to kill their own children to prevent them from being raped and taken into slavery and bondage? Dark thoughts flew through his mind, thoughts that he had never had before.

Gunfire continued to echo from the heart of Naxos; they all concurred on the direction. "I think it may be coming from the king's palace area," Euclid theorized. "From the distant echoes, the fire is at least two miles from here, but not more than three. Now, if we could hear these sounds from say a mile to the south, we could triangulate and get a better guess."

"Yes, but wouldn't it just be easier to take a carriage into the city and see for ourselves?" asked Doros, ever practical.

"And get yourself shot? No you don't Doros," Nikoleta put her foot down on that idea. "I need you, if you haven't noticed."

He put his arm around her and she appeared mollified. "I was just saying that that would be easier. I didn't mean I'd do it."

The gunfire went on for quite some time before it trailed off. Just as they were about to head back inside, Eros pointed out, "Hey, look! Smoke!"

Fire in a dense city is the most feared calamity, made all the worse by the near paralyzation of all normal city functions and the inability of men to walk. Ordinarily, a fire would bring all men, women, and children in the surrounding areas out to help fight it, forming water brigades. Bereft of women and men barely able to crawl, Mathias had a very bad feeling about this fire. Who would be fighting it?

Many of the structures were made of stone and some marble. Yet, at least half of the homes either were wooden or had wooden roofs. These were susceptible to the ravages of a fire out of control. Mathias knew that the majority of the wooden structures lay in the east side, where the slums were located. As isolated as they were here on the extreme western edge of the city, they had no fear of fire. Besides, his mansion was stone and marble with a red tiled roof.

By evening, they all knew what was happening. Horrors of horrors. A massive, out of control inferno was raging over on the east side of Naxos. The nighttime sky was illuminated in a sickly orangish glow! Smoke drifted over their mansion porch where the group stood watching the sky to the east. None said a word, their minds picturing what must be happening.

Breaking the eerie silence, devoid of expected distant shouting of those fighting the fire, Mathias said, "In time, it will burn itself out." He knew this as a certainty, only the amount of destruction was unknown. From the size and intensity of the blaze, he knew that it was huge and devastating. As they watched, a lone rider came ambling slowly up to their gates.

Eros recognized his dad and crutched his way rapidly across the huge courtyard to unlock the gates. His father's clothes were scorched, soot covered his face, his hands showed signs of burns. In an apathy, he rode silently alongside his son up to those gathered on the expansive porch. Eros helped his father dismount. He seemed to have aged twenty years, he thought. What had happened?

"She's gone," Doctor Rikos mumbled apathetically.

"Who's gone?" Eros pleaded with his father.

"Mom. Couldn't save her, couldn't. . ." his voice trailed off. Mathias insisted they get him inside, but it took some doing. On crutches, they were not able to help much and his hands and knees were rather badly burned and scraped. Once inside, the boys went to get some water boiling, while Sophia went with Aristeides, telling him where they kept their first aid supplies.

The five managed to get him out of his ruined clothes and got him washed off and his injured hands and knees cared for as best they could. If he needed anything else, Mathias hoped the doctor would bounce out of it and tell them what to do. He felt horribly ignorant of medical methods.

Mathias kept at him and slowly the story emerged, a grim one. The soldiers again attempted to kidnap some teens from homes near the king's palace area. He had taken his wife who had become ill to the makeshift infirmary at the palace and was tending her when the massive gun battle broke out. Men in the slums had finally had enough of the soldiers kidnaping their daughters and had fought back. Hundreds of soldiers had been killed, many more wounded. Likewise, with the townsfolk, though the soldiers just left the wounded townsfolk where they had fallen, refusing to help get them to the infirmary. During the battle, someone shot out a lantern and a wooden home caught fire.

The fire might have been prevented had both sides ceased shooting at each other and worked together to put it out. They hadn't and continued to kill each other for another two hours, before the fire was leaping from house to house so fast that they had to crawl away or get burned themselves. More and more wounded were brought in for the army doctors to handle as well as the six doctors of Naxos. Before long, though, the raging inferno leaped onto the wooden roof of the palace complex. No one realized this until it was too late!

Frantically, Doctor Rikos had tried to get others to help him get his wife out of the palace as well as the many other patients. However, the soldiers panicked and fled. He had tried to drag her out, but simply could not, barely escaping himself as the ceilings finally collapsed. There had been around eight hundred inside at the end. He'd hear their tortured screams in his mind as long as he lived. Somehow, he'd gotten to a horse and had come here.

Mathias found it encouraging that when the doctor finally had told them what had happened, the man had risen from apathy to grief. He thought that a release of grief might be a good thing. Eros held his father's head in his lap, allowing his dad to cry, unable to say anything helpful or even consoling. He was too much in shock over it himself.

Mathias sat down with Sophia, who whispered, "Maybe we should just leave Naxos and go somewhere else that is safer."

"Where can we go? I've a cousin who lives on a farm south of Naxos. I don't know if they are still alive or whether they could even take us all in. They might not have enough to eat either. We could try to get down to Andros and buy passage on a ship somewhere, but where would we go? If the whole country is infected, the inns along the way will not be open either. We'd have no food or shelter on a lengthy trip. Yet, dear, can we realistically continue along as we are? I just don't know," Mathias sighed. What to do? Stay? Go? If so, where? How? When? He thought, we men are hobbled up and barely able to get around and our women are nearly helpless, dependent upon us men. What should I do? What ought I do?

"Dad, can we get away from here? Go somewhere?" Persephone asked. "I don't feel safe anymore. I'm scared. At first, when I got the plague, I didn't want to live as I am, so helpless, but Eros and you and mom and everyone have been so kind that until tonight, I thought maybe somehow, someway we can make it. Now with the fire and all and the constant threat that soldiers will come in here after us, I'm scared and I don't want to live scared, not like this. Maybe before I lost my arms, I might have been able to live with it all, but not when I am like this. I can barely walk. If they come, I can do nothing to stop them nor can I even flee. Isn't there somewhere we can be safe?"

Mathias felt like screaming. All his life, he'd done everything that he could to create a safe home for Sophia and his daughters. Servants, social life, clothes, comforts, security — yet, in this moment, it had all been for nothing. The world was tumbling down around them, and he felt more helpless than his daughters and wife. He had been their point of anchor, the one fixed point upon which they could all depend. Now, they were adrift in a chaotic, tumultuous sea that threatened to drown them all with the next wave and he could do nothing, nothing at all to save them.

What did he know how to do? His mind drifted. True, his dad had left him the family business, but it had been himself, Mathias Nasses, who had expanded the cloth factory twofold capturing seventy-five percent of the Naxos sales. He had bought out the others and now owned all the grain milling operations and silo storage facilities here in Naxos. He had moved into the brass foundry industry and the imports arena. Why? What was his secret for success? Why should he be worrying about all this now? His mind reeled, yet he could not stop these seemingly errant wanderings to focus on the crisis at hand. People have needs and desires, so fulfill them, and you can make a tidy profit. Yes, that is my secret. See what they want and make that available for a reasonable price. What does this have to do with me now? I would give it all up just to get them all to safety, for this nightmare to be ended! His mind screamed; his face grimaced as if he was somehow being tortured.

"Daddy? What's wrong?" asked Persephone, who saw his face and became even more worried. "I'm sorry. I've no right to dump my problems on you, dad." Fiercely independent prior to the plague, she felt guilty about suddenly making her dad shoulder her own shortcomings and utter dependency now. After all, he'd shouldered mom all her life and now he had five women to take care of not just herself. I'm just being selfish, she thought, but then grief swelled, as once more she sensed how utterly dependent she now was and again wished that this would all end somehow. She felt like a horse whose legs were broken, just waiting for an act of kindness to put her out of her misery, for misery this certainly was.

How could he answer his dear Persephone? She, who more so than Dora and Nikoleta, was suffering from this plague from Hell — she who was more like a son, a rising star in the horse breeding and training arena, she who was so independent, breaking stereotype molds, a breathtakingly beautiful young woman who cared not to trade upon that, but insisted on making her way as a horsewoman. Now all her goals, her aspirations, her love in life — all of that had been ripped from her — shredded without even remotely asking her consent. Could this really be the end of all? He could not see how life could ever continue this way. Well, maybe for a few more days they could manage, but only a few. When their sacks of cornmeal and flour were gone, then what? Farmers could not possibly grow their crops, not hobbled as they were. No crops, no food, no food for this city of millions who depended upon the annual harvest and the daily farmer's markets. Death by slow starvation — that's what they were all facing. All his fortune meant nothing now. In fact, he had not even bothered to check on his many stores and factories around the city. Why bother? No one was interested in purchasing silk bolts from Tashien — they couldn't eat it. True, none of the women's clothing now fit them remotely. Sophia was more interested in eating than looking her best as she had done daily for nineteen years until the plague.

The plague! Everything had ended because of this damnable plague. He put his arms around Perse and pulled her close to him, allowing her to bury her head in his chest. "I'll figure something out, Perse. I promise," he whispered in her ear. What else could he say? He just could not betray her or his family. It seemed like only yesterday that he was sitting here holding her in his arms when she was barely five years old. He was stroking her long black hair while she was telling him about her exciting day — she'd been on her first horse ride. He recalled how he had made it happen after that day. That is, he'd made available the horses and trainers who had given her the training that she needed to become what she desired: a horse breeder and trainer. Make it happen, ricocheted around his mind, like some blinding arrow that one cannot see, except when its flight ends in the target. Make it happen.

"Hey, I need to try something. Everyone, listen up. I am going to go find this General Methodios and see what can be done around here. There is always the possibility that I will not come back. If I am not back by say tomorrow morning, boys, I am charging you to pack what you can and take the women out of here by wagon. Go down to the river, then go through the Cloth Factory complex, and then stay on the river road until you are clear of the city. Aristeides will lead you to my cousin's farm about twenty miles north of Naxos. It's about the only place that I can think of where you will be safe."

"Dad, what's going on? What's going to happen? Please, don't leave us," Aristeides spoke up, suddenly very worried that his father was about to be killed too.

"I've got to do something to try to stop this insanity, son. I know the general. He is a fat pig, egocentric and opinionated. Still, he's the only one who can bring some semblance of order to Naxos. I have to get him to see reason and start doing the right things. I have to get him to put in some control over his soldiers and their looting and raping. I'll probably be all right, son, but just in case, I want you boys to promise me that you'll do as I ask." Although they protested some, the four boys agreed.

In his office, which he had not left since the plague struck, General Methodios sat behind his large desk. "What's the results?" he asked an aide who came to report on the aftermath of the Great Fire.

"A quarter of Naxos is rubble, including the palace, sir. Thousands died in the fire. We believe that many became trapped trying to escape in the streets. We lost nearly all the wounded soldiers who were in the makeshift infirmary in the palace. Official count is in, sir, as you requested. We have five thousand six hundred-fifty-one soldiers left. With luck, most of the troublemakers are now dead as well. The riots were completely suppressed. What do we do with the thousands who are now homeless?"

"Hell if I know! Fools. Let them figure out their own problems. Haven't we got enough of our own to deal with?" he growled. He'd just gone over the paymaster's reports. After paying the men tomorrow, all their coins and those they had stolen would be gone. No more pay meant soldiers would soon be deserting him. That was his greatest fear. He regretted not the loss of half of his force. They had died putting down the rioters, and besides, the needed payroll was now half of what it had been. Their sacrifice had been doubly beneficial.

"Oh, one more thing, general, Nobleman Nasses is here to see you. He's requested an audience with you. Shall I send him packing, sir?"

"Hum, Nasses, you say? Isn't he about the wealthiest man in Naxos? No, send him in; he might be useful," General Methodios replied. Money, the man had money and he certainly needed money and soon.

His aide crawled to the door and opened it. Hesitantly, Mathias entered on his crutches, thinking that at least he was able to move around upright, not crawling like all the soldiers he had seen on his way to this office.

"Ah, Mr. Nasses. I am General Methodios, the new Ruler of Naxos," he said emphasizing the word ruler. He wanted to leave no doubts about his important position with the nobleman.

"General Methodios, good afternoon. May I sit?" Mathias asked politely, already he confirmed everything that he knew about this man. The general waved his hand and Mathias took a seat on the opposite side of the huge desk. "Trying times we are facing. Horrible beyond description."

"Well that's certainly true. What is it that you want?"

"I am probably the wealthiest man in Naxos. I just cannot sit by idly any longer doing nothing to help our once proud and great city. I have come to offer my assistance to you, in hopes that our new Great Ruler will help us all get back into operation once more. Surely, there is something that I can do to help you. I have money." He made a coldly calculated guess that money was the key to controlling the general. The ever-broadening grin on the rotund face told him that he'd guessed right.

"Well, this is a pleasant surprise. Indeed, I do need funds to keep the army in operation. After all, my soldiers are all that is preventing a total collapse of all law and order in Naxos. So many have given their brave, valiant lives to crushing the rebelling mobs of thugs."

"Indeed, general. How much do you need each week?"

"Five thousand gold would be ample."

"Consider it done. If you can find the Banca del Dio bank manager to open the bank, we can setup an automatic withdrawal for you. It's the least that I can do for our new Great Ruler." He emphasized the last two words, watching the obese man puff up as they registered.

"Excellent! Excellent, Mr. Nasses. At last, we are getting someplace in resorting order to Naxos."

"Yes, indeed. Say, could I possibly make a small request of you? You see, once others in the city learn that I am covering your pay, some thugs and rioters might try to attack my estate. Could you possibly station a few soldiers to guard my gates night and day?"

"Why, yes. The rabble has caused us no end of troubles. We must protect our benefactors in this our time of great need. Consider it done." He sat back looking rather pompous. A few soldiers to protect his only continuing supply of funds were minuscule.

"Thank you Great Ruler," Mathias played the man appropriately. "I know that you must be terribly busy working out all the needed plans to get our great city going once more. I assume that you have already reached the conclusion that to get this lawlessness ended, you are going to have your soldiers man some key food distribution centers around the city, doling out desperately needed supplies to the starving folks. As you probably have already worked this all out, you have certainly seen that if you can keep the people fed, they will be less likely to cause problems for you. Am I right?" Oh, how devious he was being. He knew damn well that the general had no such ideas. Yet, by his phrasing, he had just told the general what he must do immediately, but in such a way that the general could say yes he was in the process of implementing it.

"My, you are indeed most astute, Mr. Nasses. Why, yes, we were just working out those very details before you came to see me. Distribution sites scattered around the city, my soldiers handing out food supplies will definitely go a long way to restoring order. Most astute of you to have noticed this," he replied.

Mathias grinned, "Ah, very good, Great Ruler. I also suppose that you will be putting a stop to some of your more disreputable soldiers who have been kidnaping young women, carrying them off to become their whores. I do believe that a good deal of our citizens greatly resent that and have caused otherwise law-abiding folks to shoot wantonly at anyone wearing the uniform. Truly, this is so sad. They shoot innocent soldiers and not those guilty of the actual crimes."

"Why yes, I've issued such orders, but you know how it is. There is always one bad apple in the barrel. You have my word that I will root out those bad apples and soon. We do need our city back in operation once more," the general lied, but saw the nobleman's point. He had best put a stop to this practice. Even though the women of Naxos now were not worth anything but being a whore, still, far too many people had taken up arms against his soldiers because of this. And besides, they already had a barracks full of whores to entertain themselves when not on duty.

"Excellent. Well, if you need anything else, please contact me. I am so glad that I have been able to do my part, even if it is such a small thing," Mathias replied. The general offered him his hand and he shook it, fighting down his feeling of touching utter filth. Still, if the general would only do these three things, some resemblance of calm might come to Naxos.

"Thank god you are back safe!" Sophia exclaimed as Mathias entered their front door later that afternoon. All breathed a huge sigh of relief. "So what happened?" she asked what they all wanted to know. He gathered them all in their living room and related what had occurred.

That afternoon, three soldiers took up positions outside their gates. Two days later, one came to tell them where the nearest food distribution center was located. Mathias went there and returned with the first beans they had had in over a month, along with dried lamb, sugar, honey, and a number of other luxuries that they had been lacking for so many weeks. That evening, they had a feast. As the days progressed, they heard no more reports of kidnaped women and Mathias felt a little more secure. His extended family was safe enough for now.

When the end of December came and feet were restored to normal, folks everywhere cheered for joy! Men, no longer hobbled, began to get back to their jobs. Farmers were finally able to bring produce into the Naxos markets. Mathias was kept busy getting his mill operations going once more. Finally, some calm prevailed, though the situation was far from optimum.

One quarter of the city was in ruins. Those who had lived there and still were alive were taken in by other friends and families, who lived in other parts of the city. Farmer's markets reopened, but mostly men were seen on the streets along with the ever-present soldiers who no one actually trusted. Overall, women were still scared to leave the relative safety of their homes. Rightly so, unscrupulous men began opening up "private clubs" for the soldiers, where they could take their pleasure with women. They acquired their women by abducting them off the street.

About the only real businesses that reopened were those dealing with food and its distribution, along with charcoal, coal, lamp oil, and similar necessities that were needed just to barely keep a household going. The tailor shops and the dressmakers, for example, did not reopen. Neither did Mathias restart his Cloth Manufacturing plants.

On the other hand, Mathias did help his employees at his four non-opened companies find work, primarily at his mill and silos, when the autumn crops began arriving. Few men chose to work a full day. Rather, with desperate, dependent women at home, they often preferred only to be gone four hours at most, just enough to make enough to barter for the food and essentials that they needed. Mathias realized that the average person was just barely clinging to life, doing only what they absolutely had to do to survive.

Several of his fellow businessmen did begin dropping by to chat, seeking advice and sometimes giving it. All agreed that with the general running things, no one was going to stick their necks out and attempt to rebuild or actually get city services going once more. This was especially so when in February, word came to the city about there being new Monarchs now in control down by the port of Andros. Several of Mathias' business friends did send men down there to investigate the rumors. By early April, it was clear to the vast majority of those in Naxos that their country did have new rulers, beneficent ones, who were rebuilding their country. Mathias and his friends began constructing a map which marked the overall progress that the daughters of the late king were making in their attempt to retake control of Arolas. Slowly, the conquered zones began encircling Naxos until only the city remained.

Because of this, none of the other wealthy men did anything but what was necessary to survive. Soon, the two Monarchs would finally retake Naxos from this pig of a general. Then, the real recovery could begin. That the general was perfectly happy ruling over a burned out quarter of the city gave even the average person a very clear picture. It was almost as if life was more or less put on hold, awaiting the return of the two monarchs. By late April, as most realized that the monarchs' forces were slowly surrounding the city, people began talking in the future tense. As soon as the Monarchs arrive, construction will begin. When the Monarchs come, we'll see some action in getting all the stores open. When the Monarchs get here, things will be put right again. Everyone was playing a waiting game.

All except General Methodios, that is. He began to worry. He too had heard the news that the two helpless daughters of the late King Tropos had somehow managed to survive and were now appointed the new rulers of Arolas. Who had appointed them? Why would anyone appoint a helpless pair of teenage girls to run their country and not himself? Clearly, this made no sense at all. Had the whole country gone mad? Surely, it must have. He began to give his soldiers pep talks, making parodies of how the two helpless girls would manage the country's affairs. Many of them laughed at his parody. How could helpless women do anything? They knew that now women were only good for one thing, sex. Nothing else. Hell, they even had to feed their whores, an action, which they detested. Worse, they had to wash them as well, though this they did only when the stench became too annoying. After the "pleasure houses" opened up, the soldiers finally stopped feeding their hostages, allowing them to starve to death. Grim. No, their Great Ruler was right. The supposed monarchs were unfit to rule anything. General Methodios built up a strong backing.

As May approached and his scouts began reporting the total encircling of Naxos, the general began making his preparations to defeat these helpless monarchs and the foolish soldiers who backed them. Of course, he could not fathom why any soldier would possibly follow or even accept such rulers. He needed a strong, defensive position. The army barracks itself would not do. Located in the southeastern corner of the city and on relatively flat terrain, his men would have little cover. He hated the idea of having to leave his beloved office, but he knew that he simply could not hold it for long. They could be overrun by charging cavalry very easily.

Looking over his map of the city, he formulated the perfect trap. He knew the style of fighting that the other generals preferred, assuming that they were still alive and in command. "Perfect trap!" he explained to his aides. "See that the majors and captains are briefed. We deploy in the morning."

"What's the plan?" General Gyros asked, as the noisy motor-wagon came to a halt and the two young monarchs climbed out, accompanied by the Ridon twins with their long guns. "Well, our advanced recon squads report that the enemy soldiers have barricaded all roads into the city and are prepared for a fight. About our only option is to punch into them and fight our way into the city. We dare not risk use of the cannonae; we must avoid collateral damage. Er, that is, accidental civilian deaths."

"Damn, I hoped it wouldn't come to this," Ana sighed. "Are you sure that there are not any other ways into the city that are open?"

General Krates of the Third Army answered, "You are welcome to take a drive around the perimeter and see for yourselves. Of course, there are openings on the river side." By that, he meant that the far western edge of the city lay against the banks of the Pinos River. Of course, enemy soldiers heavily guarded the three bridges that crossed the river at Naxos. He added, "What General Karpos and I have been discussing is where is the remainder of General Methodios' troops? You see, by our estimates, only perhaps a thousand are guarding the perimeter. Their barracks, where we had hoped to meet them in battle, is abandoned. Before the plague, he had ten thousand under his command. Where is the remaining nine thousand?"

"Ah, good point, generals. I smell a trap — sucker our brave men into an ambush. That's what I'd certainly try to do," Callisto replied.

"Okay, generals, let us do our scouting," Ana declared. "Come on sis, fellows, let's park our bodies in our motor-wagon. You get to look after them again, fellows," she teased. Every time the two headed off to scout out the enemy positions, Seth and Spyro were given the boring job of watching over their bodies while they moved out of them and headed off to see where the enemy was located.

While the generals chatted among themselves, mostly marveling over how these two teenagers could possibly be doing that they were saying that they were doing, though they had yet to be wrong in their locating of the enemy, the two sailed over their home city. After about a half hour, the two moved back behind their bodies, animating them once more. "Oh, you're back, great Miss Spunky," Seth said teasingly to Ana as her body suddenly animated.

"Crap! You would not believe what damage the Great Fire has caused!" Ana exclaimed. "Our home, our palace — it's just a blackened shell! The roofs are gone, rubble everywhere."

"Hey, at least a quarter of the city is gone, burned to the ground!" Callisto added, quite shocked with the destruction she'd seen. The two described in more detail the destruction that the fire had caused.

Then, Ana said, "Okay, we found the main body of soldiers. There are a lot fewer of them than we expected. There are maybe about four thousand of them hold up in the rubble in the burned out section, hiding in ambush. They have so much protective cover they that if you go at them with our soldiers, who will be out in the open streets, our men will get picked off easily."

"Excellent report, Ana. If that's the case, you are right. As our men approach them from the open streets while they are hiding under the protection of the rubble, they will be able to inflict massive casualties. We'd best find a countermove," General Gyros declared.

"True, but we think that there is also something else that's planned here," Callisto interjected. "We checked on all the main entrances to the city. Your scouts are right, each one is heavily guarded, but they have their horses concealed just inside their positions. We think that when you attack them, they are to fire off a volley, mount up, and head to the burned out section, joining the others. We think that these guards' orders are to sucker your men into following them into the ambush in the burned out section."

"We have an idea," Ana added. "Let's put this to a test. Have some men try to take the lower bridge over the Pinos. If we are right, after they fire a bit, they will gallop off into the city, expecting your men to follow. Don't. Instead, have them secure the bridge. When they do, Callisto and I want to drive our motor-wagon across and check out one section that is free of all soldiers. There just might be a way to eliminate the thousand or so guards preventing them from reaching the main body."

The generals agreed and galloped off towards the northwest corner of the outskirts of Naxos to issue the orders. As the four headed to the motor-wagon, Callisto declared, "Hey Ana, it's my turn to drive!"

"Oh no, it is still part of my turn," Ana teased back, unwilling to relinquish the fun.

"Hey, what about my turn? I'm supposed to get to drive it next," Seth added.

"Me too, I think it's more like my turn," Spyro declared with a big grin.

"Age over beauty," Ana insisted, grinning at her sister.

"You pulling age on me again? That's not fair. You had your turn to drive. Now it's my turn," Callisto insisted.

"Cat fight! Cat fight!" Seth teased them both.

"Now taking wagers. Two to one on Ana," Spyro jested. Callisto swung her hips and gave Spyro a good bump, and he broke out laughing. "Spunky," he said as he guffawed. She broke into a laugh as well, yielding to Ana this time. The four piled into the motor-wagon, Spyro helping Callisto climb in the bed and then joining her.

This time, Ana drove more slowly, staying behind the advancing generals and their men. "There's the bridge and there's the soldiers waiting for ours to advance on them." She stopped the vehicle and got out. "Let's soften them up a bit, Callisto. Balls of fire, nothing is flammable around this stone bridge. As a battalion of soldiers moved into position to assault those crouched behind a barricade of wagons, the two launched a pair of flaming balls, centered on the enemy soldiers.

While their two blasts did not get more than about half of the enemy, it served the purpose that Ana had in mind. As she guessed, as soon as the flames subsided, everyone saw the survivors racing away on their horses, back down the street into the town. As their soldiers cautiously approached the smoldering wagons and bodies, the clip-clop of many horses echoed on the otherwise silent streets. They were retreating, most likely expecting the soldiers to follow them through the streets of Naxos to the prepared ambush.

"You two are doing all the work for us," teased General Gyros. "Well done."

"Indeed, most impressive, monarchs," General Karpos added, very much impressed with the presumed witchcraft, for he had no other words to describe what he'd witnessed.

"Incredible. We've taken the bridge without any casualties. Looks like you are right, they are inviting us to follow them into the city," General Krates pointed out. "Well, I'll have my men secure this area, but not follow them. We'll set up a perimeter in case they try to come back."

Seth asked, "Okay, Spunky, what's the plan now? You've taken the bridge, so what's the plan?" The three generals grinned at the teen's mannerism. General Gyros thought that one day these boys would grow up and respect their monarchs properly.

"Simple, really," Ana explained to everyone. "It would not be wise to have our soldiers heading through the city when we do not know what the situation actually is here in Naxos. There are or used to be millions of people living here. What are their feelings towards our soldiers retaking control of Naxos? Are they against us? If so, we could be sending our soldiers into a hornet's nest. Are they likely to welcome us? If so, then we could enter the city safely. We need to find out and I have a good idea how we can get a handle on that, based on what your scouts have told you, General Gyros."

"She'd make a clever general," he declared. "Astute observation. Yet, I don't see what the scouting report has to do with it."

"They reported a large section along the western side at the edge of Pinos where there were no guards, only open land. From the cloth factories in the north down to the mills in the south. If memory serves me, that is the estate of a nobleman, Nasses, if I remember right. We are going to pay him a visit. If anyone knows the true situation in Naxos, it will be him. He owns quite a lot of factories and stores in the city, if they weren't burned down in the fire," Ana explained.

"Yes, Nasses is the one. He owns the mills and the cloth factories, I remember that too," Callisto added. "Good bet he knows what's been going on. Can't get anything past the noblemen. Now, do I get to drive this time?" she teased her sister.

"Good plan, but you will be on the wrong side of the river," General Gyros pointed out. "If you intend crossing the river, then I absolutely insist that some soldiers accompany you! That could be exceedingly dangerous. Who knows, maybe there are some soldiers hold up in his estate. Captain Jude, go with them. If they attempt to cross, you are ordered to go with them and take some men with you. Do not let any harm come to our monarchs."

"Aye, sir!" he saluted, looking pleased that he would again accompany the two teens. During the past many months, he'd taken a liking to these two teens and even their unusual boyfriends, who always accompanied them.

Ana let Callisto drive this time and Captain Jude rode along ahead of them, struggling to keep his nervous horse going. The noise from the motor-wagon continued to spook his mare. Following along behind them would not be a wise move, not with the generals all watching them go. When they noisy vehicle had crossed the bridge and was at last out of sight of the generals, Captain Jude veered to the right and came up some ways behind them. Finally, his roan mare calmed down.

Now they passed by squads of soldiers, dismounted and relaxing on the banks of the Pinos. From the cloth factories down to the mills, there was no bridge. Thus, they counted themselves lucky, no imminent threat of a battle for them today, just boring guard duty. They passed by the cloth factories on the opposite banks. The great water wheels slowly rotating with the current caught their attention, though no one was actually at the three factories.

They spied a grove of trees just south of the factories. Beyond them lay rolling green pastures. At least two dozen horses grazed, though they all lifted their heads to see what was making this most unusual noise on the opposite bank. Two teens who were fishing stood up and stared over the river at them. Callisto drove the motor-wagon close to the bank and stopped it. The four climbed out.

"Hello there!" Callisto called out.

"Hi, what is that thing? You can drive it?" asked the young woman with long jet black hair. Her clothes were ill fitting. She stared in awe at Callisto and then Ana.

"Sure, made just for us women to be able to drive, men too. Called a motor-wagon," Callisto yelled back.

"Wherever did you get such a thing? We've never seen anything like it!" she called back.

"Andros. First one off the new assembly line. Soon, everyone will have them. Latest thing, especially for us women," Callisto replied as Spyro came to her side and slipped his arm around her.

Ana joined her sister close to the river's edge, several hundred feet from the pair with the fishing poles. "Say, is this the Nasses Estate? We're looking for the Nasses estate."

"Yes, I'm Persephone Nasses, my fiancé Eros Rikos. Why? Who are you? You look familiar. I think we've met before."

"Right, now I recognize you. You are Mathias' eldest daughter," Ana finally connected the name to the face. "Seen you in our court with your dad a couple times. I'm Anathia Tropos, my sister Callisto Tropos. We are your new monarchs now. Our boyfriends, Seth and Spyro Ridon."

"Wow! Yes, I remember you two too! Our monarchs? What is going on? You want to see dad?" she asked, trying to absorb this interesting news. "We saw all these soldiers over on your side."

"Great. Yes, we came to see your dad. Got anyway for us to cross the river? If not, we've taken a bridge and maybe can come around to your estate's main gates. That is, if there are no soldiers guarding it," Ana called back.

"The soldiers left. They were protecting us, but they left a while ago," she answered.

Eros yelled, "We got a boat here, I can come get you. Is that okay?"

A half hour later, Eros rowed Callisto, Ana, Seth, and Spyro over, then headed back to fetch Captain Jude and two soldiers, who insisted that the monarchs not go across alone. "Hi Persephone. I'm Ana, this is Callisto," Ana said, making sure that the young woman knew who was who. "Looks like you are surviving this awful mess."

"Only barely. For a while, we thought the world was ending, but dad has kept us alive," she replied. "Are you really our new queens?"

"Monarchs. No more kings and queens. Benevolent monarchs we are now. Say, I like your estate. Many good-looking horses. Your dad's?" she asked.

Perse fought hard to keep her eyes from watering. "No, they were mine. I was a horse breeder and trainer. I used to ride all the time." She lowered her voice so that Eros out on the river could not hear her. "I refused to be a pretty doll, a pretty wallflower like my mom. She is a Holy Woman. I was really good at raising them, training them, and showing them." She could restrain her loss no longer. Tears swelled up and trickled down her face. "Now, I can't do anything at all but be a pretty doll for Eros. None of us — we can't do anything for ourselves anymore. My dad and our fiancés have been with us all the time since the plague struck. We're utterly dependent upon them, just like you must be with your two fellows."

"Persephone! We are not helpless, far from it. We've gotten a whole lot of help from the folks up north in Velona. A woman there called Bethany has written a book telling us how to do all sorts of things. Riding a horse is a simple matter. Why, Calli and I have even driven horse drawn wagons. We had to in order to escape Naxos when the mobs broke into the palace. Seth, you go back and fetch a bunch of those books, will you please? How far away is your house?"

"At your service, spunky," Seth replied with a wide grin. He took one look at the horses and then guessed what would be coming next. Once Eros let the three men off, he hopped in and took the oars from a pooped Eros. "Gotta go get some books for your fiancé and the others. Come on; won't take a minute."

"About three miles over the pastures. We brought that wagon down — it's there over by the shed where I keep halters and hay for the horses." Perse nodded towards a small building hiding in the trees. A small wagon with a horse was tied up to a tree. "Food is really scarce so some of us fish everyday so we all can have some meat for supper."

"Okay. Well, we all won't fit in the wagon. Let's ride some of your horses up to your house, Persephone," Ana suggested.

"But we can't ride. The fellows can, of course, but I only keep halters down here, no bridles or saddles," Perse objected.

"That'll do fine. Come on, Spyro, Perse; let's round up some horses. I don't want to walk three miles just now."

The three headed to the small building and Spyro entered, returning a moment later with his hands full of halters. "How many?" he asked.

"Eight, if we can catch them," Ana suggested.

"But we can't ride," Perse protested.

"Sure we can. Calli and I are going to show you how. Which ones?" Ana insisted.

"I can get them, I suppose," Perse answered rather morosely. She began to whistle and shortly several horses came trotting up to her. She had tears in her eyes as they nuzzled up to her. All she could do now was lay her head against them, no longer able to run her hands lovingly along their proud necks.

"Spyro, Captain, put the halters on them and then tie the lead end to the halter as well. We ride by holding the looped lead rope in our teeth," Ana explained. The two set to work. By the time that Eros and Seth returned and pulled the small boat ashore, they had eight horses waiting. After depositing the pile of books in the wagon, Ana told them what they were going to do.

"No saddles, so fellows, we're going to need a little lift up, please," Ana requested, confident and going first. Seth helped her up and got the rope loop up where she could reach it and she bit down. "Okay, get Persephone and Calli up and let's go for a ride!" she said through her clenched teeth.

Before long, they headed across the green pastureland, with Eros following along behind bringing the wagon. Soon, Persephone urged her mare into a trot and then a gallop. Ana and Callisto were right behind her, while Seth and Spyro rapidly caught up to them. "Spunky gals," Seth called out. Perse was elated! The freedom of the fast ride that she thought was lost to her forever had just returned. The wind blew her long hair behind her as she and her mare flew over the grasslands. Now she shed a different kind of tears, though out in front of the others, none could see them.

When they reined up close to the back fence gate at the rear of the mansion, she called out, "I can ride! I really can ride again!" Ana grinned and showed her how to wiggle around and slide off, an awkward manner of dismounting, but it worked.

"Sure you can ride, Persephone. We are not helpless. We just have to learn new ways to do nearly everything, that's all. All this is in those books we brought for you."

Dora, who had seen them all come riding over the pastureland towards the mansion, had let everyone know what was happening and that some strangers were coming. As they dismounted, Ana recognized Mathias Nasses and his family along with several others as the group came out to greet them. She grinned. I bet they never had company coming to visit them from the river side, she thought to herself.

"My god, Perse! You were cantering! You can ride!" Mathias exclaimed, rushing to hug his eldest daughter. Then, a large round of introductions created even more excitement, as they learned that Ana and Callisto were now their official rulers.

Captain Jude hastily asked, "Sir, is your estate secure? We are charged with protecting our monarchs."

"Not any more. There were a couple of soldiers who stood guard at my gates out front, but they left mysteriously," he replied.

"Okay, Ana, Callisto, I'm going to take my men and watch the front. Call if you need us," he requested.

"Come on inside, everyone. I'll fix up some tea! What an incredible honor, monarchs. We thought that you were killed too. I am so sorry about your parents," Mathias said, leading the way, still holding an arm around Persephone. "Boys, go prepare some tea for our guests, please." Doros, Euclid, Aristeides, and Eros dashed on ahead.

"You're the famous singer, now I remember," Callisto said to the sandy blonde Sophia.

"Yes, that's me. I am afraid that is a thing of the past. We've only been barely able to stay alive since the plague struck," she replied.

"How come the boys have to make the tea?" asked Ana.

"We women are so totally helpless. Mathias and the boys now have to do nearly everything for us. Now I used to have servants to help me with everything, but since the plague, there is only Mathias and the boys. Why if it wasn't for them, we'd not be alive today," she replied.

Ana began to realize the severity of the situation here in Naxos. Perhaps none of the women in the city had learned to do anything for themselves! As they entered the Nasses mansion, Ana began to appreciate the size of the place. It was enormous. This main central section was at least five hundred feet long with spacious rooms, all elegantly decorated with many fine works of art. Not pretentious, but comfortable, she thought. Mathias did not flaunt his wealth — rather the works of the artists of Naxos were on display. At each end of this huge three-story main building, two wings nearly as long and equally tall stretched eastward towards the gates. A giant carriage house and stable building lay just to the north of the north wing.

Mathias noticed her noticing the immense size of his place. "Years ago, our whole extended family used to live here. For the last twenty or so, it's just been us, my family. The north and south wings are furnished, of course, but empty. Honestly, most of this main section is empty. I couldn't convince my lovely Sophia here to have a dozen more children." She laughed and gave him a playful bump with her hips.

He led them into the spacious, but elegant dining room. Already, the teens had brought more chairs, and Aristeides carried in a large silver tray with several ornate teapots along with cups. "Sorry, we don't deal with fancy etiquette in dining any longer," he explained. At once, the boys began setting the cups and pouring the tea for everyone.

Ana and Callisto calmly used their feet to sip their tea, shocking all ten of their hosts! "Now that *is* something! I never dreamed that we could do that," Sophia exclaimed. "All these years I could have sipped my own tea!"

"Oh dear, sorry. We didn't realize that you all had not yet figured out new ways to do things. Well, I'm glad that we brought you all copies of Bethany's Hints," Ana explained. She lied, she already guessed that none of these five women had been doing anything for themselves and was just being polite about it.

Callisto added, "We feed ourselves, though I always let Spyro here cut up my meat. Handling a knife is too tricky, unless I just have to use it. Honestly, it's just as Bethany says, it takes us five times as long to do a thing, but there is usually a way to do it. Sometimes, she says that we need to have special tools made for us. I'm not into dress making, but she's got drawings in there about how to make a kind of scissors that we can use. Honestly, she's got ways for almost everything imaginable in there."

Mathias flushed, "We've been complete fools, I guess."

"No, Mathias. You've all been forced to cope with a very difficult situation here," Ana changed the topic to what she needed to discover. "Please, can you tell us what all has been happening around Naxos since the plague struck. We need to know what the local soldiers have been doing and what they are planning now that we've surrounded the city."

Over the lengthy tea, Mathias related their story in good detail. When he finished Ana and Callisto and the twins were saddened, though not shocked. After all the despicable, horrific things that they had encountered in freeing the many smaller towns and villages during the last half year, they were not shocked, just saddened by the magnitude of the death and destruction here in their hometown.

"Your palace home is a burned out shell," Mathias added. "Please, would you honor us by staying here at my estate with us for as long as you wish? We have tons of empty rooms; two whole sections of the manor house here are empty. As you have noticed, when I married Sophia and she became a Holy Woman of the Eighth Degree, I had the good sense to change every last doorknob in the place to the lever action style."

"Thanks, Mathias, we'll take you up on your offer. We are going to need a headquarters from which to run our city and government, at least until we can get new quarters built. That might take a long time, since there are so many more important things that must be done to help all you survivors," Ana said diplomatically.

"Great. We can set aside the entire north wing as your governmental offices. You can use the entire south wing as your personal quarters, if you like."

Ana laughed, "There's only the four of us. Really, we can stay here in this main section with all of you, that is, if you don't mind and have the room. It is better that we women stay close at hand to help each other out with things."

"Perfect, we've dozens of empty rooms. We'll get some rooms fixed up. Are you going to go after that insane General Methodios now?" he asked.

"Yes, now that we know what the situation is here in Naxos, we will go back and assist our three generals in capturing these poor excuses for soldiers. I expect that many will be tried for their crimes later on," Ana explained.

"What can you do to help your generals and soldiers?" Persephone asked, a very confused look marked her angelic face. "I mean we are so helpless and so dependent on our men."

Seth burst out laughing, "Helpless? Boy do you have that wrong! These spunky gals here can probably eliminate every last soldier all by themselves! I'll tell you all about it tonight."

Persephone smiled, "I will hold you to that, Seth Ridon!"

Two hours later, the four, having returned across the river to their motor-wagon and then on to the generals, just finished capturing the last of the enemy soldiers who were guarding the entrances to Naxos. Because of the relatively small numbers at each post, Ana and Callisto joined up and used their sleep Druwid spells on them and then their soldiers moved in. The few who remained awake at each of these positions promptly surrendered. The captured men were taken back to the Fourth Army Barracks and placed under house arrest. Some twenty women, who had been kidnaped, raped repeatedly, and then left to starve to death, were found alive, though over a hundred more had perished. Ana and Callisto were furious when the details of this reached them, they swore to weed out the guilty men and see that they received appropriate punishments.

Late afternoon, they and the generals approached the blackened rubble of the burned out section of Naxos, along with their entire force, surrounding the area, but staying out of long gun range. "Look, there are some four thousand soldiers dug in there, hiding in the rubble. If we go charging in there, the odds are heavily in their favor. We are going to lose way too many men," Ana discussed the situation with the three generals.

"We can starve them out," Callisto suggested. "We have them surrounded. We can just wait until they are out of water and food."

"I wonder if they will recognize a white flag and parley?" Ana asked. She sent to Callisto, *We have the Grey Creature's blasters on us. If we turn them on the shield setting, they won't be able to harm us with their guns.* Callisto gave her a nod and a smile.

"General Methodios would be an utter fool not to at least parley with us. I'll send in a squad," suggested General Gyros.

"No, I think it best if Callisto and I did this parley ourselves. After all, if we are to be the leaders of our country, we need to earn the respect of our people. I must ask you to once again trust us, general," Ana replied sternly.

"But there is so much rubble, you ought to have someone with you to help keep you from stumbling," Seth protested. The three generals quickly agreed with him.

Callisto, who had already taken a closer look at the litter filled streets, agreed, "Right. We'll take Seth and Spyro with us. Trust us, generals. Maybe we can end this without any more bloodshed and get on with rebuilding the city. Lord knows the people here are in dire need of all kinds of assistance."

Only begrudgingly did the three finally give their consent but insisted in having an entire company nearby in case the parley went awry. The two sat down and used their feet to get the blasters out of each other's pockets. They adjusted the switch to the shield setting and replaced them back inside. "What are those things?" asked General Gyros. All the men were watching the two teens very closely. None had ever seen such devices before; they looked entirely alien to these men, which of course they were.

"A little insurance, generals. Something that we got from our Velona friends," Ana purposely hedged. Now was not the time to discuss aliens with these men, who would certainly not believe a word of it. "Seth, put your arm around me and always, always, always keep your body close up against mine. Spyro, same thing with Callisto. If they open fire on us, if you value your lives, you will continue to keep your bodies right up tight against ours."

"Oh, my, dear Ana, you know how much I do love to keep my body right up against yours," Seth teased. The two and the generals laughed at his joke. Even the two girls grinned. Seth and Spyro put one arm around each and were handed a white flag on a stick for their other hand. "Watch your step, dear," Seth suggested as the four headed down the street and into the scorched ruins of what had been an entire quarter of their city. Neither Seth nor Spyro mentioned that their home and parents had lived in here. Both wondered if their folks still lived or if their younger sisters had somehow escaped the inferno.

Before long, some soldiers revealed themselves and Ana asked to meet with their leader, presumably General Methodios. Once they were quite a ways into the zone and beyond the range of the long guns of their side, they were asked to wait. Two filthy soldiers headed off to find the general. "Good thing we had you two come along, Seth. Very tricky negotiating this mess," Ana complimented the boys for their foresight.

"Acrid smells though," Seth replied. The odor of the ruins was very overpowering. Fire blackened wall remnants poked up here and there at various heights, marking the shells of what had once been homes and shops. After standing around for nearly twenty minutes, a filthy general and a dozen captains came walking cautiously up to the four.

"General Methodios here. Who are you and what is the meaning of this parley?" the obese man spat out, totally confused at seeing two teenaged girls being supported by a pair of twins. Incongruent, yes, that's the word, the general thought to himself.

"We are your new monarchs. We are now running Arolas. Monarch Anathia and Monarch Callisto Tropos, daughters of the late king. We have retaken control of all the rest of Arolas and are now in control of Naxos as well. We've come to convince you to honor your monarchs and have you and your men walk out of here to our generals, peacefully. We do not wish to slaughter you or your men. We've lost far too many men and women and children," Ana declared.

Methodios began guffawing. "Helpless whores you are, that's about all you are good for now, nothing much else. Hell, you can't do a damnable thing for yourselves. Monarch, bah. If this is all those fools of generals can do, sending in two pathetic women, well, we'll show him. Shoot them." He ordered. A dozen long guns fired within seconds of each other. The bullets struck the defensive shields of the blasters and the lead bullets merely lost their momentum and dropped like marbles onto the blackened street.

"I would not have done that if I were you," Seth spoke as he sensed Ana chanting. The general and the dozen stared in disbelief. They'd fired at point blank range, yet nothing had happened at all. Nothing yet. Suddenly, lightning bolts came streaking down from the cumulus clouds drifting over the city. Often forking, the bolts struck each of the men who had fired on them. Bodies went flying in many directions. Great peals of thunder echoed over the city. Thirty seconds later, none of the twelve who had shot at the four remained alive. Smoke curled up from their electrocuted and fried bodies, leaving the general to face the four alone.

Seth said, "I told you that wasn't a good thing to have done, general. Now if you don't want to end up dead, I suggest that you tell your men to surrender and follow us out of here now. Very spunky, Ana. Very spunky."

The general's antagonistic, angry attitude shifted towards fear now. His legs began nervously twitching. He glanced around him, looking for a way out. His eyes drifted from one smoldering body to the next. "This cannot be! Freak of nature?"

"General, we're not helpless women. Rather, it is you who are helpless against us. If you don't surrender now, we will take our time and blast every one of your soldiers and you as well. An hour from now, we will dine, while our generals haul out the thousands of your dead carcasses. Your choice. Walk out with us or let them come carry your smoldering carcasses out later on. Makes little difference to me. Choose now, my patience grows thin," Ana grumbled.

Callisto, who had moved out of her body and took up a position high above them, spotted another bunch of soldiers sneaking into firing position. She launched a ball of flames over their position. The general spotted the blazing ball and saw another half dozen of his men shrieking and fleeing, their hair and clothing flaming brightly, though each collapsed after only a few panicked steps. The general wet his pants. Never had he seen such witchcraft, such magic. Surely, these two were demon witches or worse. How could he hope to fight demons? Maybe others would soon see that these were demon witches and kill them for him. Then, he would be right and seen as the true leader that he was.

"Okay, okay. I will do as you ask," his voice trembled as he fought for a semblance of physical control. His body was shaking very visibly now.

He yelled orders and his distant captains began relaying them. One by one, hesitant, filthy soldiers rose from their many places of concealment, dropping their weapons, and began walking out of the rubble quarter of the city. Ana and her group marched General Methodios out in front of them, further ensuring that his men got the message.

"Here you go, generals," Ana stated matter of factually. "Take him from us. Lock them all up at the barracks. Later tonight, please come by the Nasses estate. We have much to plan for the morning," Ana requested. The amazed generals took the obese general into custody, while the four headed for their motor-wagon.

"Okay, spunky ladies, it is my turn to drive," Seth declared with a gleam in his eye. He'd worked this all out in the last few minutes.

"Hey, my turn isn't done yet," Callisto teased him.

"I drive or else you have to tell us what those strange stick-like things are and how come all those guns didn't harm us. Take your pick. Which one will it be?" Seth stated, pulling himself up to his full height. Either way, he was going to get something that he wanted.

"Are you blackmailing us?" Ana suddenly realized what he was doing.

He winked, "You bet. Which one will it be, dear?" He grinned, knowing he'd get one desire.

"Okay, you drive," Ana consented. Seth laughed. He knew that he would be driving. Whatever the secret of those strange devices was, the girls were not about to divulge it just yet.

When they arrived back at the Nasses estate, the men already had supper waiting for them. Over dinner, Seth and Spyro told the others about the capture of the four thousand rebel soldiers. Then Ana commented, "Well, sis, we have finally got control of our country away from those who are out to destroy it. Now we have an enormous amount of rebuilding to do. Tomorrow, we'll have the soldiers go door to door. We need to see that each woman gets a copy of Bethany's book, find out what is needed and wanted at that home, and find out who has potentially harmed them. We will see that those guilty of crimes against our people are dealt with appropriately."

"But what about the rest of Demokritos? What about the Emperor?" asked Mathias.

"Honestly, sir, there is no more Demokritos and probably never will be again. Each of the kingdoms has grown far too large to ruled by one person. From now on, each kingdom will have its own rulers and autonomy. The centuries of the emperors and empresses are over, because we are all too large to continue down that route. Besides, the other six kingdoms are in utter chaos now. None has any rulers at all. They've unfortunately entered the Dark Ages," Ana explained.

Callisto added, "Against all odds, we've managed to save Arolas from that fate. Now, Mathias, you have an excellent opportunity to help us become a modern country and move forward to greater heights. We are going to show you some pretty darn great things tonight and like those in Andros, you and your extended family here can get involved right here at the start of it all."

"Ana, we've been reading that book since you all left. It's incredible," Persephone interrupted. "We are all going to do our best to learn. My sisters and I refuse to be helpless like our mother was all these years."

"Hey, I am going to learn too. I am sick and tired of having to be waited upon hand and foot," Sophia interjected, very much wanting to be a part of all that was happening. Her daughters and Natasa smiled.

Persephone continued, "But first, can we ask one thing of you, please?"

"Sure ask away," Callisto answered.

"Can you marry us? I mean the Church of Jehosanity is no more. There are no more priests who can marry us, and we here all want to be married. We figure that our monarchs have the authority to marry us. Please, can you do this for us?" Persephone asked, hoping that she would not have to beg, but she and the others were prepared to do so if need be.

Ana giggled, this was not what she had expected. "Okay, but it sure won't be a fancy thing. However, if we do this for you, then you have to convince your father to do the same for us."

"Do what?" he asked, not grasping what Ana meant.

"Marry us. We have no one to marry us either. So Callisto and I will marry you four, and Mathias can marry Callisto and me to Spyro and Seth," Ana grinned at Seth.

"Thought that you'd never ask, spunky," he teased her.

"Hey, I have an even better idea!" Callisto spoke up. "Come on everyone. Bring your fiancé and follow us." A bit later, while Spyro began peddling the electric generator, Callisto demonstrated the LD radio system and soon she and the whole group were chatting with me in Velona. I sent for our High Priestess, Danila West Po. Via the LD radio, she then married the six couples officially.

Although the winter was nearly on them now, Arolas alone had been saved from the Dark Ages. The two monarchs set up their government there in the north wing of his estate. Mathias began investing very heavily in these new inventions, forming companies to begin their manufacturing. Eros, Doros, and Nikoleta, the inventor, engineer, and chemist, soon became key players with Mathias. Euclid and Dora, on the other hand, began to oversee the creation of the new school system that the two monarchs established. All children from six to fourteen would be getting an education free of charge, compliments of Ana and Callisto. During the winter of 824, hundreds of plans were formed and their executions begun. The two monarchs knew that they had to bring positive change to the people of Arolas and bring

Vic Broquard

it to them quickly.

Chapter 15 Escape

I continued to check up on Pian Ling Wu and Shu Wen Chow, that is, Jemma and Fina as I used to know them in our last lifetimes. Additionally, I also began chatting telepathically with Misha Wu, knowing how terrified the twelve year old girl must be, now both armless like the rest of us, but also blind like her mother. Her terror was very acute and real, but after her feet became normal, she perked up somewhat. Yes, this was a major annoyance to Don Ho. While he was extremely pleased that his feet returned to normal, he was not so pleased suddenly to find all of his kami's feet also normal. He'd paid a fortune to have them all have the elegant tiny feet of Great Ladies.

Soon, he saw that all the Great Ladies no longer had their tiny feet either. Each of these women faced the decision to undergo once more the painful breaking of their arches and six weeks of convalescence or not to do so. For all, the decision was simple, lacking their arms, none wanted the added challenge. Life had suddenly become extraordinarily difficult to manage as it was; thus, they welcomed the bit of freedom having normal feet gave back to them.

Don Ho could not afford to have all his kami unavailable for two months and certainly not his ever-growing prize trophies, his magnificent yellow-brown eyed women. Each late evening he took extreme pride in parading them about the main floor of the Purple Palace, displaying them before his exclusive clientele. Pity that they still had not the faintest notion about what they were doing. While they knew that there must be people around the room — they often bumped into men and women seated in chairs staring at them or even some who were ambulatory — still they had no idea that they, with their fake smiles and hesitant steps, were the center of attraction. Pity that they could not witness this incredible victory spectacle. No, as much as he had truly enjoyed seeing them take such tiny, tiny steps, he refused to have them laid up for two months.

He soon found an alternative, which in his view was nearly as good — the extreme Annelise high heels. He remembered the sinking faces of the women when he told them that they would have to wear these shiny black heels all the time. Oh, how he delighted in the manner that he had set them up. "Most Honorable Ladies, it is so wonderful that your feet have, as has everyone's, returned to normal. I know how you must feel now, stripped of your Great Lady status of small feet, but please, do not beg me, for I will not inflict the pain and months of recovery in the iron casings with which you first had your feet done. Not even for my dear kami will I force them to endure that again. But do take heart. I have acquired fine sets of Annelise oxfords for each of you. They have laces and I have instructed the manservants to make sure that they also knot the bows when they tie them on your most elegant feet. I do not want a lace coming untied and potentially causing you to trip on them."

He thought, the blind fools don't realize that they will be wearing seven inch heels, forcing them to walk much as before. No, not until they first tried to stand in them did they discover this aspect. Once more, he had them parading around as before, again taking barely an inch step at a time just to keep their balance. He truly enjoyed their performance each night.

Still eleven young women were not enough. There were far more than eleven wealthy noblemen in Shansee. No, this was merely a tiny drop in the bucket of his ultimate revenge.

At first, little could be done about it. While everyone was so hobbled, virtually no one ventured out of doors, much less came to his many gambling houses or pleasure palaces. Just finding the food to stay alive had more than occupied everyone, including himself.

With the recovery of feet in December, finally men returned to their livelihoods. Commerce began to flow once more. Farmers came into the great city with their loads of produce. Fishermen brought in fresh catches. Storekeepers returned to their sometimes damaged stores and purchased more supplies to stock their shelves. Yes, it took weeks to get things somewhat back to normal. Only around the first of the year did business begin to pick up at his gambling houses and pleasure palaces. Still, with all the chaos in the streets, Don Ho began a new service: providing protection escorts to the wealthy so that they may visit his fine establishments in relative safety. This venture proved highly profitable.

This new protection escort was provided free of charge to the wealthy clientele, an added inducement for which they eagerly accepted. Once more, Don Ho found himself able to acquire additional young women to add to his every growing collection of elegant, yellow-eyed women.

"Most Honorable Ladies, I am very pleased to introduce to you your newest guest, Most Honorable Tian Le," he announced to the room of blind women.

"Please," the terrified young woman's voice called out, "I cannot see anything. I cannot walk in these shoes. The heels are too high for me to manage. Please, I beg you. What is going on?"

Once more Pian's heart sunk. Another nobleman's daughter, she knew this woman; she was nineteen and very pretty. Why was Don Ho doing this to them? As usual, Lin Li called out to Tian, and telling her that she had company and what their life was like now. For days, Pian and the others listened to the terrified woman crying almost constantly.

I kept Pian informed of the days now and she reported back that Don Ho was adding a new woman to their group on the average of one per week. Soon Xiu Zang, Xue Dhou, Soo Din, and Mei Tao had joined them, filling each new week with their screams of shock and terror and absolute fright. Most of these women Pian knew, having seen them from time to time either in her court or at elegant dances. *Bethany, there are sixteen of us now. He just isn't stopping!* She sent towards the end of January. Still, I could come up with no reasonable way to get to her, not unless we could somehow send in an army. Yet, for every action, there is a reaction.

Don Ho did not know that his actions had consequences: that for every action, there are reactions. When he took Xiu Zang into his collection of yellow-brown eyes trophies, he set into motion events far beyond his control. Nineteen year old Tao Dhou burst into the elegant estate of Most Honorable Zang, throwing protocol aside. On his way to pick up his fiancé, the lovely Xiu, Tao was about to knock when he heard a gunshot coming from inside the wealthy family's estate. "Xiu!" he called out as he dashed from room to room. Where were all their servants? Fear slowly seeped into the young lad's mind. Where was everyone? "Xiu!" He called again.

He stopped short as he set foot in their dining room, a room in which he had spent hours as a Most Honorable Guest of the Zang's. "Most Honorable Zang?" he whispered, shocked. Sitting in his chair, the older man sat slumped at a ridiculous angle. Acrid gun smoke filled the room. Half of the man's face was gone; his ornate pistol still clenched loosely in his right hand. "Most Honorable Zang?" he said again, his voice trailing to near silence by the last syllables.

Lying on the table was a letter. Ordinarily, Tao would have minded his own business; the letter was not for him, but for the Zang family undoubtedly. Nevertheless, fear for his Xiu caused him to pick it up. As he began to read, he held onto his stomach, where fear had taken hold, growing stronger with each of the lines he read, each done with perfect calligraphy. "Sold? Xiu sold? How can this be?" Tao screamed aloud. He reread the whole letter, which outlined what the man had done and more importantly what Don Ho had done, essentially accepting Xiu as a slave, gambled away by her father. Crushed, the young man charged out of the estate, determined somehow to get his fiancé back, somehow, someway.

He knew that Don Ho was a powerful man. For a week, he began collecting what information he could find out about him. He soon discovered that he owned all the gambling houses and pleasure palaces frequented by the wealthy of Shansee. He assumed that in one of these, his fiancé must be being held. But which one? It took him a week of visits before Tao received the shock of his young life. Late one evening, he saw a parade of young beautiful women shuffling with the tiniest of steps, wandering seemingly aimlessly around the main floor of the Purple Palace. As one came close to his table, he saw her eyes, yellow-brown. They focused not on him, even as the woman nearly bumped into him, as if she did not see. He gasped. Blinded! These were glass eyes! Then, he saw his beloved Xiu just entering the room. It took all of his self-control to keep from dashing over to her, grabbing her, and trying to escape with her. Such would have been most foolish, as there were a dozen bouncers standing around, just waiting for some unruly guests.

He came back the next night and took a seat where he thought that he might have a chance to be close to her when she was brought into wander among the crowd. One by one, many others were brought to this edge of the room by a young man and then nudged to begin walking. At last, a terrified Xiu appeared, guided by the same young man. As the terrified woman began taking tiny inch steps, Tao whispered, "Xiu, it is Tao. I will be rescuing you soon. Pretend that you do not hear me." For an instant, she turned her head slightly, and her faked smile flashed real, but only for an instant as her leg bumped into the side of a table.

That night, Tao observed each of these women carefully. He recognized their Princess Pian and her daughter right away. His heart sunk, even our Princess! He knew over half of these young women. The wealthy class tended to hang out with others who were wealthy, of course. He'd once dated Tian Le, but now her heart had fallen for Cheng Pan, who he also knew. Did Cheng know what had happened to Tian? A mission began to form in his mind.

He went to see Cheng. "She's where?" the twenty year old young man cried out when Tao explained what he saw. Tao related the contents of the letter the Don Ho had left the Honorable Zang, just before he'd killed himself in shame.

"Damn! Yes, that is what happened to Honorable Le. I heard that he went bankrupt. I assumed that he had sent Tian away to a place of safety. Blinded? Held as a pleasure slave? Damn, I've got to get her out of there!" Cheng's ire rose to a blinding fit. That night, he and Tao visited the Purple Palace, but Tao pointed out all the martial arts bouncers and begged Cheng not to react or do something that would alert Don Ho.

The next day, the two began visiting known boyfriends of the other young women. Slowly they found more who wanted to join up to rescue their girlfriends. The how remained elusive. To avoid suspicion, the nine men alternated days casing the Purple Palace and Don Ho's men. Soon, it became apparent that this evil, wicked sadist was extremely heavily protected at all times by a small army of fighters and thugs. Indeed, the only time they discovered that he was ever without them was the occasional evening when he came to a wealthy man's estate, leaving with yet another young woman. They were appalled to see her several days later being paraded around the main floor with the other blinded women. Of course, they found her boyfriend and he too joined their ever growing band of would be rescuers.

"Tao saw me. He's going to rescue me," Xiu whispered to her unseen companions in their unseen room, filled with many beds and couches. Here she and the others spent their days sitting on the couches. The monotony was broken by the occasional bathroom needs and the kind man who came to groom them and feed them. At least they were now being fed twice a day, Pian thought. Of course, they all dreaded the time before bed when they were escorted down the unseen steps into some large room where they were forced to walk around all by themselves. Pian was still terrified at those times, and so were all the other women, all except Lin Li who had an eidetic memory and now could walk well, unless a table or chair had been repositioned, that is.

Rescue? All ears listened — the first faint hope any of these women had had. "Yes, he is strong, he loves me, he will rescue me," Xiu replied to the other's questions. "But why he will still want me I do not know. I am now less than worthless. I cannot see anymore. He should forget me and find someone else." Her voice cracked, and Pian did not need eyes to know that she was crying once more.

Lin Li spoke up, "I know every inch of that room now. I know where the door must be to the outside world. Perhaps somehow I can lead us out of this place one night." Now their discussion took a different turn. Lin Li explained how it was that she could recall all details, all except sight since she had lost her eyes, that is.

Pian then relayed this interesting turn of events to me during my daily telepathic contact with her. I replied, *Look, Pian, Don Ho probably has a small army protecting him. It would be most foolish of these young men to try to attack the palace to get to you women.*

Yes, I think that we might only get one chance to escape. Even so, where can we go now? There is no place of safety left. Besides, we are now completely and utterly helpless in all things. We cannot survive on our own. Better that we all lose these bodies and perhaps begin again.

No need for that drastic an action just yet, Pian. However, I ought to talk with these young men. If nothing else, Eve and I can lend them a hand.

But you don't know these men. How can you touch their minds if you do not know them first?

True, very true. Okay, I have an idea. I need to meet Xiu first. Then when you all are taken down to the room to walk, when Xiu hears Tao, I can spot who is talking to her and make contact that way.

Pian chuckled, *What a roundabout way. Might work. I'll tell her about you and have her start talking. I do hope that you can see her.*

I left my body sitting on our couch and appeared over the Purple Palace. It was just where I last had seen it. I zoomed down inside it from the room. Based on the number of steps that they had to go blindly up and down each night, I had a good idea that they were being held on the third floor. I was right. I spotted a large number of kami there in other dorm style rooms, but soon zeroed in on Pian's room.

Okay, I am with you now, Pian. I touched her head with what appeared to her as a loving pat. I saw her smile. She and another woman there began talking, but all the women were listening intently.

Xiu, hi. I am Bethany from Velona. I am with you now. Yes, this is telepathy. I am going to be helping rescue all of you, but first, I need you to help me find your boyfriend Tao. I have to make contact with him and make sure that he does not do anything foolish. We do need him to help rescue all of you.

Oh please, let no harm befall my Tao. I am no longer worthy of him, but I love him still, and my heart would be so crushed if anything were to happen to him. Tell him I want him to forget me. I am now useless in all ways. He should stop his rescue attempt and find another more worthy woman.

I ignored that and sent, *Tonight when you sense him near, I will be with you. Point him out to me and I will talk with him. I will do my best to see that no harm comes to Tao.*

We chatted a bit and then I left them and began taking a good look at the place where Dita and I had been held captive. While it was still the same building, the entire third floor had been redone. The main floor layout was pretty much in tact as I remembered it with some disgust. I began counting what were likely his security forces. Damn, nearly fifty men. Breaking in here would be difficult. I moved out onto the street. More men were discretely watching the streets for several blocks. Even if they could somehow get them out, they would not get far, that's for sure.

Well, Eve and I could help with that, but where could they be taken? I knew just how much care these women were going to need. Besides having the horrible trauma of losing their arms, they also had the overwhelming betrayal of their fathers who had sold them into slavery to pay their gambling debts. Then having their eyes removed, casting already helpless women into utter darkness would make for massive layers of trauma. These women would need a whole lot of therapy sessions even to get them willing to continue to live and try to adapt somehow to live.

Here in Shansee, only the Church of God could provide such therapy. The only alternative would be to somehow get them onto the train and transported here to Velona, where I or Raffaella could deal with their traumas. To get them to the train station meant crossing half of the huge city now under mob rule. Blind, I gave them no chance at all of making such a trip. As I looked over the city, I realized that the only possible place Tao and his young men could possibly take them would be to the Church of God, where the Olin Masters might be able to protect them and give them sanctuary as they had done for us over a half century ago. I did not know where this new Church of God was located in Shansee, but perhaps Fina, that is, Shu Wen, might know. I kept referring to her by the name she had last lifetime. I was doing better with Jemma, that is, Pian, primarily because I had met Pian several times now.

I was anxious the rest of the day, anxiously awaiting Pian's contact alerting me to their next walk. Of course, there was no guarantee that Tao would be in the audience tonight or that he would attempt to contact Xiu for that matter. Actually, that contact did not occur for another two days.

"Xiu, it is Tao. Be brave, we are working out how to rescue you," a young man was whispering to Xiu as she began her most terrifying walk into the unknown room. My heart went out to these women, these incredibly brave women who had not yet totally given up and were still fighting to live somehow.

Tao. Do not react outward. I am Bethany. I am a friend of Xiu and want to help rescue these women. Yes, telepathy. Think your thoughts. You do not need to speak your words.

Who are you? What is this? You know Xiu? Please, we must rescue her and the others.

Yes, we must. First, you and I must talk.

He and I chatted for some time. I explained the situation inside the palace. He was disheartened by learning that there were so many guards inside. He already knew that there were hundreds of Don Ho's men on the streets nearby. They protected not only the Purple Palace but three other palaces and five gambling halls, all within a six block stretch along the Princess Path.

I asked him about how he could deal with Xiu once she was rescued, after all her situation would require extreme assistance. As I expected, young love swore eternal love and devotion. Well, time would tell on that one, for her needs would likely be more than he could ever imagine. He explained that he had formed a group of other boyfriends who were equally keen on rescuing their fiancés as well.

He had no idea of where they would then take their women once freed from the Purple Palace. I pointed out that once they broke the women out, Don Ho's men would certainly come after them. *We can't take them to our homes, can we?* Reality began to sink into Tao's mind. No, once rescued, they could never return to their homes. If Don Ho had a signed slave contract, some would argue that these women now "belonged" to Don Ho. Further, he certainly would launch devastating attacks on their families, just to get back his prized trophies. *Where can we take them?* he finally begged me.

The only real answer was to seek sanctuary in the Church of God for the time being. *Hey, my folks are into that,* he pointed out. I found that encouraging. I got his agreement not to make any attempts without coordinating it with me and I promised to contact him every day or so.

When I next chatted with Pian, she told me that she had explained to the others that when the great escape came, she could use some of her powers to put the men to sleep. I found it encouraging that Lin Li and Pian now thought that somehow they could get themselves and their companions to the front doors. If they could do that much on their own, it would go a long way to increase their self-respect.

Eve asked a key question: Are other women being held in the other pleasure palaces? I spent several more days hovering over the general area. As I spotted what must be another of these pleasure palaces, I began exploring it was well. While I did find a large number of kami, I found no others who appeared to have been blinded by Don Ho. As yet, I had still not even seen the man, or if I had, I'd not recognized him as such.

"We should put these places out of business," Eve declared to me one night as I was about to check up on Tao. "Put an end to them. Okay, they can rebuild, but look. The cost of replacing that plush Purple Palace will be enormous. Think of all the gold fixtures in there. That's gotta hurt whoever tries to take over the business once we eliminate this Don Ho fellow. I say, burn them all down."

"Yes, but what about the kami who depend upon them for their livelihoods?" I countered.

"Well, they should find something better to do," Eve lamely replied.

As I contacted Tao, I sensed that something was up. *Hey, we gotta do it tonight or else another woman is going to become blinded! Look, the only time we have a chance at getting Don Ho alone is when he is visiting his next victim and bringing her back with him. We've seen him doing this three times now. He's inside the house now. If he brings out another woman, we are going to take him out. Five of us have our long guns at the ready. We are not going to let him blind another woman.*

He was insistent. I floated over the area and spotted his companions hiding in bushes near the house before which sat the finest looking carriage I'd seen. Its driver was half-asleep, waiting patiently. I guessed that it must be around eight at night. The crescent moon was slowly descending in the western sky. *Okay, don't miss. I'll let everyone know to get prepared.* I had to hand it to these fellows. They'd done their homework. I rightly guessed that they had been following him for weeks, learning his patterns and movements.

Pian, though excited about the impending escape, told me that the palace was packed now. They were not due to make their walk for at least an hour or two; she had extreme difficulties now judging time. Eve joined me, and she and I began watching over the five young men. We waited. Then, the front door opened and a tall man emerged, escorting a sobbing young woman, probably twenty at most. I sure hoped the fellows were good shots or they would hit her too.

Eve was so darn tempted to take the sadist out herself that I was impressed with her patience! As the two walked down the paved walk to the waiting carriage, we saw five long guns trying to get a clear shot at the man. As I expected, he held the young woman close to him, supporting her as much as forcing her along with him. I held my breath, figuratively that is, hoping the lads would wait for the shot. At this distance, the long gun slug would go through him and into her as well. Good lads, they waited. Don Ho kindly lifted the sobbing woman into the carriage.

Bang! Bang! Five shots broke the night stillness. Several nesting birds fluttered into the dark sky. Don Ho jerked five slightly different directions as the lead slugs slammed into his body. I moved over him to make sure that he was down. Eve spotted the carriage driver reacting, grabbing a long gun stowed up in the driver's box. His head spun around his neck, as a child's top, before she pitched the dead man's body off the carriage, dropping it onto the ground near Don's. The five came running up to the carriage from their hiding places.

"Are you all right?" Tao asked the sobbing woman, who was trying to grasp what had just happened. She nodded. Tao advised, "Are there some relatives where we can take you, where you will be safe? You can't stay here." Eve and I backed off, allowing the lads to deal with this, which they did. One hopped up into the driver's box, and the four climbed in with the young woman.

Well done, Tao. Meet you at the Purple Palace around midnight, I sent. He agreed.

Eve and I then headed to the Purple Palace and hovered over Pian and the others. *Pian, the rescuers have just killed Don Ho as he was bringing another woman here to join you. She's fine and being taken to a place of relative safety with some of her relatives. The escape is on for later tonight. It is safe for you to talk about it now. No one but you sixteen are in the room now.*

Pian relayed the news to the others, "Good news! Some of your boyfriends have just killed Don Ho as he was about to bring another young woman to join us! The escape is on for tonight!" The women cheered, relieved that the man who had destroyed their lives and that of their families was dead at last. However, they were more than worried about the escape.

"But we can't see! How can we escape?" Mei Qing asked nervously.

"Don't worry," Lin Li spoke up. "I can find our way to the front doors. Just stay real close to each other and we can do this. I want out of here."

Pian, tell them someone is coming, I sent. She did and the women became quiet once more. Sixteen nervous women sat like silent statues on the couches, waiting for the unknown man to enter. It was their manservant sent to groom them for their display walk in a short while. He was a kindly middle aged man and must have once been a women's hair dresser, I surmised from the skillful way that he brushed out each woman's hair, arranging it in a perfect style that brought out the best in each of the women's appearance.

Once done, he waited until a kami entered. "It's time," she whispered. He rose and asked Lin Li to rise. He put his arm around her waist and began guiding her out of the room. Her impossible Annelise oxfords made walking treacherous, once again forcing her to take perhaps three inches a step, while he held her securely. When they reached the steps, his soft voice guided her down, step by step. When he finally had Lin Li near the side of the large room filled with men and women lounging on reclining chairs or sitting at tables listening to the melodic music, he whispered, "Remember to smile. You look your very best, Lin Li. Off you go, tiny steps," he advised, giving her a gentle nudge in the right direction.

Now totally on her own and with no arms to feel her way, no blind man's stick to tap out before her, she was reduced to taking minuscule steps, barely an inch at a time, feeling her way along by gently brushing into something with her legs, mostly. Don Ho got off lucky, a quick death. If Eve had had her way, well. . . I thought, not finishing my thought. I watched as he headed back up to fetch the next woman. I decided to stay here and keep an eye on things. I didn't see any of the young rescuers around. Good thing, I thought. They had to make their preparations, and besides they could not break in now, the palace was packed.

A half hour later, the last of the sixteen women had been brought down and sent out into the room to shuffle around aimlessly on her own, a forced smile hiding her terror or fear. None of these women could see the lecherous looks that many men had as their eyes followed them about. Even some women licked their lips as they watched them closely. The working kami were always careful to give these women a wide berth as they went back and forth, often carrying a customer's order between their teeth.

This degraded performance lasted a half hour, before the man began ushering the woman closest to the exit on out of the room and up the stairs. Still, it took almost that long for him to usher the last one out and up the stairs. That was Lin Li, who had purposely gotten herself over to the main entrance, checking it out, I suspected. At least the man had the decency to whisper to each woman as he escorted her out. "Lin Li, you did very well on your own tonight. I am so pleased, Most Honorable Lady." This time, her smile was real.

Once she was back sitting on the couch once more, he told them all, "I will return in a while to prepare you for bed. You all did so very well tonight, Most Honorable Ladies." He turned and left, leaving them alone once more.

When they were certain they were alone, Pian explained, "Now here's the plan. When the time is right later tonight, perhaps around midnight, I will put all the men we encounter into a deep sleep. Lin Li will lead us to the front door. Each man that we encounter I will put him to sleep."

"But how can we see Lin Li to follow her? How can we manage the steps by ourselves?" asked Ting Zhe. "I am so frightened of falling."

"We must feel the steps with our feet. We will not be in a rush or hurry. We go slow and take our time. Do not take a step until you are sure of it," Pian advised. She added, "One of our rescuers wanted to burn down these pleasure palaces, but I advised against that. So many of the kind kami depend wholly on the money that they earn here. Burning these places down will hurt them badly. I don't want more women to suffer."

They chatted about this aspect and agreed with her. Ting Zhe pointed out, "Kami Ying told me that she is supporting her three children with the money she is making here. If she loses her job, her children will suffer as well. It is best that we do not steal her livelihood from her or the others."

We let the women chat. I sent Eve outside to watch for the nine young rescuers, while I kept watch over the women. We waited patiently. Later on, the man servant came to undress them and put them into bed. Pian demonstrated her skills. While they could not see what happened, they heard him slump to the floor, with a little aid from me. His snoring became obvious. I gently moved him onto one of the many beds. We waited once more, though I could sense the women were getting more and more nervous and worried.

A little after midnight, Eve reported in to me. *Crowd is gone; doors are locked. Quite a few of the guards left. More came, the night shift, I think. At least twenty are inside now, maybe more. There are still many men out on the streets patrolling for several blocks. The nine are hiding in the bushes across the street waiting for the signal. Honestly, if they fire a long gun, that will bring the guards down on us like honey bees.*

Can they get to the doors below unseen?

Not a chance, far too many guards nearby. When you're ready, I'll quietly take them out so that the fellows can break in the front doors. Now's as good a time as any.

Okay, let's do it. It will probably take the women some time to get to the doors. Let the fellows know.

I let Pian know that it was time, and she whispered it to the others. "Okay, listen to Lin Li. She will go first, and Misha and I will follow right behind her. We must stay very close together so that we can follow each other. Lin Li, you get to our doorway and we'll all line up behind you."

"Mom, I am scared. I don't know if I can do this without help. I'm terrified of the steps," Misha whispered.

"I will be in front of you and Bethany will be watching over us. We must be brave, Misha," she whispered back. Lin Li rose, got her balance, and began her tiny, one inch, feeling sort of steps as she navigated around the feet of the women and the edges of the bed. Yet with her eidetic memory, she did very well indeed. She seemed to know just where her body was in relation to the objects in the room, all except the feet of the women that is. She stopped precisely at the door as if she could actually see it with her eyes, remarkable, I thought.

Pian whispered, "Now I am getting up. Misha, you too. Follow mommy. We can do this." Pian had a far more difficult time finding her way across the ten feet, bumping into Lin Li at the end. Misha, likewise, struggled mightily, but finally found her mother's body and hugged her as close as she could get, pressing her body into her mom's. One by one the other women rose, found their way over to the ever-growing line.

At last, Mei Tao whispered, "Okay, I am the last in line." Lin Li began moving slowly out of the door and down the long hallway. Each of the others followed as closely behind her as they could, often their dresses rubbing against each other. I held my breath, ready to catch any that started to take a tumble. Going so darn slowly greatly helped them, I soon realized, like a line of penguins I thought as I watched them making their way to the steps, which would be their greatest challenge.

"Hey, where do you ladies think you are going?" a voice called out. The women panicked but soon heard his body slump to the floor. I slid him out of the way. Lin Li resumed her slow march to the stairs. Twice more, a man appeared. Twice more, Pian put him to sleep and I moved him out of the way.

I had Eve join me at the stairs. Going down three flights of stairs in high heels is challenging, that's why we have handrails. Doing it armless requires very careful attention to what you are doing. Add blindness to the mix and it becomes a treacherous nightmare. Yes, I could intervene and just lift each woman safely down. Hours ago I thought of doing just that. I held off. Why?

Self-respect. These women had very little of that left now. It was taking real guts for them to get this far on their own. If they could somehow manage these steps on their own, their self-respect would definitely increase. I owed it to them to give them this chance, though Pian knew that if they could not manage, I would be able to lift them down safely. She had not asked me to do it yet and I knew why. She desperately wanted to give Misha and the others, including herself, a chance to convince themselves that they could do this difficult thing.

Lin Li whispered, "Feel each step with your foot before you take it. Go sideways, I think." Slowly, she began her descent. Her caution was whispered down the line of women. Also, each one whispered to the woman behind her when she felt the top of the steps begin. They were working as a team now.

Lin Li made it safely down and waited for Pian to touch her before moving a ways out into the main room. Two more men accosted her; Pain acted again. One failed to fall asleep and Eve promptly took care of him, placing the body with its broken neck far out of their way. After what seemed like an eternity, Mei Tao whispered, "I'm down too." Now Lin Li relied on her eidetic recall to move them over to where the main entrance should be. Compared to the stairs, this was easy; they had all navigated around the room many times now. Finally, she got to the furthest edge of the room.

I made telepathic contact with her and praised her for her leadership. *You are facing the entrance foyer, which is about twenty feet from the actual door. Turn just a little to your right. Yes, perfect. Now you are facing the doors. Hold your position until we can get the doors opened.*

Eve and I headed outside. Damn, I saw at least twenty men who could easily see the women as they left the front doors. *Keep an eye out,* Eve sent. With a passion, she set to work twisting the necks of the guards. One by one, like dominoes they slumped to the ground. Within five minutes, all the nearby guards were dispatched, and I signaled Tao to bring his friends to the door.

Of course, when I pulled on it, the door was locked. None of the nine lads knew how to pick locks. We dare not risk making a whole lot of noise breaking it down. I took a firm hold of the ornately carved doors and slowly applied increasing outward pressure. A loud snapping sound announced the fact that I'd busted the doors. Everyone held their breaths. Had the noise roused anyone? Eve and the nine stood guard outside the doors, while I went inside to protect their rear from anyone inside who might come to check on the noise that I'd made. I gave Lin Li the go ahead, and once more, the line of women began to cross the space slowly. I later learned that Lin Li was following her nose; she smelled the fresh air coming in from the doorway.

Two men, wiping sleep from their eyes, came into the room. I dispatched them rapidly, though making a little noise in the process. One day, I ought to have Eve give me lessons on neck twisting. As soon as the last women cleared the door, I followed them. Already the nine boys had their arms around their girlfriends, whispering like mad.

I sent to Tao, *Okay, now you fellows are going to have to double up, a woman on each side of you. They need your touch and guidance to walk. Eve and I'll deal with any guards. Lead the way to the Church of God, Tao.*

Kang had to let go of his girlfriend. Misha did not want to be separated from her mother, so he put an arm around each to guide them, giving a loving look at his girlfriend, Xue Dhou behind him. She couldn't see his look, which pained him. I figured a whole lot was going to pain these boys in the near future. With the lads holding them, they were able to take their normal three-inch steps now and progress was faster than before, still painstakingly slow for an escape.

Eve took point, moving far ahead of the line, twisting more and more necks. An awful lot of guards were patrolling the streets, I noticed. I played rear guard, watching for others coming at us from the rear. I saw little action at first, just one man, who I dispatched rapidly. I didn't know at the time how far we had to go, but later I learned that it was about a mile and a half to safety. The lads could not use a wagon, far too conspicuous on the streets in these unsettled times. Walking was the only safe way. That meant these women were facing taking thirty thousand plus tiny steps. I hoped that their feet and legs did not give out before we got to safety.

Time passed and the number of dead guards had fallen off as I continued to bring up the rear. Evidently, we were getting beyond the range of their assigned patrols. No, I noticed that some of these current dead wore shirts with a blue calligraphy symbol on their backs. Strange. Then, I heard it, the hue and cry coming from far back in the distance. Our escape had finally been noticed. I let Eve know and Tao as well. I doubted that they could pick up the pace any. In fact, the women's legs were starting to give out.

I spotted a dozen men running after us — more like heard them. The night was now quite dark. The moon had set long ago. I launched a ball of fire their way. As it detonated, it gave me a bit of light, and I fired off a more accurate one. Even from this distance, the party was vulnerable to long gunshots. My balls of fire naturally attracted even more attention to us. More men came out of nowhere to pick up the chase, possibly from some of the gambling halls that we had passed. I fired off another two balls, forcing them to keep their distance and hopefully not give them a chance to see us and shoot their long guns. A sort of stalemate resulted. They kept back and I didn't fire again.

After an eternity, they reached the main gates of the walled compound of the Church of God. Tao knocked on the door — pounded desperately would be more like it. Pian herself chose to address whoever opened the door.

A wooden slat slid, a face holding a lantern peered out. "Princess Pian and party beg you for immediate sanctuary. Don Ho has blinded us and has been holding us prisoners. We've just escaped but a large force is hot on our heels. Please, we need immediate sanctuary." Evidently, the gate man recognized her and the women heard the encouraging sounds of the gate creaking open. Slowly the group entered, just as a swarm of men came a little too close and I could see their bodies in the lantern light. I had no choice but to fire off another couple of balls of fire, praying that they didn't get a chance to shoot any of the women.

Once the last were inside, the gate man shut the door and slid the massive bars back in place. "Wait here, I'll fetch the master." While they waited, we heard a number of men arriving at the gates too. Soon, Master De Dhow and his wife, Nan Dia, came rushing towards the group. The lads whispered what they were seeing to the women, a good sign, I thought.

Master De Dhow saw the sixteen women with yellow-brown glass eyes. His face looked highly saddened by what he saw. He introduced himself to Pian, and she quickly related her story, speaking loudly over the noise of the men pounding on the gates behind her.

"Sanctuary granted. Nan, lead them all inside, we must see to their immediate needs." He went to the gates and opened the slit. "What is it that you want?"

"Hey, some of Don Ho's property just went through this door. We demand that you hand his women over to us. They belong to him."

De spoke softly, but with intention behind his words. "They are human beings. No human being is an object or property of anyone but themselves. No one can own another human being. Your claims are a falsehood. Be gone with you now." He slammed the slat shut.

"You haven't heard the end of this! We'll be back and storm this place and take them back anyway, killing any of you who resist us," the man yelled over the walls. De followed the retreating party.

I told Pian that we'd check back with her tomorrow.

Thank you Bethany, Eve for saving our lives. I owe you a very big one.

You would have done the same for us. Eve and I waited around the gates a little longer making sure the men left. When we were sure that they were gone, we returned home.

Chapter 16 The Walking Dead

The next day, I contacted the Banca del Dio and used my authority to freeze Don Ho's accounts. All told, he had a staggering one hundred thirty-six million in them. He definitely had been fleecing the wealthy of Shansee. I set up trust finds for the sixteen women victims; at least they'd have the funds to help them survive, about eight and a half million each, though later, this was lowered, as they wanted their funds used in reconstruction efforts.

I then made contact with Fina, rather Shu Wen Chow, of the Church of God up in Zau, the Imperial City. After telling her of the escape and rescue operation, we had a long talk. I didn't like what I was hearing, scary really, if you value human life.

Shu Wen sent, *Once people's feet returned to normal, the Emperor and Empress fled the city in secret, disbanding the army, sending them home to their families. The last vestiges of law enforcement were now gone. Yes, supplies are moving; farmers are bringing crops to market; shops are open to some extent once more. The period of starvation has lessened.*

The downside is grim. Gangs now rule the streets, fighting among themselves for control of more streets. Each one has adopted a different calligraphy design, usually drawn prominently upon the backs of their shirts. Besides enforcing their control over other gangs for their blocks, they are hustling those who live and work there, robbing them blind. One is as likely to be killed as merely being robbed these days. The overlords have once more played their power card, attempting to seize control of as much territory as they can, often now incorporating gangs into their fold. Free from all restrictions, save those they chose to enforce, these overlords are unleashing a massive reign of terror and destruction on the common folk within the zones that they control.

I just heard about an example. Overlord Yi's men entered a farming village of some hundred men, women, and children. They demanded half of their food supplies. Several men pleaded with them that if they took half of what remained, they would starve to death long before their fall crops were grown. The men laughed at them and killed them with their swords. Then, they took all their food. The remaining villagers simply sat down in the dirt streets of their village and waited for death to take them. Only one woman managed to run five miles to the next village for help. Word has only now reached Zau of this episode. Similar actions are becoming routine.

Shu went on to say, *One of the most common reactions that we are seeing around Zau now are people merely sitting waiting for their bodies to die. It seems that if the gangs and overlords take too much, the victims just give up totally, sitting around allowing their bodies to die. They do not even have the energy or will power to take their own lives. Honestly, Bethany, it is spooky to see these people who are pressed so close to death that they just sit there waiting for it to come. You cannot even talk to these people or try to help them. We tried to feed a couple and they wouldn't even open their mouths. We forced it in, but they didn't even chew or swallow. It's like they are walking dead! I thought that apathy was the bottom pit, but there are emotions even worse. Total and complete uselessness lies even lower than apathy. You give a person who feels completely useless a slight push, and they slip into dying, just sitting around waiting for death to take them. It's beyond imagination, Bethany.*

So many of the average people of Zau are already socked into fear, despair, numbness, and grief, that this latest round of savageness against them is dropping them down below even apathy. Many of the wealthier of Zau are a bit higher, emotionally, primarily because they have not had to face the same harsh mistreatment that the average person has had to face. Many had enough food stocked piled in their estates that they got by the first few months relatively easily. Still, they too are now feeling the pressure from the overlords.

Our small sanctuary here in the heart of Zau is filled to overflowing. I'd guess that now we have two thirds of the wealthier of Zau within our walls. These are the men who have the funds to finance new ventures, new businesses, to make things happen. Yet, to a one, they are terrified of taking any action at all, knowing that the overlords will just demand a goodly share. Worse, they can no longer find bodyguards to provide them protection. Even the supposed guards have been robbing them blind, jacking up their pay demands almost daily, citing increased risks each day.

Bethany, while we have a thousand able beings now, some with extraordinary powers, you might say, we simply cannot withstand this much longer. An able being cannot make it in an insane environment. I'm going to talk with Macario today, but I just don't see how we can stay here and not become overwhelmed and wiped out ourselves. We are trying to care for four thousand people in our complex here, which is designed for one thousand. We are forced to ration food to one meal a day now. Grim. I wonder how the other Churches are faring. I hope Macario can give us some guidance.

We chatted a bit longer before she had to deal with another crisis. I understood their predicament. No matter how good your intentions are, no matter how great and powerful your skills may be, thrown into a den of degradation and insanity, into a psychotic-bin, you are simply going to be overwhelmed by it all and succumb yourself. Eve, or Dita, rather and I already found this out the hard way last lifetime. As able as we are, with our telepathy, levitation, telekinetic skills, to say nothing of our old Druwid skills, she and I only managed to lose our limbs one by one, until at last completely helpless were left to freeze to death in the back of some wagon. I wondered what Macario would advise and say to her.

I then contacted Pian to see how she was doing. First thing, she wanted to connect me up with Nan Dia, the wife of their benefactor, Master De Dhow. After exchanging introductions she sent, *I want to thank you for all that you and Eve have done to rescue these women and eliminate Don Ho. Until now, he has been untouchable. He controlled over half of Shansee. Now that he is gone, his domain is starting to break up into many groups, fighting each other for bits of his pie. We all think that this is for the better, strange as that may seem.*

I told her about my conversation with Shu Wen minutes ago and asked what the overall situation was like here in Shansee. I found that they were in a very similar situation. Only now that Don Ho was out of the picture, already today more of the artists and wealthy of Shansee were flocking to their church seeking sanctuary as well. I told her that Shu Wen was going to contact Macario for advice and she agreed to do that too. She also promised to get into communication with her counterparts in Nan Yan and Lou Yang in the far north and let me know their situations as well.

A couple days later, Macario and Raffaella came by to discuss the situation with Marco, Eve, and me. Macario began, "Well, Bethany, Eve, Marco, once more it has been made painfully clear to me that a powerful being cannot long stand in a psychotic, suppressive environment. You tried to teach me that lesson centuries ago during the Great Messiah years. I failed to learn my lesson after that experience with the Grey Creatures, though you warned me them as well." I smiled; this was not quite what I had expected to hear from him though it was quite accurate.

"Until this alien plague, your and your friends' valiant attempts to bring back order into Tashien worked and allowed us to begin our work of freeing spiritual beings there. Until now, I was quite proud of our efforts there, four growing pockets of sanity and power. If this plague had not come, in a century we might have pulled it off. Now, the situation there is grim. I need to ask you three, in your opinion, is there anything that you or your friends can do at this time that would once again bring back law and order to Tashien?"

I saw where he was headed. "Can we do it again? Well, right now, Macario, I will be bluntly honest. No. With all women everywhere disabled as we are now, a lengthy period of adjustment, physical and cultural, faces both men and women. Here's the chart that Stefano and I are keeping. We believe that we have the Sea Princes and the Greenway salvaged and on track to a good survival level. Megalos, once our archenemy, is now behind us, and we've put a checkmark on their good survival level, as long as we continue doing what we have for them. Likewise, Konstantin will likely be salvaged now, but it will be very critical there probably for a year."

"The Northern Steppes and Annelise are also going to make it and perhaps a third of those in the Arad will as well. Down in Demokritos, it is not so good. I think that we are witnessing the death of that civilization, but there remains one small light of hope with Ana and Callisto in Andros, Arolas. No matter how that one turns out, Demokritos will never be the same as it was. Until recently, we had written them off. That leaves Tashien as the final mess."

"With the three provincial militias gone and the Imperial Army also dispersed, we are once again back to square one with them. Actually, this time it is far worse, Macario. Women are no longer effective as they used to be, now dealing with their own basic survival needs. Men are forced to devote drastically more of their time and energy just helping their womenfolk get by from day to day. Compounding matters, so many have already perished, millions by the reports that we've received. I am afraid that the power base that we were able to mobilize last time just is not there anymore. Worse, Macario, I don't see any other power base that we could tap into to help restore law and order."

He sighed, "Then it is a land of the walking dead."

"For now, I think so. At this time, the Dark Ages have come for that civilization and culture. Some years from now when we women have learned new ways and are confident and able once more, some years from now when the thugs in Tashien have pushed the people so hard and so low that even they know something has to be done about it all, then we can begin again to pick up the pieces there and try once more." I tried to be as optimistic as I could about it.

Marco added, "I don't think that the world will ever be strong enough to just go into Tashien with an army and take it over and install a new order there. The land is just too populous for that."

I explained, "I think that our philosophy of MMCE has a better chance of turning them around down the road." I had to explain our new term, Modernization, Mobilization, Communication, and Electrification. "Look, I have never seen a war yet that solved any of man's problems. They only create new problems along with the destruction attendant with them. MMCE offers a peaceful approach to revolution at least that is what Stefano and I are counting on this time."

Eve had been silent throughout. "I think that we should concentrate what resources we have to Demokritos. At least there, we have some slim chance of success. The population is low in emotional tones, but nowhere near as low and sadistic as Tashien."

Macario nodded, "I accept your judgment, Bethany, Marco, Eve. Demokritos it is then. I will need your help in pulling out my Church of God people and those that they are protecting. Perhaps others will want to exodus as well."

"Macario, what about Nan Yan?" Marco asked. "They are not in quite as bad a position there. If all the other church members went to Nan Yan, would their combined forces and strength be sufficient to withstand the chaos and thrive there? If so, we'd maintain at least some small hold on the country. Perhaps we'd be able to expand outward from there like we did last time a half century ago?"

"Hum, very possibly, Marco. I see what you are driving at, a foothold. Yet, Nan Yan is so isolated, there in the rugged foothills of the mountains. However, once there, the people could become trapped or cut off from the rest of the world. There is no way over the mountains and even if there was, the Desert of Desolation is impassible on the other side," Macario answered.

Eve suggested, "You know, if we could somehow traverse those steep gullies, the current train line along the coast is only two hundred miles due southwest from Nan Yan. That area is largely uninhabited anyway. Could they build a train line to Nan Yan through that countryside somehow?"

"Say, if they could, then we might be able to keep our foot in the door, so to speak," Macario replied, becoming more animated.

"I like that idea too, give us a few days to see if it is feasible," I added.

"Great. In the meantime, I will have the Lou Yang, Zau, and Shansee churches begin working out how they could safely get to Nan Yan. The two northern ones could get started soon, because they have a very long way to go," Macario replied. We left it at that and he left to begin working out how his people could move southwards.

Marco and I visited the Velona Train Yards the next morning. The elder Jules Bartolo, now fifty-seven, had married one of the West Po's, Daniella, and was given the post of New Lines Planner. He had enlisted his son, Jovanni, as his resident engineer planner. After exchanging pleasantries with my uncle and cousin, we got down to work. Marco had good recall the terrain over which we wanted to extend the line. As Bianca last lifetime, she had come riding up to Nan Yan to help rescue us and still had good recall the terrain.

Marco suggested, "We could skirt the steep sided valleys by not heading north until here, nearly due south of Nan Yan, but that is something like five hundred miles along the southern coast of Tan Loc. If we could somehow cut through these V-shaped valleys or snake along the ridge lines starting somewhere around here, you'd shave two hundred miles off the line to Nan Yan," he indicated on the large map, pinned to Jules' wall. The existing rail lines were precisely drawn on the various maps of the Sea Princes, the Greenway, the Northern Steppes, as well as the Arad and Tan Loc, Tashien.

Jules pulled on his chin, deep in thought. "Hey, dad, we should make a survey first, but with all the lawlessness there, it's going to be dangerous," Jovanni pointed out.

"Yes, that too, son. Say, Bethany, how about the cost? Usually, we would expect those in Tan Loc to cover the cost of construction. Any chance of that here and providing protection for the workers?" Jules asked. "The construction of the line heading north out of Shansee has virtually come to a halt ever since this second plague struck."

"I think that I can get the financing from Nan Yan. We can probably put locals to work; they would know the area well. As far as protection goes, Stefano would have to send along a garrison force," I suggested. "You know, the biggest concern is to get the line up to Nan Yan as fast as humanly possible so that they are not cut off as the chaos of Shansee builds up."

"Okay, if cost is not a factor," Jovanni did a quick, rough estimate on his paper, "say we need to lay three hundred miles of track. My guess is that we might have it done by the end of this year, assuming we get the materials delivered in a timely manner and encounter no major obstacles."

Jules added, "Materials shouldn't be a problem. We've tons stacked up for the Shansee spur, which are just collecting rust since the plague began. We can use them first and later replace those supplies, if and when they resume work out of Shansee."

With such encouraging words, we set to work on making it happen. A week later, Stefano sent two construction crews and five hundred soldiers along with Jovanni to get the project started. I had little trouble getting a dozen in Nan Yan to offer financial support to the endeavor. Now we waited to see what help Macario would need to get his other three churches and those to which they were providing sanctuary safely to Nan Yan.

Twenty-one year old Chan Yingkao, breathing heavily after her exhausting workout with Master Ning Dong, bowed low to her master. "Master Chan, you have adapted well," he complimented her as he returned her bow. He was the Master of the Lou Yang Olin Masters and sworn guardian of the Church of God, here in Lou Yan, Lin Yi Province. She pivoted and headed to her quarters in the overly cramped Church complex. Ordinarily after such a workout, the mind and soul of this tenth level master would be calm and serene, but not anymore! Not ever, she thought after the devastation the plague had wrought upon her! Not ever!

She no longer even attempted to silence her mind, not since the plague. Her thoughts drifted uncontrolled into the past. Chan saw again the scene she had witnessed as a ten year old girl. There was her beautiful mother being beaten and raped as the two were walking home from the market, their arms full of fish and greens for supper. She watched helplessly as her mother was horribly violated. Now time jumped; she was sitting on the floor beside her mother, who was dying from the disease that the wicked, evil man had given her. Chan watched as her last breath expired, a quiet, yet painful death; Chan would never see the unborn child. Just as well, as it would have been a bastard, unwanted by all. There and then Chan swore that she would never allow herself to be a victim of a man, not ever. She convinced her grieving father to send her for lessons with the Olin Masters.

Time slipped forward on her again as she slowly walked from the practice room with its many safety mats. It was in this very room that Chan had her first lessons. She pushed her body as hard as she could, excelling in all ways. When she was twelve, she cajoled her father into allowing her to move into this very complex so that she could study and learn more. Oh, how she had worked, her body taking more punishment than most boys her age could withstand. Some whispered that she was driven. Over the years, Chan rose to higher levels of mastery than many other students here did, so much so that when she was twenty, Chan had finally attained Level Ten and full Olin Master status. Such was almost unheard of within the school!

Early on, she had received the Church of God's therapy sessions to handle the trauma of witnessing her mother's rape and subsequent later death. Because of the therapy, it no longer truly bothered her, though she still clung to her postulate that no man would ever violate her as they had her mother. Now she could concentrate and focus her mind and her spiritual powers. That alone allowed her to begin moving up into the upper levels of Olin Master's training. Her hope and dream was to one day master the topmost level of supreme power, Level Fifteen and become a Grand Master herself. Quite what she would do then, Chan was not yet certain, but she had ideas of one day opening her own school, as had her Master, Ning Dong.

Then the plague came to this far northern province. In three days, her life had nearly been destroyed! All the highly skilled martial arts moves, which involved her arms, gone! Years and years of dedicated practice, gone! Her sole goal in life, gone! Vanished without a trace, just as her arms had that awful morning when her she rose, helpless and ruined. In an instant, Chan had gone from a very independent person relying solely on herself to one of almost total dependence upon men, for whom, with a few exceptions, she had no respect at all.

Master Ning had understood. Half of his students were as armless, as crushed, as ruined as Chan. His soft, gentle, kind, reassuring words, his endless, patient hours of practice, almost solely dedicated to his female students these past months had salvaged them, all fifty-one in fact. "Master your mind and self. Focus your intention. It is your intention alone that makes all else possible. Waver and the action fails." He had to work so much harder than before to convince these frightened, terrified students of this fact. Here in early March, he had succeeded, for the most part.

Chan had expected to be dropped from her Level Ten mastery to perhaps that of a One, but she had not been demoted; neither had any woman. Worse still for her and for all the female students was their melon-sized breasts. In the beginning, their unexpected weight and huge size had thrown all of her critical timings off. More than once, she had fallen clumsily onto the mat in utter disgrace, a fall that a Level One might make. Utterly humiliating. Instead of calling attention to the falls, Master Ning merely helped her and the others use alternate moves to execute the same task and allowed them sufficient time to practice the moves. "Always, there are many ways that one can use to accomplish what one desires."

Indeed, Chan had even surprised herself, as her legs became even more lethal and precise in their movements and punches. Further, she was now learning to focus her intention to execute her advanced kijutsu powers, which separated the Olin Masters from the many other martial arts schools in Tashien. Already as a Level Ten, she had mastered the Push. Master Ning pointed out that she could use the Push in many situations where she would have used her arms.

Chan had mastered the kijutsu Shield, Extension, and now the Fly. True, she didn't really grow wings and soar like a bird; rather this power enabled her to take such leaps and jumps, which gave the appearance that one was almost flying. Instead of being demoted because she could no longer do so many of the more basic moves, Ning had forced Chan and the other women to find alternative ways to bring about the desired effect, and now Chan was working on the many kijutsu powers she needed to learn to advance to Level Eleven!

At first, Chan felt completely humiliated to have to sit on her butt and use her feet to put things into those damnable yokes and then to have to use the yoke to carry things. Embarrassing beyond belief. With a vengeance, she had thrown herself into the mastery of the kijutsu. Now she could make things Rise and Move. Though this took extreme concentration on her part, she was more than willing to do so, if only to avoid the humiliation that the yokes signified in her mind.

Still, Chan felt humiliated every second that she was not out there on the mats, training, straining, striving to focus, and master more kijutsu. As she approached the doorway that led from the training room into the housing chambers, her humiliation rose. Doors stared back at her as if telling her, "So you think you are able? Well, I am here to show you that you are not! You are now utterly dependent on men." At least with most doors, the men around the complex always made sure that they were opened. She entered and steeled her emotions so she could face the coming humiliations.

"Ah, back from your training, Master Chan," a fourteen year old Level Two student called out. He opened the door to her quarters for her. All the male students were now twinned up with a female student and charged to look after their needs. Lian was Chan's twin now.

"Yes, I need to get changed, Lian," she said softly, fighting back emotional forces that threatened to form a torrent of tears in her eyes. She could not tie nor untie her prized Master's sash, that red band that all Level Ten's and above wore around their waists, distinguishing them as an Olin Master. She could not get herself out of the white upper tunic that they all wore, though the men had removed the sleeves and sewn the holes shut so that flopping sleeves would not become a hazard for the women. She could not get out of her own white pants either or her panties. Every time that she needed to relieve herself, she had to endure the utter humiliation and embarrassment of having Lian pull her panties down and even wipe her privates. That he too found this highly embarrassing went unnoticed. The only minor victory the women had was that by now they could at least feed themselves at meal times. From Chan's point of view, routine life had become almost intolerable, a continuous stream of embarrassing, humiliating series of obstacles for which she needed assistance of a man with arms.

Bitterly, she complained to the Counselors, "All the therapy in the world will not give me back arms that I might dress myself, brush out and braid my hair, and cook my meals." Of course, therapy sessions could not do that. However, Chan began to see that more of the most advanced kijutsu just might allow her other ways to do some of these immensely challenging things of life.

Yet, things only grew worse as spring finally came to Lin Yi Province. It was bad enough having to have Lian deal with her helplessness, he was a fellow student, but now the Church of God had given sanctuary to so many other outsiders! At least three thousand plus now crowded into their complex, designed for a maximum of barely one thousand of the Olin Masters, the Counselors, and their servants who cooked, cleaned, and handled the laundry for them. Now Chan was forced to share her small private room with others, outsiders, many wealthy men and women and children.

"Make our guests feel welcome and wanted. They have nowhere else to turn to except us," Master Ning had explained to his group of martial artists and Counselors. His eight hundred fifty members and a little over a hundred domestic staff agreed to do so. Still, agreeing to do so did not lessen the humiliation that Chan felt, when two outsiders were brought into her room to stay with her. Her room was small enough as it was, but worse, they would have to share her bed, which was large enough to sleep three, if they slept close together.

"Master Chan Yingkao, this is Most Honorable Tian and Pani Pyong," Master Ning said, as he brought the two very nervous brother and sister to meet her and see their new quarters. "They have recently lost their parents and have come seeking sanctuary with us and I have granted it. Master Chan will help you get settled in and show you where everything is located. We have almost four thousand crammed into our quarters, which ought to hold barely a thousand. While the accommodations are sparse and cramped, here I and Master Chan will guarantee with our lives that you are safe as long as you remain within our outer walls. I will leave you to get settled." He bowed to them and then to Chan, who returned his bow.

Her humiliation knew no bounds now. Here, in her most private chamber, she would have to sleep and pretend company to two outsiders, one of which was a male. She would have to have this male in her bed. It was almost more than she could bear now. Pani lowered her head and began sobbing.

"There, there, Pani, we are going to be safe now," Tian said trying hard to comfort his younger sister, putting his arm over her shoulders. Chan got a good look at the two. He was skinny and tall, perhaps six-two. He looked like a nobleman, though his rich clothes were dirty and torn. Perhaps he had been in a scuffle, she thought. Like most men, he wore his long, black hair in a single braid, which fell to the back of his knees. He could use a good washing, she noted. He was twenty-one as well. Pani was barely eighteen, armless as the rest of the women now and just as helpless, Chan thought. At least someone had altered her bright green dress with red silk bird designs to accommodate her large breasts. Her dress too showed signs of a scuffle and she wore her long black hair identical to her brother's. Well, that was to be expected now, since he probably had to care for her needs as well as his own.

Tian looked up with sad eyes at Master Chan, more than a little surprised to see that she was a woman. When he heard that they would be staying with a Master, he'd assumed that one of this power would be male. He saw a young woman his age, five-eight, with long black hair done in a single braid as his, though hers was disheveled from her lengthy practice session. Her eyes were an enchanting green and seemed to miss no detail, and her face was rounded, almost angelic. Of course, there was no mistaking her femininity. Her large bust, though hidden beneath the traditional white tunic that all the martial artists wore, was most noticeable, as was her waist, made even more accentuated by the bright red sash tied around her tiny waist. She wore white pants and slip-on shoes. "May we sit on the bed?" he asked politely, thinking of Pani, who continued to cry softly now.

"Yes, it is now your bed as much as it is mine. Please, Most Honorable Tian, sit."

"Thank you, Master Chan. I regret that we are imposing upon your private quarters. We had no choice but to come here for help," he bowed and nudged Pani to the bed.

"We are here to serve, Most Honorable Tian," Chan forced herself to say. Well, she would not have minded serving them anywhere except here in her own quarters. In the back of her mind, she felt as if her sanctuary was being violated by this man and woman.

"Please, just Tian. Alas, I am no longer worthy of being addressed as Most Honorable," he said.

She detected sorrow behind his voice, though, and curiosity made her inquire. "Say, what happened to you two?"

"My father and I are, or rather were, Purchasers," he began. Chan knew at once that this meant that he was a wealthy merchant, one whom others hire to find and acquire items for them. Whether that is swords, artwork, people, or perhaps of late just food, a Purchaser could be counted upon to locate, buy, and deliver the requested item or items. "Yesterday, our world ended, though we, Pani and I, could sense that it was coming. The Tonqha Gang has been invading our block, demanding all manner of tribute as 'protection money.' Around suppertime, they burst in upon our family dinner and attempted to rob us of anything of value. Naturally, we never keep more than small living expenses in our home; the rest is secure in the Banca del Dio. They killed our parents, after torturing them, because they found so little coins in our house. While they were beating them up, I sneaked Pani out our backdoor. They came after us, threatening to kill us as well. We ran, scrambling like dogs, over the back wall and through dirty alleys until at last we no longer heard them following us. We cannot go home now. The thugs will certainly return, if they have not yet stripped our house of anything of value."

"Pani has had some therapy sessions from your Most Worthy Church of God. It has benefitted her greatly. The plague was devastating to us all. She suggested that we flee here and seek sanctuary. I don't know where we could have gone if your Master Ning had refused us. We owe you and your Church of God our lives. Still, we arrive with only the clothes on our backs."

"I'm sorry, I didn't know," Chan replied, realizing that their grief was real and raw. "Well, my quarters will be cramped with three of us in here. My bed will be a bit crowded."

"I am so sorry that we must intrude upon you, Master Chan," he bowed his head in shame. "I have been looking after Pani's needs ever since the plague. I would be honored if I could at least assist you with whatever you also need. We both owe you so very much."

Chan could hardly refuse, since they were after all her guests. "Thank you," she replied mechanically. "Come, I will show you where the bath is located, where we dine in shifts. You will be dining with my group, the Masters. We eat first. The problem is that we, like everyone else, are having a hard time finding enough food supplies. It is grim out there beyond our walls."

Pani, who had stopped crying and allowed her brother to wipe her face, replied, "Yes, we were down to only two meals a day as well. It is so difficult for us to cook. Dad and Tian have been doing the cooking for us. What is happening to our world? Is the world ending? Surely it must be. We are so helpless now. How can we survive?"

Chan growled, "Well, I am not dead yet. They'll have to defeat me first, but yes, we are Pani, we truly are that. Come on."

Later as they gathered for supper, bathed and in clean, but plain clothes while theirs were being laundered and mended, the two followed Chan into the spacious, but plain dining room. Tian helped his sister get seated, but before he could do the same for Chan, she had already moved her chair out and had sat down. Chan sighed as Master Ning began filling his plate and his wife's then passed the bowls on around the table. She would have to ask this stranger to fill her plate, she — a Master — was yet unable to do such a simple thing. Maybe Pani was right, maybe the world was slowly endimg after all.

At least Tian was polite about it, asking her what she wanted and the quantity. Soon, Tian began holding up food for his sister to eat. Chan at least did not have to suffer this indignity. She had her kijutsu power. Much to Tian and Pani's surprise, the food on her plate seemed to rise and move into her mouth. Even her teacup served her as if my magic. The two noticed a number of other women Masters were doing similar actions.

Later, Chan took the two on a stroll around the outer walls, while the next batch took their places at the same tables. Chan stalled as long as she could, but at last, she had to face the utter humiliation of bedtime. As they entered her tiny room, Tian asked, "I usually unbraid Pani's hair and brush it for her, help her into her nightgown, and then into bed. Shall I do the same for you? I am unsure of what I am allowed to do for you, Master Chan. I mean you no affront."

"I cannot do my own hair, Tian. Please, you may do mine; only I will need it braided again first thing in the morning. I am sorry, but we have no nightgowns. We sleep naked so that we can manage more easily nightly needs that arise. I simply cannot get my panties back on once I struggle to get them off. We do have a lot of covers to stay warm." Her face was flush with embarrassment. What other choice had she but to allow this strange man to see her deformed body as it now was? Often, she needed to use the chamber pot long before morning. Humiliating.

Tian sensed that Chan hated the living arrangements as much as he and Pani did. Yet, the massive overcrowding left their hosts little choices. "You will need to light that oil lamp; it is getting too dark to see well," Chan indicated.

Tian did so and then set to work undoing Pani's hair. She eyed him from the corner of her eye, not wishing to invade such personal, private moments that the brother and sister were sharing. At least he seemed to know what he was doing with her hair, she thought. At last, he removed her borrowed dress and Chan could not help noticing her shapely form. Pani was rather pretty, she thought. If only their breasts were not so gigantic, their waists so impossibly small.

Then, Tian began to unbraid her loose braid. Well, for sure it needed redoing; her combat session today had really taken its toll. He was kind and gentle, and his hands did seem to know just what to do. Well, Chan thought, I can endure this somehow. It must be done. All too soon, he began undressing her, asking where he should place her sash, pants, and then tunic. At last, she too stood naked before the two.

"Oh my, your legs are so powerful. I had no idea they were this strong," Pani exclaimed. Chan's legs were extremely well muscled, her power weapon. "You are very beautiful," she added.

"I am most ugly, Pani. Look at this mutilated body," Chan retorted. "Disgusting and helpless."

"Oh, Chan, you are truly a beautiful young woman," Tian insisted. "Yes, like Pani, you are bearing the whole brunt of the plague. Still, the plague has not diminished your beauty. What I wouldn't give to have all women's bodies put back to the way that they used to be. Still, Chan, you shouldn't think of your body as disgusting."

"What am I to think of it then?" she retorted and moved to climb into bed. Ordinarily, she would mostly flop into bed and then struggle to get the covers over her. However, Tian quickly moved to help her lay back gently, adjusting her long hair before she lay upon it. With the two women snuggled together, he blew out the lamp and crawled in on the far side, next to his sister. There was barely enough room for the three of them in the bed. Yet, for the two, it was a bed and they could sleep in safety, something they could never do in their old home again.

The next morning, Chan allowed him to braid her hair and was amazed that he did such a fine job of it. Perhaps it would not come undone during her combat training later on. Once dressed properly, she felt less humiliated and could not wait to head off to the morning meal. Perhaps she could spend far more hours in the practice arena. Perhaps she could volunteer to spend hours with the beginners, anything to remove herself from so much humiliation.

At breakfast, Master Ning said, "We are once again running low on food, particularly rice and greens. Once again, we will have to foray out into Lou Yang in search of supplies. However, we have with us now a Purchaser who has told me that he knows where we may acquire a large supply of rice, squash, and perhaps apples. Today, I will send out a party to lay in more stores for us all. Tian Pyong will lead us to where he believes that we can acquire a large supply. Yes, we will put a dozen of our male guests to work, they will man the pushcarts and hopefully return with them very full. Master Chan, you will lead the defense force that will accompany them. Pick your men and women carefully. It is very dangerous on the streets now. I would advise not less than twenty-five accompany the twelve men."

Chan bowed, "Yes, Master Ning. I am honored with the task before me." To Tian, she added, "Bring your men and wagons to the main gate. I will join you there with my force." Chan rose and left, excited and honored to once more be entrusted with the safety of the foraging party. While more dangerous than practice sessions, it was more fun, and she could get out of the compound for a time.

She knew that she dare not pick another Level Ten to accompany her, for they were sorely needed with all the women's special training sessions. An Eight would be allowed. She picked five men and twenty women to join her, most of whom had gone out with her before. These she both liked and trusted. Still, the ultimate burden for their safety rested on her shoulders. Master Chan walked proudly to the main gate, her troop following behind her. At the gate, the gate man opened it for the party. No humiliation here, he always opened the gate.

After learning their destination, Master Chan ordered, "Okay, the men with the carts go in single file. Half of my group will form a barrier around you. The rest will form the outer barrier and I will walk point. We are heading through three gang-controlled areas to get to this warehouse. Stay alert for trouble. Questions?" Seeing none they formed up their line, and her group encircled the men with their carts. Two others took the rear guard position while she moved to the front and took the most dangerous point position herself. Satisfied, she began walking down the street, leading her party out in search of most needed supplies.

To Tian, having so many helpless women as their escort seemed strange, if not dangerous. Others behind him also whispered similar concerns that only five male martial artists were with them. He expected that if trouble came, he would be pressed into helping these women. They looked so helpless walking along with no arms or hands with which to deflect a sword or even a fist. He began to worry, what had he gotten himself into here?

They had only gone some ten blocks when a dozen thugs jumped them. From the blue calligraphy, Tian read, "Ca," their symbol. Six men, none older than twenty, swords drawn, moved out of the shadows of doorways, blocking the way in front of Master Chan. On either side of the line, three more appeared. "Hand over your money and we'll let you pass this time. Your martial arts do not scare us. You've only five to our dozen," their leader called out to one of Chan's men, ignoring her completely. Obviously, the women were not even remotely viewed as a threat.

Master Chan spoke softly, "Move out of our way and I'll allow you to live another day."

One of the female Olin students near Tian whispered to her close companion, "Rats, there are too few of them. I bet you that we will not even get a chance to attack even one."

Her companion replied, "Maybe we will get one. Fools."

"Okay, boys, take them! We'll rape the women once we've killed those five," the leader ordered and he attempted to take a swipe at Master Chan. What happened next was almost a blur. Chan pivoted on her left leg, avoiding his sword swing. Her rising right leg, bent at the knee. Just as her leg moved into position, she extended her right leg in a precision strike, focusing the full force of her kick on the man's exposed neck. His neck snapped and his body slumped to the ground. Yet, she followed on through with the motion and her body seemed to rise into the air as she pushed off from her left leg, spinning head over heels, like a cartwheel. On her downward fall, she again sharply extended her right leg, direction the full force of her blow to the next thug who had moved somewhat past her position, snapping his neck from behind.

Chan landed as if on a pogo stick, up her body flew, but her direction of travel moved her behind the other man who had rushed past her on her right side when she had faced the leader. Once more, her power kick snapped that man's neck from behind. She landed and took a running step forward and again launched a rear circle kick downing a fourth man. As her feet hit the ground, she launched into an enormous back flip, whose arc was some ten feet in diameter. As her body neared the ground, this time it was her left leg that dealt the fatal blow.

She landed gracefully and stood facing the line of men. Tian's mouth was wide open. All dozen thugs lay sprawled on the ground, dead. Only one of her men had delivered an arm thrust of death, the other men found no opponents reaching their positions. All the others gang members were handled by her outer group of women, where most had killed one thug, while she had gotten five. All twenty-five bowed in unison and resumed their positions as if nothing had happened.

"Told you we'd get none this time. Master Chan is good. One day I hope to be as skilled as she is," the original woman who had predicted that she'd not get a chance to fight whispered to her companion.

Tian followed them, but he had never seen such a display before. He was soon to see more, however. Five blocks further on, another gang whose blue symbol read "Ra" attempted to take them by surprise. Eighteen swarmed them, with six of those leaping down from a roof, intending on smashing into the flank of the point group including Master Chan. She pivoted to face the falling men and cast her kijutsu Push power. Tian watched all six men suddenly following a different trajectory as they fell, smashing hard into the wall the building, stunned momentarily. Meanwhile, she again pivoted, bringing her right leg up to her approaching attacker. The force of her power kick snapped his neck, leaving his head resting upon his shoulders as his lifeless body fell to the ground.

Again, Chan pushed off the ground the instant her left foot landed, flying in a graceful arc, rotating her body, and delivering another killing blow to the back of another's neck as she began her descent. As she again landed, she leaned far to her left as the thug's sword sliced through empty space where her body had been. As she then leaned to her right, her side forced his arm down sharply, snapping his arm, while her left leg rose to deliver the killing blow. Following through on the motion, she again cartwheeled through the air, striking another as she descended.

A man lunged towards one of the men guarding Tian. He moved slightly so that the sword thrust missed his chest, but he brought his arm up applying a power thrust at the man's exposed neck. Tian heard vertebrae cracking and the body dropped to the ground as if it were a sack of rice. Beside him, his partner, gracefully leaned to her right, allowing the attacker's blade to miss her chest, but brought her left leg on up and thrust out her foot. Her leg motion snapped his sword arm, but her foot crushed his throat and he went down.

The action was once more both graceful and swift. One minute later, the group bowed and continued their way. "Well, I did get one," the young martial arts woman whispered to her friend. Tian just could not believe what he was seeing. These women were incredible, but none more so than Master Chan, who once more killed five in the time that her companions managed to get one or two. She was a blaze of grace and power, a lethality he'd never dreamed possible.

As they neared the market district and the warehouse where Tian expected to be able to purchase the desired supplies, more trouble came their way from the "An" gang. Only this time, three of the two dozen attackers carried guns. Now Tian saw why Master Chan had brought along the five men. They needed no orders to know that their job was to deal with the guns.

One of the gunmen knew from the colors of the sashes that Master Chan was the leader and most powerful. He aimed for her from twenty-five feet away and fired. Again, Chan was forced to use her kijutsu power; her Shield deflected the lead slug upwards and out of harm's way. Meantime, one of the men dashed to the gunman, one arm deflecting the gun up and out of the way, while his other hand delivered a killing blow to his neck. Likewise, two other men eliminate the other shooters forcing their shots to go astray an instant before their other fist sank deeply into their necks.

Several of the other attackers knew martial arts moves and their best man focused on Master Chan, attempting to use a double fist strike on her head, in a one-two smash. Tian watched as she snapped her head back out of his reach while bringing her left leg up and into his neck, thrusting her power at the last instant straight into it. While his body crumpled to the ground, another man tried to circle kick her back, only she followed on through and her body flew in an immense cartwheel, landing like a cat on her feet, facing the off balance man. Her left leg came up, hitting his from the side, snapping it like a toothpick. As her body continued a sort of rolling motion, her trailing leg found his neck.

After sixty seconds, two of the attacking martial artist fled the battle at top speed. All others lay severely crippled or dead in the street. This time, Master Chan had only felled four and several of her companions had two kills each. "It seems the streets are becoming more dangerous every day," she commented to Tian. "I hope that this does not turn out to be a wasted trip." The area that they were in did not look promising for finding food supplies. She would have never come here in search of rice and greens, that's for sure.

A couple of blocks later, Master Chan and her group took up a guarding position outside the warehouse, while the dozen men went inside to make their purchases. Chan sent in two of her men with them, just in case. Now she had time to kill and began watching the people on the busy street. The sights saddened her. What had her city become?

Across the street and to her far right, a woman pulling a rik stopped. Chan watched as a well-dressed man stepped out and deposited a coin in her collection tin, strapped to her back. The woman was tied securely to the rik's pulling poles by ropes around her waist. She would be tied to her rik until someone untied her, probably at the end of the day. Her feet were swollen and sore, undoubtedly from pulling the rik through the streets barefoot. Suddenly, two teenage thugs accosted her. While one held onto the rik, the other took all of her copper coins from her collection tin. She tried to see them, but couldn't. "You won't need this. We protect you," one thug sneered at her. Both took off down the street laughing. The woman, whose legs were gaunt and thin merely collapsed onto her knees and then slumped on down, sitting in the street on her butt, rik tied to her waist. She hung her head down and waited for death to take her. The man who had just disembarked came back to her, put a gold coin before her eyes, and then dropped it into her tin. The woman did not move or rise. After sometime, the man retrieved his coin and shook his head, leaving the woman to her fate.

Shortly after this nearly opposite them on the busy street, Chan spotted an older woman, clothes in tatters, struggling with one of the humiliating yokes. From the way she was bent, Chan guessed that she carried some weight in the two balanced baskets. Two thugs came out of the shadows and taunted her. They took a bag of rice from one of the baskets. Now lopsided, she had no choice but to stop and set the yoke down. "Here, we'll help you balance it," he taunted, taking out everything from the same basket. Sugar and some greens. "Ah, still not balanced," he teased and the two removed her bag of grains and dried fish from the other side, leaving her with two empty baskets.

"Please, I have children to feed with that," Chan heard the woman's faint protest. The thugs laughed and fled with the woman's food. She sat down on the street, lowered her head, and waited for death to take her as well.

A while later, a young woman passed them by, carrying some supplies in her yoke. Four thugs jumped her. One ripped off her dress and began fondling her, while another began undoing his pants. One of the male companions of Master Chan whispered to another beside him, "She'll intervene." Both knew their Master well. Indeed, Chan flew across the street, dodging people, horses, and carts, making a bee line for the four men. As she reached the one in the rear, her left leg rose up and power connected with the back of his neck. As he dropped, she used his body as a step upwards, now rising high in to the air. On her downward patch, her leg took out a second thug. Now landing on one leg, she contracted the other and pivoted, extending the leg into the side of the man whose pants now dropped to the ground. The first thug who had ripped off her dress revealing her two well-formed breasts, turned to face the steel-faced Master Chan. He got a good look at her face, before he felt her right foot touch his neck. All went instantly black, his neck spun around and his lifeless body dropped to the ground.

Master Chan bowed to the terrified young woman, who was nearly naked now. Chan felt humiliated because as much as she wanted to pull up the woman's dress and somehow cover her, she could not. However, her two male companions had followed her across the street and they did it for her. One even made some emergency repairs to her dress, enough to get her home safely. The frightened woman managed a thank you before bending under her yoke and heading terrified on down the street. Master Chan bowed to her two fellow martial artists, the best she could do to thank them. A bow from their Master was ample payment for these two men.

An hour later, the dozen men came out of the warehouse, their twelve pushcarts piled to their brims with bags of supplies. Master Chan looked in wonder at Tian. She bowed, "Amazing. You were right. We owe you a big thank you, Most Honorable Tian." He smiled as they again formed their marching line. "Stay alert. Expect far more trouble on the return trip," she called out to her group. Once more, she took the point position, as her wedge of men and women pushed out into the streets heading back to their secure compound.

However, the carnage they had wreaked getting to the warehouse had served its purpose. None dared interfere with their slow progress through the city. By the time that they entered the gates, the dozen men were panting from the exertion. Master Chan bowed to the gate man and then to Master Ning, who came to witness their arrival. He was most pleased to see the large quantity that they had brought back with them. "Master Chan, it seems Most Honorable Tian does know his supplies. This alone will allow us another week. You have done well. Any troubles?"

"No Master, just routine thugs." She didn't mention what she had been witnessing along the streets, however. Tian raised his eyebrows, routine? He doubted that very much. He'd just witnessed incredible miracles of fighting prowess!

Later on, Master Chan passed by Tian and Pani and overheard him excitedly describing the amazing feats that he had witnessed. Pani kept staring at Master Chan all the while. Chan took it in stride. To those not trained, she knew what she did must seem magical, yet, Master Chan knew better. Hours of practice and dedication led to perfection of one's skill — that and learning to focus one's intention. Intention, that was the key to unlocking the kijutsu powers in all of us, she thought to herself.

That evening, Master Ning gathered everyone together. He stood on a balcony window high above the thousands assembled in the courtyard below. Master Chan stood beside her two guests, jammed together tightly so that everyone could hear what her mentor had to say. She knew that it was important, rarely had Master Ning gathered everyone together like this.

"Our city and province is dying. Chaos and madness sweeps through our city streets daily. Against millions of psychotics, we few thousand can hardly stand and hold our position any longer. While we are the able of Luo Yang, we are too few to withstand the death grip of so many millions intent upon succumbing. It is with the heaviest of hearts that I must announce that we must evacuate our province, but we will not desert Tashien."

"I have been in communication with the other four Churches of God. We are all going to merge into one large group. By uniting our forces, we stand a greater chance of not being overwhelmed by the madness, which holds our Tashien in its crushing, relentless grip, but also of being able to bring back law and order. Nan Yan in Tan Loc Province offers us the best chance of being able to survive and prosper. That city is the least impacted by the vice grip of insanity which holds so much of our country in its tentacles."

"It is our duty now to put our heads together and discover the means by which we may all safely make the two thousand mile journey to Nan Yan. Yes, all those to whom we have granted sanctuary are welcome to come with us. We will do all that we can to guarantee your safety and survival as well. At this time, I ask those of you who may have ideas on how we may travel this long distance with so many of us to please join my Masters and I in the dining room for a conference. Thank you all for being so understanding." He bowed to the group and went indoors.

"You should go, Tian, you know where to get so many things," Pani insisted.

"But will you manage without me, sister? I worry about you constantly when I am not with you," he replied. Master Chan sensed his concerns for her were genuine, not faked and not originating from pity, rather from a deep bond of love for his sister. She had not seen that for some time and she stared hard at this young man, when she saw that he was not paying attention to her gaze.

"Yes, you must lend a hand, brother. I will be fine. There are many whom I can ask for help if I need it. Please, you must do this for us. We must help if we can," Pani insisted.

He sighed and bowed slightly to his sister. Turning to Master Chan, he said, "I should come to your meeting, though I am not certain how much help I can provide. I will do all that I can. You have saved my sister's life and mine." He followed her into the complex of buildings, as soon as the packed crowd had thinned enough for them to walk again.

The two joined but five others. Besides Master Ning, Masters Liao, Hung, Peng Shi, and Kang were sitting at one table, dwarfed by the space. These men had masteries from Level Eleven to Fifteen, the highest of which was Master Ning. Chan felt humbled to be in their collective presence. These were her mentors, though lacking arms, Chan doubted very much if she could ever achieve the skills that these men held. Shortly, Master Ning's wife and top Church of God's Counselor, Xiu, entered and took a seat beside her husband.

While they waited to see if others might attend, Xiu complimented, "Tian, we all owe you great thanks for acquiring so much needed supplies. We can hold out now for another week." He bowed and smiled.

"Well, let's get started, shall we?" Master Ning said, convinced that this would be the planning group. "The challenge: how to get four thousand men, women, and children safely some two thousand miles more or less to Nan Yan. While some of us could walk it, far too many would be unable to do so, and we would be in constant danger from all quarters. Ideas?"

"Ordinarily," Master Kang pointed out, "we'd take carriages or wagons. In our case, we'd need a thousand wagons!"

"The Yonshu River may be our best hope," suggested Peng Shi. "Take it south past Zau and down to Giang and then head up the Yan River to Nan Yan."

"Could we take the river down to our port of Jiao and then take coastal vessels down to Shansee?" asked Hung.

"I've heard that the streets of Shansee are even more dangerous than ours," Master Ning answered regrettably, knowing that might be a safer route until they got to that southern city.

"Where would we possibly get enough river craft? We have so many with us now?" Master Chan asked. River travel, while more dangerous than sailing the coastal waters, would be drastically safer than trying to walk the whole way. It was inconceivable that they could find four thousand horses to take them.

After a long pause, Tian spoke up. "I believe in Jiao we could get perhaps thirty junkets to Shansee. This time of year, we could, for a price, get maybe thirty riverboats to take us to Giang. Or we could, again for a price, probably get our hands on fifty wagons or so. I don't see how we could get triple of any means of transportation all at one time, Masters."

"We could divide into roughly thirds and go three ways," Master Ning suggested. After more discussion, there seemed no other alternatives but to divide up into roughly three groups, each making their way to Nan Yan by sea, river, and overland.

The next day, Master Ning led Tian, Chan, and Liao off to begin making arrangements. "I must go with Tian to make sure that he is successful," he explained to the three. "Dominate kijutsu may be needed and Kang has not yet mastered it. I alone have. Perhaps we will not need it; then again, we must acquire sufficient means to take all who wish to go with us. Master Chan and Liao are along to protect us, Tian." The young purchaser smiled; three incredibly powerful Olin Masters were with him. He could not have felt safer and only hoped that he could live up to their expectations.

Three days later, as the four headed home again from making even more arrangements, Master Chan, walking at Tian's side as his bodyguard, said, "Amazing, Tian. Impressive. You sure do know where and how to get just the things that we need. How do you do it?"

"I listen a lot to what others have to say, and I used to wander the city, observing what is where. It is so simple that anyone could do it. I am afraid that there is no magic at all in what I do, quite unlike the magic that you and your Olin Masters possess."

In those three days, they had managed to make arrangements for three groups to travel. The older folks would go by boat to their coastal city of Jiao and by junkets from there to Shansee, where they would need to make arrangements to take riverboats up to Giang and then on up the spur Yan River to Nan Yan. A little over one third of those here in their Church of God would accompany Master Kang on this relatively safe route. Masters Peng Shi and Hung would lead a little more than a third of them down the mighty Yonshu to Giang and then on up the river to Nan Yan. Masters Ning, Liao, and Chan would lead the younger members of their large group overland in some seventy wagons.

A few days later, the first third slipped out of the compound at midnight, joining up with their boats around one in the morning. This avoided most all the mobs and thugs. Two days later, a little more than a third likewise slipped out in the wee hours of the morning and boarded a large number of riverboats to begin their long journey down the Yonshu. With the compound now down to barely eight hundred of the younger set, the many horses and wagons began to arrive and were stationed in the courtyard.

The men did most of the packing, though a few women struggled with their yokes and baskets, determined to help. One evening, Master Ning called them together. "Well, this is interesting. We have just been presented with eight hundred books from Velona, Bethany's Hints, it is called. I am told that this book contains thousands of hints for alternate ways and means for our women and men as well. Each of you is to pick up one and read it as we journey overland." Tian picked up three, nodding to Pani and Chan.

"We will be traveling west first and then cut south. I feel that the safest route will be to meander south as close to the foothills as possible. That far out from the major cities, we ought to encounter only local overlords. We will roll out of here at midnight. Let's all make sure that we have packed everything," he finished.

"I am honored to be driving your wagon, Master Chan," Tian whispered to her, though he didn't know why. The three were finishing stowing the last of the many items that their wagon was to carry. Beyond the sashes to be awarded to those who rose to their next level, their wagon also carried a small charcoal stove, cooking ware, water barrels, and a fair amount of food. Her helper, Lian was also going to ride along in their wagon.

Master Ning walked up to them. "Ah good you are all here. I want a word with you, Master Chan, Most Honorable Tian. First, I am leading this group because I am afraid that we'll need all the kijutsu I can muster to get us safely there. Master Liao is second in command and will bring up the rear of our long column. Master Chan, you are to follow my lead wagon and be prepared for anything. Tian will be driving, so you are free to take whatever actions are needed."

"I am honored to be behind you, Master," Chan relied with a bow.

"Now there is one other thing that I must ask of you both. Tian, I am charging you with helping Master Chan learn to master the many hints in this Bethany's Hints book. I want her to start with mastering the use of the yokes. She must be able to assist us on the trail."

Chan's face grimaced! Her eyes sank. Her mentor was ordering her to endure utter and complete humiliation! He saw her reaction and asked, "Master Chan, you may speak freely. What is the cause of your emotions?"

Chan could withhold it no longer, she blurted out, "Why are you subjecting me to this utter humiliation? Why? What have I done to displease you so? What have I failed to do? How have I offended you so badly that you would degrade me so?"

"Ah, I see. So it is humiliation that has kept you from the yokes," he stated softly.

"Yes, it is so utterly degrading, so humiliating."

"May I ask is it your pride that is so wounded or is it your dignity that is being so compromised?" he asked, those being the two key ingredients of humiliation.

"It is not pride!" she declared.

"Ah, so it is your dignity that is being stomped upon," he replied.

"Yes, I used to have arms and could carry very heavy loads. It is beyond me how I am still able to perform as a Level Ten. I do not want to be reduced even further to that of an ox, a beast of burden with those yokes," she admitted.

"Oh, I see," he said softly. Tian nodded. He saw her point, she, like his sister, was now almost completely helpless in all things but their martial arts, where she could use her powerful legs and training to deadly advantage. Master Ning continued, "So, Chan, you are then your body, a body which now lacks arms is that what you are saying?"

His words stung her almost as if he had slapped her across her face. "No! I am not my body! I am a spiritual being. If I was merely a body, I would not have the kijutsu powers that I do have," she countered.

"Oh, then it is spiritual beings who have the arms that I see hanging from Tian's shoulders there." He countered.

What game is he playing with me, she wondered. "Of course not. That is silly to even suggest it!"

"I am looking to see the dignity that is being trashed here. Your body is not you, yet it has no arms. If your body is your tool, how is it to carry things if it doesn't make use of ways and means that are available to it to perform what it must do?" he asked pointedly.

"Oh!" Chan flushed in instant revelation and realization. I am not my body. I use it, she realized. "Forgive me, Master Ning, I was foolishly being my body once again. You are right. I am merely using this body, which now does not have arms. It is the body, which must suffer any indignity, not I. I will do as you ask, Master Ning."

He smiled, knowing that he'd scored another small victory. Rehabilitating his female students was turning out to be more challenging than achieving Level Fifteen! He had been watching Chan for weeks now and knew that she was avoiding learning the alternate methods that many of the other women were using. Now he knew why and had perhaps made a breakthrough with her.

Chapter 17 Exodus

Eighty-one wagons pulled out of the Church of God complex in Luo Yang early in the morning hours of March 20, 824. By dawn's first light, they had cleared the last tendrils of the mighty capital city of Lin Yi Province. As the wagons rolled along, Pani began reading Bethany's Hints aloud for the benefit of Tian, Chan, and Lian. At least it gave her something to do, riding long in the heaped wagon bed with Lian. Chan, of course, sat in the driver's seat alongside Pani's brother, who drove them, following closely behind Master Ning and his wife and two children.

"Holy donkeys! You women can still sew?" exclaimed Tian, taken by complete surprise.

"Yes, that's what she says here. I wonder how? I'd better read on," Pani added, growing excited herself. Sewing? How could this be possible, she wondered.

"Sawing wood? Oh, I see, she has made little drawings here, which show how regular saws must be adjusted for our use. Honestly, Tian, I don't think that I want to saw wood," Pani explained. By the time that she had completely read the book to the four of them, all four were astounded at the vast panorama of possibilities for women to renew their routines of life.

"She keeps on saying have patience, take your time, and get it done right and proper. Who cares how long it takes but rather that it is done right. She must be a genius to have thought up all these things," Pani added. "Tian, when we finally get to Nan Yan, can you see if there is any way that you can import some of these new dresses that we women can manage to put on by ourselves?"

"Sis, anything for you! God, what I wouldn't give to have you able to live a halfway normal life again! I'll get some for you too, Chan," he added.

Chan blushed. Why are my cheeks so warm? Why should I let this man buy me a dress anyway? I am perfectly capable of buying my own. She muttered thanks in spite of her thoughts.

As the day waned, Master Ning pulled in around a dense patch of forest for the night. He issued orders to make camp and the nearly eight hundred of them began to figure out how to make a camp. None of them had ever camped out before. These were all city dwellers. Now the men and women had to work together as a team. Chan and Pani kept diligently at mastering the use of the yokes, loading the baskets up and then bringing the things for the two men, who got their campsite ready, firewood gathered, a fire started, and supper cooking.

Master Ning smiled as he watched them. He commented to his wife, Xiu, "Before we get there, this bunch will have learned a tremendous amount, both the women and the men as well."

She smiled, "It is finally as it should be. Yes, they, as we, are learning to get accomplished the things which must be done. This should have happened the first day that the plague came. Would things be different now in our country had that happened?" He shrugged his shoulders; he had no idea. "Oh let me at it, you know that you are an awful cook," she butted him out of the way and began dealing with the making of their supper.

He was right, after a week on the road and as they at last veered to the southwest, each wagon group was working together as a team. What had taken two hours of confusion that first night now was done smoothly and efficiently in a half hour. The men now had a deeper understanding of their women folk and the women folk found their self-respect and pride beginning to return to them. They, as had their men, discovered that they were not helpless.

In fact, Chan found herself anxiously awaiting the coming of darkness, when she would be tucked into their bedding beneath the wagons. She found the touch and warmth of Pani and Tian extremely welcome. Did he feel the same way, she wondered. Perhaps so, since now he insisted on sleeping between the two of them, with Lian sleeping on the other side of Chan. Although she closed her eyes and pretended to go to sleep at once, she found herself straining her senses to perceive Tian, who lay next to her: his breath, his smell, the warmth of his body, his gentle good night wishes. What is happening to me, she wondered.

By day, Chan as well as Lian, Pani, Tian, and even Counselor Xiu, Master Ning's wife, continued to wonder what had happened to their fellow countrymen and women. Taking the backcountry rural roads, they saw farmers tending their fields as expected here in the springtime. Yet, they seemed so lifeless, hunched over, bent as if carrying the weight of the world on their shoulders. "Where are all the women?" Xiu asked. Although city dwellers, her therapy sessions had often taken her into the countryside around Lou Yang. Always, women were seen out there in the fields lending a hand with the many chores a farmstead demanded. Yet, their eerie absence was pronounced. Even Tian and Pani noticed this detail though they had seldom been in the rural lands, then mostly accompanying their parents on trips when they were children.

"She's in yonder house. Can't do much but sit around now, since the plague came," one older farmer replied. Counselor Xiu had asked her husband to stop so she could chat with one farmer toiling in his field. Intrigued, she went up to the home, but was stopped by the closed door. Master Ning quickly moved to her side and opened it for her.

"Thanks, I'll just be a minute," she whispered. He stood waiting, looking back at our long caravan of wagons. Most were stretching their legs and watering the side of the road, grateful for a short respite from the long hours in the wagons. Xiu found the middle aged woman sitting in her rocking chair in a sort of rocking doze, while three children were scampering around the kitchen playing games. Two girls, who she guessed were between eight and ten, were very animated, their cheeks flushed from running. Their slightly older brother was playing kick the beanbag with them.

As she entered, the three stopped and looked up. "Oh, hello," the older girl said, surprised to see such a well-dressed woman standing in the doorway of their kitchen.

"Hello. I just dropped in to see if you were all right," Xiu said quietly.

"Fine, playing with Chao. Mom is resting, but that's about all she does now, since the plague came," the young girl replied.

"Well, you three go right on playing and having fun," she replied and left them, returning to her husband. As she stepped outside, the two solemnly returned to their wagon and he helped her climb back in. "Difference in emotional tone levels are at play," she spoke as if this explained everything.

Master Chan overheard her and asked, "What do you mean? Is his wife ill or something?"

Xiu turned as their wagon began moving once more. "His wife is probably fifty-five or so and is at least in apathy now. She just sits in her rocker all the time. He has two daughters who may be around ten and a son who is perhaps eight. The girls are spirited and active, I found them dashing about playing a game with their brother. With our youth, there yet remains some hope for life. I am afraid that the older women are too far down to rebound from the plague. We've seen this same phenomenon in Luo Yang as well."

"What phenomenon?" Chan asked curiously.

"The attitudes adopted by those who have fallen into grief and apathy or worse. The reality of their bodies and situation now is terribly painful to them. They believe that life has affected them terribly and that there is nothing that they can now do, that they can no longer survive what life has to offer to them. So they sit waiting for death, their minds absorbed in their past memories. The present, they cannot confront or face any longer. On the other hand, youth is generally far higher in emotional tone. The children mostly ignore the plague's effects on their bodies and continue to play and enjoy life. In time, they will adapt and flourish. Hence, with our youth, some hope for life remains," she finished her lengthy explanation. Chan sat silently, pondering the Church of God's top Counselor's words.

After rolling along the picturesque countryside for some time in silence, Tian asked, "So Master Chan, what do you have planned for the future? I mean once we get to Nan Yan and all settled in, what are you going to be doing? Get married and raise a family of your own?"

Startled from her reverie, Chan glanced at him. "My goal is still to become an Olin Master of Level Fifteen and start my own Academy. How about you?" Children? She thought, marry? Chan had never even considered either possibility, not since witnessing her mother's rape and later death. Men caused it, well one man had. Except for the Olin Masters, she'd carefully insulated herself from all men. Hence, she quickly tossed it back onto Tian.

"Me? Well, I was a Purchaser, mostly because dad was and he was grooming me to take over his business. Now I've left that behind my back. Good riddance, really. I never enjoyed doing that, not really. When we get there, the first thing I will do is get a house for my sister and me. I've promised Pani to help her as long as she needs me. Then, I'm going to see if I can find a job teaching children. I've always wanted to teach children how to do things, particularly arithmetic and math. You know, one needs to be good with figures, even housewives. I taught Pani well. Before the plague, she was a super cook, great at using math to measure out just the right amount of spices."

"He's right. I kept finding new uses for his lessons," Pani spoke up encouragingly, but then her face fell, "but that was before the plague. Now, I may never be able to cook again."

"Sis, remember Bethany's Hints. We just have to get us a new home and get you the right kind of kitchen and things to use in it. I'm sure that in no time, you will be back cooking again, sis," he replied trying to encourage her as best he could.

"Tian, I think that is a wonderful idea. Our children do need a good education," Chan found herself praising him. She leaned her head on his shoulders, but wondered why she was doing that. Then, she realized that before the plague, she would have wanted to put a reassuring arm around him, showing her support for him.

Just ahead of them, Counselor Xiu turned and told Chan, "Women will finally be all right when their first urge and impulse is to use their feet and the rest of their bodies and not their arms and hands."

That simple statement struck Chan like a lightning bolt! Until this very moment, that was precisely what continually happened with herself. When something occurred, her first impulse was to use her arms, as she had done all her life until the plague. Each time, stark reality smashed into her, bringing the reality of no arms acutely into her mind. In order to be effective in her martial arts, she had to first banish that urge and humiliation from her mind and then act. Every time she had to act, this extra step of banishment cost her a bit of reaction time, making her slower than she ought to be, making it harder to use her kijutsu powers. To Chan, Xiu's words seemed profound!

As if anticipating Chan's thoughts or perhaps even reading them, Counselor Xiu added, "In time, that will come to all women. Yet, in the young and newborns, especially, this will become second nature. Already, I saw it happening with those two farm girls back there. They will not be helpless women when they grow older. Give ourselves time, Chan, time to adjust and adapt." Chan smiled and knew that Xiu was right, only now Chan knew the truth of her situation finally. She finally stopped fighting it; her arms were gone and would always be gone now. Continuing to fight that reality was fruitless and a waste of her time and energies. She smiled and relaxed.

Later that day, Chan also realized why Master Ning had come with this group and not sailed down the river or sailed along the coast. His Olin Master skills were critically needed here. A large band of well-armed men came riding up to the group. The local overlord had heard of the coming of a large group of wagons and had sent some of his forces to intercept them and steal what they could from them. She watched and sensed Master Ning using his ultimate Level Fifteen kijutsu powers of Mass Domination. He spoke, "Olin Masters on a pilgrimage. You may pass."

One by one, the leaders of the band of fifty men repeated his words, "Olin Masters on a pilgrimage. You may pass." They turned around and rode off. Chan smiled and explained what had happened to Tian and Pani. Her student, Lian, was most impressed with Master Ning! He'd just witnessed one of the most powerful of all the Olin Master's kijutsu powers. He would never forget this day!

The fact that they were indeed a large band of Olin Masters kept them all relatively safe throughout their long overland journey. Neither bandits, thugs, or overlords wanted to pick a fight with these, the most powerful of all martial arts schools. Still, before they arrived in Nan Yan, Master Ning had to use his kijutsu over a dozen times to ensure their safe arrival.

A month into their long journey, Chan was now doing many routine actions to help her small group with their daily camp activities. She thought nothing of using her yoke and feet to unload or load their wagon. She, like Pani, began fetching firewood, holding the branches between her head and her shoulder. Pani started cooking again, and Chan began to assist her, learning to cook herself for the first time in her life.

One night after they finished their dinner as dusk slowly grew, Master Ning walked up to his student. "Master Chan, it is time for you to take your Level Eleven test."

"What? No! I have done no practicing for ages! I am not ready, I will fail," she protested, totally shocked with his statement. She had not had a practice combat session since they had departed Luo Yang, let alone practice her special kijutsu needed for this level. He must be teasing her or something.

"Come, assume the position," he said quietly and with full intention. Chan knew that she could not refuse, not a direct command. She rose and bowed formally to Master Ning. At once, Lian stopped everything and moved closer to watch. Now other students also gathered around to watch the impressive Level Eleven test. Even Master Liao, who himself was Level Eleven, came running up to watch the test. Chan felt embarrassed, for the whole school was watching her now!

"Focus, Master Chan, let go of your thoughts," he whispered to her. Did he know that her mind was a whirlwind of counter-thoughts? He must, she assumed, yet she strove to do as he asked. Unlike before, she found letting go of all these considerations seemed easy. The two bowed and the exam began.

He called for specific kicks and actions. The two looked more like a pair of flying white figures, as they both circled, kicked, and leapt high into the air, pivoting and twisting for advantageous positions. Then, Master Ning summoned a burning log into his hand. As if by magic, the log flew from the nearby campfire into his outstretched hand. Chan focused and used her Move kijutsu, sending the log back into the fire, almost as if it had never left there.

Next, Master Ning attempted to flee the battlefield and Chan used her Pull kijutsu, pulling his body back to her. After a few more flying kicks and giant cartwheel maneuvers, Master Ning began to Pull her out of her intended trajectory and into a position where he could easily subdue her. Chan focused and use her Push kijutsu, countering his action and then used her Pull again, to yank his feet out from under him, following that with a Move action, which placed her right foot over his neck. At this point she halted all action and bowed.

Master Ning hopped to his feet in a graceful motion, as if he had somehow lifted his body up by invisible puppet strings, bowing to Master Chan. He spoke clearly and loudly, "Master Chan has attained

Level Eleven." She grinned and bowed once more and cheering and applause erupted from the gathered students.

"Well done, Chan, well done," yelled Master Liao. "You did that better than I did when I passed! Way to go!"

As the group returned to their own wagons and campsites, Master Chan asked, "Master Ning, how did you know that I was ready for the test? I did not even know that I was ready or that I even could pass."

He smiled, "Ah, I observe, Master Chan. You no longer react to actions and events by trying to use your arms and hands. You now think and act with your body as it is. No longer are those counter-thoughts appearing first. So now, you can act more swiftly and precisely. If you will excuse me, my wife wants me." They bowed and she returned to their wagon.

"That was incredible! Well done, Master Chan!" Tian exclaimed, throwing his arms around her, giving her a warm hug.

Oh, how she loved the feel of his arms pulling their bodies close! Their lips were so close now. Timidly, Tian brushed his lips to hers, she didn't pull away, and he grew braver and gave her a passionate kiss. To his amazement, Chan returned his passion. When their lips parted, Chan's body felt light and electrified, her eyes, misted.

Pani giggled, "Told you so, big brother."

"Told him what?" Chan asked, as both their heads turned to see her, his arms still holding her close to him.

"That she likes you, silly."

Tian whispered, "Is there any room in your heart for a would-be school teacher?" Chan didn't reply, she wanted more of this and simply kissed him again, passionately.

In Zau, the situation in the large Church of God complex of Olin Masters grew worse. Already, Master Feng had granted sanctuary to far too many. Nearly three thousand men, women, and children had been taken under his protection. Overcrowding was acute, their one thousand students, Counselors, and domestic staff somehow found room for all these desperate people, for whom this isolated complex in the heart of the Imperial City of Zau represented survival. However, one major problem faced Master Feng.

Overlord Bin Zhou had cleverly moved in to fill the vacuum left by the desertion of the Imperial Army of the Emperor. His wife, now long dead, had given him the blessing of three able sons. All four of them were martial artists of the Lian School, where punches prevailed, not kicks. With no women to hold them down, when the plague struck, they remained unaffected, save for having to hire replacement domestic staff. Imperial soldier by imperial soldier was stolen away from the Emperor, because his and his sons' offers of employment were too good to pass up. In early March 824, Bin's forces numbered ten thousand.

In a city of nearly eight million, ten thousand was but a handful. Yet no other man commanded such a force of fighting men. Bin knew that he could not control the entire city, although he long held illusions of one day becoming the Emperor of Zau. Rather, he could have under his control any smaller area of Zau that he desired. By sending in such an armed force, none there could stand against him. Still, he could not attempt to control the whole city. "We pick our sections," he continually told his sons.

Naturally, one of their first targets had been the wealthier sections of town, which accounted for the large number of those who sought sanctuary within the walls of the Church of God. Master Feng's interference only aggravated old rivalries between the Olin Masters and the Lian School. For over a week now, around a thousand of Bin's soldiers regularly patrolled the streets just outside of the Church of God, as if daring a showdown with Master Feng.

Macario's decision that they should flee to Nan Yan was welcomed by all. However, at this point in time, they had no way to evacuate their complex. Bin's soldiers were just outside waiting for them to come out. They would have to fight their way through them, costing precious lives. Master Feng knew that his forces could not hope to defeat ten thousand. Over ten to one odds were dismal. He had to find another way to evacuate all these people. Unknown to him now, events were already in play, events that would change his situation entirely.

Across town, two twelve year old twins, each holding an apple between their teeth, ran as fast as their feet could carry them. Behind them, the "Tau" gang members chased after the two young women, intent upon teaching them a lesson that they would not soon forget, perhaps even more, since they were almost young women. The twins, Yin and Yan Jining knew precisely what they were doing, as they headed down a back alleyway, dodging around discarded refuse and the occasional dead body left lying where the person had died, though some had obviously been dumped here — limbs seldom appeared as this in real life. From their rear, they heard shouts, "Hey this is a dead end alley. We have them now!"

Both would have smiled had they not had the apples in their mouths.

Reaching their spot, a dark hole at the side of the end of the alley, holding their balance with their necks, one after the other descended the short iron stairs to the bottom of the sewer. Using their feet, they pulled on the rope, which they had tied to the iron cover, and the grating slid over the hole above their heads. Yin looked at Yan and nodded. They set off down the smelly tunnel, still clutching their precious apples. Sunlight came down only through the periodical grates on the streets above them. Although the lighting was exceedingly dim, these two knew precisely where they were heading. Without hesitation, they turned left, then right, and at last came to their Spot #12, as they called it. Here, four tunnels joined and on each of the four corners a three-foot tall platform rose, each one large enough to hold one of them. Yin and Yan climbed up on two of these platforms, where they had left a bowl of clean water. They washed off their slimy feet and then finally began devouring their hard-won apples.

Several rats soon joined them. "Yi, you must be patient," Yin said to a brown and black rat, which was sniffing the air close to her. "You can have the core when I'm done." She used her feet to turn the apple a bit more. A few minutes later, she carefully set the core down and nudged it a little towards Yi. Across the sewer on another platform, Yan did the same thing to her rat, Ti.

"I'm still hungry," Yin called out.

"Me too. Let's go to the river docks and see if we can snitch some fish or else find some scraps," Yan suggested. The two slipped off their perches and into the murky, foul waters once more. It was a long walk from where they were across the city to the river docks, but they had time enough. There was nothing else for them to do.

They had both been on their own now for almost half a year. Their mother had died when they were barely four years old. Their father, Wu Jining, pulled a rik for a meager living. When his wife died, he had little choice but to carry his twin girls around with him as he pulled his rik around the city by day. He had made a back seat compartment to hold them, and for years, they had watched the city go by as their father pulled fares throughout the city. At this point in their lives, they knew nearly every inch of the city, except the very wealthiest section.

As the twins grew older and heavier, Wu was forced at last to leave his girls at home during the daytime hours. They lived in shantytown, the slums of Zau. At first, they tried to play with the other children in the streets. Both Yin and Yan were teased and picked on so frequently, that they finally gave that up. One day, they found that they could move a sewer drain grate and decided to go exploring down below. Oh, how that had turned out. They discovered lost coins by the handfuls and often carried along pouches in which to carry their "finds." They came across daggers, knives, and even once a fine looking gem. They hocked most of their finds, using the money to augment the meager funds that their father gave them to purchase food. Their only job was to ensure that supper was waiting for him when he returned. He never knew about their subterranean adventures, figuring that they really knew how to strike a good bargain at the markets.

However, shortly after the plague struck, he did not come home. The next day, they headed off looking for him and soon discovered that he'd been killed and his rik fares for that day were missing. Only eleven at the time, they were both armless and on their own. Yes, a pile of items appeared in their home, but there was no one to install the kitchen for them. At first, the two were terrified and went outside seeking help. Quickly, they heard that a plague had come and that all girls and women were just as they were, armless.

"Now what are we going to do, Yan?" Yin asked.

"We still have some coins left. Let's use these yoke things to go get some more food," Yan suggested. Their feet hobbled, they did not fare well at all, often they were robbed of their precious bits of food and at last abandoned using their yokes altogether. They tried begging for a handout and somehow got by until their feet returned to normal. During this time, their attitudes adjusted and changed.

"Well, Yin, we are going to have to help each other now," Yan stated purposefully, as if she might be some adult. "Here, let's see if I can get you into your dress."

While it took the two ages to dress, even longer to braid their waist length hair, they had little else to do in their two-room shanty. Quickly, they adopted to wear only the loose fitting dresses, which they could pull over their heads. When their supply of coins finally ran out, they headed back into the sewers looking for more. Their years of combing the sewers of Zau had pretty much uncovered all the lost coins. Slowly starving to death, the two young girls finally resorted to petty theft from the local merchants, who had finally opened up their open-air shops along the streets once more.

Most merchants didn't mind their snitching an apple or piece of dried fish. Many pitied them and a few even offered them food. Somehow, the two got by for nearly six months. Now, however, the situation on the streets had taken another downward plunge. Gangs of thugs began wearing shirts with their calligraphy symbols painted on their backs. They roamed the streets over which they claimed dominion, harassing and stealing from nearly everyone. Yin and Yan were not immune either.

Repeatedly, they were forced to flee from these teenaged boys, often losing their precious food items in the process.

The Chi gang now controlled the streets around their home, as rundown as it was, and demanded a toll from everyone who walked by. Obviously, the two could not pay a toll and were now targets of these boys, who once had even thrown rocks at them, giving Yan a nasty cut on her forehead. Before long, they only dared to return to their home perhaps every few days and then only to clean up and wash their tattered dresses as best they could. Their sanctuary was the sewers and their friends, the countless rats who dwelled there. The rats didn't seem to mind their presence at all, especially after they left their scraps for them to eat.

"Perhaps old Zou will give us a bit of fish today," Yan speculated as they neared the river docks finally, having walked over four miles through the sewers.

"Yes, let's ask him first. He's always nice to us," Yin replied as they neared their exit grate. The two climbed up onto the platform and peered out the grate above them. No one seemed to be around and they used their feet raised up over their heads to push it aside. Yin poked her head up cautiously. "All clear." Now came the hardest part for the twins, scrambling up out of the sewer. They had to jump up as high as they could possibly go and lean over, hoping to catch their chests on the ground. Yin leaped. Using her head and with a lot of wiggling and with Yan pushing up from below, she made it. In turn, she bit down hard on Yan's dress, helping to pull her sister out next. They carefully pushed the grate closed and headed off out of the alley to Zou's market stall, where he sold the fish that he'd recently caught.

"Oh no! Get back," Yin whispered. From the edge of the alleyway, the two cautiously peered out into the busy street. Three thugs were beating up poor old Zou! The two waited until the boys left, before scurrying over to the nearly unconscious man. Using their feet and his water skin, they wiped off the blood as best they could and Zou regained consciousness.

"What happened, Zou?" Yan asked as he sat up and rubbed his aching chest and head.

"Gangs are controlling everything. They stole all the money that I earned today. What's Zau coming too? It isn't safe just sitting here minding my own business and selling my fish. The world is ending, I expect. The only safe place in Zau now is that strange Church of God, I hear. Well, little ladies, I do have one fish left, saved it back just for you. Not much, but it's all I have now."

To their delight, he began tearing off bits and feeding it to them, telling them how thankful he was that they tended to him after the beating. As they greedily ate, all three heard the noise of a fight not too far away. The same gang members who had just beaten up Zou were now bashing another merchant, only this time, they went too far and killed the man. Cries and wails went up, "You two had better get out of here quickly. More trouble is coming!" he urged them, as he gave Yin the last bite of fish. Hastily, the two rose and headed back into the alleyway.

Bang! Gunshots startled both girls and they ran for dear life. As fast as they could, they moved the grate and climbed back into the safety of the sewers. "I wonder if they were shooting at us?" Yin asked.

"Dunno, but I am getting scared, Yin. What are we going to do? If we cannot even get food anymore, we're going to starve to death," Yan speculated.

"Well, let's go back to our house and see if it is safe for us to stay there a while," Yin suggested. Late that afternoon, they climbed out of the sewer a half block from their shanty. They spied a dozen of the gang members patrolling their street. One was sitting in the entryway to their shanty. "Oh no, we can't even get into our house now," Yin cautioned, rather worried about how things were progressing.

"Let's go back and talk with Yi," Yan suggested and the two headed back to their Spot #12 and their pet rats. Well, the rats were not actually their pets, only the girls liked to think so. There, the two spent the night, chilled to the bone, sleeping on the cold stone platforms. In the morning, they again tried to slip back into their shanty home, but another boy was there watching for them. Obviously, the gang was after them now, both girls concluded.

"What are we going to do now?" Yan asked. Yin had no answer, and the two sat gloomily on their perches, while their stomachs growled for breakfast.

"Hey, old Zou said that the Church of God place was the only safe place left in the city. I wonder if they would give us something to eat. What is a church anyway, Yan?" asked Yin.

"Dunno, but if Zou says it is safe, we ought to trust him. He's been kind to us, Yin," Yan declared. In agreement, the two rose and headed off through the sewers towards the Church of God. While they had never been inside the complex before, from their many trips on the rik and via the sewers, they knew where it was located. Around noon, they had even found the sewer line that came from inside the complex. Cautiously, they pushed the grate aside and poked their heads up to have a look.

They saw a large number of mats on the ground and nearby walls. A lot of adults and kids, some girls like themselves, all dressed in white clothes, were practicing their martial arts moves. A tall man walked over to the two heads peering around just above the hole in the ground. "Hello girls. May I help you?" asked Master Feng. He bowed to them. No one had ever bowed to them and they both giggled at how silly that seemed to them.

"I am Master Feng. This is my place, the Church of God and the Olin Masters Academy of Martial Arts. Do you need a hand up? What can I do for you?"

"I'm Yin and she's Yan. Is it really true that this is the only safe place left in Zau now?" asked Yin, still not quite sure what to make of all this. None of the students paid them any attention and Master Feng seemed pleasant enough.

"Yes, I am afraid that that is so. Here within these walls, everyone is safe. I give you my solemn word on that. Are you hungry? You could use a bath."

"Yes, we're starving. Could we stay here a while?" asked Yan. She'd decided that she liked this kind man in white.

"Yes, you may both stay here as long as you like. I grant you sanctuary, food, clothing, shelter, and protection as long as you desire," he replied formally.

"Wow! Food? Okay!" Yin replied, animatedly.

"Need a hand up?" he asked.

"No sir. We can do it ourselves," Yin declared. He watched as the two helped each other up. Yin jumped, leaned over onto the ground, wiggled about, while her sister pushed from below. Once up, she caught her sister's dress in her teeth and pulled hard until Yan was also up. Together, they slid the grate back into place.

Just then, a woman in a white dress had joined him. "Hello, girls. I am Shu Wen, Master Feng's husband. I run the Church of God here. Welcome."

"Hello Great Lady. I am Yin and she's Yan. We're hungry," Yin stated the obvious.

Shu Wen smiled, "Well, you have certainly come to the right place. Come with me to the kitchen; let's get you filled up. Then, how about a bath and some clean clothes?"

"Wow, clean clothes? We can wash these if you have a bucket someplace," Yin explained, the two following her across the practice field.

"Maybe, Yin, we should take a bath first, so we can wash our feet before we eat," Yan suggested.

"Now that would be an excellent idea, ladies," Shu Wen smiled, trying hard not to react to the sewer smell from their legs.

"Okay, let's. We usually have a wash bucket to clean our feet before we eat. Do you really have a bath in here? We've never seen one, though our dad once told us he'd seen one. He's dead, you know. Someone robbed and killed him months ago. It's just Yin and Yan now," Yan explained.

"We have bath barrels in here, ladies," Shu Wen indicated with a nod of her head. "Okay, off with your clothes and into the tubs, please." Two other women entered as Shu Wen prepared to help the two young girls disrobe. To their amazement, the two sat down and helped each other out of their filthy and tattered dresses. There was room for only one person per barrel and Shu Wen and her assistants sat on chairs, using their feet to help wash them as well as undoing their braids. Both girls hair was in sore need of a washing as well. However, when they girls climbed out, they insisted on drying each other off and redoing each other's hair. Shu Wen smiled at their independence and allowed them the freedom to do as much as they could, which was a surprising amount.

After having what the girls thought was a feast, they were then shown around the complex and given a room with one of the martial artists. Bao was only a couple years older than the twins were, and she was eager to share her small room with them. The three chatted and the twins took an instant liking to Bao.

Meanwhile, Master Feng paced the courtyard, deep in thought. Seeing the girls appearing from the sewer had given him an idea. With the constant presence of the soldiers on all sides of his complex, there was no way to escape or even to make any arrangements. The girls had given him an idea.

That evening, he visited Bao and the twins. After bowing respectfully to Bao, who returned his, very much impressed with the fact that *the* Master was in her room, he said, "Yin, Yan? Which is which? You look almost identical, very pretty young women."

The two giggled; they had never been called pretty, but they liked him, for already their breasts had become quite large, though nowhere near as big as they would eventually become. Yin said, "I'm Yin. I have a dimple on my left chin. Yan has hers on the right side of her chin."

He smiled, "Well, ladies, we here have a very big problem, and I am hoping that you two could help us all out." He explained in detail what he hoped might be possible.

"Oh sure, that's nothing, Yan and I know everything down there," Yin answered a bit later. Master Feng soon heard their life's story. They were eager to help these nice people, as long as they got something to eat and could go with them. Although neither had ever heard of a place called Nan Yan, anywhere but here in Zau appealed to them.

"Thank you very much, Yin, Yan. My assistant here, Bao, will go with you at all times. She is a fighter and she will see that no harm comes to either of you," he tried to keep it simple for the girls, figuring that they probably had little or no education, which was correct. All they had were street smarts and an unfailing sense of direction.

Bao soon learned that, in many ways, these two girls could do far, far more than she could. They were the most independent women or girls that Bao had seen since the plague struck. That very night, the two began showing Bao how to get things done. They, in turn, kept asking her about how she did her fighting and Bao managed to show them a small kick in the confining, small bedroom.

Later that evening, Feng and Shu Wen began writing various messages. "Amazing pair of girls," Shu Wen commented as she finished writing out one dispatch. She sat at her low writing desk, while her husband sat at the normal desk.

"Yes, amazingly well adapted. I hope this crazy plan of mine works. We are rapidly running out of our food reserves, love," he replied, giving her a kiss on her forehead.

"Come here, you rascal," Shu Wen teased, her leg sweeping out and encircling him, pulling him close to her, as she rose. She leaned over and gave him a proper, passionate kiss.

The next morning, Master Feng put the dispatches into two different pouches and hung them over Bao's shoulders and neck, ensuring that they could not be dropped. "You know what must be done?" He'd already talked with Bao at length and she nodded.

Bao led Yin and Yan out of her bedroom and to the courtyard. Already the younger students were beginning their daily practice. Normally, Bao would have been out there with them, but today, she was on a mission! The two twins headed for the grate, and Bao was forced to move quickly to catch up with them. Without any real effort, the two slid the grate aside and began descending the rusty iron ladder. Fearless, Bao thought to herself as she stared down at the vertical descent of some six feet.

As if sensing her hesitation, Yin called up, "Hold on with your chin." Carefully, Bao emulated the actions of her two companions. While she moved downward with extreme caution, she marveled at how rapidly the twins managed the treacherous descent.

"Wow! It stinks and how can we see?" Bao asked once she was down, her feet a little under the blackish waters, which she did not want actually to look at to see what she was standing in — it could not be pleasant.

"Wait a couple of minutes. Then you can see lots better. We always do. Wait, that is. Okay, let's go. Follow us, it's this way," Yan called out after their eyes had adjusted to the dim light. Bao marveled at the girls' sense of direction! To her, it seemed that they were wandering around in a dark maze with no end, no reference points. Soon, she was completely lost, utterly dependent upon these two girls. She fought her rising nervousness with an Olin chant and attempted to keep up with these two.

Around noon, they arrived near their first destination, down by the river docks. She watched as the two climbed up onto the platform, stood up, raised one leg high each, and worked together to slide the grate aside. "It's clear," Yin whispered.

"Okay, how do I get up and out?" Bao asked, not seeing any easy way to do it.

"We always jump up and catch our chests, while one of us pushes up from below. It is too hard to climb the ladder. It's easier this way. Want us to come along?" Yan asked.

"No, you two stay here where it is safe. I'll go deliver the message." Bao jumped as high as she could, flopping down hard on her chest, just barely able to bend enough to hold herself up. Soon, she felt the upward push from the twins. A bit of wiggling and she got one leg out and then she was free. She stood and slipped the grate mostly back into place. Bao got her bearings and whispered, "Perfect. We are right where you said that we would be. Back in a short while."

Bao's keen, observant eyes took in the entire street scene before her. She needed to cross without attracting attention to herself. Several gang members were patrolling the street, these she had to avoid. While she knew that she probably could take them, a fight would only bring more of them and prevent her from her secret mission. She waited. Before long, a small commotion started. Some were attempting to rob a woman and the gang members all headed that way. Bao took her chance and darted across the street, disappearing onto the crowded wooden docks. She went straight to the Willow, a large river barge.

"I've a message for you from Master Feng Chow," she said to the captain. "Brown pouch." She hoped that he would fetch the letter. She still felt very uncomfortable sitting down and trying to retrieve it with her feet. He leaned over her and she smelled the odor of stale tobacco smoke on his breath and beard as he opened the pouch. "I'm to wait for your reply," she added.

The tall, thin bearded man opened the note and read swiftly. "Damn, I knew it was coming. I could feel it in my bones. Tell my dear friend I will see that it is done as he asks." She bowed and left, rejoining the hustle and bustle on the docks. While some men gave her a look, most were too busy hauling heavy boxes and crates to pay her much attention. She was in luck, the gang thugs were not in sight when she reached the street. Hastily, she darted across and into the back alley.

Damn, she thought. One thug had his back towards her, relieving himself near the very grate that she needed to use. Rapidly she moved to him. Raising her right leg, she pivoted in an arc, and then extended her foot just as she had practiced to many times before. His neck jerked and his body slumped to the ground. She moved to the grate and spotted the two girls who had watched the whole thing.

A minute later, she was safely down with them and watched as the two working together slid the grate back into place. "That was amazing! How do you do that? Can we learn how to do that too?" Yin asked, very much awed with Bao.

"Yes, me too," Yan added.

Bao grinned, "Sure, you can. It takes lots and lots of practice though and a lot of bruises when you don't get it quite right," she added a cautionary note. The girls giggled. Now they faced an even longer hike through the darkened sewers beneath the giant city. It was nearly suppertime when Bao climbed out to deliver the second message. This time, everything went according to plan. Most were indoors now dealing with whatever supper they could manage. Times were still tough for most, though food was becoming more plentiful now.

The three finally re-entered the complex well after dark. While the three were given a bath, several others fed them some supper. "Hey, we're having dinner in the bath," Yin giggled, most pleased with this. Besides, all three were very hungry by this time.

When they were dried off and dressed, Master Feng joined them. Bao reported her two return messages and he thanked them, giving each a loving hug, which again caused the two girls to giggle. They had not been hugged for ages and they rather enjoyed it.

The next day, Master Feng issued orders to several men who took up their usual observation posts on the roof of the complex. From here, they could keep an eye on the soldiers who were keeping an eye on them, ensuring that they remained inside. The overlord's plan was simple. Starve them into submission.

Three days later, the lookouts reported seeing a horse and rider go by holding a blue pennant. The next day, another rider came by the complex holding a red pennant. Master Feng smiled as they relayed the news. Now it was time to let everyone in on his plan for their escape.

He explained in detail his plans to his many students and colleagues, but only told their guests the key data that they needed to know. The twins sat on the mats with Bao, who was now their adopted older sister. "Thanks to Bao and our amazing two young twins here, we have a chance to escape. On the fifteenth, a large number of wagons are going to assemble on the north edge of Zau. It will be let slip that we are using the sewers to escape our compound and to travel across the city to meet with these hundreds of wagons and thus escape the city."

"With luck and a little persuasion if need be, all the soldiers out there will be sent to the far north of the city. Once they are gone, we will walk out of here and down to the river docks, where I have arranged a number of large barges to transport us down river to Giang. There, we will have to find transportation on up to Nan Yan. Our ten wagons will be loaded with whatever we can bring with us. Men, help everyone make backpacks so that they can carry what they desire to bring along with them. I am afraid that we will have a long walk to the docks ahead of us. That is the dangerous part, so each of us will be responsible for the safety of at least three or four of our guests. We will go in small groups, in hopes of not attracting too much attention."

When the three returned to Bao's cramped quarters, Yin volunteered enthusiastically, "Bao, we don't own anything, so we will help you carry your things."

"Yes, we can carry a lot for you," Yan added.

Bao was about to thank them, when Shu Wen knocked on her door. She entered supporting the awkward yoke, whose baskets were loaded. "Girls, I have some presents for you. These are your very own things." Both girls looked wide-eyed at the marvelous presents. Each had a new second white cotton dress, another pair of slip-on shoes, a hairbrush that was designed for use with their feet, a blanket, a special cup, copper dinner plate, and a spoon designed for their feet to use. Each also had a handmade cotton pack in which to keep their things. Both were elated and thanked her repeatedly, but they still promised Bao that she could put some more of her things in their packs too.

As evening fell, all was in readiness. Per his orders, all lights were extinguished. Everyone fell silent, giving the appearance that the place was deserted. Master Feng cast his powerful kijutsu spell and they waited. Before too long, several soldiers climbed the walls. One of the other Masters subtly altered the men's minds using his lesser kijutsu, while Feng continued his in full force. Several were heard hollering down to other waiting soldiers, "Hey, the place is totally empty. They have already left, probably by the sewers. Mount up; we'll take them when they climb out of the sewers where their wagons are awaiting them." Shortly after that, they heard the sounds of many horses galloping away over the cobblestone streets.

Master Feng waited a while and used more kijutsu to verify that no soldiers remained behind, before nodding to the gate man. He walked to the gate and opened it for the last time, bowing to Master Feng, who drove the first wagon load out of the gate, his family riding in the overly full bed. Groups of four or five on foot followed him, then another wagon. When the last group finally left, the gate man bowed to the complex and closed the door behind him, falling in behind this last group of four. He was to be their rear guard. He also sensed the mind of Master Feng with him. He smiled; if anything came at their rear, Feng would know about it instantly and even assist.

The walk was a long one, but the few street thugs who were active spotted the white uniforms of the Olin Masters and their martial arts students and gave them a wide berth. These were reputedly the very best fighters in all Tashien. Hence, none of the thugs even considered messing with them, not when there were so many of them and in such a long line. It was well past midnight when they arrived at the docks and found forty large barges waiting for them. Around one, the bargemen finally cast loose the many mooring lines and the huge river barges drifted away from the docks and headed down stream with the current.

Each carried around a hundred people. One man held the rear rudder pole, steering the bulky craft. Only one aft lantern was lit; they wanted to slip past the city before lighting up. The people sat huddled in the center of the open crafts, hushed in silence, hoping that no one would spot them. Master Feng was more worried about someone opening fire on them with long guns. This fear, he did not share with the others, only his wife, who was now out of her body, hovering far above the forty barges, on the lookout for trouble. Shu Wen was prepared to fire off lightning bolts at anyone who dared accost them. Her people were sitting ducks now, helpless to repel any gunfire from the shore. Luck was with them. Around two, she slipped back into her body.

"The last barge has cleared the edge of the city. It looks like we have made a clean getaway. I believe that it is now safe to turn on the lanterns and get the people bedded down," she whispered. Feng smiled and gave her a loving kiss.

Soon, many lanterns fluttered to life and the passengers struggled to get their blankets out. Bao needed all kinds of assistance. She'd never yet done this much on her own. Always before a male student had assisted her, but now she discovered that her two twins were actually helping her get her blanket out and laid out properly. Soon, all three were lying snugly together along with a hundred others. "Thanks," she whispered.

The twins giggled. Yan asked, "How come you don't know how to do it?"

Bao's face crimsoned. She was glad for the cover of darkness. "No one showed me how I could, not until you two came along. I am learning a whole lot from you. When we get to Nan Yan, I will teach you how to fight as I do. Fair trade?" Two giggles confirmed their bargain.

By the time that the party of four thousand reached Giang, Tan Loc Province, Bao had learned an enormous amount. She was now doing things for herself that she never dreamed possible before, all thanks to the twins. In fact, all these women had learned to do a great many things for themselves that they never believe that they could ever do again. It was a lengthy learning experience for all them, including the men.

Down in Shansee, with the death of Don Ho and the subsequent breakup of his monopoly over the gangs and thugs of the city, chaos erupted into the streets. Gangs fought with other gangs for control of specific streets, which both claimed to be their domain. That innocent men and women fell victim to their battles concerned them not, though it ought to have. Compounding the misery of this once great city was the late winter monsoon, which struck with a particular vengeance, almost as if in retaliation for the wickedness of men. Perhaps it was just Nature washing the blood soaked streets clean once more.

Either way, Master De Dhow began contemplating just how he could obey Macario's order to evacuate the Church of God's compound and join up with the others in Nan Yan's complex. He had nearly a thousand of his pupils, his wife and her Counselors, and their servants. Worse, he had given sanctuary to nearly every poor soul who had knocked on his gates, some three thousand. Packed into every available space, including closets, he felt more like a fish in a tin than the Master of an Olin Academy. How could he possibly get all these people safely to Nan Yan?

Make use of what you have at hand his wife had suggested. He had torrential rains. Well, that would certainly keep most of the riffraff off the streets. Not even gangs enjoyed being out in the monsoon. Rain pummeled down, as if the very heavens were unloading an ocean upon Shansee. Driven by strong winds, rain sometimes fell horizontally, and he wondered how it could ever reach the ground as De peered out his window.

Realistically, he knew that there were only three ways to get to Nan Yan. One was to take a riverboat up the mighty Yonshu River to Giang and then take the fork to the west, up the Yan River. The second was to take a wagon or carriage along the cobblestone road that paralleled the rivers. The third way was to walk that road on foot. In these torrential rains, walking was not even considered. Could he get enough wagons? Even if he could somehow pack fifteen to twenty per wagon, he'd need three hundred of them and he had three here in his complex. Riverboats seemed his only option. He donned his rain parka, kissed Nan Dia, and headed out to face the elements.

It was dark when the completely soaked Olin Master finally knocked on the gates for entry. His sour face told Nan Dia the story; she didn't need to hear a word from him. "Come on. It is a hot bath for you, then some hot rice." He didn't object and followed her to the bath barrels, feeling as morose as the raging monsoon beyond these thin walls.

De was a fiercely independent man, who kept his own council. Now he faced a seemingly insurmountable task. As he sat in the hot, steaming water, while his wife sat on her butt washing his back with a rag held in her feet, he sighed. She had endured so much, he thought, yet never once had she complained, beyond that piercing, terrified scream the day she awoke and found the terrible effects of the plague on her body. Stoic, perhaps, yet, she was their best, most skilled Counselor. She knew things that even he did not know.

As if reading his mind, but perhaps merely his mood, Nan Dia said, "Perhaps we should talk with those in Velona and see if they can be of any assistance to us. You know that they are always most willing to assist."

De sighed again, knowing that she was right. I must swallow my pride and ask, he thought. "Nan Dia, you are right, as always. I can see no way to get us all safely to Nan Yan. There are only five large barges at the docks and not enough small craft to handle all of us, even if they were for hire. When is this Bethany due to contact you again?"

It was morning when I Mink Linked to both Nan Dia and Master De. *Hi De. Nan Dia has been telling me that you are having some problems finding ways to evacuate everyone.* He outlined all that he had done and I sensed that he really wanted me to know that he had done everything that he could, thereby justifying asking for our help. Having been in Shansee a number of times across several lifetimes, I knew just what his situation there was like, regarding transportation. Once, we had taken a riverboat from Shansee to Nan Yan, but we were only a few, not four thousand.

Say, I have an idea. Can you get everyone to the train station? If so, I can have a number of trains there ready to transport you out of Shansee up the coast. We're in the process of constructing a spur line from the coast up to Nan Yan. Already, our engineers and crews are on their way there now to begin the lengthy construction project. I can send along three hundred wagons with the trains, unloading them near the construction site. Then, the trains can head on into Shansee and pick you up and bring you back there. Surely, the wagons can take you all the remaining few hundred miles into Nan Yan. Besides, the construction groups are going to need any number of wagons once they get into full production. How does that sound?

Like an angel from heaven, De replied.

A week later, a long line of four thousand men, women, and children make the four mile long walk down Tiger Street to the railway yards. Again, the local gangs dared not challenge these Olin Masters. Only three trains were needed. Each boxcar held around a hundred people all crammed inside for the twelve-hour journey up the coast. While the rains continued, at least the winds had died down. When the trains reached the construction site, there the monsoon had already ended, leaving the world sparkling in the first rays of the spring sunshine.

The construction folks were planning on renting or buying locally owned wagons for the massive building effort. When the wagons returned from Nan Yan, they kept half there for their own use. In addition, Master De sent along fifty of his Olin Master students to provide security for the engineers and workers. In the end, it worked out well for all of us.

By May of 824, Nan Yan was now home to the most powerful and most wealthy of Tashien. The Church of God there boasted nearly fifteen thousand. I hoped that this would be enough to hold a position while their country and society slowly died all around them. Could they possibly be strong enough to pick up the pieces and rebuild Tashien? I had no idea, but I hoped so. Still, if they could not, I felt confident that we could evacuate them all from Nan Yan easily.

Around then we learned that millions had died in Tashien because of the plague or its aftereffects. What scared me was that two-thirds of those were women. What would happen to a society in which women became a scarce commodity?

Well, that wasn't happening in Velona. We were experiencing our biggest-ever baby boom. Here at 42 Hampton Way, the four of us were very pregnant, expecting within a few more weeks. Yes, we still have to go to the bathroom frequently, but the mantis modifications were more apparent now than before. My suspicions were confirmed when I met with the Medical Research Foundation in middle May. They'd called and asked me to come by.

The doctors there had done a number of autopsies on recently deceased women and had some interesting results to show me. I'll spare you the gory part. They had laid out the lower skeletal structure for pre-plague and post-plague women. What a difference. Our pelvis region was significantly larger. Now they had positive proof that somehow the mantis mutation had actually increased the size of our bodies below the tiny fourteen-inch waists. Internal organs had been relocated into this enlarged space, not just compressed and squished as we used to do with those restrictive corsets.

We pregnant women were proof. Our waists still measured close to fourteen inches, yet our wombs bulged with our fetuses. "I look like an ant!" Eve commented and now I readily saw what she meant. Between our overly large breasts, extremely tiny waists, and now bulging wombs, we did look like some monster sized ants! Thank god we didn't have antennae! I had the strange notion that the mantis had wanted us to resemble their bodies.

Chapter 18 A Toehold in Tashien

April of 824 was a busy time in Nan Lan, Tashien. Olin Master Tian Li and his wife, Councilor Bi Mei Li, had to prepare to take in over twelve thousand more refugees from the three other Churches of God. Located in the steep sloped hills of western Shansee Province, Nan Lan was fairly isolated from the rest of Shansee. The only way into Nan Lan from the east was up the Yan River or the road that paralleled it. Now, however, a new railroad line was being constructed, which would soon connect them nearly due south to the coastal railroad line that ultimately led into Shansee to the east and Velona to the far, far west.

Their Church of God was located about a mile from the Princess Palace and two miles from the Low Parliament Building, where the local government now met. Nan Yan had elected a new Princess two years ago now. Young Princess Mei Lon Wu had just turned twenty-one, but she was a very shrewd politician and had gotten herself elected as their next Princess. She was in charge of carrying out the laws passed by the Low Parliament. Already she had passed the test, having dealt with the loss of her arms twice now. More than ever, she was determined to keep Nan Yan from descending into the utter chaos, which had descended upon the rest of Tashien. She depended upon her General Tao Bi to maintain order. A forty year old veteran, General Tao held the respect of his troops, some twenty thousand, and by his force of will alone had kept Nan Yan from collapsing when the alien plague struck this second time.

He often said that the first plague weeded out those people who were weak-willed. Now only the strong lived in Nan Yan. During those first two months of the debilitating plague, his pronouncement was heard over and over all throughout the city and surrounding countryside. At this time, Nan Yan was home to a half million people with a quarter more living in the surrounding villages, mines, and farmsteads that crept up the steep slopes of the foothills of the impassible mountains to the west.

Princess Mei Lon was a very attractive young woman with pale blue eyes, thick lips, a rounded face, and of course rich, black hair that fell to her ankles when un-braided at night. She had close ties with the Olin masters and the Church of God. Indeed, her fiancé, Huan Zu, also twenty-one, was himself an Olin master of the tenth level. Master Huan was often at the Princess Palace with Mei Lon. Unofficially, Master Tian had asked him to be her official bodyguard as well. That they had fallen in love only made the assignment easier.

Princess Mei Lon had risen to power by sheer will power and by making use of every aspect possible. Smart and intelligent, she was also driven, though some say wise would be a better term. Early in her life, she'd made use of her great beauty, opting for the tiny feet of a Great Lady when she was ten. Before the first plague came, she also had allowed her nails to grow to six inches, emulating the Great Women of the Past. Well, that aspect was now gone, and she did not even consider undergoing that painful operation to regain tiny feet again. No woman now did, that was outdated. Without arms, women depended upon their feet, and Princess Mei Lon had no intention of jeopardizing hers further. Still, when the occasion called for it, she allowed herself to be dressed appropriately and wore the extreme Annelise, shiny, black heels so popular throughout Tashien since the first plague.

Already she had met once with the young engineer from Velona, this Jovanni West Po, who was building the railroad line up to Nan Yan. Having heard of all these marvelous inventions of Velona, she insisted on launching a massive program to bring these modern things to Nan Yan. "We must have this electricity here in Nan Yan," she declared to Master Huan.

"I agree, my Princess. How about the running water, the telefonos, the motor vehicles, too?" he added.

"Absolutely. Nan Yan cannot afford to be in the dark ages any longer. We must move into the modern age," she pronounced. "Yet, how to do it?"

"Ah, my dearest love, that is why you were elected and not me," he teased her, before giving her a kiss. He was merely content just to be.

She appreciated this in him. When the first plague came, she had been very fortunate to have received the special therapy from the Church of God. Of course, when the second plague came and she lost her newly regrown arms, her comment was merely, "Oh no, not again. Bother."

Nan Yan was exceedingly fortunate to have such a young princess on the throne. She was full of life and the vigor of youth. She had not known failures yet, and she looked forward to the future for her people, though many older Most Worthy Gentlemen considered that she was going way too far. She ought to take a more conservative approach, they often told her. Now that she had her own LD radio, at least once a day during late April and May, she was on the line with me, asking advice on how to implement our MMCE. Yes, I had discussed our modernization plans with her, and she jumped on them, demanding them for her people in Nan Yan.

She and I arranged for the first commercial train into Nan Yan to bring samples of all our inventions along with appropriate engineers to assist her personnel in understanding their use, operations, and most importantly, how they are manufactured.

One afternoon in April, Master Tian and Bi Mei made a trip to the Princess Palace to discuss their situation with her. "Welcome, Master Tian Li and Counselor Bi Mei," Princess Mei Lon said with a warm smile. "Come, have some tea?"

"No thanks, Princess Mei Lon, this trip is a business one, I'm afraid," Master Tian replied, helping his wife into a sofa chair. Princess Mei Lon preferred to discuss business in an informal, relaxed setting. This was another one of her "inventions." Thus far, it had worked well for her.

"How then may I help you?" she said formally, realizing this was not going to be an informal chat.

"I am afraid that the situation in the rest of Tashien has disintegrated beyond tolerance. Our other three Churches of God are in a crisis. They have no choice left but to abandon their buildings. All are seeking refuge here with us in Nan Yan. I, of course, have agreed to give them all sanctuary here," he explained.

Princess Mei Lon smiled and added, "So you will need larger quarters, and you've come to me for help with that?"

Master Tian grinned. Oh, his Princess was a sharp one! She'd already ascertained his needs. "Precisely so, Princess. I am expecting twelve thousand to be arriving here in Nan Yan within the next few weeks. As you know already, our complex is overflowing. I turn none who are in need away."

"I would not expect less of you Master Tian. It would be best if they were housed somewhere near your complex. Come with me; let us look over my city map," she declared decisively. She rose and Master Tian and Bi Mei rose and followed her. Princess Mei Lon wore a tight, form fitting, blue silk dress, with a deep walking slit in the pencil dress. Here in southern Tashien, having already dealt with the first plague, women had dresses that accommodated their needs, though by now all of them had been altered by the men who had taken over the dressmaking industry. Her tiny waist was accentuated by her monster bosom. The blue dress fit snugly around her shoulders, flared out at her hips, then angled in to fall much like a pencil. Had the high walking slit not been there, she would have only been able to take the tiniest of steps. However, the slit had been added to most day dresses now, since she had to have the use of her feet. Still, on the formal occasions, her pencil dresses did not have these high slits, and she would wear her extreme heels, as dictated by appropriate fashion.

In another room, an enormous map of Nan Yan hung on the wall. "Okay, here's the Palace and here's your Church. Oh bother!" she'd tried to point the two locations out with her hands. She still had trouble with that aspect. "Oh here," she said, sticking out her tongue close to the Palace and then again at the Church of God. Both were too high for her to point them out with her foot. "Hum, looks like on the north side of your place, there are several warehouses. I wonder if those could be converted for your usage?" she suggested.

"But what about those who own them?" Master Tian asked.

"Well, they are just going to have to move. Look, with all the growth over the last fifty years, these warehouses are not now located where they ought to be. For their optimum use, they ought to be down here at the western edge," this time pointing with her foot.

"Yes, but won't that be an expensive proposition? Our Church has such little funds," Master Tian replied.

"Make you a deal, I'll get you those warehouses at no charge to you, but you then have to fix them up to suit your needs. As you know, I have great plans for the complete modernization of Nan Yan, just as soon as the railroad is completed. We must have new warehouses down at the eastern edge of the city. The relocation funds I'll take out of my budget somehow. Once I can get a full and compete demonstration up and running to show our people these new inventions, I am certain that I can find many wealthy nobles to help finance them, from which I will be able to recuperate the funds spent on relocating them. How does that sound?" Of course, she was only being polite. She knew that it would be acceptable. How could it not be?

"Thank you, Princess. I accept. Thousands will be thanking you for your kindness and generosity," he replied humbly.

"Of course they will. Say, twelve thousand are coming? I didn't know that you had so many Olin Masters in our country," she asked, now focusing on what concerned her even more than living quarters for the refugees.

"Oh, only three thousand are Olin Masters and Counselors, Princess. Some of the others are most desperate people, but many are wealthy noblemen and their families who are fleeing for their very lives," he explained. As he said this, he realized that this was precisely what she was seeking.

"Ah even more perfect! Yes, you must allow me to address these displaced wealthy men and women. I have great plans for Nan Yan and this will be an excellent opportunity for these people to invest in our future. Perfect indeed, thank you Master Tian." She was more than pleased. Vast more gold was now coming into her realm, gold that she fully intended to utilize.

Thus, when the thousands began arriving in Nan Yan, Master Tian had makeshift housing and quarters set up for them. As the new places became habitable, he moved some of those under his care into these new quarters. Master Tian intended to combine his wife's request with his own desires. That is, Bi Mei told him about the sixteen blinded women who were going to need both a constant, stable environment, much help with the task of just living, as well as massive amounts of therapy. She had already set her own goals for these incoming women and had begun planning her strategy for their therapy. He, on the other hand, for a time needed to group all the Olin Masters together. They would have much to discuss about the future. Security was acceptable, thanks to General Tao Bi. Unlike the chaos surrounding the other Churches of God, here, the environment was comparatively stable. The weak willed had been culled from Nan Yan during the first plague. Only survivors lived here to encounter the second plague. While they certainly didn't desire it, they had thus far endured it and were surviving, if only barely.

Those from the Shansee arrived first, the host of wagons pulling up to the Church of God complex. Master De Dhow lifted his wife, Nan Dia, down from their wagon. They bowed before Master Tian and Bi Mei, who stood waiting to greet these first arrivals. Master Huan Zu stood to their right, with his arm around Princess Mei Lon Wu.

"Welcome, Master De, Counselor Nan Dia. We have rooms prepared for you and for the sixteen," Master Tian said formally.

"We are most grateful, Master Tian. They are in these first wagons. After them are the many noblemen and their families. My followers are bringing up the rear. As you can see, we have one man guiding each of the sixteen. Six I have married to their brave fiancés who came to their rescue," Master De replied. Then, he noticed the dresses of the women, and asked, "How is it that you have such fine clothing for your women? I am afraid that ours are mostly in rags."

"Ah, we have adapted to our needs. We will see that all the arriving women are properly attired. First, let us get them settled and bathed. How has the food held out?"

"Just barely made it. We have tight bellies, but none is in serious condition. Again, thank you, Master Tian," he bowed once more as the small group watched sixteen men assisting sixteen women down from the wagons. From the women's unusual head movements and positions that they could not see was most apparent. Carefully, the men put their arms around the women's waists and began moving them slowly up to the Masters, Counselors, and the Princess. He added, "Extreme care must be taken with these women. As yet, we have not been able to give them the Holy Gift that they must have. Our Church was under siege and we had insufficient food." He knew the excuse was lame, but he also knew from his own experience in teaching martial arts and from his wife that the patients needed to eat well while undergoing therapy sessions.

Counselor Bi Mie escorted the sixteen women and their helpers into the specially prepared quarters. In this section, she had removed all but the essential furniture and objects, reducing the potential obstructions and thus making it easier for these women to navigate. She then met with the arriving Counselors. Meanwhile, Master Tian and Princess Mei Lon welcomed the many others, promising them a new and prosperous life here in Nan Yan. Princess Mei Lon also told them that once they were reasonably settled and the others had arrived, she would be making them a business offer.

The two sets of top Counselors from the two Churches met to discuss the cases of the sixteen women. Dia Son expressed her considerations, "Armless and blinded, these women face a most helpless existence unless we use our Advanced Therapy on them. Unless we can rehabilitate their spiritual perceptions, they are doomed to a life of mere sitting in chairs, unproductive and without the slightest rewards."

"What about the usual expansion of their body's other senses?" asked Bi Mei. "Often a blind person's other senses become heightened to help compensate. Should we not explore that avenue as well?"

"Without arms, how are they to feel?" someone asked.

Dia Son answered, "Master De has been working with a couple of them a little on feeling with their breasts. After all, ours now protrude almost a foot before our bodies. Three are now able to sense an obstructing wall or object with their breasts before they run into it with their noses. Make use of whatever appendages we have left, he suggests. Several are making significant progress sensing walls and doorways with this method, though none has yet been able to sense the slight pressure differences as they approach a wall. Even if we can assist them in heightening their body senses, I'm afraid that this combination loss is too severe to be overcome to allow them any chance at a worthwhile life."

"Then, we have no choice but to rehabilitate their spiritual perceptions so that they can see once more. This means that they will have to become stable outside their bodies as well," Bi Mei concluded.

"What about the rehabilitation of their ability to move objects so that they could feed themselves and dress themselves?" asked Dia Son. "Should we not carry it into this arena as well?"

They discussed a number of other aspects and finally decided upon a working goal of getting these sixteen women stable outside their bodies at all times, their perceptions rehabilitated, and their ability to move objects restored. None of this Advanced Therapy could begin until all traces of their more recent traumas had been fully handled. Dia Son and Bi Mei realized that they were facing an extended period of therapy sessions with these sixteen women, spending perhaps a year or more with each woman.

Under other circumstances, this would have been acceptable. Now, however, they had received orders from their founder, Macario, and his new assistant Eve to begin mass trauma handling of all women and men, to a lesser extent. Each woman so handled would be asked if she wished to learn how to deliver their Basic Therapy, the Holy Gift as it was called. The idea was to create an ever-growing pool of therapy givers and in time reach every woman in Tashien, a most lofty goal. The key problem was that at this time, only four Counselors were able to perform this most Advanced Therapy, the four head Counselors of the four churches. If their fellow counselors began to deliver hundreds of sessions each day, they would be needed to handle problems that invariably would arise, to say nothing of instructing the new women in its delivery.

They finally decided to see if the other two top Counselors could handle the day-to-day problems and training while Bi Mei and Dia Son dealt with the sixteen women. Additionally, Masters Tian and De Dhow were asked to drill the women on enhancing their awareness and sensitivity of their remaining physical body senses.

During the next few weeks as more and more of the twelve thousand arrived at sporadic intervals, the two masters worked with the sixteen women. Also, each woman received basic trauma therapy sessions twice a day.

Master De began working with Lin Li and Misha, while in the next room, Master Tian was assisting Princess Pian or Jemma as she used to be called last lifetime. Princess Pian posed a most unusual case, they discovered. "Look, I can manage very well on my own if I can ever get back outside of my body's head," she declared rather annoyed. "I am very able. I can cast balls of fire, bring down lightning bolts, put men to sleep, and all sorts of things, be anywhere I want — if I can just get back outside of my head. I have somehow gotten myself plastered in its head during all that plague mess. However, I would dearly love to learn how to levitate things as I've heard so many of you can do. That would make life a breeze for me. Is that possible?"

Princess Pian was thus scheduled for the first of the therapy sessions, and Master Tian began working with her separate from Misha and the others. Her situation was vastly different from her daughter's and the other fourteen women.

Master De explained to Lin Li and Misha who sat nervously on a chair in this unfamiliar room to which they had just been led. "Ladies, I am Master De and I am going to be working with both of you. You must learn to utilize more fully your other senses and even those that you may not have been aware that you had. The blind often learn to trust their heightened other senses, such as touch."

"Yes, but I can't touch anything anymore. I don't have any arms to touch anything," Misha complained. Surely, he could see that, she thought, he must not be blind.

"I have an eidetic memory, Master Tian. Once I have walked a place, I can recall precisely how I traversed the place and can duplicate my path," Lin Li added. "She's right, we can't feel anything anymore. If only we had our hands, we could feel our way around. Like we are, this is unbearably awful, impossible almost."

Mater Tian moved over to the two sitting women. He gently touched each woman on her forehead. Both pulled back slightly, startled by the unexpected touch. "Ah, you seem to be able to feel with your foreheads."

"Well, yes, but it hurts when I bang my head into something," Misha countered.

"I should expect that it would, Misha. You must make a more effective use of your sense of touch. Perhaps there is a mixed blessing with the plague. Your breasts are now quite large."

Misha flushed, "Of course, mine are so big. I wanted to have mine get larger, before the plague came, you know, as my mom's were. Now they are way too big, I think."

Lin Li laughed, "Misha, ours are humongous." Misha giggled.

"Precisely so. Do you realize that as you face a wall, they protrude out in front of you almost a foot?"

Misha giggled. Lin Li replied, "Yes, monsters aren't they?"

"Think about them for a second. Would it not be better to sense your approach to a wall or door with them instead of banging your nose against the door?" he asked.

"Oh, yes, I didn't think about it that way," Misha replied, suddenly catching on to what he was suggesting. "We should use them to feel our way around, kind of like tied up hands. I used to play Blindman's Touch with the other kids at court when I was littler."

"Precisely so, Misha. Use them to sense your approach to an object. While you could raise your leg and foot, moving it about to feel what lies ahead, it is not very practical when you want to walk a distance. Such is fine when you want to determine the location of your chair so that you can orient your body to sit."

"It's lots easier if someone moves me to the chair so I can just sit. I still find it is frightening to be told to sit. I can't see where I am sitting. I feel like I am falling, and I can't stop myself if I should miss the chair. I can't believe it that I am now afraid to sit down or even get into bed. I can't see where I am laying down. I am scared I will miss part of the bed and fall off and can't keep myself from falling," Misha admitted her deepest fears that had been building for weeks now.

"Exactly so, Misha. That is why we are going to help you learn new ways to sense these things. None of us wants you to be scared or afraid anymore. Now, let's see if you can rise and walk over to the wall. As you walk, sense what is ahead of you with your breasts. Think of them as your tied up hands. As you approach a wall or door, there is a slight increase in pressure as you move. The air that you are displacing bangs into the wall and creates a slight build up in pressure. See if you can learn to sense this subtle pressure change. Once you can, you will find this most helpful indeed."

To an untrained eye, these sessions with these women would have looked strange. They took small hesitating steps, moving their upper torso and thus breasts slightly from side to side, sensing for barriers. Day by day, they got better and better at it. Soon, Misha could sense the pressure difference with her breasts a bit before she felt it on her face. Emboldened by their success, now they began feeling their way around the room, touching the walls, doorframes, and doors with their mammoth sized breasts. They'd discovered a new use for them.

Meanwhile, he began working on their sense of balance. If they were to begin making effective use of their legs and feet in sensing lower objects, such as chairs and beds, they had to have good balance while standing on one foot and moving the other around, feeling the chair or bed and not lose their balance when encountering the unexpected position of the chair or bed. "Look, if someone bumps into you, you don't want to lose your balance and fall, do you?" he explained and asked. "Today, we will begin working on your balance. I do this with all my beginning martial arts students, so I know that you can do it too."

"But we can't see and we don't have arms to use to keep our balance," Misha complained. He ignored her. He tied each woman's right leg up to her thigh using a soft cloth belt, which normally his students used around their waists. Then he had them stand. "You are to remain standing for a half hour. Do not worry, Misha, I will not let you fall. Trust me."

"This is scary!" she exclaimed nervously as she wiggled wildly trying to keep from falling over.

"Of course it is, Misha, until you master it. Any new skill can be scary until you have mastered it." Later on, he then had them begin jumping their way across the room, one leg still tied up. As he expected, they found this even more frightening. Still with his constant coaching, win by win, they began to master it. True, he got a good workout using his kijutsu Push skills, gently adding a push here and there when they were about to lose their balance.

Once they mastered this with both legs, he worked with them on sensing low objects with their feet. He took them into a room that they had never been in yet, filled with a dozen chairs and couches. "Okay, Misha, Lin Li, I want you to find each of the dozen chairs and two couches in here. As you find one, you are to sit down on it and I will then give you an Okay. I will tell you that there is nothing else in here besides these." While both were now doing fairly well navigating around the rooms in which they were familiar, here was a totally unknown room with unknown objects and locations.

"But we can't see them? How will we find them?" Misha asked.

"Feel your way. You have all the skills that you need to succeed. After all, as you go through life, you will be entering many rooms that you have never been in before. You don't want to spend hours finding a chair for yourselves. You want to be able to do this rapidly. You pass when I can bring you to a new room and you find and sit in all them in three minutes time. I sighted person could do it in probably a minute or so. I will allow you additional time."

A week of practice and they met his goal. They also were working a little each day on feeding themselves. Their tables were low to the ground, as were all tables for women since the first plague came. By the middle of June, these women were now feeding themselves and moving around their section of the compound on their own. With their Basic Therapy finished and with the regaining of the handling these fundamental skills, the women were extremely proud and becoming more self-reliant with each passing day.

With Princess Pian, things improved dramatically within a week. While it took her a week to unburden and unravel the nasty series of losses, traumas, and overwhelm that she'd encountered, she was at last able to move out of her body at will once more. However, now able to see only by her spiritual being ability, she was in the same situation that I once was. Yes, we beings can see in a three hundred-sixty degree sphere around us, but that can be terribly confusing at first. Her problem was the same as mine had been, spatial distortion. What she saw as being perhaps three feet from her turned out to be some other distance, long or short. The physical universe quickly demonstrated to her that her sight was clearly wrong, as she banged into a door, for example. However, the Councilors continued to drill her on her perceptions, and by June, her spatial distortions were a thing of the past.

At this point, Princess Pian could see perfectly well and thus carry on with her own goals and purposes. She still wanted more training so that she could move objects and thus feed herself and dress herself without making use of her feet. However, she decided to put that on hold a while. "I must help with the therapy sessions for all the other women," she declared. She became the first of the sixteen to join the many Counselors who began to give their Holy Gifts to all the many women who had taken sanctuary with the four Churches of God. Incidentally, Eve and Pian now began chatting telepathically nearly every day.

Further, when Shu Wen Chow, the top Counselor from Zau finally arrived, she renewed her last lifetime friendship with Princess Pian. Shu Wen had been called Fina then, the Protector of Jemma or Pian as she is now. Thus, in June Shu Wen took over the Advanced Therapy of her old and dear friend. As a result, she relieved Counselor Dia Son and began working with the other fifteen on their advanced therapy sessions. Dia Son now took charge of the massive Holy Gift project.

By July when the new rail line finally reached Nan Yan and the first freight train rolled into Nan Yan bringing along boxcars of Velona inventions, over half of the women who had been given sanctuary with the four churches had received their Holy Gift. The results on these women were spectacular, as each had a renewed vigor for life, their inherent vitality returned to them. Many looked years younger! The overall impression was not lost on their husbands and fathers. Combine that with the massive invention show that Princess Mei Lon Wu held for them and the wealthy of Nan Yan, to the man, they all wanted in on the action. These people saw real hope for the first time in centuries.

Their combined wealth was staggering. Here in Nan Yan were now collected well over half of the surviving wealthy men and women of all Tashien! By December, Princess Mei Lon had an entirely new and wholly unexpected problem of magnitude: a drastic shortage of men to fill the thousands of new positions needed in the multitudes of new companies and businesses that had sprang up.

On the therapy side, things began to mushroom. Initially when they began their project, five hundred women were able to give the Holy Gift. On the average, each patient required a week's worth of therapy sessions to achieve the basic goal of erasure of the loss and trauma associated with the two plagues. After that, half of the women were both able to and desiring to learn how to do it, becoming trained, and joining those who were giving the Holy Gift. The other half had too many family responsibilities, such as very young children to care for, to spend the time needed to give the Holy Gift.

On the average, each month the number of women able to give the Holy Gift doubled in size. By July, one thousand were giving the week-long sessions. By December 824, their numbers had reached an incredible thirty-two thousand women giving daily therapy sessions! The Olin Masters were kept busy keeping track of the women, arranging the sessions, and the physical mechanics behind the scenes. Princess Mei Lon was now heavily involved in this as well, since they were now giving the Gift to the women of Nan Yan, having dealt with all of those who had sought sanctuary with the four Churches of God. Princess Mei Lon estimated that by the end of next March, every woman in Nan Yan would have received the Holy Gift as well as most of the men, though at least another month would be needed to finish off the men. She found it inconceivable that by March there would be two hundred fifty-six thousand women giving therapy sessions each day. Yet, those were the projected numbers.

Also in December, Master Feng Chow held a special ceremony. Master Bao had finally achieved Level 11. Her two protégées, Yin and Yan Jining, now thirteen, received their Master Level 10 belts. Also, Master Chan, now Level 12, married Tian Pyong, who became one of the first teachers in the first of many free, public schools that Princess Mei Lon began opening around Nan Yan.

When Jovanni West Po arrived in Nan Yan with the crew who were laying the last of the hundreds of miles of track, Princess Mei Lon and Master Tian were there to greet him and to thank him for his incredible efforts and skill. After the formalities were done, both offered the engineer a place to stay while he was in the city.

"Well, I think staying at the Church might be best," the thirty-seven year old blonde engineer replied. "It is closer to the end of the line where the last of the construction is being done. Besides, Bethany Angela of Velona has asked me to deliver a message to a Princess Pian Wu, whom I'm told is at your church, sir," he replied. Jovanni added, "Of course, my son will be coming with me. He's turned fourteen last week. Oh by the way, Princess, your huge order of Velona inventions is on its way. I received word that the train left Velona three days ago. It should arrive here just as we finish the rail line. Perfect timing."

"Incredible. I can't wait, Jovanni. This may well be the turning point for all of us in Nan Yan. I am intrigued by all this electricity stuff. I do hope it all works," she replied.

"Oh take it from me, it does work. The things that are being invented now are mind blowing. So many things are coming soon to help you women do many more things vastly easier. This rail line will open Nan Yan up to the whole world," he said enthusiastically, which is what Princess Mei Lon wanted to hear. She was relying on it.

A short while later, his son, Alonso, joined him. As usual, Alonso was carrying his large ball with him. He was never without it, bouncing it on the ground, and catching it. He'd come along on this trip to help his dad with the massive engineering problems, but was often bored, having no one his own age with which to play. His ball became his playmate.

Master Tian led them into the complex and showed them around a little. "The Princess and her daughter have their quarters down that hall, first door on your left. They have a small courtyard and adjoining bedroom. If you need anything, just ask someone. My wife will arrange quarters for you later today." He left and the two blonde men headed down the hall.

"Knock, knock," Jovanni said as he and Alonso stood at the open door. Just inside was a small courtyard with a bench. Princess Pian sat on the bench, feeling the sun on her face. Misha was practicing her walking, moving her breasts back and forth, and sensing the walls before she actually touched them. Both men were a bit taken aback by Misha's movements.

Princess Pian didn't turn her head, as Jovanni had expected; neither did Misha, for that matter. First, neither had eyes, so it made no difference to them. Second, even if they turned their heads, they couldn't see anything anyway. However, Princess Pian had heard their footsteps, and she could see them very well with her spherical vision, though at this point, it was still somewhat distorted. Rather than seem foolish, she opted to not move her head. "Come in, we won't bite, will we Misha?" she said. She did rise though, such was only proper for a Princess. She more or less faced the two at the doorway; Misha stopped and turned towards them, but was in fact facing some three feet to the left of the doorway.

"Hello, I am Jovanni West Po, my son, Alonso. I'm the engineer who is building the new railroad line up from the coastline to here. My son is fourteen now and is learning my trade," he said, very unsure of just how to deal with the two blind women. However, he was instantly struck with Princess Pian. She wore a bright red, silk pencil dress, which outlined her many curves. Jovanni was instantly attracted to her beauty, however. Misha wore a similar dress; hers was a bright green. Of course to the women, the color of their dress was a non-issue, save that Princess Pian still wanted her appearance to be acceptable, though she depended upon others to make it so.

"Wow, you are the person who is building the railroad. Very pleased to meet you. The railroad is what saved us all. We rode the train from Shansee to somewhere down south and then were brought here in wagons. Come on in. I think that this is the only bench. Sit with me please, Jovanni," she suggested.

Alonso didn't want to visit with the Princess; rather he gawked at Misha. He walked over to her and extended his hand, only to quickly retract it. Duh, he thought to himself. "Hi, Misha. I'm Alonso. I'm with my dad. We're engineers, well dad is. I'm only learning it now. Kind of boring; no kids to play with for months now." She turned to better face him, and he got a good look at her eyes. "Wow, Misha, your yellow-brown eyes — they really look good on you. Er, I mean, well, I wish you still had your real eyes, but they really do make you look very pretty. Er, you are very pretty anyway," Alonso stumbled his way through an awful start meeting her.

She giggled, "Well thank you, Alonso. You don't speak our language very well, do you? No, I can see that you can't. Now that's dumb, obviously, I can't see. I can hear that you don't. There, that's better. I bet it is fun building things."

"Sure is. Say, can I ask you something?" She nodded. "When we just came, you were sort of wiggling around and sort of walking. What were you doing?"

"Oh, I am supposed to be practicing my lessons. Master Tian is teaching us how to use our enormous breasts to feel for walls and things, kind of like feeling things with your hands all tied up so they can't move. I am sort of getting the hang of it, but it's hard. Still, I know that I must learn how to feel with my breasts so that I don't keep banging my nose into things. I got several bloody noses from doing just that. Here, let me see if I can feel you," she suggested and slowly moved towards him. Her moving breasts finally touched him and she then moved about his body, using them to get a sense of Alonso. At last, she said, "You must be about my height. What color is your hair?"

"Yes, we are about the same height. Blonde, yellow. Dad and I are overdue for a haircut. Not much chance for it while we were out there building the railroad though. It's down to my shoulders now. Gosh, Misha, your hair is almost to your ankles. Honestly, you are the prettiest girl I've ever met."

"Oh don't be ridiculous, Alonso. I don't have any eyes and no arms and I have monster-sized breasts. Hardly pretty," she replied.

"Misha, now you are being ridiculous. You are very, very pretty." His ball fell out of his hand and bounced on the floor.

"What's that?" she asked suddenly surprised by the unexpected noise.

"My ball. It's about a foot across. I like to play ball when I can, only there's no one to play with — not since we came here to build the railroad. Do you like to play ball?" For a moment, he thought how utterly stupid to ask that.

"I used to love it. When we got the plague last time, some of us really got into kick ball games. We couldn't throw balls anymore, obviously, but we could play kick ball. Of course, then I had very tiny feet; I was a Great Lady and could barely walk. Still we all played it a lot. I wish I could play again. I haven't had any fun at all since this second plague came. It's been just awful. My dad was killed, and then we were kidnaped and our eyes removed by that awful Don Ho fellow. I can't remember when I last had any fun at all."

"Well come on, we can try to play kick ball, Misha. I won't move and you can see if you can hit me with the ball. That's a start anyway."

"But I can't see you. Oh well, maybe I can hear you and do it. Let's try," she suggested.

Meanwhile, Jovanni sat down beside Pian. It felt a little strange when her face and eyes were not quite facing him. "I came to deliver a message to you from Mrs. Bethany Bartiana Angela of Velona. She says that I am to give you her love and a hug from her. Is that all right with you? I mean if I give you a hug?"

"Bethany? Wow. Sure I won't bite." He gave her a hug. She felt strong arms around her back once more, bringing back memories of her late husband who used to hug her similarly.

"She also asked me to see if there is anything that you really need. If so, I am to let her know. So, do you? Need anything that is?"

"No, honestly, here we are at last safe. That is the most important thing. Say, how do you know Bethany? She has been a dear friend of mine. I haven't seen her since the end of the first plague."

"She's one of my cousins. Gosh, Bethany's a very beautiful woman and Eve, well she is a gorgeous, knock-out blonde. If only I were twenty years younger — but then, I don't have a prayer with Giovanni, her husband. He is probably one of the two finest engineers and inventors in the world."

Pian chuckled, "Aye, that they are. Say, are they still keeping their hair really long?"

"Yes, down to their ankles the last time I saw them. Of course, they don't braid it like all you women do here in Tashien, though they do tie it in a ponytail at times. I bet your hair is magnificent when you let it down, Princess Pian."

She smiled at the compliment. "Say, how old are you anyway? Sorry, my vision is not so good yet. It's getting better now, but things are a bit distorted. I see in a sphere all around me, but not so well. With more therapy, they think that I will improve my perceptions. I certainly hope so, for all we sixteen's sake. It's been utter hell to be as we are now."

"Thirty-seven Your Majesty," he replied.

"Just Pian please. I have been kicked out of my Princess position so now really, just Pian. Tell me, where is your wife? Back in Velona? Do you have other children? I do so love Misha."

"She died during the first plague. She took a bad fall while I was at work. Now it's just Alonso and me."

"I'm sorry, Jovanni. I didn't know."

"Likewise, must have been terrible losing your husband."

"Overwhelming, actually. But with the therapy I've received here, I am back to battery, as they say. I hope with a bit more of it to be once more out of my head, where I can fully use my telepathy and other powers again."

"Wow, like balls of fire? My cousins can do that. Impressive," he replied.

Pian laughed, "I know. Yes, balls of fire, lightning bolts and more, but I'd give it all back just to have my eyes back and those of Misha too."

"I cannot imagine how bad it is for you and Misha. Still as beautiful as you two are, you ought to soon have suitors asking for your hands."

Pian laughed, "Silly, we don't have hands. Besides, no one in their right mind would want either of us now. Look at us, blind and helpless."

"Oh don't be silly, Pian. Balls of fire? You are far from helpless. Around you, Bethany, and Eve, I feel like I'm the one who is helpless. Besides, I meant it, you are still a very beautiful woman, and I do like how well your yellow-brown eyes match your complexion."

"It's a nice thing to say, Jovanni, but really. . ."

"Pian, I mean it! Don't sell yourself short. If you are not careful, I will be a'courting you."

"You wouldn't dare," she half teased him. Something inside Pian stirred a little. She liked this engineer. "Tell me about Velona. It has been a long time since I was last there, last lifetime, actually. Is the Church of the Three Holy Roses still there?"

Jovanni began chatting about the sights of Velona, and the two became engrossed in conversation. Suddenly, Pian stopped to listen to the kids. Misha was laughing away. Both turned to look at their children. They were playing kick ball together.

Pian choked up, tears trickled. "I haven't heard Misha laugh like that, other than after therapy sessions, for a long, long time. I can't see her too well. Is she really having fun, Jovanni?"

"You bet; she's positively radiant." He began to describe her and their ongoing game. Then, they resumed their chat about all the new things in Velona, including the trains. Jovanni quickly discovered when Pian had last been there and now knew better what to relate that was new since then. Time flew by and the dinner gong sounded.

"What's that?" he asked.

"Time for dinner. Come on, how about dining with us? We still need help eating. You are about to see just how pathetic we really are. That'll change your mind about us quickly," she replied.

"Mom, remember, we are supposed to find our own way to the dining room," Misha pointed out. "We're supposed to feel our way along with our breasts."

"Okay, dear. Let's show our guests that we at least can somehow get ourselves there. Lead on, Misha," Pian suggested, knowing that she had an unfair advantage over her daughter, though her spherical vision was still distorted. Still, she could perceive that Misha emanated a bit of pride as she slowly moved over to the door, feeling her way along with her breasts just touching the wall. Once in the hall, Misha kept her side close to the wall to allow others to pass her if they desired and to keep herself walking straight. Alonso walked behind her, followed by Pian and then Jovanni.

As they approached the large dining room, many voices could be heard, which Misha and Pian used to help guide them. Still Misha kept brushing her bosom against the wall until she felt the door jam and its opening. Several hundred men, women, and children were gathering to dine, the first shift of several here at the church.

"I'm afraid now you have to take over," Misha turned to where she thought Alonso might be, missing him slightly. "You'll have to put your hands on my waist and guide me to our seats. They are over to the left somewhere."

Master Tian motioned with his hand, pointing to four seats. Both Alonso and Jovanni nodded, put their hands around the women's waists, and guided them expertly to the seats. "Well, I can help you with your meal, Misha," Alonso said after getting her seated. "I had lots of practice during the first plague and a bit here during the second one. I helped my uncle with his daughters, you see."

The meal was hot, nourishing, and extremely satisfying. "My, I have forgotten how good a home cooked meal tastes!" Jovanni declared as they finished. "Months of trail food cooked by men whom I swear have never cooked before." Pian laughed, imagining how awful that must have been.

"We can take our tea back to our quarters, if you like. We have to vacate so that the second shift can enter and dine," Pian said, adding, "if you would still like to take tea with us. I imagine that you both have had enough of the blind folk for one day."

"Hardly, you are the most fascinating person I've met yet, Pian. I'll bring the tea."

"Alonso, can you point me in the right direction to go? We're supposed to be practicing finding our way back to our room," Misha asked. Using his hands as before, he navigated her to the start of the long corridor. "Twice now, I ended up in the wrong room. Now that is embarrassing," she admitted.

Alonso chuckled, "I bet it was. If you look like you are going to miss it, I'll give you a subtle hint, how's that?"

"Okay," she replied taking a deep breath. "Here goes. Breasts, do your thing." Once more, she began to feel her way, moving her torso a bit to the left and right, sensing for the wall and then recognizing the feel of the door jam. "This does work, you know. I haven't once banged my head or nose since I started doing it this way."

"I think that you are about the bravest person that I have ever met, prettiest too," he added.

Behind them, Pian whispered, "I'd better follow her example, Jovanni. I can't tell if this door is three feet from me, or six, or one. It's there though," she added. Like her daughter, she began feeling her way along until she contacted the door jab. Certainty came and soon she walked confidently along the hall, her side just barely touching the walls. "Now Lin Li is ever so much better at this, you know. She has an eidetic memory. Once she's walked a route, she can duplicate it with the greatest of ease. Still, like us, she is learning to feel her way along a new path with her bosom as well. It must look weird to you fellows, but it sure saves us a knock in the face. Otherwise, we have to take the tiniest of steps and try to feel where we are at by sticking our out feet ever few steps. Now that was miserable." She chatted as they walked the long path back to their room. Alonso didn't have to say a word. Misha led them to their room, though as she drew close, she again used her large bosom to feel for the door jam and door.

Once inside, Alonso complimented her, "Well done, Misha. Perfect."

"Thanks, I wasn't so perfect last week, though. Want to play ball some more? Lin Li — she's one of us — she usually comes by to chat with mom after dinner. They talk grownup stuff, boring."

"You bet, Misha. Come on, let's have some fun."

Jovanni sat the tray with the teapot and cups down and poured two cups, then sat beside Pian on the bench once more. Together, they sipped their after-dinner tea. "I didn't really know how badly I missed civilization," Jovanni said. "All these months, it's been nothing but work. Thanks for letting me take tea with you."

Pian laughed, "Jovanni, if you were not taking tea with me, I'm afraid that I wouldn't be able to take tea. I can't carry it back with me and the others are too busy with the four shifts of diners. I feel halfway civilized this evening."

A bit later, Jovanni spotted another yellow-brown eyed woman near the door. She paused, did a perfect right turn, and walked straight into the small courtyard. "Pian? Are you out here? I hear voices."

"Hi Lin Li, yes, we have guests tonight. Come sit with us, we are having tea," Pian said. Quickly, Jovanni moved the tray beneath the bench and rose.

"Tea? Wow, this is an occasion. I hear Misha and someone else. Is that a ball? I should sit between you and Pian," Lin Li asked and stated. Jovanni watched as she moved directly to the bench, turned, and sat down at the opposite end from Pian, almost as if she had seen what she was doing. As if sensing his amazement, she added, "Eidetic recall. Once I have found something, I can find it again. I'm Lin Li, by the way."

Balancing two teacups, Jovanni gave her a hug and sat down. After introductions, he helped both women sip their tea. Lin Li said, "Well, Misha sure sounds happy, Pian. I don't think that I have ever heard her so gay, except for therapy of course. Jovanni, usually I come by, and Misha and I work problems together."

"Hi Lin Li," Misha called out from her game. "This is my new friend, Alonso. He's from Velona. We're playing ball. Should I stop so we can work our problems?"

"Let's take a bit of a break, Misha. You are pooping me out," Alonso chuckled. Misha walked carefully over towards the bench but stopped before running into the three.

"What kind of problems do you two solve, Lin Li?" Jovanni asked, becoming curious.

"Shall we show them, Misha?" Lin Li asked. Misha agreed. "Okay then, Misha. Let's say that someone wants to dig a well that is circular, ten feet across, and ten feet deep. About how many cubic yards of dirt do they have to remove?"

"Hey, son, you ought to be able to work that one," Jovanni interrupted, challenging his son, who as an engineer ought to be able to do that one.

Misha had her answer, but heard Alonso whispering to himself trying to work it out and she politely allowed him to try. "Seventy-five, dad."

"Seventy-eight and a half," Misha corrected him. He flushed.

"Right, Misha," Lin Li replied. "We work all kinds of problems like that. If I have ever seen a problem, I can recall its solution. Misha and I have become very good at working with figures now. What else is there for us to do as we sit around all the time with nothing productive to do? So we have been exercising our minds. We started it back when we were prisoners and have been doing it ever since."

Jovanni could not believe what he was hearing and seeing. He began to pose other engineering type problems to the three. Quickly, Alonso dropped out, these women were far too sharp and fast for him. Besides, he was used to using paper and pencil to work them out. Both Lin Li and Misha kept coming up with the answers, though several times, Jovanni had to stop to work it out himself even to know if they had it right.

"My god, ladies! This is incredible. If you both ever want a job, I could use you both on my engineering work." Both women smiled. Misha and Alonso went back to their ball game while the adults chatted a while longer. At last, Lin Li rose to head for her room and bed.

"Thanks for spending time with us, Jovanni. I have truly felt human again," Pian admitted softly to him.

"Thanks for having me, Pian. I have enjoyed every minute of it. May I call again soon?"

"Yes, of course, but I'm sure that you have much work to do."

"Bye, Alonso. Thanks for playing with me. I really had fun," Misha said as Alonso got his ball and turned to leave.

"Bye, beautiful," he whispered and gave her a hug before following after his father.

During the next days, the two men were busy most of the daytime hours, assisting their work crews who were finishing the many months' long track laying. However, each evening they took the two women to dinner and chatted back in their quarters until bedtime came.

Once the train arrived with all the marvelous inventions, Princess Mei Lon met with Jovanni. "Mr. West Po, I have not words enough to thank you for engineering this rail line to Nan Yan for us. You have opened up the world to our, until now, very isolated city."

"My pleasure. Honestly, Princess Mei Lon, we must all do everything that we can to help women everywhere. Mankind's future depends upon us all making it go right somehow, someway," he replied graciously.

She smiled, "I like your attitude, Mr. West Po. I have a proposition for you. Would you consider staying here in Nan Yan for say another year and helping us build other rail lines up into the valley? As I see it, trains could bring down ores in volume, instead of slow wagon loads. If so, I will see that you are handsomely rewarded. Time is not on our side. The rest of Tashien is in utter chaos. Here in Nan Yan, we are the last vestiges of civilization. We must survive and to do that we must modernize or MMCE as Mrs. Angela keeps telling me over the LD radio. From the incredible inventions we've just seen, this is our salvation. Please, I will reward you most handsomely if you will stay a while longer and assist us."

"Sure, Princess Mei Lon. Glad to help. I have seen just how critical this rail line is for your people. These past months, for once in my life, I have made a real contribution. Thanks for the offer. When do we start?"

"Come here, I could hug you, if I could!" Princess Mei Lon exclaimed, he'd answered her prayers. Instead, Jovanni gave her a hug. "Tomorrow, come to the palace here and we'll hold a design and goals meeting and go from there."

At the meeting, her planners and Jovanni laid out a massive expansion program. He didn't tell them that to complete the whole project would take years, however. Late that afternoon, he visited Pian once more. Alonso had been there all day, playing with Misha when she was not getting another therapy session or training from Master Tian. He found them in their courtyard as usual, awaiting the call to dinner.

"Pian, I have some interesting news. Looks like I won't be going back to Velona anytime soon. I've accepted Princess Mei Lon's offer to stick around Nan Yan for some time, helping them construct more rail lines and all manner of other construction projects. I didn't have the heart to tell her planners that it will take years to complete all their plans, though."

"Years pop? Wow! That is absolutely great, dad!" Alonso called out. Misha's ball hit him hard as he lost his concentration on their game.

"Well, I had thought that I ought to send you back son," Jovanni said.

"Oh no, dad! You must let me stay," he insisted. Jovanni agreed.

To Pian he said, "See, you cannot get rid of me so easily. Now you are stuck with me for years to come."

Jovanni received quite a surprise, one that he really desired, but had been too shy to ask for. Pian leaned over and felt his body position with her bosom, still not certain that her spherical vision was at all accurate. Having located his body, she then gave him a passionate kiss. In return, his arms slipped around her and he returned her passion.

"What are they doing over there?" Misha whispered to Alonso, who was also distracted by Pian's unexpected reply.

"They are kissing," he whispered to her. Misha moved over to him, feeling out where his body was located with her bosom and awkwardly planted a kiss on Alonso. Taken by surprise, his arms encircled her thin waist, pulled her closer, and returned her kiss.

Thus began an interesting romance. In December, Pian and Jovanni were married, but the adults insisted that Misha wait until next February until she turned fourteen before she and Alonso could be wed as well.

As the workload of the many projects increased, Jovanni finally insisted that Lin Li and Misha join his construction company. "Look, I know that both of you have lots of training to do yet and all manner of therapy sessions, but please, how about lending a hand in your spare time? I will pay you well for your services. Good engineers are very, very hard to come by." They both agreed and began helping out with the many calculations during their spare time. Neither Jovanni nor Alonso ever moved back to Velona, though they often made visits there. Their hearts now belonged to the women of Nan Yan.

Chapter 19 Skulls, Vengeance, and Pirates

Charon Deimos sat on the hard stone floor beside the High Altar of Primo Church of Jehosanity in Axos, Thrace. Charon laughed hysterically, but there was no one present to hear his glee this seventh day after the plague had struck Demokritos in late October 823. That is not to say he was alone, no indeed. The forty year old priest was surrounded by hundreds of corpses. The floor was caked with dried blood. The Mano del Dio followed the late Cardinal's orders to the letter. "The Holy Day of Judgment has come. Prepare yea for the coming of our Lord. Assist the faithful." Assist had been taken to mean to speed things along a little. Well, Charon thought, perhaps more than a little.

His confused mind returned to several days ago. Mano del Dio, the Holy Enforcers, crawling like all men, began systematically slitting the throats of all those faithful who had taken sanctuary here in the largest and grandest church in all Axos. Evidently, they had then fanned out into the capital city of Thrace assisting many others who belonged to the Church to reach the Lord's Holy Realm. "But not me, Charon Deimos," he laughed aloud. "I am now Bishop-Prelate Charon Deimos. All this is now my domain, the domain of the walking dead!" He continued his wild, gleeful laugh. Others might have pronounced him insane. Yet, who around Axos was now not insane? The plague claimed everyone.

Pauper, king, whore, holy nun, butcher, farmer, shoe maker, sinner, Holy Woman, the plague cared not for a person's wealth, rank, position, power, or devoutness to the Church. All were struck down in one mighty strike, a blow that Charon could only conceive as having come from the Devil Lucifer himself. Yet, here he was alive and now Bishop-Prelate of the entire city. His insane laughter filled this most holy chamber, echoing off the tall arches and domes high overhead. Golden lamps illuminated the holiest of holy icons, statues, frescos, tapestries, and paintings, which adorned this, the finest Church of Jehosanity in all Axos.

Another yet lived. Thirty-five year old Capaneus Lampos, a Mano del Dio Prelate, whose blood soaked robes were now dark brown instead of sky blue, came crawling into this Holiest of Holy Inner Sanctum. He had carried out his boss' orders to the letter. A highly skilled assassin, he had had no trouble dealing with the masses, preparing them for their Path to the Holy Realm. Yet, as he finished off the very last woman, Capaneus put his own knife to his throat and found that he was unable to do it to himself! At first, he prayed that this was a profound weakness in his own personal faith and he had lain on the bloody floor crying and begging for salvation.

That's when Charon found him and gave him Holy Purpose once again. "Rise, Holy Prelate Capaneus. Lord Jehosa has been revealed unto us finally as a false god, one who does not even exist! Yet, Lucifer plainly does and we, my Prelate, are now elevated to the Highest in his realm. We have been chosen, you and I, to continue Lucifer's work here in Axos and all Tarra. Rise, Holy Capaneus, rise and accept your new position as Deacon-Supreme! Together, you and I, the Spared Ones, shall begin the Holy Work of Lucifer. Rise Deacon-Supreme, rise." Given new purpose, Capaneus rose and faced Charon at last.

"What must we do, master?" Capaneus asked, wiping his eyes on his bloodstained robes.

"We must adorn our Primo Church. Go now, find vats, and fill them with all the lye that you can find. We must prepare all of our fallen followers," Charon ordered.

Now his mind slipped to the present. There was Deacon-Supreme Capaneus methodically doing his Holy Ordained Work. Already half of the dead in this room had been prepared for Lucifer. Charon found that his hands held another skull. He crawled over to the outer wall and placed it ceremoniously beside the others. He moved back a ways and stared at the Holy Wall. Impressive, he thought. Two hundred bleached skulls lay nicely positioned facing the pews. Already outside the main arched entrance, the two had glued and arranged an arch of skulls, affixing them to the stonework, declaring this was now Lucifer's Church of Skulls.

By the time that both men's feet returned to normal, their cleanup work was nearly done. The Holy Wall of Skulls now contained thousands of the white, eyeless skulls, rising halfway up the wall. Amazingly, they now had a hundred followers. To gain membership to the Church of Skulls, one only had to bring Bishop-Prelate Charon a skull, with or without flesh still attached. Why had they gained so many followers? It was not because of the fiery sermons that Charon gave each evening just before supper. Rather these men and a few women joined out of desperation.

The Church of Jehosanity had enormous stockpiles of food supplies, from dried fish, beef, and lamb, to vegetables, to fruits. You name it and it was somewhere in their vast stores. Elsewhere in Axos, people were starving. Mobs had long ago raided the stores and warehouses in search of life-sustaining food supplies. Even the palace of the king had been sacked and the royal family slain very early in

November. In fact, the skull of the late king and queen now adorned the Holy Wall.

As word slowly spread about the resources of the Church of Bones, more and more began to bring them a skull. In return, they received the Holy Blessing and all that they could eat each evening, though they first had to listen to the often-ranting sermons of Charon. During the long, hot summer, Charon's numbers grew into the thousands. He cared not whether the skull was freshly removed from a living body or one dug up from some long forgotten grave. A skull was a skull destined to adorn this Holy Chapel of Lucifer.

By harvest time in May 824, when the outlying farmers began bringing in their harvest to sell in Axos, Bishop-Prelate Charon's forces were the undisputed controllers of Axos. Practically every thief and assassin as well as many low life men were members of his Church of Skulls. I say controllers, not leaders. His members took what they wanted and when they wanted it. None could stand against them, for by now they were very well armed with long guns, pistols, and countless bladed weapons.

Floor to ceiling in the main giant chapel as well as the smaller Holiest of Holy Chapels, skulls looked out upon the worshipers. They, however, left openings so that the grandiose paintings and statues could still be seen. Even spookier were the three dozen skeletons, which sat permanently in the front row of pews. Carefully glued and wired together, these skeletons were called the Unholy Warriors of Lucifer and were always blessed by Charon during his sermons. Many began to believe that these skeletons were indeed Holy and would come to life to protect the church and its members in their Hour of Need.

Axos, Thrace, once home to over four million inhabitants and the capital of the Kingdom of Thrace, by the winter of 824 had become a den of thieves and assassins. Estimates suggest that a million fled the city, a million or more perished, and a million are unaccounted for at this time. Worse, by May the Church of Skulls began to expand outward from Axos. The mere appearance of a crudely drawn skull on a merchant's door was now enough to cause utter panic.

Patri, Thrace: Morning, the day after the plague struck. On the poop deck of the gun ship Orion, Captain Opheles Phoros stared out at the gigantic port, devoid of all humans. A solitary dog trotted about, sniffed a barrel, and raised his rear leg. "Damn! What the hell is going on here?" he called out to his boson, who merely shrugged, staring at his own two malformed feet. They were sitting of course, unable to stand any longer. None was. The docks at Patri were the largest in all Demokritos, capable of handling forty ships at one time, though usually half that amount was in the docks on any given day. Yesterday, seven ships were being loaded, while ten were being unloaded by the hundreds of burly dockhands. Today, silence. Well, not completely silent, even from their position some three hundred yards offshore, they could hear women's terrified screams, muffled by the walls of their homes.

Nearly a million resided in Patri, the premier port city, complete with a steam train that ran due east to the capital city of Axos, Thrace, and then on to Kefall, the Imperial City of their Emperor and Empress. Shrill screams blended with the calls of the sweeping gulls and the gentle lapping of the ocean waters against the anchored Orion. The gun ship was a modified caravel with a dozen cannonae on each side. The Orion was anchored just off the docks to the north, while a sister ship, the Okeanos, was anchored three hundred yards off the docks to the south. Between them, they guaranteed the security of this huge port.

"Keep a sharp eye on the Signalman, boson. Surely they will soon let us know what the devil is going on here," Captain Opheles ordered. It was a wish, more than what he expected to happen, though he dare not say so. He had sailors and artillerymen under his command. No signals came.

After a week and still no signals and no one working the docks, Captain Opheles had to take action. Already another six ships slipped into the docks and tied their hawsers. He'd heard their captains yelling for help and even news. Only the sea gulls replied. While they were well stocked with food, their water barrels needed refilling and the weekly launch had not yet delivered them. He had to act.

That is not to say that he hadn't taken any actions for seven days. When the weird boots appeared, he'd figured out that they would allow men to stand and perhaps walk precariously on the tips of their toes. He'd ordered the artillery crews to begin practicing how to work their guns, and more importantly, he'd ordered his boson to retrain the sailors. Somehow, they had to be able to sail the Orion. Using his spyglass, he saw that Captain Nikias Machos was doing much the same with his crew on the Okeanos.

The lack of water forced his hand. "Lower the dingy. Load the empty water barrels," he ordered. Indeed, he found it exceedingly tricky to climb down the rope ladder into the small boat. These boots required precision placement on each rope so tiny were their soles. Two crewmen slipped and fell into the sea. One had yelled up to him that it was easier this way. Several sailors laughed.

Ordinarily, both captains would not go ashore at the same time. However, due to the circumstances, he'd signaled Captain Nikias to meet him ashore and together check in with the Port Authority to find out what was happening. "Okay, use the hand-wagons to carry the barrels to the central well. Holler when you have them ready to take aboard the Orion. If I am not yet back, go ahead and ferry them to the ship," he ordered and began his slow, careful wobbling steps toward the center of the expansive docks.

Captain Nikias met him there and the two continued their painstakingly slow walk to the Port Authority building, located north of the giant steam train station. Still, only their men and a few from the other caravels were around. "Where the hell is everyone?" Captain Opheles yelled angrily. The two men pounded on the main doors and then went inside to find the whole building just as empty as the docks.

"Hell, this is an emergency. Ring the damn bell, Captain," Nikias suggested. They stepped back outside. A huge bell with a long, thick pull rope stood like a silent sentinel just outside the building, a thick pole with a two-foot bell housing perched some twenty feet above the ground. In emergencies, the tolling of the bell always brought help. He pulled and the loud dong broke the otherwise quiet of the docks. He rang it for nearly ten minutes before giving that up.

Just as the two were about to head back to their ships, they heard hooves upon the pave stone streets. "Ah, now we're getting somewhere," Nikias declared. "We need answers!" Soon, a dozen soldiers rode up; thankfully, one was General Nestor himself.

"General! Sorry to bother you, but no one's been around for a week. Our feet are malformed. What the devil is going on here?" Captain Opheles asked, watching the general precariously dismount. He too wore these strange boots.

The middle aged general glanced around, satisfied that there was no real emergency to handle. "Come, let's go inside." To his men, he added, "Captain, check the docks as long as we're here. Send a rider back. No emergency this time," he ordered. The three men wobbling, arms flailing around trying to keep their balance, entered the Port Authority. The general made straight for the main office. After pulling a keg of rum and three mugs, he motioned for the two captains to join him. Seated at last and sipping the fine rum, the general outlined the situation.

The last train from Kefall had brought dire news, but the crew barely was able to drive the train and had gone home to their families. The Emperor was dead as was the King of Thrace. Rioting had begun in all major cities. Here in Patri, only his soldiers had prevented major rioting from impacting Patri. "I've given orders and posted them. Any rioters, any looters will be shot on sight! That seems to be doing the trick. I've declared martial law; the city is under my control now." Still, the two men found the news of so many dead unsettling, especially when they heard that the Church of Jehosanity had announced that the Holy Day of Judgment had come. Thousands were dead, their bodies lying where they fell.

"I have to deal with the rotting corpses, but my men are unable to dig so many graves. The ground around here is limestone. I've sent out riders scouting for someplace to hold a mass cremation, but as yet, they've not found a suitable place," General Nestor explained.

"Hey, you could load them into that rotting caravel that was scheduled to be destroyed. We could sail it out to sea and sink her," Captain Opheles suggested.

"Brilliant, captain, brilliant. I'll get my men on it today. Say, I have been doing some thinking. With our leaders gone, the whole country is heading towards anarchy. No stores are open, no markets, and no new food supplies are coming, save what we have in storage."

"Are you saying that Patri is on her own?" asked Captain Opheles.

"Sure as hell, captains, we are on our own. Now I've been thinking. We can use this to our advantage. There's a million give or take here in Patri and most are running out of food. If we can keep the population well fed, we can remain in control. If this food shortage lasts too long, then not even all my soldiers will be able to maintain control of Patri. I have a proposition for you two." He outlined his plan.

Captain Opheles grinned, "I like that plan immensely, general, but seeing as how you will be dependent upon us, who are taking great risks, we three should be equal partners, though we'll leave the land-side control up to your Judgment." General Nestor smiled, and they shook hands, forming a tripartite rulership of Patri. The general would see that the docks were ringed with cannonae as well as the outer rim of the port city. The two captains would set sail and capture nearby caravels, bringing the spoils to Patri. Their target would be mainly food supplies, but gold and gems would also be a nice addition to their men and pockets.

The next day, mounted soldiers escorted struggling dockhands down to the docks, forcing the men back to work as best they could manage. All around the docks, burly men griped and complained, as they teetered and wobbled about trying to deal with the heavy work while walking on the tips of their toes in the strange boots. A few days later, several caravels, which had been docked, were relieved of their cargos and sent on their way. After that, the ancient rotting caravel, now loaded with thousands of dead, slowly began its last voyage, followed closely by the Orion.

Early December, the Happy Prince sent a frantic LD radio message to Velona. "Help! We are under attack by Patri pirate gun ships! The Orion and Okeanos are shooting at us!" The radio went silent after that. A week later, the Happy Prince was finally able to make a follow up call, notifying Velona that its cargo had been stolen by these pirates. Patri was now a pirate town. Stefano had no choice but to order all the Velona caravels to stay well clear of Patri , Thrace. He also ordered four of Velona's gun ships to head south eventually to begin protecting our shipping in the far south. How times changed, I thought.

In Kefall, Thrace, the Emperor's City and the traditional seat of the throne of Demokritos and where the kings and queens of the seven kingdoms met, a very different scenario began to unfold after the plague struck. Some ten blocks from the Imperial Palace, the Tasa sisters had taken an apartment fairly close to their work. Melantha, twenty, and Pandora, nineteen, were cooks in the Imperial Palace, helping to prepare meals for the Emperor and Empress and their extended family. Their parents and younger brother lived about a mile away from the palace, which is why the two had taken an apartment much closer.

Neither was yet married, though Pandora was engaged to Midas Cepheus, a twenty year old moneychanger, whose store was a block from their apartment. Melantha, on the other hand, had finally been going out with Kastor Cepheus, the older brother of Midas. Kastor was a master chef at a fancy restaurant some five blocks from the Imperial Palace. He was twenty-one and had met Melantha via his brother, who some four months ago had set him up with a blind date with Melantha. Both saw possibilities in each other. However, Melantha was a bit strange for Kastor.

Melantha was fascinated with chemistry. Ever since she was a little girl and had seen the reaction of soda and vinegar, she just had to know more. Her bedroom soon became her experiment laboratory. One of the real reasons they had moved out to this apartment was so that Melantha could continue her experiments uninhibited by her parents. Plus, she now had double the space. She spent every extra copper that she earned purchasing more chemicals and compounds for her work. In fact, the two were rapidly running out of space in their apartment.

The two young women were both very level headed and hard workers. When the plague struck them, after the initial shock and waves of terror had passed, Mel and Pan began to work together to deal with their pressing needs. Shortly thereafter, the strange items appeared and the two began to see uses for them at once. Pandora had kept their pantry well stocked, so they were not in any immediate danger of starving. Yet, how actually to cook anything was their first hurdle. The second day, Midas and Kastor came crawling over to check on the two, for Midas was genuinely afraid that Pan had perhaps died.

Their apartment was really a small home. Both women were trapped inside, unable to get their door opened. "Oh Midas! Do we ever need you now! Come in, come in; ignore Mel's stuff. What happened to your feet?" Pan suddenly saw the men's feet.

The four sat on their single couch and exchanged news and fears for quite some time. The two men realized that both Mel and Pan desperately needed them around and volunteered to stay with them. For several days, the four worked together trying to survive and working out how they could. Gunfire often startled them, as well as mobs of men riding in the streets nearby. All four were terrified that the thugs would raid this small apartment home.

When they were running low on water, Midas and Kastor left to refill two barrels and to gather what news they could find. For hours, Mel and Pan sat on their couch terribly worried about them, especially when they heard more gunfire. At last, their hands and knees rather bloody from so much crawling, the two returned with more water and a whole lot of news. Ashen faces told the two women plenty.

"It's wild out there, Pan! Insane, crazy! They've killed the Emperor and Empress. No sign of any of their children or their families. The Imperial Palace has been raided, so much is destroyed. I'm afraid that you both have no jobs to return to when this is over," Kastor explained.

"Not like we are going to be able to do much anyway, when this is over, that is, not like this," Mel shrugged her shoulders.

"Dead bodies are everywhere, in streets and yards," Midas spoke up. "Probably some inside houses too, we saw plenty of open doors and no one around that we could see. It's just awful. We stopped by our folk's house. They are gone," his voiced cracked and tears began to well up in his eyes. Kastor's head fell and his grief flowed as well. Pan and Mel both wanted to put their arms around their boyfriends and comfort them, but could not. Once more, their own problems overwhelmed them both, and they leaned into their boyfriends and cried along with them. Soon, the men began to hold onto the women as tightly as they could.

Later, Mel asked, "Who killed your family?"

Kastor whispered, "Neighbors said it was Pelios. He always had it in for dad. Wish he were dead!"

Pandora sat up, "Mom, dad, and Alkios! Mel, we have to go see if they are all right!" Now both women began to worry about their own parents and little brother.

"How? You can hardly walk, Pan. Look at us, our hands knees can't take any more crawling," Midas asked.

"Come on; we need to get you both fixed up. I have just the compound to disinfect them and help heal them," Melantha declared. While the men washed off their scraped and cut hands and knees, Mel did her slow shuffle into her bedroom, which was filled with jars, bottles, and tins. She cursed. There was the tin that she wanted, but she had no hands to fetch it or to carry it to the bathroom. Then, she remembered the yokes and shuffled off to get it. By the time she finally managed to get the tin to the men, they had gotten themselves cleaned up.

Mel had Kastor open the tin, but she insisted on applying the salve with her feet. Pan finally joined them, having found an old sheet that Mel had asked for — "Rip it into four inch strips for bandages," Mel ordered. Frustrated at her inability to do such a simple thing, Midas quietly did it for her and then did the wrapping of their hands and knees.

They discussed how they could all get to the Tasa home, which was over a mile from here. While the women could potentially walk that far, hobbled as they were with these strange shoes and high arched feet, thousands of tiny steps would be needed, if their feet could withstand such an exertion. No way could the men crawl that far and no way would they even consider letting the women out of the house without accompanying them. The world had turned utterly brutal, no mercy anywhere.

"Tomorrow, we find a carriage," Midas decided. The next day, the two were able to borrow a neighbor's horse and buggy. This was the first time that the two women were able to get out of their apartment since the plague. Both found the going rather challenging — simple things such as stairs to be descended without the benefit of the handrail. Getting into the buggy was daunting until the men put their arms around them, balancing them, while they were on their knees. As they drove through the streets, the horrors of the previous days' events assailed all four of them, especially the two women.

Bodies lay seemingly everywhere, men, women, and even a few children. Twice, a pack of rats stopped their dining and dashed for cover as the buggy approached them. Had the women arms and hands, they would have covered their faces. Instead, they merely faced these inhuman sights. Their world had ended. Not a single alive person was on the streets this day other than themselves.

When they reached their family home, the boys helped them down and they tried to run up to their opened front door and nearly fell. Reduced to taking tiny three-inch steps, they wobbled precariously in their attempts to hurry inside. "Mom? Dad?" Mel called out, jerking her body wildly to keep from falling down as she took too large a step. No answer, just an eerie silence lay over the whole Imperial City. Both women had to slow way down as they negotiated the three steps onto their porch. Behind them, the men slowly crawled along, taking it very gently on their injured hands and knees.

They had reached the porch when they heard both women scream and they knew what must lie inside. "Damn!" Midas exclaimed. Kastor hung his head and continued doggedly on up the steps. Inside, they found both women had slumped to the floor, leaning over the bodies of their parents and younger brother. As soon as they were close, both put their arms around the two women and looked at the grim sight.

Mel observed through fits of crying, "They beat dad. Look at his arms; they're both broken, and his face, all bruised and puffy. Why did they rip mom's clothes off her?" Kastor and Midas both knew the answer to that one, especially since her body was lying flat on her back. They, however, had the good sense not to answer Melantha.

Pandora did. "My god, they raped mom before they strangled her! Who could do such a thing? Mom never hurt anyone in her life!"

"Looks like they were robbed," Midas pointed to the empty money-box, lying ajar beside a desk, which had also been ransacked.

"Melantha, Pandora? Is that you?" a voice called out from the doorway. The four grieving faces turned.

"Mr. Lexios! Yes, it's us. What happened to mom and dad? Who did this to them?" Melantha asked still wailing, her grief far too raw to be suppressed.

"Agathon's gang. Three days ago now. We heard her screaming, but I couldn't do anything to help her. Found them like this. I can't even get to the mortician to come," he replied as he too began to cry. All this was too much for the seventy year old neighbor, whose wife had died four days ago as well. Her body he had wrapped in a blanket waiting by their front door, if ever the mortician came. He added, "My wife couldn't handle the shock of it all. I have her ready for the mortician. If you can wrap them up, I'll see that the mortician takes them too, when he comes for my wife. That's the least I can do for you. Your folks were always so kind to us, you know." He stopped to wipe his own wet face.

Having something to do was beneficial. Mel and Pan headed into their parent's bedroom and pulled blankets off the bed using their teeth, dragging them back into the front room. While the men began wrapping them, they went to get another one for their brother. An hour later, they stood over the three wrapped forms, much as three carpet rolls sitting beside the front door. At least the rats would not easily be able to get them while they waited for the mortician's wagon to come. After thanking their neighbor, they got into the rented buggy and solemnly returned to their apartment home.

All the way home, Mel said not a single word. Nor did she for the next few days. At first, she sat and stared at the walls, giving Kastor quite a fright. He tried to get her talking about it, anything, but to no avail. At least, he managed to get her to eat and drink. That was something. Finally, Melantha spoke. Her voice was cold and emotionless. It sent goose bumps down the other three's spines. "Vengeance is mine! I shall have it!"

"What — what do you mean?" asked Kastor. Was she planning to go after the gang of thugs who had killed her parents? How could she? Before the plague, he could see her perhaps shooting a long gun at them. But now? She was so helpless, so dependent upon him.

Mel spoke again, "Vengeance is mine!" She rose and headed to their spare room, which housed her many, many bottles, vials, tins, and pouches of chemicals and compounds. Kastor crawled in after her watching her. "You best stay out of this room. It may be too dangerous for you to be in here, if something goes wrong. I have to make something. I will have vengeance!"

He refused to budge and sat in the doorway watching her. Mel began to use her feet as she once had her hands. Determination had steeled her will. Slowly, her ideas took form. She could use the one mixture that she'd discovered, but she needed a delivery system that she could handle. Her mind raced down a dozen paths at once, rejecting this one and that one at various points. At last, she saw the answer. For two days and nights, Mel worked in her room, perfecting her delivery system. Finally, she sighed; she was ready at last.

Kastor was pleased that Mel finally came to the table to dine with the rest of them. He had been feeding her as she worked. "After we eat, go rent that buggy again. Take me there. I will have my vengeance today!" She spoke with such power and command, that all three could not dare refuse her wishes. Midas stowed a long gun that he'd found in the buggy, while Mel helped Pandora get into the buggy. Shortly, Melantha appeared at the doorway, struggling to get her yoke through the narrow space. By the time that Kastor got to her to help, she had managed it. "Put my yoke and these things in the buggy too, but be extremely careful not to bump or jar that small vial there that's lying on the velvet cloth!" Melantha ordered. He did as instructed and then balanced her as she climbed up.

An hour later, the buggy was parked in an alley. At the end of the alley, Mel sat on the ground with her incredible contraption. A long tube rested on a sloped piece of brass, pointing at the door across the alleyway, the door of Agathon's home. When she finally had everything lined up, she very, very carefully picked up the tiny glass vial and even more carefully slipped it into the top of the tube. Then she slid a tiny cone of heavy paper over that end. "Light my candle, please," she said in her same icy cold voice. Kastor did as asked. She slid the candle close to the rear of the long tube.

"Now we wait. Keep an eye out for Agathon." The four waited for hours. Occasionally, they spotted some man crawling along the street, usually sliding a water bucket before him. "We are reduced to being nothing but animals," Melantha cursed through clenched teeth. Kastor wisely kept quiet.

Late in the afternoon, they spotted Agathon and two others crawling towards the house. They had heavy wrappings around their hands and knees, adapting nicely to their new mode of locomotion. They were carrying three heavy bags — the day's loot. As Agathon approached his front door, Melantha whispered coldly, "Vengeance is mine, you dirty dog!" She used her toe to push the candle even closer to the lower end of the tube.

None of the three had any idea of just what to expect. In truth, before this instant, Kastor and Midas thought that she was probably slightly crazy, what with the loss of her parents and the plague's devastating impact on her body. All that changed in a fraction of a second. The entire world changed in that same fraction of a second.

A huge burst of black-grey smoke burst out of the end of the tube, which shot like an arrow straight across the street. It made a whooshing noise, and the three thugs heard it and turned in time to see this flying tube with smoke and flames shooting out its rear heading at them. They had no time to react. The tube struck the front door of Agathon's place. What happened next would soon shock the entire world.

A brilliant, white, blinding flash occurred, followed by an enormous boom, louder than thunder in a summer's storm! Unlike conventional war bombs, there were no massive flames from gunpowder exploding. When their eyes recovered from the searing flash, the entire front of the home was gone. The largest body part that anyone later recovered from the three men's bodies was a right toe. Bloody bits intermingled with tiny fragments of wood and stone. His home had been made of limestone blocks. Only the back half of the home remained.

"Oops, I believe that I used a wee bit too much," Melantha commented to herself. "Kastor, can you please pick up the stuff here and put them in the buggy for me? My work is done here. We can go home for now." Her voice was still icy cold.

As they rode through the streets, Kastor asked, "Melantha what was that? How did you?"

"Vengeance is mine. I used a bit too much of one of my chemical mixtures, Kastor. Next time, I will use about half that amount. It is very potent stuff, isn't it? Highly effective. Agathon will rob, rape, and kill no more, not ever. However, we still have to get the rest of his gang and all those who killed your family too. And then there are those who have done similar killings to other families. We have a whole lot of work ahead of us, Kastor. I will rid this city of its evil. I swear to you, Kastor, that I will rid this city of evil!" He rightly did not reply.

By the time that everyone's feet returned to normal, Kefall had witnessed several dozen of these incredible blasts. Agathon's gang members were history as well as those who had killed the men's family and a number of others as well. The four had become quite skilled as vigilantes. They had even taken to posting signs near the public wells, asking for names of evil doers. By early January, the four had accumulated a rather lengthy list of new targets to strike. Each of Mel's strikes was done with surgical precision. She had gotten the amount of her explosive perfected. No fires ever resulted, but the devastation was always total and complete. Even a miss of a few feet mattered not in the least! Well, it only mattered if one was concerned about the size of the remaining body bits, that is. She did not. They left their calling card at each site: Righteous Vigilantes. By early January, 824, few in Kefall had not heard of that name.

Two days before the plague struck, Linos Andros, an ex-soldier now twenty-one, pulled the buggy up beside the Rare Book Store. Tall and handsome, Linos looked the part of a dashing soldier, though he had given that up last year after very nearly getting himself killed. The son of a wealthy merchant of Kefall, Linos did not want to be a merchant like his father. Where's the fun in that, he always said. To make his meager savings from his tour of duty last longer, Linos had taken on a renter, who shared the rent on their home here in the wealthy district of Kefall. He ran his hands through his thick black hair and waited.

Soon, his roommate, Herakles Laos, also twenty-one, stepped out of his shop, nodding to Linos, and locking his door. Unlike Linos, Herakles personally hated fighting. He was an historian at heart. He clutched a book beneath his shoulder and turned to the buggy. He was tall and thin, quite unlike the well-muscled ex-soldier, who often worked out at the gym. Herakles preferred to work out his brains, instead. While the two men were quite the opposites, they respected each other and had become good friends during this past year that they shared the home.

Herakles climbed aboard and Linos headed the horses off towards the gym. "Bet the girls will be ready for dinner tonight," Linos commented. Herakles smiled, of course they would be. Six months ago, during one of his frequent gym workouts, Linos had the good fortune to meet a pair of young women, Kalypso Dias, also twenty-one, and Leto Gia, a year younger. His mind slipped back to their first chance meeting. He seldom went in for morning workouts, preferring sometimes to nurse his head from a tad too much ale the night before. Yet, this one morning, he had awakened and felt the urge to use the gym. Perhaps it had been fate, he mused, as the images of that first meeting reformed in his mind.

He'd entered in his usual cocky manner and spotted these two women, who had also just entered the gym, heading for the mats. Both were around the same height, five-eight he guessed. He was all of six feet. Both had shiny bronze skin, perhaps showing a bit too much of it. They wore their hair short, far, far shorter than the current fashionable styles in Kefall, where many of the fashionable women emulated the blonde Empress with her gorgeous golden locks that fell to her knees. Both women kept theirs barely four inches long and could readily be mistaken for a man's head. They wore white pants and a white shirt with very short sleeves, low cut in the front. Both were barefoot and they chatted with each other, seemingly ignoring him. Ah, that's not something that women should do around Linos!

"Good morning, ladies," Linos purposely interrupted the two. Both turned their heads to look at him. Ah, that's better, he thought to himself. They both had pretty faces; he liked that. They nodded and continued walking to the mats. Well, that's a fine how do you do, he thought and rapidly moved to join them. "Here for a workout, ladies?" he interrupted them again, purposely putting his body directly in their path this time, so that they would have to see him and talk.

"No, we are here to do some shopping. Get lost," Kalypso declared flatly.

Leto giggled, "Good one, Kalypso, good one. I'll remember that one." Both moved to get around him, causing Linos to have to back step rapidly to stay in front of them.

"Well, I'm here to get a work out too. Since it seems that there are only the three of us here, how about joining me in a work out," he laid his best fitting line on them.

Leto gave a slight toss to her head, "Ha, you give us a workout? Dream on, mister!"

Linos took the bait. No woman had ever rejected wholly his advances, not wholly. He was too handsome to be rejected out of hand. Yet these two were doing precisely that. Could they be lesbians he wondered? Still, he just couldn't let it go. "Well, ladies, I'll tell you what. If I don't give you two both a real workout, then I will buy you both lunch at Antonio's!" Antonio's was one of the most elegant and expensive restaurants in Kefall! He estimated right, who would not play for a free meal at Antonio's.

Kalypso stopped, looked at Leto, grinned mischievously. That alone ought to have sent warning signals into Linos' brain, but he missed it. "If you fail to give us a real work out this morning, you will take us to Antonio's? Okay mister, you are on. I hope you can take it." He had no doubts that he could, after all he was a soldier, well ex-soldier, in his prime.

"Be gentle on him, Kalypso; don't hurt him so badly that he won't be able to take us to lunch," Leto cautioned her friend.

Kalypso growled, but conceded, "Darn, you do have a point. Okay, take it easy on him."

Twenty minutes later, Linos gave up utterly! These two women were incredible martial artists. A blaze of fists danced around his face and he sensed that at any time, either one could land a knockout punch. Worse, they continually flipped him down onto the mats. Their feet with their amazing kicks and sweeping circle kicks could have dropped him at any time they chose. After he gave up and admitted that they won the bet easily, he sat panting on the sidelines, nursing his various aches and pains, watching the two of them go at it. He now saw that indeed they had been treating him with kid gloves! Power swings and kicks of their legs constantly blocked each other's attempts to break through the other's defenses. Sweat poured off their bronze skin as they continued for almost an hour before finally stopping and bowing to each other.

He began clapping, "Amazing, simply amazing. I am humbled, truly humbled."

"Damn well better be," Kalypso declared breathily. "If you don't hold up your bargain, you're pulp."

"I wouldn't miss this lunch for all the gold in the Imperial Palace," he teased them.

"You better not, if you know what's good for you," Leto added. "We are the bouncers for the Dance Club just down the street. Pick us up there in say an hour. Don't be late," she added flashing him a smile. Oh how that first friendly smile electrified him. At last, I'm getting somewhere with these women, he thought.

He dressed in his finest suit and was waiting outside the Dance Club ten minutes early. He had to wear his finest suit just to gain entrance into Antonio's. Yet he was also familiar with the Dance Club, perhaps the finest dancing establishment in Kefall. Only the wealthy could afford the entrance fee. It was a private club. Inside, everything was free, naturally; their fees more than covered the owner's expenses. He'd only been inside a couple times as a guest of a friend on what was advertised as Friend's Night.

Right on time, the two women came out of a side door. Linos could scarcely believe his eyes. "Wow, you both look stunning," he waggled, as he helped them into the buggy. Both wore identical blue satin dresses, whose many petticoats billowed them out to nearly four feet. Black silk hose imported from Tashien adorned their legs and both wore shiny black high heels. They too needed to dress well in order to be allowed inside Antonio's.

The wager cost Linos fifty gold, but he had not the slightest regrets. The three hour-long, elegant lunch flew by at lightning speed. He'd learned a lot about these two women. Kalypso had seen her mother raped when she was a child, and she swore that no man would ever be able to do that to her, especially when her mother committed suicide six months later, unable to cope with life after that. Both had wanted to join the army, but were rejected solely because no women were allowed in the army. The two had been best friends since they were eight years old, living but a block from each other then. They had been studying martial arts together since they were ten, the youngest that their master would accept as students.

Three years ago, they had taken the job as bouncers for the Dance Club, after they had proven their skills to the owners. That had been an interesting day; they had to bounce out of the hall all the other six bouncers. "Males, they are all the same. None of the male bouncers ever had to do that," Leto declared slightly antagonistically.

"Well, you have to admit that nearly every bouncer is male," Linos defended his sex. She grinned, knowing that he was right. Now the two shared a large room in the club, all expenses paid. They did not begin work until four in the afternoon, which explained why they always worked out in the early morning hours. Linos also found that Leto was keenly interested in hearing about his times in the army, especially the many small battles that he had fought against the black savages of the Southlands. She was all too eager to go out with him on her nights off, Mondays. Yet, Kalypso wanted to tag along; she did not trust men much and fretted over Leto's safety.

Hence, Linos had set up his roommate, Herakles, with a blind date, accompanying them to keep Kalypso occupied so that he could court Leto. Of course, he gave Herakles absolutely no chance at all of interesting Kalypso, but if he could keep her occupied, that would be enough for him. Linos was definitely smitten with Leto.

How could Linos possibly have known that Kalypso would have fallen for the wimpy historian? Never in a million years would he have thought that could happen. Yet, it had. Kalypso had a love of history and constantly probed Herakles for more of his knowledge. So much so, that Herakles was bringing along a very special rare book that he's just acquired, a present for Kalypso this very evening.

They picked up the girls just outside the closed Dance Club and headed to a fancy diner. "Wow, you found it! Herakles, you are a genius!" Kalypso declared and gave him a passionate thank you kiss. His cheeks flushed. It was a hundred year old volume entitled, <u>The Kali Assassins</u>, a topic that always intrigued her. Of course, this bold group was long ago disbanded, passing down into the pages of ancient history. Still, Kalypso was fascinated by these women fighters, who fought for women's rights.

This was also a special night for the two men. Simultaneously, both produced rings and proposed to the two women. To their delight, both said yes. The two young coupled toasted the night. Unfortunately for them, the plague struck shortly thereafter.

Perhaps of all the women on Tarra, these two suffered the least terror and shock when they discovered the hideous effects of the plague, the loss of their arms. While they were frightened and cried at first, they soon snapped out of it. "Look, Leto. Back when the Kali were around, half of the Kali were just like us. Many of their top leaders were like us. If they can manage to do all that they did, so can us. Come on; we have to reread that book and find some clues and figure out what all these weird things are for," Kalypso declared, pulling Leto out of her fears.

"Yes, but they didn't have screwed up feet like we do," Leto protested. "We can just barely walk. How can we even move quickly?"

"Don't know yet, but we've still got quite deadly legs. Come on, Leto," she insisted.

Blocks away, the two men spent the first day trying to figure out what had happened to their feet. Late in the day, they finally began discovering the magnitude of the plague and its horrific effects on the women of Kefall. Herakles first discovered that he could at least stand on his feet if he wore the strange boots that had appeared in the middle of their living room. Walking in them was quite another matter, he discovered. Only when Linos joined him and they held onto each other could they manage to walk without constantly losing their balance. "The girls!" Linos suddenly realized that their fiancés might be in dire need of them. "We have to get to the Dance Club right now!"

"We can't possibly walk that far!" Herakles wailed.

"Right, to the rear and our buggy. We'll take it. Come on. Damn, this is unbelievably slow going!"

"Gosh, do you really think our fiancés have lost their arms like the other women around here have?" Herakles asked very worriedly. He could not imagine living life without his. How could he lift a precious book? Books were everything to him. The streets were eerily deserted. They heard wails and screams of terror coming from nearby homes as they passed by, their horses clop clopping on the paved streets of this wealthy district. Their fears grew and grew as everywhere, the plague seemed to have struck with a vengeance. When they arrived at the Dance Club, the parking lot for buggies was empty. The lights in the main floor were out. Not a sole was here, incredibly ominous, they feared.

After parking their buggy in the owner's stables, they began their slow climb up the outside stairs that led to the private quarters of the two women, on the second floor on the western side of the building. Four other male bouncers lived in separate apartments in the middle and on the eastern side of the second floor. The owner's main office lay in the middle of the floor. It took the two nearly ten minutes of precarious climbing to reach the women's door where they knocked and called out for Leto and Kalypso.

"We're here, Linos, Herakles!" the agitated voice of Leto called. "We're in big trouble. We've lost our arms and our feet are all screwed up. The door is locked and bolted. How in hell are we going to let you in?" Her voice bordered on panic now.

Through the thick door, they heard the voice of Kalypso call out. "Don't go away! Give us a few minutes to figure out how to open the door!"

Inside, Kalypso and Leto sat on their butts and began fiddling with the locks with their toes. After an eternity, the last one twisted. "Okay, try the knob now," Kalypso called through the thick door. Linos turned it and at last opened the door, very frightened by what he expected to see inside.

While shocking, Linos' training as a soldier came to the fore. "Well, it looks like you two are inviting us inside in a big way," he teased. The two women were sitting on the floor on scooting out of the way of the door. Both were completely naked. As the two men entered, the women realized their state and grasped his jest. Leto cracked a grin, the first smile since she got the plague.

"Oh my goodness, Kalypso! This is awful! Let me help you up," Herakles added moving to her side and nearly falling over himself.

"Thanks, dear. I am afraid that we really do need your help. Let me get these weird shoes on first. Herakles! What happened to your feet?" she asked, suddenly focusing on him instead of herself.

"Plague got us too, I'm afraid. My, you are even more beautiful than I ever imagined, my lovely flower of spring," he whispered. "Your hair has grown some. I do believe I like your new look, most becoming," Herakles whispered to her. Her short hair now fell below her shoulders, having grown some two feet in the last couple of days.

"Having no arms is really troublesome, but look at my breasts, Herakles! They are huge, incredibly enormous," she whispered back as he got her stable on her feet.

"Forgive me, my dearest. I had not seen them before, but they are very beautiful and most impressive. Your waist seems so much smaller than I imagined it to be." He lied of course. How could he not have seen them?

"Yes, I'm positively skinny waisted now too. Are you sure you still like the way I look? I mean if we go through with getting married, this is the way that I look now," she asked.

"I love you, Kalypso. You are not your body, but I do find your body most attractive as well. Why is it that you are both naked?" he asked.

"We had to go to the bathroom and helped each other out of our nightgowns. We hadn't yet figured how to get them back on when you came. Let me see your feet." She insisted and he held on to her shoulders and headed slowly to the couch. "We walk about as fast as each other now. Are all men hobbled like this too? Are all we women like we are?"

The men removed their boots to show them their feet and both women were quite shocked. At least they could stand on their bottoms of their toes, but their fiancés had to stand on the very tips of theirs and could only do that when wearing the strange boots. After helping them to get dressed, Linos and Herakles filled the two in all the little information that they had learned so far.

"Can you stay with us? We're really in need of help for a while," Kalypso asked Herakles. She'd never believed that she could or would ask this of a man, but she also realized their dire plight. Perhaps in time she and Leto could somehow manage like the ancient Kali women had, but right now, she felt incredibly vulnerable.

He kissed her and whispered, "I would not think of leaving you."

They spent the rest of the day examining and speculating on the pile of objects that had appeared in their front room area. They concluded that much of it was some kind of low to the ground kitchen with cookware and dinnerware. Leto was the first to figure out the purpose of the yokes. The writing desks were rather obvious. All four then worked together to fix supper.

During the next few days, the world around them took drastic turns for the worst. Gunshots became frequent, startling them each time they came. They learned that the Emperor had been killed and the palace, not twelve blocks away, had been looted. Mobs of men with long guns crawled the streets. From their high elevation vantage point, they witnessed some of the looting and shooting just down the street. Ten days into the plague and the streets around the Dance Club were littered with dead, mostly men, but a few were women and children. The four waited for the authorities to restore law and order, to come and remove the dead. Nothing happened, save more looting. Then the four saw even more gruesome sights, rats began feasting upon the rotting corpses!

For the time being, they were safe and had plenty of food and water. Twice a day, the men went down the inside stairs to the main floor. A complete kitchen lay behind the actual dance floor. Here the refreshments were prepared. At least the four were in no danger of starving, unlike so many others in Kefall.

Then, things turned even uglier. From their vantage point, they spotted thugs breaking into homes not far from them. Gunshots followed. Later in time, men came crawling out, bags loaded with loot and pulling sobbing younger women after them. They had ropes tied around their necks and were led as if they were cattle. Slowly but surely, Kalypso's ire and hatred grew and grew, a burning anger within her bosom. Still they prayed that the mayor or the King of Thrace would send soldiers to lay down the law, bring back some order, and bury the dead.

On the fourteenth day after the plague, their situation changed for the worst. The looters finally struck the Dance Club! Glass smashed and looters thronged into the main floor below their apartment. Wild yelling filtered up through the floor and the gang began tearing the place apart below them. Linos felt helpless. He didn't even have a long gun to protect them all. Kalypso had him bolt their door securely. The four huddled in one bedroom, the door shut, none daring make a sound. All prayed that these men would not be able to climb the stairs.

Then, they heard the other bouncers heading down to try to stop the looting. Gunshots startled all four of them. Kalypso guessed that was the end of her fellow workers, and the looting noise continued unabated. For hours, the four sat riveted to the floor, scarcely breathing, hoping against all hope they would not be detected. Finally, the sounds died down, but none moved until quite some time had passed since the last of the noise. Cautiously, the four made their way to the inner stairs, unlocking the door and peering down. Nothing. The men, with their arms around the women for support, ever so slowly descended, their speed dictated by their feet, not their caution.

The place was a wreck and they soon found the dead bouncers, who had tried to put a stop to the looting. "My god! We are not going to be safe anywhere! What if they come back later on?" Leto whispered, afraid to speak aloud for fear someone lurking nearby might detect their presence.

"Back up to your apartment," Linos' whispered. Ten minutes later, they sat on their couch once more. "Look, it is absolutely not safe to stay here much longer. We dare not use a light after dark. Someone will see it and know that we are here and maybe come knocking in the daytime."

"But where can we go? Is there no safe place anywhere? By god, this is the wealthy section of Kefall. Surely it is far worse than this in the other areas," Herakles said worriedly.

"Right. Where can we possibly go to hide out until they restore order?" Linos asked. Silence.

"I know where we can go!" Kalypso said as inspiration struck. "I've been reading all about the ancient Kali. They had all sorts of underground hideouts, all inner-connected below Kefall. All we need to do is find one of those entrances and head down there. I bet all those old places are still there." All four loved the idea and chatted about how this could really work well. The only problem was where could they find an entrance.

While Herakles held the book open, he and Kalypso began rereading, searching for possible clues. Linos and Leto began making their plans: what would they need to take with them and where could supplies be found?

Herakles found the key clue. "Hey, this Dance Club didn't use to always be a dance hall. Years ago, it was the old Church of the Sun God. When Jehosanity was adopted as the official religion of Demokritos, this Sun Church was abandoned and later converted into the Dance Club. According to this book, there used to be an entrance to the underground Kali lairs right here. Now all that we need to do is find it. Surely it is still there."

They chatted eagerly about this revelation and then headed downstairs to see if they could find it. There were still a couple hours of daylight left. Obviously, the vast dance floor area, which occupied the vast majority of the first floor held no secret entrances. They spent most of their time searching the kitchen area with no luck. "Is there a basement?" asked Herakles.

"A wine cellar — they have the entrance hidden behind this tapestry. Damn, no arms to move it aside," Kalypso replied, annoyed that she was once more stopped by something as simple as a tapestry.

The men held it back and the girls stepped through and then had to wait for the men to open the door. Again supporting each other, they slowly descended the stairs. Oil lanterns still burned, but low. Usually someone would refill them every few days, but no one had been here for two weeks. The wine cellar was square, twenty-five feet on a side. Against two walls, rows and rows of fine, aged, and expensive wines were stacked, neatly in wooden frames. Dust lay thick on most of the bottles. The team began searching in the flickering dim light of the lanterns. "This will never do," Herakles exclaimed. He began cleaning the first of the four lanterns, wiping out the accumulated lamp black. After refilling the bowl, he relit it. Much more light was produced. Hence, he and Linos began cleaning two more, while the two women stood watching, quite frustrated that they were unable to assist them.

"I feel so damn helpless like this," Leto declared.

"Same here. Once we get somewhere safe, we have to start figuring out how the ancient Kali did things for themselves. According to the book, they even fed themselves," Kalypso replied, just as annoyed with herself as was Leto.

In a few minutes, the place was brightly illuminated. Wine bottle labels could easily be read and the four resumed their search. "Ah ha. Here is something," Herakles pointed out. "See, this block here. It is recessed a little bit from all the others." He pushed on it, and to his amazement, it slid inward slightly. He pushed it further and loud click was heard. A five foot wide section of the wall pivoted open, revealing a dark tunnel.

Kalypso leaned into Herakles and gave him a passionate thank you kiss. Each man took down one of the lanterns and put their arms around their girlfriends. In pairs they headed into the blackness ahead of them. Soon, they spotted lanterns on the sides of the tunnel walls. Naturally, they lit them as well. "This is really, really great," Kalypso whispered. "It's like we are stepping back into ancient history."

Before long, they found a side room and decided to look around. To their amazement, they found what had to be an underground home of sorts. Dust covered everything and dry rot had taken its toll, but there was a bathroom area, kitchen area, two bedrooms, and a spacious dining room-living room combination. Many household items lay scattered about. "It's like someone lived here and just left and never came back. This would be a perfect hiding place," Kalypso declared. All agreed. As the hour was getting late indicated by their stomachs, they chose only to light several lanterns and then left.

It was dark when they finally made it to the girls' apartment. Not daring to light lanterns giving away the fact that they were here, the men fumbled around and fixed a cold meal. For the next few days, the group kept busy moving their things from the apartment to their new place underground. The looters had not discovered one room on the second floor where additional bags of dried food items were kept. These they took with them as well. The women got much practice carrying things in their yokes; both were determined to pull their share of the workload, as much as possible.

During the daytime, occasionally, they heard very loud explosions in the distance. Although they strained their eyes, they saw none of the ball of flames that were usually associated with such blasts. None knew what these explosions signified, however. Finally, the men decided that they needed to make a run back to their home to fetch their things. They'd need more clothes, since they only had the ones that they wore when they first came to the women's apartment. Both women insisted on going along to help defend the men, after all they still had their powerful legs.

While that was successful, in that they brought back a buggy full of their things, all were aghast at some of the sights. Again, twice they saw sobbing women being led off with ropes around their necks. "As soon as we get settled, we have to start rescuing those women!" Kalypso declared angrily.

It was nine o'clock, the bright sun promised a warm late spring day, perfect weather. "Come on, whore, keep up," Drastus growled at the sobbing young woman doing her best to shuffle along behind him. He gave a threatening tug on the rope around her waist, nearly causing her to lose her balance.

Doreia kept her eyes on the pavement ahead of her, trying not to think of her husband. He was lying there, bleeding from a head wound. Would he be all right? Was he dying? A half hour ago, these thugs had broken into their home, beating him to a pulp while she could only shriek in terror, helpless to stop them. "You come with us and work for us now, whore, and we'll let your pathetic man here live," Drastus had said.

His words burned her soul and heart. She had sobbed and pleadingly agreed. Oh how she had agreed. "Please, don't hurt him anymore. I'll do anything you ask, but don't hurt him anymore." That outburst had caused him to slap her across her face.

Her face still stung. "You don't say nothing unless we tell you that you can talk, got it?" She had nodded, still crying uncontrollably. She watched as he tied a rope around her waist, pulling her ill-fitting dress off her overly large bosom. None of her clothes remotely fit her anymore, not after the devastating plague. Her husband had simply got her dress on as best his could, precariously loose at the top. She had watched as the three men ransacked their meager food supplies, stuffing them into a large sack. She'd offered them all their money. They had money, since they lived in the wealthier district of Kefall after all. That only brought another vicious slap across her cheek. He'd said that you couldn't eat gold. True enough, she and her husband were nearly starving, down to their last few supplies. Now what would her husband have to eat if he still lived? Strange that she was worrying about him as she was the one being abducted into some kind of horrid slavery, but she had promised to go along with them if only they'd stop hurting her and him.

Drastus tied her rope to the wrought iron fence at another elegant home. She watched as the three men smashed their way inside another home. Doreia stood silently, tears dripping down onto her partially exposed bosom, unable to get loose, a slave prisoner. She heard the terrified screams coming from another woman, but she was numb to the woman's cries. These men had long guns and swords. All were helpless against them. She waited alone; no one was on the streets, no one except the many dead bodies. That these days one walked the streets of Kefall in great peril was now very real to her.

Bang! She jumped, a long gun fired somewhere inside the house. Doreia looked up at the stately home and saw another hysterical woman being pulled outside by Drastus, a rope around her waist as well. "You promised you wouldn't hurt them," the woman screamed, her blood mingled with her tears forming long, scarlet streaks down her bronze face.

"You didn't come when we asked, whore. Now you know your place, move it," Drastus snarled.

"I'll do anything you ask; please don't hurt me anymore," she wailed. Drastus stumped along on his toes, as these strange boots at least allowed him to walk. In fact, he could now at least walk a little faster than these pathetic women could. Well, women were now good for nothing but being pleasure toys for men. What else could they do? Nothing, he thought, as he led the next toy to the first one that they'd picked up this fine morning.

None saw the four forms slipping into position near the shrubs on the south side of the entrance marble columns supporting the ornate portico so popular with these more expensive stone homes in Kefall. Kalypso nodded and sprang into action. As Drastus stepped clumsily past her concealed position, she struck. A circle kick from her left leg caught his exposed neck. His long gun dropped to the stone walkway as did the rope. His body twisted to his left, his head angling towards the ground. Kalypso continued her body's rotational follow through, bringing her power kick back around, striking him a second time in the same spot. Bones cracked and Drastus' body was dead before it finally landed in a heap on the ground.

Without a word, Herakles awkwardly stepped out and picked up the rope, "Come with me, ma'am," he whispered softly and sympathetically. He continued leading her towards Doreia, who still stood still, petrified that others were now kidnaping them. The other three, she saw, took up positions on either side of the entrance door, now rather smashed.

Before long, the other two men came stumping out of the home, two large bags over their shoulders, along with a pair of long guns. As they spied their fallen comrade, both struggled to get their long guns un-shouldered, made all the more difficult because so much of their attention was focused on keeping their own balance on the tips of their unusual boots.

Like a pair of graceful swans, Kalypso and Leto launched a pair of circle kicks, one from either side targeting each man's exposed neck. The feet struck precise targets, the fronts of the men's necks, crushing their voice boxes, sending them falling over backwards. As they fell, Linos moved around Leto and using the butt of his long gun, brought it sharply down onto the neck of one man, snapping it, and shortly the other man's neck was crushed.

"Well, that went easier than I expected," Kalypso whispered.

"We'd best head inside. We heard gunfire. Someone may be hurt," Linos suggested.

"We're useless inside. We'll guard the women," Leto replied. Linos slowly headed inside, while the two women shuffled slowly towards the still sobbing women. "Better lend Linos a hand, Herakles," Kalypso ordered. "We'll watch over them for you. Thanks." He nodded and began slowly heading up the sidewalk to join Linos inside.

"Hi, I am Kalypso. This is Leto. We're rescuing you from these bastards. Are you seriously injured? I wish I could help your bleeding nose, but unfortunately, I can't now."

Between sobs, the women told them they were Doreia and Delia. Doreia's husband had been brutally beaten and needed medical attention. Delia's husband was shot and her infant son had been killed, his head smashed by the butt of a gun. "I agreed to do whatever they wanted. Why did they still kill my baby and shoot my husband? Why? I agreed. Why?" Delia wailed.

Kalypso spat on the ground, "With men like that, you can promise to do whatever they want, be their slave, and that will not stop their viciousness and beatings. They only understand force. Well, they will not be doing this to any more families and women. All three are quite dead, may Lucifer take their souls, if there is such a god as Lucifer."

"Please, I must see how my husband is doing," Doreia pleaded, trying to control her sobbing.

"We'll check on him as soon as we can," Leto replied sympathetically. Soon, the two men came slowly out of the front door. From the looks on their faces, Leto and Kalypso knew what the grim situation must be inside. They picked up the men's long guns and sacks of food supplies stolen from the house and slowly hobbled up to the four women. Herakles then untied the ropes from the women.

"There is nothing that we can do for them, Delia," Linos said softly, breaking the news as gently as he could, though he suspected she already guessed that her baby and husband were both dead.

"What am I to do now?" she wailed. "Kill me too, please."

"Oh don't be silly. You are alive and well. You are coming with us to a place that is safe. You are not alone. Many are in the same situation," Kalypso said unsympathetically. "Guys, we need to check on Doreia's husband in the other house. Come on."

The six slowly walked back to the other house and up the walkway. The men left the bags and guns on the porch and followed Doreia inside. A bit later, they returned with their arms around the wounded man. "He'll live; bad beating, though," Linos called out. "Back to headquarters." Kalypso smiled and began leading the way to their secret entrance fairly close to this section of the city.

A half hour, the two women were quite surprised to find themselves inside some underground tunnels. Further, they were introduced to over a dozen other women and a few men, all of whom had been rescued. "Who are you fellows anyway?" Doreia asked.

"Call us Kali II. We're following in the footsteps of the ancient Kali who once protected the Holy Women of Kefall and other women who were being mistreated," Kalypso replied. "These are their old, abandoned tunnels. Sorry about the not so good accommodations, but down here, you are completely safe. Only we know of the existence of these tunnels. Come on. Let's get you all introduced and settled in and get someone to help Doreia and Argos."

Chapter 20 Joining Forces

"We need to take out Memnon's Brothel," Kalypso declared. Finally, they had uncovered just where all the kidnaped women were being taken. "Strike the heart of the beast and the beast dies. Enough of clipping its paws."

"I agree, we must take out Memnon," Leto agreed.

"The how is all that remains to be worked out," Linos added. That, of course, was the tricky part. December's hot sun had come. Already they had their tunnels lined with makeshift beds. Some two dozen men and women, mostly, were now living here in the ancient Kali tunnels, just outside the small living chamber in which the four had settled, weeks before.

"Let us review what we know," Herakles broke the silence. "This Memnon fellow has taken over the Thales mansion. We know that he or his men raided the place and killed that whole family. Aglea, whom we rescued last week, knew them and saw their bodies lying in the yard next door. Our own observations suggest that at least ten men visit each day, presumably paying for the services advertised in the crude sign on the side of the outer gates. Linos and I could go see if we can pay our way inside. We'd get an idea of the layout and how many men Memnon has guarding them."

"Risky, dear, far too risky," Kalypso replied, she didn't want anything to happen to her Herakles, the rare book dealer who had somehow stolen her heart. "What if we went there around midnight or later, when most all would be asleep? Only a few should be on guard duty. If we can take them silently, we could go room to room. Surely, there can't be that many men in there."

"Okay, I think militarily that she is right," Linos spoke up. "We should study their late night operations first, and then decide on the best way to do it." All agreed and later that night, Leto, Kalypso, and Linos snuck out their secret wall door in the basement of the Dance Club's underground stables. Here a large section pivoted enabling an entire carriage to pass into the tunnels. Kalypso pointed out a passage in the rare book that Herakles had given her which told of the Kali using carriages to travel underground across Kefall, appearing at unusual locations above ground. Here was one of the entrance-exit locations.

By now, they were all accustomed to walking on their malformed feet. Linos walked without too much trouble, as long as he took cautious steps. The two women likewise did well as long as they took three-inch shuffling steps, which gave the appearance that they were sort of bouncing along, their ankles not bending much at all. Pitifully slowly, the three headed long the darkened streets; the odor of rotting corpses assaulted their senses until at last their noses went numb to it. Kefall was rotting away, mimicking the dead.

They took up a position across the street from the Thales mansion, a three story marble structure with an enormous entryway, where one lone man sat on a chair, long gun across his lap. An hour later, nothing had changed, except that the guard had dozed off. Kalypso changed their plans. "Come on, let's do it now," she encouraged them. Carefully, the three began their slow walk across the street. Their heels made significant noise and the three slowed down even further, attempting to move as silently as possible. Linos held his gun at the ready. If the guard woke up, he'd shoot and they would flee. At least they had agreed upon that point.

As Linos drew close, he swung the butt of his gun into the man's drooping head, and then pounded him repeatedly until the body slumped to the ground. He made sure the guard was dead before waving the women onwards. A pair of lone lanterns hung from each side of the porch. The double doors were teakwood with a pair of lion heads artistically adorning them. Linos tried the door. It was unlocked. He nodded, turned the knob, and opened it. The three cautiously stepped inside.

They were in an entry hall, coat racks lined one wall; portraits of the late owners, the other. A dim lantern faintly illuminated the hall. "We go room to room. Leave the front doors ajar in case we need to flee," Kalypso whispered her orders.

Two men were sleeping in chairs in the spacious living room. Again, Linos quickly dispatched one with his gun's butt, while Leto and Kalypso took the other out with their tandem circle kicks. They paused to see if the alarm had been sounded. All remained quiet and they resumed going from room to room. The dining room with its huge mahogany table and matching chairs held the remains of supper. The kitchen was piled high with bags of food supplies, stolen from their many victims.

Before the plague, Memnon lived in the slums of Kefall. While he had tried to get a moneylender to back his venture to open a house of pleasure, the man had refused him. That man was Thales and he swore to get even one day. When the plague struck and he learned that the Emperor was dead, his small band began looting. Pickings were slim to none there in the slums and he led his band into the wealthier part of Kefall. They had to crawl around the many dead men and women in the streets, but came at last to Thales mansion. Here, Memnon grinned. Five minutes later, it was all over; the bastard who refused to back his plans and his homely wife were dead and being dragged into the next yard.

While he and his crew were dining on the excellent food in the Thales mansion, he decided this was now his new house of pleasure. "Thales has provided us with his home. We should thank him. Oh, he is not able to hear us anymore. Oh well. Now then, boys, we need whores to populate our pleasure palace. No ugly ones, mind you. No old maids." Thus, he began to raid nearby homes, killing the men and bringing the helpless women back to his new place.

For the last few weeks, several of his bands that he'd sent out to fetch more women turned up dead. Hence, he began to station a guard outside and two more just inside the entrance hall. Until this night, all had been quiet. Business was beginning to pick up. The entrance fee was a bag of food, for food was now more precious than mere gold or jewels. Already, he'd found a nice stash of those here in the mansion.

He took the master bedroom on the first floor as his own and as his office. What had once been the children's quarters now housed ten of his band. All the women were kept in the many bedrooms on the second and third floors. Why? He loved to see the johns as they struggled up and down the stairs, eager to get their sensual pleasures. Somehow, the sight of them made him feel superior to all them! Even better, Memnon loved to see the naked women struggling to go up and down the stairs to be fed. What a sight! His dreams were filled with the many images of them, so helpless, so utterly dependent upon himself, their beneficent benefactor, and god. Yes, I am a god to these women, he thought often.

As the trio entered the hallway, they spotted a cache of long guns and a keg of powder. They took note of it and moved to the first of the two doors. Carefully, Linos turned the knob and peered inside. He saw ten men asleep on makeshift beds. Even more stealthily, he closed the door and put up ten fingers. Then, he had an idea. No way could they possibly handle ten men at once, but there was that powder keg. He moved it and placed it in front of the door.

They moved on to the next bedroom door. Linos turned the knob and opened the door, the faint light of a lantern peered out along with the sounds of crashing cans. Memnon had not lived forty years in the dog eat dog slums by being careless. He knew that he was only truly vulnerable while he was sleeping. For years, he always slept with a lantern on and he always dutifully set his trap on his door. A string was tied to a pile of cans and brass bowls. If anyone attempted to open his door, the string tipped them over, sending the lot crashing onto the floor, awakening him. "Guards! Intruders!" Memnon yelled as loudly as he could, throwing back his light covers.

"Damn!" Linos exclaimed, as he heard the ten men arising in the room they just passed. He made a split decision. "Take him. I'll take the others." He backed and headed down the hall to the other bedroom, while Kalypso and Leto shuffled into the room as quickly as they could, sizing up the situation as they moved. Memnon also glanced over at his long gun. He'd unfortunately left it leaning against his chair along with his boots. Without them, he could not stand. He dropped out of bed onto his knees, estimating whether he could reach his gun before the two bobbing, shuffling women.

Then, he realized they were helpless, pathetic women, though he had never seen these two before, and he changed tactics, drawing his sword from its scabbard slung over the bedpost. He calculated that his men could handle that one man, and he would take care of these two women, perhaps not harming them. They'd be a nice addition to his ever-growing collection upstairs. The two women continued moving towards him, and he crawled into a good position to take them on.

Linos had no choice. As the door opened before his eyes, he knew that he'd be facing ten of them. "Damn!" he said again, aimed his long gun and fired just as the first two men came out of the opened door. His bullet went through the door and into the powder keg. Boom! A massive explosion knocked him backwards off his feet, the door deflecting the intense flames.

Memnon rocked from the violence of the blast, and the two women wobbled crazily trying to stay on their feet. Then he realized that his men might not be coming and drew back to hack into these women's legs. Leto faked a kick, drawing a sweeping slice from Memnon's sword. As it flew past their position, Kalypso timed it perfectly. Her circle kick arced over the deadly blade and landed solidly on Memnon's neck, snapping it. His eyes in his now cockeyed head looked at her in shock and surprise, as his body slowly slumped to the floor. For good measure, Leto stomped on his neck, ensuring this evil man would never rise again. Then, both called out to Linos.

Deadened by the explosion, he couldn't hear a thing and struggled to get to his feet. Slowly, he moved toward the splintered door, glancing in at the two women, who had very worried looks on their faces, apparently saying something to him. "Can't hear," he yelled. They were in luck, the explosion had not started a fire, but smoldering splinters covered the floor and the opposite wall was blackened. He peered into the bedroom and saw in the dim light from distant lanterns bodies lying on the floor, none moved. The explosion had blown out the single faint lantern in their room. "All safe, I think," he yelled, as the two joined him.

"Up the stairs," Kalypso yelled to him, but he heard her not, throwing his hands up trying to signal her that he couldn't hear. She nodded and headed for the stairs with Leto following. He followed behind them. The stairs were very dimly illuminated making climbing them tricky for the two women. At least Linos had his arms to hang on to the teakwood railing of the stately mansion.

After what seemed an eternity, the two women reached the landing, where two lanterns provided just enough light for them to make out the rooms. Unfortunately, the doorknobs stopped both women. Linos caught up to them, realized their predicament, and began opening the doors, one after the other, throwing caution to the wind. After all, if there were more of his men around, the explosion would bring them all crawling. Kalypso shuffled inside and found a young woman sitting up in her bed, her eyes showed renewed fright. The explosion had wakened her.

"We're here to rescue you and get you to safety. Get up and get your shoes on so you can walk," Kalypso called out. The woman nodded. As she got up from the satin sheets of the high quality bed, Kalypso saw that the poor woman was entirely naked. "Do you have any clothes in here?" she added.

The woman shook her head. "They said that they burned them." Damn, thought Kalypso. She and Leto continued going from room to room, while Linos continued to move methodically down the hall opening the doors.

"See if you can find any of their dresses," Kalypso called out to Linos who was now near the end of the hall. As he turned to look at her, he saw the first rescued woman shuffling fearfully out of her room. Even though he'd not heard what she said, he knew what she must have asked and nodded. He headed on up the stairs to the third floor.

Leto called out, "Kalypso, why don't you start leading them down the stairs and I'll keep rousing them. If Linos or I find any dresses, I'll give a yell." Kalypso nodded and moved back down the hall, as more and more frightened women stepped slowly and carefully out of their bedrooms.

"This way, ladies," she called out and headed for the stairs. Going down was even more precarious than going up, she soon discovered.

The woman right behind her whispered, "Lean on the wall, it helps." She took her advice; still it was one very slow step at a time. Kalypso felt very vulnerable, exposed on the stairs. What if a guard entered now? She could do nothing. I have to get down, she thought, and quickly.

Twenty minutes later, his hearing partially restored, Linos came down the stairs, eyeing the long line of women. "That is the last of them. Give me a minute to reload my long gun, Kalypso. No clothes anywhere. It is warm out and quite dark." From the front where she was keeping an eye on the outside, she nodded.

She guessed that these women had suffered so much humiliation already that walking the streets at night naked would not likely bother them as it would normally. "Okay, follow me, ladies. We have a ways to walk to get to safety. Once there, we will get you cleaned up and into some clothes. Our place is secret and very safe. Come on, single file please." Leto joined her and the two took the lead, their eyes looking in all directions. Other than the stars overhead, they saw nothing, but heard a couple of dogs barking in the distance as well as the constant shuffling noise of so many heels on the pavement. They had rescued thirty women, the youngest was barely fourteen, and the oldest was thirty.

For these women, the hour's walk seemed like an eternity and their legs, so unused to walking such distances with so many tiny steps, began to give out as they approached their secret entrance in the underground parking lot. "Just a bit further," Leto called out. More than one woman was now stumbling, barely able to keep from falling.

At last, they entered the tunnel. "Everyone, we're got thirty women in dire need here, little help please," Kalypso called out, as the others began waking.

"Oh dear me," exclaimed an embarrassed Herakles, as he saw so many naked women bobbing into the tunnel. "Sheets, we need sheets at once." Several of the men rose and headed to fetch some.

Later, with the women washed and crudely dressed in whatever could be found, Leto sipped a cup of tea. "Well, Kalypso, we did it, put that bastard Memnon out of business."

"Yes, but I wonder how many other Memnon's are out there?" she replied.

With so many more to feed, the next day, the two men headed back to the mansion to grab anything useful, especially the guns and food. They took their buggy and made ten trips. Still, they had no proper clothing and the two decided to go further afield and see what all they could find.

They were gone so long that Kalypso and Leto began to worry. Had something terrible happened to them? They fretted that they had not insisted on going with them. Still they were needed here to deal with the new arrivals. Thankfully, the few men, who were here with their wives and daughters, lent their hands, constantly doing whatever was needed, especially the cooking. The rescued women had been given only the barest amount of food to keep them alive and were ravenous. Once they were well fed, they began to relax for the first time. Many cried, releasing long suppressed grief. Most told Kalypso that their husbands or fathers had been beaten and killed by Memnon's men. She did not ask them about what they were forced to do in their bedrooms. Rightly so, the trauma was too raw, too real.

It was dark when Kalypso heard the grating of the secret stone door opening. In came their buggy, followed by a wagon! "Sorry we are so late," Linos called out.

"We have dresses for the women," Herakles added proudly. He's spent quite a lot of time finding them. "We went down as far as the train station. We've brought back quite a lot of things. I stole their LD radio thing. Maybe we can call for some help or at least find out some news."

"We got more food and guns and lanterns and oil too," Linos added. "Plus, we've got some news. It seems that we are not the only ones setting things right around Kefall. Look at this, I took one of the two posted near the train station." He read the notice, "Report crimes against women to the Righteous Vigilantes. Post details here. See, they must be behind all those random explosions that we keep hearing now and then. I wonder who they are and where they are located?"

The next morning, the four read the instruction manual that came with the LD radio. While Linos and Herakles held out the antenna as per the instructions, Leto peddled the generator and Kalypso watched the dials. When the needle got into the green zone, she pressed the Talk button. "Hello. Is anyone there? We need help. Is anyone out there?" She repeated it twice, before they heard some static noise and a man's voice speaking awful Demokritos.

"Yes, I hear you. Try switching to Band 5." He repeated this twice more and Kalypso did as the voice asked. She again said her opening words, unsure what else to say.

"Ah, better. Where are you? I am in Velona, Sea Princes," the voice said, repeating the words twice. With difficulty, the four understood him.

"We are in Kefall, Demokritos. Help us please," Kalypso replied.

"Please wait a minute while I get someone who can speak your language better than I," the voice replied. She said okay and the four waited anxiously. Velona — that was far north, Kalypso knew. But how far? She had no idea.

"Hello, this is Bethany Bartiana Angela here in Velona. Hi. Who are you and what is your situation? Are you in Kefall?"

"Yes, yes we are. We've lost our arms; our feet are crippled. Our men can barely walk. The Emperor is dead; dead bodies are everywhere. Chaos is everywhere, food is scarce, and we are trying to rescue women who are being victimized by bastards. Oh, I am Kalypso Dias, with me are Leto Gia and our boyfriends, Linos Andros, and Herakles Laos. We need help," Kalypso replied.

"Okay. First, the plague has struck worldwide, Kalypso. All women on Tarra are as you are. All men have their feet pointed straight down and can only walk with those special boots. We already know that your Emperor and Empress are dead. So are a number of the kings and queens. I have sent some help to the new monarchs of Arolas. I can try to get some help to you. Just where are you located? Are you safe where you are at? How many are you, four?"

"No, we've rescued over forty men and women, mostly. We are very safe, actually. We found the old Kali Assassin's underground tunnels and are hiding in here, near the entrance. This place is huge."

"Wow. I know about them. Well done, Kalypso. That should be a terrific place to hide out. Have you found the main underground houses yet? There should be a lot of space in them."

"No, we are living in the entrance tunnel and one small side chamber."

"Hey, I have an idea. Hold on a minute while I try to contact someone who may be able to offer you some guidance. Hang on a minute. I need to use a different setting on the LD radio. I'll be right back."

After what seemed like eternity, Kalypso heard my voice once more. "Hi, Bethany here. I am sending along some of my hint books to you so you and the other women can figure out how to do things for yourselves. Also, on the line with us is Monarch Callisto Tropos of Arolas. She knows all about those ancient Kali tunnels. Callisto, this is Kalypso of Kefall."

"Hi, Callisto here. Are you really in those old tunnels? I knew them well," Callisto asked.

Her voice sounded very young. "But how could you? Are you related to King Tropos of Naxos?" she asked.

"My dad, our dad, Ana's and mine. Our parents are now dead. We've taken over control of Arolas, well at least a small part of it. To answer your other question, all I can say is that we are spiritual beings not bodies. I have lived in Kefall before and was a Kali Assassin leader myself, so I know every inch of those old tunnels. Now tell me, what is the number on the wall just outside that side chamber that you are in?" Callisto asked.

"Really? A Kali Assassin? But the book says that they were Holy Women of the Eighth Degree — armless as we are."

"Yes, I was. That didn't stop me or the rest of us. Bethany says that you have rescued a number of others, so I take it that lacking arms is not stopping you either," Callisto replied with a grin.

Kalypso smiled, "No it hasn't, just made it so terribly difficult. Leto and I were martial artists."

"*Are* martial artists. You still *are*," Callisto replied.

"Oh, someone says the number on the wall is twenty-two. What does that mean?" Kalypso answered.

"Let me think a second. It's been over a hundred years since I was down there. There used to be twenty-five side chambers with ten of them being the size of large mansions. How many still exist I don't know. Each has a number. The smallest ones are over on the far western edge of Kefall, while the highest numbers are on the far east. The odd ones lie to the north of the center of the city; the evens, to the south. The ten that you want are numbered seven to seventeen. Now listen carefully. Inside the side chamber there ought to be a small indentation on the wall about three feet high, so we can reach it with our feet easily. Press it. You should see a panel slide back revealing a map of the entire tunnel complex with the chambers identified. There are two main underground roads that a carriage can travel. One goes east-west, one goes north-south. There is even an underground stable where you can keep ten horses and two carriages. I have to run now, a battle is brewing. I'll call you on this band say tomorrow around this time, is that okay?"

"Sure! Thanks. We'll be here. We'll see if we can find that map. Bye. Did you hear what she said?" Kalypso said excitedly. That a real Kali had talked to her was beyond her wildest dreams. Yet, how could this Callisto be a Kali? They had been dead centuries ago.

"Well, it makes sense. All the secret panels have been within easy foot reach," Leto suggested. "Come on; let's see if there is such a map. If so, that will be an incredible help."

"Some say that we are immortal beings that live for a time in these bodies," Herakles explained as the four headed to search for the secret panel. "Yet, what intrigues me most is that this Callisto Tropos seems to remember her previous lifetime as a Kali Assassin. I wonder who I was if I lived before?"

"Maybe a great scholar," Kalypso suggested. "It would fit you perfectly."

Her boyfriend smiled, "Indeed, it might at that, but then I wonder who you may have been? Some great fighter perhaps?" She smiled, that too would make sense.

"Hey, where did these books come from? They were not here when we got up?" Kalypso said startled to find a large stack of Bethany's Hints stacked in their living room. The four stopped to examine them and then resumed their search for the secret panel. Leto was the first to find it. She reasoned that it was activated by raising her foot and pressing it to the stone block, raising it to a leisurely comfortable height. A four foot high, twelve foot long panel that looked like stone slid down, revealing a detailed map painted onto the recessed stone wall.

"Well, I'll be! Callisto was right. She must have been who she says!" Kalypso declared.

"Amazing, most amazing my love. This is a treasure of a find. Look at all these passages and there are the living chambers," Herakles said, even more excited than she was.

Using the buggy, the four began their explorations, lighting the many lanterns along the walls as they went. At chamber seventeen, they found a huge side set of rooms, enough to house fifty people, as long as several slept per room. A kitchen was there, along with antique pots, pans, and utensils. The pantry's contents had long ago turned to dust, but the kegs of oil were still usable as well as many bags of charcoal. The next two days were spent moving their large group down to this safe house. However, when they returned to the others with the news of their discovery, they found the women had been reading the hints book and were eager to try to learn how to do some things for themselves.

While they began the mass movement down the nearly one mile of tunnel using the wagon, Linos and Herakles headed outside to see if they could find more of the yokes that the women said that they must have if they were to be of much use. Ten trips later, they had raided a number of now vacant homes, confiscating all manner of abandoned items of the types that had magically appeared in Kalypso and Leto's apartment that second day.

Callisto did return their calls, checking in with them daily for a time and then every other day, offering suggestions as they came to her. In a way, she rather wished that she was back there helping out, but she had her own problems to handle in Arolas now.

At the end of the year, when their feet mysteriously returned to normal, all the women cheered as well as the men. Now the men were free of the plague's effects, but they also realized that the women, while they could now walk with ease and do more things more readily, were still highly dependent upon themselves.

Soon, they discovered that above ground life was slowly returning. Here and there, markets reopened, now almost exclusively run by the men. Still, they occasionally heard a powerful blast and the four decided to see if they could find out more about these Righteous Vigilantes.

Daily, the four headed to the outer world in search of clues. Kalypso reasoned, "Look, all around us now, men are doing everything, controlling everything, but not in a good way. If these people are really righting wrongs, how long can they survive when all around us up here are mean, vicious, wicked men? Gangs are everywhere, and we can barely travel about without dealing with them. Eventually, they are going to be in trouble. We must find a way to find them."

Herakles put his mind to the task. Over several days, he noted which homes or shops showed signs of a blast or explosion and plotted them. "Look, they are all within a mile radius of the Imperial Palace and on the eastern side at that. Somewhere within that circle our vigilantes must reside. That is where we should focus our search." Later he got the idea to once a day check to see if anyone had posted another plea for revenge or help at the ten locations where the posters had been nailed up.

On January 10, 824, Herakles got a break. As he was heading to check on one of the post sites, he saw an ill dressed man looking over his shoulders walking up to the spot. He tacked a notice up and then hastily departed. "Linos, follow that man. I don't like the looks of him. I will see what he posted."

A half hour later, Linos returned. "You were right. I think he is in the employ of one of the local thug leaders. Why?"

"Look for yourself," he pointed to the message. "They are laying a trap for the Righteous Vigilantes. We must make haste."

On their way back home, the two drove by the indicated address, but didn't stop. That might draw attention to themselves. "I know that house, Linos. One of the late Emperor's advisors lives there. He's in his late fifties I think, but I've forgotten his name." They saw a sign tacked to the gate that led up the short walk to the large home. It read: Orphans Welcomed Here. Both were certain that this was a trap. Linos purposely drove around the block a second time, taking note of the layout, trying to make a lasting memory of the buildings.

Once safely in Chamber Seventeen, the two outlined what they had learned and Linos drew up a sketch of that block. "If it is an ambush, I would place my men here. There is plenty of bushes to use for cover," Linos drew on his military experiences once again.

"I wish we knew how they blow up the buildings," Kalypso added. "They must walk up and plant some kind of bomb I suppose."

"We should take the wagon with us in case we need to make a fast getaway," Leto suggested.

"They always seem to strike late at night. How are we going to find them in time?" Herakles asked.

His arm around Pandora, Midas opened the door to their small apartment. They'd just returned from a long exploratory probe. Pan said, "Hi Mel, Kastor. Well, the Imperial Palace is still utterly vacant. Not a soul around there, so we still don't have our old jobs back." She and Melantha used to be cooks at the palace, before the plague, that is.

"No big deal, we can't cook anymore anyway," Melantha growled. "Here, look at this. We have another bastard at work, not ten blocks from here." Kastor held up the notice for the two to read. "Real fine bastard," she grit her teeth. "Kidnaps little girls, rapes them brutally, and then disposes of their bodies. A dozen girls already dead! Uses orphans as a cover for his wicked lust. Well, we'll have to put a stop to this bastard!"

"I don't get it," Midas shook his head. "Why little girls — boys too for that matter? What twisted minds get off on children? Why do they do that — to children? I can rather understand adults and our desires, but children? I agree, put this fellow out of our world. Midnight as usual?" Mel nodded and headed off to her small workshop to continue her preparations. Before the plague, she could have prepared her device and chemicals in just a few minutes, now it seemed like it took forever.

Around eleven, Kastor packed the launching gear in a small pack and carefully placed the tiny glass vial into a well-padded bag, slipping it over Melantha's neck. She trusted only herself to carry this powerful liquid explosive. She had invented it and knew its properties. One slight jar and boom. Double checking that they had everything, the four crept out of their apartment. Seeing no one around, they set off briskly towards the bastard's home. Mel and Kastor had already cased the place that afternoon, and she had picked out a perfect launching spot just across the street between two homes. There they could find cover behind shrubs to setup the launcher in secret.

As midnight approached, the four walked innocently down the block, occasionally eyeing the home of this evil bastard. They saw nothing out of the ordinary, though since the moon had set, the stars provided the only illumination, faint at best, but enough for Melantha to work her magic. On down the block a hundred feet, a wagon sat beside the road. They took notice of that, but apparently, it was only a man and woman setting up their open-air market for the morning. Well, Mel thought, they will sure have something to talk about in the morning.

They drew opposite of the victim's home and made a last check before sharply turning onto the lawn between the two stately homes. Now they moved quickly and rapidly got behind the cover of the bushes. Kastor took off his pack and began setting up the launch pad. Midas and Pandora kept watch.

"That must be them," whispered Kalypso to Herakles. "Get ready." Linos, who was pretending to unload the wagon, moved to her side while Leto crouched behind the wagon, watching the bushes across the street. Herakles began loading their things back onto the wagon and climbed up to the driver's seat.

Linos put his arm around Kalypso and the two strolled down the street to where they'd seen the four ducking into the shadows of the bushes between the two homes. Pretending to be lovers out for a stroll, Kalypso whispered to the unseen four, "If you are the Righteous Vigilantes, this is a trap. You have been setup. There is a bunch of thugs waiting in the shrubs next to the house. The man who lives there is innocent. We know him. Quickly, pretend you are lovers out for a stroll and come with us. We have to get you out of here!"

Kastor panicked. "What do we do? We'd best do as she says, Mel." He hastily stuffed everything back into his pack. All four were very nervous now and kept glancing over to the shrubs by the adjacent house across the street.

"Pretend you are kissing," Kalypso whispered and she stopped and planted a kiss on Linos, who flushed, hoping that Leto would not mind this. The four were chefs and moneychangers, not warriors. Faced with a sudden reversal, whether they believed this woman and a potential surprise attack from the very type of men they feared and against whom they sought vengeance, the four became frightened. Fear seeped into their minds, yet they attempted to put on a show for the unseen thugs. Mel and Pan wanted to run, to flee, and to escape. Kastor's steadying arm felt Mel's nervous shaking. Mel felt Kastor's arm trembling as well.

Just a little closer, thought Kalypso, as the four came walking towards her and Linos. It looked presentable; three young couples out for a stroll and a little private make-out session. "Oh, you fellows are out for a stroll too," she called out rather loudly, hoping the unseen thugs would overhear her. "Come help us with the market supplies, will you?" she added as an afterthought.

The four frightened faces confronted Kalypso and Linos as the six joined some fifty feet from the wagon. Kalypso turned to head towards the wagon, the rest followed her. Leto was already in the wagon bed, apparently working some supplies. However, she was actually keeping a sharp watch on the bushes just beyond the target home.

Ten more feet, thought Kalypso, now holding her breath. Leto rose and yelled, "Robbers! Look out, behind you! Robbers!"

The six glanced behind them and saw two men stepping out from the bushes. They carried long guns and were moving in their direction. "Get in the wagon bed fast!" Kalypso yelled. Am I ever useless like this, she thought to herself. Linos was being forced to help her into the wagon instead of getting his long gun ready. As she hopped into the bed, Linos grabbed his long gun, allowing the two men to help the other two women aboard.

Linos yelled, "Lie down, you will make a smaller target." Now a third man joined the two and they started to run towards them. Linos glanced at the others and made his decision. Blam! He fired off a shot and saw one of the approaching men drop to the street. "Get us out of here!" he yelled to Herakles and dove into the bed himself, just as Herakles kicked the horses into action. Bang. Bang. Two shots whizzed past him, striking wood somewhere behind him. The wagon careened to the right, and Linos rolled over into Kalypso. Herakles had made a sharp turn down the next street and the running pair was lost from sight. He made another turn to the left at the next corner and then a right a block later. At last, he headed back towards the safety of their underground tunnels, certain that he'd lost the men on foot. As he pulled into the underground parking stables by the Dance Club, Leto hopped off and used her foot to open the door and Herakles drove the wagon inside and halted.

Leto joined them just as the stone door shut. "We can get up now, it's safe," Linos said and the pile began climbing off the wagon bed.

"Where are we? Who are you? How did you know that it was a trap?" asked Melantha, still carefully looking after the vial of liquid in her pouch. Her voice cracked slightly and her legs felt like butter. She wanted to sit down, but dare not.

"Hi, I am Kalypso, my good friend, Leto, our boyfriends, Herakles and Linos. You can all us the Kali II. We are safe inside the ancient Kali Assassin's underground tunnels. Herakles spotted the man posting that message to the Righteous Vigilantes and Linos followed him and got wise to what they were planning. Evidently, you have made some enemies and they were trying to set you up."

"You — you are assassins?" Melantha asked.

"Sort of, we are trying to stop vicious crimes against women mostly," Kalypso replied.

"Well, they killed our folks and brother," Melantha explained, fighting back a sudden surge of grief. Even talking about it brought the pain and loss of their deaths back to her. Pan, Pandora, and I are sisters. Our boyfriends, Kastor and Midas Cepheus — evil men killed their folks too. No one is doing anything to stop these wicked murders of innocent people, so we did. We killed the men who killed our parents and their's too, plus a bunch more of these animals. So many innocent people have been brutalized, tortured, and murdered by these lawless gangs that we just had to do something to help."

"Looks like you stopped us from making a horrible mistake," Kastor broke in. "We just assumed that the people posting their desperate pleas for justice were being honest. If you had not stopped us, we would have become murderers too, just like those we so despise. We owe you more than our lives. Mel, we almost really screwed up there," he said softly to her.

"I'm glad that we got to you in time," Kalypso replied. "We've been very careful to only attack those who are in the process of committing more crimes. I think that we need to find a way to investigate the claims that other victims might have, Herakles, so that we don't make the same mistake that they almost did."

The group exchanged stories for quite some time and Kalypso learned that Melantha was indeed an inventor of new chemical compounds and formulas and that she had invented a powerful new type of explosive. She showed them the tiny vial that she still had with her, explaining that it was more than enough nearly to level that mansion they had intended to attack when Kalypso and her group had stopped them. Further, Kastor displayed the fancy launching pad that they used to fire a projectile to the target. The liquid was in the head of the tube, exploding when it struck the target.

Later, the news of this discovery and delivery means was relayed to Callisto and then to me in Velona. When I told Stefano about it, he insisted that somehow we just had to get a hold of this formula and delivery system. "We need her, this Melantha Tasa chemist. Figure out a way to get to her, Bethany," he ordered. I grinned, knowing that there were all sorts of uses for her incredibly bright mind. Removal of tree stumps from a new crop field was one that came to my mind.

With a three-way LD radio call, I gave them some suggestions while Callisto added hers. She promised to find a way to get to them once she had Arolas under control. Meantime, the four were added to the growing Kali II group. Melantha and Pandora moved all their possessions to one of the underground chambers. Via Midas, I made sure that she had sufficient funds to continue her experiments. He, like several other men, began venturing above ground, reopening his money changing shop.

Realistically, during the first six months of 824, about the only businesses that resumed substantial operations were those involved in the food supply industry and financial transactions. That is, the farmer's markets, gain storage, food preparations, butchers, for example, began to reappear throughout Kefall, along with the Banca del Dio's and the moneychangers. Very little else reopened. Everyone was too afraid to do much of anything beyond their homes, except attempt to keep food coming in somehow, some way. With gangs controlling the streets, few women at all ever ventured out on their own, and even men feared to be on the streets.

Quickly, the gangs and thugs realized that if they pressured or robbed the markets, those men would simply take their produce elsewhere. Hence, the few who resumed their businesses found themselves in the unique position of being guarded and watched over by the very same men who were causing all the chaos in Kefall. This once great Imperial City was now in limbo, barely doing only those actions that would keep its population alive. All were just waiting, waiting for some unknown action that would somehow make their world livable once more. For six months, it did not come.

Kalypso and Leto continued their rescue mission, however. Using information gleaned from their boyfriends and the few other men who were with them, they continued their carefully planned raids. During the first six months of the new year, more and more people joined their underground group. As always, two-thirds of the new arrivals were women, but a few were now also children.

By May 824, all around Kefall rumors flew. The Kali Assassins were back with a vengeance! Some of the pubs had dared to reopen and whispered voices there often discussed this seemingly dark side of Kefall life. I say dark side, but that was the opinion of those who committed and continued to commit acts of lawlessness and crimes against women in particular. Many others huddled in their homes thought differently. Somewhere out there in the huge Imperial City, the Kali were righting wrongs, giving them a faint echo of hope for the future.

Chapter 21 Ancient History

June 824 became baby month around 42 Hampton Way, a novel experience for us women — that is having babies and caring for them with our bodies as they were now. Lucianna and Valerio had their son, Durante Tito on June 2. Lisa and Sergio had theirs on June 7, Bartolo Sandro. Eve and Giovanni had Adona Marta on June 15, while Marco and I welcomed Bianca Sofia into this world on June 21.

Lucianna and Giovanni were the most prepared of us all; naturally, they were inventors. Me, I was just glad no longer to have to go to the bathroom every five minutes. Okay, I exaggerate, every thirty minutes. She invented a fancy baby pouch that we could easily slip our babies into and then slip over our heads to carry them around with us, cradled against our fronts. These worked extremely well, as we all soon discovered. Giovanni worked out a diaper-washing table affair, where we could both change diapers and wash them with relative ease. All the items that we needed were right there at our toe-tips, in one of the many compartments. He even had a pair of washbasins attached to it. Honestly, though, our jobs as mothers were fraught with challenges that we'd never faced before.

We were not alone; the baby boom had struck not only the Sea Princes, but many of the Greenway kingdoms as well. The roles of husband and wife continued their evolution. Marco pointed out, "You know, in the old days, a man and a woman could lead independent lives of each other. An unmarried woman could do well on her own, assuming that she had a means of earning a living. Today, the relationships between men and women have already been undergoing a huge change. There are some things that women either cannot do by themselves or find it exceedingly difficult to do or very time consuming, and they rely upon men to do these things. Husbands, fathers, brothers, all are finding that they must help the women in their lives. If humans are going to survive, men absolutely must assume more responsibility for the women in their society and lives. In a way, this is a good thing, I think."

"Gee, are you suggesting that you will be changing Bianca's diapers for me now?" I teased him. Our whole group was sitting in our living room chatting and doting over our newborns. Lisa, Lucianna, Eve, Sofia, and Marta all chuckled.

Marco grinned and teased me, "I promise to clean the really messy ones, dear." We laughed again. Indeed, we women did find such help very much appreciated. Further, all four of us were finding it difficult to deal with nursing. Trying to get our babies situated and ourselves in the right position so they could nurse was most challenging. We just couldn't pick them up and cradle them beside our huge breasts — no arms. The easiest method we soon discovered was to get our babies on a bed and then carefully get our bodies lying down beside them. Such required a whole lot of wiggling to get our babies feeding. We all soon began to appreciate the helpful hands of our husbands with this frequent need.

I had reread that letter from Fianna and Ines that had been delivered over six months ago. The mystery of the standing stones had been in the back of my mind of late and I had dug the letter out this morning and re-examined it. There was definitely a mystery here to be solved. I had been putting it off until we all had our babies and now we had. Funny how you can postulate something for the future, then forget about it, and then suddenly remember it at the designated point in the future. Well, that's what had happened.

I smiled as I thought of that group of women and girls who had somehow fled the chaos on Cymry to get that message to me. I had soon discovered that Brina and Kaie were lovers. Once they had learned from us and had begun to start doing things for themselves, I had made arrangements for their whole group to move in with Tatiana and Wanda, just three blocks down the street. Brina and Kaie were elated to find that they were not alone in their sexual preferences, and the two became very close friends with Tatiana and Wanda. Keelin and her five year old daughter Shela and Rona d'Aine and her five year old daughter Tam had much in common, while Zena was more than pleased to help her sister and niece. Having the seven new women as guests did wonders for Tatiana and Wanda, expanding their zone of responsibility. (I am always big on doing that, whenever I can.)

The Standing Stones were near the city of Brea, Cymry or West Reach, where King Lachlan Laird used to rule, and that town would be our destination. Brea lay in the Ruadan Highlands, cradled beside the Ath Mountains, which separated the Highlands from the rolling grasslands of Tewdwr. Over the centuries that I had been on Tarra, I had discovered many such ancient sites of Standing Stones, all long abandoned, all mysterious, all forgotten by humans who lived nearby. I once wondered who had built them. I still had never found the slightest clue. That they were located at power points of Tarra I had discovered. Our Druwid spells were greatly enhanced when cast there.

I also remembered seeing the vast energy beams radiating up and outward from these stones, like a roman candle firecracker of Tashien. The stones, immense and mysterious, captivated my attention this evening. I recalled where Lia Ines had said that while wandering among the stones, she had found one stone, which seemed to draw her to it. There appeared to be a sort of human form molded into it, her kind of form, like that of an armless woman. She walked into the hollow spot, seeing if her body matched the shape. The ground opened up and she fell far into the ground, though landing as if she had not even taken a step. This intrigued me. Everything pointed to yet a fourth alien group here on Tarra, perhaps a group that was far more ancient than the mantis, Greys, and plasticine Dolls.

I recalled her description of being in an underground chamber. More important was the voice that spoke to them. I pondered the meaning of the words: "Dalny? My long lost Dalny? Have you returned to me, my love?" Lia Ines related that she felt a mind touching hers and along with it an intense sorrow and the idea: "No, you are not my Dalny. Yet you so resemble her. Go now and I will look after you, you who are the image my long lost Dalny."

What did the being mean by this? Who was Dalny? I had promised myself to go check this out after I had Bianca. Well, that was now. True, she was only days old now, but how long could I delay the trip? Somehow, I felt that I dared not let this slide for a couple of years until Bianca was much older. I couldn't say why I felt this, only that I did.

Still, from what little we knew, Cymry was in complete chaos as were so many other lands since the plague. Yet they had now had nearly a year to adapt to the results. Perhaps things were improving on the island. On the chance that they had not, getting to Brea via Layamon to the south or through Moyrath to the east would be fraught with peril, far too much countryside to traverse with way too many towns. Tewdwr looked more and more inviting. Besides, there was a narrow path through the Ath that would take one right to Brea. The Standing Stones were a few miles north of there.

The last time I was in Tewdwr the land was very sparsely populated. That was my Ket Bethany lifetime. Once one traveled a few dozen miles inland, most of the land was simply rolling hills. This seemed our best course to travel, minimizing contact with towns and villages. Still with babies along who needed so much attention, travel would be challenging enough without inns along the way. We would need to bring along enough food to get us there and back. Who knows whether we would be able to purchase anything on the trip? Still going this way would only be two hundred miles or so, one way, shorter than any other route, though perhaps not as fast, because we would not have the benefit of paved roads all the way to Brea. Roads would go through towns and villages, these I had to avoid, unless I brought an army with me.

"Well, Marco, we ought to be planning a trip to check out the mystery of the Standing Stones north of Brea, Cymry. I've put that one off long enough, don't you think?" I finally said.

"I was wondering when you would remember it. When do we go?" he said with a wry smile.

"Hey, count me in," Eve, who had been watching me for a bit, quickly chimed in.

"You need an engineer along too," Giovanni added, supporting his wife.

I figured Valerio would be dying to come along, but he would do whatever Lucianna desired. No way would he leave her alone with their newborn son, just so he could go off on an adventure, no matter how badly he wanted to see some action. "We're in too," Lucianna quickly spoke up. One glance at Valerio and she just had to come along for his sake.

"Look, I believe that you may well need the services of a master detective, Bethany. Lisa and I will be tagging along with you on this trip as well," Sergio added, after glancing at Lisa, who nodded her approval as well.

Sergio then continued, "Besides, Bethany, I have been working on a plan to get us there and back safely and quickly. Back burner, so to speak, but I've been at it for months now. We need to avoid population centers this trip. Let me show you what I've worked out." He raced to his room and returned with some drawings and maps.

"We take a caravel to this point here," he pointed to an isolated stretch of Tewdwr coastline. "We take along a motor-wagon with two petrol barrels, which should be more than ample to get us there and back again. Now if you look carefully, there is another way through the Ath to the Highlands right here, some twenty miles north of the Standing Stones. I believe that we can drive the motor-wagon all the way through that pass. Actually, this route might well be the shortest one to get there."

"Now I figure that driving across the countryside we probably won't make more than about ten miles an hour. Still, that means only two days driving time to get there. Add in a day of sailing and a day to get the motor-wagon unloaded and onto the land and our things loaded, and we have four days total — one way, eight round trip. Say, we spend two days there; it's only ten days that we would be gone. Like my plan?" he said proudly.

I laughed, "Sergio! How long have you been planning this anyway? I only remembered that I needed to go there this morning!"

He gave a sheepish grin, "Well, actually, ever since we got that ancient letter from Fianna and Lia Ines. I think that this find could be extremely important, though just how I have no idea, just a feeling."

I had been estimating a month or two by horse-drawn wagons and such. Ten days sounded vastly better. Sergio showed us his sketch for a landing raft to be used to ferry the motor-wagon ashore, assuming that the caravel could not actually dock.

"So that is what that raft is for!" Giovanni declared. "He's been after me to build one and test it for months now, but Sergio would never tell me what it was for. You rascal. Here I thought that it was a design for the army to invade somewhere using motor-wagons. Gr." We all laughed.

He added, "His times are right, if and only if, the seas are calm when we attempt to ferry the motor-wagon to land. Otherwise, we have to delay a bit. Yes, I've got it built and tested, though I had to make a few modifications to the design, Sergio. Your concept is sound. So when do we go?"

"We ought to give Bethany a while to recover and get caring for little Bianca down before we go," Lucianna replied. Well, I couldn't disagree with that. We decided to set July 1 as our departure date. We women let the men take charge of making all the arrangements and procuring of supplies needed. We had our feet full of babies now.

Summer had come, the weather quite warm. Billowing white clouds danced about the crystal clear blue skies, while sea gulls dove like streaking arrows across the docks. With Bianca secure in my front pouch, I stood watching the others handling the last minute loading of our things. It felt good to be getting away from it all. Ever since the plague struck, I had been constantly dealing with one crisis after the other. Now, I was about to embark on a little exploration of my own. Plus, I would be sailing once more. You never get the love of the sea out of your veins. Well, okay, I admit it, my ocean explorations had been several lifetimes ago, but still the sea yearned for me or rather I yearned for it.

As Ket, I grew up in a small Tewdwr fishing village, sailing my own small dingy out into our bay. Now, I was heading back to Tewdwr, centuries later. Okay, we were not planning to visit any towns. Still, the land of rolling green hills seemed to call out to me. Perhaps it was just nostalgia. Probably we were wise in our desire to avoid towns in Tewdwr, after all, their accent was unique and quite thick, a hard language to learn to speak and understand. I wondered if I could even remember it or even speak it now.

"It's good for Sergio to get away from Velona for a few days," Lisa commented to me. She, Lucianna, and Eve stood beside me, their babies in their front pouches as well; all watching our men scamper about loading our fancy baby changing tables. "Still, I think he is really fascinated but this Standing Stone business. Okay, they are ready for us. Here we go, little Bartolo, we are off on your first trip on a caravel."

"Honestly, Marco, I can walk up a gang plank just fine," I whispered to him. The fellows were hovering over us like mother hens. He smiled, but still kept close to me anyway. Once on deck, we climbed on top of the poop deck, after getting the captain's permission, of course. Here, we eight watched the sights of Velona gradually shrink as the ship tacked out of our immense harbor. Once at sea, we climbed down onto the main deck. The sailing time to reach West Reach or Cymry was only a few hours, but it would be triple that as we sailed along the southern and then western coast of the huge island. Our destination was about three-quarters of the way up the western side of the island.

Before long, we spotted the tree-covered island, the southern portion known as Layamon. Soon, we spotted small fishing boats plying the waters near the land, though we stayed far out to sea. As we rounded the southernmost portion of the island where their largest port city lay, Bregia, we were shocked to see the destruction. At least half of the city had burned down. Men, like tiny ants, were rebuilding some of the warehouses near the docks. The chaos had not spared this large port.

By late afternoon, we arrived at the small bay, which Sergio had picked out. "Well, it looks different than I imagined," he commented as we all got a good look at the beach. Gulls called out to us, but the land was otherwise void of people. After a lot of discussion, they decided to go ahead with the landing in the morning.

Just after first light, we watched as the crew and our fellows struggled to get the heavy wooden raft off the deck and into the water. At last, I decided to intervene. "Let a woman at it," I teased them. Sweat poured off their shirtless bodies. Eve gave me a coy smirk. Together, she and I moved out of our bodies and over the raft. While heavy, I had lifted heavier things before. A spiritual beings' power lies in their postulates, postulates that lack any counter-postulates, that is. Soon, the raft was bobbing on the warm, blue-green waters.

The motor-wagon was lighter than I imagined, far less than the raft. While Eve and I lowered it, the fellows hopped down and quickly secured it to the raft. Eve and I decided to help guide it to shore and to be ready to hold it all up, should the raft not manage the waves. For a perilous half hour, she and I kept busy keeping it upright. Once ashore, the rest of the cargo transfer was straightforward. The captain and crew were dumbstruck. Never had they ever seen such "magic." Ah well, it was either that or risk losing our motor-wagon.

Around noon, Sergio fired up the motor and we began rolling across the beach and into the grasslands of Tewdwr. We were off finally. Bumpy. He forgot to tell us just how bumpy this ride would be. If the vehicle was going slower, I would have jumped off and walked! All of us were glad for the frequent breaks from the constant jostling. Still, we made good time, far better than a horse drawn wagon, though nowhere as smooth a ride.

As the golden sun approached the western horizon behind our backs, Sergio, taking his turn driving, had us look around for a suitable camping spot for the night. As I looked to the north across the waving grasses, I saw two distant women. I looked again, "Are they jumping up and down?" I asked Marco, who was sitting beside me in the bed.

"Hey, I think that they are trying to catch our attention. Hey, Sergio, head north," he yelled to the cab. "Two women are hailing us." The motor-wagon veered to the left and headed towards the two figures with red hair. That I could see from this distance. A few minutes later, Sergio halted and killed the noisy engine. The fellows helped us step down and we closed the short distance to the two women.

Both were barely fourteen, both had long, flaming red hair, typical of Tewdwr. They spoke with a very thick accent, but I was able to understand them. Their dresses were barely on, crudely tied across their backs. Two black and white dogs roamed beside them. (Rather than force you to attempt to grasp their thick accent, I'll translate.)

"Please, help us! We need help. My grandfather is very ill. We have no one to help us with him. Please, come and help him. Please. We have four sheep which we can give you if you can heal him, please," the slightly taller teen begged us.

"Sure, we'll be glad to help. Where is your grandfather now?" I asked.

"At her house," the other teen replied. "He's very sick. We've been trying to find someone to help, but no one is around. What is this thing that makes the noise? We heard it and came to see what it was."

"It is called a motor-wagon. My name is Bethany, my husband, Marco." I introduced the others.

"I am Ethlinn daughter of Danaan son of Connacht. She's Etain, daughter of Mor. Connacht is very ill. He's at our house. It's this way. These are my herding dogs. He's Donn and she's Bran. It's this way. Not far, please, you must save him."

I decided to walk along with them and find out more about them and her grandfather. "It is just Etain, me, and grandfather," she began as we walked through the tall grasses. Donn and Bran lopped along, running off ahead to the right and left, before circling back to her. "Last winter, Etain was over at my house, when the bad men came to her home. We heard gunfire, and when we got there, her parents and brother were dead. Danaan buried them and had Etain move in with us. We are like sisters anyway, so we liked that. Then maybe a week later, we heard horses coming and Danaan put Etain and I into our secret hole. We would be dead or captured if he hadn't. The bad men came to our house and shot mom and dad and stole most all our food. Grandfather buried them for us. After that, it was just grandfather and us. Now he's very sick and we are desperate."

"I'm sorry to hear such awful news. Has Connacht been cooking for you?"

"Yes, and he plants our garden and sets rabbit snares. We used to be doing those things, but we can't do so much anymore. Do you all have little babies? One day, we want to have babies too, but not with men. We don't want to be with men anymore. Can we have babies without men?" she asked. We chatted, but I could sense their grief lay just below the surface and didn't press them.

Before long, we spotted their small farmstead. A typical rural Tewdwr cottage, roughhewn timbers, and whose thatched roof was badly in need of repair, rose from the surrounding grasslands. A small garden plot was neatly lined with the stones that had been removed from the ground prior to planting. A small lean-too served as their barn and stable. I spotted their four sheep grazing on the grasses near the front. One thing was certain, these girls were exceedingly poor and probably in very dire straits.

At least their door was easy for us to open, a sliding wood slat was the only catch, crude but simple. Marco insisted on holding our baby, since I wanted to go inside to check on Connacht myself. Valerio and Eve joined me, following the two teens inside. The smell was unmistakable, the old man was at death's door; his body was dying. "Hello. I am Bethany. This is Eve and Valerio. How are you feeling?" I asked softly. Her grandfather was quite old, his grey hair, very thin.

He coughed, and with what seemed pure effort, he opened his eyes. In a low whisper, he said, "I am dying. Old age has caught me. Please, my girls. They have no one to look after them. Please, promise me that you will take care of them." His eyes riveted on mine. How could I refuse a dying man's last request, especially his?

"I promise you, Connacht, we will take very good care of your girls. Thank you for having taken such good care of them all this time," I whispered back, acknowledging him for what he must have done all by himself and at his advanced age and poor health. He smiled, sighed, and his eyes closed.

"He's gone," Valerio whispered, as he felt for a pulse.

I rose to face the two anxious, worried girls. "Can you save him?" Ethlinn asked, though I detected a hint in her voice that suggested that she already knew it was over.

"I'm sorry, Ethlinn, your grandfather has passed way. How old was he? Do you know?"

She slumped into a chair, the last connection she had to the whole world vanished. "Eighty-five," she said just barely audible, tears flooded down her cheeks.

"He died of old age; his body was all worn out, and yet he continued to do everything that he could for you girls. His last words were to ask me if I would take care of you two, Ethlinn, Etain. I promised him that I would do so. Come; lean on me. It's all right to grieve; he must have been a fine grandfather." Both girls leaned on my shoulders and cried.

Meanwhile, Valerio told the others waiting outside and Eve joined them, taking her baby back from Giovanni. The four men came in and quietly carried the old man outside. Their family burial plot was behind the house, quite visible still. They buried him and I conducted a brief ceremony. However, as we gathered around the site, I sensed that he was still present, looking after the two teens. I acted on impulse, I later explained to Marco and the others. I made a Mind Link between the two girls and Connacht.

I used to call this the Last Holy Communion Ceremony. Connacht, Ethlinn and Etain are here with me. You may use this opportunity to say your last farewells. I have promised to look after both girls for you. I will honor my pledge. Now I will allow you three to have your most private last moments together.

Honestly, I had forgotten just how valuable and precious this Last Holy Communion Ceremony was to the grieving members. When a loved one dies, often both the living and the deceased have unspoken thoughts that they would have liked to share. Death removes that opportunity for closure of both beings. The ceremony allows both to share their last thoughts with each other, finishing that cycle of life and death.

A bit later, when they had finished, Ethlinn asked, "Will he be okay? What will happen to him?"

"He will be fine. He is off to find a new baby body and begin a new life once more," I explained, then gave them my usual briefing about all of us being immortal spiritual beings inhabiting these fleshly bodies for a time.

When we headed back inside, Marco had gotten supper ready for us all, using mostly the food that we brought with us. He found next to nothing edible in their home, save fresh lettuce from their garden. Because of the cramped space, the fellows held the babies, allowing us women to eat first. Any concerns that I had about the teens being able to feed themselves vanished in an instant. Both began to eat ravenously, using their feet much as we did. I guessed that they had not had such a hearty, nourishing meal in a long time. Once done, we four lay down and began to nurse, while the fellows took over the table themselves.

Ethlinn and Etain sat down close to Eve and me and watched us closely. At last, Ethlinn said, "Can we learn how to do what you did for us, that Holy Ceremony? Are you goddesses? Where do you come from? You are not from Tewdwr."

"Yes, you can learn how to do it, but it will take lots of learning, lots of study on your part, but you can learn how to do it. No, we are just people like you. We are from Velona. I speak your language because one life that I had many years ago was that of a Tewdwr boy from a town called Cuch Glen, many miles to the south of here along the coast. Bad men killed my parents in that life, just like yours. I escaped with my sister in tow and we headed to Velona."

Etain giggled, "You must have forgotten it a bit, but we can understand you. The others, well, we get a word here and there. We promise to study hard. We want to learn how to do many things."

"Why are you here in Tewdwr? There are no towns around here. Glen Aran is the nearest town about twenty miles to the west," Ethlinn asked.

"We are on a mission to check out the Standing Stones in Brea in the Highlands. Say, do you have any other relatives with whom you want to go live with now?" I asked. Both girls shook their heads no.

"Honestly, Bethany, we have no one now, no one at all, except you. I don't think that Etain and I can live here all by ourselves. Before the plague came, we might have been able to do it, but not now. Can we come with you to this Velona place?"

"Of course you can come and live with us. We have a very big house. You will have to learn our language though."

Both smiled. Ethlinn asked, "Why did the gods want us to lose our arms and become cripples? I asked my father and grandfather, but they had no answer. At first their feet and ours were also twisted all out of shape, but then after a while, they got better. Will our arms get better too?"

"Girls, there were no gods involved with the plague. It is a long story." After Marco took our sleeping Bianca from me, I sat up beside the two girls and told them a very long tale. Both listened intently, though they often interrupted to ask more questions. I hoped the truth would help orient them to what had happened to us all.

Ethlinn had a curious, sheepish look her face. "Then, I am not this body here?" she asked, politely.

"No, not at all. You are you, an immortal spiritual being," I replied. The two girls looked at each other and began laughing. The more they laughed, the wilder they became.

Through fits of laughter, "This is not me," Ethlinn tried to say to Etain. Her friend, laughing just as hard, nodded her agreement. The two laughed for nearly an hour, before Ethlinn and Etain calmed down. "I want to find out more about what I am. Is this possible? It is such a huge relief to know for sure that I am not this poor body which can hardly do much of anything anymore."

"Me too," Etain added. I promised them both that this would be one of the first things that we'd work on when we got back to Velona — that plus learning our dialect. As we finally fell asleep, all crowded together on the floor of the small cabin, I realized just why the two girls had experienced such a huge relief from knowing with certainty that they were not these bodies. Interesting, I thought.

The next day we spent driving across the grasslands, climbing steadily as the towering grey Ath mountains drew ever closer. It took Sergio an hour to find the pass that he thought the motor-wagon could negotiate. Rather than gamble on getting halfway up and have nightfall, we camped on the last patch of grasslands.

The next day, we headed up the rocky pass. Unfortunately, the motor-wagon just did not have enough power to pull us up. Eve and I had to do a bit of extra lifting to get us up onto the flatter highlands of Ruadan. As Sergio expected, we were in a relatively isolated area and only passed through a couple of very small villages. Around noon, we pulled into the bowl-shaped valley where the ancient Standing Stones still stood. After a quick lunch, our group fanned out and began to look for the site that Fianna and Lia Ines had described in their letter.

With twenty-one grey granite monoliths standing in the circle, it didn't take us long to find the specific stone slab that had so intrigued those two women so long ago. One stone whose finger lay due south had a curious shape formed into its weathered, lichen covered northern side. "I found it," Sergio called out to us and we all swarmed around this stone. Indeed, it did look somewhat like our current female body shapes, almost as if a woman had pressed the front of her body into a clay statue, leaving an indentation of her body. Clearly, the form was female and had no arms or they simply were not represented, assuming this was actually supposed to represent a female body. It was simply a granite, jagged, monolithic stone, after all.

We chatted a bit about who would attempt to activate it as Fianna and Lia Ines had done before. Of course, I would try it, but everyone else wanted in on the action as well. Based on their letter, Fianna had been standing beside Lia Ines when she had pressed her body into the form. We figured one of us could accompany me. After a bit of discussion, Sergio was nominated to stand beside me, because he had the best observational skills, being the Chief Detective Inspector of Velona. I also agreed to Mind Link everyone to us so that they would be able to see what we were seeing, if anything.

Sergio pressed his body against my back and I pushed my body in close to the indentation, attempting to fill the form with my front side. He and I had the sensation of perhaps falling, but the next instant we felt solid rock beneath our feet and had the sense that we had dropped into a cavern below the Standing Stones. The others described what happened as simply one second we were there and the next instant we had disappeared from view. Marco had inspected the ground on which we had stood, but found nothing but the grass and weeds, which we had trampled while standing there.

We found ourselves inside a chamber whose dimensions we could not readily ascertain, only a faint glow came from a glowing ball some three feet above our heads. I did sense the power radiating upwards from the earth itself, the power that had always amplified our old Druwid spells. He and I saw no one. "Blue Light," Sergio whispered. His light appeared and I cast mine as well, shedding an even eerier light on the chamber.

"Hello. Is anyone here? I am Bethany; this is Sergio. Are you here, Partholan?" I called out.

"Someone's here, Bethany. I can sense another mind's presence. No body, just a being and its mind," Sergio whispered.

Then, we both felt its telepathic contact, as did the others waiting above ground. I was glad that the Mind Link was working now. *Dalny? Dalny, is that you coming back?* The thoughts came through, though the mind and being seemed ancient to me somehow. Yet, besides the thought, the heavy, heavy emotion of apathy also came through. The words seemed to come minutes between each one, though perhaps that was just how it seemed to me.

Sorry, I am not Dalny. I would like to talk with you, if I may. Who is Dalny? I have been told that you are called Partholan. Is that correct? Who or what are you? Where are you? Do you have a body like ours? I sent. It seemed that my thoughts flew like one of those MGBs, rapid firing long guns, bam, bam, bam, compared to the intensely slow apathetic thoughts we were receiving.

Partholan, yes, I am called that. Dalny is my love and companion here, only she has been gone for so long. Lost. Still I wait. I am here. You have the right form, but you are not Dalny.

Move out of your body, Sergio sent. I did so and at once saw a huge energy aura around the spiritual being called Partholan. Now, he also saw us as well and took notice of us, far more than before. My estimate was that Partholan's energy field that defined his position was perhaps fifty feet in diameter, a very dark grey field. In contrast, Sergio was whitish and perhaps twenty feet across. The others claimed that mine appeared to have a slightly yellowish tinge to the white, but I was comparable in size to Sergio.

Definitely, Partholan was low in emotional tone, apathy for sure. To me, that along with what he had said, indicated that he was suffering from some ill effects of a trauma of some kind, perhaps a loss. He had no body, nor did he appear to need one; he retained his own sense of self as a spiritual being, unlike most here on Tarra, who had long ago lost their own sense of self and identity, adopting the identity of the body, which they occupied.

Since this is an extremely key point, let me try to describe it another way. As you read this, you probably think of yourself as the identity of your body; it is your ID card, so to speak. You likely do not think of yourself as a spiritual being, but rather you are thinking about making money to pay the bills and buy food to eat or other fine things for yourself as a body, nice clothes, house, and so on. People believe that all they are are their bodies and when their bodies die, that is the end of them, ignoring what various religious beliefs might suggest. That is, as a spiritual being, such people are below death, emotionally. Okay, spiritual beings are immortal, but when they have failed too much and cannot have the simple expediency of "dying" and then being able to start all over again, they stop being themselves, a spiritual being, and start becoming the body. That is, they identify themselves as their bodies.

That was the case with our two teens, Ethlinn and Etain. They believed that they were their bodies, until I performed that Holy Communion Ceremony during which they discovered that they existed and were not their bodies, but separate from their bodies. That they were not their bodies gave them an enormous release, massive confusions of identity had blown away from their minds and thinking processes.

Here, Sergio and I saw at once that Partholan retained his own identity as a spiritual being. He was not associating himself in anyway with our fleshly bodies and had no need to be in one or controlling one in order to operate in the world around us. However, he was in apathy and thus quite close to death as a spiritual being. If he dropped slightly down, he would become a normal human, probably picking up a baby body and joining us. That is why I decided to do what I did next.

Partholan, Sergio and I are going to help you. I want you to return to when you first sensed something might be wrong with Dalny. After a long pause, he replied.

Yes, I can see it.

Good. Now move through what all happened and tell me what you are seeing, feeling, sensing, and hearing as you go along. Running a person who is stuck in apathy is about the worst going — it's slug, slug, slow and thick as molasses syrup in the winter. As we listened to him, time was moving excruciatingly slowly for Partholan, and thus us.

About fifteen hundred Tarra years ago, Dalny and I find this planet. We are so happy. Life is beautiful and we are so powerful. The place is perfect for us. Animal life is abundant as is plants. Perfect. She and I want to create our life forms, what you call your bodies. They are, as are all things, merely an illusion that is agreed upon. We create these new animal bodies, just as we had planned to do for so long. We make both the male and female human bodies bipedal. Yet, we desired to have the male animals dote and care for the female animals. So many other animals do not, you know. Some females eat their male mates once they breed. We see many other divergent examples wandering the planet. We make the male animals have arm appendages but not the females. We make the female animals bear the children instead, a division of the workload. For hundreds of years, we help our animals adapt, flourish, and prosper on our private world here.

Dalny says that our animals need a place to worship us and we make the Standing Stones so that our animals can come and talk to us. Then, our planet is invaded. Mechanical ships come bearing other animal forms with spiritual beings stuck inside them, degraded beings, Dalny calls them. We worry. Their bodies look like praying mantises only they are huge, sometimes a hundred feet long. Maybe they will leave us alone, I suggest. We watch. They are far down south where it is warmer.

Woe and alas, they capture some of our animals! We grow angry with them. We spy on them and they are doing awful experiments on our own creations! They added arms to our lovely female animals and they soon begin populating our private world with their perverted alterations. They begin to exterminate all of our animals! We fight them but they have strong energy weapons and we get stunned. When we awake at last, we witness the horrors that they and now two other aliens inflict upon our animals — they are forcing their degraded spiritual beings into our animals!

Dalny leaves here to go see what is going on with them. She reports that those spiritual beings are dead to themselves; they don't even know who they are and are convinced utterly that they are our animals! We talk a long time about how we can correct this awful thing that has been done to our wonderful animal creations. She decides to go see what she can do to blast these spiritual being thieves out of our animal bodies, while I am off to see if I can get these mantis creatures to put our creations back to the way that we created them in the first place. We both know that we cannot directly attack these aliens. Their energy weapons are too powerful for us to handle. We are going to use sneakier means, indirect attacks.

Long and hard, I work on these mantis abominations, planting the idea in their minds to put the female animals back the way we had them. Over time, I begin to see my plan is working. First, small groups were formed, though still they kept their degraded spiritual beings stuck inside our animal's heads. After a long time, they had an entire large island put back to our original forms, though their degraded beings were still stuck inside our animal's heads.

Dalny reports to me that when our animals breed, there is an enormously fine sensation emanating from their bodies, just as we had planned. We want our animals to enjoy breeding so that they can multiply and thrive. She tells me that these degraded beings have become addicted to this sensation and long for it. She believes that it helps keep them stuck inside our animal's heads. I agree and she leaves to see if she can do anything about that. That was the last time that I ever saw her.

After a long time, I go in search of her, looking everywhere, but alas, I am unable to find her. I worry, something bad has happened to her. I try again and again, but with no luck. I grieve and grieve, but still she does not return. Instead, more and more of our animals multiply and more and more of the alien degenerate beings come to occupy their heads. Woe is me. Our creations are destroyed, stolen, and perverted, and Dalny is lost.

I wait and wait and grieve. No longer am I able to move around as before. Perhaps it is because I grow old. Long ago, I discover that I can no longer leave here, our headquarters. I am stuck here. I've lost my powers. All is lost, if only Dalny will return to me. Maybe we can do something about all this treachery. You show up and here I am. He finished.

Good old Eve, as she began to hear Partholan's words, she took the initiative and contacted Macario Ines, the Guardian. About half way through all this, I felt him join our Mind Link. I was running my first therapy session on another being thar didn't have a fleshly body. I figured that Macario would lend me a hand if I got off the rails with this one.

When Partholan finally got to the end of the lengthy incident, I thanked him and had him return to the start and go through it once more. I was a bit worried about the time aspect. In the past when I gave a therapy session to someone who had undergone a loss or trauma, usually the incident's duration was fairly short, from a few minutes to perhaps a couple of days from start to finish. Here, Partholan was apparently covering a millennium-long incident. I began to see that time for spiritual beings who are not being human bodies have a different viewpoint on time than those of us who measure time against our body's lifetimes.

However, I didn't worry too much about this; the therapy was having the desired effect; the trauma and loss was beginning to lift, to erase. He was coming up in emotional tone on this second pass through the long event, I sensed his enormous grief and sadness this time, and he moved through it more quickly than before. The next pass the largest volume of anger that I had ever witnessed radiated off him. For the first time ever in a therapy session, I might have been tempted to come a cropper and get the heck out of there had the others and Macario not been right there with me gently backing me up. Wow. What an immense release of anger Partholan had. On the next pass, he slipped on up into antagonism and hostility. When he touched on boredom on the next pass, I knew we may well be getting close to the end and that the therapy process would indeed work on spiritual beings who did not have and were not in a physical body. The final pass he finally reached a level of cheerfulness, the huge reactive charge had been blown.

Only then did I realize fully what I had just done. I had reversed the downward spiral for this being. Had I not done my therapy on him, he would soon have dropped a little lower to "death" of himself, and he would have likely taken over the identity of one of our human bodies, becoming trapped as we were. I had salvaged this being, though obviously, he would need far more therapy to recover fully, but I had arrested his downward slide for now.

Well, I have a good notion about what happened to Dalny. She was so fascinated about the breeding sensation that I expect that she fell victim to that. She is probably out there right now, unfortunately being one of our own animal creations. I very nearly became entrapped in our own creations! I cannot thank you enough for saving me from eternal damnation.

You are very welcome. This therapy session is now ended. Thank you, I replied.

He now noticed all of us for the first time. *You are some of the beings who were trapped in our animal creations, aren't you? Yet, you are now free of them?*

Yes and no. Some of us are getting there. Macario here can best tell you about that. Boy was I ever glad that the Guardian was here now!

They need to feed their bodies and put them to sleep. Can you return them to the surface for a time? You and I have many things to discuss, Macario sent. He agreed and Sergio and I found our bodies once more standing above ground before the Standing Stones. I was quite startled! The sky was pitch black; the stars were shining. I smelled the aroma of supper, and suddenly my body had to go to the bathroom badly, and it was starving! How long had we been down there? My baby? By now, Bianca must be ravenously hungry.

"Well done!" Marco exclaimed, immediately helping me with my physical needs. "The others took turns feeding Bianca, she's fine. It is about midnight. We've kept supper warmed for you two. That was the most interesting therapy session that I've ever seen! Just incredible. Do you realize the magnitude of the information we've learned? The whole history of Tarra now has become crystal clear to us!"

I ate as fast as he shoveled it into my mouth. "Brilliant, Bethany, just brilliant. I hope you didn't mind my fetching Macario," Eve put in sleepily.

"Nope. Incredibly insightful of you, Eve. Perfect. I really am out of my league with this one," I replied with my mouth full.

"What I found fascinating," Sergio added, eating as fast as I, "was that the cavern area where we were at is almost entirely bare — it's just a cavern. I was expecting to see all manner of devices, you know, like those of the mantis and Grey Creatures or even the Dolls. But no, Partholan does it all by postulates, by sheer creation, not by electronic or mechanistic means. Very interesting."

"Yes, Lucianna and I are a bit disappointed by that. She and I were hoping to gain some great ideas for more inventions. Ah well," Giovanni added a bit sadly.

"So these two powerful beings originally created our bodies and the Standing Stones," Valerio mused. "That means the ancient Druwids, you remember, way back when many of us were part of that organization centuries ago, they must have retained some connections to Partholan and the Standing Stones. I remember holding our Druwid ceremonies at these stones, though no one really knew their history. They were standing there long before Alabaster Benjamin Crowley started the Druwids. Yet, he must have felt some strong bond or connection to those Standing Stones."

"Yes, but what kind of a life would our bodies have without us to guide them?" asked Lisa. "I mean, they are just animals. I don't think that I really do understand all of this."

"So Partholan and Dalny created our human bodies much as they appear today something like fifteen hundred years ago," Sergio summarized. "Along came the mantis who didn't know that they were here first and that the human bodies were their creation. They experimented on them, apparently giving arms to the females. We know that they were actually working on creating as they called them mammalian prison cells for the unwanted beings of their world and those of the Greys and the plasticine. Once they had human bodies ready, the three aliens then began implanting spiritual beings inside the heads of these human bodies, trapping us here so that we could not return to our home worlds and cause them further difficulties."

Sergio went on, "Unable to fight the advanced electronics of the mantis, Partholan took the only avenue left to him, to implant ideas in the mantis geneticists' minds to alter our forms back to his original design. He had no way to remove we entrapped spiritual beings, however. I think that he would have been satisfied to have his animal forms back again. Yet, his implanted idea took hold and the unwitting mantis began to slowly head in that direction, culminating in the recent plague. Fascinating how one idea implanted a thousand years ago trickles down through time and many minds to the present."

"Yes, but Sergio, what does he mean about our bodies being an illusion?" asked Lisa. "I know my body is solid and real. How can it be an illusion?"

"Dear, close your eyes and mock up a cat. Let's make it a purple cat so that you know that it is your creation, not an image of some cat that you've seen." She did, but several others also played along with this, getting a purple cat themselves. I knew where he was going with this and relaxed, quite full at last.

"Okay, now that is your illusion of a purple cat that you've created. Suppose that I join with you and see your purple cat. We are both agreeing on your cat, right?" She agreed. "Good, now suppose that everyone else here also sees your purple cat. We all agree that we are seeing your purple cat. Now, suppose that everyone we meet also sees your purple cat. Doesn't that mean that your purple cat is now 'real?' I mean, everyone who sees you also sees your purple cat. How is that any different from people seeing your body? Reality is merely the agreed upon illusion. Suppose that Bethany alone sees a lion roaming our campsite. All the rest of us look and see nothing at all. In her universe, she is certain that she is seeing the lion, but here in the physical world, no one else sees her lion. Would not we believe that she is a bit crazy or insane? If she kept on insisting that we were all in danger from this lion, we'd eventually lock her up or something, because she is totally out of the stream of uniform agreement upon which all the rest of us are working. So yes, our bodies, this whole world even, are an illusion, a powerful one on which each and every one of us is agreeing with constantly with every tick of every second."

Sergio went a bit further with all this. "Partholan got the mantis geneticists to eventually agree with his illusions of armless women and thus brought about a new agreed upon reality among us all. I find that absolutely fascinating, though it took him ten centuries to bring about."

All this talk about illusions created an idea in the back of my mind. However, I soon fell asleep, my body was too tired to pursue all this tonight.

The next morning, the noise of breakfast making roused me. Already Marco was up, helping the others with the morning chores. Dew hung in the air around these tall, dark monoliths, as if we were faerie folk gently touching upon sacred ground. "Ah, you're awake. Bianca needs you, if you are ready," he said quietly, as if his very voice would shatter the mood of the morning. He laid our daughter beside me and she began nursing, sucking life from me. What a feeling.

Later, my prince helped me up and took Bianca while I sat down with the others. Food smelled somehow extraordinary this morning. Perhaps it was just the atmosphere created by this place, once sacred to the "animals" that Partholan and Dalny had created over one and a half millennia ago. Macario appeared just as I finish. Once more, I wondered just how much power he had. His agreed upon body form materialized before us.

"Good morning Bethany. If you are ready, I would like you to join us below for a minute before you get on your way back to Velona," he said politely. Velona? Well, I guessed that was a subtle way of saying that we'd finished all that we could do here. At least, the mystery was solved. I rather wished that I'd known about all this over a century ago, perhaps I might have been able to avoid so much of the awful events that had happened.

He walked with me to the special Standing Stone, "I took the idea that you had late last night and discussed it with Partholan."

"Huh? What idea?" I asked. What was Macario talking about? What idea had I had? I was exhausted. Then, it came back into my mind. If Partholan had created these human bodies or animals as he called us, could he not also work his magic and give women back our arms?

"Yes, that idea," Macario said as if reading my mind. I smiled, for he probably had done just that. "Here you go." We'd arrived at the Standing Stone, and I pushed my body into the indentation in the stone and found myself once more somewhere far below the surface. I blinked and tried to adjust my vision in the dim subterranean light. I gave that up and moved out of my head further, spotting both beings.

Partholan and I have reached an agreement, Macario began. *The problem that he has been facing for over a millennia has been a slow dwindling of his powers and abilities. Originally, when he and Dalny came here, they were quite powerful and able to make their illusions quite solid. Over the years what with all that happened here, he's gradually succumbed to accumulated traumatic incidents, as we all have. I have agreed to give him our therapy that will free him from his self-made barriers. Once he has regained his innate spiritual abilities once more, he will restore all of you women's arms for a time. He will give us all time to finish our work of freeing all the trapped spiritual beings. We have convinced him that our therapy process will work faster if women have their arms back. Once we are all free, I have given him my word that we will leave Tarra and give him back his and Dalny's creations, these bodies that we are using. Additionally, we both suspect that Dalny has somehow become trapped as we are, Bethany. I have given him my word that when we find Dalny and free her from the entrapment, we will make sure that she gets back to Partholan once more. Is this agreeable with you?*

Sure, fabulous. Actually, having arms will greatly speed up the process. We are so slowed down by this it's not funny and our men have to waste much of their time helping us get by. Both will have more time to devote to therapy sessions this way. Thanks, Partholan. Honestly, if we all get as powerful as Macario has, we will have no need of these bodies any longer. I, for one, wondered just what that would be like — to operate *fully* without the need of using a body.

Thank you, Bethany, for saving me from losing my own identity. I can see now that I came perilously close to becoming entrapped just as you have been. Perhaps, Dalny and I created too good an animal here. Yet, we are not God, the Supreme Being. Though we are lesser gods, every one of us, we sometimes make mistakes. Perhaps, Dalny and I did just that.

I giggled, *These are very fine bodies that you have created, I will say that.*

I felt mirth from both Partholan and Macario. *Indeed, Bethany. I've kept you too long. Your friends are eager to get on the road. I will stay and work on Partholan now. Thanks again, you are holding your half of our bargain well.* I knew what Macario meant. While he worked on freeing us beings, I worked on maintaining a calm, planet-wide, safe environment. I wasn't so sure how calm it was now, though. Half of the population had fallen into the Dark Ages.

A bit later, I found myself on the surface again. The others were already packing, as I walked over to what had been our campsite, squarely in the middle of the Standing Stones. "What news?" Marco called out as I walked up. Honestly, I felt elated to give them the incredible news that one day we would have our arms back. When they heard this news, absolutely everyone cheered. We had scored an unbelievable victory over the devastation caused by the mantis geneticist.

"Can we still learn how to do the therapy and the special Ceremony?" asked Ethlinn.

"Of course, we will begin as we ride along today," I encouraged her and her friend. Both girls beamed. They had witnessed so many "miracles" in the last two days that their lives would be changed forever, for the good, that is.

Around nine, Sergio fired up our motor-wagon and we headed back north, retracing our overland journey through Tewdwr. Again, we tried to avoid all population centers. None of us wanted any chance encounters.

Chapter 22 Old Ways Die Hard

High Priestess Airlea Petos paced the Observation Deck of the Tower of Orthos. The warm spring day flooded her senses, bringing the scent of irises, jasmine, lavender, and sweet grasses into her nose, but most of all she felt the warmth of the returning sun. The gentle breeze ruffled her white robe emblazoned with the yellow orb of the sun and tossed her long flaming, curls out behind her. She worshiped the Sun God, as did all the women here in Orthos. Yet, Airlea was more than just a High Priestess of the now nearly forgotten Sun God — god who had been very nearly supplanted by the wildfire-spread of the Church of Jehosanity. She was a Seer, perhaps one of the last women in all of Demokritos who still had the Vision.

Airlea ran her fingers through her hair, placing it behind her once more. Her curly red hair fell to the small of her back, the only bit of vanity that she ever allowed herself. She was fifty-five now and a widow, having accurately foretold the death of her husband some six years before. Basking in the warmth of the spring sunshine, she reflected upon ancient history. Her grandmother had often told her the ancient stories and legends, particularly how busy the High Priestesses of the past used to be. Hundreds of men and women would make the long journey to the Tower of Orthos to consult the Seer, exchanging gold, silver, food, or whatever the person could afford for the chance to get a glimpse of the future, however fleeting. Farmers desired to know when to plant; hunters, the best time to maximize their hunts; nobles and merchants, what they must do to gain more wealth. Yes, even the kings and queens often came seeking guidance. All this was provided by the Seer, the High Priestess of Orthos.

In recent years, this new religion, this Jehosanity, had entered Demokritos and swept across the lands, converting nearly everyone by October 823, into its folds. Sun God temples either had been torn down making way for these new churches or merely lay vacant, weeds and vines slowly covering the white marble floors and columns. Indeed, Airlea had not had a suppliant come to see her for almost a month now. Just because no one came anymore did not mean that Airlea did not continue to See. Quite the contrary, her visions had become far, far stronger and more vivid than usual, especially during the last couple of months. A great calamity was about to befall Demokritos; she had "seen it."

The soft slapping of leather sandals upon the marble stairs intruded upon her thoughts. Airlea turned to see who was coming, as the wind whipped her long, curly hair around her oval face. She had blue eyes and high cheekbones, but was not terribly attractive; her whole body was covered with reddish freckles.

"Ah, here you are, mom," the alto voice of her daughter, Tanis, broke the stillness. The breathy sound of her voice spoke of the long climb of five stories to reach this Observation Deck. Tanis, now twenty-one, also had her mother's blue eyes and fiery red hair, but she had the robust features of her father, who had been rather handsome. While Tanis was a Priestess, she was also a fighter, who kept her hair quite short, short as a man's. Her leg muscles were strong and well defined; her arms were as stout as most men, hardened by long workouts in their combat arena. She too wore the white robes with the single large sun emblazoned on its front and back, though she always wore a short sword around her waist with daggers strapped to either leg.

"News mom. Nestor has returned and says that all four have agreed to come. They should arrive by the weekend," she reported officially. "Are you sure all this is really necessary? I mean, do we really want outsiders living with us here at Orthos?" She rubbed her hands through her short hair, her fingers massaging her scalp. She always did this when she was annoyed, a nervous habit she'd picked up from her late father. While visitors were often put up for a night especially when they came for their Seeing late in the day, Airlea had asked these outsiders to come for an extended stay. Why had her mother suggested that this should be a spring vacation for these guests? Tanis knew all the ritual prayers and some of their history. Nowhere had she ever heard of the Tower of Orthos ever hosting guests for long periods of time, especially for months. These guests were being asked to spend the whole spring here among the hundred Temple Women who lived their lives here in the huge complex.

Airlea smiled at her daughter, beckoning her to join her at the marble wall surrounding the open deck. She tossed her long hair to the wind, allowing the light breeze to drape it back across her shoulders for her. Inwardly, she sighed. Tanis took after her father, a fighter; she would never have the gift of the Sight. How can one explain the Sight to someone who cannot See, she mused. Tanis joined her, leaning over the edge, looking down on their whole complex.

The predominate feature was this five story, polished, white marble tower. Yet, below them, Tanis could see the six-foot tall marble outer defensive wall that surrounded the complex, designed to keep wild animals out. As she well knew from much experience, the wall could easily be scaled by anyone. As a girl she'd spent hours walking around and around on the top of the wall. It enclosed a stable and their main living quarters, another marble building, which housed the hundred women and the few men who lived here all their lives. Women of the Sun Temple, they were called, though many were also trained priestesses as was Tanis. These days, Tanis wondered why they even bothered. Hardly anyone still believed in the Sun God, since Jehosanity had supplanted their age old religion with its Heaven and Hell beliefs.

The two women looked down on their gardens and beyond the walls to the rolling grasslands. In the extreme distance, they could see a few farmers out tilling their fields, though many had already begun their planting. The Temple of Orthos lay on a hill, just above the flood plain of the great Vardan River, whose roots lay in the high peaks of the Katos Mountains to the east, some two hundred miles away. The mighty river divided the kingdoms of Penelopus to the north from Thallyus to the south. The main paved connecting road that joined the two capital cities, Tinos to the north and Thal to the south, lay a hundred miles further down river to the west. Yes, the Temple of Orthos was quite isolated from the major cities of both kingdoms. Rightly so, this way the Seers would not be pulled into the hectic activities of the two ruling courts, remaining aloof and separate from those who ruled the two kingdoms. Still, progress and expansion had come.

Further to the east, many mines and smelters had sprung up over the centuries. Iron ore, copper, lead, tin, gold and silver were plentiful in the foothills. Agriculture continued to expand nearly every year. Now farmers were tilling the land not five miles from the Temple. To the west, Tanis knew of three large horse farms and had often visited them to purchase quality mounts for the Temple. Her roan stallion was among the best of the best, she thought, fast, swift, and surefooted. He'd never let her down and now always came when she whistled. Tanis loved to gallop across the hills, free as the wind, though for the last two years, she'd had little time to spend on her pastime, not since she was appointed the Captain of the Temple Guards. Her obligations now included protection of the entire complex, not a light duty.

"It is good that our guests are coming, Tanis. One day, you will see why," Airlea whispered to her daughter. "Patience reveals all. The Sun will illuminate our path as it always has since the dawn of time." Tanis grinned, so like her mother to speak in riddles and hints of what was to come. Of course, the sun will light their way. How could it not? Patience, well, that was a trait that Tanis lacked — act first, there is plenty of time to think about it afterwards. That was her motto or was it her father's?

Airlea now spoke normally, asking formally, "Has Steward Rhea laid in all the supplies that I requested?"

"Yes, I double checked with her before climbing all the way up here, mom. Honestly, I don't see why we need to lay in a half a year's food supply, lantern oil, charcoal for the cooking stoves, and coal for winter's heat. Are the crops going to fail? It hardly seems like it; this spring is just perfect. Right rains, right sun. Mother Earth is providing as always," Tanis replied, hoping to fish a bit more information from her mother.

"Dark days are coming, Tanis. I wish I was wrong, but I know in my heart that I am not. We must be prepared. It will be hard on us all; we will all be tested, even you, daughter, even you," he voice trailed away, a great sadness hinted at, but not vocalized.

Tested? Well, her mother had been going on for weeks about the "dark days coming," but Tanis now heard something new. "Tested? Mom, how am I to be tested? I am strong and as fit as any man is. I know all the prayers. I know all the codes and locks. I know our current financial shape and physical means. What else is there?" Tanis doubted that any of this was what her mother was hinting at, but hoped to get her to elaborate a bit more. What dark days? What testing?

"You will know when the time comes, dear Tanis. When it does, remember to be strong. Many of our women look to you as a role model. They will take strength from you; remember that, just as I will need to be strong as well, somehow, someway. We must, so much depends upon us remaining as strong as our Temple's foundation. The Sun never fails, so must we not fail. Remember that, Tanis, remember that."

Tanis didn't like the sound of her mother's ominous words. She countered, "Well, I still have Lykou to depend upon and you have Nestor too." She was referring to her boyfriend, the great hunter, Lykou Phanes, who was also twenty-one and a proven hunter. Nestor Machos was forty-five. Both men lived here along with another five. Nestor was the official Messenger of the Tower of Orthos to the outside world. It was Nestor who had just returned from a lengthy trip into Tinos and Thal, arriving back a half hour ago.

Airlea smiled, "Yes, Lykou is a fine lad, Tanis. Still, even Lykou and Nestor and the others will be sorely tested as well. Indeed, all here will be tested. We all must prove our mettle, our strength, so that the Sun God will in time pierce the veil of the Evil Darkness in men's hearts. I fear it is coming. I fear what is coming, Tanis. Yet, I must be strong and lead us back into the light. I give you my solemn word, daughter, I will lead us back into the light, though that trip may be unexpectedly challenging for us all." She sighed and then added more cheerfully, "Come on. Let's go see to the preparations for our guests." Airlea put her arm around Tanis, who reciprocated. The two headed down the steep marble stairs to consult with Steward Rhea.

That evening, Tanis made her final security rounds of the compound, bidding good night to her two night guards. After blessing the two women fighters, she headed into her bedroom, which she shared with her companion, Melina Iris, who was a year older than she was. Melina was also her lover and she watched the young woman as she brushed out her long brown hair. Melina had style about her, Tanis knew. From the way that she cut her bangs to the fall of her hair now nearly as long as her mother's flaming locks, Melina looked every inch a beauty. She had thick lips, dark brown, mischievous eyes, and a laugh that would disarm any soul. Since they were ten, the two had shared a room and later shared intimacy as only two women can.

While Tanis was in love with Lykou, she also loved Melina as well. Such was the way of life here in this isolated Temple of Orthos. Over a hundred women lived here within these elegant marble structures, made from the finest polished marble, crafted by the best artisans centuries ago. Some of the women had sought this cloistered, holy life, escaping from intolerable life situations caused mainly by men. Most, however, had been born and raised here within these white walls. Centuries ago, noblemen often sent one of their daughters here as an offering to Sol and to gain more favorable oracles when they visited. Now that had changed. Tanis couldn't remember when a nobleman had last sent a daughter. Mostly, poverty-stricken, desperate young widows with their offspring formed the new recruit pool these days.

Melina put her ivory brush down, pivoted in her chair, smiled, and asked, "Get any more out of your mother?"

"We are to be tested, whatever that may mean," she replied, hastily changing into her nightgown. She related what little ambiguous news that she'd heard.

"Well, at least we know a bit more tonight," Melina concluded. "I wonder what she means? Guess we'll find out." She winked, and whispered seductively, "Time enough for that later. I've been waiting for you all day!" She pulled Tanis onto their shared bed, while Tanis blew out their oil lantern.

Sometime later, the two satisfied women lay facing each other. "Lykou is back. I saw him at the stables," Melina whispered.

"I know. I saw him arrive, though we've not spoken yet. Don't worry, I will ask him about us. Honestly, Melina, with one hundred plus of us and only seven men around, I'm sure that he will support us both. He's a hunter and would make a good father and husband for us."

"I hope so. I do want to be a mother one day, but I don't want to leave here to become one," she whispered.

"I know. I don't either. The world out there is vicious and cruel," Tanis replied mechanically. She had been out there, accompanying Lykou several times and she'd not liked what she had seen. The outer lands were male dominated, vicious and cruel. Women were objects of lust or so she had concluded, not like here within the sanctity of the marble walls. Such thoughts reminded her of Melina's charge. "Say, how is Zona doing?" she inquired.

Zona Rho, the thirty year old blonde widow had come here two years ago, desperately seeking sanctuary for herself and her seven year old son, Apollo. Her late husband, a nobleman of Thal, had insisted and demanded that she become a Holy Woman of the Eighth Degree solely and only so that his social standing would greatly increase, giving him more power and influence with the Church of Jehosanity in Thal. She had been armless now for over six years. Whatever possessed Zona to have ever consented to such mutilation, Tanis wondered. Her husband had become unfaithful not long after that, been mixed up in some nefarious dealings, and had been found murdered in a back alleyway two years ago. Moneychangers laid claim to his fortune, and Zona found herself destitute and helpless with a five year old son to support. Using her last gem, she had managed to get a kind farmer to bring her and her son here to Orthos. For the last two years, Melina had been charged with assisting Zona with her unique needs.

"She keeps amazing me, Tanis. She keeps trying to figure out ways to care for herself using her feet. It is so utterly hard for me to stand by and watch her struggling to brush out her hair. I have to keep reminding myself to let her do it, even though my heart aches and longs to assist her," Melina replied.

"I know how you feel, yet, she needs to become as independent as she can. I won't ever forget how helpless she was when she came here two years ago. You had to do everything for her."

Melina giggled demurely, "How well I know. Yet, just look at her now, Tanis. She is full of life and vitality; she has the sparkle of Sol in her now."

"More than me?" Tanis teased. Melina's searching lips found hers and they passionately embraced once more.

In the Royal Palace's Great Hall, King Karistaios Aikos, a fifty-nine year old widower, looked out at the nearly empty long table. His eyes fell upon his two daughters and their boyfriends, sharing a last supper together. His daughters had accepted the Seer's invitation to spend a spring holiday at the ancient Temple of Sol at Orthos. Why neither had yet agreed to marry their boyfriends was beyond him. Sophia was now twenty-two and ought to have been married already. She had the long, rich black hair and eyes of her mother, but had taken a keen interest in the running of his kingdom of Thallyus. Her boyfriend, Theron Kissos, was a year younger and an accomplished hunter. While he preferred that she marry a man with loftier ideals, the lad seemed honest and genuine, and Karistaios had accepted him, if only Sophia would consent to marry.

His eyes drifted to the other side of the table, lighting on his youngest daughter, Elissa, now twenty-one. She had long sandy blonde hair like himself and his blue eyes as well. If only she had been a son, so much would have been for the better. Elissa was determined to be an engineer and inventor! Her room was filled with little inventions and books on the design and construction of nearly everything he could imagine. If only she were a he, he mused. After all, he knew of no female engineers at all. Still, she had fixed more things around the palace than his own staff. Worse, her boyfriend, Thoth Motheos seemed to support her fully in her endeavors. Quite why, the king did not know. Women were not engineers; he knew that well. If only he had had a son, if only his lovely wife had not died so unexpectedly...

It was all Queen Frona's doing or now rather the late Empress Frona's doing, he mused for the thousandth time. When she had married the Emperor and given up her position as Queen of Thallyus, she appointed him the kingdom's new ruler, if and only if his wife also became a Holy Woman of the Eighth Degree. Sybil had not wanted to do it, but she had not stood in the way of his advancement and had yielded to Frona's demands. Two years later, she had fallen down the palace steps, smashing her head on the unyielding stone, leaving him to raise their two daughters by himself. If she had had her arms, she would not have fallen, he mused, again for the thousandth time. Well, he'd done the best that he could. Karistaios could find no faults with either daughter; both had grown up to become beautiful young women. If only they would marry and settle down. Of course, he thought almost at once that then his dinner table would be completely empty. He sighed.

Elissa chatted, "Well, this is going to be a great vacation, Thoth. You know that we are both close friends with Zoe and Amynta Haimon, the daughters of King Ares and Queen Brosia of Penelopus. They are coming on this spring vacation too. We four will be together for at least a whole month!"

"Zoe's an engineer too, isn't she?" Thoth asked. "I'm going to really miss you, Elissa."

"Yes, she and I exchange letters and ideas all the time. This is going to be a great get together, I just know it!" She sighed and added, "I know, Thoth, I'll miss you too. I suppose that you can come and visit us if you can get away." Elissa tossing an errand strand of her blonde hair out of her face as she turned to look at Thoth sitting beside her. She flashed him a coy smile. If they had been alone, she'd have given him a passionate, quick kiss, but thought better of it with the others present.

"Well, I expect that Amynta and I will get in a lot of horse riding," Sophia broke in. "Think that you can get away for a while too, Theron? It would be so great if you could be with us for part of the time. I don't think that the Seer would object."

"Don't worry, love, I'll find a way as soon as I can. I am obligated to lead a hunt this week. Some wolves have been causing farmers grief all winter. Once I handle the problem, I'll come for a visit. I'll go nuts if I don't see you at all for the rest of spring!" She grinned coyly, but also knew that she would be just as crazy if she didn't see him privately for several months. Perhaps, she thought, she ought to have married Theron before now. Well, time enough for that later on, she mused.

They planned to leave in the morning, though she knew that their friends, Amynta and Zoe, had already left over a week ago. The distance from Tinos, Penelopus to Orthos was double the three hundred miles that they had to travel from Thal. The Haimon royal family and the Aikos royal family were close — the two kings shared a common grandfather. As a result and especially after the untimely death of Queen Sybil, Queen Brosia made frequent trips to Thal, seeing to the education and proper upbringing of his two daughters. The past seven years, their daughters had made the trip from Tinos to Thal and vice versa at least eight times a year, more if they could persuade their fathers.

King Ares focused his attention on grooming his son, Adrastos, to one day take the throne from himself. Thus, he pretty much allowed his daughters to do what they desired. Brosia would see that they were proper. Amynta, now twenty-one, had shoulder length black hair and eyes, and had developed into a competent fighter. Quite why, he had no idea at all. Amynta was fair to look at, her solid body well formed; her eyebrows were quite bushy. King Ares was pleased that Amynta always wore proper dresses to dinner and to formal meetings. That she wore men's outfits at other times he graciously accepted.

Of course, Zoe was equally a mystery to the king. A year younger, Zoe also had her mother's attractive looks and hair. Actually, Zoe had never cut hers and her black hair fell to the small of her back, thought she usually wore it in a ponytail, so as not to interfere with her work. She too wanted to be an engineer and inventor. Why, he had no clue. Of course, King Ares had no idea what women actually thought or felt, for that matter. Still, Zoe also wore proper dresses as was required of her. Her room was filled with all manner of books, and she had persuaded him to give her a whole room, which she turned into her creative workshop. Yes, women would remain a mystery to him until he died. That his daughters were off on a lengthy spring vacation for several months meant that he would have some peace and quiet around the palace, time to work even harder with his son, preparing him to take over the throne, perhaps soon. He longed to retire from politics.

On October 10, two carriages pulled up to the gates of Orthos. The two groups had met up on the road two days before. Amynta and Sophia now rode together, chatting about how exciting this getaway was going to be, while Elissa and Zoe rode in the second one, discussing various theories and possible invention designs. Both were intensely interested in this new electricity phenomenon and its seemingly endless potentials and possibilities. Both women had brought along two large crates stuffed with their books, drawings, and designs; they had secretly planned for months to work together on several projects to see if they could bring them to fruition.

Two white robed women motioned the drivers to enter and pull in just to the left, where the huge stables awaited them. White columns supported an open area where the carriages parked under a protective canopy arch. The entire building was two hundred feet long and sixty wide, but only this first section was open on two sides. Patiently, though not without some apprehensions, Tanis stood waiting to greet their four guests as they climbed out of the two carriages. Why had her mother chosen these four women to stay here? Long duration guests were unprecedented, that she knew.

Elissa and Zoe climbed out first, gaping and commenting on the magnificence of their surroundings. Sophia and Amynta joined them, and Tanis recognized the unmistakable stance of a fellow fighter, she smiled. "Welcome to the Temple of Orthos. I am Tanis Petos, Captain of our Guards; my mother is our Seer, Airlea, and your host."

"The small building to the left of the entrance is the Men's House. There are only seven here, but they are not always around. The long building is the Living Quarters, where you will be staying on the second floor," Tanis explained as they began walking along the paved pathway across the green grounds. The four stared at the impressive three-story structure. One hundred feet wide and three hundred long, the marble structure was an incredible feat of architecture. Great columns rose along both the front and back, supporting a sun deck on the second and third floors. Each deck was twenty feet wide and three hundred feet long. Each inside room opened out onto these balconies. Entrances lay at either end and in the middle.

Tanis led them in the north entrance, where a long hallway lay before them, and two stairs were on either side. All construction was the same: polished white marble. "These rooms are our work rooms. Ahead at the end of this long hall is the dining room, where we take our meals." She led them through the spacious room, equipped to feed two hundred at one time. A small adjoining building to the south housed the massive kitchen and ovens and attached to that was their pantry building, now brimming with supplies.

"Your quarters will be on the second floor, rooms 201 and 202. We always double up," Tanis explained.

"Great, Zoe and I want to share a room, please," Elissa quickly spoke up. "She and I are engineers and we want to spend a whole lot of time working together."

"Fine with us," Sophia grinned, glad to be rid of her sister for a change. Amynta agreed for precisely the same reason. She too was tired of hearing engineering talk all the time.

Amynta asked, "I've done a lot of fighter training. Perhaps we can spar and exchange tips, Tanis."

"Sure. Now the Tower of Orthos is next. It is five stories and cylindrical. I hope that mom will let you up onto the Observation Deck at the top. The view is incredible from up there. Mom lives on the fifth floor; our exhaustive library is on the fourth floor. Melina and I live on the third floor along with fourteen others and there are sixteen more that live on the second floor. Our meeting rooms are on the first floor. That's where we are headed now. Mom wants to meet you four."

Tanis led them into the first meeting room, where Airlea was waiting for them. She sat on her oracle throne, a white marble dais that was positioned so that the sun shone directly on her. As the four entered, their eyes took in the awe that the Seers always took care to present to those seeking an audience. Basked in the warm glow of the radiant sunlight, her white robes nearly blinded their eyes. Her flaming red hair stood out even more so than normal. She gave the appearance of being a goddess, which made her predictions carry more weight than one might have expected. Airlea rose to welcome her four guests. As she moved out of the sunlight, the momentary spell was broken, the four blinked as their eyes adjusted.

"I am Airlea. I am so very glad that you four chose to accept my invitation for a spring vacation. Has my daughter shown you your rooms yet?" she began. Tanis shook her head no and the introductions began.

A bit later, Airlea explained, "While you are here, you are free to wander anywhere within our walls. If you wish to go outside them, please coordinate that with Tanis, who is responsible for your safety here. We rise with the sun, sing our morning vespers, and then dine together. After supper, we sing our evening vespers and then retire for the night. You are welcome to join our song. If you wish, you may spend part of your days helping with the gardening and laundry duties, but you are under no obligation to do so."

She paused and looked at Elissa and Zoe, before adding, "I understand that we have two budding engineers with us. Zoe, Elissa, feel free to continue your experiments. If you like, you can look over our complex and make suggestions for improvements. Finally, if you need something, ask either Tanis or her mate, Melina, who is on her way here to meet you now. Melina is also looking after Zona Rho. I do need to warn you both about Zona. She has lost her arms. Her husband forced her into becoming one of those Holy Women of the Eighth Degree. He then got himself killed as well as financially ruined, leaving her and her young son destitute. She found us and we have given her sanctuary."

She went on sternly, "When you meet her, please do not give her sympathy, or sympathize with her situation, for sympathy is but a mockery of actual assistance to her. Sympathy does not help her, but rather harms her mental state. Remember, anytime that someone has to have absolutely everything done for them, their sanity deteriorates rapidly. Allow her to do things for herself and only do something for her when she asks for help. She's been with us for nearly two years now and has made remarkable progress in adapting to life and regaining her self-respect. Ah, here they come now. Melina, Zona, I want you to meet our guests."

Sophia, as her sister expected, rose to the occasion, donning a ruler's mien. "Pleased to meet you both. I am Sophia Aikos. You must be Melina; I see what Tanis sees in you. I do love the way that you've done your hair." The brown bangs not quite touching her eyebrows and her long straight hair falling at the sides framed her face giving her an angelic look. She gave Melina a brief hug. Then she faced Zona, "And you must be Zona. So very pleased to meet you. I must say that you are most attractive, Zona. Honestly, at our court in Thal, you are prettier than ninety percent of the women in their fancy dresses who hang around dad's court. I think that it's downright inhuman what happened to you. I give you my word that if I am ever the ruler of Thallyus, I will make it a serious crime for what happened to you and provide a countrywide safety net to help others who are in such need. I can't imagine how you managed to get yourself and your son safely here to Orthos. Indeed, if you have time, I would like to hear your full story so that I can have a better idea of what new laws I will need to pass to help prevent further abuses to us women." She gave a surprised Zona a hug as well.

Elissa giggled and gave Zona a hug too. "My sister — she's always like that, but seriously, you are quite attractive, Zona. Don't let anyone tell you differently. Me, I am an inventor and engineer. So is Zoe here. We're on a get-away and are going to put our heads together and see what we can invent. Can we chat with you for a time? We might be able to invent some things to help you to do even more things on your own."

"Yes, we just might be able to do that, Zona," Zoe quickly moved to the pair, giving Zona a hug as well. She definitely didn't want to be left out. "I'm Zoe Haimon, King Ares Haimon's youngest daughter. My sister, Amynta and a fighter, though I've no idea why she is into the combat arts," she gestured towards her sister. "Honestly, we need to put our minds to work creating more useful things for our people."

Amynta chuckled and joined them, shaking Melina's hand firmly and giving Zona a strong, solid hug. "Well met, both of you. I don't know about Tanis here, but no one's going to mistreat me, not over my dead body. That's why I am a fighter; no one's going to make an object out of me. I've seen too much of that already. Hell, it even happened to Sophia and Elissa's mother, though they might not care to admit it. King Karistaios forced his wife to become a Holy Woman just so that he could ascend to the throne of Thallyus. You know, the Empress Frona used to be the queen there and she insisted that any queen of Thallyus would have to be a Holy Woman. Well, their mother was dead less than two years after she was forced into becoming one. She fell, unable to prevent herself from falling. Mom was gracious enough to help look after Sophia and Elissa from afar, but I swore that no man was ever going to force me to do things that I didn't want to do; no one is going to make an object out of me."

"I'm sorry about your mother, Sophia, Elissa. I didn't know," Zona finally got a chance to reply. "I could not just succumb because of little Apollo. He was only five at the time. I had to live. Thanks for the compliments, but now no man will ever look at me as an attractive woman ever again, not like this. I am so completely dependent upon the kindness of others now, but I am trying my best to do what I can. It is so hard though. Well, inventors, I could use some help," she smiled, a tiny spark of hope appeared in her dark blue eyes.

Later on, Zoe, Elissa, Zona, and Melina headed off on a lengthy walk. Melina wanted to give the two a complete grand tour of the entire complex. Airlea suggested that the two engineers might be able to see what repairs were needed and offer suggestions for improvements. Zona, on the other hand, wanted a chance to see if the two inventors really could help her. Zona explained, "Right now, my biggest hurdle is that I cannot carry anything, except in my mouth or unless someone slings a bag over my shoulders and head. I would really like to be able to carry my own things around and not have to be so completely dependent on Melina here."

"Oh great! Our first project!" Zoe exclaimed. "We will get right on it! I am sure that we can figure out something that will work well for you, Zona."

"Hey, we ought to finish seeing what all needs to be fixed around here," Elissa cautioned. "We've already seen that their rain water gathering gutters are in terrible shape. Where does the water get collected, Melina?"

She led them into the basement of the tall tower. Four great cisterns, each twenty feet across and carved from the bedrock, lay uniformly around the central stairway. The two engineers inspected these and pronounced them in good condition. Only the many collection pipes and gutters were in need of immediate repairs. Satisfied with the fresh water system, they headed outside.

"Wow, what a spectacular view!" Elissa exclaimed. The four stood by the long western wall looking down into the river valley below them. She estimated the bluff rose some hundred feet above the river plain. Stands of willows interspersed with fields of yellow buttercups and tall grasses fought for their attention as well as the white marble columns supporting a typical domed roof. "What's that down there?"

"Our broken down mill," Melina explained. "Many years ago, we used to mill our own flours and also for the surrounding farmers. It hasn't worked as long as I've been here. Have to ask Airlea about how long it's been broken."

The four gazed out over the idyllic scene for some time, each lost in their own reflective thoughts. "It is so utterly peaceful here," Zoe finally broke the silence.

"Yes, yes it truly is," Melina replied softly, as if her very words would somehow break the spell that Orthos cast upon the land.

"Because there are almost no men here makes it that way," Zona added, a trace of bitterness in her voice.

"You won't get any argument about that from us," Zoe commented. "Men, so many just make such a complete mess of everything they touch. Well, not all; Thoth doesn't. He's about the only man that I know who respects me for who I am."

"We need them for babies and their muscle," Melina added. "Give them more to control and they get power hungry. The seven that we have here are kind and descent men. I do hope the male children that some of us have will grow up to emulate them."

"Say, Melina, can I ask you a personal question? You don't have to answer if you don't want to," Elissa asked. Curiosity had finally bubbled to the surface and she just had to know. Melina nodded and she asked, "You and Tanis — you are lovers? Are all the women here, well, you know, lovers too?"

Zona gave a forced laugh. "No man would want me like I am nor would any woman for that matter."

Melina ignored Zona's bitter remark, remembering Airlea's admonition of caution. "Well, there are over a hundred women here who have chosen to spend our lives here aiding the Seer. We have only seven honest and true men around. So yes, Tanis and I are lovers. We respect and admire each other for who we are, but Tanis also loves Lykou and he, her. Tanis is torn between Lykou and me, which is why she hasn't yet agreed to marry him. I know, it is a confused tangle. As far as the others go, some are lovers and others are not. Who can predict affairs of the heart?" Elissa left it at that, she could only agree with that last.

Tanis and Amynta spent the afternoon in the sparing room. Both found they had an awful lot in common and struck up a solid friendship almost at once. Each knew moves that the other did not. After they worked up a sweat with their short sword dueling, they worked on their other approaches, hand-to-hand. Only when the half-hour supper warning bell tolled did the two finally stop. Hastily washing up, they headed off to join the others for dinner.

Lykou and Nester joined them and the four got to see Tanis' boyfriend. He looked something like a handsome wolf. His facial features were rather angular. His bushy hair was uncontrollable and he long ago stopped even trying to pat it down. He looked something like a wild man. He was a good hunter and a fighter as well, though he doted on Tanis. Nestor, on the other hand, was forty-five and appeared well dressed. At one time, he may have been a court advisor, Sophia guessed.

Over a hundred women gathered in the spacious dining room, but only filled it halfway up. The other five men apparently had wives among these women, Sophia rightly determined. They were all middle aged. She was pleasantly surprised to see over a dozen children and a few babies here as well.

Airlea rose as the ten cooks entered and took their positions behind the long buffet line set upon a number of long tables. "Good evening everyone. As you have noticed, we are hosting four guests for a time." She introduced the four who were asked to rise as their names were called out. "We have but a little time remaining for us. I have told only a few of you my whole vision. Now it is time that I tell everyone, including our new guests. I have Seen that soon we will be facing very Dark Times. Terrible times. Some may claim the end of the world has come upon us. I say that it is not so, but I can say that the times will be extremely terrible. Even men will suffer, though as usual, it will be we women who must bear the brunt of these Dark Ages to come."

"For months now, we have been laying in supplies for the future, far more than ever before. Why? I intend for us all to survive the coming Dark Ages. Sol will guide us all back into the light once more. However, we will all of us be tested, even our men. We will be tested as we have never been tested before. We must rise to meet this head on. We cannot and must not allow ourselves to wallow in self-pity, to lose hope, and to succumb despite all urges to do so. We must be strong and work together as we have never done before. We must and will survive the coming dark times together."

"These evil days will strike all of Tarra, not just Penelopus or Thallyus. The whole world will be facing the same Dark Ages that we will be facing here at Orthos. I have Seen that it will destroy forever Demokritos and the position of Emperor. Some of you have long said that the seven kingdoms have long outgrown the alliance called Demokritos; that one man, the Emperor, cannot hope to rule such highly populated kingdoms, that the kingdoms should be independent countries. Well, that day is rapidly coming, whether we wish it or not. When the Dark Ages end, the seven kingdoms will stand as independent countries. The Emperor and Demokritos will be no more, a thing of the past."

Her stern, ominous, and dark predictions cast a dark pallor over everyone present. Sophia swore later that you could hear a pin strike the marble floor. Airlea paused briefly before continuing. "Some of you have wondered why it is that I have asked these four young women to come and spend time here with us. Never before have we opened our doors to outside guests for an extended stay such as this. Some of you suspect I am using the two engineers to help repair the many things in dire need of repairs. While this is true, it is not the only reason that I have asked these four to come here. Rather, I have *Seen* the vital, critical necessity of these four women to survive their dark hours of testing."

A buzz of whispers flittered around the room, but the four just stared at each other. All this was so far beyond their wildest imaginings that they were speechless. Airlea continued, "I have *Seen* that if these four are with us, then they will find the support and strength from us to be able to survive the coming darkness and survive their dark hours of testing and will be found fit. It *must* be so; we *must* make it so. The future of the Tower of Orthos and the kingdoms of Thallyus and Penelopus depend utterly and wholly on these four women. It will be these four who are to lead us all out of the despair, evil, and chaos of the coming Dark Ages."

"We have yet a little time remaining before our testing comes. Let us all work together, assist our two engineers, and get our home in good repair. Finally, I suspect that some of you have also had visions of the future. If you have, I wish that you would join with me after evening vespers. Now let us dine on the delicious meal that our able cooks have provided for us." Murmurs filled the room as the four rose to follow the lead of Tanis, Melina, and Zona.

While the four wanted to chat about this shocking revelation, their attention was forced upon the buffet. The cooks stood behind the counter while the long line of women, children, and the few men slowly began serving themselves from the many pots, crocks, and dishes they had prepared. Zoe and Elissa kept an eye on Zona and Melina to see how the woman could handle these complex actions. Melina pushed along two trays, helping herself and Zona, who told her what she desired. Apollo came behind them, helping himself. The difficulties that the woman faced became obvious to the two.

Once seated back at their table, Zona then was able to feed herself using her feet. The four relaxed and began chatting with Tanis and Melina. "What does she mean about the Dark Ages? Why us? We are not the kings or queens? Our older brother Adrastos is in line for the throne, not us," Amynta asked, just a little worried or annoyed, she couldn't tell which. She had come for a vacation, a fun one at that.

"I don't know. Mom is a good Seer. She really does have visions of the future, though I know that they are not clear, like memories of the past are for us. She's been telling us part of all this for weeks. Poor Rhea has been purchasing vast quantities of supplies for over two months now. I don't get it either. What are we to be tested about? Fighting, that I can handle," Tanis replied.

"I don't think she means open warfare," Melina added. "All of Demokritos is going to fall; at least that's how I read her words. Surely, there is something that someone can do to prevent these dark times happening. Isn't that what the kings, queens, and the Emperor and Empress are supposed to be doing? Protecting us," she asked.

"Well, I know that dad hasn't got any word about anything bad that is about to happen. We've heard nothing about this calamity in Thal," Sophia countered.

"Same in Tinos," Amynta put in sharply. "We've not heard about anything coming. All is perfectly normal back home. In fact, we've heard nothing at all that might suggest this end of the world scenario. Weird."

"Well, Zoe and I ought to at least get to work tomorrow on getting the gutter system repaired and then have a look at the old mill down by the river. Perhaps it can be repaired as well. Really though, we had wanted to work on these new electrical devices that have been invented up in Velona," Elissa said changing the subject to one with which she was more comfortable. All this talk of her being some kind of a savior had completely unsettled her. She glanced at Zoe and saw that her friend felt the same way.

"Are you four really important in your courts?" Zona inquired. "Are you really special women?"

"Nope, Zona, we are not important or special, excepting our sisters, who want to be engineers and inventors," Sophia answered her sincerely. "It completely baffles me, why Airlea thinks that we are so important a key. Now for myself, I do try to stay ahead of all the affairs of Thallyus, but that's about all. Elissa and I do try to wear proper and fitting dresses when we are in dad's court, helping to maintain appearances for him, but that's all. I do admit that I do like to dress up and wear fancy clothes, though Elissa doesn't. This whole thing makes no sense to me at all. I am going to have to have a long talk with Airlea tomorrow; yes, that's what I must do. I'll let you know what I find out."

Amynta declared, "Tanis, we ought to practice harder. If trouble is coming, we two ought to be prepared. Lord knows what men might try to do to this place." Tanis agreed, more worried about the future now than ever before. She also agreed to see if she could get more solid facts from her mother.

During the ensuing days, the two engineers proved their mettle. Working from dawn to dusk, the two, assisted by several other women, repaired the rainwater collection system and a number of smaller projects around the complex. Then, they tackled the old mill system. The millstones and the wooden gearing were in good condition. The water wheel which harnessed the force of the Vardan River was rotten, what was left of it, that is. The two spent nearly a week completely rebuilding it. However, the two also added another wheel, one that they hoped they could use to power an electricity generator. Together, they had acquired the necessary parts and had brought them along, hoping to get a chance to experiment with this new electricity discovery from the distant northern country of Velona.

During the evenings, the two drew up detailed plans for an above ground water tower, one that would provide running water and for the modern toilets, which they hoped to get purchased and installed. Both wanted to overhaul completely the bathroom facilities here at Orthos, claiming it was completely out of date, which it was. Airlea agreed and sent Nestor off to make the purchases. In return, she insisted that Zoe and Elissa tell her how they had become so interested in engineering. Zoe explained that they were both inspired to become inventors and engineers by the stories that they had read about Enyo of Velona, the inventor and creator of so many marvelous inventions. Thus, just before the Dark Ages struck, a modern toilet system and bath was in operation here.

Sophia, on the other hand, took Airlea's warning to heart. She spent much of her days in their library, researching. She gave up on calamities, finding nothing that remotely approached the doomsday scenario, which Airlea was suggesting. Instead, she focused on political and government philosophy and spent some time discussing these with Airlea. Sophia found the few volumes imported from Velona extremely fascinating reading — especially so the small volume written by someone named Callisto that described what she called the dwindling downward spiral of the overall emotional tone of Demokritos. Using many historical facts to back up her observations, this woman's conclusions made an indelible impact on Sophia.

According to Callisto, over the centuries, their male dominated society had dropped from a pioneering spirit near its founding to one of sympathy, where it was at today. Couple Airlea's cautionary note about Zona, namely that sympathy is but a mockery of actual assistance, which Sophia instantly applied to her world and Demokritos, and she began to see the overall impact. If some catastrophe did come to all people, death was only a short drop down from sympathy, through grief and apathy. A slight push and many would succumb, she realized. This scared her. What about her dad? Would he succumb too?

Tanis did attempt to get more out of her mother that next day. "Mom, look, you need to level with me and with everyone else. If you can See what is going to happen to us, please, I implore you to tell us the whole of it. Perhaps we can better prepare ourselves for this great test that you keep talking about."

Airlea sighed, "You don't know how badly I want to tell everyone here what I've Seen! Yet,

Tanis, the Sight carries with it a great responsibility as well. If I tell you what I have Seen that's coming, the shock of it might cause even greater harm. You will know what it is about soon enough."

Tanis watched her mother closely as she talked. Suddenly, it struck her; Airlea was terrified of her own vision! She too was scared, really scared! "Mom, haven't you always told me that shocks can be lessened by having more time to get accustomed to the shock? Athena passed away last year, but we all knew that she was very sick for months. So when she died, even though we all loved her, our grief and loss was lessened because we all could see it coming for months. Not so when Iris died two years ago. One day she was fine, the next, she had died. We all took that one very hard. Mom, if you know what is coming, tell us, let us prepare for this worst thing; let us get used to its coming, then we will be better able to pass the supreme test, please, mom, please." Tanis was quite willing to beg as she had done so often as a child, anything to get more out of her mom. Times like this, she regretted that she had not the gift of Sight.

Her voice barely a whisper, Airlea said, "It's too awful, Tanis, too awful. I know that you are right, daughter, but it is going to be so awful. I keep hoping that I am wrong. Maybe I am wrong."

"Mom," Tanis declared flatly, her hands upon her hips in defiance, "whenever has your Sight ever been wrong? Huh? Tell me. Has it ever been completely wrong?"

"No," Airlea whispered. "Come here, let me hold you tightly." Tanis did, feeling her mother's arms around her. She put hers around Airlea as well. At last her mother whispered, "We are all going to lose our arms, and men will be unable to walk." Both women squeezed each other even harder.

At supper, Airlea told everyone about her vision of the near future. Across all of Tarra, these few people here in this isolated Tower of Orthos were the only ones who knew what was about to happen to them, long before the mantis released their plague. Naturally, Zoe and Elissa shifted into high gear on their inventions, working constantly with Zona for ideas. Indeed, Zona now found herself the center of attention. All the women began looking to her for ideas on how to get by, how to be able to live, if Airlea's Sight proved true.

By the time that the plague did strike, Zoe and Elissa had made two major changes in the food distribution system. First, the serving tables, which held the various pots, crocks, and such along which the women slid their trays were lowered to a height that Zona thought she could manage. Second, the two engineers, unable to lower the ovens and stoves in the kitchen, worked out a way to raise the floor by building a wooden, raised platform such that Zona could reach the cooking pots on the stove with her foot. Of course, the cooks all complained of back aches in the final days before the plague came, having to bend so far over just to do their work.

Amynta and Tanis took the news particularly hard, along with the other ten women under Tanis' command, their guards. "How on earth are we to do our jobs, Amynta? If we don't have arms, we cannot even hold a sword! If evil men try to invade us and we can't hold a sword, how can we defend ourselves?" Tanis wailed.

"It's worse than that, Tanis," Amynta added. "These days, far too many have the long guns. While I am a good shot with one, I didn't bring it along with me. Without arms, I couldn't use it anyway. Yet, men will be able to use them. We cannot possibly defend against long guns, unless we too have long guns. Maybe it is the end of the world that's coming," she added gloomily.

"Somehow, I have got to find a way to defend us here. Anyone can climb over the walls. Without arms, we women are going to be defenseless. Any man can do what he pleases with us. I'd rather die than let that happen!" Tanis cursed.

"Not entirely defenseless, we have our legs and we can certainly kick hard," Amynta suggested. "I agree, I'd rather die than let some man have his way with me. Come on, we have to figure out something."

"Flee, that's about all that we can do. We do have a secret escape tunnel that leads down to the river. We could possibly hide out in the woods, make it harder for them to find us," Tanis suggested. The two then headed off to check on the current condition of the escape tunnel, which had not been used since the founding of the complex centuries ago. Below the basement where the fresh water cisterns were located, another stairs carved from the bedrock led even deeper underground. Amynta knew at once they were entering a catacombs; the smell of dust and decaying bodies was strong.

The passageways were narrow, barely three feet wide, roughly hewn from the stone. On either side, burial niches rose from the floor to head-height. "It's quadrant-based with four walls of crypts per quadrant. This way," Tanis explained, holding her lantern high. They walked to the north end of the entrance corridor until it T-ed. She then headed due southwest until this passage also ended, joining another at right angles to this one, one which headed back northeast.

While Amynta held the lantern, Tanis fumbled with the lock and got the rusty iron door open. "We'll have to oil it," she whispered. The two looked ahead down a narrow, dark passage, filled with cobwebs. Tanis drew her sword and began a lengthy duel with the webs. A half hour later, the two women finally pushed together to open the very stuck exit door which opened into a stand of trees near the banks of the river. Both decided this exit would serve in an emergency and spent several more hours oiling the hinges and cleaning it out a bit more. Still, both were very worried about possible invasions of men and continued to attempt to find ways that they could defend the complex. All ten of her guards also added their thoughts to the mix.

Lykou found the band of women looking very gloomy. He already had a good hunch what was troubling them, Tanis in particular. "Hi Tanis. Melina said I'd find you here. I heard that you have the exit tunnel prepared."

"Well, yes, but right now, we are trying to figure out how in Sol's name we can possibly defend this place, Lykou," she replied, glad to see him. She realized that, since her mother had revealed the whole vision, she'd become totally occupied with her own problems. She'd ignored him completely.

"I know, I have been thinking about that too, Tanis. We seven fellows are going to have to take on more responsibility for your safety; there is no question of that. You are going to have to depend on us. However, I do have an idea. I don't see how we can keep invaders from climbing the walls and charging into the complex. Probably we couldn't even if you all still had your arms. It is a very long wall and so few of us to guard it. If they come inside shooting, which I doubt very much, we don't stand a chance at all. More than likely, they will be expecting helpless women. That's what I've been thinking about all day."

"Oh, so you like to think of us as helpless women, do you," she taunted him argumentatively.

"No, you misunderstand me, dear. That's what likely raiders will be thinking. I figure that you and your guards can use your feet to counter them. Come on, all of you. I have a practice room all set up. We need to train all of you diligently."

The group followed him to the combat practice room. He had fixed up some swords by wrapping them heavily with old cloths so that a strike would not harm them. "Okay, I come at you with a sword. You use your feet to deflect it and take me out. I am not a martial arts person, but I've seen such done before. Let's see if you can figure out how to do it."

The guards and Amynta spent the remaining days working out all day long. Slowly they became adept at deflecting the sword and kicking Lykou hard enough to knock him over, which was all that they needed. Prone, he could be kicked and stomped to death if need be. Still, all were rather sore and bruised when the plague finally struck.

As far south as they were, the piles of mantis-fabricated items appeared the same day that they awoke to find their bodies totally altered. Prepared as they were and with a heavy dependence upon Zona, the shocked and terrified women began to adapt. In every woman's mind, Airlea's words seemed to echo, "We are all going to be tested. We must be found worthy." Of invaluable assistance to all them was the simple fact that each woman always shared a room with another and thus was able to help each other significantly.

All them discovered that their breasts were now nearly the size of their heads, monster melons, as Tanis declared, though Melina enjoyed them. Tanis' hair now fell below her shoulders, a mass of flaming red hair like her mother's, whose hair now almost touched the floor. "I think your hair looks really good this long, Tanis," Melina told her lover. Hers, however, fell to below her knees, and she needed Tanis' help getting it into a ponytail each morning.

Similarly, Zoe's black hair now reached her ankles, while Elissa's sandy blonde hair reached her knees. Most of the women now found that dealing with their hair took vastly more time than it ever had before. Actually, nearly everything that they now did took vastly longer for them to accomplish.

The fact that their feet were also now grossly malformed was not as big a problem, as long as they wore the shoes, which came with the piles of useful items. Walking so very slowly was annoying, but not terribly debilitating. On the other hand, the seven men and the male children had a very hard time with their feet. Tanis quickly discovered that she could help Lykou walk by supporting him. As a result, Airlea assigned a woman to accompany each of the men so that they could walk in their strange new boots. All told, because they had advanced warning and because of their way of life, these hundred plus made the adaption to the plague's results as well as could be expected. Isolated as they were, news from the two kingdoms and the world in general became almost impossible to obtain. Airlea was very reticent to send out Nestor and Lykou on reconnoitering missions as she usually had done in the past. They simply waited.

Chapter 23 Dreams

General Hypatios Isodoros lay on his cot inside his office, staring at the ceiling. He'd requested the cot and his meals be brought here ever since the plague struck him down along with everyone else. While his aides were forced to crawl on their hands and knees, and his soldiers too, he refused to stoop to such a lowly position, unseemly for a man of his position, in charge of the Thallyus First Army Group. He'd sent an orderly to care for his wife and daughter's needs that first day. He remained here at his command post, though there was little that he could do except ponder the significance of the reports which trickled in from the few brave soldiers who attempted to ride into the capital city of Thal.

The Church of Jehosanity and their henchmen assassins had done a thorough job, he agreed. No longer would that church be a thorn in his side. He was still an ardent Sol believer, though of late he had begun to wonder if this might not be Hell on Tarra now. The streets were littered with the dead, though the worst news was that his king, Aikor, was dead, along with most of his palace guards. Chaos reigned for a time, but now few dared leave their homes. Hence, the rats and birds had free rein on the street's cuisine, foul smelling though it was. He was order-less and leaderless, adrift in a tumultuous sea of utter chaos. Nothing in his training or knowledge compared to the current situation here in Thal. What to do?

What to do? His men were ill equipped to patrol the streets; they couldn't walk either. He refused to take orders from the top noblemen because he did not trust them. They served their own self-interests. He served the king, but the king was dead. Wait for a new king to be appointed, that's what the manuals dictated. Yet, the manuals said nothing about the chaos in the streets. True, civil disturbances could and should be put down, but this was far beyond a mere crowd gone out of control. The madness pervaded every quarter of the city! Criminals, thugs, bullies, and sadistic men had taken over control of the entire city. What to do?

He stared at the ceiling. Maybe this was the end after all. In his fifty years, he'd never seen anything as grim and hopeless as the present scene. The carnage of a battlefield paled against the scene on the streets of Thal. What to do? Well, he had done one thing right. On the first day, sensing riots and unrest coming, he'd ordered his men to raid the armory in Thal and remove all their equipment, ammunition, and field rations. That had been a stroke of utter brilliance, he thought, bringing a brief smile to his face. His men had rations and water, while the criminal elements now had no access to their cannonae, long guns, and voluminous ammunition. That was brilliant. Yet, what to do?

He waited. General Hypatios could not figure out any reasonable actions to take. Why? All of his men were debilitated, crippled, and unable to walk. Prudence dictated that he not risk the lives of his men — his men, men that he was responsible for, men whose lives depended upon his making the right decisions. They were not at war with an opposing army to face. No need to risk his men just yet. Time enough for that when a new king was appointed. The one thing that General Hypatios knew was that he did not want any part of being the ruler, the leader of Thallyus. That was an open door inviting all manner of problems and possibly his own life. Politics belong to the politicians. Let them face the wrath of the people, not himself. What to do? Nothing.

When the new year finally rolled around, the men of Thallyus rejoiced! Their feet returned to normal finally. While women's feet also returned to normal, they still had little to cheer about; their plight was still horrific. At last, General Hypatios took action. He ordered his soldiers to enter the city and to assess the situation. The reports were grim, beyond anything he ever imagined. Disease and death lay everywhere. Many died from simple starvation. Gangs ruled the city blocks, countless gangs. Simply put, Thallyus had degenerated into a city of anarchy.

He sent out patrols in squads of two dozen men. Their first operation was the removal of the dead from the streets and yards. He had little choice but to cremate the mountains of remains. After two weeks, the streets of Thal were cleared. Next, he sent his men door to door, discovering even more dead.

On the brighter side, by February, the farmers markets had opened up once more and food became available once more, alleviating the near starvation of the general populace. Still, few women dared to venture into the streets. Gangs often kidnaped any woman they could find, taking them as their objects of pleasure. However, by March, that practice had subsided considerably as they soon discovered that they then had to attend to these women's needs or they would perish. Few wanted to assist them going to the bathroom, bathing them, or feeding them.

Early March, General Hypatios was finally able to meet with the other three generals who commanded outlying Army Divisions. Army Division One was stationed near their border with the kingdom of Thrace, while Army Division Two was positioned near the Vardan River border with the kingdom of Penelopus, leaving Army Division Three in a similar position along the Ile River border with the kingdom of Theolopolis. All three generals reported similar situations in most of the larger towns, though the smaller villages appeared to have been spared the worst of the growing anarchy. Of course, these three looked to General Hypatios for guidance. It was late fall now with winter's snows right around the corner.

Reluctantly, General Hypatios agreed to declare Martial Law throughout all of Thallyus. He gave the three generals the green light to shoot first and ask questions later, anything to maintain order. At least the fall harvest was finished and the food supplies would be ample. Still, this meant that he was now the official leader or ruler of the kingdom, the position that he had been trying to avoid these past many months.

Then it began — the nightmares. As soon as he laid down beside his wife, who needed so much help these days, he began to feel nervous. Once sleep finally came, he saw a white form, a woman in white, armless, calling to him, waving non-existent arms, beckoning him to her. He woke in a sweat. Trying not to disturb his wife, he crawled out of bed and took a stiff drink. Then a second. A bit later, he slipped back into bed. Again, as he finally went to sleep, there was that woman in white, calling him to her again.

After three nights in a row with so little sleep, he finally saw a yellow sun on the white robes of the woman. He sat up shocked, dripping wet. "It's the Seer! That's the Sun Priestess! She's calling me."

"What's the matter? Are you ill?" his wife asked, a tremor in her voice. Her life was miserable now, but at least her husband was sleeping with her ever since their feet returned to normal. That alone gave her the strength to keep on trying to stay alive. But now he was having terrible dreams; she knew he kept waking up, though she thought better of saying anything to him. He did have a temper about him. Besides, she dare not risk losing him from her bed again.

"It must be the Seer, the High Priestess of Sol at Orthos. What else could it be? She's calling out to me," he whispered, scared of how this might sound. "Don't tell anyone else what I've just told you. They'll think that I'm crazy."

"I promise, dear. Should you go? See her, I mean? Everyone knows the Seer is a goddess and has divine connections," she volunteered a generalized support.

He sighed, "If I don't, I'll never get any sleep! Damn, this is just plain crazy. Why would the Seer be summoning me? I haven't prayed to Sol in thirty years. I thought that they all more or less died out, you know with all this Church of Jehosanity religion that's so popular now."

"Hypatios do not doubt the divine. If the Seer is calling you to her, it must be vitally important. Do you want me to go along with you, dear?" she asked, hoping against hope that he would say no. Clothes did not fit her anymore. Her bosom was so huge and her waist so small that nothing fit remotely. Besides, her helplessness would only be accentuated by a long overland journey. Who would feed her, help her with her needs? Hypatios detested doing such things for her, always assigning one of his aides to help her out.

"No, it is not safe to travel, dear. You will be safe here in the barracks. I'll make sure someone is here to look after you, as always. I best go in the morning," he replied. Interestingly enough, once he had made the decision to go seek out the Seer, he fell asleep and slept soundly.

Some thousand miles northeast of Thal, General Horus Sokrates faced similar problems in Tinos, Penelopus. Tall and thin, General Horus was forty-seven, fit, and a combat veteran, well versed in army leadership. Stationed at the First Army Barracks on the south side of the capital city of Tinos, he commanded a force of fifteen thousand men. He had four other generals beneath him who commanded ten thousand men each. The Second Army was stationed across the border with Thrace near the Dark Forest border with Arolas. The Second and Third Army were stationed centrally but on either side of the Illos River, which divided the kingdom roughly in half. The Fourth Army was stationed just across the Vardan River, some two hundred miles as the crow flies from Thal.

When the plague struck, he and his forces were debilitated, as was everyone else. As soon as the magnitude of the situation became clear, he did allow a third of his men to return to their homes to assist their families. By November as the chaos began spreading, he finally had to send in armed patrols to watch over the streets of Tinos. Such did little good. Always remaining on their horses, the soldiers could do little to stop the crawling men who were looting stores. True, the looters backed off and generally hid themselves when the soldiers rode up. Yet as soon as they passed on by, the looters came back out and continued their thievery.

By the end of November, he had to order his men to begin carting the dead from the yards and streets and alleyways of Tinos. That first day, he rode out with one squad to oversee the situation, but he returned quickly; the stench of dead and rotting corpses was overpowering. Worse, his poor men, unable to walk or stand up, had to crawl and manhandle the remains, somehow loading them into the wagons.

The sight made him sick.

With the king, queen, and their heir-apparent dead and with the palace looted, in early December General Horus visited the wealthiest noble in Tinos to ask him who would be the replacement government. To his dismay, he found himself appointed to oversee martial law in Tinos for the near future. Immediately, General Horus was besieged with civilian problems of magnitude. No food. Women were being kidnaped and raped, while some were outright turned into slaves. No stores dared open and if they still had any wares to sell, no one would brave the street to visit the store.

The plight of the women of Tinos came acutely to his awareness when one day dozens of nearly naked women came to the army base begging to be let in and fed. They promised all manner of sexual favors for food and shelter and help surviving. When he spotted this group, he did an inspection and found that already hundreds of women were now living on the barracks, in virtual servitude to many of the soldiers, providing sexual favors for their basic survival needs. He returned to his Spartan office and vomited.

While General Horus had never been married, he nevertheless respected women and often dated some of the noblewomen who were single. To be seen as an escort to this General was something of a status symbol among the courtiers. He'd never married for two reasons. One, he never found just the right woman. Two, his job as Penelopus' top general demanded nearly all his waking hours. It would not be right to spend so little time with a wife, he always had argued when pressed by the women he chose to escort to the formal affairs. This, they had accepted.

After washing his mouth out and splashing cold water on his face, he stared at himself in the mirror. "What can I do about this mess?" He had no answer. Women were now so utterly helpless, so completely dependent upon men for almost everything; he just could not send the women who had come to the base back home. That would be signing their death warrants. He allowed his men to continue their practices, though more and more desperate women continued to arrive, begging for help from his men.

Still every day, wagon loads of new dead were collected and cremated. He likened the situation to that of some hideous plague. Yet, if it was a plague, the doctors could cure that. With this mess, there was no cure; none that he could see. Men crawled like dogs. Women, well, their plight seemed like utter Hell to him. Slowly but surely, overwhelmed by the totality of the situation, General Horus sank into a deep apathy.

Only when their feet miraculously returned to normal did he start to pull out of the hopelessness that he felt. With a little coaxing, he got word to the local farmers, promising them an armed guard at their open air stores if only they would start bringing food supplies back into the city once more. That arrangement worked. By mid-January, many farmers' markets reopened, but always a half dozen well-armed soldiers stood nearby, maintaining order.

At night, though, when he turned out his oil lamp and crawled into bed, the multitudinous images of the past months began to give him nightmares. He continued to see the gaunt, death-white faces of the armless women lying dead in the streets. The beaten, stabbed, and gunshot men's faces looked pitifully up at him from their sprawled forms on the ground. He slept ill.

Then, he too began to see a woman in white calling out to him, beckoning him to her. Terrified, he woke up, dripping perspiration onto his sheets. The image of her blended with the thousands of dead from the streets and homes of Tinos. She was a zombie coming after him, as if he was the only one to blame. In a way, he felt that he was, after all, he was now in charge of Tinos.

Night after night, he continued to have the same nightmare, until one night he finally realized that the woman was wearing a white robe with a golden sun. She was a priestess of Sol, not some crazed devil. At last, General Horus realized that she must be the Seer of the Temple of Orthos over by the Vardan River, one of the last Temples of Sol still in existence. She was summoning him. The next day, he put his aides in charge of Tinos and headed off to the Temple of Orthos.

Chapter 24 An Idea Can Be Powerful

"Damn it anyway!" Tanis exclaimed. It was the second day of getting used to survival without arms. The cooks had worked long and diligently to finally get a meal prepared. Now the long line of women attempted to get their long overdue dinner. The serving table had been lowered and the pots, crocks, and plates of steaming food were only a couple feet off the ground. Each woman pushed their tray along and attempted to get a plate from the stack and then to help themselves to scoops. Tanis and Melina were side by side and had finally managed to get an empty plate onto their trays. Now she was trying to get a scoop of potatoes onto her plate and she nearly fell over while doing it. If she had arms, she would have lashed out at something, anything, to relieve her frustrations.

After an eternity and many fumbles, both women managed to get food on their plates and a half cup of tea. Now at the end of the line where they had placed one of their yokes, the two sat down and precariously attempted to get their trays into the baskets. Loads had to be balanced, so each woman was paired with another and used one yoke. Several spilled their trays and curses filled the room. Down on their knees, Lykou and Nestor worked on cleaning up the spills, and finally the two began lifting the trays down into the waiting baskets for the women. "God, this is almost impossible!" Tanis declared antagonistically. "Thank, Lykou."

He looked up at her and grinned. "This is a damnable mess, Tanis. Yet, look, both of you managed to dish out your own plates. That's something." He tried his best to say something positive. After all, the room was filled with many other women all facing the same almost insurmountable problems. She managed a grin and shuffled into position to lift the yoke. With Melina shuffling along beside her, Tanis managed to get their food over to their table.

"Now how the blazes do we get our trays up onto the table? Answer me that one, Melinda," she said testily. "How are women supposed to survive like this?" she growled.

Zona, who had followed the two to the table, bringing her dinner plate along with Airlea's, said, "Well, it was not so bad when I had servants to help me with these things. Plus, here, Melina did a wonderful job of helping me. You are right, this is damn near impossible! But I'll be damn if I am going to eat off the floor like some dog!"

"We must experiment and find a way," Airlea said quietly, trying to keep her own panic under control and set an example for all the other women. "I don't think we can lift the tray without dropping it. Maybe with both feet, I can lift the plate up."

"Damn food will be cold before I can ever take a bite," Tanis growled, but mimicked her mother, sitting on the floor and using her feet to lift the plate up carefully. Melina aided by pushing it securely on the table's top. Then, the two reversed roles and got hers up. The tea mugs went up rather easily, primarily because they were only half full to avoid spills.

A bit later, Tanis grumbled, "Damn, I can't use a stupid knife to cut anything. Hell, I'll just eat it from the fork." Around her, others were displaying similar reactions to their first real meal in two days. They had simply scrounged around for quick edibles, such as bread and cheese the first day, while their cooks tried to work out how they could possibly cook a meal. Airlea knew that the seven men could potentially take over the cooking duties, but she wanted to use them for that as a very last resort. From now on, the men would be overwhelmed with many tasks that the women could not do any longer. She didn't want to add to that list any more than she had to — they had to mostly crawl or wobble wildly on the tips of their toes in their strange boots.

Slowly, as the days passed, the women began to work out ways and means of dealing with everyday life, one hurdle at a time. Overall, most of the women were either angry or hostile about the whole situation. Unlike millions of other women who woke up shocked to find themselves armless, these women knew in advance what was going to happen. As a result, they were not thrown into heavy grief and apathy upon awaking to find themselves armless. Anger at their plight was about as low as most fell, though a few hit grief for a brief spell. Here at Orthos, terror and panic screaming had not accompanied the plague as it had elsewhere. Airlea now realized that Tanis had been right, foreknowledge made all the difference.

By December 1, this tight knit group had worked out ways of getting by and now their thoughts began to drift to how the rest of the world was faring. How widespread was this plague? How many women were afflicted? At last, Airlea sent Lykou and Nestor out on a reconnoitering mission, visiting the nearby farms and villages. While the extended farming families were at last coping with the mutilations, the villagers were having more difficult problems, primarily in acquiring food supplies, since the farmers were not able to bring anything in to markets.

Upon hearing about the situation in the nearby villages, now Sophia, Elissa, Amynta, and Zoe began to worry about their parents. Their spring vacation had turned into a nightmare without end, though after a month and with the help and support of these women, the four finally were managing to feel alive again. Unfortunately, there was little that they could do to get word to their parents. Ordinarily, they would have sent off a messenger to Thal and Tinos, but now messengers could not walk. Lykou did try to send a message for Sophia when he was visiting a nearby village. No takers, they all refused to leave their homes. Sophia sighed when Lykou reported this to her, but she understood completely. Women were now so helpless; men just had to stay home and take care of them.

However, everything changed on December 10, when two wagons pulled up at their gates. Tanis cursed, "Damn! Damn! It takes my guards forever to shuffle to get to me and then I can't walk but a few inches a step to get to the gates! If we were being attacked, the battle would be over before I ever got to it!" Tanis cursed again as she nearly fell down while trying to rush to the gates; she took too large a step. Walking on their toes with hardly any heel support made walking treacherous unless she did a sort of shuffle, taking about three inches forward per shuffle. She did muse about how weird it felt when she did lose her balance and flailed around with her arms, only there were none there to flail. Strange sensation, she noted.

"Hi, I'm Yannis and this is Sophos. We're the boyfriends of Amynta and Zoe and have come from Tinos," one young man called out to her when she finally got to the gates. Both were sitting on a wagon. Behind them was a second wagon with two more young men. "They are Theron and Thoth, boyfriends of Sophia and Elissa — they're from Thal. We met up on the road here. Can we please see our girlfriends? We bear some really bad news from home."

"Sure, we all want to hear the news from Thal and Tinos. I'm afraid that here, we've all lost our arms, and all of us can now only barely walk," Tanis replied, helping her guards push the gates open with their bodies.

"It's the same everywhere that we've been. We've not come across a single woman who still has her arms. Every man's feet are somehow fused, and we can either crawl or stumble around trying to walk on our toes in these strange boots. They are kind of like what the ballet dancers wear," Yannis replied, patiently waiting for the women to get the gates open. "Are you low on food? Everyone seems to be running out of food, so we brought some along with us, just in case."

"No, our Seer had us lay in a large amount of provisions. She saw this coming," Tanis replied. "Park them to your right by the stables and . . ."

"Yannis!" Amynta called out from several hundred feet away. She spotted him as they entered the gates and she was hurrying as fast as she could, trying hard not to fall down.

Zoe yelled a hello to Sophos. Not to be outdone, Sophia called out a welcome to Theron, while Elissa squealed to Thoth. All four really missed their boyfriends, now more than ever. As soon as the men parked the wagons, all four very carefully climbed down, setting their feet or toes rather, carefully onto the ground. Holding on to each other, they headed as quickly towards their girlfriends as they could manage, which was only slightly faster than the shuffling, bobbing women. All eight were very excited to see each other.

When they finally met, the four fellows put their arms around their girlfriends and exchanged passionate kisses. Then, Yannis took it upon himself to relay the awful news. Rioters in Tinos had stormed the palace and killed their parents and older brother, looting the palace. Likewise, in Thal, looters had also killed King Karistaios. The four women's sudden loss overwhelmed them and as Yannis expected, they began crying. The four boys could do little but continue to hold their girlfriends tightly.

Quietly, Airlea joined them. Having Seen the coming of their boyfriends, Airlea was prepared and gently suggested they all go into the closest meeting room to sit down. She did her best to comfort the four grieving women, though she knew that only time would heal these wounds of the heart. Having their long-time boyfriends now with them did much to soften the news of the loss of their parents and the two's brother.

Once the four finally recovered a bit, Airlea had the boys relate all the news, none of it good. Both kingdoms were leaderless. Rioting and looting were rampant. Worse, women were being kidnaped, raped, and often turned into sex slaves, though some begged to become one, if only to have someone feed and help them survive. The stark reality of just how horrible the situation had become shocked everyone — all except Airlea and a few others who had Seen the near future. The sheer number of dead was terribly difficult for the four young men to describe. None had ever seen a dead body before and now the streets were littered with corpses.

On the positive side, having four more men around greatly helped out the women of temple, and besides, Airlea knew that now the four girls would not easily be parted from their boyfriends. Still, she insisted that the fellows allow the girls to try to accomplish a task before they lent them a hand with it. "We must learn to live and survive as much as humanly possible," she explained to the four newcomers. Curiously, the four often were stuck peeling potatoes and cutting up the meat into thousands of bite-sized pieces for the cooks.

When the end of December came and everyone's feet returned to normal, absolutely everyone cheered. Airlea celebrated, issuing a round of red wine for everyone. "At least I can keep my balance better this way," Tanis declared.

In the middle of January, Amynta met privately with Airlea and asked her, "Can you marry us? Yannis and I want to wed soon. My folks are gone and I only have him now. Can you do it for us, please?"

With a stern, matronly voice, Airlea asked, "Are you marrying for love or to have a set of hands to help you?"

"Both," Amynta sighed. "We've been in love a long time, but now I need him more than ever before," she admitted. Satisfied, Airlea consented, but as you might expect, the other three wanted to marry as well, announcing the fact minutes after Amynta and Yannis broke their wedding news.

As word of the coming marriage ceremony spread around the complex, Tanis, envious of the four, decided now was the time to marry as well. Her situation was a bit different, since she'd been with Melina all these years. She, Melina, and Lykou talked it over and Airlea agreed to their decision. Lykou would take them both as his wives. They had a three-way love triangle, since neither woman wanted to part from each other, and they both wanted and now needed a husband with arms to help them. The weddings occupied the women of the Temple of Orthos for a week, providing a strong breath of hope for the future to these hundred plus women.

As things finally settled down, Airlea decided now was the time for her to make her move. Each evening, she focused her mind and began to reach out and impact the minds of the two generals, whom the boys had said were mostly in charge of the two capital cities. Nightly, she attempted to enter their minds, implanting the idea for the generals to come to Orthos to meet with her. After many attempts, Airlea finally felt that she had succeeded; now she had to wait for their arrival. Then, she would implant the idea that she had foreseen in her vision.

On February 25, the two generals and their large escort, complete with supply wagons, met up on the long eastward road that paralleled the Vardan River, leading to the Temple of Orthos. As they rode along, General Horus broke the ice. "I kept having these infernal nightmares, until I realized that it was the Seer of Orthos calling out to me. She beckons me to come to her."

"Strange, same here. I got no sleep for nearly a week until I recognized the sun emblem on her robes. The Seer is summoning me there as well. I wonder what she wants? The situation in Thal is horrors beyond any imagination. I have instituted martial law, but I swear that it is doing no good at all," General Hypatios replied.

"Same in Tinos. We just got word that the Emperor is dead as well. I don't think that any king or queen anywhere has survived this plague and the subsequent rioting and looting," General Horus relayed a bit of the most recent news that he'd received. "It seems that our kingdoms are in our hands, general. I for one do not want to rule. It is a no-win situation. No matter what I decide or do, half will be against me."

General Hypatios chuckled, "Same here. Give me a nice tidy war any day. At least those you can win."

"Or lose," General Horus teased. "Either way, both beat the mess that we've gotten ourselves into now. Maybe the Seer of Orthos will have some answers for us. I hope so anyway." The two lapsed into a detailed conversation about the situation and events of the last few months. In many ways, the situation in both countries was nearly identical, horrors beyond horrors.

On March 1, the two arrived at the gate of the Temple of Orthos. This time, Tanis was able to run to the gates swiftly, when one of her guards came to fetch her. "Hello. I am Tanis, Captain of the Temple of Orthos Guards. Welcome to Orthos. Our Seer has said that you would be coming. If you will follow me, generals. Your men can make use of our stables and the men's house just there to your left. Sorry, I have to nod my head, no arms anymore."

"You are not alone, Captain. We've not come across a single woman who still has her arms anywhere in Penelopus or Thallyus. Lead on," General Horus said kindly, pointing out the stables and men's dwelling to his men. The two dismounted, handing their reins to one of their men and following the young woman. She led them into the main meeting room on the first floor of the impressive white marble tower. There, Airlea was waiting for them, along with the four young women from their cities. Conveniently, she already had the four new husbands bring in some tea, biscuits, and honey. They had laid everything out for her.

"Welcome to Orthos, generals. I am Airlea, the High Priestess. I have summoned both of you here. I apologize for being unable to shake your hands in welcome. Please have a seat. You recognize your princesses, I take it?" Both men recognized Amynta, Zoe, Sophia, and Elissa.

"Thank god that you are alive! We thought that you were both dead. I am so terribly sorry about your father," General Hypatios said sympathetically to Sophia and Elissa. Airlea sensed the immediate relief emanating from the two generals. Here were likely successors to the two thrones, so soon they could be relieved of their enforced roles as dictators or martial law.

"Same here, Amynta and Zoe. We all thought that you both had also perished or had been kidnaped and taken into some brothel somewhere. It is so good to see you both alive and doing as well as can be expected," General Horus added. Both men took a seat near their respective princesses. Airlea asked them to pour their tea and to help themselves to biscuits and honey, though a feeling of slight degradation seeped into her thoughts. Serving her guests was beyond her ability now, most frustrating, and humiliating.

Trying hard not to let her feelings become apparent, she began her carefully planned discussion, hoping for the best. "I have summoned you here for two reasons. First, I need to know the precise situation in both capital cities. I have Seen such horrors, but I want verification that what I have Seen has actually happened. Please, bring me up to date and spare no details. You cannot shock me, for what I have Seen happening to the women and men of our lands is beyond words, beyond any wildest imaginations."

Slowly though hesitantly at first, each general took a turn relaying the news. Airlea insisted on the graphic details, especially when it concerned women. The four princesses were aghast at what they heard! The general's estimates suggested that half of the population of each capital city had perished. Worse, far more than half of the casualties had been women and girls. For an hour, the two men relayed the awful news, ending with their declarations of martial law. Both men willingly admitted that they would rather enforce laws, not make them.

All four young women fought hard to keep from sobbing, fighting to keep their grief at bay. When the men finished their graphic report, Airlea said calmly, "Yes, what I have Seen is what has happened. Of that, there is no doubt. You see generals, all this I foresaw long before the plague came. I had our temple make advance preparations and we were not caught by surprise when we awoke to find our bodies armless."

"Yes, but you mentioned two reasons. Pray, Seer Airlea, what is the second? Surely, there is some hope. Surely it is not doomsday as the insane Church of Jehosanity claimed before they killed so many of their parishioners," General Horus astutely noted. Just because he was a fighter did not mean that he was not observant, quite the contrary. He instinctively knew that a great Seer would not summon both men here just to hear the very news that she had already foreseen.

Airlea smiled. "Yes, there is hope. The path that both countries are now following does indeed lead to the total destruction of both countries. Look, if men continue to loot, rob, pillage, rape, kidnap, and then brutally mistreat we women, what future will there be? We women are the vessels which bring forth new life, new generations. If we are destroyed, if women are forsaken, there will be no new life. Both countries will slowly die off all in one generation."

"Do you wish to see that happen? As men, do you wish to see your country wither and slowly die off?" she asked pointedly.

"No of course not, but what can we do?" asked the forty-seven year old General Horus Sokrates. "Please, don't get me wrong. I have never married, and thank the gods that I do not have a wife and daughters who have to endure this awful nightmare. Still, I respect women. As Princess Amynta can vouch, I always escort charming women to all the Royal Balls. Perhaps when I retire from military duty, the time will be right for me to wed. Still, I fear greatly that we are now spectators watching the destruction of our country and all of Demokritos, for that matter. It is as you suggest. If so many women are lost, there will be no future generations to inhabit Penelopus."

The fifty year old General Hypatios Isodoros of Thallyus squirmed in his seat and fiddled with his cup. Had this Seer seen his treatment of his wife and daughter? He knew that his conduct toward them had been less than exemplary during the first two months of the plague. But he'd had his duty to perform, he justified for the hundredth time. He cleared his throat, "Aye, I too fear that we are witnessing the destruction of Thallyus. So many women have already perished. My wife and daughter have thankfully survived, but what kind of future can they expect to have? I admit that I've had a very hard time adjusting to their needs. Still, I've seen to their care." He stopped himself just as he was about to add that they want for nothing, when he realized that was a total fabrication. It was obvious what they wanted: the same things that all women now wanted.

Instead, he added, "Kleio has just turned seventeen. She used to be a very attractive young woman who prided herself on always looking her very best. She should be looking for a husband, but now how can she? I don't dare let her out of the barracks. I have to keep armed guards around our place day and night for fear that she may be abducted and turned into a sex slave in Thal. I can see no hope at all."

Airlea smiled, she guessed that there was more unsaid by the general, but she did not want to go down that path. She refused to stray from her chosen route. "Indeed, I'm sure that you have done your best for your family. Yet, both of you fear that the two countries are now on the path of death — the death of our civilizations." She rose for emphasis, "All of you listen up. I will share a bit of wisdom with you. That which you fear you will have."

She paused a moment, allowing the simple statement to register. General Hypatios sighed, rubbing his day-old stubbled face, he replied, "Then, there is no hope. Are we to just sit back and watch our people succumb?"

Airlea grinned slyly. "Let me make this universal law more real to all of you." Tanis looked up at her mother and wondered what she meant by this. Her pronouncement "that which you fear you will have" echoed in her ears. Surely, there was more to it than this.

"When you want something, don't you feel like you are pulling it towards yourself?" she asked. "When you don't want something, don't you feel like you are pushing it away from yourself?" Everyone nodded, but what did this have to do with anything, Tanis wondered. Her mother continued, "When you agree with something or someone, are you not pulling it towards you, and when you disagree with someone or something, are you not pushing it away from yourself?"

"Well, yes, mom, but I don't see the connection," Tanis replied. Seldom had her mother shared such secret wisdom with others, but now she was doing it openly and before nearly total strangers.

"Allow me to demonstrate just how this applies to us all," Airlea said quietly. She moved over to General Hypatios and pretended to kiss him passionately, as if she greatly desired his affection. At once, he pulled back sharply, shocked at the Holy Seer's actions, his face reddened with embarrassment.

"Forgive me, General Hypatios, but you have shown us all a perfect example of how this works. You see, I attempted to pull into myself affection from the general. Yet, from his point of view, the flow going from him to me seemed to him as an outflow, which is disagreement. When you attempt to pull in to yourself something or someone, from the other side it appears as an outflow and it tries to disagree with you. On the reverse side, if I flow out disagreement towards the general, he will see it as an inflow towards himself. Thus to him, it seems that he desires me."

General Hypatios chuckled, "Well that explains a lot. Sometimes the thing that you want most totally disagrees with you when you finally obtain it!"

"And when women play hard to get, it makes you want them all the more," laughed General Horus. "Oh donkey's butt! What fools are we! I see it so clearly now. We are fearing and resisting and not desiring the destruction of our country and thus that is precisely what we will end up having!"

Airlea smiled, "Yes, precisely, generals, precisely."

"Wait a minute mom," Tanis interrupted. "Lycos and I both want each other and we are not repelled."

"Yes, the law of the universe can be disobeyed, when you know what you are doing. You are alive and sentient. You do not have to play the universe's game, daughter," she replied.

Zoe started laughing hysterically. As all eyes turned to her, she attempted to explain while laughing. "Sis, that explains so many of the young women at dad's court. They doll up and parade around with this big sign on themselves saying 'want me.' 'I'm desirable.' Yet, how many times have we seen some young lad attempt to want them only to find the women pushing them away! This explains a whole lot!" Everyone got her point and laughed along with Zoe.

Grinning, Airlea added, "Yes, it explains much, but there is more to all this. The next point is this. How many times have we all heard that we must adjust to the environment in which we find ourselves?"

"Well, yes, everyone knows that is true," General Hypatios replied. "We must all adapt to the circumstances in which we find ourselves."

"Wrong, general. Again, that is playing along with the laws of the universe. Let me ask you, after you have adapted yourself to the new situation, are you truly happy and content? Not really. Rather, we should be doing the opposite: we should be modifying our environment to suit our needs, our goals, and our purposes."

"Wait a minute!" General Horus spoke up. "General, she's right. On the battlefield, the side that alters the environment to fit their needs often comes up the winner! Priestess Airlea, you would make a fine general!"

Zoe looked at Elissa, the two nodded. Zoe spoke up, "Well, that's just what Elissa and I are planning on doing: modifying our environment to our needs. You see, as we are now, we are so helpless in so many ways. Now if we can get this newly discovered electricity thing going in our countries, then every home can have automatic lights. Just flip a switch. I'm sure that I can no longer light a candle or a lantern, but I could flip a switch. We are both going to work full out on changing our environments so that we can find ways to survive easier. I know that my sister can't ride her horses any longer, but if we can get some companies making those fancy motor-cars that Velona has, then she can drive them wherever she needs to go. Change our environment to fit our needs — that's what Elissa and I aim to do as soon as we can. Of course, we're going to need a lot of help."

Airlea smiled, "I am sure that in time all women of Penelopus and Thallyus will thank you most hardily. Yes, you are going in the right direction, Zoe, Elissa. Now for my final key point. How do we change the future?"

"Well, yes, that is the key question," General Hypatios agreed with her.

She smiled; the general took the bait. "One changes the future by changing the present. One alters what one is doing in the present and that changes the future. Suppose that you have a chicken farm, producing a large volume of eggs to sell each day. What happens if one day you decide to stop feeding and watering the chickens? When the future arrives, you have no eggs and no chickens. Surely you have seen this on the battlefields, generals."

"Absolutely, High Priestess," General Hypatios replied. "The best generals make the best changes in their present situations to obtain their desired future victory. I swear that you have the mind of a top soldier." He meant that as a compliment, Tanis thought, but knew her mother would never countenance wars.

"Exactly so. If we do nothing, then we will be watching the death of our countries. We must change the present to make a better future, one of our choosing, one which gives life, prosperity, and vitality to us all," Airlea replied. She had them all setup and ready for her ultimate plan. Would they accept it or would they reject it as being too radical?

General Horus sized up the situation. The Seer must already have a plan in mind and she must have Seen that it would work. "Please, High Priestess, what must we change?"

Airlea took a deep breath and began, "Until now, our whole society has been dominated by males, a patriarchy to be blunt. Males control the government; mostly they make the laws. As a rule, when a father dies, his property goes to his first-born son. With a few exceptions, women have little or no say in much of anything, except perhaps in the minor domestic arena. Yes, we occasionally had an Empress in charge, but as history shows, she never lasted very long, a few years at most, before she was replaced by males. Today, we see where that male domination has led us. We are at the very brink of destruction as a people and a country. If nothing is done, then perhaps those in the Church of Jehosanity may be right, doomsday has come."

General Horus interrupted, "Yes, I see your point, but what can be done about it?"

"Simple really, generals. You both have the power to pull our countries back from the brink of utter annihilation and set us on course to flourish and prosper once more. How? Now, women are terribly dependent upon those with arms to help us. We cannot be turned out into the street because our fathers have died with all his property and funds going to the eldest son. We cannot survive with men, who have proven themselves totally unworthy, to continue to lead us. It is time for a change. We must do everything possible to allow women to survive and flourish. The answer, generals, is simple. It is time that we instituted a matriarchal society."

"Women must become the new rulers. Property must be owned by the wife in the family and be handed down to her daughters. When a man and woman marry and acquire a home, the home is in the woman's name, as are the entire finances of their marriage. The woman becomes the boss. She has total say over what money is spent and upon what, not the man. In short, we empower the women of Thallyus and Penelopus, for men have already abdicated their responsible use of power. Now we absolutely must give it to women. If we do this, within a few years, I have Seen that both countries will be flourishing and prospering like never before."

"You both have your official monarchs. Sophia can rule Thallyus, while Amynta can rule Penelopus. They will make the laws that you and your men will enforce for the time being. Elissa and Zoe will have a critical role to play. Both are inventors and engineers. Under their guidance, I foresee them bringing back incredible prosperity, wealth, and greatness to both countries. While their sisters guide and control the kingdoms, these two will make it possible for everyone to both flourish and prosper beyond anything that we've seen before."

"So generals, you have a choice to make. Will you do nothing and allow the countries to perish into history books or will you become the force behind the great change that will propel both countries back into greatness once more?" Airlea finished and allowed the men to reach their decisions.

"Count me in, Great Seer," General Horus replied first. "Change must come and soon or there will be no Penelopus. Your argument is simple. As it now stands, women are doomed to a slow extinction. We must do everything in our power to assist our helpless women survive this god-awful plague. If we do not, we are doomed. I am behind you, Amynta, all the way."

"Same here, Sophia. If you think that you can handle the immense job, you have my full support. I believe that if we do not truly protect and help our womenfolk, there will be no future generations. I think that if we present this idea right, it can be done. Yet, I must ask you, are you willing to shoulder such a heavy load?" General Hypatios asked.

Sophia smiled, "You bet. I have to do it. I want to survive. I want to raise a family, but I don't want my children to inherit a dying world. I have already worked out my first law. Any man who mistreats a female in any harmful way is to be publically executed and all his possessions given over to the women whom he victimized. We'll probably need to right away execute a number of those wicked men who have been raping, kidnaping, and holding women as sex slaves. We'll make an example of them, and quickly men will change their ways; at least they may not be so overt about it. Being shot or hanged is a powerful convincer to others."

General Hypatios roared, "My dear Sophia, are you sure that you have not been a general?" All the others joined him, chuckling at her pronunciation. He added, "Yes, that would certainly and rapidly get every man's attention. As long as you have the army there to back you up, the idea would fly. Count me in. I have no respect for the kind of man who would put a woman into slavery, especially now that you are so completely helpless and so utterly dependent upon men."

Visibly relieved, Sophia said, "I'm not a general, but I paid attention to everything that went on in dad's court. Are you sure that you will be able to have a woman giving you your orders? I think that's going to be the most difficult barrier to overcome. Men are used to giving the orders, but now it must be women who give them."

"Your Highness, I am yours to command," General Hypatios bowed his head in a gallant, but polite manner. Both then grinned. He added, "Just don't make me have to make political decisions. I am a soldier, not a statesman." She agreed.

"Oh, by the way, Zoe," the general suddenly remembered. "Just as we were leaving, a delivery came for you. The teamsters tried to deliver it to the palace, but finding it in ruins, they brought it to the army barracks. I brought it along with me. It is a box from Velona."

"Eureka!" Zoe exclaimed, becoming very excited. "Elissa, it's come! I bet yours has come too." She whirled to look at her dear friend. In the process, her thick, rich black hair slipped over her face and bulging bosom. Her hair, like that of many other women, now reached just below her knees. Sophos, her husband, gently stroked it back into place for her.

Elissa whirled to face Zoe, her knee length, sandy blonde hair also flying out of place, forcing Theron to help her get it back out of her face. "Wow! Now we can keep in constant touch with each other. Sis, we got our portable LD radio sets from Velona. With them, we can talk to each other from wherever we are at! Can we go see it now?" The two engineers were so excited that they effectively broke up the meeting.

Elissa pointed out, "Now we can call Velona and ask them for some help right away. I know that it takes a half a year to get here from there, but the sooner we can get some outside help, the better. Zoe, this is the greatest, isn't it? We were sure wise in ordering them when we did. I do hope mine is waiting for me back in Thal."

A bit later, Theron and Sophos unpacked the large crate, under the exuberant eyes and direction of their two wives. Tanis, Lykou, Melina, Airlea, Sophia, Amynta, and the two generals stood watching. Airlea smiled to see such wondrous, childlike enthusiasm on the two young women's faces. Such smiles brought rays of hope to her; perhaps this would all work out somehow for the best.

To everyone's amazement, the instructions were written in their own language as well as that of Velona. With the boys pedaling the generator, much like a bicycle, the two engineers began using their feet to adjust the controls. "Zoe and Elissa calling anyone," the raven-haired woman began yelling into the microphone. After a bit of scratching sounds, they heard a voice speaking to them. The voice spoke in their own language.

"Hello Zoe, Elissa. This is Callisto Tropos, one of the two Monarchs of Arolas. Ana is my sister monarch. I am currently with an army group on the bridge over the Pinos River, right at the border with Penelopus. Who are you two? How can Ana and I help you? Where are you at now? Over."

"Yippee! It works! It works," Zoe exclaimed, jumping up and down, too excited for words. Again, her long raven locks slipped over her face and front. With a grin, Sophos adjusted her hair back for her. Meanwhile, Elissa took Zoe's place and replied.

"This is Elissa Aikos and Zoe Haimon. Our sisters are now going to be the rulers of Penelopus and Thallyus, that's Sophia Aikos for Thallyus and Amynta Haimon for Penelopus. We are with our top generals and at the Tower of Orthos on the Vardan River, which borders our two countries. Orthos is only a couple hundred miles from the Kathos Mountains. Seer and High Priestess Airlea foresaw this plague and had we four come here before the plague struck. We are alive because of her, but we need a whole lot of help. Just a second, Zoe wants to say something."

"Hi, this is Zoe. I just got my LD radio from Velona. Elissa and I are engineers and we both ordered these radios. We need all the help we can get. We have lost our arms. How has Arolas fared? Did the plague strike your country?"

Thus, on March 1, I learned of the situation in Thallyus and Penelopus. Again, I had another run of my Helpful Hints book made, and the Guardian somehow got them delivered. With the assistance of Stefano, we made all manner of licensing agreements with these two countries and sent off more equipment and models, though Ana and Callisto were very glad to send some of their prototypes to Zoe and Elissa so that they could get a start on their lengthy reconstruction tasks. For the next month, Zoe chatted daily with Callisto and Ana in Arolas and with us in Velona. Guidance was what these four women needed most for theirs was a daunting task. True, they had the backing of their country's army, but their palaces and capital cities were in complete chaos, still under martial law. My job had turned into one of global coordination of efforts.

Chapter 25 The Groundwork Is Lain

Four days before the plague struck, the Nikon family began preparing for the Royal Spring Ball to be held at six this evening. Forty-six year old Alexandros adjusted his cummerbund. He was ready, but long years of experience told him the rest of his family would consume the entire afternoon getting ready. He'd closed his general store early, cursing once more his ill luck: four daughters and not a single son. Ambrosia, now forty-five, still looked ravishing in her ball gowns, but both knew years ago that a son was not in their cards. "Dear, you can tighten my corset fully now; it's been an hour now," she called out. Dutifully, he returned to their master bedroom.

His brood of four daughters was costing him a fortune in wardrobe expenses. Nothing was too good for his women. All four took after their mother, wearing their raven black hair long, down to their waists. Indeed, the four looked remarkably similar: Adelpha at twenty-one, Adonia at twenty, Aella at nineteen, and Perse at eighteen. Yes, Ambrosia was exceptionally beautiful when she was their age and he had first met her. Though now middle aged, she still looked radiant and highly attractive. All four daughters looked remarkably like their mother, except that Ambrosia had put on significant weight these last six years. She was a big woman, big boned and robust.

Of course, his goal — okay, Ambrosia and his — was to get them married off soon. Their insistence and need for the latest in fashion dresses and accessories consumed nearly all of his profits from his store. If he and Ambrosia were ever going to save up enough for their long planned trip to Thrace, they would have to get their daughters married. Besides, Adelpha and Adonia were long overdue to marry. At least Adelpha had a steady boyfriend now, a hopeful sign. The entire family subscribed to the idea of "go to all the formal balls and look your very best," attracting the attention of Thal's finest young men. "Love will then come," Ambrosia always said. God, how Alexandros hoped this was so. It couldn't happen soon enough as far as he was concerned.

"Papa, come and tighten me up, please," called out Adelpha from her room. Once he had his wife secured, he headed off to his daughter's room, knowing that the other three would need a hand as well. "Thanks papa. Get it good and tight. You know how I must look my very best tonight. It is the Spring Ball, after all. Do my nails look okay to you or should I put another layer of polish on them?" Although he was struggling to pull her laces tighter, snugging her tightly into her fourteen-inch waistline so that her fancy new red Annelise satin dress would fit her properly, he looked over her shoulder as she held her three-inch long talons up for inspection. She had them painted the same shade as her new dress.

"They look fine, dear, as always. I don't think that you have time to waste on them. They are just fine as they are, perhaps a bit long, dear," he commented.

"Oh papa. You know that men are so attracted to such things. I *do* want to attract the attention of all the young men, especially Ammon. Do you think that he is right for me?" she asked coyly.

"Yes, dear, he is a fine young man. There, it is as tight as I can get it. I'd best see to your sisters now." She thanked him and continued brushing out her long, raven hair as he left her room.

Two more corsets later, Alexandros finally entered his youngest daughter's room. "You ready too, Perse?" he asked.

"Do I have to do this papa? I really don't want to go to the ball. I'd rather go spend some time with grandpa," Perse replied.

"How will you ever find a husband if you don't go to these social balls, dear? Come on; it isn't that bad. Perhaps tonight you will fall in love with a handsome lad. Let me get yours tightened down for you."

She stood up and held on to her bedpost while he tugged and pulled the laces tight. Perse hated to be so constrained, so uncomfortable, and yet she went along with it for now. How could she not? After all, her sisters constantly teased her about being a tomboy all her early years. At last, she had allowed her hair to grow long like theirs, and she stopped cutting her nails. She even took to painting them as her sisters did. For the last few years now, they had stopped teasing her and accepted her as one of them. That was something anyway.

Perse was still conniving. "Papa, I'll make you a deal. I'll go to the ball and dance all night if you will drop me off at grandpa's on the way home. I can spend the entire weekend with him. You know how he needs help with his work, and I'm good at helping him. How about it?"

"You promise not to complain tonight, not once all night?" he asked hopefully. He hated all the minor arguments the women of his household often had. Perse was frequently at the fore in them, complaining about this and that.

"Yes, papa. I promise," she agreed.

"Deal. You be a good girl and do this dance properly, no griping, and I'll drop you off at dad's on the way back — that is, if he will take you in for the weekend. If he is too busy, then you'll have to accept that. After all, he is getting on in age. Besides, dear, you'll be stuck wearing your ball gown the whole weekend."

"I'll manage, papa. Thanks. I promise to behave," Perse replied coyly, having gotten the best of this bargain. She'd put up with this dress and dance for the chance to spend the whole weekend with Grandpa Dio. Too bad that he lived over a mile from their home; otherwise, she could visit him far more often. At eighteen, her parents refused to allow her to walk the streets unaccompanied.

"Deal. There, you are all cinched up."

"Thanks, papa. Can you help me into the rest of the outfit, please?" she asked. The severe corset inhibited her movements. and she found it difficult to get into the rest of her many dress parts without help. Her sisters each helped each other, but they rarely helped her. Why? She really didn't know, but perhaps they still thought of her as a tomboy. Alexandros also knew this and began helping her into the rest of her elegant outfit. Black silk hose from Tashien adorned her legs. Her overskirt and bodice were sky blue satin. When he finally had her dressed, she looked gorgeous. Alexandros knew that she ought to be able to attract the attention of nearly any young man at the ball — perhaps many others as well. Actually, all his daughters would attract such attention. He kissed her forehead and returned to help his wife into the rest of her billowing outfit.

All five wore the latest Annelise style dresses, flaring out to twelve feet across at their feet. They wore the extreme Annelise high heels as well. With their long raven locks falling across their shoulders down to the small their backs and with their long talons, the five women looked stunning. Indeed, Alexandros was very proud to escort his brood to these dances. He always received numerous compliments on their beauty and grace; these comments he enjoyed, though he would have preferred to have at least one son to dote upon.

Perse listened to the idle chatter of her sisters as they got themselves ready for their big night out. While this was a major event for her sisters, Perse bit her lip, avoiding throwing snide comments towards her sisters, remembering her bargain. At last, she headed off to her mother's room to get out of earshot of her sister's banter. "Mom, you look really good tonight," she offered a bit of small talk.

Her mother was sitting at her dressing table, looking at herself in the large mirror while brushing out her hair for the final time. Putting down the brush, she rose and said, "Come here, dear Perse. Why, thank you. I always try to look my best for your father. He does so very much for us all; it is the least that I can do for him in return. Now look at you, Perse. Why, you are all grown up. You look every bit as lovely as your older sisters. You have nothing to be ashamed of there."

Remembering her bargain, Perse bit her lip. Usually, she would have retorted some snide comment about not wanting to look pretty like her sisters. Her mother must have noticed that she remained silent and continued, "Perse, my little baby, you are now eighteen. It is time that I give you your family heirloom too. After all, each of your sisters got theirs when they turned eighteen."

She opened her large jewelry box and took out a beautiful mahogany box, lined with green velvet. "Perse, yours is very special, unlike those of your sisters. I've been saving this one back you see. Now Adelpha is so into red you see, and she always detested green. When she turned eighteen, we gave her a set of rubies, which of course, pleased her very much. Likewise, with your other sisters, but you, Perse, you have strong ties to our past and your late grandmother on your dad's side. Now Aella loves white and as you know, I gave her my mother's fine set of pearls last year when she turned eighteen. But for you Perse, it is my honor to give these to you. Long ago when your Grandmother Kore Nikon passed on, I promised her that I would give these to one of her granddaughters." She opened the box to reveal a magnificent pair of emerald earrings and a matching necklace. "These were given to Kore by her mother, your Great-grandmother Korinna, whom you never knew. Korinna was one of the personal assistants to Queen Frona Aristos, who later became the Empress. She gave them to Korinna almost a hundred years ago, I expect, in honor of her dedication and service to her. Korinna passed them on to her daughter, Kore. Now, I have the honor of passing them on to you, dear Perse. Here, let me help you put them on."

Perse stared at the shining emeralds. For once, she was speechless. No finer present could she have than to be wearing her grandmother's earrings and necklace. She alone of the family had held her strange grandfather and grandmother in the highest regard. She alone doted on the now aging old man, spending all the time that she could with him and helping him with his work. Her mother had no idea how much this meant to Perse.

As Ambrosia picked up one of the earrings, Perse began to wonder how long it actually was! Emeralds set in gold fittings dangled one below the next. Her mother hooked it on her right ear and the earring dangled down, touching her shoulders! Once she wore them both, Perse felt the strangest sensations of the lower emeralds brushing against her shoulders as she turned her head. Ordinarily, she would have complained about how heavy they were, that they were going to pull her ears off. However, the combination of the new sensations on her shoulders and her awe behind their previous owners stifled all such thoughts from her mind. She was wearing earrings given to her great-grandmother by the queen herself! Ambrosia then affixed the necklace around her neck and the two stood looking at Perse's new look in the mirror. She found herself tearing up; they were so beautiful and so replete with meaning for the young woman.

Adelpha popped in to have her mother inspect her outfit. "Oh! Perse gets grandmother's emeralds. Well, that's fine with me. Rubies look better on me. Green doesn't suit me at all, mom. Oh Perse, you are going to need a new gown, one that matches the emeralds. Sky blue and the green so clash, but they do look good on you. Aren't they terribly heavy though?" she chatted away, as usual pushing Perse's buttons, hoping for a fiery outburst.

Used to her sister's slams, Perse bit her lip, remembering her promise. Spending the whole weekend alone with grandpa was worth taking the verbal cuts. After all, they were only words. "Well, yes, dear, Perse should have an emerald gown to match. We'll have to go shopping one day next week, Perse," her mother replied to Adelpha's criticism. "Come, your father is growing impatient. We should be off to the ball." They rose and Perse followed her mother and older sister out of her mother's bedroom. She fell in line at the rear, behind Aella, who also ogled over her new earrings. The five women in their billowing gowns and terribly high heels moved very slowly but elegantly down the long hallway towards their front door, where Alexandros was patiently waiting. One by one, he escorted them to their waiting large carriage, helping each climb aboard as he always did. Dressed as they were, they needed his strong hand to keep their balance and manage to climb into the carriage.

Following along behind in her usual position at the rear, Perse had a long look at her mother and sisters. Aella turned to her as they waited their turn and whispered, "It's so hard on the knees going downhill in these heels. I wish papa would redo our entranceway so that it was level at least."

"But then there would be another couple of steps to maneuver at the street side," Perse reminded her sister. Taking stairs in these gowns and heels was treacherous. More than one young woman had taken bad spills negotiating stairs without an escort. Such news was commonplace among those who went to these Royal Balls.

Around midnight, Alexandros pulled their carriage to a stop in the driveway of his father. Five very tired women were relaxing inside the ornate carriage, quite ready to get out of their constricting gowns and heels. Yet, all were very pleased with how the dance had gone, excepting Perse of course, who could have cared less about the dance and the attention fawned on her by so many young men. Rather, Perse was excited; she had endured all this in order to spend the very long weekend with her beloved grandpa.

Although her feet were aching, she said nothing, biting her lip and offering her hand to her father, who graciously helped her step down. Arm in arm, they strolled up the cobblestone walk to his dad's front door. "You realize that he might be asleep, that he might have other plans, and that he might not want you to spend so much time with him. We haven't asked him ahead of time, dear."

"I know papa, but he will, I'm sure," she replied, hoping that would be so. She had endured the whole day just for this opportunity.

He knocked on the door and they waited patiently. Several minutes later, Dio Nikon, lantern in hand, opened the door. He was in his nightgown and obviously had just gotten out of bed. "Hi dad. Sorry to make an unannounced visit, but Perse here wants to spend the whole weekend with you, that is, if you can take her for that long. Now if you have other plans, dad, or if you would rather not have her stay that long, just speak up."

"Oh my, yes, yes, come on in, Perse. Sure, she can stay with me," the old man's eyes began to sparkle.

"Now dad, do you have enough food in the house for her to stay with you? Are you sure that it's all right," he pressured the old man.

"Yes, son, yes, we'll manage just fine. Now you run along home. I'm sure the others want to get to bed soon. I'll take good care of my granddaughter, Alex. You know how I love to have her here with me."

"Okay then, dad. I'll come around sometime on Monday, if I can get away. If not, then I'll pick her up when I head home after closing the store. Thanks dad." He gave his father a brief hung, gave Perse a strong hug, and kissed her forehead. She watched as he hastily jogged back to the carriage. Both Perse and Dio waved to the four women and the two watched the carriage disappear into the dark night. Neither of them knew it now, but this would be the last time that they saw them alive.

As they stepped inside, Perse gave her grandpa a loving hug. "Thanks for having me. I've missed you so. We have four days to ourselves!"

Tears streamed down the seventy-five year old man's face. "Those earrings and necklace — Kore used to wear them — her mother, Korinna, gave them to her when we got married as a wedding present. I can't help crying, Perse, you look so grown up, so much like the beautiful woman your grandmother was." He hugged her close for a moment.

"How about I make us a cup of tea, grandpa? Then you can tell me all about these earrings," Perse ventured. The light of joy in the old man's face told her that she had said just the right thing. Although her feet were aching, she headed off to his kitchen to fix their tea. At last, sitting around his kitchen table, he began to tell her the unique history behind these earrings and necklace.

"Kore's mother, Korinna, used to be the personal servant of Queen Frona Aristos, who reigned back in the middle 740's. Queen Frona was one of those Holy Women of the Eighth Degree, you know. That's why Korinna was so important to her. She was the arms and hands of the Queen for so many years. Some say that that gift is worth at least fifty thousand gold, maybe more. We never had them appraised, Kore and I just basked in the beauty that they gave Kore. Like you, Kore looked like a queen when she wore them for me." His voice trailed off into a silent remembrance of long by-gone days.

Perse allowed him the private time. When his eyes came back to the present, she whispered, "Grandpa, I promise never to take them off. I will always wear them to honor Korinna and Kore and you too. I love you so, grandpa."

He smiled, appreciating the gesture. "You know that those earrings belonged to Queen Frona. Korinna said that she often wore them so that she could feel and sense her shoulders with them. That's why they are so long. It must have been a terrible life, you know, being armless and all that. Anyway, child, we best get to bed. Your room is just as you left it last visit."

"Okay, grandpa. You go back to bed and I'll tuck myself in. We have four whole days to get things done around here," she replied. He grinned and kissed her forehead, then headed back to bed himself. Perse sat a moment longer and then carried the lantern to her room, the spare bedroom. Indeed, it was just as she left it, bed nicely made.

Now she regretted not having brought along a change of clothes. In her constricting corset, she could not easily undress. Even if she could, in the morning, she knew that her grandfather had not the strength to tighten her corset and she couldn't get back into her dress without wearing it. "Oh hell," she muttered and plopped down on the bed, sleeping in her dress.

At first light, she rose and in spite of her aching body, headed off to fix their breakfast. She beat him to the kitchen by mere minutes. "You can relax, grandpa. I'm in charge of the kitchen for four days," she teased him.

"Bless you child, I do get tired of my own cooking. Kore was a great cook, you know. Say, you are still wearing your ball gown."

"I know, grandpa. I wasn't able to bring any clothes with me. We went straight to the spring ball and then dad dropped me off here on their way back home. I am stuck wearing it I guess."

"Dear child that must be most uncomfortable for you. Why don't you wear some of my old clothes? We've already pitched out all Kore's dresses, but at least you'd be more comfortable," he suggested.

Soon she had their breakfast ready, but within minutes of sitting down, she realized that she really did need to change. "Gosh, I guess I had best change now. With this corset on, I feel like I'm bursting but I've only eaten a quarter of what I normally have for breakfast."

"A good breakfast is the best way to start a day. I always told your father that. Come, let me help you get out of that outfit," he suggested. A bit later, wearing an old set of his pants with the cuffs rolled up and one of his work shirts that was three sizes too large for her, she returned to their breakfast, relieved, and starving.

With a good meal in their bellies, Perse asked, "Okay, grandpa. Now to work. How is the almanac coming along for this year?"

Dio came alive, more alive than his years might suggest. "Since we have the time, I am going to let you draw the conclusions this time. Come, I'll show you all the data that you and I have accumulated thus far. See what conclusions you would draw. Then, we can compare them to mine."

"Goodie, I like a challenge, grandpa. You're on," she exclaimed, growing as excited as he.

Dio Nikon was the sole author and publisher of the Thallyus Farmer's Almanac. Published once each year in the late summer, this almanac was the bible for nearly all the farmers in their country or kingdom and many nearby ones as well. It contained vital year-long weather predictions, crucial information for the farmers who had to have a good idea of what to expect during the next growing season. How much rain? How much snow? How cold would the winter be? How hot would the summer be? Drought? Wet fields in the spring? The list of questions that the Thallyus Farmer's Almanac answered were too numerous to mention. Farmers literally depended upon this little hundred page book.

Dio Nikon had inherited the job from his father, who got it from his father and so on back for five generations now. Over one hundred seventy-six yearly volumes of the book completely filled one bookcase in his front room. Additionally, the almanac contained many short, useful articles, such as the best way to preserve green beans, how to store apples through the winter preserving their freshness by wrapping each in scrap paper. During the year, other knowledgeable people submitted such articles to him and Dio would pick out the best and use them in the next year's almanac. Already, Perse had helped him choose the ten new articles for the coming issue covering the 824 growing year. All that remained was what was most critical: the detailed weather predictions.

Dio led her into his huge study, where every available space was filled with sheets of paper, dried bugs, notes, spider webs, and all manner of nature's objects. These were used to help make his yearly weather predictions, based upon keen observations of nature, and backed with the data of the past one hundred seventy-six years. Several volumes held comparison data. That is, a comparison of the predicted weather versus what had actually occurred. This alone was invaluable, for it allowed them to adjust their predictions.

Yet, in order to make such observations, he needed to be at the edge of the sprawling city, where he had immediate access to the farms, grasslands, and forests. Here, he and Perse collected specimens of caterpillars, for example, checking the bands on the wooly worms for clues. "Okay, Perse, here's the summarized data. You've seen most of it, except for the last month's data. Take your time and write out your predictions. I will go smoke my pipe until you are done."

Perse smiled, this would not only be exciting, but quite a challenge. Never before had he given her total access to everything and allowed her to make the whole year's predictions before! Perhaps he was testing her, she mused, and set to work. She examined the cloud patterns and the rainfall amounts. Hours flew by; she was so engrossed in the work that she scarcely noticed that it was past lunchtime. Dio brought her in a tray of soup and sandwiches, which finally called her attention to the passage of time.

Late in the afternoon, she finally sat back and looked over what she had written. Satisfied at last, she called for him. He smiled and read her ten pages over her shoulder, noticing that she still wore the fancy earrings, which did look a bit unusual considering she was wearing his overly large shirt and pants. "Can I see what you wrote, grandpa? How far off am I from what you came up with?" she asked as he came to the last page of her predictions.

"We know that we have predicted a long, hot, and dry summer this year," he began. "For the fall harvest, we agree, heavy overdue rains will set in early this year. We agree, farmers should attempt to get their crops harvested as early as possible this fall, by April at the latest. We agree, late April and May 824, will be a very wet period. We both predict that we will have a moderate winter and an early spring. We differ only on two points. One, when will be the first snowfall, and two, when should the first planting begin? I have the first snowfall being on June 15 and you predict June 10. I have first planting on October 1 and you have it pushed back to September 23. Those are the only significant differences. Now let's see if we can convince each other about our predictions," he suggested.

"Wow! I got everything else right! Incredible, grandpa," Perse let out a burst of glee, extremely pleased that she had done so well.

"Everything depends upon making daily observations, keeping an accurate journal of what has occurred, Perse. As long as you keep the observations made, we can make accurate predictions of the weather. Now how come you have the first snowfall almost a week earlier than I do?"

For an hour, the two explained their lines of reasoning. Both had made excellent deductions and neither managed to convince the other that theirs was more accurate. At last, they stopped to fix some supper, although they continued to discuss these tiny differences while cooking, eating, and even while doing up the dishes afterwards. Around eight that night, Perse finally won the debate. "Look at the past records, grandpa." She showed him the records from a previous year, which very nearly matched their observed data for the past year. "I am betting that history will repeat itself, grandpa." He finally conceded the two points.

As they sat on his back porch watching the spring fireflies and the fresh smell of spring, Dio made his announcement. "Perse, the time has come for me to pass on the Thallyus Farmer's Almanac to a younger person. I am going to be seventy-six soon, and my health is going downhill rather rapidly." Shock and surprise flooded her face. This can't be! She wanted to scream aloud. She could not envision life without her grandpa, without spending all her free time helping him make the many observations, wandering the land looking for bugs and clues. Perse felt like her whole world was somehow coming crashing down upon her.

"My father handed the almanac down to me when I was ready to handle it. Now it is time, Perse, that I do the same." Perse sighed, fighting back her tears, struggling not to let her disappointment show. She already knew that his health was not as good this past year. Indeed, twice she had come to spend a few days taking care of him and making the daily observations for him.

"Perse, it is with great honor and pride that I am handing over the publication of the Thallyus Farmer's Almanac to you, dear. You will publish the 824 edition; we'll use your predictions, not mine this time," he said quietly.

Taken by total surprise, Perse's mouth opened wide, but she couldn't think of any words to say. At last, she managed to squeak, "Grandpa! Me?"

"Yes, you, my Little Mouse," he replied with a twinkle in his eye. That was his pet name for her, but spoken only when they were alone together. As a little girl, she was completely taken with his study of field mice activities as they related to the weather and that had earned her this private nickname. "You are more than qualified. I know of no other person in all Thallyus who knows half as much as you do about weather prediction. Will you accept this gift, this immense burden, Perse?" he asked.

"Are you sure, grandpa? Am I really ready for it? I have so much more to learn," she countered.

"Of course you do. So have I. Dear Perse, we never ever stop learning. Life ends when one stops learning new things. Today, you've taught me to compare past data with the present. I'd forgotten that in my old age. Yes, you are as ready as I was when my father passed it on to me some fifty years ago now. Will you accept this immense challenge and burden? Millions of farmers depend upon our almanac each year. It is and always has been both a blessing and a burden, for if we are completely wrong, so many are hurt and suffer because of it. The Thallyus Farmer's Almanac is quite a responsibility to shoulder, but I am sure that you can handle it, Perse, if you are willing to do it. What say you, granddaughter?"

Perse threw her arms around him, sobbing, and hugging him tightly. "Of course, I'll do it for you grandpa," she whispered. He patted her back gently, running his hands down her back.

A bit later, he added, "You know that I tried for years to get your father interested in it, the weather, but he was always more interested in that store of his than anything else. He wanted no part of it."

"I know, dad's stuck on his store," she replied. Her mind drifted back to when she was five and had first helped him make some observations. How do you know it's going to snow next week, grandpa, she remembered asking him. After that answer, she became completely infatuated with learning all about weather prediction, constantly hounding her dad to let her visit her grandparents as often as possible. These were good memories, these times with her grandpa.

"Oh, I should mention money, Perse. I have already assigned my Banca account over to you. There is over a million gold in it, far too much for me to spend if I had three lifetimes in which to spend it. Each year, you ought to make at least a hundred thousand gold in profits from sales. Of course, the first copy must be delivered in person to the King and Queen of Thallyus. That's tradition for you." He chatted on about the little details of the publishing, but these she already knew. She merely basked in the warmth of his hug, cradling her head on his shoulders.

"Of course, you'll need to keep a home at the edge of the city. I have been forced to move to a new home four times now. Thal keeps expanding so. Before long, this place will no longer be at the edge of the city and it will be time to move once more," he whispered. She smiled, recalling how she had helped them move twice now. He added, "But at least all that moving into new homes gives me the latest in home furnishings. Why this home has one of those new fancy bathrooms." She giggled. She knew. The latest homes had a toilet built especially for women wearing their fancy ball gowns. She had made use of this invention last night and early this morning. "Why, my first home did not even have running water. Now this one here has both hot and cold running water, as long as I remember to fire up the charcoal water heater, which I keep forgetting to do," he chuckled. His memory was rapidly going, that's why he had forgotten about checking the old records as Perse had done.

Arm in arm, the two headed indoors as the early spring evening chill descended. They turned in at nine that night. The next day, the plague began, though at first neither noticed it. Both were engrossed in getting the last of the predictions written and the 824 edition ready to go to the printers. At eight the next night, they had it finished and ready to be delivered.

"Gosh, grandpa, my arms are so weak and tired! I never knew that so much writing could be so arduous!" Perse said, massaging her arms a bit. Somehow, they seemed smaller than usual, but that was impossible she thought.

"I know, my old body is aching too, Perse. Why, my feet can hardly carry me anymore. A good night's sleep will do us both wonders. Congratulations on getting out your first edition of the almanac." She smiled, hugged him, and kissed his forehead.

The next morning, she awoke and tried to get up and failed. Perse stared at her non-existent arms and let out a shriek, as did so many women that morning. Dio took what seemed forever to get to her room. He was reduced to crawling on his hands and knees.

After the shock wore off the two, Dio somehow managed to get her dressed and to fix them breakfast. The two sat at the table and he fed Perse and himself. "Grandpa, what has happened to me? What has happened to your feet? What is going on?"

"Perse, I surely do not know. If you were unaffected, why, I would have just chalked my feet up to old age. Now, I believe that is not the case at all. Something awful has happened. Besides, Perse, where did that pile of things in the living room come from? I didn't hear anyone entering my house during the night, did you?"

"Well, no, I slept incredibly soundly," she admitted. It seemed preposterous that someone could have entered the house during the night and deposited all of those things without making the slightest noise. Maybe I am just having a very bad dream and I am asleep. That must be it, she concluded. It had to be all that talk of the old Queen Frona that had triggered this awful nightmare. She wondered when she would wake up.

"Come on Perse; let's go see what we can observe with that pile of stuff in my front room, shall we?" he suggested, valiantly trying anything he could think of to get Perse's mind off the shock of the sudden loss of her arms and hands.

"But grandpa, I have lost my arms! I am so completely helpless," Perse wailed.

"Of course you are. It's quite a shocker, Perse. Still, you have your eyes and can observe and you still have your mind. Plus you can at least walk some. I cannot even stand up anymore. Come dear, let's see if we can find any clues to this incredible puzzle," he suggested, trying to make a mystery that the two of them could somehow solve together. She carefully tiptoed her way into the living room, while he crawled along behind her. Together, they sat on his couch and looked the pile of things over carefully.

"Well, those are certainly kitchen utensils, pots, pans, cups," he commented. "Unusual handles though. By golly, that thing must be a writing desk, Perse."

"Well, it could be, but the desktop is only a few inches off the ground," she replied.

"Ah, probably so that you can reach it with your feet," he mused, starting to grasp what was here in the room — means for Perse's survival.

"You mean that I am supposed to write with my feet?" she asked incredulously.

"Suppose so, Perse. Say, things are starting to fit together. I have an idea. See if you can find Memnon's book on that shelf there. If I remember right, it's rather high up on the shelves. It's called <u>A Survey of Dorota Culture</u>, I think that's its title. I can't stand up to get it, but see if you can at least find it, Perse."

"Okay, I don't see what this has to do with anything, grandpa," Perse replied, but rose tentatively onto her toes and carefully went to the shelves. After a bit of looking she found it, "I see it, but how can I get it down? I'm so completely helpless like this." Tears streamed down her face once more.

"Use your chin to pull it out. Maybe let it fall on the floor. It's a book, so it won't break. Maybe I can crawl over and get it, dear."

Perse did better than that. As the book came loose with her chin pull, she saw that she could grab it between her chin and shoulders. Holding it in a pincher grab, she awkwardly returned to the couch, dropping the book into his lap.

"Very well done, Perse. See, you are not as helpless as one might think. Now sit beside me and let's have a look see," he boosted her morale a bit.

As he flipped through the pages, the two looked at the rough illustrations. "That is a writing desk, grandpa! It looks just like the sketches there."

"I believe that you are right. It does look exactly like it. Now this wooden, V-shaped thing with baskets on each end, that's pictured here. A yoke. It allows women to carry things," he observed. A bit later, both concluded that somehow an entire Dorota kitchen was sitting in the living room as well. At last, the two had worked out what everything was for and their eyes rested upon the strange shoes, neither pair of which were in the book.

"Well, those must be for you, grandpa. Your feet don't bend at all?" she asked worriedly. For the first time, she began to see his plight. His feet were pointed downward, straight as an arrow to the tips of his toes.

"Not a tiny bit, dear. Now yours do, but your foot arch is hugely bent. These must be for you. Let me get them on your feet for you and we'll see."

"Okay, and you put yours on too, grandpa. We're in this together," Perse ventured.

A couple minutes later, Perse rose. "Well, this is lots better. I can stand more easily, but walking is still almost as bad as when I wear my Annelise heels. I can get by, I think. How about you?" He had a vastly more difficult time of it, standing like a ballerina on his toes. Perse instinctively came to his side and helped support him. Together, they found that they were able to walk a little.

After sitting back down, Perse asked, "So what does this all mean, grandpa?"

"I don't know yet, but I am hopeful. You see, as I understand that book, the women of Dorota all had no arms, probably much as you find yourself now. Yet, they created what was called Alternative Ways or Women's Ways of doing things for themselves. From reading that book, I gather that their women were quite capable of doing most everything, but in their own unique ways, like carrying things in that yoke."

He went on, "Conclusion: although you have lost your arms, some provision has been made for your continued survival as witnessed by all these critically important items before us."

"And you too, grandpa, what with your feet," she added. "But who did this and why?"

"Darn good question, dear. This is going to sound very strange, but remember a while back that we were hearing all these rumors about some kind of alien plague that struck many of the northern countries, like Velona? Rumor has it that some aliens came to Tarra and unleashed a plague."

"Oh yes, I remember hearing something about it," Perse brightened up. "The women all lost their arms, just like I have."

"Precisely, Perse. I bet anything that the alien plague has just struck us here. That must be what has happened to us, Perse. It has to be. There is no other rational explanation, is there?" he suggested.

"Well, it must be, grandpa, but I don't feel sick or anything. Do you?" He shook his head no. "I wonder if there is anything else wrong with my body?" She was still wearing her nightgown.

"Well, I suppose that we should check it out and make sure that there is nothing else that is wrong that we have missed. Let's get this new hairbrush here into your bedroom. I can help you change, if you don't mind."

"Good idea. No, I am absolutely going to need help with almost everything now, grandpa. I can't even dress myself anymore." The two slowly moved into her bedroom.

He helped her take off her nightgown and both stared at her form in the full-length mirror. "Oh my gosh! Look at my waist! My breasts! Grandpa, they are huge!"

Dio chuckled for the first time this day. "Well, you ladies are always priding yourselves on having tiny waistlines. I think that this certainly qualifies in that regard." She gave a laugh as well; her waist was smaller than her tight-laced corset now! Still the enormous size of her breasts worried her, though she was too embarrassed to mention it to her grandfather.

In the process of all this, her hair, which she had tied up into a bun while sleeping came undone. Dio finished undoing it for her and both let out an exclamation over the length of her raven locks, which now reached the tops of her ankles. "My hair! Look how it has grown! Incredible!"

"Well, you do have your grandmother's hair, Perse, though I would also have to say that your sisters do so as well. Lush, thick, and long, that's how Kore always wore hers, though I don't believe that hers was ever quite this long. Shall we get you dressed now?"

He helped her into the old pants, but then had second thoughts about the old shirt. Not only did she look strange with dangling, empty long sleeves, he pointed out that having them dangling, they might get caught on something. Instead, he turned them inside out, so that they were now in the inside of the shirt. "Thanks, I feel better now," Perse admitted, and then added, "I suppose that I ought to try to brush my own hair."

"Okay, I'll leave you to it. I have another idea that I want to check out. Holler if you need me, Perse. By the way, you are being incredibly brave," he validated her.

She flashed him a large smile and he slowly walked out of the room, holding onto the walls for balance. While Perse kicked off her new shoes and wiggled a foot into the hairbrush's unusual handle, Dio had another bright idea he wanted to explore in private. No sense in getting her hopes up only to have them dashed. She was being incredibly brave, under these circumstances, he thought.

While Perse experimented with the brush, she discovered to her amazement that she was now far more flexible than she had ever been before. That is, her nose itched and without thinking about it reached up and scratched it with her foot. Then she realized that she could effortlessly touch her nose with her toes, something that before today she could not do at all, not even get close to her nose without pulling her leg up there with her hands. A while later, Perse decided that she liked her hair this long and finally went in search of her grandfather to have him tie it back in a ponytail.

She found that he had sewn another shirt for her. He'd cut off the sleeves and sewn the hole shut. Not only did the new shirt fit better, but was more comfortable to wear. "Dear, look what I have here," he said once he'd changed her shirt. "You see, as the publisher of the almanac, you will be receiving free books from all sorts of places. They seem to think that we need them," he chuckled. "Anyway, look at this one that I got about six months ago. I've never read it, no need to, but now it may be very handy. Some woman up in Velona wrote it, Bethany's Hints. I think that it was written to help the women up there when they all got the plague a while back."

"Great. Maybe it will give us some ideas. Say, grandpa, we've forgotten to make today's weather observations!"

"You are right! All these catastrophic events have unsettled us both. Why don't you go make the observations? My poor feet are aching badly," he countered. "Oops, I need to get the door for you don't I?"

While she was outside, Dio got the observation ledger down and put it on the low desk along with a pen. "God above, please grant me this one favor. Please let my Perse be able to carry on for me in my weather work, please dear God," he whispered.

A while later, Perse returned, a bright smile on her face. She grinned when she saw that he had already gotten the ledger down for her. Now came her challenge, could she actually write down what she had observed? She knew that if she could not, then she would have to give up taking over for her grandfather. It was critical that all observations be fully documented if one had any hope of accurate predictions.

"Say, big puffy clouds, what does that mean?" he tested her, reading over her shoulder.

"Going to rain," she replied, though she knew that he knew that she already knew that well.

"Ah, but how soon and how much?" he pushed her a little, hoping to instill a bit more confidence in her.

"Probably tonight, late afternoon, early evening. Thunderstorm, I predict. The tops of the clouds seem very high. Am I right?" she asked coyly, suspecting that she was.

"Well, in a few hours we can tell if you are. Now come on, we ought to get all this kitchen stuff into the kitchen. You can practice carrying things in that yoke. I've worked out that maybe we can install this stuff without removing the current sink, stove, and counters." Unwilling to let him down, she began struggling with the yoke and moving pots, pans, cups, and such into the kitchen.

A bit later, she found him lying on his back working on hooking the new sink into the old system. "Say, can you go into the basement and find me a length of pipe about this long?" He told her where to look and Perse headed off to try it. Sometime later, she proudly returned, holding the pipe pressed against her shoulders and chin.

"Perfect, Perse. See, never toss anything away. You never know when you will suddenly have a use for something. That's what I always say." She laughed. Grandpa was a pack rat. She'd spent hours helping him organize the piles of stuff in the basement, for stuff it was, held against that future day when it might be needed. Now she saw some wisdom in this as the pipe was precisely what was needed to finish the connection.

By suppertime, he had a low counter set against a side wall. A small low stove sat at one end while a sink was at the other end. All these were barely six inches from the floor, just enough height to allow the water to drain from the sink into the existing lines. Jammed along another wall were the low shelves and her chair with rolling wheels moved easily around the workspace.

However, she saw that her grandpa was totally exhausted and near collapse. He admitted to her, "Afraid that I've overdone it today, dear. Can you possibly fix us supper? I can hardly move."

Panic struck her at first. Fix supper? Like this? Without arms? Impossible, she thought. Still, she realized that she had little choice; her grandfather looked bad. If he should die on her, she would be done for. I am so utterly dependent upon him now, she thought but began to try it. It was nearly eight that night when she finally got a meager supper finished and carried to the table. She hoped the food would help him bounce back, but he ate more like an imagined zombie, she thought. He headed off to bed as soon as he finished. He'd never acted this way before now and his age and frailty loomed large in her mind.

Around ten, she finally had the dishes done and her own clothes off, ready for bed. However, she simply could not figure out how to put on her nightgown and gave up, crawling into bed as she was. She awoke the next morning to a quiet house. Slightly spooked and thinking that perhaps something awful had happened to grandpa, she got up and tried to get the clothes on herself. Perse met with a dismal failure and headed off to see what was going on, while wearing only her shoes. Modesty be damned, she thought to herself.

She looked in on her father and saw that he was alive, his chest moved up and down rhythmically, much to her great relief. Perse headed to the kitchen to see about breakfast. Around ten she finally had something made, just as her grandfather finally rose, joining her in the kitchen. "How are you feeling today, grandpa?" she asked, a tone of worry in her voice.

He noticed that, sighing, "Well, I overdid it yesterday. I suppose that I should take it easy today. Amazing, Perse, you got us breakfast."

She laughed, "You call this breakfast? Ha. It's about all I could do and it took me three hours to make it. God, this is a horrible way to live."

"Yes, but you are living and that is all that matters to me, Perse." She flashed him a smile.

Later, she sat down, began reading the Hints book, and then made the daily weather observations. Dio mostly sat in his chair and slept. However, he did rise and made them a hot lunch. As he fed her and himself, he commented, "Well, I suppose that the next thing we must do is to try to see how widespread this plague is. Your father ought to be coming by today to pick you up. Guess we can wait and hear the news from him."

Until now, Perse had not given this aspect any thought at all. She was totally consumed with her own situation. That others might be in the same horrific mess now registered in her mind. What about her mother? Her sisters? Were they affected too? Or was she the only victim? She finished reading the Hints book as the two waited. Finally, Dio rose and headed off to make them some supper.

By evening, her father still had not come by to pick her up and both grew more and more worried. Just when Dio was about to suggest that they head out into the streets for a reconnoitering walk, the popping sounds of gunfire broke the evening stillness. "Grandpa! Gunfire? What can that mean?"

"I don't know, but it cannot be good. I think that it is best if we stay indoors tonight. Perhaps tomorrow we will be able to learn more. Do you need me to undress you?"

She grinned, "Nope that I can do. It is almost impossible to get back into them, though, but you can undo my ponytail, please." She sat up for another two hours brushing out her hair before blowing out her lantern and slipping under the covers.

The next morning, Dio was up early, and the two of them helped each other make breakfast. Once the dishes were done and with Perse dressed and her ponytail retied, the two decided to take a walk. After measuring the amount of rain from the thunderstorm, they headed into the street. His home was at the very eastern edge of the city. His backdoor opened onto a farmer's vegetable field. The grocery store, which he frequented, lay one block further north. Since they were getting low on supplies, the two decided to make a trip there.

"Oh my god! What's been happening?" Perse asked. They had only reached the street when both began spotting dead men and women lying in the street. They pivoted and looked to the south only to see more dead.

"I don't know, but I don't like it. Come, let's see about the groceries quickly," he replied. Perse detected a bit of fear in his tone, something that she seldom sensed from him. The two slowly walked another hundred feet before he stopped. "Perse, I can't make it that far. My feet are giving out on me. Please, help me get back to the house before I fall down and break an arm." His face was white as a sheet, alarming Perse even more. Dutifully, they headed back, though she prayed that he could make it all the way. How could she carry him home if he should fall? How could she care for him if he did break an arm? She very nearly panicked once again.

Only when he collapsed into his chair did she finally calm down. "I'll be alright in a while, Perse," he suggested, much as he used to suggest to his late wife. Still, he knew well the trouble that the two were in now.

"That's okay, grandpa. I will go and check on the store. It is only one block. Don't worry, I'll be careful," she attempted to alleviate his growing fears, much as she often did with her father. Now, however, the situation was vastly grimmer, she was nearly helpless and the world had gone crazy. Still, she put up the same stoic face that she found so useful with her father. "Just leave the door ajar so I can get back inside."

Off she went. Of course, her progress was pitifully slow. Her heels and feet allowed her to take only a three-inch step at the very most. She found herself more or less doing a bobbing sort of shuffle along the street. Perse soon found that the smaller her step, the more surefooted she was, and she slowed down even more, remembering how she used to walk in her Annelise heels. She realized that a fall would be very dangerous, since she had no arms to break her fall or latch on to something to prevent it.

The day was bright, the street still damp from the rain. Dead littered the street. Perse decided to count how many dead she saw down this first block. When she reached the grocery store, she'd counted twelve dead. Worse, she had passed two other homes whose front doors lay wide open. No one seemed to be living there anymore.

Perse stood outside the grocery store staring in disbelief. The doors were smashed and hanging loosely on a single hinge. All the windows were broken; glass littered the street. Worse, inside the shelves were bare. Someone had stolen everything in the store! Reluctantly, she began her long return trip back down the block. It seemed long to her now because of her painstakingly slow walk.

She had not gone far when she realized something was missing all this time: other people. Normally, the streets of Thal would be filled with men, women, and children. Yet this whole time, she'd seen no one at all. Fear crept into her mind once more and she attempted to pick up her pace. After nearly falling down, she quickly slowed back down. As she finally approached her grandfather's home, she heard the sound of hoof beats on the stone street, unnerving her slightly. "Damn, I cannot even run to get away if I need to," she cursed to herself, steeling herself for whatever fate now held in store for her. Steadily the horse approached her until at last she braved turning to face the rider.

She saw a young man sitting tall in the saddle. Two long guns were strapped across his back. He reined in as he neared her. "Miss, it is not safe for you to be out walking." His voice had a kindness to it and she decided to relax.

"I know, but my grandpa is too old and feeble to make it to the grocery store. I had to try for him," she explained.

"I've been all the way south to the Royal Palace. Not a single market or store is open. All those that carried food supplies have been looted, miss. How far do you have yet to walk to get back to the safety of your home?"

"I'm right here. This is my grandpa's place. None at all? What has happened? Has everyone gotten the plague?" she asked. Maybe he knows some news, she thought. At least then her trip would not have been a total waste.

"Strange that you recognize that it is the plague. Yes, the plague has struck. I think all of Thal is down with it. I don't know about any place beyond here, though. However, since the train and carriages are not running on the main lines, perhaps the plague is more widespread than just Thal. Many believe that this is the Day of Judgment or some such nonsense. The Church of Jehosanity went around killing off their own worshipers the other night. You be careful when you are out and about, miss."

"I will, thank you sir."

"Say, doesn't the almanac writer live here?" he asked.

"Yes, Dio Nikon. I'm his granddaughter, Perse Nikon. He's given me the task of writing the new almanacs now. I just finished the 824 version before the plague struck."

He smiled, "Well, if you need anything, we are just next door. I know that we have a wall around us, but we are the Dorota Church of God. We've a side door next to your grandfather's place. Just give a knock if you two need anything. Just be careful, wicked men now rule the streets of Thal. Law and order has broken down completely." He nodded and rode on, Perse turned and headed for their front porch.

Once safely inside, she relayed what she had seen and heard from the next-door rider. Suddenly, Dio brightened up. "Yes, that's it, the Dorota Church of God. How stupid of me. I'm slowly losing my mind, Perse. If anyone knows how the old Women's Ways were done, it is these people. Come on; let's pay them a visit. I'd give anything if they could somehow teach you those ancient Women's Ways of doing things. Then, you would have a fighting chance at life. Come on, Perse. Let's pay our neighbors a visit."

After knocking on the gates on the side wall around the church complex, the two waited patiently. After all, given how slowly everyone now moved, it would take time for anyone to answer. Several minutes later, the gates opened, and Perse recognized the tall man. He had been the rider on the street. "Hello neighbors. I thought we might see you soon. Come on inside. I am Elder Ivan Alido."

"My granddaughter, Perse. I'm Dio Nikon."

"Who is it daddy?" a small boy came hobbling along, his arms resting on his younger sister for support.

Iwan smiled, "My son, Kasper, he's six now. My daughter, Julita, five."

Julita spoke up proudly, "I have to support my brother so he can walk."

Iwan chuckled. "And you do such a very good job of it, Julita." She grinned.

He then asked, "Dio, are you the publisher of the Thallyus Farmer's Almanac? The weather forecaster?"

"Used to be. I've handed it down to Perse here. She's just put out the forecast for the 824 edition, assuming that it can ever be printed, what with this disastrous plague and all," Dio answered honestly.

"Well, I am extremely pleased to meet you and Perse finally! We've followed your forecasts. Frankly, I am amazed at how you can predict the weather so accurately. We planted the very day that you suggested and our gardens are thriving now. This is vital to us, because we grow as much of our own food here as we can so that we are less dependent upon the outside world around us. Please, allow us to give you a tour of our church and its grounds. Ah, here comes my wife now." Perse now estimated that both were about twenty-five years old. Aniela had long brown hair tied back in a ponytail, much as hers. Like herself, normal dresses no longer fit, and she wore one of Iwan's shirts. The two women looked at each other and broke into a giggle.

"Seems we both had the same idea. Honestly, since the plague came, none of our dresses fit. Marzena is beginning to make massive alterations to our old dresses, but it takes time for us to do much sewing," Aniela explained. Turning to Iwan, she added, "Marzena has taken over for me in the kitchen."

Iwan grinned, "Well done. Okay, please allow Aniela to give you a grand tour, Perse. Dio, why don't you and I sit a spell and chat? Walking is darn near impossible for we men, it seems."

"This way first. Ahead there is our huge garden. There are twenty-four of us living here now, so it takes a pretty large garden and quite a few farm animals for us to get by," she explained. "So your forecasts are invaluable to us, you see."

"Well, I just predicted a wet fall, so my advice is to harvest as early as possible this fall," Perse offered. "Say, it must have been so devastating for all of you to suddenly wake up like I did, missing our arms and hands," she made polite conversation. She did not remotely expect what Aniela reply would be.

She laughed, "Oh dear me, Perse. I've been armless since I made the decision when I was five years old. All of us here have been armless since age five. As we walk, let me tell you a bit about us." Shocked, Perse did as asked, wondering what on Tarra could ever get a woman to have her arms removed, doomed to such a horrible life.

"You see, our ancestors lived on the island of Dorota. Back then, for untold centuries, no woman ever had arms, you see. It was a religious thing. Then, back in the time of my great-grandparents, two Holy Maidens appeared, Dita and Bethany. They gave the women of Dorota spiritual freedom, the likes of which are seldom seen anywhere on Tarra. My great-grandparents were close friends of the Holy Maidens. Elder Albin and Klara Feliks were their names. The immigrated here to Demokritos, finally settling down and raising their family, bringing their special gift with them. Klara was one of the original Givers of the Holy Gift as it is called."

"Their twins, whom they named after Dita and Bethany, later married and continued the ancient traditions. Dita passed away some years ago, but Bethany is still here with us. She is now seventy-eight years old and very feeble. Later Bethany's daughter, Marzena married Dita's son, Amadei Feliks. Those are my parents; they are fifty-two and fifty-three respectively. Marzena is our top Giver of the Holy Gift here at the Church of God. To this day, we women consider it the highest of honors to forgo our arms and take up the ancient Women's Ways, complete with learning how to be the Givers of the Holy Gift. Julita has just had hers removed about three months ago, but I had been teaching her our ways since she could first walk. Honestly, Perse, once you learn our Women's Ways, you will never again feel like you need arms. I certainly haven't."

"I don't know about that, Aniela. I feel so helpless now. Grandpa and I looked at a book that talked about your Women's Ways. There were sketches of some of the things that magically appeared in his front room the day the plague struck. That's partly how we figured out that this was the plague and what the stuff was for, but he nearly died trying to install the new kitchen stuff. I have managed to somehow fix a couple of meals for us since then, but it is so hard, darn near impossible."

"Yes, of course it must seem that way to you, Perse. Please, you must spend time with us here and learn the Women's Ways. You will never regret the time spent in learning. Besides, I would like to give you the Holy Gift as soon as we can," Aniela replied.

As they passed the stables, Perse saw a teenaged woman milking a cow. "She's getting milk for our supper. See, I bet you didn't think that we could milk cows."

Perse giggled; never in a million years did she think that she would ever need to know how to milk a cow! Aniela continued, "Well, I can't say that we have not been immune to this plague. As you can see, our feet are as badly distorted as yours are, but with these shoes, we are able to walk, which is more than our menfolk can. Did your hair grow out wildly?"

Perse grinned, "Yes, it used to be down to the small of my back. Now it touches my upper ankles, almost too long, but I've come to like it long, I guess."

"Same here. Mine got so long that I almost asked Iwan to cut it, but now I am glad I didn't. He likes it long like this. Time will tell. Oh, did your breasts swell up too? Mine have become as large as my head!"

Perse giggled. "Yes, mine are humongous. None of my clothes fit anymore."

"Same here. Our waists shrank too, but only mom, Marzena, is complaining about that. You see, she prided herself on being a 'big woman.' Now she has as small a waist as the rest of us." The two women chuckled.

An hour later, the two were introduced to the extended family, as they all gathered for the evening meal. Perse noted that there were eight men, two of which were her own age. Nine were women, with Bethany being the eldest at seventy-eight. She noticed that the one young woman her age was likely betrothed to one of the teen boys, because they sat beside each other and chatted intimately when they thought no one was looking. The seven children were composed of four girls and three boys, all between the ages of four and nine.

To her surprise, the eighteen year old teen offered to sit beside her. "Hi, I'm Albin Feliks. Allow me to assist you, please. Such is considered an honor among us."

"Sure, I'm Perse. My grandpa has been feeding me since the plague struck. I have no idea how to do it without my hands. Sorry to embarrass you so," she whispered, attempting to be up front with this young lad.

"Not a problem. Say is it true that you are the new almanac publisher? The ultimate weather forecaster?"

"Well, yes, my grandfather just handed it down to me. I got out the 824 edition just as the plague struck, only now I don't know if it will ever get published, considering all that has happened."

"Incredible! Well, those of us who farm absolutely depend upon it. I am sure that in time someone will find a way to get it printed up and distributed. Any hints?" he half teased and half begged.

Perse giggled, "Okay, just one. I predict a very wet fall, so get crops harvested as soon as possible."

"Now that is useful to know! Thanks Perse." After a brief prayer led by Bethany, the extended family dove into the meal. Perse was shocked to see the utter normalcy of the giant family meal. While the men and boys did most of the passing around of the bowls and scooped out what the women and girls beside them desired, after that, each woman fed herself, chatting all the while.

Sitting across from Perse, Hanna looked up and whispered to her, "Like this Perse." She demonstrated how to use the special spoons to feed herself. She purposely did it in slow motion. Perse smiled and made a bumbling attempt to duplicate her motions. Perse also saw that the other women were actually eating at the same rate as the men who were using their hands.

Albin whispered, "Don't worry, Perse, all you need is a lot of practice. After all, Hanna's been doing it for thirteen years. Meantime, allow me."

"I feel so foolish, having to be fed like a baby," Perse whispered what she felt.

"That's what mom says is the initial reaction so many have. Trust us, Perse; a little practice with the right tools and techniques of the Women's Ways and you'll be as independent as you want to be."

"Well, I need to be that way now, especially since I have to get out the almanac each year." The two began chatting and Perse forgot about being embarrassed.

A bit later, she overheard Elder Amadei Feliks say, "So Dio, have you really handed down the almanac making to your granddaughter?"

"Yes, yes, I have. Honestly, I have been training her since she was five years old. I regret to say that I am getting too old and have actually missed two forecasts for 824 that Perse caught. It is long past time that I hand it down to younger hands, Amadei." A bit of pride surged through Perse, something that she needed at this chaotic period in her life. At least there was one thing in the world in which she excelled.

When the dinner was finished, Marzena suggested, "Guys, why don't you men take care of the dishes tonight and leave us women to chat with our guests."

Albin whispered, "Maybe I can see you later on or maybe tomorrow, Perse." He rose and began helping clear away the many dirty dishes, leaving the women to the two guests.

Marzena and Aniela took Perse with them into one side living room, while several others doted over Dio in another room. Marzena began seriously, "Perse, whether you realize it, you are a very important, key person; you are now the creator of the all-important yearly almanac. We owe you and your grandfather quite a lot. You've never been very wrong. Will you allow us to give you our most precious Holy Gift?"

"I am just getting started at this. I am sorry but I have no idea what this Holy Gift might be. I will admit that I am most desperate to learn your Women's Ways. I don't see how I can survive really without learning them," Perse freely admitted. Somehow, she felt at home with these women, even though Marzena was fifty-two.

"Our gift is a mental therapy which removes the trauma that one has suffered. Then you will no longer be bothered by the aftereffects. As far as learning our ways, we here would be honored and delighted to teach you. After all, you live right next door to us. Somehow, I believe that we are destined to teach our Women's Ways to a great many women," Marzena answered.

The relief on Perse's face was plainly obvious. "Come; let us begin your therapy right now. We are all well fed and ready to go. Now I want you to close your eyes and return to the first moment when you first had the slightest notion that something bad was beginning to happen to your body, before you awoke to discover that your arms were gone," Marzena asked.

"Well, that's easy. I am writing out the last draft of my 824 weather predictions for the almanac. Grandpa is watching over my shoulder. My arms feel like they are dead somehow," she replied.

A bit over two hours later, Perse was roaring with laughter. "I really have lived before. I really am an immortal spiritual being! There I was, a soldier, a Centurion, marching on Zargarb. How utterly stupid is war! Honestly, these cannonae are blasting around me and one goes off near me taking off my arms near the elbows. I just stand there staring at them, wondering how I can possibly live like this. I decided that I couldn't, and I am standing there waiting for another blast to end it. How funny. Well, after a while, another blast did finish off that body. No wonder I think wars are a total waste of life and men. Oh dear, Marzena! I just realized that if I had not been able to learn how to survive now, I might well have been inclined to have a fatal accident! My god, you've probably saved my life!"

"Well done, Perse, well done indeed. Our first session is over. Come; let us get something to drink," Marzena suggested.

When the two finally returned home that night, Perse was scheduled to come over just after breakfast each day. The various women pledged to teach her their unique Women's Ways and Marzena promised her additional Holy Gift sessions. However, Perse pointed out that she did need to return around noon to make daily weather observations and get them logged. She insisted on doing it, even though Dio volunteered to keep the log for her while she was learning.

As she began heading home around noon, Albin came up to her. "Hold on, Perse. I have been assigned to look after you. I am to be your arms when you might need them. Plus, dad's said it's not safe anymore and that I'm to carry a long gun, just in case."

"Well, okay. Is it really getting that bad out there?" Perse asked.

"Dad says so. I take his word. He's never been wrong yet. Say, can I put my arm on your shoulder for balance? It is almost impossible to walk much on the tips of your toes."

She grinned, "Sure, Albin, but I don't think I'm going to need much protection. I'm only going out to our back yard and perhaps into the farmer's field behind our place. Say, can I as you a question?"

"Of course, Perse, anything."

"Well, it kind of seems to me that in your group, you men take your orders from your women, rather than the other way around."

"I can see what you mean. Not really, Perse. We all work together. Each of us has an equal say because we are all equal. Well, that sure doesn't sound quite right." He flushed. "Obviously, you women are very different than we men. It is just that we both have an equal say, and if there is any real difference of opinion, we men always defer to our women. After all, they are dependent upon us men far more than the rest of the women of the world. Oops, well, that's not true any longer, is it? Am I coming out all befuddled?"

She giggled, "No, I get it. I think that is noble of your men. We do need to lean on you so heavily, you know. Say, what do you want to do with your life? I mean are you getting married soon? What kind of work do you do?" she flushed. She'd never asked a boy outright what his plans were.

He smiled, "No, Hanna is already in love with Aleksy. No, what I really, really want to do is somehow make a big difference in the way that we all live. Somehow, I want to make life's chores far easier for everyone. As yet, I have not seen how this may be done, but I have some ideas. Velona keeps turning out these incredible inventions, telephones, LD radios, even motorized vehicles, which some claim can be driven by our women folk — no arms or hands needed. Now if we could get those here, just think how much better everyone's lives would be. Why, mom could drive herself to the store and do the shopping by herself. I've heard that they have invented this electricity thing, probably comes from lightning somehow. But they can funnel it into these bulbs which make light. Just flip a switch and the light goes on. No lanterns to light. Mom has a devil of a time lighting a lantern, you see. Think how wonderful it would be for her if all she had to do was flip a switch. That's what I want to work on, but as yet, I don't know how."

"Gosh, those sound terrific, Albin. I do hope you can get them here somehow."

"Mark my words, Perse, one day I will help get them here in Thal, somehow, someway." She gave him a big smile and hoped that he would. All of those sounded like heaven to her just now.

A few days later, Amadei called the adults together. "I have just had word from the Guardian up in Velona. He says that we are on the right path. We are right in doing everything possible to help Perse. He says that we must somehow hang on for a while yet, before help will arrive. He does indicate that real help will eventually becoming to Thal, but that it may be months before it comes. Now that's the best news I've heard in ages. Real help. That's what we need here and soon."

Chapter 26 The Idea Grows

November 1, 823 came and still Perse and Dio had no word from her parents and her sisters. Each day, she spent now learning and practicing the new Women's Ways and each evening, she received additional Holy Gifts of therapy. However, it had been well over a week since her father had promised to pick her up. Of course, she would not have returned with him had he come now. She had entirely too much to learn and gain here. Rather the constant worry about how her parents and sisters were faring finally came to a head.

"Honestly, Amadei, someone's got to go check up on her folks and sisters. Her therapy is being seriously impeded," Marzena explained later that night after another session with Perse. "I know that it is risky, but we have to get her some certainty on their well-being."

"Okay, I'll take Iwan with me and check them out tomorrow morning, my love. Shall I offer them sanctuary here if they are in need?" he asked.

She sighed, "I leave that to your discretion. Honestly, there are likely a million women out there in Thal alone that desperately need our help and aid. We cannot house all them no matter how big our hearts may be."

The next morning, hope flooded through Perse as she drew out a map to her home and to her dad's store. "If he's not at home, check his store. That store is his whole life," she explained.

Perse could not concentrate on much of anything, pacing near the main entrance of the Church of God. She estimated that the riders might need at the very most an hour to travel the two miles to the house and back again. Albin waited with her, but spent most of the time sitting, allowing her to do the pacing. At last, he picked up the horses' hooves and awkwardly moved to swing the gates open, while Perse peeked out. The others slowly began assembling in the entrance courtyard awaiting the men's return.

"Oh dear god!" Aniela exclaimed as the two horses came through the gates.

"Those are not my sisters," Perse said believing that the others may be thinking that the two naked, young women sitting in front of the two men were her sisters. She'd never seen either before. What on Tarra was going on? Had they actually gotten to her house? Then, she noticed a streak of red trailing down the side of Iwan's right cheek. He'd been hurt, she surmised. What had she gotten her new friends into?

"This is Lida and that's Maia," Amadei spoke solemnly and softly. "They've been badly mistreated and we had to rescue them. Their families were killed, and they were being escorted down the street to some whorehouse. Yes, they were stripped, and were being led wearing dog collars and leashes when we intervened. Four are dead now, but Iwan took a grazing bullet. Here, hold our horses so we can dismount first." Perse said nothing, fearing the worst. She wanted to hold one of the horses, but could not. Dio quietly stepped up and held Iwan's, putting his other arm around his granddaughter. Dio suspected something just by what Amadei had not said as they arrived, but kept quiet.

Very carefully, the two men slid off their horses, their toes gradually touching the ground. Indeed, dismounting onto the very tips of your toes was quite tricky. Then, the two men lifted the terrified, shocked, humiliated, and zombie-like women down. "Get them bathed and clothed, please," Amadei said softly to Marzena, who took charge, ushering the women on into their large white stone quarters. "Iwan, you go tend to your wound, Albin, Aleksy, and I will tend to the horses." Iwan nodded, but did not make eye contact with either Dio or Perse.

"Come, you two; let's sit over there on the bench by the flower garden," Amadei added softly to both Dio and Perse. Perse offered her shoulders to both men and with their arms over her shoulders, the three walked slowly to the ornate stone bench. Yellow daffodils were in full bloom, along with varieties of tulips and irises. Once seated, Amadei sighed and began.

"There is no easy way to tell you what has happened. Only one thing is certain, Dio, Perse. All five are dead." He gave them time to react and to grieve before continuing. "We may never know fully what happened to them, but Iwan and I have done our best to determine what occurred. His store was looted. We stopped there first and found that it had been stripped bare of all food items; only pots and pans and similar household items remained on his shelves, along with things like rat poison."

"At your home, we found nearly every pot and pan and dish in the place was dirty. Evidently, your father had done the cooking and had not washed any dishes since the plague began. Also, there was nothing edible left in your kitchen and pantry. Further, we do not believe that the house had yet been raided. We did recover the women's expensive jewelry and some funds, which is a sure indicator that robbery was not involved."

A sobbing old man, Dio asked, "What then did happen?"

"We found them all lying around the dinner table. We believe that they died shortly after eating their last meal."

"But how?" Dio pushed him for more.

"Dio, there is no easy way to say this."

"Just the truth, please."

"We found a half-full can of rat poison on the stove. The pot from which he fed them smelled of rat poison. I'm so sorry to have to suggest this, Dio, but we believe that he poisoned them and himself. Knowing that they were out of food and knowing that there was no place to get anything else to eat, rather than see his wife and daughters starve to death, he chose a faster route. We believe it was a mercy killing. There may be more extenuating circumstances involved, Dio. Shortly after that, we discovered gangs of thugs going house to house, murdering the occupants, and kidnaping the younger women. We rescued two young women who were in the process of being taken away into some brothel. Their parents had been shot first; they were stripped, and dog collars fastened around their necks. They were being led like cattle down the street not far from your son's home. We intervened. Those four will not be doing that any longer. Yet, it may well be that your son knew that this was happening and didn't want your granddaughters to become victims as well. We will likely never know the whole truth, but I think that he and they chose the time and place of their deaths to avoid starvation and the vile mistreatment of their daughters."

"Thank you Amadei, thank you. Woe be unto us all," Dio sobbed. "What has our world become? Perhaps it is the End of Days. Now I am left with one granddaughter. Amadei, Amadei, please, please promise me that no matter what happens you will look after my precious Perse, please, I beg you. I am too old to. . ." his voice faltered and his hands went involuntarily up to his chest.

"Grandpa! Grandpa!" Perse wailed, sensing that something was very wrong.

"Dio, I give you my word. I will look after your precious Perse for you. Rest now, Dio. You have done a superb job with Perse. You may pass with great honor and no regrets. Accept my thank you for having done all that you could for our world and Perse. I will take over for you now," Amadei's soft, but solemn voice broke the stillness. Perse saw a brief smile on Dio's face, and then the light of life left his body. She broke down and bawled, and he pulled her head tightly onto his shoulders and allowed her to grieve.

Quietly, Albin shuffled up to the pair and sat down beside them. He'd finished taking care of the mares and had returned, overhearing most of what Amadei had said. Albin noticed Amadei's slight head nod and eye motion. He pulled the body of Dio Nikon off the bench and laid it on the ground, covering it with his own shirt.

"Perse, Albin will take you inside now. We must prepare to honor your grandfather now," Amadei whispered gently. Still sobbing, she rose, and Albin put his arms around her, pulling her head into his shoulders. Together, they stumbled their way into the Church complex, leaving Amadei still sitting on the bench.

Later that day, Dio Nikon was buried in a shallow grave in his own backyard, one of the very few who received a proper funeral during these dark times. That evening, three of the Givers of the Holy Gift began their therapy sessions on Perse, Lida, and Maia. Marzena pointed out to the others later on that Perse had more grief over her grandfather's death than she had over her parents and sisters.

Albin noticed a remarkable change in Perse the next day. Sure, she still missed her grandfather, but the emotional trauma behind the heavy loss was gone. As she made her noon observations with Albin watching over her, she stopped and sighed, "Albin, I am now all alone. I have never been so alone in my life before and now, more than ever before, I cannot live alone. There are so many things that I cannot do any more."

"I know, Perse, but you have all of us now. I promise to be with you now. After all, we have to look after the one and only almanac publisher. If we lose you, how will any farmer know when to plant and harvest?" he attempted a little humor. It worked; she flashed a smile.

"True, I carry a lot of weight on my shoulders now. But Albin, what has become of our world? I mean, how can men be doing these evil, wicked things to women? Instead of being there when we really need them, men seem to be treating us horribly. Why? What is going on? Is this all some horrid aspect of the plague illness?"

Albin mused, "Perse, I'm only eighteen so I don't know as much as Amadei. He's a genius, you know. Anyway, as far as I'm concerned, this plague is bringing out into view many men's hidden motives and attitudes. Before the plague, the King enforced the laws of Thallyus and such crimes would have met stiff punishment. Now that there is no King and the army is nullified, only the might of man makes the rules and chaos reigns. Men no longer need to hide their attitudes and desires, so now they can freely act upon them, to the destruction of society. It's as if someone has removed all barriers to men's actions. All consequences have been removed. As long as you have enough force behind you, you make the rules. Our society is being destroyed from within by these men. I say perhaps it is time for a wholesale change. For my money, we ought to put you women in charge of everything."

Perse giggled. Albin smiled; he had brought the light back into her eyes again. "Silly, don't you see that we women might become just as bad as the men are now? For sure, a game without any rules is not a playable game."

Albin roared, "Perse, you sound just like Amadei!" She grinned, taking that as a compliment. "Well, I still think that it is time to put you women in charge of things."

"Ah, there you two are," Amadei interrupted the two. "As soon as you are done here, please join us in the living room. We have some guests that have just arrived. I think this meeting may be a critical one."

"Okay, we can go now. I am done here," Perse suggested, becoming curious about having been included in some kind of meeting.

As if picking up her thoughts, Amadei added, "Good, Perse. We value you opinion in these matters as well." She blushed and wondered why he would value her views.

The date: a week before the plague struck. The place: Saint Timon's Cathedral, Thal. The occasion: the wedding rehearsal of Kalypso and Teris Isis, both nineteen years old. Teris Isis, the youngest son of a wealthy nobleman of Thallyus, had moved away from the family home in Geo, a large town some two hundred miles west of Thal along the paved road connecting Thal and the capital city of Theolopolis, Kingdom of Theos. Strong, well-muscled, blonde, blue eyed, wealthy, handsome, Teris was something of a scholar-fighter. He was good with weapons, particularly projectiles, arrows, quarrels, and of course the long gun. Yet he was also highly educated, well-versed in politics. Among his many aspirations was becoming a Senator of Demokritos up in Kefall. One day, he would help, or dictate as he often claimed, the laws of the united kingdoms of Demokritos. He advocated openly the abdication of the Emperor or rule by dictator, as he referred to their current form of government. Yes, Teris was something of a rebel, but as of now, he was not taken seriously by the Emperor or even the King of Thallyus. Most merely thought of Teris as another young hothead who had not yet found his calling in life. Certainly, his parents believed this was so.

Not so with Kalypso, who had become enchanted with Teris. She was an only child; her mother had died in childbirth when she was only three years old. Raised by her father, who was a top advisor to the King of Thallyus and who was also quite rich, Kalypso found herself constantly at the Royal Court and had now become a Royal Courtesan. Her father constantly hammered her with advice to look her best always. Enchant men and you will get what you desire from men, he drilled into her. Well, Kalypso, lacking other guidance, always took his advice.

Kalypso was one of those rare, knockout, good looking young women. Her bronze skin was blemishless and perfect. Her greenish eyes, everyone found utterly enchanting, bewitching perhaps. Many women would die to have her waist length, long blonde hair, rich and luxurious, thick and radiant as the sun. Her large lips begged all men to kiss them. Her well-formed bosom attracted instant attention, aided by the tight Annelise style, wasp-waist corset, which she had worn since she was a child. Yes, her waist was always a tiny fourteen inches, and she always, always wore only the finest satin Annelise ball gowns, complete with the matching extreme Annelise heels and expensive, imported Tashien black silk hose. Having mastered the outfit when she was barely ten, at nineteen, Kalypso glided across a room as if she were the very Empress herself. To say that Kalypso was gorgeous would be a gross understatement. Whenever she made her entrance to a room, all eyes, both men and women, stared at her image, for different reasons, naturally. Women envied her grace, beauty, and style. Men lusted for her. Kalypso relished the attention and used it to her advantage often. She was a true epitome of the Courtesan of the Royal Court.

During the last year, she had fallen in love with Teris, and he, her. This evening, they were making their final marriage arrangements with Father Urias of the Church of Jehosanity, that is, Saint Timon's Cathedral, the largest cathedral in Thal and the grandest of them all. Surrounded by priceless works of art, arm in arm, the two followed the priest into his private room back of the gold encrusted High Altar. Kalypso wore her finest light blue ball gown, which contrasted beautifully with the plush red carpeting of the cathedral. Indeed, she had so chosen it for just this effect, just as she always chose her colors to contrast perfectly with her intended surroundings. Teris, dressed in an immaculate dark blue suit with white cummerbund in prominent contrast, walked at her slow pace, quite used to the pace that her extreme heels dictated. In his mind, their slow movement only allowed him more time at her side, to bask in her exquisite beauty and charm.

Once inside his room and seated properly, Father Urias chatted a bit about how the wedding would proceed. Of course, the pair had long ago dictated just how they wanted it to be conducted. "Now then, Kalypso and Teris, as pastor of Saint Timon's Cathedral, it is my obligation and duty to verify your devotion to each other and to gain the knowledge that will guide me in this matter. Please be honest with me. Kalypso, do you love and cherish young Teris here."

"Oh yes, yes of course," she replied demurely, giving him a coy flash of her long eyelashes. Her long red nails squeezed Teris' hand, bringing a smile to his face. She sure knows how to treat a man, he thought.

"Do you love Teris unconditionally? Will you stick by him in sickness and in health, in good times and in bad? Will you support him in his endeavors and be a mother to his children?"

"Yes, certainly, Father Urias. But I must say, neither of us have any intention of ever getting ill. Why, I have never been sick in my life. Besides, we both are very wealthy, so there cannot ever be bad times for us. Yes, each of us will be retaining our own wealth, separate from each other. You see, we are going to have an absolutely perfect marriage," she replied a bit haughtily, but exuding a great confidence. She gave him a loving glance and added, "I am totally certain that Teris will become one of the greatest Senators that Demokritos has ever seen. I will be right there at his side backing him up all the way."

Apparently, the priest was satisfied and he turned his attention to Teris. "My son, do you love and cherish Kalypso unconditionally? Will you stick by her in sickness and in health, in good times and in bad? Will you support her in her endeavors and be a father to her children?"

"Of course, Father. Yes to all of those. How could anyone not love and cherish a woman of such grace and beauty? She's right, you know. For us, there never, ever will be such a thing as a bad time. Ha, we are too strong, too powerful to ever be victims of ill fate!" The priest smiled, so many young couples had such high aspirations, and yet so many fell so short of them. Ah well, now he needed to get to the real reason for this private meeting. These two were a perfect pair, wealthy, opinion leaders, strong ties to the Royal Court, prime candidates to further the Church's goals.

"I hereby give you my unconditional blessing for your coming Holy Union. Now then, have you two considered making the ultimate expression of your unconditional love for each other? By that, I mean have you considered having Kalypso become a Holy Woman of the Eighth Degree? As such, you and she would always be seated in the front rows of our church, afforded the very highest honor by everyone, a constant beacon of the unconditional love of a man and woman for all to see." He continued outlining all the incredible benefits such a status would offer them in their career, how it would promote his career even further, how so many queens and empresses had been Holy Women. He pointed out that both had sufficient wealth to totally provide for Kalypso's needs and that they would be setting a stellar example for others to follow, to say nothing of demonstrating their unconditional love for each other unto Lord Jehosa. Yes, he did his very best to convince these two prime candidates to undergo this holiest of ceremonies.

Neither of the two had even thought about this aspect. Their thoughts had naturally been on entirely different matters. "Father, please forgive us," Teris said masking his true thoughts carefully, "but we have not yet had the chance to consider this Most Holy Ceremony. Such a decision should not be taken lightly, as I understand it. Right?" He cleverly sought to gain a tiny bit of agreement from the priest.

"Oh my yes, yes of course, it must never, ever be taken lightly," he hastened to admit.

"Of course. You must please forgive us. Since we have not yet even thought about this ceremony, would you please give us some time to do so? Right now, we have so many other physical aspects of life to work out between us. You know, getting a new home, moving each of our things from our old homes into our shared home, to say nothing of making sure that our wedding plans work out properly. And then there is our honeymoon to handle. Now, Father, we are more than a little overwhelmed by the myriad of details that must be handled. May we have some time to get these handled properly, and then we may more fully focus on your grand offer of this Most Holy Ceremony?" Teris played the priest like a guitar. Kalypso also saw precisely what he was doing and fully backed him. His mastery of others was what had first attracted her to him. However, she was the only person on whom his skillful manipulations never worked, which is what had attracted him to her in the first place. Okay, her beauty also made an indelible and lasting impression on him as well.

"Oh yes, yes of course. I understand. Please, have a grand wedding and a wonderful honeymoon. When you return, we can discuss this further. I am so glad that you will consider this Holiest of Ceremonies. Our young people so need role models to follow to better achieve admittance into Lord Jehosa's Holy Realm of Heaven," he replied humbly, though certain that these two would very likely agree to the ceremony in perhaps a month or so. He just knew that he could manipulate them into agreeing to go forward with the ceremony. Besides, if needed, he could bring the matter before her father. As top advisor to the King, his support and backing would certainly add further pressure to the couple, if need be.

The next day, the young couple was wedded at Saint Timon's Cathedral in a lavish, but small ceremony. Her father was present, but none of his relations was invited. In fact, none of them even knew of the wedding. Three dozen of their close friends attended, as well as a hundred other well-wishers who had heard about the wedding and invited themselves.

Already the pair had purchased a lavish estate less than a mile from the Royal Palace. Both greatly desired to remain "close to the action." During the next few days, they dealt with moving their possessions into their new estate as well as the purchase and delivery of new furniture. The two wanted their new home to be operational before they headed off on their honeymoon to the Thallyus Hot Springs, far to the south, near the permanent ice shelf and winter vacation spa. This way, their attention would not be pulled from each other, and they could enjoy their honeymoon to its fullest. Teris and Kalypso had carefully planned every detail weeks in advance. All was to be perfect; each insisted it must be so. Both tended to be perfectionists.

The day that the plague struck, the two had completed setting up their huge estate, which boasted some twenty-five rooms. Each had their own dressing room and private study. Their master bedroom held a king-sized bed with satin sheets. Their bedroom walls were adorned with numerous paintings that Kalypso had acquired. Their kitchen had just been extremely well stocked because the two had planned to hold many parties and dances for their friends when they returned from the Hot Springs. She had teased him about having enough food to feed an army, but he had countered that they would be hosting many, many parties and dances. Both loved to dance and already had their ballroom ready to host their first dance in perhaps two weeks.

The day that the plague struck, the newlyweds spent most of the day in bed with each other. Kalypso loved to rake her long talons across his taut bronze chest and arms. He in turn pushed back her blonde tresses, planting a passionate kiss on her thick, inviting lips. Bliss, yes, the two were enjoying the bliss of their young love. All that was soon to change, however.

Both seemed unusually tired by evening and they fell asleep far earlier than either had desired or expected. When they woke, the terror and shock swamped both of them. Her scream was so loud that Teris fairly jumped out of bed. His feet no longer worked and he fell onto the floor, smashing his nose, which began bleeding wildly. "My god! What has happened here?" he screamed as he sat up, blood streaming down his face. He stared up at his bride, who was sitting up in bed. Both were naked, but she had no arms at all — her face white as her bride's dress.

Seeing the blood flowing down his face brought her back to the present. "My god, Teris. You're bleeding badly! Is your nose broken? What happened to you? Why are you sitting there? Go wash it off in the bathroom," she ordered. "Did that priest do this to us while we were sleeping?"

"My feet. Something is wrong with them. They don't bend. Look at them," he cried out, holding his pointed feet so that she could see them. "I can't bend them and can't stand or walk. Damn, I am bleeding!" Slowly, he crawled off to the bathroom, leaving a trail of blood drops on the highly polished marble floor.

Kalypso rose and got to her feet, noticing at once that her feet were also grossly altered. Now she was standing on her toes, wiggling to maintain her balance. Carefully, she moved over to their huge, ornate, mahogany, full-length mirror to observe her body. "What has happened to me? My arms are gone, but god, my breasts! They are enormous, as big as my head! My hair! It's down below my knees! How is this possible? Have we been unconscious for months and months? Hair doesn't grow that much in half a year. What is going on? What's happened to me? God, I don't want to be helpless like this! If that priest did this to me, I swear I will kill him myself!"

"How dear," the nasal sound of Teris greeted her monolog. He'd came crawling back into the room, a towel over his nose and also wiping up the blood drops as he came. "You don't have any arms now. God, your breasts! I've never seen knockers that huge before. Your hair, wow. I didn't know that your hair grew so fast. Well, Kalypso, you still look ravishing to me. Come herel let me hold you. God, I can't stand up. What in the blazes is happening to us?"

She carefully walked over to him and knelt down before him. At once, he put his arms around her and held her tightly to him. "Damn, Kalypso, you are still the most beautiful woman in the world. Except for the arms, I do like your new look. Hey, is your waist even smaller than last night?"

"I think it is. You don't mind the humongous knockers?"

"Of course not, more of you to love, but what the devil is going on here? Your feet are all distorted too, but not as bad as mine are."

"Hold me, Teris, I'm terrified. I feel so helpless like this," she whispered her inner fear to him. He responded well. A bit later, she added, "Teris! None of my dresses will fit me anymore! I don't have any clothes that will fit me, not with these huge knockers of mine. What are we going to do now? Send for a seamstress somehow, will you?"

"Come on, love. Let's see about some breakfast. Our servants ought to have arrived by now and have it waiting for us. I'll send one out for a seamstress immediately. Then, I'll send for the doctor. We have to find out what is going on here. We can't live like this."

The two slowly moved out of their bedroom and down the long hall, but the mansion was eerily silent, unexpectedly so. After all, they had already hired six staff to care for their estate, including a gardener, a cook, a stableman, and maids. Halfway down the huge hall they stopped before a large pile of foreign objects. "These were not here last night, I swear," Teris exclaimed rather surprised with discovering these foreign objects in the middle of his hallway. "Perhaps I forgot to lockup last night."

"No, I swear that I saw you locking, Teris. Someone must have broken in while we slept," she replied with the only logical answer she had. "What is all this stuff? Hey, those look like shoes that I could wear. Teris, help me into them. Hey, maybe those strange boots will help you walk on your toes."

"Okay, love. Say, I am not a ballerina."

Kalypso giggled, "Well, you may well be one now. At least try. This crawling is no good. You are banging up your knees on the marble."

A bit later, Kalypso rose and took a few steps. "Ah, this is a whole lot better, Teris. I have a bit more balance from the heels now. It is just about the same as my walking my Annelise heels. I think I will be okay walking. How about you?"

He rose, wobbling around wildly, arms flailing about as he tried to keep his balance. Kalypso giggled, "Wow, you do look sexy in those boots. Come here; put your arm on me, maybe I can give you a bit of support. Hey, if ballerinas can do it, you can too, probably just takes practice. I know that I had to do a lot of practicing when I first began to wear the Annelise heels. Practice, Teris, that's all. Come on, I'm starving. Let's find our new cook."

Once they made it to the kitchen, they found it as they had left it the night before. Their new cook was nowhere to be seen. "Damn, where is she anyway?" Teris cried out, wholly unused to having others disobey direct orders, certainly not from those whom he hired.

"Well, dear, I am starving. Fix us something. I would but I am helpless now. I know what, dear. Since I can walk, I'll go see if I can find any of the rest of our staff. They were supposed to be here long before now. It must be at least eight or nine in the morning. Do you really like my knockers?" she added still insecure about her drastically altered bosom.

"Well, I'd really like your arms back, Kalypso, but otherwise, you are even more of a knockout!" He gave her a passionate kiss. She decided that her new look was acceptable, except for her arms. They would just have to do something about them, she thought. Maybe a doctor could repair them or something. She then headed slowly off to find their other servants, while he tried to make them something to eat. There was no shortage of food, just a shortage of cooking talent and skill on his part. By the time that Kalypso returned, he had something prepared.

"Well," she said as she bumped her chair around to get it so that she could sit down, "I've checked everywhere in this building and there is absolutely no one here but us. I will say this, Teris, thank god all of our doors have the new style bars and not the old style round doorknobs. I was able to open each door with my foot. At least, I won't be trapped in a room. Say, look at this?" She raised her foot and touched her nose with it. "I am really limber somehow. I could never touch my nose that way before, not without using my arms to pull it up there. Something has happened to us, Teris. I just know it. God, how the devil am I supposed to eat?"

Teris gave a chuckle, "Damned if I know, Kalypso. I will have to feed you. I don't see any other way. Of course, I am liable to take a bite out of my lovely bride as I do it." He sat down beside her and gave her another passionate kiss. So much so, that both almost forgot breakfast.

Once fed, Teris was all for getting dressed. "Dear, nothing is going to fit me. Besides, if I have clothes on, then you are going to have to help me go to the bathroom. For now, maybe it's best if I stay like I am, at least until the dressmaker comes and can alter my dresses or at least alter one to fit me."

"Okay, walk me to our bedroom. I'll dress and then go out and see if I can find out what is going on around here."

A while later, Kalypso supported Teris, now dressed, as he went outside across their courtyard to their small stable. She provided support for him as he saddled their horse and got ready to ride out. "Hey, I'm getting really worried, Kalypso. There is no one here in case you need anything or to protect you if something happens. I will lock the gates when I leave."

"Don't worry, Teris. I can manage the door latches. With the twelve-foot tall, wrought iron fence around our estate and the spikes at the tops, that ought to keep thieves out. But you be careful. I'm helpless without you. If you don't come back, I'm doomed, dear."

Kalypso ambled back inside the huge, but empty manor house. Only the echoing clicks of her heels could be heard, as she slowly but gracefully shuffled her way down the long hall. She stopped beside the pile of foreign objects and chose to sit down on what looked like a desk, only the writing surface was down by her feet. Alone at last, Kalypso began to cry, allowing her fears and humiliations to flow uninhibited from her body. After the good cry, she felt a bit better and stared at the strange things before her. Images began appearing unbidden in her mind. She saw someone using her feet to write using this very desk. That took her by surprise. "I've never seen anyone doing anything like this," she called out to the walls, as if they might answer her.

Soon more and more images came into her mind, as her gaze went from object to object. She had images of using the wooden yoke to carry things, of drinking from the cups with the strange handles, designed for her foot, of cooking using these kitchen items. "Where the devil are all these images in my mind coming from? Am I going mad? Stark raving mad?" she called out to the walls once more. Silence greeted her.

Suddenly, she knew the truth! Data had been bouncing around her mind ever since she awoke. Finally, the pieces fell into place, revealing the stark truth to her. "My god! It's the alien plague! Oh dear god!" She now recalled reading about the strange alien plague, which had struck the far northern continent some time ago. She had written that whole thing off as sheer lunacy, but now she knew that it was not fiction nor was it an exaggeration. The alien plague had struck Thal. "Oh my god," she said yet again and knew what news Teris would be bringing back to her, assuming that he did return. She tossed her long hair back, stared down at her shoulders, and then her legs. Then, something unexpected happened.

"Oh my god!" she cried out yet again. She felt a small electrical explosion somewhere around her head. Instead of an acute headache, swarms of long forgotten images flooded into her mind, swamping her momentarily, as they took shape and form. "Oh my god," she said again and again and again, as the images rolled on, much like a motion picture. As the images finally subsided and settled down, Kalypso's personality and motor skills had totally changed!

Some might have said that she had undergone a psychic shock; others might assume that she had a psychotic break. No matter how one looked at it, Kalypso no longer had the same personality or outlook on life. As she would later learn, she had just somehow plugged in a former lifetime when she had been a Kali Assassin in Kefall, an armless assassin, out to protect other armless women who were being mistreated by men. More importantly, her finely honed, assassin skill set had returned. Teris would return to find a totally changed Kalypso awaiting him. No longer was she the bride that he had married!

Teris rode through the deserted streets, shocked by what he was not seeing! The streets should have been swarming with people, but not today. Occasionally, he heard shrieks coming from women and girls in homes that he passed. He knew what that meant. The multitudinous open-air markets were vacant. Not a single store was open. All were shuttered, as if it was midnight, not a spring midmorning. The more that he rode, the more afraid he became. At last, he decided to visit some of his close friends and see how they were faring.

He visited four before returning home. All were as afflicted as he and Kalypso. Fear, terror, and shock greeted him at every turn. As he began heading home, he finally realized what had happened. The alien plague of the northern continents had finally reached Thal. Everyone would be impacted, none spared. His mind raced down avenues of future tracks. What would happen next? He was a scholar, something of an historian, a budding politician. His thought patterns were well able to piece together possible outcomes and all paths shocked him.

So engrossed, Teris failed to pay much attention to the environment around him. He didn't see the three thugs on horseback moving to catch him, not until it was too late. "Halt. Give us your valuables and horse and we'll let you live," one large man called out, his horse blocking his path. Two others moved around to his rear. Damn, I forgot to bring my long gun, he cursed. The men did not have guns, he quickly observed, just the swords. Teris reached an instant decision. He kicked his horse and galloped through the attacker, ducking to avoid the sword strike. The chase was on!

The four horses galloped through the empty streets of Thal, the only noise to be heard, save the occasional scream from a terrified woman. The only thought in Teris' mind was to get back to the safety of his estate and to Kalypso. God, was she still okay? Had men tried to break in while he was gone? Why had he not armed himself before leaving? How stupid could he have been? The paved streets, budding trees, and bushes flew past him as he galloped for dear life.

"He's been gone a long time — too long," Kalypso fretted. Instinctively, she headed down the long hall and out into their courtyard, standing naked before the locked gate, peering out into the totally deserted street. She waited, praying that Teris would return to her. Then, she heard the sounds of galloping horses. No, make that several horses, she observed. Her senses heightened by her personality change, she knew trouble was coming her way. Soon, she saw Teris galloping towards the estate, followed by three thugs waving swords. She looked at the gate lock and knew that she could not get it opened herself. She swore another curse, but then reacted. She moved to an ideal attack position, estimating how they would enter after Teris got the gate opened. She knew that she needed to buy him some time to get the gate unlocked, so she positioned herself accordingly and waited.

Soon, Teris came riding up and leaned over, frantically trying to unlock the gate. The three thugs were right behind him, but they reined up and stared in disbelief at the naked woman standing just beyond the fence, perhaps the most beautiful woman they had ever seen before! She had precisely the intended impact on the men, who halted and stared at her, giving Teris time to get the gate unlocked. As he rode inside, they suddenly came out of their stupor and came charging in after him, determined to win far more than their intended prize!

Wham! Her right foot struck out, hitting the lead horse's neck. It reared, throwing the man onto the hard ground. The other two horses balked, their riders fought to control their disoriented beasts. Kalypso took advantage of the delay to move closer to the fallen man. She drove her right foot down with all the force she could muster squarely on the man's exposed neck. He died instantly. Now she whirled and planted a circle kick onto the next rider, taking him by surprise, knocking him from his saddle, his sword clanking away from him as he hit the hard stone of the courtyard.

The third man recovered enough to attempt to take a sword swing at her. Kalypso ducked and brought her left leg up in a sweeping kick that landed on the man's sword arm, breaking it at his elbow, his sword clanking onto the stone ground. He tried to rein his horse with his left hand. Kalypso took a breath, let out a cry that sounded like, "Hy!" She spun her body around, lifting both legs into the air, pivoting around the center of mass of her body. At the last instant, she lashed out with her left foot, striking the man in his neck; a bone crunching sound broke in upon the panting of the four horses.

Unused to the strange deformation of her feet and being out of practice by several hundred years, she missed landing on her feet and hit the ground rather awkwardly. "Damn! That hurt!" she exclaimed as she struggled to get to her feet. Without arms, it was always awkward, she remembered. The man had fallen to the ground, but she again stomped his neck and then proceeded to do the same to the other two men, making doubly sure that all three were dead and the threat to her precious Teris ended. Satisfied, she looked up at a very white-faced husband.

"My god! Kalypso! I never knew. You saved us! How? I screwed up. It's the plague — we all have that alien northern plague," he finally called out, while slowly dismounting.

"I know. I figured that one out for myself, dear. Get their foul bodies out of our estate, please," she replied, still panting from her intense, but brief exertion. "Damn, that fall hurt. I am out of practice." Seeing Teris on his knees struggling to move the men, she began to assist him, using her feet to help roll the dead bodies. She was not satisfied until they lay far out into the street from their place. "Come on; put your arm on my shoulders. You should walk back into your home, Teris dear," she ordered. He grinned, but did as asked.

Horses handled, once inside, she said, "Well, today is not a total loss. There are three less evil men alive, and we have got ourselves three more horses and tack. Not a total loss. Come on, dear. I am hungry again. We must make more plans."

"Yes dear, but how? You seem different somehow," he said as they slowly headed for the kitchen.

"I am different. That wallflower you married — I'm afraid she's gone — gone forever. Hell, it is still me, Teris, but I've changed. Don't ask me how or why, but I know that I used to be a Kali Assassin. I think it was a couple hundred years ago up in Kefall. I remember everything, particularly all the attacking moves that I used to make. I'm a deadly weapon against wicked men who molest, harm, humiliate, or hurt women like me. You will just have to get used to it, dear. This is now the way that it is. God damn everything anyway. Fuckers are going to pay for their abuse of us women, pay like they never dreamed possible." She spat on the floor but then realized that Teris would have to be the one to wipe it up later on and regretted her lack of control.

Teris was stunned by her pronunciations and outburst. He had the good sense to work on fixing them something to eat, giving him time to think. Kalypso had snapped; she'd changed, of that, he had not the slightest doubt! He'd just seen her kill three armed men right before his eyes and kill them in mere seconds and without the slightest hesitation! She was as lethal as she claimed, but she was still just as beautiful as he had left her.

"Thanks for saving my butt, love. I admit I screwed up twice. I should have gone out armed to the teeth, and I shouldn't have gotten lost in my own thoughts while returning here. Thanks. I'll make it up to you, love."

"You had better make it up to me — in bed — tonight — or else," she retorted, but a grin formed on her Madonna-like face, a mischievous one at that.

"Ooh. I like the sound of that one, love," he teased her. "Seriously, other than those three, I saw absolutely no one on the streets. No shops are open, markets are empty, women are screaming here and there, you know, terrified like. I finally visited some of my friends. They are in the same mess. On my way back, I realized that this must be that alien plague that struck the northern continents some time back. Now it's here. Probably all Thal is infected."

"Agreed. I concur. Say, all those things that were left — those are for me. Most of it is a replacement kitchen so that I can cook. Well, I seldom cook, but at least with it installed I can make something when I have to do so. You will get it installed for me, won't you?"

"Bossy aren't we?" he replied.

"I'm used to giving the orders, Teris. Back then, I think I might have been a leader or something. Sorry, dear. Please, will you see if it can be installed for me?"

"Absolutely dear, but we have other things to discuss. Sit down and let me feed us and then we can plan."

Over tea later on, Teris began, "On my way back, I began to see many future tracks that may result from this plague. You know, my education is just what I need now to foresee the future. I believe that I'm able to make accurate predictions, but none of them is good. As the week goes by, I'll have more data about the current situation and be better able to foresee the future, dear."

"I had hoped so, dear. That's one of the things that made me fall in love with you. Do go on. It is going to get really bad, isn't it?"

"Afraid so. Not sure yet how bad. One thing is certain, we need to get others in here with us, build up a defensible safe haven," he answered her. They talked for some time and both agreed that in the morning, Teris would invite all their friends to move in here with them. He knew that it had to be tomorrow, before things got so bad that travel would be treacherously dangerous for anyone.

"Now it is bed time. I need you now, big boy," Kalypso ordered huskily. Teris grinned and the two retired for the night.

The next morning, Teris rose at dawn. He asked Kalypso to stay in bed and he returned a while later with breakfast in bed for her, which pleased her. She sat on the bed brushing out her long blonde hair when he crawled in with the tray. "Breakfast in bed for the most beautiful woman in the world," he said. However, their passions overcame them, and it was a bit later before the two actually ate their breakfast.

"We have two problems, Teris. One, I have to have a way that I can open the gates by myself. If my naked body had not distracted them, you might have been killed while I could do nothing about it. Two, should I go with you today? Extra protection?"

"I believe that I can solve the first one, Kalypso. I think that you should remain here to help get our friends inside and settled, as they start coming. I won't be gone long this time, and I will go out armed to the teeth. Let's go over the exact route that I should follow. I want to get to every one of our friends in the most efficient time possible, returning here as fast as possible," he explained.

"Damn, that's a math problem, isn't it?" she asked. He nodded. "Well, let me at it. I think that I ought to be able to solve it. I think that I used to have to do things like that." Within a few minutes, sitting at her new low desk, she had traced out the route for him.

"That's what I like about you, Kalypso, sharp, bright mind," he teased her and kissed her.

"What? You don't like my goddess body?" she teased him back.

He flushed. "Well, that too," he added and both chuckled. "Back very soon, then I'll fix up a key that you can use." A little over an hour later, he returned, and not long after that, Teris had a key that she could use to unlock and lock the gate. He'd bolted a strip of metal onto the end where normally fingers would hold it and turn it. Using her toes and feet, she could turn the lock mechanism. Additionally, he put the key onto a long golden chain so she could carry it around her neck and then sit down and put it into the lock easily.

Shortly after that, their friends began arriving, bringing what they could in wagons or carriages. By nightfall, six of their married friends were now staying with them, each couple had their own room. Four unmarried fellows along with ten single women rounded out their small group. Uniformly, the women wore crude, makeshift clothes, mostly nightgowns or men's shirts. Nothing remotely fit them now. Of course, the fellows got an eyeful of naked Kalypso hovering about.

"Okay," Kalypso began, addressing the fourteen unmarried young people, "we have to deal with our problem head on. As you know, those ten of us are going to have to have a lot of assistance and you four fellows are going to have to shoulder the load. Unless you object, those of you who are dating each other, I am going to give you a private room, like our married friends." None of those eight objected. That left six women without any male helpers. "Let's try bunking three of you ladies to a room. Perhaps you will be able to help each other out somewhat. Now when you need assistance, one of the other men around here will lend you a hand. Holler and one should come at once. Fellows, if you don't come to their aid, I will boot you out of here. At mealtime, I will have each of you sitting beside one of the fellows who can feed his wife or girlfriend and one of you at the same time. It ought to work out. I think our biggest problem will be clothing for us."

"Ah, but we appreciate you just as you are, Kalypso," one young man called out. Several fellows chuckled.

Teris glared, "Don't get any ideas, fellows. I'm hers now." Even more chuckled, especially when she winked coyly at him.

Thus, at the end of the second day of the plague, these people were very safe and secure inside the locked estate of the Isis family. Kalypso was right; clothing was their biggest concern for the next few days. None of these young folks could sew before the plague came. One woman had done a tiny bit of sewing, embroidery mostly, but obviously not any longer.

"How about this?" Teris suggested. He held up some of his pants for Kalypso to try on. Both were trying to find some reasonable clothing for her to wear. She had stiff requirements. Kalypso wanted to be able to dress herself, be able to use the bathroom by herself, and be able to fight effectively, and not be hindered with her clothes while fighting. Tall order, Teris moaned yet again. "Honestly, dear, I love to see you with nothing on. You look fabulous and delicious and luscious."

"Well, that's rather obvious, isn't it," she teased him back. "While such is fine with me, but come fall, I'll be an icicle. Besides, I might become too tempting to our friends."

"You have my permission to be tempting to our girlfriends, just not our fellows," he teased her back.

"Oh I can?" she said raising her eyebrows and acting both surprised and pleased.

"Oh damn." He roared. "Okay, okay, back to clothes." Before too long, they decided that pants and a man's shirt would be the best, if they could devise some way that she could don them on her own. Several hours later and a good deal of trial and error and they hit upon a workable idea. He sewed some grab loops onto the tops of pants. Using these, she could pull them up, accompanied with a good deal of wiggling, which Teris enjoyed watching. A loop and button worked to fasten them up, especially because of her tiny waist. Once buttoned, though loose, the pants could not fall down over her much larger hips. After more experimentation, they found a loose fitting, pull over shirt of his that she could manage. At last, she felt more comfortable; she could at least deal now with her own clothing.

The two presented their results to the others. While some of the young women moaned about no longer being able to wear their accustomed fancy gowns, by the end of the day, they could at least get in and out of something on their own. It was a start, Kalypso declared as they all sat down to supper. Amazingly enough, her attitude coupled with that of Teris kept the other women's spirits up and their fear and terror at bay.

At breakfast the next morning, gunfire erupted not far from their estate. Being less than a mile from the Royal Palace, the group found themselves not far from the initial route of the looters and rioters. Cautiously, they observed the dogs crawling along the streets below them, slinging their long guns with them. Because of the high fence, their place was ignored. These men simply were unable to stand up, let alone climb the fence.

For several days, they observed gangs fighting for control of the streets as well as looting nearby homes. Often the occupants were outright slain, though frequently, the younger, fairer women were carted off, which raised the ire of Kalypso greatly. Still, with all the commotion and gunfire, the streets were far too dangerous for them to travel. Teris and friends did manage to sneak out from time to time to confiscate a fallen man's long gun and/or ammunition. By the end of the week, they had over thirty long guns in their estate. "You can never have too many long guns," Kalypso declared. Teris grinned. He needed them, but she definitely didn't.

The following week, the gunfire seemed to have moved further away from their street. Over breakfast, Kalypso stated, "Okay, now it is time for us to rescue those women who were carted off last week. Armed to the teeth, three of you fellows are to ride out this morning and see if you can figure out where they were taken. Once we know the location, we need to scout it out, and then assault them, rescuing the women. Leave none of those men alive who are responsible for their kidnaping and murder. Gang, from now on, we are going to be known as the ILS, the Isis Liberation Squad!"

"Yes, but who's our leader?" one young man asked.

"I am, stupid!" Kalypso retorted. Everyone laughed, especially the women who were beginning to regain a small token of self-respect, especially since one of them was their leader.

While the men went off in search of where the kidnaped women were being held, Kalypso took the fourteen women into the kitchen. Already the men had installed the new low facilities. Now it was time for them to learn to deal with cooking. While Kalypso had seldom cooked herself, she provided support, helpful hints, and encouragement for the three women who used to do some cooking. Everyone pitched in, trying all manner of ways to deal with the basic problems at hand. In the end, the three managed to cook a passable lunch, but needed the help of three others. Another six dealt with setting the table properly. When the men returned near noon, Kalypso declared, "Now, gentlemen, your women are back into the cooking arena. At last, we have food fit to eat." Teris roared with laughter, very relieved to be finished with the cooking detail. He discovered he did not have any skill at meal preparations.

As they sat down to eat, Kalypso pointed out, "You see, if we women work together in small groups, together, we can accomplish what one of us used to be able to do. This is at least a start of normalcy again. However, this is most definitely not the honeymoon that Teris and I had planned." All agreed and chuckled. Their morale began to climb.

After lunch, the three men left once more. That evening, Teris returned with his scouting group bearing good news. "They are being held in Saint Timon's Cathedral, of all places! They've turned it into a whorehouse! How ironic."

"Yes, but we know something about its layout, Teris," Kalypso pointed out. Now came the hard part: how to rescue the captives. The next morning, six including Kalypso, headed out to scout out the church. "Damn, I ought to be able to ride, Teris. I think that you are to tie the reins into a knot that I bite down upon."

"Guess you need a good neck reining mare," he suggested. After saddling up the most likely candidate for her, he helped her mount. She then neck reined the mare around their grounds to get re-familiar with what she had once known. At last satisfied and with Teris satisfied with her ability, the six headed out of the gates and off to the vicinity of the church. They returned later that night having watched a stream of men entering a side door and leaving no more than a half hour later. Teris had to restrain Kalypso from eliminating these men! It was obvious what they were doing. However, twice that day, a man came up to the main front doors, leading a woman, a rope tied to her neck as if she was a sheep or goat. They disappeared inside with the man leaving a short while later, often holding a small money pouch.

Over dinner, Kalypso began to put together a plan. They would strike at dusk, when the lighting within the cathedral would be minimal. The key problem was how to gain access. The place was a veritable fortress. While constructed to be a holy shrine to God, it was also an impenetrable fortress, with stone walls many feet thick. Everything depended upon Kalypso gaining entry and then ensuring that the doors stayed open while the other rushed inside.

At dusk, eight men and Kalypso arrived near the front of the huge cathedral, tethering their horses in the shadows across from the church. Six men armed with swords and long guns then fanned out, crossing the street and moving up to the front walls of the church. So far so good. No alarm was raised. Teris and Kalypso then began their slow walk across the street. They headed towards the main front, massive doors. "Kind of like we are getting married again, my love," he whispered. She flashed him a grin. She'd picked a good man to marry, she decided.

Once they stood before the doors, she gave him a nod and the other six moved up close to them. When all was ready, Teris knocked on the door. After a few minutes, it opened. "Got another one for you," he stated flatly.

The guard glanced at Kalypso and opened the door wide. "Got a good looking one this time. Great. We can use more of them." Kalypso swung her right foot up sharply into the man's throat and pushed hard against it. His neck snapped and he fell silently to the floor. As she regained her balance, Teris stepped slowly inside, his eyes glancing rapidly about, looking for the other guards. Two were located way across the huge domed room, near the side entrance. Another man was smoking a pipe nearby. Teris pretended to be ushering Kalypso inside and they moved towards him. As they did so, the other six men quietly stepped inside the front doors, their long guns at the ready. The guard looked up as Kalypso neared him, staring at this incredible beauty. Just as he was about to say something, her flying kick crushed his voice box, breaking his neck along with it.

The action caught the attention of the two distant guards who called out. Since they were raising their guns, Teris acted. He was a crack shot and proved it to Kalypso. Bang! He fired and one of the men dropped. Bang. Bang. Bang. Three shots came from behind them and the second guard dropped, his gun smashing noisily onto the carpet. Bedlam erupted from the rows and rows of pews. Women screamed in fright. Kalypso ignored their noise and kept looking for the arrival of more men. "Stay alert!" she yelled above the women's screams.

Not long after that, the back doors on their right opened, and two men came crawling into the main domed chamber. Her men fired another volley, a bit overkill she thought. She would have to instruct them later on how to signal each other as to which enemy they were intending to take out. Why waste shots? Still alert for more guards, Kalypso suggested they move out into the cathedral a bit further.

Now she could see the women. All were naked. Some were lying on the soft red carpet of the isles, their legs tied apart. Others were leaning like a dog over the pews, again with their legs and knees tied such that they could not move. Kalypso fumed, itching to get her feet into the big boss who orchestrated this vile wickedness. After no more men appeared for a couple minutes, Kalypso ordered the main doors closed and bolted. "Go make sure the side door is secured as well. We're going to have to search this whole place before we let our guard down," she ordered.

"Say boss, I've been in here some. Those two back doors, one on either side of the High Altar there, are the only way into this portion from the back. If we bolt one shut, then there will be only one way for any others to get to us."

"Excellent. See to it, please. I am going over to the right door and stand guard. We need to find the man behind this operation. He's likely hiding out somewhere," she replied.

Five minutes passed. They had the facility locked down, and all had moved over to the right door, which led into the inner recesses of the huge cathedral. "Well, looks like we are going to have to smoke the fiend out, fellows. Stay alert," she ordered.

On her signal, Teris opened the door by suddenly throwing it wide open. Bang! A gunshot came flying their way. She had two of her men lying prone on the floor, both had good shots and returned fire. Bang! Bang! Using their fire for cover, Kalypso and Teris slipped inside; he, crawling, gun at the ready. Down at the end of the long hallway, the shooter was moaning.

"Come on, he's been hit!" She moved as quickly as she dared, cursing the pitiful state of her feet. Three-inch steps hardly suited an assassin, but that was better than Teris who really needed her support to walk right. However, he surprised her by crawling ahead of her quite rapidly. He got to the man who was valiantly trying to reload using one arm only. Blood gushed from a wound in his right arm, which hung limply at his side. He wore a fancy black silk suit, a visible clue that Kalypso had her man. Teris knocked the gun out of the man's hands. "Don't kill him until I get there. Damn my feet anyway." She nearly fell down trying to speed her pathetically slow progress down the long, red carpeted hallway.

She finally reached the man, who now held his wounded arm with his good arm. He was sitting with his back to the stone wall at the very end of the long hallway. "So, you are the man responsible for all these murders and abduction and prostitution of these young women," Kalypso called out as she approached him.

"What of it, bitch? We're just keeping you pathetic women alive. You'd all starve to death if it weren't for us. We just have them payback what we men need," he retorted haughtily. Wham! Her foot connected to his privates and he crumpled in intense pain. Wham! Her leg connected with his good arm at the shoulder, dislocating it. Wham! Her foot came down on his right knee, shattering it. Wham! Now his left knee shattered from the force of her follow up strike, leaving him howling in pain.

"So now who's the bitch?" she spat on him. "You are hereby sentenced to death for crimes against women." She sent her killing blow to his neck and his screams of pain ceased immediately. Silence fell.

"We go room to room now. Probably this is all them, but before we get involved with the women, let's be damn sure we have them all. Go in pairs," she ordered.

Teris added, "And stay alert for anything that we might find useful. Food, guns, ammunition, whatever."

She nodded her approval to him. "Nice move back there opening the door and being out of the line of fire," she added. He grinned back.

A half hour later, they decided that they had the last of the men. Now they headed back to rescue the women, all of whom were tied up, in one fashion or another. At least, they had already found their shoes thrown into a pile in a back room. They would be able to walk out of here, Kalypso thought. She had a hard time confronting the horrid condition of the women though. Teris and the six moved rapidly from woman to woman untying each in turn, telling them to go over to Kalypso and see if they could find their shoes. All told, they rescued eighteen women between the ages of fourteen and twenty-five.

A bit later, one of their men reported that he found the mother-load. In a basement room, vast quantities of supplies were stored, tons of food, guns, ammunition, blankets, clothes, and more. "You know, we should confiscate this church and make it a safe haven for others," Teris suggested. Having also found the keys to the place, this was feasible. Two men went outside to the rear and found the Royal Carriage used by the Cardinal and thought what better way to rescue these women. Not long after that, they ushered the still terrified women out the side door and into this huge, plush carriage. After locking the doors securely, they all rode across the street to where they'd left their horses and then on back to the safety of the Isis Estate.

Once they were all safely inside, Kalypso spoke to the eighteen women, who were still trying to grasp what had happened to them. "Ladies, you have just been rescued by the ILS, the Isis Liberation Squad. You are now free women once more. First things first. A hot warm bath, some clean clothes, and then a hot meal. We can talk later. Please follow our women who will bathe you."

One woman called out meekly, "Thank you." Kalypso smiled.

While the fourteen women began tending to the women, Kalypso sat down with Teris. "You know, what are we going to do with all them, once we have them cleaned up and such?"

"Good question, love. We need more allies. Where are we going to put these women up for the night? How are we going to be able to feed them all? I guess we fellows can take turns with you all," he suggested.

"Hum, I guess you fellows are going to have to do a lot of feeding," she teased. "Seriously, we need more allies. But who?"

They were interrupted. "Kalypso, we are just not able to wash them properly. Can you ask our fellows to lend us a hand with them?" The eleven men, including Teris, spent the next couple hours washing the women, especially their hair, drying them off, patting dry their hair, and getting them into some clothes that would at least cover them. Then, they herded them into the dining room, where the women had a hot supper waiting. Thankfully, they had managed this on their own. Still, the men had to feed all the women, all thirty-three of them. That is, each man was responsible for the feeding of three women. Finally around ten, the rescued women were tucked in, four to a bed, in the remaining bedrooms. Fortunately, all the beds in the estate were king-sized. A very exhausted group then gathered in the dining room.

Over tea, Kalypso thanked everyone and then said, "Gang, we need more allies. We need to take these women to some place of safety where they can recover and get better care than we can give them here. All are quite traumatized by their ordeal. Most suffered the loss of their families before being led away into that hell hole of prostitution. Frankly, we are not going to be able to provide for their urgent needs. We need allies."

After a bit of discussion, one of her friends spoke up. "Say, speaking of trauma, how about that old Dorota Church of God? They are supposed to be good with trauma victims. Perhaps they can help us."

Kalypso thought this was a brilliant idea and promised to investigate this prospect the next morning. She, Teris, and one of his friends, both armed to the teeth, rode out of the Isis estate shortly after eight the next morning. They had good directions to follow, plus being located at the very eastern edge of the city made it somewhat easier to find. They reined in before the gates of the low walled compound. A sign read Dorota Church of God. Teris knocked and they waited.

Amadei opened the gates and Teris introduced themselves and explained why they had come. "Come on in. Please, let us meet with everyone in our large commons. Will you take tea with us?" Kalypso smiled; how good it was to experience real civilization once more!

Presently, Marzena and Aniela entered bringing tea in their yokes. Kalypso marveled at how efficiently and easily these women served up the tea for everyone. "We have been armless most of our lives," Aniela whispered to Kalypso, adding, "We have special Women's Ways of doing most all things. You are welcome to come here and learn our ways, my dear." Kalypso longed to do just that.

"Ah, here come the others. This is Perse Nikon, the publisher of the almanac, and Albin," Amadei introduced the last two to arrive. He then introduced them to the three guests.

Once more, Kalypso outlined the situation and what they had done yesterday. "In short, we have eighteen traumatized women who need help that we cannot provide. A friend of mine suggested that your church here might be able to help."

"Of course we will help. Please, bring them to us as soon as possible," Amadei replied. "However, I fear that there are far more women in Thal that are in as desperate need as these eighteen."

"You have my word, sir. We will continue to rescue all that we can find," Kalypso sought to convince him of her intentions.

"I'm sure that you will do just that. Now I do know some trustworthy men who might be willing to help you, that is, if they have survived the chaos," Amadei added.

"Darn, I can't write anymore! Teris, jot their names down and where we might find them, please," Kalypso asked, once more feeling slightly degraded having to ask him to do something that she used to be able to do without even thinking about it.

Perse also sensed her discomfort. She had been in the very same situation. "Kalypso, we have to learn to write with our feet. I have to keep daily logs of the weather and such. If you go slowly, you can do it, and if you use those special low desks that somehow appeared."

"I guess I will need to start practicing writing again, Perse. Is it hard to do?"

"Awkward and pitifully slow, but it can be done. I think that is all that matters, in the end, I mean, can you get something written down that you need," she added.

"Kalypso, please, when you have some time, we would love to have you come here for some time and learn our century's old Women's Ways. If you have the right tools and the right methods, there are few things that you cannot do or accomplish," Aniela once more suggested.

"She is right," Perse added. "Each day I am getting better at all sorts of things and learning how to do so many more things. It is like a miracle here. You absolutely must come and spend a long time learning!"

"Okay, I am convinced," Kalypso replied. "However, it will have to wait a while yet. We have so many women in such dire need. I cannot abandon them. When things get better, then I will come. Say, will you need food supplies, blankets, and clothing? We discovered a huge cache of these in Saint

Timon's Cathedral."

Amadei looked very relieved, Kalypso picked that up the very instant she spoke. "Yes, food supplies, blankets, clothing — such would really help us out here. We have ample for ourselves, but if we are going to support so many, many others, we will need more."

"Great. We'll bring a wagonload of women and a wagonload of supplies later today. I think if we hurry, we might make it yet today. No, I keep forgetting how dismally slow we all are now. Make that tomorrow morning. Think we can make that Teris?" she asked.

"We ought to be able to do it. If we go load up the church supplies today, then it should be a simple matter of driving them here in the morning," he replied. They chatted a while longer and then left to begin this major operation.

After their guests left, Amadei said, "Well, it has begun. Our big problem is what to do with so many, after they have received their Holy Gift and are able to live once more. Where can we house so many? If I am not wrong, this Kalypso is going to be bringing us a whole lot more women." No one had any real ideas, and they broke up, heading off to prepare for the arrival of so many who needed their help.

Just after lunch, Perse needed to make her noon observations. As usual, Albin accompanied her over to her home next door. Today, she went out into the backyard, pausing to pay her respects over her grandfather's grave. "Come on, Albin. I need to go over into the farmer's field. I have to check up on the mice family," she explained. As always, he kept his arm on her shoulder for support, as the two carefully made their way over the grass and then into the edge of the field.

"Why are you observing field mice?" he asked.

"Ok, just to gather more clues about the weather," she chatted as she looked around for signs of the mice.

"Hello. Who are you? Why are you in our bean field?" a youthful voice interrupted them. He held a corn knife in one hand and was crawling along on his hands and knees.

"Hello. I am Perse Nikon. I am now the publisher of the almanac that grandpa used to do. I'm trying not to harm any of your beans, just looking for the field mouse family that ought to be around here somewhere. Clues for the weather predictions and all that," she replied.

"Hi, I am Damon. We know your grandpa. Is that his grave? We thought we saw someone being buried here."

"Yes, he died and now I am carrying on his work."

"That's good. He was a nice old man. He used to always come over to our farmstead and chat with dad. You are welcome to come over if you want. Things have gotten bad though. Sorry about your arms. My sisters lost theirs, mom too. Now my brother, dad, and I have to do everything and we cannot keep up. Dad's afraid that we will be raising weeds this year and not vegetables."

"That's awful, Damon. How many sisters do you have? I had three, but they also died."

He smiled, "I have four sisters. Honestly, they used to do a whole lot of work. Until now, I never realized just how much they did do."

"Wow. Is there anything I can do to help you out?" Perse asked.

"Probably not. You don't have any arms either. We have to chop out the weeds with corn knives. I can't really walk, so I just crawl along, chopping out the weeds. How does your friend walk?"

"Easy, Damon," Albin answered. "I use Perse for support. Without her, I have to crawl along like you do." Damon smiled, glad to find out that Albin and he were in the same boat.

"Great. I am just about done with this field. One more row down and back. Want to come over for a visit when I am done? If you are the new weather forecaster, I'm sure dad will want to meet you. Your grandfather used to share all sorts of weather tips with dad."

"Okay, Damon. I will finish my observations here and be ready for you when you get done," Perse replied.

After making her observations, she and Albin headed back into her house so she could log them. "Are you sure that you ought to be going over to their place? Is it safe?" Albin asked.

"Well, if my grandpa used to do it, I should too. Maybe he learned some useful things from the farmer. I have to at least visit with them and see. You can come too, if you want," Perse replied.

"I have to come, Perse. I'm in charge of watching over you. I'm to ensure your safety," he said rather proudly.

"Okay, then let's get going. I bet he's waiting on us. I'm so terribly slow at this writing still." The two headed back outside into the sunny spring afternoon. She looked up at the growing clouds to the south and announced, "Looks like it will thunderstorm later this evening."

"How do you know that?" asked Damon, who had crawled back to the edge of the field, waiting for them. She explained in detail. "That's our place back there, to the east. It is about a quarter mile."

"Say, why don't you see if you can walk too? Put your arm over my other shoulder, Damon.

Maybe we can all walk there," Perse suggested.

"Well, it's hard, but at least I'm walking again. What a great idea you have Perse!"

Taking small, careful steps, the three took nearly two thousand steps to reach the large and sprawling farmstead. To Perse who had never seen a farm, the place looked gigantic in size, dwarfing anything that she had seen before. As they drew closer, Damon called out loudly, "Mom, dad, everyone, look! I am walking. We have company coming."

Presently, a younger boy and his father came crawling out of the huge barn. "Hello, I am Perse Nikon, granddaughter of Dio. Damon says that he used to come to visit you often. He died and now I am the new publisher of the almanac. This is my neighbor friend Albin."

"Please forgive us. We have to crawl now. I am Horus, Horus Paneus. Say, Damon, you are really walking. I didn't think it was possible."

"It is if you hold on to someone. Perse showed me how." Horus led them into their very large farmhouse, a stone building, much like most buildings in Thallyus. It was a three-story dwelling, though many of the upper bedrooms were currently unused. Following him inside, Perse found the five women sitting around the huge dining room table, looking incredibly forlorn and wearing very ill-fitting men's clothing. All self-respect was long gone here; they were now nothing but flower ornaments, unable to do their household chores and farm work. Perse saw at once that these older sisters had probably been doing quite a lot of the work around the farm. She guessed that Horus had lost two thirds of his daily workforce. Couple that with his having to assume all the other chores that they did, she was surprised to see that they were doing even this well.

After introducing Perse and Albin to the group, Horus introduced his family. His wife Agrea was thirty-nine, a year younger than he. His daughters were Donia, eighteen, Delphie, seventeen, and the twin of Damon, Alexina, sixteen, and Chara, fifteen. Kastor was the youngest at fourteen. "Are you really the new weather predictor and writer of the almanac?" asked Donia, who seemed the most alert and impressed with Perse.

"Yes, grandpa has been teaching me everything about it since I was five. Just when the plague came, I finished the 824 edition, though now I don't know if it will even be published," she answered.

"Say, any tips for us?" Horus asked. "Old Dio was always dropping hints for us. We always gave him some sweet corn in the fall."

Perse grinned, "Sure, I have predicted a very wet fall. So I'd get your harvest in as early as possible this year."

"Great, dad. See, she knows her stuff," Damon pointed out, though he quickly realized what he had said was rather silly. Only after they actually had the predicted wet fall would they know for sure that she did know her stuff.

"Damn, more hard luck!" Horus replied unexpectedly. "As shorthanded as we now are, I'll be lucky to get a third of the crop harvested, assuming the weeds don't claim it first. So it is the plague. Agrea thought so. We are doomed."

"Yes, it must be the alien plague that struck the northern continents some time ago," Albin pointed out.

Perse bit her lip. People were starving in Thal; food was scarce. Yet, if he didn't get his crops grown and harvested, there would be even less later on this summer and fall. "Say, I think I know a way to get you some help. There are a lot of women who need a place to stay and will likely be willing to help you with the farm."

"Thanks, but women? Sorry, we are now nothing but a huge burden for Horus," Agrea spoke up. "We cannot do anything anymore, except sit around and force the fellows to feed us."

"Honestly, Albin's people, they know alternative ways for us to do everything, really they do. I'm actually writing again and learning how to do so many other things. I bet they would be willing to come here and teach all of you too. Albin, let's talk with Amadei and see what we can do."

"Sure thing, Perse. She's right. Our women do nearly everything; we call it Women's Ways. They certainly do everything differently than we men do, but they do it. Mom cooks, cleans, bakes, scrubs, washes clothes — honestly, she does everything, only differently that I would do those things," Albin boasted a little, proud of his mother.

"Yes, but they can't feed themselves or even dress themselves," Donia protested.

"Oh sure they do that! I do admit that we do some things for them, like cutting up the meat. They can do it, but handling a sharp knife with their feet is far too dangerous. Mom uses her feet as I use my hands. Let us talk with them and see if they can help you all out," Albin suggested. "Better yet, why don't all of you walk back to our place with us and you can see for yourselves? We can get something worked out sooner this way."

"You mean crawl, son. That is a long way to crawl," Horus corrected him.

"Oh come on, ladies, let's show these two how to walk again," Albin countered. "All of you — you have your special shoes on, so come on. Let's get going. Perse, show them how we do it."

With a little more coaxing, Albin and Perse led the entire Paneus family out and down their long lane towards the back of the Dorota Church of God complex. Horus held on to his wife for dear life, but the two were managing to walk together. Donia supported Damon this time, while Chara helped Kastor. "We walk so slowly," Delphie complained.

"Quite true, Delphie," Perse replied. "Pathetically slowly, but we still can walk. Just remember to take very tiny steps. I'm most afraid of losing my balance. I've done that quite a lot. What a freaky sensation flailing my arms around to get my balance back, only there are no arms there to move. Freaky."

"Hey, I've felt that too," Alexina admitted. "Terrifying too." The young women continued to chat all the way down the quarter mile lane. Perse noticed that the complex had a back gate and Albin led them straight to it. A few minutes later, the Paneus family began to see nearly unbelievable things, as the women of the complex served up tea and biscuits, and accepted their guests readily.

After a bit of explaining by Perse, Amadei caught on to her overall idea and he took the discussion from there, giving Perse a sly wink. Although they were expecting the eighteen traumatized women in the morning, Amadei sent two of the church's women back with them. One was Hanna. Her boyfriend Aleksy went too, as well as Iwan and his six year old son, Kasper. The agreement that the men worked out was simple. The men of the complex would come over daily to help around the farm, while two of the women would begin showing the farm women the special Women's Ways. Later on, once the traumatized women were better, they would come and stay on the farm. All the women would receive daily lessons on how to do things, continuing until his family no longer needed their help. The women for whom they would provide a home would then help with the farm chores in return.

At supper, Amadei complimented Perse, "You have done wonders this day, Perse. Your idea with the Paneus family is brilliant. They have the space to house many women, and they can use our help in return. Everyone wins. Well done, Perse, well done indeed."

"Thanks Amadei, but what I really want to learn how to do is this Holy Gift thing. I want to be able to help other women over their traumas just like Marzena helped me," Perse replied.

Marzena beamed, "Well said, child. Tomorrow when the women come, we will get you started. We are all glad for the help, Perse." The smile on Perse's face told all.

Chapter 27 And Grows

As promised, around ten the next morning, two wagons arrived at the gates. One carried the eighteen women; the other was brimming with supplies. They left the supply wagon at the complex, returning with the other one. On their way back, Kalypso and Teris, along with six other men, then began contacting those on Amadei's list who could help. Within a few days, they had another dozen volunteers. These, they stationed at the Saint Timon's Cathedral, turning it into a safe haven and fortress. A large sign read: ILS Safe Haven.

Daily the situation in Thal deteriorated, and by the next week, word had spread that there was help available. The number of volunteers began growing rapidly. Soon they had two dozen, then three, then four dozen. Although half were women, still Kalypso felt that twenty-four men would be enough to hold the church against bands of thugs.

She and Teris continued their rescue operations. During these next few weeks, they averaged another ten rescued men and women. Frequently now, they rescued husbands and wives, sometimes their children as well. Many were simple rescues, in that the family was starving, long out of food. Kalypso did not differentiate. A person in need was helped. Once each week, they ferried the newly rescued down to the Dorota Church of God.

After that, the sheer number of dead bodies lining the streets began to prevent travel by wagon, besides the stench was overpowering. Kalypso began to encounter victims who were ill; cholera made its appearance. Worse, there were no doctors to be found. By December, she stopped attempting to transport victims to the Church of God, choosing instead to house them in the giant cathedral for the time being. With spring ending, disease and starvation began to rise at an alarming rate. Bodies continued to pile up in the streets. There was no place to put them, plus, it was not safe to be on the streets for any reason.

Even armed to the teeth as the ILS members were, they still found themselves occasionally being shot at as they rode down a street. Consequently, Kalypso had them never take the same route twice in a row. So far, they had been lucky, and no one had been seriously injured. Thus, with the situation so out of control, Teris finally convinced Kalypso to stay at the Church of God for a while and learn what she could. Disease and the dead had stopped them, not the evil men. At last she agreed, and on December 4 as the first days of summer came, Kalypso moved into a room at the complex. Teris remained at their estate, dealing with whatever he could.

Interestingly enough, the cathedral began to take on a life of its own. The odors of fresh baking bread and foods cooking on a stove floating through the air from the giant cathedral's attached kitchen facilities. More and more desperate people began seeking shelter and sanctuary. By mid-December, five hundred men, women, and children now called the Saint Timon's Cathedral their home. By the end of December, their numbers had grown to nearly a thousand, and space was at a premium there.

At the Church of God, Kalypso and Perse now shared a bedroom together, since Amadei was unwilling to have Perse sleep outside their complex because of the ever-growing danger. Part of the time, Perse worked with Kalypso, teaching her what she had learned to do. Part of the time, the two spent with Aniela, learning together how to do additional actions. Evenings, Perse gave therapy sessions, while Kalypso received hers.

One evening, Kalypso returned to their room laughing wildly. "Perse, I did have a psychotic break when I got the plague. I flipped out and plugged in a complete former personality that I had a couple hundred years ago! I really was a Kali Assassin up in Kefall. After I got married, I agreed to become one of those Holy Women of the Eighth Degree to help further my husband's career. Ha. As soon as he got what he wanted, he dumped me! Well, after that, I got help from the Kali and then joined them. Later on, after proving my mettle and skill, I became one of the top leaders. So when I got the plague and saw women being mistreated, I just snapped! I went crazy and just plugged in that whole lifetime. Suddenly, I knew how to fight and to assassinate. Wild. This therapy gift is fabulous. All that is now under my control. Besides, my reaction times have been cut in half! I'm better at it than I ever was. Incredible stuff, this Holy Gift."

"No kidding, that's great, Kalypso. I sure am glad that you were there to help those women. You ought to come see how they are faring now. Let's get Albin to accompany us to the farm tomorrow so you can see for yourself," Perse replied eagerly. She agreed, mostly out of curiosity.

The next morning, Hanna and Aleksy were scheduled to spend the day on the farm. Albin, Perse, and Kalypso went along with them. Hanna explained, "Kalypso, we've taught the rescued women many basic actions. Now they are working on gaining speed, practice, practice, practice. True, they all have tons more to learn, they've only gotten the very basics so far. What you will be seeing is our solution to that. Marzena came up with it. We assign three women to each task. They help each other get it done. Alone, none of them has the skill and speed to get it done in the proper amount of time. For example, a cook ought to be able to prepare a meal in an hour at most, start to finish. Left alone, these women could cook the meal, but they might require three or four hours to get it all accomplished. By working them in teams of three or four, we get the time cut down to what it ought to be."

"Just remember the vitally important thing is that all these women are now getting the job at hand actually done!" Hanna finally finished.

"So you are saying that I will have to practice things for years before I can do all the things that I used to be able to do? I mean before the plague?" asked Kalypso.

"Yes, I am afraid so. Look, it took you what, eighteen years to learn all that you could do before the plague. Now you have to relearn how to do all those things all over again. Please, give yourself a break. Give yourself some time. Besides, there may well be other things that you might like to learn how to do, such as becoming a seamstress," Hanna answered honestly.

Kalypso chuckled, "Me sew? Hardly!"

When they finally arrived at the farmstead, Horus, leaning on his wife, was there to greet them. "Welcome, Perse, Albin, Hanna, Aleksy. And who is this lovely young woman?" Horus asked. His outlook on life was totally altered from when Perse first met him. Now he was halfway cheerful. His complexion looked far better; the bags under his eyes were gone.

"Allow me to present Kalypso Isis, the woman behind all these rescued women," Hanna introduced her.

"Incredible. Such an honor to meet you. Thank you for what you've done and of course, Hanna, all of your people's incredible help. Why, these women have turned my whole farm around. It has never been this clean. The crops will be the best ever this year — all thanks to their help. Besides, they saved my whole family. I've four daughters, you know," Horus declared sincerely and honestly. "Come, let us show you around."

As they toured the farm, the many women spotted Kalypso and uniformly dropped whatever they were doing and came rushing over to see her. Well, rushing was their intention, for no one rushed, not with steps they had to take. Kalypso saw bright eyed, cheerful, active, and vibrant young women. All were healthy and eager to give her a hug in their special Women's Way, heaping thank you upon thank you on her. Hanna's biggest challenge was to get them back to their activities so that Kalypso could see how things got done with these new ways.

As they left, Horus handed Albin a large sack of fresh green beans to take back with them as the trio headed back to the complex. "Little sample for all of you. Come back any time."

On their way back, Kalypso commented, "Well, I do see what you mean, four can do what one can do in the right amount of time. That is a valuable lesson learned, Perse. I will put that one to use when I return home. Say, we need every woman in Thal, heck, every woman in Thallyus to have an opportunity to learn these special Women's Ways. Without them, they are as helpless as those Holy Women of the Eighth Degree were, dependent upon servants for everything, only now there are no servants to be had at any price. We've all lost our arms."

"Oh I agree, but how are we going to be able to teach all women, Kalypso?" Perse asked innocently.

"I've no idea at all. There are only a couple dozen of us," Albin answered, "and half of us are men. Yet, I see Kalypso's point. All women desperately need the training that our women can give. I will think about it, but it seems hopeless to me."

Around the end of December, the miracle occurred, everyone's feet returned to normal over a rather painful couple of days. Uniformly, men cheered, relieved beyond measure. They were now completely normal, healed of all the plague's effects. While women and girls were generally thankful for this small kindness, they were still mostly helpless, save those who had been rescued and helped, a tiny handful in comparison to the millions in Thallyus.

At last, General Hypatios acted, declaring martial law and sending out his soldiers to begin cleaning up the dead, rotting bodies, while dealing with the rapidly spreading diseases. For those who were starving, fresh food began to trickle back into the city. Local farmers now began to return to their market stalls, under the protection of at least two armed soldiers per farmer. Thus encouraged, Kalypso headed back to her Isis Estate to lend a hand in the recovery — well a foot at least.

In her absence, Teris made huge signs and posted them around Saint Timon's Cathedral and then around the city. With a few variations, they read: Women in need come to the Isis Liberation Squad located in the old Saint Timon's Cathedral. Kalypso grinned when she spotted the first of his signs. "Has it worked?" she asked playfully, as she rode beside Teris, heading back to her Isis estate home.

"You bet. We have almost two thousand hold up in the church. We're at capacity now. Many men are on our side, helping out, especially since we can now walk. Things are looking up for us."

"Well, maybe for you men, but not for we women," Kalypso acridly pointed out.

"Point taken. Still dear, with at least one of us back to normal, think how much better we will be able to help all of you." He tried to put it into a positive slant. "Many of us have been doing a lot of soul searching."

"I didn't think most men had a soul," she retorted, some of her residual hostility toward men surfaced again. While she had erased quite a lot of her trauma, she still had a low opinion of men in general. "Look where the rule of men has led us all."

"That's precisely what a whole lot of we men have been thinking, dear. Are you able to read my mind now?" he teased her and cleverly made her seem right. He was a politician, after all, and about to become a very good one.

She grinned, but he didn't fool her. She played along, though, "Er, no, sorry Teris. Tell me more. Say, the sun feels good. It's finally summertime."

"The way some of us are thinking now is that we ought to switch the role of rulership over to women somehow. You know best what your needs are now. Honestly, so many of we men just cannot fathom how you are able to even cope and survive. We're thinking along the lines of somehow giving power to women for a change, only we haven't worked out how this could come about."

"Well, Teris, it is just devastating, no other way to put it. I think you are on the right path. Our plight is horrendous. Without the training I got from those Dorota women, I'd still be nearly totally helpless and dependent upon you for absolutely everything. That means, dear, that nearly all women of Thal are still utterly dependent upon the men around them for damn near everything. It is almost a hopeless situation. If we do not do something about it, I don't see us ever surviving long. It may be, Teris, that we are watching the end of our civilization."

"Lord, I hope not, Kalypso. I am pledged to try to keep that from happening somehow, someway."

Kalypso spent the next few weeks sharing what she had learned from Aniela with their fourteen women friends there at the estate. Daily, she worked with them, coached them, and continually encouraged them. After just a couple of weeks, she and the men there began to see sparks of life returning to their wives and friends. At least able to cook meals, feed themselves, deal with the dishes on their own, these women began to regain a spark of self-respect. Kalypso wished that these friends could somehow get the Holy Gift as well. She saw the difference that it made, comparing her friend's progress with those women they'd rescued and who had received the gift. Still, just seeing how they could get some things done on their own was a major step for these women, she noted.

By late January, the streets were cleaned up, the epidemic of disease arrested, and many male-operated shops and stores began to reopen. Some semblance of life seeped back into the capital city of Thal. Only now, with soldiers patrolling the streets was it safe for foot traffic. At this point, the many ILS members began to see the magnitude of the devastation, as they began helping folks return to their homes. Under the supervision of patrols of soldiers, they went door to door. The soldiers removed any dead that were found, while the ILS members helped the survivors as best they could. Often that meant helping get the kitchen into better working condition for the surviving women of the household.

While the soldiers were tracking their own tallies, the ILS members kept their own. Teris and Kalypso found the numbers shocking. BP, Before Plague, Thal was home to close to four million men, women, and children — at least according to the last tax collecting records they could discover. The new AP figures suggested that perhaps half that amount still lived in the city. They had heard that some families had found a way to leave the city, staying with relatives who lived on farms or in outlying towns and villages, but those were in the distinct minority. Kalypso suspected two million had perished so far. Three-quarters of the casualties were women and children. Grim statistics indeed.

However, this also meant that nearly one home in two now lay vacant. Here in the wealthier section of Thal where the Isis estate was located and about a mile from the vacant Royal Palace, two thirds of the homes were empty, looted by thieves — the occupants, murdered. Teris took the initiative and following the guidance of Kalypso, the ILS began resettling those under their care in the cathedral into these now vacant homes. Further, the ILS confiscated all the alien objects that had been left behind, creating a massive pool of said objects, doling them out to those who now needed them. The large cathedral became a warehouse for alien objects. Anyone who needed a yoke, a cup, a hairbrush, for example, only had to visit the cathedral to obtain what they needed.

Whenever possible, Teris had at least one male member staying with the resettled women, even if the man was just dating one of the women there. Always at least four women were placed in the same home. Kalypso insisted on this, based on the knowledge that she had from Aniela. Four women working together could somehow get by. She also insisted that these folks be placed in the vacant homes in the wealthier districts. Security would be better. Soldiers were biased and would protect the wealthier sections of town before they would protect those in the slums — harsh reality, but true.

As the dog days of summer came, the last of the rescued finally were resettled into homes. The ILS members continued their monitoring activities. At least once per day, a member visited the resettled groups to check on their well-being. Kalypso insisted on these daily checks. Everyone in Thal was more or less operating on a pure survival level. That is, no one thought anything about governmental actions or reconstruction, for example. All thoughts were on where to get the next few days of food, charcoal, and so on. Keep alive. That was the prime motivation among the vast majority in Thal.

The criminal elements remained somewhat dormant, preferring to operate by covert, secret means. There were just too many soldiers patrolling the streets to be overt as they had been. Besides, their ball game had changed rules now. Food was available; no longer could they charge a gold for a carrot or apple. Those with huge stolen food stocks found much of it rotting and were selling it off for what little they could now get for it. Those who had stolen gold and gems sat back wondering what they could do with their ill-gotten fortunes, for there was little to buy save the necessities of life.

However, those who had used the chaos to kidnap women and build up large prostitution establishments now came face to face with the stark reality of just what they had on their hands: a large number of helpless women, for whom they were now having to cook, feed, bathe, and handle all their needs — the burden became intolerable. Their ill-dreamt concepts of massive whorehouse profits dried up under the necessity of the total care of their captive women, who could do absolutely nothing for themselves. The situation that these men found themselves enmeshed in was not at all what they had intended or planned for — rather the opposite.

True, with women becoming a scarce commodity, low life frequented their establishments, primarily at night now. Yet, their customers would not pay to lay with a filthy, starving, disease-ridden woman. Few were that desperate for sexual relief. The owners had to keep their kept women cleaned and fed, which meant they had to have men fetching groceries, doing the cooking, feeding the women. Others were needed to bathe them. The list of chores went on and on, all eating up nearly all their ill-gotten profits! Running a house of prostitution in this manner with captive women became pointless.

This was precisely what Kalypso greatly feared would happen. These perverted men would soon realize the futility of their enterprise and begin executing their captives. Because these operations were not openly visible on the streets, the soldiers operating under martial law knew nothing about it. Once more, the ILS stepped in to deal with the problem. Late February, while on a routine ILS patrol, Teris and his men came upon the bodies of a dozen young women. They had all been strangled. Many still had the bits of rope tied around their necks. All were naked and all had been sexually abused. Their bruised bodies told many stories. True, once alerted to this, the soldiers carted them off and buried their bodies, but that was all that they did.

Back at his estate, Teris grimly said, "Kalypso, you were right. They are killing off their captured women." He told her of his grisly discovery earlier that night.

"Damn! Damn them to hell!" Kalypso cursed. She took a deep breath and calmed down. "Okay, alert all ILS members. We need to discover the locations of all these underground brothels and raid them, before more women get murdered."

"Yes dear," he replied meekly, trying hard not to raise her ire further. The next day, he spread the word. By now, members of the ILS covered over half of the city, but few resided in or near the slums where she suspected these houses were located. Nevertheless, within days, they had located three such establishments.

"We cannot go in with guns blazing," Kalypso pointed out to the assembled ILS raiders, as they prepared to go after the first of these places. "The soldiers have orders to shoot first and ask questions later when gunfire breaks out. They'll shoot us as readily as they shoot the perps. So we must use swords and do it quietly. Teris and I will go in first and eliminate the guards at the entrance. Then you all flood inside. Two remain outside. I want no man in there to leave the place alive!"

"Hey, what about me? I'll be inside," Teris teased her. She gave him a swift kick in his butt and the others chuckled. They mounted up and headed out, with one man driving a large wagon, which she hoped would return with many rescued women.

An hour later, they halted in the shadows across from a large, rundown warehouse. As they watched, two men crept up to a side door and knocked. Someone opened the door; light beams illuminated the men for a brief instant before closing behind the two men who entered. "Okay, let's do it!" she ordered. Quietly, the party rushed across the street. Inwardly, Kalypso was grateful for how well she could now walk. At least her feet were normal, a major help she thought.

Once at the door, she hung back to one side where she could land her kicks and yet not be instantly seen by the man who opened the door. Teris knocked. As before, a man opened the door. "Five gold," he muttered rather bored with it all. Kalypso struck out with a lightning fast thrust of her leg, landing it perfectly on his neck. As he began to slump, Teris grabbed him and held on to the dead man, pretending to move himself and the doorman inside.

Kalypso stepped inside, followed by a dozen others. "What the. . ." another guard just inside the door cried out, as he spotted his fellow guard, slumping to the ground. Kalypso's kick silenced his question. Now they surveyed the scene before them. Dozens of mattresses were lying on the main floor of the warehouse. Naked women were lying on many, their legs tied spread eagle to the sides of the mattresses. Several had men over them, a disgusting sight indeed.

Two more guards stood on the opposite side. One called out and rushed up some side stairs to the second floor, while the other man drew his sword and dashed across the room to attack them. The three men looked up startled and jumped up, pulling up their pants, looking for a way to get out of here, their pleasure interrupted. Teris's sword met the guard's with a resounding clank of steel upon steel, drawing the attention of many bound women as well as the three who were frantically pulling up their pants.

Kalypso dashed across the room, followed by her other men, three of whom stopped to eliminate the three men, who begged for their lives. "We've done nothing wrong," one pleaded. His ILS attacker replied, "You've taken advantage of these poor women. Sentence is death!" Three screams echoed in the room.

"No, don't fire, you fool! You'll bring every damn soldier in the city down on us!" a well-dressed man yelled from the second story landing. A dozen men, one who held a long gun, looked down on Kalypso. "Use your swords, kill them all!" he screamed. The dozen dashed down the stairs.

She ducked as the first one swung his deadly sword at her neck. Her follow up motion brought her right leg up, striking hard at the man's exposed neck. He dropped like a stone. Steel clashed upon steel, as her men met the onrush coming down the stairs. She spotted another opening and struck one in his privates. As he doubled up in howling pain, the ILS friend sliced his sword into the man's neck, ending his pain permanently.

Teris finished off his opponent and joined the main battle. It did not last long. Within three minutes, the last of the dozen dropped to the ground. A few of the ILS nursed some sword cuts, including Kalypso. However, she ignored her slight cut and charged up the stairs, more determined than ever. Teris was right behind her; he knew what she wanted, and he did too, for that matter.

Suddenly, the man in the fancy suit stepped out from a side room, leveling a pistol at the two. Sneering, he said, "All right, take the damn bitches. Go now. Take them all and be done with it!"

Kalypso replied haughtily, "I will do just that, but only after you pay for your crimes."

"Bitch! Who the hell are you?" he called out, a slight trace of fear in his voice.

"The ILS, fool," she replied.

Bang! He fired and dashed back into his room. In a lightning fast move, Kalypso swung her torso to the left, the deadly bullet whizzed by her chest. She staggered twice to regain her balance and keep from falling. "Damn you are fast!" Teris exclaimed. "I thought that you were a goner there."

"I said my reflexes have improved. Come on; let's get this bastard." Teris lunged his body weight into the door, busting it wide open. As it gave way and he fell to the floor, she dashed inside, racing up to the man who was feverishly trying to reload his pistol, hoping for a second shot. Wham! Her right foot smashed into his privates, doubling him over in pain. Wham! Wham! She delivered to more crushing blows, breaking both his legs. He crashed onto the floor screaming from the intense pain.

Kalypso stood over him and said sharply, "Never, ever harm a woman again! Remember that next life!" With that, she stomped on his neck ending the noise.

"Let me tie a handkerchief on your thigh, dear, you are bleeding," Teris said as he came to her side.

"You need one on your arm, too, dear. Okay. Do it quickly, we need to get these women out of here."

A half hour later, they had thirty women packed into the back of the wagon. Teris covered them all with several blankets and urged them to remain quiet until they got them to safety. He helped Kalypso mount and the band of ILS rode off into the hot summer's night, taking them to the Isis estate.

The next day, all thirty women had been cleaned up, dressed in spare shirts and pants, and fed. Teris had also tended Kalypso's sword cut as well as his. Now they again loaded the women onto wagons, this time using two. They headed off to the Dorota complex where she knew that these highly traumatized women would receive the best possible care.

"Hi, rescued thirty more for you," she explained, as Amadei opened the gates for the party.

"Well done, Kalypso," he replied. "What news have you? Take tea with us?"

After helping get the women unloaded, she and Teris joined him for tea. Marzena and the others ushered the traumatized women off into their complex. Perse and Albin came running up to hear the news as well. "Hi Kalypso. You rescued some more?" she asked.

"You bet. Thirty this time. News? Okay," she replied. For a while, she relayed all that had been happening, the dead count, and generally how things were progressing.

Perse piped up during a lull in the conversation. "Albin took my 824 almanac to the publishers two weeks ago. It will be published soon, so everyone will have their weather forecast for next year after all. Isn't that great news?"

"Absolutely. I am sure the farmers will be very grateful, Perse. We need all the crops we can grow right now," Kalypso validated her. Perse smiled. "Say, we'd better get back soon. We have more women to rescue."

"Before you go, a bit of news from here," Amadei interrupted. "Once the farming men could walk again, they began visiting their neighbors. The reports that we've been getting in here indicate that those folks living on farmsteads have pretty well handled the plague. There have been only a few reports of death from them. Looks like our rural citizens have weathered the storm vastly better than we city folks have. Interestingly enough, many of the women that we've trained are now expanding out to the farmsteads close to the Paneus spread, showing the women there how to do things for themselves. I know that it is a small number, but it is a start, Kalypso, it is a start."

"That's good to hear. Impressive. You all here are saviors, really you are," Kalypso validated him and those at the complex. Then, she and Teris headed back to their place. She rode on the driver's seat beside him, frequently giving him a passionate kiss. Their ILS friend driving the other wagon behind them merely smiled at the two. He thought it was a good sign, a good omen for the future.

By March 7, the first hints of fall had come. Kalypso and the ILS had raided three more brothels. One hundred six women were rescued. On this day, she, Teris, and two other men arrived with the last pair of wagons, bringing another twenty-nine women to the complex safe haven.

Amadei insisted on holding a conference with Kalypso. "Just as soon as we get these new arrivals settled, we must have a vital talk. Please, Perse, Albin, entertain these two for a few minutes."

"Sure," Perse replied. After he left, she asked, "Oops, how am I supposed to entertain you two?"

Kalypso chuckled. "Do you dance or sing?" Both laughed.

"Er, no to the singing. I used to go to the Royal Balls though. You know, dress up in those fancy Annelise gowns and dance the night away. I do rather miss that now. Strange, but I do sort of miss it," Perse admitted.

"Well, if we wear such outfits now, Perse, why, we would then truly be helpless wouldn't we?" Kalypso answered.

"It's so funny, Kalypso. Four months ago, I thought that I was hopelessly helpless. Now I don't have any such thoughts anymore. Funny isn't it? I'm still the same as I was then," Perse admitted.

"Yes, I feel the same way, Perse."

Perse looked at Kalypso and resolved to do it. She asked, "Say, can I talk with you in private before you go?"

"Sure dear. Come on; let's go have a look at the gardens. Albin, you can entertain Teris here," Kalypso flashed him a coy smile, one that no man could refuse. He flushed.

Once they were alone among the bushes that had begun their golden change, Kalypso asked, "So what's this all about?"

"Well, my mom's gone now, so are my older sisters. I don't have anyone to talk to about, well, you know, women's things. I mean I suppose I could talk to Aniela, but she always seems to be very busy. All the women around here are so terribly busy all the time. So I thought that maybe I could, well, you know, ask you about certain things," Perse rather beat around the bush.

Kalypso could sense that she was a bit embarrassed about whatever this was about. "You and I are friends, Perse. You can talk to me about anything, ask me anything."

Perse flashed a smile of relief. "Okay, what I want to know is how do you know if you are in love with someone?" She came right out with it at last.

"Man or woman?" Kalypso asked.

"Man, silly," Perse giggled.

"Well, I thought that I'd better ask. You never know about love. Okay, well, I'm not an expert in these things. Damn, I honestly don't know how I ended up with Teris, but he is absolutely perfect for me." She chatted on, trying to explain the unexplainable to Perse. "Have you kissed each other yet?"

"Er, well no, not exactly. Is that important?" Perse asked. The two chatted and chatted, until finally Amadei called out for them. Giggling, the two joined the others, who were now having tea on the patio, enjoying the warm early fall day.

After getting the two served, Amadei began, "Okay, help is going to be arriving on March 10. I promised you that help, real help, would be coming, and I'm pleased to announce that it will be here in just a couple days. Please, do not ask how it is that I know this. It is vital that you two, Kalypso and Teris, be here to greet and brief them. They will be arriving here at our complex first, before moving on into

Thal."

"Exactly what do you mean by real help, Amadei? No, I do want to know. How is it that you know this?" Kalypso replied. "I mean, this is a matter of trust. You can understand how it is that I trust so few men these days. How is it that you know these things? Answer that first and then define what you mean by real help."

Perse held her breath. Never had she heard anyone order or demand something from Amadei. She'd never dare to do such! "Well, Kalypso, this could take quite a lengthy explanation," he replied.

If she had had arms, Perse swore that Kalypso would have placed her hands on her hips as she replied this time, "Well, Amadei, it seems that we have several days to listen." Perse was sure that Amadei would explode in anger. No one ever talked like this to him.

To her surprise and amazement, Amadei laughed. "Okay, Kalypso. Okay. You have earned the right to know the full truth. Let's see. You realize that you are an immortal spiritual being, right?" She nodded, so did Perse, involuntarily. She was listening intently.

"Well, have you ever given any thought as to what powers and abilities a spiritual being alone might have? Not your body, but you?"

"No, not really. To be honest, I'm just sort of operating a body," she replied. Perse nodded, she agreed fully.

"Yet you are not your body. Everything that a body can do, a spiritual being ought to be able to do and then a million times more. For example, can you lift your teacup up to your lips? No, not with your foot, Kalypso." She'd reactively begun lifting it up with her foot as usual now. "You lift it."

"Oh don't be silly," Kalypso retorted.

"Like this," Amadei replied. Perse stared at his cup in total disbelief. His cup rose into the air, positioned itself before his lips, while he took a sip. Then, his cup floated back down, resting at last on the table once more.

"Wow! How did you do that?" Kalypso asked. Now, he had her full and undivided attention.

"We spiritual beings can be very powerful. By using our Holy Gift, our therapy and a whole lot of practice, practice such as you have been doing with your feet, we can regain the abilities that we, as spiritual beings, once had. One of those abilities you call telepathy."

"Surely telepathy is nonsense," Kalypso added.

Does this sound like nonsense to you? Amadei's words echoed in her mind, as they did with Perse and Teris.

"Oh!" Kalypso jerked, quite shocked and startled. "Oh my!"

"Yes, I have regained my ability to use telepathy; not fully, I am still practicing it. I have much to relearn, just as you do, Kalypso. All of us here at the Church of God have much to relearn. Telepathy is crucial to my story. The founder of our church used to be called the Guardian, but now goes by the name Macario Ines. Currently, he is up in Velona working to help them there, just as we are here working to help all of you."

"One of his most important helpers is Bethany Bartiana Angela, of Velona. She is coordinating our worldwide efforts to help all people recover from the alien plague, which has left every woman on Tarra armless. She uses the LD radios that one of her close friends has invented to stay in touch with many other leaders around the world. Closer to home, she is in daily contact with two of her friends who are now running the kingdom of Arolas, namely the two daughters of the late king there, Anathia and Callisto Tropos. Those two young women, much as you, Kalypso, have retaken back control of Arolas and have appointed themselves co-monarchs. They now rule Arolas and are working hard to improve their kingdom to enable women to survive and prosper."

"Wow! Incredible news. But this thing is worldwide? All women? Everywhere?" Kalypso asked.

"I am afraid so. All women, including newborn baby girls. We are stuck with this catastrophe and must, I repeat, must find ways to survive and prosper and thrive. Ana and Callisto are bringing many of the new marvelous inventions of Velona to Arolas, such things as electricity to light homes. I've heard that they have invented a machine to clean floors. Bethany tells me that they have these motorized machines that she can drive herself anywhere. They have motor-wagons that women drive, carrying loads that would take a team of horses to pull." He chuckled, "I've also heard that Callisto drives a mean motor-wagon. Anyway, the basic idea that we are all now following is to create and get distributed as many devices as we can to enable women to more easily deal with the necessities of life."

"That's what I want to do, help bring such things to all women here in Thal," Albin butted in. "I want to get electric lights in here so Aniela can simply flip a switch to turn on the lights. My heart aches to see her trying so hard to light a lantern."

"Rightly so, Albin. The idea is first to make life easy, doable, and bearable for women and for men. Then, make it so that we have more free time so that we have time to give our Holy Gift to all women and then to men. In time, our goal is to have every man, woman, and child on Tarra as free spiritual beings, able to do all the incredible things that are native to we beings. Lofty goal."

Amadei continued, "Anyway, back to the current situation. It seems that we got a helping hand from the Seer Priestess of the Temple of Orthos, the Priestess of Sol, Airlea. Evidently, she foresaw the coming of the plague and a way for Thallyus and Penelopus to overcome the chaos. Before the plague came, she invited the daughters of both countries' kings to come to Orthos. Thus, when the plague struck and the rioters looted the palace here in Thal and others did the same in Tinos, killing our kings and queens and eliminating all official rulers, the four princesses survived nicely at Orthos."

The top general of Thallyus and his counterpart in Penelopus are now bringing the four back to their respective capitals. They will be declaring them monarchs of Thallyus and Penelopus and will be guaranteeing that they are the rightful rulers of our two countries. Interestingly enough, Zoe of Penelopus and our own Elissa are truly engineers and inventors. Those two will be bringing the fabulous technology of Velona to Penelopus and Thallyus."

"Monarchs Sophia and Elissa have an LD radio with them and talk with Monarchs Ana and Callisto of Arolas and with Bethany of Velona every day. Via telepathy, for the last of week now, Bethany has been keeping me informed on a daily basis. The last estimate is that they will be arriving here at our complex on March 10, probably mid-morning. Our new monarchs are insisting on meeting with you two personally, Kalypso and Teris. You see, I have been telling Bethany about your activities, and she's relayed it to Sophia and Elissa."

He went on, "You both are young, nineteen, and our monarchs are also young, twenty-two and twenty-one. Apparently, both of them have recently married their long time boyfriends, but those men will not be placed on the throne as kings. I am not sure what our monarchs have in mind, but Bethany says that it is revolutionary in nature. So as I said originally, real help is on its way. Only a couple more days and they will be here. Now does that satisfy your curiosity Kalypso?"

She grinned, "In spades, Amadei, in spades! Thank you. For the first time in four months, I honestly feel like I can relax a little!"

"Same here. I am very pleased that we are going to have women on the throne. I believe that is going to be a key detail," Teris added. "I just wish that there were more of you folks, Amadei."

He sighed, "There would have been millions, but the aliens destroyed Dorota first. Had they not, things might have been vastly easier, but then there is no sense dwelling on what might have been. We must deal with what we have."

"True. Well, since I am here for a couple days, maybe I can learn some more things," Kalypso added.

Amadei gave her a wry grin. "Perse, now that we've finished here, would you take Kalypso to Aniela? I believe you have work to do with the new arrivals. Was it twenty-nine of them?"

Kalypso nodded and followed Perse. Not long after that, she found herself sitting with one of the rescued women as she began giving her first Holy Gift, her first therapy session, and she was rather nervous about doing it. Several hours later when she ended this session, Kalypso felt as fantastic as her patient did. She spent the ensuing days giving as many sessions as she was allowed.

Chapter 28 And Arrives

As predicted, around ten the next morning, a large number of riders and several wagons pulled up outside the gates of the Dorota Church of God. Albin, Perse, and Teris were there waiting for them and Albin sent Teris off to let the others know their monarchs had arrived. He opened the gates, with Perse helping to push them aside, allowing the wagons to enter easily.

General Hypatios reined in beside one wagon. "Your Highness, I will leave an escort here to guard you. As planned, I will go on into town and be briefed on the current situation and check on the Royal Palace. I believe that repairs will have to be made before you can move back into your home there. I'll return here by nightfall."

"Thanks general," Sophia said. The group dismounted, while the others came out of the white marble building to greet the arrivals.

Amadei did the introductions for his group, Sophia then did the same for her group. Both Sophia and Elissa wore the white robes with the sun symbol of the Tower of Orthos, the only real clothes that fit them thus far. Sophia's long black hair had been neatly trimmed just below her knees. Likewise, Elissa's flowing sandy blonde hair had been trimmed similarly. Theron stood proudly beside Sophia, while Thoth stood beside Elissa. "Hi everyone. I am Queen Sophia Aikos, my husband, Theron Kissos Aikos. He's taken my name," she grinned. "And my sister, Elissa, and her husband Thoth Motheos Aikos. I do hope that you don't mind that I've been appointed to rule Thallyus now."

"Mind? Queen Sophia, I was prepared to beg you to be our leader," Teris declared. "Until a couple days ago, we didn't even know that you were still alive."

"Welcome to our church, Monarchs Sophia and Elissa, gentlemen. Please, let's go inside and have tea. I believe that we have much to discuss and share," Amadei suggested.

"Thanks. Let's dispense with this monarch's stuff," Sophia began. "Has Bethany somehow told you about our adventure at the Tower of Orthos?" she asked.

"Yes, I relayed it to them all a couple days ago," Amadei answered.

"Okay, then I will get right to it, without any long preamble. Elissa and I were saved by the incredible foresight of Airlea of Orthos. Otherwise, we'd be just as dead as our dad is. Our country and Penelopus too is standing on the very brink of destruction. Yet, Airlea has seen one path that we may travel to avoid this catastrophe. Elissa and I have agreed to follow her foreseen path, so has Amynta and Zoe of Penelopus. Our two countries are going to become very closely allied and linked from now on. Anyway, the path that we absolutely must follow is one of a matriarchy. Until now, men have been the ones in control of our country, our marriages, and our finances, all of it. Few women have ever held true power and then only for a brief time period. Under these circumstances, that must change. From now on, Thallyus and Penelopus will become a matriarchy; women will own the property when they marry. Women will be in charge of the family finances. When a man dies, the property goes to his wife and daughters, not his first-born son. We must do everything in our power to ensure that women can survive and thrive or the doom will surely take us all."

"Well I'll be a monkey's uncle," Teris interrupted her. "Sophia, I have been arguing this very point to everyone. Our ILS will be backing you all the way. We have built up a surprising force. We are with you. It is the only way that we men can see. Count on us."

Sophia grinned, "Man, Bethany sure knows what she is talking about! She told me that I would likely find staunch supporters when I arrived. Incredible. Thank you, Teris. I know that this is a very radical idea and will not go over well with most men, particularly the wealthy, who have always operated their own ways, but not any longer, I'm afraid. Kalypso, you should know that I have issued my first official orders just before we left Orthos. The general is now beginning their implementation. It was: any man who mistreats a female in any harmful way is to be publically executed and all his possessions given over to the women whom he victimized. We'll probably need right away to execute a number of those wicked men who have been raping, kidnaping, and holding women as sex slaves. We'll make an example of them, and quickly men will change their ways, at least they may not be so overt about it. Being shot or hanged is a powerful convincer to others."

Kalypso laughed, "Your Highness, we have already been implementing that order for months now!"

Sophia chuckled, "So I have heard. Well done, Kalypso. Now it will be done publically and not behind closed doors. Now as far as titles go, I am officially dispensing with queen. That has too many ties with the way things have always been in Thallyus. Instead, I will be called Monarch Sophia Aikos. If anything ever happens to me, Elissa will assume that role, which I know that she really does not want.

Instead, Elissa will be our Royal Engineer. While I try to hold the country together and keep us somehow surviving, we are all going to be utterly dependent upon Elissa for our future. She has tremendously wise plans to bring all the marvelous inventions of Velona to us. Our idea is to make life easier to handle for we women and thus for you men. Electricity plays a key role as do these mechanical machines, these motor-thingys. Elissa absolutely must succeed in her mission; our future depends utterly on her success."

"Now that is about as far as I have been able to plan without being here and seeing for myself the true situation. Bethany has told me that I should expect major assistance from your church here and from the ILS. Please, can you tell me what ILS is and does?"

Kalypso giggled. "Okay, it is my doing, mostly. Isis, that's my married last name now, Isis Liberation Squad. We started out with a couple dozen of our close friends. It multiplied from there." She spent a good hour outlining what all they had done and how she had somehow "plugged in" her former lifetime as a Kali Assassin up in Kefall. That Teris now counted close to three thousand most influential men and women in the ILS was viewed by Sophia as extremely vital to gain acceptance of her monarchy and matriarchal ideas. He and Kalypso had lain the foundation for change.

Next, Amadei and Marzena explained their role. While Sophia and Elissa had no reality on this Holy Gift therapy, they were in total awe at how effortlessly these women handled nearly everything in life. "My god, somehow Elissa and I must learn how to do all these things for ourselves. This is utterly incredible. We just figured that we were destined to be mostly helpless, dependent upon our fellows for most things from now on. Bethany is right; we need to be here a long while somehow."

"We insist that you stay with us for as long as you desire, Sophia, Elissa. In fact, we already know what the general will report about the palace. It has been pretty well sacked. Much work will be needed to make that place livable again. Please stay here with us for as long as you want," Amadei insisted. They agreed and chatted a bit more.

"Oh, I almost forgot. Perse, ah, yes, that's you," Sophia glanced around, still not sure of everyone's names.

"Yes, your monarchyship," she fumbled.

"You are right. That doesn't work well either. Your Highness is too much like business as usual. I know, how about just Sophia among friends and Monarch Sophia for a formal address?" she suggested. "Now then, Perse. Are you really the publisher of the Thallyus Farmer's Almanac? The one who figures out what the weather will be next year?"

"Yes, Sophia, my grandpa taught me, and I did the forecast for 824. The 824 edition is going to be out in a week or so — from the printers, I mean."

"Incredible. I do hope that we are not in for a cold, long winter this year."

"No, Sophia. An early wet fall and a relatively mild winter, I expect. We should start getting a lot of rain in a few weeks. I've been telling everyone to get their crops harvested as soon as they can."

"Terrific, Perse. Okay, our farmers depend on your almanac. I will have the general assign guards to watch over you. Your safety is vital, Perse. Where are you staying?"

"My grandpa's house in just next door to here. I do my work there, but I have been sleeping over here. Albin has been my bodyguard and hands all this time. Why?"

"I have to guarantee your safety, Perse. After all, if anything happens to you, there will be no one who can give us a proper forecast. Our farmers will be greatly harmed without their almanac. Well, this simplifies it. General Hypatios will be assigning guards to protect this complex, so I'll just have him include your house next door."

"It's time for lunch, will you please join us?" Aniela asked. As they all headed into their large dining room, Albin moved to Elissa's side.

"Royal Engineer Elissa, I have always dreamed of doing what you are planning to do, making things that will help our women live easier, better lives. I would give anything to help you with all the work. Please, will you accept my help? I'll do anything I can to help. Please. I have dreamed of this day all my life."

"Really? Wow, that's great. I didn't think I'd find any man who would take orders from a female engineer, excepting Thoth here, of course. Sure, you can be my Assistant Royal Engineer. See Thoth, we have help already. After we eat, I'll show you how to operate the portable LD radio I got. Zoe up in Pinos should have hers any day now and then we can coordinate our efforts. Thoth, this is going to work out, I just know it. Now then, after lunch, we have to get going on the real planning. We have so many projects to get started so quickly that it's not funny. Albin, you will be a very busy engineer. You can count on that."

Even as they sat down and lunch was served, Elissa continued to chat with Albin, "You see, electricity is the very key to making it all happen quickly. Now in Velona, they use these enormous steam engines to generate the electricity. We don't have the facilities to build such monstrous engines, but we do have unlimited geothermal energy, which I aim to tap. After all, their whole method of generating electricity is just making a magnetized shaft revolve — that's what they use the engines for — to turn the shaft round and round. So we are going to use Tarra heat to do the same thing. Then, we need to lay long wires from the thermal fields down south up here in a sort of grid, so that the electricity can be delivered to everyone. Of course, the wires have to be kept out of the reach of people or they will be electrocuted and possibly die. That's happened in Velona, I'm told."

"Sis," Sophia interrupted her continuous stream of explanation, "eat first, plan second."

Elissa giggled, "Okay, okay. Sorry, I do tend to get a bit carried away. Oh darn, now I get to be embarrassed again trying to eat!" she sighed, resigned to the humiliation once more. At last, she began to observe the other women, how effortlessly they were managing, and awe began to sink into her mind. These women did know how to do things after all. Bethany was not exaggerating!

After lunch, the two women watched how many things were done. Both knew that they just had to stay here quite a while. However, Teris caught up with Sophia. "Excuse me, Monarch Sophia; may I have some words with you?" She nodded and the two sat done on a couch. "Why don't you give us a few days to sort of prepare the populace for your rule? Have you given any thought about how you actually want to run the affairs of Thallyus? I'd like to help anyway that I can."

"Well, not completely. I do know that I want an open door policy, right from the start. Anyone in Thallyus ought to be able to talk with me directly. Please, go ahead and do what you can to make this a smooth transition of power, Teris."

"Okay, will do. Another thing, if you use the Royal Palace as your base of operations, assuming that it can be fixed up enough, won't its mere presence be a constant reminder of the past rulership? Maybe you should establish a whole new office — turn the Royal Palace into a museum or something."

"Teris! You are right. Yes, anyone just entering the palace will be instantly reminded of our past. I need a clean, clear-cut break with the past. A new office. Yes, that's it. Business-like, not pompous-like. Of course, the general will protest that he will be unable to protect me outside of solid palace walls and such. Surely, we can find some alternative. Okay, Teris, your first assignment as my Top Advisor: find us suitable, professional business offices."

"Your request is my command, ma'am! Kalypso and I will get on to it yet today."

"A royal museum, I like that. Thanks." Teris and Kalypso left shortly after that, they had much to ponder and offices to seek out.

"Ah, there you are, Sophia. If you will follow me, we will get started on the most precious Holy Gift for you," Marzena said in a tone that did not allow for any other response.

"But, I don't know what this is or what you want me to do. Maybe I can't do it, Marzena," Sophia babbled as she found her body following the older woman's.

Late that afternoon, laughing wildly, Sophia had experienced the incredible benefit of the Holy Gift. The fear, trauma, humiliation, feelings of helplessness and worthlessness had completely vanished. She felt more like a ten year old girl again. Even more interesting to her was what she had discovered. Several hundred years ago, she had been one of the Holy Women of the Eighth Degree. She'd been through this mess before, but back then, she'd never been able to do anything for herself, dependent upon many servants her adult life.

Her sister was waiting for her session to finish. "Well, sis? How did it go for you?" Elissa's face seemed brighter, her complexion somehow fairer.

"Wow, oh wow, sis. I've been through all this before," Sophia exclaimed.

"Me too," Elissa grinned. The two exchanged stories for a few minutes. Elissa had been an engineer in the ancient days, sent off to the Isle of Right, where she spent an armless lifetime there, still trying to invent things. "Sis, how can we get this Holy Gift done to everyone? I surely don't know, but since you are leading things, see if you can figure out a way. Incredible, isn't it?"

That evening, the two were given their first solid lessons in their special Women's Ways of doing things. They worked diligently at it, under the watchful eyes of Aniela. When it was time to retire for the night, Aniela answered Sophia's query. "Yes, Sophia, there are darn few things that we women cannot do by any means, very few. I won't exaggerate, though. Some actions take us many times longer to do than it would take a woman with arms to do. That's one reason we do prefer to have at least four of us in the same general household area, we can help each other out. For example, many of us wear our long hair in ponytails during the day. We find it vastly faster to have our fellows put our hair up for us or to have a couple of other women do it for us. Perse, for example, has Albin tie hers up each morning and let it down for her when she is ready to retire. It takes him a minute to do it at most, but with three of us women doing it, it likely takes us five minutes."

"So don't be embarrassed to have your husbands do some things for you that before the plague you would never have considered asking them to do for you. We just have to do things in different ways. Do not be embarrassed because you have to sit down on the floor suddenly to do an action. Remember always, what counts is getting it done on your own. Don't expect to be as fast at these things as we are. It takes lots of practice to be able to do things rapidly. Also, some things require special tools, particularly in the dressmaking arena. We have to have specially made scissors that we can work with our feet. Sewing is always a very slow proposition and honestly, none of us here ever do much sewing."

"Thanks, I am starting to see what you mean," Sophia replied. Elissa agreed as well.

"Ladies, I'll share one other little known fact with you," Aniela lowered her voice, a twinkle in her eye. "You remember those strange images that you first had about how to use some of those alien objects?"

"Yes, they were strange. It was like I knew that I could use the desk to write and do my engineering drawings," Elissa answered.

"Yes, those are what I'm referring to — those images, those memories Bethany had the aliens implant in their plague to give we women some clues. I'm sure that I don't know how she ever managed to pull that one off, but I have heard many stories about women valuing those as a way to get started."

"Wow, Bethany must be a powerhouse. I do hope one day I can meet her," Sophia replied. "At least we are able to talk to her on the LD radio device."

For the next week, the two sisters received a session each evening and spent half of the day learning the basics of the Women's Ways. The afternoons, they worked on their own projects, Sophia, planning how to run the country, Elissa, working with Albin and Thoth on how to best get their projects started. After that, Marzena explained that once the country was back to battery and the women could spare more time, their therapy sessions could be continued, if they desired. However, the two decided to stay here another week, spending more hours learning how to do basic actions faster and better, as well as additional actions.

The second day, however, they did take a quick tour of their old home, the Royal Palace. Both wanted to see for themselves what state it was in and if they could recover any of their old possessions. Both were appalled, each room had been thoroughly ransacked. Clothes, books, papers, and other items lay scattered on the floor, trampled by many feet, knees, and hands. They found little of value that could be salvaged.

The third day, Teris and Kalypso dropped by to take Sophia off to see a possibility for the new office building. General Hypatios and a platoon of soldiers accompanied them. "Ta da! It's the old Saint Timon's Cathedral, Sophia. From the main chapel area, you could address at least two thousand citizens, delivering speeches and such. Or we could make it a welcome arena. There are tons of spaces that make good offices and the place comes fully furnished. There is a back kitchen and a basement, which used to hold vast stores of supplies. Then there is the rectory building just behind it and a stables. Another aspect that I like is that everyone knows where Saint Timon's Cathedral is located."

"Wow, the place is filled with the most incredible works of art!" Sophia exclaimed as she entered the huge, ornate cathedral. This central area was littered and a bit dirty, having been the home of upwards of two thousand during the worst times. It would need some cleaning for sure.

"Well, the large open areas surrounding the complex is a plus," the general pointed out. "We'd have a clear line of sight of oncoming attackers. It's a solid structure and could be defended with minimal force, unless they attempted to smash in the stained glass windows to gain entry."

Elissa added, "It is not far from the old palace, centrally located in the wealthier district. There is quite a lot of working areas in the rectory where I can set up our planning rooms. Sis, I like the idea."

While none was completely sold on the church, but for now, they all agreed this would serve as a starting place. After all, they could always move to another location if this did not work out. Teris volunteered to get the ILS group here and clean the place up and make it ready for operations. Sophia suggested that he take at least a week or two to have all ready, "I need more time with the incredible women of the church." He smiled and agreed.

Later, they agreed that April 1 would be the day of action. The ILS spread the word around the city that the new monarch would be addressing the citizens of Thallyus from the new seat of government, Saint Timon's Cathedral. Further, he arranged for Sophia to make four speeches, spaced two hours apart. At ten, the wealthy and the nobles would fill the chapel to hear her. Then, she was to repeat it at one, three, and five. The last three times anyone who cared to hear their new ruler could attend, subject to seating capacity. His estimates suggested that eight thousand people could hear her first speech, a very good start.

During the ensuing days leading up to this all-important speech, Sophia had to deal with staffing. Each day, she managed to meet for a few hours with Teris and Kalypso, who acted as her front persons. "Look, we are starting from scratch. Who knows if any of dad's old advisors are still alive. Frankly, I'd rather start fresh, Teris. I insist on having at least half of our staff be women. I want us women to be very visible. Then, we will need domestic staff as well. Again, half ought to be women."

She continued her explanations, "Now as far as the actual operations go, I have definite ideas about how I am going to set this all up, Teris. First, I have always believed that one person cannot possibly know all about everything. Our kings and queens in the past attempted to do just that, surrounding themselves with advisors. No, I am going to delegate responsibility. I want a set of ministers, such as a Minister of Education, Minister of Finance, Minister of Trade. These top-level people, half of which must be capable women, will run their own departments and handle routine affairs. I will expect them to bring the more critical ones to me for adjudication, just as I will be sending orders down to them about policy that I want enacted. Each minister ought to have a strong say in the selection of their personnel as well. After all, they will have to work with them. So Teris, our first real challenge will be to find qualified men and women to become our first set of ministers."

"Brilliant, Sophia. Once the kinks are ironed out, your government should run like a well-oiled machine. Even if you are ill or need to be away for a time, everything will keep on running along just fine," Teris replied. "I love it. Let me see what Kalypso and I can do. Do you have a complete list of the minister positions that you want?"

"Of course, silly, wrote it out on our return trip to Thal," Sophia answered. "I have given this considerable thought and have bounced my ideas off Bethany of Velona. In a way, we are rather modeling our new government off that of Velona. The main thing, Teris, is that we have to find enough women who are willing to give it a try, even though now they may feel utterly helpless."

Kalypso added, "You are right about that, Sophia. That will be hardest of all, but we'll give it a go. I can be very convincing when I have to be." She grinned.

"Another thing, Teris, keep your eyes open for a dressmaker, probably have to be a male at this point. We simply must have some clothes that fit, though now, I don't have any ideas at all. Elissa and I used to always wear fancy Annelise gowns and heels, but now, if we did that, we'd be unable to use our feet effectively and thus practically helpless again. So I really don't know what to do about clothing."

"We all are facing the same problem," Kalypso pointed out. "I too always wore nothing but the finest Annelise outfits. Now, women everywhere are wearing whatever rags, shirts, and pants others can put on their bodies for them. It's rather grim. We'll see what we can find out."

"Great. Say, if you can find some, please bring them to me. Bethany says that she has a hot dress designer near her who has created fashions that we can manage ourselves. She says that her dresses are easy to put on and take off by ourselves. I surely don't know how that can be, but I trust Bethany. She will have the designer on the LD radio tell our dressmakers how to make them. Plus, she had already sent many samples on a caravel from Velona. Still it takes many months for the ship to get to Arolas' main port of Andros and Thal is several thousand miles south of Andros. They will take some time to get to us. Our best bet is to get the information directly to our dressmakers and go from there."

The following day, Sophia was shocked to discover that the Guardian had somehow gotten millions of copies of my Hints book delivered to the cathedral! All were in her language, translated from the Velona dialect. She followed my orders and had her soldiers begin mass delivery of one book for every woman and girl in the city, to be followed by delivery to all the outlying towns, villages, and farmsteads. By May, a copy of the Hints book was being read or had been read by nearly all women in Thallyus. Months later, Sophia reported to me in Velona on how vital that action had been. The Hints book had given millions of women a glimmer of hope.

Next, Sophia wrote out her speech, revised it many times, bouncing it off Teris and Kalypso as well. Why? She planned to have it printed up and then delivered to every home in Thallyus, her personal message to every citizen in the country. As Kalypso proofread the speech, she began to really relax for the first time since the plague struck. She sensed this might really be salvation coming.

On April 1, Theron adjusted Sophia's hair for her, allowing her raven tresses to fall evenly down her sides and back. She wore the same white Temple of Orthos robe that she'd worn nearly every day. She wanted to make a good impression and wearing ill-fitting shirts of Theron's was fine for every day, but not for today. All eyes would be upon her. Nerves began to get the better of her. "Theron, what if they don't approve of me? What if the men rebel against my plans? What if?"

"Love, you can what if all day and it won't do you any good. Look, you are certain of your plans. That's good enough for me. I can't come up with anything that is more workable or better, not even remotely. Relax. Look, Sophia, even if they don't go along with you, you are going to go right on ahead with your plans anyway, aren't you dear?"

She grinned, "Well, of course I am! Oh, I see what you mean. Right, expect trouble. I am flying into the teeth of those who have brought us to the brink of disaster. I guess I am ready."

General Hypatios and fifty soldiers accompanied the many wagons and carriages, as they slowly headed to the Saint Timon's Cathedral, the new seat of government of Thallyus. Everyone at the Dorota Church of God complex accompanied Sophia and Elissa. They would be part of the huge ten o'clock crowd, the first to hear her formal address and to provide moral support.

They pulled up and saw an enormous crowd of men, women, and children standing on the spacious grounds of the church complex. Hundreds of soldiers armed with long guns stood quietly observing the crowd. Teris and Kalypso met them near the rear door. "They are waiting to get in for the one o'clock speech. The place is incredibly packed right now, a half hour ahead of time. I think folks want to hear what you have to say," he teased her a little, but saw that she was nervous and backed off a little.

"Knock'em dead," Kalypso whispered to Sophia.

"Glad that you are doing the talking, sis," Elissa whispered. Thoth gave her a little hug. Both husbands had their arms around their wives giving them the physical and morale support they needed just now. They entered and headed for the bathrooms for a last minute check.

"Well, since the place is packed, I suppose I might as well start early," Sophia suggested. Theron led the way, opening the doors for Sophia and the others. The huge chapel buzzed with hushed conversations. The High Altar was covered with a blue satin cloth, late fall marigolds in two golden vases were perfectly placed at either end. Sophia stood behind the altar, her body framed by the blue and the many multi-colored flowers — Kalypso's touch, aided by Teris, naturally. Theron placed a copy of her speech on the altar in case she got lost and then Sophia stepped up before the altar to begin. She wished that she had made a practice run. Panic. Could everyone hear her? The acoustics were perfect, designed for services; she need not have worried about this aspect. Her voice carried superbly in this massive chapel.

"Good morning everyone. I am Sophia Aikos, the Monarch of Thallyus, a benevolent one, I hope. My sister, Elissa, is our Royal Engineer. These are our husbands, Theron Kissos Aikos and Thoth Motheos Aikos. Please note: I rule, not my husband. Now then, let me begin at the beginning." She took a breath, so far so good, her voice was carrying and no one jumped up to attack her.

"Some of you have probably guessed what has happened to us all. Several months ago, we were all struck with an alien plague. Yes, aliens from another world came to Tarra and unleashed this hideous plague upon our entire world! There is not a woman or girl anywhere on Tarra who has not lost her arms. A few have subsequently given birth and already know that our baby girls are also being born without arms. We here in Thal are not alone. Every woman in the entire world is facing the same nightmare situation. However, the one piece of good news is that mighty fighters up in Velona, Sea Princes, have managed to kill the alien creatures that inflicted this horrible plague upon us all. The perpetrators of this plague have been eliminated. I wish with all my heart that we could say the same about the aftereffects of the plague, but alas, we are as we are now."

"Elissa and I, along with the new Monarch of Penelopus, Amynta Haimon and her sister Zoe, were spared some of the starvation and sickness that so many of you faced here. We were the invited guests of High Priestess Airlea of the Tower of Orthos, just across the Vardan River in Penelopus. When the plague struck, these brave women cared for us until General Hypatios came to rescue us."

"At this time, we have a good idea of just how devastating this evil plague has been. Here in Thal, nearly two million of us have perished during the last four months. Worse, well more than half of those have been women and girls! As you look around today, men vastly outnumber women here in Thal. I admit that we do not have any idea how the outlying towns, villages, and farmsteads have weathered the plague. Communications are still most difficult. Yes, so many of us have lost our loved ones. Elissa and I lost our father and some aunts and uncles as well. Hardly anyone has been unaffected by this wicked plague."

"Yet, it is far, far worse than that. At this time and as many of you have been speculating, we are facing the distinct possibility of the extinction of the entire human race, not just our own country! If we allow things to continue as they have for the last few months, there will not be any women left to bring forth our future generations. Yes, we may well be facing what the traitorous Church of Jehosanity wildly claimed upon the coming of the plague: the Day of Judgment is at hand. Yes, these supposedly holy men murdered thousands of the Church's followers, shortly after the plague struck."

"We are still here. The world has not yet ended. Life is within me and within you. Some of you have already brought forth new life. The world has not ended. Yet, if we continue down the path traveled thus far, our country will disappear within a generation. We have entered the Dark Ages. Doom lies at our heels and before us, dogging our every step. A wrong move and doom swallows us. Thal will be mere dust in the winds of time, the death of our civilization."

"Airlea pointed out to me, 'That which you fear you will have.' She made this law of the universe real to me this way. When you want something, do you not feel as if you are pulling it towards yourself? When you do not wish to have something, do you not feel as though you are pushing it away from yourself?" She paused noticing that she began to get their agreement on this simplicity. She then went on, "When you agree with something or someone, you are pulling it towards yourself and when you disagree with someone or something, you are pushing it away from yourself. Where does this get us?"

"If we fear something, we are pushing it away from us, yet look at what happens to the other side. It is seeing a flow moving towards itself, an agreement, a have me. So if we fear this plague and disaster, then we will end up having it, the annihilation of our world. Another way to look at this is when we women play hard to get, does not that make you men want us all the more?" A bit of laughter echoed around the spacious chapel and Sophia smiled along with them before continuing.

"This law of the universe can be disobeyed, when you know what you are doing. We are alive and sentient. We do not have to play the universe's game. The next maxim that so many believe in is this: we must adjust to the environment in which we find ourselves. Yet that too is wrong. Again, that is playing along with the laws of the universe. Let me ask you, after you have adapted yourself to some new situation, are you really truly happy and content? Not really. Instead, we should be doing the opposite! We should be modifying our environment to suit our needs, our goals, and our purposes. Our own distinguished General Hypatios will back me up on this point. On the battlefield, the side which best alters the environment to fit their needs often comes up the winner!"

"Okay, so then how do we change the future that we are all now facing? As it stands, the future is bleak and hideous. We women apparently cannot do anything for ourselves any longer and have become dependent wholly and completely upon men and boys to do absolutely everything for us, including feeding us. Yet, you men are also facing an awful future. Are you not overwhelmed by having to do your work and all that which used to be done by your wife and somehow care for every need of the women in your life? Indeed, the present is intolerable for both men and women; we just are facing different situations. Alas, men, you cannot just give up and move to some other country and start over. All women on Tarra are affected, not just here in Thal. Do we then just give up and die as the traitorous priests of Jehosanity have done? Nay, I say. I am not about to die just yet. We will survive this, but we must alter the future. How do we change the future?"

"Airlea explained how this can be done. It is simple really. One changes the future by changing the present. One alters what one is doing in the present and that changes the future. She gave me an example of a chicken farm, producing a large volume of eggs to sell each day. What happens if one day you decide to stop feeding and watering the chickens? When the future arrives, you have no eggs and no chickens. General Hypatios told me that the best generals make changes in their present situations to obtain their desired future victory."

"Ladies and gentlemen, if we do nothing, then we will be watching the death of our country. We must change the present to make a better future, one of our choosing, one, which gives life, prosperity, and vitality to us all. What must we change?"

"Until now, our whole society has been dominated by males, a patriarchy. Males controlled the government and mostly made the laws. When a father dies, his property goes to his first-born son, as a rule. With a few exceptions, women have had little or no say in much of anything, except perhaps in the minor domestic arena. Yes, we occasionally had an Empress in charge or a Queen here in Thallyus, but as history shows, she never lasted very long, a few years at most, before she was replaced by a man. Today, male domination has led to the very brink of destruction as a people and a country. Many of you know just what some males have done during the plague, raiding homes, killing those who lived there, kidnaping the younger women, and forcing them into whorehouses. What male lifted a hand to stop this? Males raided every store in Thal, looting all of value. They raided the Royal Palace and killed our king. What male doled out food to you and your family when you were starving? What male stepped up to bring back law and order?"

"At this point in time, we women are terribly dependent upon those with arms to help us. We cannot be turned out into the street because our fathers have died and with all his property and funds going to the eldest son. We cannot survive with men, who have proven themselves totally unworthy, to continue to lead us. It is time for a change. We must do everything possible to allow women to survive and flourish so that we can bring about future generations. It is time that we instituted a matriarchal society."

"Women must become the new rulers. Property must be owned by the wife in the family and be handed down to her daughters. When a man and woman marry and acquire a home, the home is in the woman's name, as are the entire finances of their marriage. The woman becomes the boss. She has total say over the money that is spent and upon what, not the man. Sorry fellows, rent money will be spent before you get funds for a beer. In short, we empower the women of Thallyus, for men have already abdicated their responsible use of power. Now we absolutely must give it to we women. If we do this, within a few years, I promise you that our country will be flourishing and prospering like never before."

"We are not alone in making this drastic change. Monarch Amynta is doing the same thing up in Penelopus as I speak. Further, months ago, Ana and Callisto have already done the same in Arolas. Yes, three kingdoms are now being ruled by women. More will likely be following our example."

"Okay, so what are my plans? What am I going to do to change our future? I will be taking many different approaches. First of all, Bethany Angela of Velona had put together a book of hints on how we women can do many things for ourselves. She based it upon the old Women's Ways of Dorota. I have obtained enough copies for every woman and girl in Thallyus. Some of you have already received your copy. The soldiers are in the process of delivering them, so you should have yours shortly. Yes, following these hints, I am now able to feed myself, brush out my hair, write, and even mostly dress myself, plus many other things. I have to do a lot of practicing, and it does take me a whole lot longer to do things now, but the bottom line is that I am doing them for myself. Theron is finally getting a break." She grinned.

"I believe that a year from now, women will be vastly more independent and self-reliant. I will work to make it so with other plans in the works. Yet, far more must be done. We must alter the environment so that women can survive and flourish far better. To this end, our Royal Engineer will be bringing many of the marvelous inventions of Velona to our country. She is beginning with this electricity thing. I admit I can no longer light my own candle or lantern. When she gets this electricity here, I will be able simply to flip a switch with my foot and turn on electric lights!"

"Velona has motor-wagons, motor-cars, and three-wheelers called T-putt-putts. These motorized vehicles are driven by women and men too. One motor-wagon can carry more than one horse drawn wagon and travels, I'm told, forty miles an hour. With these readily available, women will be able to go anywhere that we need and buy the things our families need, groceries for example. Plus, there are many more devices that will be following these, all designed for we women so that we can more readily do what needs to be done in life."

"Yes, these devices will be expensive, but don't worry. I will be providing them to all of you at no charge. Your government will be paying for them, not you. We will need new companies and factories to turn out these new things. If you have money that you care to invest in the future, this is your prime opportunity. See me or Elissa. We have all the necessary licensing arrangements with Velona worked out. There is a bundle to be made here, if you are willing to step forward and invest."

"I give you my word that within a very few years, Thallyus will be flourishing and prosperous beyond anything that we've ever seen before! Elissa and I will make that happen! She and I are going to change the environment of women to fit our new needs. Still, we will need much help in doing so. Your help is welcome and desired."

"On the grimmer side, I have been forced to make my first new law. Any man who mistreats a female in any harmful way is to be publically executed and all his possessions given over to the women whom he victimized. The ILS has already done much to rescue kidnaped women. Still, I expect that we will probably need to execute a number of those wicked men who have been kidnaping, raping, and holding women as sex slaves. I won't stand for mistreatment of women any longer. We must survive or our country is lost."

"Finally, I know very well that men are used to giving the orders, but now it must be we women who give them. In my new government, one-half of the ministers will be women and one-half will be men. If you feel that you wish to become a part of those who lead our country, please contact me. I can use your help. While we are in the Dark Ages now, I am spearheading the drive to bring us all back into the light of day, stronger, more powerful, more vital, more prosperous, and more able than we have ever been. If you want to be a part of this revival, come see me. Thank you all for being so patient with me today."

"I'm sorry, one more thing. If you or anyone you know is able to sew and make dresses, please see Elissa or me. I have dress designs from Velona that are made so that we women can easily dress ourselves. I am frankly tired of wearing Theron's old shirts and pants. None of our clothes now fit our monster bosoms or tiny waists. Women, I promise you that as soon as I can get these dresses made, I will get one to you at no charge. Anyone who wants to invest in women's clothes making, you can make a fortune. That's a tease, by the way. Thanks everyone."

She finished and waited. Twenty-three hundred men and women packed into the huge ornate chapel sat in silence. Then, Amadei and Albin began clapping. Soon the noise of the applause and foot stomping thundered through the one holy chapel. Sophia broke into a broad smile, bowed repeatedly, graciously accepting their applause and approval. She finally completely relaxed for the first time since the plague struck. Her plan was accepted. Now the real work would begin.

As Sophia and Amynta were getting themselves established in Thallyus and Penelopus, Macario Ines, alias the Guardian, dropped by to visit with me in 42 Hampton Way. "You're looking well, Bethany. Baby's doing fine, I can tell, June right?" I nodded. "Well done on the coordination of worldwide efforts." I smiled at my very large belly, six months along.

"Thanks. Tea?"

"No thanks. I've come by to discuss something with you. As you know, Sophia and Elissa have discovered the isolated Dorota Church of God there in Thal. They've received both training in Women's Ways and the Holy Gift, that is, therapy sessions."

"Yes, they have, but so have quite a few traumatized women. How I wish Dorota were still around. We could so use their help now," I replied, lamenting the loss of the millions who lived there and who could deliver therapy sessions as well as instruction in Women's Ways.

"I know very acutely the loss. However, Bethany, what you don't know is that I have several smaller groups with Dorota ancestry scattered around the seven kingdoms of Demokritos. They are all small, carrying on the work. We built upon the work that you and Dita started on Dorota. As you know, women have all suffered a shocking loss. It seems to me that it might be possible to deal with this in a manner similar to the way that you and Dita did on Dorota."

"You mean by getting hundreds and thousands of women trained to deliver the sessions?" I asked, suddenly catching on to his intention.

"Precisely, Bethany. How did you manage it? How was it possible to coordinate so many sessions, ensuring that everyone got one? You know the situation down in Demokritos better than I. Is it even possible to make a similar attempt there or anywhere else for that matter?"

"Well, after receiving the benefits of the therapy sessions, more than half of the women then wanted to learn how to do it. It's only natural. After experiencing it, they know how valuable it is, and it's in a woman's nature to want to nurture and help others. It's certainly possible, if you have some who have a knack of training others to do it. Plus, you need some hotshot givers who are available to assist with the quirks and problems that always seem to arise. We gave the males the job of dealing with all the arrangements. In the case here, the males are already overwhelmed with everything else. I don't think you dare dump this on top of them as well. Maybe some of the women could handle the coordination and arrangements, Macario."

"Hum, how about a frank opinion, Bethany. Do you think that doing something like this is feasible in this situation?"

"Things are different now than back then. Still, Macario, still I think it is worth a try. Why not put Eve in charge of the overall coordination of it? I'm up to my ears in everything else."

"You called?" blue eyed Eve called out demurely, walking into the living room. Her rich blonde hair was parted in the middle, lay draped over her shoulders and back, just inches from the floor. Her belly was as large as mine was. We four here at our place were all due in June. Even pregnant, I thought Eve cut a striking figure.

Macario and I outlined what he had in mind. "Up here in the north, therapy sessions are nowhere near as critical as they are down in Demokritos," he explained. "Thanks to Bethany, the Dark Ages that I predicted for those seven kingdoms may well be averted in three of them. Yet, if we can get massive therapy sessions done, that may well be the turning point for those three kingdoms, Eve. Up to a big challenge?"

"Sure thing, but what do we have down there to work with? Do you want me to move down there?" she asked slightly concerned. There was Giovanni to think about; he was needed here in Velona.

"No, coordinate from here."

"Okay, that's best for me. Say, things down there are in an awful state, not as it was when Bethany and I did it on Dorota. There, everyone was doing fine in life. They had jobs; women were able to do all that needed to be done; food was plentiful. Not so down there, right Bethany?" Eve pointed out. I nodded. "So how are we going to do it?" she asked, looking at me, of course.

"Bright ideas, Eve, your turn to have some, Blondie" I teased her.

"Well, are there some women who already can perform the therapy well and deal with rough cases and train others?" she asked.

"Yes, but not many," Macario admitted. "Perhaps you and I should pay a visit to one of them, and you can get a better feel for the situation. In fact, why don't we visit six of them? That way, you can meet them, and after that, you can stay in contact with telepathy. On the positive side, Eve, at least three of the groups have one person who has regained telepathic skills. They will be able to contact you as well, after you have met."

"But I can't really travel, not as pregnant as I am," Eve protested.

Macario grinned, "I had no such idea. Bethany, will you watch over her body this afternoon? I will take her and materialize a body for her." Now it was Eve's turn to grin; this she liked. I got her body into a comfortable position on the couch and watched it slump into a sort of zombie-like state as Eve pushed off from it. Macario and Eve vanished from 42 Hampton Way. For a minute, I envied Eve. She was going to have an interesting experience, but then, I was hailed on the LD radio again. Back to work for me.

Macario led Eve to the complex main gates on the eastern edge of Thal and proceeded to materialize himself and then a body-likeness of Eve for her. "Wow! It looks and feels like me," Eve exclaimed.

"Excuse me; please watch out for my wooly worms there. Don't step on them," Perse spoke up.

She was squatting down, examining a group of six, which were making their way across the pavement heading for some bushes. "Thanks. I didn't hear you two walk up. I'm Perse and I'm studying these worms, you see. Have to get all the clues together for what the weather will be like next winter and all." She rose and tossed her long ponytail back onto her back by throwing her head, her long earrings glistening and bobbing in the sunlight of the cool early afternoon.

"Hi, I'm Eve and this is Macario. Hey, nice earrings. What have the worms to do with winter?"

"Thanks, they're a family heirloom, only I don't have any family anymore. Oh, just one more clue. I publish the almanac down here. It's my job to predict long range weather patterns so that the farmers know what to prepare for, you see." Eve didn't see, but Macario apparently did.

He said, "Going to be a relative mild winter?"

"Yes, I have already worked that out, Macario. I'm now trying to estimate the total amount of snowfall here in Thal," Perse replied.

Evidently, Macario was amused. He asked, "And how much do you estimate there will be?"

"Oh, I've not got all the clues yet, but I believe that we are looking at some thirty inches, maybe more."

Macario grinned, though Eve didn't see why. "Well, my guess, Perse, is thirty-five. Should we knock to get their attention? We've come to visit."

"Oh no bother. I'm done here. I'm staying here as well. My house is next door, but I really live here. They don't think it is safe for me to live alone. Bad times we live in now. Come on; follow me. Did you want to see Amadie or Iwan? Or maybe you are bringing Eve here for the Holy Gift?" Perse chatted innocently, as she pushed on the gates to get them back open again. "I sometimes give the Holy Gift too, especially when we get a whole bunch of victims to handle. Usually Albin is my bodyguard, but now he is off following his dream of helping invent things to help women. He comes back after supper though. This way, if you will please drop the gate latch for me? I can do it, but it's rather hard for me to do. Thanks, come on. I'll take you to Amadei."

The two followed the raven haired young woman into the complex ground. "Oh there you are, Perse. I was just coming to see if you needed anything," the fifty-three year old Amadei said walking out of the front doors of the marble building. "Oh, excuse me. Hello. Welcome to the Church of God. I am Elder Amadei Feliks."

"Wow, Feliks. I once knew Elder Albin Feliks. Any relation?" Eve blurted out. Perse, who had by now heard a great deal of the family ancestry as well as numerous fairy tales of ancient Dorota, perked up her ears. Perhaps it was the first name, however, that got her full attention.

Elder Amadei frowned, trying to assimilate Eve's pronouncement. "Well, yes, Elder Albin was my grandfather, but he's long dead. Perhaps you are referring to my nephew, Albin."

"Oh no, I knew Albin when he was a boy, growing up with me on Dorota. He lived next door to Bethany and me. Oh darn, that was nearly a hundred years ago." Eve realized her blunder.

"I am Macario Ines, the Guardian. We've spoken often."

"Oh my goodness! Forgive me for not recognizing you right off," he bowed low. "Perse! Run and fetch everyone! It's him, the leader of our church! Be quick about it!" Perse dashed off, but looked back over her shoulder twice. What was happening?

"Please, come on inside."

"Thanks, this is Eve Bartiana Angela, a dear, close friend of Bethany of Velona. Eve did indeed know your grandfather. You see, it was Bethany and Eve here who created the Holy Gift. Back then, they were called Bethany and Dita. Bethany still manages to somehow keep being named Bethany by her new parents."

"Oh my goodness! This is an honor beyond all honors!" Amadei exclaimed, nearly fainting from the shock. By now, everyone else had come rushing in to see what was so urgent. Macario once more introduced himself and Eve, allowing the shock and surprise and awe to settle down before launching into the purpose of his coming.

After he explained the basic idea that he had — of somehow training hundreds of women in their therapy methods and then using them to give sessions to every woman in Thallyus, he said, "Please realize, that it was Bethany and Dita, that is Eve, that came up with that idea back then and implemented it. I had no hand in it. Bethany and Eve worked that miracle themselves. Now I have called upon Eve to see if it can be done again here in Thal. Bethany's rather tied up coordinating survival actions with many countries."

Perse asked, "Is that the same Bethany that I talked to on the LD radio? The one who is advising Sophia and Elissa?"

Eve took over. "Yes, she's my sister this time. She's a bit overworked now. Honestly, I've lost track of all the countries that she is working with, coordinating worldwide relief efforts. So you all are stuck with me."

"Wow!" Perse exclaimed, then asked, "Say, do you know the mighty warriors in Velona who somehow killed the aliens who did this to us all?"

"Sure do, I was — oops!" she looked at Macario, unsure just how much she dared say about that.

Macario grinned, "Yes, if you must know, Eve, Bethany, I, and several others took care of the aliens; unfortunately, we did not discover their presence until after they had unleashed the plague upon us. Eve can tell you all about it later on, if she wants. Oh, her real body is still in Velona with Bethany. You are seeing an image that I made for her. Eve is highly skilled in telepathy and will be able now to contact any of you when she desires." He looked at Perse and then added, "Okay Perse, Eve here is a highly formidable fighter, one that no one ought to ever challenge."

Thinking that Macario was putting her on, she said, "But how? She's like me, no arms. How can she be a formidable fighter? Using her feet like Kalypso?"

Eve grinned, "No, Perse. I seldom now use my body. I prefer simply to twist their necks. Like this." Eve gently lifted Perse's body up and gave her neck a gentle twist. "Only I give it a sharp twist, killing them instantly."

Perse grinned and said, "Wow!" With her curiosity satisfied, Macario then directed their conversation back to the problem at hand. Eve asked a number of key questions, increasing her grasp of the situation, which was actually worse than she had anticipated. It became obvious that these folks would be unable to travel around the country, not in its current state. They would have to operate solely here in Thal.

"Well, we have treated several hundred women that Kalypso rescued. We've sent them off to nearby farmsteads to help there. Some of them might wish to learn how to do it," Amadei suggested.

"Excellent. We start by building up a core of volunteers. I will have Bethany talk with Sophia and see that these women are paid well for their services, you too, for that matter. Now then, Sophia has or will be if she has not yet, confiscated the Churches of Jehosanity here in Thal. Let's use them as our base of operations." The more Eve chatted, the better the plan sounded. With the initial details ironed out, Macario said their farewells, but Eve promised to contact them every day, even Perse, who seemed very pleased to hear that.

Macario dissolved their bodies, giving the group something to see. He then took Eve off to visit the next group. As they traveled, he sent, *Eve, you are very close to being able to materialize your own body now. A bit more drilling and a bit more therapy on what is impeding you from doing that and you will be doing it yourself.*

Terrific! But there is no one to drill me and so on.

I know, it takes one of us five to do that for you. I promise you, Eve, that as soon as we have a handle on this mess and have things going well, I'll get back to you and give you and Bethany your long, long overdue therapy.

Thanks.

They visited a smaller group who lived in a smaller town in the far northwest of Thallyus, close to the border with the Kingdom of Thrace. From there, they visited a group in Tinos, Penelopus. After that, they visited a very small group of ten who resided in the foothills of the Kathos Mountains, some hundred miles further east of Tinos. Here, Macario asked them to journey to the Tower of Orthos and there give the Holy Gift to all the willing temple women. "If I am not entirely mistaken, once that is done, you will have at least a hundred women who will want to learn and go forth on the quest of delivering the Gift to all women." That pleased the ten.

Next, they visited two groups in Arolas and urged them to get in contact with Monarchs Ana and Callisto, and then take it from there. As they started to head home, Eve asked, *What about Thrace, and the other kingdoms? No groups there?*

Yes, there are some, but the physical situation there is too dangerous for us to ask anything more of them than to somehow keep their bodies alive. Perhaps something will work out for them. But right now, they are in the Dark Ages. She didn't press the issue.

Back home, I quizzed Eve about her adventures and helped her construct a large map of the three kingdoms, placing stick-it notes of who lived where. Eve had met over a hundred people and now had to keep track of the key names.

I grinned, thankful that I did not have yet another massive project with which to handle. My hands were full already. Okay, my feet were full already.

Chapter 29 The Path Out of Darkness Begins

Fifteen years ago, Leto and Aella Menolaos and Kleitos and Daphne Monos decided to move into the eastern foothills of the Kathos Mountains far from the decadent cities. Why? Each family had two young sons and they wanted to find a safe, quiet place where they could work their Advanced Therapy on their boys and themselves as well, free from all distractions. The men were convinced that this way, they could easily get their boys to total spiritual freedom, practicing the methods that their Church founder had taught them. As mid-April came, they had been very successful, achieving many of the goals, which they had set for themselves. Aella and Daphne moved objects quiet easily now. Their boys had become veritable powerhouses, even moving huge boulders. All were stable and always located outside of their bodies. All had recovered their innate telepathic ability and their perceptions, quite keen and sharp — that is perceptions received directly not via their body's eyes and ears, for example.

Yet, these eight were quite surprised to have Macario himself appear before them, along with Eve. After explaining what they would like this group to do, Leto and Kleitos agreed to carry out his request. "Besides, it is way past time for our boys to begin to meet women their own age." Only on their infrequent trips to the nearest village some ten miles distant did the young men even see women other than their mothers. That they were going to the Tower of Orthos where over a hundred unmarried women resided only appealed to these four lads, as you might expect.

Only Aella and Daphne had reservations about the move, "Dear, we are going to have to go back to using our feet to do everything. What a big hassle," Aella complained to Leto.

"I'll make it up to you in our bed, dear," Leto half-teased and promised.

"You'd better, Leto. Honestly, this will be very good for the boys," she replied. These four adults had a strong sense of family and their obligations and responsibilities to their boys. All four boys were now exceedingly able spiritual beings, and the four parents were quite proud of them.

At the Tower of Orthos, Airlea was eating dinner, along with the hundred plus women and few men. Suddenly, she had a vision and her eyes appeared to be staring off into space. "Mom! What's happening?" her daughter Tanis whispered. Tanis was the Captain of the Guards and the security of their compound was her responsibility.

Her mate Melina tossed her waist length brown hair out of her way and whispered, "She's having a vision, isn't she?"

Lykou, their husband and sitting between the two women so that he could help them as needed, whispered, "Sure looks like it." He'd seen her have a vision a couple of times over the years that he'd been here. Lykou considered himself a very lucky man. He'd married the women that he loved. Actually, he had always loved the fighter Tanis, but she also loved Melina, so he had to marry them both — a package, so to speak. Now he'd discovered that he loved Melina as well. Tanis and her fighting skills appealed to this hunter, but the sheer beauty of Melina hit his heart in an entirely different way. Here in mid-April, he loved them both equally, something that Tanis was eternally thankful for, because she could never leave Melina, not for just a man. She and Melina had grown up their entire lives together and swore that they would never be parted, especially so since the debilitating plague so ruined their lives.

After a time, Airlea roused. "Well, that is interesting. We are going to have some powerful visitors in a couple of weeks. They will be offering us perhaps the most vital gift ever offered anyone on Tarra. We'll have to get some quarters prepared for them. Two families, dear." Although she tried, Tanis could get no additional information from her mother, despite her many pleadings. Her mother merely tossed her head, adjusting the fall of her flaming red, curly locks, which she had Lykou trim back to waist length. Most women here had theirs cut back to waist length, making their hair more manageable. Tanis and her guards had theirs rather short, they had to be prepared to defend the tower somehow.

Three days before the foreseen visitors were to arrive here in the middle of the fall, around noon Airlea had another vision. "Oh my god! Tanis! Tanis, where are you?" she called out. The redhead Seer was at the top of her tower, gazing out across the fall landscape. Reds and browns predominated, with a touch of orange and hues of yellow. In the distance, she saw farmers harvesting crops, like tiny ants moving ever so slowly over the rolling hillsides. She sensed her daughter was near, hence the hasty scream. Pat, pat came the distinctive sounds of sandals on the stone steps leading to the roof of the five-story tower and her observation station.

"Mom! Mom! What's the matter?" a breathless Tanis exclaimed as she raced up the steps as fast as she could, paying close attention to her movements. Tanis, as many other women, still felt the acute loss of her arms, especially when she needed to keep her balance. Her mother rarely yelled for her, and her stomach tightened, a little afraid of the unknown.

"Tanis. Good. I just had another vision. Men are heading this way to attack us, they are intent upon having their way with our women! They have guns. Tanis! We must prepare somehow. We cannot let them get to us."

"Damn! Okay, mom, I'm on it. How long do we have?" Tanis felt her heart skip a beat then fear tightened up her stomach.

"Few hours at most, maybe less. They are coming by horseback." Seldom had Tanis seen her mother actually afraid. Not even with the coming plague vision had she displayed fear or terror, rather a stoic determination to survive. Fear distorted Airlea's face and her body actually trembled slightly.

"Okay mom, get to your room. I'll spread the word, lock all inside doors. Make it harder for them to get to us." She leaned into her mother and rested her head against her mother's, the best she could do to display comfort. Then, she dashed back down the stairs, again cursing her missing arms as she twice nearly fell, bouncing her sides off the stone walls.

She headed to the large gong, which they sounded when an emergency arose. At least Lykou had reworked the mallet. She sat down and pulled the mallet back. He'd mounted it in a sling so that anyone could simply pull it back by any means that they could and let it go. Bong! Bong! Bong! She let it sound three times before struggling to her feet, once more cursing her pitiful form. Before the plague, she and her ten guards could easily have taken three men. Now, she dare not think what might happen.

Women began rushing outside in answer to the gong. Her ten guards came running. Lykou, who had been repairing harnesses in the stables, also came racing towards the gong, located between the tower and the huge women's dormitory. "What's wrong?" he yelled.

"We're about to be attacked by three men with guns," Tanis yelled. Many curses echoed her own utter frustrations. She waited until a rather large number of women had gathered, before she told everyone what Airlea had just foreseen. She issued orders for everyone to go to their rooms and lock all outside doors and then their own bedroom doors. "Make it as hard as possible for them to get at you."

As the women scattered, relaying her orders to the late arrivals, Tanis, Lykou, and her ten guards jogged to the main gates. "Lousy timing," Lykou called out. "Nestor is off on message errands and most of the other men are out purchasing local farmer's harvested grain for our winter. Damn, damn, damn."

"Tanis, how are we going to stop men with guns?" one of her guards asked her as they stopped before the open gates and watched as Lykou shut them and slid the heavy locking timber into place.

Tanis thought rapidly. "Look, they are going to be forced to scale the walls to get inside. Probably they will attempt to scale it somewhere near these gates. They ride up and find the gates barred. They will probably try jumping off their horses onto the marble wall's top, probably close here to the gates. That's what I'd do, because it's easier than climbing them from the ground level."

"She's right. We will have one instant in time to take them and that will be as they just reach the top. They can't have their long guns at the ready, since they'll be using their hands to crawl up," Lykou continued down his wife's line of thought. "Once they are on top, they'll be able to see the layout inside, but we need to be hidden. That way, their guard will be down and they'll then scramble down. Again, as they do, they will be vulnerable for an instant. After they fire, they again will be vulnerable while they reload."

"Half of you take up a position over by the men's dorm, and the other half with me at the stables," Tanis ordered. "We'll rush them from behind."

"Right, dear. I'll get all the long guns together and take up a position near the edge of the women's dorm. From there, I can get a clear line of sight to most of the front wall. I'll try to pick them off as they climb over," Lykou suggested. "I promise you, Tanis, I won't let these beasts harm you." He gave her a reassuring kiss and raced off to get a number of long guns, while the eleven women looked around for good positions to hide and yet be able to rush to attack them from the rear.

Soon, the dozen lay in waiting. Tanis had to face her own dark thoughts. She dare not say anything to the other five guards who were not far from herself. What could she say to them? They were pathetic excuses for guards now; she knew it, they knew it. Now their worst fears had materialized — their worst fears since they first heard the plague was coming from Airlea. Slowly a dark black mental mass moved in around Tanis's head, her mind clouded.

The sounds of three horses broke the stillness of the crisp fall early afternoon, bringing Tanis's attention out of the black cloud in her mind to the brilliant white walls of the stables. She heard voices. "Locked. Over the walls men. This is going to be the easiest lays that we ever had." Another gruff voice laughed and said, "Hope there's no hags here." Tanis strained her ears to hear where the horses were moving to alongside the walls. She thought two were somewhere on the stables side of the gate. The other must be on the men's dorm side. She heard the sliding, grating sound of boots on the marble walls.

Bang! Lykou's long gun fired. "God damn, someone shot me!" yelled a voice over the roof of the stables. "I see him, back there by the huge building. Let him have it!" another voice yelled. Bang! Bang!

For what seemed an eternity, long guns fired in succession, both from Lykou and from overhead. She heard a thumping sound and then another. Were they jumping down to the ground? From her hiding place, she could only wait. Wait until she saw their backs and then and only then did she dare attack, as pathetic as it would be. Thump. She saw a wounded man fall to the ground just in front of the stables. Then she saw a man with one arm dangling at his side, still holding a pistol in his other hand, his long gun abandoned. He walked past the stables heading towards Lykou.

Tanis acted. She flew from behind her barrel and smashed her body into the man, knocking him over onto the ground, as well as herself. Her five guards were right behind her and she rolled to her left and saw Lykou at last! God, he was not moving! Anger and terror swept over her. Her guards began stomping the fallen man's head and neck. One moved over to a second one, who had landed just to the left of the gate, badly wounded. From the corner of her eyes, she saw the other five guards stomping on the third fallen man. Tanis struggled to the feet and raced across the courtyard to Lykou. Her shock and terror mounted with each step. Blood. She saw blood — a red pool shown in crystal sharp contrast with the white stone of the courtyard. "Lykou!" she heard her voice call out, sounding so utterly distant, unreal.

She got to his side, Lykou lay sprawled on the hard stone, face down, unmoving. "Lykou! Lykou!" Her helplessness crescendoed, and she just screamed, "No!" Soon two of her guards joined her. One sat down and rolled him over, revealing two chest wounds. He stirred and his eyes opened slightly.

"Tanis. You are safe?" he whispered and then coughed up blood.

"Yes, we are safe. Lykou, don't die. You can't die on me. I love you, Lykou. Lykou," she screamed as if by sheer willpower she could keep him from dying.

"I love you, Tanis. Tell Melina I love her too," his voice died off. His eyes closed, his chest stopped moving.

"Lykou! Lykou. I will. Please, Lykou, don't die on me. Lykou. Someone help us, please. Help him," she wailed, feeling utterly helpless to help her lover in his hour of greatest need. She didn't notice the many women who slowly came out to see what had happened and now gathered in a large circle around her and the body of Lykou.

Airlea, tears trickling down her face, moved through the crowd to her daughter's side and squatted down beside her. Oh how she wanted to put her arms around her daughter, to comfort her in her tragic loss. "He's passed on, Tanis. He is our hero. He and you and your guards have saved all of us from these monsters."

"Mom! He can't die! He just can't!" she wailed, the dark cloud in her mind seemed to expand larger and larger.

"Come, let us figure out how we can bury him with our highest honors," Airlea gently suggested.

One of her guards said, "We'll take care of the beasts and get their horses into the stables, High Priestess." The ten headed back towards the gates. Tanis finally rose, her eyes mostly blinded by her flowing tears. Anger swept over her and she ran over to the fallen man whom she had tackled. Though he was already dead, Tanis jumped and jumped onto his head, smashing it with all her might. Her guards looked downcast, but understood and allowed her to vent her anger, though the man's head was completely pulverized when Tanis finally broke down completely, sitting on the ground and crying harder than she had ever cried in her whole life.

She didn't see a woman carrying a sheet up to Lykou's body. She didn't see Airlea ask the ten young boys to lend a hand, removing his ring and personal effects. She didn't see Zona's eight year old Apollo help the other boys in rolling him over onto the sheet. She didn't see the ten boys working together to drag the body on the sheet across the huge courtyard and into the Tower. She didn't see their mighty struggle to get him down the stairs to their underground catacombs. Nor did she see their mighty efforts to get his body raised into the first empty niche close to the ground that they could find.

Melina, crying almost as much as Tanis, pushed her body into that of her lover's and got Tanis to rise. "Come," she fought hard to say and began pushing Tanis toward the Tower. An eternity later, she got Tanis into their room. The two sat on their large bed, laid their heads on each other's shoulders, and cried together.

After sometime, Tanis whispered, "His last words were, 'Tell Melina I love her too.'" Together, they let their grief flow. By suppertime, several other men returned with wagons full of grain sacks. Further, with the mill repaired by the two engineers, they had worked out a contract with many neighboring farmers to grind their flour later this fall. Yet, all this meant nothing when they heard the awful news.

Neither Tanis nor Melina wanted anything to eat when the dinner bell sounded. They merely sat together, their eyes bloodshot. After the meal, Airlea gave a long eulogy for Lykou, and then they all headed to the catacombs where Airlea conducted his funeral. Tanis and Melina barely heard a word that she said, however. Somehow, the two found themselves back in their bedroom, which now seemed to utterly empty, their husband and lover, Lykou was gone. Slowly the stark reality of his eternal absence became apparent to both women, who lay down finally. Sleep finally came to both.

Melina perked up some the next morning, but Tanis did not. Try as she might, Melina could not get Tanis to rise and get some breakfast. At last, she left, leaving Tanis still lying on their bed wearing the soiled clothes that she had worn yesterday. Tanis had sunk into a deep apathy. Later, Airlea came to visit her daughter, but was unable to rouse Tanis at all.

Just as she had foreseen, the visitors finally arrived around noon. Tanis could not be roused from her room to greet their guests, her apathy now quite solid, though Melina had brought her a little food from time to time. Instead, Airlea stood with the ten guards to meet the two wagons as they rolled into her complex. Six men and two women arrived, though she had not known their numbers, she was surprised to see so many men, young men at that. All six men had bowl-cut hair, typical of those living on the distant frontiers of the foothills, far from civilization. The two women who looked to be her age also had short hair, trimmed short, not even reaching their shoulders. Practical women, she thought as they pulled up.

"Welcome to the Tower of Orthos, I am High Priestess Airlea and the Seer. We have rooms prepared for you. Normally, my daughter, Tanis, our Captain of the Guards would be showing you around, but she is indisposed. You see, we were attacked two days ago. One of our few men here, Lykou was killed. He was the husband of Tanis and Melina. I'm afraid that Tanis has taken this rather hard. If you will allow the guards here, they will show you the stables and to the quarters that we've fixed for your stay. Once you are settled, Zona and Melina will give you a guided tour and then we can meet formally."

Leto raised his eyebrows. "You knew of our coming? Thanks. Your complex here is most impressive. I am Leto Menolaos. My able wife, Aella, our two sons, Phil and Thanos. This is Kleitos and Daphne Monos and their two sons, Seth and Titos. I am sorry to hear of your great loss. If we could have gotten here sooner," he suggested.

"Yes, the death of Lykou might well have been prevented," Airlea finished his thought. "Please, take time to get familiar with where things are at. We can talk fully in a few minutes. I'll have tea prepared." Both bowed to each other, and her guards nodded towards the stables.

Having handled their team, the eight were joined by Melina and Zona. Apollo tagged along, curious about the newcomers and to help open doors for his mother. "Hi, I'm Melina and this is Zona Rho and her son, Apollo. We're supposed to show you around and then take you to Airlea."

"I'm sorry that you lost your husband, Melina," Leto said softly, testing the depths of her grief.

She sighed, "He was the first man that I even loved even a little. Now I am terrified that I've also lost my lover, Tanis. She's not come out of our room since that day. I can't get her even to eat much. I can't lose her too." She fought hard to keep her swelling grief from sweeping over her.

Zona came to her rescue. "Yes, tragic loss for both women. So few men can be trusted you know. This is called the men's dormitory; hardly any rooms are in use. Nestor is our messenger man and lives here. The other five men live with their wives in the main dormitory. We are putting you up in two large adjacent suites."

While the six men dropped off their many sacks and the two women sat down their yokes whose baskets were also full, Phil made polite conversation, "So Zona, you've lived here all of your life? Is your husband around?"

He didn't expect the answer he received, "Ha! That bastard got me to become a Holy Woman of the Eighth Degree right after we married. He then managed to squander his fortune and get himself killed, leaving me destitute and with Apollo here to raise. I fled the city and came here. These women here have saved my life, especially Melina and Tanis. Melina took me under her wing for years, helping me learn to get by somehow. Then, this damnable plague came, and we are all doomed now. I'd thought that at least Tanis and Melina might have some chance after Lykou married them both, now that's gone as well. Life sure can be a bitch, can't it?"

'I'm looking after my mother now," Apollo spoke up proudly.

Phil grinned at the boy, "I am sure that you are doing a fine job of it. Zona, as pretty are you are, I am surprised that you didn't have men beating down your door."

"Oh they tried to beat it down, but not the way you are thinking! No one wants a helpless Holy Woman and now it is completely hopeless. We're all doomed. Honestly, Phil, I think that we are really witnessing the end of humanity, though maybe the two monarchs, Amynta Haimon and Sophia Aikos, can slow the end down some. Look, Tanis was a very competent fighter before the plague. Now she can hardly do a damn thing to protect herself, let alone the rest of us. I am shocked that men have not raided this complex before now, raping us all or worse. Honestly, Phil, we are living on borrowed time."

Melina recovered her poise and led them to the women's dorm, showing them where meals were served. "We have evening vespers and then all of us dine together. Long ago, we had to eat in shifts of two hundred at a time. Now, all of us only fill the place about half full. Grim."

"We and Airlea live in the Tower proper. The first floor are the meeting rooms. Tanis and I have our own room on the third floor. Our library is on the fourth, while Airlea and her priestesses live on the fifth. This way, please," Melina indicated with her head, then tossed her head from side to side to get her long brown hair away from her face once more.

Airlea was waiting for them. Two teapots and two plates of biscuits and two jars of honey sat waiting them on the table. In her white robes, her flaming red hair flowing down her sides, she looked every bit the Seer and High Priestess that she was. Zona was surprised as Phil helped her into her chair, even adjusting the fall of her long brown hair. She noticed that all these men helped the other women similarly. Strange, she thought.

"Welcome once more. If you will serve us, please. I admit that I can no longer be the hostess that I once was. I am now most pathetic at serving, but we women here have at least learned to feed ourselves mostly. As you have guessed, I have foreseen your coming. Although I do not know your underlying purpose, I sense that it is of vital importance to not only us, but to all of Penelopus and Thallyus. Please stay as long as you desire. We have plenty of food. Ordinarily, we are totally safe here. The recent attack on us was the first in some ten years. I do hope that it is the last, but in these dark days, perhaps that is merely wishful thinking."

"Thank you for your hospitality, Airlea," Leto replied politely. "Indeed, these are harsh times. I am amazed at your skill in foreseeing the future. Yes, we are here to help as we can. We offer you and all here our Church's Holy Gift. It is a therapy, which handles tragic loss and trauma. You will find that all of us are highly skilled in our methods. Normally, we would prefer to have women performing the Holy Gift to other women, as it was done on Dorota. However, Kleitos and I have only sons. Yet, I assure you that they are highly skilled and will do a very good job of it. While we could chat more, Airlea, I believe that I speak for us all. We would like to get started on this at once."

Airlea nodded and Leto continued, "I understand that your daughter Tanis has suffered a tragic loss and is doing poorly. We ought to attend to her immediately. I understand that Lykou was also the husband of Melina as well. She should be handled soon as well, though I am afraid that I don't quite understand these relationships."

Airlea smiled, "There are over a hundred women living here in near isolation from the rest of the world. Many have very good reasons for doing so, such as Zona here. If the truth were told, you will find over half of the women who live here have suffered atrocities at the hands of men. Thus, many women here have formed close relationships with other women. Tanis and Melina have grown up together, inseparable since they could first walk. Lykou wisely married them both; Tanis and Melina would not have had it any other way. I am proud of the way that Melina had handled this tragic loss, but I foresaw that my daughter would not be so lucky. I hope and pray that she can recover from the horrible death of Lykou."

"I give you my word, Airlea, we will not leave until she has fully recovered. Now then, I think it best if Seth handles her. Of all our sons, he's the best fighter. Titos, you handle Melina here. Phil, take Zona. My dear, you handle Airlea," he nodded to his wife, Aella. Thanos, you make a complete list of everyone who is here at the Tower of Orthos. We don't want to miss anyone. Daphne, Kleitos, and I will find ourselves three other women. Let's get started, shall we?"

"What do you need to do this thing?" Airlea asked, unsure of what they intended to do.

"A quiet room where the session will not be interrupted. Thanos will also provide security for the complex, in case more attacks come. You will find all of us more than capable of defending this particularly beautiful complex," Leto replied.

A short climb later and Melina led Seth and Titos to her bedroom. As she opened the door, Tanis still sat on the edge of their bed in the same position in which she had left her hours ago now. Melina had no idea what to say and so said nothing.

"Okay, Melina, let us use your chairs there by your dresser," Titos said softly. He adjusted her chair for her, though she didn't know why he'd bother. "Now I want you to close your eyes. Good. Let's go back to the first moment when you had any idea that your husband Lykou was hurt."

Meanwhile, Seth looked over Tanis. He saw a robust young woman, very fit, strong, powerful legs. She had the same fiery red hair as her mother, but hers was much shorter as fitting a fighter, he thought. His eyes missed nothing as he assessed his patient. He suspected what she must have felt when Lykou died during their desperate attempt to defend the whole complex. Her loss of fighting skills must have devastated her enormously, he concluded. She was just sitting there, staring off into space, apparently not even noticing that they had entered. He sat down beside her and stared off into space as well, duplicating her as best he could. He waited patiently.

Before long, her head turned slightly, her eyes looking at this strange man sitting beside her. He did the same exact actions only mirror image-wise. She had a sort of questioning look on her face. He made the same expression. At last, she spoke, "Who are you?"

"I am Seth Monos. Close your eyes, please. Let's return to the first moment when you suspected or saw that Lykou was hurt during the recent attack," he said softly, but with full intention. She did so and Seth was off and running.

Nearby, Melina had already re-experienced that tragic day several times. "Like I keep telling you, men are just no good. If they don't rape and hurt you, they just get themselves killed when you most need them," she said. Titos asked if there were not something similar to this that happened earlier. Melina, he soon discovered, had the "aliens" clumped together with "men." She now began to go through the loss of her arms during the plague. He thought that this was fortuitous; they'd tackle what he most needed tackled, the plague trauma.

Over an hour later, Melina had already gone through the plague's trauma a number of times. Titos began to see the effect that Airlea's advance warning had had on Melina, greatly lowering the traumatic shock. He made a note to point this out to his dad later on. With Melina looking for something even earlier in time that was similar, Seth got Tanis to go earlier, back to the plague trauma. Already, he had heard over and over Tanis proclaiming how pathetically helpless and useless as a fighter she now was. He understood her completely, a highly trained fighter now unable to fight. Of all of his extended family, he could most empathize with her position.

Melina had returned to an early childhood incident. She recounted how her father had beaten up her mother when she was three years old, very nearly killing her mother. He had stormed out of their home and somehow managed to get himself killed in a drunken bar fight. Penniless, her mother had brought her here to the Tower of Orthos, seeking sanctuary. Two days later, her mother had died from her beating and Airlea had taken her under her wing, becoming her substitute mother. She and Tanis had roomed together ever since then.

Seth knew that Tanis was very low on food and probably sleep, thus he kept it slow and didn't push her in the slightest. His intention was to get enough trauma eased off so that she could eat well and get some sleep. When the dinner gong sounded, he and Titos ended off. Melina felt a lot of relief, but Titos knew that there was a whole lot more to go with her.

"Thank god you are awake, Tanis. You gave me a fright," Melina exclaimed as she saw that Tanis was back in the land of the living.

"I feel a little better, love. Who exactly are you fellows anyway?" Tanis asked, as Melina got up to lead them down the tower stairs and over to the women's dorm for dinner.

"I am Seth Manos, my brother Titos. We have a small farm in the high foothills way to the east of here. We came to help all of you," he replied.

"We are pathetic now. You really can't help us, except to perhaps put us out of our misery. I couldn't even do a goddamn thing to help our dear Lykou when he was wounded. All I could do was sit there and watch him die," Tanis replied, though she was not crying anymore.

"I know — such a feeling of utter helplessness. There is nothing worse for fighters like ourselves," Seth replied diplomatically, but with a purpose. She took the bait as he had hoped.

"Are you a fighter?" she asked, as the four joined many others walking across the courtyard to the dining room.

Titos spoke up, "Yes, he's the best of all of us. Kicks my butt all the time." Seth grinned. Titos also understood what Seth was attempting to do, pull Tanis more out of her shell of grief and loss.

"Say, after supper, I can show you one of my prized possessions. I have a Velona-made sword that was used in the First Crusade for Spiritual Freedom. Not only is it a historical relic, but it is an incredible sword. Would you like to see it?" He knew already what her answer would be. What fighter could possible reject such an offer?

"Wow. That is incredible. Sure, I would love to see it, even if I can't hold it anymore. How on Tarra did you ever get your hands on that?" Tanis asked, a tiny spark of life returning to her.

"Need any help dishing out your plate?" he asked, as they finally were able to push their trays into the long buffet serving line.

"Tanis, I forgot our yoke," Melina spoke up. Both women realized that without it, they couldn't get their tray from the line over to their table.

"Okay, Melina, just this once, I'll carry your tray for you," Titos risked teasing her. She smiled and relaxed a bit. He thought, so far so good. She was stable after the session.

They took their usual positions at the table, sitting beside Zona and Apollo, who was not old enough to carry her tray plus his own. Zona looked incredibly bright and her eyes sparkled, Melina noted.

Zona commented, "This therapy thing is incredible. I never ever knew that there was so much pain when they cut off my arms! God, did that ever hurt, but I was unconscious, but I still felt it somehow." Although she'd been run through that operation many times, it was still lifting. She then laughed wildly. "My husband is standing over me after the operation was done and while I am still unconscious. 'Well, that takes care of her. Zona is now my pretty flower. She won't be able to interfere with me anymore. She'll be a nice, pretty wife, totally helpless as she ought to be.' What an evil thing to say! No wonder I hated all men after that. Even the darn doctor agreed with him and so did the priest who was there with him! Men!" She roared with the laughter that comes from the relief of a heavy trauma.

Airlea was also extremely happy that afternoon. While she did not tell others what she had found, Aella was quite pleased with her progress. She also suspected that with further sessions, Airlea's Sight would be greatly increased.

In their morning session, Melina went back through the beating death of her mother once more, and then Titos kept asking her for something even earlier. "But I was only three. How can there be anything earlier?" she protested.

"Well, have you got some images there, some strange pictures?" he asked, knowing that she did. He could easily see them, but that did no good. She had to spot them for herself.

At last, she admitted that she saw a bluish thing, and he began running that earlier one. All of a sudden, she shrieked, "I killed him! I killed the bastard!" She began roaring with laughter as she related the whole thing to Titos. She had a twin sister and lived with their parents on an isolated farmstead, some fifteen miles from the nearest village. Their father often got drunk and beat up his wife and the twin girls. One time, he had beaten both girls so badly that their right arms suffered a compound fracture two inches below their right elbows. He'd also beaten their mother horribly, and she was unconscious; her spleen had ruptured, though no one knew it at the time. He'd fallen into a drunken stupor, leaving the bleeding twins howling in pain, scared out of their wits.

The next morning, he was sober once more. Of course, he was remorseful, begged his wife and daughters to forgive him, promising he would never lay a hand on them again. Of course, they didn't believe him, because he'd said those very words over a hundred times to them now. Worse, his wife was still unconscious and the twins were drifting in and out. Both of their lower arms were now infected, the bones protruding like branches of trees in the dead of winter. Now his voice took on that of the loving father, explaining the seriousness of the situation and that he had no choice but to amputate their lower right arms, which he proceeded to do. When the twins awoke to find their right arms gone below their elbows, they shrieked and cried, but soon found that they felt far better than before. Now their attention turned onto their mother, who looked ghastly and was still unconscious. Their father was tending her constantly. She died a day later. The twins recovered and for several weeks, he'd remained sober, helping his daughters constantly and changing their bandages daily.

Weeks later, when they were fully healed, he again took to drinking and once more tried to use the twins as a punching bag. This time, Zona had had enough. When he came staggering over to her to slap her around, she took the butcher knife in her hand and stump and stabbed him repeatedly. "After that, it is just my sister and me. We lived our whole lives there together after that. No wonder I only wanted to really be with Tanis this life!" She laughed and laughed. Suddenly, she shrieked, "I lived before! I am not my body. Oh my god, I am a spiritual being!" She roared once more, heady on the significance of this revelation. Throughout the rest of the day, Melina laughed and told everyone she could find about this amazing incident.

By evening Airlea, Zona, Melina, and several other women were laughing, their immediate therapy completed. At dinner, Leto explained to Airlea, "Our immediate goals with you, Melina, and Zona, for example, have been met. We want to remove the plague trauma and that is done. Now this is only the tiniest of benefits that are achievable with further therapy sessions, Airlea. I give you my word that if you wish more, once we have given our Holy Gift to all the women of Penelopus and Thallyus who desire it, and the men, secondarily, we will return to your Advanced Therapy."

"Thank you, Leto. That is as it must be. Our women must have this gift of yours. The gift is giving us back life and vitality, which we must have to survive," Airlea answered.

Tanis, on the other hand, was encountering a very different set of traumatic incidents. Today, she had discovered three earlier lifetimes in which she had been a fighter. In each of these, she had a male body and was involved in a combat situation, twice as a Centurion. All three times, she had been badly wounded and unable to continue to fight. In one, her back had been broken and she lay on the ground, paralyzed and unable to hold a sword as her enemy came up to her and put her out of her misery. That she too had lived before became quite real to her, but the intensity of her feelings and pains had not lessened. She had more to face yet, especially as Seth noticed that she continued to say, "I'm so helpless; everything is happening at the same time."

That night in their room, Seth pointed this out to his father. "Yes, dad, she's still going on about being helpless. More importantly, she keeps saying that everything happens at the same time. That's going to have a tendency to pull all of her traumatic incidents and pile them up right on top of her in the present."

"We can see it — a black mass around her head. Keep at it, son." Seth grinned; he had no intention not to keep at it. Besides, he was taking a liking to Tanis, seeing her as a kindred spirit.

The next morning, Seth resumed by having Tanis go back through the last trauma before asking her if there was a similar one that happened even earlier than the one that she was re-experiencing. "Well, I sure didn't live very long those last three lifetimes. Everything is happening all at the same time. I'm pathetic and helpless," she replied with a resigned sigh.

"I understand, Tanis. Let's see if there is something earlier that is similar," he coaxed her gently. She yawned and yawned. Seth smiled; at last, she is yawning, he thought. Until now, she just had not yawned much at all, which was a sure indicator that the unconsciousness of a heavy trauma is lifting. Finally, she began to see something else among the swirling blackness around her head.

"Oh, it's night. I am on a horse. I think I am a captain. Yes, I'm leading a patrol up in Arolas, I think. You know, against the wild raiding horsemen of Vladimir. Yes, We're riding along. Suddenly, we are set upon. An ambush. My horse rears, I fall hard on the ground. Damn, broke both my arms. They are swarming on us from all direction. I hear steel upon steel. I am trying to get up. Have to issue orders. My men are falling. My sergeant is saying, "Damn, everything is happening at once. We're helpless now." I am helpless. I can't get to my feet. My arms — I try everything I can to not move them! The pain shoots up my arms. A bearded horseman runs up to me. I am helpless as he stabs me with his spear. I am so helpless. It is all happening at once."

He had her go through it a couple more times. All of a sudden, Tanis jerked straight up in her chair, her eyes wide open. "I've had this before! Seth, I've had this therapy before! I think it was back in 640 or so! Wow! I was an artist, but the Church of Jehosanity captured me and encased my arms in this metal thing. When I was rescued, my arms had withered and were dead. A woman named Jenna ran this same kind of therapy on me. Just like you are doing. Wow. I felt so alive after that! I got married and was a fabulous dancer. I've been through all this before! Seth, I feel so serene and peaceful now. Incredible!"

"Well done, Tanis. I believe that we'll stop our session now," he replied smiling.

"Come on, I want to show you something, Seth," Tanis said, her eyes shining. Her complexion had cleared. All traces of the horrid loss gone, and she looked young and vibrant once more.

"Come on, follow me," she teased him, as she rapidly climbed the stairs of her tower.

"Where are we going," he said playfully.

"Up here." She walked out onto the observation platform. "Look at the view. This is one of my favorite places. You can see the whole world from here. Look there," she pointed with her head. "I like to ride across those hills in the springtime. There are thousands of buttercups in bloom. Wow, Seth, I am way outside of my head right now. This is the most incredible feeling. I feel so big, so powerful. I feel like I can almost reach out and touch those hills, the grass."

He noted that she was indeed three feet from her head, above and behind it. Knowing that she was a fighter, Seth decided to take a chance. "Okay, I am right here with you. Go over to those hills and touch them, why don't you? Yes, like that, see, you are doing it."

Oh my god! I am touching the grass. Look! It moved where I touched it! Did you see that, Seth? Is this real?

Sure it is real, Tanis. You are a spiritual being, and you have incredible powers; we all have, only over these long eons, we have had too many traumas and have forgotten how to do so many of them.

Wait a minute! I am hearing this in my mind. God, there are our bodies way back there. They look so small. How can I be hearing you? How are you hearing me? I can feel the grass. How is this possible?

We beings used to know how to use telepathy to communicate. We used to be able to move around and do many things and never needed a fleshly body with which to do them. You are now actually doing some of the things that you have merely forgotten how to do. Simple. Let's head back to our bodies. Just decide that you are above your head. Hey, wait for me!

Now back at their bodies on the observation deck, Tanis had tons of questions for Seth. "Yes, I will be giving you more Advanced Therapy sessions so that you can be able once more. We fighters have to stick together."

"Thank you, Seth! Thank you. Oh! I just remembered my name back then, Zeta Seppina d'Aine. Wow!" Tanis bubbled with enthusiasm. "Seth! I have never felt so alive! This is incredible!"

"Come on, let's go find Leto. He's in charge of these therapies. We'll need his okay to do more," Seth explained. She gave him a quizzical look. "We're supposed to help all you recover from the plague trauma. You and I want to go far beyond that."

"You think I can? I know I can. Wow, I just realized that I don't need your opinion. I know that I can learn to do many things now. I just know it," Tanis exclaimed with more certainty than she had ever known possible.

They found Leto taking a break from his session with another woman. After checking her over and listening to them both, he said, "Very well done, Tanis. What would you say to your learning how to perform the therapy sessions and then spending part of each day helping other women and part of the day with Seth working on your Advanced Therapy?"

"I'd like that very much. I want to help. I had this therapy back around 640 when I lost my arms before, up in Barcella, I think it's called. This therapy gave me my life back to me then, just as it has done this time. I simply must know how to do it so I can help others, but I do need to learn how I can do more myself. I actually felt that grass and it was two miles away!" Tanis bubbled with unfettered enthusiasm.

"Perfect, Tanis. You and Seth have my permission to continue into Advanced Therapy sessions, but not today. Instead, you are to enjoy your tremendous gains. After supper, Aella will begin to teach you and several others how to perform the Holy Gift. It is not hard to do at all," Leto replied. He added, "Seth, why don't you take Tanis for a walk and enjoy the beautiful fall afternoon. You both have earned it."

Leto seemed very pleased with the results, Seth thought. They bowed and he did as requested. As they headed out into the courtyard, they spotted Phil playing ball with Apollo while Zona watched. Tanis had never seen Zona smiling as much as she was now. Zona saw them and commented, "Look at Apollo! He's actually having fun for the first time in I don't know how long! Phil is a natural with children. Apollo should have a father. I can see that now. I simply cannot play ball with him, not as I am."

Tanis grinned and replied, "Zona, you should have a husband as well. You look years younger now. I've never seen you so happy."

"I am, truly, Tanis, I'm happy. I can't ever remember being this happy, not ever. It must be this Holy Gift. I'm to learn how to do it tonight. I want to give it to every woman I possibly can!" Zona explained. "After all, it *is* something that I can do. I only hope that I can do it well."

Just then, Melina caught sight of Tanis. "Tanis! Over here," she gaily called out. "Over here. Come join us if you have time." She and Seth jogged over to the front gates, where Melina, her long brown hair was being tossed about in the gentle fall breeze, stood beside Titos. "Wow, love, look at you! You look radiant, Tanis!"

"I do? Great. I feel like a goddess or something. What's up?" she asked.

"I'm supposed to show Titos our mill setup. Airlea wants him to make sure all is ready for the farmers who will be bringing in wagons of wheat and oats in a couple of days. Want to come with us? Say, you'll never guess what I'm doing after supper," she said more excited than Tanis could ever recall her being. She didn't wait for Tanis to guess. "I'm going to learn how to do this Holy Gift thing so I can give it to others too. Isn't that fantastic? I'm sure that if you ask them, Tanis, they'll teach you too."

"I have already asked. I'll be there too, after supper. Seth and I are supposed to be going for a walk, though I surely don't know why," she replied. "We'll follow you two." The four walked out of the gate and down the sloping path to the mill, about a quarter mile down the riverbank, where the Vardan River flowed.

As they walked, Tanis acted on instinct. "So, Seth, did you leave your wife and family back at your place?"

Seth laughed, "I'm not married. No women where we were living. Mom and dad and the Menolaos family moved us out of the town into the wilderness of the foothills of the Kathos when I was five and Titos was four. They wanted to raise us in an environment free from distractions so that we could get as much Advanced Therapy as we wanted. Actually, all eight of us got it. So Tanis, I have not had the pleasure of having my arm around a woman in my life. I hope that you don't mind and that I'm not too awkward at it. I'm afraid you may find our social skills lacking."

"You lived out there in the wilderness all by yourselves?" she asked rather surprised.

"Yes, but it was worth it, Tanis. My brother and I have had so much of our native spiritual abilities restored that I don't know where to begin with them. Macario Ines, that's the founder of the Church of God, has laid out a walk-able path to compete rehabilitation of us spiritual beings, a path to total freedom and truth. All eight of us have been walking that path, though none of us have yet reached its end."

"I'd — I'd like to walk that path with you, Seth," Tanis admitted.

"Honored to have you at my side," Seth replied.

As Leto and Kleitos expected, nearly every woman who received the Holy Gift also wanted to learn how to deliver it and wanted to see that every woman had a chance to receive it. By mid-May as fall neared its end and the first snowfall the season was expected any day now, the last of the women's therapies was finished.

The eight, plus Airlea, Tanis, Melina, Zona, and the steward of the Tower, Rhea, met in the main meeting room on the ground floor of the tower. Leto outlined what his objective was. "We have been asked to somehow deliver the Holy Gift to every woman in Thallyus and Penelopus who desires it, secondarily, the men as well.”

“Please, you must let us help you,” Airlea broke in. “It is part of the path that I have foreseen. It is a role that we women here must play.”

“Your help is most welcome, Airlea. We will not be able to succeed without it. The question with which we have been wrestling is how to go about it. We have concluded that we must divide ourselves into two groups, one for each country. We should begin with the two monarchs and those who are helping them restore order to the countries. Once we have gotten everyone in the capital cities of Thal and Tinos, then we can expand outward,” Leto explained.

“But we’ll need an army of you to reach all the women,” Airlea countered.

“It is our hope and prayers that many of the women who receive the gift will want to learn how to do it and join with us, as all of your women have,” Leto answered. “Eve, who is Macario’s assistant, is coordinating all of our efforts. It was she and her friend Bethany who taught the women of Dorota how to give the Holy Gift. That is their name for our Basic Therapy. She believes that we can somehow build up an army of Givers of the Holy Gift here in our two countries, much like she and Bethany did on Dorota. That’s the plan anyway.”

Airlea smiled, “So far, this much I have Seen, Leto. As our army of volunteers goes out among our people, they must have a way for people to recognize that they are Givers of the Holy Gift. Rhea and Nestor have worked this out. Rhea, show them, please.”

She rose and used her foot to remove the lid of a small box. “Based upon the symbol of your Church of God,” Rhea explained, “Nestor and I had these made.” Leto held up a small golden broach with a golden sun shining in the center and rays emanating outward from it. A thin golden chain held the broach. “I do hope it meets with your approval. We’ve had enough made for everyone who can now give the Holy Gift. If each wears it, then anyone can tell at a glance that here is one of the very special people who can give them this miracle of life. If you like it, we will order many more to be made.” Rhea was quite proud of her secret work on this project.

“Perfect, dad. Women everywhere will be able to tell our Givers easily,” Phil added his encouragement.

“Brilliant, Airlea, you are a keen leader in your own right. Accepted, we will go forth with these as our symbols, though how will we pay for them?” Leto asked.

“The Tower of Orthos is paying for them,” Airlea answered with a grin. “How can we not? We are going to play our part, our role in salvaging our people. That’s settled. Now then, Tanis, you and Melina will go with the Monos group. Zona will go with the Menolaos group. We’ll divide our women fifty-fifty. Rhea, I, the ten guards, and the few families with men will remain behind here to keep the Tower safeguarded and to run the mill. Plus we will slowly give our Holy Gifts to the local farmers, expanding outward from Orthos. Further, as Leto and I discussed, you are likely to encounter some women who have become insane or completely psychotic. Please send them here to Orthos where we will look after them and give them a distraction free environment where in time they may recover.”

Airlea continued, “In a few days, a large number of coaches will be arriving from Tinos and Thal. The monarchs are providing you with transportation to their capitals. Your main problem will be obtaining clothing for winter. None of our clothing fits, and we have been wearing our summer robes far beyond the summer. I am afraid, Leto, that if our women must be bundled up in pants and warm boots, that you and your sons will have an awful time caring for us. Honestly, we are so dependent upon men now it’s not funny,” she openly admitted this fact, which until now she had not, though it was plain to everyone.

“We will take only the very best of care of your women, Airlea,” Leto promised. She smiled, knowing that they would, though now, she could not envision these six men dressing over a hundred women each morning.

Each monarch sent seven large carriages to bring them to their capital city, along with an escort of two dozen soldiers to ensure their safe passage. The captains in charge of this trip had carefully worked out their route, based heavily upon inns along the route, which could handle fifty plus guests each evening. This restriction meant long days in the carriages, sometimes upward of sixteen hours. Even so, the inns were now staffed with mostly men and young boys, because few women had been able to return to their jobs as waitresses, barmaids, cooks, and maids. Always, the innkeepers were harried, their faces grim and gaunt from overwork and wild attempts at staffing. Often, very young boys were now serving the meals. That the majority of women had not been able to return to their former employment hit home to all these travelers.

Often Tanis rode along with Seth when it was his turn to drive his family’s wagon. Likewise, when Titos’ turn came, Melina sat beside him in the driver’s seat. These two couples chatted to each other about their lives, hopes, and dreams. As farmsteads passed, they often saw a few women out in the fields helping the late fall farmwork. This stood in sharp contrast with the women in the towns and cities, hardly any of which they saw either on the streets or in the inns.

Also, Tanis insisted on helping protect the wagon and carriages from bandits, though Seth didn't think that they would be bothered, not with so many soldiers accompanying them. While this turned out to be the case, as they rode along, Seth continually challenged Tanis, though. "See that rock over there," he pointed out a large grey boulder. "See if you can toss that one, dear."

"What? Like this?" she teased him back as she lifted it and gave it a nice toss. Tanis had regained her ability to move objects and, as I learned later, had begun to use this as her primary attack mode, tossing enemy bodies with wild abandon. While her telepathic skills were still rather limited, her lifting skills were not. She was on par with Seth, who was continually impressed with her.

"Hotshot," he teased her back. "Say, I've been meaning to ask you, Tanis, I know that your husband has only recently been killed and that it may be too soon for you, but have you considered dating other men yet? Melina too, for that matter."

"Wow, Seth," she was taken by surprise with this question. "I know analytically that I lost Lykou just weeks ago, but now that seems like lifetimes ago. I am not the same person that I was back then. Isn't that just strange? I mean I am more me now. Does that make any sense at all?"

"Sure does, Tanis."

"You know, when I laid down beside Lykou, I felt safe for the first time since the plague came. I knew that I had arms ready to help me, to protect Melina and me. Although I knew Lykou for years, perhaps I just hurried up and married him so that I would have his arms always with Melina and me. Security. Yes, she and I loved him, but there was also a security feeling there too that we both got out of it. That's kind of selfish of us, isn't it?" she admitted.

"Oh, I don't think I would go so far as to call yourselves selfish. I can't imagine how awful it really is for you. Objectively, yes, I can see how difficult things are for women, but it's as if I am on the outside looking in as opposed to being on the inside and being one of you women trying to survive somehow. How does the old saying go, walk a mile in my shoes?" he replied.

"Yes, but then you and your family are the most able beings that I have ever heard of. Sometimes I think that none of you even need a body," she replied.

He laughed, "When we finally reach the end of the path, the end of our Advanced Therapy, that is precisely right. Can you keep a secret?" he asked, a twinkle in his eye and a grin on his face.

"Sure, what?" she nudged him, wondering what secret.

"Before we came to your tower, Macario and Eve visited us. I swear, Tanis, that Macario has no need for a human body at all. He just materialized body forms for them to talk with us because we would feel more comfortable talking with him that way. Honestly, I still agree with him. I much more enjoy taking with you, Tanis, than I would talking to — well, what many would call a ghost or some such thing."

"He can create a real body? Like ours?" she asked amazed.

"Yes, I even shook his hand! It felt like anyone else's hand that I've ever shook. Absolutely amazing. I couldn't tell any difference from his versus yours, Tanis."

"Bet his had arms, though," she teased and they both laughed.

"Eve's didn't," he added. "She's a knock out blonde. Her hair falls down to her ankles even, but that's assuming that is the way she actually looks. Mind you, I've never seen her before."

"Say, I didn't really answer your original question, did I? Well, Seth, when I am around you, I feel different. It's more than a safe feeling; it's more as if somehow I am whole again. Does that make any sense to you?"

"Yes, same with me, you, Tanis, make me feel whole and complete somehow. Strange, isn't it? We've only just met and under the most difficult of times, yet I feel whole around you too. I don't have that feeling when I am with any of the other women, just you, Tanis. What does this mean? I admit, I haven't been around women my life. That's one of the drawbacks of living such a hermit existence."

"I'm glad that you did — live the hermit existence, because you are so able as a result. It is part of what makes me feel so whole with you. That doesn't make any sense, really, does it?" she admitted, trying to sort out her feelings.

"Two peas in a pod?" he suggested.

Tanis sighed, what the heck, go for it, she thought to herself. She leaned over and kissed Seth. His arm slid around her back, and to her delight, he returned her passionate kiss. Thus, a new romance began amid the ruins of another.

On June 3, 824, they arrived in Thal and took up residence at Saint Timon's Cathedral. After a whirlwind round of meeting Monarch Sophia and Elissa and their ever-growing staff, the fifty-four began giving their therapy sessions to all of those women. Around the same time, Leto and his party began doing the same thing to Monarch Amynta and Zoe and their staff in Tinos.

Eve now had added the number of trained therapy givers to each of her sticky-notes plastered on her huge wall map of Tarra. "Well, Bethany, it has begun well in Thallyus, Penelopus, and Arolas. This just might work like we did it on Dorota." I complimented her on her good coordination work and I hoped that it would.

Chapter 30 A Naval Affair

Early February of 824, Stefano and I met with Vittorio West Po. He and I had received one too many requests for help from Annelise, Arolas, Megalos, and many Sea Prince sectors. The Patri pirates had been getting steadily bolder in their actions. They'd gone from the mere stealing of cargos and valuables to the actual sinking of ships. At first, the two gun ships fired salvos across the bows of merchant ships, forcing them to stop and be boarded. By January, they were actually damaging the shipping. The last straw was the actual sinking of an Annelise ship with the loss of all hands on board — a ship carrying a cargo of clothing!

We got a break in some ways. Before the plague, while each of the seven Demokritos kingdoms had their own small fleets as well as many independently owned ships, the Emperor had one hundred caravels for his use, plus ten gun ships. The two Patri gun ships were part of the ten, on permanent assignment in Patri. The other eight were scattered across the seas, as were the vast majority of the hundreds of his caravels. By February, most of these had finally returned to their home ports desperate for new orders amid the worldwide chaos.

When Alexio and his group joined up with Ana and Callisto in Andros, he temporarily assumed the position of Emperor. Here in the port city, he setup shop, the temporary Imperial Court. His self-appointed task was slowly to disband the assets of the position of Emperor. Since ultimately these assets came from the seven kingdoms, his idea was to return them fairly to the kingdoms. With three of the kingdoms landlocked and with three of the coastal kingdoms in anarchy, the division was problematical. Ideally, he would have preferred to sit down with seven rulers and work out an agreeable division of the assets. With the widespread anarchy and chaos, this was impossible.

Thus, he made his own decisions. He gave one gun ship to each of the other six kingdoms, ignoring Thrace, which already had two of the ten. The remaining two he gave to Arolas, figuring they needed all the protection they could get, since they were the only coastal country on the road to recovery. He assigned the three landlocked country's gun ships to protect the coastline of Arolas so that those country's merchants could have safe ports to dock and ship goods overland from Andros, Arolas. The merchants he divided equally between the seven kingdoms, with each receiving fourteen merchants each, Arolas getting the extra two. However, until he heard from landlocked Theos, he temporarily allowed their ships to be controlled by Arolas.

His problem lay with the gun ships. Would they dock at their respective home ports or would they attempt to join up with the Patri Pirates, adding to the problem on the high seas? By February, he had the answer. The gun ships of Alia and Phindos decided to disobey Alexio, and their captains joined up with the pirates, doubling the pirate fleet. Thus far, Arolas kept the pirates from entering their coastal waters or interfering with their shipping. However, no merchant ship was safe entering the waters of Thrace, Alia, or Phindos or go anywhere near there.

I pointed out, "Well, Arolas simply cannot spare their gun ships to attack the pirate ships. Their mission is critical: safeguard our many key shipments of materials into Andros. Not only is the situation in Arolas fragile, but so is that of Thallyus and Penelopus. They are hanging on by threads."

"Looks like we are going to have to intervene on everyone's behalf," Stefano concluded. "I sure hope this does not escalate into a war between us."

"If it does, you will have more than half the world backing you, Stefano. These pirates have to be stopped or there is no chance of pulling those kingdoms out of the Dark Ages that they've created for themselves," I pointed out.

Vittorio added, "Besides, there are dozens and dozens of caravels which are scheduled to sail to Arolas in the very near future. If you don't act, I will have no choice but to send our gun ships along and that gets to be expensive."

"Yes," Stefano replied, running his hands through his hair in frustration, "but wooden ships are particularly vulnerable to their gun ships. If our gun ships get damaged, it's three months sailing to get back here. And that is assuming that they can get re-supplied along the long trip."

"Point very well taken," Vittorio agreed. "Say, I have an idea, Stefano. It's a bit on the expensive side and will require some adjustment of planned shipping schedules, but it might drastically reduce the risk to our ships in the engagement. The Grande Pistola II is due for its sea trials next month. We could put a rush on it. Assuming that works out, we need a re-coaling station ideally around Megalos. We can send a coal tender caravel on south and use it to resupply on the return voyage. It's just that we are getting slightly ahead of the worldwide re-coaling stations that have been planned. If Bethany can work out something with the Monarch of Megalos for the re-coaling station somewhere in that area, I believe that we can get the Grande Pistola II down there in two months."

"Brilliant, Vittorio! Why didn't I think of that?" Stefano asked.

"Cause you have far more important things to handle than keeping track of our maritime activities," Vittorio teased him.

"Excuse me, but what's the significance of the Grande Pistola II?" I asked, completely ignorant of this ship.

"It is a byproduct of the Second Crusade, Bethany. We thought that we ought to have a metal steamship gun ship. It has taken quite a while to build her, back-burner project," Stefano explained. "The key factor is that with her, these pirate caravels will be at a severe disadvantage. The steamships go twice as fast, and the caravel cannonae supposedly will be almost ineffective against the Pistola's metal hull, saving lives. That was the plan, saving lives and ships. Okay, Vittorio let's see if we can make this work. Of course, the liability is that if it does work, other countries will then begin trying to make one of their own. That's just the way history has gone. Every time we get a more powerful weapon, another country goes all out to duplicate it. Escalation. I was hoping to save this new weapon for a more critical situation, Bethany."

I nodded, catching on at last. "Well, Stefano, if we lose Arolas, we've lost the whole of Demokritos. I'm willing to take that risk."

He smiled, "Me too. MMCE at work again. Vittorio, get on it. Bethany, let's you and I contact Monarch Aminta and see about getting a permanent re-coaling station set up down there somewhere."

Within two days, we'd worked out a very good deal for both countries. Our new metal steamships required periodic re-coaling stations. That was their primary deficiency, limited range requiring the necessity of taking on more coal approximately every five thousand miles. Vittorio was slowly working out such stations worldwide, in anticipation of more and more of our new metal steamships coming online. We were merely pushing all that somewhat ahead of schedule.

The run down to Megalos was well over a thousand miles. Yet, if the ships could top off there, they would then have enough to reach Demokritos. However, if they also were re-supplied at sea, they would be able to operate for some time in the waters down there. In order to return, they would need to resupply in Andros. That also had to be arranged, but we were certain that would not be a problem.

Vittorio met with us three days later with good news. "I've talked with the ship's two designers. They assured me that she is sea worthy at this time. However, the remaining work and field testing will require that the designers make the voyage as well, dealing with the last bit of work and testing. They need to bring along a crew of ten workers with them. Per law, a war ship must have your okay, Stefano, to allow civilians on board in when it is sailing to war, which this trip actually is doing."

"Okay, I'll sign off on that," Stefano readily agreed.

Vittorio pulled at his three-day old stubble. "You realize that one of the two designers of the Grande Pistola II is a woman, don't you? Engineer Marinella Lina?"

"Damn! I forgot. Yes, she was instrumental in developing the new gun systems, wasn't she?"

"Precisely. Her inventions are key here. She has to go along, unless you want to delay sailing for another month while all the testing and kinks are worked out here. The mechanical engineer, Bernardo Battista needs to go along to take care of the engine and drive system," Vittorio pointed out.

"Is she up to the challenge of being at sea so long and yet being effective?" Stefano asked.

"No choice, she has to be or you have to delay at least a month, maybe longer if problems arise that need handling," he replied.

"Has she been told? Is she willing to go?"

Vittorio grinned, "You don't know those engineers! She is insisting that she goes along."

"Okay then. Is she married? If so, her husband ought to go along to help her with what she may need," Stefano decided.

"That was her only stipulation," Vittorio added. "I know, this is likely to be a rough assignment for any woman to tackle just now, but she really has a right to go. She designed the gun system. She and Benardo have spent the last seven years of their lives working exclusively on this project."

"Okay, let's go meet her and give her our support and permission," Stefano suggested.

He and I headed to the Eastern Shipyards, where the Grande Pistola II was undergoing the final preparations. My first view of our newest steamship was breathtaking! Silver in color, she was triple the length of the caravels with which I had so much experience. At first, I was startled to see no masts! Silly me, she was powered by two enormous steam engines. The main desk was flat and smooth, with a secure railing to keep one from falling overboard. Two-thirds of the way down her deck rose the control tower, which they called the bridge. Two smoke stacks rose above this. I saw three metal gun turrets sticking up above the main deck, two in the front of the bridge and one behind it. A long grey gun barrel protruded some distance from each turret.

Workmen and dockhands were scurrying all over her, finishing up the last bits of construction and loading her with the supplies needed on the long maiden voyage. The yard foreman directed us to a group off to the sides and we headed there. Four men and a woman were playing ball with an improvised merry-go-round! Neither Stefano nor I could believe our eyes as we walked up to them. One was obviously the captain; he wore a uniform, navy blue, complete with the familiar captain's hat that I had often seen before. The woman was standing on a ladder looking down on top of the contraption while another man in a white uniform was spinning the merry-go-round. Two other men sitting on the device were rolling a large ball towards each other. He and I couldn't believe what we were seeing.

The captain recognized Stefano as we neared and halted the motion; the others stopped and looked up at us. The man in white got off and joined the captain, jumping to attention. "Captain Archangelo Arturo, sir!" He saluted his commander-in-chief. "Artillery Captain Bartolo Gostino."

"At ease men. Bethany Bartiana Angela. We are looking for Chief Engineer Marinella Lina," Stefano responded. The woman's face cringed, and she hastily stepped down from her makeshift ladder. Her brow wrinkled in a deep frown.

"That's me, Monarch Stefano. Now, look, sir, I simply must make this trip! You've forced us to move up our timetable by over a month. The guns are simply not ready for combat action yet, not without these trials and adjustments. You must allow me to sail and continue this critical work, sir." Marinella's words came out like one of those rapid firing long guns, bang, bang, bang. "We still have major directional problems to solve."

She was a tall woman, probably in her early thirties. Her brown hair was cut very short. I could see that she spent little time with it, mostly just a fluff. She wore a man's shirt and pants, though she wore flats similar to mine, easy to take off when she needed her toes. From her tone, she had guessed that Stefano would refuse to allow her to go because of her sex and her lack of arms, deadly on a moving ship at sea. Marinella was making her case as strongly and rapidly as she could, figuring this was her very last chance at it.

Stefano put up his hands. "Whoa, whoa, Chief Engineer! I dropped by to make sure that you really did want to go and if so, give you my formal permission for you to go on this long voyage, that is, if Captain Archangelo has no serious objections." She stopped abruptly and stared at him, not believing that she heard him correctly.

"You are not against my going?" she finally asked in disbelief.

"No, not if you want to go and feel that you are able to handle it."

"Thank you sir!" I suspected that if she had arms, she would have saluted him! Her relief was instant. The frown lines vanished.

"I must admit that I didn't expect to see you all enjoying play time, though," Stefano grinned, pointing to the makeshift merry-go-round.

"It's not play. I'm showing them the very serious problem that remains as yet unsolved," she explained. "You see, we've got six-inchers now, and they shoot their shells nearly two miles." Apparently, she saw the blank non-comprehending look on my face.

Captain Bartolo interceded, "Let me explain, Mrs. Angela. The previous cannonae that were used by ground-based artillery were four-inchers, meaning the diameter of the inside of the barrel was four inches, and therefore the shells fired were four inches in width. Their maximum range was under a mile, if you could elevate the barrels sufficiently. The guns of this size are too large and unwieldy for use on our caravel gun ships. There, they use three-inchers, lots of them, but none can be elevated but a few degrees. Hence, the old mode of combat was to fire a series of these in a broadside fusillade and hope some shells would smash into the target ships. This meant that the two ships had to be fairly close to each other, no more than say eight hundred yards."

"Now Chief Engineer Marinella's guns are six-inchers, an amazing piece of design on their own. They can lob a shell that is twice what any other gun can shoot and lob it over two miles! We ought to be able to take out these four pirate gun ships without their even being able to get a single shot off at us."

"Two miles?" I asked, that seemed incredible to me. Now men could be two miles from each other and kill each other! Wars, I hated them.

"Yes, precisely so. Accuracy is our main problem. This problem first became known with our four-inch cannonae. Sometimes a shot missed the target. Most assumed that this was due to inaccurate gun sights, a miss-alignment of the barrel, an imperfection in the barrel itself, or even human error in lining up the shot," he explained. "During our initial field tests of the first six-inchers, the problem grew in magnitude and must be solved."

Marinella interrupted him. "Yes, we must solve it before we have to use the guns in combat. The whole point of my invention is to save the lives of our men by sinking the enemy vessel before it can even fire on our ship and men. That means firing from two miles away, where this problem has become a major factor. I have finally figured out what is causing it, and I was showing the fellows here what it is all about with this improvised merry-go-round. Believe it or not, it is our spinning Tarra that is causing the shells to miss."

"She is an absolute genius," Artillery Captain Bartolo praised her. "She's right. The errors of our shots are due to the spinning of our world. Absolutely amazing. You ought to see this for yourselves. Stefano, you take my place on the merry-go-round. Mrs. Angela, you climb up on the ladder and watch. The spinning merry-go-round represents Tarra. The ball represents one of our artillery shells in flight. Stefano, once it is moving, try rolling the ball straight across the platform. It will not go straight; it will curve off course and end up at one of us. Come on, this you have got to see."

I climbed up and leaned over to watch. As Captain Archangelo pushed the merry-go-round at a good clip, Stefano tried to roll the ball straight, but it kept veering off course, allowing Bartolo or Alberto to catch it. The experiment done, Stefano and I were most impressed, and Alberto introduced himself; he had been totally forgotten in all this, Marinella's husband. Alberto, it turns out, was a photographer. He'd taken the camera invention of the DEA and expanded upon it, making large-sized images. As it turned out, when they returned from this mission, Alberto had captured some amazing images of the combat and ship. He published them in the first photographic images book ever printed, but that's another story.

Marinella continued. "Based on my observations that this effect is due to the rotation of Tarra, then the problem is quite complex. The magnitude of the effect will be dependent upon the latitude of our ship and the direction that it is firing. Furthermore, the effects ought to be the opposite once we get below the equator. No one has worked out the mathematics of all this, so I am facing having to devise some empirical tables that Captain Bartolo can use to make slight corrections when he takes aim. Of course, in the heat of battle, he has to be able to calculate these corrections very rapidly. That is why we wanted another month of field trials before we launch."

"You see, up here, if he fires a shell due east, the motion of Tarra will shove the shell off course to the south. If he fires due northward, the motion of Tarra will shove the shell off course to the east. I suspect that we will find these reversed when we get way down there to fight the gun ships, because Demokritos is way below the equator. Still, it is only my guess, since we've never fired our cannonae that far south," she explained.

"Now I designed the gun turrets and the loading machinery, and we can safely state that we believe there will be no problems in those areas. So far, they have worked flawlessly, allowing Captain Bartolo to get off a shot every minute, an amazing rate of fire, considering each shell weighs close to forty pounds. I could not have done it if it weren't for Bernardo's amazing steam power. He designed the engines, you see," nicely sliding some of the praise off on her compatriot. Both had spent seven years on this single project.

"Say, would you both like a tour of the Grande Pistola II?" Captain Archangelo asked, changing the subject. While he appreciated the demonstration at hand, he had no grasp of what they were saying. We took him up on his offer. To say that I was amazed is an understatement.

The ship was compartmentalized. That is, each section had sealable doors in case one section sprung a leak. That way, one leak would not sink the ship. The spaciousness was incredible. I could see now how she could carry so many times more than one of our wooden caravels. The living quarters were also spacious. Each crewman had twice the personal space as on the caravels. There was a large recreation room, perfect for games. The galley was large and the dining area could serve a hundred men at one time. He also pointed out that she carried three LD radios onboard. One belonged to the engineers and was for their own use, allowing them to communicate to their staff back here in Velona, should problems arise. The ship itself had two; one was for backup emergencies only. I could only say that sailing in her would be the height of luxury compared to the many voyages I had in the older caravels. Plus, she had a normal cruising speed of thirty miles per hour, twenty-four hours a day, independent of what the wind was doing! Just incredible, I thought.

On February 12, 824, the Grande Pistola II steamed out of Velona on her maiden voyage. Many of us watched her depart, curiosities roused. Besides the engineers and their work crews, the ship carried one hundred crew. Once this shakedown cruise was finished, she would normally carry a crew of one hundred fifty men and perhaps women. Now I could see why Stefano and Vittorio were working so hard on their ten year plans to build many more of these metal steamships. They would rapidly replace our aging wooden caravels.

On April 12, the Grande Pistola II docked in Andros, Arolas. Her arrival there was met with great pomp and ceremony, on specific orders by Ana and Callisto. None here had ever seen one of these new steamships, and its size alone was impressive. Still, they had to take on coal, one of the primary reasons for the stop. Secondly, Captain Archangelo had to meet the other four Arolas gun ship captains and make their attack plans. Thirdly, Chief Engineer Marinella had still not been able to work out fast, empirical tables for the artillery captain to use in combat. She needed accurately measurable misses from which to construct her tables, wholly undoable, she discovered, while at sea.

During the sailing time, Ana and Callisto had been in daily conversations with both the engineers and Captain Archangelo, working out their long-range plans for this offensive. All agreed that somehow the gun ships of Arolas had to be involved so that this did not seem like an invasion from Velona, that they were there only to assist Arolas in bringing some law to the high seas around southern Demokritos. Since Ana and Callisto were making their home and offices at the Nasses estate, naturally, they discussed the details of this most welcome help from Velona. The pirates had already sunk one of their caravels three weeks ago, and Callisto was rightly angry about that.

"I do hope that they can get their guns to work right," Callisto said, "because if so, they can blast the enemy long before the enemy is close enough to shoot back. I'd hate to lose one of our gun ships. They are sorely needed if we are to maintain law and order on the high seas around here." The extended Nasses clan then began asking her lots of questions about this marvelous new ship made of metal and powered by coal and steam. When she tried to explain about the targeting errors that were plaguing Marinella, both Dora and Euclid spoke up.

"What exactly is their problem?" Euclid asked.

"How is it that they are missing their targets? That should be a simple math problem," Dora asked. Callisto shrugged her shoulders; she had not the faintest idea. However, the next morning when she called the ship for a progress report, she asked to speak to Marinella.

"Hi, Callisto here. Say, I have two sharp math folks here with me. They have been asking me about the problem that you are having with hitting targets. Of course, I haven't the faintest notion about it, so can you explain what it is to them, please? This is Dora and Euclid Masses Kleides."

"Hi, Marinella here. Do you really understand math?" she asked, not quite knowing what their educational level or knowledge might be, just strangers on the other end of the LD radio. Often, she'd run across folks who claimed to be sharp with math, only to find that they were more of arithmetic whizzes. Soon, however, she found the two actually were grasping the effect that she was outlining. Dora even suggested to her that it ought to be latitude dependent, and Euclid added that the effects should be opposite below the equator. She had not yet mentioned this! The three discussed the details for nearly an hour before Callisto finally had to cut them off. That was near the end of February. By the end of March, Dora and Euclid came to Callisto with pages of detailed equations, which were incomprehensible to her.

"We believe that we have worked out the solution for Marinella," Dora said modestly. Hence, Callisto insisted that Dora and Euclid come with them to Andros to meet the Grande Pistola II when she arrived. There, they could sit down with Marinella and see if in fact they had. It was worth a shot, Callisto thought.

As the world would shortly discover, Dora and Euclid had just invented three-dimensional geometry, which now provided accurate solutions to numerous engineering and design problems! Their breakthrough in math accelerated new inventions during the next twenty years.

After the monarchs and friends had a tour of the ship, Marinella, Dora, and Euclid sat down in her workroom to go over what they had worked out. Meanwhile, Callisto met with Captain Archangelo and her four gun ship captains. She did the introductions. Captain Ikaros commanded the Dragon's Fire, Captain Kastor commanded the Punisher, Captain Midas commanded the Perseus. Captain Praxis commanded the Revenge.

"But your ship only has three guns, compared to our twenty per side," Captain Ikaros pointed out. Surely your new ship will be severely out-gunned!"

"They have only three-inchers. Ours will blast them out of the water from two miles away," Captain Archangelo explained.

"That's preposterous! No cannonae can shoot that far, let alone hit anything at that distance!" exclaimed Captain Kastor.

"Let me assure you, captains, not only is this true, but each gun can fire a round every minute. Let's see your crews top that."

"But how is this possible?" asked an incredulous Captain Midas. "I have drilled my crew and they can fire a round every two and a half minutes at their very best."

"The loading is all done by mechanical means. The gunner simply lifts the shell and inserts it into the rear breach. All else is automated, driven by our steam power," Captain Archangelo tried to explain. "You simply must see how this is done."

Just then, Marinella joined them, "Excuse me for butting in, captain. It seems that Dora and Euclid have solved our problem mathematically! Could we possibly conduct a test firing to see if their equations actually work properly? If so, then in a few days, I believe that I can work out firing tables for Captain Bartolo to use in combat situations, sir."

"Yes, Captain, let's have a demonstration," Captain Ikaros added, the three other captains nodded their agreement.

"Okay, Marinella. Callisto, we will need a target towed out to sea perhaps a mile and a half. Of course, it's going to be hit, so make sure that it is expendable," he grinned.

The next day, a half-rotted coastal fishing vessel now lay anchored a mile and a half off the port of Andros. Marinella explained, "This has to be a carefully controlled situation. We are looking to verify the accuracy of Dora and Euclid's equations. Hence, the Grande Pistola II is still at anchor, minimal sea motion. The target is stationary. Hence, we are plugging in the distance and angle of firing and computing the correction factor that their equations predict. Since we are docked, we will be firing only the rear gun. Yes, I know that this is a highly contrived situation, far unlike the real combat situations you will be facing. We are just trying to see if the equations are right. If so, then we can proceed. If not, then I will attempt to use the empirical values that I have been working on so far, which I know are only a wild approximation. We've done so little firing here south of the equator."

Everyone headed up onto the main deck and then climbed up the tall bridge. From here, they could look out over the stern and see the action. All the men had their spyglasses with them and began to search out the small silhouette of the target. "This is an impossible shot!" declared Captain Ikaros. "Hundred to one shot."

"No, thousand to one shot," Captain Praxis insisted.

"If you will excuse me, I need to join Artillery Captain Bartolo now and verify the calculations." Marinella left the men and Callisto watching from the bridge. A bit later, a whistle sounded and Captain Archangelo picked up a tube.

"It conducts our voices through these tubes down to the engine room or to the guns. Yes, Artillery Captain Bartolo?" he said formally, mostly because of the presence of the other four captains and the monarch of Arolas.

"Yes, you have my permission to fire when ready," he yelled into the tube. Everyone watched. Cah-boom! A huge explosion shook the ship as the giant six-incher fired a single salvo. A giant plume of gun smoke slowly rose from the angled barrel. Everyone felt the whole ship recoil slightly. He hastily added, "They are using an explosive shell so that we can pinpoint the detonation point."

Far out at sea the shell came arcing down its trajectory, slamming into the rotting fishing boat. A brilliant flash was seen in the many spyglasses. After they involuntarily blinked, the vessel was nowhere to be seen. Upon later inspection, they found bits of boards drifting in the vicinity where the old ship had been.

"Incredible! I don't believe it!" yelled Captain Ikaros. The other captains added their wild exclamations to his. A bit later, a smiling Chief Engineer Marinella climbed back onto the bridge.

"Their equations worked perfectly! I do believe that we have this firing problem licked, sir. I will begin work on the tables for Artillery Captain Bartolo immediately," she reported the obvious.

"Monarch Callisto, we simply must have some of these new ships! Think of the power. With these we can enforce law and order on the seas," Captain Praxis begged her.

"As soon as it's practical for us, we will get some! You can count on it!" a very enthusiastic Callisto replied. "Incredible Captain Archangelo, incredible. Now I am not so worried about sending my four ships with you. Impressive beyond description. I do hope it goes this well with the pirate ships."

By June, a small book was published and worldwide distribution began. It was called <u>Three-dimensional Geometry</u>, by Dora and Euclid Nasses Kleides. It was extremely well received and highly praised in Velona, of course.

On April 16, the Grande Pistola II and the four Arolas gun ships left the docks of Andros, bound for the southern coasts of Demokritos. The game was afoot. Now their job was to locate the raiding pirate gun ships. A week later, they neared the border of Arolas and Thrace. Here, Captain Archangelo had no choice but to depend upon the other four captains. He was in unfamiliar waters and had no idea where the enemy ships may be.

The captains frequently stopped at the small fishing villages and questioned the fishermen, looking for last known sightings. They hailed many small fishing boats, asking the same thing. Slowly the picture emerged that the Orion and Okeanos were trolling the seas some thirty miles out from Patri, looking for caravels who were trying to bypass this danger zone.

Rather than look for a needle in a haystack, Captain Archangelo used another tactic. He fanned a gun ship out to his port and starboard sides, sailing parallel courses but four miles from him. With spyglasses, each ship could see him. He had the other two take similar position from these two. Thus, his sweep covered a swatch of some sixteen miles. Surely, one of them would spot the two ships soon. He wished now that he'd brought along four more LD radios so that he could easily keep in touch with the four and they, he. However, they had to make due with maritime flag signals. On April 25, the Punisher and the Dragon's Fire both spotted a gun ship dead ahead of themselves. After raising the flags, both captains turned hard to starboard, retreating from the approaching gun ships. Both captains were loathed to turn tail, but Monarch Callisto had given them a direct order to do so, if at all feasible.

"Battle stations! Battle stations!" barked Captain Archangelo. At first, the two enemy ships raised sail to pursue the two fleeing ship, but then the huge steamship caught their attention, and they began to frantically turn around to flee. "All ahead full!" he yelled into the speaker tube to the engine room, and soon thick clouds of black smoke belched from the twin stacks. He felt the Grande Pistola II lurch forward. Now he had them; he was certain. His ship could travel more than twice as fast as the enemy could, and the winds were not strong this afternoon.

He watched as one fore gun turret moved slowly to port, while the other one turned to starboard. Good, he thought, they are getting a bead on our prey. He picked up the tube to the firing room and yelled, "Fire whenever you have a firing solution, Artillery Captain!" Now all he needed to do was to continue straight ahead. He knew that he couldn't alter course, as that would throw off the firing solutions. Besides, he had no need, both enemy ships were sailing parallel courses back towards Patri, he guessed.

He took note of his four companion ships. They had now all reversed course and were sailing on an intercept course to the Grande Pistola II, though they were being rapidly left hopelessly behind. He waited. Cah-boom! One fore gun fired, the ship lurched to starboard as the port facing six-incher fired its first salvo. He trained his spyglass on the retreating gun ship, the Orion, he thought. Cah-boom! The second fore gun fired, shoving the ship slightly to port; the massive smoke cloud puffing out of the starboard pointing gun appeared and rapidly expanded. He wished that there were not so much smoke, for it kept interfering with his vision.

He spotted the bright flash of the exploding shell on the Orion and focused his attention onto its effectiveness. Yes, the ship had taken a hit, but at this distance, he could not tell how serious it was. He turned to see the effect on the companion Okeanos, but had missed the explosion, yet he thought that he could see some damage to her as well. Cah-boom! The port facing gun fired again and not long after that the starboard one fired its second round as well. Once more, both struck the ships. The Orion no longer seemed to have its main masts, he thought. There was too much smoke surrounding the Okeanos to tell what was happening to her.

Two more salvos erupted. "Damn this smoke. I can't see a blasted thing," he yelled. His companions on the bridge also were watching with their glasses. One said that he could no longer see the Orion. "Where? Where did it go? It could not have just vanished," he yelled. "Damn smoke anyway!" At last, he had no choice but to yell into the engine room tube, "Ahead one eighth. Right full rudder. We are going in for a look at the Orion. Send out the signals for the other ships to check on the Okeanos," he ordered.

When they slowly steamed over to the last known position of the Orion, they spotted debris: planks and timbers floating in the water, including her figurehead. They spotted the upper torso of a sailor, but little else. The Orion had been sunk. By now, the four other gun ships were circling the last known position of the Okeanos. A flag message declared her sunk but that they were picking up one survivor. An hour later, the four caravels dropped sail and coasted alongside the Grande Pistola II, and all five captains shared the news. All five cheered Artillery Captain Bartolo, when he and Marinella arrived on the bridge to see for themselves what the results had been. They'd lost sight of both ships after the third salvo.

Before long, the hundred crew members also came on deck, yelling and cheering wildly. To Bartolo's and Marinella's dismay, they picked them both up and danced them around the deck, heaping all manner of praise upon them. Alberto quietly took a picture of the celebration. He had been snapping pictures the whole time and managed to frame one of the Orion just as the second shell detonated, creating what was to become a most famous photograph indeed.

After dinner with the four captains onboard as his guests, the five decided to sail into the port of Patri and see if they could get the other two gun ships to duel them. Now they would also be facing the four-incher coastal batteries that rimmed the largest port city in all Demokritos, Patri. Repeatedly, Captain Archangelo reminded the four to keep their ships out of coastal battery range.

On April 25, they spotted the picturesque port of Patri ahead. It was nearly the same size as the old port of Velona, before the eastern addition had been made. Patri was huge. While many caravels were docked, very little actual shipping had been done since the plague struck Thrace. As ordered, the four caravels hove to about a mile from shore, just barely out of coastal battery range. Locating the two gun ships was easy. Both were anchored at opposite ends of the port, about a quarter mile from the docks, but under the complete protection of the coastal batteries. From these two positions, they controlled all access to the large port.

He ordered the maritime flag messages be hoisted, demanding the immediate surrender of the two gun ships. Now he waited to see their reactions. From this distance, he could easily see their reactions and decided to slowly close the distance, risking entering the outer ranges of the coastal batteries that lay to the north side of the main port. After some twenty minutes, he had his reply. Four coastal batteries opened fire on the Grande Pistola II, while both gun ships began raising all their sails.

Captain Archangelo yelled into the tube, "Take out the coastal batteries first." Several giant water splashes rose around the ship as the distant guns hunted for the right range. "All stop!" he yelled to the engine room, his idea: make the firing solutions easier. Keep the ship mostly stationary. The two fore guns began firing. Unlike the coastal batteries, which had to fire all manner of bracketing rounds until they experimentally found the right combination, Marinella's fancy targeting system allowed their first salvo to hit the batteries onshore. After five salvos, the coastal batteries that had been trying to hit them all fell silent. One enemy ball had finally struck them, making a slight dent in the port side near the water line.

Now the stern gun fired. Shortly after that, one of the forward guns fired. Three salvos later, only wreckage of the enemy gun ships floated on the surface. "Damn, these six-inchers are murder on wooden caravels," Captain Archangelo noted to his fellow officers on the bridge. "Okay, have the flags raised. Send them ashore and let them work out their peace treaty," he ordered. He then yelled to the firing room, "Keep aim on the other coastal batteries. Fire at will if they attempt to fire on our approaching caravels."

The Dragon's Fire drew close to the docks and lowered a dingy. A pair of sailors rowed ashore. An hour later, the two men rowed back. He spotted the flag message from Captain Ikaros. Peace. Head home, they read. He waited until all four ships had passed the Grande Pistola II before he gave the full astern order. He intended to back out of coastal battery range before turning around. To his amazement, their reverse speed nearly matched the caravel's forward speed. Yes, he thought, these new steamships were worth every bit of gold spent on them!

That evening, all five captains dined aboard the Grande Pistola II, joined by all the engineers in a joyous victory celebration. Via LD radio, Monarch Callisto received a full report. At last, the shipping lanes of the world were free of pirates. Now critical commerce could begin to flow without fear once more. One big problem solved. On July 1, 824, the Grande Pistola II docked in Velona, and we gave everyone our own victory celebration. A new era in naval combat had just been ushered in. Eve and I wondered how soon it would be before other countries had their own versions of the Grande Pistola II — far down the centuries, we hoped. When someone invents a better weapon, others soon duplicate it, and the arms race never ends.

Chapter 31 The Centurions

Yes, temporary Emperor Alexio cheered along with everyone else when the Grande Pistola II and the four Arolas guns ships docked in Andros. One of his two huge problems in the disbandment of the old Demokritos Emperor rulership had been handled. Now the vast number of ships owned by the Emperor had been disposed of properly. All that remained was the Imperial Army.

The Demokritos army controlled solely by the Emperor had always used the Centurion model of one hundred soldiers per legion. The last figures that Alexio had seen suggested that his father had commanded one hundred five legions. Some were scattered, at least one was stationed on Megalos and one somewhere in the Southlands. No one knew what had happened to these and mattered little. His problem was with the remaining one hundred three legions, that is, some ten thousand combat-ready men, fully armed and with many cannonae. At least the numbers were smaller than some fifty years ago when the Emperor had three hundred legions. His father's attitude of giving the people what they wanted had reduced the Imperial Army by two thirds. Why? People didn't see the need for a huge army when there were no wars or even threatening countries at hand. Instead they wanted more wine, more ale, more gold, less taxes, all of which his father had furnished.

Where were these many legions stationed? That was what he truly did not know for sure. He'd never paid much attention to it; his father's aides had always taken care of such minor details. He did know that one legion was posted near the coast in Arolas where the Kathos Mountains reached the sea. Their assignment was to protect Arolas from the occasional raiding parties from Vladimir. These hundred men were still at their post, mostly bored.

Additionally, he knew that at least ten legions were stationed somewhere within each kingdom, though in recent years, their numbers had been steadily dwindling. Except for the revenue gained by so many nearby soldiers spending their pay locally, most kingdoms really didn't want Imperial Centurions on their land. Each kingdom maintained their own army. General Gyros sent a party to the Imperial Garrison in Arolas, down along the coastal border with Thrace. However, they returned saying that the barracks there was totally deserted and had been for months. No one knew when they left nor where they might have gone. Evidently, they had departed when most people were remaining indoors.

Similarly, by April, Thallyus and Penelopus could find no trace of the Imperial legions that had been garrisoned in those kingdoms. Of course, the new monarchs were very relieved to find them long gone. Not so Alexio. Before he could officially and ethically step down as Emperor, he had to see to the disbandment of the Imperial Legions. The only thing that he did know for sure was that the majority of Imperial Legions were stationed in Thrace, though not all were in Kefall, the historical seat of the Emperor and his throne.

As of April, we had little word from Thrace, save only the frequent communications from the Kali II, as they now called themselves. The small band of vigilantes lived in the long abandoned Kali assassin tunnels that ran for miles beneath Kefall. They were staying alive and doing well, continuing their attempts to rescue mostly women in dire need. However, one of them, Melantha, was a bright chemist and had invented some kind of new highly explosive compound, so powerful that a small vial of it could level half of a stone building. From a strategic point of view, Stefano and I agreed. We could not let that compound fall into the rebel's hands. Somehow, we had to get a force to Melantha and bring her and those who wished to safety. Stefano really wanted to get his hands on that formula!

With the pirates of Patri, Thrace handled, we now began to see if there was some way that we could get to these people, Melantha in particular. Unfortunately, Kefall was smack in the middle of the lawless kingdom of Thrace, many hundreds of miles from the borders of Thallyus, Penelopus, and Arolas. How could we get safely to them?

Commander General Ares Mokrates dismissed his aides for the evening. The instant that the door closed, he ducked into his side room where he had three washbasins at the ready. Just as fast as he could, he lathered up both hands, rubbing and scrubbing them frantically. After rinsing them, in the first bowl, he moved to the second basin, repeating the task, only a little less frantically this second time. After rinsing again, he sighed and repeated it one more time, finally drying his hands off. He had just shaken the hands of his subordinate generals, all ten of them. Duty demanded that of him, but he knew that duty did not extent to having one of them infecting him with some nasty disease, such as leprosy. Once dry, he poured out some aloe salve and rubbed his raw, reddened hands. There, that was that. Now he could eat his dinner with peace of mind.

Disease in an army spells death. It said so right there in his army manual. By god, he would not stand for disease within his ranks. Hell no. He commanded the entire Imperial Strike Force, which now numbered one hundred five legions, not counting the cooks and various support personnel. Everyone knew his standing order: all sick people are strictly quarantined, period. No exceptions, not ever. His goal was a simple one: be ready for a surprise attack. Never be caught with your uniform down. He was even known to conducted surprise emergency drills just to gauge the readiness of his Imperial Army, his prized Centurions.

He was glad finally to get off his feet. Today had been awful; his feet had ached badly. Must be the new boots, he told himself. Changing into his old pair right after lunch had not helped. Now, eating alone so that no one could possible infect him, his feet felt much better. After dining, he carried the tray to the main door, emptied out the three basins and refilled them. "Be prepared," he muttered to himself before turning in for the night.

The next morning Commander General Ares awoke to the full effects of the plague. After falling down, he examined his feet. "Oh dear god! I have been inflicted with some horrible disease!" He crawled to his door and yelled for an orderly. Within an hour, he began to grasp the magnitude of the plague. His mighty invincible Imperial Legions were infected, down to the last man, the last cook, the last orderly!

He washed his feet furiously for an hour to no avail. Then, he had to stop; his ten subordinate generals insisted upon a high-level conference. Forced to crawl like dogs, the ten generals entered his office, thankful to finally sit down. Ares had no choice, "Generals, our situation is extremely grim. Per the laws, this constitutes a National State of Emergency." None offered any resistance, and he continued. "That said, we must open the sealed orders of our Emperor." This was the part that he detested. He had not only to get down on all fours and crawl to the wall safe, but he actually had to undo the combination lock! Lord knows what diseased people had handled it last. Worse, he could not wash his hands until these generals finally left.

He retrieved the sealed envelope. Returning to his seat at the front of the table, he said, "Notice that the seal is unbroken." He opened the orders and read them aloud.

If you are reading this, our beloved country, Demokritos, has come under a life-threatening attack by aliens to our land. The Imperial Legions are our last and only defense from these invading aliens. I am placing the fate of our nation in your hands. Your final orders are to stay alive, maintain your battle-readiness, and fight to the last man when the alien forces reach your base. If you are reading this, I, your Holy Emperor, am lost. Thus, I leave the fate of our nation, our people, in your hands. You will determine whether Demokritos is lost or if it survives. Do not fail your Emperor or our people.

He neglected to say that it was signed by the man who had been Emperor over a hundred years ago. That did not matter. Their Emperor had not gotten word to him; the alien enemies must have already killed him.

"We should seal this base. No one goes in or out," one of his generals suggested. He agreed, insisting on a total lock down. Another suggested fielding their many cannonae around their huge complex, located at the Fork. The Fork was just east and a bit south of Kefall where the two wide paved roads connected and then headed on into Kefall. One fork headed southwest to Alia, one fork led northeast towards Arolas, the main road led on through Thrace and eventually forking again, heading into Penelopus and Thallyus.

"Yes, this will be our final lines of defense. Shore up our walls. Place your cannonae such that each can provide covering fire. We will hold this base against all enemy attacks! It is our final duty to Emperor and country," Ares declared.

"Should we not send out a patrol to check on what is going on in Kefall? Check on our Emperor?" another general asked.

"We need every man possible to defend our position. If the attack does not reach us in a few days, then we can send out patrols to see if the enemy's location can be ascertained," he ordered. After a more discussion, he dismissed them, eager to wash his hands, which had been contaminated by the filthy lock of the safe, to say nothing of the floor and the other generals.

A few miserable days passed without event. At last, Ares sent patrols into Kefall. One returned swiftly with news of the plague. Another returned after that with the news that riots had broken out all over the city. Finally, he received word that the bodies of the Emperor and Empress had been found. Now he was totally convinced that Demokritos was under a hellish attack by alien enemy forces. You must realize that his idea of alien forces meant that some other country's army had launched an all-out invasion of Demokritos. He had no idea about creatures from other worlds.

Daily, his orders remained the same. Be prepared for the assault on the Imperial Barracks at any time, night or day. Most of his generals suspected to see a nighttime assault and thus had more guards on duty during the nights. No attack came, however. After several weeks, all the generals began to believe that the enemy had perhaps landed in Patri and were slowly making their way up to Kefall. This made perfect sense. Well, when they arrived here, they would show these invaders a thing or two. More time passed.

Each day, five times per day, Ares triple washed his feet and then triple washed his hands. His idea was somehow to wash off this massive infection and to keep it from spreading to his hands. In fact, many of the generals were very worried about this aspect. With women having lost their arms altogether, such only fueled their wild ideas. Secretly now, more than one of his ten generals began thoroughly washing their own hands periodically. If they lost their hands or arms as the women folk of Kefall had, they would be helpless to stop this invading army of aliens. That was their greatest fear, that they'd lose theirs and be helpless to stop the advance of the invaders.

One month after the plague struck, they were joined by the remaining Imperial Legions, who had been garrisoned in other kingdoms. Led by majors, they too had opened their secret, sealed orders, and had packed up everything, making for the Imperial Compound here at the outskirts of Kefall. Having the additional legions bolstered everyone's morale some. Still they waited for the inevitable assault.

In late December, Commander General Ares let out a hoop of joy! "It worked! I've finally washed the infection from my feet! I can walk again! The enemy's diabolical infection has worn off before their army could make its way overland to us. Now we have a chance!" Quite a few other aides and generals were of the same opinion, having been caring for their feet these past two months. That all men's feet returned to normal didn't register in their minds as important. That they were once again the most potent, effective fighting force on Tarra did.

Thus embolden, he sent out patrols in many directions, hoping to hear word of just where the enemy army was located now. He received all manner of disaster reports, untold thousands dead in the streets of Kefall, for example. Yet no scout reported seeing their opponent. Many began to believe that there was no invading army. Worse, many of the young men had wives and families. As they began to hear how widespread the plague had been and that all women had been so horribly affected, they longed to go to their homes to assist their wives and families. Of course, such would be desertion in a time of war. Penalty: shot instantly. Thus, as January rolled on and summer's heat increased, worried soldiers began slipping over the barracks walls, usually late at night. Often, they would ditch their emerald green uniforms just on the other side of the walls to avoid further detection.

Adding to the confusion, many of those sent out on patrols now came back with various illnesses. Primarily, cholera and dysentery began sweeping through the ranks of so many men who were living so close together. Naturally, Ares washed himself off nearly every hour now. His hands were slowly growing raw. The doctor's warnings to thoroughly wash before eating to help prevent the spread of disease only fueled his psychosis, and even more of his generals were also following suit. With the first signs of fall coming in March of 824, his legions had to be continually reorganized, because so many men were missing, dead, or ill. He now counted barely thirty legions all total.

Daily, he tried to install morale in his subordinates, claiming that any day now the great battle would be raging for their country. Few believed him any longer and even more quietly deserted. Sentries now completely ignored even the boldest scaling of the walls by the deserters. By April, barely ten legions remained. Then, on April 21, Commander General Ares found no breakfast waiting for him. He called out and no one answered. At last, he left his quarters, the first time since the plague struck. All around him, the huge compound was totally deserted. He raced from barracks to barracks and found some who had died of their illnesses. Ares became convinced that the aliens had come during the night, slaying his men. He swore that he would defend to the last man, meaning himself. Several days later, a passing farmer found his dead body draped over a cannonae.

Thus, the once mighty Imperial Army vanished into history. Alexio finally learned of its fate in the middle of April, when he accidentally ran into a former legion major who he knew and heard what had been going on. The major had finally managed to return to his home in Naxos, only to find his wife and family deceased; they'd died in the great fire, which had destroyed a quarter of the city.

Finally, Alexio walked up to Ana and Callisto. "I hereby dissolve the Demokritos Empire. The position of Emperor is now history. Each kingdom is now responsible solely for themselves."

"On behalf of the kingdoms, Alexio, we thank you," Ana replied with a grin and nod.

"Hey, now I can get on with my life!"

"So what are you going to do now?" Callisto asked.

"Honestly, I don't know. Lend a hand in the reconstruction process, I suppose. How can I not help?" She grinned. "Callisto, I have been thinking about this whole disaster thing. When I fled Kefall, I could not have been more desperate to save my family. What saved us all were the local farmers and their families. They took us in, gave us shelter, and often fed us as well. I did not expect such kindness or charity, and they gave it to us freely. I want to give something back to the farmers of Arolas. About the only thing that I'm good at is planning. I was thinking that perhaps you and Ana might allow me to work on the rural electrification program for Arolas. Let me see what I can do for those who helped us survive."

"Alexio, you got it. Flavio and Alexia can help you and Io work on this project. MMCE we call it, Modernization, Mobilization, Communication, and Electrification," Callisto agreed, and Alexio, Io, Flavio, and Alexia set to work, beginning with setting up the RME program, based initially in their shared home in Andros. Rural Mechanization and Electrification soon became a reality across southern Arolas. They coordinated with me in Velona, and I kept referring them to the appropriate contact people. In the process, I learned a lot about planning.

Considering that steam engine plants would have to be the source of electricity generation across the south of Arolas, they decided on placing five such plants strategically located to serve the whole southern portion. These plants depended upon coal in quantity, dictating steam engine trains to deliver the coal. Thus, a rail line had to be constructed, and they chose to make it parallel the existing main paved road from Naxos to Kefall. The generating plants were located uniformly along this line. Engines and cars had to be acquired, rail lines built, coalmine contracts established, to say nothing about building the plants themselves and equipping them with the great machines. All this was need to create the electricity in the first place. Then, the power needed to be transported over wires attached to poles throughout the whole five zones with spurs branching off to each farmstead. That brought the power to the farmer, but that alone was only a potential. Next, each farmstead had to be equipped to make use of the new electrical power. That is, the homes had to be wired, light fixtures and switches installed and so on. All this and it only brought them electric lights!

Only then could the new inventions be added, such as the sweeping machine to clean the floors and the clothes washing machines. Those, however, also required both running water and some kind of sewer system. The way that he began organizing all these dis-related components and the work force required to install them was fascinating for me to watch. Since they would be stringing lines anyway, he added a telefono system into the mix. Cleverly, Alexio created a working model of the end product, using the first steam powered electrical unit that arrived in Andros in May. By June, the four were able to have an entire city block totally fixed up with his model RME homes. At that point, all the key personnel and their families were given live demonstrations of just how labor saving this would be for women and thus for men.

Beyond just a morale booster, many individuals saw the importance of the whole project, including those of their two monarchs. That they also saw great fortunes to be made also nudged them to invest. New companies sprang up to meet the ever-growing demand. Across Arolas, Thallyus, and Penelopus, the MMCE and RME began to take on a life of their own, growing almost exponentially from the early winter months of 824.

Down in Penelopus and Thallyus, the engineers that I had sent arrived and began assisting Zoe and Elissa in this monumental expansion of services. The two women were right; they could harness the Vardan River and the geothermal energies commonplace around the city of Geo, some hundred miles west of Thal. By the summer of 825, that is, March, two of the planned ten power generating plants were operational sending electricity to both Thal and to Tinos. From this point on, it began to grow exponentially.

One of the key moves that Alexio and the monarchs did to push these massive plans through so quickly was to mobilize the ex-Centurions, who had deserted the Imperial Legions in Kefall, returning to their homes in the various kingdoms. Here was a labor pool that was both fit and strong — young men eager to make money. That they also saw the desperate need for this, having returned home to see firsthand the terrible results of the plague on their wives, girlfriends, fiancés, and family members only fueled them to work all the harder on the projects.

Additionally, the monarchs utilized many of their country's soldiers on these projects as well. Yes, some were kept patrolling the borders with the anarchy countries of Thrace and Theos, but well over half were put to work on these public works projects. Further, the once lucrative war industries now found themselves with virtually no orders for more weapons, armor, guns, ammunition, cannonae, and so on. While some owners attempted to wait out this shortfall of new orders, many began retooling to begin to help meet the incredible demand for wire, poles, coal, iron and steel, and fabrication plants that were needed to create this RME and MMCE boom. Those who switched their operations rapidly began expanding. By the summer of 825, nearly all had finally ceased making products for war and were making products for survival. Personally, I thought that this incredible turnaround was extremely positive.

Thus, with the dissolution of the Imperial Legions in Kefall and with the many projects beginning to come to life, I began to turn my attention on those trapped in Kefall, the Kali II and more importantly Melantha and her new explosive compound. How long could they remain underground? Here in May of 824, they had been living in the tunnels beneath Kefall for nearly three-quarters of a year. How long could they possibly hold out? I needed someone who was familiar with those tunnels and the only person that I knew who did was Callisto.

The latest reports from the Kali II indicated that finally a Thrace General Thebes had begun taking back control of Kefall. He and his men arrived from the borders and found the streets filled with rotting corpses. He had little choice but to declare martial law and thankfully had his men clear the streets. Still, five thousand soldiers in a city that once held millions was insufficient to maintain law and order. He found that when he entered the city in late January, countless fractions vied for control. Over a hundred individuals now had sufficient men and guns to enforce their arbitrary rule. Essentially, the city was divided into a hundred zones of power, constantly battling each other to either hold on to what they had or to expand their zones. General Thebes did the only thing he could, since his men had not been paid for a couple of months. He bargained with those in the wealthier districts of Kefall and became their overlord. For a monthly price, he and his men guaranteed the safety of those districts, and mostly ignoring the others.

Further, word had now trickled into Kefall about the situation in the capital of Thrace, Axos. Bishop-Prelate Charon of the Church of Skulls had taken nearly total control of the city. By all reports, the man was insane. His followers who now ran the city were primarily thieves and assassins. Worst, they were expanding their vice grip control to the suburbs of Axos and even as far as five miles out of the city! Conditions there were beyond dismal and daily, Kefall saw refugees from Axos quietly arriving in their city, bringing nothing but the clothes on their backs as a rule. Those that made it to Kefall were small in numbers, relating that many of their neighbors had fled to smaller outlying towns and villages within Thrace.

I studied my maps again. Some seven hundred miles separated Kefall from the border with Arolas, but the main paved road traced this route. It was nearly twice that to the borders of Thallyus and Penelopus. Any rescue, I reasoned would have to come from Arolas. Based on the petrol consumption of our motor-wagons and the round trip distance, I estimated that they could make it if they carried four fifty-gallon drums of petrol along with them. Motor-wagons were still a premium in Arolas, since they were just starting to come out of the factories now, but in very small numbers. Much as I hated it, motor-wagons were not going to solve my problem, horse-drawn wagons were the only real possibility, taking two weeks to travel such distances.

Callisto and I often discussed the situation in Kefall. Thankfully, she came to me, volunteering to lead a rescue mission. "After all, I'm the only one who knows where those secret Kali tunnels are located. It has to be me leading the party. Spyro will go with me, and I have the Grey Creature's blaster, so I'm not likely to be shot or anything." We agreed on the principle of her leading the rescue.

Stefano suggested that they mount three of the MG long guns, those that rapidly fire a rain of deadly bullets, onto the lead wagon. If they ran into real resistance, they'd have a fighting machine, so to speak. She took along two dozen wagons and fifty of her soldiers, but they didn't wear their uniforms. Callisto did not want them being identified as soldiers from Arolas. Less potential troubles, she thought. No one would think that they might be an invasion force from Arolas. The only trouble: it was nearly winter now. The first significant snow was expected any day.

On June 1, Callisto and her band halted at the rim of the steeply sloped Lonki Basin, the boundary between her kingdom and Thrace. Already the ground was spotted with white, though most of the recent snow had already melted. Ten of her troops rode on out before them, while Spyro drove her in the lead wagon, along with six men manning the three MG long guns. "How much trouble do you think that we're going to have, dear? Highway robbers too?"

"I am hoping that the cold will keep them indoors. A lot depends upon how much traffic we encounter on the road. Lots of travelers and wagons, then expect thieves a plenty. If not, we may run into only a few bandits," she replied.

"Well, I think that once they see fifty men with long guns, they will leave us alone," Spyro stated his hypothesis. They pushed on until they estimated they'd made fifty miles, before camping. That was her plan, fifty miles each day, more or less arriving in Kefall on June 16.

They met no one on the road that first day, but then they did not expect to meet many travelers this far from the heartland of Thrace. Inner-kingdom travel had fallen off to a mere trickle ever since the plague came. When they approached a town or village, Callisto continued to move out of her body and to check out the place ahead of their passage. Thus, the overall picture of the situation in Thrace slowly became clear. Typically someone had come to power in each and now exercised their own laws and whims upon the town. Uniformly, she saw barricades and guards near the main road entrances. As a result, they began to look for alternate routes, generally taking back roads around these larger villages and towns.

Traveling a lot at night, Callisto began noticing something unusual with a fair number of farm houses here on the side roads, something that was completely absent from those farmsteads just off the main paved road. A dim lantern hung in a front window, but obviously, those who lived there had gone to bed hours ago. It was after ten at night, some six hours after dark. Callisto began paying attention to this seeming anomaly. Not every farmstead had a night light on, perhaps half at most.

On the third evening, long after dark, their advance riders encountered fellow travelers — actually, terrified travelers, who had not expected to come upon such a large group of men. As her advance men reported that they had company, Callisto called out, "Let them pass, captain. Spyro, hold our lantern up a little higher so I can see them better, please." He did so and she shortly saw five walking through the light snow towards her lead wagon. She could sense their fear. "Hello, you have nothing to fear from us. We will not bother you folks," she attempted to put them at ease, if possible. As they entered her light, she concluded rightly that this was a family. The husband led the way, walking hesitantly towards them, his eyes darting from man to man. His arm was around his daughter. Callisto guessed that she was perhaps twelve years old. Behind them, a son had his arms around his mother and another sister, likely a couple years younger than her older sister. The man carried a large pack over his back, while the others had a small sack strapped to their backs, rolled bedrolls peering out of them.

"You, you are not bandits? You are not going to capture or hurt us?" the man asked, his eyes still drifting from armed man to man.

"No, we are on a long trip and travel a lot at night because we think that it's safer. Besides, the towns we've bypassed so far are very unfriendly. We're due for a break. Would you care for something hot?" Callisto asked.

He looked at his wife and she nodded. Callisto ordered someone to start up their small, portable charcoal stove and fix a large pot of tea and heat up their stew. While the family gathered around the stove, absorbing the welcomed heat, the husband opened up, "Yes, the main road isn't safe to travel any longer. We're following the Underground Road. I'm trying to get my family to somewhere that will be safe."

"What's the Underground Road?" she asked. She found the answer fascinating. The situation in many towns and cities had become so untenable, that many were fleeing. If one were caught on the open roads, men were often killed and women captured. As a result, many of the farmers now offered temporary sanctuary for those fleeing the tyranny. Most all traveled by night for safety and the farmers who were sympathetic, left a lantern on in their windows. Thus, those fleeing could take sanctuary in their barns and were usually fed in the morning. Further, many of the local farmers knew of other farmers around them who were willing to take on extra help, thereby assisting the resettlement of the desperate families.

As the days passed, Callisto continued to see clear evidence of the Underground Road. They continued to encounter other families fleeing the nearby towns and cities. As a result, the grim reality of life in Thrace became clear to her, though there was little that she could do about it. The closer that they came to Kefall, the more difficult it became to find ways to bypass the more densely inhabited zones.

As they entered the suburbs of Kefall, they ran into their first combat situation. Ahead, the main street was blocked, and ten armed men accosted her ten advanced scouts. Callisto heard her captain warn them, "Move that wagon, and allow us to pass. We outnumber you five to one. See the lead wagon? There are MG long guns aimed at you." She didn't like the attitude of the townsman, but the man did signal him men to pull one wagon aside to allow them to pass.

"Spyro, pull our wagon off to the side. We'll let the others pass and act as a rear guard. I don't trust them," she ordered. After the last wagon passed the barricade, the townsmen closed the gap. Just when Callisto thought perhaps they would be reasonable, they opened fire upon her wagon, now at the rear. Several aimed for her and Spyro, as well as the three men manning the MG guns. Her men just could not believe that somehow all ten shots missed them. In fact, they had not missed, but the Shield setting of Callisto's blaster worked its magic. Her ten mounted men and the three MG long guns returned fire. The battle was over in less than a minute; all ten had been killed or wounded. Quickly, Callisto had Spyro caught up to the others. She and her advance men resumed their lead position, though all kept their guns at the ready, watching the buildings and windows. Nothing further happened. She was quite relieved to leave this suburb behind them.

Ahead she saw the outskirts of the northeastern Kefall proper. "Wow, it sure has grown some."

"What'd ya expect? Been a hundred years since you were here, spunky," Spyro exaggerated. "See the fellows that we're supposed to be meeting around here anywhere?"

Chapter 32 The Rescue

A week before the plague struck, Olympia Oma's Boarding House in the heart of Kefall, some two miles from the Imperial Palace, was a bustling place. Olympia was a forty-five year old widow who ran an impeccable boarding house, nearly always filled to capacity. Matronly in attitude, Olympia ran a tight ship, as she often stated. The portly woman, proud of her large build, proud of the success of her boarding house, whose reputation had even enticed many foreign visitors to stay at her place, barked, "Xerxes, make sure that we are well stocked. And don't forget, tonight's meal should be your roast duck. We need our guests to be well fed. They perform again tonight, you know. You can't play well on an empty stomach."

Xerxes, her twenty-five year old cook, smiled, "Of course, madam. We've some fine birds for the meal. You forgot that Isabella has given me box seat tickets for their performance tonight."

"Yes, of course, but honestly, Xerxes, the symphony? I didn't know that you were interested in such things. Perhaps, it is our young guests that have enthralled you?" she teased him with a sly innuendo. Olympia was referring to some of her guests from Velona. She did not get the chance to chat further; she spied Icaros, a twenty-nine year old brass foundry worker, who had just entered the front door. "Icaros, don't forget to remove your dirty boots. Alexina has just cleaned the carpets today." Icaros grimaced but did as she ordered, no sense getting on the wrong side of Olympia. This boarding house was ideal for him — a touch of class in his otherwise rather drab existence. Besides, he enjoyed dining with so many fine looking young women.

Olympia took brief note that Icaros followed her orders and then spotted Alexina coming in the door. "Ah, Alexina, you'll need to change Ammon's bedding after dinner. It seems that he's managed to soil them once again."

"Yes ma'am," the twenty-year old woman nodded. She was a working guest here. Weekdays, she worked as a seamstress and was saving every copper to one day open her own dressmaking establishment. She worked for her room and board here at Olympia's, being a maid of an evening and on the weekends. This had allowed her to be already halfway towards her postulated goal of one thousand gold, enough for her to rent a small storefront, purchase the cloth bolts and sewing supplies. Another two years and her childhood dream would finally become a reality. She nodded to the portly matron and headed to her room to change for dinner.

Olympia checked her bun and remembered another detail. She always wore her long brown hair in a neat bun. Besides being out of her way, she thought that it made her look more in control of her staff, more business-like. "Jonus. Jonus, where are you?" She headed off to the basement in search of her combination handyman and security man. Jonus was thirty and a jack-of-all-trades, as he liked to tell others, frequently, especially at the dining room table. "Ah, there you are, Jonus. Tomorrow, I need you to fix the handrail on the stairs; it is getting loose. We cannot have our guests tripping, now can we?"

He'd spotted that the base post had a little give in it, hardly anything to worry about. Yet from long experience, he knew that he dare not tell her such. Not Olympia. This woman had the knack of being able to issue more orders than a general, he thought. Still, she ran one of the finest boarding houses, and he was thankful to be living here in the heart of the wealthier district of Kefall, so close to the Imperial Court. One day, he expected to be "discovered" and offered a far better paying position, perhaps even at the court itself. He replied dryly, "Tomorrow, I will fix it, ma'am." She nodded and headed off to see if the dinner table was properly set, having the utmost confidence that the post would be repaired. Olympia never doubted for a second that one of her orders would be failed to be carried out. Her confidence level was so high that no one dared disobey her.

Later, they gathered around the large dining room table for supper, as chef Xerxes served up another superbly cooked meal. Few chefs could compete with him, and Olympia's tastes in food required the talents of only the best of chefs. Food was her remaining greatest pleasure in life, though her rotund body did not really need such. Besides Icaros, Jonus, and Alexina, all of her current guests were present as well. Ammon with his impressive black moustache sat across from her, as always. He was the Director of the Royal Imperial Symphony and a bachelor and a reputed womanizer. He'd already tried to seduce the foreigners but had failed. Still, he continued to try to get Olympia's affections, failing as always, though he took it as a personal challenge now. While the other young women had a valid excuse to reject his amorous pleadings, they were married, Olympia did not; she was fair game. Two years now and he still not even had a slightest kiss from her, a dashing blow to his overly large ego.

Sitting at the end of the table were her foreign guests, who called themselves the Basari Quartet. The four were from Velona, though Olympia had not the faintest notion of where that country lay, merely somewhere very far to the north. She had learned that these highly skilled, highly sought after musicians were here in Kefall on a tour. They had taken their name of the academy where the four had perfected their amazing musical skills, the Basari School of Music. As Olympia understood them, which was somewhat difficult as their command of her language was rather poor at best; they had been schoolmates and had joined their talents together upon graduation. They had to be famous, that she knew, because the news of their coming last month had been the talk of the whole neighborhood.

A young and wealthy nobleman, Leon Stantinos, a thirty-three year old, unmarried, fine arts promoter, had been instrumental in arranging for the Basari Quartet to spend two months playing at various musical concert halls here in Kefall. More importantly for Olympia, Leon had now made numerous visits to her boarding house during these past six weeks, bringing so much attention to her establishment that she now had a waiting list for room bookings that was twenty-five long! This was unheard of in her many years of running her boarding house!

Director Ammon asked, "Well, are you ready for tonight's performance? I didn't hear you practicing it today." He had an accusing tone in his voice.

Aldo Arantos looked up and glanced at his wife and their two friends, then replied, "Director, we know the Gloria by heart. Please, keep the tempo down. We feel that you not do the work justice when you rush it." Aldo was twenty-five and their harpsichord player. He had nicely trimmed brown hair and plaintive eyes and sensitive hands. He was also rather thin. Olympia always thought, the man needed to eat more, and she continually insisted so at the dinner table.

His wife, Natasha, was twenty-three with fiery red, curly hair that draped far below her shoulders. She had a slightly brownish hue to her skin and one of the two strangest accents, only barely able to make herself understood by Olympia. She had fiery eyes to match her hair and a temper to match them both, though her temper was only directed towards all things musical and then only when what was being done did not suit her opinion on how it should be done. At those times, Director Ammon had learned to go along with her, not only to shut her up, but also because more often than not, she was right! Natasha played the cello.

Her skin tones matched those of Mrs. Vasili Rostov, their twenty-two year old horn player. Indeed both women's strange, thick accents baffled Olympia, so different from the other two. Vasili had thick, straight, black hair that fell to her waist, though her bangs over her forehead gave her more of a pixie look, Olympia thought. Mrs. Isabella Fluente, also twenty-two, had long, slightly curly brown hair that fell well below her shoulders. She played several sizes of flutes and a horn-like instrument called a cornetto, which was fingered more like the flutes but blown like a horn. Isabella had very sharp, pale blue eyes that never seemed to miss the slightest detail. Isabella and Aldo definitely came from Velona. Olympia had met several from that country over the years, and these two matched the others, from skin tones to accents. Not so with Vasili and Natasha.

Although Olympia did not know this, Vasili and Natasha's parents came from the Northern Steppes and were ambassadors to Velona from the Czar. The young girls had heard the incredible music in Velona's concert halls and had insisted on learning to make such music of the gods. After spending eight years studying at the Basari School of Music, they had achieved their dreams. Both had entered the school when they were barely nine years old. After three more years, all four of these musicians had achieved critical acclaim. Two years ago, they took an opportunity to tour the world, playing in many countries.

Their first lengthy engagement had been in Shansee, Tashien, leaving there just before the first alien plague struck there. They spent three months playing concerts on Megalos, before making the long trip to Annelise, where they spent almost a year. The Annelise kept extending their contract, until at last, they had to honor Leon's requests to stop delaying and come to Demokritos and Kefall. Six weeks into their two-month tour, Leon had already offered them an extended contract, much as Annelise had done. The four had accepted the extension, looking forward to playing another four months of concerts here.

Two other local young musicians also stayed here. Kore Leto, a blonde twenty-five year old viola player, replied to her Director's question, "I've played this piece since I was ten, sir."

"Same here, Director," Lysandra Liz added. She was twenty-one and blonde. She was the second violinist. Only one man stood in her way of becoming the youngest first violinist in the history of the Royal Imperial Symphony and the first woman to achieve that esteemed post. The post also held the title of Concert Master, leading the symphony when their Director was absent, which was too frequently as far as many were concerned. Already Director Ammon had tried to seduce both women but had failed, both claiming that they were engaged. That was a fib on their part. They'd learned from other musicians that this was an acceptable way to divert his unwanted attention.

After dinner, the musicians headed to their rooms to change. Vasili and Isabella shared a bedroom, as did Aldo and his wife. Likewise, Lysandra and Kore. The others had their own bedrooms. The six musicians insisted on doubling up. Olympia understood why Lysandra and Kore moved in together, for it kept Director Ammon at some distance. Well, she had given him unequivocal orders to leave the two women alone. She assumed that Vasili and Isabella had the same idea, though she often wondered where their husbands were and why they were not staying with their wives. She'd inquired about this, but the women had been vague in answering. Olympia had the notion that perhaps their husbands had not even accompanied their wives on this long trip. Still, both women wore very beautiful wedding rings, nearly identical, intertwined, golden roses with a small diamond between them.

In their room, Isabella and Vasili changed into their black concert dresses, but not before giving each other a passionate kiss. They were married — the ceremony conducted at the Church of the Three Holy Roses in Velona just before heading off on this very lengthy world tour, much to the displeasure of their parents. They'd kept their relationship and marriage to themselves, though Aldo and Natasha both knew. "Let's knock them dead tonight, love," Isabella whispered.

"You got it," Vasili replied with a grin. Dressed in simple black gowns with black silk hose, the two slipped into their shiny black high heels. All the women were obligated to wear nearly identical black dresses, hose, and the five-inch heels. The men wore black tuxedos. While their white cummerbunds and shirts added a bit of contrast, the women wore a white silk sash around their waists. After brushing each other's hair, the two women picked up their instruments and headed down the stairs.

Already Leon Stantinos had arrived. For weeks now, he insisted on picking up the quartet personally, transporting them to the elegant concert hall in his great carriage. The other women accompanied Director Ammon in his carriage. Tonight, Xerxes had been invited by Leon to share his private box seats, and the chef looked a bit out of place, wearing his only suit, contrasting sharply with the well-dressed Leon.

The Royal Symphony Hall, built some twenty years ago, had cost a fortune, paid for by the Emperor, whose ruling philosophy was "give the people what they want." Well, many nobles had asked for a new concert hall and he'd obliged them. Plush red carpeting covered the entire floor. Two hundred lanterns in five large, gold, ornate clusters illuminated the concert hall. Fifty private box seats lined the outer rim. Leon's box seat was the first one on the right, from where he could see the orchestra very well indeed. The sound would have been better at the rear center box seats, but he chose this one, preferring to see the players and their intricate movements. Xerxes had never been to a symphonic concert before and was most impressed. Leon took pleasure in chatting with this chef, explaining about this passion of his life.

As the curtains pulled back, the one hundred member orchestra appeared, seated in the center of the stage. The Basari Quartet was positioned off to the left side of the stage, right below Leon's box seats. Behind them stood twenty-five male singers; off to the right of the orchestra stood twenty-five female singers. First up tonight was Alekto's Gloria, a piece written by one of their own countrywomen who had immigrated to Velona and become one of the most famous symphonic composers in history. Director Ammon walked on stage and the huge crowd began their usual welcome clapping. He bowed, took his position, and raised his arms. Satisfied, he set the tempo and the music began.

The resounding one-two tempo of the combined orchestra set the mood instantly, then the vocalists entered, singing, "Gloria! Gloria! Gloria! Glory to God on the Highest." Xerxes had never heard such sounds; goose bumps electrified him. By the time the long piece ended, he felt that somehow he had ascended to heaven or something similar. He joined the others as they gave a standing ovation, clapping wildly, stomping their feet, and even whistling. After the intermission, they played one of Alekto's symphonies, which featured solos by the various members of the Basari Quartet. The mood created by the bass flute playing of Isabella sent chills through Xerxes.

Leon was so taken with just how much Xerxes enjoyed the performance, he invited the chef to accompany him tomorrow night to the Black Cat Nightclub. "Wear this suit, nothing fancier. I'll let you in on a very little known gig. Let's see how you like this one."

"Thanks! This is just incredible. I'm going to have to come to all these concerts. When is the next one?" Xerxes asked. It was next week, but it never occurred because of the plague.

The next evening, Leon picked up Xerxes again and drove them to the ritzy nightclub. Again, Xerxes had never been here before, way too expensive for him, but Leon picked up the tab. The nobleman had taken a liking to this superb chef. The room was dim. Some fifty tables filled the room, with some additional tables set back against the walls. A raised platform held the musicians. Xerxes was very surprised to see Isabella and Vasili quietly walk on stage. This time, the two wore simple day dresses and flats, gone was the elegance of the concert hall. Several hundred people were sitting at the tables, drinking and smoking. Each table in the center had a candle lantern in the center, and waitresses moved among the clientele, serving drinks.

"This is called jazz. They take a tune, which many may know, as a starting point. Then — well, you just got to hear them," Leon tried to explain the unexplainable to Xerxes.

Vasili played her horn, a rather low, soft sound. Isabella had two flutes with her; one was the bass flute that she had played last night. She also had the cornetto as well. Ignoring the crowd and seemingly everything but themselves, the two began to play. Xerxes liked the beginning tune, but soon they began improvising and twisting the melody, stretching notes here and there. The women communicated a mood, Xerxes thought, an introspective, thoughtful, yet highly emotional mood. He felt like crying at points, as if he'd lost the most precious thing in his life. Other times, he felt like he was sailing on clouds. He swore that their two-hour gig lasted only a couple of minutes!

The crowd definitely loved them and applauded loudly when they finished around nine. Leon signaled the women and soon the two musicians, carrying their instrument bags, joined them at the table. "Incredible! I was almost crying and then felt like I was floating in the sky," Xerxes said as the two women smiled and sat down. Leon had already ordered up them a pitcher of dark ale, the women's favorite.

"Thanks, Xerxes, glad you enjoyed it," Isabella replied. Vasili allowed Isabella to do most of the talking for them, because her command of the Demokritos dialect was marginal at best, but she smiled. "We play these clubs for our own selves, you see. It is a time that we can lay back and make our own sounds, our own moods. That others like them too is fine, but we do these gigs for ourselves, kind of like a treat, you know."

Xerxes grinned, "I understand you — like the chocolate mousse that I fix for myself. Well, I sure wish I'd known about these gigs before. I won't miss any more of them, you can count on it."

Sipping the mug of dark ale, Isabella smiled, "Glad that you enjoy them. We are supposed to play here again in five days."

"How did you two ever learn to play like that anyway? I've been meaning to ask you that for some time now," Leon inquired.

"We've been playing together since we were ten. Every now and then, you know, a couple of musicians rather get on the same wavelength. Well we did. We always know just what the other is thinking or feeling — makes for real tight playing," Isabella tried to explain.

"Ya, that's what it takes, tight, being real tight," Vasili added, finally willing to say a few words. "Music is our lives."

"Right, there's no better way to say it. She and I live to make music," Isabella explained. "Our lives are our music."

"It's been my greatest pleasure to have somehow managed to get you and the others in your quartet to come to Kefall. If I had my way, why, I'd somehow keep you here forever," Leon teased the two, who grinned. "But I suspect your husbands would object mightily." The two women chuckled, glancing briefly at each other.

The next day, the plague struck. The women's arms ached and seemed very weak that whole day. Undaunted, Olympia continued issuing her orders, "Jonus, please lend Alexina a hand with the laundry. For some reason, our arms are aching. Perhaps, there was something wrong with the duck last night."

"Can't she do it? All right, all right, I'll lend her a hand," Jonus grumbled. "I'm a handyman, not a laundress, ma'am." Olympia frowned; she didn't like the backtalk, but headed off to the kitchen to press her latest idea about why their arms were so aching today. It had to be food, she concluded.

"Xerxes, what was wrong with the duck last night? We're all displaying symptoms today. Was it bad? Did you cook it enough or what?"

"Ma'am, I assure you that my duck was cooked to perfection!" he defended himself. "I chose those ducks myself. They looked healthy to me. I swear it is not the duck." Xerxes didn't like anyone criticizing his cooking and he put on a hurt face. Olympia took the hint and left the kitchen.

At dinner, the women's arms were even weaker and seemed thinner somehow, but that was not possible. Worse, their feet also ached, but not as badly as the men's feet. All had a grumpy meal and everyone headed to bed early that night. Xerxes even let the dishes go until the morning. His feet were throbbing from having stood on them all day long. Of course, he stood on them every day and this made no sense to him.

The next day, screams filled the boarding house, as the women awoke, shocked by their horrible situations. "Help! Jonus, Xerxes! Help me!" screamed Olympia, "Get in here immediately!"

"My god, Natasha!" Aldo exclaimed. His look of horror was mirrored and added to by his wife. She just sat in their bed beside him and screamed and screamed, while he held her tightly in his arms.

In the room across the hall, Lysandra and Kore added their hysterical voices to the cacophony of terror, shock, and fright. He heard the screams of Vasili from the room next to theirs. At the time, he didn't realize what he didn't hear, however.

Vasili and Isabella sat up beside each other in their bed, shocked, terrified, and panicked. Vasili began screaming wildly, forcing Isabella to put her attention onto her mate instead of herself. She longed to put her comforting arms around her lover. Isabella knew how desperate the young woman felt, but she couldn't. She noticed their monster breasts, and those being the only upper appendages she had, Isabella began moving her melons against Vasili's body and her breasts as well, trying to get Vasili's attention somehow, someway, anyway. "Slap her face." The words appeared in her mind. Someone once had said that was how you handled someone who was freaked out, but she could no longer do such a thing. She tried to say soothing words and continued to rub her breasts against her lover's body. "Vasili. Vasili." She wanted to say that it will be okay, but knew that it would never be okay, not ever. Their lives may well be over now.

At last, Vasili began to calm down, and she leaned into Isabella, pressing her breasts against her lover's. Her screams gave way to uncontrolled sobbing. "What's happened to us?" she sobbed.

Isabella's tears came now; she couldn't withhold them any longer. "We've got the plague. You know, that awful plague that we heard had struck Velona last year. It's now come here; we're infected now. I still love you, Vasili. I won't ever leave you. We must be brave."

"I — I can't! How can we live like this? Our music! Our music! Oh god, no, no, not this," Vasili now realized the ramifications of their illness.

"I don't know, I surely don't know, Vasili. We got to find a way to get home, I think. Let's get up and see how badly we are harmed." She struggled to her feet, Vasili, still sobbing to herself, also struggled to get out of their bed and stand on her toes.

"Our feet too?" Vasili wailed. "We can hardly stand! "What's happened to our breasts? Isabella, look at the size of them!" She now stopped crying and began to compare here mutilated body with her lover's. "Our waists? What happened to them? Do you feel all right? Are we missing some organs too?"

Isabella, glancing from herself to Vasili, answered, "Well, I feel okay, I don't hurt anywhere. Our waists — they are so tiny, but our pelvises seem much bigger to me, don't you think? Such hips! I hope that we're not missing vital organs! Dang, it's hard to stand on just my toes. I have to sit down. Oh! My hair!" She finally noticed her hair, which had slipped off her back, covering much of her front. Her brown hair fell to her knees. Leaning over, Vasili's long black hair slipped over her shoulders as well, falling just below her knees too. Both women sat back on the edge of their bed. Their faces were white, eyes bloodshot from the crying, unable to provide the comforting touch to their partner as they used to do and now so desperately desired. All that Isabella could do was to rub her mate gently with her breasts, which now protruded out nearly a foot.

Vasili flashed a slight grin, "I can't believe that we now have to caress each other with only our boobs. What have we become? Our lives have ended, Isabella, haven't they? We're as good as dead now, aren't we? We've lost the most important thing in our lives, our music. What's left for us now? Why didn't they just kill us? Why are they torturing us? Are they sadistic beasts?"

"I don't think that we are dead just yet, my love. We probably ought to be. After all, how can we exist without our music? I don't think we can, but I still love you more than even our music, Vasili. Maybe that is what counts now, that we love each other still," Isabella suggested.

"I do love you, Isabella. I do," Vasili whispered and rubbing her breasts against Isabella's. She added, "We are now both pathetic and helpless, aren't we? I never dreamed that I could only touch you with my breasts. Pathetic. We can't do anything for ourselves. How will we even eat or get our clothes on or even brush our hair? We should have just died. We can't live like this, can we?"

"We have to live, Vasili. We just have to and somehow get back home. Look, we heard that everyone back home got the plague and they somehow survived. Well, we did hear that quite a few did died, but most somehow got by. We have to be brave and survive, Vasili, we just have to. We've lost our music, but I just cannot lose you too, Vasili. I don't know what I would do if anything ever happened to you. You are the whole world to me, dearest, everything."

"You too," Vasili whispered and leaned over, planting a loving kiss on her wife. Just then, Aldo opened their door.

"Excuse me, are you — my god, you are affected too. Natasha has lost her arms too. I figure none of you will be able to open your door now. Want me to leave it open?" Aldo asked. He was white as a sheet. Shock and fear lined his face.

"Thanks, we can't open it anymore. Why are you crawling?" Isabella asked, noticing how awful he looked. He showed them the situation with his feet, and Isabella told him that she thought this had to be the alien plague finally coming this far south.

He agreed and then said, "Weird, but you have a pile of strange things in your room too. We do too. If you want, come into our room. Natasha is taking this really badly."

Now the two noticed the pile of strange things, shoes, desks, hairbrushes, and dinnerware lying in one corner of their room. They tried on the shoes, found to their relief that they could stand more easily, and they headed to console Natasha. They found her sitting on the bed sobbing, deep in grief. Although they sat beside her and did their best, Natasha seemed not to even sense that they were there. Aldo put the new shoes on his wife's feet and then tried on the special boots, but was only barely able to stand in them, wiggling and wobbling wildly. He gave that up and sat down on the floor. "Whatever are we going to do now? We're going to die, aren't we? We're going to die." Natasha apparently heard that and cried even harder.

Isabella took charge, "Damn it anyway! We are not dead yet. We need to find a way to get back home to Velona. Look, if our friends could somehow survive this plague while we were gallivanting around the world, then sure as heck we can too! I don't know how we can do it, but we must, we just must, somehow we must, Aldo. Hey, how is everyone else? Maybe the others were not affected; do you suppose it is just us that have gotten infected?"

They now moved over to the doorway and spotted others coming up the stairs. Icaros and Janus were crawling up the carpeted stairs; their feet looked like Aldo's. They spotted the frightened and ghastly face of Alexina standing at the bottom of the stairs, her shiny black hair draped down her sides to her knees. Xerxes, struggling to somehow stand and walk in the boots, came up behind her. His face was pale; his cheek muscles, taut. He looked up at the four and at Alexina beside him and his face sagged even further. Just then, Director Ammon opened his door. He looked awful and was on his hands and knees too. He said not a word, but crawled over to the other two musician's room, knocked a warning tap, and opened it.

The sobbing of Lysandra and Kore told all there. "Damn!" Ammon said. "Damn!"

At last, Icaros and Jonus reached the door of Olympia and Jonus knocked. "You took your damn time! Come in, I am dying! I need help; there is not much of me left!" Olympia screeched, her terrified voice was an octave higher than normal. Hearing that, Isabella cracked a slight smile. The woman was portly before and probably now was much thinner and imagined the difference they would soon be seeing.

"Just look at me! My arms are gone! They've cut away my whole belly! There is hardly anything left of me now! Help me, Jonus. Help me right now," she ordered in her usual voice, the shrillness now gone.

"Ma'am, help you with what? You seem to be all right. Can you get up?" the man replied somewhat annoyed with her. After all, he was dealing with his own problems right now.

"Send Alexina to me. She can get me dressed, Jonus," she ordered.

"Sorry ma'am," Jonus replied. "She's got no arms either."

"Well, then see if Lysandra or Kore can help me dress," she ordered.

He shook his head. "All of you women are the same — no arms and monster knockers. Men cannot even walk anymore. Just look at my feet, will you?" Jonus complained.

"Oh don't be silly, Jonus. You have your arms. Now come here and get me dressed! Xerxes? Xerxes, if you can hear me, for heaven's sake, get our breakfast ready right now!" Olympia ordered.

"Yes ma'am," Xerxes called up from the bottom of the stairs. Isabella watched him put his arm around Alexina and had her follow him into the kitchen. It's good that he isn't leaving her alone right now, she thought to herself.

"I will see if I can get Natasha dressed and then I'll come lend you two a hand," Aldo whispered to Vasili and Isabella. He and Natasha disappeared into their room. The two moved back to their bed to sit down and wait, feeling utterly helpless, a feeling that was only going to grow by leaps and bounds for quite some time after this.

Shortly, the two heard their matron calling out, "Oh this is beyond disgraceful! Nothing I own fits me. Oh the heck with it, Jonus. I'll just have to eat in my nightgown. After breakfast, Jonus, I want you to go find a seamstress and bring her here to alter some of my clothes!"

"I can't walk, Olympia. It will have to wait," he replied becoming slightly more antagonistic to her. Soon he crawled past their door followed by Olympia, taking tiny steps, trying hard not to fall down. Indeed, her portly frame was drastically altered, down to the same twelve-inch waistline as the other women had. Her hair was down to her knees and not up in her usual bun. Actually, Isabella thought, the woman looked rather attractive now. She had lost significant weight.

"What can we wear? No clothes will fit us too? Can that be?" Vasili whispered worriedly. "We can't have all these men seeing us in our thin nightgowns!" Her modesty came to the fore. Using her feet, Isabella struggled to open their clothes drawers, while Vasili opened their clothes closet. Both were desperately looking for something that Aldo could put on them. Both soon realized the utter futility of it, nothing would fit, their monster breasts could not be gotten into anything that they had.

Vasili sank back onto their bed, crying once more. "Now we get to be utterly humiliated as well. We ought to just died, Isabella." Her lover gave up as well and sank down on their bed beside her, her head hanging low.

Aldo poked his head in, "Nothing fits Natasha anymore. I put one of my shirts over her nightgown. It's better than nothing. Want me to do that for you too?"

Vasili raised her head, "Please, Aldo, please. This is so humiliating." He nodded and returned shortly with two of his long sleeved shirts. After turning the sleeves to the inside, he put one on each woman. Across the hallway, Director Ammon took the hint and enjoyed himself while he put one of his shirts on Lysandra and Kore, who both looked positively miserable. Dressed as much as possible, the group headed down to the dining room.

Alexina looked forlorn and humiliated, sitting in the nightgown, which left nothing at all to one's imagination. Icaros and Jonus both were eyeing her, especially her breasts. Olympia looked awful, but sat in her usual chair at the head of the table. "Jonus, Icaros, stop staring at her and go help Xerxes. You two can set the table, since Alexina cannot any longer."

"Hell, I don't know how to set a table. I didn't sign on to be a waiter. I'm your handyman," Jonus replied. Icaros, however, began to crawl out to the kitchen, and Jonus begrudgingly followed him. Isabella began to notice a change in Olympia. The woman was used to giving orders and having them be carried out, without her even thinking about them again. Now, she was getting a lot of flak, and she definitely looked flustered, on top of everything else.

"What has happened to us? It cannot be bad food," she said to no one in particular.

"We've gotten the plague, I think," Isabella offered her explanation. The woman grimaced; the terrified look returned to her face. Only when Icaros returned crawling in with bowls and cups on a tray that he pushed before him did that look modify.

"Well, it's about time. From now on, you men are going to have to do everything for us, you know," she pointed out the rather obvious.

"Maybe not, there is a whole new kitchen in there. Bunch of replacement things, stove, sink, chair on wheels, low cabinets. I think that maybe you are to be cooking," Jonus added following Icaros into the room. Isabella thought that he was either teasing her or poking fun at her, she couldn't tell which. "If you like, after breakfast, I can install it, ma'am." He knew darn well that Olympia never cooked — at most, she heated tea water. That's why she had hired Xerxes; she never did like her own cooking.

"Well, we'll see about it after breakfast," she replied somberly. Soon, Xerxes crawled into the room, sliding several trays in front of him. Now the women faced their next hurdle. "Jonus, you are going to have to feed me," Olympia ordered.

"Sorry, I have already promised Lysandra here that I would feed her," he replied. Isabella thought that he took pleasure in deflecting her order.

"Well, someone has to feed me, damn it! I certainly can't do it myself! Ammon, be a gentleman and come feed me," she requested.

"I was going to feed Kore," he answered a bit testily, but saw that Icaros was already sitting beside Kore and Alexina. "Oh all right. Seriously, we have got to figure a way out of this mess."

Xerxes sat between Vasili and Isabella and fed them, while Aldo fed his wife. All the women felt mortified and humiliated, but realized they had no other choice. Isabella had a hunch that things were going to get much worse. She was not wrong.

After the meal was finished, Olympia began pleading, "Jonus, you just have to go find us a doctor and someone who can alter our clothes. Please, Jonus," she begged.

"I would if I could walk. I can't crawl for miles," he replied.

"I am supposed to work at the brass foundry today. I'll see what I can do on my way," Icaros promised.

During the morning, Olympia was now begging and pleading to get the others to help her out, to handle the laundry and dishes among other things. Isabella noted this change in her.

Icaros returned not long after he'd left. He related that not a soul was on the streets. No shops were open. Further, his hands and knees were bleeding from his brief trip.

"Whatever are we going to do now? Who will help us?" Olympia's voice was now saturated in sympathy. "We are so helpless like this. Jonus, Icaros, Ammon, I have never been so helpless before. I need you men to change our dirty sheets and wash them. We are going to need more groceries. You just have to help me. I need you so," she exuded, begging for their sympathy, which she really did not get back. The men were concerned with their own problems.

By supper, Olympia slumped into a deep apathy. She had given up, no longer giving out any orders at all, merely sitting in her chair at the dinner table like some child's doll, waiting for someone to animate her. While Isabella was musing over this rapid degeneration of Olympia's mental condition, she saw Director Ammon take advantage of this.

"Ah, fair Olympia. If you will allow me to run the boarding house here, why I will look after your needs," he proposed. She merely nodded. From this point on, Ammon now took charge of the boarding house and began bedding Olympia. He'd scored another victory in his lengthy list of conquests, only this time, he'd obtained a wealthy boarding house for his own.

Embolden by Ammon's actions, Jonus began working on Lysandra. "Dear, this is so awful for you now. If you will promise to be mine, I will look after all your needs from now on. You are a beautiful young woman. I will treat you right." Isabella doubted that very much.

Lysandra sobbed, "Okay, I promise. I cannot possibly hope for anything more, not any more. I am completely helpless and I certainly am not worthy you or anyone, Jonus." He smiled and kissed her passionately. Isabella saw Lysandra cringe and then accept the horrible fate that had befallen herself. She too sat around in the depths of apathy after that.

Not wanting to allow this prime opportunity to pass, Icaros made a play for Kore, who likewise agreed to be his woman in all ways. "I have no choice, I am completely useless now," she whimpered. All three men led their women off to their bedrooms for some pleasure, leaving the stunned group still sitting in the dining room.

Alexina whispered, "I'm just as helpless as they. Like all of you, I've lost everything. My dreams — they are shattered. I was going to open up my own dressmaking shop next year — be an independent woman. Now, that's beyond utterly hopeless. I thought that all I had to do was save up enough money. Well I very nearly have the money now. A whole lot of good that will do me. Xerxes, don't you dare get any ideas about me!"

"Have no fear, Alexina. I have never fully trusted those fellows, especially their music director. It seems he's gotten greedy now. I can't believe that all three of them just gave up as they did. Vasili, Isabella, I promise to help you all that I can and see if somehow we can get you back to your homeland. Alexina, I'll help you all that I can too. I admit, I know nothing about being a maid. Perhaps you can tag along with me and talk me through what must be done."

"Thank you, thank you," Alexina replied, greatly relieved about this small aspect. Isabella could sense the woman's enormous relief.

That evening when Isabella and Vasili headed into their bedroom for the night, Isabella sat down at their low desks and experimented, trying to jot down some notes. "What are you doing, my love?" Vasili asked, at last becoming a bit curious, pulling out of her own doom and gloom thoughts.

"I want to somehow jot down what we saw happen today. I think that it is somehow very important. You see, Olympia was in charge here. It was her boarding house. When we first came here, she gave orders and she just knew that they would be carried out. Then, she started getting resistance and had to put more force behind her orders. After that, she began requesting the cooperation of others to get her desires met. When that began failing, she began pleading to get her desires carried out. When that failed, she tried to use all the force that she could muster, which admittedly now is virtually nothing. When even that failed, she resorted to trying to illicit sympathy for her to get them to carry out her wishes. When even that failed, she dropped into that lifeless state in which she is now stuck, like a deep apathy. I think this series is an important one."

"That is interesting, love. Do you think they will come out of it? How come you and I and Alexina didn't get that way?"

"I don't know, Vasili. Maybe they will be better tomorrow and wish they had not gone along with those men's desires. Come on, I got some scribbles down. That will have to do for now. Shoot, dear, I can't brush your hair for you anymore."

"Well, we can rub our breasts against each other, what else is there for us now?" she replied sorrowfully.

The next day, Isabella noted that Olympia, Lysandra, and Kore had perked up a little bit. Well, at least they cried a lot, instead of sitting like rag dolls. Icaros again went out to see if he could get help or find out what was going on. He returned with really bad news. Later that day, gunfire erupted in the streets nearby, adding to the bad news. Isabella noted that with each bit of bad news that the group received, Olympia, Lysandra, Kore, and even Natasha to a lesser extent, began shrinking back into themselves once again.

Just after supper, Leon Stantinos came knocking at their door. His face was white as a sheet. He too came crawling inside, joining the group as they sipped their after dinner tea. "Oh thank the gods that you are still alive!" he said, looking at the quartet members.

"Alive yes, barely. Not much of us left, I'm afraid," Isabella replied before the others could. While meant as a bizarre jest, Leon knew what she meant by the remark, because it was far, far more that their mere loss of arms. Their music had died as well. He crawled over and took a seat on an empty chair, finally feeling human again.

"It's madness out there, complete chaos, unbelievable insanity," he said, thankful for a cup of tea, compliments of Xerxes. "I've come from home, Madam Olympia, could I possibly trouble you for a room?" She mumbled something inaudible.

"Well, she is now under my care. She's given the ownership of the boarding house to me now, seeing as she can no longer do anything at all for herself," Director Ammon spoke up. "You need a room?" he asked curiously.

"They've murdered my folks, ransacked our home. I can't stay there now."

"Oh dear god, Leon! What happened?" Isabella asked, her attention going outward onto Leon instead of inward on herself, a fact that she also noted.

"We were running low on food. I went out in search of supplies, taking our carriage. It took forever, though. No shops are open. I had to call in a whole lot of favors, but I finally managed to get a friend of mine to let me in his shop. He told me that the rioters have killed the Emperor and ransacked the Imperial Palace as well. I rather went nuts myself and I'm afraid that I bought half his store. Well, a wagon load at least. I got all sorts of things, including long guns. Anyway, I had a hard time driving the wagon both there and back here, for that matter. So many dead lie in the streets. When I got back to my home about a half hour ago, I found looters crawling away from our home. None of our guards or servants has been there since the plague started. I went inside and found my parents had been shot. They were defenseless. They had no chance at all. I was planning on coming over here tonight anyway to see how you all were managing, but honestly, I need a place to stay now, and I brought all the supplies with me."

Greedily, Director Ammon smiled and then said with a snide smile, "I am so sorry about your misfortune, Leon. As they say, one man's misfortune is another man's fortune. Yes, you can stay here in exchange for your supplies. I am sure that we can find some bed somewhere for you. Perhaps you could share Alexina's bed. We men are trying to stay with the women now. You know, to assist them with all their many needs."

Alexina miss-interpreted Ammon's intent. "Please," she pleaded with Leon, "will you stay with me? I am so completely alone and helpless now. We women cannot do anything at all now. It is devastating. Please, sir."

"I would be honored to help all of you women. Yes, Alexina, you can count on me. I do think that we ought to get the supplies inside and the doors barricaded. We may be next on the looter's hit list."

Isabella was watching where her attention seemed to be focused as well as her mate's during the discussion. She had noted that when the bad news was relayed, she found her attention sliding inwards towards herself, almost as if the world was collapsing in upon her. Yet, when he mentioned some good news, such as the supplies and that he was here to help them, her attention moved outward from herself. She saw a similar reaction in Vasili's eyes as well. Most curious, she thought, resolving to jot down this observation as well.

As the women stood watching the men crawling in and out, slowly unloading the wagon, Isabella realized the purpose of the yokes, which until now remained a mystery. She retrieved one from her room and had the men load the two baskets up. "By golly, it mostly works. I am helping a little bit. Come on, Vasili, grab one, and let's help them with this," she suggested. They were not very effective, since yokes were not made to negotiate the many doorways between the front door and the kitchen. Still, they were able to take a bit of the load off the men. Alexina and Natasha joined them. However, Olympia, Lysandra, and Kore merely sat at the dining room table, staring at the teacups, not even making the slightest attempt to sip from them.

By the time that they finished, the men's hands and knees were raw and bloody. Isabella so wanted to tend to them, but again watched like some spectator as her attention came slamming inward on her own helplessness. Well after dark, Ammon, Icaros, and Jonus led their zombie-like women upstairs to their bedrooms, calling it a night.

The others gathered around the living room. Leon asked, "What has happened to those three women? They seem to barely be alive." Isabella explained what had happened, and Leon grimaced more than once.

"How is it that you four are not like them? Surely, you have lost even more than they have; well, I guess that's not true. Lysandra and Kore were musicians too," he asked.

"I don't know. I've been seeing all sorts of interesting things going on. I think that they are important somehow. Someone needs to know these, but I'm not exactly sure who," Isabella replied. "I do feel safer with you here, Leon, and all the long guns. Do you think that looters will come here? We've hardly anything of value, excepting for our instruments, which we'll never be able to play again." Just saying the words was all that it took. Grief swept over her and tears flowed once more. Likewise, Vasili and Natasha cried involuntarily, but so did Alexina, realizing again that also meant her sewing career.

Days passed excruciatingly slowly for the group, now constantly on the alert near all the downstairs windows. The men each had a pair of long guns beside them as they watched armed looters crawling around the street. Daily the situation grew worse as now they spotted men hauling off young women whom they were kidnaping. This gave all the younger women even more of a fright. Isabella made Leon promise to shoot them if they were in danger of being kidnaped and led off like some farm animal. He gave his word, but inwardly knew that he would die first; he could never shoot these young women, not ever.

After many fearful days, the looters moved on to other streets and theirs became quite once more. Hazarding a look outside for the first time in weeks, Isabella saw dozens of dead men and women lying where they had fallen, in the streets, on their steps, on their lawns. Again, she observed that somehow, the world was collapsing into her, she felt tiny and insignificant. Still, as the day progressed, the world moved ever so slowly back out away from her.

Xerxes got creative. He knew that fresh supplies would likely not be available for some time. Somehow, it was up to him to ensure that what they lasted until they could be certain more food could be obtained. Hence, he put all of his skills to use, preparing their meals. Soups became more watery, though with the extra dashes of herbs and spices, no one even noticed. Late December, Leon finally figured out what Xerxes was doing and on the quiet praised him for his culinary work. The chef wanted to know when more food could be had, but Leon had no idea either.

Then, one day everyone's feet began aching and Xerxes only made one meal that day, unable to stand and cook long enough. The next day, the men actually cheered, their feet had miraculously healed somehow. Isabella and the others did not share their elation, though. Yes, they could walk fine now, their feet were back to normal, but they were still just as hopelessly helpless as before.

To say that they were helpless at this point is not altogether accurate. It began with Isabella and Vasili, who began to see that somehow they could use their feet and the alien utensils to manage to feed themselves. That they could finally lift their own teacups to their lips did wonders to their morale. Quickly, Natasha and Alexina followed their lead. Olympia, Lysander, and Kore did not. Their emotional and physical situation had not changed at all, still behaving as if they were zombies.

The group was relieved to see the soldiers finally removing the dead from the streets. None was happier than Xerxes when finally they spotted farmers' wagons bringing in produce to markets. He and Leon headed off at once to replenish their meager supplies. Slowly, things improved food-wise, but little else improved. They did learn more news of what had happened. Somehow knowing that all of Demokritos had suffered the plague, that all women were still armless, did little to boost their morale.

As summer drifted into fall, Leon began to go out more often, searching for news and searching for a way to help get the quartet back to their homeland. Gangs now ruled the streets. Each demanded a toll to pass safely through their zones. Of course, if the soldiers were present, they slipped into the shadows. Leon wisely timed his trips to coincide with patrols of soldiers. While he learned all manner of news, he could find no way to get them safely out of Kefall, let alone out of Thrace and on a ship bound for Velona. Worse, word now came of the Church of Skulls and their evil ways in Axos, the capital of Thrace and a city through which they would have to travel to get to Patri. Yet even Patri was not safe, renegade soldiers and sailors had turned that into a pirate den. No Velona ship would ever dock there again. Leon had never felt so utterly frustrated in his life. Always, he had been able to find some way to achieve his goals, but in this, he felt defeated.

In April, he began hearing of the actions of the Kali Assassins, who had somehow reappeared right out of ancient history. Once more, these Kali were somehow rescuing women in dire need. Slowly, he began to wonder if this might be the answer. At last, he decided to act and posted a message, hoping that somehow one of these mysterious Kali Assassins would see it. Each day after posting it, he returned to see if there was an answer. Finally, someone had scribbled a few words: here noon Tuesday. That was tomorrow. He returned home excited, but decided not to get their hopes up and remained quiet about it. After all, it could all be some diabolical ruse, an attempt to kidnap more women.

He stood around the message board at noon. Men and soldiers were moving up and down the street, though barely a twentieth of the activity that used to be here before the plague — and no women were in sight. He had not seen a woman on the streets all this time, he noted. A thin man walked up to him, holding a book. Somehow, the man looked familiar. "Fine fall day. Looking for the Kali?"

"Yes, don't I know you? Haven't we met before," Leon answered. He glanced at the book in the man's hands and added, "Laos Bookstore. Don't you run the Laos Bookstore?"

"Why yes, I did. Herakles Laos. Store's gone now. Looters. Made a complete mess of it and now no one is interested in buying a book."

"Leonidas Stantinos," he held out his hand.

After shaking, Herakles said, "Walk with me." Leon did so. After a bit, he said, "So you have need of the Kali?"

"Yes, desperately!" Leon related the whole situation. "I have just got to find a way to get these people to someplace that is safe and then find some way to get them back to their homes in Velona. I owe it to them; after all, they came here at my request."

"There is a totally safe place where they can stay and even get a message to Velona. Perhaps they would like to contact their parents and husbands," Herakles suggested.

"Please, Herakles, how can I make this happen? I have money. I will do anything that the Kali want," Leon begged for the first time in his life. Afterwards, he realized that he actually was begging this man and he wondered why.

"Tonight at midnight a wagon will come to the boarding house. Be ready," Herakles said calmly. "We will meet later under better circumstances." He nodded and moved off down the street. Leon watched him go, too elated to move. He spotted another man slipping out of some shrubs, two long guns over his shoulder. Quickly this man nodded to Herakles and the two joined up, disappearing from sight rapidly. Leon headed home as rapidly as possible, though he still had to merge in with the soldiers, avoiding the gangs on the streets.

"Ladies, I've finally got good news for you. I've found a safe place for you and a way for you to communicate to your family back in Velona. I admit I have no idea how that communication is done, but there is a possibility of somehow getting you back to your Velona."

"Wow! That's the best news in months," Isabella replied. "When do we leave? Tell us about it."

Leon looked around. Ammon had gone out; Icaros was at work at the brass factory; Jonus was off at the farmer's market. Olympia, Lysandra, and Kore were in their rooms sitting in chairs doing nothing but staring off into space. The others gathered around the dining room table. Xerxes brought in the fresh pot of tea he'd just made and Leon explained. "The Kali Assassins have returned, helping out women in dire need. It's as if ancient history has come alive once more. I've just met with an acquaintance who is somehow involved with them. It is arranged. Tonight at midnight, the Kali will come here with a wagon and take us away to safety. He promised that you would be able to contact your parents and your husbands, Isabella, Vasili. I bet your husbands are absolutely frantic with worry." Both women flushed, but said nothing.

They chatted a bit longer, pushing Leon for more details. "Well, I am game," Aldo said. "Anything has to be better than being cooped up in this boarding house. Natasha, we are at last maybe getting a start on going home."

Alexina spoke up, "Leon, can I go with them? I want out of here too. From all that they've told me, Velona has to be a better place to live than here. I know that I'm useless and helpless, but at least I won't live in fear every darn day. Please, can I come?"

"Of course, Alexina, of course you can."

"Hey, how about me? I bet they could always use another chef in Velona. Can I come too or is it limited to only women?" Xerxes asked.

Leon scratched his head, "Well, I don't see why not, Xerxes. He didn't say that men were not welcome. After all, Aldo is going. Sure. Let's try it. We shouldn't say a word to the others. I don't like Ammon, Jonus, or Icaros. Agreed?" All agreed readily; none had any respect for those three, not any longer. "Well then, we ought to get packing before they get back. Alexina, I'll help you pack first, then I'll come help you both, Isabella, Vasili." Leon felt alive for the first time in months.

A half hour later, Leon knocked and entered the women's room. They had tried to pack some of their things, but mostly had failed. "I'm here, what needs to be packed besides your instruments? I know, but take them with you anyhow. I insist." He packed their musical instruments, stands, and sheet music for them.

"Well, I bet your husbands will be overjoyed to hear from you both," Leon said cheerfully. Both women flushed red and said nothing. Leon looked confused, "But your rings?"

At last, Isabella spoke up, "Yes, they are our wedding rings, Leon. *Our* wedding rings." She emphasized the word. Poor Leon simply did not catch on to her meaning. "Okay, Leon, Vasili is my husband and I, hers. All right? There, we admit it, but please don't say anything to the others."

"Well, I'll be! I never — wow. Okay, mum's the word. Congratulations, by the way."

"Why? For what?"

"For following your hearts," Leon replied honestly. Both women grinned; his reaction was not quite what they had expected. He then added, "Okay, if the Kali ask you about contacting your husbands, you can say that we just got word that your husbands died as a result of the plague. That ought to be very believable."

Both women moved close to him and planted a kiss on his cheeks. "Thanks, that's clever," Isabella whispered in his ear.

Xerxes served a fine meal and the evening hour passed as boring as it had been for months. The other three men soon took their women upstairs for bedding, leaving Xerxes to deal with the dishes. Leon and Aldo helped him out as usual. Then they retired for the night as well. Around eleven, Leon, Aldo, and Xerxes quietly began carrying the few bags down to the front door. Leon then stood guard on the porch while the other two escorted the women down. As midnight came, all seven stood quietly on the porch, hearts pounding with excitement and anticipation. As usual, Leon had his long guns at the ready. Even Xerxes held one, though Aldo refused. He had never shot one before and preferred to help the women, leaving any fighting the others.

Right on time, they spotted a wagon moving slowly towards them. Five black cloaked people walked along side, three carried long guns. As the wagon approached, one cloaked figure stepped forward and whispered, "All set? All of you are coming?" The voice startled all seven! It was a woman's voice! Beneath that dark cloak was a woman, just as helpless as they were, Isabella thought. Quickly the men began loading the wagon with the bags and then helped the women aboard, climbing in beside them last. The woman then spoke for the second time. "If we encounter trouble, do not fire your guns unless one of us asks you to do so. Sit back and relax. You are in the arms of the Kali now. Okay, so two of us don't have arms," she teased him. In the darkness, Leon thought that he saw a broad grin on the woman's face.

Slowly and quietly, the wagon moved on down the street. Leon had a million questions flashing through his mind. How long would this ride be? Where were they going? Instead, he helped cover the women with the blankets that he found in the wagon. It was fall now and the late night air was very chilly, especially since the women had no proper clothing. At last, he leaned back and watched the nighttime city pass by.

Suddenly, three men jumped out of the shadows, pointing long guns at the party. "Halt. What have we here?" one man said. As Leon and the others turned to look, their stomachs knotting in a rush of fear, the two women acted. In a flash, they whirled and unleashed their deadly kicks. Two of the men fell to the ground, their necks broken. The third man dropped his gun and raced off into the night. The other three men with long guns and dark cloaks had not moved an inch. One man nodded and their driver continued down the street.

"Did you see that?" Xerxes whispered.

"Yes, but I don't believe it," Leon whispered back.

"Those were the women, right?" whispered Isabella. Leon nodded affirmatively. Now he knew that the Kali Assassins were back in business, and he wondered where they had been for the last century plus.

An hour later the wagon pulled into an underground parking stable and headed up to a stone wall. Leon looked about totally confused. Surely, this was not a place of safety! One of the men pushed on the wall, and they heard a low grating sound. A black space opened up and the wagon entered. A bit later, the wagon stopped and they again heard the grating sound. Then the men began uncovering lanterns, and the seven saw that they were underground somewhere. Two men removed the cloaks from the women who walked over to the wagon as it began moving again.

"Hello, I am Kalypso and this is my dear friend, Leto. We are the leaders of the Kali II. You are now our guests here in our underground lair. It is very safe down here. You have lots of company. We've rescued close to a thousand now, mostly women and children, but some men, obviously. We have one of those LD radio sets and tomorrow you can talk with Bethany Angela of Velona. She can get word to your relatives. Oh yes, we'll give you each one of Bethany's Hints books. They will give you tons of help on how to do things for yourselves."

"We've sort of figured out how to feed ourselves," Isabella replied. "Thank you for rescuing us. How can we ever repay you?"

"Dunno on that one," Kalypso answered. "Just figure out how to get by pretty much on your own, that will be reward enough. We women are doomed if we do not learn new ways, that's for damn sure. The hints book will give you many clues, and many of the other women down here can help you as well. Honestly, we are doing surprisingly well."

"Ah, here you are at last!" Herakles stepped out of a side chamber as the wagon came to a stop. "Welcome, I see you've met my charming wife Kalypso?" Leon shook his hand once more, very surprised indeed. Surprise followed surprise, all very pleasant ones at that, as they saw their new living quarters and others like themselves who had been rescued.

Kalypso had followed my suggestion, though, and kept the highly traumatized women isolated from the main group and especially from contact with the men. Hence, they didn't meet this far larger group for some time. The next morning, Isabella and Aldo got to chat with me, hastily outlining their tragedy and begging for a way to return to Velona.

Isabella resolved something in her mind and spoke up, "Bethany. I have observed something that I think is vitally important somehow but I don't know who to tell it too. In case I can't ever get home again, can I at least tell it to you? Then if I don't make it, someone will have the information." I agreed and she related her observations.

"People start out in control of things; they issue commands and orders and just know that they will be followed. Later on, they start getting some back flash and balking and now they are not sure their orders will be carried out. They drop down into requesting cooperation from others to get them to carry out their orders or commands. If those get balked too much, they drop down into pleading to get the others to follow them. When that doesn't achieve the results, they drop down further and use all manner of force to get them to follow their orders. When even that doesn't work, they drop into asking and begging for sympathy, hoping the others will be sympathetic to their needs and help them. Finally, if that doesn't work, they give up and become zombie-like. That's what happened to three of our friends. They ended up zombies and are still that way, just sitting around staring at nothing all day long. This must be important somehow."

"Incredibly good observation," I pointed out, amazed at what the musician had seen.

"There's more. You know normally a person thinks of their world as being so big. If someone hits them with bad news, their world rather collapses inward on them; their attention shrinks inward. If good news comes, their world expands outward once more, their attention goes out toward the world. I think that is important too," Isabella added.

"Well of course, it is," Kalypso broke in. "As a fighter, we have to keep our attention far out there in the world around us. Bad things, bad news, attacks on us, all that tends to collapse our attention down towards ourselves or even smaller. A skilled fighter must not let that happen or you get hit. That's how Leto and I are so good at what we do. Hardly anything can drive our attention inward during a battle situation. That's an obvious point, Isabella."

"Thanks Isabella. Those are important and I will relay them to those who can use them," I replied.

Kalypso broke in, "Say Bethany, she has a point. That's exactly what we're seeing a whole lot down here now: zombie-state. Here in Kefall, above ground, that's primarily the way that most women are acting. It's as if they've totally given up. Women are accepting any awful situation, saying this is all that they are worthy of any more. It's a terrible state, Bethany. Plus, there is hardly any point in us trying to rescue them now. All they do is just sit here doing nothing at all for themselves. Should we start killing off all the men in Kefall now?"

Leon butted in, "Please don't, Kalypso. There are still a few of us out there who want to help." She grinned at him and shrugged her shoulders. After a bit more discussion, once more I promised to send some help to them as soon as possible. Now I had even more reasons to get someone to the Kali in Kefall.

The night of June 15, Kalypso, Leto, Linos, and four other men sat in a wagon, bundled up against the cold. At least it isn't snowing, Kalypso thought to herself. To get here to the edge of Kefall, they had had to bust through two gangs, which had placed roadblocks in an attempt to extort tolls for passing through their section of Kefall. Kalypso had no intention of paying them, and she and her party left a trail of dead hoodlums marking their passage. They waited. At last, she heard the creaking of wagons and hoof beats on the paved road. She and her group threw off their blankets and climbed out of the wagon, ready for action.

"If this is them, mind your manners, Leto, Kalypso. One of them is supposed to be the Monarch of Arolas," Linos whispered a cautionary note to his wife and friend.

"She'd better not be a wuss! I don't think I can take anymore those," Kalypso whispered back antagonistically. Soon they spotted ten riders with a trail of wagons disappearing down the dark street.

As the lead rider approached them he called out, "Cold is the night."

"Colder is the day," Kalypso answered the prearranged password. "The Kali here. Follow us, be prepared, we had to fight our way through several gang blockades to get to you. I suspect that they will be better prepared on our return trip."

"Let me notify Callisto," the man said and rode back to the lead wagon. He soon motioned for the Kali to drop back.

"Hi, I'm Callisto and this is my husband, Spyro. Our wagon is armed with three of the fancy rapid firing MG long guns. If you run into more resistance, please drop back and let us handle it."

"Kalypso here, leader of the Kali, my second, Leto and her husband, Linos. So you are the Monarch of Arolas?" she asked. It was too dark to see much of the woman. Kalypso desperately wanted to appraise her, but just could not see well enough to do so. Still, she didn't like outsiders giving her orders.

Sensing the woman's resistance, Callisto added, "Well met, Kalypso, Leto, Linos. Please let us handle any further trouble. You are far too valuable to risk on our behalf. Your people here in Kefall really need you."

Well, at least she has that right, Kalypso thought. There's certain to be trouble; guess we can sit back, and see just what these folks are made of, she concluded. "Okay, then, but we had to fight our way through two road blocks getting here. They will surely be re-enforced now." Linos signaled his driver who pulled their wagon in line behind Callisto's. Linos and his men rode on ahead with the ten scouts of Callisto's, while Leto and Kalypso walked along side Callisto's wagon.

"Want to ride with us?" asked Spyro.

"No, it's a death trap for us. We can't fight if we're in a wagon," Leto explained.

"That's quite true, Spyro," Callisto backed up Leto. "You can't execute lethal circle leg kicks if you are in a wagon. It's too damn hard for us to get out of the wagons easily, dear."

"Cool. I'm surrounded by spunky gals. Who could ask for more?" Spyro teased her. To Kalypso, he added, "You fight with your feet, and she fights with her spells. Nice combo." Kalypso and Leto didn't know what to make of this and so said nothing.

A half hour later, they turned a corner onto the main east road that led towards the Imperial Palace. Ahead the roadblock that they had smashed their way through had been rebuilt. A dozen lanterns illuminated the area. Many long guns were pointed their way and the riders halted immediately. "Damn, idiots rebuilt it. Well, looks like we have a bit more trouble to handle this time," Kalypso whispered.

"Leave them to me. I don't want any of us to get shot," Callisto whispered and began to concentrate.

"What's she doing?" whispered Kalypso. They should be taking defensive action at once, before the thugs started shooting. Precious time was being wasted.

"Watch," Spyro whispered back, and the six men in the wagon bed behind him uncovered their MG long guns and prepared them for a battle.

Suddenly a giant ball of fire exploded in the midst of the thugs with guns, who were hiding behind the wall of wagons. Then another exploded to the right of the first and then a third one billowed out blazing flames to the left. Men screamed, fleeing in all directions, their clothing a mass of flames. Seconds later, the street went dark once more, though here and there parts of the wagons were burning.

"What the devil?" exclaimed Kalypso.

"What just happened?" Leto gushed. Callisto's ten scouts moved ahead and began move two wagons out of the way, then gave a hand sign to move out.

"No one messes with my Callisto. She can also bring down lightning bolts and put men to sleep too," Spyro answered.

"Well, that ought to keep them from bothering us any further," Callisto added. "Like I said, leave them to me. Come on, let's get going, Spyro."

As they moved past the remains of burning dead men and bits of wagons, Kalypso whispered, "How did she do that?"

"Dunno," Leto whispered back. Six blocks further on, Callisto repeated her rain of fire, determined to not let any harm come to the Kali and to get her group safely underground before dawn came. An hour later, they entered the underground stables next to the Dance Hall.

"Wow, it is all coming back to me, Spyro! This is it — the eastern entrance to the Kali tunnel system. That wall ahead there, it moves aside. There's a stone push lever off to the right about three feet from the floor, where I can reach it with my foot! I've used this entrance dozens of times, usually riding in my carriage. I wonder what ever happened to that carriage?"

Leto looked at Kalypso; both were very impressed. Surely, this young teenager did know all about the Kali, though they had no real grasp of how she could know all this. "Yes, she's right. I'll open the secret door," Kalypso whispered and quickly moved ahead of the horsemen.

Spyro was very impressed with the secret door. "Super spunky!" he whispered.

"Keep going in a straight line. We'll uncover the lanterns once all the wagons are inside and the door shut. Take no chances," Kalypso whispered.

Minutes later, with the door to the world shut, the lanterns on, winter cloaks and coats off, and the introductions done, Callisto and Spyro sat in the small chamber that Kalypso had first discovered some eight months ago. Herakles provided hot tea and bread to the assembled group, consisting of the Basari Quartet group, Kalypso, Leto, Herakles, and Linos. Also, she had asked Melantha, Pandora, Kastor, and Cepheus to join them. While the hour was late, this arrival and meeting was the most important event in the last eight months, as far as the Kali were concerned.

"Are you really the Monarch of Arolas?" asked Melantha.

"Yes, Ana and I are co-monarchs right now. She's a year older and a bit more skillful at organizing things, while I am a bit more of a fighter," Callisto admitted.

"A bit, dear?" Spyro nearly choked on his tea. She flashed him a grin.

"Is it really as bad as here? All over the world, I mean?" asked Isabella. While they heard reports, here was someone from the outside world. She put more stock in direct observations than what others merely said.

"Let me tell you a story," Callisto launched into a detailed account, though much was not firsthand knowledge, but what she had learned from me. Sometime later, she wrapped it up, "So Velona and many of the northern countries are doing very well, all things considered. The two key problem areas are Demokritos and Tashien. Ana and I have gotten Arolas back on track to a possible recovery. Monarchs Sophia and Amynta are doing the same in Thallyus and Penelopus. I am afraid that at this time, Alia, Theos, Phindos, and Thrace are pretty much lost causes. Anarchy is running rampant in these countries, the conditions are deplorable."

"So it isn't going to get much better here anytime soon, then is it?" Kalypso asked what she had been fearing for months now.

"I wish I could paint a better picture for you all here in Kefall, but I'd be lying if I did. Give us time in Arolas, Thallyus, and Penelopus, and things will be vastly better for everyone, not just we women. Bethany's MMCE will work miracles, if given enough time to be fully implemented. After all, Dorota was once thriving and prosperous. Women there didn't know that they were ever supposed to have arms."

"Yes, but they also didn't have any arts, no music either," Isabella pointed out, caustically.

"Right, very true, but then they didn't have all these new inventions which enable us to do things more rapidly and have the free time to explore the arts. Now I could tell you all kinds of stories about the old Laird foundation up in Velona, but that's ancient history now," Callisto replied.

Cocking her head to one side, Vasili looked at Callisto and asked, "But Velona has a thing called therapy, don't they? Won't that somehow help us? Isabella and me? And all the rest of us?"

She hadn't mentioned this and was a little surprised by the question. "Yes, now that you mention it, yes. The problem is finding enough people who know how to do it. Always before, why they had enough to handle the occasional trauma victims, but now, jeesh, everyone needs it, not just us women, though we need it far more than our men do. I know that Bethany and Eve are working on some way to get us all the therapy that we need. Still, I surely don't know how they are going to manage that. In Arolas, Ana and I have a small group of women in Andros who are just now getting started on delivering therapy sessions to the women there. Ana and I are pledged to see that all the women in Arolas get the therapy that they need. I'm surprised that you have heard about this, Vasili."

"I don't know how I know, but I know," Vasili replied timidly.

"Well, therapy isn't going to get us our arms back, so what good is it really? So that we feel better? Ha! We're still doomed," Kalypso countered.

"She's right, you know, Vasili, Natasha, and I will never be able to make music again, so what's the point?" Isabella added her sarcastic feelings to the mix.

Callisto decided to change the topic. "Well, we've brought along a lot of supplies for you, ammunition, guns, food, blankets, and a spare LD radio. We've got two dozen wagons and figure that we can take at least three hundred fifty back with us, without having to acquire more wagons."

"I guess the question for us is do we go with you or do we stay here?" Kalypso replied. "Well, let's sleep on it. I'm very tired. We've fixed up bedding here for all of you. We have the others on down in two of the larger chambers; the highly traumatized women are being kept separate from the rest of us. They seem to get worse when our men are around them."

The next morning, Raffaella Ines appeared, standing beside Callisto. "Wake up, dear. I'm here. Please tell the others that I came along with you and was asleep in the wagons." Callisto struggled to sit up, waking Spyro.

"Whoa, who's this?" he asked rubbing the sleep from his eyes, wishing that he could have slept in this morning. Well, if they turned off the lanterns, it would be dark and he could go back to sleep. Callisto introduced her and repeated the fib that they were to tell.

"Spunkier and spunkier!" he replied, helping Callisto into her modified man's shirt and pants.

"What are you doing here?" Callisto asked.

"Field research for Macario. Still, what I do depends upon the other's decisions. Say nothing about me until I volunteer, okay?" They agreed and headed into the side chamber to rouse the others and figure out how to fix something to eat.

Melantha was waiting for them. Cepheus had already fixed breakfast for the bunch. She and Pandora were sitting on the stone bench, while Midas was still carrying trays to the stone table. "Hi, we're all packed, we have our own wagon," Melantha volunteered to Callisto as she and Spyro walked in. They introduced Raffaella and dove into the pancakes and eggs with a relish.

"How did you ever get eggs?" Spyro inquired.

"Kalypso and Herakles do all right at the markets," Melantha replied. "When I get to Velona, will they really let me have my own chemistry lab? Do all the experiments I want to do?"

"You bet. Probably they will have it all arranged and waiting for you, Melantha," Callisto encouraged her.

"Mel, just Mel," she asked.

"Just Pan here too," Pandora added.

After they ate, Herakles joined them, asking them to come with him to the first large chamber quarters where hundreds of the Kali now dwelled. Although it was a half mile, they decided to walk it, stretching their legs after spending the last two weeks cooped up in the wagons.

As they arrived, they spotted a wagon with the bags of the Basari Quartet folks, who were waiting patiently to leave. Callisto and Spyro entered, while Raffaella hung back behind them, observing the many people gathered here.

Kalypso spoke first, "Callisto, we are most grateful for the supplies and help. Leto, Linos, Herakles and I have decided that we want to stay here. Somehow, we four want to be around in case we can really help others. If we just abandon Kefall, others who may need the Kali will be badly disappointed. We feel responsible for our people. I hope you understand. If things get too bad, we'll make our own way to Arolas. We promise."

"Admirable of you four. I fully back your decision. We find it hard to desert our fellows in their times of need," Callisto replied.

Clearing his throat, Leon spoke up, "Alexina, Xerxes, and I will go with you, but with your permission, we'd like to settle somewhere in your country. There, we are going to see what help we can assemble and put together to help our people here in Kefall and Thrace. If we can get ourselves access to one of those LD radios, then we can keep Kalypso up to date and coordinate our efforts. Somehow, we have to set things to rights here. I'm sorry, Isabella, we had planned to go with you to Velona, but we three feel we just have to find ways to help here. We are not fighters, but I will be more useful trying to arrange help and aid from Arolas and perhaps even Thallyus and Penelopus. I hope you will not be terribly disappointed with us, Isabella."

"I understand, Leon. We just cannot begin to thank you enough for all that you have done for us," she replied, giving him a kiss on his cheek.

Kalypso retook control of the discussion. "Our problem is figuring out who to send along with you. I would like to send three hundred of those who are doing rather well. There are a fair number of children with them. Living underground is no way for children to grow up. We debated long last night. We'd love to send the five hundred traumatized zombie women with you, because they are a real burden on the rest of us. However, we feel that we owe the ones who are doing better to have a chance at a life."

"That's fine with me," Callisto replied. Raffaella moved up to her side. "Oh, this is Raffaella from the Church of God, one of the very able therapy givers; she came along with us."

"Hello, I came to see what I can do with your traumatized women. I will stay as long as I can to help get them back to battery. First, however, I will be giving you and Leto therapy sessions and then your other women who are staying and are doing well. Once I have all of you helped, then I will be tackling the zombie women. Somehow, I need to find a way to bring them back from the depths to which they have sunk."

They chatted a bit longer, while those who were going began carrying their few things to the many wagons. Meanwhile, Callisto's memories of her lifetime here in these very tunnels continued to flash by her and she got an idea. "Kalypso, will you come with me? We'll be gone at least an hour. Can we ride a couple of horses? It's a ways that I want to go."

"I can't ride a horse. Perhaps a wagon?" she answered rather annoyed with a suggestion, which she found impossible.

"Oh sure you can. Spyro, go saddle up some horses," she ordered.

"I'll come with you, dear. If you can sit, I can lead your horse," Herakles suggested.

A half hour later, Spyro had four horses ready, having tied the reins together on two of them. Callisto demonstrated how it was done, but accepted Spyro's help getting mounted. Not to be shown up, Kalypso had Herakles help her up, and she bit down onto the reins, emulating Callisto. "Okay, here we go," Callisto said between clenched teeth. Spyro and Heracles held up lanterns and they were off.

Spyro was amazed; his wife seemed to know just where she was going, down one tunnel, taking side tunnels here and there. At last, she pulled back on her reins and stopped. "Okay, the steps are still here. Spyro, help me down please. I can do it, Kalypso, but it is such a pain, so damnably awkward." While Herakles was left holding the reins of their mounts, Callisto headed up the steps. Spyro carried a lantern for the three.

"Here we are. These steps used to lead up to the mansion that I used to live in when I was head of the Kali. I'd slip down these stairs when I needed to become Kali once more. I left something here, though I don't know if it is still here. See this stone here." She pushed it with her foot. A grating sound echoed in the stairwell, revealing a secret compartment.

"By golly, they are still here. Spyro, that bag, careful with it. I suspect it has rotten badly." He reached in, and sure enough, the leather disintegrated in his fingers, revealing sparkling stones.

"Wow, gemstones, lots of them," he exclaimed. While he pulled the stones out and began making a pile of them on the floor, Callisto explained.

"I left this stash here in case I ever needed to make a fast getaway. Never did and they are still here. Kalypso, I am giving these to you to help you finance your Kali," she said.

"Wow, this is a fortune!" Spyro added, having gotten the last one out and staring at thirty gems.

"Yes, probably around a hundred thousand gold worth."

"Thank you! Incredible! We can certainly use this! Are you sure? Don't you need them yourself?"

"No, I have all the funds I need. Besides, consider this a gift from the ancient Kali to the modern Kali," she grinned. Kalypso beamed and tried to hug her. Callisto lifted her leg up and pulled her close, showing her how they could now hug.

"I don't know how to thank you. Besides the gift, you've shown me that I can ride by myself. Maybe we women are not as helpless as we think."

"Yes, that's the idea. We really aren't. It's just like Bethany says, we have to find different ways to do things."

The four returned to find that the group had the wagons loaded and were ready to leave. As they were finalizing their plans, Raffaella took Callisto aside. "Bethany has asked me to give you an order from her."

"What? Bethany's giving me orders now?" Callisto faked a hurting tease. "Sure what's she want done?"

"She wants you to give the three musicians therapy sessions as soon as feasible, especially Isabella and Vasili. She has some kind of intuition that this might be significant, though she hasn't said just what."

"Okay will do. Maybe while we are riding along once we get to the safety of Arolas," Callisto agreed. She hugged Raffaella and joined Spyro on her wagon. Right behind them came the musicians and then Melantha's group in their wagon.

As before, Kalypso and her group escorted them through the streets of Kefall until they reached the open road. Spyro was surprised to discover that it was probably ten at night when they exited the tunnel and rolled out of the parking stables. It was also snowing heavily. While that kept the gang members inside and they had no nasty encounters leaving Kefall, it forced the Kali constantly to hide their tracks in the snow.

On July 5, they rolled into the Nasses estate in Naxos, the temporary seat of the government of Arolas. For the first time in nine months, Leon felt relaxed and in familiar territory. Being a wealthy nobleman and living here with the extended family of Mathias Nasses, he fit right in and began to explore the many projects, which needed financing. Before long, he and Mathias became close friends.

Xerxes, constantly complaining about the quality of the meals being served, was given a chance to cook dinner at Ana's insistence. One meal later, Ana begged him to become the Royal Chef of the Monarchy, an offer he could not refuse!

Also, once Leon saw that things were really vastly better here, asked Ana to marry Alexina and himself. The two had fallen for each other, and Leon insisted that they marry, though Alexina still felt that she was unworthy of him. She too needed therapy, Ana observed.

After getting everyone settled, Ana and Callisto began to give Vasili and Isabella therapy sessions, honoring my request. They began their parallel sessions just after lunch and both ended around three hours later and with similar results.

Both women came out of the rooms laughing wildly. Vasili had just discovered that she had been Lia Ines Amir, while Isabella discovered that she had been Taliesin Amir, the famous bard. Lia had been armless back then and yet had been a fabulous singer and dancer. The two were madly in love that whole lifetime. So much of their lives this lifetime suddenly made sense to them. The day that they had met, both were instantly totally in love with each other, despite both having female bodies. Now they knew why they were always so close, each knowing what the other was thinking and feeling. So much of their lives made sense to them now. They laughed and laughed as all manner of little confusions, embarrassments, and humiliations by others blew off them. Even more interesting, they no longer had to keep their marriage a secret from others. Over the large group who now dined together, the two explained that they were lovers and were married. Now they had nothing to hide, nothing haunting them, unseen in the backs of their minds.

"You can thank Bethany, Isabella. She literally ordered us to give you two therapy sessions," Callisto said as they ate.

Isabella cocked her head curious, "Just who is this Bethany Bartiana Angela anyway?"

Callisto explained, and then she and Ana suddenly realized the significance. "Oh my god! Isabella or Taliesin, Bethany, she was your father, Ket Bethany! She's often wondered what all happened to you two. She just got that letter that Vasili or Lia and Fianna wrote to Bethany. They've gone off to explore the Standing Stones there in the Highlands of Ruadan. It took a couple of centuries for that message to get to her."

"My dad! Well, I'll be! All these memories are coming back to me now, a flood of them, Vasili. How about you?" Isabella asked.

"Swimming in them. Gosh, two centuries? Yes, I remember it now. Weird thing happened there. I wonder what she found there?" Vasili asked.

"Well, next time we chat on the LD radio, we can ask her," Ana replied. "Right now, I think that she and her friends are on their way there to explore that mystery. We are not to contact them unless it is an emergency. Meantime, tomorrow we should get Natasha handled and then get you on your way to Andros. We've got caravels coming from and going to Velona frequently now," Ana added. "You should be back in Velona by November at the latest."

That night as Isabella and Vasili retired to their bedroom, their passion and love for each other reached a new height. Isabella whispered, "Well, my love, this time neither of us has arms or hands."

Vasili replied, "Nope, but we do have these monster boobs. Make do with what we have, dear." Soon their passions exploded, their love, their special bond had transcended the centuries.

Chapter 33 Raffaella and Eve Take Action

After Callisto and her band left Kefall, Raffaella went to Chamber 23 as it was known. Here she found the severely traumatized women that the Kali II had rescued. This group of women unfortunately did not recover, according to Kalypso and were being isolated from the many others who formed this underground community. According to Kalypso's count, there were five hundred three such women. Obviously, these were now becoming a terrible burden on the others who had to tend to their every need as well as their own.

Although Raffaella did not speak of this to the others, Macario and she had discussed this at length before she came. Why? Their existing therapy, the so called Holy Gift, did not work on people who were so badly traumatized. If the person was unable to return to the time of the trauma and recount what had happened to them, the trauma could not be erased. Macario and Raffaella had predicted that they would have severe problems with two very different types of patients: the zombies as here in Chamber 23 and those who were constantly committing crimes against women and humanity as a whole. Thus, Raffaella's goal was two-fold: study these zombie cases, and see if she could work out a handling of them so that they too could be salvaged somehow.

As she walked slowly among the women, she observed their state. Zombie-like was an accurate description. They sat or laid, generally motionless, staring into space. They ate only if food was inserted into their mouths, drank only when water was poured into their mouths. They were well below a general apathy but not yet actually dying. It was almost as if they were useless in all ways. "Well, Kalypso, I guess it is time that I see what I can do. I'll take this one here; they appear all the same."

"Her name we believe is Io. Good luck with her. I'll leave you to it then. Holler if you need something and one of our group will come," Kalypso replied. She shook her head, thinking that honestly there was nothing that could be done for them. Perhaps death would be a blessing for them.

Raffaella sat down beside the woman on her bed. She wore the typical makeshift clothing that they all wore down here, a discarded man's shirt and ill-fitting men's pants. Because these women didn't even let anyone know when they needed to go to the bathroom and just went in their clothes where they sat or lay, Kalypso had ordered them all to be put in diapers, as if they were babies. This helped the caretakers a great deal. Io smelled; she was in need of a bath. She had blue eyes and long blonde hair that was in need of a good washing and de-tangling. Gently, Raffaella adjusted her perception band and zeroed in on the woman's mind. If nothing else, she wanted to see what the woman was seeing in her mind, thinking about if anything, or feeling.

She was appalled when she finally realized what was happening with Io. She was totally in the past, staring at some horrible traumatic incident, but not really seeing it. She was encased in a grey-black mass, hundreds of traumatic incidents spanning centuries were all piled up into one enormous mass, the many colors merging into a grey-black smudge. The woman was simply psychotic now. Her thoughts were unbelievably slow. For example, if she were saying a sentence, the woman was going at the rate of a word every minute of time. Io had virtually no attention on the present world around her. Perhaps Macario was right; better let them die and pick them up in their next lifetimes.

No, wait, she thought. The woman did have some tiny amount of attention on the present. Raffaella noted that she was sitting almost in the exact same position as Io and Io was now beginning to notice her. Raffaella had an idea. Take what you find and build upon it. She continued to sit motionless. After several minutes, Io turned her head towards Raffaella, who decided to mimic Io, turning her head to face Io. She noticed now that Io had a wee bit more attention on her. Io blinked, Raffaella blinked. Io's right shoulder made a funny twitching movement, so she duplicated the motion as best she could.

After twenty minutes, Io's motions became larger, and Io finally spoke, "What?" Raffaella noticed now that Io had even more attention coming out of the massive mental blackish mass and on to her. Somehow, she had to get more of Io's attention into the present time, and she had an idea.

"Feel the floor with your feet," she commanded. After giving Io some time to do so, she thanked her for doing so and repeated the command. After five minutes, Io became even more responsive and even began replying that she had done so. She continued with that same command repeatedly. A half hour later, Io brightened up noticeably.

"There is a floor there," Io said, as if she had never seen it before.

"Very good, Io. Now look at the wall," Raffaella changed to the sight sense, but quickly saw that was not working. "Touch the wall," she modified her command, helping Io to rise and move a foot to the wall. Io leaned into it, her large breasts pushing hard into it. Raffaella continued with the touch sense, and in a few minutes, Io became even more alert; more of her attention was here in the present. Now she changed to the opposite wall and had Io move over to it, repeating her touch command. An hour later, she had Io moving around the room, albeit slowly, touching walls and stone benches and chairs and tables with her bosom, hips, or legs.

Finally, Io volunteered, "There is a room here isn't there? Who are you? Do I know you?"

"Yes, there is a room here. I am Raffaella. I've just met you today. Now then, let's sit down. Good. I want you to see if you can remember a time when you were really, really happy." This was pay dirt, Raffaella thought. If I can get her to remember something that is pleasurable, then maybe after enough of that, we really could get the Basic Therapy to work on her.

It took Io nearly five minutes to recall eating a chocolate pie when she was a little girl. After thanking her for remembering it, she asked for another time when she was really, really happy. After an hour, all sorts of pleasurable times came back to Io, and she was now smiling, hungry, and in dire need of going to the bathroom.

After making sure Io's needs were met and that she was well fed, Raffaella gently moved over into the basic trauma therapy. The constant raping and torturing she endured at the hands of the men was right there, the most recent thing that had happened and which had ultimately been the straw that broke the donkey's back, so to speak. She'd had her psychotic break at that time. When dinnertime came, she ended the session, just as Kalypso returned with many others to feed and care for these women.

"Wow! It's a miracle! Io's awake and rather alert!" she exclaimed totally shocked at the difference between Io in the morning and Io here at suppertime. Io even flashed her a smile and said thank you as Raffaella helped feed her. Once fed, Io fell asleep, exhausted.

Back in the next chamber, Raffaella talked with Kalypso. "Well, I have had a major breakthrough. I believe that we can salvage all these women, but it is going to take a huge effort on our part."

"What must we do?" Kalypso asked. Raffaella pondered the question for some time. If she had hundreds of therapy givers — but she had none, only herself. She looked up at Kalypso, looked into her eyes.

"You would like to really help these women, don't you?"

"Yes, why else would we have risked our lives rescuing them?" Kalypso thought that a silly question.

"Okay, let me address all of your people, tonight yet." A half hour later, Raffaella stood before some six hundred men and women.

"Today, I have brought one of the zombie-like women out of her trance. While there remains days of more work to be done with her to get her back to battery, she is at least no longer a zombie. Actually, zombie is a poor choice of words. These women have suffered a psychotic break. They are insane, stuck almost wholly in past traumas that they have had happen to them. It is like all that pain, fear, and loss is piled into one giant mass in their minds, absorbing nearly all their attention and awareness. Thus, to us, they seem to be zombies. But they can be brought back into life again, just as I did today with Io."

Many cheered and the men clapped. "The problem is that I can't do this alone. I spent all day and have barely gotten one woman back into the land of the living at least partially. I need probably several more weeks to get her fully handled. At this rate, I'll be at it for years, and you will be burdened with their care at least that long. So I am asking all of you for your help. Tomorrow, I will show all of you women what must be done and how to do it. There are about four hundred of you women here. If we women do this starting tomorrow, then in a day or so, these women will have been pulled up to at least where Io is at tonight. Of course, your few men will have to deal with absolutely everything else, cooking and such. We all will get a work out, but we can salvage these women."

"Once we have them recovered sufficiently to start caring for some of their own needs, I will teach you all how to deliver the therapy sessions, which will actually erase all such trauma. As a reward, I will see that each one of you, both men and women get your own traumas handled, and then we all can fully handle these women. What say you? Are you willing to give it a try?"

It was unanimous. They were fed up with the incredible workload and burden of caring for these women. They were willing to try anything to get them recovered. Hence, the next morning, Raffaella began outlining what needed to be done, keeping it simple. Mimic whatever the person was doing until they got the woman's attention. Then have the woman touch the floor. Once they really perceived the floor, then have them move around the chamber touching other things, never leaving a specific object until the woman actually had really, really felt it. Finally, when they actually had the woman talking and brightened up, ask them to remember a time when they were extremely happy, repeating that until the woman was very bright, at least comparatively.

Off the four hundred women went, first thing after breakfast and feeding these women. Raffaella moved about the chamber offering advice and encouragement where needed. Around noon, the hundred men along with some fifty boys brought in trays of lunch and helped feed everyone. When they returned with dinner, the results were most encouraging. At least two hundred of the women were now talking with those who were feeding them and even helping with the handling of their bodily needs. The remainder was in far better shape than they had been in the morning.

The second evening, all five hundred plus women were at last talking with their care givers and back in the land of the living. Thus, the next morning, Raffaella began instructing the volunteer therapy givers on just how to do it. After lunch, she turned them loose on the first three hundred and began circulating among the many sessions, doing her best to monitor all them at once. Raffaella was a very capable being and actually managed to span her attention across all three hundred sessions at one time, a feat that she later reported to Macario, who was quite impressed with her ability to do so.

Six weeks after she arrived, the last session was finished with the expected laughter that accompanied the full erasure of the chain of traumatic incidents. Every man, woman, and child had their basic plague-caused or related trauma fully handled. The life and vitality of each had been restored in spades. Naturally, this group of nearly a thousand now viewed Raffaella as a goddess. From her viewpoint, she now had about eight hundred who were fully capable of taking a psychotic person and restoring life to them, an amazing feat, which Eve fully noted on her ever-growing pile of sticky-notes on her world map.

However, during July, via Kalypso, we learned that the Bishop-Prelate Charon of the Church of Skulls in Axos and his band of assassins and thieves were now threatening Kefall. Emissaries had reached the western edge of the city, threatening all manner of madness unless their demands for gold and skulls were met.

"Look, we simply have to do something about that madman and his men before it is way too late, if it isn't already," Eve declared. "Can't we use that explosive of Melantha's and blow that damnable church to smithereens?"

"What about all the art works in the church? And the gold. Such really ought to belong to the survivors of Thrace and Axos," I suggested. "Besides, Eve, there is just no way that we can reach Axos overland. Look at the immense difficulties just getting to Kefall."

Macario replied, "We must consider what is going to do the greatest good, the greatest benefit for all the people of Thrace. I agree, these men have to be stopped before they completely destroy what little is left of Thrace."

"We could go wring necks," Eve suggested her usual solution. "Get all of us together like our raid on the mantises and go wipe them out."

"We could do that perhaps," Macario answered thoughtfully. "However, there is this to consider. Those beings would then go get another baby body. There is no guarantee that they would not just continue their criminal ways in their next lifetime. If possible, I would like to get to them this lifetime, only we need a way to get them to desist in their harmful ways. I have an idea. Let's continue this later on. I need to see someone." He left Eve and me in rather a mystery and said no more before vanishing.

"One day, I want to be able to do that!" Eve declared. "He did say that I was close to being able to do it, you know, create bodies at will. I wonder who he is going to see?" We speculated on this for a while, but had no actual plausible person in mind.

In a cavern beneath the standing stones in the Highlands of Ruadan, Cymry, Macario appeared. *Partholan?*

Yes, Macario, I am here. Has Dalny been found?

Not yet, but we are most hopeful that she will be found in time. Our plan is beginning to work.

That is good to hear. I took your advice and have been monitoring my animals. You and your beings are right; this sudden loss of their upper appendages on the adult females is catastrophic. I bear the suffering of my female animals. When we created them, there was no such pain and suffering. The mantis beings have inflicted this incredible evil upon our animals. Yet, the very young ones are doing well, just as the young did when we created them. I am becoming hesitant about re-inflicting such pain and trauma upon our female animals again.

I understand, Partholan. Perhaps we do not need to give the females back their arms as we had thought. Our plan appears to be working better than I had ever hoped. Let us table that decision about the female's arms for a while. Allow us to continue our work. We can re-evaluate the progress later on.

Thank you. I am most willing to wait to avoid inflicting such pain upon my creations.

Yet, Partholan, we have a most serious situation which is threatening both of our plans. Down on the southern continent, on the western portion, in a city called Axos in a country called Thrace, many of the spiritual beings occupying your male animals are destroying the other female animals and the lives of nearly all of your animals who live there. We call them thieves and assassins.

For quite some time, Macario described the situation down in Axos. *We are seeking a handling of these at this time. Some have suggested the destruction of these male animals, but you and I know that this is merely forcing them out of the male animal bodies, while killing your creations. It does nothing about those spiritual beings who are perpetrating their evil upon so many of your other creations. We do not have the means to go there with other of your animals and somehow contain them, preventing them from committing further evil acts.*

Ah, so you have come to ask their creator for help, he picked up Macario's purpose instantly.

Yes.

I have seen some of those of whom you speak. Your spiritual beings there are below their own deaths. They have lost all trace of their own selves and believe that they are my male animals. Yet, they insist on punishing other animals and controlling them. Macario, I can go two ways on this. I can give them a push further downwards and convince them that their identity is now that of a single cell in the animal's body. With such a tiny sphere of operation and influence, they will remain completely and forever harmless, forgotten to the entire universe. Or, I can alter their animal bodies in a way that they will find it impossible to continue perpetrating their evil on my other animals there. Which would you prefer? I prefer the first, for they are not deserving of salvation, but of being damned to spent the rest of eternity controlling and operating a singly, microscopic cell.

Let's go with the second choice. After all, they are our responsibility. I would like a chance at salvaging them as well. If I cannot, then you may have them.

It will be as you wish. After a slight pause, he added, *There, it has been postulated.*

Down in Axos, there was no massive explosion, no visible destruction, no sudden deaths, and no bodies suddenly vanishing. All of those actions required the use of physical universe energy in one form or another. Partholan merely postulated the desired effect and it occurred, because he was once more able to make his postulates stick. His decisions now altered the physical universe as they once had, specifically here on Tarra.

Macario reappeared in our home. "Well, I just wanted to let you both know that the situation in Axos, Thrace, has been handled by Partholan and me. Expect no further trouble from those assassins and thieves."

"Partholan? Wow! great. What did you two do to them? Blow them up? Wipe them off the face of Tarra?" Eve asked eagerly.

"He has handled them in a way that may make it possible for us to one day salvage even those criminals there, Eve. Blowing them up is not the best way. I think Partholan has a much better notion of justice than instant body death. Besides, he is loathed to harm his animal bodies. After all, your bodies are his creations," Macario answered her.

He left and Eve and I were still in a mystery about just what they had done. I could see his point. The evil actions were not caused by the male animals, that is, our human bodies, but by the degraded spiritual beings who were currently residing inside those body's heads. Why punish the animal for something the being was doing? Still, I longed to know what the result was. I passed along the information that the Axos Church of Skulls situation was handled, but of course could not give them any concrete facts.

Fifty year old Urias Zoraster II paced his study trying to work out a solution to the latest crisis. BP, that is Before Plague the term that they now used to refer to their lives before the chaos came, he had been a wealthy capitalist of Axos. His father, Urias Senior, had made a fortune in business and had bestowed his vast experience and wealth upon his two sons, Urias and Phil, and had helped his daughter Alekto's husband, Aison Gidios, who was also the son of a wealthy nobleman of Axos, do well himself. Phil had taken control of the Zoraster Industries over in Patri, while Urias remained here in Axos where he had been looking after his parents. The elderly Urias Senior and his mother did not survive the chaos of the first two months of spring.

The Zoraster estate and huge manor house was located in the heart of Axos, a mile from the Royal Palace, surrounded by many others of the wealthiest of Axos. He, like his father, held to no religion, certainly not this new Jehosanity, which had so swept through Axos and Thrace. He saw their church leaders as merely competing capitalists, out to control as much as possible, and make as much money as possible.

His wife Iris was forty-nine with gorgeous blonde hair, which Urias loved to draped over himself when they were being romantic, which was even more often AP (After Plague). Living here in the huge manor house were their married children and their grandchildren. They had three sons, but no daughters. Xenocrates was now thirty, Ikaros was twenty-nine, while Damon, their youngest just turned twenty-eight. Their respective wives were Korinna, Diona, and Doris. Between them, the three had seven children ranging in age from nine year old Loukas to the five year olds, Demetra and Jude.

When his sister Alekto Zoraster, forty-eight, had married Aison Gidios, forty-nine, Urias Senior had insisted that they make this huge manor their home. There was plenty of space to go around, he'd said. If the truth were told, Urias Senior wanted to keep his only daughter close to him. The Gidios clan was one of his business rivals. Alekto had a son and daughter. Alexio, twenty-eight, was now married to Deila and they had two children, six and five. Alekto's daughter was Andromache, who was now twenty-five, with rich, long brown hair. Unfortunately, from Alekto and Aison's point of view anyway, Andromache was something of a rogue and had taken as her partner Dianthe Metra, twenty-four with long, silky black hair. While officially the two women were not technically married, they acted as though they were, having lived together for the last eight years. The two owned A & D Ball Gowns, a small company that made only the finest in ball gowns. They were the principal designers and seamstresses of their company.

Urias continued to pace his study as he had so often, since the plague struck without warning. He could not help reflect back on his many decisions, which had kept his extended family and many others alive for the past nine months, against all odds. Like his father, he was something of a pack rat. All manner of things filled their huge basement. When the plague struck and fresh food supplies became almost impossible to get for two months, they were able to live off the huge stockpile that he and his father had stowed away for some rainy day. True, towards the end of those months, they got very tired of the same things for breakfast, lunch, and dinner, but they had food, where so many others had not.

When the plague struck, his parents dropped into apathy and Urias Junior took control of the extended family, making all the key decisions. BP, his three sons were constantly arguing with him over nearly everything, claiming the old man was behind the times, was incredibly dumb and narrowminded. Well, AP, his sons now considered him an absolute genius! He smiled as he recalled the three of them heaping praise on him several months ago. His first action had been to identify correctly what was happening that first day when all the women woke to find themselves armless and the men unable to walk. He'd remembered reading some book about the plague that struck way up in the northern hemisphere somewhere. It had taken some doing on his part to retrieve the book stuck near the top of his floor to ceiling bookshelves. That little book, Bethany's Hints, had now been read cover to cover, its binding was broken, and many pages were loose.

Additionally, because of the book, which he had to read to most of those in this manor house because they didn't read Velona dialect, the women began to see how they could make use of all the strange items almost that very day. Nine months later, the many women around the mansion were doing far better than just about any other woman in Axos.

When the plague started, his sons insisted that General Agamemnon, who controlled the twenty legions stationed in and around Axos, would be providing for their security as well as the king's. A week later, they heard that the palace had been sacked and the entire ruling family slain. Shortly after that, they heard that General Agamemnon had disbanded the twenty legions, sending the men home to care for their own families and had then shot himself in the head.

Next, his sons insisted that the Emperor would send his Imperial Legions down from Kefall any day to restore law and order. They never came, and in January, they heard that there was no Imperial Army any longer and no emperor either. This news crushed his sons and now they believed their father was an absolute genius.

When the looting began, Urias realized that these wealthier neighborhoods would be prime targets. Consequently, he sent his sons to all their neighbors, arranging a block-defense group. When the looters began to appear, they found this whole area armed to the teeth and fighting as a unit. For months, this single block had been left alone, while so many others were sacked.

AP many of their friends and associates decided to abandon Axos, moving out into outlying towns, villages, and even some farms, where they had relatives. His sons reported that many of those attempting to flee had been attacked, robbed, and many were killed, their younger women kidnaped.

When the looting began, Urias and his sons made a secret night trip to one of his warehouses, bringing back a wagon load of guns and ammunition. Later, he doled some out to their block neighbors for their block defense.

He also knew that obtaining fresh drinking water would be a crucial need. Hence, he had his three sons help him build a massive rainwater collection system. Always now, they had a dozen large barrels of drinking water available.

Slowly, the Church of Skulls began taking over total control of the city. Often the thieves and assassins went door to door, demanding to see all the younger women who lived there. The prettier ones they simply kidnaped and the women became their chattel. Until now, their strong block defense had kept these wicked men away.

Still, they had to deal with them. The only active business in all Axos for the last seven months was that of the farmers markets. Daily, outlying farmers brought in supplies. The sale of which was watched over by the thieves of the Church of Skulls. Rather than harass the farmers, they chose to deal with those buying food. Either each person gave a portion of what they had just bought or they gave gold coins and gems to the Church of Skulls representatives.

The Banca del Dio did not reopen AP. The bank manager knew that without outside deliveries, the bank would soon run out of coins, which its customers would surely be demanding from their accounts. Also, even if they did open, the Church of Skulls would be waiting to rob those who made withdrawals as they left the Banca.

By August 1, hardly anyone had any coins or gems left to purchase food, and a barter system had sprung up in the absence of money. Of course, the Church of Skulls was delighted when citizens began trading long guns for food. Bit by bit, Urias watched his neighbors becoming more and more desperate, selling their guns for food during July.

Fleeing the city now was impossible, although many of their neighbors tried it. His sons often reported finding their wagons looted, and the men and boys killed, the women nowhere to be seen. Of course, soon all the dead bodies would disappear, their skulls and bones adorning the Church of Skulls.

What did Urias have to handle today? They had just received a dispatch announcing that the Church of Skulls was demanding two young women from his home to come serve them at their church. Failure meant instant, all-out attack. His sons had long ago boarded up the lower windows and claimed that they could hold out for quite some time. He had visions of his manor being besieged like some castle or palace. Without food, they could not hold out for very long. There had to be another way. He was not about to surrender any of the six younger women here. He assumed that they did not mean the small girls. What to do?

Suddenly, he had a flash of insight. He raced through his floor calling out for Xeno, Ikaros, and Damon. Aison, that is, Alekto's husband, and Alexio, her son, also joined his three sons. "Well dad, what have you dreamed up this time to get us out of this mess?" asked Xeno.

"A trade. Come on, we need to dig up the family burial crypts! We will trade them skulls instead of our wives!"

Ikaros laughed, "Well, it's not like our dead are going to need their skulls anymore."

When morning came, Urias had a dozen skulls in a large sack sitting near the gates. In case they didn't accept his trade, all the men took up covering fire positions, while their small boys were nearby ready to reload fired weapons for their fathers. Around ten, a dozen men rode up before the locked gates of his estate and dismounted. All drew their long guns and then advanced to the gates. Taking a deep breath, Urias stepped out to meet them, hoping and praying that they would accept this trade, buying them more time to come up with a better solution.

In case this failed and in the event that the men could not hold them, Urias had all the women and girls safely stowed in a secret chamber off the basement. If these evil men actually got into the manor house, they would find it empty. Still, what would become of their women after that, Urias dare not think. Their leader came up to him and snarled, "Okay, we're here to take two of your young women. Bring them out for us to choose."

Urias began his pitch, "How about a substitute trade. Instead of our women, how about taking these dozen. . ." His voice trailed off as he stared in utter disbelief at the sight before him.

As the thief made his demands and his eleven men grunted their approval, the twelve men heard in their minds, *Thou shalt never again harm a woman or man or child*. Immediately after that, their arms completely vanished without a trace. Their dozen long guns fell to the ground breaking the stillness of the winter's morning. Shock and fear flooded the men, then their screams pierced Urias' ears, so loud was the volume. They turned to get to their horses, but were unable to grab the reins, let alone mount. They horses moved away and the terrified men began to run off down the street, still screaming wildly.

"Dad! What the devil did you do to them?" Xeno called out, stepping out from his hiding place. The other men joined him.

"I — I — I didn't do anything. Their arms — they just vanished!" Urias rubbed his eyes and pinched himself to see if he was still real.

"I'll get their guns and horses," Xeno took charge. He and the younger men opened the gates and began gathering up the guns and dozen horses, leading them into their stable.

Fearing the worst, Urias and Aison raced into the mansion and opened the secret door. Both feared that the plague had returned and men were now going to lose their arms as well. They just had to get the secret door opened and their women out. If they lost their arms, the women would be trapped inside!

For over an hour, the extended family sat in the dining room, sipping tea. They discussed repeatedly what they had seen, and their fears that the plague was now affecting men as well as the women. Just in case, Urias made sure that all the food was put either on the floor or down as low to the ground as possible.

Iris pointed out, "Dear, you have not lost your arms yet. I don't see any more yokes appearing. I think that if you are going to lose yours, yokes ought to appear somehow. They did with we women." Urias sent everyone on a thorough search of the mansion looking for additional yokes. None were found.

After lunch, Xeno and Ikaros decided to saddle up and see about visiting a market. In the saddlebags of the thieves they had found a cache of coins and planned to use them to lay in more fish and dried vegetables. Armed with a pair of long guns each and bundled up against the late winter's cold, they headed off to the nearest market square, about three blocks away. Most of the snow had melted off roofs and the paved streets. This winter, they observed no snowmen in the neighboring yards. Few dared venture out AP.

At the market stall, a number of other men were there picking over what was available. The two looked around. What they didn't see made an impression — none of the thieves and assassins was present, waiting to steal from those who came to buy life-sustaining food. As they made some purchases, they asked about the missing men.

The farmer laughed, "You should have been here! That was the best entertainment that I've ever seen. Five of 'em was here as I setup. Soon as the first couple of men showed up, they tried to take their cut. All at once, their arms completely vanished! Gone, poof. Not there! Their guns fell onto the stones over there, but my customers took them. The looks on their faces! Serves them right for all the misery that they've caused us all and your women too, I hear. None of the Skulls have been back here since then. Amazing, don't you think?"

Xeno certainly thought so. "Let's check out some others around here, Ikaros."

"Yes, what do you make of it? Plague again?" he asked.

"If it is, why are only the Skull members being affected by it? It can't be in the food we're getting. We've been getting it from all over," he replied. The two bounced ideas and theories off each other, though none sounded plausible. After visiting ten markets and three gang-controlled blocks now devoid of gang members patrolling the streets, they headed home.

"I don't understand what's going on," Xeno's wife, Korinna said, she, like the others, was confused. "Your arms are still okay, Xeno?"

"Strong as ever, dear. The farmers who came into town today seemed unaffected too, as were those who came to purchase food. I just don't get it."

"Well, perhaps this new plague is impacting only the Church of Skulls members," Urias theorized. Perhaps something in their church or food or water is causing it. Whatever it is, I'm all for it! Tomorrow, let's see if the thieves are back at it. Whose turn is it to make supper?"

"Ours, dad," Damon and Doris said in unison. Each evening, one husband and wife prepared the evening meal. Lunch and breakfasts were more or less help yourself, though Urias and Iris often baked bread loaves for everyone.

"Dad, is it safe enough for Dianthe and I to take a walk around the grounds," Andromache asked Aison. "We've got cabin fever."

"Who doesn't?" her mother, Alekto, broke in. "We've been virtual prisoners in our own home for almost nine months now!"

"I'll go with them, dad," Alexio volunteered. "Want a stroll too, love?" he asked his wife, Delia. She jumped at the chance, though it was cold. The sun was low in the sky, though they all knew spring was just around the corner. He helped fasten a heavy cloak over Delia. Meanwhile, Andromache and Dianthe went to their room and returned with their winter cloaks gripped between their teeth. Alexio smiled. "You must really be hungry, sis, if you are planning to eat your cloak," he teased. Andromache let hers go and swung her hips into him, playfully.

"Just put it on for me, big brother. My wife's too, please," she replied and took another opportunity to impress upon him that she considered Dianthe to be her mate.

A bit later, the four headed outside for a bit of chilly fresh air. Though brisk, the moist air felt good in their lungs. Alexio shouldered his long gun and led the way out past their gate, making sure that no thieves or gangs were prowling around.

Two blocks away in what used to be the Andrastos estate, Athena struggled to get out of her bed. She was twenty-two and had been kidnaped and forced to live in this house of prostitution. Her long blonde hair stank, and she wished she had had her late father cut it short after the plague came. She had always loved long hair and had allowed herself this small bit of vanity after the plague struck her. Three weeks ago, the Skulls had raided their home, killing outright her mother, brother, father, and her boyfriend. She and her sister were soon joined with a dozen other young women as the Skulls turned her home into a brothel. After their first rape, her sister just gave up and had died four days ago. Well, the lifetime of these women was not good — that fact she'd learned from the other dozen women. Apparently, the Skulls had to keep kidnaping more women to replace those who died. Well, if they fed their women properly, they might have stood a chance, she thought.

Athena was starving. Breakfast, lunch, and now dinner had not come. Well, neither had the raping men, she thought, and was grateful for that bit of kindness. She had heard men screaming, terrified voices earlier. Athena prayed that someone was coming to rescue them, but thus far nothing had happened. No one came into her room.

Naked, she looked around the dimly lit room, the sun must be low, she guessed as she found her shoes. At least they allowed them to keep their shoes. She tossed her head back and forth several times to get her blonde hair behind her somewhat and headed to the door. She said a small prayer to her father for having the good sense to remove all their fancy gold-plated doorknobs and install simple sliding bars in their place. Athena listened at the door, heard nothing, and used her foot to open the door. Women were not allowed to leave their rooms unless one of their captors was with them. Several had violated that rule and had been beaten on their legs.

The second floor of her home here was devoted to bedrooms, ten of them. Here is where the women were kept, though two rooms held two women each. She stared down the long hall, silence. Seeing no one around, which in itself was highly unusual, she walked quietly down the long hall to the stairs and carefully peered down them. Still no one. At last, she decided to investigate, willing to suffer another beating if only to know what was going on with their captors. She knew which boards creaked and was able to move silently down the steps.

As she peered into the hall the first floor, she heard voices coming from the kitchen. Where were all the men? What was going on? She had to know, and she crept down the hall, scarcely daring to breathe for fear of being heard and then beaten again. The living room was empty, so was the dining room. At last, she neared the door to the kitchen. She paused and strained her ears to hear what was being said.

"We got to get help. We can't do anything now. We're as bad off as the whores."

"Aesop should have been back long ago. Maybe they aren't coming back. Maybe we ought to get the Bishop to send us some more men."

"Well, at least there have been no customers yet. Hell, what are we going to do if some come? I'm freaked out and starving."

"What about the whores? They've not been fed all day now. Soon they are going to be protesting at least. What'll we do then?"

"Hey, Aesop ought to be back anytime soon and bring us help and re-enforcements. They've just got too!"

Athena just could not fathom what they were so afraid of, and she hazarded a peek around the doorframe. Her eyes nearly popped out! The four men were sitting on chairs as completely armless as she was! Their empty long sleeves hung down at their sides. The four looked terrible and extremely frightened and worried. She quietly backed up and headed back upstairs.

Their captors now had the plague; she concluded the obvious. Now they were as helpless as their captive women. More importantly, Athena saw a tiny window of opportunity — if she and the other women could get out the front door before this Aesop returned with more men, they had a chance to get free! She began going from room to room telling the other eleven women what she'd seen. "Can we really get out of here?" whispered a friend of hers, Diona.

"I think so. Dad replaced all the knobs," Athena answered. "It's cold outside, but I don't see how we can do anything about that. I'd rather freeze and get away than stay here and be raped again tonight. God damn men anyway!" she swore. One by one the others agreed; somehow they had this one chance to escape the perpetual misery they'd been forced to endure.

In single file, Athena, followed by Diona and then the others, crept down the stairs. Athena went slow, hoping not to raise the alarm or fall. AP, falling was always on these women's minds when going down stairs, though it had lessened when their feet returned to normal. Athena opened the front door as slowly as she could, making no noise. It creaked slightly as she pushed it out. She held her breath, but heard no reaction and she headed outside.

One by one, the other women joined her. It was cold and they began shivering at once. Now where? Athena whispered and started jogging, hoping the exercise would provide a little barrier to the cold. Where could she run to? What now? Were they free only to freeze on the streets? She decided to jog until she dropped. Suddenly, she saw three cloaked women and a man just inside an iron gate. She recognized the estate as belonging to a noble family and decided to take a chance. "Help! Help us! Please!" she stammered from the cold.

"Oh god! Alexio look!" Andromache exclaimed. "Get the gate open fast! In here! In here! Quick!" she yelled to the women.

"I'll fetch the men," Delia decided to go for help and headed back inside. Alexio undid the lock and swung the gates wide open.

Andromache and Dianthe hovered over the women like mother hens. She said, "Come on, this way, inside fast. Are there more of you? It's safe here. God, you must be freezing! Come on, follow us!" She and Dianthe began jogging to the door. Aison came out and reacted quickly to the shocking surprise. Holding the door open, he motioned the women inside. Andromache and Dianthe led the dozen straight into the living room and over the floor grating from which very warm air billowed up from the coal-fired furnace in the basement. The shivering women crowded together over the heat.

Soon the entire extended family came into the room to see what was going on. "Oh dear god," Iris exclaimed. "Urias, get the hot water tubs going immediately. We have to get them warmed up and bathed at once. Korinna, Diona, you start hunting around for some clothes for these women. Doris, Delia, Alekto, Andromache, Dianthe, you're with me. Let's get these women warmed and cleaned up. Their hair is a mess. Quick, quick. Aison, you get the boys to help fix these women a hot meal. Move, move," Iris was always quick to respond to emergencies. Athena greatly appreciated her words; maybe they had actually escaped their captors.

An hour later, dressed in warm clothes that really didn't fit though they cared not, the dozen women sat around the large dining room table, allowing the men to feed them. Athena told them what she had seen and she and Diona explained what had happened to them, how her family had been killed, and her home turned into a whorehouse.

"Tomorrow, Athena, we'll take our guns and go over there and roust all them out of there. Then, we'll see what we can retrieve for you. Yokes, brushes, cups, clothes. We'll see what we can find for you. Well done on your escape! You are totally safe here; we've kept the Skulls out."

The next day, hundreds of armless, pathetic men went randomly from home to home begging for help. The oppressed people didn't even open either their doors or gates or they simply stared at them in disgust. After another day, the braver men began rounding these men up and sending them back into their Church of Skulls. A week later, all of those who had been so brutalizing the city were forced to stay in their "sacred church." Once a day, men brought leftover food all dumped together in buckets and left them at the doors for the dogs to fight over.

More importantly, hundreds upon hundreds of women were located and rescued, though many were so terribly traumatized by their long ordeals that they merely sat and stared at nothing. Eventually, they were housed together in an empty manor house and cared for by volunteers in the hope that one day they might recover.

During this recovery period, a squad of soldiers from Patri came to relay orders and requests from the General who ran the port city. While his pirate scheme had been ended, he still ruled Patri with an iron fist. He also conducted business with the Church of Skulls. When these soldiers began to attempt to mistreat those they encountered, they too instantly became armless! Freaked out, frightened, and terrified, most managed to ride back to Patri. For another couple of weeks after that, the general's soldiers were spotted on the outskirts of Axos, watching and waiting. Several made overt actions towards some of the townsfolk with the same devastating results, the loss of their own arms. After that, no more soldiers came to Axos.

While no one entirely believed that the men of Axos were now being infected with the plague as the women had, outsiders dared not risk it. Thus, Axos and its suburbs finally became calm and free of the suppression they'd been under for nine months. The question now became how did they pick up the pieces? Many opted to do nothing, waiting to see if they also lost their arms.

A week after the end of the reign of the Church of Skulls, one of their surviving neighbors came running over to the Zoraster estate. "Urias! Urias, I must have a word with you," Aias exclaimed.

Urias and his three sons came rushing to their front door, now freed from the barriers placed there during the siege. Even their gates were left open during the day. From the crinkled lines on his neighbor's face, Urias knew something terrible had happened. Were the Skulls back? "Aias, what's the matter? What's up? Are the Skulls back again?" he asked rapid fire.

"No, no, nothing like that or maybe it is. It's terrible. It's my son, Urias, he's only six years old," Aias tried to explain.

"Cadmus?" Urias asked thinking of the man's ten year old son.

"No, Dion, he's turned six now. Urias, we have to warn every man in the city!"

"About what? Aias, calm down, what happened to Dion?"

"He and his sister got into another one of their petty squabbles this morning. You know how kids are," he beat around the bush. Urias sensed that he was trying to find a way to avoid deep embarrassment. "Well, they argued and Dion, he slapped Alexia in the face. Then I heard him screaming in terror. When I got there, his arms — Urias, his arms are gone too, just like Alexia's! It's just awful, he didn't mean anything by it — just a child's horsing around, Urias. We have to warn everyone."

The four did just that, cautioning all men in the manor house and particularly all their many children. Xeno's seven year old Adonia teased her older brother, Loukas, "Now you *have* to do what I say or you will lose your arms too, just like Dion! Ha. Ha."

"Adonia, that will be enough of that!" Xeno declared. "Your brother has been looking after you for the last nine months. I promise you that if you goad him into hitting you and he loses his arms, you will have to do everything for yourself after that. Look, Adonia, treat your brother right and he will treat you right. You need him as much as he needs you." Adonia pouted a little but agreed. She knew well what kind of a mess she would be in if Loukas wasn't always helping her out.

Over tea, Urias suggested, "This is more serious than we thought. Mixed blessings."

"Dad, if we men retake control of Axos, aren't we in jeopardy of losing our own arms? I mean some of the harsh decisions that must be made might not sit well with some women. I'm scared of trying to try to help lead Axos or even our block," Xeno admitted.

"It's scary dad," Ikaros also admitted. "What if something we do is misconstrued?"

"I don't think any man is going to take such a gamble, dad. Please don't ask me or do it yourself," Damon added.

Urias looked at Aison, whose hair had the first streaks of grey coming. He'd aged considerably since the plague. Aison shrugged his shoulders, "We have too much to risk, Urias. You and I have to continue to hold our families together."

His son, Alexio hastily spoke up, "Hey, I agree. I have Delia and the kids to think about, Urias. If I should lose mine, it'd be a total disaster. Our wives and children are dependent upon us."

Feisty Andromache tossed her head back and forth, getting her long brown hair out of her face. She looked at Dianthe and nodded. "Well, isn't this just like men? Bring chaos down upon us and then not lead us back out of it. Hell, I don't have any more arms to lose. I'll do it. Besides, brother, you do have kids to worry about. I like my niece and nephew, and I don't want to end up having to support them, not when I am like this. I'll do it. Someone has to lead and make the hard decisions. I've nothing to lose. Maybe it is time that we women actually lead our country, and I don't mean the pretend leading that so many of our past queens have done."

"Great sis, I'll support you," Alexio hastily replied before she could change her mind or have anyone veto her suggestion. "Dad, can't you start pulling some strings to get Andromache appointed our leader?" He wanted to get this resolved as fast as possible, getting himself off the hook. He, like the other men, was getting more and more worried about some accidental goof that would cause his own arms to disappear. Although in the past he had always looked upon her as weird because of her sexual preferences, just now he pretended that he'd always been totally behind her.

Urias saw potential in Andromache's suggestion. "Andromache, are you willing to do this? To be the leader of at least Axos and maybe more? It is quite a load that you are shouldering."

"Well, it's a cinch that men got us into this mess. Notice that there wasn't one woman in the Church of Skulls band, not that they could have done much if there were some. I can't really blame you fellows now, though. Honestly, I feel sorry for our neighbor's son. He's so young and look at the life that he is facing. Beyond the physical limitations that we face, he's going to be carrying the stigma of having been nasty to women all through the rest of his life. He can never live it down. One look at him and everyone will know. I feel sorry for him; he's just a kid. Well, look, Urias, someone has to step up and lead us. Dianthe and I cannot possibly reopen our business, not like this," she shrugged her shoulders. "So we might as well make a difference elsewhere."

"Okay, Andromache, I'll give you my full support. Aison, you and I ought to visit the nobles who are still around and see if we can get a consensus on this right away. Someone has to start putting in some order around Axos fast. Your daughter has always been feisty and fighting for what she believes in, even if the rest of us don't share her views." He nodded to Dianthe. She wondered when the men would finally accept her and Andromache as mates and smiled as she suddenly realized that they no longer had to fight the Church of Jehosanity on their lifestyle. That church was history.

Aison pointed out, "She and Dianthe have had managerial experience. Their A & D Ball Gowns was very successful BP. But she is going to need men to help back her up. Perhaps, you and I could be her advisors. I think for the time being we don't even need soldiers to help keep order. The fear of the plague will be enough to keep men in line."

"Okay, Aison, let's get to work. I'll canvass what's left of our block, you take the next one," Urias suggested. The two left to begin laying the groundwork.

After a few minutes, only Andromache and Dianthe remained at the table. Both were still struggling to sip their tea, when two of the rescued women walked into the room. Athena kept glancing from side to side, making sure that they were alone, her light blonde hair flowing gently from side to side. Diona's long brown hair contrasted sharply with Athena's, but now that they had been cleaned up and their hair fully brushed out, their waist length tresses looked very impressive. Andromache and Dianthe had let their brown and black hair continue to grow, exercising a bit of vanity AP. Ankle length now, both were rather proud of theirs. There was so little to be proud of AP thus far at least.

"Hi Athena, Diona," Andromache greeted the two women, who were a couple of years younger than she was. "Your hair looks really nice now that we've got all the tangles out and conditioned again." She noticed Athena's nervous glances, though, and wondered if Athena would ever overcome her fears.

"Thanks, we owe you and everyone here our lives," she replied, glancing at Diona, who nodded her head slightly, encouraging Athena.

Glancing at the floor first, Athena finally raised her eyes to meet those of Andromache's. "Can we ask you two something?"

"Sure, ask away."

"You two are, well, sort of like married, right?" Athena finally uttered what she and Diona had been whispering between themselves for a week now.

"You bet we are. No way to get married though," Andromache answered wondering why Athena was asking about this.

"She does the husband role mostly," Dianthe added with a wry smile. "But sometimes I do too. We love each other. Isn't that what a marriage is all about? In sickness and in health? Well, it's permanent sickness now and we'll never be parted."

Athena smiled, "Then is it okay for Diona and me to be mates too? I mean, neither one of us ever wants anything to do with a man! We even cringe when one touches us. Are you able to help each other enough to get by? That's what we were worrying about — having to have a man around to help us get by. You two seem to be able to do so many more things than we."

"We have Urias to thank for that. When the plague struck, he found a Bethany's Hints book and read it to all of us. I'm afraid we've rather worn it out, but we'll go over it with you now. Loads of clues in it. But, Athena, I have to be honest with you. Until now, if we had not had all the men around here helping us, we would both be dead."

Athena looked crestfallen. That she and Diona would have to find a man to care for their needs made their skin crawl and their stomachs tighten up in utter disgust and revulsion. Andromache realized what must be going through Athena's mind and added, "But that was then, when it wasn't safe for man or woman to be outside. Now, things will be different. We don't have to fear evil men any longer. Hell, let them try something! I'll cheer when their arms fall off! So I am very hopeful that now we, Dianthe and I, will be able to better get along on our own as we once did." The relief in both women's eyes and faces told all. "Come on, you two; let's go read that really helpful book. It was written during the first plague by a woman somewhere up in the northern hemisphere."

On August 1, 824, Andromache Gidios was appointed Monarch of Thrace. The largest problem that she faced that very day was the total lack of coinage or money. No one in the city had any left; the Skulls had long ago stolen the lot, though the farmers who came with their produce did receive some. Her first official order was to send a number of men and women into the Church of Skulls where the thousands of pitiful armless men were now forced to live and bring out all the valuables they had looted from the people of Axos. Andromache and Dianthe went along to see for themselves how much was there.

Several assassins attempted to kick the men and Andromache, cursing them. However, Andromache had the last laugh. Each man who lunged at her to kick her, found the leg which was about to strike her suddenly vanishing! After ten men suddenly became one-legged, all resistance to them ceased. As her men began bringing out the coins, gems, jewelry, and other valuables, she was utterly shocked by the amount. A dozen wagons were needed to haul it all away.

The next day, she began distribution. "Each head of a household, whether it be a man, woman, or even a child are to immediately receive a hundred gold coins worth of money so that they can purchase food and supplies from the farmers." She also asked those who were going door to door handing out the pouches of coins to make a head count of how many people were still alive, how many heads of households were now women, and how many were children living on their own somehow.

However, what shocked her was on the same day that the first of the coins were handed out, thousands upon thousands of Bethany's Hints books translated into their dialect appeared beside the many money wagons! Thus, a book was also handed out to each woman and girl that they could find in Axos.

A week later, the massive distribution task was done. Andromache stared at the results. Two-thirds of their BP population was gone! Some reportedly had fled to the surrounding towns, villages, and even distant farms. Still, the numbers were shocking. Men outnumbered women two to one in Axos.

The Royal Palace was uninhabitable now. So Urias and Aison found an abandoned manor house two doors down and helped her set up her temporary Monarch's Offices in that building. She had to deal next with building up a staff and then begin tackling reconstruction tasks, which were enormous to say the least. She focused solely on Axos for the time being. Patri with its ruling general and thousands of soldiers and the Imperial City of Kefall to the east with its gang-ridden streets would have to wait.

On August 5, Xeno returned from a scavenging expedition to the Royal Palace and brought back an LD radio for Andromache. After their whole group read the operations manual, Xeno fired it up, and Andromache made her first call, asking if there was anyone out there listening. I was quickly informed and hopped onto my LD radio and began to chat with the new Monarch of Thrace. Naturally, I promised her all manner of aid and assistance, if only we could figure out ways to get it to her. Axos was deep inside Thrace from Arolas, Penelopus, and Thallyus, but only some few hundred from Patri, which was still under the iron grip of the general.

I also wondered how many of the surviving women were so badly traumatized that they could no longer function. I hesitated to call them zombies, as had Kalypso in Kefall. Now, Andromache had far bigger problems with which to deal. I decided to wait on this until she mentioned it.

Based on my suggestions and the hints book, Andromache had her dad and brother install the low to the ground kitchen in their new manor house. She and Dianthe had their things moved into their new home and Monarch Office building. One section became their living quarters, while most of the first floor she devoted to the business of running Axos. Based on my suggestion of four women living together, she invited Athena and Diona to move in with them. "Look, it will be just us two like-minded couples. We will need to work together if we're to manage without having men around," Andromache explained. After a week of experimentation, the four realized this was quite feasible. Hence, the young monarch issued a proclamation that if women did not have a husband or others to look after them, they would be given a home and three other women roommates. By September, two dozen homes now housed only women and girls. Some of the larger homes held eight.

Chapter 34 Evolution of Women's Apparel

Some countries experienced a vastly different reaction to the plague. In Annelise, where fashion was king, one quarter of their economy was devoted to the construction of clothing with many other industries providing support, such as the manufacturing of satin and cotton bolts, needles, thread, and buttons. In the days immediately after the plague struck, the entire economy of Annelise shut down over night. Half of the clothiers were women. The men did their best to learn to walk in the strange alien boots and did their best to assist their womenfolk. The casualty count from the plague was minimal, just ten had died.

Unlike so many other countries, chaos did not break out in Annelise, primarily because there were virtually no criminals in the country. This startling fact became clear to me many months later. Essentially, crime in Annelise was nearly zero. With a total emphasis on proper, elegant dress, what was there to steal? A dress? No, those spiritual beings that were dramatizing criminality had simply not stayed in Annelise, a most curious fact.

However, their economy came to a crashing halt, save only the food production and distribution side, which amounted to another quarter of their economy. King Niels Ryker and Queen Malena faced a crisis unheard of in the long history of Annelise, a crisis that threatened the very foundations of their nation and culture. "My god, Niels, not a single dress of mine will fit me!" exclaimed forty-one year old Malena, once she recovered from the initial shock of the plague. Millions of women and girls throughout Annelise echoed her words repeatedly.

During the first two months, the numerous tailors were pressed into service making drastic alterations to women's dresses. King Niels' response was to get all women's dresses altered to fit somehow. "Somehow, someway, we must have our women properly dressed!" That had been his standing order issued throughout the land on the second day after the plague struck. Of course, once everyone's feet returned to normal, a more permanent solution had to be found. With half of their population now utterly dependent upon the men, the situation became more and more critical as the weeks passed.

Finally, King Niels turned the matter over to his wife, Malena. "Dear, I believe that for the time being, you are ruling Annelise. We men have failed you, our lovely women. It is time for you to lead us out of darkness, my dear."

"That is good of you, my love. Yes, we women have to work this one out. Obviously, you men simply cannot handle it. You deal with suits just perfectly. Now it is up to us women to deal with our unique situation."

Their son, Jorgen looked at his mother. He was twenty-one with the same jet black hair as his father. Like his father, Jorgen sported a fancy moustache and sideburns, the latest in style here in the capital city of Hodenhagen. His fiancé Agnethe was twenty with wavy, blonde hair that, after the plague, reached her knees. They were to have been married in January, but because of the dress problem, they agreed to delay their wedding until she could have a proper wedding dress made, one which was fitting for the future queen of Annelise. Jorgen was the single heir to the throne. He said, "Okay mom, I'm behind you. Please, find a solution fast. Agnethe and I really want to marry, she needs me now more than ever before."

"Dear, you are already helping her with everything. Relax. I assure you that we women will have this monumental catastrophe licked in no time. Besides, son, her waist is now just perfect, fourteen inches, the often sought and seldom attained ideal of perfection," Queen Malena replied.

Her daughter, Princess Kristen giggled. She was twenty now. Unlike her mother who had long wavy brown hair that reached her knees by virtue of the plague, she had light blonde hair, wavy as well. Like her mother, hers also touched the top of her knees. Kirsten was a bit flighty, Jorgen thought, never making up her mind. For a time, she wanted to be a musician. Then, it was a seamstress, now she was trying her hand at dress designing. "Yes, Jorgen, you are really being most helpful to Agnethe. I am sure that she needs your help. I only wish that I had a boyfriend now."

"In time you will, dear," her mother advised her. "Besides, you are barely twenty. Now then, Jorgen, go fetch Agnethe please. We women need to put our heads together." Jorgen chuckled. Well, he thought, they can still do that. He left to bring his bride-to-be to the throne room.

Soon he escorted Agnethe into the room, helping with her chair. All three women wore their drastically altered ball gowns. While they still wore a corset, these had been altered to merely fit snugly and provide garters to hold up their fine, black hose. All three wore the expected Annelise extreme heels and all three had long ago perfected the elegant gliding style of walking in which they seemed to float across the room, taking but the tiniest of steps. Naturally, their men took the time to dress them and to handle their personal needs while they were so dressed. Royalty had to set an example for the other women of the country.

True, they all had copies of Bethany's Hints, thanks to Macario, who had them translated into the Annelise dialect, millions of copies printed, and delivered to the King. They had appeared not long after the plague struck. Yes, when they were not formally dressed, the women did do some things for themselves, such as brushing out their hair at night. However, court protocol dictated that they look their very best during the daytime, which also meant that wearing these outfits. Hence, they depended upon their men for most everything. "Gentlemen, if you will leave us now, we will get started. Niels, do be a good fellow and stick around and take notes for us, please." He smiled, he'd already guessed that she would ask him to do so, since she was wearing her seven inch, black heels which he so loved to see her wearing. She walked like an angel in them, he thought. He also prayed that she could solve this, the worst crisis in Annelise history.

The three women chatted a bit before Kristen had a very bright idea. "Say mom, why don't we call in the four top dress designers and makers of Annelise? Perhaps with so many brilliant minds, the solution will become apparent."

"Excellent idea, we should call it the First Women's Fashion War Council. After all, this is tantamount to war having been declared upon us by these despicable alien creatures. Niels, make it so, jot that down. Say, we have many of the fashions from Velona in storage. Perhaps we should have one of their designers as a part of our council. After all, Velona is leading the way to recovery worldwide and they are very good allies." Queen Malena declared, liking her phrase "after all," for it sounded so definitive.

The first meeting was scheduled for January 15 to be held there at the Royal Palace in Hodenhagen. This gave the four dress designers time to travel from their homes to Hodenhagen, located in the middle of Annelise. Niels arranged for their LD radio to be moved into the large working room where Malena decided to hold the council meeting. During the days leading up to their first meeting, she had Niels and Jorgen bring in all the many dress designs of Velona and put them on display as well.

At nine that morning, trumpeters played a fanfare for each of the couples while their husbands escorted their wives into the War Council Room, as Malena began calling this huge room with the long oak table and soft, purple chairs. Actually, it was their purple room, where guests often waited to meet with the king and queen.

The doorman announced, "Hedvika and Hans Gustavo of H & H Clothiers of Viborg." The forty-eight year old woman with long black hair glided into the room, her husband's arm securely around her thin waist. She wore her elegant, green satin ball gown, which flared out to fourteen feet at the floor. It fit her poorly, but the same could be said for all the women. All felt horribly disgraced at having to wear such ill-fitting dresses, but this was a national crisis of unparalleled proportions. She managed to keep a smile on her face as she glided across the polished wooden floor. All the women wore similar dresses; all wore the extreme heels as appropriate to the occasion. All now had hair that draped to the vicinity of their knees. Hers was brown.

"Zabrina and Hagen Jutta of Z & H Clothiers, Hodenhagen." Zabrina was thirty-five with black hair and strong, angular facial features, accented by the blue satin gown. She was all work and no nonsense, though she glided superbly across the floor to her seat, assisted by her husband.

"Ingjerd and Johan Knute of Knute Clothiers, Barborg." Ingjerd was thirty and had blonde hair; her gown was cherry red. Her eyes sparkled. She was something of a flirt and was extremely pleased to have been asked to take part in this historic war council. She expertly glided over to her seat.

"Agda and Halvor Morten of A & H Clothiers, Bjorg." Agda was thirty-nine with platinum blonde hair that had greatly increased in thickness and body since the plague. Hers was the longest hair, now an inch above her ankles. Her dress was pink satin.

This morning, Queen Malena wore her brown satin gown, while Kirsten wore her sky blue satin gown, and Agnethe wore her dark blue satin gown. Once the women were seated, their husbands bowed to the Queen and retired, joining Jorgen in the billiards room. Niels had to remain to take notes and assist the women as needed. He dialed up the LD radio and soon everyone heard the voice of Mrs. Tatiana Torellini of Velona.

"Thank you for inviting me to take part in your historic war council," Tatiana said over the radio.

"Okay, then. We are all present for this opening session of the First Women's Fashion War Council. Indeed, this is a war council, for the wicked, evil alien creatures have indeed declared war upon us women, in an attempt to rob us of our elegance and fashion, which we most cherish. We are civilized women, and we will not and must not fall victims to this evil plague. I have called upon the foremost women's dress designers in the world. Together, we will defeat the chaos and utter disaster these aliens have inflicted upon we women," Queen Malena began her carefully rehearsed opening remarks.

"Tatiana, we have along the side of this room all the sample fashions from Velona. I believe the vast majority are your designs. Please feel free to add your thoughts, opinions, and ideas when you desire. Now then, let me lay out the ground rules for this war. In short, ladies, there are none. We must and shall win this war!"

"Now then, for Tatiana's sake, since she cannot see us, I will describe how we are dressed. I know the look is utterly pitiful. We are all horribly humiliated to be wearing these ill-fitting gowns, grossly altered by our menfolk, but we cannot go naked. Now then, since this is a formal meeting at the Royal Palace, we are all wearing traditional ball gowns." She described each gown to Tatiana, all billowed out to fourteen feet at the floor. All wore the extreme heels, as the situation would not permit a lesser height. Tatiana then told them what she was wearing, one of her simple dresses, which she could put on herself. It had pull straps and loops and had hook and eyes going up the front so she could manage it herself.

Then, the women got down to the business at hand. As the noon hour approached, Kirsten summarized the goals that they had all agreed upon, "Women are armless now. Yet, we women fulfill many different roles in our lives and society, from bearing and raising our children, to working women, to running our homes. Until the war, which has left us armless, we women could wear our typical gowns, with slight allowances in the width at the floor and our heel heights. The fabric and the width of the hoops allowed for our different occupations and needs. For those women who assisted on farms, theirs were barely five feet at the floor. At the other extreme, when we women attend formal functions, such as balls, our gowns span fourteen feet. There are times when a woman wants, desires, and needs to look the very best that she can. Yet there are times when a woman needs to be more practical. Now with the alien's modifications, we are facing a crisis."

Kirsten continued, hoping that her father could keep up with her. She was talking rather rapidly. "At this time, we women are forced to use our feet in lieu of our hands. This has a major impact upon our lives and our ability to perform our usual and normal actions. However, there are several other side results that must also be taken into consideration. First, women's waists are now frequently fourteen inches around, a size once considered the ideal feminine form. Thus, the restrictive wasp corsets are no longer needed to reduce waistlines, though we do agree that we may need them to hold up our stockings and fancy black hose. Second, women's busts are now impossibly large, with most breasts protruding an intolerable foot from our chests. Third, our pelvis and hips have expanded quite noticeably. The combination of all three has made alterations of our current dresses nearly impossible."

Kirsten finished, "Our solution must deal with all women and all their needs, which we all agree vary greatly, often within even a day's time. At times, we need the use of our feet, particularly at mealtime and at work. Other times, we need to look our very best at formal affairs. Our solution must be workable, in that we women must be able to dress ourselves. There, have I missed anything?" She hadn't and they adjourned for lunch.

The seven women then rose and tossed their heads from side to side, sliding their long tresses back over their shoulders. Gracefully, the seven began their very slow angelic glide out of the War Room, down the halls to the dining room, where their husbands had gathered already.

At one o'clock and after their men had helped them with restroom needs, the seven women glided back into their War Room. Now the real work began. Tatiana opened the afternoon session. "One of the benefits of my simple dresses is that we can easily don them. I call them simple day dresses, but they are not practical for more than wearing around the house. Certainly, they are not designed for the working woman, though I do admit that lacking anything else, women are wearing them to work here in Velona. Now here in Velona, for dances and elegant affairs, besides wearing Annelise ball gowns, the strapless slinky gowns have always historically been quite popular among the women who were armless. As you may know, over the years, Velona has been home to a number of unfortunate women who lost their arms for various reasons. These women have always loved the bare shoulder look and the pencil thin, form-fitting design of these dresses. They say that this style shows off their curves the best."

She continued, "From my own personal experience, I can tell you that my mate just loves to see me in these slinky gowns, really sexy she says. However, when I wear it, I am dependent upon her to both dress me and to assist me, as I no longer have the use of my feet. This is also the same situation that all of you are facing at this very moment. While you are wearing your fancy gowns, hose, and heels, you are dependent upon your men for most everything. Still, I do believe that we women should have such gowns. There are times that I am perfectly willing to relinquish my independence of action, allowing my mate to assist me with everything. Sexy. We women must be allowed to make that choice, to look really fancy and sexy, though that means we will be dependent upon our mates. We must be allowed to so chose when we desire."

"Oh, I believe that is an absolute must!" Zabrina replied. "I see your point, Tatiana, and it is a good one. We women must be in the driver's seat to choose when we wish to relinquish our remaining freedom of action, the use of our feet — relinquishing it when we desire. That means that we need regal, elegant, sexy gowns for these occasions. You will get no argument on this point. We in Annelise would rather die than not look our very best when we need to do so."

"We need to also have practical outfits, too," Kristen pointed out. "How can we get good looking outfits when we must have complete freedom of action with our feet? Certainly we cannot do so when we wear our ball gowns nor with the slinky dresses."

"We must design a variety of outfits, aligned for the purpose we women find at hand," Agda suggested. Now the real work began. Soon, they all agreed that the pull loops that Tatiana had invented must be an integral part of each garment. That way, either the woman could put it on herself or another woman could assist her, alleviating the constant problem of having to have a man dress them.

Mechanically, buttons were problematical. While easy before the plague, at this point, the designers rejected them as fasteners. Tatiana's hook and eye adaption that ran up the front of her day dresses looked too inelegant for continued use. She'd adapted them from the Annelise ball gowns, in which they were used to fasten the overskirts and underskirts to the bodice. Ribbon and string ties along with belts were likewise rejected as the fastener of preference. While another woman could, with difficulty, manage to fasten a belt on another, men were now needed for tying anything.

All the designers had been experimenting with the new zippers that the tailors were now beginning to use on men's pants. These would solve many fastening situations if only a way that a woman could manage them could be found. They set their husbands to work on seeing if some mechanism could be found by which a woman could pull up a zipper and pull it down by herself.

Over dinner one evening, Hagen Jutta showed the women some sketches that he'd made. "We put large loops on the zipper's pull bar. Now you only need to get the loop over the hook on this machine. Once hooked, you use your foot to pull the rope downward and it pulls the zipper up. To unzip, you use this other side where when you pull the rope downward with your foot, the device pulls the zipper down." The concept seemed sound, so during the daytime, the men set to work making prototypes of Hagen's machine and modifying some dresses that the women could use to experiment with to see if it was actually feasible.

On January 20, the women began experimenting with the Zipper-Upper as Hagen named his invention. All were delighted with the ease and workability of the device, though they suggested some slight modifications. Hagen then relayed details of its design and construction to Tatiana, who relayed them to Lucianna, who brought her a working model a few days later.

Now the designers set to work in earnest. Zippers would form the main means of fastening now. For several days, ideas flew hot and heavy — different designs for different situations that women worldwide now faced. Women working on farms in the winter now had stylish long pants to wear that would keep their legs warm and give them the freedom of motion that they needed with their legs and feet. Skirts were invented as an alternative that was easy to don by themselves. Most fell to their ankles, as none of the women wanted to show off bare legs. Tatiana added pleats to them adding to their attractiveness. Form fitting blouses based upon the bodices of the ball gowns came into being, zipped up the back with the new Zipper-Upper.

They altered the look of the slinky gowns primarily by adding a long back zipper. Adjustments for their massive bust lines were made to the ball gowns. Tatiana learned another reason that the Annelise women so preferred their ball gowns. They hid a woman's pregnancy from view quite nicely. In Velona, Tatiana had a ball designing new garments, as she sat at her low desk in her simple day dress. In Hodenhagen, the women still wore their ball gowns and were having a rougher time making their drawings. Although they knew that they ought to be wearing something other than these formal gowns to do their work, none dared mention it.

On January 25, a young man came to the Royal Palace, seeking an audience with the War Council. Word had spread everywhere about their meeting and he thought that this was a perfect time to make his pitch. Anders Gard was twenty-one, with shoulder length black hair. He'd spent his last coins on this new suit, knowing that at the Royal Palace, one must be well dressed. Anders was a shy man. His looks were barely average; his nose a bit too pointed. His mind, on the other hand, was bright. King Niels was still taking the official notes of the meeting, so it was Jorgen who met him as the guards walked the young man and his large box into the throne room. Some twenty minutes later, Jorgen and Anders entered the War Room.

"Excuse me, everyone. This is Anders Gard, an inventor. He has made a machine that I think that all of you women should see." Jorgen winked at his sister, while Anders open the large box and began setting up his invention.

"What is it, Anders? Speak up son," King Niels ordered.

In a shaky, nervous voice, Anders began to explain. "I know how awful this plague is on us all.

My sister is a seamstress and obviously her budding career is in jeopardy now. So I invented this little machine. It is a mechanical sewing machine that sews as well as she used to be able to sew. It can be operated by one woman herself, but sewing goes faster if two are working it. Let me demonstrate. You sit here; the working surface is only six inches from the floor, making it easy for you to position the fabrics to be sewn together." He awkwardly began to use only his feet to get to sample pieces up on the head.

"This is the needle and the guide. It will sew a half-inch seam. When you have it all lined up right, you hold the pieces with one foot and slowly pedal this foot pedal with your other foot, like so." The seven women watched him fascinated. As the pedal went up and down, the needle pierced the material and rose up again, leaving behind a perfect stitch. He pedaled several times and then stopped so that they could see the result: a perfectly straight, evenly space series of a dozen stitches.

"Oh my goodness! It actually sews! Can I try it?" Kristen begged, suddenly seeing a way that she could actually sew.

Anders rose and Kristen sat down. "Please, Anders, push my hoops down so I can see what I am doing." Rather embarrassed, he did so. A few minutes later, Kristen shrieked, "This actually does work! Wow! Incredible!"

"Here, Kristen, let me have a try," Zabrina insisted, nearly shoving Kristen out of the chair. Kristen slipped on her heels, rose, and stood beside Anders, watching Zabrina try it. Again, he pushed her hoops down so she could see what to do. The women had to slip off their heels to operate it, but even with their fancy hose, their feet could operate the machine, as long as Anders positioned the material for them. If they had the use of their toes, he would not have had even to do that much for them.

One by one, they all tried it out. Tatiana was green with envy, but could only listen to their wild exclamations about how wonderful this machine was. Obviously, this invention was critically needed and in large numbers. While the women experimented with it, King Niels had Jorgen take over for Anders, and he took the inventor aside.

"Son, this invention of yours is going to save our country. We must get them mass-produced immediately. You have a company formed for this?" he asked.

"Er, no, Your Highness. I — I spent my last gold on this suit so that I could come to you and show you what I have invented to help our women," he admitted. No sense hiding the fact that he's spent every copper he ever earned on his inventions.

"Son, this is a nationwide — no a worldwide crisis that we are facing. Please allow your country to back you in this. We must get these being manufactured immediately and in large volumes. You leave that to me. Your country will cover the startup costs, son. Meantime, you will please stay here at the palace with us. I will send for my aides and we'll get the ball rolling on this invention yet today!"

"Thank you, Your Highness," Anders managed to squeak. This all came as a shock to him. He figured that he might be asked to make a few of these machines, enough that he might be able to make a little money from them. A whole company was beyond his imagination.

A bit later, they rejoined the women, Niels having Anders relieve Jorgen. "Well, ladies, Anders and I have worked it out. We will begin construction of these machines yet today. In the meantime, I am insisting that Anders stay at the palace with us."

"Great dad!" Kristen exclaimed. "Tonight, after supper, Anders, will you please show me how it works with two of us? This is just incredible, maybe I can become a seamstress after all. I'd given all hope of that up, you see, after I got the plague." He flushed and agreed to show her.

When a country is threatened by war, so many immediately step up to the plate to help defend the country from attack. In this case, the actions taken by so many men were almost unheard of in Annelise. Within a week, a plant had been built in Hodenhagen and the first of the Gard Sewing Machines was completed. A year later, these machines were found all over the world, though most were commonly now called simply a Gard. The second machine made was packaged and sent off to Tatiana, though she did not receive it until early June. She also received copies of the many different designs that they had all been working on to date.

Of course, Lucianna just had to see it and her first action was to modify it to make use of a small electric motor, eliminating the foot pedal. The motor was controlled by the woman's shoulder, pushing against a lever.

On February1 , the First Women's Fashion War Council released their recommendations for women's fashions. For those special occasions when a woman wanted to look elegant and place herself under the control of her mate, there were the modified ball gowns and slinkys. For winter days and heavy work, there were pants and blouse combinations. For everyday around the house, blouse and skirt combinations were needed. In all, their formal proclamation outlined a set of four very different types of outfits that every woman should own. Accompanying heels remained the same, five, six, or seven inches, though buckling straps replaced the tied laces on many of the styles, such as the oxfords. Women simply couldn't manage the laces. By themselves, they could not manage the buckling straps either, but another woman could fasten them for them.

Along with the War Council's recommendation came King Niels' proclamation. The king would be providing each woman in Annelise with one set of the four outfits at no charge. While it depleted his treasury, it assured him that soon the catastrophe would be over.

February 1, the War Council ended and the designers headed home to begin advance planning to implement their designs. With the expected arrival of the Gards, they would be able to begin producing fine clothing for the most desperate women of Annelise. For the rest of the year, King Niels ordered all tailors to assist the many dressmakers in making these new outfits. As more and more Gards were made and delivered, the less the men had to assist their counterparts. Pattern cutting remained to be solved, however.

King Niels insisted that Anders continue to stay at the palace and continue to work on inventions to assist the seamstresses. To that end, Kirsten began to spend most of her days with Anders. Working together, the many problems and barriers that women faced while attempting to make an outfit were discovered. Anders finally solved a major problem: how could women cut out the pieces from the cloth bolts. He invented a foot cutter, essentially a sharp blade on a frame with a leather strap. The woman slipped her foot into it, much like a shoe. The blade was perpendicular to the shoe and she could slide it along the material on a cutting board.

Later on, he invented a pinning machine that pinned up the hem of a dress or skirt, uniformly to boot. Again, the woman pushed it to the next spot and pushed a lever, which inserted a pin into the held fabric. While a slow operation, women could now deal with this necessity.

In March, Jorgen was able to wed Agnethe. She wore an elegant white ball gown wedding dress, one of the first of the new style, which nicely fit her form. Kirsten, wearing another of these new gowns and her extreme heels, insisted that Anders accompany her and assist her with her many needs during the wedding day. In truth, she was smitten with this young man and wanted his company at all times.

In April, Kristen realized that Anders was so shy that she would have to make the first move. She asked him to marry her. He admitted that he'd fallen in love with her, but dared not show it, because she was a Princess and he a simple inventor.

"Oh don't be ridiculous, Anders! You have single handedly saved our whole country with your sewing machine!" she declared. In May, they were wed as well and in June, she opened her own dressmaking shop, based there at the palace. Incidentally, a few years later, Anders was an extremely wealthy man as Gards took the world by storm.

In mid-October, we received a very pleasant surprise. Princess Mia of Viborg dropped by 42 Hampton Way, accompanied now with her assistant, Anja, who assisted her with her needs. Of course, Princess Mia wore her usual extreme heels now with buckles instead of laces and her ball gown of sky blue satin, fourteen feet across at the floor. She looked elegant, and the new style dress certainly showed off her form. She brought four huge crates with her. As she glided slowly into our living room, we knew that she was wearing those tall heels. "In honor of what all you and your friends have done for us, the King and Queen have sent me to deliver a small token of our whole country's gratitude." She explained to Eve, Lucianna, Lisa, and me about the four key styles for women's needs. She had cleverly gotten our measurements from Tatiana, who now made all our dresses and for our mothers as well.

"We didn't know whether you would prefer the ball gowns or the slinkys for your elegant, regal, formal affairs, so we made you each one of each. Tatiana told us your favorite colors too," she giggled. "Of course, you will have to help each other into these elegant dresses, since the fine, black silk hose prevents us from using our toes, naturally. Anja helps me dress, you see.

Marco and the fellows somehow managed to get the four large crates inside and we women had a very enjoyable time that day. They also had new tuxedos for our husbands, which pleased them. Each of their suits would have sold for five hundred gold or more. Interestingly enough, Princess Mia had decided only to include the six-inch and seven-inch heels, rejecting the lower five-inch ones, claiming that we all were far too important women to be seen in such lower heels.

That evening, we had our fellows dress us up in each of our new outfits. Marco loved my new bright yellow satin slinky gown. Gosh, was it ever tight fitting, showing off prominently my shapely body. His hands continually slipped up and down my sides, "Love your new look, dear."

"Yes, but you don't have to try to walk in these extreme heels either," I teased him.

"That's why I love to see you in them. I get to keep my arms around your waist all the time."

I gave him a passionate kiss and whispered, "You don't need an excuse to keep your arms around me, silly."

Princess Mia stayed for a week with us and visited with Tatiana as well. She also explained that she would be back each year with more fashions for us. How could we turn down receiving such a wonderful thank you?

Chapter 35 Heavy Darkness Descends on Phindos

The Kingdom of Phindos lay south of Alia and west of Theos. The North Range of mountains was rich in ores, and beyond which lay Alia, but there they were known as the South Mountains. Whaling and fishing the cold waters of the South Seas accounted for half of their products. The large port of Filantos was the hub of their fishing industry The capital of Pirgos lay five hundred miles inland, where the headwaters of the Crima River flowed northward, cutting a deep gorge through the mountain range, the Gap, as it was called. From there, it flowed on through the heart of Alia, before dumping into the ocean north of Preveza. Hundreds of years ago, Pirgos was the center of gold mining and quality gem cutting, but now the mines had long ago played out. The capital now focused on being the farming hub of central Phindos.

The country's rulers were King Agathon and Queen Adelpha Kadmos, forty and thirty-nine respectively, coming from a long line of Kadmos rulers of Phindos. Agathon was known for his vicious temper and sadistic tendencies. Adelpha, a Holy Woman of the Eighth Degree, was perhaps even more sadistic than her husband was. Couple that with an acid tongue and you have the recipe for a very unhappy domestic life. Mind you, not for those two adults, but for their children and servants, for obviously Holy Women were surrounded with servant women to care for their needs and to satisfy their requests — orders and demands in the case of Queen Adelpha.

The couple had three children. Adonia was their eldest, now twenty. Adelpha hated Adonia for many reasons, not the least was the fact that she had her at a very young age and the delivery nearly cost Adelpha her life. She never forgave her daughter for that. Adonia hated her parents with a passion, ever since they forced her to become a Holy Woman of the Eighth Degree when she was barely ten years old. She'd refused to obey her mother's orders to slap her tutor for some imagined indiscretion. As a result, they'd had her arms removed, saying that now she would appreciate Adelpha and treat her mother with proper respect. Adonia was a lovely young woman who had long, thick, straight black hair, which continually annoyed her mother, who had stringy, thin blonde hair. For Adelpha, Adonia's good looks and hair were a continuous reminder of her own shortcomings in the beauty department.

Next came Alcestis, who was nineteen. She had her mother's thin, blonde hair and as a result, kept hers cut rather short. She too was now a Holy Woman, primarily because she had begged and pleaded with her mother to allow her to be just like her. Alcestis, unlike Adonia, did everything she could to please both their parents, going along with everything they asked. Secretly, though, Alcestis was in love with a young courtier and counted on his stealing her away one day soon.

Finally, from Adelpha's view at least, she gave Agathon the son that he demanded. Theo was now eighteen with his father's thick black hair. He lacked his father's forcefulness. Rather, he was a browbeaten coward, kowtowing to all the sadistic requests of his parents, including slapping Adonia silly whenever Adelpha requested she be slapped for having made a nasty remark. Adonia was constantly at war with her parents, so Theo got a lot of practice in hitting her. Although his hands inflicted the stinging pain on her face, she held her mother responsible, not him. He was just cowardly following orders, believing that one day he would become king.

The rulers had two advisors, Stavros Kietos, fifty, and Sophokles Akios, forty-three. Stravros' wife had died during childbirth many years ago. Since then, he had never remarried, preferring wenches at the more exclusive clubs around Pirgos. He was a well-known figure about the darker circles and frequently made arrangements for sadistic sexual episodes for both the king and queen, who took particular pleasure in together working their ways on the same woman or man. Sophokles, who went by Sop, had never married, for his intention was on amassing wealth and power. He saw families as sucking the very life blood out of men, who were forced to work to provide for them and which gave back little in return. He always ignored the sadistic adventures of his lieges and was well remunerated for doing so.

Of course, with three Holy Women in the palace, servants were plentiful. The queen, for example, had six women attending her, though often Agathon and Adelpha would sexually molest one of them of an evening, particularly when they were bored. Well paid, the six endured their mistreatment. Alcestis, their charming daughter as Adelpha continually pointed out when Adonia was present, had three women looking after her many needs. However, Adelpha's six servant women were all young and attractive, and she made sure that Alcestis' three women in waiting were homely. Not a chance would Adelpha feel eclipsed by her daughter.

Adonia however had only one servant to help her with life's needs, Philomena Lis, who was also twenty. She had long brown hair and blue eyes Kind and considerate, she always treated Adonia with the greatest of care. Although not homely, she was a stutterer and around Adonia's parents, her stuttering was most pronounced. Philomena had come to be Adonia's caretaker when they were both fourteen. Her father, a widower, was something of a drunkard, and often Philomena received beatings, which the next day he swore that he would never do again. Thus, she leapt at the chance to get out of her house and into the palace. Though life here in the palace was harsh, Adonia loved her and treated her as her best and only friend. In this Royal Palace, the only real love present was that between Adonia and Philomena.

Last year, her loyalty to Adonia had been horribly tested. Adonia had gotten into yet another argument with her parents, who wanted her to come join their sadistic sexual escapades. She had flatly refused to do so. Agathon flew into a fit of rage and ordered Philomena's left hand be cut off. Adonia sat with her night and day until she had healed — the two often crying together, sealing their unspoken bond of love between them. Adonia was taught that open rebellion on her part would be taken out on the one person in the world that she cherished, Philomena.

Still, Adonia refused to obey her parents' requests that she believed were wrong. True, she did go along with those that she felt were acceptable or even the right thing to do, though the latter seldom occurred.

Of course, fashion played a paramount role with all women of the court, none more so than the queen and her daughters and their servants. If you were a woman, the only way that you would be allowed to enter the outer gates of the Royal Palace was if you were wearing the finest of Annelise outfits. Adelpha, angered at the loss of her figure after three years of bearing children, had worn ever restrictive corsets until she had her waist back to a proper sixteen inches around, two inches smaller than before she became pregnant with Adonia. All women were required to wear the exotic satin ball gowns imported from Annelise. Adelpha's was, naturally, the largest in diameter, covering some sixteen feet in diameter as it touched the floor. Her daughters' gowns had to be fourteen feet at the floor, while the servants, ten. No exceptions were allowed.

Yet, after Adonia's outburst had cost Philomena her left hand, the sadistic natures of her parents were only fueled even more. It was now a week before the plague struck, lunchtime. Gathered in the Great Hall, the family ate together, with each Holy Woman being assisted, that is fed, by one of their servants. As usual, Philomena was having a hard time dealing with her own meal and Adonia's. Agathon spilled some wine and it seeped down onto his magnificent black moustache and onto his well-trimmed goatee. "Damn it!" he curse and reached for his napkin, then a grin formed and he looked over at Adonia. "Daughter, get over here and lick the wine from my moustache and beard, please." His voice was cold and covert.

"Use your napkin, father. That's what they are for," she replied slightly sarcastically.

"I've had just about enough of your insolence, Adonia. Obviously, cutting off Philomena's hand has not been enough. Well, I ought to have realized that she's just a servant. Your mother and I have devised another method to teach you manners."

"Don't you dare hurt Philomena!" she cried out.

"No, that has not been enough to get you to change your ways. No, we've worked out a better way. In fact, you will be our test subject to see if it works," he insinuated. Adonia felt a twinge of cold fear in her stomach and refused Philomena's next bite of the roast duck. "Actually, dear daughter, you should feel very pleased with what we've devised." Now she was worried, she did not like the sounds of this. Often it meant the two had hatched up some new torture to send her way. Life was bad enough as it was, forced to wear this outfit, which kept her waist at eighteen inches around.

He went on, "We've been cleaning out one of the attic storage rooms and came upon the most exquisite pair of earrings ever. They are very ancient and special. Sop here has done a bit of research on them, and apparently, they were discovered centuries ago on some island. The myth suggests that they were made by some ancient race, now long dead. Sop had their value estimated, and frankly, we were not surprised. They are worth at least a half million. So Adonia, never say that we do not lavish you with presents. No, these earrings are just incredible, you will enjoy them."

Somehow, Adonia just knew that she would not enjoy them, even though his words sounded like she was getting a high honor, a valuable present. Alcestis looked crestfallen. Adonis was going to get a royal present and she was not. A pouting look filled her pretty face, but her parents failed to notice it.

He continued, "We have just acquired a special corset for you and dresses to fit. After lunch, we will get you into your new outfit and earrings. I do so hope that you appreciate them both. However, knowing you, Adonia, if you make so much as even a single complaint about either of them for the next month, or even one little peep, we will have the doctor pull out all of your teeth! That ought to curb your incessant complaining. Yet, your mother has begged me to go further this time, considering the expense that we have gone to this time, Adonia. So if you make a bigger scene, complain loudly, we will have the doctor replace your eyes with glass eyeballs. What you cannot see, you cannot complain about! I think your mother's idea is positively a brilliant one. My only regret is that we should have thought of this years ago. Think of all the bickering and complaining that we would not have endured had we swapped your eyes with glass eyes years ago. My, oh my. Well, that's the deal. A little complaining and you lose all of your teeth. Big complaining and you also lose your eyes as well. At last, Adelpha, we will have some peace around here." Alcestis looked a bit pale. Theo grinned, sensing that Adonia was about to be silenced for good. Sop ignored the whole scene, while Stavros began to calculate the odds of Adonia remaining silent.

After finishing lunch, Adonia was marched into her mother's room, where they had prepared everything for her that morning. Adonia now realized that this was not a spur of the moment reaction, but had been well planned, probably for days. Her fears only grew as they stripped her of her clothing, piece by piece, until she was standing naked before her parents. Well, she breathed deeply, thankful for this brief respite from the corset. She kept her mouth shut, however. Now her father began putting a new corset on her. She thought it looked a bit small but soon knew what was happening.

"Now this corset has plenty of steel in it and in a couple of minutes when I get it tight, your waist will be twelve inches around. Don't worry; the new emerald green dress was made for your new waist size. But also, your breasts are still way too small, so this one will push them up a bit. Now exhale like a good girl." Twelve inches? Adonia wanted to scream no! She could only barely manage eighteen; twelve would be impossible. She would not be able to breathe! Tighter and tighter, the corset became as her father relentlessly pulled on the heavy duty laces. At least he knew the proper way to tighten a corset; years of assistance to Adelpha had taught him well. "Breathe out!" he ordered and even punched her in her belly, forcing more air out of her lungs. Just as she began to pass out, he finally stopped and began tying them off. "Now then, you will not be allowed out of your new outfit for the next entire week. You will sleep in your dress and heels. To make sure that Philomena does not try to get you out of it in secret, I have wired it shut and padlocked it. Only I have the key to unlock it. You will remain in this outfit for a whole week. If you behave during that time, I will consider releasing you for a breather." She then passed out.

She awoke sometime later to discover that they had gone ahead and finished dressing her in her new clothes. "Ah, you are awake now. I might also add that we have affixed your new Annelise heels with padlocks as well. We don't want Philomena helping you out of your new shoes either. Now then, we have also affixed your new, most exotic and most expensive earrings. Their design does not allow for them to ever be removed. After all, we do not want you to have them fall off accidentally. You have no hands to pick them up with, you see. Now then, remember the bargain: no complaints, dear daughter. Philomena will escort you to your room where you can examine your new look in detail. I must say, I am very, very pleased with how you now look, dear child. However, I so do look forward to hearing you complain a lot about this. I believe that you would look even prettier with glass eyes. Just in case you are curious, here are the ones that I picked out myself. I chose them to match your earrings and dress, emerald. So you can make your loving father very happy indeed by complaining a whole lot. Please do, Adonia. Please do."

Adonia could barely breathe. Her ears hurt for some reason; the earrings felt heavy; her shoes seemed a bit too tight. He indicated to Philomena to help her stand up to leave, which she did using her good hand. Adonia wobbled a bit, her heels were higher than she those she normally wore and realized that they had put her into the extreme heels, not the usual six-inch ones that most women wore here in the palace. With Philomena holding her tightly, the two moved very slowly out of her parent's quarters and to her own. They had to stop five times so that Adonia could catch her breath and avoid fainting yet again!

Only in the safety of her suite of rooms did they dare speak at last. "O-oh h-h-how a-a-awful!" Philomena exclaimed. Adonia stood before her mirror. The earrings caught her attention first. They were huge, made of oblong jade pendants secured by heavy gold fittings. A round golden disk had been punched into her ear lobes and a thick gold loop went thorough it holding the gigantic and heavy earrings. From the central point at her lobes, six separate sets of dangling gold and jade dropped down, each set containing six large, oblong pieces of jade. The lowest two levels of jade rested on her shoulders and the upper part of her breasts, now pushed upwards by the corset. Her lobes were pulled downward so hard that they appeared double in size. When she turned her head, she felt that the earrings were about to pull her ears off!

Her waist was shockingly small, made all the more dramatic by the sudden flaring of her billowing dress just below her hips. However, the corset had so many metal stays in it that Adonia could not bend at all, except at her waist. As she tried to breathe, she found that the corset did not give even a fraction of an inch. "T-They s-said that you need to take frequent shallow breaths, Adonia. Maybe like a dog panting. Please don't faint on me. I have such a hard time getting you back up with only one hand."

When alone and calmed down, Philomena normally ceased her stuttering. Adonia flashed her a smile. Getting Philomena to not stutter when they were alone together had been one of the two women's most significant achievements, one which made Philomena feel really proud. "I will try not to."

"The heels. Can I sit and see them?" A bit later, Philomena held a mirror just so and by looking into the full-length mirror on the wall down into the mirror that she was holding for her, Adonia finally saw her new shoes. They were emerald green oxfords, with metal bands locked by a padlock. The heels were as she suspected, the extreme variety, ones in which one could only just barely walk and only if one were very careful. Well, the Annelise Princess who came by nearly every quarter always wore them. Glide across the floor, she always said. Well, if the princess could somehow manage them, Adonia thought that she could, if only to spite her parents! No, the impossibly tight and painful corset — that would be what would likely cost her her eyes next. The earrings — well they would just likely tear her ear lobes off. At least then, her parents would be done messing with her ears.

"They make it," she ran out of air and took another shallow breath, "almost impossible," another breath, "for me to walk." Gasp, "I can barely," gasp, "talk now."

"I know. Talk short words and sentences. That might h-h-help," Philomena suggested. However, Adonia instantly knew without turning that someone had entered. She had stuttered. Slowly, she turned in the chair to see her brother standing in the doorway.

"Knock, knock, sis. I came by to see how you look. Wow, your waist seems tiny. Bet that is uncomfortable. But your earrings, holy cow! They drop all the way down to your knockers, sis. Now for once I think dad goofed. You are wearing a fortune, sis. I wish he'd give me a half million. Heck, I'd be happy with a quarter million. You should have seen the look on Alcestis' face when dad said how much they are worth! Priceless. Now she's begging dad to get her an identical pair. If he does, I am going to ask him for something too."

"You should." Gasp. "I can't even," gasp, "talk hardly." Gasp. "I can barely," gasp, "walk now." Gasp. "My ears are," gasp, "going to rip."

"Gosh, sis, you can't breathe can you? Wow. Well, I will mention that to dad. I doubt that he will loosen it, though. You know dad. It is all your own doing, Adonia. You should play along with them like I do. You don't see dad picking on me or on Alcestis, now do you? It is all your own fault." He turned and left.

"It is not your fault. It's your wicked parent's fault," Philomena said once she was sure that he could not hear her. "I think that you and I ought to get you used to this new torture. You should practice walking, you know, like the Annelise princess does. She manages."

"But she has," gasp, "arms!" She wanted to say more, but couldn't. Talking was too difficult now.

"I know, but you must try. You must not complain. Did you see those glass eyes he had? I was terrified that he was going to rip your eyes out right then! I am scared, Adonia. I think since he has the glass eyes, he will find some reason to use them on you. You must be very careful now."

"I can't live," gasp, "if I can't," gasp, "see."

"I know. Let's work hard not to give him any reason to do that to you. I love you so, still." She leaned over as best she could in her tight corset and the two kissed passionately. Then, they spent the afternoon practicing walking, which wore out her knees. Only with a great effort were they able to get her to the Great Hall for dinner. Her feet and knees ached; her chest felt mercilessly crushed; her ears throbbed unrelenting. However, she kept her mouth shut and did not speak. She couldn't really. She had to focus all her attention on trying to eat and breathe at the same time. She couldn't hold her breath long enough to chew and swallow a bite of food.

"Well, I see our daughter loves her new outfit and earrings. How pleasant it is not to hear her complaints at the supper table," Agathon sneered. "I do hope that you start complaining soon. These fancy glass eyes cost me a pretty copper." She wanted to curse him, but simply could not, not without choking to death on the meat that she was trying hard to chew. Her parents threw at least two dozen jabs at her during the meal, but she simply did not respond. At last, he said, "Well, Adelpha, I do believe that we have solved our wayward daughter."

Nighttime gave her no relief. She had to sleep in her complete outfit, darn near impossible. By the fourth night, she at least managed to doze off a bit, before the pain and intense pressure in her body woke her again.

The night before the plague culminated, at dinner in the Great Hall, Agathon said, "Dear Adonia, look what we found in the attic. My grandaunt Adonia Kadmos, and your namesake by the way, apparently had a dark skinned servant from somewhere in the far north. Someone did an oil of her. See?" He held up a portrait of one of the Utu Princesses with the huge top and bottom lip plates for her to see. "Now I was thinking, Adonia. The look of this woman is so erotic, so exciting, so enticing, that your mother and I are thinking seriously about adorning you with a similar look instead of the glass eyes. After all, what fun is there if you can't see anything anymore? If we can give you such impressive lip plates, I believe that's what they are called, why then I doubt that you could talk understandably. That might be preferable to the tight corset that we have you wearing now. What do you think, dear? Would you exchange your corset for such impressive lip plates? Of course, you can have them in any color of your choice. Green I suppose would be your best choice so that they would match your earrings. Now on the other hand, perhaps we should give the lip plates to Philomena, since she is your servant and the woman in the painting was her servant. Besides, she stutters so badly that no one can understand her anyway. What do you think, dear? Would you like them or should we give them to Philomena? You choose."

Adonia wanted to scream, but the corset made that impossible, especially when eating. Her sadistic father was taking an enormous amount of pleasure out of making her choose which one of them would be tortured next! Philomena went white with fear. Damn you to hell! I won't give you the satisfaction of watching me make your filthy choice, she thought to herself. She then fainted and fell out of her chair. She came too to find herself lying on her bed, Philomena fanning her with one of their small, accordion fans.

"You are safe now. They left us here."

"Did he choose?" she asked and gasped.

"Not yet. We are safe a little longer. Can we go to bed soon? My arms are so weak and tired. I can barely fan you, my dearest love."

"Yes, you go," gasp, "to bed now." Gasp. "I am all right," gasp, "lying here." Gasp. "I love you." Gasp. "Somehow we will," gasp, "find a way out," gasp, "of this mess." Gasp. "I promise you," gasp, "somehow we will."

"I — I sent a message to my brother's friend tonight. I hope you will not be mad with me."

"Of course not."

"I asked him to write a fake letter from your uncle Alex. The letter will beg King Agathon to send you and me down to Filantos to assist him with designing the Spring Ball. If the king believes it, maybe he will send us down there. Then, we can make an escape and hide out with a friend of my father's. He's a whaler and is gone a lot of the time. We should be safe there."

"Philomena!" Gasp. "That's brilliant!" Gasp. "That might work!" Both women now had the faintest glimmer of hope as Philomena climbed into her bed in the next room. Normally, she would have climbed in with Adonia, but now that she had to sleep in this huge dress, she couldn't.

The next morning, everyone was awakened by women screaming from all parts of the palace. So many were screaming that no one took notice of Philomena's panic screams, except Adonia, of course. When the princess came into Philomena's room, she found Philomena sitting up in her bed as armless as she was. Adonia found that she could breathe normally now, just not bend easily. Her feet ached almost as if they were broken somehow. Her breasts had enlarged so much that they had completely popped out of her dress. She didn't notice her hair had grown two feet, though. Philomena likewise had a tiny waist, breasts as large as her head, no arms, and her feet were horribly distorted as well. Adonia sat down on the bed beside her and the two leaned into each other and cried.

Sometime later, Theo came crawling into their room on his hands and knees. "Hell has come, maybe the end of the world. I've come to let you out of your dress, sis. Dad's orders. Every damn woman in the palace has suddenly grown enormous boobs and has lost their arms. Every man's feet are like mine. They don't bend anymore. None of us can even walk. Has to be the plague, that's what Sop is saying. I believe him. There you go sis. You can thank me later."

"Thanks, Theo. Can I beg you to at least put our nightgowns on us? Please? Let us have some slight modesty left." Adonia begged him and he relented. During this change, Adonia finally noticed that her hair had grown and now reached down to her ankles. Her feet were also distorted but because she had been wearing her Annelise extreme heels, they had kept the foot modification from taking place fully. Still, the only way that she could walk was to continue to wear those same heels. After he had gone, the two found the pile of alien objects in her common room, and Adonia manage to help Philomena into the pair of shoes that fit her. Now the two headed for the Great Hall, where she suspected that everyone was now eating breakfast.

The family was there, only breakfast wasn't. Her father didn't notice them entering. He was talking with the palace Captain of the Guards and his advisors. Adelpha and Alcestis were chatting about the incredible growth of their hair and marveling over the size of their breasts. Adelpha then said, "This is absolutely incredible. Look at my waist. So utterly perfect in all ways. Why, I never thought that I could get down to a twelve-inch waist, Alcestis. But we both are! We will just have to have new dresses made for us immediately. Already your father just loves my breasts! It is a holy miracle, that's what I say."

"But mom, our servants are like us now too. Who are we going to get to care for our needs?" Alcestis asked very worried.

"Oh don't fret so, dear. I'll have your father go acquire some new servant women who do have arms. Probably have them later this afternoon. Don't worry. We look spectacular now. Just perfect. It's a miracle."

She spoke loudly to get Agathon's attention. "Dear, do get rid of our helpless servants this instant. Send them home or something and send someone to get us new servants. And send someone to the kitchen. We are way past breakfast time, dear."

Hearing that, Adonia and Philomena quietly left the room, terrified that Philomena would be sent back to her abusive father! While they discussed ways around that awful event, more and more news began coming into the palace. Adonia, realizing this was likely to occur, left Philomena in her room and headed back into the Great Hall, sitting quietly and listening to everything that was said. During the day, she found out more and more — all of which was frightening and anything but good.

Around noon, Sop managed to get a number of bread loaves to the table along with rounds of cheese. Cleverly, Adonia bit into one loaf and then quietly left the room, taking it back for Philomena and herself. She returned and did the same with an entire cheese round. The two then worked together to eat, each one holding the bread or cheese solidly while the other tore off bites to eat. Then, Adonia headed back to listen in on the many conversations.

Sop managed to create supper — an awful tasting stew. The men had no choice but to feed the women now. Agathon helped Adelpha, Theo helped Alcestis, and Sop fed Adonia. Adelpha, once finished, said, "Sop, put the rest into pans and take them to the many women servants. They can eat out of the pans. I don't want you having to feed them. They are such a liability now. We simply must send them all home tomorrow." He nodded and crawled back to the kitchen to carry out her wishes. Adonia followed him and watched as he scooped piles of the ill-made stew into shallow pans.

"I'll take one for Philomena, Sop. I'll carry it with my teeth," Adonia suggested. He held it up and she bit down hard. Slowly, she made her way back to her room and struggled to sit it down without spilling it on the floor. "I am so sorry, Philomena. They said that you have to eat it from the plate. I wish there was some way I could feed you like you did me all these years."

"Thanks for bringing it. I'm starved. I'll eat somehow. Any news?"

"Lots and it's all bad. The plague, that's what it's being called, it's struck everyone in Pirgos. They say that all women are now as we are and that all men are like Theo and have to crawl; their feet can't bend anymore. As much as mom wants new servants, she isn't going to get any anytime soon. I think that we are safe for a while longer. They say that no stores have opened and that hardly anyone is on the streets, only a few men riding horses. Sop reported that some are saying that this is the Day of Judgment coming, that we are all going to die soon. I don't believe that rumor, though."

Their chat was interrupted by distant popping sounds. Both concluded rightly that it was gunfire. Their room steadily darkened while they chatted. "Knock. Knock, sis." Theo's voice broke in on them. "Come to light some lanterns for you. Sop's orders. From now on, the lanterns stay on day and night. We men can't be bothered continually lighting them for you. Things are getting bad out there. I heard that some are rioting. What else can all that gunfire mean, eh?" He finished lighting four lanterns in her commons room. They would also dimly illuminate their neighboring bedrooms and he crawled out to light more lanterns in the halls.

Hunger satisfied, the two headed into her commons room to examine the pile of strange objects. Images came into their minds as they began to see uses for the things. When they spotted the hairbrushes with the leather straps, both giggled and began to experiment on each other's hair, using their feet as the images in their minds suggested.

"I do love your hair this long, Philomena. It looks really good on you," Adonia complimented the sole person whom she loved. Philomena's fell below her waist now. An hour later, with their hair sort of brushed out, the two decided to get some sleep. However, Adonia insisted that they sleep in her bed from now on. Wiggling and squirming, the two got themselves into bed beside each other and snuggled up. Their passions took over. They kissed and did their best to give each other some pleasure.

The next morning, Adonia headed to the Great Hall to see if she could fetch something for them to eat. Philomena was still too terrified of Adonia's parents even to leave their quarters. She, as Adonia, was helpless to prevent further sadistic actions, and she was sure that they would take advantage of her total helplessness, just as they had Adonia's last week.

She found her family, advisors, her mother's hairdresser Sel, and a number of guards already there. As before, a light breakfast lay on the table, help yourself style. She heard one guard reporting to her father, "Yes, I have confirmed it. The Cardinal has declared that this is the Day of Holy Judgment come finally. His men have been going around the city killing the faithful of the Church of Jehosanity. Can't tell who has shot who, though. Rioters and looters have done their fair share. A lot of the stores with jewelry and gems have been looted already."

"Idiots, our city is filled with idiots," the king exclaimed. "We're in a crisis and they want gems!"

The guard continued, "Most shop owners are not opening up because they are hard pressed to help the wives and daughters — at least this is what some of my men heard when they checked up on a number of owners. The women of our city obviously now need the constant help from the men in their families. We've a real calamity on our hands, Sire."

Agathon grumbled, mostly concerned that there were no women servants to be found for his wife. "This is becoming a major problem, Adelpha." She nodded grimly, waiting for him to decide what to do next.

"Yes and a messenger has just delivered this for you, Sire," the guard added, handing him a sealed letter. Absentmindedly, he opened it, his attention still on how he might get someone, anyone with hands to wait on his wife's needs. He read it hastily and laid it out on the table for Adelpha to read.

"Well, send her packing!" Adelpha said with a wry smile. "One less to have to deal with. Besides, let him deal with her acid tongue."

He smiled, "And ruin all our fun?" His grand plans for her subsided amid this calamity. He sighed and said, "Well, you are right. We've got more problems now that we can handle." He looked up at Adonia. "Adonia, start packing your bags. It seems your uncle wants your services down in Filantos." He sneered and let out an evil chuckle, as if he knew something diabolical that she did not. Adonia feigned surprise, but dare not protest, not now, not with all that was going on. "Get a carriage ready to take Adonia and her servant to the port," he ordered another guard, who crawled off to see to the king's order.

Adonia turned to rush back to her room with the incredible news that she and Philomena were getting away. She saw three churchmen in their sky blue robes crawling into the room. They stopped just inside the main doors. One called out, "The Last Days of Judgment have come. Prepare to greet Lord Jehosa in his Holy Realm of Heaven." The men were heavily armed and, as he finished, his two companions raised their guns. Adonia screamed. Gunfire erupted. She was closest to the men and the acrid smoke burned her eyes; she tripped and fell, which probably saved her life. For what seemed like eternity, Adonia heard the loud bangs of gunfire from all around her, then silence.

Coughing from the smoke, she struggled to get back onto her feet, her lungs aching from the smoke, her eyes burning, and she could not even rub them, only continue to blink feebly. She heard her mother cry out, "He's been shot! Get help here fast!" Someone bumped into Adonia and she fell once again. She stayed down this time. The air was easier to breathe down near the floor. She tried to wipe her eyes with her knees. What had just happened? Who was shot? In spite of everything, she discovered that she just had to know. She waited as the smoke slowly began clearing. Men were crawling around like ants, she thought.

Then, she finally saw the aftermath. "King Agathon is dead," Sop declared. "Your Highness, there is nothing more that we can do for him." Her mother was at his side, but not weeping, she observed.

"Theo's gone too," Stavros declared. "Damn Mano del Dio."

"Well, I am the queen! I give the orders around here now. Any objections? Good! Send word to the Army generals. I want every damn last priest and guard of the Church of Jehosanity executed today! Bring me the Cardinal's head on a platter! Get the dead guard, the king, and my son carried out of here. Take them to the State Room. We'll deal with a funeral later on. This is war and by god, I aim to win!"

Several began crawling to the fallen men, dragging their bodies across the floor. "Someone help my pathetic Alcestis get up. Get a grip on it, daughter!" Adonia struggled to her feet, unwilling to be seen as helpless. Her sister was sobbing uncontrollably, lying in a heap on the floor near her dead brother's body, now being slowly dragged away from her.

"Sop, Stavros, we have plans to make. Agathon's not done anything that has been effective in handling this fiasco. We will!" As soon as order returned to the room, that is, the dead had been removed and the smoke mostly gone, Adelpha, her two assistants, and the Captain of the Guards moved back to the Great Table and sat down. "Sel," she called out to her quailing hair dresser, "be a good boy and make us all some tea. You are now appointed to be my handmaiden. I think that will suit you perfectly."

Adonia looked over at the young man. Sel smiled effeminately, most pleased with his sudden promotion. He crawled off to carry out his orders. "Now then, we have to help our people get a grip on this catastrophe. No one is working because they are all stuck at home caring for their wives and daughters, right?" Sop nodded. "Well, that is bringing the universe to a standstill. That we cannot have. With so many dead in the streets, we simply cannot allow that to continue."

Sop advised, "If there are hundreds of dead in the streets, Your Highness, that poses a serious health risk. We cannot afford an outbreak of serious illness on top of everything else."

"Of course not. The bodies must be removed," she concurred. "Where do we take so many dead? Who can dig so many graves at one time?"

"We could drain the obsolete Roc Pond, dump them in there, and later cover it up," Stavros suggested.

"Brilliant, Stavros. You heard him, Captain. Have the army soldiers begin scouring the city for the dead and dump them in the old Roc Pond. Have them use their cannonae to blow a damn hole in the retaining wall and let the water join the Crima River. Now how do we get the shops open again?"

No one said anything, but Sel did bring them their tea. Adonia sat down, hoping that someone would help her have some tea. How she had missed her morning tea! Besides, she still needed her mother's consent to this trip, her escape. Sel held the cup for Adelpha. Sop did the same for the still whimpering Alcestis. At least Sel had put a full cup before her. She bent over and her heavy earrings banged on the table, but she was able to sip a little by herself.

"Well, gentlemen, it seems to me that the crux of the problem is all our helpless women and girls."

"Yes, Your Highness," Sop agreed, but had no idea how to deal with it. Obviously, men and boys had to care for the women in their families.

"Well, someone's got to get a handle on this. I will! Okay, I will set limits on the number of women or girls one man or boy will deal with. Let's see. I have it. In any family, only one daughter will be allowed. Any family who has more than one daughter shall have the excess daughters removed. Let the parents decide which daughter they will keep. Have the soldiers remove the excess daughters. That will reduce the number of women that must be cared for. Draft that up as an official proclamation. One daughter per family. Now if there is no husband, but some son serving as head of the household, he is allowed a wife. Get rid of other females in that household. Issue a second proclamation. Men must return to work. They are to set out pans of food for their women and allow their women to deal with their own problems for now."

"Yes Your Highness. That might work to get them back to work. What shall we do with all the women and girls that we remove from their homes?" Sop asked.

Adelpha looked at Stavros and smiled wickedly. "Have the prettier women, say between eighteen and twenty-five, brought here to our dungeons. I have some plans for them. The rest, take them to the Roc Pond and dump them in with the rest of the dead. Use your imagination; get rid of them. Get rid of all the excess women here in the palace too."

Alcestis began crying wildly, interrupting the meeting. "Alcestis, what *is* the matter with you?" Adelpha sneered caustically. For once, Adonia was relieved that her ire was not directed at her, as it usually had been for as long as she could remember.

"You are going to kill me, mom?" she wailed.

Adelpha looked at her favorite daughter and then at Adonia. Adonia spoke up quickly, "Mom, uncle wants me to come to him. I will leave as soon as the carriage is ready. Then, you will only have one daughter around."

"Well, you have a point for once, Adonia. Agreed, just don't ever come back here, you understand me? If you do, I will have you dumped into the Roc as well. Stop blubbering, Alcestis. Your sister has saved you from the Roc."

"Now then, Sop, we must think ahead. Have the soldiers go at once to the Granaries and the Royal Stores. Load up all the grain and food supplies and bring them here into the Royal Palace. If I am not mistaken, soon everyone will run out of food. They will pay royally for a sack of flour. We will have the supplies and will make a fortune. We'll divide our profits into quarters, one for each of us three and one we'll use for rebuilding efforts and payments to our army soldiers. What do you two say to that?"

Adonia watched their greedy eyes nearly pop out. Adelpha knew precisely how to control the two advisors! Like lap dogs, both men readily agreed to that proposition.

"Might I also suggest that we send out riders throughout Phindos to see just how widespread this plague is?" Sop asked.

"Precisely. Make it so," she added.

A guard came crawling in to make another report. "Your Highness, there are so many dead men and women littering the streets, the Royal Carriage will not be able to leave until enough have been removed. The driver has asked that the trip to Filantos be delayed a day or two." Fear seeped back into Adonia's stomach once more!

"So be it. Adonia, your trip is going to be delayed. However, I don't want to see you making use of any of the men here at court. You deal with your own damn needs yourself. Either that or join the others at the Roc."

"Yes, Your Highness," Adonia for once used her title — anything to keep her from having second thoughts! She bit down on a loaf of bread. Holding it in her teeth, she slowly shuffled out of the Great Hall.

Later, she held it for Philomena, who tore off bites ravenously. Then, she told her lover all the horrible news. Philomena said, "When I heard all the gunfire, I thought that you were killed. I cried and figured we had both met our end. Do you think she will let us actually leave when the roads are cleared?"

"I think so, Philomena, if I can keep from antagonizing her until then. She's got far more serious things on her mind now." The two then decided to see if they could somehow pack some of their things to take with them on the trip.

Late that afternoon, Adonia heard the faint sounds of women crying and screaming. While she wanted to go see what was going on, she followed Philomena's advice and stayed put until it was suppertime. "I'll see what I can bring back for us." She shuffled slowly off to the Great Hall, getting there as the others were beginning to assemble. She sat as far away from her mother as possible and waited.

Sel began dragging a pot of stew over to the table. One by one, he served up everyone, finally filling a pan and sitting it before her. He then went to Adelpha's side and began feeding her. Sop begrudgingly fed Alcestis. Adonia had no choice but to try to eat from her pan like a dog. Well, she had suffered worst indignities. Sel was definitely a better cook, she thought.

After diner, Adelpha said, "The doctor has arrived. Stavros, care to join me? Adonia, you are ordered to join me in the dungeons. I want to show you something." Fear swamped her again. Was her mother going to go back on what she had promised? Her legs trembling, Adonia followed her mother, as the women and crawling Stavros headed to the dungeons. She dare not say even one word.

The doctor was already present. Adonia saw that her mother now had two dozen young women held in the dungeon cells. All were naked, except for the shoes, which they needed to be able to walk. Their terrified looks spoke volumes. Adonia now realized that many women and girls had probably already been murdered by her mother's soldiers! She felt nauseous and nearly lost her supper.

"Adonia, dear. I wanted you to see what your father and I had planned for you. Honestly, he was just waiting for the right time to do this to you. He would have done this sooner, but he so enjoyed seeing you struggling all last week. Too bad the plague came. Well, now we have others on which to experiment and get it right. Okay, doctor, let's see your handiwork in action. You do want your thousand gold, right?"

"Yes, Your Highness. All is prepared. This way." He led them to the far end of the dungeon, where three women lay unconscious on wooden tables. "Which do you want which done to?"

"That one, her eyes. That one, her teeth. That one, her lips." Adelpha nodded her head in three directions. "Come, Adonia, see what your father had planned for you. Alas, he could not live long enough to see the fruits of his brilliant ideas. Well, I've decided that after you have antagonized your uncle and he sends you back here, I will have these done to you. Watch what you have so far escaped having done to you."

As Adonia watched, the doctor removed one young woman's eyes, replacing them with the emerald glass eyes, the very ones her father had shown her last week! Adonia gagged and vomited up her supper. She missed watching the doctor pull out the second woman's teeth, but saw the blood oozing from her mouth afterwards. That was nothing compared to the blood that flowed from the third woman's lips, as the doctor carefully slit her upper and lower lips, inserting the two lip plates, pre-made to the right dimensions.

"See, I have three play toys for my amusement now, Adonia. Can you imagine how much pleasure your father would have had to see you with all three? Oh my, that he would. It is such a shame that he didn't think of these years ago! Ah well, I must not antagonize your uncle, so you may go. Just remember, if you ever return back here, dear, I promise that I won't have you killed. I'll see that you get all three of your father's last brilliant modifications." Adelpha took great pleasure in seeing the look of horror on Adonia's face. Adonia turned and shuffled as quickly as she could out of the dungeon.

Back in her room, she cried for a long time. Philomena tried to hold her, but could only lean her breasts onto her lover. At last, Adonia got control of her emotions and related what she had witnessed. Philomena cried too. Just then, someone knocked on her door. They looked up to see a young palace guard at the doorway.

"Excuse me Princess. I am Akantha. I am to drive you to Filantos. I have the carriage ready now. I am told that a path will have been cleared by tomorrow evening. We can leave any time after that. Just tell me when you want to leave, Princess."

"Let's leave the very instant that they tell you it is clear," Adonia said, sniffing to clear her nose. "Can you get a pile of food to take with us, Akantha? I don't think that we'll be able to stay at any inns. Probably none will be open, if the plague has gotten to the other towns too."

"Wise idea. And water too. I'll load us up a bunch. Do you need a hand packing anything?" The offer of kindness surprised both women. They agreed and he helped them, packing what little they had that they thought might be useful. None of their clothes fit at all and Akantha promised to see if he could find some large shirts that they could wear over their nightgowns. "Blankets. I'll bring some of them too." Akantha was very helpful, Adonia thought.

When he left, both women were extremely hungry. Adonia shuffled through the darkened halls to the Great Hall, hoping to find something edible there that she could bring back for her and Philomena. Only one dim lantern illuminated the Great Hall, still she headed to the adjoining kitchen area, looking for anything she could find. She latched onto a loaf of bread. That would have to do for now, she thought. Just as she was about to leave, she heard the sounds of crawling men coming, and she hid in the kitchen.

Soon she recognized the voices of Stavros and Sophokles, speaking in hushed tones.

"The woman's gone too far this time. I can see that we need to reduce the number of helpless women in any given household. That part is practical. But this, this is even too sadistic for my stomach," Stavros whispered.

"Agreed. She's allowing her sadistic impulses and drives free reign. Lord knows what she will dream up next. We, Stavros, we might be next. At least with the king, we had a buffer from her," Sop whispered back.

"Yes, but we cannot just kill her. We need her if we are to run the country," Stavros pointed out. "As long as she lives, she is the lawful queen and our liege."

"True, we lose her and we lose our cozy, profitable positions. As long as she lives we are safe. I see what you mean, but it could well be us next in one of her fits. What can we do about it? We need her alive."

"We do at that, alive, but that's all. I have a plan, Sop. She'll be alive all right, but she will not ever again hinder us," Stavros hinted.

"I'm game, what do you have in your diabolical mind?"

"A taste of her own sadism. The doctor is still here. I will make the arrangements. I'll slip it in her breakfast tea. You don't need to know the details." Stavros sneered wickedly, "She'll get a taste of her own ideas. Trust me; we will have an alive queen that will not bother us any longer." Adonia heard them shaking hands and then leaving. She waited until she was certain that they were gone and not coming back before she shuffled her way out and back to her room.

Adonia did not quite know how she felt. They were plotting against her mother; yet her mother had mistreated her all her life. No love lay between them, merely hatred and loathing. Indeed, somehow Adonia had barely escaped these latest tortures herself. She decided to say nothing, except to Philomena, of course.

Curiosity got the better of her and she was at the Great Hall in time for breakfast. The doctor was speaking when she arrived, "Ah well, there are just too many germs down there in the dungeon, Your Highness. I am afraid that the surgery has become infected."

"Well, no problem. There are many more to use. Take them to wherever you think will be better. I want some play toys alive. That's all that matters."

"Yes, Your Highness. It will be so today."

"I feel so sleepy. I must not have gotten enough sleep. I am so excited about these three women! I wonder how the blind one is faring? Is she terrified? So delicious, I can't wait to lick her." Adonia cringed; her heart went out to the poor young woman who now could not see on top of everything else!

When she looked up at last, her mother was out cold. The men ignored quiet Adonia, carefully dragging the queen out of the room. She again bit down on cheese, took that back for Philomena, and then returned for some bread. On her return trip, she saw two guards dragging the dead bodies of the two women who had had their teeth pulled and lips sliced. Evidently, both had gotten an infection and had died, she thought. Now the two only had to wait until the evening, and they may yet escape this nightmare palace.

At lunchtime, she decided to see if she might obtain something for them to eat. She found everyone but her mother already eating. She sat down and Sel crawled over and put a cold cut sandwich on a plate for her, then crawled back to continue helping Alcestis eat hers.

"Doctor's left. He'll be back in the morning, but he says that all went well this time. Shouldn't be any infections," Stavros said. "She was awake when he left. We'll check on her after we finish lunch." He turned to the two princesses. "Ladies, your mother has suffered some serious side-effects from the plague. The honorable doctor has done his best. We want you to come and visit your mother on her sick bed after lunch. He's assured us that she will recover just fine. I'm sure that she will want to see you both." He sounded very polite, yet covert, Adonia thought.

After eating, the two princesses followed the two crawling men. "Sel, you come too, your liege will have need of your services," Stavros called back. Dutifully, Sel began crawling rapidly to catch up, following behind the two young women. They headed to their mother's chambers and found her lying on her bed, still in her nightgown. Both women gasped at the sight of their mother.

Her lips had been split, and she now wore the same lip plates that the poor young woman had worn yesterday. Her eyes were gone, replaced with a pair of red glass eyeballs. In her partially open mouth, they saw she was missing all her teeth and the front half of her tongue. "Sel, you are to gargle her every hour with this disinfectant, doctor's orders," Stavros ordered the gaping young man.

"Queen Adelpha, your lovely daughters are here to see how you are doing. Would you like to say hi to them?" Stavros sneered viciously. Their mother made some strange, unintelligible noises. For the first time in her life, she saw pale terror on her mother's face. She thought perhaps revenge would seem good, but she felt sick at her stomach instead.

"Princesses, you will not say anything about this other than your mother had some bad side-effects from the plague or you will find yourselves like your mother. Understood?"

Alcestis squeaked, "Yes." Her legs gave out and she fainted. Adonia nodded and left, leaving the men to deal with her sister. She heard Stavros speaking as she slowly shuffled away.

"Adelpha, you will nod your head yes when we ask something of you. If you do, Sel here will be your constant attendant, pleasuring you as you desire."

"But you know that I don't rise around women," Sel pleaded.

"Use your damn fingers on her, Sel, unless you want a similar fate. She is your responsibility now. Keep her pleasured and happy and you will be rewarded nicely," Stavros added.

"Perhaps we ought to do the same thing to Alcestis, Sop. It would appear more plausible if both looked the same — bad side-effects of the plague," Stavros suggested, pulling his chin. "She's unconscious now, doctor's returning later on. Perhaps we should also to it to Adonia."

"We best leave her go to her uncle's place for now. We can have her done when she comes back. No sense getting him antagonized," Sop suggested. Now she was out of hearing range and she found that she felt a pang of pity for her mother and her awful plight. Her poor sister, was she next? Adonia knew that she just had to escape!

She told Philomena what had happened to her mother. "Serves her right! Adonia, what's going to happen to all those other women in the dungeon? Are they going to murder or torture them too?" The more that the two speculated, the more that they knew they had to do something to help those women. They guessed that soon those women would just be murdered and dumped in the Roc. A plan slowly formed in Adonia's mind.

Around ten that night, Akantha came to their door with good news. "Princess Adonia, they have enough streets cleared that we can get out now. I have stored food and water in the carriage. When do you want to leave?"

"Now! You go wait for us at the carriage and we will join you shortly," she said. He nodded and crawled off. "Come on, it is worth a try. Everyone should be sleeping now or at least not paying much attention to us, Philomena." The two women stole down the halls and headed down the long stairs into the dungeon. One dim lantern, black with lampblack, provided the only light. They spotted two cells, each with ten women in them.

"Incredible, the doors are not even locked!" Adonia whispered. "Come on, I'll pull this one open, you get that one open. Ladies, we are going to try to set you free. Don't make any noise. Head on out the way that they brought you in here. Once you reach the courtyard, stand close to the carriage there. When we leave in the carriage, you walk as fast as you can behind us, and with luck, you will walk right on out with us. After that, I surely don't know what to suggest. They're murdering so many women it's not funny."

The twenty women whispered their thanks and did as she asked, slowly shuffling their way out of the main entrance to the dungeon, which led to the courtyard, not the winding stairs the two had descended.

"Help," a faint voice called out to them, as they watched the last woman start her three-inch steps toward freedom. They turned to see another open cell. The young woman with the emerald glass eyes was standing askew to the door, a pleading look on her face. "Help me, please," she called once more. Adonia and Philomena shuffled over to her as fast as they could, which was pitifully slow, Adonia thought.

"We can't just leave her," Philomena whispered.

"I know, but she can't see and we don't have any arms to guide her. I know, I am going to grab your hair in my mouth and sort of lead you along. Philomena, you give her directions when we get to any barriers or steps." The woman had beautiful red hair, slightly wavy, and it fell to her knees. Adonia squatted down, grabbed a mouthful of hair, and rose. She gave a gentle tug and the woman began trying to take hesitant steps. The next fifteen minutes were the longest and hardest minutes ever for the two. The poor woman, unable to see, no arms to feel her way, and crippled up feet forcing her to walk on her toes, had a very frightful time. Philomena constantly had to direct her, "A bit to the right. Now to the left." She could not get the direction of motion right. She had no way of seeing what that was, save the gentle pull on her hair, which was somewhat confusing. The flight of stairs went better than expected, though, one "felt" step at a time.

By the time that they reached the carriage and the waiting Akantha, the twenty women had moved in close behind the carriage, keeping very still. Akantha whispered, "What's going on?" when Adonia appeared and drew close.

"I am setting them free. Please help us get her aboard the carriage; we have to take her with us. The rest are going to follow us out the gates, so go very slowly, please, Akantha. They are going to murder these women or torture them," Adonia pleaded, hoping the very young soldier would go along with her.

She need not have worried, for he had a younger sister whom he loved.

His hands lifted Adonia into the carriage, then Philomena, and then the blind woman. Adonia held her breath. Would anyone stop them? Were they really going to escape this palace of horrors? After an eternity, the carriage began moving, slowly. She relaxed slightly. He was going slowly enough, she hoped. The main gates were already opened in anticipation of the carriage's departure. The two sleepy guards noticed the women following right behind the carriage, but they had no orders concerning them and assumed they were with Akantha and the Princess. Once they cleared the gates, Adonia heard them slam shut and the heavy bars dropping into place across the gates. Now, the carriage picked up speed and the two looked worriedly out of the windows. The streetlights still worked, and she saw the twenty women begin to scatter slowly.

"What's that smell?" she asked.

"Dead bodies, I think," the blind woman answered. "My uncle died and wasn't found for two days last summer. His place smelled like this. Are we safe? Where are we? Are we moving somehow?"

"I think we are almost safe. I am Adonia Kadmos and this is my lover and dearest friend Philomena Lis. I was a Holy Woman and she used to care for me. Philomena's grand plan is saving all our lives. We are supposed to be heading to the port Filantos. I have no idea what we can do once we get there though. She made up a lie saying that my uncle needed me there. We would not be safe around him either. He'd just send us back to the palace. Right now, we just want to get as far away from the palace as we can."

"They made my dad choose which of his daughters to give away," the woman volunteered. "I was the oldest and he thought that I would be the most likely to be able to get by on my own. He didn't know that they were going to kill us. I should have gone ahead, said yes to his proposal, and gotten married. Then, none of this would have happened. It's all my fault."

"None of this is your fault. Do you love him or did you have reservations about him?" Adonia asked.

"I didn't trust him completely. I'm Alexis Kimos, by the way. What will happen to me now? I am beyond help, really."

"You are with us now. We'll do our best to look after you. Look, we are finally getting to the edge of the city," Adonia sounded a hopeful note, but quickly realized that Alexis couldn't see what she was seeing and bit her lip lightly.

Once they were clear of the city, the carriage stopped, and Akantha open the door. He explained, "We made it this far. Should be smooth sailing now. Let me cover you all up with the blankets before we get going on the long haul."

After making sure that they'd stay warm on this cool spring night, he got back up, and the carriage headed off at a good clip this time, while the women dozed off.

Three hundred miles lay between Pirgos and Filantos along with numerous towns and countless villages. After passing through the first one, Akantha knew he was in for major problems with this carriage. Dead littered the streets forcing him to turn around and retreat. He then took some back roads around the town. He realized that the plague was even more widespread than those in the palace suspected. Worse, the dead didn't get that way by themselves. He was a soldier. Someone or many someones were shooting them and that didn't bode well for him. The Royal Carriage would be a prime target, he thought. He put his military training to use.

He thought to himself, "If I travel sixteen hours each day and we make four miles an hour, allowing for all the detours, I should make the port in five days. I brought along enough food for three of us that long, but we've another mouth to feed. I can ration it. We'll be okay on food. It's probably best if I travel after dark as much as possible. So I will find some safe place to pull over during the day. They can yell if danger comes while I sleep. That ought to work. Say, I wonder why they didn't send an escort along with us? If I were the Captain, I certainly would have sent along a squad at least, especially in these times. Wonder why he didn't? I should have asked about that, but then I'm only a private. Not my place to second-guess orders. Still, why didn't he? It is obviously a quite dangerous trip, what with all the rioting going on."

Then, it hit him hard. They wanted something to happen to her, the princess! There was no other plausible answer. The manual, which he had studied, had a hard and fast rule. Send along back up if there is any potential for threats. They had not and this certainly qualified as a serious potential for threats, for nearly every town they passed through was a threat! That could only mean that they intended to let something bad happen to the princess! As he realized this, he also realized that he himself was expendable bait! They had calculated that they would be attacked and the princess killed or worse. He would be the enemy's obvious first shot! Now he began seeing gunmen lying in wait behind every turn, behind every large tree and bush. Akantha was spooked.

He drove all night long, finally parking the carriage far off the main road, hidden from view by a thick grove of bushes. Here the horses had some early spring grass and a small stream bubbled nearby. He carefully climbed down and opened the carriage door. "We're stopping so I can get some sleep. I think this is going to be a very dangerous trip. Ladies, I am putting you three in charge while I sleep. If you see any kind of trouble coming, wake me up. I think that we should do most of our traveling at night. Let me fix up some grub for us. I'll keep it simple so maybe you can help yourselves during the day while I sleep."

While he slept beneath the carriage, the three women sat nearby on a blanket. Water, bread, and cheese lay beside them. "Philomena, you have saved us all," Adonia said.

"Not really, Adonia, I just got us out of the palace. Whatever are we going to do once we get to the port? Eventually, he's going to ask us for directions to your uncle's place. What will we tell him then?" she replied.

Philomena spent the hours brushing out Adonia's hair and Alexis' hair as well, saying that she had much experience doing it, though none while trying to use her feet. With all the time to kill, she kept at it, and Adonia returned the favor when she was done.

"There, Alexis, your hair looks very nice. You have such pretty red hair," Philomena said soothingly.

"It grew so much longer," Alexis commented and then her face grimaced. "What does it matter now? I am beyond being even helpless." She began crying again. Neither woman knew what they could possibly say to Alexis and so said nothing. The day passed slowly into night and into day. To the women, it seemed as if they were in a time loop. Sleep, wake, and sit. Sleep, wake, and sit, on and on.

Akantha continued to go around all towns and villages, using the back roads. Not even getting lost a couple times caused him to worry. No way was he going to attempt to go through a town, and he kept his long gun at his side along with his two pistols at all times. The closer he got to the port, the more that he worried. He would have to negotiate the city streets there, if he were to deliver the Princess to her uncle's place.

It was early dawn, quiet and peaceful. Akantha halted the team for a moment on the hilltop. Below him stretched out the wide coastal valley some five hundred feet below this last ridge line. Sea gulls carped, climbed, soared, and dove over the sprawling port city of Filantos, home to a quarter million people. Its outskirts lay some ten miles ahead, but even from here, he could see the sprawling suburbs; outlying towns dotted the landscape between this ridge line and the eastern edges of the port city. The rocky field fences wove a seemingly random patchwork quilt of farmstead plots, built from the limestone removed from the very fields that they now enclosed. Few trees could be seen anywhere below him. Years ago, the last of the coastal valley trees had been cut down and hewn into the many caravels and local fishing boats, for which Phindos was famous. Now the needed large timbers were being imported from far inland, as they were in all the ports of Demokritos. The pervious Emperor's huge push to build the world's largest caravel fleet had denuded the coasts of the kingdoms. Still, it was an impressive sight and the lad had half a notion to wake the women so they could see it as well.

As soon as that idea came to him, he rejected it. One was blind and would surely start crying again. No, better to leave well enough alone. His problem was now how to safely get from here to there, he mused. The paved road ran straight through the many 'burbs' of Filantos.

Too many chances for an ambush. From this viewpoint, he had another brilliant idea. He could angle to the south, bypassing the urban growth areas and come into the city from the southern coast. He jiggled the reins and the weary horses moved on once more. They too smelled the fresh sea air and knew that their journey was nearing an end.

It was nine in the morning when he finally reached the Coastal Road, a narrow paved path that paralleled the coastline from the Ice Sheet in the extreme south up on into Alia, and from there, all the way into Patri, Thrace. "Wake up ladies, we are about to enter Filantos from the southern Coastal Road. You can see the ocean off the left side. I will be needing directions in about twenty minutes, but we'll stop for breakfast first, if you like."

Zeno Zacharias was forty-two and Filantos' Harbor Sheriff, a position he took very seriously. He answered only to the mayor, and except in national emergencies, his word was law here in Filantos. His son, Than, twenty-one, was following in his footsteps and had recently been promoted to Chief Deputy Sheriff. Zeno commanded a group of one hundred deputies and Chief Deputies. Their job was to ensure the security and safety of the port city on out to the start of the 'burbs.'

When the plague struck, he'd ordered half his men on duty. As word came to him that the men of the Church of Jehosanity were responsible for all the gunfire and were murdering citizens, he'd called them all back to active duty. Than had worked out a protection schedule of twelve hour shifts, with two-thirds of the force dealing with the dawn to dusk hours. Already, his men had killed half of the churchmen before they could kill the many people on their lists. Than had quickly discovered that these men had lengthy lists of families and were systematically going down the list killing those families. Zeno reckoned that their fast action had saved close to a thousand lives.

Of course, riffraff had tried to take this opportunity to rob unattended stores and shops. Zeno had given his deputies orders to shoot looters on sight. By this time, all serious looting had come to a screeching halt. Still the many dead posed serious problems, but the mayor's fast thinking handled it. He'd requested the local soldiers to collect the dead and put them on barges. Nearly one thousand bodies had been buried at sea now, deposited in the frigid waters of the South Ocean.

Still, the deputies needed to patrol the streets. With nearly all shops remaining closed and with no farmers coming into town with their wares, the unattended stores were prime targets still. This morning, father and son, armed with two long guns and six pistols, rode side by side along the southern edge of the port, speculating when the fishermen would set sail once more. Never in anyone's memory had virtually no boats set sail to ply the nearby waters. The thriving fish market was completely deserted, a sign of just how bad this plague was.

Not far from them, two men lay on the ground, long guns at the ready, hiding behind bushes near the Coastal Road. "Hey, look. Here comes something."

"Yeh, I see it. Looks like a royal coach! Damn, there must be something mighty valuable inside that one. Shall we risk it?"

"Yeh. Only one soldier driving, maybe more inside, though. If not, we can take him with one volley. If it's empty, we can hock that coach; it'll bring a pretty copper!"

"See any deputies around?"

"Nah, we'll be quick about it. One volley, get to the carriage, and drive it away. If the deputies show up, we can say that we heard gunfire back down the road. Pretend it's our carriage, because in a minute, it will be our carriage!" Both men laughed; this one was going to be too easy!

Bang! Bang! Two shots rang out. Akantha lurched forward, and then slumped over to his right. He tried to reach for his long gun, but couldn't. He drew a pistol and fired in the general direction from where the shots came from, very visible from the small black powder clouds rising from the bushes a hundred feet ahead. One slug smashed through the back wall of the carriage, narrowly missing Alexis' head. "What's happening?" she screamed, her terror-filled darkness again sinking home.

"Akantha! Akantha!" Adonia called out, but the lad did not answer, though the carriage continued to move forward, albeit slowly. Bang! The young soldier fired blindly once more, he had one more pistol at the ready, but the pain from his wound finally got to him. He passed out.

Zeno and Than kicked their horses and headed towards the gunfire. As they came riding up, they spotted the carriage and saw no driver. Two men were now crawling out from the bushes, long guns at the ready. "The deputies!" one called out, frantically trying to turn around. Bang! Bang! The two lawmen fired, grabbed a second pistol and fired another round. Both bandits were hit and had dropped their guns as the two men rode up to them.

"Than, go stop that carriage, I'll take care of these two."

"You got it dad." He urged his horse on ahead. Bang! Bang! He smiled; those two had robbed their last carriage. Than liked this job! He came up to the carriage horses, leaned over and grabbed a hold of the left horse and called out, "Whoa, whoa there. Whoa." Both horses finally stopped. "Soldier, are you all right?" He saw the bleeding soldier slumped over in the driver's seat. Then, he heard women's voices calling out from inside the carriage, moved his horse to the left window, and peered inside. He saw three young women. "Are you ladies all right? The soldier is hurt. Not sure if he is alive or not."

"We're okay. What happened?" Adonia asked, fearfully.

"You're safe now, ladies. Couple of bandits tried to steal your carriage. Lot of that going on since the plague started. Good thing we were on patrol. I'm the Chief Deputy Sheriff and the Harbor Sheriff himself is with me. You are safe now. I am going to check on your driver." He moved out of view of the window and very carefully dismounted. When not on horseback, he, like all men, could only barely walk in the strange boots. He and his dad had bravely tried them on and could walk a little bit in them, wobbling around wildly. It beat crawling on all fours as so many men did. Yet, dismounting was the hardest part. Once down, he tied his reins to the carriage as his dad rode up.

"Checking on the soldier now, dad. Some women are inside, unharmed. Shook up, but okay." He climbed carefully up and felt a pulse. "He's alive, but wounded. Best get him to the doc at once. Want me to drive?"

"Hold on a minute, son. I'll tie our horses to the carriage and ride with the women and find out who they are and where they are going." A couple minutes later, Harbor Sheriff Zeno climbed carefully into the carriage and called out to Than.

"Ladies, Harbor Sheriff Zeno Zacharias. My son, Than, Chief Deputy Sheriff. May I ask your names and where you are headed? After we drop the wounded soldier off at our doctor's we'll take you to your destination, if it's in Filantos, that is."

"I am Adonia Kadmos, my dear friend Philomena. Alexis Kimos. My mother had her blinded. Please sir, can you help us."

"Princess Adonia?"

"Yes sir."

"Well, I'll be. Yes, we can help you. Please, what is going on in Pirgos anyway? Has the plague struck there too? What news?"

Adonia decided to trust the Harbor Sheriff. What else could she do now? Slowly, she began relating all that had happened to them. Zeno cursed several times and had her repeat the official proclamation about having only one daughter per household. That Alexis had been taken away and scheduled to be killed shocked him, but he really swore when he heard that thousands of women and girls had been taken from their homes, murdered, and dumped in Roc Pond. He was livid with anger.

As she finished, the carriage halted before a limestone block home with a red and white spiral post in front of it, the symbol that this was a doctor's home. The Harbor Sheriff climbed out and helped his son lift the wounded soldier down. Together, they dragged him up to the doctor's door. A bit later, they continued dragging him inside the home. The three women waited wondering what would happen to them next. Where would they go?

"If someone can get these monster earrings off me, we can sell them and use the money to buy us a house. But how will we be able to live?" Adonia suggested. Philomena shrugged her shoulders. Perhaps all this had been mere useless folly on their part. Perhaps there was no escape possible. Alexis certainly believed so. She considered her life over now and prayed death would soon take her.

After what seemed an eternity, the two men came back outside. Adonia saw that they were sort of walking, not crawling, though they seemed precarious on their feet. Than climbed back into the driver's seat, while Harbor Sheriff Zeno climbed into the carriage.

"Princess, my son has come up with a bright idea. We're going to check it out now. We cannot put you up at an inn. They are all closed due to the plague. Now the old Church of Jehosanity might have put you up, since you used to be one of their Holy Women, but that church is no more. Murdered many of their parishioners here as in the capital. Fortunately, we stopped them before they could get very far down their lists of names. So finding you some place that is both safe and where you can be helped is a bit of a problem right now."

"But my son has an idea. I don't want to get your hopes up yet. We'll just have to see. There is a Dorota Church of God here at the southern edge of Filantos. They just might be able to take you in. When I was a boy, the Church of Sol would have taken you in, but alas, those Jehosanity folks wiped them out. Shame, really, when it comes down to it. Ah, we here we are. I will go and see if they will give you sanctuary, Princess Adonia. Keep your fingers crossed." His face flushed, "Sorry, I didn't mean to offend you." She had no fingers to cross. He hastily climbed out, nearly falling as his toes hit the ground a bit too hard.

"Careful dad. Want me to tag along?"

"Yes, we walk better if we hold on to each other. Make sure the team is tied up."

Adonia stared out the window. What a picture perfect place, she mused. The white-grey-yellowed limestone buildings, typical of all the buildings in Filantos, had weathered well. The red tiled roofs contrasted nicely. A white marble, pillared fence three feet tall outlined the spacious estate, once home to a wealthy merchant perhaps. A sprouting vegetable garden lay on the south side of the grounds, while a beautiful shady flower garden with four-foot tall ferns covered the north side. A lawn swing hung from an octagonal gazebo in the front, not far from the spacious marble columned front porch that ran the whole length of the two-story manor house. The call of many sea gulls drew her attention to the rear of the estate. They had a beach! A stone path led down to the sandy beach. A small wooden dock rose on marble pillars rising from the lapping blue-green waters. She decided to describe the place to Alexis to pass the time.

At last, she spotted them coming back outside the front door. Also, two older couples and two younger couples followed them; the men had their arms over the women. She realized now that the women were providing support for the men so that they could walk. All were moving just as slowly as she had been. The plague had struck here too, no doubt. The women wore relatively plain cotton dresses, but these dresses actually fit the women's bosoms, which, Adonia noted, were just as large as hers.

As the men approached, she overheard them. Zeno was saying, "Good. I will spread the word to every household about the Queen's Proclamation. With some clever temporary juggling, folks might be able to fool the soldiers if they come to carry out the order. I think many will be very furious over this one. Trouble will come of this, you can count on it."

"Good. Civil unrest can only come from this. Meantime, we'll take care to keep the presence of the Princess here a secret. Only you and we know, and we'll keep it that way," one of the older men said.

"Thanks, Telamon, I owe you one," Zeno said.

"No, we owe you one. Spread the word; save the many daughters of Filantos. That's more than ample payment," the man replied. Adonia felt hopeful.

"Dad, I'll check on them as often as I can," Than added.

"Ah, Princess, they have agreed to give you and your companions sanctuary here at their estate. Princess Adonia Kadmos, this is Elder Telamon Makedon, his wife, Chara. Elder Thales Platon and his wife Danae. They will be caring for your needs. Their son, Kreon Makedon, his wife, Hera, and their daughter Doris. Their son Niki Platon and his wife, Iola, and their son Aesop. And their daughters Ariadne Makedon and Desma Platon. I'm sorry, but I don't remember the names of your companions, Princess Adonia."

"Please, just Adonia please. My dear friend Philomena Lis and the woman we rescued, Alexis Kimos. My mother had her eyes removed. She's in a very bad situation, but we just couldn't leave her when we freed the other twenty women. I don't know if they were able to really get to safety or not, but we did get them out of the dungeon and out of the main gates. Thank you for helping us. We are in a bad way. If you can get these monster earrings off me, they are supposed to be worth a half million gold. You can use it to help pay for our needs."

"Why, I've never seen such earrings before," exclaimed Chara. "Come on; let's get you three inside and cleaned up. Are you hungry?"

"Yes, we have not been eating well for many days, not since the plague struck," she admitted. The men helped the women out.

Kreon put his arm around Alexis' shoulders, "Hello, Alexis. I'm Kreon. I'm going to lead you inside for a warm bath and a good, hot meal. How's that sound? You have lovely, red hair, very impressive." He had a soft, kindly voice, just what the frightened woman needed now.

"I can't see anything. I'm scared of moving. I'll trip and fall or worse," she admitted.

"Nah, I won't let you. Next step, lift a little higher, the flagstone is a little higher there. Yes, that's right. You are doing just fine. I wish I could say the same for us men. We have to walk on the tips of our toes, you know. Our ankles don't bend at all. Strange, isn't it? You are doing fine, Alexis." He continued to talk gently to her, interspersing guiding instructions just before she needed to compensate. Adonia relaxed, feeling that they would take care of Alexis. She wanted to, but of course could do nothing to help her.

Thus began a day of pleasant and unexpected surprises for the three women, who discovered how able the women here were. Hardly anything had to be done by their husbands, shocking Adonia, who had never been able to do a darn thing for herself. Philomena, on the other hand, began to see some hope ahead. Perhaps, she could also learn how these women were managing to do nearly everything.

Over a delicious, hot meal, during which Kreon, Niki, and Telamon helped the three women eat, Elder Telamon explained the history of their Dorota religious sect. Their parents had not immigrated to Hieras Anubis some fifty years ago, choosing instead to remain here in Filantos. After the meal, Chara, Danae, and Hera began therapy session on the three, with Chara, the most experienced, handling Alexis, who proved to be in the worst mental state.

That evening, Telamon removed Adonia's massive earrings, much to her relief. Next, the three women got their hair trimmed. All the women here had brown hair and kept theirs between shoulder length to waist length. Adonia and Philomena had theirs cut back to waist length, while Alexis had hers cut back to shoulder length. For sleeping arrangements, Adonia asked if the three could share one bedroom. She didn't want to be parted at all from Philomena, and she wanted to stay close to Alexis, at least for the time being. That night, the three women got their first sound, relaxing sleep in a long, long time. Adonia's fortune had most definitely taken a turn for the better.

Chapter 36 In Phindos, For Some, the Darkness Grows

It was November 10, 823, very close to the start of the warm summer in Phindos. The flagrance of blossoming flowers filled the air, masking the putrid stench of death. General Kratos, his knees heavily wrapped, crawled into the Royal Palace at Pirgos, Phindos. As much as he hated to be seen crawling before his lieges, he had to answer the summons of his Queen. He had heard a rumor that King Agathon had passed away, but that the Queen Adelpha still held the throne along with Princess Alcestis gave him some hope. Although he knew of the sadistic nature of the queen, he, like most others in power, made allowances for her behavior. After all, she was their queen. With anarchy breaking out citywide, especially the despicable actions of the Church of Jehosanity going around murdering their most ardent followers, he needed orders and soon.

Forty year old General Kratos thrived on order. Everything in its proper place. Events should go as planned, especially if he had a hand in their planning. Now chaos seemed growing by the day. Palace guards were issuing what seemed terrible orders: that a man was now only allowed to care for one woman and at most one daughter. Excess daughters were seen being taken away by the palace forces. This he knew and had been worrying about for several days now. He had a wife a year younger, a nineteen year old son who had just received his commission as a captain in the Phindos Legion, and three daughters, Iona, Iola, and Iantha. Iona was eighteen; Iola, seventeen; Iantha, sixteen. With four women at his home now in dire need these last few weeks, only because he was a general and could order others to lend him a hand had they gotten by. He knew that he simply could not handle the life needs of the four. However, he dearly loved his wife and three lovely daughters.

Ever since hearing of the Royal Proclamation, General Kratos began trying to find a way around the decree. Laws were laws. If the palace guards came to his home, he knew that he would have to follow the letter of the law. For the first time in his life, that scared him, the man who thrived on order. Iona had a boyfriend and he figured that he could send her to him. His brother owned a farm just outside the city. Iola could be sent there, since his brother had no daughters, just three sons. Then, he would be able to follow the letter of the decree, but he hoped that it would not come to that.

The doorman, also on his knees, announced in a loud, clear voice, "General Kratos." He crawled into the Throne Room. What he saw shocked him. Queen Adelpha sat on her throne, quite naked, except for her shoes. All women now had to wear the strange shoes that had appeared. No, it was not her lack of clothing that shocked him; rather it was the four-inch disks that protruded from her upper and lower lips. Both lip plates drooped heavily, giving her a strange appearance indeed. He quickly saw that her bright red eyes were not her own, that her sockets held unmistakable glass eyes, pretty ones though. Yet her long blonde hair was artfully draped over her shoulders, partially covering her enormous breasts.

Sitting on a smaller throne at her left sat Princess Alcestis. Like her mother, she had similar lip plates protruding out from both her lips. Two front teeth on the top and bottom were gone, and the lip plates were held horizontal, butting up tightly against the remaining teeth. Her eyes were glass as well, emerald green in color. Her long ankle length blonde hair was also artfully arranged, draped over her bronze huge bosom, hiding her privates from view.

At last, his gaze drifted to the king's throne. He recognized Advisor Stavros Kietos sitting there, a pleasant looking smile on his lips. To his right, Advisor Sophokles Akios sat, looking pleasant but not smiling.

"Ah, good morning, esteemed General Kratos. Thank you for coming. As you can see, the plague is having some awful aftereffects on some of our women. Still Queen Adelpha lives, likewise Princess Alcestis. We must be grateful for that, mustn't we? Yes. As you are guessing, I and Sop here are now controlling Phindos on behalf of Queen Adelpha and her daughter. Queen Adelpha is having a most difficult time of it and has given Sop and me total authority to run Phindos until she recovers. Isn't that right, Queen Adelpha? Please nod your head for General Kratos. Show him that you have delegated this responsibility to us, our beautiful queen."

He looked at the pitiful queen and she nodded her head, "Yes." Stavros added, "And she has further stated that if she perishes from this plague, then Princess Alcestis is to assume the throne and that Sop and I are to follow Princess Alcestis' rulership and assist her in running Phindos. Isn't that right, Princess Alcestis? Please nod your head for General Kratos, dear."

Trembling slightly, Alcestis nodded her head, though she had no idea which direction she was facing. Her world was entirely black. Her mind drifted back a few days, she was standing over her mother's bed, looking at her mother's horrible mutilations. Queen Adelpha's horrible glass eyes, stared mercilessly up at her as if taunting her. Her lips stretched out with those awful disks, her missing teeth, and her gurgling attempts at speech made impossible by her missing tongue shocked Alcestis. She saw herself vomiting on the floor, then escorted to her room by Sel, her mother's hairdresser. Now she was sitting at the dinner table in the Great Hall, naked and humiliated, though Sel had shown her how she could lean over and get her long blonde hair to fall between her legs before she sat down, hiding her privates from the glaring eyes of Sop and Stavros. She'd felt so tired that night and awoke to eternal darkness!

Her lips ached and she realized she too wore those hideous lip plates. Her eyes were gone, replaced with the emerald green ones that Stavros had intended for her sister's eyes. At least she still had most of her teeth and her tongue was still there. She heard the soft voice of Sel and tried to speak, but found no one could understand her anymore, not with the four-inch disks between her two lips. She'd cried, oh how she'd cried.

Days had passed, but only mealtimes indicated any passage of time. The awful images in her mind repeated themselves over and over like some hideous nightmare from which there was no awakening. Alcestis knew that there would be no wakening for her, not ever, not ever again. She cried.

Music, dance music was playing at dinnertime. She heard Stavros order her mother to rise and to dance. "Alcestis, you rise and dance with your mother, please," the distant voice of Stavros collided with the nightmare images. Someone was lifting her up onto her feet, forcing her to move. Her breast felt something warm and soft, her aching lips touched something. She realized that she must be touching her mother. Hands pushed her head onto her mother's shoulders. "Dance, come on, dance for us." Words floated into her ears, barely registering over the nightmare images in her mind, which seemed far more real than anything else.

"Nod your head yes, Alcestis. Let the general know that this is your wish too, my Princess," the cold voice of Stavros finally pierced her agony. She nodded her head if only to get that hated voice to go away.

"There, General Kratos, our Queen and Princess are in full agreement. We have their full and unequivocal backing. Now then, we wish to honor the late king's last decree. For now, let our women go naked, since none of their clothes even fit them. It is nearly summer and the weather will be hot as usual. Surely by fall, the tailors will have found a solution for our women."

"Yes, sir, it will be followed," General Kratos agreed. He hesitated about suggesting that the women wear overly large men's shirts. The timing was not right and he held his mouth firm.

"The king also insisted that we get our men back to work. Having nothing open, no stores, no commerce, no nothing is crippling our city. I know that we can only crawl now, but surely you can see what will soon happen if men cannot find any groceries. A starving population will soon go completely out of control. We'll have even more chaos in the streets."

"I could not agree more with you, Stavros," the general replied.

"Our late king was right. There are only two reasons why the men of Pirgos are not going to work as usual. One, they have to crawl. Two, they have to stay at home caring for their wives and daughters. Well, kneepads handle the first, as you so rightly have done, General Kratos. Yes, even I find it humiliating to be reduced to crawling like some dog. Still, I cannot walk on my toes; I am not one of those gay ballet dancers. So crawl we must."

"Yes, sir," the general replied. He had a feeling about the second reason, but waited to hear the words from Stavros.

"The second can be handled as the king instructed. In each home, a man may have a wife and/or one daughter, but no more than one woman must he be caring for. That way, he can afford to leave the woman alone while he works. After all, none of us will die if we have nothing to eat for say eight hours, now will we? Hungry, yes, but we must allow the women to suffer if our men are going to get back to work. After all, our women are now completely helpless and wholly dependent upon men. So they must make a sacrifice as well, if we are going to keep Phindos running. Certainly you will agree with me, general."

"Yes, of course." There, he had the order verified and in no uncertain or vague terms.

"Now then, since we all agree, here is what I need our powerful army to do at once. I simply do not have enough palace guards to deal with the crisis. I am hereby mobilizing the entire Phindos army. You, General Kratos, are put in charge of the four army groups." He handed him a set of documents. "These you can present to the other three generals to prove that you have been given this high honor and the authority to carry out the Throne's wishes."

"Now then, there are three actions I need your soldiers to take starting as soon as you can get them their orders. First, visit all of those treasonous Churches of Jehosanity and execute any cardinals, priests, and their henchmen that you find. They are behind the assassination of our king. We simply will not stand for such treason against the throne of Phindos. Second, continue the task of clearing the dead from the streets and homes of our city. Our palace guards have begun that work, but the numbers have overwhelmed our few guards. Third, as your soldiers go from home to home, enforce the throne's orders that men are to return to work at once and physically remove the excess women and girls from their homes by any means your men see fit."

"Yes sir, it will be done at once," the general replied. At least order was coming back to the city. The world needed order, of that he was certain. "Sir, what are my men to do with the excess women?"

"Bring them here to the palace and our palace guards will deal with them. You need not concern yourself with those women. Obviously, our queen and princess need much assistance now. I'm sure that some of these excess women will jump at the chance to serve their queen and princess." The general nodded and left to carry out his new orders, pleased with his promotion as well.

Later that day after he sent word to the other three generals to come to Pirgos at once for orders from the throne, he met with his aides and majors. After outlining the new orders and receiving congratulations on his promotion, discussion began on the one man-one woman decree. As he suspected, his aides and majors balked at removing women and girls from their homes, just to get the ratio at that home in balance. These soldiers knew well that if they truly implemented this with an iron hand, eventually the whole country would rebel and civil war would breakout. That Stavros did not see this concerned the general. His opinion of Stavros dropped considerably.

"Look men, we are caught between the hammer and the anvil on this one. If men do not return to their jobs quickly, food riots will break out citywide. By reducing the workload at home, men will be able to return to work. Yet, in forcibly removing their wives and daughters, that too will eventually cause riots and civil war. Here's how we can handle it, gentlemen. After your soldiers explain what is needed and if the men to women ratio is out of balance at that home, then have the soldiers make some suggestions. Perhaps the husband has some relatives where the excess women and girls could be taken. If not, perhaps a boyfriend will take over responsibility for a daughter. If not, maybe a neighbor whose balance can support another woman can be persuaded to take responsibility for the daughter. Have your soldiers do all that they can to help the husband deal with getting the ratio in balance as our king has ordered. Only if all fails are they to remove the excess women and girls from their homes. In that case, they are to bring them to the Royal Palace. I believe that they will be given positions in the court, assisting our queen and princess." This accommodation his aides and majors could support.

Late that afternoon, the legions began taking positive action. General Kratos had ten thousand soldiers under his command. Within a few days, the other three generals would add another thirty thousand. General Kratos felt confident that soon the chaos of Pirgos would be under control at last. Order would be restored and civil unrest and the potential of a civil war abated.

That evening, General Kratos received word that the palace guards were searching for Princess Adonia. Apparently, she had gone missing and a reward of a thousand gold was being offered for her safe return. He gave this detail considerable thought, as it seemed to him wholly impossible for a princess to be "lost," especially since Princess Adonia almost never left the Royal Palace. He found this most curious.

Kassandra Istrates, sobbing, was led to the wagon, joining three other older women and a baby girl. The soldiers had left her father no choice. She had to go with them. They had pleaded that her fiancé was a captain in the army and was supposed to return any day now. "She can perhaps be offered a position as a servant to the queen until he returns," the soldier said sympathetically.

An hour later, the wagon pulled into the Royal Palace and palace guards helped them down. One man sat on a chair in the huge courtyard, observing the women. He gestured at Kassandra who was twenty-two with long, curly brown hair and sad blue eyes, red from crying, as were all these women. One guard brought her up to the man. "Would you like a position as one of the queen's attendants-in-waiting?"

She didn't like the icy tone of his voice. "My fiancé is due back anytime now. He is a captain in the army. We are to be married, please let me go."

"Well, then, the best thing for you to do is attend our queen until such time as he returns," the man said. Seeing no alternative, she nodded and allowed herself to be led into the palace proper. Glancing over her shoulder, she saw the others being escorted deeper into the palace, though she didn't know, they were being herded into the dungeons. Perhaps this won't be so bad, she thought as she was led into a private chamber. A bit later, Sel came crawling in with a tray of food and fed her. He chatted friendly enough and even brushed her long curls a bit. Later, she felt terribly tired and fell asleep. The last thing she remembered was his hands carefully laying her down on the soft, plush bed.

She awoke to throbbing pain in her lips. Kassandra wiggled out of bed, looked at herself in the mirror, and screamed. Both her lips had been slit and four-inch disks inserted in them, braced against her teeth. Two upper and lower teeth had been extracted to allow the disks to fit tightly against them, protruding straight outward, parallel to the floor. She also noticed that she was naked, except for her shoes.

Stavros entered her room, "Ah, there you are, Kassandra. My, you look lovely today. No, don't try to talk; no one can understand you. Unfortunately, you are suffering more ill effects from the plague. However, you can still be the queen's attendant. By order of our late king, all women in the court are to be naked, until we can have new, proper clothing made for all women in Phindos. Now if you will follow me, I will take you to the dining room where the queen and her other attendants awaits you. Please, don't try to speak; no one can understand you — the disks, you see."

Terrified and sobbing, Kassandra followed him into the Great Hall. "I am afraid that Queen Adelpha has passed away from the plague. Our new queen is her daughter, Alcestis, who is sitting there at the head of the table. She has unfortunately lost her eyes as well to the plague, so she really does need the help of her attendants to get around. Please take a seat with the others, breakfast will soon be served." She saw eleven other young women like herself, ranging in age from around eighteen to the mid-twenties. All wore similar four-inch lip plates in their lips, including the queen, whose eyes looked a strange emerald green.

"Your Majesty, ladies, permit me to introduce your newest attendant, Kassandra Istrates."

"Allow me to arrange your hair, my lady," Sel said softly as she got to her designated chair. He draped it across her such that when she sat down, much of her was covered. She felt very grateful for this bit of kindness. "I will be feeding you, Kassandra, but you will have to wait your turn. There are so many of you now." His voice sounded highly sympathetic.

She still had not been fed when Stavros and Sop had finished. They rose and left. As they reached the doors, she overheard Sop's hushed voice say, "Stavros, I don't like this. When is it going to stop? Haven't you got enough. . ." The voice trailed off out of hearing. She wondered what he meant.

After more waiting, Sel finally began feeding her, which was difficult at best with the lip plates. She ate ravenously, however. When he finished with her, Sel said, "Okay my ladies. It is time to escort our lovely Queen to her chambers. You know what to do, so please show Kassandra the ropes. I'll see you all later on. I have such a mess here to clean up."

Queen Alcestis rose, and Kassandra could not help but notice the terrified expression on her face. How could she even walk, Kassandra wondered. The other young women rose and took their tiny shuffling steps over to her. Several pressed their bodies to the queen and slowly they began moving her across the room. One young woman made an unintelligible noise at her and motioned with her head. Kasandra fell in line behind them.

In the Throne Room, Sop continued his argument, "I tell you Stavros, this is getting out of hand. What if someone finds out what you are doing with these women? It's bad enough murdering the excess women and girls, but torturing them like this?"

"No one is going to find out, Sop, not if you and the doctor and Sel keep your mouths shut. Besides, the Black Boys Club is still closed," Stavros added. Sop knew well what that club was about: boys being tortured and sodomized by club members. He'd never been there, but its reputation was widely known. The late king and Stavros had been often seen there.

Cleaning up the rest of the left over dishes in the room, Sel over heard them talking. He began to worry. He was expendable, if Stavros ever needed to take action. Besides, his heart went out to these tortured women, Alcestis most of all. Still, he was powerless to do anything except make them as comfortable as possible among this den of sadists.

Captain Diomedes Athion had seen enough of the effects of the plague. He had been in command of a group of soldiers who went door to door here in Pirgos, executing the Royal Decree. He'd seen the women being loaded onto the wagon and had seen them being dropped off at the Royal Palace. Fear crept into his mind. What had happened to his fiancé Kassandra? He had been under strict orders for weeks now and had no chance to visit her father's home to check up on her. He swore when he got to her, he would marry her and get her out of harm's way. Her dad had three daughters, and surely, Kassandra would be in dire jeopardy.

Sunday evening he finally was given private time finally. He mounted his horse and headed to the Istrates home. As he crawled back to his horse and struggled to mount it; his eyes teared over so badly that he could not see to mount. Finally, wiping his eyes on his shirt three times, he could see and climbed into the saddle. He was too late; soldiers had taken her off to the palace three days ago now. He clung to the faint hope that Kassandra had been offered a post as one of the queen's attendants. He had heard rumors that most of the women had been killed, deposited in the mass grave site along with all the other plague victims.

Captain Diomedes reasoned thusly. Well, if they have killed her, then all is lost. I have no way of searching the mass grave. Even if her remains were there, I'd never find them among the thousands there. My best chance is to see if she is now a Lady in Waiting. If so, perhaps I can plead my case before the queen and get Kassandra back. Yet, how do I get to see if she is at the palace?

He chided himself. "Damn it, Diomedes, you don't get to be a captain by being indecisive. You are a captain in the Phindos army. Bluff your way in the palace. See for yourself if she is there." He kicked his horse into a trot, heading for the Royal Palace.

He was wearing his uniform, and he sat tall in the saddle as he approached the palace guards on duty at the entrance. "Halt," one said as he rode up.

The guard saw at once that he was a captain. Diomedes merely said, "Official business." The guards motioned him inside; he nudged his horse through the gates. He had only once before been inside these gates, when he'd accompanied his major. At least he knew where the stables were located and he headed to them. There he carefully dismounted as a stable hand came crawling up to him.

"Staying long or should I bed him down for you?" the man asked.

"Bed him down," the captain said in a stern, official sounding voice.

"Here, you'll need these," the stable hand said, handing him a pair of kneepads. He thanked the man and headed off, acting as if he were on official palace business. His problem was a simple one: he had no idea where anything was. Crawl like you are very important and know what you are doing, he thought to himself. It was November 25. Unknown to the captain, he was entering a hornet's nest.

Alcestis felt herself being fed her dinner, kind Sel, she mused. I can't live like this, she thought. Hell, that's all I can do now: think! I have to get out of this somehow, but how? Later, she felt her attendants pushing her body along the long halls to her room. God, this is no way to live. I am better off dead than like this. She felt the women pushing her. God! No, I will fall! She panicked but could say nothing intelligible. She heard several voices trying to speak, but could not understand them either. She lost her balance and fell onto her bed.

Lying there, it came to her in a flash. Falling. She could fall down. True that was her greatest fear now, falling down because she could not see nor had arms to feel her way along. She saw the long stairs that led down into the dungeon in her mind. Involuntarily, she tried to smile, but her tight lip plates held no trace of it. She waited. All was quiet. She took a deep breath and struggled to get to her feet, wobbling wildly to get her balance, made all the more difficult because she could see nothing.

Using her memory of her room and the palace, ever so slowly, Alcestis began to shuffle her way out of her room, bumping into the walls and feeling her way to the door. Thank god, it was now always kept open. An eternity passed until at last she convinced herself that she had actually found the long, winding stairs that led to the dungeons. Alcestis stood there a moment then took a deep breath. Suddenly, it all seemed so ludicrous, so funny to her that she started to laugh. Her lip plates deadened even this minor expression of emotion, bringing her back to the present. She took another breath and stepped forward. As she anticipated, her foot did not find the floor and she began falling. She had the strangest sensation of flailing her arms around wildly, but nothing happened. Then pain, sharp pain appeared in her lips, her nose, and then her forehead. Real pain. Then nothing. No pain. She was shocked that she could once more see, if only vaguely. Down there was her body lying dead on the steps to the dungeon. Yet here she was looking at it. "I am not that body?" she thought, rather confused. Then a command appeared in her mind, "Go get another baby body." She shot away through the heavy stone walls as if they were as thin as air, heading off to find a pregnant woman somewhere in the city.

She didn't hear the cries of a palace guard who had discovered her body. She also didn't hear the other events, which happened around the same time. Sel was only a hairdresser, but he was not stupid. At dinner, he noticed that Stavros seemed to become rather tired shortly after eating. To Sel, this seemed most unusual. He'd seen similar reactions many times now, beginning with the late queen herself. Always it meant that Stavros had drugged their food, preparing them for his sadistic operations later that night. Now Stavros himself seemed to be displaying the same symptoms. He glanced at Sop and noticed that he seemed particularly alert and was covertly keeping an eye on Stavros. Perhaps he even had a slight smile on his face. This was not good, he thought to himself.

When Stavros headed off to bed directly after dining, Sel knew something was afoot! He himself became afraid. At least, he had not yet taken the time to eat himself, having to feed the queen and her dozen attendants first. Don't take a bite, Sel, or you'll end up dead too, he told himself. He worried that Sop would say something to him, like hurry up and eat yours before it gets cold, but Sop ignored him, as he ignored the women. Maybe he wasn't the target tonight, he hoped he was right.

A while later Sop left, and Sel hurried the women up, making sure that they got Alcestis to her room safely and they to their nearby bedrooms. Then, he quietly headed down the halls to see if he could see what was happening with Stavros. He spotted a captain crawling his way. "Can I help you, captain?" he asked.

"I've a private message for the queen. Can you direct me to her chambers, sir?" Captain Diomedes said very formally and forcefully, as if he were completely in charge of some battle. Well, in a way, this was his battle, his own and perhaps Kassandra's too.

Sel didn't question the man's authority; he seldom did. On ordinary nights before the plague, he might have made a play for this young, handsome man, but tonight, far more sinister ideas occupied his mind. "Down that hall; first door on your left. The queen's bedroom is on the right; her attendants are to the left." He headed on down the hallway. Soon he got to Stavros' bedroom. The door was open a crack; a dim light came from inside. He sneakily looked inside. There was Sop leaning over the sleeping man. He was pouring some kind of liquid into the sleeping man's mouth. Sel's nose detected a sickly sweet odor, and he knew what that liquid must be! Quietly, he backed up a ways, fearing that he would be assassinated next; surely, he would be if Sop saw him at the door!

Somewhere in the distance, a man began yelling, "The queen has fallen. She is dead. Help, help, someone help!" A moment later, Sop appeared crawling out of the door, a grim smile on his face. He saw Sel and their eyes locked. This is it, Sel thought.

Sel acted, "Sir, I've come to tell you and Stavros that our queen has somehow taken a very bad fall down the stairs. You both must come quickly. Send for the doctor, please." Only later would Sel realize that his fast thinking probably saved his life.

"Oh my god. What a night, Sel. I've just found Stavros has died in his sleep. Now the queen too? Dear god, what next?" Sop said, faking genuine concern. "Come Sel; let's see what has happened to our queen." Dutifully, Sel followed Sop.

A bit later, the two men arrived at the steps to the dungeon, where a dozen palace guards sat around, staring at the lifeless body of their queen. "One calamity after another. Stavros died in his sleep and now the queen too has passed on. Well, it is just as well. The plague had so destroyed her life. Take her body down to the courtyard. Tomorrow, we'll send her to the grave where her mother is buried. Also, send someone to drag Stavros there as well. I'll be in the throne room. Send someone to fetch General Kratos for me.

Sel followed behind Sop to the throne room, the older man completely ignoring the hairdresser. Sop crawled up to his usual chair and lifted up his bottle of wine, which he always kept here. "Sel, please take the dozen attendants down to the wagons. We'll take them away as well. Without a queen, we have no need of them anymore." Sel nodded and turned around to leave. Sop drank deeply and then began choking, wildly clutching at his throat. Foam came out of his mouth, as Sel turned to see what was happening. Sop's eyes bulged. He gasped and then slumped lifeless back on his throne room chair.

Sel headed off to the attendant's room as fast as he could go. If nothing else, he would carry out this last order and get those poor women out of the palace before anything else awful happened. He entered and found Diomedes holding onto his beloved Kassandra. Both were crying. "What have they done to her?" he wailed.

Sel said, "We have to get these women down and into a wagon at once. All hell is happening. We have to get them out of here before the general gets here, if not, they'll probably be killed too. Ladies, come on, follow me if you want to live," Sel said uncommonly bravely.

"What do you mean?" asked Diomedes, his red, swollen eyes looking at this hairdresser. Still, he crawled alongside him, the dozen women shuffling to keep up.

"Look, their lips just didn't happen that way. The sadistic advisor Stavros had them done that way. He drugged them and his doctor friend did it while they were out. He's also done the same thing to the queen and the princess, only with them, he had their eyes removed too and the all queen's teeth pulled out, plus had her tongue cut off. A bit ago, the Queen Alcestis fell down the stairs and died, probably suicide, since we put her to bed hours ago. Then I saw the other advisor Sop poison Stavros; he's now dead. I just came from the throne room where Sop went to wait on your general to come. He drank from his usual wine bottle and it contained poison. I think Stavros did it. He's dead too. Soon, the guards will discover all this and lord knows what will happen next. Right now, my last orders were to get these women into the wagons and out of the palace. Of course, his intention was that they would be taken to the mass grave, killed, and dumped in there. I don't know what we're going to do, but I aim to get these women safely out of the palace. Are you with me? I could use the help." He slowed down as they approached the doors leading out into the huge courtyard.

"Damn! Okay, I am with you. Kassandra, I have to save you," Diomedes replied. They couldn't go far wrong following the orders to get the women out of the palace. "If anyone challenges us, let me do the talking. I'm a captain."

"I know and a handsome one at that," Sel winked at him, unable to completely restrain himself around this handsome, virile lad.

It seemed like an eternity crossing the vast open space to the stables. At any moment, Sel expected to be challenged. Yet, only when they reached the stables did the stable hand and a palace guard come crawling to meet the group. "Hitch up a wagon. Sop's orders, we're to remove these women from the palace immediately," Captain Diomedes ordered sternly, using his typical captain's commanding tone, one that allowed no back flash.

"Yes, captain. Right away. Do you want your horse saddled too?"

"Well, no. I'll drive the wagon and bring it back. I can get my horse then. I don't trust this hairdresser behind the reins," Captain Diomedes said. The stable hand and the palace guard both chuckled. Evidently, Sel had tried to hit on them at one time or other, he thought. Perfect, it played into their hands. A half hour later, the women were loaded and the wagon rolled on out of the palace. As they turned a corner, he spotted General Kratos and several others just entering the gates.

Sel did too and prophesied, "All hell is about to break lose now! I am glad that I am out of the palace. Well, captain, what do we do now? Sop did not explicitly tell me that the women were to be killed." He tried to sound a hopeful note. Yet, if the captain did want to take them to the mass grave, he knew that he could do nothing to prevent it.

"I'll be damned if I am going to let my Kassandra be killed, hairdresser. None of you women should be so mistreated. Right now, I sure as heck have no idea what we are going to do. With those mutilated lips of yours, you will stick out like a plum in a pie. We have to get you to some place where you can hide and be safe."

"Count me in on this!" Sel said. "I want to be safe too, you know. Where are we going to go? Nowhere in this city is safe anymore. Too many soldiers around."

"Okay, we leave the city. Perhaps we can find a nearby farm where we can spend the night and try to figure this out. I will be going AWOL, so soon they will be out looking for me too. I can't stay here in Pirgos either," Diomedes added. "One thing is for sure, Sel, we need to get some clothes for them and supplies. We're going to be hungry and thirsty by morning. I wish we had blankets for them; Kassandra is shivering already. Damn them anyway."

An hour later, they left the last home of the city behind them and ahead lay farmlands. They were going nearly due east now on the main paved road that led to Theolopolis, Theos, and then on to Thal, Thallyus. "We have to get off the main road, we patrol it heavily," Diomedes said, more to himself. He took the first side road to the south. After a couple of miles, he veered to the west. By now, Kassandra was shivering badly and valiantly tried to tell him, but neither he nor Sel could really understand her. Sel asked if she was too cold and she nodded yes, her lip plates clapping together adding a strange soft sound to the night.

"Okay, my love. We'll just risk the next good barn that we come to," he sighed. A half mile later, he turned down a farmer's lane. The farmstead was dark and he made straight for the barn. He insisted that Sel get down and open the doors, shutting them once he drove the wagon inside. He finally risked lighting one wagon lantern. In the dim light, he looked for anything that might be useful. A haystack was the only thing that he saw that could be used to keep the women warm. Carefully, he and Sel got each woman down and then had them climb into the hay. Carefully, the two men covered the women up. The two looked around for other useful items, but found little. At last, the two men joined the women.

A cock crowed at dawn, startling both men. Sel had never heard one and was a little afraid of what it might mean. "Relax, Sel. Help the women. I'm going to go talk to the farmer and see if we can get a little help." Sel crawled back into the hay. He was not a hero.

Diomedes crawled to the door and opened it a crack. By the early morning light he saw that the farm appeared rather deserted. No farm animals. That fact struck him as important. He crawled to the front door and listened. Silence. He knocked once. Twice. He waited and knocked again, figuring that it might take some time for the occupants to crawl to the door. Perhaps they had to get dressed first. Finally, he decided to open the door. The odor of rotting flesh assaulted his nose and he knew what must lie inside. Death. He slowly went inside.

He found the farmer and his wife and three daughters lying on the sofa and chairs in their living room. He'd been dead for some weeks, he estimated. Already, he'd seen enough of death to last him a lifetime. Diomedes was not a religious man, but he did take a few minutes to cover each one with a blanket. Then, he opened all the windows he could find. The early morning breeze brought the myriad smells of late spring into the home, temporarily flushing out the scent of death. This would have to do. He yelled out of one window, "Sel. Sel, bring them all inside. There is no one alive here. There is food here, if we can cook it."

By the time that Sel and the dozen shivering women entered, he had the kitchen stove roaring, and the women moved to the heat nodding their approval, since they could now longer smile. "Ah, now this is more like it," Sel said with a bit of gusto. "Let me at it, I've been fixing most of the meals at the palace for a couple of weeks now. See if you can find the women something they can wear."

An hour later, Diomedes had dressed each woman in a heavy man's shirt. He put women's panties on them and then got them each into long pants. While none fit them, they would at least stay warm. Kassandra tried several times to tell him how thankful she was, but she just could not make herself understood. Sel called out, "Come and get it. Food's up."

Diomedes got a quick lesson in just how to feed Kassandra. She could not drink from a teacup; he had to spoon the tea in between the lip plates for her. She felt miserable and he sensed her emotions. "It's all right, Kassandra. I don't mind feeding you. You are still the love of my life." She leaned her body into his, unable even to kiss him.

An hour later, the two men had each woman well fed. "I'll put their hair up for them. They will find traveling far easier with it up rather than down and getting in their way. Their hair is so beautiful. Ladies, I would never cut it — such fine, long, beautiful locks — you should be proud of your hair." He didn't add that there was so little else for them to be proud of.

As he worked on them, Diomedes did the dishes and then began rummaging round the home. "So what's the plan now, Diomedes?" Sel asked as he worked on Kassandra's golden locks.

"I think that we ought to get as far away from here as we can. If we can make it to say Filantos, maybe we can hop a ship to somewhere safe. There's enough of what we need for that journey lying around this farmhouse, but we're going to have to hide the women from prying eyes along the way. One look at their faces will shock anyone. They'd remember us forever after one look. We can put a canvas cover over the wagon and they can hide beneath it when it is light out or when someone approaches. We must avoid the towns. No telling how many soldiers will be there or if they will be looking for us. If I get caught, I'll be shot as a deserter."

"Well, handsome, you better leave your uniform here then," Sel teased him. They spent the rest of the morning gathering up what they needed, preparing the wagon for the long journey. To assist in their illusion, they nailed a canvass cover over the wagon bed, creating a safe hiding place for the women, covering the canvass with a layer of hay. Thus, to others it would seem as if they were carrying a load of hay. They stowed charcoal, a small cook stove, blankets, cooking gear, silverware, water skins, and plenty of easy to fix food. Sel insisted that they bring along plenty of dried beans, rice, lentils, fruit chips, and even dried vegetables. Each morning, Sel put out another batch of dried items to soak all day. By dinnertime, they were ready to be cooked. Finally, around one with the women safely beneath the canvas, Sel and Diomedes headed their wagon back down the farmer's lane.

"Would have made a nice safe place," Sel lamented.

"Except for the smell of the dead and that Eventually the soldiers would visit the farm. Then, where would we be?" Diomedes replied.

For two weeks, they traveled the backcountry roads, spending long hours on the trail. Diomedes headed nearly due west and finally they reached the coast, some fifty miles south of Filantos. They headed up the coast road now wondering what lay ahead. Could they get a boat? Where could they go? Arolas perhaps? That kingdom seemed far away.

On December 15, they entered the southern edge of Phindos' largest port, Filantos. They had stayed off the main coastal road, preferring to ride along the coast as much as possible, bypassing the smaller towns just south of the port. That afternoon as they entered the city on the street closest to the shore, they came upon a quaint limestone home. A simple sign out front said Church of God.

"Well, let's stop here and see if we can get some information," Diomedes suggested. He and Sel carefully climbed down and began crawling up to the front door. Just as they neared it, the door opened and a man stepped out. Sel noticed that he was walking fairly well in the strange black boots that all men now wore. Perhaps he was a dancer before the plague, he thought.

"Hello, welcome to the Church of God. I am called Telamon. May I help you?"

"Yes, we have come a long ways, sir. We need information. Is it safe here in Filantos? Has the plague struck you? Are there many soldiers about?" Diomedes asked.

"Come inside. We can talk more freely," he said. They followed him inside.

As Sel crawled inside, he saw all the others standing in the living room looking at him. His eyes nearly popped out of his head! "Princess Adonia? Is that you? Are you really alive? Oh thank god that you are safe! You look really well." All eyes turned to her and she flushed.

"Yes, Sel, I am doing better than really well. I am so utterly alive! And Sel, I am able to do many things for myself now. These people are beyond incredible. But Sel, what are you doing here? Have they found out where I am? Are they on their way to get me again?" Suddenly, she realized what the implications of the Royal Court's Hairdresser's appearance here might mean.

"Oh dear lord no, honey! We're escaping and rescuing a dozen horribly mistreated by those sadists. I hate to be the one to have to tell you this, but your mother is dead and so is your sister, Alcestis. On the other hand, those two sadistic advisors, who took over control of Phindos and so badly mutilated your mother and sister and the women we've rescued — they are now dead too. Each managed to poison the other. While they were doing that to each other, Captain Diomedes here and I got the other dozen mutilated women safely out of the palace. They were going to murder them like all the others. Kassandra is his fiancé, you see. We're desperately looking for some place that is safe for them and us. We are on the run, so to speak."

Telamon spoke up, "Sel, I saw only you two. You speak of a dozen women? Pray, where are they?"

Grinning at just how well their concealment plan had work these past weeks, Diomedes answered, "We have them in a concealed compartment in the wagon out there. We stopped here hoping to find out what the situation is here in Filantos and if we could perhaps find a boat that could take us and the women to somewhere that it would be safe, where the plague has not struck."

Telamon laughed, "Captain, that's going to be hard to do. This time the entire world has gotten the plague. There's not a woman on Tarra who is unaffected; even newborn baby girls are just like their mothers. Pirates now control the high seas from here all the way up to Arolas. You couldn't possibly get a ship to take you anywhere right now. For now, you best stay here with us and let us evaluate the condition of your fiancé and the other women. If no one is watching, let's get them safely inside. I expect that they could use a bath and their hair washed and a good hot meal."

With the coast clear, Sel and Diomedes helped Kassandra and the eleven other women down from the wagon. One by one the women shuffled their way down the sidewalk and into the picturesque limestone home. As they saw so many others just inside, to a woman, tears began trickling down their cheeks, humiliation and embarrassment crescendoed. "Oh my god!" whispered Ariadne. Iola, Desma, and Hera echoed her shock and surprise. All four were nearly the same age as these twelve. "How utterly awful," she added.

"Come, come, dears, it is not as bad as it looks," Chara came to the women's rescue. "You are safe here. Now come along. We've a hot bath for you all and then a good home cooked meal. Girls, stop your gawking. Lip plates adorn princesses of a tribe somewhere in the northern hemisphere and are considered a thing of ultimate beauty. Why, one of our very own queens used to have several servants with lip plates far larger than these. Ladies, think of yourselves as being princesses." She attempted to put a different slant on their physical mutilations. Of course, it did little for the traumatized twelve.

While the women as well as Adonia and Philomena headed off to take care of the new arrivals, Telamon sent Niki off to bring Harbor Sheriff Zeno Zacharias and his son here at once. The others began unloading the wagon, stowing everything in the attached stables. Perfect timing, that task done, Zeno and Than came riding up with Niki.

"Serious business, Zeno, Than. Let's go inside," Telamon suggested. A bit later, the men sat around the large living room and both Sel and Diomedes related what had happened. Only the blind woman, Alexis Kimos was present, sitting quietly in her corner of the room. The two young children were out back playing on the beach.

Alexis suddenly spoke up, "They will have a harder time of it than me. I can't imagine life without being able to speak. Are the disks really four inches across?"

"I know you," Sel noticed the quiet woman at last. "Weren't you one of the first women the Queen Adelpha tortured? How did you get here?"

"Yes, Adonia rescued me. I'm sorry. I have no idea how we got here. I couldn't see anything," she answered him as best she knew.

"Well, you are looking far, far better than when I last saw you, Alexis. You are quite a beautiful woman. I just love the way you wear your hair." Her beautiful, thick red hair still flowed down her sides to her waist. She had it cut shorter so that she could manage better.

"Thank you, Sel, is it?" she replied. He nodded, then realized his gaffe and said yes.

A bit later, Chara marched the dozen women in to join the large group. Dressed in simple dresses borrowed from the younger women here at the complex, their hair washed and now drying, they at least felt more human. While Zeno and Than tried to keep from gasping and staring, Diomedes on the other hand burst out, "Wow, Kassandra, you look great. Say, this is a church isn't it?" Telamon nodded. "Can someone here marry Kassandra and me right away? We were going to get married several weeks ago, but the plague came, and I couldn't get away from the army barracks."

"Now? Today?" asked Telamon, a bit surprised by such a request.

"Absolutely, before anything more happens to us."

"Okay, but first, let's allow our sheriff to get all the facts. Zeno, any more questions? I know the women would like to tell you their stories, but now, they are not really able to speak understandably," Telamon replied.

"Dear, we women have already been working on that a bit. Since our dialect relies so heavily on the backs of our front teeth and our lips, with their lip plates, most of the sounds are too mumbled to make out. However, we have worked out some. Everyone pay attention. When the make this sound, ee, that means they need help going to the bathroom. The a-u sound means thank you. The oo sound means that they are hungry and would like some food. The ah sound means that they need some help and you'll have to work out just what that may be. So we at least have a start," Chara explained.

"Telamon, I believe that I have all the facts that I need. I will talk with the mayor and you can count on his issuing orders that anyone found harming our women will be executed. What was done to these women is just plain criminal, especially so since the plague. Son," he looked at Diomedes, "you are to be commended in what you have done for these women. I assume that you will be staying here in Filantos now, here at this safe Church of God?"

"Yes, it seems that there is no safer place that I can take my love to, Harbor Sheriff."

"Well, then, how would you like a job as a Filantos Sheriff? We could use more dedicated men like you."

"But I am an army deserter now," he protested.

"Perhaps in the general's eyes, but not in our eyes. If you take this position, then Filantos will back you all the way. The mayor has some pull yet, son. Trust us."

"Okay, Harbor Sheriff. I accept. I'm broke. I left everything behind when we fled. Kassi and I are going to need some money." The two shook hands and Zeno told him where to report in the morning. Then the two left. The large group headed to the dining room. Once supper was finished, Telamon conducted a simple wedding ceremony for Diomedes and Kassandra. Once that was done, the younger women escorted the new arrivals to the various bedrooms. Many were now going to have to double up, though Adonia, Philomena, and Alexis still shared one large bed. Adonia had kept her word and made sure that Alexis was always with them, though she had a feeling that might not last for long. During the past month, a young gardener had taken a fancy to Alexis. Every evening, the two took long walks around the church grounds, often along the beach. Adonia saw them kissing once, when Than had taken her out for a walk.

Chapter 37 The Path Out of Darkness Appears

Finally alone, Chara, Telamon, Danae, and Thales met to discuss the new arrivals. "Honestly, Telamon, it is going to have to be you and Thales who run therapy on these dozen. I'm certain that you will need telepathy to have any idea what they are saying. Honestly, we tried while we were bathing them. No luck, we can get maybe one word out of ten at the very most. Those lip plates are completely debilitating their speech. Perhaps it might not be so in some of those northern languages, but just try immobilizing your lips and saying something. It is just awful."

"Agreed, Chara. We'll work on two each day. Meantime, you, Hera, and Danae continue to work on Adonia, Philomena, and Alexis. All three are doing very well and it will not be too much longer before they will be prime candidates for advanced sessions. I'll have Kreon and Niki work on Diomedes and Sel. Iola, Desma, and Ariadne will have to watch the children and deal with the many chores for a time," he concluded.

Thus began the many therapy sessions. Already Adonia, Philomena, and Alexis were quite alive and vibrant, and the therapy sessions were digging into all manner of other things that had happened in their lives. The trauma of the plague had long ago been fully erased. The two men had their immediate loss and suffering alleviated within a few days and Diomedes then spent most of the daytime learning the ropes of being a Sheriff of Filantos, a job he rapidly discovered he truly enjoyed. Unlike soldiers, his new position required him to assist others in need far more often than apprehending criminals.

As he had for a month now, Than dropped by to visit with Adonia each evening after supper. Likewise, Ammon, the gardener came to visit with Alexis, usually taking her out for a stroll along the beach, where he could describe all the magnificent flowers and shrubs for which he tended. Chara suspected that two romances were well underway, but the close connection with Philomena might be a problem and she decided to do something about that if she could.

As the days passed, Telamon and Thales, using telepathy to help them understand what the women were saying during their therapy sessions saw a pattern emerging. All twelve women were unable to face the pain of their most recent mutilation of their lips and instead found the painless loss of their arms vastly easier to confront. As a result, both men decided to work this aspect of the twelve first, getting that horrid loss and grief erased. As Telamon pointed out, "The removal of times of severe loss and grief beings back vitality and cheerfulness rapidly."

Two weeks after they arrived, all twelve were bright and vibrant once more, but still were pinned down by their lip plates. Now the two tackled these times of real physical pain trauma, which were buried beneath the drug-induced anesthesia — the drug that they had been given mixed in with their dinner. Just before they sat down to work their first two women, Thales suggested, "You know, Telamon, even if we remove the pain trauma, the lives of these women will be miserable at the very best. Unable to speak and looking so weird, they may well relapse as they try to merge back into society."

Telamon rubbed his face in frustration. "I know, I've been thinking about their futures ever since I first saw their actual condition. Thales, you and I are simply going to have to take these twelve and Adonia and her two companions far into Advanced Therapy. I know that we've had to put our children's continued Advanced Therapy on hold since the plague came. It's been one thing after another, but we can have Chara and Danae take over for us, they can lead and drill them a good ways. Perhaps when our wives have taken them as far as they can, you and I will have these women handled and can resume with our children. What do you say? Give it a try?"

"Hera and Desma have both been begging me to expand our works to many of the women of Filantos. They would rather see the loss trauma handled on the women of our city before they get pushed on up the line further. If all our feet were not so lamed up, things would be so much easier. Okay, I say let's go for it and see if we can get those twelve back their innate spiritual skills of telepathy. A human is not human if they cannot communicate with others by some means, but I still think that we ought to get Adonia as able as possible, Telamon," Thales added. "After all, she is our remaining princess and heir to the throne, at least at this point she still is."

"Agreed. Okay, I'll let Chara and Danae know our decision. Let's get to work on them. We've a long path to follow if we are to lead those twelve back to lives worth living again," Telamon replied.

They didn't get far at all that day, January 1. Everyone's feet began aching badly, both men and women's feet. The next dat, the men rejoiced, their feet were back to normal. While the women greatly appreciated their feet's recovery, it was relatively minor, but at least walking became safer for them. On January 3, they finally were able to begin the sessions on the twelve, but with a slight change in their plans. Sel volunteered to handle all their cooking as well as look after the children. Hera had explained that she and the others wanted to start giving their loss therapy to the women of Filantos. Sel was very eager to back them and volunteered to do their chores around the complex, freeing them up so that they could. He had experienced the benefits and wanted others to have them, especially the women.

Now Hera, Iola, Ariadne, and Desma began inviting their friends and neighborhood women in for therapy sessions. They put Kreon and Niki to work on scheduling and arrangements so that they each could handle three women a day. Meanwhile, Chara, the more experienced of the two older women, began working exclusively with Alexis, while Danae alternated between Adonia and Philomena, alternating sessions between them.

Chara's first major hurdle with Alexis was to get her perceptions vastly increased, not her physical body's perceptions, but her innate spiritual perceptions. Chara drilled her on creating a mockup of simple objects at first, a broom, for example. She had her turn it red, then green. She had her put it above her, below her, to her right, and so on, moving it all around. As she became better able to do these creations, Chara then had Alexis begin to put various emotions on the object and then to feel and perceive those emotions coming back at her from the objects, such as a broom which emoted sadness or anger or cheerfulness. On and on she drilled Alexis. Now she had stone houses whose roofs were upside down radiating happiness back to her. She had Alexis plant enthusiasm on mocked up horse drawn wagons which drove up the sides of houses and then had her feel the enthusiasm coming from it. After doing these mockups for nearly a week, gradually becoming wilder and wilder, suddenly Alexis saw the room in which she was sitting!

She saw the room not with her body's eyes — those were long gone. Rather she saw the room, she, the immortal spiritual being which was now located just in back of her head. The phenomenon rather startled her at first, but Chara continued working her. The more they drilled the clearer became Alexis' direct perceptions of the world around her.

One evening, Alexis shocked Ammon, the gardener, when he came to take her for their usual evening stroll at sunset. "Ammon, I see why you like to bring me out here. The sunset is magnificent. Just look at the delicate hues between the sky, the clouds, and the sea. It is beautiful."

"Alexis? How? You can see this? For real? Yes, yes, it is exactly so!"

"Yes, Ammon, Chara is working a miracle with me. I can see you, Ammon, I see you, but not with my body's eyes. I am not my body. It is true, what she says. I am a spiritual being and I can now see directly without needing a body's eyes. Each day, my vision gets clearer and clearer. At first, everything was so awful looking, so distorted, but now, tonight, it is so clear. You, Ammon, look so handsome to me." She leaned into him and gave him a passionate kiss. Watching the two as she often did from a rear window, Chara smiled, knowing that she was making terrific progress with Alexis.

Danae's progress with Adonia and Philomena followed a different track altogether, though the therapy process was in many ways similar. After weeks of drilling and then therapy sessions to remove the barriers that came up as a result, both women were actually lifting a spoon up from the table and putting it into their mouths and then back down again. They were moving the objects themselves without the use of their bodies. She began by having them spot a dust mote in the sunlight streaming in the window. Next, she had them giving the dust mote a shove. Often as they attempted to perform the action asked of them, mental traumas appeared, dictating to the women the "reasons why" this was impossible. These traumas were then handled in the usual manner and then Danae had them back attempting that action once more. Weeks passed but now the two proud women were actually moving a spoon around.

The next step was to put something in the spoon, that is, food. Before long, Adonia and Philomena shocked many of the women by feeding themselves using their new skills and not using their feet. Chara and Danae then had to point out to everyone but their children that they too could do the same; Telamon and Thales had long ago given them much Advanced Therapy sessions.

"Mom! Why haven't you been feeding yourself this way all the time?" asked her daughter Iola.

"Yes, mom. How come you haven't? I mean it is so miserable eating with our feet and you don't need to," her other daughter, Ariadne, asked.

"Because, daughters, it is not wise for us to shock and amaze others who cannot do these things themselves. Often it creates a fear of us in others. Having my lovely daughters afraid of my powers is the last thing I would ever want to do. Besides, you all do just fine with your feet; we all do. It is our ancient Dorota heritage. Your father assures me that he'll help you both achieve these advanced skills too, if you really want them."

"You're right mom. So many other women are in far greater need of just having the awful traumatic loss of their arms handled. It gives them back their enthusiasm for life. That's more important right now than us lifting our spoons," Ariadne stated. Chara smiled, her daughter was right.

Each a spiritual being has their own unique set of barriers that keep them from using their innate powers. Normally, the Advanced Therapy as taught to them by Macario Ines, took the route of least resistance. That is, by working with the person, the skill most easily recovered was dealt with first, and then, the one with the next least resistance. In the cases they faced now, they didn't have years to spend on the twelve women. Rather both men had one specific goal in mind, the rehabilitation of the women to use telepathy to communicate their thoughts and ideas and wishes to others, bypassing the lip plates' barrier to speech. With some, the barriers were huge and required a lengthy amount of time to achieve. With others, telepathy came back to them more readily. Kassandra was the first to cross that barrier.

One evening when Diomedes came home, as usual, he gave her a hug and kiss. *Thank you for saving me and bringing me here. I truly love you, Diomedes.*

"What? Did you just — I thought I —," he looked at her wide-eyed.

Yes, I can talk to you this way now. Isn't this fantastic?

"Unbelievable! Fabulous! Oh Kassandra, this is indeed a holy miracle!" He picked her up and twirled her around the room, so great was his excitement and joy.

Within a week, all dozen were now "talking" via telepathic implantation of their thoughts into others. However, they were yet not able to "hear" others thoughts. Chara and Danae had not been working toward that goal yet. Their sole goal now was to make the twelve able easily to communicate to others.

Thus, when Eve and Macario contacted Telamon in mid-April, the group here in Filantos had their women in very good shape. So much so, that when the dozen women with lip plates heard about Telamon's ideas to greatly expand their Basic Therapy to as many women as possible, they volunteered as well, insisting that they be taught how to deliver this Holy Gift, as it was called by these Dorota descendants. Incidentally, all had also picked up basic skills and were doing many things for themselves now, emulating the methods of the Dorota Women's Ways.

The twenty-one women here began their first public therapy program. Kreon and Niki were in charge of making the arrangements, finding the women, and getting them transported to and from the complex. Telamon and Thales supervised the women and helped when they ran into difficulties that they could not handle or had problems. By May, word began to spread about the miraculous therapies being conducted at the Church of God here in Filantos, Phindos.

Chapter 38 The Coming of Darkness Over Alia

The Kingdom of Alia lay south of Thrace, where the Lonki Basin was the natural boundary between the two countries. Alia was a sea faring nation and made its fortune in the shipping industry. Whale hunting for oil and fishing brought in a stable income for many, while the rich ores of the Southern Mountains, which formed the boundary with the Kingdom of Phindos to the south, allowed a bustling metallurgy industry as well. Though the smallest of the seven kingdoms, Alia boasted of the highest per capital income per person of all the kingdoms, before the plague that is. Wealthy, yes, prosperous too.

King Aeon Stathis came from a long line of Stathis rulers, who had held on to the throne for several generations now. Aeon had ascended to the throne five years ago, handpicked by the Cardinal of the Church of Jehosanity, but only after he married Katherine, then eighteen, and then only after she agreed to become a Holy Woman of the Eighth Degree. Thus, the Cardinal guaranteed the church's ultimate control over the throne of Alia, just as they continued to do in many other kingdoms. Aeon had shoulder length blonde hair and blue eyes, sporting a well-trimmed beard. Yes, Aeon was a handsome king, perhaps the most handsome king ever in Alia.

Queen Katerine was also very pretty, handpicked to become Aeon's bride on her eighteenth birthday and a Holy Woman the day after that. She was inches taller than Aeon, very noticeably taller when she wore her Annelise extreme heels, which was nearly all the time now. Katerine had thick, but slightly curly, long blonde hair, which her servants always draped perfectly for her, falling down to her waist, held tiny by the tight Annelise corset. Yes, Katerine always wore the traditional Annelise ball gowns, preferring various shades of red, which accentuated her thick red lips, her beautiful bronzed skin, and her blonde tresses. She too had enchanting blue eyes.

They had a daughter nine months after they were married. Barbara was now five years old. Aeon had named her Barbara, a derogatory name that she would carry with her throughout her life. Why? She was different, too different for Aeon. Barbara had raven black hair, shiny at that, and black eyes. Surely, she could not have been conceived by Aeon and Katerine; Aeon insisted that Katerine must have somehow been unfaithful to him. As a result, since the birth of the black haired girl, he had not slept with his queen. True, he tolerated her and treated her with the courtesy and respect due to a Holy Woman of the Eighth Degree, but that was all. No intimacy. In lieu of his love, Katerine gave all her love to Barbara, doting on her constantly.

By the age of five, Katerine also knew that Barbara was somehow very different. She sometimes talked of strange things that could not be; of lives and adventures she could not possibly have had as a five year old girl. Of late, she caught Barbara doing very strange things, bending a teaspoon as if by magic. Still, Katerine love Barbara unconditionally.

At their court, General Atlas Erebos, a proven general at thirty-five and as yet unmarried, held the ear of King Aeon, who usually followed the general's advice. Katerine hated the general, who seemed to believe that Katerine was becoming the downfall of his king. He treated her with disdain and disgust, whenever no one else was around. Mistreating a Holy Woman would be punished severely by the Church of Jehosanity, who valued these women who helped them control the kings.

The night that the plague struck hard, as usual, Katerine's servant women undressed her and helped her into her loose fitting nightgown. Then, they pulled back the satin sheets for her. After brushing her hair and that of Barbara, her servants left. Following their traditional nighttime routine, Katerine climbed awkwardly into bed, slipping into the sheets. Barbara came over and repositioned her mother's beautiful, long hair for her. She blew out the lanterns and climbed in beside her mother, pulling up the sheets, tucking her mother into bed.

Normally, Katerine would now tell Barbara a bedtime story. Tonight, Barbara spoke up, "Mommy, did you notice how weak their arms were tonight? They could barely undo your corset. It took two of them to do what one used to do. I think that their arms are getting weak like mine. Did you see that my arms are smaller around? I thought that my arms were supposed to be getting bigger and stronger."

"Well, now that you mention it, dear, why yes, it did seem a little strange. Do you feel all right? Should I send for the doctor?" Katerine became a bit worried, lying there in the dark. Was Barbara getting sick?

"No mommy, I feel fine, just my arms are so tired. Mommy, when you had arms, did your arms ever get weak and tired on you?"

"No dear. This is very strange. Perhaps tomorrow they will be strong once more. If not, let's visit the doctor. He might know what is wrong. Do you want a story dear?" She did and Katerine told her a long goodnight story, ending when her daughter was sound asleep. Katerine then drifted into sleep, thinking about what her daughter had observed.

The next morning, Barbara woke Katerine. "Mommy, mommy look! Look at me! Now I am just like you! See!" Katerine woke and struggled to sit up. She wished for the millionth time that she could just rub her eyes, but of course, she couldn't, not for the last five years now. She looked over at Barbara who was also sitting up. Her arms were gone! She blinked and looked again. Empty sockets stared back at her, but no scaring as she had on her shoulders. Katerine screamed for help.

"Why are you screaming mommy? Now I am just like you. Isn't this fine?"

"Well, yes dear, but this should not be happening. It should be done when you are married and become a Holy Woman of the Church of Jehosanity. Something is wrong here."

"Mommy, look at your breasts! Wow. Will mine get that big too?"

For the first time this morning, Katerina looked at her own body and cried out. Her lovely breasts had somehow grown enormously, beyond anyone's wildest imaginations. They, like every other woman on Tarra, were the size of her head. She called out for her servants repeatedly. Finally, she got out of bed, only to discover that her feet were somehow changed; she could only stand on her toes. Barbara, likewise, stood only on her toes. Their feet could no longer go flat. Katerine called out again, but still no servants came. Now she noticed her hair, her beautiful, shiny, slightly curly blonde hair fell to just above her ankles, shocking her further.

"Wow! Mommy, look at my hair! It's grown much longer too. Isn't this just great? Now we look so much alike." She turned and noticed her daughter's hair also fell to her ankles, but she also saw that even as a five year old girl, Barbara's breasts had already begun to grow, years before they should have. Something awful was happening, Katerine was now convinced of it. She yelled and yelled, and still no one came.

At last, Barbara said, "Come on mommy. Let's go see what is going on. I wonder why they are not answering you. Maybe something has happened to them too."

"But dear, we cannot open the door. It has a knob and we have no hands."

"Look, mommy. I can do it for us. Come on; I want to see what is going on." Barbara walked slowly and carefully to the door. As Katerina followed, she saw the doorknob turn, as if by magic. With the door open, the two moved into the outer room, which by now should have four of her servants awaiting her and tending to her needs, dressing her and Barbara, brushing out their hair, and so on. The room was empty of people. Her gown from last night lay where the servants had left it.

"Something is not right. Let's check on them." The two walked across the room to the door to the servant's bedrooms. They had their own private quarters, just off hers, so that they would always be at hand to assist her with her many needs as a Holy Woman. Again, Barbara opened the door for them. Katerine was not prepared for what she saw. "Mommy, they lost their arms too!" Four terror-stricken women stared back at her. They were standing staring at themselves in their mirrors. All looked as helpless as Katerine and Barbara. Their bosoms were monstrous in size; their hair had likewise grown several feet.

"Ladies, come with us. We must find out what has happened here. Come," she ordered. The four young women obeyed, too shocked to say much of anything, and too filled with horror and fear. The next room that they came to was the Queen's drawing room and living room combination, where Katerine spent much of her day, when she was not required to sit on the throne. In the middle of the floor lay a large pile of foreign objects, including five pairs of strange shoes.

"Mommy, what is all this stuff? How strange. Look, there are some shoes. Why, those look like they will fit me. Let me try them on, mommy." A bit later, all five older women took Barbara's advice and slipped shoes that fit them on. "See mommy, I told you that it is easier to walk with the shoes on, but I can't take very big steps without wobbling. Can you?" Barbara's childlike enthusiasm kept the five older women from a total panic, and that was her intention. The five year old knew well that something awful had happened and that there were probably worse things yet to see. Barbara was not your typical five year old girl!

As they shuffled slowly out of the Queen's quarters, they discovered the plight of all the men. As they stood beside the King's quarters, Aeon opened the door. He came crawling out on his hands and knees, his feet no longer working. He stared at the women and cursed.

"Aeon, please, please, we need to use the chamber pots desperately. Can you please help all of us out of our nightgowns, please, this once?"

"What has happened to all of you? I can't stand. Bend over a bit more." Aeon pulled each woman's gown off. "There, now go relieve yourselves. I'll be damned if I am going to do that for you too. I have got to find out what the devil is going on." He began yelling for his aides and then the guards. No one came, so he crawled on out of his personal quarters.

Sometime later, the women, still naked, unable to dress themselves, shuffled slowly into the dining room, hoping to have someone feed and dress them. Along the halls, they saw several guards, crawling along, their feet horribly miss-shaped as well. They found Aeon in the dining room, stuffing himself. "Aeon, please, can you dress us or get someone to dress us? We are starving too. Can you possible feed us, please?" Katerine asked and pleaded. Now was not a time for modesty. They needed help with everything, she knew; that's why she had four servants for the last five years. Only now, her servants were as helpless as she and Barbara were.

Aeon laid out several round loaves of bread, two large chunks of cheese, and started to pour a glass of milk. Then he changed his mind and filled up several pie pans with the milk. "There ladies. Help yourselves. I don't have time to feed you. We are in a crisis of magnitude. Fend for yourselves." He then crawled on out of the dining room.

Katerine thought that hunger makes one do what one must do to eat. Tossing her long hair back as best she could, Katerine sat down and began tearing off bites of the bread. Barbara followed her and her servants did likewise, for all were too hungry to protest much. That they ate like some mongrel dog made an indelible impression in Katerine's mind.

Finally full, Katerine suggested that they go to the throne room. Surely, the king would be there. "Maybe we can get some answers and get him to send someone to help us dress," Katerine suggested, although she really doubted that Aeon would do much for them. While he had when they were first married, he had stopped shortly after she became pregnant. With Barbara's birth, their relationship effectively ended. All was mere show now. The women slowly shuffled the long halls to the throne room.

King Aeon sat on his throne, while six of his advisors sat nearby. A number of guards stood on their hands and knees, some were crawling out past the women on their way to carry out orders, while they passed by another on his way to the king. The men were talking, so Katerine thought it best to take her seat on her smaller throne, her servants moving close to her where they usually stood. Still shocked and numb, they endured the humiliation of standing there naked, except for the shoes, which enabled them to walk better.

"It's everywhere, Aeon. We have frantic reports coming in from all quarters of the city. People are demanding to know what happened and what you're going to do about it. The city is at a standstill," an aide explained. "I got here as fast as I could, but the streets are practically empty. The markets are vacant, no one's there. I heard so many screaming women on my ride here it's not funny. My own family is afflicted as well. What is going on? What do we tell them?"

"That's what I pay you men to know!" Aeon cursed angrily. "Leave me. Go find out the cause of all this. Where's General Erebos anyway?"

"On my way, sire." The aide began crawling out of the room.

Aeon looked up, "Oh. You are here. What do you want now? Can't you see we are in crisis mode?"

"We need someone to dress us," Katerine said softly.

Aeon was about to say, go have your servants do it, but bit his lip instead. One aide took pity on her and spoke up. "King Aeon, I believe that we have a more serious problem here. I mean look at the size of the women's breasts. I mean no disrespect, Queen Katerine. But the sheer size — none of their dresses have any chance of fitting them."

One of her servants bravely added, "Sire, he's right. Nothing that we have will fit us. We will have to have massive alterations done to the tops."

"Well, send for the seamstresses, will you?" Aeon ordered.

The aide spoke up, "Sire, they've lost their arms too. There is no one to alter their dresses. I think that you are going to have to address that problem as well. All the women in Levkos will be having this problem in common. We need to address this topic as well."

"Damn, one problem after the other. Well, hell, this one is easy. Issue a Royal Decree. From now on, all women in Alia will go naked, except for their shoes. It seems that they can put on their shoes. That solves that problem in a hurry. It is spring and the hot summer is coming, they should be all right. There, problem solved. Write up that decree and let's get it posted. Man, we have far worse problems with which to deal than stupid dresses."

"Yes, Your Highness. I will see to it. Ah, here comes the general now."

Katerine decided it was time to leave. She rose and her small group followed her back to her quarters. Here, her servants broke down completely, crying and sobbing. Katerine had no idea what to say to her servants. "It will be all right in time. We can get by somehow." She was about to say that as long as they had servants to care for their needs, being a Holy Woman was not the end of the world. Now she began to see it differently.

"Mommy, my hair needs brushing. Yours does too," Barbara broke in on her private thoughts. The two went into their own quarters and Barbara retrieved a couple of hairbrushes from the pile of objects, carrying them between her teeth. With little else to do, Katerine watched as her five year old daughter experimented with the brush, using her foot in the leather loop. Soon, the girl was managing a crude job of brushing out her mother's very long blonde hair. Embolden by her daughter's attempts, Katerine reciprocated. For the first time since becoming a Holy Woman, she attempted to do something herself.

Time passed. At dinnertime, Katerine decided to brave the dining room once more. They were all hungry. Likely all the men would be there, and perhaps one or more would be kind enough to help them. Like four zombies, her servants followed Katerine and Barbara through the halls to the dining room. She was right; Aeon and five aides and General Erebos were sitting at the table. The smell of stew filled the air, along with a strong, dark ale.

"Excuse me, but would one of you be kind enough to help us get some supper?" Katerine asked politely, praying that one of them would feed them.

"Throw some stew in pie pans for them," Aeon ordered. An aide did as asked. The king added, "Forget the spoons, man, they haven't hands to use them." The aide nodded and placed the pie pans on the table for the women. "Issue another decree. All women must feed themselves from now on. Use pie pans."

"Yes, Your Highness. We do have critical problems to solve. Queen, you must understand that there is now rioting in the streets. Looters are crawling about, ransacking shops right and left," the aide explained.

"Aye, my soldiers now have orders to shoot looters," the general broke in.

The women sat down and attempted to eat from the pie pans. At least they were being fed, Katerine thought. That was a small step. Just as the men had finished eating, two men dressed in the sky blue robes of the Church of Jehosanity came to the door, two Mano del Dio. One said, "The final Days of Judgment have come upon us all. Prepare yea to enter the glorious Gates of Lord Jehosa's Holy Realm of Heaven!" He raised his long gun and fired. Bang! The shot echoed in the dining room. The women screamed. Acrid gun smoke filled the room. Katerine saw Aeon lurch backwards and then slump onto the table, dead, a round bullet hole in his forehead.

"Damn you!" screamed General Atlas Erebos. He drew his pistols and fired. Bang! Bang! Both Mano del Dio men jerked and lay still, bullet holes from their chests seeped blood onto the marble floor. The room was now hushed as the magnitude of the assassination struck everyone.

General Erebos calmly said, "Well, that's that. The damn church has assassinated the king. Guards, summon my captains at once. Close the palace gates. No one but my soldiers is allowed inside the palace. Shoot any that try and shoot to kill! Gentlemen, our king is dead. We are in a riotous crisis. I am hereby assuming total and complete control of Alia. You will follow my orders or you will be shot. Do I make myself clear? I have limitless supplies of bullets."

"Yes, general," an aide whispered.

"Good. Aeon's orders still stand. Let the women of Alia go naked for the time being until we can get this mess sorted out. We men have vitally important work to do than to bother with feeding helpless women and girls. Aeon's order to feed them in pie pans stands. It is quite workable. You ladies are managing, I can see that. Good. Then that's settled."

"But general, isn't it morally wrong for women to be seen naked in public, to have to eat like animals?" an aide asked. Of Aeon's aides, he had been the closest to a friend that Katerine had here in the palace.

"Look man. This is a crisis of unparalleled magnitude. We are far, far beyond mere right and wrong. As of now, right and wrong really have no meaning. Look, the king's been assassinated. I cannot be responsible for even myself anymore. I'll shoot on sight anyone who stands in our way. It's martial law from now on. Get those carcasses out of my sight! Tell my captains that I'll be in the throne room. We have work to do fast." He scooted his chair back, got down on his hands and knees, and crawled out, spitting on the dead men.

Katerine led her group back to their quarters, but only after several men dragged the two Mano del Dio assassins out of the way. Her servants once more followed her; all four acted as though they were in some kind of trance, not caring about anything any longer. By now, their rooms were dark, and there was no one to light their lanterns. "Come, Barbara, let's go to bed early," she suggested.

"How will I tuck us in, mommy?" she asked. The two wiggled around and finally used their teeth to pull the sheets up. Barbara snuggled up to Katerine, who for the millionth time longed to put her arms around her daughter.

Katerine pondered what she ought to do now that Aeon was dead. Her parents lived across town. Perhaps she could return there, but she could not walk such a distance. Ask the general? She decided that would not be wise. Now, she was totally at his mercy. At any moment, he could refuse to dole out even pie pans of food. She had Barbara to think about now. No, she must not do anything to cause the general to look her way. Learn more. Yes, she thought that is the only thing that I can reasonably do now. Be quiet and observe. Perhaps my folks will come for me when they learn the king is dead. On that, she rested her faint hopes.

Days passed. General Erebos began asking her to come sit on her throne beside him during some meetings. "It is nice to see such beauty around us, and besides, you are the queen," he explained.

"But what am I to do?" she asked.

"That's a stupid question. You obviously cannot do anything, except look as pretty as you can. Your presence lends a bit of credulity to my position as commander in chief. Thus, she began attending his mid-morning briefings, sitting on the cold throne, naked and humiliated. Yet, she listened. Alia depended upon merchant shipping. All that had come to a halt. That some gun ships that had gone rogue up by Patri, Thrace, did not help at all. At least the dead bodies were being carted away by the soldiers. Each day, one captain reported on the number of dead that were found the previous day. Hundreds died each day.

Soon food shortages became a problem. General Erebos was ahead of that game. Early on, he sent his men to confiscate all food supplies from all storage warehouses, piling the goods up here within the palace. Now he began to dole out food rations. In return, his soldiers were authorized to take whatever they desired. One captain asked if that meant sexual favors; he replied affirmative. Alia was used to providing vast quantities of marble, stone blocks, building materials, and granite slabs. However, the demand for these evaporated into nothingness. Nearly all trade halted. The only people who were really still working in the city were the soldiers, who continued to dole out food rations, while taking in return whatever they desired. Misery piled on top of misery. Any that protested were simply shot, becoming just another number in the next day's tally of dead.

Mid-November, the general brought word to Katerine that her parents had been killed by robbers. He promised her that the culprits would be found and shot. She was crushed by the news. Not so much because she had strong bonds with them, but rather it dashed her only hope of rescue from her dismal life at the palace. Already one of her servants had stopped eating and had finally died. She had given up completely and was merely waiting to succumb. At last, death took her.

This upset Katerine even more. At last, she broke down and began crying. Barbara snuggled up to her. "I feel so betrayed! So powerless, so helpless. What can we do now?" she wailed.

"I know, mommy, I know. It is really, really bad, isn't it," her five year old daughter answered in her childlike manner.

"Yes, yes it is really bad. Barbara, whatever are we going to do? With grandfather and grandmother gone, I have no one I can turn to for help. I have some uncles and aunts that might take us in, but I have no way to get word to them. If we could get a carriage to take us, we might be able to visit them, but I don't think it is safe for us to be out on the streets. It is all so completely hopeless, so hopeless."

"The general is not a very nice man, is he mommy? Daddy wasn't either, but now he's gone." Katerine didn't answer. She felt so powerless, so weak. "Mommy, we are just going to have to help ourselves," she declare stoically and with a determination often found in the very young who have yet to be told "no" often enough.

The catalyst came the next day. General Erebos and three of his men came to her quarters just after breakfast. "Queen Katerine, I am seeing that your servant women get better homes and living arrangements. Obviously, they are not really of any use as your servants any longer." He snickered. "They are in need of servants themselves. So I've found better home for them. My men will take them now. As for you, Queen Katerine, while there are no clothes that will fit you or any other woman right now, we have come across some jewelry that I believe will enhance your incredible beauty. Red has always been your color. I admit, red does you justice, perhaps now more than ever before. Please, allow the jeweler, who has come at my call, to adorn you with these extremely expensive rubies. Later, please join me in the throne room. Oh yes, we found some similar emeralds for little Barbara. We all know how she does so want to look like her mother." He smiled wickedly, turned, and crawled out of her chambers.

"Your Highness, if you will merely sit, I will put these prize earrings on you as ordered. I must say, they are worth a fortune. Never have I had the honor of handling such treasures. Indeed, my queen, you will be wearing earrings worth at least a half million, maybe more." He held them up so that she could see the incredibly beautiful and valuable earrings. A four-inch gold circle held five chains of large red rubies, each affixed in a golden basket with each flowery basket hanging from the next. All told, each of the five chains held seven large rubies in their ornamental baskets. "Here we go. Now I need to apply a little heat, please do not move. Ah, yes. There we go. One more, there." Katerine sensed his competence, suspecting that he'd adorned many women through the years. Now she recognized him, he was one of Alia's finest and most wealthy jewelers. "Now they will seem a bit heavy, I'm told. You do not have to worry about losing them. Per the general's orders, I have sealed them on your ears. They cannot easily be removed, so you need never fear losing such priceless earrings. Why don't you have a look, while I fix up your daughter's pair?"

In the past, Katerine had a fondness for jewelry. If she were being totally honest, one of the reasons that she had consented to marry Aeon at the Cardinal's request was the expectancy of wealth and expensive jewelry. Well, for the most part, she had not been disappointed, though it had been her servants who had to adorn her with them. Oh, these were heavy, she thought as she rose and long too; they draped down onto her shoulders and pulled her lobes down noticeably. Still the brilliant flashes of red did accentuate her rich blonde hair and complexion. They were indeed very stunning. In other times and in other circumstances, she would have been ecstatic over such a royal gift. But now — what did these imply? Was the general seeking to bed her? Was she supposed to show him gratitude, likely sexually? Was he planning to make her his queen? She felt revolted by such thoughts.

"Mommy, mommy, come look at mine!" Barbara called out. The jeweler has stepped back, admiring his handiwork. She sported a similar set done in emeralds. "Yes, a matched set. One with rubies, one with emeralds. In a few years, she will grow some and they will not hang quite so low on her chest, Your Highness. Does she not look like a true budding spring flower?" he complimented her daughter. Katerine bristled; she was only five years old, far too young to be wearing such earrings and such heavy ones at that. Yet the look on Barbara's face melted her misgivings.

"Honey, they look beautiful on you. Now you and mommy look just alike. Thank you sir." He started to say something, but apparently thought better of it. He quietly crawled out of their room. Barbara went to the mirror to see how she looked in her new earrings and was very pleased for a while.

As Katerine prepared to go to the throne room as asked, Barbara whined, "Mommy, these are too heavy for me. My ears are hurting. Can you take them off me?"

"I know honey. Mine too. I can't take them off. Not even the general. They are made so that we cannot take them off. They are terribly valuable. That's why they are fastened so well. Perhaps if you lie down they won't ache as much. I have to go to the throne room. Come get me if you need something."

As she shuffled slowly into the room, General Erebos stared long at her, watching her body as it moved, her huge breasts bobbing gracefully, her magnificent earrings reflecting a sparking reddish glow amid a sea of blonde hair and bronze skin. Katerine had seen that look before, lust. She wished that she could have somehow said no to his orders to wear these earrings. "You look radiant; such beauty is rare in the world. Please have a seat. Ah, here come the morning's news."

It was not good. Word had come. The Empress and Emperor had been assassinated. Neighboring Thrace was in complete turmoil; no one was in charge. The plague had evidently struck all Demokritos now. The other two neighboring kingdoms of Phindos and Theos were also in chaos. "Well, things are worse than I imagined. We are going to have to beef up our border patrols to protect Alia. I would not put it past some of the other generals to attempt a land grab right about now. After all, everyone knows Alia is one of the wealthier kingdoms," General Erebos speculated, forgetting about Katerine for the time being. Quietly, she rose and left unnoticed by all the worried men.

Katerine found Barbara lying on their bed. She sat up and asked, "Did the general try to kiss you mommy?" That was as close as she could express what she thought the general's actions might be to her mother.

"No, but he got distracted by other things, and I slipped away. We must get out of here, Barbara. It is growing more dangerous for us by the day. We don't want him to share our bed, now do we?" Barbara shook her head, her earrings flying about making a slight tapping noise as the various gold baskets and emeralds banged together.

"No, mommy, never. I know where we can go, mommy."

"Maybe we could try my uncle, if he still lives," she said wistfully.

"I know where we can go, mommy. We can be safe there."

Slightly annoyed, Katerine said, "Okay, okay, Barbara, where?"

"The Dorota people. Their church place. Remember hearing about them? At the ball. We heard people talking about them. They don't have arms too. We would be safe with them. Please, mommy, can we go to them soon?"

"Oh! I remember — the followers of the old ways. Most all of those people left our country almost fifty years ago. You are right; we did hear that a few had refused to go. Where did we hear that they were staying? Oh, I wish that I'd paid more attention!"

"I remember mommy. They live at 20th and Vine. I remember because I am not allowed to drink wine yet, but I am when I am twenty, which is four times my age. Tomorrow is my birthday; I'll be six, but I won't get any presents this year, will I?"

"No, I am afraid that you won't. 20th and Vine? Are you sure? That's quite a ways from here."

"We can walk, mommy," she suggested. Distance has so little meaning when one is almost six.

"I suppose that we have no choice, but it is so far to walk. Okay, we walk. Now how are we going to get out of here? We can't just walk out of the palace gates. I am sure that the soldiers will not let us.

Once the general finds out that we tried, he'll surely lock us up in our rooms."

"Like naughty boys and girls?"

"Yes, dear. We will have only one chance. How can we get out of here?" she sat down on the bed, thinking hard.

"Mommy, how about daddy's secret way? He showed us it last year. Remember?" Katerine knew what she meant. The palace had a secret tunnel exit in case of dire emergencies. Aeon had proudly shown it to them last year, when it was opened for cleaning. The entrance was in the throne room, though she had no idea where it led.

"But it's dark in there. How will we see our way? We cannot carry a lantern with us. If only you still had your arms, Barbara, we might manage." She sighed; it seemed so hopeless once more.

At supper, General Erebos sat their pie pans before them as usual, but he dallied before Katerine. To her humiliation, his fingers began rubbing small circles around her enormous breasts. His face held a wry smile and lust filled his eyes. Thank god, Katerine thought, he won't do anything around a child. He leaned over and kissed her forehead, then left them alone. Once he was gone, Barbara looked up from her pie pan and whispered, "We have to go now, mommy, don't we?" Katerine nodded, she had no choice. Stay, and she would become the sex slave of the general. How long would he delay taking her? Probably not much longer. Katerine resolved to leave that very night.

She knew that she could probably open the secret door. Aeon had merely pressed a certain stone inward. That she could manage. Yet how they could find their way in a pitch-black tunnel she had no idea. She had no choice but to try. Either that or give up entirely, which she could not; she had Barbara to think about now. After dinner, the two lay down and waited. When Katerine thought that it must be midnight or later, she roused Barbara. "Okay, we must be very, very quiet. No one must hear us leave."

"Oh boy, this is exciting!" The two stole out of their chambers. Since the plague struck, no one had ever closed their doors. In fact, wedges beneath the doors kept them open. No one wanted to deal with opening doors for the women. Quietly, the two shuffled down the long halls to the throne room. As expected, a lone lamp-blackened lantern dimly illuminated the familiar room. They walked over to the secret door's entrance. Both remembered which stone Aeon had pressed. Katerine bent down and pushed on it with her head. Harder and harder. At last, with a low grating sound, the stone moved, and the entrance door swung open. A black hole greeted them. She began to have second thoughts now. Once inside and the door shut, they would be in complete darkness, unable to see anything at all.

"Mommy, we can do this. It will be like playing blind man's bluff!" Barbara sensed her mother's growing fear and tried her best to calm her.

"But we don't have any hands to feel our way along," Katerine expressed her growing fear. "What if there are steps? How will we find the stone to move to open the exit?"

"We can still feel with our feet and bodies, mommy. Come on; let's do it!" her enthusiasm bolstered Katerine's confidence a little, enough to try. After all, the worst that could happen is that they would get trapped inside. Well, she could always yell until someone came to rescue them. Of course, she knew that after that, she'd be a sex slave to the general forever. Perhaps it would be better just to die trapped inside. The two stepped into the secret tunnel.

"Let me do it, mommy," Barbara whispered. Katerine, fighting her growing terror of the coming blackness, allowed her daughter to push on the stone. The grating sound came once more, and then blackness, total and complete blackness. For a moment, Katerine panicked. "It goes this way mommy," Barbara called out, bringing her back to her senses.

"Go really slowly. Follow me." Katerine took perhaps one-inch strides, praying that there were no stairs. Stairs were always a challenge for women wearing the fashionable Annelise extreme heels, even more so for a Holy Woman of the Eighth Degree, and terrifying if one was also blind. Soon, though Katerine found a use for her huge bosom. She began to use it as an early warning beacon. They touched the cold stone before her face could smash into the walls. She managed a grin as she realized this, though no one could see it.

Each step was small and tentative, for any step could bring the start of stairs. Time passed, and at last, she felt stone in front of her. Using her massive bosom as feelers, she began to explore the hard blackness and found the tunnel had turned. "This way," she whispered. Much later, she again encountered a stone barrier. Once more she explored it, seeking the next change in direction. This time, she found none. Twice she covered the entire area until she was satisfied that they had reached a dead end. "This must be the end of the tunnel. Somehow we have to find the stone to push to open the door."

It was sheer guesswork. Katerine estimated the height of the entrance stone latch and began pushing against stones that seemed to be the same height. How long she pushed, she could not tell. As she was about to give it up, a stone moved a little. "I think I have it!" She pushed her face into the stone even harder now, praying this would work. The wall before them slowly swung outward, fresh air seeped in, a refreshing breath from the intense staleness to which they had become accustomed.

Outside, Katerine saw the dawn's twilight. It was mid-spring and quite chilly. Naked, both began shivering, but she focused first on shutting the secret door. Now she had to get her bearings. Where were they? Soon it would be daylight. They dare not walk the streets in the daytime. They'd have to find a place to hide out until nightfall, she was certain of that. They had come out along a side wall of a warehouse in an alleyway. They walked out into the street and spotted a street sign. At last, Katerine knew their location. A bit later, she found a deserted alleyway and the two entered it, finding a hiding place behind a large pile of discarded crates. Both sat down on the cold ground, shivering. "Here, cuddle up to mommy. I'll try to keep you warm. We must sleep now."

Ill was her sleep that day. Constantly fearing a chance discovery, chilled to the bone, and quite hungry, she dozed on and off. Midday, though, it did warm up substantially. After sundown, she finally decided it was time to begin their long walk to 20th and Vine. She guessed that they had four miles to walk.

As they shuffled along at barely three inches per step, Barbara occupied her mind by working out how many steps they had to take. "Mommy," she whispered, "we are going to have to take eighty four thousand steps! My feet are hurting."

"I know dear, this plague has mutilated our feet. Be grateful that our feet are not as bad as the men's feet are. If they were that bad, we'd not even be able to crawl. It takes arms and hands to do that. Come on, we must get there tonight somehow."

Even with frequent breaks, their feet and legs began to ache mercilessly. Still, both were determined to get to these people before dawn. Just as the twilight came, they approached 20th and Vine. Both were now almost stumbling with each step. "Just a little more, just a little more, just a little more," Katerine said trying to encourage herself as much as Barbara. A wrought iron fence surrounded a small marble two-story building. As usual, a stable was attached to the home. Katerine used her foot to open the gate and the two headed up the long granite paved sidewalk.

At the door, she paused. "We don't even know if the Dorota people live here, not for sure. What if they don't?"

"Maybe we can ask for directions," Barbara suggested.

"Damn, I cannot even knock on the door!"

"Let me mommy." She used her head to bang on the door a few times. She waited a bit and then banged again. Katerine heard noises inside and then saw a dim light coming from inside the window.

"Someone's coming," she whispered. A moment later, the door opened. A man in pajamas stood there holding an oil lantern up. He appeared to be in his mid-thirties. "Excuse us, sir. We are looking for the Dorota folks. We think that we heard that they live somewhere around here. Can you help us?"

"Yes, the Dorota people who did not leave fifty years ago," Barbara added.

The man lowered the lantern and look squarely at the six year old. "You must be Barbara."

"Yes sir. I am six now."

"Welcome, Barbara! We have been waiting for you. And this must be your mother?"

"Yes sir."

"Welcome, welcome. Come on inside. Come. You have found us. You must be freezing. Quick, inside. Eleni, it's Barbara at last. Quick, heat up some water, bath water. Rouse the others. Come inside. You are safe now." Katerine did not know what to make of this greeting, but did as asked. He shut the door and began turning on more lanterns. Safe at last? Shivering wildly, her legs gave out, and she slumped unconscious to the floor.

She awoke to find herself in a warm cotton nightgown and tucked into a warm bed. Rising up with effort, she found a middle aged woman sitting on a chair by her bed. "Ah, you are awake at last. I am supposed to get you to eat as much of this chicken soup as you desire. You'll soon have your strength back. I am Eleni."

She sat up, worried, "Where's Barbara?"

Eleni smiled, "She's outside playing with our children. Now you must eat." The woman used her foot to lift up a spoonful of soup. She found herself ravenously hungry and finished off the bowl. Only when she was full did she realize that Eleni was feeding her using her foot.

"There now, feel better? If you are, let's get you up and dressed. Everyone wants to meet you."

"But I have no clothes," she protested.

"You can wear one of my dresses. Helen has already altered our dresses to fit our strange body forms. It's the result of the plague, you know. Of course, these won't be the fancy dresses that you are used to wearing at the court. These are practical ones that we women can put on ourselves, but I'll help you into it this afternoon." The dress was a simple cotton one, red. She suspected that Barbara may have helped pick it out. First though, Eleni helped her slip into some cotton panties, showing her how she could pull them up or down herself, using her toes and the four large loops that were sewn into the waistband. The dress had similar loops where toes could hold on while a leg lifted it up. The front was open from the waist on up and a line of hook and eye fasteners running its length. Eleni showed her how easily she could fasten or unfasten them herself. "We are very independent women around here, you'll soon see. Come on, everyone wants to meet you."

She rose and looked at herself in the mirror. "I look human again, thank you Eleni. I feel human too."

Katerine followed the woman into the large living room. Apparently, they all knew that she was coming, the room held six adults. As she entered, Eleni, paused by the window. "Have a look." A very big smile formed on Katerine's face, one that had not been seen for a very long time. There was Barbara dressed in a similar dress dashing about the front yard with five older children. They were all playing kick ball. Barbara was laughing and dashing about — the girls moved more quickly than the boys who walked on the tips of their toes in strange boots.

Someone called the children and the six headed into the living room, joining the group of adults. Eleni beckoned Katerine to sit on the couch beside her from where she could more readily see everyone else. The children clamored in, though in slow motion. Their cheeks were flushed and smiles lit up their faces. They sat down on the floor around their parents.

The man, who she recalled had let them inside, spoke first, "Please, why don't you introduce yourself and your charming daughter first. Then, we'll introduce our group."

One of the young girls piped up, "You're our queen aren't you?"

Her mother hushed her, "Io, hush. Let her speak."

"Yes, I am Queen Katerine Stathis. Aeon, the king, was murdered by the Mano del Dio. His top general is in charge. We had to escape. He has become a tyrant and threatened to take me, well, I won't say more. Yes, Io, I was a Holy Woman but now I have been betrayed by the church, and I won't go near them ever again. Barbara is my daughter; she's just turned six. It was her idea that we come here, seeking help. I just don't know what we are going to do now. The world has somehow gone mad. My parents are dead, and we have no one to turn to for help."

"You came to the right place, probably the only safe place in all of Alia for you," the old man spoke. "I am Elder Homer Manasses." He was sixty, with mostly white hair, though his eyes were riveting, giving him the appearance of being all-knowing. "We are all descendants from our immigrant parents who came here from Dorota many years ago to help spread the Holy Gift to others. As you know, fifty years ago, a lot of pressure was put on all families who had armless women among them to migrate up north to a place called Hieras Anubis. You see, as descendants from Dorota and ardent followers of the old ways, our women chose to be like our ancestors, and they make their choice when they are five years old."

"Anyway, when the time of the exodus came, our Supreme Elder asked me to stay on here in Alia. My purpose was to be here to recover two others who had become temporarily lost from our flock. You see we are spiritual beings and for a time inhabit these human bodies. Some years ago, we recovered Yanni here and have been waiting for six years now to recover Barbara, your daughter. Have you not noticed that she is a most able young girl?"

"But more of that later. I am lax in my introductions. I am the leader of our small group. My wife has passed away some five years now. This is my son, Jude Manasses and his charming and able wife, Eleni." Both were thirty-five. He had his father's black hair and demeanor, the kind of face that sees all and knows all. Eleni was rather ordinary looking, with a luxurious, long black hair, trimmed nicely at her waist. Their son was Triton, a tall, wiry lad of fifteen. Their daughter was Hermina, now fourteen. Both had their parents' raven hair. She wore hers straight and long, just like her mother, trimmed at her waist.

"This is Midas and Helen Drastus." They were a year younger and both of these had the typical Alia brown hair. While his was cut short, Helen had hers trimmed shoulder length. She had an infectious smile, which never seemed to leave her. Their son was Myron, now fifteen, likewise tall and thin, a rapidly growing teen. Their daughters were Io at fourteen and Isis, who was twelve. Both young women had their parents brown hair. Io had hers waist long, while Isis kept hers shoulder length.

"Finally, this is Yanni Argos, the newest addition to our fold." He was twenty-five and rather handsome. "His wife passed away in childbirth."

"I'm so sorry, that must have been awful for you," Katerine spoke up.

"Yes, but thanks to these people here, I survived and am now doing well. You just have to experience their Holy Gift. It will make a new woman out of you. Actually, I used to be a part of the Dorota Church of God. When my old body died, I picked up a new baby body, but well, I goofed and picked the wrong parents. I cannot tell you how grateful I am that these folks were kind enough to wait around for me."

"What's this about Barbara?" Katerine asked. How did her own daughter fit in with these people whom she had never met and only once even heard about?

"Barbara was one of us and a very able person. Have you not noticed that she is far more than a six year old girl?" Elder Homer asked.

Suddenly all manner of little things stood out in Katerine's mind. Barbara spoke up, "Sorry mommy, but I love raven hair not blonde, and so I changed it. I hope you don't mind."

"No dear, you look beautiful to me as you are," she grinned.

"I belong here. I'm sorry mommy. I was supposed to have given you the Holy Gift, but I forgot."

Elder Homer added, "Yes, when her previous body died, she was supposed to rejoin us and have Hermina's or Io's or even Iris's body. Alas, she chose to delay getting a new baby body and then she chose you to be her mother. Hence, we had to continue to wait for her to come to us. Unfortunately, we still cannot get her to explain why she deviated from the plan."

"And I am not going to say why now either," Barbara pouted. The expression on her face, Katerine had seen many times, usually with both arms folded across her chest in a defiant pose. "The time is not right," she added.

"Yes little one," Elder Homer replied.

"And don't call me little one! I'm really big!" she added. Katerine chuckled, that was just like her Barbara.

"Now then, the first thing we must do is to begin teaching you both how to fend for yourselves," Eleni finally spoke up.

The next week was a revelation for Katerine. Constantly, she found herself facing normal life actions, which, since becoming a Holy Woman, she could never do again. Under their guidance and coaching and direction, she began doing them again, beginning with feeding herself and even cooking.

Each day, Eleni gave her therapy sessions, the Holy Gift. As she began to re-experience and erase the emotional and physical trauma of having her arms amputated six years ago, the pain did not fully erase. Then, she discovered something that had happened to her even earlier. Two lifetimes earlier, she had also been a Holy Woman of the Eighth Degree. When she ran through that one, the whole pain and emotional sorrow vanished. Roaring with laughter, Eleni had no choice but to end this session. She came out laughing and laughing, bumping into Yanni.

"Excuse me, Yanni. Once is enough, twice is entirely too much. No, even once is too much," and she laughed and laughed.

"Come walk with me," he suggested. He led her around their backyard, which had high bushes surrounding it, giving them much needed privacy.

"I feel so alive now, Yanni! I feel like a little girl, somehow."

"Yes, the Holy Gift has that benefit. It brings life, which has been stunted by pain and trauma back into us once more. I'm so glad to see you laughing. You're the most beautiful woman that I've ever seen. It's good to see you happy."

On the tenth day since they arrived here, Elder Homer called for a group meeting. "Well, the situation has become more serious. Katerine, I hate to tell you this, but General Erebos is furious that you left the palace. He has his soldiers out scouring the city for you. He has put a bounty on those who are harboring you. It is no longer safe for us to stay in Levkos. As they say, it is time that we abandon the sinking ship."

"I'm so sorry! I've brought this on all of you." Katerine was near tears. She'd just formed strong bonds of friendship and now they were in danger of being shattered. Her friends, murdered.

"It's not your doing, Katerine. We have always planned to leave, once Barbara returned to us. No, the real question before us and the one that we all must answer is where do we go?"

"Well, we could head to the Northern Mountains and hide out there," suggested Yanni. "I can hunt for fresh meat. Hope you all like venison."

"That option may have been a good one before, but with our feet the way that they are, walking in rocky, mountainous land will be nearly impossible," Homer countered.

"It's no good trying to flee into Phindos or even Theos; both countries are in a similar mess as Alia. I think that is out. How about going to the seacoast and hiding out there? We could at least fish and have something to eat," suggested Jude.

"Yes, obtaining food is rapidly becoming our number one problem. The soldiers are getting stingier and stingier with their handouts," Homer added.

"And more demanding. Soon, they'll want to bed us," Eleni added with disgust.

Helen spoke up, "We have to think of Katerine's well-being now. No matter where we go in Alia, someone is eventually going to recognize her. Few can forget a woman as beautiful as she is. Someone's bound to recognize her, and then we'll have to take drastic actions."

"What about going over to Thallyus or even Penelopus?" suggested Myron. "I know it is thousands of miles. Oh, yeh, no food. Forget that one."

They discussed other ideas before Jude offered a viable alternative, "Say, what about leaving Demokritos entirely? There are small groups of old Dorota folk over in Annelise. There we would be totally safe and can ride out this disaster in peace."

"Two things hinder that, Jude," Midas pointed out. "One, how the devil do we get there, and two, you know that they have the strictest dress code in the world. Our women will be really constrained there."

Jude grinned, "I can solve one. I just remembered that the Annelise Spring Trading Ship is due in any day now." For Katerine's benefit, he explained, "Each quarter of the year, several Annelise ships visit our largest port, Preveza. They bring along the latest in the coming season's fashions to trade. They ought to be here with the summer's offering about now. I am sure that we could purchase passage to Annelise. Look, with this plague and the chaos, they will probably make no sales at all. I suspect that they will be more than glad to accept some paying customers."

"It sounds like heaven to me," Eleni spoke up. "Look, we all know how nuts they are on proper clothing and how restrictive it will be for we women, but if the other Dorota groups who live there can bear it, so can we. I am all for trying this option. I'd rather face a little discomfort and difficulty than the uncertain and deadly chaos over here. Every time I hear horse's hooves on the streets, I get a twinge of fear that they are coming and will harm us all. Please, let's give Annelise a try." The other women agreed with her and thus it was settled. Katerine noticed that the men took the women's advice. Strange, she thought, so unlike the world that she had known.

Once the decision was made, Katerine was surprised at how quickly they packed to leave. The next evening, they had three wagons loaded with their things and began their three hundred mile journey to the coast. They chose to leave at night, sneaking out of the city, avoiding the potential witnesses who might recognize the queen. Yannis drove one wagon and Katerine sat beside him. The many children took turns riding in the various wagons, chatting and playing mental games. They pushed hard, on the road for sixteen hours at a time, though with some rest breaks. Much of the time they chose to travel at night, it was safer.

On November 25, they pulled up to the docks of Preveza. Several fishing boats plied the shallow coastal waters, but only a few. "Where are all the fishing boats?" Jude wondered. Normally, hundreds would be out on the waters. Two large caravels were docked along with the single Annelise coastal vessel called a dahabea. The dahabea was about a quarter of the size of the caravels, with one main mast far to the aft of center, sporting a lateen sail on a long boom attached high atop the mast. A tiny spinnaker hung off the rear and was used for steering and stabilization.

Captain Grenen, immaculately dressed in a blue suit with twin tails and white cummerbund, greeted Jude as he walked onto the main deck. Katerine held her breath, but soon the broad smile on the tall man suggested he was very pleased to have paying passengers. Shortly, Jude returned to the wagons. "It is all arranged. Come on; let's get aboard. His crew will load our things for us. Oh, their Princess Mia Jorgen is below and in terrible shape from the plague. I suggested that we might be able to help her or at least assist her. He was very relieved to hear that. Oh, yes, he said hold on to the railings, fellows, it is terribly difficult to navigate the moving ship in these boots. He's already lost one sailor overboard on their trip here."

Yanni put his arm on Katerine's shoulder and his other hand held onto the railing. Together they attempted to navigate the dahabea. Likewise, the other men held onto the shoulder of a woman and the railing. Since Myron helped both Iris and Barbara, Katerine relaxed and concentrated on not falling down, since she was balancing for Yanni as well as herself. With extreme caution, they safely made it below deck. Because cabin space was limited, they would have to bunk together in the cargo hold as a group, surrounded by the crates of unsold clothing.

They found Princess Mia Jorgen sitting at the long dinner table in the galley, fore of the cargo hold. Her eyes were bloodshot; her clothing, a complete mess. Her fancy Annelise ball gown no longer fit her huge bosom. Someone had cut holes in the back of her top and laced it shut with twine. However, most of her breasts hung out of the dress, whose top was built for a drastically smaller bosom.

"Oh, forgive me. I am a total mess now. Nothing fits. All is lost! I cannot even go ashore. I look so awful. I can't bear to be seen in public like this. We can't sell anything this trip! What has happened to the world? Has it all gone insane? I am so helpless like this that I can't bear it." Then, she noticed the simple dresses that these newcomers wore; they fit and looked far, far better than the mess that was tied onto her.

Eleni said softly, "Would you allow us to dress you in one of our dresses? I know that ours are so crude compared to yours, but at least they fit. We have had to make drastic alterations to them."

Princess Mia brightened up at once. "Oh, please, please do! Thank you ever so much. I am sure that when I get home, our dressmakers will have found a solution to this awful mess. I am Princess Mia Jorgen, by the way. I live in Viborg. I'm eighteen. I was supposed to get married when I get back from this trip, but now, I am sure that my boyfriend will not want me. I am so helpless, just like you are. It is this plague. It struck us while we were on our voyage here. It was just awful. One sailor fell overboard and died. Just awful, but then I expect that you have seen things just as bad. Is it as bad as they are saying? I mean in your cities? Are people actually starving? It is so utterly awful, you know. Someone ought to do something about it. I know that I would; only I'm sure that I don't know what that might be. Oh, yes, this dress does fit me well. How did you do that? You don't have any arms?" She finally realized that Eleni and Helen had just undressed her and put her new light green dress on her.

Katerine had the feeling that they were going to be chatted to death on this voyage. She wasn't wrong about that detail. As soon as the ship set sail, Eleni began therapy sessions for Mia, who finally erased the shock and terror of the plague's effects on herself and felt a million times better.

It was a long voyage from Alia to Viborg, Annelise, several thousand miles. Hence, they got language lessons and very lengthy chats from Mia. They arrived in mid-December. All during the voyage, Eleni and Helen worked with Katerine and Mia, teaching them all manner of Women's Ways of doing things, made all the harder by the constantly rolling ship. Io, Hermina, and Isis did the same for Barbara, though Katerine saw that Barbara was a natural; she picked everything up extremely rapidly. Often, she only needed to be shown how to do something once and she had it down pat, unlike Katerine, who had to practice and practice.

As they neared their destination, Princess Mia doled out fancy Annelise suits to all the men, her way of thanking them. "Now you will have no trouble when we dock. We women are a mess. Perhaps they will have it all sorted out and we will be able to be properly dressed once again." She chatted on, while the men tried to figure out how to dress themselves in these fancy suits. "No, you have the cummerbund upside down, Jude," she called out, not missing a step in her chat.

They all had permanent invitations to come and spend days with her at her estate on the edge of Viborg anytime. If her wedding was still on, which she gravely doubted, they were all invited, and she promised to send word to them if it was. Jude attempted to tell her that any man worthy of her would not be put off by the after-effects of the plague. If he was, he was not worthy of her. This boosted her self-esteem significantly, realizing that it was the truth. At last, they heard the gulls and felt the ship heading in to dock.

Princess Mia ordered several carriages for them and instructed the drivers on where to take them. All experienced relief when the harbor master informed them that due to the plague, their women's dresses were acceptable for now. After giving Princess Mia a farewell hug, the small group boarded the carriages and headed off through the cobblestone streets of hilly Viborg. They saw men out attempting to navigate the sidewalks, hanging on to anything at hand, walking bravely on their toes. Few women were seen, though.

The Dorota Church of God, Viborg, was located near the western edge of the city, cradled against the back of a wooded hill, very picturesque. A black iron fence surrounded the large estate, and the grounds was well tended, with shrubs and flowering plants dotting the perimeter, very artfully laid out by the previous owners of the estate. The manor house was a four story, brown brick home, quite large and very well maintained.

"Welcome, welcome, especially Queen Katerine Stathis. It is a great honor to host the Queen of Alia and her charming young daughter. I am sure that you will be quite safe here in Annelise, quite safe indeed." Their leader was a tall, robust man, who instilled confidence by his mere presence. Katerine felt totally safe and secure for the first time in a very long time.

Chapter 39 Help for Katerine and Annelise

Katerine's refuge, the Church of God, was located near the western edge of the city, cradled against the back of a wooded hill, very picturesque. The manor house was a four story, brown brick home, quite large and very well maintained.

Jude and Eleni Manasses and their children, Hermina and Triton, had brought Katerine and Barbara here. Along with them were Midas and Helen Drastus with their three children, Io, Iris, and Myron. Of course, Yanni Argos came too, the handsome lad who constantly assisted Katerine. Upon entering the manor house, they were met by the Viborg Church of God, their hosts.

Julie Jaeger was the matriarch of the group. She was sixty-five now with very grey hair and a widower for many years. She was the mother of the two middle aged wives, Andrea and Hilda. Axel and Andrea Ansgard, in their middle thirties, had a son Becker, sixteen, and a daughter Berit, fifteen. Erik, thirty-seven, and Hilda Gustavo, a year younger, had a daughter, Hedda, now seventeen, and son Halder, who was fifteen. From the moment they were introduced, Katerine could tell that the teens were obviously engaged to each other; the boys kept their arms around their girlfriends the whole time.

Jude introduced his group and gave a very lengthy explanation of their situation and that of Katherine. "Of course, you are all welcome to stay here for as long as you like. We have plenty of unoccupied rooms," Julie explained. "I've been in touch with other church leaders across Tarra. I am afraid to say that the plague had struck everywhere this time and no cure is expected, unlike the last one which struck up north."

"Oh dear! Are all women like us now? Everywhere?" Katerine burst out, shocked beyond belief to hear that this plague was worldwide. Nowhere was safe now.

"Yes and no, Katerine," the matronly woman smiled and replied. "Yes, from all that I've learned even baby girls are born like yourself. Here at our church we women voluntarily gave up our arms when we turned five, in keeping with the ancient ways of our ancestors from Dorota. To be quite honest with you, Queen Katerine, I've never missed them. We have our own ways of doing things. We will gladly teach them to you, dear. Why, in no time you will be doing everything that you used to do for yourself."

Katerine flushed. "I'm sorry. I gave mine up too, five years ago, when I married my late husband. Holy Woman of the Eighth Degree. That was the worst mistake of my entire life. I don't know how I could have been so stupid."

"That's okay with us, Queen Katerine. Nevertheless, we will show you how to do all the things demanded of us in life. Yet, I must admit to all of you, that we women here in this house have, in some ways, welcomed the coming of this plague."

The shocked look on Katerine's face caused Julie to smile and explain further. "You see, you are now in Annelise. Outsiders call it the fashion insane country. You probably have heard about this land, where you must be dressed for the most regal occasions just to step outside your door. Katerine knew that she was not really exaggerating. Four times a year, one of their princesses came to her court bringing along the latest in fashions. She'd heard all about this country, where women always wore restrictive corsets in an attempt to attain the waistlines that all women now had. Indeed, for the past five years, she had worn only the finest of Annelise outfits and was intimately familiar with their extreme heels and giant hoop dresses. She began to see why Julie had this opinion now.

Julie continued, "We women use our feet where others use their hands. Being so constrained in their official outfits, why we women became as helpless as you must have been in your court, Queen Katerine. Thus, we seldom went outside for that very reason. Since the plague struck and since seamstresses cannot make new gowns nor alter the now terrible fitting ones, King Niels Ryker has relaxed all restrictions on proper clothing for the women of Annelise, until such time as proper new clothing can be designed. Men, however, must still be properly dressed at all times, of course."

Only now did Katerine finally actually notice the clothing that the women were wearing. Julie wore her hair in a bun. She had on a satin gown, which had been altered to fit her new needs. The many pleats did tend to flair the dress out near her feet a little. She noticed that all the other women also wore satin dresses, which had been nicely altered to fit their now tiny waists and massive bosoms. Obviously, they had already found a seamstress to do the work, she thought, incorrectly. Yet, none of the women wore the restrictive corsets, no need. Their dresses looked elegant, yet manageable and comfortable as well. Perhaps Yanni would help her into one soon, she thought.

As if picking up her thoughts, Julie added, "Yes, Queen Katerine, Andrea here is a fine seamstress. She made all the alterations to our day dresses that we are wearing. Having lived here so long, we all are in love with the feel of fine satin. I'm afraid that in a little way, we've gone native." She grinned at her jest. "Of course, our biggest problem, and that of our men as well, are our feet. However, I have heard from my contacts in the north that perhaps very soon now all of our feet will heal up and will return to the way that they were before the plague. None too soon for us, I can tell you that, Queen Katerine."

"Just Katerine, please, everyone. I don't feel much like a queen now. Our feet will get better? Now that is something. It is so hard for everyone to get around, but then I have spent the last five years in those extreme Annelise heels, so I honestly am quite used to walking like this."

"Of course you are, Katerine. Now then, we have some business to discuss among us all," Julie's voice turned serious. "Many of us have been given quite a lot of Advanced Therapy, far beyond our Holy Gift, which, by the way, Katerine, we will be giving to you starting tomorrow. Here in this manor house, we all are spiritual beings and some of us have progressed to what outsiders would call very advanced states of being, able to do some amazing things that we all once were able to do. I for one have had my telepathic abilities recovered. That is how I know so much of what is going on in the world. I have contacts with a great many people worldwide. I am also able to move lighter objects. When we dine, Katerine, please do not be shocked to see my silverware apparently levitating my food up and into my mouth. I am actually doing it. So are my daughters Andrea and Hilda. Since the plague came, we have been working on this very skill with their daughters, Berit and Hedda, so that they may eat far more easily as well. Mind you, the teens are still novices at it and sometimes drop their spoons. They just need more practice, drills, and therapy and they will have it mastered."

"Axel and Erik are very good at moving far heavier objects and are working on getting their telepathic skills restored. They still have quite a ways to go, I am afraid. Interestingly enough, the four teens are doing remarkably well with such skills. What I am saying is that around this manor house, we do not hide what we, as spiritual beings, can do. Not unless outsiders are here, then we all behave ourselves." The four teens all giggled.

"Why is that?" Katerine asked, most curious. Was she in the house of some gods?

"Imagine that you found yourself around people who could levitate anything, for example. Would you not tend to be afraid of their powers, that they could do something that you could not?"

"Oh! You're right. While I might think it was really great when I first saw it, I can see myself worrying that they might cause me problems," Katerine replied.

"Yes, we try not to blow other's reality to smithereens," Julie said graphically. "Now then, I must ask you, Jude, to tell us here where your people are at with the advanced skills."

Jude sat straight in his chair. Evidently, this was important, Katerine thought. "With two exceptions, we have been following the path laid out by our church founder. Except for handing life's bumps, we did not begin therapy formally on our children until they were ten, though of course, the girls had their arm surgery fully erased within days of having it done. Triton and Myron are already into the beginnings of Advanced Therapy, while Io and Hermina are ready to begin it. Iris still has a ways to go; she's only twelve. When our parents died, we four adults lost our Advanced Therapy giver and have been on hold ever since then. I am able to control other people's bodies to a limited extent while Eleni and Helen are both very good with moving small objects. Midas can move rather heavier ones."

"Excellent, I will see that you both can resume your Advanced Therapy while you are here with us," Julie replied. "Now then, the two exceptions?"

"Ah, yes, well when the others left Alia, we were asked to delay a little longer to pick up two of our abler flock. Yanni here, we finally located about two years ago. We've been working with him and have him back to where he was last at in his Advanced Therapy. Yanni is able to control others, lift heavy objects, but he has not recovered his telepathic skills yet. He is stable outside his body though if he is hurt bad enough, he still gets pulled back into its head. We are still working on that aspect," Jude explained.

Katerine looked at the handsome Yanni as if she had never seen him before. "You never said that you could do all that," she said quite surprised.

He grinned, "You never asked and I've had no need to use them. I promised that I would look after you and I meant it, Katerine." She gave him a big grin.

"The second exception," Jude continued, and now Katerine listened to his every word, "is Barbara here. She goofed up and ended up moving into the wrong baby body. We had to wait around until she came to us. Barbara formerly was a very able being, quite powerful, though we will likely need to do a bit of remedial drilling with her to get her back to battery. She was a powerhouse mover, able to lift enormous weights; she could control other's bodies, and still is always outside her body and has very good perceptions. Her problem is that she has been living among the normal humans for the last five years, who have no idea of their own spiritual identities or abilities. In short, Barbara has had a rough five years. Still, she managed to get her mother and herself to us when the chaos came to their palace home. She tells quite a story about it all," he grinned at Barbara who sat proudly as though she were the most important person in the room. In a way, she was or would be very soon now.

"Mommy, does this mean that now I can lift my spoon and feed myself without having to have someone do it for me?" she asked.

Julie answered before Katerine could, "Yes, of course, Barbara, you can do whatever you please around us. All that I ask is if we have outside company don't spook them," she grinned at the six year old girl. Barbara grinned right back at her.

"Now then," Julie resumed control of her meeting, "we will get you all to your new rooms and show you about the manor house. Yanni will be staying with Katerine and Barbara for the time being, until Katerine can handled her own basic needs. Katerine, tomorrow we will continue your therapy as well, plus all of us will continue teaching you our ancient Women's Ways of doing everything that you used to do before you became a Holy Woman, perhaps even more things. I bet that you never sewed before." Katerine flashed her a smile; how did she know that she wondered and then realized that she had just had that very thought and Julie had simply picked up her thought.

"Thank you all for your incredible kindness. All this is almost too much to believe, thank you," Katerine replied.

Each day after that, Katerine saw new surprises, but none made her happier than those of her daughter. "Mommy, look at this!" Barbara proudly moved the heavy couch around the living room for her mother.

"Amazing, dear. Hug!" That became her daily battle and she soon learned how to hug properly, using one leg. She had never felt closer to her daughter.

Two weeks later, and Katerine felt very alive; her face shone like a candle in the night. The pain and trauma of her surgery was gone, as well as the many shocking losses when the plague struck. All her fears, worries, and problems had vanished, as if they had never been there. "Now, it's time to work on your Advanced Therapy, Katerine," Julie said and Katerine was ecstatic. Perhaps she too could regain abilities; at least she now knew that she was an immortal spiritual being. She had seen six of her former lives while erasing the pain and traumas thus far.

Even more shocking, by mid-April, Barbara was fully rehabilitated to her former level of abilities as a spiritual being. As it turned out, she had been one of Macario's more advanced members. She now began giving Julie and the other adults Advanced Therapy sessions. At the same time, Katerine was very proud to be able to lift her own fork and spoon at the dinner table. She was actually feeding herself without using her feet. Though a bit wobbly in her motions and with a few accidental spills, she did it and received praise from the other women, including the teens who had finally gotten this down pat. Yes, dinnertime around the great table was a most interesting sight. Spoons and forks floated over plates, scooping up the food, floating up to opened women's mouths. Teacups rose to the women's lips, seemingly of their own accord. Katerine realized that if outsiders saw such a display, they would indeed be shocked and later become terribly afraid of them.

An aside, both Barbara and Katerine continued to wear their long, dangling earrings, worth a fortune each. Katerine loved the feel of the rubies on her shoulders as she moved her head about. Besides, they blended perfectly with her long blonde hair, which she now kept waist length. Barbara's emeralds looked magnificent on her, contrasting very well with her long black hair, which she also kept waist length, emulating her mother. Even though neither Barbara nor Katerine now really needed Yanni's hands at night, Katerine insisted that he sleep with her.

One night mid-April after Barbara had drifted into sleep, she finally admitted to him, "Yanni, I love you. I never thought that I would ever fall in love again, but I have. That's why I still want you close to me."

He rolled over a bit and kissed her. "I love you too. I was waiting and hoping that I might have a chance with you. You are an incredible woman."

Incidentally, they were married on May 1, 824. The next day after they spoke of their love for each other, Barbara gaily announced, "Mommy and Yanni are in love with each other. I heard them last night."

"How could you, dear? I know you were sound asleep," Katerine whispered, slightly embarrassed.

"That was my body, mommy. I am never asleep, not any more. I hear very well." Katerine gave her daughter her usual big hug, and she began to wonder if Barbara ought to have her own room. Then she realized that walls and space meant nothing to Barbara; so much for privacy, she thought.

Later that day, Eve and Macario dropped by or rather materialized there, requesting a conference with Julie, who insisted that everyone hear what the founder of their church had to say. She well knew Macario, Eve discovered, and Julie alone truly appreciated the significance of Eve, one of the founders of the Holy Gift. Once she explained this fully to the others, they too looked at Eve with great awe and respect.

After hearing what Eve and Macario desired to try, Julie agreed. "We have everyone here pretty well along to fairly stable points. I believe that I speak for us all. We'll do our best to train others and expand our basic Holy Gift. You may count on us."

"Please, can you teach me how to do it too," Katerine insisted.

"Of course, dear. Tomorrow," Julie replied.

Not long after the two departed, a soldier dropped by handing them a lengthy announcement. "Evidently, they've worked out new clothing for women," Julie explained as she read the lengthy article. Some groaned.

Hedda complained, "Not those awful corset and monster dresses again!"

"No, I do believe that the King and Queen have come to their senses. This time they wish to be more practical. Looks like they will be giving each woman in Annelise four free outfits." Everyone crowded around to see the series of outfit sketches.

"Well, that's better," Hedda calmed down. "We won't have to always wear those impossible ones. I do like those new slinkys. Mom, can I have that kind instead of the hoops?"

"Yes dear, but I think you will find walking in those slinkys most challenging, dear. We will see."

Here at their church, Julie had twenty-one who could deliver the Holy Gift, though nine were males. She thought better of letting the fellows work the women. Hence, she had Axel and Erik deal with the scheduling and arrangements and record keeping. The other seven men began working with the males of Viborg, while the twelve women began working the women.

Interestingly enough, Katerine's first patient was none other than Princess Mia herself. Katerine was picking up where they had left off during the voyage. "I want to be the best that I can be. I'm getting married as soon as I get the first of these new dresses," she explained. A week later, Princess Mia had an entirely different viewpoint on life. While always a talkative person, now she found herself so full of life that she felt like she was exploding — her words.

In mid-May, she personally brought the four new outfits to the twelve women and insisted on explaining all about them to the gathered women. "A definite pattern is emerging here," she chatted away. "It seems the older women prefer the elegant ball gowns with hoops, while we younger women prefer to try out these new slinky dresses. Honestly, Hedda, you simply have to wear the extreme heels with your new slinky. You can't walk otherwise. Trust me, I know, I experimented with all three heel heights. You tend to trip if you try to wear only the five-inch heels. But to tell you the truth, I am getting both the ball gown and the slinky. I like them both, you see. It is so hard for me to decide which I like best."

The women all received a ball gown or a slinky, complete with all the necessary undergarments and hose and newly designed heels to match. Everyone was very pleased to receive the vastly more practical pants and blouse combinations as well as the around the house blouse and skirt combinations. Katerine did wonder though whether these more practical outfits would really become popular with the Annelise women.

Chapter 40 The Strange Case of Alexina Phanes

Midas Phanes was a bronze maker, who fabricated all manner of bronze household items. Competent, Phanes Bronze was a profitable business, prior to the plague. Situated in the middle class section of Levkos, Alia, his shop was a block from his home, a respectable stone structure, a bit small for his family, however.

His wife, Mina, was a year younger than Midas. Thirty-five, she had light blonde hair and blue eyes. Her face was angelic which had attracted Midas to her some sixteen years ago. They had five children, before the miscarriage, which ended Mina's childbearing years. Airla was the eldest; she was fifteen. Ambrosia came next at fourteen. Their eldest son, Kastor, was thirteen. Their youngest daughter, Alexina, was twelve, and their youngest son was Jude who was eleven. All the children shared their mother's light blonde hair and her blue eyes. All except Alexina, whose eyes were the palest blue, which enchanted those who looked at her, a perfect match for an angel, her mother often said.

The plague struck them particularly hard because they had no extensive food supplies; Mina preferred to shop each week. Plus, Midas' income, while substantial, never seemed enough to meet their large family's needs. Near starvation level around November 15, Midas and Airla left to find vitally needed food. Midas returned with a pushcart of food, having sold Airla to a man who offered him the best deal in food supplies.

Pinching and tightening their belts, especially since no one had come to Phanes Bronze since the plague began, they made it through December 1, when their feet returned to normal. Still no one bought any bronze wares, and Midas took Ambrosia with him in search of food once more. Again, he returned with a pushcart, having traded Ambrosia for their survival. At last, some business came, and in January, he barely had enough to keep them alive.

It was early January; the dog days of summer lay just ahead. Hot, humid, and hungry, tempers flared. Jude picked on Alexina as he did nearly every day. "You are just an object, Alexina."

"No I am not!" she yelled back antagonistically.

"Are too!" he yelled even louder.

"Am not!"

"Are too!"

"Am not!"

"Are too!"

"Am not!"

"Mom, for heaven's sake, shut Alexina up!" Kastor finally yelled at Mina, who was trying her best to figure out how to do some cooking, though Kastor was doing most of it for her.

"Alexina, shut up! You too, Jude," she yelled at the two.

"Mom, tell her that she is just an object, a thing that dad owns," Jude sneered back.

"Oh all right. Alexina, Jude is right. We belong to your father. He owns this house, he owns his shop, and he owns us. After all, he had to sell your sisters just to have enough food for the rest of us. Men own women now. We can't live without them. We depend utterly upon them. We belong to men, dear. Now go play," Mina pointed out the now prevalent view among the majority of women who had survived the plague this long. She had cried when Midas told her that he would have to sell Airla if they were to have food again, but what other choice did he have? None.

Alexina pouted for a few minutes, ignoring Jude's incessant teasing. "I own you, Alexina. You have to do what I say."

"Do not."

"Do too."

"Do not!" she raised her voice.

"Do too!"

"Do not!" she yelled.

"Do too!" he yelled back.

"Do what?" Midas yelled above his kids. He'd just walked in, tired from a long day's work.

"Daddy, Jude says that he owns me. Tell him that he doesn't," Alexina.

"Jude, I own Alexina and your mother. One day when you get a wife, then you will own her and any daughters she has. There, that's settled," he grumbled.

Miffed, but not done, Jude complained, "Dad, I told her that she had to do what I say. She says she doesn't. Tell her dad."

Midas grumbled, "Alexina, you do what your bothers ask when I am not here. If you haven't noticed, you can't do much of anything by yourself. You depend on me and your brothers, so with all that we do for you, it is only fair that you obey us. That's the law around here."

Alexina pouted. A while later, she said, "Daddy, tell Jude that I am a person, not a thing."

"Of course you are a thing. Now go play and leave me alone."

The next day, Jude got into it again with Alexina. This time, he waited until after supper when his father was home. "See, dad told you that you are a thing."

"Am not. I am a person just like you are," she retorted.

"You are not like me. You are helpless. You don't have any arms and I do, so there," he countered.

"I am too a person," she declared flatly, planting her feet apart for emphasis.

"Are not."

"Am too."

"Are not!"

"Am too!" Now they were yelling loudly once more.

"Damn it, Alexina, shut up! Look, persons have arms. We've always had arms. You and your mother do not have arms, so you are not a person, you are a thing now. Live with it, for heaven's sake!" her father shouted her down.

Alexina got into another shouting match an hour later. This time her father slapped her to shut her up. "Look, Alexina, I have about had enough out of you. You are the prettiest of my daughters. However, you cannot be sold until you are fourteen, but when you are, I expect that you will fetch twice as much as your sisters. So be proud that you will bring us such a large amount of gold."

That night, Alexina decided that she should run away. Her plan was simple: leave here and go to some place where girls were persons, not things or objects, where she wasn't owned. She packed her few things into her two yoke baskets and waited until everyone was asleep before making her move. It was challenging, but she got to the front door and sat down, working the latch with her feet. At last, she stepped out into the dark night. She had no idea which way to go and so just started walking.

An hour after sunrise, her father found her. He'd discovered her missing when he rose and had sent his boys out searching for her as well. She'd gone over a mile before he caught up to her. "What in heaven's name do you think you're doing, girl?"

"I'm going away to where girls are people and no one owns me," she declared flatly.

"You belong to me, Alexina, at least for another year and a half. Just as soon as you turn fourteen, I'll sell you." He put the struggling girl into his wagon and took her home.

Later that day, Jude teased her mercilessly, and they got into five shouting matches, which ended only when Kastor had enough. He slapped her hard and sent her into her bedroom, where she and her sisters used to sleep. Two beds were always empty.

She tried to escape again that night and the next night. On his way home from work, he stopped by his old friend, Doctor Morpheus, for some advice on how to handle Alexina. Over a pitcher of ale, they discussed it. "Well, you need to do something to slow her down a bit, to put her into her place. I have an idea. You are a bronze worker; make her a pair of bronze earrings that hang down onto her shoulders. Good and heavy, that'll slow her down."

The next evening, Doctor Morpheus accompanied him home and assisted in piercing her ears, making sure that no infection would result. Already he had learned his lessons in that very thing, having lost so many women at the palace. "Daddy, these are way too heavy for me. They are pulling my ears off," Alexina complained bitterly. At least they were shiny. He'd fashioned ellipsoidal lobes and connected each two-inch lobe with bronze wires to the ones above and below it. A loop, which could not easily be undone, went through each ear lobe. Three of the lobes hung from it. Below that row, another three hung, and another three below that, and three more below that. The bottom two sets rested on her shoulders, banging around whenever she moved her head.

"Daddy, these hurt me. Please take them off," she begged, tears in her eyes.

"Nope, these will convince you to stay home and be a good girl. Obey your brothers when I'm gone. I'll not lose all that gold that you'll fetch, my little angle, when you turn fourteen!"

The next days were misery for her. Jude teased her relentlessly now and her ears hurt — a continuous dull, pulling pain. Whenever she turned her head, she felt like she was about to pull her ears off. This could not be avoided either, because her long light blond hair that fell to her knees continually slipped off her shoulders onto her face, forcing her to toss her head to get it back. Jude flatly refused to tie it into a ponytail for her.

Her arguing matches continued, even louder than before, if that was even possible. Midas grew more and more annoyed with her conduct. "At least she is not running away anymore," Doctor Morpheus consoled him over a pitcher of dark ale one late afternoon.

"If only she would shut up. She argues all day long or so Mina says. Got anything else in your bag of tricks to silence her?" Midas asked.

"Let me think on it, Midas. I believe that I do indeed."

A day later, Doctor Morpheus again met with Midas for an after work ale. "I have an idea that will definitely shut her up. I've heard that this was done down in Pirgos, Phindos. Here's a history lesson for you." He pulled out a book with several pages marked. "Years ago, our queen and even the Empress at the time had three servants, Utu Princesses they were called. Here are some drawings of what they looked like. There used to be some oil paintings of them around somewhere, but who knows where those are now. We could do something like this. She certainly would not be able to speak afterwards, but she doesn't really need to speak, does she?"

"No, her damn voice is so shrill and piercing. This would certainly stop her from arguing, but what about her sale value? She's promising to be even prettier than her mother and certainly the prettiest of my three daughters," Midas asked.

"Well, considering the novelty of it, Midas, if we do this right, it might just add to her sale value. Knocking out her teeth would lower her value; look at these sketches. No, we need a better design. I've made some sketches. I think if you make it from polished bronze and put a concave curve at the base, matching the curve of her gum lines, then that would support them out horizontally without having to remove her teeth. Best make them very thin and lightweight, though. Too much weight and they would droop which would not look good, I think. What do you think about this?"

Midas stared at the drawings of the Utu women. "Let me think about it, Doctor Morpheus."

Morpheus added, "Then, there are these rings around their necks which apparently have stretched their necks. I can find no details on their making, though. In my opinion, if we also added the neckbands, those would keep her from bending her neck at all. That should make everything far more difficult for her, make her more tractable, and obey you and your sons."

While a buyer could remove the heavy earrings if he chose, the lip modifications would be permanent. The neckbands could possibly be removed. He was counting on making a large sum from her sale in a little over a year from now and didn't want to jeopardize it.

He came home to another round of noise. "Do so!" Jude's voice bellowed as he neared the front door. Their yelling could be heard outside their home.

"Do not!" Alexina's shrill voice retorted angrily.

"Do so!" He opened the door and came inside.

"Do not!" she shrieked.

That settled it. He didn't even bother to ask what the argument was about this time. Midas had enough of her constant bickering. He visited the doctor on his way to work and told him to do it. Later, Doctor Morpheus dropped by his shop around noon with some detailed drawings of how the disks ought to be made, emphasizing once more that they needed to be very thin and lightweight. Midas altered his work plans for the rest of the day, focusing on making the pair. Since these would be highly visible, he wanted them to be of the highest quality, so as not to detract from her resale value. He even adorned their centers with dolphins, stamped into the thin metal. Next, he fashioned a number of highly polished bronze rings, though he didn't know how many would actually be needed to completely encase her neck. Better have some extras, he reasoned.

Doctor Morpheus dropped by the following day to inspect his handiwork, giving Midas his okay. "Here, slip this into her juice tonight. When she falls asleep, bring her to my office." He handed Midas a small vial and Midas handed him a sack with the bronze objects he'd fashioned.

Again, not an hour after he returned home that evening, Alexina was in yet another shouting match, this time with her older brother, Kastor. His resolve firmed even more solidly, and he went into the kitchen and fixed Alexina a cup of juice and then poured the vial's contents into the juice and mixed it up. He smiled. I will have peace in this house yet, he thought.

An hour later, he carried the sleeping daughter into the doctor's home office. "Put her down on my operating table. I've already boiled all the bronze, so they are sterile. We must be terribly careful about infections. From all that I've read and from my experience, an infection is the only thing what we need be careful about in this operation. It won't take too long, but I think that you should put the neck rings on her first. We don't want to bang into the cut lips."

It took him a half hour to meld the rings around her neck. Each ring had to be carefully bent and then the joint bonded lightly. He got five rings around her neck until at last there was no play or give among them. The neck rings were now solid, as if formed as one piece. "In time, her neck may stretch perhaps, making them looser, but who knows for sure," Doctor Morpheus stated. "Now for the messy part. My slits have to be done just wide enough for the plates to be held securely in place. A tight fit is a must." After careful measurements and some calculations, he began, erring on making the slits too narrow, each time extending them slightly, but uniformly, on each side until at last the top plate slipped firmly into place. As predicted, it was held securely and would be perfectly horizontal when she was upright. Then, he did the same to her lower lip.

An hour later, both men wiped the blood off themselves and her face. "I'll need to keep her here for a couple of days until they heal. We can't risk an infection, Midas." He agreed and thanked his friend profusely, promising him a share in what she would bring in another year and a half.

Alexina awoke midmorning. Her lips hurt and she tried to get up her usual way by bending her neck. It didn't budge. She could not help but see the shiny bronze disks protruding out from her slit lips. She wiggled and finally rose and called out shrilly. "Help! What's happened to me?"

Doctor Morpheus came in to see. "Ah, you are awake, Alexina. Don't bother trying to talk; no one can understand you now. You see, your father has had quite enough of your constant arguing. He and I did this last night." She screamed and danced from foot to foot, but soon calmed down.

"I got to go pee!" she said, but she could not even understand her own words! Repeatedly, she tried to tell the doctor what she needed to do. He smiled and kept saying he couldn't understand a word she was saying. At last, she squatted down, and he got her intention.

Later, he fixed her some breakfast, sitting it before her on a low table, which women who came for treatment sometimes used. "There you go. You have to learn to feed yourself once more. Midas will not want Jude to constantly have to feed you, so see what you can do."

"But I can't bend my neck," she said, but it wasn't even intelligible to her. Her neck immobilized, she had a very hard time of it, especially with the interference from the four-inch disks. When she bumped them, her lips sent a bolt of pain through her face. She cried and cried, but finally managed to eat a little.

"How can I talk now? How can I tell dad what I need?" Alexina continually tried to speak to the doctor. She tried and tried, but simply could not even understand herself. Then, she got up to move around and discovered that the rings were so tight that she could not turn her head! To look left, she'd have to shift her body. More misery, and she cried for some time. Her hair now drifted over her face and she had to swing her whole body just to get it to shift back across her shoulders. She cried again. At last, she accepted the doctor's suggestion to go lie down a while. She drifted into a deep sleep, aided by a potion he's slipped into her food. While she was asleep, he cleaned and poured sterile water over the healing slits.

That night, Midas dropped by on his way home from work. "How's my little golden angel tonight?" he asked as he admired her new look. She definitely looked golden.

"Daddy, I can't talk. I can't move my head. Why did you do this to me? I can hardly do anything anymore," she wailed, but she knew he couldn't understand her; she certainly couldn't.

"Ah, now you won't be arguing with your brothers anymore. No one can understand a word that you are saying. Doctor, what a brilliant idea. It certainly works.

"But I can't live this way," she tried to protest.

He teased her, "What's that you are saying, my golden angel?" She repeated it, knowing it was no use. "Oh, I get it. You are thanking me for it. You just love your new look." She tried to shake her head no, but couldn't even wiggle it. At last, she pivoted her body trying to say no.

Midas and Morpheus decided that she should stay here until the cuts had healed. Neither wanted to risk an infection, not with such excellent results. A week later, when Midas came to bring her home, he brought her a new dress, a golden dress that matched her ornaments well. Actually, it was not a new dress; no one had made a new dress since the plague began. Rather, he had shopped around and found a used one that was a bit too large for her. This was feasible because her bosom had not yet begun to fill out much, though in the next two years, explosive growth would be the situation, as it was since the plague.

"There you are my pretty golden angel. You look stunning. Look at yourself in the mirror."

She did and shrieked. "I look like some kind of freak!" she exclaimed, but knew it wasn't understood at all. Midas then took her home. Her humiliation was enormous as her brothers and mother stared and gawked at her.

"Metal mouth," Jude began a new tease. "Metal neck." She cried and cried. She tried to tell her mother how awful this was, but nothing she said could be understood. Jude kept saying, "Alexina, what did you say?" Repeatedly, he egged her on, loving every minute of her humiliation. At last, Mina herded her off to her bedroom and brushed out her hair for her, taking the time to examine closely what had been done to her daughter.

"Well, you don't have much choice now but to behave, Alexina. After all, you have no one to blame but yourself. Your constant arguing and bickering have brought this on yourself. We are dad's things now. I do hope that you have learned your lesson."

"Mom, how can you say that? I am a person, so are you," Alexina said, but knew that it was hopeless. Even she didn't understand a word that she had said.

"There, there, Alexina, no one can understand you anymore. You might as well be silent now.

You must admit that your father did a superb job with the bronze work. Very artistic."

"I hate it! I can't talk. I look like a freak. I can hardly move," she complained, the sounds coming out sounded more like a cat's snarl than words.

Life quickly became unbearable for Alexina. If Jude had harassed her before, that was nothing to now. "Hey metal mouth, metal head. Come here; you got a mess to clean up." Jude called out.

True, she was supposed to clean the floor, but unable to move her neck, doing so was nearly impossible. Jude snickered and laughed at her awkward attempts. At last, she did the only thing left, she screamed as loudly as she could. Instead of arguing with Jude, she simply screamed. No one could understand her anyway, but she at least got her protests acknowledged.

In the back of her mind, she hoped that Midas would hit her so hard that she'd die and be done with this. She simply refused to become an object; she continued to say that she was a person, only now, no one knew what she was saying.

At last, Midas had enough. One evening, he put her fancy, though ill-fitting, golden dress on her, brushed out her hair, and took her out with him. "What are you doing with me? Where are you taking me?" she said, knowing it was pointless. She was unintelligible now and would always be so.

It was early February and the late summer flowers were in full bloom, adding to her colors. Her bronze skin, light blonde hair, golden dress, and highly polished bronze made her look almost angelic. A number of men passed by them and Alexina watched them gawk and stare at her. She felt even more miserable. At last, they entered some house, where a well-dressed man was apparently expecting them. He looked like a foreigner, she thought. He wore a well-tailored navy blue suit and polished black shoes. His hair was black and he had a handlebar mustache that curved upwards. He eyed her closely, moving from her left side to her right side, musing to himself.

He spoke in a soft voice, "Indeed, a most unusual young girl. You were not lying about that, downright amazing. I don't believe that I have ever seen someone quite like this. She cannot talk you say?"

Midas said, "Alexina, say something to this nice man."

She wanted to seal her lips, but of course couldn't. "All right. Please, sir, help me. Look what my dad has done to me. Help me. Get me out of this." The man smiled, and she knew that he didn't get a single word that she'd said.

"Right, wholly not understandable. Well, that is a good benefit. She can't talk back. Still, as I said, she is two years too young. In my club, they must be of age, Midas."

"Yes, but she will be so in a year and a half. She should start filling out anytime now. That's what her mother says. She's a wise investment in the future, one of a kind and so angelic. I call her my golden little angel."

"Most appropriate indeed. Okay, I'll take her, but mind you only seventy percent of what you are asking. I will have to support her for a year and a half before I can get any profit from her. Seventy percent — take it or leave it."

"Deal." Midas agreed. The man handed him a large money pouch. "Okay, Alexina, you now belong to Hans here. You are now his property. Mind your manners. He might not be so kind and patient as I have been to you." He turned and left.

Hans put his hand around her back and pushed her forward into his living room. "Sit, let me look at you. My, such a fine looking young woman you will be in say two years. I am Hans. If you do as I say or as my matron says, why, we will get along just fine. You will have plenty to eat and have a warm home for the winter. Agreed?"

"No, I am a person! You don't own me," she yelled, but it sounded like gibberish. So she just screamed. She expected that maybe he would just slap her, but he didn't. He pushed her into a bedroom and shut the door. A small lantern illuminated the room. At least she had a clean bed, she thought.

She soon learned from listening to conversations that Hans was in Levkos on a "purchasing" trip. A while later, she found out what he was purchasing, young women between eighteen and twenty-three, women he planned to take back with him to his whore house in Preveza! The next day, she met the matron, a large woman, perhaps forty. While she didn't have arms, she certainly was bossy and knew her business. Later that day, three young women were introduced to her, his recent purchases.

"Ladies, we are heading to your new home in Preveza. There, you will have the finest sheets on the finest of beds. We serve you only the finest in foods. As long as you do what is asked of you, your lives will be well cared for, I promise you. Now, I've got our things packed; it's time to go. I have my carriage waiting out front." At last, Alexina realized that this was a boarding house. The carriage was expensive. She'd never ridden in one before and for a time was satisfied with her new life.

Soon though, her humiliation continued. The four women stared at her and asked her all sorts of questions. She tried to tell them what had happened, to answer their questions but to no avail. She simply could not articulate anything that could be grasped. Worse, her neck prevented her from simple headshakes for yes and no. She had to move her entire body to make such gestures. She broke down and cried for quite a while.

By the time she got to the port of Preveza, she had been gawked at and stared at by so many men and a few women that she became numb to being a freak. The Cat Club read the sign in front of the building before which the carriage finally halted. Inside, she found that he had not lied. Her bed had silk sheets though she would have preferred something other than red for its decor. Nightly, she heard the other women engaged in acts with men who came and went all evening long. She had a good idea what that meant and what would be happening with her when she turned fourteen. At last, Alexina decided that it was time that she end her miserable life. Unable to do it herself, she worked out a plan to get Hans to do it for her.

Screaming as loudly as she could, she began a concerted effort to drive Hans as nuts as she had her father. After a week of it, Hans finally had enough. He looked terribly angry when he burst into her room after one of her screaming episodes. Here it comes. I am ready, she told herself, bracing for a painful slug with would put her out of her misery. Hans reached back to deliver the killing blow, but he stopped and looked at her. She did not expect what he said.

"Say, Alexina, can you write?"

"Yes," she replied and then bent up and down at her waist, hoping he would understand.

"Good." He left and returned a bit later with one of the low writing desks, along with paper and pencil. "Sit down, Alexina. Please tell me what it is that you really want." She looked at him questioningly. "Yes, Alexina. What is it that you truly desire?"

She sat down but found it harder than ever to write. She couldn't bend her head and could barely see her toes over the protruding lip plates. She decided to tell him the truth. She wrote: I am a person, not an object. No one owns me. I want to go to some place where I can be a person and not a thing. I will never, ever be a thing. I will not be owned.

Hans picked up the paper and read it, twirling his moustache absentmindedly. "So, is this the truth? You are a person and will never be my prized employee?" She bent at her waist several times, indicating yes. "I see. So this is why you are screaming so? You will keep on screaming until I either kill you or get rid of you or send you somewhere where you can be a person, is that it?" Again, she bent up and down vigorously, trying to emphasize yes, though she thought that this might then be the end of her misery.

Instead of hitting her, he smiled, "Well, I have been had, that's for sure. I admit that you are incredibly unusual looking as well as pretty. In another couple of years, you could have been my star attraction, bringing in a small fortune each night. Ah well. It looks like your father has gone to extreme lengths to break your spirit and even I have given it my best. Well, a loss here and there is to be expected in my trade. Say la vie as they say."

He looked her straight in her pale blue eyes. "Okay, Alexina. If I promise to send you to a place where you can be a person and not a thing, not owned by anyone, will you promise to be a well behaved young girl until you get there?" While she didn't know what that really meant, it sounded like heaven, and she bent up and down rapidly. He smiled.

"All right. You keep quiet for now. I will need to make the arrangements. It is a long sea voyage to get to this place, but once there, you can be a person. No one will own you. Acceptable?" Again, she bent up and down, hardly daring to believe him.

A week later, Hans put her into his carriage, and they rode down to the docks. He escorted her onto a strange looking ship. The men looked like Hans, white skinned, not bronze. All were well dressed, not what she had imagined sailors to look like, but then she had never seen a ship or sailors before. All the sailors stared at her as the two walked onto the main deck. Alexina bore the humiliation. What else could she do?

"This is Captain Jorgen. He will be taking you to your special place. It is a long voyage and he will be stopping at many ports before he get you to your destination. You be a good girl, be well behaved, and he will treat you right and take you there. All right? Promise?" Alexina bent up and down rapidly. He smiled and handed a scroll to the captain. "Give this to them when you dock and take her onshore. Her name is Alexina Phanes." He handed the captain a money pouch, bowed, and left.

"Well, this way, Alexina," he said kindly, but Alexina panicked. She didn't understand his language! He quickly realized this and spoke crude Demokritos. "Well, we ought to be a teaching you our language on the voyage, you'll need it."

The novelty of having such a strange looking girl on board soon wore off. While he did teach her a few words of their language, whatever it was, they were mostly single words: food, pee, sleep, wash. Soon, she was left mostly to herself. There was little to do in the stuffy cabin below deck. With her neck immobilized, she couldn't use her head to help her keep her balance on the rolling ship and found walking far too treacherous to attempt. Still, she was patient, clinging to the faint hope that one day, she would reach a land where she could be a person and not someone's thing.

She did not know it but this ship was an Annelise coastal trading vessel. Several months went by along with at least a dozen stops at ports. Each time they docked, she expected the captain to come and get her, but he didn't. Finally, around May 1, 824, he entered her cabin, "Alexina, I thought that you should know that once we load this cargo, we will be sailing to your new home. We should be there by the end of the month." She bent-nodded as best she could. Long ago she had given up trying to smile; her lip plates prevented all such motions.

As he left, he turned and said, "The island is called Zeederland." She understood most of his words now. Though they had pretty well left her alone these many months once her novelty had worn off, she had been listening to the crew. Slowly she began to understand more and more of their language, but she had no idea that it was Annelise that these sailors spoke.

Chapter 41 Zeederlund, the Land That Time Forgot

Captain Jorgen stood on his deck, calling out orders to his six crewmen, as they began navigation of the narrows at the opening of the Nebelzee, a large circular bay, some fifteen miles across. This narrow opening from the South Sea into the Nebelzee was located in the middle of the island of Zeederlund and faced due south. This lost island lay in uncharted waters some five hundred miles due east of southern Annelise. No other landmasses were within a thousand or more miles from this solitary and remote island nation.

The Nebelzee was actually a volcanic crater basin filled mostly with fresh water near its north shore though saltwater predominated here at the southern narrows entrance. Here in late May, fall was nearly ending. In a couple of months, the sea would become a solid ice sheet, preventing all passage by the Annelise coastal vessel. Zeederlund stretched some hundred miles from east to west, but only fifty, north-south. At the northern edge of the central Nebelzee rose the northern rim of the extinct volcano. This rugged mountainside was called Altenhorn. Here many mines yielded diamonds, rubies, emeralds, plenty of gold and some silver, which is why a very few adventurous Annelise captains traded here. Zeederlund was not on any charts or maps. These few captains kept the location of this island a secret because they made lucrative profits from each trip here.

On either side of the narrow entrance lay Vesterborg and Osterborg, two port cities with a population of around ten thousand each. Fifteen miles plus due north at the opposite edge of Nebelzee was the capital city of Zeederlund, Altenborg, nestled between the shores of the lake and the sharply rising Altenhorn. Captain Jorgen once sailed around the island and counted twelve cities all about the same size, but Altenborg was the only inland city he'd seen. Many small fishing boats plied the waters off each of the eleven coastal cities and he had to take care navigating through the narrows to avoid the small craft from the twin port cities, separated by the two mile width of the narrows here at the southern edge of the island, fifty miles from either end of the island.

While the population of Zeederlund no doubt was thriving, each trip here filled Captain Jorgen with trepidation. These people were weird and strange. He never felt more uncomfortable around people as he did here. Yet, the profits from one trading trip exceeded ten of his normal coastal runs around Annelise and Demokritos. Money was Captain Jorgen's drive in life, the more, the better. Still he and his crew always felt highly ill at ease while docked in Altenborg.

As his ship moved slowly across the inland lake with bits of ice near its shores, he spotted several carriages following the roads that paralleled the coastline of the Nebelzee. Some were going south from Altenborg to Vesterborg, some going the other way. On the eastern side, some were heading south to Osterborg and some going the other way. All these carriages looked strange to his eyes. The driver's box was low to the ground, not high as they were in Annelise. Further, the bench seat sloped back at a sharp angle. Even the carriage boxes themselves were much lower to the ground that those of Annelise. The wagons were similarly strange to his eyes. Besides the strange shape of the driver's seat, the wagon beds themselves were low to the ground, barely a foot of clearance.

In the far distance, he could see the rolling hills awash with late fall colors. Far ahead, the dark mass of the half-moon shaped Altenhorn rose prominently. He did know that all the fabulous gems and gold came from this volcanic peak. He smiled, imagining the profits that he would take back with him in a few days.

At last the hawsers where tossed and the ship secured to the docks. Captain Jorgen and his men could not help but stare at the people, though this was their twelfth trip here. Each time, the culture shock hit them, as it also did to those on the docks, who often stared back at them. Yes, Captain Jorgen and his men were dressed in their fine blue suits with twin tails and highly polished black boots. As true Annelise, they always looked their finest.

On shore, the dockhands were similarly dressed in fine brown suits with twin tails and polished black shoes. However, the dockhands were women and their suits had no sleeves — they never had had them, not since his first trip here. Even more shocking in their eyes, they spotted the typical elegant ball gowns in a wide array of springtime colors moving on the streets not far from the docks, but these were men! The women had haircuts that looked much like his own, while the men's hair styles were quite long, many falling to the small their backs!

One woman dressed in an immaculate blue silk tuxedo walked prominently towards his ship. "Hail Captain Jorgen isn't it?" she called out.

"Well met Harbor Master Lise. I bring the usual cargo, but this trip I have a young woman for you. One moment while I fetch her. I also have a note for you," he replied. Well, she has changed little, he thought as he went below to fetch Alexina. Her bosom looks like it might explode from her shirt and her waist is as tiny as our women's.

A couple minutes later, he lifted Alexina up the stairs, not chancing a fall at this point. His arm behind her back, he nudged her across the deck, across the gangplank, stopping before the well-dressed harbor master, who was staring wide-eyed at Alexina. From the corner of his eyes, he spotted many of the other dockhands pausing to stare at her as well. "Harbor Master Lise, this is Alexina Phanes. This note, I was told, will explain. I am to give her to you." He handed her the scroll, though he felt very ill at ease handing a scroll to a woman who had no hands with which to accept it.

Deftly, her husband glided forward to accept it from his hands. He wore a billowing gown of yellow and pink, but from his slow movement, he guessed that the man was wearing the extreme heels that women of Annelise wore. His black hair lay nicely down his back. "Why thank you so much, Captain. Dear, allow me," he said as he opened the scroll and held it so that she could read it.

Harbor Master,

This is Alexina Phanes, the golden angel. She is thirteen and greatly desires to be her own person. She has a relentless drive to be in control. I believe that she best belongs with your people. She certainly does not fit in with ours.

Hans Stern, Cat House

Lise looked up at Alexina. "My, you are a strange one. Can you even speak young lady?"

"I have veen trying to learn your language. No one can understand anything I say vack hove in Alia, vut yours coves out vostly okay," Alexina tried to say very slowly. In this Annelise dialect, her b, m, p, and v sounds all came out the same, like a v. Most all other sounds were fairly understandable. "Vlease, I want to ve a verson, not a thing. Can I ve a verson here?"

Lise smiled. "Well, you most certainly can, Alexina. In spite of your ornaments, I am able to understand you. Very well, Captain. I'll take charge of her. Now do you have your cargo manifest? If so, you may begin unloading at once. I'll take your manifest and Alexina to the Monarch and return with your payment. Satisfactory?"

"Perfect, Harbor Master Lise. Thank you." He turned to his crew, "Well, what are you waiting for? Start unloading."

"If you will come with me, Alexina, I'll take you to our Monarch. She will know what to do with you. My, you are so overdue for a haircut! And that awful dress! You must get into a respectable suit at once. Come, Ludwig dear, we are off to the Royal Court." Her husband put his arm on her shoulders, and the three began moving very slowly away from the ship.

"Why are we walking so slowly?" Alexina asked. "Why are you dressed like a wovan and she, like a van? Where av I?"

Ludwig answered, "I can only walk slowly in my elegant heels, see?" he paused a moment and pulled his billowing dress back so she could see the high heels that he was wearing. "Tiny steps, I glide like an angel for my dear Lise. You are in Zeederlund, of course. We are all wondering why you ever allowed these pervert men to put you into a man's dress? Outrageous! Well, the captain and his men as just as outrageous, aren't they dear? I mean wearing women's clothing in public! Shame on them. They look positively terrible in those women's suits, don't they dear?"

"Of course, Ludwig. Preposterous, I'd say. But then they are outsiders, Ludwig. We must make allowances for the weirdos of the world, that's what our Monarch says," Lise replied.

"Still, allowing her hair to grow so very long like a man's — why, that's almost criminal, I say. Don't you worry one bit, Alexina. We'll soon set all this to rights. Ah, here is our carriage, Alexina."

Lise moved him to the door and opened it with her foot. Then, she positioned herself so that he could keep one arm on her shoulders while he daintily climbed inside. Lise whispered, "Mind our manners. We women always help our men inside. Now then, in you go." As Alexina moved to the low step, she saw another woman wearing a brown suit with sparking buttons appear near the front.

Lise spoke, "To the Royal Court, please." The woman driver nodded and turned to climb into her driver's seat.

"Does she drive the carriage?" Alexina asked quite surprised.

"Why of course she does. We never have our beloved men drive wagons or carriages; it is uncivilized of women to do so. We honor and cherish our men. Climb aboard. The Monarch is waiting."

Alexina looked out the window as the carriage moved slowly through the cobblestone streets of Altenborg, heading to the Royal Court. She noticed that most buildings were made of black bricks and were only one story high. Their grey slate roofs contrasted nicely, but the wooden doors and window frames were painted in gay colors, adding spice to the dark buildings. All were well kept, and many had ornate flower boxes out front and bunches of marigolds were in full bloom adding even more color.

She saw many shops go by and people. Lots of men, women, and children, though she was still shocked to see the men all wearing fancy and obviously terribly expensive ball gowns and the women all wearing different colored suits. Uniformly, the women had very short haircuts, which she often saw on men back home, while the men's hair was always extremely long, varying from below the shoulders to their waists. Inside the carriage, she observed Ludwig. His nails were several inches long and painted a nice red color. How strange, she thought. Are men, women and women, men here, she wondered.

Soon they pulled up into a long U-shaped drive. In the center of the U, a row of cherry trees stood. On either side, rows of late fall blooming flowers were growing in perfectly straight rows with the taller ones closer to the low cherry trees and marigolds closest to the cobblestones. She saw two women dressed in brown suits sitting on their butts, tending the garden with their feet, gathering the fallen leaves. Out the other window, she got her first look at the Royal Court of their monarch.

Actually, the Royal Court consisted of four single story, large brick buildings. Only the ornate gold work hinted at the royal nature of this complex. The carriage stopped at a huge set of double doors, huge so that men wearing their enormously billowing gowns could pass through without crumpling their dresses. Two women dressed in red guard uniforms stood at either side of the doors. One came over to the carriage and used her foot to open the door for Lise. "Good day, Harbor Master," the guard said in her mellow alto voice.

Lise got out first, and then positioned her shoulder for her husband to lean upon as he wrestled with his billowing dress and extreme heels. Once he was out, Alexina followed him. Of course, both guards stared at Alexina, but she stared right back, having never seen such well-dressed guards, women for sure, but how could they guard, she wondered.

Both women opened the huge doors with their feet, and Lise led them inside, Alexina at her side, while Ludwig followed gracefully behind his wife, as was fitting and proper when entering the Royal Court. Just inside, a woman wearing a very elegant black tuxedo stepped up along with another man who wore yet another beautiful ball gown. His black hair was draped over his shoulders falling below his waist, which Alexina now saw was quite small around, but nowhere near as tiny as all women's waists were now.

Lise said, "I have another Annelise ship's manifest for the Monarch, and this young girl has been left for us."

"The monarch is free and can see you now," the steward explained. Turning to the man, she indicated to Lise, "Lund is her personal secretary. He will take you to her now." She bowed to Lise, who returned her bow.

Lund wore an enormous ball gown, some fifteen feet across at the floor. He walked even more slowly than Ludwig, though Alexina could not see his shoes. Still, he walked with supreme grace, gliding across the stone floor. Ahead, another two women guards dressed in similar red uniforms used their feet to open another pair of wide double doors, and Lund moved on into the throne room.

Alexina's eyes blinked. Gold furnishings were everywhere; even the many lanterns hanging from the ceiling were gold plated. Great tapestries hung on one wall, while statues of men and armless women stood close to the opposite wall, with large oil paintings interspersed between them. Ahead, she saw nine men, women, and a two year old baby. They had just returned from lunch and were about to go their separate ways when they entered. Lund announced them, "Your Majesty, Harbor Master Lise Jorgen and her husband Ludwig and guest. She has an Annelise ship's manifest for you and a note about the young woman." He bowed, nodded to Lise, turned, and elegantly glided on out of the throne room.

Monarch Andrea Alten wore a very expensive white silk suit, with the usual twin tails. Her blonde hair was cut very short. Alexina guessed that she must be around forty. She quickly took her seat in a raised, plush purple chair. Everyone except the baby stared at Alexina and again she felt nervous and ill at ease.

"Hello, I am Monarch Andrea Alten, ruler of Zeederlund. My charming husband, Anders. Dear, be a good fellow and fetch that manifest for me. I really don't want to take off my shoes now. I'm rather stuffed from lunch. Ate too much again. Honestly, Lise, if we don't, how will we ever get our waists back again. Ah well."

Anders retrieved the manifest and the scroll, holding the scroll for his wife to read. "Well, Alexina, is it?" She bent-nodded. "Well, you are safe with us here. Of course, you can be a person. Everyone here in Zeederlund is a person. I cannot imagine the brutality of the outer-worlds! Honestly, they ought to be drawn and quartered for so mistreating you, such a good-looking young woman. The nerve of them to fail to cut your hair! Why, it's as long as men's hair, how awful for you. I just don't know how you could have endured such torture and being forced to wear such a crude man's dress. How humiliating for you! Well, dear, we will get you properly fixed up in no time."

"Thank you, your vajesty," she said, completely shocked that the monarch thought that the horrible mistreatment was not cutting her hair and making her wear this dress, the nicest that her father had ever given her.

Lise spoke up quickly, "Her fancy ornaments do not permit her to make the b, m, p, and v sounds."

"I see. I'm sure that we'll all understand you just fine, Alexina. Now let me present my family. You've met my handsome husband, Anders. These are our children. Our youngest is Princess Hedda; I believe that she is about your age." Hedda also wore a white satin suit with the same highly polished black leather slip-on shoes that the other women wore. Hedda smiled and bowed to her.

"Our son Johan, he is fourteen now." Johan had very long blonde hair, very long fingernails also painted red. He wore a white satin ball gown with spanned fourteen feet as it reached the floor. He also wore very long, dangling earrings with rubies, emeralds, and diamonds, which sparkled in the light from the lanterns.

"Most pleased to meet you, Alexina," he said politely, curtsying to her, which she thought very strange indeed.

"Our daughter Iduna, who is fifteen." She also looked like her mother and was dressed in a similar white satin suit with the same shiny black slip on shoes.

"Don't worry, Alexina, we'll get you properly attired soon. It must be so awfully embarrassing to be wearing such a rag of a man's dress and forced to have such long hair. We'll have you fixed up in no time."

"Our oldest son, Halder Knut. He has married Jutta Knut and this is their two year old daughter, Kristen. Jutta is my Minister of Mines, a most important and powerful position in my government. Halder is very lucky indeed to have married such a fine woman."

Both nodded to Alexina. Princess Hedda spoke up, "Mom, can Alexina stay with us, please? She can study with our tutor, Julie. Please mom? Iduna and I will look after her."

"Yes, Hedda, I do think that would be wise of us. She will need a lot of education quickly, I suspect. Alexina, occasionally, we do accept men and women from the outer-world here in Zeederlund. Always, they need to learn our culture, and true, occasionally we send some of our men and women who just do not get along with us to the outer-world as well. Please, accept our hospitality in helping you become an active, productive person in life."

"Thank you, Your Vajesty. That's all I have ever wanted, to just ve a verson like everyone else."

"Well, I am sure that you will be a very fine person here, Alexina. Anders, please work your magic on her hair. As soon as he is done, Hedda, Iduna, you see that she is properly bathed. Johan, go find a proper white satin suit and shoes for her," Monarch Andrea ordered. She slipped off her shoes and took the manifest documents between her toes. "Jutta, let's take a look at this and then you can fetch their payment."

Quietly, Halder picked up their baby and glided out of the room. Anders, Hedda, and Iduna led Alexina out of the throne room by a side door. "We're going to our private quarters in the next building attached to this one. Don't worry, I'll show you around once we have you cleaned up and looking all proper."

"Yes, and this way, we get out of having to do our afternoon lessons," Iduna giggled.

"Yes, but if I know Julie, you will pay for it tomorrow," their father chastised them. A bit later, Anders had Alexina sitting in his hairdressing chair. "I'll have you know, Alexina that I do everyone's hair in our family. I'm quite good at it. I'll have you looking perfect in no time at all. Our girls will get you bathed and you will finally feel human again. Say, I do like your fancy ornaments. They look good on you, brass I trust? Gold would be way too heavy."

"Thank you, sir."

"Just Anders, Alexina." Even with his long nails, Anders worked quickly. Before long, he held up a mirror so she could see. "There, you look just like Hedda and Iduna, three prefect models of excellence in hair. Now then, girls, get her cleaned up."

An hour later, bathed and dried, the three began to get her dressed properly. Working together with their feet, the two princesses slipped white satin panties on Alexina. She noted that there were large loops, which the girls put between their toes to pull them up on her. She quickly realized that the women worked together to get themselves dressed. Next, they slipped a silk camisole up her legs and over her already overly large bosom, which would hold it up nicely. Then, they called for Johan. "We women usually dress ourselves this far and then allow our menfolk to put our shirts, pants, and coats on us. While we could do it ourselves, it just takes too long. Besides, the fellows like to do it for us and we let them," Hedda explained.

Johan came gliding in, moving awfully slowly, Alexina thought and wondered what his shoes looked like. He was very gentle and got her sleeveless satin shirt on and buttoned, before putting on her satin pants. All in white, she too looked like the two princesses. He fastened her white satin coat on her and allowed her to slip her feet into the shiny, black slip-on shoes. "There you go, Alexina. If I do say so myself, you look very regal, very proper, very elegant."

"Thank you. I have never worn such fine clothes," she admitted. She noticed that he nearly lost his balance trying to rise. "How cove you walk so slow?"

"Oh, these shoes of mine. Here, I'll show you." He pulled up the front of his enormous satin gown, revealing his thin, black hose, and ballet style boots, the kind that the aliens had left when the plague struck.

"Oh vy, didn't your feet heal uv? Ours all did," she asked.

Johan grinned, "Oh sure they healed up, but around here, we fellows think that these boots are really sexy. Our women agree and so many of us still wear them. Bit tricky at times, though. Don't you think I look really good in them?"

The two princesses giggled. Hedda said, "Of course, silly boy. You look sexy enough to attract any girl, little brother." He flushed. "Come on; let's show you around. You can have the spare bedroom next to mine."

"Can I tag along? It is not often that we have such pretty young women guests here," Johan asked.

"Oh I suppose so, unless Alexina doesn't want to go so slowly."

He looked at her pleadingly. "Sure, you can cove along," Alexina suggested. His eyes lit up, and a smile creased his lips.

"Well, as the oldest, it's my duty to give you my shoulder, Johan," Princess Iduna said offering him her shoulder for support. She looked at Alexina, "We women must always help our menfolk, you see. We want them to look elegant and handsome for us and so it's only fair that we assist them. They do have many challenges in those restrictive outfits. He can't hardly bend, if you haven't noticed."

"Well, I do have a respectable waistline now," Johan explained proudly. "I've been wearing tight corsets since I was six. You have to, if you want a waist as small as mine."

"Didn't you have trouvle when the vlague cave?" Alexina asked.

"Cave?" he looked quizzically at her. "Oh, came. I get it. Well, those were strange days. We men had our feet frozen into a point. Had to learn to wear these fancy boots. Now many of us really do like them and women find them erotic. Nothing much happened with you girls though."

"Don't be silly, Johan, our hair grew like weeds, and we had to have dad cut our hair right away. Our waists shrunk down to man-size, but we mostly just had our menfolk seamstresses rework our pants. It was our breasts that grew enormously, you see. All the men seamstresses on Zeederlund were kept very busy for a time, altering every woman's shirts. Most annoying, Alexina, to be going around with improperly fitting clothing for almost a week. Just awful," Hedda explained most seriously.

"Vut didn't you lose your arvs with the vlague like I did?" she asked.

"What? Alexina, women on Zeederlund have never, ever had arms, not in a thousand years," Hedda pointed out a bit surprised by such a silly question.

Iduna added learnedly, "Hedda, remember your lessons. It is said that women in the outer-world have grotesque arms like our men. Remember the rumor that we heard last fall that the women out there were losing their arms in the plague."

"Oh yeh, now I remember. You had those awful arms, Alexina? How terrible that must have been for you! They must have gotten in the way of everything! How dreadful! Well, you're with us now. You'll see, arms are nothing but a nuisance. Just look at all our men and how they get in their way with everything."

Johan defended himself. "Yes, but just look how quickly we can cut your hair, how fast we can get you properly dressed, sis. Look how quickly some of us make new suits for you."

"Well, I guess you need them to help you manage such fancy ball gowns," Hedda admitted.

"Boys are supposed to look sexy, silly. How else will you ever attract a girl?" Iduna added with a wry grin.

As they toured the four adjacent and connected brick buildings, Alexina got a quick lesson in this new culture. It seems that the women ran everything, did all the work and jobs that men in Alexina's world did. Meanwhile, the men did most of the work that women in the outer-world did, caring for their families, cooking their meals, shopping, cleaning, scrubbing, and caring for their young children. At last, Alexina realized that here in Zeederlund, the roles played by men and women were exactly reversed. Yet, Alexina could not fathom just how the armless women could possibly manage to do all the work, including building all the brick homes. She would be learning about that soon, however.

The last room that they visited was the tutoring room. "Ah, here is my new student," Julie exclaimed enthusiastically as the four walked into her room. Julie Jost was twenty-six and married to Henning who cared for their two small children. Her room here was filled with bookshelves, crammed with volumes of various shapes and sizes. Alexina noted that there were a number of low to the ground desks, reminiscent of those back home, but there were also desks designed for the men and their expansive gowns. A chalkboard was fastened to one wall.

"I do love your ornaments, Alexina. Most impressive. Don't worry; tomorrow we will begin your lessons. We'll start with a review of our long history, that way Alexina will know more about us," Julie explained. Hedda and Iduna looked relieved; they would be reviewing things that they already knew.

"Julie really knows her stuff," Johan bragged a bit, smiling at Julie.

Later they headed to an adjoining building where Anders had dinner waiting for them. Alexina learned a bit about social etiquette. The women always pulled out the men's chairs for them, assisting them to get seated properly. The table was divided into two halves; the men's side was taller than the women's side, which was low to the ground. After Alexina got herself seated beside Hedda, Andrea bowed her head and said a brief prayer. "Dear God, we thank you for your bounty and for our loving husbands who graciously prepared our evening meal." She looked and said, "Dig in."

As Alexina watched, the three men helped themselves first, finally passing the bowls with foot handles on to Andrea. She marveled at how skillfully the women managed the entire dining process. "Mom, can I have ornaments like Alexina's? They look really good," Hedda asked, filling her plate.

Andrea merely replied, "We'll see, dear."

Very quickly, the group found that these pretty ornaments were a severe liability, horribly limiting Alexina's ability to eat, and she couldn't possibly drink from a cup. Worse, although she had perfect posture, she had extreme difficulty leaning enough to get a spoon of food up to her mouth. Getting it inside the plates was even more challenging. Once there, she had to lean back in order to chew and swallow it. She had a devil of a time spooning her milk into her mouth.

At last, Andrea said, "Johan, please lend Alexina a hand. She is having such a hard time of it. Her fancy ornaments are making eating so terribly difficult."

"Yes, mother. My pleasure," he grinned and rose. Gliding effortlessly around the table, he came to her side and began feeding her. Now she merely sat straight as an arrow and was able to eat far more swiftly.

"Thank you, Johan," she whispered.

Sipping their after dinner tea, Andrea and Jutta picked up a pair of long necked pipes. Anders and Halder kindly lit them for the two women. "Ah, nothing like a fine after dinner smoke," Andrea declared.

"Men don't smoke," Hedda whispered importantly to Alexina. "Mom says we can once we get married."

Puffing a small round cloud, Andrea asked, "Alexina, about your ornaments. May I ask you why you chose them? They seem to be giving you enormous difficulties. Do they make outer-world men more attracted to you?"

"No! Vy father did these to ve as vunishvent vecause I kevt trying to ve a verson and he wanted ve to ve his thing," she admitted, and tears long held a bay, came despite her efforts to suppress them.

Andrea sat up straight. "Child, are you saying that your father did this to you as punishment?"

"Yes," she whispered sorrowfully.

"Oh dear God. I'm so terribly sorry, Alexina. We all thought that you chose to wear such unusual looking ornaments," she admitted her error.

"Vlease, can you get thev off ve?" she asked, knowing that was highly unlikely.

"Yes, Alexina, we will do our best in the morning. Perhaps we should all get some sleep now."

Alexina followed Hedda and Iduna to their bedrooms. "We help each other out of our suits," Hedda explained. "Golly, I thought that your ornaments were fabulous. I am sorry, I didn't know."

"It's awful, veing like this," she admitted. "I can varely do anything now." The two princesses sat down on their butts and began removing each other's suits. Alexina watched and tried to help but unable to bend her neck or see over the lip plates, her attempts were useless. The two girls undressed Alexina and made sure she got safely into bed. She slept in her camisole and panties on the finest bed that she'd ever slept in or even heard about.

After breakfast the next day during which Johan again helped her eat, two women dressed in brown suits arrived, carrying two large bags over their shoulders. Andrea explained, "Ah, thanks. We need to see if these hideous ornaments can be removed from Alexina. Dear, these are some of our metalworkers, very competent at their craft. Relax, you are in good feet."

They had her lie down and the two removed their bag, sat down, removed their shoes and then began taking a close look at Alexina's strange ornaments. "Brass, soft metal," one said. "We can get rid of the earrings swiftly. Cutters please." The second woman scooted over to a bag and began rummaging through their tools, finally bringing out the strangest looking cutters Alexina had seen. Often she's seen her father's tools in his shop, but now she realized that those were made for hands, not feet. These cutters had foot loops and were operated by bringing one's feet closer together. The first woman used her feet to place the cutting blades precisely over the ear loops. Then, the second woman pressed her legs together and Alexina heard a snapping sound.

A moment later, and the first woman carefully pulled the loop out of her left earlobe. A couple of minutes later and the second earring was gone. "Well, that was the easy part. Her neck rings are more challenging. We need to study them." For an hour, the two women carefully studied the rings, having Alexina turn over several time. It was hard to lay on her stomach though, her lip plates banged into the floor, forcing her to have to bend upwards at her waist, difficult to do for more than a brief time. At last, one woman said what Alexina hope and prayed for, "If we can get this third one off, the rest will be easier. This third one offers us the best chance, but her plates are in the way. Let's get something under her, perhaps on a couch."

Alexina ventured, "Vayve Anders could revove thev vore easily, he has hands."

"Oh don't be silly, Alexina. We women wouldn't think of asking our husbands to do something that we are perfectly capable of doing. Just be patient, dear," Andrea replied.

Three hours later, the two women had the third ring removed without hurting their patient. At last, her neck bent a little. and she could turn her head. Again, Johan helped her with lunch, and then the two metalworkers were back at it again. Finally, at suppertime, the last of the rings was removed. Alexina was extremely happy to have them off. As they dined, she was far better able to cope with feeding herself, though the lip plates still made things most difficult for her. Able to bend over now, she was able to eat.

The lip plates could easily be removed, but the slit lips were the real problem, as the metalworkers pointed out. Hence, the next morning, Andrea sent for a doktor. She and her nurse arrived. The doktor wore a white suit and his nurse wore a white ball gown. She had the nurse remove the plates, and they, as well as the royal family, looked at the situation; her lips drooped down like rubber bands. Dangling like this, the doktor pointed out that she could easily get them caught on something and rip them off. "Please allow me so study this situation for a while, Your Majesty. Never in all my years have I ever seen anything like this. In the meantime, keep on wearing the plates. It is far safer for her that way. However, Your Majesty, do not get your hopes up too far. We may not be able to do anything for her."

"Vlease try. I don't want to ve like this," Alexina begged her.

"I know dear," the sympathy rolled from the doktor. "I will see what I can possibly do, Alexina, but sometimes there may be nothing that can be done."

"Okay, then I think that Julie wants you four in the study room," Andrea hinted. After the four headed off to begin their lessons, she asked, "Doktor, is there nothing that can be done? Well, I didn't think so. A piercing of that magnitude. . ."

"Some doktor has taken a knife to her lips, cutting long slices and then inserting the bronze plates. From the looks of the incisions, it had to be a doktor. The cuts have long healed up, so there is no just removing the plates and suturing the halves together. If she goes around without the plates, she is likely to get the lip loops caught on something and ripped. If she wants the plates gone, we could surgically remove the loop lips, but then she would look almost as strange. Those are the obvious solutions, but let me see what else may be done."

"Thank you, doktor. That's all we can ask." She walked her to the door.

"Well, finally I get you students back in my study room," Julie began. Hedda and Iduna giggled. They knew well that they had been cutting classes, but Alexina was a good excuse. "Okay, I know that Alexina cannot read our language nor write it. Don't worry, Alexina, we will remedy that deficiency in the coming days. We will start with ancient history of Zeederlund and then cover our geography."

Using her foot, she pulled down a book from the shelves, pressing it tightly with the side of her head against her shoulders. At her low desk, she retrieved it with a sweeping motion of her legs, grasping it and placing it on her desk. Alexina marveled at her skill — her motions seemed totally smooth and natural, as if she had been doing this all her life. Alexina then remembered that Hedda had said as much, but she didn't yet quite believe it. Women all had arms before the plague, she was certain of that. Julie then began to read aloud and Alexina was soon fascinated by the story.

It seems these people and the Annelise were once the same group of people. Over a millennia ago, the outer-world was populated by men and women. From the dawn of time, men were born with arms and women were born without them, yet it was the woman who gave forth new life from her body. Around one thousand years ago, a warring rift occurred between many of the tribes of the outer-world, which Alexina now understood mean her oval continent, which included Demokritos, Vladimir, and Annelise. Lise and Zabina were two clan matriarchs whose tribes fought against the savagery of neighboring tribes. The two clan matriarchs decided to separate their clans from the constant fighting and bickering among the many other tribes. They led their people on what was called the Great Exodus, leading them to the promised lands where they could dwell in peace. They worshiped a god called Partholan. However, both Lise and Zabina insisted that their people dress in the finest clothing so that Partholan would know at a glance that they were the truly advanced and civilized humans. On this, they both agreed and they called their new home Annelise.

Once homes had been built and crops planted, Lise and Zabina began their grand plan to properly clothe all their people. Over the next twenty years, the dress and suit designs rapidly evolved into more and more exotic and extreme designs, until at last, Zabina and some of her clan rebelled, saying that the men should be wearing the dresses and manning the home front, not the women, who wanted to lead and produce. After a bitter argument, Zabina took those of her clan who accepted her views on the Second Exodus, sailing eastward whereon they came upon Zeederlund and settled down.

Following the guidelines set forth by Zabina, men stayed at home, caring for their children, cooking their meals, washing their clothes, making their clothing, and in general nurturing their families. The women, of whom Zabina became the first monarch, took charge of the country. They did the farming, the making of the bricks, the making of tools, the construction of their homes, the barrel making, the construction of wagons, the laying of roads, even the building of boats and fishing. Under Zabina's guidance, the women became the breadwinners of their families.

In those early years, Zeederlund imported most of its cotton, linen, and satin from Annelise. In doing so, the exotic and extreme clothing designs were also imported, but modified for the opposite sex. Men strived to look handsome and desirable by wearing ever more intricate and constricting gowns, ever higher heels, allowing their hair to grow as long as possible, as well as their nails. Of course, the latter was impacted by the chores that the man had to perform.

It is said that under Zabina's reign, the Great Stone Circle north of Altenborg was built, where special ceremonies are still held today marking the beginning of the four seasons. However, the Great Rift occurred after the death of Zabrina and those of her generation. Essentially, the sailors no longer knew the route from Annelise to Zeederlund and vice versa. All contact with Annelise ended around that time period. Yet, enough trade had transpired that the people on Zeederlund thrived and multiplied down through the ensuing centuries, though there was no contact with the outer-world.

A hundred years ago or so, an Annelise coastal ship was blown off course by a severe storm and stumbled into Zeederlund. Once they discovered the vast amount of gems and gold to be had in trade, word slowly spread, though these captains kept the knowledge and route to Zeederlund a closely guarded secret to protect their future profits. What those on Zeederlund found most curious is that the evolution of their dress styles and designs so closely matched those of the Annelise! Trade goods consisted of some clothing and shoes, but more of cloth bolts from which dresses and suits could be made. In addition, many of the modern inventions found on Annelise were traded, toilets being a prime example. Until fifty years ago, chamber pots were the norm or outhouses on the farms. The ship that brought Alexina also brought along two of the new sewing machines and an LD radio. A lengthy document also outlined numerous other marvelous inventions that were being planned for Annelise, things like electricity and steam trains, and motorized vehicles, all of which intrigued Monarch Andrea.

Julie asked, "Okay, who can tell Alexina the motto that Zabrina instilled into all of our many women workers, the motto that we all still cling to even today?"

Hedda's foot went up; Julie nodded. "Take your time and do it right." She grinned, knowing that at least she got this one right. Studies were not her strong suit.

"That's right, Hedda. Around here, Alexina, you will find that every working woman follows that code. If you are doing something, do it right. You will find that no one is worried in the slightest how long it may take to get a thing done. All that your family and anyone else care about is that it is done right and properly. Yes, we recognize that men with their awkward arms might be able to do some things faster and easier than we, but why bother them when we can do it ourselves. We need them in their nurturing roles."

"Like changing smelly diapers," Hedda broke in, wiggling up her nose and looking at Johan.

He smiled, "Sis, I don't mind that at all. I've changed some of yours, too." She flushed, that didn't quite go as she had planned.

"We want our men to look really fantastic and elegant and sexy, too," put in Iduna, with a wry grin.

"We try our best," Johan teased his older sister.

"Stop it you two. Hedda and Alexina are still a bit too young for such nonsense. Now then, on to basic geography. Who can tell me the approximate population of Zeederlund today?"

Johan spoke up, "Two hundred thousand." Julie nodded.

"Who can tell me how many large cities we have and their names? Point them out on our map for Alexina please," she requested.

Ah, geography, that was something Hedda enjoyed. She stood and walked to the big map. Using her right foot, she began naming them and pointing them out for Alexina. "Here in the center bottom half is the Nebelzee, which freezes over in the winter and we go ice skating, sledding, and skiing on it. Here is the tall Altenhorn. Right here is where we are, our capital city, Altenborg. Down here where the

Nebelzee touches the ocean are Vesterborg and Osterborg. To the east of Osterborg along our southern coast are Veenborg, Svenborg, and Ahren-ostborg, which is the easternmost port city. Going west along our southern coast from Vesterborg are Heideborg and Ahren-Vestborg, there at the western most tip. Continuing on up the northern coast from there is Ringborg. Havenborg lies almost due north of here, the northernmost city on the coast. Then come Kampenborg, Storeborg, and back to Ahren-ostborg again. Ta da."

"Excellent Hedda. During our practice session coming up, I want you to drill Alexina on them, until she can rattle them off and point them out to you rapidly," Julie requested. "Each of these large cities has about ten thousand people living there. When a city gets this big, traditionally, the monarch encourages future growth in smaller towns. Alexina, none of us likes to be living in a city that has more than ten thousand inhabitants. It gets too crowded. Space shrinks; we value our space."

"Wow, vack where I cove frov, vy city had villions of veovle living there. Yes, it is terrivly crowded there, vefore the vlague, I vean. I don't know what it is like now," she replied.

"Millions?" Hedda exclaimed in utter disbelief. "Do you live on top of each other?"

Alexina laughed for the first time since the plague. "No, silly. The city is vany viles across, it is really very vig."

After supper was finished, Monarch Andrea asked Alexina to come chat with her and Jutta. "Any news avout vy livs?" Alexina asked hopefully, repeating it twice because too many key consonants ended up like v's.

"No, I am afraid not yet. I am acting as your Monarch now, Alexina. I need to ask you some questions, please answer them honestly, as best you can. You see, I am facing a big decision with the outer-world. From our view, those in the outer-world are crazy and wrong about the roles of women and men in a society; at least we believe this is so from our conversations with the few that we have allowed to join our country and from the few ships that sometimes come here to trade. Here, we believe that it is the woman's role to lead, to work, to provide life's sustenance for her family, while the man's role is to nurture and care for the family. Seldom will you find a man forced to get a job to earn money to feed and clothe his children. Even when a wife dies, most men are asked for their hand in marriage by another woman — of course, after a respectable period of mourning has been observed. True, a few men love to sew and make clothing and a few love to help the doktors with saving lives, but most are stay at home fathers. Certainly, there is more than enough for them to do to run our homes efficiently."

"All of this is completely loony in the outer-worlds, where women's and men's roles seem to us to be reversed. Goofy, goofy, goofy," she added.

"And their men often fight bloody wars and battles, we're told," Jutta pointed out. "Here, there is no crime or fighting. What would be the point of it? Certainly, we women have arguments and disagreements, but always some compromise can be reached, even in the worst disagreements. Even our men do not actually fight. Well, sometimes they get a bit carried away and slap each other, but that's as aggressive as they get."

"Right, Alexina. I know that you are only thirteen, but does this seem to you to be an accurate description of your former land and people?" Andrea asked pointedly.

"Well, yes, vov ran our household, cooked our veals, and raised us kids. Dad had his vronze vaking shov and worked all day to earn the voney for our favily. Ven have gone insane after the vlague cave. They vurdered so vany veovle, vodies were everywhere for a while. Dad really got vean to ve after the vlague cave," she explained, though she had to say it a couple times because of the confusion of the many vowels.

"I see, then the stories that we've heard a true," Andrea sighed — her decision was all the more difficult.

"Why do you ask?" Alexina asked.

"You see," Jutta spoke up, "the men in the outer-world seem to value very highly our gem stones and gold. Over the years, we have seen an ever-increasing number of their trading ships coming to Zeederlund. They have guns and armies of soldiers with guns. We are beginning to fear that some of them could sail into the Nebelzee and conquer our country and we would be almost powerless to stop them, certainly against guns our few guards could do nothing."

"And, apparently these new LD radios are being sent all over the outer-world, allowing people to talk to others from very far distances. We fear that soon the whole outer-world will find out about us and come to conquer us, making us into slaves, much as your father tried to do to you, Alexina. On the other hand, there are these incredible rumors of all manner of marvelous inventions being made in some place called Velona. From what we have heard, Zeederlund could really make good use of them. As our monarch, I have a responsibility to bring these that would be most useful to our people. Yet, I am afraid that in doing so, I will bring the slave masters here as well. I face a most difficult choice."

Alexina relied naively, "Well, if Velona is vaking these varvelous things, surely they cannot be slave vasters. Vefore the vlague, vy father was vaking all these really nice vronze works. He only turned wicked to ve after the vlague cave and no one vought anything frov hiv any vore and we had no voney to vuy food."

"She does have a point, Andrea. If these people are making all these incredibly useful sounding things that would make people's lives more comfortable and productive, surely they would not also be slave masters," Jutta pointed out.

"You both make a good point. Let's do it. Jutta and I have studied the manual that says how to use this LD radio device. Alexina, would you help us with it, please. Someone has to pedal the machine to make it work," Andrea asked.

Alexina was very eager to help. Soon, she was pedaling away, while Andrea and Jutta went down a checklist of actions, switching various knobs and dials on the small machine. At last, Andrea began speaking, "Calling Velona. Calling Velona. Does this thing work? Calling Velona."

After a minute, crackling sounds echoed in the room followed by a man's voice. His accent was so horrible that Andrea could scarcely understand him. "Please wait a minute until I get someone who speaks your language." He repeated it a couple times until Andrea and Jutta figured out what he was saying. They waited patiently while Alexina continued to pedal the machine, generating electricity, Jutta explained. None of the three actually knew what that meant, however.

Roused from bed, I said sleepily into my microphone, "Hello. This is Bethany Bartiana Angela of Velona here. Are you still there? Can you understand me? Are you speaking Annelise? Come in please." I'd just gotten to sleep and was yawning, as Marco slipped his arms around me, kissing my neck.

"Yes, this is Monarch Andrea Alten. We are here. We are not from Annelise. We've just received one of these LD radios and have been told that your outer-world makes many marvelous inventions that would be most helpful to my people," she replied hesitantly.

"Hi Monarch Andrea. Yes, yes, we do — many great inventions to help women and men live better. You are speaking the Annelise dialect. What is your native tongue? I speak many languages. If I speak yours, you might find it more convenient to converse in your native language."

I heard three women chuckling. "Just Andrea. No need for formalities. This is my native language."

"But you are not in Annelise?" I asked becoming confused.

"No, we are not, though our ancestors came from Annelise. Our country is called Zeederlund."

My eyes were suddenly wide awake! Marco became very alert as well. Zeederlund? During the course of our many lifetimes on Tarra, we'd been just about everywhere, one time or other. Neither of us had ever heard of Zeederlund!

"I'm sorry. I do not know of Zeederlund. I'm looking at a large map of Tarra, but I don't see anything called Zeederlund. Is there another name that your country goes by?" I thought that this was likely the most logical explanation.

"No, since our ancestors came here over a millennia ago, it has always been called Zeederlund. We do not have much contact with the outer-world, not until a ship from Annelise came here about a hundred years ago. Still, only a few of them come here each year," she explained. Now we were definitely keenly interested!

"Yes, we can provide you with all manner of useful inventions and/or we can send along some engineers who can help your own people learn to manufacture these things yourselves. Of course, many require raw materials that you might not have available in your country. Our trading ships cover the whole world and can provide what you might lack in raw materials," I explained. "The only problem that I can foresee is that we do not know where your Zeederlund is located. Is your country adjacent to Annelise or part of what we thought was Annelise, east of the mountain range?"

"I'm sorry. I truly do not know where Annelise is located. Actually, no one in Zeederlund knows where any of the outer-world is at. As I said, our only contact comes from the trading ships, which claim they come from Annelise. I believe that they do; their sailor men are always well dressed."

"Well, then it is unanimous. We don't know where you are and you don't know where we are. How very strange. Interesting problem we have," I replied.

"The cavtain told me when we left the last Annelise vort that we would arrive here in about a vonth," Alexina volunteered what little she knew.

"Can she repeat that? I didn't quite get all the words?" I asked.

She did so, but it was no better, and Andrea then repeated it. "I'm sorry, but Alexina was brought here along with this LD radio. She was badly mistreated, and we've given her a better life here, where she can be a person, as she says. Honestly, the brutality of men in the outer-world is why we certainly want to avoid such outside contact as much as possible."

"I can understand that. Since the plague, the men in some countries have taken to badly mistreating women and men for that matter. I assure you that here in Velona none of that goes on. Our men treat us very well indeed. I'm sure that the same is true in Annelise, but it certainly is not the case in the kingdoms that used to be Demokritos," I explained, hoping to reassure her a little.

"I vas in Alia," Alexina added. "Very vad there. Vy dad had vy livs sliced and vut these vig vronze disks in thev. I cannot say anything in vy language, no one can understand ve at all, vut here in Zeederlund, I can sveak their language vretty well."

"Oh my lord! Not those infernal lip plates again. I understand, Alexina. I really do. I think that you are speaking very well."

"Thanks," Alexina replied, trying to smile, but her face remained expressionless as always.

"Well, she has given us a clue to your location. A month from Annelise can only mean sailing eastward. We have nothing on our maps there but vast ocean. I think I can figure out a way to find your country, Andrea."

"That is good then," she replied. "My Finance Minister wants to ask you something. This is Jutta."

"Hi, say, if you send these marvelous things to us, what do you wish from us in return?"

"Ah, well, what do the ships from Annelise take back from you?" I asked, hoping to gain some clues as to what they might have as resources.

"We have a lot of gem stones and gold and some silver. They prefer gems and gold."

"Well, if you have those to spare, they will be just fine with us too," I replied, thankful that we did not have to work out some more exotic means of exchange.

"Say, may I ask how your women are doing since they got the plague which struck everywhere on our world?" I probed a bit. Obviously, Alexina needed therapy and soon, but I wondered how the other women in Zeederlund were faring. I was not expecting the answer I got. In fact, I was shocked.

"A minor annoyance. Our hair suddenly grew a couple feet, almost the length of some of our men's hair. Of course, we women all got our hair cut back to our usual crew cuts. Also, our waists shrunk, annoying some of our larger women, plus our breasts — well, they are enormous. Our dressmakers had a workout making the needed alterations in our shirts, pants, and suit coats, but we women were soon perfectly well dressed within a week. Our men are such good seamstresses. My husband put in sixteen-hour days getting our suits fitted to us — that's me and my two daughters. The plague didn't do much for them, except their feet. Well, that's not entirely true, for a time we women had to wear shoes similar to those that our men always wore, prior to the plague. You know, very high heels. Now we are all fine, back to our polished slip-ons. However, some of our men have continued to wear those strange boots and have become as accomplished in walking in them as they were in their extreme heels. Nothing had to be done to their fancy ball gowns, though. Our men caught a break there. They didn't have to make any alterations to their gowns. How about your people in Velona?" she asked.

"Er, didn't your women also lose their arms?" I asked. Suddenly, my mind was traveling down several different paths — her words were so confusing.

"Oh don't be silly. Women of Zeederlund have never, ever had those useless upper appendages that the men have. Not ever, not in the millennia plus that we have been here. Oh, may I ask did you have arms that were lost like Alexina?" she suddenly realized that might be the case.

"Yes, to be honest with you, Andrea, all the women on Tarra had arms before the plague came, except for your women, I guess. The plague has been most traumatic for the women of Tarra. Your women have never had arms? Not ever?" I asked completely baffled as to how this could possibly be.

Andrea launched into a brief ancient history lesson, while Alexina smiled; she already knew this from Julie's lessons. "Fascinating, Andrea, fascinating history." I decided to explore a bit, "You've no records of huge insects harming your people?" She said flies were their biggest insects. "On one northern island, their doktors amputated the arms of their baby girls at birth. Their women had no idea that this was being done and were convinced that they were born that way."

"Such brutality! Well, I assure you that our doktors do not ever do such a thing! Our girls are born without those useless appendages. I know, I have seen my two daughters born and my two sons. They came out with their silly upper appendages, while my charming daughters came out without them. Besides our doktors are women and pledged to save and heal, not brutalize, like the doktor did to poor Alexina," she replied.

"We are very civilized here in Zeederlund. Our women pride themselves on looking their best always in very nice suits. We work hard and provide for our families. Our men are very nurturing; they do an excellent job at raising our families, cooking, cleaning, and maintaining our households. They too always look their best in their billowing ball gowns and high heels and long hair."

I began to get a very strange idea about this new country. "So your men do not build your houses, pave your streets, and mine your gem stones and gold?"

"Oh don't be silly. Of course not. We women would never, ever even suggest that a man do something that we could do ourselves. We women do all the work, bringing in the paycheck so to speak.

However, we do allow those men who wish to sew to make dresses and suits. Some even like to make shoes for themselves and for us. Women tolerate that much work outside our homes by our men, but not much more. It would be wholly uncivilized and inhumane for us women to let our handsome men do such things. Their skills lie in supporting us and our families in the home. Is this not the case in Velona?" Andrea asked, becoming convinced that it must not be, rather that Velona was indeed like what she suspected the outer-world was like, wholly uncivilized. I began to think we had another amazon country.

"No, here in Velona and in most of the rest of the world, we women by and large nurture our families and our men do the major work. Well, that's not wholly true. In Velona and some other countries, women also do quite a lot of work as well. I think that we have two societies with different cultural values." We chatted about our two societies for quite a while, before she voiced her real worry about this new outer-world contact and trade with us.

"Yes, Andrea, I understand your concern fully. Since you women run everything, if men came with long guns, you would not have any chance at all of defending your country. As you say, the slave masters could conquer Zeederlund with little effort. I simply will not stand for that. I know our monarch Stefano West Po will not stand for it either. There is another country which is run by women who fear the very same thing will happen to them, now that they have lost their arms to the plague. We have sent a strong force there to help defend them. Please, allow we in Velona to work out a way to guarantee the safety and autonomy of your country against any who would try to attack and conquer or enslave you."

"I don't know how you can do that, but your words bring gratitude and relief to me. That is my greatest concern. I fear that in bringing these marvelous inventions to my people that I will also bring about our downfall by evil outer-worlders," Andrea admitted.

"I promise you that we in Velona will not let that happen to you." Marco whispered something in my ear and I nodded. "Can you tell me what your country looks like? That way our people will know it when they see it." She did so. We arranged to chat again tomorrow evening my time, afternoon, hers.

The next morning, speculation ran rampant among us. "If their ancestors are as old as they claim, they must have been Partholan's original creations that somehow the mantis creatures missed altering with their arms creation program," Sergio concluded. "We are obviously looking at a culture and society that has been isolated from the rest of Tarra for nearly a millennia. Fascinating. Women run everything? How can they make stone buildings?"

"How can armless women build houses?" Lisa wanted to know.

"Those women must have immense pride in what they accomplish," Lucianna added. "I know I would if I could somehow build a house without the use of my arms!"

"Well, they are just as overboard on clothes as the Annelise are, only in reverse," Marco put in. "Guys, can you imagine wearing those corsets and huge gowns and incredible heels?"

"Oh, I think that you would look terrific in one," Eve teased him. I grinned.

"Yes, but, dear Eve, are you willing to cut your hair really, really short? I think not," he had the last laugh.

Marco and Sergio decided that they would take off and go see if they could locate Zeederlund. Eve decided that she wanted to go as well. In the back of her mind were therapy sessions. Did they need them? Alexina certainly did, but the other women were an unknown. Meanwhile, I headed off to have a long talk with Stefano, who as I expected was excited and elated that a new, undiscovered country had been found.

Around noon, Marco joined Stefano and me for lunch. "We found Zeederlund. It is almost exactly due east of Annelise out in the middle of absolutely nowhere, some fifteen hundred miles from Annelise, the closest land mass to them. Wild. We three took the time to explore their island a bit. You are right, dear; it is a mirror image of Annelise. Just take the women's apparel and put them on their men and take the men's suits and put them on their women and you have their scene. Yes, women do all the work there. Most amazing. They have all manner of strange tools and machines that enable them to build a brick home. However, we didn't see one structure that was more than a single story tall. It is an island, really. Sergio estimates it is one hundred miles long and fifty at its widest near the center. A huge inland sea or lake connects to the ocean. I checked, it is deep enough in its center to support a caravel. Their docks will probably be too small, though."

"Incredible, just incredible," Stefano said. "Who would have thought that when I got up today, a whole new country would have been discovered? One that wants to open up trade with us as well. Incredible. Yet, Bethany, I already have a pair of caravels loaded with the sample inventions. I've been keeping a pair stocked and ready to sail. We keep on getting these new contacts, so I'm prepared. They can sail today."

It was my turn to say, "Incredible, Stefano." He looked very pleased at how well his foresight and planning had become.

"It will be hard to protect them from attack. They are so distant from us," Stefano pointed out.

"However, I have an idea that might work. I can issue a formal proclamation to all countries saying that Zeederlund is under our protection. I will declare total war on anyone who attacks them or anyone who harms them. A deterrent is what we need here, a strong deterrent." Later that day, he drew up the first Defense Treaty of Velona. After discussing this with Andrea that evening, I gave him the okay. He then sent copies of it to every country leader on Tarra on August 1, 824.

The more that we discussed this unusual situation the more that we eight felt that we needed to see this country first hand. "Look, centuries of adaption could well yield us invaluable clues and ideas for our women," Sergio pointed out.

"They could well have inventions that we could use or adapt for our needs, Bethany," Lucianna argued.

"Besides, someone ought to represent us, not just the couple of engineers that we are sending along," Stefano added. He'd dropped by to discuss this with us, and he wanted personally to tell Monarch Andrea Alten that two caravels with the inventions would be sailing shortly.

"Who could we send," I asked. "I'd love to go, but I'm up to my ears in coordination work."

"Look, Lisa and I will go," Sergio suggested. "Right now, your Chief Detective Inspector has almost nothing to do. Crime is at historic lows. Lisa and I are not really needed here. Either she or I can give Alexina her needed therapy."

We agreed and waited for Andrea to call via the LD radio. Right on time, she made her connection to us. "Hi Andrea. Good news. Monarch Stefano wants a word with you first," I replied.

He told her about the Defense Treaty and that it would likely be a strong deterrent. Most countries respected the might of Velona, though our army right now was very small and mostly used to help people in the city proper as well as our smaller towns. He also told her that later tonight two caravels would set sail bringing her samples of the inventions. "I will send along two of our engineers who can assist your engineers. I'll also send along a trade representative who can work out trading deals between us and any other countries who manufacture some of these goods."

She was quite pleased. I then said, "I will send along my brother and sister-in-law. They will be able to give Alexina the therapy that our women truly need. Plus, they can help with many other things that arise. However, Andrea, what about the differences between our cultures? There is the matter of clothing and the matter of who does what. I suspect that when your dockhands see the sailors from the Annelise trade ships, there is a lot of gawking and staring. I would suspect that it will be worse as our people will be staying with you for some time."

"Surely your people dress well and civilized," Andrea hinted. I knew from experience with the Annelise that we had significant differences of opinion on what constituted well dressed.

"By your standards, Andrea, I would have to say that our people wear clothing that is comfortable and practical for what they are doing. Yes, we do dress up in outfits that we think that your people wear on an everyday basis. By that I mean we are familiar with Annelise dress codes. Am I correct in simply reversing who wears what?"

"Well, yes, I believe that is appropriate. If your women do not wear nice suits, they will simply not be respected. Likewise, your men, though some small tolerance has been granted to the Annelise sailors who insist on wearing women's suits," she explained.

"I understand. Could our people purchase appropriate clothing from you when they arrive?"

"Absolutely."

"Good. Let's go that route. Our women prefer to wear their hair long. Will your women not respect them if they have long hair but otherwise wear proper suits?" I asked. I knew that Lisa would not like to have her hair cut much shorter than it was. As Sergio's Protector, she kept hers rather short, not even touching her shoulders. Still, I knew that she would not want to cut it all off, unless she had to do so. We chatted and reached reasonable compromises.

Sergio and Lisa headed off to pack, including a pile of necessary baby items. Little Bartolo was now almost two months old and was off on his first ocean adventure. Stefano sent along as his trade representatives, Lucinda and Vito West Po. Vito had adopted Lucinda's last name, for political reasons. Both were eighteen and were available for such an extended voyage. However, Sergio and Lisa would have to teach them and the engineers the Annelise language during the voyage. Lucianna and Giovanni sent along two of their engineers and inventors, Beni Molo and Lene Sorensen. They were twenty and engaged to be married. She was of Annelise descent, that is, her parents had moved to Velona five years ago, primarily so their daughter could put her inventive talents to work at the DAE. Thus, she spoke Annelise well and was very familiar with their dress code and customs, though where they were heading, everything was in reverse.

Their plan was to sail there, unload the cargo, and have the caravels sail over to Annelise and pick up return cargo bound for Velona. We had enough caravels sailing the seas that we could reroute one to pick them up when they were ready to return.

The two caravels set sail with the high tide that night. I learned that the captains stopped in Megalos for supplies and water. From there, they set a great circle course for Zeederlund, using Marco's location of the island. This cut their sailing time down to three months, arriving in early October 825, where spring was well underway. During the voyage, Lene advised the men to let their hair grow as much as possible so that they would better fit in with the locals.

Chapter 42 Culture Clash

"The Mid-fall Ball is coming this weekend, Alexina. You just have to go. Everyone goes; it's loads of fun," Hedda explained. The girls were on their study break. She was more animated than usual. She lowered her voice to a whisper, "We are thirteen now, so we can ask a boy to be our date. I've had my eyes on Nelson since I was eleven. He's agreed. great, huh?"

Alexina grinned, only nothing physical occurred. "Who is Nelson?"

"Oh a handsome fellow. You'll meet him soon enough."

"Well, sis, I'm asking Morten," Iduna interrupted. "He's a whole lot more handsome. He has such long brown hair! Have you seen how long his nails are too?" She giggled.

"Well, he *is* two years older. Nelson will grow some, I'm sure of it," Hedda retorted. "Say, we have to find someone for Alexina to take to the ball." She suddenly realized that Alexina needed a boy as well. "Hardly anyone our age goes to the ball by themselves. Only the younger girls do. You *have* to ask someone, you *must*, Alexina."

"Vut I don't know anyone hardly," she protested, "and I don't know how to dance."

"We can teach you. There's time," Hedda insisted. "We can get Johan to help us." She called out to her brother, "Johan, you'll help us teach Alexina to dance, won't you?"

"Sure, sis," he replied. Alexina noticed that his eyes brightened up when he was asked.

"So who has Johan asked to the vall?" Alexina asked.

Johan's face flushed and the two girls giggled. Hedda explained, "Boys almost never ask a girl out! Girls ask the boys, silly. Gosh, I can't recall any boy asking a girl out. They'd have to be terribly desperate to do that, so utterly embarrassing, you see."

She didn't see, but asked, "Johan, has anyone asked you to the vall?"

Johan didn't get a chance to reply. Iduna broke in, "That overbearing pig Malena is always asking him out, but he keeps refusing her. I would too, if I was him. She is too bossy. Jordis has taken him out a few times, but she has such a pimply face though. She's nice enough, but Johan likes the gardener's daughter, Hilda, but she's the prettiest girl around and doesn't pay much attention to Johan."

His face flushed with embarrassment of having his love life tossed about without his consent; he interrupted her, "Well, maybe one day Hilda will ask me out. You'll see. And I haven't agreed to go to the ball with Malena. I might just not go this year," he pouted in defiance of his sisters.

"Johan, how avout going to the vall with ve? I don't know hardly anyone. Vlease," Alexina asked him. As ugly as she now looked, she couldn't bear going to the ball with a stranger.

"I would be highly honored to accompany you to the ball, Alexina," he replied, his eyes brightening up, and a big smile seemed to say "so there" to his sisters. "I won't disappoint you, Alexina," he added, though she didn't quite know what he meant by that. His sisters flashed him a frown however.

"Well, I'm going to ask Julie if we can teach you to dance this afternoon. That will beat having to study all afternoon," Iduna concluded and headed off to find Julie.

Just then, Andrea walked into the parlor where the kids were taking their study break. Her face radiated just how annoyed she was. "Honestly! What can possibly have happened to the Annelise? This is an utter disgrace."

"What is mom?" Hedda asked, becoming curious. Johan looked up, equally curious. Seldom had he seen his mother so annoyed.

"Oh, come on children, I'll show you. We've just finished unpacking all these supposedly new fashions from Annelise. Now mind you, Alexina, the Annelise have everything backwards, forcing their men to wear women's clothes and their women to wear men's clothing. Well, we just always reverse their mess, but this time — well I have never seen such abominations. Whatever can they be thinking?"

"What do you mean, mom? Are the new suit designs really that bad?" Hedda asked.

"Oh no, they have changed very little, if at all. No, it is the new men's fashions. Despicable, risqué, why, I wouldn't be seen with a man wearing some of these! Just look at their proposals!"

"Anders, dear. Hold up some of those, please," she asked. He held up the new style skirts and simple day dresses and blouses.

"Oh dear lord, I wouldn't ever be seen in that, mom!" Johan burst out. "Not only are they ugly, but they are hideous looking!"

"That's not all, son, look at this proposed alternate ball gown, at least that is how it is labeled," Anders added. He held up one of their new slinky designs.

"Good lord! Would you look at that tiny thing?" Johan gasped at the opposite extreme from his dress.

Anders said, "Well, it certainly would show off our curves, son. I bet walking in it would be more challenging than our gowns." To his wife, he added, "Dear, in this one, everyone would be able to see our shoes and our steps would be highly visible. Might you find that a little enticing?" He flirted with Andrea, who melted a little.

"Well, I'd have to see how you looked in one, love," she replied.

Hedda quickly explained to Alexina, "Dad always sets the men's styles. Every man looks to dad for the latest fashions. That's part of his job as husband to the monarch, you see."

"Johan, come son, let's try on one of these new slinkys for your mother. We will absolutely reject these others. Now their true ball gowns are just not up to our high standards; they've reduced the hoop sizes. Intolerable," he suggested. Carrying several dresses, the two men glided slowly out of the room.

Andrea added, "Well, you must make allowances when they try these on. Ignore the ill-fitting bosoms. When dad reworks the dresses, he'll make them to fit men's forms, as they should have been made in the first place. Honestly, the Annelise have everything completely backwards!" Alexina wished that she had had a chance to see the Annelise, but then she was below decks and miserable at the time.

An hour later, the two men returned wearing the ill-fitting dresses to show how these would look on men. Each was holding on to the other, taking even smaller steps in their ballet boots, which were now highly visible, as were the shapes of their bodies. There was just barely enough ease in the slinkys to allow them to cross their legs but no more. "We will have major problems with the smallest of stairs," Anders informed Andrea.

Andrea moved around looking at her husband and son from several angles. After a couple of minutes, she said decisively, "Indecent, Anders. If you fall, how will you even get up?"

"Only with extreme difficulty, dear. Our manhood keeps becoming indecently visible. Perhaps on their women these might be more appealing to the eye by virtue of your body's extreme curves. I just don't see how we could possible wear these in public. I don't see how we could modify them to be pleasing to your feminine eye, dear."

"You are right, as always, when it comes to men's fashions. We'll reject these new slinkys too. What possible use could you make of their new ball gowns? Such small hoops," she asked.

"None, I'm afraid, unless we use them for small boys. Certainly, no adult man would be caught dead in such small hoops. They would work for boys between five and perhaps ten, though. It'd give them a bit more variety from which to choose," Anders suggested.

"Okay, then we'll accept only those then, but in limited quantity. The next Annelise shipment that come, I will refuse payment for all but these gowns," Andrea concluded.

Johan whispered to Alexina, "As soon as I change out of this and put on my dancing shoes, we'll start on your dancing lessons." She flashed him a smile, but again nothing changed on her face.

A while later, he rejoined the girls, who were already walking Alexina through the basic moves. Hedda was reminding her, "Remember, you are leading him, but you must take what seems to you to be very tiny steps. Your partner will only be able to take very small steps at one time. Oh, here's Johan. Brother, show her your dancing shoes so she can see why she has to be so careful when she leads you."

He raised his huge hoop skirt, showing off his shiny black extreme heels, while smiling proudly at Alexina. He glided to her side, put his arm over her shoulders, and the four continued with the dance steps.

Alexina had never been to a ball before and was in utter awe, ignoring all the many stares that she got. The dance was held in one of the adjoining buildings where the enormous hall occupied the entire building. The musicians were all men and nearly five hundred couples packed the hall. Johan wore a blue satin gown what was sixteen feet across at the floor, wider than most others were. True to his word, he made Alexina the envy of many her age at the dance, including Hedda and Iduna. Her bronze face and complimentary lip plates contrasted sharply with her white satin suit and blouse, with its ruffled scarf tied around her neck where ties were worn by men in other countries.

Near the end of the dance, the lights were lowered and the couples danced very close to each other. She loved the feel of his strong arms around her, feeling a comfort that she had long missed. Then, Alexina spotted many women kissing their partners. How could she even kiss anymore? Panic rose, but his arms moving gently up and down the back of her suit coat dissolved her fear. She looked Johan in his eyes and carefully touched her protruding lips to his. Hot heat flashed through her body as he returned her kiss. Her body felt so strange, but then the music ended and the men applauded. The dance was over.

"Thank you for a fabulous evening, Miss Alexina Phanes," Johan said softly and most politely.

"I've never had so vuch fun in vy whole life vefore, Johan. Thank you!" she whispered back.

"I know a secluded place nearby, very romantic," Johan suggested.

"Let's go see it," she whispered back. Slowly, the two walked out into the formal gardens behind the dance hall. Here among the carefully tended gardens, Johan stopped. Fragrances from dozens of varieties of flowers drifted into their noses. He held her close and waited hopefully. Alexina finally realized that it was her position to make the first move. Again, she touched the leading tips of her lips to his and their passions flowered.

Later, he whispered, "You are like the flowers around us, rare and beautiful, Alexina." She flushed and smiled, though nothing visible occurred. Young love began to blossom between the two.

The next day, Julie began their lessons, by saying, "It is time that you girls begin to study lessons in the areas in which you wish to work. Iduna, of course, is in line for the throne and will be studying management and leadership principles. Johan has already decided to follow his father's example and become a dressmaker and tailor. So, Hedda, what is it that you wish to learn to do for work? Alexina, we will make allowances for you, since you are so new to Zeederlund and have few ideas of the types of employment that are available here."

Hedda sighed exasperated, "I don't know, Julie. The only thing I'm good at is geography. Maybe I could be a mapmaker. Maybe when we get all these new inventions from Velona I'll have some other ideas."

Julie smiled, "All right, then. For now, mapmaker it will be. Let me get you your new textbook." She found the one that she was looking for on her shelves, pulled it partially out, catching it between her shoulders and neck, then pulling it off the shelf. She leaned into Hedda who took it between her shoulders and neck, carrying it over to her desk. While the three kids began studying their respective books, Julie took Alexina aside and the two read over the exhaustive list of potential jobs available in Zeederlund.

"Woven do all these things?" she asked in disbelief.

"Yes, women and men, both are encouraged to be what they desire, to strive to achieve their goals in life, subject only to doing no harm to our people, that is," Monarch Andrea replied, as all heads turned to the doorway where she had just entered an interrupted them. "Of course, some wish to be something which is beyond their abilities and some do change their minds. Yet, we are all free to choose our paths in life. What path do you wish to choose, Alexina?"

"I don't know. I just wanted to ve a verson, not a thing. Now I av allowed to ve a verson, vut I don't know what else I should ve. I — I av looked uvon to ve the vrovider in a favily, like vy father, vut I don't know how to do that or vuch of anything yet," Alexina admitted. "Vayve I will just let you and everyone else down."

"Dear, you are young and have not grown up among us. We cannot expect that you should be ready to make such an important decision just yet. Give yourself time. I think that you ought to take some time to travel around our city here and perhaps down to the coast. See for yourself how we live our lives here. It will do you good to see so many possible paths that you could follow. Johan, you will escort Alexina around our city and down to the coast. Show her around; let her see for herself so many rewarding careers."

"Sure mom, delighted to do so. When can we leave?" Johan grinned, realizing that he would have the opportunity to be close to Alexina for many days.

"Tomorrow will be soon enough. Take a coach, have Anja drive you; she is our best carriage driver. Give Alexina a grand tour, allow her to meet and chat with whomever she desires, son. Mind you, be on your best behavior, son."

"You can count on me, mother," he hastily added. "Come on, Alexina, we best make some plans on what to take with us. Hedda, may we have one of your fancy maps, please?" he asked, but he was prepared to beg her if she refused.

A bit miffed that she was not given the opportunity to travel about, Hedda turned up her nose, but relented. "Well, I suppose that you will need one brother. Just you mind your manners with Alexina, because she doesn't know all of our customs yet."

He raised his arm and Alexina realized that was a hint for her to come to his side so that she could provide a shoulder for him. "Thanks," he whispered, as they moved slowly out of the room. "We should bring along a complete change of clothes. Mom ought to be giving you a money pouch so you can pay for our expenses. It would be unseemly if I were to be seen paying innkeepers and such."

"I av suvvosed to do that, vay for what we need? I don't know if I can handle a voney vouch or even get the coins out. I av afraid that I'll just evvarrass you, Johan," she admitted and she started to worry once again.

He stopped and whispered, "If you can't, you can always pretend to be busy with something else and ask me if I would do it for you. That's also acceptable, just look busy though."

"Thanks!"

The next morning, Alexina had a folding bag containing a second suit packed along with a small bag of her few personal things. Hedda thumped on her door, "Johan's ready for you, Alexina. Oh, you are supposed to carry your things and some of his. Use a yoke," she gave last minute guidance, wondering how many goofs Alexina would be making. Well, maybe Johan could cover for her, she thought.

"Oh, I didn't know that," she answered, sitting down to maneuver her bags onto a nearby yoke. One thing she knew, yokes were everywhere, sometimes a dozen in one room. Her suit bag was far too heavy, and she struggled to get her load down the hall to Johan's room. He was waiting for her, wearing a yellow satin gown. "Oh, how av I to carry that vuch?" she exclaimed, seeing that he had several large bags.

"Put this one opposite your big one — this smaller one opposite yours. I'll carry my small bag," Johan advised. Men always carry one personal bag, you see. She struggled with the bags and finally got them stuck in the baskets. As she raised the yoke, it was far heavier than she expected.

"I don't know if I can carry this vuch," she said nervously. "It is unvalanced."

Johan put his arm on her shoulders and helped her keep the heavier basket from dragging along the floor. "Thank goodness we go slowly. This is really hard to carry," she whispered, noticing quite a lot of the palace staff were eyeing them as they traversed the long hallway to the main doors.

"You are doing marvelously well, Alexina. Good job," he whispered encouragement to her. Once outside, she had to sit the baskets down a moment to catch her breath. Anja, wearing a brown cotton suit with a white blouse, came up to them and nodded.

Anja said, "So we are to do a grand tour of the city. This will be fun. Alexina, put his bags inside the carriage, and then I'll show you how I drive the carriage. If you like, you can ride up front with me for a while. The view is much better than from inside the carriage."

It took her ten frustrating minutes to wrestle the bags up and into the carriage. Anja suggested that most used their teeth to help, but Alexina quickly gave that up, because her lip plates just didn't allow her to use her mouth for much of anything, hampering her ability to accomplish some tasks more readily. Finally, she lent Johan her shoulder so he could climb safely into the carriage. "What avout the yoke?" she asked.

"Leave it. Someone will take it inside where it will be ready for whoever needs it next. Climb on up beside me," Anja suggested. "Use your chin against the rail there to help keep your balance, child."

"Why is the seat so slanted?" she asked.

"Watch, see how we drive," Anja pointed out, as she took one set of reins in around her left ankle and another, her right.

"Vut wouldn't it ve easier to have a van drive the horses? This looks so hard," Alexina asked.

Anja laughed. "Such a silly idea. Why on earth should we have our charming, handsome men in their gorgeous dresses do what we can do for ourselves? Such an outer-world idea. Oh, I'm sorry, Alexina, I forgot that you came from out there. It must have been so utterly uncivilized."

They toured the city and Alexina saw a large number of working women. Men were on the streets as well, often carrying bags of groceries to their homes. She focused on the women, of course, and saw so many wonders that she could scarcely believe her own eyes. Of particular interest was their half-hour stop to watch a new brick home being build. Dozens of women worked together. One was the architect who directed the bricklayers. Intricately assembled scaffolding allowed the women and their yokes to carry bricks and mortar up to the current layers being set. Specially made towels allowed them to use their feet to do the actual brick laying, though always they worked in small groups, each woman providing assistance to the overall action to be done. While a single man could slop on the mortar, place the next brick, align it, and tamp it down, four women worked together to get each brick laid.

Now Alexina began to see why all the buildings looked so very much the same, the women followed the same tried and true construction methods. Repeatedly, she saw women performing what she had always considered men's work back home in Alia. It wasn't that in Alia women didn't work, rather just not these types of jobs, especially since the plague. The reality between the world that she grew up in and here became rather poignant in her mind. She felt more like an outsider than ever before.

Towards evening, they pulled up to an inn. Once Anja halted the carriage, she whispered, "Alexina, after you get down, grab one of those yokes by the door there. After you open the carriage and assist Johan down, load your bags onto the yoke. The doorwoman will open the doors for you as you lead him inside. I'll take care of the carriage and perhaps join you for dinner, if you like."

"Thank you. I don't know if I can vanage it, vut I will try. Thanks." She used her chin to help her get safely down, though Anja whispered to go slow and sure, that there was no rush.

She went up to the doorwoman, nodded, stepped under a yoke, and swiftly took it to the side of the carriage. She opened the door with her foot and leaned close, as Johan's arm rested firmly on her shoulders. From his smile and motions, she knew that he really did need her assistance disembarking. Managing the giant hoop skirt while wearing such a tight corset and impossibly high heels made this simple action challenging, she thought. Once he was down, she noticed that he had cleverly repositioned their bags close to the door. Still, she had a difficult time getting them down and into the baskets. Finally, after what she thought an eternity, she lifted the heavy load. She felt Johan's arm softly alight across her shoulders, steading the yoke. Slowly, the two moved to the door, which the doorwoman proceeded to open, timing it perfectly.

"Where do I go now?" she whispered. "I have never veen in an inn vefore."

"Move across the room to the man behind the counter. We need two rooms, unless you would like to share one with me."

"Can I? Is that vervitted?"

"Sure, I am supposed to be showing you around. Anja will keep her mouth shut."

"Good evening miss. I say, such fine lip ornaments! I've never see such before. How may we help you?" the man in the green gown asked.

"One roov, vlease," she said three times before he understood her properly.

"Supper and breakfast, I presume?"

"Yes, vlease. Oh, and a second roov for our driver, vlease."

"Two gold, miss."

Alexina had never tried to get coins out of a pouch before, and Anders had tied it to her belt. She sat down and did her best to untie it. She nearly gave up when it finally came loose. She fumbled with her toes and managed at last to get one between her toes. She tried to lift it up to the outreached hand of the innkeeper, but it slipped. He cleverly caught it and waited patiently. Alexina felt her face must be beet red with embarrassment by now. This was all so hard, but would have been trivial if Johan has just done it for her.

Now she had to get her shoulders under the yoke again and then support Johan. "Which way?" she whispered. He cleverly guided her to their room. She'd not even remembered what room number the man had said.

A half hour later, they headed down to dine, just as Anja entered. It had taken her this long to deal with the horses, though two inn stable women had assisted her. Johan told her what room she was in and she promised to join them as soon as she washed her feet.

She was surprised to see a woman was their waitress. When she brought their meals in a yoke, she was even more awed to see her sit down and maneuver the table settings and food onto the table using her feet. She did have a hard time reaching the higher table where Johan sat. Again, Alexina couldn't see why a man didn't just do this waitress job; it would be so easy for him and was obviously quite a challenge for women. Still, the whole operation seemed nearly automatic for the waitress, who didn't seem to mind it at all.

When the two were finally alone in their room together, Johan began his lengthy process of undressing. "Don't worry. I always sleep in my corset and kickers. You will see nothing unseemly. Let me help of your suit. No one will be the wiser." At last, Johan was free of social restraints and could help her a little.

"Thank you. This has veen so overwhelving to ve."

"I know, but you did very, very well, dear." He leaned over and touched her lips gently with his.

After he pulled back slightly, she leaned over and touched his lips with hers. "I cannot even kiss any vore," she said sadly, a tear welled up in her eye.

"There, there, the touch of your lips is so gentle, dear. I relish your touch."

"Really? It is not a vorver kiss at all."

The week passed slowly, with each day bringing more and more incredible sights to her eyes and mind. More and more she wondered why the men did not take it upon themselves to do so many things that they left for the women to struggle with, for she only saw their herculean efforts as just that. She really was an outsider; she was becoming increasingly convinced of it.

When they returned, Monarch Andrea met them and asked, "Well, Alexina what do you think of our country? How was your trip?"

"The country is very veautiful. The veovle are very friendly and kind, everywhere we went. Vut what I don't understand is why ven don't do sove of the harder jovs for the wovev."

Monarch Andrea was wise. "Well, let me put it to you this way, Alexina. In your world as it now is, could you or the women of your country make your own living independently? That is, without having a husband or man around to help you?"

"No way. Not at all," she replied.

"Yet, here in Zeederlund, we women are truly independent. We can get by without the need to rely heavily upon men to do things for us. We are not dependent for our survival upon men, nor are they heavily dependent upon women. Though we all admit that most of we women hate to cook and do housework and men enjoy doing both. It is a good match, don't you think?"

"It is going to ve very hard for ve," Alexina admitted.

"I know, dear, I know. We will do all that we can to make it as easy for you as possible."

As the days dragged on, Alexina became more and more moody, though her face could not show it. People only saw the shiny, four-inch bronze disks protruding from her mouth, stretching what was left of her lips. This, she was thankful for — after all, these people here were being incredibly kind to her. Still, she couldn't figure out what job she could do or wanted to do. At least her lack of common facial expressions kept others from frequently asking her what was wrong.

As the Winter Solstice neared, preparations were made for the royal family's trip to the Stones. "We pray first and then we sing and dance," Hedda explained the essence of their holy day. "It is the start of winter. Time for fun, well for we kids, that is. At least we don't have to study much. Julie takes time off to spend with her family. She usually takes them down to the beach. We can go ice-skating, if you like. Do you know how to skate?" she asked.

"No, I have never veen to lakes," she replied. "Is it hard for us to skate?"

"The men, well they can really go fast over the ice, but we women, we go slower because it is hard to keep our balance. It is a lot of fun; trust me. I'll show you how," Hedda volunteered. "Say, what's the matter with your ornaments? Alexina, they are drooping down a whole lot these days."

"I don't know. They are sovehow loose."

Hedda took charge and summoned their doktor. Alexina didn't like what he had to say. "Over time, Alexina, your lips are stretching some. To keep them straight and from becoming a huge problem for you, we ought to make larger disks or somehow enlarge yours. I'll send for a friend of mine, she'll be better able to give us an answer."

A few hours later, Alexina was asked to lie down, while Cecilie began to examine her disks and lips. "I am a very fine quality metal worker, Alexina. You are in good feet with me." After a careful examination, Cecilie pronounced, "Your father did an excellent job in crafting these plates. I believe that we do not need to make new ones. Rather, there is enough metal around this area that I can pound thinner, which in turn will make the disks larger around. It will be trial and error. Your job is to let me know when they are as tight as they were originally. That way, they will remain horizontal on you and not be drooping as they are now. I can see how they make eating very difficult for you. I'll have you fixed up just fine." She encouraged the young girl.

She went to get her tools, returning with her yoke heavily laden with her portable anvil as well as tools, most of which had leather foot pockets in which she could insert her feet and use them to pound the small ball-peen hammers against metal and anvil. She spent two hours tap-tap-tapping around the bronze plates, being careful not to touch the edges, which were concave to support her lips nor the central artistic patterns her father had made. At last, both plates were quite tight again and protruding horizontally. Alexina found eating easier once more. However, her plates were now about four and a half inches across. Although she said nothing, she began to fear that they would have to be continually made larger and larger every half year.

The day before the celebration, Alexina helped the other women make their preparations. She made numerous trips with yokes, carrying baskets of food and drink out to the carriages. Hedda carried blankets. Finally, Andrea announced that it was time to leave and Alexina went to lend her shoulders to Johan. She found him wearing a bright purple gown this time, "I didn't know that you liked vurvle," she said as they moved slowly down the hallway.

"It's the traditional color we use for the celebration. See, there's dad in his purple gown," he replied. Indeed, Anders, his arm over Andrea, was moving towards the doors a little ahead of them. "Hi, Jutta, Halder," he added, as they came out of another door. He too wore a purple gown and carried their two year old girl in one arm while he held on to Jutta for balance and support.

"I heard about your plates, Alexina. Cecilie did a good job on them. They look great," Jutta complimented her.

As they stepped outside, Johan whispered, "I am wearing my ballet boots just for you, Alexina. I will need to be holding on to you all the time. That's why I am moving slower than normal. I do hope you like them on me. This will be a fun festival, after we pray first, that is. I wanted you to be proud of the way I look today, since it is one of our most holy holidays."

"Aren't they hard to walk in? Vy dad had to try it after the vlague cave. He couldn't. I don't think I ever saw anyone avle to walk in thev, until I cave here, that is," she replied.

"Oh I had to practice hours and hours. Now I do fairly well, but we will be on rough ground out there at the Stones. And there is the slippery snow to contend with. I hope you don't mind my holding on to you?" he smiled at her.

"Oh no. Vlease, I don't want you to fall."

"Oh that would be bad. It is so hard to get back up while wearing this outfit and heels. Slow and easy does it, my pretty lady." She smiled involuntarily at the compliment, but nothing happened except that she again realized that nothing happened.

They rode north through Altenborg and soon the road began climbing up towards the sharp volcanic peak known as Altenhorn. Even from this distance, she could see small mining roads leading down from the rugged peak. They pulled up along with dozens of other carriages. Alexina struggled to get the door opened and then stepped down, leaning her shoulders in for Johan. This time, she noticed, he did indeed put pressure on her as he awkwardly and a bit clumsily climbed out, made difficult by the shoes he was wearing just for her. Fortunately, there was little snow on the ground.

Already, Hedda had gotten her yoke out and had both baskets filled. She whispered secretively, "He's doing this just for you, Alexina. I think he has a crush on you and wants to look sexy for you." Again, she flushed and smiled, though only she knew that she was smiling.

Minutes later, struggling under the weight of the yoke with full baskets and Johan leaning heavier than normal on her, she began to follow the others. "What is this vlace with the stones anyway?"

"You remember your history lessons? This is where we worship God. Simple ceremony, really, just saying thanks and all that. The real fun comes with the music and partying afterwards. It usually goes on until long after dark. I do hope my feet can hold out that long for you," he answered.

The rocky, uneven ground made her going slow and that of Johan even more precarious. He wiggled and wobbled quite noticeable, but he continued smiling for her. He intended to make an impression on Alexina this outing. Then, the twenty, tall, basalt monoliths appeared, arranged in an enormous circle. She saw at least a hundred men in purple dresses accompanied by even more women, dressed as she, in white suits. Already, Monarch Andrea had chosen their spot on the ground and Anders was struggling with laying out blankets, made challenging because of his huge hoop skirt. "Let's go beside them and I'll get our picnic diner ready for us, Alexina."

By the time that they made it to the others, Anders had a blanket laid out for them. Johan very carefully squatted down, allowing the hoop to collapse on top of itself. At last, he let go of her. Now she sat down and began handing him their many items that had been jammed into her baskets. All the while, Alexina kept glancing at the Standing Stones. Finally, someone announced that it was time, and Johan rose, pulling on her shoulders so hard that she nearly fell down herself. Then, they followed the others. Since the other men moved a little faster than they did, she guessed that only Johan was foolish enough to wear such inappropriate boots. Still, she admired him for wanting so badly to please her.

At last, she got a good look at the stones. Somehow, they felt familiar, as if she had known them all her life, though she had never seen such things! So engrossed in them was she that she never heard the prayers of offering delivered by Monarch Andrea. "Come on, the others are heading back to the blankets to eat," Johan broke in on her swirling mind. "Told you these stones are really great."

"So faviliar. Can things you've never seen ve like really faviliar to you?" she asked as the made their slow way back.

"I surely don't know. Come on, I get to feed you this time, part of our customs." For once, she was more than willing to let him do just that. Around them, the other men were doing the same thing as well. "We are honoring you women and all that you have done for us since the last ceremony," he explained.

"It's delicious. Did you cook it?" she asked.

Pride swelled across his face, "Yes, I cooked it especially for you, my dear."

She flushed and smiled, but of course, he saw no smile. He found her hard to read, going mostly with what her eyes said. A bit later, he added, "When we dance, remember I can only take very tiny steps, but all the better to be close to you," he winked and smiled.

Although the music was enjoyable and the dances easy for her to do, for Johan moved hardly at all, she continually kept turning her eyes over onto the dark stones. So familiar, she thought, somehow. All the way home, she saw the images of the stones in her mind and then again as she finally fell asleep that night.

The spring days were more fun for all. Picnics, swimming, walks in the parks, games of croquet on their lawn — all entertained the young adults. True, Alexina got to see even more occupations that she could enter, such as lifeguard, though she had no idea at all how she could possibly rescue someone who was drowning. Swimming was a nightmare for her; she continually tried to use her arms, which were not there. In fact, for these many months, this was her biggest hurdle: she continued to attempt to use her arms, but reality continued to thrust itself upon her instead.

Early November 824, our two caravels slowly made their way up the center of the Nebelzee, sounding all the way. By the time that they neared the docks, thousands of people stopped to stare at these — the largest ships that they had ever seen! Their arrival caused quite a stir. All Altenborg knew of their arrival, though it was highly anticipated by Monarch Andrea. The interplay between being interested versus being interesting became quite pronounced, that is the interplay between being cause and being an effect.

"Gosh, their hair is even shorter than we anticipated," Lisa observed. The six stood on the main deck as their caravel carefully sounded its way into the unfamiliar waters of the Nebelzee. She, Lucinda West Po, and engineer Lene Sorensen had their fellows trim their hair short. Of course, Lisa always did keep hers short so that it didn't interfere with her Protector duties. Lene had her attention on her engineering inventions and plans and didn't wish to spend the time that longer hair demanded of her.

Still, Lene agree, the women of Zeederlund certainly had short hair, a couple of inches long at most, she observed. "Well, their suits will be just fine to work in, no problems there, Lisa."

"My god! What about us men?" Vito West Po exclaimed. "Those are men I see in the distance, right?"

Beni Molo, the second engineer, commented, "Oh my goodness. It is as Mrs. Angela said; the roles are reversed. The men are wearing women's dresses and the courtly ball gowns of the Annelise at that! However will I ever be able to get my work done wearing that, Lene?" She shrugged her shoulders.

Sergio, their leader, spoke up, "Well, remember gang, here the women are the bread earners and the men take care of their families. Exactly the opposite of us, where women often nurture the family unit. There are bound to be innumerable culture differences, and we best follow theirs as much as we possibly can. This island country is not like the amazon women of Konstantin. Here men are not brutalized; rather they've merely switched roles in life."

"If the women do all the work, how are we going to get all of our cargo unloaded and setup?" Beni asked.

Sergio answered, twiddling his moustache, "Beni, if these women are used to doing what we men do in our culture, we must assume that they have their own unique ways of dealing with this. I heard that their women actually have built all the buildings we are seeing in the distance. They look like stone to me."

"Incredible, Sergio," Lene broke in, "I know my limitations now as a DAE engineer and designer. I just cannot fathom how I could possibly build a stone home myself. Even before the plague, I would have been hard pressed to do it, but could have done it. Now, doing something like that is beyond my imagination, and I have a good one or I wouldn't be one of the DAE's representatives here."

"She's good, Sergio," Beni validated her and she smiled. He added, "Love, if I have to wear outfits like those, I am going to need plenty of your advice!" She was of Annelise descent and spoke that language well.

"Don't worry, dear, I certainly will." She added with a wry smile, "Now you fellows will see what we women put up with when you want us all dolled up for dances and parties. The shoe will be on the other foot." The three women chuckled, and Sergio faked a moan in protest.

As the docks drew close, Beni pointed out, "This is good. We are likely to find deep waters all the way up to their docks. This is the remnants of an ancient volcanic crater. Those distant, black mountains are the northern rim of the crater."

"Where are the south rim and the other sides?" asked Lucinda.

"Probably blown to bits in the volcano's last eruption. Don't worry, I suspect this one has been dormant for a millennia," he advised.

As the crew tossed out the thick hawser lines to the women dockhands, wearing brown suits with white blouses, they all watched to see how these women could deal with mooring the caravels. Also, Lisa pointed out that three carriages had just pulled up. Each was driven by a woman driver, and the carriages looked far lower to the ground than those in Velona. Sergio watched fascinated by the dockhands, who acted as if they had done this action all their lives. Using a foot, they wrapped the lines around an ankle, and hopping, they dragged the lines around the huge mooring timbers. Six women per line then began pulling on them together, inching the caravel up tight to their dock. He was amazed to see how the women used their feet to tie the securing knots. Even the crew stared in wonder.

One woman stepped forward, "Welcome to Altenborg. I am the Harbor Master, Lise Jorgen. Can you understand our language?"

"Well met, Harbor Master Lise, I am Sergio Bartiana, my wife Lisa. Representatives of Velona, Lucinda and Vito West Po. Our engineers, Lene Sorensen and Beni Molo. Yes, we all speak your language, but probably not too well."

She grinned, "Wild accents, but understandable. I understand you have quite a lot of cargo to unload at this time. Can your ships deposit the cargo onto the docks or do you need us to unload it for you?"

Sergio looked at the captain who nodded. "Yes, they have cranes that can lift the crates onto the docks. Will your dockhands be able to handle it from there?"

"Of course, why wouldn't we be? That is good. Have them begin unloading, and I'll give the orders for the hands to get them loaded onto wagons. Our teamsters will take them to the Exhibition Hall for now. It is by the Royal Palace where you will be staying. If you who are coming aground will please follow me, I will introduce you to Monarch Andrea Alten."

As the six followed Lise, the many dockhands eyed the strangers closely, muttering comments about their weird dress styles. "This is our Monarch Andrea Alten, her husband, Anders, and her daughter Iduna, heir to the throne." She then introduced the six. "They will be unloading the cargo now, and I'll see that it gets to the Exhibition Hall."

"Thank you Harbor Master. Well done. If you will join us, I have carriages that will take us to the palace, where we have rooms prepared for you. Iduna will take four with her and two may come with me," she said graciously. Eyeing Anders, Sergio and Lisa followed the two, while the other four followed Iduna to the second carriage.

He estimated that his ball gown's hoop was at least fourteen feet across at his feet. From his slow pace, he guessed that he was perhaps wearing those extreme heels so popular in Annelise and with many fashionable women in Velona as well. His waist looked small and he assumed the man was wearing a tight corset as well. Anders had brown hair that fell to the small of his back and Sergio was thankful that he and the other men had allowed theirs to grow during the three-month voyage. His fell significantly below his shoulders and would likely be acceptable fashion here.

After exchanging pleasantries and asking about the voyage, Monarch Andrea asked, "Well, Lisa, your hair is bit long for us, but yours, Sergio is acceptable. Of course, there is the problem of dress codes. As I understand Mrs. Angela, your Velona is backwards with men wearing women's apparel and women, men's. Since you are going to be staying here with us for some time, you will find acceptance of our people much more readily if you dressed in our styles. Though by no means do I wish to force you to do so. . ."

Sergio replied diplomatically, "Of course, Monarch Andrea. As long as we are your guests in Zeederlund, we should dress as your people do. It would be terribly rude of us to insist on wearing apparel that your people would find controversial. However, we will need some guidance on what to wear, and where we may purchase appropriate dress. We certainly should pay for our new clothing."

She looked at Lisa for confirmation. "Yes, he's correct. In Velona, often, but not always, our men take control of situations. I understand that here it is the women who take charge. If you are uncomfortable with Sergio and the other fellows speaking openly first, please say so and we will try to make appropriate allowances while we are here."

She laughed, "Well, I can see that there are going to be innumerable cultural differences between us and the outer-world. I should ask if you and your fellow women are as knowledgeable as your men on these affairs are? Are you allowed to make the critical decisions?"

Lisa replied, "The two engineers, Beni and Lene, are equals, though their expertise differs greatly. On some things, it would be wise to listen to him. As far as the trade negotiations are concerned, it is Vito who must make the final decisions, Lucinda is more of a housewife, similar to the role of your men here, I believe. Sergio is most competent and very able; back home he holds a powerful position and I am his Protector. That is, it is my duty to guard him against all enemies and threats. He is one of the keenest observers in all Velona. Will this be tricky for you and your people?"

Andrea smiled, "Well, it seems that a compromise is in order. Our people will have to accept Sergio, Beni, and Vito as valid speakers, if they will dress appropriately as our men do."

"Accepted, Monarch Andrea," Sergio agreed.

"Please, just Andrea. Around here, we do not dwell on titles."

Anders spoke up, "Well, Sergio, I was so hoping that your men would agree to wear proper men's clothing while you are here. I and my son are excellent dress makers and tailors. We make all the clothing worn by those at the palace. We would be honored to outfit your party. In anticipation of such, Johan and I have prepared and gathered together much of what will be needed. Unless you have distinct preferences for colors, we will get your party presentable in no time. Since you will be staying with us, the women's suits should be white, unless the engineers would prefer something darker that doesn't show the dirt as readily."

Lisa replied, "Thanks, Anders, that would be most welcome. White is fine for Lucinda and myself. Lene probably ought to be dark, since she and Beni will be doing quite a lot of setup work to get all the many items we've brought to you fully operational." He nodded understandingly. She grinned at Sergio, "As for my husband here, I'd love to see him in a bright red gown, if that is an acceptable color." He chuckled.

"Ah, excellent choice," Anders winked at Lisa.

"Vito probably would like a rich blue, since that is the predominate colors of Velona's rulers. Beni's ought to be dark as well, is black acceptable?" she asked. It was and then the palace came into view.

When the carriage stopped, Sergio and Lisa watched carefully the unspoken protocol that was being followed. Andrea opened the door and stepped down first, leaning back inside so that Anders had a shoulder to support himself as he very carefully descended the low step. Lisa then emulated her, though now, Sergio certainly didn't need her shoulder.

As they surveyed the four large, interconnecting buildings that comprised the Royal Palace, others came out to meet them. The huge gardens lay behind them while the buildings stretched out before the group. Princess Hedda was introduced followed by Johan. "Our Finance Minister, Jutta Knut and her husband Halder and their daughter Kristen. This is our guest from Alia, Alexina Phanes." After the introductions and brief words about who was in charge of what among the six, Andrea, Anders holding on to her, led them inside and showed them to their rooms and where the bathrooms were located.

Anders said, "If you will all relax and bathe, Johan and I will come around with proper outfits for you all. It is customary in our country for men to dress our women. While they are perfectly capable of dressing themselves, it is an honor for men to do this for them. If you are not comfortable with this, please say so and we'll make other arrangements."

"Thanks, Anders, that will be most welcome. I would love to have a real bath after three months on the caravel!" Lisa said heartily. Her sentiments were echoed by the others.

"Once you are bathed and dressed, we will give you a complete tour of the palace," Andrea explained.

Two hours later, Lisa, wearing a white satin suit with twin tails and a lacy sash tied under her collar, started at Sergio as he, holding onto Anders for dear life, came slowly into the room. "Wow, Sergio, you look scrumptious! Really hot, dear." Anders grinned — his work was appreciated, he felt.

"Dear, I certainly hope so! I can't breathe and I can't walk," he complained.

"Oh don't be silly, we women do this for you fellows back home all the time. Here, hold onto me. Remember, dear, small steps." He faked a grimace and Anders chuckled, leaving them until the grand tour.

Slowly the two headed out into the hall to check on the others. Sergio whispered, "Beni is going to have an awful time doing what he must do. We're going to have to get his arrangements altered. Lene is not going to be able to do all of his work for him."

"I figured as much. I think that we can work out a compromise with Andrea for him," she whispered. "At least you won't have a hard time allowing me to do the leading, dear." He flashed her a fake moan and gave her a kiss. She whispered, "Just you wait until I get you in bed tonight."

"Don't we look weird," Vito commented as he held on to Lucinda as they joined the others. Beni just grumbled about not being able to do his work.

"Ah, you are ready," Andrea said as she came looking for her guests. "My, you all do clean up well. Your men look positively civilized. Come, this way, the teamsters are bringing the first of your crates here. The Exhibition Hall is this way."

All six got a quick education in load handling by the teamster women of Zeederlund. Essentially, when the caravel's crew unloaded a crate onto the docks, the women had it set down on a rollers base — a four foot wide six foot long wooden contraption with ten bars spaced evenly down its length. Each bar held a dozen metal rollers, a disk with a hole through which the bar passed. Thus, a couple of women could push the crate along the rollers base or by fastening the crate to its frame and push the whole thing along on the many rollers. By using a series of block and tackles affixed to a large yoke-like base — the number of pulleys varying depending upon the weight to be lifted — one woman could easily lift the crate.

"Absolute genius!" Beni exclaimed as he watched the women unloading the wagons with the yoke-cranes, as they were called, placing the crates on the rolling base. Lene began the first of hundreds of engineering sketches that she would ultimately bring back to Velona. She realized that the knowledge these women possessed could greatly benefit all women in the world, men too.

Lene, between sketches, explained, "Monarch Andrea, Beni and I will need several days to get everything unpacked and assembled. The motor-wagon, for example, had to be broken down into a couple of parts for shipping, since we brought along so many inventions. Our caravels are only so big, you see. Once we have everything setup properly, we will give you and everyone who is interested a complete presentation."

Andrea, her daughters, and Jutta wandered off with the two engineers, chatting about just what all they had brought. Lucinda and Vito followed politely after them.

"And you must be Alexina. I am Sergio Bartiana, my wife, Lisa, our son Bartolo." The young teen had remained a bit hesitant with the arrival of the strangers. In truth, she felt self-conscious about her unusual appearance. While she had grown accustomed to those here in the palace, these were strangers from far off Velona.

"Yes, that's ve. I hove you can understand ve well enough," she said shyly.

"Sure, we knew a couple of women who had lip plates similar to yours. Both just could not talk at all well in the Demokritos tongue or ours in Velona. However, the Annelise dialect makes drastically less usage of the lips in forming their sounds," he replied.

"I just wanted to ve a verson, not a thing," she said. "Were they avle to ve a verson?"

"Oh my, yes, Alexina. Right now, about half of old Demokritos is in a bad way with their women as well as Tashien. Unfortunately for you, Alia is part of the bad ones. Women are treated as people nearly everywhere else, though of course, there are always some bad apples in any city who mistreat their women," he explained.

"Lisa and I came here purposely to give you our gift of therapy, which women who have suffered this horrible plague really need."

"I av okay, really, vut can it do anything for vy livs?" she asked.

Lisa answered, "We'll just have to see. At least any residual trauma that you may have can be erased. Now, Sergio is much more skilled at doing our therapy than I am. However, if you would prefer not to have a man giving you your sessions, I will be glad to do it."

"I don't vind, though I don't think I need it. I just wanted to ve a verson, not a thing," she replied. They chatted while they slowly walked to join the others.

An hour later at the first state dinner held in honor of their special guests from Velona at which the many ministers who aided Monarch Andrea in running Zeederlund smoothly were introduced. Sergio, Vito, and Beni found themselves at the center of attention and gossip. They were bombarded with questions. How do you like wearing proper, civilized clothing? Do men and women in the outer-world really wear the opposite clothes? Don't you feel more natural now that you are wearing clothing that men are supposed to wear? Do men really do all the work that we women do here, and if so, what is left for women to do to earn their own self-respect and keep? Vito, half expecting this, was prepared and played his role as perfect diplomat.

Lisa and Lucinda were bombarded with questions from the women ministers. Don't women have a true say in the governing of their countries? How can your women possibly be content with only doing a man's work, caring for the family? Now honestly, look at your men now; aren't they just incredibly handsome and sexy in their proper dresses? Do you women *really* just primarily do domestic chores?

Lisa and Lucinda were quite thankful that Lene was with them. "Oh not at all, some of us are engineers and inventors. Many of us have very good jobs with the DAE company, that's the Dianna-Arsenio Enterprises named after perhaps the two most famous inventors in Velona. Now myself, I am keenly interested in the new electricity and all the uses to which it can be made. My fiancé, Beni is mostly interested in the steam engine power systems and the uses to which that can be put, you see. While we have very different interests, we complement each other."

She chatted on, "Besides, from what I have seen here today, your women have invented so many highly useful machines to allow us to do so very much more than we women of the outer-world. Honestly, you have been at it for over a thousand years, I'm told, while we women of the north have only had a couple of years to deal with our lack of arms. Please, you must allow us some years to create such workable machines as you have here. Already, Beni and I have begun to sketch some of the remarkable machines and tools that you have created here to allow you to do things unheard of in Velona."

Thanks to Lene, by the time for after-dinner tea, the six were accepted, based heavily on the fact that Lene seemed to fit their ideas for the role of women in society and that we have had only a few years to deal with being armless. While Lisa sensed that none of these women could honestly imagine what their lives would be like if they had arms, she did see that they accepted the short time span explanation for it seemed to make sense in their minds.

The three men, however, just could not get used to chatting solely about domestic issues, which was about all that Anders and the other husbands chatted — that and fancy dresses and shoes. Johan wondered why more of our men did not continue wearing the exotic ballet boots given to the by the aliens. "Our women and girlfriends find them so sexy on us," he explained.

While the two engineers worked on setting up the large demonstration of the inventions that they brought, Vito and Lucinda began their work. First, they needed to establish just what the resources of this island actually were and on what their economy was based and how it operated. Vito was under strict orders from Stefano and me to not take any actions until he fully understood the underpinnings of this country.

It didn't take long for Beni to discover that the island was the result of an ancient volcanic eruption shooting through many sedimentary rock formations. This meant that on the western side of the island, large coal seams had been upthrust by the eruption. Surface mines in this area produced the coal that was used for heating and cooking. The rich soil provided abundant crops and pasture lands for horses, cattle, and sheep, though all three species were vastly different from those we had in Velona. The horses were smaller, on par with those found in the Northern Steppes, except here they had thick, shaggy manes to help them through the cold winters.

On the other hand, their ancient history was Sergio's second interest, after of course the handling of Alexina. These people still had religious ties to Partholan, one of the two original creators of the animal species, which we call humans. Chatting with Julie who was very knowledgeable on their history, he learned all that was known about those early days. Unfortunately, most was stories told down through the ages until someone began writing them down nearly five hundred years after the fact. However, he did glean a key piece of information from Julie, which these people did not know because of their limited knowledge of the rest of Tarra.

Sergio speculated that originally, their ancestors actually sailed from the Western Continent and probably passed this very island on their way to the Southern Continent's eastern shores, now called Annelise. Thus when the Second Exodus came, Zabina led her group eastward back to Zeederlund, which they already knew existed. This made much more sense to us, because this remote island was so far from Annelise that it would have been a miracle for Zabina to have otherwise found it. It was a month's sailing from Annelise.

On the second morning after their arrival, Sergio began therapy sessions with Alexina. "Alexina, I know that this is not your primary language. I also speak your language fairly well."

"Yes, vut you won't ve avle to understand ve if I sveak it," she explained, worried that this would become a problem for her again.

"Alexina, you must trust me. If you find that you cannot fully describe something to me in Annelise, please say it in your own language. I will be able to understand you. Trust me on this point. I have known other women who had lip plates such as yours and I was able to understand them anyway. Trust me on this." She agreed, but did not believe him at all, because she couldn't understand a word that she said in her own language.

They began with the first moment that she could contact when her father had slipped something into her drink to knock her out. The first time through it, she slipped right over the whole time that she was unconscious and having the operation, wading through all the after-effects, pain, and fear that followed until she arrived here in Zeederlund. After ten passes through all of this fear and travail, she began to unravel the period of unconsciousness, beginning with her father's work in putting on the many rings around her neck. After a couple more times through it, she contacted the heavier pain of the slicing of her lips and finally got the doctor's pronouncement. "There, that will keep her quiet and under your control now!"

While Alexina experienced a good deal of relief, the trauma failed to erase fully. On the fifth day of therapy sessions, Sergio asked for an earlier trauma that was similar. She immediately went to having her ears pierced and the monstrously long and heavy brass earrings inserted. While she experienced even more relief, the traumas still did not erase. Alexina just continued to say, "I want to ve a verson, not a thing."

In their bedroom that night, an exasperated Sergio said, "If I hear her say I just want to be a person one more time, I think I'll scream. Honestly, how can any of us *be* a person? We can be a bricklayer, a farmer, a teamster, a wife, a leader, a soldier. What she is really trying to say is that she wants to be accepted in society around her as a person with her own goals and purposes in life and not be someone's sexual slave."

"Of course, dear, but you know that you simply cannot tell her that. It would be an evaluation of her and one of the worst possible things you can do for someone. She has to find this out herself," Lisa pointed out.

"I know, I know. I am sure that that phrase is the key to unlocking her whole trauma case. Tomorrow, I aim to use that phrase to blow her case apart," Sergio declared.

The next morning, he ran Alexina through the earrings trauma once more and then asked her for something that was both earlier in time and similar. She could find nothing. "Okay, Alexina. I want you to start saying over and over I just want to be a person. Can you do that?"

"I just want to ve a verson. I just want to ve a verson. I just want to ve a verson." She shrieked, and un-phased, Sergio continued to run her through what had just come up, an earlier trauma incident. (To avoid confusion, I am correcting her b's, m's, p's, and v's.)

"I'm floating around. Down there, I see my body. It's dead. I'm pulled towards the white light. I fight it, but I can't stop being pulled into it. I hear an order to get a new baby body. I fly through space and swoop down on my mother. She is having a baby. I go into its head. I just want to be a person again. Now I am a person again," she related to Sergio.

After a couple more times through, Alexina became cheerful about it and began laughing. "I am not a body! I am me! I have lived before!" she exclaimed her startling, eye opening revelation. Sergio end that session for now. After lunch, Alexina had slipped from her cheerfulness back into sadness, and Sergio knew that there was far more here to be faced. He picked up where they had left off.

After repeating the phrase a few more times, Alexina found something even earlier. Soon, she began laughing. "I saw them! I'm a servant in the Queen's Court in Alia. She has three brown skinned women from somewhere in the far north. They have even larger lip plates than I have! Neckbands. They wear the same neck rings that I had on. They're very kind to my Queen, very bright, very smart, but they do not ever speak. They can't speak, as I can hardly speak. So that's where my dad and the doctor got the idea from! Wow! I remember now. They're Utu Princesses." Again, Sergio had to end the session; she was just too cheerful and happy to continue, reveling in her discovery.

Sergio knew that there was far more to all of this. He'd seen into her mind and saw a huge black mass of unseen trauma lying there. Thus, he was not surprised to find that she had once more sunk down in emotional tone by the next morning. Still, that she was improving by large strides was clearly visible to all those in the palace.

The next morning, Sergio again had her repeat that phrase of hers. She ran headlong into the black mass, just as he had hoped. She began speaking in her native language, and he had to use telepathy to understand what she was saying, her speech was simply unintelligible, just as Dita and my speech had been when we had the lip plates.

Sergio wiped the sweat off his face when they finally ended for the day. Alexina was just too exhausted to continue. She had run square into the mantis creatures and had an traumatic incident in which the mantis and their machines electronically blasted her, apparently scrambling all her memories. The inability to place one mental image after or before the next one in sequence had driven them both off the rails that afternoon. Still, both had stuck to it until she became too tired to continue.

For two more days, the two continued to unscramble this massive trauma incident until at last they had it pieced together. In the end, it was simple, she ran into the mantis. They had electronically zapped her, swept an electronic beam of some kind over her memories, convincing her they were in total chaos. When she was completely confused, they ordered her to get a new baby body. When it died, she was to follow the white light, report to them, and then go get another baby body.

"I feel a thousand vounds lighter now," Alexina exclaimed as they ended the session. "Now I can ve a verson." While she was cheerful, Sergio was not! There was that damnable phrase coming out yet again! He knew more must lay behind this still.

The next day, they continued from where they had left off. Alexina continued to find more incidents in which she had attempted to battle the mantis creatures, though in these earlier ones, she had not been so badly harmed. Mostly, she had been zapped unconscious and awakened to find herself in the ocean, at which point, she promptly said I must be a person and took off to get another baby body.

During their evening session, while repeating that phrase yet another time, the earliest time on the chain of traumatic incidents appeared. Once more, the vocabulary she had of the Annelise language was insufficient and she spoke in her own tongue. Sergio simply continued with his telepathic connection to grasp what she was saying to him.

"I don't understand this at all. How can this be?"

"Just tell me what you are seeing as you go along, Alexina."

"I am just a being. I don't need or use any of these animal bodies. I think that I somehow helped make them. He and I are making them for this world. Then, the mantis came and started altering our creations. Plus, oh my god!" She began laughing hysterically. It was several minutes before Sergio was able to find out what she had seen and realized.

"One day, I accidentally had a sensory beam on two of our animals who were breeding. I felt these incredible sexual sensations coming from their bodies. I got hooked on it and secretly decided that I wanted to be one of these persons so I could experience that incredible sensations. I told Partholan that I was going out to put an end to the mantis messing with our creations, but really, I was going to grab one of our animal bodies and experience that sexual sensation. I got hooked on it, like a drug, so to speak." She continued to laugh and laugh.

All the next day, she continually broke into fits of laughter. Her vitality returned, Alexina was a new "woman" after that. More importantly, everyone in the palace saw the incredible changes in her and began wondering about this new therapy that Sergio was delivering. Perhaps there was something to it after all.

A day later, Alexina confided in Sergio, "I kevt saying that I wanted to ve a verson. That is ridiculous. You can't ve a verson. You *can* ve a doctor, a fishervan, a housewife. What I was really trying to say is that I want to ve accevted as a verson and not as soveone's slave. God, it is a viracle that I didn't end uv in soveone's whorehouse. If so, I would have vrovavly vecove addicted to it and truly lost vyself covvletely! You have saved vy life, Sergio!"

She then sat up like a rocket. "Sergio! No wonder I was attracted to the Standing Stones at the cerevony here. Our vase was veneath one of those vower voints, sovewhere uv north! I wonder what havvened to him? Vartholan, that is."

Sergio smiled. "He is still there waiting for you to return to him. Bethany and we found him. He was in bad shape, almost to the point where he too would have become convinced that he was one of your animal bodies. We are giving him therapy sessions, just as I have been giving to you. He is recovering his true spiritual abilities once more. I give you my promise that we will continue to work with you as well, so that you can regain the abilities that you once had. May I contact him for you and let him know that we have at last found his Dalny?"

"Yes, that is what I called vyself. Dalny. Vlease, vlease let hiv know that I av here. I av no longer worthy of hiv, vut I long to see hiv once again."

Sergio contacted me, and I contacted Macario, who contacted Partholan, who came to me. I took him down to Sergio, who presented Alexina to him and we left them alone for a time. Whew, what a lot of vias on that line. Hovering over Sergio, I resisted the temptation to tease him about his bright red dress. Instead, he filled me in on what he'd discovered with Alexina.

Dalny! Oh how I have longed for this day. I have missed you more than I can possibly say.

Me too, but I have failed you, Partholan! I — I lied to you. I went off to get one of our animals so I could enjoy their sexual sensations and I was hooked on it. I did fight the mantis creatures several times, but I always lost. Now I am so unworthy of you. I have lost all of my abilities. I cannot even move much out of its head.

I was nearly to that point myself. Bethany and Macario — they have rescued me. Their therapy — it has been restoring my native skills and abilities. You must let them help you some more. I will beg them to continue working with you so you can regain all that you have lost too, my precious Dalny.

Will they do this for us?

Yes, these are the spiritual beings that the others dumped here on our world, forcing them into the heads of our creations. Now, Macario is getting those spiritual beings salvaged and back up to where they no longer need our creations. One day, he says that he will have all the beings freed and we can have our creations back.

We must find a way to help them, Partholan. I was lost utterly until Sergio came to me, giving me his therapy. I own him everything. We must help them and this Macario.

You are right. We must do this. Now that I have found you again, I am able to come and visit with you anytime I want. I will be with you as often as I can. You talk to Sergio and I will talk with Macario. We will help them somehow, my precious Dalny.

Thus, on November 8, 824, Dalny and Partholan were reunited after all these centuries. Now came decisions. Partholan suggested to Macario that he might be able to create arms on the female bodies now. However, Macario decided against it. Why? Three reasons. One, Partholan and Dalny had created the original females as they now were and Macario didn't what them to undergo another round of losing their arms again. Second, with all the new inventions coming out of Velona and with the incredible mechanical means being employed by the women of Zeederlund, he wanted to give these a chance to fully take hold throughout the world. Third, the Church of God therapy project, the giving of the Holy Gift, was beginning to look like it might just work, getting millions onto the path that led to total spiritual freedom. He feared that if women regained their arms, the urgency of getting others onto the path and getting them to walk it would be lowered significantly. Thus, the two decided to allow more time to pass.

Alexina now had to make a decision. Sergio explained, "Yes, Alexina, Lisa and I can train you so that you can deliver these Basic Therapy sessions which are called the Holy Gift. However, this therapy is limited in that the person must have some physical pain and unconsciousness or severe losses to which it can be applied. Here in Zeederlund, there is very little of that, most people here are doing well in life, the complete opposite of the outer-world. Thus, these people here need someone who can provide them with a much more advanced form of therapy. Neither Bethany nor I are so trained. Macario will be sending some others here who are and who can help free these people here."

Sergio continued, "As far as yourself is concerned, yes, I will continue to help you erase any other traumas that we can discover. However, you, like me and Lisa, need what is called Advanced Therapy in order to recover our forgotten spiritual abilities. That is what Macario has been giving to Partholan. Bethany ran his first session, removing the huge loss trauma that he had over losing you, Dalny. After that, Macario took over with Advanced Therapy."

He went on, "Your Queen Katerine is now delivering therapy sessions. She is in exile in Annelise, having just barely escaped with her life when the chaos of the plague struck Alia. She has with her a number of people who are giving her Advanced Therapy. If you were to return to Annelise and join up with her, your queen, I am sure that you would be able to get your Advanced Therapy there on a routine basis. While you could opt to return to Alia, with your lip plates, speech will become a huge barrier and the country is still in complete chaos. In Annelise, you would be far better off."

"That is encouraging, I could helv vy Queen. Here, I av very vuch still an outsider. I av suvvosed to ve looking for a vrofession. Hedda and Iduna are already working on learning theirs, vut I don't want to ve doing what I velieve is a van's work. I've watched vany of the vrofessional woven here and so vany of thev vake use of their teeth in gravving sovething. That I can't do anyvore. Here in Zeederlund, I av really just veing suvvorted vy all these kind ven and woven. I think that it is right that I join vy Queen Katerine."

Thus, in early November, Sergio and Lisa notified me that they needed to take Alexina back to Annelise. From there, the two could return to Velona at last.

Meanwhile, a week after they arrived, Beni and Lene had everything set up and reassembled. Sergio and Vito were very impressed with the professionalism displayed by Beni and Lene. He allowed her to operate and display most of the inventions. First, they used our old toy steam train that used to go around our house at 42 Hampton Way. This was the prototype for the much larger trains, which were far too difficult to transport this far, to say nothing of the heavy tracks, which would have to be laid just to demonstrate the concept of steam powered trains. With our prototype, Lene gave everyone rides around one of their buildings and was a terrific hit.

Lene then drove them in the motor-wagon, which was just as impressive. She followed that with the T-putt-putts. Beni then explained the concept of the steam powered electric generator and fired it up. Lene had installed temporary lights in the Exhibition Hall and had Andrea flip the switch, which turned them on. The electric vacuuming machine was a hit with the men as was the clothes washer, which had a temporary water supply and drain hooked up so that it could work. The telefono system was also a big hit.

While Sergio was off delivering therapy, Vito and Lucinda were working out trading arrangements. Beni and Lene continued to give complete demonstrations to hundreds of other key personnel. Messengers were sent to the other towns and their leaders and staff began to arrive for a demonstration as well. By the end of November, at last all the key personnel in the country had seen the incredible inventions.

When Sergio and Lisa announced that they would soon be heading back, Beni and Lene wanted to stay. Beni explained, "Look, here we are vitally needed. They need our help in getting all these new inventions working and factories built. We've so much ground work to do here that we simply must stay for a couple more years." They gave Sergio two hundred fifty sketches to take back to Giovanni and Lucianna.

Lene added, "Monarch Andrea has promised to marry us next month. Isn't that great?"

Lucinda and Vito also decided to stick around for at least another year. They wanted to help get everything worked out properly with Velona's newest trading partner. "Besides, we have an LD radio with us and can let you all know if anyone tries to invade Zeederlund," he pointed out.

"We love it here," Lucinda added. "Unlike the constant hustle and bustle of Velona, here, everything is quiet and laid back. People are so kind and friendly, and there is no crime at all. They don't even have a policeman in the whole country." Sergio later pointed out to me that overall, Zeederlund was almost a cheerful society, always in mild interest as a group. That contrasted sharply with the incredibly low emotional tones of Alia, for example, and Tashien, where people were only a shade above death.

When Alexina announced that she would be returning to her world with Sergio and Lisa, Johan was the most upset. He had fallen for her, but his young love was also tempered by his own observations. Johan was well aware of her inability to latch onto a professional career path from which she could support a family. Because of this, he accepted her decision and praised her for it, telling her that he thought that she had made the right decision. Still, he wanted her to succeed and brought the metalworkers who had enlarged her plates for her back to the palace once more.

"I see that your plates are drooping again, Alexina, so I invited the metal workers back to enlarge them again. It won't do for you to go away to a new place with them drooping so badly. Plus, I wanted to give you a going away present. They are going to give you a set of tools so you can make these alterations whenever you need them done. Who knows if you can find anyone in the outer-world who can do this properly for you. I want you always to be at your best, Alexina. Remember me always as I will you."

"Thank you, Johan. You have veen the vest to ve," she replied, touching her lips to his, the best that she could do to kiss him. The metalworkers showed her exactly what to do and how to do it. They even insisted that she enlarge them this time by herself, under their expert guidance. When she finished, her plates were now about five inches across, almost year after she had her surgery. What a year this has been, she thought. I came from the depths of despair to salvation. Now I must learn to do this for many others, she resolved.

On December 1, 824, a caravel docked to unload more materials for the beginning work of the enormous MMCE plan that Vito and Andrea had worked out. Two of Macario's Church of God members, both women, came with them, laying the groundwork for the church's therapy work on Zeederlund.

Three days later, the caravel set sail with Sergio, Lisa, little Bartolo, and Alexina aboard. Destination: Viborg, Annelise, then on home to Velona. Once the ship set sail, Sergio, having born the laughter of the crew over his women's dress, finally got to change out of it and into his own clothes. Unfortunately, having worn those heels for so long, it took nearly a month before he could really plant his feet flat on the deck.

As they relaxed on deck, Sergio commented, "You know, those Zeederlund folks may have something in their societal arrangement, Lisa. It is darn hard for women in our society to care easily for their babies and young children. In their society, the men easily do these things. I wonder if that played a role in the evolution of the Zeederlund society?"

"You have a valid point, dear. I don't know what I would have done without your constant help with Bartolo," Lisa replied.

On January 1, 825, Alexina joined up with Queen Katerine in Viborg, Annelise. There she began to receive her Advanced Therapy, while she joined them in giving the Holy Gift to countless other Annelise women.

Chapter 43 Heavy Darkness Over Alia

During this time span in which Katerine and Barbara found refuge from the chaos in Alia at the Dorota Church of God, Viborg, back in Alia, General Atlas Erebos had taken charge, declaring martial law as expected of him in a crisis. For him, everything now was beyond right and wrong; it was rule by his soldiers, who took what they wanted and doled out lifesaving food to the populace. By official decree, most women the capital city of Levkos and the port of Preveza, went naked. Clothes no longer fit and the general saw no way to alleviate the situation. Most women never ventured out of their homes anyway and often convinced their husbands to at least put their nightgowns on them, very unwilling to be completely naked.

The situation only grew darker and darker, for men and especially for the women there. For a long time, I felt powerless to assist these people. The last we heard, General Atlas Erebos was ruling Alia, having declared martial law shortly after the plague struck.

General Erebos, now thirty-six, stormed around the Royal Palace. Queen Katerine and her despicable offspring had entirely vanished without a trace. One by one, his soldiers crawled up to him to report. "Damnable woman anyway! Where can she have gone? One of you aides must have secreted her out of the palace last night. Which one of you did so?" he demanded of the six older men, the aides of the late King Stathis.

All six denied any part in the disappearance. Two aides, who were more closely allied with her and whom General Erebos suspected of having done the deed, not only denied it, but went so far as to suggest that the general himself had disposed of her and her five year old daughter. "Look, she rightfully owns the throne of Alia, not yourself," one had declared. That was his last declaration. General Erebos fired both of them, though he resisted having them shot. They might yet hold a clue to her whereabouts. For months, he ordered soldiers to spy on their actions, hoping that one of the two would lead him to her.

In the meantime, he ordered a citywide search for Queen Katerine. Soon, however, his attention was forced upon the rioting and looting taking place within the capital city of Levkos. "Damn them all. We are in crisis mode!" he yelled to his majors and the remaining four aides. "We are beyond right and wrong. Hell, there is no more right and wrong. There must be and will be order around here! My orders are that any and all looters and rioters are to be executed on the spot!"

"But General Erebos, perhaps some of them are out of food and are just trying to get something for their families to eat," one of King Stathis' aides replied.

"We will setup food distribution centers. Majors, let's review the map and establish a dozen such locations. The men who need food can crawl there and get some. Have your men finished getting a hold of all the storehouses?" They had. In Alia, food was now doled out to those who came to one of the twelve distribution centers. Most were located in farmers' market squares, now devoid of the farmers.

Looting continued, though at a slower, more cautious pace. The thieves merely waited until the soldiers left an area before breaking in and taking what they desired. At least the dead bodies did not pile up in the streets as they had in so many other kingdoms. By December, the general gave up on finding Queen Katerine. She had apparently either died somewhere or disappeared completely. No trace was ever found of her.

However, aides now began bringing additional problems to his attention. Many had been contacted by concerned citizens, especially the noblemen. "Damn the stupid women! If they all want to become Holy Women of the Church, why, let them! We have vastly more serious problems to solve or we will all perish!"

"So what are your orders?" one asked.

"Proclamation One. All women will put their own clothing on or go naked. Two, all women will at least feed themselves. We cannot have our valuable men being pulled away from their vital duties just to feed and dress them. Hell, there are no dressmakers who can make clothing to fit them anyway. They will just have to tough it out like the rest of us. If they cannot cook their own food, then they can wait until some husband can."

Dismally and slowly, life continued in Alia. A mile and a half from the Royal Palace, Nobleman Olympos Stathis, the brother of the late king, lived in a huge manor house. The stately grounds covered three acres; an ornate iron fence surrounded it, though it was decorative and did not offer protection. For that, he depended, prior to the plague, on a dozen bodyguards and a handful of servants and staff for his family's protection and needs. Olympos was the wealthiest man in all Alia, now that his father had died and also his brother, the king. The entire Stathis empire fell into his hands, along with its vast wealth.

Indeed, the throne of Alia had long been in the Stathis family. However, Olympos was more interested in making money than ruling, which is why his brother had become king. Short lived, he thought.

Somehow, Olympos kept his family alive during those first two debilitating months of the plague. He had insisted that some of his guards and staff return, staying here in his manor house. They were told to bring along their families as well. Thus, well-armed and with sufficient men around, the looters gave his three acres a wide berth, especially after they shot and killed a dozen men who tried to loot the estate.

Melita, his wife of some fifteen years and herself being thirty-four, struggled mightily with the debilitating effects of the plague. She had always worn only the finest dresses, doing her part to cast Olympos as being the very best in Alia. Before the plague, she wore her wavy brown hair rather long, but now it reached to the small of her back as well. The two had four children. Orpheus was sixteen and the undisputed heir to the entire Stathis empire. His three daughters, Niki, fifteen, Antheia, thirteen, and Andromeda, twelve, were promised substantial dowries when they married another nobleman chosen by Olympos. To date, he'd found no suitable suitors for his daughter's hands and now they had none to give. Perhaps this was just as well, since he really didn't want to give up so much money for their dowries.

Niki had long black hair with charming eyes. Antheia's wavy hair was light brown, like her mother's. Andromeda's dark brown hair was perfectly straight and thick, parted down the middle. Since the plague, all the women now kept their hair trimmed at the small their backs. Olympos decried the official proclamations, however. He saw to it that the four women were at least wearing some clothing, mostly their loose fitting nightgowns for now. He and Orpheus helped them to eat in a civilized manner, defying both official proclamations.

The sole serious problem facing Olympos was financial. Since the plague, none of his businesses reopened. Some had been looted, and he lost all stock in those. Most of his employees did not report to work, at least during the first two months. When their feet returned to normal, he was very hopeful that finally, his many businesses would revitalize and begin making money once more. Such was far from the case!

No one wanted to buy fancy jewelry, one of his more profitable businesses. While his gold and gem mines reopened, no one was buying the gold or gems. Worse still, no foreign orders came to him from the port city of Preveza or from anywhere else! Before the plague, the per capita income of Alia was the highest of any of the seven kingdoms. Now that changed dramatically. An economic crash of unparalleled proportions ensued.

True, the farmers did well, as did coal miners. Even the bronze makers had some orders for new housewares coming in. The whalers still found a demand for their oil and byproducts, and the fishermen found steady work. Before the plague, these were some of the lowest, menial of trades, the "relatively poor" of Alia. Countrywide, this economic downturn struck with a vengeance. Thus, Olympos took the position of we'll just hunker down and ride out this storm.

Still, he continued to send messages about the plight of the women of Alia to the aides of the late king. He retained a power position with them, since he had had a hand in getting them their positions with his brother. Many owed him favors of magnitude. Thus, the plight of the women of Alia continued to be brought up during meetings with General Erebos.

"Okay, let's get some young, pretty women back here in the Royal Palace," the general finally assented. "They sure as hell cannot actually do anything, but we'll give them token positions on the staff. That ought to appease the noblemen."

In March of 824, Niki, who had just turned sixteen, received an official appointment as a Royal Attendant to the Court of Alia and a stipend of a hundred gold a month. Each day, Orpheus drove his sister to the palace and picked her up each evening. No woman dared walk the streets of Levkos alone. There were too many reports of women being abducted, though no one had any proof of who was behind the kidnappings. Though he didn't like to, Orpheus also dressed his oldest sister in her nightgown each morning and brushed her hair for her, after feeding her breakfast, which one of their new manservants prepared.

Niki soon complained about her pointless job. "Dad, all I do is sit around, look pretty, and smile. They don't have me doing anything at all."

"Well, dear, that is understandable isn't it? What can you do now?" he replied somewhat bitterly. Taking care of his four women was slowly taking its toll on him, though he loved his wife and three daughters.

Niki frowned; he was right. She couldn't actually do anything anymore anyway. "But dad, at lunchtime, they throw everything into a pie pan and make us eat it as if we are dogs. They don't even feed us," she protested further. Perhaps he could do something about this humiliation that she faced daily along with two dozen other young women, all of whom were Royal Attendants to the Court of Alia.

Dutifully, Olympos began making such suggestions to the aides, who in turn reported this to

General Erebos. As expected, he did not take kindly to "these incessant, irrelevant problems of the women." "Look, we have far more serious problems in Alia. While some men are back at work, the vast majority are still idle. Forget the damnable women, will you!"

When others began reporting the kidnaping of women, this he also completely ignored. "Look, that makes one less woman who is hobbling a man. Good riddance," was his reply.

By April, enough of the wealthier of Alia had put enough pressure on the general that he finally set aside two hours each day for public input. At these sessions, anyone could come before him and plead their case. Of course, just as soon as he relented and began holding these sessions, he regretted it. Women's issues continued to dominate. The many men who came tended to always ask for assistance with the needs and well-being of the women in their lives.

One afternoon, Doctor Morpheus came to speak with the general. "Sir, I have heard that you are having problems with the women of Alia."

"Well, you have heard that right! Damn creatures just don't shut up. They simply cannot see that we are facing monumental problems here in Alia, problems that dwarf their petty ones," General Erebos replied, suddenly becoming curious about this mild-mannered doctor.

"Well, sir, there is a way around the problem with the women. I brought along an old drawing," he replied quietly. He showed the general the drawing of the Utu Princesses from the old Royal Court. "If we construct them out of brass, this will put all of our metalworkers, coal miners, and ore smelters back to work big time. With these in place, I do not believe that they will be able to speak any longer."

"Ah ha! I suddenly see your key point! No speaking, no more bugging their husbands and fathers. Brilliant, Doctor Morpheus, absolutely brilliant. If I order all women to be so adorned, think of all the work for our metal industries! Why, they would have work for a year or more just making them!"

"Indeed they would. Sir, if we also set some of the cheaper gems into heavy brass settings for long, dangling earrings, this would aid our gems industry as well. Look at these drawings."

General Erebos smiled. He already knew what they ought to look like, because he'd given two pairs to the missing queen and her daughter. Oh how he like their appearance, and how the two women had complained about their ears nearly being pulled off. That would give the women something to think about! Anything to stop them from interfering with the men of Alia who must get back to profitable employment and soon!

Doctor Morpheus added, "I know that you have issued orders for women to eat out of a pie plate. However, with these ornaments, that will become impossible, I believe. Now in this old book, it alludes to the fact that women of that Dorota place use their feet to feed themselves. You should also issue just such an order, make it mandatory." He showed the general another passage, thankful that he had done his homework so thoroughly. The general was being more receptive to his notions than he had ever imagined.

"Ah ha! See, they are not as helpless as they all claim to be. I knew it! They are just trying to kill off the productivity of our valuable men! We need to act on this at once. Let's see. Yes, let's equip our twenty-five Royal Attendants to the Court of Alia. Let them set an example for all to follow. A showcase. Yes, how soon can you be ready to equip them? We should do them all at one time. Less complaining to endure," he suggested, imagining the bitter complaints he would receive from the others if only one were done at a time.

A week later, Doctor Morpheus arrived back at the Royal Palace in his buggy. He brought along twenty-five sets of the brass and cheap gemstone ornaments. By making them all with standardized dimensions, he had been able to farm out the contracts to many of the brass makers and jewelers. Plus, he had already learned a whole lot about the process. First, with the queen's teeth removed, the plates had drooped and looked ugly. With her daughter, the removal of her upper and lower two front teeth had allowed the plates to protrude horizontally, which looked attractive and like the old painting and drawings. Yet, with the modifications done to Alexina, all was perfect, no teeth needed to be removed, simplifying the process.

When all was ready, General Erebos assembled his Royal Attendants. "Ladies, tomorrow when you come here, you are to be prepared to stay here a week before returning home each evening. During that time, I will be presenting you each with some very special and valuable ornaments." While Niki asked just what these ornaments were, the general refused to answer, frowning at her. By now, she knew not to press the issue with him. She had seen enough of his fiery temper and outbursts.

The next morning, they were given a morning tea, laced with a knockout drug. Soon after that, Doctor Morpheus, two jewelers, and two bronze workers began their work. The jewelers punched small holes in the women's ear lobes, inserted the bronze rings and melted the joint to prevent their removal. Then three dangles were likewise affixed to each ring. Each dangle held a series of four gemstones surrounded by some ornate bronze work. Once attached, the bottom three rested on the woman's upper chest.

As a jeweler finished a woman, the bronze workers took over, bending the highly polished bronze rings around the woman's neck, sealing the joint, this time extremely well with hot metal before applying the next ring. The last ring then applied the actual vertical pressure, holding the neck nearly immobile, giving them the appearance of having an elongated neck, pressing down hard against their shoulder blades.

When they finished a woman, the doctor worked his magic. Using sterilized methods and knives, he set to work slicing their lips. Knowing the precise dimensions, since all the lip plates were made to the same specifications, this went rapidly. Guesswork was eliminated. By noon, he'd finished with the last woman and proceeded to clean up the bloody mess he'd made.

"I'll keep them sedated today and give the wounds time to heal up a bit. Of course, their reactions might be a bit wild at first, general," Doctor Morpheus explained.

That evening, he roused Niki first, since he'd done her first. Niki struggled to get up, but her usual motions didn't work. Her neck wouldn't move; her lips ached and throbbed in pain; she felt a dull pain in her ear lobes. Her eyes moved down and saw the shiny brass upper lip plate. Slowly she realized that somehow her lips were now around these four inch in diameter disks. She shrieked loudly.

"Here let me help you sit up. You might be a bit groggy from the sleeping drought that I gave you to spare you the pain of the minor surgery," Doctor Morpheus explained. He put his arm behind her neck and helped raise her up from the bed. As Niki came to a sitting position, her long, heavy, dangling earrings suddenly pulled their full weight on her ear lobes, distorting them somewhat as the cool metal and gemstones came to rest upon her upper chest. Each weighed about a pound. She shrieked again.

"What has happened to me? What have you done? My lips hurt badly. These earrings are too heavy. I can't bend my neck," Niki gushed out rapidly. Suddenly, she fell silent. She could not understand a single word that she had just said! Shock flooded over her youthful body like a tidal wave. What had he done to her?

"I'm sorry. Niki isn't it? I didn't understand a single thing that you just said. Want to try again? Here, let's show you how beautiful you now look with these fabulous new ornaments." He helped her up; though her legs shook, she was certain that her legs wouldn't hold her. A six-foot mirror was fastened to the far wall here in the women's quarters. He moved her into its view.

Niki repeated in a trembling voice, "What's happened to me? What have you done? My lips hurt badly. These earrings are too heavy. I can't bend my neck." Her shock and terror grew so much so that her legs nearly gave out as she saw her reflection in the mirror. "I can't speak anymore," she added, realizing the truth. The large metal lip plates prevented her lips from forming nearly all their words. Only strange sounds came out of her mouth. She couldn't even move her head. The neck rings held her head in a vice, forcing her to move her body to see from side to side or to bend at the waist to see downward. Worse, the disks blocked her forward line of sight, forcing her into a sharp bend just to see her feet. She screamed and began crying profusely.

"There, there, Niki. This is all for the best you see. I still cannot understand a word that you are saying. No one can now. Men will no longer be affected by things that you say. Your lips will heal in a few days and then you can go home," he explained, catching Niki as her legs finally did give out. Until this moment, Niki never realized that her language made extensive use of her lips. He carried the fainting woman over to her bed and sat her down.

Just then, General Erebos entered. "Ah, I see they are waking up, doctor. How are the results? My, she does look attractive — all that bronze so matches her complexion."

"Niki, tell the general how you like your new ornaments and earrings, please," Doctor Morpheus requested.

Sobbing, she said, "Horrible! I can't speak anymore. I can't move. What have you done to me? I can't live like this. I am a freak!" Of course, she couldn't understand anything that she had said; it was all guttural sounds. Words could not be made out at all.

"Why, perfect, Niki! I can't understand a single thing that you are saying. Now no one can. Perfect. Doctor, I am completely amazed. Well done indeed." He looked at the sobbing teenager and added, "One more thing Niki. From now on, you are to feed yourself using your feet. The women of Dorota used to have no trouble at all doing so, and I can't see any reason that you women cannot follow their example." He turned sharply on his heel and left the room feeling an immense weight had been lifted from his shoulders.

He went to his office in what used to be the king's private chambers and drafted a letter and a formal proclamation. Two of his captains copied the letter twenty-four more times. In part, it suggested that the parents of the woman could bring in more expensive gemstones for her earrings and they would be installed at no cost for them. Also, gold could be substituted for the brass in their earrings, if the gold was also provided. The proclamation was very carefully worded.

Women's Adornment and Ornamentation Project One

When called, all women and girls aged five and up are to be brought to the Ornamentation Centers to receive their new and fancy ornaments. At that time, they can bring along any particular gemstones that they desire to be set in their new and exotic earrings. A total of thirty gemstones can be brought, though more can be accommodated if longer earrings are desired. Additionally, if the woman desires to substitute real gold for the bronze in her earrings, bring along thirty-two ounces of gold as well.

The government of Alia will defray the expense of the ornaments, but only inexpensive gemstones and brass will be used for her earrings.

This is a mandatory order for all women from five on up. No exceptions, no extenuating circumstances will be considered. We want our women to be stunningly beautiful.

Anyone resisting this order when a specific woman is ordered to the Ornamentation Centers will be shot. No exceptions. Protest and you may expect to be summarily executed. We are facing the worst crisis that Alia has ever faced. Together, we will survive and overcome all obstacles.

General Atlas Erebos

With numerous copies of the proclamation made, he had his soldiers begin posting them throughout Levkos. During May, he and his aides began the operation. A dozen centers were constructed strategically located around the city. Contracts and specifications were drawn up and given to every bronze worker in the city, though it took many weeks to reach all them. Likewise, all jewelers were given similar contracts, with payment funds drawn on the main Alia account with the Banca del Dio. Subsidiary contracts were sent out to the mines and smelters and to those working the coalfields. By June, production at the centers reached their maximum capacity, each one handling two dozen women every other day, though all women had to remain at the centers for five days until the doctors were convinced that no infections had arisen.

The day that Niki and the two dozen others were allowed to return to their homes, the formal proclamations were posted. As the women sat around the palace dinner table this final evening before being sent home, General Erebos commented, "My lovely Royal Attendants, you all look positively stunning. My compliments on your new looks. I must say that I did not realize what a difference this has made in your postures! You all have perfect postures! Incredible. Well done, my ladies."

"We can't move or eat," Niki tried to say, but gave up as her words were no better than before.

"What's that you are saying, lovely Niki? You too are very pleased with your new ornaments?" General Erebos could not refrain from teasing the poor teen who could not even shake her head no.

Unable to bend their necks and with their central forward vision blocked by their lip plates, the women found trying to even see the plates of food before them nearly impossible. Only with much trial and error and numerous spills did they even manage to get a little food into their mouths.

That night when Orpheus came to pick up his sister, he cried out, "Oh my god, Niki! What have they done to you?"

Crying, she tried to explain, but there was no way that she could speak understandably. She cried all the way home and then some, as her parents and sisters were just as shocked as Orpheus had been. She did show her father the letter that the general sent along, though. It was tied to her waist.

"My god Niki. Now we know what that proclamation is all about. This is horrible," Olympos said.

"Dear, you can't let them do this to us," Melita shrieked, pressing her body against her daughter's as Niki continued to cry.

"We can't protest this dad. You'll be shot! Then what will happen to us all?" Orpheus added, becoming afraid that his dad might just defy the general and his thousands of soldiers.

"Olympos! We can't live like this," Melita shrieked, becoming almost as afraid as she had been when she got the plague. "We won't even be able to talk anymore! Poor Niki can't even speak now, my poor baby."

"I don't know dear. Let me think about it. Surely, they will not be able to do this to all the women. There are hundreds of thousands of women and girls in Levkos to say nothing of all the others around our kingdom. Surely, this will end soon," he added hopefully.

Meanwhile in his office, General Erebos looked over his estimates. He had already allowed the two dozen Royal Attendants to return to their homes for the first time since getting their ornaments. It was just too much trouble to deal with their needs at the palace. His mind began coldly calculating. With each center at full production, three hundred sixty women would be handled per month. Assuming twelve such centers, over four thousand women would be handled each month. "Damn, that will be four years before we handle all the women in Levkos alone! Well, we must add more centers; add them in the surrounding towns as well and in our largest port city too."

"Say, I am going about this the wrong way. Let's see, I'll keep the monthly center's production of three hundred sixty. Now given the rough number of women in Alia, I need how many center-months?"

He jotted down some figures. Ah, to get this project completed in say one year, I need to have nine hundred twenty-five centers going. Well, that's not possible, not in such short a time span. So let's see if we cannot bring another couple of dozen centers online each month. Take a bit longer than a year to do all this, but the problem of our women will be handled. Moreover, just look at the incredible spurt in our economy this project will generate! Incredible number of jobs. Yes, indeed." He sat back and smiled, although he had no idea such rates of production would not physically be possible.

"Plus, I have one other thing going for this project. Having been a general all these years, there is one law of this universe that I truly know. If someone tries to run away from something, they end up just pulling it in on themselves. You bet many men and women will be trying to flee from this, resisting it like mad, but that only means that they will indeed pull it right in on themselves, just as surely as my match will light if I strike it on this surface. I win."

He grinned and added, "Besides, the women do look quite stunningly unusual and have incredibly good posture. Makes their monster boobs look even more prominent." He chuckled. "Maybe it is time for me to take a wife after all. That would look even more presentable to the people — if I did, that is. One thing is for sure, I would never get any talk back." Again, he laughed to himself.

Later that night, Olympos entered his daughter's bedroom, where she was still sobbing quietly to herself. "Dear, I wish I could undo all this, but I cannot. I have no skill with metals and even if I take the disks out, your lips would be in danger of catching on things and ripping, causing you even more pain. However, I feel at least I owe it to you to make your earrings worthy of you. I'll send along the gold and some gemstones worth thirty thousand. At least you can be proud of your earrings. How does that sound?"

"They are too heavy, daddy," she tried to say, but wasn't understood. She bent at her waist making a small yes nod of her head, her earrings banging against the bronze rings around her neck. He followed through on his promise, sending the gold and gems to the palace later the next day. Ten of the other women also returned with replacement gems and gold. It took the jewelers several days to replace Niki's earrings. What none knew was that the new earrings weighed even more than the bronze ones, much to Niki's dismay, though now her earrings were worth a small fortune. The many red rubies looked very striking, however.

General Erebos planned well. Some four thousand women were handled that first month and all came from the upper classes. Why? He anticipated that the noblemen would offer the greatest threat to the program. Once the general population saw that these men and women were following the new law, the others would fall in line. Besides, the only threat to his martial law rule would be these very noblemen, who could possibly band together and appoint a new king and queen. So far, the chaos had prevented all such meetings. Once their women were handled, the noblemen would be more under his control permanently. General Erebos had taken a liking to running the country.

A week after Niki first returned home, a soldier delivered the dreaded orders to Olympos. Melita, Antheia, and Andromeda were ordered to the Ornamentation Center tomorrow morning. The soldier said, "We will bring a carriage by for them at ten. They will be returned in five days, properly ornamented. If you wish to substitute gold or gems, have them ready by ten tomorrow. Resist and we have orders to shoot to kill, sir." He saluted and left the speechless Olympos standing in his doorway.

His wife and two daughters began crying and pleading with him, but he ignored them. "Look, if I or Orpheus gets killed, then how will you four survive on your own? But I'll not have you wearing those trashy bronze earrings. I'm off to the bank. At least you can be proud of your earrings." Once outside his home, Olympos began crying himself. For the first time in his entire life, he felt utterly powerless. Before the plague, he was in control of an enormous business empire, perhaps one of the most powerful men in Alia. Now he was reduced to utter helplessness. He cried all the way to the Banca del Dio.

The next morning, he gave his wife a loving farewell kiss and hugged each daughter. "You three be brave. Show them that you are true noblewomen. Hold your heads up proudly," he whispered what little encouragement he could to the three sobbing women as they were led out of their home. Outside, three soldiers slowly lowered their long guns. They had been pointed his way in anticipation of resistance. He knew that they would not have hesitated to fire if he had protested in any way. "What has our country come to?" he said to Orpheus. "What have we become?" He was truly a defeated man this morning.

Niki returned home to a nearly deserted home that evening. As expected, she began wailing and crying for her mother and sisters who would now be as crippled up as she was, unable to even communicate their basic needs. "There, there, Niki. At least you are still alive. Somehow, we will get through this. I promise that we will always help you eat. Come on; let's keep on working out how best to get food and drink into your mouth," Olympos suggested.

Already getting liquids into her was their biggest concern. Unable to drink from a cup any longer, all liquids had to be painstakingly put into her mouth one spoonful at a time. Her plates kept interfering with this and it took a bit of coordination on both their parts to get a cup of tea down.

"Dad, I can't live like this," Niki tried to say. Garbled sounds came out and she broke down and cried yet again.

"Come here, my pumpkin. Rest your head on daddy's shoulder," he said softly, remembering how he used to cuddle her when she was only four years old. She did as asked, feeling the comforting arms of her father around her. Slowly, her sobbing subsided.

Later once Niki was sleeping, Orpheus glared at his father. "How could you allow these fiends to do this to my sisters and mother?" He spat at Olympos, but failed to hit him. "You are the most pathetic father in the world!"

"What in heaven's name do you expect me to do? Shoot ten thousand soldiers with one long gun? Am I to siege the Royal Palace with my one gun?" he pleaded with his son for understanding, but found none.

"You could have done something — not just let them take them away to mutilate them. Hell, Niki cannot even communicate to us anymore. She is more miserable now than when she first got the plague. What kind of a life can she ever have now? Or my other sisters and mother? You've condemned them to abject misery!" He stormed out of the house without waiting for a reply.

He headed over to his girlfriend's home. Orpheus was in love with Athena Drastus, a pretty, black haired teen his own age. She had thick lips, a round face with thick eyebrows, and eyes that penetrated him. Now he feared for her safety as well. The Drastus mansion held an extended family consisting of the two Drastus brothers, their wives, and children, plus their sister, her husband, and children. Since the plague, they had banded together for mutual support. Olympos had not actually told Orpheus not to marry Athena, but had not encouraged it either. While the Drastus clan was noble, they were not the most influential in Alia.

"Good god son! Olympos did nothing to stop them? Melita, Antheia, and Andromeda — all three besides poor Niki?" Kimos Drastus exclaimed when he heard the awful news from Orpheus, who clung to his girlfriend Athena.

"Nothing. They had guns," he added in a meek, half-hearted defense of his father.

"Well, just let them try to take our women and daughters!" he exclaimed. "We'll be ready for them!" His wife, Delpha was forty. Their eldest son was Acteon at eighteen. Next came Athena at sixteen, then Adonis who was fifteen, and then Kleto, their youngest who was fourteen. Staying with them was Kimos' younger brother Aesop who was thirty-nine. His wife was Katerina, who had just turned forty-four. Their eldest was Alexius, who was nineteen. Doris was eighteen, and Anatol, thirteen. Kimos and Aesop's sister was Chara, now forty. Her husband was Aias Gidios. Their eldest son, Aison was eighteen. They had two daughters, Diona, who was twenty, and Chloe, who was seventeen. Aison was dating Doris and Acteon was in love with Chloe. Cousin marriages were not uncommon in Alia.

Five days passed fretfully for the two. As usual, Orpheus drove their carriage to the Royal Palace to pick up Niki, but both were disappointed when they returned home and their mother and sisters had not yet been brought home. They hoped that five days would somehow be lessened. At dinnertime, Orpheus helped Niki to eat.

In anticipation of their return the fifth night, Olympos prepared a feast, sparing nothing. At least, he thought, they would have a filling, healthy meal. He suspected that they would not have eaten much for the last five days, though he had no way of knowing. Niki couldn't tell him about her ordeal.

As they were eating, the soldiers arrived, depositing the three women on the Stathis doorway. They left immediately. Sobbing, the three women were helped inside by the two men. "You are safe now," Olympos attempted to console his wife and two young daughters. All three looked like Niki. Their necks were immobile; their bronze lip plates protruded out the same four inches as Niki's. At least Melita's earrings were pure gold with embedded diamonds. Antheia had emeralds in her settings, while Andromeda had red rubies, her favorite gems. That was something anyway, he thought. At least, they had made use of the gems and gold he'd sent along. The three sobbing women sat down at the table and allowed Olympos and Orpheus to feed them. From the way that they ate, both knew that the three were extremely hungry.

True, all three tried their best to relate what had happened to themselves, how awful it had been and now was, but only strange sounds came out. Of course, this only made them cry even more. After dinner, Melita did her best to show Olympus what she and her girls wanted: a long, hot bath. Finally, he figured it out and began helping them with it.

Meanwhile, Orpheus left to go visit his girlfriend and to tell them that the three were back. He spared no details about just how awful their plight was. Kimos was furious and livid with anger. "Look at this!" He handed Orpheus a document. Now he understood why Athena was in her room crying her heart out. Tomorrow morning, all the women of this home were to be taken away to receive their ornaments. "They'll not get our women and daughters without a fight!" he declared angrily.

"Right, we Drastus will not give up easily!" Aesop cursed and promised. "Lend us a hand, Orpheus. We have a dozen long guns to get loaded and primed. We'll prepare a siege defense."

Later Orpheus kissed Athena, who came out to see him one last time. Her lovely eyes were red and swollen. "You'll be all right, Athena. At least your dad and brother are going to put up a fight, unlike my pathetic father. You'll see, it will be all right."

The next morning after Orpheus dropped off Niki at the Royal Palace, he took a different route home, stopping by the Drastus mansion expecting to see them all safe and the soldiers driven off. Instead, the front door was smashed to pieces. He had a sickening feeling in his stomach as he dismounted from the tall driver's seat and headed inside. Nothing prepared him for the bloody carnage inside.

His eyes first spotted the dead bodies of the three men, Kimos, Aesop, and Aias. They were lying in various positions near the remnants of the door; long guns lay scattered about. The acrid smell of gunpowder still lingered in the air. "Athena? Anyone?" he called out, fearing the worst now.

"Over here!" Adonis screamed. Behind a couch, Orpheus saw the teens Adonis and Kleto frantically trying to help Acteon and Aison. Both were wounded and bleeding, but still alive. Nearby, the lifeless corpse of Alexius lay with a gaping hole in his forehead. Young Anatol came into the room struggling with a heavy pot of boiling water. His face was white as a sheet.

"They took all them. We put up a fight, but dad wouldn't let us young ones fight. But after the gunfire, we both kicked the soldiers as they dragged our sister and mother out of their bedrooms," Adonis explained. "Can you help? Acteon and Aison are wounded. What are we to do now?" While Adonis was scared and shaking, he still retained some presence of mind. After all, he was now the eldest at fifteen.

"Come on; let's get them into my carriage. Let's take them to our house. Maybe dad will be able to help save them. Come on," Orpheus replied, unable to think of anything else to do.

A half hour later, he pulled up at his own side door, yelling for his father. A bit later, with the aid of the teens, Olympus had the two wounded older teens inside and lying upon the kitchen table. Both were unconscious now. Adonis had already relayed what had happened while they struggled to carry the wounded teens inside. Olympus got water boiling and finally spoke, while waiting on it.

"Well, we dare not go find a doctor. If the general's proclamation is the law, surely the doctor would report this and then soldiers would come here to finish off their work. We're going to have to tend to them ourselves, boys. Let's see what we can do for them." He examined both and saw that they were hit once in their shoulders. No sign of an exit wound could be seen on either teen. "The bullets must still be inside them. We're going to have to dig them out somehow." As he began to probe, Orpheus gagged and quickly left the kitchen.

Melita, Antheia, and Andromeda watched quietly from the side of the kitchen, but then Melita tried to say, "Okay, boys, let's leave Olympos alone." She regretted her attempt as soon as she heard her own garbled voice. Though Adonis and Kleto looked up, they obviously had not understood her. She used her body to push them out of the room and into the living room where Anatol was sitting on a chair crying. Orpheus soon joined them; his face was bleached. He'd lost his breakfast. She made a moving motion with her body toward Andromeda and then a similar one to Antheia. She sat down beside Adonis and leaned in to him, the best that she could do to comfort the young lad. Her motherly instincts were still not wholly destroyed. In spite of her own mutilations, she still felt the urge to comfort the young teen. Andromeda and Antheia emulated their mother's actions. All three were surprised when the boys put their arms around them, buried their heads on their shoulders, and began crying.

Olympos only knew one basic medical fact: always keep everything completely sterile. He'd learned this detail from the doctors who had attended the births of his four children. This he followed slavishly as he began working on the two wounded teens. It is good that they are unconscious, he thought, as he clumsily dug around trying to find the bullets and then extract them. A feverish hour passed before he had both patched up. Covered in blood, he came out into the living room.

"Well, I got the bullets out and have them patched up. I think that they both will survive, but I could use a hand getting them to the spare bedrooms, fellows," he reported, trying to sound optimistic. Eagerly, the teens obliged and soon had the two lying on soft beds.

After cleaning up, Olympos made a pot of tea and sat down to think. Adonis and Kleto came into the kitchen. "Thank you for saving them," Adonis said softly.

"Most welcome son. So they took all seven of them, eh?"

"Yes, now what are we going to do?" he asked.

"Well, as I see it, boys, you cannot continue to live in your manor. Look, there are just three of you youngsters left, and seven women will be returning in five days. I don't see how you three can manage to care for all seven," he began. Orpheus and Melita joined them.

"Dad, Antheia, Andromeda, and Anatol are sitting with the two wounded boys in their room now. They'll come get us if something happens to them," his son broke in. He added humbly, "Dad, I guess you are not all that stupid. I'm sorry."

"Thanks son. I was just telling the boys here that they are not going to be able to handle all seven women when they return. I think that the only reasonable thing to do is to have them all move in here with us."

"Really? Gosh, thanks, Mr. Stathis," Adonis replied, grateful for the unexpected kindness.

"Cool, dad. Then I can look after my Athena," Orpheus added with a grin.

"Right. Second, your fathers did not send along gold and gemstones with the women did he?"

"Er no. They fought the soldiers instead," Adonis replied. "Why?"

"Well, look son. Your women are noblewomen. The earrings that they are being given by default are wholly unworthy of their status. At least they ought to be wearing expensive gems and real gold settings, not the polished brass substitutes and cheap stones. Okay, what are their favorite colors? I'll visit the Banca del Dio and get the appropriate stones and gold to the Ornamentation Center for them. At least they can be proud of their earrings."

Around one, he delivered two heavy sacks to the center. Inside, one he had seven bags of gems with a label denoting the name of the woman. The other sack held all the gold; it was extremely heavy. When he returned to his home, he then sent the teens over to the Drastus manor to start bringing their key possessions over to his estate. This menial work would give the boys something constructive to do, he reasoned.

Earlier that same morning, one of General Erebos' aides, following the general's orders, watched the women as they were brought into the center. For the last week, he had been making the rounds every other day to each center, observing the women being brought in to receive their ornaments. This morning, his eyes rested upon the twenty year old blonde named Diona Gidios. Her huge breasts were firm and quite perky. Her face was angelical; her deep-set eyes added to her charm, he thought. Her lips were full and her nose perfectly formed. Her long blonde hair was thick and lustrous. Her legs were well muscled and toned. A fine specimen, he thought, and he rushed off to notify the general, after issuing an order to delay a bit on putting Diona under.

Later that morning, General Erebos rode up to the center on his grey stallion and dismounted. Wearing his finest uniform covered with medals, some made especially to his orders, he strode prominently into the center, the aide following behind at a safe distance. "Well, where is she?" The aide moved up and took the lead, taking him into the waiting room, where four young women were still awaiting their sleeping drought.

"Ah, you must be Diona Gidios," he began, looking her over from head to toe. She was wearing a nightgown. Though thin and revealing, at least she was covered. She dared not say anything, for here was the very man who was responsible for all the mutilation of the women of Alia. His men had just murdered her father and her uncles and brother and cousin.

"Yes, you will do just fine. Diona, I want to marry you and make you Queen of Alia. If you agree, you will sit upon the throne of our country as its queen, the most highly respected and powerful woman in Alia. What say you to my proposal?"

Diona was shocked. Never in a thousand years did she expect to hear such words, not after his men had murdered six of her family. Waiting here for her turn to be mutilated beyond description, she had only a single thought in her mind: how to murder the general — the man who was cause, the man who was responsible, the great butcher himself. All the time that she had been waiting here in fear, that had been her only thought: how to get revenge on this man who lived in the fortified and heavily guarded Royal Palace. That she could be queen and thus live with this butcher inside the palace seemed to her to be the chance of a lifetime for her to seek her cold revenge!

She found her voice speaking, though she felt so remote from it. In fact, these would be the last words that she would utter intelligibly. "I would be most honored, sir."

"Excellent, my dear Diona. As soon as you have your ornaments, you will be brought to the palace and become our queen. I will see that all luxury is prepared for your arrival. Until then," he bowed to her, pivoted sharply on his heels, and left. Later, his aide brought the supplies in for her new earrings. Gold and rubies. However, the general insisted that she have five sets of dangling tiers not the usual three, setting her off for all to see as their queen. Finally, an aide drafted a letter and sent it off to whoever still resided at the Drastus manor, declaring that Diona would become the new Queen of Alia and reside at the Royal Palace instead of returning home in five days with the others.

The evening that the women were to be returned, Olympos and Orpheus were there with the three Drastus teens. Although they remained in the background so as not to alert the soldiers of their presence, they knew that the three teens would be overwhelmed with the six women and their new needs. Sometime after the dinner hour, a carriage pulled up, escorted by three soldiers who were well armed. The six sobbing women were helped out of the carriage and deposited on their steps that led to the shattered front door. Then, the carriage and men promptly left.

"Come on inside," Adonis urged. The six obeyed, still crying and looking helpless and humiliated beyond words. Their lives, they thought, were completely and utterly ruined. Once safely inside, Olympos uncovered a lantern, revealing himself and his son. Immediately, Orpheus ran over to Athena and hugged her tightly.

"Okay, ladies. As you know, I am Olympos Stathis. All is not as bad as you may have thought. While Aias, Kimos, Aesop, and Alexius are dead, I have saved Aison and Acteon. They are recovering from their wounds at my place. Your sons and we have moved all of your things over to our place. All six of you are going to come and live in my mansion with us for the time being. We will be looking after you all."

"Thank you so much for saving my son," Chara tried to say, but not even she could understand what she'd just uttered, bringing on more bitter tears. Several others tried to speak as well, and Olympos' heart nearly burst as he heard them trying desperately to be understood.

"Okay, the soldiers are gone. Orpheus, go bring our carriage around to the front. Let's get these women home. We have hot baths waiting for you and a hearty meal," he explained. Several nodded their heads by bending at their waists, their long, heavy earrings clanking into their neck rings.

Once safely inside his manor house, he led them all into their large dining room. "Okay, here's how it will go. From now on, Orpheus you are responsible for Athena and all her needs. Son, you will be with her at all times. Acteon, you are with Chloe. Aison, you are paired with Doris." The three smiled and their girlfriends also tried to smile, but of course, nothing was observable; their lip plates stifled all such expressions.

He continued, "Adonis, you are to look after Niki. Kleto, you are to help Antheia. Anatol, you are to be with Andromeda. I will look after Melita, of course, and Chara, Delpha, and Katerina. I know, I will have my hands full," he made a stab at a jest. "Boys, first thing, let's get them well fed. After that, it's bath time. Somehow, we will all make this work out for our women. We simply must, fellows, we absolutely must, somehow, someway."

The women once more attempted to say something, but were unable to make themselves even remotely understood. As they began dining, he asked Chara, "Did you know that your daughter Diona has agreed to marry General Erebos and become the Queen of Alia?"

"Yes, they told me. How awful. I don't know why she could have possibly agreed to that," Chara tried valiantly to say. Realizing her speech was unintelligible, she resorted to bending at the waist, indicating yes. Several others also nodded yes.

"I can't imagine why she would have done that," Olympos said, more to himself than anyone else. "Maybe she did it to save your remaining sons," he speculated. Again, Chara, Delpha, and Katerina made a nod motion. He left it at that for the time being, having planted some rational reason for Diona's acceptance, one that allowed the women some tiny measure of comfort. "Well, Diona will make a fine queen," he added.

"But she won't be able to speak or do anything," Chara protested and then became silent. It is so hard not being able to say anything anymore, she thought, and fought hard from breaking down yet again. She was rapidly becoming emotionally drained of all life and vitality.

Once fed, as the fellows began spooning in their after dinner tea, Olympos announced, "Okay, I have been giving this considerable thought. Our womenfolk must have some way to communicate their most basic needs to us. Melita and I have worked out a starting point. When you women need to go to the bathroom and need our help, make an ee sound, as in pee. When you are hungry, make an uu sound. When you need any kind of help, make an aa sound. That will at least alert us to something." Had they been able to smile, he'd have seen a room full of smiling women. It was a start at least.

That evening as he sat in his living room holding his wife close to himself, he said, "You know, Melita, with so many women living here with us, we simply have to get dresses to fit you women. Honestly, it must be horribly embarrassing for Athena and the others. We can see everything beneath their flimsy gauss of a nightgown."

Melita said something and then wiggled a bit at her waist, her earrings clanking lightly off her neck rings in a yes motion. He grinned, "Well, tomorrow, I guess I am just going to have to teach myself how to sew." She grinned, but nothing visible occurred. "Besides it is wintertime and you ladies must be constantly freezing." Now she did make a serious waist bend, indicating a hearty yes!

While everyone began adapting to the new circumstances of life, Olympos began trying to work out how to modify the many dresses that the women used to wear before the plague struck. He worked first with the heavier winter outfits. In July, he finally got Melita's favorite red satin ball gown reworked and got her dressed in it. Melita even insisted on wearing her high Annelise heels as well. While smiles were forever gone from the women's faces, the light the shone from Melita's eyes, as she appeared before the whole group finally dressed as she had been accustomed to before the plague came. This, Olympos would never forget!

Once he had worked out how to do the first dress, the others followed more and more rapidly. By the end of July, all the women were now wearing their fancy, heavy winter gowns. They looked like humans for the first time in almost a year, excepting of course their ornamentations. Still, their morale rose a little.

Orpheus and Adonis began frequenting their local pub of an evening, in search of news. In August as winter was ending, the news became interesting. This Women's Ornamentation Project was certainly producing results in the economy of Alia. The gold and gemstone mining arena, smelters, gem cutters, jewelers, and bronze makers were thriving like never before, to say nothing of the other areas whose production was vastly increased to help support them, such as coal mining. Still, the basic economy was dismal in all other areas. Virtually nothing was being imported or exported. No orders from other countries came in or went out, for that matter. Eighty percent of the Stathis enterprises were still not even open.

One evening at the pub, Orpheus ran into an acquaintance of his, Dorieus, who now worked in the Ornamentation Tabulation Office. "Well, the project is taking off well now," he said over a pitcher of ale. "We've hit the ten thousandth woman mark already. A new center is being added each week now. Still, it is a monumental project."

"Yes, but how can people stand for such horrible mutilations of our women?" asked Orpheus.

"Oh, you have to admit that they do look just as attractive as before, maybe more so, don't you think?" a half-drunk Dorieus replied. "My sister doesn't give me anymore backtalk. Now that is something. Besides, who can go up against the whole army of Alia? I say, Orpheus, just admire our beautiful women and let it go at that. Are you still dating Athena? I heard that her dad tried to stop the soldiers and was killed."

Later when he reported what he had learned to his dad, Olympos requested that he continue to inquire about the numbers periodically. He himself began to keep a record. Olympos also took the teen boys to the Banca del Dio and arranged for their parent's accounts to be transferred to the boys, dividing Kimos' assets between his three sons. While he also wanted to provide for their wives and daughters, such was impossible, for they could no longer write or even speak their wishes. From now on, the women would utterly dependent upon their men for every aspect of their lives. As much as he abhorred this, he could see no alternative.

September 824 came, bringing with it the rejuvenating springtime. It also brought even more desperate times for over half of the male population of Alia. Now out of work for nearly a year and with no prospects of their former employers reopening their businesses, these men reached the breaking point. The only thing keeping them from open rebellion was the constant threat imposed by the soldiers who patrolled the streets and from the generous handouts of food supplies by the soldiers. General Erebos rightly realized that if they were not fed, they would revolt and that he could not afford.

He tried to force closed businesses to open. Without a single customer, he quickly realized that was pointless. The redeeming feature was the thriving and mushrooming Ornamentations industry, which was now rapidly escalating. He began issuing proclamations ordering unemployed men to take jobs in these areas and those supporting the main production work. For a time during the spring, Olympos and his group were immune to these new odious orders. He had funds and really didn't need to work, not just yet.

More orders continued to get issued from the general as the spring led into the summer. The proclamations became even wilder. Now Olympos began to grow increasingly worried. His guess that the general was rapidly running out of money with which to pay the salaries of his soldiers was accurate. New taxes were levied against the wealthy. Young unemployed men were now being ordered to join the army. At last, with the threats from the general about to reach the young teenaged men upon whom the women were so utterly dependent, Olympos finally had to act. Over supper he announced, "Tomorrow, we are picking up everything and moving to Axos, Thrace. We simply have to get out of Alia before the insane general forces our teens into his army. There is no way that by myself I can help eleven women."

The next day, they loaded up three carriages with food, blankets, water barrels, long guns, and other meager supplies. It took far longer for the fellows to get their exodus planned and wagons loaded than he expected. Suppertime loomed as the last of their items was packed. At night on November 1, the sixteen set out on their long overland journey of some five hundred miles. Soon, Olympos realized that leaving after dark was a brilliant idea. Almost no one was on the streets of Levkos to stop them, harass them, or possibly attempt to rob them.

Although it was late spring, the weather was warm that first night. The women all wore their gowns and were able to stay warm. Their perfect posture forced upon them by their neck rings kept them from sleeping much, however. Still, they endured it, fearful of the consequences in Alia. Once on the main paved road that led from Levkos straight northeast across Alia, over the lip of the Lonki Basin, down into Thrace, and on into Kefall, the three carriages made excellent time. Traveling some fifty miles each day, they reached the Lonki Basin rim on their third day.

He trusted no one in Alia. Besides, inns were still mostly closed. They camped out, fixing their meals over an open fire. While the men slept on the blankets beneath the carriages, the women remained inside, doing their best to sleep while sitting rigidly upright. Even if they had wanted to complain, the women had no way to communicate such. They bore their misery stoically. What else could they do?

Once safe inside Thrace, Olympos began stopping in smaller towns both for supplies and for information on what was going on in Thrace. News from the other kingdoms rarely was heard in Levkos. Since the plague, most all outside contact had been lost utterly. As they traveled deeper into Thrace and finally took the spur road towards Axos, the news shocked them all. Olympos returned to his group and explained what he had heard.

"This is unbelievable, but many are swearing to it. Only Axos is a safe haven in Thrace. Some general is controlling Kefall and the northern parts and another general is playing dictator down in Patri, their large port. In Axos, thieves and assassins gained control of the city and ruled it ruthlessly. Something about skull collecting. I really didn't follow that bit. However, evidently in the Axos area, there is some strange after-effect of the plague. It only seems to affect men, you women are still safe. I received the sternest and most sincere admonition. Fellows, whatever you do, from now on, do not do or cause any harm or even threaten any woman or girl in anyway. If you do, your arms will vanish just like has happened to our women!"

Gasps echoed, even from the women. After some additional discussion about this weirdity, he continued, "Evidently now they have a new monarch, a twenty-six year old woman called Andromache Gidios."

Chara gasped and tried to speak, as did Chloe. "I know mom. I'll tell them," Aison broke in. "If this is the right Andromache Gidios, she is our second cousin. I haven't seen her and her family for ten years or so. I was eight when we last saw them. I think that we should go see her as soon as we can, Olympos. If she is our cousin, she will be able to help us out, I'm sure of it."

"Well, that's the best darn news ever!" Olympos declared, visibly relaxing for the first time since the plague began. More than likely, help was days away, he thought.

On November 10, 824, the three carriages rolled into Axos, Thrace. They stared at the sights on the streets in disbelief. Women were out shopping for food, carrying their items in the baskets of their yokes. Small children were playing kick ball in the streets, little girls were equally represented, dashing about, dodging the balls with the boys. They saw a distinct absence of men, however. Not a single soldier was spotted anywhere. However, they could not help noticing that nearly every other homes was boarded up, uninhabited at the present. Olympos wondered if the city could have lost that many of its people.

Although was late afternoon, he decided to see if it would be possible to meet this Monarch Andromache Gidios. If so, then perhaps she could recommend somewhere they could safely stay. Even if she was not their cousin, perhaps she could still make a recommendation, he felt. He asked for directions to the Monarch Office building, which another had said now served as her palace. Before long, they pulled up beside what had once been a nobleman's estate. A simple sign hung outside that read Monarch's Office.

"Well, this is it. Why don't Aison and I go in first and check it out?" he suggested to Melina and Chara. He wanted to spare them the awful stares that they now received whenever anyone saw them. Both women bent at their waists, indicating yes.

The two men walked up to the front door and knocked. Soon a long brown haired young woman opened the door. "Hello. Can I help you? The Monarch's Office has closed for today. It is nearly suppertime."

"I do hope that you can. I am Nobleman Olympos Stathis from Levkos, Alia. This is Aison Gidios. We believe that Monarch Andromache Gidios is his cousin. We are most desperate, my lady. Could we please have a brief audience with Monarch Andromache? It is most urgent, please?" he actually found himself begging, something that he never used to do before. Well, times had changed. If begging brought him an audience and help for his extended family, so be it.

"Sure come on in. I am Diona Zoraster. She and her wife, Dianthe, and my wife, Athena are fixing supper. I'm sure that she will want at least to say hello to her cousin. Follow me. All this first floor area is our monarch offices. Mine's over there," she nodded her head off to the right. "Our living quarters are on the second floor, though this place is utterly huge." They followed her up an elegant marble stairs. The odors of supper hung in the air. "Andromache, your cousin from Alia is here and wants to see you. He says it is most urgent." They had entered the large kitchen. Both men gaped at the two women sitting on chairs with wheels cooking over the stove, which was barely six inches off the floor.

The long, brown haired Andromache pushed her chair around and rose to reply. "I'll take over for you," Diona offered.

"You do look sort of familiar," her alto voice began, as she stared at the eighteen year old lad.

"Wow, you've certainly grown up. I was only eight we last met at a large family outing, Andromache," Aison replied.

"Well, come here and give me a hug," she said with a welcoming grin. He did so. "This is my wife, Dianthe. Isn't she a beauty? Anyway, you've met Diona and this is her wife, Athena." A pretty blonde woman turned and smiled at him.

"Oh, excuse me. This is our savior, Olympos Stathis, his brother used to be the King of Alia."

"Pleased to meet you, Olympos. Hug?" she suggested. He did so. "So what brings you all the way from Levkos? How goes things down there? Up here, we are finally setting things to right after that devastating plague and the Church of Skulls slaughter of our people."

"It is beyond all imaginable horrors," Olympos tried to find words to explain it all. "There are fourteen more of us waiting in our three carriages. We seek sanctuary for a time, Monarch. Our plight is, well, most desperate indeed."

"Well, sixteen of you? Wow. I think, Dianthe that we are going to need a much larger supper! Please, Olympos, bring them all inside. At the very least, they must be starving," Andromache ordered.

"Monarch Andromache," he started to say.

"Oh just Andromache. Save the monarch stuff for formal meetings in the office downstairs."

He grinned. "Okay, Andromache. There is something that you must know before we bring our many women inside. I don't know how to explain what has been happening in Levkos."

"Oh, come on. Let's go down and I'll just meet them myself. Sometimes, a picture is worth a book of words. I've certainly found that is so. Come on, Olympos, Aison. Say, how is your father and mother?"

As they walked down the stairs, he replied, "Dad's dead. Shot by the soldiers who came to take away our women. Kimos, Aesop, and Alexius were killed then too. Olympos here saved me and Acteon, because we were shot as well."

"Oh I am so sorry for you. Chara must be devastated." She didn't quite see why he suddenly had tears streaking down his face. Perhaps she'd reminded him of his father's death, she concluded.

Olympos open the carriage door and began helping them out. "Oh my god!" exclaimed Andromache as Melita struggled to step out of the carriage, constrained severely by her immobile neck and her lip plates blocking her forward-below view. Several more times Andromache repeated her exclamation as the other women and teens disembarked, but only with difficulty. "Come on inside. You are completely safe here. Oh my dear god," she added, leading them up her short path to the front door.

A bit later, she led them into their huge dining room where the other three joined them eager to meet the new arrivals. Likewise, all three emitted squeals of shock and dismay at the sight of the seven women.

"This is my wife, Melita, our son Orpheus, our daughters Niki, Antheia, and Andromeda. This is Chara Gidios, her son Aison and daughter Chloe. Her other daughter is Diona, but she is the supposed Queen of Alia now and is as bad off as these are. This is Delpha Drastus, her son Acteon, daughter Antheia, and sons Adonis and Kleto. This is Katerina Drastus and her daughter Doris and son Anatol. Forgive me, but I don't remember all of your names yet, I am a bit out of sorts," Olympos apologized.

"I understand. I am Monarch Andromache Gidios, my wife, Dianthe. This is Diona and her wife, Athena. We four have unconventional marriages. Perhaps you have heard of what happened here with men who had been harming us women?" She related what happened to men who harmed women in Axos.

"Serves them right," Dianthe added. Honestly, we have a terrible time of it now, but your women — gosh, it's so awful! Can they speak? Please, tell us what is going on in Alia."

"I can speak, but no one can understand me," Chara braved embarrassment once more. She felt that their hosts deserved to hear just how bad their plight actually was.

"I — I didn't get even one word," Andromache whispered to Olympos, fearing to embarrass Chara further.

"None of us can understand a single word that they say. It is most pitiful; they cannot even tell us of their needs. We here have become pretty attuned to their needs and are getting good at guessing what they need," Olympos explained. "Orpheus, what was the tally when we left on the first of November?"

"It was just under fifty thousand women who have been mutilated like our women. It's called the Women's Ornamentation Project. Their goal is to make every woman and girl from five on up into very helpless people, just like ours. When we left, they are doing this to another seven thousand plus women each month, but it is growing. They keep adding a new Ornamentation Center, as they are called, every week or so. By now the total women they've mutilated is likely closer to sixty thousand. They may well hit their goal of one hundred thousand women by year end."

"Good god! No one can stop this butcher?" Andromache asked, horror lining her face.

"No, General Erebos is ruling the country with an iron fist. Their three husbands and Alexius tried to stop them from taking their women and daughters and were brutally murdered in their own home for trying. He's made a whole country's economy based on the construction of these massive earrings, neck rings, and lip plates. Virtually all other economic activities, other than food production and distribution, has been shut down since the plague began over a year ago now," he explained.

"At least he is doling out food to those men who are out of work still and have run out of money to purchase more," Orpheus added. "If he didn't, I think the whole country would revolt. Now he is trying to force every unemployed man into his ever-growing army. That's why we just had to flee. If we teens are conscripted, dad cannot take care of my fiancé Athena and all the rest of our women."

"We can't even get married. All the churches seem to have vanished," Aison added.

Andromache grinned. "So Orpheus here wants to marry Athena? Who is your fiancé, Aison?"

"The gorgeous Miss Doris, of course," he replied, looking proudly at her. She flushed and smiled, but the smile was invisible, naturally.

Acteon spoke up, "I want to marry Chloe."

Adonis, not wanting to be left out, added, "Niki and I want to get married too. I am now sixteen, so we are old enough."

Andromache, grinning even more broadly, turned to the teens and asked, "Do you want to marry these fellow? Are you in love with them?" All four waist-nodded, though their grins did not materialize.

"Well, as Monarch of Thrace and Axos, I can marry couples. All I ask is that they both are in love with each other, just as Dianthe and I are and Athena and Diona are. It's love and caring that make for a good marriage, that and respect and understanding. If your parents agree, I can wed you, but there's time enough for that."

"After dinner, I want to show you our LD radio. We are in daily contact with many others who are helping us recover big time." She began chatting about me in Velona and the other monarchs of Demokritos. She explained that a new road was just finished connecting Arolas to Axos, going from a port in extreme southern Arolas straight here. Soon, she expected all manner of new inventions and prototypes would be arriving. Already, the remaining few wealthy nobles had begun laying the foundations for the new industries and manufacturing plants.

Later that evening after the men helped enlarge the volume of supper that the women were preparing and assisting the women dine, they did up the dishes. At last, Andromache led them downstairs to the LD radio room. Although Dianthe was going to pedal the generator, Aison volunteered, allowing her to stand beside her mate, who explained roughly how the device operated. Before long, I was chatting away with them.

I admit that I was dismayed beyond belief to hear that at least sixty thousand women were so mutilated. After careful questioning, I concluded rightly that these women were given the same treatment that Alexina had been given, hobbled beyond imagination. Now I had a new and desperate situation to handle. I felt an urgency not felt before, each month that I delayed, another ten thousand or more women would be permanently mutilated. Here in November 824, for once, I had no idea what I could possibly do for these people. Their split lips were permanent.

Chapter 44 Darkness Over Theos

The Kingdom of Theos lay southeast of Thrace, where the Lonki Basin was the natural boundary between the two countries. The Ile River on the east separated Theos from Thallyus, while the Marhsa River on the west separated Theos from both Phindos and from Alia. Far to the south lay the permanent Ice Sheet, a land continually snow covered year round. Close to the Ice Sheet lay the premier vacationland and town of Trikala, famous throughout all Demokritos as a winter wonderland.

Heavy forest and open, rolling crop lands provided grains and timber for the ship building trades in the other kingdoms. Copper, tin, and iron mines dotted the northern portion of Theos. Some of the gemstones found in Theos were the finest in all Demokritos. Still, metallurgy accounted for over a quarter of their gross products. All manner of household bronze, tin, and copper items were shipped regularly to the other kingdoms. Still, mere mention of Theos brought Vacation Land into most people's minds.

The capital city of Theolopolis lay some two hundred fifty miles north of the Ice Sheet and some seven hundred miles from the border with Thrace far to the north. Theos was ruled by the Patra clan, as it had been for hundreds of years now. King Deimos Patra, a great nephew of the legendary Queen Athena Patra, ruled and had so for many years now. He was sixty-five and his white hair was falling out, bit by bit each day. "One day, I will be entirely bald," he often complained to his wife, a Holy Woman of the Eighth Degree, Erika, who was sixty-two. Her hair was also thinning and grey streaks added to her personality, Deimos insisted. She had a bark that all heeded, a commanding tone of voice, and she was a recognized domestic force around the palace.

Their four children were grown now. Dimitrios, their eldest at twenty-five, was the dashing heir apparent. He'd been promised the throne for years now, groomed by his father for the post. He was married to a Holy Woman, Mina, who was a bit homely and a year younger than he was. They had been childhood friends, and Dimitrios had insisted that she marry him, over his father's protests. He had long held out for Dimitrios to marry a noblewoman of means. However, Queen Erika insisted that Mina become a Holy Woman or they would refuse to allow them to marry. Mina was now expecting their first born.

Their son Dion was twenty-three, a dashing young man, carefree and something of a gambler. He knew that he'd never gain the throne, so why waste time worrying about it when the world was full of exciting things to do. He took his parents advice and married a wealthy noblewoman, Aella, who was quite good looking and had already become a Holy Woman. She'd rightly calculated that as a Holy Woman, she stood a better chance of netting a man of great means. Dion filled the bill perfectly and she ensnared him with her grace and beauty. They had been married a year now.

While their marriage plans for their sons had somehow worked out for the best, King Deimos and Queen Erika had big problems with their two daughters. Elektra was now twenty-one and ought to be married, perhaps even by a couple of years. She kept her auburn wavy hair shoulder length, and her hazel eyes caught men's attention. Elektra at least always wore the accepted Annelise gowns and heels, and she at least tried to look her best at all times, even though she was a passionate book lover and spent all her time devouring every book that she could find. Her room now held over four hundred volumes. Frankly, Elektra was not interested in any of the men that she knew. She had rejected a dozen "arrangements" already, much to the chagrin of her parents.

Their youngest daughter, Xenia, now twenty, kept her brown hair cut very short, as short as many men. Indeed, Xenia was now a competent swords-woman, a fighter. Always wrestling with her older brothers and often besting them, she grew up as a tomboy. Now twenty, she still acted more like a son than a daughter, which caused constant friction in the family. Her older brothers teased her relentlessly; her parents chided her daily. They even went so far as to attempt to arrange two marriages for her. Both attempts failed, when Xenia told the respective suitors that if they ever tried to kiss her, she would cut off their balls. Both suitors had quietly slipped away, much to the disappointment of her parents, who could not figure out why the nice young men vanished so quickly.

This past year, they had put their feet down on Xenia. Erika ordered, "Xenia, you will come to meals dressed in your elegant Annelise gowns and heels or you will not be served the meal. I have issued the orders and you know darn well that they will be followed." Ever since then, Xenia had no choice but to have her servants quickly dress her just before meals. She hated wearing such horribly restrictive outfits, as she called them, and she took an inordinate amount of teasing from her brothers over it.

Two days before the plague struck, at dinner, the large extended family gathered around the beautiful oak table in the Royal Dining Hall for supper. Xenia, forced to wear her green satin gown, sat beside her sister, Elektra, who wore her favorite pink satin gown. Both were opposite their parents. To the right of their dad, Dimitrios and Mina sat — she wearing her yellow gown. To the left of their mother sat Dion and Aella — she wearing her bright red satin gown. The three men were in a good position from which to feed their loving, charming wives.

"Oh lookie, Xenia's wearing her dress again. Guess she wants to eat," Dion teased her, knowing that Xenia could do nothing about it. Had she not been bound tightly in the corset and wearing impossible heels, he'd of never opened his mouth, because she would have attack him. However, constrained as she was, he was free to tease her mercilessly, which he did. Aella smiled at his jest. Xenia fumed.

Dimitrios then took the opportunity to get in a dig. "I say, father, the Royal Spring Ball is coming up in a few weeks. You could always hold a raffle. Whoever holds the winning ticket will marry Elektra or Xenia. Lord knows, they will never find a man to satisfy their needs. What do you think?" King Deimos smiled, actually liking that idea.

"Won't work, though, not unless we tie them two up," he replied. "No, your mother and I have a far better idea." Xenia and Elektra did not like the sound of that. It usually meant some new disastrous plot against their wishes. "Go ahead dear, tell them about it." He deferred to his lovely wife, whose tongue was far sharper than his was.

"Daughters, since you simply won't get married and keep on rebuffing all suitors, your father and I have decided that you must be made more desirable to men, proper and noble men, that is. So we have asked the Cardinal and have received his okay just today. Next week, you both will become Holy Women of the Eighth Degree. Then, vastly more men will seek your hand in marriage."

"Mom! We won't have any hands to seek!" Xenia screeched. "If I can't fight, I'd rather be dead! You want me to run away from here? Is that it?" She rose to leave the table, but took too large a step in the Annelise extreme heels and fell flat on her face, adding to her humiliation. White with the shock of the sudden news, Elektra rose and helped her sister regain her feet, no small matter in these outfits. Arm in arm, the two left the dining room, Elektra whispering to her sister to take smaller steps.

"Damn them anyway, Elektra. I don't want to be a cripple, a useless, helpless person like mom, Mina, and Aella."

"Neither do I. How could I hold a book to read it? I think that they are just trying to scare us, Xenia. As I understand the Holy Woman Ceremony, it has to be done with the expressed permission and consent of the woman. If we don't agree to it, I don't think the Church is allowed to do it. I think they are just bluffing," Elektra tried to calm Xenia's fears.

As they approached their rooms, Xenia, near tears, hugged Elektra. "Thanks sis. You are probably right. I just played into their hands, didn't I?" The two stood there hugging for a minute, before heading into their own rooms, which were next door to each other. Xenia paced her room, still wearing the Annelise outfit. While her sister was probably right, as she usually was, still, she was not totally convinced and decided to act accordingly. That night, she packed a large bag with her most cherished things, her many weapons, and added a change of clothes and hairbrush.

The next day, she visited the Banca del Dio and made a substantial withdrawal, mostly in gems, though. The heavy money pouch she stowed in her escape pack. Then she asked Elektra to pack an escape bag, just in case, hovering over Elektra until she did so.

"Good. If they do attempt to cut off our arms, you and I will be out of here in a flash, sis. Don't worry; I will protect you. I'm as good a fighter as most men are, sis."

"I know, Xenia, I know. Come on, we best get you changed for supper. My arms seem so tired today it's not funny."

"Yes, I know what you mean, that money pouch seemed far heavier than it ought to be. Ah well, I hope supper goes better tonight." In fact it did. Their parents seemed to have totally forgotten about their threat. The men seemed grumpy, complaining about their feet hurting them, but their wives chatted normally. Xenia found it to be one of the more pleasant dinners in long while, even though she felt totally constricted and ill at ease in the tight clothes. Both sisters felt tired and retired early that night.

They awoke to discover the aftermath of the plague. Both young women began screaming as they awoke, but no one came. Elektra got out of bed and nearly fell over, struggling to keep her balance on her toes, and then hurried into Xenia's room. She too had finally gotten out of bed and stood wobbling precariously on her toes. The two sisters stared at each other and gasped, then began wailing, collapsing on Xenia's bed.

Finally, their father came crawling into their room on his hands and knees; his face was white as a sheet. "Oh dear god! Not you too!"

"Daddy, why did you cut off our arms? I hate you! I hate you!" Xenia screamed out all her horror and shock, as if her words could kill.

"I didn't Xenia; we were just threatening you. My god, what has happened here? All our servant women — their arms have vanished! Your breasts are like your mother's — grotesquely monstrous. Your feet are all crippled as your mom's, but look at my feet! I cannot bend them nor can I even stand up. Your brothers are like mine. All the men in the palace are affected too. What calamity has befallen us? Is this the end of days come upon us? You stay here. I have to get us all help. I have to get the doctor here fast." He crawled out of their room, leaving the two terrified women sitting on Xenia's bed. Shortly after that, their mother came cautiously into their room, walking very, very slowly, trying hard not to fall or lose her balance. Like them, only her toes were on the floor, making walking treacherous.

"Oh dear god, not you too!" She moved over to the bed and sat beside her daughters. She wanted to put her arms around them, to comfort them, but could only lean on them, her huge breasts bumping into theirs.

"Mom, what has happened to us? I can't live like this," Xenia wailed.

"Be brave, Xenia, be brave. Somehow, we can. I've always depended on our servants, so has Mina and Aella. You will see. It will be all right somehow," she tried to sound brave, but knew it would not be all right. All of her servants were the same as her daughters. She'd sent out one of the guards to check on all the other women in the palace, but he had not returned yet.

As they sat waiting for something to happen or someone to come, Erika said, "Well, look on the bright side, you won't have to wear those corsets any longer, not even me. My waist is so tiny now. I can't believe it is this small. Look at yours, daughters."

"Mom, my hair is itching my shoulders," Xenia complained. "I hate it this long."

"Look at mine. I'm sitting on mine," Elektra whispered and tried to adjust it by tossing her head around until at last it settled at her sides. "Mom, what are we going to do if there are no servants to help us?"

She sighed, "I truly do not know, daughter. I truly don't know. Yet, your father will think of something; he always does you know. I am sure that soon all this will seem like some really bad dream."

After sitting for some time, Erika said, "Well, girls, one thing positive, none of us will have to get out of our nightgowns today. Heck, with breasts this large, none of our dresses are gonna fit us. I'll have to call in our seamstress."

"But mom, what if she hasn't any arms too?" Elektra pointed out, beginning to grasp what must have happened.

"Oh surely she is fine. She lives five miles from the palace, dear."

"Mom, I think this is that alien plague that struck up in the northern continent last year or so. I think we've all gotten the plague, just like they did," Elektra suggested. She'd read all about it in one of her books.

Sometime later that morning, their father discovered the first of the piles of alien objects. Not long after that, the others spotted more and soon the women tried on the shoes. "Wow. These sure do help noticeably," Erika commented and encouraged her daughters and daughters-in-law who had now joined them.

"Don't worry, Elektra, Xenia," the young and pregnant Mina tried to sound a hopeful note. "Just as soon as we can get some servants, everything will be okay. It is not so bad when you have servants to help you."

Elektra grimaced, "You don't get it do you? There aren't going to be any more servants. It is the plague! All women are like us. There is no one with arms to help us now." Mina looked very pale, and Elektra wished that she had not sounded too gruff and harsh. After all, her mother, Aella, and Mina were in the same boat as she, though by choice years ago.

Aella decided to bolster up Xenia. "Now you can make your brother feed you like he feeds me." Xenia finally flashed a half smile.

Around noon, they gathered in the dining room, Dimitrios had made lunch for everyone. "Kind of crude everyone, I am not a cook. Come on; let's dig in. Elektra, you sit here and Mina there. I will feed you both. Dion, you get Aella and Xenia, and if I hear one snide comment about our sister, I'll bash your head in. God, this is really bad."

After lunch, the men headed to the throne room. Reports finally began coming in to the King. Things deteriorated rapidly as the day drew on. So far, no one had found an uninfected person in Theolopolis, but only a portion of the large city had been searched. There was no one on the streets, no shops were open, no farmers at the markets, nothing but a nerve wracking silence punctuated by distant screams of terror from women.

For the evening meal, Dimitrios had their cook standing beside him, telling him what to do. He and she decided on a stew, something hearty and easy for him to fix. He'd found some old crutches that he'd use ten years ago when he had broken his right leg. Now he used them to get around and stand. True, the strange boots helped, but this way, he felt more confident. Additionally, the entire dining room slowly filled up. King Deimos invited everyone in the palace to dine together, because it was simpler this way. Even the guards were present and pressed into feeding many of the servant women. Some had begged to be taken to their homes and families, and Deimos agreed, just as soon as they finished supper.

Queen Erika's lifelong servant cried as she said her goodbye, "I am so sorry, Erika, but as you can see, I can no longer do anything at all for you. I must go home and get my husband to look after me now." King Deimos watched as all their long time servants requested to be taken to their homes in the city. At last, only a few of his guards remained. He'd already sent his advisors home to see to their own family's needs.

Just then, two Mano del Dio men came crawling into the room. They sat up and struggled to get their long guns in position. One man called out, "Holy Women, Lord Jehosa's Holy Day of Judgment has come upon us all. Prepare to enter Lord Jehosa's Holy Realm of Heaven." Bang!

A shot rang out even as the first man finished. The bullet missed King Deimos and lodged in the table in front of him. Bang! Bang! More shots startled those in the room. And then more shots. Now the guards were firing back. The room quickly filled with thick acrid smoke from the black powder. Elektra coughed and screamed, feeling utterly helpless. Xenia tried to fight back, but her arms just were not there. She slumped back into her chair, totally defeated.

"Help, Dimitrios is hurt!" Mina cried out in panic.

"So is Dion, please help me," wailed a terrified Aella.

"Damn, damn, the world has gone insane," Deimos bellowed. "Damn smoke, I can't see a blasted thing. Quick, attend to my sons. Who else is hurt? I can't see anything in this smoke."

A guard called out that he was hit, while another rather moaned. Several guards crawled over to the king's two sons. As the smoke began to clear, aided by a quick thinking guard who opened a couple of windows, King Deimos saw the aftermath, as did everyone else. The two guards sitting beside his fallen sons shook their heads and everyone knew what that meant. Mina and Aella began sobbing uncontrollably. Queen Erika had the good sense to have Elektra and Xenia help her usher the grief-stricken wives out of the dining room and into her quarters.

While the two women continued to sob wildly, Erika's grief manifested itself and she joined them. Likewise, Elektra, but Xenia still sat there in a total daze, defeated, all life gone from her. Why bother even crying? It was the end of days that had come.

Much later King Deimos joined them, a broken man, his spirit, his life gone, as if the hand of God had reached out and stolen it from his body. He was now a mere shell of a man. He sat there waiting for death somehow to take him. At last, Queen Erika took charge. "Girls, take Mina and Aella to your rooms. Have them sleep with you tonight. Come on. Let's get everyone to bed. Tomorrow we will grieve more."

Like an automaton, Xenia rose, and Aella, still crying quietly to herself, followed her. Likewise, Elektra motioned for Mina to come with her. As she left, she heard her mother trying to get Deimos up and into bed. "What's the use? All is lost. There is no future and now only the past," he moaned.

The next day was darker than the previous one. King Deimos, after constant chiding from Erika, finally threw some bread and cheese onto the table for their breakfast. He was a dead man walking, no ambition, no hopes, no dreams left, nothing remained, save the welcome embrace of death, but he was too apathetic to do the deed himself. Eventually, his aides crawled in and reported that wide spread looting was under way, but the constant popping sounds of gunfire had already alerted them to that fact. Half of the palace guards had left their posts, returning to care for their own families.

"What are your orders, King Deimos?" an aide finally asked.

"Why ask me? I don't know. There is no more future. Life has ruined me utterly. Even our Church of Jehosanity has betrayed us in our hour of most desperate need. They have taken my sons from me. I am powerless now."

"Sire, we must do what is right and just," he suggested.

"What is right and what is wrong? I surely cannot tell the difference anymore. Was it right to murder my sons?" The aides then left quietly.

As the day progressed, King Deimos continued to do nothing more than sit in his chair still at the dinner table, his bit of bread still untouched. The sounds of gunfire grew louder by the hour and Queen Erika grew more and more worried. What staff still remained, she wondered. How many guards? Were the gates closed or opened? At last, she decided to act. She began her slow shuffling walk around the palace, searching each room for anyone present. Closed doors were insurmountable barriers, so she stood before those and just yelled. At last, she found their gay hairdresser, Heracles.

"My queen. Do you need a hair trim? I have borrowed these crutches and am now able to get around much better."

"No, please head to my quarters. That's an order, son."

"Of course, Your Majesty. I'm on my way now."

She continued her rounds and finally found another guard. "Doros, to my quarters now." He began crawling along. As she pivoted to continue her search for more, she heard a loud scream echoing through the halls. It was Mina. "Damn, what is happening now?"

She and Doros moved as quickly as they could back to the Queen's chambers. They found Heracles, Aella, Elektra, and Xenia standing beside Mina, who was lying on the couch. She was in labor, but it had to be a miscarriage. She looked pale and terrified. Queen Erika needed a doctor now more than ever before, but none was around.

"Of all the times — well, Heracles, see if you can heat up some water. What are we going to do?" she asked rhetorically.

As if in answer, gunshots rang out. Very close this time, shocking them all. Erika took charge. She looked at her daughters and then at Doros. "Doros. Are you loyal to us? Will you do precisely as I ask of you?"

"Of course, Your Highness. What do you want me to do? I know nothing of women's matters here," he looked at the pale Mina on the couch.

"I want you to take my daughters and Aella out through the secret passage in the throne room. Elektra can show you the way. It comes out in the stables across the avenue. There, hitch up our carriage and take them out of the city. Head for Trikala. Take them to our winter home there. Elektra knows the way. Guard my daughters with your life, Doros. Will you swear to me that you will do this?"

"I solemnly swear, Your Highness."

"Thank you, Doros, thank you. I will never forget this. Please slap Xenia on the face for me. I have to snap her alert." He looked at her quizzically; surely, she didn't mean he should hit her own daughter. "Slap her now. There is no time to waste." He did so. Xenia, startled out of her melancholy and self-pity, looked up, and into the present. For the first time today, she saw the here and now.

"Xenia, take your sister and Aella to our winter home in Trikala. Guard them as best you can. You are the fighter of our family; now fight for us, daughter! Go quickly; the looters are already at the palace gates. Run." Xenia, hearing the sounds of gunfire so close, suddenly snapped out of her apathy. She headed off to her room, begging Doros to help her.

"Grab that bag. Okay, come on. Follow me. We'll go the back route to the throne room. The looters will be in the main courtyard. It will buy us sometime. Come on, Aella, Elektra. Move it."

"I'm coming as fast as I can, but we are so slow," her sister complained.

Heracles came crutching back carrying a steaming bowl of water and several towels, spilling a good deal of it with his awkward motions. "I'm here, my queen. What do we do now? Oh, she looks bad, doesn't she?" Blood had now soaked the couch where she lay. Her eyes were shut, her skin, pale. She still breathed, but weakly.

"See if you can wash her off down below, please. I will try to help with my feet as I can. Deimos, will you please lend us a hand?" Several men wearing masks over their faces and carrying pistols came crawling into the room. "Well? Can't you see we are tending a woman in labor?" Queen Erika said caustically. Bang! Bang! Erika felt a shooting pain in her chest and then the complete freedom from her body. She drifted up above the palace and realized that she was a spiritual being. Then she knew that she needed to find a new baby body, but where in this chaos?

The four made it to the throne room and soon were inside the tunnel. Doros lit a lantern and then shut the door behind them. "We should be safe now, ladies. Follow me." He continued his crawling, and the three women shuffled along behind him. At least he still had Xenia's and Elektra's bags slung across his back, and for this she was thankful. Was there anything in her bag of weapons that she could use to help protect them? She thought about this as they walked slowly through the secret escape tunnel.

By the time that they reached the exit and the stables, Doros' knees were bruised and bleeding from so much crawling on the hard, unforgiving stone. Next, he had to harness the two horses to the carriage. Xenia, long used to such actions, felt pangs of helplessness. She could easily do this, if only she still had her arms. At last, she said, "Doros, let us help as we can. I can lead the horses with my teeth. Sis, come on, lead the other one. His knees can't take much more of this."

The two managed to lead the two horses into position, but Xenia could see no way that she could assist Doros with the harnessing. Instead, she used her teeth to get her precious bag into the floor of the carriage. Then, she saw some pots lying around. She had the two women pick them up and put them inside as well. "Look around and see if there is anything else we can use. We will probably have to be camping out. Damn, we need blankets."

She soon spotted Elektra and Aella carrying horse blankets and smiled. They were at least dealing with that aspect. She continued looking for anything else in the stable that might prove useful. Using her teeth, she carried a tin water bucket over to the carriage. By the time that Doros had the team ready to go, the women had retrieved quite a number of useful items. Acting as independently as she could, Xenia was determined to get into the carriage by herself. With a lot of unusual motions and wiggling, she managed it. Elektra and Aella followed her motions, taking pity on the bleeding knees of Doros. All three women knew just how much they were depending upon this young soldier!

"Thanks, my knees are about gone. Okay here we go. I have my long gun with me and lots of powder. I am going to make a break for it. I won't be stopping for anything until we are clear of Theolopolis. Hunker down women. We're off and running," he exclaimed with a bit of boyish enthusiasm. This was his first real adventure, and he was rather excited about it — a very special mission for the Queen herself! He felt very important now.

They raced through the streets occasionally bouncing one or more wheels over dead bodies, which lined the streets at random intervals. Gunfire seemed all around them or so Xenia guessed, but she really could not see well from inside the rocking carriage. Besides, she was bouncing around, unable to grab a hold of anything. Elektra looked positively miserable as she fought to keep from crying, Aella too, for that matter. Both were also feeling the heavy loss of their arms and hands now.

After what seemed an eternity, the bouncing stopped and the ride became sooth. "We've cleared the edge of Theolopolis, ladies. We're really on our way now," Doros called out to them. At last, Xenia relaxed. Damn, she thought, we are still wearing our nightgowns!

They traveled the rest of the day. Xenia estimated that six days of travel would be needed. Where could they get food occupied much of her thoughts. After running into similar chaos in the first town that they came to, Doros now chose to take back roads around each town, bypassing potential hostilities and threats to his passengers. Yet he too was hungry and wondered where they could get something to eat. Plus, it was spring and the nights, cool. He'd checked on them once and saw that they had somehow covered themselves with the blankets. Good for them, he thought.

Late that night, he pulled off into a thicket of trees. A small stream provided a good drink for the tired horses. He allowed them to graze and he dozed himself. At dawn, the women woke and Doros again helped them as he could. All were quite hungry, but had to settle for a drink. Having no cups or glasses, they all had to drink from the tin pan that Xenia had brought along. Then they began traveling once more. They had to have some food, Doros thought, but how?

As the next town appeared on the horizon, he had an idea. He halted and began outlining his idea, talking through the backside of the driver's seat. "In case I don't make it, I will leave the reins tied together and looped over the foot bar. Maybe somehow you can drive yourselves, if I am killed." Xenia had no idea how she could possibly drive the carriage now, as helpless as she was. Still, she liked Doros' foresight. He drove the carriage to just outside the town, near the army guardhouse. He helped Xenia up into the driver's box before beginning his long crawl into town.

His plan was simple, report to the local army guardhouse. Plead his special assignment and ask for some supplies. Either they would give them to him or not. The real question: would he be allowed to leave? He had no written orders. It was just his word. After what seemed an eternity, Xenia saw Doros crawling his way back to them, a bag slung over his back. She grinned; he had to have been successful. As he came closer, the smile on his face looked sweet to her.

A bit later, he held bread and cheese up for the women inside to eat. Xenia volunteered to sit topside with him, because it would be too hard for him to get her down easily and his knees were now bleeding badly once more. A half hour later, he climbed up and they got under way once more. As they rode along, he held the bread and cheese for her to eat, helping himself as well. Fed, he then chatted about the local news that he had picked up. The story was pretty much the same, although looting was minimal in these smaller towns. Still the dead mounted, as so many people just gave up entirely.

"Bandits are likely to be our biggest threat. Report of robberies of travelers have become commonplace, though the number of travelers has dropped to near zero now. I think many were in transit when the plague struck, Xenia." That worried her again.

Slowly the days passed and they drew closer to their goal, but the daily temperatures also dropped the closer that they got to the Ice Sheet. Their meager food supply now gone, the four resolved to make it by tightening their bellies — that is, just drinking water when they stopped. Doros insisted they always carry a bucket full inside the carriage. Two days from their destination, Xenia began to think ahead. There was a fatal flaw in her mother's plan. Their winter house was a safe haven, true. However, there would be no food supplies there, just an empty house. Only in the winter would the caretakers stockpile food supplies in advance of their yearly visits. With all the stores closed and no markets, the caretakers would be unable to even buy food, assuming that the caretakers were actually around during the spring and summer months.

When they stopped that evening to rest, Doros lifted her down. She took this opportunity to chat with her sister about what lay ahead. "You're right, sis. There isn't going to be any food there. I know that the caretakers usually take off in the spring to plant their crops and take care of their own home. I don't even know where they live. We are going to arrive at an empty house with no one there to help us at all."

"Where else can we go that is safe?"

"Let me think, sis." Elektra was a storehouse of facts and information. Few in all Demokritos had read as widely as she had. Surely, in all that she had read there just had to be something useful. As she drifted off to sleep, it came to her in a flash. She sat up. "Sis, sis, I got it. There is an old Dorota Church of God on the western edge of Trikala. Let's head for there and ask for sanctuary. I bet they will help. Their women are Holy Women too, so they know our needs and can help us. I bet they can."

"I could hug you, but I can't anymore. Way to go sis. I'll never tease you about your book reading ever again." Elektra smiled, very pleased that she helped even a little bit.

The next morning, Doros asked if Xenia wanted to ride topside again. "Sure, why not," she called out and did her best to climb up herself. He only had to steady her. Going up with someone steadying you is easy. Getting down is quite another story, especially if you have no arms for the person on the ground to hold. She had been dismounting by mostly falling onto him, he catching her with his hands, just beneath her huge breasts — awkward at best if not somewhat embarrassing.

With any luck, they should make the resort late today, she thought. Safety lay just ahead of them. Xenia felt happy for a change, sensing that her luck was changing. The day was pleasant enough, though she was chilled with only her rather dirty nightgown to keep her warm, which it didn't. She regretted not having brought a blanket up here with her.

As they approached a stand of stunted oaks, two men suddenly rolled out into the middle of the road. Two long guns were pointed at them! Doros reached for his, which was positioned to his left. As he did, the highway robbers both fired their guns. Xenia saw the two puffs of black powder smoke envelop the prone men. Wham. Something slammed into the back of the bench just to her left. Doros lurched and slumped over. From inside the carriage, Elektra screamed and Xenia gave Doros a little nudge back with her leg. As he slumped back, blood oozed rapidly from his chest. His eyes were closed. "Damn you!" Xenia screamed. Fortunately, Doros always left the reins tied together and around the metal foot cross bar. Xenia picked the wad up in her teeth, yelled, and moved her head as much as she could, slapping the reins on the horses back. At once, they responded, moving into a trot from their leisurely walk.

She drove them right over the two men, the carriage wheels crushing each man, while jostling Xenia nearly out of the driver's seat. She frantically tried to control the horses, but soon relaxed a bit, they were staying on the paved road. She waited, knowing that eventually they would slow down of their own accord. When they finally did, she chanced letting go of the reins, hoping that they would continue to plug along the road.

"Are you all right sis? Doros has been shot. I think he might be dead," she yelled loudly.

From inside, she heard Elektra crying. "It's Aella. She's dead. Shot in her head. What happened? Are you okay? I'm okay." Xenia yelled back a quick description of the robbery attempt. Then she put her full attention on trying to control the team. Fortunately for her, they were totally grooved in on following on down the paved roadway, and she didn't have to do much at all, except occasionally encourage them to keep on at it. Late in the afternoon, she spotted the outskirts of the vacation town ahead, Trikala at last. Her family had come here nearly every winter since she could remember.

She was on familiar ground, except she had to steer the horses and make turns to get over to the far eastern side of town. As the first turn approached, she pulled the reins to her right as hard as she could, but without hands, the horses just didn't get the signal. At last, she gave up and pulled back hard. This, the horses were very willing to do; they stopped. "Are we there?" Elektra called out.

"I can't turn the horses, so I stopped. We're at the first corner coming into town; no one is around. Can you get out? I don't think I can get down by myself. Maybe you can walk ahead and lead the horses somehow."

Elektra fiddled and fiddled with the door latch and finally got it opened. She sat down on her butt and carefully scooted out the door and slipped to the ground. Xenia watched as her sister hit the ground and then wiggled and wobbled her torso wildly trying to keep from falling down. At last, she caught her balance and looked up at the slumped Doros and her sister. "Can you get down some way?"

The step rungs led vertically up the six-foot side of the carriage. Going up, she had Doros pushing her body into the side. Without his pushing, she couldn't get down that way. Now she looked at the front. "Hey, hold the horses still. I am going to try to come down inside them and between them." She carefully slipped down from the box hoping that she had aimed her feet right to land on the hitch bar. She did but her tiny feet slipped off and she went on down, landing hard on the ground. "Ouch!" She lifted one leg over the bar and then squeezed her way through the horse's rear, joining her sister standing in front of the team. "That was tricky. Come on, you grab the reins over there and I'll get this side; maybe we can lead them the rest of the way."

It worked and the two slowly led the team through the needed turns of the streets. Both were shivering, though. The Ice Sheet was a quarter mile south and the air quite penetrating through their thin nightgowns. An hour of tiny steps later, they stopped before a small estate on the western side of the town. A three-foot tall marble column fence outlined the perimeter. A white stone, two-story, square building lay before them. A smaller stable adjoined the home off to their left, south.

"Spooky that no one is out on the streets," Xenia whispered, as if their very voices might bring more trouble on top of them. "Are you sure this is the right place?"

"Yes, silly, see the sign, Dorota Church of God. We're here. Come on. Let's see if anyone still lives here. If not, then we'll have to think of something else and fast. I'm f-freezing," Elektra whispered. The two walked up the paved sidewalk to the front door. Unable to knock, Elektra tapped on the door with her toe.

After several more taps, a middle aged man opened the door. He seemed friendly enough. Xenia said, "Hello. Is this the Dorota Church of God?" He nodded. "Sir, we have come seeking sanctuary. Robbers tried to stop us and shot our driver soldier and our sister-in-law inside the carriage. We're starving, freezing, and desperate. Please, can you help us?"

"If your driver was shot, how did you get here?" he asked.

"I drove us. Doros left the reins tied around the foot bar so I could manage, but we had to walk them once we got to Trikala."

"Theodra, we have guests in need," he called out. "Please, come inside. We have to be a bit cautious these days. I'll take care of your carriage. I am Zenon Pyrros and here comes my wife, Theodra." To her, he said, "They've asked for sanctuary. They are freezing in those nightgowns and hungry. Warm up the tub and let's get them cleaned up before supper. Tell the boys and Ptolmey that I need them outside."

The women noticed that he wore the same strange boots and had to walk on the tips of his toes as well, but he seemed to be more skillful at it. Theodra came shuffling in, wearing the same alien shoes that the young women wore. She wore a warm cotton dress that had been altered to fit her large bosom. She was a big-boned woman, one who most definitely did not like the new tiny waistlines that the plague left in its wake. She also had a deep voice.

"Good grief! You shouldn't be going around here in your nightgowns! You'll freeze to death. Follow me, ladies." They did as asked. Down a long hall, they arrived at a large bathroom, where most fixtures were low to the ground. Soon another older woman joined them. Theodra was forty-four. Althea was forty-one and short. Both women had brown hair that had been recently trimmed fairly short in an easy to care for style. Then two other young women joined them, introducing themselves as Sofia and Penelope; they were twenty-two. They too had brown hair, but wore theirs long, about halfway down their backs. They were thin compared to the two older women.

"Don't the fellows have to bathe us?" asked Xenia, confused by the presence of the four armless women.

Theodra gave a hearty laugh, though friendly. "Land sakes, no! You must be one of the plague's victims." They nodded. "We follow the old Dorota ways. We've not had arms since we were five. We do everything our own way, Women's Ways, they are called. You are in good feet now," she jested. Xenia flashed a brief smile.

An hour later, they were washed, dried, and helped into one of Sofia's and one of Penelope's dresses. "Yes, I had to alter these after the plague struck us," Theodra explained. "I don't mind the big boobs, but I hate this infernal tiny waist. Ah well, Sofia and Penelope love the small waists, but they don't like their breast sizes. No accounting for tastes, I say," she and the young women chuckled.

Sofia added, "We like our hair longer too. It's sexier in bed. We're married, you see. Come on, you have to meet our husbands and see our three year olds."

They headed to the dining room, where the men had already gathered. Zenon explained, "Mother, we went ahead and dished out your meal for you. Come on in and sit down. It's all set. Newcomers, can you feed yourselves or do you need assistance?"

"How can we possibly feed ourselves?" asked Elektra. He smiled, and motioned to the young men who helped get the two seated where they could handle their needs.

"I am Zenon Pyrros, Theodra, my wife, Aminias, my son, his wife, Sofia, her son, Aison." All nodded to the two. He continued, motioning to the other older couple, "This is Ptolmey Platon, his wife Althea and their three sons. First is Kronos and his wife, Penelope, and their daughter, Alekto." Both children were three years old. "Kronos is their oldest." He was twenty-three. "Their sons Judas and Hektor." Judas was twenty-two while Hektor was a year younger. Both were not married and helped the two women at the dinner table.

"I am Elektra Patra and my sister Xenia," she introduced her sister, since she was the eldest.

"Wait a minute, did you say Patra?" Ptolmey asked, very curiously.

"Yes, we're the daughters of King Deimos." Elektra had hoped that they might not make the connection to throne. It might make them reconsider having given them sanctuary.

"By golly, I thought that I recognized you two. I've seen you around town during the winters.

How is the rest of your family? What's been happening in the capital? What brings you here?" he asked.

"Dear, let the poor things eat. We can always talk later on," Althea complained. He smiled and the meal began. Both women ate rapidly, for they were very hungry indeed.

Finally filled up, Elektra did the explaining, outlining what had happened. Their brothers were dead, Aella too. They suspected Mina had died and from the gunfire as they left, they expected that their parents too had been killed. Ptolmey cursed, "Damn, then no one is running the country now. This has gotten way too serious for my liking."

"Well, ladies, you have sanctuary here for as long as you like," Zenon said softly. "We'll have rooms fixed up for you later tonight. I've brought your packs inside, Xenia. The horses are stabled and fed. Don't worry about food, we're well stocked — Theodra's doing. This time, she is right; we need to be well stocked. Things are a bit crazy around here. I expect it will get worse before it gets better. Since you are not familiar with Women's Ways of doing things, I've asked Judas to look after you, Elektra, and Hektor to look after you, Xenia. Anything you need done, just ask them. Tomorrow, I've asked the women to begin teaching you their ways of doing things, which we call Women's Ways around here. I've got work to do, so I'll leave you in the hands of the boys." He nodded and left.

"Why don't you boys take the girls outside and get some fresh air? We'll clean up the supper dishes," Althea suggested.

"Go ahead brothers, Aminias and I will carry everything to the kitchen for mom," Kronos added. This satisfied the boys, who asked the two if they wanted some air.

"Walking is so darn hard, but we manage," Judas said to Elektra as they slowly headed for the door. Outside, the sweet, humid smell of spring hung in the chilly air, though the nearby Ice Sheet kept things on the chilly side. A bit of fog now hung in the early evening air. Both women finally totally relaxed, sitting quietly on the porch swing. Life seemed normal once more. Everything had been just a horrid nightmare, that is, until they needed to itch their noses and couldn't. Then, it all came back, including their extensive losses. Tears welled in their eyes.

Inside in the study, Zenon and Ptolmey discussed the situation in which they now found themselves. "We have to give the girls sanctuary and assistance. No question of that, but will there be consequences? We have our own women to think of; we're messing in state affairs, Theos affairs, Ptolmey, not our own affairs. We have no orders from the mother church."

"I know, I know, not since they blew up Dorota, wiped them all out. We know that there are some of us still scattered around Demokritos, but we are too few. At least Elder Manasses over in Alia still has old orders to follow. Lucky him. I say our path is clear on this one, Zenon. If it is the alien plague again, it's likely all over the world this time. We have no place to evacuate to, no place of safety. It's going to be bad everywhere. None of these kings has any idea how to govern. Mark my prediction: they'll all be wiped out in a matter of days of the plague's striking. Who's going to rule then?"

"Thugs, generals, dictatorial men seizing power," Zenon answered his life-long friend. True. We agree, our mission is to stay alive and keep our women alive through all this, even our two new princesses. Our question is how best do we do this? Should we gamble on another move? If so, where?"

"If we stay here, we have ourselves a pretty good setup. Yet, with the two princesses, eventually someone around here will recognize them, just as we did, Zenon. Then what? Lord knows. We could attempt to disguise them or perhaps keep them isolated in this house, minimize contact with the outside world. At this point, they'd go along with whatever we ask of them. They are about as desperate as possible. I think personally that another move is out of the question. You heard the kind of troubles that they ran into just coming the few hundred miles down here. The chaos has only begun. It will get much worse. I think we have to make the best of it here in Trikala," Ptolmey replied. "I think our chances are still pretty good here. After all, we are at the Ice Sheet, which is nothing more than a popular vacation spot. With the plague, no one is going to be even thinking about taking a vacation, probably not for years. We should remain isolated down here. That is, unless there is something political going on with these princesses which we know nothing about."

"You are likely right; a move at this point would be suicide. We're stuck here, unless we travel along the ice sheet. That might be our only real safe passage from Theos. Yet, that only gets us into Thallyus or perhaps to the foothills of Kathos. That would be a long journey with no dwelling at the other end. Let's keep that one as our last resort if things go badly for us here, Ptolmey." His friend nodded agreement. "So we have the princesses. If I remember them, one is into books and the other is something of a tomboy fighter, though obviously the Patra line has been ended. Neither seems like a candidate to take over the throne. I think there may be no political fallout concerning them. The question is do we allow them free run and likely to be recognized or do we keep them in isolation or possibly somehow disguise them? Which will it be?"

"This we should decide tonight. As far as we can tell, no one has seen them enter Trikala. We have the opportunity to keep it that way for now. However, lord knows how many more desperate women will find their way here, but then that is one of our basic purposes in life, Zenon. I for one would prefer to put it to the women and let them make the decision. That's always best, allowing self-determinism to rule. Shall we put it to them tonight or first thing in the morning?"

"Morning, they've been through a lot. Give them a good night's rest."

"Sleep well?" Zenon asked the young women the next morning as they joined the small group for breakfast.

"As well as could be expected," Xenia answered. "The reality of these last days is only now sinking in hard, I am afraid." He nodded and the group dined — the two young men once more feeding the two princesses. Once the meal was done, Zenon did what had to be done.

"Ladies, we must ask you for a decision. Let me explain. Our goal here," he waved his arms encompassing the extended family, "is to somehow survive the chaotic turmoil that is sweeping Theos and likely the whole world. We aim to survive this, along with our wives and daughters. We've agreed to support both of you as well, as if you were our own daughters. However, you two have to make a decision. If others here recognize you, then that opens the possibility of many, many more bad things happening to you and to us with whom you are living. To avoid that, you could always remain indoors. If you are not seen, you cannot be recognized, and no one knows that you are here. You and we would be safer. Yet, we do not have the right to order you to remain within the house — that would be rather like being in a prison. Another possibility is that when you go outside, we could somehow disguise you so that no one would recognize you, but that would mean that you could not then contact your friends or even go to your family's winter home."

Xenia decided to answer first. "Sir, I don't know why anyone would want anything to do with us. Our brothers were going to inherit the throne, not us. We're not prepared for that, and neither of us would seek it ever. Still, to be honest with you, we are both terrified right now. We are so utterly helpless. I was a fighter and now I can't even hold one of the many weapons that I put in my run-away bag, which you kindly carried to my room last night. I am a pathetic excuse of a person, completely dependent on all of you to stay alive. If anything were to happen to you, my dismal, worthless life would be over. Perhaps it should have been already, who can say. For my part, I'm willing to stay inside or if I go outside, go in some kind of disguise. I have no friends, and dad's winter home is just a house, nothing more to me. How about you, sis?"

"Same with me. I'm so helpless. I need you all more than you can possibly know. The only thing that I wish is that I had my books with me. I miss reading already. I won't go outside without a disguise, only I know that I can't put the disguise on myself. Please, don't do anything to put yourselves at risk because of us. Already Aella and Doros have died because they were with us. I don't want anyone else to die because of us. Please," Elektra added in a propitiative manner.

"Good. So be it. We will put together some kind of disguise when you want to go out. I believe that Theodra and Althea would like to take you aside to receive our Holy Gift. Ladies," he signaled their wives who led the two women to small side rooms.

Theodra and Althea had not been idle. Based upon the different things that the two young women had told them had happened, they realized that they now had two rather tough and balled up trauma victims on their hands. There was the shocking loss of their arms and other physical body modifications, their view of similar changes on those around them, the sudden deaths of their brothers, the general rioting, their father's insanity, the miscarriage and likely death of their sister-in-law, the likely death and loss of their parents, their fleeing days including starving and freezing, the death and loss of their driver and their other sister-in-law. The trauma was mixed up in one grand mess, which had to be sorted out, and each one traced back to the earliest occurrence, most likely in former lifetimes. They let it be known that the princesses would definitely not be given training in Women's Ways until their traumas were well on the way to being handled. Now the two women began to do just that for Elektra and Xenia.

During the weeks of therapy, Elektra began a voyage of self-discovery. When Aella was shot in the carriage right at her side, the surge of complete helplessness overwhelmed her. As that trauma was run, she discovered that lifetimes ago she had been a husband who had lost his wife in childbirth. He stood over her body and watched the life drain from her face and eyes, unable to do anything to prevent it. Right there, she had made the decision that she was quite useless. When she spotted that decision, the whole feeling left her, replaced by cheerfulness.

Later on, in handling the loss of her two brothers who were shot by the Mano del Dio, she discovered that one time she had been a small boy riding in a carriage with his parents. Bandits stopped the carriage and killed both parents, leaving him and his little brother just sitting there watching, unable to do anything. Right there, she'd reached the decision that she didn't know what to do and that reading books would give her the knowledge that she needed. Laughing, she knew why she had such a passion for reading books and little else.

Finally, in handling the trauma of losing her arms, she discovered that she had once been married to an abusive husband who had often beaten her. He'd broken her arms, making her completely helpless for a time. During this period, he had taken to slapping her face hard and punching her. She had firmly decided right then that you just cannot trust men at all, not ever. Laughing wildly, she said, "No wonder I refused to even consider getting married this life. I just knew that I should not trust men! Well, that's a stupid thing to do. Don't trust abusive men is more like it." At last she was free of the aftereffects of the time of the plague. She was vibrant and alive once more.

Xenia presented an even tougher situation. As Althea got the therapy rolling, the first thing that she struck was Xenia finally openly admitting that she felt strong attractions to women, not men. She was scared of being not normal and had hidden it, never acting upon her inner urges. Her admission of this brought on an even bigger grief than the loss of her brothers and their wives. Couple that with her total dedication to being the best fighter possible and Althea really had her work cut out for her to handle this trauma victim. Xenia kept insisting that she just had to be a capable person, pointing out how she had to take over driving the carriage and getting her sister to safety when the highway robbers shot poor Doros.

Try as she might, Althea kept running into stone walls with Xenia. Tracking back the loss of Aella, Xenia ended by realizing that she had a secret crush on her brother's wife and that she just had to protect her, getting her safely away from the palace, though she had failed at that. Her loss of her brothers ran light. They were men and supposedly capable of defending themselves. They should have been there protecting their helpless wives, sisters, and mothers. Yet, they did not. Her father ought to have taken charge, gotten the women to safety. Yet it had been her armless mother who had to step in and give all the orders while he "pretended" insanity, according to Xenia. "I should really be loving women. What's to love in men, tell me that?" an antagonistic Xenia retorted. "I really am a woman lover, aren't I? I should embrace it, not hate myself because of it. I must do something. It's as plain as my monster boobs. I should do something about it."

As Althea continued the sessions, the phrase "I should do something" kept coming up. Finally, she grinned, that was the key. "Xenia, repeat the phrase, I should do something." The young woman did, several times in a row and then let out a blood-curling scream. Althea knew the trauma case was now cracked. "What do you see?" She was off and running on the key trauma that was locking up the whole situation.

It took over twenty times through the traumatic incident before all the details came out, and layers of pain and unconsciousness lifted with each pass through it. At last, the complete event became clear, and the many decisions Xenia had made lifted from her life. She had been a ten year old boy on an outing with his family and a neighbor family. He had an older sister who was best friends with the other family's daughter, whom he had thought very pretty indeed. A band of men had attacked them, and he'd watched the two fathers dueling with the six men, while his mother had held him close to her, along with his sister. The other wife did the same with her daughter. Xenia had stared at this beautiful young girl and seen the fear and terror in her eyes and on her face. Then, both fathers had been mortally wounded. His own father's dying words as he handed his sword to him was, "Protect the women, son. Do something." He'd taken the sword and watched as five men finished off the other husband and moved towards the ten year old boy.

There he stood a few feet in front of his mother, who was still clutching his sister to her bosom. Beside her, the other mother clung to her beautiful daughter. Only the boy stood between them and the now five wickedly grinning men. Men were no good, he'd thought. Yes, he'd tried to fight, but he'd never held a sword before, and they hastily subdued him. Though he'd kicked and bit and struggled, his efforts had been useless. They killed the two older women and then raped the young daughters, forcing him to watch to see how it was done. He'd lashed out once more and they beat him and then raped him as well. When he awoke, he stared at the pretty neighbor girl who now lay half-naked and dead beside him. She was so pretty still. The boy had then gotten to his feet and looked at everyone lying there dead. Somehow, he had survived, though he had many wounds. He had no idea where he was at or how to get back to town and had died of his wounds later that night. He'd leaned back against a tree and stared at the lifeless neighbor girl until he too died. During the whole event, he'd made many, many decisions and conclusions that had stuck and entrapped him in lifetimes after that.

When the last of the buried details finally emerged, the relief that Xenia felt was beyond description. She began uncontrolled laughing which did not stop really for almost a day. All sorts of small things set off another round of laughter. For example, she suddenly saw Hektor for the first time, that is, she really made eye contact with him. Noticing that he was rather cute, she said, "You are rather handsome, aren't you?" and roared with laughter for another half hour.

Later, Althea admitted to Theodra, "Xenia was the toughest one that I have ever had to handle. Please, give me the simple, oh he cut my arms off traumas!" Both women laughed. Althea had truly given another Holy Gift. Only now could the two princesses be taught their special Women's Ways of their ancestors.

In Theos, the Dark Ages came down hard in late 823. With the fall the government in Theolopolis, Theos, and the death of King Deimos Patra and Queen Erika, the situation became one of total lawlessness. The average family had run out of food; looters had stolen nearly all food supplies from the many warehouses. Most dared not leave their homes; gangs crawled about the city like ants. Vicious and cruel were their ways. By December 1, most families were so desperate for food that they began to deal with the gangs who promised food for a price. A gold piece for a bag of beans became the standard. Exorbitant prices were paid so that their families could somehow avoid starvation.

With the Banca del Dio closed along with all other stores and shops and no farmers bringing in any food and with no shipments of fish from the coastal kingdoms arriving, the gangs quickly collected all the available gold, silver, and copper coins in circulation. Now they began bartering, accepting weapons, armor, horses, and even a young woman in exchange for precious bags of life saving food. The dead continued to pile up on the streets and outside the homes in Theolopolis. Nearly a quarter of the population perished before feet returned to normal around the end of December and farmers began returning with their crops to sell.

The smaller towns and villages of Theos faired significantly better due in part to the mayoral system of government of Theos. When the plague struck, the mayors used their authority to commandeer the food supplies and began a distribution system. Thus, for the most part, outside the capital city, families survived those first two terrible months.

As soon as feet returned to normal, General Herodes led his army of twenty thousand soldiers into Theolopolis. At first, he was overwhelmed and dismayed by what he and his men found. Rotting corpses made the very air almost un-breathable and disease was running rampant. General Herodes moved into a tone of anger as he dealt with the impossible mess. He issued martial law and orders to shoot to kill anyone who gave them any kind of trouble. During January, as the slow recovery began, he ruled with an iron fist. By February, he had order restored, his order anyway, and the surviving nobles asked him to continue to rule the country for the time being.

His rule was heavy handed and merciless. There was only his justice to be had, and his was always severe, always ten times stronger than it need be. He had no idea that this would eventually lead to a civil war.

Chapter 45 A Light in Trikala, Theos

Down in the resort town of Trikala and unknown to those in Theolopolis, Princesses Elektra and Xenia were surviving. Their massive trauma had been erased and both felt more alive and well than they had their entire lives. The Holy Gift worked miracles with these two, much to the skills of Theodra and Althea. Ptolmey and Althea's two youngest sons, Judas and Hektor had become fond of Elektra and Xenia and were always with them, assisting them with their needs.

With their therapy finished, Xenia had her brown hair trimmed back to shoulder length. No sense in cutting it short as she had before the plague, since her fighting days were over now. Besides, Hektor liked it this long, claiming it was like silken threads. Well, he was a bit romantic in nature, she discovered, but more important to her, he loved fighting, which had been her passion.

On the other hand, his brother Judas hated fighting and was a budding historian. His room held fifty books on the topic — books he's spent the last eight years finding. Most were well worn from many readings. Of course, Elektra was enamored with Judas, as reading had been her sole passion for so long now. She kept her brown locks trimmed to waist length, which Judas enjoyed, since the other women of the Church of God here kept theirs rather short, except for Penelope and Sofia. Penelope was the wife of his older brother, Kronos, and Sofia, the wife of Theodra's son. Theirs were also waist length.

With their therapy sessions now officially ended, at breakfast this early December morning, Theodra said, "Okay, now that summer has officially arrived, it is time that Xenia and Elektra learn our many Women's Ways. They have to be able to care for their own needs, just as we do. We will be teaching you the ancient Dorota Women's Ways, handed down to us through generations."

"Does that include learning how I can fight again?" Xenia asked seriously and then chuckled. "I'm sorry, Theodra. I know that's forever lost to me. Just teasing."

"Well, Xenia, I will give Hektor that assignment, if that's okay with his father." She looked at Ptolmey, who grinned.

"Sure, son, your task is to turn Xenia into a lethal war machine."

Unable to tell if his dad was serious or not, he protested, "But dad, that's impossible. I mean look, she's got no arms anymore. Surely you are making a bad joke at her expense." He looked apologetically at Xenia, hoping she'd forgive his ill-fitting jest.

Except for Althea and Theodra, everyone was surprised by Ptolmey's response. "Son, haven't you let learned that absolutely *nothing* is impossible for our women? Where there is the will, our women will find a way, son. Haven't we taught you anything? Haven't you ever actually looked at your mother and sister? Good grief, Hektor. No, I am not kidding around here. Your job is to train Xenia to fight again. You may only stop when she has decided that she can do as much as she would like to be able to do. In the process, son, you may learn more about women than you do now." He flushed beet red. Women were women in his youthful mind. He'd always looked at women outside of the Church of God as normal, while Theodra, Althea, Penelope, and Sofia were the anomalies.

He looked across the table at Xenia, "Dear, it will be difficult for you, but persevere and you may yet fight again. Nothing is impossible, though it will test your mettle, your resolve, to their limits."

"Well, I don't see how I am to hold a sword or a long gun, Ptolmey. Okay," she sighed. If there was even a slight chance that she could at least sort of defend herself, she had to try, "I'll give it my best, sir."

The first month of summer, Elektra and Xenia spent most of the daytime working with the four women, Theodra, Althea, Sofia, and Penelope, as the four went about their daily tasks. Cooking, cleaning, scrubbing, laundry, and making the beds — all had unusual ways to be learned and mastered. As the days passed, the excruciatingly slow actions gradually began to speed up; the actions began to become second nature to the two young women. During the afternoons, they helped the four with their gardening duties, pulling weeds, picking the berries as they ripened and later the fresh green beans. Also, they helped out with the many flowers that Althea and Theodra insisted on having around their small estate.

The first evening that Hektor and Xenia met to begin relearning how to fight, both stood and stared at each other for a moment, then simultaneously broke into a laugh. "I haven't the slightest idea how we can do this, Xenia," he admitted.

"Neither do I. I can't hold my sword. God, I used to be so darn good with it. I didn't really like the long guns, because with them, you kill from such distances. I like to face my foe right up front. I think those that use long guns are basically cowards," she replied.

He grinned, "Point taken. I'd not thought of it quite like that, Xenia. I guess that we are going to have to forget about arms."

She laughed, "That's rather obvious, isn't it?" He flushed and nodded. "I guess we have to work with my legs and feet, unless you think I can head butt or something," she volunteered the only thing she could think of that might help.

"Okay, see if you can kick at me," he suggested. Before long, he built her a dummy body to practice kicking. As the days went by, the two of them continued experimenting with ways and means. He made a padded wooden sword and pretended to be attacking her while she first tried to avoid getting whacked by the sword. Later, she also tried to somehow attack back. All of this would have gone far, far faster and better if either had had any marital arts training so commonly found in Tashien. Often she fell flat on her butt. Yet, Hektor insisted that she get up herself, since her opponent certainly would not be helping her get back onto her feet again.

After one particularly rough session, when they finished, Xenia leaned over and gave Hektor a passionate kiss. "Been meaning to do that for a long time," she whispered.

Shocked at first, he melted and threw his arms around her, embracing her as well. That was the first display of their growing affection for each other. After that initial kiss, they opened up to each other.

During the days, the men worked with other men of Trikala trying to keep their small town surviving, by helping each other out somehow. Crawling was, of course, the normal mode of locomotion. However, as the summer wore on, everyone's feet returned to normal and with that, shops reopened for business and farmers began bringing their produce into town once more.

Here at the Southern Ice Sheet, the vacation wonderland, the crime scene in the large cities did not occur. One had to be hardy to live here where winters were so cold, and the snows quite deep. Summertime was the off-season, so only the locals were here. Nearly half of the homes were empty, boarded up until the winter season of tourists and vacationers arrived. This year, they expected few would be coming here. One afternoon in mid-January, Zenon walked into the heart of Trikala to visit the mayor. As he strolled down Main Street, he noted that now quite a few women were out on the streets, their alien yokes balanced over their shoulders. He smiled; it was so good to see the women active once more. He had no idea that such a sight was now very rare throughout Demokritos.

"Hi Mayor Karpos," he said as he entered the mayor's office.

The slightly overweight mayor looked up from his papers. "Things are definitely improving here in Trikala. I hope that by winter, the food crisis will be a thing of the past. Wonder if we'll have many vacationers coming this year."

"My guess, hardly any, mayor. Say, what about our Summer Festival? Is it on this year or are we cancelling it?"

"I hate to be the one to cancel it, Zenon. It has been our local tradition for centuries — a time for fun for just us. With our feet back to normal and our women sort of adapting, I am inclined to go ahead with it anyway. Of course, we've lost three of our musician — women, you know."

"I agree, it will be a big morale booster," Zenon concurred, glad to hear that it would not be canceled.

"Say, you play the fiddle, don't you?" Zenon nodded. "What say you to taking the place of poor Ambrosia who can't play hers anymore? Think we can find a couple more replacements?" The two chatted a while longer before Zenon agreed and left.

On the evening of February 15, mid-summer, some five thousand locals who lived here year round, gathered at the enormous Dance Hall in the southern half of the town. Most women were still nervous and apprehensive about going to the dance, but at the same time, they greatly desired this bit of normalcy.

At the Church of God where they had been keeping Elektra and Xenia's identity hidden, more or less, Althea worried about the two princesses being recognized. "Look, what's going to happen if they are recognized? They have been here nearly every winter during vacation time since they were little girls. Someone is bound to recognize them, Ptolmey."

"Introduce me as Hektor's fiancé," Xenia suggested.

"And me as Judas' fiancé," Elektra added, "after all, we are, well almost anyway."

"Would you really marry me if I asked you?" Judas asked a bit surprised with Elektra's reply.

Coyly she answered, "I don't know, Judas. You've never asked me."

"Okay, I'm asking you now. Elektra, will you marry me?"

"I thought that you would never ask, Judas. Of course, I will. I love you so!" She kissed him sealing her decision.

Taking a hint from his older brother, Hektor asked, "Xenia, will you marry me? I love you more than I can say."

"Of course, I will, though I was beginning to think that I was going to have to ask you, Hektor," she replied. Throwing his arms around her, both their passions released for a minute.

"Say, I have an idea," Elektra suddenly perked up. "This is a church here. Why don't we get married immediately, before the dance? Then if anyone asks, you both can say that we are your wives. That will be even better. No one here will think that the Royal Princesses will be marrying local men."

"We aren't worthy of you?" Judas asked suddenly worried about the whole thing.

"Of course you are, Judas. It is that in normal times, everyone expects princesses to marry noblemen at the court. No one would expect what we are doing. It ought to work."

After everyone was dressed in their best outfits, Zenon performed the two wedding ceremonies. Then the men, with their arms around their wives, escorted them through the streets of Trikala to the huge dance hall. The two younger children, Aison and Alekto held on to their father's hands as well. Both were now four years old. Actually, Alekto had no arms, rather her father, Ananias, had his around her.

The dance did wonders for everyone's morale, especially the women of Trikala. However, those of the Church of God now became acutely aware of the differences between themselves and the other women of Trikala. While all the men wore reasonably nice suits, the women's dresses were awful. Most had cords tied loosely across their backs of their dresses to accommodate their now massive bosoms, while their waists were horribly baggy, designed for waistlines sometimes double what they now were. In sharp contrast, the Church of God's women dresses were properly fitting and the envy of nearly every woman here. Constantly, they were asked how their dresses had been made.

Further, the men uniformly had to assist their womenfolk with everything from holding their punch glasses to feeding them the cookies and cake slices. This evening, both Elektra and Xenia actually realized how much better they had adapted than the ordinary woman of Trikala. "We need to show the women here exactly how to do things for themselves," Elektra whispered to Althea, who nodded. Such was clear to her as well.

Near the end of the dance, Mayor Karpos got everyone's attention. "Before we end our delightful evening, Pastor Ptolmey Platon of our local Church of God would like a word with you, especially with our womenfolk. Ptolmey?" he waved in the man's direction.

"Hi everyone. Yes, we of the Church of God would like to give back something to all of you kind folks who have helped us so much over these many years. Our women, as you know, have always been armless, following the ancient traditions of our ancestors from Dorota. As a result, our women have developed what we call their Women's Ways of doing all the normal things that they must do in life. We could not help notice so many of you women noticing their dresses. Yes, my wife sews and made the alternations you've seen here tonight. Better still, she dresses herself. I can't recall when I last had to dress her." This pronouncement made quite a stir among men and women alike.

"So we wish to share our special Women's Ways with all the women here in Trikala. Starting tomorrow, we will begin doing just that. Second, we have all suffered enormous losses because of this diabolical plague. Our Church has a special Holy Gift that we will also be sharing with all the women here as well. Perhaps you have noticed how alive our women are, how cheerful and enthusiastic they seem. Well, they are and it has much to do with our Holy Gift. In the ensuing days, we will give our Holy Gift to any woman in Trikala who wishes to receive it. Thank you all for helping us all these many years." After a round of applause and thank you's the final dance of the evening began.

"Well, we certainly now have a big project on our hands, Ptolmey," Althea said as they walked home.

"Dear, you keep forgetting that you don't have any hands," he teased. The whole group roared with laughter.

"Hey we want to help too," Elektra then said. "Can you teach us how to do the therapy? Xenia and I want to help too."

Theodra agreed as long as both women continued with their efforts to learn the many Women's Ways, and if Xenia continued her fighting lessons with Hektor each evening. Both agreed.

It took a few days for them to work out the ways and means of fulfilling Ptolmey's promises. Kronos was put in charge of record keeping of the learning of Women's Ways. He made a list of all the homes. During the mornings, the six women, in teams of two, went to a specific home to teach and coach the women there in their unique methods. Kronos kept track of what was taught to what home.

Ananias was in charge of keeping track of the scheduling of the therapy sessions, making sure each woman who wanted it arrived safely and on time. During the afternoons, the six women ran their therapy sessions on six women. Zenon and Ptolmey acted as supervisors, handling any difficulties that arose, especially with Elektra and Xenia who were handling their first-ever sessions. After a few weeks, they had so little to do that they began taking a man each afternoon, giving him their Holy Gift as well.

After two week of this, Zenon and Ptolmey had hard figures on how well the therapy was going. On the average, each woman needed about five days to fully deal with the loss trauma of their lives. Unlike their loftier goal with Elektra and Xenia, here they only wanted to remove the loss trauma, which alone would bring back enormous vitality and enthusiasm to these women.

Zenon declared, "At six women handled every five days and with about twenty-five hundred women and girls to handle, this project is going to take us over four hundred days to complete! And that's ignoring the men."

"We have to find a way to get more women trained to deliver the therapy sessions, that's all," Ptolmey concluded.

Upon checking, they found that half of the women who had finished their therapy wanted to learn how to do it, to give back such incredible and profound help to other women. Thus, they began training those who wished to help them with this enormous task. When Eve and Macario contacted Ptolmey, they found that he had already gotten nearly a hundred women trained and giving daily therapy sessions. Furthermore, it was working.

Ptolmey estimated that by mid-winter or July, they would have all the women in Trikala handled and certainly by spring have all the men finished as well. Eve and Macario realized that their idea of massive therapy sessions was entirely possible and quite feasible here, as long as there was no chaos around them. It would not be practical to attempt to deal with Theolopolis at this time, life there was at the basest survival level. Life was a living horror in that city.

Chapter 46 Baby Boom and Therapies

In late June 824, Tatiana called and asked if Marco and I could come over to her house after dinner. I thought that she sounded a bit nervous on the telefono. Around seven with little Bianca in her pouch slung over my head, he and I walked the three blocks to her home. "Hi, come on in," Wanda said as she opened the door for us. Wanda looked fit, I thought as we entered. The women from Cymry were staying with them and I sensed a real warmth radiating from their home. Visions of the horrid state of disrepair from my first visit here during the first plague returned to me. What a difference between then and now.

"Hi Bethany, Marco. Come on in; take off your cloaks. Tea?" Tatiana welcomed us as we entered her living room. Her blonde, wavy hair fell to the small of her back, having grown considerably with this second plague. She seemed vibrant and alive, so why this strange meeting I wondered.

Marco hung up our cloaks and we said hello to the others. Brina's black hair was nicely done, falling below her shoulders now. She looked bright, a sparkle in her eyes. Likewise, her mate, Kaie, also looked well, and her blonde hair was now the same length as Brina's. Their hunting days were over with the coming of the plague and now the two wore fashionable dresses designed for them by Tatiana. At a small low table, Keelin smiled, looking up from the Words letter game that she was playing with her daughter Shela. Rona d'Aine and her five year old daughter Tam were also playing; rows and columns of words covered the board. Zena was watching them play, but took a seat beside Brina, Kaie, Wanda, and Tatiana. Marco and I sat across from them. He had laid Bianca down so she could nap for a while.

Tatiana already had the teapots waiting for us, along with cups. Using her foot, she began pouring and I noticed how skillful she had become. Well, these days it was become skillful or perish for we women. After some polite pleasantries, Tatiana explained, "Wanda, Brina, Kaie, and I have been working for Stefano doing the baby survey as you probably already know."

"No, sorry, Tatiana, we don't. I've been preoccupied with other matters. Tell me about it," I asked, becoming more curious about what she wanted to ask.

"Stefano wants to know how many babies have been born since the plague struck the first time and how many women are now pregnant now. He needs this to help plan for our future," she explained. "Well, we're just about finished now. Do you realize that nearly every married young woman in Velona is either pregnant or has just had a baby? Stefano's calling this the Incredible Baby Boom. We've added two hundred thousand new babies to the population of the sector."

"Wow, so many! I had no idea, but then that was one of the objectives of that first plague," I replied, genuinely surprised at the numbers.

"Yes, we have talked with the Church of God's Elder Lucio and he says that over a million folks lost their bodies when Dorota was destroyed. So many others perished elsewhere during that first plague that I don't think we will ever know precisely how many died. Anyway, according to Lucio, all these spiritual beings must get another new baby body. Hence, the boom in babies," she explained further.

"Well, that is true. I guess Marco and I are doing our part to help," I teased.

"Yes, you have Bethany. With Shela and Tam around, we are seeing everyday just what we are missing and Bethany, and we want to do our part too," she said with a bashful grin. I raised my eyebrows, not quite grasping what she was suggesting.

Tatiana saw that I was missing her point and came right out with it. "We five, we each want to have a baby too. We want our own children and to do our part in helping make new baby bodies for all those who have perished from the plagues."

"You mean all five of you want to become pregnant and each have a baby too?" I sought clarification. Well, with their unusual marriages such would be rather hard to achieve.

"Yes, exactly so," Brina added. "But we don't want to play whore to get ourselves pregnant, though. We want to choose our baby's fathers, more or less. You know, bed someone we like and trust and admire, not just any man we can find." She flushed and became quiet.

Tatiana's face was also quite flushed. She suddenly came right out with it, "Marco, we would like you to sleep with each one of us. We will not ever expect anything more from you afterwards. I mean we won't expect you to help us raise our children, nothing like that. Just help us get pregnant."

"Yes, Brina and I will act as surrogate fathers," Wanda hastily added. "We have more than enough funds to see that all our children lack for nothing. Lucio examined all five of us and said that Tatiana and I are not too old yet to bear children. We can do this and we five really want to have children of our own."

Poor Marco, was he ever on the spot! "I like all of you, really I do," he stumbled, flushing red as well. "But if I were to father five more children, honestly, I would feel responsible for them as well as my little Bianca here. I don't think I could just ignore children for which I am the father."

"We figured that you might say something like this," Tatiana replied with a sigh. "This is a crisis, so many have lost their bodies and need new ones. We want to do our part too. What if you and Sergio and Valerio and Giovanni each bedded us? Then, none of you would know who the actual birth father was," she suggested hopefully.

"That's what Lucio suggested," Wanda added. "Then, you four could always come around and see the babies anytime, but no one would really know who really is the father of which baby. Please, you must help us do our part."

"What about taking in some orphaned children or babies?" I suggested an alternative.

"We thought about that, Bethany, but that is not helping to create more babies for the many spiritual beings in dire need," Tatiana explained.

"Well Tatiana, Brina, Wanda, Kaie, Zena, can I have a little time to think about this and talk to the other fellows and our wives?" Marco asked as diplomatically as possible.

"Sure Marco. Take all the time you need," Tatiana replied.

Later that evening, we eight discussed their proposal. Our four husbands all expressed similar feelings and were reticent to do this. Since Lucio had a hand in it, Marco asked him to drop by. Again, he materialized into a solid body for our sakes. After a lengthy discussion, we saw his reasoning — so many of his fellows who had lost their bodies on Dorota still were desperate for new baby bodies. He added, "Look, do this for me. I will guarantee that the five only have daughters, no sons. Considering their situation, that would be optimum. Please, fellows."

During the next couple of weeks, Marco, Giovanni, Valerio, and Sergio took turns with the five women. After that, all became pregnant as they had so carefully planned and greatly desired. April 825 became baby month around Tatiana's home as five girls were born as promised. True, we four women lent the new mothers a whole lot of advice, though our experiences were barely ten months along.

In June 825, our four babies were now a year old, walking, crawling, and talking a storm. We four mothers were kept busy, but their two grandmothers gave us tons of help with them. Interestingly enough, that very month, all six of us found ourselves pregnant once more! Yes, our mothers surprised us, Sofia saying, "Well, your father and I have a big surprise for you kids. You are going to have another little brother or sister!" So much for our mothers being too old to have more children. Tatiana's latest estimates indicated that Velona had now added nearly four hundred thousand to its growing population. We were experiencing a real baby boom.

Stefano needed this key data so that he could plan for their futures. Even his wife got pregnant once more as well. After checking with the other Sea Prince monarchs, he found that Velona was not alone in experiencing the baby boom, though our numbers were double those of the other sectors. None of us were surprised by that, however, Velona being the leader in so many ways. Stefano had plans drawn up for many new schools, promising that in four years there would be enough schools to handle all the new children. Incidentally, we were expecting our second babies sometime in February and March 826.

In July 824, our four children were now thirteen months old and growing like weeds. Mom kept saying wait until the terrible two's arrive, but without arms with which to deal with them, I thought that the terrible ones had arrived! That all changed once we had returned from our investigations on Cymry at the Standing Stones.

Hi mom. Macario says that it is time for your Advanced Therapy.

What? Bianca? Is this you?

Yes, mom. My little body doesn't speak so well yet. Let's do it this way, please. We will have a session for you each day. I am also doing your mother and Marco once each day. All four of us one year olds are going to give everyone here Advanced Therapy each day. You all have more than earned it. Don't worry, Macario will be monitoring us four in case we need his help, but I don't think that we will, mom.

Eve came rushing into my room. "Bethany! Adona is going to give me and Giovanni Advanced Therapy!"

I grinned, "Great, Bianca here is going to do us too. The real question is how are we going to find the free time for a session." Our two babies giggled. Thus, beginning in late July 824, our four parents and we eight began to receive regular Advanced Therapy sessions, usually a two-hour session each day, sandwiched in between our hectic schedules.

Not long after that, dinnertime around 42 Hampton Way became most unusual. Forks and spoons and cups seemed to float up to our mouths as we all began using our spiritual lifting abilities instead of making our body's feet do the chore.

I will never forget July 21, 825. That evening, we were all sitting around our large living room chatting after dinner, while the new dishwasher of Lucianna's dealt with the dishes. Eve said proudly, "Gang, look what I can now do." She materialized a duplicate body. We stared in disbelief as we saw two gorgeous looking Eves standing before us. Giovanni went over and hugged each one.

"Oh no, Eve! I can't tell which one of these is you, dear!" Giovanni exclaimed. We all had to go touch them both. As far as my feet could tell, both were living bodies!

"I am both, dear. Isn't two of me better than one of gorgeous little old me?" one of the Eve bodies said coyly. The other Eve body added, "I certainly think so." We all laughed.

"This isn't all, gang. Look at this." Suddenly, one of the Eve bodies had her arms back! This greatly impressed us all and again, we all had to touch them to verify that they seemed real. As far as I could tell, her body had her arms back again.

"Of course, I won't go around with arms just yet. That would create too much upset with other women. Soon, I expect that all of you will be able to do the same. Macario did say that I was close to being able to materialize a body and he was right. Now I can go anywhere I want and I don't have to bring my body along with me. I can just mock up a duplicate one when I arrive. Way super great!" Eve proudly exclaimed. We all agreed on this point.

For the first time in a very long time, I felt that the future was incredibly hopeful. Beings were beginning to become freed of the necessity of having these fleshly bodies here on Tarra. True, only a handful was as capable as Eve now was, but overall, this was monumental in impact. Macario's Advanced Therapy would work. We could become free and able spiritual beings again. We just needed time, time and those few who could deliver the Advanced Therapy.

Macario did later tell us that the four beings who took over our four new baby bodies last June were four of his more able followers. Now it began to make sense to us all. As far as the outside world was concerned, 42 Hampton Way was once again the home to four very precocious children who were in their terrible twos. This helped offset the darkness that had descended in other parts of the world.

Chapter 47 The Saving of Phindos

As has often been said, General Kratos thrived on order. Everything in its proper place. Events should go as planned, especially if he had a hand in their planning. Awakened in the middle of the night for more chaos in the Royal Palace was not order nor planned. It was November 25, 823 and after midnight, making it actually the 26th. "Do be careful, Kratos," his wife Io whispered as he struggled to get his pants on and then the awful boots and mandatory kneepads and gloves for crawling.

He had already gotten around the terrible orders that a man was now only allowed to care for one woman and at most one daughter. He had sent his eldest daughter, Iona, off to live with her boyfriend. He'd sent Iola off to his brother's farm just north of the city, where there was an excess of boys. Only sixteen year old Iantha now lived here at home. So far, he'd stayed within the letter of the laws. Still, years of watching the depravity of the Royal Court and the king's advisors made him sick. Now this early morning summons bode ill, he thought. Some new trouble is brewing. He had no idea that in minutes he would be the ex post facto leader of Phindos!

He arrived at the palace around two in the morning, but didn't pay any attention to the wagon leaving as he entered the gates. As he crawled through the main doors, having ridden his horse across the courtyard shortening the distance he had to crawl considerably, he was met by a captain of the palace guards who reported that both advisors and the new queen were dead. She had somehow fallen down the stairs, striking her head on the marble stone. Both advisors appeared to have been poisoned. Speculation suggested that they had poisoned each other.

"Okay, I hereby declare martial law. I am now running the country until further notice. Secure the palace. No one goes in or out. I will return in the morning, and we'll get this all sorted out, captain. Good night." He saluted and crawled back to his horse. A half hour later, he crawled back into his bed with Io, whispering, "Well, now I am running Phindos. Fancy that, the sadists have all killed each other."

The next day, General Kratos rescinded all previous proclamations and orders since the plague began. Officially, he declared martial law. He drew up a posting that said all looters and rioters would be shot on the spot. No exceptions. By now, his subordinate three generals and their thirty thousand men arrived in Pirgos. He assigned one general to deal with the dead, ordering them to go house to house in search of more dead as well. A second general and his army was ordered to go door to door, inquiring on the well-being of those who resided there. He needed an honest appraisal of just what the situation actually was. The third general and his army was ordered to visit all the Churches of Jehosanity and retrieve any gold, gems, and food supplies that might be stashed away for needy times. Certainly, these were needy times.

He sent his own men out on food scavenging routes. Their orders were to bring back to the Royal Palace whatever stockpiles of food they could find.

Late that first afternoon, he began hearing back some reports of the house-to-house canvass. Soldiers had come across several establishments, which were holding women captive, whorehouses to be more specific. Several of the women had pleaded with the soldiers to rescue them. They did not because they had no such orders. General Kratos fumed, imagining one of these women was his own daughter, which of course she wasn't. He exploded. "Okay, from now on, anytime you come across a woman or girl who is being held against her will, she is to be rescued and returned to her home. Those responsible are to be summarily shot. Let's close down all the whorehouses throughout Pirgos for now."

He scratched his chin and had another idea. "Say, let's set up a hotline here at the Royal Palace. Anyone who wants to report a kidnaping, a mistreatment of a woman, or a rape is to come to the palace and report it. Send out squads to investigate and apprehend those responsible. If they are guilty, they are to be executed. I will not stand for any more of these things, not while I am in charge around here!" He appointed the Captain of the Palace Guards as head of this task. He also added a line that said anyone wanting to report any other troubles or problems should also bring them to the palace. "Son, your men are to take careful notes of what is reported and bring the list to me once each day. I will be at the First Army Barracks. This palace is not a secure place. My army barracks is highly defensible."

Within days, he discovered vast food stockpiles had been stored in the many Churches of Jehosanity. The number one problem was starving, desperate families. Hence, he issued another proclamation. Anyone in need of food supplies were to report to one of the Churches of Jehosanity scattered around the city. He put one general in charge of securing these places and doling out food to those who needed it. There would be no charge for the food.

By early January 824, order had been restored to Pirgos. With everyone's feet returning to normal, the situation rapidly improved, at least for the men. General Kratos insisted that the Banca del

Dio assign himself as a signature on the Kingdom of Phindos bank account and began withdrawing pay for the forty thousand soldiers.

Now he felt like addressing the secondary problems facing the city. Women had a clothing crisis. Men had no time to go to work, since they had to stay home to care for the women and girls in their families. Many homes had only women living in them now, the men there having been killed. These were most desperate women indeed.

He began to issue more proclamations. First, until dresses could be altered, women were to wear men's pull over shirts and pants. He had his soldiers round up all known tailors and gave them orders to go house-to-house and alter the women's dresses to fit them satisfactorily.

Second, he established citywide work hours for men: nine to eleven in the morning and one to four in the afternoons. Every worker was to report on Monday to their previous jobs. Of course, he realized that probably half of the workers would have nothing to do there, but it was a start. He needed the men to realize that their women could survive a few hours without their constant attention.

Third, he followed up on several suggestions from women. Apparently, most homes had a replacement kitchen appear along with the alien shoes. One entire army group was ordered to go home to home and assist the occupants in installing these kitchens.

Forth, he began to draw up a citywide tally of all homes which had too few or no men in them to support the women there. By February, he saw the magnitude of the problem and began forming up women's dorms, as he called them. Essentially, he confiscated abandoned mansions and moved these women and a few men or boys into them, making a sort of communal living arrangement for them. He then assigned soldiers to assist each mansion as needed. By the end of February, over one thousand of his soldiers were now tied up dealing with these domestic duties, keeping these women and girls alive and surviving.

Around February 1, one of the palace guards finally reported back to the general. He'd been given a special assignment the day after their feet had returned to normal. This soldier knew Princess Adonia well. His task: search the mountain of dead for any trace of the princess. "Look, soldier, Adonia just disappeared from the palace one night. While I would not put it past the sadists to have had her killed and her body dumped, I don't think that happened. The last time that I saw her, she was being totally ignored by the queen and her advisors. Shortly after that, the queen herself was tortured, so I find it a bit curious that Princess Adonia just vanished. She alone fought against her parents' sadistic ways. Perhaps the bright woman found a way to escape the palace. Certainly, her handmaiden also vanished with her, and she was never without Philomena. I need to know one way or the other. Is she dead or did she somehow escape?"

While the soldier had the worst two months of his life, digging his way through the mountain of dead bodies piled up for a mass burial, he carried out his orders. After getting ill twice in the process, he finally reported, "General Kratos, I have not found the body of Princess Adonia nor her handmaiden Philomena, sir. Unless they were buried in some unknown location, they must have somehow escaped the palace during all the confusion."

"Well done, Captain Hermes, well done indeed! Yes, you have more than earned your promotion," he added. The private saluted sharply; he'd just received a huge promotion for his efforts.

"Okay, Captain, I'll be assigning you a squad to command today. Your new orders are to search all of Phindos if you have to, but find me Princess Adonia. I absolutely must speak with her."

"Yes sir!" He saluted and left to celebrate his incredible promotion. General Kratos had a good idea of just what Hermes had been through for the last two months. If a soldier was willing to do that, he was just the man to continue the search. Besides, with this huge, unprecedented promotion, he would continue the search relentlessly and get the job done.

As fall came here in February, groups of noblemen began seeking an audience with him. Obviously, they wanted control of the country turned over to them or to be allowed to appoint new rulers. Considering their track record on those they had chosen to lead the kingdom, General Kratos wanted no part of that. He had had more than enough of sadistic leaders. "Gentlemen, the kingdom is still in dire straits. I will not consent to release my martial law just yet. Only with my forty thousand soldiers am I able to keep order here in the capital city. We have yet to tackle the rest of the kingdom. You ought to concentrate your efforts on rebuilding your many businesses. Get our people back to productive work." He had a valid point and for months, they did not press the issue further. After all, he was seeing to it that their homes were safe and secure and that food was available. That he also had cancelled all tax collection for the entire year also influenced them to remain quiet.

By May 824, the fall harvest was complete. The city granaries were full; stores, well stocked. Sufficient coal and oil and charcoal supplies were available. Now General Kratos decided it was time to see about the rest of the kingdom. He sent one army and its general off to visit all the northern towns and villages and bring law and order to them as needed. Another was sent off to the east. A third was sent to the west. His own army continued to patrol Pirgos proper.

Around the same time, Eve asked me, "Say, Bethany, do you suppose that we can get an LD radio to Filantos, Phindos?" She went on to explain that she'd learned that Princess Adonia Kadmos was with the Church of God there in the port city and that they were all beginning to deliver massive numbers of Holy Gifts to the people there. "I think that she is the rightful leader of the kingdom, and they could use all the support that we could give them."

I agreed and went to see Stefano. Sure enough, he already had two caravels docked in Andros, Arolas fully loaded with all our sample MMCE items. "I have been waiting to come to the rescue of another kingdom, Bethany. As soon as this pair gets their sailing orders, I have another pair loaded and ready to set sail. You get the countries ready for salvaging and I will have the MMCE things there," he grinned. He was again quite proud of his advanced planning.

"I could kiss you," I teased him.

"You'd better not or my wife will have your hide," he teased back. "Okay, I'll give the captains their sailing orders: delivery to the Church of God, Filantos, Phindos. I expect that they will be there by June 1. How's that?"

"Perfect," I replied. Now I needed to establish contact with Princess Adonia. Good old Macario came through once more. That evening, he, Eve, and I materialized before their large seaside estate just after suppertime there. Telamon and Thales had been informed of our coming earlier and they were anxiously awaiting our visit.

Actually, their entire extended family and group were extremely anxious and pleased. The founder of their church was paying them a visit, to say nothing of the two women who created the Holy Gift in the first place back on Dorota. Seldom had I been seen by others with such reverence and awe. It rather surprised me.

Princess Adonia was charming and now very able in her own right. Except for the glass eyes, one could not tell that Alexis was blind. The dozen women with their lip plates were equally quite able, using telepathy to talk with us. I did learn that they had already had them enlarged to four and a half inches to keep them from drooping down precariously. For once, as tea was served, I was very surprised to see all the teacups moving apparently of their own accord up to the lips of the women — spoons of tea in the case of the twelve women with the lip plates. I realized that these Church of God folks had really done an amazing amount of Advanced Therapy on the fifteen women for which they had originally provided sanctuary.

Chara and Danae outlined their progress thus far. Danae explained, "As of today, we have one hundred more women who are giving daily Holy Gifts. Kreon and Niki are handling all the record keeping, appointments, and transportation of the women. We've adopted the policy of spending a week with each woman that we assist. Besides giving her the Holy Gift, we also go through the basics of our Women's Ways with them."

Chara added, "Over half then want to help us and learn how to do it as well. We could have more volunteer if we could somehow pay them so that they could help their families get by while they were off giving their Holy Gifts. Our immediate goal is to attend to every woman in the greater Filantos area, that's roughly one hundred fifty thousand women."

Macario then explained about my Hints book and promised that sufficient quantities would be arriving shortly. After taking a round of applause and thanks for having written my book, I then launched into the Velona MMCE program, explaining in detail how it could well salvage a whole country.

"This is incredible news, Bethany," Adonia replied. "I can see where this program could save our country. Right now, only a small portion of our people is back at their old jobs, fisherman, farmers — those upon whom we are depending just to survive from day to day. Our whole economy is trashed at this point. This MMCE thing could well turn everything around."

"Dear, perhaps we should open up communications with General Kratos," her fiancé Than Zacharias suggested. To us, he explained, "General Kratos took over control of the kingdom, Pirgos really, after the sadistic folks in power assassinated each other. Honestly, from what we have seen and heard, thus far, the man has been holding the capital city fairly well. All of his proclamations that we've received here in Filantos have been honorable and valuable, quite the opposite of the evil ones that first appeared after the plague struck. Perhaps it is time to meet with him."

"Well, Than, that's probably wise, but with the state of inns and towns, it is not wise for us to travel to the capital just yet," Telamon replied. "Now if he can be persuaded to come here, then I say let's chat with him."

I added, "The other monarchs are getting their wealthier nobles involved with the financing and manufacturing of the MMCE products. Perhaps you will be able to do the same here, Adonia. When the two caravels arrive, the best idea is to allow the two engineers to set up a test demonstration site. Then, bring all those key persons to view it. Trust me. They will be incredibly impressed with all the inventions and advancements. Once you have the LD radio, you can then chat with the other monarchs, Ana, Callisto, Sophia, and Aminta. I'm sure that they will be able to give you lots of suggestions and guidance."

As we prepared to leave, Macario said, "Telamon, Thales, Chara, Danae, Kreon, Hera, Iola, Niki, Ariadne, Desma, you have my sincere thanks for a job incredibly well done with these women. Adonia, Philomena, you have also done very well indeed. I am proud of what you have achieved already. And Kassandra and your group, words cannot express how proud I am of you twelve, who have overcome the biggest hurdle imaginable."

We owe it all to Chara and Danae and the others here. They gave us back our very lives. We were all ready just to die when we came here, she sent to us. *We owe them more than we can ever repay. We will not rest until every woman has received the Holy Gift, sir.* Eleven others nodded; their smiles were invisible, dampened out by their lip plates.

Hundreds of thousands of copies of the Hints book appeared the next day and distribution began at once. Than used the sheriffs to deliver them to each home, but many men came themselves to the docks to retrieve copies for their wives, daughters, and fiancés sooner than Than could get them delivered.

The Church of God members continued to work their magic, spending a week with each scheduled woman. Often, they also spent time training them on how to deliver the gift and adding them to the following week's schedule. Around the end of May 824, over one thousand women had received the Holy Gift and were now doing extremely well. Demand for the gift spread like wildfire throughout Filantos.

The mayor recognized the vital nature of this project and offered fifty gold per week for those women who would take time off and deliver the gifts. The last few days of May were spent training up an additional five hundred women who had already received the gift, but had been unable to volunteer their help. With the funds available, their families could now afford to get by without them for a time. The mayor liked the idea of having another thousand women helped each week in June. "By golly, we are making definite progress with our women," he declared to Telamon.

That same evening, Captain Hermes rode up to the Church of God. He and his men had finally located Princess Adonia. By now, many in Filantos knew of her because of what she and the Church of God were doing. Rather than alarm the church members, he rightly decided to visit them by himself. It would be less threatening for her, he reasoned correctly. He dismounted and knocked on their door.

"Hello. I am Captain Hermes. I would like to speak with Princess Adonia, please." Telamon had opened the door, having spotted the soldier arriving. He was a bit hesitant, but realized that perhaps this was for the best. He could not see any other soldiers around, just this one man.

"She and her fiancé are walking on the beach. I'll take you to her." As he stepped outside and began walking around the porch and down to the beach, where Than and Adonia were strolling, he added, "Mind you, do not harm or harass or bother her, if you value your life."

"I promise, sir. I just wish to talk with her briefly," Captain Hermes replied.

"Adonia, this is Captain Hermes. He wishes a word with you," Telamon called out and the two walked up to the pair.

"Hello, Captain. I'm Adonia. What do you want?" she asked politely.

He grinned, "Finally. I have actually found you! You would not believe what I have been through to find you. Well, maybe you would. Anyway, General Kratos has had me looking for you since January. He desperately wishes to speak with you. Is there any chance that you would be willing to return to the capital with us?"

"None, captain. I am far too busy here. I am helping them deliver the Holy Gifts to all of our traumatized women. If he wishes to talk with me, have him come here. I suspect it is vastly easier for him to travel than for a woman. Are the inns back in operation yet?"

"Er, not really. Okay, I'll tell him. I suspect that he will come here at once to meet with you, though I have no idea what he wants."

"Tell him that I will be expecting him. I too would like to chat with him. Tell him that from what I have seen from here in Filantos, he has been doing an admirable job running our kingdom," she replied.

Seeing that this meeting was going well, Telamon invited the captain inside for tea and a chance to show him the dozen mutilated women. He wanted the captain to appreciate fully the magnitude of the tortures inflicted upon the women of the palace court. One incredibly wiser captain left several hours later. He was dismayed at the condition of the twelve women with their debilitating lip plates, but even more astounded with their ability to plant their thoughts directly into his mind. That all these women were somehow levitating their cups and spoons also blew his mind. He had much to report to General Kratos. Not knowing the general's intentions, Telamon wanted the general to realize that these women were now not only able but powerful.

On June 1, the two promised caravels arrived, filled with all manner of inventions and two engineers. The mayor arranged for them to have a whole warehouse in which to setup their many demonstrations. They needed a week to get everything reassembled and back into working order. They even had one small portable steam engine to provide electrical power for the many inventions.

On Sunday, the two engineers gave their first demonstration to the many Church of God members, including Adonia, along with the mayor, his staff, and the Harbor Sheriff and many of his men. To say that it was a hit would be a gross understatement. In fact, the two engineers found themselves giving the demonstration three times a day for the next three weeks! Nearly everyone in Filantos wanted to see for themselves, especially their womenfolk. "We just *got* to have these here!" was the most frequent comments they heard repeatedly.

On June 20, General Kratos arrived with Captain Hermes and a whole legion of soldiers on horseback. However, he took his captain's advice and just the two of them rode up to the church to speak with Princess Adonia. After the many introductions and his witnessing of the dozen with lip plates and the others taking tea, he was dutifully impressed with them, compliments of Telamon, who had insisted on making darn sure that he fully understood the power that these women represented now. He still didn't know the intentions of the general, but he was not about to allow anything bad to happen to any of them. Far too much depended upon these women now.

At last, they left Adonia alone with General Kratos. She began, "Well, from what little we have seen and heard here in Filantos, you have been doing a fine job of running things. The awful sadism of my parents and their advisors is over now for good, I hope."

"Yes, I simply could not stomach it any longer. I believe that I have stamped all such activities out in the capital. I must apologize for not getting to Filantos sooner, but the crisis in the city of millions has kept us incredibly busy until the last couple of months. At this point, my soldiers are fanning out to the smaller towns and villages setting things to rights there," he replied.

He cleared his throat. "The reason for my visit, Princess, is that by our laws, you are entitled to be our leader, our queen. The throne of Phindos is yours. I have been stalling the many noblemen who have been pressuring me to allow them to regain control. Personally, I am not very inclined to allow them that power. Look at all the sadists that they have elected to run our kingdom in the past. I just won't stand for it any longer."

He went on, "Back when the plague started, I was informed that you somehow went missing. Everyone rather forgot about you after that. I figured that you had the smarts to get yourself out of that den of sadists. I've been searching for you ever since. Say the word and the throne is yours. You have my full support and the support of our army of forty thousand. By the way, the Banca del Dio has accepted me as a signatory on the kingdom's accounts. However, I have only withdrawn funds to pay our soldiers, Princess."

Adonia bit her lip. Becoming Queen of Phindos was the last thing that she wanted to do right now. "General, come with me. I want to show you just what we are doing here in Filantos." He agreed. He was given the opportunity to watch how the Women's Ways worked and got to witness a Holy Gift session, carefully timed so that he could see the woman as she finally erased the plague's trauma. He chatted with women who had received her gift, her lessons, and her Hints book. Then, he was given a complete demonstration of the incredible MMCE inventions hosted by the two Velona engineers. To say that he was impressed would be an understatement. He begged and pleaded for her somehow to give this Holy Gift to his wife, Io, and his three daughters, whom he had been protecting these many months.

Although she talked all this over with Than, both agreed that she had to assume the mantle of ruler. She agreed, "Okay, I will accept the rulership of Phindos. However, I will be our Monarch not queen. There will be no king. For the time being, I will rule from here, so that I can continue my Holy Gift sessions and supervise the MMCE program. You, General Kratos, will continue to run Pirgos, handling the daily affairs. I'll send along an LD radio so you can chat with me anytime you desire and vice versa. You send your wife and three daughters here, and I'll see that they get their gifts and training immediately. Plus, I want you to meet with all the wealthier nobles. Have them come to Filantos to see this MMCE demonstration. I'll then get them onboard. With their backing and funds, we are going to get these inventions widespread throughout Phindos as rapidly as we possibly can."

She went on, "I will continue to see to it that all women who want to learn how to deliver the Holy Gift are given the chance. Over time, we will have an army of them and will be able to deliver the gift to every man, woman, and child in our kingdom. Once that is done, I will return and sit on the throne. Is this acceptable to you?"

He gave her a big, strong hug. "Absolutely, Your Majesty! Absolutely. But what about your security here? How can we protect you from assassins and the like?"

"You don't need to, general. Look, we both know that living in the palace is like being in a prison, and assassins can get to me. My parents and their advisors are a prime example. No, I will not live in a prison, separated from our people. I will be among them. If some assassin wants to shoot me with a long gun, there is nothing that you could do about it anyway, even if I was in the Royal Palace Throne Room. If they try something closer, they will be dead. Look." She lifted the general up, moved him rapidly across the room, and then brought him back before her body.

His mouth waggled, but he was speechless. She added, "If you were threatening me, I would have tossed you far away like a rock. We are very able to protect ourselves, excepting of course the surprise long gun shot by cowards. You worry about other things, okay?" He agreed.

During July, the middle of their winter, over a hundred wealthy men and a few women made the journey to Filantos. Each was dutifully impressed with the incredible inventions of the MMCE program. All praised Monarch Adonia for her foresight in arranging to bring these to Phindos. She gave them the enormous task of getting them somehow into production and implemented.

She quickly discovered that she needed someone who was an excellent planner to coordinate the many different projects. Obviously, the infrastructure had to come first. To her utter astonishment, Kassandra and her new husband Diomedes volunteered. With such things, it turned out, she excelled! By spring when things really got into motion, her new Minister of Planning, Kassandra and her Assistant Minister, Diomedes, began their massive coordination efforts. True, when a new person first met the Minister of Planning with her now five inch in diameter lip plates, they were hesitant. However, her incredible presence, bright mind, quick thinking, and keen grasp of all aspects of planning wowed them, to say nothing of her using telepathy to communicate to them soon turned them into ardent supporters. By summer, when Kassandra walked into a room, everyone paid very close attention to her and not because of her incredible looking lip plates!

With Adonia's access to her kingdom's finances, she was able to pay each Holy Gift giver fifty gold a week. During the fall and winter, their numbers continued to grow exponentially. By mid-spring, October 824, the Church of God in Filantos now had some twenty thousand women delivering therapy sessions each week. All the women in the greater Filantos area had received their gift and they were now fanning out across the countryside. Most had their husbands along with them and helping with the scheduling and physical arrangements. True, the Church of God could have had far more therapy givers by now; it was just that they could not deal with so large and expansive group of women.

Telamon estimated that in three years, they would have given therapy sessions to everyone in Phindos. However, he, Adonia, and the others wanted it to happen sooner than three years, but even trying to manage twenty thousand women givers at one time was boggling their minds. Surprisingly, in late July, the eleven lip plated women stepped up offering to help.

One of them, Alekta, suggested. *Look. We eleven have given this some serious thought. Suppose that we organize our people this way. The basic unit is a legion of one hundred, half men and half women. The men handle the administration lines while the women give the sessions. We make up one thousand of these legions, giving us fifty thousand therapy sessions going each week. Next, we make up a Company Unit composed of ten legions. The Company Unit would have ten men and women in it. The women handle the tougher cases while the men handle the coordination of the ten legions. We need a hundred of these Company Units. Next, we make up a Division Units, consisting again of ten men and women to control and direct ten of these Company Units. We need ten of these Division Units. There are ten of you and eleven of us plus three with Adonia. That is twenty-four of us to direct ten Division Units. Once we have that going, we could expand until each one of us is controlling a Division Unit. If we could get that many people involved, so that each of us was controlling a Division, we'd be giving one hundred twenty thousand sessions each week. At that rate, we'd get to everyone in a year.*

"Brilliant, Alekta! Positively brilliant!" Telamon exclaimed. "This is the answer I have been searching for! Incredible! How about you eleven being the first of the Divisional commanders? The rest of us will work on the training of new women and getting them organized into legions and pulling out the best for the Company and Divisional Units."

Thanks to Alekta, they finally had their organizational design, one that would work. Of course, most women and men would not participate from the beginning to the very end. That would take them away from their homes, families, and businesses for over a year. In the end, the new recruits made up for those who had to leave.

In October 824, Stefano and I placed a checkmark in the done column for Phindos. We'd gotten another country salvaged.

Chapter 48 The Civil War of Theos

The recruiting sergeant looked the frightened family over. He pointed to a gangly lad who looked to be perhaps eighteen. "You'll do. You are ordered to join the army. Move over there," he pointed to a half dozen other young men that he'd already recruited.

"But I have a wife and baby to support," he protested. "You can't take me, they cannot live without me."

"Tough luck. We all have to make sacrifices. Now move over there."

"I won't. You can't make me. I have to support my family," the lad protested loudly.

"Okay, have it your way," the sergeant replied. Turning to one of his squad members, he said, "Shoot him."

Private Kyros looked at him. He knew the lad; he'd played ball with him when they were children. "Sir, I can't. He has a family to support."

"Shoot him. That's an order private!" the sergeant yelled at him. Still Kyros refused to raise his long gun. "Arrest him for treason," he yelled. Quickly, two others grabbed Kyros' arms, pinning him. The sergeant repeated his shoot order and another private obeyed. Blam. The women screamed. The young father dropped to the ground, a bullet hole quite visible in his head. Blood splattered on his wife's face and that of his young infant son, who were standing behind him. She shrieked and dropped down to lean her head on him, almost squashing her infant in the baby sack across her chest.

A half hour later, another father was murdered while trying to prevent the recruitment of his eldest son. Then, with a wagon load of new recruits and Kyros tied up and in the wagon as well, the recruiting army squad headed out of the village. A couple hours later, they stopped for the night. The soldiers forced the new recruits to make camp and prepare their meal. Once they ate their fill, they allowed the recruits to devour what little was left, laughing all the while. Adding insults to the mix, they forced the recruits to wash up the dishes as well.

Then they made them all climb back into the wagon. "You'll sleep in the wagon tonight, recruits. Army life, get used to it," the sergeant ordered. They grumbled and complained, but what new recruits wouldn't, he thought. "These are hard times," he recalled his general explaining.

As full dark came here in the late fall, the new recruits began shivering. They were not even given blankets. One sentry was posted. When Kyros thought the soldiers were asleep, he whispered to the new recruits, "I'm getting out of here. Anyone with me? Only one sentry." Many nodded and one untied his hands. "You all stay put," he whispered. When the sentry's eyes were looking away, cautiously he climbed out of the wagon. It was a simple matter to sneak up behind him. The sentry was half-asleep anyway, just waiting to be relieved. Wham! Kyros hit him over the head with a fire log and caught his body before it could fall and rouse the others. He took the man's long gun and knife.

Slowly, he stole over to the other sleeping men, five plus the despicable sergeant. He brought the butt of the gun down hard on the sergeant's neck, killing him instantly. One by one, he moved down the line and repeated his action. Three minutes later, he called out, "Okay, they are all dead. Come and grab their guns, money, and horses. Put their stripped bodies in the wagon. We can't take that with us. It is army issue and would be recognized at once. We'll burn it and the bodies."

A half hour later, the six plus Kyros had armed themselves, confiscated all of value, and torched the wagon which now held the corpses. "What do we do now?" one lad asked.

"Good question. You might sneak back to your village, but be alert. Everyone there knows that you were taken away by the recruiter. If the army men come back and ask questions, you are sure to be found out. Even though you had no hand in killing these bastards, you'll still be blamed. However, you could take your family and move to another village tomorrow. Or if you want, you can join up with me. I aim to go after more of these despicable excuses for soldiers."

Three joined him and three headed back to the village to take their families elsewhere before the army missed these men. As Kyros and his three new recruits rode off into the night, one asked, "What do we do now? Where will we get any food when what we've taken runs out?"

"I'm going to join up with the Free Militia, if I can find them. They are around somewhere. They have been giving General Herodes absolute fits for a month now. Out here in the country, you can identify yourself as a Free Militia man and most farmers and villagers will give you lodging and food for a night. They hate the general and his soldiers as much as we do."

General Herodes had staffing problems as the year 824 rolled along towards winter. Originally, he commanded twenty thousand soldiers, that is, some two hundred legions. When the plague struck, he ordered all the outlying legions who were closer to the borders with other kingdoms here to Theolopolis to help guard the capital city, where millions lived. However, as the plague's effects were so devastating, he began losing men. Some got sick and died while handling all the dead bodies lying around the streets of the huge city. Others began quietly deserting, heading to their own homes and families who were obviously in great need. Before he became alert to the desertion problem, he had lost five thousand men! Now he had standing orders that any deserter was to be executed immediately. This slowed the pace down dramatically, though not entirely. Now soldiers so inclined picked more opportune times to desert, as had Kyros.

Quelling the riots and looters had cost him a thousand casualties, though half would recover in time, he hoped. Yes, he had a staffing problem, which he first attempted to solve by posting Soldiers Wanted posters around the huge city. He got no takers.

Then he began sending out his recruiters who went door to door, picking able young men. Those who refused to be drafted were shot, as well as any others who tried to stop them. That worked for a time, though the recruits turned out to be nearly worthless as soldiers. The noblemen who continued to support him as the temporary ruler backed his actions. Obviously, the soldiers were the only thing standing between them and utter chaos. Still, the general wisely did not try to recruit from the noblemen's families, not at first anyway.

They recruited from the poorer sections of town. This did not go well either. After a number of men were shot, the general discovered that his recruiting units were subject to ambushes and the entire squad murdered either en route to a new selection site or returning from one with a wagon load of new recruits, who also disappeared. Finally, he sent his recruiters to the outlying towns and villages, hoping this would fill his ranks. It didn't.

"What? The whole recruiter squad has disappeared? That is not possible! Send out a whole scouting party. Find them, damn it!" General Herodes bellowed. His major saluted and spun on his heels, then smartly walked out.

Captain Kakios ordered, "Well, you heard the major, mount up. We ride immediately. Find the lost recruiters." He saluted his major and mounted his mare. Here in Theolopolis, he took point leading his twenty men as they rode impressively through the streets heading south. However, once clear of the city an hour later, Captain Kakios dropped back, sending a private to take the point position.

Why? Theos had vast tracts of forests, which were ideal for ambushes. Better waste a private than a captain, he thought. Still with twenty men under his command, he hardly expected any real trouble. Rather he began pondering just how he ought to go about finding the "lost" recruiters. He knew the sergeant well, a tough, no nonsense man. No way would he ever consider deserting the army as so darn many of the younger soldiers did these days. Captain Kakios was a career soldier, having spent the last ten years serving under General Herodes. Now twenty-eight, he looked back on his career as being worthwhile for the most part, up until the plague struck that is. For the last eight months now, things continued to slide downhill as far as he was concerned.

While he did not always agree with the general's position or orders, he respected them. The army was the only thing standing between utter chaos and anarchy and law and order now. The king and queen were long dead as well as most of their advisors. Their sons and heirs were gone as well, compliments of the Church of Jehosanity. For a time, he pondered just how that church could have issued the orders to kill all their most prominent followers. That made no sense to him.

Late in the afternoon, they entered a village and made inquiries. Yes, the recruiters had passed through here two days ago, but had neither stopped nor recruited here. They pushed on down the road, entering another patch of tall oak trees.

Bang! Bang! A volley of long guns broke the stillness of the woods. Birds took flight all around them adding to the confusion. Smoke puffs appeared on both sides of the road. Four of his men fell to the ground, while the others grabbed their guns and returned fire, adding to the noise.

"Cease firing! Cease firing!" Captain Kakios ordered. His men were shooting wildly, hitting leaves and trees. Other than that first volley of shots, he'd seen nothing else. While his men reloaded their guns, several dismounted to check on their casualties. All four were dead. Hastily, he ordered a burial detail and confiscated their personal possessions and doled out their equipment to four others and tied their back packs onto the four empty saddles.

An hour later, they rode onwards. Towards evening, once more gunfire broke out. This time, three more of his men were hit. Again, whoever was firing did not stick around for a second shot as his men returned fire towards the locations of the visible powder puffs. Since the hour was late, they made camp here, burying two more, and attending the shoulder wound of the third man. Quite a few of his men grumbled about these blatant attacks, but there was nothing that he could do about them, except press onwards.

Midmorning, they came across a burned out wagon and stopped. "Damn, that is definitely one of ours," Captain Kakios observed. A private pointed out that there were human remains inside its bed and they estimated six bodies had been burned. Once more, they dug a grave, putting the combined remains into one hole. Well, this was a quick trip, he thought. Obviously, the recruiters had been ambushed and killed. Worse, their horses, guns, and supplies were taken by the enemies. He knew the general would be spitting angry when he made his report.

After a light lunch, they mounted up and headed north back to Theolopolis. Now the men held their long guns at the ready. They would not be taken by surprise a third time. In fact, the point man rode several hundred feet ahead of the main group. Bang! Bang! Another volley of four shots rang out. Once more, his men returned fire, aiming at the general locations from which the powder puffs hung in the air. Four more of his men died this ambush. He had lost half of his whole squad and with one too wounded to fight.

Two hours later with their fallen buried, they hit the road once more. Several now carried two long guns, one in hand and one over their shoulders. The ten were getting very edgy now, especially since two men were tied up leading the string of ten horses. Nothing further happened and they eventually pitched camp just outside the village that they had passed through before. His men were getting edgy now.

Sipping coffee, he pointed out, "Look there cannot be more than four rebels out there attacking us. They fire and leave. If they try it again, after they fire, whatever you do don't fire blindly back. Your new orders are to charge full speed towards the powder trails. Look, they need a couple of minutes to reload. If you charge into them, they cannot reload and will be sitting ducks." This appealed to the men whose morale was sinking rapidly.

In the morning, they headed out once more, beginning by riding through the village again. As they entered, a young woman ran out in the street in front of them and began yelling at them. "You took my husband. Now how am I supposed to survive? I have no one to help me. I'm starving. You soldiers are supposed to be helping us. Why are you killing us? Tell me that? Why? Why? What am I supposed to do now?" She ranted on and Captain Kakios tried to lead his men around her, but she kept backing up and putting her body in his way. "Why? Why? How am I to live now? Tell me, tell me."

At last, he had no choice but to push on ahead through her, knocking the helpless woman onto the ground. As his men passed by her, he turned in his saddle to see if she was all right. The woman did not get up. "Damn!" he thought to himself. He'd just run down a helpless woman. Well, she just wouldn't get out of the way, he justified. We need more soldiers, but probably the general was wrong to be conscripting married men, whose wives depended upon them, he considered. Soon the village was left behind them.

Around noon, again four gunshots rang out as they entered another dense patch of forest. Four more of his men fell off their horses. Their point man was well out in front of them; he turned in his saddle, saw that only four men plus the wounded man and Kakios remained mounted. He kicked his horse into a gallop on down the road, deserting the army, saving his own life. Four soldiers did as ordered and charged into the trees where they thought the fire had come from, their guns leveled ready to fire. Captain Kakios dismounted along with the wounded man and moved over to check on the four fallen men. Damn, there was nothing he could do for them. He was not a doctor. Watch over them, private," he ordered, remounted and headed off after his other four men. He heard more gunfire and was optimistic that his strategy had worked.

Behind him, he heard a horse take off at a gallop. Turning, he saw the wounded man fleeing for his life, another deserter, he thought. He reined in quickly. His four men lay dead on the ground, where they had fallen! Evidently, either their enemy had more than one long gun at the ready or there were more than four of them, he couldn't tell which. For the first time in his life, Captain Kakios was spooked! He was alone; all twenty of his men were dead or gone. It was just him against his unknown enemies.

Self-preservation kicked in. How long had it been since he'd heard the last volley of shots? Too long. By now, they could have reloaded and were taking aim at him! He whirled his horse around and kicked her into an all-out gallop, heading south, back towards the small village, where the woman who had been trampled by him and his men lived. He feared for his life now. He continually looked back over his shoulder, expecting to see a bunch of men galloping after him. After all, he was a prize target, a full captain. He saw nothing coming, but then he realized that if he entered the village, angry relatives of the woman might try taking a pot shot at him as well. He certainly would not be welcomed there either. He veered off the road to the east and headed across country, putting some miles between himself and his imagined pursuers. At last, he halted, his horse well lathered and in dire need of a rest.

He listened but heard no sounds of pursuit and relaxed. He began to think of what he ought to do now. If he could somehow return to Theolopolis, how would General Herodes react to hearing that he had lost his entire squad without ever having seen their enemies? He knew that he would be court marshaled at the very least, demoted if lucky, executed if not. However it went, his career in the army was over.

His world came crashing down on him. The trampling of the woman loomed large in his mind. Suddenly, all the general's orders that he had felt were wrong flooded over him. He knew he had been a willing participant to actions that were harming the very people whom he had pledged to protect! His self-respect crumbled utterly. He felt less than worthless. For a moment, he pulled out his pistol and pointed it at his head. Damn, he just couldn't pull the trigger. That image of the trampled woman loomed large in his mind. Was she dead? Seriously injured? Somehow, he had to know what had happened to her. Well, he could not ride into that village dressed as he was — a soldier. He dismounted and began rummaging through his saddlebags.

Fortunately, he still carried around some old work clothes, which were needed when he did some dirty work, such as carting off the dead bodies after the plague. The knees were pretty well worn out, but serviceable. He changed his clothes and tossed his uniform aside. He'd never wear that again. He looked himself over and ripped off the army insignia from his tack and bags. Satisfied that he now was not identifiable as a Theos soldier, he mounted up again. He headed back to the village, intent on finding out about that woman.

It was getting dusk as he entered the village. He guessed perhaps some five hundred lived here. A few men were milling around just outside the local pub. He headed there. "Hello," he said and dismounted. "Serve good ale here?"

"Sure do."

He nodded. "Say anything exciting happening around here today? I heard some gunfire in the distance as I came down the road." He tried to probe them for information.

"Nah, all quiet here."

"That's good these days. Any of those darn soldiers around? Do I need to be alert?" he asked.

"Some came through here earlier today. Ran Xene down they did."

"Wow. Is she all right? Was she hurt?" he asked what he desperately wanted to know.

"Fool of a woman darn near got herself killed. They took her back to her home, last house on the right."

"Well, I'm thirsty." He excused himself and went inside for an ale to keep up the pretense and to think about what to do next. Kakios decided that he ought to drop by her house and see how she was doing. When he came back outside, the men had left. He led his horse on down the street, looking for the last house on the right. Her home was in dire need of repairs, that was a certainty.

It was now dark, but he saw no nights on. He hesitated then took a deep breath and knocked on the rickety door. He knocked a second time then realized that she might be having a hard time getting to the door. Women were now so darn helpless and fragile, he thought. At last, a small boy opened the door. "Hello. Is Xene home? Can I see your mother?" He just assumed that this four year old boy was her son.

He opened the door and called out, "Mom, some man is here. Wants to see you."

"Tell him I can't get up right now." He nodded to Kakios; obviously, he'd heard her.

Kakios came on inside and followed the boy as he led him into the small, darkened home. The woman was lying on a front room couch. A five year old girl wearing a tattered dress sat on the floor beside her. "Hello. I am Kakios. I heard that you stood up to the soldiers today and got trampled. I thought that I might come by and lend you a hand, see if you needed anything, ma'am."

"My leg aches. I can't stand on it. Please, sir. Can you light our lantern and somehow fix the kids something to eat? We've hardly anything to eat though. Matt, you and Ambrosia show him where the lantern is at and our kitchen. I am Xene."

"Certainly. Come on, Matt, Ambrosia, let's get some lights on, and get you something to eat," he replied. Matt led him over to a table and pointed out the lantern. He lit it and then Ambrosia called to him, telling him here was the kitchen. He lit another two lanterns there and began to look around for their food supplies.

"We got beans," Ambrosia explained. He didn't find much else. She had not lied; they were indeed in dire straits.

"Wait here, Ambrosia. I'll be right back." He went outside to his horse, retrieved his trail bag of food, and brought it inside. "Let's see what I have in my pack. We want something besides beans." She watched him pull out his carefully wrapped dried food and became excited. So much food!

He cut up some dried bacon, added that to the beans, and then took out four fish slabs. He fired up their stove and set to work. A while later, he asked, "So where do we dine, Ambrosia?" She giggled and led him into their small dining room.

"I sit here, mom sits here, and Matt sits here between us so he can feed us," she explained. "Where will you sit?"

"Oh, I'll sit by your mother so I can help her, I suppose. Where's the plates?" he asked.

"Over here, Matt usually carries them, one at a time. He's only four you know. Mom and I can't carry them anymore, not since we got sick. Did you get sick too?"

"Sure did. See my pants? Nearly wore holes in my knees."

"So did daddy, but then the soldiers came and took him away. He got killed after that. Now it is just us, though Alex sometimes comes by to help us a little. He runs the only store in town."

He got the table set and the food carried over. While the kids sat down, he went to check on Xene. "Food is ready. Can you make it to the table? I can carry you, if need be."

"My leg. I can't stand on it. Maybe you can hold me and I can sort of hop. I was very foolish today, standing in front of those soldiers. I got what I deserved. Ouch. They said it is not broken, just badly bruised. Thank you for helping us, Kakios." He got her seated.

"I'm sorry. I have not been around women — I mean since you lost your arms. You have to tell me what I need to do."

"Watch me," little Matt said, as he lifted a bite of fish up for his sister to eat.

"Where did all this food come from?" asked Xene, shocked to see a real slab of fish on her plate.

"My pack. I just added a bit to your beans. Tomorrow, I'll see what I can fetch from your grocery store."

"You don't have to do that. Somehow, we'll manage. You look rather familiar. Do you live on a farm around here?" she asked.

Kakios sighed, eventually she would realize that it was he who had run her down. He decided to come clean. "I ran you down out there on the street today. I am deeply sorry for having done that to you. I truly am so sorry."

"You — you were their leader! I thought I recognized you. Why? Why run down a helpless woman? Why are you here now? Are you going to beat me up or rape me?"

"No, no, I am truly sorry. I was leading the squad, and I just wasn't thinking right. We soldiers are supposed to be protecting you folks, not hurting you. My whole squad is dead now, except for two who deserted. Ambushed four times. Now I am a deserter. I just cannot any longer support General Herodes and his foul orders. So now, I will probably have a price on my head. Yet, I just had to come back to find out how you were doing and to help you a bit. Please, I mean you no harm. I know that there is no way, but I really want to make amends with you for what I've done. Please." He held another bite of fish up to her mouth.

She accepted the bite and stared at him long and hard, then chewed the fish. At last she said, "Apology accepted." She looked him over, seeing a twenty-eight year old man, strong and robust, with short brown hair and blue eyes. He had a weather-beaten face and was in need of a shave. He was not particularly handsome, but had a solid look about him.

He saw a rather plain woman with waist length brown hair and brown eyes. Her eyebrows were bushy, but she had a presence that commanded his attention. Here was a woman who spoke her mind and took action on her beliefs. She added, "Thanks for the fish and bacon. We haven't had meat for almost a month now."

When they finished, she said, "Kakios, this is so embarrassing for me, but can I please impose on you to help me go to the bathroom? I can't stand and I really do have to go. God, what has become of us women? We ought to have just died when the plague came."

"Just tell me what to do, Xene. I'm glad that women have survived. Our whole civilization depends upon you women. No women, and we're extinct." He helped her with this and then got her changed into her nightgown. He learned that until tonight, they had been sleeping in their clothes, since Matt had too difficult a time trying to dress them. Slowly the harshness of their lives became real to Kakios. He tucked the children into bed and then spread out his bedroll on their living room floor and turned in himself.

The next morning, he was roused by the children and had them help him fix them some breakfast. Xene limped out of her room and watched this strange man as he fixed their food. He did have a way with her children, she mused. "Morning, Xene. You are feeling better?"

"Aches, but I can walk. Thanks."

By the light of day, he saw the abject poverty that this family was enduring. Their home was in need of major repairs. Her husband had been killed several months ago, and they had been struggling, just barely staying alive since then. After breakfast, he headed off, got them a large supply of groceries, and then set to work repairing things right and left.

As he finished, Xene, who had been watching him all day, said, "Thank you, Kakios. I feel so awful that I can no longer do much of anything for my family. I am so helpless now, but somehow we managed to stay alive. So what are you going to do now that you have deserted the army? Won't they hunt you down and shoot you? What about your family?"

"Honestly, I just do not know what I am going to do. Yes, if soldiers find me and recognize me, they will execute me. My parents are gone now, plague. I've made the army my career since I was eighteen. Now I am out on my own. I have no idea at all what I am going to do. I just knew that I had to come back and make amends with you for what I did to you. Other than that, I don't know. I cannot stick around here too long, though. Soldiers will undoubtedly return within a few days looking for what happened to my squad."

"The Free Militia got them, I expect. They operate around these parts, striking a blow for all of us. Honestly, the army is causing us more harm than good."

"They are certainly being effective. Say, do you have any place you could go where you would be better off?"

"My parents have a farm down near Trikala, but I have no way to get us there. It is too far to walk."

"Say, what about I take you and your family there? The army's arm does not stretch that far. I ought to be safe way down there as well."

"Would you? That would be the kindest thing imaginable. I hate to dump myself and kids off on my parents, but right now, I have no one else to turn to for help."

"It would be my honor to take you there. Let's get planning. Don't suppose that you folks have a wagon?" They didn't of course, so he spent the last of his money purchasing a one-horse wagon and plenty of supplies. The family had little to pack, little in the way of possessions, but he made sure that they had plenty of blankets. Winter was just around the corner; the nights would be cold. A day later, he packed their breakfast pans and dishes, lifted both children up and into the wagon, and then helped Xene climb aboard as well. She flashed him a big smile and sat down beside her children, who watched as he tied his horse to the rear of the wagon. Then they were off on a two hundred mile journey southward.

They had gone but ten miles, approaching another village when gunfire erupted from just ahead around a bend. Heavy forest prevented Kakios from seeing what was happening. He pulled their wagon off to the side of the narrow rutted road. "We'd best wait here for a bit," he explained to Xene. She nodded, huddling her two children close to her. Gunfire grew louder. Six men came galloping around the bend, ordinary men, he thought. Perhaps fellow travelers, he considered. Maybe not, each carried a long gun.

As they cantered past the wagon, one called "Look out!" Kakios reached for his long gun. Just as he was bending to pick it up, six soldiers cantered around the bend. They spotted the other six ahead of them and fired another volley. Pain shot through Kakios' head, darkness fell. Bang! Bang! More shots came from close at hand, but Kakios was only dimly aware of the sounds, the last thing he heard.

He came to. It was dark still. His head throbbed. Something cold pressed against his head. Slowly consciousness returned. He was lying on the cold, hard ground. A crackling fire cast eerie flickering lights. Kakios tried to sit up but his head forced him back down, throbbing mercilessly. Little Matt moved the cold, wet rag back onto his forehead. "What happened?" he whispered.

"Mom didn't wake up. They put her into the ground," the four year old replied. Now Kakios saw the boy's eyes were red; he'd been crying. A sniffle got his attention. He looked a little to his left and his eyes focused on Ambrosia, who was still crying softly to herself. Both children were sitting on either side of him. They were in some kind of camp out of doors — that he knew.

"Ah, awake at last, Kakios. The kids told us your name. I'm Bion. Sorry about your loss. Xene was killed by the damnable soldiers, who just shot at everything on the road. Wrong place at the wrong time. You are incredible lucky, grazing shot on you skull. A half-inch lower and we'd have buried you too. We got them all, thought. That whole squad of soldiers is history now. Welcome to the Free Militia camp. Got some stew if you are up to eating."

Damn not Xene too, he thought! He looked at the two children who now had no one at all to look after them. "Come here you two," he spread his arms open. Both Matt and Ambrosia laid down beside him and rested their heads on his shoulders, his arms encircling both, holding them tightly. Both children really needed comforting now that was plainly obvious to him. "I guess I get to be your father now. Somehow, I'll take care of both of you."

Later, Kakios got up and brought some stew back for three to eat. As he fed Ambrosia, her desperate situation was even more acute in his mind. What could he do now? He had no idea where Xene's relatives lived. He'd failed to learn her last name even and neither child knew. They'd only known their village. "Can we go home now?" she asked.

"Yes, I don't know where else we can go, Ambrosia," he replied with a heavy heart.

When he finished eating, he felt better and Bion came over again. "Feeling better I see. Say, Matt here says that you used to be a soldier. Is that true? We could always use experienced men in our battle with the evil soldiers."

"Yes, I used to be a captain. Now I am a deserter too. I cannot stomach what General Herodes is doing any longer. I was trying to get Xene and her children to safety. Guess I blew that one."

"I take it that Xene and you were not married? These children aren't yours?" he asked bluntly.

"No, I was helping her. Our soldiers had recruited her husband by force and he was killed. She was all alone trying to survive with her two children. Now they have no one but me. I've promised to raise them," he answered. He felt too ashamed to tell him how he'd run her down in the street.

"Commendable. We all have to do our part — helping our women and children. So what are your plans now?"

"I suppose the only reasonable thing is to return to their shanty home in the village. At least the kids will have a roof over their heads. Why?"

"I've a girlfriend there. I'm sure that she will be willing to help you look after them. Consider joining up with the Free Militia, we could use a well-trained soldier like yourself. Think about it. We can talk more in the morning when we go into the village. You will find that there is a whole lot of support for us, the Free Militia, that is. Even in Theolopolis."

A few days later, Eudora, Bion's girlfriend, waved goodbye to the group of Free Militia men. She moved the two children into her home not far from their shanty home. She was twenty and determined to do her part. Her father ran the blacksmith shop and was also an ardent supporter of the Free Militia. Kakios had given both Matt and Ambrosia a big hug, promising to return as soon as possible. "Kill all the bad soldiers," Matt had asked, and he'd promised the lad that he would do just that.

As winter came in early June, the civil war escalated. General Herodes fumed; his recruitment plans had ended up in the loss of an additional five thousand soldiers, men he could ill afford to lose. He was down to barely ten thousand men or a hundred legions now. "Okay, to hell with the outlying towns. We will keep Theolopolis under law and order," he barked to his majors. "Send out six legions to patrol the streets. Surely, nothing can happen to a hundred men at one time. We'll root out these filthy anarchists! Kill every one of them and anyone who gets in your way." Six majors saluted and left to carry out their designated sweeps of the capital city.

As one legion marched out of the barracks on the east edge of the huge city, a beggar, dressed in rags and a heavy cloak to ward off the light snow that was falling, tipped his hat. Further down the street, another man tipped his. Rapidly, word of the progress of this legion spread down this major street. About a mile distant, Kakios got the word that a legion was coming this way. "Okay, you all know the drill. Wait until I fire and draw their attention. Make sure that they get nicely deployed with their backs to you before you open fire," he ordered. His plan was simple. He slipped across the street, three long guns strapped across his back. Rapidly, he climbed up to the building's roof and carefully moved into position on the red tiled, sloping roof. He placed his three long guns strategically along the backside of the roof, one at either end and one in the middle. He moved to the far end where he would take his first shot. Kakios' plan was devilish. He would take three shots at the marching soldiers. Naturally, they would fan out and begin shooting back at him, taking what cover they could find.

Normally, that would be the end of it. Many shots would be wasted trying to hit the soldiers hiding behind wagons and the like. Instead, Kakios had the rest of his band of Free Militia on the opposite side of the street on the rooftops there. They were to wait until they had clear shots at the backs of the soldiers. Then, they would take a heavy toll on the legion from behind. Now he pulled his cloak over him and waited. Patience. This was the hallmark of the Free Militia. They were infinitely patient, waiting for just the right opportunity to attack, and then always with odds in their favor. They had to; they were greatly outnumbered, perhaps as much as ten to one. At least for the last week, the Free Militia men who were operating in the outlying towns and villages had been slowly coming into Theolopolis this past week, because the general had halted all of his dreaded recruitment activities. This, Kakios felt, aided their battle, allowing them to amass larger numbers for any given skirmish.

A half hour later, he spotted the bright uniforms of the men walking point just coming into view. He cocked his gun and waited. Before long, he spotted his prime target, the major who was riding his horse and surrounded by his hundred men. A captain was also on horseback. Kakios smiled, that man would be his second target. He took careful aim and fired. Leaving the gun barrel sticking up over the roof peak, he slipped down below the edge and began rolling across the red tiles. While it was awkward and uncomfortable, he dare not risk standing up; he'd be spotted easily. Rather, he wanted his gun's smoke to draw their attention and counterfire.

Bang! Bang! Shots began smashing into the tiles around the gun's position, but Kakios was now twenty feet from it, picking up his second gun. Carefully, he raised his head enough to see below. Ah, his shot had found its mark; the major was on the ground, and several men were dragging his body out of the way. A squad was providing counterfire while several other squads backed them up; the others scrambled for cover. He spotted the captain issuing orders and fired a second time.

By the time that he reached his third gun, bits of red tile were flying all around the roof as bullets flew hot and heavy. Kakios waited this time; he wasn't suicidal. As bits of tile rained down on the street below and slid down the backside not far from him, he finally heard his militia firing. Almost at once, they stopped firing his way and he hazarded a peek. Many soldiers lay in the street, shot from behind in the first two volleys from the militia. His trap had worked to perfection. Now he picked his last target carefully, drawing a bead on the sergeant who seemed to be issuing the most orders. Bang, he fired and then slid back down, bringing his gun with him. Now he hastily rolled over the roof, picking up his other two guns. He slide down and landed on a second floor porch. Hastily, he reloaded all three guns and then slipped on down to the ground. He pulled his cloak over him, hiding his guns and headed off down the alley. Carefully, he peered around the corner, looking back on the street scene.

Fifty remaining soldiers were hastily retreating the way that they had come. Ten others dropped their guns and were running away, deserting the army. Some forty bodies lay dead or wounded in the street, red streaks covering the light dusting of snow, which continued to slowly descend from the gray clouds overhead. One by one, the Free Militia men appeared on the street, coming down from their rooftop positions. Kakios gave the signal, and they moved out into the street, confiscating weapons and supplies and making sure each of the fallen were dead. Ten minutes later, the Free Militia disappeared into the side streets once more.

Two other Free Militia groups also took action that day with similar results. General Herodes lost almost two legions of men out of the six he sent out on patrols. He was livid with anger when the reports came in of the three attacks.

During the ensuing week, another three legions were lost in similar ambushes. Unfortunately, Kakios and his men were running low on power and shot. He'd already devised a clever plan to acquire more. The last attack, he had his men confiscate the uniforms of those they'd killed. Now resting in an empty warehouse, compliments of a nobleman, who had also stored a goodly amount of food and blankets there, he waited for an opportunity to put his plan into action. General Herodes still had five thousand cavalrymen left among his ninety-five legions. If he were the general, he'd stop wasting his few remaining foot soldiers and start using the cavalry, who had mobility on their side. Within the town, the cavalry were not as useful as in the open countryside.

Later, General Bion came to meet with General Kakios; both were now officially Free Militia generals, having earned the title by their constant successes. "My guess is that he has at best forty-five hundred foot soldiers, and most of those are in guard stations. He's got to start using his elite cavalry soon," Bion theorized.

"Yes, they will be far more difficult to eliminate. The best tactic will be to ambush them out in the forests. We need a way to draw them out of the city," Kakios suggested. A bit later, the two came up with a plan. It took a week of coordination to get to the other members of the Free Militia. Their organization was quite loose. On June 20, Kakios put his plan into action.

General Herodes now had large cavalry patrols roaming the city. General Bion arranged for a number of volunteers to stage an appearance of a mass group of militia cavalry. This was all a show just to get the attention of a couple of cavalry legions. Meanwhile, wearing their confiscated army uniforms, Kakios led a hundred of his militia into the First Army Barracks. They entered unchallenged and headed for the armory. Most of the foot soldiers were out on patrols within the large city and well over half of the cavalry as well, leaving only a token force guarding the barracks. Quickly, General Kakios had his men load up their five wagons with powder and shot and some replacement long guns. Then, he began spreading kegs of gunpowder around the huge warehouse. Only a few of their cannonae were still here in storage, General Herodes had most all them in defensive positions around the barracks compound, just in case the Free Militia chose to attack the base. Of course, these men were not so foolish as to make such a suicide attempt.

Once his men had returned to the main gates, Kakios dropped a torch onto the small powder line and mounted. He cantered up to his men, saluting the two guards at the gates. He joined his column and headed off into the snow-covered street. Boom! Boom! Massive explosions shook the city as the remaining ammunition detonated. Brilliant flames shot skyward like some immense fireworks display. Kakios grinned, so far so good.

Several streets later, his men swapped places with other Free Militia men, who drove the wagons off to resupply many different groups. Meanwhile, Kakios and his men rode to a back alley, where they dismounted and quickly changed their clothes, discarding the army uniforms. Now they headed for their prearranged meeting place, where the fake militiamen were waiting. Once they arrived, one by one the fake men melted back into the normal street traffic. Some of these were mere boys, perhaps ten years old. Some were old men, but all wanted to do what they could to help stop the tyranny that held Theolopolis in a vice grip.

Kakios and his men prepared for their critical role as bait. The question was: would General Herodes take the bait?

Shock and anger seethed and fought for dominance in the general's mind. The Free Militia had gone too far! They'd just destroyed his entire ammunition dump, severely crippling his entire army. His fist smashed into his desk, knocking half the papers onto the floor. "Damn them to hell!" he shrieked, as if by his mere fist he could crush them.

Soon other reports came back from his cavalry units. The Free Militia were now mounted and assembled on the southern edge of Theolopolis. Estimates suggested that they numbered several hundred. At last, General Herodes smiled, "Now we have them! Idiots. This is just what we have been waiting for. So they think that they are now strong enough to take us, well, now we can crush them once and for all! Majors, send out all the cavalry legions. Go after them. Do not return until every one of those Free Militia men is dead. Ride hard; smash them. Take no prisoners. Shoot anyone in your way. Hell, shoot anyone that even looks like they might be a militiaman! Revenge shall be most sweet!"

It took over two hours for all the fifty legions of cavalry to pack up, assemble and then ride out, heading for the southern edge of the city. As always, the local townsfolk sent along plenty of advanced warning to General Kakios and his men. At last, he gave the signal and his large band mounted up and headed out of Theolopolis, going south. His task: be the bait and lead bands of the enemy cavalry into ambushes along the way. Additionally, they also knew that the cavalry would be extremely low on powder and shot, while their forces had just been completely re-supplied, thanks to their raid on the armory.

The Free Militia dared not fight a conventional battle with the soldiers. Instead, as always, they picked their battlefields with care, preferring ambushes. A quick strike and then melt into the countryside. General Kakios and his men were the bait, leading the cavalry legions to their doom, they all hoped. About five miles south of Theolopolis, the first of many, many ambushes occurred. After Kakios and his riders passed, the other Free Militia men waited for the first of the cavalry legions, hot on their trail, to pass by their position. Soon, gunfire erupted behind them and they reined in to await the result.

Shortly after the gunfire ended, a militiaman rode up to relay the news that this first legion was wiped out. A dozen had deserted and the rest were dead. Kakios waited a while, giving the men time to mount up, move further down the road, and reposition for the next ambush. For several days and through one town, the ambushes continued, slowly eliminating the massive number of General Herodes' cavalry.

However, on July 1, General Kakios received word that the cavalry had been so angry when they enter the small town that they had murdered half of the townsfolk for no apparent reason. This did not bode will with him. Innocent men and women were being ruthlessly killed by these cavalrymen. He wondered how those men could possibly live with the atrocities that they were committing. He sent word ahead to the next village warning them to evacuate or stay indoors.

Again as bait, he waited until the cavalry closed and then galloped on down the road, leading the now encouraged cavalry into the next ambush location. What he didn't know was that several legions had joined up and were riding as a larger unit, far too many to be wholly eliminated by this band of Free Militia. As before, the trap sprang, but he soon found an entire legion galloping after him firing as they rode! Hastily, his men cantered down the snow-covered road, hoping that the other band of militia were already in their positions a couple miles ahead. He had no way of knowing, however.

Just as the cavalry closed upon his men, the firefight ambush broke out again. He had no choice but to whirl around and order his men to open fire on the charging cavalry. Lead flew in all directions. Powder plumes covered the open space of the road; tall trees lined the road, containing the smoke until at last nothing could be seen. A bullet smashed into his left arm and he lost his long gun. It fell uselessly onto the snow beneath his horse's feet. Pain shot through his arm, but Kakios continued to rally his men.

At last, he saw a friendly face emerging from the dense smoke. "Got them. You can head on out, general. Damn, you're hit!" Kakios slumped in his saddle, fighting to keep from passing out. He awoke, his arm ached. He was in a room, a bed. Men were present, talking. He passed out again. He awoke again, now he was in a wagon. It was cold out and they were rolling along. Snowflakes floated down and he noticed the blankets covering him were covered with a thin layer of the white stuff. Matt and Ambrosia were lying beside him. He tried to rise, but his left arm seemed to have problems. Then, he noticed most of his arm was gone and he panicked.

"You are alive, that's what counts," a woman's voice said from off to one side. Both kids roused and he turned to see Eudora's face. The twenty year old woman's face looked grim, but stoic. "They had to cut it off; bone was shattered they said. If you wake up, you are supposed to be all right, but. . ." her voice trailed off.

"Where are we? What's happening?" he managed to whisper. His throat was parched; his stomach growled. How long had he been without a meal? How many days had passed?

Eudora answered, "Aias is driving us south. We had to leave the village. They said that the soldiers are killing everyone in the villages that they come to, so we had to leave. Aias is one of your men. He volunteered to drive you and us to safety." He learned that he had been unconscious for three days and that they had been on the road for two of those.

Matt held a water skin up for him to drink. Ambrosia handed him a pot of cold stew with her foot. Kakios sat up and ate his fill. Although cold, he thought it delicious. "You must have been really hungry," Ambrosia giggled.

"Aye, really hungry. That was very good. Did you make it?" he asked her. She giggled again.

"Of course not, silly. I don't know how to cook yet. Eudora made it."

He looked at Eudora, who blushed. "Well, Aias cut up everything for me. We all have to do what we can, even if it is such a small thing."

He grinned and thanked her. Then, he dozed again. Gunfire roused him with a start. "What's happening?" he asked struggling to sit up. "Hand me my gun, someone." Definitely, a battle was taking place not far behind them. The noise was near at hand. Eudora told him his long gun was stowed beneath their blankets at the far right of the wagon. Kakios hastily dug through the mountain of blankets until he felt his gun. He brought out and discovered how awkward it was now going to be; his left arm was only about six inches long and still too sore even to touch the gun. He propped the gun between his knees, pointing it to their rear. He knew that he would have only one shot, in the rolling wagon; he'd never get it reloaded with one hand.

He waited, along with the other three, while Aias continued to push the horses even harder. Now he noticed that Aias had his horse tied to the rear of the wagon. Smart fellow, he thought. Patience, he kept telling himself, patience. Before long, he heard galloping horses headed towards them. Then the familiar uniforms of the Theos Army cavalry came into view. Four men were chasing after them or so it seemed to him. Patience, patience, he told himself again. None of the four raised their guns, which he took as a good sign. That didn't last long. Two of them raised their guns forcing Kakios to act. He aimed as best he could and squeezed off his only shot. Bang! One of the two who was attempting to fire on them pitched out of his saddle.

Aias twisted around, aimed at the other, and fired a bit wildly, missing the three remaining riders. Bang! One fired towards them, and Aias lurched off the wagon, smashing into the ground, rolling over and over across the snow covered ground, leaving a red stripe in his wake. "Damn!" Kakios exclaimed. He realized that no one was driving the wagon now and somehow he had to get into the driver's seat.

He struggled up and managed to get over the back seat and up front. The reins were looped around the brake handle, and he grabbed them with his right hand. Looking over his shoulder, he saw more riders coming up from behind. Bang. Bang. More shots broke the winter wonderland. Well, they missed me, he thought as he continued to keep the horses going. Eudora called out, "They shot the cavalrymen! Hurray!" Soon, two of the First Militia came galloping up and passed the wagon, then leaned over and helped Kakios slow them down. Finally, the wagon came to a stop.

"Sorry about your driver, sir. There are just too many of them for us to stop all at once. Will you be all right now?" the young lad, barely sixteen asked. Kakios assured him that he would be.

"Okay, I'll leave you to it. We'll take your extra horse. We need it, if that's okay with you. Just keep on going south as fast as you can. The cavalry is not stopping for anything," he said and the two neck reined their horses about and trotted back down the snow covered road. Kakios slapped the reins on his horses and got the wagon moving once more.

A few minutes later, they were alone once more. Snow continued to fall; already six inches covered the ground and road. The white-cotton covered trees looked pretty, as if nature knew not the problems of man. Eudora asked, "What are we going to do now? Can you drive, Kakios?"

"So far so good. Where were you heading? We'll look for help in the next town."

An hour later, they rolled into a village of some thousand people. Chaos greeted them. Everywhere, people were frantically packing up supplies and their families. A mass evacuation was in progress. Kakios pulled up by one man who looked like he might be one of the Free Militia men. "Evacuating?"

"Right, keep on going, sir. General Herodes' cavalry are on their way and are killing everyone in the towns they pass through. It's not safe to stay here." He nodded and moved on down the packed main street. Most were fleeing to the east or west, he noted. Further south lay the Ice Sheet, completely inhospitable, thought the vacation town of Trikala was there. At the edge of the town, he pulled up. A young woman was frantically trying to get anyone's attention; a five year old girl was at her side.

"Ma'am, what's wrong?" Kakios asked.

"Aias. He's in the militia, but he was supposed to come and help me leave today. He's not here and everyone's leaving. Please, help me, please," she begged.

Eudora described the man who had been driving their wagon and the woman paled. "That's him. What's happened to him?" she wailed.

"He was killed trying to save us," Kakios replied as gently as he could. "He died a real hero."

Her reaction was instant grief. Kakios climbed down and helped her into the wagon followed by her daughter. "Eudora, Matt, see if you can get her covered up. I'll go inside and grab what I can." He tied the hitch line to a fence post and ran inside. He grabbed blankets and several pouches that the woman had managed to fill. He cursed his awkwardness; still he could touch nothing with his heavy, blood-soaked left stump. He managed to get the things added to their wagon and decided not to press his luck any further. He climbed up and got the horses going again.

Few were heading due south, and he thought this might work in their favor. Soon the noise and chaos of the town were left behind. Only the quiet sobbing of the woman broke the stillness. Sometime later, she finally spoke, "Thanks mister. I'm Leda and she's Io." The others introduced themselves.

"Sit back and relax, Leda. I'll protect you and Io with my life."

"Is she your wife and these your children?" Leda asked, figuring this was another family fleeing from the tyranny.

He chuckled, "No, Eudora is the wife of one of our generals. The kids are sort of mine now. Their parents were both killed by the soldiers. I'm looking after them now."

Eudora spoke up, "He's General Kakios of the Free Militia, but he got badly wounded fighting the cavalry. He's lost his arm; it was awful."

"Ex-general now. Can hardly do a thing with only one hand," he replied, disgustedly.

"Well, that's one more than we women have," Leda replied. He kept quiet. Indeed, their lot was drastically worse than his was. He bit his tongue and drove onward.

As darkness came, they were nowhere near any town or village, so he found a likely spot where the forest opened up. Here he pulled over and climbed down. "Guess we can camp here. I'll see about finding us some firewood, and then I'll make camp. You all stay put."

After tying up the team, he did just that, lugging some dead wood and making a crude campfire circle. To his amazement, Eudora and Leda had already somehow managed to get themselves down and, using their teeth, were carrying the cooking gear and food sacks over to where he was about to light the fire. Matt, Ambrosia, and Io were getting the needed items out from under the blankets and over to the edge of the wagon for the two women. Eudora looked up at him, "We're not completely helpless. If you can cut up some more potatoes and fish bits, I'll add them to the stew pot."

He went about the many camp chores, allowing the others to do what they could. He was very surprised at what all these two women did for themselves. Later, as they sat down to eat their tins of hot stew, he was prepared to have to feed the four of them, perhaps with Matt's help. "Like this, Ambrosia," Leda demonstrated for her, having pulled her boot and sock off. She used her toes to grip a spoon and began to eat. Eudora followed her lead. Ambrosia looked at Io, who was also feeding herself, and emulated them as well. Leda looked up at an astonished Kakios and added, "We're not completely helpless."

"I am truly amazed. Well done," he replied and genuinely meant it. He later did the dishes as best he could and then helped everyone get back into the wagon. He spread the blankets out over everyone, urging them to huddle up together for warmth. At last, he crawled in on the outside, so that his stump would not touch them. At last, sleep came to them all.

Breakfast consisted of reheated stew, the last of it. He had to help the four relieve themselves, afterwards making sure that their pants were secure. Once they were safely in the wagon and well covered up, he broke camp. Soon, they were back on the road once more. From his knowledge of Theos, the next town would be Trikala, the vacation wonderland. Well, it was winter, the traditional time that many visited Trikala. This year, no one was vacationing. The road was still deserted.

To help break the monotony and ward off the cold, Kakios began chatting with Leda and Eudora. Leda's grief was very raw. Somehow, someway, Kakios felt that he had to make up to her and Io for the heavy sacrifice that Aias had made to save him and the kids. Just now, he didn't know how except to get them to a place of safety. Surely, someone in Trikala could take them in and provide temporary shelter. Keep their hope alive, he thought as he continued to keep them chatting.

Late afternoon, his heart sank. They were on a long straight patch of road not far from Trikala, when he heard the sound of many horses coming up from behind them. Eudora cried out, "Soldiers are coming! They have guns, Kakios!"

He slapped the team into a gallop. "How many?"

"Twenty or so," Leda yelled back. "What do we do?" She sounded terrified.

Kakios knew that he could not fire his gun. It took all his strength with one hand to control the horses. "Lie down flat in the wagon!" he yelled back. That way, their shots would be unlikely to hit them or the kids. In turn, he slipped down as low as possible in his seat, only the top of his head was visible from the rear. Only a lucky shot would get him now, he reasoned. His only hope was to outrun them, get into the town ahead of the cavalry, and then hope that there was Free Militia in Trikala or some men who would help stop the cavalry from their murderous rampage. He felt a pang of guilt. Likely he was bringing death to many of those who lived in the vacation land, but he had little other choice now.

Bang. Bang. Gunfire erupted, several shots whizzed past him, ricocheting off trees, which dropped clumps of snow, or puffing into the snow covered ground on either side of the racing horses. White foam sprayed from the two horses as they dashed madly along the road. The wagon slide off to the right and then the left as he valiantly tried to keep control of the horses with his one hand. Crouched down, he used his legs to keep his body from being slammed to the left and right. The only thing saving them was the gravel beneath the half-foot of snow.

Why were these soldiers shooting at them? Surely, they could see they carried nothing but two women and three children. While he used to be their enemy, now he was just a casualty of their war, almost useless as a woman was. So why were they trying to kill them? His mind just could not grasp a plausible reason. It seemed insane, crazy.

The cavalry steadily gained on the careening wagon. Just as the riders pulled within a hundred feet of its rear, the first home of Trikala appeared. He'd made it into the vacation town here at the permanent Ice Sheet, the southernmost extreme of Theos. "Oh hell!" he exclaimed. Dozens of men, women, and even a bunch of children were on the main street, carrying packages or just playing in the snow. Several snowmen lined the sides of the street. "Get out of the way! Flee! Bad soldiers are coming! Look out! They are shooting everyone! Flee for your lives!"

Zenon and Ptolmey were walking down main street, having just finished their coordination work and afternoon session. They had heard distant gunfire and became alert. They saw a wagon coming into Trikala going dangerously fast, nearly out of control. Its driver seemed in an unusual position, barely visible. A squad of Theos soldiers with guns in hand were galloping behind it, almost parallel with it. A couple of them again attempted to fire at the wagon, their bullets landing in the snow-covered street, narrowly missing a woman and several children who were putting the finishing touches on another snowman.

The two leaders of the Church of God acted. Zenon cursed, "Damn soldiers! They are liable to hit the kids. We must stop them!" Both acted, using their spiritual skills. For a brief instant, they became a cavalryman, causing its body to drop the long gun and rein in his horse. Ptolmey also took over Kakios for a moment and began to rein in the lathered, exhausted horses. The wagon flew by their position, but one by one, the cavalrymen reined in, halting not far from the two men.

Kakios found his team stopping finally and quickly jumped out, running up to the two men, who were now facing the twenty cavalrymen. "Look out you two. They are going through every town, killing whoever is there! They are nuts," he yelled to the two men, as he came up to them from behind them, all the while slipping and sliding through the snow.

In his mind, Kakios felt, *Relax, you are safe here,* but he didn't believe it. "They have come all the way down from Theolopolis and have been killing everyone in the towns and villages. You must get to safety before they start shooting again," he yelled breathlessly. Now he saw that they had somehow all dropped their long guns, though they still had several pistols and swords around their waist belts. Strange.

"Is this true? Have you been shooting men, women, and children in the villages and towns?" Ptolmey asked softly.

Their sergeant moved closer, trying to figure out why on Tarra he had dropped his long gun. Why had his men done so? Perhaps they needed to be reloaded. He drew his pistol and stepped forward. Suddenly, his hand dropped his gun into the snow. He stared in disbelief and quickly drew his spare. It too fell into the snow. He drew his sword only to find it momentarily lying in the snow, half covered. He felt the urge to speak out and did so. "We are under orders from General Herodes to kill every last First Militia men and absolutely everyone who stands in our path, man, woman, or child."

"Ah, I see," Ptolmey replied. Kakios noticed that now a large crowd was gathering, forming a huge circle around them. The middle aged man spoke softly, "And just how are an armless woman and a child a threat to a stout, strong, cavalryman such as yourself?" He noticed behind him with his spiritual being vision that two women and three children were struggling to get out of the wagon. He saw no armed men in the wagon, only the wounded man whose left arm had been amputated above his elbow.

"Well, they were ahead of us on the trail. That makes them a serious threat," the sergeant attempted to find some justification. Now that this man pointed it out, why were they firing on this wagon? "We've been ambushed time and time again on our long ride down from the capital city. These people must be involved in the ambushes." There, that seemed reasonable, if only he had not dropped his guns and sword.

The mayor had come up to see what this confrontation was all about. He had heard the sergeant's reply to Ptolmey's questions. "Ptolmey, I believe that we should arrest these men and hold them until we can prove or disprove the charges against them."

"You do not have the authority to arrest us. General Herodes is in charge of Theos, martial law.

When he finds out about this, you will be shot!" the sergeant replied testily, reaching for a pair of pistols in a soldier's waist belt who was close to him. Again, he found his hands dropping each as soon as he retrieved them. One by one, each of the other soldiers drew their pistols and swords, only to drop them into the snow at their sides.

"I agree, mayor. Have your men escort them to the holding building. Make sure that they do not have further concealed weapons on them. Then, retrieve their weapons from the snow, we don't want our children finding them and accidentally getting hurt with them," Ptolmey replied.

Quickly, the mayor and his staff began doing just that, the soldiers balked but dared not challenge the several men who drew their pistols and pointed them at cavalrymen. Once the twenty were being escorted away to the holding building, Ptolmey and Zenon finally turned to the one armed man behind them. "Hello. I am Ptolmey and this is Zenon. We run the Church of God here in Trikala. I see that your wound needs attending to at once. Your women and children also need attention. Please, come with us. You are safe here in Trikala."

"Yes," Zenon added, "let's get them back on your wagon, and I'll lead your exhausted horse and wagon to the safety of our church and get everyone attended to immediately. You shouldn't gamble on an infection in your arm there. When was the last time someone changed your bandages?"

"Thank you. We are most in need. I am ex-general Kakios of the Free Militia and ex-captain of the First Army. I have been trying to rescue these women and their children from the slaughtering of Herodes cavalrymen." They walked to the wagon and helped them back aboard. Just as Ptolmey and Zenon moved to the front to begin leading the wagon to their place, the sergeant pulled a dagger from his boot. Xenia and Hektor were walking back from their therapy sessions and were in the wrong place at the wrong time. The sergeant whirled and put the blade against Xenia's throat, a move that he shouldn't have done.

She brought her knee up sharply, grinding it into the man's groin and leaned back sharply, avoiding his blade. She spun on her left foot and brought her right foot up and thrusting it into the man's neck, snapping it. The sergeant dropped to the ground. "Well done, dear. Who are these men anyway?" asked Hektor.

"Apparently, they are General Herodes cavalrymen under orders to kill townsfolk," the mayor replied. "Search the rest of them. Kill any that try anything. Are you all right, Princess Xenia?"

"Sure, not a scratch. Weird, why would General Herodes be out to kill our people?" she asked. The mayor shrugged and suggested that they ask the newcomers for news.

When they arrived at their church-home complex, Ptolemy and Zenon had just helped the newcomers down from the wagon. "Penelope is making dinner, Xenia. See if she has some water boiling. I need to change Kakios' bandages and check on how it is healing. Hektor, take the women and children in to the bathroom and see that they get a nice hot bath and some clean clothes." To the newcomers, he added, "Everyone else will be coming home within the hour, so we'll deal with all the introductions then. Meantime, let's get you all cleaned up and his bandages changed."

Zenon led the horses and wagon to their stables, while Ptolemy took Kakios into the kitchen, where Xenia was bringing their first aid kit to the table, holding it between her neck and shoulders. "Does he need something to bite on?" she asked. "That looks ugly." Ptolmey had begun unwrapping it. Kakios fainted, so it didn't matter.

Around six, he came to and found his group had been bathed and were wearing good fitting dresses. Plus, a whole lot of others were here as well. "Ah, welcome back to the land of the living, Kakios. It is healing. I took the liberty of draining it. We'll need to change your dressings every day for a while," Ptolmey explained. Then came a long round of introductions.

He was shocked to discover Princess Xenia and Elektra were still alive and looked extremely healthy. Elektra asked, "So Kakios, Leda and Io and Matt and Ambrosia are not your wife and children. You are looking after them?"

"Yes, I promised their mother, Xene, that I would care for Matt and Ambrosia. First, she lost her husband to the soldiers, and then she was killed by them as well. A few days ago, after I was wounded and lost my arm, Leda's husband was driving us all to safety when the cavalry killed him too. I've promised to look after her and Io as well. Honestly, how can I not? They've done so much for me and Theos."

Leda spoke up, "If you two are our princesses, can't you fire or do something about the evil General Herodes?"

With increased spiritual abilities and skills come increased responsibilities, not just for their usage, but social responsibilities as well. Elektra and Xenia sighed; they'd been ignoring this aspect for months, focusing on delivering lifesaving Holy Gifts of therapy. Now finally, they both realized that they also had responsibilities to their country.

"I am not sure how the rulership of Theos falls to either princess," Hektor spoke up.

"Well, the throne has been in our family for quite a long time. Usually, Hektor, the nobles will allow a deceased king's children an opportunity to ascend to the throne," Elektra replied. "It's well documented in all of our history books. In this case, the nobles probably don't even know that we are still alive, so they are allowing the general to run the country."

"Well, sis, one of us has got to take control of Theos," Xenia added. "I vote for you. After all, you are widely read and very knowledgeable while I am mostly a fighter by nature."

"Maybe we could share it somehow. First, we have to get there and stay alive. Then get rid of this general and then get the nobles to back us," Elektra stated decisively.

"Well, you cannot go it alone. We have pretty well finished therapies here in Trikala. We ought to go with you," Ptolemy decided. "Zenon and I have discussed this at length. Althea, Judas, Hektor, Kronos, and Penelope will accompany the two princesses. Alekto comes of course." He was referring to their three year old daughter. Zenon and the rest will begin expanding our Holy Gift to others fanning outward from Trikala, getting the locals around here first, and heading across the southern portion of Theos. We'll work on Theolopolis proper and make sure nothing happens to Elektra or Xenia."

"Gosh, dear, if you become the queen, I hope you don't plan for me to become the king," Judas spoke up suddenly. He now realized that his wife may take control of Theos, but he had no wish to be the king.

Elektra laughed, "No, I just need you to be my arms. I doubt that this will work out, but we'll see. If we can just get the killing stopped, I'll be happy."

Kakios and the others began receiving their needed therapies the next day. Elektra decided that she wanted his expertise when she headed to the capital and asked him to come along. Eudora also wanted to come, if only to hear any word from her husband, Free Militia General Bion.

Thus, they prepared to leave mid-July. A slow week later, their wagons finally reached the edge of the great city of Theolopolis. Along the way, they found evidence of many mass graves off to the sides of the road. On several occasions, they also found blood stained snow as well, more evidence of brutal fighting from the civil war. At the edge of the city, a dozen armed men rode up to them.

"Hello, strangers. We are members of the Free Militia. Please use extreme caution when traveling within the city. We are still routing out the evil soldiers who went on a murdering spree," one of the men cautioned them.

"Can you get word to General Bion? We need to speak with him. It is most urgent. We have his wife here with us," Ptolmey replied. The young lad sent a rider off to fetch Bion while they decided to wait here for him. The men got a fire going and heated up some hot tea to ward off the winter's cold. Once more, the day promised more snow.

Two hours later, General Bion and twenty of his men rode up. "General Kakios! Good to see you again. Our plans have worked. Eudora!" He leaped from his horse, slipping twice before reaching her. The two hugged and embraced for a moment.

Ptolmey then began the lengthy introductions. "My god! Elektra, Xenia! Everyone thought that you were dead as well! I am so sorry about your family."

"Yes, Xenia and I escaped just barely. We've been down in Trikala with the Church of God, who have saved us. Now, I am going to try to assume control of Theos and put this wicked General Herodes out of control. Has he really ordered the murder of our citizens?" Elektra asked.

She got more than she bargained for by way of a response. Bion outlined his nearly year-long reign of terror and brutal killings, all in the name of "order." He added, "Kakios and I worked out a plan that drew his cavalry out of the barracks. We lost a hundred brave men and quite a few innocent villagers, but the plan worked. Those few cavalrymen that you got in Trikala are the last of those legions. The rest are dead or deserted. That leaves General Herodes holed up in his barracks with only a few troops. We surrounded his barracks and over several more weeks, one by one most of those men also deserted. Four days ago, we launched our assault. I am pleased to report that the general is dead. He died defending his barracks with the last hundred of his most ruthless followers. Now the city is free from his tyranny, but we are hard pressed to fill the vacuum. The nobles are giving us the most trouble. Just be very cautious in the city."

"Is the palace still safe for us to set up a new government?" Elektra asked.

"Well, the main gates are destroyed and the place has been ransacked, but with our help, I'm sure it can be made habitable once more," Bion replied.

"Okay, escort us there and let's get things organized a bit," she requested.

An hour later, they pulled into their family home, the Royal Palace. Indeed, looters had done their best to trash the place, but true to his word, Bion brought in fifty men to help clean things up and make it habitable once more. They had also found vast warehouses of food supplies, the general's private horde. Some of these they brought in for the palace needs and the rest Elektra set up as a free food bank for those in need.

During the massive cleanup project, a militiaman discovered a new LD radio system. Since Ptolmey had been staying in touch with Eve via telepathy, he knew the significance of the radio. "Please, Elektra, Xenia, you should use this radio immediately and call for help from Velona and our neighboring kingdoms. Trust me. I believe that real help can be had."

A bit later, I began a lengthy chat with Elektra and Xenia, via the LD radio. Also, Monarchs Ana and Callisto of Arolas, Sophia of Thallyus, Amynta of Penelopus, and Andromache of Axos, Thrace, joined us, congratulating Monarch Elektra Patra Platon on her ascension to the throne. They offered their support and aid. We discussed the matriarchal reorganization being adopted in the other kingdoms and Elektra decided to implement it here in Theos as well. The MMCE program was critical, I explained. Lines of supply to Theos would be difficult from Velona. Andros, Arolas was still the nearest seaport, thousands of miles from landlocked Theos. As a result, Monarch Sophia agreed to send a convoy of MMCE items and several engineers to Theolopolis immediately. Velona would then unload a similar batch of MMCE items in Andros and send them overland to Sophia. Stefano then ordered another two caravels loaded with MMCE items to set sail for Andros.

Following everyone's advice, Monarch Elektra arranged a big meeting with all the nobles who cared to come. She outlined her position as the new ruler of Theos and her MMCE plans, along with the Church of God's plans to give all women the Holy Gift as soon as possible. Further, she encouraged the nobles to invest heavily in this new technology, promising them a big return on their investments as well as this being a way for all women of Theos to survive vastly better. "We will have the MMCE things here by the first of spring. After you see these things for yourselves, then let's all work together to get this project going. If you cannot wait, Monarch Sophia of Thallyus has extended an offer for you to come to Thal and see them for yourselves right now."

Monarch Elektra put the security of Theos into the hands of her two generals, Bion and a very surprised Kakios, who expected to play no role now that he had lost his arm. "Don't be silly, Kakios, you still have a good arm and hand. That's one more that Xenia or I have." He flushed and agreed to accept the post. As he's promised, he continued to support Leda and her daughter Io, along with Matt and Ambrosia. That spring, the two wed and provided a lasting family setting for the three children.

When the spring MMCE items arrived around September 1, 824, Stefano and I put a checkmark in the salvaged column for Theos. While we were a little bit optimistic, we felt justified. Thus far, MMCE was working well in the other kingdoms. October would see Phindos also salvaged. Only parts of Thrace and Alia remained to be handled.

Chapter 49 Thrace Recovery

That an idea can be more powerful than the gun again proved itself in Thrace during the second half of 824. Monarch Andromache Gidios was extremely pleased with the MMCE expo that our two engineers put on for her and her extended family. Naturally, Urias Zoraster, her wealthy uncle, and her dad, Aison, jumped at the golden opportunity, throwing their huge financial backing behind the gargantuan project. The two immediately setup another demonstration for several other of the remaining wealthy who were still residing in Axos.

Now came the hard part, planning just how to implement these many new inventions and projects. Already they had a stream train, which ran from the port of Patri to Kefall. However, both regions were still in chaos, controlled by generals and under their martial law. Only the middle section of Thrace where Axos lay was under Monarch Andromache's control. Vast quantities of raw materials needed to be brought into the companies in and around Axos and new factories built. By November, the plans were finalized and contracts had been sent out.

Urias suspected that the many orders for coal, iron ore, copper, tin, poles, for example, would startle those in the chaos areas, particularly Kefall and Patri. Soon, the wealthy there would be wondering what was going on in Axos. Andromache knew that communication was the key. If the people in these two sections of Thrace could somehow find out what was happening here in Axos, the middle swath, then they would likely desire to be included.

Thus, in November, she sat down at her writing desk and began laboriously composing a letter outlining her rule and the MMCE program that she was implementing in Axos. "Damn, Dianthe, my mind goes at ninety miles an hour and my foot barely makes a half mile. This is ridiculous." She sighed, fighting back tears of depression.

"I know, love, but at least you can read what your foot is writing. I do hope with more practice we can write faster. We are getting better with our cooking, so maybe there is a little hope that our writing speed will improve," Dianthe replied, leaning her body to the right and left to get her ankle length black hair back over her shoulders again. Both women had allowed their hair to continue to grow, their only remaining source of vanity. The plague had removed all else, from their point of view anyway.

"But two days to get one long letter written? Honestly, this is so hopeless, Dianthe," Andromache replied. "Why did we have to get this infernal plague anyway? So many died as a result."

"I know, love, but I can't wait to get our place electrified. Then, we can have a clothes washing machine and a vacuum sweeper, to say nothing of electric lights. I wonder how soon we will get them here?" Dianthe asked.

"Well, when all the demos are done, they are planning to wire up our house first. We can then showcase the new things. Things are already starting to arrive via the new rail line from Arolas. That is likely to be a godsend for us. I wonder if we will be able to get all the raw materials that dad is hoping to acquire to get the huge undertaking started? If the rest of Thrace doesn't come through, that rail line will be our only access to what we are going to need."

"Quite true. At least we have the best protection imaginable. If any man tries to harm a women, they lose their arms too. Are you telling about that in your letter? You should. Put the wrath of the gods in it." Both women chuckled.

Andromache added, "Well, I explained that detail, but added that I did not know how widespread that effect actually is. Besides, by now, we ought to have heard if it was also happening in Patri or Kefall." This reminded her of the plight of her cousin and others who had just arrived from Alia. "I guess we can count our blessings that we were not treated like my cousin. God, those lip plates prevent all speech and they can't even bend their necks. Every little action that we can do, Dianthe, those poor women can't — well nearly all. They can't even sip tea or eat by themselves. Bethany's Hints are almost useless for them."

"I know, it's painful to watch them struggle just to nod yes or no. The only thing that is positive is their fabulous earrings. They are worth a fortune, but they look so heavy. I bet even those are troublesome to wear," Dianthe replied.

"Well, at least their husbands are taking it in stride. I found it highly encouraging that they all wanted to marry their fiancés. Honestly, if they had just forsaken the women, we'd have to hire some folks just to help them with daily life. I guess we can count our blessings, my love."

"True, this had caused me to change my opinion of men." Andromache giggled; she knew what it had been. Dianthe added, "Before it was all men are pigs. Now it is most all men are pigs." Both women laughed. After the plague, both women had hardened their opinions of men, well most men anyway.

Near suppertime, Andromache finally finished the long letter and Dianthe had given her approval of it. She picked the pages up between her teeth and headed for an adjoining office, here some of her staff had their desks and offices. Speaking between clenched teeth, she asked, "Io, will you take these to the printers? Ask them for fifty copies as soon as they can."

Io agreed and Andromache leaned forward as Io took them between her teeth. Io was eighteen and very pleased to have a job in the new government, even though it was mostly errand running thus far. Still, she had a daily job, which was far more than most women of Axos. Besides, she liked working for Andromache, who treated her with great respect. Her mouth free, Andromache commented, "Damn annoying to have to carry things around in our teeth. God, this life is becoming annoying." Io grinned and nodded. She struggled to get her dispatch pouch open with her feet and at last got the pages stuffed inside. Andromache helped her get the large leather loop around Io's head and Io headed out the door to carry out the errand.

Dianthe joined Andromache and the two headed up the long stairs to their private quarters, where they lived along with their close friends, Athena and Diona, and the many recent arrivals from Alia, whom she had granted sanctuary. "At least your uncles are fixing our meals now. That's something," Dianthe commented. Indeed, this small thing gave the four many extra hours each day to work on running the country instead of fixing meals, pitifully slowly. Now, the two had to face the lip plated women with immobile necks again. God, Andromache thought, how those women must be suffering, unable even to speak.

Eve and I knew that we had to get some able Church of God members to Axos to help Andromache and now the refugees from Alia as well. Eve took my advice and paid a visit with Raffaella who was wrapping up her studies of the zombie-like women in the tunnels of the old Kali Assassins up in Kefall. Raffaella had worked her miracle therapy and well over one thousand women were back to battery, so to speak. By early August, they had finished all the therapies, at least the basic ones. Now they faced the problem of what to do with so many women who were living in the old Kali tunnels beneath the city.

Eve and Andromache chatted via the LD radio. While the young monarch had no idea what this Holy Gift therapy was all about, she sympathized with her fellow countrywomen stuck in the tunnels beneath Kefall. With a number of men and children there as well, Andromache agreed to provide them all homes of their own in Axos. Because so many had died in Axos, vast numbers of homes were still vacant. She took Eve's advice and allowed for at least four women per home, more if the dwelling were larger. Hence, the problem they all faced was how to get these people safely transported from Kefall to Axos, some three hundred miles to the west of the Imperial City.

In late August, the trains began running once more, due solely to Andromache and her MMCE programs that initiated commerce again. The rail lines in Thrace were still in their infancy, with the single main line running from the port of Patri through Axos and on up and ending in Kefall. However, Andromache was able to arrange one special train run on August 25. The Kali II escorted one thousand two hundred ten people through the tunnels to the train station. These men, women, and children were those who wanted to take this opportunity at renewed life. The mass movement was a bit tricky and done in the middle of the night to avoid having their exit location widely seen by others. The Kali II ran protection for the folks until they could board the train. By that evening, the train pulled into Axos where Andromache met them with a large number of wagons.

It took her small staff nearly a week to get them all resettled in their new homes. She'd thought ahead and had a week's worth of groceries stored in each home along with the fully equipped low to the ground kitchens. Thus once placed in their new homes, the folks were able to begin living on their own once more.

Raffaella now had a massive organization problem: how to get a thousand Holy Gift sessions going. While she had the women trained to deliver them, she did not have transportation or anyway to get the women patients found and connected to the giver. She found herself having to establish the Church of God in Axos and Thrace from scratch. She spent a day surveying the city, looking for building possibilities. She needed a large building, preferably which had a lot of small rooms where the therapy sessions could be conducted. While there were plenty of warehouses, those would be too crude. She could not help but see five abandoned Churches of Jehosanity, along with the one that had become the Church of Skulls. She decided that the two closest to that area of Axos where the thousand plus had been resettled would work well.

Andromache agreed to let Raffaella have the two for her new Churches of God, though the monarch still had no idea why Raffaella was so eager to start a new church. Hadn't the last one, Jehosanity, proven to be traitorous? Still, she went along with Raffaella's request. On September 10, Raffaella was ready to get the therapy sessions rolling. She decided to work Monarch Andromache and her large extended family first, for obvious reasons. She would handle Andromache personally, though it was difficult for the monarch to squeeze in time from her hectic schedule to sit down and receive her therapy.

Five days later, Andromache knew the incredible benefits of this Holy Gift. "It truly is a Holy Gift, Raffaella. I had no idea how valuable and vital this would be. Honestly, all women of Thrace need to get it. Is this even possible?" Raffaella grinned. She now had what she needed here in Axos, the full support of its leader.

Raffella replied, "It is the goal of our church to see that every woman and then man in Thrace receives our Holy Gift. Yes, it will take time, but we will succeed. Those thousand women whom you've brought here from Kefall and given homes are all set to begin giving their special gift. It would help them if somehow they could get a small payment each week to help them pay for their own food and such." Andromache agreed and beginning the third week in September, each of Raffaella's one thousand givers of the Holy Gift began receiving fifty gold each week as compensation for their precious work.

For the next month, Raffaella was extremely busy working out the massive coordination of this project, training the new women who wanted to learn how to deliver the Holy Gift, and handling the minor problems that always arose during sessions. In the other kingdoms and countries, small church groups already existed and most had several who were skilled in giving Advanced Therapy and who dealt with these many issues in their lands. Here, everything fell onto Raffaella to handle. Soon she saw that she would absolutely have to have some assistance.

Unfortunately, there really was no one to lend a hand. Hence, she turned to Andromache's extended family. Her cousin Damon and his wife Doris volunteered to help, along with her brother Alexio. These three who knew the city well were given the enormous task of record keeping, advance scheduling of patients, and their transportation. Raffaella then picked the ten most competent of her women and appointed them the trainers for the new women who wanted to help others after they received their Holy Gift. By October, she only had the task of overseeing the many ongoing sessions, helping when troubles arose. Finally, she had the enormous task somewhat manageable, though she and Eve continually were on the lookout for additional Church of God personnel who could come to Thrace to help.

On November 11 when the large group arrived from Alia with their women so helpless and in dire need, her orderly world took another spin. Eleven women had debilitating lip plates, neck rings, and huge, heavy earrings. Their plight was horrific. Raffaella knew that as soon as she met them at Andromache's home; she'd lightly touched the minds of several of them.

She, Eve, Sergio, Lisa, and I all Mind Linked to discuss Raffaella's current situation. Why? Alexina Phanes. They had finished her therapy and we used her situation as a guide.

Sergio advised, *Removal of the neck rings is critical. Once that was done, she had vastly improved range of motion. She also wanted the heavy earrings removed, but with your new ones, their earrings are incredibly valuable and they might not want them removed. The lip plates require periodic enlargement, every six months or so. If not, their lips will have stretched from the pressure of the plates and the two plates will begin to droop badly. When that happens, her eating becomes vastly more difficult. It is far too dangerous for the plates to be removed; her lip loops keep getting in her way and look even weirder.*

What has saved the day for Alexina was learning to speak Annelise. It seems that that language is about the only one on Tarra, which can be spoken mostly intelligible by someone who has these lip plates. There are a few vowel sounds that come out the same, but she is understandable anyway. She has had Advanced Therapy and will be getting more once she gets over to Viborg, Annelise and joins up with her Queen Katerine and the Church of God there. Levitating her food makes eating much more doable. Still, I don't see how you can give eleven women that much Advanced Therapy.

Raffaella replied, *Good tips. No, it is far worse than eleven, Sergio. From what they are reporting, at least sixty thousand women in Alia are in the same situation with thousands more being similarly mutilated each month. It is an epidemic of huge proportions in Alia. How were the neck rings removed?*

Sergio briefed her on this detail, based upon what he had learned from Alexina and the others there in Zeederlund. Raffaella promised to look into this at once. This she did the next day, bringing two bronze workers to Andromache's Monarch's Office and home. The two men began examining the neck rings of the eleven women. After two hours of close examination, both men shrugged their shoulders. "Raffaella, there is no way to remove these rings. They have been carefully bonded at each joint where the two ends of a ring meet. See here, molten metal has completely bonded the ends together. Each ring is now a solid ring."

"Can't the bond be heated and the ends separated?" she asked.

"Sure when the women are dead," one man replied. "The heat that would be needed to partially liquefy the bonding metal would give the women an extremely serious, if not fatal, burn. Plus, it has to be done at least five times to get all the rings off their necks. By that time, they would be dead. The burning pain would just be too great. Whoever did this must have been under orders to make the rings unremovable at all costs. Great workmanship, though. Very, very well done, I might add."

Eleven women's hopes were crushed. Although she checked with the women, none wanted their expensive earrings removed. They were the least of their problems. After dismissing the two men, Raffaella offered them a little hope. "Ladies, another one of your countrywomen, Alexina Phanes, has had all this done to her. Quite by accident, she was forced to learn the Annelise language. As it turns out, even with her lip plates, she can speak quite understandably in Annelise. While I'm told a couple of vowel sounds turn out the same, for the most part, she is quite understandable when she speaks. Hence, I am going to see if we cannot get someone here to teach you and your husbands and sons the Annelise language. With luck, in a few months you will be able to speak and communicate again. That is something at least." Several waist-nodded vigorously and she knew that was probably a key point with them all, unable to speak at all.

Two days later, a fifty year old woman named Aglea came by their home. Olympos paid her handsomely to begin teaching his whole group Annelise. All sixteen threw themselves enthusiastically into the task of learning a new language. Almost at once, hope began to spring from the eleven women, who discovered that they could speak this dialect. Raffaella vowed to give them therapy sessions once they could speak well, giving her time to see what else could be done for them.

During the late summer, that is, December 824, the MMCE planning turned towards the implementation phase. Vast quantities of supplies were ordered from all over Thrace. Large contracts for coal and iron ore suddenly gave miners and teamsters more work than they could handle, their first real employment in over a year! The wealthy of Patri and Kefall and other outlying areas took Andromache's offer to come and visit her MMCE demonstration of the future that she was implementing for Axos and possibly all of Thrace.

Many of these men, she soon discovered, were hesitant to come to Axos for fear of losing their arms. "Look, you lose your arms here only if you harm or threaten a woman or girl. If you are nice to us, nothing will happen. Obviously, all the many men you see here are doing just fine." She tried to put them at ease on this point. After seeing the demonstration, they became convinced that her intentions were powerful and to be supported.

"If you want in on the ground floor of this huge project, you can invest and perhaps ultimately make a fortune. However, if you want these things for your areas, you are going to have to agree to my rule. The general in Patri must turn over control of the southern part of Thrace to me and cease his pirate ways. Likewise, in Kefall and the surrounding areas, you are going to have to get the many ruthless gangs under control and cease harming women. If you do this, I will include your areas in our advance planning for MMCE."

A week later, General Nestor arrived to view the demonstration personally. The wealthy nobles had returned and virtually ordered him to come and see for himself what all was happening in Axos. He was shocked to see so many women walking the streets, the markets open as they had been before the plague. Indeed, Axos had returned to normal, quite unlike Patri. The demos convinced him at last. "Monarch Andromache, I hereby return control of Patri to you. I have done my best to keep the chaos of the plague under control. Please do not judge me too harshly." He tried valiantly to not appear the greedy, wicked dictator that he had been for the last year.

"I suppose that you have made a tidy profit during this past year, from all the stories that I have been hearing from Patri," she said coyly. "Unless you have murdered or ordered the execution of innocents, all can be forgiven if you start investing your funds in the reconstruction of Patri and the surrounding towns and villages. If so, I will get Patri and you involved in the MMCE project immediately. In time, Patri can become as electrified and automated as our capital Axos."

General Nestor agreed and promised his full cooperation. She sent her cousin Xenocrates and his family back with the general to see to the coordination of their efforts. Within days, the usual train runs between the port city and Axos resumed for the first time in over a year. By the start of the new year, Xenocrates reported that Patri was indeed coming around. It was now safe for Korinna to walk to the markets with her yoke to buy fresh produce.

Kefall was more problematical. Hundreds of gangs controlled the city and the wealthy had little to no control over them. Hence, Andromache asked General Nestor to bring his many troops to Kefall and put the gangs out of business. By February, he had done just that and Kefall finally returned to some kind of normalcy. The Kali II finally returned above ground, helping with the reconstruction and MMCE efforts.

Thus, in February 825, Stefano and I put a checkmark beside Thrace. We considered it salvaged and on track to prosperity once more. Only Alia remained lawless and in its Dark Ages, and of course

Tashien, which we had pretty much been ignoring. That country was too huge and too out of control just now.

Chapter 50 Alia Has to Be Salvaged

That an idea can be more powerful than force boggled my brain during late November and December of 824. I needed an idea, but could only see force. The Alia situation was hideous to say the very least. Tens of thousands of women were being horribly mutilated under the guise of a twisted "beautification" program of one General Erebos. I needed an idea to counter this disgusting situation. I had the eleven women now under the care of Monarch Andromache of Axos, Thrace. These I could experiment with to see if I could come up with a counter move to make their lives at least livable. Currently, they and their menfolk were getting a crash course in speaking a foreign language, Annelise, which was the only language thus far that we knew someone with lip plates could speak and still be mostly understood. Eve and I had our own taste of the lip plates fiasco in a former lifetime and thus we had good reality on just how these women were suffering.

Humans thrive on communications; relationships demand communications. Knock out the ability to communicate and you've knocked out a person's beingness in life. That's just what this General Erebos was doing to the women of Alia. Suddenly, half of their population could no longer communicate, assuming women still accounted for half of their population. Perhaps I was exaggerating the numbers, but his plan was to do this to all of Alia's women. The savagery of some men still amazed me. Eve was all for twisting his neck, but I pointed out there was no one to take control of Alia after that and even more chaos would ensue. We needed to find a solution quickly, but none was obvious.

April 20, 824, Diona Gidios awoke from her anesthesia, Queen of Alia now. Her lips throbbed; her ear lobes felt like they were being ripped from her ears. She couldn't bend her neck, though she tried. The rings were so tight that she couldn't even turn her head a quarter of an inch! She struggled to rise, made incredibly awkward by the rings. Her ears now took the full weight of the six very heavy dangles; the bottom gems and gold settings rested just above her breasts. "Help, I can't move much. My lips hurt," she called out. A sudden wave of panic swamped her; she could not understand one word that she'd said.

Doctor Morpheus came over to her as she sat on the edge of the table. "Ah, Queen Diona, awake at last. My, I must say your earrings are extremely expensive. I don't know of another woman who has earrings as spectacular or as costly as yours. You must be very proud of them. Now don't try to talk. We cannot understand you, but then you don't have anything to say anymore — that's important, that is. You will feel a bit woozy for a while yet. I'll get you a drink later on. Oh, I am supposed to show you how beautiful you now look. As our Queen, you will be expected to look your very best at all times." He held a mirror up and Diona got her first glimpse at her new look and was shocked, simply put.

She was twenty years old. Her knee length blonde hair looked lush, lustrous, and thick as always, contrasting with the many red rubies in her earrings. Per the Official Proclamation, she was, as were all women when in public, naked, the general's orders. Her huge breasts were firm and quite perky. Her face was angelical; her deep-set eyes added to her charm. Her once full lips were now stretched around the pair of four-inch, bronze lip plates. At least her nose remained untouched, perfectly formed. She felt a bit more comfortable as the doctor draped her thick hair over her chest, somewhat hiding her breasts. She spotted a pair of Annelise extreme heels, shiny and black sitting near her feet. At least she would be wearing shoes, she thought, though why she would take any comfort in that eluded her now.

No, the major thought that rushed through her mind now was, "I have to kill General Erebos. I will get revenge for the murder of my family and uncles and cousins."

A bit later, Doctor Morpheus returned with a glass of water and a spoon. Diona was introduced to the extreme difficulties that she would be having eating and drinking from now on. He lifted a spoon of water up and she opened her mouth. The plates opened sufficiently to allow the spoon to get barely inside her mouth. Unfortunately, lips are most useful when liquids are being ingested. Water trickled out of her mouth, between her teeth. Though she reflexively tried to use her lips to keep the liquid inside her mouth, of course, they didn't move. She couldn't even raise her head back a little, Diona was forced to bend back at her waist to get her mouth elevated so that the water stayed in her mouth.

"Although you women are supposed to learn how to feed yourselves, Diona," the doctor explained, "until your lips are fully healed, someone will help you. We cannot risk you getting an infection, now can we?" She felt more and more miserable by the moment.

The second day, General Erebos dropped by to see how she was doing and how she looked. "Ah, perfect job, good doctor! Queen Diona, you look just fabulous. Your new ornaments are fantastic. You will be setting a very fine example for the other women of Alia. My, yes you will. You are a very beautiful young woman, our queen."

"I am going to kill you," she replied, knowing that he could not understand her. Just saying the words made her feel a little better, a slight comfort.

"Ah, I'm so sorry, Queen Diona. We men just cannot understand you any longer." He gave her an evil grin and left.

"Now you ought to get used to putting your pumps on and taking them off by yourself, my queen. I'll let you practice that. From now on, when you want to walk somewhere, you must wear your shoes. We must be civilized, mustn't we?"

"What you've done to me isn't civilized at all!" she retorted.

"Oh, you are saying that you love your new shoes? Glad that you like them." He then left to check on the other women.

She found getting her shoes on quite a challenge. She couldn't bend her neck and seeing over her lip plates and massive bosom was impossible. Her lower vision was completely obstructed. To see her feet while sitting perfectly erect, she had to twist her body slightly to one side and use peripheral vision to see the extreme heels. Well, at least she had some experience in walking in them, but always she had her arms securely around her dance dates when she wore them. Walking in them was treacherous and challenging. In her current state, walking in them was a nightmare. She knew that no one would be putting their supporting arms around her very thin waist. "I need to practice. I have to be able to get around if I am going to kill General Erebos," she said to herself, ignoring that her speech sounded like gibberish.

The next morning, she was asked to join the general and staff for breakfast. "After you dine, my queen, Paris here will show you to your new queen's quarters." Paris Kraytos was a private, but he was also the best chef in the army. Naturally, he was ordered to cook for the general and his staff. Dining with the general was the chef Paris, Major Perseus Monos, and Major Stefanos Ronios. Diona waited a bit to see if one of these men would help her and found them ignoring her. She sighed and took off her shoes and tried to figure out how she could possibly feed herself. Unable to bend so that she could see the table, again she had to sit slightly sideways just so that she could even see the plate and teacup before her. She tried to pick up the spoon between her toes.

The men had finished eating before she even got the spoon between her toes. "I'm sorry, Queen Diona, you are going way too slowly. You must eat more swiftly, but then perhaps you prefer not to eat such large breakfasts. Paris, will you show our queen to her quarters and then bring her to the Throne Room. She will take her seat this morning as our queen. Make sure that she's there in forty-five minutes," General Erebos ordered.

"Yes, sir," Paris saluted. He motioned for Diona to rise. While she was starving, she had no choice but to follow him. Maybe, she thought, the general will see that it was impossible for her to do this and have someone feed her.

Paris was not accustomed to walking with a woman who wore the extreme Annelise heels. Diona was forced to take very tiny steps, more like a shuffle than a walking step. He kept moving ahead of her. Diona knew that she must walk with extreme care. She could do little to regain her balance, not even bending her head. "Slow down, I can't walk this fast," she said, frustrated with Paris, but he couldn't understand her at all.

She found her new quarters luxurious though, as befitting the queen of Alia. These were Queen Katerine's old quarters, but Paris had cleaned up the room nicely for her. She noted that besides the large living room, a servant's bedroom lay just adjacent to the living room. Her bedroom door and the servant's bedroom door both opened into the very elegant and comfortable living room. She noted the couches and chairs were designed for women wearing their enormous hoops. Though she didn't really enjoy wearing them, she found herself wishing that she had them on now. Chilly goose bumps trickled up and down her legs and back.

Right on time, Paris led her into the Throne Room, where General Erebos motioned for her to take her seat on the plush queen's chair, again designed for a woman wearing a sixteen-foot hoop skirt. She felt a bit dwarfed sitting in the wide chair, but she did as asked. However, she bent low at her waist to get her thick, blonde hair to slide over her sounders before she sat down. At least her hair would cover her a little and provide a bit of warmth.

With little else to do but sit, Diona began to listen to the men. With her debilitating lip plates, she no longer had to worry about her facial expressions. Her face was motionless and expressionless. Major Perseus was about twenty-five, she guessed, with blonde hair. Under other circumstances, she thought he would be handsome. Soon she learned that he was responsible for the palace staff and security.

Major Stefanos was thirty, again she guessed, with black hair and strong facial features. He had a scar across his forehead and she found herself wondering how he'd gotten it. Major Stefanos handled the city patrols and the economic factors for the general.

During the morning, a nobleman named Simonides Ridon came to report on how the economy was faring. This new Ornamentation Project, he explained, would most definitely put many men back to work. At least, the nobleman bowed to his new queen and said, "Queen Diona, you look extremely beautiful. Such fabulous earrings. I've never seen the likes of them. My wife only has three dangles on each of hers. I used diamonds, but your rubies really go well with your blonde hair, Your Majesty."

Later that morning, nobleman Telemon Phoros came to report on the mining industry's response to the new project. He also reported on the number of bronze workers in the city. She had no idea that there were so many. He too praised her earrings and said that she looked very attractive. "I am going to kill General Erebos," she said to him, knowing that he could not understand a word that she said. He presumed that she'd made a remark about her earrings and added that he'd given emeralds for his wife's new earrings.

By lunch, she was ravenous. Still she could not easily get the spoon in her toes. She tried to eat her food like a dog, but could not find a way to get her head down to the table and gave up that idea. She ended up finally getting the spoon between her right toes but by then everyone else was done. "Let her have some practice. I don't need our queen on the throne during the afternoons, Paris," General Erebos gave her a break.

After a long while, she managed to get her first bite onto her spoon. Getting it up and into her mouth was quite another challenge. More than once, she dropped either the bite or the spoon. At last, she stopped trying and just cried. "How can I kill the general if I cannot even eat?" she wailed. Paris, who had been watching her discretely, took pity on her and fed her the lunch. "Thank you," she said.

Although she didn't know it, Paris then reported back to the general, "Sir, I do believe that it will be nearly impossible for her to feed herself." He went on to explain the extreme difficulties that she was having.

"Okay, in the past, our queens had their servants. So let's get our queen say four Ladies in Waiting. Perhaps they can feed her," he suggested. He decided that he liked seeing women around the table at meal times.

That evening, Paris once again fed her, but General Erebos explained, "Your Majesty, tomorrow we will have four Ladies in Waiting who will stay in your quarters with you and assist you with eating and the like. Never say that we men do not understand you women and your problems."

The next morning after Paris fed her, General Erebos had Major Perseus bring in her four new Ladies in Waiting, otherwise, her servants. Dora Zenobia was a nineteen year old blonde with light blue eyes. Her face was fairly plain, but full. Rubies contrasted with her knee length hair. She looked a bit frightened, but then all four looked scared. Tisiphone Psyche was twenty-one with raven hair that reached to her ankles, thick and straight. Her black eyes shone with her inner strength; she was a fighter by nature, taking this new assignment seriously. Her earrings had many diamonds in them. Xanthe Minos was twenty with light brown hair that fell below her knees. She had green eyes and a roundish face. Emeralds figured prominently in her earrings. Rhea Sappho was twenty-one with curly brown hair that fell to just above her knees. She also had rubies for her gemstones. All were naked, but like Diona, had managed to get their hair over their shoulders covering somewhat their front sides. All four also wore similar black Annelise extreme heels and were just as uncomfortable as Diona wearing them.

"Okay, my ladies in waiting, your task is to assist your queen. Help her eat, do her hair, whatever you women need to do," General Erebos ordered. "Now, Queen Diona, please show your Ladies in Waiting to their quarters. Get them settled. They will be required to feed you at lunch." Diona saw what had to be fear in their eyes. She suspected that until now, none of these women had ever been able to feed themselves.

She rose and took what was a comfortable pace for herself, barely two inches a shuffling step. The four followed her. Once they were shown to their bedroom, they gathered in her living room. Diona waist bowed to Dora and said "Dora." She repeated the motions in turn to the others, saying, "Tisi, Zanthe, Rhea." The women heard the sounds "or, is, an, and ea." She repeated it and now the four realized that she was saying their names and repeated everyone's names as well. All five were smiling with their minuscule victory, though nothing was visible. Now with the four sounds plus "ia" for Diona, the five could recognize when one was addressing them.

"What do we do now?" asked Tisi, but realized none could understand her. She took the initiative. She walked over to one of the new style hairbrushes and took off her shoes, picking it up with her right foot. Hopping on one leg over to Diona, she conveyed the idea that she wanted to brush Diona's hair. She sat down and the four women began experimenting doing their queen's hair. Between the four of them, they did get Diona's hair nicely brushed for the first time in over a week. Diona realized that they all had to work together to get by, and Diona picked up one of the brushes and began doing Tisi's hair. At once, the other three got the idea and began helping her with the task. By noon, all five had their hair done, but following Diona's physical motions, they all arranged their hair to drape over their front, hiding their breast and privates as much as possible.

A gong sounded the advance warning for lunch. The five struggled to get their heels back on and then followed Diona to the Royal Dining Hall. They found that they were all seated together, opposite the men. The four set to work, trying to figure out how to feed their queen. With all four working at it, they did manage to get food and drink into Diona's mouth. At least the general allowed them to stay after the men left so that they could feed each other. Diona insisted on helping feed her new friends as well. A comradery between the five women began at this meal. All five saw that by working together, they could get things done for themselves, though it took enormous amounts of time to do them.

When evening came, all five helped each other brush out their hair and even get into bed, though Tisi who was the last one up had a most difficult time of it, since there was no one to help tuck her in. Still, the luxurious bed, satin sheets, and elegant quality of everything in their rooms made all five feel a bit like a queen.

Now Diona began to start thinking about just how she could manage to kill General Erebos. He only required her attendance in the Throne Room during the morning hours. The rest of the day was hers, though she spent a lot of it helping her four friends, for friends she considered them, not servants or Ladies in Waiting. Each began to depend on the other for their survival. Still, how to do the deed festered in her mind.

First thing I must do is familiarize myself with this palace, she thought. Although walking was most difficult and treacherous, she was very determined. During the next weeks, she began exploring the whole palace and its many rooms. Stairs led to the basement levels and to the second floor, where the general and his men had their private rooms. True, their bedroom quarters were on the first floor, but they had private rooms on the second as well. One day, she came shuffling into one of these upper rooms, which was not currently occupied. She spotted a pistol on a dresser and made for it. With one shot, she could accomplish her mission, she thought. Now how to use a pistol occupied her mind. She had no arms or hands. She took off her shoes to see if she could find anyway to use the pistol with her foot. She could sort of pick it up between her toes, but could not hold it and nearly dropped it on the floor before she let go. "Well, pistols are out. No way can I ever use that to kill him," she said to herself, ignoring the fact that her words sounded like gibberish.

She headed back to her room, but now faced going down the stairs. Going up was far easier, but going down gave her a fright. Unable to bend her neck, forced into perfect posture and with her lower-forward vision blocked by her lip plates and bosom, she had to carefully feel for each step, made all the more difficult in her extreme heels. One miscue and she'd take a horrible fall, unable to break or impede it in any manner. Still, she did not give up, but continued her survey of the entire palace.

As April ended and May dawned, the late fall temperatures began to drop. General Erebos, always eyeing his five distractions, noticed that they were all beginning to chill. "Damn, well I thought by this time, women would have worked out ways to clothe themselves. Major Stefanos, what are we going to do about this next problem, eh? While I admit having them go around naked was pleasing to the eye and *most* practical, the weather is getting chilly, and winter is around the corner. We can't have them freezing to death, unseemly for our queen. I'll give you the task of figuring out something. Major Perseus, you lend him a hand. Surely, there are enough clothes in this palace to outfit hundreds."

Indeed there were, Queen Diona had already discovered a huge room filled with all manner of dresses. Some were quite old, having belonged to many previous queens and staff who had occupied the palace in years gone by. The problem facing the two majors was two-fold. First, whatever they chose for the five women, the outfit had to keep them warm. Second, they knew the general's mind. The women ought to be able to dress themselves in the clothes, although Perseus pointed out that the first time they ought to dress the women.

"Look, we are likely going to have to try a whole lot of things on them. Lord knows what we can find that will even fit them," Perseus pointed out. The two men were about to dive into the massive clothing piles when they were summoned by the general again. Both men rushed to the Throne Room, where they saw nobleman Telemon Phoros there along with another man, whom they did not recognize.

With a wry smile, General Erebos explained, "Ah, incredibly good timing, as I was just saying to our esteemed Phoros here. He has, as many others have also already pointed out, seen that our women are simply going to have to start wearing some clothing, now that winter is nearly upon us. True, when spring comes, they can again forego clothes, making their lives simpler to manage. Still, we cannot have out queen and women of Alia freezing. He's rightly noted that our many tailors are still mostly unemployed; few men are purchasing new suits, though the army continues to need new uniforms regularly. Nobleman Phoros has proposed that we employ our many tailors by having them adapt women's dresses for their current needs. He's brought along his personal tailor, Mr. Diomedes here. Please have him accompany you and allow him to help you outfit our beautiful queen and her servants."

The middle aged tailor followed the two majors to the huge old clothing room. Both majors were very relieved to have someone who knew something about dressing women. The three men surveyed the clothes room. All were the fancy Annelise ball gowns, though the hoops varied in diameter from twelve to sixteen feet across. Mr. Diomedes pointed out that the queen always wore larger hoops than her servants and that this tradition ought to be upheld. However, he was not stupid; he now had to feed his own wife and daughter, who had yet to be adorned with the new fancy ornaments as the general had decreed. He rightly concluded that with the neck rings, the women would have an even harder time managing tasks. He suggested that the queen wear the fourteen-foot style while her servants would wear the twelve-foot hoops.

Of course the real problem lay in the fitting. The bodice tops had to be greatly modified to accommodate women's mammoth breasts and extremely tiny waists. None of the corsets really fit at all well, but now they were only needed really to hold up their fancy stockings and he could make do with the smaller ones that were here. "The bodices will have to be completely remade," he pronounced. Major Perseus then brought the five women into the clothing room and the tailor took their measurements, comparing them to some of the articles he'd pulled out for them.

"It's a pity that we cannot ask them what color of dress they would prefer," he pointed out. "Well, we shall just have to use our own good taste and pick colors that bring out their best looks." He chose a cherry red satin gown for Queen Diona. She tried to protest that she could not manage a thing in such a gown, but her words were gibberish and the tailor mistook them for her agreeing with his choices.

Later that day, Major Perseus offered a suggestion to the general, "Sir, we have located dresses that the tailor believes he can adapt to their needs. However, we are both in complete agreement. The women will be wholly incapable of dressing themselves, as you require. However, sir, I have an idea. We have so many men currently unemployed. Why not appoint some of them as Women Dressers. Put them in charge of dressing the women of Alia. I know that such would provide limited hours of employment, probably a few in the morning and evening. Perhaps, they could also be charged with feeding the women as well, since we've seen the extreme measures that are needed by our queen and her Ladies in Waiting."

"Well, I don't like it totally, major. Look, there is no question that we need to get every man back to productive employment, but what a total waste of manpower, dressing and feeding the women. Still, I can't let them freeze to death. Okay, let's do it. We'll have unemployed men begin dressing women and feeding them for two hours in the morning and two in the evening, but only from May through September. Once spring comes, the women will once more go naked and have to feed themselves. Perhaps by next May the women will have it all worked out for themselves, and we'll have our men back to full employment," the general declared positively. It seemed workable for now. That some of these men would end up robbing the homes in which they were employed did not occur to him, nor that the women wouldn't be able to tell their husbands who the guilty person was.

It took Mr. Diomedes a week to get all the dress modifications completed. Major Perseus interviewed a number of unemployed young men who leapt at the chance to dress and feed the queen and her servants. Most were looking for a way to avoid being conscripted into the growing army of General Erebos. Major Perseus was cunning and chose a twenty-one year old effeminate hairdresser to service the women of the palace. Eros Euclid had rather long brown hair for a man and spoke with a lilt. That he preferred the company of men was plainly obvious to Major Perseus. Eros was perfect, the general thought. He would not have to worry about indiscrete sexual relationships going on here at the Royal Court.

When the tailor was finished, Eros began working full time at the palace. "Ah, my fair Queen Diona, finally you will be wearing a magnificent red satin gown! I just hated it when all you women were forced to go naked. So uncivilized. Now Eros is here. I want you to know that I really do understand women's apparel and how to make you all look your very best, as befitting our queen. Oh yes, Your Majesty. You are in good hands now. I will not let you down."

An hour later, Diona was finally dressed for the first time since the plague had struck nearly three quarters of a year ago. She felt warm finally! However, the price that she and her servants had to pay to be warm was almost more than she could bear: trussed up in a tight corset limited her mobility even further. While the fine silk hose was welcome on her legs keeping them warm finally, now she had no use of her toes. Plus trying to get around in the fourteen-foot hoop skirt was almost unmanageable. Torture upon torture she endured, continuing to swear aloud that she was going to kill the general. Poor Eros took her unintelligible noises as confirmation that she greatly approved of his work.

When Eros had finished getting her completely dressed and her hair draped perfectly, she looked at herself in the full-length mirrors. Well, she looked rather pretty, she thought, as long as she ignored the lip plates and neck rings. Her extremely heavy earrings did go well with the dress, though she would have preferred something other than cherry red. Now she had to learn to deal with life actions all over again, unable to see where her feet were located, buried beneath the fourteen-foot hoop skirt. Worse, she had no hands to assist her with her dress when needed. Still, she continued planning her murder of the general, who now more than ever, had to be killed.

In June, she made a clandestine trip to the kitchen where Paris cooked their meals. Here she found all manner of knives, many of which would serve nicely to carve up the general, she imagined. She found an appropriate butcher knife and began working out how she might manage to steal it. Later, she told herself, she'd worry about how she could possibly use it. Constrained as she was in this gown, this was a small feat. Balancing on one foot, she managed to remove her right heel. She swung her leg up, got her toes around its handle, and tried to lift it up. She lost her balance and nearly fell down, trying to find some part of her body that she could move to counter herself. At last, she was stable again, but the knife was simply too heavy for her to lift. She sighed and worked on getting her heel back on her foot without falling down. Now she realized that if she did fall, she might not be able to get back up on her feet in this confining dress. More worries flooded her mind. Stable finally, she stared lovingly at the butcher knife, which would do the job, if only she could somehow get it back to her bedroom. There, she could practice with it and perhaps find some way that she could wield it.

Then she had a bright idea. If she could come here during the night, she might be able to grab a hold of it with her teeth. Embolden by the prospect of obtaining the knife, she headed back to her room. The trip took her nearly a half hour and countless tiny steps. At least all the doors in the palace were permanently barred open, but she wondered how long that would last.

That evening after supper, Eros came to undress her and her Ladies in Waiting. He seemed nice enough, she thought, chatting away about the silliest of things. God, women were being brutally tortured and he was worried about a small rat in her hair. Still, she appreciated his help, without which she and her four friends would be doomed. He helped her into her nightgown and tucked her into her bed, pulling up the covers for her. Then, he repeated the process for her four ladies. Finally, her rooms became quiet for the night. She waited, sometimes biting her tongue to keep herself from falling asleep, which her body continued to attempt.

When she thought the hour was very late, she struggled to sit up, no small feat in itself. From her sitting position, she could now get to her feet. Damn, the stone floor was cold. She considered putting on her heels but decided against it. Besides making noise, they would greatly impede her freedom of motion. She'd have to suffer cold feet. Stealthily, she crept out of her bedroom, listening for any sounds. Hearing nothing, she moved on out of the queen's quarters into the long hall. Still no one was about and she headed off for the kitchen.

While the place was quite dark, she was able just barely to make out the butcher knife right where she saw it earlier. She opened her mouth as wide as possible and bent at her waist, getting her lip plates over the handle, and then bit down onto the wooden handle. Carefully, she pulled it loose from its cradle and felt elated. She had the knife at last. She turned and headed back to her room, hoping and praying that no one would see her with the knife. Luck was with her, she decided as she crept back into her room, the blade still in her mouth. Now she had to find a place to hide it, a place where no one was likely to find it and a place from which she could retrieve it later. At least they left one lantern burning and she had a little light.

Beneath her bed came immediately to mind, but she quickly realized that she might not be able to pick it back up from the floor. She decided to keep it somehow at head height, where she could use her teeth on its handle. Her walk-in clothes closet might work. She found a back corner with a ledge where shoes were stored, all too small for her to wear. Carefully, she inserted the blade between the shoes, its hilt sticking out a bit. This would have to do for now, she thought and headed back to bed, her feet feeling like a pair of numb icicles.

She fell asleep dreaming of stabbing General Erebos in his heart, if he even had one. The next day, Diona couldn't wait until Eros tucked her in for the night. All day, the knife and how to use it was in her thoughts. Late that night and for the next week, she retrieved her butcher knife and experimented on her bed with it, in case she dropped it. Of course, she dropped it frequently. After one long frustrating week, she finally gave up. She could find no way to wield the instrument of death. Her bodily motions were just too constrained by the lip plates and neck rings. For days afterwards, she was severely depressed, until she decided that she simply had to find another way to kill the evil general.

She thought about using a rope to strangle him, but gave that up, she could not use her mouth and teeth and had no way to tie it off or tighten it enough to throttle him. She toyed with the notion of driving her seven-inch heels into his head, but soon discovered that she could not keep her balance well enough even to attempt it. She imagined using a pillow to suffocate him, she imagined herself pushing him down the stone stairs, but saw him always using his arms and hands to thwart the attempt.

During evening meals, General Erebos now began to have a group of six musicians play for him. "It's just like our late king used to do," he announced. One thing led to another. Before long, the general made Diona dance with him and then her Ladies in Waiting. Dancing in the extreme Annelise heels was problematical for normal women. In these women's case, it was treacherous and exceedingly difficult.

More than once, they lost their balance completely and the general was forced to grab them to keep them from falling over.

The winter dragged on slowly for her. She continued her explorations and one day discovered a length of rope. Carefully she stole out of her room that night and retrieved it. For hours each night after that, she sat in her bed trying to work out some way to use it to strangle him. She even managed to make a slipknot in it, but was unable to take that plan any further.

Spring came. In October, General Erebos formally declared the season of dresses was over. Women were to go naked once more and must feed themselves again. Diona and her four friends took this with mixed blessings. Grateful to be freed from the confining dresses, they hated to be naked and worse, they were back to their awkward and feeble attempts to feed each other once more.

A breakfast, one October morning, General Erebos was uncommonly cheerful. "Your Majesty, I am so pleased to announce that we've hit the forty thousand mark. That is, forty thousand of our finest women in Alia have now received their proper and most impressive ornaments. I feel that we ought to have a spring celebration. On Saturday evening, we are going to hold a formal ball here in the palace for all the nobles and their wives and families. My queen, you will be center stage, showing off your magnificent earrings." Then, he saw her drooping lip plates. Similarly, her four Ladies in Waiting had drooping lip plates as well.

"Well, Doctor Morpheus is right. Your lip plates have become too small. Fear not, Your Majesty, I will summon a bronze worker today to get your beautiful ornaments enlarged. We cannot have your royal good looks diminished by drooping lips, now can we?" he sneered a little.

By late afternoon, the five women's plates had been properly enlarged and now fit very tightly. Once more, both plates were perfectly horizontal to the ground. Diona's lips felt tight and stretched, but she could do nothing about it, no one could now. She was grateful for their enlargement, eating had become nearly impossible when they were so drooped. At least now she could eat, though her vision was slightly more obstructed.

As the time for the ball came, Eros brushed out each woman's hair, arranging it artfully across their backs. Naturally, Diona insisted on leaning forward and wiggling as best she could to get her long hair back over her front side, hiding as much of herself as possible. "No, no, this will never do, Your Majesty. You look so much prettier with your hair across your back." He undid her efforts. After three such episodes, she gave up and allowed her hair to drape down her back.

Soon, Major Perseus came to fetch the women for the ball. General Erebos wore his finest uniform, complete with numerous patches and badges and pins for valor. "Here you are, my queen. You look positively stunning this evening. Come, stand beside me as we greet our guests." She had no choice but to slowly move to his side near the entrance door. Opposite, twenty musicians were warming up. She wondered if the other women who would come would also be humiliated and naked.

Before long, the thousand men and women began arriving. The women were miserable, naked but wearing the extreme Annelise heels as dictated by the general's proclamations. The men seemed either excited by their women or embarrassed, about fifty-fifty, she thought. One by one, they were introduced to Queen Diona, who had to bow at her waist as each man was presented to her. Each woman was asked to press her body against hers in a womanly welcome, their metal necks clanking, their earrings bouncing lightly off each other. She saw grief, humiliation, and embarrassment in every woman's eyes as they touched bodies in a welcoming hug, less the hug part. Yet she also saw something else in their eyes, something that she could not yet put into words. That would come later.

The dance itself went well. The music was uplifting and upbeat. Still, the women were mostly unable to dance properly, if at all, in these heels and so constrained. Her feet were aching by the time that the dance ended. More than one woman leaned upon their husbands as they exited, she noted. Diona had no one to lean on and very carefully made her way back to her bedroom, more determined than ever to somehow kill this wicked, sadistic general.

Now that she had her freedom of motion restored, that is, sans the confining hoop ball gown, she continued her palace explorations. She spent most of her time wandering the upper floor, peering into long unused rooms, looking for additional ideas. She had overheard Paris talking about how the late king's advisors had managed to poison each other. Diona reasoned that if it had happened the way that Paris described, then neither had time to get rid of their bottles of poison, unless they had used it all on their victim, that is. She wondered where those men's private rooms had been, but of course, she could not ask anyone for directions.

During this time, Tisi and Rhea had not been idle. They managed to convince Major Perseus to move the special low to the ground writing desks into the queen's living room. By pushing at them with their bodies and making unintelligible sounds with their voices, he'd finally realized what they wanted and moved them for the ladies. Now Tisi and Rhea began experimenting with writing by using their toes. Proudly, they showed Diona their first attempts. Scrawling lines covered the pages, but one could make out the words. Embolden by their actions, all five spent their afternoons learning to write with their feet.

Where do you go in the afternoons? Tisi wrote for Diona.

In search of something that I can use to kill General Erebos. My sole goal is to get revenge for what he has done to my family and all of us. Diona wrote back. After they all read it, she used her foot to toss it into the fireplace.

Finally, the five women had a way that they could speak to each other and lengthy written conversations began. The five women bonded together as never before. Tisi and Rhea began helping Diona search for the means to carry out her execution of the general.

In November, General Erebos announced that as of now, all the women associated with the nobles and wealthier of Levkos, Alia, had received their ornaments. At this time, they were expanding to those women in the middle class. Over fifty thousand women had received their gifts. The economy was rolling along now. Bronze workers had more work than they could do each day; the gem cutters were kept busy; the jewelers became backlogged setting the stones into the fancy ornaments. Supporting industries were booming. General Erebos felt all was going well, though many men still remained unemployed. Hence, he began ordering those men to join the army or go to work at specified locations about the city where more help was needed with the ornament making process.

In December, Major Stefanos reported that some families were fleeing Levkos. "Fine with me. Less men to have to worry about," General Erebos replied.

Later that very day, while exploring, Diona came across what had to have been one of the aide's rooms. She found a small vial in the commode next to the bed. It had a label on it, but she didn't know what the word meant. However, the skull and crossbones warning symbol suggested poison. Carefully, she retrieved the vial with her toes and considered how she might carry it back to her room. She dare not put it in her mouth as she had the knife. Instead, she managed to get the vial above her ear, her hair helping to hold it secure. Walking gingerly, she made it safely back to her room and put it on the shelf in her closet.

She had long ago found the library up on the second floor. Now she headed there, with Tisi and Rhea in tow. She'd written the name on the label and asked for their help in tracking down what it was. The library held hundreds of books, neatly arranged on floor to ceiling shelves, lining three of the walls. A large window made reading easy here. A long table held a few of the books recently viewed by unknown readers.

Now the three women began searching for a book that might tell them what the vial contained. Diona hoped that it would also give her enough information to know if there was enough left to do the job, to kill General Erebos. Several volumes looked promising. However, the women had to get them down and later put them back up on the shelves. Otherwise, someone might discover that someone had been researching poisons and take preventative measures.

Ordinarily, we women would pull a volume partly out with our feet, latch onto it between our heads, necks, and shoulders, carrying it to the table. However, the three could not move their necks and had to devise other means. Cleverness won the day. Tisi brought Xanthe and Dora to help them. By strategic placement of chairs, two women, while lying on their backs on the chairs and using their feet, caught the volumes as the other three lowered them.

During the process, Tisi realized that an enormous amount of information on the history of Alia and the running of the country was stored in volumes of chronological logs. She pointed this out to Diona as well. While her basic purpose was in learning what this poison actually was and its effectiveness, she began to see that other even more interesting material was here to be read. So did the other four as well. Beginning this day, all five spent as many hours that they could each day here in the library, reading voraciously.

Tisi continued to discover interesting facts. She tried valiantly to point these out to the others, but their lack of speech was a severe problem. They resorted to an 'uh' sound to get someone's attention and then pointing with their toes to the interesting passage. All five became utterly fascinated with the hitherto unknown or undisclosed secrets of the kingdom and its ruling. For example, Diona learned that General Erebos got his topmost army position because he had helped the late king cover up some sadistic affairs that he had had, which ended in the deaths of those he sexually molested. Some of these occurred before he had met his wife and took the throne. Interesting and fascinating reading absorbed their daily afternoons for weeks.

Yes, Diona learned that the vial did contain a powerful poison and that in all likelihood there was more than enough to poison General Erebos. However, she had yet to figure out just how she could get it into his drink. Because of its taste, the book recommended it be mixed with wine or similar beverages, which would mask its slightly bitter taste. Had she arms, General Erebos would already be dead. During their morning breakfasts and sessions in the Throne Room, she carefully observed the general and his habits. Seldom did he drink wine at these times. Yet, she noticed that there were empty wine bottles around, so someone was drinking wine at some point. Diona took a big gamble and quietly wandered past the general's bedroom later in the evening, hoping and praying that the man would not take her actions as perhaps desiring his attentions. His door was closed.

However, one morning she walked past it and the door was opened. Since she knew that he was likely at breakfast, she peered in and saw an empty wine bottle. Unfortunately for her, he wasn't. "Oh, I suppose that you are looking for me. I know, breakfast is waiting for us, Your Majesty. I have such a headache this morning. Too much wine last night. Don't stand there, come on in." She felt very vulnerable and nervous but had little choice but to shuffle into his room.

"Well, you look very pretty this morning, Your Majesty. More than I can say about our country. I've been trying my best, but I just don't get any respect. They want everything to be back to normal months ago and, hell, it is never going to be back to normal, not ever. Everything has gone so far beyond mere right and wrong — you know what I mean?" He looked at her. "Oh hell, you can't even talk now. No matter, I prefer it this way. You women and your petty problems are the very least of my worries. Look Your Majesty, I have given you very expensive and gorgeous ornaments. What more can I do to adorn the women of Alia? Tell me that one. Clothes don't fit. You've no arms to fend for yourselves. At least I have you looking very attractive. I've never seen such fabulously good posture as we saw at the spring dance. Our women of Alia all have perfect posture, and by god, you all look beautiful. Now that is something. Besides, adorning all of you has given a huge spurt in our economy, giving thousands of men jobs and money coming in again. So you see, Your Majesty, you women are actually helping your men of Alia."

He seemed satisfied with his justifications and walked her to breakfast. As she shuffled slowly along, he added, "You know, our little talk was a good one. I feel better. Say, I have been ignoring your needs some. Why don't you drop by my bedroom this evening after supper and share some wine with me?" It was more of an order than a question and she began to worry about his intentions. In fact, she worried about it all day, even writing out to her four friends what had happened. They wrote her that they were worried for her safety, and Tisi even suggested that he would rape her.

One very scared Diona shuffled slowly up to the general's room around seven that night. "Ah, there you are, Your Majesty. Come on in, I won't bite. I've taken the liberty of pouring us each a glass of wine, though I figure that I'll have to spoon yours for you. Come, have a seat on my couch beside me. Let us toast the success of our Women's Ornamentation Project." She did as asked, moving to the couch and sitting down. She made sure that she bent at her waist so that her long hair draped over her front side, hiding her privates as much as possible before she sat down. That was the best that she could do, and Diona resigned herself to her fate, swearing once more to murder this wicked man.

"He took a sip of wine and then spooned a sip up and into her mouth. Wine! Damn, it tasted good, she thought, unable to recall the last time that she had wine. Must be well over a year now. She bent-nodded her approval, hoping that he'd give her more, which he did. "Tonight, my queen, we are celebrating. Today, Major Stefanos reported that we've just ornamented our hundred thousandth woman of Alia! Isn't that just incredible?"

Diona sighed, such a hideously large number of mutilated women! How could he so totally ruin the lives of so many women? He misinterpreted her moan and added, "Yes, I am so glad that you agree. Here's another sip. Yes, probably five times that many men now have well-paying jobs again. Five to one, that surely is a great benefit. Each woman ornamented provides for five men's livelihood, most worthy of you women, Your Majesty."

After more wine, the general's fingers began to seek out her bosom. While she tried to say no, he couldn't understand her and mistook her protests for agreement. "Don't worry; it would be immoral of me to bed you. We are not married and you are our queen. Still, I owe it to you at least to give you some pleasure. I do like to pleasure women, you know." For an hour, his fingers did just that. Diona was extremely grateful that he did not rape her or try to have his way with her. His actions were at least acceptable, she thought. Half-drunk, she finally staggered back to her room, where her four friends wanted to know what had happened.

You have access to his room now and his wine bottle, Tisi wrote out. Diona smiled for the first time in a long time, though nothing appeared on her face due to the debilitating lip plates. She slept soundly as well, thanks to the wine.

Unbeknownst to me, Eve had already taken matters of Alia into her own hands. For days now, she had been spying on the Palace in Levkos. She had discovered that Queen Diona and her four friends had been spending hours reading and learning from the extensive library on the second floor. Cleverly, she had indirectly been calling their attention to various books to read, hoping that they would learn enough to be able to run the country. Eve also had stealthily read the surface thoughts in Diona's mind. Eve knew that Diona's driving passion was to kill General Erebos, and she understood the reasons behind the monarch's drive. She's witnessed his soldiers murdering her father, uncles and cousins, though she didn't yet know that two had survived thanks to Olympos and his fast actions.

Eve was amazed that Diona was not using her mutilations as the driving force to kill the general. Rather all this ornamentation mutilation of women was entirely secondary, though it was in the minds of the other four, who sought his death for this reason. Eve further realized the magnitude of the problem facing Alia. She knew that soon Diona would work out the means to poison General Erebos and she had no doubt that Diona would be successful. While Eve could have killed the man at any time, she had not for the very good reason of just who would step in and take over control of Alia afterwards. If you kill your power leader, someone else invariable comes in to fill the vacuum left by his absence. Often one would only be replacing one tyrant with another. That alone kept her from wringing the general's neck these past few months.

Eve quickly realized that just as soon as Diona was successful in her quest, the country would once more be leaderless. Already the chaos and destruction, particularly with respect to their women, was devastating. Their economy, which had been the best in Demokritos, was now nearly destroyed, kept going only barely with all the ornaments being constructed, a pitiful excuse for an economy. Once Diona committed her deed, all hell would again break loose in Alia, threatening even further the pitiful state of so many of their women.

Hence, she knew that she had to be extremely careful about taking drastic actions and yet had to prepare for the aftermath of Diona's vowed revenge on General Erebos. Education, she felt, would play a key role, which is why she spent so much time nudging the five women towards specific volumes in the library. Eve was elated when she and the five finally came across the legally binding laws of succession for the rulership of Alia.

The laws stated unequivocally that if the king's wife should die, he was free to marry another woman, who would become Queen of Alia. Should the king die, the laws stated that the queen would retain her throne and rule subject to the following:

Should the reigning queen not desire to retain her throne, she may abdicate and the Noble High Council shall elect a new king.

Should the reigning queen remarry, he then becomes the king, but subject to the approval of the Noble High Council who may reject the king if he is found to be insane, mad, or incompetent.

Should the reigning queen be insane or mad or incompetent, she may be removed by the Noble High Council, who then elects a new king.

Should the reigning queen not fulfill her duties of governing Alia, she may be removed by the Noble High Council, who then elects a new king.

Nowhere did the laws state that the queen must be able to speak. This idea Eve gently placed into Diona's and her friend's minds. Tisi wrote, Diona, you would then be our legal queen and can rule Alia. You could then put a stop to the mutilations of women!

I'd have to write it, Diona wrote hesitatingly, adding, but how would I get the men to obey me? Tisi shrugged her shoulders. Eve pondered this one as well. While she could write out her orders, would men follow them? That was the key question. Eve also knew that if Diona kept the throne, she would have to purge out of the court all those men who had been behind this brutal mistreatment of women and those who had supported it. Further, the affected women would certainly want justice for the soldiers who murdered their husbands and friends who had tried to prevent their being taken away to be mutilated. Also, those who did the dirty work would need to be brought to justice. This would be a very tall order for Diona unless she had staunch supporters from the moment she became sole ruler.

Eve began looking at possible future tracks. First, she examined what might happen if Diona was successful in poisoning the general. She was surrounded only by other soldiers here at the palace. She'd get little support from them. The moment that the general was eliminated, Queen Diona would need immediate and powerful supporters or she would be swept away in the resulting chaos. Eve doubted that the Noble High Council would automatically back Diona. The poor woman could not speak and was able only to barely function at all. The likely results seemed dismal to Eve. What to do?

Even worse were the day-to-day conditions of these five women's lives. Reduced to being barely walking dolls, the humiliation and loss of self-respect was acutely noticeable to Eve. She knew that a woman likes to care for her own needs and appearance. Forced to go around naked, forced to wear the extreme Annelise heels, and only just barely able to keep their hair brushed by doing each other in teams, these women operated only on the barest, basest level of hygiene, almost on the last legs of their basic nurturing nature. Yet these five continued to operate and had not yet given up, sitting around waiting for death to take them as so many in Tashien had.

This detail piqued her interest. Why had they not yet succumbed as those in Tashien had? She observed the five further, most curious about this detail. Then she spotted it. These women were sympathetic to each other's plight and awful situation. They had dropped down from the stark fear and terror into a sort of numbness to their own plight, but were still being sympathetic to the other's situation. Absolutely anything at all was far better than nothing and hence they had accepted their debilitating mutilations, it was something at least. Eve realized that for these women, even pain was better than absolutely no sensations whatsoever! What had driven these women so low and to such depths were simply the dual snakes and whips of betrayal and ridicule!

Their ultimate trust and faith had been utterly shattered, driving their awareness of the universe around them inwards, until all that they could sense and perceive was their own helpless, miserable situations. If that was not enough, subsequently they were subjected to total ridicule by the men around them, who put their naked bodies on public display, removing the last shreds of their own personal modesty and values. It came as no surprise that they were very numb people. What had pulled the four out of their pits of depression had been living and caring for Diona, their queen. She was like themselves and a bond of sympathy had formed between them.

Eve also realized the magnitude and significance of Diona's goal: to kill General Erebos, the symbol of their oppression. She theorized that her steadfast, tenacious hold on this goal had kept Diona relatively sane and alive. Her four friends had adopted this as their chief goal as well, providing the five with a reason to survive. On the other hand, Eve knew that this was truly a false goal. Once they met their objective and the man was dead, they would then simply crumble. A woman is as alive as she has goals for the future. Beyond this destructive goal, these women had no further aims for which to strive. What to do?

Eve was certain of one thing. She had to have a new goal that was acceptable and somehow achievable both ready and waiting for Diona and her friends the moment that Diona achieved hers. She didn't worry that the remaining soldiers would determine that it was Diona who had poisoned their general. Obviously, in their minds their queen was merely a helpless doll, incapable of nearly any real action. Eve didn't fear retaliation against the five women. She feared their own loss of goals and thus their reasons for living. "I am right in having them get the idea that Diona has a legal right to rule Alia once the general is gone," she said to herself. "Okay then, Diona is going to need some real help and backing once she is the sole ruler. How can I make that happen?" she asked herself.

Olympos and his extended family certainly would back her. He was still a wealthy nobleman, but his and the Gidios families were in Axos right now, trying to help their eleven women deal with these debilitating mutilations. Were there others who would back Diona, she wondered. Eve had a positive route to follow.

For a week, she began appearing in various homes throughout Levkos, starting with what appeared to be the wealthier, more expensive homes of the capital city. Yes, she was spying, invading their privacy, though she did not make herself visible to the occupants. Eve never was much on the privacy issue, and she just had to know what the true situation was like outside of the palace where General Erebos kept the queen. She found that most of the families were defying the official proclamations in that the men dressed their women and cared for their now many needs. She found that encouraging. Undoubtedly, they would go along with Diona if she immediately rescinded the general's proclamations. Still, she found the many soldiers of the general going about their duties, taking more women each day from their homes to the Ornamentation Centers.

Eve also discovered that the soldiers were now into the working class portions of the city, having already mutilated the women of the wealthier class. She found another action occurring with frequency: upon receiving the notice that their women would be taken the following day, families began departing the city, leaving empty homes with most of their possessions behind. More and more, the soldiers arrived to take the scheduled women off to the centers only to find the home completely empty. She began to wonder just where these families had gone.

This intrigued her and she decided to monitor the situation more closely. She spotted several families leaving the city and decided to follow them. Many were on foot, carrying packs on their backs. A few led women on horseback with saddlebags stuffed with what they could carry with them. More often than not, they were heading up the north road that led to their largest port of Preveza. Given this clue, she moved on up to their port city and began observing there.

During the next couple of days, Eve discovered a very interesting fact. As families entered the outskirts of the port city, they were met by small groups of soldiers. These men then escorted the families into town and into a large building. Later, others escorted them out of this place. Following one family, she observed the two soldiers leading them to a home, before the two soldiers returned to the large building. She slipped into the home to see what was going on with this family of five only to discover that they were starting to set up house there. Interesting.

Eve moved back to the large building and eavesdropped on the conversations there. Incredibly, the soldiers were giving these newcomers sanctuary and homes here in Preveza! She spied a little more and discovered that they had a list of vacant homes and were doling them out to the new arrivals. Evidently, these were the homes of those who had perished during the plague. This was obviously in direct defiance of the general's proclamations. Now Eve really became interested and followed the soldiers, looking for their headquarters.

Towards the end of the day, she was rewarded for her diligence. The major running the sanctuary office reported to the Second Army Barracks and its General Thebes Nophios, a young man in his thirties. "Sir, we housed another six families from Levkos today."

"Excellent, major. Good work," the general saluted his major. "I don't know how much longer we can keep this up, but Levkos' loss is Preveza's gain."

"Sir, might I ask how we will be able to prevent the Ornamentation Project when it hits here?" the young major asked.

"You can ask, but I cannot answer," the general grinned. They saluted and the major left.

Another aide entered. General Thebes looked up and the aide reported, "Sir, all the doctors have been monitored today. As yet, none have taken any actions. We have confiscated the brass worker's products as ordered. They griped and asked just how many bullet casings we need anyway. I had to laugh though. We've got enough brass stored up to last us through two wars now."

General Thebes grinned, "True, but as long as they have no brass to use on our women, they cannot continue their Ornamentation Project here in Preveza." He sighed, "Still, you are right, Eventually we will have little options but to allow them to resume their evil works on our women. Either that or openly rebel and you know what that means."

"Well, we've stockpiled as much as we can. We'll be ready to take them on. Honestly, we certainly will have many young men of the port more than willing to take up arms with us. We ought to outnumber Erebos' forces greatly. He can't possibly send all the First Army here, because he needs them to maintain order in Levkos."

"True, but I hate to start a civil war. So much bloodshed," General Thebes replied. After the aide left, the general also left his office and Eve decided to follow him. He entered his private quarters and she was surprised to see that the general had a family. Well, she just wasn't expecting such. He had a wife and two young daughters and a son, who was eight. During the day, the boy was obviously caring for his mother and sisters, but now General Thebes took over, cooking their supper and helping his family, just like ordinary folks, Eve concluded.

Chapter 51 Salvaging Alia

Eve returned to our home in Velona that night, a plan forming in her mind. "Tomorrow, I am going to play god in Alia," she announced playfully over supper. "Has Stefano got another MMCE set of caravels near Alia? I think that am going to need them really soon."

The next morning, Eve materialized a body that looked like hers which was still here at our home, sitting on the living room sofa. Her new body appeared in an alleyway close to General Thebes' office. She walked boldly out and headed to his office. Eve only got some fifty feet before two sentries accosted her. "Halt. What are you doing in our barracks, ma'am?" one young lad asked.

"I have a personal message from Queen Diona Gidios for General Thebes Nophios. Can you take me to see him, please?" Eve asked, flashing them a coy grin. They were obviously not used to seeing a young woman walking on their private grounds. Eve, however, had mocked up a body that appeared to be of Alia descent. Her skin was bronze but other than that, her new body looked like hers back home, her hair falling almost to her knees. She wore our typical Velona dress. The two sentries led her into the general's office.

General Thebes blinked twice, not believing his eyes as Eve walked into his office. She surmised that women never met him here directly. Ah well, she was now being a god so she could do as she pleased, she concluded. "Sir, she claims to have a personal message for you from our queen." He saluted the general who reciprocated. The two stood by the door, an aide was sitting before the general's desk.

General Thebes looked at Eve. "Well?" he said, not sure if he believed what he was seeing.

Eve began, "Well, General Thebes, this is a very private message, for your ears only." Eve didn't believe in subtleties or beating around the bush. He looked her over a second time and decided that no matter what, Eve was not a threat to him. How could an armless woman be a threat? He dismissed the three and Eve took the aide's seat without waiting to be asked.

"Now then, general. I come directly from your Queen Diona Gidios. You may call me Eve."

He smiled, this young woman was in her teens and quite brash, he decided. "Well, Eve, what is the message?"

"Queen Diona has become aware of the fact that you are defying General Erebos' Ornamentation Project and doing all that you can to provide a safe haven for those who are fleeing his tyranny in Levkos, giving the fleeing families a home in which to start over. She believes that your confiscating of the bronze output is a brilliant move. No bronze, no debilitating ornaments. She wants to extend her personal thanks to you and your men for all of your efforts to date." Eve dropped enough clues for the general, if he was bright, to sense that perhaps the queen was against General Erebos and his Ornamentation Project. Getting started with this would be the toughest part, she guessed right.

"Well, we are doing what we can here in Preveza," he hedged his words. "Many nobles and those in power believe that this project of his is not going to solve the monumental problems facing Alia today." He was hedging.

Eve continued, "Indeed, Queen Diona also believes that this is so. Alia was facing hideous problems, but the General's Ornamentation Project has mushroomed the problems tenfold or more. A hundred thousand plus women are now nearly helpless dolls, wholly unable to care for any of their needs, unable to even speak. It has become a monumental fiasco and disaster of monumental proportions and must be stopped at all costs."

"Well, she won't get any disagreement with that from the people of Preveza. Just what does our Queen Diona propose to do about it? I understand that she was one of the first to become an Ornamental Doll herself." He was being purposefully noncommittal.

"Queen Diona is not as helpless as one might imagine. She is looking for allies to step in and both maintain order and help her get Alia on the road to true recovery the very moment that General Erebos is, shall we say, out of the picture. At the present, his soldiers control Levkos with an iron fist and they take their orders from him. When he is gone, she desperately needs someone that she can trust to take over instantly the control of those troops so that another 'General Erebos' does not immediately step into his shoes," Eve replied, becoming more specific.

She continued, "At this time, Queen Diona has the total support of the other monarchs of the kingdoms of Demokritos, along with the full and complete backing of Velona. All are poised and ready to send all manner of aid to Alia, the very moment that it is safe to do so."

"Well, indeed, if this be true, Alia has never had such good news. Yet, how am I to know that you speak the truth and that this is not some scheme of General Erebos to entrap me? You see my position here. I am obligated to follow his orders, since he is my superior officer."

"Of course he is and you have been following them to the letter. Of course, if there is no bronze available, the women of Preveza cannot undergo their Ornamentation Project. Clever of you. She also realizes the extreme position that you are in here. Her plan is simple. If you will swear allegiance to her and follow her orders, she will appoint you to succeed General Erebos as the Supreme Commander of Alia's Armies, once General Erebos is out of the picture, so to speak."

"I cannot turn down a promotion, but obviously I will do nothing to harm my superior officer. That would be treason and I would be shot. However, if as you are saying, something happens to General Erebos, then obviously someone must step in to maintain law and order. I would be shirking my duties to the Throne of Alia if I did not do as our Queen asks of me," he replied, trying hard not to put himself into a position of treason. He still did not trust Eve and rightly so.

Eve smiled. She had what she wanted. "Excellent. Queen Diona does not wish to put you into a position of treason or into a compromising position. You may count on that. If you leave today, how soon could you and the men that you would like to bring along need to get to Levkos? Timing will be the most critical factor, you see. She cannot act until she has a replacement general ready to step in and maintain law and order when General Erebos has passed away. She cannot afford even more chaos and evil to befall our country."

"Well, I do need time to make some arrangements for my own family during my absence," he hinted. "This plague has been utterly devastating to our future plans, but then I expect that it has been so for everyone. Allow me a week to reach Levkos."

Eve replied, "Yes it has for every woman in the entire world. Still, in other lands, women are finding that they can do nearly everything that they used to do only using different means. Both myself and Queen Diona write with our feet now."

He grinned, "That's amazing. You can actually write with your feet? Well, maybe so," he conceded. Abruptly, his tone changed to one of deep sorrow, "Io was going to open her own dressmaking shop, but that's all gone now — wiped out in an instant. She used to be a fabulous homemaker and loved raising our kids. Even that's gone. It's no wonder husbands are seldom away from their homes these days. Our families are so dependent on men now."

"General Thebes, once Queen Diona gets things going properly, your wife will be able to see just how she can still open her dressmaking shop as well as take care of your home. We women just have to learn new ways of doing our things and have you men make us the proper tools that we need for our work. Trust in your queen to bring these about as swiftly as possible," Eve couldn't resist giving him some encouragement.

"Surely you jest!" he exclaimed, taken by complete surprise and astonishment. Then, his tone dropped once more. "But our queen is an Ornamental Doll. By orders from General Erebos, the Ornamentation Project has begun here in Preveza. They began with the rich families of our port. Several hundred women and even little girls were ornamented before the bronze supplies ran too low for them to continue it." He refused to come right out and say that they were purposely finding ways to defy the proclamation orders. "We've all seen these Ornamental Dolls, for that's what they are being called around here. Unable to speak, unable to turn their heads, and barely able to eat, these poor women are now nothing but Ornamental Dolls. None of us can see anyway that these ornamented women and girls can do anything at all for themselves. They just sit around and look pretty; their husbands and sons have to look after their every single need. We've seen this here in our port. Those poor women and even little girls — their lives have been destroyed. So I ask you, how can our queen possibly be doing anything at all? I am sure that General Erebos isn't lifting a finger to help her."

"It is perfectly true; none of them can speak the Alia dialect anymore. However, it has been discovered that they can speak Annelise, only a couple of sounds cannot be deciphered. Hence, Queen Diona will be working hard to get linguists to teach the Ornamental Dolls to speak Annelise and those who are around them. That way these women will be able to communicate once more," Eve explained, though she had yet to actually meet Diona personally, let alone discuss all this with her.

Eve continued, "You are right, Queen Diona can do very little all by herself now, but she has four Ladies in Waiting. By all five working together, they are able to feed and dress themselves and thus have some semblance of normalcy. I am sure that in time, these women will be able to find ways to cope with their sadistic mutilations. Well, I had better be returning to the queen. One week it is then. Queen Diona will send for you at that time. Until then, she would appreciate it if the bronze supply remained too low for more ornamentation," Eve hinted. He smiled and nodded. Eve left his office, using her foot to open the door.

She walked down the street and ducked into an alleyway. Noticing that no one was around, she un-mocked her fake body and moved over the Royal Palace in Levkos, ready to deal with Queen Diona. She found her and her maidens struggling with lunch. General Erebos sat across the table from the five women, along with his small staff. None even noticed the naked women and their feeble efforts to feed each other.

Eve fought hard against just twisting the sadist's neck right now! Her flash of anger diminished. He needs to be taught a lesson, she decided. However, she also knew that Queen Diona needed to exact her revenge on the man as well. Indeed, her thirst for revenge was what had kept her going these many months. Still death was letting him off far too easy, Eve thought. Suddenly, Eve had a bright idea, left the Royal Palace, and hovered high over the huge city.

I could start searching the records of the girls who have been made into Ornamented Dolls, but that could take a long time. That is just agreeing with the laws of the universe. Let's see. I should be able just to know the answer. Ah, pervade the city. That's the answer, Eve thought. She expanded her awareness, looking for her precisely defined target.

A few minutes later, Eve felt exhilarated, *Just knowing the answer is so vastly easier! Wow. I am going to have to do it this way all the time!* She'd found what she sought. Absolutely a perfect situation! She made contact with the sobbing girl, barely five years old. Little Pandora readily agreed with Eve's idea, begging for it to happen sooner and wondering if Eve was a goddess or something. *Sit tight, only seven more days,* Eve placed in Pandora's mind.

Back at the Royal Palace, Eve waited for the five women to enter the library. Right on schedule, with careful and tiny steps in their heels, the five came into the library to continue their afternoon studies. Eve materialized her fake body in the hall, taking great care that no one could see her suddenly appear. Satisfied, she strode into the library, ready to tackle Diona's situation.

"Hello, I am looking for Queen Diona," Eve said as she entered, slightly annoyed that she wore a dress while the five were naked except for their extreme Annelise heels. Well, she couldn't undo this slight goof on her part. The twenty year old blonde pivoted in her chair, unable, of course, to just turn her head. She saw a nicely dressed young teen with very long blonde hair standing in the doorway. Eve's body looked to be of Alia descent, down to the bronze skin tones. Diona nodded by bending at her waist. At once, Tisiphone and Rhea, the two older young women, rose and positioned themselves between Diona and Eve, the only protection that the twenty-one year old women could think of doing to help Diona.

"I am here to help all of you. My name is Eve. In case others might ask about me, let's say that I am a distant cousin of yours, Queen Diona."

"But we cannot speak and be understood," Diona valiantly spoke the words, though the sounds were completely unintelligible as speech. She wanted to let this newcomer know their awful state and that she would be unable to help her.

"I understand, Diona. None of you can speak any language on Tarra, excepting one. Take heart Diona, we have found one language that you can speak and be understood except for a few sounds. Another young woman of Alia has discovered that she can speak the Annelise dialect and be well understood. That language does not depend much on lips to form their word sounds. With some language learning, all of you will be able to speak and be understood just fine," Eve explained. While the women's faces remained mostly expressionless because of the lip plates, their eyes shone a bit brighter. Eve continued, "In the meantime, you can write with your feet and I can read what you write."

Eve sat down across from the five and helped get some blank papers before their feet. "Now then, let me begin with a long story." Eve talked for well over an hour, beginning with the root cause of the plague. She covered the MMCE efforts being implemented in the other kingdoms, along with the Church of God's therapy assistance and the important role that Velona was playing in the salvaging of the kingdoms of Demokritos.

"Two caravels will be docking within a week or so in Preveza, bringing the sample MMCE items and engineers to help you begin a massive implementation here in Alia. All the other kingdom's monarchs are prepared to send you all the help you need and assist you in your efforts to restore Alia to freedom and prosperity once again. An LD radio system will be here in about a week and you can stay in daily touch with all the other monarchs, Velona, and even Annelise as well. True, until you learn the Annelise dialect, someone can do the actual speaking for you, reading what you have written with your feet for them to say or ask."

Diona tried to say something but frowned. She struggled to write a couple of words for Eve. "General Erebos won't allow it. He must die. I must kill him."

After reading it, Eve answered. "Of course, Diona, that treasonous, sadistic bastard must be eliminated. General Thebes Nophios of Preveza will take his place. Right now, General Thebes is stalling the Ornamentation Project in Preveza by consuming all the brass that is being produced there, making useless ammunition shells out of it. So far, his stalling action is working; no women have been ornamented for quite a few weeks now. I have talked with him, and he is willing to swear allegiance to you, Diona, and back you all the way the very moment that Erebos is slain. However, we must give him a week to get here to Levkos with his men. Then, Erebos will be removed and General Thebes can take his place, backing you as the sole monarch of Alia. I will send for him to come to you as soon as Erebos is removed."

"I will handle all the coordination needed. I'll make sure that you are successful in your self-appointed task with Erebos," Eve suggested. "On a lighter note, Diona, your family and the others are safe in Axos, Thrace. They are at the court of Queen Andromache, learning to speak the Annelise language right now. If you like, I can arrange for them to return here to lend you a hand in getting law and order restored and the huge problems of Alia solved."

Diona bent-nodded vigorously, though her face remained expressionless. Eve added, "I'll see that they also bring with them a large number of Bethany's Hint books, one for every woman and girl in Alia." She went on to explain about the book and how valuable the other women found it. "Unornamented women can learn how to do just about everything, just using different ways to do them, assisted by special tools to help them." Eve elaborated for some time, giving them some hope for the future.

What about us? We can't do much at all, Diona slowly scratched out in large uneven letters.

"Yes, I know. The ornaments are very debilitating. Your parents and Olympos have been researching ways to remove the neckbands with Monarch Andromache's help. So far, no luck. The bronze makers have been unable to remove them without harming the women. Still, they are working on it. It seems your bronze workers here in Levkos have done too good a job with them. In time, I am sure that solutions will be found. First, you must learn to speak Annelise. At least then you will be able to communicate once again until other things can be worked out," Eve explained.

"Oh, one more thing, an Annelise princess is bringing a huge load of their new fashions to trade with you. Finally, they are making clothing that we women can manage to put on ourselves — clothes that are practical," she added.

We help each other, Tisi wrote out.

"Yes, Tisi, that is what we women must do now, help each other. In Velona where they have had more years of getting adapted to the plague's aftermath, they have found that four women working together can accomplish what one used to be able to do by herself. So you five should continue to work together," Eve answered her. Tisi bent nodded her agreement.

Diona wrote slowly, What should we do now?

"Why not put your heads together and start writing down your first official proclamations? I'm sure that you want to put a screeching halt to this Ornamentation Project and to get women somehow dressed. Don't forget to promote General Thebes Nophios as your Supreme Commander of all Alia's armed forces." The young queen bent nodded.

They chatted a while longer before Eve left, promising to check on them each afternoon here in the library. Out in the deserted hallway, Eve's body simply vanished and her body in Velona, which was still lying on the sofa, animated. After supper, she had a lengthy conversation with Monarch Andromache, Olympos, and Diona's mother, Chara. They agreed to leave for home the next day, bringing as many supplies to Diona as they could manage.

Over the supper table, Eve announced, "Gang, I have a big problem. How do I teach something like two hundred thousand in Alia to speak the Annelise dialect?" Well, that was certainly a conversation stopper. Many voices asked, "Why?" Eve explained what she had been arranging in Alia. "Six more days and they will be ready to be salvaged; only how can we teach so many women and their families how to speak a foreign language very rapidly?"

After many ideas flew around the table, mom suggested, "You know, they ought to have a little dictionary with simple sentences and questions in their language followed by the Annelise equivalent. That way, they could look up what they wanted to say and then sort of see how to say it."

The underlying problem was how the language sounded, its phonetics. Eve liked the idea and set to work on making one up. Macario agreed to get it published in large volumes and somehow delivered to Monarch Diona, once she took over control of Alia. Again, I did not ask him how he could possibly do this, considering it was just by magic. However, with all the Advanced Therapy that I was now getting, I began to realize how he was doing these things with my Hints book.

The next morning, Eve called down to Viborg, Annelise, to chat with Queen Katerine. "I am about to free Alia from the tyranny of General Erebos. As you have probably heard, he's caused well over a hundred thousand women to be mutilated as Alexina was. So many women now are in desperate need of our therapy, Katerine, to say nothing of more than double that number who have to learn to speak and understand the Annelise tongue or these poor women will be wholly unable to communicate anything."

"Surely you don't want me to retake the throne of Alia," Katerine wanted to know. Eve sensed that Katerine felt her worst nightmare returning, having to rule Alia herself, something that she did not wish to do.

"No, they have officially appointed Diona Gidios as their queen. She is willing to assume the mantle of monarch. Considering what she has been through, I think it best to allow her the chance. As one of their Ornamented Dolls, she will command their attention and hopefully, their respect for persevering in spite of everything thrown at her," Eve replied.

Her voice echoing the great relief that she felt, Katerine replied, "Excellent. I ought to back her up, Eve. If you say that it is safe for us to return to Alia, we will. I'll talk to Jude and Midas about returning too. If they agree, we could form a Church of God in Levkos and get the Holy Gift being spread everywhere. But, Eve, what about the hundred thousand women who can't even speak? I know that Alexina's therapy was aided by the fact that she'd learned to speak Annelise beforehand. With these women, they can't speak. How can we run their sessions?"

Eve replied, "Well, they did it by telepathy to the eleven others down in Filantos. Still, I see your problem. Your group only has a half dozen who could possibly use telepathy to run the therapy session — far too few to deal with a hundred thousand plus women and girls. I think that they will have to learn Annelise first before they can receive therapy."

Katerine agreed, adding, "The real problem is how can so many suddenly learn a foreign language quickly. It's as if each home needs a private tutor or something. Let me see what we can work out here. I'll call you back tomorrow."

Eve was quite surprised by what Katerine had to say the next day. "Okay, Eve, my group will head for Alia within a couple of days and we'll see that the Holy Gifts are given. Plus, I have some good news to share. As you know, General Erebos has completely ignored the problem of proper fitting clothing for the women in Alia, ordering them to go naked. Obviously, a whole lot of simple dresses must be made for them as well as learning the Annelise dialect. If the treasury of Alia can afford fifty thousand a month, I can get one hundred men and women of Viborg who are willing to come to Alia for several months. They will go home to home, providing language lessons and sewing up dresses for the women there, using the new sewing machines to speed their construction. If Alia is totally broke, perhaps Velona can float me a personal loan and I'll pay their wages and somehow pay Velona back."

"I will check on it. However, Katerine, if the funds are lacking, I will pay their wages myself!" Eve declared. "What a brilliant idea, Katerine. Perfect. Make it happen. I will relay this terrific news to Monarch Diona today. She will be elated. Thank you very much!"

"You are welcome, Eve. It is the very least that I can do for my homeland and people, but what are we really going to do for the hundred thousand Ornamented Dolls? Can't the neck rings be removed somehow?" she asked.

"So far, no go on that. Olympos has nearly every metalworker in Axos on it, but to no avail. It seems that the bronze workers were very thorough in carrying out General Erebos' orders. They used molten metal to fuse the joining seams. Only reheating them to the melting point will work, but that will surely kill the women in the process. Still, Olympos is working on it. I don't hold out much hope, though. Perhaps you will be able to help those women find other ways to adapt and get by," Eve suggested.

"Oh by the way, Eve, I have remarried. Yanni Argos proposed and I accepted. I am now Katerine Argos."

"Well congratulations! That's great. Are you two planning on starting a family?" Eve asked coyly.

"I am not an old maid yet!" Katerine teased. "Yes, we are. Barbara is excited about having a little brother or sister too. Okay, I'll make the arrangements and let you know when the large group is ready to set sail for Preveza, Alia. Say, can I ask one question? How are you getting rid of General Erebos?"

Eve chuckled, "I'll let you know in a couple of days. Diona insists on obtaining her own revenge. I think that in doing so, such will help her regain her own self-respect and that of many of her fellow countrymen and women. To learn that an Ornamented Doll eliminated the sadistic bastard will play well throughout Alia. It may give heart to the hundred thousand plus who have fallen victim to his wicked ways."

During the ensuing days, Eve continued to materialize in the hallway just outside the library each afternoon. She kept the five updated on all the progress being taken on their behalf. None of the five could comprehend how so many people that they did not know could be so generous to themselves and the people of Alia. Diona wrote, Thank you, Eve. You are an angel. You are saving us and Alia. How can we ever thank you?

"By bringing hope, prosperity, kindness, and mercy back into Alia. Now then, let's see how your first proclamations are coming along," Eve quickly changed the subject.

The day before the proposed elimination day, Eve checked up on the host family that she'd discovered earlier. All was still going according to her plans. Diogenes Dotos, twenty-six, was a miller by trade. He worked at ABC Millers, a large milling plant on the eastern edge of Levkos, a mile from his home, a modest limestone single-floor dwelling. Diogenes was considered lower middle class by the wealthy of Levkos. He made enough money grinding grains to support his growing family but with little extra. Because of his daily access to the mill, his family survived the plague fairly well. Always there was flour available, though during the worst times they made do with oat flour.

His wife, Ambrosia, twenty-five, tended their home and children. She also used to raise vegetables in a garden plot behind their home, before the plague, that is. She wore her brown hair short and fluffy, easy to manage. After it grew some two feet during the plague, she wanted Dio to cut it back to its usual length, but he talked her out of it, claiming she looked good with her hair flowing to the small of her back now. Helpless, she agreed — anything to keep Dio happy, she thought, desperately depending upon him for everything at the onset of the plague.

They had two children. Dion was six and now looked after his younger sister, Pandora, who was five and whose brown hair was down to her knees. Pandora loved her long hair, about the only thing that she still liked about her body after the ravages of the plague had struck. Still, like her mother, she didn't just give up. She and Dion continued to find ways to play during the day and slowly she began adapting to getting by without her arms.

Already they had seen many of the new Ornamented Dolls, as the women were now being called. The whole Dotos family was shocked and appalled by these women, who could no longer speak and who looked miserable and even more helpless than Ambrosia and Pandora were. When the notice came a few days ago giving them time to prepare for the Ornamentation Procedure, they were shocked and terrified. Pan had screamed, "Mommy, I don't want to be like them! Please, don't let them take me away and do this to me." Ambrosia could only cry, as did Dio, who had heard of many men being outright murdered when they attempted to prevent their wives and daughters from being taken to the Ornamentation Centers.

Ambrosia had extenuating circumstances that the doctors could not ignore. She was pregnant and due any day now. If she were to undergo the procedures while pregnant, she could well go into labor right in the middle of the sensitive operation. Nevertheless, following the general's orders, both Ambrosia and Pandora were escorted out of their home on the morning of February 24, 825, and taken to their local Ornamentation Center. Obviously, Diogenes had no funds to provide fancy gems or gold for their ornamental earrings.

At the center, the doctors sighed and realized that Ambrosia's surgery would have to be delayed, but that evening they put Pandora under to begin her operation. Halfway through her daughter's operation, Ambrosia gave birth to a baby girl, whom she called Io. After they saw mother and daughter were doing fine, they then put Ambrosia under to give her the requisite ornamental surgery as well, claiming this was most timely indeed.

The afternoon of February 24, Eve appeared at the library. General Thebes was in position at the edge of the huge city and waiting for the word to report to the Royal Palace. Now Eve had to see that Diona accomplished her long-planned assassination of General Erebos. "All is ready, Monarch Diona. General Thebes is in position and awaits your summons. Do you still want to go through with this yourself?" she asked.

"Yes!" Diona said, but then was once again painfully reminded that her speech was unintelligible. She bent-nodded vigorously to make sure that Eve knew how much this meant to her.

"Okay, then it is time. You four stay here. I will go with Diona and make sure she is safe and gets it done," Eve ordered. Diona rose and began her slow shuffling walk to her room. Wearing practical flats, Eve had to walk extremely slowly to keep pace with Diona in her extreme heels. She smiled, those heels would soon be history, she guessed. Eve knew that she had to allow this woman to carry out her mission on her own. Eve could not just do it for her. Still, she intended to provide unseen assistance if needed. The general's body had to die tonight for her plan to work.

Eve almost cried as she watched the pathetic, awkward motions that Diona had to make just to retrieve the vial of poison. Oh, how she wanted to reach out and lend her some assistance, but continued to allow the woman to manage for herself. Only once did Eve have to put a hasty pulling beam onto the vial to prevent Diona from dropping it, though the young monarch did not realize that Eve had done so.

A half hour later, they finally entered the general's room. There was his wine bottle. Luck was on her side, the bottle had been opened, probably the night before. Only with a great effort and some incredibly precarious moves was Diona able to get the cork out. Eve resisted the urge just to pull it out for her, though she made sure that the poison all went into the bottle, helping it along a bit when the liquid tried to drip down the bottle's side. "Shake it a bit," she urged, watching the two fluids mix into a lethal combination. She added a bit of an extra push to the cork as Diona managed to get the cork into position. Unable to bend her neck at all or to see over her lip plates and massive bosom, the task was incredibly difficult for Diona. Still, she gave it her all; this was her one and only chance to avenge the death of her father and uncles. She was determined not to fail them.

A half hour later, the two headed out of the room. Eve had already made sure that everything was just as the general had left it the night before. She held her breath, hoping that no one would suddenly appear in the hallways and corridors. Eve was prepared for a sudden surprise, though. She left nothing to chance, for the salvation of Alia depended on this all working according to her plan.

After Diona returned to the library, Eve whispered, "It is done. I will return later tonight and act as your messenger to Thebes." Eve apparently left, but in fact merely un-mocked her fake body in the hallway. She hovered around the women and again watched them go down to supper. As she watched the general, Major Stefanos reported, "Well, come Saturday, General, we will have passed the one hundred fifty thousand women handled mark. We are up to handling twenty thousand per month now and increasing rapidly. We may well make the end of the year goal of ornamenting every woman in Alia. Congratulations."

"Ah perfect. Notice the superb silence from the other side of the table." He nodded to the five women. "This has been a terrific idea of mine, perhaps the best yet. Our commerce is growing; men are back to work — well, mostly. How goes conscripting of those men still out of work?" he asked. The two men chatted over the duck dinner.

When they finished and the major left for the evening, Eve placed a thought into General Erebos' mind. He rose, "Well, my beautiful queen, ladies, I bid you adieu for tonight. I am retiring to my room to celebrate. Yes, another ten months and the project will be complete. You women do look very pretty and acceptable now. Good night my lovely queen." He bowed and left the five who were valiantly struggling to feed Diona. After she was fed, then they had to continue the process for the other four. Dinner always took them five times longer than the general and his staff took to eat.

Eve followed the general as he entered his private quarters. She watched as he picked up his wine bottle and poured himself a large glass. He took off his boots, lay back on his couch, and began sipping his fine wine. Eve waited patiently. If she had had a body, Eve would have grinned. Nothing like this had been attempted before, but she felt confident that she could pull it off. One thing was certain: she wanted this man to taste his own medicine!

Foam came from the general's mouth. Eve realized at once that the amount of poison Diona had put in his wine amounted to a gross overkill. A few drops would have worked, but she'd put in the whole vial! Eve watched, as the shocked being called Erebos realized that he was poisoned and was rapidly dying. He tried valiantly to rise and get help, but failed, slumping back onto the couch, clutching his throat. Eve made sure that the wine bottle fell and shattered on the floor. She did not want someone else drinking from this poisoned bottle.

As expected, the general's body died quickly. Eve latched onto the spiritual being who was Erebos and picked up his wild stream of thoughts and reactions, none good, of course. Then, just as the mantis implant activated, which would order him to go find a new baby body and start life over once more, Eve latched on to him. *Come with me, your new body is prepared and awaiting you!* She was total intention, total postulate in her command. Erebos had no choice whatsoever; he had to follow her.

Eve led him to the Ornamentation Center. Meanwhile, she reached out to Pandora. *Pan, are you ready to have your new body now?*

Yes! They did it to me, didn't they? Now it's all crippled up and can't even bend or speak! Yes, I am ready. What do I do? Pan replied.

Here, feel this baby body. Yes, like that. Hang on to it. Perfect. There you go. Your mom is calling you Io now. I hope you like that new name. Thank you Pan for giving up your old body.

It's so tiny. Oh well, in a few years it will be as big as the old one was. Thanks, Eve.

Eve pulled Erebos down to the bed on which Pan's five year old body lay now in a drugged state. *Here is your new body. Move into its head. Here, yes, latch on to that,* Eve sent.

Mostly blind, Erebos did as ordered, feeling for the head and latching onto its motor controls. Wham! A huge surge of pain struck him, energizing his holding beam, pulling him solidly into the body's head, like some huge magnet pulling a sword onto itself. So strong was the pull that Eve knew that Erebos would be wholly unable to extricate himself from the five year old body! Worse, he was almost at once pulled into the drug mental mass and he went unconscious, out like a light.

Eve looked down on the mother and her two children. Her baby Io was doing just fine. Ambrosia was now ornamented and would have an awful time of it, Eve knew. After all, just caring for her own child was more than challenging and she'd needed Giovanni's help often. With those heavy earrings, lip plates, and neck rings, motherhood would be almost a nightmare, requiring the constant assistance of others. Ah well, this reign of terror was stopped now, but one hundred fifty thousand women would suffer its effects for the rest of their lives.

She looked down at the five year old girl, Erebos' new body, Pan's old one. Eve grinned, even though she had no bodily form now. The general was now going to have to live a very long lifetime in the manner in which he had forced so many women to endure. Eve had chosen the youngest possible girl to maximize the years that Erebos would have to endure the taste of his own sadism! Eve had never felt as pleased with herself as she did at this very moment. Then, she took off to meet up with General Thebes.

She spotted him and materialized her body form once more. Then, she walked into his encampment asking for him. Shortly, she was led to his tent. "Ah, right on time. Is it done?" he asked, still not really believing that the general was dead.

"Yes, Monarch Diona has done it. She requests your presence immediately at the Royal Palace. I can lead you there if you don't know the way," Eve replied.

"I know the way to the palace. I am sorry, but we have no carriages with us."

"No problem. I can ride a horse as well as anyone. Just tie the reins together." After seeing his disbelieving stare, she added, "We women bite down on the reins and can neck rein quite nicely. Honestly, you know as well as I that hands are not needed to ride a horse." He grinned and issued his orders.

A soldier brought up a horse for her and tied the reins as asked. General Thebes himself held the mare steady as Eve mounted up, awkwardly however. Normally, she'd just lift her body up, but now tried to do the action with just her body. One day, all this silliness won't be needed anymore, she thought to herself. She bit into the reins and called out, "Let's get going."

It took them a good hour to traverse the nearly deserted streets of Levkos. Few ventured out after dark; most had to stay home to care for their women and daughters. They entered the palace unchallenged by the night guards, who were used to seeing soldiers coming and going at all hours. General Thebes noted this, however. What a lack of security, he thought. Anyone could get hold of a uniform and ride into the palace unchallenged! Well, if he were the Supreme General, he'd put a stop to this breach of security.

After dismounting, Eve led the general and his six men across the courtyard and into the palace complex. She went straight for the queen's private chambers, where Diona and her four friends were waiting patiently. All five were extremely nervous, so much could go wrong!

"Monarch Diona, allow me to present General Thebes Nophios. General, your monarch Diona Gidios." Diona rose and waist bowed to him, cursing for the millionth time that she was utterly naked before a man. At least her long blonde hair now partially covered her, as it always did when she leaned forward, her only means of gaining a slight bit of modesty.

"Your Majesty! I am honored to meet you. I wish this were under better circumstances. I am told that General Erebos is dead?" he said as a question, still uncertain of the true situation.

"Yes," Diona replied, before she realized that her speech was incomprehensible. She hastily waist nodded and began her slow shuffle out of her room. Since Eve followed her, General Thebes and his men moved in behind the two, her four friends followed discretely behind them. She led him to the general's private chambers, which used to be the king's quarters. There lay the dead general, most definitely poisoned. "See, I told you so! I killed that awful bastard who killed my dad and the others! I hope he rots in hell!" she gushed, regretting that she had once more spoken. Her words were not even understandable to her own ears.

She turned and made her slow way back to her chambers, where she had a stack of papers ready. She handed him the top one. He read: I am the lawful Monarch of Alia. As such, I hereby promote you to the position of Supreme Commander of Alia's Armed Forces. Do you swear your undying loyalty to me and to follow my orders?

"Yes, Your Majesty. I do so swear! This is incredible! Did you poison Erebos yourself?" he asked as the reality finally sank home.

She bent nodded vigorously, preferring not to vocalize gibberish again. She felt embarrassed that she had lost control back in his room and made a fool of herself. Obviously, she could no longer speak.

She handed him the next paper. He read: Put a complete stop on the Ornamentation Project countrywide. Arrest those who have been mutilating our women. Post the following proclamations countrywide as fast as you and your men can.

"You have my complete support on this one! I've been consuming all the brass that is made in Preveza so that they can't perform the damnable operations on our port city women. I will do this with gusto, Your Majesty!"

Using her foot, Diona handed another paper towards Eve, who clumsily took it between her teeth and then got it with her foot. Eve grinned, it read: Please explain the MMCE and all the aid that we are going to be getting to General Thebes for me. I can't write that much. Eve chuckled and began a very lengthy explanation.

In the middle of it all, Majors Perseus and Stefanos came into the queen's chamber. "General Thebes! What a surprise to see you," Major Stefanos called out, interrupting Eve. "We heard from the guards that you arrived. General Erebos is in his quarters for the evening."

"General Erebos is dead. I am your new Supreme Commander. Go see for yourselves." To two of his men, he added, "Go with them and make sure that they don't do anything. Then, arrest both of them.

I'll visit with them later. Eve, sorry about that interruption. Please continue, this is the best news that I've heard since the plague came!"

"But he was alive just hours ago — at supper," Major Stefanos objected. General Thebes ignored him and Eve did likewise, continuing her long explanations.

Meanwhile, Diona awkwardly wrote out a new message. "Paris Kraytos, the cook, helped us. He should not be punished. Major Perseus was guarding the palace only. Major Stefanos carried out most of Erebos' orders."

After glancing at her paper, he smiled, "Understood, Your Majesty." After Eve finally finished, the two majors came back, insisting on an audience with General Thebes.

"General, we were just following General Erebos' orders," Major Stefanos protested. "Did you kill him? Looks like he was poisoned."

"I'll have the palace searched for the assassin," Major Perseus added. Both men looked extremely nervous, but Stefanos was definitely very worried. He kept fiddling with his pockets and belt, and then running his hands through his hair.

"I prefer to call the person who poisoned that sadistic excuse of a person a national hero, gentlemen. How many of our citizens has he ordered murdered? How many of our women have been turned into utterly helpless Ornamented Dolls, eh? A hundred fifty thousand? How many women have suffered incredible humiliation and embarrassment by his foul proclamations? You should have arrested him yourselves a year ago!"

"But someone assassinated him," protested a worried Major Perseus. "I don't know how he could have gotten by my guards at the gates."

"Idiot. We all entered unchallenged. Anyone could have entered here and poisoned him. Yet, stop fretting, major. Your own monarch here did the deed. She deserves the highest praise that we in Alia can give her. Monarch Diona by herself poisoned the evil man. We'll discuss your security tomorrow, major. Rather at this point, it is Major Stefanos who ought to be very worried. I ought to have him executed this evening for high treason against the women of Alia!"

"But I was only following orders! She can't even speak. How can she lead us? She ought to be shot for poisoning our general," Stefanos protested madly. His eyes glanced around the room, looking for an escape route, calculating his odds against the six guards of the general.

"Major, you are inches away from being executed by my own hand! Watch your tongue and what you say from this instant on! Following orders is no excuse for such treasonous behavior. If you want to live, you will cooperate with me fully and immediately."

"Yes sir," he saluted his commanding officer. His legs felt very weak; his knees trembled. Sweat began pouring out of his facial pores, though it was not that warm.

"Monarch Diona is reduced to writing out her orders now, thanks to you and Erebos. Here, read her first proclamation." He handed him the paper outlawing the Ornamentation Project. "Now then, you are the one person who handled the overall project. I want to know where all the centers are located, who is in charge of each, and how we can guarantee that no more women are operated upon without their consent."

Major Stefanos began outlining the overall project and its organizational makeup. "Okay, Major Stefanos. I'll send a dozen guards along with you. It is your first task to see that all such operations are ended immediately. For every woman who undergoes the Ornamentation Project beginning at dawn tomorrow, you will lose a finger. If you run out of fingers, I'll take toes after that. Do I make myself perfectly clear, major? No more women are to be ornamented without their consent." Turning to Monarch Diona, he added, "Some women may wish to undergo the ornamentation project. If they want to do so of their own freewill and choice, we should allow them to do so. The choice should be the woman's alone."

Diona cringed, but her face didn't show it. She hastily scrawled out, "Why?"

"You've been isolated here at the palace, cut off from interacting with our people, Your Majesty. With all the noblewomen and the wealthier ones as well now ornamented, many others see this as a status symbol and want to become ornamented themselves, if only to gain such status and perhaps to better fit into our population," General Thebes explained.

Major Stefanos quickly added, "He's right. Here in Levkos, as far as we could tell, a hundred thousand women more or less died directly from the plague and its aftermath. Another two hundred thousand women have simply vanished from the city; presumably, they have moved to other towns and villages or died elsewhere. Our initial estimates suggest that Levkos had around a million women and girls prior to the plague. At this time, nearly one woman or girl in five is an ornamented. All the wealthier and nobles aged five and above are ornamented here in Levkos. These women are the status symbols of Alia; they are the ones that many others look up to for guidance. What we are now observing as we are into the middle working class women is that many are desiring their ornamentation, seeing it as *the* thing to do, seeing as how all women are pretty much helpless objects now. So if they actually want the ornamentation, they ought to not be denied it."

Eve saw something else underlying his explanation: the safety of his own fingers and toes. Once a woman was ornamented, she would be unable to explain that she had not wanted it done to herself, thereby getting Major Stefanos off the hook.

Diona began her fumbling attempt at writing once more. At last, she bent nodded to General Thebes, who retrieved the paper from the floor, saving her from having to do so. He read it aloud. "Declare a moratorium on the Ornamentation Project. Any woman who wants it done to herself can come to me and explain why she wants it. I can then okay it, if I choose."

"Perfect, Your Majesty," General Thebes replied with a smile. "See major, our monarch is wise and can issue the proper orders, even though you and your sadistic general made it impossible for her to speak her orders aloud."

Major Stefanos groveled, "Perfect, Your Majesty." His words sounded hollow, though. He was still in shock over the incredible events of the evening. "Some of our centers are in outlying towns, Your Majesty. It will be impossible to reach them before dawn in order to stop the day's operations." He was still maneuvering to keep his fingers, Eve noted.

"Well how long will it take to get all the centers shut down?" the general asked.

"A week at most, though a day or so here in Levkos."

"Okay, my aides will go with you now to make sure that you obey the monarch's orders. At the end of the week, I want an accurate count of the total number of women who have been ornamented throughout Alia. Is that understood, major?"

"Yes sir. I can do better. We've kept accurate records of those who have been ornamented: names and addresses, sir. I can have a copy of that extensive list for you by the end of the week."

"Good. Now get going yet tonight. Tomorrow, I will draft our monarch's new proclamations and with your help, we will get them posted all over Alia. Dismissed, major," he ordered. The two saluted and several guards accompanied Major Stefanos out of the queen's chambers.

"Major Perseus, get rid of Erebos' body, burn it. He is not worthy of a burial, cast his ashes in some pigpen somewhere. Ah Paris, you are still here," he noted.

"Yes sir! I am a good cook, sir," he saluted.

"Be a good man and rustle up some tea and a snack for us all. Your Majesty, let's adjourn to the dining room for tea. We can go over the other papers there. I am famished. My men will assist your with your meals and your needs. Do you have any clothing at all to wear?"

Diona moved her body left and right, indicating no. The only clothing they had were those awful billowing Annelise ball gowns which made their lives even more miserable during the past winter. She did not want to be wearing that again. Worse, she couldn't even write while wearing that dress. "Damn, you can't even shake your head no. Damn Erebos to hell! Well, tomorrow I will send out men in search of something for you to wear. I do hope that promised Annelise ship comes soon! It must be unbearable for you women to go around naked."

As they walked slowly to the dining room with General Thebes carrying the stack of papers, he added, "Back home, I made sure that my wife and daughter were always dressed, defying the general's orders. Your Majesty, if you can bear it a little longer, I promise you that we will soon set things to right."

His eyes didn't miss the five women's action of bending forward, allowing their long hair to drape over their front before they sat down. He saw why they did so and even helped Tisi adjust her hair so that it covered her better. Soon Paris came bustling in with a tray and hot tea. He returned a second time with a second tray of biscuits, honey, and cheese. Several soldiers entered and were ordered to feed the women. For the first time since arriving at the palace, Diona actually began to relax. Perhaps life would indeed become better, she thought.

After a lengthy, mostly one-way chat, the general walked them back to their quarters and even asked if they needed help getting into bed. Diona turned left and right, such kindness she had not been shown for ages. After the five finished brushing out each other's hair, Diona climbed or rather fell into bed. Lying there, she suddenly realized how badly she had missed her mother, sister, and brother, who were now on their way here. Until now, she had totally blocked her past from her mind, focusing totally on finding a way to kill Erebos and to stay alive. She cried silently to herself. Somehow, if her mother were here, she would feel safe again. Quite why, she had no idea. After all, her mother was in just as bad a shape as she was now.

Eve returned home when the monarch retired for the night. However, she realized that she would have to return first thing in the morning to be available to help her out, at least until others arrived who could talk and assist her. A very sleepy-eyed Eve hastily explained to me and the rest of us what she had done with the sadistic man. "Yes, Diona poisoned him and had her long sought revenge, but my revenge is even better. She's only five, so she or he now has to face living sixty or more years as an

Ornamented Doll. May he stew in his own pot." I chuckled. Leave it to Eve to come up with some remarkable justice.

The next morning, Pan awoke; the anesthesia had worn off. Her lips throbbed in pain. She had to go pee badly and tried to rise. Erebos tried to use arms, but Pan had none. Only with extreme effort was she able to sit up in bed. She saw the four-inch lip plates blocking her forward and below vision; she felt her lack of arms. Her neck couldn't move, not even a fraction of an inch, forcing her to make drastic body movements just to see around herself. Her earrings felt like they were about to pull her very ears off her head. Suddenly, Erebos realized that his new body was that of a small five year old girl, now completely helpless. Pan shrieked and cried out in terror and fright.

Her mother and her newborn girl were lying on the bed beside her, though Pan didn't even know that she was her mother. Poor Ambrosia awoke and joined Pan with her shrieks. A doctor came running in. "Ah, awake at last. My, you both look just perfect. Now we need to be careful with your lips for the next few days. Once they've healed, you can return to your home. Pan, you now have a new little sister. Her name is Io. Ambrosia told me before her own ornamentation operation began. She is fine and healthy. Now I am sure that you both need to use the chamber pot. I don't want you up and walking today. Just call out and someone will attend to your needs. I will see that a light breakfast is brought to you both soon and someone will help little Io nurse a bit later."

Pan felt humiliated to have this strange man helping her naked body use the pot. Her mother felt such even more so, but was utterly dependent on the help. Ambrosia knew that she could not take care of her own baby, let alone herself now. Somehow, little Io had to survive. Perhaps somehow Io could avoid this awful ornamentation mutilation.

Pan just cried and screamed for some time. At last, when an aide began feeding her spoons of chicken soup, she had to shut up. Now she faced how terribly difficult eating would become, soup kept trickling out of her small mouth; her lips could not hold anything inside and her missing front baby teeth only made matters worse. Lean back, the aide suggested. Well, that helped, she discovered. Once fed, Pan laid back and began crying again. Erebos was in the unusual position of having full recall of his life as the general but now was inside a five year old girl's body, doomed to the utter torment and hell that he had created for over a hundred fifty thousand women of Alia. As he realized this, he or she bawled uncontrollably for quite some time. At last, Pan stopped crying. Her mouth felt like dry leather; she desperately wanted a drink, but as she began talking, trying to tell a nearby aide what she needed, she discovered what she already knew; her words were completely unintelligible. Her misery began to pile up on her now and she cried yet again.

"Ah, you want to be tucked in again," the aide came by, completely missing what Pan desired, a drink of water. She sobbed even more, realizing how hopeless it would be to tell anyone what she desperately needed or wanted. In a flash, it dawned on her what exactly she had done to the women of Alia. She called out, "I didn't mean it," but of course, not even she could understand the sounds that her voice made now. Pan realized that no one would ever know that she had not meant it and she began crying once again. By the action of denying what she had done by saying that she had not meant it, the next morning, she awoke having forgotten completely her former lifetime as General Erebos. She'd negated her own previous beingness, and now she was merely a helpless little girl in pain and unable even to communicate her basic needs to anyone.

Five days later, the miller Diogenes Dotos welcomed his wife and two daughters home. As promised, the soldiers brought them up to his door shortly after breakfast. "Oh my, Ambrosia! You did it, Io is her name?" he asked excitedly as he took the infant in his arms from one soldier. Unable to speak or nod yes, she bent at her waist to indicate that was the name she'd given her new daughter.

"Oh, she is perfect, just like her mother and little Pan too!" he exclaimed, happy to have them back with him. Both were wearing the same nightgowns that they had worn when the soldiers took them away. That they were not naked as prescribed by General Erebos and his proclamations wasn't observed by the young miller. Once they were inside and the soldiers shut out at last, Dio added, "My, let me look at you Ambrosia. You look stunning, dear." He gave her a kiss on her cheek after giving up trying to figure out how to kiss her on her lips as he always had done. "Pan, you look just like your gorgeous mother." He gave a one-arm hug to his daughter while Dion simply stood and stared at the both of them.

The two parents headed into the kitchen, leaving Dion still staring at Pan. "You look really weird, Pan. Does it hurt?" he asked.

With her earring chains hanging down onto her chest, Pan bent nodded but it felt as if her ears were being pulled off. Involuntarily she said, "Yes, everything hurts." As soon as she spoke, she wished that she hadn't, for she only made strange sounds.

Dion crinkled up his nose, "Can't you speak anymore?" Tears flowing again, Pan moved her whole body left and right. Again, her earrings, like pendulums, threatened to pull her ears off or so she thought, as they moved left and right, clanking into her neck rings. Pan felt both terrified and confused.

Who were these people? She'd never seen them before. Evidently, this boy was her brother and the man, her father. Was this her house? Everything was totally unfamiliar. She'd never seen this place before. Pan stood rooted to the spot where she stood.

"Come on; let's play. You can still play can't you?" Dion asked. Again, she risked having her ears pulled off and bent nodded yes. Although she had no idea if she could play or what Dion had in mind, she remained hesitant. Did she even have a room? If so, where was it? Did she have any toys? Well, she thought, I certainly can't play with them now. Pan was miserable. Her fears grew as she realized that she needed to go to the bathroom. How could she even tell them that she had to use the pot and soon?

Diona was awakened by a knock on her door. "Your Majesty, are you awake?" a man's voice called out.

"Yes," she replied, but wished that she hadn't. Embarrassed by her strange sounds, she tried to rise up. After a bit of a lunging struggle, she sat up in her bed. A soldier with a moustache smiled at her. He appeared to be around thirty she thought; his face seemed friendly enough.

"I am Sergeant Kastor. I'm to look after your needs and those of your Ladies in Waiting. You needn't worry. I've been caring for my own wife and daughter since the plague struck us so hard." His voice sounded kindly, matching his facial expressions. Probably he was sympathetic, she adjudicated. He continued, "We've searched the palace during the night and found the Royal Clothing Room. Of course, hardly anything will fit you women properly anymore, not since the plague. None of my wife's clothes fit either, but we made do. I've found some things that may work. Can I assist you now?" She tried to bend nod, but doing so while sitting in her bed was difficult.

"Forgive me, Your Majesty, but I've not been around the Ornamented Dolls before. I'm told that you cannot speak and be understood. Is this true?" Again, she replied that it was so, allowing him to hear her garbled voice sounds, completely unintelligible.

"Thought as much. How about saying yes and then no for me. That way, I can tell which is which. Then you can just make those sounds and I'll know what you mean," Sergeant Kastor suggested. Reluctantly, she did so and then realized that as awful as her words sounded, this was better than trying to bend at her waist or move her body from left to right to indicate yes or no. She smiled but her face did not show it.

A bit later having helped her to use the chamber pot, he helped her get into panties and then a simple day dress. She guessed some servant must have worn it. It fit rather poorly, but at least she was covered. She slipped into her extreme heels and waited while he repeated his actions with Dora, Tisi, Xanthe, and Rhea. All five women looked at each other and smiled. Such simple kindness they had not known since they were taken away to be ornamented. Naturally, their smiles were not visible.

"There you go, all set. I believe that breakfast is waiting you. If you need me later on, just send for me. I will be around every morning and evening to assist you and at any other time you need help," he explained. Again, Diona smiled and then began her slow walk to the dining room.

As promised, five soldiers were already there, waiting to help them dine. General Thebes sat at the lower end of the large table and insisted that Monarch Diona sit at the head of the table, where General Erebos had always sat. Her friends sat on either side, a soldier interspersed between them to assist them. Paris walked in carrying a large tray.

"Ah good morning Your Majesty! I've prepared a fine breakfast for you. Sometime we need to discuss what you wish to have for your meals — you know, your favorite dishes and all that," Paris said, setting the tray down and arranging the plates and mugs before the soldiers who would be feeding each woman.

"Very good, Paris. I'm sure that our monarch will let you know soon," General Thebes broke in. "Right now, we have more important business to handle. We've reconnoitered the palace during the night so that we know what is where. The first thing we must decide upon is where you wish to hold court. You know, meet with us, hold your meetings, and receive the nobles and those who wish to see you. We need to make that space highly defensible. Who knows what riffraff might decide to do? I take your security seriously, Your Majesty," General Thebes added. He went on, "Once we make that decision, I'll see that your writing desks are taken there along with plenty of paper and pencils. Also, since writing is the key here, I have sent men out in search of more of these special writing desks. I would like a desk in each of the rooms that you frequent. You must have a way to communicate to us at all times, Your Majesty."

"Oh yes, I nearly forgot. I am supposed to ask you to say yes and then no so that I can learn to recognize your words. We realize how difficult it is for you women to move your bodies to make such an indication," he continued. "Paris, you pay attention to her words too."

Dutifully, Diona said the two words in succession a couple times. Yes was more of an "ah" sound, while no came out more like an "oh" sound. "Got it, Your Majesty. From now on, when it is appropriate, please just say the two words and we'll learn to understand you." Diona smiled and said "Ah," pleased with his attempts.

"Now then as far as which room to hold court in, I would like to recommend that you use the old King's Throne Room. It is the largest of the meeting rooms and the most defensible as well. The Queen's Throne Room is likely going to be too small. Is this okay with you or should we try using some other room? Oh, say yes, if the King's Throne Room is okay with you." He was still just getting the hang of asking her questions that could be answered with a simple yes or no reply.

"Ah," she replied and he nodded his approval. Perhaps this will work out, Diona thought.

He looked at his teacup for a moment and then raised his eyes to hers. "I have one small favor to ask of you, Your Majesty. Would it be possible for my family and those of several others who will be assisting you and your Ladies in Waiting with your needs to move into some of the guest rooms here in the palace? I really don't want to be away from my wife and family any longer than I have to — same with Sergeant Kastor and a couple others."

"Ah," Diona replied. It would be good to have other women around and children too, she thought.

"Very good, Your Majesty. We all do greatly appreciate your kindness," General Thebes replied. Diona began to have some real hope for the future; finally, she was being treated with kindness and respect.

Eve's task this morning was to bring an LD radio to Diona. I insisted that Diona get into contact with the other six monarchs and us in Velona today. It was imperative that this new monarch know that the other women rulers were behind her, even if she couldn't speak understandably to them. Besides, I knew that the MMCE caravels would be likely docking in Preveza sometime today. Hence, Monarch Diona had to know of their arrival. Everything depended upon the MMCE project to rescue Alia's economy before their winter set in.

This particular LD radio set had been ordered by their king over two years ago now and had been collecting dust on its crate in a warehouse in Preveza. It had arrived shortly after the plague struck. With the king dead and most communications gone, the crate had been left alone. Still, I was aware of its existence and had taken a devious route to getting it delivered to Diona. Essentially, I placed the thought to send the crate on to the Royal Palace in Levkos into the head of the warehouse foreman. Okay, I had to implant that thought before he took action and arranged for its shipment. It was due at the palace around noon and Eve arranged to make her appearance with its arrival.

The wagon pulled up to the gates and the two guards checked his bill of lading before allowing him to enter. Eve materialized in the shadows and walked up to the wagon. "Ah, it has arrived. Will you kindly put the crate on a pushcart for us," Eve asked the driver. A soldier and the driver did as she asked. "Thanks, we should wheel this directly to our monarch. She is anxiously awaiting this." The soldier nodded and began pushing it.

A few minutes later, Eve walked into the King's Throne Room followed by the soldier and crate. A sign over the entrance read Monarch Diona Gidios. "Hi everyone. I hope I haven't missed anything. The LD radio is here. Can someone unpack it for us?"

Diona wanted to greet Eve and she momentarily forgot and said, "Hi Eve. I am so glad that you came. There is so much to do." As soon as she said this, she regretted it. Once more, the reality of her situation came slamming home to her; her words were unintelligible. Hastily, she wrote out a shorter greeting for Eve.

"You bet we do, Diona. We certainly have to find a way to get you all to learn to speak the Annelise dialect quickly. Then you can be easily understood. Now this is a portable LD radio, LD for long distance. The instructions should be in your language. It's pretty simple. Someone pedals the generator, which makes the electricity to power the set. You set the dials to the frequency of the site that you wish to talk to and then you push a button with your toes to talk. It automatically plays what the others are saying. You and I can easily operate it, Diona," Eve explained.

"But I can't speak," Diona protested and quickly wrote that on a paper.

"Say, we can understand her yes and no sounds now," General Thebes broke in. "This morning, we had her say the two words, and now at least we can understand those two words when she says them. It is a small step, Your Highness." He looked at Eve and asked, "Is it really true that she and our Ornamented Dolls will be able to speak Annelise and be really understood? Please, we need no false hopes here."

Eve realized that he was being protective of his monarch. "If the timing is right, perhaps we can have Alexina talk a bit with us, that is, if anyone here can understand the Annelise dialect."

"Well, I do a little bit. Have to, what with all the Annelise Princesses docking quarterly with their cargos of clothing and shoes to trade. One of my men does speak it fairly well; he's the one who often deals with the crew of the Annelise ships when they dock in Preveza," the general explained. Eve realized that this man was keen witted, and he'd come prepared to verify all that he could.

With the LD radio now out of its crate, Private Thad was assigned to be the permanent radio operator. Eve helped him get it all set up and then said, "Okay, we call Velona first. Bethany and Monarch Stefano West Po are awaiting our call. She will set up the conference call to the other six monarchs of the other kingdoms."

Soon Private Thad was calling out to Velona. "This is Levkos, Alia calling Velona. Come in please." He followed the written script before him. Diona hovered as close as she dared, trying to position her body so that she could see what he was doing.

After a bit of crackling, my voice came through. "Hi, this is Bethany Bartiana Angela of Velona. We read you loud and clear, Alia. I have our Monarch Stefano with me here. Is Monarch Diona present?"

"Yes, she is right here and so are Eve and General Thebes," Thad replied. "This is incredibly great! Velona! Half the world away from here!"

"It sure is," I replied. "Diona, can you say something please? I know that it won't be understandable, but I would like to hear your voice anyway. Eve tells me that you can write out your questions and answers and Thad can relay them to us."

"Yes, hello Bethany, but I cannot even understand what I am saying," Diona obeyed. I wanted to make sure that she was present and so that I could recognize her voice. I smiled, now I could make telepathic contact with her if I needed to do so.

"Hello Monarch Diona. This is Stefano West Po. Our MMCE caravels have landed in Preveza about a half hour ago. All of our ships carry one of these portable LD radios with them so we and they can stay in touch. The two engineers accompanying the many items will be able to demonstrate their use, instruct your engineers on how to reproduce them, and even negotiate the manufacturing rights for you. Essentially, Velona is making all of our marvelous inventions to help women survive better available to any country who wishes them. We are accepting as payment only a small tithe on each item that you produce. The idea is to keep the cost of these as low as possible so that every woman on Tarra can afford them. You will see what I mean when our engineers make their demonstrations. The monarchs of the other six Demokritos kingdoms are already plunging ahead with the manufacturing of these things. They can tell you about them themselves shortly. My best advice to you would be to get as many of your wealthy men and women to supply the startup funds necessary to get the manufacturing of these many things going as quickly as possible."

Diona wrote out, Thank you! Thad relayed her message.

Meanwhile, I had dialed up the other monarchs and also Katerine Stathis, now Argos, their previous queen. Alexina was with her, ready to add her advice to the mix. One by one, I introduced Diona to the other monarchs, asking her to say hello even though her words couldn't be understood: Anathia and Callisto Tropos of Arolas, Andromache Gidios of Thrace, Adonia Kadmos of Phindos, Elektra Patra of Theos, Sophia Aikos of Thallyus, and Amynta Haimon of Penelopus.

"Hi Diona. Callisto here. Say, wait until you get to see the motor-wagons and the T-putt-putts! We can drive them anywhere at almost forty miles per hour! What a blast. You control them with your feet. You are going to love them!" Diona had no idea what these things were but Callisto's enthusiasm was more than encouraging.

Ana interrupted her sister, "Ana here. These motor vehicles run on something called petrol. Right now, we are conducting a huge survey of all our kingdoms looking for more sources of this oily stuff. If your kingdom doesn't have any, don't worry. Arolas does and we can run a pipeline to Levkos for you. Say, all we monarchs ought to get together and visit, say during the winter lull in all the helter skelter activities. How about it, gang?" The others agreed and Ana said she'd make the arrangements and get back to everyone.

"Hi cousin. Andromache here. Wow, who would have thought we both would end up our country's monarchs, eh, Diona? Wow. Well, I sent your mother and her large group off to Levkos. They ought to be arriving in about five more days. They are driving some of the new motor-wagons. Chara loves to drive them, so I'm sure that you will too. I guess that we monarchs had all better brush up on our Annelise dialect so we can chat with you, cousin. When you are able to chat, let's get together. I haven't seen you since we were little girls. My wife, Dianthe would love to meet you. And say, you just have to get some therapy from the Church of God! It is absolutely life-changing, cousin."

"Hi Diona, Elektra here. I am sending a large shipment of poles to you to help you get a start on the electricity distribution. I know that Alia has pretty well used up its supply of tall trees making all the caravels, so I am contributing what I think you will urgently need."

"Hi Diona, Adonia here. I'm preparing a large shipment of iron to help your new companies out with some of the critically needed materials."

"Hi Diona, Sophia here. Like Adonia, I'm sending a large shipment of copper to you. All these new gadgets need copper wire, so this will help you get started making all these really useful things."

"Hi Diona, Amynta here. Andromache is right; you just have to get some of the Church of God's therapy sessions. They've salvaged so many of our women. I think Eve knows a whole lot about it and Bethany too. Anything you need to help get Alia back on its feet, just let us all know and we'll do our very best to help. Gosh, it must be just awful to be unable to speak, but Bethany has told us that once you learn to speak Annelise, we will be able to understand you. Thank goodness for that! We will all make darn sure that we can understand Annelise when we meet this winter. Do they really call you Ornamented Dolls?"

"Yes, they do," Diona replied, but hastily wrote out: We are as helpless as a doll. We just look pretty and can hardly do anything for ourselves. That was General Erebos' plan, to make us all completely helpless and unable to speak. Now everyone calls us Ornamented Dolls. Somehow, this has to change. Thad read her words for the others.

"Well," Sophia exclaimed, "my advice is to issue proclamations." She outlined her beginning ones, namely that any man failing to help a woman or girl or harming them would be shot on sight and so on. Her enthusiastic words brought a smile to Diona's face, but, of course, it was not visible. The women chatted for quite some time before signing off.

"Hi, this is Katerine Stathis, your previous queen. I am in Viborg, Annelise now, but I will be returning soon to help with the Church of God and their therapy sessions. I am so glad that you accepted the throne, Diona. I surely do not want that kind of responsibility. I greatly prefer giving women our needed therapy sessions. I escaped just after the plague struck when General Erebos was about to rape me. I have another of our countrywomen here with me, Alexina Phanes. She was ornamented like all of you. I think she might have been one of the first to get hers. Her father wanted to shut her up, of all things. Anyway, I'll let her chat with you now. I look forward to meeting you in a month or so."

"Hi, Alexina here. I have to sveak in Annelise. I was covvletely helvless until they were avle to get the neck rings off ve. Bethany and Androvache have told us that they can't get yours off safely. That's horrivle. We vust keev on trying to find a way. With the rings and earrings gone, I av doing vretty well on vy own now. Only a few sounds I can't vake. Are you getting this?"

General Thebes looked at his fellow soldier who quickly translated what she had said. He added, "Her b's, p's, m's, and v's all sound the same, like v's. Otherwise, I understand her completely. It is a miracle!"

"Yes! Yes, Alexina! My aide here understood everything you said! It is a miracle! I did not believe Eve when she said that our Ornamented Dolls would be able to speak again," General Thebes replied.

Alexina added, "Good. Katerine and I will ve vringing a couvle hundred ven and woven vack with us to helv teach everyone Annelise. That will helv lots I av sure!"

Diona quickly wrote out, "Thank you, Alexina, for saving us Dolls!" Thad relayed her message.

After they signed off, I announced, "Okay, I have made a connection to our engineers in Preveza. They have a Major Letos on the line with them. General Thebes, you need to issue orders to get the MMCE things and personnel brought to Levkos as fast as humanly possible. Here, I'll turn you over to Major Letos," I explained. Getting all these marvelous MMCE things to Diona was my top priority now. With them, she could begin to get the wealthy to begin financing the many, many projects that had to be started fast to get Alia's economy going in the proper direction as soon as possible.

Interestingly enough, General Thebes not only did just that, but he also issued orders for them to bring along his own family and those of several others, including Sergeant Kastor's as well. He also ordered a thousand of his troops to accompany them. Major Letos suggested that they would arrive around March 1, some four days hence. General Thebes smiled broadly.

Our lengthy conversations finished, a private reported that a huge pile of books had mysteriously appeared in the courtyard. He had brought one of each with him to show the general. Eve broke in, "Ah yes, this one is called Bethany's Hints. In it she gives hundreds of clues about how we women can use alternate ways to do all the things that we need to be able to do for ourselves, like feeding ourselves. These are meant to be distributed to every woman and girl in Alia as soon as possible. I know that these hints are not designed for the Ornamented Dolls, Diona, but perhaps some of the hints will give you some ideas about how you can do some things for yourselves anyway. Now the second one is designed for the Ornamented Dolls and their families. I wrote this one myself. It is a little book that shows commonly used sentences in your language and the corresponding way it is said in the Annelise dialect. The rest of it is a big dictionary of all the words that I know in Annelise. It is only a start, though you really do need to hear how the words sound, I'm afraid. Maybe it will help."

General Thebes broke in, "Well, let's examine them over lunch. It's time. Diona, a number of nobles have heard of the death of General Erebos and have requested an audience with you. I suggested that they return around one. Is that all right with you?"

"Ah," she replied with an unseen smile. Everyone headed off to the dining room. Eve glanced at the four Ladies in Waiting and though she could not see a smile on their faces, their eyes shone with hope for the future. Now if I could just figure out a fast way for these women to get their therapy, Eve mused as she followed them.

General Thebes ate quickly and excused himself after an aide entered and whispered something in his ear. Meanwhile, the six women enjoyed their lunch. With the men helping them eat, the five concentrated on just eating without the benefit of lips to help keep their food inside their mouths. For once, they actually took pleasure from the mealtime. Eve only ate a little, claiming that she was still full from breakfast. When the five finished, they spent the remaining time before their one o'clock session perusing the two books. All five quickly realized that the yokes that had appeared at the time of the plague were meant to be used by themselves to carry things. Diona wrote a note to that effect, asking General Thebes to see if some yokes could be found for themselves.

The Hints book says that we can carry things cradled in our necks, but we can't bend our necks, wrote Diona for Eve. "I know, Diona. You are going to find many hints that you Dolls will not be able to do the way that the book suggests. The best advice that I can give you is not to give up hope, but to work together as a fivesome and see if you can invent other ways to do things. In fact, we ought to start making a hints book for you Dolls. There are so many of you that we ought to see what we can invent. I'll make you a deal. As you and others figure out ways to do things, write them down and I will see that they are published as a Dolls Hint book. How's that?" Eve suggested.

"Ah," Diona answered, indicating yes as best she could vocalize.

"You know, back in Velona, the rule was to always try to room four women together. That way, they could help each other. Always that proved highly successful. In fact, many years ago, special homes were built for them. Around a communal, large living room, four annexes were built to house the four families; they looked like a giant plus sign. That way, the women could help each other during the day and yet still have the privacy with their families at night," Eve pointed out as her memories returned of those days.

We should do something like that here in Alia, Diona wrote out. Tisi added her "ah" as additional confirmation.

"Excuse me, Your Majesty," General Thebes broke in, having quietly entered the dining room. "I need to speak to Eve in private before we meet with the nobles. If you will come with me, please, Eve," he added rather sternly. Eve rose and followed him into a side room out of hearing of Diona.

"Eve, just who are you anyway and how are you getting here into the palace? I ask because I have been a bit suspicious of you since we first met. The guards at the gates definitely did not see you enter today and yet you are here. The LD radio came and shortly after that you were reported as walking up to the wagon seemingly from out of nowhere. Yesterday, no one saw you leave through the main gates either. A week ago, no one actually saw you leave our port city. Then, there is the mysterious appearance of these hundreds of thousands of copies of the books. Poof. They just appeared in the palace courtyard. So I ask again, just who are you and what are you?"

Eve sighed. This was the major problem that we nearly free spiritual beings were facing now. With our incredible abilities regained, compared to those still stuck in their heads, we were supermen or gods. Worse, as Macario warned us, if we flaunted our abilities in public around those who do not even realize that they are an immortal spiritual being, those people will begin to become afraid and terrified of us and perhaps even attack us or work against us, thinking that we were the enemy. Either that or they might begin to worship us as gods. Eve had been careful, but not careful enough. She always was a bit headstrong.

"The identity that I have is Eve, Evelina Angela Bartiana. I am married to Bethany's brother, Giovanni, one of the top inventors and engineers of Velona. We have a year and half old daughter, Adona. We live in Velona. While Bethany is working with all the countries of Tarra on getting themselves stabilized and the MMCE programs in operation to make life more livable for the women of Tarra, I am working with Macario Ines who founded the Church of God. Our goal is to bring the critically needed therapy to every woman, man, and child on Tarra. I have had quite a lot of Advanced Therapy now and have regained an enormous amount of my own spiritual abilities."

"You see, we are all immortal spiritual beings, inhabiting for a time these fleshly bodies. Of course, this may not be real to you at this time. The vast majority of people on Tarra at this time are not even aware anymore that they are spiritual beings, believing themselves to be their bodies, which seem very real to them. When a person gets our beginning therapy, the vast majority come to realize their true nature, their true selves. Advance Therapy goes far beyond just relieving the hideous emotional trauma and pain and unconsciousness that we've all suffered because of the plague. It gives us back what we have lost, incredible abilities."

"Some of us can use telepathy to communicate. Others can lift and move objects, telekinesis some call it. Others can see without using their body's eyes. Some can even create a physical body that is indistinguishable from yours. While these are indeed powerful abilities, with them comes the need to assume more and more responsibility for our fellow man."

"Look, it is now about a year and a half since this hideous, debilitating plague struck us all. During all those weeks, only two people here in Alia actually took some responsibility for the people of this country: you and Diona. Even your previous queen, Katerine, chose to leave Alia, but she has subsequently assumed a great deal of responsibility for the people in her new city of Viborg. Now she is heading back here to help deliver the needed therapy to the people of Alia. Just you two. During that time, many have died, and worse, Erebos has very nearly made life impossible for the Dolls. What is going to happen if all the women in Alia are so debilitated that they cannot even live life? Women bring forth your new generation. With your women gone, your entire country will become nothing more than a footnote in the history books."

"I saw what Erebos was doing down here in Alia, via the nobleman Olympos, who was forced to take his extended family and flee to the safety of Axos, Thrace. Considering how widespread the Doll Project was becoming, I just had to act, to assume some more responsibility for all of you in Alia, general. I discovered that Diona was focused solely on murdering Erebos to obtain justice for his orders that resulted in his soldiers murdering her father and uncles, who only wanted to prevent their daughters and wives from becoming Ornamented Dolls, very nearly completely helpless and with very little future to look forward to. If she went ahead with her plans, after Erebos was slain, then what? Even more chaos would result and more than likely the Doll Project would have continued on its merry way until all women of Alia were helpless Dolls. I saw that you were against this sadistic mutilation of women and asked you for your help, which you readily gave. So here we are. We three are all working to salvage Alia and help the country get back thriving and prospering once more."

General Thebes looked doubtful. "So you are saying that you have some supernatural powers that allow you to just come and go as you please?"

"I can do many things, general. I am not this body. In fact, this is just a mocked up body that I created to sort of better blend in here in Alia. After all, would you have given me your trust if I appeared to you looking like I really do with my Velona body?" Eve countered. "Here, this is what my body back home really looks like." She un-mocked her bronze skin body and made a duplicate of hers back home. "See? I can just be anywhere I need to be and once there, create an acceptable body for everyone to view."

"But is it real?" he protested.

"Pinch me, touch me," she teased him. "Ouch, not that hard," she countered his sharp pinch, though she had to mock up the pain that ought to have been there with such a pinch.

"But shouldn't you be in Velona taking care of your daughter?" he asked.

"True, it is not optimum for me to be spending so much of the day down here, but your needs here far outweigh Adona's. Bethany and our parents are helping out with her."

"Okay, but what is it that you are hoping to do down here with us? How can you possibly do anything for Diona and the other Dolls?" he countered.

Eve sighed, "General, I will be bluntly honest with you. I really do not know yet. There are so darn many mutilated women here in Alia, okay, Ornamented Dolls. You see, when the numbers were small, we, I mean other Church of God therapy givers, were able to find resolutions for those women. For example, with Alexina Phanes, once the neck rings were removed and she learned Annelise, they were able to give her therapy sessions. In fact, she is now receiving much Advanced Therapy sessions so that she can move objects. If she can do that, then she will be able to feed herself and do many things which usually require the use of one's teeth, which she can't, of course, use, not with those lip plates."

Eve continued, "You are not alone in having sadistic men taking advantage of the plague and its chaos. Down in Phindos, over a dozen women were also given the lip plates. There, the Church of God members, not yet knowing that women with lip plates could be able to speak the Annelise dialect, opted to give them Advanced Therapy so that those women could use a limited form of telepathy to communicate their thoughts to others. That worked out incredibly well, and all of those women are now very highly competent therapy givers, actively working on the women of Phindos, salvaging them from their traumas from the plague. It took them a considerable amount of time to get these women able to regain their limited telepathy skills."

"Over in Tashien, one sadist there took a different approach. He removed young women's eyeballs, replacing them with glass eyes and then paraded these helpless women around his pleasure palace. Well, again, we intervened and rescued those women. Once more, they received Advanced Therapy. After all, armless and blinded make an almost impossible condition to survive. Again, after a long period, they are regaining their spiritual abilities to see without the use of a body's eyes. So far, two of them are now able to see quite well and are able to live productive lives once more," Eve explained.

"But here, general, we are dealing with over a hundred fifty thousand women who have been turned into Ornamented Dolls. This time, we can't even get the neck rings off them, which would at least give them a great deal of flexibility. As you know, they are almost completely helpless now."

General Thebes asked, "Can't you just give them a whole lot of the Advanced Therapy?"

"There are perhaps a few dozen people on Tarra who can deliver this Advanced Therapy. Even if we could somehow get them all here in Alia, what's a few dozen compared to a hundred fifty thousand plus? No, the first step has to be to get the Dolls and their families to learn to speak Annelise and to get them into some kind of livable situations. Once that is done, Katerine and her group of Church of God members will be able to start in on giving them all the Basic Therapy sessions, which will remove the traumas they've suffered, returning a vitality of life back to them. Yet, truthfully, just how much of an independent life an Ornamented Doll may be able to have I just do not know, general. Yet, I aim to do everything that I can possibly do to help them get back to battery."

"Well, I am behind you on this first step. I read a little from the Hints book. Is it really possible that my wife can learn how to sew dresses again?"

"After she gets the proper new tools that she needs and gets a lot of practice with them, I am sure that she can do it. If she can get her trauma erased as well, I *know* that she can, if she still wants to do that, general."

"I will hold you to that, Eve. Come on, we are almost late. Those nobles will be arriving soon and likely will be causing Diona trouble," he replied. The two headed for the Monarch's Office, the old King's Throne Room, where Diona and her friends were already waiting for them.

Diona stared at Eve and then wrote: What happened to your skin? It's all white. You sick?"

Eve flushed. She'd forgotten to un-mock the copy of her Velona body. "Er, General Thebes suggested that I remove my disguise. I am from Velona, after all. You see, I thought that if I looked like a citizen of Alia, everyone would accept me better than if I looked like a stranger. He's convinced me to look my old self." That was a close one, Eve thought to herself.

"Ah," Diona said, just as a soldier entered announcing the arrival of a group of six. Diona recognized them but had no way to tell Eve who was who. Three were the heads of three noble houses and the other three were some of the wealthier men of Levkos. Although Eve did not know it yet, two had frequently met with General Erebos during the past year and a half and had helped implement the Ornamentation Project, namely Simonides Ridon and Telemon Phoros. Ridon took charge, evidently their spokesman.

Monarch Diona sat on the large throne with a pile of papers at her feet. General Thebes sat on what used to be the queen's throne, smaller and to her left. Eve sat on a chair to the right of Diona, while her four Ladies in Waiting sat on chairs just behind her. Two soldiers with long guns stood guard at the door as a third soldier led the six men into the room, motioning them to the group of chairs sitting before the rulers.

"Well, this is certainly a surprise. You are General Thebes?" Ridon began talking. His voice held a wisp of contempt perhaps, but he certainly glared at Diona.

"Yes, Mr. Ridon. Your Monarch Diona Gidios, sir. Our guest from Velona, Mrs. Eve Angela, and the monarch's Ladies in Waiting," General Thebes introduced his group.

"Yes, I am familiar with Diona. General Erebos was kind enough to make her his token queen. Of course, now the nobles will elect a new king," Ridon replied. "Obviously, Diona is a mere Ornamented Doll now, though I cannot fathom how she could possibly have killed General Erebos. Have you looked into possible assassins, general?"

"Let me make this *perfectly* clear, Mr. Ridon. Diona *is* your monarch and *is* running the country. There has been a change in how Alia's leaders are elected. Monarch Diona has the full support and cooperation of Alia's Armed Forces. Yes, Diona was able to poison the sadistic, evil General Erebos, and she has put an end to this despicable Ornamentation Project, which has so ruined the lives of over a hundred fifty thousand of our women."

"But she is nothing but an Ornamented Doll now, a totally helpless Ornamented Doll who cannot even speak nor do anything at all for herself. I ought to know, my wife and daughter are Ornamented Dolls now, helpless in all ways, able to do nothing at all but sit and look pretty for we men. Surely, this is some kind of jest, a joke. You are pulling our legs, eh general?"

"Do I look like I am jesting, sir? Just for the record, while the Ornamented Dolls cannot speak our language anymore, it has been discovered that they can speak the Annelise dialect fairly well. Once our project to teach the Ornamented Dolls and their families to speak Annelise, you will find our Ornamented Dolls able to communicate with us once more. However, she certainly can write. Now, writing is her main form of communication with us," General Thebes responded. He added very seriously, "I would advise you to treat her with the respect due our monarch, sir."

"But she is an Ornamented Doll," Ridon protested again.

"We are in the process of obtaining justice for the hundred fifty thousand plus women who were brutally turned into these helpless Ornamented Dolls. Many of their fathers, husbands, and brothers were murdered by soldiers who were taking the women and girls off to be ornamented. We are investigating these and I assure you that those who have murdered our innocent civilians will be punished. However, many others not in the military have played key and important roles in this brutalization of our women under the guise of the Ornamentation Project. We will be looking into that arena soon," General Thebes pointed out.

Eve noticed that Ridon and Phoros began to squirm slightly. Diona wrote something on paper, but it took a minute for her awkwardly to get it written out. General Thebes read it aloud. "Mr. Ridon, I was present at a lot of the meetings you and Mr. Phoros had with General Erebos. I know that you in particular were a staunch supporter of the Ornamentation Project, that you facilitated many aspects of the project, making them happen swiftly for the general. What kind of a person would do this to women and girls — turn us into nearly helpless Ornamented Dolls?" General Thebes raised his eyebrows; this was news to him. He added, "Well, now that is interesting, Ridon. So you assisted the general in a most substantive way, eh?"

"Well, he was in charge of Alia. Our men were out of work. Hardly anyone had gone back to work after the plague struck. Our women were complaining constantly. At least now, they wear fabulously valuable earrings, look stunning, and no longer complain. Besides, look what a boost it has given to our economy. Our men are at productive work once more," Ridon began to justify his actions. Fear had crept into the fiber of his being, Eve noted. He'd dropped his hostile contempt attitude and was definitely afraid now.

Diona hastily began writing once more, causing a hushed silence to fall in the room. At last, General Thebes read, "Productive work? Ridon, what work will there be once you have turned all women in Alia into helpless Ornamented Dolls? Are the men going to spend all their time just looking after our needs? I doubt that very much. Rather once the project is done, everyone will be totally out of work once again, only this time, half of Alia will be utterly and completely helpless Ornamented Dolls!"

She wrote another note. General Thebes smiled as he read it and proceeded to follow her request. Since she had not the luxury of time on her side, Diona had opted to quote verbatim Monarch Sophia's speech and proclamations when she took over control of Thallyus in April of last year. She had scratched out Thallyus and substituted Alia along with similar minor changes. General Thebes read the very lengthy speech.

"Alia is standing on the very brink of destruction, brought to its knees by the plague and very nearly pushed over the edge by the Ornamentation Project. The other kingdoms have seen this happening in their countries and have found the one path that could be traveled to avoid this catastrophe. I am now closely allied with the six other monarchs of Demokritos. The path that we absolutely must follow is one of a matriarchy. Until now, men have been the ones in control of our country, our marriages, our finances, all of it. Few women have ever held true power and then only for a brief time period. Under these circumstances, that must change. From now on, Alia will be a matriarchy, women will own the property when they marry, and women will be in charge of the family finances. When a man dies, the property goes to his wife and daughters, not his firstborn son. We must do everything in our power to ensure that we women can survive and thrive or the doom will surely take us all."

"Over a year ago, we were all struck with an alien plague. Aliens from another world came to Tarra and unleashed this hideous plague upon our entire world! There is not a woman or girl anywhere on Tarra who has not lost her arms. A few have subsequently given birth and already know that our baby girls are also being born without arms. We here in Alia are not alone. Every woman in the entire world is facing the same nightmare situation. However, the one piece of good news is that mighty fighters up in Velona, Sea Princes, have managed to kill the alien creatures that inflicted this horrible plague upon us all. The perpetrators of this plague have been eliminated."

"At this time, we still do not have a good idea of just how devastating this evil plague has been. We are still examining the records made by General Erebos. At least two million of us have perished and maybe a whole lot more. Worse, well more than half of those have been women and girls! As you look around today, men vastly outnumber we women here in Alia."

"Yet, it is far, far worse than that. At this time and as many of you have been speculating, we are facing the distinct possibility of the extinction of the entire human race, not just our own country! If we allow things to continue as they have for the last year, there will not be any women left to bring forth our future generations. Yes, we may well be facing what the traitorous Church of Jehosanity wildly claimed upon the coming of the plague: the Day of Judgment is at hand. Yes, these supposedly holy men murdered thousands of the Church's followers, shortly after the plague struck."

"We are still here. The world has not yet ended. Life is within me and within you. Some of you have already brought forth new life. The world has not ended. Yet, if we continue down the path traveled thus far, our country will disappear within a generation. We have entered the Dark Ages. Doom lies at our heels and before us, dogging our every step. A wrong move and doom swallows us. General Erebos and his Doll project very nearly spelled the total end of Alia as a civilization."

"Many believe that we now must adjust to the environment in which we find ourselves. Yet that too is wrong. Let me ask you, after you have adapted yourself to some new situation, are you really truly happy and content? Not really. Instead, we should be doing the opposite! We should be modifying our environment to suit our needs, our goals, and our purposes. On the battlefield, the side which best alters the environment to fit their needs often comes up the winner!"

"Okay, so then how do we change the future that we are all now facing? As it stands, the future is bleak and hideous. We women apparently cannot do anything for ourselves any longer and have become dependent wholly and completely upon men and boys to do absolutely everything for us, including feeding us. Those of us who have been turned into Dolls are in even far worse shape. Yet, you men are also facing an awful future. Are you not overwhelmed by having to do your work, and all that which used to be done by your wife, and somehow care for every need of the women in your life? Indeed, the present is intolerable for both men and women; we just are facing different situations. Alas, men, you cannot just give up, move to some other country, and start over. All women on Tarra are affected, not just here in Alia. Do we then just give up and die as the traitorous priests of Jehosanity have done? Nay, I say. I am not about to die just yet. We will survive this, but we must alter the future. How do we change the future?"

"One changes the future by changing the present. One alters what one is doing in the present and that changes the future. If we do nothing, then we will be watching the death of our country. We must change the present to make a better future, one of our choosing, one that gives life, prosperity, and vitality to us all. What must we change?"

"Until now, our whole society has been dominated by males, a patriarchy. Males controlled the government and mostly made the laws. When a father dies, his property goes to his firstborn son, as a rule. With a few exceptions, women have had little or no say in much of anything, except perhaps in the minor domestic arena. Yes, we occasionally had a Empress in charge or a Queen here in Alia, but as history shows, she never lasted very long, a few years at most, before she was replaced by a man. Today, male domination has led to the very brink of destruction as a people and a country, acutely so by General Erebos and his Ornamentation Project. Many of you know just what some males have done during the plague, raiding homes, killing those who lived there, kidnaping the younger women, and forcing them into whorehouses. What male lifted a hand to stop this? Males raided every store in Alia, looting all of value. They raided the Royal Palace and killed our king."

"At this point in time, we women are terribly dependent upon those with arms to help us. We cannot be turned out into the street because our fathers have died and with all his property and funds going to the eldest son. We cannot survive with men, who have proven themselves totally unworthy, to continue to lead us. Now that you have turned over a hundred fifty thousand of your women and girls into even more helpless Dolls, it is time for a change. We must do everything possible to allow us women to survive and flourish so that we can bring about future generations. It is time that we instituted a matriarchal society."

"Women must become the new rulers. Property must be owned by the wife in the family and be handed down to her daughters, acutely so if she is a Doll! When a man and woman marry and acquire a home, the home is in the woman's name, as are the entire finances of their marriage. The woman becomes the boss; she has total say over the money that is spent and upon what, not the man. In short, we empower the women of Alia, for men have already abdicated their responsible use of power. Now we absolutely must give it to us women. If we do this, within a few years, I promise you that our country will be flourishing and prospering like never before."

"We are not alone in making this drastic change. All six of the other kingdoms have already done the same thing!"

"Okay, so what are my plans? What am I going to do to change our future? I will be taking many different approaches. First, Bethany Angela of Velona has put together a book of hints on how we women can do many things for ourselves. She based it upon the old Women's Ways of Dorota. I have obtained enough copies for every woman and girl in Alia. The soldiers are in the process of delivering them. Yes, following these hints, an armless woman can learn many alternate ways to do nearly everything that she used to be able to do before the plague. However, we Dolls are in even more trouble, as most of these hints are impossible for us to do. We cannot speak yet nor use our teeth nor even bend our necks. We will work hard on finding ways around our incapacitation. The first thing is to learn to speak Annelise, which I am told we will be able to do and be understood. I have arranged for a large number of tutors from Annelise to come here and begin teaching us Ornamented Dolls and our families how to speak again. Give us time to work out new ways for us Ornamented Dolls."

"I believe that a year from now, ordinary women will be vastly more independent and self-reliant. I will work to make it so with other plans in the works. We Ornamented Dolls will likely take far longer to become independent, if ever we can be. Yet, far more must be done. We must alter the environment so that we women can survive and flourish far better. To this end, my allies in Velona are bringing their numerous and marvelous inventions to our country. Within a week or so, we will be holding demonstrations of all these incredible inventions. The nobles and wealthy will be some of the first to view this spectacular demonstration."

"Velona has motor-wagons, motor-cars, and three-wheelers called T-putt-putts. These motorized vehicles are driven by women and men too. One motor-wagon can carry more than one horse drawn wagon and travels, I'm told, forty miles an hour. With these readily available, we women will be able to go anywhere that we need and buy the things our families need, groceries for example. As yet, I don't know if we Ornamented Dolls will be able to manage those, however. Plus, there are many more devices that will be following these, all designed for we women so that we can more readily do what needs to be done in life."

"Yes, these devices will be expensive, but don't worry. I will be providing them to all of you at little to no charge. Your government will be paying for them, not you. We will be needing new companies and factories to turn out these new things. If you have money that you care to invest in the future, this is your opportunity. See me or General Thebes. We will soon have all the necessary licensing arrangements with Velona worked out. There is a bundle to be made here, if you are willing to step forward and invest. Already the Houses of Stathis, Drastus, and Gidios have pledged a fortune for these new developments."

"I give you my word that within a very few years, Alia will be flourishing and prosperous beyond anything that we've ever seen before! I am going to change the environment of women to fit our new needs. Still, we will need much help in doing so. Your help is welcome and desired."

"On the grimmer side, I have been forced to make my first new law. Any man who mistreats a female in any harmful way is to be publically executed and all his possessions given over to the women whom he victimized. Soon, the soldiers will make a thorough search of Levkos looking for those who are in the present time mistreating women, kidnaping, raping, or holding women as sex slaves. I won't stand for mistreatment of women any longer. We must survive or our country is lost."

"Finally, I know very well that men are used to giving the orders, but now it must be we women who give them. In my new government, one-half of the ministers will be women and one-half will be men. If you feel that you wish to become a part of those who lead our country, please contact me. I can use your help. While we are in the Dark Ages now, I am spearheading the drive to bring us all back into the light of day, stronger, more powerful, more vital, more prosperous, and more able than we have ever been. If you want to be a part of this revival, come see me."

"Soon we will have new clothing from Annelise, dresses that ordinary women can put on themselves, though I do not know if Ornamented Dolls will be able to do that themselves yet. We will have Annelise language tutors for the Ornamented Dolls. The other monarchs have promised all manner of aid both physical and financial as we begin to modernize with the inventions of Velona. I have an LD radio system that allows me to talk with those in Velona and all of our other monarchs at any time, though at this time, others must speak for me as my speech is not understandable as yet. I write and someone reads it into the radio system for me."

The wealthier men nodded and voiced their agreement with her speech the very moment that General Thebes finished. Mr. Phoros was non-committal, while Mr. Ridon still vacillated between hostility and fear. Diona had watched him carefully as General Thebes read her lengthy speech, and now jotted some more onto another paper. Again, he picked it up and read it aloud. "Mr. Ridon. The choice is yours. You can back me and join us in the restoration of Alia or I can make very sure that General Thebes begins a very exhaustive investigation into just what your role has been in the mutilation of us Ornamented Dolls. Which will it be?"

Behind Diona, Tisi whispered, "Ah!" Eve grinned and thought, damn, Diona has a sharp mind!

Mr. Ridon fidgeted. "How do I know that a month from now you will again come after me for my part in keeping Alia alive this past year? Assuming it isn't just what you might have wanted."

Again, Diona awkwardly began writing on another paper. After a couple of minutes, General Thebes read it aloud. "I have already killed the one man ultimately responsible for the Ornamentation Project that mutilated women, namely General Erebos. We will still be looking for the soldiers who murdered men and boys who tried to stop them from taking their women away to be ornamented. However, Mr. Ridon, unless you have murdered men or women, raped, beaten, kidnaped women, or savagely mistreated women, such as throwing a helpless woman out of her home for whatever reason, I have no plans to punish or otherwise seek retribution from those who had little choice but to carry out Erebos' orders. What good will it do to kill all of our doctors who performed the surgery or the bronze makers who entombed our necks or the jewelers who made these monstrous earrings? None at all. We need everyone working on valuable projects for everyone's future survival. Again, it is your choice, Mr.

Ridon."

Eve thought, brilliant move, Diona. Excellent reply! She was becoming more and more confident that Diona was perfect for the job of monarch of Alia.

"Well, I will hold you to that, Your Majesty. You may count on the House of Ridon to assist in Alia's recovery. Exactly what are these new inventions all about?" he asked and Diona breathed a sigh of relief, though only Eve picked it up. To the others, Diona's face, as that of all Ornamented Dolls, was mostly expressionless, due to the lip plates.

Eve took the stage at this point. "If you will allow me to answer this one, Your Majesty — I am your Velona representative until the demonstration and engineers arrive." Diona made her ah sound and Eve launched into a lengthy description of all the devices. She noticed that the three wealthier men were keenly interested in all that she had to say. The noblemen were less interested, but did see avenues for potential profits. It was late afternoon before they all left.

Eve then said, "Well, I must be returning to my own family in Velona. I will stay in contact with you via the LD radio and I can return here whenever I am needed. Just let me know."

"Say, Eve, may I ask you one question?" General Thebes asked. "In reading Monarch Diona's speech, I could not help notice that passage about valiant fighters in Velona killing the alien creatures. By chance, do you know these fighters? Were you one of them?" Diona and her four friends looked at Eve, eyes wide.

"No need to lie to you, general. Yes, I know them. I was one of those who killed the three alien creatures. Never mess with Eve is a motto that many in Velona follow," she teased jokingly. To Diona, she said, "I'll let General Thebes tell you a bit more about me. Bye for a while, I'll stay in touch and can return when you need me." Purposely, Eve un-mocked her body and reappeared behind her body's head in Velona. Diona and the others simply saw Eve vanishing, poof, like some magic trick. General Thebes was impressed and began a lengthy explanation of what he'd learned from Eve.

On March 1, General Thebes finally received the documentation about the Ornamented Women. All the many centers had finally ceased operations, at least for now, though some women would be kept for another four days before being taken home as usual. "Incredible, at least they kept a precise tally. Every woman or girl is listed along with their address, Your Majesty. The final count is one hundred seventy-five thousand four hundred fifty-two Dolls. Damn, it took longer to get all the centers to stop than we thought! What I cannot believe, Your Majesty, is that per your orders, any woman wishing to become an Ornamented Doll must first seek an audience with you. Can you believe this? Women are signing up to have just such an audience with you! Already the list contains fifty women who want to get your permission to be ornamented! Have they lost their minds?" He was quite distressed.

Diona wrote, They have been helpless since the plague first struck them. They see that being an Ornamented Doll as a way to be like myself and the other women of wealth and status — a way to have men legally tend to their needs. Erebos was wise when he had us done first; we are the fashion setters. Now those of the middle class are seeking to gain the perceived status that we Ornamented Dolls hold. If we do not allow some who wish to become Ornamented Dolls, you can expect underground Ornamentation Factories to spring up. Let's pick two of the best centers and allow them to continue a limited basis for now. Keep an eye out for underground Ornamented Doll Factories please. Stamp them out. He agreed.

She also wrote, Once these ordinary women read Bethany's Hints and start to experiment with them, I truly hope that they will begin to recover some of their self-respect and begin to do things for themselves. If so, they will not want to become an Ornamented Doll. I hope and pray that is so. He grinned and gave her a hug, unable to do what he desired, to shake her hand.

Chapter 52 Alia Begins to Recover

On February 28, 825 following Monarch Diona's orders, soldiers began making deliveries of Bethany's Hints to every female in Levkos and delivering Eve's small dictionary to every Ornamented Doll as well. Further, following Monarch Sophia's suggestions, she had the soldiers examine the women's living situation in each household. Specifically, they were looking for potentially lethal circumstances, such as way too many women to handle versus the number of hands available in the home to care for their needs, especially so in Ornamented Doll homes. While Alia's reactions to the plague had been different from that in Thallyus, Diona still worried that some women may be in untenable living arrangements. Were there whorehouses where kidnaped women were kept? She didn't know. Certainly, General Erebos and those working for him had never mentioned such things.

Also per Monarch Andromache's suggestion, the soldiers were to compile a list of vacant homes. So many had perished during the last year and a half that some homes were certainly going to be found unoccupied. These might become useful if large numbers of women needed homes where their care could be managed. Additionally, they were to note whether the replacement, low to the ground kitchens had been installed in each home.

After breakfast, while General Thebes worked with his staff on the massive distribution project, Sergeant Kastor escorted a bronze worker into the queen's quarters. All five women's lip plates were drooping substantially, making it more difficult for the soldiers to feed them. It was time to enlarge them once again. Light, rapid tapping of the ballpeen hammer against the bronze disks and the small anvil echoed through the grey stone walled chambers. He made quick work of the task of enlarging the circular disks, though he was careful not to alter the shape of the concave surface, which butted up against their gums and front teeth. However, Diona accepted his suggestion of slightly enlarging that surface so that it would provide a lager base and help support the plates in a horizontal position. When he finished, the five women's plates were now about five inches across. Diona noted that they were enlarging at a rate of about an inch a year and she wondered if they would ever stop stretching. She took a deep breath and tried to banish that dread, for she had more than enough to worry about just now.

With their drooping plates handled, Diona then asked her four companions about their own families. The five exchanged a flurry of written notes. She already knew that her four Ladies in Waiting had been confiscated from their families, much as she had been. Having been isolated from their families for over a year now, none of the four knew what their family home conditions were now like. Diona did learn that the four came from upper middle class homes and that their fathers, prior to the plague, had been wealthy merchants. Having a daughter become a Lady in Waiting at the Royal Court was viewed by them as a big step up in the world.

Tisi wrote, Dad was very pleased with my selection, but he was also very pleased because he would not have to provide a large dowry should I marry. Cheapskate!

Ditto, wrote Rhea.

Even my boyfriend abandoned me when I got ornamented, Dora wrote.

I never had one and now I never will, wrote Xanthe, adding to Dora's reply.

None of us will now. What man would want us like this? Dora theorized.

Tisi added in large letters, I don't want a man now! Not ever.

Why? Diona wrote.

Tisi wrote, Cause not one man came forward to help us in our hours of need. Not one rescued us. Not one helped us with Erebos. They either all made these horrid ornaments or did nothing to stop them from torturing us. Not one is helping us now, not really. Eve is and the other monarchs, but not our men. The soldiers are following orders. Thebes is helping but because he is the most powerful man in Alia now and he wants to keep his own family from becoming Ornamented Dolls.

Rhea added, Diona, it is just us five now. We have to stick together to survive somehow. It is just us. Like Andromache and Dianthe. We should really be mates like they are — remove men from our private lives.

Well, I have grown very fond of all of you, Tisi admitted. I don't ever want to be parted from any of you, though I don't know how we can pleasure each other, not as we are. I would love to try, if you like. She flushed but her face remained expressionless.

Tonight, Diona wrote hesitatingly. All five smiled and then giggled; the last was understood between them.

Around noon, reports began arriving and shortly after lunch so did rescued women! Diona's request had been extremely wise. The soldiers had begun uncovering homes in which women were in very dire straits indeed. By the end of the day, they reported only three homes had the replacement kitchens installed. Thus, Diona issued orders for everyone to install these kitchens, using the soldiers where needed. She wrote, Yes, even here at the palace, Paris. I want the possibility to fix myself something to eat occasionally. He grinned and agreed to oversee the project, primarily so that the new kitchen did not interfere with his "grande kitchen."

The first of the rescued women arrived just as they finished their lunch. "General, Your Majesty, a wagon has arrived with some Ornamented Dolls. You must come immediately," a soldier interrupted. At once, Diona rose and her four companions did likewise. While General Thebes headed off after the private at a good clip, the five made their way excruciatingly slowly down to the courtyard, their extreme heels clicking on the stones. When they arrived, a young woman was lying on a blanket on the ground. A doctor, the general, and three soldiers were attending her. Four young children sat in the wagon watching. All five were Ornamented Dolls, Diona quickly observed. Slowly she shuffled up to the prone woman, who must have been in her mid-twenties. She, like the four girls, had long blonde hair, but the woman looked emaciated and she had severe burns on both legs.

"What happened?" Diona asked instinctively, but her words were unintelligible. Instant frustration appeared on her face, mostly masked by her large lip plates however.

General Thebes did not need to understand her words. To him, her simple question was obvious. "My men found her in her home. According to the records, her wealthy husband was murdered when he tried to prevent her and her daughters from being taken three weeks ago. She had a nine year old son who tried to care for the five when they were brought back. Evidently, there was some kind of kitchen accident — a fire or a dropped pan of boiling liquid. My men found the decomposing corpse of the lad and the mother is severely burned. She and her daughters probably haven't had much to eat for weeks and are nearly starved. It doesn't look good for the mother."

Just then, the woman, obviously in great pain, tried to say something, but it was unintelligible. Diona cursed as did the doctor. "Wait, ma'am, are you saying that you want us to take care of your children?" General Thebes made a guess at what the woman was trying to say. Damn, he's good, Diona thought. I should have realized that must be what she is trying to communicate to us.

The woman said, "Ah," which everyone knew was a yes. Diona inwardly thanked Sergeant Kastor for having gotten this bit of communication worked out with her and her four friends. At least everyone around the palace knew "ah" and "oh" meant yes and no. Diona's eyes met the woman's. Diona then bent nodded yes. From the corner of his eyes, General Thebes saw her motion and spoke up, "Yes, Adelphe, Her Majesty will look after your children. We will treat them as our own."

Diona smiled. What a kind gesture and from the heart as well. Later she wrote a thank you note to Thebes. She bent nodded vigorously, backing up his words. The dying woman's eyes met hers and Diona felt that she received eternal gratitude from Adelphe — all that from her eyes. Adelphe exhaled and her eyes closed for the last time. Gently, the doctor covered her face with part of the blanket, symbolically signifying her death. Diona moved over to the wagon and saw the four sobbing young girls, four Ornamented Dolls, thin and emaciated.

"Okay, Diona, let's get them into the dining room and get them fed immediately," General Thebes took charge. All four were so weak that the soldiers had to carry them, following after Diona and her friends. Although to Diona, it seemed like hours to get them to the dining room, it was only a few minutes, and she hurried as much as possible in her extreme heels. All five hovered around the four girls as Paris brought out bowls of chicken soup. He'd already received word to whip up some broth from the doctor. While several men began feeding them, another soldier gave them the official report.

"The youngest has just turned five, she is called Alekto Angelos. Next is six year old Dorcia. Then comes Kore who is seven. Ariadne is the eldest; she is eight. They have been ornamented some twenty-three days now, according to the reports from the Ornamentation Center."

"You are in safe hands now," General Thebes spoke softly. "You will be living here at the Royal Palace with your Monarch Diona, who will be looking after you in place of your mother. I am so terribly sorry about your mother's death and your father's too, and your older brother. Do you understand me?"

Ariadne nodded, though tears continued to trickle down her cheeks, but she gulped at each spoonful of soup that came anywhere near her mouth. "Slow down, Ariadne; there is plenty of soup. From now on, you four will never be hungry again," he consoled the four. Ariadne smiled, but realized it was not visible, so she bent nodded a little.

Children are resilient, Diona soon discovered. Once the four were fed, they came to life, chatting away, completely oblivious to the fact that no one could understand what they were saying, not even themselves. Diona wrote out, Let's get you a bath and into some clean clothes. You will be staying in our rooms with us. Sergeant Kastor read her words to the girls, and Tisi and Rhea went with him to help the girls. As they rose to leave, Diona noted that the girls were now able to walk on their own, an encouraging sign.

Each wore a filthy nightgown and their long blonde hair was rather ratted, but all four looked remarkably like their mother. All had new lip plates and the bronze neck rings; all had identical massive earrings with red rubies, similar to those worn by Dora and Rhea, complimenting nicely their yellowish hair and blue eyes. Like all returning Ornamented Dolls, each wore the extreme heels, but theirs were fastened on with tied laces. Diona knew that neither she nor they could take them off without the help of hands. She sighed as she watched the five year old Alekto valiantly trying to walk in such heels, taking wobbling, small steps, emulating her older sisters. Criminal, Diona thought.

Now she had other concerns, General Thebes again whispered to her, asking her to head to the courtyard. More wagons were soon to arrive. He explained that he had advanced notice that more women were on their way here. Diona, Dora, and Xanthe made their slow way down to the courtyard; all three hoped that this time would not be so grim, so deadly. Thus began a long afternoon for Diona.

Two wagons slowly pulled up to Diona and the general, carrying a dozen women and girls, along with three small boys. Diona gave a sigh of relief; these were merely armless women, not more Ornamented Dolls. They comprised four families whose males had all met with death by various means. The three small boys had been doing their very best to keep them all alive. General Thebes, of course, gave them a welcoming speech and sanctuary here at the palace. These he put up in the guest lodgings, sending along soldiers to assist them in getting settled in, bathed, and fed.

No sooner had they been handled than another wagon brought another family of Ornamented Dolls into the courtyard. A mother, three daughters, and two teenaged boys comprised this needy family. Her husband had also been shot trying to prevent their ornamentation. This family was also put up in the guest rooms, since the boys insisted that they could care for their mother and sisters, if they had a little help. Again, Diona wrote out a quick welcoming sentence, insisting that they stay here in the palace for the time being. The mother looked extremely grateful or so Diona thought from the look in the woman's eyes.

Two more wagons brought another fifteen women, girls, and small boys into the courtyard just after some soldiers led the Ornamented Doll family off to the guest rooms. Diona was thankful that these were merely armless women and not more dolls. Again, she gave them sanctuary, but wondered how many more would be arriving. The situation out there in Levkos was worse than she had imagined. "You were very wise, Your Majesty, in having our men on the lookout for disasters in the making," General Thebes praised her between wagon loads.

By late afternoon, she had given sanctuary and thus life to twenty Ornamented Dolls and fifty other women, not counting the small boys and teens among them. However, around four, General Thebes had to have her finally meet with a dozen younger women who were insisting on undergoing the Ornamentation Project, though the list of those wanting to meet with the monarch to get her permission had now grown to well over a hundred women!

She and the general met with these dozen women in her office, the old King's Throne Room. After she sat down, a soldier escorted the twelve women into the room. They ranged in age from eighteen to thirty, Diona guessed. General Thebes began, "It is our understanding that you all wish to become Ornamented Dolls. Is this correct?"

All said that it was. One woman began, "Yes, we most certainly do. Every woman who is *anything* has had it done. We feel left out, ostracized even for not having it done yet. You *must* allow us to have it done, please, we *beg* you."

Awkwardly as usual, Diona wrote out, Have you read Bethany's Hints book yet and tried out some of the hints?

Six had not. She wrote, Look, by following the hints, you will be able to do most everything for yourselves that you used to be able to do. It takes patience and practice, I am told. You do not have to be utterly helpless women as we Ornamented Dolls are. Almost none of the hints can we Ornamented Dolls actually do. I order you to go read the Hints and try them out. Later, if you still want the ornaments, you may return and make another request. Somewhat downcast, the six agreed and left.

Diona wrote, Do you really realize just how awful it is being ornamented like we are? We are very nearly helpless women. We cannot even speak. We can barely communicate our needs to others. The general read it for her.

"Yes, but my boyfriend is wealthy and wants to marry me as soon as I am an Ornamented Doll. All the noblewomen are Ornamented Dolls. I want to have that high status too. Besides, I will raise his status too. He promises to see to my every need. We are madly in love too. Please, you must let me do it," the eighteen year old brown haired young woman pleaded.

Diona wrote, But it cannot be undone. Once you have it done, you must live like this for the rest of your life. I can tell you that living like this is a nightmare.

"Maybe for you," the young teen replied. "But you are not married. I will be, he will look after all my needs. He has money and can afford it. I want to look like you, our Monarch, Your Majesty. We all do.

You look fabulous and we want to look fabulous as well. You must allow us to look like you."

The other five pleaded similar arguments and could not be dissuaded. Diona wrote, conceding the argument at last, Okay, bring your fiancés or husbands here tomorrow and let them affirm what you are saying. If they do, then I will grant your request. All six looked elated, thanking her and promising to return at one tomorrow.

"I told you so," General Thebes remarked as the two headed off in response to the supper gong.

The four small girls looked remarkably better at dinner. Their hair was nicely brushed, and Sergeant Kastor had found them something to wear, though the dresses were very ill fitting. Diona noticed that they ate with some enthusiasm. She jotted a note to General Thebes that asked him to take the girls back to their house so that they could retrieve their more valuable possessions and to see if they had any relatives who were capable of taking them in. He chuckled, "I knew that you were going to ask me about that. Already my aides have looked into their situation. Her family has more or less vanished from Levkos and her husband was an only son. I think that we are stuck with them, Your Majesty." She grinned, but quickly realized he couldn't see her smile. She cursed to herself again.

After dinner, Diona wrote out, We should organize the regular women into groups of at least four families and give them one of the empty homes in which to live. Make sure that the new kitchens are installed in the house and that ample food supplies and things are there for them. Using Bethany's Hints, they are supposed to be able to fend for themselves in units of four.

"My thoughts exactly, Your Majesty. Still, I think it prudent to leave at least one soldier there with them for the foreseeable future to make sure that nothing goes wrong," he replied.

She bent nodded and added, "Ah."

"Tomorrow, Your Majesty can meet my wife and family. I have really missed them," he added. She smiled, but realized that he couldn't see that expression and so merely bent nodded again.

After sipping tea, or rather having it spoon fed into their mouths, the nine retired for the evening. Diona and her four friends led the four orphans back to their plush quarters. The girls tried to chat, ignoring the fact that neither themselves nor the others could understand them now. Diona wrote out, Can you write?

Ariadne wrote in very clumsy block letters, A little. Kore can write her name. What is going to happen to us? Will we go to sleep like mom?

Oh, how Diona wanted to talk to these girls, but none of the nine could say anything understandable. She wrote, We will be your mothers. You will live with us now. However, only Ariadne could read what she wrote; her three younger sisters looked at the words and chatted incomprehensibly. At last, the five began their awkward nightly ritual of brushing out each other's hair. Soon, the girls got into the act as well, trying out their feet with the brushes for the first time since the plague had come. When it was time for sleep, Diona took Alekto to bed with her, while her friends took the other three with them. Tomorrow, she would see that better arrangements were made. Certainly, the four ought to have their own room with four beds somehow.

March 2 turned out to be a hectic day around the palace. Midmorning, a wagon brought the four children's possessions to the palace. Tisi and Rhea accompanied the four to their home and acted as spokespersons or rather spokes-writers for the girls, helping them retrieve what they wanted. Then, shortly after noon, Olympos and his group arrived at the palace, bringing Diona's family back to her. Late that afternoon, the engineers from Velona arrived, along with over a thousand more soldiers, escorting General Thebes and Sergeant Kastor's families and a dozen wagons loaded with the MMCE equipment.

The girls brought their favorite blankets, a few favorite dresses that no longer fit, not since the plague had come, hairbrushes, several dolls, and even a ball, though why they brought a ball Diona had no idea. Still, having their own blankets and dolls made them quite happy. Meantime, Sergeant Kastor orchestrated a rearrangement of the Queen's Quarters. Two of the Ladies in Waiting's beds were moved into Diona's room and placed together forming one monster-sized bed that would sleep all five women. The remaining beds in the other room were pushed together similarly so that the four orphans could sleep in one bed. With his help, the four arranged their blankets, dolls, brushes, yokes, and such, making this their own private room. Diona noticed that they now seemed more alive than yesterday, and the girls seemed to be very pleased with their new arrangements. At least Diona hoped this was so. How awful it must be for the four girls to lose both their parents and brother while they were helpless Ornamented Dolls, she thought.

The noontime reunion was quite emotional for all. Olympos Stathis had brought the three families back safe and sound. He also brought along Herodes Odotos, a twenty year old linguist, hired while they were in Axos to teach the three families to speak the Annelise dialect well. Herodes was being very well remunerated for his lengthy stay with the families. While none of the women in the three families was fluent in Annelise, at least they could say some five hundred basic words. Still, such had not been enough for them to be able to receive therapy sessions yet. The women were fairly well dressed with dresses that at least fit them properly. All wore flats, not heels.

"Mom! Aison! Chloe!" Diana exclaimed as she moved precariously swiftly to greet her family. Chara moved her body hard into her daughter's and swung her foot around Diona's waist, the best she could do to hug her, fighting back tears of joy. Her sister, Chloe, joined them and her brother, Aison, put his arms around all three.

"Well done on killing Erebos," Aison praised her. "Oh, my wife — sis, I got married! Doris is the most marvelous woman." Chloe said something in Annelise and he added, "And Chloe got married to Acteon here." Diona looked over at the Drastus clan.

Acteon smiled, "You're stuck with me as your brother-in-law now, I'm afraid. Chloe and I got hitched. We're going to have a baby too!" he added proudly. Diona looked at her sister, who bent nodded, though she also said something in Annelise, which Diona didn't understand.

Delpha Drastus, now forty-three, nodded her approval. Her other son, Adonis spoke up, "Our sister, Athena here has married Orpheus, but then you probably suspected that they would hitch up. Kleto is now fifteen." He was referring to his younger sister. The other widow, Katerina Drastus, now forty-five, nodded to Diona. Her eldest daughter, Doris snuggled against Aison, and Diona thought that her brother had done well. She always had liked Doris. Anatol was still shy, she noted, recalling that his older brother had died trying to prevent their being taken to the Ornamentation Center.

Finally Orpheus, his arms around Athena, said, "Dad saved us all, Diona. Niki says that she doesn't know how you could have possible stood up to Erebos. She was petrified whenever she was around him before you were taken by him." Orpheus was now seventeen, and Niki was sixteen. Olympos and Melita's two younger daughters, Antheia and Andromeda chatted away in Annelise, but bent nodded to Diona.

Diona moved aside, sat down, and wrote out, Thank you very much for saving my family and the others, Olympos. Her brother read it aloud for the group.

"Thank you, Diona, for getting justice for dad," Aison added. "How on earth could you possibly have killed him?"

She wrote, I poisoned him. Everyone chuckled.

"Well done, sis," Aison grinned.

"This is Herodes Odotos, a linguist," Olympos broke in. "I've hired him to teach us all to speak Annelise. Already our women can speak a little bit. It is remarkable, but we can finally understand our womenfolk, Diona. He will be teaching you as well, at least until you can find someone else if you prefer. You simply must learn to speak Annelise, and then you can finally communicate again and not have to write what you want to say."

Diona then introduced her four friends, though General Thebes was kind enough to do the talking for her so that she didn't have to write. Then, the four orphans were also introduced. Diona wrote, Mom and all of you — you are welcome to stay here at the palace if you want.

"We need to fix up our estates, sis. I will make sure that we all come to visit every day. We have lots to talk about. I just wish that you could learn Annelise soon; it has to be terribly hard on you to have to try to write everything. Mom can hardly see the paper on which to write. She and Chloe have to kind of look sideways, like you do," Aison explained.

Come around five for supper, please, Diona wrote and the general extended his welcoming insistence on that as well. Olympos agreed for the four families. After more hugs and well wishes, they left to return to their four homes and figure out how to get their lives going again. Meanwhile, Diona had to get ready for the arrival of the engineers from Velona and to meet the general's family. Plus, the six women who wanted to become Ornamented Dolls had returned, their husbands or fiancés in tow, begging for her permission to be ornamented. Reluctantly, she and General Thebes had little choice but to grant the six permission; the men seemed enthusiastically behind the women's choice to become Ornamented Dolls. Diona tried one last time to convince the women not to do it, that it was permanent and could not be undone if they discovered it was horrid. They didn't listen to her; their minds were made up long ago. Six more underwent the operation the next morning, adding to the total number of Ornamented Dolls in Alia. More would certainly follow, but Diona hoped that their numbers would be few.

The large group from Preveza arrived. General Thebes introduced his wife Io to Diona. Io was thirty, with long brown hair and was very attractive. His eldest daughter looked like her mother; Thalia was ten. Dora was nine and had her father's hair and face. His son, Alex, had just turned eight and looked proud, intent upon following in his father's footsteps becoming a general himself. He played with toy soldiers all the time that he was not helping his mother and sisters. Diona saw at once that theirs was a loving family and why General Thebes had resisted the Ornamentation Project.

Then, the two engineers from Velona were introduced. "Your Majesty, I am Engineer Gino West Po, a distant cousin of Monarch Stefano West Po. This is my assistant engineer, Miss Alessa Blanco." He was twenty-nine with black hair and a thin, wiry frame. She was twenty-five with brown hair, cut short and easily manageable. "She's also part inventor and works for the big invention company, the DAE," he explained. "We will need perhaps a week to get everything assembled and setup for the demonstrations."

Diona wrote out, Thank you for coming. You can stay here at the palace. General Thebes will see to your needs. Dine with us each evening, if you like.

The general sent an aide to assist the two in determining what space was needed for their demonstration setup. They borrowed a warehouse not far from the palace. After a little discussion, the general sent along fifty soldiers to assist the two in setting their demonstrations up. Their added labor allowed the two engineers to make their first presentation days sooner, on March 5.

The supper that evening was quite large and boisterous, at least for those who could speak. Diona was exceedingly happy; so much was going so right now. She enjoyed her family's company enormously, even though she could not chat with them. She observed that they did speak short sentences in Annelise and knew that she just had to learn and soon.

Towards the end of the lengthy meal, Io came over to Diona and asked, "I have read Bethany's Hints during the lengthy trip here. Is it really possible for me to learn to sew dresses again?" Diona answered with her partially understandable yes and wrote a message to General Thebes asking him to contact me in Velona and have Io chat with me about just that. Io looked very pleased and was ecstatic when I finished talking with her later that night. I had given her back some hope for her future, if only she could somehow get one of their metalworkers to make her the right tools. I already knew that the new sewing machines were on their way from Annelise along with Katerine.

That evening when Diona and her four friends returned to their private quarters, they found the four orphans totally engrossed in playing a game with their ball. Still hobbled with the extreme heels, the four could barely move around and then only with care. Nevertheless, they were playing kick ball, attempting to hit each other with the ball. They were laughing and gay when Diona and her friends entered. Of course, none of the nine could speak to the others, but Ariadne came up to Diona and pushed on her body, trying to get her to come play with them. She caught on to the eight year old's request and soon the five joined the girls and their game. Diona discovered that while it was most challenging to play in their heels, it was thoroughly enjoyable. For the first time in years, Diona and her four friends just had pure fun, no strings attached.

Later they tucked their four orphans into bed, and Tisi squatted down and pressed her lips and disks onto the cheeks of each girl, the best she could do to give them a good night kiss. Diona and the others followed Tisi's lead. All four girls beamed, though only their eyes showed it.

The five then brushed out their hair and awkwardly got into their very wide bed. Tisi made the first advance and soon all five worked on giving each other some loving attention, so long denied to the five. They were an inseparable team now. No men were in their lives, not even distant prospects, nor did they desire men right now.

The next day, Herodes began giving them lessons in how to speak the Annelise dialect. More women were brought in by the soldiers and given sanctuary at the palace. Half of these were Ornamented Dolls who were in dire straits without men in their lives for one reason or another. Some of the men had been killed or died, while some had abandoned the women and girls, which angered Diona some. More women requested an audience with her so that they could be allowed to become Ornamented Dolls as well. Thus, Diona was kept busy dealing with one situation after the other.

That evening, Sergeant Kastor brought flats in for the four orphans to wear. He'd searched the palace high and low for ones that would fit their small feet. However, to his dismay, all four tried to reject them. At last, with Ariadne doing her best to write, Diona found out why. The orphaned girls knew that they were now considered elegant Ornamented Dolls and wanted to look the part, which included the extreme heels. After all, Diona and her friends wore them, the four girls wanted very much to look like the five. Diona was able to convince them to wear the flats when they wanted to play and got a compromise from the four, though it did not last for very long. The small girls were determined to look like the five older women.

At last, the demonstrations were ready. Alessa proudly drove the motor-wagon, motor-car, and T-putt-putt around the warehouse, showing the non-Dolls that driving was now very easy to do. Io was elated and begged General Thebes to get one of these noisy ones for her own use. Alessa privately told Diona that she would work with herself and her Ornamented Dolls in a special, private session so see if it was even possible for the Ornamented Dolls to drive them.

The electricity demonstration was a sure winner. Diona was able to operate the washing machine and the floor sweeper herself, much to her surprise. She could easily manage the light switches as well. The telefono, however, was problematical for the Ornamented Dolls, until they could speak Annelise. The next day, the two engineers began a lengthy series of demonstrations for the nobles and the wealthy of Levkos. Already the Stathis, Gidios, and two Drastus families were fully supporting these new projects, particularly financially. The other wealthy men and women and the remaining nobles also saw the incredible benefits that the MMCE program offered. Now they began meeting with the engineers to work out how to begin.

Diona had another chat with Monarch Sophia via the LD radio. After that, she appointed Tisi to be her Minister of MMCE Planning and Rhea to be her Minister of Finance, taking advantage of both women's inherent skills. Tisi could organize things well, while Rhea was good with figures. Sophia explained that efficiently running a country required acquiring a competent set of top-level ministers who had the authority to run their own areas without direct and constant intervention on the monarch's part. Xanthe became her Minister of Resettlement, dealing with the empty homes and women in dire need. Dora was always interested in the arts, so Diona appointed her the Minister of the Arts.

After more consultations, she appointed her brother Aison to be her Minister of Shipping, an arena sadly in need of reorganization. Their huge fleet had been mostly idle for a year and a half. She appointed Niki Stathis to be her Minister of Education, giving her the challenge of establishing a free education to all children of Alia from six through fourteen, complicated because of the dual language nature now facing them. She appointed Io, the general's wife, to be her Minister of Clothing, giving her the challenge of rebuilding their entire apparel industry, though she would have to wait a few more weeks until Katerine brought the new designs and equipment from Annelise. Io was incredibly pleased with her appointment as was her husband. Next, she appointed the raven haired Athena, now the wife of Orpheus, to be her Minister of Ornamented Doll Skills, giving her the huge challenge of seeing what could be done for the many Ornamented Dolls as well as what possible things they could do for themselves. She also appointed Sergeant Kastor's wife, Aella, to be her Minister of Women's Ways, charging her to help work out ways and means that the non-Doll women of Alia could do things for themselves.

Diona realized the vital nature of the MMCE program and that the generation of electricity would be the key factor in making all else work. Hence, she appointed Olympos Stathis to be her Minister of Electrical Works. However, she also knew that Mr. Ridon had to have a role. If left out, he would cause trouble. She appointed him, much to his complete surprise, to be her Minister of Transportation, charged with getting extensive rail lines established throughout Alia. He was most pleased with the appointment. Similarly, she appointed Telemon Phoros to be her Minister of Communications, charging him with establishing a countrywide telefono system and getting LD radios in every town with a population of five thousand or more.

In short, her goal was to get all these projects started before the winter snows came in July. That way, she reasoned, the people of Alia would have some hope to carry them over the winter season. By the time that Katerine and her large convoy arrived on March 20, Diona had actions occurring on many fronts. Still, she was bothered with at least a dozen more women becoming Ornamented Dolls each week, whom she simply could not dissuade from undergoing the irreversible procedure. By the end of March, another sixty women had become Ornamented Dolls. On the other hand, at the time of Katerine's arrival, she could at least speak a few words that were understandable.

The same was true of her adopted orphans, who picked up the new language far faster than she did. Still, Diona's great pleasure came each evening after dinner, when she and her girls played a game of kick ball in her quarters. After which, she tucked them into their bed and gave them a good night kiss of sorts. Now she could say "Goodnight" and "Love you" to the girls, who reciprocated, calling her their "Mother," which pleased Diona, who suspected that she would never have children of her own. What man in his right mind would desire a helpless Ornamented Doll? That some of the men who had come to back up their wives, daughters, and girlfriends in getting her permission to become Ornamented Dolls eluded her thoughts about this.

Katerine had been gone for almost eighteen months when she finally landed in Preveza, Alia. Already she noticed changes, changes for the better. Some women were actually on the streets using yokes to carry produce home from the markets. Men, carts, and wagons bustled around the city, though mostly they were transporting the fall harvest. Still, it was a positive change, she thought. While most watched from the decks of the six Annelise coastal vessels, Jude, Midas, and Yanni went ashore to arrange transportation from the port to the capital city. However, the men discovered that they were expected and returned shortly, accompanied by a major and a squad of soldiers.

"They've already arranged for our transportation," Yanni explained. "They want us in Lekvos pronto. A legion is accompanying us. What a change, dear."

Soon a large number of wagons began lining up on the docks and the passengers began disembarking. Crews worked the derrick cranes, unloading the cargo, depositing loads directly into waiting wagons. Because she had brought along two hundred Annelise men and women who were under contract to teach the Ornamented Dolls and their families the Annelise dialect, they had to travel by wagon. There were not enough coaches to be had, though the major insisted that the Church of God folks ride in the four carriages.

Yanni explained, "They want us in Levkos fast. The major said that they would be pushing the horses to get us there in four days at most. They have arranged for three inns to put us up each night, but the major said that we'd be getting in late. His men will be providing food stops along the way. Nothing like red carpet treatment, eh dear?"

Katerine and Barbara chuckled. "Not like when we left, mom," her daughter replied.

Four days later as they rode through the streets of Levkos, the city was definitely not like they had left it. The city was bustling with activity, though at least half of the traffic was soldiers going about their assignments on behalf of their monarch. Still they did observe a fair number of empty homes or businesses along the way; some were boarded up. As their carriages pulled into the palace courtyard, halting near the main entrance, a small crowd hurriedly came out to greet them. The many wagons bearing their trade goods from Annelise and the two hundred linguists pulled in behind them.

Katerine took charge of the introductions, as her Church of God group walked up to the General, though she could not tell from all the Ornamented Dolls which one was her monarch. "Welcome to Levkos, I am General Thebes Nophios and this is our monarch Diona Gidios. I believe that you and I met once when you were our queen."

Although she had been forewarned about the sheer number of Ornamented Dolls, seeing so many of them, including her monarch standing before her, all with perfect posture, massive earrings — many worth a small fortune — protruding lip plates, and immobile necks rather startled her. Yes, while she had grown accustomed to Alexina and her lips, the Ornamented Doll phenomenon was shocking, made all the worse because she knew that these women could not yet speak intelligibly, save for a few words that they had learned from Herodes.

She was introduced to Diona, her various ministers, and the large extended families, as well as the four adopted orphans. Diona managed to say, "Welcove Katerine," in Annelise, a small first step. She in turn introduced the Church of God members starting with her husband, Yanni and her daughter Barbara and Alexina. Then she introduced Homer Manasses, Jude and Eleni Manasses and their teens, Hermina and Triton. Next, she introduced Midas and Helen Drastus and their teens Io, Iris, and Myron. "This is Princess Mya Rolf, who has brought a huge selection of the very latest Annelise fashions designed for we women, along with their latest invention of a sewing machine. Finally, behind me are two hundred volunteers from Annelise who have come to teach their language to those of you who need it." She felt awkward saying Dolls or Ornamented Dolls.

General Thebes picked up on her hesitation. "It is all right to just say Dolls or Ornamented Dolls. We all do around here. It is not derogatory or demeaning. It is what it is. Worse, women and girls still pester Monarch Diona daily, begging to become Ornamented Dolls. My soldiers will escort the Annelise to their quarters here in the palace. We do have room for them all, though it will be a bit tight. Monarch Diona has a complete list of the Ornamented Dolls and their addresses and has taken the liberty of working out schedules for the volunteers. Honestly, she wants to thank you very much for having brought them."

"Yes, thank you, Katerine," Diona spoke slowly and carefully. She grinned, but it was not visible.

"After they are settled in, when the gong sounds, we will all dine in the Royal Hall this evening, where everyone can be seated at one time," General Thebes continued. "We have rooms prepared for all of you in the main complex. If you will follow us, we will show you to your rooms and my soldiers will begin unloading your things."

By the time that they were shown to their rooms and had their bags brought in, the dinner gong sounded. Katerine and the Church of God members observed the women closely during the evening meal and light discussions afterwards. The few women, who were not Ornamented Dolls, Io and Aella, in particular, did their best to carry the table conversation for the women of Levkos. It was plainly obvious that the Ornamented Dolls said virtually nothing. That they were severely constrained in the motions that they could carry out became acutely obvious. Often Diona would have to turn her body just to look at the person who was speaking to her while she ate. That they had to be fed by soldiers only added to the overall dismal picture, though Alexina was able to feed herself like Katerine and the others from Annelise. True, Alexina had to be far more careful in her motions, but she had the full use of her neck, which the Ornamented Dolls certainly did not. That the Ornamented Dolls also all wore the extreme heels that made walking slower and more difficult was not lost on her as well. The stark reality of the Ornamented Dolls finally sunk home to these Church of God members.

After the lengthy meal and table discussions, Barbara headed off with the four orphans to go play kick ball. Ariadne tried to show Barbara how to play, but she couldn't make herself understood. Hence, Barbara simply used telepathy with the four allowing them to chat with her as they played. The game was pretty much lopsided, since Barbara was wearing flats and the four, their extreme heels. "Why do you wear such heels?" she asked.

Ariadne thought, *Because we are now* Ornamented *Dolls. We are very grown up. All the* Ornamented *Dolls wear them. All the important women of our country are* Ornamented *Dolls and we are too now. How come you don't wear them? Do you want us to find some for you too?*

Although Barbara's body was going on seven now, she was totally aware and knowledgeable, a very able spiritual being — just with a small body. She saw the signs of heavy and massive emotional trauma sitting over the four girls, guessing it was the deaths of their parents. She presumed that there was also a lot of pain associated with their ornamentation process.

Consequently, Barbara rightly responded to Ariadne's questions, realizing this was likely their valiant attempt to remain somehow alive. "Yes, you all look quite beautiful now. Even your monarch is an Ornamented Doll too. I am not an Ornamented Doll, so I don't wear those heels. When I grow up, maybe I can wear them then when I dress up. We brought along a whole lot of fancy clothes. Maybe tomorrow you will get some satin dresses to go with your shoes." All four brightened up, grinning broadly, though their faces didn't show it. Barbara did not need facial expressions to know this, however. They went back to their game.

After dinner, Katerine led Diona and General Thebes into the old King's Throne Room, now known as the Monarch's Office. "I have to show you the secret door. It saved my life and Barbara's too." At last, she had the opportunity to pass along the knowledge that otherwise might have been lost. Diona thanked her repeatedly for showing her the door. The general did likewise.

Later, the Church of God members met in Jude's room for a battle conference. "My god, this is worse than I imagined it would be," Jude began. "I mean we all know how hard it is for Alexina, but these women — my god, they can barely do anything."

"Did you notice how the Ornamented Dolls barely said anything all evening? Only a couple basic words were understandable," Eleni pointed out the obvious.

"They have to learn to sveak Annelise like I did," Alexina explained. "I know, not veing avle to sveak is the very worst thing ivaginable for thev. At least they have soveone to helv thev eat. Those neck rings vake everything so hard to do."

Helen added, "Diona's earrings look like they are pulling her ears off her head! But I guess that must not be a problem or she'd have had them cut off."

"I suspect that they haven't done that because the earrings are extremely valuable, gorgeous, and add to the mystique of the Ornamented Doll image," Katerine guessed.

"Mom, how are we going to give them the necessary therapy?" asked Hermina. "Do we wait until they can speak well? He did say that there was nearly two hundred thousand of them now!"

Iris interjected, "Didn't Eve say that they used telepathy to conduct the therapy sessions on women with lip plates down in Phindos?"

Eleni and Helen looked at their respective daughters and Helen replied, "Yes they did and it was effective, Iris, but they numbered a dozen not two hundred thousand. Midas, what are we going to do?"

Elder Homer spoke up, "It is obvious. Look at the broad picture. Alia's key leaders are Ornamented Dolls with a few men and ordinary women. If Alia is to survive, these key people must become more able and clear thinking. The real question for which we as yet do not have an answer is to what extent will the Ornamented Doll's physical limitations dampen their ultimate ability to lead their country forward?"

"What exactly do you mean by this, dad?" asked Jude.

"We've seen the two opposing views of the Ornamented Dolls at the state dinner tonight, son. Her Minister of Transportation, Mr. Ridon, most definitely holds the Ornamented Dolls in complete disdain and disrespect. I am certain that he feels that such women are completely and utterly helpless and useless, not deserving to be a leader in any way shape or form. On the other hand, that women and the men in their lives are still begging Diona to be allowed to become Ornamented Dolls themselves shows that a large group of people view the Ornamented Dolls in high regard. It's not whether being an Ornamented Doll is good or bad, rather it is that others are looking up to them as role models. Both points of view are most definitely present in Levkos," the sixty-one year old man explained.

He continued, "So if the Ornamented Dolls by virtue of their physical constraints are found to be unable to effectively lead, this government will fall. Yet, if the Ornamented Dolls are able to be successful leaders, more women will want to emulate them. I must admit, I find their physical limitations incredibly damaging. Only with a very large amount of our Advanced Therapy will they be as physically capable as the ordinary man of Alia is now. They will have to be pushed up to being able to do nearly everything using mostly the innate powers of a spiritual being just to compensate for their physical limitations. That is a very tall order, considering that we are dealing with two hundred thousand of them."

"It takes one to make one," Barbara broke in on the adult conversation.

Homer smiled, "You are quite right, Barbara. It takes a freed spiritual being to make another.

There are eleven of us not counting Katerine and Alexina. If we are to do it ourselves and if we allow a year of Advanced Therapy, it will take us eighteen thousand years to handle the two hundred thousand women. We are going to have to find another approach here." They all chuckled, though Katerine thought that it was obviously going to be doomed to failure from the get go.

Eleni offered another thought, "Say, we are forgetting what our primary mission must be here. We need to erase the trauma suffered by the men and women from the plague. Additionally, with the Ornamented Dolls, we will likely have a little unconsciousness and a bit of cutting pain and shock to handle beyond that. Let's not get the cart in front of the horse. Our primary objective is to have the plague trauma and that endured with the Ornamentation surgery eliminated across Alia. That must come first. Secondarily, the Ornamented Dolls and their unique situation can be addressed."

"True, but shouldn't we do more than that for the Ornamented Doll leaders, Diona, for example," Helen asked.

Homer answered, "Yes, you are probably right, we should do more for the Ornamented Doll leaders, but only as we focus on the broader picture. We must focus on making those that are able even more able if we are to stand a chance here. Diona and her small group of Ornamented Dolls have already proven that they are far more able than one might expect. Look, she assumed a high level of responsibility in eliminating the sadistic general who was leading the country into ruins. Similarly, General Thebes has also assumed a large measure of responsibility as well. I am not entirely sure about her other Ornamented Doll ministers, but the simple fact that they are attempting to fulfill those duties is in their favor."

"Okay dad, then the question becomes do we start right away with the Ornamented Dolls and use telepathy to run the sessions or do we tackle ordinary women who can speak?" Jude asked.

"Well son, counting Diona, there are seven Ornamented Dolls to handle, five men, and two ordinary women. That handles her ministers and Thebes, her current government. Obviously, they will take some time to handle. I can see no option other than to make the other Ornamented Dolls learn to speak Annelise well before we tackle their cases in general. Of course, there will have to be some exceptions. Olympos will want his family handled, as will several others. Still, we must begin on the ordinary women as soon as possible and then train many of them to build up our pool of therapy givers as rapidly as possible. Let's give the Ornamented Dolls at least three-quarters of a year to build up their language skills before we tackle them in volume. By then, we ought to have a large number of other women trained and giving Basic Therapy sessions. How does this sound to you?" Homer asked. "Fourteen need handling at once and there are thirteen of us, though I expect that the five men will take far less time."

"Yes, dad," Jude pointed out, "but you know as well as I do that they are going to want their families and relations handled too and insist on it. Where do we draw the line?"

Midas pointed out, "Another thing to consider is that the Ornamented Dolls may well be mostly physically helpless, crushing their self-respect. In Phindos, the women with the lip plates have become some of the very best therapy givers. Obviously, that occurred only after they had Advanced Therapy so that they could use limited telepathy. Wouldn't this give these Ornamented Dolls something highly useful that they could contribute to their society: therapy giving?"

"I can't sveak our language," Alexina offered her viewpoint, having sat quietly listening to the others. "I will ve useless unless I have sove who can understand Annelise. If I could send vy thoughts to another and hear their answers in vy vind, then I could helv the Dolls. With our norval woven, if I could just send vy covvands into their vinds, I could helv thev."

Triton stuck up for her, "She's right. We've just been giving her routine Advanced Therapy. If you work on just having her place her thoughts into another's mind, then she could deliver therapy to the ordinary women. A bit more work and she could receive their thoughts and then she could work with the Ornamented Dolls too."

"He's right, dad," Myron also stuck up for Alexina. Though they had only known her for about three months, both boys liked her a lot, though not romantically. Io and Hermina had the two boy's hearts already. "Just how difficult and time consuming is it to just get someone to be able to use telepathy? If it isn't too long, do the Ornamented Dolls. Given them a real reason to continue to live and contribute something of great value."

Eleni decided to try another angle. "Say, we know that Macario and several others who are totally free or nearly so can alter what we consider 'reality.' We know that a long time ago, both Bethany and Eve had lip plates similar to these in many ways. He healed their lips; he even regrew their arms, if the stories were true. What about trying to have the hot shots in our Church of God come here and undo the Ornamented Dolls? Put them back to ordinary women?"

"Yes, why not try that?" Helen added. "Undo this awful mess that these women are enduring. Why, then our task would be far easier. If he could do it for those two, why not all these women?"

"Can that ve done? That would ve favulous!" Alexina added.

"Yes, from our point of view, it would be most convenient," Homer answered. "However, such would be doomed to failure. I know how our hearts go out to these people, but you know as well as I that it would ultimately fail. Why? You can't give a person something of great value without their having somehow earned it or performing an equivalent exchange. It is the factors of responsibility, ethics, and exchange. When a person receives something that they consider of great and vital value, their sense of honor and responsibility and ethics demand a fair exchange in return. For lifetimes, Bethany and Eve have been working flat out to make Tarra a safe place for us to work our therapy. Hence, they more than earned their 'gifts' from Macario. As we have already seen in Annelise, more than half of the women that we treat immediately turn around and learn to give it to others and so do. Exchange. If Macario just magically undoes all that has been done to the Ornamented Dolls, while at first it will seem fantastic, soon they will realize that they have been given a precious thing without any way for them to repay it back. Their self-respect will crumble further, many may even begin down the criminal path of give me, give me. Besides, Diona has already told us that probably a quarter of the women actually desired getting their ornaments. Undoing their ornaments would be a crime against their self-determinism. No, while this would seem to be the right thing to do, ultimately it is the wrong thing to do."

"I have to earn it, don't I?" Alexina asked.

"Yes, that is the route to total freedom, Alexina."

"Vlease, you know that I want to helv and how good I have veen helving woven in Annelise with vasic theravy. Here I can only helv those who can sveak Annelise, which is hardly anyone," Alexina pleaded.

"Don't worry, Alexina. You are one of us now and we will find a way to put you to work," Homer consoled her. "It is just that if Macario and others gives these two hundred thousand women the gift of undoing their ornamentations, they would be making a welfare state, a give me-give me state, which would eventually lead those two hundred thousand into a loss of self-respect and into criminality."

"Yes, a welfare state is akin to death of a civilization, dad," Jude countered, "but isn't that just what *has* already happened here? A huge welfare state where all women are helpless, requiring men to attend to their every needs? Even if some pick up Bethany's hints and start back doing things for themselves using Women's Ways, that still leaves two hundred thousand who are not likely to be able to do much of anything at all, the Ornamented Dolls. Won't this still be mostly a welfare state even then?"

"You see the magnitude of the problem facing Diona here in Alia, son," Homer countered. "As they now are, the Ornamented Dolls are almost totally helpless, dependent upon men for nearly everything in life. In short, they are on welfare. Worse, it is two hundred thousand of the top women of Alia on welfare! Think of the resources that they will be consuming: all the men have to be pulled off other more productive endeavors of the MMCE programs just to keep these women alive. Worse, if these men are not independently wealthy, in time they too will require a handout when they no longer have funds with which to purchase food and other necessities. In a twisted way, General Erebos saw this situation arising and attempted to handle it by making Ornamented Dolls out of the dependent women. By shutting up the women, that is, making them unable to communicate, that would allow the men can get back to work, if only to make all the ornaments. Instead, that created even more chaos and confusion among the working men. That plan didn't work, mind you, but he certainly saw that having half of their population totally dependent upon the other half just to live each day is suicide for a country. He chose the wrong solution. Too bad that he didn't take the route of working with women to uncover alternate ways for them to become productive members of society again."

"I see your point. We simply must get to the average woman of Alia, get her rehabilitated and learning alternate ways to do what she must. If not, the whole country is doomed. I can see that clearly now dad. Yet, what about the two hundred thousand Ornamented Dolls? I can't see how our Women's Ways will be of very much use to them. Are they not going to be the welfare albatross of Alia?" Jude replied, still concerned.

"Yes they most certainly are, son. As much as my heart goes out to these women, we simply must handle the millions of normal women first. Only then can we spend the huge amounts of time working with the Ornamented Dolls to get them up to a point where they will not be so utterly dependent upon men with arms for nearly everything."

"I know that you are right dad," Helen replied. "It's just so hard. My heart goes out to those poor Ornamented Dolls, whom I know we could help enormously."

"For the want of a few, the many must suffer," Midas added. "We have to avoid that and make it for the want of the many, the few must suffer. Diona will think that we are heartless, Homer."

"Perhaps so, perhaps not. She has a strong sense of responsibility in her. Diona may well see the actual state of affairs and see that this is the right path to follow," Homer suggested, sounding a hopeful note.

"If you could just find a way to get the neck rings off thev safely, they could vanage vuch vetter," Alexina added her thoughts to the mix.

"I am certain that they will continue to try to do just that, Alexina. I'll speak with Diona first thing in the morning," Homer concluded their discussion, leaving their next day's schedule open as yet.

The next day after breakfast, Homer took Diona aside and the two had a lengthy chat. Diona was most surprised and frankly amazed. He used telepathy with her so that she could merely think her thoughts and questions and not have to struggle mightily to write them down.

I really don't know what the real benefits of your therapy might be, Homer. However, I am aware of the welfare situation that I face. If you believe that you and your people can get our normal women back to leading productive lives and not so completely dependent upon men for everything, then that would be a miracle and help me save Alia from its destruction. I agree, no matter how this therapy goes with my ministers and me, I will insist that the other Ornamented Dolls learn to speak Annelise well before they are eligible to receive your therapy. Is this agreeable?

"It most certainly is, Diona."

Okay. Please, I like Diona much better than Your Majesty. He grinned and promised to tell the others.

"Excellent. We need to begin with yourself and staff yet today. Shall we say right after lunch?"

During the morning, the major emphasis was on getting the two hundred linguists off to their first homes, though two stayed here at the palace to work assist Herodes. Diona ordered everyone who did not have a critical action to perform to join one of the three language sessions. So began the massive Annelise language training for over four hundred thousand people, the largest language training ever conceived or executed on Tarra. Everyone who had any connection to an Ornamented Doll had to learn to either speak or understand the Annelise dialect. Eventually, many beyond these women and their extended families also learned to understand spoken Annelise, such as the farmers and shop keepers, with whom these Ornamented Dolls would eventually interact down the road of recovery.

Homer himself took Diona into her first therapy session. Alexina took General Thebes because he could understand basic Annelise due to his long contacts with their princesses who came quarterly to trade apparel with Alia. Only Mr. Phoros was left out of this first round of sessions.

Diona's case began slowly, her abduction and ornamentation surgery was still quite charged up and she began running it, starting with the breaking of the news that she and her family would be taken away that next day. She ran routine, Homer noted, except for one small detail. She kept saying, "Men simply cannot be trusted with any kind of power; they abuse it and harm women." Rather, she thought this and he received it as if she had said it. Certainly, he could see how she could reach that conclusion, that decision, because of the ornamentation process and the murder of her father and others who tried to prevent their being taken away and mutilated. Of course, he did not really expect this traumatic incident to erase.

Still, he kept her at it until she recovered all that was said and felt while she was unconscious for nearly twenty-four hours during the surgery on her lips and afterwards. Diona was very surprised to see that she could recall everything that was said and going on around her while she was drugged unconscious. "So being unconscious is not really unconscious! Incredible."

She had a good deal of relief from the long afternoon's work and he ended for suppertime. *Thank you, I feel much better, but you can see why men simply cannot be trusted with any kind of power, don't you?* she thought.

"You are welcome. Yes, I see your point. We will continue tomorrow. I believe it will soon be time to dine," Homer answered.

Everyone was quite enthralled with their therapy session and none objected to spending the whole next day at it. Diona and her staff cancelled all their meetings, postponing them for the weekend. After breakfast, Homer resumed with Diona. He ran her through the ornamentation surgery one more time and then asked her if there was something similar and that had occurred earlier in time. Sure enough, she began running the debilitating plague, just as Homer calculated. It was a no-brainer. She was a woman who had lost her arms to the plague. Thus, that shock, trauma, and terror was right there to be handled, and it was similar to the ornamentation surgery.

Naturally, that whole episode was full of fright, terror, and loss. After a number of recountings, her tears began to flow. Her loss was severe, her terror real, most vivid. After a break for lunch, they continued going over this one all afternoon, reducing it piece by piece. More than once, Diona let out scream of shock or terror as she re-experienced all that she had endured when the plague struck, leaving her a helpless invalid or so she claimed. Again, she continued to insist that men simply couldn't be trusted with any kind of power. As the supper hour approached, Homer was again forced to end off for the day, leaving her feeling much better, having gotten off a whole lot of emotional trauma, though there was little actual pain associated with the plague. Homer secretly thanked the mantis for that small kindness.

Over supper, General Thebes was laughing at nearly everything anyone said. Alexina had finished his Basic Therapy, removing all the plague's trauma on him. He'd discovered that he'd lived before and been a soldier before. Over a century ago, he'd been in a war up in the Arad and Zargarb and had his feet blown off in a cannonae fusillade. Unable to walk, he just laid there in massive pain until another cannonae blast killed his body. He also took every opportunity to praise how great Alexina was in giving her sessions. She smiled, but it was invisible to most.

The next day, Homer picked up where they'd left off, running Diona through the plague times once again, before asking her if there was something earlier in time and that was similar in nature. After a bit, she saw a bluish mass and began dealing with this one. *Oh my god, I have lived before. There I am, a young woman. Shit, there is my husband. He's telling me he just got a major appointment in the government. That's all,* she sent. Homer grinned, knowing certainly that this was not all. He had her go through it once more.

Oh, I wasn't a courtesan! Oh shit, he poisoned me to get rid of me so he could marry a proper courtesan! Damn, I was only thirty-three! See, you just cannot trust men with power! He ran her through it a few more time, reducing the effects of the poison on her body. She realized how she knew that she could easily kill General Erebos with poison. This incident had given her the knowledge that it would work, which it had.

Of course, this one didn't fully erase either. Homer actually didn't think that it would, though it was interesting. Again, he asked for something even earlier in time. She looked and looked, finding nothing. He had her go back over the poisoning incident once more and then asked for an earlier one. After a long pause, she exclaimed, *I am sitting in something. It is huge, completely surrounding me. It's all over me. I'm buried in it!*

A bit later, Diona began to unravel what had happened. She realized that this trauma had been affecting her whole life. *Oh my god! I was doing all this before! Ruling Alia. I was Melita Stathis, our queen and leader. Damn, the men murdered all of our husbands and many of our children in a massive fireworks explosion at a factory! I am an armless Holy Woman of the Eighth Degree back then. I was left helpless and in charge of Alia. Oh my god, I knew Bethany and Eve! They saved us all back then! God, they are saving us all again right now! No wonder I have never ever trusted men in power since then!* Diona began laughing and talking like mad, forgetting entirely that her words were unintelligible. Homer smiled and allowed her to continue laughing and chatting. He knew that the huge black mass hovering over her had completely vanished. He could no longer see it. His job with Diona was finished for now.

At supper, she was still laughing and chatting, ignoring that others couldn't understand what she was saying. At last, she wrote out, Everyone just HAS to get this therapy! None of her ministers disagreed. They all had just as big wins as she had. She wrote another note, We Ornamented Dolls just have to learn to do things ourselves somehow. I feel fantastic but my body's limitations are huge. We all must learn to speak Annelise fast!

Io declared, "I bet I can sew somehow. Thebes, get someone one to make me those tools drawn in the hint book, please!"

Princess Mya Rolf took this opportunity to make her bid for their attention. "Speaking of sewing, I really do want to show you all the great fashions and tools that we in Annelise have invented," She had her therapy and knew how important it was for these rulers to get theirs. Now that it was finished, she wanted to execute her mission.

"First of all, last year, we in Annelise held our First Women's Fashion War Council to try to solve the disaster that the plague has inflicted upon we women and our fashions. Let me say that we've been very fortunate in having invented some most useful tools. First, there is the Zipper-Upper, which allows us women to both zip up our dresses ourselves and unzip them. Then, to help make dresses in volume, we have the Gard sewing machine, which I will demonstrate shortly. In addition, he invented the foot cutter, essentially a sharp blade on a frame with a leather strap. The woman slips her foot into it, much like a shoe. The blade is perpendicular to the shoe, and she just slides it along the material on a cutting board. Works far better than scissors ever did. He also invented the Hemmer, a pinning machine that pins up the hem of a dress or skirt. It's operated by a foot. Simple and effective. So Io, there is now no reason you cannot get going making dresses for everyone."

"Now for the new designs, Your Majesty. We have created four totally different types of outfits, though here at your palace, you might not want some of these. Remember, some have been designed for working women. All of our new designs come with loops on each garment so that we can use our feet and toes to pull them up or down, as the case may be. We've made extensive use of zippers as fasteners and every home must have at least a Zipper-Upper for each woman and girl. We have them in all public restrooms as well — standard equipment now for such places. I'm sure that you will want them everywhere as well, once you see how easily you can manage zipping yourself up and down. Oops, I am not sure if the Ornamented Dolls will be able to do it themselves, but your helpers ought to be able to do it for you."

Princess Mya was just as fast a talker as Princess Mia Jorgen. She continued at a rapid pace, "Now for the designs. For those special occasions when a woman wants to look elegant and is willing to place herself under the control of her mate, we have two very different, most elegant styles: a modified ball gown and a slinky. The ball gowns only have a five foot in diameter hoop skirt, which we have found is quite manageable ourselves. However, we will still make the usual ones, that are twelve, fourteen, and sixteen feet across for those very special occasions, but we've found that we need a lot of help with the hoops. Now the slinky is quite exotic. It hugs your body's form quite tightly, showing off all of our feminine curves, which you must admit that we all have now, thanks to the plague. For your use and those of your ministers, I recommend either one of these styles."

"Now for working women and for winter days and heavy work, we have pants and blouse combinations. You probably are not much interested in those. However, for everyday around the house, that is, very informal settings such as when you are not going to hold court, we have the easy to put on blouse and skirt combinations, which come in a wide variety of colors and shapes. As far as heels are concerned, we women can no longer tie our shoelaces, so we've replaced them with buckling straps. We usually have another woman fasten them for us, because it is a bit difficult to buckle them while wearing some of our fancier dresses, you see. The heels now come in three heights: five, six, or seven inches, though we usually recommend seven for formal court wear. The women wearing the lower height are usually wearing them while working on their jobs, you see."

She chatted away, "Now I have brought with me several of each new invention and five dozen of each type of outfit. I would dearly love each of you to try them on, experiment with the Zipper-Upper and see how readily these new dresses can be put on and taken off. Annelise wishes each of you to have two of the formal dresses and a pair of the everyday ones, if you so desire. Of course, matching heels also come with the dresses. After you have tried them on and made your choices, I will be ready to take orders. I am sure that your apparel shops will want to make many such purchases. Now, Your Majesty, women of Alia can finally and finally be dressed properly instead of the ridiculous nightgowns and such that you have been forced to wear, to say nothing of the ill-fitting attempts to modify existing dresses to our new, exotic female forms."

By this point in time, General Thebes, Olympos, Orpheus, and the other men had quietly left the throne room. I wonder why? Princess Mya's helpers began opening the crates, laying out the apparel as well as the inventions. Diona realized at once that the pants outfits and the skirts would not be appropriate for herself and her ministers, excepting, as Princess Mya suggested, while lounging around on off days. Hence, she wrote, We need to look good and to be able to still write. When he had us wearing the old ball gowns, we couldn't write.

"Ah, yes, well, that is only going to be temporary, I expect. Just as soon as you learn our language, you will not need to write anymore. Alexina is perfectly understandable. I would recommend then that you try on the slinky style. Perhaps have one of the five foot gowns for your balls and such," Princess Mya suggested. "Of course, with the slinkys you need to wear the seven inch heels; there is just so little ease in them, form fitting and all that. How about your four girls?"

Ariadne hastily sat down and wrote, Please, we want to look like you too. Diona had not the heart to say no. Soon, she, her four little girls, and the other women were trying on the slinky style dresses. While their neck rings kept them from maneuvering properly to use the Zipper-Upper themselves, they could easily manage it for another. Hence, this minor problem was rapidly solved, much to the relief of Princess Mya, who was holding her breath. She had no idea what these Ornamented Dolls could manage to do for themselves. She had another lengthy speech ready to deliver just in case the Ornamented Dolls were unable to even help each other into the dresses. Somehow, she just had to make this sale.

The Ornamented Dolls became rather enthused with the slinky dresses. They were made from satin and really did hug their curves extremely tightly. Princess Mya and her helpers assisted the Ornamented Dolls with their new heels, though, since they could not manage the buckles themselves. Princess Mya explained, "In Annelise, we always have someone else buckle our shoes for us. Way too difficult for us to manage, so this is perfectly normal, Your Majesty." She hoped this would allay Diona's concerns about the heels. "Besides, wearing them, you all will have more incentive to learn to speak Annelise," she teased.

"Wow, look at how I look!" exclaimed Diona as she looked at herself in the mirror. Several others said similar words, all ignoring the fact that it sounded like gibberish to the others. "I look incredible!" she added. "Wow, Tisi, look at you!" She saw her friend in a bright red slinky looking at herself in the mirror. Tisi pivoted a little to look at Diona and uttered something as well.

"Mommy, look at me!" exclaimed Ariadne who now wore a similar colored slinky as Diona, complete with matching heels. Diona pivoted to see Ariadne and smiled. The eight year old looked very nice in her dress, so did the other girls. Princess Mya ignored the unintelligible utterances, which now came with increasing frequency. She correctly guessed that the women were very much pleased with their dresses and looks.

Three hours later and many dresses, blouses, and skirts tried, Princess Mya closed her sales. Not only did the Ornamented Dolls look fabulous in the slinkys, so did the normal women. Io was in love with the new style, promising to learn to sew and make more. She said, "Just as soon as women see us in these, Diona, they are going to demand similar dresses! Princess Mya, you must see that Alia gets a large delivery of these very soon indeed." Diona added her "Ah" to Io's suggestion.

Although Diona tried on the lower five-inch heels, her legs hurt too badly to wear them. She realized that her legs had already adapted well to the extreme heels that she had been wearing daily for the last eighteen months. She noted that her four friends also couldn't wear the lower heels either and relaxed about this detail. Although she wanted her four orphans to wear the lower heels, they refused, demanding to look like her. After all, since they were now Ornamented Dolls, she could not refuse their request.

When Princess Mya finally left, Diona and all the women now had three slinkys each, a five-footer ball gown, two sets of blouses and skirts, and heels to match. Of course, they all had the necessary undergarments to go with them as well. The women were extremely pleased with the dresses and thanked the princess repeatedly. Now they felt like women once more. Going around naked had been the height of humiliation. Wearing ill fitting, crudely altered dresses was not far behind that. Each woman looked stunning in her new dress. Their spirits rose even higher. Diona knew that before spring came, every Ornamented Doll and every woman needed a completely new and proper wardrobe. If they did, they would feel human again and go a long way in the recovery of their self-esteem.

Princess Mya had brought along over four hundred outfits to sell. These were rapidly purchased by Olympos, the moment that he saw Melita slowly walking up to him wearing her new blue satin slinky. "I'll make them available for the first four hundred Ornamented Dolls," he gaily advertised.

Diona wrote, "How soon can hundreds of thousands of these slinkys be delivered?"

"We are so very short on satin. We've had to make dresses for all our own women too," Princess Mya explained. "We've taken to reusing the satin in our old outfits. That has helped ease the shortage a good deal."

Diona wrote, "Please take back with you all the old dresses in our clothing room. None fit us and there is a mountain of satin there."

"Thank you. I will do so. When I return, I will deduct the satin from your cost. It will save a good deal of funds." Diona grinned, but it went unobserved.

When Diona and her ministers held court the next day, all wore their new outfits. The dresses were an instant hit and orders and request came flooding in to the palace. Olympos sold out his four hundred dresses in less than three days. He made no profit, however, selling them at his own cost or a little less. He wanted to do his part for the Ornamented Dolls.

However, when wearing the slinkys, it was impossible for the women to make much use of their feet and legs in the Women's Ways of doing things. The Ornamented Dolls couldn't do them anyway, so that this limitation was not a problem. Diona merely raised her foot and the nearest man would unbuckle her shoe so that she could write. Still, all the women worked even harder on learning to speak Annelise.

Chapter 53 Alia Becomes a Done Checkmark

As April 825 rolled around, the fall harvest was going strong. General Thebes reported that every home in Alia now had the low to the ground kitchens installed. Every woman had her own copy of Bethany's Hints and every Ornamented Doll had Eve's Dictionary as well. Diona's ministers were extremely active, often conducting three major meetings a day. Planning was starting to bear fruit with the first of the many new constructions set to begin in a week.

However, Diona knew very well that everything hinged on the normal woman of Alia beginning to take care of her own needs and that of her family as much as possible, according to Bethany's Hints. Adding to the confusion was the return of those families who had abandoned their homes in the city during Erebos' reign and were now returning to Levkos, only to find in a few cases others now occupying their old homes. This situation was deftly handled by Diona, one on one. Usually, she was able to find other housing for those that she had placed in the unoccupied home. Still it was a bothersome waste of valuable time and energy.

Aella's job of working out Women's Ways and then disseminating the knowledge broadly was Diona's primary concern in early April. Vast manpower was tied up just looking after wives and daughters — manpower that would be urgently needed on real production activities come spring, if not sooner. Aella also worked closely with Io, who was dealing with the clothing and apparel situation of Alia. These were the only non-Dolls on Diona's staff, and she placed a high value on their work.

Io, now armed with the newly invented dressmaking tools from Annelise, began experimenting with sewing. As she worked out the best ways and means, she relayed these to Aella, who began disseminating them to other would be seamstresses. Aella and Io began conducting workshops in Women's Ways and soon discovered that other women had not been completely idle. Many began giving Aella additional tips on how a woman could accomplish something.

Winter was just around the corner; late May often brought the first snowfall the winter, which officially began in June. Few women in Alia had decent clothing to wear and almost nothing for winter use. Annelise promised a huge delivery of women's apparel by early May, paid for from Alia's treasury. Diona had as yet to have her Minister of Finance, Rhea, work out how to recoup the cost of the shipment. However, in early April, Alia and Diona received a welcome surprise.

The world famous Alexa Shoe Company of Velona, at my behest, sent a million pairs of their latest styles of women's boots to Alia. Yes, I covered their cost. Their designs, based upon women's needs discovered during the First Plague, now had leather tips above the heels so that a woman could more easily slip the boot off her foot. Otherwise, they were the same old, extremely well made, solid, fleece lined, sturdy boots. Of course, they came with various heels, varying from flats to three-inch heels to five, six, and even seven-inch heels. I rather guessed that the Ornamented Dolls had been wearing the seven-inch heels for quite some time now and that their calves had adjusted, meaning that their feet could no longer go flat. Hence, a fifth of the shipment had these extreme heels. The majority, however, were flats or three-inch in height. My gift was greatly appreciated. Diona wrote me a very nice thank you letter and had followed my suggestion, distributing them at no charge to the women. She did have a short note inserted in each box saying these were compliments of Bethany Bartiana Angela of Velona. In June, via the LD radio, I learned just how valuable this gift had been to the women of Alia. Only a few wealthier women had ever owned a pair of Alexa boots. Now a million women had a taste of pure luxury and the finest in footwear for the winter.

The second surprise came from Io herself. As she began preparing for winter, she, as had all women here, found winter coats a huge problem. The past winter, all women had dealt with heavy coats that did not fit. First, they all had sleeves, which got in the way. Second, they all did not close across their now massive bosoms. Third, the buttons made it impossible for a woman to close her own coat or take it off later if someone buttoned her up somehow. Io needed to solve this critical problem. Using her new Gard sewing machine, she began experimenting, using older, non-satin clothes in the large obsolete clothing room. She devised a clever, heavy cloak, comprised of several layers of material, wrapped around a woolen lining. The cloak fastened primarily at the neck using an oversized hook and eye, borrowed from the building industry. She could easily use her foot to fasten and unfasten the hook. She added another two further down the front, which could be closed if needed.

She was extremely proud when she demonstrated her new design to Diona and the rest of the women at the palace. Furthermore, Diona was able to fasten the cloak herself, though not without a significant struggle. Still, she could do it, though most Ornamented Dolls preferred to allow a non-Doll to help her into her cloak. While there was nothing fancy about the cloak, it was very warm and women could handle it. With Diona's backing, Io rushed it off to the many tailors of Levkos to get them mass-produced and sold before the colder portion of winter struck.

Meanwhile, the tailors had already begun to branch out, making copies of the new Annelise blouses, pants, and skirts for the average woman. Former women seamstresses were also beginning to return to their old craft, but more Gard sewing machines were desperately needed before they could make significant quantities. Hence, Diona subsidized the tailors and seamstresses. She paid for half of the tailor's cost in producing a garment, as long as he sold it for a price that was lowered by the amount of her subsidy. She paid three-quarters of the cost to the women seamstresses as an encouragement for them to keep at it, allowing them to sell their products at the same price as the tailors, giving them a substantial profit on each garment.

When the Annelise shipment of new dresses finally arrived, most of the stock was meant for the wealthier women, who, almost without exception, were Ornamented Dolls, save those who had lived in outlying towns or the port city, where the Ornamentation Project had not been fully implemented. However, Diona also knew that here in Levkos, many middle class women had been also turned into Ornamented Dolls as well. These women would be unable to afford the elegant Ornamented Doll dresses that she and the wealthy were now wearing. Hence, she again subsidized the sale of these fancy dresses to every Ornamented Doll who could not readily afford their rather expensive cost. She received numerous thank you letters for this action.

By wintertime, more and more women were finally seen walking the streets of Levkos. Finally, they had clothing that they could wear and be warm as well. Diona counted this as a small victory.

In contrast, Athena, her Minister of Ornamented Doll Skills, was having a far rougher time. She and her small staff that she chose sifted through the many suggestions for the removal of the neck rings. She'd made that one of her top priorities, based on Alexina herself. However, by mid-April, she realized that there was likely going to be no safe way for the removal of the rings. Already one woman had died when a man had tried to remove hers by sawing them off. He'd accidentally cut her jugular vein in the process.

At last, Athena concluded that the rings would be a fact of life for the Dolls, just as the lip plates were. Resigned to the fact that they would be permanent, she then redoubled her efforts at working out what she began calling Ornamented Doll Skills, adapted in part from Bethany's Hints. By her own experimentation, she discovered that cooking a meal was still possible. Once she had it worked out, she ran an experiment in which she and Io each prepared the same meal. To her dismay, but not unexpected, the two found out that it took Athena three times as long as Io to cook the same meal. Worse, Io complained that it took her five times as long to cook it now as it had done so before she got the plague. Still, Athena was pleased that a Ornamented Doll could still cook.

Feeding remained a significant barrier. Athena had a special spoon made, one with an extremely long handle. As the lip plates continued to enlarge, the handle had to be long enough to reach into the woman's mouth. Still, an Ornamented Doll trying to feed herself was problematical. Unable to bend her neck and forced to sit in perfect posture, her lower vision partially obscured, an Ornamented Doll had to sit slightly askew and use peripheral vision just to see her plate. Then trying to use a spoon in her foot was almost insurmountable. Still, as Diona already knew, another Ornamented Doll could feed an Ornamented Doll. That was possible. Thus, Athena finally wrote up her recommendations for feeding an Ornamented Doll, which required either another Ornamented Doll or another person. She was quite frustrated that she could not even help herself to a drink of water anymore.

Her husband Orpheus came to her rescue. "Dear, I have an idea that might allow you to drink anytime that you want." The next day, he brought his contraption into the dining room and set it up. Essentially, on a raised platform he had a cup with a hole in its bottom. A long tube was affixed to the hole. At the other end, the tube went through a large wooden block. Above the cup was a pronged catch, which would hold the tube's end above the cup's brim.

"Okay, dear. To help yourself to a drink, use your foot to lift the wooden block and lower it into your mouth. The water should flow down and into your mouth. When you have enough, raise the block up higher than the cup. Try it." She did so and got way to much in her mouth, spilling it over her face and dress. But the basic idea worked.

"Needs some refinements, like slower flow, dear, but it works."

"Ah," she replied grinning invisibly. After further experimentation, his invention worked well. While it looked strange seeing this towering cup contraption sitting beside her at the table, she was able to drink water, juice, tea, anything liquid all by herself and without making a mess of it. Diona requested one for herself and then ordered one for every Ornamented Doll in Alia. Orpheus allowed his dad to deal with the manufacturing aspect of his invention. By winter, every Ornamented Doll was able to drink by themselves, as long as someone filled their cups for them. Most homes had several, one containing water while the others were used at meal times. Here in the palace, the four girls now drank their own milk at meal times, much to their pleasure.

Athena decided to continue going down the list of domestic duties that a woman was likely to perform, analyzing which were somehow doable and which were not. As always, she began using Bethany's Hints as a starting point for a given task. Picking up clothes and carrying them to the laundry basket was doable, though the Ornamented Dolls were unable to use their teeth and had to make very awkward motions to pick things up from the floor using their toes. Perfect posture was not all that it seemed, Athena grumbled. She was able to do the laundry and take the sheets off a bed, again devising alternate means than just using one's teeth as we often did. Athena quickly realized that everything would have to be done with her feet and toes. Making the bed became quite a challenge. Having four working together on this task worked well, but one Ornamented Doll alone could do it, if she allowed herself an hour or so to get it done.

Some things proved entirely too difficult to manage. For example, getting the food off the stove and transported to the table, dishing out one's food — these just could not be done by an Ornamented Doll. Likewise, washing dishes was almost undoable, unless one spent an enormous amount of time at it. Vast patience and incredibly awkward motions were required, simply because of the obscuration caused by the lip plates and the inability to bend one's neck.

On the other hand, Bethany's Hints of sitting on one's butt and using one's feet to sweep or scrub a floor was doable, just as the hint suggested. However, the special brushes with leather foot loops were mandatory. Most preferred to wait and see if the fancy vacuum sweepers would pan out as they had in the demonstrations.

Athena wrote a small pamphlet outlining all that she had learned how to do. She included detailed drawings where needed. Diona had it printed off and distributed to every Ornamented Doll in Alia. Meantime, Athena continued to see what else an Ornamented Doll might be able to accomplish. The results on the domestic side were not too great. An Ornamented Doll would always require someone to feed her and to deal with the dishes and the carrying of the dishes to and from the table. Diona sighed; no way could an Ornamented Doll be allowed home alone during the daytime. An Ornamented Doll would always require some kind of help just to survive. Diona cursed loudly, but smiled afterwards. No one could understand what she'd just said.

Armed with this vital data, although Athena would be continuing her exploration of Ornamented Doll's Ways, Diona had to act. Every household with one or more Ornamented Dolls had to have a helper present whenever the men of the household were away. Damn, she cursed again, that was assuming that every household with Ornamented Dolls even had men in them! There were almost two hundred thousand Ornamented Dolls at this point, and each needed an assistant just to survive. Well, Diona already knew that in her heart the very day that she awoke as an Ornamented Doll that she would be mostly helpless in life. Athena's research only confirmed her view.

Diona sat down and began writing out the official notices that she had been dreading having to do for weeks. She sighed, but she could see no other option available to her. One notice she sent to all the Ornamented Dolls, thankful that accurate records had been kept during the Ornamentation Project. It read:

Fellow Dolls,

After significant research into just what domestic activities we can do, I've prepared a little booklet, Athena's Ornamented Doll's Ways outlining them. Soon, you will have received your copy. Yes, we are severely limited and there is no way around the fact that we must have assistance with many things, most notably eating.

Hence, by official proclamation, I am ordering every home that has one or more Ornamented Dolls residing there have an Ornamented Doll Assistant. The rule of thumb is: one Ornamented Doll Assistant is required per every two Ornamented Dolls living in the household. You may have more, if desired, but no Ornamented Doll Assistant is to be assisting more than two Ornamented Dolls.

They will be working from eight in the morning until six at night, but only six days a week. Presumably, your husbands and men can assist you on the remaining day, usually Sunday when no one is working.

The agreed upon salary for an Ornamented Doll Assistant is fifty gold per week. The assistants will be women only. If you are unable to afford the assistant's salary or paying it would create financial hardship, please contact me, the Minister of Ornamented Doll Skills, Athena Stathis, and other arrangements can be made for their salary.

These she had copied and delivered by the soldiers. Next, she wrote out a job wanted advertisement and had copies made and widely distributed throughout Levkos. It read:

Women of Alia, a new working position has just been invented: Ornamented Doll Assistant. After conducting significant research into the realistic capabilities of Ornamented Dolls, it has been found that Ornamented Dolls require a personal assistant to assist them with domestic duties, particularly at mealtimes. The usual job hours will be from eight o'clock in the morning until six at night, six days each week. Meals will be provided at no cost to the assistant. The pay will be uniformly fifty gold per week. Women must be at least twelve years old to apply. Nearly one hundred thousand Ornamented Doll Assistants are needed urgently. Training will be provided at no charge to the applicant. Contact the Minister of Ornamented Doll Skills at the Monarch's Office if you are interested.

Between the two, she hoped that the manpower loss situation would be handled. Well, it might be if only the average woman would begin to do things for herself. Diona wondered if she could so order them, but decided against it for now.

Around the dinner table, her proclamations became the topic of conversation. "Do you really intend to have an Ornamented Doll Assistant for every two of you Ornamented Dolls here at the palace?" asked General Thebes.

Diona attempted to reply in her beginning Annelise. "Yes, I cannot have your ven continuing to feed us. They are needed on vore ivvortant things."

He smiled, "Damn, you are right, you know. I do appreciate this, Diona. You are going to need quite a few women assistants, thought. One for every two of you?"

"Yes, vore, if needed," she replied. She decided to hire a dozen assistants, and at least two should be young girls to help her four girls. While not all of her ministers dined with them, when they did, there would be enough assistants around to help, she thought. Of course, the assistants would also have to learn basic Annelise so that the Ornamented Doll could communicate her needs to her assistant. She'd forgotten to mention that in her advertisement.

Diona was not surprised at the response to her ad. Many young women had already had their careers and futures virtually wiped out by the plague. The promise of fifty gold was a lifesaver, a very significant sum for the needy women of Levkos. Within days, over a hundred applied and began a short training period with Athena, who showed them what kind of things were most likely needed, helping them eat, assisting them with meal preparations, and filling their drinking cups. She also taught them a few basic words in Annelise, hoping that they would start to pick it up on their own or that the Ornamented Dolls, who had begun their language lessons, would work on teaching them. Otherwise, she explained, the Ornamented Doll would have to write out her needs.

By early June, Diona was satisfied with the Ornamented Doll Assistants program. Almost sixty thousand women had joined the program and miraculously it was working out. Here at the palace, the four girls had Donia and Agape as their assistants; they were twelve and thirteen respectively. In addition to helping the girls dine, they often played with them.

Diona's Ornamented Doll Assistant was a young woman named Airlea who was twenty-one. While she had a son who was five, she desperately needed the extra money. Times were tough and Airlea worked hard to please Diona. Her friends had Delia and Hera, twenty and eighteen respectively, to help them dine. The Ornamented Doll Assistants at the palace knew that they were extremely lucky to be in the service of their monarch and did their very best to make life more livable for the Ornamented Dolls. At their first mealtime on their first day on the job, all the assistants were nervous. After all, they had no arms either and would have to use their feet.

As she reported for work that first day, Airlea asked Diona, "Why did you want women to be your Ornamented Doll Assistants and not men who have arms and hands? They can do a much better job of feeding you."

Airlea didn't yet know Annelise, so Diona wrote out: Because this is something that women can do. We need our men working to get electricity plants going so we can all have electric lights, telefonos, and vacuum cleaners. We need them to build the motorized vehicles that we women can drive around by ourselves. These new inventions from Velona will allow all us women to have a much easier time in life. That satisfied Airlea, who later relayed it to the other Ornamented Doll Assistants.

The Church of God was not idle either. Once the key members of the monarch's staff had received their therapy sessions, Homer and his group began working with the ordinary women of Levkos. While in other countries, many of the wealthier women were handled first so that they could in turn learn how to do it and lend a hand with it, here they could not; they were all Ornamented Dolls. Hence, the common folks were handled first. After a woman had received her therapy, erasing the plague and any subsequent trauma, she was asked to learn how to deliver the therapy and offered fifty gold per week for her services. Many had family duties that prevented their participation right away, such as infants and small children. Yet, week by week, the number of Givers of the Holy Gift, as it was being called, grew steadily.

At last, Homer asked that Diona establish a Minister of the Holy Gift to help keep the process running smoothly. Women had to be scheduled a week ahead, records kept, and so on. As he expected, the process slowly began mushrooming. By June 1, a thousand people were being handled each week and almost half of those wanted to join up for a time afterwards, giving this precious gift to other women.

As the heavy snows of winter came, Stefano and I decided to place the checkmark in the done column for Alia. While vast amount of more work needed to be done, we both felt that they were on their way. We could see nothing on the horizon that might threaten their recovery, as long as the MMCE project constructions commenced in the spring. The only reservation I had was Diona's report that still she was forced to allow another twenty women to become Ornamented Dolls each week. On June 1, 825, Alia had one hundred seventy-five thousand six hundred seventy-two Ornamented Dolls. At least there were only twenty more made each week. Perhaps the numbers would soon fall off. Many, I learned were women who were marrying men who held important positions and they saw this as a way to advance their husband's status. Ugh.

Chapter 54 Partholan Intervenes

July of 825 was a time of morning sickness around 42 Hampton Way; at least it was for a few days. We six women were all pregnant once more, including our mothers, but our four two year olds quickly ran therapy sessions on us, eradicating that unpleasant side-effect. We all were due sometime in February 826. I was still very busy, daily fielding LD radio calls from all over Tarra. Usually, I was the go-between and was able to connect the caller with someone who could directly respond to the person's needs.

After we finally decided to checkmark Alia as salvaged, Eve and I sat down before our best known world map on which we'd drawn in Zeederlund. "Well, we now have salvaged and have therapies going in all the countries except four," I pointed out.

"Vladimir, Volksholm, West Reach, Tashien, and all but the extreme southern end of the Western Continent," Eve called out. Vladimir was isolated between two mountain ranges, which separated them from Annelise to the east and the kingdoms of Demokritos to the west. We had been there briefly centuries ago and found wild, generally nomadic horsemen living there. None of us had ever been to the home of the Axemen, Volksholm, in the cold, far north. Little was known of their civilization at all. The island off our northern continent, Cymry or West Reach, was still more or less out of communication with the main land, deep in the throes of their own brand of chaos. The natives of the jungles of Wanakan had vanished without a trace, presumably moving back into the deeper parts of the jungles of the Western Continent. We also knew that there were some small villages along the northeastern coast of the continent, but little else was known. Tashien, well, we all knew the horrors going on there. "Chaos factorial," Eve declared. Certainly, Tashien, with the sole exception of Nan Yan, was in the throes of their Dark Ages. Perhaps these other places were as well.

Until now, my method of salvaging a country depended upon helping those people within a country who reached out for assistance. That is, I was passively helping as opposed to going to a country and putting in or bringing order. I allowed the people living there to begin to pull themselves up out of the mire and then supported them all the way, as opposed to my going there and forcibly pulling them up. Now I was beginning to consider that I might have to intervene directly in these five lands.

The ringing of our telefono interrupted our discussions. Mom called out, "Bethany, Stefano for you." I rose and headed to the living room, where ours hung on the wall. Mom grinned and I wondered what he wanted. She was definitely getting more able; the receiver end floated in the air over towards me and I latched on to it, floating it to my ear, grinning back at her. Yes, mom was definitely getting more and more able as a spiritual being, and I made a note to thank little Bianca, who was now two years old and running mom's and my therapy sessions. Yes, it rather blows one's mind to sit across from a two year old and have them run Advanced Therapy on you.

"Hi Stefano. Bethany here. What's up?"

"You had better get down to the docks as fast as possible. I don't quite know what to make of this. Just come, please," he ended up begging me.

"Come on, Eve, to the docks. Something is up; he didn't say what." She and I raced out of the house to our T-putt-putts. By now, we were experts with them, and in a minute, we left the front gates noisily behind, roaring down Hampton Way. Okay, we appeared to be reckless drivers, but we were honestly in total control as we flew down the streets, dodging the other traffic and vehicles. We arrived at the docks in about five minutes.

As we climbed off them close to where Stefano was standing, we saw why he'd called us. A greyish colored man stood on the edge of the docks, his arms folded across his chest. He wore only a loincloth, but he was a giant. I estimated that he was twenty feet tall and extremely well-muscled, his grey form glistening in the morning sunlight. Work at the docks had halted; everyone stared up at this spectacle.

"Partholan!" I exclaimed, as I recognized the being, not the body. All of us failed to see the Axeman long boat docked just behind him.

"Wow!" Eve added.

His voice bellowed, "Bethany. Good to see you again." Of course, coming from a body that large, nearby windowpanes rattled. Eve and I walked on up to him. "Macario said that you prefer talking to a solid form. This is the one that I used to use a millennia ago."

"Cool. It's just a bit big for us," I hinted. As we watched, his giant form shrank down until he was our size, with a proportionate decrease in his voice's volume, thankfully. "Yes, that's better. What can I do for you?"

"My people on Cymry need help. Axemen need help. They both are ready for your aid," he replied. Only now did we both see two burly Axemen standing behind him, their long boat with many others docked behind those two.

"Well, would you all like to step into my office?" Stefano broke in. "I'm Monarch Stefano West Po. My offices are not far from here." He definitely did not want to be left out of this one. The whole city would be buzzing over Partholan's appearance this evening.

"Yes, we all need to talk, though I find talking so incredibly slow," he replied.

Show off Eve and her big mouth interjected, "We have become really able now. Try us, Partholan." Wham, he did just that. In one instant, the entire purpose of his surprise visit flooded into our minds at a rate that was almost impossible to absorb.

Humbly, Eve answered, "Okay, you win. Perhaps just a little bit slower, Partholan."

The gray man broke into a hearty laugh. "You are doing better though, Eve. Come, for the sake of the Axemen, let us talk this out." Eve grinned, pivoted, and strutted towards Stefano's nearby office; the rest of us followed her lead.

Chapter 55 Just as Likely as Berwyn's Girls

In Dunloy Caern, Tewdwr, Cymry, two days before the plague struck, Berwyn Goronwy hauled his small fishing boat ashore. After securing it alongside of fifty others, he hefted his day's catch over his shoulder and began his two-mile walk home. The fishing village of Aran Glen cradled the large cove, home to perhaps five hundred. Just two miles further inland and atop the rocky bluff overlooking Aran Glen and the vast western sea lay Dunloy Caern, a town of some ten thousand people. Many men in Dunloy Caern kept fishing boats down at Aran Glen.

Berwyn's fortunes were often discussed in the local pubs. The forty year old, red headed man and his red headed wife, Angwen, frequently became the topic of gossip. Why? They had five red headed daughters and no sons. Many thought that was most peculiar and the odds of such happening were frequently used in other arguments. "Just as likely as Berwyn's girls" had become the catch phrase for all manner of unlikely events among these people. Yet after so many years of ribbing, the family had become mostly immune to it. After all, what could they do about it? Five daughters was what they had begat.

Tegan was the oldest, followed by Rhiannon, Megan, Nesta, and Carys. Their respective ages were sixteen down to twelve. After the rough birth of Carys, Angwen found that she could no longer bear more children, dashing forever Berwyn's faint hope of having a son. Of course, the five girls all had flaming red hair and except for split ends trims, their hair had never been cut. Carys often teased Tegan about her hair because it was the longest, falling to her thighs. All had freckles like their mother; yet they were all rather attractive with round faces and greenish eyes.

There were around twenty-five hundred homes in Dunloy Caern and half that number more shops and businesses. The wealthier lived near the hundred-foot rocky bluff that overlooked the small fishing bay far below. Their homes were stone cut granite, both large and plush. The poorer section of town lay on the western edge, where the homes were built from stones removed from farmer's fields and mortared together. Thatched roofs predominated in these single story dwellings. At the very western edge of the town lay the Goronwy home, a modest stone and mortar home. Because he had no sons and now that his five daughters were teenagers, Berwyn could barely make ends meet. Consequently, behind their home, he had prepared a large garden spot, painstakingly digging the rocks from the ground and using them to make a foot-tall wall around their plot. Angwen and the girls raised all their fresh vegetables here and seldom bought produce in the markets.

Just beyond their home, many farmers tilled the land. The green hillside was covered with twisting, stone fences outlining each farmer's plots. However, Berwyn also had a small stone half-shed in which he kept fifty sheep. The half-shed was enclosed on three sides with a roof, but totally open on the other. Here the sheep took shelter in bad weather. Daily, Tegan and Rhiannon led the flock out of the pen and walked them two miles to some rolling, green grasslands, so widespread throughout Tewdwr. Their border collie, Lyn, helped the girls manage their flock.

In the spring, Berwyn sheered the sheep, and Angwen and the girls spun it into wool and later sold it for cotton bolts from which they made their dresses. Hand-me-down dresses were the rule in this household, though the girls seldom complained. They were good at needlework and always took the time to adorn their own white cotton dresses with lively and bright designs, usually quite colorful indeed.

To help make ends meet, Berwyn also went fishing at least three times a week. Most of the catch Angwen and the girls dried, storing it for the wintertime. The entrails were dumped on their garden patch, enriching the rocky soil. Berwyn did light carpentry for other families around the town, usually twice a week earing extra coins, which the family needed. During the summertime, the girls took long walks far inland, returning with baskets of berries. Later in the fall, they brought back baskets of various nuts, all stored for the winter. Industrious family? Yes.

Tegan, being the eldest, often took charge of the girls, making their plans and seeing that their work or tasks were done both timely and correctly. Carys did the most complaining, always wanting to play with the other children her age. Megan was into the local gossip and frequently spent time gabbing with other teens and their neighbors, often neglecting her chores, much to Tegan's dismay. Still, their family was close-knit, unlike many others around them. Then, the plague struck, changing everything.

The day before, the six complained of extremely tired arms. Carys swore that her arms were much shorter and thinner, but Berwyn insisted that was just her imagination. Angwen's shriek of stark terror woke the five teens that awful morning. Space was at a premium in the Goronwy house. Of necessity, the five teens shared the largest room, though each had a narrow bed and their own chair, dresser, and clothes wardrobe. Their parents slept in the small bedroom off the living room, while their room adjoined both the dining room and the kitchen-pantry.

Her mother's screams woke Tegan up. She used her arms as always to push herself upright in bed. Today, nothing happened; her body didn't move. She tried it again, still nothing. Then she looked at herself. Her arms were completely gone, as if she had never had them. She screamed, waking her sisters, who momentarily also began screaming. Although they were not paying attention, screams could also be heard from more distant homes around theirs to the east. Amid the cacophony, Tegan heard a loud thump, as if someone or something heavy had fallen onto the wooden floor. "Dad?" she began yelling, cancelling her general screams. "Shut up. Something else is wrong!" she yelled to her sisters. Mechanically, the four obeyed her. "Dad?" she yelled again. She heard some kind of sliding noise above her mother's continuous shrill screeches. Then their door opened. She expected to see her father standing there, but he was on his hands and knees, blood flowed from his nose.

"Oh my god! Not you girls too?" he wailed and collapsed onto the wooden planks of their floor. Tegan struggled to get out of bed. As she put her feet onto the floor, she discovered that they too had been altered, twisted into some strange U-shape. Still, she could stand. The other four also struggled to their feet.

"What's happened to us? My arms are gone. My feet are weird," Carys called out the obvious. "But I can stand up too. What happened to my arms?"

"Come on, dad's bleeding!" Tegan ordered, and she made her way carefully over to him. She bent down to help him, but had no arms or hands to do anything at all and she began crying at last. Hearing Tegan crying caused all the others to begin bawling as well. After all, if Tegan could not handle this, they certainly couldn't. Tegan was always in charge. Her dad rose and sat up, holding his nose.

His nasal sounding voice said, "I fell over. My feet are broken somehow. Your mother has no arms too. Come, see if you can get into the kitchen where there is more light. I'll bring your mother." He turned and crawled off to their smaller bedroom, leaving a trail of blood drops behind him. The teens walked very slowly and carefully into the kitchen, where the early morning sunlight brightened up the room. Once there, they looked back into the dining room and saw a huge pile of foreign objects lying in the middle of the floor. Naturally, the teens went to inspect them. They were busily examining them, when Berwyn led their mother into the room, on their way to the kitchen.

Angwen was hysterical. At least she had stopped screaming, Tegan thought. "Partholan has come for us! I just know it. He is taking our bodies piece by piece down into the Underworld! Berwyn! Can you see him? Where is he now? Is he going for my legs next?" She continued on hysterically claiming all manner of ills were befalling them. Now the teens could see their dad's feet, which were pointed downward and inflexible. He could not walk on them, unless he stood on the very tips of his toes, which he couldn't. Hence, he crawled.

He paused to look at the large pile of objects in the middle of the room. Then, he just sat down and stared off into space. Tegan was an intelligent young woman. Her mother was carrying on about the Underworld. She'd never seen such and didn't believe a word of it. Rather, she was intrigued by the strange objects. The teens saw six yokes of various sizes, hairbrushes, writing desks, and of course all the kitchen items. Then they spotted the shoes. All five dove for the shoes, commenting about how weirdly shaped they were. It was not hard for them to see which ones belonged to which teen; their feet were different sizes.

"Well, now this is better," Tegan proclaimed as she stood up. "Come on, get yours on somehow. I feel more secure in them and my feet have stopped hurting."

"I bet that we have gotten the plague!" Rhiannon suddenly burst out. "It's just like the carnival ladies were telling us last month." She was referring to the annual carnival that came to town, putting on a show. One of them had told them all manner of wild stories about the alien plague that had struck Velona and elsewhere last year.

"You're right, sis. That must be what has happened to us," Tegan concurred.

"But I want my arms back. I have to go pee," Carys complained. "Badly," she added. Tegan was about to rebuff her and tell her to go pee by herself when she realized that Carys would not be able to get her panties down by herself. Now she also had to go.

"Come on, all of you. We have to help each other with the pot," Tegan ordered. The five teens shuffled slowly into their bedroom and followed Tegan's example of removing another's panties with her teeth. "Don't you dare pee in my face, Carys," she ordered.

All were wearing their baggy nightgowns. As Rhiannon helped Tegan remove hers, Tegan noticed that her bosom seemed heavier and larger than she remembered. "Sis, see if you can also pull my nightgown over my head for me." The two struggled, and quickly Megan and Nesta joined Rhiannon. Together, they got Tegan's off.

"Oh my god! Tegan! Look at yours!" exclaimed Megan, shocked to see her older sister's now massive breasts.

"My god! They are as big as my head!" Tegan exclaimed.

"Help me see mine," Rhiannon asked. Before long, all five had their nightgowns off and were staring at their breasts and those of their sisters.

"Look at me! I've got real big ones too," Carys exclaimed excitedly. Secretly for weeks, she had been looking at her small breasts, hoping that they would get bigger like Tegan's. Now Tegan's were giant melons and her small ones were vastly larger as well, pleasing the youngest teen. Now Carys noticed Tegan's hair. "Tegan! Your hair! Look, it has really grown!" the twelve year old announced.

All noticed their hair now. Uniformly, everyone's hair had grown two feet. Their flaming, slightly curly locks fell down to their ankles. "Wow!" Tegan uttered.

"Way great!" Carys added, glad that hers was now as long as Tegan's.

"We'd better see if we can get our dresses on," Tegan suggested. "Wait, they won't fit over our breasts anymore. We will have to alter them."

"But how? Our arms are gone. We can't do anything anymore," Rhiannon protested, realizing just how helpless the five were now.

"Damn!" Tegan said without thinking.

"I'm going to tell dad that you cussed, Tegan," Carys teased.

"We'd better see if we can slip back into our nightgowns. I think that we are all going to have to help each other into them," Tegan explained.

Later, they joined their parents in the kitchen. Angwen now sat on a chair in complete shock. She was at least silent now. Their dad looked oblivious, staring at the ceiling, humming a dance tune. "Dad! Dad! Wake up! We need help," Tegan cried out, bumping lightly into him with her leg.

"Huh? Help? Oh!" he snapped back into the present. "My god, what has happened to us all?"

"We think it must be that plague the carnival women were talking about last week. Remember, dad?" Tegan said.

Coming more to the present, he replied, "Yes, I suppose that would explain it. Damn, we have the plague! This is a disaster! How you all must be suffering! God, you have lost your arms and are helpless now, like your mother. This will ruin us utterly. Whatever will we do now? They said that there was no cure for it, didn't they? Will it get worse? Will I lose my arms too? Will your feet freeze up like mine? If so, you cannot even crawl! Maybe I should crawl off to the doctor's. Maybe he will have something that will help."

"I don't think so, dad. Remember what they said?" Tegan replied. "What is all that stuff in the dining room for? In the pile, we found good shoes that help us walk. There are still two pairs of shoes left. I think that they are for you and mom."

"Help you walk? Now that is encouraging. Okay, let's go see," he suggested, getting back down on all fours to crawl.

As their father tried on the boots, the girls began seeing uses for the many items. They were always curious anyway, now even more so. Until this moment, they had few personal possessions. There just wasn't funds available for anything other than necessities of life. Here was a huge pile of things and their inquisitive natures took control. One by one, they ascertained the use or purpose of item. "We're supposed to carry things with these yokes," Tegan suggested.

"These must be our new hairbrushes. Look, our feet go into the leather loops," Rhiannon guessed.

"Looks like we have a whole new kitchen, but everything is so low to the ground," Megan pointed out.

"Maybe so we can use our feet to reach the pots and stir something," Nesta elaborated. So it went, the five rapidly worked out that these items were supposed to make life possible for themselves now. Berwyn was unable to stand or walk in the boots and gave up, preferring the stability of crawling. After fixing everyone some breakfast and allowing his girls to see if they could somehow feed themselves, he attempted to feed Angwen, who was almost oblivious to the world. She just could not accept the stark new reality thrust upon her.

After eating, the girls headed outside to see if anyone else had the plague. They could not do the dishes, and their dad promised to do their usual chore. The five walked very slowly out of their house and into the street, shuffling along with the tiniest of steps. Tegan suggested that they listen to their neighbors, if possible. When they returned, they told their dad that they were the only ones outside. Further, they had heard scary noises from every house they had passed. All agreed that likely the whole town of Dunloy Caern had come down with the plague.

By suppertime, Angwen had finally begun speaking once more. "He's coming, you know. The Lord of the Underworld is here. He is in the shadows. He is everywhere now. First, it is our arms. Next, he'll be taking our feet or maybe our legs. He wants us to suffer, don't you know? He's been here for quite some time. Maybe years, only we didn't recognize him. He's in the shadows so we can't see him." She rattled on about secret things and soon no one listened to her any longer.

The next day, Berwyn spent the day installing the new kitchen, using the available space along one wall. He was loathed to remove their old stove, oven, and sink. He did move their many supplies to the lower shelves and put some into the new cabinets that rested on the floor. Still, he did the cooking and chores for everyone. The third day brought no further changes. Legs were still as they were. Hence, Berwyn decided to crawl around outside to see if he could learn any news. Tegan had him wrap heavy towels around his knees, which allowed him to do more crawling over the paving stone streets without tearing up his knees more than they now were.

He returned hours later and backed up Tegan's notion that the whole town was infected. "We have plenty of food, so we can hole up here for weeks," he outlined his only idea. Sit tight and hope that help would come. Tegan didn't buy this idea. According to the woman at the carnival, whole countries were infected last year, not just a small town. She doubted very much that any help would becoming at all.

On the third day, Tegan said, "Dad, we must get the sheep to pasture. By now they are starving."

"But how can you?" he asked, his eyes watering again.

"We only have to walk them. Besides, Lyn can herd them. He knows the way," Tegan explained.

He knew that she was right. They had to be fed and watered. "All five of you go. Help each other."

They found walking was terribly slow now and precarious. More than once, Tegan found herself losing her balance and flailing around with her arms, which were not there. "That's so weird," she explained.

"I know. I keep trying to use my arms. It seems like they are there, but they aren't," Rhiannon added. With the help of their dog, the five got the sheep watered and the two miles up to their pasture area.

"Spooky," Carys whispered as they brought the flock home near sunset. The once bustling streets were eerily quiet. All day long, they had not seen another person outside.

"On the fourth day, a few neighbors came outside. The men ventured only a short distance from their homes, but several women braved the treacherous walking to check on their closer neighbors. Slowly word spread that everyone was infected. Many kept asking if more body parts had disappeared. None reported losing anymore, which Tegan took as a promising sign.

As the days passed, their mother continued to rant and rave about invisible creatures, secret societies, secret gods, and the like. On the tenth day, Angwen rose and seemed normal; she put on the special shoes and went outside for a walk. However, she said nothing to Berwyn or her girls, though they pestered her with questions. Angwen shuffled slowly and precariously through the streets of Dunloy Caern, heading for the eastern edge and the homes of the wealthier folks.

Tegan and Rhiannon decided to follow her. "What is mom up to?" Rhiannon asked.

"I don't know, but I don't like the way that she is ignoring us," Tegan replied.

Angwen took an hour to get to the very edge of town. She stood near the edge of the tall, rocky cliffs. Far down below, the ocean waves rushed onto shore only to seep back out once more. Sea gulls called, the day was cloudy, and rain was coming, as it usually did here in Tewdwr.

As Tegan and Rhiannon got closer, they heard their mother call out, "Lord of the Shadows, you will not get me! I know you. I see you. You can't have me!" She took another step forward and fell off the cliff. Tegan and Rhiannon watched in horror as their mother dropped from their sight. A bit later, they heard a loud smashing sound and knew that their mother had died from the fall. Shocked, the two headed home, unable even to cry.

Once inside, Berwyn asked why their faces were ghastly white. Tegan mechanically told him what they had seen. Only then, did their tears finally start to flow; their dad held him in his arms and cried as well.

In the days that followed, the girls continued to hear horror stories of other men and women who jumped off the cliff, though mostly it was women who committed suicide. After that, some of their neighbors began to run low on food. It was well known that the Goronwy family always stockpiled food, since they had so little funds to purchase more during the cold, harsh winters. Daily some desperate man would come by and beg Berwyn for a bit of fish or grain. Always, Berwyn sent the man way with something to help tide the man and his family over. "Better days will be coming," he continually told those who came to beg. Tegan didn't believe him. How could days be better?

Finally, Mayor Bledig ordered the able-bodied men with boats to crawl down to the bay and go fishing. "Look, we are all running out of meat. You have to bring back a large catch and share it with everyone equally," he ordered.

"I don't see you crawling down there and going fishing," one man called out. The mayor ignored him. Berwyn did his duty, but wrapped towels around his knees before leaving near dawn.

"Don't worry about us, dad," Tegan encouraged him. "We can cook our breakfast and lunch.

We'll try to have supper waiting for you when you get back. Catch lots of fish."

Fifty men joined him that first day. Most had bloody knees when they returned that night. The catch was good, and Berwyn had brought back a large sack of fish. However, Mayor Bledig and his rich men confiscated all but one fish, allowing him to bring that one home to his girls.

"That's not fair! He didn't do a damn thing to catch the fish!" Nesta complained bitterly. All five agreed and Mayor Bledig became the topic of conversation for days afterwards. Yet, things only got worse.

By December, half of the town was dangerously low on food. That half, of course, were the wealthier, who had always been able to purchase their supplies from the other half and the outlying farmers. Now, no farmers had come since the plague. Mayor Bledig and his armed men came crawling to the Goronwy home demanding large quantities of their food. "You are obviously hoarding food that we need. Hand it over, Berwyn," he ordered. Against six guns, he could do nothing. However, these men had never been in their home and didn't know where they kept their yearly supplies. All that they stole were the small amounts that they had taken out of their underground root cellar.

After that, they took Tegan's advice and took pains to hide their food supplies in various places around the house, including at the bottom of each girl's clothes chests. Later, Mayor Bledig ordered him to go fishing twice a week, even though winter was coming and the waters were now dangerously cold. Soon the bay would be iced in for the long winter. Again, all that he had to show for his entire day's work was one fish, a small one at that.

When January came, everyone's feet returned to normal. Finally, farmers braved the cold and snow to bring part of their harvest into town. Berwyn was never so grateful to see the farmers as that first day. All the pressure was off him and they settled down to enjoy the wintertime inside their home. Of course, Berwyn knew that come spring, he would be in big trouble. So did Tegan. Somehow, they needed to lay in another ten cords of firewood or else purchase a load of coal for the next winter. They needed to plow and plant their garden. They needed to lay in a large supply of fish for the next fall, gutting and drying them. They needed to sheer their sheep, card the fleece, and spin it into woolen thread to sell. Nuts and berries had to be gathered and turned into jams. So much work to do just to be ready for the next winter, but now Angwen was gone, as were the five girls' arms, leaving Berwyn to do the work of seven.

"Dad, somehow we must learn to do what we used to do, we must dad, we must," Tegan pleaded. Carys didn't see how they could, but all five promised to do their best.

When spring came and the snows melted, the town came alive once more in a grim sort of way. Many bodies were found below the cliff and a mass grave was prepared for all those who fell. Additionally, a sizeable number of other dead were carried out of homes and transported down the hill, buried in the mass grave. Mayor Bledig formally announced that one thousand three hundred sixty-two had died since the start of the plague. One thousand one hundred six of them were women. Most of the men were above fifty years old.

During the winter, men dressed the women in their homes. The common cotton dresses laced up their backs. With the massive bosoms, the laces just barely spanned the gap. Although very ill fitting, at least they were dressed. By springtime, the five teens had finally worked out how to work together to lace and tie their own dresses. Slowly but surely, they were becoming independent once again. Yet, they had no idea that they alone of the women in Dunloy Caern were doing all these things. The other women and girls still had the men in their homes doing everything for them. Necessity drove these five.

With the return of warmer weather, the girls were out and about nearly every day. Bit by bit, other women and girls appeared as well. Megan resumed her gossiping activities, learning all manner of "secrets." These, she shared with her sisters each evening as they took turns brushing out each other's long hair.

Often one or more of the girls were seen using their yokes to transport either food supplies or wool spindles to and from the stores. Slowly, other women began to grasp the fact that they too could carry things this way. By fall, Tegan reported seeing six other women out on the streets using their yokes to carry produce.

However, all was not rosy for others in the town. One evening, Carys reported, "Did you know that they found old Cledwyn dead inside his home today?"

"No, how did he die?" Berwyn asked.

"Don't know, but they also found his wife and two daughters and son dead too. They think that he died a couple weeks before they did," Carys enthusiastically added.

"How can they tell that?" asked Tegan in disbelief.

Her dad answered, "His body was probably more decayed than theirs, Tegan. Like the fish that we sometimes find on shore."

After this, Tegan began keeping track of other deaths. She was surprised to learn that townsfolk were still dying. At last, it dawned on her. If the man of the house died, the women who also lived there would slowly perish because they were unable to do anything for themselves. However, she had no time to go from house to house trying to convince the women there that they could do many things. She and her sisters were constantly busy from dawn to dusk. Tegan pointed out, "We are spending at least five times longer doing the same things that we used to do."

"Yes, but you are doing them, Tegan. Kids, always remember that, you are doing them," Berwyn complimented them. "I don't care how long it takes, just that it is getting done. I am very proud of you all. Without your constant help, we will be in bad trouble this winter. I, too, am working as hard as I possibly can. Somehow kids, we will make it, we must."

Like Tegan, Rhiannon's curiosity was roused by the unexpected deaths. She decided to start keeping a record of them. Whenever she went to the markets, she made discrete inquiries. By the time that the winter of 824 began, she looked at her tallies. Another sixty men and boys had died, but more importantly, four hundred six women and girls had perished as well! Even more curiously, most all these came from the wealthier families on the east side of town. Hardly anyone had died here on the west side. Rhiannon didn't quite know what to make of all this, except that way too many women were perishing. That would soon change.

As the first snowfall came, Berwyn came home more solemn than the girls had ever seen before. "From now on, girls, never, ever leave this house!"

"Why? What's going on, dad?" Tegan asked, growing concerned. He'd never said such a thing before.

"Mayor Bledig and his gang are kidnaping women and taking them," he replied hesitantly.

"Taking them where? Why? What is he doing that for?" Rhiannon asked.

"There is no easy way to tell you this. He's setup a whorehouse in the old Wynn house."

"Why?" Megan asked.

"It seems that the rich of Dunloy Caern have lost many of their women. Men have needs and the Mayor is capitalizing on those needs — despicable. I've heard that he's taken Atwan and Isolde."

"Can't the rest of you go rescue them and free them?" Tegan asked.

"They have guns and we don't. I want you girls to promise me that you will stay indoors from now on, please," he begged. The five reluctantly promised to do so.

Things got worse however. A few days later, Berwyn returned home early. He had been tending their flock of sheep and shouldn't have come back until dark. "What's wrong, dad?" Tegan asked, fearing the worst.

"Major Bledig just stole our whole flock of sheep! Said that they needed them for meat this winter. I couldn't stop him; they had six long guns on me. Maybe it is time for us to leave here," he said solemnly.

"Where would we go?" Megan asked. He shrugged his shoulders, having no idea where they could go, particularly in the winter when travel was difficult.

Instead, he put his skills to work making their front door secure. He fastened a heavy wooden bar across it, which the girls could manage to put in place by working together. Each night, he put it in place before they retired. For a time, they felt a little safer. Berwyn did not. He continued to fret and worry. His girls could be kidnaped and forced into a life of forced prostitution, something he feared more than his own death, but what else could he do? He had no gun, just knives used in fishing and carpentry.

For the next few days, he mysteriously left the home, but insisted they bar the door once he had left. "Only open the door if I knock three times, then twice, then once. Don't answer or say a peep until you hear that knocking pattern. Who knows what they will try to do to get at you girls? Play it safe, okay?" He made all five promise, no matter what they heard through the door.

After he left, Carys asked fearfully, "What does he mean by no matter what we heard through the door?"

Tegan sighed, "They might be torturing him to make us let them inside here."

"Why would they do this to us? We haven't hurt anyone?" Nesta asked.

"They are men, that's why," Tegan vented. "Men cannot control what's in their pants. They think they can bed us anytime they want."

"Even that cute Alun?" asked Carys, not quite believing her older sister. Surely all men were not wicked and evil.

Tegan shrugged. "Right now, who knows? Dad is really scared. Haven't you noticed? I've never seen him this worried, not even when mom was having such a hard time giving birth to Aled who died before he was born. Dad is really frightened, Carys."

"I'll kill any man who tries to bed me!" declared Rhiannon.

"How?" Megan wanted to know. "We are kind of limited in what we can do now."

"I don't know, kick them in their privates really hard, maybe," she growled, realizing that Megan was right. Against men with arms, what could they do to stop them?

Tegan added, "She's right, kick them there and then when they are howling, we jump them and kick them and stomp them to death. That's what we'll do! Work together; we are a team." Her sisters all promised to do so.

As the slow winter days dragged onward, Berwyn continued to go out occasionally for more news. He told them that several of the kidnaped women were found dead below the cliffs. He didn't reveal that they were found naked, though. "Emlyn and Nye are forming a defense network, but I don't see what pitchforks can do against the mayor's guns," he announced one day. "They took young Glenys yesterday. Elgan was killed trying to stop them." He also told them that he found a dozen other men and young boys at the bottom of the cliff. All had been shot.

A week later, he reported that Emlyn and Nye had gone into hiding and that his wife Ceiwen and Nye's eldest, Almeda, had been taken. Slowly as the winter progressed, more and more evil news reached the ears of the five sisters. Doom hung over the Goronwy home just as the dark, snow filled clouds hung over Dunloy Caern.

Then in early April as the ice in the bay began to break up, the long anticipated, greatly feared knock came upon their door. "Berwyn, we've come for your daughters. Be a good fellow and save yourself. Open up and you won't be killed like the others," Mayor Bledig's harsh, bass voice broke the girl's soft chatter around the kitchen stove. They were attempting to bake more bread. Berwyn grabbed a butcher knife in his right hand and a sharp fish-gutting knife in his left.

"You girls go to your room. Bar the door," he ordered. They scampered across the kitchen, heading for their room as fast as they could run. Berwyn didn't answer the mayor.

The frightened girls heard pounding on the front door. Tegan whispered, "Please door, hold!" For a time the door did hold. Through the stone walls, the girls heard the men talking.

One man said, "We could smash in the windows."

Another suggested, "We could smoke them out. Climb onto the roof and plug that chimney."

"Nah, too dangerous. Might fall. This is one of those thatched roofs, way too dangerous," someone else answered.

The mayor's voice broke in, get that log over there, we'll smash down the door. Come on; put your worthless backs into it!" Shortly after that, the girls heard heavy thumping on the door, then the sound that they dreaded: wood splintering.

Berwyn was ready for them. He stood at the side of the door. When the log finally splintered the door, a man with his long gun held in his hands poked his head inside. Berwyn plunged the fish knife deep into the man's neck, severing his jugular vein. He dropped his gun, letting out a terrified noise, which sounded like a cross between a gurgle and a muffled scream. He slumped to his knees and then collapsed over the remains of the door just inside.

Meanwhile the others outside saw Berwyn's arm and thus his location. They couldn't shoot him through the thick stone wall to the left of the door. "Rush him boys!" the mayor ordered. Berwyn took a deep breath. He heard a man beginning to run and he tried to time it right. As the man came rushing through the door, he had to watch his footing over the dying man. Berwyn struck again, plunging the butcher knife into the man's belly. The man twisted but Berwyn held on to the knife, which now ripped through the man's guts like a fish. He went down, his insides flopping bloodily on the wooden floor. However, the action had exposed Berwyn. Three gunshots rang out, hitting the man. His body involuntarily jerked in three slightly different directions and then slumped onto the pile of dead or dying men. One of the shots had entered his forehead; Berwyn was dead before he landed on the gutted man.

"Drag'em out of the way. Let's get what we come for, boys," the mayor's harsh voice broke the stillness, scaring the teens even more. What had happened to their dad? They heard dragging noises, and then booted footsteps entering their home. Suddenly, their bedroom door burst open. Carys screamed.

The men rushed in, but the girls put up a fight. Kicking and screaming, the five girls were slapped around, grabbed, and tossed over the men's shoulders like sacks of grain. Still they kicked and screamed, yelling for help from the other townsmen all the way across the town to the mayor's very large stone home. Many faces peered out of windows, even few doors opened a crack, but no one came to their rescue. Tegan cursed them all, "Damn all of you to Underworld. May Partholan take you down with him!"

Still wiggling, screaming, and kicking, the five teens were carried inside and tossed unceremoniously onto the floor, bruising them severely. Then the door slammed, leaving them in the dim lantern light of a very large room, filled with beds close together. They stopped screaming and began sobbing, but soon noticed seven other young women sitting on nearby beds. All were naked.

"It'll be all right, at least they feed you," one older woman whispered. Tegan recognized her. She was Almeda, a twenty-three year old mother who lived with her family three houses down from theirs.

Raelyn, who was a good friend of Tegan's, whispered. "She's right. They at least feed us twice a day, Tegan. They killed Almeda's husband and son. Have you seen my dad? Mom died last year."

The offer of news brought the sobbing teens out of their grief slightly. Carys asked, "Why don't you have your clothes on?"

Raelyn replied, "They took them off us and there is no one to put them back on us. Besides, they take us away at night and rape us, sometimes several times a night. But they do come and feed us twice a day. Bastards!"

"What's the matter with Myfanwy?" asked Rhiannon, who had looked at the seven women and saw the twenty-two year old just sitting and staring into space. She wasn't even aware of the arrival of the five new red heads.

Almeda answered, "They killed her husband and threw her baby over the cliff. She's been like that ever since. She doesn't even eat, but they like to rape her the most, probably because she's the prettiest woman in Dunloy Caern."

"Why don't you escape? Run out of here?" asked Tegan, who was becoming more and more angry. Her grief had given way to open hostility. Somehow, these bastard men had to be punished.

"We are helpless, just as you are. Since the plague, we can't do anything at all," Raelyn answered her. Tegan sat there utterly dumbfounded by her reply. She and her sisters were anything but helpless.

Just then, the door opened and a man came in carrying a pot and a pitcher. "Food time, whores," he said gruffly. One by one, the women lined up on one bed. He spoon fed each woman one bite at a time, going down the line. When he reached the end, he went back and gave the first woman in the line her next bite. The sisters just stared in compete disbelief. "You five had better get in line if you want anything to eat. When the pot's empty, that's all there is." Dutifully, the five joined the line, though they saw that Myfanwy never opened her mouth as he brought the spoon up to her lips. After a brief pause, he move on down to Tegan, who accepted the food.

"God, this is horrible. Who the hell cooked this mush?" she declared, but decided not to spit it out.

"Don't like it, you don't have ta eat it, whore," he replied gruffly.

Once done, he left, shutting the door. Now the women chatted at length with the new arrivals. Tegan decided to learn all that she could about this place and what went on, though it shocked her to hear such things.

That evening, men entered and took several women out of the room. One was Tegan. She discovered that most of the rooms in the mayor's large home had been converted into bedrooms. Her clothes were removed and left with the others. She was pushed back onto the bed by the mayor. "Okay Tegan, isn't it? Well, I am going to initiate you into my lucrative brothel personally." He began to strip before her.

"You bastard! May Partholan take you to the Underworld!" she cursed him. As he neared the bed, she spat on him, which only made him angrier. As he tried to come down upon her, she kicked him in his privates as hard as she could. The mayor doubled over in pain. She struggled to her feet and began stomping on him. Just then, the door opened and two men entered. They slapped her silly, grabbed her, throwing her over their shoulders. Kicking and fighting, they threw her back into the holding room, calling her a bitch.

"What happened?" asked Rhiannon. Her sisters gathered around Tegan. She told them what she had done and the five laughed. Megan found the water pitcher and began washing off her sister.

"You will have some bad bruises where they slapped you, I'm afraid. I got your nose to stop bleeding, though," Megan explained.

A while later, the mayor opened the door. "Tegan, you and your sisters will get no food for a week until you learn to behave!" He slammed the door shut.

True to his word, when the man returned the next day with the pot of food, he refused to feed the five. At least that night, no one came to take the sisters away and rape them. However, by now the five were starving. "Okay, when it gets late, I am going to go out there and get us some food!" Tegan declared.

"But you can't! We are helpless," Raelyn countered.

"I most certainly am not helpless! Impaired, yes. Helpless, no way!" Tegan replied.

"I'm coming too, you need help," Rhiannon declared.

When they thought that everyone was asleep, the two rose and went to the door. Using their feet, they undid the latch and peered out. No one was around. Off they went, sneaking around the large home. "Follow your nose," Tegan whispered. Soon, they found the kitchen and pantry. They spotted the filthy pot, which the man had used earlier to feed the others. However, they also found the mayor's private stash of the best food. Tegan grabbed a whole loaf of fresh bread and Rhiannon bit down into a whole round of cheese. Satisfied, the two headed back to their room. Megan opened the door as they came tiptoeing back inside with their find.

578

While the five took turns eating their fill, the other women watched in disbelief. "Come on; you can have some too. It's lots better than that filth they feed you," Tegan offered.

As the days went by, the bonds between the captives grew stronger and stronger. Tegan and Rhiannon continued their nightly pantry raids, bringing back more and more food, which actually helped the others regain their strength. Tegan also began to sabotage things. She sprinkled one man's gun powder into the cold stove. She poured a bit of water into another man's powder bag. Rhiannon got in on the fun, putting some oil down several gun barrels, wondering what would happen when they fired them.

The next morning, they awoke to an explosion as the stove blew up when the man started the fire. He was badly burned and the mayor just had him tossed over the cliff, joining the pile of bodies left there during the winter. Not long after that, Myfanwy died in her sleep; she'd starved herself to death. Her body was carried out and tossed over the cliff as well.

Fortunately for the sisters, business was dying off. Spring had come and the usual customers now had to deal with springtime chores. The mayor had tried to rape Tegan again and met with a similar fate. This time, his men severely beat her before tossing her back into the bedroom. That night, Tegan began praying to Partholan. "Please hear my prayers, mighty Partholan. I need your help."

Two houses down from the mayor's lived the widow Euren Yestin and her son Rees, who was twenty. Her husband had died in a fall just after the plague came. Rees was now caring for his mother in his place. Rees reported, "Mom, they've taken the Goronwy sisters this time — all five of them. Shot Berwyn dead."

"Damn Bledig to Partholan! He has always been kind to us Rees. Those girls of his — they deserve better," she replied growing even angrier with the mayor.

"I know mom, they have always helped us out with food when we were desperate last year. What can we do? His men have all the guns in town," Rees answered. He didn't like the mayor's brothel any more than his mother did. Worse, the mayor's actions had been anything but kind and honest, ever since the plague came. "He's taking advantage of everyone in the town, getting rich and fat off the rest of us."

"I know, son, but what can we do about it? Those poor girls. The little one, she isn't even of age yet is she?"

"I think that she might be, mom. I think that she might be fourteen now," he replied.

"Well, we owe something to Berwyn, Rees. Somehow we have to protect his daughters from the mayor's ravages." Both agreed but the how remained the problem.

That night, Euren had a bright idea. "Rees, I am going over there. I have an idea of how we can protect the five from being raped!"

"How mom? Don't go getting yourself killed!"

"I won't, son. You stay safe yourself. Don't do anything foolish until I get back. This might or might not work out."

Meantime, Raelyn began educating the five sisters. "Look, the men are total pigs. If you are not wet and ready when they rape you, their actions just rip you apart. Five women have already died because of being badly torn and then getting infected. Here's what we have to do each evening." The five girls got a rapid, but pleasurable introduction to self-preservation against the brutality of the rapers.

One night, the door opened and two men stood pointing long guns at the women. The mayor stuck his head inside and ordered, "All you Goronwy kids, come with me now!" Against long guns, Tegan knew that they had no chance. Dutifully, they obeyed, though Tegan felt more confident. All five were going together, so perhaps together they could overpower the man.

"In you go, all of you. If you hurt her, there will be hell to pay on your part!" the mayor spat on them.

Prepared for the worst, the five entered the bedroom and the door slammed shut. The forty year old widow lay on the bed. "Come on in, kids. Do you know me?"

"Yes, we gave your son a bunch of food last year. You are Mrs. Yestin. What are you doing here?" asked Tegan, quite surprised to see her here in this place.

"I've come to try to save you girls. We owe you and your dad more than we can repay. Your generous food gifts kept us alive last year. Now come sit by me. Here's what we have to do." She outlined her plan. It was quite simple really. She would pleasure each of them and they, her. "Make sure that we make lots of moaning noises," she added. "I'll go first, because I suspect none of you have ever bedded a man." Tegan nodded and the five paid close attention. Okay, the soon found that they really enjoyed this pleasure time and their moans were not all that faked. After an hour or so, Euren called out that she was finished and the men with the long guns led the five back to their bedroom.

"Well, you must have a way with them," Mayor Bledig commented as she walked out of the room.

"Just as I thought, mayor. You have picked the wrong women. They are lesbians. You'll probably have to kill them if you are to bed them.”

“Damn! Who could have known? Well, I suppose I ought to — five women together. Just as likely as Berwyn's girls coming back to haunt me. Hell.”

“I have an idea. Why don't you make them my personal toys? Let them be my personal pets? Of course, I'll pay your fee each night. How's that?”

“Well, Mrs. Yestin, that would be most considerate of you.”

“Excellent. Just make damn sure that no man spoils them for me or the deal is off.”

“I give you my word. No man will touch them as long as you pay their fees.” She nodded and left, satisfied that she was keeping her pledge to Berwyn.

During the early summer, Tegan continued to pray to Partholan every night, as the other women were occasionally taken away to be raped yet again. Still, the five continued to make their nightly excursions out into the house, causing as much mischief as they could safely manage. Later they heard that two of his men had died when they fired their long guns, which had somehow managed to explode in their faces, most mysteriously. They overheard the mayor cursing, “Damn, that is just as likely as Berwyn's girls!” The five chuckled to themselves.

Another voice said, “Maybe it's them damn girls. You know you have Berwyn's girls here. Maybe they have jinxed us, boss.”

That night, Tegan began to worry again and prayed to Partholan for help. To her utter shock as well as the other women in their bedroom, a grey giant of a man, hairless and well-muscled suddenly appeared in their room. His head touched the ceiling.

“I am Partholan. I have heard your prayers, my daughter, Tegan. You and your sisters I have found most worthy. I hereby grant your salvation. Men of Tewdwr shall no longer threaten you, not ever again. In return, I am appointing you, Tegan, Rhiannon, Megan, Nesta, and Carys as the sole rulers of all Tewdwr. I will let all within Tewdwr know that you are their new leaders tonight. May you five rule our land with justice and honor. Fear not, no man can ever again harm a woman of Tewdwr. So says Partholan.” With that, he vanished as suddenly as he came.

That night across all of Tewdwr, everyone was suddenly awakened and heard the booming voice of Partholan in their heads. *From this moment on, no man of Tewdwr shall ever mistreat or harm a Tewdwr woman. If they do, my justice will be instantaneous and final, for I am Partholan! From this moment on, Berwyn's Daughters of Dunloy Caern shall be the sole rulers of all Tewdwr. Follow their rule and all will be well. Disobey them and my justice will be instantaneous and final, for I am Partholan!*

Outside their door, the captive women heard the mayor. “What the bloody hell was that? What have those bitches done now? Come on; let's get them,” Mayor Bledig cried out. They heard footsteps coming their way. Their bedroom door burst open and the mayor and two of his men with long guns stood looking at the five long-haired red heads. “You bitches,” he cried out. “Shoot them now!”

Tegan prepared for the worst. At least she might find solace and her father now. A long gun shot ought to be swift, she thought. Nothing could have prepared these women for what happened next. At that instant, the three men's arms completely vanished. The two long guns fell loudly onto the floor. Two more of his henchmen came rushing up, and their arms vanished as well. The five men stood there completely shocked. Slowly stark terror flooded over them as they realized that they too were now as helpless as the many women that they had victimized. Screaming wild curses, Mayor Bledig came running over to Tegan, intent upon kicking her to death for what she had done. As his legs came up to kick at her, both his legs vanish. What little remained of his body crashed onto the floor — a head and torso was all that remained of his body. He shrieked in terror more wildly and loudly than any woman had done when they awoke from the plague. The women just stared in utter disbelief at what remained of their slave master.

All around Dunloy Caern, lights turned on. Men and women rose. Some additional male screams echoed around the town, seeping in through the windows and cracks. Tegan finally rose and stared down at the man who had caused so much suffering in her town. “Well, Mayor Bledig, it seems that you are getting a taste of your own medicine. We are now all free, ladies,” she announced to the group of kidnaped women.

“What about the cook fellow? We haven't seen him yet,” Raelyn pointed out. She still did not trust her eyes. Perhaps this was all some fantasy, some hallucination.

Just then, their cook came out of his side room, pulling up his pants. “What the hell is going on here? What have you done this time, Tegan?” He stared at the shrieking mayor, or rather what was left of him.

“Shoot her! Shoot her, before she damns you too!” Mayor Bledig screamed.

He reached down for a long gun. His arms completely vanished! His shrieks joined those of the mayor. He turned and fled out of the now opened door. “Well, I think that is the last of them,” Tegan suggested. "Come on; let's see if there is anything good to eat. I am tired of that slop that they've been feeding us. Come on; we'll show you how to feed yourself." The group of eleven young women walked out of their prison bedroom together, heading for the kitchen.

Just then, others appeared at the doorway. "My god! Tegan, are you and the girls safe?" exclaimed a very worried Mrs. Yestin. Her son, Rees, was at her side. "We saw armless men running out of here as we came up, which is just as likely as Berwyn's girls. No offense, Tegan."

"I swear that we saw Partholan, Tegan!" Rees said excitedly.

"We did too. He was here! In our bedroom!" added Raelyn.

Three other young men, panting from running, came up behind the Yestins, stepping inside the front door. They were Nye, Emlyn, and Pedr. Tegan recognized them, recalling her father had told them that these men were resisting the mayor and his treachery, but had been forced into hiding by the mayor's men. Emlyn called out, "Tegan? Are you all right? We had a vision. The armless thugs of the mayor are running madly around the town."

"Hi Emlyn, Nye, Pedr. Yes, we're okay. Partholan answered my prayers. We're saved at last," Tegan answered.

"Are you really our leader now, Tegan?" Emlyn asked curiously.

"I don't know."

"That's what he told us, sis. We five are supposed to be the rulers of all Tewdwr now," Rhiannon added. "How are we going to do that?"

"At least we're out of this hell hole," Megan added. "What's left of the mayor is back in our prison bedroom. Go see for yourselves. Sure is weird, but it's fine with me. How many men and women has he had killed anyway?"

"We lost count, Megan," Emlyn admitted.

"At least a hundred, probably many more," put in Nye, "including my dad and sister." The five newcomers walked into the bedroom to look at the mayor. All were shocked, but pleased to see how the mayor was now suffering for his crimes.

Nye commented, "Well, this is better than just killing him, Tegan. Way to go. He cannot even move. Serves him right for what all that he has done. The plague was bad enough for us all and particularly you women, but what he did to us all after that pales. The bastard!" He spat on the helpless mayor, who continued to squirm on the floor, limbless.

Emlyn then said, "My god, you are all naked. Come on, fellows, we have to get them into some clothes!"

"We can dress ourselves, Emlyn," Tegan explained and they all headed into the bedroom to find their dresses.

"But how? You have no arms," Nye pleaded.

"I need help, Nye. I can't do anything much," Raelyn volunteered. All the others agreed with Raelyn, except for the five sisters. While the small group watched, the five helped each other into their dresses, struggling to get their long hair on to the outside.

"Here, Tegan, at least let me lace up your back for you," Emlyn said kindly. Tegan allowed him to do so.

"Okay, we have been fed pig swill for months. Let's see if we can find something better to eat in the mayor's private stock," Tegan suggested. She led them into the pantry.

"So this is where you two were always stealing that fine stuff from," Raelyn commented as her eyes took in all the quality food supplies he had stored away.

"We don't even have this much, mom," Rees commented. "He's been hogging all the best food in Dunloy Caern for himself!"

"Here, let us cook you all some bacon and eggs," offered Nye.

"We can cook just fine, only not on this high stove," Rhiannon protested slightly, unused to having someone else cook for her.

As Nye began to cook, he asked, "What do you mean, Rhiannon? We fellows have been doing all the cooking since the plague came."

"Didn't you fellows install that low kitchen for your moms?" asked Tegan in disbelief.

"Huh? Well, no. Mom couldn't use it if we did."

"Now that is just plain silly, Nye. Of course, we can cook on the low kitchen stove. Dad installed ours right away, and we've been cooking and doing the dishes ever since," Rhiannon explained, much to the complete disbelief of everyone else present.

"This I have got to see, Rhiannon. If so, then we ought to get the stuff installed, fellows," he added.

Thus began several days of surprise and shock for the residents of the town. The five sisters quickly discovered that they alone had adapted and were doing their usual household and gardening chores. All the other women had been content to do nothing, convinced that they were truly helpless now. Likewise, the men in their lives thought the same thing. As a result, the five constantly had to demonstrate how they had learned other ways to do things. Tegan realized that now the whole town was really looking to the five of them for guidance and leadership.

Nye, Emlyn, Pedr, and Rees scoured the town and rounded up all the armless men, well over a hundred of them. Raelyn pointed out that many of them had been paying the mayor to rape them. A few had been mistreating their own wives and or daughters. However, as they were rounded up, well over half of them chose to make a sudden dash and dove over the cliff to their death below. "What do we do with these men and the mayor?" asked Emlyn.

Tegan looked them up and down. It had only been a couple of days and already the men looked and smelled awful, having gone to the bathroom in their pants. They were a sorry lot, she thought. Nye suggested, "We ought to just push them off the cliff and be done with them."

"Aye, they deserve what they got. No, Partholan wanted them this way so let's let them live this way. Put them ten men to a house and let them get on with living their lives. Just be sure that a low kitchen is installed for them. They can live as we do now," Tegan decreed.

"What about the mayor?" asked Nye. "He really is helpless."

Tegan asked around to see if there was anyone who wanted to care for him. There were no volunteers. Just as she was about to suggest that he be thrown off the cliff, a cousin of his agreed to take him in. However, two days later, his cousin threw him off the cliff as well, claiming he was just too foulmouthed to have around any longer.

Tegan and Rhiannon now faced squarely the problems of the town. So many women were now alone or had hardly anyone to look after them. Almost half of the town had now died, one way or the other. Based on their own experience, they decided that at least four women should be living in the same house, regardless of the number of men who lived there. Thus, for the next week, the townsfolk began moving each other around to attain Tegan's goals for them.

Everyone absolutely insisted that the five sisters should move into the old mayor's home, which was the largest home in the town. Nye and the other young men quickly cleaned it out, made needed repairs, including knocking out the temporary walls that enclosed the brothel room, and installed the new kitchen. Since their new home would hold at least a dozen or more, they asked Mrs. Yestin and Rees to move in with them. Nye and his ten year old sister Tegwen, joined them. Emlyn and his mother and sister gladly accepted the sister's offer to move in with them. Raelyn, Eirian, and Briallen came too, since their entire families had perished.

For the next week, the sisters traveled from one home to another, demonstrating how they did the usual things of life for the women there. Slowly the women began to catch on and a little hope returned to the women of Dunloy Caern. Shortly after that, riders from two neighboring towns arrived asking to meet with the new rulers. Now the sisters had entirely new problems facing them and began to worry that they might not be able to deal with more than their small town.

Chapter 56 Brina Cerdwin of Bregia, Layamon

In Layamon, the plague struck hard. Most of the towns of Layamon were constructed of wood, since timber was cheap and plentiful. During the first few weeks of the plague, over half of the towns and villages experienced an "accidental fire." In these towns with their close-set, wooden homes, fire was feared second only to a plague. Half of the towns burned to the ground, as did Nuadilan, where over half of the population perished in the conflagration. Their large port city of Bregia was not spared the ravages of fire. When the flames subsided during a downpour, half of the city was destroyed. Even the few stone buildings had their roofs and floors destroyed, leaving grey stone shells protruding against the blue sky.

In the years before the plague, young Brina Cerdwin, the youngest daughter of one of the wealthier men in Bregia, the sixth of their children, was much of a tomboy, to her parents and siblings disdain. Galloping over the countryside at all hours of the day, sword fighting with any who would practice with her, Brina demonstrated her fiery strong will, defying her parents and their attempts to turn her into more feminine pursuits. When she turned eighteen, her father put his foot down on the swordplay, swearing that any man caught sword fighting with her would be shot. Undaunted, Brina took up the martial arts, having discovered a master who had recently settled in Bregia. At twenty, Brina was as well muscled as any man and a highly skilled horsewoman, swords woman, and martial artist. She was comely, with pale skin, enchanting blue eyes, and of course as blonde as her mother was. Her alto voice added to her charm, though she wore her hair nearly as short as a man did.

Enter Weylin Dunn, the twenty-three year old son of the king, the richest man in the kingdom of Layamon. For years, Weylin had his eyes on the perky Brina, but had failed utterly to win her heart. His first date with her was a disaster, and she refused to go out with him after that. Undaunted, Weylin was now more than ever determined to make Brina his wife.

At this time, the Church of Jehosanity had extreme influence over the king. The Cardinal often dictated actions that the king then executed. No one knew just why this was so, though many speculated that the Cardinal was somehow blackmailing the king. You know how rumors go. Still, Weylin had befriended the young Cardinal and at last sought his advice on how to net the fair Brina.

The Cardinal, resplendent in his magnificent purple robes trimmed with pure gold, said wisely, "Weylin, netting Brina is extremely easy. Rather you should be more concerned about keeping her."

"Huh? What do you mean? She won't even go out on a date with me anymore," the young man replied.

"The king and her father can come to some kind of arrangement that will force her to marry you. That can be arranged in a day or so. No, my friend, it is the keeping of Brina that will be your greatest challenge."

"Ah, I had not thought of an arranged marriage! Brilliant, positively brilliant. What do you mean by keeping her?" he asked, now catching on to the line of reasoning of the Cardinal.

"She is a strong willed woman, used to having her own way. While she will protest the arranged marriage, once the knot is tied, she will make your life an utter hell. That is, of course, unless you are the type of fellow who desires the woman to be in utter and complete control of your life and actions."

"Oh don't be silly! No way would I allow her to control me; she is the woman, not I. Oh!" Suddenly, Weylin realized just what the Cardinal meant. "Oh," he repeated himself. "Is it all then hopeless? Should I give up the love of my life?"

The Cardinal smiled. He finally had the king's son just where he wanted him: finally under his control. He was about to score yet another victory for his Church of Jehosanity. "There is a way." He purposely lowered his voice, adding a bit of mystery and secrecy to his words.

Weylin bit completely. "Please, please, tell me the answer. How may I keep her once I have married her?" The Cardinal bent low and whispered something into his ear. A grin formed on Weylin's face, growing larger and larger. At last, he said, "Let's make it so!"

"I will speak to the king tonight and to Mr. Cerdwin on the morning. Visit me tomorrow afternoon and we will finalize the details. Of course, this will cost you a bit of money, but what is money compared to true love, eh, my fine Weylin?"

As was her wont, Brina went out for a long ride the following morning and thus missed the Cardinal's visit with her father. When the family gathered for the evening supper, her father said, "I have an announcement to make. Tomorrow, Brina will marry the king's son, Weylin, at the Church of Jehosanity. All the arrangements have been made."

Brina choked, splattering wine across the table. "I will not marry that pig of a man, father! How could you do this to me?"

"Money, power, influence. You will be joining our family to that of the king. One day, you will become our queen, Brina. It's settled. Prepare yourself. Do not try to run away; I have guards posted. You'll be at the church at ten tomorrow if I have to have you dragged there by your heels. This is utterly final, Brina."

Brina shrieked, cursed, and ran off to her room, crushed. That her own father would do such a thing appalled her. She calculated her chances of escaping and saw there was none. Guards were already beside her door and below her window. Later on, her mother entered and insisted that she bathe and start getting prepared for the morning. Brina collapsed and allowed her mother's servants to bathe her and dry her off. She didn't protest too much being forced into the very tight corset that always accompanied the fancy Annelise gowns, which she had no choice but to wear on formal occasions. In preparation for the morning, she had to sleep in it so that it could be fully tightened in the morning. Twice during the night, she looked out her window, but several guards were there, pacing back and forth. She opened her door a crack, but saw three guards standing beside her door. There was no escape possible. She cried herself to sleep.

Her mother's servants finished dressing her, tightening her corset until she nearly fainted. She wore a white satin gown, which billowed out fourteen feet, and they forced her feet into the dreaded Annelise oxfords with the impossible heels. After the servants tied them off, she simply could not take them off herself. Unable to bend enough, she couldn't reach the laces without help, and she knew no one would take them off, not until long after the wedding. A miserable Brina was escorted off to the Church of Jehosanity to be married at ten, though her movements were pitifully slow, and she kept her arm securely around that of her father's the whole time for fear of falling down.

The wedding was short but elegant. Brina heard nothing of the words; her attention was focused solely on her own personal misery. She refused to say a word during the ceremony, but the Cardinal spoke for her anyway. Weylin looked his finest in his new suit, bought for the occasion yesterday. At the reception, Weylin did explain a little. "My love, dad has given me the Hillwood Estate for our own palace. It is huge and expansive. You will love it there. However, first, we will be taking our honeymoon on Megalos, seeing the magnificent sights there. I promised the Cardinal to bring back some artworks to adorn our church and to see if I can somehow obtain the autograph of the Pope himself. We will have a grand time before we return to our new home."

"I will kill you, Weyin, for what you've done to me," Brina finally managed to speak, though she nearly fainted from saying so much in one breath. Her corset was killing her now, and she could scarcely breathe anymore.

"I do so love you, Brina. I hope one day you will love me too," he said. Later he brought her another glass of wine. That was the last thing Brina remembered before she awoke up onboard a caravel far out at sea. She was still wearing her wedding outfit, complete with the impossible heels.

"What happened to me? Where are we? I have to use the pot. Get me out of this dress," she said rapid fire, coming to her senses. She felt like she had a hangover.

He helped her use the pot, but refused to get her out of her dress. "Dear, we left so quickly to catch this ship in time, and besides, I didn't know what clothes you wanted to bring along. Don't worry. We can get you any clothes you desire on Megalos before we see the sights."

She tried to stand up, but in the dress and heels, on the rolling ship, she simply could not keep her balance. She spent a miserable three weeks lying around in her wedding dress, pure torture, which Weylin seemed to enjoy. "Look, if I take it off, you will have to go around here naked. I know the sailors would love that!" She flushed and endured her torture, planning ways to kill Weylin just as soon as she could.

When they finally docked, Weylin offered her another cup of wine to celebrate their landing. She accepted and that was the last thing she remembered before she woke up to massive pains in both her shoulders. She tried to rise, but her arms didn't seem to work. She looked down at her tightly bandaged shoulders and shrieked as loudly as she could. They had cut her arms off. Now she realized that she had become a Holy Woman of the Eighth Degree and totally against her will!

The doctor who answered her cries was sympathetic and began assisting her with her needs. "You will be a bit woozy for a time. The pain will subside. The surgery went well, and you will have almost no scarring." He chatted on and Brina just cried her heart out.

At suppertime, Weylin appeared, bringing her supper. "Ah, you look wonderful, Brina. I am to feed you now. Not too much according to the doctor. Once you are healed, we will see the sights of Megalos, my love."

"I will kill you!" she spat.

"I hardly think so now. Here," he lifted a bite of food to her lips. She was ravenous and opened her mouth to eat the delicious steak.

Per the doctor's orders, Brina was not to wear constricting clothing for another month after her wounds healed, allowing her time to get used to being armless. Thus, Weylin dressed her in a simple cotton dress and did live up to his promise to show her the sights of the Holy Cathedral where the Pope held services in Constanza City. Shortly after that, they boarded a caravel bound for home.

They arrived home in September of 823, weeks before the plague struck. Hillwood Estate was everything that Weylin had said it would be. Sporting fifty bedrooms and all the requisite additional rooms to support many guests, the grey stone manor house was four stories tall, sitting on four acres of grasslands and formal gardens. It was near the western edge of the port city of Bregia. An attached stable could hold a dozen carriages at the same time. When they arrived, Weylin's father had already hired a rather large staff for his son. Vast stocks of food and wine were in the pantry. Gardeners cared for the lawn and fall flowers.

He had hired the necessary servants for Brina. The Bran sisters, Seanna and Shayla, twenty-one and twenty respectively, and Fionn Anwell, also twenty-one, were expecting her and were prepared to attend to her every need, which would be nearly everything. Brina's father and mother had purchased a dozen fancy ball gowns with all the accessories to go with them, giving Brina a completely new wardrobe, though they did not know that she would be returning a Holy Woman. Even if they had, it would have mattered little to them. Additionally, the king had hired a superb, young chef, Enys Condon, who at twenty had already made a name for herself as a chef around Bregia. To attend the horses, young Tristen Kearney had been hired, twenty-three. He knew horses well, having grown up with them around himself all his life.

When the carriage brought the new couple up the long ornate drive to the manor house, Tristen was there to greet them. He took an instant liking to his new Lady of the Manor, helping her down from the carriage before Weylin remembered that he was supposed to be doing so. No matter, he thought. Once inside, she was introduced to her new attendants and told that Fionn, Seanna, and Shayla were all very experienced at handling the needs of a Holy Woman.

"Now then, take Brina to her new quarters, bathe her, and get her dressed for supper. Remember, she is to always be wearing one of the ball gowns, as fitting a right and proper Holy Woman," he ordered.

"Yes, Your Lordship," Seanna replied. "This way, My Lady." Brina fumed, she'd been comfortable for the last month, as much as possible, she thought. Now she was about to be tortured beyond belief once again!

Brina allowed her ladies to bathe her and didn't protest their dressing her. She took a liking to these three young women. She was now twenty-two, only a year older than they. The three were kind and gentle with her, though they commented about how strong and muscular her legs were. Trussed up in the terribly restrictive Annelise outfit with impossible heels, they escorted her down the long hallway to the spacious dining room. Already Weylin had had his fill of feeding her and ordered her servants to deal with these issues. He sat proudly at one end of the oak table so that he could gaze on his beauty at the opposite end. Her three servants sat on either side of her. Brina felt miserable, but found the women did a vastly better job of feeding her than Weylin ever had. She was thankful for this tiny bit of kindness.

Weylin had already given up bedding her. Every time that he had, she had just lain still like a sack of potatoes, unmoving, unfeeling. She never responded to his amorous advances. Now that they were home, he stopped entirely, preferring to sleep in his own bed, some distance down the hall from hers and her servants. He was content to gaze upon this beautiful flower, which was his, as was this fabulous estate. Life was now perfect for Weylin.

Shortly after their arrival, Brina had certainty that she was not yet pregnant. "Thank god for small favors," she exclaimed.

"Why do you say that, My Lady?" asked Seanna.

"I hate that bastard! I've sworn to kill him. Look what he did to me — cut my arms off and ruined my whole life! I'll kill him. I swear I will!" She let her anger pour out.

"But My Lady, he has given you such a wonderful place to live. This is a mansion — so many servants. You have money now and can buy anything you want. You have the finest dresses and clothes money can buy," Shayla added, confused.

"Money cannot by me my arms back nor can money buy my love. My dad forced me to marry the pig. I could not even escape and run away. He had my room guarded night and day. Weylin drugged me at our wedding, carried me onboard the ship to Megalos, and drugged me once we were there. I had no idea at all that he wanted my arms cut off. I awoke to find them gone. Now do you see why I want that pig of a man killed?" she vented the last of her anger.

After that outburst, her three servants now understood her and what was going on in this mansion. The three did not like the situation in the slightest. Unbeknownst to Brina, Fionn also told all this to the stableman, Tristen, who also became quite sympathetic to Brina.

One day when Brina finally came outside on her own while Weylin was gone, Tristen came up to her. "My Lady, allow me to escort you, please. A fall would not be a good thing." She allowed him to put his stabilizing arm around her.

"I am forced to wear these awful heels. I can barely walk in them when I had arms. Now it is almost impossible, but I did want to see our grounds. This is a lovely garden, isn't it?"

"Yes, perhaps the finest in all Bregia or even Layamon for that matter. My Lady, Fionn has told me your story. I want you to know that I will forever be on your side. Anything that you ever need done, just ask me," Tristen confided in her.

"Thank you, Tristen. I will remember your offer, though I don't think that you would kill Weylin for me, now would you?"

Tristen chuckled, "No, I have never killed anyone nor do I intend to do so. I don't know how to use a gun, but I am very good with horses. I love them and they love me. Horses are so much better than most people, don't you agree?"

"Absolutely. Before I was abducted into this marriage, I used to go for long rides, even at night. I was good at it, but now I probably cannot ever ride again, except in a carriage. Damn Weylin to Hell, if there even is such a thing."

During the next two weeks, these five became good friends: Brina, Fionn, Seanna, Shayla, and Tristen. Weylin was gone most of the daytime hours, and Brina merely had to look pretty for him at the supper table, which she found acceptable, though it didn't dissuade her in the slightest from wanting him dead for what he'd done to her.

Then the plague struck hard. Her three servants' shrieks roused her and she climbed out of bed as best she could, moving into the adjoining rooms where the three had their own private bedrooms. "Oh my god! He's done it to you too!" Brina exclaimed. As she went from room to room, she found all three women as armless as she was. Then she saw Weylin in the hallway, down on his hands and knees. Blood dripped from a cut on his head.

"Damn it, what's going on? My feet are paralyzed. I can't stand up. Get your servants here at once," he ordered.

"They can't. You've cut off their arms too!" she cursed at him.

"The hell I did! I haven't even seen them since suppertime. Hell, I'll go see if the other men are around. You can take care of your servants now."

"How the hell can I do that? You cut off my arms, you bastard," she let it all out now.

He turned and gloated, "I arranged for the marriage. Your father loved the money he got for you, thinking that one day you will be the queen. The Cardinal and I arranged the Holy Woman thing as a sure-fire way to keep you under my control after your dad gave you to me. Now you are my wife and you cannot do a damn thing about it. You are mine forever. Now go take care of your screaming servants, Brina!"

She snapped. Her dad had betrayed her; Weylin had betrayed her, and even the despicable Church of Jehosanity had betrayed her. "No way in hell are you going to control me, you bastard!" In an instant, she recalled her martial arts training. She didn't need arms to be lethal. This moment now was one of the very few times that she was not encased in those awful Annelise outfits, barely able to move. She wore only a thin nightgown. Brina acted, venting her long built up hatred of this man. She dashed to the man slowly crawling away on all fours. She brought her right leg up and thrust it down on his neck. It snapped and he dropped to the floor, paralyzed from the neck down. He looked up at her and saw the fire of righteous vengeance in her eyes. Weylin saw her foot rise again and then blackness flooded over him. He became semi-conscious as he floated high over Bregia. What's happening to me? He wondered, and then he felt the all-powerful urge and drive to go get a new baby body and fled.

She turned and headed back to her servants who were still screaming, terrified beyond belief. Brina could relate to what they were going through, since she'd been there only weeks before. "Fionn, get up, come to my room, and sit on my bed, dear." She repeated her words in the other two women's rooms. Before long, the three sobbing women were sitting helplessly on the edge of her bed, while she pushed a chair closer to them.

"Weylin said that he did not do this to you. For once, I believe him, but he is now dead. I got my revenge on him. His feet were all paralyzed or so he claimed. Something is going on around here, but I don't know what it is."

"How can we live like this? We have no money to hire servants," Seanna wailed.

"You are with me now. I will pay for servants for us all. I promise I will look after all of you. Wow, what else had happened to you three?" She noticed their massive breasts for the first time.

Fionn looked down and shrieked yet again. "My god! My breasts are bigger than my head! Oh no, Brina! Look at yours," she exclaimed.

Only now did Brina look at her own body. "My god, they are enormous. My waist — it's smaller than when I wear that damnable corset!"

"Shayla! Your hair — it seems much longer," her sister pointed out. Both sisters had raven hair and bushy eyebrows, quite attractive young women. They wore their hair a bit on the long side, draping down to the middle of their backs. Now their tresses fell to their knees.

Fionn, a brunette, wore hers shoulder length. Now it fell to the middle of her back. Brina glanced at hers. During the past two months, Weylin refused to let her have her hair cut short like she always had it. As a result, hers had also reached to just below her shoulders. Weylin had complimented her on its length, but she'd ignored him. Now hers too fell to the middle of her back.

"Look at our feet!" Brina had been tiptoeing around, thinking that was because of having worn those extreme heels for so long. Now she noticed the awful U-shape in her arches. Only her toes could touch the ground. The other three were similar.

"I've got to use the pot," Seanna suddenly wailed, feeling utterly helpless now.

Brina took charge, "Come on. I'll help you all and you can help me. If we use our teeth, I think we can pull each other's panties down and then up again." She was right. That was the beginning of the foursome cooperating on handling their needs by themselves.

A half hour later, the four headed off on a search of the spacious mansion, looking for the other staff, which ought to have been here by now. Chef Enys always arrived by seven at the latest, but they found the kitchen empty. Nothing had been prepared for their morning breakfast, though none thought about eating now. Sometime later, they arrived in the huge living room area and saw the large pile of foreign objects. Brina spotted the unusual looking heels first. Soon all four were relieved to find that wearing these most unusual heels did make their feet feel vastly better, and they could maintain their precarious balance somewhat better.

"Well, I don't know what the rest of this stuff is for, so let's keep on looking for the staff. Surely, they ought to be arriving anytime now," Brina took charge. The four shuffled along the main hall to the front doors. Hillwood Estate was a new building and thus had the newest style doorknobs — latches or bars would be a better description. Brina used her foot to push the latch down and then pushed it open. Fresh air greeted them, though it was somewhat chilly, this being the end of October.

Absolutely no one was around. The main gates were still locked shut from last night. "Well, Tristen ought to be here. He lives in the stables, come on," Brina ordered. Shivering slightly from the cold, the four moved carefully and slowly over the cobblestones of the walkway to the stables. "Tristen? Tristen, are you here?" she called out.

"Yes, My Lady, but I have a really big problem right now. Just a minute." Soon, he opened the door. He was down on all fours.

"Oh my god! What's happened to Fionn, Seanna, and Shayla? Did someone cut your arms off? What day is it? Have we all been drugged or something? Come on in; you must be freezing in those gowns."

The three began sobbing again, but Brina explained what little she knew, observing that Tristen's feet were also somehow weirdly paralyzed.

He said, "I found these boots beside my bed when I got up. I'm still trying to get them on. They are almost like a ballerina, I think. I am sorry, My Lady, I might not be able to walk in them." He tried to stand and wobbled precariously.

"Here, put your arm around me; maybe I can steady you. Shayla, you get his other side, please." Between them, Tristen was able to walk somewhat, and they headed back inside the mansion and warmth. Brina led them to the body of Weylin.

While they stared, she explained, "I used my feet. I have had some martial arts training. Somehow we need to get his body out of the house and into the street where he belongs with the filth of the city."

"If my feet were not paralyzed, I maybe could carry him," Tristen suggested.

"Well, let's roll him. Come on, sit down and push him along," Brina took charge again. Foot by foot, they rolled his body down the hall and to the front door. While Brina held the door open, they pushed him outside. A half hour later, they had the body rolled down the long lane and at the main gates. Tristen had the keys, and while holding on to Brina for balance, he opened the gates. Again, she sat down and helped them push the body out into the street. All struggled back onto their feet and looked around.

They heard random screams and wild yelling coming from various directions and spotted another dead person lying in the street as well. Just as they were turning around, Tristen heard horses coming and they turned to face the street, hoping to catch some news. A blue robed rider came up to them, carrying a long gun. Brina had seen these folks before; she knew that it was a Mano del Dio enforcer for the Church. The man had blood splatters on his robes, which got the immediate attention of Brina, who was to the left of Tristen, helping to support him on his feet.

"The Holy Day of Judgment is upon us. Prepare yea to enter the Holy Kingdom of Lord Jehosa," he rattled off, then his eyes lighted upon the dead Weylin and he stopped. "Oh, Weylin has already been taken to Heaven. Good." He leveled the gun at Brina. Both she and Tristen realized the man's intentions.

Tristen acted first; he whistled and the horse reared, just as he had anticipated. The gun went off and its bullet struck Tristen, who dropped to the ground hard. The man lost control of the horse, and Brina dashed towards the horse, yelling loudly. With wild motions, the rider tried to stay mounted but slid out of the saddle. She knew he must not be an experienced horseman. As he hit the ground, Brina was over him. Down came her foot on the man's neck, ending his miserable life, she thought. She stomped on his neck several more times to make doubly sure. Meanwhile the horse headed on inside their gate, spying several of their mares in the stables.

"Damn, Tristen's been shot," she said the obvious, as she turned around. Her three companions panicked, unable to do anything to help the young man. Brina glanced around for other riders. Seeing none, she closed the gate and used her teeth to turn the key in the lock.

Talking through her teeth, she asked, "Fionn, take the key from me and carry it into the house." Shaking from the shock of the near death experience, she did as asked, though she nearly dropped it. Brina knelt down beside Tristen. It was a shoulder wound, but he had to be treated she well knew. "Okay, we have to get him inside. Shayla, you and I are going to have to support his weight. Tristen, pull on me. You have to get to your feet! Come on; you have to!" Brina insisted, cajoled, trying everything she could think of to get him conscious and up on his feet.

After nearly pulling her over, Tristen managed to rise, holding heavily onto her. His wounded arm, he draped over Shayla. Slowly, they made their way back to the huge house. Once inside, Brina asked Seanna to see if she could somehow lock it and then join them in the kitchen.

Tristen didn't make it that far, collapsing in the hallway, unconscious. Brina didn't hesitate. She sat down and began pushing him along. Fionn and Shayla joined her and a while later had him on the kitchen floor. "Okay, we need to boil some water, find some bandages, and figure out how we are going to get the bullet out of his shoulder," she explained.

"But we can't do any of that, Brina. We lost our arms. We're helpless like you are," Shayla wailed.

"Look, we are not helpless, not totally. I've just killed my second man in an hour; we've helped him walk; we've locked our gates and gotten the body out there and his in here. It's damnably hard, but we don't have a choice. If we do nothing, Tristen dies and then where will we be? No arms around here at all. We simply have to find a way to do these things. Come on. Let's put our heads together, ladies. We have to."

"I know where the towels are kept. I can carry them in here between my teeth," Shayla offered.

"I know where the bandages and first aid things are stored. Weylin showed me that when I came to work last week. I can probably carry them here too, in my teeth that is," Seanna volunteered.

"Okay, Fionn, you and I have to get water boiling. Come on, let's do this," Brina ordered. Large pots and pans hung from hooks in the well-kept kitchen. If one had hands, fetching one down was simple. Brina and Fionn stared up at them. At last, Fionn started jumping up and down, a most precarious move on her part. Her head struck a pot knocking it from its hook. Both the pot and Fionn came crashing to the floor; she had lost her balance.

"Good thinking, Fionn. Now for some water," Brina complimented her friend, for she now thought of her as a friend, not as a servant any longer. Using her teeth, she carried the pot over to the sink. Sitting on the sink, she was able to get her feet onto the pump, but had a whole lot of trouble raising and lowering the level. Finally, water came out. Carrying the heavy pot over to the stove was even more difficult and both women held on to the metal loop with their teeth, shuffling together slowly over to the stove.

Lighting the stove was extremely tricky for the women. The other two joined them, bringing a towel and bandages. Both left to bring in more, while Brina and Fionn studied their current problem. Fionn managed to get some firewood logs inserted with her feet. While she was doing that, Brina looked around for a way to start the fire. She found lamp oil, flint, and steel. Three trips were needed to carry them over to the stove, by which time Fionn had enough wood in it. Working together with their feet while lying with their backs on the floor before the stove, the two managed to spread some lamp oil over the wood.

"Okay, you hold the steel bar over the stuff with your feet, and I'll use my feet and try to strike the flint on it," Brina suggested. After several failed attempts, she finally got it to spark. After two more tries, the oil ignited, and they barely got their feet out in time. "Okay, you blow on it and make sure it gets going good. I have to find something to dig the bullet out of his shoulder with," Brina requested.

Fionn laughed, "At last, you have given me something that I know I can do." Both women chuckled. It took all four of them working as a team to extract the slug. Fionn acted as director, telling each what to do and how to move. Shayla acted as their excess blood swabber, while Seanna used her feet to keep the wound as open as possible for Brina to dig into it with the end of a paring knife. A half hour later, using leverage on the knife blade, Brina finally extracted the lead slug, having actually made the hole far worse in size by her clumsy efforts.

"Does anyone know anything about doctoring?" Brina asked.

"I know a little," Seanna replied. "We should let it bleed to wash the wound clean before we try to bandage it up. I think that is all we need to do. Gosh, I hope it doesn't get all infected or anything." After letting it bleed some, Seanna suggested that they also pour some of the now cooled boiled water over it to wash off some of the blood. They did so, making a mess on the floor. At last, they began to attempt to bandage him up. First, they shoved his body several feet away from the bloody mess on the floor. While Seanna held the large bandage in place over the wound, the others used their feet to try to wrap it around his chest. This they failed at doing completely. However, they had it tight enough that the bleeding subsided and they decided to leave it at this. When he woke up, perhaps he could finish wrapping it around his chest.

"What a mess we've made," Fionn said as she looked at the floor. All four worked together and managed to mop the floor with the rest of the water and towels. It was noon when the four sat down on chairs and looked at Tristen.

"Good going, friends! A job well done!" Brina complimented them.

"Yes, My Lady, we did do that, though I don't know how we managed," Fionn replied.

"Hey, no more of this My Lady stuff. From now on, you three are my closest, dearest friends. We are in this together. I could never have done this without your help. Friends to the end, okay?" The three grinned.

"I'm starving. I wonder what happened to us. I don't think that the doctors did this to us. There are no bandages or anything. Our arms are just not there. Unless we have been unconscious for weeks, wounds don't heal that fast," Seanna mused.

"Right, it took many weeks for my shoulders to heal. I know that we haven't been unconscious that long, though our hair growth might suggest otherwise. No, something else is going on. Our monster breasts and feet and all those strange things in the other room — it must be something else," Brina added.

"The plague!" exclaimed Shayla, suddenly remembering the strange tales from the mainland from over a year ago. She hastily relayed what she had heard had happened over in Velona and Fortress d'Grange. All four now felt that this was what had happened, the plague had struck them.

"I bet the whole city is down with it," Brina mused. "Remember hearing all those distant screams? If so, that would explain why none of our other staff reported here to work today."

"That means we are really on our own, Brina!" Fionn added.

Bread, cheese, and water comprised their meal. Each woman took a turn at holding the object with her feet, while the others bit off bites to eat. Full at last, they headed off to inspect more closely the pile of objects. Now Brina began to see the images in her mind and pointed them out to her three friends. They too recognized the images in their minds, and all four began to see the uses for which these things were intended. Every item present had its use. To verify that they were right, they four used the yokes to begin carrying the kitchen items into the kitchen where they belonged, all except for the heavier items, such as the low stove and oven. Then, they pushed their four desks into the large study, where Brina thought that they would most likely need a way to write. They took their hairbrushes to their bedrooms.

Later that afternoon, they heard a moan and headed to the kitchen. Tristen was rousing at last. "What happened? Oh, I got shot! Brina! Is she. . ." he stopped. Brina was looking down at him.

"You are in the kitchen. Sorry, but we just could not get the bandage wrapped around your chest. We boiled water, sterilized things, and got the bullet dug out." Brina explained.

"How could you have possibly done all that?" he asked dumbfounded.

"We did. I don't know either, but Brina said that we must or you would die. Please, don't die on us. We need you, Tristen," Shayla begged him. He sat up and finished wrapping the bandage around his chest, though Brina used her foot to hold it in place as he struggled with one hand to tie it off.

He got to his feet and slumped into a chair. "God, it hurts."

"Sorry, we probably cut you a lot trying to dig the bullet out, Tristen," Brina explained.

"My Lady, I owe you my life," he said weakly.

"Just Brina now. You are my friend, Tristen. We are all just friends here now. No more My Lady stuff. We have all gotten the plague."

He smiled. "Food, I am starving. I have to try to fix you all something."

"We ate a bunch of bread and cheese. Here, we'll let you finish it off. We can worry about cooking something later on," Shayla suggested.

After they helped him eat, he seemed to perk up a bit. "Hey, if we all really do have the plague and it has spread throughout Bregia, things could get dangerous out there. Already some guy has tried to kill you, Brina. We ought to make sure that this house is securely locked up."

"You are too weak and besides you can't walk. We'll go check on the doors," Brina suggested. A half hour later, each woman returned from one of the four doors into the huge manor house. All had been locked the night before; at least Weylin had done something useful. Now the five felt safer from the ravages that might be on the streets.

"I should probably go lie down in my bed in the stables," Tristen admitted.

"You will do no such thing! From now on, you will be sleeping with us." Brina flushed. Her words didn't quite come out the way that she intended. "I mean that you are one of us now. You can have a room close to ours. You can have Weylin's if you want, but I'd like it if you were closer, like right next door to our four bedrooms, Tristen."

He grinned, "Who can turn down such an offer to sleep so close to four beautiful women," he teased them a little.

"Oh get real! We are hardly beautiful now. Just look at us, no arms, monster boobs, microscopic waists, screwed up feet," Brina pointed out.

"Well, my feet are even more screwed up than yours, but I am glad that I don't have the monster boobs though," he replied. All laughed, though it hurt him to laugh. He grimaced a little. The women helped him rise and walk to the bedroom next to their four, and he gratefully plopped on the bed. Soon, he was asleep.

"Say, we still have the fire going a little. While it is going, we should see if somehow, someway, we can really cook something for supper," Brina suggested. The four headed to the kitchen to see what they could devise. All four realized that with the low kitchen, they might just be able to cook a meal. With the high kitchen at hand, it was problematical. In the end, they just dumped everything into the pot and let it all simmer away for hours.

"How are we going to actually eat?" asked Fionn. "I mean before — we all had to feed you, Brina. Now who is going to feed us? Tristen might, once he heals up a bit."

"We feed ourselves. I think that is what the strange images in my mind are saying. What have we to lose?" Brina suggested.

As the sun slowly sank, the four women began ladling the mixture out of the pot. Brina was sitting on the counter using her foot to work the ladle, cradling it between her toes. Fortunately, the other end was bent in a semicircle so that she couldn't readily drop it. Two women working together held the plate between their teeth, carrying it over to the table. After four plates were set, the four sat down and attempted to use the new funny looking spoons that had come with the alien items. With effort, they managed to feed themselves, though all four realized at once that the table ought to be far lower. That way, they could manage this much more readily.

Brina suggested they take a plate to Tristen, in case he woke and was hungry too. She carried the plate between her teeth to his room, while Shayla carried a fork and Seanna, a spoon. Then, the four retired to their rooms — well to Brina's room.

"We ought to brush out your hair, Brina," Fionn began what had been their nightly ritual. "Damn, we can't even do that!"

"Hey, these new brushes — let's try them," Brina suggested. "Here, let me try you first, Fionn." Quickly, all four women discovered this was possible, but Brina was the first to realize that if three worked together on one woman's hair, it went faster and better than trying it alone. A half hour later, it was quite dark and they were finished.

As each woman headed for her bed, Fionn said, "Brina, thanks for saving us. I awoke more terrified than I have ever been in my life. I thought that the whole world had ended and that I was a helpless woman as you were. Now, I have some hope. We really did do some amazing things today, didn't we? I mean maybe we aren't completely useless and helpless." The others agreed with her.

The next morning, they checked on Tristen. The plate that they left for him was empty, but he was sleeping soundly. The four headed to the kitchen for a light breakfast. Brina asked, "Ladies, do you have family of your own? I mean maybe I am keeping you here when you ought to be returning to your own families."

"Our folks would have already come for us if they could," Seanna replied. "They probably have the plague too."

"Same with mine, but I've been out on my own for a couple of years, working as a servant for a Holy Woman. She was really old and died though," Fionn added. "I think that you are stuck with us, Brina, unless you want us to go or something."

"Good god, no! Please, don't go, not unless you have to. Working together, we are able to do things. Without you all, I'd be sunk utterly," Brina explained. "I just don't even know much about you and your families and all that. None of you are married?" All shook their heads. One by one, they chatted about their lives, sharing their personal situations with each other. Brina did likewise.

By the fourth day, Tristen was feeling much better and joined them for breakfast, though he used only one arm as he crawled into the kitchen. Brina insisted that from now on, when he wanted to go somewhere, he lean on Brina and one of the others. They chatted and briefed him on what they had observed. Gunshots were still being heard here and there. All knew trouble lay in the streets of Bregia. Tristen promised to help get the kitchen things installed when his shoulder mended. However, Brina insisted that they help him, for the sooner they had the kitchen going the better. Hence, that fourth day, all five worked together to get the job done. Tristen was amazed at just how much the four were able to do to help him with the task, and he wisely complimented them frequently, bringing much needed smiles to otherwise frustrated faces.

Late that afternoon, Seanna said, "I cook tonight. If I have to eat one more of Brina's mushes, I will vomit." She was jesting of course, and they all laughed. Seanna had done some cooking before with the older Holy Woman. They discovered that she was good at it as well, appointing her permanent chef, unless Enys showed up sometime.

By the end of the first two weeks after the plague came, the five had bonded well together. Daily, the women discovered more ways to do things that needed to be done, including changing their bed sheets and doing the washing. Today, they decided to venture outside and see if they could get any news about what was happening elsewhere in Bregia. They knew instinctively that the plague must be widespread. None of the two dozen staff had yet reported here for work.

"What's that smell?" asked Brina as the five stepped outside.

"The dead, I think," Tristin suggested. Once they opened the gate, with Brina supporting him on his left and Seanna on his right, they moved out into the street. Both bodies still lay just where they had left them. However, as the five looked up and down the street, they saw many more dead. Rodents were scurrying here and there, sampling the bodies. They found it revolting. Not a soul was outside, even though the day was sunny but chilly.

The women were chilling rapidly. Tristen decided there was nothing to be learned here and headed them back inside, making sure the gates were secured again. Inside once more, he said, "Perhaps it will be best if I ride a horse out there and see if I can learn anything." Brina hated to see him go. To her, it seemed that the world had become terribly dangerous, but their lack of news seemed even more critical now. Just what were they facing? Worse, all four were constantly cold. Winter was coming and nightgowns were a poor substitute for a warm dress.

After warming up, Brina and Seanna helped support Tristen as he walked out to the stables to saddle up his horse. Just as they were trying to work out how to keep him on his feet while he lifted the saddle, they heard shouting coming from the front gate. Slowly, the three moved to the front of the stables to see. "Oh my goodness! That's my sister, Morgandy. Come on. Morgandy," she yelled, "we're coming!" Their pitifully slow pace ground on Brina's nerves; this was pathetic. What if there was an emergency? It would be all over before she got there.

She relaxed a little as she saw her younger sister sitting on a horse with a soldier just outside their locked gates. There was no emergency just now, she thought. As they drew close to the gates, she saw that Morgandy looked terrible. Blood covered her nightgown. Her long curly hair was a mess. Dirt covered her face, but she didn't appear to be wounded. No bandages were visible. The soldier looked equally down and out. His uniform was filthy and caked with bloody patches. Well, the blood is not fresh, she observed, and relaxed a little. While Tristen unlocked the gates, she saw that Morgandy's eyes were bloodshot. She was definitely in grief. Something had happened.

The soldier said, "We best not talk out here. Gangs are everywhere, looting and killing. We just dodged another group three blocks from here. Best get inside quickly."

"Ride into the stables, sir," Tristen suggested. "We'll join you as quickly as we can, which is pretty darn slow these days." As the horse entered, the three walked the gates shut and he locked them. They turned and made their way back into the stables, out of sight from the street.

"I got her up behind me, but only with extreme difficulty," the soldier said as the three approached him. He'd just ridden inside and was waiting patiently for them to reach him. "I don't know how I can get her safely down."

"Sort of fall towards me, My Lady, and I will do my best to catch you," Tristen suggested, removing his arms from around the shoulders of the two women, and bending his knees. Although he looked clumsy and awkward, he reached his arms up. Morgandy leaned over and mostly fell off the horse into his arms. He lost his balance and the two collapsed onto the ground, albeit rather softly. "Got you, more or less. Damn feet anyway," Tristen said, helping her back to her feet. "Okay, you are next," he said to the soldier. He was able to support the soldier somewhat better, and the man made it to the ground without falling. He slumped down to his knees, explaining that he could not walk in the boots.

"It is the biggest disaster I've ever seen. Men cannot even walk," he said. "Thanks, young man. Maybe the world is ending after all. Captain Bran Bryce." He held out his hand to Tristen.

Tristen said, "Hello sir. I am Tristen Kearney, Brina Cerdwin, and Seanna Bran. We can walk if we have our arms around the women for balance, but it is painfully slow going. Beats crawling, sir." Brina and Seanna moved to support Tristen.

"Captain, put one arm around me," Brina ordered. "Morgandy, you stand to his right and let him put his other arm over your shoulders. We can walk you into the house." Slowly the five walked the cobblestone path to the front doors. Curious, Shayla and Fionn were just inside watching the proceedings, and they opened the door for the five. "To kitchen, everyone," Brina ordered.

Once safely in the chairs, the captain relaxed, but Morgandy began bawling. "Sis, they're all dead! Murdered. Church fellows did it." Through her wails, her story slowly emerged, though Brina had to ask pointed questions to get at some of the details. The day after the plague struck them down, Morgandy was in the bathroom when she heard strange voices and heard lots of gunfire and screams and yelling. Terrified, she peered out of the bathroom to see three blue robed churchmen with long guns searching for others. She saw their cook coming to see what the commotion was all about and watched helplessly as one of them shot her in the head. Morgandy had then sense enough to hide behind a washtub. One man stuck his head in the bathroom, but didn't see her. Morgandy waited for a long time before venturing out. All was deadly quiet.

She found their parents and their other brothers and sister lying in pools of blood. Helpless though she was, she went to each to see if they would wake, but they were lifeless and no longer breathing. She lay beside her mother, waiting for someone to come to help her. Days passed. At last, starving, she decided to go for help, though she had no idea where she should go at first. She wandered through their home looking for a way out of it. At last, she found the back door was ajar and at last was able to get outside their home.

She headed for the streets, but there were so many dead lying around that she spooked and had hid for a time, watching. No one stirred. That's when she thought of trying to walk to Brina's new estate. The captain had come along and found her. Since he was coming here anyway, he insisted that she ride with him.

Captain Bran took up the story from here, far more coherently. "Our general is in Nuadilan now, at least I think so. When the plague struck, the major was with the king. The gunfire alarmed me, and I managed to get them to saddle my horse. I went to report to the major. I found my boss had been killed along with the king and his entire family. Two men from the Church of Jehosanity were also dead in the palace. I put two and two together and surmised that the church men had assassinated our king."

"It took me several days to get my men to clean up that mess. Meanwhile, I sent most home to their families. This plague is just devastating, particularly so for our women, who are now incredibly helpless. Then I waited hoping for a message from the general. None came, though I did send out scouts to several nearby towns. By all reports, the plague is wide spread, though I cannot say for sure if it has struck all of Cymry, you realize."

"Okay, if the king is dead, who then is next in line, I asked myself. We need a leader fast. I reasoned that the king's son, Weylin, was the heir to the throne. Hence, I decided to find him. After searching his offices and the palace thoroughly, I decided that he must have been at his new estate when the plague struck. I headed here to inform him that he is now our ruler. Brina, that now makes you our queen, Your Majesty." He saluted her.

"Weylin is dead. You certainly don't want him running things," Brina dashed the captain's hope for finding the rightful ruler. "He was evil. He had my arms cut off without my consent!"

"Oh, really? I thought that you had just lost them as everyone else has with the plague. Dead? Damn, now who is our ruler?" he replied, crestfallen.

"Doesn't that make Brina here our queen still? She is Weylin's wife and therefore queen," Tristen commented.

The captain brightened up, "You are right. Brina, you still are our queen, until they elect a new king! Your Majesty, what are your orders?"

"Stay alive until some help comes, silly," Brina replied. "Look, the general will know what to do and can bring our army to help restore order around Bregia. It is only a couple days ride from Nuadilan to here. He ought to be bringing help soon, don't you think?"

"True, he has most of the army with him, I suppose. I am sorry Your Majesty. I really don't know where the bulk of our army is located. We only had a small garrison here in Bregia. We've never been under attack nor are we likely to for that matter. We have all Layamon between us and any enemies."

"Okay. How is your wife surviving?" she asked.

"Sorry, Your Majesty, I am not married. My fiancé is, well, she's taking this rather badly. I think that she has gone mad, but maybe that will pass. She is living with her parents."

"Okay. How about guns? Have you secured all your guns and ammunition? We've heard lots of gunfire in the streets. I certainly don't want more of that falling into their hands. Oh, and just Brina. I don't like Your Majesty. Just Brina, please."

"Yes, Your — Brina," he corrected himself awkwardly. "I regret to inform you that the supply depot has been looted already. Whatever guns and ammunition the general had stored there are gone."

"Well isn't this a fine ta-do!" Brina replied, a hostile note in her voice. "Okay, then it seems that there is very little that even a king could order now, is there?"

"Well, no Brina, I guess there really isn't much. Without soldiers to back up orders and carry them out, not much at all."

"Okay, so our job now is to stay alive and well until help comes. Surely help will come sometime," Brina replied. "Until then, since you don't have a place to stay, you may stay here with us."

"Thank you, Your — Brina. I pledge my life to protecting you, our queen!" he gallantly bowed.

Brina smiled, "All right then, first things first. Are you both hungry?" Of course, they both were. While Seanna began cooking, the others helped the two bathe. Tristen found some clothes of Weylin's for the captain to wear while his uniform was washed. The three women worked on bathing Morgandy, who was particularly filthy and still sobbing quietly to herself.

While Seanna took what seemed forever to fix the meal, it took almost that long for the three women to handle Morgandy, particularly her ratted blonde hair, which fell below her knees now. By the time that Brina, Fionn, and Shayla had Morgandy cleaned up and presentable in one of Brina's new nightgowns, the food was ready.

Morgandy had slowly come out of her self-sorrows and had observed that her sister and her two friends had been able to care for her. She discovered that Seanna had somehow managed to cook a hot meal that was actually quite good. These actions were not missed by the captain, who commented as they sat down to eat, "This is incredible! She cooked the meal all by herself. I would not have believed it possible if I had not seen it. Amazing."

"They bathed me and did my hair, no small feat in itself," Morgandy added.

"Of course, sis, we are not completely helpless, though at first, I admit that we all thought so. These past ten days, we four have been finding all sorts of unusual ways to get things done. We'll show you, sis. First, watch us and see how you can feed yourself. Bet you didn't think you'd ever be able to do that again, did you?" Brina pointed out. Morgandy was both shocked and surprised to discover that she was rather able to manage for herself. Tristen did aid her a little, as she slowly got used to the motions that she needed to do.

That evening, disaster struck Bregia, though the root cause was not known until years afterwards. Thieves breaking into a warehouse in search of food accidentally knocked over an oil lantern, spilling its oil onto the wooden floor. The flames rapidly spread, and the three thieves were unable to put it out and fled for their lives. By early evening, the entire warehouse was a raging inferno, billowing smoke clouds rose high into the air. The smoke caught everyone's attention, as they sipped their evening tea before bed. All went to the eastern windows to look and saw the orange glow in the sky, great sooty tendrils arched skyward, illuminated by the flickering of the giant flames far below.

"This is not good," the captain announced. "The fire fighters are as crippled as I am. How can they possibly fight the fire?"

They could not and no one even tried. By morning, the whole city was engulfed in a smothering smoke cloud. The fire spread rapidly, consuming more than half of Bregia before it burned itself out at the docks. Thankfully, the prevailing winds were to the south during those few days. However, many, many people of Bregia fled for their lives during the four days that the fire raged. Many said that if the winds shifted, the whole city would be burned to the ground. Brina didn't worry too much, however. Her mansion and estate was on the far western edge of the city and sat back far from the street and nearest buildings. Besides, her roof had tiles not thatch. She had no doubt that her mansion would escape the inferno. At the time, they had no idea that a similar scenario was playing out at over one quarter of all the towns and cities in Layamon, during November and December.

Adding to their misery, as soon as the fire died out, heavy snows came, covering everything with a foot of snow, turning Bregia into a white chaos of charred remains. Only a quarter of the population of Bregia remained in the city and they were sorely tested in the coming months. After the heavy snow came, Brina sent Tristen and Bran out to look for survivors who were in dire need. Any found were brought back to her estate and given sanctuary. Because they were still crippled, their explorations were severely limited, but they did bring a dozen women and a few men back with them.

Fortunately, one of the men was a tailor. He had never made a dress before, but Brina and the women were desperate for something to wear to stay warm. He began to make them crude slip on dresses, using the massive amounts of cloth from all her many new ball gowns. At least, they were finally able to stay warm.

When January arrived, their feet returned to normal and they all celebrated this most fortuitous event. Brina realized that men were complete free from the plague's effects, while the women were still quite helpless for the most part. Still she did do her best to educate the dozen women whom they'd rescued. Slowly, these women caught on as well. At last, Brina felt confident in sending Tristen and Bran out on scouting missions, looking for those in dire need.

What kept the remaining quarter of Bregia's population alive during the winter was their raiding of whatever food supplies remained in the now vacant homes and shops spared by the fire. Brina gave Bran an order to have the few men who were here lend him a hand in locating and removing the dead bodies that littered Bregia's streets, yards, and homes. She suggested that they be dumped into the shell of the old Church of Jehosanity. Hampered by the deep snow, this task took them until spring to accomplish, at which time, their remains were burned.

Additionally, Brina had Tristen and Bran bring a dozen women from their homes to her mansion for training. Brina had seen enough women's reactions to the plague to know that nearly every woman had just given up and was "being helpless" in all ways. Hence, she had a few at a time brought to her place, where she and her friends demonstrated the various ways that they had worked out to accomplish domestic activities. After a few days of practice, the two men took the women back to their homes. During the long winter months, this not only gave the women something to do, but it also guaranteed that come spring, the remaining women in Bregia would not be useless. If a recovery was possible, women would have to play a role in it, Brina reasoned.

When spring did come, at least two hundred women were able to perform some domestic chores around their homes. True, it was a far cry from the nearly thirty thousand women and girls who still remained in Bregia. Originally, the port's population was close to two hundred fifty thousand. Now they had barely sixty-five thousand still living here. Brina's spring orders were simple: clean up as much as possible and stay alive. She still held out hope that help would come. Surely now that travel was possible, men would come to help rebuild the vital port city. Help did not come.

Instead, gangs of thugs began making their appearance. By the end of summer, women were being kidnaped and held in houses of prostitution. For a woman to be seen on the streets of Bregia was an open invitation for some man to abduct her. Several tried to gain access to Brina's estate, but the captain and several other men with their long guns persuaded the thugs otherwise. Mostly, the gangs left Brina's place alone, thankfully.

"If only we had the army here," Captain Bran lamented. "I just hate not being able to put things right." Brina sympathized with him, yet there was little that they could do except continue to be on the lookout for those in need and bring them to her estate. During the summer of 824, more and more women, girls, and men called her estate home.

By fall, Captain Bran absolutely insisted on traveling to Nuadilan and other outlying cities. "Look, we absolutely have to have help here. Perhaps I can find where the army has gone and bring them back." He was so insistent that Brina had to give him permission to go, though she feared for his life.

He returned in late October a changed man. "It is all over, Brina. Nuadilan is gone. Burned to the ground. I saw human bones lying everywhere in the debris. Sickening. It is the same everywhere, towns burned halfway to the ground. Only the farmers are still doing well. In what's left of the towns, gangs control everything, just like here in Bregia. Women are constantly being kidnaped and forced to live in brothels. It is more horrible than I can possibly say." After he gave his report to Brina, Captain Bran was so depressed that for days he just sat and stared at the walls.

Fearing the worst, she made a thorough survey of their food supplies. Already they had laid in a large supply of dried fish along with what other dried meat they had acquired from nearby farmers. She believed that they had sufficient grains, vegetables, and dried fruit to hold them over the winter. Tea, however, was almost gone. No ships had docked; they couldn't, not until the burned out docks could be rebuilt. At least we can survive the winter, she thought, if we can just get more firewood. She gave Tristen that task.

Now she began to ponder the situation with the women here in Bregia. Once the snows came, most travel would cease until spring. Perhaps, they could get enough men together and raid these brothels, freeing the women and eliminating the evil men. At least she hoped so. Surely, there were enough good men around to form up vigilante groups to carry this out. She approached Captain Bran with her plan.

"No good, Brina. The thugs have vastly more guns than the rest of us. You are sentencing your volunteers to death," he shot down her only plan. Now Brina was in the dumps. What else could she do?

"Perhaps we can keep an eye on these places," Captain Bran suggested. He saw how crushed Brina was and attempted to provide some slight hope. "At least then when we can muster the proper forces, we'll know where they are located."

"And you'll know the men who used those women. They are just as guilty, paying to rape a woman," Brina cursed, wishing she had her arms and sword. She could extract justice then. Well, perhaps not against guns, she admitted to herself.

"Desperate men do foolish things," Captain Bran attempted to justify.

"Against a woman who no longer even has arms to push him off her? No, I say desperate men do wicked things. Mark my words, one day they will pay for their actions. Is it not said that for every action there is a reaction?" Captain Bran bowed his head.

He kept his word and continued to scout out the locations of the brothels. Brina kept an accurate record, and he was amazed that she was able to write a little using her feet and those low desks. On their side was the winter of 824. Bregia received almost a record amount of snowfall, burying the port city in nearly two feet of snow. Very few men even attempted to venture outside, and then only for short distances. Late March of 825, the snow slowly began to melt, but it was nearly April before the muddy streets were passable easily. The heavy mud made walking difficult and messy. The Great Fire had ruined even the cobblestones, cracking and up heaving them as well.

In April, the kidnaping began once more, though infrequently. A number of dead young women were found tossed near the ocean. Captain Bran theorized that some of the kept women had perished during the winter and were merely dumped there. Twice, he spotted a kidnaping occurring and was able to kill two of the bearded men, rescuing the two young women.

"Will this never end? How can we begin to rebuild our city when these vile creatures continue to destroy us?" Brina exclaimed utterly disgusted.

That night Partholan appeared in her home, appointing Brina the Monarch of Layamon. He promised that any man harming a woman in anyway would face his wrath. Of course, the hundred plus men, women, and children now residing in Brina's mansion were greatly awed by this appearance. Some believed it was only a mass hallucination they witnessed.

The next day, Captain Bran and Tristen went to check on one of the whorehouses. "My god! It is true!" exclaimed shocked Captain Bran. Streams of women were coming out of the large home, once the house of a wealthy family. Their clothing was in tatters, what little of it they wore. More like zombies, Tristen suggested. Both men began ushering the women towards Brina's place. Soon, Tristen ran on ahead to alert her of the coming of nearly two dozen dazed women. Brina issued orders, but now there were so many men and women staying in her place, that she didn't have to worry. Many hands and feet would begin caring for them at once. She then raced along with Tristen back to where Captain Bran stood just outside the large, once elegant, home on the eastern side of Bregia.

"Ah, you're here. Your Majesty, I counted twenty-five women. I hope they will make it. Shall we head inside and see what's what?" he sounded an encouraging note. "Maybe that wasn't a dream after all." He was referring to the visit of Partholan.

Inside, Brina found some fifteen men, all as armless as she was, only they were just now experiencing their own shock and terror, much as the women had the day of the plague. Their wailing pleas for help fell on deaf ears. The three turned around and left the home, making sure that the door was firmly latched. Old style round doorknobs would be a bitch for them to open, Brina thought. She was right.

Captain Bran led them to the next location. Here they had to open the front doors. They found eighteen women in the hallway attempting to get out. One told them that the men were helpless now and could not get themselves out of their own bedrooms. Tristen led these women back to Brina's, while Captain Bran and Brina headed to the next location. Same story. This time Brina led nineteen women back to her place, while Captain Bran headed to the last known place of prostitution. Later, he led thirteen more women to safety.

Similar scenes occurred throughout Layamon that day. Many of the armless men were killed by the male relatives of the women whom they'd victimized. Brina did not even comment upon hearing of this, however. She had her attention on the women and how she could possibly help them recover.

Chapter 57 Partholan's Request

Seated in Monarch Stefano's office, Partholan spoke first. He outlined the savagery that some men had done against women in Tewdwr and Layamon in particular. His vengeance was parallel to what he'd done down in Axos, Thrace. Eve smiled and complimented him for such a brilliant postulate. "That is vastly superior to just wringing their necks," she added.

"Ah, not quite as good as the one that you invented for General Erebos in Levkos, Alia," he replied.

Eve grinned. "So you heard about that one."

"Yes, clever. I have appointed two women as monarchs of Tewdwr and Layamon. The five Goronwy sisters, led by the eldest called Tegan, will run Tewdwr. Brina Cerdwin will be the monarch of Layamon. The Highlands of Ruadan fared better. I helped a man called Fergus d'Aine recover from deadly wounds, though it took six months of convalescence for him to heal fully. He was first in line to the throne, as I gather in these matters. He shall be the king there."

"He lives? Incredible. His wife and sister are here in Velona, three blocks on down the street," I replied. "She will be elated to hear that Fergus is alive."

"Without my intervention, he would not be, Bethany. Further north in the Dark Forest, the Axemen have fared well, facing the plague with firm resolution and defiance. They needed no assistance from me. However, I have brought two Axemen with me." Only now did he introduce the two bearded, burly men, who had sat quietly through Partholan's long story.

"This is the leader of the Axemen in Cymry, Bjorn Valdr. This is the leader of the Axemen of Volksholm of the far north, Einarr Dagfinrr. Einarr wishes to speak first," Partholan said.

Einarr rose and bowed to we three and then to his kinsman, Bjorn, and to Partholan. I realized that in his land, it was customary to rise when speaking to a group. He began, "I have come to Velona to request your aid for my people. The plague has been devastating to our women, who have still not recovered. We have heard that here in the south, you have ways that our women could use to begin to live their lives once more. I have come seeking such aid as you can give."

"More than that, I need one question answered honestly. For us, the answer is, how do I say this, most critical, most crucial. Will our women's arms return one day as they have done here in Velona some years ago?"

"I am truly sorry, Einarr, I really am. After the First Plague, we were able to create a way to undo it, to re-grow our arms. This Second Plague, I regret, simply cannot be undone. We women are doomed to have no arms. Our female children are born without arms, though I expect that you also already know this. I am so sorry. This time, I too am helpless to undo the devastation the plague has caused."

"It is as many of us have thought. This is the way our women will always be. Then, my trip here still has meaning. We have endured two winters now. The toll that it has taken on our women is beyond words. If our people are to survive, we must abandon our homes in the north and seek warmer lands, lands where we may be able to partake of the strange and marvelous inventions of Velona. All those in Volksholm are preparing to move to the south even as we speak. What remains to be decided is what we must do to obtain the lifesaving things of Velona and where we may resettle in peace. We cannot afford to go to war to obtain new lands. The Plague has greatly reduced our numbers. Bjorn has offered many of us a new home in his Dark Forest. Yet, we are too many for his land. I have come to ask for your help. Is there a place where we may resettle and live in peace and not forsake our customs and ways?"

"There is the whole northern part of the great Western Continent," Stefano answered. "However, I would not recommend that land. It is too distant from us. You see, Einarr, we in Velona are making all of our incredible inventions available to all countries and people who desire them. This plague is a world crisis, not just one country's. We all must work together if we humans are going to survive. So I would prefer that you and your people move somewhere closer. Let's see what we can come up with, shall we? We do not know what your people actually need in terms of a new country or land."

"Snow in the winters, access to the ocean, and forests for timber to make our homes and long boats," he replied.

I had an idea and had Stefano and Eve take them on a demo tour of some of our inventions. I asked Eve to discuss the possibility of giving them our Holy Gift therapy. Meanwhile, I fired up Stefano's LD radio and had two lengthy talks with two kings. When I returned, the two Axemen were extremely excited about our electricity and the most useful machines that used it. Eve had just finished giving them her talk about our therapy.

"Good news, Einarr. I have two places that fit your needs. I discussed your situation with the kings of Westfold and Calgary, Greenway. Both kingdoms border on the sea, just east of Cymry. By and large, these coastal areas are sparsely inhabited, primarily by small fishing villages. About fifty miles further inland the heavy timber of the coastal range gives way to the vast fertile fields, which are being heavily farmed. Both kings are offering you and your people sanctuary in their countries, as long as your people swear fealty to the new country and obey its laws. Further, both kingdoms are advancing on their electrification program, so our inventions will soon be usable in both countries. I'd say that this is perfect timing."

"Then our people could settle in three locations and yet be but a short ways from each other. I like that," Einarr replied. "Thank you, Mrs. Angela, thank you."

"Ah, now for my last request," Partholan broke in, "I need you to send immediate aid and guidance to Brina and to Tegan. Fergus could also use the aid, but his lands are not in such dire shape as Tewdwr and Layamon. Can you get help to them in days? I am afraid that they are in extreme need of assistance."

"Absolutely, Partholan. Let the two women know that help will be there in, let's say, two days. We'll get right on it," I replied, glancing at Stefano, who nodded my way.

"In that case, I will leave you now. Thank you for saving my Dalny. She is doing well and is helping our animals survive better," Partholan replied and left the room, vanishing entirely at the door. Impressive exit, Eve thought.

"Eve and I need to see what we can get arranged for the two women. Stefano will help you two make all the necessary arrangements. Hopefully, we will see each other soon," I said goodbye to the two burly men.

Back home, Eve headed off to chat with Macario. We needed more Bethany's Hints, translated into the thick accent of Tewdwr, into the Layamon dialect, into the Highlander's variation, and into that of the Axemen. I didn't know anyone now who actually spoke the language of Volksholm and wondered how Macario would manage that. Meanwhile, I had to find a caravel that could sail in one day for West Reach and then find folks to send.

"Look, no one speaks the thick Tewdwr dialect better than you, Bethany. You should go there first. You can run everything else you are doing via LD radio. You are on it most of the time," Sergio advised. Everyone was now getting into the act, trying to find immediate assistance as requested. Finally, West Reach was reachable and hopefully salvageable.

"Okay, you are probably right. We need keen, observant eyes on the ground there to work out accurately what is needed and how it can be done," I agreed, seeing little other options. Tewdwr was perhaps one of the roughest languages to learn. I swear they hated vowels!

Neither Lucianna nor Giovanni dared make the trip. Both were totally overloaded with invention works in progress. The DAE had tripled in size in just the last year alone, putting another five hundred women to work as well. "How about Lisa and me going to Bregia? We can speak their dialect fairly well," Sergio suggested. Hearing no objections and with few other options, I agreed.

I headed over to tell Rona d'Aine the fabulous news. "Hi, come on in," Zena said, as she answered my knock.

A minute later, I had Rona, Zena, and now eight year old Tam sitting down across from me in their living room. "I have just had the most fantastic news for you. Partholan has just visited with us — tell you about that later on. He told me that he saved Fergus' life, though it took him six months to recover fully. Fergus is alive and Partholan has made him King of Ruadan! Your husband is alive!"

Rona fainted. A bit later, recovering from the shock, I told her that we were sailing for West Reach in two days and were prepared to take them with us. "Can you three be packed by them?"

"My god, Bethany! I can be ready tonight! We thought he was dead. He looked dead — took an awful fall and was shot," Rona explained.

"Aye, he looked very dead, lassie," Zena added.

"I want to see daddy!" Tam exclaimed excitedly.

"Okay, pack up what you want. Give a telefono call when you are ready. We'll make the arrangements," I summed it up. "What about you four? Interested in returning to Layamon?"

Kaie replied for the four. "No way. We love it here in Velona. This is now our home. Besides, here we are accepted; back there, she and I would be ostracized for being married, maybe even run out of town. No, we love Wanda and Tatianna." I grinned, the four made a perfect group of women, I thought.

Back home an hour later, I got busy on the telefono. I needed engineers and soldiers, the latter not so much for our protection, though I knew Stefano would insist on sending some along for just that reason, but to supply manpower, hands in other words. Actually, I needed two complete sets, one for Layamon and one for Tewdwr. Finding some to go to Bregia was relatively easy to locate. Many also spoke their dialect because prior to the plague, nearly all the trading for West Reach went through the port of Bregia. Finding people to go to Tewdwr was a challenge. Few even spoke their thick dialect.

After spending almost all day on the telefono, I located the key personnel that I needed. Many years ago, some families from Tewdwr had immigrated to Velona. Alessandra Cesarino's grandmother came from there. Likewise, Adona Boldovino's grandfather had come from a fishing village in Tewdwr. Both women spoke the basic language, albeit crudely, if my recollection of the dialect was to be trusted. Both were married and all four worked for the DAE as engineers and inventors. Such luck, they were the only two out of the thousands employed there that spoke the language. I also found Captain Dario Doro whose grandfather had been part of the army that was sent to Tewdwr many years ago to help defend the land from the King of Layamon's aggression war. He too spoke it crudely.

Thus, at last I had my basic crew. Now to the packing. Stefano only had one set of MMCE demonstration equipment loaded on a caravel. He continued to keep at least one set loaded at all times, just so that he could take advantage of surprise salvage requests, such as this one. He never ceased to amaze me — what an organizer he was. We decided to take it to Tewdwr first, since we all knew that Bregia was still in ruins. They had not rebuilt the port since the Great Fire shortly after the plague came. Rebuilding would be their first actions, not the MMCE. My plan was that after we gave the demo in Tewdwr, the caravel would then take it on down to Bregia.

When we arrived in Tewdwr, we found that it was like stepping back into time some two hundred years. Perhaps we just were no longer used to a rural farming and coastal fishing culture. No town was larger than perhaps ten thousand people and the whole population of Tewdwr had now dropped to just over two hundred thousand, but only seventy-five thousand or so females. Tewdwr had never had any countrywide rulers, preferring to have a mayor run each town or village. At least half of the population could neither read nor write, compounding our problems there. We had very little infrastructure to work with when we arrived.

Still, Tegan and her sisters were amazingly well adapted, I found, including placing at least four women and girls in one dwelling. My first actions were to help the five sisters organize. Tegan's only ruling concept was that of a mayor. Building on that, I suggested that they continue with that basic unit, though she insisted that all the towns and villages elect a new mayor who had to be a woman. Nearly all the mayors either had turned against women as had Mayor Bledig or had turned a blind eye to the mistreatment of women in their towns.

Once that was done, the mayors themselves traveled to meet regularly with the five redheads in Dunloy Caern. At these meetings, Tegan and her sisters outlined what needed to be done next. After a few months, this became a workable solution.

Our engineers worked out an overall rail line plan that called for a coastal line running from the north Dark Woods along the eastern coast down to Bregia and then on up the western coast through the towns of Tewdwr. A spur line would run north into the Highlands of Ruadan. In Tewdwr, Velona had to provide the funds for most of the construction and MMCE projects since these people were quite poor by our standards.

Coal was plentiful and near the surface in the foothills of the Ath Mountains. Fuel wasn't a problem. The engineers decided to place quad electrical generators just outside Dunloy Caern. From here, the power lines would run northward and southward. Spur lines fanned out into the countryside servicing the outlying, non-coastal villages. This became a doable project.

The motor-wagons were a huge hit, not only with the women, but also with the men. Able to transport more than five times their usual wagon loads, they would also be a time saver as well. Tegan and her sisters preferred these to the simple T-putt-putts, since each town or village was easily walked on foot, unlike the huge city of Velona.

To handle the illiteracy problem, I had Tegan establish a school in every town and village. All children from six to fourteen were to attend. However, she also made provision for night school so that adults who wanted to learn to read and write had the opportunity. Again, a lot of the funding for this project came from Velona out of the Laird Foundation, this time.

On the therapy side, Marzia Michela began her work, though Marco and I pitched in as much as possible. She began, of course, with all those now living in Tegan's home. Even though the five sisters wanted to help give others therapy too, they had to forego that in favor of running the country. However, Mrs. Yestin and her son Rees, Nye and his sister Tegwen, Emlyn and his mother and sister, Raelyn, Eirian, and Briallen formed the initial core of therapy givers. The men handled making the arrangements, travel, and record keeping, while the women gave the sessions. By the end of September, they had given the gift to all of Dunloy Caern and were now expanding out to other towns and villages, aided by another twenty women and six men.

Marco and I returned to Velona on October 1, just before the icing of the bays would prevent our leaving until spring. While there were vast amounts to be done, Tewdwr was well on its way to modernization. We picked up Sergio and Lisa on our way home.

598

In Bregia, the first task that they faced was the rebuilding of the docks and city. Since the Great Fire, most were quite leery about building more wooden homes. Sergio had them lay out a new city, using as much salvaged stone from the several Church of Jehosanity shells in the burned out section of the city. Where it was not possible to use stone, Sergio advised them to allow for very wide streets. Triple what they had been. Thus, the streets provided something of a fire wall, should another catastrophic fire break out. The rebuilt towns and villages were now going to be significantly larger in physical size as a result.

He and Lisa, along with their engineers, helped them plan for four power-generating plants. One would be outside Bregia. The other three would be spread out across the middle section of Layamon. Additionally, they took frequent trips to visit Fergus d'Aine and helped him establish two power plants to service the highlands.

When they left, they and their engineers estimated that within four years the MMCE projects would be complete island-wide. Now if things would just stay settled for these four years, real hope for a better future was possible, especially for the women of West Reach. When we returned in October, Stefano and I placed a checkmark in the done column for the island. We also put one on Volksholm.

During that summer, a mass migration of the Axemen occurred. They divided into roughly thirds, establishing new towns and villages in the Dark Forest of West Reach, in Westfold, and in Calgary. Their new sites were distant from the existing settlements, but the kings added their towns to their own MMCE programs. Electrification would soon reach them as well. I expected that some of the Axemen would likely refuse to leave their ancestral lands, but that was their choice to make. At this time, I had no idea how many Axemen remained in the inhospitable far north. Right now, my concern was with the many, not the few. All told, our summer of 825 had been a productive one.

Only Vladimir on the Southern Continent, Tashien, and the majority of the unknown Western Continent remained in the Dark Ages.

Chapter 58 Be Careful What You Import

In Levkos, Alia, Aikos Ptolema was widely known as the importer of the exotic. His storefront was both elegant and filled with tastefully displayed expensive merchandise from all over Tarra. One display case held the Earrings of the Ancients or so the sign read. He'd acquired these monster jade and gold earrings from travelers of the north who claimed that they had come from some far distant island in the middle of the North Ocean. Another case displayed blowgun and darts from some tribe of the mysterious Western Continent. Along the side wall was a stuffed paca, whose soft wool was slightly discolored from the oils of many fingers who simply could not resist touching it. He had Highlander bastard swords of unparalleled quality. The name of the store did not communicate what lay inside, Ptolema's Imports.

If you had the money and wanted something, you went to Aikos and made your request. If you and the shrewd man reached an agreement, Aikos guaranteed delivery of said item, no matter the cost, distance, time involved, or difficulty in obtaining said object. In 802, Aikos was notified that a superb statue of a golden dragon was on the market in Shansee, Tashien. It was said that its ruby eyes were each the size of a fist and its body was pure gold. Aikos submitted the winning bid of one million gold on behalf of the Queen of Alia, who was intrigued by the rumors that the dragon gave its owner enhanced sexual powers. With an item this exotic and expensive, Aikos took no chances. After all, once the Banca del Dio money transfer was completed, it was his, but the dragon was in Shansee, many thousands of ocean miles from Alia.

Hence, Aikos made a secondary deal for someone to both guard and bring the prized dragon home to Alia. He hired a competent, young martial artist named Wie Lon Dong to accompany the dragon from its owner's home all the way to Levkos. Wie Lon was married and Aikos agreed to allow his wife, Mie, to come with him, particularly since she was also trained in the martial arts. He figured that he gained two guards for the price of one. As it turned out, it was money well spent.

Thieves made an attempt to steal the dragon while it was being transported to the docks. Wie and Mie thwarted that attack, though several of those hands doing the actual transportation were killed. Later, on the short overland journey from Preveza to Levkos, a large band of thieves also attempted to hijack the dragon. At the time, no one knew that these men were hired by the Queen of Alia to steal the dragon for her so that she could get a refund from Aikos as well as the dragon. Again, Wie and Mie successfully thwarted the surprise attack, though this time six of Aikos' men died. When Wie presented the dragon safely to Aikos, the man was extremely grateful and pleased with Wie's performance. So much so, that Aikos felt that he owed him a favor.

Now it just so happened that Wie and Mie had not just taken this long ocean voyage for money. Both had heard wild stories of exotic outer lands. Both had acquired the "explorer's bug," and they wanted to travel Tarra and see the outer world for themselves. Now that they were finally in Levkos, Alia, one of the wealthiest kingdoms of the huge country of Demokritos, they wished to stay here a time, seeing the sights, learning all that they could.

Aikos offered Wie a job as guardian of his store, located in the heart of Levkos. Further, he bought a semi-rundown combination storefront and home that was located directly behind his store and gave it to Wie as part of his payment for his services. Both sides were completely pleased with the deal. Wie had his first, very own home and an income for doing almost nothing, while Aikos had perhaps the best store protection money could buy in Alia.

As the years went by, both young families began to have children. At the time of the plague, Aikos had a son, Aesop, who was nineteen and had been married for a year, and identical twins, Psyche and Kassandra, who were fifteen. The two were impossible to tell apart unless they wore something that gave their identity away. As children, they were always pulling gags on their parents by switching hair ribbons, for example, thereby confusing their parent's orders. "But you told Psyche to do it, mother, I'm Kassandra."

Wie and Mie also had children. Their oldest was Alexus De Dong, seventeen at the time of the plague. The parents decided that it would be best if their children had both a local Demokritos name as well as a Tashien one. That way, if and when they returned to their homeland, their children would have a traditional name. Next came Roxane Bi, who was fifteen, and then Selene Dai, who was fourteen at the time of the plague. However, the story really begins years earlier when the twins were barely ten years old.

Wie and Mie had worked wonders on their rundown place, converting the storefront into a martial arts studio. By 808, they were giving lessons to others, though they accepted few students. One day while accompanying their parents to his store, the twins had wandered out back and discovered martial arts lessons in progress. Both twins stared at the students, enamored with the flying kicks and the seemingly impossible feats that the students were performing. When their dad finally found them, both were watching the lessons more intently than anything he'd ever seen them do. Of course, they begged him to allow them to take lessons too and thus it began for Psyche and Kassandra.

Almost from the very day of their first lessons, Aikos saw a wonderful change in the twin's attitudes. They were taught honor and righteousness, to think before you act and speak. After that, he backed them all the way in their training. Additionally, Mei was something of a linguist herself. She picked up languages as one might pick up loaves of bread, or so Wie claimed. Further, she believed in teaching others not only to read and write, but to also speak and write other languages as well. By the time of the plague, the twins were not only able to read and write perfect Demokritos, but also they were very conversant with the language of Tashien, Velona, and Annelise as well, though they were only just beginning their study of our language.

Psyche, Kassandra, Roxane, Selene, and Alexus were very close friends. The twins were usually over at the Dong home, a mile from their father's fancy manor house. As long as Wie escorted the twins, Aikos allowed them to spend as much time there as they desired. After all, he knew well that Wie was the reason that he had two extremely educated and very well behaved and mannered daughters. Long ago, they had ceased playing their childish gags on their parents.

The week before the plague struck Alia, Psyche, Kassandra, and Roxane proudly stood in their white robes, as Master Wie presented the three with their Black Belts. Each bowed to him as he tied theirs around their waists. "Most honored to present your Black Belt, Psyche Ptolema," Wie said formally.

She bowed and replied, "Most honored to accept the responsibilities that come with it Master Wie." He repeated this twice more. Then the three erupted into cheers and excited jumping. "We did it, Kassi, Roxane! We made it!" Psyche said exuberantly. Mie then offered the three a traditional tea to celebrate their achievement.

"Don't worry, Selene, you will earn your Black Belt very soon now, I can tell," Psyche encouraged her. Last year, Alexus became the first to reach this, the highest level of training that Wie could teach. Selene sighed, but joined in the party atmosphere, she knew that she still had not quite fully mastered the flying circle kick.

Wie had often told them about the other schools in Tashien and in particular, the incredible kijutsu powers that many of the masters there possessed. "It sure is a real bummer that we cannot learn more from you, Master Wie. Are you sure you cannot teach us some kijutsu powers?" Kassandra pleaded for the umpteenth time.

He grinned, "I cannot teach what I do not know. It was most unfortunate that Mie and I came to your country when we did, for I was about to be taught those things."

Psyche grinned, "Glad that you did, otherwise we would not have become Black Belts!"

Mei smiled, adding, "And I would not know so many languages and we would not have seen so many different things that this land offers."

"I think that we all ought to make a trip to Tashien, Wie and Mei, and we all can learn kijutsu together," Kassandra suggested. "Wouldn't that be just great? We have enough money that we can pay for everyone's passage, but we should wait a little until Selene is also ready." Selene looked very pleased.

Interestingly, the twins had long ago chosen to emulate the way that the Dong's wore their hair. None of the Dongs ever cut their long, thick black hair. However, the men wore theirs in a single braid, while the women wore theirs in a double braid. Wie also had a black moustache. All had roundish faces and a yellow tint to their skin. In contrast, the twin's skin was more bronze in color. Their hair was not as thick as the Dongs but it was just as black. They took after their mother. After beginning their lessons when they were ten, they allowed their hair to continue to grow. While even Selene's was longer than theirs was, Psyche was pleased that theirs now touched the small their backs. Both twins had brown eyes and thick eyebrows. Their faces were somewhat angular giving them a slightly fierce or wild look, which they liked since they were fighters now. All the children's bodies were physically fit, well-toned and muscled from the constant strenuous, daily workouts.

Their happiness and lives came to an abrupt and crashing halt when the plague struck late in 823. Their mother, Chara, had been a Holy Woman of the Eighth Degree, which is why Aikos was so pleased that his twins ceased playing gags on her and suddenly became responsible children, helping her out around the house. When the two awoke to find themselves as armless as their mother, they were tremendously shocked, shrieking in terror and crying for hours.

"Look, Psyche, Kassi, this is not the end of the world! Your mother has been without hers since we were married over twenty years ago."

"Twenty-two, Aikos," Chara amended his comment. "I've done well, have I not, girls? We are so very proud of you twins. Nothing can change that."

"But mom, we can't do our martial arts anymore," Psyche screamed. She felt that she had lost the only thing in the world that really mattered.

"Now we can never learn kijutsu, not ever!" wailed Kassandra.

Aikos knew better than to touch this subject. Instead, he said, "I will get you both some of the very best servants in Alia, just as soon as I can walk."

"But dad! We are completely helpless right now! I got to go pee," Psyche wailed as loudly as Kassi.

"Calm down, Psyche. I'll help you. This crawling is tearing up my knees."

Poor Aikos, he had more to handle than he'd ever imagined. None of Chara's servants came nor did any of his personal staff. Even his son had not come by to say hello. For the first time in his life, he was in a real pickle. What none of the women around him knew was that for the very first time, he realized what he had put his wife through for the last twenty-two years! He had been the one to encourage her to become a Holy Woman, based primarily on the queen's advice. Until this morning, he really didn't fully comprehend his wife's misery; he'd always provided her servants who handled these very needs what he was now handling in triple! Yes, he was embarrassed helping them with this very private action.

By evening, his knees were quite bloody from all the crawling around. However, after being fed supper, the twins had finally calmed down. The stark reality of their situation had been faced. At last, they began to turn their attention outward instead of inward. Both were quite startled to discover just how huge their breasts had become; none of their clothes fit, not remotely. That their waists were quite small made no impression on them. They were not interested in wearing fancy ball gowns, though they did so on occasion. Rather what really brought the twins back into the present with their attention turned outward was their hair. As they began to relax, they let their hair down, intending on having their dad brush it out, though they didn't expect him to braid it for them.

"Kassi, your hair! It's grown a whole lot!"

"Yours too, Psyche. Wow. It is falling to our ankles! I bet ours is now longer than the Dongs! I can't wait to compare lengths," Kassandra replied. "Say, I think I saw a brush in that pile of junk in the front room. Come on; let's check it out. We can see if mom's hair has grown too. Dad's sure hasn't, though. Strange."

Presently, they stood before the pile. "Hey, those are shoes. Let's try them on, maybe they will help us stand. My feet are aching from standing on my toes," Psyche suggested.

"Hey, perfect. Lots better, though I bet we can't walk much in them. I wonder why our feet are not like dad's? Maybe they were headed that way and somehow stopped. His sure are paralyzed," Kassandra wondered aloud. "Come on, we need to get mom to put this last pair on, then she can walk better. Damn, take minuscule steps, Psyche!" Kassandra wobbled wildly, swinging her non-existent arms to catch her balance. "That's really, really weird! I keep moving my arms. It even feels like I have arms, but there are no arms there. Weird, sis."

"Wow, we can barely walk! It's more of a shuffle than a walk. You're right; we're barely able to move, but at least our feet don't hurt now. I'll take the shuffle over aching feet any day."

Their mother returned with them and tried on the other pair with equal benefits. She then left to tell Aikos about the strange boots that must have been meant for him. "There are three hairbrushes, at least I think that's what they are. Do our feet go in them?" Psyche asked.

"They must. We don't have arms or hands to put in those loops. Come on, let's give it a try on each other or should we see if our legs can reach our own hair?" asked Kassandra.

They experimented on their own hair, and to their amazement both found that they were far more flexible than they ever had been before. "Wow, look at this, Psyche. I can touch my nose. I can even put my foot behind my head."

"Well, so can I. I used to do that but I had to use my arms and hands to pull them up there. Now it is so easy. You know, that must be a clue that we are supposed to be using our legs as our hands from now on. I wonder if mom was always that flexible?" Psyche wondered.

"How so?" asked Chara. Returned with Aikos crawling on the floor. He'd wrapped heavy towels around his knees now. After they showed her how flexible they now were, Chara sat down to test her legs.

"Wow, you are right. No, I was never able to touch my nose. If I really had to, I could almost touch my waist, but just barely. Well, now I can itch my own nose," she pointed out. While their dad began trying on the boots, the twins began experimenting with their now vastly longer hair. They quickly discovered that their hair was thicker and stronger than before, perhaps because of its remarkable new length, they assumed.

As they brushed, they became aware of the images in their minds. Before finishing their hair, they began experimenting with the other objects. They realized that the yokes would allow them to carry things. Kassandra was the first to suggest that they might be able to write using the low desks. Aikos groaned, he'd just realized that a completely new kitchen had to be installed. He groaned even more as he tried to stand on his toes like a ballet dancer, flailing his arms around wildly. "I think I'll stick to crawling," he grumbled.

"Psyche, let's see how these yoke things work and carry some of the kitchen stuff to the kitchen," Kassandra suggested.

"That is a good idea, Kassi," her father suggested. "Save my knees some. I'll get someone to install the kitchen tomorrow, if you women think that you would somehow be able to use it. I won't hold you to it, though. It is probably impossible for you actually to cook. After all, there have been many Holy Women like your mother and none of them have ever cooked that I know of, how about you dear?"

"No, none of my friends can cook at all. Aikos, we cannot even feed ourselves, so how could we cook? Yet, why else should all this kitchen stuff be here?" Chara replied.

The twins began carrying loads of pots, pans, cups, and silverware towards the kitchen. Just then, their front door burst open and two men in blue robes came crawling inside. How rude, Psyche thought. Then they saw the long guns!

"Holy Woman, Lord Jehosa's Day of Holy Judgment is upon us. Prepare to arise to Lord Jehosa's Holy Realm of Heaven," one said. The other man fired. Bang!

Psyche and Kassandra acted. Although they were severely limited, their many hours of training kicked in. Psyche lunged her yoke into the other man, whose gun misfired, its bullet lodging in one of the desks instead of Aikos. Then, two circle kicks arced at each man's neck. Wham! Wham! Both feet connected and both pushed outward as their misshapen feet touched their targets. Two necks snapped nearly simultaneously, both men dropped to the floor dead.

Aikos screamed, his reactions were so slow compared to his twins. "Chara! Chara! What is going on? Chara? My god, Chara!" The twins looked at their fallen mother, who was bleeding profusely; a large blood pool surrounded her chest. Aikos was crawling through the blood, getting to her side. As fast as they could, the twins moved over to their folks, a sickening feeling tightening up both of their stomachs, simultaneously, as many things always had. They were identical twins and often just knew what the other was thinking.

"Chara, Chara, hang in there. Kids, get some towels," he said. Why towels, the twins did not know. Instead, they bent down close to their mother.

"I love you, Aikos," she whispered.

"I love you too, Chara. Please, don't die. I will crawl to find a doctor, just don't die on me!" he wailed. The twins watched as she stopped breathing; the light in her eyes went out; her body stilled. Both knew that she had passed, but Aikos didn't and kept cradling her head, talking softly to her.

"Dad," Psyche whispered, "mom's gone." He looked up at her. She saw giant tears obscuring his eyes, and then he bawled, rocking his wife's head with his own body. The twins sat down and joined him, allowing their grief to flood over them like water over a falls.

Time passed. At last, Aikos recovered a little. He crawled off and later returned with a sheet and towels. Silently, he wrapped up his wife and began to drag her to their backdoor. The twins saw what he was trying to do and shuffled over to him, sat down, and helped him by pushing with her feet. "I must bury her properly. She loved to sit in our garden. We'll put her to rest there, not in that damn cemetery of Jehosanity!"

It took them several hours to bury her and darkness had fallen before they finished. Next, the three pushed the two dead assassins out of the home and into the street, but not before Aikos thoroughly searched them, confiscating their guns and other valuables. When they got back inside, Aikos finally spoke, "Thank you for killing your mother's assassins. All of your training has been put to the best use that I can think of — damn that church to Hell!"

"Dad, we ought to clean up the front room. You go get yourself cleaned up and Kassi and I'll clean up," Psyche suggested, her sense of responsibility kicking in once more.

He nodded and crawled off to the bathroom and then his room. A bit later, they heard him breaking into another long sobbing session. Meanwhile, Psyche stared at the bloody mess on the floor. "How are we supposed to clean this up, Kassi? Me and my big mouth. Mom always had us clean up messes, but now we are as helpless as she was."

"I know, but dad's breaking down. We just have to, Psyche. We must do this. I'm worried about dad." Between them and after tossing out a number of ideas, they used their yokes to bring in buckets, water, and rags. Although they spent an hour at it, often stopping to get their incredibly long hair out of the way of the mess, they finally got the blood cleaned up and the floor dried. At last, they too headed for their bedroom, unwilling to ask their dad to do anything more for them tonight.

Using their feet and teeth, they helped each other out of their dirty nightgowns. Both decided not to try to get into another so that they could use the pots by themselves. At last, they sat on the edges of their large bed. The two had slept together since they were little children. The twins began brushing out their hair, once again marveling at its incredible new length. Unspoken between them, they left their lantern burning, knowing they could not relight it if needed. "We even have to invent new ways to get into bed," Kassandra whispered, as she tried to use her arms to pull down the covers.

"More like flopping into bed," Psyche whispered, hitting the bed rather hard. Wiggling, they used their teeth to pull their covers up, snuggling up to each other as usual. Now their massive bosoms kept them further apart than they were used to being; they giggled and then grew passionate with each other.

The next day, they arose, filled with the same twin shocks of the day before. Again, the fact that they were missing their arms was driven acutely home. Reactively, they used their arms to try to get out of bed and to the chamber pots, which brought tears to their eyes. This morning, though, they didn't scream, just cried quietly to themselves. "We're just like mom," Kassandra whispered. That brought another round of crying, memories of their dead mother came vividly into their minds. An hour later, eyes red, the twins had finally stopped sobbing and were ready to face their world and somehow eat, but they were naked. With great difficulty and clumsiness, the twins managed by jumping, jerking, twisting, and pulling with their teeth to get themselves into a clean nightgown. "Nothing else is going to fit," Psyche pointed out.

They found their house strangely quiet as they came out of their room at last. It was already midmorning. Sounds of gunfire came through the windows and walls, but they were distant, Kassandra pointed out. However, the noise brought back their memories of their mother's assassination yesterday and both sat down in the living room and cried again. Later, their father came crawling out of his room. His eyes were bloodshot; he had not shaved; he looked awful, the twins thought.

In a voice almost devoid of all emotion, he slowly and softly said, "I will get you some servants today." He continued crawling to the kitchen. After looking at each other, no words were necessary, for they often shared the same thoughts, they rose and shuffled after their father, upon whom they now thought that they were utterly dependent.

At first, they believed that they were now useless in the kitchen and contented themselves, sitting on chairs watching him mechanically go through the motions of fixing some breakfast. After he served up the food, both insisted on trying to use their feet to eat. Their father sat staring at his own plate for the longest time before he began to feed himself. "Dad, you have to eat," Psyche whispered to him. He obeyed like some mechanical doll.

They figured they couldn't do the dishes now and left them, following their father into the front room. Kassandra whispered, "Dad, if you can get the new kitchen things hooked up, maybe Psyche and I can do the cooking for you." She was afraid to talk any louder, for fear more unknown men would come charging into their home, guns blazing. Aikos merely sat there and stared vacantly at the new things on the floor.

A little after noon, even more gunfire erupted. "It's getting closer," Kassandra whispered. Just then, they heard a familiar voice crying out for help. "Dad! That's Aesop's voice. Dad! Aesop is in trouble."

Kassandra and Psyche jumped up and raced to the front door, forgetting the awful condition of their feet. Both women fell forward, flailing their missing arms like mad. They landed with an awful thump, but avoided smashing their faces on the floor. That woke Aikos up. He began crawling towards them, then heard Aesop's cries. While the two struggled awkwardly to regain their feet, he passed them by, reaching the door and continued on outside. A bit later, shuffling pitifully slowly now, the twins joined him, staring at the sight before them.

Their brother had managed to get his carriage hitched up and get his new wife, Diona, up and into the carriage. Obviously, he'd driven here, seeking help from his folks. However, the gangs roaming the streets had intercepted him. A dark red patch outlined his left shoulder. Blood. He'd been shot. Worse, he kept calling for Diona, who was inside the carriage, but she was not answering. The twins felt a huge knot growing in their stomachs, as their father managed to get to the carriage door. Aesop struggled to get himself down from the driver's seat without breaking his pointed feet. His knees were also bloodied from extensive crawling.

The twins watched helplessly as Aikos lifted Diona down from the carriage. She seemed lifeless too, they thought. Then they saw the huge red stain on the front of her nightgown and knew that she'd been shot as well. He shook his head slowly and the twins knew what he meant. Aesop wailed no, no, no, over and over as he crawled up to the two on the ground beside the carriage door. He cradled Diona's head and rocked back and forth, sobbing and cursing.

Finally, Aikos said, "Let's put her beside your mother, Aesop." The two began dragging her to the backyard, leaving the twins standing there by the carriage, shocked.

At last, Kassandra whispered, "Let's get the carriage into the stables." They experimented and finally using their teeth on the harness, they tugged and pulled, convincing the horses to follow them into the stables. Once inside, they decided they could do nothing further and headed after the men.

Around two, Diona was buried, and Aikos tended the gunshot wound to his son's shoulder. They learned that he'd planned to bring his wife here and join up, figuring more hands were better. On his way, he passed by the import store and found rioters looting it. Wie was trying to protect the store, but there were just too many looters. He'd told Wie to save himself. As he left, some of the rioters had opened fire on the fleeing carriage. Obviously, one shot had gone through the thin sides and struck Diona in her chest. One had hit him in his left shoulder.

Unable to get a doctor, both because of the lawless streets and his inability to walk, Aikos had no choice but to doctor his own son. He tried and tried, but he could not get the bullet out. At last, he gave up and bandaged up his son's shoulder as best he could. He hoped and prayed for the best.

The next day, Aesop was awake. He talked much, but was feverish. He kept telling his dad that they needed to lay in a stock of food. Late in the afternoon, a soldier came by with some news as well. "Yes, it is the plague. Everyone's got it. The king is dead, murdered by that damn church of his. Martial law is in force; we are putting a stop to the rioting. If you need food supplies, we are rationing it." He indicated where he could get his rations.

The next day, another soldier came around with some of the initial proclamations. Women were to feed themselves somehow and to go naked. Clothes didn't fit them, so men were to stop babying them and get back to work somehow. Aikos couldn't, Aesop was growing more feverish by the day. Although he would not admit it at first, he began to realize that the wound was infected.

As the days drifted by, more silly proclamations came out, including only one woman per man in the household. Well, there were two men here now, Aikos claimed, and begged the soldier to fetch a doctor. No doctor came, but one soldier suggested that he staunch the wound with a red hot poker; that's what was done to wounded soldiers in the field. With little else he could do, Aikos attempted to do just that. The weakened Aesop screamed and passed out; the stench of burning flesh permeated the home for hours. Aesop did not wake up and died several days later. The three buried him beside Diona and Chara.

Grief filled the Ptolema household after that. Now half of the family was dead. Poor Aikos became horribly depressed and barely functioned at all. Yet, he had to act; they were running out of anything to eat. Finally, he used Aesop's carriage and headed off to the food ration center. The twins hoped that getting out would bring him around; they prayed it would be so. They needed him now more than ever before; their whole world was crumbling around their feet.

Getting out at last roused the middle aged man. Their home was in the wealthier district and soldiers patrolled these blocks vigorously. He filled the carriage with the rations he was allowed, a bit more than most since he was rather wealthy and widely known. On the way back, he decided to see what was left of his storefront. Looters had smashed in the windows and doors. They'd taken the items that contained either gold or gems, leaving the rest. Who wanted a stuffed paca? Many other items remained and were valuable before the plague. Now they were likely worthless, since you couldn't eat them nor trade them for food. As he stood amid the ruins of his store, Wie Lon Dong walked in.

"Forgive me Master Ptolema. I have failed to protect your valuable store."

"You have not failed me, Wie. Aesop told me what happened. There were just too many thieves with guns. Aesop is dead, Chara is dead, Diona is dead. They are all dead. Our world is coming to an end," he said apathetically.

"Never have I seen such anarchy, Master Ptolema. What of the twins? Roxane and Selene have been asking about them."

"Alive, but armless as their mother was, so helpless now. Are all our women so utterly helpless, Wie?"

"It would seem so, Master Ptolema. Mei, Roxane, and Selene are as your lovely wife was. Have you gotten the low kitchen installed yet? It seems that our women are somehow able to use it to do some cooking."

"No, Master Wie. I have not the skills to do it."

"Ah, then I shall come with you and help." He climbed in the carriage, and Aikos had no choice but to bring him along with him to his place. Four hours later, the men had the low to the floor kitchen hooked up enough to function. Using the yokes, the twins managed to carry the new rations from the carriage into the kitchen and got them stowed in the cabinets resting on the floor.

After that, Aikos said, "Master Wie, you may take the carriage as yours. I know that you do not own a carriage and we can only crawl now. So use it to get your family food rations."

"Thank you so very much, Master Ptolema. Thank you." He bowed and Aikos crawled off to his room, exhausted and depressed.

For the first time, the twins got the chance to talk with their master. "How is Roxane and Selene?" asked Psyche, assuming the worst.

"They are as you, armless. I see that you are finding ways to continue with life, much as they are.”

“Pathetic, Master Wie. All of our goals are gone, dashed forever, aren’t they? Our martial arts dreams are shattered. One day we were Black Belts ready to learn kijutsu and the next we are reduced to pathetic, helpless women, unable to do hardly anything at all, let along spar,” Kassandra declared the obvious, and what had so crushed the twins.

“Ah, it would seem so, but looks can be deceiving. Did you not use your kicks to stop the assassins from killing your father?”

“Well, yes, but we took him by surprise — a freak happenstance, Master Wie,” Psyche explained how she viewed it.

“There is no happenstance, no chance, only actions you take. Have you forgotten all of your training?”

“Well, no, of course not, only we have no arms and cannot do much of any of our moves,” Kassandra spoke the obvious, slightly annoyed that he would think that overnight they would forget their many years of training.

“Have you not been feeding yourselves, brushing your hair?”

“Well, yes, we had to,” Psyche replied, growing more annoyed.

“You do not have hands and yet you do these things which you used to do with your hands?”

“That’s rather obvious,” Psyche replied acidly.

“Ah, I see, alternate ways of brushing your hair and feeding yourselves do not matter then?”

“Of course they matter,” Kassandra protested.

“Why not find alternate ways to perform and execute your martial arts moves?”

The simplicity of his idea hit home to both teens. “Wow! Is this possible, Master Wie?” they said in unison, having both gotten the idea and the hope that it offered at the same instant.

“I believe that is so. Roxane and Selene are praying that this is so. I wish that you could come by and train each day with them. Now that I have a carriage, I will take you back and forth and protect you. I am sure that Master Ptolema will grant his permission. I will come for you tomorrow after lunch and we will begin.”

Both teens rushed him. They wanted to throw their arms around him and hug him tightly, but could not. Instead, they pushed their bodies hard into his, forcing his arms to encircle and hold onto them.

The next afternoon, Master Wie had to dress the twins in their white sparing uniforms, tying their black belts around their small waists for them. When they finally entered the Dong home and arts studio, Roxane and Selene were elated, anxiously waiting for them. Even Alexus was pleased to see them return.

“Dad says that we might be able to find other ways to execute our moves,” Roxane explained. “We’ve really, really missed you both!”

“Please, Psyche, Kassi, you have to help me,” Selene added, “or I will never, ever get my Black Belt. I just have to earn it somehow. Gosh, your boobs are as huge as ours!” She changed the topic.

“Wow, your hair! Selene, it’s almost touching the ground,” Psyche finally noticed the changes in her friend.

“Mine and mom’s are below our feet now,” Roxane added. “Dad and Alexus have to braid it for us and tie it up. I still don’t want it cut. I might lose some of my strength — at least, that is what everyone always says.”

Mei added, “It is said that cutting one’s hair removes some of one’s power, but that is merely an old wives tale I think. Still, ours is incredibly long now. I am so sorry about your mother and brother. How is your father taking it?” They chatted a while before the teens headed into the padded studio to train.

“If our feet were not so messed up, we might have a chance,” Roxane complained.

“At least you can stand, sis,” Alexus complained. “I am almost useless like this.”

The five teens worked hard, but were constantly frustrated with their physical limitations. So many of their hard-learned skills were lost to them. Nevertheless, Master Wie kept them at it all that afternoon. Somehow, he had to give them hope. During the next two weeks, he wracked his brain for ideas of alternate moves. “Look, the objective is to throw your opponent. While using your arms is the easy way, there must be other ways.” Sometimes in tears because of their failures, they continued to make feeble attempts.

After the grueling sessions, Mie prepared tea and a biscuit called a scone, filled with berries or honey. These times, the small group chatted, particularly about the great Olin Masters of Tashien. More and more, it sounded like the only real hope for the children was for them to all go back to their homeland. That the Olin Masters had the greatest and most powerful kijutsu only escalated the twin’s desires to make that lengthy sea voyage.

Then, in late November, more disasters befell the Ptolema family. The Ornamentation Project began to pick up momentum. The twins, fortunately, were only vaguely aware of the project, concentrating all their energies on trying to find alternate moves and regain their Black Belts. True, they did not actually lose their Black Belt status per se, rather they felt that until they could somehow accomplish all that had been on their mastery test, they were not Black Belts.

Aikos, however, was aware of the Ornamented Dolls, as they rapidly became known. He did some traveling to his store and began meeting with other wealthy men and nobles. Thus, he saw firsthand the devastating results of General Erebos' project. He also learned of the deaths of several wealthier men and boys who tried to stop the soldiers from taking their wives and daughters off to the Ornamentation Centers. Alone in his empty bed, his mounting losses festered in his mind. He'd lost the love of his life; he'd lost his only son and heir. Now he was about to lose even his own daughters, whose lives would be beyond awful. He saw that they were beginning to become alive once more because of their constant training with Master Wie. For that, he was eternally grateful and even bequeathed a small fortune to Master Wie in his will. However, he knew that his daughters would become hopelessly helpless, beyond even Master Wie's help once they were forced to become Ornamented Dolls. Their lives would be utterly ruined.

What could he possibly do? He already knew that he could not flee the city. Travel right now was nearly impossible. Besides taking two armless women out of the city would be beyond his abilities, he could only crawl and they could barely walk. The only idea he had lay in the fact that he was allowed to provide the Ornamentation Center with both the gold and gemstones to be used in their new earrings. He knew that the Ornamented Dolls were unable to speak. Hence, if anything were to happen to him, the twins would not be able to retrieve any of the vast fortune he had in his Banca del Dio account. Without him, they would be penniless and starve to death, unable to withdraw the funds he'd accumulated. Thus, he devised a clever plan: put a goodly share of his wealth in the twin's earrings. To that end, he made a trip to the Banca del Dio and made some arrangements.

Late November, the soldiers came to give him advance warning. "Mr. Ptolema, it is time for your twins to receive their prized ornaments. We will be arriving on Monday to take them to the Ornamentation Center. Of course, you may provide the gold and gemstones to be used in the making of their gorgeous new earrings, sir. Resist and we have orders to shoot to kill."

"I understand. I have made the arrangements and have already sent their gold and gemstones to the center," he replied, his voice was the saddest that it had ever been. All hope and life drained out of the man. That night, he had to explain to his twins what would be happening to them on Monday. Worse, they really didn't know what all was involved with the Ornamented Dolls, and he tried to explain it to them. Regretfully, he just could not bring himself to describe fully what the results would be. He did tell them very carefully about the value of their new earrings and how they were to use them to pay for their upkeep, should anything happen to him. He stressed this repeatedly.

Greatly annoyed and argumentative, the twins left to visit a distant cousin, who they'd heard had become an Ornamented Doll. At least she lived in the wealthy section of town, heavily patrolled by the soldiers. Their lives were not in significant danger as they shuffled along for over a mile on foot. To say that the twins were appalled at what had happened to their cousin would be an understatement. Fuming, cursing, and condemning their father when they finally returned, Psyche screeched, "Dad, how can you let them mutilate us so? We won't be able to do anything at all after this, nothing. Those poor women can do nothing but sit around and look pretty! Everything has to be done for them. How could you let that happen to us?"

He could not answer them, merely lowered his head in shame and cried. The twins ranted and raved their outrage, which soon turned to fear. They went to their room and tried to figure out what they could do to avoid being taken away. They could not run away, they could barely walk. Fight. That was the only avenue left to them. "Kassi, we fight to the death! We can't live like our cousin. I'd rather be dead, so we fight and take as many of the soldiers with us as we can."

"Right, Psyche, we'll make them pay!"

Aikos was not a fool; he made a coldly calculated guess what his daughters would do on Monday morning when the soldiers would come for them. He wrote out a long letter addressed to Master Wie Lon Dong, placing it where the man would surely find it when he came around noon to pick up the girls. He loaded the three long guns that he had — two from the assassins who had killed his wife. He was prepared at last and waited for Monday to come. He rose early and made his twins a good breakfast, insisting that they eat. That was at six in the morning. As the eight o'clock hour approached, the twins took up their positions on either side of their front door.

"This is it, Kassi. Let's do this!" Psyche whispered.

"Right. I'm ready." Kassandra replied. Across the front room, Aikos waited for the doom, which he thought now was inevitable, to arrive. Unknown to the twins, he had all three long guns hidden beside him on the couch. The dreaded knock came. He did not answer, he simply couldn't. His hand grasped one hidden long gun. Maybe the twins would give it up and go along peacefully with the soldiers. After all, the Ornamentation Project demanded that all women of Alia become Ornamented Dolls. Eventually all women would be Ornamented Dolls.

The doorknob turned and two soldiers, long guns at the ready, poked their heads in, one calling out, "It's time, we've come for Psyche and Kassandra Ptolema." They saw Aikos sitting on his couch, apparently harmless. Then the twins struck, using their circle kicks precisely aimed. Both soldiers were struck in their necks and dropped paralyzed to the ground, dying slowly. Outside, six more soldiers, having met some resistance before, were prepared. The twins were now visible and they rushed in en mass. Under orders not to harm the women, they could not shoot the twins, who continued to make circle kicks at them. Using the butts of their guns, they sought openings to crack the women on their heads. Blam! Aikos shot one of the soldiers in his head. He dropped to the ground, adding to the mess at the doorway.

Psyche landed another killing blow, but the lights went out. Another soldier took advantage of her exposure and rammed his gun butt into her head. Blam. Another shot rang out. Kassandra saw that her father had shot one of the soldiers and briefly took heart. He had not deserted them as they had expected. However, another soldier fired back, and she saw her father drop the second long gun that he was raising to shoot a second soldier. He slumped onto the floor. Then, the lights went out. Her momentary distraction gave another soldier time to whack her on her head. The soldiers picked up the two twins. They left their four dead companions where they fell, intending to return later to remove their bodies. Soon, their wagon rolled off to the Ornamentation Center.

Around noon, Master Wie pulled up in front of the Ptolema home and saw the open door and dead soldiers. As fast as he could, he climbed down, landing a bit too hard on the tips of his toes. Even though he wore the boots as protection, he grimaced from the shooting pain in his feet. He crawled up to the men and saw that the four were dead; three had broken necks, one a gunshot to the chest. Crawling over their bodies, he spotted Aikos lying on the floor, two long guns beside him. A pool of drying blood seeped out from beneath his chest. He called out, but got no answer. He crawled up to his benefactor and checked for signs of life. None.

"Damn, what has happened here? Psyche, Kassandra?" he yelled. No answer. He crawled off towards the kitchen and then spotted a letter lying close to Aikos. It was addressed to him! He went to the letter, opened it, and read. "Oh my god!" he exclaimed several times before he finished it. He read it again before crumpling it up and stuffing it into his pocket. He lowered his head and cried. He wept for his friend Aikos and more so for his twins.

His grief was interrupted. A group of soldiers arrived and began carting off the four soldiers. One asked, "Will you be here when the women are returned, sir?"

"When will they be returned?" Wie managed to ask and not sound so grief-stricken.

"Friday around ten, sir." He promised that he would be here. He just had to, that he knew. Once the soldiers were gone, he took the carriage home, showed his family the letter, and returned with Alexus to bury Aikos beside his wife in their back yard, which was rapidly becoming a family cemetery plot, he thought.

"We can put the twins up in the storage room," Mei suggested. "We must look after them, Wei."

"According to Aikos, all women will be getting ornamented. I think his plan merits our consideration. He wrote that we are to move into his home. He thinks that when they come for you and our daughters, they will find our home abandoned and thus believe that we have fled the city. He thinks that this way, we may save you from this terrible thing. It is my decision; we shall follow his advice. He has never been wrong with us. I believe him. We simply cannot have this happen to you or our daughters, Mei."

Quietly, the Dongs packed up their things and moved everything they owned over to the Ptolema home. By Friday, there were no signs that their old home was inhabited any longer. Master Wie hoped and prayed that this would stall the ornamentation of his own family. When the wagon brought the sobbing twins home, the Dong family was there to greet them. All were shocked beyond words at what they saw.

Psyche awoke. Her head hurt; her lips felt stretched, and a throbbing pain shot through them. She tried to rise up as usual, only her head and neck didn't move. Her eyes saw the bronze disk with the etched dolphins that forced her slit upper lip out into a four-inch circle. She panicked and forced herself to sit up, though it took a great effort. Her sister was lying in the narrow bed beside her. She screeched in terror as she saw how her sister looked, knowing that was how she now appeared as well. Bronze neck rings encircled her neck. She was unable to move her head at all. Even to turn her head, she would have to move her entire body! Drool seeped out of her mouth, and she tried in vain to keep it inside by pressing her lips together. They no longer worked, and the ooze slid down the sides of her face.

Her yells brought the doctor to her, but not before she yelled to Kassandra, "Kassi! Wake up! Look what they have done. . ." She stopped abruptly! Her words were completely unintelligible.

The doctor stepped up to her and examined her lips. "Yes, you are healing just fine. You've been out for twenty-four hours. Someone will come by and feed you light broth today. We'll start you on solids tomorrow. If all goes well, we will send you home Friday morning after breakfast. Ah, your sister is waking up." He repeated his often-said speech for her, ignoring her screams of terror and unintelligible words.

Sitting up, Psyche now felt that her ears were being completely pulled off her head. So heavy were her new earrings that her lobes were quite elongated. Any moment, she felt they would simply pull her ears right off. She screamed and cursed the doctor, who mistook her words as saying that she approved of her new Ornamented Doll look. She screamed even more; Kassandra added her lungs to the noise.

He left them sitting up in bed. Kassandra tried to talk to Psyche but she could not understand a single word that she said. Psyche replied, and Kassandra realized that they could not even speak any longer, adding a new dimension to their woes. Shortly a man came with two bowls to feed them. At first, the soup trickled out of their mouths, their lips no longer kept anything inside their mouths. He was experienced with this, and said softly, "It helps if you lean back a little. Liquids stay in your mouths that way."

Both teens spent the rest of the day in abject misery, alternating between sobbing and outright crying. Now they were beyond helpless, unable even to ask the kind man for a drink. Even the simplest thing now became nearly impossible for them to do, such as using the pots beside their beds. They couldn't move or bend their necks; they couldn't see over the obstruction of the lip plates or their massive bosoms. At last, Kassandra was able to help Psyche use hers and then Psyche helped her sister. They chatted a bit as they always did, but simply could not understand what the other was saying, which brought on another round of sobbing and crying.

At night, they could not even use their teeth to pull their covers up any longer. Besides not being able to bend their necks to reach the covers, their teeth were totally out of reach because of the protruding bronze disks. Both resigned themselves to a life not worth even living anymore. When Friday came, both were more like zombies than teens. Deep apathy had set in, and they allowed their bodies to be moved around at will by the soldiers. Kassandra was not even able to warn Psyche that their father had died trying to help them stop the soldiers. She anticipated returning to an empty home, there to die, unable to do anything at all, including eating.

The soldiers lifted them down from the wagon and helped them up the walk to their front door. One knocked. Kassandra wondered why they bothered. Their dad was dead and no one would answer. "Just put us inside and leave us to die," she said unintelligibly. Imagine her shock when Master Wie opened the door and beckoned them inside!

"Oh dear god! What have they done to you?" exclaimed Mie as she got her first look at the twins.

"They've completely ruined us! Please, just kill us now," Kassandra begged Mie.

"Damn, they cannot even speak!" Master Wie added. "It's just like Aikos said in his letter. This is beyond inhuman!"

"We are going to look after you both. This is so horrible, Psyche," Roxane exclaimed, her heart nearly bursting.

"I don't care about becoming a Black Belt anymore, Kassi. I will devote my life to helping you," Selene added, her sympathy knowing no bounds.

"Come and sit down, kids. Let me see if I can at least get those awful neck rings off you," Master Wie took charge. For a brief moment, a little hope started to form in the twin's minds. That tiny spark was dashed a bit later as he announced, "Damn, the rings cannot be taken off! The bastards have fused the two ends with molten metal! May they rot in hell. May the dragons eat their minds!" Neither twin had ever heard Master Wie so angry or swear. They wondered if there were dragons and if they did somehow eat minds.

Master Wie calmed down and then said, "Kids, Alexus and I buried your father beside your mother. He died trying to prevent the soldiers from taking you. He killed at least one soldier. Honor his memory now." Psyche, who had not yet known this, began crying. The last of her hope was banished forever. Kassi cried because she had tried unsuccessfully to tell Psyche this for days.

He allowed them time to grieve, before continuing. "You father was a most wise man. When I came to fetch you for the afternoon training, I found the dead soldiers and Aikos. He knew that I would find him and left this letter where I would be sure to find it. Please, allow me to read it to you. Nod if this is okay with you." They couldn't nod, but bent at their waists, their huge, heavy, but gorgeous and highly valuable earrings swinging and then banging slightly on to their neck rings.

He read, "Master Wie, it is with the saddest of hearts that I write this final letter to you, my old friend. Little did I know so many years ago that hiring you to protect the Golden Dragon would become my only hope for the future." Her father then explained all that he knew about General Erebos and his Ornamentation Project, including just how terribly debilitating the Ornamented Dolls actually were. "Unable to speak and only just barely able to move, the name Ornamented Dolls is most appropriate, doomed to a lifetime of sitting and looking pretty, for what else can they possibly do now?"

"I wish with all my heart that your wife and lovely daughters can somehow avoid this most awful and terrible mutilation. The general must truly be a sadist. When my daughters are returned here, they will need constant care. I wish that you and your family will move into my home and care for my daughters. If you do, there is a strong possibility that when the soldiers come for your wife and daughters, they will find your home deserted and believe that you have died or fled. They will not expect to find you have moved into my home. That is the best chance that I can give you, my old friend, to avoid this sadistic mess. In that such might not work out, I have transferred one million gold into your personal account. Use it for whatever purpose you desire, but I urge you to use it to help Mie and your daughters to somehow escape this country which has become beyond evil."

"Since my heir and son is dead, I leave everything else to my daughters, but now they will be unable to speak. I fear that they will not be able to get any money withdrawn from the Banca del Dio, since they cannot be understood any longer. Hence, that they may not be penniless, I have put a fortune into their new earrings, taking advantage of this offer. Each pair of earrings will hold around a million in gemstones, not counting the quantity of gold in the settings. They are to use these funds when no other funds are available to them."

"Daughters, know always that your mother and I loved you both so very much. Keep us in your hearts if you can. I simply cannot face seeing you mutilated as the Ornamented Dolls that I saw the other day. I will do my best to die with honor and not disgrace you. I am truly sorry that I was not a stronger father. I have failed to protect everyone that I love. I am ready for death now, for I can do no more in this world. Goodbye my twins."

Both twins choked up again and began crying, unable to contain their grief any longer. The whole world had gone mad, and they were the victims, so crippled up that they could not even kill themselves and be done with it. No, they would have to endure this masochistic life thrust upon them by powers beyond their control. They cried and cried.

Later, Master Wie and Alexus fed the twins their lunch. During the afternoon, Wie decided to give the twins time to readjust to life. He had already decided that if they were to have any remote chance at all, he had to know what they were actually capable of now doing. Wisely, he left that for the morning.

The next day after breakfast, he said, "Okay Psyche, Kassi, it is time that you and we determine just what is and is not possible for you to now do. You and we must know your limitations if we are to help you properly. We have never seen anything like the way that you are, so please be patient with us. Let's begin by seeing if somehow we can understand you when you say yes and no. That way we can at least ask yes-no questions of you."

That worked well, they were able to distinguish between the two sounds the twins made. Next, he checked their range of motion. Neither could move their heads a fraction of an inch. Thus, they had to turn their body to look in different directions, a severe limitation, he thought. At least their feet and leg flexibility was unaltered. They could easily touch their lips and head with their toes, though they wobbled precariously while standing and doing so. The heels only provided limited support to their toes. At least this was unchanged, while he and Alexus could not walk or stand much at all. This he pointed out, bringing a slight smile to their faces, which they now realized no one could see anymore.

"Well, it seems that you both now have perfect posture," he pointed out. Both shrugged their shoulders; this mattered not to them. He experimented with eating, ascertaining that they were unable to sit squarely at the table and see their plates and special spoons. If they sat slightly askew, they could see them, but then trying to use the spoon to pick up food became nearly impossible, their legs didn't bend enough to allow such strange contortions. No human's legs would, he pointed out. He also noted that the special alien spoons did not have a sufficiently long handle to easily allow them to both hold the spoon in their toes and get the business end into their mouths around the four inch plates. This, he decided, he could perhaps remedy with longer shafted spoons.

Further, they continued to slobber. Liquids seeped out of their mouths unless they had their heads tilted slightly back. Drinking, he realized would be a serious problem. They tried pouring water into their open lips over their plates, but it went in all directions, though a little actually made it into their mouths. He removed the plates and now things went far better for them, eating-wise, except that their lip loops, as he called them, dangled from their mouths. These got in their way continually and would be dangerous, since they could get caught on all manner of protruding objects, ripping what remained of their mouths wide open. He put them back in, "We take them off only if it is absolutely necessary, kids. One rip and your whole mouth could be torn apart."

"How about helping each other eat?" he suggested next. Finally, they found something that they could do, albeit drastically slower than before and full of spills. "With practice, kids, it will be possible for you to feed each other. As for drinking, I am afraid you will have to use a spoon instead. While I might be able to bend the lower plate some, making a sort of trough, I don't recommend it, except as a last resort. As long as you can spoon water, milk, and tea, I would like to go that way."

"Can they brush their own hair?" Mie asked, getting into the personal details. It was incredibly awkward, but they were slightly able to perform this task. Again, Kassandra took the initiative and began doing Psyche's hair, showing them that they could do each other's far better than their own. She then discovered that they could not take down or up their own panties. Mie said, "Anything that we can do using our teeth, they can no longer do, Wie. We will have to dress and undress them ourselves. No way can they wipe themselves, so we'll have to do that or let them do each other."

Next, she killed two birds with one action. She had them try bathing in their large tubs. They needed a bath from their five days at the center anyway. Could they somehow bathe themselves? That also did not work well, for they simply did not have enough range of motion with their feet and legs to compensate for the total loss of bending their necks and using their teeth. Perfect posture even in the tubs had severe drawbacks, she noted. However, it was possible for each to somewhat bathe the other, they discovered.

Of course, braiding their hair fell to Wie and Alexus, as it had since the plague came. None of the women and teens could do their own hair any longer; their toes were just not that flexible; toes were just not fingers.

While dressing them, Kassandra said, "Please, just kill us and put us out of our misery." Mie cursed, unable to grasp what Kassi was saying.

"Hey mom, maybe they can learn to write," Selene pointed out. "We got all those low desks. They must be meant for us to use to write. Why don't we all see if we can do that. If they can learn to write, they can talk that way, mom."

"Brilliant, Selene!" Mie replied. Now all the women headed to the living room, where Wie had put all the desks, unable to figure out any other useful place in which to put them.

For several hours, the women experimented with writing with their feet. The twins again found that seeing over their plates and bosoms impossible, but they discovered that if they leaned back far enough, they could see their feet and thus write. At first, their letters were huge and ill formed, but Mie could still read what Kassi wrote: Kill us.

"Oh don't be silly, Kassi. We won't kill you. We just have to find more alternate ways for you, that's all. Give us time; heck, my writing is worse than yours." She lied, but Kassi didn't realize it.

The next day, Wie decided to see how the twins could manage with some of their martial arts skills. He dressed them in their white robes and tied their black belts securely. Then, they all headed down the stairs. He had converted their basement storage area into a mat covered arena. A new problem suddenly raised its ugly head. Obstructed as their lower front vision was, both teens nearly panicked as they hit the stairs. Going down stairs was a huge challenge, and they went mostly by feel, excruciatingly slowly, compared to the very slow descent of Mie. At least, she could see where she was placing her feet; the twins could not.

Once down, he removed their plates. "If you take a spill with these in place, you will shatter your heads and mouth, probably also knocking out most of your teeth." Both grimaced at that thought. As they began their session, the twins found that some leg motions were still possible. Their circle kicks and punches were still highly effective, and they both took a little heart from this. Perhaps not all was totally gone.

After an arduous workout, Mie commented to Wie, "They all need kijutsu, don't they?"

He sighed, "Yes, ladies, there is no escaping the fact that you all could benefit enormously from kijutsu powers. Still, I believe that Selene can master her Black Belt, and Roxane, you can use alternate moves to equal your training. Twins, I just don't know, but we have nothing to lose if we try, do we?"

During December, their daily workouts were the only thing that kept the twins from emotionally just giving up entirely. Bit by bit, their feet and leg skills improved, but they were now a long way from the skill levels of both Roxane and Selene, who could use their necks and head, particularly when it came to balance. At last, Wie got a bright idea. The twins had to develop a better sense of balance, far beyond that of Roxane and Selene, though they both could greatly benefit from it as well. He explained what he was going to do and why.

Then, he made each teen stand on one foot, while he tied up the other foot. Now the four had no choice but to try to keep their balance while standing on one foot. Okay, they were standing on their toes with the slight additional support of the tiny heel about a half inch beyond the base of their toes. Wobbling and falls were quite common, and he and Alexus had to help them up frequently. Many days later, his training began to work. The four were far more able at maintaining their fragile balance. If only their feet were normal, Wie mused.

January 824, came bringing one day of painful feet to everyone. After that, all their feet returned to normal — a cause for celebration among all them. None paid much attention to the fact that their waists had filled out a couple of inches. Now the teens could walk normally and maintain their balance vastly better. Wie continued with his balance training, because he saw where it could lead them. After a couple more days, he then had the four teens hopping around with one leg still tied up. The twins were just as able as his daughters to do this; their neck restriction did not come much into play with hopping. All four grasped where this was all leading them and worked hard at it, ignoring their many tumbles.

By mid-January, he had the teens begin trying to knock each other over while hopping with one leg securely bound up. This added a bit of excitement into the mix. For once, the twins were not severely limited and banged into Roxane and Selene with some enthusiasm. All four saw where this was heading: maintaining their balance while in combat!

During the evenings, Mie had all the girls and herself practicing their writing skills. After all, if the twins ever stood a chance at being able to communicate beyond yes and no, it would be through writing. As January closed, all were definitely picking up this necessary skill.

Mid-March 824, all four were once more working on devising alternative means of meeting their Black Belt requirements. The skill of keeping their balance under extreme conditions had paid off handsomely, Master Wie noted. Now Roxane and Selene were making solid progress, week by week. Even the twins were coming along nicely. He talked to Mie in confidence. "If they can master the Black Belt, we owe it to them to take them to the Olin Masters and beg them to teach them their advanced levels. The kijutsu powers will make their lives livable, especially for the twins." Mie agreed with him, pointing out that they now had sufficient funds to make such a trip.

In April, the twin's lip plates were drooping badly, making everything far more difficult for them. Thankfully, a note from the Ornamentation Center came notifying them that they could expect this stretching phenomenon to occur and that they only needed to come to a center and the problem would be fixed. Wei and Alexus drove the twins to the center, explained what was wrong, and were told to wait. A man took the twins into a back room. When they returned about an hour later, their plates were again horizontal the ground once more. When the two looked them over to see what had been done, they realized that the plates had been enlarged to about four and a half inches across. Later, the twins wrote that a bronze worker had pounded them out, making them larger. They also wrote that the man said they would need this adjustment every six months or so. Kassi wrote: How big will they become? No one knew the answer to that one.

By June, their writing had improved so much that it was quite legible and they could do it fairly swiftly, all things considered. At last, Psyche wrote a lengthy note to Mie, whom the twins had now adopted as their mother in lieu of Chara. She asked: Is it all right that Kassi and I pleasure each other at night in our beds? Yes, it was an embarrassing question to be sure, but the twins had no one else they could ask and they trusted Mie now.

Mie flushed. She suddenly realized that the teens were depending upon her as their replacement mother. "Yes, it is fine to give each other some pleasure. Perhaps one day you will meet a pair of handsome young men, fall in love with them, get married, and raise your own families. Then, your husband and you can share in this joy and pleasure of life. Feel free to ask me about anything you want."

The twins smiled, but the gesture was invisible. Now they relaxed at night and enjoyed the pleasure the other gave them, for they had so little pleasure in life now.

In July, Mei made a startling discovery quite by accident. More and more talk was heard about forcing unemployed men into the army just to give them jobs. Now, she and Wei began discussing seriously about somehow returning to Tashien. As a result, she thought that all the kids should learn to speak some languages that she felt they might encounter on such a trip. "We will likely have to stop in Annelise, before we make the long trip north of there to Tashien. We should learn to speak a little Annelise, just in case we have to spend some time in that country. Once we get to Tashien, you must all be able to speak our native language — well at least read it and perhaps write it, in the case of our twins." She had begun to talk of "her twins" now, and the twins really appreciated such.

The twins had long since given up any attempts at speech excepting the occasional yes or no sounds. As Mie began their lessons, she encouraged them to practice along with Roxane, Selene, and Alexus. She even made Wie take part as well. "This is how you say: Hello, my name is Mie. Now each of you in turn repeat it. I'll tell you how to say your name next."

Each spoke up in turn, fumbling their way through the unfamiliar sounds of the Annelise dialect. After each had a turn, Psyche decided to say it as well, not wanting to be left out. "Vy nave is Vie."

"Oh my god! I heard that, Psyche. It was mostly understandable!" Mie cried out shocked.

Kassandra quickly spoke the phrase as well. The twins looked at each other and smiled, invisibly of course.

The more phrases that she taught, the more phrases the twins learned to say. Soon, it became obvious to Mie that the twins might well be able to speak in the Annelise dialect! To Psyche and Kassandra, this seemed like a miracle, offering them some real hope that one day they could communicate with their adopted family again!

Despite her enthusiasm, Mie decided to try the Tashien language. After all, if they were ultimately to go there, the twins would have to at least be able to understand that, even if they could only respond in Annelise. To her complete amazement, they could vocalize Tashien as well. She tried several other languages that she knew, but struck out completely. Their Velona dialect, for example, was completely unintelligible. She spent hours trying to figure out why this was. Then, she hit upon it. In Tashien and Annelise, the basic sounds, the phonetics, were not made with the lips but primarily with the placement of the tongue inside the mouth. With the Demokritos and Velona languages, most of the phonetics involved the lips and not so much the position of the tongue. Hence, the twins would be able to speak somewhat both the Annelise and Tashien languages!

So vital was her discovery that Wie allowed the kids half of the day to be spent on learning language skills and the other half on their martial arts skills. The twins threw themselves totally into the language lessons, seeing the strong possibility that they could finally communicate easily once more.

In August, Selene finally succeeded in her dream. She passed the Black Belt test! Everyone jumped for joy, pressing their bodies into hers in unbridled celebration. With immense pride, Master Wie bestowed Selene's black belt upon her, tying it around her waist.

"I did it! I did it! I did it!" Selene called out once the formal portion of the ceremony ended. Soon, Roxane reached her level as well. By the end of August, the twins were also there as well, achieving something that they thought was impossible. Somehow, they had worked out alternate ways to achieve every one of the Black Belt goals.

"Now we can go to Tashien and seek out the Olin Vasters," Psyche spoke in Annelise. Everyone understood her too.

"You must learn the languages a little better first," Master Wie cautioned them.

Secretly, he now spent the mornings while they were with Mie searching Levkos for the ways and means of doing just that. One day while he was searching, he found an advertisement asking for men to train to be able to enlarge lip plates. It seemed that now so many needed theirs enlarged that it was putting a strain on the usual bronze workers who were hard pressed to keep up with the weekly demand for their new products. Wie realized that if he took the twins to Tashien, he would have to be responsible for enlarging their plates when they needed it. He signed up to be so trained. A week later, he was a licensed Lip Plate Expander, as the profession was now being called. Ten gold later, he had his own tools: a small anvil and ballpeen hammers.

At home, he taught Alexus how to do it as well, figuring that it would be wise for both of them to know how to enlarge the disks. The only downside was that he now had to make house calls on Ornamented Dolls who needed theirs enlarged. Still, this had to be done and he did it, knowing that he could care for the twins and their needs, if they could somehow get to Tashien.

Travel was still limited. Few inns had reopened, though more were doing so, if only so that men could avoid being conscripted into the army. A job kept them out of the army. If they did not take many possessions with them, they could travel in one carriage down to Preveza, the port city. Well, he had a carriage and he had money that they could use to purchase new things. Yet, would the critical things that women needed be available in other lands? Were there yokes there? Low kitchens? He just didn't know. If they started to bring along many items, then they'd need more than a simple carriage.

Late at night, he continually shared each day's findings with Mie. She pointed out, "Dear, you are forgetting one critical thing. We women need clothes to wear. Nightgowns and martial arts robes will not get us very far, especially in the winter. If we are going, somehow we have to have some warm clothing."

"No wonder General Erebos keeps saying that all women should go naked in the warmer months! What are we going to do about warm winter clothing dear?" he asked, somewhat red-faced. He had not thought about this aspect at all. The women almost never left the house. Women were almost never seen on the streets, and he did not consider it safe for them to be outside.

Mei decided to ask the twins if there were any dresses around the house. At least this would be a starting point. Psyche replied, "Yes, vov has lots of fancy dresses. We do too. None fit us any vore."

"Neither do ours, dears. Let's check them out, shall we?" Mie asked.

The twins had two fancy ball gowns with all the accessories and several day dresses, which they usually had worn all the time before the plague. None remotely fit their altered bodies, however. Their mother had six fancy gowns and four day dresses, none of these looked promising either. There were plenty of nightgowns, which is what they had all been wearing.

"I used to be able to do a little sewing," Mie said with a sigh. "Now that's impossible."

At last, Wie decided that the only real solution was to dress them in some of their father's old shirts and pants. At least they would be warm, though the women would need the assistance of the two men to dress and to use the pots when needed. With clothing handled, Wie then decided to see about funds. He and Alexus took the twins to the Banca del Dio.

"Our women here speak Annelise. Does anyone here speak it?" Master Wie asked politely at the main desk. Luck was on their side. One teller actually had an aunt from Annelise and he spoke it a little.

"We want to transfer a villion frov our account to our account in Shansee, Tashien, vlease," Kassandra requested of the teller. She had to repeat it three times, but the teller finally understood, repeating back that she wanted to transfer one million. She gave them her father's account, and a bit later, the man returned with her receipt, offering it to her, before realizing his goof. Besides being a woman without arms, she was an Ornamented Doll, even more helpless. Wie took it politely for her and thanked him. He then transferred his own sum and taking out some gems and coins to help pay for the trip and traveling money.

When they got home, both looked at the receipt closely. "Vy goodness, we have over twenty villion left! Dad was rich!" Kassandra exclaimed.

By October 1, the group was finally ready to make their move. However, Wei took two hours to enlarge both women's plates before they left. Now their lip plates were five-inches across, somewhat dismaying both teens. "When will they stov stretching?" Psyche asked. Wie did not have the heart to tell her that in all likelihood they never would.

The next day, soldiers came by to ask if the two men were employed. If not, they were to join the army. "Yes, I am a licensed Lip Plate Expander. My son will be traveling to his new job in Preveza tomorrow, sir." That seemed to satisfy the soldiers who left. Their appearance sealed their move. Tomorrow they had to leave Levkos or risk Alexus being conscripted into the army.

They packed their few things, fully planning on being able to purchase what they needed when they arrived eventually in Shansee, Tashien. The men loaded the bags and then helped the twins manage to climb into the carriage. "Getting out again will ve vuch vore difficult for us," Kassandra pointed out. Alexus rode topside with his father. Inside, Mie decided the four teens ought to practice their language skills. It would help pass the long days of travel.

Chapter 59 Be Careful Whom You Meet

Before the plague came, Kapaneus Phalos led a double life. He was the caretaker and groundsman for the Church of Jehosanity of Edessa, a small town about fifty miles from Levkos and on the road to Preveza. He was forty-five now and in the employ of the Queen of Alia. Often when she needed something sadistically erotic arranged, she called upon Kapaneus, who never failed her. Sometimes even "spent" bodies of young men and women simply vanished without a trace under his expert hands, for a hefty price from Her Majesty.

Kapaneus knew that her erotic tastes went in for the truly exotic, and thus he was always on the lookout for something new and unusual. Already, he'd made a small fortune working for the queen. One day while performing his maintenance duties around the Church of Jehosanity, he stumbled upon a secluded, locked room, deep underground. From the thick layer of dust upon the floor, which he ought to have swept up, he knew that no one had been down here in many, many years. He felt confident in picking the lock to see what was kept inside. He'd picked nearly every other lock in the church already, sometimes discovering only religious junk, as he called it. He certainly did not believe all the church mumbo jumbo.

Inside, he found a lantern and proceeded to light it. His eyes lighted upon all manner of strange looking devices. "What do we have here?" he whispered to himself. He didn't know it then, but he had stumbled upon the church's repository for all manner of torture devices invented over the ages — devices that the Pope had sworn had been destroyed, but had been sent here to this secret depository on the off chance that one day they might prove useful once again.

Each device was identified with labels and an instruction manual of sorts lay beside the device. He found two benches used by the Confessore who strapped their victims to the bench, put their hands and fingers into the clamps, and proceeded to cut off their fingers or even hands. The instructions said that this would cause the victim to confess to the crimes for which they were found guilty. It had been outlawed centuries ago. "Useful, but not practical," he mused. He knew of no real use for cutting off someone's fingers or hands. They'd probably bleed to death, he thought. He moved on.

Three heavy metal encasements caught his attention. The instructions read: place ring inside person's mouth, then clamp head unit shut and secure ring to head piece. Clamp arms behind and across their upper back and secure in back clamps. Pour molten lead onto the bolts, permanently encasing the victim. "Now this sounds erotic enough for the queen herself, though she doesn't need to encase them permanently. She ought to have a whole lot of fun with this one." He moved on, after reading that the device had been outlaw even further in the distant past.

He came across another strange looking contraption: Lucifer's Daughter's Silencer. He read the instructions. Slice lips top and bottom according to these dimensions. Insert disks. Insert headpiece. Adjust head screws to hold framework solidly in place around head. Adjust blindfold bolts so that eyes are held shut tightly. Insert bolt into center holes of lip plates. Tighten securely. Adjust earplug bolts until firmly against ears. Shake. If any give is found, tighten accordingly. Once no give or play is found, pour molten lead to secure permanently. Lucifer's Daughters cannot see, hear, or talk, and you will be safe from their spells.

"Now this is darn interesting. I bet the queen could find any number of uses for this one!" he said to himself. An aside note: here in Velona, we had thought all these torture devices that the church had used at one time in the past had been destroyed, or so the popes had assured us. Obviously, the popes had other ideas and had put them into a secret repository.

He found many other items, but none as exotic as these were. Kapaneus then closed the door, locked it, and began his floor sweeping. Now he began to make big plans for their use. Surely, the queen would pay handsomely for the use of these items. The church would never miss them. Obviously, no one had been in that room in at least a half century, he thought. "I should test them to make sure that they work," he thought. A wry, evil grin pierced his unshaven face.

In Edessa, the Xandros family was one of the wealthier ones. Specifically, Kapaneus had long had his eye on young Xenia, who was now fourteen. However, she had rejected his advances repeatedly, which annoyed him no end. He chuckled as an idea formed in his mind. "I do need to test these before I go to the queen with them, now don't I?" He laughed sadistically.

That night, he put his ill-conceived plan to work. He'd spied on Xenia frequently and knew that she loved to spend Thursday evenings playing cards with her girlfriends. Nothing ill ever happened in Edessa, home to some five thousand people. Hence, she was allowed to walk to her girlfriend's home. So were all of her friends, for that matter. Kapaneus filled a small bottle from a larger one that he "borrowed" from the Mano del Dio's room while he cleaned it. He then replaced the large bottle back into the assassin's room. He'd be none the wiser, and Kapaneus would be the benefactor of the Mano's assistance.

He went to a secluded location, which from previous stalking times he knew that she would have to pass, and hid himself in some bushes. Now he only had to wait. He grinned evilly. Around ten, the young Xenia came walking along, her five-inch heels clicking on the cobblestones. She was in a particularly gay mood; she'd won the card game this evening and felt on top of the world. Xenia wore a six-foot hoop skirt beneath her satin gown. Her parents insisted that she be sixteen before they bought her larger ones or permitted her to wear higher heels. Still, these Annelise style oxford knock-offs were fine, tied nicely on her feet. Her curly brown hair bobbed up and down as she walked along.

Suddenly, a rag was over her nose and mouth. She tried to call out, but her voice was muffled. In seconds, she felt faint and weak. All went dark. Kapaneus picked up the unconscious young woman, glanced about to make doubly sure that no one saw him, then headed rapidly to the church. He let himself in with his key and took her down the many flights of stairs into the long unused basement. Setting her down for a moment, he lighted a lantern, picked the lock, carried the lantern inside, and then carried Xenia inside before closing the door.

Now he set to work following the instructions for the encasement mask. He had a bit of trouble getting her arms crossed above her back and into the metal restraints. Finally, he had them properly aligned and closed the latch, securely binding her arms behind her. Then, he inserted the mouth ring and fitted the head encasement, securing the bar attached to the ring to the encasement. After making a few more adjustments and making doubly sure that all was perfect, including the metal blindfold bolted to the head encasement, he sat her down in one corner and looked at his handiwork.

"Damn, this sure works extremely well! Incredibly so, if I so say so myself. Okay, now for her food and water." Carefully, he placed two large bowls before her and attached a chain to the head encasement, which would prevent her from moving more than five feet from the back wall. He didn't want her messing around in here, perhaps mixing up the instructions for some of the other devices. Satisfied, he waited until she awoke from the ether. She moaned a little and regained consciousness. She tried to move, but her arms were completely immobile behind her back. She tried to talk but felt a large O-ring between her teeth; she could only make incomprehensible noises.

"Ah, fair Xenia. You are mine finally. Yes, you are imprisoned in an iron encasement or so it is called. You can call out all that you desire, but there is no one who can hear you at all. I have placed a bowl of food and a bowl of water just in front of you." She made some awful noises. He added, "Oh I understand. How are you to eat? Well, lap it up like a dog, once you find it. Don't worry. You can't get the metal blindfold off you. The whole encasement is bolted shut quite tightly. I'll return tomorrow and then we can play. I'm sure that you'll not reject my advances this time, my sweet Xenia." He laughed; she uttered a wailing noise. He left the room, blowing out the lantern and locking the door behind him.

For the next two days, he tormented her, but he was very careful to make sure that she found the food and water. Then, the plague struck. It was several days before Kapaneus could crawl into the church to check on his prize. He brought along a goodly supply of food this time, fearing that it would be some days before he could return. He was right. Looters with guns scoured the church here in Edessa, stripping it of its golden ornaments and artwork. After that, the church was deserted, and no one came again. No one had bothered to remove the many dead whose decaying corpses filled the church rooms and hallways.

Kapaneus grumbled; the queen was dead — he'd heard that news. Besides, the world was ending or so many said. Certainly, things were vastly different now. Women had all lost their arms to the plague. Ah, but he had his own private play toy tucked safely away. At least once a week he made the long crawl to the basement room to enjoy himself and to make sure that she had food and water. Each time that he came, he found the water gone as well as the food, so he knew that she was eating and drinking. He enjoyed playing on her misery, for misery it was for poor Xenia. Although she did not know it, she also got the plague. Now her arms were actually gone, but long ago, she'd lost all feeling in them and didn't know that they had vanished. She did experience a hideous pressure around her chest as her bosom quintupled in size, eventually bursting the bodice top and freeing her from that crushing pressure. At least her corset no longer bothered her, though she didn't know why. It just felt loose. She tried to stand up and managed it, then explored how far she could move, barely five feet. At last, she stayed close to her food and water, though eating was a nightmare of lapping.

As the new year moved into summer, Kapaneus tired a little of his toy and a new plan crept into his mind, aided by what he'd just heard. General Erebos had ordered all women to become Ornamented Dolls. Just what were they he wondered. In late July, the first Ornamentation Center came to Edessa, and the orders went out to ornament the noblewomen and the wealthy first. This pricked Kapaneus' interest. He applied for a night janitor at the center. and because of his former experience as a church janitor, he got the job. Imagine his elation when he saw the first Ornamented Dolls being made!

A week later, Xenia's older sister, Ariadne who was now seventeen, was brought in along with eleven other women. He looked down on the unconscious woman with her huge earrings, enormous lip plates, and bronze neck rings and grinned evilly. What a marvelous addition she'll make, he thought, especially since they are sisters! Already helpless, she would be easy to capture now. Carefully, he made his plans. On the night before she was to be released, the doctor pronounced her lips healed sufficiently so that no infections were possible and that she could go home in the morning. The poor woman could only make unintelligible sounds now. No one saw the janitor in the back of the room grinning wickedly.

Late that night, he put the rag over her nose and the sleeping woman fell into a deep sleep. It was a simple matter to lift her up and carry her out of the center. No one was on guard, only a night nurse was even awake. He took her to the church and down into the basement room. "Oh hello, Xenia. I thought that you needed some company, so I have brought your sister to you. I need a few minutes to get her all fixed up." Xenia let out a noise that sounded like a scream, but he ignored it.

Tonight he tried out the Lucifer's Daughter contraption. It took him a lengthy time to drill the holes in the lip plates without hurting her healing lips. But the bronze was both soft and thin, and he managed. Carefully following the instructions, he began assembling the device. He followed them to the letter. Finally, he gave the head unit a jerk and nothing moved, not even a fraction of an inch. He sat back and admired his handiwork. Ariadne awoke and let out an unintelligible noise. She could not see, speak, move her lip plates, nor hear. Well, that was not true; she could barely hear muffled sounds. A man was speaking.

"Ah fair Ariadne, so good of you to come and join your charming sister. I bet that you've missed her a lot. It's been over six months since you've seen her. Well, she's right here with you, but I am afraid she cannot make much more than a noise, like yourself." Both women made as loud a noise as they could, completely unintelligible.

As he stood there admiring his handiwork, he suddenly realized that Ariadne would not be able to feed herself nor drink. She couldn't do either before he had abducted her for that matter. With the contraption on her, she couldn't see or hear. How was she going to be fed or given water? He had not thought of that. Consequently, he decided to undo the metal blindfold of Xenia and unchain her.

Xenia now saw her sister and screamed even louder. "There, there, that is no way to welcome your sister to our very private place, now is it, Xenia? Now I want you to listen carefully. Xenia, as you can see, your sister's life depends on you. You must feed her and give her water. I have brought you these long handled spoons, which I'm told the Ornamental Dolls need to feed themselves. So you must now use your feet to feed your sister food and drink. It will be tough, but I have left her plates open enough for you to get the spoon into her mouth. I will return tomorrow to see how you have fared. You both look quite beautiful, I might add. Enjoy yourselves, my pretties." He left, but did leave the lantern on.

Xenia stared in terror at her sister. How could she possibly feed her? Tears streamed down her face as did her sister. She tried to say comforting words, but the ring in her teeth prevented her. At last, she moved over to her sister's side and began trying to figure out how she could use her feet with the spoons. At last, Xenia had a purpose. After months of total isolation and sensory deprivation, now she had her sister to care for and who was more helpless than she was. Somehow, someway, she had to get food and water into Ariadne's mouth. Surely in time, someone would rescue them, though at this point, she'd lost all hope of that, but with Ariadne missing too, maybe someone would come.

One thing was certain; sadism had really taken root in Alia and not just around the throne in Levkos. Actions sometimes have far-reaching consequences. True, a citywide search began, as the few soldiers looked everywhere for the missing young woman, but since they had shot her father who tried to prevent her from being taken away, there was little effort made. Besides, it also solved their problem of just where to take her the next morning. They were under orders not to leave an Ornamented Doll in a vacant house where there was no one to care for her needs. Again, Kapaneus escaped detection and began to enjoy his private toys.

In early October, Kapaneus overheard news that frightened him. The old, abandon church was going to be torn down, and its stone work reused to build more Ornamentation Centers, which would benefit all working men of Edessa or so the army proclamation stated. He had to move his prizes to a new, safe location. Kapaneus knew that he only dared move them at night. After around eight, no one was out of doors, not in such a small town. He could safely walk them down the streets to his new safe house, a small manor house that he'd spent most of his savings on earlier this day.

Around six, he ducked into the church for the last time. He went down the stairs two at a time, happy as a lark. Nothing could go wrong; soon he would have them moved into his own basement, where he could play with them as often as he desired. Entering, he announced, "Tonight, my pretty women, we are moving to a new home. I have gotten us a fine new house. I promise you that it will be much warmer than these cold stones and less stinky as well. Now, Xenia, I'll leave your blindfold off you if you promise to help lead your sister and cause me no trouble. I can't easily remove her eye blocks, so I'm depending on you to help lead her. Nod if this is all right. If not, I'll put your blindfold back on and lead you both myself.

Xenia nodded yes and then shook her body from side to side trying to say that she didn't want the blindfold back on. "Now it is cold out there on the streets. I am going to put your heels back on your feet and then put some on Ariadne's," he explained. He put the five-inch heels back on her feet, making sure the laces were tied tightly so she could not get them off. Then, he did the same to Ariadne, only her heels he had stolen from her home yesterday. Hers were six-inch oxfords. He had wanted her higher extreme heels, but those had no laces, and she could easily take them off. These, she could not.

He helped both women rise. Holding the lantern, he said, "Okay, my fair Xenia, up the stairs you go. I'll lead your beautiful sister. I'm right behind you, so don't try anything stupid. If I have to let go of her, she will fall and kill herself. You don't want that, now do you?" Xenia moved her torso left and right, the best she could do to indicate no. Her head, neck, and upper torso were still encased within the metal enclosure. Although terrified of falling herself, Xenia began going up the dimly lit stairs, thankful that they were going up and not down.

Even more terrified, the blinded Ariadne continued to try to walk, stumbling on each step. She would have fallen on each stair step if Kapaneus had not been holding on to her. After an eternity, she dimly heard him say that they were on the level street at last. Pivoting her body around, Xenia saw familiar streets, the first she'd seen in a year of captivity. The air smelled so good; it was fresh, but chilly fall air. The feces-filled dungeon had almost deadened her sense of smell. Slowly, their heels clicking on the cobblestones, the women moved down the middle of the street. Xenia prayed that someone would look out their window, see them, and come to her rescue. She thought of yelling, but knew that she would not be heard; besides, he might hurt her sister.

"Well, dad, we sure misjudged the distance, didn't we?" Alexus commented as darkness fell. This was their first day on the road from Levkos. While they had an early start, neither had any real idea of the location of the towns with inns nor the distance their carriage could make in a day. Now it was well past dark, but they finally entered the outskirts of the town of Edessa, some fifty miles from Levkos.

"At least we made a good distance today," Wie commented back. He called out loudly, "Ladies, we are entering Edessa at a last. Won't be long now before we get to an inn. Hope there is one, though."

"Dad, what's that ahead of us? Women? What are those metal things on their heads?" Alexus asked, baffled by what he was seeing in the dim light.

Kapaneus panicked, he heard horses coming up from behind him. "This should not be happening! No one is out at night. Oh hell!" His first inclination was to run, but he realized that he'd hobbled both women by forcing them to wear high heels, they could not go much faster than they were going, especially the blinded Ariadne. What to do?

"My god, what have they done to those poor women?" Alexus asked his father, who clucked to the horses, which picked up speed, rapidly overtaking the three. One woman, who seemed entirely encased in a metal shell, turned around and cried out. Although it was only noise and not words, her meaning was clear; she was in trouble. At that instant, the man broke into a run, abandoning the two women. Wie pulled up beside them and gasped at what he saw.

Wie made a snap decision, he said, "Did that man who is fleeing do this to you?" Both women made strange noises and waist nodded affirmative.

"I'll get him dad; you help the women," Alexus decided to go into action. Besides, he didn't have the reins. He leapt from the driver's box and hit the ground running. The man turned to look and see if they were after him and saw a man running after him. Although he poured on the speed, he was no match for the athlete. Besides, he had not run in years. Alexus caught up to him and placed a hand on a precise spot on his neck. Kapaneus felt his legs go limp. His body dropped helplessly to the ground. Alexus caught his breath and pulled the man up to his feet. He undid the man's belt and tied his hands behind him, then led him back to the carriage.

Still not a soul was on the streets. Wie dismounted and came up to the women. "My god, what has he done to you?" Both made noises, and he saw at once that without tools, he could not free either woman. "Come on, ladies. I'll take you to an inn, and there we'll get you out of these weird devices." They nodded and he led them carefully to the carriage doors.

"Oh my god!" Mie exclaimed; the teens joined her with various other expressions. "Wie, get them inside. We have to get these horrible things off them!" While getting Xenia into the carriage was relatively easy, her blind sister was problematical.

"I am going to lift you into the carriage, miss." She liked the gentle sound and relaxed. Wie lifted her up and got her inside, then helped her to sit down. By then, Alexus arrived, dragging the protesting Kapaneus behind him. "Walk him, Alexus. He doesn't deserve to ride." They drove on down the street until they found a lantern illuminating a sign, Inn. Wie stopped and went inside. A short while later he returned, the innkeeper and a soldier in tow.

"We found this man ushering these women down the street," Wie explained. The soldier took custody of the protesting man, while the innkeeper looked in on the women. "Do you recognize them, sir?" he asked.

"My lord, yes! Them's Xenia and Ariadne Xandros. Xenia went missing over a year ago now. Ariadne went missing maybe six weeks ago. Her father was killed when they took her to the Ornamentation Center. They've no others to look after them. Bring them on inside; my god they stink!"

"Okay, I will pay for their keep here, as well as my party," Wie said politely. "I believe a bath will be needed as soon as I can get them free, innkeeper."

"Indeed. I'll also rustle up some leftover supper. Though it's late, I need all the business I can get. These are mighty hard times. What has Kapaneus done to these poor women anyway? He should be drawn and quartered, that's what I say. Wait until the town hears about this in the morning!" He chatted about this news all the way inside his inn. Nothing like this had ever happened in Edessa. True, the church folks went on a killing spree after the plague came, but this was even wilder.

Ariadne was unable to do much walking and Wie simply carried her inside to the large room that the innkeeper hastily made available. Wie's party was the largest he had had since the plague and he stood to make a goodly amount on their stay. Once everyone was inside and as many lanterns lighted as could be found, Wie and Alexus began to examine the contraptions. The soldier soon joined them, adding his curses to the mix. A screwdriver and pliers were all that would be needed, Wie ascertained. He retrieved both from his small tool kit, designed to enlarge lip plates. He and Alexus set to work on Xenia first. In a half hour, the woman was finally free, though her jaw was in terrible shape, sore and almost frozen open.

"Off you go to the hot bath barrel, Xenia. That should help you feel better," Wie said politely. Mie and the teens ushered the frightened girl to one of the two tubs.

"My arms! My arms are gone! So are yours!" Xenia attempted to say; her voice was unsteady and the words were barely understandable; her jaws barely moved. While she stepped into the tub and the women began to scrub her feces covered lower body, Mie explained about the plague and its horrible effects. She also explained about the Ornamented Dolls, which her sister had become. The poor teen was a year behind the times; she'd missed an awful lot of what had happened. Her mind tried to grasp so much in so little time. At last, she gave up and bawled.

Meanwhile, the three men worked on Ariadne's contraption. "We must be careful with hers. We don't want accidentally to poke out her eyes or ears nor do we want to tear her lips, so easy does it. I wish we knew the order in which to undo this mess," Wie said softly.

"Dad, let's undo the lip plates first. That way, if it jiggles, it won't hurt her lips any," Alexus suggested. A few minutes later, those bolts were undone and her plates were free to move. Next, they carefully unscrewed the bolts pressing the leather pads onto her closed eyes. At last, she could see, and she blinked and looked around, terrified. While Alexus and the soldier began unscrewing the ear plugs, Wie examined how the frame was fastened together. Soon, he had the two men support the frame while he began undoing specific bolts. An hour after they began, Alexus removed the head contraption from the Ornamented Doll. Now she was free, but she was still in an eternal prison, unable to speak to her sister, unable to do much of anything except cry.

Xenia, now out of the tub and being dried off, stared at what had become of her sister. "My god, Ariadne!" she wailed, realizing that her sister looked like the two teens who were helping dry her off. Her sister continued simply to cry as she was helped into the second tub of warm water.

Mie dressed Xenia in one of her nightgowns and Wie led her to the main room where warm food awaited them. The soldier followed them, bent on asking Xenia what had happened to her and verifying they had the right man. Her jaws were still not closing and Wie began to massage them. After some ten minutes, they closed finally, much to her gratitude. While Wie fed her the hot stew, the soldier asked her about her ordeal. He was soon satisfied and left, promising her that Kapaneus would pay for his hideous crime. She took comfort in that, but she had so many questions. So much had happened.

"A whole year had passed? The plague? Mom's dead? Dad, too? What will become of us now?" she wailed, her grief finally overcoming her again. Wie allowed her to cry. A bit later, Alexus and the others came into the room, leading Ariadne. Again, Xenia looked at her sister and cried even harder.

Alexus fed Ariadne, who seemed famished. Although no one knew it, she'd lost ten pounds during her captivity. Poor Xenia had not been able to get enough food in her mouth. Later, they took the two rescued women into the rooms that the innkeeper provided, and Wie and Roxane slept beside them, ready to help them if they needed anything.

When the morning gong sounded the call to breakfast, the men dressed the women and walked them back into the spacious dining room. Unfortunately, fifty people were there to see for themselves.

Word had already spread. While Alexus and Wie began feeding the two, the mayor of the town pulled up a chair close to Xenia and Wie; at least she could tell him what had happened. She did, of course. Then, the mayor explained about her mother and father.

Master Wie decided to extend an offer. "Mayor, as I understand it, these teens are now orphaned and have no one to look after their needs." He nodded grimly. "Sir, I have money and am willing to take them with me and to look after them as if they were my own daughters."

"Would you? Now that is a big relief. We've been trying to figure out how we could manage to care for them. You know, General Erebos and his proclamations that only one woman per man is allowed. We simply don't have the men available here in Edessa to care for them, not without breaking the law."

"I understand. I am transporting these two Ornamented Dolls to Preveza where they have a man each to care for their needs," he lied. "Plus, we have several others who will be taking on these others. There is plenty of room for Xenia and Ariadne. I guarantee that they will get the best of care."

"Deal, son!" The mayor shook Wie's hand vigorously, greatly relieved of this unexpected burden. Further, no one had mention his failed attempts at locating either women when they mysteriously disappeared. Wie was very careful not to mention it.

Later, as they were getting ready to leave town, Wie took Xenia to their small Banca del Dio. There, he set up an account for both women in their own names. The banker quickly divided their father's account into halves for the teens. Wie suggested that the proceeds from the sale of their home go to benefit the town, which the banker was quick to accept. Xenia smiled for the first time.

On their way out of town, they stopped at the Xandros home, allowing the girls to bring what belongings they desired. Both men went inside with them and gathered up what they wished to bring along. It was not much. Clothes didn't fit, but they did bring nightgowns, hairbrushes, and some jewelry of their mothers. Around ten, they finally left Edessa behind them.

Inside the now crowded carriage, Mie began explaining to Ariadne that if she learned to speak Annelise or the Tashien dialect, she could make herself understood. Thus, Xenia and Ariadne began lengthy language lessons, passing the endless hours of carriage riding. When they stopped for a picnic lunch, Xenia said, "Master Wei, thank you for saving us and for taking us in. We promise to do what you say."

"You are most welcome. Just do what is right and just, and we will all get along just fine." Xenia grinned, taking a liking to this foreigner.

"Where are we going? Preveza? Is it safe there?" she asked for her benefit and her sister's.

"To be honest with you, Xenia, it is not safe for women to be in Alia. General Erebos is in charge, and he has ordered that all women become Ornamented Dolls just as your sister is and Psyche and Kassi are. I do not want that to happen to my wife and daughters. I don't believe that you want it to happen to you either, right?"

"No! It is so horrible." She gave a sympathetic look to her sister, who began to cry again.

"Right. So we are going to Preveza all right, but we are then going to try to get a caravel to take us somewhere else where it is safe for women to live in peace," he explained. She agreed with that, and they finished eating and continued down the paved road to Preveza, a little over a hundred miles further north and a bit west.

Several days later, they arrived in Preveza and took rooms in one of the better inns. At least, they would stay in relative comfort, Wie decided. Once they were settled, he and Alexus left to scout around a little. Meanwhile, the women continued with their language lessons. Mie felt strongly that this would give the grieving teens something constructive to do. Additionally, the other teens were constantly showing the new arrivals how they could accomplish some things on their own.

A few discrete inquires later, they learned that General Thebes, who controlled the port under martial law, was quietly stalling the Ornamentation Project. The two men breathed a sigh of relief. They could afford to spend some time here attempting to book passage to Shansee. They visited the Harbor Master first, inquiring about shipping that might be bound for Shansee. Unfortunately, since the plague struck, no caravels were going that far away. In fact, most were idle. Little sea commerce was transpiring in Alia, which they both found utterly amazing, since before the plague, such commerce was Alia's lifeblood.

For a week, they toyed with the idea of hiring an idle ship to make the journey. To that end, they visited several docked ships. Wie found them all most unsatisfactory. Smelly and ill maintained, they did not look sea worthy for such a long voyage. He had no intention of losing his party at sea.

Further discussions with the Harbor Master yielded little additional information, until Wie kindly slipped the man a dozen gold coins. "Well, since you are so insistent, we have heard that the Ace Iron Company is expecting a shipment of ore in here on a Velona caravel sometime this month."

"Ah that sounds much better. How much to have you contact me when that ship arrives so that I may make appropriate inquiries of her captain?"

"Another ten and I will make sure that you are informed in a most timely manner, sir." Wie handed the man the additional coins. The two headed back to the inn. Now all they could do was wait and hope that nothing further arose. If it did, Wie needed a backup plan. He and Alexus began working out how they might travel overland to another country. Thrace was their only real choice, neither wanted to go back through Levkos just to go on to another country. Alexus made sure that their carriage was always ready to go on short notice. They settled in and joined in with the language lessons.

Late October, the Golden Scallion docked in Preveza. True to his word, the Harbor Master sent word to Wie. He and Alexus headed to the docks at once. As they arrived, they saw dockhands beginning the arduous task of unloading a cargo of ore. They walked up to the ship's gangplank. Wie was unsure of the proper protocol. He'd last been on an ocean ship nearly twenty years ago. "May I speak with your captain?" he asked a crewman.

"Aye, I'll fetch him," the man said, but Wie barely understood his Velona dialect. He wished that Mie was with him now for sure. Shortly, a tall, thin man wearing a blue uniform came to the other end of the gangplank.

"You wanted to see the captain? I'm Captain Tom Weatherspoon."

His Demokritos was poor, Wei noted. "Can we come aboard and discuss a matter, captain sir?" He introduced himself and his son. He had to repeat it twice before Tom smiled and motioned them aboard. He led them into his fancy cabin and offered the two a drink, which Wie refused. He didn't drink.

"I am afraid that I don't quite understand your Demokritos speech very well, captain."

He laughed, "That's understandable. I don't speak it very well. How about the Velona dialect?" the captain tried.

"My wife speaks it fairly well or so she claims. How about Annelise?"

"Not much better than Demokritos, I am afraid. Say aren't you from Tashien?"

"Yes, do you speak that?"

"Now we are cooking," Tom replied using the Tashien dialect. "I've done far more trading with Tashien than Demokritos." At last, the two men had a language both could speak fairly well.

"I'll get right to the point, captain. I wish to purchase passage for my party to Shansee, Tashien. I am willing to pay whatever is a fair price."

"How many are in your party, Wie?" he asked.

Wei had to count them. "There are nine of us, two men, seven women, but three are Ornamented Dolls and need our assistance."

"Well, this is a cargo ship, but you are in luck, Wie. We do not have any return cargo yet. Times are in the Dark Ages down here. I plan to go over to Annelise next and see if I can rustle up a cargo there. In any case, we have to go to Annelise to resupply. We are so far south now that we need a complete resupply to make it back into the northern waters. I'm afraid supplies are so scarce in most Demokritos ports these days that we can only acquire enough to make it to Annelise. I believe that we can make a deal that suits us both. If I get Annelise cargo, it will be clothing, which will not take up too much space. If not, then it is on to Tashien anyway. If you are willing to pay a hundred a head, you have passage to Tashien."

Wie handed him gems worth a thousand, telling him to keep the change. After shaking hands sealing the deal, he called out, "Bosun, prepare cabins for nine. We have travelers this trip!"

"Aye, aye, captain, nine it is," a voice called out from below.

"Bring your party on board say November 1, Wie. We'll be ready to sail around then." Wie agreed and told him where they were staying. Alexus and Wie walked off the gangplank elated. At last, they were making real progress!

On the first, Wie brought them all to the docks in his carriage. All the ship's hands stared at the three Ornamented Dolls as they very carefully negotiated the gangplank. Wie kept his hands around Ariadne's waist making sure that she kept her balance. He was certain that Psyche and Kassi would have little trouble, but she was barely holding her own, breaking down in fits of crying at least once each day.

"My god! This is almost inhuman what they are doing to their women here in Alia," Captain Tom commented as Psyche and Kassandra boarded and neared him. "Our women have lost their arms too, but doing this too them — why this is just plain sadistic! How can they do anything at all?" he asked.

"Yes, it is very hard for us to do things, vut we do vanage sovehow. Ariadne has just becove a Ornavented Doll and she is having a vost difficult tive of it," Psyche answered him.

"Hey, you can speak after all! I didn't think that you could. I understand your Tashien, ma'am!" Captain Tom replied.

"We cannot sveak our own language, vut we can sveak Annelise and Tashien, that's all though," Kassandra added.

"Well, welcome aboard the Golden Scallion, ladies. Cabins are below. Will you need a hand with the stairs?"

"Ariadne will, vut we should ve avle to vanage," Psyche replied.

When Wie got aboard with the slightly frightened Ariadne, who was very unsure of her footing, Captain Tom realized that he might have made a mistake in their quarters. "Mr. Wie, we had intended to put your party up in the four main deck cabins. The galley where we dine is below in the cargo hold. The stairs are pretty steep. I'm wondering if perhaps we should make some makeshift bedding for your party down in the cargo hold? Then they wouldn't have to go up and down the stairs much. Or maybe you would prefer bringing them their meals up from the galley? The poop deck cabins are far more comfortable, but they only sleep eight. One person can triple up in a hammock or can sleep in the hold."

Wei decided, "Let's try the cabins first. Alexus and I can bring their meals up. If that doesn't work out, then we can make other arrangements."

"Excellent. The boson will show you to your rooms. My crew will load your things shortly. What about your carriage? Is that to come too?"

Wie smiled. He had not even thought of that. "No, I gave it to the Harbor Master. It is his now. Thanks."

Shortly, the nine stood cramped in the narrow hallway, four doors opened into the cabins. Wie said softly, "Mei, you and Ariadne take this room. She will need the most help. I will sleep in a hammock with you to help. Alexus, you and Xenia take that cabin and you are to help her as needed. Psyche, Kassi, you take that cabin."

"I know dad. Selene and I get the last one. We'll be okay," Roxane broke in.

The rooms held two bunk beds and a small desk and chair. Drawers in the desk also served as the wardrobe cabinet. Before long, crew members brought their bags, depositing them in the hall. Wie doled them out to their owners, who attempted to stow their things. The Ornamented Dolls and Xenia had a most difficult time with this, unable to use their teeth to carry their things. They'd brought along no yokes. Even if they had, they would not have even fit in the narrow hall here.

Before long, Captain Tom offered to give Wie and Alexus a guided tour, while his crew made last minute preparations. "High tide is in an hour. We sail then. Now here in my cabin is our LD radio. With it, I stay in daily contact with Velona and our Shipping Minister, who knows were ever last one of our ships is at every day, everywhere in the world. If we run into trouble, I can call for help as well. Nice safety factor, eh?" Next, he led them below decks into the main hold and showed them the galley and dining area. To avoid seasickness, their cook had already brewed a special pot of tea. He suggested that they drink a cup before they set sail. The two men carried the tray of cups and spoons back up the stairs, noting that it would be a challenge for any of the women and nearly impossible for the Ornamented Dolls.

Tea consumed, the Golden Scallion drifted loose from the docks, slowly tacking clear, before hoisting the mainsails. While Psyche and Kassandra wanted to watch, they felt more secure in their cabin. The ship seemed to be very unstable beneath their feet. Only Wie and Mie had ever been on board a ship before and that was twenty years ago for them.

December 1, the Golden Scallion docked in Andros, Arolas, to pick up more supplies and particularly water. With the heat of summer now upon them, everyone was drinking a lot onboard the "sauna" called a caravel. Thus far, the voyage was interesting. Captain Tom LD radioed into Velona their current position at sunrise and sunset. Wie found this encouraging — that others would know where they were at twice a day. Captain Tom, a talker type, spent hours telling his passengers all the news of the last couple of years. Right away, he found the Alia folks were news-starved, having heard nothing about the rest of the world since the beginning of the plague.

Wie and his group found his alien plague story a bit farfetched, but at least it was an explanation. He told them about the ongoing recoveries of many of the old Demokritos kingdoms. In particular, he pointed out that six had now become matriarchies and that women were their monarchs. Arolas was the first to begin the walk back into prosperity. He told them about many of the incredible inventions, though he had no real concept of this electrical stuff only that it worked somehow.

"Look, we will be taking on water in Andros. You can have a day of shore leave. I am sure that you will be able to see many of these inventions first hand. I don't know if either of their monarchs will be there, probably they are in Naxos," Captain Tom suggested.

What a contrast in ports, Wie noted. As his party walked off the gangplank, ten ships were either loading or unloading. Andros was busy. Even more interesting were the three motor-wagons, which were being loaded directly from caravels. They took a stroll through the streets and got to see three women driving their T-putt-putts, their baskets loaded with sacks of food. As they approached an open market, a dozen women were shopping using their yokes to carry their purchases. "Things seev so norval here," Psyche commented to her sister.

"The yokes — they really are needed, aren't they?" Kassandra asked. She watched as a woman sat hers down, sat herself down, and used her feet to examine some melons. A bit later, she struggled to put one in her basket, scooting a bit on the ground. Then the woman retrieved a coin pouch. While the twins watched, the woman finally was able to retrieve a coin, handing it to the busy farmer. "It took her avout five tives longer that it used to take us vefore the vlague," she noted.

"We can do it, that's what is ivvortant. We can do it," Psyche declared with resolve.

"*They* can do it, sis. *We* will have a harder tive of it," Kassandra pointed out the huge difference between them and normal women.

"Amazing," Xenia added. "Women are doing things. I didn't think that it would be possible, but I am seeing it. Sis, maybe there really is hope for us."

"Hove so," Ariadne hazarded speaking a little in Annelise. She was still very timid about even trying to speak in public. This was the first time that she was really out in the public eye, she felt very self-conscious. Everyone was looking at her and the twins, but the twins didn't pay the onlookers much attention. There was just too much of interest for them to see.

Having seen firsthand that it was safe for women to be on the streets, Master Wie decided to treat them to a fancy meal. While the inns were still trying to get back to battery, several people on the street recommended Kleto's Inn. Around noon, Wie took them into the best inn in Andros. Their waitress came up to them, "Party of nine?"

"Yes, we are on shore leave from the Golden Scallion. We are fleeing the chaos in Levkos. Women seem to be everywhere here in Andros, amazing. In Levkos, a woman doesn't dare walk on the streets. You never see them outside their homes," Master Wie explained.

"We are still learning new ways to do things. Our monarchs are leading the way. Monarch Ana always dines here when she is in town. I am still learning myself. What strange ornaments those three are wearing. I've never seen such things," she said, staring wide-eyed at the twins and Ariadne.

"The sadistic General Erebos has ordered all women to become like these women. They are called Ornamented Dolls, or Dolls for short. Most of the Ornamented Dolls are now completely helpless," he explained.

"Wow! That's awful. Can they eat? I mean with those things in their lips?" she asked, leading them to a most unusual looking, oblong table.

"Only with extreme difficulty," he explained. "None can feed themselves, their vision is too obstructed, and they are unable to turn their heads or bend their necks. It is quite a challenge."

"Why is your general doing this?" she asked in disbelief.

"Evil men have evil ideas. What an unusual table," he commented as they arrived at what was to be their table.

"Oh, I'm sorry. We women prefer eating from tables that are low to the ground. You have so many women that I'm seating you here. The women sit on the low side, you men are to sit on the high side. But if you need to sit beside the three Ornamented Dolls, I can make other arrangements."

"No, we can make this work. Ariadne, you sit next to me. I'll help you," Wie decided. She did as asked. He and Alexus went from woman to woman, adjusting their chairs for them.

"Mind if we watch how you do things? None of us have any ideas how you are able to do so many things," Mie asked.

"Not at all! Please, do so. Haven't you read the Bethany's Hints book? After all, most of us will be watching the Ornamented Dolls. We've never seen anything like them. Such incredible earrings."

She sat down on the floor, produced a pad and pencil from her low pocket, and began taking their orders. All went with the house special. The women watched how she did this, completely amazed. A short while later, she brought their orders using her yoke. Wie noticed why the tables were so far apart, for it gave her room to maneuver with her yoke. The women watched in amazement as she served them. She sat the yoke in position, sat herself down, and used her feet to lift one plate up, sitting it before Mie. She shifted her position, took one out of the other basket, and sat it before Selene. Only then, did she get to her feet and move the yoke. She was serving every other woman, the spacing of her yoke.

"I know I'm slow, but I'm doing it," she pointed out to the women who were watching her every move. "The hard part is lifting it up to the men's side. I still have a whole lot of trouble with serving men. That's why I really wanted to serve your party." She grinned.

When she got to Wie, she moved very slowly, balancing the plate carefully as she lifted it up with her feet. As it reached the edge of the table, Wie deftly slid it over for her. She smiled. "Wow, that's incredible!" Roxane exclaimed.

"Here, I brought you a Bethany's Hints book. I will see if I can get you some more before you go. We've got lots of them around now," she said as she finally lifted a book up, placing it before Mei. They all thanked her.

Wie took care as he fed Ariadne, making sure that she was not embarrassed. She was nervous; all these people were staring at her. Psyche and Kassandra took turns feeding each other, but also felt a little uncomfortable. So many were watching their every move.

When they finished, the tables turned once again. The women watched how their waitress handled receiving Wie's coins to pay for the meal. She sat down, picked a coin up, and tucked it in a pocket that was nearly at the bottom of her dress. Convenient, someone had thought of everything, Mie thought. After pocketing the coins, she went to the barkeeper and repeated her actions, depositing one coin at a time on the top of the counter. She kept the very generous tip the Wie gave her. "Thank you for helping educate our women," he said as he gave her the extra coins. She smiled, grateful for the tip.

As they were about to leave, two other women came over and gave them two more Hints books. "Now that was absolutely amazing!" Roxane exclaimed as they hit the streets again. "I would never have believed it, not in a million years. We can do things. Did you see how she had pockets sewed near the hem of her dress? We must make adjustments, that's all."

"And a whole lot of practice," Xenia added. "Maybe I can learn to live again. You too, sis." Ariadne merely said ah, meaning yes, but her tone suggested anything but yes. The group headed back to the ship, the women wanted to explore the three books that they'd received. Wie was most pleased; the women had just received a huge boost of hope. He also noted that nearly all the women that they'd seen were young. Not one was over thirty. Where were all the older women, he wondered. What he didn't yet know was the simple fact that the younger women were adapting readily, while the older women were having a much more difficult time adjusting to all these new ways of doing things.

The seven women spent the afternoon in their cabins reading the Hints book. "We can sew? I don't believe it!" Roxane exclaimed.

"We vrovavly can't sew. See, she is vaking too vuch use of teeth and vending, Kassi, Ariadne" Psyche pointed out to her sister and to Ariadne.

The afternoon was very well spent. Ideas flooded into their minds, so many different ways to learn. More importantly, they saw that women were actually far, far from helpless, if they just allowed five times more time to do something, used alternate ways and means, and in some cases had the proper tools.

At suppertime, Captain Tom notified them that their water and supplies were loaded and they would sail at high tide, around four in the morning. "We will sail about one and a half thousand miles, stopping at Grenen at the eastern edge of Annelise. There, we will load up on supplies before heading north for thousands of miles. You can have several days in port, if you like, but they will probably insist that you wear proper clothing. You know the Annelise — clothing freaks." Wie chuckled, thanked him for the data, and relayed it to the others. No one felt the ship slip out of the harbor in the early morning hours.

A week out of Andros, Captain Tom became worried. It was noon and the skies to the north and east of them grew steadily darker and darker. The winds picked up. He issued storm-rigging orders and sent a message to the passengers. A crewman called out from the hallway, "Heavy storm is coming. Stay in your cabins. Prepare for a rough ride." The landlubbers didn't quite know what this meant. Worries predominated among the nine. Soon they felt a huge surge hit the caravel, it rolled heavily to one side before righting itself. Sheets of rain followed that. Inside, the nine rolled heavily to one side and then the other side. All stayed in their beds, though the women had a difficult time of it. Their bodies tended to roll with the ship and they had to keep their positions by propping their feet against the wooden edge of the bed and the side of the ship.

On deck, Captain Tom knew that they were in trouble. This was a major blow that had sprouted up, perhaps even a hurricane. The winds continued to shove the caravel closer to the shoreline, thwarting his attempts to head her into the winds. Lightning crackled, thunder rolled across the giant waves. The Golden Scallion rose high in the air only to plummet as the bottom fell out of the swell. Worse, the ship was still losing distance from the shore, dangerously so. It had been pushed and shoved several miles already, worrying the captain, who was lashed to the tiller. He had to make a decision soon, but either way, the choices were fraught with peril.

If he did nothing, the hurricane would soon push them ashore, crushing the ship. If he hoisted a bit of sail in an attempt to tack further from the shore, either the rigging or masts would likely not stand the gale force winds, with equally devastating results. He opted to attempt to keep from being run aground. Only with the greatest of effort were two crew members able to run up two forward jibs. Moaning and creaking from the strain, the masts held and he swung the wheel, heading the ship back on a tack that would begin to pull them further from the shore. Now the caravel broke into the raging swells even harder, threatening to splinter its hull. The pressures being forced upon the ship were near the breaking point, still it held together.

Black skies obliterated the noontime sun. With flashes of lightning, he could catch only the briefest of glimpses of the shoreline off to his right. Captain Tom felt encouraged; the land was farther away with each sighting. Luck was on his side, he thought. "Hang in there baby!" he called out to his ship.

Now he tried to determine which side of the hurricane he was facing. Was the eye dead ahead? If so, they'd have to go through all this again, only this time they'd be blown far from land. Well, that would certainly be safer, he thought. He double checked his two crew members. They gave him repeated thumbs up signs, indicating that they were roped securely to the ship. Good, he couldn't risk a man going overboard now. That would be a death warrant in these seas. How long would it blow?

Lightning flashes revealed a monster wave rolling unstoppably towards their port side. "Damn!" he screamed. "Big one!" he yelled hoping his men could hear his warning over the cacophony of roaring noise. His luck ran out. The wave crashed over the ship. He heard timbers cracking, ropes beyond taught snapping. His own body flew from the wheel even though his hands were gripping them with all his might. Underwater, he flew across the deck and nearly had his mid-section severed when his own safety line reached the end of its play. He fought hard to keep from involuntarily exhaling. He'd drown if he did. Wait. Wait. He forced his mind to think. Now he felt the heavy pressure of the seawater lessening — the wave was passing over him and soon it would be just a memory. Air! Sheeting rain pelted his face. How great that felt. He exhaled and inhaled deeply, thankful to be alive.

The caravel was leaning heavily to starboard now, making his attempts to regain his footing and drag himself back to the wheel nearly impossible. Lightning flashes revealed his worst fears. Both masts were gone, snapped off like toothpicks near the main deck. The heavy rigging still held both masts and were now dragging them down, threatening to pull what was left of the caravel under the seas. One more huge wave and the masts would win. He had to cut the lines. He yelled his orders to the two crew, hoping that they were still alive. He grabbed the stern safety axe and struggled to get to the nearest rigging. Chop. Chop. Holding on to whatever he could, he swung the axe into the remnants of the rope rigging.

He heard other chopping sounds and took heart. At least one had heard and was helping. Eternity. That's what it felt like to Captain Tom, an eternity of chopping. At last, the two masts drifted off, the caravel was free, she rolled back somewhat, though she was still leaning heavily to starboard. Now he faced the greatest challenge in his career. The hurricane was driving the ship ashore; his only weapon was their rudder. Somehow, he had to keep the ship from being destroyed as it hit the shallows! He spun the wheel and rudder, praying this would be enough.

"Eyes on the shore!" he yelled to the two crew. Both knew what he meant. Their remaining job was to call out the distance to the land. They also knew what their fates would be, but they had faith in Captain Tom. For several minutes, estimated distances were relayed to him, and he still fought with the rudder to minimize their rapid closure and doom.

"Bay! Bay! Bay!" screamed a crew member. Captain Tom also trusted his men. They were nearing a bay. That meant slight protection and possible salvation. He spun the rudder the opposite direction, and the ship righted itself even further, the wind and sea driving it from behind now, directly into the bay. "Starboard! Starboard! Starboard!" the crew screamed as loudly as possible. He spun the wheel in the opposite direction. The caravel responded sluggishly, leaning heavily to starboard once more. Then they struck shallow waters, and the caravel keeled over sharply to starboard and did not right itself. Again, the force of the sudden stop threw him bodily from the wheel. He hit hard into the railing. Darkness swept over him; he went unconscious.

In their cabins, the passengers were tossed one way and the other. They heard what sounded like breaking wood. Fear and panic swept over them, though Wie did his best to keep Ariadne as calm as possible. After an eternity, the ship seemed to stop fighting the seas, and they all calmed down a little. Then, suddenly it rolled starboard and stopped so suddenly that Psyche was nearly thrown into a sitting position. Selene and Roxane rolled out of their bunks and landed on the side of their cabin walls, bruised. Alexus held on to the terrified Xenia and cushioned their fall and subsequent slam into their walls. The hideous rolling and pitching ended, though the caravel still rose and fell a little. The ship remained at a forty-five degree angle from its usual upright position. None of the passengers dared move! They waited and prayed.

Now they heard footsteps out in the hallway, Xenia wondered how anyone could walk on such a slant! Voices. The storm muffled words, but hearing voices was encouraging. More voices and a dragging sound came from their hall. The boson called out, "Passengers, are you all right?" One by one, the nine voices called out yes. "Captain has taken a blow to his head. Got us safe in a bay. Lost the masts though. Sit tight; we can ride the hurricane out safe enough now."

They did as asked. "I think the wind might be dying down some," Mie suggested to Ariadne. She was too scared to reply.

Sometime later, the lights came back on, and the wind and rain died down. A crewman called out from the hall, "Storm has passed. We made it. We'll get you all out and ashore as soon as we can. Stay put for a while longer." Wie yelled an okay.

Chapter 60 Shipwrecked

"I hove they get us out of here soon; water is coving in," Kassandra pointed out the obvious to her sister. Both were sitting precariously on the slanted edge of the bottom bunk bed.

As if in answer, their door opened and fell back against the outer wall. "Time to go ashore ladies. We're going to help you all the way." Walking on a steeply sloping floor is difficult if you have arms and hands to help. Captain Tom, nursing a first-class headache, knew the women would find it nearly impossible, especially the Dolls. Hence, he rigged up a rope and pulley sea rescue basket to lower them down the askew main deck and into the long boat. First, though, he had to have his men get them out of their cabins and down the hall to the doors. Strong arms encircled the teens and steadied them as they struggled to climb their floor to the hall. In the hall, he had them put one foot on the floor and the other foot on the side wall. Now they could at least walk down the hall. At the doors, another crewman helped each in turn into the sea rescue basket and then others hoisted them up into the air.

Their view of the ship was dismaying to say the least. Splintered posts were all that remained of the two tall masts. The ship was lying on its side in shallow water. The shore was perhaps a hundred feet further off. They were lowered into a long boat safely and easily, they thought. "I don't think the shiv will ever sail again," Psyche said to Kassandra when she was positioned beside her sister and they watched the men bringing the others, one by one.

"At least we are not at the vottov of the ocean," Kassi replied.

A half hour later, all nine were safely aboard and two crew joined them, rowing them to the shore. They spotted Captain Tom hustling on shore, preparing their makeshift quarters. He waved to them and continued working some ropes taught. Once the longboat landed, the crew lifted each woman safely onto the solid, but soaking ground.

"I see that you have survived well. That was a full blown hurricane, ladies. Now that is something to write home about! I have set up tents here which will serve as our temporary housing until repairs are made. This way," he said.

The passengers had one tent and the crew, a second. Cots with blankets were inside theirs. "Where are we? Can we help?" asked Wie.

"Well, my guess is that we are somewhere near the Vladimir town called Tanja which is about halfway across that country. Can't tell if we are east or west of it yet. I'll need to take some star sightings tonight. As soon as we get things established, yes, we could use all the help we can get. Masts will be our major problem. Main thing now is to get camp setup. It will be nightfall soon. Tomorrow, if I can get the LD radio dried out enough to work, we can radio for help. No need to worry. Even if I can't get the radio to work, help will come. They knew our morning position. If they cannot contact us in a day or so, they will send out search vessels. We are quite visible and they knew our route. Rest assured, help will come. Now then, any chance you folks could rustle up some dinner for us all? I can use the cook's help with other things."

"Yes, point us to the food and pans," Wie replied. The two men looked at their surroundings in hopes of finding some dry wood. Unfortunately, all that they saw was rolling fields of green grasslands somewhat flattened by the hurricane. Not a tree was in sight. The cook came ashore bringing a load of charcoal, lamp oil, and pots and pans. He pointed out the water barrel and bags of food supplies. He also pointed out that the captain had saved them from certain death. Maneuvering into this tiny bay had been the only thing that had kept the ship from breaking up as it hit shallow waters. The cook thought this had been a miracle.

Alexus took charge of digging a fire pit, while Mie and Wie examined what could be cooked easily. He followed her suggestions. After Alexus got the cooking coals going, Wie threw stew ingredients into the pot and carried it to the coals. "Now we take over, Wie," Mie insisted. She and the teens took turns stirring the large pot.

As the sun began to sink in the west, the large group sat down on blankets to a picnic-style stew and tea. The crew offered Mie a full time job as their cook, much to the dismay of their cook. She took that as a compliment. When darkness fell, the passengers retired to their tent. "I like sleeving on solid ground vuch vetter," Psyche declared. Everyone agreed, especially Ariadne, who finally felt safe.

The next morning, they reheated the leftover stew for a fast breakfast. Over tea, Captain Tom informed Wie that Tanja must be somewhere to the west of their position. "We will be taking stock of the ship first. Once we have that done and know what will be done in what order, we'll let you lend a hand, Wie." He nodded.

While the women contented themselves with making a stab at doing the dishes, Alexus and Wie lent them a hand. Afterwards, they sat down to do their hair. After that, Alexus and Wie moved aside from the women to have a private talk. Both were worried that the ship was beyond repair, especially since there seemed to be no trees anywhere around here. They chatted about the possibility of walking back to Andros, but decided that might be a last resort if help didn't come.

The morning was sunny, promising to be another hot one, the beginning days of summer. Already the nearby grasses had begun rising towards the sun, life continues on, Wie mused. He was broken from his reverie by the sound of thunder. He looked at the sky, pure and blue. He glanced at the horizon and saw twenty-five horsemen riding over the western hills toward them. "Alert everyone, we have company!" He and Alexus moved over to where the women were sitting on blankets on the ground. They stopped chatting and rose to watch the riders too. Wie glanced at the ship, Captain Tom and his men were all on board, the riders would be here long before they could get back. Wie took charge.

"We don't know if they are friendly or not. Xenia, Ariadne, fall behind us. Alexus, you and I take either end, Psyche, Kassi, you are in the middle. Defensive positions," Wie ordered. The two teens did as asked, moving behind the others and wondered why bother? Two unarmed men to protect seven women? It seemed hopeless to them. Once more, fear crept into their minds. Everywhere they went, men seemed to want to harm helpless women, they both thought.

"My god! They are all just boys," Mie commented as the group drew close. Boys with swords drawn, Psyche noted, but said nothing. Her eyes rapidly swept over the group. One could not have been more than ten years old. One looked to be perhaps her own age, he moved a little closer. While the boys looked over the nine and then glanced out at the ship, most focused upon Psyche, Kassandra, and Ariadne. Well, she was used to that; she was an Ornamented Doll after all. Ornamented Dolls were supposed to attract men's attention and look pretty, at least according to General Erebos anyway, she thought.

The older boy said something to Wie. His language was strange and he didn't understand what the lad was saying. The boy repeated it, Wie concluded. In desperation, he looked at Mie for help. "Sounds like Galt, that minor language of the horsemen of the Northern Steppes," she replied to his glance. "I'll try." She said a brief greeting in all the languages she knew. One by one, the boy continued to shake his head indicating no. In desperation, she said the only two words that she knew in Galt. A smile replaced the frown on the boy's face. He replied with a rapid fire of speech, which Mie didn't understand at all. "Well, it is close to Galt. I said please and thank you in that language and he responded. Now what do we do?"

Mie was very observant, but then so were all the martial artists. She noticed several of the boys looking now at their bags of food, plainly visible near their fire pit. "Wie, use your hands and make like you are eating. Point to them and see if they are interested in eating some of our food." He made eating motions, following her suggestion.

At once, several boys smiled and duplicated his. They pointed to their food bags and made more eating signs with their hands and mouths. Wie nodded and moved towards the bags. The boys all dismounted and rapidly joined him, holding out their hands. Wie now saw that they were all thin and probably very hungry. He made cooking motions and the boys all grinned and nodded. He added more charcoal and began fixing another pot of stew, but had Mie and the girls do the actual stirring as before. Wie carefully observed the boys. It was obvious that they were very hungry, if not starving for a good meal.

"The cavtain is coving," Psyche said, noting that the boys glanced at her and shook their heads. They didn't understand her either. As he and his crew approached, the boys reacted. Wie expected that they would retreat and or cower from the men. The opposite happened. All drew their swords, forming a line around the women cooking the food.

Captain Tom didn't draw his sword or his pistol. "I see that we have company. Boys. Let's see if I can speak to them."

"You know their language?" Mie asked.

"Not exactly, but I have known a few from the steppes. I've heard the language spoken here in Vladimir is similar. Do any of you know it?" Everyone replied that they didn't, so he tried it.

"Hello. I am the ship's captain. These are my passengers. Our ship ran into a bad storm," he said slowly, as if picking his words carefully.

The older boy looked at him with a wince and said, "You speak strangely, but we know. A boy saw your ship during the storm. We thought it was destroyed and came to salvage food. Woman is making us food. We are very hungry. You have food to trade perhaps?"

"Whoa, too fast. Say again slowly, please." The boy did so and the captain translated what he said.

"Great! Captain, ask him to call off his words for the things that he sees here and point to them as he says them. I can get a fast language lesson. Everyone pay attention to his words for the objects.

Then, we have to work out the action verbs of their language," Mie requested, taking a turn stirring the pot.

The boys thought that this was great fun, especially when the women began repeating his words for each object. Slowly, the language barrier was cast aside. An hour later, Mie and the teens watched the boys devour the stew ravenously, even asking for more.

While they were eating, Captain Tom asked, "Tanja that way?" pointing to the west.

Several nodded that it was. One added, "Two miles." Well, they guessed that was the distance measurement. Both Wie and Captain Tom had the same idea, someone ought to go into Tanja and see if help could be found there. Wie insisted that he take his group into the town.

"Okay, I am obviously needed here to get the ship fixed up and the radio working. You be careful. If we have not heard back from you by nightfall, we'll come in there with our guns blazing and cutlasses rattling." Wie grinned but did not think that would be needed; the boys seemed friendly enough.

After Wie made his intention known to the boys, they made two attempts at communicating ideas. First, they wanted Wie to bring along the food bags. Second, they thought that the women ought to ride their horses, while they led them. Wie convinced them that the women preferred to walk, after the harrowing experience on the ship. Captain Tom said to take the food bags, the cook could bring more ashore on their next trip. "Look, the one thing that we have is plenty of food," he pointed out.

Some of the bags were hoisted onto the saddles, but Wie carried one. Since the women were walking, the boys decided to lead their horses and more language training ensued. Slowly, Wie and his group picked up more and more of their words. Psyche and Kassandra, and Ariadne to a lesser extent, were disappointed because they simply couldn't make the proper sounds and knew that they would not be able to speak directly to them.

Captain Tom had related all that was known about Vladimir to the group the previous evening. While some of the facts seemed correct, Wie was beginning to wonder about all them. The outside world's data on these people was very out of date, few traders ever stopped in their tiny ports. The facts were sketchy at best.

Vladimir was a land was relatively dry steppes, cradled between the Hagan Range on the east and the Katos Mountains on the west which were tall and blocked most of the rain. The people who lived here were horsemen and nomadic for the most part, though they had four coastal permanent towns. They were a brutal and warlike people. With few trees anywhere in Vladimir, they only had the smallest of fishing boats, and those were very few. Hence, their raiding parties — unable to cross the mountains or travel by sea, occasionally they rode up the coast to attack, pillage, and rape the women of the towns nearest the border. These riders would not sacrifice their prized horses just for a raid. Of their leaders, little was known except that they got their positions by being the strongest and best horse combat riders. Rumors, unsubstantiated, suggested that these rulers had sorcerers who advised them, powerful men who possessed terrible spells. Just what the spells might be, there was no definitive statement.

The largest of the coastal towns was called Tanja. The land itself was sparsely grassed, rolling hills, reminiscent of the Northern Steppes. As far as he knew, Tanja's population was perhaps fifty thousand and was a step backwards into time and civilization. The buildings were crude adobe for the most part, which made sense if trees were scarce here. The number of stone buildings one could count on one hand, these were the larger structures. Yet all them looked like rundown shanties, Captain Tom later stated. The streets looked like they had never been cleaned since they were built.

The people wore leather and horsehair-woven clothing. Women's dresses were supposedly decorated with gay colored embroidery, while the men's tended to be plain. Hair, all wore theirs long, suggesting that haircuts were unknown here. Brown was the dominate color. As far as leaders were concerned, they were organized into tribes or clans. The leader held the title of Kopon and was reputedly the strongest fighter. His wife was called Koponess, though her duties were unknown.

As Wie and his group crested a hill and looked down on Tanja for the first time, everyone felt as though they had stepped back three centuries in time! Crude beyond belief was their instant opinion of these people, but that soon changed. Tanja had perhaps ten thousand adobe homes with some larger buildings scattered among them, sprawled over many square miles along the coast and stretching inland even further. The streets were dirt, but they did see a handful of stone buildings.

As they approached, they saw boys and girls in very large numbers making adobe bricks while others were using stacks of dried bricks to create new homes hastily on the edges of the city. Thousands of girls were stomping in the mud, mixing the dried grass and mud. Some girls carried a pair of buckets of water from the ocean to the mixing site. The boys were forming the adobe into bricks and laying them out to dry.

"We make new homes," one boy proudly said to Wie, pointing out the industrious children. As they neared, Wie spotted a few older teens who appeared to be in charge. Strange, he thought. Where were the men and women?

As they approached, the first group, they saw that both men and women never cut their hair, but the boys had theirs tied back in ponytails. The girls' hair reached to their knees and they had to toss their heads continually to keep theirs out of their faces. Psyche wondered why they didn't tie theirs back as well. The workers stopped and stared at the newcomers, especially the three Ornamented Dolls. The older boy called out, "They bring food." Almost in unison, smiles broke out and they were cheered. The in-charge teens had to yell to keep the children from stopping their work and mob the newcomers.

"We go meet Holy Mother now. Take her food," the teen explained. Now they entered the dirt streets of Tanja and got a closer look at their clothing and appearance. The people wore leather and horse hairwoven clothing. The women's dresses were decorated with gay colored embroidery, while the men's tended to be plain. None seemed to fit anyone properly; some pants were too short, others too long. Some boys passed them by, pushing a cart filled with dried horse manure, a staple for their fires, the boy explained. Charcoal was harder to find. Other boys pushed along carts loaded with berries and nuts, delivering small wicker baskets of these to homes along the street. However, to Mie's eyes, every child that she saw looked half-starved.

Near the center of Tanja, the riders stopped at one of the rare stone buildings, a single story building with an attached stables. A few horses were inside. "Come, meet Holy Mother now," the teen leader insisted. They followed him inside, as one boy held the door open for the nine as they entered. Mie thought, "Polite at least."

The first room they entered was an official meeting room, very large in size, with a number of crude wooden tables pushed together to form a long one. The chairs were made of wicker and actually were rather soft. Various trophies lined the back wall. On the opposite side of the long tables sat two more chairs. A woman whom they estimated was in her mid-thirties met them as they entered. A gangly boy in his mid-teens stood at her side. He carried a long gun and a sword; both looked bigger than he did.

(Although they were still working out the language barrier, I will fill in the gaps rather than deal with the broken phrases.) "Welcome strangers. I am called Holy Mother Anezka. My son, Evzen. My daughter, Zelenka is out supervising home constructions. My husband, Radek, is out leading a hunting party. During the storm, a ship was seen about to hit land. I sent out the party to see if we could salvage any food or useful things. I guess you must have been aboard."

Wie replied that they were and introduced his group and had to answer many questions about the Ornamented Dolls, naturally. Anezka was appalled as she learned that these girls were wearing their decorations not as fashion but as torture. The introductions finished, Anezka offered her guests honey mead, and Evzen brought in the drink, three mugs, and a bunch of pie pans. He poured a small amount in to each, sitting them before his mother and their guests. The men received the mugs, the women, the pans.

"Food is so very scarce, please accept this humble offering," Anezka said meekly. She leaned over and began licking her mead. Selene watched her and then emulated Anezka. Quickly the others followed suit, but Wie asked for spoons for the three Dolls, explaining that they had to be fed by spoons because of the lip plates. That bit of embarrassment aside, Wie turned the topic to where were all the men. Was the town leader still called a Kopon? What they heard shocked them more than anything that they had ever heard or experienced. I was appalled when I later heard about it via the LD radio!

Before the plague struck, Vladimir had a population approaching two million. Now their best estimates suggested only three hundred thousand remained. Over a million and a half had so far perished and more were expected to perish as well! To understand what happened, you must understand their culture before the plague. These were a nomadic people. The men, fierce warriors and master horsemen, hunted the plentiful wild game, while the women were primarily the gatherers, foraging for what the grasslands had to offer, berries, nuts from the few groves of trees, roots, herbs, and honey. They never stayed too long in one location for obvious reasons. However, they had begun to settle down in coastal towns. By the time of the plague, there were four towns scattered widely along their long coastline, of which Tanja was still the largest.

When the plague struck, the women could no longer do any of their critical activities, which helped sustain life on the grasslands. Nothing was gathered. They could no longer cook or maintain their homes nor could they sew new clothing or mend torn ones. Men, crippled and unable to walk, were faced with a crisis and they responded poorly.

At first, according to Anezka, the men attempted to do everything that they had been doing plus everything the women had been doing along with caring for all their women's needs. That lasted barely a week! Angry and depressed, the men began fighting each other, claiming rights to what the other had, primarily food stores. One tribe fought another, but at least they fought on horseback far from the dwelling sites. During that summer, battles were a constant fact of life.

Boys were forced to gather what they could and to also cook, feed, and care for the women and girls in their encampments. Still, many of the older women refused to eat and sat waiting for death to take them. The opinion of many was that more of their body parts would be disappearing, as Death was stalking the land. All manner of wild superstitions and rumors ran rampant throughout the grasslands that summer.

Then came the winter. The remaining men continued to battle each other, while women and children were left to fend for themselves. Freezing cold and nearly no food stockpiled for the winter was devastating. Nearly all the older women simply gave up and died of the cold and lack of food that long cruel winter.

By springtime, few adults remained alive. Anezka and Radek were the oldest people in Tanja now. However, the children and teens were better able to adapt to the drastically altered conditions of life. They retained a vitality of life that the older folks lacked. Here in Tanja, Anezka took charge this spring. Now everyone called her the Holy Mother, because of her efforts to keep them all alive.

She had taken the few remaining men and the older boys and organized them into hunting parties, sending them out in search of meat. She had gotten the girls to begin making use of the yokes, brushes, and cooking utensils, though she had no idea what the low stoves were for or the desks. They preferred their own soft wicker chairs and had abandoned the hard ones with strange wheels on their legs. She sent the smaller boys out with the girls to forage and gather, filling the baskets of the girls. During the spring and summer, slowly food was had, but not nearly enough. All were going hungry a little.

In the other coastal towns, Anezka organized them along similar lines, establishing the oldest woman there as that town's Holy Mother. Then, she sent out riders scouring the land for the hundreds of nomadic settlements, begging them to come to one of the towns, if they wanted to live. Her riders found hardly anyone alive who was over thirty years old! Thousands of small boys and girls jumped at the chance for food and life. Many were still finding their way into Tanja even now. More homes had to be built to accommodate them; hence, the big push here at the end of summer to get more adobe homes built.

Anezka put at least four to six women and girls in the same home, along with at least four boys, never less. While she insisted the women do what they could, the boys and their hands were needed desperately by the women for many things, including getting them dressed each day. They had a huge surplus of horses now and the teenaged boys had built an enormous corral south of the city. If nothing else and times got bad enough this winter, Anezka would slaughter them for food. Somehow, someway, she wanted her people to survive the coming cold winter months. Desperation filled these people's daily lives, that and a strong will to survive. Vladimir had become a country of children!

"We have extra food with us," Wie began to respond to their needs. "Let me go back to our ship and see how much we can spare. Do you have any wagons to carry supplies back here?"

"Really? Extra food? Your country must be so rich! Yes, I can send the boys back with you and a wagon. Your women can ride there. Please, you must come and stay with us. The storms may come again. Your huts are too thin and weak, my boys tell me," Anezka replied.

A half hour later, Wie helped the seven get aboard the wagon and they rode the two miles back to the ship and campsite. As they drew near, all were surprised to see some progress. Captain Tom was on land now; the ship was upright. A small mast had been strapped to the remains of the main mast, and a small sail was just being taken down.

"Got her upright and off the bottom," he announced as the wagon pulled up. Radio is in our tent, drying out. Should be able to use it tomorrow, with any luck. What news have you brought?"

"Grimmest that I have ever heard. They are dying of starvation," Wie began. He hastily related all that they had heard from Anezka.

"Oh for heaven's sake! Kids? Starving? No adults? We have to do something, Wie! We'll tighten our belts a little on our eating. Let's see about getting this wagon loaded. Boys," he called out to his crew, "one more trip yet today." Near dusk, the heavily loaded wagon rolled into Tanja. Wie sent along a message that his group would come to the town tomorrow with even more food, if it could be spared.

Meantime, Captain Tom worked on the LD radio. Around nine that night, his boson peddling the generator, he finally got it working. "Golden Scallion calling Velona Shipping Ministry. Emergency Call." He repeated it twice before an operator answered.

"Golden Scallion. You're behind in reporting your positions. A search party is set to sail in the morning to look for you. State the emergency, please."

"Caught in a hurricane, lost both masts, shoved ashore two miles east of Tanja, Vladimir. Need masts, sails, and rigging. Got ship afloat and ready for repairs. Will try to move her into Tanja's harbor tomorrow."

"Roger, I will inform Andros rescue caravels and have them bring masts, sail, and rigging. Food and water holding up? Casualties?"

"Okay on both. Say, I also need to talk to whoever handles countrywide dire emergencies. It is a matter of life and death for thousands," Captain Tom said. Wie and eight others nodded. Somehow, they had to get help for these people.

A bit sleepy-eyed, I was asked to join this call. Captain Tom briefly outlined what had happened to his ship, and then he put Wie on the LD radio, much to his surprise. He'd never spoken over one before.

"Master Wie Lon Dong formerly of Levkos, Alia."

"Hi, Bethany Bartiana Angela here," I replied, wondering what this was all about. Alia — perhaps he had more Ornamented Dolls who were in trouble. I asked, "You have Ornamented Dolls with you who need help?"

"Yes, but no," he was slightly confused by my inadvertent misdirection.

Then, I heard a girl's squeal and a voice said in Annelise, "Are you the Vethany who wrote the Hints vook?" From her mispronunciation, I suspected that she was another Ornamented Doll.

"Yes, I am. Wie, please, tell me all about yourself and this dire emergency. Take your time. After that, please tell me all about yourselves. She is one of those Ornamented Dolls, right?"

"Yes, that's Psyche. Okay. First, the emergency. Our plight pales in comparison." Wie then talked for about a half hour, outlining in detail all that he had learned, ending with the Golden Scallion sending a wagon load of their supplies to Tanja, which he felt was a mere drop in the bucket of their huge needs.

"On dear god! Almost two million dead? Only children left alive and starving? We have to get real help to then immediately! Tom? You still there?" He was. "Okay, I will make calls tomorrow to Ana and Callisto, the monarchs of Arolas, and see if I can get some kind of large emergency food shipments to Vladimir as soon as possible. I will also arrange for an adult rescue and advisory party to get there as quickly as manageable." He said that would be extremely wise.

"Wie, do you or any in your party know anything about farming?"

"No, I am afraid that none of us have such skills. I teach martial arts and I was taking my family and those that we have adopted to visit the Olin Masters. The last I knew, some were in Shansee, Tashien."

"Glad that you said that, Master Wie. All the Olin Masters are now in Nan Yan. Shansee has become gang infested and the chaos and violence has driven them out of there. All are holed up in Nan Yan. You should go there. We have a spur railroad line that runs from the coast up to Nan Yan. Captain Tom ought to know where that is and can take you there instead."

"Thank you so very much," he replied politely.

"Okay, I will make LD radio contact with you tomorrow with further information, say around noon." We signed off and I found that everyone in the house was now awake and waiting expectantly to hear what this latest emergency was all about. Over tea and biscuits, I related the awful news from Vladimir. Eve and I took the news rather hard. We both recalled our visit there many lifetimes ago. As explorers, we discovered Vladimir and spent time in Tanja even. Apparently, the town had not gown much in these past centuries. Well, they were a nomadic people.

"If these are only children, Bethany, they cannot continue to be hunters and gatherers and nomads," Sergio pointed out. "Somehow they are going to have to change their way of life. If they are all now living in those four towns, they will quickly deplete all wild game within reach and all the berries and such. They are in real trouble!"

Lucianna added, "Darn, if they are all children, they probably can't even read and write. Your Hints book will be useless for them. They are going to have to be shown how to do things by other women." I had already guessed that would be the case. I certainly did have a monster problem to handle.

It was early summer, far too late to plant crops. Worse, they had no plowed fields and had no idea how to raise crops. They were just children after all. What could possibly be done for them, I wondered. I chuckled, two centuries ago, I would have just sent every available Loremaster down there to educate them in the art of growing things and animal husbandry, but Druwids were now ancient history as well. I realized that their needs were so great that one country alone could not possibly handle them. Early the next morning, I got on the LD radio and began making calls.

First, I chatted with Ana and Callisto, who as expected were also shocked and appalled at the disaster happening in the country next to theirs. True, an impassible mountain range separated them, and in the past, the fighters of Vladimir raided some of their coastal towns. Yet, a country full of children with almost no adults to help them struck a motherly chord in us women. We had to help. They promised to send as many caravels with grain and farm animals as could be spared and send them within a week or two at most. "If they can get by until the end of December, our food should arrive by then," Ana explained. "I'll call the other monarchs here and see if we can all put together timely shipments after that, keeping the food coming until spring arrives."

That was a good start. I called up the other monarchs of the Sea Princes and the ten kingdoms of the Greenway, beginning with Barbe Barcella. To my surprise, Barbe offered to send them four of the new steam powered tractors, with plows and wagons. "One tractor can do the work of dozens of oxen teams and in far less time too. One per town — that ought to allow them to plow a very large amount of ground. Maybe the Greenway can provide seed for them to plant," she suggested. Vito promised to send loads of coal to fire their engines and perhaps an electrical plant.

Right in the middle of my calls, the King of Annelise called me. Ana had talked to him and he pledged to send over loads of children's work clothing and four teams of tailors and dressmakers, along with the equipment that they needed to make more clothes. "By golly, we'll have those hundreds of thousands of children properly dressed and proud of themselves!" I chuckled at his attitude. Well, it just might help, I thought.

Their real hope lay with the farmers of the Greenway. I was not disappointed. Uniformly, every kingdom responded with open hearts — they were just children after all. By the end of December, I had pledges of five hundred Greenway pioneering families who had volunteered to go down to Vladimir and help them learn the ways of farming. It would be late fall there before most arrived, but they would need months to learn their language and make appropriate plans for the spring planting. Pieta and Solamina donated many caravels of lumber to build barns and sheds for the planned livestock. In short, nearly every northern country and those in the far south pitched in to help in some manner.

Wie, elated to hear that aid was coming, chatted with Anezka. He learned that there was quite a lot of gold, silver, and gemstones there. However, everyone left such behind when they headed for the towns. You cannot eat them, she pointed out. Unlike their deceased adults, they prized such not at all. Wie explained that those items would be highly acceptable in trade for all the help that was being sent to them. She promised to send out groups to scavenge what they could find. There were mines in the far north, she explained, though none now knew precisely where they were located. Wie began to realize the depth of the loss of their knowledge and culture that had occurred in a little over a year, almost beyond belief.

The third week in December, Ana and Seth arrived along with the caravels in Tanja. She wanted to see firsthand what was going on and had accompanied the ships. One brought the new masts, sails, and rigging for the Golden Scallion's repairs. Additionally, a caravel moored close to the shores of each of the four towns, unable to dock, for they had no docks. Each brought crates of food and some farm animals: cows, chickens, and sheep mostly. Ana now realized that docks had to be built and radioed for a work crew and an engineer to come and start building a caravel dock. I had forgotten that detail, duh.

"Are you really *the* vonarch of Arolas?" asked a wide-eyed Psyche as she greeted Ana and Seth as they landed.

Ana grinned, "You betcha. My sister and I share the throne. Wow, I've never seen Ornamented Dolls, Psyche. I am sure glad that you are able to speak Annelise. I hope mine is good enough for you to understand."

"What's she saying? What're you saying?" asked a baffled Seth. He hated being left out of conversations. Both Psyche and Kassandra giggled at him. Ana translated for him.

"There is no way to get those neck rings off you?" Ana asked.

"No, that is a very vad thing. We can get vy vetter if the rings were off," Kassandra added. "So vany things are so hard for us this way. We cannot use our teeth like the Hints vook says."

"Damn that man!" Ana couldn't restrain her curse. "He has to be stopped. I'll see what I can do, but I guess we'd better help these children first. What men do, honestly," she added exasperated.

Ana and Anezka spent the day dealing with organizational matters. Even unloading the caravels was challenging because of the lack of a dock and manpower. Crates had to be ferried from the caravels to the town via small boat. However, the men that Ana brought began dealing with the construction of a permanent docking facility that could hold two caravels, on either side of the single dock platform.

Late that afternoon, Anezka's husband and five other men came galloping into the outskirts of Tanja, where all the adobe brick making and new home construction was taking place. Radek yelled, "Sound the gong! Raiders are on our heels!" He and his five continued through the streets toward the main stone building where Anezka and the others were holding their planning session. The children dropped everything and began fleeing in all directions, like ants when their hole is uncovered.

Bong! Bong! Bong! Ana and Wie looked up from the drawings that she had brought and were studying on the table. "What's that?" She knew something was wrong. Anezka looked frightened.

"That is the alarm. Men, adults, are about to raid us again! Come, you must hide quickly! All of you!" she gushed fearfully.

"Hold on, what's going on? I thought all the adult men were dead," Wie asked, just as confused as Ana and the others.

Anezka tried to explain while urging them into a semi-secret room. "There are still small roving bands of older men. They occasionally come into the city to take young girls and steal our food. Mostly, they do it in the winter, but occasionally, they come in the summer. Come on; we must all hide from them."

Ana and Seth ignored that order. "Well, it is time that we teach these men a lesson that they will never forget. Seth, get our men together with their long guns!"

Master Wie added, "We are martial artists. We will stand and help, but please, take Xenia and Ariadne to safety."

Just then Radek came bursting in the room, out of breath and sweaty. Ana, Seth, and Wie took defensive postures, along with his students, prepared for the worst. He barked urgently, "Who are you? Anezka, ten raiders are coming; they are hot on our trail! Get to safety."

"Radek, these people have come to help us. She's the Monarch of Arolas! These others were shipwrecked, but have brought help and food to us. He's my husband," she hastily explained, still trying to get the others to follow her.

Radek looked shocked and was momentarily speechless. Ana spoke up, "Radek, pleased to meet you. You say that there are only ten men coming? Do they have long guns or just swords?"

"Swords and a few pistols," he answered hastily, motioning everyone to follow Anezka to their hiding places.

"Okay, where will they come at the town? From the south?" Seth asked.

"Yes, due south, following hot behind us. Should be here within a couple of minutes. I alerted the kids making adobe, and they have fled to find what safety they can. We must get you into our hiding place quickly. We can't have anything happen to a monarch; my god, that will bring more disaster upon our kids!"

"Radek! I am more than capable of defending myself. Don't be silly. I had to help retake Arolas from wicked men with long guns. Okay Seth, fetch all the men, arm them, meet us at the south edge of the town. Come on; probably not a moment to lose, Wie," Ana exclaimed, heading for the door.

"But. . ." Radek protested.

"Xenia, Ariadne, go with Anezka," Wie ordered and opened the door for Ana. His group followed them. Radek looked at his wife, gave her a quick kiss, and trailed outside after these fool hardy people, protesting that they would be killed or worse.

Ana ran through the almost deserted mud streets. Here and there, another teen was running to the relative safety of their home, hoping that the adult raiders would not search their home. With so many homes, the raiders would never get into each one. They would search a couple, take a few older girls, sacks of food, and then leave. That's what they had always done.

She halted at the construction site and decided this was not a good place to defend because there was too many things on the ground to get in their way. Adobe bricks lay everywhere, baking and drying in the late afternoon sun. "Out there, we'll make our stand, Wie. Spread your fighters out on either side of me. Seth and the others will join us and build up our flanks," Ana ordered and took charge.

Mie and Wie moved to either side of Ana. Psyche and Kassandra moved close to Mie, while Alexus, Roxane, and Selene moved to stand beside Wie. Ana added, "Okay, I want one man left alive. I will send him back out there with a message for any other raiders." Wie grinned, and agreed, if possible.

Soon, they heard the thunder of horses upon the grasslands. Then bouncing heads appeared just over the rolling hill to the south of them. The riders and their horses became visible as they loped over the land towards Tanja. The riders were spread out leaving at least ten feet between each of them. "Rats, they are too far apart for me to wipe them all out in one shot!" Ana declared. Wie and his group had no idea what she meant. However, they heard men coming from their rear, and Wie felt more hopeful about the outcome.

When the riders were about a quarter mile distant, Ana began chanting. Shortly her ball of fire spell detonated. The startled group saw a thirty-foot sphere of flames appear centered on the middle rider and engulfing him and the riders on either side. When the flames disappeared, three horses galloped off in random directions, their riders were nowhere to be seen at this distance.

Twice more, she shot her balls of flames, felling another six riders. Four more wild looking men reached their position, but Wie and his group took their horses by surprise, yelling some kind of sound that Ana had not heard before and leaping in front of the horses, which spooked, forcing their riders to either dismount or to attempt to control their mounts. As Ana prepared to put men to sleep, the martial artists became a blaze of action. Those on the ground, the women quickly dispatched with powerful leg kicks, all aimed at necks. For those still mounted, Alexus and Wie used their fists, punching precise locations on exposed legs. Ana heard bones snapping and cries of sharp, intense pain from these men, who then fell off their horses.

"Spunky!" Seth called out. "I protest Ana, you fellows didn't leave any of them for us to fight!"

He sounded definitely annoyed, Psyche thought, as she backed up from the finished fight, which had lasted barely a minute. She turned to see two dozen men with long guns standing behind Seth, all panting for breath, having run all the way through the town from the docks.

"Are you a Sorceress?" asked a shocked Radek, rubbing his eyes. He was similarly astounded at the fighting prowess of Master Wie and his women, but the three incredible balls of flames had shocked the young man.

"I suppose that you can call me that," Ana admitted. What else could she say? "Come on; let's get back to the others. Seth, see if any are alive. I ought to send them back out there with a warning about ever raiding the towns."

"Yes dear, but I doubt that any are still breathing," he teased her.

As they walked back, Wie bowed to Ana, "Such powerful kijutsu you possess. It is my goal to have the women under my care to learn such from the Olin Masters. Then, they will be better able to take care of themselves."

"Master Wie, I think that is an admirable, worthy goal. I hope that you can succeed in your quest," she replied, her mind on other matters. What else *didn't* they know about Vladimir?

After a lengthy discussion, Ana did not discover anything else. She radioed her discovery to me and to Callisto back home. Callisto sent twenty-five soldiers and their families to help guard Cazin and another group to defend Tulsa, while the King of Annelise sent a small group to protect the town of Moztar, closest to their border. Ana also had Callisto send along the families of the twenty-five soldiers that she'd brought with her. They would remain behind indefinitely and protect Tanja from further wild-man aggression.

Slowly the pieces began to fall into alignment for the long-term survival of Vladimir. Ana returned home three weeks later, after ensuring the many repairs to the Golden Scallion were finished. Her estimate was that if enough help and supplies came to help them through the winter months of June through August, then the coming farmers from the Greenway would be able to get a large number of crops planted and by fall, there would be no further food shortages. However, rebuilding a solid foundation for the country would take years. Only if the many children could be educated would they ultimately pull out of the near destruction of their whole country. With the notification that many had set sail from the Greenway kingdoms, Stefano and I decided to put a checkmark in the done column for Vladimir here in February 825. However, we planned to keep a sharp eye for further troubles down there. Having an LD radio in each of the four towns would help. I complimented Lucianna and Giovanni for having invented them and for having made these highly useful radios so widespread!

Master Wie and his group set sail on February 15, 825, bound for Nan Yan, Tashien. While the voyage took three long months, it was uneventful. However, during the long months, Xenia and Ariadne learned to speak both the Annelise and Tashien languages. When the group arrived in Nan Yan on May 20, 825, the whole group spoke the Tashien dialect fairly well. He had them as prepared for the Olin Masters as he could. However, in March, he had to enlarge the women's lip plates once again. Psyche and Kassandra sported five and a half inch plates, an inch larger than Ariadne's, who cried as she observed how much more her vision was being obstructed.

Me, I now began to focus my attention onto Tashien, the last country still in their Dark Ages. Somehow, these people had to be salvaged as well, though now, I had no clue how that could be brought about. Direct intervention? Perhaps.

Chapter 61 Nan Yan and We Take Responsibility

Late March of 825, spring came to the western foothills of Tan Loc Province and the garden city of Nan Yan. Everywhere flowers thrust upwards, signaling the annual rebirth of life. This year, the human population also experienced their own rebirth of life and vitality, though many claimed it was a Holy Miracle. The last man who lived in this city of a half million had just finished receiving his Holy Gift. Princess Bi Mei Li declared a week's festival to celebrate this incredible lifesaving achievement, due wholly to the Counselors of the Church of God, who now numbered some sixty thousand women, though many worked only part-time giving Basic Therapy sessions.

During the second day of the festivities, Princess Mei Lon Wu called for a Summit Meeting, requesting the Olin Masters leaders, the four top Counselors, General Tao Bi, and Jovanni and Alonso West Po, who represented the engineers. Masters Tian, Feng, De, and Ning sat beside their Counselor wives, Bi Mei, Shu Wen, Nan Dia, and Xiu. Opposite them, sat Jovanni and Alonso, while Princess Mei Lon and General Tao sat next to them.

"This is indeed an auspicious day. I've asked you here for a meeting of minds and to plan the direction that we need to take. First, let's hear from our counselors, without whom this day, this week, would not be possible. It is like a rebirth of our people here in Nan Yan," the princess explained. She wore her red silk pencil style dress and had her long hair nicely brushed and shiny, looking her best for this all-important meeting.

The four counselors looked at each other and allowed Shu Wen to speak for them. "Well, as you know, we have sixty thousand women in our force to deliver the Basic Therapy. Another twenty thousand, more or less, are willing to lend some help on an intermittent basis. Many have small children to look after. Now we must look to delivering our Basic Therapy to those in the outlying areas and towns of the valley. Of course, we need to get Overlord Dong Lo's permission before we can go too far up the valley. The question is more one of an organizational one. How do we get our givers to those who need to receive it and such matters?"

"How goes it with the sixteen blinded women?" the princess asked.

"Princess Pian and Misha are pretty much finished with the level of Advanced Therapy that we agreed that they simply had to have to be able to live useful lives. The other fourteen are doing well. By summer, we believe that they will also be finished. The big barrier is that there are only four of us who can deliver this Advanced Therapy. However, Nan Dia has suggested that these sixteen women ought to be able to deliver some Advanced Therapy themselves once they are finished. We will be exploring that as an option. If it works out, then we will begin a regimen of Advanced Therapy on those who are most worthy of it at this time."

"Excellent. My heart went out to those sixteen women when I first met them. Okay, then, what resources do you need to begin moving outward from Nan Yan proper," the princess asked.

"The women need to be paid. We need wagons to transport them, men to make the arrangements, to get the patients and the counselors together at the appropriate times, to keep accurate records, and to deal with keeping everyone properly fed and a roof over their heads while they are away from Nan Yan. Also, of course, they must be fully protected by our Masters."

Princess Mei Lon smiled. She had anticipated as much. Turning her attention to the Olin Masters, she asked, "So what is your martial arts situation now?"

Master Tian chuckled, "Situation? Well, we have eight hundred three who have achieved the Master Level 10 or higher. We have another eight hundred twenty who are still training and learning the lower levels. Speaking for my colleagues, we have never had so many in our academy. I believe that there are enough of us to fully protect the counselors as long as we are not spread out too thinly."

"Indeed, we are getting more coming to us asking to learn than we have ever had in the past. We believe this is in large part to the Basic Therapy that they have received. Yet, if it is the defense of Nan Yan that concerns you most, My Princess, we are strong enough to defend our city from an invasion of overlords to the east."

"Yes, that is a concern of mine. I certainly do not want anything to interfere with our incredible progress here. As our counselors fan out to the south, east, and north of our city, soon they will enter lands under the control of these warlike overlords," she replied.

She looked down to Jovanni. "How are our MMCE plans progressing, Master Engineer Jovanni?" She had long ago bestowed that title on the blonde man from Velona.

"I came prepared to give you a full report, Your Majesty," he began, nodding to Alonso, who handed out some graphs and papers to each person, though he allowed the men to arrange them for the women to view.

"As you know, the rail spur line from the coastal line is completed and daily trains are making their runs from here to the rest of the world. We have a dozen side lines to route cars to the manufacturing facilities and warehouses here in the city completed as well. Now we are ready to begin the valley expansion. We feel that we should head on up the valley to the west where so many critical ore mines are located. However, Overlord Dong Lo controls this territory. We need him aboard the MMCE project yet this spring. If so, our estimates suggest that by winter all the needed spur lines to the west will be in operation, allowing the critically needed ores to reach the new manufacturing plants ten times faster than now, maybe more."

"Similarly, by winter the spur lines that are to fan out towards the east from here ought to be finished. Well, at least in the local area that is under Nan Yan control, that is. Velona will be sending along three tug engines and a hundred cars later this summer. The tugs will be most useful here, shuttling a few carloads from the mines to the factories and such, just what we need here. So the steam train project is nearing completion."

"A dozen motor-wagons have already arrived and are in use. We expect another two dozen more to arrive later this summer by train. By fall or winter at the latest, we anticipate the first of our locally built motor-trucks to be finished and ready to be driven from the new factory. If so, they tell me that they will be able to manufacture fifty more each year, as long as the raw materials arrive in a timely fashion."

"The construction of the power plant is still going strong. As most of you know, we are building a dam of sorts on the Yan River just west of the city's edge. We are using water flow to turn the electrical generators, a very cheap way to make the electricity. We have one of the five planned generators now in minimal operational status. The palace here should be electrified by early summer, along with the Church of God buildings. If this goes well, by fall, we will bring all the generators online and have at least a quarter of the city powered. I hope by next summer to announce that all homes and facilities in the city proper have electrical power."

"The telefono system is being brought online in tandem with the electrical power," he explained. He chatted for another half hour on the rest of the MMCE improvements that were either ongoing or planned for this construction season. Most of the materials were being imported from the various Sea Princes and their mushrooming manufacturing facilities. Two steam powered tractors were also due to arrive this summer and a "let's see how this will work" project was in the planning stages to see how it would work on the outlying farms.

"The wealthy men and women are financing this expansion. We have more funds available than we can spend now. Our biggest problem is one of manpower. With so many projects going on, there just are not enough workers to be had. It is further complicated by the fact that every one of the companies and work crews are now rejecting any applicant who has not had their Basic Therapy. From my own observations, that is extremely wise of them."

"How so?" asked the princess. Many eyebrows rose. Tashien was filled with men who could work. Until this instant, manpower was never an issue.

"You see those who have had their therapy make better workers. Some are saying they are a thousand times better than those who have not yet had it. Without the therapy, the men are apathetic, take little or no responsibility for their actions, and are dangerous to have around. Accidents happen with those men. One wealthy man who is running one of our new factories has said that one of those who have had therapy is worth a hundred who haven't, and he refuses to hire those who have not yet had it. They work harder and even take the initiative when something is not quite right."

"Still, we need thousands more workers, but those will have to come from outside Nan Yan. That means that somehow you all are going to have to get those men their Basic Therapy soon, counselors. Please, we need the manpower," Jovanni pleaded his case. He was desperate for more men, many more men.

"Right now, insufficient manpower is holding back much of our MMCE expansion projects to say nothing of our production lines," he added for emphasis. After all, this was supposed to be a problem resolving session. He thought so anyway.

"This is more serious than I thought. We simply must have the MMCE project meeting no obstacles. I see it as the savior of our land," the princess stated dryly. "Okay, do we concentrate on pushing up our valley first before we fan out to the rolling hills east of here? Do we do both? Will the therapy givers be able to work in both directions at the same time?"

"The upper valley should come first; we really do need their mineral resources pronto," Jovanni broke in. "If there is a choice to be made here, go west and let's get our entire valley in order before we fan out to the east."

"He is right. Militarily, we need to remove the overlord at our rear before we tackle the lower lands," General Tao advised. "Give the order and we can move on Overlord Dong Lo."

"Well, I wish there was a peaceful solution. We can ill afford to lose men in battles just now," the princess replied. "Are we all in agreement that we tackle the upper valley first?" She found unanimous consent on this point.

"If the army is to move on the overlord, the Olin Masters will assist. We may be able to keep the casualties down," Master Tian added.

"I don't want any, if it can be helped. Though if he has been mistreating the people in the upper valley, he must be held responsible for that," she added.

"That is the crux of the matter," Master Tian replied. "These overlords have almost by definition been ruthless to those that they rule — over-lord," he emphasized each half of the word.

Counselor She Wen spoke up. She was remembering her previous lifetime as Fina a Protector and how in Velona the Santi del Dio had established some policies for recovery. "If the overlord has committed atrocities against his people, he should be given the opportunity to make amends broadly. I suggest that the amends project be something along the lines of personally paying for the MMCE project in his territory."

"Assuming that he has enough funds," Nan Dia added. "What do we do with him if he does not? More broadly, what do we do with all of those who are being criminals? Surely, we are going to run into many of those the further that we expand outwards. Here in Nan Yan, those who were suspected of being criminals, the hardcore ones, simply fled the city rather than have their crimes exposed in therapy. Yet, if one does not come clean in a therapy session, he cannot ever get well and recover. Therapy in such cases is useless and wasted and yields no benefits to the patient unless he or she does come clean."

"That's a simple one," General Tao answered. "We execute them."

Counselor Xiu chuckled. "Ever the ways of soldiers and leaders. You forget one salient point, general. You are dealing with an immortal spiritual being, not a body. If the person is being a criminal and you execute his body, when he gets his next body, what is to prevent him from following in his former ways?"

"That at least pushes the criminal problem off for some eighteen years or so," General Tao justified. "Pragmatic solution. Deal with them twenty years later on. By then, we may be much stronger."

Shu Wen smiled, "For now, we will accept the general's pragmatic solution. However, we here all have a good idea of the terrible things that have and are being done to others in Tashien. I believe that the Church of God will have to find a better, permanent solution to the problem of the criminal. To that end, I will contact Eve and Macario about this matter. Perhaps they will be able to give us a better solution. Until then, the general is right. We have to stop the criminal from continuing to harm others or all is lost. If it currently means executing their body, at least the immediate danger is removed from our society, though by no means can it be considered handled. In their next life, they may be even worse to our society."

General Tao added, "We may not have too big a problem with Dong Lo. From the reports that I've seen, he has not been a ruthless leader, not by the standards we've seen in Shansee and elsewhere. Perhaps we should meet with him and discuss the matter."

Everyone seconded this idea and Princess Mei Lon agreed to send for him and discuss the situation with him. She thought that this would be an excellent opportunity to see if she could use her powers of persuasion to bring him aboard without resorting to physical force. When the meeting ended, she did just that — wrote out an order requesting his presence.

Four days later, Overlord Dong Lo rode into the palace grounds, along with a small armed escort that he thought he needed to guarantee his physical security. He was forty-five, well-muscled, and an excellent swordsman, but he also had a fiery temper. He often thought of himself as infallible and therefore was the right man to lead the western valley peoples.

"Greetings Princess Mei Lon Wu. I am here as requested. How may I be of help to you?" He thought the best offense was to pretend that she somehow needed his aid in some matter. That point of view lessened the impact of having been sent for by her, eroding her control over him, or so he thought. Although annoyed when he first read her summons, he decided to see what the trip might bring for himself. Why did Nan Yan suddenly need such vast amounts of iron, tin, copper, and other metals? Was a war eminent that he didn't know about?

"Thank you so much for coming on such short notice, Dong. I am sure that you could not miss all the new constructions occurring around Nan Yan as well as our new railroad lines. Pray, come with me. I would like you to see what I am bringing to our territory. Then, we can talk." Princess Mei Lon was shrewd. She gave him a royal tour of the demonstration center where Jovanni had all the marvelous inventions operational, including a small portable electricity generator powered by a petrol motor. She allowed him to turn on the light switches and he was quite surprised. After a thorough tour, she showed him how to drive the demo motor-wagon and turned him lose with it, asking him to take himself on a tour of the city.

He returned just as she anticipated, grinning with a boyish smile, sold on the value of these petrol-run machines. When he returned, she had several of the wealthier men of Nan Yan present waiting to be brought into her throne room when the time was right. "Now then, Dong, you can see why we need all the ores that we can get. This year, we will begin manufacturing these vehicles right here in Nan Yan ourselves. Our power plant will be operational later this year. Hopefully by next year, all the houses in Nan Yan will have electricity and lights."

"So what has this to do with me?" he asked.

"I would like to extend this opportunity to get in on this incredible modernization right here at the grassroots, Dong. We want to extend the rail lines into your valleys, right up to the mines. We want to get this electricity thing into all the homes in the upper valley as well. We want to make motor-wagons readily available to all those who could use them in your territory."

"That is commendable, my princess. Yet, what is the price that I must pay for all this? Is it true that over half of the wealthiest men and women of all Tashien are now in Nan Yan?" he asked. This one rumor had most intrigued him for the last year. If so, Nan Yan was in an incredible position of power and he desired some of that for himself.

"Yes, well over half of the wealthiest families of Tashien have fled here to Nan Yan during the last year. Perhaps more will come. Wealth has little meaning if chaos lies all around you. Most discovered that you couldn't eat gold and gems. As to what you must do, it is simple. Lend your complete assistance with our programs, adding to them, as you deem suitable. Lend your financial backing as needed."

"But am I then to relinquish the control over my lands?" he asked what he considered the key question. If so, the price would be too high. He'd become just another wealthy man and the Princess would end up running his lands.

"No, not unless we find that you have been harming your people more than you have been helping them survive this plague and collapse of our civilization. If you have been a despot, then I would have no choice but to have you removed from power. To date, I have not heard horror stories from your lands of any brutality towards your people on your part. Rather, I believe that we should work together. I would like you to meet with some of our new company owners and discuss how you and they can work together to bring all these marvelous inventions to your lands."

"Well, in that case, I am listening," he replied, very relieved. She summoned the dozen men and three women and introduced them to Dong. As they started chatting, she quietly left the room, preferring to let them hash out their own bargains and deals. Later, she invited Dong to supper with her and Jovanni there to discuss engineering plans and objectives. Dong was totally sold on the whole MMCE project and quite eager to become a part of it, especially since he would retain his leadership role of his lands, the upper valley system.

Princess Mei Lon smiled after he left that night. So far, she calculated that she had achieved a bloodless coop. Overlord Dong Lo was backing her — now, if only they did not discover signs of atrocities against the people of the upper valley. She hoped and prayed that they would not. In the ensuing months, they did find some disgruntled men and women who were not pleased with Dong and his iron-handed rule. However, comparatively speaking, all such things were relatively minor. He had done what he could to maintain law and order amid the chaos of the times.

Thus, Jovanni was given the go ahead to get dozens of projects started in the upper valleys west of Nan Yan. Princess Mei Lon hoped that by next spring much would have been completed so that they could begin to fan out to the east, reclaiming more and more of Tan Loc Province and Tashien.

On May 15, 825, the Golden Scallion pulled into Spur Port, the name given to the single dock there at the bay where the main coastal railroad line that ran all the way to Shansee met the northern spur line that led to Nan Yan. The engineers had built a small caravel dock close to the rails, capable of handling two ships at the same time, one on either side. A crane could lift the cargo from the holds, placing them directly on railroad cars for transport.

Captain Tom shook hands with Wie and Alexus. "This is goodbye, I guess. We sure have had an exciting voyage." Wie agreed as he helped the seven women off the ship and onto the docks, where a steam engine and cars were awaiting them. Captain Tom had been in LD radio contact with us as usual and, via Velona, the train had been asked to wait a day for their arrival. Yes, I had already seen to the transfer of their funds from the Banca del Dio of Shansee to one in Nan Yan. All was waiting for them. I owed this group much for what they had done for the children of Vladimir.

The engineers enjoyed showing off their steam belching engine and train to these newcomers, none of whom had ever seen one before. Besides, they also got a good look at the three Ornamented Dolls.

As the train made the gradual bend around the eastern spur of the jagged ridge line, the great city of Nan Yan became visible to the passengers. The deep Yan River that flowed down from the far western mountains, bisected the city, before heading eastward, eventually joining the huge Yonshu River which emptied at last into the ocean at Shansee. None of the passengers had ever seen this foothill city, and they stared in awe at the picturesque scene before them.

Green, rugged, and steep sided ridges formed the northern and southern sides of the fifty-mile wide lush valley. Contrasting sharply were the multicolored buildings, rising helter skelter from the brown stone, rolling lands of the city. Oranges, reds, blues, greens, and browns predominated, though some yellow trim was present as well a dash of black. Although Master Wie and Mei had been born in Shansee, they had never been to this far western city and were just as amazed at the incredible sight as the many teens.

The streets thronged with people of all ages. Wooden wheeled riks carried passengers, men pushed small carts, and a few donkey-pulled wagons wove their way through the crowded streets. Most noticeable of all were the many women bearing their yokes over their shoulders, their twin baskets carrying all manner of items, though most often food supplies.

Once the train halted at the main station, Master Wie led his band onto the bustling platform. Already crews of men began unloading several boxcars ahead of their sole passenger car. On unfamiliar ground, his eyes sought out someone to ask for directions. Then his eyes met those of Master Tian Li. The men exchanged customary bows.

"Welcome Master Wie Dong. We have been expecting you. I am Master Tian Li of the Li Olin Master Academy of Nan Yan, though all the other Olin Masters have now established their schools here as well. Do you have baggage to fetch?"

"No, we came with what we could carry and little else. We must purchase what we will need. Allow me to introduce my wife," he replied politely. One by one, he introduced his family and the teens under his wing. "All the children except Ariadne and Xenia have achieved their black belts, the highest that I am able to train them. We came here hoping that they might be accepted in your academy for advanced training."

"Yes, I am sure that you will be able to find what you need here in Nan Yan. Our city is returning to normalcy finally. Come, I will lead you to my academy and our Church of God. My wife, Bei Mi, and many others wish to meet you. Unless you have other plans, we would be honored if you would stay with us until you get settled into life here in Nan Yan," Master Tian explained, adding, "Besides, my wife wants to see that you get your Holy Gift just as soon as possible."

Now housed at the academy, which adjoined Bei Mi's church, Wei's group began three weeks of testing, therapy, and education. Unfortunately for the teens, they experienced a dose of culture shock. Life was so different here, plus their language skills often failed them. They were immensely impressed with the higher-level academy students, whose kijutsu seemed boundless. As expected, their therapy went according to Bei Mi's expectations. All had significant traumas to eradicate, especially the twins and Xenia and Ariadne. She allowed three weeks of therapy for these four and a week for each of the others. Bei Mi's estimates proved accurate to within a few days. The four were the roughest cases that she had yet to handle, far worse than the sixteen blinded women, who had not had the long duration tortures these four had endured.

During these weeks, Master Tian carefully examined the three Ornamented Dolls, sharing his observations in private with Master Wei. Finally, with Master Wei's consent, he met with all them. "Psyche, Kassandra, Ariadne, I wish to report my findings to you, in particular. I have the power to remove your neck rings without harming your bodies. Yes, my kijutsu is quite powerful, though several of the other Olin Masters are my equals. Anyone of us could remove them." He saw the light of hope suddenly appearing in the three teen's eyes, and he knew that he was about to extinguish that light. It would be up to Bei Mi's skills to restore it.

"However, if I were to safely remove your neck rings, your bodies would be in dire peril of suffocating. Allow me to explain more fully. You have been wearing them for nearly two years now and have been unable to use any of your body's neck muscles at all. As you may know from your training, muscles left unused atrophy. I have examined your necks for several days now and that is precisely what has happened to your neck muscles. They have withered and shrunk for lack of use. If I were to remove the rings, you would find that your necks were similar to that of a newborn baby. Yet your heads are much larger than the newborn. In short, you would not be able to hold your head up and it would flop in all directions beyond your control. Your own head would pinch off your windpipes and thus suffocate your bodies. We might be able to minimize the effect by making you lie in bed motionless until your neck muscles regained their strength and mass. Yet, that could take many months, and someone would have to watch over your bodies night and day to prevent accidental suffocation."

Psyche spoke up, "I don't think that we want to do that. We are alive and okay as we are. It's just that we cannot do vuch at all, the liv vlates keev interfering with everything, even vore than the neck rings. We were hoving that kijutsu would helv us do norval things vetter, you know, like eating."

Master Tian bowed respectfully to Psyche. "You have wisdom beyond your years, Psyche. Then we shall leave the neck rings alone. I am afraid that we can do nothing about your lip plates. While none of us has any doubts that kijutsu would be of great assistance to you three, we also feel that fighting kijutsu would not serve you nearly as well as spiritual kijutsu."

Ariadne spoke up a bit hesitatingly though, "You vean like the vany vlind woven who have the glass eyes vut can now see even vetter than we can see?"

"Precisely so, Ariadne. Fighting kijutsu is but a tiny fraction of the powers that we spiritual beings possess. The Church of God and their Advanced Therapy can help each of us recover our native powers. My recommendation for you three is to pursue as much Advanced Therapy as you can. Therein lies your salvation. I have spoken of this to Bei Mi and she agrees with me."

Roxane spoke up, "Master Tian, if Psyche and Kassi are not going to get advanced martial arts training, then Selene and I don't want to either. We four stick together, always. Besides, we have already agreed to start learning how to deliver the Holy Gift. We six all want to help others who need it, right Xenia?"

"Yes, this is the most precious thing that I know," the young teen replied eagerly.

"Yes, as long as they can understand us, I want to helv others too," Ariadne added.

"Well done to all of you," Master Tian acknowledged the six young women, bowing respectfully to each. "I should let you get back to Bei Mi then." They bowed to him and file out of his meeting room, heading back to the counseling rooms.

"Thanks for sticking with us," Psyche whispered to Roxane. "I know how vuch you were counting on learning kijutsu."

"We're going to be a team, us six. I just know it," Roxane replied. "Somehow we are." Soon, they were back working on learning how to deliver Basic Therapy sessions.

Poor Master Wei. He just did not know what to make of this. Here he'd brought them all the way here hoping that the teens would get the advanced training that he knew would make their lives livable. Yet, the Olin Master was denying them that. While the therapy was okay, he didn't yet know just how powerful it could be. He decided to have a long chat with Pian and Misha, the two incredible women with the yellow-brown glass eyes. How was it that they could actually see out of them? He intended to find out.

"Well, now this is extremely fascinating," Sergio mumbled in his usual Chief Detective Inspector's tone. It was late June 825. He and I were having a midmorning tea break. Only yesterday, I had pronounced Alia salvaged. Mom and Sofia were getting their morning's Advanced Therapy sessions delivered by our youngsters. Lisa was off giving another Basic Therapy session and Marco was grocery shopping for our extended families. It was his turn, though he grumbled about it slightly. Both Sergio and I had a short breather in our otherwise hectic schedules, though I did keep an ear on the LD radio. I was expecting a report from Ana and Callisto later this morning and then one from Alia.

I bit, "Okay big brother. I'm game. What is extremely fascinating?"

He gave me a wink and said dryly as if relaying the most ordinary of news. "I know how the alien bacteria worked its magic on women's physical bodies and how it can be instantly undone, sis. Want your arms back?"

"What? Really? How?" I exclaimed, forgetting completely about the LD radio.

Sergio was pleased with the effect he'd created on me and answered, "It's very simple actually, once you know how human bodies are formed. I suspect I even know how Partholan and Dalny created our ancestral bodies."

"How? You didn't answer my question, big brother." I feigned a bit of annoyance.

"Something has to hold the space which the body's matter occupies, particularly its bones. You see, it all has to do with the forming and holding fixed a space, sis. Each bone, each joint in our fleshly bodies has tiny golden balls defining its space thereby fixing it in space. These balls are located at each movable joint in our bodies. The body then fills this space with its fleshly matter and bones and stuff. Move the balls closer, the space shrinks, and the body then shrinks the bones and flesh to fill that smaller defined space."

He saw my confused look and changed track. "Imagine this rubber band here represents your big leg bone. My fingers at each end represent the golden balls, which demark the outer boundary of the bone. Now I move one of the balls out like this." He stretched the rubber band a little. "The bone and flesh occupies the space defined by the balls, but as the space is now slightly larger, the bones and flesh expand to fill the space. Now I move the balls closer and the bones and flesh shrink so that the space defined by these balls is filled. This is the underlying principle behind the construction of fleshly bodies:

thousands of these little golden balls which anchor the physical structure, holding it in place."

"For want of any name, I call them anchor balls because they are anchoring the space of the body. Move them around and the fleshly body adjusts itself to occupy the altered space formed by these anchor balls. Look at my body this morning." He stood up beside me and motioned for me to stand beside him.

"Hey, have you grown?" I asked, a bit surprised. I was a tall young woman, but now he was at least four inches taller than he used to be. He grinned as he saw that I saw his new height.

"Yes, I have moved my leg's anchor balls apart about four inches last night. Now this morning, my lower legs have altered to fit the new dimensions. Lisa didn't appreciate my having done this, so now I have put them back to where they were. By suppertime, my body ought to be back to where it was, height-wise, that is. I had to experiment. Now I've shown that altering the positions of the anchor balls causes the fleshly bodies to adjust to fill the altered space. While we were having tea, I inspected your anchor balls around your shoulders."

"But I've got no arms left, Sergio. Those anchor balls must have been removed or something."

"Well, I thought that at first, sis. That would explain the loss of arms. No arm, elbow, and finger anchor balls equals no arms, and the body would respond. However, I was quite surprised a moment ago to find that is not what has happened. All of your arm's anchor balls are still there."

"Sergio! This makes no sense. If they are still there, then why aren't my arms there too? Aren't they filling the space demarked by the anchor balls? How can you see them anyway?"

"Oh, you just look for them. No, the bacteria did a clever thing, sis. It collapsed all the many anchor balls of each arm on top of each other. You have what appears to be a single anchor ball right in the middle of your shoulder socket where your upper arm bone would begin, if you had an arm there. They are all piled up on top of each other. That's what the bacteria actually did to your arms, collapsed all the many anchor balls of the fingers, wrist, elbow and so on into one spot at the shoulder socket. All that has to be done for you to get your arms back is to push those anchor balls back out to where they originally belonged. Honestly, sis, the tiniest push would do it. Plus, the same thing has happened to those which demark your breasts and waist. A slight push and your breasts would reduce to what they ought to be. A slight push and your waist would swell back up to its proper size."

"That's almost too incredible to believe, Sergio."

"I know. The proof is in the doing. I need to actually give someone's a push and see what the results will be. Of course, then the woman would suddenly have her arms back, sort of defying the trend nowadays," he added. He looked at me coyly and continued, "Check on mom later today. I used her as my guinea pig. Her arms ought to be appearing rapidly, but she doesn't know that I did this yet. After all, if I am all wrong and nothing happens, I sure don't want to give her another upset."

"Thoughtful. She's had it rough."

"Right. I chose her because if it works, she can start playing her violin once more. We both know how important that is for her. Music was her life. If it works, she will have her arms back to battery. Also her monster boobs will be gone. I know that she doesn't like them."

"None of us women do, brother. Only you fellows must like them," I teased him. He flushed a little.

"More of you to love," he justified hastily, before changing the topic. "If it works, then we have a serious matter to discuss with Macario and the Church of God."

"How so?" I asked, not tracking with his sudden change of topic.

"Look, now, worldwide, you are giving women Basic Therapy. That is, you are getting millions of women and some men onto the track of therapy, which will eventually set them free as all of us here at 42 Hampton Way have become or very nearly so. The women's horrible loss of their arms has been sort of a catalyst for the explosive growth of the Church of God and its therapy or Holy Gift. Every woman has very nearly the same trauma that must be erased, critically so and rightly so. If soon all women worldwide suddenly have their arms back, that may well cause them no longer to want to get their Basic Therapy. It might even undo all the new matriarchal governments just now being established in Demokritos and Megalos. The world could go back to the way it was before the plague, which would greatly impede the rapid spread of the Church of God and its attempts to free all us spiritual beings."

I saw his point. "Ah, you are right. If we women suddenly had our bodies restored to pre-plague conditions, then there would be little drive to get Holy Gifts. Plus, men would no longer be as solidly behind having women ruling their countries and lands. Good point, brother. Damned if we do and damned if we don't." I felt frustrated, so close and yet so far.

Later at lunchtime, mom looked shocked. "Honey, can you help me out of this dress? Something is very wrong with my body." Both Eve and I followed her into her bedroom. We both could see that her dress no longer fit her properly. Her waist seemed to be bursting out while her bosom seemed darn near flat, folds of loose cloth draped over her chest. Plus, the sides of her dress bulged. Although I knew what must be happening just out of our sight, Eve did not and she looked as spooked as mom did.

"Oh my god! My arms are coming back!" Sofia exclaimed, both shocked and extremely pleased.

"Bethany! Look! The plague's effects are going away!" Eve added her surprise to mom's.

"Mom, you are almost back to normal. Terrific!" I added a comforting comment, waiting for the shock to subside a little.

"My arms work! Incredible! Kids, are yours coming back too? This is a miracle. What a relief!" mom declared, feeling herself with her arms. Slowly a grin appeared, "I do hope your father won't be annoyed with my breast reduction." We three laughed. Her melons were almost back to their usual size. I helped her find one of her old cotton day dresses from pre-plague days. Then, we rejoined the others and our children — all of whom had heard about mom and were sitting on the sofas in the living room. Speculations ran the gamut, though Sergio said nothing, trying hard to keep a straight face.

"Look at me!" mom declared excitedly, waving her new arms about as we three joined the others. "Looks like the plague is not permanent after all."

I gave Sergio one of my stares that told all. Sheepishly, he spoke up, "Mom, it was my doing. I needed a guinea pig to experiment up. Looks like it works just fine. Pretty darn fast, I might add."

"What?" she exclaimed. All eyes turned onto my older brother. His face flushed. Serves him right, I thought, for keeping this a secret.

Just then, Macario and Raffaella materialized in our front room. Eve had summoned them before she knew that Sergio was behind the "cure." Both looked at mom, and Macario commented, "Well?"

"My doing, Macario. I've figured out just what the plague bacteria actually did to our bodies. I calculated that it could easily be undone and tried it out on mom, though she didn't know that I was going to try to undo the plague's effects on her. Sorry mom, I didn't want to get your hopes up only to have them dashed."

"So when are you going to fix us all up?" asked Lisa pointedly. If she had arms, she'd of had her hands on her hips, challenging him.

"That's just the point," Sergio answered in a noncommittal manner. He looked at Macario and Raffaella.

"Let's hear what you found out and how you fix them up, Sergio," Macario spoke up. I couldn't tell how he felt about this surprising development. His face was expressionless. So was Raffaella's for that matter.

"Okay. Last lifetime as Cosima, I figured out that growing bodies can be called upon to regenerate. We know that much physical damage to a fetus can be repaired while it is in the mother's womb. I correctly worked out how to convince the physical body to continue that repair once the body has been born. I extended my research to the bacteria and its effects on us all. Just how did simple bacteria manage to eliminate arms, as if they were never there, to say nothing of the other physical body alterations? I spent weeks observing my physical form as well as the women in my life. Just what were the differences between our forms since the plague?"

"I took my guidance from our resident engineers. Something must be providing the framework upon which our bodies hang. At first, I incorrectly thought that this would be our bones. However, once I became able enough to mock up a visible, operational body, as all of us now can thanks to the Advanced Therapy we've been given, I saw that was very shortsighted of me. What holds the bones in place? I keep coming back to the simple fact that before you can have an object, before you can mock up anything, you have to create the space, which it will be occupying. Without space, the object cannot come into being — the mockup cannot be created. Thus, I reasoned that something must be creating and holding the space in which our physical bodies reside and began looking for it."

"Last week, I spotted the little golden anchor balls, as I've named them. Surrounding each of our body's bones and form are these small golden round things. The bones, for example, exist within the space defined by them. I found these most curious, since they cannot be seen with our body's eyes. Only if you look with your native spiritual being vision are they visible. I began messing around with mine. While moving those that are defining my body's stomach area, I managed to give myself a bad fright and stomachache. However, I did discover that if I stretched those that were defining the space of my big upper leg bones, those bones grew rapidly and I was two inches taller for a time last week — four inches this morning." Lisa gave him a glare.

"Fascinated, I began studying my own arms and the golden anchor balls that define them. I lengthened my fingers for a few hours, and I shortened them. Most curious. Yet, there are a large number of them, which define the spaces occupied by my arms. When I looked over Lisa's body, I found all those anchor balls completely missing. Of course, I rather anticipated that. At first, I theorized that the bacteria simply destroyed those anchor balls. I needed to test that theory."

"Three days ago, I visited the morgue to do a bit of experimentation. I did not want to risk permanent damage to our own bodies, you see. I performed some experiments on corpses. I destroyed the golden anchor balls around its thumb. The thumb vanished! Worse, even though I put some new replacement golden balls back, its thumb did not reappear. Next, I smashed into a pile of golden bits several others that formed a finger. That finger then appeared completely smashed, as if someone had hit it with a hammer! I tried to reform the smashed anchor balls, but the body again did not respond. Either the body was incapable of reforming because it was dead or, once destroyed, the anchor balls cannot be repaired. Further, replacing the body's anchor balls with mine failed and were rejected by the body."

"You didn't smash up your own hands to figure that one out, did you?" asked Lisa, aghast. She had suddenly leapt ahead from his conclusions to the next logical experiment.

"Er, no dear. I am not masochistic. If my body doesn't accept its own repaired anchor balls or accept my replacements, then my body would be permanently damaged. I've put that one on the back burner for now. Instead, I discovered that you women have one anchor ball that we men do not have. It is located right in your shoulder's sockets, where your arms would begin. I thought that this was most interesting and took a closer look. That's when I made my breakthrough discovery. What appears to be a large, single anchor ball is really a large bunch of anchor balls all piled up on top of one another!" He paused to let the significance of his discovery sink into their minds.

"So that's when I got the idea that perhaps all that the bacteria actually did was to move these balls on top of one another. This collapsed the space for the body's arms and thus the arms, having no space in which to exist, disappear. Naturally, I wondered what would happen if I pushed them back out to where they might have belonged? Of course, that raised another huge problem. There are hundreds of them all piled up. How am I going to know which one goes where and at what distance from the others? At first, I thought this would be an insurmountable problem. There is no blueprint to follow to put them back in place. If I got their positions wrong, you might have hands attached to your shoulders and upper arms attached to that ending with lower arms where your hands ought to be." Everyone grimaced at that imagined mix-up.

"So I decided to experiment a little on mom. Just a little, mom," he gave her a quick glance. "That's when I discovered the remarkable healing powers of our physical bodies once again. If you give that compressed pile of golden anchor balls a little shove, kind of like cracking pool balls, they all fly outward and back into their original locations! That was the most amazing thing to see. A tiny shove and presto, they flew back to where they belonged. A half-day later, mom's arms have reappeared! Ta da!"

"Hey, I see the anchor balls that you are talking about," Lisa suddenly exclaimed. "A little push?" she added. "Oh my!" Her eyes opened wide. "It's working! They flew out like cracked pool balls! Incredible. Wow, they now look like the space that my old arms used to have! Oh, I feel a little funny in my chest and stomach."

"Hey, which ones are you talking about?" I asked, suddenly seeing a large number of golden spheres around my own body.

"Hold on, ladies!" Macario's deep voice spoke commanding our attention. "Let's think this through before you all act. If you suddenly are back to normal, every woman on Tarra will want the same."

I stopped short of giving mine a push. "True. Sergio," I said, "the only way to restore our arms and bodies is to have one of us who is really able and who can actually see the balls give them a shove. That means that the few of us will have to visit every woman on Tarra to give them their cure!"

"Ah precisely," Macario pointed out. "Sergio, you have come upon the cure for our women. Yet, just how are you going to deliver the cure to every woman in the world? As soon as word spreads that a cure has been found, as soon as others begin to see women with their arms back, every woman will be demanding the cure for themselves and their children."

Sergio looked a bit sheepish. "Er, I was hoping that you would have the answer for that one, Macario."

"Plus, Dalney and Partholan have already decided that they did not want to put their female animal forms through this awful conversion a second time and thus he has not made any attempt to undo the plague's effects as yet," Macario explained.

"I know, but women ought not to be forced to live such tortured lives without arms," Sergio justified.

"True, big brother," I replied. "Yet, there are other things to also consider. If women worldwide regain their arms and become normal once more, what will happen to the new governments, which have accepted women as their rulers? The kingdoms of Demokritos, Megalos, for example. Will this not have a tendency for the men in those lands to retake control of the countries from their women rulers, thus undoing all that we have been working toward, MMCE and all that?"

Eve spoke up for the first time, "Further, if women regain their arms, then they will be far less likely to seek out the Holy Gift from the Church of God worldwide. We are just now getting into the explosive growth, where thousands of therapy sessions are being given daily. That is the first step toward getting those beings onto the path to total spiritual freedom. Won't this bring all that to a crashing halt? Isn't getting all us beings free a higher goal, a more important goal than our regaining our physical body's arms again?"

Sergio squirmed, seeing her point and mine too. She added, "Exactly how are you going to visit every woman on Tarra to give her anchor balls a push?" He squirmed even more, and I knew that he had no answers for these serious considerations. He'd only wanted to do what was right for the women in his life.

Raffaella spoke up, "Well, Sergio, there are about a hundred of us now who could see the balls and give them a push. We could advertise the cure as being a byproduct of having received the Church of God's Holy Gift. We have records of every person who has received the gift thus far. While it might take some time, we hundred could pay a visit to those who have already received therapy and undo the plague's effects on their bodies. That would certainly provide an impetus for all other women to receive the Holy Gift. Macario, do we have the numbers to be able to meet such a huge demand for Basic Therapy?"

"Not really, but we can make it work, don't you think so, Eve?" Macario asked.

"Well, perhaps," Eve answered hesitantly. "As long as many women continue to want to learn how to do it and to then give therapy sessions to others and as long as some of the men also either volunteer time and help or funds to help keep us going, probably we can make it. It is the help factor rearing its head. Our therapy is the most valuable thing anywhere. Although now we are giving it away free, eventually, the receiver realizes that he or she is getting something of immeasurable value and knows that they must contribute. Payback is a must. Considering this awful emergency situation, payback is usually volunteering to learn and to give others sessions."

"In the southern countries, we are making excellent headway. I don't know the full story up here in the northern hemisphere, though," Eve added.

"We have not yet mobilized like you are doing down south, Eve," Raffaella admitted. "If we are going to have to meet this new demand, we're going to have to get the avalanche going up here, Macario — like Eve has done down south."

She added, "I think that we should sponsor Sergio's cure for the plague. It will become the weenie."

"Huh?" I replied, not quite following her.

"The prize. The thing that everyone seeks in a game, Bethany. You see, if women see that by getting the Holy Gift the effects of the plague are eliminated, that will drive nearly everyone to at least obtain the Holy Gift, thus getting them onto the path to total spiritual freedom. We are being given an excellent opportunity here to drive all women onto that path, though not necessarily all men. Within a few years, the numbers of beings on the path could number in the millions. Macario, we must make use of this opportunity here in the north, just as Eve is doing down south. However, we ought to get Partholan's agreement before we do this."

Macario agreed and shortly Partholan joined us, his huge grey form filled the sofa across from us. He materialized a body for our sakes. After being briefed on Sergio's discovery and the many ramifications of it, he agreed. "I have been observing Dalny-Alexina. Her life would be immeasurable assisted if her body's arms were returned. She and I now agree; it was a mistake to have created our animals the way that we did. While the original forms served their intended purposes over a millennia ago, in today's world, female forms should have arms as the males do."

He went on, "However, we must free all the trapped beings who currently occupy our animal creations. I agree with your proposal to give arms back to those who have undergone your Basic Therapy. You will have led them to the path to freedom. From there, it will be their responsibility to walk it and to assist others in making it. To be bluntly honest, Macario, some of these trapped beings are not going to make it. Those whom I have punished in Axos, those Skull worshipers, for example — those beings have sunk almost beyond reach. In time, they will have sunk so low that they will actually become one of our animals, having no life force of their own, no will or awareness of themselves. At that point, they will be indistinguishable from the life energy of our original animal creations and cease to be a problem for us, as their highest awareness will be that of monitoring and controlling the bodily functions such as the heart beat and digestion process."

"Wow," I whispered. That a being could sink so low was something that I had not considered before.

Sergio spoke up in the lull. "So was I right in my observations of the golden anchor balls, Partholan?"

"Indeed, Sergio, that is how Dalny and I constructed our animal forms so long ago. They anchor the physical form by creating the space to be occupied by the bones and muscles. There are thousands of them in one body. I too have seen that the bacteria merely collapsed the many, which formed their arms. Over a millennia ago, she and I knew that the animal forms that we were creating would have a challenging existence. We built them with the basic postulate that the anchor balls would tend to return to their genetic blueprint locations, if disturbed. You are right, give them a push and they will automatically return to their original locations. The physical form will follow them rather rapidly."

Sergio smiled smugly. He'd been right. "Say, what about those women who had lost their arms prior to the plague? You know, those Holy Women down in Demokritos — they had theirs removed surgically."

"I am afraid that their anchor balls are gone — destroyed, when their appendages were cut off," Partholan answered. "You cannot give them new anchor balls, as you have discovered, Sergio. Any given animal body will not accept other anchor balls than their own. We designed them that way to avoid all manner of other complications."

"Ah ha. I rather thought so," Sergio replied. "Say, what about Alexina and her lip plates. They slit her lips and inserted those awful plates. Can anything be done about that?"

"Alas, I am afraid not, Sergio. The anchor balls that define her lips and mouth have been shattered, broken into pieces by the physical damage done to her lips. While the pieces could be pushed together, they will never reassemble nor will her lips suddenly become whole once more as if they had not been cut. She had suggested that once she has enough Advanced Therapy, she will have her animal lips removed and then create a mockup of what her lips used to look like and make that visible to all others, thereby presenting a 'normal look' once more. But it will just be her mockup that is seen; her animal body will be without lips. Still, hardly no one would be able to tell the difference." Eve and I realized this was what Macario had done for us when we had those awful lip plates. True, we could not tell that his new illusion was not our real lips put back as they had been.

"Damn, so lost anchor balls and smashed anchor balls yield a permanent body alteration," Sergio both cursed and summarized. Partholan nodded. "Well, those hundred fifty thousand women in Alia are doomed with their lip plates, damn that general and his sadistic ideas!"

Partholan added, "When they finish their Advanced Therapy, they will have no further need of the bodies anyway. Get them freed, that is the answer, Sergio, get them freed."

Macario spoke up, "That's our objective. Do you realize that when the plague arrived, there were sixteen of us who were freed and now there are one hundred of us? More are in various stages of Advanced Therapy. Soon, we will number two hundred of us. We are making more progress in the last couple of years than in all the centuries before! There is real hope now that we can make it, if we can just keep the world calm for some years."

"I am working on that one," I grinned and replied. "My job, keep the world safe so you all can go to town on freeing us all. Now, we've only one *known* area that is still in the Dark Ages — most of Tashien. They are isolated, for the most part, and are not likely to bother the rest of the world too much. Things elsewhere are now stable. As long as MMCE continues along at a good clip, I think it will stay that way. The real unknown is the status of the western continent. Other than the southern tip, it is a big unknown. Also the status of the Southlands is unknown, specifically the interior lands there."

"Do you need to go to Tashien to help them out?" asked Macario.

Eve spoke for me, "The last time she and I did that, we met with sadism and disaster. Got our bodies tortured and wiped out. Going there is an awfully risky business right now."

He chuckled and changed the topic. "Okay, then let's work out a plan to get all the women who have been through Basic Therapy to have the plague's effects undone. Sergio, I'll need you to train the other ninety-nine of us quickly. We'll have to make it known that only the effects of the plague can be undone. Arms lost prior will not be reappearing. Let's get this going rapidly. Meanwhile, Raffaella and I had better get Eve's program going full speed here in the northern lands."

"You bet! If we don't, we're going to be swamped with women demanding therapy if only to get their arms back," Raffaella added.

The next day, we held a massive Mink Link, though many chose to materialize a body directly in our front room. The occasion: Sergio's announcement and training of the one hundred able beings in how to undo the plague's effect on women's bodies. After a bit of amazing discussion, the real problem of how to implement this worldwide was tackled. After much discussion, Eve's plan was adopted. Each would coordinate their efforts in the lands where they were now operating. Since accurate records had been kept of everyone who had received Basic Therapy, each woman would be visited and her anchor balls adjusted. With so many having received it, the process would necessarily take some time to complete fully. Many here volunteered to aid those who had a large backlog of women to visit. Eve promised to handle the coordination between them all, much to everyone's relief.

Bei Mi of Nan Yan took me aside for a chat when we were finished. "Say, I need some advice. I have three of the Alia OrnamentedDolls under my care now. Master Wei brought them to Nan Yan in hopes that they could get advanced Olin martial arts training so that they could use kijutsu to help them survive better. Of course, with their relative immobility and lips, they cannot receive such from him. It would be far to dangerous for their health. Instead, we are working on giving them Advanced Therapy. Yet, these teens are like fish out of water in Nan Yan. Everyone, quite naturally, looks upon them as freakish with their strange ornaments. Is there some way that we could get them to return to their homeland?"

"Yes, Alia has been salvaged. Homer Manasses is leading the Church of God there. Let me speak with him and get back to you, Bei Mi," I replied.

All over Tarra on June 25, 825, celebrations rang out, though it would take far longer for the words to be implemented. Later in Nan Yan, Bei Mi called for a meeting of all the many women who were delivering the Holy Gift, along with Princess Mei Lon Wu and her staff. Her announcement was rather simple, yet profound. "I've called all of you together this morning to hear the best news ever. One of our most able Church of God members, Sergio Bartiana, Bethany's brother, has discovered a cure for the plague's effects on the women of Tarra." She allowed the large group time to absorb this incredible news before continuing.

"Unfortunately, the cure must be administered by one of us who has mastered Advanced Therapy. There are only some hundred of us who can do this. It will take us time to get to every one of you. During the next few days, we will be going down the list of every woman who has so far received our Basic Therapy and administering the cure on her. Once that has been completed, we will routinely see that each woman gets the cure when she completes her Basic Therapy. Once again, our friends in Velona have come through with a cure, though this time the cure requires special treatment by the ablest of spiritual beings." After a rousing round of yelling and cheering, she continued.

"When your name is called, please come to see one of us four Top Counselors. We who will be delivering it to all of you. Thank you." She carefully stepped down from the small raised platform amid an even louder round of cheering. Now came the hard work, she thought.

Late afternoon, Psyche and Kassandra finally heard their names being called out by Master Tian, who grinned at them as they stood up reactively. "You have more than earned your cure, twins," he whispered as they passed him. Both grinned back, but their expression wasn't visible, of course.

"That's all?" Psyche exclaimed after doing little more than stand before Bei Mi. First, the counselor had asked her if she also wanted their massive breasts returned to their normal size and waist restored too. Both said that they wanted to keep their melons and tiny waists because that would help direct other's attention away from their lip plates. People still stared at them and they didn't like it, though they were no longer troubled by such attention. As it turned out, they were not alone. A fair number of women desired to retain their massive bosoms and tiny waists. In Annelise, most women chose to keep their narrow waists and many also wanted to retain their bosoms as they now were. Why didn't that come as a surprise to me, I wonder?

"Yes, that does it, Psyche. Once you both have completed your Advanced Therapy and training, you will be shown how to also do this for other women," she explained. "However, girls, I need to meet with you and all of Master Wei's family — your whole group. Please meet with me just after supper." She said no more and after thanking her, both left, chatting about this experience.

"My shoulders tingled sort of," Roxane indicated to the twins. All were dining together and discussing this momentous day. "I couldn't tell if anything was really happening, of course. How about you, sis?"

"Same here. It felt like an itch is all, a fleeting one. Did you all want to keep your big boobs?" Selene replied.

"We Ornamented Dolls did. It gives strangers sovething else to look at instead of our livs," Psyche exclaimed. "I wonder why Vei Vi wants to sveak to all of us. Vaster Wie?"

"I have no idea at all, Psyche. I guess we will find out soon enough. I am so happy that you all will get your arms back. Tears of joy keep coming. This is my third handkerchief." He dabbed his eyes again.

A short while later, the nine gathered in her office, where she kept her LD radio. She didn't keep them waiting any longer. "I've asked you here because I have received an urgent message from your new Monarch of Alia, Diona Gidios and her Church of God leader Homer Manasses. Incidentally, your new monarch is an Ornamented Doll, just as your three are. It seems that she poisoned General Erebos and has taken over control of your country, freeing your people from his tyranny. She has begged Homer to return to Alia from Annelise, where he and your former Queen Katerine had fled for refuge. They are desperate for more therapy givers. She and Homer wish to speak with you over the LD radio here."

Master Tian operated the controls and soon the group heard the crackling voice of another Doll, unmistakable. She spoke Annelise, though not well. "Hello, I av Vonarch Diona Gidos. Hover is with ve."

After spoken introductions, she continued. "I av calling to veg you to return to Levkos and Alia. We need your skills with the Church of God's Holy Gift and Advanced Therapy. We have over a hundred-fifty thousand of us Ornavented Dolls here who desverately need your helv."

Homer explained further. "We have had to delay giving the Ornamented Dolls Basic Therapy because they are unable to speak intelligibly. We have most of them on a crash course learning to speak Annelise. Only when they can speak well can we hope to understand them well enough to be able to deliver their therapy, which they need far more than the normal woman. Diona and I are begging you nine to return to Levkos and lend us your help. Please, there are so many Dolls here, please."

Psyche glanced at her companions and spoke for them. "Yes, we will return as fast as we can. One hundred-fifty thousand? Vy god, so vany!"

"Thank you, thank you," Diona replied. Her voice sounded relieved, Kassandra thought. They chatted awhile longer before the Diona needed to hang up to attend to other matters.

Bei Mi then explained, "I have arranged for you to take a train to Spur Port tomorrow morning. At the small port there, I am told that a caravel from Velona will be waiting to take you straight to Alia. I am also told that the voyage will take approximately three months, which is perfect for you seven women. Bethany's daughter, Bianca, will be coming with you to give you Advanced Therapy and to train you in its delivery. Bianca said that while three months might not be enough to complete your Advanced Therapy, it would certainly be enough to get all nine of you well along in it." Now the small group really did have something to talk furiously about — especially since time was short!

The next morning, the three Ornamented Dolls were actually crying, they were so elated. As promised, their arms had returned, and for the first time in two years, they no longer felt so completely helpless. Now with difficulty they could at last feed themselves and take care of their own personal needs! Miracles were happening all over Tarra this day. Of course, dresses had to be hastily altered, but Mei promised to alter their clothes during the trip. She could once more sew! The very happy nine waved goodbye to their new friends as the black smoking engine hooted and slowly began to chug-chug out of Nan Yan.

Late that afternoon, they boarded a caravel that was waiting for them at Spur Port. Three months later, they arrived back in Alia. Although Bianca's body was barely two years old, she mocked up a form of a ten year old girl when she appeared before them on the caravel. At sea and without any of life's usual distractions, Bianca found that their Advanced Therapy went many times faster than it had while back in Velona. "Yes, I av five feet vehind vy head," Psyche answered her as the teen's first Advanced Therapy session began.

By the time that they arrived in Levkos, Alia, Psyche and Kassandra had had to have their lip plates enlarged again to alleviate their massive drooping. Ariadne's were enlarged as well. The lip plates of the twins were nearly eight inches across, while Ariadne's were about seven. Still, as very able beings, they didn't worry about mere fleshly body difficulties any more. They could now do many things that people only dreamed of being able to do — the very least of which was to give a woman's anchor balls a slight push. With their great language skills and their ability to use telepathy, the nine began the massive project to give the many Ornamented Dolls of Levkos their initial Basic Therapy sessions. If the Ornamented Doll could not fully communicate what was happening, they could use telepathy to help transcend the language barrier. They had their work laid out for them: one hundred-fifty thousand plus Ornamented Dolls were in desperate need of their therapy, after which they would be given their arms back.

Here at home, the demand for the Church of God's Holy Gift grew enormously as the news of the newfound cure spread like wildfire. At 42 Hampton Way, we all found ourselves pressed into service, helping give therapy sessions every day. Still, I had to spend some time on the LD radio, coordinating actions and needs among the various monarchs of Tarra. Eve also spent long hours coordinating the overall efforts of so many Churches of God. Without telepathy and the ability to appear there in person, so to speak, the tasks would have been beyond our abilities. Still, strange as this sounds, we got much work done during the nighttime when our fleshly bodies were asleep. We simply mocked up a substitute one and carried on with our work. However, I still had one major worry that continued to gnaw away in the back of my mind: the rest of Tashien beyond Nan Yan.

Chapter 62 The Rise of Philosophies

The chaotic fall of law and order in the Imperial City of Zau, Wontun Province, was catastrophic. Not only had the mighty Imperial Army dispersed, but also their Princess and their High Parliament. With the mysterious vanishing of the entire Olin Masters, who took over half of the wealthiest of Zau with them, only chaos remained. This, the largest city of Tashien, fell into the utter depths of Dark Ages.

Older women unable to cope with their loss of arms simply gave up and waited for death to release them. Street gangs took over control of city blocks, demanding everything imaginable from those who lived here. At least by January 824, food became available once more, though it was fought over and doled out by the many gangs. Trying to stay alive was the chief objective of millions.

Overlord Bin Zhou stepped in during the chaos. A ruthless man, he had been forced to bide his time during the last twenty years while their Princess and the elected High Parliament enforced and dictated the laws. Often, Bin railed against such a system. "Look, you cannot have a bunch of idealists inventing laws and a woman ordering the army to enforce them. You need a strong leader." He never added — which was himself. As he watched the slow destruction of Zau, he began taking action. First, he made offers of employment to the deserting Imperial Army men, offers that were hard to refuse. Food and money became excellent inducements, for few had either these days. Slowly, his forces grew until at last he estimated that he had enough to begin his reign over Zau.

Shortly after the Olin Masters vanished, he posted notices around the city that he was now in control of Zau. Overlord Zhou was their sole leader. Any resistance to his orders or his soldiers would be met with the ultimate force. Gang leaders had to submit to his rule and orders or else. After twenty public executions of protesting gang leaders, the remaining hundred or so gang leaders submitted, but only begrudgingly so. Thus for a short time, the common man found that any law was better than anarchy.

Yong Chi was twenty-five when the plague struck. He ran his father's bookstore for his ailing parents. His wife, Qian, assisted him and took care of their five year old daughter, Ni. Shocked at his distorted feet upon which he could no longer walk and the dire situation of his wife and daughter who were now completely helpless in all ways, Yong sat for days staring into space. Then, it struck him. Acceptance. At last he rose, "Qian, we must merely accept what has happened to us. Come, I will fix us something to eat." Qian and Ni had long stopped crying and were sitting beside Yong, waiting for death to take them. They had nothing to eat for two days, not since they had awakened to the effects of the plague.

"We can do nothing, Honorable Chi," Qian whispered. "We are as helpless as babes."

"Yes, you must learn to accept this, Beautiful Qian. We must all learn merely to accept what happens. That is the answer. Accept it. Do not fight it. We cannot win. Only by accepting what happens can we retain peace of mind and heart."

"But Honorable Chi, we can do nothing. Ni and I are completely helpless in all ways," she protested.

"Yes, that is so, Beautiful Qian, Lovely Ni. Accept it as so. You are completely helpless in all ways. Accept the fact that you are. When you do so, it will not be a problem for you any longer."

"But daddy, I don't want to be helpless," Ni whimpered. "Make them give me my arms back, please."

"Ni, you must accept the fact that you no longer have arms — that you are completely helpless. Only then can you find peace of mind. I will be looking after you and your mother now, just as other fathers must do so."

Qian sighed and sank at last into apathy, accepting her fate. From that moment on, she did not attempt to do anything for herself, allowing Yong Chi to do it for her or accepting the fact that it would not be done. She did admit that she felt better; she was no longer protesting and fighting against the effects of the plague. She protested nothing, accepting whatever came her way.

Ni, however, did not, though she soon saw that overtly protesting brought no results from her father. All the ways that she had used to control him had vanished. Her coy, pleading smile, which used to bring a smile to his face and his agreement with her request, now did nothing at all. Her temper tantrums went unnoticed and she gave them up as well. After a week of trying all manner of ways to get her father to help her failed, she pretended to emulate her mother's acceptance of all things. Pretended was the key word. She went along with her father's orders, but continued to look for other ways and means. In her mind, she saw all sorts of uses for the strange objects, which had appeared in their small living room located behind the bookstore proper.

When her father was not present or looking, she began experimenting with them. She found that she could brush her hair and carry things with the yoke. Using her feet, she was able to manage to feed herself. Thus, while her mother barely got enough to eat, Ni was always swiping enough food to satisfy her growing body.

That soon ended when the food supplies dried up. Outside the bookstore, chaos prevailed. Into the chaos, Yong Chi began explaining his revelations to others. "But Yong, we are starving! We have no food. My children are growing weaker by the day," one man railed.

"Yes, Bo, it is the same everywhere. You must relax and just accept this as fact. Acceptance will free you of your woes and worries and cares. All of you, this is the answer. Worry and fear only eats at your heart and mind. It drives others to the madness that we see all around us. Over there, the thugs are beating that poor man. We all must learn just to accept this. Acceptance. Do not fight it. It is and we cannot change it. Yet, we can retain peace, if only we accept it."

Repeatedly, Chi delivered his message. One by one, others began heeding his words, finding their fear, terrors, panic, and worries vanishing, replaced by an unfeeling apathy, which they found more palpable than the constant knots in their stomachs and fear in their minds. Many began calling this new way Chi-ism. Slowly during the crisis, the concept of Chi-ism's Acceptance of All Things spread.

In March of 824 when Overlord Zhou took forceful control of Zau, he soon learned of this new philosophy of Chi-ism. He grinned as his aides explained it to him. Put the population into an acceptance of all things, an apathy, and his rule would be a breeze. He summoned Yong Chi to his court, now held in the old Imperial Palace where the Empress and Emperor used to rule.

"Welcome Most Honorable Yong Chi. I am Overlord Bin Zhau. I have heard of your new philosophy of life. Come, please explain it more fully to me," he said cunningly. For a half hour, he sat patiently listening to Yong outline his method for obtaining peace of mind and heart. Chi's words differed little from what his aides had reported, though.

"Excellent philosophy, Most Honorable Chi. I am hereby ordering your Chi-ism to be the official religion and guiding philosophy for all of Zau! I am giving you the charge of spreading your words of great wisdom all over our great city. Through acceptance, our people will become strong and prosperous once more!"

Yong fought to quench a rising pride and elation. "I must accept this as what is," he told himself repeatedly. His fortunes improved. Overlord Zhou saw to it that he had plenty of food delivered to his home each week and that armed guards patrolled nearby his bookstore. Overlord Bin was no fool. If the whole city or at least a majority of it would adopt Chi-ism, then his rule would be supreme and unchallenged. This was much superior to the hangings of the gang leaders, which he had been forced to do to get them under control. That there would be dire consequences to having the whole city in apathy escaped him utterly. He was used to ruling by force, and he saw Chi-ism as a way to minimize that, endearing him better to the population.

By the summer of 825, the ramifications of Chi-ism had spread everywhere in this city of millions. On the river docks, workers were unloading a cargo of fresh fish when the crane's main rope broke. The dockhands merely accepted this and left the cargo to rot. Half of the city's riks no longer were operational. When one broke down, the owners merely accepted this and sought other employment if such could be found. No one took any responsibility for anything anymore. Bit by bit, the infrastructure of Zau began to break down. Sewers plugged up and was accepted by all. A water well's pump broke down. It was accepted and the folks who depended upon the well now walked ten blocks further to get their daily water supply. Disease sprang up, but few sought medical care, merely accepting this as well. Thousands continued to die each week, and their bodies were generally left on the streets, ignored by the acceptance policy of Chi-ism. Overlord Zhau had no choice but to order his soldiers to make weekly trips throughout the city, carting away the dead.

Slowly but surely, Overlord Zhau was being forced to take over control of every aspect of the city. During the summer, he had his soldiers now watching over and even assisting the unloading of river vessels, issuing orders to correct anything that went wrong, which often did these days. Daily, he found himself up to his neck in city problems caused by the people's acceptance of whatever was, though he did not realize the actual cause. Instead, he condemned his people, "I have a city filled with nothing but ignorant, moronic idiots!"

He had a far worse problem, however. The exodus of so many of the wealthier of Zau caused a severe financial collapse. These men and a few women had been providing the financing of many city projects, to say nothing of their business enterprises. With these people gone and their money with them, there was little financing of new projects occurring. True, their abandoned businesses were taken over, often by some of their employees, the severe lack of money at the highest levels of the city reverberated downwards. Virtually no new projects were started in those two years. What little capital remained, Overlord Zhau confiscated for his own needs, paying his mighty army, which now numbered some forty thousand strong.

At last, he had to order iron coins to be issued, replacing the gold coins, which had become quite scarce by the summer of 825. The poorer folks accepted this change; Chi-ism again proved its worth or so thought Overlord Zhau. However, among others, this became a severe warning sign that a total economic collapse was imminent. Said iron coins were not accepted by anyone outside of the city, including the farmers upon whose produce the city depended.

Outside Zau, the fertile countryside with its numerous farming towns, villages, and hamlets fell under the control of Overlord Yi, a brutal man in his forties. Long had he sought to be known as the supreme leader, perhaps even the Emperor, but until the plague came, he had been forced to remain on the sidelines of Wontun politics. Slowly marshaling his forces, he was prepared when the plague-caused collapse of their government came at last. At once, he and his men began seizing control of the towns and villages just outside of Zau. He made his headquarters in Ningo, a town of ten thousand, some fifty miles west of Zau. Here, in his carefully guarded rural estate at the edge of the town, he commanded his ever-growing forces.

He grew his forces by sending out patrols to outlying villages. There, they abducted into his army all promising younger men, usually by force. Few joined his army willingly. This was even more apparent after the plague struck hard.

In the village of Longdon, Li Ning had turned twenty-three. Li was the village blacksmith and thus one of the most listened to men of the thousand who lived here, some fifty miles further west from Ningo. He had a homely wife and a son and daughter, who were now six and five years old, respectively. While they were all terrified, shocked, and traumatized by the plague as were the other villagers and nearby farmers, Li and the villagers persevered, due in large part to their mostly independent ways and the close proximity of farms and a small river that provided fish, supplementing their diets.

By spring 824, word had spread everywhere of Overlord Yi's men raiding the villages. All the young men of Longdon now had yet another fear, a growing one, that of being abducted into the overlord's army. "But how can we survive this?" one young man asked of Li, who was shaping a new pair of horseshoes for the man. Several others stood nearby, eager to hear what wisdom their able blacksmith might bestow.

"Non-resistance is our answer. Look, if they come for you, Bo, and abduct you into his army, your wife and daughter are doomed. Who will look after them and feed them? Our women are so utterly helpless now. They will perish. Yet, if you resist the overlord's men, they will most certainly kill you. We've heard how they did just that in Yan. If so, once more, your wife and daughter are doomed and will perish," Li explained, as he hammered away.

"I am doomed either way. Is that what you are saying?" the lad asked. Now all the other young men paid close attention. Surely, this was right.

"Yes, either way, Bo, when the soldiers come for you, your family will have been sentenced to death. So, Bo, the choice is yours to make. Do you want to lose your own self-respect and allow yourself to be abducted into the overlord's army so that you can be ordered to do the same thing to another young man such as yourself in the next village or do you wish to retain your self-respect? It seems to me that you have only two choices, if the overlord's men come for you."

Bo spat onto the red hot coals. Steam puffed up. "Damn, I will not become a soldier only to repeat this slavery in the next village!"

"Right, Bo. We must practice non-resistance. Let them come. We will not resist them and fight against them. That would cause the soldiers to murder the whole village. Instead, we turn the other cheek to the soldiers. Let them kill you, but you will retain your self-respect and not allow yourself to be forced into doing similar actions to other villagers. This way, you can die with pride, and your wife and daughter can likewise die with pride in you — that you did not allow them to take you away and force you to do wicked things to other villagers in turn. All will die with great pride and honor."

Li went on, "If a man strikes you, justly or unjustly, simply turn the other cheek and go your own way. Be true to your own goals, my friend. Forsake not your own goals out of fear of being struck down by evil men. That's what I have to say, Bo. Non-resistance is the key."

"Yes, but," Bo complained, "won't the others in our village knuckle under when they see me getting killed for refusing to be abducted into the army?"

"If the whole village also does not resist and does not go along with them, they would be utter fools to kill us all. Look, do we not provide them with food, cloth, grains, and horses? Do we not provide them with leather goods and even ironworks? If they kill us all, who will they then get to provide them with these things?" Li replied. The others around the two nodded their agreement. It seemed both logical and practical. "True, a few will die before the soldiers realized that force will not prevail here. Those few will have become heroes, for they will have saved the other young men in the village."

Early April 824, the resolve of the village of Longdon was so tested. A group of two dozen heavily armed soldiers of Overlord Yi rode ceremoniously into the village. As anticipated, they began rounding up all younger men, pushing them out into the center of the street. Blacksmith Li was the last to be shoved out into the street. The leader barked, "You men have been selected to become soldiers in the mighty Overlord Yi's army. You will march with us now."

Bo spoke up. "We will not do so. You may kill us here, but we will not go with you. We will not become soldiers of the overlord."

"What? You dare defy me and the mighty overlord?" the leader barked. "This is your last chance. March now or I will execute you myself!" Bo didn't move, not even when the leader rode up to him and sliced Bo's head off. That alone alarmed the leader. Always before, such men would at least cower or try to flee. This man stood defiantly to the end. "All right, who is to be next? You will all move out now," he ordered, certain that this example would have served its purpose. Such had always worked in the other villages before now.

To his amazement, no one moved. He murdered two more men and still no one moved, not even the slightest. Li spoke up, "Sir, you ought to think about what you are doing here. None of us will go with you. We are all prepared to die on the spot. You see, we have wives and families who are utterly dependent upon us. If you take us away, you are dooming our families to death. If you kill us here in the street, you are also dooming our families to death. If you continue to slay us all, who then will you get to provide you with food, grain, gold, horses, swords, and all the other things that our village produces? Go ahead and slay us all, but then return not later expecting to obtain that which we men ought to have produced for you."

The leader grimaced, realizing that he had better not kill off this whole village, not without the consent of Overlord Yi. Instead, he yelled, "I will report this to the overlord. We will be back. Perhaps he will order the destruction of your whole village!"

"Go ahead and destroy us all. Then, he certainly will not get food, grain, gold, horses, and swords from Longdon," Li replied softly but firmly. The soldiers galloped out of the village. Li and the others buried the three fallen young men. Afterwards, the entire village gathered to decide what to do. Many thought it was prudent to send some of their wives and children to their relatives who lived on nearby farms. Two days later, half of the village had been abandoned as a safety precaution. The town's seneschal ordered Li Ning to take his family to his wife's father's farm.

"Look, Li. If they do come back and wipe the village out, we need you to help rebuild it. Without a blacksmith, the village is doomed. Besides, we need you to spread your ideas to the other villages. The overlord cannot destroy all villages. Eventually, he will realize that doing that would be cutting his own throat. You must go, Li. Go now."

With a heavy heart, Li hitched up his small one horse wagon and took his family to her father's farm. Two days later, they all saw a huge cloud of smoke on the northern horizon. Indeed, the overlord had sent his men to burn down the village. As asked, Li then returned to help rebuild their village. However, word of his philosophy had already been spread by the many others who had also left. Each day, some representative of a surrounding town, village, or hamlet came to learn of his ideas. Soon this philosophy was named Ningism, a philosophy of non-resistance, of turning the other cheek, of dying with self-respect intact. Only one other village was burned to the ground before Overlord Yi had to change his ways and cease abducting young men into his army by force of arms.

At last, he had little choice but to obtain new recruits by offering them power, money, and positions. Instead of demanding villagers give him their young men for his army, he now demanded more goods and gold in trade. Again, Ningism was applied, though his soldiers now merely took what they desired. No one offered any real resistance to their thievery. Still, the overlord realized that he could not take too much from any one village, since that would also spell the doom of that village. He had to plan very carefully just what his men were to steal from each town and village. Thus, much of his day was wasted in such planning.

He continually eyed Overlord Zhou in Zau proper, his only real enemy. The further outlying areas of Wontun Province also had their overlords, but they were all weaker than he was. Yet, as the months went by, he began to see that the conditions within Zau were worsening. When the iron coins came out, he knew that now he had a real chance of laying claim to the highly prized Imperial City! He renewed his efforts at soldier recruitment.

Though at first glance Ningism appeared to be saving the day, the idea of just turning the other cheek, of non-resistance, allowed many women and children no chance at survival. Many died as a result of their husbands being killed or abducted. More died when their husbands were lured into the army with the promise of gold. While some did sent part of their wages back to their families, the women were helpless and could not fend for themselves or eat the gold. They died as a result, though some were taken in by other relatives, putting an even larger burden on those menfolk.

Up in Linyi Province, the four Elemental Towers took control of the land and their capital city of

Luo Yang, building four new temples there. Originally, the Elemental Towers were located in the nearby western city of Quanhao, some hundred miles west of Luo Yang. The priestesses, who held the ultimate power in each of the four Elemental Towers of Earth, Air, Fire, and Water, were shocked and terrified with the effects of the plague. However, their menfolk, highly skilled martial artists, stepped in to assist them.

Among them was Feng Lian, the thirty year old High Priestess of the Temple of Earth. Shocked beyond belief with the sudden loss of her arms and of becoming so utterly helpless and dependent upon her husband for nearly everything physical, Feng began to pray and meditate, seeking for some answer to this catastrophe which had so totally destroyed their government. Even the wealthier and the Olin Masters had now deserted Linyi Province. Was this really the end of the world? Had the gods ordained this as the time of ultimate destruction? She needed answers. Her fellow High Priestesses of the other Elemental Towers likewise had no answers, only questions.

Feng sat in her inner sanctum, her legs crossed. She thought, I must blank out all thoughts from my mind. I must forsake the fleshly realm of this unholy world. Already part of my body is gone. Earth has shown me that I cannot even feed this pathetic body any longer. The answer must be in letting go of my body and all that is in this earthly world. Quiet my thoughts. I am nothing.

At first, Feng found this was hard to do. Stray thoughts entered her mind, attracting her attention. Her legs cramped, but she had no arms to massage them, and she continued to attempt to ignore them. Finally, her mind went quiet, and she obtained a relative peace that she had not known before, but had glimpsed at times while performing her many Earth ceremonies.

Elated with her newfound revelations, she began spreading the word of the Lian Meditation, as it became known throughout Linyi Province. "Forsake these earthly bodies, for they cannot even feed themselves any longer. Forsake all worldly goods as these are mere disguises of the truth. Meditate and cast all thoughts from your mind and you shall be free from this earthly world!" So she began to preach her newfound wisdom.

Amid the chaos and crumbling culture of this northern province, the ideas of Lian Meditation began to be seen as an answer to an otherwise miserable existence. Through Lian Meditation, one could achieve a lasting peace or so it was claimed. Many began to come to the Earth Temple to learn how to perform this meditation. Most were women, as one might have expected.

Quieting one's mind is most helpful and beneficial. Thousands upon thousands who took up Lian Meditation began experiencing this peace, but unknown to Lian, her route to salvation was booby-trapped. The way out of the physical universe is not through denying it, denying all use of physical force. By denying the physical universe, she began to give it an even greater force over her life! That from which you run takes you prisoner in the end.

By early 825, Feng no longer experienced the deep peace of mind when she meditated. Instead, horrible images began to appear in her mind, terrifying ones, filled with horrors, pain, unconsciousness, and death. She had no idea that these were her many past deaths that she was now seeing, periods of utter and complete immobility. In one, she sat frozen in place as a sword severed her head. In another, a massive hammer crushed her skull much like a watermelon, though she tried with every ounce of her being to keep her brains from exploding outward. In another, her body was being burned in a fire.

Often now, her meditations were abruptly ended with her shrieking in panic, wildly trying to avoid the flames, the hammer, the sword. To those around her, she seemed to be going mad. She talked of strange things happening to her, things which her husband could not see. "Ants! Bo, ants are everywhere! Get them off me! They are biting me to death," she shrieked one afternoon. Try as he might, Bo could see no ants in her sanctuary, giving him a scare. Was she going mad, insane?

On June 8, 825, Feng screamed and fled from her sanctuary, fleeing the flames, which she saw were burning her alive. She raced out of their temple and through the streets of Luo Yang, screaming wildly. At last, she dove into the Binz River and drowned herself, putting out the intense, flesh-searing flames. As she rose above the waters, she saw her lifeless body floating helplessly in the waters below. The command to go get another baby body flooded her mind, swamping the flaming images. She instantly and reactively obeyed the implanted command that the Plasticine Doll Creatures had installed in her mind centuries ago. Over the months, many others who practiced Lian Meditation, denying the physical universe, also perished, though few ever found the connection between their deaths and the meditation.

Chapter 63 Aberration Unhandled, Returns

Surgeon Peng Ang was forty at the time of the plague. In his teens, he'd studied with the best surgeons of Zau. He'd acquired the very best texts on surgical procedures, a series of volumes by the most famous surgeon of all Tashien, Doc Yi. Now he had his own hospital and staff, a small one, however. He chose to practice only on the wealthier of Zau, allowing lesser surgeons to deal with the poor, who often could not pay for their lifesaving operations. He had three surgical nurses and three orderlies, who tended the patients in recovery. At the time of the plague, his Banca del Dio account totaled nearly five million gold.

His small complex in the heart of the wealthier district of Zau was equipped with the very best equipment and surgical tools. Many he had hand-made following the guidelines set down by old Doc Yi in his textbooks. However, he was shocked utterly by the appearance of his three highly skilled nurses, who showed up terrified, shocked, and armless, begging for his help. The nurses were in their teens and lived onsite in very comfortable back quarters. Why? Whenever an emergency arose, Doc Peng insisted that any needed operation be done immediately. Only on Sundays were his nurses allowed to return to their homes for the day. Similarly, his three male orderlies were allowed a day off, though usually they stayed on the premises only when there were patients at hand.

He had not yet married, primarily because he had never found the "perfect woman." He could not actually define the perfect woman, if asked, however. He just had the feeling that he would know her when he met her. Something was always not quite right about the many women whom he'd met during his life thus far. What was wrong with any one woman, he simply could not put into words. It was just a feeling that he had. Still, his long hours kept him busy to say nothing of the hours that he spent reading his texts, which were now dog-eared from so many re-readings.

The shock of seeing this three nurses standing before him with their arms completely gone unnerved him and shocked him heavily. For several minutes, he could not tell the difference between the nurses crying before him and images in his mind, so real they were. In a flash, he knew what the form of the perfect woman just had to be.

"Please, Doctor Peng, you must help us! We can't do anything. We're so helpless. What has happened to us?" the nineteen year old Ting pleaded, finally pulling his attention to the present.

"I'm sorry, nurses. It must be the plague. My own feet are demolished. I cannot stand. What is it that you need done right now?" he asked, admiring the beautiful oval face and blue eyes of Ting. It was as if he'd never seen her before now. Perhaps he hadn't.

He crawled after the nurses and helped them with their personal needs, even going so far as to prepare breakfast for them all. Only one orderly was present and after feeding and somehow dressing his nurses, he asked him to take the women back to their homes. "Look, you three will be of no use to me as nurses any longer." While that was the truth, now was the wrong time to say so bluntly. All three wailed uncontrollably, their lives were ruined utterly. Their plight was lost to him, however. He also asked his orderly to visit the other two orderlies and tell them that their services would not be needed until he sent for them directly. Somehow, he had to get by without his three surgical nurses. Something in old Doc Yi's texts came to mind and he felt confident that he could do so.

Later as he sat pondering the images sketched in one of the texts, the orderly returned with Ting. "Doc, her home has burned down. Apparently, her parents knocked over a lamp and the house caught fire. She's got no place to stay, so I brought her back here."

Poor Ting's eyes were bloodshot from crying. Her whole universe had collapsed this eventful day. "Yes, of course, Ting may stay here with me. Go now and see to your family, son. If and when I need you and the other orderlies, I will send for you." He bowed and left Doc Peng with the still sobbing Ting.

"Come Ting, you can stay with me. I will look after your every need now. Come; let's get you back to your bedroom, shall we? How about a nice cup of hot tea? Old Doc Peng will make it better somehow, though I must crawl."

After making and serving them tea, he put Ting to bed. Ideas swarmed in his mind. Well, no one would want surgery for some time, he concluded, not with the plague's effects. A grand plan formed in his mind. Images of precisely what must be done appeared, and he set to work implementing them. Little but planning was done those first two months. Crawling made leaving the complex futile. He was fortunate in that he had a well-stocked pantry, due in part to the sometimes lengthy stays that his recovering patients needed. His feet returned to normal in January and now he put his long, well thought out plans into action.

An unused storeroom became the new bedroom. He equipped it fully, though the mattress lay directly upon the floor, just as in the images in his mind. Besides, no noise coming from this room could be heard much beyond its walls. With the arrival of the handmade leather equipment, Doc Peng was ready to put his plan into action. Having looked after Ting for the past two months, he felt that she had precisely what it took to become his perfect woman. Now he intended to put his plan to the decisive test. Could he make a perfect woman out of Ting? Little did she know what was about to happen to her. Until now, her employer was very carefully attending to her, and she was extremely grateful. Still, she could not fathom what would become of her life now that she was so helpless.

At breakfast the next morning, Doc Peng held her teacup. "Ah, drink up beautiful Ting. This is our finest oolong. I surely don't know when we will be getting more of it. The stores are out of most everything these days. Perhaps this fall the tea plantations will bring us a new supply, do you suppose?"

"Yes, perhaps. Women used to harvest tea leaves. Will the men be able to do that now? We women cannot do anything for ourselves anymore," Ting replied innocently. "You have been so kind to me, Doctor Peng. I wish there were something that I could do in return, but now I can't even assist you with your operations anymore. I am so useless I could just cry."

"Please don't do that, beautiful Ting. Yes, that is now denied you. Still, we must look to the future and find a new path that you may travel. You have your beauty still."

She yawned. "With these huge breasts and armless? Come on, Doctor. You and I both know that no one will ever desire me. I think that you might be doomed to be caring for me for the rest of my life. Such a burden on you, Doctor Peng." She yawned again. "I don't know why I am so tired this morning." She dozed off. The drug produced its desired effect. Carefully, he lifted her up and carried her into his operating room, where he had all his needed tools carefully laid out. This would be his greatest challenge, a major operation without nurses, but he was determined, even driven, to do this. He was about to create the perfect woman out of Ting.

Six hours later, he finished with the last of the bandages and surveyed his work. "Well, that went perfectly! Incredible. Already Ting looks like the perfect woman for me!" He gently lifted her up and carried her into her bedroom, tucking her in, before returning to clean up the operating room. Next, he prepared a light broth for her, laced with a measured amount of painkiller. Then, he carried the tray into her room and sat down beside her bed to wait.

Sometime later, she awoke, sensing massive pains in both her legs. She tried to rise and found her legs were missing just below her knees. "There, there, Ting. I have saved your life. You fell, tore up, and shattered both of your lower legs. Thank god that I was there with you or you might well have died! Here, I have made this recovery broth for you." He put the spoon to her lips, and she accepted it. Her throat felt like she'd swallowed sand! Her mind reeled, trying to take in this awful news. She couldn't remember falling, only blacking out. Mentally, she substituted what must have happened. Somehow she'd fallen, taken a very bad spill. Both legs were shattered. Well, she knew that there was nothing that could be done for a completely shattered bone. She'd assisted the doctor with two such cases already. He'd had to amputate them in both cases. She was about to break down once more when the dose of pain killers hit her, and she drifted into a deep sleep once more, imaging how she must have fallen.

For a week, she drifted in and out of consciousness. Always, she awoke to find the kindly face of Doctor Peng looking down at her. Always, he was there with lifesaving food. He was indeed caring for her every need, she thought, in a sort of muddled fashion. Eventually, he lowered the dosage and allowed Ting to regain full consciousness.

"How are you feeling this fine morning, Most Beautiful Ting?" he asked.

"A bit groggy, but otherwise okay. What am I to do now? My legs are gone! I can barely move at all! Oh Doctor Peng, you should have just let me die!" She began crying.

Wiping her tears for her, he replied, "There, there, Most Beautiful Ting. It will be all right. I have decided that I will marry you so that I may care for all your needs for the rest of our lives. We have enough money to help you with everything. Besides, while you were sleeping, I have been doing some research." He lied; he'd prepared everything long before he attempted the operation. "I believe that we can find a way for you to walk again. There is hope, my beautiful Ting, yes there is."

Ting had no choice at all. She was beyond helpless now and she knew it. Marry her? Well, she dare not say no, for she was completely and utterly dependent upon his kindness now. Her parents were gone, and she had no one else to turn to, even if she could somehow get out of here, which she now could not. She resigned herself into the care of her employer and the man who had and was saving her life. Why he was doing this for her she could not fathom.

By March, her wounds had fully healed and he prepared her for the next step. "I have had these special boots prepared just for you, my beautiful Ting. With them, I do believe that you may be able to walk once more, albeit slowly and carefully." He laced the leather boots tightly against her thighs. At the lower end, three inches of padding lay between her leg and the heavy leather pad, which was sufficiently solid to allow her to stand. He carefully lifted her out of her bed and sat her gently onto the floor. "First, you must learn to keep your balance on the leather pads."

Ting waved her non-existent arms about wildly as she fought to stand upright on her two stubby legs. "I can't! I can't! Don't let go of me!" she cried panic stricken.

"I will never do that, my pretty Tian. You must use your head to help keep your balance now." He also realized that her long hair would be getting in the way, since it was now two feet longer than her body while standing. However, he dare not cut it shorter. No one in Tashien ever did that! Cutting one's hair was tantamount to cutting off one's life or so superstition suggested.

Holding her, he got Ting to take her first clumsy steps, leading her into her new specially prepared bedroom. Here the mattress was on the floor. A special chamber pot had been made to his specifications, one which in time she might be able to use by herself, if only she could learn how to walk in these special boots. He even had a special table, which rose barely six inches from the floor, where they could sit and dine together. As they slowly made their way into the new bedroom, he explained, "I had all this made especially for you, my beloved, beautiful Ting. Once you learn to walk, you will be able to get around our room here on your own. I am certain of it. I read all about such things in my many texts. You will see, my darling Ting."

"You did all this for me?" she asked incredulously.

"Yes, nothing is too fine for my beautiful, charming, loving wife, Ting." What could the poor young woman do now? She gave him a tentative kiss and that evening, they consummated their marriage.

By July 824, Ting was able to get out of bed on her own, to use the chamber pot, and to walk to the low table, where they always dined together. Yes, it took her endless squirming and vast amounts of time to move the few feet to say nothing of the enormous effort on her part to do so, but in the end, she managed these tiny things. She felt victorious in that at least Doctor Peng didn't have to do these things for her. Besides, she knew that she couldn't do anything else for herself but these few, tiny actions. She was completely dependent upon him and she knew it. In turn, she did her best to please him. After all, she reasoned, he was doing everything for her.

Doctor Peng's mind raced these days. Somehow, he felt as if he had written the Doc Yi texts himself! Quite why he had such strange notions, he didn't know. Still, he knew what was on every page as well as many other things. One thing wasn't in the texts — the surgical instrument that he recalled using, one that made surgery extremely easy, handling the healing process at the same time as it performed the cutting. This lifetime, he had to resort to using sterilized saws to cut through the bones. Yet, his mind was filled with memories of the tool that he had used back then. Suddenly, he recalled the two women who had taken it away from him! Their names came to mind unbidden: Bethany and Dita. They were strangers, he remembered. Somehow, they had taken it away from him and killed him, but his body's actual death by their hands remained unseen in his mind, hidden away. By August, he put all such thoughts out of his mind. He now had the perfect woman and his life was complete.

During the last six months, he had to perform some emergency surgeries, once a week at most, for few could afford his services. Dutifully, he trained one orderly to assist him, promoting him to a nurse. Occasionally, he invited a few very close friends over to dine with him and his wife. Soon, many in Zau had heard of the tragic story of Ting and how well she was now getting along. Indeed, she was very beautiful and charming, though she was always soft-spoken when others were present besides Peng, of course. That was because she was always naked. No clothes would fit her, and with clothes on, she could not fend for herself in the slightest.

Early September, a very wealthy man came by his surgery complex. "I am looking for Doctor Peng Ang," he said. Peng noticed that he wore perhaps the finest silken suit that he'd ever seen. His shoes were so shiny that they reflected part of the room in them as the doctor glanced down at them.

"I am he. What brings you to my surgery complex?"

"Allow me to introduce myself. I am Chi Cheng. Perhaps you have heard of me?"

"Forgive me, but I seldom get out. My work consumes my time," Peng replied gracefully.

"I own the Purple Citadel, the finest pleasure palace in all Zau."

"I'm sorry. I've heard of the Purple Citadel, but I have never been there. Just so little time, what with all the surgery," he lied graciously.

"I understand. I have heard that you are perhaps Zau's greatest surgeon."

"Well, I probably am," he answered truthfully, though he had no intention of supporting such a claim. Why bother?

"I am told that you have saved the life of a woman and that she now gets around on her leg stumps."

"Well, yes, she was my nurse. She took a bad fall after the plague came, shattering both her lower legs. They had to come off or she would have died. I saved her and have made her my wife so that I may care for her many needs. Would you like to meet Ting?" He never passed up an opportunity to show off his "perfect woman." His ego would not permit him to do otherwise now.

"I would be delighted to meet her!" He led Chi into her special bedroom and introduced him. After some polite conversation, the two returned to his office. "Indeed, she is a magnificent woman. Now then, I am satisfied of your skills, Doctor Ang. I have need of your services. I am afraid this is something of an emergency. I am prepared to pay you whatever you deem appropriate for your services."

"Oh dear me! An emergency! Why didn't you just say so right away? We've wasted precious time! Time is our enemy, you realize," the startled doctor pointed out.

"Bring your bag. I will take you to her and you can see what the situation actually is. Perhaps I am exaggerating the severity of the problem. Perhaps not. I cannot afford to get this wrong. My carriage awaits us now." After kissing his wife goodbye, he grabbed his small black bag and followed Chi out to his carriage. He was impressed with the carriage! Real gold adorned it. Even the latches were pure gold, hardly practical, the doctor thought.

Five minutes later, they arrived at the Purple Citadel, a huge four-story brick building, ornate in all ways. Golden ornaments were everywhere. The carpeting was plush and purple. However, Doctor Peng had little time to absorb the view, as he rushed to keep up with Chi, who led him to the third floor.

Pausing before a door, he explained, "The patient is my very best kami, Yan Yu. Of late, she has been being obstinate and refusing to service our paying clientele. They pay five hundred gold to bed her, you see. At last, she gave us no other option but to tie up her legs, as you will see. In the past, this has worked out well. However, someone forgot to untie her and hence the problem." He opened the door and escorted the doctor inside.

He got a swift odor of opium, which hung in the air. The room was spacious and beyond any conceivable elegance of the doctor's. Lying on a purple silk bed was a very beautiful young woman of twenty-one. Her legs were crossed behind her back and tied with a thin silk scarf behind her head. In this position, her body lay upon her legs. Only her tied feet could be seen just behind her head. Her rich long black hair lay draped across her massive bosom, partly covering her privates. From her eyes, he knew that she was currently drugged on opium. Well, that was a good idea, he surmised as he saw the problem immediately. Her legs had turned a deep purple; her circulation had been cut off for far too long.

"Well, is this serious or not?" Chi asked softly.

"Yes, most. If you untie her legs, she will be dead within a couple of minutes. The only chance she has to live is if we can amputate both legs immediately," Doctor Peng replied honestly. He'd seen something similar several years back. A man had come in with one leg busted up and his blood flow had been cut off. Unfortunately for him, someone managed to get the blood flow returned to the leg just as they carried him into his surgery center. The man died even before he could operate.

"What will you need? Can you save her?"

"We must very, very carefully get her back to my operating room. If we do not jar her at all, I can remove her legs safely, and she will make a full recovery," he gave his optimistic diagnosis.

"Let's make it so, good doctor," Chi replied, summoning several men. To be on the safe side, Doctor Peng tied two ropes around each leg, as close to her hips as he could reach, forming a tight tourniquet. Carefully, two men carried her down and into the waiting carriage. Five minutes later, they carried her into his surgery center, placing her down on his shiny metal operating table. He insisted that Chi remain in the waiting room, while he hastily prepared for the lengthy surgery at hand.

Six hours later, his capable hands finished bandaging her up. She was alive and doing as well as could be expected. In fact, she'd lost very little blood, a good sign, he thought. He asked Chi to come and inspect his handiwork, and he explained how she would need to be looked after for some time to come. "It will be many weeks before she is fully healed, but she should be just fine in time. Will she be staying here with me?"

"I'd prefer to take her back with me. Can you come by each day to check on her?" Chi asked. Doctor Peng agreed and watched as the two men carried her back out to the waiting carriage. Once they left, he headed to Ting. He'd seldom left her alone for so long. However, she was doing fine, though quite worried about him. Over dinner, he explained what had happened and what he'd done.

"My god, Peng. She will be even more helpless than I am! At least I can sort of move about a very little bit. She won't even be able to do that much."

"I am sure that Chi will take very good care of her. He seems to care deeply for her, just as I do for you, my love."

Early November, Doctor Peng pronounced Yan Yi fully healed. He had made very sure that she had almost no noticeable scarring on her front side. He wanted nothing to distract from the woman's inherent beauty. Chi was extremely pleased with the results as well, paying Doctor Ang a very handsome sum indeed. Peng also noted that Chi kept Yan fairly well doped up on opium, though. Probably that was just as well, he thought. It would keep her trauma reactions minimized. However, he could not help noticing that Yan Yu looked even more like the "Perfect Woman" of his dreams.

Early December, Chi Cheng once more visited the doctor. "How is Yan adapting to her situation?" he asked, setting a cup of the finest oolong before the impeccable Chi.

"Extremely well, doctor. In fact, that is the reason for my visit. She has become the most sought after woman in the Purple Citadel! Men are paying a thousand for the opportunity to spend the evening with her. I would never have guessed that."

Peng smiled; he could not help adding, "Ah, she is the Perfect Woman."

Chi smiled, suspecting that he had the good doctor right where he wanted him. "Yes, that she is, the Perfect Woman." Both men grinned, but for vastly different reasons! Chi saw gold, Peng saw beauty.

"That is the reason for my visit, doctor. I would like your services from time to time. I wish your help in creating more of these absolutely Perfect Women," Chi proposed. No beating around the bush — either the doctor was in or was not. If not, he could be forced into participating. Men always had a weakness that Chi exploited.

"Ah, she certainly is the Perfect Woman. Makes me rather wish I had one too," Doctor Peng admitted. "Okay, count me in. I will leave a legacy of having been the man who created the world's most Perfect Women ever!"

Chi smiled, "Ah, that is superb of you, good doctor. About your fees?"

"If we can do this in a non-emergency situation, how about ten thousand per woman?" Peng suggested, cutting his figure in half from what Chi had paid him to save Lan Yu.

"How about eight thousand, and I give you one of the Perfect Women of your choice, excepting Lan Yu, of course," Chi countered. "No emergencies."

"Agreed. Will it be one for one?" Peng asked.

Chi frowned. What did the doctor mean by this? "You want a woman for each one that you do for me?"

Peng chuckled, "Well, I suspect that would be too much to ask. How about one whenever I am ready for another one, but never more than one per five that I make for you?"

"That is agreeable with me. When can you start?"

"Will tomorrow morning around nine be suitable?" Peng asked. The two men shook hands and Chi left, having made the deal of the century in his opinion. Soon, he would have the most exotic women imaginable with untold gold rolling into his pockets! Already he was the richest man in Zau, but he kept that a closely guarded secret — his ultimate weapon against Overlord Zhou.

On the other hand, Doctor Peng was back in business, performing the same sadistic operations on his patients as he had done in a previous lifetime, one that Dita and I had ended. Aberrations, which are not handled, viewed, and erased, simply continue onward in subsequent lifetimes. Peng was back to his old ways, the mutilation of women according to his own twisted sense of "beauty." Of course, now he needed to work out the details of just how he would be able to look after the new Perfect Women" that he anticipated acquiring.

The next morning precisely at nine, Chi's carriage arrived. As before, his two helpers carried a semi-conscious woman into his operation room. Chi introduced her. "Doctor Peng, this is Zhen Du, she is twenty now. I am afraid that she has had a wee bit too much opium this morning, haven't you, Zhen?"

"More?" the woman moaned a little. Doctor Peng looked her over. As nearly all of Chi's kami women, she had lustrous, shiny black hair that reached her ankles. She had a round face, thick lips, and thick, bushy eyebrows. Like Yan Yu, she was extremely pretty. He didn't ask about her past or if she desired the surgery. Such was irrelevant in his twisted mind. What woman would not wish to become a "Perfect Woman?"

Around three that afternoon, he finished and called Chi to view his newest addition. As before, Doctor Peng had done a superb job with his surgery. "My compliments, Doctor Peng. Will you be making daily visits as you did with Yan Yu?"

"Most definitely. I would never trust my handiwork to other hands. I will be there around ten. You may transport her now," he replied. "When may I expect another to do?"

"Let's give her time to fully heal. Around the first of February, I will have another for you to do plus one for you to keep for yourself."

"Will I get to choose which one I am to keep?" he asked.

"Naturally, Doctor. That would only be fair," Chi replied. He didn't mention that the women would be hooked on opium.

Peng had two months to make his own preparations for his new "Perfect Woman." While the physical preparations were minimal — she could join Ting — his main problem was how to present his acquiring another "wife" without upsetting Ting. He always could hold the threat of removing the remainder of her legs should she object too vehemently, he thought.

As the appointed time drew close, he prepared Ting for what was coming. "My dear, I believe that I will have to rescue another woman who will be in even worse shape than you are, my love."

"How could anyone be in worse shape? I can barely move at all," she asked slightly perplexed.

"I am afraid that she has lost all of her legs. I need to rescue her because she would otherwise be forced to become a prostitute. I cannot stand seeing that. I must rescue her, don't you think, my love?"

"Oh dear god! She is completely helpless. How can she even live that way?"

"Only with someone who is kind, who respects her, and who appreciates her great beauty, such as we, my love. Would you be terribly upset if I have her join us? She is going to need a whole lot of our love, attention, and affection."

Although Ting didn't quite know what he meant, she could only agree. "Oh my yes, she will need all that we can give her. Yes, you must rescue her, Peng, you simply must. I don't know how much I will be able to help her, but I will try."

"I am sure that you will, dearest Ting. We must make her a safe haven here."

As promised, on February 1, 825, Chi arrived with two drugged women. Both were twenty years old, and both had exceptionally pretty faces. Although the opium tended to influence both women noticeably, Peng liked the attitude of Wen De better than Shu Lon and chose to keep Wen. First, he performed the operation on Shu Lon and then allowed Chi to take her back to the Purple Citadel. After fixing a quick meal for himself and Ting, he then put Wen De out and duplicated the operation, finishing late that night. He took special care to make his stitches as tiny as possible, not wanting any ugly scars to mar her exquisite beauty. After making sure that she would not awake during the night, he retired to the bed he shared with Ting.

"Well, my dearest Ting, I have rescued her just in time. However, she has an additional problem; she is addicted to opium."

"Oh dear, that is really bad, isn't it?" Ting replied aghast. What more could be wrong with the poor woman?

"Yes, I am afraid that once she has recovered enough, we will have to get her off opium. I don't think that is anyway to lead a life, being high on drugs, do you?"

"Oh no, not at all. But can you get her off opium? I've heard that it is terribly addictive."

"We will try, my Ting. We will try. I suppose that if we cannot, we will have to make do."

"Where did she get addicted — to opium, I mean?" Ting asked curiously.

"I rescued her from the Purple Citadel. I believe that she was a kami there. They must have gotten her hooked on opium so that she would greatly desire pleasurable sensations," he answered honestly.

"That's so sad. I mean I was a highly skilled nurse before the plague wiped me out and then I took that bad fall. She had a choice in life. Why did she want to become an object of men's lust?" Ting asked even more curious.

"I don't know. Perhaps when she has recovered we can find that out." He gave Ting a loving, passionate kiss, ending her questions.

The next morning, he carried the gorgeous young woman into their special bedroom, placing her on the bed beside Ting, who got her first look at the poor woman. "She's my age, Peng, barely twenty, I guess. She is so helpless, Peng! I mean I am helpless, but she won't be able to even move at all!"

"I know, dear. She is going to need all the loving care that we can give her now. I have to get us more supplies now. If she needs something, pull the cord as usual, love." He was referring to the clever pull cord, which, via a system of pulleys, rang a bell near his operating room, alerting him that Ting needed his assistance. She pulled it with her teeth and head. He added, "She is very pretty, is she not?"

"Yes, but she is so helpless, Peng. What kind of a life can she have now?"

"We must help her have a good one, Ting. Back in an hour." He gave her a kiss and Ting struggled mightily just to get herself up into a sitting position so that she could watch over the unconscious woman. It took her almost herculean efforts to move herself about, but she realized that poor Wen De would be unable to move at all! Tears trickled down her cheeks as she watched the woman lying there. Unfortunately, she had no way to wipe her own tears unless she fell back down on her bed face down. If she did that, it would take her at least a half hour to regain her sitting position. She at least could do that, but poor Wen De would be unable even to do that. She cried again.

Over the next week, Doctor Peng slowly weaned Wen De from the painkillers, though he kept her opium intake about what Chi had been giving her. Only then did she finally regain sufficient consciousness to realize what had happened to her. "Miss Wen De, I am Doctor Peng and this is my darling wife, Ting. We have rescued you from the clutches of the Purple Citadel, where Chi had your legs removed."

"Oh dear god no!" Wen shrieked as the stark realization of her new condition slammed home into her consciousness. Once she calmed down a little and Peng had wiped her wet face, she murmured, "What happened to me? Where am I? I can't move at all now."

"Chi wanted you to be like his Yan Yu, a sex slave, as I understand it. I managed to get you out of his clutches."

"Please, kill me. I can't live like this. I can't do anything now. It is beyond hopelessness. Please, just kill me."

"Oh dear me no, most beautiful Wen. You are gorgeous and so full of life. You are young. Ting and I will be looking after your every need now. Ting used to be my nurse before the plague came. Then she took a bad fall and shattered her lower legs. Still, she and I have found ways for her to live. We are married now. We will make sure that you are well cared for and lack for nothing," Peng explained.

"I lack my legs and arms! I can't move at all. Please, put me out of my misery. Oh! I need a hit. Opium, please, please, I beg you! I can't stand this any longer."

"Oh my. So soon? How do you normally get your opium?" Peng asked.

"A pipe, please. I must have it now. Please, I crave that release. Please, please," she begged him, forgetting all else.

Unfortunately, Peng lit up a pipe and held it for her to inhale. The fumes filled their small bedroom, and both he and Ting received the effects as well. Soon, sexual urges drove all three of them. Satisfied, the three lay beside each other. "I promise you, Wen, that I will look after your every need now. I will marry you as well." He rambled on, still a bit under the influence of the opium. He also realized that he would have to find an alternative way of giving her a fix or else risk getting addicted himself. However, perhaps that would not be so bad, he thought. Ting did seem to enjoy it immensely, he observed.

When he left the room, he whispered to Ting, "If she needs it, please see if you can find some way to pleasure her. I think that Wen will need it badly — the aftereffects of the opium," he added. He didn't say what he really had in mind, however. If Ting could get used to pleasuring her somehow, perhaps Wen could reciprocate, and the two women could pass the time far better when he was not present.

Two months went by swiftly as Wen healed from the surgery. Peng built her a special sloped chair so that she could sit up at a forty-five degree angle during the day. This she readily accepted as she then felt more like a person again. Still, she continued to need an opium fix at least once a day, followed by her intense demands for sexual pleasuring, which both he and Ting found that they simply could not refuse her. She begged and pleaded until they at last yielded to her desires. What else could they do? The woman could experience little else in life now, Ting justified.

In April and May, Chi brought another two women for Doctor Peng to handle. Both were barely nineteen and quite pretty, though neither had the ravishing looks of Wen De, he thought. Qian Ni Lun and Mei Fan he handled nicely. Later on in July, he brought in two more, once more giving Peng his choice of the two women. This time he chose the lovely Fang Zu over Juan Hong, primarily because Fang was a year older than Juan. Once more, he explained to Ting and Wen that he was again about to rescue another woman from the clutches of the Purple Citadel.

When he added Fang Zu to his collection, he unwittingly sealed his own doom. Already, Ting was becoming suspicious. Bit by bit, Wen was remembering what had happened to her, as she gradually received lower and lower doses of the opium. By early September, Fang had recovered fully from the surgery and was now also being heavily pleasured and slowly being taken off opium. Peng was extremely proud of his three "Perfect Women" and spent long hours each day with them, tending to their near constant needs. Always he left them with their hair nicely brushed out and draped over their privates. Still he had given no thought to dressing their naked bodies, for such would hide their perfect forms, he thought.

At the Purple Citadel, Chi Cheng had problems of his own now. He found that his six exotic women required constant care, constant watching. True, when their services were requested, he made a fortune. However, with the iron coins now in circulation, all the gold pretty much dried up, and so few could afford the women's affections. All around him, he saw signs of a financial collapse, which would ruin his lucrative business. He did not ever intend to accept the vulgar iron coins as payment for the kami's special services, but he did accept them for the main floor general entertainment; that he had to do, but certainly not for his six special women, his perfectly exotic women. Still, their care began to cost him more than the income that they produced. In truth, he realized that he had been swayed by some sadistic impulses, but for the life of him, he could not say from where these cravings had come. This bothered him, but he would soon have a far greater worry. Unknown to him, Fang Zu was married.

Before the plague struck, Fang Zu was a rising star in the Imperial Ballet. Her grace and beauty brought the traditional Tashien dances alive as never before. Just eighteen, many predicted that this young star would become the most famous dancer in history. Nobleman Kang Zu, then only twenty himself, had fallen in love with her and she, he. While Fang was highly focused on her art, Kang was just the opposite.

The eldest son of the wealthy Zu family, he had yet to find his niche. Most claimed he was still sewing his wild oats. As a youngster, his father had sent him off to get training in the martial arts, thinking the regime would help the young boy keep a level head. He was always playing tricks on nearly everyone. Unfortunately, though he demonstrated skill in the martial arts, his heart was not in it, and he dropped out. He took up horse training and breeding at fourteen, raising several prize horses, but gave that up within two years, though he still kept his horses even today. He tried his hand in the performing arts next as an actor. Again, he demonstrated a knack for getting into the persona at hand, though many claimed that he was merely a con artist, playing tricks on others. That's when he first met Fang, who was then barely sixteen. He fell in love with her as he watched her gracefully dance. Never had he seen such life, such vitality in these traditional dances. He was hooked and proceeded to court the young and beautiful Fang.

At first, she wanted nothing to do with him. Her friends claimed that he was nothing but a con artist. She could do much better than Kang. Still, he persisted. A year before the plague struck, her parents ran into a bit of financial difficulties. Kang stepped in without being asked and paid off her parent's debt, close to twenty thousand gold. When she asked why he did that, he replied, "It's only money. Your parents are good folks. They just got a rotten deal, that's all." After that, she took more of an interest in him, wondering if there was more to Kang than a mere con artist.

Her parents ran a book publishing company. That gave Kang another idea: he would become a writer. Four months before the plague struck, his first action novel was published and became an instant hit. Nonstop action kept his readers enthralled, unable to put the book down. Elated with his success as a writer, he proposed to Fang who accepted. A month before the plague began, they were married in a lavish ceremony and moved into a new estate located on the northern edge of Zau, where he had sufficient pasture for his six horses. Luck or foresight, he could never decide which, but their panty was well stocked when the plague struck, devastating both of them. "You can still dance, my dearest love," he continued to encourage her during those first two months.

In December, he finally was able to make a trip to check on his parents and hers. At once, he saw the danger in driving Fang through the streets in his carriage. Looters and rioters roamed the streets here in the wealthier section of Zau, though some Imperial Soldiers did attempt to run them off. That fateful day, they discovered to their horror that both of their families had been slain by the rioters and their family homes looted! After that, Kang refused to allow Kang out of their house. He purchased a number of weapons to protect their estate, and he also handled the funeral arrangements. Later, when the Banca del Dio reopened, he handled their affairs, setting up an account for Fang, transferring her parents' funds into hers. Likewise, he did the same with his parents. Between them, they had over five million gold in the bank, enough to survive anything, both concluded. Neither knew how wrong that would prove.

Conditions deteriorated rapidly. Looters attempted to invade their estate and Kang fought them off using his long guns. In the process, he was also shot and took a bad fall. Poor Fang was helpless to assist him, but he managed to get himself to a close friend who was a doctor. With his shoulder wound bandaged, he returned home, but his strained back kept him nearly bedridden for several months. Kang also had several friends who had joined the Church of God, swearing that their therapy was more of a miracle. As the chaos grew, he wanted to visit the church and find out for himself, but his back prevented him from doing so. When he had recovered, he found that well over half of the remaining wealthy, the entire Olin Masters Academy, and Church of God had simply vanished! Their academy was empty!

This so unnerved him that he spent all his time when away from the estate trying to find out where they had gone. By now, Overlord Bin Zhou restored some semblance of order, and the chaos seemed to subside for a time. Still Kang refused to allow Fang out of their fortified estate, and he, himself, left only when he had to purchase more supplies and check to see if anyone had any news about the Church of God or where the Olin Masters had gone.

Early July 825, disaster struck the Zu's. He had received word that an acquaintance had news of the Church of God and the Olin Masters. Later Kang cursed himself for having left Fang alone for several hours that day. Still, he finally heard the news that he had been seeing for nearly two years. He learned of the mass exodus of the wealthy, the Olin Masters, and the church. They were now in Nan Yan far to the south. Apparently, they were surviving extremely well. Reports of miracles were now coming out of there. Somehow, women of the Church of God were regaining their arms, undoing the effects of the plague! Armed with the best news ever, he dashed home to tell Fang and found her gone, abducted. Signs of a struggle led from the front room all the way to the main doors. Crushed, he frantically dashed to neighboring houses, begging for any clues about what had happened.

One elderly man told him that three of Chi Cheng's thugs had come and taken Fang away in an expensive carriage, most likely to the Purple Citadel. Crushed, he returned to his estate and collapsed on the couch. Running his hands through his hair, he tried to think of ways that he could rescue his wife. At last, he decided to visit the Purple Citadel and see if he could at least see her there. Somehow, he had to find where she was being kept. Was she being forced into becoming a kami? That notion disgusted him.

Shocked with what he saw when he entered, Kang knew that finding her quickly was not an option. The place was heavily guarded. Rightly so. The sheer amount of gold fixtures was incredible. To get into the place in proper fashion he had to dress in his finest suit. He persisted, visiting it every day, spending as many hours there as he could. At last, he realized that he was really casing the place. He had to check out every kami, which took him well over a week. She was not among them. Then he learned of the exotic kami of the third floor, and he took a chance and spent a thousand for a visit with one.

To say that he was shocked when he was led into the main meeting room was an understatement! Five strange looking, sloped, heavily cushioned chairs on rollers faced him. Sitting in them were five young women, rather what was left of them! None had any arms or legs! Their lush long hair draped demurely over their massive bosoms, reaching the floor. The faint odor of opium hung in the air, and he could tell all five were under its influence. Each woman was particularly attractive; their faces seemed angelic. Chi explained to the shocked Kang, "Here are the exotic beauties. Look them over and take your pick. You then wheel her into the plush bedroom, lift her onto the satin and silk sheets, and enjoy her wiles. The assistant here will watch the time for you and let you know when your two hours with her are done. If you wish an opium pipe as well, let him know. I assure you that these women live only to satisfy your sensual needs." He bowed and left Kang still staring wide-eyed at the five women, all of whom seemed to be moaning for his touch.

Kang picked Yan Yu and pushed her chair into the bedroom. Never had he seen such an elegant room. Even the chamber pot was made from gold. "Lift me on the bed and drape my hair over you, please hurry. I need your touch, please. Touch me. Rub me. I need it so badly," she whispered from her opium daze. No way was Kang going to have intercourse with her, but he did as she asked, giving her a pleasureful time, which he noted did satisfy her cravings. He left her almost asleep on the bed. He was sick at his stomach. Where was Fang? Had this wicked, sadist done this to Fang as well? Where was she? Think man!

Later as he was leaving, Chi joined him. "Did you find them absolutely exquisite?"

"Well, yes, most unusual." He had a flash of an idea. "Say, I only saw five of them. Do you have more to choose from?"

Chi smiled, "Actually, in a couple of months another beauty will be ready to service you. Right now, she is healing."

"Would it be possible to see what she looks like? I mean a taste of what's to come? I have half a mind to visit these women frequently." Kang played Chi like a harp. Money. Thus far, he'd seen no other man come to the third floor during his many visits checking out the working kami. "Would a hundred allow me a sneak peak, so to speak?" He dangled a money pouch and Chi accepted.

"Yes, your desires are my command." After counting the coins, he led Kang into a side room where Juan Hong was heavily sedated, heavily bandaged, recovering from her surgery two weeks ago.

"Ah, you have excellent tastes in women, Chi. Surely, she will be an incredible addition to the five," Kang replied, relieved that she was not Fang.

During another few trips to the Purple Palace, Kang dropped some gold and acquired a little more information. "Say, I heard that Chi brought in two women, but only one is on the third floor. Where is the second lovely young woman?" For a hundred gold, he learned that Chi had given her to his associate. Now Kang had to find the associate, which proved even more difficult, since no one would answer that query.

As he continually watched the comings and goings of the Purple Citadel, he spotted a man carrying a doctors bag entering around ten each morning, leaving within a half hour. Now he realized that some doctor would also have to be involved, preforming the abysmal surgery for Chi. Perhaps he was the associate. Kang followed the man and discovered where Doctor Peng Ang lived and worked. For days, he discretely watched the surgery center. He saw no one entering or leaving, save the good doctor, who always locked up when he left. The man certainly had a low volume practice, he thought.

One day as he watched and saw Doctor Peng leave for the Purple Citadel, he decided to see if he could break in and have a look around. As he was contemplating this, he realized that if his wife was inside and had undergone this evil, sadistic surgery, he could not just take her away with him. Rather she would need constant medical attention until her wounds healed. He had seen this doctor's work and saw that the five women bore no visible scaring, except on their backsides; he must be competent at his work, albeit sadistic and wicked. "If she is in there, I have to wait until she has recovered before I rescue her," he whispered resolutely to himself. He knew he would be unable to care for her wounds. He had no medical training at all.

His youthful pranks finally paid off. It took him less than a minute to pick the lock on the doctor's door. Quietly, he stepped inside. He went from room to room, discovering the operating room, the waiting area, and the recovery room. Then, he found a locked pair of side rooms and listened at the door. Inside one, he heard two unfamiliar voices talking, but could not make out what they were saying.

He heard nothing behind the second door. Steeling himself for the worst, he picked that lock and peered inside. It was all he could do to maintain his self-control. There lay his wife, the lovely Fang, heavily bandaged. Her legs were gone and she was unconscious, probably sedated with painkillers, he thought. He fought hard from rushing inside and taking her away with him. Only with every ounce of will power did he manage to pull back and relock the door. A minute later, he stepped outside and locked the main door. He had only crossed the street when the doctor's carriage came down the street. It had been a narrow escape, but now he knew the worst had happened and where she was. He went home a distraught, destroyed man.

After downing four dark stouts, he cursed, "Those two must pay for what they have done to Fang. Hell, and to the other women as well! I will make them pay, somehow I will!" He downed another stout.

The next day, slightly hung over, he began to work out his options. No way could he attack and kill Chi, the man was inside a fortress and heavily guarded. The doctor, well he could be handled easily and Fang rescued when her body had healed. The mad doctor would pay dearly for what he had done to these women, Kang so swore. But how to make Chi pay? Now that was the real question, for undoubtedly it was Chi who had abducted the women and probably paid the doctor to perform the surgery.

Then his mind focused on what Fang's life would be, once he rescued her. He bawled like a baby for over an hour before it suddenly struck him! If he could get her to the Church of God in Nan Yan and if the rumors he'd heard were true that the women there got their arms back, at least she would not be completely helpless! "That's it! I have to get them all to Nan Yan! I must!" he yelled to the ceiling.

With that bit of hope returning, he began to focus on how to make Chi pay. He knew that the only thing that was important to Chi was money. His revenge had to center around relieving Chi of his wealth, but how? Ah, all his years of being something of a con artist had not been wasted. He began working out a clever, devious plan.

That afternoon, he put his plan into action. First step, get a job at the Banca del Dio. With his talents, that was easily achieved. While the work was terribly boring, he spent that first week learning how the bank handled funds. He paid particular attention to the transfer of funds process and asked numerous questions, under the guise of a learning new assistant, which for all purposes he was now.

That evening he visited the Purple Citadel as was his usual wont. During the evening, Chi came up to him. "Are you ready for another visit to the exotic floor, Most Honorable Kang?"

"Ah, this evening, I am content here watching the lovely kami and enjoying the marvelous music. Say, let me know when that new beauty is ready for work. I'd like to be her very first customer, if you know what I mean," he said coyly.

Chi winked and smiled. "Your wish is my command, Most Honorable Kang. It is likely to be another month. Surely, you do not wish to wait that long before your next visit. Do you not find them most exotic?"

Kang realized something. Chi was attempting to induce him into spending another thousand gold. Well, what with all those worthless iron coins circulating these days, he could see why. "I've promised myself to wait for the lovely Juan — she is so incredibly beautiful. Surely, many of these other fine honorable men here will partake of the exotic women; surely, they will. If not, well, perhaps I could be persuaded." He was pumping Chi for information.

"Business is off. The iron coins. Worthless trinkets. So few of us have real money these days. It is becoming impossible to run a business in Zau anymore," Chi replied.

"Absolutely. Iron coins. Who ever heard of such a thing? Worthless utterly. Just between you and me, I really don't see how you can afford to keep those exotic women. Their constant needs must be costing you a fortune. But then, you do get ample rewards from us customers, right?"

"Oh yes, a fortune. Had I known how costly their upkeep would be, I might not have ever entered into this. With these ridiculous iron coins, I'm losing so much money with these exotic women that I wish I'd never gotten into them," Chi admitted, testing the waters with Kang.

"I couldn't agree with you more, Most Honorable Chi. I'm in the horse business. It costs a fortune to raise a high quality mare or stallion. Now I'm to sell them for pieces of worthless iron? Hardly. Yet, what can we do? I suppose that your situation with these incredible women could be far more easily handled than my horses," Kang set him up.

"Indeed, I see your point, Most Honorable Kang. Selling a fine horse for worthless pieces of iron — that must really hurt."

"Yes, so I'm not selling them. I have enough gold to ride this downturn out, you see. I will not part with my horses for iron coins. You know, perhaps you could sell your exotic women for gold."

"You've taken the words right out of my mind, Most Honorable Kang. I have given this considerable thought. While I could just kill those beauties and eliminate my overhead, such would pain me deeply to do so. If only I could find someone who would swap gold for the women, then I would be out from under the dung pile. I don't suppose that you would be interested in making such a trade?" Chi felt out Kang.

"Well, you know how much I do treasure them. Yet, I do not know what must be done to care for their needs. Perhaps if I could be educated into the proper methods of assisting them, I would be in a better position to make an offer."

"Of course, if you would like to purchase them all from me, I would provide all necessary instruction and guidance. I'll even throw in all their needed physical things, such as their specially built chairs. Would you consider ten thousand a woman?"

"Incredible. Only ten thousand? Now Most Honorable Chi, that *is* a bargain! Are you sure that you would not be taking a severe loss with such a price? I would feel terrible if you were," Kang sympathized.

"Oh dear me, no, no that would be a fair price as far as I am concerned. Are you willing then to entertain purchasing all six at one time?" Chi asked, scarcely believing his luck this evening.

"Sixty thousand is a mere pittance for me. Yes, I would only consider purchasing all the exotic women. I do have a fine estate where their unique needs can be fully handled and where they and I can achieve the ultimate in pleasures." Kang offered Chi his hand, and the men shook hands, sealing the deal among gentlemen. "Shall we meet at the Banca del Dio tomorrow, say at eight in the morning? I can have the funds transferred to your account at once."

"That would be most generous of you. I would point out that the latest addition, Juan, shouldn't be moved for another four weeks, according to the doctor."

"Perfect. That will give me time to learn how to care for them from you and to make the necessary arrangements at my estate. Unless they require very unusual things, a month should give me more than enough time to make advance preparations before they move from here. Should I give you some donation for their upkeep for this coming month?"

"No, that is the very least I can do for you for coming to my rescue. Sometimes we do make mistakes in life. This has been perhaps the worst mistake that I've made."

"Only because of the drastic downturn of our economy, Most Honorable Chi. Iron coins will destroy everything, mark my words. Now is the time to invest in gold, I'm sure of it," Kang replied.

The next morning, Kang met Chi at the Banca del Dio and submitted the financial transaction. After shaking hands and promising to visit the citadel this evening, the two parted ways. Once out of sight, Kang walked two blocks to where he'd left his carriage, climbed inside, and donned his bank employee disguise. Then, he drove to the staff lot and entered the building to begin his day's work. He was scheduled to begin at nine and took a moment to clandestinely examine the transfer paperwork. After memorizing Chi's account number, he headed to his new work desk to begin work. Later when no one was looking, he looked up Chi's account password and memorized that. Even later that day, he stole a look at Chi's account summary, while filing another person's summary to which he had to add another hundred that the man deposited. He grinned.

Later that evening, he got an education from Chi's exotic women assistants. He never dreamed of just how much care each woman had to have! Now he saw that just caring for the needs of these six women would be a full time job! No wonder Chi wanted to divest himself from them. Still, he was resolute, determined to get all these brutalized women safely to Nan Yan where he hoped and prayed the Church of God could somehow, someway, by some magic give them arms again.

As the days progressed, so did his plans. He discarded taking them overland by wagon. The journey would be long and hazardous. The only real option was to go by river and that would require a boat, a dedicated boat. To that end, he purchased a boat under an assumed name and wearing a different disguise. Bit by bit, he began outfitting the river craft to suit his needs, adding plenty of soft bedding, food supplies, a charcoal stove, and so on. Then he uncovered a fatal flaw in going by river. The incessant rocking and rolling of the boat would knock the women off their special chairs. They were helpless to do the slightest thing to prevent it from happening. He sold the boat and began working out an overland route.

As the sparrow flies, he had just over twelve hundred miles to travel and one major river to cross, the Lian River. Before the plague, he might even have considered such a route, but not now, not with the Imperial Army gone and chaos running the land. No, his problem was overlords. These power hungry men now controlled the land, raiding and taking what they wanted. Overland travel was anything but safe. Just beyond the mighty city of Zau lay the lands controlled by Overlord Yi, a vicious man rumors suggested. He had to avoid the overlord's soldiers.

He ruled out stopping at inns along the way because of the exotic nature of the women would only beg for trouble and stares, maybe worse. Besides, the main roads would be patrolled by the overlords. No, he would have to travel by the back roads. He sighed; he knew that meant camping out each night. Further, that also meant he dared not stop for food supplies in towns. His women companions would attract far too much attention. As despicable as so many men had become, he dared not gamble that none would try to take advantage of the helpless women, who could now do nothing for themselves to fend off unwanted advances. The more that he saw just how pitiful these women's daily lives would be the more that he knew that he had to get some kind of justice for the women. His resolve hardened further.

The next day, he purchased a long wagon and equipped it with mattresses on which the women could lay. As he was picking up the wagon, he saw a handwritten notice posted on the side of the building. It was a missing person notice. Qian Ni Lun had disappeared several months ago. A reward was offered for any news of her. Suddenly it hit Kang hard. All these women must have families or other loved ones who missed them! After driving the long bed wagon home, he rode over to the indicated address: Lun's Weaving. He entered the small storefront and found only one man about his age there, sitting at a floor to ceiling loom, weaving. A number of tapestries hung on display. He rose. "May I help you?" the weaver asked.

"Yes, I saw your notice about a missing Qian Ni Lun."

"Oh my god! Have you seen her? What can you tell me of her? She is my sister!" Lines of intense worry creased the otherwise pale face.

"Yes, I am in the process of rescuing her. Please sit down. This is going to be awful news for you, but she is alive at least," Kang replied. How do you tell someone that their sister is now a mere head and torso? As he related the news as gently as he could, when he described her, the twenty-one year old weaver completely broke down.

"There is hope for her yet, Cheng. I have heard that in Nan Yan, the Church of God can restore women's arms, undoing the plague. I'm planning to take all the women there and do whatever is needed to get their arms restored. If that happens, she will not be so utterly hopeless." He outlined his plan of overland travel. Of course, Cheng asked why not go by riverboat, since that would be faster and safer. Soon, he too realized the futility of that; the women would be unable to handle the boat's motions.

"May I come with you?" Cheng asked when Kang had finished. "You say that you will need one wagon to carry the women; surely you'll need a second one to carry the supplies. Please, you must let me come and help care for my sister!"

"Of course you may. Truly, I do need a second wagon. I will purchase it tomorrow and together, we can outfit it with what we think we will need. Do not worry about money, I have plenty to spare," Kang pointed out. He rightly assumed that the weaver had little. What he didn't know then was that Cheng was an excellent planner. Soon, he left the outfitting of their supplies entirely up to the weaver. Meanwhile, he had another vital mission: find out if the other women had any family as well.

Two days later, he visited the husband of Yan Yu, the first woman to have been mutilated well over a year ago. Jian Yu listened to the tale of what had happened to his kami wife before he replied. "Serves her right. I should never have married a kami. Worst mistake of my life. Well, good riddance to her, I say. Let her figure out how to care for her own needs now. She's all yours. I wash my hands of her!" Kang left the man totally shocked. How could a husband so desert his wife when she was in such dire need? He shook his head sadly; he couldn't fathom why Chi or Peng had done what they had done to the women either. Insanity. That could be the only reason.

A few days later, he knocked on the door of another estate that was now quite rundown. Windows were broken; the door was half off its hinges. The place looked deserted, but soon a small figure peered out at him through the crack of the half-opened door. His eyes met those of a small boy. "Hello son. Did a Mei Fan live here?"

"Where is she? She's my sister," the ten year old boy relied very softly. His voice trembled; he was very much afraid.

"I am rescuing her soon. May I come in?" he asked politely. "I won't hurt you."

"You aren't going to take me away, are you? You aren't going to shoot me?" the fearful boy asked.

"No, I most certainly am not going to hurt you. Are your parents here?"

The lad opened the door, which made loud creaking noises, threatening to fall off its hinges. As soon as he stepped inside, the odor of rotting flesh stung his nose. He pointed to his parents who had been dead for some months now, shot in their heads, execution style, Kang thought. "The men did this when they took my sister away," the boy whispered. Kang chatted with the lad for a time, learning that he was called An Fan and was ten years old now. He had been surviving on what food had been in the home, but was now catching and eating rats. Kang gathered up what was salvageable of the boy's things and took him home with him.

Hours later, cleaned up, in fresh clothes, and well fed, An's fears began to subside and be became more talkative, though his voice was always quite soft. "Mei doesn't have legs anymore? She lost her arms in the plague, when my feet were broken. My feet got fixed up, but her arms didn't. If she doesn't have her arms or legs, how can she do anything?"

"She can't, An. She is going to be depending upon you and me to help her with everything. Are you big enough to help your sister when she most needs it?"

"Oh yes. I am big now. I will help her. When can I see her?" he asked eagerly.

Several days later, Kang was able to locate the fiancé of Shu Lon. Hu Die was a gunsmith, and he too had put up missing person posters around his area of the huge city. Kang had discovered his posters quite by accident. He intended to purchase a supply of long guns and ammunition for the trip and had come to the gunsmith shop. As he arrived, he spotted the posters and recognized the name.

"Yes, Shu Lon is my fiancé. She is twenty and a most beautiful young woman. Even though the plague cost her her arms, we were still planning on getting married this month. Alas, she vanished without a trace months ago." He explained what all he had learned, before asking, "So how do you know about my Shu?"

"This is going to be truly hard on you. Please, sit down and let me explain," Kang said sympathetically. "She is alive, but. . ." As gently as he could, he outlined what had happened to his fiancé — at least as much as he knew for a fact, filling in the missing pieces as he guessed they must have happened.

"Oh dear god! Cut off her legs? Damn! Damn those bastards to hell! I will kill them myself!" Hu's anger rushed outward like a volcano and Kang knew enough to let the man vent. After Hu calmed down a little, Kang outlined his grand plan and the faint hope of salvation that the Church of God held for the women, if only he could get them there to Nan Yan.

"I'm coming with you!" Hu declared, not even allowing for a no on Kang's part. "I will supply lots of guns and ammunition. "Tell me your plan. When do we strike? When do we leave?" The man's anger sublimated into the arena of action. He was ready to leave yet that night! "Can I see her tonight?"

"We must wait a bit longer. Two more women are not yet fully healed from the sadistic surgery. Only when the doctor releases them can we make our move. Until then, it is best that we make our preparations. We must leave the very night that I rescue them. Much in the way of justice will depend upon our leaving yet that night." Kang then put Hu in touch with Jian. Between them, they continued making the many preparations and took over looking after An, giving him chores that he could manage. Meanwhile, Kang continued to don his disguise and work at the Banca del Dio. Further, he used the bank's resources to see if he could locate the families of the other women.

Alas, one by one, he scratched them off his list. The other women's parents and close relatives had perished, either during those first two awful months or from the street violence that had ensued during the last two years. At least Kang was able to transfer all of those family funds into new accounts for the women. He sent their funds down to the Banca del Dio in Nan Yan.

On September 1, 825 when Kang dropped by the Purple Citadel after work, he discovered that the time was at hand. Chi grinned broadly, "Doctor Peng has finally given us the okay on Juan. She is ready for service now. Her wounds have healed fully. I must admit that there is even less scarring on her backside than the others. I believe the doctor is getting more skilled with each operation. How soon will you like to take possession?"

"Will tomorrow evening be acceptable?" Kang asked. The two men chatted a bit. Since they were hooked on opium and desperately needed four fixes a day, Chi sold Kang a three-month supply for the women.

"I will have the opium and the women ready for you tomorrow evening. You will need to purchase nothing to attend to their needs. However, I will tell you this. Make sure that they get their opium doses regularly. If you do not keep them high, strange things happen with them, most unpleasant things. Such is not the result of the opium. I am not talking about withdrawal symptoms. Rather it is something strange and weird that happens to them. I've never seen the likes of it before. Yet, if you keep them on opium regularly and, vitally important, you keep them well pleasured, it keeps the wildness at bay completely."

Kang had no idea what Chi was talking about, but carefully marked his words. He knew that he would somehow have to get the women off opium, but this other strange thing? Well, he'd just have to deal with it when it appeared in the women. He promised Chi that he would take the very best of care with the exotic women, which seemed to please Chi. Kang detected that Chi was reticent to be losing his women, but the economics of their keep precluded keeping them any longer.

Later that night, he dropped by his compatriots. "Tomorrow evening, the rescue begins. I will take the long bed wagon and return with them. After we get them here to my place, we need to leave shortly after that, so have the other wagons ready to go."

"But what about justice? I want to kill those who did this evil," Hu protested.

"As I have been saying all along, leave that to me. When I arrive with the women, justice will have been completed. Trust me. I will explain fully once we are beyond the city's edge and on our way.

Trust me a little longer, Hu." Hu swallowed his anger, figuring that if he did not like Kang's justice, he could obtain it for himself later on.

At the Banca del Dio the next morning, Kang set to work implementing his long planned revenge against Chi. The man had indeed been behind perhaps the most sadistic actions against women that Kang had ever heard, but he also took extreme measures to see that the exotic women were well cared for. Moreover, he had arranged to give them to another instead of just having them killed. Kang reasoned the man had earned the right to not be killed for his actions. Instead, Kang intended to make the man ultimately responsible for these women's lives in the future. It was probably just a pipe dream that they would somehow be able to have their arms back. No, they would need constant care for the rest of their lives and that would cost a substantial sum of money. Money would be Chi's penance for his evil actions.

Transfers of one hundred thousand or more were very carefully monitored by the bank. Smaller amounts were routinely handled. He set to work. As of this day, Chi had one hundred ten million gold in his account. By the end of the day, he would have barely five million left, most of which would soon be spent in wages and other monthly expenses of Chi's businesses. He'd carefully analyzed Chi's spending patterns and knew just how much to leave so that all current and near future transactions would occur without any problems. He even left a five percent cushion as a margin of error.

He opened up nine fictitious accounts, locating them in Shansee. Into these, he made numerous deposits of blocks of fifty thousand gold. Then, he opened up nine new accounts in Nan Yan in the names of the nine women, using their names as the account and 4me as their passwords. Again, he made numerous transfers from the fictitious accounts into these nine real ones. Then, he placed these into the ready to go bag, resealing it when no one was looking. This bag contained the transfers that had already been approved and were about to be picked up by riverboat courtier, taken down to Shansee, and from there off to the rest of the world.

Next, he prepared fake transfer papers, placing the one hundred five million gold into another fake account. He marked those as completed, borrowing the official stamp from another clerk whom he cleverly distracted for a time. These papers he then placed into Chi's official account folder. Thus, whenever anyone came to look at what happened to Chi's funds, they would retrieve these fake papers. If they tried to locate the funds, they'd find none. Additionally, Kang added a safeguard. Faking Chi's handwriting, he inserted a letter of explanation, allegedly addressed to the Banca's president. In the letter, he explained that he was sending this money to the nine women whom he had brutally mutilated, outlining in detail what he had done to these women. Thus, if Chi attempted to get to the bottom of his missing funds, both he and the Banca's personnel would see the letter admitting his guilt and complicity. Kang figured that might just be enough to force Chi to withdraw any protest on his part, if only to keep that incriminating letter from becoming widely known.

After he left the Banca, he handed a note and a gold coin to a small boy. The lad would be delivering the sad note to the Banca when it reopened in the morning. It announced that Bo Dhu had been found murdered in the streets last night and would not be coming to work any longer. Back at home, after changing out of his Banca disguise, he donned his fancy suit, stuffing a special bag into the long bed wagon. He drove to the Purple Citadel and parked in the back alleyway. It was dark when he finally entered the front doors, where Chi was patiently awaiting him.

After some last minute words, Chi had his men carry the naked women sitting in their special chairs down to the wagon. Then they carried down numerous blankets and covered the women. Kang was grateful that Chi had taken the precaution of giving them all a heavier dose of opium. All were in dreamland and oblivious to what was going on with their bodies. Chi's men then carried down the bags containing the needed opium, the women's hairbrushes, and few other possessions. At last, the two men shook hands. "Best of luck with your new harem, Kang."

Kang smiled, "Yes, I have the best of this deal. Such fine young women who only know how to please a man. I will be in heaven." Chi looked extremely pleased, confident that he had disposed of the women in a humane fashion. Kang climbed aboard the wagon had headed off. Once well beyond the Purple Citadel, he stopped and changed clothes once more, donning the disguise of an elderly man. After making sure the women were covered and out of sight, he drove the wagon on over to Doctor Peng Ang's surgery complex.

He picked the lock and stole inside. A startled Peng looked up at the stranger who suddenly appeared in his kitchen. "What? Who are you? I thought I had locked the door. Please come back tomorrow." His voice sounded both surprised and annoyed. He was preparing dinner for his three captives, though he called them his wives. As anticipated, the presence of an elderly man did not unduly alarm the doctor. One swift martial arts move, and the doctor was out cold on the kitchen floor. Kang tied him up and placed him on the man's operating table in the next room. Now he went in search of the captive women.

He found them in the locked room where he had previously heard two women conversing. There was his beloved wife, sitting in one of those special chairs. Alongside of her was Wen De. Sitting on the mattress was Ting, who still had her upper legs. They were encased in strange leather booties. "Who are you?" Ting asked. The other two women barely glanced at him. Oh, how Kang's heart ached to see Fang so utterly destroyed.

"I am here to rescue my wife and the rest of you." Only now did Fang raise her head, recognizing his voice.

"Kang? Is that you?" Fang spoke up, the tiniest spark of hope in her otherwise apathetic tone.

"Yes, my love. I'm rescuing you at last. I'll have you out of here shortly."

"But Doctor Peng said that these women had taken bad falls and he had to remove their crushed legs," Ting protested.

"Don't be silly. He is a sadist. He cut them off for his own pleasure and for money. I have a wagon full of other women who Chi Cheng of the Purple Citadel paid Peng to cut off their legs for him. You have been lied to, Ting."

Poor Ting. All along, she had buried all her many doubts about what Peng had been telling her. Her own nurse training she had ignored, wanting to believe him. The alternative was too shocking to believe or to bear. After all, she was completely dependent on the doctor. Ting began to cry as the suppressed facts burst forth from the dam in her mind. She knew that this old man was speaking the truth.

"Ting, I will be looking after your needs. When I come back in a minute, please let me know what things in here we must bring along with us. Back in a minute, Fang. Then we are off to safety." He didn't wait for their reply; he just had to get out of the room for a minute. Seeing his wife like this had completely unnerved him. He returned to the doctor who had regained consciousness and was squirming to get free.

"Doctor Peng Ang, you have been found guilty of committing the most heinous crimes of brutality against helpless women. Your penalty is not death, for that would be too good for you. Rather, you will never again be able to work your sadistic methods on another woman."

"But I made the Perfect Women! They are perfect in every way," Peng protested. Surely, this man could see that. His women were absolutely perfect!

Rage flooded over Kang. Perfect? His mind recalled the last time that he had been at the Imperial Ballet and watched his wife dance. That was perfection, not this shell, this torso and head that remained! He reactively punched Peng out cold once more. He rummaged through the doctor's tools and found the right item. Two thrusts and it was all over, the man's bloody eye balls lay beside his head. He cut the bonds restraining the man. "If I was a doctor, I would amputate your hands instead, then you could never perform your wicked surgery again. Instead, without eyes, you cannot perform your evil surgery. I must settle for that, plus your entire bank account, some six million gold. It will help compensate Ting for your sadistic brutality towards her." He spat on the unconscious man and headed for the women.

Ten minutes later, he had Fang and Jian in their chairs sitting beside the others. He was surprised to see that Ting was able to do a tiny bit of walking on her own. She had him bring along several items that she could manage to use, if only with extreme difficulty. "I can sit. Are you really rescuing us? I, we are so utterly helpless."

"Yes, I will explain more when we get to our estate. We must hurry. We will be leaving Zau later tonight." He covered them up and climbed into the driver's seat. Thirty minutes later, he pulled into his estate, where Hu, Cheng, and An impatiently waited. They had two other heavily loaded wagons ready to go as soon as Kang gave the word.

Kang pulled up and dismounted as the three rushed up, holding lanterns, eager to see their loved ones. "I am afraid that most of the women are heavily drugged on opium now, but you can at least see them. I warn you, this is the worst imaginable sight." He pulled back the canvas cover, revealing the nine women.

Cheng and Hu both broke down and began bawling. Hu wailed, "My god! There is hardly nothing left of them!"

Surprisingly, An crawled up into the wagon and went to his sister. He gave her a hug and a kiss, though she barely moaned, so drugged was she. Not to be outdone by a ten year old, both men did the same to their wife and fiancé. Meanwhile, Kang discarded his old man disguise and then gave his wife a long, passionate kiss.

"Kang, please just kill me now. I am so useless, so worthless. Please put me out of my misery," she whispered pleadingly. "I am a horse with a broken leg. I cannot survive. Please put me out of my nightmare."

"I love you, Fang. We will survive somehow. Look, I have heard that in Nan Yan at the Church of God — they can somehow magically get you your arms back. That would be fantastic. Maybe they can also get you magically your legs back. We are going there now. Please, let's try that first. I cannot kill you. You are everything in the world to me, Fang."

"But I am — well okay. I — we have to have some opium soon, Kang. Peng was going to give us some with our supper. It's getting bad for me right now. I have to have it. So does Jian. Please, please, we have to have it now," she relented and begged as the massive cravings once more overwhelmed her, driving all other thoughts from her mind.

"They do need it soon," Ting added. "I used to be a nurse. Trust me. They must have some soon. I don't, but they do. Please, I do hope you have some or they will likely die without it."

Following the instructions from Chi, Kang prepared what he thought was the right amount. He lit the pipe and held it for Fang, who deeply inhaled as if her very life depended upon it! Her reaction was somewhat starting to Kang and the other two men. Within a couple of minutes, both Jian and Fang had finished their pipe. Now both women were moaning and begging to be pleasured.

"This always occurs. About all that we can do now is experience pleasures of others touching us. If you have any love for her and sympathy for our pitiful existence, you just have to pleasure her now and all of us. Please, Kang," Ting explained.

"We have to get going soon," Kang objected. He was too embarrassed to think about having sex with his wife now.

"Look, I can move around a very little bit and can do it for them," Ting volunteered. "If you are serious about getting us away, then you should get going. I'll do what I can for them, but please, later on, will you do it for me? Honestly, Kang, we are really nothing at all now but sensual toys. No arms, no legs. We and they can only experience sensual pleasures of someone else's touch."

"Okay, Ting. Thank you. We must get out of Zau before dawn comes or there may be hell to pay. Fellows, let's get these wagons going."

Hu placed four loaded long guns in Kang's driver's box, before climbing aboard the second wagon. Meanwhile, Cheng and An climbed onto the third wagon. Hu slapped his reins and led the way, Kang followed behind him, while Cheng brought up the rear. The three wagons moved down the quiet, deserted streets. Soon, they left Zau behind them. His estate was very near the edge of the once Imperial City. However, they had to get to a more southern side road out of town. The main road led straight towards Overlord Yi's town.

Kang knew that these first few hours were the most critical. The two overlords kept a tight watch and control on this border zone between their two territories. They simply had to avoid all the overlord patrols and night watchers. Kang knew many of the back ways just outside Zau from his horse breeding and training days. He used to ride these back roads daily and he had thus carefully plotted their initial route of escape. As he rode along in the dark of the early evening awaiting the rising of the late moon, he said a silent prayer to the gods. "Please, let us pass safely, if not for our sakes, for the women's."

Chapter 64 Flight to Safety

For eight long hours, the three wagons rolled slowly along, making but two miles per hour to avoid jostling the sleeping women. Luck was guiding them as they traveled dirt rut trails of the back countryside. In the moonlight, they saw passing farms and patches of forest, but no soldiers. At dawn's twilight, Kang estimated that they had made sixteen miles, still well within the lands controlled by Overlord Yi. Yet, he knew that they would have to stop soon, if only to handle the women's many needs. He called out to Hu, and soon Hu led them into at thick patch of forest, stopping beside a tiny stream.

Here out of sight from the rut track and the eyes of others, they made camp. He pulled back the canvas covering, exposing the women to full view. They were rousing from their deep sleep, as he had anticipated. Hastily, Kang began educating the other three on just what would have to be done for the women. One special chair held their common chamber pot. Each woman in turn had to be lifted from her chair and placed on this one so that she could go to the bathroom. Care had to be taken to keep their long hair out of the way, since their hair now stretched several feet below their bottoms. Still, no one dared defy tradition and taboo and cut the women's hair shorter.

"They have to be repositioned into a different position every two hours or else they begin to get all manner of sores developing on their bodies," Kang explained. "We need to get some nourishing food in them and then give them their needed opium. Clothes don't fit them. Besides, there is a purpose in their being naked. We have to be able to see the early signs of a sore developing. If we see one, we are to rub this aloe salve on the spot at once. Such is a sign that they have not had their body position moved often enough. We probably should have taken them out of their chairs during the night. So let's lay them on the blankets after we potty them."

Kang lifted his wife up and carried her to the potty chair, as the men began calling it. He was embarrassed at first, for he simply had to put his hands beneath her breasts to support her, as he waved her slightly to get her hair out of the way. He realized that the others would be equally embarrassed but he also realized that soon they would find this common place and think nothing of it. After potting her, he examined her backside, noticed that it was a little reddish, and knew that he ought to have stopped during the night to put her onto the mattress instead of leaving her in the chair all night long.

It took him several minutes to handle all eight women. Meanwhile, Ting insisted that she could manage herself. From the corner of his eye, Kang watched Ting. She used her head and very awkward body motions to rise onto the leather booties. Throwing her head this way and that, she managed to take tiny steps to her special potty. Kang saw that Ting alone of the women could do a few things for herself, and he complimented her on her actions. Ting flashed him a smile, the first smile he'd seen from these nine.

Once pottied, the women seemed alert and aware of their surroundings. It was just as Chi advised; at such times, the women would be lucid and clear-headed. He also told Kang that such would be fleeting at best, for soon they would be hungry and then quite desperate for their pipes. Kang took this first lucid period to explain to the women what was happening to them.

"Guys, this is Yan Yu, Zhen Du, Shu Lon, Wen De, Qian Ni Lun, Mei Fan, Juan Hong, Ting Nun, and my wife, Fang Zu. Ladies, this is Cheng Lun, the brother of Miss Qian Ni, Hu Die, the fiancé of Miss Shu, and An Fan, the brother of Mei Fan. Ladies, I'm sorry I couldn't find any of your other relatives. Many perished during the plague and the chaos afterwards. I have rescued you from the clutches of Chi Cheng and Doctor Peng Ang. We will be looking after your every need for the time being. Our plan is to take you to Nan Yan in the Tan Lon Province. There, I have heard that the Church of God is somehow able to get women their arms back. I will do everything in my power to have that happen for all of you. Perhaps they can magically get your legs back, I just don't know. Anyway, that's the best idea that I have. Don't worry. If that doesn't happen, you will be well cared for and lack for nothing in your care."

"I have gotten justice for all of you from both Chi and Peng. Chi has donated around eleven million gold to each one of you nine women. Yes, when we reach Nan Yan, the Banca del Dio has an account for each of you in your own names. Your password to access your millions is simply 4me. Peng will never again be able to mutilate another woman. I put his eyes out. Now he can spend the rest of his days in deserved darkness for his crimes against you women."

"How? How did you get us away from Chi?" Yan Yu asked, her voice trembling a little. She was chilling, hungry, and fighting the cravings, which were making their appearance again. She desperately wanted to know before she rejoined her nightmarish dreams once more.

"The whole economy of Zau is collapsing. Few now can afford the steep price that Chi was charging for your services. In short, you were bankrupting him. I struck up a bargain with him and paid a pile of gold to 'purchase' all of you from him. He values money more highly than you women. In short, I suckered him into the deal. I have been called something of a con artist, but this time it has paid off handsomely. Now we best get you all fed and then the pipes. If you ever need something, you only have to ask one of us."

He could see that all eight were now fighting the cravings bravely. Yan Yu spoke hesitatingly and rather embarrassedly, "After we get the pipes, will you be pleasuring us? Honestly, that is all that we can do anymore. We crave pleasurable sensations. If you can't, if you lay us on the mattress and position our bodies right, maybe we can pleasure each other. We just have to have it or we go nuts with desire. Please, sir."

"Don't worry, Yan. We'll manage this somehow. I wish that you were not addicted to the opium, though. I wonder how we can get you off it?" he replied.

Meanwhile, Hu and Cheng had breakfast ready and now the four began feeding the nine women. Kang was very thankful that he had help, as he realized just how much care these women had to have. With breakfast done, the eight's cravings began to become more than they could bear. Working as fast as he could, Kang prepared four pipes and they soon got the women their needed fix. Just as soon as they finished the pipes, all began moaning to be somehow pleasured. This was the most embarrassing moment the four had yet faced! Such things were always done in private with one's wife or perhaps fiancé, but never out in the open with everyone else watching, especially a ten year old boy!

Ting saw their hesitation and barked, "Look, damn you. You took us and them. Now you have to fulfill your promises to see to our needs. They just have to have this. Use your fingers if nothing else. Men!" she cursed. "Either do as you promised or arrange the women so that they can do each other." Red faced, the three men began using their fingers, running them along the women's torsos. An watched and emulated their movements on his sister, determined to somehow give his sister what she really needed. Soon, the men found that physical sex was not needed or required of them in order to satisfy the women; the mere touch of their fingers running long their bodies worked wonders. Once the women drifted off into a dreamy sleep, Kang did the same to Ting, who finally lost her anger, melting from his touches.

With the women now sleeping, the men met to discuss their next move. Hu suggested, "We are deep in Overlord Yi's territory. Perhaps it would be best if we traveled at night. Few will mark our passage that way. We can hold up during the daylight hours, as long as we can find a forest in which to hide." All agreed with his analysis.

"Okay, we have to get some sleep ourselves. However, the women need to be repositioned every couple of hours. Let's have one of us stand watch in two hour shifts during the day," Cheng suggested.

"I can do it," An spoke up. "I can sleep at night and watch over things in the daytime." In the end, they heeded his suggestion. Although one of the men rose to reposition the women every so often, mostly the men slept by day with An watching over them all. He slept soundly during the long night rides.

At noon, they all woke up and repeated the entire process, placing each woman on the potty chair first, then in her own chair where she was fed and given the pipe. Then they were repositioned on to the mattress and pleasured into their dreamland of sleep once more. Again at suppertime, they repeated it all in an identical manner. This time, they left the women sleeping on the mattresses when they finally began to head on their way once more.

As Kang was affixing the canvas cover over the top of the long bed wagon, Ting whispered, "Can I sit up front with you for a while? We can talk. I'd like to see a little even though it is dark." Kang agreed and carried her up to the box seat. After sitting her down, he tied a sash around her waist, securing her to the backrest. If he hit a bump, he didn't want her falling; she had no way to keep from falling over and getting hurt. Next, he adjusted her hair over her front side, hiding her privates as best he could, and then wrapped a warm blanket around her. While the early September days were warm, the nights were chilly, especially for the naked women, who had to be kept wrapped in warm blankets.

At last, the wagons began to move once more. Hu continued to take only the dirt rut tracks, heading westward or southward, whichever appeared next. This time, the men remembered to stop twice during the night to reposition the women on their mattress.

Ting spoke softly, "I was a complete fool, you know. I knew better, but hid the truth from myself. After all, he did treat me very well. He even said that he married me, but there was no ceremony or minister."

"You did what you had to do to survive, Ting," Kang replied.

"I suppose you are right. I really don't want to die, but I also don't want to live like this. Then again, I am far better off than the others are. At least, I can move a very little bit; they cannot move at all," she admitted.

She looked at Kang and then added, "I wanted to talk to you about us. I was a nurse, before the plague, that is. I know something about medicine and surgery. I've noticed something peculiar about them and me. You see, I still have a wee bit of mobility left. I know, it takes a huge effort on my part to move a tiny bit, but I can do it. You can't imagine how wonderful it is to be able to potty myself. Anyway, the others are immobile while I am not. I think that has something to do with their mental states."

Fascinated, Kang replied, "Interesting. Please, continue."

"After I lost my lower legs, I began to have nightmare images in my mind, scary ones. However, when I do get them, I have this overwhelming urge to move! I have to move, to get away from it somehow. I know it sounds totally wacky and crazy, but it is very real, too real almost. It's as if I'm drifting into another time and place and the only way out is for me to physically move, to change my position and location somehow. As long as I do that, no matter how hard it is for me to do it, I feel a huge, huge relief, and the images subside in intensity, though they are always there. Even now, they are there in the back of my mind, only I sort of ignore them."

"What kind of images are they?"

"The kind that create nightmares, I expect. I see dead or dying bodies. I see battle scenes. One time, I saw someone falling off a tall cliff to their death. Just all manner of crazy things, as if time is standing still on me somehow, and the only way out of them is for me to change my body's position or location. If I do that, they subside. If I don't they just get worse and worse until I do move my body somehow. Crazy, isn't it?"

"No, but then I don't know anything about the human mind," Kang answered honestly.

"Well, when Peng first got Wen, she was only on the after surgery pain killers at first. Now normally, after a week or so, we take the patients off them and they do just fine, though sometimes we do give them a sedative to help them relax and get some sleep. Peng tried to do that with Wen, you see. It didn't work as we expected."

She went on, "Wen began having similar nightmares that I have. She would scream and yell about falling, about having to get out of the way of the sword that was cutting off her head. Oh, some of them were wild. Obviously all were just nightmares, but I noticed that no matter what she did, she could not change her location or position of her body. She is immobile, fixed, and rooted to one spot. She cannot move or change on her own anymore. I think somehow that has an awful lot to do with all this."

"I think I see what you mean, Ting," Kang replied. "When your body is dead, you cannot move; you're immobile. When someone is about to cut off your head, you frantically want to move out of the way, to change your location. You have to or your head gets cut off. I see a connection here. The women are immobile and cannot move at all. Somehow, this is bringing into view all manner of nightmares where they have to move or die. If they can't move, they are again immobile in a dead body. No one wants to be immobile in a dead body! God, everyone will do almost anything imaginable to avoid that."

"Yes, they change, change, change, move around, duck, dodge, anything to get out of the way," Ting continued. "Change is the key word here. Change. If they cannot change, they are stuck in the unchanging part, the immobility, the death, the dying."

She added, "That's what I believe happened to Wen. She became swamped and overwhelmed by all the nightmares of dead and dying bodies and was and is completely immobile, unable to change her body and thus unable to change her mind's images." She lowered her voice, "When they do that, they are completely mad and insane. Wen was. She was screaming at the top of her lungs! It drove Peng and me nearly out of our minds! He had to give her a sedative just to quiet her down. Man, can she ever scream! A stark and utter terror scream, blood curling scream."

"Well, the next day, Peng went to consult with another doctor, or so he said. I now suspect he went to see Chi because he came back with a lot of opium. He said that her body was craving opium now and that was the cure. I didn't believe him for a second, but again, I forced that idea out of my mind and agreed with him. Well, it sort of works. As long as you keep her doped up and sensually pleasured, the nightmares tend to stay in the background somewhat."

She went on, "I thought you ought to know all this because you suggested that you wanted to get the eight off their opium addiction. If you do, you will be facing what we originally faced with Wen. Her screams will torment you like you cannot believe."

"Damn! That's awful news, Ting. I am glad that you told me all of this. We are damned if we do and damned if we don't! Hell, what has Peng done to all of you?" Kang cursed again.

"Made us helplessly immobile," Ting whispered.

"I wonder where those nightmare images are coming from anyway? Children's stories?"

"I doubt that, Kang. I know the ones that I see, the ones that I keep at bay, I've never seen before I lost my lower legs. Honesty, Kang, I have seen quite a lot of trauma as Peng's nurse. Many dead, many who died. None are like the images that I have at bay."

She changed the topic slightly, "I just want you to know that he wasn't always a sadistic surgeon. When I first began, he was very kind, sensitive, and caring. He was one of the best surgeons in Zau."

"But what caused him to become so sadistic and evil? My god, cutting off women's legs after they already are devastated with the loss of their arms from the plague — that is beyond criminal It's utter madness," Kang gushed.

"I think it had something to do with the plague. After I showed up with no arms, he changed — almost overnight. Shortly after that, he cut off my lower legs. Something about me having no arms triggered something in him, I am sure of it, only I have no idea what it was. The plague did things to all of us," she rationalized.

"Can't disagree with that!" Kang grinned and Ting returned his smile. "Well, I still wonder where these mind's images come from? I wonder if all the eight and you have the very same images or if they are different? I heard something about the Church of God dealing with people's minds and traumas. If I had not been shot and hurt my back, Fang and I would likely be in Nan Yan with them. We were planning to seek sanctuary with the Olin Masters and the Church of God, before I got hurt. When I recovered, they had gone, vanished without a trace. I spent a very long time finding out where they went. Nan Yan."

"Interesting. Well, I can tell you that I don't believe that mine and Wen's are alike, though obviously, I can't see her mind's nightmare images. It's just from what I heard her scream about, I think they are different from mine. The topic seems similar, you know, dead and dying type of things," Ting added.

"I wonder where these come from? If each person's are different, where did they come from? I know that we all have imaginations, but no one really imagines such awful things as you are saying that you women see. Maybe they are hallucinations."

"Opium does that, gives hallucinations. No, Kang, these nightmare images are different than hallucinations. I got a dose of opium smoke when Peng was first working with Wen. I saw hallucinations, things that really were not there. Those images are very different that the nightmare ones. The scary ones seem so utterly real. I swear that Wen's were more real than the real world around her at the time. That is scary. I can't imagine anyone just imagining these nightmares on their own," Ting declared.

"Well, if they are not hallucinations and you are not just imagining them from events and things you have seen in life, then what the devil are they?" Kang asked, more of himself than her. He went on, "What if, Ting, they were images of former lives that we have led? That would explain them. If we have lived before this life, then surely those bodies would have had to die somehow."

Ting chuckled, "If I have lived before, then I sure had some awful deaths." Kang chuckled too.

"I wonder how we could tell if we had lived before, I mean?" he asked. "I can only recall a couple of events when I was maybe three or four years old. I can't remember much earlier than that. How about you?"

"I remember being on a swing with mom. I must have been four at the time. No, I can't remember anything earlier than that either," she answered. "Still, it is an interesting theory, Kang. We would be reliving our own deaths again. Not good."

"I bet the Church of God will have an explanation, if only we can ever get you all there," Kang suggested hopefully. "In the meantime, we really do need to get them off the opium if possible. Yet, if these nightmares become too much for them to handle, then what? The trigger is their immobility. I wonder if there is something that we can do about that?"

"I surely don't know. They are only a torso and a head now." That was a grim assessment, but the truth, the awful truth, Kang thought, hardly alive at all. Still, he refused to give up hope.

"Say, can I ask you something, Kang?" Ting asked coyly. He nodded. "I can understand why you would come and rescue your wife, but why did you spend all that money to get the rest of us? We are just dead weight for you. We are slowing you all down on your escape. It is all that you can do to handle our needs. Why didn't you just leave us or as they asked, put us out of our misery? Is it that you think of us as Perfect Women much as Peng did? You can have a harem of us now, and there is nothing that we can do about it."

Kang sighed and answered, "You all are alive. You are women in the most dire need that I have ever heard about. I just could not leave you all there. I cannot abandon you when you need my help. You are all fellow human beings, after all. I know that there are many men who would take advantage of you. That was what Chi was planning to have happen, make a fortune off you by selling your services to despicable men. I'm sorry, but I just could not let that continue. I value life and people, not gold. I even value horses. All these are mine. I raised them from colts and trained them myself. As long as there is life within you women, I will do all that I can to help you survive somehow. I know I'm placing an unreasonable faith in this Nan Yan Church of God thing. But I did hear from other travelers that they actually saw women there who got their arms back. I could not live with myself if I didn't get you there and try it. If it fails, then we will all put our heads together and see what else we can devise. I'll not abandon you as long as I live, Ting."

"Thank you, Kang. Fang has chosen her husband well."

"Thanks Ting. I'm sure that one day you will find just the right man for you too."

"Don't be silly, Kang. I'm barely more than a torso now myself."

"Your body certainly is, but I just feel that you aren't. I have to believe that we're more than these mere bodies, Ting. Look, when I met Fang, I saw the most beautiful ballet dancer imaginable. She could bring the dance to life; she made it alive somehow. Now, her body is just that: a torso and head. If I believe that is all there is to Fang, what hope is there left? She just has to be more than a body, but right now, it's all buried beneath the grey cloud of the opium. If I can just get her off it and also keep those nightmares that you spoke of from her mind, you'll see just how beautiful and bright she really is, still is."

"Okay, I see your point. I'll lend you a hand with it." She crimsoned. "Sorry, I mean I'll give you all the guidance I know."

"No need to apologize, Ting. It's perfectly fine for you to lend me a hand. We both know what you mean. Where do we start?"

"Lower the amount that you give them each time, but do it gradually, not all at once." They discussed how much he was using in the pipes and agreed upon the next slightly lower amount for their morning's pipe. Not long after that, they halted for a few minutes. While Kang carried Ting back and helped her get covered up for the night beside the other women, Cheng and Hu carefully turned each woman onto her right side for the next few hours. Much later on, they stopped and put them onto their left sides. In the wee hours, they again stopped and put them onto their stomachs, propping their heads up with pillows.

As the first hints of dawn peeked over the eastern horizon, Hu again looked for a good location to camp and spend the daylight hours. Once again, they entered a stand of forest, but this time the sun had already risen and the women were becoming desperate for the potty. Hastily, they made camp. Kang began handling the women, while the others worked as fast as possible to get some breakfast ready.

"Kang, I'm really addicted to the damnable opium. I wish I wasn't. I can't even enjoy your company much like this," Fang whispered to him while he was helping her with the potty.

"I know love; we're going to start weaning you off the opium starting this morning. I know that it may be really hard for all of you, but please give it your best shot," he whispered back. The two passionately embraced briefly, before he quickly had to handle the next woman. While the group ate their rushed breakfast, Kang explained to the others that they were going to work on getting the women off opium by lowering the dosage gradually.

"But we freak out," Wen called out. "It was horrible. I saw such awful things."

"I know, Ting told me about that, Wen, but hang in there. We will think of something. There has to be a way around it," he offered what little hope he could.

"We could also try holding back the pipes a bit longer each time," Ting added. "I've heard that is also useful. Stretch it out more while they are lucid."

"Do it, dear. Make us wait longer this morning, if we can," Fang begged. The others nodded their acceptance, though they were already beginning to feel the dreaded cravings seeping into their bodies. After the women were fed, Fang could no longer hold the cravings back. "Kang, we need it now. I can't stand it. I have to have some now. Please, I beg you. Light the pipe for all of us now, please," she begged.

Kang, Cheng, and Hu looked at Ting. "Make them fight it a little longer. It is just the drug cravings that are talking to you," she advised.

"Okay, pipes come after we get the breakfast dishes done, ladies," Kang pronounced. The eight women moaned, begged, and pleaded all the while the men did the dishes. Kang felt his heart would break if he did not give in, but continued glances towards Ting helped him steel himself for what had to be done if ever they were going to get off the drug. All eight gulped in the first hit from the pipe as if their very lives depended upon getting that precious smoke into their lungs. All eight coughed, losing most of it in their desperate attempt to inhale the opium. By the second puff, they had calmed down a bit. The pipes went out sooner than the eight anticipated though, but they said little about that. Rather now, they all wanted to feel the ecstasy of sensual pleasures upon what was left of their bodies. A half hour later, the women drifted off into dreamland. The men left them in their special chairs, covering them up from the chilly morning air and crawled into their own bedrolls. An proudly took up the guard position, though Ting was now awake as well, and she kept watch over the women too.

Whereas the women did not come out of their daze until near lunchtime the day before, this day, because of the lower dosage, all eight were awake and talking an hour earlier. By the time that noon came, they were already feeling the intense cravings once more. Kang again made them eat lunch and wait on the cleanup work before lighting their pipes. Late afternoon, the women roused even sooner than expected, their cravings growing strong well before the men rose to fix supper.

With the eight women already pleading and begging for the pipes, Kang had to do something.

"Fang, look at that magnificent oak tree there." He pointed it out to her, and she did as asked. He noticed that for a brief instant, Fang took her attention off her cravings. Encouraged, he quickly rearranged all eight chairs to face outwards. He began pointing out things in the distance, trees and boulders mostly. All eight looked out at the forest around them and became much quieter. Kang realized that this action was making a difference. With his assistance, they were holding off the cravings, though he knew that eventually their cravings would get the better of them. Just when his assistance began failing, Hu brought over the hot meal, and the four began feeding the nine and themselves. Once more, it took nerves of steel to refuse the women their pipes while they did up the dishes and got the horses ready for the long night's ride.

This time at Ting's urging, the men arranged the women such that each could use her mouth to pleasure the woman beside her. Ting whispered, "This will give them something to do to help each other out. I think it might be good for them — you know, to help another out, even if it is such a little thing. You should get the wagons going soon. I'll call out when we need you again." Kang kissed her forehead and did as asked. Soon all nine were on their sides and doing their best to pleasure the woman they faced, and the wagons moved out on their third night of travel. Kang estimated that by dawn they ought to be clear of the lands directly under the control of Overlord Yi. Yet who controlled what lay ahead of them none knew. Hu's estimate agreed with his: they would need at least seventy-five days to make Nan Yan, seventy-two more after this evening.

Hu led them into another forest patch well before dawn. He couldn't see another patch that they could reach before daylight came. None wanted to take any unnecessary risks, not this close to Zau, some fifty miles behind them. Even though it was still quite dark, the women were awake and chatting during their lucid period. Long before dawn came fully along with breakfast, they would be fighting off their body's intense cravings — this Kang now knew. Thus, he continued to have them notice things around them in the real world. Each time he did this, he noticed that doing so greatly aided them by bringing their attention to the world around them, not allowing them to look inward.

Day by day, their lucid periods lengthened. Each day, he was able to put off the pipes a bit longer, though always eventually their cravings got the better of them. Still he and Ting knew that progress was being made. Around noon on the tenth day of their slow withdrawal from opium, Fang suddenly began frantically screaming, waking everyone, spreading a bit of momentary panic through the group.

"I can't move! I can't breathe! Help! Help!" she cried wildly. Although she had no appendages, she still managed to shake what remained of her body a little. As Kang rushed into the mattress-covered bed of the wagon to get to her, he saw her shaking, wildly moving her head about gasping for air.

"What's wrong, Fang?" he called out, as his arms encircled her shoulders. "Fang, it's me. What's wrong?"

"Help me! I'm drowning! I can't move! Help, I'm drowning! Somebody, help me, help me!" Fang screamed, still causing her torso to shake by violently tossing her head around wildly. Indeed, she seemed gasping horribly, as if her lungs were filling with water. She wasn't aware of Kang at all. In desperation, he picked her up, putting his left arm securely around her tiny waist, holding her up. He climbed out of the wagon with his panic-stricken wife in his arm. Her long hair fell nearly touching his ankles.

"Fang, look at that tree!" he commanded. She apparently didn't even hear him as she continued to fight against drowning with an immobile body. He used his right hand to push her head toward the tree. "Now look at that horse," he ordered. He did sense a slight attempt to obey on her part, though her screaming hadn't lessened. "Now look at that wagon." Her head turned perceptibly. Encouraged, he continued asking her to look at things in the world around them.

After a couple of minutes, her screams finally lessened, much to the relief of everyone else. By now, all were extremely upset and scared for her. Whatever was happening to her? Kang continued asking her to look at objects. After ten minutes, she ceased struggling and actually answered him. "I see it." After a few more objects, Fang seemed to be all right and had completely calmed down. He noticed her body was actually sweating heavily, though the air was still barely comfortable here in mid-September. He quickly took her back to the wagon and sat her down, drying her off so she would not get a sudden chill.

"What happened to you?" Kang finally asked her.

Sobbing now, she answered, "That was so real, Kang. I was drowning and I couldn't move. I couldn't swim or use my arms or anything to stop it. I couldn't breathe. It was horrible. Kang, it wasn't real, was it? There's no water here, except for that little brook, is there?"

"No, you were not really drowning, Fang. It was in your mind, I think."

"But it was so real, Kang. It was so utterly real! I was drowning. I know it. I couldn't move! I was completely helpless to keep from drowning! Hold me, Kang. Hold me for a while, please," she sobbed. He did so.

Ting spoke up, "Kang, that's just what happened with Wen. Doctor Peng's only choice was to give her substantial amounts of opium after that." He nodded, he'd already guessed as much. While the others now set to work on making lunch, Kang continued to hold onto his wife, rubbing her torso and shoulders, easing the tension out of them for her. He glanced over at the other seven and noticed that several more seemed to be fighting something, Wen in particular.

Just as lunch was about ready, Wen lost it completely or so Kang thought. "No!" she suddenly shrieked at the top of her lungs. "No! No! No! Help me, somebody please! I can't move. The sword will kill me, please, someone, help me! No! No! No! I have to get out of the way! I can't move! Oh dear god, no! Not like this! I don't want to die. No! No! No!" She screamed and tried to move her head out of the way of the invisible sword. They saw her trying desperately to move her body and head, but of course, she couldn't. Her torso seemed to be writhing in a wild attempt to dodge the sword. Kang sat Fang down in her chair and picked up Wen, much as he had Fang. Once he got out of the wagon and stood up, her long hair also fell to the ground and then some.

Once more, he tried the same tactics with Wen as he had used successfully on Fang. "Look at that tree." She wailed and screamed, not even hearing his command. He moved her head a little and gave another command. Poor An just covered his ears to drown out her high pitched screaming; he couldn't stand it any longer. Hu and Cheng, although taken by surprise, decided to continue with the lunch and began feeding the others. Both hoped and prayed that the other six would not suddenly have a similar episode. They shoveled the food into the women as fast as they could.

By the time that the women finished their lunch, Kang had gotten Wen calmed down somewhat. Her body was also drenched in sweat, and he dried her off and also gave her torso a massage. While he then fed her and Ting, Hu and Cheng lit up the pipes for the others, though giving them still a bit less opium. A half hour later, the women, who were now lying on their sides, finished pleasuring each other and had drifted into the opium daze of sweet dreams.

"You fellows try to get some sleep, I'll pleasure Wen for you," Ting volunteered. Kang was most grateful for her help and thanked her, receiving a flashing smile from her. The weary men fell into a troubled sleep, much needed.

Their rest didn't last as long as the days before, however. Around four in the afternoon, they were once more rudely awakened by the screams of both Fang and Wen. Kang and Hu jumped up and began to handle the two. Unfortunately, Yan Yu also began screaming wildly this time. "I can't move. They are going to get me. Help me, someone, help me! I can't get away! Help! Help! Oh god, no! Help! Someone, please!" Her screams added to the cacophony of ear shattering noise. Cheng had no choice but to go to her and emulate Kang's actions with her.

If the three of them were not enough noise, now Zhen Du lost it. She began screeching, but hers was nearly ear shattering in volume. With no others left to deal with Zhen, Ting bravely made the attempt. Awkwardly, she tossed her head about and got to her legs, then wobbled slowly to Zhen, where she sat down. She commanded Zhen to look at a tree, pointing to it with her head. The woman ignored her and Ting, frustrated that she had no arms to assist the woman, did the only thing that she could. Using her head for balance, she gave Zhen's head a push with her left stump, very nearly falling over herself. Then, she ordered Zhen to look at the wagon's side.

Ting had no idea if she would be successful or not. Bravely, she continued, inwardly cursing her own physical condition. She was a trained nurse, now almost unable to perform her life-saving actions. Although she continued, she too began crying at her own misfortune and condition. Still, she kept at it with Zhen, who was in terrible condition. She hoped and prayed that none of the others would lose it right now. She couldn't take any more of the screaming.

A half hour after it began, Fang calmed down. One by one, the others did so as well. As Kang sat the dried off Fang back into her chair, he picked up the soaked Ting and dried her off. Her tears had soaked her face, chest, and breasts. "You were superb, Ting. Very well done," he whispered to her and gave her a loving kiss. She looked up at him with her deep blue eyes, and he saw just how grateful Ting was for his small act of kindness to her.

Later as they began breaking camp for the night's travel, Ting asked Kang if she could ride up front with him for a while. The eight were now in their dream lands. Again, he tied her securely with a silken sash, and they rolled out on the next leg of their overland journey. As they rode along following Hu's wagon, Ting began to chat.

"Thanks for the validation, Kang. I admit, I really, really needed it. I felt so awful, so useless, so helpless back there with Zhen. I have never cried so much, really, I haven't. It's all just coming out of me now and I can't stop it."

"That's understandable, Ting. Let it come out, as it will. After all, you have suffered a tremendous, irreplaceable loss as well. Your whole life has been mostly destroyed, taken away from you without your consent. I will help you all that I can, Ting. We need you and your skills."

"Yes, but Kang, what are we going to do when all eight of them start screaming at the same time? It is bound to happen, probably soon I would guess. Look, four collapsed this afternoon. By morning, it might be six of them or all eight who completely lose it. Maybe we are doomed to failure. Maybe we should keep them doped up until we get to Nan Yan. Maybe there others can help us with them."

"I thought about that, Ting, but I don't want to give up on them just yet, not if we don't have to do it." They rode along in silence a bit.

Ting began again, "It is amazing that you found a way to pull them out of their temporary insanity or madness or whatever this is. Having them look at things in the present is working, though it takes time to get them to do it. How did you ever think of that?"

"Don't know, just seemed the thing to do. Whatever they are seeing in their minds cannot be real, certainly not where we are. So I figured I'd try to get their attention onto the real world. You really did do an outstanding job with Zhen, Ting. Well done. I know it was awfully hard on you, but you did it and that's what counts in my book." Ting flashed him a big smile.

After a few minutes of silence, she asked, "Do you suppose that their madness will ever end? I mean supposing that we do get them off opium. Won't their madness just continue? They are still totally helpless and immobile, which is what seems to be triggering their overwhelming madness. I've been thinking, what is going to happen after they are off it? Why should their bouts of insanity suddenly cease? With Wen, hers didn't and that's why Peng turned to opium. Are we not just setting ourselves up for a nightmare mess with all eight of them going mad at the same time and all the time — once they are off the opium, I mean?"

"Ting, I hope and pray that isn't going to happen. God help us if that is the outcome. We will have lost all eight of them. They cannot stay hooked on opium the rest of their lives," Kang answered.

"I wonder if there is something else that we could do to help them stay in the present time with us and not drift off into their mental madness images," Tang mused. "That seems to me to be the crux of what you are doing when you have them look at the trees, wagons, and things. You are causing them to look at things in the present."

"You have a point there, Nurse Ting. This is a clever way to put it, yes, get them to focus on the present. What else can we do to help them do just that?" he replied, encouraged by her astute observation.

"Sorry, not much of a nurse anymore, not since the plague took my arms. Still, thanks, Kang. Well, let's put our minds together on this. Keep their attention on the here and now. Well, dancing certainly would, but that's out. Talking doesn't have much effect at all; we've tried that to no avail. Say, I wonder if there ever have been any quad amputees around? I know I've seen several who have lost an arm or leg. They have phantom pains in their lost limbs, but none has had this madness thing. I don't think we women had it either when we lost our arms in the plague. I was devastated, but I didn't go insane or mad because of it, just experienced a horrible loss, which I probably will never get over. I didn't go mad either when I woke up to find my lower legs gone either, for that matter. Crushed, hopeless, lost, wishing I was dead — I felt those acutely, but no madness overcame me. I don't really understand what or why they are acting the way that they are. I can see no medical reason for their insanity."

"I accept your observations and conclusions, nurse. You are the expert in such matters here, not me. I've never heard of anyone having lost all their arms and legs. I can't imagine anything more awful than that, though. Still, why that should cause mental insanity is beyond me. So what else can we do to help them focus on the here and now?"

"Dunno, how about singing? That they can do. We have to stick to things that they can do, which pretty well rules out nearly everything!" Ting pointed out.

"Hey, that's a good idea. Singing. We'll try that next. If we could dare travel during the daytime, we could open the cover and have them look at the countryside as it goes by. Terribly risky, though," he added.

"Keep that one as a last resort. If they start screaming and others are around, we could be in real trouble, to say nothing about running into overlord soldiers," Ting pointed out.

"So far, we have been extremely luck. Twice, Hu has run into a small river that we could not cross without heading west to the nearest town, crossing there. I am worried that we'll have to go through a large city in order to find a way across the Lian River that borders Tan Loc Province. That could spell real trouble for us," he pointed out. They rode on in silence. When they stopped to rotate the sleeping women's bodies, Ting joined them. She was now exhausted.

Around four in the morning, the blood curling screams from Shu Lon startled Kang. "Help! Snake! I'm being crushed! I can't move. Help! Someone, help me! I can't breathe. It's crushing me! Help! Help!" She started gasping as if she really couldn't breathe. Kang reined in and dove for the wagon bed, wondering how the constrictor could have gotten into the wagon. Perhaps it had slithered in while they were not looking. He hoped the others were not already dead!

Even in the pale starlight, he saw no snake coiled around Shu. She was having a bout of her madness. Her screams woke everyone else, but Kang ignored them and picked Shu up and climbed off the wagon. At once, he tried to get her to start looking at things around them. In the starlight, little could be seen. He persisted and a half hour later had her calmed down. Hu pointed out that they were out in the open and just had to get going soon. The other women were also fighting their own demons; Kang saw it in their eyes from the pale starlight.

"Okay, let An see if he can drive this wagon. I'm going to ride back here and see if I can keep them calm somehow," Kang ordered. Soon, An had the wagon moving, though Cheng, riding behind them, kept a sharp eye on the ten year old boy. An did a remarkable job of it though.

Meanwhile, Kang began rubbing Wen and Fang's bodies with his hands. His touch seemed to help them. As soon as he thought another woman was about to lose it, he switched off worked on her some. Ting caught on to what he was doing and had him position her beside Fang. She then used her leg stumps and mouth to touch Fang, giving her present time sensual stimulations, which aided her to keep her focus on the present and not her scary mental demons. Before long, poor Kang was handling four women at once, using both his feet as well! Then the other three began to lose control as well. In desperation, Kang repositioned the eight women into pairs and ordered them to begin to pleasure their companion's bodies. He continually had to tell them to do so, though. Before long, they responded, much to his relief, and he and Ting finally sat back to catch their breaths. The near disaster had been averted. Never was Kang so glad to see a dark patch of forest ahead! Around five, Hu halted and the three men quickly made camp.

After quickly helping the eight to potty, he placed them into their chairs. "Okay, ladies. It is sing along time. I want each of you to sing as loudly as you can. Let's give Hu and Cheng some entertainment while they cook your breakfasts," he both ordered and suggested. At first, they were hesitant, fighting to keep their mental demons at bay as well as their opium cravings. Still they obeyed and with Kang's constant encouragement, they opened up, singing loudly. Ting smiled; she saw that it was working. Now they had one more weapon in their arsenal to help combat this strange madness, which the eight were desperately fighting.

On September 13, Counselor Bi Mei contacted Eve. *Hi Eve. Say, I've come across an unusual situation here in Nan Yan. It sounds like something that you or Bethany might have done or had a hand in.*

What's that? Eve replied.

I just got word from the Nan Yan Banca del Dio that the strangest set of transactions has just occurred. Nine women have just had new accounts opened up and substantial funds transferred into them. All accounts have the same password.

So what's strange about that? Why is the Banca telling you about them? Eve wondered.

All the nine listed their addresses as the Church of God, Nan Yan. I've never heard of any of the nine women and neither has anyone around here. They asked me about the women because of the highly unusual nature. All told, the accounts hold close to one hundred eleven million gold!

Holy cow! Wow, that's a sum, Eve reacted.

Right. It sounded to me like one of the actions that you or Bethany used to take to make someone pay for their crimes against women.

Not us this time. It sure is strange.

More so, since the Banca president cannot backtrack to find out where the funds originated. It seems some records are missing.

Hey, since these are women, we ought to investigate. I'll come to you and we can chat more about this. It's a mystery that has my interest, Eve replied. A few minutes later, she materialized a body resembling hers back home and gave Bi Mei a welcoming hug.

"Hi, here's the list of names. Yan Yu, Zhen Du, Shu Lon, Wen De, Qian Ni Lun, Mei Fan, Juan Hong, Fang Zu, and Ting Nun. Recognize any of them, Eve?"

"Nope. Not a one. Wow, one hundred eleven million between them, incredible."

"Yes, and they are supposed to be living here in my church! That's what is bothering me, Eve."

"Perhaps they advanced transferred their funds. Many travelers do just that," Eve suggested.

"That is the only explanation that makes any sense, given that no one here has ever heard of these nine women. Yet, where did this money come from? The Banca man could only say that it appears the funds came from somewhere within Tashien. At first, I thought that perhaps these women were coming from New Xin over your way, but the transfer suggests that is not the case."

"Let's assume that we are not dealing with fraud here," Eve began, thinking rapidly.

"Right, the Banca president is taking all necessary precautions. If someone tries to withdraw the funds or touch the funds in anyway, he will alert us. He's temporarily frozen those accounts until we get to the bottom of it," Bi Mei added.

"Wise move. Okay, assume that we have nine women who are on their way here then. Say, what about their husbands or men? Any new accounts in men's names? Surely, they would be traveling with a fair number of men," Eve asked.

"Nope, none at all in the last month, just our own local folks."

"Well, they cannot be traveling across Tashien alone — not nine armless women — not in these times. Such would be madness. They'd never make it." Eve pointed out.

"Now you are seeing what I am seeing, Eve. Frankly, I am worried about this. While it could be some kind of elaborate hoax or con, if it is not, we have nine relatively helpless women traveling to Nan Yan from somewhere out there in the countryside which is deep in the throes of the Dark Ages. Here, have a look at my Tashien map, Eve. It's been fifteen days since the transfer. By riverboat, they could have originated from as far north as Zau or possibly even Luo Yang, considering that it is a down river float. Fifteen days and they could have sailed here from Shunkou, but perhaps not from Jiao or Ning on our eastern coast."

"That encompasses a tremendously populous zone, Bi Mei. Could they be coming overland, perhaps?" Eve suggested.

"Nine armless women, alone, walking, subject to every overlord soldier between here and there? Hardly likely, if they wanted any chance at all of making it here. See what I mean? Strange indeed, this mystery."

"What about coming up from Shansee?"

"By river, they could have come from nearly anywhere in Tan Loc Province and be here by now, Eve. I thought of that already."

"What about a collection of wealthy noblewomen making an escape from up north somewhere?" Eve asked.

"Thought of that too. The Olin Masters brought so many of the wealthier men and women when they came here. I checked with many of them. No one has ever heard of these women, with one exception."

"Ah, now we are getting somewhere," Eve grinned. "Holding out on me, eh?"

Bi Mei smiled. "Not really. One nobleman from Zau thinks that one name on the list might be familiar to him. He once saw an Imperial Ballet, which featured an up and coming young dancer. He thinks that her name was Fang Long, but there is no Fang Long on the list, just a Fang Zu."

"Oh, close but no bananas, eh?"

"Right. I checked further and found several others who remembered that young, talented dancer, but they could not recall her name. Still, there must be hundreds of thousands of women with the name Fang in Tashien. It is a common name at that."

"Okay. Assuming this is not a prank, nine armless women traveling to get here must be taking a huge gamble traveling in this chaotic land," Eve concluded. "We ought to see if we can locate them and see exactly what their condition actually is."

Bi Mei smiled, "Precisely. I'm very tied up here running the show. There are only a few of us who can give the Advanced Therapy, and I really can't be spared now. Since you are my immediate boss, I called you."

Eve grinned again, "So you want me to see if I can magically find these nine women?"

"Yes, Most Honorable Evelina," Bi Mei made a teasing, humble bow to Eve. Both broke up and laughed.

"Okay. Will do. Any ideas how I go about finding nine unknown women?" Eve asked.

"Nope. But then you are my boss; you are expected to know such things," Bi Mei teased Eve, who merely said "Grr."

Bi Mei left Eve; she was already nearly late for another therapy session appointment. Eve paced the small room, thinking hard. She decided that she had no idea and returned to our home and rounded up Sergio, Velona's Chief Detective Inspector. She outlined the problem to him.

"Intriguing mystery, Eve. Mind if I tag along on this one?" Sergio replied. Eve's grateful look answered him. After a moment's thought, he spoke again, seriously, "Eve, this all has the feel of a man. I am theorizing that a man was behind these transfers. Look, outside of here, armless women, especially so in Tashien, are very nearly helpless. A whole lot of devious work was done to make the transfer and to hide its origin as well. There has to be a man behind it, a man with arms and a whole lot of inside knowledge and talent as well."

"Okay, I am ignoring all possibilities of fraud here. Let's assume this is a valid situation. Why would a man transfer over a hundred million gold to nine women, divided nearly equally?"

"Dunno," Eve replied.

I had come in and overheard most of their conversation. I could not help but butt in, "Because these women were somehow brutalized by someone, and the man is now trying to provide financial support for these nine victims."

Sergio smiled, "Precisely so, Bethany. Precisely so. We have nine women who were somehow harmed and some man has had the wherewithal to attempt to make amends or to guarantee that these nine women can survive. Considering the magnitude of the sum, they must have been badly mistreated."

"Shades of the Purple Palace," Eve declared, recalling our previous experiences in Shansee.

"Precisely, Eve," Sergio replied.

"Okay, so how do we find them?" she asked. I wondered that too. I searched my training and had no idea how.

"Well, while you all were gabbing, I was off thinking, Eve." I hadn't realized that we were gabbing! Damn, Sergio had an incredible mind for detective work, I realized once again. How could Lisa keep up with him, I wondered.

He went on, "The women, we have no way to trace. We know nothing at all about them. Rather, I believe the way to find them is to focus on the man who is ultimately behind them, the man who arranged the transfer of funds. Find him and he can lead us to the women. Now then, we can possibly find him."

"Oh good grief, Sergio!" Eve stamped her feet. "We know nothing about him either!"

"Oh no, my pretty Eve. We most certainly do know quite a lot about him. To do what he has done, he must have a very strong bond with the women. He must have strong emotions about what was done to them. If perhaps he is even traveling with them, his emotions will still be very raw and acute. We can attempt to home in on that," Sergio declared, speaking as if the entire problem had already been solved and the women found. Both Eve and I were completely lost. It was almost as if he just spoke a foreign language to us.

"Okay, come on, let's plop these bodies down and go find them now," he ordered. Relieved, we did as asked. We three soon hovered above Nan Yan.

Wow, they sure have built much since we were here, Eve sent. Truly, I was also impressed. We could see the steam engines puffing smoke into the clear sky.

Okay, imagine you are that man and that you are with these most needy women and that you have already gone to extreme measures to get to safety. Focus on that emotion that you are feeling. Good. Now we fan out and expand our awareness. Sense for that very emotion. It should be intensely strong. Off we go, Sergio sent. I did as asked, but perceived nothing at all. I suspected Eve didn't likewise. We both put our faith in the Chief Detective Inspector.

This was strange. I was attempting to perceive a spiritual being that I did not know, solely and only by trying to pick up the emotion that I imagined that I would have if I were in his shoes, trying valiantly to get nine brutalized women to the safety of Nan Yan.

Oh, this will take forever this way. Come on; let's get a few miles up in the sky, Sergio sent. We complied. I have to hand it to Sergio; the being is positively brilliant. We had only been three miles up in the sky for five minutes at best before he sent, *Bingo. Eve, Bethany, sense what I am sensing?*

God, that is strong! Intense worry and fear for women. Okay, got it. Let's check it out, Eve sent. Now that he had pointed it out to me, the raw emotion was easy to perceive. We followed him as he zoomed to the north and east, on about a forty-five degree line from Nan Yan. My weak geography got a boost as I spotted the Lian River, which I knew marked the northern border of Tan Loc Province. We continued diving and on the same heading for many miles and then zoomed down towards a patch of trees amid a patchwork of small farms. I spotted many men out in their fields, probably harvesting this time of year. All were several miles from the patch of forest towards which we descended.

It was around noon. This time, the singing had failed to keep them all from their temporary insanity. Fang believed that she was drowning, Wen was trying to keep her head from being chopped off by a sword, Shu was gasping as she felt her chest constricted by the large snake, Yan couldn't move or get away from her tormentors, while Zhen tried to fight off her attackers though she couldn't move to do so. Mei Fan added to the cacophony screaming about not being able to breathe from the intense smoke. At least, she intermittently had bouts of severe coughing that interrupted her wild screams for help. Overwhelmed, Kang, Hu, Cheng, Ting, and even An tried to work with one of them to get them to see things around them in the present time environment.

As Sergio, Eve, and I zoomed in on the three wagons, the sight that we saw and heard was most unnerving. Six women were screaming loudly. Three men were holding a woman, an arm around their waists. None had any appendages, most shocking. Yet, the men were pointing out trees, wagons, and the cook stove to the women. At first, we thought the men were somehow harming the women, but almost at once, we realized that they were trying valiantly to calm them down and bring them into the present. I spotted another woman who at least had her upper legs using them to do something similar to another of these women, while a small boy was trying hard to get another woman's attention onto the side of the wagon. Two other women were shaking and trembling in their strange looking chairs, about to lose it as well.

Calm them, Eve sent us two. Together we radiated a large flow of affinity to the entire group. Almost at once, the two who were about to break down seemed to regain a bit more control. With the others, their screaming lowered in volume, and they began to obey better the commands that they were being given. *Let them finish the process,* Eve sent us. While we hovered invisibly above the small assemblage, the afflicted women rapidly let go of their demons and calmed down. I sensed a huge relief from the three men, the one woman, and the boy. *Okay, we had better materialize a body and go find out what's going on,* Eve suggested.

Drying the sweat off Fang, Kang exclaimed, "Whew, that was a wild one! Good going, Ting, An. Thanks for helping. Good going Qian Ni and Juan, you kept yours at bay this time."

"Kang! We have company!" Hu called out, scrambling to get to his pile of long guns.

"Hello. We mean you no harm. We are unarmed," Sergio called out, as we three slowly walked up to the rear wagon following the path they had taken to enter this secluded spot. Both Eve and I had mocked up armless bodies, thinking that we shouldn't shock these people's reality too badly. Nevertheless, we three did look quite strange to these people. We were obviously foreigners and didn't look at all like someone from Tashien, although we spoke their language fairly well for foreigners.

"Who are you? Where did you come from?" asked Kang, stepping forward to meet us and prevent us from getting too close to the second wagon where the nine women were now sitting in their special chairs and also looking at us.

"We come from the Church of God in Nan Yan. Counselor Bi Mei asked us to see if we could find nine women," Eve began. "By any chance is anyone here called Yan Yu or Zhen Du or Shu Lon or Wen De or Qian Ni Lun or Mei Fan or Juan Hong or Fang Zu or Ting Nun?" The look of complete shock and dismay on the three men's faces told us instantly that we had found them.

"How do you know their names? How could you possibly have found us? Yes, those are the women in the wagon there. I am Kang Zu. Fang is my wife. This is Hu Die, Shu's fiancé. This is Cheng Lun, Qian Ni's brother. He is An Fan, Mei's brother."

"We are very glad that we found you. Do you need any help? I assume that you are trying to get them to Nan Yan and the Church of God there," Eve asked.

"Yes, that is our hope and destination. I don't know how you found us, but we are in big trouble. Our only hope is that in Nan Yan, the Church of God there can somehow magically get our women's arms back. We are from Zau. The nine have been brutally mutilated, and we have rescued them and are trying to get them to Nan Yan," Kang explained. He decided to trust these three strangers. He saw nothing alarming in them or threatening. Besides, he could use some help. He looked at Hu and Cheng, then added, "We are kind of short on time now. The women are hooked on opium, and we are trying to get them off it. We have to get lunch made fast and the women fed. Then, we give them a lower dose of opium. After that, they are pleasured and will go to sleep again. We need to sleep some too, since we have been traveling only during the night."

"Okay, let me lend you a hand with making lunch," Sergio suggested. "Meanwhile, Kang, why don't you let Eve and Bethany here help you with the women. Perhaps you can tell them your full story." Hu and Cheng headed off to fix the lunch with Sergio following them, striking up a mild conversation with them. An followed behind the three.

"I've got to dry the sweat off them so they don't chill," Kang said, as he returned to finish with Fang. Eve and I followed and began drying off another pair of the women, using the towel with our feet. Kang noticed us and smiled. "Hey, you two are pretty clever with your feet."

"Have to be. We don't want to be totally helpless," Eve replied. After the six were dried off, Eve asked, "How come they don't have any clothes on?" Kang quickly wrapped each one in a blanket.

"We cannot find any clothes that will fit them. Besides, caring for them is easier for us this way. We were told to constantly look them over for red sores appearing and to put salve on them right away."

"I used to be a nurse," Ting spoke up in his defense. "Bed sores are commonplace with the bedridden."

"Makes sense. Good plan," Eve replied, validating them. She was satisfied that they were not naked for other, more prurient reasons.

With the women temporarily handled, Kang sat beside his wife and began relating their story. Partway through it, the others brought a hot lunch over to the bed wagon, and we all pitched in feeding them. Kang continued his lengthy tale, even outlining that the women would have enough money in Nan Yan to support themselves if need be.

When he finished, I said, "Well, now we can tell you better how it is that we came to look for you. The Banca del Dio has indeed gotten the money that you transferred. However, the sheer size of the amount raised a red flag with the president. Since all nine listed addresses as the Church of God, he discussed this with Bi Mei, the head of the Nan Yan Church of God. She didn't recognize any of the nine and asked us to investigate. We assumed that you were not going by riverboat, since you ought to have already arrived in Nan Yan by now, based on when the bank transfers were dated. With a good deal of luck, we found you."

Eve took up the discussion now. "You are absolutely right in wanting to bring them to Nan Yan and the Church of God. We have a powerful therapy that we are working on all men and women to remove the trauma caused by the plague. Recently, we are now able to undo the effects of the plague on the women of the world, though we only do this once the trauma has been erased from their minds."

"So you are saying that our women can get their arms magically restored?" Kang asked, hoping that he had heard right.

"You bet they can. However, their legs were amputated and those cannot be brought back," Eve added. "I'm truly sorry about that, Kang."

"It will be miracle enough if they can have their arms back. Then, they have a chance at a descent life," Kang replied. "Hear that, love, you will be able to have arms once more, just as soon as we can get you there."

"Yes, but I don't think I can make it that far, Kang. It's coming on me again. Got to have a pipe, please, please," she begged. Eve and I both recognized the opium craving and saw at once that this reaction was very different from the madness, which we saw when we arrived.

"Best give them a bit for now, Kang. Then we can talk some," I advised. Eve already gave me a glance that said she concurred. We both had been in these women's position the last time that we were in Shansee.

After the women were handled once more, Kang, Cheng, Hu, and Ting wanted to find out more from us. Ting began by asking, "You are foreigners. Yet you are here in the backcountry of Wontun Province. I heard no horses coming, though the women were making far too much noise. Still, I see no horses. How could you possibly have found us and how did you get here?"

"How is it that you seem to know so much about the physical conditions of the women?" Kang added.

"Long story. Bethany, I will let you handle this one," Sergio grinned and teased me. How could I honestly answer such questions?

"We are some of the elite members of the Church of God. We are from Velona, Sea Princes, far to the west of here, on the other side of this dog bone continent," I began. "We of the Church know that each of us is an immortal spiritual being. Through the therapy that our leader has discovered, we are able to regain the native abilities that each of us once had. All of we beings are immortal and have inhabited many bodies. Through the millennia of accumulated traumatic experiences and our own conclusions, we have slowly lost the vast majority of the abilities that we once had. Through our Advanced Therapy, any spiritual being can regain them once more. We three have done so."

"Eve and I have been in a similar circumstance as the women here, having had sadistic men amputate appendages and hooking us on opium as well. With the help of others, we were able to break that addiction and become free of its lingering aftereffects. Thus, Eve and I know firsthand what these women are going through, at least in part. Both of us agree that the methods that you are using to get them off opium are correct and will accomplish your goal. You are right; they must be off opium before our therapy will be completely effective on them."

"Well, that's good to hear. Ting is a nurse and has been invaluable in helping us with it," Kang sighed, obviously greatly relieved.

"That was the easy question to answer. The harder ones are how we found you and what it is that you are seeing right now. Sergio was the one who was able to find you. He realized that we could home in, so to speak, on the emotions of the man who was behind the rescuing of the women. Based upon the amount of money that you were able to obtain for the women, you, Kang, must have had very strong feelings about the women. Sergio and we were able to perceive that emotion and zoom in on your physical location in the world. A being can perceive many things that our mere bodies cannot." Now came the tricky part.

"What you are seeing are not our real bodies, but forms that we have created so that we can communicate easily with all of you. Our real bodies are sitting on our front room couch back in Velona. We are able to appear anywhere we desire and mock up an illusion of a body that seems completely real to others. One day with enough Advanced Therapy from the Church of God, you all may be able to do similar things," I put in a plug and offered them some hope.

"So you are not really here?" asked Kang, not quite understanding me.

"My body isn't, but I am. Just as you are right here viewing this area from inside your head, we are here as well. The difference is that we are able to make very good illusions. Look, all of you, close your eyes and mock up a black cat." I paused until they each had one. "Perfect. That is all that we are doing, except that we are able to have everyone else see our mocked up black cat."

"But you were able to touch us and help with the women. And your bodies aren't real?" asked Hu.

"They are real enough so that you cannot tell the difference unless we wish it." Sergio broke in. "Now the problem that you are facing is that you have a very long way to go overland and it is likely to be very dangerous for you. Thus far, you have been both fortunate and wise to travele during the night. Few are outside long after dark. Yet, if you could travel by day, the women could look out at the countryside and that would help keep them focused on the present time and not on their dreamlands. However, you are quite right; such would ordinarily be far, far too risky and dangerous. We must lend you a hand in getting these women safely to Nan Yan, where the Church of God there can begin their healing therapy on all of you."

"All help is welcome," Kang replied. "We very nearly lost it all there, just before you came. The women seem to be fighting some strange mental demons. Ting and I suspect it somehow has to do with their utter immobility — their inability to change their locations. Does this make any sense to you?"

We had Kang and Ting give us a full explanation of their observations. Ting also explained what Doctor Peng had to do when Wen's demons began appearing, that is, to put her on opium. "It shut her up, but she became an opium addict," Ting added.

"We need Macario," Sergio volunteered. Eve and I agreed with his assessment. Fighting the women's opium addiction would be a huge challenge for these men. Just as big was the challenge of physically getting them to Nan Yan and safety. Their mental demons, as Kang called them, were far beyond their knowledge to handle. Put all three together and they had no chance of success. Besides, as we zoomed down on them, we spotted a number of soldiers following their wheel tracks, though they were still some distance away. Wisely, Sergio had not yet mentioned that nasty fact to the three men.

After insisting that Kang get some much needed sleep with us standing guard, Sergio summoned Macario and soon he materialized a body near us. We four walked out of earshot of the wagons and explained in detail what we'd uncovered here. "Look, they all are not dramatizing demons," Macario pointed out. "Qian Ni and Juan have not yet displayed such actions. Just because one loses ones arms and legs does not mean that mental insanity arises. However, you are right in summoning me. What you are observing firsthand is a most unusual phenomenon. Total, complete immobility, that is, no movement possible, means that one is fixed in location, in space. One cannot change her location if she desires. When one's body dies, the body is then fixed in location and immobile, as far as the spiritual being is concerned. When have you ever seen a dead body get up and move around? Thus, these women woke up to discover suddenly and shockingly that they are completely without the means to move or change their body's location in space. That alone is a hideous traumatic event, but it also tends to bring back otherwise hidden memories of past times when they put out a huge effort to change their position and failed or were unable to move out of the way of a certain death."

He went on, "As you know, our goal is to increase the self-determinism of the person, the being. Of course, along with that comes an increase in their own personal responsibility as well, contrary to what many suspect might happen. Here, the women woke up and found themselves as they now are. That was an other-determined action completely against their own survival. Their demon situations are similar situations in which their own self-determinism was completely overwhelmed. All they see is the other-determinism wiping them out. The physical condition of their bodies is mimicking the past circumstances and thus bringing the past mental images into their present — a now equals then proposition. Yes, the past traumas are being so accentuated by their body's physical conditions that they frequently cannot tell the past from the present. When their demons are active, as far as they are concerned, then is now, and there is no now but then."

"The opium is dulling those past memory recordings and pulling their attention onto a distortion of the present by vastly enhancing their physical sensations that they get from their bodies. The question is really what can we do to help them? That is a good question. If they were not hooked on opium, we could run therapy on their 'demons' and free them from that past trauma. The opium addiction prevents us from doing that. We'd just get them into the traumatic incidents when their body's cravings would kick in, overwhelming them. Thus, we cannot erase that severe trauma while they are still hooked on opium. The first priority is to get them off the drug."

I broke in, "But what do we do when their demon's kick back in? Apparently, this is happening with greater and greater frequency as they lower the amount of opium the women are getting. It's a 'gotcha' situation; we need them off opium so that we can erase their trauma, but we have to keep them on opium so that their traumas don't drive them utterly insane in the meantime."

Sergio added, "Plus, their men have to get them across at least another thousand miles of hostile, enemy territory. I've not told them that already some soldiers have picked up their trail. Make that a third devastating problem here."

"What about just giving them back their arms," Eve suggested. "That would certainly ease the physical burdens on the men as well as the women."

"I've considered that, Eve," Macario answered solemnly. "While we could easily do just that, trust me, it will not handle their past traumas. Whether they now have arms will make little difference on the repeated bouts of temporary insanity. Worse, if they have arms and hands, it will make them more difficult for the men to control when they are temporarily mad and doing wild things. They could even help themselves to another opium fix when the fellows were sleeping. Addicts do incredible things to get their next needed fix."

"No, the best course to follow is to make the present time reality stronger than that that their demons create in their minds. That will help keep their mental trauma at bay and show them that they can exercise some control over their own minds. Right now, they likely have concluded that they can control absolutely nothing by themselves. That is, they consider that they have no self-determinism left; all is being other-determined for them. Without even the slightest ability to move or do anything for themselves, you can see why they would make or believe such a conclusion. We must devise more ways to allow them to see that they have some self-determinism left, that they can control their minds and their demons a little bit, that they are bigger than their problems. If we can do that, such will even help them get off the opium as well, killing two birds with one stone, as the saying goes."

"However, Sergio has a valid point. They are going to need constant around the clock protection from the soldiers and such, along with direction and route guidance. I've picked up the fact that none of the men actually knows the way to Nan Yan. They are just heading southwest and hoping for the best," Macario pointed out.

We agreed with this assessment. "So what do we do and how do we do it?" Eve asked directly the very question that was on my brother's mind and mine.

"They must travel by day so that the women can spend time looking at the sights. That will help keep them in the present time a little bit better. Trying to sleep during the daylight hours and trying to sleep through the night is adding to their misery. They need to be on a normal person's schedule — awake days, sleeping nights. Kang and his companions have already seen the right path to follow when their 'demons' begin to appear. Give them an assist by pointing out things around them; give them physical stimuli such as a massage. Get them to talk about anything, except how they are doing and their condition. Give them less opium during the daytime hours and keep on reducing the amount given," Macario issued his suggestions.

"Plus, we are going to need to have several of us with them day and night. They are now in the middle of nowhere, as far as the Church of God is concerned. We cannot get the Olin Masters here soon enough to be of much use. Some of us will have to ride guard over them at all times."

I asked what was bothering me. "If Eve and I are here to help them, dare we appear with arms? Without them, if we pretend to act as armless women, we will be mostly useless to the men here. If we had arms, we could relieve them of their constant care of their women. If we just use our native abilities, I am afraid that we will look like goddesses or something to them, perhaps even freak them out."

"Right on the native abilities. That will certainly be detrimental to their already fragile mental health. If they were into the martial arts, then you might get away with saying it was kijutsu powers. I guess the only option is to appear with arms, Bethany. Perhaps that will give them some hope for the future for themselves as well. Of course, we cannot regrow their missing legs, for what's been done to their bodies is done," Macario answered.

He added, pulling his chin in thought, "Now then, one more thing. I've seen the men's memories of just how wild the women's immobile insanity bouts have been and just how difficult it has been for them to control those episodes. I've looked at Juan Hong, who has yet actually to dramatize her madness, though she has come close. There is no doubt at all that the immobile insanity bouts are far worse than the opium cravings for the men to handle. Further, if they occur during the daytime while they are traveling, their screams will upset those within hearing distance, potentially bringing even more problems onto the men and women."

Eve broke in, "You don't think that we and they will be able to keep the women sufficiently in the present time to avoid more of these immobility insanity outbreaks?"

"No, Eve, I don't. As we have been talking, I've been looking at their mental states, weighing one option against another. Mind you, it is purely a guess on my part. Even though I can see what they are seeing — the images of death — there is no way that I can gauge just how they will react to them or even interpret them or even the degree that they even perceive the images. All I can do is give my best educated guess, which I have done. Eve, I believe that we ought to try a different strategy with them."

We were all ears. Seldom have I been privy to such detailed analysis of people's therapy situations. He continued, "These women have another traumatic incident which has been lying mostly swamped by both the opium addiction and the immobility insanity traumas of former lifetimes."

"I get it!" Sergio interrupted. "The surgery, right?"

Macario smiled, "Yes, Sergio, their surgery. The mad doctor's surgery on them had been lying mostly dormant, wholly swamped by their heavy immobility trauma incidents, which became highly charged up when they woke up from their surgery. That trauma was allowed to reactivate upon them, and then instead of being handled, it was muffled by the opium. Now, however, they are getting about half of the opium that they were on to deaden the immobility trauma. Of course, now that trauma has once more come to the forefront and is dominating them. Yet, there still is the most recent surgery trauma. We all know that the more recent the trauma, the stronger its effect seem to the person, though that trauma is really getting its force from all the earlier similar traumas that the person suffered. I expect that if the surgery trauma were allowed to surface fully, then it might take precedence over the immobility trauma."

I asked, "I'm not sure what you mean, Macario. Will they then be in severe pain?"

"No, that will likely remain suppressed. Rather, they are more likely to heavily dramatize and act out the command value of the words that were spoken in their presence during their operation. The doctor was himself highly aberrated and very likely laid in some powerful command phrases quite by accident while he was performing the surgery. If I am interpreting these right, the women will respond to the command phrases rather like puppets."

"But isn't this not a good thing to do?" I asked.

"Lesser of two evils. If we get them to Nan Yan, Bi Mei can handled their therapy and salvage them. The key is to get them there. I believe that if we allow the command phrases of the surgery to come forth, they will force the immobility traumas to the background," Macario explained. "Now the command phrase will go something like 'I am a Perfect Woman.' They will be insisting upon the men believing that they are the essence of perfection and extremely highly desirable and will require constant proof of such. The men will need to make love to them, frequently, I am afraid."

"Oh good grief!" declared Eve, somewhat disgusted.

"Look at it from another point of view, Eve," Macario pointed out. "As they are now, they believe completely that everything is being determined for them by others and that they can cause nothing at all, being so helpless. That is, they have no self-determined actions that they can take, since all is being determined for them. They are at total effect, which is precisely what the immobile traumas are all about — being at total effect. With the Perfect Woman commands operating, they will believe that if they can get the men to make frequent love to them, then they are being a slight cause and not an effect, you see. Increase their apparent self-respect and you increase their responsibility levels and decrease the impact and effects of their immobility traumas."

"I see what you are driving at, Macario. Clever," I validated his astute observations.

He smiled and added, "Allow Juan and Qian Ni to vocalize their opinions, then Fang will back them up, and Shu will then insist on it as well, bringing them all into the command dictates of their surgery trauma. I will leave it to you to explain this to the men and to get them to fulfill the women's needs. I must now arrange for others to come and relieve you. We'll set up a group to be here and watch over them. I think two of us at one time is sufficient. You can summon others if something arises beyond your control. Considering how busy we all are, perhaps four hour shifts each day will be tolerable. We'll need six shifts and a dozen all total."

I volunteered, "Hey, count us in. Our kids will want to help too, so we're twelve right here. No need to bother all the others. I sure wish we had more than a hundred of us now."

"Thanks Bethany. Yes, so do I, but this is greatest number of freed spiritual beings that we've ever had by a factor of ten. Give me a bit more time and we'll be closer to two hundred. Bethany, thanks to you and your companions, I can now see that our route to freedom is brilliantly lit for us all! Well done, gang. I must get going. Don't hesitate to holler if something else comes up." He vanished and we set to work watching over the sleeping group during the afternoon.

Around four that afternoon, Sergio handled the soldiers who came too close to their hiding place among the patch of trees. He got them to decide that they were merely following some farmer's wagons, and they turned around and headed back the way that they had come. Meantime, the women roused from their opium induced naps, lucid once more.

"Say, I am thinking clearly once more," Juan Hong spoke up while Kang was helping her use the potty chair. "You know, ladies, we really *are* Perfect Women now, highly desirable, highly sought after by men."

Qian Ni quickly added, "She's right! She is really right We *are* Perfect Women, perfect in all ways. I just know it! Kang, Hu, and Cheng should desire us above all other women. We are Perfect Women."

"Hey, you're right, Qian Ni, Juan! I just realized what you are saying is precisely right! We are the *only* Perfect Women," Fang spoke up. All the others were now nodding their agreement with Juan and Qian Ni. "Kang, what is the matter with you? Why have you been avoiding making love to your absolutely Perfect Woman? I'm your wife, and now I *am* a Perfect Woman. You should be making love to me all the time and yet you have not."

"Same with you, Hu," Shu broke in. "I'm now *absolutely* the Perfect Woman. You must make love to me all the time, you simply must. Now I'm *worthy* of marrying you, Hu. I'm finally the Perfect Woman. We all are. Hu, you must make love to us all. We are Perfect Women now; you simply must!"

"Yes, Kang, you must make love to us all. We are all the essence of perfection now. We are Perfect Women. You must; you simply must!" Fang insisted.

"You too, Cheng," Yan Yu added. "We are all Perfect Women, and we simply must have you honoring us by making love to us all the time! Look, it is Chi-ism in action. We all are now fully accepting that we are Perfect Women. We accept that and so must you, Cheng. You too, Hu and Kang. You must practice Chi-ism and accept the reality that we are Perfect Women and not dishonor us. If you men do not make love to us all the time, then you are dishonoring us Perfect Women. You are disgracing us and what we Perfect Women stand for. You must start making love to us and show us that you too accept us for what we now are: Perfect Women, perfect in all ways. You three simply must."

"Kang, you must also make love to Ting. I know that she is not quite the Perfect Woman yet, but she is very nearly so. Please, do not dishonor her. She has done so very much for us all. Please, you must consider her a Perfect Woman too and not disgrace her or us," Fang pleaded, glancing at Ting several times.

"Yes, Kang, Cheng, Hu, we accept that we are now absolutely Perfect Women. We all are. Now you simply must honor our exalted status as Perfect Women by making love to us or you will be totally insulting us, humiliating us, dishonoring us, and disgracing us!" Zhen added her thoughts to the discussion.

"My brother, although I'm now a Perfect Woman," Qian Ni broke in, "it would not be proper for you to make love to me, since I'm your Perfect Sister. I will allow you not to have to make love to me, my brother. So you will not be disgracing me if you do not. However, if the others do not, then I will be utterly disgraced as a Perfect Woman."

Eve and I looked at each other. While the women seemed totally lucid and not talking from the influence of the opium and not from their immobility traumas, I began to suspect what Doctor Peng Ang had been saying to the women while they were unconscious as he amputated their legs. Buried beneath all that pain and unconsciousness probably lay these very words that all eight were espousing. He probably told them that they were now going to be absolutely Perfect Women, highly desired by all men. Yet, these women now believed that they were in fact perfect. All the women were finally lucid enough to make a tiny attempt to *cause* something and not be a total effect as they had been. If the men rejected them now, then either they would be hit with all the suppressed pain from their surgeries or their immobility traumas would take control of the women once again.

I intervened, "Yes, ladies, there is no doubt whatsoever that all of you are now Perfect Women. However, even Perfect Women need to eat. Let's allow your men here to fix supper first. You see, we've decided to begin traveling by day from now on and sleep during the nights. There will be all night for love making." One by one, they all accepted this, since they were hungry.

While Kang, Hu, and Cheng worked on fixing supper, I explained to the men what Macario had suggested. Hu replied, "Then, we must accept what is reality now, Kang. I don't understand why they should think that they are now somehow Perfect Women, but if we play along with that idea and if it keeps their madness at bay, I will do so. I just cannot take much more of their screaming. Shu's voice is piercing and shrill. I keep thinking that she is about to die on me. Anything is better than their madness. Earlier we very nearly could not calm them down. If they should have another bout of that madness during the day while we are traveling, think of how much trouble that could cause us! Everyone will think that we are murdering the women!"

They discussed the situation and reached an agreement to follow the women's wishes. However, they decided to put blanket barriers separating the long bed wagon into thirds so that they would have a semblance of privacy. Kang agreed to handle Fang, Ting, and Juan. Hu would handle his fiancé Shu, Wen, and Qian Ni. Cheng agreed to take care of Yan, Zhen, and Mei. Kang suggested, "Well, we can hold one in either arm while the other is on top of us. Fang wishes to be on top so that she can kiss me better. She says that she can move her head and do that, so I will give her the chance to do so. I do feel ashamed to be doing this to the women, though. Yet, if it keeps their madness away, I must or we are doomed." The others agreed.

Once the women were fed and told that the men would love them at nightfall, we were all very much surprised at their reactions — or rather their lack. While the men did the dishes and cleaned up the campsite, not one of the women complained about needing opium! True, we three could see that they were fighting the cravings, but they said not a word. Further, their eyes were bright with anticipation, keeping the immobility insanity also at bay a while longer as well. Macario appeared to be right in his assessment. The women felt that they were somehow being self-determined a little bit by getting the men to make love to them and that was just enough of an edge for them to keep both their cravings and insanity pushed off from the present. I wondered how long that would last. Surely, their opium cravings would soon kick into high gear.

"Don't worry, Kang, one of us will be here all night long. We guarantee you that we will protect all of you while you sleep," Sergio assured him and the other two. He also got the ten year old An nicely tucked into his bedroll near the fire, and he sat beside the boy, telling him a bedtime story. Soon An was sound asleep.

Eve and I kept watch and quietly observed from a distance. So far, everything went extremely well. Finally around ten at night, the women just had to have their opium fix. Kang gave them a little less than before and soon they were all sound asleep. During the night, Lisa and Valerio came to replace us. Once home, we found that everyone had worked up a scheduling board of who would be on guard duty and for what hours. Our children took the night shifts while their little baby bodies were sleeping. Wise move, I thought.

Sergio and I took the early morning shift, partly so we could see how the night went and the day travel would go. The women looked perky and lucid at breakfast, chatting among themselves about how great it was to be respected as Perfect Women. When the wagons were ready to roll, I sat back with the women, while Sergio sat up front with Kang. He also was out looking ahead of us for signs of trouble and so that he could better direct Hu.

The men had the women sitting in their chairs, but wrapped up in blankets to stay warm. All were positioned so that they could see the countryside as the wagon rolled along. At first, I got an earful about how great it was to be a Perfect Woman. I soon got their attention off that and onto the fall colors, the checkerboard farmsteads, and the few men out working them. I pointed out the rustic, but relatively crude homes and the smoke clouds curling into the blue sky, mingling with a few clouds. I kept a sharp eye out for signs of the appearance of the immobility madness and opium cravings, but the women were valiantly fighting both urges amazingly well.

By the middle of the morning, we passed through a small village. Mostly men were visible on the streets, going about their duties. I was surprised with the women's attitudes. All nine held their heads up proudly as befitting the Perfect Woman. Incredibly, all were acting their commanded roles. A couple of soldiers moved to intercept us, but Sergio again implanted ideas in their minds, and they walked away, allowing the three wagons to pass unchallenged. Around noon, they stopped for a brief lunch. Still the women were keeping the demons and opium cravings at bay, when Valerio and Lisa came to replace us. I rather wanted to see how the women would fare during the afternoon as well, but I had other duties calling me back to Velona.

Later that afternoon, Lisa and Valerio returned. "Well, they are still keeping their demons and opium at bay. Pretty darn amazing. It is as if life has returned to these women somehow, but it is a fake aliveness, though. Perfect Women. That must be what the doctor said to them repeatedly while he was cutting them," Lisa commented. I agreed.

"Valerio had to handle twenty overlord soldiers. I think the best policy is to just have the soldiers go away, rather than fighting them," she added.

The next morning, Sergio and I took our turn once again. This morning, I asked the women if perhaps they would like their hair cut much shorter, perhaps only as long as their torsos were. "Oh no! We are perfect as we are, that would cut off much of our vitality," Fang replied, shocked that I would even suggest such a thing. "Perhaps you could brush out our hair. We want it full so that it can be draped seductively over our perfect bodies, not braided, please," she added. Ah well, I did as asked — anything to help them kept themselves in the present time and not dive into the past or yield to the cravings.

A wild month it became. Numerous overlord patrols challenged the party. Twice, combat could not be avoided, but our fellows did a quick job of handling the soldiers, tossing them several miles away from the wagons as opposed to killing them. Three times, they had to stop in a larger town to resupply. We were fortunate that no one could tell the actual condition of the women in the wagon, who were bundled up from the increasingly cold weather. Finally, on October 15, 825, the three wagons rounded a bend and the magnificent city of Nan Yan appeared before them. The women cheered and the three men were greatly relieved. Somehow, they had managed to get the women to safety and to the one place in the world, which offered them some hope for the future.

The women saw it differently, though. They were utterly convinced that they were Perfect Women now and that all men ought to treasure them and care for their needs willingly. Upon meeting Bi Mei, Fang insisted, "We don't need therapy, Bi Mei; we are Perfect Women now! We could use a bath and have our hair brushed out nicely. We don't need clothes; nothing will fit us. Besides, we want men to see our absolutely perfect bodies." Ah well, now the women became Bi Mei's problem. If not before, now it was very real to me. When a person is in pain and unconscious, words spoken in their vicinity can have tremendous impact on their subsequent behavior, and our therapy is the only way out of the mess.

Chapter 65 From the Ashes

During the winter of 825, the engineers, Princess Mei Lon Wu, and General Tao met to discuss their spring offensive. Expansion was the key — that, the princess knew well. Besides, the brutality that was occurring in northern Tashien was appalling. She met with the Perfect Women and nearly cried. Worse, that Overlord Bin Zhou was issuing iron coins instead of their usual gold indicated an eminent economic collapse up in Zau.

During the fall, she had sent spies out to assess the situation throughout eastern Tan Loc Province, preparatory to her planned expansions in the coming year. While the rice lands to the south were mostly unchanged as they had remained for perhaps several centuries now, Shansee to the south and the rugged hills to the north posed new problems. Opium. Life had become so difficult, so unrewarding, that many turned to opium for their only pleasure in life. The trade had quadrupled over what it had been prior to the plague.

The poppy plants were grown in the rugged, but fertile, hills from just north of Nan Yan all the way up as far as the Jan River in Wontun Provence. The dealers funneled their final product down the Lian River, which formed the border between the two provinces. When it joined the mighty Yonshu River, boats could rapidly carry the opium up to Zau or down to Shansee. The Opium Hill Overlords, or drug lords as General Tao now called them, ran a slave population, forcing everyone to work the poppy fields. Only a few inhabitants were left to handle the usual farming, barely producing enough food and a good deal had to be imported from the southern regions.

"We can easily expand eastward as far as the Yonshu and south to the ocean," General Tao pointed out on the map. "Our spies report the few overlords there are most interested in the newfound economic wealth of Nan Yan. Going north of the Yan River, we must deal with the extremely hostile opium overlords, who are making a large profit and who are not interested in what we have to offer. We cannot go into Shansee proper, not without a whole lot more force than we can muster now. We might be able to isolate Shansee and push on eastward to the ocean, though, thus cutting off their opium supplies coming down the Yonshu. Of course, they will react to that."

Jovanni, their resident Master Engineer, broke in, "Just remember, we cannot expand faster than the Church of God can deliver their Basic Therapy to those in the areas that we take over. Workers who have not had it are nearly worthless, causing more trouble than they are worth." His memory was vivid. A recent accident had cost a worker his leg, when a crane's line came loose, dropping a heavy crate onto his leg. The crane operator had not had Basic Therapy and was following Chi-ism, allowing what is to be, accepting it. Instead of taking immediate action, he merely allowed what will be to occur. He was fired immediately, of course, but the damage was done.

"Right," Princess Mei Lon replied absentmindedly. She was thinking about a far more serious problem. At last she spoke what was on her mind. "Gentlemen, what are we to do with the criminal men whom we find when we take over these new lands? Perhaps half of Shansee has turned to crime. Certainly, the northern opium overlords have. Do we just kill them?"

General Tao answered, "I have given that some thought, Princess. A century ago, they would have been banished to the northern ice province of Dong. Perhaps, we should re-instigate such a policy. Few now dwell there, not since the mass exodus to New Xie. I doubt that the Church of God has the capabilities of handling such large numbers of criminals at this time."

"Say, I like that idea, General Tao. We can send them there via coastal prison ships, avoiding the hostile lands between here and there. Well, that is a big load off my mind. Let's plan to do so with all the criminals that we encounter. That will get them out of our way permanently."

Jovanni spoke up, "Okay then, I recommend that we extend the rail lines on a arrow lines towards Giang, Shansee, and towards Zau. From Giang, we can run a line to the coastal city of Shankou. That will give us access to the four largest cities in the lower half of Tashien."

"How soon?" the princess asked.

"Depends on how fast the Basic Therapy can be given to the men. Giang, probably by next fall. Shansee, maybe by the following spring," he answered. "We have few engineering obstacles to overcome this time, mostly rivers."

"Okay, then let's get down to the hard planning," she replied. Together, they began to draw up coordinated plans. Of course, everything depended upon the women who would volunteer to deliver Basic Therapy sessions. They were planning to reach perhaps twenty million people during the next year. That they all could receive it would be nearly impossible, but that did not keep them from attempting to bring MMCE and a new civilization to those now in the throes of the Dark Ages in southern Tashien.

Angelo Corelo of Zargarb moved to Shansee back in 810. He and his brother, Hovani, ran Corelo's Imports in Zargarb. So intrigued by the incredible items coming from Shansee that they decided that one of them should move there and be the purchaser of even finer items for their blossoming business. Then twenty-five, Angelo agreed to go. As many foreigners were, Angelo was most impressed with the refined society of the wealthy of Shansee, who chose to ignore the poorer sections of the city. A year later, he fell in love with Ai Bi Dhoz, and married her.

"Tell me again how you met mom," his daughter Marzella, now fourteen, asked. The plague had struck Shansee for the second time. During the first plague, Ai Bi had taken a bad fall and had died. Outside, the monsoon raged, while inside their modest home in Da Nang, a small village just beyond the borders of the ever-growing Shansee, the forty year old Angelo sat beside his daughter's bed. He'd been caring for her every need since the plague struck and by this time, his knees were swollen from so much crawling. His son, Jian, thirteen, sat on his bed, covertly listening in because he didn't want to appear sentimental and womanish.

Marzella's skin was lighter than the normal resident of Tashien, but she had her mother's rich, long black hair and her squarish face, thick eye brows, and piercing black eyes. She was overly tall for a woman of Tashien, getting that from her father, who stood six-six. Now she too had gotten the plague for the second time only this time it had been far worse. She'd cried over the enormous size of her massive breasts, the awful skinniness of her waist, thought she didn't complain about her hair having grown so much that it now fell six inches below her feet. Prior to the plague, Marzella considered herself very attractive, taking after her gorgeous mother. Now, her self-esteem had plummeted to rock bottom.

"Ah I well remember that day in June. It was shortly after I arrived and took a room at the old Santi Inn. I was out on a buying spree and I came across a quaint shop that specialized in fine gold watches. There I first saw her, an angel I swore. Long, lustrous black hair, piercing black eyes, she actually spoke to me! I thought my heart would explode. I'm afraid that I said some stupid things, but Ai Bi didn't seem to care. We chatted and she suggested that we take tea."

"Well, I followed her like some puppy dog, and Ai Bi wove her spell over me. I was hooked," Angelo said with a sigh and a strong pang of loss. Ai Bi was gone some four years now. "I'll never forget our first date, Marzella. I bought her an orchid for her red silk dress. As we danced, we both became intoxicated with the headiness of that flower. Oh, how her eyes shone on me. I felt like I was a king or emperor whenever I was in her presence. Your mother was the epitome of grace and beauty, Marzella. You are so like her."

"Oh don't be silly, dad. Like this, I'm not only helpless as she was in the end, but also grotesque. Just look at me!"

"Marzella, never think less of yourself. Your body is not you. You are full of life, love, and beauty," Angelo attempted to build up her self-esteem, which had collapsed utterly with the arrival of the plague. He kissed her and pulled the covers up over her shoulders. The raging monsoon consoled the them as they slept.

Jian was a tall, gangly lad of thirteen. Already he was a black belt. Angelo insisted that his son know how to protect himself. However, Jian was far more interested in the long gun and had two of his own now. Jian prided himself on being a crack shot, and he had also invented a sighting device for them. Essentially a small telescope was mounted to the gun, allowing him to hit a bulls eye from nearly six hundred yards away. If accuracy was not an issue, he could at least hit a large target from a mile away.

With his children asleep, Angelo took stock of their provisions, thanking his good fortune. After the fiasco of the first plague, Angelo had always kept his pantry extremely well stocked and not just for the yearly monsoons that struck. Now with the second and even more debilitating plague upon them, he and his two children had sufficient food to last them for several months, he concluded. Satisfied, he went to bed as well.

With the education of his children having fallen solely upon himself with the death of Ai Bi, Angelo concentrated on instilling survival values in them. "Always look out for your sister. Remember, family is the basic unit. Never desert family. It is a man's duty to provide for the women in his life. Life is precious. Never doubt your own self. Be true to your own goals. Always be truthful and honest, for anyone can lie; only the brave and honorable can afford to tell the truth."

In January, their feet returned to normal, but Marzella insisted on wearing her extreme heels primarily so that her long hair didn't touch the ground. Like everyone in Tashien, she would rather be dead than cut her hair! Rarely did she consent to having it wrapped up in a bun, and few ever wore theirs this way in this country, though now Angelo was forced to braid hers for her. Of course, hobbled by her choice of shoes, Marzella needed even more assistance, particularly when walking.

The situation in neighboring Shansee rapidly deteriorated, and violence began to spill over into these surrounding suburbs. By late January, Angelo knew that he really needed to make a trip to Hun

Ho, a smaller town some twenty miles west of Shansee, where Ai Bi's parents lived. He had promised to bring their grandchildren for monthly visits, and they were very overdue. Worse, the plague had likely deprived the older family of much needed supplies. Hence, when he left Da Nang bound for their grandparents in Hun Ho, Angelo loaded their carriage with provisions as well.

He was right, but the situation in Hun Ho was grim. Overlord Nanguros was making his bid for power in the lands surrounding Shansee. Twice he had raided the village, abducting young men for his ever-growing army and demanding the village provide his men with food. Already hundreds had died, including their grandmother. Angelo found the old man nearly starved to death, merely waiting to join his wife, whose decaying body still lay on the bed where she had died. He'd been physically unable to handle her burial.

Quickly, Angelo and Jian buried her and fixed a good meal for the seventy year old man. After spending two weeks nursing him back to health, they returned to Da Nang. Nevertheless, Angelo promised to visit every other week and bring food, which pleased the old man. Unfortunately, the situation deteriorated rapidly in the ensuing weeks and months. It was not until March that Angelo dared make another trip to his children's grandfather. Again, loaded with what food supplies he could gather, no small feat in itself under the wild conditions that Tan Loc Province was now experiencing, the three headed the twenty miles to Hun Ho.

Several bands of Overlord Nanguros' soldiers stopped them twice and confiscated most all their supplies. Fearing that they might harm Marzella, Angelo wisely hid her beneath a pile of bedding that they were taking to their grandfather. Only because Jian was still too youthful looking prevented the men from abducting him into the overlord's army.

When they finally got to the village, Angelo was shocked. Nearly half of the village was now dead or missing. Their grandfather was dying; he'd given up all hope. He whispered to Angelo, "They forced me to sign over my Banca del Dio account to Overlord Nanguros. Now I have nothing left to give to my grandchildren and my sons. They have forsaken me, cursing me for my folly, but I had no choice."

"It's all right, grandfather. It is only money. We don't need it," Jian whispered. He liked the kindly old man, always had. He had always told him the greatest stories, far better than any that Angelo had told. Tales of Emperors and Empresses and mighty armies and battles pricked the young teen's interest many time more than stories about great finds of silken bolts and gold watches.

Angelo decided to stay here for a while and look after him. After all, he was his wife's family. While Jian and Marzella sat listening to their grandfather describe what had been happening with the overlord soldiers, Angelo went outside to see how the village was faring. Many knew this outsider as Bin Dhoz's son-in-law and accepted him as one of them. Soon, Angelo heard far more horror stories than he was prepared to hear! Person by person, the picture became clearer to him.

Around the supper table that night, Angelo finally told his children the true situation. "Overlord Nanguros has abducted all men between fourteen and twenty-five into his army. Any that resisted were shot and killed. He's stolen most all the food from the villagers and shot all who resisted. He told the few remaining adults here to round up all the rest of their food for his men and that they would be back for it in four more days. Worse, he's forced every family in the village to sign over their Banca del Dio accounts to him, leaving everyone here penniless. Three-fourths of all homes are either deserted or only have children in them, trying to somehow survive."

"Tomorrow, we are going to try to do something to help them, kids. I don't know what, but we simply cannot leave children to survive on their own without any food or means of getting by. We have to help them. Kids, if anything should happen to me, I want you to promise me that somehow you will get to Zargarb and my brother. He will look after you. I will never sign over my Banca del Dio account to this butcher of men and women. I have plenty of money in the bank and so does my brother. Jian, promise me that you will look after your sister and get her to safety. Tashien is crumbling; nowhere will be safe. Somehow, you two have to get out of this god-forsaken country. Promise me, Jian," Angelo insisted.

"Of course, dad, I won't let anything bad happen to Marzella. You can count on me," Jian replied, feeling about ten feet tall. At last, he was getting some real responsibility.

"Dad, nothing is going to happen to you, is it?" Marzella asked. All this evil talk had begun to strike a chord of fear in her mind. Until now, she'd only been concerned about her own horrible condition; the aftereffects of the plague had left her nearly helpless, dependent on her father. From his tone and words, she began to sense that he felt he might not be around much longer. Then who would look after her and her every need? Her silly younger brother? Perhaps that scared her even more.

He was always into guns and fighting, coming home stinking of sweat from his martial arts training — all of which turned her off. She, on the other hand, had always tried to look her very best as befitting a Great Lady, just like her mother had been. Worse, all that had been stripped from her, leaving her world a desolate wasteland. No ladies were usually seen out of doors, not since the plague. There had been no social gatherings, no dances either, for that matter. It was as if everything that she valued in life had been ripped from her, just as her mother had been taken too. She was left with a shell of a body, unable to care for herself, unable to be the Great Lady that her mother had been. Thus, she clung to her father for dear life, and now he was suggesting the one remaining anchor in her pathetic life might also be suddenly taken from her. This scared her deeply, though she could find no way to express this in words.

The next day, the village held its first communal meeting, in which everyone who was still alive assembled in the village's sole inn. Angelo was appalled as he stared out at the frightened, nearly hopeless crowd. Their aged grandfather was the only remaining village elder. Five middle-aged men also remained along with seven women. Over fifty children ranging in age from barely a year old to around thirteen huddled behind the few adults. Many were filthy and most were starving, eagerly drinking the last of the ale that remained in the inn.

Angelo took charge. "Thank you all for gathering here today."

"What are we going to do? The overlord will soon be coming for the last of our food. Our children will starve to death," one middle-aged man asked.

"We must somehow save the children," Angelo replied. "We should go from house to house, gathering up anything that is edible. Let's bring it all to one place and hide it from the overlord. We should also gather all the children into one place and see that their needs are met. The older children should look after the younger ones and the girls as well."

"But where can we hide the little food that remains?" a woman asked.

"Where they have already looked and where they would not expect to find any food," Angelo answered.

"We can store it in my basement," the teens' grandfather spoke up. "They've already searched my house and will not likely search there again. They've taken everything I own last time."

"Good idea. Let's put the children up here in this inn. There is plenty of room," Angelo added. "Okay, let's everyone get to work. Kids, you round up your things and bring them here. Jian will help you organize into survival units, with one older boy in charge of say ten younger ones and girls. We adults will go house to house seeking anything that can be eaten. Later on, we'll bring cooked food here to feed everyone." While there seemed little hope, at least they did as asked. The promise of food did much to bolster the morale of the many children, however.

Going home to home proved rather a successful action. While no single home had much left, by combining what was there with what was in the other homes, Angelo realized that they really did have sufficient supplies to feed the children for perhaps an entire month. After that, he planned to bring in more from his village by carriage. Perhaps he could rent a wagon as well. That evening, the children got their first nourishing, hot meal in over a week.

Jian had gotten them all organized into five larger groups and everyone had a good bed here at the inn. Their morale rose that night. Just before bed, Angelo spoke to the many children. "Look, when the soldiers come, I want all you leaders to make sure that the older girls are well hidden in their bedrooms. The soldiers may try to take them away into slavery, so I'm counting on you boys to make sure that the older girls are not found. You six older boys are in charge. Jian will lead all of you. Somehow, you children have to survive this. If anything happens to us adults, Jian knows where you can go to find safety. Now get some sleep, kids."

Around noon the next day, some twenty soldiers entered the village, bringing one large wagon with them. The remaining adults sat quietly around the tables in the inn, waiting for whatever the soldiers would do. Most had already accepted their fates and were mostly in apathy, very different from the previous day when Angelo had fired them up, getting them to make one last ditch attempt to save the many children of Hun Ho.

In the end, it went as Angelo suspected it might. Finding no food waiting for them, the soldiers beat the remaining men, who said nothing. After that, the men went randomly house to house and found nothing edible, seemingly backing up what they beat out of the men. Furious, the leader of the soldiers ordered the remaining men to be shot and the inn searched. Bang! Angelo felt a sudden wave of intense pain in his chest and blackness swept over him. He didn't feel the floor hitting his body as he fell from his chair. The women shrieked and were carted off, thrown into the wagon. They'd become sex slaves for the overlord's soldiers for as long as they lived, which was not expected to be very long. Deep in apathy, the women did not protest; most were just waiting for death to take them out of their misery. None lived for more than a couple of weeks.

After that, a few soldiers went searching the rooms of the inn, but found nothing but huddled, frightened children. These they left alone, for they were of no importance whatsoever. An hour after they entered Hun Ho, they left for the last time. Jian raced down the steps two at a time from his room. He had not even helped Marzella up from beneath her bed where he'd shoved her and covered her up. "Dad!" he cried and raced to his father, who was bleeding profusely, though not yet dead.

"Take care of Marzella. Get them to safety. Promise me," he whispered.

"I will dad. Please don't die, you gotta live." He pleaded and even punched his father, demanding that he not die on him. After a couple of minutes, he finally realized his dad was dead. Around him, the other five older boys, the other leaders, stood staring at the seven dead men, wondering what to do.

"What's going to happen to us now?" one whispered, scared to break the silence, half expecting the soldiers to suddenly reappear and shoot them too.

"We have to get them carried outside and somehow buried," Jian also whispered. "We don't want the other children to see this. Come on, let's do it."

In her room, Marzella called out, "Jian, help me. I can't get out from under the bed. Jian? Jian?" Silence. For the first time in her life, Marzella felt truly scared and forsaken, completely alone, but totally responsible for her own self. Wiggling, she managed to get herself out from under the bed. Quickly, she headed down the stairs, being as careful as she could in her extreme heels, though her hair did brush along the steps behind her. She saw Jian beside her father and tears swelled in her eyes. Soon, she could no longer see clearly, and she sat down in the nearest chair and sobbed. She was alone, like the other children now, alone and forsaken. She cried, pitying her awful situation.

"Is your father dead too?" the soft voice of thirteen year old Cai whispered. She and the other three thirteen year old girls had come down to see what had happened. All four stood beside Marzella, watching the older boys drag the dead men out of the inn.

"Yes, we are all alone," Marzella whimpered.

"No you are not alone, Marzella," Chan whispered consolingly. "You have us. We are with you, Cai, Feng, Li, and me. We must help each other now."

"She's right, Marzella. Me must. Say, I wonder if now we can use those yoke things that appeared when the plague came?"

"Huh?" Marzella mumbled, not grasping what Chan was saying.

"When the plague came, we found shoes, yoke things, and all sorts of stuff in our houses. Our parents forbade us to have anything to do with them. They said that they were evil, but how can a wooden yoke be evil? We all have images in our minds about how to use them, but our parents would not hear of them. Didn't you have any images? We all did," Chan explained. Li, Cai, and Feng quickly agreed with her.

"Well, I did, but I didn't pay them any mind," Marzella answered, remembering her father's admonition to always speak the truth.

"We all think that we are supposed to use the yokes so that we can carry things," Chan added.

"We are supposed to use the hairbrushes with our feet, we think," Li added her thoughts.

"We've all been comparing ideas since the plague came. Can we use these things now?" asked Li. "We might be able to even feed ourselves with those spoons and strange mugs."

With no adults now telling the girls that they could not make use of the objects, the four older teens insisted the fellows help them retrieve all the alien items that they felt they could somehow use. Half of the day was spent gathering up yokes, brushes, mugs, spoons, and other useful items from the many homes. A few had been tossed in the village garbage dump and several yokes were rescued from there as well. "You can actually use these?" Jian asked his sister.

"We are going to try. After all, Jian, there are too many of us for you fellows to manage on your own. We older girls are just going to have to help somehow," Marzella replied with a newfound enthusiasm. She and the four older girls then proceeded to help the older boys carry all the stored food from the hiding place in their grandfather's basement into the inn. Although the boys struggled to make supper, the girls constantly gave them directions. None had ever cooked a meal before, but many of the girls had. Thus, they began to take charge of meals. However, the boys had no idea how to install the low to the ground kitchen items and thus had to follow the girls' cooking instructions.

After a week of getting used to surviving on their own, several local farmers came into the village to see what had happened. Chi-ism had taken hold, and most of these men merely nodded and said that the children would have to accept what was. Jian glared at these farmers; he was not about to accept this situation. However, the farmers did agree to occasionally bring what produce and supplies that they could afford into the town for the children, especially so with milk for the very young. In trade, they began stripping some homes of usable lumber for use on their farm buildings. Jian wondered what would happen when the buildings were torn down, what could the kids trade then?

In June 824, he decided that he must return to their home in Da Nang and at least get their things. He really wanted to retrieve his two long guns. Here, they had only found three guns and little ammunition. Thus, he and Bo, another thirteen year old boy, hitched up Angelo's carriage and headed off to Da Nang. Of course, Marzella had given him verbally a long list of her things to bring. "Hey, our place might have been robbed already, sis," he'd countered, making no promises to bring back her things.

Jian was lucky. He avoided all the patrols on the way there, and their home had thus far escaped being ransacked by looters. He and Bo spent most all the night loading the carriage with anything either thought might be useful. The first things that the boys packed were all their stored food supplies, which were quite a lot in fact, enough to see the children through another two months. Soon, they realized that a second trip would be needed, and they spent the night.

In the morning, a number of neighbor children came by asking what had happened to Jian and Marzella. Of course, Jian took time out to tell them all the sordid news and of the death of his grandparents and father. To his surprise, several of the neighbor kids were in a similar situation. Overlord soldiers had been periodically raiding Da Nang, and their parents had been killed or abducted. Jian could not resist a six year old girl's begging for him to take her and her little brother with him. Thus, two more children joined the village of children.

However, soon word began to spread of a safe haven for children, especially orphans. Whenever Jian returned to fetch more things, more children approached him, begging to be allowed to come with him. By August, for twenty miles around Hun Ho, the children knew that if they were in need, they could find sanctuary in Hun Ho. Just ask for Jian. Child by child, their numbers grew. By September, over two hundred children were holed up in Hun Ho's inn. Yes, the inn was now getting very crowded, but none minded. They were safe, had enough to eat, and had a roof over their heads. Besides, the girls were rapidly learning various ways to deal with their own needs and life, using many of the alien objects. Their self-respect soared.

Jian and several of the older boys had turned fourteen by September and were officially of age. Being the eldest, they took on more and more responsibility for the care of the younger children. Already, Jian had helped them amass twenty-five long guns and plenty of ammunition. All swore that if the soldiers ever came to Hun Ho again, they would shoot them! However, none did. Half of the homes were mere shells by now, stripped of siding and heavier timbers. Hun Ho looked more like some abandoned ghost town than a sanctuary for children. Still, Jian and the older boys worried about food supplies. Soon, the winter monsoons would come again. Where would they get more to eat and how?

Three newcomers had some ideas. Two brothers and their sister chatted with Jian. Lian Ho, who had just turned fourteen, suggested, "We know where the overlord stores all the food that he steals from the farms and villages around Shansee." Jian took a liking to this young teen; she had cleaned up nicely, thanks to Marzella and her girlfriends, who had given all newcomers baths and clean clothes, as could be devised. Lian had pretty blue eyes and a coy smile that melted his heart.

Her brother Pheng added, "We can take you there. It is a warehouse at the edge of Shansee, on this side. We can steal back some food they've stolen from everyone else."

Pheng's words pulled Jian's gaze off Lian's face, though she continued to smile at him, which Jian took as a very good sign. Jian said, "Surely they will have it heavily guarded."

Giu, their twelve year old brother, spoke up, "Yes, but we know some secret ways to get inside. We used to play there when it was empty. We can easily get inside."

"Okay, I like this idea. Even better, we should go during the monsoon. No one goes out in the monsoon rains unless they have to. The heavy rains will give us cover. We're going to have to get us some wagons, though."

Lian disagreed, "Not really, there are always a bunch of wagons inside. I know, we snuck in there to see what they were doing. That's why we know they are storing food inside. We can take their wagons."

"Well, I guess that is a good idea. We probably aren't stealing them, because they already stole them from other towns and villages, including ours here. We're just taking them back," Jian justified.

"Good. We can go as soon as the rains come," Lian declared.

"Wait, you can't go, Lian," Jian protested.

She stomped her foot on the wooden floor of the inn. "And just why not? I've been in there many times. You think that I am just a helpless girl? Is that what you think?"

Jian flushed; this was not going at all the way he had hoped. "But you don't have any arms and hands."

She stood tall and right in front of his face, "So what?" She was so close that he could smell her freshly washed skin.

"But, but," he stammered, unsure how to reply. The last thing he wanted to do was to upset her.

"Well, maybe your sister is helpless, but I surely am not helpless! I just do things differently than you do, Jian. I've been through this plague thing before, and I've figured out ways to do the things that I must do. So, either I'm going or the Ho's stay here. I'm the boss of us kids, now that mom and dad are gone."

"Okay, okay, you win. You can come along," Jian relented, though he hope that she meant what she was saying and would not hamper their raid on the food warehouse.

"That's better. I'm going to go help them wash up our filthy clothes now," Lian replied and headed off to lend some help to Marzella and her group who were now acting as mothers to the younger children. After all, they were the oldest and several were of age.

By the time that the November monsoons swept over all the southern regions of Tan Loc Provence, their food supplies were dangerously low. Jian hitched up his carriage. Covered with an oversized adult rain poncho, which certainly didn't fit him, Jian climbed into the driver's box, while Lian, Pheng, and Giu climbed inside. His friend Bo wanted to come along, but Jian insisted that he stay behind. "Look, if anything goes wrong, you are to take my place as leader, Bo." The two shook hands.

Even the horses protested being out in the torrential rains, but they did as he commanded. Jian went slowly, barely able to see the road. The rains flew nearly horizontal, obstructing daylight vision of everything except a few feet ahead. Already, the road was covered with inches of water. Jian wondered if the returning wagons would get stuck in the mud. He resolved not to over load them, just in case. It was nightfall when he finally drove through the streets of his hometown of Da Nang. For a moment, he entertained the notion to spend the night at his old home here at the edge of the town, but decided against it. They needed to raid the warehouse during the nighttime and Da Nang was only a few more miles from the edge of Shansee and the warehouse. He pushed on, but began wondering what they would do if the warehouse was now empty.

Around ten at night, he finally saw what appeared to be the outline of buildings ahead. He halted and called down to the others, "I think we are at the edge of Shansee now." Shortly, Pheng, also draped in an oversized poncho, climbed out and up to join him.

"Yeh, that's it. Go left now. We are close," Pheng replied nervously. He'd never been a thief before. Besides, men with guns would surely be guarding the place.

A few minutes later, Jian reined in rapidly. The sides of a building suddenly appeared out of the dark before him. Only the vertical rain coming off its sides alerted him to the obstruction. The rains continued to fall nearly horizontally. "We'd better lead the horses now," Pheng suggested. He climbed down, trudged through the accumulating water, and began leading the team, feeling his way along the side. Once on the backside, they got a respite from the rains. Here they parked the carriage and the other two climbed out.

"Okay, Guo and I will go around the warehouse and see if there are guards and all that. We'll meet you at our secret entrance. Lian will lead you, Jian," Pheng suggested. Before Jian could protest, the two boys headed off in opposite directions, staying close to the sides of the large warehouse.

"This way," Lian whispered, bending to keep her balance as the winds struck her once she moved beyond this side. She stopped beside what appeared to be a firewood shelter and stepped inside. Using her foot, she pushed on the back wall the warehouse. To Jian's surprise, the wall gave way. "Doggy entrance. We found it while playing hide and seek around four years ago. We'd best wait for the others before we go inside."

Jian guessed that the boys returned in around five minutes, though he had no way to tell precisely. "One horse is tied up in the warehouse shelter. There are six more in stalls in the stables nearby," Pheng advised.

"Okay, in we go, but be as quiet as possible. We need to find that guard first," Jian ordered. Lian ducked into the doggy hole before he could stop her. Gusty, he thought. He followed her, hoping that it would not be pitch black inside.

They were in luck. Several lanterns hung from the eight by eight vertical beams supporting the roof. Three wagons sat in the middle near a pair of double doors. To the right of the doors were a couch, table, and chairs. A man was dozing on the couch, about two hundred feet from their location at the back end of the warehouse. On either side of them lay many crates of food, nicely stacked on shelving. Jian thought that there was enough food here to feed an army! The overlord was hording the food, while others starved. For an instant, he wished that he could somehow distribute all the food to those who needed it. He banished that thought and focused on the single guard.

He motioned for the others to stay put. Using his skills, he slowly closed the distance between himself and the guard. If only the guard didn't hear him until he was close enough. Ten feet from the dozing man, his foot broke something underfoot, perhaps a twig or piece of dried wood. The guard rose and spotted him. He reached for his long gun and Jian had seconds to act. He rushed forward and used his hands in a one-two blow to the man's face. He jerked back, dropping the long gun. The guard pivoted and tried to shake off the pain. Jian followed through with a sweeping kick with his right foot, knocking the air out of the man, who didn't expect such an attack. Gasping, he drew out a dagger and swung it wildly before him, intending to keep Jian at bay while he caught his breath. Jian dodged and slammed his palm in hard on the man's neck. He heard bones cracking and the man dropped to the ground. The fight was over. The soldier was dead.

"Wow! Are you a martial artist?" asked a very impressed Lian, who had come running up along with her brothers to lend him a hand.

"Yes, black belt. Come on; we need to see if there are any other guards around," he whispered, picking up the man's gun. A quick check yielded no further guards. "Okay, let's start loading the wagons. We'll take two of them."

"Why not all three?" asked Lian.

"Cause there is only three of us who can drive the wagons, and one of us has to drive the carriage." Jian felt like a dope saying the rather plainly obvious.

Once more, Lian stamped her feet and shoved her body close to his. "Idiot. I'm not helpless. I can drive the carriage if you fix the reins for me. I've done it before, just ask Pheng."

Pheng nodded, unwilling to get involved. He knew his sister had quite a temper and wisely chose not to interfere when she was in this mood. "Okay," Jian whispered, hoping she'd back off. She did.

Lian ordered, "Now then, we should load the wagons evenly, just in case one gets lost or something. It will be a bad idea to have all of our meat in one wagon. Let's spread things around evenly. I'll find the right crates, and you fellows load them. That I can't do." Jian smiled. He liked her ideas, and quickly they began working as a team. Lian searched among the shelves and spotted what she wanted. The three boys each took a crate of that item and put it into the wagons.

It took them an hour to get just what Lian decided that they needed. Jian made sure that none of the wagons was loaded above its sides. Then, they strapped canvass coverings over the load. Finally, they dimmed the lanterns, and the three boys headed out to fetch the horses from the stables. After bringing them inside and closing the bay doors, they turned the lanterns up and began hitching up the horses. This took them nearly a half hour to do, because only Jian really had any solid idea of how it was done. His carriage was far easier to hitch up than these wagons.

When all was ready, Pheng slipped out the doggy door along with Lian. He helped her up into the driver's seat and then tied the reins together around the footrest board that ran the width of the carriage. If she lost the reins, they would not fall to the ground. Finally, he wrapped them around each of her legs. "Meet us out front," he whispered. He waited until he was sure that she could get the team started, before he ducked back in the doggy hole.

They turned out the lanterns and opened the bay doors. After the last wagon left, Jian stopped and secured the doors. Perhaps with luck, the theft would go unnoticed until the morning. He then took the lead with Lian on the carriage coming behind him, followed by Guo and then Pheng bringing up the rear. Again, the torrential monsoon rains blasted their faces, like a thousand stinging mosquitoes. This time, they were heading obliquely into the rain, making it even harder to see where they were going. Only when Jian finally saw the familiar buildings at the eastern edge of Da Nang did he relax a bit. He knew where he was at last. Now if only they could make it back to Hun Ho and not get lost or stuck in the mud!

Going slightly into the stinging rain was three times more difficult, Jian soon discovered. He had to go even slower than before just to be sure that he kept the horses on the road. Occasionally, he glanced behind him to make sure the others were still with him. He barely made out Lian and the carriage and hoped that her brothers were behind her. After an eternity, the pale dawn came, though the monsoon did not let up. It wouldn't — not for weeks now. He decided to stop, make sure all was okay, and that the two boys were still with him.

"Why are we stopping?" Lian asked, as he came trudging through the two inches of water that covered the road and lands around them.

"Just making sure we are all here," he yelled above the noise. The two boys grinned and said they were okay. Jian also noticed that their passage was completely obliterated by the rain. Encouraged, he resumed their travel and found the going was easier in the dim light of the day. Around noon, they finally pulled up before their inn home in Hun Ho. All four desperately needed to use the chamber pots and allowed the other boys to begin unloading their precious cargo.

"You are soaked!" Marzella exclaimed as Jian entered the inn and rushed to find an available pot.

"Yes, but we did it," he called out.

"Jian, please, little help here. I gotta go badly," Lian called out, struggling to find a way to get the oversized poncho off her.

He rushed to her and got the poncho off her. "Gosh, you're soaked too."

"Please, get me out of these clothes so I can go. Forget modesty. I've been holding it all night!" she exclaimed.

Marzella soon came up to them carrying a couple of towels between her teeth. Jian took one and dried off Lian, who gave him a big smile. Marzella then ushered Lian off with her to help her get dressed into something dry. Shivering, Jian realized that he too needed to get dried off and into warm clothes as well.

A half hour later, he stepped out of his room that he shared with the older boys and watched as the many children were still bringing in all the crates. Bo had already handled the carriage and was now dealing with the first wagon. Seeing Jian sticking his head out of the door of the inn, he called out, "Good going. I got the horses stabled. Looks like we now have three new wagons. great! I'll get them stabled up, Jian."

That evening, the two hundred fifty-three children had a victory celebration party! Never had they seen this much food at one time. Marzella estimated that they would have enough to last them until spring came. Of course, everyone wanted to hear all the details, and Jian had to tell the story for all the others.

Later, Lian came up to Jian. "You were impressive fighting that soldier. He had a gun and a dagger, you know." She smiled coyly.

Embolden, he replied, "Well, you and your brothers sure knew what you were doing. Hey, I never did see just how you managed to drive the carriage."

"I used my feet, silly. As I keep telling you, we girls have to do things differently than you boys. But thanks again for helping me out of those soaking clothes."

"No problem. I am really impressed with what all you can do, Lian. Maybe you can show Marzella how to do some things."

"I have been, silly. Thanks for taking my brothers and me in here. We were hoping and praying that you would. Life in Shansee is almost unlivable anymore." The two chatted for some time, although it seemed mere minutes to Jian. He didn't know why, but he like being this close to Lian. She then asked, "Say, would you mind giving my legs a massage? They are sore from all that driving. My back is too. I admit it. I rather overdid it, but I wanted to help."

"Sure thing, Lian. I am astounded that you could drive the carriage, let alone through the monsoon." He began massaging her legs and then her back too. "You don't give up easily, do you?"

"No, do you?" she replied, sighing from the relief flooding through her sore limbs.

"Well, no I guess I don't either," Jian admitted. He justified, "I do have to look out for my sister."

"I have to look out for my brothers," Lian replied, indicating another knot in her leg for him to work out.

Both began saying simultaneously, "I promised. . ." They stopped and looked at each other, surprised that they had been saying the same thing. "You first," Jian suggested.

"I promised my father when he was dying that I would look out for my younger brothers," she admitted.

"Same here, I promised dad that I'd get Marzella to safety."

"But she's older than you. She should be looking out for you," Lian replied, a bit confused. Then she got his meaning. "Oh, I see. You think that just because I don't have any arms anymore that my brothers should be looking out for me, is that it?"

He flushed, "Well, I suppose so. Marzella was so dependent upon dad and me — you know, after the plague and all."

Lian relaxed, "Okay, I get it. Well, not all of us girls intend on remaining helpless and dependent on you fellows. Sorry, Jian. I refuse to be utterly dependent like my mother was. She was a Great Lady, you know, small feet and all that. All she ever wanted to do was to look her best for dad. She tried to get me to follow in her footsteps, but I found hers too small for me. That's a joke, by the way."

Jian grinned, suddenly getting her jest. "Yes, mom was a Great Lady too. That's what dad found so intoxicating about her. Dad came from a foreign land, Zargarb, Sea Princes. I suppose that I can see why he found mom so charming. Great Ladies do look highly attractive."

Lian pouted, "So you are only interested in Great Ladies who can barely even walk?"

Jian flushed, "Well, not exactly, Lian. I mean that I can see why dad fell for mom. She was very beautiful and charming. Dad was always telling us stories about Zargarb. One day, I'd like to see those strange animals that he calls pacas."

"Well, that's better then. Tell me about this strange land. What is it like?" she asked. The two chatted away for quite some time, before Jian realized that it was way past time that he headed off to the kitchen to help the older boys fix the meal for the large troop of children.

"Thanks for the massage, Jian. Say, you don't need to rush off this time. Come on; I think Marzella has a surprise for you," Lian said with a wry smile. He helped her up, and they headed off to the inn's kitchen, where Jian was indeed quite surprised.

"Hi little brother! Surprise," Marzella called out. Bo and the other older boys were just beginning to carry the large pots into the dining room. Marzella and the four other older girls were just finishing up. The kitchen looked very strange from the last time that he'd been here cooking. While they were gone, the older boys had worked to install a lower height kitchen. Although they really didn't know just how to do it, they had managed to get most all of it working in some manner. Jian was shocked and nearly as pleased to discover that the older girls had now managed to cook the entire meal themselves. "We did it! We four actually cooked the whole meal!"

Jian gave his sister a big hug, and then hugged the other three very pleased teens as well. "Incredible, sis, ladies. Incredible!"

"See, I told you that we are not helpless dependents, Jian," Lian added with a grin. "We've been planning this for days."

His friend Bo spoke up, "We did our best to install the things that they said they needed. It looks crude, but everything mostly works, Jian. We had to do something while you were gone."

"Well done, fellows, well done," Jian answered. A few minutes later, the large gathering of children began commenting that this stew was the best tasting stew ever. Jian flushed, knowing that he was not a chef, while Marzella and her three friends beamed. At last, the four had really begun to contribute in a big way to the survival of the group.

A few days later, Lian and Marzella were having a private chat, while working on trying to find ways to mend the rags that the children called their clothes. "Bo kissed me last night," Marzella admitted.

Lian grinned, "He's handsome."

Marzella giggled, "I know. I got goose bumps when he did it. Are we supposed to get them? I wish mom were here. He must like me, don't you think?"

"That's for sure, Marzella. Have you seen how he is always looking at you when you two are in the same room? I think he's mad about you. Do you like him?"

"You bet. But I don't want to seem too forward. Besides, just look at me now. My breasts have gotten almost as monstrous as mom's were. God, they are huge now. I can't see why Bo would really be interested in me, not when I look so awful. He should wait and find a real woman, not one as helpless as I am."

"Oh don't be silly, Marzella. All women are like us now. No one has arms and look at my boobs! They are even larger than yours are, monsters. So really, where is Bo ever going to find a woman as we used to be? Nowhere. Besides, you are very pretty. Stop putting yourself down, Marzella. You are a fine person, really you are. Bo would be a fool not to court you."

"But I'm not a Great Lady like mom was. He deserves the best. Bo is really cute and smart and strong," Marzella countered.

"Hey, you are the best, Marzella. Look, it was you and your brother who have saved all these children from starvation and death, including my brothers and me. Didn't you have screwed up feet when the plague first came?"

"Well, yes, our feet were all bent weirdly. I could only walk if I wore those alien shoes."

"Okay then, your bent feet were almost like mom's small feet, when she was a Great Lady. Did you like how you could barely walk in them?"

"No, it was awful. Such impossibly small steps," Marzella admitted. "But all the Great Ladies are so fashionable, Lian."

Lian giggled, "Point taken. Yet, I don't want to have to walk that way all the time."

"I know. That's why I began wearing those extreme heels after my feet got better. They are almost like having small feet."

"Good point, Marzella. I see what you mean. You could choose to look like a Great Lady whenever you wanted to, makes sense. I never thought of it quite like that. You're right; we need a choice. Say," she grinned coyly, "do you know if Jian likes me? Your brother is awfully cute too."

Marzella giggled, "Haven't you noticed? Ever since you four got back with the food, he is always watching you when you aren't looking. I think he really likes you."

"No. He is? Oh," she flushed. Lian asked, "Can you find out — I mean without actually telling him that I'm really interested in him? You, you don't mind if I like him, do you?"

"Of course not, Lian! You've saved my life, showing me that I can still do nearly everything! I owe you tons. Besides, I think he's prefect for you, Lian."

Later that night while the two were brushing out their hair before bed, Marzella giggled, "He's smitten with you, Lian!" Both giggled. "I think that you might have to make the first move, though. Jian is terribly shy with girls." They chatted for quite some time.

In March when the rains ceased and the earth began sending forth spring life once more, the old farmer whose plot was just at the south edge of the village came to visit. Jian, Bo, and the four other older boys met with him in the dining room of the overcrowded inn.

"Fellows, my wife and I want to thank you for helping all these children," he began. Jian thought that the farmer must be at least sixty maybe more. His hair was nearly grey and his weathered face must have witnessed many a spring and hot summer. "The soldiers have taken away my boys and I am just too old and tired to farm any longer. I want you kids to have my farm. I can tell you how to take care of it, plant this year's rice crop, and how to milk the three cows. I just can't do all that work anymore. If you don't want it, then so be it. I'll see if my neighbors want it. I've got no one left to inherit my farm."

Jian jumped at this opportunity. Soon, the older children were spending their days with the old man, learning many things. By April, they actually had the crops sewn. Milk was now plentiful for the younger ones, though the older ones still drank it sparingly. "Things are really looking up, Lian," Jian whispered to his girlfriend later that night. The two embraced, though a couple of younger children who were watching them went "euh!"

Chapter 66 Flight

By the early summer of 825, the situation in and around Shansee had deteriorated further. Overlord Tao Tian had just taken over control of the city finally, having had slain well over twenty thousand men who had stood in his way. Many of these had been the gang leaders, who had taken control during the time of the plague when Don Ho ruled expos facto. Now consolidating his army, his recruiters combed the city, abducting in to his army young men between sixteen and twenty-five. Resist and you'll be shot became the constant words spoken by his recruiters.

Housing for his army was simple. He took over the vacated estates of those who had fled. Besides living in luxurious mansions appealed to the young soldiers, who saw this as an added inducement. Why? Their pay was in copper coins and rumors suggested iron coins would soon follow once the supplies of copper were exhausted. The dozen Banca del Dio's secretly sent their records and remaining assets out of the city via train to Nan Yan. Now they officially closed their doors for two reasons. Most of the younger men who worked in the banks, having taken over for the women who could no longer perform teller's jobs, had been forced into the army. Secondly, there were little new funds being deposited — no gold for months and little silver. Thus, when Overlord Tao raided the Banca's hoping to find treasure in their vaults, he found the vaults opened and empty.

With Overlord Nanguros controlling the lands surrounding Shansee, very little food supplies made it into the city these days. His men charged a stiff tax on every wagonload of farm produce that entered the city. Likewise, Overlord Tao charged an equally high tax on all the fish products being sent out of Shansee. Fish had slowly become the only readily available source of protein in Shansee, and many began to try to grow produce in their yards, if they had such.

On the other hand, through many street fights and clandestine raids, Xiong Fu finally achieved his goal: the opium czar of Shansee. He'd been a subordinate of Don Ho and had battled many others for control of the man's opium trade when Don Ho mysteriously died. One by one, he and his thugs managed to eliminate the competition. Now Xiong Fu controlled all the opium distribution in Shansee. His supplies came in via riverboat from northwestern Tan Loc Province and southwestern Wontun Provence.

By the summer of 825, his situation took a strange turn. With almost all gold gone from Shansee's population as well as gemstones, his customers sought other ways to pay for their next bag of the drug. Xiong saw this coming, however. At first, he allowed men to trade their women for drugs, as long as the women were young and marginally attractive. These, he traded to the pleasure palaces, forcing the women into the kami trade. Soon, those palaces were overrun with new kami and fewer and fewer could even afford to make use of these pleasure palaces. Xiong then began selling the women to the various houses of prostitution in the slummier sections of Shansee. Unlike the well cared for kami, these women were ill-treated and, as a rule, did not survive more than a few months at most. Hence, for a time, Xiong had a viable market for the many young women being traded for the men's opium.

He knew that would not last for long, and soon his addicts begged for their next bag of opium, offering to trade anything at all for their next fix. He began to accept more valuable merchandise, such as fine chairs, fine guns, fine china, and even silverware. These, he sent back to his suppliers as payment for the drugs that they delivered to him. He also sent a fair number of women as well.

Thus, the summer of 825 became known as the Summer of Starvation. Xiong stepped in and began giving small pouches of opium to the common men in the slums. Quickly, these men also became hooked on the drug, trading anything of any value to his dealers, many of whom had been recruited from the gangs of thugs who controlled the many streets of Shansee.

Yet, Xiong was not stupid. He knew well that soon few would have anything left of any value whatsoever to trade for their next hit. Further, he could read the telltale signs of the impending overlord battles coming. As far as he was concerned, it mattered little whether Overlord Nanguros or Tao won. The prize was a defeated city full of starving, worthless people, over half of which were now hooked on opium. At least, he thought, they can take pleasure in their dreams while their bodies slowly starve to death. No, the winner would win nothing of value at all. Instead, Xiong began planning his secret exodus. In the beginning, he had counted on banking all of his profits in the Banca del Dio. If so, he merely had to travel elsewhere and have his funds transferred there. Now that plan was dashed; they were closed. Bankrupt, some said.

Xiong knew that he would have to take his wealth with him when he left the city for good. Chairs and china simply could not be transported. Hence, he slowly accumulated what gems he could get his hands upon by any means possible. When the time came, he could carry them with him onto the steam train out of Shansee. However, he hedged his bets. If the overlord wars somehow cut off the trains, he needed an alternative way to flee the city. Going upriver was out, that only led to further chaos. No, he'd need a sea worthy ship to take him far from Tashien. Day by day, he continued his preparation in secret.

The children of Shansee suffered the most during this incredibly Dark Age. Slowly their parents succumbed, one way or another. If their dads were not abducted into the army, many became hopeless opium addicts, forsaking all, even trading off their wives and young daughters for their habit. Mostly left to fend for themselves, thousands of desperate children roamed the streets in search of any morsel to eat, either for themselves or for the girls that they were watching over. Yes, it was the smaller boys who ultimately took responsibility for their female siblings, whether older or younger than themselves.

Many children died of food poisoning from eating rotten food. Others fell ill to the diseases, which now ran unchecked throughout Shansee. Yet, many began hearing of the children's sanctuary in Hun Ho, some twenty-four miles west of Shansee. With the coming of the warmer weather, many small groups of children began to make their way to Hun Ho. Walking on foot and without food or water, many never made it to the promised sanctuary. Still, over time, hundreds did make it, bringing vital news of the tense situation in the huge city.

The news grew more and more ominous with each passing day that summer. Jian and Bo constantly worried about the anticipated war between the overlords. Hun Ho was far too close to the city for comfort. On June 6, disaster struck these children.

Bo was out in the fields helping the hundreds of children who were all lending a hand working the fields. Of course, vipers were a huge problem in the rice paddies. Already six smaller children had been bitten and died as a result. Bo took it upon himself to do what he could for the kids who worked the fields. If all went well, they would harvest enough food to get them through the winter. At least that was the hope of Bo and Jian.

Suddenly, Bo heard the thunder of horses and sounded the alarm. A dozen of Overlord Nanguros' soldiers came galloping up, swarming through the ruins of Hun Ho. Charcoal had long been used up. True, they had gone house to house confiscating all the charcoal, but now the kids had been burning the larger timbers of the shells of the homes. Only the inn remained untouched. Two soldiers stopped to search it hastily. Finding only smaller children in droves, they hastily left them and joined the others, who had ridden out into the fields. Jian had seen them coming and had ordered all the older children hidden — those who might be subject to abduction into the army or taken as prostitutes. Hearing the horses leaving, he took his two special long guns and headed outside to follow them. He feared for all the older boys working the fields.

He was right to be worried. The soldiers spotted several older boys and attempted to abduct them into their ranks. All resisted and, as Jian drew closer, gunfire erupted, scattering the boys like chaff in a strong wind. He saw he dear friend Bo dropped by a soldier's gun. Anger seethed through Jian. He sat down and took aim. He was six hundred yards from that man, but he knew he could get him. Bang! He fired and then rolled to a new position. His shot was true; the soldier fell off his horse, dying as he landed.

With all the other gunfire, his shot was not perceived. Jian took heart. Bang! Bang! Bang! He fired as rapidly as he could. Each shot felled another soldier. With over half of the band dead, the remaining five wheeled around, trying to grasp what was happening. Who was shooting them? Jian got off three more deadly shots. Fear flooded over the last two soldiers who still had not located Jian, hiding among the tall plants of the field. Bang! Bang! His last shot dropped the final soldier, but not until he was nearly eight hundred yards away. Seeing no more soldiers, he got up and raced to where he'd seen Bo fall.

He sat down and cradled his dear friend's lifeless body. Tears streamed down his face. Sometime later, Marzella and Lian came running up, and his sister shrieked and broke down. The love of her life was gone. Lian did her best to comfort her. The four older boys quickly got the survivors back into the safety of the inn. Ten of the boys had died, including Bo. Near sunset, Jian finally returned to the inn. He had buried all the boys and burned the soldiers' bodies. They now had another dozen long guns, ten horses and tack, though such could not compensate them for the loss of the boys.

"Marzella's taking this hard," Lian whispered to Jian as he entered the inn. "She's in her room, crying. I saw you take out all the soldiers, Jian. You were so far away from them. How did you do it?" she asked what many of the older ones had been asking all afternoon.

"My special long guns. I invented a special sight that allows me to shoot from a very long distance away. I miss Bo already. Damn those soldiers! It isn't safe around here anymore, is it Lian?"

"No, and it will probably get worse if the overlords go to war with each other," she replied. He agreed and went to console Marzella. He put his arms around her, and she leaned her head on his shoulders and cried heavily once more. Wisely, he said nothing, for what could he say? Nothing would bring his friend back.

The next morning, he held a group meeting. One thousand two hundred three children crammed into every available space in the inn's dining room. "Okay, we are going to have to send out watchers in all directions around here. We will use the ten new horses. Ten of you will ride out about two miles in all directions and keep watch. Hide yourselves well. If you see more soldiers coming our way, you are to get back here as fast as possible to warn us in time. I and some others will lay a trap for them, if they are not too many for us to handle."

He described in detail what he wanted done and had many more volunteers than he needed. Soon, ten rode off and for a time, everyone felt a little safer. At least if more soldiers came, they would have a little advance warning and could hide better. Here in the inn, the boys had made a fake wall in the basement where the older girls and boys could run and hide when trouble came. Thus far, no one messed with the younger children.

"We are going to have to evacuate Hun Ho," Jian explained to Lian, while he sipped the tea that she had made for him. Marzella sat quietly beside him, her eyes still bloodshot.

"Where will we go?" Lian asked.

"My dad told us to go to Zargarb, but that is too far and I don't know the way. I think the only way we can go is west. Many be we can hide out in the foothills. If we go far enough west, we can leave all the towns behind us. Maybe there we all would be safe," he replied.

"But how can we take all thousand of us? What will we eat?" asked Lian, already making plans for the evacuation that she knew would one day happen.

"We've got three wagons and a carriage. We probably can also use the three wagons on the farm as well. If we load them down with food and water, we can walk away from here. At least, we'll be able to eat," Jian suggested.

"Well, we better do it soon," Lian suggested. She was very worried about the ill turn of events. Besides, if the soldiers found her, she would either be raped or sold to some whorehouse. Her life would be over and she knew it. So did Marzella and the other girls who were thirteen or older.

Jian moved the wagons up to the inn and during the daytime, he and the older girls supervised loading them with food supplies. They left room on top for a large quantity of yokes, without which the girls would be unable to carry anything to help. At the end of the day, he had the three wagons covered with canvas and ready to go.

The next day, he brought up more wagons from the farm. Several other farmers donated some of theirs and Jian now had six more wagons to load. Around noon, one of the ten spy riders, as the kids called them, came galloping into Hun Ho, very excited. "Riders are coming! Riders are coming!" the lad called out.

At once, they older girls began heading everyone back inside the inn, taking cover in the basement hiding places as well. The older boys did their best to hide the wagons, while Jian queried the spy rider. "Three riders are coming from the west. They are on the back roads. I didn't see any guns, but they were pretty far away. I came as fast as I could," he gushed. After complimenting him, he sent him back out to keep watch again. Jian fetched his two long guns and took up a position in the ruins of a home. From his vantage point, he could cover the entire entrance to the inn. Three other boys took up nearby positions with a pair of long guns apiece. The idea would be to shoot as many of the soldiers at one time as they could. Now Jian could only wait patiently. Nevertheless, his mind raced. Had he been too slow evacuating Hun Ho? Doubts flooded through his mind. At last, he put his martial arts training to good use, quieting his many counter-thoughts. He waited.

"What do you make of that kid who was spying on us, Yan?" asked Yin as the three rode along the mostly deserted dirt road. Yin, Yan, and Bao were on a secret, special mission for Master Feng. Their task: infiltrate Shansee and see what the situation was in the city. While they were now healed of all the plague's adverse effects, many thought that sending women with arms on this mission would be too risky. However, that these women could also deliver visible proof to those that they met that salvation awaited in the Nan Yan Church of God more than offset this. Besides, Bao was now a Level 12 Master herself and the twins, Yin and Yan, were Level 10. If anyone could find their way around a city, it was these twins, who grew up in the city sewers. The twins were now of age, fourteen, and Bao was sixteen. Already they had visited many smaller villages and hamlets, to say nothing of remote farmsteads, where they spread the word about Nan Yan, giving real hope to the women they met and hope of an economic recovery to the men. They had decided to approach Shansee from the western edge and had to go through Hun Ho, reputedly a tiny village. Some twenty miles further east and near the edge of the city, they planned to hold up in Da Nang and gather news before entering the city proper.

"Dunno. Seems like he is maybe ten years old at the most. He sure lit out fast when he first saw us," Yan replied.

"I don't think we need to worry about him. Overlords don't use children, not that anyone has ever hear tell of — 'course, these days, who knows," Bao added. "We should be getting close to Hun Ho, if that last farmer was right in his directions."

"Hey, another day and we ought to be spying on Shansee," Yin changed the topic.

"Wonder what we'll find?" Yan added. As always, these twins seemed a bit uncanny to Bao. Each always knew what the other was thinking. Bao smiled, remembering when she'd first seen these two twins. Precocious, yes, but lovable. She had begun their training and had seen them all the way through Level 10. Now at night around their campsite, she was training them on Level 11 kijutsu skills. Yin and Yan were very able students. Bao had no doubts that one day they would achieve total mastery of the Olin Masters.

Several more times they spotted that same boy watching them, but now he seemed to be retreating as they moved forward — a definite change in his tactics, Bao noted. Still, he seemed harmless enough. An hour later, they spotted Hun Ho ahead and soon rode into the village from the west.

"My god, what happened here?" Yan gasped, staring at all the shells of homes. Chimneys rose like tombstones.

"All the wood had been ripped off," Yin added.

"Hey, only one building is still intact. That must be the inn," Bao pointed out. "Let's stop there and see if anyone is around. I wonder what happened to Hun Ho? There is supposed to be a thousand people living here. Are they all dead?"

They pulled up before the inn and dismounted. Jian watched the riders closely. As they dismounted, he received a shock. These three were women! They also had arms and hands! That they also did not have massive bosoms, he noted but didn't think much about. Women with arms. Where did they come from? What did they want here? They did not seem to be armed so he rose and stepped out of his hiding place.

"Ah, here comes someone now," Yin noted.

"He's got long guns. Watch out," Yan pointed out.

"Remember, be friendly," Bao cautioned them.

"As long as he's friendly," Yin insisted. "He's kind of cute."

"Our age, I'll bet," Yan added.

"Hello. Who are you? Where did you come from? How did you avoid the plague?" Jian asked, very surprised with the teens. He guessed that the identical twins were his age at most, while the other was maybe a bit older than his sister was.

"I'm Yin. She's Yan, she's Bao. We come from Nan Yan. We got the plague same as everyone else, but the Church of God in Nan Yan has a cure for it. Got our arms back. So who are you and what awful thing happened to Hun Ho? Only the inn is left, at least we think that's an inn."

"Jian Corelo. Long story, but we are sort of under the gun timewise. There is going to be a war between the two overlords happening around here soon, and we have to evacuate as quickly as possible. Come on. I'll take you inside and you can talk to the others. I have to keep on loading the wagons." He lowered his guns, and the other boys came out of their hiding places, joining them. He stepped inside and gave the all clear signal. Soon the many children began reappearing.

More and more kids crowded into the dining room area. Yin, Yan, and Bao blinked, hardly believing what they were seeing — so many children and of all ages! At last, Lian and Marzella pushed their way into the room.

Jian introduced them and said, "Look sis, Lian! They have arms again and are saying that there is a cure for the plague! I've got to hurry up and get the rest of the wagons loaded in case the soldiers come soon. Talk to these three and find out how all of you can get this cure." He would have loved to stay and heard their answers himself, but he knew that soon those men he'd killed would be missed and many more would come looking for them. He had to be ready to evacuate everyone as quickly as possible.

"How many children are in here?" asked Bao.

"One thousand two hundred three. All are orphans; many came from Shansee. Jian and I started this refuge for us children last year. More and more keep on coming here seeking sanctuary. Soldiers came the other day and killed ten kids, but Jian killed all ten soldiers," Marzella explained.

"You're kidding? One thousand two hundred three kids and no adults?" asked Bao in disbelief.

"We have a count-off, if you want to hear them," Lian explained. "We do it so that we don't accidentally forget someone. We have ten three year olds; those are the youngest. Bo was the oldest boy, but the soldiers killed him the other day. We older ones are looking after the younger ones."

"How could Jian kill ten soldiers by himself?" Bao probed, still not grasping the complete picture.

A young lad spoke up, "He knows martial arts, but he was too far away for that. He used his two special long guns." Several others agreed with him. Another added that he hid in the grass and the soldiers couldn't see him.

"He's got his own invention on his guns that allows him to shoot accurately over a very long distance," Marzella attempted to explain it further. "I admit that I don't know any more than that. We older girls were hiding in the basement to avoid being taken away by the soldiers. They have not yet bothered the younger children, not yet anyway."

Lian added, "But that will likely soon change. There is about to be a big war between Overlord Nanguros and Tao. Tao controls Shansee and Nanguros controls all the lands around here. The latest kids to find us from Shansee tell us that the soldiers are about to go to war with each other. You had best come with us. We are escaping to somewhere to the west where we can be safe. Is Nan Yan going to be a safe place for us? Do they really have a cure for the plague there? I had to breathe in some gas last time, but I couldn't smell it. Is that the way it is this time?"

Bao looked at the many, many faces watching her and her companions. She noticed that every face was clean. Even their clothes were clean. However, most clothing was beyond worn out, patches upon patches and ill-fitting at best. The kids were obviously making do with whatever they could find. Most had no shoes. At last, she answered, "Yes, Nan Yan is the safest place in all Tashien for you kids. Totally safe. All the Olin Masters are there ensuring it, along with the princess, General Tao, and his men. That is where you have to go. Can some of you tell us what has been happening around here? Hun Ho is in ruins."

Eagerly, the children began telling the three new arrivals everything, though the older girls had to maintain order, allowing each child to contribute his or her ideas and tales. Lian excused herself, because she and several others had to get their supper going if they were to eat on time. Yin and Yan decided to follow them and lend them a hand, though they allowed the armless teens to ask for assistance when they needed it. Both twins knew all about self-respect and self-reliance. "So you older girls do all the cooking?" Yan asked.

"Yes, ever since the older boys managed to rig up the kitchen for us, but we ran out of charcoal and now have to use what wood still remains on the ghost homes," Lian explained, as Yin lit the stove for them.

Jian and the older boys finally got the last of the wagons loaded up, nearly emptying the basement pantry of their remaining food supplies. Also, they had loaded up a fair amount of timber to burn in cooking fires. One wagon carried the timber and all the cooking gear, though most of that would have to be loaded at the last minute. Another wagon was completely stuffed with blankets for sleeping, though Jian suspected that they simply would not have enough to go around. Still, it was summer, and as long as the weather held, this shouldn't be too bad a problem.

No, he was far more worried about running out of food and whether all the children could manage to walk that far. Nan Yan seemed impossibly far away. He already planned to put the youngest children in the carriage; they'd get to ride, but most would have to walk on foot.

Bao stepped outside. "Hi, Jian. Can I have a word with you please?" She'd decided that it was time to level with Jian, who appeared to be the leader of the children.

"Sure, I've just finished loading the wagons. I need a breather. We have to be ready to leave soon, probably in the morning," he replied.

"Your sister tells me that you are a martial artist," Bao began.

Jian smiled, that seemed like an eternity ago. Was it even real? He remembered how his training had saved his life when the soldier in the warehouse tried to stab him with a dagger. "Yes, I got my black belt from the Tishi Academy, but that was years ago."

Bao bowed to a fellow artist, surprising Jian, who reciprocated. She explained, "I am Level 12 of the Olin Masters Academy. Yin and Yan are Level 10 's. Pleased to meet you." Jian bowed even more respectfully.

"Wow! Three Olin Masters! Incredible. Welcome. Say, we heard that they all moved to Nan Yan."

"Yes, we evacuated Tashien when our survival was threatened. With our help and that of others, we've made Nan Yan a place of survival, and it is now thriving and far more prosperous than before the plague came. We three are on a mission for the Olin Masters, but we now realize that part of our mission is completed. We have a good idea what the situation is here near and in Shansee. We would now like to offer you our assistance in getting the children safely to Nan Yan."

"I would be honored for your help. We have over a thousand children, most orphans, to get to safety. I'm afraid most will have to walk there. We've enough food for over a month, I hope. The smaller ones can ride in my carriage. I have ten other horses; the boys are fanned out around here and will give us a warning if the soldiers are coming our way. Say, is it true that the Church of God can help our girls get their arms back? I'd give anything for that."

"Yes, the church will give all of you their Basic Therapy, after which all traces of the plague's ill effects will vanish. Arms will reappear, almost as if by magic as far as I am concerned. Okay, how soon do you anticipate the soldiers will be returning here to Hun Ho?"

"No idea. We killed their entire patrol the other day. Eventually, they will send out another patrol to find out what happened to them. If they send only a few, I maybe can take them out before they kill any more children, but it is my hope that we can be long gone when they next appear here."

Bao squatted down and made a sketch in the dirt. "Look, we now have a steam train railroad line going from the coast up to Nan Yan here. Shansee is here and Hun Ho, here. We should make for the coast and the railroad line, using the back roads, avoiding all towns."

"Why? How will we get to Nan Yan? Following the railroad line?" Jian asked.

"No, the Olin Masters will have a train there to meet us, and the children can ride to Nan Yan in style and very quickly. If these overlords are going to fight it out, nowhere around here will be safe. My guess is that we can travel in an arc something like this, making the railroad after around twenty-five miles."

"But how will they know about us and have a train there? How will we pay for the train ride?" Jian protested slightly.

"Kijutsu. My master contacts me each day, and I relay what we've found out. You will not need to pay for the ride. By rescuing and providing for these thousand children, you have more than earned a simple train ride to safety."

"Thank you and thank the Olin Masters for me. Twenty-five miles is not that far, maybe three days. We can't push some of the children too hard. Some are not in very good shape after their ordeal in Shansee. Many came here half-starved, but we don't have enough food to really fatten them up, so to speak, though we've done our best to see that the youngest have had some milk," Jian explained.

"You are welcome, Jian. Perhaps we should leave some of the food that you've pack here in case other children find their way here later on," Bao suggested. "I will have the Olin Masters send some men to look after any more children who make it here to Hun Ho."

"Fantastic. I was actually a little worried about leaving here. We get more children wandering in every few days. If we leave most of the food, then far more of the littler ones can ride. Perhaps we can make it in just two days. Okay, we should get everyone to lend a hand unloading the wagons yet tonight. I guess we older boys got our exercise today loading them up," he teased. Bao nodded and promised they'd lend a hand with it.

The ten outrider spies returned for supper. Another ten rode out after dinner. Jian wanted to take no chances with the escape set for tomorrow morning after breakfast. During each of the four shifts of dinner, he explained what would be happening the next morning. Each time he added, "Our three Olin Masters will be leading us down to the railroad line. From there, we will be taking a steam train all the way into Nan Yan and safety. We will try to have all children under six ride in the wagons." Of course, they responded with cheers, clapping, and stomping.

By morning, everyone was on edge. Three of the spies had returned with grim news. Thousands of soldiers were massing barely ten miles from Hun Ho, forming lines that were miles long. Jian expected the boys were exaggerating a bit. Nevertheless, the long anticipated major battle had arrived. Hastily, the thousand plus children pitched in to get breakfast done and the things that had to be brought along to prepare their supper stowed in the wagons. Few had any other real possessions, save the girls who now had hairbrushes, yokes, and such. A few yokes could be carried, but the rest could not. Many girls sighed as they realized that once more they would be mostly helpless, unable to carry anything. Still the prospect of getting to this incredible Nan Yan and safety more than offset their annoyance.

The littlest children were packed into the comfortable carriage, which Lian insisted on driving. "Look, Jian, I am not helpless and I want to do my part. If there is any trouble, we are depending on you boys to protect us. So the least I can do is drive the carriage."

Jian gave her a quick kiss and she flushed. After helping her up, Marzella began escorting the littlest ones out and into the carriage. Bao lent her a hand, lifting the three year olds up and inside. All told, they got ten three year olds and seven four year olds into the carriage. It was packed, but the excited kids didn't mind. "Remember to tell Lian if you have to go potty," Marzella reminded the little ones. She still thought that one of the older girls ought to have ridden with these.

Two food wagons and one loaded with cooking supplies and one loaded with blankets moved to the front. They would lead the way. The carriage followed them. Three other wagons were loaded with the rest of the four and five year old children. They were packed in tightly, but that was better than making them walk so far.

Jian had the ten spies join Yin and Yan. Together, they would scout ahead and lead the entire group. Bao promised to lag behind and keep a sharp eye out for anything coming after them. Now the real work began for Jian. He had the kids begin to line up in rows of five. Each row was to walk just behind those in front of them. Some two hundred rows later, the last five fell into their walking places, making a line that was nearly eight hundred feet long. At last, Jian climbed aboard the lead wagon and they were off at last.

As they left the small town, the open rice paddies dominated the scene, with stands of bamboo forests dotting the landscape. Occasionally, a thicker patch of trees appeared on their left or right side. Mostly, rice paddies covered the nearly flat land as it did all around the greater Shansee area. Vast quantities of rice came from these many fields. Yet, the fields also contained quite a lot of water and Jian paid careful attention to the dirt road that snaked its way along between the fields. Why? Vipers were often found either in the rice paddies or on the higher ground where the dirt road ran. With so many barefoot children walking, a viper would spell death probably to many children, considering they were walking so closely together. Often he would halt the wagon to encourage a snake to move out of the roadway.

About two miles later, far off to their left lines of soldiers were spotted. Thankfully, none were facing them, though at first, many children became scared that they were about to be slaughtered by the soldiers. Even Jian was very uneasy with so many soldiers barely a mile from them. Although they continued to watch the seemingly endless line of gun toting soldiers, so far they were being ignored.

That did not last long. Soon, Jian spotted four riders galloping towards them. Bao spotted them and moved on up following an intercepting course. She placed herself between the long line of children and the oncoming soldiers. As they approached, she readied her most powerful kijutsu spell. As the four reined in before her, her illusion triggered. "A child slave labor patrol," the man called out to Bao, who seemed to be a man in their eyes. She nodded and the man sneered, neck reined sharply. The others followed suit and headed back to their skirmish lines, satisfied that these children were no threat to them.

"What did you do?" Jian called out to Bao as she rode up to him.

"Convinced them that we were a child slave labor party. Worked nicely. Keep on going; don't stop if more come our way," she advised, before dropping back to her rear guard position.

"It's okay. Don't panic," Bao repeated as she passed the long line of children. Most were attempting to be brave, but more than one were nearly ready to break ranks and flee. "We are doing fine." At last, she reached her rear guard position. Ideally, she would have liked to sneak up on the battle lines and watch what happened. The Olin Masters certainly would like to have a firsthand look at what was about to happen. However right now, the children had become her priority.

They had gone perhaps three miles when the sounds of gunfire erupted in the distance. Firecrackers, that's what the kids called them, and Bao had no intention of convincing them otherwise. "Keep on walking, kids. It is a long ways from us. We are in no danger," Boa yelled to the line of nervous children ahead of her. She certainly hoped that was true. If the battle somehow flowed to them, she knew that she could not stop the kids from fleeing in panic into the rice paddies. With so many vipers around, many would be bitten. She decided to slowly move up the line of children and attempt to instill calm.

At last, she reached Jian. His face told her everything. "Yes, the battle between the overlords has begun, Jian. We are likely in no danger. The gunfire is at least a couple miles away from us, and we are putting distance between them and us as we speak."

"Yes, but what if the line falls back. We're right in the way of them," he said what he had been fretting about since he first heard the firecrackers. He had both of his long guns now at the ready, Bao observed.

"The kids are taking it in stride, Jian. If you like, I could double back and keep watch on them and give us advance warning if their lines start to fall back towards us," she suggested.

"Hey, would you? That would be great. Perhaps the Olin Masters would also like you to observe the battle," he suggested.

Bao grinned, "You read my mind?"

He shook his head. "No, I am just as curious about it as you are, Bao. Go ahead, but don't lose sight of us. Thanks."

A half hour later, Bao reined in at a good vantage point, just inside a small grove of tall bamboo. Remaining mounted, she edged to the front and peered out at the scene before her. As far as she could see, men were fighting. Dead littered the ground. Most chose to simply stay on their mounts and fire their long guns as rapidly as they could. None was particularly fast reloading, she noted. None appeared to want to get any closer than the couple hundred feet that separated the opposing men. Instead, they just kept firing, reloading, and hoping that they were not shot in the process. After a couple of minutes, she observed that none of the men were really into the fight, but were merely going through the motions. The soldiers were in apathy, mechanical zombies firing away at the opposing zombies.

She watched the battle for about fifteen minutes before retreating, rejoining the caravan of children a half hour later. Bao took care that she was not spotted, though. She worried that someone might think that she was a deserter and come after her, which would lead them straight for the defenseless children. She need not have worried though. Along the line, the company leaders had their hands full issuing mostly unheeded orders to the dwindling ranks. Overlord Tao Tran had far more soldiers that Overlord Nanguros, but only a quarter of his were mounted. The rest plodded through the rice paddies, knee deep in the waters, destroying the young crop as they trudged through them. More than a few died from viper bites, however.

Overlord Tao's battle plan had been a simple one. Push out to engage the enemy and have the massive numbers of foot soldiers push on through any break in the enemy's lines. With a bit of luck, his men on foot would be able to encircle the enemy, finishing them off. That done, they would begin systematically raiding the towns and villages that had been under Overlord Nanguros' control, confiscating badly needed food supplies for Shansee. However, Overlord Tao had a backup, contingency plan. If his forces lost the battle, his riverboat was loaded and ready to sail up the Yonshu River to Giang. From there, he would either hold up at his dead parent's estate or continue upriver to the Lian River. There he would decide whether to head up the Lian to the foothills and relative safety or to head to the eastern coastal city of Shankou, where he seek sanctuary with that city's overlord, who owed him a favor.

Overlord Nanguros had a plan too. Although he had only a hazy idea of what life had become in Shansee, the lure of controlling such a huge, wealthy city drove him onwards. He knew that Overlord Tao's army had few horsemen and most would be on foot. His plan was to form long lines of mounted soldiers and avoid charging into the enemy. Rather, his men would stand fast and fire continuous volleys at the enemy. Once the few mounted enemy were dispatched, his troops would simply massacre Overlord Tao's foot soldiers. That done, he would ride victoriously into Shansee and be seen as a conquering hero, freeing the city from the oppression of Overlord Tao. That he was just as oppressive as Tao never entered his thoughts. He too had a contingency plan. If by chance his strategy failed, he would retreat to his family estate. From there, wagons carrying his amassed booty would take him into the western foothills where the opium overlords dwelled. With the amount of money that he would be bringing them, all would vie for his services.

Around noon, Yan dropped back to the lead wagon. "Hi Jian. Looks like the battle is giving us a big break. We've not encountered a single soldier all morning, but then they are not likely to be out here in the sticks. We'll be veering to the right shortly. The dirt track dead ends a mile beyond the junction ahead. There are an awful lot of snakes around these rice paddies, aren't there?"

"Thanks for the head's up. Yes, sure are. So far, we've been lucky and no one has been bitten." Slowly the sounds of the distant firecrackers died down. Around one, they took a long rest break, doling out water, some bread, and dried fish to the kids. By two, they were back on the road once more. Progress was a bit slower than Jian had hoped; the kids were tiring and would need more frequent rest stops, he concluded. What he dreaded most would be stopping for the night. So many mouths to feed — the fellows would have to do the cooking now. Worse, he still didn't know how they would be able to sleep in safety. The only idea he had was to simply camp out right in the middle of the dirt track and hope that no one came along.

In their favor were the long days. Around six, they finally halted and made camp right in the middle of the road. On either side, rice paddies stretched as far as the eye could see. Smoke curls drifted up here and there from the few farmsteads. Thus far, they had met only one aged farmer and his donkey carrying a load of produce towards a distant village. Hastily, the older boys began stoking a fire and preparing their supper. Lian and Marzella looked on, giving Jian advice on the cooking. Others kept the children more or less organized. Organized chaos dominated dinner.

"What are we going to do about the snakes?" Marzella asked Jian, as she watched him and several other boys doing up the dishes. "I don't feel safe sleeping on the road."

"We'll have to post guards," he decided. "Dole out the blankets, but have groups sleep close together. All have to be in the middle of the road. We'll keep lanterns going and take shifts watching for snakes."

Bao overheard them and broke in, "Wise move, Jian. Snakes will be attracted to the body warmth of the children. If you have enough kids watching the sides of the road while the others sleep, we should be okay."

While Jian and the others began making the arrangements, Bao met with Yin and Yan. "We are going to have to stay awake tonight and keep a sharp eye out for vipers attempting to join the sleeping children."

"Figures," Yan replied.

"We thought so. We've seen a lot of them today. Of course, we never saw them in the city, but out here in the rice paddies, they seem to be everywhere. No wonder so many farmers die from snake bites," Yin added.

"Right. If anyone spots one, come get me. I'll use kijutsu to move the snake safely away," Bao ordered. Both bowed to her, signaling their acceptance of her orders.

The night watch as it became called among the kids proved a wise move. Guards walked up and down on either side of the sleeping kids all night long. Several vipers attempted to partake of the warmth offered by the thousand sleeping children, but Bao carefully moved each one away from the sleeping kids.

Breakfast was also more like controlled chaos. Instead of an early start, they were unable to get going until close to nine that morning. Unlike the previous day, their second day went without incident. However, the kids were dead tired by evening. Yin and Yan estimated that they would make the railroad line by noon the next day. Once more, the older ones stayed up all night guarding the younger ones.

At noon, Jian shook his head in utter disbelief. When they finally reached the coast and the railroad tracks, there was an enormous train just waiting for them. How could the engineer possibly have known that they would appear at this precise spot, he wondered. As if guessing his thoughts, Yan whispered, "Bao has good kijutsu. Her doing. Me, I am going to sleep the whole way to Nan Yan," she yawned heavily.

"But we'll miss all the scenery," Yin protested, but also yawning. "Come on; let's start getting them aboard."

Those with arms were kept busy for quite some time helping all the children climb into the twenty large boxcars. At least, there was ventilation openings through which they could peer out at the passing countryside, Jian thought. After the thousand plus children were safely stowed, the engineers lowered a ramp, and the carriage and wagons were driven up onto the flat cars and tied down for the trip. Around three that afternoon accompanied by a loud whistle from the engine, the train began to move.

"We did it, Jian," Marzella said to Jian. The relief in her voice told all.

"Yes, amazingly we did it," added Lian, who leaned onto Jian's right side, while Marzella leaned onto his left side. All were sitting with their backs to the side of the boxcar. Dozens of other children were with them, most scrambling to get a peek at the outside world. None of the thousand plus children had ever been on a train before. Only a handful had even seen one, for that matter. This was all new to them and they were appropriately excited about it.

On June 15, 825, the thousand plus orphans of Shansee arrived safely in Nan Yan. They were met at the station by Master Tian Li and his wife, Counselor Bi Mei, along with a large party of helping hands. Bao quickly pointed out who they were to Jian, Marzella, and Lian. Thus, the three were very much in awe by their welcoming group.

After bowing and shaking his hand, Master Tian told the three who had masterminded this escape, "Words cannot describe how grateful we all are for what you and your many others have done. Children are the future of Tashien, and by your own actions, you have saved a large part of the future. Well done, all of you. Most impressive." Coming from the top Olin Master, Jian was flabbergasted. He'd only done what was right and honest. Yet the master thought highly of them.

Shortly, they were taken to the Olin Academy building, given a bath, and presented with proper fitting new clothes and shoes. Many had never had such fine garments before and were most impressed. After a good meal, hundreds of women began giving the children their first Basic Therapy sessions.

By July, all the children had finished. More importantly, all the girls had their arms back, the full effects of the plague undone. Interestingly enough, both Lian and Marzella decided to keep their massive bosoms and tiny waists a while longer. Now that they had arms, they wanted to see how they would look in their new clothes. Yes, Bi Mei had the Banca del Dio transfer all of his father's account into two accounts, one for Marzella and one for Jian. Their first action was to go shopping for fine clothing. Jian insisted that Lian get precisely whatever she desired in the way of dresses. He'd proposed to her and she had accepted.

The Banca del Dio president spent long hours attempting to track down any funds that the other children's parents might have had on deposit in Shansee or neighboring towns. At least a hundred children wound up with some funds of their own. Most, however, did not. Still, most all the older children were quickly employed by one of the many new MMCE companies, who desperately needed competent workers. Others were trained to deliver therapy sessions and joined those who were being given a salary to continue delivering Basic Therapy to those who needed it. Their expansion project had moved into high gear and daily more and more women and men were brought under the protection of Nan Yan.

On July 15, Jian and Lian were married. Thanks to Marzella, both young women now looked like Great Ladies, complete with form-fitting pencil dresses highly accentuated by their large bosoms and extreme heels, which did give them the appearance of having the traditional small feet. Jian merely said, "You two are total foxes!" Both women beamed, proud of their new look and appearance.

As Marzella explained to Lian, "Now we can have the best of all worlds. We can be Great Ladies when we desire and ordinary comfortable folks when we need to be. This is utterly perfect!"

Still, Jian wondered whether he should honor his father's dying wish that he take Marzella on to this Zargarb. In the end, he put it off for a time. There was far too much work to be done here in Tan Loc Province. He felt a strong responsibility to continue to help those in dire need.

After they helped the children disembark when they arrived in Nan Yan, Bao, Yan, and Yin met briefly with Master Tian. When the train left the next day, the trio was aboard, along with fresh provisions. The three had a new assignment: find out what happened with the huge battle. Who won and what was the current situation — these needed answering, for already the MMCE project was moving out eastward from the Nan Yan valley system, slowly heading towards Shansee. Everyone needed to know what the precise situation there now was.

When the trio finally arrived back at the battlefield, they were shocked and dismayed. Local farmers had no choice but to attempt to deal with the dead. Close to two hundred thousand men had been killed. Few wounded survived, as there were no doctors to patch them up. Wounds got infected and men continued to die for weeks afterwards. The rice paddies were mounded with the dead.

The winners of the battle turned out to be the local farmers, who suddenly came into possession of thousands of horses, tack, guns, and clothing. The farmers, who were all too old to be soldiers, began selling these in local villages and in Shansee as well. However, Bao made many deals with them and acquired well over twenty thousand horses and guns for General Tao back in Nan Yan.

After chatting with many farmers and many direct observations, she concluded that neither side had won the battlefield. However, now some farmers were beginning to venture into Shansee to sell their produce. Long afterwards, they learned what had finally transpired.

Seeing his army nearly wiped out, Overlord Nanguros quietly fled the battlefield. By the next morning, he and a huge wagonload of booty headed north and west into the opium overlords' territories, there to purchase a new start. Overlord Tao, seeing his vast army wiped out, quietly left the battlefield and before nightfall was sailing upriver towards Giang, taking a large pile of accumulated wealth with him. Later, he too disappeared into the lands controlled by the opium overlords.

In Shansee and the surrounding lands, nearly all the younger men were now dead. Old men, infirm men, and children remained, along with most desperate women and girls. With the main workforce destroyed, the situation within the once mighty city degenerated even further. However, Bao was under definite orders not to enter the city. Such would be far too dangerous for her and her two companions.

Chapter 67 High Country Drug Overlords

Ancient traditions were kept alive in the high, rugged country of western Tan Loc and Wontun Provinces, where the long, narrow Lian River divided the lands in half. In the eastern portions, the lush green hills were home to vast numbers of silk farms, honey farms, cotton, grains, and all manner of animal husbandry. Farther west, the rugged, jagged hills produced gold, silver, copper, iron, coal, and gemstones. Amid these lush lands of plenty lay the vast poppy and marijuana fields as well. These lands were the home of the drug overlords, fierce and independent men who for centuries successfully defied Imperial Authority.

Attempts to force these men to submit to the Emperor or Empress or of late the High Parliament met with continual failure. Why? These ruthless, vicious men controlled the delivery of the life-blood of Tashien, from basic foods to meat, eggs, cloth, honey, both precious and valuable metals, and gems. Sadistic some said, but these overlords were honorable to their own code almost to a fault.

Their code was a simple one. They had but one rule: unquestioning loyalty to the overlord. To question an order from an overlord yielded an instant and painful death, usually by being publically drawn and quartered by horses. Seeing a disobeyer being tied spread eagle between four strong horses and watching the horses gallop off in the four cardinal directions went a long way to strengthening this rule. Seldom was an offender simply beheaded. That set no example to others who might stray. On the other hand, those who were faithful in all ways were richly rewarded.

These drug overlords kept alive the most ancient of traditions of Tashien. Some claimed that these went back to the dawn of time. The overlords themselves always wore the finest of bleached white silken suits, with diamond cufflinks. Each wore a pair of diamond stud earrings, the larger the stones, the wealthier the overlord. All overlords and powerful men sported long, drooping moustaches, the ends of which fell below their chins. These men wore their never-cut hair tied behind their heads in a ponytail, never braided. Only the farmers and laborers wore theirs in a single braid.

These powerful men also kept alive the ancient tradition known as the Yingchan, roughly translated as the Golden Angels. Part of the Great Lady tradition found so widespread throughout all Tashien prior to the plague stemmed from these incredibly looking women. True, the practice of binding women's feet had been supplanted by the vastly simpler procedure of simply breaking their arches and forcing them to heal into the deformed small feet. Six weeks of wearing the iron boots yielded a small-footed woman, replacing years of tight foot binding used centuries ago. Prior to the plague, any woman of merit had small feet and wore the high arched extreme heels that forced her to take the tiniest of steps. That she also needed the strong arm of her husband to navigate the hilly terrain only added to their mystique and fame.

Yet, Yingchan meant far more than mere small feet. Each woman prided herself on her brightly painted fingernails, the longer, the higher her standing. The wife of an overlord always had at least six-inch long talons, usually painted bright red. They wore their hair parted down the middle of their heads, each half tied in a ponytail that draped down each side of her head. Still all this was but a fraction of Yingchan. These women had golden eye disks that were inserted over her eyeballs, giving the appearance of the woman having golden eyes. A very tiny central hole allowed her a small amount of vision and always only straight ahead. Yes, these women could just barely see.

Each Great Lady also had a golden circular disk inserted in her ear lobes. From these disks, a three inch golden bar hung horizontally. From the bar were hung six strands of six tiers of oblong golden ovals, set with prized gemstones. These magnificent earrings echoed the wealth of the Yingchan's husband or sponsor and were always a foot in total length as measured from the horizontal bar. Most earrings weighted between two and three pounds, due to the large amount of gold in them. Their heavy weight continually stretched the earlobe hole, and every few years, a larger circular disk had to be inserted. The oldest Yingchan's disks were often nearly five inches in diameter and worthy of great pride. Further, each side of their nose was pierced with a golden stud. Hung between each earring and the nose stud was a golden, lattice veil, dropping four inches down from the woman's nose, covering her mouth. Around their necks, a trio of golden rings supported a four pound gold and gemstone encrusted necklace.

Thus, to gaze upon a Yingchan was to gaze upon a golden angle indeed. Wearing contrasting colored, form-fitting, silken dresses with their black, high arched, extreme heels, these women drew everyone's admiration and attention, as befitting a Great Lady. However, these women also had one other aspect that in modern times was rigidly enforced by the overlords. They could not speak. Centuries ago, these drug overlords eliminated any protests and complaints from these Yingchan. At birth, women who were destined to become Great Ladies had their tongues removed. If a woman found herself elevated to this high status later in life, her tongue was removed at that time. Thus, no overlord or wealthy man ever heard the slightest complaint from these Yingchan, and to date, no Yingchan had ever been drawn and quartered for disobeying an overlord's order. Why? The average Great Lady wore between a half million to several million worth of gold coins! Besides, they could not speak beyond making an "ah" sound, meaning yes, and an "oh" sound, meaning no.

Just prior to the plague, Overlord Mag Tazau was one of the most powerful drug overlords. His base of operations was in the large town of Nag Tasha, located in the hills close to the Lian River in Tan Loc Province, and some seven hundred miles nearly due north of Nan Yan. The long arm of his control extended to within two hundred miles of Nan Yan to the south, on up to the Lian River to the north, and from the impassible mountains of the west to five hundred miles to the east of Nag Tasha. His was the largest of the drug lord controlled lands.

His wife, the gorgeous Li, prided herself on her seven-inch red talons and her impeccable Yingchan appearance. Her jewelry was once appraised at three million gold. She had an angular face and kept her lips a matching cherry red. She wore a dark blue eye shadow, which only added to her mystique and attractiveness, for she prided herself on being the best looking Yingchan in all of her husband's land.

She had born him both a son and a daughter. Meng was nineteen before the plague came and was Mag's undisputed heir-apparent. None dared disobey the teen, who was as impeccably well dressed as his father was. Some also said that he was just as sadistic as his father, but none ever said such outside of their homes, for that would be enough to be drawn and quartered! Meng had some martial arts training while he was growing up and now frequently used crippling moves on his opponents.

Their daughter was Dai, then eighteen. She was even more beautiful than her mother was, having extremely bushy, black eyebrows and very long lashes. Her face was almost squarish. Like her mother, she had six-inch long, bright red nails and painted her lips to match, but she was always careful to keep her nails an inch shorter than her mother's. It would be an affront to Li for Dai to appear more beautiful than her mother was. She too wore a blue eye shadow, enhancing her native beauty even more. Her gold and gemstone encrusted jewelry was appraised at two million gold, and she had her ear lobe disks enlarged several times before her eighteenth birthday. Hers were now over three inches in diameter. Unable to speak since birth, she was long used to not being able to speak, for Great Ladies never spoke.

At this time, Wu Shenyan was wooing Dai. Wu was a year older and a well-trained martial artist, who often beat Meng, much to Meng's anger. Yes, Wu had captured the eye of Overlord Mag. Here was a young lad who Mag felt was both worthy of his Great Lady daughter and of becoming one of his Seconds in command of his vast Opium Empire. He dressed himself appropriately and constantly professed his undying love for Dai. Although she could not speak, she made her love for him visible to the handsome, strong, and able young man.

Two days before the plague struck, Wu dined with the Tazau family. Proudly, he sat beside the beautiful Dai, the golden doll of his dreams. He watched as she carefully leaned forward to be able to see her plate from the near pin hole circles in her golden eye disks. Her highly practiced motions with her long fingers, exaggerated by her six-inch nails deftly picked up a bite of juicy steak. As she lifted it up to her mouth with her right hand, her left nails lifted her golden veil back enough to allow her to delicately place the morsel into her mouth, between her bright red lips. Wu marveled at how skilled Dai was, considering how hindered her actions were.

Across the table, Meng glared angrily at Wu, whom he'd failed to defeat yet again today during their fighter practice session. While he had dispatched all the other men of his father's garrison, Wu consistently defeated him, bruising more than his ego. With the meal finished, Wu assisted the nearly blind Dai to rise. Putting his strong arm around her waist, he escorted her out of the plush dining room. She flashed him a smile, though she could not see him. Of necessity, she had to bend her head slightly downward so that she could barely see the floor ahead of her. Wu matched her tiny steps of three inches. "Would you honor me with an evening walk, Most Honorable Dai?" he asked politely. She flashed him a smile and nodded her assent, her long, huge dangling earrings bouncing lightly against her chest.

An evening walk was the two's usual time together. The Tazau estate was huge and elegant. Nothing was too expensive to be found here. However, the plush carpeting, which looked as fine as that found in the most elegant of pleasure palaces, made her walking extremely challenging. Without his steadying arm, she would have been unable to negotiate the soft, thick, brown pile. She'd often tried on her own, but found her inability to see much at all and her tiny feet a combination for a fall.

As the sun set ruddy red over the distant hills, she wished once more that she could speak to her lover. All Dai could do was to turn her head so that she could glimpse his face and then point her long talons to the western sky. "Ah, yes, such is nature's beauty, but it pales compared to the beauty standing at my side, my dearest Dai." She grinned and leaned into him, putting her arms around him. She pressed her thick lips against his, but the golden weave of her golden veil kept their lips from actually touching each other. "I love you truly, my Dai." She uttered the only word that she could, making an "ah" sound.

For an enjoyable hour, the two strolled around the paved courtyard of the estate, taking in the intoxicating odors of the late summer flowers. Mag employed five gardeners to guarantee that no one's estate would be more adorned than his was. Neither noticed Meng glaring at them from the shadows.

Overlord Mag also had a harem of young beauties. These concubines were also Great Ladies or Yingchan. Every overlord kept a harem as well as their wives. While they often enjoyed these young women's company and sexual favors, the harem also served the needs of his Seconds and other important guests. Often after a meeting and lavish dinner, Mag would make the young women of his harem available for an enjoyable evening for his male guests or Seconds.

Overlord Mag had been steadily adding to his harem of Yingchan. At the time of the plague, he had four of the most beautiful young women that he'd found throughout his vast lands. All had come from much lower status; some were mere farmer's daughters. He made his choice based solely on their inherent beauty. Yes, each of these four was even prettier than either his wife or his daughter, the cream of the young maidens in his vast territory.

Binan was his most recent addition, added only three months before the plague came. She was a rural farmer's daughter, and he had remunerated the man a thousand gold for the loss of his daughter, primarily because the man had willingly offered him his daughter. Usually, the father would protest slightly that she was needed to help on his farm or in his business, though not enough to warrant being drawn and quartered. However, Binan was having a very hard time adapting to having become a Yingchan.

Although what remained of her tongue had healed, as well as her broken feet arches, she often was found crying to herself. While the golden ornaments that she wore were worth a half million gold, she had an awful time caring for her own personal needs. Unused to being almost blind, unused to having such tiny feet, and unused to the incredible heaviness of her earrings and the barrier of her golden veil, Binan was most miserable. She often fell while walking which only made life more difficult for her.

The other three young women had similar difficulties, primarily with seeing and walking, but they had been Yingchan for at least a year now. Several had been so for five years. These included Chichong, Danyin, and Huachun. While these four women were well treated and lacked for nothing, their lives were miserable, and worse, they could not tell anyone about it, which only intensified their misery.

Then the plague struck them all. The earlier plague had not reached this far north. Thus, this was everyone's first experience with the devastating plague. Wu's heart went out to the terrible plight of his love. Poor Dai, bereft of her much-needed arms and hands, was now completely helpless, as were her mother and the four harem women. With the men crippled up as well, Overlord Mag and his son, Meng, along with his two Seconds, Yi Huhe, and Jinan Sha, spent their days totally engrossed in attempting to continue control over his opium dominion. While Wu ought to have also been involved, he begged, "Most Honorable Mag, please allow me to assist your wife, daughter, and harem women. Without their arms, they are most helpless. Surely, we cannot allow such magnificent Yingchan to perish or suffer."

Distracted by his own crippled feet and the disaster threatening his very opium empire, Mag agreed. "Wu, I charge you to care for our Great Ladies. I simply cannot afford to give them the time and assistance that they need. If anything bad happens to them, I will hold you responsible."

"I will not fail you, My Lord, Most Honorable Mag," Wu bowed low. He had no intention of failing him, for such would also be failing his beloved Dai, who now needed him more than ever before. He quickly discovered that the six women absolutely had to have him supporting them while they attempted to walk. Without their arms to help them keep their balance and unable to see much of anything, they simply could not manage to navigate within the huge estate. Thus, Wu had little choice but to don the strange alien ballet style boots and learn to walk in them.

Seeing Wu somehow managing to walk on his toes in the strange boots, Overlord Mag and Meng had to do so as well. Soon, he ordered his Seconds and other soldiers follow suit. Thus, Overlord Mag slowly managed to get his operations continuing once more. However, he now had to hire a chef and other domestic staff men to replace the women who could no longer perform even the most basic of duties. Somehow, the whole group managed to survive the first two months before their feet returned to normal.

Overlord Mag held a victory celebration the very day that he was at last able to walk upright as a man once more. That the Yingchan women's feet also returned to normal, that is, before they had their feet turned into small feet, caused Overlord Mag much concern. At first, he insisted that these women now wear extreme heels, though he saw that in flats, the women were finally able to walk on their own.

The horrible experience that Mag suffered with his crippled feet hardened him, though some say that it merely re-enforced his sadistic streak. On the quiet, he ordered his shoemaker to use the alien boots as a model and fabricate similar boots made from pure gold for the Yingchan. However, the gold proved too soft, and Master Jinnan worked on a blend, retaining the desired golden color. The goal was to make the golden women even more golden. After all, they simply could not even protest, and besides, the men had learned to walk in them. Further, he decided that the metal boots should not be removable, but fused tightly to their feet. That way, there would be no opportunity for them to remove them or even desire such.

It took the master shoemaker, Jinnan, nearly three months to create the desired boots with strength enough to withstand constant wearing and yet would not permit any movement of their feet below their ankles or their removal. Each boot had to be form-fitted and molded to their feet. His first experiment on a wooden form of a foot resulted in the scorching of the wood. Most of the three months had been spent upon working out a way to mold them without burning the women's feet. He knew that if he did that, he'd be drawn and quartered!

His process infused steel and gold together, with the outer surface primarily gold. On April 1, 824, Master Jinnan began his shoeing work on the six Yingchan. Overlord Mag had kept this whole idea a complete secret from all the women and even from his son and Wu. His son was already looking for a proper woman for himself. Overlord Mag had given Meng carte blanche to canvass his territory for the perfect woman for himself. After all, his son ought to have only the very best woman his lands offered. As of this date, Meng had found three candidates, but had not yet made his choice.

"My fine Yingchan, it is with the greatest of pleasure that I have found another way to honor you and make you all even more golden. Master Jinnan will be fitting you with new golden boots. No longer will you need to deal with those imported extreme heels. Now you will have boots that are totally appropriate for Yingchan, golden boots, and very expensive at that," Overlord Mag explained to his wife, daughter, and the four harem women. Wu had brought them to the shoemaker's building, two at a time, his arms around the women, supporting and guiding them, for their sight was so limited.

"Come, Wu, let's allow Master Jinnan to do his work," Overlord Mag sneered and ushered Wu outside.

"What kind of golden boots will they have?" Wu asked, suddenly having a bad feeling about this. Perhaps they were merely gold plated shoes.

"I have to compliment you, Wu. You were my inspiration for them. You were the first to demonstrate that we could walk in those strange alien boots, walking on our toes. In your honor, I'm calling them Wu-boots. Master Jinnan has made them out of an alloy of steel and gold, steel for strength and gold, of course, to match their many adornments. Now they will look even more magnificent! I will be counting upon you to help them learn to walk in their new boots."

Wu felt a surge of panic sweeping into his stomach. Learn to walk in them? What did he mean? Surely, he would not be making these helpless women have to walk on their toes as the plague had forced the men!

A half hour later, Master Jinnan came to his door and announced, "I have your daughter's new boots on her. If you will escort her back to her room, I will work my magic on your wife, Overlord Mag. I believe that you will find your daughter's new boots most satisfactory."

Both men followed the shoemaker inside. Dai was crying softly to herself, but sitting in a chair. Wu stared at her feet and saw a golden pair of ballet style boots, very similar to those that he had had to wear. Their surface was uniform and the same shiny golden color of her earrings and other jewelry. Dai turned her head so that she could barely see her lover from the tiny golden eye openings. Her face communicated her fright and terror to Wu. Now she would be even more helpless, unable to walk, she thought.

"My compliments, Master Jinnan. They are just perfect, matching her earrings precisely. Don't worry, Wu, they cannot be removed. No need to have to deal with putting on and taking off their shoes any longer. One less thing that we must do for them now. My most beautiful daughter, let's see how well you can stand and walk in them. After all, you've seen us men walking in them for a couple of months, so you know very well that you can do it too. Now you will be even more beautiful than before, my darling," Overlord Mag commented. His face showed a slight touch of covertness.

Without arms, Dai knew that she simply could not do this on her own, though she also knew that she had to try. Perhaps if her father saw that she could not even stand without help, he would have them removed. She tried to stand up and began to fall. Wu jumped in and caught her before she fell, though Dai was frantically trying to flail her missing arms to keep from falling. Holding her tightly, Wu whispered, "Take small steps, my love. I won't let you fall." Tears covered her tiny eye holes, and she couldn't even see where she was being led, dependent utterly on Wu.

By the time that Wu finally got her into her bedroom and safely sitting on her bed, a servant came up to him to tell him that he needed to escort Great Lady Li now. Overlord Mag was waiting impatiently for Wu to return. "This is awful, Dai! I will speak with your father tonight and see if I can't get him to see reason and have them removed." Dai nodded, still sobbing and quite scared.

Scared, terrified, and crying — uniformly that was the reaction of the other five women when they were asked to stand by themselves in their new golden boots. Each time, Wu had to make a herculean move to catch them before they fell and hurt themselves. It took the poor women over a half hour to make the short trip from the shoemaker's shop into the grand estate and their room.

When dinnertime came, it took Wu almost an hour to get all six women walked from their room into the dining room. However, Overlord Mag merely watched each woman's awkward movements as she entered the room. A most pleased expression appeared on his face each time. Wu's heart sank, as he finally sat down beside Dai to feed her. While Meng and the two Seconds fed the four harem women, Mag fed his own wife, thoroughly enjoying her helplessness and inability even to say a single word in protest. Finally, Wu realized just how sadistic Overlord Mag actually was!

For the first time in a very long time, Wu lost his self-control. "Mag, how can you do this to these poor women? Already, the plague has left them completely helpless. Before the plague, they were only just barely able to get by on their own and still needed help walking. They can barely even see. Now they have lost their arms and cannot do a thing for themselves. With these unremovable boots that force them to walk on their toes and even unable to bend their ankles, you have gotten them so crippled up that their lives are going to be a horror. Surely, you can see this for yourself and have Master Jinnan remove these debilitating boots of his. We needed our arms just to keep our balance while walking in those alien boots. The women have no way at all of keeping their balance in them."

Challenged as he was, Mag's face turned livid. "You dare to challenge my brilliant idea to make our Yingchan even more beautiful? You disappoint me, Wu. After all that I have done for you, now you have the audacity to disgrace me before my own supper table and before our fabulous Yingchan and my wife! Wu, you give me no choice. Meng, arrest Wu; throw him in the dungeon. We have no choice but to publically draw and quarter him tomorrow morning!"

"You fiend from Hell! You vile, wicked old man!" Wu lost it completely and spat onto the man's table, the worst possible offence, save spitting in his face. Wu would have done that except his position at the table was too far from the Overlord's. Meng rose to carry out his father's orders. His face radiated the most pleased look that Wu had ever seen on the young man's face, and he realized that Meng had long considered him is personal enemy. Meng knew that at last he would have his revenge on the man who consistently humiliated him in every combat practice session for as long as he could remember.

"Be brave. I will rescue you, Dai," Wu whispered hastily to Dai, who sat immobile, trying to grasp what was happening around her. She could only just barely see the others across the table and could do or say nothing on behalf of her lover, Wu. Now she couldn't even stand by herself. She wanted to tell him that she would try to be brave and that she would wait for all time for him to come back to her, but she could only make an "ah" sound.

Wu knew that his singular outburst of anger had now cost him everything that he had been working towards his whole life and that of his one true love. Instantly, he quelled his anger and allowed his life-long training to return. Timing his move precisely, just as Meng made his move to subdue him, he struck. One swift thrust of his fist blocked Meng's attack, while his other hand grabbed Meng's arm and used the man's forward momentum to his advantage, giving him a pull. Meng went flying past Wu's chair, landing hard on the plush carpeting. Wu bolted to the door and flew out of the estate as fast as his legs would carry him. Evening darkness was falling, and he decided to use it to his advantage. Within a minute of his miraculous escape from the dining room, the overlord guards armed with long guns and swords came bursting out of the estate and into the streets of Nag Tasha.

Immediately, they launched a hue and cry, demanding the arrest of the traitor Wu Shenyan. Wu quietly ducked down a deserted alleyway. He soon found the right roof and climbed up onto it, lying flat against the red tiles, completely out of everyone's sight. Now he had time to think of his next move. Wu knew that he would now be a hunted man, that the overlord's soldiers would begin searching for him. Knowing Overlord Mag as well as he did, Wu knew that the man would never give up the search, not even if months went by.

Where could he go? Five hundred miles to the south and east stretched the lands under the vice grip of Mag. He'd never make it out alive going in those directions, yet only those directions offered him safety and a chance to make a new life for himself. But he didn't want a new life! He needed to rescue Dai. Only with her could he even think of making a new life! He could go north, but crossing the Lian River would be fraught with difficulties. Surely by dawn, sentries would be guarding all the ferry crossings, looking for him. He could not swim, so north was out. He could go west, climbing deeper into the foothills, perhaps even reaching the tall, impassable mountains, but what was there for him? The life of a total hermit? No, he needed Dai, somehow. Where could he go? Where could he go?

He heard the hue and cry taken up by more and more men on the streets of Nag Tasha below his perch on the rooftop. Well, they'd not find him up here, he thought. Think, man, think! Perhaps it was his last thoughts of the mountains that triggered his memory. Not far from Nag Tasha, high upon the ridge line sat the holy monastery of Taschi, home to a clan of holy monks. These celibate men spent their whole lives in near total isolation from the world around them, safe within walls of stone. Their monastery was impregnable. Several times a year, a group of the orange robed men would bring their pushcarts loaded with gold into Nag Tasha, returning to their eagle's perch laden with food supplies. Never had anyone ever heard one of these monks speak so much as a single word. They quietly paid whatever price the vendor chose to charge for their purchases.

Perhaps he could seek sanctuary with these holy monks, he thought. If so, he would not be too far from his beloved Dai, since their monastery was only about three miles from the southern edge of the city, perched high on the ridge line. "Yes, this has to be the answer," Wu whispered to himself. He waited for the dead of night to arrive before making his escape from the city below him.

Around one in the morning, the noise of the searching soldiers died down and Wu slipped down off the rooftop. Using all of his skills, he maneuvered through the back ways of the town of some fifty thousand, the largest in the overlord's territory. Cautiously, he followed the well-worn track up towards the Taschi Monastery. Around three, he stood directly below it.

Perched much like an eagle's nest, the Taschi Monastery was about two hundred feet above the rocky ground, a grey stone citadel high atop a giant ledge right at the steeply sloped ridge line, so commonly found here in western Tashien. These razor-backed ridges rose steadily higher until at last they touched the impassable mountains, the teeth of the mountains as they were sometimes called. A single rope hung down from far above. In the starlight, Wu could see no way up the ridge to the monastery. At last, he took a deep breath and pulled on the rope. Far above him, he heard a single gong from a bell sounding. He dare not sound it a second time, for fear the soldiers might be alerted and come looking for him. If so, he would be trapped with nowhere to flee.

After what seemed an eternity, he heard a squeaking noise coming from far overhead. Soon, he spotted a wooden box being lowered slowly and took heart. Someone had heard him and was coming to greet him. A half hour later, an empty box rested upon the ground before him. Unsure what this meant, he decided to climb into it. After a moment, he felt the box moving beneath his feet, swinging clear of the ground. Someone was pulling him up to the monastery and he relaxed for the first time this evening.

At the top, the box stopped level with a wooden floor. A monk wearing an orange robe locked the mechanism, though he was breathing heavily from the exertion. "Thank you. I come seeking sanctuary. The overlord wants to kill me. I am Wu Shenyan."

The orange robed monk said nothing but bowed to him and gestured for him to follow him, which Wu did. A short distance from the elevator mechanism, the monk motioned for him to enter a small room. Inside was a crude bed and blankets. Again, the monk motioned to them and Wu entered. The monk closed the door. A small candle provided the only light. A great tiredness came over Wu at last; the adrenalin of the flight was gone, and he did as indicated. He laid down on the hard bed and soon fell asleep.

It was well after dawn when the door opened and another orange robed man motioned for him to come with him. Dutifully, Wu rose and followed him. They followed a twisting, narrow stone passageway into a dining room. Crude wooden tables and chairs filled the stone cavern of a room. Oil lanterns hung from the ceiling and sunlight entered from three sides — open aired, windows. One aged monk sat at one table, and the man who had led him here motioned for Wu to join the other one. Wu did so, sitting next to the monk.

"I am Most Venerable Peng, the leader of the Taschi Monastery. I am told that you seek sanctuary here." Wu hastily outlined what had happened and why, begging for a place to stay.

"I give you sanctuary here for as long as you desire. Please do not expect the other monks to speak to you. We have taken vows of total silence, for words are not necessary to become one with the world around us. I will speak with you, should you desire speech."

Thus began Wu's new life. He wanted to contribute something of value to these men who were saving his life. Soon, he found himself spending part of each day helping three monks mine a small vein of gold. He learned that the gold would be spent in Nag Tasha for their needed food supplies and other necessities of their frugal lifestyle.

Evenings, he struck up serious conversations with Most Venerable Peng. "I betrayed my love, Dai. I have left her utterly helpless and even unable to walk. For that, I am eternally doomed, am I not?"

"I am sure that she is still awaiting your promised return. You did tell me that you told her that one day you would rescue her, did you not?"

"Well, yes, I did. If I rescue her, where can I take her where she would be safe? Besides, there are four other young women there that also ought to be rescued from the sadistic overlord."

"Ah I see. You have promised to care for their needs too?"

"Well, not exactly. I was looking after them for several months when no one else would. I guess I really do need to take responsibility for them as well, don't I? After all, who else will?"

"I see. And what will you do if you have the women under your care?"

"I don't know. Try to get those awful boots off their feet, maybe more. They are being forced to wear such very restrictive adornments. Maybe I can free them from those too."

"Ah, I see. And in doing so you would remove their highest honor as Yingchan, what makes them Great Ladies?"

"Well, shouldn't I?"

"Have you asked them if they want to give up that which makes them some of the most honored and beautiful women in Tashien?"

"Well, no, but. . ."

"Traditionally, they, like we, do not speak, though ours is by our own choice. Stripped of their golden adornments, they would be both armless and unable to speak, and have nothing of honor remaining."

"Oh, I didn't think of that. I guess I need to ask them first. But how? They cannot speak."

"Then, you must learn to speak for them. As I understand the Yingchan, they can answer yes or no."

"Yes, that's right. Dai can at least say those two words. Well, really, they don't sound like words. They are just two distinctive sounds that they make. How do I learn to speak for them?"

"You must learn to know what they are thinking and so repeat that to them."

"But how do I do that?" The monk shrugged his shoulders, leaving Wu in his own mystery.

Days later, Wu asked, "If I can rescue Dai, can I bring her here for a time, until I can figure out a way to get her to safety?"

"Ordinarily, we do not take women into our monastery," Most Venerable Peng answered. "However, here we are dealing with the most honorable women of all Tashien. The Yingchan tradition is one of our most ancient ones. Such women have made the most supreme sacrifice to represent the golden angels for mankind. For these most honored of all women, we will make an exception. Yes, if you can rescue her, she may stay with us for a time. However, no one must know that you have brought her to us. We do not want to battle the overlord and his men, though we could hold out here for a very long time."

"I give you my word that none shall know it." Now Wu had some slight hope. How to rescue her would be his greatest challenge. Could he also rescue the other four? He knew that he had to try before the sadist came up with additional tortures for the helpless women.

As spring moved into summer, Overlord Mag began expanding his opium dealings. He received more and more requests for additional supplies coming ultimately from the larger cities, especially Zau and Shansee. His men began going from farmstead to farmstead, forcing the poor farmers to stop growing their usual crops and to plant poppies instead. Many protested and were instantly killed.

He gave his son, Meng, the authority to force more men into the opium production facilities, to force more and more farmers into the business of poppy growing. Further, he ordered a massive buildup of his own armed forces, calculating that with the rapidly increasing demand for his product, other overlords might attempt to confiscate some of his lush growing lands. During the summer and fall of 825, the oppression of Overlord Mag grew steadily. Many young men who protested slightly were killed outright, but some continued to object. Often their protests centered on the women in their families, women who now needed help with nearly everything.

Undaunted, Overlord Mag ordered all women to take up their yokes and lend their men a hand with the opium production. At least they could carry water, chemicals, and product about, relieving the men from those duties. Now Meng began forcing otherwise helpless women into the opium production operations, adding to the oppression sweeping over the entire lands west of the mighty Yonshu River.

In July, Meng finally found the ideal woman to become his wife. Love played no part in his decision, simple physical beauty. As he raided one village to acquire a dozen more workers in their production facilities in Nag Tasha, he spotted the nineteen year old Luan Jing. Raven haired, round faced, with thick eyebrows, she reminded him of his mother in many ways. She was exceptionally pretty, far above the norm, even though she was a mere farmer's daughter and dressed in patched rags. Her eyes shown like beacons and her lips were thick and full. It was all that Meng could do to keep from bedding her right then and there. Instead, he told her, "You are coming with me. I am going to make you my wife."

Poor Luan dared not resist or even protest him. She knew that he was the overlord's son. If she did, he'd outright kill her, just as he had done to her brother, who last week had refused to join the overlord's army. If she had known what this would ultimately mean for her, she might have chosen otherwise and allowed herself to be slain that very day. Instead, she allowed him to lift her onto his saddle. He climbed up behind her and headed home. After dismounting and lifting her safely down, Meng called out to Mag, who came walking up to his son, to find out how the day's orders had gone.

"Dad, Luan Jing here is my choice for a wife. Doesn't she have tremendous potential? Gorgeous beyond belief," Meng proudly announced.

Mag grinned, finally his son had chosen. Well, she was exceptionally pretty; his son had good taste, but why had he waited so long to make his choice? "Excellent, son. Welcome Luan Jing into my family. We will soon get you cleaned up and into proper, fitting clothing. Nothing will be too fine for you, my new daughter-in-law. Rich will be your attire from now on, and you will want for nothing or I will have my son's head."

While Luan wished that he would have his son's head right now, the idea that she would be richly attired and want for nothing greatly appealed to her. Already devastated by the plague, she had depended on her brother for nearly everything. During the week since his slaying, she had her helplessness and dependency brought into sharp relief. Perhaps if they helped her, this would not be so bad. At least, Meng was not an ugly pig of a man. He was rather handsome, though he did not have his father's good looks.

Mag then said, "Okay, Meng. Take her into the bathroom and get her bathed. Then, when you have her dried off, give her some wine to help warm her up. We don't want her to get a chill before dinner." He gave his son a sly wink, though Luan had no idea what it meant. A real bath sounded fabulous to her. She had not had one since the plague struck her. Wine, well she had never tasted such luxury, only the crude honey mead that her father made each fall with the bit of honey he secretly kept back from the overlord's men who came to confiscate his products.

Meng did as ordered and gave Luan a good bathing, even undoing her braids and washing her hair. He noticed that hers, like the other women's hair, was exceptionally long, thick, and lustrous, a byproduct of the plague many claimed. Certainly, it was long enough; hers fell below her feet a couple inches. He smiled, realizing that once she was in her golden boots, her hair would not touch the floor any longer. After drying her off and examining her firm, but huge breasts, much to her discomfort, he poured her a glass of red wine and held it to her lips. Eagerly she drank it and felt a strange warmth in her stomach. A while later, she felt drowsy and then blacked out. Meng carried her to the back room where their local doctor was waiting, having been summoned from his home before he could eat his dinner or feed his own wife hers.

At least, this will be a quick one; probably can get home before the meal goes cold, he thought to himself. Remove one tongue, slit two ears and insert the golden disks. Won't take but a jiffy, he thought to himself as he set about the task. Staunching her bleeding tongue took a bit longer than he might have desired, but he did a good job of it. Her ears went quickly. Mag slipped him a coin pouch and he left, hurrying home to his dinner.

Now Master Jinnan worked his craft on her feet, which went far faster than it had before. By now, the shoemaker was most experienced with these golden boots. After that, Mag brought in several jewelers and provided the necessary gold and gemstones for his son. Although Meng had quibbled over the estimated value of his new bride's jewelry and ornamentations, Meng had conceded the issue. Luan would be wearing a million gold worth. He could later add on more once he was in charge and not his father. Then, he could make her worth ten million, surpassing even his mother's jewelry value.

Last upon the scene was the family dressmaker, who fitted her with a form-fitting red silken gown, which he claimed brought out her intense beauty. Both Mag and Meng stood over the sleeping woman, admiring the incredible transformation from peasant's daughter into a venerated Yingchan. "Thanks, dad. She is absolutely, incredibly perfect."

Mag smiled, that she was. He began to envy his son's choice. Luan was far prettier than his own wife, daughter, or the four in his harem. He cursed himself for not having come across her before now. Secretly, he made a vow once more to search his lands for such incredible beauties. Where there's one, there has to be more, he thought.

By morning, Luan woke to discover her new condition. She shrieked and woke Meng who was sleeping by her side. She tried to speak and gagged instead. Luan was shocked, terrified, and freaked beyond all imagining. She couldn't see, well only just barely. A tiny pinhole of light reached her eyes. Her tongue was missing and she could not communicate anything to this man. Worse, the sheer weight of her earrings drove her almost mad as Meng helped her into a sitting position. At last, Meng got her to stand up, and she realized what her feet were now like — she was wearing boots similar to those that her father had tried to wear when the plague struck. He quickly gave them up, claiming it was impossible to walk in them. Now she wore similar ones, only she couldn't even move her ankles. Her feet felt like they were enclosed in unyielding steel. Luan could not stand on her own, but Meng realized that would likely be the case. He kept his steadying arms around her and said, "Come on, my lovely Luan, it is time for our wedding ceremony. You look ravishingly beautiful. Your red silk dress does you justice. After the ceremony, I will introduce you to the others, and we will dine on the finest of food."

Luan tried to say some things, but made only strange sounds, crushing her self-respect even further. Wobbling wildly on her toes, she would have fallen many times had Meng not kept her upright. Her feet were aching by the time that they entered the room where the ceremony was going to be held. Oh, how she desperately wanted to sit down, but Meng insisted she stand during the whole ceremony. Fortunately, it was quite short, and soon, Meng lifted her face golden lattice veil and kissed her lips. She did not respond, however. She was too terrified, too much in shock, and too much in pain to care.

Like a zombie, she allowed herself to be led into a dining room. Luan was never as glad for a chair as she was when Meng finally helped her to sit down. She struggled to see who was present, but the pinholes made even that most difficult. She felt food being pressed against her lips and opened her mouth. Oh, how she was hungry, but she found that eating without her tongue an awful challenge. She prayed that all this was a mere nightmare and that she would soon awaken. Her ears throbbed; she felt that at any moment her ears would be pulled from her head. Luan had never felt so utterly miserable in her life; this dwarfed even the plague. At least then, she could walk and speak. This was far, far worse.

Over after dinner tea, Overlord Mag explained to Luan, "Now my dear Luan, you have become a true Yingchan, one of the rare golden women. Everyone will treat you with only the utmost and highest respect, for you are a Most Honorable Yingchan. The magnificent jewelry that you are wearing is worth a million gold, a huge fortune. After tea, Meng will stand you before a mirror so that you may gaze upon your stunningly beautiful image."

Meng did as asked by his father. He stood her before the mirror in their bedroom. Luan struggled to see out of the tiny pinholes. She saw a golden version of herself, complete with a most exotic red silk dress. At last, she realized fully what had become of her. She now had golden eyes that allowed her only a tiny glimpse of the world around her. Finally, left alone in her bedroom, Luan began to cry, unleashing all the terror and grief, which filled her so. Life as she had known it was over; this she fully knew now.

As the dog days of August came, Wu finally worked out a plan to rescue Dai from the clutches of the overlord sadist. Based on the last time he had seen her, he knew that she would be unable to walk and only just barely able to see. No way could she walk out of the estate, let alone walk across the town. Traversing the rocky trail that led to the base of the ridge, which held the monastery, was beyond even her remotest possibility of negotiating on the tips of her toes. No, he had to come up with a different way to get her safely here. Then inspiration finally struck.

The night before the monks in their orange, hooded robes planned to walk down from their monastery and into town to make their purchases, Wu took a pushcart, robes, and several other items and was lowered down to the ground by a silent monk. Stealthily, he made his way through the sleeping town towards the overlord's estate. He'd gone over his plan a thousand times in his mind, seeking always to better it and to find its flaws. He knew the layout of the estate completely, for he had almost become a Second in command. Stealthily, he snuck in a back way, where food deliveries were made during the daytime.

He hid the pushcart behind some shrubbery, which was just as he had last seen it. The gardeners always did their job perfectly. Mag would execute them if they did not. Wu counted on this aspect. There wasn't any originality or self-motivation behind any of the overlord's many servants and men. He slipped out of his shoes and hid them as well. Silently, he slipped past the sleeping guards and into the estate proper. Only a few dim lanterns provided nighttime illumination — Mag's orders. Soon, he stood before Dai's bedroom door. He paused and listened.

He heard her sleeping peacefully and slipped inside. Quickly, he moved to her bedside. She was still wearing her red silk dress. The men found it easier to allow the women to sleep in their dresses rather than changing their clothes each night. He moved close to her ear and whispered, "Dai. Dai. Wake up. It is me, Wu Shenyan. It is time for you to be rescued. Dai, Dai, wake up." Her eyelids fluttered and she opened them. A tiny bit of light reflected off her shiny golden eyes. She turned her head towards him. "Yes, it is ne, Wu Shenyan. It is time to set you free. Be very quiet. I will carry you, my love." Her eyes opened wide, and she struggled to glimpse him through her tiny pinholes, but gave it up. She could not and it was too dark. She felt his arms around her and felt herself being lifted up into his arms. She said a prayer to whatever gods were listening to help Wu rescue her.

Having plush carpeting throughout the estate helped him greatly, muffling totally his heavier footsteps. Soon, he had her outside and past the guards. Carefully, he sat her down in the pushcart. "I have to push you out of the estate, and then I will tell you more," he whispered. Moving extremely slowly, Wu pushed the cart out of the estate and into the deserted streets of Nag Tasha. When he had put a considerable distance between them and the estate, he pulled into an alleyway behind a bakery. Here he stopped and whispered the rest of his grand plan. She nodded that she understood, and he then helped her lay down in the pushcart. Gently, he covered her up with a blanket, hiding her body completely. Next, he retrieved a dozen loaves of bread that he had brought from the monastery and laid those over the top of the blanket. Now he waited for the dawn, hoping and praying that all would go as planned.

At dawn, twenty-five orange robed monks came into Nag Tasha making another of their frequent food supply trips. With his orange hood pulled up, Wu began slowly pushing the cart out of the city and up the long track to the monastery. He went slowly, mimicking the slow, deliberate motions of the other monks. Before long, several other monks caught up with him, forming a line as they approached the wooden basket that would raise them into their monastery. Although impatient, Wu waited his turn, hoping not to hear a hue and cry. At last, he pushed his cart into the empty basket and felt it move free from the ground. "Only a few more minutes," he whispered to Dai. At last, they reached the top and he wheeled his cart out of the box. Today there were three monks working the contraption and they bowed to him as he exited the box. He returned their bow and pressed onwards, following the agreed upon route that Most Venerable Peng had suggested. Soon, he found himself before a door to a side room. This would be their room now, for as long as they desired to remain here. Once inside and the door shut, he tossed the stale, dried bread aside and helped Dai to her feet.

"We are safe now, my love. We are inside the Taschi Monastery. Most Venerable Peng has granted us sanctuary for as long as we desire it. You are free of him finally, my darling Dai. Let me look at you! How I have missed you!"

Their room was barely fifteen feet on a side, but it did have a high window open to the outside world. Sunlight entered, illuminating the room. A single bed and one table with two chairs were the only furniture. A single candle would provide nighttime illumination, should such be desired. Finally, Dai could finally see through her pinholes. She looked around awkwardly, finally locating Wu. She moved to him and pressed her lips to his, ignoring the golden veil of gold that kept their lips apart. She had no other way to express her love and gratitude.

Their embrace was interrupted by a knock on the door. Wu left Dai standing beside the bed and opened it. "Good morning Honorable Wu. I see that you have been most successful."

"Please come in. Dai Tazau, this is our benefactor, the Most Venerable Peng, who runs the monastery." Peng bowed to Dai, who moved her head slightly, attempting to locate him. Spotting him at last, she too bowed, her long earrings bouncing over her chest as she raised her head.

Wu suddenly realized that he had left her standing on her toes without himself there to support her. "Dai, I am so sorry. I forgot and left you standing without me being beside you to hold onto you. I'm coming," he hastily moved to her side and slipped his arm securely around her tiny waist.

Peng chuckled. "Most pleased to meet Most Honorable Yingchan Dai. You must forgive Honorable Wu. He does not yet know how to read your thoughts. Wu, she does not need you to hold onto her. She can stand by herself, isn't that right, Most Honorable Yingchan Dai?"

"Ah," Dai said with a big grin. She nodded, her earrings again bouncing lightly off her chest. She wanted to make that idea known for sure.

"But. . ." Wu began, allowing his arm to let go of her.

"Most Honorable Yingchan Dai can also walk by herself, right?"

A big grin formed behind the golden veil. "Ah," she said extremely pleased that he had asked her that, and again she nodded to make doubly sure that Wu understood that she could now walk by herself, though only very limited amount.

"But. . ." the confused Wu uttered.

"Most Honorable Yingchan Dai is most proud of her achievement. She has spent long hours practicing and is most pleased that she is now able to walk for you, Honorable Wu. Is that not right, Most Honorable Yingchan Dai?"

Dai really smiled now, both uttering her yes sound and nodding. Somehow, this aged monk really was reading her very thoughts! She longed to tell Wu about how many hours she had spent learning to walk in these golden boots. She had done it for him, intending to be able to walk out of her father's estate when Wu came for her as he promised. Although she knew that she would have no way to tell Wu what she had done, she could at least show him that she could now walk some. That had been her only plan, but now this monk was almost reading her very thoughts.

"Ah, it is her present to you, Honorable Wu. Is it not?" Peng asked Dai. Again she smiled and nodded. She pivoted slightly on her toes to face Wu and to be able to see his face instead of Peng's. She nodded to Wu.

"Never have I had such a most worthy present as this, dear Dai! Thank you, thank you for this, my love," Wu finally managed to say to her. Again, Dai smiled broadly beneath her golden veil, nodding her head slightly to Wu.

"It is as I have been telling you, Honorable Wu. You must learn to read Most Honorable Yingchan Dai's thoughts and repeat them for her to verify them as accurate. Only then will Most Honorable Yingchan Dai truly be happy, as she can in that way communicate her deepest thoughts and feelings for you, Honorable Wu. I shall leave you to practice that. Please join me for lunch when the gong sounds. We will dine after the others have finished." He bowed to both of them, turned, and left.

"I am so proud of you, Dai! I can't imagine how hard you have worked to learn to walk in those golden boots. Nothing pleases me more than to see you able to walk on your own and not remain as helpless as Mag intended. May I see you walk?" Dai flashed him a very proud smile. This was precisely what she had wanted to do for him since first kissing him when they entered the room and he had sat her down on her feet at last.

She bent her head down, her earrings rocking gently over her large bosom. She had to get her pinholes in the right position so she could see where she was going. Then she began to take her tiny steps, just as she had done around her father's estate. Wu watched as she moved extremely slowly, measuring each step carefully. Without arms to catch her balance and only her head and earrings to do that, Dai had to be careful. Her breakthrough had occurred when she realized that her very heavy earrings could also be used to help her keep her balance while walking on the tips of her toes in these unyielding golden boots. Her face displayed yet another smile as she remembered how proud her father had been when he first saw her walking on her own. He had thought that she was doing this for him, but she was doing it for Wu and that dichotomy had even caused her to smile back then.

She wanted to explain that she could only go very slowly and only over smooth surfaces, and that she had not yet managed any steps or stairs. However, she could not figure out how to communicate that to Wu. Perhaps he would read her mind instead.

"Magnificent, Dai, magnificent. You can walk. I can see that you must go very slowly and carefully. Are you using your heavy earrings to help keep your balance? Is that why now and then you are tipping your head to one side or the other?"

"Ah," she uttered and nodded, trying hard not to break her concentration. Walking took every ounce of her attention. Worse, she had moved so far around the room now that she lost track of where Wu was located. She dare not turn her head to look unless she stopped walking. Dai had not yet been able to turn her head away from the floor before her and continue to walk without falling down. He saw her hesitancy and called out, "This way, my love. You are walking beautifully! Incredible." When she had finally returned to him and stood before him, Dai at last looked up into his eyes, smiling proudly. Now Wu had seen that she was not totally helpless, that she could walk on her own.

"Can you go up and down stairs or steps yet?" he asked. She shook her head no and made her unique sound. "Okay, got it. I bet rough surfaces are out too, right?" She nodded her agreement with that too. His arms slipped around her waist, steading her. He leaned over and the two kissed once more. "Will you marry me, please, Dai?" She nodded that she would. "Really soon?" he added. Again, her bright smile and nod told him yes. Suddenly, Dai's whole life had changed from an awful nightmare into one filled with bright prospects of real hope and love. She swore that she would be the very best Yingchan just for him.

A while later the gong sounded and Wu said, "That's the dinner gong. Is it alright with you if I put my arm around you and lead you to the dining room?" She nodded and he did so. He had not realized fully just how slowly she did walk until now, while he was walking with her. Even when he had worn those alien boots, he had been able to move a bit faster. He realized that he both had arms then as well as clear vision. She barely could see anything at all, making it all the more difficult for her.

Entering the dining room, Peng called out, "Here, come sit beside me that I may bask in the beauty of the Yingchan. Together we may speak freely." Wu sat her between himself and Peng. Then, he began the arduous task of feeding her. I say arduous, because it required a bit of coordination on both their parts and some dexterity in getting her golden veil lifted at just the proper moment. As always, Dai had to pay close attention to her eating. Her lack of a tongue made it far more difficult. Peng probably realized this, as he ate quietly, saying nothing until they began their after lunch tea.

"I suppose, Dai, that I should work on trying to get those awful boots off your feet. We can also remove those heavy earrings and the golden veil as well," Wu began. "But I don't know what they did to your eyes. I am hesitant to mess with them, my love, but I will try if you like."

Dai gave him a frown, but he didn't understand. Peng spoke up. "Ah my son, you still have much to learn about reading your fiancé's mind. She does not wish anything to be removed from her body."

Wu gave him a shocked look, but Dai did nod affirmatively. "You see, Dai is a Most Honorable Yingchan now, one of the most revered women in all Tashien, and carrying on one of our most ancient traditions. To remove her golden ornaments will be removing her highest honor, leaving her as a mere common woman who cannot speak. Such would ruin her self-esteem completely. Am I not right, Most Honorable Yingchan Dai?" he asked. She made her yes sound and nodded vigorously.

"Further," he said with a twinkle in his eye, "I suspect that she has pledge herself to being the very best Yingchan possible for you, being the very best that she can be, giving you the highest honor that she is able to give."

Again, Dai nodded vigorously and made her yes sound. "You see, her goal in life is now to be the very best Yingchan that she can be, just for you. Do you really want to take all that away from her? If so, she would be far less than an ordinary woman, one who cannot speak, ignoring the plague's effect of losing her arms as well."

"No, Dai! I don't want you to give that up, not unless you yourself desire it. Forgive me my love. I just presumed that you would. I should have asked you before making such pronouncements." She flashed a smile in his direction, although now she could not see him. Her pinholes were focused on Peng.

"That is good, Honorable Wu. You are learning, perhaps a bit too slowly. Now then, you have told me that you wish to be married. Is this still so?" This time, both nodded affirmatively. "Good. But tell me, Honorable Wu, will you take Most Honorable Yingchan Dai as she now is — a Most Honorable Yingchan and not attempt to make her into something that she is not?"

"Yes, I promise, dear. I will never make you do something that you do not want to do, not ever. I love you as you are or as you may later choose to be. Have I said that right, Most Venerable Peng?"

Peng smiled. "That is not for me to answer but for the beautiful Dai." She pivoted awkwardly in her chair and moved her head around slightly locating Wu at last. She smiled and nodded vigorously, adding her yes sound. He leaned over and kissed her lips through the golden veil once more.

"Ah, you see, she agrees with you. If it is your wish, I will marry you when you choose."

Wu smiled, "I am ready right now. How about you, my love? Are you ready for Peng to marry us right now?" She grinned as broadly as she could, nodding so vigorously that her earrings swung wildly about her head. Peng smiled and proceeded to do so right then.

He had them rise and stand together. He gave them his blessing and encouraged them to always communicate and work out any disagreements that always seem to arise in a marriage. He charged them to take care of each other through good times and bad ones and when they were healthy and when they were ill. Finally, he charged Wu never to fail to help the Yingchan with her many needs, no matter how busy he might become. Finally, he allowed them a kiss to seal their marriage. After that, the two headed back to their room.

Wu quickly got an education in just what her unique needs actually were. Before, he merely escorted them and help her eat. Now he had to manage all of her other needs, beginning with figuring out that she desperately needed to go to the bathroom the moment they entered their room. Later, when he had her undressed and lying in their wedding bed, as he lay down beside her, she tried to tell him something else. After several trying minutes, he at last worked out that she wanted him to lift her golden veil, laying it over her upper face and eyes so that their lips could touch each other. Finally, the two lovers were finally able to become man and wife.

Weeks past and day by day, Wu became more and more skilled at "reading" his wife and her needs. Often, he was able to anticipate them now. Finally, the topic of the other harem women arose. "I wish to rescue them as well, my love, but in doing so, I will be obligated to also look after their every need as well, at least until we can get them into a new, safe world, where they too may find a loving, kind husband." Her reaction was confusing and he didn't quite get what she wanted desperately to tell him. He tried numerous variations, such as that she didn't want him to do that, that she would be jealous of his helping these other women, and so on. At last, he admitted defeat and begged Most Venerable Peng to lend his aid. "Look, I just have to figure out what she is trying so hard to tell me."

With Peng present, Wu quickly explained what he wanted to do and the many things that he'd said trying to understand what her objection was all about. Peng could see that both were frustrated and decided to help the two out. "Most Honorable Yingchan Dai is trying to tell you something else about the harem women. Let me see. Is there more than four harem women now?"

Dai nodded yes, but hesitantly so. She knew Yuan Jing, Meng's wife, wanted desperately to get out of that horrible marriage and mess into which she had been thrown. While she was not a harem woman, she was like Dai, a Yingchan now.

"Ah, I am close but yet miss the mark. It is another Yingchan that you are concerned about?" Peng asked. Dai nodded vigorously, sensing that he was getting closer. "You see, Honorable Wu, this is more like a game of charades. We must make guesses until we find it. Is this other Yingchan your mother?" he asked. Wu thought that must be it, that she wanted her mother rescued as well. Dai shook her head no vigorously, her earrings banging wildly from side to side.

"Ah, we are getting closer. She wants another Yingchan rescued, but it is not her mother and not one of the four in his harem. Thus, another Yingchan must have been added since you were there, Honorable Wu." She nodded yes vigorously. Peng smiled broadly.

"See, we hit the mark. Now we must determine who this new Yingchan is. Is the woman a harem woman? No, well is she someone's wife? See, now we are zeroing in rapidly. We must guess whose wife, Wu."

Wu had a flash of insight. "Meng! Meng finally found someone and got married?" Dai broke into a huge smile of relief. She made her yes sound and nodded, bouncing her earrings over her chest and then her back. "How can we possibly guess her name?" he asked becoming frustrated once more.

"Perhaps her name is not now the important thing," Peng replied. "Dai, is she the only other additional Yingchan who is living in the overlord's estate?" She nodded affirmative. "See, there you have it."

"Say, Dai, does Meng love her, I mean real love, like we share?" Dai shook her head violently no, her earrings really flying about her head this time. "Does the Yingchan love Meng?" She duplicated her violent no response. "Okay, you want me to rescue her as well?" Dai nodded yes, finally pleased that he understood her finally.

"Say, this really does work! It is like a child's charade's guessing game. I have learned a lot, Most Venerable Peng."

"I am pleased. And yes, we would be honored to house these Yingchan here until you can find a way to get them to a place of safety," Peng replied.

"Well, I ought to be able to get one or two more out the same way that I got Dai out of there. However, Eventually, they will discover how I am doing it. I must come up with a better plan, my darling."

Dai made a noise and he realized the guessing game had begun again. "You have an idea or comment about the rescue attempt?" he asked. She nodded. A half hour later, both were very pleased that he finally asked, "You want a plan which will keep your father and brother from believing that the Yingchan are still alive? That way they would stop looking for you and them." She grinned and nodded yes, proud that Wu was catching on. Perhaps they really could communicate well this way. She had even more hope for their future.

Unfortunately, Wu could not think of any good plan to rescue five women at one time. He knew that he would need to have a wagon to transport all five at once, though. Borrowing a bit of gold that he had helped mine, he donned a disguise and went into Nag Tasha to buy a horse and wagon. Next on the southern edge of Nag Tasha, he found an elderly man who agreed to stable the horse and wagon for him until he needed them. He claimed to need the wagon to carry produce in from some farms from time to time. The old man was glad to obtain a bit more spending money with which to purchase more food for his ailing wife. That was as far as his planning went for nearly four more months.

In early November, fate took a twist in his favor. The constantly growing, heavy demand for processed opium had grown so much that two shifts of workers were kept constantly busy. Around nine that fateful night, a fire broke out in one of the processing buildings close to Overlord Mag's estate. The raging fire was clearly visible from their monastery's eagle eye's position. Suddenly, Wu knew how he could rescue all five at one time! Kissing his wife goodbye and telling Peng his plan in brief, he was lowered to the ground in the wooden box. He dashed to the wagon and soon had the horse harnessed. Within fifteen minutes, he reined in the wagon, concealing it in the dense bushes just behind the estate. He quietly moved through an opening and crept up to the backside of the estate.

Fire was the single most feared event in any town in Tashien. If left uncontrolled, it would spread, perhaps burning down the entire town. He knew that Mag would be close to the fire, ordering his men. Likely, all available men would be out there fighting the fire, leaving him his key opportunity to rescue all five at one time. Stealthily he crept in the back entrance and stole through the house. The women were not in their bedrooms, unless he'd moved the harem to another location, which he doubted. Mag was a man of habit. Cautiously, he went from likely room to room. He did gather up five dresses, however, four from what had to be the harem room and one from Meng's room. At last, he spotted the six women standing in front of the front room windows, watching the men fight the fire, which was now a raging inferno.

While he hated to do this, he knew that he had to. He crept up to Li Tazau and gently thumped her on her neck, knocking her out. He kept her from falling, sitting her into a nearby chair. Of course, the five women heard the noise and slowly attempted to turn and try to see what was going on near them. Their pinhole sight aided him. Before they could really see him and Mrs. Tazau, he spoke to them softly.

"It is me, Wu Shenyan. I have rescued Dai. She is quite safe. I have come to rescue all five of you. Do you want to leave here for a place of safety? Nod your heads if you do." All five nodded. "Can you walk to the back entrance?" Four nodded. Yuan did not; she was the new woman, Wu noted. "Okay, you four walk there while I carry her." He carefully picked up Yuan and carried her out of the room. Being as quiet as he could, he carried her outside and into the wagon. There, he laid her down and covered her with a blanket. "Please be as still as a mouse."

He headed back to the entrance. None of the four had yet reached the door, and he picked up Binan and carried her outside, placing her beside Yuan. After then bringing Chichong safely to the wagon, the other two had finally reached the door. He carried each of them to the wagon but left the outside door opened. Lastly, he tossed the five dresses into the small stream that ran just beyond where the wagon was parked. Satisfied, he climbed aboard the wagon and headed around the edges of Nag Tasha. Some fifteen minutes later, he stopped below the monastery and rang their gong.

When the box settled on the ground, he carried three women into the box, sitting them carefully on the floor. After another tense time, the box again settled on the ground, empty. He carried the other two, sat them in the box, and waited until they rose into the air, before returning to the wagon. A few minutes later, he had the horse back in its crude stable, and at last, he headed for the box himself. Around eleven, he finally stepped out of the box, safely atop the monastery. He had done it, rescued all five women. A monk led him to the women, who were sitting at a long table with Dai smiling broadly at them. He knew that she wanted to tell them so many things, but of course was unable to do so.

He also realized that the monks had been very thoughtful. The five women were sitting side by side across the table from Dai, and he sat down beside her. Now the five women could see her and him with little fuss. He spoke slowly, allowing the women to have time to move their heads about, locating him at last with their pinhole vision. "Hi again. I am Wu Shenyan and my new wife, Dai. Yes, we are married now. She and I have rescued you, and now we are all safe in the Taschi Monastery high atop the ridge where the overlord cannot reach us. Further, in all likelihood, Mag and Meng will soon believe that you five perished trying to run away from the threat of the fire, drowning in the river behind his estate. Yes, I dropped one of each of your dresses into the river. Tomorrow they will likely be found and you will probably be considered to have perished, if we are lucky. If so, they will never search for you again." Five wide smiles told him everything.

"Now then, four of you know me well, but I don't know you," he looked at the new woman. To her, he added, "We'll work that out in a bit. First, for your four, Binan, Chichong, Danyin Chou, Huachun, you are Most Honorable Yingchan, the most revered women in Tashien. Yet, Overlord Mag has so horribly mistreated you, by forcing you to have sexual relations with many of his guests. Such conduct on his part is inexcusable and unforgivable, particularly because of your highest of status. I give you my solemn word that I will do everything in my power to prevent that from ever happening again to you women, the Most Honorable Yingchan."

The four bowed to him, the best that they could do to thank him. He continued, "As I have said, I will be looking after your needs now for a time. With my wife's help, we will make your lives as pleasant and good as we can. Ultimately, Dai's and my goal is to get you all safely out of here to some place where you will be utterly safe, where you will receive the highest respect that you deserve as Yingchan, and where true love may come to you, as it has between Dai and myself. I admit that I do not know where this place may be or how we may get there, but I will always be trying to find it for us all."

"Next, Most Venerable Peng has taught me that I must learn to read your minds so that we may communicate with each other. I am still a mere novice at this, as Dai will attest. Still, she and I are beginning to succeed. We call it our charade game, in which I make guesses and she tells me if I am right or wrong. Sometimes, it does take me a long time to work out what she is telling me or rather what she wants to tell me. Yes, it was Dai who told me that I must also rescue our mystery Yingchan here. Dai was able to tell me that she was the unwilling wife of Meng and that there was no true love between them as well." The four grinned; this they must have found extremely interesting and lent credence to what he was saying about communications, he correctly assumed. Wu thought that he saw a tiny spark of hope appearing on the four women's faces.

"Finally, I wanted to compliment all four of you for having worked so very hard to learn to walk by yourself in your golden boots. As you know, I was banished and threatened with instant death because I dared stand up to Mag and tell him that he should not have done this to your feet. Still, I am extremely pleased that you Great Ladies have had the courage to learn to walk in them. As you four know, I had to do the same thing when the plague struck me, but I had the aid of my arms and sight, which you did not. I am extremely pleased with your courage." Again, the four cracked a big smile. He knew that he had scored a point with these women. What he did not know was just how hard it actually had been for these women, though he would soon get a tiny taste of that with Yuan.

"Now then, for our mystery lady. While all of you know her name, I do not. So we must play our charade game and guess her name." Yuan finally flashed a small smile. He sensed that she was still quite traumatized over the whole ordeal that she had recently undergone. "Now I have worked out a way to do this. Rather than trying every woman's name that I can think of, I am going to be methodical about it. Hopefully, I can learn her name faster this way — unless I got phenomenally lucky and guessed it on my first try," he teased them. All six chuckled at his jest. He began guessing the first letter of her first name, having her nod when he reached it. Just a few minutes later, he knew that she was called Yuan. A few minutes more and he had her full name, Yuan Jing. The young woman breathed a huge sigh of relief. Somehow, this was the most important thing that she wanted Wu to know, her name.

Next, he verified each woman's age. Yuan and Binan were now nineteen. Danyin was a year older, Huachun was twenty-one, while Chichong was twenty-two, the oldest of them all. Dai was twenty and Wu, twenty-one. As he finished, a monk came to escort them to their new rooms. Peng had arranged for the group to occupy three small bedrooms close to each other. Wu and Dai had one for themselves. Wu then allowed the five women to choose their own roommates. The two older women chose to bunk together, and the three younger ones decided to room together. "Don't worry. I will be helping each one of you with your daily needs. Just be patient, for I have to help all six of you now," he grinned. He knew he would be quite busy at certain times during the day and evenings, but that they were now living free from their torture made up for it in his mind.

That evening when he finally was able to tuck Dai into bed and crawled in beside her, she wanted to tell him something. They spent a half hour before he got her idea. "Yes, Yuan is an incredibly beautiful young woman, Dai. Don't worry your pretty head. It is you that I am in love with." He lifted her golden veil up, laying it gently over her eyes and their lips met.

Beginning the next morning, Wu had his hands full dealing with the six women and particularly Yuan. She refused even to try to stand up on her own. Fear and terror radiated from her when Wu asked her to stand. "Ah, you are afraid that you will fall if you try to stand up by yourself?" She nodded and began crying. After a bit more guessing, Wu found out that she didn't know how she could stand. She couldn't see or keep her balance well. He had her locate her two roommates and asked the two to show Yuan how they managed to get to their feet from a sitting position on their shared bed. Thus began a long workout for Wu.

After breakfast, he and the women began a lengthy chat session. In truth, Wu made wild guesses until he homed in on an idea and the women made their two yes-no sounds. He learned that Yuan had only been a Yingchan for barely four months and was still traumatized about it. Further, she wanted no part of it. He soon learned that she wanted to undo all of it, though she knew nothing could be done for her absent tongue. A bit more guessing led him to the fact that she did not want to be a Yingchan and was begging him to help her get rid of everything that had been done to her body.

"Okay, Yuan, I give you my word that I will do all that I can to undo all that the sadist did to you. However, I have no idea what they did to your eyes to make them golden. If I do something wrong with them trying to fix them, I could permanently blind you. Please, you must wait until I can find a doctor who can look your eyes over and figure out how to undo it, if there is any way to do so safely. I'm not a metalworker, and I can see no way to get the metal golden boots off you right now. However, again, I promise in time to find a metalworker who can do so. I will not rest, Yuan, until I have your body back to as close to your original body's condition as possible. If we are really lucky, the only thing that cannot be undone is your tongue. Just give me the time I need. For now, let's leave the earrings and other jewelry in place. They are worth a fortune and now belong to you. Perhaps they can be used to help provide for your needs when we finally get you to a new, safe place to live. In the meantime, it will help us all if you can be brave and see if you can learn to stand and walk a little on your own."

She sighed, but agreed. At least, he's promising to try, she thought. However, listening to all this, the other four Yingchan harem women began to have second thoughts about remaining as Yingchan themselves. They realized that if they could somehow be normal women once more, with all the wealth contained in their jewelry, they might be able to live far more productive and useful lives. As they now were, their lives were a continuous series of miseries, with little hope for anything better. They'd always be very dependent upon others for nearly everything, which the four hated more than anything else. The plague had very nearly done them in, but this sadistic mutilation was almost more than they could bear. Wu agreed to help the four as well.

That night, Dai was most troubled. After an hour, Wu finally worked out what Dai wanted to say to him. She was torn between remaining a Yingchan so that she could be the best possible wife for Wu. At the same time, she could not help but desire the freedom of just being able to be a normal woman again, even if she couldn't talk. Thus, she was torn between her two desires.

"My dear Dai, I love you no matter what you chose to do. You should do what is the best for you. I will back you up all the way." Dai still looked perplexed, and he added, "Look, there is plenty of time for you to make your decisions. Now we are stuck here in this monastery with no way that I can see to flee safely from here. In time I will find a way, so you don't have to make any decisions right now." Dai sighed, thankful for the gift of time. She knew that if she had not lost her arms, she would chose to remain a Yingchan, for she had been one for ages. Dai had even learned to walk in these new golden boots, just as Wu had. She could tolerate them, if only she had her arms back so that she could do things for herself.

Between assisting the women and doing a bit of gold mining for the monks, Wu's days were filled. Nevertheless, he continued to try to invent a way to get them all to safety. He broke the problem down. First, where was this imaginary place of safety?

Mid-November, Wu finally asked to speak to Most Venerable Peng. "I see that you are quickly learning to read the minds of the Yingchan," the old monk said, sitting down with a cup of tea.

"Yes, but my current problem is where will be a place of safety for these women? I've thought about it for days now. Tashien is in shambles. I cannot think of any city where these women would be safe from harm."

"Ah, yes. It would seem so."

Wu thought that was not particularly helpful, so he tried a different approach. "While they are safe enough here, we cannot continue to impose upon you and your monks. However, they would be safe within an Olin Masters Academy. Besides, they might be knowledgeable enough to help me undo the things that have been done to the women. I know that they often grant sanctuary to those in need, and we are in need, that's for sure."

"Ah, yes. That would be a wise choice, Honorable Wu."

At least Peng didn't shoot this idea down, Wu thought. "The only problem with that is that I know for a fact that the Olin Masters have abandoned their academies in Zau and Shansee. I have no idea where they have established their new academies."

"Perhaps I can help with that. We have heard that they have all gone to Nan Yan some five hundred miles south of here, as the eagle flies," Peng replied.

"That's great! Nan Yan is where we must head. Great. Er, now I have to figure out how I can safely get them there. Thank you, Most Venerable Peng." The monk nodded and Wu left to tell the others that he'd at least worked out their destination.

The next day, the first heavy snowfall of the season dumped over a foot of snow on Nag Tasha. That effectively ended any chance that Wu had to flee the monastery before winter came. The high country would be snow covered until spring. The women had no winter clothes and couldn't possibly walk in the snow in their golden boots. Even if he could carry them to and from a carriage, two weeks travel would be beyond their endurance in the cold. For sure, they could not stop at inns along the way. With jewelry worth millions, they'd be robbed at the first inn they came to. At least Wu had time to work out travel arrangements for the spring.

On December 1, Wu noticed a large number of riders coming up the snow-covered road into Nag Tasha. From his eagle eye view, he could not mistake the banners of several other neighboring drug overlords. Each brought hundreds of their own soldiers with them. Obviously, some key meeting was about to take place, and he wished that there was some way that he could listen in to what was going on.

Times had definitely taken a turn for the worst. Meng asked, "Dad, surely you are not going to accept iron coins from Zau or Shansee — are you? They are worthless."

"Not on your life! We've been producing more opium this past year than in many years combined. We have met the dealer's demands for more product. But this — this is robbery! I won't stand for it. I'm going to call for a Overlord Council. Let's see if the others have been made similar offers. We need to present a unified front, son. That's how it's done. If one overlord accepts worthless iron coins for their opium, then we're all doomed."

"I understand, dad. Damn, I wish Yuan had not drowned. I would have loved to have shown her off to the other overlords," Meng replied.

"Hell, I lost my entire harem too, son. They must have thought that the fire was about to engulf the estate and tried to flee. We know that they can barely walk, so they must have lost their balance and fallen into the river. Shame about the millions that we lost on their gold and gemstone jewelry. Has anyone discovered their bodies yet?"

"No dad. We've rather given up the search for now. Eventually their bodies will float to the surface. No moneychanger will accept any parts of their jewelry, if someone tries to rob their bodies. I've threatened all them in Nag Tasha and several surrounding towns. Any chance that we can get some replacement Yingchan before the overlords come? Will they be bringing their Yingchan with them?"

Mag grinned, this would be his son's first meeting with most all the other drug overlords. "More than likely they will, Meng. We will lose face if we do not have more than my wife to show off. Point well taken. There is still time for us to rectify the situation. Son, it is time that you have a harem too, especially with the significance of this council. We are going to need four women quickly. I should have acted sooner on this, son, but other events are just coming too swiftly these past months. Okay, check with our Seconds. Put your heads together and round up four young women. There is no time to get their agreement or anything else. If they look suitable, kidnap them and bring them here. I'll make the arrangements to have them made into proper Yingchan when they arrive."

"Great, dad. Okay, I'm on it!" Meng saluted his dad and rushed off to find his dad's two Seconds.

"Sorry about your wife," Yi Huhe said, when Meng told him and Jinan, his dad's two Seconds, what was needed immediately.

"Yes, well, no great loss to me. Dad took the hit, financially, unless we can find their bodies and recover the gold and gems. However, you heard about the proposed Overlord Council, so we have to get four women today, if possible."

"Okay, what are the criteria that Overlord Mag is looking for?" Yi asked.

"Hey, two are going to be mine. I'm getting a start on my own harem. Well, dad wants them between eighteen and twenty-five, but I want them between eighteen and twenty-one. No old ones for me," he teased Yi and Jinan. Both men chuckled along with Meng.

"What about married women?" asked Jinan.

"They will do too," Meng answered.

"What if they have already had children?" Yi asked.

"Oh hell, we're desperate. Take them anyway, but let's see if we can find four without children first," Meng concluded.

"Hey, remember those twins that we passed up when we were looking for Yuan?" Yi proposed. "They weren't half bad looking and were single the last time that we checked."

"Great! Two in one shot. We'll fetch them. Need two more," Meng decided. The three men discussed other possibilities, recalling their lengthy search of nearby towns and villages when they were helping Meng find one to be his wife. Before long, they had agreed on the four new women. While the Seconds saddled up their horses and issued orders for a carriage and two dozen soldiers to accompany them, Meng reported to his father. "Got the four picked out, dad. Yi, Jinan, and I will go get them now."

"Let the Seconds deal with the women. I need you to run an important errand for me. I just got word that there is some kind of trouble brewing in Shachang. Take a hundred soldiers and go straighten out the mess there, son."

"All right! Some action! I'm on it," he bolted out of the room, eager to get in on some real fighting and not mere kidnaping of helpless women. Meantime, Mag left to make the needed preparations, rounding up both doctors who he had used before and four jewelers as well. Finally, he had Master Jinnan fire up his hearth. They'd need their golden boots soon. One thing was certain: the other overlords would get to see his marvelous extensions to the ancient tradition of the Yingchan. He gave a snide smirk as he imagined their faces when they saw his Yingchan. Besides, he had other ideas for these new Yingchan. Times were taking a bad turn and Mag wanted to be fully prepared, just in case.

Late that afternoon, his Seconds returned, dropping off the now unconscious women at Mag's estate. "Any trouble?" he asked, as his men carried the drugged women inside, pausing briefly so their boss could catch a glimpse of each woman.

"Not much, twin's father had to be shot, but the other families seemed greatly relieved to have us take their daughters," Yi answered. "I take it these will do?"

"Yes, I've seen prettier women, but these will do nicely. Thanks, go get some grub." He turned and followed the last man inside. All four women wore mostly rags and were rather dirty. Well, he thought, that was to be expected. Few have enough men to care for their women. I'm doing these four a great service indeed. Quickly, his servant staff stripped the women and then bathed their unconscious bodies, giving Mag a chance to examine them in detail.

The twins, Zhu and Zhen Yun Zi, were nineteen, with oval faces and thick eyebrows and long lashes. Both also had thick lips, naturally curved in a smile. These, he decided to take for his harem. Smiling women would be a nice touch. Both were just nineteen. Yan Zhou was also nineteen and Ting Sha was twenty. Both were a tad on the short side, but attractive. These would be fine for his son, he concluded.

Dried and dressed, the women were laid out on tables for the doctors, who now set to work. One handled the women's tongues, while the other dealt with the slits and punctures required to support their jewelry and handled their eyes. Having performed this procedure so frequently, the men made rapid progress and finished the four up in a little over an hour. Next, the jewelers arrived and plied their trade on the four women, though this time, each woman would only sport a half million gold worth of gems and gold in their ornaments. Finally, his servants sat each woman in a chair to allow Master Jinnan proper access to their feet. His work took nearly three hours to complete. Once done, the drugged women were given a last minute check up by one of the doctors and then carried to their beds in the old harem room.

Mag assigned two servants to look after their needs when they awoke and then retired for the night with his wife. He explained to her, "Now tomorrow I need you to begin helping the four new Yingchan learn how to walk as well as you, my love. Soon, we will be hosting all the other overlords, and I want them to really admire you and your skills." She smiled and made her yes noise.

Zhu awoke to a massive pain in her throat. She tried to get up, but the unexpected weight of her heavy earrings pulled her back down. Her feet felt funny and wouldn't bend; they were pointed downward. She felt something over her lower face and lips. Zhu opened her eyes wide but only saw a tiny pin prick of light. She cried out and discovered that the front portion of her tongue was gone, and she screamed. Soon three other women's screams drowned her out. Zhu, Zhen, Yan, and Ting awoke from their drugged sleep to find themselves turned into Yingchan, though they did not know that detail yet.

Much later on, I would learn firsthand the shock, terror, pain, and panic these four felt that early winter morning. The servants worked with them, handling the chamber pots, gargling out dried blood, and then feeding them. Later in the day when they had calmed down, Mag and Meng joined them.

"Ladies, I am Overlord Mag Tazau. My son, Meng. You four have been given a very great honor. I have turned you into Most Honored Yingchan, the golden angels. Each of your jewelry is worth a half million in gold, so you can be very pleased with your appearance indeed. Zhu and Zhen, you will be in my harem, Yan and Ting will be in Meng's. The only thing that we ask of you right now is rapidly to learn to get to your feet and to walk around my lavish estate by yourselves. Our servants will be helping you with that as well as my Yingchan wife, the lovely Li. Now then, it is time that you rise and see yourselves in the full-length mirrors. You will lack for nothing at all and always be wearing the finest silk dresses."

Zhu and Zhen tried to say that they could not even stand up in these boots, but only unintelligible noises came out, and they shut up quickly, totally shocked at their complete helplessness even to speak! One by one, a servant helped them stand and walk to the mirror. Quickly, all four realized that they could not move their eyes, and that in order to see out of the pinholes, they would have to bend or turn their heads. However, they did get a look at their new appearance, beginning with their eyes, which now looked like shiny golden orbs. The smallest of pinholes in the center allowed them a minimum of vision. All four screeched and cried, but could do nothing else about it. Worse, their feet were aching, and yet the servant continued to make them walk around the room. All four wanted to just die, but sadly no longer had any means to do so. The women were about as miserable as they could be and still be alive.

During the ensuing days, each was forced to continually learn to walk on their own. Mag was insistent that by the time of the council, these women had to put in their appearance by walking into the meeting room on their own. Thus, his servants really had little choice but to continually force the terrified women to practice. They had but a few weeks to master this or else. December 1 came rapidly.

Chapter 68 The Drug Lords' Plans

As each overlord and his party arrived, Mag and Meng were there to greet them. Most arrived in their private carriages and had brought at least one Yingchan with them; usually she was their wife. Proudly, Li stood by her husband's side as their guests dismounted and carried their Yingchan inside. Uniformly, all the overlords were greatly impressed with Li and her golden boots. They were fascinated by the fact that she had no tongue, their Yingchan were traditional and could speak. They typically wore the imported extreme heels, however, since the plague had wiped out their small feet and then restored them to normal. None had wanted to undergo another six weeks with their feet broken and allowed to heal inside the metal shoes — although they probably would have done so, if they had not lost their arms. Even the visiting Yingchan were impressed with Li and her skills.

At dinner that first night, on cue, the four new Yingchan were marched into the dining room and forced to find their own seats, all on their own. While they wobbled terribly and very nearly lost their balance several times, each finally made it to their seat, where their servants finally began to help them. Mag pointed out that they were brand new Yingchan and that their walking skills would soon be improving. Nevertheless, several overlords inquired about the golden boots and how they were made.

The next morning, the real meeting began. Overlord Bao from north of the Lian River was the second most powerful man present. Only Mag was more powerful and controlled more land and opium production. The other ten overlords came from just beyond Mag's territory to the east and south of his huge area. Bao was the key man, Mag knew, for he supplied Zau with a good deal of its opium.

Bao opened the meeting. "Well, it's become an even worse chaos in the Imperial City. As you may know, many of the wealthier class somehow escaped Zau, taking their wealth with them. Traitors. We've now learned that they have resettled in Nan Yan, south of here. To be frank, the money supply has all but dried up. They are now issuing worthless iron coins!"

"Yes, they are trying to pass them off as legal tender for their opium," another overlord added.

Another overlord from the south broke in, "Same in Shansee. The wealthy relocated to Nan Yan. Worse, the two overlords there have just fought a huge battle for control of Shansee and both lost! My spies tell me that hundreds of thousands died in that massive battle. Now no one is running Shansee."

"It just gets grimmer and grimmer," Mag pointed out. "I've called you all here today so that we may meet this challenge to our businesses head on. I for one will not accept iron coins for my opium. Period. End of deal." All eleven others seconded him and Mag relaxed. At least they could present a united front on this point.

"Hey, what about women? I've had several of my dealers offer to trade women for opium. At first, that sounded intriguing, but then we have to waste huge amounts of manpower just taking care of the women, who as you all know very well are totally helpless since the plague struck. Has anyone heard of a cure coming?" another overlord asked. "Hey you, refill my tea," he ordered a servant who was sitting quietly on the side lines.

Wu simply could not resist listening in on this likely important overlord conference. He'd donned a disguise and had joined the many other men who were temporarily hired to handle the many extra guests. He got himself appointed as tea servant, and his job was to sit quietly in the room, refilling the overlord's cups when needed. Humbly, he did as requested. No one paid him the slightest attention. Why should they? He was but a lowly servant and a bent-over one at that. Wu took his seat once more. His mind was racing since he discovered that they had taken four more women and turned them into Yingchan as well. Worse, he knew the twins and their father.

"Hey, actually, there is a cure for the women. Down in Nan Yan, the Church of God is somehow working miracles, giving women back their arms, undoing the plague's effects on them," another southern overlord reported. "Some of my spies have actually seen women with their arms back. "But I have far worse news, if I may, Overlord Mag?" Mag nodded and allowed him to speak. This was news to him. Perhaps his wife could get her arms back. If so, his life would be far easier, but then he had taken a liking to her current helplessness.

"The Princess Mei Lon Wu and her General Tao Bi are slowly conquering neighboring lands. My spies have reported that come spring, they plan to push eastward and north into my own lands! They are definitely out to conquer all of Tashien. My spies have never been wrong on their moves yet. Gentlemen, this is a very serious development. Alone, I have not sufficient soldiers to withstand an all-out siege by General Tao. He is one of the most ruthless generals ever!"

"God damn! Is the whole world going nuts?" Overlord Mag cursed. All this was news to him. "First we have to deal with iron coins, then we are to take women in trade, and now we face General Tao and his glorious ambition to conquer all Tashien? What the hell is next?"

The meeting temporarily broke up into eleven men all talking at once. For most, this was shocking news! All were aware of the iron coin situation, but that General Tao of Nan Yan was out to conquer their very lands and put them out of business took most by complete surprise.

Wu used every ounce of self-control to maintain his distant, stone face. That there was a cure for the women was the very best news ever! That these people were then going to attack the drug lords and put them out of business — this was almost a miracle! Further, he knew they had the entire Olin Masters behind them too, for they were in Nan Yan as well.

At last, Mag restored order. "In light of this shocking news, I have an idea, gentlemen. We agree, no iron coins for our opium. No women. Rather, let's trade for equipped soldiers. If they want their opium, then they must send us equipped soldiers in trade." Again, they all began talking at once, totally in favor of Mag's brilliant idea. After some discussion, they agreed upon the price of a pound of opium: twenty equipped soldiers. The opium would be sent when the soldiers arrived.

That settled, the attention then turned to the planned spring offensive. "I cannot possibly hold out against General Tao's forces! I simply don't have the manpower that you have, Mag. What am I to do?" Nine other weaker overlords added their "me too's" to his protest.

Overlord Bao spoke up, "Look, we have a vastly better chance of defeating Tao's army here in the hills than we do down there on the wide open plains. Look at what happened to the two armies around Shansee? Decimated. While I feel deeply for my fellow drug lords, your territories simply cannot be easily defended. Mine and Mag's here can be, but not your far eastern lands, Mag — too flat, too open. Our best chance to put down General Tao is to join our soldiers together and fight from the higher ground, perhaps even here, Mag. Nag Tasha is highly defensible from attacks from the east and south."

"But what about us? Are we to just flee our own lands?" one protested.

"Are we being cast to the wolves?" another asked.

Mag was a shrewd man. He played out the scenario in his mind rapidly. If these eastern and southern drug lords were left to defend by themselves, General Tao's forces would likely crush them. He would then be in a very untenable position and likely lose control of his own vast lands. "Gentlemen, stand alone and we all lose. We must present a united front. Bao is right, we cannot, even with our combined might, hope to defend the relative open lands to the south and east. Instead, I propose this. I will welcome any of you into my lands; bring your entire army here. If we all join forces and defend this higher ground, this ridge land, then together we can defeat this egomaniac general. Once that is done, I will lend my own forces to help drive the last vestiges of Tao's forces from your lands."

Bao added, "Yes, I will muster my forces just across the Lian River. When Tao sweeps into these hills from the eastern flat lands, we will ford the river and come at his rear, cutting off his supply lines, surrounding him. Together, we will cut him and his army to pieces."

Mag immediately knew what Bao was really saying, however. The man would actually take a clever wait and see approach. If things went ill for the defenders, he would keep his own troops from the battle. Yet, if Mag and his forces were winning or could easily win if Bao stepped in, then Bao would. None of the other overlords detected this subtle move on Bao's part.

While the nine overlords discussed Mag and Bao's generous offer, Mag reached a decision. He waited until the nine finally agreed to his terms. When they did so, he said, "Okay. We need to setup a war room. I have a large-scale map of my lands. We can setup a defensive line, and I will assign towns and villages to each of you overlords. You can move your households and armies into those areas. I will move mine out, turning control of those towns over to you and your men. I will be depending upon you to hold these positions. As you move up to these new positions this winter, bring all the young men you can press into service with you." This they liked, and the meeting adjourned so that the overlords could discuss this extremely bad news with their own men and Seconds.

Wu found himself summoned to bring tea to the assembled Yingchan. He had the opportunity to see how the traditional Yingchan were treated. None of the visiting ones had been mutilated like Li and the others. All were chatting merrily, wishing that Li could talk to them. They were fascinated by her golden boots and really did want to find out how she managed in them. True, none could see well through their pinholes, but before the plague, they got by rather well anyway. Wu realized that it was only Mag's sadistic perversions that had turned a centuries old tradition of great honor into a terrifying nightmare. He resolved to find a way to rescue these new four.

As he served the women, Wu noticed a ten year old boy sneaking a peek into the room. Curious, he'd not seen any children about before, but now with all the guests, he concluded that Mag was pressing everyone into service. Still something about the boy held his attention. What was he doing? From the corner of his eye, the lad was staring at one of the women. His eyes followed the path of the boy's and lit upon Yan Zhou. No question about it, the lad was watching her closely. Why? Then he saw it; the boy's face closely resembled Yan's. He wondered if that was possible — could this boy be related to her? He decided to keep an eye on the boy.

Later that afternoon, he saw the boy snatch up a sharp knife from the kitchen and walk off with it. Not good. The boy was more than likely to get himself killed. Carrying yet another tea tray, Wu followed the lad, though he had to make several stops and lost sight of him for a time. A half hour later, Wu spotted the boy. He had the knife hidden behind his back and was walking slowly towards the one man who stood guard just outside the room where the Yingchan were sitting. Wu moved as quickly as he dared, without divulging his bent, old man disguise. As he neared the boy, he saw that the knife hand was trembling and Wu moved closer. He whispered, "That would not be a good idea just now. Follow me, please." The lad looked terribly frightened but saw what appeared to be a very old man, barely able to get around. He slipped the knife under his shirt and followed Wu.

When he got to a quiet corner, he whispered, "Are you trying to rescue one of those women?"

Stumbling over his words, the nervous ten year old replied, "Yes, but please don't give me away. They took my sister. I have to free her."

"I know, son. Is it Yan Zhou?"

"Yes, how do you know that?"

"Observation. Now is not the time to rescue her, son. There are too many soldiers around. Besides, have you seen her feet and eyes? She can just barely see and can only walk a very tiny amount in those boots, which cannot be taken off. If you really want to rescue her, you will come with me. Together we will rescue her at the right time and place."

"Please, you have to help me rescue Yan, please," he whimpered.

"I give you my word. Now then, what is your name?"

"Jie."

"Okay, Jie. Carry on with your assigned work. Ditch the knife somewhere. You'll be killed if someone finds it on you. We won't need it to rescue her. I'll find you later tonight, and we can work out a good plan, son."

"Okay." He left, tossing the knife behind a couch. Wu breathed a sigh of relief and then continued with his assigned chores. He learned nothing else useful the rest of the day, though he still kept an eye out for Jie.

Around eight, all the temporary staff began lining up to leave. A steward was handing out their pay, and Jie came up to Wu and fell in line behind him. A bit later, the man handed Wu a silver coin and said, "Tomorrow morning at eight." Behind him, he heard him say the same thing to Jie. Together, they followed the many others out of the estate into the snowy evening. As they walked away from the estate, Wu pointed out all the soldiers on guard duty. He wanted Jie to realize that the place was very heavily guarded now and that a rescue attempt would be utter folly. Jie got the message.

"Where are we going? I am getting cold."

"No talk. Just follow me." An hour later, the boy stared up at the box that came descending from high above the two. Yes, Jie enjoyed the elevator ride up into the monastery. A bit later, while eating a late snack, Wu told Jie what was going on and introduced him to the other six whom he'd rescued. Jie finally relaxed and began to gab to the six, though they could not do more than nod yes or no.

With Jie occupied, Wu went to find the Most Venerable Peng. "I am so sorry to have waken you, but things have taken a turn for the worst."

"Please sit down and tell me why you are so worried, Honorable Wu." He did so, spilling all that he had seen and overheard today. "I am scared that they might even send soldiers up here to gain a better spot to fire down upon General Tao's forces," he ended with his great fear.

"So now you know a whole lot of news, my son. What do you want to do with it? Worry not about the monastery. We will not allow them up here."

"Honestly, Most Venerable Peng, I need to rescue those four women, get this news to General Tao in Nan Yan, and get the women there. Everyone is saying that the Church of God there can give our women back their arms somehow. If there is any chance of that at all, I must get the women there."

"I do not know this General Tao of whom you speak, but I know that the Olin Masters would not be backing an evil general. We must assume that this general is an honorable man. Thus, I agree with you. You must take this news to him before the spring comes. Let me ponder this tonight. Get some sleep, Honorable Wu. By the way, if I were you, I would not gamble on your disguise another day. You were very fortunate today, but tomorrow you might not be so lucky. Now that you have the news, your priorities must change."

"I understand, but I must also rescue those four Yingchan. I've given my word to Jie." He bowed and returned to the women and the boy.

Mag studied his large map. Teacups represented the towns, which he had donated to each of the other overlords. All had agreed to begin evacuating their stronghold, moving their forces to the designated towns, digging in, and preparing for the spring offensive. They had guessed that they had at most three, maybe four months before General Tao would begin his invasion. Meng was with him.

"Looks good dad. I don't see how anyone could get through all that."

"Son, this battle will bring glory to us all. I am getting too old for battlefields. I want you to take our forces and setup our major defenses in Xian. We both know that most of the other overlords will crumble when General Tao hits them, but I am putting all our resources with you. You will stop them. I've no doubt of that. When you do, your position as the dominate overlord of the highland will be cemented. None will ever challenge you after that. This is your opportunity to fulfill your destiny in a way that I never had. I had to build up to where we are today, one drug deal at a time. Son, I'm giving you the leadership of all the drug overlords on a golden platter."

"Dad! This is incredible! Yes, I see your brilliant plan. I defeat General Tao, retake all the lands. We'll be the supreme overlords! Thank you! I will not fail!" Meng had never shown such enthusiasm, Mag noted. They shook hands.

A week after the conference ended and the overlords left for their home to begin their own exodus and war preparation, Meng proudly led a thousand soldiers and twenty supply wagons out of Nag Tazau. Already messengers had been sent, pulling all their soldiers from their assigned stations back and down to Xian, a town about fifty miles to the south of Nag Tasha. There, a long ridge provided a magnificent natural barrier some ten miles long. Entrenched on the ridge line, General Tao would be hard pressed to dislodge his forces. A few days after that, another thousand support personnel also left Nag Tasha as well, leaving the town with only a handful of guards and of course, the opium workers, who were finally given a long respite. Mag suspected the opium purchases would plummet, and he was right. Orders fell by more than half; few dealers could provide equipped soldiers as payment.

Overlord Mag knew better than to believe in the grand plan that he devised. The handwriting was more than plain. With the total collapse of the economy of both Zau and Shansee, demand for their product would dry up drastically. True, orders still came in from more distant cities and towns, but the volume there was far smaller, barely enough to survive on and still keep operational. No, Mag knew that the days of his highly profitable opium business were over.

Further, he knew both of the two generals whose armies had fought for control of Shansee. If they had eliminated each other, then the drug overlords would stand little chance of defeating the better supplied army of General Tao. It might take three months, maybe even half a year, but eventually, General Tao, backed by the Olin Masters, would crush their defenses and capture all his territory. Would he then attempt to cross the Lian River and push on into Wontun Province? That, Mag decided, he could not predict. It was logical for the general to attempt to gain total control over his own province, Tan Loc. But did he have visions of becoming a self-appointed emperor? Mag did not know nor did he care.

Long had Mag prepared for just such an eventuality. Jinan was off with Meng; Yi, he sent eastward to arrange any further opium deals, under the guise of shortening the time to get equipped soldiers to the battlefield. It was typical for him to be down to a skeleton crew for the duration of the winter season. With the deep snow cover, few would be traveling, unless they had to. It was time — time for Mag to retire from this business. At least, he had given his son a chance, though he would not have placed any wagers on it. The real question that he had to answer was did he take his golden angel with him or not? What to do with Li? She had been faithful to him all these years, but since the plague, she had become a total liability. That she could barely walk was not an issue. Without her arms and hands, she now depended utterly on others.

Worse, if he took her with him and if it became necessary for him to become anonymous, having her with him would announce his presence to the whole world. A golden Yingchan was exceedingly rare, seldom, if ever, found much beyond the highlands. If he ended up in the great coastal port city of Shankou, she would instantly attract everyone's attention, and thus by association, to him. No, she couldn't speak and could be trusted with any secret. Rather her golden looks would spell his doom. Besides, he could always obtain new women. He didn't lament the loss of the monetary value tied up in her jewelry or even that with the women who had drowned. What were a few million gold to Mag? Nothing but mere change. No, his real wealth he had been secreting away for the last fifteen years. Much of it now resided in Shankou, where the weather was much warmer in the winter, heated by warm ocean currents from the south. No, Li must remain here, he decided with a sigh.

His mind fixed on his objective, Mag made his preparations. "Li, I have to make a lengthy business trip to the east. I will be gone for quite some time. Our brave son will be protecting us from the attacks from the south. You will be quite safe here. I am leaving you safe with our estate steward and your servant men. When I return, Li, I will bring you the very latest in fashionable dresses, nothing but the very finest for you, my love." She searched for his face and then kissed him through her golden veil. He slid his arms around her and held her close.

The next morning, he quietly emptied out his safe and re-locked it. Before the plague, he would have been quite worried about Li becoming overly curious and opening it herself. If she discovered that the metal briefcase was gone, she would know that Mag had abandoned her. Now she had no arms and could not open it. Although she could not speak then or now, she would have been able to write and thus explain his absence. Now, she could not even do that, if by some unknown means the safe was opened by another. No one would have any idea that he had simply retired from the business. His goal was to vanish without a trace. The briefcase contained ten million, spending money in gold and a number of extremely valuable and large gemstones. The bulk of his funds, now amounting to just over a hundred million, was stored in secret locations. Mag did not trust banks.

He climbed onto his private sleigh. His faithful driver would come with him, perhaps all the way to Shankou. He took two of his best fighters along as well; both were faithful bodyguards. All three were highly skilled martial arts fighters and crack shots with the newer long guns. He looked under the blankets and nodded. The dozen guns were at the ready in case of trouble. He climbed into the passenger seat and nodded to his driver. Slowly, his sleigh moved down the snow-covered streets, as he took in his last view of Nag Tasha.

From his eagle eye perch, Wu saw Meng leading the troops out of the town, heading south. Later he spotted an equally large group following them. Curious, he continued to keep watch on the city whenever he had the chance. When he had to work in their mines to help pay for their stay, he had Jie keep watch. Around nine, Jie came to him extremely excited. "Wu! Wu! Come quick. Overlord Mag is leaving on his sleigh!"

Both dashed through the stone corridors to the observation window. Wu spotted the sleigh. Mag was definitely leaving town. From all the bags piled on the sleigh, Wu concluded that he intended to be gone for some time. "Perhaps now is the time that we rescue your sister and the others," Wu suggested.

Jie became even more excited. At last! He had been waiting for a whole three weeks now! "When do we go? Now?" he asked.

"Bit more patience. Nighttime will be best." Recognition filled Jie's face; he nodded affirmatively. Now Wu had to think quickly. The snow would make their tracks quite visible.

He also saw several other wagons carrying long crates coming into town and had an idea. Hastily, he donned his old man disguise and headed down the elevator, leaving Jie to watch over the women. He had a good guess where the teamsters would take the wagons. Most supplies came into Mag's huge warehouse in the center of town. Wu made for it, arriving as several men were unloading them. Standing around hunched over, adding his own grey breathy steam to the chilly winter air, Wu listened in on their conversations.

"'Cuse me. Some work for a poor old man and his grandson, perhaps?" Wu said brokenly and pleadingly.

"You want some work?" one burly teamster asked.

Wu nodded energetically, "Yes, yes, for me and my ten year old grandson."

"Got six food crates to be unloaded. Be at Mag's estate in an hour. Steward will give you orders," the man said. Turning to his companions as Wu nodded appreciatively and backed away, "Well, that's a bit of luck. What with everyone heading to Xian, we were going to be stuck unloading these six crates. What luck, eh?" Several chuckled.

An hour later, Wu and Jie arrived at the estate with his wagon. The steward looked relieved as the pair walked up to him. "Bao said you were after some work?" Wu nodded. "Good, I have six large crates that need to be unloaded, and the goods stored on the panty shelves in proper order. Silver each when you're done with it."

"Please, kind sir. May we have the wooden crates instead? Firewood is scarce. I haven't the strength to chop any more, and my grandson is too young. We work for the crates?"

A snide grin pierced the man's face. "Crates it is then. No rush, take your time at it. This way." He led them to the back pantry, which was near the very back doors, which Wu had used to escape with the previous harem women. Their harem bedroom was three doors on down the hall from the panty to the back doors. Wu thought this was a most convenient, perfect setup. The six large crates were stacked in the middle of the panty, whose shelves were rather empty. Much had been taken south with the soldiers. "Each shelf is labeled. Uncrate the supplies and stack the goods where they belong, neatly mind you."

"Oh, yes, yes, but this will take some time to do," Wu nodded eagerly, rather like a puppy.

"I don't care if it takes you all day and half the night. Just do it right. I'll check back on you from time to time. Crowbars are over there. Get to it and the crates are yours when you are done, old man." Wu nodded eagerly once more. He and Jie set to work, carefully opening the top crate.

When they were alone, Jie whispered, "We're going to take them out in the crates? Right?"

Wu smiled, bright lad. "You'll bring the wagon around to the back doors and we'll load them when we are done. Go slowly. We need to finish this after supper. Do a very good job; make everything neat and proper."

The two worked slowly all afternoon long. Twice the steward came by to check on their progress. Because the new packages were very nicely stack and in their proper places, the steward more or less forgot about them. Late afternoon, several cooks came by, picking out things for the evening meal. Both sat quietly on a crate, staying completely out of their way. They were on the last crate when they heard the small group having their dinner in the dining room, some five doors on down the long hallway. Wu kept one eye on the hallway, anticipating seeing the four women being brought back to their bedroom. At last, he saw two servant men leading the virtually helpless women down the hall to their room.

He had Jie sit on the last box, as if he were exhausted. "Let me know when the two men leave their room," Wu whispered. Shortly, Jie signaled Wu, who took a quick verification glance. Not long after that, a sleepy steward made his last visit to them.

"Ah, just about done. When you finish, bring your wagon around to those back doors there. You can load your crates there. Just be quiet about it. The women will be sleeping. When you are ready, a guard will see you out." Wu nodded and the steward left.

They took another half hour to finish up, dragging it out as long as they dared. With the estate now very quiet, Wu and Jie began carrying their crates down the hall, making a long line of them. Wu and Jie then stole into the harem room. The four were not yet asleep and Jie whispered to Yan, "Yan. Yan, it is Jie. We've come to rescue all of you."

Wu whispered, "Please be absolutely quiet. I will be putting you into some crates, carrying you out of here on a wagon. Make no sounds or we'll be caught!" They managed a nod, straining their heads to try to see who was here. In the dim candle light, they simply could not manage it. Wu's strong arms lifted Yan and carried her out of the bedroom, laying her gently inside one crate. Jie covered her up with the lid, and they quietly carried the crate to the doors and went back for the next. Five minutes later, all four women were lying in crates, much like a coffin, though they could not quite perceive it. Wu purposely stacked the two empty crates on top of the four, then sent Jie to bring the wagons around back.

One guard sleepily came to check on them, opening the top crate to make sure that it was empty. He grunted and walked to the panty, took a quick look around, and returned. "Hurry up and get those loaded so I can go to sleep."

"Yes, honorable sir, but we are tired. Give us a few minutes, please," Wu said, feigning exhaustion. He grunted and headed back to his station at the front doors. Quickly, Wu sat the two empty crates aside and lifted the far heavier ones first, with Jie's help. They moved as quickly as they could. When they were about to carry the last two crates out, the guard returned and again opened the two crates. He nodded and allowed them to finish loading the two empty ones. Just as soon as the two stepped out with the last one, the guard shut the door and locked it. Once loaded, the two climbed aboard, and Wu began driving them away from the estate.

Now was the critical moment, Wu thought. If the guard checked in on the women, the game would be up. It would be obvious to the guards that they had stolen the women away in the crates and would soon be after them. He purposely ducked down side streets, merging his wagon's tracks with hundreds of others. At last, he made for the winding track that led to the monastery. Wu was nervous as he waited for the wooden box to alight on the snow once more. Carefully, he lifted each shivering woman out of a crate and sat her in the box, explaining to the frightened woman that they were soon going to be warm and safe. He sent Jie up with the four women, while he took their wagon back to where it was being stored. When he returned, still no alarm had been sounded. He loaded the crates into the wooden box and climbed in, pulling the signal rope. Slowly, he was lifted up into the monastery. "Brought you some extra firewood," he explained to the silent monk who was working the winch. The man bowed and Wu dashed off to find the women and Jie.

He found them together with his wife and the other Yingchan. The four newcomers were wrapped in warm blankets, sitting on the edge of Dai's bed. She and the others were sitting on the chairs, though some were leaning on the table. Jie was gaily chatting away, telling his sister all about what he'd bravely done to rescue her. She had tears trickling down her cheeks and was trying hard to see her little brother, nodding here and there. "Oh, here he comes now, Yan. This is Wu Shenyan, Dai's husband. He's really the one who did most of the work rescuing you."

Yan tried hard to see Wu, but until he spoke, she couldn't locate where he was. The candle light made vision difficult anyway. Combined with the women's pinhole vision, seeing was nearly impossible. "Hello Most Honorable Yingchan. I am Wu Shenyan. As Jie has undoubtedly been telling you, we have rescued you from the clutches of Overlord Mag. You are safe now. We are in the Taschi Monastery for the time being. Most Venerable Peng has granted us all sanctuary. As soon as I can, I will be taking all of you to Nan Yan. There, we have heard that the Church of God has a way to restore your arms to all of you.

Alas, I do not know how your tongues can be made whole again. Nor do I know how to remove your golden eyes or those awful boots. Yet, there is hope for us all in Nan Yan. The powerful Olin Masters have all gathered there as well. It is my hope that somehow, someway, much can be done for you women. I give you my word that I will always be here to help you with your needs."

"If you wish to remain golden angels, we will always look after you. If you wish to return to as normal as possible, I will do all that I can to make that happen too. In Nan Yan, we can all start out on a new path in life. Now then, we know one of your names, Yan Zhou. Dai and I, along with the five other Yingchan have worked out a way for you to communicate with us. We call it the charades guessing game. We will show you how it works by finding out from you three what your names are."

A half hour later, Wu introduced Zhu Yun Zi, Zhen Yun Zi, Ting Sha, and Yan Zhou to the others, Binan, Chichon, Danyin Chou, Huachun, Yuan Jing, and Dai Shenyan. Still mostly unable to see each other properly, the women bowed in the general direction of each other. Then, Wu helped each of the newcomers into a warm bed, tucking them in, before he finally returned to his own room and Dai. As he lay beside Dai, he quickly told her how it had all gone as planned and she relaxed. A bit of a guessing game later, Wu deciphered her thank you for having rescued the four new Yingchan.

If he was busy caring for the six women before, now with ten Wu was constantly busy for half of each day tending to their needs. Jie helped some with his sister, of course. He found that the four were still extremely vulnerable, unsure of everything, and quite scared. They had not had time to adapt to their situations at all well. Most still tried to speak though all their sounds were unintelligible. Wu's heart went out to these four as they tried bravely to somehow endure their continuing nightmare tortures.

Most Venerable Peng reached a decision. Wu and his rescued Yingchan just had to be taken to Nan Yan. If the rumors that the Church of God there could restore the women's arms were true, their lives would be immeasurable helped. Besides, Wu had invaluable information for the army there. While Peng seldom took sides in man's petty squabbles, he knew the brutality and hardship that Mag had inflicted on his people, and now he knew the depths of the man's sadism ran deep. To pervert so horribly one of Tashien's oldest traditions was a sacrilege in his mind. Peng was a good judge of people; he had sixty years of practice. When he heard from Wu that Mag had left in a loaded sleigh, leaving his Yingchan wife, Li, behind, he suspected that the sadist was deserting Nag Tasha for good. He also knew that Wu on his own would not be able to figure out a way to get these Yingchan to the safety of Nan Yan, at least not until spring's warm weather melted the snow, and perhaps not even then, since Wu might have to wait until the conquering army cleared out Mag's soldiers. If the honorable Yingchan were to be taken to safety before then, he would have to lend a hand and interfere in worldly men's affairs. Had it not been for the fact that there were ten Golden Angels here, ten Yingchan, he simply would not have acted. Most Venerable Peng still held true to the ancient traditions. He decided to act on their behalf.

He was about to summon them all when he heard the gong sound. Someone else was asking to be lifted up into the monastery. Slightly worried that it might be the Overlord's men come to search for the missing Yingchan, Peng scurried to the elevator room to see for himself. Already the monk was pushing the heavy capstan with four protruding spokes slowly around, the thick rope wrapping itself around the capstan, raising the box up the hundreds of feet. He peered down and saw a man in a heavy parka. He did not look like a soldier and allowed the monk to continue to bring the man up. This time he stood patiently waiting to greet the man.

"What an incredible view, Venerable One," the young man bowed respectfully to Peng. "I am Kang Yun Zi. The overlord's men have kidnaped my sisters, and I have taken up a Holy Quest to find them and rescue them. I seek sanctuary for one night, that I may warm up and rest in total safety, before I continue my Holy Quest. I have traveled long and far and am in dire need of a good sleep."

"Sanctuary is granted. I am Most Venerable Peng, leader of the Taschi Monastery. Only I am allowed to speak. We monks have taken vows of silence. Words are not necessary to life. What is the name of the sisters whom you seek?"

"Thank you, Most Venerable Peng," Kang bowed low in deep respect for the aged monk. "Their names are Zhu and Zhen Yun Zi."

Peng smiled, "Ah, then perhaps your Holy Quest is at an end. If you will follow me, I will take you to them. Honorable Wu Shenyan has only just rescued them from Overlord Mag's estate."

"What? Here? Rescued? Are they well? Have they been mistreated? Are they all right?" Kang gushed forth question after question, unsure which he needed answered first.

"They are alive and well, though you will not find them as you last saw them. Mag has given them both a Most High Honor and a most evil torture. You will find that they are now Golden Angels, Yingchan."

"Oh! Yingchan? Golden Angels? Indeed, they are then to be highly honored," Kang replied, trying to fathom what could possibly have happened to his twin sisters. Yingchan were extremely rare and greatly respected. But what did he mean by evil torture?

As if anticipating Kang's thoughts, Peng continued. "Please prepare yourself. Mag has cut off their tongues that they may no longer speak."

"Oh dear god, no! Oh god no! The butcher!" Kang's anger rose, but his long years of martial arts training kicked in. He knew anger would defeat him. He fought to control his seething emotions.

"Mag has also added Golden Boots to their feet, boots which cannot be removed. They are modeled on the alien boots that we men were forced to wear after the plague struck us down," Peng added. "Take heart, Kang, they are learning to walk now. Their silence is not the end of the world. Look, we monks do not speak, and we survive very well, so shall they, Kang. Life is not in the sounds that we make, but in our hearts and minds and the actions that we take."

Peng continued, softening the blow to Kang. "Wu has learned that the Church of God in Nan Yan has been somehow restoring the arms and hands of the plague victims. He is planning to take all the rescued Yingchan there and see if this can be also done for them. If so, their lives will be restored to them, and they can be our Most Honored Golden Angels."

They entered the dining room, where Wu and Jie were still dealing with feeding the ten women. Both looked up at the unexpected arrival of Peng and the parka covered stranger. Kang gasped in horror and rushed to his twin sisters, whom Wu was attempting to feed them their breakfast. "Zhu! Zhen! My god! What has the butcher done to you?" Kang exclaimed, throwing off his parka and going to their sides.

Both women recognized his voice, but could not easily turn to see him. Struggling on their toes, they attempted to swivel in their seats towards his voice, moving their heads this way and that trying valiantly to get their pinhole vision onto their older brother. Wu softly pointed out, "Sir, their vision is terribly restricted. We believe that they can only see out of tiny pinholes in their golden eyes. It will be easier for them to see you if you are across the table from them."

Kang ignored him, hugging Zhu and then Zhen. Tears flowed down each woman's cheeks, and they tried to speak rapid words, but even Kang was shocked to hear completely unintelligible sounds coming from beneath the golden latticework veils that covered their lower faces. Wu also saw tears coming from this stranger and concluded he was either their husband or brother or a close relation.

Peng stepped in, "Kang Lun Zi, Honorable Wu is right. Your sisters can see you much better if you will take a seat across from them." Mechanically, Kang obeyed and watched as his golden sisters struggled to get straightened in their chairs once more and to locate him. He called out to them and that helped the twins zero in on him at last. Still, the twins tried to speak to him, but soon gave up, crying all the harder.

"Welcome, Kang. I'm sure that your sisters are extremely glad to see you," Wu began. "We sort of have developed a way that we can communicate with the Yingchan. Pretend that you are playing a child's charades game and make educated guesses. They can nod yes or no. I think that Zhu and Zhen want to know if you are all right." Both twins nodded yes.

"Yes, I'm fine. I came as soon as I heard that you had been taken. I followed the soldiers here to Nag Tasha, but I'm exhausted and hungry. It isn't safe for me to be seen in the town, so I came here to seek a good night's sleep before breaking into the overlord's estate to rescue you both. Alas, I'm far too late. Can you ever forgive me?" he pleaded.

Both twins tried to say something again and Wu stepped in. "Are you trying to say that you forgive him? That it is not his fault?" Both nodded vigorously. "See, they are still able to communicate, Kang."

Wu and Jie helped the twins finish eating, while a monk brought food and tea for Kang. Wu continued to assist the twins and Kang in their urgent need for communication and understanding. At last, Kang calmed down and begged Wu to tell him everything. Wu and Jie continued assisting the ten women, while outlining all that had happened. By the time Wu finished, the women were sipping their tea, and Kang actually was helping Dai with hers, emulating the actions of Wu and Jie.

"Honorable Wu Shenyan, I am eternally grateful that you have risked your life to rescue my sisters. It is a debt that I can never repay, though I will dedicate my life to trying. Zhu, Zhen, I swear to you that I will find this butcher of women and make him pay dearly for what he has done to you."

It took Wu a couple of minutes to work out what both tried to say in response. Neither wanted him to get himself killed. With the gold and gems of their extensive jewelry, they would be able to get by, especially if they could get their arms back.

"Wu, this butcher of helpless women must be stopped. Look, he's already done it to nine women in just the past year or so. How many more women must be brutalized before he is stopped? This is something that I must do myself to uphold our family's honor. The Yun Zi's have been in this valley since ancient times. It is said that our great-great-great grandmother was a Most Honored Yingchan herself. Since those times, our family has had high honor. Now Mag Tazau has completely tarnished our family's honor. I must kill him if I'm to regain our family's honor. Surely, you all understand that. Do not worry about my safety, for I have been dodging Mag's soldiers since I was a little boy."

"Wu, I must again entrust the safety of my sisters into your hands. Get them to safety in Nan Yan. I do not know if this Church of God can help them or not, but please try to help them. Zhu, Zhen, I will return to you there, my Golden Angels, my Yingchan. I will return with our family's honor intact. If by some miracle that you can get this horrible plague's effects undone, then you can truly be Golden Angels, Most Honored Yingchan, and bring incredibly high honor to our family once more."

Although Wu tried to talk Kang out of this plainly suicide mission, he had to admire the man's convictions and courage. He swore once more that he would do everything possible to get them all to safety and to the Church of God in Nan Yan. He also saw that Kang was nearly asleep on his feet. A few minutes later, he helped Kang get his sisters to a bedroom, where he laid down with them for a long overdue sleep. As Wu shut the door, Kang lay with a sister in either arm. They were resting their heads on his shoulders. Zhu mouthed a "thank you" to Wu and he nodded.

It was now nearly ten the next morning, and he'd spent two hours plus handling the ten women as they rose to face the new day. Wu jested to Dai that if he had four more Yingchan to take care of, then he would be spending his entire day at it. She giggled at his jest, but wished desperately that she could take care of her own needs. Dai felt so utterly helpless like this.

Around eleven, Peng summoned Wu to his chambers. "Honorable Wu, you must get the Yingchan to Nan Yan. Have you figured out a way this can be done?"

Wu sighed. "No, Most Venerable Peng, I admit defeat. There are thousands of enemy soldiers blocking our way to the south, to say nothing of where we might spend the dozen plus nights of the long journey. We certainly cannot stay at inns along the way; the women would surely be robbed of their jewelry. How they could withstand the cold winter I'm ignoring, as well as how we could bring along enough to eat and even cook it. I admit that I feel defeated. I'm letting them all down, but I will continue to try to figure out a way that it can be done. Please give us a little more time here, Most Venerable Peng," he pleaded for a time extension to their sanctuary here in the monastery.

"Do not worry, Honorable Wu. I am not canceling your sanctuary here. Rather, I have decided that we Taschi monks are obligated to help the Yingchan get to Nan Yan and the Church of God there. They can be proper Yingchan if they can have the plague's effects undone by the church. That is why we monks must lend a hand, to give the Yingchan the opportunity that they deserve as our rare Golden Angels."

"That is most generous and thoughtful of you, but how can you help?" Wu inquired.

"We monks have long lived here near the foothills of the great mountains. Often in the summer days, we have hiked the mountains. Here all is still, free from the hands of man. Quite stimulating. You ought to wander there sometime yourself. However, more to the point. During our extensive wanderings into the mountains, we have come across a high mountain path that meanders along from far to the north to far to the south. None of us has ever walked its complete distance. However, we have discovered strange caves located periodically along its path. If we accept that aliens caused the plague, then perhaps we can also accept that these very aliens carved these caverns from the bedrock of the great mountains and dwelled there for a time. Who can say?"

"The caverns do contain strange beds, quite large by our standards. Over the years, monks have stayed in them and have brought in some charcoal and food, storing them there for a rainy day or when some stranded climber might be in dire need. Wu, I believe that you can make the journey to Nan Yan via our secret mountain path, spending the nights in these large caverns. We can provide you with a sleigh, food, charcoal, lanterns, and warm blankets. I have made a crude map to guide you. I caution you, do not attempt to travel during a snow storm or blizzard."

"Incredible! There is a mountain trail that leads from here all the way down to Nan Yan?" Wu asked utterly surprised. No one knew that such a thing existed.

"Indeed there is — at least, we believe that it may go that far south. I would only ask that you continue to honor your pledge to the Yingchan. If there is any way that they plague's effects can be undone, then see that is done so that these Most Honorable Golden Angels can safely be the Yingchan and not be just another batch of completely helpless women. While they are most distraught about their inability to speak, with their hands restored, they can write and care for their needs and those of their families, bringing the highest honor to their families and carrying forward the most ancient of traditions of all Tashien. We must give them the opportunity to be true Yingchan, worthy of our greatest respect and admiration."

"I swear to you, Most Venerable Peng, that I will do my utmost to see them succeed. I will leave no stone unturned." He bowed low to the old man. Never had he been more grateful for a solution to a problem than now. That there was a way he could get to Nan Yan without fear of running into enemy soldiers at every turn was truly amazing.

"I will make the arrangements and speak to the women at supper tonight. I suspect that you will find the Yingchan are in need of your assistance once more, Honorable Wu." They exchanged bows and

Wu headed to the women's rooms. As he neared the one with the twins and Kang, he saw Zhu and Zhen wobbling on their feet, struggling bravely to leave their bedroom. Kang was sound asleep now.

"You need me?" Wu asked, causing the twins to raise their heads, attempting to locate him in the dim corridor light. "Over here. You are walking well. Potty?" Both nodded, and he moved beside them, putting his arms around their waists to steady the two. By the time he assisted all the women, the lunch gong sounded, and they all headed to the dining room at their very slow pace.

Over lunch, Zhen wanted to say something to Wu. As he fed them, he worked on figuring it out. At last, he got it. Zhen wanted to tell him that they found walking on the hard stone floor easier than the plush carpeting of the overlord's estate. Both grinned when he finally got it.

At supper that night, Peng explained the plan to get them all safely to Nan Yan. Even Kang, who had finally risen, thought this was a brilliant idea. Except for the treacherous, snow-covered mountain path, they would have no fear of detection from the thousands of soldiers.

Peng then spoke directly to the ten women. "My Golden Ladies. Our ancient traditions hold the Yingchan in the highest regard, respect, and honor. Yet, I also know that those traditions have been horribly perverted in your cases. A woman is supposed to make the choice to become a Golden Angel of her own free will. You were not given any choice. Yingchan are not supposed to have their tongues removed or wear such difficult shoes either. The alien plague's effects have turned this into a never-ending nightmare for you. Yet, all of you have shown remarkable bravery and courage in dealing with this."

"The Taschi Monastery has given you sanctuary and is providing you with a means to get safely to Nan Yan. Why? It is our fondest wish that somehow the Church of God there can undo the plague's awful effects on your bodies. If that happens, you will be helpless no longer. You will be able to care for your needs and those of your families. As Golden Angels, you will be able to bring the highest honor to your families and the greatest respect for yourselves. Do not let the inability to speak be a burden. We monks have all taken vows of silence and yet we live just fine. Speech in not what is important. It is what is in your hearts and minds. It is in what actions you take. With your arms restored, you can write what it is that you may wish to say. Thus, we monks wish that if you are able to have the plague's effects undone, that you will decide freely to become true Yingchan, following our most ancient of customs. We are not insisting that you do so, but it is our wish that you will deeply consider it. In the chaos of these times, we must maintain a hold on our most cherished and ancient traditions or lose our own heritage for all time. Just consider it wisely before you make your decisions. That is all we ask of you. If the church cannot undo the plague's effects, then by all means, take what actions are necessary for your survival."

The women bowed their heads to him, signifying that they understood him. Kang also thanked him. "Sisters, I am entrusting Wu with your care for a little while longer. I must go after Mag Tazau this evening. He already has a good head start on me. If I delay longer, I may never be able to find him and bring him to the justice that he so deserves. I promise that I will join you both in Nan Yan just as soon as I possibly can. I will bring honor back to our family, Zhen, Zhu. I promise. I love you both." He gave each a warm hug and kiss. He shook Wu's hand and then bowed low to Peng, before leaving. Wu didn't say much, figuring that they would never see Kang again. Going after the most powerful drug lord was a recipe for death.

That evening, Peng gave him the hand-drawn map, and the two talked long into the night about the path and caverns. The next morning, the monks had gathered their supplies, but surprising Wu, they did not go down the elevator! Instead, Peng led them all down another long tunnel. "I am sorry to have to make the Golden Angels walk so far, but it cannot be helped. We have another way out of our monastery, a secret exit, far from the town and on the other side of the ridge. There the sleigh is waiting and some of the supplies have been loaded for you."

Walking nearly two miles on their toes very nearly did the women in. By the time that they arrived at the cave's mount and the waiting sleigh, all ten were wobbling wildly on their feet, kept from falling only by the men's arms around them. Now Wu saw why Peng had brought the other monks along with them. While the monks could have carried the women, Peng was showing them that they could walk this distance, enhancing their own self-respect. As Wu lifted each woman into the sleigh, he fastened a hooded, fleece-lined cloak about them. They sat in three rows. He and Jie covered up their feet with blankets and then wrapped more around them. Only their golden clad faces were visible to the outside world. The sleigh was quite sturdy and was pulled by two horses. Wu gave Peng a goodbye hug, and he and Jie climbed aboard. Waving farewell, Wu clucked to the horses, slapping the reins over their backs. Off they went over the snow covered ground, high upon the southern ridge, opposite the monastery.

Their first objective was to locate the first of the caverns somewhere high above their current position. According to the map, it lay some fifteen miles up the hillside. He and Jie studied the map, and Wu appointed Jie the official map-reader and navigator, which pleased the young lad. Again, he was doing something important to help his older sister, Yan. From their seats, the bright sun reflecting off the white snow allowed them the best vision they'd had in quite some time. Although their field of view was quite small, they could turn their heads and take in the breathtaking mountain scenery. There's would be a pleasant ride, if a cold one.

Wu pushed the horses that first day. He knew that he had to locate the cavern before the sunset. If not, he had no idea how he could possibly find it in the dark. Higher and higher they climbed, the horses' steam rose from flared nostrils. The rugged, snow-covered mountains loomed steadily taller, until at last they completely dominated the scene. Since they were heading due west, by late afternoon, the sun was gone behind the peaks. Dark shadows formed, turning the scene from idyllic into an ominous one. Just as Wu was starting to get worried about having to find this first cavern in the dark, Jie called out, "There, I see it. Just up there. Bit further. A big black hole." Even the women moved their heads about, trying to see what Jie was seeing. As Wu got even closer, they finally located the dark hole; it entirely encompassed their tiny field of vision.

As Wu finally got the sleigh up to the opening, he found that there was indeed a wide ledge leading to both the north and south from the cavern's mouth. It was snow-covered as he expected. He drove the horses into the dark cavern, stopping when the skids hit the dry stone floor. "We made it!" he called out. Turning around, he saw ten smiling faces looking in his general direction.

"Jie, lanterns out first. Then, let's see what we have before we attempt to bring the women inside." The cavern was huge and had three giant lobes off the main entrance. In the one to their left, they spotted an enormous bed, complete with sheets and covers!

"They must have been giants!" Jie exclaimed. The bed would hold all them.

"Okay, let's get them in here, and then you feed the horses while I rustle up supper," Wu suggested. That was delayed a bit, for the ten needed the potty first.

An hour later, the ten, still wearing their warm cloaks, sat in a line on the bed, while Jie and Wu fed them. Later, Wu helped each one out of their cloak and into the bed. All twelve of them slept in their clothes, huddled together for warmth.

Over breakfast the next day, Wu and Jie again studied the map. They guessed that these caverns were about thirty to forty miles apart. With the short days, they had to make haste or risk traveling in the dark. Wu wanted to avoid that if he could and explained the situation to the women as they ate their breakfast. Later, while the men loaded the sleigh, Wu saw that the women were actually walking around, trying to get a good look at the cavern and its strange contents. While he would have loved to spend time seeing what all was here, he felt the pressure to get going as quickly as possible. He feared greatly being out there on that precipitous ledge path in total darkness and snow. One misstep and the fall would surely kill them all!

Thus began their planned fifteen-day journey through the mountains down to the mountains west of Nan Yan. Three of those days, they had to hole up and wait out snowstorms. However, none of the women minded at all, for now they could wander about the caverns, looking at all the strange alien things. Not even Jie dared touch anything; he feared being turned into a toad or something. He thought that the caverns reeked of magic, the evil magic of the aliens who had given everyone the plague.

Chapter 69 Countermeasures

Kang found his sleigh right where he had hidden it. After feeding his two horses and watering them, he made doubly sure that his long guns were primed and ready for action. At last, he climbed onto his sleigh and headed in a cross county arc to reach the northern edge of Nag Tasha. There he hoped to pick up Mag's sleigh trail, based on what Wu and Jie had told him.

"Justice, not revenge," he reminded himself of his mission. After an hour, he finally picked up a single sleigh heading due east. What was Mag's mission? Where was he going? Kang knew from Wu that he'd sent his son and army south to Xian, there to defend against the coming spring offensive. He knew that the other more vulnerable drug lords were evacuating their lands, bringing their armies into the more defensible towns of Mag's lands. So what was Mag's mission now? Why leave home? Due east led nowhere, merely paralleling the Lian River, which lay some ten miles further north. He was heading into the lower, less defensible rolling farmlands. Why? Why alone with only three men with him? Kang had more questions than answers as he followed the well-defined sleigh tracks.

Late in the afternoon, he spotted where they had spent their first night, camping out in the open! How strange, he thought, but the signs on the ground were unmistakable. A campfire, bits of discarded food — even some now-frozen, tossed, cold tea lay clearly visible on the ground. Kang decided to press on until the last possible minute before making camp. Later as the moon rose, he could see well enough to continue and did so until the wee hours of the morning, when he finally stopped and napped while sitting in his sleigh. After a warm breakfast and tending to his horses, he continued following the trail.

Like an arrow in flight, the path that Mag was taking was straight east, deviating only to bypass the towns along the way. There were plenty of farmsteads where he could have pulled in for the night, but Mag avoided these too. Well, perhaps that was to reduce the risk of having a distraught farmer skewer him while he slept. Towards the end of the second day, Kang now realized that he was traveling faster than Mag, perhaps twenty-five percent faster. That only meant that Mag's sleigh was heavily loaded — probably with food, he concluded. Embolden by the prospect of catching up with him, Kang pushed on even harder, traveling as long as the moon was available to help him.

The twelfth day, Kang felt sure that he would catchup with Mag any day now! He had to be making for the Yonshu River. That evening he reached a small village on the banks of this mighty river. His sleigh could go no further. The snow cover was too thin to support the sleigh. He halted just outside the town, picked up his long guns, and walked on into the village. He spotted the sleigh parked outside a store. Kang's heart raced. At last! He steeled himself for the showdown and entered the store.

"Hello, just closing up for the day," the shopkeeper called out. "Can it wait for the morning?"

Kang looked around and saw no one else present. "I saw that sleigh outside."

"Ah, you want to purchase it? It is a fine sleigh. I have the horse that goes with it too. Make you a fair offer, son."

"Er no. What happened to the man who owned it? Didn't he get here in the last couple of days?"

"Well, as a matter of fact, he sold it to me only this morning. I admit that I got an amazingly good deal on it. I'll sell it to you very cheap," he replied, eager for another sale.

"Where did he go after he sold it? Didn't he have three other men with him?"

"He asked about getting transportation across the Yonshu. Why?"

"I'm keeping you from your supper. I'll check with you in the morning."

"Okay, you do that. Fair price, mind you." Kang left and headed down to the riverbank. A dozen small boats were pulled up on the banks. The dark river was more than a mile across here, cold and dark. He spotted a couple of riverboats away to the north and south. Which way did he go? No one was around and it was getting quite dark. Kang had no choice but to walk back to his own sleigh and make camp at the edge of the village.

The next morning, he was at the riverbank shortly after sunrise. Quietly, he began asking the fishermen and soon learned that another fellow had been asking about passage across only yesterday. A few coins in the right hands and Kang found himself talking to the ferryman.

"Sure, took those fellows across yesterday. Wanted to know where they could buy a carriage." Kang slipped another coin into the man's hand. "Told them that there was only one carriage over there, belongs to old man Bao."

"Can you take me and my horse across?"

"For a price, three gold, unless your horse spooks, then it'll cost you five." Kang handed him the three coins.

"Back in a short while." He loaded all that his horse could safely carry and then abandoned the sleigh and the rest of his gear. Kang had little choice. He would not be able to rent another carriage and would have to travel on horseback. Well, perhaps this is just as well, he thought. I can go faster and make up the lost time.

An hour later, he tied a blindfold over his horse's eyes and led him onto the ferry. Another hour later, he led the horse off onto the other side. Handing the ferryman another coin, he asked for directions to old Bao's place.

"Pleasure doing business with yea. If you need passage back, just light that lantern there." Kang thanked him and mounted up, heading for old man Bao's place, where he hoped to pick up the trail.

He found the farmstead without incident. However, the place seemed deserted, though he called out several times. At last, he began looking for tracks. He found recent carriage wheel tracks leading out of the man's barn. He then decided to ask Bao if Mag had given him any idea where he was headed. Perhaps he'd asked Bao for some directions. He knocked on the door, but got no answer. Since the door was already open a crack, he pushed it open and called out. "Anyone home?" Still only silence. At last, he entered the farmer's home but soon wished that he had not.

Bao and his wife were both dead, a gunshot wound to their heads. They had been executed! Kang cursed and sat down to think a bit. He made up his mind and walked to the barn. Sure enough there was another horse there. He rode back to the river and lighted the lantern. However, he had unloaded his horse back at the barn and his plan now was to fetch the rest of his supplies and let the villagers know that they had been shot.

He was delayed for an hour by the local sheriff and had to take him over to see the remains. While the sheriff examined the bodies and house, Kang loaded up the second horse with the remainder of his supplies. He left twenty gold with the sheriff to cover the cost of the old mare and finally headed off, following the carriage tracks. As he rode along, he estimated that Mag was now almost two days ahead of him again. Traveling on horseback, he ought to make that up quickly.

Although Mag was still traveling eastward, he now followed the main roads and passed through the towns and villages along the way. Kang cursed. This would slow him down, since he would have to make inquiries in each town if he were to have any idea which way Mag went. Three long days later, Kang found himself looking at the rugged Bleak Hills, a natural barrier before the land opened up into the bowl shaped lands of southeastern Wontun Province. Ahead lay the huge port city of Shankou. Mag must surely be heading there, Kang concluded and made straight for the city of some ten million inhabitants, prior to the plague, that is.

Chaos and the Dark Ages had also arrived in Shankou. Gangs controlled the streets, but Kang had a decided advantage, he was on horseback. Few dared to challenge him, especially when he kept one long gun cradled in his free hand. Had he come all this way only to lose Mag among the millions of Shankou? If he only knew what Mag was planning — some slight clue, he thought. Then it struck him. Mag would need an inn. Knowing the overlord, he would not settle for anything less than the best and safest inn. A few more coins later, Kang found himself at the Orange Teacup Inn. Now he had to make a decision. Should he gamble that Mag was staying here or not? He could take a room and watch for him, but if he had the wrong inn, he could miss Mag entirely.

He decided that Mag was a creature of habit and he took a room, paying fifty gold for one night, a rather exorbitant sum he thought. Well, he got a hot bath, fine meals, and a luxurious, large bedroom, fully carpeted. Most of the time, Kang sat in the bar, keeping an eye on those coming and leaving. Late that night, Kang spotted Mag and his three men entering the inn. Mag carried a steel-colored briefcase and headed on up to the suites, while his three accomplices headed for the bar.

Kang tried to listen in on the men's conversation, but the noise of the many customers prohibited him from hearing much of what they were saying. He did overhear one man complaining that they had three more days of this running around to do. Kang found this encouraging.

Kang was up early and had his breakfast, paying for another three days. While he was eating his meal, Mag and his associates came down to dine as well. After finishing up, he quietly left and got his horse from the stables and took up a position not far away. An hour later, the men came to the stable where a carriage had already been hitched. One man took the driver's seat, while another sat beside him, holding a long gun across his legs, ready for action. Mag and the third climbed inside, and they rolled out of the inn's stables and into the crowded streets.

Kang noticed almost no women were on the streets. Prior to the plague, they would have accounted for half of the traffic. He was soon glad that he'd chosen to ride once more. Frequently he spotted thugs strong arming men on foot. A bit later, he witnessed a man being stabbed and his money pouch stolen. Later a gunshot jerked him to attention. Off to his right, someone shot another man, yet no one seemed to care. Others passing by simply ignored the wounded man and the shooter, for that matter. What had become of Shankou, he wondered.

After an hour, the carriage pulled up at a store, and Mag entered alone. Sometime later, he came back out, again carrying the silver briefcase. He climbed in and the carriage continued on its way. Kang fell back a couple of blocks so that the men might not spot him. Later, he donned a different hat. During the day, Mag continued to make more stops. Each one lasted an hour at most and each time he carried that briefcase inside and back out again. What was the man up to? Kang could not invent any reasonable theory. The shops seemed to have nothing to do with each other. A tailor's shop, a blacksmith's shop, a sundry goods store. Mag's actions seemed completely random, save for his constant briefcase that he took inside with him and brought out once more.

In frustration, Kang headed back to the inn to eat a late lunch and try to think. He knew that he could not shoot all four men at once. As soon as he fired at one of them, the remaining three would be all over him. No, he had to find a way to get Mag alone without his bodyguards, if that were what they were. Yet, his curiosity was roused. What was in that briefcase? What was the man doing? Over a dark stout, he pondered this.

Mag could not be recruiting more soldiers for the coming battle with the forces from Nan Yan. Shankou was too distant from Nag Tasha for that. They were well over a thousand miles from Nan Yan as the eagles flew and almost that far from Nag Tasha for that matter. Besides, none of the places he visited seemed remotely connected to soldiering. Could he be after more women to brutalize? Kang discounted that one as well. None of the shops he'd seen was connected to women, and none was doctors either. Yet, whatever Mag was doing, it had to be important.

He was into his second stout when Mag and his men entered. This time, Mag asked the floor manager to lock his briefcase in the inn's heavy iron safe. Ah, whatever was in it must be valuable, Kang thought. It could not be gold; any real volume would be quite heavy, and Mag showed no signs of struggling to carry it. If not gold, then perhaps gemstones? That seemed plausible. Was Mag delivering gemstones, trading them for some additional war supplies? If so, what did a tailor have to do with equipping an army? Now if he visited an armorer or a weapons maker, that would be a plausible theory, he concluded.

Then he had another thought. Perhaps Mag was collecting on debits. He might be calling in outstanding loans he'd made to others so that he could acquire more money with which to better equip his soldiers for the spring battle. For a time, Kang favored this theory; it made much more sense. However, he then wondered about that too. He reasoned thusly: Mag must have countless millions. Look, he can afford to dole out two million worth on a day's notice to turn his sisters and the other two into Golden Angels. Each one's jewelry must be worth at least a half million. With that kind of petty cash, Mag must have untold millions that he could spend. Why would he be going around collecting outstanding loans here in Shankou, of all places?

What was unique about Shankou anyway, he wondered? It was the second largest port city in Tashien, second only to Shansee in the distant south. Jiao to the north up in Linyi Provence was slightly smaller. Shankou was a seaport and a departure port for very large volumes of sea trade. Was Mag planning on taking a sea voyage? If so, then he would miss the spring battle for sure. Why would he do that? What was happening that was so darn important that he'd miss the most important battle in his life? Kang chuckled. He'll likely be losing that battle, if Wu gets through and alerts General Tao to Mag's defensive plans, he thought.

Then, it struck him. Of course! Mag already knew that come spring, his forces would lose the battle and that the forces of Nan Yan would take over his territory. Mag was planning an exit! He was planning to leave — not only leaving Nag Tasha, but perhaps even Tashien itself! If he were doing that, he'd be collecting all of his assets, probably cashing them into lightweight gemstones! That briefcase could certainly hold a whole lot of large stones worth a fortune. Suddenly, all Mag's actions became clear to Kang. The man was making a clandestine exit from Tashien, throwing his own son to the wolves and his wife as well! In that case, he would discard the three associates too, when he no longer needed their protection. Kang smiled, that would be when he would have his best chance to get justice. He finished his stout and went to his room for a nap. He'd had too much stout.

After supper, he reasoned that Mag still had two more days of errands to run. Hence, he decided to investigate the port proper. Slipping the Harbor Master a few coins yielded significant information. The Pearl was scheduled to set sail at high tide in three days. Of course, four other ships were also scheduled to sail that same day, though more would be expected as that date drew closer. What the Harbor Master thought a bit strange cost Kang another couple of coins. The captain had unloaded his cargo and offered the load to another captain. The Pearl was making a passenger run or so the captain claimed. A couple more coins and the Harbor Master's lips were sealed, he'd never seen Kang.

On Mag's theoretical last day of visiting shops, Kang decided once more to follow them. He assumed that at some point, Mag would separate from his three men. Once he was alone, Kang would strike. No longer did he fear reprisals. He'd seen men shot and stabbed in the crowded streets, and no one took any notice, save to get themselves out of the way. Again, he rode his horse and kept his long gun at the ready. Only carriages and horsemen were able to navigate the streets with relative impunity, he noted.

Mid-morning, the carriage pulled up beside Wuhan's Jewelers, an upscale establishment. Just as the carriage came to a halt, a shot rang out. Blam! Kang startled, reined in his horse, lifted his long gun up, and tried to focus on where the shot had come from. He saw a puff of smoke coming from the alleyway across the street, but saw no signs of a shooter. Dozens of men on foot scattered, some walking briskly, others flat out running from the area. Kang saw the bodyguard of Mag's fall off the carriage, while the other one jumped out of the carriage brandishing his long gun, looking wildly for the shooter. The driver picked up the dropped long gun and looked towards the alleyway.

Nothing further happened and the driver dismounted. He and the bodyguard examined the fallen man. Evidently, he was dead, Kang surmised. They left him in the street. Finally, briefcase in tow, Mag climbed out, nodding to the two men and entered the fancy jewelry shop. At least, the second bodyguard pulled his fallen companion over to the side of the street before taking up a defensive position, while the driver held onto the team of horses. Both were quite nervous, Kang observed, their eyes darted from person to passing person. Nothing further happened and he relaxed, tying up his horse and pretending to be examining its hooves for stones.

An hour later, Mag opened the door and peered out. After a quick look around, he stepped out and moved quickly to the carriage. Bang! Another shot rang out, this time it came from a different alley, one a block further down the street. The second bodyguard dropped to the ground. Mag dove inside the carriage, while the driver frantically climbed up into the driver's box and furiously kicked the horses into a gallop. Kang slowly mounted and followed, though he kept back a good distance. What was going on now? Was this a random shooting? Hardly, anything was taken. If it had been a robbery attempt, which would have made sense, since he was at an expensive jewelry store, why had the shooter or shooters not taken them all out? Why wait an hour to take the second shot? Kang ruled out a gang. Had it been a group of thugs, they would have taken the carriage out and then easily shot Mag. No, Kang reasoned that there was a single shooter and a patient one at that. He'd taken a surprise first shot, moved to a new location, and then waited patiently for the second shot. Further, he had taken out the two bodyguards, leaving only the driver and Mag.

Why had he not taken out the driver first? That would have forced one of the bodyguards or perhaps even Mag to drive? None of this made any sense. Even more confusing, they stopped at another tailor's shop not six blocks away! This time, Mag made a dash from the carriage into the store, while the driver stayed in his box, but hunkered down presenting as small a target as possible. Figuring the Mag would be an hour in the shop, Kang wheeled his horse around and returned to the original shootings. He saw gangs of thugs stripping both bodies clean of their possessions, including their clothes and boots! Soon the dead men were left lying in the street in their underwear! Kang turned into the first alley and began looking for clues about the shooter.

Near the corner, he found small drops of blood but little else. He then rode over to the next alley from which the second shot had come. Curiously, he found several additional blood drops on the ground, but no trail leading away. Cautiously, he rode back to the tailor's. After pondering the blood, Kang concluded that the shooter must be wounded and had stood in one place for a long time and that the blood loss was small. Was someone else looking for revenge? Or was this a random attack by some desperate man? Well, if the shooter stayed his course, the driver was next on his hit list. Kang stayed keenly alert, but nothing happened.

Kang tailed the two the rest of the afternoon. Mag visited three more stores. The only thing that Kang was able to ascertain was that the briefcase was now rather heavy. Mag was definitely favoring it, switching it with heavy heaves from arm to arm as he walked. Perhaps he did have gold in it after all. Kang followed them back to the Orange Teacup Inn, always staying back a block. He watched the carriage pull up by the main entrance to the inn. Bang! Another shot rang out, and his driver fell into the street from the tall driver's box, his body raising a puff of a dirt cloud as it hit. Instantly, two doormen raised their long guns and took up defensive positions. Mag opened his carriage door, pausing a moment. One doorman waved his hand while keeping an eye out for the assassins. Mag raced from the carriage inside the inn, but no further shots came.

The doormen signaled other staff, and soon the body and carriage were moved, the carriage taken to the stables behind the inn. Kang now rode up and went past the inn, heading for the alley from which the shot had come. Again, his eyes spotted three blood drops on the ground. Now he headed for the stables himself. As he dismounted, the groomsmen were all talking about the shooting, raising all manner of speculations. "Did'ja hear about the shooting a bit ago?" one asked him as he dismounted, handing the groomsman his reins.

"Hear a shot. Anyone hurt?"

"Yeh, a driver of yonder carriage was killed. Sure is strange, you think that they would have tried to rob them afterwards, but I guess our doormen scared them away."

"Say, are we safe inside the inn?" Kang asked.

"Sure, only three ways in. Front doors have two guards on them, day and night. Then there is the door you have been using, from the stables here into the inn. De is on that one now. Then there is the servant's entrance in the back. Bo is there, so no one can get by us. You're safe once you get inside that's for sure."

"Hey, that's not totally true," another grooms-boy interrupted him. "Tell him about the six assassinations that have occurred here." The first groomsman flushed and rapidly added that extra detail. De nodded to him as he let Kang in the door. Kang returned the nod and allowed his eyes to get more accustomed to the dim light of the hallway. Ahead was the stairs to the suites; to the right lay the side entrance to the dining room and bar and front entrance. He spotted Mag coming his way and stepped back, allowing him to pass. Mag took little notice of him. He'd just finished complaining to the manager about the shooting of his driver, raising hell over the lack of security in the inn. The manager looked very flustered and began barking orders to his staff. Kang also noticed that the briefcase appeared to be quite heavy now; Mag was favoring it considerably as he climbed the carpeted steps to the long hall. Kang followed a distance behind him and saw that he entered Room 202. Kang was surprised to see that his room was next door to Mag's! Well, perhaps he could confront the man in his room and obtain his long sought justice. Best wait for night, Kang thought.

In his room, he washed up for supper, tidied up his appearance, and then headed down for the elegant meal. He'd paid enough for the fine dining, he thought. A little later Mag came down to dine as well, still carrying his briefcase. Kang decided that it must be extremely valuable for Mag never to let it out of his sight. He finished the roast duck long before Mag, and Kang slowly walked out of the dining room and back up the stairs to his room, pondering his next move. Soon, he must strike a blow for justice. Halfway down the hall, he spotted a tiny drop of blood on the carpet, and the hairs on his neck bristled. He didn't have his long gun on him. Every sense alert, he headed to his room, though looking for more drops. He saw nothing further; perhaps a servant had cut their finger. Still, he felt nervous. Could the shooter be inside the inn at this very moment?

If so, the shooter must be after Mag as well! In Kang's mind, the sadistic drug overlord had made enemies of probably thousands of men, all of whom would want to see him dead. Perhaps one of them was also after him. Kang steeled his mind. "He's mine! I aim to get justice!" he whispered to his walls.

A little later, he heard Mag enter his room. Well, that was normal; perhaps he could sneak in there in the middle of the night and obtain his long sought justice. He heard voices and then a thumping sound! To the best of his knowledge, Mag ought to be alone now; his three companions were dead. Had he acquired another? What was that thumping sound? He strained his ears, hoping to pick up further sounds. He had half a notion to go barging in there and see what was going on. Perhaps if it was nothing, he could explain it away by saying he was worried since the assassination a short while ago. He'd made up his mind to give that a try when he heard further muffled voices, and he put his ear against the wall trying to make out what was being said.

"Drink!" Kang made out one word. Well, the tone indicated the speaker had intense hatred behind that single word. This didn't sound good at all. What if someone were poisoning Mag? "Damn, I'll be denied my justice!" Kang whispered angrily. He grabbed his long gun and took action. He opened his door. All was very quiet. There were few guests in the inn. At fifty a night and in these time, he could see why. He moved to Mag's door and spotted yet another blood drop on the carpet. Damn, the assassin has him. I have to intervene, Kang thought. Long gun at the ready, he opened the door to Mag's suite. He had expected the door to be locked, but it opened easily. His eyes took in the scene rapidly, but he was also shocked and surprised.

"Put the gun down. Come in. Lock the damn door behind you. I don't know who you are, but I'll kill you if you make one wrong move," the middle aged man spat out. Intense hatred and anger filled his voice, though he kept his volume down. Kang also detected several hints of intense pain in his words as well, as if it hurt him terribly to speak. Kang stared into the barrel of a long gun and did as asked, locking the door.

The assassin was sitting on Mag's bed. Mag was sitting in a chair with both his arms securely tied to the arms of the chair. His feet were bound together. Blood oozed from his eye sockets! The man had poked them out! Blood gushed from his mouth, and Kang almost gagged when he saw the remains of Mag's tongue lying on his crotch. He raised his eyes to the assassin.

"Don't know who you are." The assassin grimaced in pain, spat up a little blood onto the bed. "You a friend of Mag?"

"No, I came to seek justice. Mag has butchered ten women, and I am sworn to obtain justice for the women," Kang answered truthfully, eyeing the assassin. His shirt was soaked in blood; he had a nasty chest wound. Part of a crude bandage was visible near the top of his shirt. He had to be the one who had killed the other three men, Kang concluded.

"If you don't interfere, I won't kill you, then." He coughed again. "He's mine. Do as I say or I will kill you." Cough. "I've already killed three of his men and I surely won't hesitate to shoot you." Cough.

"I only came for justice for the women," Kang repeated. His mind was calculating his odds. He could make a move to disarm the man. One swift blow would likely do him in, but he was not fast enough to avoid the gun aimed at him. At this range, the man, although his arms were shaking, couldn't miss. Kang decided to play along for the time being. "What do you want me to do?"

He coughed again and pointed the gun barrel off to his right. "Take those ropes and tie them around his arms, about an inch above his wrists. Make them tight, tourniquets." Kang picked up the ropes and figured out what the assassin had in mind. Tourniquets — he was going to cut off Mag's hands! Still he kept the long gun pointed directly at him and Kang obeyed, making very sure that the ropes cut off all circulation in Mag's hands. As he did so, he spotted an empty vial on the floor. The assassin saw him noticing it and added, "Drugged him so he won't make any noise." He coughed up more blood.

Mag's hands slowly began to change color as the blood flow to them ceased. "Move back to the door." Kang obeyed and watched the assassin carefully move to inspect the ropes. Satisfied that they were stopping all blood flow to his hands, he sat back on the bed, grimacing in pain and coughing up more blood. Kang moved closer and sat on the floor in front of the two men. He decided to present a non-threatening position. He knew that he could still act swiftly when the time was right. What would happen next, he wondered.

The assassin reached for a hunting knife strapped to his right leg. It was already covered in blood and Kang assumed that he'd already used it on Mag's tongue. However, the assassin was terribly weak now and he dropped the knife. Groaning, he tried to pick it up and gave up, sitting back in great pain. Kang decided to stall.

"May I ask who you are and why you are doing this to Mag? I too want to bring him to justice for the many crimes that he has committed against helpless women."

"He's mine. He's betrayed me, stole most all my money, took my land, stole my only daughter on her wedding day, mutilated her, and murdered her fiancé too. He's mine. I'm making him pay for all the evil that he's done to me. You have to wait your turn at him." He coughed up more blood. "Name's Bao Nan."

Kang began to recall all the names of the ten women whom Wu had rescued. Perhaps one was this man's daughter. "Say, was her name Binan?" he asked.

"Bi Nan," Bao corrected him and coughed up more blood once more. "Blinded her, cut out her tongue, ruined her life." Cough. "She was already helpless after the plague came. Li wanted to marry her anyway. Mag destroyed her whole damn life. Now he will pay dearly." Cough.

"Hey, Mag took my twin sisters too and mutilated them in the same way. A friend of mine has rescued all them. He's rescued Bi Nan too and is taking them to safety in Nan Yan. Look, we've heard that the Church of God in Nan Yan is able to undo the plague's effects. We hope that Bi will get her arms and hands back soon. Your daughter is alive and doing well. I think that she needs you, Bao."

"She still can't see and can't speak, barely able to even eat. Her life is destroyed. Better that she just died and got her horrible life over with." He coughed once more. Kang saw that he was weaker now than when he'd first entered the room.

"We need to get you to a doctor," Kang suggested.

"Nah, I'm done for. Gotta cut off the beast's hands yet. Make him suffer like he's made my Bi suffer." Bao coughed hard again.

"You need a doctor," Kang suggested again.

"No, I told you." Again, he attempted to get to his knife and failed. He was reluctant to let Kang get too close to him. Bao didn't trust Kang. Anyone could say anything to anyone.

"How did you know Mag would be here in Shankou?" Kang tried a different approach. Besides, he was curious.

"He's a blasted coward. Always has his men do his dirty work. Been watch'en the situation in the highlands. War's coming soon," he said, pausing to cough again. "I knew Mag well. We were partners once, before he betrayed me. He doesn't trust the Banca and stashed his wealth around Shankou. He was fleeing Tashien, you know. I knew that when it got grim in the highlands, he'd light out here. I've been waiting for him to show up. I knew a couple of places where he stashed his loot. Missed him a couple times, but got him today."

A bit later, Bao revealed, "Booked passage out of here on the Pearl. Leaves at five this morning. He was going to fly the coop, bastard. Now he won't fly any coop. He'll suffer just like my Bi is suffering." He fell silent for a time. Mag's hands had now turned black and looked ghastly.

"Damn, I ain't going to see this through," Bao admitted a few minutes later.

"You might, if we can get you to a doctor soon," Kang suggested again.

"No. I mean I am getting too weak to cut the miserable man's hands off."

"You may not have to. The doctors will have no choice but to amputate them when they see him. Look how black they are getting," Kang pointed out. "Let's get you out of here and to a doctor."

"No, we will wait." He coughed again. Bao was definitely getting weaker by the minute.

After a long silent pause, Kang asked, "Who shot you or stabbed you?"

"Street thugs. Killed them both though. Still was able to get Mag, curse his soul."

Minutes later, Bao asked, "You believe in this new Chi-ism that's goin' 'round? Accept what is and all that?"

"No, a man has control of his life. That's what my martial arts teacher taught me," Kang replied.

"Good man. Chi-ism is for fools, I say."

A bit later, Kang tried a different approach. "If you are going to let yourself die here in this room, do you have any message for me to take to your daughter Bi?"

For the first time, Kang saw a brief flicker of a smile on his grimacing face. "Yeh, tell her I loved her and have made Mag pay dearly for his treachery and butchery. Tell her to find a way to end her misery too."

"I promise that I will relay that to her when I see her again. Are you sure you don't want me to fetch a doctor? We could use my room next door. I can take you with me back to your daughter."

"Can't you see I'm dying? Never make it. No, I aim to see this through. Mag has to lose his hands too. You have to stay until it's done. Don't trust you to not bring in a bunch of guards."

"Can I attend to your wound then?"

"No, I don't trust you. You stay back or I swear I'll shoot you too." Bao glared at him and coughed again.

Kang had little other choices. No way was he going to take a gamble and get himself shot. His sisters were depending upon him staying alive to help them. There was no point in getting himself killed trying to prevent further injury to the sadistic man who had caused so many women so much pain and constant suffering, ignoring all the countless others he'd harmed. No, he could wait it out. Eventually Bao would pass out. Then he could act. The minutes passed by slowly, but they passed.

An hour later, Kang suspected that Mag's hands had now long passed the point where they could be saved. When the doctors got to him now, they would have no chance to save them. Bao would have his revenge after all. Kang continued to wait patiently.

It must have been nearly midnight when Mag began coming around, moaning slightly. Bao tried to get up and collapsed onto the floor, dropping his long gun. Slowly, Kang rose and moved to the man's side. His fingers felt for a pulse. While he found one, it was only just barely. Bao was dying rapidly now. Kang finally acted. He picked up the silver briefcase from the floor where Mag had dropped it when he'd entered his bedroom suite. Damn, it was heavy, but Kang did not pause to check what was inside. Rather, he unlocked the door and closed it. Not a soul was around. He ducked into his own room and packed his gear, stuffing the briefcase inside his heavy pack.

After making sure that he left nothing behind, he headed down the stairs. The night manager and a bartender were the only ones up, save some night guards. He checked out, claiming he had to catch a ship, which was to sail at high tide.

"Ah, you still have a couple of hours then," the manager replied.

"In that case, I'll have another stout for the trip. Have the stable hands saddle my horse, please," Kang replied. He took his time downing the stout. After the young lad came in to tell him that his horse was ready and he tipped the lad, he went back up to the manager.

"Excuse me. This is probably nothing at all, but earlier tonight, I heard some strange noises coming from the room next to mine. If whoever is staying in that suite doesn't come down for breakfast, you might send someone to check on them. Thank you for a fine stay. I will recommend the Orange Teacup Inn to my friends."

"Will do. Have a safe voyage, sir," the manager replied. Kang took the stable exit and soon rode out into the dark streets of Shankou. It was three in the morning and hardly anyone was about. He made straight for the docks and the Pearl. He looked the ship over and decided it was seaworthy, though he'd never been on a ship before. It just looked okay to him. He walked up the gangplank.

Several crewmen were doing odd jobs, getting ready to sail. The captain stepped out of his quarters and asked, "Who are you? What do you want?"

"Ah, well, it's like this. The man who hired your ship is not going to make it. He's had a rather unfortunate accident. He sent me to take his place. Perhaps you have heard of the shootings at the Orange Teacup Inn last evening?"

The captain grunted. He didn't like this at all. He'd sacrificed a paying cargo to take a single passenger. "How do I know that he isn't coming?"

"He knows when you are to sail, right? So when he doesn't show, then you know I'm telling you the truth."

That satisfied the captain, who Kang took an instant dislike to and steeled himself for more trouble. "Well, what about our pay?" he asked.

Kang thought quickly. "Look, you would not have off-loaded your half-loaded cargo and given it to another captain on a mere promise of a paying passenger. You don't strike me as a fool. He's already paid you handsomely for the trip."

Kang saw the man's reaction and knew that he'd caught him in a lie. "Well, all right then. If he doesn't show at sailing time, we'll take you instead."

"Good. Where shall I wait?" The captain motioned for him to sit near the main mast. Kang did so, but continued to carry his pack in one hand. He un-slung one of his two long guns, and sat down, the gun across his knees, the pack at his side. The hour passed slowly. At last, several other ships set sail, and Kang knew that it was past time to get going. In the east, the pale light of the predawn cast shimmering shadows on the undulating waves.

"Okay, seems you are right. Set sail boys. Untie the lines; let's get going," the captain barked his orders at last.

Kang rose, holding the gun in one hand and his heavy pack in his other. His second long gun was still slung over his shoulder. "Excuse me, captain. The one thing that my boss didn't tell me was our destination. Where are we headed?"

"Shansee. Take the first cabin on your right. It's next to mine. Food is in the galley. If you get sick, use the damn bucket in your cabin."

"Thanks. Say, how many days will it take to get to Shansee?"

"About a week, if we don't run into any monsoons."

"Any way to get to Nan Yan instead? I'll pay you extra," Kang suggested. He knew that Nan Yan was hundreds of miles inland, but he wanted to know if there was anywhere closer than Shansee. After all, by all rumors Shansee was in total and complete chaos at this time.

"There's a new port at the rail spur, Spur Port it's called."

"How much?"

"Another two hundred, if the monsoons are over."

"Okay, I'll let you know later on," Kang replied and headed off to find his cabin. The cabin was sparse and relatively crude, very different from the utter luxury of the Orange Teacup Inn. Still, it would have to do. Once inside, he laid his long guns aside and opened up his heavy pack. He still had plenty of dry rations. He didn't fully trust this captain or the crew. There was little to prevent them from attacking him and stealing his things. Heck, they could simply drug his food. Kang decided that he'd only eat his own rations for now. He'd grown rather paranoid since he arrived in Shankou and for good reasons.

Finally, he decided to have a look at his funds to see if he could scrape up the two hundred gold. He let out a sigh of relief; he had three hundred and some change left. He counted out the two hundred and put the rest back into his pack. Sitting the pouch aside for the captain, he took out the briefcase.

It was very heavy, and at last, his curiosity had to be satisfied. It was locked and he didn't have the key. Still, it was a very simple lock and using his knife, he easily picked it. He carefully opened the lid. His eyes saw plush red velvet. He lifted the wadded cloth and stared at a huge pile of gemstones of all colors, sizes, and shapes. All were quite large. While he had only a scant knowledge of the value of gems, these seemed vastly larger than the few that he had ever seen. The smallest stone that he could readily see was many times larger than the largest stone in any of the ten women's very expensive jewelry. He guessed this was a fortune, but had no idea how big. Carefully, he shut the lid and re-locked it. He stuffed the briefcase deep into his pack, putting his food and spare clothes on top of it.

Whatever this is worth, I'll divide it up among the ten women. At least, they will have the funds to provide for their own care in Nan Yan, he concluded. Then he laid back using his pack as a pillow. A week — he had to keep alert for another week.

"Oh dear me! The assassin has struck again and right under our very noses!" the distraught manager exclaimed when the porter came to tell him the awful news. "Looks like Mr. Tazau managed to mortally wound the assassin, but not before the assassin was able to hurt him. Don't just stand there; fetch the doctor at once! You there, untie the man, but don't touch those ropes around his arms. His hands look just awful. God, that's his tongue there! I can't take any more of this!" He left quickly before he vomited.

A half-hour later a doctor examined Mag. "Well, no doubt about it, his hands will have to come off. Get him to my office at once." Several strong arms lifted the sobbing man and carried him out of the suite. Blinded and still gagging on the drying blood in his mouth, Mag felt panic, a terror far worse than anything he'd ever known. What had his former business partner done to him? Why? He was so close to getting safely away, just a few more hours.

An unknown time later, Mag smelled something. A rag was over his face and nose. He tried to speak but heard only strange garbled noises. More waves of panic flooded over him, but he rapidly drifted into unconsciousness. Later, he awoke. His mouth felt better, though the remainder of his tongue hurt. Perhaps they sewed it back on, he thought in his foggy state. However, his wrists ached and throbbed with a pain that he'd never felt before. All was pitch black. He couldn't see anything, but he tried to feel his hands and wrist. Nothing. He panicked more and tried to sense them. Slowly, he realized that his hands were missing; they were gone too. He screamed and tried to talk, but only made unintelligible noises.

"There, there, Mr. Tazau, is it? You're safe. I've managed to save your life. I couldn't save your hands, of course. The assassin poked out your eyes, but I've found a lovely set of green glass eyes. They do look acceptable on you. I couldn't do anything about your tongue, however. We'll take good care of you until you heal. Do you have any relatives that can care for you after that?"

Mag made some awful noises. "Here, let me get some chicken broth in you. Mind you, you will have some difficulty with eating now." He nearly choked trying to get his tongue to work, because it wasn't there. Wave upon wave of panic spread through him. What had happened to him? Why? Why did Bao Nan do this to him?

In a flash, it hit him. He'd stolen Bao's fortune. That same day, he'd interrupted Bi's wedding to take Bi Nan into his harem, turning her into a Most Honored Yingchan. His men had to kill her fiancé though, because he had protested too much and tried to stop his men. So why was Bao so angry with him? He'd made Bi into a Golden Angel. Surely, the man could see that he'd done a fabulous thing for him partner. Honestly, he'd even spent a fortune on her jewelry.

Then, it registered. In a way, he was now like Bi, unable to see, unable to speak, and with no hands to help himself with any of his needs. He was now like the Golden Angels, minus all the gold and jewelry and thus value. What was going to happen to him now? How could he even survive? As soon as he was healed, then what? Six weeks later, Mag was turned out into the streets of Shankou and left to fend for himself. No one ever knew what happened to him after that.

January 1, 826, the Pearl docked in Spur Port, and Kang was more than ready to leave the ship. He'd been sick half of the time, but had insisted on eating his own provisions. His feet welcomed dry land! Spur Port had been steadily growing in size and importance. Trains seldom ran on into Shansee any longer. Not only was it not safe but there was no reason to go there. Nearly all commerce had ceased after the devastating battle last year. Kang was able to purchase a ticket on the next train to Nan Yan, but would have to wait a day for it to arrive from New Xin. Although his funds were almost gone, he managed to be able to pay for a room. After a bath, he felt like a new man again.

When the steam train arrived, Kang, who had never seen one before, was shocked. The engine alone totally dwarfed a person. The two engineers looked tiny way up there in the cab! A dozen boxcars were loaded with supplies. Several flat cars held numerous tall poles. At the rear was a single passenger car, and he was directed to it. A number of men and women joined him for the short run up to Nan Yan. Kang found himself staring at the women, though. None had the monstrous breasts or tiny waists that the plague had caused. All had their arms and hands. He was quite shocked and surprised indeed.

"Haven't see women back to normal yet?" one middle aged woman asked him.

"Sorry for staring, ma'am. No, I've come from far inland. So it is true. The Church of God in Nan Yan is able to undo the effects of the plague?"

"Yes, it is a miracle. You must get their Basic Therapy too, just as soon as you get to Nan Yan. I was on a buying trip for my husband," she replied. The two began a polite chat. "We should be there in sixteen hours. My name is Lin Li Sun, by the way."

"Kang Yun Zi, but Nan Yan must be five hundred miles north," Kang exclaimed.

"Oh yes it surely is that, maybe more, but the train goes fast. Well, not so fast on this run, in and around all the ridges and hills. I think they say that it goes only thirty miles an hour, not the usual forty," she explained. Kang was awestruck with the incredible speed. He'd taken many days to travel such a distance, which was reduced to mere hours now. What was happening to the world, he wondered.

Suddenly he noticed her eyes. They were yellow-brown and made of glass! "My god, I didn't realize that you were blind, Lin Li! I am so sorry!"

She smiled. "Oh yes, I do still get compliments about the color of the glass eyes, but I am hardly blind, Kang. I see perfectly well, just not through the glass eyes, that is." She began to explain about the Church of God and spiritual beings. Kang was extremely fascinated and listened to her every word. He also learned that she was a valuable assistant to the Most Honorable Engineer of Nan Yan, a Jovanni West Po, who had married an ex-princess, Pian Ling Wu of Shansee. Kang was very impressed indeed.

"Say, since you are well connected, perhaps you can tell me how I might contact a General Tao. I have vital, critical information on the placement of the drug overlords' soldiers and their planned defense. I simply must see him as soon as possible and warn him."

"Not a problem. I'll take you to him when we get to Nan Yan. I stay in the palace with the engineers, Princess Mei Lon Wu, and the general. Stick with me. I'm sure he will be most appreciative. We are trying hard to bring civilization back to Tashien, one small area at a time." She chatted on about their MMCE program and how she was helping to work out the more complex mathematics of their construction problems.

Hours passed quickly for Kang. Six hours later, the train stopped. "Ah, our rest stop. We are allowed off for fifteen minutes to grab a bite. Come on; let's get something to eat. I'm starving." She put her arm around his. At first, Kang thought that the blind woman was asking for some help in navigating the car and such. Soon, he realized that she was seeing just as well as he. A man and a woman operated a small food cart at the small station. The engineers were taking on more water and coal, he noted as they joined the line to purchase something to eat. "Allow me, my treat, Kang," Lin Li offered.

"Thank you. I admit that I have spent nearly all of my funds getting here." A while later, the train's whistle sounded and Kang carried their snacks onboard, while they both took in the splendid scenery. Dark rain clouds were rolling in again, however.

After they finished their small meal, they chatted more. Kang was fascinated by Lin Li; she was both beautiful and highly intelligent, he noted. "So how did you learn about the drug lords plans?" she asked.

"Now that is a long story, Lin Li."

She chuckled, "Well, we still have about ten hours to go. Surely, you can tell me all about it in that time." She disarmed him completely. Soon, Kang found himself telling her all about it, beginning with his discovery of the abduction and mutilation of his twin sisters and the death of their father who had tried to prevent it.

"My god! These Golden Angels, these Yingchan — they actually exist?" Lin Li said very surprised. "I thought that they were just legends of our distant past."

"No, that tradition is still kept alive in the deep highlands, though only the sadistic Mag Tazau has ever perverted it, mutilating those women. Of course, only the very, very wealthy could possibly afford to have a Golden Angel. The ten that were rescued — each one's jewelry alone is worth a half million gold. Some are several times more than that."

Lin Li was very much impressed and Kang continued his lengthy tale. "What? This Wu and the child are bringing them here to Nan Yan through the high mountains full of deep snow? That is impossible!" Lin Li was suddenly horrified for the women.

Kang had to explain in even more detail about the monk's discoveries of the alien caverns and trails. He then went on about his role and the obtaining of justice for the women. Finally, he wound up his tale, "Never was I so glad to set foot on dry land as I was back there in Spur Port! I am not a seaman. Now, I have to get all the data to General Tao at once. It is only January, so he has time to make counter-plans, I hope."

"This is incredible, Kang. You and Wu are heroes. You know that? Everyone else would have just left those women. None would have even bothered to get the information to General Tao. You really are a hero."

"No, I am just getting justice for my poor sisters. However, I neglected one detail, Lin Li. I peeked into Mag's briefcase. It is filled with the largest gemstones that I have ever seen. I will divide it between the ten Yingchan. That way, they will have enough funds to support themselves and their huge needs. Honestly, Lin Li, I was crying when I saw how my darling sisters have to live now. They are so helpless, can hardly see anything at all, and are just barely able to walk. This is the very least that I can do for all ten of them."

"How very noble of you, Kang. I'm sure that your sisters really love you. We must get all this to General Tao and Counselor Bi Mei of the Church of God. They will know what to do," Lin Li advised. Finally night fell, and the two fell asleep in their cars, Lin Li resting her head on his shoulders.

They arrived in the early morning on January 3. Kang was visibly impressed with the sights of Nan Yan. The new motor-wagons, the putt-putts, the electricity phenomenon — all combined to make an incredible impression on Kang. Still, Lin Li continued to surprise him. She was met at the station by Jovanni himself, who asked if she had acquired all their needed supplies. She had. "We have to get Kang here to see the general and Bi Mei immediately," she insisted.

To Kang's amazement, he did not doubt or question her further. "Hop in. I'll take you there right now. Pleased to meet you, Kang." Kang knew that he was a foreigner and Jovanni added, "I come from Velona, Sea Princes, originally. However, both my son and I have married two fabulous local women and are now residents of Nan Yan. They were blinded too, just like Lin Li. You know, the attractive yellow-brown glass eyes. Well, I got the better deal. Princess Pian Wu is the greatest woman in the whole world." Jovanni chatted on about his wife, while navigating the throngs in the streets, arriving shortly at the palace.

"Say, you will have to join Pian and me for dinner, Kang. Won't take no for an answer. Lin Li, you come too and make sure Kang here doesn't get lost. She has an eidetic memory. Did she tell you that?" Lin Li flushed; she hadn't.

Once parked, Jovanni led the two into the palace and straight into the princess' office. "You two sit here and I'll round them up," he insisted.

A bit later, Princess Mei Lon Wu entered. She too had her arms back and now really looked the part of the Princess of all Nan Yan. At her side, General Tao strode impressively.

"Welcome to Nan Yan. I'm Princess Mei Lon Wu. General Tao Bi. I'm told that you need to see us both immediately?"

"He most certainly does!" Lin Li spoke before Kang could reply. "You should both sit down and take tea. His is a long story and a very, very important one for us all!" Kang flushed. He only wanted humbly to relay the data, but Lin Li was making this sound so extremely important.

Over tea, Kang retold his story. As expected, he was interrupted several times, just as Lin Li had. That the Yingchan existed shocked them both. That Wu was bringing them here via the high mountains and alien caverns and trails was shocking. However, as he had expected, his detailed information on the drug lords' defenses against his spring offensive was taken very seriously. General Tao realized that Kang was right; there had to be spies among them.

He'd barely finished when Bi Mei entered. "You needed me?" she asked. After more introductions, Kang once more had to relay his entire story. "Oh my. Yingchan. Mutilated. Damn Mag Tazau! Alien caverns? Okay, I need Bethany right now!" Poor Kang looked mystified. What was she talking about?

Lin Li whispered, "Bethany is one of the churches leaders. She is in Velona, but Bi Mei is using telepathy to contact her. If I know Bethany, she'll be here in a few seconds. She knows a whole lot about those alien caverns!" To Kang's complete surprise, I materialized a body that looked like my very pregnant self. The others were no longer surprise by our sudden appearances.

"Hello, sorry about shocking you with my arrival, but I must know more about these alien caverns! Please, I hate to do this to you, but can you start at the beginning once more?" I asked.

Humbly, he did so. An hour later, he finished. "Excuse me, but can I ask something of you folks?" Kang pleaded.

"Oh sure. Ask away," Princess Mei Lon replied.

Kang dug out his briefcase. "This is the briefcase I took from Overlord Mag Tazau, the sadistic man who so mutilated those ten women, the Yingchan. It contains some very big gems. I'd like someone to get them appraised and to get Banca del Dio accounts opened up for the ten Yingchan. Whatever it is worth, divide it up ten ways for the women. When they get here, they will need funds just to stay alive. Please, can someone do this for me?"

Princess Mei Lon took the briefcase and opened it up. "Oh my god!" she exclaimed. Everyone else rushed to look too, except Kang. They were just gemstones to him, something to keep his sisters alive.

"I'd better see to this, Princess! I'll take it to the Banca del Dio personally, under heavy guard! Son, this is a fortune!" General Tao left at once.

I asked Kang a number of questions, trying to flush out more what Wu was doing. Unfortunately, he really had little more to add. We chatted for a while longer, waiting for General Tao to return. He had a huge grin when he walked back in. "Son, I got a rough estimate. The final figures will be days in coming. The Banca folks suggest that there is at least two hundred fifty million in gems in that case. It is the largest collection of gemstones that anyone has ever seen! The ten women will get at least twenty-five million each. Incredible, son. Are you sure that you don't want a little of that for your trouble?"

"No sir. It is for my twin sisters and the others. I can make my way in the world," Kang replied humbly. Lin Li was even more impressed with him.

Chapter 70 Rescue

While the others had their lunch, I began making some plans. It was the dead of winter; the snow cover on the distant mountains was very deep. I had no idea how many of these caverns existed, nor any idea that a sort of trail existed between them. One man and a boy were trying to bring ten very helpless women through all that. It seemed impossible. Surely, they must be in deep trouble, if not dead already.

"We need to send out a search party to look for them," I advised.

"But surely no one can get through the deep snows of the mountains," General Tao countered. "Travel in the mountains proper in the summer is extraordinarily risky at the very best. In the winter, it has to be suicide. Avalanches. One slip and down the mountain you go. They are probably dead or frozen already. Besides, if you don't know their route, how could you possible find them?"

"Kijutsu, general," I replied. Here in Tashien, the unexplainable can be explained and accepted by the mere mention of that word.

"Oh! I forgot. Yes, by all means, use your kijutsu powers. That is the only way that you could find them up there. Kang, do not be too disappointed if we find that they have not survived the cold and snow. Even in the summer, such a trip is fraught with untold dangers, but in the winter," he didn't finish his sentence.

"Please, I must help too," Kang pleaded.

"Let's look at the maps I have of the upper valley and mountains," Princess Mei Lon suggested. Everyone crowded around her map boards in her office. The details grew sketchier and sketchier as one moved closer to the mountains proper. She pointed out with her long red nail, "Finzau, here, is the last known village at the end of our valley. Probably take at least a week for us to get there overland, Bethany."

"Okay, I am going to get some others on it with me. We'll search for them. I have a good idea where we can begin our search. Kang, we will be using our kijutsu powers. If we find them, we will use our kijutsu to bring them directly here. How about you helping them fix up a place for them when they get here?" I suggested.

"Bring them directly to the church complex," Bi Mei ordered. "Kang, you can return there with me and help us set up a space tailored to their needs. I am sorry that we don't really know precisely to care for them. So we will be depending upon your guidance to get things setup for their arrival. I am sure that Bethany will be able to find them in a day or so and bring them back here at once. Their kijutsu is very powerful, Kang."

"Hey, can't he come by my place for dinner? I've already invited him," Jovanni complained.

Bi Mei laughed, "It seems our resident engineer is fast on the draw." Everyone chuckled. "Okay, Lin Li, can you come by and pick him up in time for Jovanni's dinner? He's new to Nan Yan and doesn't know his way around yet. Meantime, this afternoon, he can help us get all setup for the women." That was agreeable and Bi Mei led Kang out of the palace to her waiting motor-wagon. One amazed man arrived shortly at the large complex.

"That is my husband's compound, the Olin Masters Academy. To the right of it is our master Church of God. We have many rooms available now. It's been modernized considerably. This way," she led him inside. He soon got lost in the maze of rooms and halls.

"Now here is a typical bedroom quarters. Please turn on the light so we can see better."

Kang looked around and flushed, "Er, I'm sorry. Where are the lanterns?"

Bi Mei flushed. "I'm sorry. I forgot that you don't know about electric lights. That switch there by the door — yes, flip it up. See?"

"Wow! Magic lights. Incredible."

"Not magic. Electricity. Have Jovanni show you the electricity generation plant of his. Now then, will a room such as this work for the women?"

"Yes, they have been sleeping three to a bed. That way, Wu or Jie can help them potty more easily. Where do you keep the chamber pots?"

Bi Mei laughed. "We are modernized now. Look in that small side room. There is a bathtub and a toilet and running hot and cold water. It was designed for us women before we regained our arms. You know, when we used our feet for everything."

"I see. This is marvelous, but these women can't use their feet. Their golden boots can't come off."

"Oh right. You said they are like the alien boots that our men had to wear?" she asked.

"Yes, only made out of gold. Well, they look golden, but gold is soft and these are not. They are very hard and sturdy and do not allow them to bend their ankles in the slightest. They walk very, very slowly."

"I see. Will they be able to walk from their beds to the bathroom with some help?"

"I think so. How far is the dining room from here?"

"Way too distant, I am afraid. Let's see if we can find some closer rooms, shall we?" A while later, they decided on using five rooms, those closest to the dining room. Next, Kang helped her carry extra bedding into each room and then all manner of sundries, including hairbrushes.

One room was set aside for Kang and his twin sisters, that way he could care for their needs, which he insisted upon doing. Bi Mei then brought him some clean clothes and ordered him to take a bath and get familiar with how the modern system worked, including the light switches. "Lin Li will come for you. When she arrives, she will phone. That device there is called a telefono. When it rings, you pick it up, talk into that cone, and put that one to your ear to hear. She will then come and get you so that you don't wander around here aimlessly. It's a big complex. At once time, we had hundreds upon hundreds of women staying here. Once we were able to undo the plague's effects on them, they were able to return to their own homes. Now we bring newcomers here for their therapy and send them home when that is done and their arms are back."

"Then it is really true. My sisters and the others will be able to get their arms and hands back?" he asked.

"Absolutely, unless they were amputated before the plague. We can undo the plague's effects only, but that happens after they finish erasing the trauma that they have suffered. You need to get your therapy too, Kang. I know; do the women first," she grinned.

"Absolutely!" he replied.

"If you run into troubles, pick up the telefono, and when you hear a voice, tell them about it. The women will direct you. I have to run now. Catch you later on, Kang."

"Thank you for everything. My sisters cannot speak now, so I am thanking you for them too." She nodded and left Kang to explore the marvels of the MMCE.

Bi Mei had her own problems. Ten women crippled up and unable to speak meant a very nasty combination. Only very advance therapy givers could possibly handle these ten and only by using telepathy. They would be rough cases indeed to handle. Further, they would have to be given Advanced Therapy, at least enough so that they could send their thoughts into another's mind. Counting herself, they had four who could give such sessions. She'd have to beg Eve for some extra help. Besides, she was still dealing with the torso women, as she called them. "God, the brutality of men!" she declared as she walked to her office.

Meanwhile, I rounded up the gang and explained the serious situation that had arisen. When I finished, Sergio commented, "Well, it shouldn't be too hard to locate ten spiritual beings. There is none that we know of in the mountains, so it should be easy to find them, even if they are in the caverns. We know where a few of the plasticine dolls had their caverns, but apparently we missed seeing a whole lot of them, to say nothing of the fact that they have a walking trail connecting them."

"Yes, but also stay alert for more of their weird devices. The world has seen enough of those things," I added, recalling the man who became invincible while wearing their helmet and armor. Eve recalled the surgical knife apparatus that the mad doctor had used to perform his sadistic surgery on women and us too. She knew what I meant. If there were more of those things around, they must not fall into the wrong hands. Tashien did not need another Golden Warrior. Apparently, there were already enough sadistic doctors.

The eight of us left our bodies in our beds that night. Eve and I took them all to the town of Nag Tasha and we easily spotted the monastery. Yes, I thought that it was most impressive and particularly beautiful. We headed up the back valley and soon homed in on the first of the plasticine doll's caverns. Sergio did a quick inspection and pointed out unmistakable evidence that they had been here some days ago. Off we went, the eight of us fanning out, attempting to discern a trail left by a sleigh, a possible plasticine doll-made trail, or another cavern.

Before long, we spotted another cavern. Once more Sergio discovered that they had been here as well. Outside, deep snow covered the mountainside. Any tracks left by the horses and sleigh had been covered up, though we began to discern that beneath the heavy layer of snow, there was a trail or path most likely made by the dolls centuries ago. On we went.

"What — what — what are we going to do?" asked a shivering Jie. For four days, Wu and his party had been stuck here in the tenth cavern. They had finished off the last of their food. Now the remaining charcoal had been burned just trying to keep the ten women warm enough to survive. Wu had them all in the one bed and covered with every bit of cloth that could be found, while he and Jie tried to figure out what else they could do.

The problem had been the snowstorm, which arrived four days ago. Four feet of new snow had obliterated all signs of the faint trail that they had to follow. Worse, just outside their cavern, a huge bank of snow threatened to start an avalanche. Wu correctly guessed that if they attempted to leave in the sleigh, the vibrations would be enough to trigger the avalanche, wiping them out. They'd tried yelling as loudly as they could, but that was not enough. They had tried throwing stones, but again, to no avail. He'd decided to wait it out a day or two. Perhaps the snow would start sliding of its own accord. The sun had melted some of the snow above them, and at first, this seemed a likely event. However, four days later, the avalanche still had not begun, and the mound of snow continued to threaten them. Now they were becoming quite desperate. They had to make the next cavern complex if only to find a bit more food and firewood or charcoal. Yet, if they took the sleigh out there, they'd be caught in an avalanche.

Wu estimated that they were about a hundred miles north of the valley system in which Nan Yan lay. Three more caverns at most and they could try to head down the valley into Nan Yan. The ten were holding up as best they could. None complained, though they had no means by which to complain. Unable to speak, their eyes hidden behind golden eyes, only meager facial expressions and their shivering bodies presented outward signs of their intense discomfort.

"I have another idea Jie. We must get that avalanche started. Rocks failed, but what if we made a snowman?" Wu suggested. Jie gave him a funny look. Perhaps Wu was going mad, the ten year old boy thought. "Hear me out. When you start rolling a snowman, you start with a small ball in your hand. As you roll it around, it accumulates more and more snow, growing larger and larger."

"Oh, I see!" Jie suddenly exclaimed. "I get it. Okay, let's try it." The two headed outside once more. Climbing carefully, they maneuvered up the mountainside just beyond the cavern's mouth. Here, the sun had been melting the snow pack, though it was now just starting to dip over the mountain peak, casting long shadows over the white landscape. Both began making snowballs and rolling them down the snow pack. After a dozen tries, they had ribbon streaks going down the sloping bank. Then, one of Wu's began to grow in size. Jie pointed it out and they both stopped to watch.

Larger and larger the ball grew as it gained in speed. Then a crack appeared in the huge bank. "I think it is working!" Jie cried. Wu crossed his fingers. A minute went by then without warning the whole snow bank gave way, sliding in slow motion downwards, gaining speed with each passing second. Soon it thundered away, knocking more and more snow below it into its mass. The avalanche shot down the mountainside growing in speed and magnitude. Several more nearby banks gave way and joined the downward plunge. Both cheered and scrambled back down to the cavern. At the edge, they saw the faint outline of their path once more. Tomorrow, they could resume their treacherous journey!

Inside, Wu told the ten women the good news, but did not uncover them. "I am most sorry, but we have no more food or anything to burn for a fire. We will have to stay warm until the morning sun comes up. Then, we will be on our way once more." Several made some unintelligible noises, which he took to be cheering or merely adding their thank you support. After checking on the forlorn horses who had nothing to eat or the last three days, the two crawled in with the women, adding their warmth to the ten.

Eve was the first to locate the tenth cavern. *Hey, I found another cavern. Bingo. There are twelve spiritual beings here. Yes, I sense their bodies. We've found them!* The eight of us entered the cave, and I sent them a message to materialize bodies for the benefit of those inside.

"Hello. Anyone in here? Wu? Jie? Are you here?" I called out. The eight of us walked our bodies just inside, passing by the horses and the sleigh. "Anyone here?"

"Huh? Voices? Hello?" Wu called out. "Jie, stay here, I will go see what this is. Perhaps, we are dreaming. No one could possibly know that we are here."

A moment later, a sleepy man fully dressed and with a heavy parka on came out of the left side cavern area. He stared at us eight in disbelief. "Hello. Wu Shenyan?" I asked. He nodded mechanically. Okay, I admit, we erred; we forgot to mock up heavy winter coats for our bodies.

"Kang Yun Zi sent us out to look for you. I am Bethany Bartiana Angela." I introduced my companions and added, "We are using our kijutsu powers. These bodies that you are seeing are not ours, which are back home in Velona. We've come to see if you need some help."

He bowed to us and said, "We have been very nearly done in by an avalanche. Jie and I finally got it to slide, freeing the path so we may continue our journey. However, we have been stuck here for four days and now have no food and no more firewood. I'm afraid that the women are getting very cold. Please, if you can provide heat?"

Lucianna and Giovanni were extremely excited. They had the chance to examine the plasticine doll's caverns in detail. Giovanni said, "Okay, Wu, give us a few minutes to figure out their controls. I think there is a way to get light and heat in here." Wu looked dumbfounded so I chatted a bit more with him.

"Sorry, we didn't bring any food with us. Lucianna and Giovanni are inventors and engineers. If anyone can figure out how to operate this installation, they can. Kijutsu powers, you know," I explained.

"Oh, yes. You must be powerful Olin Masters," Wu replied, trying desperately to put our appearance into some graspable context, some frame of reference that he could comprehend.

"Yes, very much like the Olin Master, but perhaps with even more powerful kijutsu," I added. "Is any of the women ill? Anyone hurt?"

"No, just cold and very hungry," Wu answered.

"Okay, Bethany. Some of us can go back to Nan Yan and bring food and water back up here," Valerio suggested. I agreed and he, Sergio, Lisa, and Eve headed back to Nan Yan to do just that.

"What does he mean? How is this possible?" asked a confused Wu.

"We have powerful kijutsu. We can move objects. They will move a basket of food up here from Nan Yan. Kang has arrived there and told everyone about you and the ten women. We are with the Church of God and here to help by using our kijutsu to look for you."

Just then, bright lights suddenly turned on, fully illuminating the entire cavern complex. Giovanni called out, "Now that's a whole lot better, unless everyone really wants to sleep. Lucianna is working on the heat in here. Bit longer, please."

"How did he do that?" asked Wu.

"Wow! Can I see too?" asked Jie, who had crawled out from the massive pile of blankets and covers, unable to restrain himself from seeing what was going on. I introduced us to the boy as well.

Just as I finished, I knew that the heat was on. I detected a strong infrared component to the light. Had the bright lights been off, Wu might have been able to see a very deep red glow covering the entire cavern space. Lucianna's voice called out, "Got the heat on now. It will be warm in here soon. Holler if it gets too hot in here."

"I feel heat! Where is it coming from? I see no fires?" asked Wu.

Lucianna walked up proudly and explained, "It is coming from the walls, which are now generating infrared rays, like sun rays, only not so bright. Heat rays might be a better word. We'll soon be warm in here. The aliens liked it warm, but I don't know why. Bethany, can Giovanni and I do some exploring while we are waiting?"

"Engineers!" I teased them, bringing a smile to Wu's face. "Sure, only be careful what you turn on."

"Gosh, I am starting to sweat in this parka!" Wu exclaimed, taking his off. So did Jie. Now the women began to stir. "Excuse me, I must help the women get up and take off their heavy cloaks. We have piled everything we could on them to keep them from freezing. Please, do not be so startled by their appearance. It is very hard for them. They cannot speak; the butcher cut off their tongues."

"Yes, Kang told us all about the. Yingchan, is that the right term?" I replied. Wu nodded and he and Jie began removing the mountain of covers, blankets, and bits of cloth that they had mounded over the women. Before long, they had the ten sitting up on the sides of the large bed, cloaks removed, and warm for the first time in four days or longer. We didn't ask if they had been cold before they became trapped in this cavern.

Rather we four were completely shocked and nearly blinded by the reflected light off their massive amounts of golden jewelry. Huge earrings dangled down below their chests. Their hair, parted in the middle, was tied with bands on either side of their heads, draping down over their bodies, un-braided. A golden mesh or cloth like veil hung down from either earring and was attached also by a stud on either side of their nose. The veil hung down to an inch below their chins. Even more dramatic were their eyes, solid gold orbs faced us. But we soon realized that the reason the women were moving their heads slightly was that they were trying hard to see us out of tiny pinholes in the center of the unmoving golden eyes. Our eyes followed their plague altered massive bosoms and tiny waists, covered with fine silk dresses, pencil style. At last, I saw their golden boots, fused as if one piece onto their feet. They appeared to be similar to those alien provided ballet boots that the men had to wear when the plague struck, only these were made of gold. I saw at once that they could not move or bend at their ankles. I was more than a little shocked at their appearance.

Wu explained, "A true Yingchan is a most honored woman. Evil Mag has so perverted them. They should have their arms and hands, which the plague destroyed, and they should have their tongues. They should have small feet, not these awful boots in which they are only just barely able to walk. Yes, a Yingchan is a most honored woman, but Mag has mutilated these women. I am sworn to bring them to Nan Yan in hopes that somehow the miracles we heard are true, that they can somehow get their arms and hands back. If so, they can survive. Is it so? Can this Church of God undo the plague's horrible effects?"

"Absolutely, Wu, ladies. Thousands of women in and around Nan Yan now have their arms and hands restored to what they were before the plague came. Our breasts and waists can go back to normal too. The only things that cannot be undone are those that have been surgically removed. I am afraid that your tongues cannot be replaced, honorable Yingchan. Yet, if you have your hands back, you can write what you wish to say," I explained, giving them much needed hope, not knowing that I was nearly paraphrasing what the Most Venerable Peng had told them just before they left his monastery.

I continued, "Yes, there have been many men who have done very evil things to some young women of Tashien. In Nan Yan, you will get to meet some women who were mutilated far worse that you have been honorable Yingchan. After these women lost so much to the plague, evil men then cut off their legs, leaving them mere torsos and then turned them into opium addicts and sexual toys. They've been rescued. One day, they will have their arms back, but unfortunately not their legs. In time, honorable Yingchan, your situation will be much better, trust us." Wu bowed and bowed, happy to hear these encouraging words.

Just then, the others arrived. I was surprised. Not only had they brought along a large amount of hot food, but they also brought Kang with them! "Kang? Is this really you?" Wu burst out as the five walked in from the main entrance.

"Yes, Wu! Most incredible! They flew me here! Picked me up and the hot pot and we flew through the sky! Never have I heard of such kijutsu as these Church of God members from Velona have! Zhu! Zhen!" He saw his sisters sitting on the edge of the bed, straining to try and locate him. Both now awkwardly struggled to stand up, and he rushed to them and flung his arms around both, hugging them tightly and also keeping them from falling on the hard stone floor. "We brought hot stew for you, though it might have chilled from the flight. I was flying! Really, I was flying through the air!"

"Come on, gang. Let's get the hot stew in them before it gets too cold," Eve interrupted. "Wu, you must show us how to feed them, and we'll all lend a hand." Soon, we each had a Yingchan to feed, lifting her veil with one hand, while holding the spoon to her lips. I quickly realized that we had to use their sense of touch, because they simply could not see much at all from their tiny pinholes. We all caught on quickly though, and the warm food was very much what these women really needed. Their bodies were very low on energy as Eve suspected.

At last warmed and pottied, the women were good to go. "Okay, it is time that we take you all down to Nan Yan. Counselor Bi Mei is waiting there for you with warm baths and beds," I explained.

"But we cannot see the path at night," Wu protested.

"Kijutsu, Wu. Let's get everyone bundled up against the cold and then all of you into the sleigh. Unhook the horses; we'll bring them along later. We eight will fly you down to Nan Yan lickety split. Kijutsu powers."

"Hey Wu, this will be great! But bundle up, the wind gets terribly chilly. Wait til you all see this!" Kang gushed out.

While Sergio wanted us to just lift the women from the bed and carry them into the sleigh, I sent him a hold on that. Instead, we followed Wu's lead. He put his arm around Dai's waist, and together, they began walking extremely slowly towards the sleigh. Kang did the same with his sisters, one around each arm. Jie followed them with his sister, Yan. The rest of us assisted the others in a similar manner. As we slowly walked the women to the sleigh, Wu pointed out, "See, they are not completely helpless. They are most brave and can walk, though it is easier for them if we steady them on longer walks such as this." I noticed that they all had proud faces, and they were able to do at least this small thing for themselves. Eve noticed it as well and telepathically pointed it out to the rest.

Once everyone was snugly tucked into the sleigh and well covered against the chilly air, we eight picked up the sleigh together and began flying them down towards Nan Yan, much like some enormous eagles. Even the women let out wild exclamations. We were definitely giving them something to talk about in future times, well at least write about in the case of the ten. An hour later, we deposited the sleigh at the front gates of the Church of God. Bi Mei and a dozen others were there waiting on us; Eve had sent her a telepathic message of our estimated arrival time.

"Welcome to the Nan Yan Church of God, Most Honorable Yingchan. Please, come inside. We have warm baths prepared for you and warm beds ready as well! You honor us with your presence," she bowed to the ten women, whom the men and some of us were helping get out of the sleigh. Whether she was shocked by their golden appearance, I could not tell. She allowed the men to assist the Golden Angels to walk inside the church. Although it was a very long way for the women to walk on their toes, they did so as a matter of pride. Once they reached their bedrooms, Kang began to show Wu what to do to operate the baths, and we left them to the able care of Bi Mei.

We eight huddled briefly. "Look, we need to not only bring the two horses down, but also search that place and all the others for alien artifacts," Eve pointed out. Lucianna, Giovanni, Valerio, and Eve headed back to continue the search and to bring back the horses. The rest of us headed on home.

When I awoke the next morning, I found another of those golden armor and helmet outfits sitting on the front room couch, along with another of those special surgical blade affairs that the doctor had once used on Eve and me. Apparently, the gang had been right about the artifacts and had brought them back with them. Later that morning, Eve pointed out that they still had not finished searching that first cavern. Oh brother, how many more of these things were out there? Naturally, I sent the two engineers back to the caverns to look for more of these alien artifacts.

Back at the Church of God, Bi Mei began working out just how they could handle these new ten women's trauma. "Talk about being swamped," she exclaimed exasperated with having more brutalized women dumped on her plate. "What do we know? Well, in other lands, Eve has pointed out that their average emotional tones are perhaps at anger or slightly higher. There, the women's plague trauma is being handled in about a week of near constant therapy sessions. Here in Tashien, we have had two types. In the greater Nan Yan area, we've been lucky and had a relatively higher emotional state with durations of therapy similar those of the other countries. However, as we have expanded outward into the normal population of Tashien, the average emotional tone is closer to apathy. Those cases are taking five to six times longer to handle the trauma of the plague. Thus, our overall progress is vastly slower, consuming five times our resources. If that is not bad enough, we keep getting these awful cases!"

"The torso women are starting to improve finally. Their conviction that they were Perfect Women as torsos only has finally been cracked. Yet, they still refuse to allow us to give them their arms back yet. They thus need constant care, and we have had to dedicate women to assist them with everything. From your estimates, they have at least another couple of months to go before we can declare their Basic Therapy completed, ignoring the fact that they ought to potentially receive Advanced Therapy soon, especially if they continue to desire to be the way that they are, Perfect Women."

Nan Dia pointed out, "Look, we knew that if we allowed them to sit on the conviction that they were Perfect Women, then they would be able to keep the immobility incidents of their past lives at bay and keep them off opium. Thus far, that is working perfectly. Eventually, they will cognate on just why they are holding onto the Perfect Woman idea so strenuously. Give them and their therapy a bit more time."

Bi Mei agreed and continued, "Now we have another ten most unusual cases. As you know, they can't speak, no tongues. They can barely walk. I don't see that we again have any choice but to restore their arms at once."

Shu Wen spoke up, sighing, "I agree, Bi Mei, we don't have much choice with these ten. I think that we ought to have the Olin Masters look at their feet and eyes. Perhaps the boots and their golden eyes can be removed. If so, that would give them freedom of motion and the ability to take care of themselves. But I agree, we will have to use telepathy to even begin to conduct a therapy session. That means the four of us once more are going to be overloaded."

Nan Dia and Xia agreed. Nan added, "How about we ask Eve for some assistance? As I recall, there are now about two hundred worldwide that could help us out."

"Okay, I'll do just that. Of course, the liability is that others may not have quite the cultural knowledge of our people," Bi Mei pointed out.

The next morning, the Yingchan heard the gong sound for breakfast. All this was so new and foreign to them. Electric lights, running water, bathtubs, and toilets — all were so foreign to them. Combine that unfamiliarity with their minuscule vision and you can appreciate their extreme nervousness as they began to face their first day in Nan Yan. Their men and several women were there to assist them in walking the relatively short distance into the dining room. Around a hundred women and children along with a few men were already there. Naturally, these Golden Angels became the intense focus of everyone in the room. Fortunately, the ten could only barely see a tiny fraction of the room at one time from their pinholes. Besides, they needed what little vision they had to see where they were attempting to walk.

The ten were positioned near the nine Perfect Women, who still sat in their slanted chairs with wheels. After the ten were fed along with the nine, the two groups of women were introduced to each other.

"Hello. Very pleased to meet such Most Honored Yingchan! I'm called Yan Yu. We're called Perfect Women because we have neither arms nor legs. Thus, we're perfect in all ways. You're also so very beautiful! Your jewelry must be worth a fortune. We can see why you're called Golden Angels. Wu, your wife is most attractive, but I so wish that she could speak."

Wu smiled, "Yes, my Dai is most beautiful, Yan Yu. You are very pretty yourself. We can see why you are so perfect, but don't you want your arms and hands back?"

"Oh no! Then we would not be Perfect Women. We'd be just like ordinary women, only we wouldn't have any legs. It is so very much better this way, but at first, we had so many problems." She began to tell them all about their mental demons and their need for opium to counteract them.

Dai and the others moved their heads around trying to get a good look at the Perfect Women. Dai made a strange noise. She was shocked and appalled to see these women were in far worse physical shape than she was. In a way, this really did help the ten Yingchan's mental state. They felt far less like victims. Surely, these nine were in vastly worse condition than they were, especially if they somehow magically got their arms back. Dai promised herself not to make any further fuss and to do her very best to lessen the burden that she knew she must be on Wu. The others had similar reactions and made similar conclusions. While they didn't realize it, this was precisely what Bi Mei had in mind for them first thing this morning.

That settled, the nine Perfect Women were wheeled off to their morning therapy sessions. The top four Olin Masters then entered and bowed respectfully to the Yingchan. "I am Tian Li, the Olin Master of Nan Yan. My fellow masters, Feng Chow, De Dhou, and Ning Don. We have also brought Doctor Tran. If you will permit us to inspect your feet and eyes, we will see if anything can be done to assist you. The doctor also wishes to make sure that your health is good. Nod if this is acceptable to you." All did and the five men began their examinations. Specifically, the doctor was asked to see if he had any ideas about their golden eyes: how they were made and if there was any safe way that their vision could be restored.

The doctor was thorough with his examinations. The Olin Masters used their combined kijutsu probative powers to get a good feel for the construction of their boots and the condition of their feet inside them. They found that these boots had been made to fit each woman's foot precisely, leaving not even the tiniest gap where bath waters could seep in between their legs and the sides of the boots. They realized rather quickly how they had been made and fastened to their feet. An alloy of gold and probably steel had been used forming a sort of cast around their feet. Next, the nearly cylindrical shell was bent tightly closed, encasing their foot and rising part way up their calves. Once this was done, probably while the alloy was cooling, the shoes retained their inflexible shape. The joint where the two halves met had a tongue and grove mesh, so that when they were closed, a tight seam resulted. Next, molten gold was poured down the seam, ensuring that the seam could not be forced open, thus sealing the boots on their feet permanently. The designer had been wise in making sure that water could not seep inside them from their calves. Yet, if their feet ever swelled, they would have no room in which to expand, which was a distinct disadvantage.

All four concluded that to remove the boots would be a very long and arduous challenge. First, the sealing gold would have to be completely removed from the tongue and grove seam, which was over a foot in length. Once done, it might be possible to pry the boots apart at the seams. Yet there was no guarantee that this could be done without further injuring their feet or toes in the process. Had they the option of reheating the boots, the prying action would be easier, but the feet would be toast in the process.

That analysis concluded, the four focused on the actual state of their feet inside the boots. Here the situation had taken a grimmer turn. Those who had worn them for the longer time now had fused foot bones. Even if the boots were removed, their feet were more or less calcified into this en pointe position. There was hope that the four newest Yingchan's feet had not yet begun to calcify significantly, but none for the other six. Thus, removal of their golden boots was a moot issue. With a sad heart, Tian explained their findings in detail to the women. Bi Mei, who was watching them from a distance, kept a close eye on their reactions to this disheartening news.

Because they had seen and listened to the nine Perfect Women earlier, none of the ten had any particularly awful reaction to this news. They attempted to put on a brave face. At last the doctor finished his examinations of the women.

"With one exception, the women's overall health is remarkably good!" he began attempting to be as upbeat as he could. "However, all have suffered a good deal of tooth decay. I am afraid that whomever has been caring for their needs has neglected to brush their teeth often enough. Well, these four still have teeth in relatively good shape, but the other six are going to need some dental work. In light of their golden images, I would suggest using gold for their dental work." Several smiled, more gold would only add to their image.

"Now then, as far as their eyes are concerned, several have developed a slight eye infection, but that can easily be cured I believe. Unfortunately, I am still unsure how their eyes were done. It does seem that their eyeballs have been encased in a golden sphere or partial sphere. I cannot find the outer edged of that sphere. I'm afraid that if I probe any further to find its edge, I may permanently damage their eyes. I believe that they were fitted with spherical caps over their original eyeballs. If so, the outer edges of the sphere must have been forced together to fit tightly around the balls. How this may have been done I surely do not know. Unless I can see how it was actually constructed and put on their eyeballs, I would never risk making any attempt to remove them. One false move and they could be permanently blinded, I'm afraid. Is there any possibility that you can find the person who made and installed these? If so, then they may be of more help in removing them."

"May I go ahead and attend to their eye infections now?" he asked. Given the go ahead, he put several drops into their eyes. "I will repeat this each day until the infections are cleared up. We should get their teeth looked after as soon as possible." Of note, ten days later, the women sported golden caps over their front teeth and many of their molars as well. The low-grade pain that each had been feeling in their mouths vanished completely. Their smiles were now also golden.

When the doctor and the Olin Masters left, Bi Mei, Shu Wen, Nan Dia, and Xiu then made telepathic contact with the women, four at a time. After explaining their kijutsu, which the women accepted as an explanation for this phenomenon, the four followed an agreed upon dialog with the women.

Dai, we usually help plague victims undo the plague's effects once the woman has finished her Basic Therapy. In your case, we will perform this action now before we begin your therapy so that you may be better able to care for your own needs. If your arms and hands were lost to the plague, they can be recovered in just a couple of days. Do you wish to have them back? Bi Mei asked.

Oh yes! Yes! Yes!

Okay. There, I have used my kijutsu on your shoulders. Within two days, your arms and hands will be as they were before the plague took them. Now the plague has also shrunk your waists and greatly expanded your breasts. Each of these effects can also be undone as well. Some women prefer not to have one or more of these undone. It is your choice. You do not have to make it now. Many women take a wait and see approach. We can undo the effects later, if you desire. What do you prefer?

As expected, the ten were so happy to be getting their arms restored that they chose to wait on the rest, which had no real bearing on their abilities to care for their own needs. Physical appearance was the very least of these women's worries at this time. Not being utterly dependent on others for everything in their personal lives was.

"Okay, the next step is to get you all fitted for some new dresses. Soon you will have arms again and these dresses will no longer work," Bi Mei explained to the group. "Since you are Most Honored Yingchan now and since money is no object, I have instructed the dressmakers to fashion new dresses for you from the finest silk that we have available to us at this time. They will make the dresses patterned off the ones that you are now wearing, unless you have other desires." All shook their heads no and she continued, "Good. What remains will be your individual choice of the color of your dresses. I'm instructing the dressmakers to make each of you five new dresses. Shortly, they will bring you color swatches and allow you to make your choices." Smiles behind golden veils rewarded her for her kindness.

"We will wait until next week to begin your Basic Therapy. We want your eye infections cleared up first and your teeth handled. We also want to give you time to become adjusted to having your arms back and such. If you need anything, don't hesitate to ask us." Dai mouthed a thank you and Bi replied, "You are most welcome, Dai."

The four left the ten when the dozen dressmakers entered, carrying a basket of color swatches, paper, pencils, and tape measures. "Well, that went as planned. I do believe that these women will be far easier to handle in therapy than I first supposed," Shu Wen commented to her three High Counselors.

"Yes, with their arms back, much of their utter helplessness will have been handled. True, they can't see well at all and walking is treacherous, but other than that, they are in remarkably good shape," Bi Mei concluded.

"Still, running the whole session via telepathy is going to be a drain on we four. Any word from Eve yet?" asked Xiu.

"Yes, she will be sending us some help soon. She didn't say exactly when, though. I guess it is time to get back to the Perfect Women again." The four smiled and headed off for their sessions.

"No, for the hundredth time, Bi Mei, I don't what my arms back," Fang replied. "I am a Perfect Woman. Yes, I know that we've been through that operation many times. I know what the mad doctor told me, 'Now I am a Perfect Woman.' Yes, yes, but honestly, Bi Mei, I *am* a Perfect Woman as I am now. Kang Zu loves me; we now have the greatest sex ever. He tilts my head back so my long hair flows down my back, he lays down and puts me on top of him. My breasts are large enough so they hold my head up from him enough so I am in complete control of kissing him. Everything is just perfect. Hey, we went to the dance last week. I met so many wonderful people. Kang and I danced the night away. I'm so very light that he can easily carry me in one arm. I put my head on his shoulder and we danced all night. Everything is really just perfect. Shu Lon Die and her new husband Hu are also in total agreement with us. We are really just perfect as we are. What we all want now is to get Advanced Therapy so that we can have kijutsu and be able to move objects. Then we will be able to care for our own needs and keep our perfect body forms. Please, can't you understand this? All of us, we are just prefect as we are. We don't need to be changed. The others already have found boyfriends too. It's not like we are helpless invalids anymore. We are all alive and quite happy and content with ourselves as we are."

Bi Mei was quite frustrated with Fang and the other Perfect Women, the torso women as she called them. At first, she had erased all the demon traumas the Fang had had, former lifetimes of traumatic and painful deaths. Next, she had dealt with all the opium effects, the drug induced traumas.

Finally, she had gotten Fang and the other women to re-experience their long and painful surgeries. Each woman had eventually uncovered the precise words that the sadistic doctor had uttered to them, which installed the concept that they were now Perfect Women. Bi Mei had then expected the usual to happen. With the source of the idea revealed as merely the aberrated words said by another while they were helpless, unconscious, and in great pain, then they would laugh mightily and no longer have any desire whatsoever to remain a "Perfect Woman." To her and her three top counselors, uniformly this had not happened. Well, it had with Ting Nun, the nurse who still had the upper half of her legs. Her body would soon have its arms restored and her breasts back to their usual size. Not the other eight torso women. All continued to insist that they were Perfect Women as they were. Again today, Fang continued to insist, frustrating Bi Mei even further.

Finally, she had no choice but to consult Macario for help. These eight women had been the first cases that she simply could not handle. He joined with her mind and she explained again all that had been done and the current situation. Macario listened to her with undivided attention. Finally, he answered her. *Look, Bi Mei, we aren't here to superimpose our ideas of ideal life on others or our opinions on how one should conduct and live their lives. Ours is to help them erase the traumas they've experienced and to drill them on regaining their native skills, erasing the trauma barriers that come up while drilling. You're evaluating for her and invalidating her. We don't tell others what deity to worship or even how to worship. We don't tell people how they should live their lives. We don't tell others what they are to think. We don't interfere in their own self-determinism unless their actions are causing more harm than good. Are you not trying to enforce your own ideas of what kind of physical bodies these women ought to have upon them?*

Yes, but...

Perhaps in due time with more handling, they will decide to change their minds about what they wish their bodies to be like. Then again, they might not. If you are confident that you had helped them fully erase the operation trauma, then I suggest that you get on with their Advanced Training, focusing on their ability to move objects.

Am I really doing that? Forcing my ideas of a perfect body off on them? I guess I am, Macario. Damn!

Don't fret about it. I will drop by later tonight and give you and your three counselors a session to help you four out with this. Meantime, have at it.

Thanks. I don't know why we have been so blind, Macario.

We'll find out tonight.

"Okay, Fang, onto Advance Therapy it is. Now I want you to mock up a blue ball out in front of you. Okay, now change its color to red. All right. Make it green. Good. Move it to the left of you five feet. Fine. Now move it to the right of you five feet. Oh, it's stuck over there to your left? Okay, then. . ." Off she went with Fang's Advanced Therapy.

Eve sent our four children to help Bi Mei. While their bodies were going on three years old now, they were all very able beings and eager to help. They spent their days in Nan Yan, but Eve insisted that they return at night so we could enjoy their company as well.

By March, the ten Yingchan had finished their Basic Therapy plus a little of Advanced Therapy as well and were now being trained so that they too could deliver it, that is to use telepathy to "talk" to another. With their arms back, all ten were able to take care of themselves without needing help from another. Although they could only just barely see and barely walk, these deficiencies now seemed rather unimportant to the Golden Angels as they were now commonly called. That they could handle their own bodily needs and deliver this priceless therapy to others was what mattered most. They just allowed more time to move from place to place and to do what they needed to do. Their lives and vitality had been restored to them, and they were determined to give such gifts to other women. They had just enough Advanced Therapy so that they could send their thoughts to another's mind and thus communicate finally. For these ten, this alone was a huge miracle, and it allowed them to be able to deliver therapy to others.

As far as the Perfect Women were concerned, with the heavy focus on the drilling of moving objects, by March, the eight were actually doing so. Many admired how they now levitated their forks and spoons up to their mouths to eat. They even lifted their own bodies up from their beds, sitting them into their special chairs. More than one person was spooked to see these women in their chairs rolling along the halls with no one pushing them. They were uniformly happy women, but continued to insist that they were perfect in all ways.

During this time span, work continued on the planned spring thrust out into the eastern and northern portions of Tan Loc Province. This was to be a coordinated effort between the army, the MMCE engineering staff, and the Church of God. First, General Tao would secure an area. Immediately, the

MMCE staff would begin to implement all the modern improvements, such as electricity and provide any needed relief supplies, such as food and doctors. At the same time, the army of therapy givers of the Church of God would begin systematically giving everyone Basic Therapy. In the case of the women, when it was completed, their arms returned. On paper, the plan seemed sound, but would it work, providing a smooth transition of power and ways?

When the snows finally melted and General Tao finally began marching his army out from Nan Yan, they found that he could retake territory far faster than the MMCE crews and the Church of God members could handle. Thus, he was forced to go at what he considered a snail's pace. Eventually, he began to use some of his forces to "convince" farmers to plant edible crops and not poppies. He left a garrison force in an isolating oval some thirty miles from Shansee, effectively cordoning off that huge hot spot. By the end of summer, his forces controlled all the lands to the mighty Yonshu River to the east and northward to the defensive lines of the drug overlords. In August, his forces had gone far, far beyond the areas being handled by the engineering staff and the Church of God members.

He met with Princess Mei Lon Wu and representatives of the other groups to decide what to do. "The drug lords have positioned their armies just as Wu Shenyan has told us. They've built up a defensive line cordoning off the most defensible hill country north of us. The question now is do I attack them or hold until next year? Already, my lines have gone far, far beyond the rest of yours."

"We can build up the infrastructure only so fast," Jovanni explained. Perhaps by next summer at the very earliest will we finally catch up to your positions!"

"Yes, it will be at least that long for us as well," Bi Mei added. "It is just way too difficult to attempt to coordinate more than about fifty thousand therapy givers at one time."

"Well, I can attack now and clear out all the drug overlords out of Tan Loc Province, retake all lands up to our border with the Lian River. That would provide a natural barrier from the other overlords across the river in Wontun Province. That would give us a far more defensible perimeter, river barriers on all sides, except the zone around Shansee."

Princess Mei Lon asked, "General, what would you prefer to do? What is the safest route to take?"

"Attack now, secure all lands up to the Lian, princess."

"Then, I vote that we do just that," she replied. "Jovanni, what is the biggest barrier that your engineers are facing? What will it take to get more infrastructure built sooner?"

Jovanni chuckled, "Money. It always comes down to money and men, that is, workers who have had their Basic Therapy. We have to order all manner of supplies and that takes money. Already, the wealthy of Nan Yan and other towns are stretched thin. They've invested nearly everything they have. True, in time they will be reaping huge rewards, but now, we have to wait for some of that to come back before we can spend it."

Bi Mei spoke up, "With us, I think that we are going to have to create some additional Churches of God. We've been talking about it all summer. I think that we can take some of the best therapy givers and give them their own churches out there in the eastern portions of Nan Yan. This is the only way that we can see for us to manage such an enormous expansion."

Later when the Golden Angels and the Perfect Women heard about the shortage of money, all ten decided to invest the vast majority of their funds. They divided it among the engineering departments and the Church of God. By fall, work had begun on building four new churches and staffing them as well. They were spread out evenly, based on population density, of the newly controlled territory. Jovanni quickly quadrupled his orders for supplies and equipment, promising by next summer to have MMCE throughout these now controlled lands.

Thus, on August 10, 826, General Tao launched his planned invasion of the drug overlords of northern Tan Loc Province. His soldiers were well paid, had their Basic Therapy, and were anything by apathetic zombies so commonly found in the overlord armies. Further, he did not intend to enduring the type of slaughter committed by the warring overlords around Shansee. His objective was to capture these lands with the minimum cost to his own forces. He lived up to his reputation as a ruthless general. Rather than send in his troops in a massive charge, he chose to use artillery. For the past several years, he'd been purchasing cannonae from various countries. He also made use of Tashien rockets as well.

For the first days of the battle, his forces fired hundreds of rockets into the midst of the enemy lines. Devastating cannonae barrages fired in tandem with rocket bombardments. When he finally ordered his cavalry to advance on the enemy positions, they had little to do except mop up actions. All fight had gone out of the defenders, who were not already dead, wounded, or who had not routed, fleeing for their lives.

In one week's time, he had taken out all the defending overlords and their armies. Many of the overlords and their top men fled across the Lian River. That could not be prevented; General Tao would deal with them later. His army confiscated a large amount of equipment, which he planned to use in the further expansion of his army. A small amount of gold and gems was also recovered.

Of more interest were the other Yingchan that were found as they captured the various overlord strongholds. Most were the abandoned wives of the overlords. These women, General Tao kept together where some of his men could assist them with their needs. The last Yingchan they found was Li Tazau, Dai's mother, nearly alone and forgotten in Mag's empty estate in Nag Tasha. General Tao then sent the ten Yingchan back to Nan Yan and the Church of God there. He had no other way to help them.

"Mother? Is that really you?" Dai wanted to call out as the women were slowly entering the church. She could only make unintelligible noises however. Wu had told her that she had been rescued and another ten Yingchan were to arrive soon. Dai wanted to run to her mother, throw her arms around her, and hug her tightly. Yet, she struggled to spot her mother, and she was forced to wave her arms wildly as she tried her best to hurry and not fall down. Her fast motion seemed more like slow motion, however. Wu spoke for her and for Li.

Li was half-starved and very weak. She was on her feet and walking very slowly only because a kindly soldier was holding her upright. "Li, here is your daughter, Dai, my wife now," Wu explained, taking a hold of Li from the grateful soldier. At last, Dai reached her mother and both moved their heads slightly to glimpse each other. Big smiles appeared beneath the golden veils. Dai threw her arms around Li and hugged her tightly. Wu added, "Yes, Li, Dai has her arms back. Soon you will have yours as well."

Li nearly collapsed, and Wu carried her to her new bedroom. He and Dai bathed her, dressed her in clean clothes, and then fed her. At last, feeling a tad stronger, Li sat looking Dai over, from head to toe. Tears trickled down Li's face, and Wu tried to handle the communication between the two, but failed. Fortunately, Bi Mei came to talk with Li, and she formed a Mind Link between mother and daughter, allowing them to talk to each other for the first time since Dai was a little girl. They had much to share.

On the other hand, Bi Mei was pleasantly surprised to discover that the other nine Yingchan had normal feet. They could also see drastically better. Their golden eyes did not have pinholes, but holes about a quarter of an inch, allowing much improved sight. Further, they all could speak. They were "proper" Yingchan, Bi Mei soon learned. While these women were angry that they had been captured, they also felt utterly betrayed by their husbands who had fled, leaving them at the mercy of the conquering army. Their emotions were quite mixed, even more so now that they realized that here they could get their arms back and be normal Yingchan once more.

While the Church of God was now once more overloaded, General Tao now had to change strategies. The vast territories now had to be thoroughly searched for remnants of the enemy army. An accurate assessment of the situation facing the conquered towns, villages, and farms had to be made. A defensive perimeter had to be established in order to protect all the MMCE workers and the Church of God workers. Plus, the many poppy fields had to be burned to prevent reopening of opium factories.

By the middle of the fall, the massive survey was finally completed. The results were staggering, but not unexpected. Few women over fifty remained alive, victims of the plague and constant neglect by their husbands who were overworked, beaten, abducted into the armies, or outright killed. Many women were in very poor physical condition; proper nutrition had been difficult to obtain. In sharp contrast, very few men between eighteen and thirty were found, because they had been pressed into armies, the drug trade, or murdered for protesting. Older men were now doing the work of two just in order to survive and maintain what remained of their decimated families. Only the teens and children fared halfway decently.

A sharp contrast in emotional tones was sharply visible. The older were primarily in apathy, having long ago given up nearly completely, accepting whatever came their way. The children had not yet been so oppressed. In fact, for the first time ever, they had been mostly neglected by their parents, who struggled just to keep everyone alive. The boys had taken responsibility for the girls in their families or sometimes their neighbors. This was particularly so in the many families who were missing one or more of their parents, which was more than half of the homes.

Given the unique circumstances of this huge new territory of Tan Loc, the MMCE folks and the Church of God decided to take a different approach. The children could be handled rapidly through their Basic Therapy. With the young women back to battery swiftly, they and the boys could be pressed into helping with the reconstruction efforts, while the Church of God dealt with the apathy cases of the adults. By November, the result of this change in strategy was definitely working out. The teens threw themselves into the many MMCE projects, eager to bring these marvelous inventions to themselves and their families. For a time, the engineers were hard pressed to keep up with the demand the children generated.

Every farmstead was visited to make sure that they had seed grains for the spring planting season. Many did not, having been forced to eat even that just to stay alive. Hence, much seed was imported from the Greenway, arriving in plenty of time for the 827 planting season. Meanwhile, the heavier construction projects, such as building new electricity generation plants and new railroad lines were done by the regular MMCE work crews. By the end of the 827 work season, Jovanni anticipated that a rail line would reach the second largest city in Tan Loc Province, Giang, located at the fork between the mighty Yonshu River and the Yan River which originated in the upper Nan Yan valley. Another main line ran north through what had been the strongholds of the drug lords. A large number of shorter branch lines would T into these two main lines, servicing many smaller towns.

Further, a survey team accompanied by a regiment of cavalry began exploration of the many east-west ridge lined valley systems to the north of Nan Yan. They were searching for potential new sources of coal, iron, copper, and other raw materials vital to the continued expansion of the MMCE projects. When the snows finally forced them to return to Nan Yan, over a dozen new sites had been found. Now they had to find the manpower to open up these new fields, a difficult challenge to meet. The magnitude of the loss of so many younger men was being sharply felt in Tan Loc Province.

The question being asked the winter of 826 was this. Should General Tao release some of his soldiers to satisfy the intense demand for strong, young men to work the mines and heavier construction or should he keep them ready for either defense or offensive actions next year? In the end, they reached a compromise. General Tao would drastically scale down his next spring offensive and release over ten thousand men who wanted to work the heavier construction projects.

As Eve and I looked over the grim statistics that slowly came in to us in Velona from Tan Loc Province, we realized a significant detail. While the stories of a few women were horrific and while so many women suffered horribly from the plague and the aftereffects, which were often the neglect of them by the men in their lives, the actual numerical losses suffered by the younger men of Tan Loc Province dwarfed those of the women! So many had simply died, frequently by a gunshot or stabbing, and often they had been either murdered or been killed while being a soldier. Throughout the vast majority of Tan Loc, young women now outnumbered their counterparts by two to one. Only in the greater Nan Yan valley system were the numbers in parity. This loss of a generation of manpower was only now becoming acutely felt in Tan Loc Province.

Chapter 71 Economic Collapse and the Desert Dwellers

Bao Trong took a wheelbarrow full of the newly minted iron coins with him. He and his family were desperate for food. His wealth was long gone now, spent largely on his opium addiction and gambling habits. Half delirious part of each day, he was roused by his wife and children begging him for food, anything that they could eat. Sadly, he returned home with a single loaf of bread in his now empty wheelbarrow. All around the once mighty Imperial City, people were slowly starving to death. Gold and silver coins had all but vanished, some said into the pockets of the drug overlords. Some said it had all gone to the pleasure palaces, while others claimed the gambling houses took away all the gold.

Overlord Bin Zhou didn't care what anyone believed anymore. He'd solved the money problem by minting iron coins. His soldiers then forced everyone to accept them as legal tender. Of course, he had no inkling of economics. The merchants accepted the worthless coins for what they would bring to them when melted down and made into horseshoes, wrought iron fences, and so on. By March 826, a loaf of bread from the baker cost a wheelbarrow of the metal coins. Although the population was forced to use these coins as tender, everyone thought that they were worthless and thus continued to demand large and larger volumes of them for any given item being purchased.

Worse, the outlying farmers, who depended upon bringing their products to the once lucrative markets in Zau, now began to take other items in trade or exchange. A black market barter system slowly began evolving. As the spring came, bartering finally came to the Imperial City. To understand what began to occur, one must grasp the situation that millions of farmers in the eastern breadbasket country had after the plague struck them. Geography now plays a vital role in grasping what was happening. The Yonshu River runs north-south through Zau. Two thirds of Wontun Province lies to the west of the river, while one third runs down to the eastern ocean. This top agricultural zone stretched from about a hundred miles west of the huge river and extends eastward down to the coast and the large port of Shankou. So what happened to the millions of farmers?

Each farmstead usually was home to an extended family, sometime numbering up to thirty men, women, and children. Labor intensive, a third of the farming work was done by the older women, though some women remained in the homes handling the necessary domestic duties, which was why they were not doing half of the work around the farms. When the plague struck, suddenly one third of the work was no longer being done. Worse, the men how had to spend long hours each day helping their womenfolk. The result was simple, production crashed to only about a third of what it was in the pre-plague days. Hurt worst were the larger cities whose tens of millions utterly depended on timely shipments from the many farmers.

Suddenly faced with having to accept iron coins in payment, they began charging exorbitant amounts of coins based on their perceived worth of that much iron to themselves and their farms. In turn, those who processed the raw products also tacked on their fair share, resulting by March of 826 of a loaf of bread costing a wheelbarrow full of iron. Quickly, that became unworkable, they had more raw iron now than they could ever use and they began bartering on the quiet.

Soon, they took advantage of the desperate city dwellers. Perhaps taking advantage of is too harsh a word. The farmers began to accept older boys and teens in exchange for significant quantities of their products. In turn, these boys and teens were then required to work on the farms, helping to product larger crops and such. While some claimed that they were being turned into slaves, in fact very quickly the bartered kids had a very different idea about it. They were well fed and had a dry roof over their heads. The farmers knew that if they were to be worth anything to them in the fields and other heavy work, the kids had to have their strength and health. Thus, the "slaves" were very well cared for and soon were extremely happy with the deal. Most had been slowly starving to death in the city. Now they could eat their fill and so were most pleased. As youngsters, they learned the needed skills rapidly and became good workers for the farmers. Everyone won on the farms. Overlord Bin saw this as a benefit as well, since thousands of starving older boys and teens were leaving the city. This meant fewer mouths to feed and fewer troubles for their families. Hence, Overlord Bin intentionally overlooked the whole barter system. That he was ruling over a dying city never occurred to him.

The new seat of true power slowly shifted to the port city of Shankou, with its ready access to a vast fishing fleet. By the summer of 826, the Imperial City of Zau, once home to nearly thirty million, now had but a third of that. Worse, virtually all the nobles and wealthy were gone. Some had immigrated to Nan Yan. A few finally left the city to go stay with relatives in other outlying towns, villages, and farms.

Many had become opium addicts and squandered their wealth, eventually dying of starvation along with their helpless wives and children. Two of every three homes were vacant and had long ago been ransacked for anything of value to trade for food. Now others were slowly dismantling them using the wood for firewood in the wintertime.

Overlord Yi controlled the lands to the west of the Yonshu River, that is, the crop lands portion. As he watched the slow disintegration of Zau, he realized the mistakes that Bin Zhou was making and attempted not to make the same ones in his lands. As a result, by the summer, his soldiers were now actually protecting the farmers, not harassing them.

The remaining drug overlords who controlled the highlands along the east-west Lian River that bordered on Tan Loc Province also had problems. With the total loss of the southern drug lord lands last year to General Tao's forces, they were the sole producers of opium now. However, almost none of their shipments were paid in gold as usual. There was none to be had, save that which was being mined, and that was closely hoarded by the miners. They saw where the economy was rapidly heading and took action. One by one, these drug lords ceased their operations and quietly moved elsewhere, their huge bankrolls secure in many Banca del Dio accounts. Some never made it to their final destinations and were never heard from again. Most headed eventually into Shankou, the last thriving metropolis in plague-stricken Tashien.

What of their soldiers and the farmers who grew their poppies? They were left to fend for themselves. By the summer of 826, most farmers were plowing under their fields of poppies and frantically attempting to get some kind of cash crop in before the fall, hoping for a late fall this year. Most of the soldiers had been abducted from towns, villages, and farmsteads. These men quietly returned to their original homes.

General Tao's 826 offensive was to bring the second largest city of Tan Loc Province under his control, Giang, and to extend his control towards the eastern ocean as far as possible. Slowly, he discovered that the drug overlord armies across the Lian River were disintegrating. He took advantage of this by reducing drastically the number of his soldiers guarding the river crossings, pulling them into the actual battles far to the east. Thus, by the end of the 826 season, his forces controlled all of Tan Loc Province except for a hemisphere thirty miles across centered on Shansee in the far south.

Geographically, just north of the semiarid poppy fields of the drug lords lay the great desert of Xi, stretching nearly a thousand miles from the mountains down to almost a hundred miles west of the Yonshu River, where fields were fertile once again. The desert began about a hundred miles north of the Lian River and reached up to the Jan River Valley, of which the last town was Mong Yu, from where the Golden Warrior came a century before. Roughly five hundred miles wide and a thousand miles long, this zone received little rain, cut off from both the southerly winds and the northern winds by the extreme heat of the Desert of Desolation and the impassable mountains.

Yet here in this arid land other ancient traditions still were followed. Among these was the post of local Seneschal or the local ruler. He, as most of the darker yellow-skinned inhabitants of the Xi, carried on the tradition of Lunula, which derived its name from the crescent-shaped area of the fingernail. That is, the higher one's status in society is, the longer are one's fingernails, with the Seneschal's nails being the longest of all. The length of a man's nails reflected the degree of physical labor that he performed. The lowly farmers and blacksmiths, for example, kept their nails as short as possible, they could not afford the luxury of long nails, which would impeded their work or broke readily as they worked. On up the ladder of less work and higher wealth and social standing went men's nail lengths, until one reached the local Seneschal, whose nails were always at least six inches long or longer. Naturally, he never did any real physical work with his hands; rather, he was supposed to be using his mind and brains. At least that was the traditional interpretation of Lunula.

The women of each family also allowed their nails to reach the same lengths as their family elder, though the women often painted theirs. Various shades of red were the commonest colors used. Those of higher social status also painted their lips and wore a deep black eye shadow as well. Women also wore a shaka or headdress. Much like a skullcap, these contained and reflected the wealth and status of the woman. The shaka of the wives of the Seneschal were made from gold and formed a mesh over their heads, draping down over their ears, foreheads, and down their cheeks, touching their shoulders. Made from pure gold, the shaka were heavy and in the more expensive ones, contained rubies, sapphires, and diamonds. Even a simple, married village woman wore a shaka, given to her as a combined wedding present. Her family provided the base shell of gold and the husband donated enough gold and gemstones as befitting her new social status.

While the shaka were magnificent jewelry in and of themselves adding to the beauty of the women, they were also practical. If a woman lost her husband, she could live off her shaka, by slowly removing gems or bits of gold as needed. Additionally, those of the lowest standing still braided their long hair, often tying it up into a bun to keep it out of their way while working. Those women of slightly higher standing on up never braided their hair, but allowed it to fall wide and full, often draping it across their front and not down their backs. The shaka was perfectly suited to this different hairstyle. In fact, a woman would be disgraced if she were ever seen I public without her shaka on her head. Women only removed them when they were washing their hair.

When a young woman reached puberty, one by one she had her teeth pulled and a golden tooth inserted. Thus, most all adult women all had a golden smile. Rare was a Xi region woman who had tooth decay problems. Men who had such troubles also had gold tooth replacements when needed.

Additionally, the ancient practice of binding one's feet, while outlawed throughout Tashien centuries ago, was still practiced here in the wilds of Xi. Shortly after birth, a girl child had her feet broken and the front half was bound back over the top of her foot so that her toes touched the front of her ankle. Long bandages were kept wrapped tightly around the girl's feet for the rest of her life. When she was old enough, special tiny, soft covered shoes were given to her, and she was helped to learn to walk in them. I say walk, but hobbled as they were, only just barely could they manage a few steps on their own. It was common practice for their husbands to hold them securely when they had to walk any significant distances, especially for those of the highest social standing.

Not all girl babies had their feet bound, however. Only those girls born into a family, which was halfway up the social ladder, had theirs bound, for one of high standing would never marry a woman whose feet were not tiny. Those whose feet were not bound were never to gain higher standing, unless they underwent a very painful operation on their feet as an adult. Seldom did that happen.

The women wore brightly embroidered, white cotton dresses for the most part, while men wore white, loose fitting shirts and pantaloons fastened a few inches below the knees. All shoes were soft skinned. The men's were more like sandals, well suited to the hot, desert sands. Silk garments were never worn.

The desert environment was hot and dry. Consequently, during the day, if a person was to be outside, they wore a white, hooded, cotton robe. For the women with their heavy gold shaka, this was critical to keep the searing heat off the metal that clung to their entire heads. Although the robes were unisex, one could always tell a woman from the gold hanging down her face and cheeks, if not from her feet.

Goats and sheep predominated in the Xi region. Dates and figs were harvested along with honey and exported as well. In the more distant ridge line hills, men mined for gold and gems. The villages tended to be centered on an oasis, where water seeped up from beneath the ground. Every village had its own Seneschal, whose word was law. Transportation was mostly by camel, though there were a few horses near the edges of the Xi region. The leader of a camel caravan was of sufficiently high status. Thus, he wore his nails about two inches long, and their wives were the lowest status women whose feet were bound. These men knew the land and were depended upon to move goods and people from village to village. Without their superb navigation sense, all would be lost, hence their status.

Of course, in the families with bound feet, domestic help was always at hand to assist these higher status women with household menial tasks. Meal preparation and clean up, house cleaning, laundry, and similar chores became the responsibilities of the working class woman, who were called the zhenhui. The women with bound feet were called the xanqiao, the refined, elegant, artful women. This is not to say that the xanqiao were lazy and did nothing. Rather, these women, who made excellent use of their hands, did all the magnificent embroidery found on both men's shirts and women's dresses. They also sewed the women's dresses as well. The xanqiao also were the village teachers and taught all the younger children up to the age of twelve. Many of these women were also superb singers. Friday nights, they performed some of the many historical songs for the village Gaoshi, a song and dance festival designed to instill the honoring of the ancient ways into everyone's mind and heart.

Among the women, then, a simple division of labor separated women based primarily on whether she had small, bound feet, which dictated which type of work she was able to handle. In contrast, among the men of Xi since all were inherently capable of work, fingernail length and thus status became the dividing principle. Common laborers had no nail length. Merchants kept theirs extending at least an inch. The Seneschal of the village allowed his to reach at least six inches as his work was mental, planning for the survival of his village, adjudicating disputes, and other administrative duties.

Because of the weekly Gaoshi, which everyone attended, the ancient traditions were kept alive and present in everyone. They heard these songs of history all their lives. It was a great social affront not to be present at the Gaoshi. This is the primary reason why the traditions outlawed elsewhere in Tashien were continued here in Xi. This is also why their society was a fairly closed one, and few outsiders were allowed into their desert region. Communications with the outside world beyond the desert was kept to the bare necessities. Most trading went through their largest town of Yutshu, home to ten thousand and at the southeastern gateway into the Xi. Here, traders brought in items to swap for gold and gems. Hardly anyone dared to venture further into Xi, especially Imperial Soldiers. Without a camel caravan leader, their chances of survival after one hundred miles was zero. Water was only found at the random oasis villages. Unless one knew the precise locations of these, he or she was doomed. Few dared go further than Yutshu. Thus, the ancient peoples of Xi were rather autonomous, although still part of Tashien and the Empire.

The modern invention of the long gun had come slowly to Xi, though never replacing the saber and curved stiletto dagger their warriors carried. Although these people were not warlike by nature, they fiercely defended their desert lands from outsiders. More than once, the sun-bleached skull of an invader was found — his body buried vertically in a sand pit with only his head above the sands. Ants and other vermin were left to strip his skull clean, while the relentless sun cooked the man's brains. Such warning signs dotted the outer perimeter of Xi and were carefully heeded by most men who valued their lives.

Deep in the Matag Ridge Line Valley some hundred fifty miles west of Yutshu lay the rural village of Matag, the namesake of this extensive valley desert system. Home to nearly a thousand, Matag was a thriving village before the plague struck them hard. Two hundred fifty adobe homes lined the hard packed sands of this oasis village, roughly oval occupying a square mile of the valley floor. Centrally located, the crystal clear waters of the three hundred foot, circular pond was the life hub of the village, as such water sources were for all villages of the Xi. First Street paralleled the edges of the pond and was the most important avenue of the village. All the villages were laid out in a similar fashion, with the key avenue encircling the oasis. The side closest to the pond held no houses, providing public access to life giving water. On the opposite side were the homes and businesses of the most important people of the village.

Concentric elliptical streets fanned out from First Street, with spoke side streets connecting them. The lowest in status lived on the outermost street. Here many of the common laborers lived as well as the village guards, who would be first in line to protect the village from any outside attack or threat. The homes were constructed from red-orange adobe bricks. Square, each single story structure supported a domed ceiling, which was painted to reflect ancient gods, the nighttime skies, and artful scenes of the world, all done using gay colors. Indeed, one often relaxed by lying down and admiring the magnificent overhead paintings.

Village life was centered on the Seneschal. Matag's Seneschal Shi Yushube, forty-five at the time of the plague, had the first home on First Street, next to the traditional open aired theater where the village met on Friday evenings for the Gaoshi song and dances. Shi was the official leader of Matag and the most highly respected man of all. His wife was Qing, forty-four. She was perhaps the most highly skilled embroiderer in Matag and many prided themselves on wearing one of her creations, either a dress or a shirt. She also led the Gaoshi each Friday night and taught school in the theater, though she had recently been transferring her teaching duties to her eldest daughter, Shan. Shi kept his nails nicely manicured at six inches from his fingertips, a respectful length. He wore his long black hair in a single braid and spouted a very long moustache, whose ends now fell some six inches to either side of his mouth, a most dignified length. Shi was a stickler for tradition and protocols as befitting the village leader and arbitrator. His ultimate goal was to lead the village to greater prosperity and survival potential. Qing's shaka was huge and filled with many rubies and emeralds. Its sidepieces fell to the tops of her breasts. Her golden smile always captivated everyone, for her lips always appeared to be smiling, even if she was not intentionally doing so.

Their son, Tian, was twenty-three and cut a dashing figure about the village. Groomed to succeed his father as Seneschal, Tian's nails were also six inches in length. Two years before the plague struck, he had defied tradition slightly by marrying the woman he loved, Ting Yang, the daughter of the village caravan owner, Peng Yang, whose home was on Second Avenue, just northeast of the theater, quite close to the Yushube home. Ting was the lowest of the social classes who still had bound feet. Had she not, Shi would have forbidden the marriage as far beneath that of a future Seneschal. They had a baby girl now, Wen. Often, Peng Yang and his wife Mata were found visiting with the Yushube's, related strongly now by the fortuitous marriage of their daughter. Indeed, marrying the future Seneschal had elevated Ting's social standing enormously. Wholly unprepared for this new status, Qing took Ting under her wing, teaching her what she would need to know when her husband became the village Seneschal.

The Yushube's had two daughters, Shan, twenty, and Shu, eighteen. Both looked remarkably like their mother, with oval faces and strong facial bones. As befitting their high status, they and their mother wore their nails six inches long as well, painted bright red. Each woman's shaka was almost as heavy, long, and lavish as their mother's shaka. Of course, they had bound feet as well. Shan had recently begun taking over her mother's teaching duties at the theater, right next to their home. Shan was betrothed to Jian Wie, the twenty-one year old son of their next door neighbor, Medan Wie, the village finance minister, whose nails were a respectable five inches. He was fifty and his wife was Xue, forty-six and the village calligraphy expert. None could make characters like Xue. Jian had also taken over one of his father's duties, village historian, which allowed him to keep his nails at five inches also. Although

Shan's were six inches, he kept his shorter than hers out of respect for her higher status. With the wedding only months away, Medan Wie and his family were also frequently in the Yushube home.

The youngest daughter, Shu, was eighteen, bright eyed and clever for her age. She was dating Pengdu Pong, the twenty year old son of Liang Pong, the village food supplier, whose house and store was next to the Wei's home. The forty-three year old man had the terrific responsibility of ensuring that there was sufficient food available for all families in Matag. Everyone shopped for their food supplies at his large store. His home was adjacent to the shop. His foot bound wife, Yudu, was forty and acted as his assistant, for running the store was more than a full time occupation and a most vital one at that. One day, his son Pengdu would take over operations from him, a highly respected position. His nails were always at least four inches long, though Yudu allowed hers to extend some five inches as befitting her higher status than his. She was a cousin of Shi Yushube. Liang had an eighteen year old daughter, Shesong, who was the dearest friend of Shu's. Ever since childhood, the two girls were inseparable. Thus, the Pong family was also frequently around the Yushube house as well.

With so many women in the Yushube home, he had three hired assistants to deal with the mundane home chores. Lindi Nag was their thirty year old cook, wife of Boan Nag, the house builder. Her ten year old daughter, Caili, was always with her, while their eleven year old son, Dag, was always with his father. Lindi was an excellent cook and her duties included the shopping, meal preparations, and cleanup work. She and her daughter wore their nails one inch long, quite respectable for a cook.

Next, Juli Jiaon, twenty-four, was the personal assistant to Qing, Shan, and Shu, helping them with whatever they needed done. Often, she helped them walk longer distances, such as the few hundred feet to the theater. Juli had a six year old daughter, Caibi, who was always with her. Her husband was Dechen Jiaon, twenty-six. He was the village painter and artist responsible for the finest of the home dome paintings. Their five year old son, Gang, followed his father around from painting job to painting job. Both Juli and Dechen kept their nails two inches long, for he was a famous, skilled painter of some renown.

The Yushube's also employed a maid, Chani Pheng, twenty, who handled the cleaning of the home, the laundry, and similar activities. She was married to one of the village guards, Hojie Pheng, twenty-one. Coming from a slightly higher status family, her nails were two inches long, but his were only one at most. Hojie was a strong, skilled fighter, though he preferred his saber to the long gun.

Thus, before the plague came, there were always many people coming and going from the Yushube home, in addition to those who came to seek the Seneschal's assistance on some matter of importance. Qian always played the role of smiling host, her lips always gave such an appearance, her golden teeth only adding to the overall effect created by her huge shaka with its many rubies and emeralds adding vivid colors as well.

Just before the plague came, late Friday afternoon, Juli, her arm around Shan, opened their door, leading Shan inside. Shan had walked several hundred feet home from the theater, where she'd just finished the day's lessons for twenty children. Her feet, like the other bound feet, were barely five inches in total length. Her heel proper was two inches and supported her weight. What was left of her arch and foot was barely three inches long, her toes just barely touching the front bottom of her leg. This three-inch portion helped her keep her balance somewhat, but it was painful and terribly awkward to walk such a distance on her own. She depended upon Juli to help her with this long a walk. Her long, thick black hair was a bit tangled from the light breeze and was draped perfectly over her front side falling to just below her knees.

"We're home, mom," she called out well in advance of her actual arrival in the family living room where a number of soft couches provided the usual perches for the bound footed women. Setting aside her current sewing project, Qian used her long nails to gently lift up her long bushy tresses so that she could rise to greet her daughter. Always rising on her own was a tricky maneuver to retain her balance and avoid teetering too far forward and thus falling. After a bit of wiggling adjustment to her standing position, she began walking towards the door though which Shan would soon be entering. Her steps were tiny and carefully made, and Qian now let her lovely hair fall straight down her front, adjusting its fall slightly while using her arms to help her keep her balance on her tiny feet.

Shan met her about halfway across the room. She could move slightly faster because of the support provided by Juli. Mother and daughter met and hugged each other briefly, while Juli quietly slipped her other arm around Qian to help support her as well. While the two women made their slow way over to the couches, Shan gaily explained, "I do so like teaching the children, mom. Such bright faces are uplifting, especially when you see that they have understood something for the first time." Her golden teeth shone brightly outlined by her cherry red lips.

"Ah, yes, dear. I find that I am missing that too. Perhaps, I ought to have given you my embroidery job and kept my teaching position," Qian replied, flashing her golden smile as well.

"You wouldn't dare!" Shan feigned a shocked look. Both women chuckled as they approached their couches. With Juli still holding them, they turned around and used their long talons to gather their hair before their bodies, then carefully sat down, arranging their hair nicely before themselves. "Juli, could you please bring me my hairbrush? I am afraid that the wind has messed mine up a bit this afternoon."

"Yes, Miss Shan. Might I also suggest that I bring your mirror and lipstick? You might want to freshen up before Jian arrives for supper," Juli hinted. Shan flashed her a huge, golden smile.

While Juli went to fetch them, Shu and Shesong, arm in arm, came walking slowly into the living room. "Hi sis, how went school today?" Shu asked her older sister, as she and her girlfriend continued to make their slow, careful way into the room, heading for a vacant couch. Long ago, the two had learned that by holding on to each other, they both could walk fairly well, without having to depend upon personal assistants. Both teens enjoyed this small bit of freedom that this offered them. Shu was slightly shorter than her sister was, and Shesong was noticeably shorter. The teen's shakas also looked rather different, with Shu's being as huge as her sister's was, while Shesong's, although long, lacked many of the rubies and emeralds of the Yushube sister's shakas. Additionally, Shesong's nails were much shorter than the bright red talons of the sisters.

"Oh I do love it so, sis! How was your day? Is Pengdu coming by tonight?" Shan asked demurely, teasing her younger sister slightly and raising a flush on Shesong's cheeks, who was always a bit flustered when her older brother was around Shu. She didn't yet have a boyfriend; perhaps that was the root cause for the teen's fluster.

"I hope so. He promised to walk me and Shesong to the theater tonight. He'd better come," Shu replied, as she and Shesong reached a couch and carefully turned around. Using their hands and long nails, the two gathered up their long hair moving it out of their way and sat down, adjusting it before them once more. Both teens had already touched up their makeup, anticipating their dinner guests. The four chatted and later watched Shan as she skillfully adjusted her makeup and brushed out her hair.

Shan had barely finished when Juli announced that Tian and his wife Ting had arrived. All four skillfully rose, anticipating their arrival. Soon, Tian and Ting entered. While Tian held his lovely wife supporting her slow walk, she held on to their little girl, Wen, who was nearly two. After the perfunctory bows all around, Tian helped his wife and baby get seated on another couch, while the two teens slowly moved over to have a good look at Wen and play with her a bit, relieving Ting for a few minutes.

Juli again called out, announcing that Jian and Pengdu had both just arrived. Shan's heart skipped, and she again rose, making sure that she looked her best. Shu flushed and rose to meet her heartthrob as well, likewise, adjusting the fall of her bushy hair with her long talons. Shesong merely giggled and continued to ogle at Wen. Both young men entered and bowed to all the women in turn, before going over to their girlfriends and kissing them lightly on their outstretched hands. At once, their arms encircled their waists, giving the two much needed support as they continued to stand on their heels in their soft soled shoes.

"You smell like dates," Shu teased Pengdu, who grinned. He'd been dealing with a load of dates all that afternoon. All began chatting, until Shi finally entered. At once, everyone bowed respectfully to the older man, who returned their bows.

"I have two more marriages to perform next week," Shi announced. Their talk now focused on the two young couples. Shan, Shu, and Shesong wanted to hear all about the couples' plans. He was saved from this by Lindi's supper call. The men put their arms around their women's waists and began the slow walk into the dining room, still chatting about the two weddings.

When dinner was finished, Peng and Wen Yang arrived, along with Medan and Xue Wie and Liang and Yudu Pong. All were going to the Gaoshi together this Friday night. The four older men began chatting about the day's news as they often did, allowing their wives to make last minute adjustments to their appearance.

"Got in a load of dates today. Looks like a fine crop this year," Peng reported. His caravan of camels had deposited their loads at Pong's store.

"Fine dates, Peng," Liang added. "Took Pengdu all afternoon to get them on the shelves. "Good crop. Where did you find them?"

"Up by Yutix. Got a good price for them."

"Isn't that close to the Valley of the Fallen Beasts?" asked Medan, the historian turned financier.

His son, Jian nodded, while Peng replied, "Yes, about ten miles further up that valley."

"Well, it is good to hear that crops in Xi are doing well this fall," Shi commented. "We will not have to worry about shortages this winter. I heard that the honey crop was exceptional this year. One of the honey producer's son's is getting married next week, so I got the inside scoop." Shi flashed his long nails accordingly.

"We're ready," Qian announced, walking slowly back into the living room, now filled with smoke from the many after-dinner pipes of the four older men. At once, the men moved to put their arms around the various womenfolk, and slowly they headed off to the theater, some hundred feet north of the Yushube home. The husbands and other children of their three servants also met their wives just outside, escorting them to the Gaoshi as well. As they approached the theater, the streets were filled with others, since all thousand residents were headed there at the same time.

The theater had a main stage, one step up from the street. Looking outward and north from the stage, rows of adobe seats rose higher and higher. The bound footed women and their families were seated in the lower rows, while those women with normal feet took the higher seats. Seating was also delineated by the lengths of fingernails, with those with the longest nails sitting closer to the stage and those with the shortest nails sitting in the topmost rows.

Several musicians took their seats on the stage, along with Qing and several other singers. Four women and three men composed the vocal portion, with the men supporting the standing women as they performed. The first half of the performance covered the traditional songs, which helped infuse their cultural heritage in the young. Qing sang and danced superbly, though dance meant something different than one might imagine. She moved her hips, arms, and upper body with grace and seduction, akin to belly dancing. Her feet remained fixed, of course.

The second half featured dance music. Many couples danced, including many bound footed women. Holding on tightly to their men, the women were able to move about in small steps, which is good since each row was rather narrow. Actually, the theater adobe levels had been designed with the restrictions that these women faced. This part of the evening, all young men and women looked forward to all week long, and romances blossomed frequently at these communal gatherings. Further, it was the one time during the week that anyone of any position in their society could ask anyone of any position for a short dance; marital, nail, and feet statuses were cast aside for two hours each week.

"We'll hold Wen, Ting, so you and Tian can have this next dance," Qing said to her daughter-in-law, who flashed her a big thank you. Tian readily handed her his daughter and whisked Ting off her feet. None of these thousand had any remote idea that this would be their last enjoyable Gaoshi! Two days later, the entire village was suffering horribly from the alien plague!

The women lost their arms and major status symbol, their long nails. Their breasts seemed to have exploded in size, while their hair grew another two feet, most now touching the ground easily. That their waists were tiny was hardly noticed by the women, save the larger women, who grumbled about that as well. The women who had normal feet now found themselves with feet so distorted that they resembled those with bound feet, save that they now had to wear the special alien high-heeled shoes that appeared mysteriously in their homes. Those with bound feet found that their small bit of arch, which had been the front of their feet and on which they had depended to help keep their balance while standing, had become grossly bent, so much so that now they neither could stand on their heels nor could they stand on their bent down arches. That is, with their feet so arched and curved downward, the front of their arches touched the ground and they could not bend them up enough to get their heels on the ground as they normally did. The bound foot women suddenly were unable to stand or walk! The alien shoes simply did not fit the shape of their feet, not even remotely.

The men's feet were pointed straight downward, thus they could not stand up either. They could crawl, which they began doing. Fortunately, the women's dresses were short enough that the bound footed women could move around a little on their knees and were not immobile because of the plague.

That first day, after the terror-filled screaming died down, Shi and Tian began helping the women in their home. At least the women's dresses still were serviceable. Their bodices were laced down the center. With their huge melons now protruding enormously, the men were still able to tie the laces, though much of their cleavage was plainly visible through the wide-open laces. Still, I think across all of Tarra, only these women still had serviceable dresses after the plague struck.

"My god, Shi, what has happened to us all?" the terror-filled voice of Qing asked as he tied off the laces of her dress and began straightening out her hair with his long talons.

Pale faced and quite shaken, Shi could only reply lamely, "I don't know. Surely, our servants will come soon. When they do, I will go and see if I can find out."

"Daddy, we are helpless!" Shan wailed. "Do something, please!" his terrified daughter wailed.

"Keep calm, sis. Help will soon be coming," Tian replied. "Dad, I've got to help Ting and Wen. They are still in our bedroom." He left, crawling quickly to help his own wife and baby.

The servants did not come, and Shi found himself facing the daunting task of preparing his extended family something to eat. With his long nails, this was challenging, all the more so since he'd never cooked a meal in his life! After the two men fed the four women, Tian and Shi decided that they had to do something.

"Look dad, everyone in Matag is going to be looking to us for answers. What are we going to tell them?"

Shi pulled on his moustaches. Never had any Seneschal ever faced such a crisis. "I don't know, my son. I don't know. First, we must find out why our servants have not come this morning. Perhaps this has happened to others. Tian, I am charging you to go check on our friends and our three servants and their families. We must get a handle on the situation. How many are effected. Surely not everyone. This is some kind of supernatural event, I think. The gods must have struck us down."

"You can't be serious, dad! Gods striking us down?"

"How can you explain the sudden loss of our women's arms, the unnatural growth of their breasts, and the distortion of all our feet? Go and see how others are faring. We cannot leave the women alone now, for they are so very helpless. My god, no arms at all. Where did they go? What could have possibly caused this? I just don't know. Go now, find out what you can," Shi ordered.

After Tian left, crawling on all fours, Shi reentered the living room where the four women were now sitting on their couches. All were still shaking from fear, their faces wet from crying. However, they were also staring at the large pile of alien objects in the center of the room. Shi finally decided to have a good look at the objects. "Qing, we have four hairbrushes with strange leather-like loops on them. What are the loops for, dear? Any ideas?" he asked.

Shan answered instead. Her father pointing them out to her had just jogged some strange images in her mind. "Dad, maybe we are supposed to put our feet through the loops." He brought each woman a hairbrush and slipped off their ill-fitting soft soled shoes, kissing each woman's toes as tradition dictated, honoring the woman. "Wow, mom! Look at me! I can touch my nose with my foot. Never could do that before," she added. All four began experiencing just how more limber they actually were. Soon, they got their feet into the brushes and began experimenting. Before long, they discovered that it was far easier to brush someone else's hair than their own.

"Well, I wonder about these boots," Shi commented holding up a pair of the ballet alien boots. "I wonder if they might fit you better, Qing?" He brought them over for her and tried them on her feet. Her feet only went about half way down into the boot before becoming tight. Her foot was twice the thickness of a normal foot, because her feet were folded over on top of themselves. "At least I can get these on your feet, love. I know you would be standing on your toes, so to speak, but let's see if you can stand up in them." She tried her best to get to her feet. Shi had to adjust her hair for her so she could even try. He also had to hold on to her as she wildly tried to get and keep her balance.

Soon, she smiled, "I can stand, Shi. Maybe if you hold onto me, I can walk a bit." After some experimenting, Shi and Qing discovered that she could actually walk almost as well in them as she had on her own feet before the plague. However, there were only two pairs of the boots. Although Shi realized now that they were probably meant for Tian and himself, that Qing could now at least stand and walk convinced him that she should have them, not the men. He put the second pair onto Shan's feet and then helped her stand and walk too.

"I will find both of you some of these strange boots too," he promised Shu and Ting. "We have lots of kitchen things, at least they look like such. I wonder what these items are for?" He held up a long handled spoon. They all ate with bamboo sticks imported from the outer lands. He held up obvious pots and pans, but had no idea of what the yokes, desks, and chairs with wheels on them were for, let alone the replacement stove and oven.

"Daddy, I have strange pictures in my mind," Shu spoke up. "I see women without arms picking up things with their toes and putting them into those basket things and then carrying the yokes across their shoulders. I think that women are to use those yokes in place of their arms, only daddy, how can we do that if we can't stand up anymore?" She broke down and began crying once more. Shi never felt so utterly frustrated and helpless in his life.

A while later, Tian returned, extremely pale faced. "Report son? Are our servants on their way now?"

"Dad — dad. This has happened to everyone in Matag, we think. Whatever this is, it has affected everyone, men, women, and children alike. Dozens have been asking me what has happened and for help. I told them that we were on top of it and would soon tell them what to do. Dad? Please, dad. You have to know what we are to do!" He saw the blank look on his father's face and all hope left him. He added, "Medan and Jian will be coming to see you soon. I bet everyone in the village will be coming here soon, though. Everyone is scared out of their minds, dad. What are we going to tell them?"

Shi shrugged his shoulders. Tian then spotted the four women, including his wife working on brushing out each other's hair, and he went over to lend them a hand.

"Hey, Tian, we can sort of do this ourselves. Can't do much else, though," his wife interceded. Ting added, "You can check on how Wen is doing. I can't get to her."

Just then, others entered his home. Medan, Jian, and Pengdu came crawling into the room. Their faces were ashen as well, though the two younger men brightened up when they spotted their girlfriends sitting on their usual couches, attempting to brush each other's hair. "Shi, we have to talk. What is happening to our village? Tian says it has affected everyone. What are we to do?"

Shi pulled his moustaches with his long nails. He knew that he had to take quick, effective action. The village depended upon his guidance, though just now he felt certain that he had no ideas at all. He was the Seneschal; he had to lead, but lead where? How?

"You are the historian. Search your records. Find out what has happened to us, Medan. Now then, we can do some things. Notice our women. They are able to do some things for themselves, I've discovered. Notice how they can help each other, but not themselves so readily. I believe that for the time being, we need to get at least four women in the same home with each other so they can help each other. Also, we need to gather up all those strange ankle boots. The women's feet can fit part way down them, and with the boots on, they are able to stand and walk a little, with help, naturally. Without the boots, they can't walk at all. So we need to gather up all them and get them distributed to the bound footed women of Matag."

He continued, "Shu has some images that may help the normal footed women. Apparently, using their toes, they can pick up things and put them into those two baskets. By putting their shoulders into the yokes, they can then carry things in the baskets. Crude, but Shu believes that it will work. Only our bound foot women cannot; they have no toes with which to pick up anything, let alone be able to walk carrying the yoke thing. We haven't really figured out what all the rest of this stuff is for, or where the pile has come from; maybe someone else will know."

Within a few days, Shi set an example for the whole village. His home, though spacious, was now crowded. He had the Yang's, the Wie's, and the Pong's move into his home. Additionally, he had the three servants bring their whole families here as well. Eleven women, ten men, and their children now called the Yushube home their home.

All the bound foot women now wore the ballet style boots and were just barely able to stand in them and walk a little, though men had constantly to assist them. They could not manage on their own yet, and the other non-bound footed women valiantly attempted to walk in the extremely high heels of the aliens. However, Shu was right, normal women were slowly adapting to using their feet and toes in conjunction with the yokes to carry things around. Bit by bit, uses were discovered for the remaining items, though many were unhappy that they would not be able to use them. For example, the calligrapher, Xue, having discovered that the desks were for writing, lamented that she had no toes with which to write. In fact, the bound foot women were in dire straits, almost unable to do much for themselves at all, since their feet were useless.

Shi decreed that women were never to be left unattended. Always at least one man or teen had to remain at home to assist the women living there. This became very practical in that it allowed the other men to return to some semblance of normal village life, handling what had to be done.

Before long, Lindi began to figure out how she could possibly cook again. Shi asked a laborer to come and install the kitchen items. After Lindi began experimenting with the new devices and finally was able to prepare a meal once more, Shi ordered the installation of all these kitchen items. With normal footed women now staying with bound footed women, life slowly progressed from a total disaster into some semblance of livable lives, especially since many men were able to perform some work to keep things going.

In the ensuing days following the plague, many wondered why it happened and what had caused it. Shi was a cool head. He kept Medan and Jian working on searching for any kind of historical reference or cause, meanwhile, he redirected all such queries to him off on to the steps that they could take to continue to survive.

In January when feet returned to normal, the men were elated at first. Normal footed women also were pleased that they could now walk as they had before. The bound footed women were thankful to wear their own slipper shoes once more, making them more surefooted than when wearing the awful ballet style boots. More importantly, for days after that, everyone, particularly the women, continually expected to find their arms somehow back as well. When that did not happen, many women became quite depressed. Their lives were miserable, even more so because of their now extremely long hair, which was often a foot longer than they were tall. Without arms to deal with it, they had difficulties even standing up without stepping on their hair. Of course, in Tashien, no one would ever consider cutting it shorter, and the women of Xi never wore theirs braided, always bushy, full, and draped across the front of their bodies. Lacking arms, they couldn't even tie it up. Most men had no idea how to help them with their hair, and besides, their shakas prevented more usual solutions.

By February 824, the caravans began to traverse the entire desert regions once more, bringing needed replenishment to the local food merchants. Liang Pong was kept extremely busy now, since his wife was no longer able to assist him much at all. His son would have helped more, but Shi had him helping Jian who was scouring every known source, seeking an explanation or a cure.

In March, the common idea that pervaded Matag was that the women suffered from some kind of demonic illness. Many claimed that only eating powdered god bodies would cure them. More than one man begged Shi to send a caravan off to the Valley of the Fallen Beasts and bring back some of the bones of the ancient gods. While Shi discounted this folk remedy, by June, he had little choice. Three quarters of the village was demanding that he take some action to help their women.

"Okay, okay. I will lead the caravan to the Valley of the Fallen Beasts," Peng agreed. "Who are you going to send there?"

Shi replied, "Pengdu, you know a lot about food. You go and prepare the bones. Jian, you know a lot about our history and legends, you go as our historian. Hojie, I want you to go with them and protect the caravan and the personnel. Take as many guards as you deem necessary. I will help look after Chani while you are gone."

"I am honored to do this," Pengdu bowed, very pleased that the Seneschal chose him.

Jian added, "Most honored to serve." He glanced at Shan who beamed at him. If nothing else, he wanted to prove to Shi that he would be a good and faithful husband to Shan. Likewise, Pengdu smiled at Shu. Although they were merely dating, he was thankful for this opportunity to prove to the Seneschal, her father, that he was worthy of dating his daughter.

Shan spoke up, "Dad, I am going with Jian."

"What? Shan, no, it will be too hard a trip for you to make."

"Look, Mata always goes with Peng on his caravan trips. She has bound feet, as do I. If she can do it, I'm sure that I can also. Besides, Pengdu can make a sample and I can try it. If it works, we'll be able to bring back enough for everyone." She ignored the fact that Mata could also try it and Shi missed that detail. "Please dad? I am so useless like this. I want to try to do something to help. After all, I'm the Seneschal's daughter."

Shi relented and gave his permission. Hojie added two more guards to be on the safe side. The men broke up to discuss their plans. Meantime, Mata did her best to toss her hair out from beneath her feet, then carefully lurched her body to get on to her feet. Still wobbling a bit, she said, "Shan, come with me, please. We need to talk too, if you are really serious about coming along." Shan leaned her head forward and to the left and right, swinging her hair out from beneath her feet. She too leaned back and lurched forward attempting to get to her feet was well. Life was especially tough for these bound foot women since the plague. Just rising from a chair without the use of their hands left them with little grace and a whole lot of wild wobbling, wiggling of heads and torsos around to steady themselves. At last, the two women slowly shuffled to the room where Mata and Peng now slept.

"Look, we sit for long hours on the camels. It is hot and sweaty. The nights get cold, and we must take care to avoid the scorpions and snakes, especially at night. It is not a thing to be taken lightly, Shan. Honestly, Shan, you have lived the sheltered life of the Seneschal's daughter. Taking a long caravan trip is not going to be easy for you," Mata cautioned her. "Now that we women have been so afflicted by the gods, even a caravan trip is a most difficult challenge for bound women. We are so useless. If you come, think of the difficulties that you will be adding to poor Jian, who has so many other worries now — what with the finding and proper grinding of the ancient bones. If you are coming along only to be with Jian, I would urge you to reconsider. Young love is one thing, Shan, but have you really considered that Jian might now not really want to marry you? After all, we have lost our arms and have become so completely helpless and useless, we cannot even use our feet in place of our arms as the normal women have begun to do."

Shan fought back a surging urge to cry. No, she hadn't thought that Jian might now not want to have her hand in marriage! Hand? She had none now. Mata was right. She was so completely helpless and useless! The only task she could do by herself was to brush out another woman's long hair! Her lovely hands and six-inch nails were completely gone, taken away by angry gods, leaving her with nothing at all. She couldn't even put on her makeup to look her best. Gone was her budding skill with needlepoint. Now she depended upon others for everything, even feeding her and occasionally helping her push one of her golden teeth, which had come loose, back into its socket.

For a moment, her mind drifted back to that day when she was thirteen and had gotten her golden teeth. She remembered chewing on some bitter leaves and her mouth had gone numb. True, she felt nothing more than the heavy pressure and pulling — that and a whole lot of blood. The replacement teeth being pushed in — ah, that was a nice warm sensation, she recalled. The teeth were heated, she remembered. Well, that was the trouble with all the gold teeth replacements — they often came loose and had to be pushed back into place. Now she couldn't even do that, so embarrassing to have to have Jian do it for her. She also remembered how heavy her mouth felt once the numbness had gone — that much gold was far heavier than the teeth she was born with, but now she scarcely noticed their heavier weight.

No, Jian could not possibly want to marry her now, not as she was, a pathetic cripple, of no real use to anyone. Still, she had to save face. Fighting for control of her eyes, Shan answered, "I must go. I am the Seneschal's daughter. He cannot go; he is desperately needed here in Matag. I must go in his place to represent our village and his honor."

"Well, then you will need one of these hair sacks that Peng fixed up for me. Our hair, particularly so since the god's afflictions upon us, is just too unmanageable. He puts my hair into the sack and ties it to the back of my shaka, before he puts my white robe and hood on me. Then, my hair does not get in the way." Mata leaned over and bit down on one sack, wobbling wildly to keep her balance while leaning. She carefully turned and tilted her head, handing it to Shan, who opened her gold encrusted mouth to take it from Mata. She then shuffled over to a bedpost and carefully laid it on the post where she could more easily pick it up.

Shan asked, "So why do you continue to go with Peng on the caravan trip?" Having had a moment to regain her composure, Shan went on the attack. Obviously, Mata was as useless and helpless as she was, yet Mata always went with Peng. Why?

Mata sighed heavily. "Yes, I too am afflicted by the gods for reasons that I know not. Yet, I must continue to accompany Peng, my husband. Before, I did the cooking and dishes, kept the camp for his company. I was most useful, but now I am as the mouse caught in the eagle's claws. I can but wiggle and do nothing of any use to anyone, save as you pointed out, brush your hair at night for you. I even need Peng's help to go to the bathroom without peeing on my dress. Shan, I go with Peng because I must. He will lose much face if he has to leave me behind for another man to look after my needs in his place. I cannot also bear him having even more disgrace because of me. Our son is long married and has his own family to handle. Ting now has little Wen and Tian. Peng cannot bear to ask Tian also to care for my needs while he is away for so many days. Such is too much to ask of any man. Thus, as useless and helpless as I am, as much of a burden as I am to him, I go with him so as to not make myself an even larger burden for Peng."

"Then we must both do our duties," Shan replied stoically, steeling herself for what must surely be coming. Mata nodded, with this she could wholeheartedly agree, and she flashed Shan a golden smile of mutual understanding. Shan bent over, picked up the sack, and slowly wobbled her way out of Mata's room, heading for her own room. What had started out as a perfect opportunity to spend some time alone with Jian had now become her death knell. Jian would see just how awful life would be if he went through with their marriage plans.

That night, Shan cried herself to sleep. She finally realized fully that the God's Affliction really had destroyed her life. Until this moment, she had held out some hope of a future. Now she knew the future was so terrible that it was not worth facing. When she woke somber face the next morning, she also knew that she had to put up a stoic front for her father's sake. She was the Seneschal's daughter. "But damn little more," she whispered to herself as she struggled to get her helpless body out of bed and await someone to help her pee and dress. Pathetic beyond pathetic, she thought to herself. Worse, she knew that by herself she had no way to end such a pitiable, miserable life. She could only go on enduring it and the total humiliations that came her way. She was the Seneschal's daughter and always would be.

"Morning, love. Ready to get ready for the trip?" an excited Jian asked after knocking on her door politely. After holding her long hair out of her way so she could relieve herself, he then struggled to get her into her cotton dress. Again, he was so unfamiliar with handling her terrifically long hair that he continually fumbled with it. If only she still had her arms, she could have held it for him. At last, he tied the laces over her massive bosom. "Mata says that I am to put your hair into the bag and tie it to the back of your magnificent shaka. Okay?" Shan nodded, wondering how awful she would look at breakfast.

An hour later, with his arm around her waist supporting her, Jian led her out to the waiting lines of camels. Peng and Mata were already there, Mata sitting on top of a camel, stone faced. Peng pointed to another sitting camel and Jian led Shan over to it. His strong arms lifted her up and positioned her on the leather and cloth saddle. He double checked her hood to make sure the bow was still tied securely. The women especially had to wear a hood over their golden shakas when out in the blaring, searing sunlight of the desert. Otherwise, the metal would heat up, becoming unbearably hot. "How do I hold on?" Shan asked as a bit of panic struck her. The camel lurched as it rose to its feet, nearly knocking her from her position. She found herself wildly flailing around with her non-existent arms, trying frantically to hold on and not fall off.

Peng's soft voice called out, "Do not worry, Shan. You will not fall off. Squeeze with your legs if you feel off balance." Peng, Jian, and Pengdu got on their camels. Peng lead Mata's camel, while Jian led Shan's. Shan realized that she was now forcing Jian to have to lead hers; she couldn't even ride without his help. More humiliation swept over her.

Pengdu mounted his camel behind hers. Hojie and two other guards with their sabers and long guns brought up the rear. Each of the others led supply camels. Eight people and fourteen camels headed off into the mid-morning sunlight, leaving the sparkling, blue waters of the oasis behind them. The day promised to be another hot one, as most days in Xi were.

Shan felt a bit of excitement replacing her feelings of humiliation. This would be the first time that she had ever left Matag. She realized that she had lived her entire life in this small village! Now she was about to see more of their world.

Out on the baking desert sands of Xi, Shan began to feel the searing heat upon her head and hoped that she could endure this. She steeled herself. If Mata could, then so could she. Great dunes appeared, orange-red, with beautiful, graceful waves flowing down them, as if they were the waters of the Gods. For a time, Shan took all this in; it was so new to her, so beautiful.

Later on, Jian and Pengdu swapped the camels, which they were leading. Jian then moved up alongside her. "Holding up, Shan? Hot one, isn't it? You know, I've never been this far from Matag before. This is all new to me."

"Me too, Jian. I've never left Matag before. How strange it is to say something like that. We've lived our whole lives in that small village and yet there is a whole world out here," she replied, still marveling at the beauty of the desert around her, though she was sweating heavily now, particularly around her head. Her shaka felt as if it was melting her head, squashing it under its heavy weight.

"Yes, quite right. I've been studying all our history and legends, reading about the world, but seeing it, well, it's quite different than I imagined," Jian admitted, slightly daunted. "It is so big!"

"Say, why do so many think that eating powdered god's bones is going to cure us?" asked Shan. She noticed that Mata was now paying close attention to their conversation. She was just in front of the two.

"In the Valley of the Fallen Beasts, it is said that the gods struck down the many dragons which used to decimate our world, devouring us, much as we devour goats and chickens. It is said that the God Long brought forth all manner of dragons to wipe us from the face of Tarra. Then the God Jie Li Meng came forth and struck down these mighty abominations of Long's, burying them in that valley. Some now believe that if we eat of these bones, we will gain some of the ancient dragon's vitality and strength and power. Yet, I do not see how this can be so, since the dragons are dead, long dead. How this will bring forth women's arms I cannot foresee. Yet, so many believe this is so that we must at least try," Jian explained the reasons behind this journey.

"Well, I will give it a try. I hope I don't get sick from eating old bones," Shan replied. "Surely there must be a better explanation for our God's Affliction."

"I should think so, Shan, though I have as yet been unable to find it. Certainly, our most ancient legends talk of the mighty Gods. It is said that they lived on high with the eagles. Legends speak of their enormous powers. One says that the Gods were displeased with man and in their wrath, so they turned the fertile valleys of Xi into this great desert, and then told man to live here and to be faithful to the ancient ways or the Gods would turn the rest of the world into a great desert as well. Yes, the ancient Gods must have had great powers indeed."

"Do you really believe that there were ancient Gods?" Shan asked. "I've never seen any signs of them around."

"Ah, and what would those signs be? Our women's God's Afflictions perhaps?" he suggested.

"Well, true. For what else could have caused my arms and hands to just vanish like that?" Shan replied. "What else could have caused my breasts to grow so enormously? Perhaps, though, something has merely put us to sleep for a very long time without our knowing about it. Then while we were all asleep, they cut off our arms and did the other things to us."

"How can you think that?" asked a curious Jian. This was an entirely new theory to him, one that he'd not heard before. Perhaps the Seneschal's daughter knew something more. Well, that could surely be true, for she was the village leader's daughter and knew so very much, he thought.

"Simple, Jian. You have to look at all that happened to us. Look, my hair grows some each year, but this time when I went to bed, I woke up to find it had grown some two feet. That must mean, based on how much it has been growing all my life, that I was out or unconscious or asleep or whatever for a *very* long time. I think that someone operated on us women and you fellows too, for that matter, and they kept us unconscious until our bodies fully healed. Then, we woke up," Shan explained her private theory. In her mind, it fitted better with what she knew to be true. Broken feet took weeks to heal. Both men and women had healed, but grossly malformed feet, as though someone had broken them and forced them to heal in that grotesque shape.

"Wow, Shan! I never thought about that! You are right. Mom's hair grew two feet too. Her hair has never grown that much as long as I can remember. Perhaps we were knocked out by some all-powerful Gods. Wow."

Pengdu, listening in, interrupted, "Hey, if that was so, why didn't our hair grow two feet? And how about our beards, Shan? We men ought to have had a two-foot beard when we woke up. None of us had any more than what we would have expected for one night."

"They could have shaved us, Pengdu," Jian backed up Shan and her incredible theory.

"Yes, I suppose so. God, I hope they did not cut my hair! I wonder if I have lost some of my vitality? How can I tell, Jian? You are the historian. How can we tell if we've lost some of ourselves by having our hair cut?" Pengdu asked.

"Don't know. Wow, I wonder if I am weaker than before?" Jian speculated.

This sobering thought occupied the minds of the men for some time, and they rode along in silence. Jian began to wonder about his loss of vitality and life force. If so, he was unworthy of the lovely Shan! As much as he loved and respected her, if he were less than himself, he didn't dare marry her. She deserved far more than a weakened, shell of a man.

As the sun sank behind the far distant mountains, Peng halted at Mag Hu, a bowl shaped arena in the side of the desert ridge line on their left. Another caravan had already stopped here for the night as well. Before they halted, Peng dismounted and visited the other caravan. He came back smiling. "It's Hu and his bunch. It will be safe for us to camp here with them. Circle the camels there," he pointed to one side of the bowl.

Shan panicked as her camel slowly dropped to its knees and then lay on the ground. Again, she flailed her arms, frantically trying to keep from falling off. Jian helped her off and her legs felt a bit weak — his too, for that matter. Red faced, he whispered to her, "I am sorry, Miss Shan, I am so weak. It must be because they cut my hair."

"Mine are like butter, Jian. Please help me sit before I fall down," she whispered back.

Peng came up to them. "Okay, time to set up camp. Don't worry, first timers. You'll soon get your camel legs." Shan wasn't so sure about that. Frustrated and feeling humiliated, she and Mata sat on a rock watching the men set up camp and prepare their supper. Across the way, the two spotted three women in the other camp. They were using their yokes to help and were actually cooking the men's meals. Obviously, they were not bound footed women. Still, seeing these women actually helping only made Shan's depression worse. Even Mata seemed effected by the scene playing out while they could only watch. Shan saw visible evidence that, unlike normal women who could still do useful work, she was pathetic, unable to do anything at all to help. She could only sit and watch while their men did everything. Just a few feet beyond them, three other women were busily struggling with making the men's supper. She knew that Jian deserved far better than her pathetic self.

Later, Jian fed her and afterwards she sat around the campfire watching the men wash up. She felt more like crying but suppressed it by looking up at the brilliant stars overhead. Shan felt grimy now. The sweat had dried, leaving a thin, crusty grim over her entire body. However, she dare not ask Jian for a bath. How could he do it out here? The only water was in those precious goatskins they had brought with them. Shan was miserable.

Later, Jian came and sat down beside her. This time, he did not put his arm around her as he often had done back home. Shan noticed this subtle change. Now he is really seeing just how worthless I really am. He's seen those other women who are still able to help, and he is having second thoughts about me. Well, that is good then; I don't have to tell him otherwise, she thought to herself.

I am so weak. I've lost some of my life force when they cut my hair, Jian thought to himself. I am so unworthy of Shan. I should not encourage her any further. Surely, she can see just how weak I now am. She can't possibly desire me, not when I'm like this. He too stared at the stars and said little. Sometime later, Peng handed out the blankets and Jian made Shan as comfortable as possible, making sure that she was well covered from the chilly night air. He turned in beside her. Unlike previous nights, he had not kissed her. In the dark, she finally allowed her tears of woe to come. No one could see her now. She thought, this is good; he has seen that I'm a worthless woman now. I love him dearly, but I must allow him to find a real woman who is not completely helpless, so utterly dependent up him for everything. The newness of the camping experience kept her awake long after she heard Jian sleeping soundly. She also heard Peng and Mata making love and turned her head to peek.

Even in the starlight, she could see that Mata was lying on top of him beneath their shared blankets. Good for her, she thought. Morning came unexpectedly; Shan decided that she must have fallen asleep. Quickly, the men handled the two women's needs and then left them sitting beneath a blanket while they fixed breakfast. The early morning air was chilly, but that would soon change out here in the Xi desert.

Mata whispered, "It is the only thing that I can now do for Peng. Saw you watching us last night." Shan flushed red. "Think nothing of it, dear. Sex. It is the only thing I can do for Peng. I'll give you a tip. If you are on top, your breasts will keep your head up so you can kiss him properly, and you can make him feel good. Use your shaka. Rake the ends over him. Peng likes that stimulation."

Shan nodded, thinking, so that is all that I'm good for now, a man's sex toy. Well, so be it. I can't do anything else for him. He needs to find a better woman, no question of that. Before long, the women began to be fed their breakfast.

Peng chatted, "Well, boys, hopefully your legs won't be mush this evening like they were last night. Riding all day long takes some getting used to, but you'll soon catch on."

"I ought to be a lot stronger," Jian protested. "Haven't you noticed that you are a little weaker since the God's Affliction came upon us all?"

"Er, no, Jian. I am as strong as ever. Why? Are you weaker? I have heard all sorts of complaints, but never that we are weaker."

"Well, they probably cut at least two feet off our hair. That's how much the women's grew, so ours must have too. You know, they knocked us all out, cut off their arms, and broke our feet. Bodies take time to heal from that, at least a couple of months. I figure we must all have been knocked out at least two or maybe three months," Jian explained.

Peng roared with laughter. "Oh brother, now I have heard the best one yet, Jian. No offense son, but that ranks up there with the best of them, doesn't it, Mata?" He continued to laugh much to Jian's embarrassment. He had it all worked out.

"Look, son. None of us is any weaker or stronger, for that matter. I know that no one messed with my hair. It was still braided at the base of my head. If it had grown two feet like the women's did, someone would have had to re-braid it after they cut it."

"Well, maybe they did so while you were unconscious," Jian pointed out hopefully.

"Not a chance of it. The last time I braided it, I was in a damnable hurry and botched it a bit, got an awful knot in its end. Same goofy knot was there when I woke up with my feet screwy. So no, nobody cut my hair. Somehow, ours didn't grow while the women's did. Besides, who would have taken care of all the animals for that long? We would have noticed that the season had changed if we were out for that long. Didn't happen, sorry Jian," Peng explained.

Mata added, "Jian, everyone's legs get rubbery when they ride all day and are not yet used to it."

"Then I am not weaker somehow? Not lost some of my virility?" Jian asked.

Peng chuckled, "Son, I highly doubt that! Now let's get these women aboard. We've a long way to go today if we are to make the water hole before dark."

As Jian helped Shan rise and walk to the camel, he whispered, "I'm sorry Shan. I thought that I was weaker now and undeserving of you. How silly of me. Forgive me, my love." He gave her a passionate kiss.

"But Shan, you need to find a normal woman, not a bound footed one like me. I am the one who is so unworthy of you. My god, Jian, I can't do anything at all for myself. I feel horrible that I can't even help you with anything at all. Look at those women. Even now, they are using their yokes to carry things to their camels. I can't even do that little for you. You must forget about marrying me and find a more worthy woman. I can hardly even walk." There, she had said it. She knew that she finally had to come out with it — all the more so since Jian was still passionate about her. She had to give him a chance to back out and find a better wife.

Jian didn't say anything. He was shocked at first, and then her logic hit him. It was true; the bound footed women were virtually helpless, save perhaps brushing out another's hair. He just didn't know what he could say. After getting her onto her camel and over her fright of falling off, he got onto his. Peng gave the orders and they hit the trail once more.

"Look, you could hardly walk ever since you were a baby. Nothing new there, Shan," he pointed out. "You never felt this way before we all were afflicted."

"Yes, but I had arms and could do many things. Now I can't. I'm helpless. I can't even kill myself and be done with it all!" Shan declared her darkest thought, bringing it into the sunlight.

"Well, don't you even try, Shan. I love you. Look, even your feet went back to normal. We just have to wait a while longer, perhaps. Or else we find a cure. That's it, Shan. We must find a cure."

"You think eating some dead bones is going to cure us?" she asked in disbelief.

Jian looked at Pengdu then her. "No, not really, but we have to lay that strange rumor to rest. That's why your father sent us on this silly trip. We will show them that is just a fairytale. Then, we can set about finding a real cure. Shan, I won't ever stop until I find a cure for you."

Shan relaxed. He sounded so hopeful; maybe there was a cure. Still, her own dark thoughts returned, but she said nothing more.

Chapter 72 Blinded and the Search

They rode all that morning, stopping when the sun reached the zenith for a quick lunch and break at the Hanging Rock. Shan marveled at how this huge rock, twice the size of her home back in Matag, could balance perfectly on a thin, tiny point without falling over. Yet, balance it had, for centuries. Jian told everyone the ancient story of the Hanging Rock, while Peng worked on handing out cheese and bread to the men.

Just as Jian finished his story and was offering Shan a bite of cheese, disaster struck them. Carefully aimed rocks suddenly came flying at the men. Jian took a rock to his head and he slumped unconscious on top of Shan. She looked around and saw all the men now lying on the ground, knocked out. Only she and Mata were unharmed.

Ten foreign looking men came out from their hiding places; several led a group of horses, ill-suited to the desert travel. All were filthy and unshaven for at least a week, Shan thought. All had long guns. Although she was helpless, Shan called out, "Who are you? Why did you hurt our men? Leave us alone."

One man, far better dressed than the others, walked up to her, eyeing her up and down. At last, he spoke, "I am Overlord Meng, the Ferocious. We've only knocked them out. If you want us not to kill them where they lie, then you both will do as I ask."

"What do you mean?" Shan asked lamely. She ought to have said something stronger, but panic was rapidly overtaking her mind. She felt sick at her stomach.

"You will come quietly with us. If you do, we will leave these men alone. If you scream and make a fuss, we'll kill them. Savvy?"

"Please don't kill them. What do you want?"

"I'll tell you later. Coming peacefully?"

"Yes, but you will have to help us, we can't walk," Shan lied, hoping to gain a tiny potential advantage with these strange men. They were not desert dwellers, of that she was certain. The only overlords around here lay far to the south over a hundred miles or more. Those were the opium drug lords, she realized. Her father had sometimes spoken of their savagery and addiction to the poppy. Strong hands lifted her up and sat her on one of the horses. Mata was carried to another one. Before she knew what was happening, the band of men mounted up and began riding out of this secluded, shady area, back out into the broiling sun.

As they rode along, none spoke. She did notice that the leader Meng constantly looked at some small device in his hand. Afterwards, he indicated a direction. Why he needed that, she didn't know. Obviously, they were heading south. Any desert dweller could tell that. After a time, Meng noticed her noticing him, and he satisfied her curiosity. "It is a compass. It tells us the direction to travel. Without it, we would be lost in this god-forsaken desert." Shan filed that away for future use.

She also noticed that the horses were not fairing so well. By late afternoon, the men and the horses were near heat exhaustion. Apparently, Meng also realized this and called a halt. While the men set about making camp near the ridge line, Shan noted that from this height, they could see anyone coming for several miles. If Jian came after her, they'd be spotted long before they could get here. After sitting the two women side by side, Meng brought them a drink. "Here, take a good long drink. You need it." Eagerly, the thirsty women drank their fill. A bit late, Shan began to get drowsy and panic once more began to flood into her mind. Her stomach knotted, but before she could try to say something to Mata, she fell into a deep sleep.

"Okay, doc, they are out. Do your work and be quick about it. When you are done with them, they won't give us any more trouble. Stay alert men. Those nomads we knocked out might do something foolish," Meng ordered. "Now make with the food."

It must be daytime, Shan's fussy mind tried to focus. There was light. Her head felt overly warm. She tried to sit up, but found her legs were somehow not as free as they ought to be, as if they were encased in something. She tried to focus her eyes, but could see almost nothing, except a little straight ahead. As she sat up, her ears felt like something was pulling them off! Something metal hung from her nose and dangled across her lips. What was going on?

"Ah, you are awake at last," she heard the voice of Meng. A chill went through her body. "Now then, do not worry. Both of you are now my harem of Yingchan, my Golden Angels. You see, there is going to be this drug overlord conference, and they are all bringing their Yingchan along with them. Well, I wanted mine to be extra golden. Your skin color is very different from the women in my land, just to the south of Xi. We've spent two lousy weeks in this god-forsaken desert, and you two are the first women that we've seen. Well, you both will do for now. You are now my Yingchan. Here, have a look, if you can even see yourselves. Doc, hold up the mirrors. You know better than I how they can see now."

The doc held a mirror in just the right position for Shan to see her reflection. "You see, you are our Golden Angels now. I have put golden eyeballs over each of your eyes. Yes, you can only see out of that tiny spot in the very center. I believe that you will need to move your heads to see anything. The golden eyes don't move. They cannot be taken out, so don't try, not that you could, mind you. Now look at your incredible earrings, golden lattice veil, and huge necklace. Yes, we've left your marvelous head pieces intact. That will only add to your exceptional beauty as Golden Angels."

Meng interrupted him. "Ladies, your earrings, veils, and necklaces are worth a half million gold. That's why they are so heavy; they are worth a fortune. We've dressed you in our traditional red silk dresses, so now you actually look like proper Yingchan. You can thank me for having given you both the highest honors that we can give our women."

"But we can't see. Our ears are being ripped off," Shan complained bitterly. She lowered her head trying to see the bottom of the dress and why her legs were not working properly. Bright red silk came into view. Her new dress hugged her entire body like a restrictive sheath, clear down to her feet. Well, perhaps if she were standing, there would be enough give for her to walk. Her steps were extremely short anyway, just a few inches at a time, if she were to keep her balance. Still, she could only see a tiny fraction; her field of view was only a few degrees wide, and Shan found that she had to move her head in order to see what she ought to be seeing normally.

Shan saw that she was sitting near the edge of a small drop off, a rocky one at that. Meng was standing in front of her as she looked towards her feet, leaning over her slightly. Meng ordered, "Okay boys, start breaking camp. I'll get a reading here on my compass and we'll head back home at once." He leaned over a bit more, doing something with his compass. Just what, she had no idea, but Shan reacted.

Quite why she did what she did, afterwards she couldn't say. It was just intuition that struck. Unable to see much of anything except her legs and feet and the bent over man whose hands were on the compass, she swung her feet upwards sharply, striking his hands, sending the compass flying through the air. Meng made a valiant attempt to catch it, but he was taken by total surprise. The compass flew out over the drop off. Shan heard a shattering noise as it struck the rocks below. Meng bellowed and cursed, but stopped just short of bashing her head in with his boot.

Still cursing her, he stomped around madly. "Damn it! Damn it! She's broken the compass!"

"Boss, we can still find our way back, right?" a shaky voice asked from somewhere behind her.

"Hell, we had better. We can't get lost. It must be that way," Meng answered. Shan detected a note of uncertainty or hesitancy in his voice. The men began discussing their opinions on the direction they needed to go to get out of Xi.

Meantime, Mata fought to gain control of her mind, reeling from the discoveries, particularly that she could no longer see. Well, that is not quite true. She finally won her panic battle. She was looking to the west, but her field of vision was a few degrees at most. Still, she took heart in what little she did see. As she listened to the men arguing over the direction to go, she mentally thanked Shan. Her action might have saved them.

Mata spoke up. "Sir, I can't see you, but I can hear you, Overlord Meng. We are desert people, and we know the desert. Look in whatever direction I am. I can't see very well any more. Tell me, is that an orange dust cloud that I'm seeing. Perhaps not, I can't see well at all."

"Yeh, well what of it? You're not *supposed* to see well anymore. You have golden eyes to match the rest of you that is golden. Yes, it is orange. Why?" Meng finally deigned to answer the woman. She was probably in her forties, he guessed, and ordinarily far too old for a Yingchan, but after spending so darn long in this god-forsaken desert, he would take any woman. At least, she too looked quite different and even perhaps more like his idea of a Golden Angel, since her skin was more golden than his people's skin color.

"That is a sami, a dust storm, sir. It will be on us in short order. You should get yourselves and us prepared for it," Mata answered him, still not taking her tiny vision off the cloud. She was making an educated guess about its speed, hindered considerably by her lack of vision. If she was right, a big if considering what little she could now see, they had at most a half hour to prepare.

"Mount up boys, we'll outride it," Meng ordered. Fools, thought Mata. She felt her body being lifted up, but she couldn't see what was happening to her, except her ears felt like they were being pulled off her. She was sat across the lap of some sweaty smelling man on a horse. She saw Shan also being lifted up and sitting in front of Meng. The women's legs in their tight fitting red silk dresses dangled over the left side of the horses. She relaxed; their backs were to the oncoming sami. She smiled, but no one noticed it.

Shan tried to turn her head enough to see, but could not. She felt like a sack of grain now. Mata and Shan were desert dwellers and frequently had been in sami, which blew through Matag at least once or twice each summer. She felt the wind coming on her back and relaxed as well. She would be protected, that is, her face, nose, and what was left of her eyes. Shan began to recall what she had seen of her eyes in the mirror minutes ago. Golden, yes, her eyes were all golden, entirely so, but if that was so, how could she even see a thing? She concluded that she hadn't gotten a good look at her eyes.

The riders had not gone but a mile down from the ridge line into the sandy desert below — the worst thing that they could have done, had they bothered to listen to or ask Mata. Wham! Blinding, cutting sand driven by a forceful wind slammed into them. Chaos erupted as man and horse fought the stinging sand. Shan felt herself falling or rather sliding from the horse, and she tried her best to catch herself as she fell. Unable to see, her legs held tightly together by the silk dress, she hit hard on her heels and fell over. She rolled over onto her stomach, closed her eyes, and waited. She heard another thump and guessed Mata had joined her on the ground. Wild whinnying from the terror-stricken horses and yells from the men added to the cacophony of sound. She heard some of the men also dropping to the ground, but soon only the shrieking wind could be heard.

"My head! What happened?" Jian moaned and staggered to his feet. A bit of dried blood was on his hand as he pulled it back from the side of his head. The others were rousing, and Jian went from each to each, checking on them. All were alive, holding their heads. "Oh god! The women! They're gone! Peng. Get up, Shan and Mata are gone!"

"Don't move, Jian," Hojie called out, struggling to get to his feet. "Let us look at the ground around us first. Clues, Jian. Damn, my head hurts. You fellows all right?" A chorus of yes's trickled in, one after the other, while Hojie began leaning over the ground. He walked slowly around the last known location where he remembered the women were sitting.

"A bunch of men with horses have taken the two women," he announced at last, sending shock waves through Jian and Peng. "Must be outsiders from down south. No one in Xi uses horses, certainly not this far into the desert. Horses are a bad liability. Water is at a premium in our land. Come on; let's get the camels ready and go after them. They won't get far, and they have left us a clear trail to follow. It must be three, so they've a good head start on us." The men mounted their camels and followed Hojie. Both Peng and Jian trusted Hojie, for security was the man's specialty, though they had apparently walked into a trap that Hojie had missed.

Sometime later they stopped, while Hojie surveyed the ground around the ridge line. Below them, a dust storm raged, but here on the higher rocky ridge line, they felt only a strong, hot wind. "Look, there's four small pools of blood," he pointed out.

"I'll kill them if they've hurt Shan!" Jian swore. He asked, "How bad do you think they are hurt?"

"Can't say; it's not a whole lot of blood though. From the horses, I'd say they stopped here for a couple of hours or so," Hojie answered.

"Couple of hours? That's good, isn't it?" Peng asked.

"Yes and no. Yes, in that they cannot be but a few miles ahead of us not. Bad, in that their trail leads down into yonder sami," Hojie replied. All the men stared at the swirling orange cloud that totally obscured all vision of the valley below the ridge. "We have no choice but to wait it out. Sami is about done anyway. We ride as it begins to break up. Tie cloths over your faces." The men did as ordered.

Around four, off to the west about a mile or so, Jian began seeing rock formations through the orange dust. Hojie gave the order, "Okay, let's ride. It's breaking up." Down into the howling, stinging dust storm the men rode, the camels braying but obeying. It was as if they too knew the storm was subsiding. A few minutes later, they came across the kidnapers. Their horses had spooked and half had injured themselves while running blinding about. The others had so much orange sand and dust in their eyes that they could not see and just stood looking like forgotten, forlorn beasts. Hojie counted ten men partially covered in the sand. Two bright red dresses had to be their women. Hojie gave a hand sign to his three guards. Like silent assassins, the four crept up to the men and slit their throats, one by one. Several tried to rise and fight, but their eyes were caked over, and they were mostly blind, dying shortly thereafter. Once the men were dispatched, Jian rushed to Shan, while Peng ran to Mata.

"We're here. Shan. Are you okay? The men are dead. Oh my god! What's happened to you?" Jian had rolled her over and saw her humongous earrings, veil, and golden eyes. Peng let out a similar cry some ten feet from him.

"Jian? Jian? I can't see much. I have sand in my nose and mouth. Can hardly talk. Water," she whispered desperately. Quickly, the men acted. They poured water into the women's mouths and had them spit it out. Once cleared, they had the women snort water as well, until they had coughed up all the sand and cleared their noses from it. Fortunately, both women had known what to do and had mostly been able to protect their faces from the driving, relentless sand storm, aided by the golden veils in fact.

At last able to drink and then to speak, the two told the men what had happened to them, at least what they knew. "Okay, fellows, carry them back up to the ridge line. We'll make camp there for tonight. The rest of us will put these beasts out of their misery. Search every man; bring all their stuff up to the ridge. Find the women's dresses and their robes. We didn't see them back around the ridge where they stopped earlier this afternoon. We have to get them out of those dresses. They are made of silk, if I am not mistaken, deadly in the desert heat," Hojie ordered.

A while later, sitting with her back to a rock, Shan began crying. "Jian, Jian, I can't see much of anything. What have they done to my eyes? Why are they golden? My ears are being ripped from my head. Help me please?" she wailed.

"We will, we will, just hang in there a bit. Hojie may know what to do. Try to just rest a bit, Shan, please," Jian asked. He had no idea what was going on. She had golden eyes, that much was apparent as well as the huge earrings and necklace. Peng removed Mata's necklace, so Jian followed suit. Both men began studying the complex earrings, but saw no way to unfasten them.

Finally, Hojie and his men and Pengdu came back, leading the camels, now loaded with what they had taken from the dead men, left to rot in the desert along with the pitiful horses. While Hojie's men began unloading and setting up camp, he knelt down beside the women at Peng's request, "Can you see how we can take these earrings off them?"

"Don't know. Looks like we will have to cut them off. Here, use your knives. If that main loop really is gold, you ought to be able to cut through it. Gently or you'll tear their ears. While you get them off, I'll get some water boiling. Then, we can remove those ear lobe plugs and wash out their wounds. In time, I think they will heal fine," Hojie ordered. As the two men got a closer look at just what the situation was, Jian and Peng decided against it.

"Shan, the metal loops are way too close to your ears. If I do any cutting, I will likely rip out your ears. I can't undo the golden veil either. It is attached to two studs in either side of your nose. Somehow, they are fused on to the studs. I think it best that we wait until we get back to the village and let the shaka maker see if he can safely remove them," Jian explained, his heart sinking. Again, he was failing his love who was counting on him. Peng agreed with Jian's analysis. It was too dangerous to try to use a knife on them.

Soon the smells of supper filtered into the women's noses. Hojie finally agreed with the two men's conclusions. "Yes, ladies, it will be far safer if we wait. Your ears are not in danger, only your eyes. We'll see what can be done about them in the morning." Resigned to being miserable, the two women allowed themselves to be fed.

That done, it was nearly dark. Although both women's shakas had filled up with sand and their heads were now orange, there was nothing more that the men could do for them in the dark. Peng and Jian slept close to the two that night, watching over them like mother hens. In the morning light, while Hojie and crew fixed breakfast, they helped the women out of the red dresses, only to discover that their whole bodies were caked in the fine orange dust.

Jian called out, "Hojie, they are caked in it! We have to get them a bath."

"Already thought of that. Masai is not too far from here. We'll make for there. Should get there around noon, right Peng?" The caravan owner nodded, thankful that he didn't have to do the critical thinking now. His only concern was for his wife.

"I've never felt so dirty in my whole life, Jian. I can't see you unless I turn my head. Can you fix my eyes at least?" Shan asked. As the men fed the women, they all took turns examining them closely.

"It looks like they have somehow put a golden shell completely around their eyes," Jian noted.

"Ah, that small black spot, that must be the hole out of which they can see," Hojie pointed out. "Can you move your eyes around?" he asked. Shan tried, but nothing happened. It was as if her eyes were glued in place, immobile.

Mata began explaining again what she remembered the men saying. Yingchan, Golden Angels, finally registered with Jian. "It's an ancient tradition. It's in our scrolls." He went on to describe what little he could remember having read about them.

"Well, I am not the finance minister, but those earrings, veils, and necklaces must be worth what the man said, a half million each. You two have inherited a huge fortune for your suffering," Hojie commented.

"I just want to see again. Please help get these things out of my eyes," Shan pleaded.

The men examined both women closely and sat back defeated. "It's almost as if they had taken out their eyes and put a sphere of gold around them," Jian pointed out.

"Well, that's impossible, unless they are dead," Hojie pointed out. "They only had a couple of hours to torture the women. Let's have a thorough look at their possessions. Perhaps that will give us a clue."

They rummaged through the collected packs. Finally, Jian discovered the doctor's pack and found what they were looking for. Another huge set of earrings, a veil, and a necklace were carefully packed in a velvet bag. Another bag held four hemispherical, golden shells, each with a small central hole, perhaps an eighth inch across at most. Around the outer edge, small pie shaped pieces of the sphere had been carefully cut. Among the other items in that pouch was a strange, handheld type of pliers. The golden shells fit nicely in the opened pliers. Now Jain saw how the golden eyes were installed on the women's eyes. While someone held their eyes opened, with a golden sphere in the pliers, one merely closed the pliers, bending the edges together securely clamping the sphere around the eye ball. He demonstrated, closing one of the golden spheres with the pliers, making sure that both women could see him doing it.

"So how do we get them off their eyes?" asked Hojie.

Jian felt sick at his stomach. "The ends are bent around the backsides of their eyes. There is no way at all of getting them off that I can see. My god, I don't see how anyone could ever get them off them without ruining their eyes in the process! Dear god, what have they done to you two?"

Shan panicked. "I can hardly see. Come on; there has to be a way, please?" she begged.

Mata took a deep breath, trying hard to fight her rising panic. "Shan, we can see a little. You saw him close the pliers; the metal has closed around our eyeballs. There is no way to get behind them and pry them loose without crushing our eyeballs. At least, we can still see a little bit. That's better than being totally blind, I hope. Peng, say that's so," she pleaded.

"Yes, my dearest Mata. If you can see even a little bit, that's better than being blind completely. We will get by somehow, I promise you," Peng held onto his wife and said what she needed to hear now. In any case, Peng brought all of the doctor's things back with him with the faint hope that someone in the village might be able to figure a way to get them off the women safely.

Hojie found an iron poker and a bag of gold dust. "Hey, I see how they fused the earrings and veils on the women. Heat up this poker and use a little gold dust. Melts and fuses the joints. We really are going to have to wait until we get back to the village, ladies. I'm sure that the shaka maker can find a safe way to remove them."

Hojie then ordered, "Come on. We have to get them to the water hole at Masai soon. They'll bake with all that sand still stuck in their hair and all over their bodies." Soon they were back on the trail once more. Shan was even more frightened sitting her camel this time. Left alone and in daylight, she saw really just what her new limitations actually were and felt terribly sick at her stomach. Mata too put on a brave face, but riding along, she had to turn her head just to see what was all in front of her.

As predicted, around noon the party arrived at the small watering hole known as Masai. Scarcely six feet across, the blue pool did help support a half dozen date trees and four palms. Masai was often used to water sheep and goats from nearby shepherds, as well as a camping ground for caravans that passed through this area of the Xi. Hastily, the men made camp, and soon, Jian and Peng had the women undressed and their shakas removed. Carefully, they led the women out into the cool waters and began giving them a vitally needed bath. Their hair needed washing even worse. After an hour's work, both men were satisfied that they had gotten all the dirt out of the women's hair. Carefully, they carried the women out of the pond, their long hair bunched up on their chests.

Sitting them in the sun, they dried them off and began the lengthy pat-drying of their hair. By suppertime, the dry heat of Xi had completely evaporated all the water, and the men then brushed out their hair for them, replacing the shakas on their heads afterwards. Of note, Shan's shaka completely covered all but the bottom five inches of her dangling sets of earrings. This restrained her earrings from swinging wildly as she moved her head around to see. Mata's was shorter and did little to prevent her earrings from swinging around wildly, adding to her fears that they were pulling her ears off. A few minutes later, dressed in their now washed and dried white dresses and with their white robes on, the men fed them their supper, chatting about where they were and how far they had yet to travel.

Both women said little, save to thank them for giving them a bath and washing their hair. Both had been embarrassed and humiliated to have been forced to sit naked in the sun before the men all that afternoon while their hair and dresses dried. Yet, nearly blind, they could not have done any of it for themselves. Still they felt the acuteness of their enforced nakedness, and had their circumstances been any better, they would have tried to avoid it somehow.

Sitting side by side around the campfire while the men were cleaning up, Shan whispered to Mata, "I feel like a prisoner in my own body now."

"Dear, I do too. Why did they have to nearly blind us? Aren't we bad off enough?" Both women cried silently to themselves.

Later when Jian laid Shan beside him and got her covered up, he whispered, "Shan, I will dedicate the rest of my life to finding a way to get those golden eyes off you without hurting your eyes. I swear this to you. I will never, ever stop trying." She whispered a heartfelt thank you to him, but she just knew that he would never find a way. The image of the pliers closing on that golden sphere burned in her mind now and would forever haunt her; she just knew it would.

The next morning as they broke camp, Hojie spoke to Shan and Mata. "Ladies, it is my fault that you were taken and harmed. My Seneschal placed his faith in me to protect both of you and I failed in that task. I will honorably accept my fate when I get you safely back to our village. Although I have proven myself not to be fit to be your guard, until I can be replaced by the Seneschal, I have no choice but to continue this mission. However, if you wish, I can return you now and allow others to make this journey to the Valley of the Fallen Beasts."

"Hojie, it isn't your fault. You rescued us from death at their hands. None of us saw the trap that they laid for us. Please, let's continue. How close are we to the valley?" Shan said, encouraging him. After all, she and Mata were now more dependent upon him and the men than ever before.

"I will ask Peng," he bowed and left. Shan detected a note of apathy in his voice; he had failed her. Well, she knew well how he must feel now. Still, he had rescued her and she needed him. She also resolved to put in a good word for him to her father when they returned to Matag.

Three days later, they entered the far western Valley of the Fallen Beasts. Only Peng and Mata had been here once before. They had been in the vicinity on a caravan run and had taken a slight detour to see it briefly. Here the valley floor was only two miles wide, and the rocky, steep sides of the ridges to the north and south were commanding and not traversable by camel. Over time, strong winds had barreled down the valley from the distant mountains, blowing loose sand away and carving out strange curved features in the rock of the valley floor, revealing what appeared to be bones.

After dismounting and securing the camels, the group fanned out to examine this amazing sight close up. Shan struggled along as best she could, Jian's arms holding her steady as her heels attempted to navigate the uneven valley floor. She constantly moved her head about, catching a glimpse of where her next step would land, but also trying hard to see these white bones of beasts, which were exposed by the winds.

"Jian, these must truly be dragons! It must be huge!" she exclaimed, nearly stumbling again.

He caught her and replied, "Yes, my love, this one must be at least sixty feet long. At least that's my guess from what is exposed. It may well have been far longer, because its back half must still lie beneath the floor."

"Wow. Incredible. It could easily have eaten me whole!"

"Indeed, it could probably swallow a horse without any problems. These dragons are huge!" Jian added.

"Jian, this must prove that there are Gods looking out for us. They killed off these monstrous beasts for us. If they had not, why, we'd of all been eaten alive!" Shan declared.

"I do believe that you are right, Shan. There must be Gods. How else can we explain the deaths of so many monster beasts?" Jian agreed with her sound reasoning. Even one of these beasts could easily devour their entire village in just a few days, if it were hungry enough, he thought.

Mata asked, "Peng, how many of these great beasts are there?"

"I have no idea. They seem to stretch on as far as the eye can see. Maybe hundreds of them," Peng answered.

"I do wish I could see better. I can't see more than a little bit at a time," she complained.

"Take all the time you like, Mata. We're going to set up camp here for a few days," Hojie ordered. "Pengdu, do your thing while my men set up camp. Remember, everyone, there is no water around these parts."

"Where do I start?" Pengdu complained. "Jian, which one should I try first?" Jian and Shan continued their wandering and sightseeing until they found one that they liked. Pengdu got out his tools and began chipping off a piece of the bone to grind in his mortar. "These bones are hard as stone! My goodness, how could we ever have killed one?"

"We couldn't, that's for sure," Shan declared, though she had little notions of combat.

"You are right about the Gods, Shan," Pengdu declared. "There must be Gods to have killed all these great dragon beasts for us.

Finally exhausted from the walking and sweating from the midday sun, Shan needed to sit down. After getting her properly positioned to sit down, Jian exclaimed, "Dear, you are about to sit on what must be one of its teeth! Dear god! It's almost half the size of your whole body, Shan!" She turned around to look and added her exclamations to his before sitting down. Now she could slowly move her head, taking in a sort of panorama of the area around her.

"This is like powdered rock!" Pengdu explained as they later sat around their campfire about to eat supper. "I've mixed it with a bit of broth. Gentlemen, if you will give each woman a cup please?"

"Honestly, Pengdu, do you really thing eating ground rock bones is going to help us get our arms back?" Mata declared incredulously. "I don't believe it at all. It sounds ridiculous."

"Yes, but the Seneschal is depending upon us to at least try it and put the villagers' demands and hopes to rest once and for all," Shan declared flatly. "Jian, I'm ready to drink it." He lifted up her golden veil and held the cup as she sipped. "Yucky, it does taste like powdered rock, Pengdu!" She wrinkled her nose, but continued to drink it all. After that, she enjoyed the meal far better than other nights.

The next morning, the men gathered around the waking women to see if they could detect any changes in their bodies. Alas, neither woman felt any different. No arms had mysteriously appeared. After breakfast, they strolled among the bones once more, while Pengdu took another sample from another likely candidate.

For three days, the group stayed in the Valley of the Fallen Beasts, while Pengdu made sample after sample for the women to drink. Nothing happened to the women, and at last, with their water supply running low, Peng decided that they had best leave for home.

"At least we've put that fairytale to bed," Mata declared.

"Yes, but what about the Gods who slew these beasts for us. They must be around here somewhere," Shan observed. "Where would Gods reside?"

"Probably up there where people never go," Jian pointed to the dark mountains, which rose high on west of them. These ridge-lined valleys rose up to the very base of the impassible mountains, just as they did all up and down Tashien.

"We should go up there and search for the Gods, Jian. I'll bet anything that up there somewhere are the very Gods who have afflicted us so badly," Shan declared.

"Yes, but wait. If the Gods are up there and we go there, won't they do even more harm to us all? Look at what they have already done to you women," Jian protested.

"True, but maybe we can talk to them and get them to see just how awful it is for us. Maybe we can ask them why they did this to us. Maybe we can find the reason why we women all deserve to be so Afflicted. We can find out what we did wrong. We can promise never to do it again, if they will give us back our arms," she continued throwing out serious reasons to go looking for the Gods.

The entire group began discussing Shan's ideas. They made sense. "Look, if we can find the Gods who caused our women to be so Afflicted, then we can find out why and what they or we have done wrong to so displease the Gods. We can make amends somehow and get our women's arms back," Peng concluded. "We have to follow this lead. Look, gang. If we return having dis-proven the villagers' ideas about these bones, when they hear Shan's ideas, they will be insisting that we follow down that path, track down these Gods and find out why and how we can get the Gods to reverse what they have done to our women. If we go back now, we are just going to have to come right back here and pick up where we left off. That's wasting weeks of valuable time. I say we continue to follow Shan's leads."

After more discussion, everyone agreed to continue. "We must have more water and food supplies. As far as I know, there is no water available anywhere in the Valley of the Fallen Beasts," Peng pointed out. "Some of us will have to return to the nearest village and replenish our water skins and purchase additional food supplies. I can lead some of us there, but there is no reason to put our women through any additional hardships. Jian and Pengdu, you can stay here. We'll leave one guard behind as well. With the little water and food that remains, you should be just fine for a few days."

"They should move the camp further into the valley, out of sight from here. After all, if any others come here, we don't want them spotting them," Hojie advised. "Further, at the village, I will arrange to send word back to Matag of our plans. The Seneschal must know what we are doing next."

By noon, they had moved the camp four miles further into the valley. Plus, Hojie positioned them behind a jagged out-thrust where they could not be easily seen from further down the valley. Around one, Peng and the others left, leaving only two camels for the five of them who were staying behind, one for each woman. If an emergency arose, the women could ride.

"You were incredibly brave and clever to have destroyed the overlord's magic compass so he could not find his way out of Xi," Jian chatted with Shan. "Very clever of you. Because of that, in time we would have caught up with them, as they rode in circles in the desert. That's one reason I love you so, Shan. You are so clever and bright."

"But — well, I was desperate. I don't even think that's what I was thinking when I did it."

"It sure helped," Mata pointed out. "They headed off in the wrong direction after that. I knew if Peng was not dead, he'd eventually find us. Good thinking, Shan." She flushed, that was not what she was thinking. Rather, she'd just wanted to lash out at the man who did this to her. Still, she saw the wisdom in her intuitive action.

They chatted a while and then took to wandering around their area, looking at the bones that were visible. Each tried to imagine what they must have looked like. The sheer size of the beasts made that nearly impossible. Soon, the five became bored and spent most of the time merely trying to stay out of the direct sunlight by moving into rocky crevasses which temporarily blocked the scorching late June sun.

At first, the two women complained about their terrible eyesight at least a dozen times a day. By the time that Peng returned on July 2, both had ceased mentioning it. Obviously, nothing could be done about it now. Shan's interest now lay on finding their ancient Gods. Surely, the Gods had seen how well the desert people of Xi had continued to follow some of the ancient ways, but perhaps she had not allowed her nails to grow long enough. Perhaps that was the reason the Gods Afflicted her. All manner of wild ideas floated in and out of her mind, reasons why the Gods were displeased with her and the other women of Xi. Perhaps, she had an awful thought, the Gods were displeased because they no longer followed the ancient Yingchan tradition! At least the evil drug lords still honored that tradition. Maybe that was the very reason she had been Afflicted. Well, she steeled herself as she thought, when I see the Gods, they can see that I am now a Yingchan and maybe restore my arms.

To the five's surprise, Peng had returned with an additional twenty camels loaded with water skins, food supplies, and even a hundred feet of rope. "I added ten more oil lamps and a keg of oil too," he pointed out. "Now we are a well-armed expedition. We shall begin our search for the ancient Gods first thing in the morning."

A week later, they finally climbed up and out of the Valley of the Fallen Beasts onto the lower sides of the impassible mountains. The view was spectacular, and here they spent an hour just taking in the view, allowing extra time for the women to take it all in. For these people, this was a once in a lifetime opportunity to see what few, if any, had ever seen before. Jagged ridges fell away from the mountains as far as the eye could see, all up and down the line.

Curiously enough, Peng had occasionally paused to collect gold nuggets. The eroding winds had carved out the bedrock, leaving the heavier nuggets behind. By the time that they reached the mountain proper, he'd accumulated twenty pounds of gold nuggets. "We won't have to worry about mining for gold for new shakas for a while. Probably got enough for three or four of them."

After studying the terrain, they decided that the Gods must live far higher up. This close to the beginnings of all the western valley systems of Tashien would be too close to the millions of people for the Gods. There only seemed to be one easy way on up — a V-shaped valley or gorge appeared to climb far higher up the imposing mountains. Lacking any other direction, they headed on up this one. As it rose sharply, the men had to go on foot, leading the camels who began to protest the climb.

On August 1, 825, the high mountain valley began rising steeply. It had narrowed to almost a crack, just barely wide enough to allow the camels to pass. Had the floor been rock strewn, they would not have made it. Centuries of snow slides had pushed any loose rock on down and out into the Valley of the Fallen Beasts. Just when Peng was about to suggest that they give it up, the gorge ended. To either side, a twenty-foot wide, level ledge disappeared going north-south. Peng had kept silent about just how they could have possibly turned the camels around had he decided to retreat. He didn't have any idea so tight was the fit.

"What is this?" asked Jian as he stumbled out of breath onto the ledge, leading Shan on her camel behind him. He moved south following Peng, leading Mata's camel.

"Don't know, but make room for the others. Keep close to the western side. God, that drop off to the east is a sure killer!" Peng pointed out the obvious. Shan gazed out over the side from atop her camel and felt sick at her stomach. The drop-off fell over a thousand feet down!

"How utterly strange," Jian commented as one by one, the others appeared on the wide ledge. "This is like a highway along the top of the mountains."

"Hardly the top, Jian. We are a long, long way from up there," Ping pointed out the obvious fact. "Still, to my eyes and senses, this ledge does seem like a path or highway, Jian. Most peculiar, though I have never been in any mountains before. Is there anything in our historical records about something like this?"

"Not that I recall, Peng. I wonder how far it goes?"

"Don't know, but we really don't have any choice but to follow it, do we?"

"This must be the God's Highway," Shan declared ardently. "I can't see it well, but what I can see, it sure does look like a road or path. We must have entered God's Realm and this is his highway, like Jian says!"

Everyone quickly bought this explanation, for it certainly did look like a road. After a brief rest, Peng led them onward for several miles. Although it twisted and turned, it hugged the side of the mountain, neither rising nor falling! This convinced them even further that this was God's Highway. Just as Peng was mulling over how they could safely make camp along this ledge without someone falling over its edge in the dark, an enormous hole opened up into the mountain just to his right.

"My god! What is this?" he exclaimed. As he and Jian stood and stared into the blackness, Hojie came up to them to see what the holdup was all about.

"Let me go inside first and see if it is safe. There could be wild animals inside." He went back to his camel and returned with two men. All carried lanterns and had their long guns at the ready. They walked into the cavern. Its entrance must be at least twenty feet tall, Jian estimated and six wide. Soon the three figures began talking loudly. Peng and Jian picked up, "It is absolutely huge in here. See any creatures? No, keep your eyes open."

Tense minutes passed, while Shan sat on her camel, her excitement building. This just had to be the home of the Gods! It just had to be so. What else could possibly explain the highway and now this — this enormous cavern? Already she could no longer see the three men; they must be deep inside. Panic struck her. What if they encountered the God? It should be herself that faced the God to ask why and how and what they could do to make amends for their transgressions. After what seemed to her to be an eternity, the three reappeared. Their faces looked ghastly, and they were most certainly spooked.

"It's safe. No wild animals are inside. It must be the Home of the Gods! Come on in, light all the lanterns," Hojie said in a trembling voice. Shan moved her head a bit and saw that his arm was shaking a little. What was inside? She had to see!

"Oh my god! We are right! This must be the home of the gods!" Shan exclaimed as she was led inside on her camel. Hojie looked ashen as he held the camel and got it to kneel and then lie on its stomach. Jian carefully lifted her off, setting her gently on her small feet, but holding her tightly. In the dim light, he knew that she would have an even harder time seeing.

"There are at least three side chambers. Go look at that one first," Hojie pointed to the leftmost side chamber. One by one, the others lit their lanterns and all headed to see what Hojie meant.

"Oh my!" Shan exclaimed abruptly. "Jian, is that a bed that I'm seeing?"

"Oh dear! Yes, it is a bed, but it is the largest bed that I have ever heard of — who — who ever sleeps here must be a giant!" he replied, his face becoming almost as ashen as Hojie's. The bed was fifteen feet long and twelve wide! It still had bedding on it, but a layer of dust suggested it had not been used in a long time.

When Jian pointed out the dust, they all began to relax a bit. Obviously, they had stumbled into the home of the Gods, but the Gods had not slept here for many years. Jian helped Shan to the bed and got her sitting on its edge. Mata soon joined her. "We have got to take care of the camels and get more lanterns on and supper going," he explained. "Hojie is off making doubly sure that no one is here."

"You were right, Shan! There are Gods around," Mata whispered, as if the very Gods were listening to her right now.

"Yes, Mata. Somehow, someway, we must have displeased them, which is why we women were so badly Afflicted. I wish we could talk to the Gods and ask them what it was that we did that so angered them. We must have done something really, really bad, don't you think?"

"Yes, but what could it have been, Shan?" Mata replied totally lost. "I've never cheated on Peng. Maybe it was because we have long ago abandoned the Yingchan, do you suppose? Honestly, I only know what little your mother sings about them, the Golden Angels. Maybe we have angered the Gods because we don't have Yingchan anymore and the drug lords do."

"I don't know, Mata. I heard from dad who heard it from other travelers that the God's Affliction has affected everyone in Tashien, including the people who live in the hills south of Xi, where the drug lords live. Maybe we were supposed to have many Yingchan in our village. Maybe those of us with bound feet were also supposed to be Yingchan as well. That could be it. Dad says that those in the outer lands have long ago forsaken our ancient traditions. Maybe this is why we were all Afflicted."

"You might be right. We have to find the Gods and ask them. I hope that I am brave enough to face them, though," she admitted.

"We will. We both will face the Gods and ask," Shan declared.

After they ate supper, the group decided to put off further exploration until daylight came, to preserve their oil. The bed was so large and so comfortable that they decided they would sleep in it. However, Hojie and his guards decided to sleep on the floor close by. If anything came after them in the night, their bodies would be in the way, providing some protection for the women and others in the bed.

They woke with the rising sun, which cast its strong rays into the caverns. All realized that by noon, the light would drastically dim down as the sun passed the zenith and no longer entered the huge entrance directly. They would have to resort to lanterns after lunch. Thus, early mornings became their best times for their searching.

After even a few minutes of wandering around in the better light, all concluded that without a doubt, this had to be the home of the Gods. Further, by all signs, the Gods had not been here in quite some time, perhaps since they Afflicted everyone in Xi. While dust covered everything, it was not the vast amounts that they expected to see if the place had not been used for say a century. Rather, their best guesses suggested a far shorter time, likely since the Affliction struck them.

In one chamber, they found many crates stacked up. Hoping they might contain food, several were opened. However, all contained very strange objects, which our engineers later verified were electronic devices, which emitted the energy beams that had kept the general population of Tashien so badly depressed in emotional tones, allowing none to rise above anger and hostility. After examining several of these crates, they left the remainder untouched, figuring rightly that they only contained more of these God Things, as they began calling the electronics.

My worst fears were realized. They discovered another set of the Golden Helmets and Shields, along with the accompanying sword. Many years before, a young man had discovered these, had put them on, and ended up slaughtering thousands of soldiers while seeking his lost love. The Golden Warrior he had been called. Hojie examined these objects carefully. Thank god, he did not attempt to put them on. If he had, he would have been unable to get them off himself. It took our engineers to figure out how to get the Golden Warrior out of his!

They found a stash of gold ingots however. While they were not particularly interested in it from a monetary standpoint, it did drive their speculations! "Why would the Gods want so much gold?" asked Shan.

"There are no legends of our ancestors giving gold to the Gods," Jian pointed out. "Never has our history stated that we sacrificed gold to the Gods. The only references to gold in the oldest legends are the Yingchan and our shakas. 'Dress forth the chosen one in gold that she may become your Golden One, your Yingchan.' That's what the scroll says."

"Do the Gods want us to make more of us as Yingchan?" Shan asked, questioningly.

"Dunno, but there sure is a whole lot of gold here. Probably enough to adorn a hundred women like you and Mata are adorned," Pengdu pointed out.

"Do you suppose that the Gods Afflicted us because we have forsaken the ancient tradition of the Yingchan?" Shan asked. Many shook their heads.

"That could explain it, possibly," Jian answered in a non-committing manner.

After looking at the items that were in plain sight, the group began looking into not so obvious things. All wanted clues. Hojie was the first to turn the lights on in the cavern complex accidentally. "What happened? Has the Gods shown up?" screamed Jian. Even Shan very nearly peed her pants when the bright lights came on.

"It's only me! Hey, come look at this! Magical light! Push this and — oh! They go off," Hojie yelled to the others. Hastily, he pushed it again and the place was flooded with daytime illumination. After everyone saw the button and how he did it, they turned their attention to the high ceiling overhead.

"Where's the sun coming from?" asked Pengdu, confused.

"I don't see any openings in the roof," Jian added.

"Told you, it must be magical or something," Hojie confessed. He had no other answer for the light's existence.

Embolden by the clear visibility, they searched through things more thoroughly. With most of the items that they found, they had no clue as to its use or purpose. However, during their third day of searching, Jian came across a concealed drawer, which slid out of the cavern's wall. As he looked inside, pleased with his cleverness at finding this drawer, he saw several more of the golden eye ball spheres! These had substantially larger holes in them and he reasoned that the wearers would be able to see better than Shan and Mata could. Besides a dozen of these, he also saw a long cylinder affair with ten buttons on it.

"Hey, Shan, come look at what I found in here," he asked. Slowly, Shan walked on her heels over to the drawer. "Look," he pointed. She bent over and moved her head around a bit, piecing together the contents of the three-foot long drawer. Her field of vision could not take in the whole drawer at one view.

"Those must be more golden eyes, Jian!" she exclaimed. As they talked about that, Mata and several others joined them to have a look at what he'd found.

"Now this clinches it," Jian pronounced. "These *are* the Gods whom our ancient legends tell us brought us the Yingchan, bound footed women, and Lunula."

"Say, Jian," Shan proposed, "do you suppose that our shaka custom comes originally from the Yingchan? I mean like Mata and I are, we can barely function at all. Perhaps, our ancient ancestors turned these veils and massive earrings into the easily worn shakas. Women easily wear shakas, but these earrings and veil are just awful. Every time I move my head, my ears feel like they are being pulled off. I bet anything that our ancient ancestors turned Yingchan into shaka to make life fantastically easier for us women."

"Shan, that's brilliant," Jian exclaimed. "I bet that is exactly what happened way back when!"

"So there is no doubt of it; the Gods here are the same as our ancient Gods," Shan declared positively. "Look, they may have even made or invented these golden eye spheres that so cripple Mata and me."

"Yes, but Shan, there are none of those special pliers that the doctor fellow had — you know, to clamp the spheres around your eyes so that they can never be removed," Jian pointed out.

"Perhaps they are in the drawer somewhere. I can't see very well. Surely, there ought to be at least one pliers here. Maybe there is a way to removed them too, Jian. That would make sense. Nothing harms gold, so when a Yingchan died, the Gods would want to remove them and reuse their golden eye spheres," she suggested.

Mata pointed out, "If she is dead, it wouldn't matter if the Gods needed to tear out her eyeballs just to get the golden spheres back."

"Hum, true, Mata," Shan conceded. "Say, what if a Yingchan got sick or something or what if the Gods decided that another woman should have the golden spheres. Then, they would want to remove them from one of us who was still alive. Maybe they had a way to undo it."

"Maybe they have a way to undo the Afflictions too," Mata suggested.

"I think that we are getting warm, closer to the solution," Jian pointed out. "We know that the Gods have these here. It remains for us to find out how they installed them and removed them. Perhaps that will give us a clue about the Afflictions as well. Back to work, everyone. Search high and low."

Try as he might, Jian found nothing else in the drawer and no other secret compartments. However, there was that foot long cylinder with the buttons lying in the drawer. At last, he picked it up. Had I been there, I would have let out a screeching warning! That was the surgical knife instrument that the mad Doctor had used on us to amputate appendages, cleanly and easily! However, I wasn't there and couldn't stop the curious Jian.

He studied it for a time. Each button had a unique, but foreign symbol on its surface. Talk about luck! Jian had twelve possible buttons that he could have pressed. Several would produce the amputation knives used in surgery. The one he pressed caused a three-dimensional image to appear before his eyes, emanating from the cylinder. "Hey, Shan, come look at this!"

She bent over to look and saw the same holographic image. "Look, those symbols in the image are on the cylinder — on the buttons," she pointed out.

"You are right. That one looks promising," he suggested and touched the image of the button within the image itself. Instantly, the three-dimensional image changed. There was writing, if that was the proper term for all the symbols that appeared, but also there were small pictures within them. "This looks like a procedure guide, instructions to follow."

"Yes, but look at what it is doing! It's cutting off someone's legs!" Shan gushed, dismayed with what her limited vision was showing her. She continually moved her head slightly, trying to see the whole three-dimensional image.

"I'll try another one," Jian suggested. "Hey, look at this one, Shan. See, it is being held against the body where an arm should be. Then, way down there, it shows the body with its arm. You don't suppose that this is the cure for the Affliction, do you?"

"I don't know, Jian. It looks promising. I wonder if we dare try it?" she asked. Part of her wanted nothing to do with this God device. Another part of her desperately wanted her arms back. The two chatted about it for a bit. Shan finally made up her mind. "Look, I came along on this trip so that we could test out possible ways to undo the Affliction. I ate all those powdered bones of Pengdu's and that did nothing. Now we find this thing here, which certainly belongs to the Gods. From the pictures, it looks like it might work. I don't think that we have any real choice. We have to try it on me and see if it works."

"Oh no! What if it does something else even more horrible to your body?" Jian protested. Mata, Peng, and several others, overhearing their discussion, joined them and a serious discussion began. Some agreed with Shan, that they should try it, while others were extremely hesitant.

"Look, what if it actually does work and undoes your Affliction, Shan? Then, the Gods return and see that you and we have undone the Gods Affliction. Won't that make the Gods terribly angry and smite us all down? Turn us into bones in the Valley of the Fallen Beasts?" Peng pointed out.

"What if it does something else really awful to you?" Mata added.

After more discussion, Shan won out. "Look, our whole mission coming here was to find a solution to women's Afflictions. We have to try it. I will be the guinea pig this time. If something horrible happens to me, all I ask is that one of you puts me out of my misery. I may not even be able to talk, so just do it. I don't think I can live if I am missing any more parts."

"Yes, but what if the Gods are angry with us?" Peng insisted on his critical point.

"Tell them it was my idea. Look, Peng. We have already established that the Gods very likely caused women's Afflictions because we had all forsaken our own ancient traditions, especially the Yingchan for us. The outsiders have forsaken bound feet and even the Lunula too. Mata and I are now proper Yingchan, right? At least as best we know from our history legends. So perhaps the Gods will not be angry with us, because we have returned to the ancient Yingchan tradition."

"Well, that does make sense, Shan," Peng gave her that point. "We all have forsaken Yingchan centuries ago at least. There is no doubt that you are a Golden Angel now, your captors said as much. If we believe them and what little Jian can recall the Yingchan, then you are a proper one. Maybe then the Gods will relent and not be angry with us for undoing the Affliction."

They discussed it further and finally all agreed. Shan ought to give it a try, for that was her purpose in coming along in the first place. Her argument about now being a Yingchan assuaged their fears of the Gods' retaliation on them. While everyone watched, Jian carefully pushed the proper button. A round sphere appeared at the end of the cylinder. A low humming noise could be heard. He touched it to her armless left shoulder.

"It tingles," she said. "Kind of like someone is tickling me. Anyone see my arms appearing yet?" No one did.

"Well, maybe I'm doing it wrongly," Jian suggested, turning it off and bringing up the informational images once more. He looked them over along with the others who looked over his shoulders. At last, he determined that perhaps he had and tried it again, this time on both shoulders.

"Still nothing happening, just tickling, Jian. I guess it must not be doing what we had hoped," Shan said with a letdown sigh.

"Well, it was worth a try," Jian added. "Back to the searching everyone." The hopeful group disbanded, each returning to what they were doing before.

"Thanks for trying, Jian," Shan whispered, and she headed back to the bed to sit down and think. Besides, she'd been standing on her small feet for too long, and they were aching. Jian went back to his experimenting with the images of the cylinder.

A while later, he spotted another button and realized what he had found. He leaned over the golden spheres and pressed the button. One of the golden eye spheres flew up and into the hollow spherical receptacle that had appeared at the end of the cylinder. A bit later, pressing the next button, the vaned outer edges slowly closed, as if encasing an eyeball. That sequence ended. He'd discovered the Gods' pliers. Quietly, he experimented further. Soon, a huge grin filled his face; he'd just reversed the plier's operation. The golden spherical shell had returned to its previous state!

He hadn't said anything about this discovery for good reasons. He felt that Shan was entirely right in her deductions. The women were Afflicted because they had for so long abandoned the most ancient traditions of the Yingchan. Given that and the possibility that at any time the Gods could reappear, to keep the Gods from smiting down them all into the Valley of the Fallen Beasts, Shan and Mata had to be true Yingchan, at least as best they knew what Yingchan had been. If he removed her golden eye spheres so that she could finally see properly and the Gods returned, they undoubtedly would be quite angry with them all. Further, if by some lucky chance, they stumbled upon a way to undo the Affliction and Shan had her arms and hands back and was not a Yingchan any longer, surely, the Gods would smite them down in a rage. Yet, if she was still a Yingchan, they could plead for forgiveness, demonstrating that they were honoring their women as Yingchan now, pacifying the Gods' ire. In Jian's mind, it was vastly more important for Shan and Mata to have their arms back than to have the golden eye spheres removed or even the annoying jewelry. Hence, he kept this discovery to himself and continued to seek a way to undo the Gods' Affliction.

A bit later, Hojie called them over to see his latest find. "The Gods use a metal rope. Look at this," he held up a large coil of copper wire. All believed it was the Gods' version of a rope, knowing nothing of Velona's discovery of electricity. So it went the rest of that day. After supper, Hojie turned out the cavern's lights, and they again turned in for the night.

Everyone was awakened by Shan's yells. Jian panicked, figuring the Gods had returned and were about to turn them all into stone. Shan was sitting up in the monster-sized bed. Jian stared at her. There were her arms, just as he remembered them the last time that he'd seen them. Poor Shan just could not see all them and continued to try to move her head to see portions of them.

"Praise the Gods! Shan! Your arms! They're back!" Jian exclaimed, more excited than he had ever been in his life.

"Touch them, see if they feel real! I cannot believe it, Jian. They feel like my arms, but maybe not. Everyone, please check them out. I just cannot see them well enough to tell if they are really real or not," Shan pleaded, again feeling horribly constrained by her eyes.

Everyone began feeling her arms. "Ouch!" she exclaimed. Hojie had actually pinched her upper arm.

He flushed, "Had to do that. Looks real enough to me, Shan. Can you move them properly?" She swung her arms this way and that.

"God, I never thought that I would so love my arms again! Jian, this means that what you did yesterday did work, only it took a day! God, I am starving, like I haven't eaten for days!"

"Perhaps your body had to grow them and that's why you are so hungry," Peng proposed.

"Do me soon," Mata yelled above the others.

"As soon as we eat, Mata, I'll do it to you. If we are lucky and on the right track, you should have your arms back by morning too!" Jian boasted.

"Oh, I can walk ever so much better," Shan added as she headed for the huge table where they had their meals. For the first time since the plague struck, Shan was able to feed herself without any assistance from Jian. Mata was dying with envy and insisted Jian do her the very instant he finished eating. He complied.

"Well, I can feel my way around even though I can't see very well. Oh, this is heaven, fellows," Shan continued to bubble over, expressing her immense relief repeatedly. Later, Shan insisted on taking over washing the dishes and fixing their meals. Although her very long nails were bothersome and made these tasks challenging, Shan didn't care in the slightest! She had her arms back and that was all that mattered.

Over supper tea, Jian decided to reveal what else he'd discovered and allow her to decide on their next step. "Honey, I have found the cylinder's buttons that both install the golden eye spheres and more importantly, the buttons to remove them, safely, I believe. The question is," he began.

Shan interrupted him, intuitively knowing what he was about to say. "We've just undone the Affliction that the Gods put on me, and Mata too most likely by morning. What if the Gods return and find that we've undone it? If we are right and the reason we were Afflicted in the first place was our abandoning the ancient ways, specifically those of the Yingchan, then the Gods have an honest right to be very angry with us and even cast us into the Valley of the Fallen Beasts. Yet, if I remain true to the Yingchan, we can say that we have seen the errors of our ancestors and have returned to the ancient ways of the Gods. Then, they may forgive us. What do you think?"

"As much as I would love to see you able to see properly, at least you can see some. Having your arms back is so much more vital. I wouldn't like to gamble with the Gods. If you can bear it, I would like you to remain a Yingchan for a while longer, just in case the Gods return. Perhaps our men's lives depend on it," Jian answered.

"I agree. I love you so, Jian. I would feel just awful if the Gods took their anger out on you solely because I gave up being a Yingchan too. I can get by this way. It is not fun or easy, but with my arms back, I can do all that I used to be able to do. I am no longer a helpless woman; now I am worthy of you once more, Jian."

"Shan, you have never stopped being most worthy of me," Jian protested. She leaned over, found his face by using her hands, and kissed him through her golden veil.

The next morning, Mata was wildly excited. Her arms had reappeared as well. After everyone checked her arms, they celebrated, and Shan fixed them breakfast. Over tea afterwards, Shan and Jian explained about his other discoveries.

"Look, we can return to our village and undo the Afflictions of our women," Shan began, waving her long talons for added emphasis. "The question that we face is this: are we supposed to turn all women into Yingchan before we use the cylinder on them to give them their arms back or not? We must go to the other villages too. Is there supposed to be one Yingchan per village? Or are all women supposed to be Yingchan? I fear the wrath of the Gods if we make a miscalculation here, for surely our forsaking of the ancient tradition is what so raised the ire of the Gods."

"Now that, Shan, is a very good question," Peng answered. He turned and addressed the others, "She raises a vital point. Do all women need to become Yingchan or perhaps only one or two per village? If we get this wrong, who knows what future ire the Gods will manifest upon us all? Those first two months were terrible for us men. We dare not make a mistake on this one."

"I agree," Hojie added his thoughts, "we dare not get this one wrong. After all, if Shan is right and we were Afflicted because we abandoned the ancient ways of the Yingchan, then if we don't get this right, the next Gods' Affliction could be far worse. So how do we know which the Gods desire? All women, a few dozen women per village, just one per village or even two or three?"

"This seems to be a question for our village historian," Peng suggested. "I have no idea which is the right choice. Jian?"

"I wish that I had access to all the ancient writings. I agree, we must get this one right or by our actions of undoing the current Affliction, we may bring down a far worse Affliction on our people," Jian admitted.

"Think, Jian, what do you remember about the ancient legends?" Shan insisted on prodding him a little. She was certain that he knew the answer. He was their historian.

"Well, the legends didn't ever say that all women everywhere had to be Yingchan. Heck, there probably isn't that much gold in the whole world," Jian admitted.

"Well, that's a start. Not all women. Makes sense, not all of our women are bound footed. Not all have the same length nails either," Peng agreed with him.

"Yes, Peng, but about half of us in Xi are bound footed," Mata pointed out. "I honestly don't think that there is enough gold to make such elaborate jewelry for half of us women. I know a lot goes into the shakas, but most shakas are smaller than Shan's. Take mine, for instance. It has about half the gold that hers has. Still, there is a whole lot of gold in our Yingchan jewelry, a half million worth, if those vile men are to be believed."

"Very possibly they are right — a half million. Look how dense and heavy each dangle is and how many dangles there are in the earrings alone," Peng pointed out. "Plus you add in the veils and then their three neck rings and the attached monster sized necklace and you probably do have a half million. Shan's shaka, minus the rubies and emeralds, probably has a hundred to two hundred gold in it."

"Two hundred. Dad once told me that," Shan interjected. "But wait, the shakas are often handed down. Part of mine was my grandmother's shaka. Dad added on to it some."

"She has a point," Jian backed her up. "You see, we just keep handing the shakas on down to our relatives and each adds a bit more gold or gems to it, making it their own. Never have we gone out and mined enough gold at one time to make a large shaka from scratch. They evolve over the centuries. That must mean that the Gods do not want us to make every woman into a Yingchan. Even if we took all the Gods' gold back with us, there would not be enough to make every woman into a proper Yingchan."

"He's right. While there is perhaps a hundred pounds of it, Shan's Yingchan jewelry must total at least ten pounds. So there's enough to make ten Yingchan at most here," Hojie pointed out.

Pengdu added his thoughts to the mix. "Say, even if you decide that each village must have one Yingchan, how are we going to make all this jewelry and stuff? I doubt that most villages would be able to scrape up enough gold to make even one set like Shan's. They are definitely going to need some gold to even make one Yingchan. Perhaps we should consider taking the Gods' gold with us and dole it out to each village to help them make the Yingchan jewelry that they will need."

"Good idea. We could leave a lengthy note for the Gods, telling them what we are doing and planning. Surely they can read our writing and will know that we mean to honor the ancient ways as we undo the Afflictions of our women," Hojie suggested.

"So what we are saying is that we believe each village should have one Yingchan present?" Jian asked for clarification.

"Yes, I think that we can manage somehow to make one per village, assuming that we help them out with the extra gold that they will need for the jewelry," Shan answered. "Only one problem: there are only a few of the golden eye spheres here."

That set them back a bit. Even Jian knew that the Golden Angels had to have golden eyes; that was inherent in their description in the ancient legends. Hojie came up with an idea, "Look, surely the Gods have a way to make more of those spheres. They must have a way to make the gold into those bars, so they must have a way to make the spheres from some of that gold. We just haven't located that device yet. I think that we need to focus our search for some device that turns raw gold into the golden spheres." On this, they all agreed and the search began once more. This time, all were focused on a single objective.

A day later, Hojie found the molds that the Gods used. Several were in the shape of the ingots that they had found. Two were obviously meant to form the golden eye spheres. Now armed with a means of making more spheres and the necessary jewelry for proper Yingchan, the group felt far more comfortable.

The next day, while Hojie and his men began loading up the camels with the things that they were going to take back with them, Jian wrote out a very lengthy and careful explanation of just what they were doing and why. To be on the safe side, he signed his name to it and Shan added hers. After all, if the Gods wanted to take revenge on their undoing of the Afflictions, then the two of them wanted that retribution to fall on themselves alone, not their friends and others in their village and the rest of Xi.

"Dear, it looks like we have taken it upon ourselves to visit every woman in Xi and undo their Affliction," Jian pointed out.

Shan flashed him a smile, "Yes, we have. I'm so glad that you are helping me with this. It's going to take us a good while to do all this, but it must be done, Jian." He gave her a kiss through her golden veil.

They left the plasticine's cavern around September 1, heading back down the steep gorge which slowly widened out until it reached the demarcation line, where the rugged, steep ridges began. Reaching it on September 7, they looked back and were shocked to see a blanket of heavy white snow covering the mountain side where they had been.

"We are one lucky batch of travelers," Hojie commented, while Shan and Mata strained to see the whole scene. "A few more days in the caverns and we would have become snow bound and unable to get back down until spring. We'd have starved to death long before that happened! We are incredibly lucky!" None disagreed.

As they rode along, Peng insisted that the two women hide the fact that they had their arms back. No need to raise expectation levels of whomever they came across just yet. They had too many problems to resolve first. Thus, with the white robes covering them, the two allowed the men to lead their camels for them again. However, when they camped in the open country, they did the cooking and dishes. Several times, they stayed in a village, camping near the water pool. Here, they did their best to hide that they had their arms back. In time, if all worked out, Jian and Shan would return here and work their miracle on the women of the village.

Mid-September, the group finally arrived back in Matag, receiving a warm welcome, though they were still hiding that they had their arms back. Once inside the Yushube home, the two women took off their robes, revealing all. Shi and Qing both gasped at the sight of their daughter. Her younger sister, Shu, squealed. While their golden appearance was shocking and distressing, their arms and hands elicited the wild reactions of joy and hope.

Shu exclaimed, "Shan! What happened to you? Can you even see? How did you get your arms back? Can I get mine back too? Pengdu, you have to help me get mine back right away? Aren't your ears being pulled off? I don't think she can see, mom."

"Well, I think I would rather have my arms than see. Dear child, what happened to the both of you? How? Was it the powdered bones after all? We got Hojie's message," her mother, Qing asked.

"Are you really blinded, Shan? Can you see anything? I'm so thankful that your arms seem like I remember them," Seneschal Shi asked. Meanwhile, all the others were firing similar barrages of questions at both Shan and Mata, rapid fire — so much so that neither woman had a chance to answer. They continually moved their heads about trying to see everyone who was here, but they could only focus on a portion of a single face at a time. This only added to the rapidly forming assumption that they were blinded by their golden eyes, which did attract almost as much attention as their arms did.

Shan tried to give each person a hug, but gave it up. Her feet couldn't support such rapid movements, and she couldn't see well enough to walk without banging into those who were thronging them. Seneschal Shi restored order quickly, "Everyone, everyone, please. Let's only ask Shan one question at a time. Please, she must sit down before she falls down. Jian, get her to her couch; I don't believe that she is able to do that herself. Please, let's let them sit and tell us all about it. Yes, that's her couch. You sit with her, Jian. Peng, escort Mata to that one. Oh, it is so good to see you all back safe and sound. We were most worried about all of you. Please, dear daughter, tell us how you were able to get new arms and whether the rest of our women can get new ones too. I think that is the most important news of all time."

"Yes, Mata and I can see, but only just barely. Everyone, we have exciting and incredible news to share. We did it! We found where the Gods dwell and have brought back many things with us. We believe that we have a way for all of we women to undo the Gods' Afflictions," Shan began. "It is rather complex. I believe that it is important to explain what happened first. Mata and I got kidnaped by a drug lord who came into Xi to find some women to turn into Yingchan. He told us that the drug lords still follow the ancient ways of the Yingchan, the Golden Angels. We don't know why he didn't take some of the women in his own lands and wanted us instead." She outlined what had happened to them and how they had been rescued.

"Shan, this is awful! You really can't see hardly anything?" her sister asked, interrupting her. Shan explained as best she could and heard many sympathetic comments from the other women, though she couldn't see the women now.

"We can only see about this much at one time," she held out her hand in a narrow V cone, which only brought more wails of sympathy and astonishment.

"But this is really important, when we were rescued, Mata and I really had been turned into Yingchan. Our earrings, veils, and necklaces are supposed to be worth a half million, but I guess Medan can inspect them and tell us if that is even right," Shan continued.

She told about their experiences in the Valley of the Fallen Beasts and the total failure from eating the powdered bones. "We were so close to the mountains and obviously the Gods must dwell in the uninhabited mountains. Well, we just had to continue the mission that you sent us on dad." She described their arduous climb up the mountain and their incredible discover of the Highway of the Gods. "We knew that we were getting close to the Gods," she went on and then described their discovery of the Gods' Cavern Home.

Everyone was so interested in this that Shan swore that she could have heard a pin dropping on the floor. She did her best to relay all that they had seen and done, though many gasped when they heard the incredible dimensions of the bed of the Gods. That ten humans could sleep in it at one time filled them all with awe and a tremendous respect for their Gods who must be absolute giants!

"Now you have to understand what we worked out. We strongly believe that the reason the Gods afflicted us all — why we lost our arms — is that we have all forsaken the ancient tradition of the Yingchan." Several gasped and she went on, "Thus, the Gods have given us a warning. Hojie estimates that the Gods were last in the cavern around the time that we were all Afflicted, so that ties in too. Jian then discovered the Gods' Cylinder and he is a genius! He figured out how the cylinder can both install our golden eyes as well as remove them safely. Without this cylinder of the Gods, our golden eye spheres cannot be removed by us without destroying our eyes, blinding us permanently. He also discovered that this same cylinder can undo the Affliction the Gods cast upon us. He used it on me and on Mata. Look, we have our original, very own arms back, though I admit that my nails are now in dire need of attention.

I've been cooking and washing dishes with them."

"Here is our dilemma and our solution. If we are right that the Gods grew angry with us for having forsaken the ancient ways of the Yingchan and Afflicted we women, then if we use this cylinder of the Gods to undo what they have done to us, the Gods will rightly be sorely angry with us and perhaps Afflict us far worse than we now are. So we reasoned that we need to show the Gods that we are returning to the old traditions of the honored Yingchan, and hopefully, the Gods will see that we have learned our lesson and not punish us for having undone their original Affliction on us women." Many nodded, seeing the logic of her reasoning. It seemed quite sound and logical. Furthermore, the women now had a solid reason why they had lost their arms, something that they didn't have until now. Honestly, that was perhaps the biggest thing on every woman's mind throughout Tarra: why did I lose my arms? This line of reasoning seemed the complete answer to the women of Xi, for they had centuries ago forsaken the tradition of the Yingchan, substituting the shaka in its place, for a shaka was a mere head dressing, and the Yingchan was debilitating for the woman.

Shu spoke up, "Sis, are you saying that we all need to become like you are? I mean a Yingchan just so we can get our arms back?" She was worried, as were several other women. Shan and Mata looked like they were very restricted though nowhere near as bad as they were without their arms.

"We thought about that, sis. We don't think so." Sighs of relief echoed around the room. "You see, if Medan verifies that it takes a half million in gold just to make our needed jewelry, there isn't that much gold in the whole world to adorn all the women in Xi. No, we have thought long and hard about this. We are gambling that the Gods will be content if just one or two women in each village become the traditional Yingchan for the village. At least we hope that the Gods will be content with just one or two from each village." Shan detected visible relief. Well, they had a right to be, the severe restriction of her eyes made everything so terribly difficult and challenging, to say nothing of her ears and difficulties holding the veil up so she could eat.

"We went further. There is not likely to be enough gold in any village to make all the needed jewelry for even one Yingchan, so we brought back the Gods' stash of gold to help. Also, there is the problem of how to make the needed golden eye spheres. I admit, they are most awful to have on, I can only just barely see, and my eyes don't move anymore so I have to move my head around all the time, very annoying, but it must be done if we are to be proper Yingchan for the Gods. Jian found the gold molds and he believes that we can use some of the Gods' gold to make more of the golden eye spheres too. He and I think that we will be able to make at least one Yingchan for each village. Once we have a village Yingchan made, then we think that it will be safe for us to restore the arms of those women in that village. At least that is our plan. Since Mata and I have chosen to remain Matag's Yingchan, we can get started on undoing our women's Afflictions soon. That is, dad, if you agree with us and give us your consent to do this."

"Shan, you and Jian have shown the greatest wisdom that I have ever known!" Seneschal Shi replied finally. "I can find no fault in either what you have done or in what you have reasoned. It would seem to me that you have uncovered the truth of it all. At last, I can see why we were so afflicted and why our women did not regain their arms as we all did with our feet. Our feet were merely a warning, which none of us heeded. Had you not discovered all this, our women would remain Afflicted forever more, for I would never had uncovered why the Gods had done this to us all. Yes, you must work your magic on our women here in Matag. If it is successful and we incur no further wrath of the Gods, I will visit the other villages of Xi and explain the situation to their Seneschals. Together, we will help each village prepare a Yingchan of their own, and once she is done, you may work your magic on the other women of that village. In time, we will have undone the Afflictions upon all of Xi."

"Do me first!" squealed Shu, who hastily added, "Does it hurt much?"

Shan grinned. "No, it sort of tingles, that's all. Can we unpack our things first? I can't do it, though. I can't see well enough to do it. Jian does it. A day later, your arms are back just like they were before that awful day."

Half expecting the women to be very anxious to have it done, Jian had carried his precious sack in with him. "I can do it to all of you right now. By tomorrow, we can see if it will work outside of the Gods' Cavern Home. We've never tested it outside of there, so I warn you; it might not work. If it doesn't, then we will have to make pilgrimages to the Gods' Cavern Home and do it there on you." Shu looked terribly anxious. Seeing her sister and Mata with their arms back had raised her hopes to a pinnacle. That it might now work became a crushing blow to her.

All eyes focused on the strange cylinder in Jian's hand. He went up to Shu and activated it. "It tingles," Shu giggled. One by one, Jian touched it to the shoulders of the other women in turn, Qian, Ting, Xue, Yudu, Lindi, Juli, and Chani. He did the little girls last: Wen, Caibi, and Calli.

"Tomorrow, we shall see if it has worked," Jian declared.

The group began chatting about all that they had heard, allowing the men to bring in all the things that they'd brought back with them. For an hour, it was more like a children's show and tell game. Though Shan and Mata could only barely see the others, briefly catching a glimpse of them as they darted into and out of their tiny line of sight, they could sense the awe and excitement of the others. Shan kept her fingers crossed all that day and night, hoping that they would all have their arms back the next day.

Excited shouts told all as dawn came. All were elated and overjoyed to find that their arms had returned. In fact, none could notice any difference from the last time that they had seen them. Even their fingernails were exactly as they had been, much to Qian's pleasure. Word spread quickly and Seneschal Shi held a special Gaoshi meeting the next evening, with Shan and Mata sharing center stage with him, along with Jian, of course. After making a few introductory remarks, commending his daughter and the village historian, he turned the meeting over to Jian. He explained in detail what had happened and their deduced logic along with the immense significance of the Yingchan. Seneschal Shi then explained their plan, emphasizing that no woman would be forced to have her Affliction removed, if she feared the wrath of the Gods later on if she did so. As expected, every woman and girl there wanted her arms back.

One by one, the women stepped up to Jian, who used the Gods' Cylinder on each of them. Uniformly, everyone was extremely excited, especially the younger girls and all the bound footed women, who like Shan, had been completely helpless since the coming of the Affliction.

The next morning told all! Seneschal Shi declared the day a holiday; every woman and girl in Matag had their arms back. September 17, 824 became a Holy Day after that. Of course, Seneschal Shi knew that they had their work cut out for them now.

Soon word would spread to all of Xi, and everyone would be demanding the cure for their women. Thus, the next day, he sent messengers to the four nearest villages, requesting a visit by their Seneschals. On the September 20, he met with the four leaders, who were shocked, amazed, and surprised by what they saw and heard. As expected, all desperately wanted the cure for their women and worked with Shi to make that occur as soon as possible. Seneschal Shi laid out the ground rules, keeping them as simple as possible. "First, you must create one Yingchan for your village. She must choose to do this of her own free will for her village. She must be a bound footed woman. Your village jeweler must come here and fabricate the necessary jewelry, based upon that worn by Shan and Mata, our Yingchan. Yes, we can help with the needed gold. Once the jewelry is ready, send word to us and we will come and prepare her as an honored Yingchan. When she is prepared, have your women and girls line up and one by one, Jian will work his cure upon them all. It takes about a minute per person, so it will not take long to do them all. A day later, their arms should be back to normal."

"But it will take time to make such elaborate jewelry," one protested. The others concurred.

"It can't be helped. If we restore their arms and you do not have a Yingchan for your village and if the Gods return and see this, their wrath inflicted upon you and your women will make their present Afflictions look like nothing at all!" Seneschal Shi warned them. That handled it. Fear of an even more wrathful God convinced them all. Soon, work began on making four new sets of Yingchan jewelry. Starting on October 20, Jian and Shan began visiting these four nearest villages, spending three days in each. Seneschal Shi sent along fifty guards, nearly all that were in Matag, to ensure the safety of the two. First, Jian inserted the golden eye spheres and then had the village doctor insert the ear pieces. Their jeweler then worked his magic, including the sealing of the joints by more molten gold so that the earrings, veil, and neck rings could not be easily removed or come off by accident. That took nearly a day to accomplish, ending with Jian touching the new Yingchan's shoulders with the cylinder.

The second day, their new Yingchan proudly displayed off her arms and ornaments to her village. One by one, Jian worked his magic on the others in the village. The two stayed around until the next day to make sure that all the women had gotten their arms back, which they had. Then, they traveled on to the next village. By November 1, four villages were finished, and Seneschal Shi summoned the next four nearest villages' Seneschals to Matag to begin another round.

One of these four, Gong, was much larger, having a population of ten thousand. The Seneschal there thought that one Yingchan might be too few and requested and insisted that four be made for Gong. At least, he volunteered to supply the extra gold needed for their jewelry.

By March 1, 825, thirteen towns and villages of Xi had been handled, counting Matag. Two had populations approaching ten thousand and each of those had four Yingchan each, bringing the total of the Golden Angels of Xi to twenty. By the following March of 826, forty more towns and villages had been handled, with another fifty to go, including their largest town of Yutshu, whose population approached thirty thousand. Sixty more Yingchan had been made, bringing their numbers up to eighty. Five more larger towns opted to have four, while another five desired two each. The problem facing everyone now was a shortage of gold. They had used up the supply of gold taken from the cavern, though Jian kept one gold bar back to use to make more golden eye spheres. Now the orderly process slowed down, as the remaining fifty towns sent out men to search for more gold. Some even began to melt down the shakas — anything to make the needed jewelry so that their village could get the cure.

One might have suspected that many would attempt to steal the device from Jain. No such thing happened. All were highly superstitious now. The men remembered their nightmare two months when they could only crawl. The wrath of the Gods was ever in their minds, as they looked upon the women in their lives. None dared incur any further wrath, especially since those who had received the cure were now doing just fine. The Gods apparently were satisfied with the Yingchan. No need to anger them further, just find ways to get the needed gold.

Chapter 73 Traditions and Truth

"Bethany, we have a big problem on our hands," Eve got my attention on March 1, 826. I was nursing my newborn baby boy; all of us had recently given birth. She and Lucianna, Giovanni, and Valerio had been slowly but surely locating all the plasticine doll caverns along the paved roadway in the tall Tashien mountains. The monks had been right; there was a whole series of caverns carved into the mountains periodically along the roadway, which they had also built, allowing them freedom of movement along the western border of Tashien. True, they had found the supplies that the monks had put in some of them, though much had been used by the fleeing band that we'd rescued just a couple months ago.

Because of all the supplies that the four had found, we were certain that the plasticine dolls had done a resupply job when they dumped the last of their unwanted spiritual beings on Tarra at the time of the second plague. Would they be back? We had no idea. However, the four were doing their best to remove all the electronics, weapons, armor, and of course those cylindrical surgical tools, which had been used by unscrupulous doctors to cut off women's arms and legs. We dare not let any of the armor and weapons fall into someone's hands. We'd already seen what one Golden Warrior could do and didn't want a repeat performance. Eve and I also had the misfortune to taste the surgical knife as well. Thus, they were in the process of finding all the caverns and removing the dangerous items.

"Okay, what is our big problem this time?" I asked, having no idea at all what she was referring to, but she was worried, that much was certain.

"We found another plasticine doll cavern."

"Yes," I half-acknowledged her. They had been on this project for nearly a month now.

"Some people have been in this cavern for quite some time. They slept in the monster bed and rummaged through absolutely everything in the place, including the secret compartments and drawers. Loads of camel dung is in the entrance chamber. Valerio's wild guess is that they were there at least a couple of weeks."

"Was anything taken?" I asked, suddenly having visions of another Golden Warrior slaughtering all the overlords and their armies throughout Tashien, perhaps even wiping out the stronghold in Nan Yan!

"You bet."

"Not the helmet and shield?"

"No, thankfully not those, or the sword. They rummaged through all the electronics crates, but we don't think that they took any of that stuff. They took the gold stash, naturally, but they also took the surgical knife and a bunch of miscellaneous things of no importance. Bethany, we could have another mad doctor on our hands, out amputating women's appendages making more so called Perfect Women! We have to do something!" She was highly animated over this. You would be too if you had once been a victim of the mad slasher.

"Okay, where and when were they there at the cavern? What clues do you have?" I asked.

"Well, we may have gotten a break. The cavern is located above the desert of Xi region in western Wontun Province. From what I can see, it is an isolated, desolate region with few inhabitants. Perhaps the mutilations will be confined this time. Valerio estimates the camel dung has been there at least a year, give or take a few months, he said. Perhaps, it will not be too difficult to locate the mad doctor this time," Eve suggested hopefully, though I could sense her deep concern and worry. She added, "We found a parchment with writing on it, but we can't read it."

"Well, I guess we had better take some swift action, Eve. How can we find who took the surgical knife?"

"Dunno, but I bet Sergio can help us. Permission to form a search party?" Eve said teasing me, as if I were a general. After all, this was my province; hers was handling the massive global therapy sessions.

"Permission granted private," I teased her back. We both grinned. Later that day, Eve, Sergio, Valerio, and Giovanni headed off to see what all they could figure out. I looked after Eve's body and baby that afternoon.

Arriving at the cavern, Valerio pointed out the signs he'd discovered. "Let's follow the trail of camel dung as far as we can. That ought to point us in the right direction more or less." The four had mocked up their bodies to facilitate chatting.

"Let me get a good feel for those who were here," Sergio asked. He spent time sensing the cavern, especially the bedroom area. "I think that a party was here. Some women were with them as well. One had her monthly period, I believe. I might be able to home in on her, but we'll see. Lead on Valerio."

Their bodies disappeared and Valerio led them outside and down the obvious gorge that the mysterious group had used. Since they had not come across any other trespassing at the more southern caverns, they had come up from either this one here or perhaps one further north. He pointed out more camel dung and was convinced this was the route taken. Before long, they sailed over the Valley of the Fallen Beasts. The trail continued down this valley, but the four stopped to marvel at all the exposed ancient remains. *What a really great place this is! I have to come back and study this place later on!* sent an excited Valerio.

Eventually, they left the zone with the bones behind them. Now the year old trail became confused. Here dozens of tracks and trails led off in many directions, rather like a woman's fan. Studying the camel dung piles within a few mile radius, Valerio decided they should follow the one that ran mostly eastwards. Eventually, it too was crossed by many others, and they spotted a number of oasis with small villages surrounding them. A quick glance revealed the women here were still armless, as expected. Eve guessed that it might be years before the Nan Yan group could reach out to them with their Basic Therapy and arm restoration.

I'll take it from here, Valerio. We now know that they were heading more or less east and can rule out about a third of this desert that's behind us. I am going to see if I can home in on that woman I sensed in the caverns. I might not be able to, but it's worth a try, Sergio sent. I'm always amazed at his keen powers of sense. I guess that's partly why he remains Velona's Chief Detective Inspector. For a time, they moved mostly eastward but slightly to the south as well. Eve took a position high above the desert so that she could observe their overall location within the desert region. Valerio remained closer to the ground, still hoping to find more clues from the camels, though he was doubtful that he'd be of any more use tracking them. The trail was far, far too cold for reasonable tracking. Besides, the desert winds had now obscured much that was older than a few weeks.

From Eve's vantage point, they had covered about half the length of the desert when Valerio sounded the alarm. *Gang! Come down to this oasis village quick!* All three joined him nearly instantaneously, hovering just above a village of perhaps a thousand people and some two hundred adobe homes, all with domed roofs.

My god! The women all have arms! Eve sent shocked. None of us expected this. Only we few beings who had a lot of very Advanced Therapy were able to undo the golden anchor balls and restore women's arms, breasts, and waists. Yet, here somehow these women had their arms back. *Look, they still have the monster boobs and probably tiny waists, though I can't tell that well with those loose fitting dresses. We just have to find out what is going on here — how did this happen. We've had no reports of arms returning to normal as our feet did.*

Well, that means they must have had the plague. The other women that we've seen out here in the desert still don't have arms. Why is this village unique? It warrants further study, Sergio sent.

Eve contacted me and I appeared beside them. I was just as surprised as they. *Wow! You are right. They likely have had the plague. We do need to check this out. Probably the smartest move would be to mock up a male body similar to one of theirs and go chat with some of the women. Perhaps they can tell us what's going on. Maybe they never lost their arms. That's the most likely scenario.*

I'll do it, Sergio insisted. While we watched, he materialized a body not unlike the men that he saw working in and around the village. He appeared just beyond visibility from the village and walked on into the oasis. Several women were doing their laundry close to the clear waters of the pool. He decided to see if they would chat with him. As he slowly approached them, a man stepped out of a home and accosted him. The man carried a sword and looked the role of a guard.

"Hello stranger. Welcome to Changjin."

"Ok, hello. Just passing through your village. Say, I cannot help but notice that those women have arms. In my village to the south, none of our women do. Did they not lose theirs?"

The man grinned, "You haven't heard then. Yes, ours lost theirs in the Great Affliction as well, but Seneschal Shi Yushube is helping all our women regain their arms. You see, we were Afflicted by the Gods because we forsook the ancient traditions of the Yingchan. Now we have returned to those ancient ways, and our women have had their arms restored."

"Now that is a Holy Miracle indeed! We have not heard of this before. Where might I find this Seneschal Shi Yushube? I owe it to my village to discover what we must do to help our poor women," Sergio asked.

"You may find him in Matag. He will tell you what your village must do. We are so proud that we now have our own Yingchan. Now the Gods will be most pleased with us and afflict us no more."

Sergio only got rather vague directions to Matag and had to walk out of the village some distance before the guard stopped watching him. Of course, we had overheard his entire conversation and now had a better idea. We materialized bodies and discussed his findings. "What the heck is a Seneschal?" I asked.

"Dunno, but I got the feeling that he or she must be some kind of official of the village," Sergio explained his hunch. "Yingchan, aren't those the Golden Angels, the women who have golden eyes and can hardly see at all?"

"Right," Eve pointed out, "plus they have to wear extremely heavy earrings and golden veils, which made life totally miserable and impossible for them when they lost their arms. Are they making more of them here? I'll crucify those men!"

"Calm down, Eve," Valerio cautioned. "We still don't know how these women got their arms back. Obviously those Yingchan that were rescued needed the Church of God to get them their arms back. Something isn't adding up."

"Ancient traditions must somehow play a role in this. We're going to need a whole lot more data. How do we find this Matag village?" I asked.

"It is in that general direction. Come on, let's see if we can find this Matag place," Sergio advised. We unmocked our bodies and took off once more. A while later, Sergio spotted another village. Its women too had their arms back, though their breasts remained gargantuan. He decided to see if this village might be Matag. It wasn't but we were definitely getting closer. This time, Sergio got better directions, and a short while later, we finally found Matag.

Again, we estimated its population to be no more than a thousand, with some two hundred-fifty adobe homes. Thus far, all the homes appeared to be constructed quite similarly. All had domed ceilings, which we found rather unusual. Now came the hard part. We needed to find out what was really going on here in Xi. That we were also looking for a surgical knife had long ago taken a back seat.

"Look, we can't go barging in here asking pointed questions. If we appear as if we are one of them, we will be easily found to be fakes. We know nothing of their culture and manners. While our bodies may look like theirs, they will know that we are vastly different," Sergio pointed out. We were again materialized out on the desert sands some distance away.

"True. Obviously, they have found some way to undo the plague's effects, at least with their arms. The Church of God needs to know all about that method for obvious reasons," Eve pointed out.

"But we can't go in there and just ask them," Valerio broke in. "This must be a closely guarded secret. They are highly unlikely to reveal it to outsiders. Bethany, you've had a lot of experience making first contacts with foreign cultures. What's the best way we should approach this?"

"Sincerity and honesty works best," I replied. "We should be just what we are, emissaries from the Church of God. We are checking on how others are getting by since the plague. We are helping those that we can, and we should see if they need anything or any help. That is how I would start. Also, we all should not go; too many of us will appear more like a threat. Fellows, I think you ought to remain hidden. Women are less likely to be perceived as a threat."

"Do we show up with arms?" Eve asked.

"I think so. After all, the church is using that one big selling point right now. Oh, Eve, mom's looking after our babies." I had forgotten to tell her that, after all, I was supposed to be doing that for her. Well, it's hard to keep me away from something like this!

A bit later, Eve and I materialized copies of our normal bodies wearing our easygoing Velona dresses. Together, we walked on into the village. At once, our different colored skin and dresses got everyone's attention. Women stopped what they were doing and stared at us. Men, too, did the same. Even some children playing in the streets ceased their games to watch two very strange looking women walking into the village.

"Hello. We are looking for Seneschal Shi Yushube. Can anyone direct us to him?" I asked, hoping my southern Tashien accent would get me by here. We'd heard very little of their speech thus far.

A man who was handling some camels stopped and walked up to us. "Greetings strangers. I am Peng Yang, the village camel caravan leader. I will take you to him. You have come far?" he asked, eyeing us closely.

"Yes, we are from Nan Yan and from Velona," I replied.

"Nan Yan? That is across the world from here. Such a long way to travel alone with so many dangers on the road, but this Velona, I have no knowledge of such a place. It must be a small village in Tan Loc?"

"Actually, it is a huge city much farther away than Nan Yan is from here, Peng. I am called Bethany Bartiana Angela. This is Eve Bartiana, my sister-in-law."

"Welcome to Matag. Ah, here is the Seneschal's home. He is a very busy man these days."

"We are not familiar with your customs. What is a Seneschal?" I asked. "We do not want to accidentally offend him."

Peng smiled, "He is the village leader in all things, our most important man." He opened the door and we entered. "Ah, Juli, these strangers from Nan Yan have come to see Seneschal Shi. Could you take them to see him?" To us, he said, "Juli is the personal assistant to both his wife and daughters, one of whom is our most honored Yingchan." He bowed to us and we returned it, which seemed to please him and he left.

"If you will follow me," Juli said. "He is meeting with two other Seneschals now. I will take you to meet his wife and daughters and let him know of your arrival when he is finished with his most important meeting." We entered a large living room filled with several couches and chairs. Overhead, we saw the central portion of the high dome and were incredibly impressed, so much so that we didn't see the women at first.

"Most Honored Yingchan Shan, Qian, and Shu, these are some visitors from Nan Yan," Juli announced us, bringing our attention down from the incredible scenes painted on the dome overhead. We saw a middle aged lady sitting on a couch doing some embroidery work. We could not miss the fact that her nails were six inches long. On another couch sat the Yingchan, the Golden Angel, who was in her early twenties, another slightly younger woman sat on a third couch. All three had nails that were six inches long; all were painted bright red. Obviously, Qian was the mother and these, her two daughters.

"Welcome to the Seneschal's home. I am Qian. This is our Most Revered Yingchan, Shan Wie, my eldest daughter, and this is my youngest daughter, Shu," the older woman stopped her needlepoint and rose, wobbling slightly on her feet. We now saw that all three had very tiny feet, very tiny. From the shape of their tiny shoes, that is the large bulge on top of their feet, we surmised that they had bound feet. Either that or they had some gross foot malformations, which made their feet twice as thick as a normal foot. We bowed before her and I introduced us.

Yingchan Shan rose even more carefully. We saw her moving her head this way and that, obviously she could not see at all well and was trying to locate us. We moved before her so that she would have little difficulty seeing us and bowed to her, and she, us. However, she still had to move her head up and down to see all of our bodies.

Shu also rose and we bowed to her as well. "Please sit across from me," Shan asked. "That way I can perhaps see you better. You are indeed strangers here." We did as asked. She was a most unusual woman, but all three were as far as we were concerned. They all had a golden mesh skull cap with enormous dangling lobes of gold falling to their shoulders along the sides of their faces and other lobes or meshes falling to just about their eyebrows. This was our first experience with shakas. They had their hair parted in the middle beneath the gold caps, had it brushed out, and draped over the fronts of their bodies. These were the first women we'd seen in Tashien who did not braid their long hair. I admit, Eve and I liked their hairstyle, because it was very similar to ours. I believe Shan also detected this similarity.

Both Qian and Shu wore makeup; their eyes were shadowed in black and their lips were red, matching their nails. Shan noticed us noticing this and added, "Alas, I'm no longer able to see well enough to put on my own makeup. So I choose to wear none, like yourselves." We gazed at her seemingly immobile golden eyes and detected a small hole in their center. No wonder she could see very little at one time. All three women's shakas were embedded with rubies and emeralds. In addition, Shan wore massive earrings whose bottoms rested well over the tops of her huge breasts. Hanging from her ears were five-inch long golden bars and the many tiers of oblong golden dangles hung from those. A stud embedded in either side of her nose held the golden lattice veil that stretched from her ears across the lower part of her face, falling several inches below her chin.

"Forgive us for staring, ladies, Yingchan, but we have never been to your land before, never been in one of your homes, nor have we met your people," I began honestly. "There is so much for us to see and understand and all at once too!"

Shan grinned, "Please, just Shan. We are indeed then honored to welcome such guests into our home. My father, Seneschal Shi will be most pleased as well. Juli, send for some tea please. Bethany, we too are most curious about you. I hope you will not mind our staring at you as well. Your skin is so very different from ours, your eyes, so blue. Eve has such gorgeous yellow hair. Our hair is always black, you see."

"Yes, we actually come from even farther away than Nan Yan. We come from a country called Velona," I replied. "May I ask you some questions about yourselves? I am afraid that I may have too many," I grinned.

Shan smiled. Qian spoke up, "Dear me, of course you must, if this is your first time in Xi. Please ask. If we find them offensive, we will tell you so, but you must also allow us to ask you about yourselves as well."

"Of course, are your feet bound?" I asked first.

"Yes, here in Xi, half of the women have their feet bound at birth. We are very proud to be carrying on this most ancient of traditions. We know that the outsiders have made such illegal, but we do not recognize their laws here. For us, a bound footed woman is highly prized for the beauty of her small feet," Qian answered. "Do you not have such customs in this Velona?"

"When we want small feet, we wear shoes with very high heels that give the appearance of small feet. That way we can have them when we desire and be able to walk normally at other times," I replied honestly.

"Ah, you mean like those strange shoes that appeared here when the Gods Afflicted us over a year ago," Shu eagerly jumped into the conversation.

"Yes, they are very much like those alien shoes that we had to wear for a time," Eve replied and Shu nodded.

"I think that is commendable of you, that you can have small feet when you desire. So many in Tashien do not even care about such important details, you know," Qian replied.

"Say, we have recently heard strange rumors from some visiting caravan masters that down in Nan Yan the Afflicted women have regained their arms," Shan asked what was most on her mind since hearing that we were from there. "Is such true? Have they also begun honoring the ancient tradition of the Yingchan, which most all of Tashien has forsaken centuries ago?"

Just then, Juli brought in the tea tray, sitting it before Qian, who began pouring the cups. Rather than make her struggle on her tiny feet, we handed the cups to her daughters and then ourselves. "Seneschal Shi Yushube," Juli announced. We turned to see the man at last. His moustache caught our attention immediately, its ends falling nearly six inches below his lip. Then, we noticed that he too had six inch long talons. He bowed to us, and we, he. He took a cup from his wife and sat beside her in such a way that he could get a good look at us. We quickly introduced ourselves and said where we were from.

"Please forgive me, but I could not help but overhear my Most Honored Daughter Yingchan Shan asking you two most important questions. I too would be most grateful to hear your answers."

"Yes, it is true that in Nan Yan and the surrounding towns the women have regained their arms, their breasts are back to normal as well. It is a long and most worthy story, and we would love to share it with you," I replied seeing an opening. Shi nodded eagerly, I could tell that he really wanted to know all that we knew about Nan Yan.

However, Shan spoke up first, "Father, it would be impolite for us to not tell them our story first. They are our honored guests from far away."

"Yes, Most Honored Yingchan, you are right as always. Forgive me, I am getting too hasty in my old age. There is so much happening now in Xi, and I can barely keep up with it all. Yes, we should tell you about ourselves first. However, it will soon be dinnertime. If you would care to dine with us, we can exchange stories after dinner. Besides, we really ought to have our village historian, Shan's husband, here with us. He is most knowledgeable of our history and will be most anxious to hear of yours."

"Excellent. Thank you. May I ask, is it polite to stare at your ceiling? We've never seen anything like this before," I asked.

Pleased, Shi said to look all that we desired. Shan explained, "When we get anxious, nervous, or worried, we lay back and look above and relax and calm ourselves. It is beautiful, is it not?"

"Incredibly beautiful!" We chatted a bit more and then were introduced to Jian, her husband, and Shesong, Shu's fiancé. After that, his son, Tian, came home, with his wife and daughter, Ting and Wen. After dinner, Peng and Mata also came. I recognized him as the camel driver who led us here. Soon, we learned of the interrelationship among these people as Shan proudly told us her tale. As she spoke, I sensed an enormous amount of pride among all these people. I soon found out why.

Shan explained how they had gone off in search of a cure for their Afflictions and had been kidnaped by the drug overlord. She described how they had turned both her and Mata into Yingchan, intent upon taking them back to the overlord's lands. I found it fascinating how she managed to escape. She went on to describe how they had eaten the ground up bones, though none of them seriously expected it to do anything at all.

"So you see, there we were having proved that the bone powder did nothing. We reasoned that it had to have been the Gods who so Afflicted all of we women, for certainly no man had done so. We worked out that several months had not passed by during that first night, though our hair grew some two feet." She explained how they came to that conclusion. I saw that these people were quite intelligent. "So it if the Gods had Afflicted us all, then there had to be a reason why, and we wanted to find a real cure for our women's Afflictions. Obviously, the Gods do not dwell among us, for none of us has ever recalled seeing one of the Gods. Now we were close to the impassible mountains, and we knew that no one lives up there, but that would be a perfect place for the Gods to dwell. Hence, we decided to give that a try, to seek out the Gods where they must dwell."

She went on to describe how they found what they called the Gods' Highway far above the timberline, a wide ledge on which even a wagon could travel. This confirmed our suspicions that they had been the ones who stayed in the cavern.

Jian added a bit, "You see, we had forsaken the ancient tradition of the Yingchan centuries ago. It is my belief that our ancestors substituted the shaka for the Yingchan. My Shan and Mata are having a most difficult time because of their limited vision. I believe that is why our ancestors modified the traditions."

"Plus, it does feel like I am about to have my ears pulled off my head," Shan added with a grin. So we believe that the Gods grew angry with us for having forsaken the ancient ways of the Yingchan. Thus, the Gods Afflicted all of us, but later restored our feet as a sign that all could be forgiven if we repented our mistake. At the time, we just didn't quite know that it was the Yingchan that was our mistake. We worked that out when Jian found the Gods' Cylinder."

Jian took over the story for a while, explaining how he discovered the secret drawer and the pile of unused golden eye spheres. He had looked in vain for a tool by which the spheres could be pinched around the eyes and how at last he'd discovered the cylinder's images. Though he could not decipher the writing, he was able to make sense of the images. He explained that he found the sequence of buttons to press to install a golden eye sphere and how to remove them safely. "At first, I did not tell this to Shan, although I had promised her that I would devote my life to finding a way to remove her golden eyes. She had already decided that she must remain a Yingchan to help show the Gods that we understood their message, their warning to return to our ancient roots and traditions. Then, I discovered how to bring her arms back!"

"Yes, it tickled. A day later, my original arms and hands reappeared, just as they were before the Gods' Affliction struck me," she explained. "Now we were convinced that we had the solution. If we took the Gods' Cylinder with us so that we could undo the Gods' Affliction upon all our women in Xi, then to avoid further enraging the Gods, we needed to show them that we were now honoring the old ways. I chose to remain a Yingchan, so did Mata. Having our arms and hands means far more to us than our sight. With our bound feet, we were very helpless, unlike the other women whose feet were normal. With heavy hearts, we could only sit and watch them learning to use their feet in lieu of their hands. Even the Gods' shoes would not fit our feet. We have no use of our toes as the others did and found ourselves utterly dependent upon the others. So you see, our arms and hands are far more valuable than our sight."

"We then had to decide upon whether all women of Xi were supposed to become Yingchan or whether only a few. In the end, Jian and the others proved that there was not enough gold in the world for all women of Xi to become Yingchan. Hojie did some calculations and showed that if we took the Gods' gold bars and used them to help the others make the needed jewelry, we could make one Yingchan per village. That is how we began our rescuing of the women of Xi. Each village provided one volunteer to become their Most Honored Yingchan. We helped them with the needed gold to make her jewelry modeled after ours. When the jewelry was ready, Jian inserted her golden eye spheres, and their doctor affixed her jewelry. Then, Jian used the Gods' Cylinder on her to bring her arms back."

"Each time it worked, arms reappeared a day later. Once the women in the village saw that their Yingchan now had her arms back, they lined up and Jian restored theirs. We always wait another day to make sure that all their arms do come back, which they have. We take all this as a positive sign that we are doing the right thing and that the Gods will not be angry with us and Afflict us far worse."

Seneschal Shi added, "Yes, now some of the larger towns decided that they ought to have more than one Yingchan, just to be on the safe side. With over ten thousand living there, I tend to agree with them. Most of those towns chose to have four. We've been at it constantly for over a year now. As of today, fifty-three towns and villages have been handled; all women there have their Affliction removed. There are eighty Yingchan all told now. However, we still have fifty more towns and villages to handle, but we have run into a snag. There is insufficient gold to make their needed jewelry. The whole process has slowed while the hunt for more gold continues. Some are melting down their shakas to help."

"So you see, Jian and I are helping all our people to get over the Gods' Affliction. I believe that it is working, since the Gods have not struck us down or given us another new Affliction," Shan finished.

Seneschal Shi added, "We have not had any trouble, though at first I thought that we might. Everyone respects the Gods and refuses to risk a worse Affliction. Many women have been extremely patient, waiting for their turn. I just hope that we can find enough gold to finish the task properly. If we cannot, then we must decide if we dare restore a village without their having their own Yingchan."

Eve and I, and the fellows who were invisible and listening in to all this, understood why these people were so proud. They had been selfishly working true miracles for their people. True, they were seeped in ancient traditions, but not all that far wrong on the details. Three godlike beings, not one, had been around Tarra. Now I faced my greatest challenge: how to relate our truths in a way that would be understood and not seem to contradict or invalidate their heartfelt and "logical" beliefs.

"Our story," I began cautiously, "begins with good gods and bad gods. Tarra is a large world and there have been several sets of gods worldwide. Your Gods stayed pretty much around Tashien. The evil gods decided to Afflict all the people of Tarra, not just their own worshipers. Yes, what you are calling Gods' Affliction, the rest of the world is calling an alien plague. Different people call it by different names, but it was the same worldwide. Women lost their arms, their breasts enlarged, while their waists shrank, and their hair grew two feet. Both men and women's feet were malformed. Yes, the affliction was worldwide." I saw that this was both new and interesting to them.

"Some of we gods fought back against the evil gods, and we rid Tarra of them for now. Who knows if they will come back anytime soon? Yet, the awful damage had been done, though in their haste to cause all humans pain and endless suffering, they made some mistakes. One was our feet, which have all returned to normal. Some of we good gods banded together and formed the Church of God worldwide, one branch is down in Nan Yan."

"The Church of God has created a Basic Therapy which erases both the emotional trauma and the physical trauma of the plague or Affliction. Once that is gone, the effects of the plague or Affliction are gone; women's arms return to them. The Church of God in Nan Yan is working very hard to give their Basic Therapy to every man, woman, and child in Tashien, but as you know, Tashien is huge and large parts are still in complete chaos. True, they are making great strides in wiping out the drug overlords, eliminating the vast opium trade, which so destroys people's lives."

"Eve here is coordinating all the many Churches of God worldwide in their efforts to reach as many people as possible with their life-salvaging therapy. She and I both want to thank all of you sincerely for taking it upon yourselves to help your women recover from the Gods' Affliction here in Xi. We count you among the few on Tarra who genuinely want to help all the other people who have been Afflicted as you have been."

"We have come to lend you our help — the help of all the remaining good gods on Tarra. As you may have sensed, while your arms have returned to normal, the heartache, sadness, feelings of loss and desperation, even pain from the Affliction are still with you, perhaps as ghostly reminders in your minds. Our therapy will help you erase and wipe out all such unwanted emotions and aches and pains. We give this to all of you and your people freely, asking nothing in return except your help to help others with this if you so desire once you have experienced its incredible miracles in your own lives."

"We agree with your analysis of the current situation, Seneschal Shi. The lack of gold will be causing major problems in getting to the remainder of the people of Xi in a timely manner. We can help. Eve would like to bring in some of the other good gods from Nan Yan and elsewhere and get their therapy sessions going. After each woman has received hers, her arms will return to normal. Meantime, we realized that many of your villages would prefer to have at least one Yingchan there, just in case the Gods return and your assumptions are correct: that they wanted you to return to the forsaken ancient tradition of the Yingchan. If you allow and assist the Church of God to come and deliver their lifesaving therapy to all of your people, we will guarantee you that you will have enough gold to create all the necessary jewelry for any new Yingchan that the villages deem necessary. We can provide as much gold as you need as soon as you are actually able to make use of it." I was purposely tossing out two misrelated ideas. Shi picked up on the second one quickly.

He replied, "We are just now hearing rumors from Nan Yan. So these rumors are then true? The Church of God is able to restore the Afflictions of our women?"

"Absolutely, Seneschal," Eve answered him.

"That is a miracle in itself. And if we allow this church to come here, they will not try to remove our Yingchan or dissuade us from following our ancient traditions?"

"Not in the slightest, Seneschal. Your beliefs are your own. The Church of God never, ever touches those. They are yours and yours alone. No, we simply help each person erase and eradicate the traumas that they have endured and suffered," Eve answered him honestly.

"That is good. And you can provide us with all the gold that we need? It is quite a lot. Just look at the amount that my daughter wears."

"Yes, all the gold that you need for such jewelry can be brought here very rapidly by the good gods. Just let us know how much you need and can use at one time, and it will be here within a day's time," I answered.

He looked at Jian, who quickly spoke up. "We took about a hundred of the Gods' ingots. To finish our task of reaching all the villages, we believe that we will need twice that amount. As you suggest, we can't use all of that at one time," he grinned. "Where would we store such a pile? No, right now, another fifteen ingots would be enough for us to work on getting the next four towns and villages ready for their Yingchan and the healing of their women's Afflictions."

"I'll see to it that you have it shortly," I replied. Valerio jumped on it. He appeared over Velona and the warehouse in which we were storing all the plasticine items. He grabbed fifteen ingots, appeared over Matag, and materialized the pile before a very startled Seneschal!

"My god! I don't believe it!" Shi exclaimed, rushing to the small pile and examining it. Jian did likewise, followed by Peng.

"It's gold all right, heavy too," Peng gushed excitedly, convinced that he had just witnessed a god miracle.

"As I said, let us know and the needed gold will be brought to you swiftly. Often, it may not be this swiftly, since some of us gods will be giving the lifesaving therapy sessions at the time we get your next gold request. Still, it will be here within a day for sure," I replied confidently.

Shan had been quiet through much of my storytelling. Now she spoke up, "May I ask a question?" Eve and I nodded. "Are you both some of the good gods of which you spoke? You surely must be, since you are not from our land, Xi, and you just appeared at our village and came on foot. No one can cross the desert of Xi on foot, unless they carry a lot of water skins and know the routes between the oasis and watering holes."

"You may consider that Eve and I are good gods, Shan, though in all honestly, many years ago, we were just like you, a normal person. Through the therapy of the other good gods, we have risen in our capabilities and abilities until today we may seem to others as if we are gods. We do not consider ourselves gods, though. We just want to help all other people become as able and capable as they can be. In many ways, we are just like you and Jian; we have a strong desire to help others and are doing all that we can to do just that, like you two are doing here in Xi." I answered as truthfully as I could.

"And yet you want nothing from us? Not even worshiping you?" Jian asked amazed.

"Heavens no! You start worshiping us and we will depart. You don't want others in your village to start worshiping you, do you?" She flushed and said no, likewise Jain. "No, there is only one small thing that we desire from you, Jian. When you are completely finished using the Gods' Cylinder, we would like you to return it to us. You see, while you are using it for good, others in the past have stolen these cylinders and used them for evil. They used them to cut off women's arms and legs, mutilating them in their sadistic ways. You may have noticed some of the other symbols and images. Some of those were used by some of your evil countrymen to wreak mutilation and torture on other women of Tashien. We stopped them, but not until many women were brutally and permanently harmed. So when you are completely finished using it, we would like to keep it out of the reach of evil men. If you ever need it again, let us know and we can give it back to you for another round of use. We just do not want one of these Gods' Cylinders to ever again fall into the hands of evil men."

"That is most acceptable," Jian bowed to me.

Shan asked what was troubling her the most. "Bethany, are you suggesting that we do not need to continue the ancient tradition of the Yingchan? That I should stop being one for our village?"

"Have you not decided that if the Gods return, then they will see that you have taken up the long abandoned ways of the Yingchan that your people forsook so long ago? In this way, the Gods will be pleased and not be angry with what you have done, undoing the Affliction on your people, and give all of you a far worse Affliction."

"Well, yes," she replied.

"Then that is what you should do. You should always follow your own counsel, Shan. Do what you believe is the right thing to do," I replied careful not to invalidate her or to force off my own opinions onto her.

"While it is hard to be like this, a Yingchan, if the Gods do return, I do not want them to be angry with us for removing their Afflictions upon us. If I am a Yingchan, then perhaps they will not be angry. I could not live with myself if they came back and struck down our people because we undid their Affliction and continued to forsake the ancient traditions of the Yingchan, which they wished us to follow," Shan answered honestly. I bowed to her respectfully and she smiled, greatly relieved.

Eve then said, "Within a couple of days, I'll return with some others from the Church of God to begin giving all here in Matag therapy sessions. Yingchan Shan, you may find that after you have received yours that you may greatly desire to learn how to deliver it to others as well. Giving these therapy sessions to others is something that any bound footed woman can most easily do and reap many rewards as you will soon see." Shan smiled and thanked her.

I decided it was time to go. "It is getting late, and we have imposed upon your hospitality long enough. Eve will be back soon and give you ways to contact us whenever you need our assistance. It has been our honor to have met all of you, and especially you, Yingchan Shan and Jian." Everyone began bowing to us, and we returned them. Eve decided that we should merely vanish from our chairs, adding to their conviction that we were the good gods. And so we did. I hoped that was the right thing to do.

Seconds later, we all were back at our home at 42 Hampton Way. Giovanni spoke up first. "Hey, while you were all dancing around them, I believe that I have figured out why the plasticine dolls wanted the Yingchan."

"Okay, I give up. Why?" I replied. I admit I was curious. Why would anyone want that much heavy gold jewelry, golden eyes, and all that?

"Gold is an extremely good conductor. It is just too expensive and rare to use much in our electrical inventions. With that much gold on them, it ought to act as a sort of receiver, picking up what is sent from some of their electronic devices. Combine that with the Yingchan's inability to see much at all, and she would then have her mind wide open to the electronic 'messages' sent to her from the plasticine dolls. I bet anything that the Yingchan were the conduit for the delivering the messages and orders to her people from the dolls."

"Brilliant idea," Eve agreed. I grinned; it sounded plausible and was probably right. Through the village Yingchan, the plasticine dolls could work their control over the whole village, especially if the Yingchan were held in positions of high honor. Wonderful control mechanism, I thought.

The next day, Eve went to visit Bi Mei in Nan Yan to tell her about the people of Xi. "Oh no, not more Yingchan!" Bi Mei said exasperated. "Well, at least they can speak. You realize that we've had to give those ten Yingchan Advance Therapy just so that they can communicate? Well, now they are all off giving Basic Therapy sessions now, so it wasn't a wasted effort. How many did you say?"

The two discussed the situation in Xi and the two came to an agreement. The following day, Eve, I, and four others headed to Matag to begin delivering Basic Therapy to Shi, Shan, Shu, Jian, and Mata. It took us nearly two weeks to get all them into good shape. Of course, Shi and Jian were finished within a week, and we added Ting and Shesong to the mix, Shesong was the dear friend of Shu's and also had bound feet. Once they were done, just as we expected, the women all wanted to learn how to deliver the therapy themselves, none more so than Shan, who had truly found her calling in life. We spent another week training them and watching over their beginning sessions on the other women of the extended household.

Meanwhile, Bi Mei had a long talk with the ten Yingchan, and Wu, Kang, and Jie. Bi Mei explained what had happened in the desert of Xi. Already there were over eighty new Yingchan there and more being made each month.

Can we go there and establish a Church of God for them? We can relate well to other Yingchan, Dai Shenyan sent to all them.

"Yes," her husband, Wu, added, "please, let us do this thing. We can really help them, and this is something that Dai and our friends can do to help repay you for all that you have done for us. That Dai and the others can now talk to me without their tongues is a holy miracle that we all want to repay."

We can do it, Bi Mei, Zhu Yun Zi sent.

Really, we can, Zhen Yun ZI sent.

"Where my sisters go, so go I," Kang added.

"Are you sure? Life will be very primitive there. No electric lights, no fancy bathrooms. It will be hard for you to walk in the desert sands, Yingchan," Bi Mei cautioned.

Please let us try. If we cannot do it, then we can return somehow, Dai sent.

Mid-April 825, the ten Yingchan and the two men and the eleven year old boy were taken to Matag. Yes, we "flew" them there in the now useless sleigh. It made quite a sight as the sleigh floated down from the sky with ten brilliantly shining Golden Angels onboard. Well, we were supposed to be the good gods to these people, I rationalized, again hoping we were not making a big mistake by openly displaying "magical powers."

Eve did the introductions. "These ten Yingchan were brutalized by the drug overlords. Each has had their tongues cut out so that their complaints could not be heard. Each was forced to wear these specially forged boots, modeled on those that the aliens left for the men when the Affliction struck them. They always have to walk on their toes now since the boots cannot be removed. However, all ten can communicate by placing their thoughts into your minds. Thus, they can deliver our therapy sessions very well. All have been doing so for some months now."

"This is Dai Shenyan and her husband Wu. This is Zhu Yun and Zhen Yun Zi, twins, and their brother, Kang Yun Zi. This is Yan Zhou and her little brother, Jie. This is Ting Sha, Hua Chun, Danyin Chou, Chi Chong, and Bi Nan. All these will be giving therapy sessions and Dai and Wu will be in charge of setting up on official Church of God here in Matag," Eve explained.

Shan asked, "Oh my. Are we Yingchan supposed to have our tongues removed and to wear those special boots too? We here in Xi have long ago forsaken the Yingchan tradition and have lost all knowledge of just what all we are to be. Will the Gods be displeased if we still have our tongues and do not wear those golden boots?"

Oh no. Evil men forced us to become Yingchan against our wills. Hence, they did not want us to complain in the slightest about our mistreatment. Also, they did not want us escaping from where the drug lord kept us, so they forged these boots on our feet. They make walking almost impossible so that we could not flee them. We do not think that either are part of the ancient ways of the Yingchan, though none of us know for sure, Shan, Dai answered her, placing her thoughts into all of those present. Of course, hearing her in their minds greatly surprised everyone, who held the ten in an even higher awe and great respect.

"Okay, I think that we ought to research ancient records, Jain, and find out if we Yingchan are missing anything that the ancient Yingchan had that we don't have," she replied.

By May, this arrangement was working wonderfully. The average person greatly respected the

Yingchan and that gave them a sort of altitude when they ran their therapy sessions. Curiously enough, any person who received their therapy from any of the Yingchan completed their therapy in record times! If given a choice, any villager chose to receive their therapy from a Yingchan over anyone else!

By the end of summer, all one thousand inhabitants of Matag had finished their Basic Therapy. Around three hundred women, most were bound footed, had been trained to deliver it as well, and were ready to head to the next village. Another two hundred normal women also knew how to deliver it and had done so, but were needed to keep the village running. Wu and Kang now began to work out the logistics needed to quickly move so many women to the next village and swiftly handle everyone there.

What worked out well for them was having a cadre of five hundred men and women. They then came to a village, which had already been cured by Jian and Shan. There they delivered Basic Therapy to the inhabitants, finishing off the normal sized village in about a month, before moving on to the next.

However, in each of these newly finished villages, another cadre of two or three hundred volunteers were trained and then sent on to deal with another village. One of the ten Yingchan joined up with the new group to ensure that the Yingchan in the next village received her therapy from another Yingchan.

In a parallel operation, Shi, Jian, and Shan, when she could, continued to visit other villages, preparing that village's new Yingchan and then restoring all the women's arms there. Because of the delays caused by the manufacturing of the needed jewelry, they were only able to handle a couple of villages each month. Still, great progress was being made on all fronts.

Near the end of the year, Kang married Yan Zhou in a simple ceremony in Matag. The other seven unmarried Yingchan now had steady boyfriends as well. For the ten tortured women, life had begun to fully blossom for them. Eve estimated that by the end of 826, everyone in Xi would have had their Basic Therapy. Many would be clamoring for Advance Therapy. Another chunk of Tashien was now out of their Dark Ages.

Chapter 74 Criminals

By 826, the situation in the cordoned off Shansee became critical. Once a vast city of some thirty million, between the two plagues and the Dark Ages, which descended after the second plague, barely eight million remained. All were poor; all were under thirty years old. The older men and women had succumbed, while the younger men had been abducted into the overlord's army and had died in the giant slaughter just outside the city. The few nobles and the very wealthy had long ago fled the city, leaving it to its fate.

Gang lords controlled the streets, each clearly marked with numerous characters or symbols of the gang who controlled it. Women dared not go outside without being escorted by strong men. As a result, many slowly starved to death. Traveling from one part of the city to another meant crossing many different gang controlled sections and was terribly risky. Only well-armed men made such an attempt or those competent in martial arts.

Yet women and girls now accounted for three quarters of the remaining population! Gone were all the fit young men, lost in the overlord's great battle. The gang lords were often barely teens themselves, and the average age of everyone in Shansee was now fourteen! True, there were many middle aged women which had raised that average somewhat higher, but Shansee was now run primarily by those in their early teens. A few older men were around, but many of them were unfit for the army, the lame or otherwise incapable of fighting. Several of these seized control by befriending the teen gang lords. By manipulating the youthful leaders, they exercised the ultimate control over what was left of Shansee. Impressionable youths often emulated these older men, who now called themselves Dons or supreme rulers.

Don Cao, now forty, controlled the docks area via his many street gangs. His gangs tightly managed all fishing and catches. No one from any other part of the city was allowed near the docks, let alone to go fishing. In turn, they traded fish for rice, which came in from the other two thirds of the city. Don Fengli and Don Hubon controlled the middle and northern thirds of Shansee, respectfully, and via their gang lords, often raided the rice farms within the thirty mile unoccupied zone that General Tao had established. They traded rice for fish.

Money as a means of exchange had virtually disappeared. True, the three Dons had confiscated what little gold, silver, and gemstones remained in Shansee long before 826 came. Barter now was the means of exchange and young girls and women were sought after in trades for food. The old Santi Fortress converted into an Inn was Don Cao's home and office now. The top floor from which much of the city could be observed became his private harem. Yes, Don Cao collected women, though he insisted that each new addition was at least of age. He refused to accept any girl not yet fourteen. As the monsoons struck in early January 826, his harem numbered fifty women.

He kept them on the top floor in one of the spacious suites. Here they spent all their time, save when Don Cao brought one into his bedroom for the night's pleasure. They were kept naked for a good reason. There was no one to tend to their needs, let alone dress them. Besides, naked they could handle the chamber pots by themselves. At meal times, pie pans were brought to them, and they had to feed themselves any way that they could, usually like a dog, since the wooden sticks were unusable by the armless women. At least, there were sufficient hairbrushes around, and the women spent most of their hours grooming each other, in hopes that Cao might pick them for a night in his bed. Yes, little humanity remained among those living in Shansee. Stay alive by any means was their single operating principle.

Most of the gang lords emulated the Don by keeping their own harems as well. The poor young girls were treated more like rats in a cage, but none dare defy the Don's iron clad rule: women must be fourteen to be in a harem. The conditions of these young girls were even more deplorable. Malnourishment and sickness thrived, many died every day throughout Shansee, their bodies normally just dumped into the Yonshu River, to float on out to the ocean.

Don Cao had a bum left leg, which made waking a chore for him. Whenever he needed to travel, some of his gangs would pull his rik while others surrounded the rik protecting him. Often, he would not appear on the streets for days at a time, preferring the company of his harem women. No one knew what had happened to his family, and he never mentioned that they ever existed.

The opium and hashish supplies had long ago dried up, and many addicts died from their hideous withdrawal symptoms. Even charcoal for cooking or even coal was now nearly vacant in the city. In lieu of this, vacant homes were cannibalized for anything burnable. There were many homes available, and everyone was confident that they could last for years before this heat source was gone.

Don Fengli, thirty-eight, controlled the middle section of Shansee at the start of 826. He had run an import-export storefront before the first plague. However, he specialized in covert exports, frequently guns and opium. A sickly man, he was as covert and as sneaky as they come. He'd never married, but now had built up a harem of some thirty-six women, which he kept in the back portion of his store-home complex. He too found that the only way to handle so many women was to keep them all naked so that they could care for their own needs and not try to escape. At meal times, he dumped their food into a long set of trays and let them feed themselves any way that they could. Unfortunately, several had attempted to escape even though they were naked. He solved that problem by making them wear the old alien ballet style boots that the men received when the plague struck. He devised a clever padlock on each boot so that the women could not use their teeth to untie them and take them off. That stopped all their attempts to flee.

Don Hubon, thirty-six, controlled the northern section of Shansee, what had once been the wealthier section of the city. By this time thoroughly looted on many occasions, most of the estates were quite trashed. He took over one of the better ones and making it his base of operations. Originally, the wealthy lived in this section, but as time went on, many orphaned children fled here, trying to escape the ruthless gangs of the poor southern section of

Shansee. This was ideal for Don Hubon, who was an avowed homosexual, preferring young boys when possible. Many younger boys fled the slums, bringing along their sisters, who now depended upon them to survive. Clever Hubon established large communal homes for the many refugees, making it appear that the girls and young women would be well cared for up here. In many ways, that was true, but the boys paid the price for their sister's survival.

As the conditions continued to deteriorate, the remnants of some families attempted to flee the city on foot. If they could survive all the street encounters until they reached the edge of the city, then they had to walk some twenty miles across the soggy, snake infested, rice fields until they ran into General Tao's garrison forces. Usually, these soldiers escorted the refugees into nearby towns, where they could receive their therapy and begin life anew. However, word of whether they had been successful never reached those that they left behind, adding their fears that anyone leaving the city was murdered by the general's forces.

Shansee had become a city of animals, barely staying alive. For most, all hope had long ago vanished and many who were above their teens were just waiting to die. Only the children still had any real life within them.

In January 826 during the monsoons, the three Dons decided to meet and form some agreements to benefit themselves. They picked the old Princess Palace, totally ransacked dozens of time. Bare walls and smashed furniture was about all that remained. The three chatted at length about their situations, revealing as little of their actual power base as possible, each hoping to gain a slight advantage over the others.

After several hours, the topic changed. Don Cao said, "Say, how soon do you suppose General Tao will come marching into Shansee taking over control of everything? I hear that he is utterly ruthless."

Don Hubon chuckled, "Probably for you two. I think that he goes hard on criminals; that's what I've heard. Several of his riders posted notices on the northern edge of the city before the monsoons came. Here, read it for yourselves." He handed them one of the posters he'd saved. In essence, it said those who were found guilty of crimes would be sent to Dong Province, the ice land.

Cao and Fengli cursed, knowing that would be their fates. "How soon do you suppose that he'll come charging in here?" Cao repeated his question.

"Probably not until spring comes. Soldiers and long guns do not fare well in all this rain, but come spring, I bet he'll be coming full on us," Don Hubon replied, hoping to gain an edge over the other two.

"Makes sense," Cao replied with a grunt.

"You two ought to be out of here before then," Don Hubon suggested with a sly grin. If nothing else, he had hoped to implant just such a notion in his two rivals. If they left, why, then he would be the only one in charge when the general came. He could show him how well he was treating all the many girls and young women in his section. Perhaps if he even had time, he could send out his boys to rescue other girls and particularly other young boys, bringing them into his section.

After a bit more discussion and agreeing in principle on trading fish and rice between their sections, the meeting adjourned. "A private word with you," Don Cao whispered to Don Fengli, who pretended to have a loose shoelace, all the while watching Don Hubon as he left. Satisfied that they were alone, Don Cao said, "Look, we both have a fine collection of women. Yet, more and more, mine are growing restless. I fear that they might try to escape from my tower. How are you able to keep yours from fleeing?"

Don Fengli chuckled. "You know those weird alien boots that we men were supposed to wear when the plague first came — well, I scrounged some of those up and put them on my ladies. That stopped their escape attempts."

"Ah, splendid idea, Don Fengli. I'll have to try that. I've given up beating them up and slapping them around; it didn't really work."

"No, just hobble them up some. Well, I best be going," he bowed to Cao and left, his large group of young gang members swarming around him to ensure his safe passage back to his tower at the extreme southern edge of Shansee, near the docks.

Don Fengli had not been entirely honest. True, he had force the women into the boots, but many of them quickly found ways to untie them using their teeth, complaining bitterly that they could not walk in them. Later, he tried locking them onto their feet. Those locks had cost him plenty. Yet even those had failed. The women took to smashing the heels off, though walking was still problematical in the remnants of the boots. Now he had devised a better plan, but was awaiting delivery of their new boots. Any day soon now, he thought to himself as he left the abandoned palace grounds.

Don Fengli's harem was kept in his converted living room, in which he'd placed thirteen beds, forcing the women three to a bed. One corner held a number of chamber pots, while another corner held the long trays in which food was thrown twice a day. Several large pails held drinking water. Little else was in the room except for the thirty-six women. He at least made sure that they had plenty of hairbrushes, and once a week allowed them the use of the bathtub, but they had to bathe themselves any way that they could.

He had a cook who did a good job of meal preparation, given the awful lack of most spices and any real variety of foods. Fish and rice were their staples, and there were only so many ways those could be prepared. His name was Bo.

He had a number of guards posted around the perimeter of the store providing his security. Don Fengli conducted his daily business in his old storefront. Of course, his own bedroom was equipped with all the finest bedding that he could find while raiding the many abandoned homes. In truth, one would say that his bedroom was most elegantly done. Each night, he picked one of his harem to spend the night in his bed with him.

Li-an was the ringleader of the resistance movement within his harem. Twenty-three, she had lost her husband in the fighting and had been taken prisoner shortly thereafter by Don Fengli. The man had good taste. He could afford to be choosy what with so many women around. All thirty-six were attractive, including Li-an, but she had risen to anger from the pits of grief over the death of her husband. For nearly a year now, she had been trying to escape the harem of Don Fengli any way that she could. Thus far, he had stymied her at each turn.

Li-an had become good friends with three other women and the quartet continued to plan ways to escape this place. Chan was twenty-one and a widow too. She'd also lost her daughter. Fang was nineteen and still grieving over the loss of her young husband who had been abducted into the overlord's army and had died last year in the great slaughter outside Shansee. Hui was only fourteen, barely of age and a recent captive or arrival to his harem. Her brother and keeper had been killed by Don Fengli's street gangs, and she had been brought to him. Quite young and attractive, she was immediately added to his harem. Her grief and anger was quite raw; she was very bitter at this time.

All felt that they had achieved a victory of sorts, having destroyed those impossible alien ballet boots that he'd forced them to wear to keep them from trying to escape. Now the four were continuing to plan ways to flee this prison house. "We make a break for it once the weather gets warmer. We go by night when there are few men in the streets," Li-an explained.

"Where do we go?" asked Hui.

"Out of the city. I've heard rumors that there is a general and army that is close to Shansee. We must make our way to them. I'm sure that they will help us somehow," Li-an insisted. They continued to work on the details, of which how to open the doors was the most difficult one. He'd beaten them, almost cracked their ribs, but still the four continued to plan their escape.

Two days later, the metalworker brought his creations to Don Fengli's store using his pushcart to transport the thirty-six pairs of shoes. While he'd had strange orders before, none had been this bizarre, but the promise of fifty pounds of rice in payment meant his family could survive far better than they had the last four months!

"Perfect, perfect. Let's get them on my harem now," Don Fengli sneered, pleased with the new shoes. These would guarantee they would not be escaping him anytime soon.

"But we can't even stand up in them," Li-an complained as they began putting the torture shoes on her feet. Made entirely of steel, only the bottoms of her toes touched the ground in the tiny V-shaped shoes. The arch was huge, even higher than the women who had their arches broken and reshaped into the common small feet that had been a trademark of the Great Ladies prior to the plague. The high heel was a tiny spike where it touched the ground barely an inch behind the rear of her toes. To prevent breakage or bending of such a tall heeled spike, a metal wedge reinforced the heel for three quarters of its length, later measured at a little over seven inches tall. An ankle band wrapped around her ankle and was locked into place. Molten metal was then poured into the lock and into the small hinge on the other side, preventing any possibility of the shoe's removal.

"Do your best, my dear Li-an," Don Fengli sneered.

"But these are higher than our Great Lady heels used to be when I had my small feet four years ago. We won't be able to walk in them," she continued her protests. The other women either reacted similarly or had no reaction at all. Many of them had long ago dropped into a sort of sub-apathy about everything in life. These women had no reaction at all, sitting on their beds watching their feet being iron shod and showing no emotions at all.

"Oh such exaggerations, Li-an. Come on; let's see how you stand in them. They are quite enticing, are they not? Quite indestructible too, I might add." Poor Li-an, she tried to stand and very nearly fell over. In order to stand, she had to keep her knees bent. He snickered and left the women to get used to their new shoes. Besides, he had more critical things to begin planning.

Left alone in their new misery, Chan wailed, "How can we ever escape in these? All our planning and practicing is for naught, now we can't use our feet to turn the doorknobs to get out of here."

"We'll need to devise another plan, that's all," Li-an said determinedly.

"But I can't even walk and only barely stand," Fang added.

"Come on; we had better start learning how to walk in them," Hui suggested. As she stood, she nearly fell over and then actually did when she tried to take a step in them. Li-an could do nothing to help the young teen get back up and could only watch the poor woman struggle wildly.

After some experimentation, Li-an finally worked out a way to move while wearing them. Taking a step was tantamount to falling, especially with no arms to catch herself or help with the balancing act. Instead, she shuffled her feet a few inches forward at a time. Though hard on her knees, she could move around the room, albeit slowly. "We must all practice this," she declared, once she made it around the room one time. She was still determined to escape from this sadistic bastard.

The women handled, Don Fengli began to make his own escape plans. He was certain now that he had to be out of Shansee by spring or he'd be captured by General Tao and his forces, which were sure to enter the city once the weather cleared and warmed. Until last week, he had always planned to take his personal harem with him when he left, along with his cook and his right hand man, a lad barely sixteen. As he sat in his room sipping tea, he realized that taking them with him was merely a dream. He could not leave by carriage, and the roads would surely be blocked. That left two ways out: north by riverboat and north by coastal vessel.

His problem was that he was in the middle of Shansee, far from Don Cao and the coast and docks. He'd never get past that man and his gangs, let alone be able to hire a coastal ship. That too was out, leaving the riverboats as his only option if he were to flee the city. While he could possibly get a few women onto the boat with him, handling their needs and food requirements would be impossible. Besides, stealth may well be required. While he had always promised both the women and two men that he would be taking them with him when the time was right to evacuate the city, he finally realized he simply couldn't. However, he dared not tell them that, especially his two most trusted men. He would need their undying loyalty until he was actually gone. His plan would be to fool them as well as the harem women.

During February, he, via his assistant and gangs, arranged for a riverboat to take them north and out of Shansee. In secret, his assistant loaded food supplies onto the boat, a little at a time to avoid raising the suspicions of his youthful gang leaders. At any point, his gangs could turn on him and he knew it. He had stopped telling himself that they needed him as much as he needed them. The rapid collapse of the entire city these past three months had shown him the error of his earlier thinking. While the needed food supplies were being stowed bit by bit onto the boat, he began consolidating his possessions and wealth, deciding what he could take with him.

He had amassed a large number of fine paintings, but these were far too bulky for transport. He sighed when he realized that he'd have to leave these behind — such a waste. He had many fine clothes, though many did not fit him properly. These, he'd gathered up from ransacking vacant homes. He decided that he would sort through these and take only the best. One night in late February, he brought Li-an into his bedroom for his evening's pleasure.

She shuffled her way into his room exceedingly slowly, trying hard to keep her balance and not take another tumble. Already she and many other women had innumerable bruises from falling while walking in their bedroom. While Don Fengli enjoyed himself at her expense, her eyes spotted all the clothes in piles. She realized that he was sorting them and what that meant: he was planning to flee the city fairly soon.

After the man laid back satisfied with the evening's pleasure, Li-an asked him, "Is it getting close to the time to leave Shansee, my Don?" She'd mustered up all the charm that she possibly could, a tall order considering she utterly loathed and detested the man. "Is the great battle coming soon to our streets?"

He sighed. He'd miss all this — pleasure from so many and varied women — all at his momentary whims. "'Fraid so. Word has it that the evil army will come charging in once the rains let up and spring comes. You know soldiers. They don't want to fight when soaking wet — can't keep their powder dry. Guns rust."

"I see that you are already packing. Make sure that you take your finest clothes, my handsome Don," she suggested, playing her role as best she could.

"Yes, but I can't take everything."

"What about us? You promised that you would take us with you," she asked what she really wanted to know. Somehow, someway, she had to avoid being hauled away with this wicked, evil sadist. Pretend just a little longer, she told herself.

Don Fengli sighed, "Oh how I always wanted to do just that, Li-an, but the way it looks now, I just don't see how. Even I, Don Fengli, may not even be able to get myself out of Shansee safely." He lied, of course. His boat was now well stocked with food and waiting his arrival. "I may have to run and dodge the soldiers, could be a running battle. I just don't want to see you lovely women being shot by the soldiers."

Li-an's heart leaped. He was not planning to take her and the other women with him after all! What an incredible stroke of good fortune, after all the latest misery that had come their way. Suddenly completely new plans swam before her eyes. "Sure, my handsome Don, you will not let us fall into the butchering hands of the wicked, lustful soldiers. They will rape us, beat us, and turn us into their slaves. Oh, Don, you can't let that happen to us, please you just can't." Again, she turned on all her charms, her pleadings for ultimate sympathy.

Running his finger over one of her huge breasts idly, he mused, "Well, you have a point there, Li-an. I know you and I sometimes were at odds, but none of you deserve to be brutalized by the general's soldiers. Lord knows how wicked those men are. Why, they take whatever they want, when they want. No one can stop them as they pillage."

"Please, you must find a way to keep us from the ravages of the soldiers," she pleaded.

"Okay, Li-an. That's the least I can do for you women who have been so kind to me all these many months," he agreed, unwilling to have other men tasting his carefully chosen morsels. He watched the attractive young woman slowly hobble her pathetic way back to the harem bedroom. She looked so inviting, he thought as he watched her struggling to walk in the metal heels that he'd had made for them. So damnable sexy, he thought, his perverted mind racing once more. He didn't regret hobbling them so badly, not for a second. They no longer attempted to escape, and besides, he had more important things to handle: his grand escape. He did not intend to honor his promise to help the women avoid the soldiers. He'd only said that to Li-an to make her feel better. After all, where could they go to avoid the soldiers? Nowhere in Shansee would be safe from them when they came charging into the city. No, safety lay in evacuating the city, and there was no way to get the women out easily. Of course, there would have been ways, if he really wanted to go to all that trouble and expense, which he didn't. Why? He knew that he could acquire more women when he settled down in another city. Women were now helpless cattle, easily acquired. They had become a means of exchange in these harsh survival days.

As Li-an made her awkward way back into the bedroom, she now knew two facts. One, Don Fengli was planning to flee Shansee soon, taking his most valuable possessions with him. Two, he would be abandoning his harem women. She knew the man did not ever intend to do anything to help them. He'd just leave them here in the bedroom to starve or be taken by the raiding soldiers.

This she explained to her three compatriots in detail. "But if he leaves us here, what will happen to us?" asked a frightened Hui.

"We'll probably starve to death long before anyone finds us," Chan pointed out, spitting on the floor while picturing the Don's head lying there.

"If we don't do anything, that is exactly what will happen or worse!" Li-an replied. "Stuck in here with all the others fleeing, we'll starve. Imagine what will happen if some of the gangs come in here and find us. Being raped by the Don is one thing, but being gang raped by all those thugs is unbearable. God help us if the looting soldiers find us. No, we have to plan our escape and time it when the Don leaves."

"But he promised to take us with him. He promised always to feed and care for us," Fang pointed out.

"And just how has he done any of that, I ask you?" Li-an angrily retorted. "Here we are, locked in a living room, fed twice a day like cattle in a trough, drinking from a bucket like a horse, and hobbled so that we cannot even walk. That's taking care of us? Ha!"

"We should make him pay for what he's done to us all," Chan spoke up.

"Damn right he should pay for what he's done to all of us," Hui agreed.

"We must gather facts. Each of us must keep our eyes open for clues. We have to know when he is planning to leave and what he is taking," Li-an advised. The four talked in hushed tones, working out just what they could do to escape when the time was right.

The last week of February, the rains died down and the weather warmed. Already early flowers poked their way into the light of the world, as if ignorant of the suffering and plight of the desperate humans who shared the land, the city called Shansee. Yellows and reds predominated in the unkempt lawn just outside their window on the world. Later that day, the women heard hushed talking in the Don's bedroom. Li-an carefully made her way over to the door and put her ear up to it, hoping to hear what was going on — perhaps he was leaving now.

"We make our break tonight around midnight," Don Fengli whispered. "After supper, bring our big wagon around back. When it is good and dark, I will load my things into it and meet you both at the riverboat around midnight. You two will go to the gang lords' meeting tonight after supper. Take them the last of our wine and that twenty pound bag of rice. Offer to cook them a meal, compliments of me. That will ensure that they will not be on the streets and on the prowl. Both of you leave there around eleven, that should give you more than enough time to get to the riverboat before I get there. I'll meet you there around one, and we'll head upriver then. By dawn, we should be clear of the army lines and on our way to safety and a better life up north."

"But Don, you'll have no protection, no one to guard your back," his second in command protested.

"Can't be helped. I'm depending upon you two to keep them all occupied so I can make a clean get-away. I'll be all right; hardly anyone is out that late at night. Just be sure you two get to the boat by one in the morning. I can't wait much longer than that. We have to slip past the soldiers during the dead of night."

"Okay, boss. You can count on us, but what about the women?"

"I'll leave them in their room. Can't take them with us. Besides, we can get as many women as we want these days. A sack of grain for a woman is the going rate. They will be a present for the soldiers when they ransack the place." All three chuckled and Li-an grimaced; they were throwing her and the others to the wolves, the ravages of wild soldiers.

Li-an whispered what she'd heard to the others. "Just as soon as the two leave and Don starts carrying his bags out to the wagon, we make our move."

"How? We are trapped in here. Besides, we cannot even walk in these iron shoes," Chan protested. Li-an bit her lip. She had to do something soon. She stared at the round doorknob, wishing it would open of its own accord. Hui volunteered to listen at the door while Li-an sat on the bed and thought.

It was dark now, probably eleven. They had been brought no supper, so that idea of Li-an's was gone. Overpowering the cook when he came was out. Hui whispered, "I heard the two leaving, Li-an. It's just Don, I think he is carrying things down the steps and out to the wagon."

"Okay, I have an idea. We have to get this door opened. Hui, I'm going to put my breast on this side of the knob, you put yours one the other side. I'll try to push down while you push up. Together, we'll try to turn the knob. Chan, you get down on the floor and put a heel under the door. As soon as we get it turned enough, you see if you can pull it open," Li-an ordered.

A frustrating half hour passed, as the three women worked on getting the knob turned. Occasionally, they heard Don passing by, as he carried his bags down and out to the wagon. At last, the latch clicked and Chan pulled the door open an inch. Li-an pushed it open with her chest and peered out. Only one more saddlebag lay on the Don's bed, the one in which she had spotted him stuffing his gold coins and gems into last week. As quickly as they could, the four slipped out of their room and into his. "What about the door?" Hui whispered. "He'll see it."

"I'm counting on it," Li-an whispered back. Here, we hide just inside his door. When he comes back, he'll see the door and look inside. That's when we rush him and attack him."

"How?" asked a baffled Fang.

"With the only weapon he's left us, our steel spiked heels. Kick him in his privates. Use our heels like daggers somehow," she advised. They waited. Li-an saw that they would have to move at least four feet before they could hit him in his back as he stood before the harem door. In their hobbling shoes, that meant taking many tiny shuffling steps. At any time, he could turn to see them and their game would be over. Well, not if she could kick him in time, she thought.

A minute later, she heard his heavy footsteps returning for this final bag. She also realized that he would be ready to leave over an hour before he said that he was leaving, and she guessed he was planning to abandon the cook and his second in command too. They'd get to the riverboat only to find that it had sailed long before they got there. Don Fengli was betraying even those two who had been loyal to him all this time. She steeled herself; this was it.

Don Fengli was excited; adrenaline flowed. This was it, his long planned great escape from Shansee. He'd stowed ten bags with his best clothes and scavenged valuables. All that remained would be to grab his very heavy saddlebags stuffed with all the gold and gems that he'd managed to obtain this past couple of years. "What?" he exclaimed as he approached his bedroom. He spotted the open door to his harem bedroom and stared at it for a moment. Cautiously, he walked to the door, pushed it the rest of the way open and looked inside at his naked harem, perhaps for the last time. How had they gotten the door opened? With their steel heels, he thought that he had finally hobbled them so there was no way that they could use their feet to open the door, which unfortunately had no lock.

The four women shuffled forward with their two-inch footsteps, trying hard to be quiet and as fast as possible without falling down. Li-an had only gone two feet when Don Fengli heard their steel heels on the wooden floor and turned around to see them. Li-an struck. She kicked at his privates as hard as she could, driving the steel point of her right foot up and inward with all the force she could muster. She lost her balance and fell to the floor, but her kick served its purpose. Don Fengli doubled over in pain, howling like mad. Chan and Fang continued to shuffle around Li-an's body. Fang got to him first and began stomping down on him, driving her spiked steel heel into his body. Chan got to him and joined her, but on their second stomp, both lost their balance and fell hard to the floor. Hui brought up the rear, carefully shuffling between the fallen bodies.

Don Fengli was crying out in pain, clutching his privates, but bleeding from several puncture wounds delivered by Chan and Fang. Hui took aim and stomped down. At the last moment, Don caught her movement in the corner of his eye and attempted to move out of the way of her deadly heel. Unfortunately, he moved right into its path and her heel slammed into his ear and on into his brain. Hui lost her balance and fell on top of the other three women, adding to their misery as well.

All four tried to get out from under each other and onto their feet. Without arms and the easy use of their feet, the four made awkward, pathetic attempts, but finally each got back up to their knees and looked at Don Fengli. "I think he's dead," Li-an suggested, giving his body a slight push. It didn't respond.

"Okay, let's get everyone out of here and down to the wagon," Li-an ordered.

"We should take his money saddlebag," Chan insisted.

"Okay, Chan, you and I will see if we can carry it. You two, get the others moving. We have to get out of here fast," Li-an ordered again.

Hui laughed, "Fast? You're joking, yes? I can't believe that we killed the sadistic pig."

"Come on; who knows how long we'll have before someone comes. If they find we've killed Don Fengli, they'll kill all of us too," Li-an pointed out.

Minutes later, she and Chan stood beside the bed staring at the heavy saddlebags. It had taken them that long to get to them. Already their knees were aching from the walking. Li-an leaned way down and Chan took the bags between her teeth trying to lift them. After a good deal of struggling, at last the bags slid over Li-an's shoulders. Although she had to lean to her right, the bags stayed on her shoulder. She guessed that it weighed twenty pounds. As she began her slow shuffle out of the bedroom, her knees bore the brunt of its added weight. It was all that she could do to carry the bags and not fall down.

Fang yelled at some of the sub-apathy women. "Look, Fengli is dead. As soon as the other men get here and see that, they will kill you. If you want to live, get up and come with us now!"

Already, Hui was leading ten other women down the hall, rather like shuffling penguins, none able to take more than a two-inch shuffle without falling down. All had their knees bent; none could stand upright in these overly tall heels. Li-an wondered if their knees would give out before they could even get out of the house.

Li-an focused on keeping her balance and not falling. Step, step, step. Oh how her knees ached, threatening to give out at any moment. Ahead of her two women's knees did give out, they went tumbling onto the hard floor of the hall. "Okay, take a bit of a break. Come on; you have to get back up. If they come, they'll kill you," Li-an called out, watching the poor women, who had begun to cry, struggling desperately to get back up to their knees.

She began to wonder what had the whole world come to? Was this life now? Women reduced to helpless, hobbling creatures, unable to do anything for themselves? Was this what life now would always be? A life completely not worth living at all, a life of being nothing but a sexual toy for men? If so, was it even worth living? Why even bother trying any longer? What was the point? Her husband was dead. Her two children, dead even before they could do more than walk. Well, they had it good; they didn't have to live to see the depths to which life had sunk. She felt good about that at least. Her babies had not had to suffer long. Was there any point at all in their futile, pitiful attempt to get out of this house in which they had been held captive for over a year? Li-an began to sink into the depths of depression, barely noticing that the line of women began to move once more.

It took them a half hour to reach the six steps that led to the back door and freedom from this house. Now they all faced going down the stairs, make almost impossible by their debilitating steel heels and lack of arms. If fact, it was so scary that Hui, taking the lead, decided to sit down and go down them on her butt. The others followed her lead. "Thank god that he left the door opened!" she called out to Li-an. Hui's enthusiastic voice brought her slightly out of her moodiness. They could get outside at least.

The wagon was parked about thirty feet away at the side of the dark alley. The team was tied to a hitching post. Hui led the line of women towards the wagon, but their legs continued to give out. Women kept falling down, but many refused to get back to their feet and attempted to crawl their way to the wagon. Li-an thought that her knees were going to give out completely; each step was a staggering challenge to keep from collapsing like the women ahead of her, made all the worse by the twenty pound saddlebag still slung over her shoulders.

Hui reached the wagon, sat on its rear board, and was able to pivot her body to get into its bed. Don Fengli's many bags of clothing lay in the bed. She decided against throwing them out; they would give the women something soft to sit on. "Come on; sit on the rear board and get into the bed," she encouraged. When Li-an finally made it to the wagon, sitting down never felt so good! Her knees ached and her legs refused to work any longer. Her feet had long ago become numb with aching pain.

Hui used her teeth to help Li-an unload the heavy saddlebags. Free of its weight, she felt so much lighter. Hui whispered, "How are we going to drive the wagon?" Li-an had no idea. If she were to be fully honest with Hui and the other women, she never truly expected to ever get this far. As she watched the remaining women making their pitiful way down the walk to the wagon, she nearly cried. She'd gotten them all this far, but now what?

Hui suggested, "Li-an, I can climb down and untie the horses from the post using my teeth. I suppose one of us can walk ahead of the horses and lead them down the street."

"Hui, we can't walk much further in these heels. If only he had not crippled us up so, we could do just that."

"Well, I will at least untie them while the others are getting aboard. We'll think of something, Li-an, we have too."

As she watched the teen doing her best to untie the reins, she realized that perhaps they could hold the reins in their teeth and drive the wagon that way, perhaps. Her knees aching, she struggled to get past the women and over the low backboard into the driver's bench. Chan and Fang soon joined her. Hui carried the reins up to them and all leaned over, trying to grab them with their teeth. After some ten minutes of effort, they had the reins and Hui joined them, though it took her another three minutes to accomplish this tiny task.

"Maybe we can wrap them around our legs," Chan said between her teeth, realizing this was not going to work. Five more minutes passed before reins were secured around Chan's left leg and around Fang's right leg. Holding the whip in her teeth, Hui banged the horses on their rumps, while Li-an did her best to encourage the horses to get moving. As the horses slowly began to walk, whispered cheers came from the women in the wagon's bed. Li-an turned around to see their smiling faces. She counted them.

"Looks like six didn't want to come," she said.

"Sorry, I couldn't get them to move," Chan whispered.

"Which way do we go? Now what?" asked Hui.

"Keep heading west; get us out of the city," Li-an suggested, shivering from the chilly spring night air. Behind her, the women were also freezing and were using their teeth to open various bags looking for some way to stay warm. Soon, they worked together to get a couple of canvas covers over themselves, hoping for a little protection.

"I-t-t's c-c-o-o-o-l-l-d," Hui chattered. Li-an's teeth were chattering so badly that she dare not talk. They had come so far against such odds, only to freeze to death as they escaped! She was out of ideas and resolved to die here on the wagon.

Ning Jon, now twenty-four and blind since birth, had been a happy man before the first plague struck Tashien years ago. He'd managed to make a living buying and selling cloth bolts from his three-room home, one being his small storefront. Miracles of miracles, he'd met a Great Lady, Lin, and she, wonder of all wonders, had married him. Their daughter, Juan, was only three when the first plague struck and thus didn't remember much from that period. Her mother had taken a bad fall, striking her head on the doorframe, dying hours later.

After that, life was hard for the widower, who somehow managed to carry on, raising Juan by himself. As long as every object in his home stayed in the same location, Ning managed well. He and Juan got by, though more recently, she was becoming more and more his eyes to the world. Then, the second plague struck. Those first two months had nearly cost both of them their lives from starvation.

As the chaos steadily grew, Ning and Juan began to find better ways to survive. He was very adept at getting around in the total darkness and that became the single most important factor why they were still alive in March of 826. For over two years, they never had a light on in their home. During the day, they kept the small home locked and shuttered. No one ever saw anyone around the place. Since it was virtually a shack anyway, no one ever bothered to ransack it. Who wanted bolts of cloth anymore? During the daytime, the two huddled together in a dark closet, sleeping.

At night, late at night, the two came out and wandered the streets. Juan would look for anything that might be edible, and Ning would pick it up and carry it back to their tiny sanctuary. There, they use a bit of charcoal to heat up the food and then eat their main meal of the day, usually around three in the morning when no one would be the wiser. All during the chaos, the two had continued to survive unnoticed and unmolested.

Ning had just picked up part of a discarded apple, when he heard the sound of horses coming their way. Juan whispered, "Dad. I see a wagon coming our way. It is going very slowly. What do we do?"

"Find a place to hide and see who they are? Which way?" he whispered back, his voice full of concern for her safety. She was his whole life now. He lived only so she could.

"Over here, dad, behind some barrels." She pushed him in the right direction. Once he crouched down, Juan made sure that he was hidden and they spied on the wagon.

A bit later, she whispered, "Dad! Four naked women are sitting in the driver's seat. They are really shaking. I think that they are freezing. What do we do?"

"Where are the men?"

"I don't see any. They look terrible, dad."

"Okay, let's stop them and see what we can do. Lead me, please." She pushed him out in the street as his stick lightly tapped the cobblestones.

"S-s-s-o-o-m-m-e-e o-o-n-n-e i-s-s s-s-t-o-o-p-i-ing u-u-s," Hui tried to say. She needn't have, for the horses stopped of their own accord. A man was in their way with his hands up, their signal to stop anyway.

"Hello. Do you need help?" Ning said softly, afraid that hidden men might hear them and come rushing out.

Shivering and chattering, Li-an asked for help. "Dad, the whole wagon is full of freezing, naked women," Juan pointed out. "We have to help them."

"Where are the reins, Juan? See if you can get me to their reins. I can lead them and you lead me. We'll take them to our back alley." Shaking violently, Li-an suddenly realized the man was blind and the little girl was acting as his eyes. She wanted to call out, but couldn't; she was so cold. The wagon went another block before turning into an alleyway that was pitch black, nestled between buildings, which blocked most light. Soon the wagon stopped.

The man walked through the blackness as if in broad daylight. She heard a door opening. The girl's voice spoke. "You can get down now. Dad has brought you to our house. Come on inside before men see us, please."

"W-w-e-e are too cold. Can't walk anymore," Li-an tried desperately to explain.

The soft man's voice whispered, "Okay, I will lift you down and carry you inside one at a time. Just be quiet." Li-an felt the man's hands feeling her body. At first, she felt repulsion — a man was again touching her nakedness, but she swallowed hard. Perhaps, he would help. She felt him securing his arms below her large bosom and up she went, over, and down. Her legs, now completely fatigued and shaking from the cold, wouldn't support her, but the man must have expected it and lifted her back up. Soon, she was inside a completely black room. "Sit here. Don't move please," he said. She sensed him leaving her.

One by one, Ning found another woman and carried her inside. By now, their tiny living room was very cramped. "Juan, I count thirty women, right?"

"Yes dad. Best get the charcoal stove going to get them warm," she replied. "We don't dare light any lights. That will bring the thugs down on us," the six year old explained to the shivering women whom she could not see, but could hear.

Warmth never felt so good to Li-an and her group. While the stove began to warm up the small home, Ning made trip after trip, bringing all the sacks inside. Finally, with Juan's help, he covered the horses and wagon with several canvas tarps that they found in the wagon. Their hope was that no one would find them during the day. They headed back inside their house and locked their door. The small charcoal stove in their kitchen-dining room cast a faint light into the living room, allowing Le-an to see a little, as well as Juan.

The blind man said in a whisper, "Always whisper. We do not want the thugs to find us. I'm sorry, but we have so little food. I will try to heat up all the tea that we have left for you. I'm blind. My daughter Juan is my eyes. We only have a very small home. We sleep in the bed in this room, and eat and cook in the kitchen. My old storefront is the only other room. While it is crowded with all of you, it is safe if we do not make any noise. We sleep during the day and are about late at night, looking for food that we can find along the streets."

One of the other women spoke up, "We found a sack of food in the wagon. You can use it if you can find it."

"I'll look for it, dad. You get the tea going. They are freezing," Juan said. Li-an noticed that she was wearing a crude sack-like dress, but it kept her warm.

An hour later, Juan guided her dad into the cramped living room. He had to make several trips to bring in everything. Sitting before Li-an, he explained, "I am sorry, but we only have four teacups. I will feed each one of you in turn, but I cannot see, so you will have to help me a little to find your mouths."

Although the women could barely see in the incredibly dim light, Ning managed to feed them and to get a cup of hot tea in them. Between the charcoal heat and the food, the women warmed up at last.

Li-an said, "Thank you for rescuing us. We are escaping from Don Fengli. We can't walk. He's hobbled us in these steel shoes with heels so high that we can only just barely walk a tiny bit."

"Oh this is awful. May I feel your feet and see what I can sense? Maybe I can find a way to take them off," he asked.

Li-an allowed him to touch her legs. His light fingers felt her legs and then moved on down them to her feet and shoes. She saw a very shocked look on his face as he felt her shoes slowly and carefully. "They are locked on?" he asked.

"Yes, and they poured hot metal on both sides of the strap so that the strap cannot come off," she answered.

"I'm afraid I haven't the skill or the tools to remove them. Still, I can perhaps make you some clothes." He explained about his former business and then set about doing just that. Meanwhile, with little else to do, Li-an, Chan, Fang, and Hui took turns telling them about their long captivity and eventually their own life stories. Juan helped her dad and chatted with the women as well. Until now, it had always just been Ning and her, and Juan really was enjoying all their company.

Before long, Ning slid a sack-like dress over Li-an. "It should be warn; it's velvet. I kept it short enough so you can go to the bathroom by yourselves. Juan manages that well. By morning, I'll have you all dressed." Li-an marveled at how rapidly the blind man worked. She soon realized that he knew the precise location of everything, but the many women and recently mounded bags of the Don's were making it difficult for him. Juan kept giving him directions when he moved around the packed living room.

By dawn, a bit more light entered the room and Li-an got a good look at their benefactors. Juan wore a bright red sack dress and looked very much like a bright six year old girl, who was un-phased by the chaos around her. Ning was about her own age, rather handsome, with a long moustache with four-inch tails on either side of his mouth, giving him a rather fascinating appearance. His eyes, however, were completely grey.

With the women finally dressed and with several bolts of cloth covering them as bedding, Ning sat down before Li-an. "You four are the leaders, right?" Li-an said so, and he went on. "I have been thinking. We can't stay here any longer. There are too many of you and we have no food. It will be impossible for me to scavenge enough food for all of you. I can barely find enough for Juan and me. We have no choice but to see if we can use your wagon to leave Shansee and make for somewhere that we will be safe. I have a cousin who lives on a farm, but it is forty miles west of here. If he still lives, perhaps we can stay with him. He has tools and may be able to get those shoes off you. Is this acceptable to you or do you have other plans? Perhaps to find your husbands and family?"

"My husband is dead, so are my two babies. All of our families are gone, Ning. Your plan is a good one. If you don't mind helping thirty helpless women, we would very much appreciate your help and kindness. We can't do anything ourselves and can barely walk."

"I am so sorry about your husband and babies. I miss my wife terribly, but I live now only for my beautiful Juan here. Tomorrow night, if the wagon is not discovered, we will flee Shansee. Now it is time to sleep."

The gangs of the middle section of Shansee had much to handle that next day. The cook and second in command waited until nearly dawn for Don Fengli to arrive. At last, they ordered the riverboat to set sail, assuming he'd been killed. "He ought to have sent word if he was delayed," the cook said as they got underway, hoping to get to a place of safety. At least, they would have a volume of food that they could trade later on.

The gang lords discovered the dead body of their boss the next morning and ransacked what was left in his place. Now they fought among themselves for control over the others. Their added chaos and infighting kept anyone from searching that back alleyway, though in all likelihood, it would not have been searched anyway.

That night, Ning found that the women could walk a little, and he got them all onto the wagon. He wrapped them all up with bolts of cloth to help them stay warm. They took the saddlebags with the treasure but left all the other bags in the Jon home. He also stowed their small charcoal stove and remaining charcoal, along with what little food remained. It would have to get them by, he concluded. He had Li-an and Juan sit up front with him. Although he could handle the reins, he couldn't see and needed their guidance to drive the team. They left the alleyway around midnight, and by dawn, the city of Shansee was behind them.

Juan and Li-an began describing the farmlands to Ning as they rode down the dirt road westward. Rice paddies dotted the landscape, which was incredibly flat. Occasional thickets of tall bamboo appeared here and there, but there were few trees. Those had long ago been cut down and used for building materials in Shansee.

Although they took frequent rest breaks, they traveled all day long. With little else to do but give Ning an infrequent order to go more left or right, Li-an began chatting with the father and daughter, sharing stories about their lives in better times. Now Ning began to understand Li-an's physical reactions last night. "I sensed horror, humiliation, and abject disgust from you when I touched you last night, lifting you down from the wagon and also later when I felt your shoes. Now, I understand why that is so, Li-an. What you have endured is beyond description, horrors no woman should ever have to suffer. It is these dark times in which we find ourselves. In a way, I'm glad that I cannot see such horrors; feeling it and sensing it is horror enough. I only hope to get my precious Juan to a place of sanity and safety, if such can even exist anymore."

"I-I didn't mean to react that way, Ning. You and Juan have saved our lives, but. . ."

"I understand, Li-an. No need to try to explain. Perhaps one day we can leave this all behind us. Somewhere out there, a better world surely must exist. We must find it, Li-an," he replied. How could he be so optimistic, she wondered. With all the horrors and chaos around them, how could such even exist?

Around dusk, they approached an army checkpoint. Li-an feared the worst. "It's the soldiers. Now we are doomed, Ning. There are so many and they have horses. We cannot get past them. I see countless guns. One is waving to us. I think he wants us to stop," she called.

"A few more feet dad. Now, pull back and stop," Juan said expertly guiding her father up to the line of soldiers, who pointed long guns at them.

"Hello. Where are you going? Where are you from?" a soldier asked.

"Excuse me, sir. I am a blind man. We're fleeing from the chaos that has befallen Shansee. This is my daughter and thirty women who have been most horribly mistreated. We're going to my cousin's farm to seek sanctuary there."

Juan whispered, "A man whose uniform is different is walking up to these ten men. He is speaking now."

"Okay, another load of refugees. All right. You are to go to Wuhanchang. There is a refugee center in that town. You will be given shelter and food. The Church of God will give you therapy. Once that is completed, the women will have their arms restored and then you can be resettled as you desire."

"Thank you sir. But I am blind. I do not know the way to this town," Ning replied honestly. "We have almost no food, but we do have a little charcoal. Can you give directions to my daughter? She can guide me. Is it possible for us to trade for a little food to get us to this town?"

"Sergeant, take them to the mess line, see that they are fed and bedded for the night. Sir, tomorrow, a soldier will drive you to Wuhanchang and make sure that you are taken to the Church of God there. It is a miracle that you haven't driven the wagon off the road into a rice paddy before now!" They thanked him, and a man crawled up, sitting beside Ning. He took the reins from him and drove the wagon a few more miles.

A large mess line served nearly a thousand soldiers. Lines of tables covered the patch of ground cradled between nearby rice paddies. There they had their first solid, well-balanced meal in well over a couple of years. Full and sleepy, they were given blankets and slept soundly that night. Morning's light brought breakfast, something none of these had in over two years. Soon, though, they were on the road again. This time, they all sat in the wagon bed, allowing the soldier to drive them.

Wuhanchang was a town of around ten thousand, down by half from pre-plague days. However, already half had received their Basic Therapy. The Church of God in Wuhanchang was now under the control of one of the Perfect Women, Fang Zu Die, and her new husband, Hu Die. Already, they had made a lasting impression on the folks of Wuhanchang. Seeing the armless, legless woman moving about and objects moving about her, most concluded that she was a goddess of some kind, which she took in stride. After all, she was still insisting that she was the Perfect Woman, refusing still any attempts to restore her arms or shrink her breasts. Yet, she, like the other Perfect Women, had become very competent therapy givers, and Bi Mei had at last assigned her to one of the mushrooming new Churches of God.

The wagon halted before the new Church and Ning and the soldier helped the women out. He did not have the patience to walk at the speed of the women and went on ahead to make their arrangements. Ning, with his arm around Li-an's waist, led them in their pitiful slow shuffle into the church. Li-an insisted on giving him directions, and he made sure that she didn't lose her balance. Juan followed at their side, just in case her dad needed more explanations. The soldier came back out, just as they were about to enter. "Everything is all set. Just go on inside, the Church Counselor will see you now and take care of you." He left, and Ning heard him riding off on his horse, which had been tied to the back of the wagon. In they went.

Sitting in her slanted chair, Fang Zu watched the slow shuffle of the long line of women entering. Inwardly she groaned. Indeed, this batch of refugees was in terrible shape. Kang, sitting beside her, had already begun to copy down their names, as provide by the soldier, and arranging coming sessions for them as well.

"Welcome to Wuhanchang's new Church of God. I am a Perfect Woman, leader, and top Counselor here," she began formally.

"Dad! She's got no arms or legs!" a very excited Juan exclaimed. Li-an looked both dismayed and shocked, as did the other women.

"No, I most certainly do not have either. I have absolutely no need for such appendages. I'm absolutely the Perfect Woman as I am. Now then, you must be Ning. How long have you been blind?"

"Since I was born, ma'am. I'm seeking a place of safety for my daughter. I don't understand. I thought that the soldiers said that the women would be able to regain their arms somehow, as they did after the first plague," he replied, suddenly frightened that poor Juan and the others were about to lose their legs as well!

"Oh they most certainly will have the opportunity to regain their arms, if they so desire, once we finish their therapy sessions. Those will erase all the emotional trauma that you have suffered and any painful incidents as well. Just because I am a Perfect Woman, is no reason that I should try to force another woman to become a Perfect Woman like me. Now then, those steel shoes have to go, unless you women are enamored with them."

"Please, take them off us somehow," Li-an begged and explained all about them.

"Well, congratulations ladies on a job well done in seeing that Don Fengli was stopped from harming more women. Well done indeed. Okay, as I said, shoes have to go. If you ladies will please sit down, I will get them off you now."

Although not understanding her, the thirty women struggled to sit down without falling down. Ning sensed the trouble that Li-an would be having and put his arms around her, lowering her gently. "Dad! She's floating through the air!" an even more excited Juan whispered to her dad.

"She really is, Ning!" Li-an confirmed it for him. She saw utter disbelief on his face.

"Of course, I fly around. How else would a Perfect Woman be able to get around? Who needs legs anyway? Such a nuisance." Fang Zu landed beside Li-an, Ning could smell her flagrance and sensed her close proximity.

"Dad! Those metal straps — they just flew off their shoes!" Juan tried to explain what she was seeing. "Now the shoe is slipping off her right foot."

"I am sensing the condition of your foot, Li-an. It is as I suspected. Your leg and feet muscles have been adapting to the shoes. We are going to have to lower your heels gradually, unless you want to tiptoe around until you can at last get your feet flat on the ground. Hu, how about fetching the shoemaker Bao? We're going to need some intermediate heels for these women or they are not going to be able to walk much. Now then, here goes the other one, Li-an."

"How did you do that?" asked Li-an, shocked and surprised with the total ease that they had come off her feet.

A shoe and broken strap floated up before her face. Fang pointed out, "See this tiny line here, I dissolved the metal bond here rather like cutting it with a knife. On the hinged side, I merely cut through the metal strap, leaving the sealed hinge intact. Now then, stretch them a bit, but if you stand up on them, you will see what I mean about your calves needing time to stretch back out." Ning helped her up and she again wobbled. While she was able to lower her heels a little, but no way would they touch the floor. If she tried, she was risking tearing and ripping her leg muscles.

Within an hour, the women were fitted with five-inch heels. Even these stretched their calves almost to a pain threshold. Next, they were all sent to a bathroom and given baths. Once dried, they were given new and proper dresses, while several women brushed out their hair and re-braided it for them. By then, it was time for dinner. Again, they all ate well. Many women who had arms fed the thirty. These were some of the volunteer therapy givers, they later learned.

After supper, each was taken into a small room and given their first therapy session. Bit by bit, the thirty-two lives were restored. Counselor Fang Zu kept them all housed together as a group. One evening, Ning asked, "Li-an, sometime when you are up to it, I would really like to see your face."

"What do you mean? I thought that you were blind," she replied slightly startled.

"He means to feel your face. Dad 'sees' by feeling. It won't hurt, Li-an," Juan explained in her six year old manner.

"Oh, I see. Sure, sometime," she replied, hesitantly.

A month later, these tough cases had finally finished their Basic Therapy. These women had an enormous amount of emotional trauma to eradicate from their lives, thanks to Don Fengli. That evening, Li-an joined Ning and Juan, whose arms had already returned to her. She and her dad were sipping tea, trying to decide on what they were going to do now.

"Hi Ning, Juan. Mind if I join you?"

Ning rose, "Please do, Li-an." She marveled that he had even gotten the chair for her although he couldn't see and she'd just walked in. Sitting beside him, she said, "Do you still want to see my face?"

Ning flushed, "Yes, Li-an, if you don't mind." She felt his gentle touch outlining her face, nose, and cheeks. "Wow, you are a beautiful young woman indeed, so matches your voice. Such a high-spirited woman. There is power in your face."

"You can tell all that?" she teased him. Juan giggled. At last, she could stand it no longer, she leaned a bit further and kissed him.

"What?" he finally said when they parted. Juan giggled even more.

"Ning, I have really fallen for you. We're supposed to be figuring out what we all want to do now. You know part of Don Fengli's treasure belongs to you and Juan. After all, if it hadn't been for you two, we would be dead."

"I am glad that you like me. Yes, I fear that I may be hopelessly in love with you, but surely you don't want to be with a poor blind man, Li-an. You are so beautiful."

"You see a hundred times better than most men do with two eyes. What say you and I open up another cloth shop? I've just finished my Basic Therapy. I am supposed to get my arms back tomorrow."

"Can we dad?" Juan asked eagerly.

"Well, I don't know about the money. It takes some to get started. Are you sure, Li-an? All that I know is cloth. Not a very exciting life."

"Of course I am sure, Ning. But there is one small thing I need to ask you." She leaned over and whispered something in his ear. He flushed and whispered back. She smiled and said, "Okay, I will keep them just for you, Ning." He smiled and gave her another kiss.

"What did you two just say?" Juan asked. Neither replied. Li-an delayed having her bosom reduced to what it had been, something that Ning appreciated.

Undaunted, Juan said, "Well, I still just don't see why Counselor Fang Zu thinks having no arms or legs at all makes her a Perfect Woman. Do either of you know why she thinks that?" Neither did, but by now, they knew, as all others who met her, that Fang Zu was something of a goddess flying around in that strange body of hers. That viewpoint they could accept.

The other story that came out of Shansee ahead of the army's move into the city was equally grim. Don Cao, who had taken over possession of the Santi Inn, the old Santi del Dio Fortress, kept the women he took in trade for food locked into a penthouse suite on the eastern half of the fifth or top floor. His private quarters was the western half that overlooked the city proper. Thus far, he had accepted fifty women in trade. Young and good looking had been his sole criteria for picking them from the many that others had tried to trade. His problems were twofold. Their upkeep was slowly draining his resources. The women continued to be belligerent towards him, their great benefactor, and they continually tried to escape.

Of course, they never got far from their room. Once, though several had made it to the long, back spiral staircase. None ever tried the main stairs, however. He'd tried beating them, slapping them silly, even denying them meals. Nothing had worked. Hence, he broken down and asked Don Fengli at the conference. What a novel idea, he thought. Make them wear the alien ballet boots that the men had attempted to wear during those first two months of the plague. Well, he knew that he had been unable to walk in them and had continued to crawl.

His latest attempt to keep them from straying had been interesting, though not fully successful He'd undone their braids, allowing their long hair to fall and drape over their naked bodies. Lacking arms, their hair continually got in their way, continually causing them problems. Frequently, they stepped on their own hair when they tried to walk, slowing them way down. Unfortunately, when they ate their meals by lapping up the food from the trays on the floor, food got into their hair. Messy, yes, but at least they were slowed way down.

Now if he could combine the two, Don Cao figured that would totally take care of his little problem. He needed time to plan his escape from Shansee, uninterrupted time, that is. Where could he acquire said boots? That was the key question that he faced the day after the conference. While there were discarded boots galore, most were far too large for the women's feet. At last, he hit upon the solution: boy's boots. He sent his scavengers, the local gangs out to find a hundred pairs. Surely, out of that number he could find some that would fit his fifty women.

Wen Bi, twenty-five, was the ringleader of the women. Like the other women, she'd already suffered the loss of her husband and small children. She had been a hairdresser before the plague and a Great Lady as well. Now she had lost everything, reduced to being a whore in Don Cao's harem. Yet, Wen was a fighter; she'd used to do the hair of the Princess and was used to having others respect her. Her current situation was untenable at best. Only the fact that she had two frugal meals a day kept her going.

Chandai was twenty-four now, a calligrapher of some renown before the plague. Her family gone, she had been captured and bartered for food. Although she was devastated with the plague's effects on her love and talent, calligraphy, she entertained notions of learning how to do her art using her feet and the special low desks. Don Cao took that last hope away from her and she deeply resented that, swearing to get revenge on him. Chandai had become Wen's best friend and saw herself as second in command of the women.

Jiao Hong Li just turned twenty-one, having spent the last eighteen months in the harem. She'd been married barely three months when the plague struck and her soldier husband had been killed, as had been so many young men of Shansee. Before the plague, she was just beginning to make a small name for herself as an interior decorator. Her contract with the Princess to redo a royal bedroom had put her name on the map. She deeply regretted that the plague ended her chance at fame. Jiao had pushed her way into being the third in command, taking no back talk or sass from the other women.

The youngest of the leaders was the very recent addition of Ying Ya, barely fourteen. The youngest woman in the harem, she was also the most flexible and adaptable. Wen quickly saw that Ying had a very sharp mind, one that grasped complex ideas rapidly. She never took no for an answer, which more often than not had resulted in her body being badly bruised. Indeed, her legs were black and blue when Don Cao had brought her into his harem. She had lush black hair and enticing, charming eyes, and a smile that captivated him. Ying was not averse to using her sexuality to gain her way. Wen took the youngster under her protective wing.

Over half of the women, though attractive physically, had now sunk into the sub-apathy band and were merely going through the motions of living. They were waiting for death to take them out of their misery, for misery their lives had become. Another quarter of the women were merely in apathy, their bodies going whichever way that forces pushed them. The remainder lay between grief and sympathy. Only the four were above that level, which is why they had assumed the role of harem leaders.

Already many had griped and bickered at Wen because her belligerence had cost them dearly. With most of the women's hair at or below their ankles and no longer braided, it constantly was in their way. They tripped on their hair, sat on it, and even got it caught in the chairs. Even trying to get into bed caused them untold grief just trying to get it out of the way so they could lie down without laying on it. Many took every opportunity to tell Wen, "Look what you've done to us."

She of course yelled back, "Look stupid. I didn't undo your braids! That sadist did!" Her antagonism only created more friction among the women. On the other hand, Ying did her best to help. By the time that Don Cao entered their room that day with the massive pile of boots, she had gotten the hair of several who had complained the most re-braided, albeit crudely.

"What have we here? Trying to undo your punishments?" Don Cao sneered and rapidly loosened the women's hair again. Ying's four hours of work were gone in under a minute.

"Easy come, easy go," Ying sneered back at Don Cao, who didn't quite get her meaning at all.

"Now then, there will be no more escape attempts. I've got new shoes for you all." As he and his henchmen began fitting and tying up the boots, the women naturally protested wildly, but Don Cao merely grinned his usual covert smile. He was enjoying every minute of the women's suffering. Best idea I've ever had, he thought, imagining how they would suffer. Shoot, he knew that he couldn't walk in them, and he had arms that flailed about wildly when he'd tried.

After he left the women alone in their new misery, one said, "Now look what you've done to us, Wen!"

"Bitch! I didn't do this. He did. Get your facts straight, woman," Wen replied, trying hard to keep from breaking down completely. This new barrier was almost insurmountable.

"Well, we have to try. If we can't, maybe we can still get around on our knees," Ying suggested, trying hard to find something positive about their new predicament.

Jiao suggested, "I took dancing lessons when I was young. It is possible for us to walk on our toes. In the ballet, it is called en pointe, if I remember it right. I was only eight though. Come on; we have to try and learn how to do this." Bravely, she tried to get to her feet, standing with her legs slightly apart and her knees bent, trying hard to keep her balance. "It was lots easier when I had arms," she admitted, finally sitting down.

Wen was determined not to let this latest setback keep her from trying to find ways to escape. She tried to walk and kept the others making attempts, though many just gave up and tried to crawl, an action made most difficult because their hair kept getting in their way. Wen soon realized that escape would be impossible unless they somehow got their hair tied up and these awful boots off.

Mid-February, the women got a break. One of the sub-apathy women accidently broke her heels. Soon, others began breaking off as well. Don Cao was so involved in making his own plans that he decided to abandon hobbling of his harem. Wen actually thanked him when he removed hers, and Don Cao felt very pleased with himself as a result, falsely believing that he'd finally earned the respect of his harem women. Pity I can't take them with me, he thought. Immediately, Ying began showing Wen, Chandai, and Jiao how to braid hair using their feet. True, all four had to work together, but they had all the time in the world to do it.

"Okay, so how are we going to escape?" Ying asked, satisfied that they now had removed all barriers impeding their flight from the Santi Inn.

"Well, we need to get the door open. There is the back circular stairs and the main stairs. He has lots of guards along the main stairs, so I think it best to try the back stairs," Wen suggested.

"Yes, but he does have guards there too," Jiao pointed out. "One guard can recapture us all."

"Gosh, you mean that you all don't really have a way out of here?" Ying asked incredulously. "I thought that you knew a secret way out of here." She sounded disappointed for a minute, and the other three sighed; she was right. For all their scheming and planning, thus far, they really had no workable plan. Unworkable plans abounded.

"Well, in that case, it is up to me," the teen declared. "Now let me think. I've studied a lot of history. I was going to try to become a palace historian, but that's obviously gone now. This is the Santi Inn, right?" Wen nodded. "Sorry, they brought me here at night and I didn't get a good look. I thought it might be, but wasn't sure. Okay. Did you know that originally centuries ago the Santi del Dio of Velona, Sea Princes, built this tower and fortress? That's when Shansee was first opened up to foreign trading. Well, sort of, they allowed the Santi to trade and they needed a secure dock deep enough to handle their big caravels."

"What's all that got to do with us now?" asked Wen, slightly annoyed that her shortcomings on their escape plans had been laid bare.

"Well, the Santi del Dio were awfully powerful and smart. They always had a secret way out of their fortresses and castles. Look, if the Emperor chose to, he could surround this fortress back then and starve them out if he wanted to. You know, if they did something to upset him or whatever. They would be too smart to have no contingency plan for fleeing the tower and fortress if it were besieged."

"Oh, so you are saying that there is a secret way out of here?" Wen asked, catching on to Ying's speculations.

"Most likely they did. Now as far as I know, the owners of the Santi Inn never knew of any secret passages. Surely, they would have had them blocked off if they did. Security of their guests and all that," the teen chatted on. Ying loved to chat. "So that means the old secret exit must still be here — secret still, of course. All we have to do is find it." She nodded her head as if to punctuate her declaration. She would have put her hands on her hips in a triumphant gesture, if she still had them. For a moment, she regretted that she didn't.

"Brilliant, Ying! How do we find it?" Wen complimented her and wondered aloud.

"Well, if these two penthouse suites were where the leaders resided — which makes sense — even today, Don Cao resides here and besides, these were the most expensive rooms when the Santi Inn was in business," Ying chatted away, not finishing her original thought, having gotten completely sidetracked.

"So if?" Wen nudged the somewhat flighty teen back on track. Obviously, these two suites were the best in the tower.

"Where was I? Oh, so the leaders up here would need a secret way down and out."

"Why?" asked Jiao. "Couldn't they just go down the stairs?"

"Not if the fortress was under attack and the enemy had breached the walls. They might have retreated upwards fighting all the way. As I understand fighting from the books that I've read, the one with the higher ground has the advantage. They'd slowly retreat upwards, so when they got to the top, they'd have no way out. The Santi would have made allowances for that. I say they must have a secret way out from up here. It is either in Don Cao's suite or on this one," Ying concluded.

"Okay, it sounds plausible," Wen agreed. "Where do we look and what are we looking for?"

"That's a good question," Ying conceded. "Well, it must be well hidden since it hasn't been discovered all these years. We should start looking."

They began a thorough study of their huge penthouse suite. Their windows overlooked the old Santi docks, whose wooden planks had now rotten away, though remnants remained, marking its location far below them. Off to the east, bamboo forests and flooded rice paddies dotted the landscape along with the shoreline and the many delta islands where the mighty Yonshu River emptied into the ocean. Circular in shape, the head of their many beds butted against the outer grey walls close to the windows.

Ying quickly ruled out most of the visible outer walls, for there just wasn't any room for a concealed stairs. However, the north side had a wooden wall that enclosed a huge walk-in closet, currently empty, save some spare bedding sheets and blankets. If there was going to be a secret exit, Ying decided that it had to be somewhere inside the closet.

Before long, Ying noticed a peculiarity in the outer walls. Along the inside of the closet beginning at the eastern corner where the teakwood wall touched the outer walls of their bedroom, the curved stone walls inside the teakwood wall the closet seemed somehow slightly different. "Come on, let's measure this," Ying exclaimed becoming excited.

"Measure what?" asked Wen.

"You start at the outer wall there where the teakwood closet wall starts and see how far it is to the main entrance of the closet. I will do the same thing here on the inside," Ying explained.

A bit later, Wen said, "I got about twenty feet, Ying."

"Funny, I get a few feet less. Let's swap and measure each other's sides and see if you and I think there is a difference," Ying suggested, growing more excited by the minute.

"Well, this inside outer wall is definitely a little closer than the outside," Wen concluded. "Is the secret stairs behind it somehow?"

"Yep, we've found it. This is a fake outer wall going around the entire back side of this huge closet. Now all we have to do is find its entrance," Ying concluded.

For several days, the women looked and studied the inner wall without finding any secret way into the stairs that they knew had to be behind this stone wall. Wen began to think that its entrance must be in Don Cao's room, which would only complicate matters, if it were. They would need to search his room too. Towards the end of February, they got an excellent opportunity. They overheard Don Cao talking about needing to go out to the docks that afternoon, arranging a bunch of gang guards to protect him.

When he took off down the stairs, Wen and Jiao sat on the floor and used their feet to open the door. This they had down pat, having done it many times before, always getting themselves into trouble with Don Cao as a result. Now the four sneaked into his suite. Jiao stood near the window keeping watch. "I see him. He's surrounded by a pile of boys. They are walking over to the docks. Start your search."

Wen noticed many bags were sitting in one corner, as if packed for some trip. Many of his suits which he had hanging in his closet were gone. Evidently, Don Cao was planning some kind of trip. She realized that he must be planning his escape from Shansee before the city was attacked by the soldiers.

Quickly, Ying determined that the outer walls inside his closet were also about three feet short as well. The three searched for any lever or way to open a secret door in his closet, but found nothing at all. At last, the four headed back to their room, defeated yet again.

"It must be here in ours," Ying concluded. "It just has to be here. Let's look again." They did, but soon they all gave up, except Ying, who was convinced now more than ever that it must be in here somewhere. It had to be well hidden, she concluded, so as not to have been found by the Santi Inn owners or any of the multitudes who had stayed in these penthouse suites over the years.

Ying began to study the actual grey stones very carefully. Finally, she noticed that one stone didn't seem to have any mortar around it. Using her foot, she pushed it. To her amazement, it began to slide inwards. "Hey, Wen! Come here, look at this!" she called out.

Wen, Chandai, and Jiao came rushing into the walk-in closet, just as Ying began pushing on it harder. When the stone had moved in about six inches, a section of the wall swung back towards the outside. The opening was close to the teakwood closet's wall. A gaping black hole appeared. All four stared inside. In the very dim light entering the closet, they could see stone steps heading downward. The passage was barely three feet wide. A layer of thick dust covered the first steps along with many cobwebs.

"I could kiss you!" Wen exclaimed.

Ying flushed, "Please don't. I've found it. It's full of cobwebs and spiders, yucky. Oh well, it goes down, but I wonder where it ends up at?"

"We don't dare follow it now. If Don Cao comes in our suite, he's sure to notice some of us are missing and raise the hue and cry. We're only going to get one chance to use it. We best choose the time wisely," Wen stated factually. "I wonder how we close it?" That they couldn't figure out in the dim light. Instead, they moved some blankets more or less to hide it from view. "Don't say anything to the others until we are ready to move. One of them might give it away to Don Cao," she advised. The three agreed, but Ying held her head high; she had done it. Now they could escape, though she wondered where it came out at the other end.

Wen now began to work out how they honestly could escape. Could they manage to go down those steps in the total darkness? How could they possibly see to find their way out at the other end? Even if they surmounted that, they would be outside without any clothes or shoes. This time of year, the nights were chilly. Of course, then where could they go? Surely, not back into the city. She decided that perhaps they could somehow wrap a blanket around each other to stay warm. That seemed slightly feasible. She set her mind to solve the light problem, which seemed most important now.

On March 3, Wen again heard voices coming from Don Cao's room. As usual, she and her friends put their ears against the door to spy on the conversation. They recognized the cook's voice, "Okay, I'll go with them, but are you sure that you want to be left alone in the fortress? Surely, someone ought to remain on guard in case the gangs get through ours and come after you."

"No, I'll be perfectly safe. Just make sure the doors are locked. I will leave my lanterns going in my window all night. If they go out, then I am in trouble; come running. How's that? Just make sure our gangs kill all of our rivals. Don't take any prisoners. We sure as hell don't want to feed them," Don Cao replied.

"All right then," another youthful voice agreed. "You can count on us Don! We'll kill all them Fengli gangsters!" The meeting ended; they heard footsteps heading down the stairs, though they also heard muffled sounds from Don Cao. It sounded like coins banging together.

Just as they were about to back away and discuss what was happening, they heard Don Cao talking to himself. "Ho, ho, ho, away tonight I go. No one will be the wiser, though they may be the miser." He seemed unusually cheerful, if not downright silly, Wen thought. It sounded as if he was about to make his escape. However, the sound of the coins intrigued her. If they fled as they were, they would need gold to pay for their way. Evidently, he was packing his gold and planning to depart while his many gangs were off fighting the other Don's gangs. Clever, she thought. It'll probably work. Then, she felt the pangs of the hideous injustice done to her and all these women. If he left, she'd never get justice for the abuses he'd committed against her and the others. He'd get away with rape and kidnaping, among other crimes.

Wen snapped. "Help me open our door," she whispered angrily. None dared counter her. Jiao and Ying sat down and used their feet, opening the door a crack. "You stay here," she whispered and crept out of the room into the hallway.

Peering into his room, she saw his many bags stacked near the door. He was stuffing a bag of gems into a duffle bag. Convinced that he was indeed fleeing Shansee, she steeled herself to get her justice. Her life and the other women demanded it. He finished and began picking up several of his clothes bags. She ducked into the darkness of the hallway far from the stairs. Don Cao came out and headed down the steps, taking them two at a time. She then ducked into his room and surveyed the scene. His clothes were tossed all over; these he was abandoning, she concluded and ducked inside his closet. A bit later, he returned to carry more bags down the stairs. She ventured a peak out of the window and saw a pushcart near the front door. He was leaving; she was convinced of it now. How could she stop him?

Again, he returned and took the last of his clothes bags down. Only the money duffle bag remained. Whatever she was going to do, she'd have to do it soon. Her mind raced. Don Cao came humming into the room. "Well, penthouse, it has been swell, but now it is time to depart." He picked up his last bag and headed out into the hall. Wen raced silently after him. As he got to the top of the stairs, she rushed up behind him and gave him a solid kick in his upper back with her right leg. He dropped the bag and swung his arms wildly, trying to keep from falling down the stairs, most unsuccessfully, since he was taken by complete surprise by her shove!

He fell down several steps and lay still. She darted down them after him, unwilling to let him get away. Above and behind her, she heard their door opening; her friends were obviously coming to see what was happening. Don Cao, lying in a jumble halfway down this first section of stairs, looked up to see the fire and rage burning in Wen's eyes. "You bastard! This is for all the rapes!" She stomped down on his neck. Although he tried to raise his arms to block it, she was faster than he was. A loud snapping sound echoed through the stairs and hallway. Don Cao departed his current lifetime.

"What have you done?" asked Jiao. "Kick him again and again!"

"He's dead," Ying commented. "Good riddance, I say."

"He's got his money in this bag. We have to take it," Wen said, bending down and trying to lift it with her teeth. It was not too heavy, and she barely managed to lift it up and quickly carried it into their bedroom. "We have to escape now!" she told her three companions. "Blankets, lanterns, hair. Remember the plan. Ying, get the door opened."

"Ladies, it is time that we make our escape from here. Don Cao is dead. I killed him for all his crimes against us, for all the rapes and tortures. We're going out through a secret door. You can come with us if you want to leave here."

"But where will we go? We have no clothes. What will we eat? Here, they feed us twice a day, which is more than I had before I was brought here," one woman asked. Many agreed with her. Wen finally admitted that she had no idea where they would go or what they could eat.

Ying joined them. "Okay, it's open but pitch black. We have to carry a lantern somehow. Ideas?"

"That one with the handle — one of us can carry it between her teeth. Let's wrap our hair first, then the blankets," Wen ordered. Already Jiao and Chandai had wrapped their long braided ponytails around their necks, and they helped the other two with theirs. Then, they helped each other wrap a blanket around each other, draping it over their shoulders. While loose, Wen hoped that they would more or less stay. Ying bit down on the lantern handle, while Jiao used her feet to get it down from the wall. Then, Wen bit down on the moneybag, and they headed into the dark stairs. None of the other women chose to go with them. Most were afraid of leaving secure meals and a warm bed behind; half no longer cared whether they lived.

Jiao, bringing up the rear, pushed on the door, and it swung closed. "Hey, gang, I got the door closed. No one will be following us or even know where we've gone. Guess the other women don't want to escape with us."

"I hate spiders," Ying called out through her clenched teeth. "This is really hard. I don't know if I can hold the lantern all the way."

Through her teeth and following behind her, Wen said, "You have to. This bag is heavy too."

"We can relieve you if you need us," Chandai called out. "I don't think anyone has been down here ever. Look at the dust."

"And all the spider webs. I'm glad I'm not in the lead," Jiao added from the rear where she could just barely see where to step next.

Down the foursome went, moving as rapidly as they dared. Poor Ying got the worst of it, running through constant webs. "At least there are no rats," Jiao encouraged from the rear. Wen noticed that they were going around and around the outer walls. As they descended, she spotted no other entrance points or exit points, for that matter. Just as well, they didn't want to exit onto another floor. They'd be trapped inside the inn.

"Anyone have any idea how much further we have to go?" Jiao called out. "I'm lost. What floor are we around?"

"Dunno, we're going around the outer walls," Chandai replied. As they descended, the air grew cooler and cooler. "I heard running water; you see anything?" she called out, but wished she hadn't. Wen and Ying were struggling to keep the lantern and bag from falling.

At last, Ying could carry it no longer. She stopped and sat it down, nearly dropping it. She and her blanket were covered with cobwebs. Her jaw ached, and she moved it around. Wen followed suit. "My jaw is paralyzed," she exaggerated. "Where are we?"

"Dunno, but it keeps on going down. I hear water though," Ying said. They took turns adjusting each other's blankets, which by now were quite loose and in danger of falling off them. That done, Jiao and Chandai slipped in front of the two, who backed up a few steps, allowing them to take the lead for a while. After a bit of struggling to get the lantern and moneybag in their teeth, Chandai led the way on down. Soon an ugly green mold covered the walls. Here and there, water seeped through the tiny cracks in the stonework. Wen concluded that they must be underground somewhere. They pushed on and soon came out alongside a sewer trough that led from somewhere inside Shansee. They had a foot wide path to follow above the flowing sewer water. However, rats also shared their path. The light froze them momentarily, before they scurried on down the tunnel ahead of them.

"I think I hate rats," Wen whispered, thankful that she was not in the lead. "It cannot be far to the ocean," she called out encouragingly. She was right. Before long, Chandai halted. Ahead of them, the tunnel opened into the night sky, the sewer flowed on out and into the ocean. They heard the waves lapping against the sandy shoreline. Fresh salt air filled their lungs and all breathed deeply, free at last. The two in front had sat the lantern and bag down and were trying to orient themselves as Wen stepped beside them.

"Well, now we have a choice. We can make our way westward and hope that we are not spotted walking along the shore or we can go east and take our chances with the river delta," Wen pointed out.

"If we take the lantern, someone is likely to see it and us," Chandai pointed out.

"Without it, we can't see much," Jiao protested, unwilling to lose the little light that they had. Once out, she knew that they could not possible light it, even if they had hands. They had no matches.

"I vote left, away from the docks and Shansee," Wen said. "I don't want to be caught right away. Let's take our chances on the delta. I know that there are supposed to be many vipers around this area, but probably no people. Maybe we can find some kind of shelter until morning. Maybe in the bamboo thickets." The others agreed, and Chandai blew out their lantern with a heavy heart. However, their eyes had adapted to the darkness, and the stars appeared between the cloudbanks. At least it isn't raining, Wen thought. After securing their blankets once more, Wen got the bag between her teeth, and Ying led the way out along the sandy beach, going slow, and looking for snakes.

"I think I must hate snakes even worse than spiders. I feel like I have a thousand spiders crawling all over me," Ying whispered.

"If it is warm tomorrow, we can all take a bath in the ocean," Wen suggested, mollifying the teen's worries a little. They walked on in relative silence. Often, they stopped to switch bag carriers. The women's jaws were aching; fatigue set in faster now, since each had been carrying weight between their teeth. More and more frequently, they had to stop and switch. About a mile from the sewer tunnel, they came across a bamboo thicket. Exhausted from their ordeal and with their adrenalin gone, Wen decided they should spend the night here. They pushed their way into the thicket and made themselves a sort of nest out of their blankets, huddling close together to stay warm. Before long, the four fell into a deep sleep.

Hunger and the dawn woke the four. "Well, here we are in the bamboo. So what now?" Ying asked, as she got up to stretch. Never had she had such an uncomfortable sleep, but she was free. As she stared out of the thicket towards the ocean, Ying felt both lost and out of her league. Why had all this happened to her — to everyone? Her sometimes jovial disposition evaporated, as she gazed on the desolate world about her. Off to her right, the once great city of Shansee was rousing, but to what? More chaos, destruction, and death? "I've just figured it all out. The world has gone mad," she said with a defiant nod.

"What's mad?" a sleepy-eyed Jiao asked, struggling to sit up. "I feel like I've been punctured all over. Oh, I slept on gravel."

"Oh nothing much, just the whole wide world, that's all," Ying said rather cynical. "We got out of there, but what's the use? The rest of the world is just as mad as Shansee."

"Come on girls. We best get up and going," Wen advised.

"Where Wen? Did you ever stop to think where we could go?" Jiao asked pointedly, Ying's depression rubbing off on her as well. Hungry, filthy, covered in cobwebs, and her feet caked with sewer muck, stark reality struck Jiao as well.

"That way. We have to find somewhere that is safe for us to live," Wen ordered. "When it warms up, we take a dip in the ocean. Come on; the sooner we get going, the sooner something will happen."

Chandai chuckled, "Now that's the first sensible thing I've heard. Something is sure to happen to us out here. Snakes, quicksand, and rice paddies — until we hit the delta. Then its mud and impassable waters. We should have gone the other way and risked getting caught again. Ah well, I'll grab the bag first, if my jaws don't fall off." Wen had already dragged her filthy blanket out of the thicket and was trying to dust it off, shivering from the chilly spring morning air.

Quickly, the three joined her and began helping each other get theirs wrapped around them. "Okay, let's follow the beach," Wen ordered and led the way. They walked for several miles, taking turns carrying their precious moneybag, though out here in the middle of the delta region, it wouldn't do them much good. Inland, poor rice farmers struggled to survive, but at least they had food — had being the operative word here. Raided repeatedly by the youth gangs of Shansee, all their crops and farm animals had been taken from them, leaving them in as bad a plight as those in the nearby city. The women knew that they could get no real help inland and continued along the beach. Twice, though, they had to duck for cover as a small fishing boat came into view. None dared be spotted. They'd had their fill of men and their lustful ways.

Late afternoon, the sandy beach gave way to muddy banks. They were entering the vast swampy delta land where the mighty Yonshu River emptied finally into the ocean. Here at its mouth, the delta region stretched over thirty miles wide, filled with hundreds of small, mud islands, barely above the water level, but teaming with wildlife. Finally, the four were faced with walking through one of the muddy water flows just to get on to the mud island ahead of them.

"We're going through that?" Ying questioned.

"Better ideas? If we can somehow get past the river, there has to be small coastal towns where we can buy clothes and food and maybe a room. Come on, ladies," Wen encouraged them. Slipping and sliding, they made their way into the muddy waters, hoping and praying it wasn't too deep. When they reached the other side, their bottom halves were caked with slimy, brown mud, compliments of the Yonshu. They crossed another two before they hit a bottom filled with quicksand or mud, they couldn't tell which.

"Damn. What are those women trying to do anyway? Blankets? Hell, they are going to drown, Chen," one brother said to the other.

"I guess we have to intervene, Dan," the other Yuz brother sighed. They poled their makeshift raft towards the struggling women.

"Stop struggling! You are only making it worse. Yes, stop wiggling," Chen called out, as they poled swiftly to the women in danger of drowning. One by one, the young men pulled each woman out of the mud and onto their raft. In the process, they lost their blankets, but Jiao managed to hang on to their moneybag in spite of it all.

"My god, they are totally naked!" Chen exclaimed as Dan pulled the last one on to the raft.

"Help us, please," Wen pleaded.

"Yes, but please don't move. Just lay still or you will capsize our raft. Guess we have to take them to the shack, Chen," Dan said. The terrified women lay still, covered with mud, their hair thick with the river mud, rescued from certain drowning by the strange appearance of two ill-dressed young men. Wen didn't know what to think. Had they now gotten themselves into an even worse predicament?

"Thank you for saving us," Wen said quietly, but politely.

"Yes, well, we really don't want the company, but we couldn't just let you drown yourselves. I am Chen Yaz, my brother Dan."

"We weren't trying to drown ourselves. We are fleeing Shansee," Wen tried to explain.

"Hold that side, Dan. Talk later, yes. Okay, Dan, I'm pushing as hard as I can. Whew, there, we've cleared it. Hang on ladies; we've a bit further to go," Chen replied. Having just gotten the raft over a shallow spot, they were out in the main current again. "If we don't get this right, we'll all end up out in the ocean and that will be the end of us all."

She turned her head a bit to see the men. They were poling the raft with long bamboo poles, sweat dripping from their flexing arm muscles and backs. She saw that the raft took a good deal of effort to control, and she lay as still as she could, thankful that she was on her stomach, though this was an uncomfortable position and for her friends. The roped bamboo floor of the raft was uneven and bit into her body at uniform intervals from her breasts to her ankles. She saw that the raft was only just above water, a mere quarter inch separated her face from the muddy waters.

After an eternity, Chen called out, "Ah, home sweet home. Hang on, just about there." All four women turned to look at their destination. Wen's heart sank. It was little more than a bamboo shanty out in the middle of nowhere. The raft hit the land hard and Chen jumped off and tied a rope to a bamboo pole in the ground. "Okay, ladies, one at a time, get up and onto the land. If you want, I'll carry that bag for you." Jiao allowed him to take the bag. She was so covered in mud, as was the bag, that she dare not put it into her mouth again.

"We know, it is not much to look at, but it is warm, dry, and we have a patch of fresh water here too," Dan explained. "I think that we'd better get you cleaned up first. Follow me. Chen, get what towels we have and the last of our soap. They are really going to need it."

He led them around the backside and there was a small sandy beach. Here the ocean touched this outer island. "In you go. I'll strip, come, and help you bathe, unless you can do it yourselves."

"Please Dan, we really can't do it ourselves. Thank you and your brother for helping us," Wen said politely.

"God, we'll never get clean!" Chandai exclaimed looking at her friends. They looked incredibly muddy. They waded out and found the water warmer than expected, but they didn't complain; it was fresh and clean at least. Soon, Dan wearing his underpants came out to them and began sloshing water over them, then undoing their hair. Shortly, Chen appeared and joined them. An hour later, all four were finally clean. Their hair had taken the longest to get mud-free. They walked back onto the sandy beach, and Chen produced four bamboo logs for them to sit on while the men dried them off.

"I'm sorry, ladies, we haven't been around naked women much, but you don't seem to be too embarrassed by all this," Chen ventured to ask what he had been thinking for some time.

"Long story," Wen replied, acting as their spokeswoman. "We've been kept naked and in Don Cao's personal harem for over a year. We escaped, though I killed the bastard before we made our escape. We are beholding to you for saving us back there. Thank you."

"No problem. We are deserters of sorts. The overlord tried to abduct us into his army, but we lit out of town instead. We've built this shanty and have been living off the land since then. Been over a year, but there is plenty of food, if you are not picky about it. We'll trade you food and a place to stay for the news," Chen suggested.

"Yes, come on, let's get them inside and warmed up. We have to find them some clothes, Chen. They can't go naked — it isn't right. Mind you, we find you are all attractive. It isn't that — I mean — well you shouldn't be going around naked," Dan replied getting embarrassed.

Their shanty was built for two, thus once inside, space was at a premium. Chen had them sit on their single bamboo bed while they rummaged through a couple of large sacks. A while later, the women wore overly large white cotton shirts and baggy pants. While Chen heated up the last of their tea, Dan began the lengthy drying and brushing of their hair. He worked on Jiao first; he rather fancied her and saw that Chen was interested in Wen. As Chen held a cup up for Wen to sip, he said, "Well, that's the last of our tea. Don't know when we can find someone to trade for more though. Times are grim for the local farmers, what with all the gangs robbing them blind. They don't find us out here, though. You are the first to find us, Wen. How about telling us your stories?"

After serving each their tea, he started in doing Wen's hair, which she greatly appreciated. It had been more than a year since anyone had done her hair, Don Cao never did. Wen relaxed and began telling the men all about their nightmare months of captivity, rape, and mistreatment. Both boys were appalled and shocked.

Later, they told their story, which was altogether short and brief. Their parents had not survived the aftermath of the plague, leaving them to look after their younger sister. That all ended when the overlord soldiers came to abduct them. They hid and their sister was beaten, but she did not reveal their hiding place. She later died of her injuries. They had packed up all that they could carry and snuck out of Shansee in the middle of the night. They came to this region because few lived out here. In time, they found this location was ideal and built their bamboo shanty. They caught fish, crayfish, snakes, and other furry creatures, trading them, until the last few months, with the local farmers for rice, vegetables, and tea. Now even the farmers had nothing left to eat, and the men were getting by on the last of their meager stock of rice and dried fruits. Still, fish was always plentiful.

Once the women's hair was properly braided for the first time in over a year, they felt almost human again. Chan and Dan fixed supper and shared it with the four. "Wow, what is this? It tastes really good," Ying said.

"Snake. It does, though most people wouldn't try it. Glad you like it," Dan replied.

"I hate snakes," Ying stated factually.

"So do we. They are all over the place around here. Have to be constantly alert for them, but they don't bother you unless you bother them," Chen added.

"Well, ladies, we do have a problem," Chen then began. He knew that he would have to address this topic eventually. "What are we going to do with you? You've eaten us nearly out of all our pitiful food reserves."

"We wanted to get to somewhere that is safe for us to live," Wen answered, "but like Ying says, the whole world has gone mad. Where can we go? I am so sorry that we ate so much, Chen. You should have said something."

"No, you are our guests. I admit, our home here isn't much, but what we have is yours. You would do the same for us, if the tables were turned," Dan interjected.

"He's right. Not everyone in the world has gone mad. We haven't forgotten what it means to be civilized, though it's rather difficult for us out here," Chen continued. "Say, we recently heard from old Bao that folks in Nan Yan are doing really well, plenty of food and work and no overlords. Maybe it's time that we take a gamble and give that city a try."

"I like the sound of that!" Wen replied. "But how can we possibly get there? It is way inland and far, far to the west."

"There is a train line, though I don't know if trains still run. If we could get to it, perhaps we could flag down one and ask them for a ride to wherever. Probably can take us to somewhere along the coast and from there we can maybe hitch rides north to Nan Yan," Dan suggested.

"Yes, but Wen says that she's heard some general has Shansee encircled and is camped maybe thirty miles all around the city. We don't dare get caught in that mess, they'll abduct us into that army," Chen protested slightly.

"We can use old Lee's boat and sail around Shansee to maybe fifty miles away. That ought to get us to safety," Dan suggested.

"Good idea, but what can we trade Lee to get him to take us that far?" Chen asked.

Wen decided to take a gamble. "Look in our bag. Take what you think would be fair to Lee. We need safe passage to this place."

"Oh my goodness! No wonder you were clutching this bag for dear life! Look, Dan! They are richer than richer!" Chen exclaimed. Dan couldn't believe his eyes either. At last, Chen took two gold coins out and re-fastened the women's bag. "This ought to convince him to take us that far. We'll make him bring along some food as well, though we can fish as we go," he added.

Sleeping arrangements were cramped. Three of the women slept in the men's bed, while Wen slept between the two men on the floor, using all the rest of their bedding. The next morning, Chen headed off in their raft to find Lee, while Dan fixed the last of their food for the women's breakfast.

Around ten, the old wooden junket appeared just off their sandy beach. Chen poled their raft from the junket up to the shore. "He's agreed, and we're ready to take the plunge back into the world. You all ready?" Dan packed their few belongings, and the two men made two trips out to the junket, not wanting to risk capsizing the raft by taking all six of them as they had to do yesterday.

Old Lee was in his fifties, a salty seaman, who still made his living hauling what cargo he could find between smaller fishing villages along the southern coast of Tan Loc Province. He avoided the city proper, because he hated city-dwellers and spun numerous yarns as they made their way slowly past Shansee, two miles off to their right side. Later in the afternoon, he produced some dried fish, bread, and cheese. "I brought along a special treat seeing as how you paid in gold. No one has paid in gold for some time, excepting those where we're headed. I found these last trip: pickles, real pickles! Haven't had them since before the plague struck." The men held them as the women bit into them, marveling at how great they tasted. None could remember the last time that they had a simple pickle. Suddenly life was taking a wondrous turnabout.

At sundown, they were only halfway there. The sleeping accommodations were crude, but a huge step up from their previous nights. Jammed into six hammocks in the smelly cargo hold, the men had to help each woman into theirs and out again in the morning. Old Lee had stayed at the helm all night. "Land ho," he called out sleepily. Hungry, but content, the six stood on deck and watched as the small port of Yingnan slowly grow in size as the junket floated towards it.

Later as Chen and Dan helped the four women safely across the crude boards that served as a gangplank, a young harbor master walked up to them. Waving to old Lee whom he apparently knew, the man bowed to the six and said, "Welcome to Yingnan. I am the harbor master of our humble, little port. I take it Lee has no other cargo to unload?"

"Right, just us. We fled Shansee. Is there an inn where we may stay temporarily? Is there any work to be had around here? Dan and I need to find work soon so we can help our guests here," Chen asked.

"Ah, refugees. Our Princess is very particular about this. You must first come with me to the Church of God and obtain your Basic Therapy before you will be allowed to work. Once your women guests have finished theirs, they will have their arms back. Until then, the Church of God will provide a room and meals for you."

"What? There is a cure for the plague? Wen! Did you hear that? Lead on, harbor master!" Chen exclaimed highly animated.

"Oh yes, haven't you heard? No, I guess not. Shansee is still beyond the Princess's reach. Yes, the Church of God is working miracles — such a wonderful day when my wife and daughter's arms and hands reappeared. I do admit that our Church of God here is rather small, but then so is Yingnan." As they walked through the streets of this small seaport and rail line, they spotted many women running their errands as well. The six stared at them. The women looked perfectly normal, no monster bosoms, arms, and hands as ever. Tears trickled down Wen's cheeks. For a moment, she thought of the other forty-six women who had refused a chance to escape. Would they ever have the chance to become normal women again?

"Here is our humble Church of God," the young man said, opening the door to what appeared to be nothing but an old warehouse. It did have a strange symbol on its front. Just inside, a young man sat at a desk filled with ledgers. He looked up and rose as the harbor master entered. "Got six refugees from Shansee for you Lyle. They've just arrived on old Lee's junket. This is Lyle Cummings; he'll take good care of you." He bowed and left.

"Welcome, welcome to our new church. Yes, my wife and I are in charge, and we will make sure that you are well cared for. We are nearly finished giving our precious therapy to everyone in Yingnan and the surrounding areas and are gearing up for the anticipated waves of those in dire need from Shansee later this spring. We'll have you all fixed up in no time. First, may I have your names and city or place of birth?"

They rattled off their names and Shansee. Lyle wrote their names in one of the ledgers. "May I ask why you need to write this?" Wen asked. No one had ever bothered to write down her name before.

Lyle looked up with a smile. "We are doing our very best to make sure that no woman or girl is overlooked and given a chance to be cured of the plague and the terrible traumas they've been forced to endure. Plus, the men here will not be able to find work until they have received their Basic Therapy. Although most employers are quite desperate for young, strong, and willing workers, they've seen the huge difference that Basic Therapy has made. Frankly, they just refuse to hire anyone who has not had it. Simple economics. I'm an engineer, by the way. I came to this country to help with all the new engineering projects and fell in love with your country, customs, and people. Pardon me if my command of your language is not the best yet. My wife, whom you will meet shortly, is still working with me on speaking properly. She is the most charming woman that I've ever met, Counselor Zhen Du Cummings. She's our top therapy giver."

"We are perfectly able to work now, Lyle, but we will do as you wish. Please allow us to continue to help our four guests. They came to us in dire need, and we have promised to look after them as long as they need us. It is the least that we can do, since we failed to help our sister, who gave her life that we may live another day," Chen explained.

"Of course, we always honor refugee's requests when possible. At meal times, many women are volunteering to help. They will be most willing to help you with your four guests' needs at any time. They also give the miracle therapy sessions as well. We are still ramping up for the expected surge in Shansee refugees, so expect a lot of construction messes. Let's get you some rooms, a hot bath, some clean clothes, and a decent meal, shall we?"

Just then a side door open and the six saw the strangest sight that they had ever seen. All six stared in complete disbelief, which slowly turned into awe. Zhen Du came floating into the room on her special slanted back chair, which was hovering about three feet above the floor. The woman was pretty, but she had no arms or legs. Her lush, black hair was not braided, but lay draped across her plague-created, massive bosom, falling down below her special chair. Her eyes were bright and her smile, huge.

"Ah, our new refugees! Great. I am Perfect Woman Zhen Du Cummings and the head Counselor at our new Church of God. I will make sure that you get your needed therapy quickly. Lyle, have you introduced us yet?"

"Just getting to that, dear. This is my incredible wife. Yes, she was severely brutalized by a sadistic doctor, but now she is as she claims, a Perfect Woman, and a brilliant therapy giver, I might add. Dear, these refugees somehow managed to escape from Shansee. Old Lee brought them here in his junket — wise move. This is Chen and Dan Yuz. Wen Bi, Chandai, Jiao Hong, and Ying Yu. Chen and Dan wish to continue to care for the women. I was about to get them settled. Care to come with us, dear?"

"You bet. We are just getting ready for the anticipated big influx of refugees from Shansee. You see, the Princess and General Tao are expected to take over Shansee soon and bring desperately needed help to those who still live there," she explained. Seeing the shocked looks on the six faces, she added, "Yes, that mad doctor cut off my legs, but that has really been of great benefit to me, once I got over the helpless madness and opium addiction foisted off on me. Therapy has returned to me my ancient powers. I can move anything anywhere anytime. Who needs to make use of body appendages to do such? So slow and cumbersome. I've chosen to remain a Perfect Woman. Let me know if any of you want to also become a Perfect Woman."

"No! I cannot imagine being so utterly helpless!" Wen exclaimed shocked by such a notion.

Zhen grinned. "Soon, you will see that you are not a body and possess great kijutsu. Anything that anyone can do with their arms, hands, legs, and feet, I can do myself, only ten times faster and much better. I have found arms, hands, and legs a total impediment to my abilities to get things that I want done. Just ask Lyle here. But I do understand your initial reaction. Mine was vastly worse, horrified I was. That was then, before I had Advanced Therapy. You see, we can restore anything that the plague caused, but we cannot restore things that man has caused to our bodies. The sadist cut off my body's legs and thus they could not be restored. Having only arms would so totally interfere with what I want to do, so I've never bothered to have them restored. I honestly don't need them. Both Lyle and I like the mammoth breasts, so I kept them too. Now then, we would love to hear your stories, but let's get you all settled in first."

"Since you fellows wish to continue to assist your women companions, we will be putting you into these two adjoining suites. Ladies, you do not have to have the fellows tend to your private needs. Many of our volunteer women would love to help you with those personal needs. Like everyone else who has suffered the plague, I too have endured the humiliation and embarrassment of having to have men handling my most private needs. It is time that we women take back what is left of our modesty and humanity," Zhen Du stated matter-of-factually.

Three women came rushing up at that moment. "Ah, this is Mei, Li, and Lona. They will help get you four cleaned up. Fellows, you can clean up in your adjoining room. Mei, bring them all to the mess hall when they are ready. See you all for a nice chat in a short while," Zhen Du added, before bowing her head and sailing off in her chair, doors opening before her as if my magic. Lyle showed the men their quarters and left them to clean up.

An hour later, dressed in new clothes, the two men knocked on the women's door. Mei let them in, "If you wish, you can help us braid their hair. Wen said that you both did a good job of it before. Come on in." Both men were surprised to see that the four women were now bathed and dressed in nice looking dresses, simple cotton, but quite complimentary.

"Wen, you look fabulous, allow me to finish your hair," Chen said with a smile.

She flashed him a smile too. "Thanks to you and Dan and these kind women, I feel almost human again. Please, you did such a good job on my hair before."

A half hour later, Mei, Li, and Lona led them down a long hall to the mess hall. Mei explained as they walked, "There are a hundred of us volunteers doing the therapy around here now. Most are out of town handling the nearby farms and small villages. Still, Counselor Zhen Du and Lyle will be joining us and a few more who are handling the last of our town's women, who had it particularly rough during the plague years. Zhen Du is simply the best! She has such powerful kijutsu, even greater than the Olin Masters, it is said, though none of us has ever met one of those most powerful masters. They are all in Nan Yan now, did you know that?" Mei chatted away, eager to share what news she had.

Over lunch, the six shared the storied of their lives. Lyle took notes, Wen observed. When she asked about it, Lyle explained, "We are amassing data about just who has acted criminally since the plague struck. The criminals must be brought to justice and held accountable for their actions. My compliments, Wen, for bringing that beast Don Cao to justice for us. I sent word to General Tao to expect to find your other forty-six women who are still captive in the Santi Inn. He'll see that they get immediate help."

"Thanks," Wen replied, easing her mind about their plight.

When they finished eating, all six received the first of their therapy sessions. Zhen Du insisted on handling Wen herself. She whispered to Lyle, "I want to make sure that Wen gets the best possible therapy because she really deserves it. She brought him to justice and got the others out of the inn." Lyle smiled; he had already guessed that his marvelous wife would do just that. Zhen Du was a stickler for insisting the women who demonstrated a fighting attitude get the very best treatment for their valor and bravery.

Two weeks later, they finished their Basic Therapy, Wen being the last to finish up. She had endured the most trauma of the six. The two men were done in only a week and spent the second week exploring their options. Lyle had them convinced that they could thrive well in Nan Yan, where there was a shortage of sharp young minds and strong arms. Both wanted to see all these new MMCE inventions and learn about this electricity thing, which offered so much promise to all.

During that second week, the six discussed their plans together. "Look, we really like you four and want to help you get settled into a new rewarding life," Chen explained. "We would be most honored if you would allow us to help you four get settled in Nan Yan. From all that we've heard, Nan Yan has become the renaissance of our country, and we want to become a part of that."

"But we have money," Wen replied hesitantly. She really liked Chen, but.

"We don't want your money, Wen. Our honor depends upon making our own way. Use your funds to get yourselves established. Perhaps open your own interior decorator company, Jiao," Chen answered. "We like you and want to be a part of your lives," he admitted.

The four agreed and the six worked on making their move to Nan Yan when the women's therapy was finished. Of note, six months later, Chen and Wen were married, as were Dan and Jiao. All six lived in one large home in Nan Yan. The brothers became trained electrical workers and began their own businesses. Likewise, the women each opened their own small shops as well. For these six, life had indeed blossomed from the pits of the Dark Ages. However, the four women also became volunteer therapy givers as well.

As more and more men and women received Basic Therapy throughout Tan Loc Province, the therapy givers began to discover an increasingly larger number of criminals. Since the Princess demanded that every man receive the Church of God's therapy before they could be certified to be employable by the MMCE projects, men with seedier backgrounds tried to slip through the process. Good record keeping on the part of the church thwarted all such attempts, and the therapy givers weeded the undeserving out easily. It seems that the truly criminal minds simply did not get great benefits from the sessions, because they constantly withheld what crimes they had committed.

Also, as more and more received their sessions, the givers kept accurate records of evil-doers who showed up in their patients histories, but only those who caused them harm in this lifetime. All this was passed on to General Tao who took effective action as he had promised. While the Church of God could redeem the criminal elements, they refused to do so now, preferring to handle the truly needy. The general merely shipped the criminals off to Ning in the ice province of Dong.

As his forces began their takeover of Shansee, the sheer number of criminal elements rose sharply. At least one boat sailed for Ning each day almost for the rest of the year. Weeding out the evil doers took time, but with the now many smaller branches of the church helping out, the salvage operation ran fairly smoothly.

The general conditions within the city were so bad that the soldiers shipped off each new batch of refugees to one of the dozens of churches, where they were housed, fed, cleaned up, and given new clothing. Then, when their bodies were well enough, therapy sessions began. As criminal elements appeared, they were shipped back with the returning soldiers. Still, it took many months to reclaim all the once huge city.

During this time, many attempted to flee to save their own skins. Shankou was the most popular destination, being just across the Tan Loc Province border. By the end of the year, that port city had added nearly a hundred thousand more men and teens, nearly all male and of a criminal bent. The already high murder rate in Shankou rose even higher.

By the end of 826, General Tao had secured the last remaining areas of Tan Loc Province. However, millions had yet to receive their needed therapy and the rebuilding of Shansee was only in the planning stages. With so much of the city in shambles, the Princess decided the wise thing to do was to rebuild the whole city, implementing MMCE citywide. During the winter season, the evacuated young were given training and education. Come spring, they would become the backbone of the reconstruction efforts. The Princess and her engineers estimated that it would take them at least five years to rebuild Shansee totally. Yes, it was an ambitious project, and she hoped that it would eventually become a shining star of MMCE success. Already Nan Yan held that distinction. On the bright side, this project would provide steady employment for many years for anyone who wanted to work.

The delays forced General Tao to delay his planned spring offensive across the border into the drug lords' territories of Wontun Province. Late summer, his forces at last crossed the Lian River into those highlands. By now, the drug lords themselves had fled. With so very few able to pay for opium and hashish, there was no profit to be had. His sweep was swift and met with little resistance. Again, the Church of God was stretched to its limits to provide for all the needed therapy sessions. The general was conquering territory faster than the church could keep up with him.

In 828, he moved on Zau and Shankou. The Imperial City of Zau was pretty much in the same state as Shansee, far to the south, home to starving children and street gangs. The overlords had also abandoned the area. Iron coins had been a dismal failure there, leaving the economy destroyed. The wise had headed south, begging to be allowed into Tan Loc Province as refugees. In Shankou, as his forces made their move on that port city, and those who could fled by boat northward.

While the coastline along Wontun Province was huge, those fleeing Shankou knew better than to land at one of the many smaller cities there. Soon the general would be sweeping through them as well. Many tried to put in at Jiao, the largest port of Linyi Provence, just north of Wontun Provence. However, there the four elementals had secured their grip on the province and refused to accept refugees coming in from the south. Such boats were turned away, forcing them to go further north to Ning, in Dong Province, the ice land. Here, they found refuge, but the conditions there were abysmal to say the least.

As my days stretched into weeks and then months and then years, I slowly began to relax. Finally, the world was settling back down into a stable state. Macario was producing freed spiritual beings at a rate that we never dreamed of when we first began. With a few exceptions, the various countries were now prosperous and thriving. MMCE had really taken hold worldwide. Modernization and industrialization had played a vital role and was continuing to do so. Agricultural production in the Greenway was at an all-time high, with much being shipped to Tashien.

The alien races had no idea just how resilient the human spirit can be. We bounced back from their plague vastly stronger than before, with thousands now in the category of free spiritual beings with all their native abilities restored. I was becoming more and more convinced that nothing could stop us now from achieving our ultimate goal: total freedom for every spiritual being on Tarra, each with their full native abilities restored.
The End.

Other Books by Vic Broquard

Without Warning (fantasy)

The Trident Series: (fantasy)
Volume 1 The Trident and the Book
Volume 2 The Trident and the Scepter
Volume 3 The Trident and the Resurrection

The Adventures of Elizabeth Stanton Series: (science fiction)
Volume 1 The Evolution of the Path
Volume 2 The Great Messiah
Volume 3 Of Kings and Queens and Troubadours
Volume 4 Chaos in the Aftermath
Volume 5 Power Plays
Volume 6 Age of Exploration
Volume 7 Abducted
Volume 8 The Emperor and Empress
Volume 9 A Job Worth Doing
Volume 10 Degradation
Volume 11 The Second Crusade
Volume 12 When Worlds Collide
Volume 13 Dark Ages

The Lindsey Barron Series: (fantasy)
Volume 1 The Rod of the Apocalypse
Volume 2 The Board of Governors
Volume 3 The Crown of Moses
Volume 4 Dominus for President
Volume 5 The National Health Care Program
Volume 6 States Justice
Volume 7 Cross and Double-cross

Zoran Chronicles Series: (fantasy)
Volume 1 A Dragon in Our Town
Volume 2 Dragons, Power, Courts, and War

Planet of the Orange-red Sun Series: (science fiction)
Volume 1 When Kingdoms Fall
Volume 2 Dark Ages
Volume 3 Age of the Towers
Volume 4 Difficillis Exitus
Volume 5 Age of the Lords
Volume 6 The Renegade Tower

Volume 7 Rebellions
Volume 8 The Aliens Return
Volume 9 Power Struggles
Volume 10 Guilds, Genetics, and Gods
Volume 11 Magi, Witches, Swords, and Superstitions
Volume 12 The Voyage of the Eagle's Seed
Volume 13 Eagle's Seed and Origins
Volume 14 Justifications
Volume 15 Responsibilities

The Return of the Wizards: Twelve Companions – The Making of Wizards (fantasy)

www.ingramcontent.com/pod-product-compliance
Lightning Source LLC
Chambersburg PA
CBHW081526120726
47907CB00016B/2435